CW01073100

(3rd edition)

AHISTORY

AN UNAUTHORISED HISTORY OF THE *DOCTOR WHO* UNIVERSE

LANCE PARKIN & LARS PEARSON

mad norwegian press

Des Moines, IA

Also Available from Mad Norwegian Press...

THE GEEK GIRL CHRONICLES (ESSAY COLLECTIONS)
Chicks Unravel Time: Women Journey Through Every Season of Doctor Who

Chicks Dig Time Lords: A Celebration of Doctor Who by the Women Who Love It
(Hugo Award winner, 2011)

Chicks Dig Comics: A Celebration of Comic Books by the Women Who Love Them

Whedonistas: A Celebration of the Worlds of Joss Whedon by the Women Who Love Them

THE ABOUT TIME SERIES
by Lawrence Miles and Tat Wood

About Time 1: The Unauthorized Guide to Doctor Who (Seasons 1 to 3)
About Time 2: The Unauthorized Guide to Doctor Who (Seasons 4 to 6)
About Time 4: The Unauthorized Guide to Doctor Who (Seasons 12 to 17)
About Time 5: The Unauthorized Guide to Doctor Who (Seasons 18 to 21)
About Time 6: The Unauthorized Guide to Doctor Who (Seasons 22 to 26,
the TV Movie)
About Time 7: The Unauthorized Guide to Doctor Who (Series 1 to 2, forthcoming)

OTHER SCI-FI REFERENCE GUIDES / CRITIQUE BOOKS / ESSAY BOOKS
Queers Dig Time Lords: A Celebration of Doctor Who by the LGBTQ Fans Who Love It (forthcoming)

Space Helmet for a Cow: An Unlikely History of 50 Years of Doctor Who
by Paul Kirkley (forthcoming)

Running Through Corridors: Rob and Toby's Marathon Watch of Doctor Who (Volume 1: The 60s)
by Robert Shearman and Toby Hadoke

Redeemed: The Unauthorized Guide to Angel by Lars Pearson and Christa Dickson (ebook only)

Dusted: The Unauthorized Guide to Buffy the Vampire Slayer
by Lawrence Miles, Lars Pearson and Christa Dickson

Wanting to Believe: A Critical Guide to The X-Files, Millennium and The Lone Gunmen
by Robert Shearman

Copyright © 2012 Lance Parkin and Lars Pearson.
Published by Mad Norwegian Press
www.madnorwegian.com

Cover & interior design by Christa Dickson.

ISBN: 978-1935234111
Printed in the United States of America.
First Edition: November 2012.

mad norwegian press | des moines

TABLE OF CONTENTS

The following *only* catalogs main story entries for each adventure; some stories occur in muliple time zones, and hence have more than one page number listed. For a complete listing of *all* story references, consult the Index.

Some stories proved undatable and lack main entries; for a list of these, consult the None of the Above section (page 747-749).

All titles listed are *Doctor Who* stories (or were supplemental comics made for *Doctor Who Magazine*) unless otherwise noted. BBV and Reeltimes Pictures stories include a notation of the particular monster or *Doctor Who* character they feature. For more on the designations used in the Table of Contents, see the Key on page 29.

TABLE OF CONTENTS

TABLE OF CONTENTS

TABLE OF CONTENTS

TABLE OF CONTENTS

TABLE OF CONTENTS

TABLE OF CONTENTS

TABLE OF CONTENTS

TABLE OF CONTENTS

TABLE OF CONTENTS

ACKNOWLEDGEMENTS

Lance wishes to thank... A great many people have been involved with this book. This is the fifth version. The first - *The Doctor Who Chronology* - was produced by Seventh Door Fanzines. It covered the television series. The second - *A History of the Universe* - was published by Virgin in 1996, and covered the television series plus the New and Missing Adventures up to *Happy Endings* and *The Sands of Time* respectively. It proved very popular. Nearly ten years on, the third version was published by Mad Norwegian Press, and covered roughly twice as many stories as the Virgin edition. This is the second update of that.

Thanks first and foremost to my editors at Virgin - Mark Jones, Rebecca Levene and Simon Winstone - and, for the Mad Norwegian versions, my co-writer Lars Pearson.

Thanks to the many other people who have offered information, comments, help, material, corrections or just said nice things. In alphabetical order, these are: Ben Aaronovitch, Nadir Ahmed, Keith Ansell, John Binns, Jon Blum, David Brunt, Graeme Burk, Andy Campbell, Andrew Cartmel, Shaun Chmara, Mark Clapham, Finn Clark (big, big thanks for his comics expertise), Paul Cornell, Alex Dante, Jeremy Daw, Martin Day, Zoltan Dery, Jonathan Evans, Michael Evans, Simon Forward, Martin Foster, Gary Gillatt, Donald and Patricia Gillikin, Craig Hinton, David Howe, Edward Hutchinson, Alison Jacobs, William Keith, Andy Lane, Paul Lee, Steve Maggs, Daniel O'Mahony, Steven Manfred, April McKenna, Iain McLaughlin, Adrian Middleton, Lawrence Miles, Steve Mollmann, Kate Orman, David Owen, David Pitcher, Andrew Pixley, Marc Platt, Jon Preddle, Justin Richards, Gareth Roberts, Trevor Ruppe, Gary Russell, Jim Smith, Robert Smith?, Shannon Sullivan, Dimity Telfer, Richard Thacker, Lynne Thomas, Michael Thomas, Steve Traylen, Stephen James Walker, Peter Ware, Martin Wiggins, Gareth Wigmore, Guy Wigmore, Alex Wilcock and Anthony Wilson. I'm genuinely sorry if I missed anyone.

Thanks most of all to the innumerable people involved with the production of *Doctor Who*, in any and every form ... past, present and future.

Lars wishes to thank... First and foremost, a shout-out is due to Lance - for his vast *Doctor Who* knowledge, writing skill, professionalism, humour and for putting up with manic phone calls in which I desperately needed to puzzle through (say) the terraforming of Mars. I've learned a hell of a lot from working with him. In fact, it's only now - eight years (!!!) after Mad Norwegian was given the honour of taking up the reins of *Ahistory* - that I've finally achieved the threshold of having written half the text you're holding, which is to say that you have to run damn, *damn* fast if you want to keep up with Lance Parkin.

Big thanks are also due to Christa Dickson, not just for the tremendous cover and overall design of this Third Edition, but for being patient with my mood swings in the time it took to complete the text therein. You know how the partners / spouses of coaches have to exert extra understanding with their stressed-out, doom-slathered mates during sports season? Now imagine that, but that it essentially goes on for two and a half years. Similarly, Robert Smith? and Josh Wilson went to exceeding lengths to keep me at least half-sane, and a man could not ask for better friends and colleagues.

A great many people assisted with my research, but I seemed to most often approach the highly prolific Simon Guerrier, Jonathan Morris and Gary Russell for help, so thanks to them for their insightful responses. Big thanks to everyone at Big Finish - particularly Nicholas Briggs and Jason Haigh-Ellery - for their continued enthusiasm and support for this project. Thanks to our beta-testing team (Barnaby Edwards, Stephen Gray, Steve Manfred, Cody Quijano-Schell and John Seavy) for the number of times that they saved us from ourselves. Valued research help was also given to me by Andrew Cartmel, Martin Day, Stuart Douglas, Paul Ebbs, James Goss, David Richardson, Eddie Robson, Alan Stevens and Damian Taylor. I'm sure I've failed to mention someone, for which I'm desperately embarrassed.

Appreciation in one form or another is due to Sophie Aldred, Jeremy Bement, Josh Bertaki, Jim Boyd, Graeme Burk, Dan and Allison Chibnall, Gwyn Cox, Jen M.F. Dixon, Sacha Dzuba, Marc Eby, Sigrid Ellis, Laura Gerald, John Gibney, Brandon and Kelli Griffis, Toby Hadoke, James Houston, Maggie Howe, Shari Hrdina, Hannah Hudson, James and Renee Juneau, Matt Jesson, Al Kennedy and Paul O'Brien at the House to Astonish podcast, Paul Kirkley, Shawne Kleckner, Michael Lee, Catherine Lowe, Shaun Lyon, Dylan Lyons, Cameron and Stephanie McCoy, Sylvester McCoy, Tiff Morgan, K.O. Myers, L.M. Myles, Dave Owen, Lars Pearson (no relation, but you can imagine how schizophrenic our Facebook discussions can seem), Chris Purcell, Cassie Sampson, Robert Shearman, Katy Shuttleworth, Deborah Stanish, Lynne Thomas, Jason Stormageddon Tucker, Peter Ware, Cathleen Young (God, the blueberry muffins this woman makes; that's not a euphemism, by the way) and that nice lady who sends me newspaper articles.

This book seeks to place every event referred to in *Doctor Who* into a consistent timeline. Yet this is "a" history of the *Doctor Who* universe, not the "definitive" or "official" version.

Doctor Who has had hundreds of creators, all pulling in slightly different directions, all with their own vision of what *Doctor Who* was about. Without that diversity, the *Doctor Who* universe would no doubt be more internally consistent, but it would also be a much smaller and less interesting place. Nowadays, fans are part of the creative process. Ultimately, we control the heritage of the show that we love. The authors of *Ahistory* hope people will enjoy this book, and we know that they will challenge it.

A total adherence to continuity has always been rather less important to the successive *Doctor Who* production teams than the main order of business: writing exciting stories, telling good jokes and scaring small children with big monsters. This, as most people will tell you, is just how it should be.

Doctor Who has always been created using a method known as "making it up as they went along". The series glories in its invention and throwaway lines. When the TV series was first in production, no-one was keeping the sort of detailed notes that would prevent canonical "mistakes", and even the same writer could contradict their earlier work. It's doubtful the writer of *The Mysterious Planet* had a single passing thought about how the story fit in with *The Sun Makers*... even though they were both authored by Robert Holmes.

Now, with dozens of new books, audios, comic strips, short stories and a new TV series, not to mention spin-offs, it is almost certainly impossible to keep track of every new *Doctor Who* story, let alone put them all in a coherent - never mind consistent - framework. References can contradict other references in the same story, let alone ones in stories written forty years later for a different medium by someone who wasn't even born the year the original writer died.

It is, in any case, impossible to come up with a consistent view of history according to *Doctor Who*. Strictly speaking, the Brigadier retires three years before the first UNIT story is set. The Daleks and Atlantis are both utterly destroyed, once and for all, several times that we know about. Characters "remember" scenes, or sometimes entire stories, that they weren't present to witness, and show remarkable lack of knowledge of real world events or events in *Doctor Who* that happened after the story first came out.

"Continuity" has always been flexible, even on the fundamentals of the show's mythology - *The Dalek Invasion of Earth* (1964), *The War Games* (1969), *Genesis of the Daleks* (1975) and *The Deadly Assassin* (1976) all shamelessly threw out the show's established history in the name of a good story. Their versions of events (the Daleks are galactic conquerors; the Doctor is a Time Lord who stole his TARDIS and fled his home planet; the Daleks were created by the Kaled scientist, Davros; Gallifreyan society is far from perfect and Time Lords are limited to twelve regenerations) are now taken to be the "truth". The previous versions (the Daleks are confined to one city; the Doctor invented the "ship" and his granddaughter named it before their exile; the Daleks are descendants of the squat humanoid Dals, mutated by radiation; the Time Lords are godlike and immortal barring accidents) have quietly been forgotten.

However, it would be unfortunate to write a book so vague that it becomes useless. Firm decisions have to be made about where stories are placed, so this book contains abundant footnotes that lay out the evidence pertaining to each story, and to explain each story's placement in this chronology.

In some cases, this is simply a matter of reporting an exact date spoken by one of the characters in the story (*Black Orchid*, for example). In others, no firm date is given. In those cases, we attempt to look at internal evidence given on screen, then evidence from the production team at the time (from the script, say, or from contemporary publicity material), then branch out to cross-referencing it with other stories, noting where other people who've come up with *Doctor Who* chronologies have placed it. What we're attempting to do is accurately list all the evidence given for dating the stories and other references in as an objective way as possible, then weigh it to reach a conclusion.

For a good example of this process at its most complicated, look for *The Seeds of Death* or *The Wheel in Space*. You may not agree with the years we've set, it might make your blood boil, but you'll see how we've reached our answer.

This book is one attempt, then, to retroactively create a consistent framework for the history of the *Doctor Who* universe. It is essentially a game, not a scientific endeavour to discover "the right answer".

All games have to follow a consistent set of rules, and as we attempt to fit all the pieces of information we are given, we have to lay some groundwork and prioritise. If a line of dialogue from a story broadcast in 1983 flatly contradicts what was said in one from 1968, which is "right"? Some people would suggest that the newer story "got it wrong", that the later production team didn't pay enough attention to what came before. Others might argue that the new information "corrects" what we were told before. In practice, most fans are inconsistent, choosing the facts that best support their arguments or preferences. *The Discontinuity Guide* (1995) has some very healthy advice regarding continuity: "Take what you want and ignore what you don't. Future continuity cops will just have to adapt to your version".

BASIC PRINCIPLES

For the purposes of this book, we have worked from the following assumptions:

• Every *Doctor Who* story takes place in the same universe, unless explicitly stated otherwise. The same individual fought the Daleks with Jo on Spiridon, Beep the Meep with Sharon, the Ice Warriors with Benny in London, became Zagreus in the Antiverse, blew up Gallifrey to prevent Faction Paradox taking over the universe, saved Rose from the Autons and married River Song.

For legal, marketing or artistic reasons, it should be noted that some of the people making *Doctor Who* have occasionally stated that they don't feel this to be the case. However there are innumerable cross references (say, Romana being president of Gallifrey in both the books and the audios) and in-jokes that suggest very strongly that, for example, the eighth Doctor of the books is the same individual as the eighth Doctor of the Big Finish audios - or at the very least, they've both got almost-identical histories.

• The universe has one, true "established history". Nothing (short of a being with godlike powers) can significantly change the course of history with any degree of permanency within that universe. The Mars attacked by the Fendahl is the Mars of the Ice Warriors.

• We have noted where each date we have assigned comes from. Usually it is from dialogue (in which case, it's quoted), but often it comes from behind-the-scenes sources such as scripts, publicity material and the like. It is up to the individual reader whether a date from a BBC Press release or draft script is as "valid" as one given on screen.

• In many cases, no date was ever given for a story. In such instances, we pick a year and explain our reasons. Often, we will assign a date that is consistent with information given in other stories. (So, it's suggested that the Cyber War mentioned in *Revenge of the Cybermen* must take place after *The Tomb of the Cybermen*, and probably after *Earthshock* because of what is said in those other stories.) These dates are marked as arbitrary and the reasoning behind them is explained in the footnotes.

• Where a date isn't established on screen, we have also included the dates suggested by others who have compiled timelines or listed dates given in the series. Several similar works to this have been attempted, and we have listed the most relevant in the Bibliography.

• It's been assumed that historical events take place at the same time and for the same reasons as they did in "real history", unless specifically contradicted by the television series. Unless given reason to think otherwise, we assume that the Doctor is telling the truth about meeting historical figures, and that his historical analysis is correct. (It has, however, been established that the Doctor is fallible and / or an incorrigible name-dropper.) When there's a reference in our footnotes to "science", "scientists", "history" or "historians", unless stated otherwise it means scholars and academics from the real world, not the *Doctor Who* universe (they are usually invoked when *Doctor Who*'s version of science or events strays a distance from ours).

• Information given is usually taken literally and at face value, unless there's strong reason to think that the person giving it is lying or mistaken. Clearly, if an expert like the Doctor is talking about something he knows a great deal about, we can probably trust the information more than some bystander's vague remark.

• *Ahistory*'s version of Earth's future history is generally one of steady progress, and as such stories featuring similar themes and concepts tend to be lumped together - say, intergalactic travel, isolated colonies, humanoid robots and so on. If the technology, transportation or weaponry seen in story A is more advanced than in story B, then we might suggest that story A is set in the future of story B. We also assume that throughout future centuries, humans age at the same rate (unless told otherwise), so their life spans don't alter too dramatically, etc. A "lifetime" in the year 4000 is still about one hundred years.

• All dates, again unless specifically stated otherwise, work from our Gregorian calendar, and all are "AD". It is assumed that the system of leap years will remain the same in the future. For convenience, all documents use our system of dating, even those of alien civilisations. The "present" of the narrative is now, so if an event happened "two hundred years ago", it happened in the early nineteenth century. On a number of occasions we are told that a specific date takes place on the wrong day: in *The War Machines*, 16th July, 1966, is a Monday, but it really occurred on a Saturday.

• We assume that a "year" is an Earth year of 365 days, even when an alien is speaking, unless this is specifically contradicted. This also applies to terms such as "Space Year" (*Genesis of the Daleks*), "light year" (which is used as a unit of time in *The Savages* and possibly *Terror of the Autons*) and "cycle" (e.g. *Zamper*).

• If an event is said to take place "fifty years ago", we take it to mean exactly fifty years ago, unless a more precise date is given elsewhere or it refers to a known historical event. If an event occurs in the distant past or the far future, we tend to round up: *Image of the Fendahl* is set in about 1977, the Fifth Planet was destroyed "twelve million years" before. So, we say this happened in "12,000,000 BC", not "11,998,023 BC". When an event takes place an undefined number of "centuries", "millennia" or "millions of years" before or after a story, we arbitrarily set a date.

• A "generation" is assumed to be twenty-five years, as per the Doctor's definition in *Four to Doomsday*. A "couple" of years is always two years, a "few" is less than "several" which is less than "many", with "some" taken to be an arbitrary or unknown number. A "billion" is generally the American and modern British unit (a thousand million) rather than the old British definition (a million million).

• Characters are in their native time zone unless explicitly stated otherwise. Usually, when a *Doctor Who* monster or villain has a time machine, it's central to the plot. On television, the Cybermen only explicitly have time travel in *Attack of the Cybermen*, for example, and they've stolen the time machine in question. It clearly can't be "taken for granted" that they can go back in history. The Sontarans have a (primitive) time machine in *The Time Warrior*, and are clearly operating on a scale that means they can defy the Time Lords in *The Invasion of Time* and *The Two Doctors*, but there's no evidence they routinely travel in time. The only one of the Doctor's (non-Time Lord) foes with a mastery of time travel are the Daleks - they develop time travel in *The Chase*, and definitely use it in *The Daleks' Master Plan*, *The Evil of the Daleks*, *Day of the Daleks*, *Resurrection of the Daleks*, *Remembrance of the Daleks*, *Dalek*, *Army of Ghosts*, *Doomsday*, *Daleks in Manhattan*, *Evolution of the Daleks*, *The Stolen Earth*, *Journey's End* and *Victory of the Daleks*. Even so, in the remaining stories, we've resisted assuming that the Daleks are time travellers.

• Sometimes, stories occur with the sort of impact that means it seems odd that they weren't mentioned in an earlier story. For instance, no-one from *The Power of the Daleks* and *The Moonbase* (both shown in 1966) recalls the Daleks and Cybermen fighting in *Doomsday* (shown in 2006). For that matter, when the Doctor and his companions refer to their past adventures on TV, they rarely mention the events of the Missing Adventures, Past Doctor novels, comic strips or Big Finish audios. (There are exceptions, however, usually when a writer picks up a throwaway line in a TV episode.) In *Doctor Who* itself, this may point to some deep truth about the nature of time - that events don't become part of the "Web of Time" until we see the Doctor as part of them... or it may be simply that it was impossible for the people making *Doctor Who* in the sixties to know about stories authored by their successors - many

of whom hadn't even been born then.

• And, in a related note, few people making *The Tenth Planet* (in 1966, depicting the distant space year 1986) would have imagined anyone in the early twenty-first century worrying how to reconcile the quasi-futuristic world they imagined with the historical reality. Whenever the UNIT stories are set, it was "the twentieth century", and that's history now. Some of the early New Adventures took place in a "near future" setting, which is now the present day for the eleventh Doctor, Amy and Rory. We've therefore accepted the dates given, rather than said that - for example - as we still haven't put a man on Mars, *The Ambassadors of Death* is still set in our future. There's clearly a sensible reason why the "present day" stories made now look like our present day, not *The Tenth Planet: The Next Generation*. The in-story explanation / fudge would seem to be that most *Doctor Who* stories take place in isolated locations, and that there are agencies like UNIT, C19 and Torchwood tasked with keeping alien incursions covered up. This paradigm has broken down over time, however, given the sheer number of public events involving aliens in the new series, *The Sarah Jane Adventures* and (to a lesser degree) *Torchwood*.

• There are still errors of omission, as when a later story fails to acknowledge an earlier one (often in other media) that seems relevant. No-one in *The Christmas Invasion*, for example, notes that it's odd Britain is making a big deal about sending an unmanned probe to Mars, when there were manned UK missions there in the seventies (in *The Ambassadors of Death*) and the nineties (*The Dying Days*). As with Sarah in *School Reunion* remembering *The Hand of Fear* but not *The Five Doctors*, there's got to be an appeal to clarity in storytelling. With so many *Doctor Who* stories in existence, it's almost impossible to tell a new one that doesn't explicitly contradict an earlier story, let alone implicitly. The reason no-one, say, remarks that the second Doctor looks like Salamander except in *The Enemy of the World* is the same reason that no-one ever says Rose looks like the girl who married Chris Evans - it gets in the way of the story, and doesn't help it along.

THE STORIES

This book restricts itself to events described in the BBC television series *Doctor Who*, and its original full-length fiction, audio plays and comics; the spin-off series *The Sarah Jane Adventures*, *Torchwood*, *K9* and their full-length fiction, audio plays and comics; and any spin-off books, audios, comics and direct-to-video/DVD films involving characters that originated in the above, and were used with permission by their rights holders (see Section No. 4 below). To be included in this Third Edition of *Ahistory*, a story had to be released before 31st December, 2011.

This is not an attempt to enter the debate about which stories are "canon" (although we have been compelled to make such determinations at times), it is simply an attempt to limit the length and scale of this book. There are two types of information in this book - evidence given in TV stories, and anything provided in another format - and these are distinguished by different typefaces.

1. The Television Series. Included are the episodes and on-screen credits of the BBC television series *Doctor Who* from *An Unearthly Child* (1963) to *The Doctor, the Widow and the Wardrobe* (2011), the *K9 and Company* pilot episode (1981), *Torchwood* (2006-2011), *The Sarah Jane Adventures* (2007-2011), the *K9* TV series (2009-2010), and extended or unbroadcast versions that have since been commercially released or broadcast anywhere in the world - there are few cases of "extended" material contradicting the original story.

Priority is given to sources closest to the finished product or the production team of the time the story was made. In descending order of authority are the following: the programme as broadcast; the official series websites; official guidebooks made in support of the series (*Doctor Who: The Encyclopedia*, etc.), the *Radio Times* and other contemporary BBC publicity material (which was often written by the producer or script editor); the camera script; the novelisation of a story by the original author or an author working closely from the camera script; contemporary interviews with members of the production team; televised trailers; rehearsal and draft scripts; novelisations by people other than the original author; storylines and writers' guides (which often contradict on-screen information); interviews with members of the production team after the story was broadcast; and finally any other material, such as fan speculation.

Scenes cut from broadcast were considered if they were incorporated back into a story at a later time (as with those in *The Curse of Fenric* VHS and DVD). Not included is information from unreleased material that exists, is in release but was kept separate from the story (for instance, the extra scenes on the *Ghost Light* DVD) or that no longer exists (such as with *Terror of the Autons*, *Terror of the Zygons* and *The Hand of Fear*). Neither does the first version of *An Unearthly Child* to be filmed (the so-called "pilot episode") count, nor "In character" appearances by the Doctor interacting with the real world on other programmes (e.g.: on *Animal Magic*, *Children in Need*, *Blue Peter* etc.).

2. The *Doctor Who*, *The Sarah Jane Adventures* and *Torchwood* books, audios and webcasts. This present volume encompasses the *Doctor Who* New and Missing

Adventures published by Virgin (1991-1997), the BBC's Eighth Doctor Adventures (1997-2005), the BBC's Past Doctor Adventures (1997-2005), the BBC's New Series Adventures (up through *The Silent Stars Go By*, 2011), the *Torchwood* novels (up through *TW: The Men Who Sold the World*, 2011), all of the Telos novellas (2001-2004), the four *K9* children's books (1980), and a number of one-off novels: *Harry Sullivan's War*, *Turlough and the Earthlink Dilemma* and *Who Killed Kennedy*.

The audios covered include *The Pescatons*, *Slipback*, *The Paradise of Death* and *The Ghosts of N-Space*; the BBC fourth Doctor mini-series (*Hornets' Nest*, *Demon Quest* and *Serpent Crest*); and the extensive Big Finish *Doctor Who* audio range... its monthly series (up to *Army of Death*, #155), the Companion Chronicles (up to *The First Wave*, #6.5), the eighth Doctor audios initially broadcast on BBC7 (up to *To the Death*, #4.10) and various promotional audios (up to *The Five Companions*).

The Big Finish Lost Stories, which adapt unmade TV scripts for audio, have been included (up through *The Children of Seth*, #3.3) because Big Finish, while having no formal policy regarding the Lost Stories' canonicity, isn't averse to the Lost Stories being cross-referenced in obviously canonical adventures and - very tellingly - considers Raine Creevy (from the audio adaptations of the unmade Season 27 stories) as "real" as any Big Finish companion. Without an express directive to keep the Lost Stories in a separate continuity, the cross-pollination with the established *Doctor Who* audios will only increase over time, so it seemed fair to include them.

The BBC webcasts *Real Time*, *Shada* and *Death Comes to Time* (the last one somewhat controversially) are also included, as well as the webcast *Torchwood* story *Web of Lies*.

A handful of stories were available in another form - *Shakedown* and *Downtime* were originally direct-to-video spin-offs, some Big Finish stories like *Minuet in Hell* and *The Mutant Phase* are (often radically different) adaptations of stories made by Audio Visuals. *Ahistory* deals with the "official" versions, as opposed to the fan-produced ones.

This volume covers two stories that appear in two different versions, because they were told in two media that fall within the scope of the book and were adapted for different Doctors: *Shada* and *Human Nature*. Those have been dealt with on a case-by-case basis. *Doctor Who* fans have long had different versions of the same story in different media - the first Dalek story, for example, was televised, extensively altered for the novelisation, changed again for the movie version and adapted into a comic strip.

We haven't included in-character appearances in nonfiction books (e.g: the *Doctor Who Discovers...* and *Doctor Who Quiz Book of* series), and *Make Your Own Adventure/ Find Your Fate*-style books where it's impossible to determine the actual story. It was tempting, though.

3) The *Doctor Who* comics, including the strip that has been running in *Doctor Who Weekly / Monthly / Magazine* since 1979 (up through "The Child of Time", DWM #438-441), along with all original backup strips from that publication, and the ones from the various Specials and Yearbooks. With a book like this, drawing a line between what should and shouldn't be included is never as simple as it might appear. Including every comic strip would include ones from the Annuals, for example. This book doesn't include the text stories that *Doctor Who Magazine* has included at various points during its run.

There's a relatively straightforward distinction between the *DWM* comic strip and other *Doctor Who* comic strips: while it's the work of many writers, artists and editors, it also has a strong internal continuity and sense of identity. This book, in all previous editions, has confined itself to "long form" *Doctor Who* and there's a case to be made that the *DWM* strip represents one "ongoing story" that's run for over a quarter of a century. The *Doctor Who Magazine* strip has now run for longer than the original TV series, and most fans must have encountered it at some point.

That said, this book excludes *DWM* strips that are clearly parodies that aren't meant to be considered within the continuity of the strip. The same logic applies to spoofs like *Dimensions in Time* and *The Curse of Fatal Death*. For the record, the affected strips are "Follow that TARDIS!", "The Last Word" and "TV Action".

DWM has reprinted a number of strips from other publications over the years. We have tended to include these. The main beneficiary of this is *The Daleks* strip from the sixties comic *TV Century 21* (and *DWM*'s sequel to it from issues #249-254).

It's certainly arguable that the *DWM* strip exists in a separate continuity, with its own companions, internal continuity, vision of Gallifrey and even an ethos that made it feel quite unlike the TV eras of its Doctors. This certainly seemed to be the case early on. However, this distinction has broken down over the years - the comic strip companion Frobisher appeared in a book (*Mission: Impractical*) and two audios (*The Holy Terror*, *The Maltese Penguin*); the village of Stockbridge (from the fifth Doctor *DWM* comics) has featured in various audios starting with *Circular Time*; the audio *The Company of Friends* incorporated characters from different book and comic ranges; and for a number of years the strip and the New Adventures novels were quite elaborately linked. In the new TV series, we've met someone serving kronkburgers (in *The Long Game*, first mentioned in "The Iron Legion") and the Doctor even quoted Abslom Daak in *Bad Wolf*.

The strip tends to "track" the ongoing story (the television series in the seventies and eighties, the New Adventures in the early nineties) - so the Doctor regenerates, without explanation within the strip and on occasion during a story arc. Companions from the television series and books come and go. Costume changes and similar details (like the design of the console room) do the same. It's broadly possible to work out when the strip is set in the Doctor's own life. So, the first *Doctor Who* Weekly strips with the fourth Doctor mention he's dropped off Romana, and he changes from his Season 17 to Season 18 costume - so it slots in neatly between the two seasons. There are places where this process throws up some anomalies, which have been noted.

Also included are the *Doctor Who* comics produced by IDW for the American market; the *Radio Times* comics featuring the eighth Doctor; the comics that first appeared in *Torchwood: The Official Magazine*; and the *Torchwood* and *The Sarah Jane Adventures* webcomics.

4) Spin-off series featuring characters that originally appeared in *Doctor Who* (whatever the format), and were used elsewhere with permission by their respective rights holders.

This needs some explaining... *Doctor Who* is a very unusual property in that, generally speaking, the BBC retained ownership of anything created by salaried employees, but freelance scriptwriters working on the TV show in the 60s, 70s and 80s (and the novelists working on the books in the 90s) typically wound up owning the rights to any characters they created. Infamously, this has meant that writer Terry Nation (and his estate) kept ownership of the name "Dalek" and the conceptual property therein, but the BBC retained the rights to the likeness of the Daleks, which were created by staff designer Raymond Cusick.

This is very counter-intuitive to how other series work - a world where *Star Trek* is so divided (say, with one person owning the Klingons, another owning the Horta and another owning Spock, while Paramount continues to retain ownership of Captain Kirk and the *Enterprise*) would be unthinkable. Nonetheless, over the years, the rights holders to iconic *Doctor Who* characters and monsters have licensed them for use elsewhere, and - unless given reason to think otherwise - their use in a non-*Doctor Who* story seems as valid as any BBC-sanctioned story.

The spin-offs included in this volume are:

• The Bernice Summerfield novels, audios and novella collections, featuring the Doctor's companion who was first seen in the New Adventure *Love and War* (1992). Benny was the lead of the Doctor-less New Adventures novels published from 1997 to 1999; Big Finish took over the license afterward, and has produced Benny audios, novels, short story anthologies, novella collections and one animated story. The first five Benny audios were excluded, as they were adaptations of New Adventures novels.

• BBV audios and films featuring licensed characters such as the Sontarans, the Rutans and the Zygons.

• Big Finish spin-off series (*Cyberman*; *Dalek Empire*; *Gallifrey*; *Graceless*; *I, Davros*; *Jago & Litefoot*; *Sarah Jane Smith*; and *UNIT*).

• *Faction Paradox* books, audios and a comic; featuring characters and concepts first seen in the EDA *Alien Bodies* (1997).

• Iris Wildthyme audios and (as of 2011) one novel; a character seen in the original fiction of Paul Magrs, and who first appeared in *Doctor Who* in the *Short Trips* story "Old Flames" and the EDA *The Scarlet Empress*.

• *Kaldor City* audios, spun off from *The Robots of Death* and the PDA *Corpse Marker* (1999).

• *Minister of Chance* - undatable audios featuring the lead from the webcast *Death Comes to Time* (2001-2002).

• *Miranda* comic, from the character seen in the EDA *Father Time* (2001).

• Reeltime Pictures direct-to-VHS/DVD films, featuring the Sontarans, the Draconians, etc.

• *Time Hunter* novellas, featuring characters from the Telos novella *The Cabinet of Light* (2003), and also involving the Fendahl and the Daemons.

Despite this volume's efforts to be inclusive whenever possible, there are also some significant omissions:

• Comic strips released prior to the advent of the *Doctor Who Magazine* strip, including the *TV Comic* and *Countdown* strips. There are some profound canonicity concerns with these strips, plus there simply wasn't the room to include them.

• Short stories, whether they first appeared in annuals, *Doctor Who Magazine*, the *Decalog* and *Short Trips* anthologies or any of the innumerable other places they have cropped up.

There are a few exceptions to this... anthologies were included if they were a rare exception in a full-length story range (say, the *Story of Martha* anthology published with the New Series Adventures novels). Also, information from the Bernice Summerfield and Iris Wildthyme short story anthologies were included if they were so interwoven into continuity elsewhere that omitting them would have been confusing. The prime examples of this are the Benny anthologies *Life During Wartime* and *Present Danger*, as well as the occasional nugget taken from the Iris Wildthyme short story collections published by Obverse. Similarly, information from *Faction Paradox: The Book of the War*

(itself a guidebook) was included if it directly pertained to characters or events prominently featured in other *Faction Paradox* stories (for instance, the background of Cousin Octavia, the lead character in *FP: Warring States*).

• Short stories from the *Doctor Who Annuals*.

• The Big Finish stageplay adaptations (*The Curse of the Daleks*, *The Seven Keys to Doomsday*, *The Ultimate Adventure*) were excluded out of canonicity concerns. It was tempting to make an exception for *The Ultimate Adventure* and its sequel audio, *Beyond the Ultimate Adventure*, as they are more compatible with the established timeline, but both were finally omitted - even in a book as large as this - for reasons of space.

• Unlicensed "cover series" with actors playing thinly veiled counterparts of their *Doctor Who* characters, such as Sylvester McCoy starring as "the Professor" in the BBV audios.

• Proposed stories that were never made, including the sixth Doctor story *The Ultimate Evil* (abandoned after the Season 22 hiatus and, unlike many of its contemporaries, never adapted for audio) and *Campaign* (a Past Doctor novel that was commissioned but never released by the BBC; it was later privately published).

• The 2003 *Scream of the Shalka* webcast, which debuted Richard E. Grant as the ninth Doctor and was then superseded with the advent of the new series. This story was previously included in *Ahistory*, but has been excluded because the sheer preponderance of material establishing the Eccleston version as the ninth Doctor means that almost nobody at time of writing (not even the *Scream of the Shalka*'s creators) accepts the Grant Doctor as canon.

• Stories that were explicitly marketed as being apocryphal, such as Big Finish's *Unbound* series featuring different actors playing the Doctor.

On the whole, the television series takes priority over what is said in the other media, and where a detail or reference in one of the books, audios or comics appears to contradict what was established on television, it's been noted as much and an attempt made to rationalise the "mistake" away.

The New Adventures and Missing Adventures built up a broadly consistent "future history" of the universe. This was, in part, based on the "History of Mankind" in Jean-Marc Lofficier's *The Terrestrial Index* (1991), which mixes information from the series with facts from the novelisations and the author's own speculation. Many authors, though, have contradicted or ignored Lofficier's version of events. For the purposes of this book, *The Terrestrial Index* itself is non-canonical, and it's been noted, but ultimately ignored, whenever a New Adventure recounts information solely using Lofficier as reference.

Writers' guides, discussion documents and the authors' original submissions and storylines provide useful information; we have, when possible, referenced these.

KEY

The following abbreviations are used in the text:

BENNY - A Bernice Summerfield book or audio

BF - The Big Finish audio adventures

DL - *The Darksmith Legacy*

DWM - *Doctor Who Magazine* (also known for a time as *Doctor Who Monthly*)

DWW - *Doctor Who Weekly* (as the magazine was initially called until issue #44)

FP - *Faction Paradox*

EDA - Eighth Doctor Adventures (the ongoing novels published by the BBC)

IRIS - The Iris Wildthyme adventures

KC - *Kaldor City*

K9 - The *K9* TV show

J&L - Big Finish's *Jago & Litefoot* audio adventures

MA - Missing Adventures (the past Doctor novels published by Virgin)

NA - New Adventures (the ongoing novels published by Virgin, chiefly featuring the seventh Doctor)

NSA - New Series Adventures (featuring the ninth, tenth and eleventh Doctors)

PDA - Past Doctor Adventure (the past Doctor novels published by the BBC)

SJA - *The Sarah Jane Adventures*

SJS - Big Finish's *Sarah Jane Smith* audio series

TEL - Telos novellas

TimeH - *Time Hunter*

TV - The TV series

TW - *Torchwood*

TWM - *Torchwood: The Official Magazine*

In the text of the book, the following marker appears to indicate when the action of specific stories take place:

c 2005 - THE REPETITION OF THE CLICHE ->

The title is exactly as it appeared on screen or on the cover. For the Hartnell stories without an overall title given on screen, we have used the titles that appear on the BBC's product (*An Unearthly Child*, *The Daleks*, *The Edge of Destruction*, etc.).

The letter before the date, the "code", indicates how accurately we know the date. If there is no code, then that date is precisely established in the story itself (e.g. *The Daleks' Master Plan* is set in the year 4000 exactly).

- "c" means that the story is set circa that year (e.g. *The Dalek Invasion of Earth* is set "c 2167")

"?" indicates a guess, and the reasons for it are given in the footnotes (e.g. we don't know what year *Destiny of the Daleks* is set in, but it must be "centuries" after *The Daleks' Master Plan*, so it's here set it in "? 4600").

- "&" means that the story is dated relative another story that we lack a date for (e.g.: we know that *Resurrection of the Daleks* is set "ninety years" after Destiny of the Daleks, so *Resurrection of the Daleks* is set in "& 4690"). If one story moves, the linked one also has to.

- "u" means that the story featured UNIT. There is, to put it mildly, some discussion about exactly when the UNIT stories are set. For the purposes of this guidebook, see the introduction to the UNIT Section.

- "=" indicates action that takes place in a parallel universe or a divergent timestream (such as *Inferno* or *Battlefield*). Often, the Doctor succeeds in restoring the correct timeline or erasing an aberrant deviation of history - those cases are indicated by brackets - "(=)". As this information technically isn't part of history, it's set apart by boxes with dashed lines.

- "@" is a story set during the eighth Doctor's period living on Earth from 1888 (starting with *The Ancestor Cell*) to 2001 (*Escape Velocity*). During this period, he was without a working TARDIS or his memories.

- "w" refers to an event that took place during the future War timeline (a.k.a. the War in Heaven, not to be confused with the Last Great Time War featured in New *Who*) in the eighth Doctor books, and which continued in the *Faction Paradox* series. Events in *The Ancestor Cell* annulled this timeline, but remnants of it "still happened" in the real *Doctor Who* timeline, just as *Day of the Daleks* "still happened" even though the future it depicted was averted.

We've attempted to weed out references that just aren't very telling, relevant or interesting. Clearly, there's a balance to be had, as half the fun of a book like this is in listing trivia and strange juxtapositions, but a timeline could easily go to absurd extremes. If a novel set in 1980 said that a minor character was 65, lived in a turn-of-the-century terraced house and bought the Beatles album *Rubber Soul* when it first came out, then it could generate entries for c 1900, 1915 and 1965. We would only list these if they were relevant to the story or made for particularly interesting reading.

We haven't listed birthdates of characters, except the Doctor's companions or other major recurring figures, again unless it represents an important story point.

Before our universe, others existed with different physical laws. The universe immediately prior to our own had its own Time Lords, and as their universe reached the point of collapse, they shunted themselves into a parallel universe and discovered that they now possessed almost infinite power.[1]

Rassilon speculated that the beings Raag, Nah and Rok had created and destroyed many universes.[2] **Before the creation of the universe, the Disciples of the Light rose up against the Beast and chained him in the Pit. It was theorised that the Beast would go on to inspire archetypes of evil on many planets, including Earth, Draconia, Skaro (where it was rendered as the Kaled god of war), Damos, Veltino and Vel Consadine.**[3] Abaddon, a grey-skinned creature that apparently hailed from the same race as the Beast, and its opposite number, the blue-skinned Pwccm, were respectively champions of the Light and the Dark - capricious beings of pure halogen that warred against one another, and in time would use the Cardiff Rift to traverse dimensions.[4]

The third Doctor once almost accidentally sent the TARDIS into the void before the universe started.[5]

The Entropy Sirens were born and "danced" before the first hydrogen atoms combined. Their ability to live in our reality was greatly diminished as nucleo-synthesis silenced the universe's scream of creation.[6]

The second Doctor tricked the Vist into travelling back to the start of the universe... where they fell off the edge of it, tumbled into the universe that existed beforehand, and became trapped in a formless, timeless dimension.[7]

The Dawn of Time

The universe was created in a huge explosion known as the Big Bang. As this was the very first thing to happen, scientists sometimes refer to it as "Event One".

> "Among the adherents of Scientific Mythology [q.v.] the element (Hydrogen) is widely believed to be the basic constituent out of which the Galaxy was first formed [see EVENT ONE] and evidence in support of this hypothesis includes its supposed appearance in spectroscopic analysis of massive star bodies." [8]

The Time Lords of Gallifrey monitored the Big Bang, and precisely determined the date of Event One.[9] **The Doctor claimed to have been an eye-witness at the origins of the universe.**[10]

> "The dawn of time. The beginning of all beginnings. Two forces only: Good and Evil. Then chaos. Time is born: matter, space. The universe cries out like a newborn. The forces *shatter* as the Universe explodes outwards. Only echoes remain, and yet somehow, *somehow* the evil force survives. An intelligence. Pure *evil*."

The evil force retained its sentience and spread its influence throughout time and space. It became the entity that the Vikings would call Fenric.[11]

---

1 *All-Consuming Fire, Millennial Rites, The Taking of Planet 5.*
2 *Divided Loyalties.* These are the Gods of Ragnarok seen in *The Greatest Show in the Galaxy.*
3 *The Satan Pit*
4 *TW: The Twilight Streets.* "The Light" presumably bears some affiliation with the Disciples of the Light who imprisoned the Beast (*The Impossible Planet*), although *The Twilight Streets* references the Light-Dark conflict as only having run for "millennia". Abaddon appears in *TW: End of Days;* Bilis in the same story almost seems to imply that Abaddon is the "son" of the Beast. The point is unclear, however, especially as "Abaddon" is also given as an alias of the Beast itself in *The Impossible Planet.*

THE CARDIFF RIFT: The ninth Doctor, Rose and Jack's discussion in *Boom Town* about the Cardiff Rift (a central feature of *Torchwood*) seems to indicate that it predates events surrounding it in *The Unquiet Dead* - the Gelth "used" rather than "created" the Rift, and it was only "healed" afterwards. References to the "darkness" might mean that Abaddon is trapped in the void seen in *Army of Ghosts* and *Doomsday*, with the Rift merely providing access. Going just by what's on screen, Abaddon's presence might be what weakens space-time in the Cardiff area, facilitating the creation of the Rift in the first place. *The Twilight Streets*, though, specifies that Abaddon wasn't imprisoned there until 1876.
5 *Island of Death*
6 *The Demons of Red Lodge and Other Stories:* "The Entropy Composition"
7 *The Forbidden Time*
8 This appears on the console screen in *Castrovalva.*
9 *Transit.*

THE AGE OF THE UNIVERSE: The date of the creation of the universe is not clearly established on screen, although we are told it took place "billions of years" before *Terminus.* Modern scientific consensus is that the universe is about fifteen billion years old, and books that address the issue, like *Timewyrm: Apocalypse* and *Falls the Shadow,* concur with this date. In *Transit,* the seventh Doctor drunkenly celebrates the universe's 13,500,020,012th birthday (meaning the Big Bang took place in 13,500,017,903 BC). *SJA: Secrets of the Stars*

One ship managed to travel to the dawn of creation, albeit by accident. Terminus was a vast spaceship built by an infinitely advanced, ancient race capable of time travel. The ship developed a fault, and the pilot was forced to eject some of its unstable fuel into the void before making a time jump. The explosion that resulted was the Big Bang. Terminus was thrown billions of years into the future, where it came to settle in the exact centre of the universe.[12] The universe was created when the time-travelling starship *Vipod Mor* arrived at this point and exploded.[13]

The Urbankan Monarch believed that if his ship could travel faster than light, it would move backwards in time to the Big Bang and beyond. Monarch believed that he was God and that he would meet himself at the creation of the Universe.[14]

TIMELESS[15] -> The eighth Doctor piloted the TARDIS back to before the Big Bang, hoping to avoid a myriad of parallel realities by entering the correct history from the very start. Chloe, a small girl from a devastated planet, arrived onhand. Jamais, her time travelling dog, aided the overstrained TARDIS in reaching London, 2003. The Doctor's party re-visited this era when Sabbath and Kalicum, an agent of the Council of Eight, attempted to seed an intelligence gestated within a heap of diamonds into the start of history. The Doctor failed, and the intelligence became part of the fabric of the universe.

The diamonds allowed the Council of Eight to map out events throughout the whole of history.[16]

Insect-like "forces of chaos" fed on the debris of the Big Bang, just as they would feed on the collapse of the universe.[17] Eleven physical dimensions existed at first, quickly collapsing down to the five dimensions familiar to us. The other dimensions came to exist only at the subatomic level.[18] Beings named the Quoth evolved inside atoms and were the size of quarks.[19] The Sidhe came to exist in all eleven dimensions.[20] The remaining six dimensions became the Six-Fold Realm, and each of the six Guardians represented one such dimension.[21]

As the universe was formed, an eight-dimensional "radiating blackness" infused space and time. Eventually, the Unity of the Scourge evolved in this darkness.[22] **The Weeping Angels, also sometimes called the Lonely Assassins, were as old as the universe or very nearly. They were quite nice where they hailed from, but developed into quantum-locked hunters who turned to stone if seen.[23] The "weeping angels of old" were known to Rassilon.[24]**

The first few chaotic microseconds of the universe saw extreme temperatures and the forging of bizarre elements that would be unable to exist later. This was the Leptonic Era, and one of the bizarre elements created was Helium 2.[25]

Time and Space as we understand them began as these bizarre elements reacted with each other and cooled.

The Shadow, an agent of the Black Guardian, claimed to have been waiting since eternity began in the hopes of obtaining the Key to Time.[26] The Master attempted to kill the newly-regenerated fifth Doctor by sending him backwards in time to a hydrogen inrush early in the universe's history.[27] Matter coalesced, elements formed.[28]

---

claims the universe is "13 billion" years old. *The Infinity Doctors* establishes that the Time Lords refer to the end of the universe as Event Two.

10 The Doctor reads the book *The Origins of the Universe* in *Destiny of the Daleks*, and remarks that the author "got it wrong on the first line. Why didn't he ask someone who saw it happen?". The tenth Doctor also claims to have seen the creation of the universe in *Planet of the Dead*.

11 *The Curse of Fenric*

12 *Terminus*

13 *Slipback*. This is a clear continuity clash with *Terminus*, and a discrepancy made all the more obvious as *Slipback* was broadcast within two years of *Terminus* and was written by its script editor, Eric Saward. If we wanted to reconcile the two accounts, we could speculate that the *Vipod Mor* explosion was the spark that ignited the fuel jettisoned in *Terminus*.

14 *Four to Doomsday*. Monarch never achieves this goal.

15 Dating *Timeless* (EDA #65) - This occurs at the universe's start.

16 *Sometime Never*

17 "Hunger from the Ends of Time"

18 In *An Unearthly Child*, Susan defines the fifth dimension as "space".

19 *The Death of Art*

20 *Autumn Mist*

21 *The Quantum Archangel*

22 *The Shadow of the Scourge*

23 *Blink*

24 *The End of Time* (TV)

25 *Time and the Rani*

26 *The Armageddon Factor*. It's possible this is just hyperbole on the Shadow's part.

27 *Castrovalva*.

EVENT ONE: The term "Event One" is first used in *Castrovalva* to mean the creation of "the Galaxy", but in *Terminus* the Doctor talks of "the biggest explosion in history: Event One", which he confirms is "the Big Bang" which "created the universe". There are a number of stories where the writers definitely confuse the term "galaxy" and "universe", and a number of others where they seem to. Rather than rule which is which, this book

The Epoch claimed to be from the dawn of time, and that they would meet Bernice Summerfield there.[29]

"The Dark Time, the Time of Chaos"

The Time Lords from the pre-universe entered our universe, and discovered that they had undreamt-of powers. They became known as the Great Old Ones: Hastur the Unspeakable became Fenric; Yog-Sothoth, also known as the Intelligence, began billennia of conquests; the Lloigor, or Animus, dominated Vortis; Shub-Niggurath conquered Polymos and colonised it with her offspring, the Nestene Consciousness; Dagon was worshipped by the Sea Devils. Other Great Old Ones included Cthulhu, Nyarlathotep, the Gods of Ragnarok, Gog, Magog, Malefescent and Tor-Gasukk. Across the universe, the earliest civilisations worshipped the Great Old Ones.[30] Not even the Time Lords knew much about them.[31]

The Celestial Toymaker was from the old times, "a spirit of mischief from the infancy of the universe". He was a hyper-dimensional being with a whole fragment of real-ity to himself, but had to obey the rules laid down during the "childhood" of the universe.[32] The Toymaker survived a catastrophe that destroyed his home universe. He carried a part of that universe within him, and so was exempt from the natural laws of our universe. As the Toymaker's universe receded from our own, it pushed back his personal time and extended his life. The Toymaker would live for millions of years - at first he helped life to prosper for hundreds if not of millennia, and created ships, cities, continents and entire planets. He then grew bored, destroyed what he had created... and found destruction as tedious as creation. To distract himself from the endlessness of existence, he amused himself with the chance and uncertainty found in games.[33]

The beings known as the Ancient Lights had existed before the Big Bang, and controlled many of the other beings in the earlier universe in accordance with the laws of astrology. They discovered they had great powers in the new universe, and influenced the development of astrology on many worlds. The Zodiac on Earth would have twelve signs; on Ventiplex, thirteen; on Draconia, seven.[34]

will list what was said in the stories, noting the more egregious examples, rather than ignoring them or trying to rationalise them away.

28 *The Curse of Fenric*

29 *Benny: Epoch: Judgement Day*

30 *All-Consuming Fire, Millennial Rites, Business Unusual, The Quantum Archangel, Divided Loyalties.*

31 *White Darkness*

THE GREAT OLD ONES: Novels such as *All-Consuming Fire, Millennial Rites, Business Unusual, Divided Loyalties* and *The Quantum Archangel* state that many of the godlike beings seen in *Doctor Who* have a common origin. These Great Old Ones are also referred to in *The Infinite Quest*.

The Great Old Ones were a pantheon of ancient, incomprehensible forces created by horror writer H.P. Lovecraft, and adopted by the novels for this purpose. Perhaps the most well-known of Lovecraft's creations, Cthulhu, had already made an appearance in *White Darkness*. *The Taking of Planet 5* uses Lovecraft's characters, but has them as fictional characters brought to life by Time Lord technology.

Other *Doctor Who* entities explicitly referred to in the books as Great Old Ones include - but aren't limited to - the Intelligence (*The Abominable Snowmen, The Web of Fear, Millennial Rites* and *Downtime*), the Animus (*The Web Planet, Twilight of the Gods*), the Nestene Consciousness (*Spearhead from Space, Terror of the Autons, Business Unusual, Synthespians™, Rose, The Pandorica Opens*), Fenric (*The Curse of Fenric*) and the Gods of Ragnarok (*The Greatest Show in the Galaxy, Divided Loyalties*). Gog and Magog (or beings with the same name) appeared in "The Iron Legion" comic strip.

The Doctor claims in *Ghost Light* that Light is "an evil older than time itself". From the context, this appears to mean that Light arrived on Earth before human history started, not that he existed before the universe's creation, but he might also be a Great Old One.

The Great Old Ones in the audio story *The Roof of the World*, and the "Old Ones" mentioned in *Tomb of Valdemar* and *Beyond the Ultimate Adventure* don't seem to be connected to this grouping.

32 *The Magic Mousetrap*

33 *The Nightmare Fair*. The Doctor says the Toymaker has lived for "millions" of years, but it's somewhat presented as his speculation about the Toymaker's origins. *The Quantum Archangel* and *Divided Loyalties* establish that the Toymaker is both one of the Great Old Ones and one of the Guardians, meaning he's actually much older than that.

34 *SJA: Secrets of the Stars*

35 The White and Black Guardians are first referred to in *The Ribos Operation*. *Divided Loyalties* says there are six Guardians, adding Justice, Crystal and unnamed twins to the two from the television series. The same book establishes that they are members of the Great Old Ones, and also states that the Guardian of Dreams is the Celestial Toymaker. *The Quantum Archangel* assigns them their colours and adds the Gold Guardian (counting the twin Azure Guardians as one entity).

36 *Divided Loyalties, The Chaos Pool.*

37 *The Coming of the Terraphiles*

38 *Synthespians™*

39 Chronovores first appear in *The Time Monster; The Quantum Archangel* and *No Future* clarifies their role.

40 *The Masque of the Mandragora, Enlightenment, Falls*

Six almost-omnipotent beings, **the Guardians, existed from the beginning of time. They were the White Guardian of Order and the Black Guardian of Chaos**; the Red Guardian of Justice; the Crystal Guardian of Thought and Dreams; the twins, the Azure Guardians of Mortality and Imagination; and the Gold Guardian of Life. They formed the upper pantheon of the Great Old Ones.[35]

Each segment of the Key to Time, which was forged near the end of the universe, represented a particular Guardian.[36]

The universe was able to constantly regenerate itself when the Cosmic Balance between Law and Chaos was maintained. Miggea was the Queen of Seirot - in the great fight between Law and Chaos, when the Archangels of Law fought the Archangels of Chaos, she represented Law. The Doctor remarked that the battle was "a bit Miltonian... only without all that religion". This was the Battle for the Balance, but Miggea's pursuit of Law was ruthless to the point of being evil.[37]

Shug-Niggurath died giving birth, causing the whole planet Polymos to absorb its offspring, the Nestene Consciousness. The Nestene Consciousness went on to colonise many planets, including Cramodar, Plovak 6 and the Reverent Pentiarchs of Loorn.[38]

The Chronovores existed outside the space-time continuum, consuming flaws in its structure. They weren't constrained by the laws of physics.[39]

The first of our universe's native entities - such as the Mandragora Helix, the Eternals and the grey man's race - **sprang into being.**[40] The Mandragora Helix was old even when this universe was born.[41] It claimed to have escaped the Dark Times, and to have created a new home in a nebula, in the heart of "beautiful chaos".[42]

The Time Lords would come to worship some of the more powerful Eternals, such as Death, Pain, Vain Beauty, Life and Time. Certain Time Lords entered a mysterious arrangement to serve as the "champion" of one or more of these Eternals.[43]

Sentient micro-organisms named Meme-Spawn were said to have originated at the dawn of time. They drifted through galaxies for millennia on end, absorbing every spoken language they encountered.[44]

Over the first few billion years, the first stars were born. Planets and galaxies formed.[45]

The oldest question in the universe, hidden in plain sight, was "doctor who?"[46]

? - THE PANDORICA OPENS[47] **-> Planet One, the oldest planet in the universe, had a cliff of pure diamond with fifty-foot letters from the dawn of time - the very first words to be recorded. The words read "Hello Sweetie", and had been placed there, along with a set of space-time co-ordinates, by River Song. The eleventh Doctor and Amy found the message and, as instructed, travel to Stonehenge in 102 AD.**

Xaos was the oldest planet in the known galaxy.[48]

? "The Life Bringer"[49] **->** The fourth Doctor freed Prometheus, a member of a hyper-advanced race resembling the Greek gods. From their vast city, they were co-ordinating the re-engineering of the lifeless galaxy, moving black holes and stars. Prometheus had been imprisoned for releasing the "life spores" before Zeus was satisfied that they would grow into "perfect peaceful loving creatures". The Doctor helped Prometheus escape with a sample of imperfect life spores, and Prometheus headed for another planet to spread them once more. The Doctor was unsure whether he was watching the distant past or the distant future.

---

the Shadow.

41 "The Mark of Mandragora"

42 *Beautiful Chaos* (p210). The Doctor also cites the Helix as being from "the Dawn of Time".

43 The Time Lords' gods were mentioned or seen in a number of New Adventures such as *No Future, Set Piece* and *Human Nature.* The seventh Doctor was often referred to as "Time's Champion". Mortimus (the Meddling Monk) is "Death's Champion" in *No Future,* and the Master is hinted as the same in the audio *Master. Vampire Science* has the eighth Doctor as "Life's Champion", and in *The Dying Days* he declares himself to be "the Champion of Life and Time". *Happy Endings* establishes Life's parentage (see that story). In *Seeing I,* Life appears as a cat.

44 *The Gemini Contagion*

45 The prologue to *Timewyrm: Apocalypse* is a brief history of the formation of the universe, and it follows the modern scientific consensus.

46 *The Wedding of River Song*

47 Dating *The Pandorica Opens* (X5.12) - No date given. The Doctor and Amy's reading of the message could happen at any point after the words are carved. This may be the same Planet One that Sebastiane lived on in *The Doctor Trap.*

48 "Warrior's Story". It's unclear if this means it's home to the first known civilisation or physically the oldest planet. As Planet One (seen in *The Pandorica Opens*) is the oldest planet in the *universe*, not just the galaxy, it's older than Xaos.

49 Dating "The Life Bringer" (*DWM* #49-50) - The Doctor puts it best: "As I still don't know whereabout in time we are, I suppose I'll never be able to puzzle it out... if that was Earth I found him on... or if that's Earth he's

On many worlds, sugars, proteins and amino acids combined to become primordial soup, "the most precious substance in the Universe, from which all life springs".[50] Hundreds of millions of years later, the first civilisations began to rise and fall.

Jelloids from the binary quasars of Bendalos were the longest-lived race in the universe, and many think they were the first living creatures.[51]

Thirty thousand million light years from our solar system, the first civilisation came into being. The beings were humanoid, and developed for ten thousand years before wiping themselves out in a bacteriological war. The grey man and his race saw all this, and he constructed the Cathedral, a machine "designed to alter the structure of reality". The grey man's race had been extremely dualistic, but Cathedral formed ambiguities and chaotic forces that ran throughout the universe, breaking down certainty. Its interface with physical reality was the Metahedron, a device that moved from world to world every eighty thousand years, remaining hidden.[52]

The slug-like Teuthoidians originated from near the beginning of time, and were among the universe's first space-faring races. Owing to a fold in hyperspace, some of their number interacted with the universe's final moments on the planet Chaos.[53]

? "Voyage to the Edge of the Universe"[54] ->
Commander Azal launched a mission from Damos that reached the edge of the universe. There he merged with a version of himself from another universe, gaining infinite power... but couldn't decide which universe was his to return to. Nearby, beings faced the same dilemma... one had waited for ten thousand years, another for twenty-five thousand years, another seventy-three thousand years.

Legend held that Valdemar was the Dark God captured and destroyed by the advanced and philanthropic Old Ones, after centuries of the biggest war in mythology. Following this, the Old Ones vanished. The Time Lords ranked this as the sixth greatest mystery in the universe. The fourth Doctor and Romana later learned that the Old Ones had punched a hole into the higher dimensions in an attempt to study them, and unleashed a hole that grew and grew, warping reality. Valdemar was the last of the Old Ones, and had entombed himself as a way of containing this reality-warping.[55]

What remains of the ancient races suggests awesome power - many had great psychic ability and matter-transmutation powers that were almost indistinguishable from magic. All considered it their right to intervene in the development of whole planets, and to destroy such worlds if they failed to match up to their expectations. Comparatively primitive races worshipped immortal beings such as Light and the Daemons of Damos as gods. The legends and race memories of many planets contain traces of these ancient civilisations. Horns have been a symbol of power on Earth since man began, and beings of light have been worshipped.

Nothing lasts forever, though, and these great races gradually disappeared from the universe.[56]

New societies sprang up to replace them, and soon the universe was teeming with life. In the late twentieth century, the Institute of Space Studies at Baltimore estimated that there were over five hundred planets capable of supporting life in Earth's section of the galaxy alone.[57]

heading toward." The story is set either in the distant past before life as we know it began, or the distant future after it died out. A character called Prometheus appeared in *The Quantum Archangel* - he was a Chronovore, a race first seen in *The Time Monster*, so it would seem to be a different individual.
50 Primordial soup appears in *City of Death* and *Ghost Light*; the quotation comes from the latter story.
51 *The One Doctor*
52 *Falls the Shadow*
53 *The Chaos Pool*
54 Dating "Voyage to the Edge of the Universe" (*DWM* #49) - The story occurs before the Daemons become extinct, seemingly at the height of their empire. The rocket is nuclear-powered, which doesn't sound terribly advanced, although it does get them to the end of the universe. This can't be the same Commander Azal as in *The Daemons*, for obvious reasons.
55 *Tomb of Valdemar*. The Doctor repeatedly asserts this was "a million years" ago, but others call it "aeons".
56 *The Daemons*. Light appears in *Ghost Light*.
57 *Spearhead from Space*
58 *The Infinite Quest*
59 *The Forbidden Time*
60 "WHEN THE UNIVERSE WAS HALF ITS PRESENT SIZE": The phrase, uttered by a Time Lord in *Genesis of the Daleks*, has no clear scientific meaning and should probably be considered a figure of speech, the Time Lord equivalent of "as old as the hills". Then again, the universe at various points is referred to as having edges, a centre and corners, which suggests a discernible "size".
61 "Agent Provocateur"
62 *Lucifer Rising*
63 *Zagreus*
64 *The Beast Below*
65 *The Quantum Archangel*
66 The robot is seen in *The Five Doctors*, *World Game* and *Beyond the Ultimate Adventure*. *The Eight Doctors* says that it comes from a time when "the Time Lords

The Dark Times
and the First of the Time Lords

"There was a time when the universe was so much smaller than it is now. Darker, older time of chaos. Creatures like the Racnoss, the Nestenes and the Great Vampires rampaged through the void."

The *Infinite*, a spaceship that could grant your heart's desire, came from this time. It was later lost to legend, and used to be inhabited by one of the Great Old Ones.[58] Many races evolved before the Time Lords.[59]

The first humanoid civilisation in the universe evolved on the planet Gallifrey, and mastered the principles of transmat technology while the universe was half its present size. They became the first race to master Time. Some legends said the Time Lords existed far in the past; there was some evidence that they lived in the present, and some say they come from the future.[60] Gallifrey was born before the Dark Times.[61]

See the section on Gallifreyan History for more detail.

As the Gallifreyans were the first sentient race to evolve, they established a morphic field for humanoids, making it more probable that races evolving later would also be bipedal and binocular. Non-humanoid races only evolved in environments that would be hostile to humanoids.[62] Rassilon ensured that only humanoid lifeforms survived on many planets, primarily to prevent the Divergents from existing. He used biogenic molecules to restructure the dominant species of sixty-nine thousand worlds.[63]

Time Lords were around before humanity evolved.[64] Evolution on Gallifrey, as on many other worlds, had been accelerated by the mysterious Constructors of Destiny.[65]

A civilisation devoted entirely to war developed the Raston Warrior Robot, then vanished without trace.[66] The Caskelliak were created as weapons of war, and were tasked with polluting and destroying entire worlds. Their creators perished in a war that they had initiated.[67]

The Time Lords explored space and time, making contact with many worlds and becoming legends on many others. Rassilon's experiments created holes in the fabric of space and time, which unleashed monsters from another universe, including the Yssgaroth.[68]

The Time Lords unwittingly loosed the vampires on the universe. Until the Time Lords hunted them, vampires fed off mindless animals to service their needs. They later resorted to feeding off other beings.[69] **Seventeen known worlds, including Earth, have stories of vampires.**[70]

The vampires enslaved whole worlds until the Time Lords defeated them.[71] **The vampires were immune to energy weapons, but Rassilon constructed fleets of bowships that fired mighty bolts of steel and staked the beings through the heart. The Vampire Army was defeated, and only its leader, the Great Vampire, survived by escaping through a CVE into the pocket universe of E-Space.**[72]

The origins of the Time Lords are obscure, but in the distant past they fought the Eternal War against the Great Old Ones and other invaders from outside our universe, beating them back and imposing Order. Science and Order supplanted Magic and Chaos as the Time Lords mapped, and so defined, the universe.[73] The Time Lords were the first to map "the web of time".[74]

The Carrionites lived at the "dawn of the universe", and discovered a means of manipulating reality - using words as science - that resembled magic. The Eternals found the right word to banish the Carrionites "into deep darkness", and nobody thereafter knew if they were real or imagined.[75] The Hervoken, a race with the ability to shape matter and time, fought a war with the Carrionites millions of years ago. They were eventually banished from the universe by the Eternals.[76]

The vast biomechanical complex known as the Event Synthesizer began operating.

"Since the dawn of time, the synthesizer has produced the ordered vibrations of the cosmos... creating events in a logical, harmonious sequence to flow into the main time-stream."

---

were young". *Alien Bodies* mentions a Raston cybernetic lap-dancer, and Qixotl claims that the ancient legend is just the manufacturer's marketing ploy.

67 *The Ring of Steel*, which describes the Caskelliaks' creators as "an ancient race".

68 *The Pit*, and further explored in *FP: The Book of the War*.

69 According to a highly suspect account from the vampire Tepesh, part of a historical simulation in *Zagreus*.

70 *State of Decay*. Vampires appear in that story, *Blood Harvest*, "Blood Invocation", *Death Comes to Time, The*

Eight Doctors, *Goth Opera*, *Jago & Litefoot* Series 2, *Managra*, *Project: Lazarus*, *Project: Twilight*, "Tooth and Claw" (DWM), *UNIT: Snake Head*, *Vampire Science*, *World Game*, *Benny: The Vampire Curse* and *Gallifrey: Annihilation. The Vampires of Venice* featured "vampires" that were disguised fish people. Vampires also appear as a part of the holographic record in *Zagreus*.

71 *Project: Twilight*

72 *State of Decay*

73 *Cat's Cradle: Time's Crucible*

74 *Gallifrey: Weapon of Choice*

75 *The Shakespeare Code*. Eternals were seen in

It was built by the people of Althrace, who were known to Rassilon, to simulate the effects of a white hole.[77] The last form of magic to survive was psionics.[78]

During this war, the great Gallifreyan general Kopyion Liall a Mahajetsu was believed to have died. He actually survived, and vigilantly watched in secret for signs of the Yssgaroth's return. He would deal with the threat of such an incursion in 2400.[79]

This war may or may not be the same conflict as the Time War, in which Time Lords from a generation after Rassilon fought against other races developing time travel. The conflict lasted thirty thousand years. The Time Lords wiped out many races during this time.[80]

One such race was the Charon, who were capable of warping space, and whom the Time Lords destroyed before they ever existed. One Charon survived this and created its own clockwork mini-universe. Another unnamed race used Reality Bombs to disrupt the control systems of time machines. A few of these weapons sur-

vived hidden for billions of years.[81]

The Doctor witnessed the horrors of the Time War. At one point, the Time Lords were attacked by an unnamed race in retaliation for something they hadn't yet done.[82]

The Time War ended with all threats to Gallifrey contained, or so completely destroyed that no evidence remained to suggest they even existed. Time Lords were encoded with genetic memories of their ancient enemies and were compelled to destroy any survivors. The Time Lords were ashamed of the Time War, to the point that they deny it ever happened.[83]

Mr Saldaamir, who would become a friend of the Doctor's father, was the last survivor of the Time War.[84] There was a Celestial War in which the Ooolatrii captured at least one primitive TARDIS.[85]

Two galaxies collided in deep space, triggering a stellar collapse that created the Silver Devastation: a vast sector with nothing but dead suns and dark matter, and looked like a huge silver sea in space. Myths about the Silver

---

Enlightenment.

76 *Forever Autumn*

77 "The Tides of Time"

78 *So Vile a Sin*

THE ETERNAL WAR: On screen, we learn that the Time Lords fought campaigns against the Great Vampires (*State of Decay*), that they time-looped the homeworld of the Fendahl (*Image of Fendahl*), that they protected other races from invaders (*The Hand of Fear*), that they maintained a prison planet that contained alien species (*Shada*) and that they destroyed huon particles and the Racnoss (*The Runaway Bride*). In the New Adventures, particularly *Cat's Cradle: Time's Crucible*, *The Pit* and *Christmas on a Rational Planet*, this was the Eternal War in which the forces of rationality and science defeated the forces of superstition and magic.

79 *The Pit*

80 *Sky Pirates!*, *The Infinity Doctors*.

THE THREE TIME WARS: This is not the Last Great Time War between the Time Lords and the Daleks that's the backdrop to the 2005 television series. In the *Doctor Who Annual 2006*, Russell T Davies states, "There had been two Time Wars before this - the skirmish between the Halldons and the Eternals, and then the brutal slaughter of the Omnicraven Uprising, and on both occasions, the Doctor's people had stepped in to settle the matter." Although they don't mention those specific incidents, the books concur that there were indeed two previous Time Wars - one in the ancient past (which, to avoid confusion, we might term the Ancient Time War, although it's not a term used in the stories themselves) and the War against the Enemy in the eighth Doctor's future (which has become known in *Faction Paradox* circles as the "War in Heaven").

81 *Sky Pirates!*

82 *Heart of TARDIS*

83 *Sky Pirates!*, *The Infinity Doctors*, *Heart of TARDIS*.

84 *The Gallifrey Chronicles*

85 *The Crystal Bucephalus*

86 In *The Game of Death*, the TARDIS data bank says that the galaxies collided "over a hundred billion years ago" - that number was presumably derived from the year in which *Utopia* takes place, but if so, the Devastation must be somewhat younger than that. (If the two numbers were equal, it would mean that the galaxies collided at the universe's very start, before galaxies had formed.) The Face of Boe is said to hail from the Silver Devastation, and the Master/Professor Yana was found there as a small child (*Utopia*). Why dead suns and dark matter look silver is not explained.

87 "Mortal Beloved"

88 *The Forgotten Army*

89 *Castle of Fear*

90 *The Time Warrior*, *Horror of Fang Rock*.

91 THE PROGRESS OF THE SONTARAN-RUTAN WAR: The length of time we're told the Sontarans and Rutans have been fighting is wildly inconsistent. It's "ten centuries" before "Pureblood"; been raging since before Time Lords had a civilisation in *The Infinity Doctors*; "six million years" according to *FP: The Eleven-Day Empire*, "thirteen million years" according to *FP: The Shadow Play*; "fifty thousand years" according to *The Poison Sky* and The *Taking of Chelsea 426*.

We hear a number of status reports from the battle-front of the Sontaran-Rutan War over the course of the TV series. Both sides have periods of success and failure, but implicitly, the Sontarans visit Earth far earlier and far more often than the Rutans. Earth is some way from the front lines (but close enough to strike the enemy using their most powerful emplaced weapons), with the Sontarans between us and the Rutans. According

Devastation suggested that it was populated by the mutant survivors of the two galaxies, or refugees from the Old Time, or monsters from another universe, or that it was just a bottomless chasm in time and space.[86]

The storm raging at the edge of the Proxima system was hundreds of light years across, and was "older than worlds, older than stars". It was the largest storm in the universe.[87]

Several million years ago, a race of carnivores ate rotting meat in the swamps of Malmatine 5, and evolved into Space-Boars capable of space travel. A herd of them travelled around the universe for twenty thousand years before excreting the mass that became the Cassetia asteroids.[88]

Ruta III was an ice world, and the Rutans evolved with no resistance to heat. The Rutans weren't natural chameleons, but instead were "shameleons" who adopted the ability to shapeshift.[89]

The Sontarans and Rutans were involved in "eternal war".[90] The origins of the conflict between them was lost in the mists of time and was the subject of much propaganda. Much later, the Rutans blamed the war on the Sontarans for attacking the Constellation of Zyt, which the Sontarans claimed was retaliation for a Rutan attack on Holfactur, which the Rutans said had been the base for attacks on the Purple Areas of Rutan Space, which in turn was revenge for an attack on Mancastovon. The war escalated, and it would rage, ebb and flow across the entire galaxy for many millions of years.[91] The Sontarans would acquire six million years of experience with warfare.[92]

Around the time the war started, the Sontarans became a clone race. Their greatest warrior, Sontar, had defeated the Isari. He was the model for all future Sontarans. To increase efficiency, the Sontaran body was simplified. All non-clones soon died. The leader of the Sontarans, always called General Sontar, had the memories of all previous General Sontars.[93] The "pureblood" Sontarans were originally less squat, with long hair and five fingers.[94]

to "Pureblood", when Earth becomes a spacefaring power, its territory borders the Sontaran Empire, but it's in neither human nor Sontaran interests to pick a fight with each other.

It's also worth noting that in *The Time Warrior*, Linx states "there is not a galaxy in the Universe which our space fleets have not subjugated", and Styre talks about invading "Earth's galaxy" in *The Sontaran Experiment*. Sontarans and Rutans are both prone to boasting but, even so, a war fought across one galaxy is already incomprehensibly vast, and one suspects the writers - as happens on occasion elsewhere in the TV series - are confusing "solar system" with "galaxy".

We never hear about either the Sontarans and Rutans coming into conflict with other space powers. From this, we might infer that Skaro, Draconia, Telos and Ice Warrior territory are all located on one side of Earth, the Sontarans and (a little further away) the Rutans lie in the other.

In Ancient Egypt ("The Gods Walk Among Us"), Earth is a suitable place for the Sontarans to "outflank" the Rutans (given both sides' use of rhetoric, this might suggest that the Rutans are making a major advance).

In the Middle Ages (*The Time Warrior*), Earth is of no strategic importance, but the Sontarans send a reconnaissance mission there. A pair of Rutans conduct cloning experiments on Earth in 1199 (*Castle of Fear*). The Sontarans and Rutans both have fighter squadrons. Then in the seventeenth century ("Dragon's Claw"), the war is being fought close enough to Earth for a Sontaran ship to crash there.

By the early twentieth century, the Rutans are losing the war. They had dominated the Mutter's Spiral (our galaxy), but now were beaten back to the fringes (curiously, mention of their withdrawal from Mutter's Spiral happens as early as *Castle of Fear*). Earth is of strategic importance. In the late twentieth century (*The Two*

Doctors), Earth is "conveniently situated" for the Sontarans' attack on the Rutan-held Madillon Cluster.

As humans spread into space, they encounter the Sontarans and find themselves caught in the crossfire ("Conflict of Interests", *Lords of the Storm*). Humanity and the Sontarans sign a non-aggression pact in 2420.

In Benny's time, the Rutans made great advances, and even manage to devastate the Sontaran homeworld. Following the Doctor's intervention, the Sontarans survive to serve as a buffer between humanity and the Rutans ("Pureblood"). In 2602 (*Benny: The Bellotron Incident*), the Sontaran-Rutan war dangerously approaches Earth's trade routes.

There is a demilitarised zone between the later Earth Empire and the Sontarans. The Rutans directly attack the Sontaran homeworld (again) circa 3915 (*Sontarans: Conduct Unbecoming*). The Sontarans lose a war to the Federation in the sixty-third century, and their Empire soon lies in ruins.

Then in the far future (*The Sontaran Experiment*), a Sontaran invasion fleet is poised to invade Earth (the story says "Earth's galaxy", but see above), which is of tactical importance. The Doctor says there's a "buffer zone" between human and Sontaran territory. At some point after that (*Heroes of Sontar*), the Sontarans achieve a victory on the planet Samur, but then suffer defeats owing to a flaw in their cloning process, and are forced to consolidate their forces within the Madillon Cluster.

The war ended three hundred thousand years before the end of humanity, resulting in the greatest demobilisation in universal history (*The Infinity Doctors*). Far, far in the future, the two races apparently merge (*Father Time*).

92 *FP: The Eleven-Day Empire*

93 *The Infinity Doctors*. The war has lasted as long as the Time Lord civilisation.

The Time Lords colonised planets such as Dronid and Trion. Sharing their secrets with lesser races, though, led to disaster. Evolution on Klist was reversed, and the civilisation on Plastrodus 14 went insane.[95] **Eventually, the Time Lords recognised the dangers of intervention when their attempts to help the Minyans resulted in the destruction of Minyos.**[96]

The Time Lords interfered on Micen Island, resulting in chemical and biological warfare and the destruction of the entire civilisation. The Time Lords built the Temple of the Fourth on the ruins, and codified the Oath of the Faction. They scattered in repentance for what they had done.[97]

The Time Lords remained content to observe, but monitored the universe and tried to prevent other, less principled races from discovering the secrets of time travel.[98] **They occasionally sent out ambassadors and official observers.**[99] **They also attempted to enforce bans on dangerous technology.**[100]

For more information on the history of the Doctor's people, see the Gallifrey section at the end of this book.

The Ancient Past

Before life evolved on other planets, the Exxilon civilisation was already old.[101] Other races such as the Raab of Odonoto Ceti, a race on Benelisa and the Cthalctose of 16 Alpha Leonis One evolved.[102] The Vondrax were among the universe's oldest sentient races.[103]

(=) THE NOWHERE PLACE[104] **->** More than fifty billion years ago, a dominant life-form evolved on Earth and would develop space travel in future. However, a mishap occurred during the race's first attempt to journey out of the solar system. A missetting of the spaceship's coordinates - when paradoxically combined with the energy of a nuclear missile strike in 2197 - resulted in the engines getting caught in their own time warp. The hyper-spatial equivalent of a Möbius Strip was created, and ripped the entire race out of space and time. They were consigned to the realm known as Time's End: a point at which all cosmic laws were invalidated.

Other dominant species would evolve on Earth, but the original race - consumed with madness and jealousy, and using the insane logic of Time's End to its advantage - subverted each race's bid for space travel. Each new race was erased from history, made to suffer continuously in the matter-crushing forces of Time's End. Billions of Earth-born species were snared in this fashion.

The original race tried to capture humanity, but the sixth Doctor ventured into Time's End and reprogrammed the original race's spaceship coordinates into a linear fashion. The nuclear strike from 2197

94 "Pureblood". The Doctor's assertion that the Sontaran/Rutan war started "ten centuries" before can't be right, as it would mean it started in the 1500s - in other words, after *The Time Warrior*. Other stories place the start of the war far back in Earth's prehistory.
95 *The Quantum Archangel*
96 *Underworld*
97 *Death Comes to Time*
98 *The War Games*
99 *The Two Doctors, The Empire of Glass.*
100 *Carnival of Monsters, The Empire of Glass.*
101 *Death to the Daleks*
102 *Frontier Worlds, The Taint, Eternity Weeps.*
103 TW: *Trace Memory*
104 Dating *The Nowhere Place* (BF #84) - The Doctor dates a tool of the original species - a mysterious door in 2197 - as being "more than fifty billion years old". This is a scientific absurdity, given that the universe is no more than fifteen billion years old.
105 *The God Complex*
106 Dating *A Death in the Family* (BF #140) - The Doctor tells Hex that they've arrived, "billions of years before your time, billions of years before your sun's time... the universe is a baby". Scientific consensus is that Earth's sun formed about 4.6 billion years ago, so this is some time prior to that.
107 *A Death in the Family*. Hex arrives on Pelican in

"local year 1871 AC", and the older Doctor takes the Handivale away in "local year 2192 AC". Although it isn't said, "AC" presumably means "After Crash" (of the timeship *Pelican*).
108 Dating *Eternity Weeps* (NA #58) - It is "six billion years ago" (p3).
109 Dating "Time Witch" (*DWW* #35-38) - Brimo was imprisoned "at a time before the Earth was formed" according to the opening caption. She says she was imprisoned for "millions of years", but even that might be an underestimate - the Doctor's encounter with her could well take place at any time in this timeline. Her situation inside the black hole is very like Omega's in *The Three Doctors* (and *The Infinity Doctors*), although there's no indication she's trapped there.
110 *Genocide* (p279).
111 *SJA: Prisoner of the Judoon*
112 *Inferno*
113 "Billions of years" before *The Runaway Bride*.
114 *Peacemaker*. The Racnoss were an ancient race, around before the Earth formed. Even if the Movellans were not the historic foes of the Clades' creators, the Doctor seems comfortable implying that the Movellans existed many billions of years ago. *A Device of Death* and *War of the Daleks* have different (and also mutually incompatible) accounts of the origins of the Movellans.

destroyed the vessel rather than creating the Möbius Strip, which obliterated the original species. Time's End was either nullified or moved. The dominance of humanity and its time-stream was assured.

The planet Tivoli was home to one of the oldest civilisations in the Milky Way; the mole-like inhabitants there endured because they capitulated to all invaders, and became the most invaded planet in the galaxy. Their anthem was *Glory to [Insert Name Here]*.[105]

c 7,000,000,000 BC - A DEATH IN THE FAMILY[106] ->

Billions of years before Earth's sun was active, a planet existed with Earth-like conditions. It became the home to English-speaking humans aboard the timeship UNS *Pelican*, who named the planet after their vessel. In the two millennia to follow, their descendants established the Handivale: a living, never-ending tale that was recited by a succession of Storytellers. Remembrances of people who had died were included in the Handivale, and were thereby said to survive in the afterlife.

Evelyn Rossiter (née Smythe) was transported through time to Pelican and lived with the people there. Two years later, she found the wreckage of the original timeship. Five years after that, she had a seat on the ruling Counsel.

An older version of the seventh Doctor left Hex in Evelyn's care as part of his ongoing struggle with the Word Lord - a linguistic being from a reality governed by language instead of physics, and who travelled in a Conveyance of Repeating Dialogue in Space-Time (CORDIS). Hex became Evelyn's ward, and read a fictional account of Ace into the Handivale, creating a linguistic version of her in 2028.

At least six months after Hex's arrival, Evelyn suffered a mortal heart attack while lecturing at Pelican University. The seventh Doctor and Ace arrived with the comatose Captain Stillwell of UNIT, who had within him the future version of the Handivale. Convinced that the Word Lord posed a threat to all living matter in the universe, Evelyn consented to have the Handivale transferred into her from Stillwell. She became the last Storyteller, and as she died, the Handivale died, and the Word Lord trapped within the Handivale died also.

About three hundred and twenty Pelican years after Evelyn's passing, the older seventh Doctor was given the contemporary Handivale so he could "combat great evil" with it. He became the Handivale's Storyspeaker, trapped a younger version of the Word Lord within the living story, and then sealed himself inside a Gallifreyan sarcophagus that would came to reside in the archives of the Forge.[107]

c 6,000,000,000 BC - ETERNITY WEEPS[108] ->

Jason Kane used a time ring to reach 16 Alpha Leonis One, the home of the Cthalctose. He met the Astronomer Royal, who had detected a black hole in their solar system and provided force field technology. Jason was placed in a stasis field and watched the Cthalctose civilisation develop for five hundred years. The Cthalctose attempted to contain the black hole, but eventually could no longer power the force fields. Unable to save themselves, they built a device, "the Museum", that could convert another world to resemble their own. This entailed using a terraforming virus that would generate sulphuric acid, which was present in the seas on their homeworld. The Cthalctose launched the Museum out of their solar system, and the forces of the black hole destroyed 16 Alpha Leonis One. Jason Kane's stasis field failed and he returned to 2003.

? - "Time Witch"[109] ->

Before the Earth was formed, Brimo was imprisoned in an eternity capsule for attempting to dominate the planet Nefrin. She watched civilisations rise and fall, and when Nefrin's sun went nova, the capsule fell into the resulting black hole. Once there, she entered a realm where her thoughts became reality.

Later, the TARDIS was torn apart and the fourth Doctor and Sharon were pulled into a dimensional rift to Brimo's domain. The presence of the TARDIS started draining Brimo's abilities, and the Doctor fought a battle of wits with her, finally trapping her by getting her to imagine the eternity capsule. Restoring the TARDIS aged the Doctor and - more noticeably - Sharon by four years.

As Earth's solar system formed from dust, the Tractite named Kitig arrived through time via a time tree. As Kitig intended, this destroyed the time tree at the cost of his own life.[110] **The Veil, reptilians who could take command of other beings' bodies, were conquering worlds "when Earth was little more than a ball of superheated gas".**[111]

Earth formed billions of years ago.[112] **The Time Lords "got rid" of huon particles, which were capable of unravelling atomic structure.**[113]

An unknown race came under threat from an enemy - perhaps the Racnoss, the Null or the Movellans - and so designed the Clades, ruthless intelligent projectile weapons that bonded with their users. The Clades won the conflict in a matter of months, and went dormant for some centuries, their mere existence warding off potential threats. Eventually, the Clades found they lacked purpose without war, and destroyed their creators, leaving their star cluster burning. They became mercenaries, and would encounter the Doctor on Sierra Secundus, Tannhauser and New Mitama.[114]

4,600,000,000 BC - THE RUNAWAY BRIDE[115] -> The Time Lords and the "fledgling empires" all but eradicated the Racnoss: spider-like monsters who were born starving, and devoured entire planets. Four point six billion years ago, as the tenth Doctor and Donna witnessed, Earth formed around one of the last of the Racnoss ships. Without the huon particles needed to revive the Racnoss within, the creatures would sleep until the twenty-first century. The Empress of the Racnoss also survived, and retreated to the edge of the universe to hibernate.

When the Earth was formed, the Blessing - a space set between two rock edges, and possibly alive - was established as a secondary "magnetic" pole that ran West to East, exiting at the future locations of Singapore and Buenos Aires. Humanity would develop a symbiotic relationship with the Blessing, which transmitted a morphic field that encompassed every person. Anyone living in a two-mile radius of one of the Blessing's access points had a life expectancy equal to the average life expectancy of humanity.[116]

While the Earth was still forming, the Time Lords were in negotiations with the Tranmetgurans, trying to organise a planetary government and end the war that was ravaging the planet. The Hoothi - a fungoid group-mind that lived off dead matter and farmed entire sentient species - attacked Tranmetgura, introducing their dead soldiers into the battle. War broke out, and two thirds of the population were killed. The Hoothi harvested the dead, taking them aboard their silent gas dirigibles. When the Time Lords sent an ambassador to the Hoothi worlds, the Hoothi used him as a host and attempted to conquer Gallifrey. The Time Lords counter-attacked, and the Hoothi fled into hyperspace. The Hoothi vanished from the universe.[117]

The father of the Osirians, Geb, said that he was around "when the world burned the skin to touch it". He claimed to have torn open the Earth with his hands, and pulled his offspring - including Osiris, Sutekh and Nephthys - from it.[118]

A plague wiped out Curcurbites - machines that were fuelled by the blood of their enemies. The last of them fell into the magma of primeval Earth.[119] When the Sol system and its sun were new, and before life formed on Earth, a young space explorer passed nearby and activated his remote viewer. The device connected with a dimension that had no time, life or death - it was an empty darkness that hungered. The explorer died, and his ship eventually drifted into the Cardiff Rift.[120]

The universe passed the point when it would naturally collapse. It was sustained by the people of Logopolis, who opened CVEs into other universes.[121] When Earth's moon was in its infancy, a black, spherical rock from another galaxy crashed onto its surface. The alien bacteria on the rock would remain dormant for 3.9 billion years.[122]

Three billion years ago, carvings were made of the Great Old Ones on the planet Veltroch.[123]

c 3,000,000,000 BC - VENUSIAN LULLABY[124] -> The Venusians were an advanced race, surprisingly so since all metals were poisonous to them with the exception of gold, platinum and titanium. Their cities were crude, with the buildings in cities such as Cracdhalltar and Bikugih resem-

---

115 Dating *The Runaway Bride* (X3.0) - The Doctor and Donna witness the Earth's formation.
116 *TW: Miracle Day*. Jack says, "The world's been turning for over four billion years", in rough approximation with the age of Earth as given in *The Runaway Bride*.
117 *Love and War*
118 *FP: The Judgment of Sutekh*
119 "Tooth and Claw" (*DWM*). The Curcurbites know of the Time Lords.
120 *TW: Long Time Dead*
121 *Logopolis*. It's unclear when this happened, but there have been "aeons of constraint", and an aeon is a billion years.
122 "3.9 billion years" (pgs 120, 146) before *Heart of Stone*. The rock must have impacted the moon long before it started orbiting the Earth (*The Silurians*).
123 *White Darkness*
124 Dating *Venusian Lullaby* (MA #3) - The Doctor tells Ian and Barbara that they have travelled back "oh, about three billion years I should think".
125 *Interference*
126 "Billions of years" before *The Day of the Troll*.

127 "A thousand million years" before *Spearhead from Space*. This date is confirmed in "Plastic Millennium".
128 *Auton 2: Sentinel*
129 "A billion years" before *The Caves of Androzani*.
130 *The Impossible Planet*
131 "The Stockbridge Horror"
132 "4x10(2d8) yrs" ago, according to *The Gallifrey Chronicles*.
133 Dating *City of Death* (17.2) - Scaroth and the Doctor both state that the Jagaroth ship came to Earth "four hundred million years ago". Contemporary science has a number of estimates of when life on Earth started, but all are far, far earlier than that. *The Terrestrial Index* takes that as a cue to set this story three and a half billion years ago.
  SCAROTH OF THE JAGAROTH: In *City of Death*, we actually *see* Scarlioni, Tancredi and four other Scaroth splinters: an Egyptian, a Neanderthal (the one some fans think looks like Jesus - the DVD commentary notes that Julian Glover thought the same), a Roman and a Celt (although most reference books, including the earlier versions of this one, describe him as a Crusader),

bling soap-bubbles made from mud and crude stone, but the civilisation lasted for three million years.

By measuring the day, which got steadily longer, the Venusians calculated that their planet was dying. For tens of thousands of years, most of the Venusians were resigned to their fate. Most of the Venusian animal species had become extinct: the shanghorn, the klak-kluk and the pattifangs. To conserve resources, Death Inspectors killed Venusians who had outlived their useful lives. Anti-Acceptancer factions such as the Rocketeers, the Below the Sun Believers, the Magnetologists, the Water-breathers, the Volcano People and the Cave-Makers believed that they could escape their fate, but the majority saw them as cranks.

The first Doctor, Ian and Barbara visited Venus at this time, just as the Sou(ou)shi arrived to offer the Venusians a place within their spacecraft. The Sou(ou)shi were vampires, and wanted to consume the entire Venusian race as they did the Aveletians and the Signortiyu. The Venusians discovered this with the Doctor's help and destroyed the Sou(ou)shi craft. The debris from the ship entered the Venusian atmosphere, blocking some of the sun's rays and lowering the planet's temperature. This prolonged the Venusians' existence for another one hundred generations. The consciousness of the Sou(ou)shi survived and travelled to primeval Earth.

w - Time Lords from the future launched an unmanned warship to destroy Earth, the original homeworld of the Enemy. The ship travelled at sublight speeds, and three billion years would elapse before it arrived there in 1996.[125]

A plant-creature, Sphereosis, fell to Earth and grew beneath the soil.[126] **The Nestene, a race of pure energy, began their conquests a billion years ago.**[127] Nestene gestation chambers were established on many worlds - including Earth - long before intelligent life evolved on them.[128] **Around this time, the last seas dried up on Androzani Minor in the Sirius system.**[129] The Scarlet

system became home to the Pallushi - a mighty civilisation that would last a billion years until it fell into a black hole.[130]

The TARDIS was possessed by an elemental alien around 1983 and travelled back five hundred million years. Here the alien revelled in the forces of primeval Earth. The TARDIS returned, but the alien was free.[131]

The Great Provider began its intergalactic conquests four hundred million years ago.[132]

Life on Earth

c 400,000,000 BC - CITY OF DEATH[133] **-> An advanced race - the callous Jagaroth - wiped themselves out in a huge war. The last of the Jagaroth limped to primeval Earth in an advanced spaceship. The ship's pilot, Scaroth, attempted to take his vessel to power three - warp thrust - too close to the Earth's surface and the spacecraft detonated over what would later become the Atlantic Ocean.**

Scaroth was splintered into twelve fragments and materialised at various points in human history. He would influence humanity's development for tens of thousands of years. This culminated in the building of a time machine in 1979, which he used to return to the past in an attempt to prevent his ship exploding. The fourth Doctor, Romana and their ally Duggan prevented Scaroth from changing history.

Earth was a barren volcanic world, but it had already produced primordial soup, and the anti-matter explosion acted as a catalyst. Life on Earth began.

The explosion of the Jagaroth ship left a radiation trace that the Euterpians detected many millions of years later.[134]

Life evolved much as palaeontologists and geologists think that it did.

---

in that order, in the flashback at the start of episode three.

Further examination of this story can account for all twelve Scaroth splinters, assuming that none of them live for more than a century, and that they acquire Scarlioni's antiques while they are new. One Scaroth version (presumably the Neanderthal that we see) demonstrates "the true use of fire"; a second gives mankind the wheel; a third "caused the pyramids to be built" (we see this one both as a "human" Egyptian Pharaoh and as a Jagaroth on an ancient Egyptian scroll); a fourth caused "the heavens to be mapped"; the fifth is an ancient Greek; the sixth is the Roman that we see (a Senator, or possibly even an Emperor); the seventh is

the Celt that we see; the eighth gives mankind the printing press (presumably, this accounts for why Scarlioni has more than one Gutenberg Bible); the ninth is Captain Tancredi; the tenth is an Elizabethan nobleman (who obtains the first draft of *Hamlet*); the eleventh lives at the time of Louis XV (and is presumably the splinter who purchases the Gainsborough that's just been sold at the start of the story - he's named as Cardinal Scarlath in *Christmas on a Rational Planet*), and the twelfth is Carlos Scarlioni.
134 *Invasion of the Cat People*

Earth was home to a species of malignant wraiths that resided in the "lost lands". It was said that they hailed from the dawn of time, but these creatures, who resembled evil fairies, had their origins in humanity's children. They came to reside backwards and forwards in time, became invisible to detection and took to murdering people in their sleep. They had control of the elements, and were especially protective of their own: children named the "chosen ones".[135]

Werewolves were among the oldest races on Earth. The werewolf Stubbe claimed to have been around at the Earth's creation.[136]

Around two hundred and sixty million years ago, the Permians - skeletal, lizard-hipped carnivores, bound together by a bioelectric field - were top of the food chain on Earth. They had a degree of intelligence, and the ability to mentally guide other creatures. They consumed electrical energy from living things, and were so efficient as predators that they wiped out 96% of life on Earth. With food becoming scarce, the Permians fed off each other. The last few of them went dormant and became fossils.[137]

In the 1970s, Dr Quinn discovered a colony of reptile people living below Wenley Moor in Derbyshire. They were the remnants of an advanced lost civilisation, and had spent many million years in hibernation. Quinn mistakenly believed that they came from the Silurian Period, and had a globe showing the Earth as it was before the great continental drift, two hundred million years ago.[138]

c 200,000,000 BC - "Time Bomb"[139] -> The Time Cannon of the Hedrons sent the sixth Doctor, Frobisher and TARDIS from the year 2850 far into the past of Earth. This was the destination for all the genetic impurities of

that world - including many dead bodies that went on to influence genetic development on Earth.

The seventh Doctor watched the first Lungfish walk on a Devonian beach.[140]

The Age of the Dinosaurs

One hundred and sixty-five million years ago, dinosaurs started to emerge on Earth.[141] In a different galaxy from Earth, which had become known as Home galaxy, a number of advanced races made contact and reengineered themselves so that they could interbreed. They developed advanced artificial intelligence technology. The People and Also People constructed the Worldsphere: a Dyson sphere that completely enclosed the star Whynot, with a surface area six hundred million times larger than that of Earth. The regulating intelligence of the Worldsphere became known as God.[142]

An unnamed race created the Omnethoth, a sentient weapon that could alter its physical state, to conquer the universe. The Omnethoth killed its creators, seeded the universe with colonisation clouds and went dormant.[143]

While dinosaurs walked the Earth, the Millennium War was fought across the galaxy. The Constructors of Destiny had created the Mind of Bophemeral - the ultimate computer and the most massive object ever built - from black holes, blue dwarfs and strange matter. Bophemeral, though, went insane within instants and destroyed the Constructors. A thousand races, including the Time Lords, Daemons, Euterpians, Exxilons, Faction Paradox, Greld, Grey Hegemony, Kastrians, Maskmakers of the Pageant, Ministers of Grace, Nimon, Omnethoth, Osirians, People of the Worldsphere, Uxariens, Rutans and Sontarans

---

135 *TW: Small Worlds.* Jack says the fairies are "from the dawn of time" - it's possible that he's speaking metaphorically, although in truth the fairies reside "backwards in time" and might pre-date humanity, even though they hail from it. Mention of the "lost lands" might suggest that they held more of a foothold on Earth until Scaroth's spaceship sparked humanity's birth. It might be far simpler, however, to assume that their development coincides with that of mankind.
136 *Loups-Garoux*
137 *The Land of the Dead*
138 *Doctor Who and the Silurians*
  CONTINENTAL DRIFT: According to scientists, continental drift is a continuing process. In *Doctor Who*, there's evidence that it was a single event. The Doctor talks of "the great continental drift, two hundred million years ago" in *Doctor Who and the Silurians*. In the broadcast version of *Earthshock*, the Earth of sixty-five million years ago looks like it does today. Continental drift was a reality according to *Invasion of the Cat-*

People. In *The Ark*, the Earth of ten million years hence also looks exactly like contemporary Earth, although we saw the continents devastated in *The Parting of the Ways*, and *The End of the World* acknowledges that technology was used to arrest continental drift.
139 Dating "Time Bomb" (*DWM* #114-116) - "Earthdate 200 Million Years BC", according to the caption.
140 *Transit.* This may be a dream sequence or an allegory.
141 In *Earthshock*, the Doctor states that the dinosaurs existed for "a hundred million years or so" and died out "sixty-five million years ago", which is in tune with scientific consensus.
142 *The Also People.* No date is given, but the People fight in the Millennium War in *The Quantum Archangel*.
143 "Millions of years" before *The Fall of Yquatine*. The Omnethoth also fight in the Millennium War according to *The Quantum Archangel*.
144 *The Quantum Archangel.* The Millenium Wars (consistently misspelled with one "n") were a feature of the

fought the Mind of Bophemeral and its drones. The planets Kastria and Xeraphas were devastated in the war, but Bophemeral was defeated. The Time Lords and People time-looped Bophemeral and the Guardians intervened, using the Key to Time to erase all knowledge of this War.[144]

c 150,000,000 BC - THE HAND OF FEAR[145] **->** On Kastria, the scientist Eldrad built spacial barriers to keep out the solar winds that ravaged the planet. He also devised a crystalline silicon form for his race, and built machines to replenish the earth and the atmosphere. Once this was done, he threatened to usurp King Rokon.

The Kastrians did not share Eldrad's dreams of galactic conquest, and so Eldrad destroyed the barriers. The Kastrians sentenced Eldrad to death. As killing a silicon lifeform was almost impossible, they constructed an Obliteration Module and sent it out into space, beyond all solar systems. The Module was detonated early at nineteen spans, while there was still a one-in-three-million chance that Eldrad might survive. The Kastrians elected to destroy themselves and their race banks rather than lead a subterranean existence. Eldrad's hand eventually reached Earth in the Jurassic Period, where it became buried in a stratum of Blackstone Dolomite.

(=) 150,000,000 BC - "Time Bomb"[146] **->** The sixth Doctor and Frobisher returned to the distant past from 2850 to discover that the Hedrons were disposing of bodies in this era, too. History might never be restored.

The Vardon-Kosnax War was meant to run fifty years, but disruption to history meant that it lasted three hundred.[147]

140,000,000 BC - TIME-FLIGHT[148] **->** The planet Xeraphas was the home of the Xeraphin, a legendary race with immense mental powers. It was rendered uninhabitable when it was caught in the Vardon-Kosnax War. The surviving Xeraphin came to Earth, hoping to colonise the planet, but they suffered from radiation sickness. They abandoned their physical forms, and became a psychic gestalt of bioplasmic energy until they were able to regenerate. The Master became trapped on Earth five hundred years after this and attempted to harness the power of the Xeraphin Consciousness.

Building a Time Contour Generator, the Master kidnapped a Concorde from the nineteen-eighties, and used the passengers as slaves in an attempt to penetrate the Xeraphin citadel. He was defeated when the fifth Doctor, Tegan and Nyssa followed him back through time and broke the slaves' conditioning.

About one hundred and thirty million years ago, the Plesiosaurus became extinct. Before this, the owner of a MiniScope kidnapped one of the species.[149]

The Doctor visited Earth at the time of the dinosaurs. He reckoned the Cretaceous Era was "a very good time for dinosaurs".[150] Professor Whitaker kidnapped various dinosaurs using his Timescoop.[151] The Rani visited this period and collected tyrannosaur embryos, one of which almost killed her later. She also expressed an interest in reviving the era with a Time Manipulator.[152] Millions of years ago, a Surcoth explorer was lost on Earth. His body eventually fossilised and was discovered in 1855.[153] The tenth Doctor and Martha visited the Cretaceous, and a tyrannosaurus chased them.[154]

Due to the Doctor's sabotage of his TARDIS on the planet Magnus, the Time Lord Anzor was sent on a slow ride back to an earlier era of time. The Doctor thought that

early *Doctor Who Weekly/Monthly* comic strips, but this would appear to be a different conflict.
145 Dating *The Hand of Fear* (14.2) - The Doctor identifies the rock in which Eldrad's hand was discovered, and twice tells Eldrad that he has been away from Kastria for "a hundred and fifty million years".
146 Dating "Time Bomb" (*DWM* #114-116) - The caption reads "Earthdate 150 Million BC".
147 *Neverland*. The war is referred to as over by *Time-Flight*. The Vardons are probably not the Vardans seen in *The Invasion of Time*. A Kosnax appears in *Cold Fusion*.
148 Dating *Time-Flight* (19.7) - The Doctor informs the flight crew of the second Concorde that they have landed at Heathrow "one hundred and forty million years ago". He states, correctly, that this is the "Jurassic" era, but then suggests that they "can't be far off from the Pleistocene era", which actually took place a mere

1,800,000 -10,000 years ago. *The Seeds of Doom* gives a more accurate date for the Pleistocene.
149 *Carnival of Monsters*. The Doctor states that the Pleisosaurus "has been extinct for one hundred and thirty million years". The MiniScope presumably captures its specimens in a Timescoop like those seen in *Invasion of the Dinosaurs* and *The Five Doctors*.
150 *Doctor Who and the Silurians, The Happiness Patrol*.
151 *Invasion of the Dinosaurs*. Whitaker tries to take Earth back to a "Golden Age," but there's no indication that this is the age of the dinosaurs, which would hardly be an Earthly paradise for humans. He uses dinosaurs to scare people out of London.
152 *The Mark of the Rani, Time and the Rani*.
153 "Cuckoo"
154 *Made of Steel*. The two dinosaurs seen are apatosaurus and tyrannosaurus, from the Upper Cretaceous.

Anzor could spend his time trying to bully molluscs and pterodactyls, and studying Mesozoic slime molds.[155]

Davros believed that any similarity between the Kaleds and Thals on Skaro was entirely superficial, and that their last common ancestors, if they ever had them, existed in the Planistavian Age, not long after life evolved on the planet. Thals were descended from urvacryls, a type of water snake; Kaleds from clam-like creatures. His evidence for this was that the two species' internal organs were completely different and that while there was a 50:50 ratio of male and female Kaleds, seven male Thals were born for every female.[156]

(=) c 100,000,000 BC - "A Glitch in Time"[157] -> The seventh Doctor and Ace arrived at a nexus point in Earth's history, the Cretaceous, and immediately met a team of time-travelling dinosaur hunters. Despite the Doctor's objections, they were convinced they were part of history and couldn't change it. They shot an early mammal... and a team of reptilian time-travelling hunters materialised to hunt apes. The two parties fighting inside the nexus cancelled each other out, and both returned to their respective futures.

(=) The paleontologist George Williamson tested his newfound time travel abilities by observing dinosaurs. Williamson's presence encouraged some saurian lizards to start walking upright and gain an evolutionary advantage, creating a parallel timeline. A dimensional doorway opened in Siberia, 1894, and some advanced saurians went through it. The timeline was erased due to the Doctor and Williamson's actions in 1894.[158]

(=) 80,000,000 BC - BENNY: THE SWORD OF FOREVER[159] -> A botched use of the Sword of Forever flung Bernice eighty million years back in time, where she was eaten by an intelligent velociraptor. The Sword destroyed Earth, but Benny's use of the item in 2595 re-created Earth's timeline.

c 65,000,000 BC - EARTHSHOCK[160] -> Sixty-five million years ago, the dinosaurs became extinct when the anti-matter engines of a space freighter that had spiralled back through time from 2526 exploded in Earth's atmosphere. The fifth Doctor's companion, Adric, died while trying to prevent the disaster.

Bernice Summerfield didn't know what had killed off the dinosaurs.[161]

c 65,000,000 BC - BENNY: THE ADOLESCENCE OF TIME[162] -> The freighter impact caused a giant dust cloud to settle on the Earth's surface, and released all manner of psychic forces. A race of reptile-people continued to reside on land and in the sea, even as their winged sister race farmed fish on a chain of islands floating above the devastation. The psychic forces slowly altered the reptiles' brains. A worm-monstrosity sought the blood of a time traveller, and - after reconstituting Benny's time ring - brought Peter Summerfield back through time. Peter misguidedly triggered warfare between the flying reptiles and the worm's misshapen minions, the worm-callers. The flying reptiles' farm belt was destroyed, and they started looking for food on the surface with their kin. Peter realised his mistake and asked the worm to return him to the future; the reptiles subsequently built a statue that regarded him as an abomination and a destroyer.

155 *Mission to Magnus.* The Doctor says that Anzor's TARDIS has been dispatched back to "the beginning of time," but his subsequent comments about the things Anzor might encounter there suggest he didn't mean the term literally. The Mesozoic era started 250 million years ago, and ended about 65 million years ago.
156 *I, Davros:* "Corruption". This is a cheeky explanation for why the male Thals so outnumber the females in all three of their TV stories. The Planistavian Age was "a hundred million years" ago according to Davros.
157 Dating "A Glitch in Time" (*DWM* #179) - It's "the Cretaceous," so between 145 and 65 million years ago.
158 "Several million years" before *Time Zero.*
159 Dating *Benny: The Sword of Forever* (Benny NA #14) - The timeframe is given.
160 Dating *Earthshock* (19.6) - The Doctor dates the extinction of the dinosaurs, and confirms that the freighter has travelled to that era, back "sixty-five million years". In the original TV version, the pattern of

prehistoric Earth's continents are those of modern-day Earth. A correction was attempted for the DVD release, where an effects option allows the viewer to see an updated special effect. However, the correction itself is historically awry, as it features the super-continent Pangea, when the proper configuration should be somewhere between Pangea and the present day.
161 *Benny: Epoch: Judgement Day*
162 Dating *Benny: The Adolescence of Time* (Benny audio #9.2) - The blurb says that the story occurs "many years" after the freighter collided with Earth (*Earthshock*) and enough time has passed that only one of the characters involved is old enough to have remembered the impact. The story helps to bridge the freighter impact with the rise of the Silurians; it's implied that the "psychic forces" released by the collision helped to develop the Silurians' third eyes, and the relocation of the flying reptiles to the ground presumably unifies the reptile-people into a single society. See the When Did The

(=) & 64,999,500 BC - THE BOY THAT TIME FORGOT[163] **->** The fifth Doctor's application of Block Transfer Computation in Victorian England made real his subconscious desire that Adric should live, and enabled Adric to enter new course computations into the freighter's computer before impact. The vessel still grounded itself on Earth, but Adric survived.

Adric found that the Cybermen's alien computer - which he named Star - could act as a psychic booster and make his ideas manifest. He created giant spiders that, using the crashed freighter as a foundation, built a City of Excellence. He also manifested millions of giant scorpions, who chanted Block Transfer Computations in "counting houses". This "song of the scorpions" sustained Adric beyond his normal lifespan - he lived for five hundred years as the scorpions' king. The scorpions ate all the reptiles in this era.

The Doctor, Nyssa, novelist Beatrice Mapp and faux adventurer Rupert Von Thal arrived from Victorian England in search of the hijacked TARDIS. The scorpions' bloodthirsty progenitors spurred a rebellion against Adric. Rupert was killed, but Adric used Star to relocate himself and the Doctor's remaining party back to Victorian England.

In Adric's absence, this timeline was sealed off into its own bubble of existence.

Sixty million years ago, a meteorite containing some Xylok - crystalline lifeforms - crashed to Earth and was buried.[164]

c 50,000,000 BC - THE COMPANY OF FRIENDS: "Benny's Story"[165] **->** A time fissure briefly relocated the eighth Doctor and Benny to the distant past on Epsilon Minima. During a lion attack, the Doctor lost some buttons and the TARDIS key - in future, both would get buried in a coal seam. He also located the fissure, enabling him and Benny to return to her era.

A hundred thousand years before the Silurians, the Earth had been ruled by "gargantuan entities".[166]

The Age of the Reptile People

On Earth, some reptiles had evolved into intelligent bipeds. There were three **distinct species: the land-based Silurians, who built a great civilisation in areas of extreme heat; their amphibious cousins, the Sea Devils; and a winged race.**[167] **There were different races of Silurians, "cousins" to one another.**[168]

Silurian civilisation started as scattered clans, which were eventually united by Panun E'Ni of the Southern Clan, whose deeds were recorded in the Hall of Heroes. Panun E'Ni was deposed by Tun W'lzz, who freed the enslaved tribes to create a united Silurian civilisation.[169]

Silurians had advanced psychic powers, which seemed to be concentrated through their third "eye". They had telekinetic and hypnotic abilities, could project lethal blasts of energy and establish invisible force fields. Much of their equipment was operated by mental commands, although the Silurians were also known to use an almost-musical summoning device. Much of Silurian technology appears to have been organic. The Silurians domesticated dinosaurs, using a tyrannosaur species as watchdogs. They constructed the Disperser, a device capable of dispersing the Van Allen Belts.[170]

They used brontosaurs to lift heavy loads, and dilophosaurs as mounts. They communicated using a sophisticated language that was a combination of telepathy, speech and gesture. They had Gravitron technology which allowed a sophisticated degree of weather control. They travelled in vast airships.[171]

The Silurians had technology far in advance of humanity in 2020, including methods of energy generation and water supply.[172] Their science was more advanced than human technology of the late twenty-first century, with particle suppressors and advanced genetic engineering. They also created creatures such as the Myrka, a ferocious armoured sea monster. Silurian law prevented all but defensive wars, but the

Silurians Rule The Earth? sidebar.
163 Dating *The Boy That Time Forgot* (BF #110) - Adric claims to be "more than five hundred years old", so that long (give or take) has passed since *Earthshock*.
164 *SJA: The Lost Boy*
165 "Fifty million years" before *The Company of Friends: "Benny's Story"*.
166 *All Consuming Fire*
167 *Doctor Who and the Silurians, The Sea Devils, Benny: The Adolescence of Time.* See the When Did the Silurians Rule the Earth? sidebar.
168 According to the Doctor in *The Hungry Earth.* This line accounts for the physical differences between the

Silurians in that story and their previous appearances, and presumably also accounts for the differences between the Silurians in *Doctor Who and the Silurians* and those in *Warriors of the Deep* (and, by extension, the winged race in *Benny: The Adolescence of Time*).
169 *The Scales of Injustice*
170 *Doctor Who and the Silurians*
171 *Blood Heat*
172 According to Eldane in *Cold Blood.*

Sea Devils had elite army units and hand-held weaponry, and the Silurians built submarine battlecruisers.[173] Silurian bioengineering technology was usually only seen on jungle planets.[174]

The Silurians lived in vast crystalline cities with imposing architecture.[175] One estimate is that their technology was three or four hundred years more advanced than Earth in the twentieth century. A provision of Silurian law was to execute members of different castes who mated. Strict laws also prevented experiments into genetic engineering and nuclear fission.[176]

Turtles existed at the time of the Sea Devils, much as they do in our time. Sea Devils didn't eat meat.[177] The Silurians worshipped the Great Old Ones, with the Sea Devils venerating Dagon in particular.[178] They also worshipped a lizard "devil god", Urmungstandra.[179]

The Prime Serpent was a Silurian deity.[180] The Old Ones visited Earth when man was just an ape.[181]

> = The Silurian scientist Mortakk performed illegal genetic experiments. He was tried and executed before the great hibernation.[182]

The Silurians saw apes as pests who raided their crops, and developed a virus to cull them.[183] Silurians also ate the apes, using Myrkas to hunt them.[184] Apes were caged and tortured.[185] The Silurian warrior Restac and others of her group hunted apes for sport.[186]

Silurian scientists detected a rogue planetoid, and calculated that as it passed by Earth, it would draw away Earth's atmosphere and destroy all life on the surface. The Silurians built hibernation shelters deep underground to survive the catastrophe.[187]

The Silurians' preparations took twelve years. Silurian hybrids were sent to Shelter 429.[188]

? - "Twilight of the Silurians"[189] -> Apes in the wild were beginning to organise into packs and attack vulnerable Silurians. One ape, Kin, had emerged as a leader and was captured. Many Silurians viewed the threat of the approaching moon as a scare story, but new calculations revealled they were merely five days from disaster. Led by Kin, the apes escaped by rebelling against their captors.

? - BLOODTIDE[190] -> The surface of the Earth became a freezing wasteland. The Silurian scientist Tulok genetically augmented some of the apes to improve their flavour, and as a side-effect they also become sentient. As the Silurian Triad entered hibernation, Tulok was banished to the surface for the crime of illicit experimentation. He was rescued by his friend Sh'vak. They went to the hibernation chambers, and sabotaged the controls so that most of the species would not revive when planned.

The entire Silurian civilisation went into hibernation, they planned to sleep for thousands of years.[191]

The Silurians retired to their vast subterranean hibernation chambers, but the catastrophe they had predicted didn't happen - instead, the rogue planetoid settled into orbit around Earth and become its moon. Because the Silurians' hibernation mechanism was defective, they failed to revive as planned. In the Silurians' absence, the apes began to evolve a greater degree of intelligence. Before long, the only trace remaining of the reptile people were the race memories of these first hominids, the ancestors of mankind.[192] Through the millennia, the family of the Silurian scientist Malohkeh monitored the evolution of the apes as they became human.[193]

The planetoid was the moon containing the Museum of the Cthalctose. The gravitational forces wrecked havoc on

173 *Warriors of the Deep*
174 *The Hungry Earth.* The implication is that Silurians lived in jungle areas, although the next episode, *Cold Blood*, suggests they lived in deserts.
175 *Blood Heat, The Scales of Injustice, Bloodtide.*
176 *The Scales of Injustice*
177 "The Devil of the Deep"
178 *All-Consuming Fire*
179 *The Crystal Bucephalus*, named in *The Taking of Planet 5.* The name was spelled Urgmundasatra in *Benny: Twilight of the Gods.*
180 "Final Genesis"
181 *Tomb of Valdemar*
182 "Final Genesis". This is set in a parallel universe, and it's unclear if Mortakk also lived in ours.
183 *Doctor Who and the Silurians*
184 *Bloodtide*
185 *The Scales of Injustice*
186 *Cold Blood*

187 *Doctor Who and the Silurians*
188 *The Scales of Injustice*
189 Dating "Twilight of the Silurians" (*DWW* #21-22) - It's "millions of years before history began". There's a note to the effect that the Silurians are also known as Eocenes.
190 Dating *Bloodtide* (BF #22) - It's set at the time the Silurians are going into hibernation, "over a million years ago", and "ten years" after Earth's surface has become uninhabitable. In *Doctor Who and the Silurians* and *The Scales of Injustice*, it's stated that the Silurians don't revive because Earth's climate stabilises below the levels the Silurians set. In *Bloodtide*, Tulok claims he prevented the reactivation, and the Doctor finds evidence of his sabotage.
191 *Cold Blood*
192 *Doctor Who and the Silurians*
193 *Cold Blood.* It's unclear if Malokeh's family remained awake the whole time, or periodically woke up to check

WHEN DID THE SILURIANS RULE THE EARTH?: There are a number of contradictory accounts in the TV episodes and the tie-in series of when the Silurian civilisation existed, and it's impossible to reconcile them with each other, let alone against scientific fact.

A lot of the dating references are vague: *Doctor Who and the Silurians* says the Silurians "ruled the planet millions of years ago". *The Scales of Injustice* states the Silurians existed "millions of years" and "a few million years" ago, but also uses the term "millennia". *Bloodtide* says it was "many hundreds of thousands of years ago" and "over a million years ago". *Eternity Weeps* shows the arrival of the moon in Earth orbit. However, it's inconsistent with its dating, stating that this happened both "twenty million" (p127) and "200 million" (p117) years ago. In *The Hungry Earth*, the Doctor says that a Silurian is "300 million years out of [her] comfort zone".

Ironically, the one thing we can safely rule out is that the Silurians are from the actual Silurian Era, around 438 to 408 million years ago. Life on Earth's surface was limited to the first plants, and the dominant species were coral reefs. The first jawed fishes evolved during this era. If nothing else, in terms of *Doctor Who* continuity (according to *City of Death*), this is before life on Earth starts. It's Dr. Quinn who coins the name "Silurian" in *Doctor Who and the Silurians*. Despite the name being scientifically inaccurate, everyone at Wenley Moor - including the Doctor - uses it. We don't learn what the reptile people call themselves, but the Doctor calls them "Silurians" to their face and they don't correct him. The on-screen credits also use the term.

In *The Sea Devils*, when Jo calls the reptile people "Silurians", the Doctor replies, "That's a complete misnomer. The chap that discovered them must have got the period wrong. Properly speaking, they should have been called the Eocenes". Yet the Doctor never uses the "correct" term. The novelisation of *Doctor Who and the Silurians* (called *The Cave Monsters*) called them "reptile people", and the word "Silurian" only appears as a UNIT password. The description "sea devil" is coined by Clark, the terrified sea fort worker in *The Sea Devils*, and the term appears in the on-screen credits for all six episodes. Captain Hart refers to them as "Sea Devils" as though that's their name. For the rest of the story, the humans tend to call them "creatures" while the Doctor and Master refer to them as "the people".

By *Warriors of the Deep* and *Blood Heat*, however, the reptiles have adopted the inaccurate human terms for their people. *Bloodtide* starts with a flashback where Silurians refer to themselves by that name in their own era. In *Love and War*, we learn that the Silurians of the future "liked to be called Earth Reptiles now", and that term is also used in a number of other novels. The designation "homo reptilia" that crops up in a number of places is scientifically illiterate. In *Blood Heat,* the Doctor uses the term "psionsauropodomorpha".

In *Doctor Who and the Silurians*, Quinn has a globe of the Earth showing the continents forming one huge land mass, the implication being that it's the world the Silurians would have known. *The Scales of Injustice* follows this cue. Scientists call this supercontinent Pangaea, and date it to 250 to 200 million years ago. Again, this seems too early, as it predates the time of the dinosaurs.

That said, while most fans have assumed - and the tie-in media stories have often stated - that the Silurians come from the same time as the dinosaurs (around 165 to 65 million years ago, according to science, *Benny: The Adolescence of Time* and the Doctor in *Earthshock*), there is no evidence on screen that the Silurians were contemporaries of any known dinosaur species. In *Doctor Who and the Silurians*, the Silurians have a "guard dog" that's a mutant, five-fingered species of tyrannosaur that the Doctor can't identify, and in *Warriors of the Deep,* we see the lumbering Myrka. Likewise, while it seems obvious to cite the extinction of the dinosaurs and the fall of Silurian civilisation as owing to the same events, it's not a connection that's ever made on screen. Indeed, we know from *Earthshock* that the dinosaurs were wiped out in completely different circumstances than the catastrophe that made the Silurians enter hibernation.

The key plot point with the Silurians' story is not that they existed at the time of the dinosaurs, it's that as their civilisation thrived, the apes who were humanity's ancestors were mere pests. The Sea Devil leader in *The Sea Devils* says "my people ruled the Earth when man was only an ape". *Bloodtide* says the Silurians ruled "while humanity was still in its infancy", and goes on to specify that the apes at the time were Australopithecus. The earliest evidence for that genus is around four million years ago - which ties in with the date for the earliest humans in *Image of the Fendahl*. Although *Doctor Who* continuity has established that humanity dates back millions of years more than scientists would accept, it doesn't seem to stretch anything like as far as the Eocene, 55 to 38 million years ago.

We don't know how long Silurian civilisation stood. One solution to the dating problem might be to say that it lasted for tens or even hundreds of millions of years, from before the dinosaurs (and surviving their extinction) through to the time of the apemen. But, all accounts have the reptile people as a technologically-advanced, innovative, stable and centrally-controlled civilisation. When they entered hibernation, they were merely "centuries" ahead of the twentieth century humans. This would seem to point to a civilisation lasting thousands of years rather than millions.

We have to conclude that the Silurians and apelike human ancestors were contemporaries, and that Silurian civilisation ended long after the time of the dinosaurs. There are more than sixty million years to fit the Silurians in, then, including the Eocene period that the Doctor cited in *The Sea Devils*. It seems most likely, though, that the Silurians flourished for a few millennia at some point in the last five to ten million years.

Earth, destroying many Silurian shelters. Race memories of this event survived in human mythology as a great flood.[194]

The Birth of the Cybermen

There have been a number of accounts of the origins of the Cybermen.[195]

Millions of years ago, a twin planet to Earth - Mondas - was home to a race identical to humanity (indeed, Mondas was an old name for Earth). Mondas started to drift out to the edge of space.[196]

It soon became clear that the Mondasian race was becoming more sickly. Their life spans were shortening dramatically and they could only survive by replacing diseased organs and wasted limbs with metal and plastic substitutes. A new race was born.[197]

"Mondas had a propulsion unit, a tribute to Cyber-engineering - though why they should want to push a planet through space, I have no idea." [198]

Mondas had been created by the Constructors of Destiny to research collective intelligence.[199]

? - "The Cybermen"[200] **->** On Earth's twin planet of Mondas, the Silurians created monsters: the all-devouring Titan R'lyeh and the giant Golgoth, the distillation of the greatest reptilian bloodstock. The Silurians eventually imprisoned them.

Mondas spun away from the sun, but was still habitable. The Silurians became tyrants, the unquestioned rulers of the world and augmented the apes to make cybernetic servants. Eventually, the reptiles were driven into hiberna-tion by worsening conditions.

After a thousand years, and the Millennium Winter, the Cybermen had evolved from the augmented apes. They destroyed their former masters and set out to conquer the planet, but soon discovered - when they accidentally released R'lyeh - that they were not the only surviving creations of the lizard kings. A lost Cyber-mission returned as phantoms, then the Cybermen fought necromantic Sea Devils and their deity, Golgoth. He created a son, then destroyed himself and the Cybermen in a battle lasting forty days and nights. The Cyber-civilisation fell.

Mondas and Marinus were the same planet.[201]

? - THE KEYS OF MARINUS[202] **->** The people of the planet Marinus built the Conscience: a machine that originally served as an impartial judge, but eventually became capable of radiating a force that eliminated crime, fear and violence for seven centuries. Yartek, the Voord leader, learned how to resist the Conscience, and thus his followers robbed and cheated without any resistance. The scientist Arbitan deactivated the Conscience, hiding the five micro-keys needed to operate it around the planet; this prevented the Voord from using the device to control the population.

The first Doctor, Susan, Ian and Barbara arrived on Arbitan's island. They recovered all the keys on Arbitan's behalf, but returned to find that Yartek had killed Arbitan and taken control of the Conscience. Ian tricked Yartek by giving him a facsimile of one of the keys, but once it was inserted into the Conscience, the duplicate broke under the strain. The Conscience exploded, killing Yartek.

progress, just as it's not explained why they didn't bother waking the other Silurians at any point after they realised the Earth was habitable once more.
194 "Twenty million years, give or take" before *Eternity Weeps*, according to Benny.
195 See The Creation of the Cybermen sidebar.
196 *The Tenth Planet*
197 *The Tenth Planet*, and elaborated in *Spare Parts*.
198 According to the sixth Doctor in *Attack of the Cybermen*. The implication seems to be that Mondas left the solar system deliberately and under its own power. However, *Spare Parts* shows the propulsion unit first being used at the far end of Mondas' journey.
199 *The Quantum Archangel*
200 Dating "The Cybermen" (*DWM* #215-238) - "The Cybermen" strip covered the early history of Mondas. It places the creation of the Cybermen in the Age of the Reptile People, which may or may not support the date for the creation of the Cybermen less than five million years ago given in "The World Shapers" (see the When

Did the Silurians Rule the Earth? sidebar).
201 "The World Shapers"
202 Dating *The Keys of Marinus* (1.5) - There is no way of dating this story in relation to Earth's history, but taking the comic strips into account, it has to happen before "The World Shapers". As it's set on Mondas, the only place it can fit is after the first fall of the Cyberman civilisation seen in "The Cybermen".

There's confusion within the chronology of the story - Arbitan seems to state that Yartek is at least thirteen hundred years old (as the Conscience was built two thousand years ago, and Yartek broke its conditioning after seven centuries). Arbitan has been working to upgrade the Conscience to defeat the Voord, and he and his followers have hidden the micro-keys around the planet, but there's no indication of how long Arbitan's been at work. Arbitan is mortal and feeling the effects of old age, and there's nothing to suggest anyone on Marinus has anything other than a normal human lifespan.

THE CREATION OF THE CYBERMEN: The origin of the Cybermen (in our universe, at least) has never been depicted on television, but the broad facts were established in *The Tenth Planet*, with additional information in *Attack of the Cybermen*.

DWM has offered two distinct origins, Big Finish a third. (The creator of the Cybermen, Gerry Davies, pitched his own origin story for television in the eighties, and this was reprinted in Virgin's *Cybermen* book.)

The three origin stories that were made might seem to contradict each other, but none of them contradict what we learn on TV. They can, with a little imaginative licence, all be reconciled with each other.

"The World Shapers" appears to diverge the furthest from the television account, roping in the planet Marinus and making the Cybermen the descendants of the Voord from *The Keys of Marinus,* but the story doesn't contradict anything like as much as it seems. The Voord are human underneath their wetsuits, and they become Cybermen to survive global environmental collapse. It would mean Marinus is Earth's twin planet - which is a stretch, but not an enormous one. (We know from *The Keys of Marinus* that it's a planet where humans, wolves, chickens, grapes and pomegranates can all be found.) The issue of Marinus/Mondas leaving the solar system isn't addressed, but neither is it ruled out.

"The Cybermen" strip in *DWM* takes fan speculation that links the Cybermen and Silurians, and is more consciously mythological in tone.

Spare Parts has, perhaps, the most orthodox interpretation of what we're told in *The Tenth Planet* - the civilisation on Mondas is roughly the equivalent of the mid-twentieth century, with a sickly population surviving in subterranean cities. Mondas travels into interstellar space, and as it does so, the population need to take existing medical technology to extremes to survive. Note that for a third time, an established *Doctor Who* race is part of the Cyberman recipe, as here the fifth Doctor's physiology provides the template for the future Cybermen.

These stories can be placed in order. The *DWM Cybermen* strip comes first - it's the only one that depicts Mondas leaving its original orbit. Not only that, it establishes that there's a period of three thousand years when Mondas settled into a new orbit where the Cyber-civilisation has collapsed and an advanced, fragmented human civilisation dominates. This is an ideal place to fit *The Keys of Marinus* and "The World Shapers" - all it needs is for (some of) the humans on Mondas now to think of their planet as "Marinus".

Again, this seems like a stretch - and, of course, it isn't what any of the writers intended or planned. But there *are* elements of Marinus technology in *The Keys of Marinus* that look remarkably like remnants or precursors of Cyber-technology: the Conscience itself is based around the idea of negative emotions being eliminated to create an ordered society and is built with "micro circuits"; the Troughton era Cybermen had hypnotic and sleep-inducing technology much like that of the city of Morphoton; in episode three, Darrius' experiments, like those of the Voord in "The World Shapers," have increased the "tempo" of nature; there's a group of soldiers frozen in ice; the Voord and Cybermen are the only two monsters the Doctor's ever met who were human once, have handles on their heads and wear wetsuits.

So... Mondas settled into its new orbit and became known as Marinus. Within a thousand years, the Conscience of Marinus was built and soon came to control the population. For seven hundred years, the planet knew total peace. Then Yartek learned how to resist the Conscience's influence - it's hard not to picture the second Doctor breaking Cyber-hypnosis in *The Wheel in Space* and *The Invasion*. The Voord's physical appearance might mean they've found some remnants of the legendary Cyber civilisation. They haven't abandoned emotions in favour of logic and the good of society, though - ironically, it's rather the opposite. If Yartek is part-Cyberman, it might explain why he apparently lives at least thirteen hundred years. Neither is it a paradox that Yartek manages to resist the Conscience - yes, the Conscience should have quelled his urge to break the conditioning if his intent was purely malicious, but it could have been an accident or motivated by... well, the fairly uncontroversial belief that having free will is a good thing. (The Doctor says as much at the end of *The Keys of Marinus* itself, and in many other stories.)

"The World Shapers" sees the Voord consciously evolving into Cybermen to survive sudden environmental collapse. We have to speculate to join the dots, but it's not a wild thing to do. The surface of Mondas is, once again, uninhabitable for humans. The *DWM* "Cybermen" strip explicitly states it also leaves its new orbit. The Voord understand the problem and are ready for it - they now achieve their aim, and take control of the planet (presumably there are at least some other survivors), and build subterranean cities (or merely extend them - their base is already underground in "The World Shapers"). Perhaps the most highly-evolved Voord - the ones who had become the Cybermen at the end of "The World Shapers" - became the Committee from *Spare Parts*.

Spare Parts itself is set later - how much later isn't specified - when the people of Mondas are used to their sickly, subterranean life. Without the Worldshaper, while they know their destiny, the early Cybermen have had to learn the science of cybernetics gradually - until the fifth Doctor comes along, at any rate.

? - "The Cybermen"[203] -> Three thousand years after the fall of their civilisation, the Cybermen were legends to the humans that ruled Mondas. Once again, the planet's orbit decayed. All life on the planet was extinguished, except for the reborn Cybermen.

? - "The World Shapers"[204] -> The sixth Doctor, Peri and Frobisher landed on a deserted area of the ocean on Marinus. They discovered a TARDIS and its dying pilot, who whispered "Planet 14" before dying, his regenerations exhausted. His TARDIS was an ostentatious new model that told the Doctor they had been sent by the High Council to investigate temporal disturbances.

Time had sped up on Marinus. The new TARDIS returned to Gallifrey, the Doctor and his companions to their Ship. The Doctor remembered hearing about Planet 14 in his second incarnation, but not the context. The travellers headed to the eighteenth century to meet up with Jamie McCrimmon - his companion at the time - to see if he remembered. As they left, a Worldshaper ship arrived at Marinus - Worldshapers reformed uninhabited planets, but were banned years after the Yxia system collapsed.

The Doctor's TARDIS returned a week later than it left... but the planet was a now rocky desert. The Voord captured the Worldshaper and used it to rapid-evolve themselves and sculpt time. They were becoming the Cybermen. The Doctor and Jamie sneaked into the Voord base and met the future CyberController. Jamie sacrificed himself, aging to death to destroy the Worldshaper. Time accelerated so that geological processes occurred in front of the Doctor's eyes. The effect died down, and the Doctor emerged from the TARDIS to find a group of Time Lords present.

Marinus had become Mondas. The Doctor lobbied for the Cybermen to be prevented from coming into being, but the Time Lords told him things were in hand.

A sect from Mondas, the Faction, believed in total conversion into cyborgs. They were at odds with the mainstream, who viewed the technology as a last resort. The Faction left Mondas for Planet 14.[205]

? - SPARE PARTS[206] -> The fifth Doctor and Nyssa arrived on Mondas when it was at the furthest point in its journey away from the Sun, on the edge of the Cherrybowl Nebula, "a crucible of unstable energy". Civilisation survived under the surface of the planet. Mondas was rife with diseases like TB, and "heartboxes" were common for cardiovascular problems. Mondas was ruled by a bionic group mind, the Committee, who were building Cybermen

203 Dating "The Cybermen" (*DWM* #215-238) - It's "three thousand years" after the previous strip.
204 Dating "The World Shapers" (*DWM* #127-129) - The story is set no more than five million years in the past, as the Time Lords calculate that the Cybermen will become a force for peace in that time, and they haven't even by our far future.

The Doctor mentions the Fishmen of Kandalinga, from the first *Doctor Who Annual,* and the TARDIS initially lands on a platform very like the one seen in the illustrations from that story. However, as the name suggests, that story was set on Kandalinga, not Marinus.

WHEN WERE THE CYBERMEN CREATED?: It's unclear when Mondas leaves the solar system. In *The Tenth Planet,* the Doctor says it was "millions of years" ago. The Cyberman Krang says it was "aeons", and an aeon is a billion years. But the Mondasians were "exactly like" humans when Mondas started to drift away. As the land masses of the "twin" planets of Earth and Mondas are identical, it seems logical that life evolved in the same way and at the same rate on both worlds (we have to gloss over the fact that aliens such as the Daemons and Scaroth accelerated human development on Earth, but presumably not on Mondas).

"The World Shapers" sets the origins of the Cybermen within five million years of the present day - the Time Lords, at least, believe the Cybermen will be a force for good five million years after their creation. David Banks, in both his *Cybermen* book and his novel *Iceberg,* dated Mondas' departure to 10,000 BC. *The Terrestrial Index*

concurred. Banks suggested that the "edge of space" was the Oort Cloud surrounding the solar system. The audio *Spare Parts* contradicts that, saying that Mondas reaches the Cherrybowl Nebula, and states that Mondas left orbit because of the moon's arrival. *Real Time* says Mondas left "millennia" ago. In a story outline for a proposed sixth Doctor story, *Genesis of the Cybermen,* Gerry Davis set the date of the Cybermen's creation at "several hundred years BC". *Timelink* notes that as the Fendahl planet was the "fifth" twelve million years ago, Mondas must have already left its orbit by that point.

Over the years, a number of fans - including the first two versions of *Ahistory* - have speculated that the Mondasians and the Silurians were contemporaries, linking the disaster that put the Silurians into hibernation with the one that threw Mondas out of its orbit. There's little to either support or contradict this in the stories themselves. The Cyberman design seems to echo the Silurian third eye at the top of the head, but the Cybermen clearly aren't cyborg Silurians. Not only are we told in *The Tenth Planet* that the Cybermen "were exactly like you [humans] once", the same story shows them with human hands, not reptilian ones. "The Cybermen" strip in *DWM,* though, ingeniously solves that problem by depicting the Cybermen as descendents of apes augmented by the Silurians.

The Virgin edition of *Ahistory* suggested that Mondas was subject to time dilation, explaining why the Cybermen weren't more advanced. *Timelink* and *The*

capable of working on the desolate surface of Mondas. The Cybermen were engineering a propulsion system to deflect Mondas away from the Nebula.

A scan of a tertiary lobe in the Doctor's brain suggested solutions to various organ rejection problems that had plagued the planet's Cyber-program, and the Cyber-templates were augmented with this new design. The Doctor realised he could do little to prevent history from unfurling as planned.

During the Miocene Era, around twenty-five million years ago, the rocks on which Atlantis would later be built were formed.[207] Certain minerals that caused blue grass to grow would not be present in Wales for twenty million years.[208] Twenty million years ago on Earth, Creodonts - a cross between a hyena and a bear, and the largest mammalian predators ever to walk the planet - went extinct.[209]

The Origins of Man

It's unclear when humanity evolved, and it depends on one's definition of humanity. Some estimates have men walking the Earth six million years ago. The scientific consensus in the 1970s was about four million.[210] The

Osirians helped a race of giant insects to build a civilisation on Mars, but became bored with them. The insects died out as other forces emerged on Mars.[211]

Twelve million years ago, on a nameless planet in our solar system that no longer exists, evolution went up a blind alley. Natural selection turned back on itself, and a creature - the Fendahl - evolved which prospered by absorbing the energy wavelengths of life itself. It consumed all life, including that of its own kind.

The Time Lords decided to destroy the entire planet, and hid the fact from posterity. But when the Time Lords acted it was too late, as the Fendahl had already reached Earth, probably taking in Mars on its way through. The Fendahl was buried, not killed. The energy amassed by the Fendahl was stored in a fossilised skull, and dissipated slowly as a biological transmutation field. Any appropriate life form that came within the field was altered so it ultimately evolved into something suitable for the Fendahl to use. The skull did not create man, but it may have affected his evolution. This would explain the dark side of man's nature.[212]

The Doctor visited Mars before it became a dead world.[213]

Death of Art reached the same conclusion. However, the continents on Mondas are exactly like those on Earth, so this theory doesn't account for the identical continental drift, assuming such a thing affected the ancient Earth in the *Doctor Who* universe.

205 "Ten thousand years" before the novel *Iceberg*, which uses the same dating system as David Banks' book *Cybermen*. This schism is the given explanation for the difference in appearance - and apparent lack of contact - between the Cybermen from *The Tenth Planet* and *The Invasion*.

206 Dating *Spare Parts* (BF #34) - There is no dating evidence in the story itself. It takes place when Mondas is at its farthest point from Earth and the implication is that the return journey will be much faster than the outward one, as it will be powered. *Spare Parts* could, then, take place a matter of decades before *The Tenth Planet* (and further evidence for this might be the Mondasian society of *Spare Parts* resembles Earth's in the mid-twentieth century).

That said, while it's never quite stated, Mondas seems to have left the solar system within the lifetimes of the older characters, not the "millions of years" the Doctor spoke of in *The Tenth Planet*. There's no indication that Mondas immediately set course for a return to the solar system. We know that the Cybermen didn't attend the Armageddon Convention (*Revenge of the Cybermen*) and that the Convention was signed in 1609 (*The Empire of Glass*), so that they were a force to be

reckoned with by the seventeenth century.

It therefore seems fair to speculate that the Cybermen piloted Mondas around the galaxy for a long time (certainly millennia) before finally returning to their native solar system.

207 *The Underwater Menace*

208 The presence of blue grass in *The Hungry Earth* tips the Doctor off to the presence of Silurians.

209 *Forty-Five*: "False Gods". The terminology is a bit off here; creodonts were an entire order of mammals whose members included the Megistotherium, said to be the largest mammalian predator.

210 When asked in *Autumn Mist* when humanity evolved, the Doctor says "the accepted figure's about half a million years, though its really nearer six". It's only one suggestion that human origins in the *Doctor Who* universe stretch further than conventional scientific wisdom would have you think. According to *Image of the Fendahl*, the Fendahl skull arrived on Earth twelve million years ago, just as the first humanoid bipeds evolved - this is eight million years before Dr. Fendelman had believed.

211 "Millions of years" before *FP: Ozymandias*. Presumably, these are the Martians wiped out by the Fendahl. It may also be a *Quatermass* in-joke, as *Quatermass and the Pit* depicted insectoid Martians who had become extinct millions of years before.

212 *Image of the Fendahl*

213 *The Creed of the Kromon*, which we might retroac-

c 12,000,000 BC - THE TAKING OF PLANET 5[214] ->
A Celestis outcast became concerned that the Celestis base of Mictlan might attract the Swimmers - beings large enough to crush the universe. The outcast hoped to destroy Mictlan before this occurred.

Using a Fictional Generator, the outcast brought the Elder Things from HP Lovecraft's work to life in Antarctica. This attracted Time Lord shock troops from the future, who slaughtered the Elder Things and subsequently readied a fleet of War-TARDISes. They intended to break the time-loop around Planet Five, hoping to use the Fendahl trapped within against the Time Lords' future Enemy.

A wounded TARDIS created a time fissure that would later be exploited by Professor Fendelman. The time-loop was breached, but this actually released the hyper-evolved Fendahl Predator: a Memeovore, capable of consuming conceptual thought. The Memeovore consumed Mictlan, and thus destroyed the Celestis, before the eighth Doctor banished it to the outer voids.

By now, the planets Delphon and Tersurus had developed their unique forms of communication.

The first true human became aware of herself and immediately developed a sense of self-doubt. The Scourge had established themselves in our universe.[215] It was believed that the 001 variant of Amethyst icosahedral plas-

mic virus No. 9007/41 came to reside in humanity during mankind's earliest evolution. Each human possessed one dormant particle of the virus, and passed it to their offspring.[216] The owl evolved on Earth around this time.[217]

Ten million years ago, a derelict primitive TARDIS from the war against the Vampires began orbiting the planet Clytemnestra. Human colonists from the Earth Empire of the thirtieth century would mistake it for a moon, and name it Cassandra.[218]

The Vo'lach feared that as the universe was constantly expanding, its matter would one day be exhausted. They constructed the Spire - a tower that would extract matter from the future and deposit it into the past - to prolong the universe's lifespan. From the moment of its activation, the Spire was a temporal paradox: if too successful, it would rob the Vo'lach of the motivation to build it in the first place. Two Planetcracker missiles came back in time from the twenty-sixth century and resolved the paradox by damaging the Spire, reducing its efficiency.

Upon finding that the missiles were of Vo'lach design, the Vo'lach became alarmed that their descendents were conquerors. Rather than let this occur, the Vo'lach committed mass suicide.[219]

The Carnash Coi, monstrous entities from a distant galaxy, conquered Earth six million years ago. Their violent empire self-destructed, and one of their citadels sub-

---

tively think is referring to *The Judgement of Isskar*.

LIFE ON MARS: The Fendahl couldn't have wiped out all life on Mars, as the Ice Warriors come from Mars and lived there at least from the time of the Ice Age on Earth (*The Ice Warriors*) until the twenty-first century (*The Seeds of Death*) and apparently far further into the future (*The Curse of Peladon*). It should be noted that in *Image of the Fendahl*, the Doctor only speculates that the Fendahl attacked Mars.

As it happens, *Image of the Fendahl* is not the only occasion that the show seemingly ignores the existence of the Ice Warrior civilisation on the Red Planet. *The Ambassadors of Death* has manned missions to Mars that don't encounter the Ice Warriors (yet they *do* meet another alien race there - one that's not from Mars itself). *Pyramids of Mars*, as the name suggests, has the Doctor and Sarah visiting a pyramid on Mars and never mentioning the Ice Warriors. We never see UNIT encounter the Ice Warriors, although *Castrovalva* has the fifth Doctor mimic his previous selves, and seems (unless, in his post-regeneration confusion, he's just marrying together two unrelated elements) to refer to an adventure with the Brigadier and the Ice Warriors. In *The Christmas Invasion*, UNIT knows that there are Martians, and that they don't look like the Sycorax. Humanity hasn't got as far as Mars by *The Seeds of Death*, explaining why they don't know about the Martians. It's harder to explain why Zoe, who is from a

time when the solar system has been explored, is unaware of them.

Some fans (as well as sources like the FASA roleplaying game) have concluded that the Ice Warrior civilisation was subterranean - a view that's practically taken for granted in the books and audios, even though there's no evidence for it on screen. The books and audios have made further attempts to explain why the Ice Warriors are not well-known to future humanity. In particular, *Transit* featured a genocidal war fought in the late twenty-first century between Earth and Mars. Its vision of most Martians leaving the planet - with a few left behind as an underclass to the human colonists - is depicted in later stories such as *GodEngine* and *Fear Itself*. (EDA).

Benny Summerfield is an expert on Martian history, but most accounts have her believing that the Martian civilisation is a dead one (or at the very least, that there are no Ice Warriors on Mars itself).

The Dying Days attempted to reconcile some of the UNIT-era accounts by depicting a Martian culture influenced by the Osirians, who are disturbed by a British space mission (and there's a fleeting reference to the aliens from *The Ambassadors of Death*). As it's set in 1997, it would explain why UNIT know what Martians look like in *The Christmas Invasion*, and some fans have interpreted the line in the TV episode as a reference to the book.

merged itself off the coast of what would become Alaska. The Carnash Coi within slept, dreaming of future conquests.[220] **The people of Trion were so horrified by an infestation of Tractators, it became embedded in their race memory.**[221]

Five million years ago on Earth, the climate of Antarctica was tropical.[222] Millions of years ago, an advanced civilisation on Betrushia built an organic catalyzer to test species for survival traits. The catalyzer exceeded its design and threatened all life it encountered, causing the inhabitants to build an artificial ring system that constrained the creature to Betrushia.[223] The people of Kirbili wiped themselves out millions of years ago.[224]

Millions of years ago, the neighbouring worlds of Janus Prime and Menda - respectively inhabited by giant spiders and a race of humanoids - ended a war. They agreed to build a doomsday device as a deterrent against further hostilities, and constructed a device that, if needed, would move a moon of Janus Prime and a moon of Menda into parallel orbit around the Janus system's sun. A hyperspace link between the two moons would then turn the sun into a black hole. The spiders wiped out the Menda humanoids anyway, but not before the Mendans seeded Janus Prime with isotope decay bombs. This made the spiders devolve into savagery, leaving the doomsday device untouched until 2211.[225]

By the time of the Pliocene on Earth, the Martian civilisation equivalent of the Industrial Revolution had already taken place.[226]

c 3,639,878 BC - GENOCIDE[227] -> A group of Tractites arrived from the future using a time tree. They established a colony on Earth, which threatened to wipe out humanity and give rise to a future where the Tractites controlled the planet. The eighth Doctor, aided by Jo Grant and Samantha Jones, tried to prevent this. Jo obliterated the Tractites and their colony with a laser cannon, preventing the aberrant future. The Doctor's Tractite ally Kitig stayed in this period to carve messages in rock for Jo and Sam to find 1.07 million years hence. At the end of his life, Kitig travelled back in time to destroy the time tree.

Three million years ago, civilisation had started on Veltroch.[228] When the People of the Worldsphere were young, their metaphors were powerful enough to restructure reality. In this manner, the concept of the "inner world" was seeded throughout the universe, and came to hollow out and reshape interior of the planet later known as Tyler's Folly. This facilitated the creation of Mankind Expects Pain, However Much It Seems To Outsiders (MEPHISTO), a conceptual entity who represented the need to feel pain even in a utopia.[229]

2,579,868 BC - GENOCIDE[230] -> Captain Jacob Hynes, a genocidal UNIT member, arrived through time with a virus intended eliminate all mammalian life on Earth. Jo Grant and Sam Jones prevented him from releasing a deadly prion, and some primitive humans killed Hynes. A message from the eighth Doctor's Tractite ally, Kitig, enabled Jo and Sam to find the buried TARDIS and locate the eighth Doctor 1.07 million years in the past.

? 2,500,000 BC - FROZEN TIME[231] -> The Martians gave one of their number, Arakssor, a life sentence because he wanted to lead his people to war. Arakssor and about twenty of his followers were frozen in Antarctica, with a group of Martians watching over them. The guards were betrayed and Arakssor's warriors broke free. A firefight led to everyone involved being covered in ice - the seventh Doctor was present, fell into freezing water and went comatose. Sediment congealed around him in the centuries to follow, and he would remain frozen until 2012.

---

214 Dating *The Taking of Planet 5* (EDA #28) - It is "about 12 million years ago" (p71). The Elder Things aren't the same as the Great Old Ones seen in Lovecraft's work, so there's no direct clash with this story and the Great Old Ones seen elsewhere in the *Doctor Who* novels.

Delphon was mentioned in *Spearhead from Space*, Tersurus got a mention in *The Deadly Assassin* but didn't appear until the Comic Relief sketch *The Curse of Fatal Death*. According to *Alien Bodies*, the Raston robots (*The Five Doctors*) are built on Tersurus.
215 *The Shadow of the Scourge*
216 *Blue Forgotten Planet*
217 *Just War*
218 *So Vile a Sin*
219 9.25 million years before *Benny: Ghost Devices*.
220 *Lurkers at Sunlight's Edge*
221 *Frontios*. Date unknown, but it's long enough

before the twentieth century that Turlough has the race memory, but doesn't otherwise seem to know the Tractators by name.
222 *The Seeds of Doom*
223 *St. Anthony's Fire*
224 *The Quantum Archangel*
225 *The Janus Conjunction*
226 *The Dying Days*
227 Dating *Genocide* (EDA #4) - It's 1.07 million years before 2,569,868 BC.
228 *The Dark Path*
229 Millions of years before *Benny: Down*.
230 Dating *Genocide* (EDA #4) - The precise date is given (p260).
231 Dating *Frozen Time* (BF #98) - The Doctor, upon his revival, says he was frozen "millions of years" ago. There is no evidence that Arakssor's imprisonment bears any

w - Godfather Morlock of Faction Paradox studied a South American missing link that was two million years old.[232] A humanoid race sent probes out into the galaxy to build transference pylons capable of teleporting people between solar systems at the speed of light. Ninety-nine percent of the probes failed, but the remaining 1% allowed the Slow Empire to be established.[233]

The Ulanti developed a technique called "bioharmonics", wherein they transformed their entire planet into a musical instrument and produced a natural melody using the biological rhythms of their ecosystem. The Ulanti homeworld was an unspoilt wilderness, and its music was incredibly sublime. Nonetheless, the Ulanti died out two million years ago. Some of their music would survive in ancient alien scripts in the archives on Nocturne.[234]

A million years ago, the Mastons of Centimminus Virgo became extinct.[235] The Hoothi made the first moves in their plan to conquer Gallifrey. They enslaved the Heavenites, keeping them as a slave race and turning their planet into a beautiful garden world.[236] The Tralsammavarians died out.[237] The planet Wrouth was an enormous diamond with a monetary value in excess of the number of molecules in the universe. For a million years, the planet had been defended by war asteroids. In that time, it attracted a number of attackers, including the Daleks (driven away by the Doctor and Captain Nekro) and the Gantacs.[238] An entity said to be "the spirit of the trees, the life force of nature" came to slumber in what

would become Wells Wood in Stockbridge. A pagan cult came to worship this Green Man, a.k.a. Viridios.[239]

The Ice Warriors of Mars had space travel a million years ago.[240] Around the same time, diamonds were formed in the remnants of a Jovian planet in the Caledonian Reef.[241] **The earliest splinter of Scaroth gave mankind the secret of fire in his efforts to accelerate human development.**[242]

The Thal civilisation had begun half a million years ago on Skaro, and writings survive from this time.[243] A quarter of a million years ago, the Monks of Felsecar began collecting objects and information.[244] **Two hundred thousand years ago, *homo sapiens* - "the most vicious species of all" - began killing one another.**[245] As man evolved, the alien entity that the TARDIS dropped off on primeval Earth was summoned. It took human form and existed "on the edge of fear", always seeking the TARDIS.[246] The Lobri were created in the collective unconscious of primitive mankind. They were xenophobia incarnate, living symbols of our fear of the alien.[247]

The planet Hitchemus was 7/8ths covered by ocean, and the shifting climate there threw the genetics of the indigenous species of tigers into flux. A generation of tigers was born hyper-intelligent and built a weather control system. However, the tigers' progeny lacked the increased intelligence of their parents - presumably as a survival mechanism to prevent the tigers from over-developing their limited resources. Before passing on, the intelligent

relation to Varga's mission (*The Ice Warriors*), and it could substantially pre-date it.
232 *FP: The Eleven-Day Empire*
233 "Millions of years" before *The Slow Empire*. The Empire lasts "two million years" once it has been set up.
234 *Nocturne*
235 *Slipback*
236 *Love and War*
237 *A Device of Death*
238 "A million years" before "Invaders from Gantac".
239 Viridios claims to have slept for "a million years" before *The Eternal Summer*. In real life, Viridios is a Celtic deity whose name means "Green Man" in the Celtic languages and Latin. Altar stones to Viridios have been recovered from Roman Britain; in *Doctor Who* terms, though, there's no evidence that Viridios-worship went any further than the Stockbridge area, with the Doctor describing it as "highly localized".
240 *The Dying Days*. They would send an expedition to Earth, as seen in *The Ice Warriors*. Its loss presumably convinced them to use their scarce resources another way, and put them off conquering our planet.
241 *Synthespians™*
242 *City of Death*. The earliest known use of fire was around 700,000 BC. Supporting this, the "second splinter" of Scaroth seen on screen is presented (somewhat confusingly) as a Neanderthal.

243 Measured from *The Daleks*, in which the Doctor says that the Thal records "must go back nearly a half a million years".
244 *Love and War*
245 *The War Games*
246 "The Stockbridge Horror"
247 "Ground Zero"
248 "Hundreds of thousands of years" before *The Year of Intelligent Tigers*.
249 *The Ice Warriors*. Arden states that the Ice Warrior Varga comes from ice dating from "prehistoric times, before the first Ice Age". Arden's team have discovered the remains of mastodons and fossils in the ice before this time. In *Legacy*, the Doctor states that Varga "crashed on Earth millions of years ago". *Timelink* favoured that Varga's ship fell to Earth in "10,000 BC"; *About Time*, acknowledging the vagueness of the evidence, said it was some undetermined point between "1,000,000 BC" and "8,000 BC".
250 According to Benny in *The Dying Days*.
251 *An Unearthly Child, Ghost Light*.
THE FIRST ICE AGE: According to *Doctor Who*, the Ice Age was a single event around one hundred thousand years ago. In reality, there were waves of ice ages that lasted for hundreds of thousands of years as the ice advanced and retreated. We may now be living in an interglacial period. *An Unearthly Child* seems to take

tigers built a hidden storehouse to preserve something of their developments. A generation of intelligent tigers would sporadically be born from time to time, with multiple generations of instinctive tigers in-between.[248]

The First Ice Age and Cavemen

A Martian ship crashed on Earth, and became encased at the foot of an ice mountain.[249] Ice Warrior spaceship designs changed little after this time.[250]

One hundred thousand years ago on Earth, the First Ice Age began. By this time, two rival groups of intelligent primates had developed: Neanderthals and *homo sapiens*.[251] Another group, the Titanthropes, became an evolutionary dead end. They possessed more intelligence than Neanderthals, but were more hostile and killed themselves off before the emergence of *homo sapiens*.[252]

The being named Light surveyed life on Earth for several centuries during the Ice Age. Ichthyosaurs were included in Light's catalogue, as were the Neanderthals. The Doctor visited a Neanderthal tribe and acquired the fang of a cave bear.[253]

The Daemon Azal wiped out the Neanderthals. Race memories of beings with horns and their science survived in human rituals. Light had preserved a single specimen - Nimrod - and a few individual examples of the race survived for tens of thousands of years.[254]

c 100,000 BC - AN UNEARTHLY CHILD[255] **-> The first Doctor, Ian, Barbara and Susan met a prehistoric tribe struggling to survive "the great cold", and was in the throes of a leadership struggle between Kal and Za. Ian

made fire, and the leadership dispute was settled in Za's favour when Kal was exposed as a murderer.

c 100,000 BC - THE EIGHT DOCTORS[255] -> The eighth Doctor observed his earlier self.

> **(=) 100,000 BC - TW: THE MEN WHO SOLD THE WORLD**[256] -> CIA agent Rex Matheson was thrown back in time from 2010 by a Ytraxorian Reality Gun. A caveman, Bent Low, confronted him.

The super-assassin Mr Wynter altered events so that the rogue CIA operative Cotter Gleason was displaced to 100,000 BC instead. Bent Low killed Gleason, and used the man's meat to feed his family.

The Cold, a form of intelligence, evolved in the Siberian ice. It became dormant as the planet warmed, but would emerge in the savage winter of 1963.[257] The Gappa - a race of telepathic hermaphrodites from Hydropellica Hydroxi, on the far side of the Milky Way - hailed from a cold planet with at least six moons. They became so adept at hunting their prey, they consumed each another until only one remained. Some Modrakanians transported the last Gappa to a snowy portion of Earth, but their spaceship disintegrated. Fire-wielding early humans drove the Gappa underground, where it was buried in an icefall. The tenth Doctor and Martha, having defeated the Gappa in 2099, recovered the bodies of the Modrakanians for burial.[258]

The box entity that the sixth Doctor flung into a space-time tear in 1965 fell into "the distant past", and arrived on a desolate asteroid. In the ages to follow, a spaceship

place at the end of the Ice Age: the caveman Za speaks of "the great cold" - although this might simply mean a particularly harsh winter. Similarly, the butler Nimrod talks of "ice floods" and "mammoths" in *Ghost Light*, and he's one of the last generation of Neanderthals. In *The Daemons*, the Doctor says that Azal arrived on Earth "to help *homo sapiens* take out Neanderthal man", and Miss Hawthorne immediately states that this was "one hundred thousand years" ago.

252 *Last of the Titans*
253 *Ghost Light*
254 *The Daemons, Ghost Light*. Science tells us that the Ichthyosaurs actually died out at the time of the dinosaurs. In *Timewyrm: Genesys*, Enkidu is one of the last Neanderthals. In reality, Neanderthals only evolved about one hundred thousand years ago and survived for about sixty thousand years, until the Cro-Magnon Period.
255 Dating *An Unearthly Child* (1.1) and *The Eight Doctors* (EDA #1) - Ian confirms in *The Sensorites* that the story is set "in prehistoric times". (*An Unearthly Child* itself never explicitly states that it's set on Earth, rather

than another primitive planet.) Now that we know that the production team called the first televised story *100,000 BC* at the time it was made (the title appears on a press release dated 1st November, 1963), dating the story has become a lot less problematical. Anthony Coburn's original synopsis of the story also gives the date as "100,000 BC".
The first edition of *The Making of Doctor Who* placed the story in "33,000 BC" (which is more historically accurate), but the second edition corrected this to "100,000 BC". *The Programme Guide* said "500,000 BC", *The Terrestrial Index* settled on "c100,000 BC". *The Doctor Who File* suggested "200,000 BC". *The TARDIS Special* claimed a date of "50,000 BC", *The Discontinuity Guide* "500,000 BC - 30,000 BC". *Timelink* says 100,000 BC. *About Time* leaned toward a date of "not much earlier than 40,000 BC".
256 Dating *TW: The Men Who Sold the World* (TW novel #18) - The year is given.
257 *Time and Relative*
258 "A hundred thousand years" before *Snowglobe 7*.

crashed on the asteroid and the box entity merged with a young boy to become The Wishing Beast. It subsisted off hapless travellers for three centuries until the sixth Doctor and Mel defeated it.[259]

The Galyari evolved as an intelligent lizard race that was descended from avians. They sought to overrun the homeworld of the Cuscaru, but the Doctor obtained the Galyari's Srushkubr, the "memory egg" deposited on every colony world. He destroyed it when General Voshkar of the Galyari refused to withdraw. This released a dose of neural energy that would taint the descendants of the Galyari present for generations. The Galyari later became nomads aboard a fleet of spaceships named the Clutch.[260]

The Doctor's role in this affair made the Galyari regard him as "the Sandman", a legendary killer of Galyari children. The threat of the Sandman's return helped to keep the Galyari's aggression in check.[261] The Witch Guards, an amorphous gestalt that absorbed their opponents' attributes, began operating as mercenaries.[262]

Scaroth, the Fendahl and the Daemons all continued to influence human development until the late twentieth century.[263] At some point mankind will become embroiled in a conflict with the Leannain Sidhe, an energy-based race dimensionally out of phase with humanity, existing in all eleven dimensions rather than the "visible" four but sharing the same planet. A truce between the two races will eventually be reached.[264]

The Gubbage Cones were the dominant empire in the galaxy.[265] The Master had a Vortex Cloak stolen from the ruins of the Gubbage Cone Throneworld on the edge of the Great Attractor.[266]

The ozone layer of Urbanka collapsed around 55,500 BC. The Monarch of the planet stored the memories of his population, some three billion, on computer chips which could be housed in android bodies. Monarch built a vast spacecraft and set out for Earth. The ship doubled its speed on each round trip, and the Urbankans landed and kidnapped human specimens.[267]

It was thought that mankind made the Great Leap Forward from animal to human around 50,000 BC. Humans started burying their dead, and created art and money.[268]

The P'Shiem created millions of mechanical beings - the Omicron - to explore different worlds via the Cardiff Rift, and then pool any information they gleaned pertaining to history, geography, science, society and technology in a tesseract fold. The Rift proved so hazardous that only one Omicron survived to the twenty-first century; the P'Shem themselves died when a monstrous creature came through the Rift and ate their world.[269]

The Flurrgh and the Wfflmibibiki initiated a long-lasting war with each other.[270]

259 "The Vanity Box". Events on the asteroid take place in *The Wishing Beast*.
260 *Dreamtime*
261 More than a hundred thousand years before *The Sandman*.
262 "A hundred thousand years of conflict" before *Heroes of Sontar*.
263 *City of Death, Image of the Fendahl, The Daemons*.
264 *Autumn Mist*
265 "Seventy thousand years" before *The Crystal Bucephalus* (p34). The fungoids on Mechanus in *The Chase* were named "Gubbage Cones" in the script but not on screen.
266 *The Quantum Archangel*
267 *Four to Doomsday*
 MONARCH'S JOURNEY: There is a great deal of confusion about the dates of Monarch's visits to Earth, as recorded in *Four to Doomsday*. The story is set in 1981. The Greek named Bigon says he was abducted "one hundred generations ago [c.500 BC], and this is confirmed by Monarch's aide Enlightenment - she goes on to say that the visit to ancient Greece was the last time the Urbankans had visited Earth. Bigon says that the ship last left Urbanka "1250 years ago", that the initial journey to Earth took "20,000 years" and that "Monarch has doubled the speed of the ship on every subsequent visit."
 This is complicated, but the maths do work. The speed only doubles every time the ship arrives at *Earth*, perhaps because of some kind of slingshot effect. Monarch's ship left Urbanka for the first time in 55,519 BC, it arrived at Earth twenty thousand years later (35,519 BC), the speed doubled so the ship arrived back at Urbanka ten thousand years later (25,519 BC), it returned to Earth (15,519 BC), the speed doubled and the ship travelled back to Urbanka (arriving 10,519 BC). Monarch returned to Earth (in 5519 BC), the speed doubled once again and the ship arrived back at Urbanka (in 3019 BC). The ship made its final visit to Earth around 519 BC, and now the trip back to Urbanka only took 1250 years. The ship left Urbanka (731 AD) and reached Earth in 1981.
 However, this solution leaves a number of historical problems - see the individual entries.
268 *TW: Miracle Day*. The advent of money occurred a lot later than this, though.
269 "Fifty thousand years" before the 2008 portion of *TW*: "Rift War".
270 Fifty thousand years before *Benny: The Infernal Nexus*.

Cavemen Days

Cave paintings on one Mediterranean island date from the Cro-Magnon period, forty thousand years ago, demonstrating that a primitive human culture had developed by this time.[271] Around 35,500 BC, the Urbankans kidnapped the Australian Aborigine Kurkurtji and other members of his race.[272] An Onihr captain took charge of a vast Onihr ship thirty thousand years ago. The same captain would seek to acquire time-travel technology on Earth, the twenty-first century.[273]

29,185 BC (24th May) - ONLY HUMAN[274] **->** The ninth Doctor and Rose arrived from the twenty-first century, on the trail of a "dirty rip" time engine. They quickly discovered a group of researchers from the far future who were monitoring the local Neanderthal tribe. Rose accidentally married the prince of the caveman tribe, Tillun, while the Doctor discovered that Chantal - one of the time travellers - had engineered fearsome Hy-Bractor creatures. She planned to release them, changing history to wipe out the inferior *homo sapiens*. The Doctor defeated her.

The Neanderthals died out around twenty-eight thousand years ago.[275] A "framily" (friends who become like family) took up residence inside a space-faring Ghaleen.[276] The T'Zun began space conquests around 23,000 BC. They defeated the fungoid Darkings of Yuggoth, but their genetic structure became corrupted and they mutated into three subspecies.[277] The energy fields of the dormant Permians influenced the early Inuit legends.[278]

Two Krynoid pods landed in Antarctica in the Late Pleistocene Period, twenty to thirty thousand years ago. They remained dormant in the Antarctic permafrost until the twentieth century.[279]

The older religions on the planet Vortis claimed that "the light" made the universe and the sky, but a being named Pwodarauk made time and the ground so that things might wither but also grow. The first Menoptera, Hruskin, went to Pwodarauk and described the world she envisioned for her offspring. They agreed that slaves would build the temples for the light and raise harvests while the Menoptera enjoyed themselves, and so Pwodarauk made the Zarbi.[280]

Humans hunted centaurs (an "extremely unpleasant lot") to extinction.[281] Around 16,000 BC, Sancreda, a scout of the Tregannon - an alien race with great mental powers - was marooned on Neolithic Earth.[282]

Around 15,000 BC, the Urbankans returned to Earth. They kidnapped the princess Villagra.[283] Circa 13,000 BC, the Canavitchi of the Pleiades begin conquering neighbouring star systems, building an empire that would eventually stretch over seven galaxies.[284]

The being named Martin was born on Frantige Two, a dull planet and home to a species with an extraordinarily long lifespan. He would live fourteen thousand years into the twenty-first century.[285]

Circa 9000 BC, Traken outgrew its dependency on robots.[286] Around 8000 BC, the Euterpian civilisation died out.[287] Around the same time, the Jex from Cassiopeia started their conquests. They would eventually dominate several galaxies, including a planet in the Rifta system

---

271 Peri has just turned down an opportunity to visit the caves with her mother at the beginning of *Planet of Fire*. Although filmed on Lanzarote and named as such in the story, in real life Lanzarote was nowhere near any ancient Greek trading routes.
272 *Four to Doomsday*. Bigon states that Kurkurtji was taken "thirty thousand years" ago. Examples of Australian Aboriginal art that are at least twenty-five thousand years old survive.
273 *Trading Futures*
274 Dating *Only Human* (NSA #5) - The Doctor and Jack calculate the precise date.
275 According to the Doctor in *Only Human*, which doesn't take into account the two survivors he met in *Ghost Light* and *Timewyrm: Genesys*.
276 Thirty thousand years before *The Song of the Megaptera*.
277 "Twenty-five thousand years" before *First Frontier*. Yuggoth is another reference to H.P. Lovecraft (it's his name for the planet Pluto).
278 "Twenty-five thousand years" before *The Land of the Dead*.

279 *The Seeds of Doom*
280 *Return to the Web Planet*. "Pwodoruk" is the name the Optera give to the Animus, evidently taking after this legend.
281 "Thirty thousand years" before "A Fairytale Life".
282 "Eighteen thousand years" before *The Spectre of Lanyon Moor*.
283 *Four to Doomsday*. Bigon claims that Villagra is a "Mayan". Although the Doctor boasts of his historical knowledge, he then suggests that the Mayans flourished "eight thousand years ago", but the civilisation really dated from c.300 AD - c.900 AD. The Urbankans, though, don't visit Earth after 500 BC. It would appear that Villagra must come from an ancient, unknown pre-Mayan civilisation.
284 "A dozen millennia" before *The King of Terror*.
285 *The Tomorrow Windows* (p256).
286 "Eleven thousand years" before Nyssa's time, according to *Cold Fusion*.
287 "Ten thousand years" before *Invasion of the Cat-People*.

where the Doctor encountered them.[288]

The wolf-like Valethske had worshipped the insectile Khorlthochloi as gods, but the Khorlthochloi believed the Valethske were becoming too dominant. They destroyed the Valethske warfleets, and released a plague that devastated the race. The Khorlthochloi later abandoned their physical bodies for a higher plane of existence. A threat to their new forms made the Khorlthochloi try to reunite with their bodies, but this proved impossible, as the bodies had become too independent. The threat killed the Khorlthochloi's minds, but their bodies lived on as sedate herds of giant beetles.[289]

About ten thousand years ago, the inhabitants of a dying planet encoded everything about their world - including genetic information on its plant life, animal life and inhabitants - onto a crystal. This was dispatched via a slow-travelling spaceship to another solar system, where the crystal would rebuild their civilisation. Half the races in the universe coveted the crystal, and its transport was obliterated. The Doctor acquired the crystal, but its magnetic fields prevented it from undergoing time travel. He deposited it for safekeeping in Earth's past; various royalty would guard it for millennia.[290]

Around ten thousand years ago, humanity developed the wheel - with a helping hand from Scaroth.[291] The leaders of the Silence claimed to have ruled the Earth "since the wheel and fire".[292]

Legends spoke of how the Ice Warriors built an empire on Mars out of snow. The Doctor suspected that they found something - a malevolent entity that lived in water and *created* water - and used their might and wisdom to freeze it in the underground glacier in Gusev Crater on Mars.[293]

The Ice Warrior Civilisation Collapses

Flowers last grew on Mars around ten thousand years ago.[294] The tenth Doctor and Martha visited the Frozen Castles of the Ice Warriors.[295] **The Ice Warrior language had the dialect Ancient North Martian.[296]** Some Ice Warriors were herbivorous, others ate glacier fish from the polar regions.[297]

> (=) Martians were superstitious about Pandas, owing to a legend from the dawn of their history, which said that a Panda deity visited them in a scarlet chariot from the stars.[298]

c 8000 BC - THE JUDGEMENT OF ISSKAR[299] -> Mars had prospered as a world of builders, craftsmen and farmers for twelve thousand years. The whole of the planet was criss-crossed with waterways, and while the Martians had learned to hunt, they didn't fight one another and had yet to experience warfare. The Martians thought themselves protected by their gods, and had a gift economy in which

---

288 "Ten thousand years" before *King of Terror*.

289 "Many thousands of years" before *Superior Beings*.

290 *The Veiled Leopard*

291 *City of Death*. Scaroth says that he "turned the first wheel". Archaeologists think that mankind discovered the wheel around 8000 BC.

292 *Day of the Moon*

293 *The Waters of Mars*. A deleted scene said that the Martians left Mars because they could not beat the monsters from that story, the Flood. Nonetheless, because the scene *was* omitted, it's unclear within the fiction if the Flood was frozen after the Martian ecology went into decline (*The Judgement of Isskar*), or in one of Mars' polar regions beforehand.

294 *The Waters of Mars*

295 *Wishing Well*. This could have been at any time, but here it's assumed that the Doctor and Martha visited when the castles were at their height, rather than in ruins.

296 *The Waters of Mars*

297 *The Silent Stars Go By, Thin Ice,* respectively.

298 This appears to be true, if nowhere else, in an alternate dimension in *Iris: Enter Wildthyme*.

299 Dating *The Judgement of Isskar* (BF #117) - This is the backstory to the downfall of the Martians, and (for some of them) their forced relocation from Mars.

Exactly when the Martian ecology goes into decline is open to debate - on screen, the only real clue is the Doctor's claim (*The Waters of Mars*) that flowers last grew on the Red Planet "ten thousand years" ago; such flora would seem unlikely once the toxic Red Dawn (*Red Dawn, The Judgement of Isskar, Thin Ice*) becomes a factor. Another approach would be to consider if Varga's ship (*The Ice Warriors*) crashed to Earth before or after Mars was devastated, but so little is said of Mars itself in that story, it's hard to make that determination.

300 *Deimos/The Resurrection of Mars.*

301 *The Judgement of Isskar*, based upon the history of Izdal given in *Red Dawn*.

302 *Demon Quest: A Shard of Ice*. This may be a reference to *Pyramids of Mars*.

303 "Ten thousand years" before *Meglos*.

304 This is suspected to have occurred "twelve thousand years" before *Benny: Secret Origins*.

305 At least ten thousand years before *Benny: Genius Loci*.

306 *TW: The Sin Eaters*. Date unknown, but this is presumably early on in each race's history. Proto-Indo Europeans settled Norway toward the end of the third millennium BC; Ireland has been inhabited for about nine thousand years. Pryovillia is the home of the Pyroviles from *The Fires of Pompeii*.

water and other goods were offered for free; a strict code of honour demanded that something be given in return. Alien visitors were rare, but not unknown. A town on the Martian equator was home to a pyramid that had taken nineteen thousand masons, six hundred carpenters and forty-six overseers to complete.

The fifth Doctor and the living Key-tracer Amy visited Mars during the second quest for the Key to Time. The segment was undergoing decay and formed a gravity well through the middle of Mars, generating earthquakes and boiling away the canals. The Doctor and Amy left with the segment, preventing it from forming a black hole. The warped gravity eventually corrected itself, but the Martian environment was left permanently altered. Millions died as earthquakes and hurricanes persisted for thirty years. Some Martians left their world during this time.

As Mars' ecology went into decline, some Ice Warriors entered hibernation in caverns on the Martian moon of Deimos. Another group went to sleep in the asteroid belt.[300] The Martians who remained on Mars wanted to rebuild their world, but Lord Izdal concluded that the cause was lost, and that the Martian atmosphere could no longer filter out deadly radiation. To prove this, Izdal gave himself to the Red Dawn - the time of day when the atmosphere was the most toxic. Izdal's sacrifice, as witnessed by the magistrate Isskar, convinced the Martians to abandon their homeworld. Isskar himself entered cryogenic suspension, hoping to exact revenge upon the Doctor for his role in Mars' decline.[301] The Doctor visited the tombs on Mars.[302]

In the Prion system, the Zolfa-Thurans developed a powerful weapon. When the Dodecahedron, a power-source, was aligned with the giant Screens of Zolfa-Thura, an energy beam - "a power many magnitudes greater than any intelligence has ever controlled" - was formed. The beam was capable of obliterating any point in the galaxy.

Zolfa-Thura fell into bloody civil war, and everything on the planet's surface except the Screens was devastated. The Dodecahedron was taken to Zolfa-Thura's sister-planet, Tigella, where the Deons worshipped it.[303] A crystal sculpture was made of Arincias, one of the lost gods of Atlantis.[304]

Two factions of evolved spiders lived on the planet Jaiwan: the Alpha spiders were a federation of cultures, but the Omega spiders - calling themselves the Laughing People, a.k.a. The Way of Life that Works - sought to eradicate the Alphas. The Omega spiders diverted an asteroid toward Jaiwan, then sabotaged the Alphans' efforts to deflect it. The Omegas went into hibernation, intending to ride out the devastation and awaken to claim the planet, but some Alphans survived in cryo-sleep.[305]

Jack Harkness suggested that Norwegians, the Scottish, the Irish, the Danish and the Icelandic all had a bit of alien inheritance, owing to a spaceship that crashed in Iceland. The ship had been looking for volcanoes, and originated from somewhere near Pyrovillia.[306]

Around 6000 BC, the humanoid Thains, arch-enemies of the Kleptons, died out.[307] Circa 5900 BC, the inhabitants of Proxima 2 created the Centraliser, which linked them telepathically.[308] **Around 5500 BC, the Urbankans visited Earth for the third time. The Urbankans kidnapped the mandarin Lin Futu, along with a number of dancers.[309]** A new "framily" formed inside a space-faring Ghaleen that the sixth Doctor and Peri would encounter.[310] The Mogor, a warlike race, lived on Mekrom.[311]

The "hammies", inhabitants of Tollip's World, developed a symbiotic relationship with a type of indigenous flora: the Trees of Life. The Trees engineered a virus to wipe out some ape-like predators, but this killed all animal life on the planet. The hammies merged their bodies with Trees, waiting for the virus to burn itself out, but the slow-thinking Trees forgot to revive their charges.[312]

---

307 "Ten thousand years" before *Placebo Effect*.
308 "Eight thousand years" before *The Face-Eater*.
309 *Four to Doomsday*. There is no "Futu dynasty" in recorded Chinese history. The Doctor has heard of it, however, and claims it flourished "four thousand years ago". The date does not tie in with the details of Monarch's journey as described in the rest of the story. Archaeologists have discovered a piece of tortoiseshell with a character from the Chinese alphabet on it that is seven thousand years old, so it seems that an early Chinese civilisation was established by that time, and the timescale does tie in with the dates established by Bigon.
310 Ten thousand years before *The Song of the Megaptera*.
311 "Six thousand years" before "Echoes of the Mogor".
312 "Eight thousand years" before *Benny: The Tree of Life*.

The planet Trion founded colonies on other worlds, forming an empire. Science and technology drove the ruling Clans, who developed a vacuum transport system that revolutionised on-planet travel. Non-Clansmen incorporated cold fusion into their spaceships.[1]

The Time Lord passing as "Jane Templeton" - unwilling to face her punishment on Gallifrey for meddling with human history - piloted her dying TARDIS into Earth's sun, inadvertently causing a small shift in the Earth's axial rotation.[2]

Ancient Egypt

Seven thousand years ago in the Nile delta, Egyptian civilisation was flourishing. A variety of extra-terrestrials visited Egypt around this time, and were seen as gods. The Egyptian god Khnum was either one of the Daemons or a race memory of them, and Scaroth of the Jagaroth posed as an Egyptian god and Pharaoh, building the earliest Pyramids.[3]

The Osirians

By 5000 BC, the highly-advanced Osirian race had influenced the cultures of many planets, including Earth, Mars, Youkali (the scene of a devastating battle between the Osirians and Sutekh) and Exxilon.[4] A final generation of the giant insects aided by the Osirians hatched in 5000 BC.[5]

Some Osirians were as powerful as decent-sized planets. Many of them bore different animal heads to keep up appearances, and to reflect their biodiversity. Osiris founded the Osirian Court, which existed in its own timeframe - its past and future could interact in varying ways with different eras of different planets, including the Homeworld of the Great Houses.[6]

Sutekh married his sister Nephthys on the same day that Osiris cut the court off from history.[7] The Osirians had a slave force of more than two billion - nearly one billion of those in the inner court alone - and had influence on six hundred and sixty worlds.[8]

The Osirians constructed the Ship of a Billion Years - a formidable vessel that would pass through the noospheres of different planets, and facilitated a "thousand year cruise" of the gods. The Ship was powered by Ra: a miniature sun that the Osirians, even mighty as they were, revered. Four Osirians (Osiris, Sutekh, Upuat and Kepri) were designated "the divine shields of Ra" - they could tap Ra's energies to defend the Ship. Ra's voice spoke through the Lady Nut, and it was said that no man could reach the throne of Osiris without earning passage on the Ship. Whichever Osirian sat on the throne could receive the loyalty of the Ship, but had no jurisdiction over it.[9] The Ship was forged inside a star, and had a hull of solid gold.[10]

Osirian technology depended on magnetic monopoles, and the Osirians built a power relay system on Earth. The Sphinx was carved from living rock, and made to serve as a dispersal point. The Osirians then left instructions on how to build pyramids to serve as receptacles for their power. They either constructed similar pyramids and a Sphinx on Mars, or found a religiously fanatical group to do it for them.

The face of the Sphinx originally had perfect alignment with the path of the sun, but this became imperfect as the angle of the Earth altered over time. Also, sand would periodically cover the Sphinx and fog the reception. The

---

1 "Nine thousand years" before *Turlough and the Earthlink Dilemma*. *Kiss of Death* also mentions Trion's colonies.
2 *Forty-Five:* "False Gods". In *Doctor Who* terms, this accounts for why ancient calendars denote a difference in the rising and setting of the sun. As this event is recorded on the box of hieroglyphs in Userhat's tomb, "Jane" must chronologically kill herself before Userhat acquires her TARDIS.
3 *The Daemons, City of Death.*
4 *Pyramids of Mars. Return of the Living Dad, GodEngine* and *The Quantum Archangel* contain the further references.
5 *FP: Ozymandias*
6 *FP: Coming to Dust, FP: The Ship of a Billion Years.*
7 *FP: Words from Nine Divinities*
8 *FP: Coming to Dust, FP: The Ship of a Billion Years, FP: Body Politic, FP: Words of Nine Divinities.*
9 *FP: The Ship of a Billion Years*

10 *FP: The Judgment of Sutekh, FP: Body Politic.*
11 All according to the Doctor in *The Sands of Time* (p233-235); he says the Sphinx was built "between eight and ten thousand years ago" (p234).
12 *The Sands of Time* (p235).
13 *Pyramids of Mars*
THE DEVIL'S IN THE DETAIL: Both *Pyramids of Mars* and *The Satan Pit* feature a god-like being - Sutekh and the Beast, respectively - who is said to be the inspiration for the Biblical Satan. The two of them even sound the same (purely because Gabriel Woolf portrayed Sutekh and voiced the Beast). *The Daemons* also features a devil-like being, but no-one in the story quite says that he's Satan - it's just that the Daemons have inspired myths of powerful horned beings. Finally, *TW: End of Days* has another creature named Abaddon that's apparently of the same race as the Beast in *The Satan Pit*.

The Beast and Sutekh do not appear to be the same

Sphinx was equipped with a mental pulse that would influence individuals to dig it out.[11] The original face of the Sphinx on Earth was that of Horus.[12]

The Osirians fought a war in our solar system. Sutekh, also known as the Typhonian Beast, destroyed his homeworld of Phaester Osiris and left a trail of destruction across half the galaxy. Sutekh became known by many names, including Set, Sadok and Satan.[13]

Sutekh was instrumental in the downfall of his brother Osiris. There were at least two accounts pertaining to Osiris' overthrow and Sutekh's eventual defeat.[14]

In the first account, Sutekh and his sister Nephthys captured Osiris and sent him into space in a capsule without life support. Sutekh and Nephthys tracked the body of Osiris to Egypt and totally destroyed it. Osiris' sister-wife Isis looked for her lost husband, and the remains of his mind endowed themselves in the mind of her spacecraft pilot. This psi-child became Osiris' son Horus.[15]

Along with seven hundred and forty of his fellow Osirians, Horus located Sutekh on Earth, trapping and sealing him in a pyramid. Nephthys was imprisoned in a human body and mummified. Her mind was fragmented, the evil side placed in a canopic jar.[16]

w - c 5000 BC - FP: OZYMANDIAS / FP: THE JUDGMENT OF SUTEKH[17] **->** The second account of Sutekh's defeat pertained to the War in Heaven. An assembly of more than seven hundred Osirians gathered on Mars, which was still under Osirian jurisdiction, to render a final judgement concerning Sutekh's claim to the throne of Osiris - whom Sutekh had secretly killed and buried near Mount Vesuvius in the eighteenth century. Sutekh now challenged his rival to the throne - Cousin Eliza of Faction Paradox, who was endowed with Osiris' biomass

and calling herself Horus - to a fight to the death.

Cousin Justine of Faction Paradox brokered a deal with the Osirians. The more than seven hundred Osirians that historically defeated Sutekh were instead dispatched to the Homeworld of the Great Houses, and "dealt with" the living timeship Lolita. Justine and Eliza separately laid a trap for Sutekh that, at the cost of Eliza's life, severed Sutekh's neural connections and psionic centres, leaving him paralysed. It was believed that Sutekh had lost his challenge, and he was imprisoned beneath a pyramid. As before, history recorded that the Osirians had bested Sutekh.

Corwyn Marne and Abelard Finton had travelled back from 1764 to aid the Cousins. Finton returned to the eighteenth century, but Marne remained trapped on Mars.

The Pyramid of Mars was built to house the Eye of Horus, and the Osirians set up a beacon there to broadcast a warning message. The Egyptians worshipped Horus and the other Osirians. Even Sutekh was worshipped by many on Earth, and the Cult of Sutekh survived for many thousands of years. The influence of the Osirians brought on the unification of the Egyptian kingdoms, and the local humans were genetically enhanced, becoming taller and with increased mental capacity.[18]

The Doctor was at the prayer meeting when an Egyptian goddess was sealed in the Seventh Obelisk.[19] **The Anubians resembled creatures from Egyptian myth. K9 freed them from the mind control of the Huducts, and earned their almost godlike reverence. After K9 left, the Anubians used the mind-control technology of their former oppressors and to conquer races that apparently included the Sea Devils, Alpha Centaurians, Mandrels, Aeolians and Jixen.**[20]

An Egyptian legend held that Ra the sun god chose to

---

being - not if the Beast truly was imprisoned before the universe began, and only released in Earth's future - but the two beings' stories do contain parallels. Much of human mythology in the *Doctor Who* universe seems to be a mish-mash of dimly-remembered ancient encounters with alien races. It therefore seems possible - and forgivable - that people have elided legends of the Beast and Sutekh, although the extent of this isn't clear.

14 Respectively given in *The Sands of Time* and Series 2 of the *Faction Paradox* audios.

15 *The Sands of Time*. Egyptian mythology can't decide on Horus' exact relationship to Set; *The Sands of Time* (pgs 142, 158) solves this by making Horus a "psi-child" of Osiris, which simultaneously makes him Sutekh's brother and nephew. The Cult of Sutekh also appears in the New Adventure *Set Piece*. In the scripts for *Pyramids of Mars*, the name Osirians is also sometimes spelt (and

is always pronounced) "Osirans".

16 *Pyramids of Mars*, *The Sands of Time*.

17 Dating *FP: Ozymandias*, *FP: The Judgment of Sutekh* (*FP* audios #2.5-2.6) - The story ends in accordance with Sutekh's status in *Pyramids of Mars*.

18 *Pyramids of Mars*, *The Sands of Time*.

19 *The Big Bang*. This could happen at any time, but it has an Osirian ring to it.

20 This happened "generations" before *K9: The Curse of Anubis*, with the Huducts ruling the Anubians for millennia. K9 did this at some unknown point before *K9: Regeneration* (possibly while working for the Time Lords). We see pictures of the races the Anubians conquered, not their names. The Anubians resemble the Egyptian god Anubis, and their technology, design, written language and imagery all looks Ancient Egyptian. There's no suggestion they've been to Egypt or even Earth before, though, and so they could well be

live amongst the people as a human. Ra transformed his "divine eye" into Sekhmet the Powerful One, the Avenger. She killed Ra's enemies, but continued the slaughter until Ra ordered his high priest at Heliopolis to dye seven thousand jars of beer with pomegranate juice, then to pour it onto the ground. Sekhmet drank from what she thought was a lake of blood, and became stupefied. She was imprisoned in trisilicate, the hardest form of salt in the galaxy, as its negatively charged atoms weakened her. She was bound under four blood locks; three sealed her in space, the fourth in time. Sekhmet was blasted into space and was finally entombed on the planet Peladon. The Doctor suspected that Ra eventually died.[21]

Dilvpod Tentacle wrote a story that was later adapted to become *Peter Pan*.[22]

The Doctor saved billions of lives by restoring the rotting "soul" of the homeworld of the Weave: creatures who existed as flexible protein ribbons, and had numbers for names. He declined to accept a reality-warping Glamour as a reward, but took a young Weave, 6011, for a jaunt to see a star system being born before returning her home. After the Doctor left, the xenophobic Tahnn conducted a war against the Weave. One Weave ship, the WSS *Exalted*, crashed to Earth with the Glamour aboard. The local tribe thought the ship a gift from the sky gods and buried it, and the Glamour extended the lifespan of one of them - Owain - to watch over the Weave.[23]

The troll-like Vykoids stood only seven centimetres tall, and were frustrated because the universe didn't take them seriously. They developed tools of conquest: assault vehicles and a Time Freeze that immobilised the larger races,

enabling the Vykoids transport them to slave planets. The Vykoid machines of war caused chaos across the galaxies.

The Ninety-Ninth Vykoid Expeditionary Force came to Earth, expecting to capture Triceratops and Diplodocuses for use as beasts of labour. Instead, the Force entered cryo-sleep in Svalbard, the Arctic, within one of their conveyances: a mechanical mammoth.[24]

Around 3600 BC, a Sontaran ship landed in Ancient Egypt. Its pilot was worshipped as the Toad-God Sontar and set the natives to work building an ion cannon emplacement. The Sontaran planned to outflank the Rutans with it, knowing that the Rutan counter-strike would destroy the planet. A priest learned of these plans, and had Sontar entombed.[25]

The TARDIS came to be represented in some Egyptian hieroglyphs.[26]

Around 3500 BC, the Trakenite living god Kwundaar re-engineered Traken's sun to become a vast computer - the Source - which regulated the climate, provided energy, stored information and destroyed all who were evil. With the Source performing such duties, the people of Traken had no further need for a god and exiled Kwundaar from their star system.[27] An empire ruled by a family of Primearchs collapsed when their final leader - Ceatul XVI - fought to the death with another race.[28]

A group of Pyroviles - stone creatures animated by internal magma - crashed into Vesuvius and were obliterated on impact. Their particles mixed with the volcano's inner core.[29]

On a three-sunned planet in the fourth galaxy, the males of an unnamed race used their group mind to subjugate

a race influenced by the Osirians.

21 Variously said to occur "thousands of years" and "countless millennia" before *The Bride of Peladon*. In Egyptian mythology, Sekhmet was a daughter of Ra and a warrior goddess of Upper Egypt, although she was sometimes regarded as a more vengeful aspect of Hathor. Her cult was particularly dominant in the twelfth dynasty (1991 BC to 1802 BC), only a few centuries before Erimem's time. The "dying beer with pomegranate juice" story comes from a myth focused around an annual Sekhmet festival, although this has Ra dying the entire Nile (which turns red every year when it fills with silt).

The Curse of Peladon says that trisilicate can be found on Mars, where Sutekh was imprisoned, so it makes sense that the Osirians would use it to bind Sekhmet. It's not entirely clear, though, if Sekhmet was deliberately entombed on Peladon or if she was blasted into space at random and happened - very coincidentally - to wind up on a planet loaded with trisilicate, the best means of restraining her. Sekhmet's claim that she "created" the desert and set Sutekh to rule over it can probably be excused as propaganda, as with talk that she's

the "Queen of the Osirians" (if she is, it's probably only by virtue of the rest being dead).
22 "Several millennia" before Barrie wrote *Peter Pan*, according to *The Tomorrow Windows*.
23 "Six thousand years" (pgs 149, 178) before *The Glamour Chase*.
24 "Several thousand years" before *The Forgotten Army*. The Vykoids must be working from wretched intelligence, if they came to Earth expecting to find T-Rexes, Triceratops and Diplodocuses some tens of millions of years after they died out.
25 "The Gods Walk Among Us". The archaeologists estimate that the tomb is "five thousand five hundred" years old in 1926, so it was built around 3574 BC.
26 The TARDIS is plainly seen in some hieroglyphs in *Love & Monsters*, even though the Ship would not be represented as a phone box icon under such a language system. Egyptian hieroglyphs were in use from 3200 BC to 400 AD.
27 "2523 years" before *Primeval*.
28 "Millennia" before *Benny: A Life in Pieces*.
29 "Thousands of years" before *The Fires of Pompeii*.
30 "Thousands of years", if not more, before *The*

their females. One female formed a mental circuit with the enslaved women and attacked the men's gestalt - the males killed the revolutionary's body, but her consciousness survived in other women. The females prevailed, but feared the power their leader had amassed. Her mind was isolated, and her severed head was deposited on Earth.[30]

Alien Centuripedes bred in oak forests on Earth for thousands of years.[31] The Vam existed as a universal force that could wrap itself around a sun, eradicate entire planets or destroy an entire warfleet. It killed billions, excreting its waste as oil.[32]

> (=) The eleventh Doctor, Amy and Rory took photographic evidence demonstrating how the temporal anomalies in Swallow Woods were making people avoid that area as early as the Bronze Age.[33]

Ancient Mesopotamia

c 2700 BC - TIMEWYRM: GENESYS[34] **->** The human race had developed from hunters into city-dwellers, and had irrigation. In the Middle East, walled cities were built and a warrior aristocracy developed. The earliest human literature was written at this time, and commerce had begun between cities. The deeds of one warrior-king - and his contact with extra-terrestrials - soon became legend.

Gilgamesh refused the advances of the alien Ishtar, who had crashed near Uruk. Ishtar went on to the temple of Kish, taking the form of a metal snake woman, and had a vast temple built. The seventh Doctor, Ace and Gilgamesh travelled to the mountains of Mashu and led Utnapishtim, a member of Ishtar's race, to his prey. Ishtar infiltrated the TARDIS computer, and the Doctor ejected her into the Vortex... inadvertently turning her into the Timewyrm, a creature foretold to herald the end of the universe. The Timewyrm became capable of independent travel through space-time. The Doctor and Ace pursued her.

The Great Pyramids

Around 2650 BC, Zoser was one of the first Egyptian Kings.[35]

c 2610 BC - "The Forgotten"[36] **->** The TARDIS materialised in Menkaure's Pyramid, the smallest of the three being constructed at Giza, and the first Doctor, Ian, Barbara and Susan were immediately arrested by Egyptian soldiers. The travellers were taken to the Pharaoh Menkaure, and accidentally foiled an assassination attempt on Pharaoh's life. In the confusion, they made their escape.

Sutekh and Osiris were depicted in paintings in Menkaure's Pyramid.

c 2566 BC - THE DALEKS' MASTER PLAN[37] **->** The first Doctor, Steven and Sara Kingdom were pursued to the time of the construction of the Great Pyramids by both the Daleks in their time machine, and the Monk in his TARDIS. The travellers escaped during a pitched battle between the Daleks and Egyptian soldiers, but the Daleks and Mavic Chen successfully recovered the Taranium Core the Doctor had stolen and returned to the future.

c 2560 BC - BENNY: THE GREL ESCAPE[38] **->** Bernice Summerfield, Jason Kane and Benny's son Peter, in fleeing from a pack of time-travelling Grel, briefly visited the Great Pyramid of Khufu in ancient Egypt. Anubis, the Egyptian god of the dead, had full knowledge of Peter's life to come - and told Benny that her son was unworthy to enter the kingdom of Heaven.

A race of crocodilians ruled the planet Sobek, an old imperial world founded on centuries of slavery. The aristocrat Snabb deemed the ruling prince of Sobek as too corrupt and led an uprising; the ensuing war devastated the

---

Suffering. The "fourth galaxy" could be a reference to the home of the Drahvins in *Galaxy 4*, and for all we're told, the exiled woman might hail from their race. Interestingly, both the Drahvins and the race in *The Suffering* have culled the males of their population.
31 *K9: The Last Oak Tree*
32 "Millennia" before the 2009 portion of *TW: Risk Assessment*.
33 *The Way Through the Woods*. In Europe, the Bronze Age lasted 3200-600 BC.
34 Dating *Timewyrm: Genesys* (NA #1) - The Doctor says the TARDIS is heading for "Mesopotamia, 2700 BC".
35 "City of Devils"
36 Dating "The Forgotten" (IDW *DW* mini-series #2) - It is "most likely around the twenty-sixth century BC". Menkaure ruled in the late twenty-sixth century BC, although historians can't be sure of the exact dates. In

the Doctor's personal timeline, this is after *Marco Polo* but before *The Aztecs*. He already knows of the Osirians.
37 Dating *The Daleks' Master Plan* (3.4) - The three time machines land at the base of a "Great Pyramid" that has nearly been completed. This might well be the Great Pyramid of King Khufu (Cheops in Greek), one of the Seven Wonders of the World. John Peel's novelisation of the story names it as such, and also says "Khufu lay in his final illness" (p72). Khufu died in 2566 BC; the Great Pyramid was built over a twenty year period, ending around 2560 BC. *The Terrestrial Index* pins the date at "2620 BC"; *The Discontinuity Guide* offers a wider range of "2613 BC - 2494 BC". *Timelink* says 2635 BC.
38 Dating *Benny: The Grel Escape* (Benny audio #5.1) - The story takes place in ancient Egypt, and it's entirely possible that the Anubis seen here was an Osirian.

planet. A few royals escaped with "the great Skull" - a molecular data encryption system containing all of Sobek's memories and history. In time, it was concealed in a sanctuary on Indigo 3.[39]

Around 2350 BC, the inhabitants of Uxarieus had used genetic engineering to become a psychic super-race powerful enough to come to the attention of the Time Lords. They built a Doomsday Weapon, a device capable of making stars go supernova. The Crab Nebula was formed as a result of testing the device. Soon, though, radiation began leaking from the weapon's power source. It poisoned the soil and the race began to degenerate into primitives.[40] The space explorer Moriah conquered Krontep and built a civilisation there. He left the planet shortly after his wife Petruska killed herself. Their descendants, including King Yrcanos, would rule the planet for millennia.[41]

Around four thousand three hundred years ago, the Chinese were making the first astronomical measurements with Scaroth's help.[42] Over four thousand years ago, an elemental "burning" entity was worshipped by various cultures on Earth. It was known as Agni the fire god in India, and Huallallo to the Peruvians.[43] **Four thousand years ago, the Futu dynasty was flourishing in China.**[44]

The Time of Greek Myth

On Earth, the classical Greek gods were long-lived beings with psionic abilities. They had forgotten their origins. Some of them believed they were aliens, although Hermes came to suspect they were an early mutation of humanity. Zeus, Poseidon and Hades were the oldest of the gods, although they were not yet five thousand years old.[45]

A psychic parasite from space was mistaken for the goddess Artemis, and fed off the people's greed. The priests

serving the parasite rose up and bound it in a circle of iron within its temple. The creature's presence gradually made some of the women in the area psionic.[46]

The Chronovore Prometheus and the Eternal named Elektra broke an ancient covenant to sire the Chronovore Kronos. The Guardians spared the half-breed's life, but sealed him in a trident-shaped crystal prison and threw it into the Time Vortex. The crystal came to simultaneously exist on many worlds.[47]

Five hundred and thirty-seven years before the fall of Atlantis, the priests of that land captured the god Kronos. At this time, a young man called Dalios was king. Kronos transformed a man, one of the king's friends, into a fearsome man-beast: the Minotaur. After this, the King forbid the use of the Crystal of Kronos, for fear of destroying the city.[48]

c 2000 BC - FALLEN GODS[49] -> The Titans had evolved at the bottom of the sea. Most left to live in the Vortex, but some remained on Earth as humanity amused them. Humans bound these Titans using special crystals. The Titans could manipulate time, and were compelled to grant the people on the island of Thera four harvests a year. They ended a war between Athens and Thera by stealing life energy from the Athenians - which was taken to be a plague - and using it to extend the lifespan of the elite on Thera.

Fiery demon bulls attacked Thera, and King Rhadamanthys believed that Athens was seeking revenge. However, the Titans themselves were causing the attacks, hoping the king would free them to repel the "invaders". Rhadamanthys was killed, and his son Deucalion succeeded him. Deucalion felt the Titans' abilities had been used unwisely, and ordered their crystals scattered far and wide, curtailing their power.

The blessings the Titans had bestowed on Thera were

39 *The Skull of Sobek*; see the dating notes on this story. It's not entirely clear if Sobek's downfall triggered a migration of its culture to other planets, or if the crocodilians had dealings with other species beforehand. If the former is true, the crocodilians must have immense lifespans, as the prince and Snabb are still around ten thousand years later. The fact that Snabb spends a full century scouring one sector of space for the Skull somewhat supports this notion, as does the fact that he only eats once a year (which suggests a slow, life-extending metabolism).
40 *Colony in Space*. The date isn't given, but this is when the Crab Nebula was formed. It was first visible on Earth from 1054.
41 Unspecified "thousands of years" before *Bad Therapy*.
42 *City of Death*. Scaroth says that he caused "the heavens to be mapped", and mankind's first star maps were

made in China around 2300 BC.
43 "Over four thousand years" before *The Burning*. The entity is drawn to Earth as the result of events in Siberia, 1894, in *Time Zero*.
44 According to the Doctor in *Four to Doomsday*.
45 *Deadly Reunion*. It's suggested the "gods" were the product of the Daemons' experiments.
46 "Thousands of years" before *The Hounds of Artemis*.
47 *The Quantum Archangel*
48 *The Time Monster*
49 Dating *Fallen Gods* (TEL #10) - It's "the Bronze Age" (p91). This is a retelling of the creation of the Atlantis as related in *The Time Monster*.
50 "Nearly four thousand years" before the 1974 component of "Agent Provocateur".
51 "The Curse of the Scarab". The casket is "four thousand" years old. The fourth year of the twelfth dynasty

stolen from the future. In the times to come, the island would experience barrenness and a volcanic eruption.

Around 2000 BC, Pharaoh forbade his daughter, Hentopet, from seeing her suitor, Temhut. The giant cat-like creature Bubastion, an agent of the Shadow Proclamation sent to oversee the forward development of Earth, manifested in response to Hentopet praying to the goddess Bast. Hentopet deceived Bubastion into attacking Pharaoh's associates, giving Hentopet the opportunity to kill her father. Pharaoh's death meant Bubastion had failed in his mission, and so he cursed Hentopet and her servant Sheeq to immortality.[50]

In the fourth year of the twelfth dynasty, around 2000 BC, Kephri the beetle god was one of the seven hundred forty gods that captured Sutekh. It was given an area of Egypt as a reward, but wanted the whole of Africa. Horus had it sealed in a casket, where it would wait, plotting revenge for four thousand years. The Doctor witnessed at least some of these events.[51]

The true meaning of the burial mound containing the WSS *Exalted* had now been forgotten. Rumours and myths about it would circulate for four thousand years.[52]

c 2000 BC - "The Power of Thoueris"[53] **->** The eighth Doctor easily defeated the "third rate" Osirian - the hippo-like Thoueris - while on holiday in ancient Egypt. Thoueris was devoured by crocodiles.

c 2000 BC - THE SANDS OF TIME[54] **->** Tomb robbers entered the pyramid of Nephthys, breaking the canopic jar that contained her evil intellect. The Egyptian priests sought a pure vessel to contain it and chose the fifth Doctor's companion Nyssa, sealing her in a sarcophagus

until the 1920s.

At around the same time, Cessair of Diplos, a criminal accused of murder and stealing the Great Seal of Diplos, arrived on Earth. She would pose as a succession of powerful women over the millennia, while her ship remained in hyperspace above Boscombe Moor in Damnonium, England. A stone circle named the Nine Travellers was set up, and subsequent attempts to survey the circle proved hazardous.[55]

The warrior Ravage captured the throne of the planet Amital, but was defeated by republican forces. He was turned into stone and imprisoned on Earth; twelve sentries transformed themselves into rock to monitor him.[56]

The Arcasian Lights were visible from Earth four thousand years ago.[57] In 1936 BC, the Emperor Rovan Cartovall of the planet Centros became bored with his imperial life. He disappeared without a trace, and took the immense palace treasury with him. His younger brother Athren succeeded him to the throne. The mystery of Rovan and his missing treasure became legendary.[58]

An alien race - possibly as an experiment, possibly as part of a battle - released two viruses, Fear and Loathing, into Jupiter's atmosphere. They remained there for millennia, grappling with each other for supremacy.[59]

In 1758 BC, the "goddess" Demeter gave birth to Persephone, the future beloved of Hades. The Greek gods passed into legend, and some attempted to live quiet existences among mankind.[60] The seventh Doctor helped the people of Wrouth defeat the Daleks "in '38".[61]

would be around 1988 BC. *Pyramids of Mars* placed the imprisonment of Sutekh "seven thousand" years ago, but this dating does coincide with the dating given for events of *The Sands of Time*, perhaps suggesting that the Osirians maintained some sort of presence in ancient Egypt for millennia.

52 Dating "The Power of Thoueris" (*DWM* #333) - No date is given, and this is clearly not the height of Osirian power, so it's been placed at the same time as events of the backstory for "The Curse of the Scarab".

53 "Four thousand years" (p21) before *The Glamour Chase*.

54 Dating *The Sands of Time* (MA #22) - The date is given (p57).

55 *The Stones of Blood. The Terrestrial Index* dated Cessair's arrival on Earth at "3000 BC", but this contradicts the Doctor and Megara, both of whom claim that only "four thousand" years have elapsed since Cessair came to Earth.

56 *SJA: The Thirteenth Stone.* There's no evidence that

the practice here of turning alien convicts into rock has any relation to *The Stones of Blood*.

57 *SJA: The Lost Boy*

58 "Five thousand years" before *The Ultimate Treasure*.

59 "Thousands of years" (p236) before *Fear Itself*.

60 *Deadly Reunion* (p115). The first part of the book takes place in 1944, and Persephone says she is three thousand, seven hundred and two years old.

61 "Several millennia" before "Invaders from Gantac". The Daleks do not appear to have been created until after this point, so the ones referred to here must be time travellers.

1500 BC - THE SLITHEEN EXCURSION[62] -> The tenth Doctor, having promised to show ancient Greece to June, a twenty-first century university student, diverted to look into a temporal anomaly in 1500 BC. King Actaeus told the Doctor and June that a group of Slitheen, who originated from circa 34,600 and were running time-travel package tours for other aliens, had ruled the region since before his father had been born. The Slitheen had provided food via molecular repurposing that kept the people from starving, and in return demanded a small number of humans compete in games for the tourists' amusement. The Doctor had the sinking feeling that the Slitheen's intervention was part of established history, and that the visiting aliens were the basis for the creatures of Greek myth. He also realised that earthquakes were being generated as a side-effect of the Slitheen's temporal drives.

The Slitheen were scheming to accuse one of their clients, a fish-tailed humanoid named Cecrops, of corporate espionage, but Actaeus sacrificed himself to destroy the Slitheen's temporal drives. The resultant explosion destroyed the island of Thera, the modern island of Santorini. The Doctor taught the Greeks some farming techniques, and then took everyone home - except Cecrops, who was thought dead in his native era, but instead became the legendary founder of Athens. Three of the Slitheen were made dormant inside some stalagmites, and wouldn't revive until the twenty-first century.

The Fall of Atlantis

c 1500 BC - THE TIME MONSTER[63] -> The Master arrived in Atlantis, claiming to be the emissary of the gods. King Dalios didn't believe the stranger, who seduced his wife, Queen Galleia. The Master and the Queen plotted to steal the Crystal of Kronos. King Dalios died of a broken heart, and the Master seized power, proclaiming himself King. Queen Galleia, filled with remorse, ordered his arrest. The third Doctor and Jo were present as the Master released Kronos the Chronovore, and Atlantis was destroyed.

Some Atlanteans survived beneath the ocean, off the Azores.[64] The Daemons would later claim to have destroyed Atlantis.[65]

(=) ? 1500 BC (fourth month) - BENNY: YEAR ZERO / BENNY: DEAD MAN'S SWITCH[66] -> The Epoch were beings who created alternate timelines to observe and alter the progression of life itself, largely to eliminate potential threats to themselves. Earth's solar system, and particularly Bernice Summerfield's ability to "see the truth" of reality, posed a danger to the Epoch. They decided to evaluate her - then either eliminate her from all potential timelines, or at least choose which version of Bernice would confront them.[67]

Following her defeat of the Deindum in 2610, Benny found herself on Raster - one of twenty inhabited worlds in a timeline restarted by the Epoch. It was currently the fourth month (springtime) of Year 54. All knowledge of anything before Year 1 had been eradicated. The Great Leader, a computer, further obscured the past by regularly assigning new names to the people and places of the twenty worlds. Studying history or archaeology warranted a death sentence. Bernice thought that only about three

---

62 Dating *The Slitheen Excursion* (NSA #32) - The year is given as "1500 BC" on the back cover and page 25. Real-life renderings of the founder of Athens (Cecrops I) do, in fact, depict him as a human with a giant fish tail for legs. Events here are unrelated to the fall of Atlantis.

63 Dating *The Time Monster* (9.5) - The traditional date for the fall of Atlantis is around 1500 BC, and the Doctor states on returning to the twentieth century at the end of this story that it was "three thousand five hundred years ago". *The Terrestrial Index* and *The Discontinuity Guide* both suggested the traditional date of 1500 BC, the FASA Role-playing game claimed 10,000 BC. *The TARDIS Logs* included the presumed misprint of 1520 AD. *Timelink* goes for 1529 BC.

64 *The Underwater Menace*

65 *The Underwater Menace, The Daemons*.

THE FALL OF ATLANTIS: We hear of/witness the destruction of Atlantis in three stories: *The Underwater Menace, The Daemons* and *The Time Monster*. In *The Underwater Menace*, the island in question is in the Atlantic, and in *The Time Monster*, "Atlantis" is another name for the Minoan civilisation in the Mediterranean. In *The Daemons*, Azal warns the Master that "My race destroys its failures. Remember Atlantis!". *The Terrestrial Index* attempts to explain this by suggesting that the Daemons supplied the Minoan civilisation with the Kronos Crystal. This might be true, but there is no hint of it on screen.

66 Dating *Benny: Year Zero* (*Benny* audio #11.3), *Benny: Dead Man's Switch* (*Benny* audio #11.4) and *Benny: Epoch* (box set #1, contains *The Kraken's Lament*, 1.1; *The Temple of Questions*, 1.2; *Private Enemy No. 1*, 1.3; *Judgement Day*, 1.4) - These six stories occur in a central alternate reality (and two subsidiary realities) as crafted by the Epoch. Three years elapse between *Dead Man's Switch* and the *Benny: Epoch* stories, with Benny in stasis. In *Judgement Day*, she returns to her native era in a timeless state while the universe ages around her, which very much suggests that the Epoch's timeline/s are located in the past. Rightly or wrongly, Benny suspects this is the case as early as *Year Zero*. In *Epoch: Judgement Day*, she tells a robot attendant in 2616 to

dozen stars existed in this reality.

Benny sought answers at the capital of the twenty worlds: the planet Zordin. She arrived there after spending three years in stasis aboard a spaceship...

(=) & 1503 BC - BENNY: EPOCH (THE KRAKEN'S LAMENT / THE TEMPLE OF QUESTIONS / PRIVATE ENEMY NO. 1 / JUDGEMENT DAY)[66]

-> Benny awoke in Year 57 to find that Zordin looked like Earth... and that just three months beforehand, the Great Leader had just renamed the planet "Atlantis". The world was an amalgamation of elements from Greek mythology - Minotaurs were "commonplace", and winged horses, Pegasii, could fly to great heights. Benny spent a few weeks assisting Acanthus the Tale-Smith.

Two secret historians - Leonidas and Ruth, a priestess of Poseidon - recruited Benny to conduct an examination of the Underground, potentially the remains of a previous civilisation. They confronted and destroyed the Great Leader, hoping to end its clandestine manipulation of the twenty worlds.

More alterations occurred to Atlantis per the Epoch's design. Many citizens were revised into law-enforcers named Hierophants, and the temple of Ando offered a two-for-one sale on blessings. Leonidas and Benny became lovers; the next day, Leonidas and his fellow Historians were changed en masse into Hierophants. An erasure wave wiped out Atlantis...

... but Benny and Ruth awoke in a pocket reality from which the Epoch observed the timelines they'd created. The Epoch gave Bernice a final test: she was shown a Jurassic era-timeline and a Victorian era-timeline, with a Benny and Ruth in each of them. The Epoch-Prime reality Benny was to deduce which timeline was genuine, and delete the other two.

Benny deleted the Jurassic timeline, and threw the Epoch off balance by deleting the Epoch-Prime reality. Before its eradication, Ruth forced Benny into a stasis capsule. Ruth perished as Benny, held in a timeless state, returned to her native era, the year 2616.

The Ikkaban Period of Yemayan history was in progress around 1500 BC.[68] The Great Sphinx was now buried up to its neck by sand. It mentally influenced the young Thutmose, who was on a hunting trip, to dig it out.[69]

Two Time Lord students visited Earth as part of Academy History Module 101, hoping to study Osirian cosmic influence. A freak surge in the Vortex damaged their TARDIS, preventing them from returning home. They were worshipped as the gods Amun and Thoth, but "Amun" died in an uprising. Thoth escaped, but their TARDIS was disguised as a shabti figure - a representation of servants who wait upon royals in the afterlife - and was stolen by Userhat, one of Amun's servants. Thoth spent several lifetimes searching for his tomb.[70]

Erimem

Erimemushimteperem, "Daughter of Light", was born to the Pharaoh, Amenhotep II, and one of his sixty concubines, Rubak.[71] She had three half brothers: the eldest, Thutmose; Teti; and the youngest, Mentu.[72] When Erimem was a child, her father trapped the Great Old Ones in a pyramid in the Himalayas.[73]

Erimem's father, Amenhotep II, defeated a rival king and came to possess the alien crystal that the Doctor had deposited on Earth many millennia previous. Amenhotep II also claimed one thousand slaves and the rival king's sister as a wife, but he prized the crystal most of all. It was regarded as a diamond and had many names, but became known as the Veiled Leopard because it almost seemed to

---

not recite everything that's happened in the "last however-many-millennia..." while she was in stasis.

Benny's unsubstantiated deductions aside, it's never resolutely established in what era, subjectively speaking, the Epoch timelines exist. Big Finish producer Gary Russell (who took over the Benny audios from John Ainsworth after *Dead Man's Switch*) confirmed that the dating was left vague, and that, "the Atlantis Benny knows [in *Benny: Epoch*] could be any time from real Atlantis to Victorian times, or indeed the twenty-fifth century". With that in mind, this clutch of stories have been arbitrarily placed as rough contemporaries of the Atlantis seen in *The Time Monster*.

67 The background to *Benny: Year Zero*, given in *Benny: Epoch: Judgement Day*.

68 *SLEEPY* (p102).

69 As theorised by the Doctor in *The Sands of Time*

(p234); the fifth Doctor and Peri visit a chamber *under* the Sphinx in *The Eye of the Scorpion*, so if Thutmose did dig out the Sphinx, he'd finished his work prior to that.

70 *Forty-Five*: "False Gods". Howard Carter says that Userhat's tomb was sealed "three thousand years" prior to 1902. In real life, Amun was a patron deity of Thebes, and rose to prominence in the eighteenth dynasty (1550-1292 BC). The cult of Thoth gained notoriety somewhat before this, when its base of operations - Khnum - became the capital of the Hermopolite nome (a "nome" being an administrative district in ancient Egypt).

71 *The Eye of the Scorpion*; Erimem's father is named in *The Roof of the World* and *Erimem: The Coming of the Queen*.

72 *Erimem: The Coming of the Queen*

73 *The Roof of the World*

glow, and possessed odd spots that looked like leopard markings.[74]

c 1401 BC - ERIMEM: THE COMING OF THE QUEEN
[75] -> Amenhotep II had recently won a war against King Gadamere of Mitanni, and even after the final battle ordered the small fingers cut from the hands of five hundred Mitanni captives, and another five hundred of them taken as slaves. Pharaoh desired an alliance with his former rival, and arranged that his son Mentu should marry Gadamere's daughter Miral. The Mitanni sought revenge, and although a plot to install a puppet ruler as Pharaoh failed, Miral killed Erimem's brothers. For this treachery, Pharaoh killed Gadamere, and Erimem slit Miral's throat and stabbed her through the heart. Some months later, Hyksos mercenaries attacked the Pharaoh's chariot escort, and Amenhotep - standing his ground to prove his divinity - was killed. Erimem became ruler of Egypt.

When her father died, Erimem ordered priests to place the Veiled Leopard inside Amenhotep's bandages as he was prepared for burial. The diamond was later separated from his body, possibly owing to graverobbing, and would become one of the world's most famous jewels.[76]

c 1400 BC - THE EYE OF THE SCORPION[77] -> A starship containing prisoners crashed near Thebes, and a stasis box holding a dangerous gestalt energy being broke open. It began possessing local mercenaries. The fifth Doctor and Peri joined forces with Erimem to defeat it. Following this, Erimem joined the Doctor on his travels; Fayum, a junior council member, became Pharaoh in her absence. The face of the Sphinx was damaged, and Peri whimsically issued orders that it be reconstructed with Elvis' features, confident that Napoleon's troops would damage it in the late eighteenth century.

1366 BC - SET PIECE[78] -> Ace arrived via a space-time rift in Egypt during the rule of Pharaoh Akhenaten. She served as a bodyguard to Lord Sedjet, and eluded the robotic Ants pursuing her. After burying the TARDIS for Benny to find some centuries on, she escaped through a rift to nineteenth century France.

The shapeshifting Vondrax subsisted on the tachyon energy generated when probabilities compressed into parallel timelines. They fashioned and dispersed spheres, the Vondraxian Orbs, to harvest such energy. The Vondrax spent centuries collecting their energy-laden Orbs, and almost inevitably caused a slaughter at each retrieval zone. One such massacre occurred in Egypt, 1352 BC.[79]

The Monk helped build Stonehenge using anti-gravity lifts.[80] The Ragman had been born at the other end of the universe as a psionic force. It had travelled on Earth in a stone, drawn to the power inherent in Earth's ley lines. The rock containing the Ragman was incorporated into the stone circle at Cirbury, and the creature was dormant.[81]

Classical History

The Doctor claimed to have met Theseus.[82] The eleventh Doctor took Amy to the Trojan Gardens.[83] The Rani was present at the Trojan War, extracting a chemical from human brains.[84]

c 1184 BC - THE MYTH MAKERS[85] -> Captured by the Greeks outside Troy, the first Doctor was given two days to come up with a scheme to end the ten-year siege. He rejected the idea of using catapults to propel the Greeks over the walls of Troy - if only after Agamemnon insisted that the Doctor would be the first to try such a contrivance - and came up with the idea of using a wooden horse containing Greek troops. Vicki left the Doctor and Steven's company to marry

---

74 *The Veiled Leopard*
75 Dating *Erimem: The Coming of the Queen* (BF New Worlds novel #2) - Erimem is 16 according to the blurb and pages 6-7; she's 17 when she meets the Doctor and Peri in *The Eye of the Scorpion*. In the real world, Thutmose (here named as Erimem's half-brother) ruled Egypt as Menkheperura Thutmose IV from about 1400-1390 BC, and historically - as in the *Doctor Who* universe - he was the son of Amenhtep II. His death as reported in *Erimem: The Coming of the Queen* is a fairly significant deviation from history; writer Iain McLaughlin had privately decided that Erimem's successor to the throne, Fayum, would get renamed and become the historical Thutmose. While this seems like a fairly convoluted way of going about things, nothing especially rules it out either.

76 *The Veiled Leopard*
77 Dating *The Eye of Scorpion* (BF #24) - The Doctor estimates the date as "about 1400 BC" from hieroglyphics; in the real world, it's unclear as to whether the reign of Amenhotep II ended in 1401 BC or 1397 BC. Peri's claim that Napoleon's troops damaged the Sphinx's face (historically, they arrived in Egypt in 1798) owes to an urban legend that they used it for target practice. The Doctor doesn't correct Peri on this point, but there's otherwise no evidence that Napoleon's troops perpetrate the crime in the *Doctor Who* universe. In the real world, at least, erosion is the far more likely culprit.
78 Dating *Set Piece* (NA #35) - The date is given as "1366 BCE".
79 *TW: Trace Memory*
80 *The Time Meddler*. The earliest parts of Stonehenge

young Troilus; she re-named herself "Cressida". Katarina, one of Cassandra's handmaidens, joined the Doctor on his travels.

Vicki and Troilus married, but the Trojans came to believe that she was cursed or possessed. While Prince Aeneas and the main party travelled onward, Vicki and Troilus settled in Carthage. They had two children - "two young heroes", as Vicki called them.[86]

1164 BC - FROSTFIRE[87] -> Vicki wept alone one day, and discovered the Cinder - all that remained of the phoenix she had encountered in 1814 AD - amongst her tears. She contained it in an oil lamp, and kept it beneath the Temple of Astarte. It amused her to call the Cinder "Frosty", and to visit it and share memories of the Doctor.

Knowing that the phoenix would devour Earth if it hatched again, Vicki cared for the Cinder - and thereby set up a loop that would end its cycle of rebirth. The Cinder would remain in Carthage until the nearby city of Tunis arose. It then became part of Captain McClavity's Collection of Curiosities in the nineteenth century - and then travelled back with Vicki again to ancient Troy.

Troilus was supervising the building of a new quinquereme.[88]

A Vondraxian Orb wound up buried in the Arctic on Earth.[89] The Sorshans let the hostile Lom past their planetary defence shield, then reactivated it and released a biological toxin - deliberately killing themselves and their planet to prevent the Lom from spreading.[90] The Doctor was given a copy of the *I Ching* by Wen Wang.[91]

Thousands of years ago, the Exxilons were "the supreme beings of the universe... Exxilon had grown old before life began on other planets". Bernice Summerfield once wrote, "There are half a dozen worlds where the native languages develop up to a point, and then

are suddenly replaced by one of the Exxilon ones."

Worlds visited by the Exxilons include Yemaya and Earth, where they helped to build temples in Peru. The Doctor visited one of these temples, and examined the carvings there. On their home planet, the Exxilons created one of the Seven Hundred Wonders of the Universe: their City, a vast complex designed to last for all eternity. It was given a brain to protect, repair and maintain itself, and thus it no longer needed the Exxilons, who were driven from the City and degenerated into primitives.

The City needed power, and began to absorb electrical energy directly from the planet's atmosphere. The City also set an intelligence test that granted access to those who might have some knowledge to offer it. Over the centuries, a few Exxilons attempted the test, but none returned.[92]

Mawdryn and seven of his companions stole a metamorphic symbiosis generator from the Time Lords, hoping to become immortal. Instead they became horrific undying mutations, and the elders of their planet exiled them. Their ship entered a warp ellipse. It reached an inhabited planet every seventy years, allowing one of the crew to transmat down to seek help.[93]

c 1000 BC - PRIMEVAL[94] -> Kwundaar launched a bid to reconquer Traken. He engineered an illness for Nyssa, knowing the fifth Doctor would seek out Shayla, the greatest physician in Trakenite history. Kwundaar then implanted a psychic command in the Doctor's mind, getting the Doctor to deactivate Traken's defences. Kwundaar's forces consequently invaded the planet, but the Doctor tricked Kwundaar and harnessed the Source's power for himself. The Doctor thus became the first Keeper of Traken. He reactivated the defences, which destroyed Kwundaar, then abdicated. Shayla became the second Keeper.

---

were built around 2800 BC, but the final building activity occurred between 1600-1400 BC.

81 *Rags* (p160).

82 *The Horns of Nimon*

83 *Vincent and the Doctor.* This presumably means the gardens of ancient Troy.

84 *The Mark of the Rani*

85 Dating *The Myth Makers* (3.3) - The traditional date for the fall of Troy is 1184 BC, although this date is not given on screen.

86 *Frostfire*

87 Dating *Frostfire* (BF CC #1.1) - The audio booklet concurs on a dating of 1184 BC for *The Myth Makers*, and the back cover dates *Frostfire* to 1164 BC, something that is reiterated within the story itself.

88 *Frostfire.* A quinquereme is an oar-powered warship,

and was developed from the earlier trireme. It was in use from fourth century BC to the first century AD.

89 "Three thousand years" before the 1953 component of *TW: Trace Memory*.

90 "Three thousand years" before "The Grief".

91 *Timewyrm Revelation* (p14). Wang was the last king of the Shang dynasty.

92 *Death to the Daleks.* The Peruvian temples influenced by the Exxilons are around three thousand years old, so the collapse of Exxilon civilisation must be after that. In *SLEEPY*, Benny detects Exxilon influence in the Yemayan pyramid, dating from around "1500 BCE".

93 *Mawdryn Undead.* The ship has been in orbit for "three thousand years" according to the Doctor.

94 Dating *Primeval* (BF #26) - It is "three thousand years" before Nyssa's time.

The Baroks were humanoids with heads like those of goats. They were an advanced species who, each hunting season, would turn into wild, ferocious cannibals. They finally developed a ritual to siphon away their bloodlust - each tribe of Baroks would nominate a "scapegoat" into whom they could project their violent tendencies. The scapegoat would be driven into the wilderness, enabling the tribe to refrain from tearing itself apart. When a "cosmic" catastrophe befell the Barok homeworld, the surviving tribes dispersed throughout the galaxy.[95]

A spaceship containing some Hervoken crashed to Earth in what would become New England in America. In the millennia to come, the ship psychically influenced people to build the town of Blackwood Falls over it.[96]

The Shaydargen were a race of space pioneers. One of their spaceships crashed in Snowdonia, Wales, where the ten surviving crewmembers lived out their natural lives. Their craft remained buried in a mountain as the crew died off, and an empathic artificial entity created to meet their needs went dormant.[97]

Three parasitic Gorgons arrived on Earth through a portal, and inspired the legends of Medusa and her sisters in Greek mythology. They took human hosts - one of them was killed, and a sisterhood devoted to Demeter protected the remaining two. The Gorgons lost the talisman that would re-open the portal.[98]

On the planet Avalon, a technologically advanced race created a system that focused solar energy to deflect the large number of asteroids in their system away from their world. They also built thought-operated nanobots that allowed them to affect matter and energy. This discovery prolonged the race's existence but made their lives futile. They drained the machines of energy, but it was too late. Their civilisation fell, and the natives regressed to being reptilian cephlies, lacking all ingenuity.[99]

The Doctor met the Queen of Sheba.[100] **The cybernetic organism Horath ruled the Dark Empire, a period of tyrannical galactic rule. Horath crushed many civilisations, but was finally banished to another dimension. A portal leading to Horath was sealed below the standing stones in the village of Whitebarrow.[101]**

Evidence found by Professor Horner in the twenti-

95 "Thousands of years" before *Scapegoat*.
96 "Millennia" before *Forever Autumn*.
97 "Millennia" before *SJA: The Shadow People*.
98 "Three thousand years" before *SJA: Eye of the Gorgon*.
99 "Thousands of years" before *The Sorcerer's Apprentice*.
100 *Other Lives*. The Queen was a contemporary of King Solomon, who lived circa 970-928 BC.
101 "Three thousand years" before *SJA: Enemy of the Bane*.
102 *The Daemons*
103 *The Song of the Megaptera*. The Biblical book of *Jonah* is set during the reign of Jeroboam II (786-746 BC).
104 *K9: Dream-Eaters*. No date is specified, and the information that the obelisk dates to "Celtic" times doesn't pin one down.
105 *Seasons of Fear*
106 Dating *Benny: Walking to Babylon* (Benny NA #10) - The year is given.
107 *Option Lock*. Pythagoras lived 580-500 BC.
108 The fourth Doctor name-drops Sun Tzu in *The Shadow of Weng-Chiang*, and the seventh Doctor and Ace refer to meeting him in *The Shadow of the Scourge*.
109 *Set Piece*, during the "Fourth Century BCE".
110 Three thousand years before *Benny: Tempest*.
111 *Benny: The Empire State*. The legend of the Stone claims it's "about three thousand years old", and Benny (speaking from 2607) says it has existed for "the whole of recorded human history". Braxiatel concurs, but also says he was inert as the Stone "for a couple of millennia". In *Benny: The Judas Gift*, Bev Tarrant says Braxiatel spent "three thousand years asleep".
112 *The Daemons*, *City of Death*.
113 "One hundred generations" before *Four to Doomsday*.
114 *The Vampires of Venice*. Records suggest that the Olympic Games were first held in 776 BC.
115 *The Spectre of Lanyon Moor*. This would be around 440 BC.
116 *Enlightenment*. Pericles died, age 70, in 429 BC.
117 *Robot*. Alexander lived 356-323 BC.
118 *The Keys of Marinus*. Pyrrho lived c.360-270 BC.
119 *The Slitheen Excursion*
120 *Omega*. This would have been around 350 BC.
121 *Horror of Fang Rock*, *Logopolis*.
122 "Voyager"
123 *City at World's End*, *The Two Doctors*. Archimedes lived c.287-212 BC.
124 *Island of Death*
125 *Eye of Heaven* (p181). Eratosthenes lived c.276-194 BC.
126 *Cat's Cradle: Witch Mark*
127 "The Crimson Hand". Depictions of Zephyrus and Hyacinth (a target of Zaphyrus' love, and killed by him when Hyacinth favoured Apollo) date back to the fifth century BC.
128 Dating *Benny: The Oracle of Delphi* (Benny audio #6.5) - The year is given. Historically, the plague that struck Athens in 430 BC returned in 429 and 427 BC.
129 *Benny: Epoch: The Kraken's Lament*
130 *The Fires of Pompeii*. Presumably this refers to the original Sybil, at Delphi.
131 "Three thousand years, give or take" (p51) years before *Benny: The Doomsday Manuscript*.
132 *TW: The Sin Eaters*. The year isn't given, but the historical record suggests that eruptions occurred at Etna in 396 BC, 122 BC, 1030, 1160 (or possibly 1224),

eth century suggested that pagan rituals took place at Devil's Hump at around 800 BC.[102] The Doctor met the Jonah of legend - a confirmed vegan with white and wrinkled skin.[103] **The Bodach attempted to send humanity permanently to sleep and feast on its dreams, but the plan failed. The crystals the Bodach needed - the Eyes of Oblivion - were set on an obelisk that ended up buried outside London.**[104]

Around 600 BC, a Nimon scout arrived on Earth and was killed by his own sword by Mithras, who was later worshipped throughout the known world as a result of his deed.[105]

570 BC - BENNY: WALKING TO BABYLON[106] ->

Benny pursued two Worldsphere rogues (!Ci!ci-tel and WiRgo!xu) and their drone (I!qu-!qu-tala) down a time corridor to ancient Babylon, and met a linguist, John Lafayette, who had fallen down the corridor from 1901. I!qu-!qu-tala curtailed the rogues' goal of triggering war between the People and the Time Lords, and terminated the corridor after sending Benny home. !Ci!ci-tel was killed, but WiRgo!xu and I!qu-!qu-tala travelled across the world with the Babylonian priestess Ninan. The Time Lords returned John to his native time.

The Doctor was present when Pythagoras discovered the connection between mathematics and the physical world.[107] Around 500 BC, the Doctor met Sun Tzu at least twice and discussed the *Art of War*.[108] The Doctor replaced Sun Tzu as the Chinese emperor's military advisor but wasn't terribly effective, as he kept holding conflict resolution seminars rather than fighting.[109] The Way of Drell, a religion devoted to universal harmony, was founded in the Mother Temple on Karnor.[110]

After Irving Braxiatel left the Braxiatel Collection in 2606, he wanted some "me" time and facilitated his transformation into a rock: the Stone of Barter. It became a legendary item that was passed between nomadic tribes, and enabled a literal exchange of qualities such as intelligence, knowledge and paranormal abilities.[111]

Ancient Greece

The Daemons and Scaroth both influenced ancient Greek civilisation.[112] The Athenian philosopher Bigon lived in Greece around two thousand five hundred years ago. In Bigon's fifty-sixth year, the Urbankans kidnapped him. For the first time in their visits to Earth, the Urbankans encountered resistance.[113]

The eleventh Doctor thought that Amy and Rory might like to visit the first Olympic Games as a wedding present.[114] The Doctor visited Athens and saw the Parthenon being built.[115] **The Eternals kidnapped a trireme of Athenian sailors from the time of Pericles.**[116]

The Doctor met Alexander the Great[117] and Pyrrho[118], possibly on the same visit.

The tenth Doctor planned to take June to Greece in 480 BC, but they ended up in 1500 BC instead.[119] The Doctor met Praxiteles, who sculpted the Venus de Milo.[120] **The Doctor visited one of the Seven Wonders of the Ancient World: the Pharos lighthouse.**[121]

The first lighthouse was built at Alexandria; Astrolabus provided the fire of its lamp. Within a year, starships began to land. "The city had become a crossroads in time. Past and future had conjoined - sorcery and science now walked hand in hand." The aliens stole Astrolabus' charts. Alexandria fell, destroyed by a sea monster.

> "It was then that Voyager came... from the realms of old time, from the dawn of myth... the very spirit of legend."

Astrolabus attempted to navigate the timelines, but the disturbances were too great.[122]

The first Doctor and Susan met Archimedes, and **the Doctor acquired his business card.**[123] The third Doctor visited Athens and spent time with Archimedes.[124] The Doctor taught the playwright Eratosthenes at least some of his craft.[125] The Doctor wrote many of the Greek Classics.[126] He judged that Zephyrus, the Greek god of the west wind, was "a lovely bloke, bit of a swinger. Should have seen what he did to poor old Hyacinth".[127]

430 BC - BENNY: THE ORACLE OF DELPHI[128] ->

Benny and Jason travelled back in time to ancient Greece, hoping to consult with the Oracle of Delphi pertaining to future events concerning the Braxiatel Collection. The Oracle, a.k.a. Lady Megaira, had gained the gift of prophecy from the Stone of Barter. She unleashed a plague upon Athens as vengeance against the patriarchy for their treatment of women, but herself fell victim to the illness. Benny and Jason distributed a plague-vaccine, and returned home. During these events, Benny met Socrates and Plato.

Benny thought that Plato was a "miserable old git who talked a lot of rubbish".[129] **The Doctor met the real Sybil, "a hell of a woman" who could dance the Tarantella and had "nice teeth". She had a bit of a thing for the Doctor, but when he told her it could "never last", she replied, "I know."**[130]

A spaceship fell onto the planet Kasagrad. Rablev, the chief engineer of King Hieronimes, tried to harness its power and capture the throne, but the ship's atomic stacks overloaded, killing thousands if not millions. The people believed Rablev's arrogance had offended the gods, and sealed him in the ship. His lost tomb became legendary.[131]

Jack Harkness once fled a lava flow emanating from Mount Etna on a goat cart.[132] The Doctor met Aristotle, who whittered on about bees.[133]

323 BC (May to 13th June) - FAREWELL, GREAT MACEDON[134] **->** The first Doctor, Ian, Barbara and Susan met Alexander the Great during his final days. One of Alexander's generals, Antipater, tired of Alexander's refusal to return home to Macedon and led a conspiracy to eliminate the king and replace him with another general, Selecus. The conspirators' actions led to the deaths of those in line to succeed Alexander: Cleitus, Calanus and Hephaestion. The Doctor's party was implicated in the deaths, but Alexander judged them innocent - especially after the Doctor and Ian respectively proved their worthiness by walking barefoot on hot coals and winning a wrestling match.

Alexander fell ill (or was poisoned) and refused treatment upon learning from the Doctor's group that his dream of uniting the entire world was destined to fail. Antipater's plot was exposed, and Selecus killed Antipater to keep his own treachery secret. Within minutes of Alexander's death, his remaining generals started squabbling over his throne. Ptolemy aided the Doctor and his friends in making their getaway, and pledged to improve upon the city of Alexandria - and to build an immense library there in Alexander's honour.

The Thousand Year War on Skaro

On the planet Skaro, the Thals and the Kaleds went to war. During the first century of the conflict, chemical weapons were used, and monstrous mutations developed in the Thal and Kaled gene pool. To keep their races pure, all Mutos were cast out into the wastelands that now covered the planet. As the war continued, resources became more scarce for the foot soldiers - plastic and rifles gave way to animal skins and clubs, but both sides developed ever-more potent missiles. The war would last for a thousand years until there were only two cities left, protected by thick domes.[135]

Ancient China

The Great Wall of China was built around 300 BC.[136] As a young boy, Qin Shi Huang found a spaceship bearing an alien: Meng Tian. Huang used Meng Tian's knowledge to unite China's warring states and become its first emperor.[137] **At the time the Ch'in dynasty ruled in China, the Eternals kidnapped a crew of Chinese sailors.**[138] At some point, the Celestial Toymaker's games became interwoven into the fabric of Imperial China.[139]

1669, 1928, 1949, 1971, 1981, 1983 and 1991 to 1993.
133 *Survival of the Fittest.* Aristotle lived 384 to 322 BC.
134 Dating *Farewell, Great Macedon* (BF LS #2.1) - The year is given at least three times. The Doctor's group spends some "long weeks" with Alexander before leaving on the day of his death, which is cited as "June 13th". (A solid claim, although his passing is alternatively ascribed to the 10th or the 11th.)

Many of the events in *Farewell, Great Macedon* are drawn from historical accounts, but extreme liberties have been taken with the timeframe, and entirely disparate events have been rolled into a single narrative. Cleitus is thought to have died about five years before Alexander (in autumn 328 BC), Calanus about a year and a half beforehand (in late 325 BC), and Hephaestion some months beforehand (in autumn 324 BC) - here, they all perish in a matter of weeks. Calanus and Cleitus died in circumstances similar to those described here, but Hephaestion likely died from typhoid fever, and here succumbs to a snake bite. Antipater is rumoured to have orchestrated Alexander's death, while the historian Plutarch rejects this idea, and it's equally likely that Alexander died from natural causes. Either way, Antipater isn't implicated as having anything to do with Cleitus, Calanus and Hephaestion's deaths. Nor did Antipater die at Selecus' hand - he was, in fact, named regent of Alexander's empire and given control of Greece before dying from an illness, after returning to Macedon in 320 BC.

135 "A thousand years" before *Genesis of the Daleks*.
136 *Marco Polo*
137 Or so the artificial version of Huang claims in "The Immortal Emperor". Huang was born in 246 BC.
138 *Enlightenment*
139 *The Nightmare Fair.* Imperial China started in 221 BC; the Toymaker's involvement could have happened at any point until its end, in 1912 AD.
140 Dating *The Emperor of Eternity* (BF CC #4.8) - The evidence is confusing when weighed against the historical accounts. The Doctor specifies that it's "210 BC", within a few days of the Emperor's death (on September 10th of that year), but the meteor incident that prompted the slaughter of Dongjun is historically dated to 211 BC. It's possible that the meteor event happened a year later in the *Doctor Who* universe, but it's equally likely that the Doctor has just gotten the year wrong.

THE FIRST EMPEROR OF CHINA: Qin Shi Huang (who ruled under the name "First Emperor" from 221-210 BC) is featured in three *Doctor Who* stories, in three different formats: the novel *The Eleventh Tiger*, the DWM comic "The Immortal Emperor" and the audio *The Emperor of Eternity*. All are reasonably reconcilable if one is flexible as to the final fate of the original Emperor. For all that we're told, the real Huang might, as history claims, have simply died after ingesting a series of "immortality pills" that gave him mercury poisoning - but that his mind was copied (by both Meng Tian and the Mandragora Helix, for entirely different purposes)

c 210 BC - THE EMPEROR OF ETERNITY[140] -> The TARDIS materialised in space, and deflected a meteor toward China. Li Si, a chancellor to the Emperor Qin Shi Huang, regarded the meteor landing as a bad omen and had the people of Dongjun put to death lest they speak of it. The second Doctor, Jamie and Victoria arrived in the village ten days later. Li Si captured the travellers and the TARDIS, but Qin - who had been masquerading as a monk - was saddened to learn the atrocities committed in his name and gave the Doctor's party permission to leave.

In 210 BC, an alien intelligence copied the minds of Qin Shi Huang and two of his generals into a stone engram. They would remain dormant until 1865 AD.[141]

c 210 BC - "The Immortal Emperor"[142] -> The tenth Doctor and Donna saw the Great Wall of China, and found that Emperor Qin Shi Huang's first general - Meng Tian - was an alien who had built an army of terracotta robots. Following an assassination attempt, Meng Tian had given the Emperor an artificial body. The Emperor learned of Meng Tian's plans to conquer Earth and slew him - but in doing so became inert and destroyed his palace.

The Jex brutally subjugated the Canavitchi, killing two-thirds of them. The Canavitchi successfully revolted, and swore to eradicate their former masters.[143] Two thousand years ago, Varan Tak from the Anthropology Unit on Oskerion was marooned in the asteroid belt when his

spacecraft was damaged. He began collecting specimens from Earth.[144] The Star Abacus of Beta Phoenii 9 was destroyed by the Paragon Virus in 87 BC.[145]

Ancient Rome

101 BC (January) - 100: "100 BC"[146] -> The sixth Doctor and Evelyn, mistakenly thinking they'd gone forward to 100 BC instead of backwards to 101 BC, arrived as the parents of Julius Caesar hailed the birth of a girl, Julia. The travellers wrongly concluded their "previous visit" had altered Julius' conception, causing him to be born with two X chromosomes. They attempted to "go back" in time, hoping to put history back on course.

101 BC (October) - 100: "100 BC"[147] -> The sixth Doctor and Evelyn happened to meet Senator Gaius Julius Caesar the elder and his wife Aurelia - the parents of Julius Caesar - and left upon realising that love was in the air.

They returned after an erroneous trip back in time, convinced that their presence had delayed Julius' conception, causing him to be born a girl. They eventually realised that they'd witnessed the birth of Caesar's sister, and that Julius hadn't been born yet. Aurelia, suitably in the mood, lured her husband into bed.

The Doctor met Julius Caesar.[148] The eighth Doctor, Fitz and Trix defeated Thorgan of the Sulumians. He had been planning to prevent the signing of the Treaty of

---

beforehand. In *The Eleventh Tiger* (p267), the first Doctor concurs with this, saying that the "Emperor" he meets is a duplicate of the original's memories "in a personality matrix", and isn't the genuine article. (That, certainly, would explain why the Emperor is portrayed a lot more ruthlessly in *The Eleventh Tiger*, and seems very intent on obtaining the immortality that he forsakes in *The Emperor of Eternity*.) Similarly, it's possible that the "Emperor" in "The Immortal Emperor" is nothing more than a robotic construct crafted by Meng Tian, who wants to remain the power behind the throne once the original Huang has died/otherwise become unavailable. The robot might even *think* he's the genuine article, although it's admittedly an oversight on Meng Tian's part to leave out a failsafe that would prevent his faux Qin Shi Huang from becoming outraged and killing him. The only remaining stumbling block is that the tenth Doctor claims ("The Immortal Emperor") that Huang just disappeared one night and that "no-one knows how he died" - something that isn't true in real life, as the first Doctor knows (*The Eleventh Tiger*, p267 again).

Whatever the case with Huang, it's possible that Meng Tian built the terracotta army (found in real life in 1974) as robots that collect dust after Meng Tian's

death until the Mandragora Helix makes use of them in 1884 (in *The Eleventh Tiger*), once the stars align as it requires.

141 "Two thousand years" before *The Eleventh Tiger*.

142 Dating "The Immortal Emperor" (*The Doctor Who Storybook 2009*) - It's "a couple of centuries BC", at the end of the First Emperor's reign.

143 "Two thousand years" before *The King of Terror*.

144 "The Collector"

145 *The Quantum Archangel*

146 Dating *100*: "100 BC" (BF #100a) - The Doctor attempts to go forward nine months in time from October 101 BC, but appears to instead go backward by the same amount. Julius Caesar's older sister Julia was indeed born in 101 BC. Nothing is here said about Julius' *other* older sister, who was also named Julia, and is only mentioned in the accounts of the biographer/historian/gossip monger Suetonius.

147 Dating *100*: "100 BC" (BF #100a) - The month and year are given, and are extrapolated from Caesar's birth on 13th July, 100 BC. The story title was doubtless intended to tie into Big Finish's 100th audio release, but is deliberately misleading in that - as the Doctor and Evelyn figure out - they were never in 100 BC.

148 *Empire of Death*, and evidently a separate occa-

Brundusium.[149] **At the height of the Roman Empire, the War Lords lifted a Roman battlefield.**[150] The Celestial Toymaker abducted a Roman legionary.[151] The second Doctor, Jamie and Victoria attended a gladiator fight in ancient Rome, and Victoria was appalled by the violence.[152]

One of the splinters of Scaroth was a man of influence in Ancient Rome.[153] **The Doctor visited Rome, met Hannibal and Cleopatra, and was very impressed by the swordsmanship of Cleopatra's bodyguard.**[154] The captain of Cleopatra's guard was a "friend of a friend" to Ace, and taught her the art of sword fighting.[155] **The tenth Doctor mentioned meeting Cleopatra,**[156] and was familiar with the size of Cleopatra's bedchamber.[157] According to the Doctor, Cleopatra was a pushover.[158] with "the grace of a carpet flea".[159] Iris Wildthyme's companion Panda said Cleopatra was an "incorrigible woman".[160]

10 BC - STATE OF CHANGE[161] **->** After watching Cleopatra's barge on the Nile in 41 BC, the sixth Doctor and Peri had decided to travel a little way into the future to follow the history of Rome. The Rani compelled a Vortex entity, Iam, to copy the Doctor's TARDIS console, but this also duplicated a section of the Earth around 32 BC, creating a flat disc-shaped world. The TARDIS console was duplicated and came to rest on the copied Earth,

where it was regarded as an Oracle.

With information from this Oracle, the Roman Empire made great advancements. The battle of Actium went against Octavian and Agrippa because they faced opponents with steamships. Electric lighting, airships and explosives were developed. The culmination of this technology was Ultimus, the Roman Empire's atomic bomb programme. Capable of kiloton yields, Ultimus could destroy any known city. Cleopatra's three children - Cleopatra Selene, Alexander and Ptolemy - ruled as a triumvirate.

The Doctor defeated the Rani's plans, and convinced Iam to relocate Terra Nova into the real universe. It settled into an unoccupied sector of space.

Anno Domini

The Doctor claimed he was at the original Christmas, and "got the last room" at the inn.[162] The Doctor took Leonardo da Vinci back to the very first Christmas in Bethlehem, so Leo could study the local light and colour for his adoration painting. Leonardo was fearful of visiting Christ's manager, so he and the Doctor had a slap-up dinner before returning to the fifteenth century.[163]

sion from *100*: "100".

149 *The Gallifrey Chronicles*
150 *The War Games*
151 "The Greatest Gamble"
152 *The Colony of Lies*
153 *City of Death*. He's listed as "Roman Emperor" in the script, but it's possible he's a senator or other Roman of rank.
154 The Doctor has already visited Rome on his travels before *The Romans*. He mentions Hannibal (247-182 BC, he crossed the Alps in 219 BC) in *Robot*, and Cleopatra (68-30 BC) in *The Masque of Mandragora*.
155 *The Settling*
156 *The Girl in the Fireplace*
157 *Ghosts of India*
158 *The Wedding of River Song*
159 *Loups-Garoux*
160 *Iris: Enter Wildthyme* (p83).
161 Dating *State of Change* (MA #5) - The Doctor thinks that it is "the year 10 BC, approximately" (p41). The Cleopatra of this world died around 15 BC (p45). Terra Nova is part of the universe's timeline by the end of the story, yet despite its prosperity and technological advantage over the proper Earth, it's never heard of again.
162 *Voyage of the Damned*
163 *Relative Dimensions*. The Doctor mentions that this was "right about Zero BC/AD", although estimates of

Christ's birth year by historians generally range from 6 BC to 6 AD.
164 Dating *TW: Exit Wounds* (*TW* 2.13) - The year is given.
165 *Planet of the Dead*
166 *Matrix*. The Wandering Jew was a shoemaker or tradesman who mocked Jesus on his way to the Crucifixion, and was reportedly condemned to walk the Earth until the Second Coming of Christ. There is little Biblical evidence for this, but records of the legend go back to the thirteenth century.
167 *The Slow Empire*
168 *The Resurrection of Mars*. Caligula ruled 16th March, 37 AD, to 24th January, 41 AD, presuming this meet-up happened during his reign as emperor.
169 Dating *Iris: The Two Irises* (Iris audio #2.3) - It's during Caligula's time as Emperor (37-41 AD).
170 *Demon Quest: The Relics of Time*
171 Dating *Demon Quest: The Relics of Time* (BBC fourth Doctor audio #2.1) - The Doctor says it's "nearly two thousand years earlier" than the present day. A Celt says Julius Caesar invaded "almost a century ago", and it's referred to a couple of times as "the first century". Although "Claudius" is actually a shapechanging demon, it would seem to be later in the year that the Doctor knows the real Claudius came to Britain: 43 AD. However, Mrs Wibbsey dates this story to 46 AD in *Demon Quest: Starfall*.

27 AD - TW: EXIT WOUNDS[164] -> Jack Harkness' brother, Gray, forced Captain John Hart to bury the immortal Jack beneath the future site of Cardiff. He would remain trapped until 1901.

The Doctor remembered the original Easter.[165] Joseph Liebermann, who would encounter the seventh Doctor in 1888, claimed to be the Wandering Jew of legend.[166]

The Doctor visited the court of Caligula.[167] The Meddling Monk and his companion Lucie Miller met Caligula.[168]

c 39 AD - IRIS: THE TWO IRISES[169] -> Iris Hilary Wildthyme - a projection of Iris' bus - and Panda visited Caligula's Rome for a toga party and some tai chi.

In the spring of 43, the Romans invaded Britain. They were led by Emperor Claudius, who was in Britain for a total of sixteen days.[170]

46 AD (winter) - DEMON QUEST: THE RELICS OF TIME[171] -> The fourth Doctor and Mrs Wibbsey arrived on the trail of the TARDIS' spatial geometer. A group of Celts considered Mrs Wibbsey a soothsayer, and she went into a trance, displaying knowledge she couldn't possibly possess. This convinced them to attack a rival tribe, which had a "wizard" and "monster". The next morning, the Doctor and Wibbsey went to the village and discovered that the monster was an elephant and the wizard was a disguised Emperor Claudius, who had run away from his army for a quiet life. Except... "Claudius" was not the genuine article, but the shapechanging Demon luring the Doctor and Wibbsey through time.[172] As the two British tribes made their peace, "Claudius" entered a dematerialisation chamber in his dwelling and vanished. The Doctor rescued the elephant from the hungry Celts, and the TARDIS headed for its next destination: the Moulin Rouge.

The Iceni, a Celtic tribe led by Boudicca, razed many Roman-occupied British towns to the ground.[173] Roundstone Wood in England always "stayed wild"; in ancient times, it was considered bad luck to collect wood there. The Romans in Britain stayed clear of it.[174] Iris Wildthyme claimed that Salome did the fan dance

with the Doctor's scarf.[175] A great earthquake in Vesuvius in 62 AD released some of the Pyroviles from their ancient slumber. The eruption of Vesuvius in 79 AD caused a rift in time that retroactively gave some of the young girls of Pompeii the gift of prophecy. Some of their number formed the Sybiline Cult. The TARDIS' arrival was foretold in the Thirteenth Book of the Sybiline Oracles.[176] The Pyroviles were unable to return to their homeworld, Pryovillia, because it had been stolen by the Daleks for their reality bomb.[177]

Pliny the Elder gave the Doctor some smelling salts.[178] The Celestial Toymaker took some inspiration for his games from the Roman Coliseum.[179]

64 AD - THE RESCUE[180] -> The TARDIS landed on the side of a hill and toppled from it.

64 AD - BYZANTIUM![181] -> The TARDIS had materialised just outside Byzantium. The Romans mistook Ian for a contemporary Briton and granted him some respect as a citizen of the Empire. Ian helped the Roman General Gaius Calaphilus and his political opponent, city praefectus Thalius Maximus, to settle their differences. Calaphilus and Maximus united efforts to purge corruption from the city, instigating a period of reform.

The first Doctor met the scribes Reuben, Rayhab and Amos, and helped them to translate the Gospel of Mark into Greek, producing a version that complemented the writings of Matthew the tax-gatherer.

Returning to the TARDIS, the travellers discovered that the Roman Germanicus Vinicius has found the TARDIS and taken it to his villa near Rome. They followed it there...

64 AD (June to July) - THE ROMANS[182] -> The first Doctor, Ian, Barbara and Vicki spent nearly a month at a deserted villa just outside Rome. Becoming bored by the lack of adventure, the Doctor and Vicki travelled to the capital. Captured by slave traders, Ian and Barbara were sold at auction. Ian escaped, but ended up as a gladiator in Rome. Barbara became the servant of the Emperor Nero's wife, Poppea, and the object of the Emperor's attentions. The Doctor, meanwhile, was pos-

---

172 *Demon Quest: Sepulchre*
173 *Human Nature* (NA)
174 *TW: Small Worlds*
175 *The Blue Angel*. Salome lived in the first century AD.
176 "Seventeen years" before *The Fires of Pompeii*.
177 Said to be "over two thousand years" before *The Stolen Earth*, although in truth it's slightly less than that.
178 *Paradise 5*. Pliny the Elder (23-79 AD), author of *Naturalis Historica* (*Natural History*) wrote about smelling salts.

179 *The Nightmare Fair*
180 Dating *The Rescue* (2.3) - This happens right at the end of the story, as a literal cliffhanger. The date is established in *The Romans*, but *Byzantium!* establishes that the TARDIS crew have another adventure first...
181 Dating *Byzantium!* (PDA #44) - This story takes place immediately before *The Romans*.
182 Dating *The Romans* (2.4) - The story culminates in the Great Fire of Rome. The TARDIS crew have spent "a month" at the villa.

ing as the musician Maximus Pettulian (despite a complete lack of musical ability). When the Doctor accidentally set fire to Nero's plans to rebuild Rome, the Emperor was inspired. As Rome began to burn, the four time travellers returned to the TARDIS.

A Dalek arrived in Roman Britain from the Time War, with orders to imprint the population with the Dalek Factor. Its capsule malfunctioned, and it was only able to release a tiny amount of the Factor before being buried.[183]

Volcano Day

79 AD - THE FIRES OF VULCAN[184] **->** The seventh Doctor and Mel arrived in Pompeii, just as Mount Vesuvius became active. The TARDIS was trapped in the rubble of a collapsed building, preventing their escape. The Doctor managed to antagonise the gladiator Murranus by beating him in a dice game. The Doctor and Mel escaped to the TARDIS just as the volcano erupted, destroying Pompeii and the surrounding area.

> (=) Temporal distortion resulted in an alternate history where Vesuvius took much longer to erupt, and the city's populace evacuated in their boats.[185]

The tenth Doctor and Martha had some "unlucky business" at Mount Vesuvius.[186] Valnaxi refugees hid themselves and some of their works of art in a warren on Earth, to prevent destruction by their enemy, the Wurms.[187]

79 (22nd-23rd August) - THE FIRES OF POMPEII[188] **->** The tenth Doctor and Donna arrived in what they thought was Rome, but which turned out to be Pompeii, the day before the great eruption. The Doctor told Donna that Vesuvius erupting was a fixed point in time, and so they couldn't save the doomed people. They learned that the Pyroviles intended to convert all of humanity into stone creatures, and so used the Pyroviles' own technology to engineer the historic eruption of Vesuvius, destroying them.

Twenty thousand people died in Pompeii, but Donna persuaded the Doctor to save the family of Lobus Caecilius, a marble trader.

> (=) Had the Doctor and Donna not intervened, the Pyroviles would have created a Pompeii-based empire that would have overthrown Rome and encompassed the whole world.[189]

Six months after the eruption, Caecilius and his family had set themselves up in Rome, and had an altar dedicated to the Doctor, Donna and their temple: the TARDIS.[190]

102 - THE PANDORICA OPENS / THE BIG BANG[191] **->** Projections made by a number of alien races indicated that the Doctor's TARDIS would explode in such a way that would destroy history. All universes were threatened. A coalition of alien races, brought together using the Cracks in Time for travel, sought to prevent this and laid a trap that the Doctor couldn't resist. Psychic blueprints were taken from Amy Pond's house in 2010, and used to construct a vault under Stonehenge - Underhenge - in 102 AD. Within the vault was placed the Pandorica: a fabled prison rumoured to contain "a nameless, terrible thing, soaked in the blood of a billion galaxies", but which was actually patterned from one of Amy's childhood storybooks, *The Legend of Pandora's Box*.

The alliance against the Doctor included the Daleks, Cybermen, Sontarans, Terileptils, Nestenes and their

---

183 Archaeologists date the site to "about 70 AD" in *I am a Dalek* (p24).
184 Dating *The Fires of Vulcan* (BF #12) - The story ends with the eruption of Vesuvius.
185 *The Algebra of Ice* (p15).
186 *Made of Steel*. It's not specified that this was during the famous historical eruption.
187 "Two thousand years" before *The Art of Destruction*.
188 Dating *The Fires of Pompeii* (X4.2) - The date is a matter of historical record. The Doctor claims he's been to Rome "ages ago" before during the great fire, a reference to *The Romans* - but as we've seen, he's made a couple of other trips to the city.
189 *The Fires of Pompeii*. According to a vision the High Priestess of the Sybilines has of the "Pyrovile alternative" timeline.
190 *The Fires of Pompeii*
191 Dating *The Pandorica Opens* and *The Big Bang*

(X5.12-5.13) - The Doctor says it's "102... not am, not pm, AD". The real Cleopatra, as is mentioned, has already died (in 30 BC).
The Cybermen seen here warn that "all the universes are deleted", which is in keeping with their having the Cybus logo (meaning they're from Pete's World). However, they now have Cyberships, teleportation and their heads sprout tentacles and can operate independently - all of which seems more advanced than the Cybus models first seen in *Rise of the Cybermen/The Age of Steel*. Those Cybermen discarded the whole body apart from the brain, but the faceplates of these newer models open up to reveal bone skulls, and hunt for "organic components". The conclusion is either that the Cybermen seen here are the first from *our* universe seen in the new series (having melded the Cybus tech with their own), or that they're from the future of Pete's World.

Autons, Drahvins, Chelonians, Slitheen, Sycorax and their roboforms, Haemo-goths, Zygons, Atraxi, Draconians, Hoix, Judoon, Uvodni, Blowfish, Weevils and Silurians. Autons posed as Roman soldiers, as patterned from *The Story of Roman Britain*. The conspirators also used Amy's psychic residue to bring Rory Williams back to life as an Auton - he was unaware that he wasn't human.

The Underhenge broadcast a signal: "The Pandorica is opening." Per instructions that Vincent van Gogh left on the painting *The Pandorica Opens*, River Song arrived at Stonehenge and posed as Cleopatra. She summoned the eleventh Doctor and Amy, and they all examined Underhenge and the Pandorica.

A vast fleet of diverse starships appeared above the Earth - a Dalek fleet (a minimum of twelve thousand Dalek battleships), Cyberships and four Sontaran battlefleets. River attempted to relocate the TARDIS to aid the Doctor, but was taken to the year 2010 instead. Rory's Auton programming activated, and he mortally wounded Amy. The Doctor insisted that he wasn't responsible for the destruction of the TARDIS, but the leaders of the alliance sealed him in the Pandorica. The TARDIS exploded in 2010 anyway.

The Doctor travelled back from 1996, and had Rory free his past self from the Pandorica. They put Amy's body in his place, knowing that the Pandorica would keep her in stasis, healing her when it obtained a sample of her future DNA. Rory remained behind to guard the Pandorica - he would do so for nearly two thousand years, spurring the legend of the Lone Centurion.

In 118, the Pandorica was taken back to Rome under armed guard.[192] The Vondrax killed many in Syria, the second century AD, while retrieving one of their Orbs.[193]

120 - THE STONE ROSE[194] -> The tenth Doctor and Rose arrived in Rome, hoping to explain how a statue of Rose from the second century ended up in the British Museum in the twenty-first. They discovered a GENIE from the year 2375 and captured it, preventing the damage its reality-altering powers could cause.

> (=) The eleventh Doctor, Amy and Rory photographed a Roman-built road in England that had been diverted around Swallow Woods.[195]

Jack Harkness attempted to sell tickets to horse racing in second century Rome to the Cephalids, but they didn't understand the concept.[196] On a visit to Condercum, the Doctor debated military ethics with a group of Romans fighting the Caledonians.[197] A group of third-century Romans was kidnapped by Varan Tak.[198] The Romans drove the Celts from their lands. Gallifreyan intervention allowed King Constantine to pass into the parallel world of Avalon. Even while sleeping, Constantine ruled Avalon for two thousand years.[199]

A Roman legionary fell through the Rift to arrive in twenty-first century Cardiff.[200] The planet Quagreeg developed in the Sirius system as a marsh world that was a source of the rare metal telmonium, and was home to a race of unpleasant reptilians. One reptilian - later named the Sepulchre, after St. Sepulchre's Church - developed within its mental landscape overlapping recreations of London in various time periods. The Sepulchre used dimensionally transcendental beams to transport various humans into the London-recreations within its mind, and did so with a Roman legion.[201] Ptolemy was immune to the Doctor's psychic paper, meaning he was a genius.[202]

> = On one parallel Earth, later designated Roma I, the Roman Empire enjoyed a golden age as successive Emperors Nerva, Trajan, Hadrian, Antonius Pius, Marcus Aurelius, Avidius Cassius, Septimus Severus, Publius Septimus, Claudius Gothicus, Domitius Aurelianus and Diocletian ruled wisely. The Rhine and Danube were crossed, and the Germanic peoples fled East; they spent centuries fighting the Huns, Vandals and Ostrogoths. Rome was free to concentrate elsewhere. Constantine conquered Asia.[203]

192 *The Big Bang*

193 *TW: Trace Memory*

194 Dating *The Stone Rose* (NSA #7) - The date is given.

195 *The Way Through the Woods*. The Roman invasion of England began in 43 AD, and formally ended in 410.

196 *Only Human*

197 *Ghost Ship*

198 "The Collector"

199 *The Shadows of Avalon*

200 *TW: End of Days*

201 *Dead London*. The "lost legion" that's used to populate the Roman London is presumably Rome's notori-ous Ninth Legion, whose real-life disappearance has led to much speculation. Sources claim the legion went missing as early as 117 AD, although it's possible it occurred later. Tellingly, the Ninth isn't listed amongst the legions active during the reign of Marcus Aurelius (161-180), so it was presumably "lost" prior to that. Films inspired by this historical oddity include *The Last Legion* (2007) starring Colin Firth, and *Centurion* (2010) starring Dominic West, with Noel Clarke in the cast.

202 "Ripper's Curse". Ptolemy lived 90 to 168 AD.

203 *FP: Warlords of Utopia*. In our history, Commodus succeeded Marcus Aurelius in 192, and was the first in

Around 200, the Doctor defeated a silicon-based life form called the Ogre of Hyfor Three - its foot ended up in the British Museum.[204]

The Demon Melanicus was a native of Althrace, a member of the race of Kalichura. He sought to conquer the advanced culture, generating legends of gods and demons. His armies were defeated and Melanicus fled to third century Earth, where he came in a dream to the tyrant king Catavolcus. Melanicus bestowed great power on him and the secrets of time travel.[205]

c 275 - "The Futurists"[206] -> Valente and Secundus, two Roman soldiers fighting in Wales, saw a green fire in the sky. The energy enveloped Valente. Shortly afterwards, the tenth Doctor and Rose arrived from 1925 and defeated the alien Hajor, who were attempting to master Time.

The Doctor challenged Fenric to solve a chess puzzle. Fenric failed, and the Doctor imprisoned him in a flask, banishing him to the Shadow Dimensions.[207] By the end of the third century, the Old Silk Road to and from Cathay had been opened.[208] The Cult of Demnos had apparently died out by the fourth century.[209]

(=) In a potential timeline, the Daleks used time machines to invade Roman Britain in 305.[210]

(=) 305 - SEASONS OF FEAR[211] -> The Roman Decurion Gralae worshipped Mithras, and had made contact with the Nimon, who posed as his god. They granted Gralae eternal life in return for his making sacrifices to them.

The eighth Doctor met Gralae at this time. Between now and his next meeting with the Doctor, seven hundred and fifty years later, Gralae would become known as "Grayle" and spend eighty years repenting with monks. He married twelve times, all his wives dying of old age while he stayed young.

The eighth Doctor sent some Nimon from 1806 to here, and rallied the Roman troops to wipe them out. He then rewrote history by buying out Gralae's commission before he met the Nimon.

A time warp briefly sent a Roman soldier to the late twentieth century.[212]

325 (May) - THE COUNCIL OF NICAEA[213] -> The Roman Emperor Constantine held a conference in Nicaea so bishops could settle issues of dispute within the Christian Church. Among other concerns, the assembled council sought to decide the matter of Christ's divinity. The deacon Athanasius believed Christ was divine, but the

a long line of weak and/or short-lived Emperors. Roma I's Emperors were all historical figures, and potential Emperors. Claudius Gothicus did rule and scored notable military victories, but died of plague. In Roma I, he survived to rout the Germanic tribes. Diocletian also ruled in our history.

204 *The Stone Rose*
205 "The Tides of Time"
206 Dating "The Futurists" (*DWM* #372-374) - It is "the late third century".
207 "Seventeen centuries" before *The Curse of Fenric*. The novelisation likens this contest to an ancient Arabian tale that takes place in "the White City".
208 "A thousand years" before *Marco Polo*.
209 *The Masque of Mandragora*
210 *The Time of the Daleks*
211 Dating *Seasons of Fear* (BF #30) - The date is given.
212 "The Tides of Time"
213 Dating *The Council of Nicaea* (BF #71) - The year is given. The Doctor says the TARDIS has landed "a few days before the council is set to begin", but Athanasius more accurately says it is "the night before the council starts". Historically, the Council opened on 20th May.
214 *Eye of Heaven* (p181).
215 *Iris: Enter Wildthyme*
216 *Timewyrm: Apocalypse*
217 *Time and the Rani*. Hypatia of Alexandria, a neo-

Platonic philosopher and mathematician, lived circa 370-415 AD.
THE RANI'S TIME BRAINS: The Rani kidnaps eleven geniuses before we see her plans nearing fruition in *Time and The Rani*. In the televised version, only three of these are named: Hypatia, Pasteur and Einstein. The rehearsal script and the novelisation both mention three more: Darwin, Za Panato and Ari Centos. The novelisation also states that the Danish physicist Niels Bohr is kidnapped.
218 "The Tides of Time". The date is given - this is the opening battle of the Millenium (sic) wars. See the main entry (c 1983) for more.
219 *Memory Lane*
220 *The Vampires of Venice*
221 *The Big Bang*
222 *Day of the Moon*
223 "Millennia" before *Point of Entry*.
224 The Darksmiths' origins go back "countless generations" before *The Colour of Darkness* (p49), and are here arbitrarily estimated as fifteen hundred years, in accordance with at least a millennia passing after the Darksmiths were commissioned by the Krashoks (presuming said "millennia" has happened concurrently from the Darksmith's point of view). There's no mention of the colonists of Karagula being human.
225 "Millennia" before *The Pyralis Effect*. Gallifrey is in

presbyter Arius held that Christ was subordinate to God. Erimem found Arius to be honourable and aided his cause, threatening to derail history. Tensions mounted, but the fifth Doctor encouraged Constantine to defuse the situation with his oratory skills. In accordance with history, the Council adopted Athanaisus' views.

The Doctor was ejected from the staff at the Library of Alexandria after he misshelved the Dead Sea Scrolls.[214] Iris Wildthyme paid a visit to the library at Alexandria.[215] The Doctor saved two Aristophanes plays from the destruction of the Great Library of Alexandria.[216] **The Rani kidnapped Hypatia to become part of her Time Brain.**[217]

In 375, Mongol hordes swept into central Europe... and were wiped out by Nazi tanks.[218] The Doctor suggested that the joke "What's the most ruthless thing in the bakery... Attila the Bun!" was much funnier if you had known the man.[219] **Venice was founded by refugees from Attila the Hun.**[220] **In 420, the Pandorica was taken from Rome during a raid by the Franks.**[221] **The Roman Empire fell; both the Doctor and Rory Williams witnessed it.**[222]

The world of the Omnim was lost when the resonances they created shattered it. Remnants of the Omnim's mental energies existed in a few fragments, one of which became rogue asteroid D35XQ2.[223] The original colonists of the planet Karagula found the heat of its twin suns unbearable - some went underground and became the Darksmith Collective, practitioners of the dark arts. They learned to break and reassemble reality, moulding time and space much like a child would play with wet sand. For centuries, the Darksmiths accepted commissions to make "impossible, wonderful frightening things".[224]

Energy beings, the Pyralis, swarmed throughout the constellation of Kasterborous and were defeated after a century-long war. They were imprisoned within a temporal void for millennia, even as their obelisk-shaped dimensional gateways remained dormant on some worlds.[225]

In 514 AD, warfare broke out on the planet Q'ell. The Recruiter, a device created to destroy the Ceracai race, extended the war as part of its programming. The conflict would last until the twentieth century, and cause at least 2,846,014,032 casualties.[226]

= On Roma I, Roman Emperor Justinian was crowned Emperor of India. By the time of his death, he was also Emperor of America. The Romans had discovered the continent and the Native Americans, like so many previous civilisations, were keen to be togafied.[227]

In the seventh century, Lord Roche's TARDIS crashed in England and died on impact. One of the Furies trapped within starved to death, but the other survived until the Ship was discovered in 1999.[228]

c 600 - TW: "Rift War"[229] -> The Cardiff Rift briefly transported Jack Harkness and Gwen Cooper back in time. Their duplicitous ally Vox went through the Rift and guided them back home.

The Doctor caught a huge salmon in Fleet and shared it with the Venerable Bede (who "adored fish").[230] Bede made the Doctor the Dean of Westminster Abbey.[231] The *Necronomicon* was written by Abdul Al-Hazred, a mad poet of Sanaa, in Damascus around 730.[232] **Around this period, Monarch left Urbanka for the last time.**[233] **The Rani visited Earth during the so-called "Dark Ages".**[234]

The Galactic Heritage Foundation emerged as an organisation to halt alien property development on planets with indigenous populations. In the eighth century, the third princess Tabetha of Cerrenis Minor spent a weekend in Lewisham. Despite her finding it all a bit gauche, Earth was accorded a low-level ranking of Grade 4, which put it under the Foundation's protection.

With planets under such development bans selling for cheap, the Frantige Two native named Martin purchased a hundred or so worlds for next to nothing. Among his acquisitions, he bought the planet Earth for a few thousand Arcturan ultra-pods from a Navarino time-share salesman going through a messy divorce. The Navarino threw in the rest of Earth's solar system for free.[235]

Kasterborous, and it's not impossible that the unnamed race that defeated the Pyralis was the Time Lords.
226 *Toy Soldiers* (p208). The novel takes place in 1919, and the war on Q'ell has been going on for "fourteen hundred and five years" by that point.
227 *FP: Warlords of Utopia*
228 *The Suns of Caresh*
229 Dating *TW: "Rift War"* (*TWM* #4-13) - Jack "reckons" from the carbon buildup in some grass that he chews that it's "around 600 AD, slap bang in the middle of the Dark Ages".

230 *The Talons of Weng-Chiang*. Bede lived c.673-735, although he never went to London, only leaving Jarrow once to visit Canterbury.
231 *Companion Piece*. This is a neat trick on Bede's part, as he died in 735 and the building of Westminster Abbey didn't start until 1050.
232 *The Banquo Legacy*. It was attributed to the Silurians in *White Darkness* (p89).
233 *Four to Doomsday*
234 *The Mark of the Rani*
235 *The Tomorrow Windows*

The Doctor defeated the Tzun at Mimosa II in 733.[236]

= "Sideways in time" on an Earth where the truth about King Arthur was closer to the myths of our world, a future incarnation of the Doctor was known as Merlin. During the eighth century, Arthur and Morgaine fought against one another, despite their childhood together at Selladon. The Doctor cast down Morgaine at Badon with his mighty arts.

Eventually, though, Morgaine was victorious and Arthur was killed. The Doctor placed Arthur's body and Excalibur in a semi-organic spaceship, and transferred it to the bottom of Lake Vortigern in our dimension. Morgaine imprisoned the Doctor forever in the Ice Caves, and went on to become Empress of the solar system.[237]

Godric, a swordsman in the age when Arthur ruled, found the Holy Grail in a freshwater spring. A wood dryad seduced Godric into her tree, where he slept until 1936. The Doctor claimed to have taught Lancelot how to use a sword at King Arthur's court.[238]

The Birth of the Daleks

The planet Skaro was the birthplace of the Kaleds and the Thals, and had formerly been home to such wiped-out races as the Tharons and the Dals. Skaro had two moons: Falkus and Omega Mysterium.[239]

& 683 - I, DAVROS: INNOCENCE[240] **->** The Kaleds and Thals had warred with each other for centuries, and neither side remembered what started their conflict. Davros was born to an influential Kaled family - his mother was Lady Calcula, a personal assistant to Councillor Quested, and his father was acknowledged as Nasgard, a senior military officer. Quested was actually Davros' biological father. Davros' half-sister, Yarvell, was in the Military Youth. A House of Congress governed the Kaleds.

When Davros was 16, Calcula murdered her husband and his sister, Tashek, to keep secret the truth about Davros' parentage. Brogan, a major, was framed for the crime and executed. Davros' interest in science grew, and

he brutally subjected his tutor, Magrantine, to radiation to understand its effect on living tissue. He also killed Quested in a domestic dispute.

& 696 - I, DAVROS: PURITY[241] **->** The Kaled-Thal war experienced a hiatus that some called the Unsigned Truce. The increasing chemical pollutants and radioactivity on Skaro mutated the Varga plants: flesh-eating vegetation that was formerly rooted in the ground, but now gained the ability to walk and hunt its prey. The name "Varga", as deciphered from old cave paintings, came from the old Dal word for "devourer".

Davros had enlisted in the military because his family's long tradition of service demanded it, but he longed to join the Scientific Corps. To win reassignment, he complied with the wishes of the Supremo, a high-ranking Kaled official, that he investigate an advanced Thal weapons facility. Davros' team destroyed the facility, but Davros alone survived the mission. Calcula discovered that Yarvell, now a peace supporter, feared Davros' potential for destruction and had warned her allies about his mission. Seeing her daughter as a threat to Davros' advancement, Calcula drowned her. A Thal infiltrator was blamed for Yarvell's death, and Davros joined the Scientific Corps.

& 709 - I, DAVROS: CORRUPTION -> The environment on Skaro took a turn for the worse. There hadn't been a summer for three years, nearly all animal life was extinct, and what little wildlife survived was in the Lake of Mutations, formerly known as Drammakin Lake. Now established within the Scientific Elite, Davros developed a blast ray with a range of three miles - its use consumed enough energy to power the Kaled city for seventy-three years, but a shot from it obliterated a fortified Thal command facility.

The Supremo became wary of Davros' ascent and desire to eradicate the Thals entirely, and sent an underling - Section Leader Fenn - to wreck his equipment and kill Calcula. She stopped Fenn by subjecting them both to fatal doses of radiation. Davros learned of the Supremo's involvement in his mother's death, and blackmailed him - henceforth, the Kaled Science Division would have autonomy, and the Elite could requisition any and all resources. Councillor Valron was framed for Calcula's murder.

---

236 "Twelve hundred and twenty-four Terran years" before *First Frontier*.
237 *Battlefield*. The archaeologist Warmsley thinks that Excalibur's scabbard dates "from the eighth century".
238 *Wolfsbane*
239 *I, Davros*: "Purity". In *The Daleks*, the Dals are cited as being forebears of the Daleks.
240 Dating *I, Davros: Innocence* (*I, Davros* #1.1) - Davros is currently 16, so it's thirteen years before *I,*

Davros: Purity. Yarvell's name is doubtless a play on "Yarvelling", the creator of the Daleks according to *The Dalek Book* (1964) and the *TV Century 21* comic.
241 Dating *I, Davros: Purity* (*I, Davros* #1.2) - Davros was 16 in *I, Davros: Innocence*, and he's now 29; we know this partly because the product blurb says he's "approaching thirty", and because his sister (two years his elder, according to *Innocence*) is cited as being 31.

ARE THERE TWO DALEK HISTORIES?: There are a number of discrepancies between the accounts of the Daleks' origins in *The Daleks* and *Genesis of the Daleks*. In the first story, the original Daleks (or Dals) were humanoid, and it is implied they only mutated after the Neutronic War. This version was also depicted in the *TV Century 21* comic strip, where the Dalek casings are built by a scientist called Yarvelling and a mutated Dalek crawls into a casing to survive. Whereas in *Genesis of the Daleks*, we see Davros deliberately accelerate the mutations that have begun to affect the Kaled race (a process the Doctor calls "genetic engineering" in *Dalek*).

Fans have attempted to reconcile these accounts in a number of ways. Perhaps the most common nowadays is to completely dismiss the version in *The Daleks*, and declare the Thal version of events to be a garbled version of the true history seen in *Genesis of the Daleks*. This would mean that the Doctor's comment that the Thal records are accurate is wrong - which isn't too difficult to justify. The idea that Skaro's civilisation lost knowledge following a nuclear war and that the two races would have subjective, propaganda-driven history is tempting... but it *doesn't* explain why both the Thals and the Daleks in *The Daleks* believe in exactly the same version of events, especially as they've had no contact with each other for some time. It's also suggesting that Skaro's historians are so incompetent that they can't tell the difference between a war that lasted a thousand years with one that lasted a day.

Another possible explanation is that the Doctor changes history in *Genesis of the Daleks* - before then, history was the version in *The Daleks*, afterwards it's the *Genesis* version. This is tempting, because altering history *was* the Doctor's mission, after all, and he says at the end that he's set the Daleks back "a thousand years". *The Discontinuity Guide* suggested that in their appearances after *Genesis of the Daleks*, the Daleks are nowhere near as unified a force as they had been before. Morever, Davros - who previously wasn't even mentioned - plays a major part in Dalek politics. *The Discontinuity Guide* credits all of this to the Doctor changing history - looking closely at the evidence, though, the Doctor hasn't actually made much of a difference. The Daleks are an extremely feared, powerful and unified force in the first of the post-*Genesis* stories (*Destiny of the Daleks*), and it's their defeat to the Movellans after that story which weakens them. In other words, no alteration of the timeline need be invoked to explain the change in the status quo. Perhaps the clincher is that *The Dalek Invasion of Earth* still happens in the post-*Genesis* stories - Susan remembers it in *The Five Doctors* (indeed, she's been snatched from its aftermath), and *Remembrance of the Daleks* contains references both to the Daleks invading Earth in "the twenty-second century" and to events on Spiridon (*Planet of the Daleks*). That's before factoring in the dozens of references to pre-*Genesis of the Daleks*

stories in the novels, audios and comic strips featuring later Doctors.

All told, it looks like the Doctor setting the Daleks back a thousand years in *Genesis of the Daleks* is part of the timeline we know, not a divergence from it - again, they still invade Earth in 2157, not 3157. With that in mind, it's interesting to note that the 60s strip has the Daleks developing space travel very soon after they take to their mechanical casings, but that this happens a thousand years after the end of the Thousand Years War (which we would later see ending in *Genesis of the Daleks*). If the Doctor hadn't been there, the Daleks would have developed space travel very soon after *Genesis of the Daleks*, and so the Doctor - as part of the original timeline - *has* set them back a thousand years.

There's a second problem: We have to reconcile the fact that *The Daleks* shows a group of Daleks confined to their city on Skaro and wiped out at the end, while all the other stories have them as galactic conquerors. Nothing in any *Doctor Who* story, in any medium, accounts for this.

The FASA roleplaying game and *About Time* both explain the discrepancy by theorising that soon after *Genesis of the Daleks*, there's a schism between Daleks who want to stay on Skaro to exterminate the Thals and those who want to conquer other planets. The FASA game names them the "exterminator" and "expansionist" factions, and states that the exterminator Daleks never leave Skaro, eventually wither on the vine and end up confined to their city - finally dying out in *The Daleks*. (In this scenario, spacefaring Daleks later recolonise their home planet.)

In *About Time*'s version, the "exterminator" Daleks do venture beyond Skaro, but only on limited sorties - like the invasion of Earth - and they're not galactic conquerors. There's nothing on screen to suggest an early divergence in Dalek history, and only a line in *Alien Bodies* (p138) supports it. *If* this was the case, it seems the spacefaring "expansionist" Daleks completely broke contact with the Daleks on Skaro. Adding speculation to speculation, we might infer this schism was because the Daleks on Skaro continued to mutate - indeed, perhaps they become the humanoid Dals mentioned in *The Daleks*, a different race altogether. Given what we know of Dalek history, it seems unlikely that this was an amicable arrangement, so there could have been a Dalek civil war of some kind.

While we're speculating, we might wonder if the Thals joined the Dals in their efforts to rid the planet of Daleks. Following this, the Dals and Thals lived together in (relative) peace on Skaro for a long time - until the Neutronic War, placed in this guidebook in 1763. The spacefaring Daleks eventually return to Skaro somewhere between *The Daleks* (?2263) and *Planet of the Daleks* (2540).

It might be straightforward, then: the "expansionist"

continued on page 83...

Fifty years before the end of the war between the Thals and the Kaleds on Skaro, the Kaleds set up an Elite group, based in a secret bunker below the Wasteland. It was run by chief scientist Davros, the greatest mind Skaro had ever seen.[242]

& 709 - DAVROS / I, DAVROS: CORRUPTION[243] ->

Although he continued to develop weapons - one of which sunk the entire Thal Navy in a day - Davros had come to realise the war was futile. Prolonging the war with the Thals and using increasingly deadly weapons would mean that soon Skaro would become a dead planet. He believed that no other world could support life, and it was impossible to end the fighting, as both races would inevitably compete to exploit the same ecological niche. Logically, the Kaled race could not possibly survive.

One of his research students, Shan, came up with what she called The Dalek Solution, a plan to reengineer the Kaled race to survive the pollution on Skaro. Fearing that Shan would become a more brilliant scientist than him, Davros framed her for treason and had her hanged.

Davros was greatly injured, and the only survivor, when the Thals shelled his laboratory. He was given a poison injector to kill himself, as none of the Kaleds could bring themselves to put Davros out of his misery. At that moment, Davros realised how weak the Kaleds were and how true power was being able to grant life and death.[244]

Davros was crippled, but survived by designing a life support system for himself. He created energy weapons, artificial hearts and a new material that reinforced the Kaled Dome.[245]

& 759 - I, DAVROS: GUILT[246] ->

Lieutenant Nyder successfully rescued Davros when the Thals briefly captured him, and thereby became his trusted aide.

Davros demanded that the ruling Council of Twelve make all Kaled children the property of the state, so his biological experiments had access to the widest available stock. The Councillors unanimously voted against Davros, and so he killed them, attributing their deaths a faulty heat exchanger. Davros took charge until a new legislative body could be elected, and instigated a mandatory "child protection program" to oversee any Kaled younger than five.

Davros successfully developed a Mark I travel machine - based upon his own life-support chair - that would house the form he believed the Kaleds would eventually mutate into. He and Nyder looked on as the first "Dalek" - a Dal word meaning "gods" - switched on and came to life.

? 760 - GENESIS OF THE DALEKS[247] ->

Davros succeeded in selectively breeding an intelligent creature that could survive in the radiation-soaked, environmentally desolate world of Skaro. Using the Mark III Travel Machines, the Daleks could live in virtually any environment. The Time Lords foresaw a time when the Daleks had become the supreme power in the universe, and sent the fourth Doctor, Sarah and Harry back to the Daleks' creation. They gave the Doctor three options: avert the Daleks' creation; affect their genetic development so they might evolve in a less aggressive fashion; discover some inherent weakness that could be used against them. The Doctor destroyed the Daleks' incubator room and entombed them in their bunker; he reckoned he had set Dalek development back a thousand years. He believed the existence of the Daleks would serve to unite races against them.

---

242 *Genesis of the Daleks*
243 Dating *Davros* (BF #48) and *I, Davros: Corruption* (*I, Davros* #1.3) - Events pertaining to Davros having Shan killed are told in flashback in *Davros* and expanded upon in *Corruption*. Davros claims in *Genesis of the Daleks*, "Many times in the last fifty years, factions of the government have tried to interfere with my research here" - "here" indicating the Kaled bunker and the work of the Scientific Elite. It seems reasonable to assume that said fifty years pass between Davros schisming the Elite off from the Kaled government (as happens in *Corruption*) and *Genesis*. That matches with Davros being 30 when he's crippled in *Corruption*, but his being "an old man" - owing to his life-support systems, which make him the first Kaled to enjoy a natural (if one can call it that) lifespan in ten generations - in *I, Davros: Guilt*.
244 *Davros* and *I, Davros: Corruption*, drawing on sources such as the novelisations of *Genesis of the*

Daleks and *Remembrance of the Daleks*. The circumstances of how Davros came to be in his life support system are never given on screen - it's described as "an accident", which doesn't directly support the idea that it was a Thal attack.
245 *Genesis of the Daleks*. There's no indication how old Davros was when he was crippled, or how much time passed between the accident and *Genesis of the Daleks*.
246 Dating *I, Davros: Guilt* (*I, Davros* #1.4) - The story ends with the Mark I Dalek coming to life. The Daleks seen in *Genesis of the Daleks* are Mark III, so some time must pass - probably just weeks or months, but possibly some years - between the audio mini-series and the TV story.
247 Dating *Genesis of the Daleks* (12.4) - The date of the Daleks' creation is never stated on television. *The Dalek Invasion of Earth*, *The Daleks' Master Plan* and *Genesis of the Daleks* all have the Doctor talk of "millions of years" of Dalek evolution and history. *Destiny of the Daleks*,

continued from page 81...

Daleks are the ones with slats in their mid-section, the "exterminators" are the ones with bands (as seen in the first two TV stories, *The Space Museum* and the *TV Century 21* strip). However, the Daleks in *The Chase* are based on Skaro and are out to avenge the defeat in *The Dalek Invasion of Earth*, so that would also seem to be the "exterminator" faction (unless the first order of business when the "expansionists" return to Skaro is to go after the man who twice inflicted crushing defeats - and so wiped out - the "exterminators").

Alternatively, it could be that the Doctor changes history in *The Daleks* - his first encounter with them might affect Dalek development. We know from *The Evil of the Daleks* and *Dalek* that the Daleks can be altered by contact with aliens, particularly time-travelling ones. Their first contact with the Doctor in *The Daleks* might have been the catalyst that set any Daleks that survived on course to conquer the universe and challenge the Time Lords' supremacy. Again, though, there's no evidence from the series that this is the case - and every Dalek on Skaro appears dead at the end of *The Daleks*.

Ironically, the *one* thing fans seem to agree on is that the Doctor is simply wrong in *The Dalek Invasion of Earth* when he said *The Daleks* was set "a million years" in the future. At the time, it was the television series' own attempt (and in only the second Dalek story!) to explain the discrepancies in Dalek history, but virtually nobody credits the Doctor's statement now.

So... reconciling the account given in *The Daleks* and *TV Century 21* with *Genesis of the Daleks* may not be as difficult as it appears, but merely needs a little *speculation* to smooth things over. The Thousand Years War ends in *Genesis of the Daleks* with the Kaleds wiped out and the first Daleks buried underground. These Daleks either leave Skaro to become galactic conquerors or they simply die out. For the purposes of this chronology, it's been assumed the Doctor set the Daleks back a thousand years, so no Daleks leave Skaro at this time. Six hundred years later (according to *The Dalek Outer Space Book*), the Daleks evolved... meaning the blue-skinned humanoid Daleks (or "Dals"). We could speculate that the Dals are mutated Kaled survivors, or perhaps Dalek mutants who've escaped from the buried bunker.

A thousand years after *Genesis of the Daleks*, Yarvelling builds a "metal casing" that looks like Davros' Mark III travel machine - even though it's not exactly the same design (the mid section and colour scheme is different, matching the ones from *The Daleks* and *The Dalek Invasion of Earth*), it's too similar to be a coincidence. Perhaps Yarvelling has based it on a design from history that he knows will scare the Thals, although it seems more likely he's got access to ancient records of Davros' work, or maybe he's even managed to excavate an old Dalek casing from the Kaled bunker. The Dals

also develop the Neutron bomb, which goes off (deliberately according to *The Daleks*, accidentally according to the *TV Century 21* strip) and all but wipes out life on Skaro. A mutated Dal - the creature predicted by Davros' experiments, perhaps even a thousand-year-old survivor of those experiments - crawls into one of the casings, and becomes the sort of Dalek we're familiar with.

Very quickly, these Daleks develop a thirst for galactic conquest, the early days of which are recounted in the *TV Century 21* strip. At some point, apparently soon after *The Dalek Invasion of Earth*, there's a split - one group of Daleks completely abandons Skaro to become fearsome conquerors elsewhere in the universe, another group becomes confined to their city and dies off in *The Daleks*. Eventually spacefaring Daleks return to Skaro and reoccupy their planet, sharing it with the Thals, at least for a while (as seems to be the case in *Planet of the Daleks* - although, ominously, there are no Thals seen on Skaro in later TV stories).

The Doctor's interference on Skaro spared thousands of worlds from enduring the Dalek wars. The Time Lords calmed the resulting time disruption.[248] **At some point, at least a thousand years later, the Daleks developed space travel and began their galactic conquests.**[249]

The Hornet Swarm, a hivemind of tiny insects ruled by a powerfully telepathic Queen, drifted through space. In the early ninth century, the Swarm accidentally ended up on Earth. They would develop plans to conquer it.[250]

c 800 - "Doctor Conkerer!"[251] **->** The seventh Doctor invented the game of conkers.

The Book of Kells - a collection of manuscripts including the four Gospels, and which would become regarded as Ireland's greatest national treasure - was created in an abbey founded by St. Columbia on the island of Iona. Vikings raided the abbey, and the monks fled to Ireland and Scotland, taking the Book with them.[252] The Vikings regarded the alien Vostok - who came to sleep beneath the polar icecap - as "the gods of the ice age".[253]

The first Doctor was present when a fire ravaged Charlemagne's library.[254]

> = On Roma I, the Roman Emperor Carolus Magnus, that Earth's Charlemagne, defeated the Vikings.[255]

The tenth Doctor rescued Charlemagne from the clutches of an insane computer.[256] The Catholic Church founded the Library of St John the Beheaded in the St Giles Rookery, a notorious area of Holborn, London. The library contained unique, suppressed and pagan texts, including information on "alternative zoology and phantasmagorical anthropology".[257]

The imprisoned Fenric still had influence over the Earth and the ability to manipulate the timelines. He summoned the Ancient One - a powerful Haemovore - from half a million years in the future. Over the centuries, the Ancient One followed the flask containing Fenric. It was stolen from Constantinople; Viking pirates took it to Northumbria. Slowly, the Ancient One followed it to Maiden's Bay.

By the tenth century, a nine-letter Viking alphabet was in use, although the later Vikings used a 16-letter version. Carvings in the earlier alphabet claimed that the Vikings were cursed, and they buried the flask in a burial site under St Jude's church.[258]

Merlin banished the Demon Melanicus from our universe. Melanicus waited a thousand years for an opportunity to escape the black, formless void.[259] Viking legends referred to the Timewyrm as Hel.[260] The seventh Doctor, Ace and Bernice were at an Angle settlement when the Vikings attacked it.[261] The Doctor met the Anglo-Saxon king Alfred the Great and his cook Ethelburg, "a dab hand at bear rissoles".[262] The Doctor became known as Shango

---

however, suggests a much shorter timeframe of "thousands of years", and Davros has only been "dead for centuries". The Daleks seem to have interstellar travel at least two hundred years before *The Power of the Daleks* (so by 1820), although *War of the Daleks* suggests those were time-travelling Daleks from the far future.

The dating of *Genesis of the Daleks* in this chronology is derived from the *TV Century 21* comic strip (for full details, see the dating notes on "Genesis of Evil" [1763]).

248 *A Device of Death*

249 *The Dalek Invasion of Earth*, and most subsequent Dalek stories. Again, taking what the Doctor says at face value, the Daleks are set back a thousand years by the Doctor in *Genesis of the Daleks*.

250 "Twelve hundred years'" before *Hornets' Nest: Hive of Horror*. The *Hornets' Nest* series sees the Doctor travelling through time to meet the Hornets, so that he encounters them in reverse historical order.

251 Dating "Doctor Conkerer!" (*DWM* #162) - No date is given, but it's set at the time of the Vikings.

252 *The Book of Kells*. This is historical, and dates to the ninth century.

253 *TW*: "The Return of the Vostok"

254 *The Drowned World*. Charlemagne ruled 768 to 814. The library fire isn't historical, and is writer Simon Guerrier's way of establishing a "missing" *Doctor Who*

story concerning the great works that went absent from Charlemagne's archive, as specifically inspired by *The Name of the Rose* by Umberto Eco. In Eco's book, a library inside a monastery is said to own works by Aristotle, etc., that were formerly housed in Charlemagne's court library. Real-life scholars aren't quite sure, though, what works Charlemagne's library may have contained.

255 *FP: Warlords of Utopia*

256 *The Unicorn and the Wasp*

257 The Library of St John the Beheaded was mentioned in *Theatre of War*, and made its first appearance in the following NA, *All-Consuming Fire*. In that book, we learn much about the library, including the fact that it has been established for a "thousand years" (p15). The library still exists at the time of *Millennial Rites*. In *The Empire of Glass*, Irving Braxiatel acquires manuscripts for the library (p245).

258 *The Curse of Fenric*. The Ancient Haemovore arrived in "ninth-century Constantinople" according to the Doctor. Ace says the inscriptions are "a thousand years old".

259 Melanicus has waited for "a thousand years" before "The Tides of Time". It's tempting to link the void he was in with "Hell", the gap between the worlds in *Doomsday*. Merlin here is the Merlin from our universe,

the thunder god of the Yoruba tribe when he demonstrated static electricity.[263]

During the second quest to find the Key to Time, the White and Black Guardians found that their powers were greatly diminished. The Black Guardian transported the fifth Doctor and Amy the Key-tracer to the location of the next Key segment - ninth-century Sudan - then crashed there himself, four decades prior to their arrival, in a spaceship. The Black Guardian became Lord Cassim Ali Baba, and sired a son named Prince Omar. He partnered with a stranded Djinn - a race of collectors who went from world to world in search of profit - to repair the spaceship and leave Earth. Meanwhile, the weakened White Guardian lived as the Legate of the Caliphate of Baghdad.[264]

The master vampire Gabriel Saunders embarked upon a breeding programme that developed the Ruthven family into formidable monsters protected by bone spikes, but could pass as human. Saunders hoped to create a prey worthy of being hunted by him, possibly even one that offered the chance of ending his undead existence.[265]

c 855 - THE DESTROYER OF DELIGHTS[266] -> The Black Guardian, a.k.a. Cassim Ali Baba, had spent two years amassing enough gold to hyper-compress into a warp manifold - the last component needed to restore his grounded spaceship. Upon its creation, the compressed gold shard became incarnated as the fifth segment of the Key to Time. Prince Omar killed the Djinn, and - along with forty others - plundered the treasures in the Djinn's spaceship. The ship self-destructed upon the Djinn's death, and the fifth Doctor and the Key-tracer Amy acquired the segment.

Romana met the Black Guardian while trying to answer the Doctor's distress call, and transported him in her TARDIS to the planet Chaos in the far future.[267]

c 885 - "They Think It's All Over"[268] -> The eleventh Doctor, Amy and Rory attempted to see England play Germany in the 1966 World Cup Final, but instead landed in Wemba's Lea, a Saxon area marauded by the Vikings. Henghist, the son of King Ragnar, killed his father as a means of spurring the Vikings against the Saxon. The Doctor and Rory forced the Vikings to retreat after besting Henghist in a penalty shootout.

The Cup of Aethelstan was made in 924 as a gift from the first King of England to Hywel, king of the Welsh. The Doctor visited Aethelstan's court around this time.[269] A group of benevolent space travellers landed in Japan and were killed by the scared natives. The ogre-like, animated mannequins - the Otoroshi - built to aid the travellers were incorporated into a holy shrine.[270]

Marshall Sezhyr founded the Ice Army, and united the nations of Mars, when the planet was in peril. He successfully defended the City of Chebisk against the rebel Dust Riders, and also fought the Kings of the Blood Gullies. Sezhyr's banners flew in a hundred Martian cities and on the planet's moons, but such was his tyranny that thousands of dissenters were killed. His mind survived his physical demise, encoded into his body armour.[271]

A thousand years ago, a new Keeper of Traken was inaugurated. The Union of Traken in Mettula Orionsis had enjoyed many thousands of years of peace before this time.[272] The family of Vislor Turlough owned a planet in a system where wealthy Trions established stellar retreats. A millennia later, these were abandoned at start of the Trion civil war.[273] Some space-faring races plundered more primitive species to create Gelem warriors - fierce cannon fodder soldiers, each created from an amalgamation of five living bodies. Gelems were used in the first battles of the War of Five Hundred Worlds, but were banned by the Pact of Chib in the eleventh century.[274]

---

a recurring character in the *DWM* strip, not the future Doctor who will pose as Merlin in a parallel universe (*Battlefield*).
260 *Timewyrm: Revelation*
261 *Sky Pirates!*
262 *The Ghosts of N-Space*
263 *Transit* (p204).
264 "Forty years" before *The Destroyer of Delights*.
265 "Over a thousand years" before *J&L: The Ruthven Inheritance*.
266 Dating *The Destroyer of Delights* (BF #118) - The back cover says it's the "ninth century", which is reiterated within the story. It's cited as the time of Caliph al-Mutawakkil, who ruled 847-861 AD. These events presumably serve as the inspiration for "Ali Baba and the Forty Thieves" and other stories contained within *One Thousand and One Nights* (vaguely dated by scholars to

the ninth century) - but curiously, neither the Doctor nor either of the Guardians comments upon this.
267 *The Chaos Pool*
268 Dating "They Think It's All Over" (IDW *DW* Vol. 2, #5) - The Doctor initially says they are "a thousand years" too early for 1966, so it's 966. Then he says it's the "ninth century", so it's the 800s. It's then established that Alfred the Great is king - he ruled from 871 to 899, and it's after the Doctor met him in such a capacity.
269 *Planet of the Dead*
270 "Centuries" before *The Jade Pyramid*.
271 "Ten hundred years" before *Thin Ice*, during the "Third Martian Polar Epoch".
272 *The Keeper of Traken*
273 *Kiss of Death*. The palace that Turlough's family owns is "almost a thousand years" old.
274 *Ghosts of India*

c 1001 - EXCELIS DAWNS[275] -> Numerous civilisations had come and gone on the planet Artaris. The populace was mostly relegated to communities living on mountainsides for defensive purposes. A nunnery emerged on Excelis, the highest mountain on the planet.

The fifth Doctor landed on Artaris and met the warlord Grayvorn, who was on a quest for "the Relic", a powerful artifact and purported gateway to the afterlife. The Doctor also met Iris Wildthyme, who couldn't remember how she ended up there. Grayvorn found the Relic, which was shaped like Iris' handbag, but he went missing. The Relic's energies inadvertently made Grayvorn immortal.

1006 - THE BOOK OF KELLS[276] -> The TARDIS fell down a temporal wormhole to Ireland, diverting the eighth Doctor and Tamsin from their journey to Charisima Maxima - a pleasure world with billion-year-old forests. A new incarnation of the Meddling Monk, with Lucie Miller as his companion, tried and failed to repair his faulty direc-

tional unit. As the Monk's TARDIS dematerialised, it backfired and scorched *The Book of Kells* - ruining its cover, and charring its pages. The Doctor hid the *Book* under some sod, knowing it would be recovered eighty days later.

The Doctor saved Aethelred the Unready from what would have been a fatal fever.[277] An amoral Time Lord used a twenty-fourth century flood controller to turn back the tide for Canute, giving him great influence. The Doctor set history back on course.[278] The Doctor talked philosophy with the ruler of Ghana, King Tenkamenin.[279]

Around one thousand years ago, Martin instigated a get-rich-quick scheme that entailed the washed-up actor Prubert Gatridge posing as a god on planets that Martin owned. This seeded "selfish memes" - philosophical concepts that led each world's populace to destroy themselves. Each genocide lifted the Galactic Heritage Foundation's development ban, allowing Martin to sell the worlds at fantastic profit.[280]

---

275 Dating *Excelis Dawns* (BF *Excelis* series #1) - The story takes place a thousand years before *Excelis Rising*.
276 Dating *The Book of Kells* (BF BBC7 #4.4) - The year is given. The loss and recovery of "the great Gospel of Clumnkille" - thought to be The Book of Kells - is recorded in the Annals of Ulster, although some historians date the Book's disappearance to 1007, not 1006.

The Doctor only acknowledges his encounters with the Monk in *The Time Meddler* and *The Daleks' Master Plan*, and seems to overlook their meetings in the tie-in media. Along those lines, he claims to have regenerated "several times" since they last met, and the Monk's directional unit - stolen by the Doctor in *Master Plan* - is still faulty. Then again, the Doctor describes the Monk as "someone I thought was dead", which doesn't describe how matters are left in *Master Plan*, but is a reasonable interpretation of the Monk's encounter with the seventh Doctor in *No Future*.
277 *Seasons of Fear*. The meeting is also mentioned in *The Tomorrow Windows*. Aethelred was king of England, and lived from circa 978 to 23rd April, 1016.
278 *Invaders from Mars*
279 *Transit*
280 *The Tomorrow Windows*
281 *Bunker Soldiers*
282 *The Ghosts of N-Space*
283 *Terror of the Zygons*
284 Dating *Hornets' Nest: A Sting in the Tale* (BBC fourth Doctor audio #1.4) - The Doctor says it is 1039. It is midwinter.
285 *Seasons of Fear*. The date is given, and it is exactly seven hundred and fifty years after the Doctor and Charley met Decurion Gralae.
286 A thousand years before *K9: Aeolian*.
287 Dating *The Time Meddler* (2.9) - The story takes place shortly before the Battle of Hastings (14th

October, 1066), the Doctor judging it to be "late summer". The Doctor discovers a horned Viking helmet, although the Vikings never wore such helmets.
288 *The Daleks' Master Plan*
289 *The Company of Friends*: "Mary's Story"
290 *SJA: Lost in Time*
291 *SJA: The Time Capsule*
292 *Vampire Science*. Joanna says she was born before the end of the first millennium, but also on the day William the Conqueror died, which was in 1087.
293 "A thousand years" before *Paper Cuts*.
294 *Benny: The Judas Gift*
295 Dating *TimeH: Deus Le Volt* (TimeH #8) - The year is given. Historically, the siege was broken on 2nd June; Honoré and Emily seem to arrive two days beforehand. "Reynald" appears to be loosely based on Raymond IV, the Count of Toulouse (circa 1041/1042-1105). He was an associate of the soldier/mystic Peter Bartholomew, who claimed to find the Spear of Longinus during a church excavation that occurred in mid-June. Faked or not, the "discovery" is credited with motivating the crusaders against their foes.
296 *Benny: The Gods of the Underworld*. Venedel has crawled back to having a feudal society circa 2100, so the Argians' millennium of decline presumably concludes before that point.
297 "A thousand years" before *Kursaal*. Given the timeframe involved, the humanoids weren't of Earth descent.
298 *The Big Bang*
299 *Rat Trap*. The castle and the Treaty are fictional. The Doctor seems awfully keen to enjoy the celebration of the Treaty, considering the conditions of this period make it a less-than-ideal holiday stop.
300 *Spiral Scratch*. This was in "the twelfth century".

During the building of the Cathedral of St Sophia, a casket fell from the sky. It was believed to contain an angel and was placed in the catacombs.[281] In 1033, Clancy's Comet was mistaken for the Star of the West, sent to commemorate the millennium of the crucifixion.[282] **A monastery was established on the site of Forgill Castle in the eleventh century.**[283]

1039 (Midwinter) - HORNETS' NEST: A STING IN THE TALE[284] **->** The fourth Doctor visited Tilling Abbey in Northumbria to investigate what he suspected was the earliest activity of the Hornet Swarm on Earth. He discovered that the nuns had been besieged by fierce dogs for three months, and that their Mother Superior was a pig that had been possessed by the Queen of the Swarm. The Doctor realised the Queen was trapped because the nuns freely sampled the products of their distillery, and the Hornets couldn't possess a person if they were drunk. The Doctor left, but only after being bitten by a dog - the new host of the Queen - that had also got inside the TARDIS. The Doctor put the TARDIS into the Vortex, taking the Hornets away from Earth. They would materialise in 1768.

> (=) During his time in the Godwins' court, Grayle was once bishop of all Cornwall. The Doctor defeated Grayle's plan to stockpile plutonium for the Nimon, and rewrote history to prevent Gralae from making contact with the Nimon in 305 AD.[285]

Edward the Confessor's reign was one of the Doctor's favourite times and places.[285] **The Aeolians were wiped out in the Centaurian Catastrophe.**[286]

1066 (late summer) - THE TIME MEDDLER[287] **-> Landing on a beach in Northumbria, the first Doctor, Steven and Vicki learnt that the Monk - a renegade from the Doctor's own people - was planning to destroy a Viking invasion with futuristic weapons. Harold's army would be fresh for the Battle of Hastings, and after defeating the Norman invasion, Harold would usher in a new period of peace for Europe. The Doctor foiled the Monk's plans, and removed the dimensional control from the Monk's TARDIS, stranding him.**

It "took a bit of time" to fix, but the Monk resumed his travels.[288]

The eighth Doctor and Mary Shelley met King Harold at the Battle of Hastings.[289] **The Shopkeeper implied that he possessed the arrow pulled from the eye of King Harold after the Battle of Hastings, although some said the king wasn't shot in the eye at all.**[290] In 1066, debris from Haley's Comet damaged a spaceship from the planet Persopolis, causing it to crash to Earth. The components of a powerful Persopolis construction device were separated,

and the ship's occupant, Janxia, went into stasis.[291] Joanna Harris, a future geneticist and vampire, was born.[292]

The White Emperor, the first of the Deathless Emperors, came to rule on Draconia. He tyrannically conquered fifty-two worlds and formed an empire that would last a millennia; scribes said that owing to his actions, the suns ran purple with blood. Each successive emperor was designated by a colour, which came to include gold, green, pearl grey, blood purple and dusk blue. As each emperor neared the end of his reign, the Draconian priesthood slowed his metabolic functions and placed him in Imperial Heaven - a tomb orbiting Draconia. The priesthood could then call upon the emperors' wisdom as needed.[293]

Early in his reign, the First Emperor used The Judas Gift - a gauntlet that detected treachery in those who wore it - to determine that one of his nobles, Lord Salak, was a traitor. Salak was executed. As he had duelled left-handed, fighting with one's left-hand became a mark of shame on Draconia. Only royals were deemed "trustworthy" enough to exercise such a privilege.[294]

1098 (31st May to 2nd June) - TIMEH: DEUS LE VOLT[295] **->** The time-travelling Honoré Lechasseur and Emily Blandish investigated mysterious events at siege of Antioch, 1098. Honoré's actions inadvertently enabled the crusaders to open the city gates, triggering a massacre. Reynald - the former Earl of Marseille, whom the crusaders had branded a traitor - had become the core of the Fendahl, but Honoré and Emily helped to prevent the creature from manifesting. A "warrior preacher" named Peter suspected Reynald's lance of being the Spear of Longinus - the weapon used to pierce Christ's side as he was crucified - and used it to rally the crusaders against the Muslims.

The militaristic Argians destroyed all knowledge on many planets, including Venedel, Zerinzar and Athrazar. The Argians were undone by their own arrogance, and, over the course of a millennium, their empire fell apart.[296] Humanoids bearing the Jax - a sentient virus - settled on the planet Saturnia Regna. They built a cathedral, but were killed by indigenous wolves. The virus adopted the wolves as its new hosts and retreated into the cathedral, awaiting the arrival of more humanoids.[297]

In 1120, the Pandorica was the prize possession of the Knights Templar.[298] The Treaty of the Marshes was signed at Cadogan Castle in 1123.[299]

Two bright green children were seen in Wulpit in Suffolk, and viewed with suspicion by an angry mob. These were actually alien Lampreys.[300] "Smart implants" - devices that could turn those fitted with them into dust - were outlawed under the Hexen-Brock Treaty. The Doctor prevented the assassination of Janakin Brock by a

Tamaranian death-squad, who used the implants in a war against the Pashkul.[301]

The order of the Knights Templar was founded in 1128.[302] The Canavitchi claimed responsibility for founding the Knights Templar.[303] The Doctor rode with the templars in Palestine. Elsewhere, the Templars recovered the Imagineum, a mirror-like device built by an ancient race of extra-terrestrial alchemists. It could create a dark duplicate of anyone who looked into it.[304]

The Doctor saw the completion of Durham Cathedral in 1133. Sir Brian de Fillis built Marsham Castle in Yorkshire in the twelfth century. The knight went mad, believing his wife was haunting him.[305]

1139 - THE KRILLITANE STORM[306] **->** The tenth Doctor found that people in medieval Worcester feared the legendary Devil's Huntsman, who had made a number of people disappear recently. He quickly identified the culprits as the Krillitane. The Doctor met an Ertrari bounty hunter, Emily Parr, who was seeking to capture Lozla Nataniel Henk: the man who had killed her father a month ago. Henk and his associates had captured a giant Krillitane, the Krillitane Storm, and were milking it for its oil. A Krillitane ship arrived, and although the Doctor drove the combating factions away, the Krillitane Storm died. Parr turned Henk in for the bounty, and decided to go to university.

During the twelfth century, the Convent of the Little Sisters of St Gudula was founded with Vivien Fay posing as the Mother Superior.[307] In the same century, the Doctor saw the King of France, Phillippe Auguste, lay the first stone of the Louvre.[308]

Genghis Khan

The Doctor delivered Genghis Khan.[309] Susan was familiar with Genghis Khan.[310] **The Doctor claimed to have heard Genghis Khan speak.**[311] **The Master implied that the Doctor *was* Genghis Khan.**[312] **The hordes of Genghis Khan couldn't break down the TARDIS doors.**[313] The Doctor suspected that Genghis Khan told him that villains liked to keep record of their villainy.[314]

Around 1168, the Aztecs left their original home of Aztlan and became nomads. They took a holy relic, the Xiuhcoatl, with them.[315] **The other end of the time corridor formed by the timelash was in 1179 AD.**[316] The Borad was disgorged from the timelash and quickly killed by operatives of the Celestis, the investigators One and Two.[317] In 1190, Stefan, a Crusader, lost a game to the Celestial Toymaker and became his agent.[318]

c 1190 - THE CRUSADE[319] **->** The first Doctor, Ian, Barbara and Vicki saved Richard the Lionheart from an ambush, and became embroiled in court politics. Richard planned to marry his sister Joanna to the brother of Saladin, the Saracen ruler, but Joanna refused. The Doctor was mistaken for a sorcerer and the TARDIS crew narrowly escaped.

Richard the Lionhearted tutored the Doctor in use of the broadsword.[320]

c 1191 - KRYNOIDS: THE GREEN MAN[321] **->** The Earl of Godfrey and his supporters dispatched two Krynoids that hatched in the English woods.

---

301 "Eight centuries" before *Freakshow*.
302 *Sanctuary*
303 *The King of Terror*
304 "End Game" (*DWM*)
305 *Nightshade*
306 Dating *The Krillitane Storm* (NSA #36) - The year is given.
307 *The Stones of Blood*
308 *The Church and the Crown*
309 *Tragedy Day*. Genghis Khan was born circa 1162, and died in 1227. The seventh Doctor must have delivered Genghis, as he claims in *Thin Ice* that he's never delivered a child before - but does so in that story, here, and in *The Settling*.
310 *An Earthly Child*. It's possible that she met Khan at the same time her grandfather delivered him.
311 *The Daemons*
312 *Doctor Who - The Movie*
313 *Rose*
314 *Borrowed Time*. Either Khan or Al Capone told the Doctor this.

315 *The Left-Handed Hummingbird*
316 *Timelash*
317 *The Taking of Planet 5*
318 Two accounts of Stefan's game are given, in *The Nightmare Fair* and *Divided Loyalties*. Both versions have Stefan serving with Barbarossa, but the former story has him losing a game of dice to the Toymaker after wagering a Greek family. *Divided Loyalties*, however, says that Barbarossa drowned after Stefan bet the Toymaker that Barbarossa could successfully swim the Bosporus.
  The account is slightly at odds with established history. Frederick Barbarossa was made Holy Roman Emperor in 1155, and died in 1190 after being thrown from his horse into the Saleph River in Cilicia (part of modern-day Turkey), whereupon his heavy armour made him drown in hip-deep water. As if that weren't enough, one chronicler claimed the shock additionally made Barbarossa have a heart attack.
319 Dating *The Crusade* (2.6) - A document written for Donald Tosh and John Wiles in April/May 1965 (appar-

The Middle Ages was the native time of Justin, a knight who would help the fifth Doctor fight Melanicus - and would later be canonised.[322] Hubert, the earl of Mummerset, died in Palestine while serving with King Richard. A hapless herbalist's apothecary took his place, and spent seven years in a Saracen prison before escaping.[323] **K9 met the real Robin Hood.**[324]

The village of Stockbridge was named after a bridge over the river Stock, which dated back to medieval times.[325] The Lokhus, a creature from the universe after ours, fell to Stockbridge and went into a chrysalis stage.[326]

1199 - CASTLE OF FEAR[327] **->** The Rutan Empire was withdrawing from Mutter's Spiral. Two Rutans took up residence in Stockbridge Castle in Mummersetshire, and began cloning experiments, hoping to clone Rutans in human form for use as cannon fodder. The fifth Doctor and Nyssa defeated the Rutans, a.k.a. "the demons of Stockbridge Castle", nine months later. One Rutan clone, Osbert, survived; his offspring in Stockbridge had some

Rutan inheritance, but this became more diluted with each generation.

These events influenced the names of local establishments such as the Green Dragon Inn and the Turk's Head, and originated the legend of St. George - in reality the apothecary masquerading as the earl of Mummerset - besting a dragon. Future residents of Stockbridge remembered the Rutans' defeat - and the Doctor's role in it - as both a hereditary memory and a mummery performance.

The alien Berserkers were active on Earth in the thirteenth century.[328] **Whitaker's Timescoop accidentally kidnapped a peasant from the Middle Ages.**[329] **Scaroth possibly posed as a Crusader.**[330] **Around 1205, a man was boiled in oil for the entertainment of King John.**[331]

In the early thirteenth century, a Khameirian spaceship was rounding Rigellis III when a Yogloth Slayer ship attacked and damaged it. The Khameirian vessel crashed to Earth and destroyed the chapel at Abbots Siolfor, home

---

ently by Dennis Spooner), "The History of Doctor Who", stated that the story is set between the Second and Third crusades, with the Third Crusade starting when Richard's plan fails.

Richard is already in Palestine at the start of the story, indicating a date of around 1190. Ian claims in *The Space Museum* that *The Crusade* took place in the "thirteenth century", but this seems to be an error on his part. The *Radio Times* and *The Making of Doctor Who* both set the story in the "twelfth century". *The Programme Guide* gives a date of "1190", *The Terrestrial Index* picks "1192".

320 *Leviathan.* The Doctor might well have taken lessons from Richard in some body other than his first (*The Crusades*), at an unspecified point in Richard's life.

321 Dating *Krynoids: The Green Man* (BBV audio #33) - King Richard is on the throne. Mention is also made of stories pertaining to the Saracen - a sign, although not a guarantee, that it's during the Third Crusade (1189-1192).

322 "The Tides of Time" doesn't specify at what point of the Middle Ages Justin comes from. However, a mercenary in *Castle of Fear*, set in 1199, has met Justin and gives a correct description of him.

323 "Seven years" before *Castle of Fear*

324 *K9: The Last Oak Tree.* This possibly, but not necessarily, happened when K9 was travelling with the Doctor.

325 *The Eternal Summer*

326 "The Stockbridge Child". The accompanying illustration suggests this was during medieval times.

327 Dating *Castle of Fear* (BF #127) - The back cover and - within the story - the Doctor agree that it's 1199. *Plague of the Daleks* reiterates that *Castle of Fear* occurs

in the "twelfth century". What's perplexing is that the Doctor determines the year to which he and Nyssa must go based upon a statement that one of the Stockbridge residents makes in 1899 - "It's the year when the ant by the lion was slain." It's a reversal of the real-life phrase "when the lion by the ant was slain", denoting how King Richard was fatally shot by a boy wielding a crossbow, who was angered because Richard had killed his father and brothers. (Richard was shot on 25th March, 1199, and died on 6th April.) Even more strangely (unless this is a deliberate choice as part of the story's comedy), the Doctor here says that the "ant" refers to Saladin - in real life it does no such thing, as Saladin died in 1193.

This adventure originates the tale of St. George and the dragon, the earliest text of which dates to the eleventh century, although George himself dates back to at least the seventh century. The Green Dragon Inn is mentioned in "The Tides of Time".

For benefit of non-UK readers, "Mummerset" is a deliberately awful depiction in plays and films of a West Country accent. Twelfth-century Stockbridge is said to reside in Mummerset; "The Tides of Time" says that the modern-day Stockbridge is in Gloucestershire.

328 *SJA: The Mark of the Berserker*

329 *Invasion of the Dinosaurs*

330 *City of Death.* Most fans have interpreted the last of the four Scaroths we see as a Crusader, although the DVD says it's a "Celt". Although Julian Glover plays both Richard the Lionheart in *The Crusade* and Scaroth in *City of Death*, it doesn't seem likely that Scaroth posed as King Richard.

331 "Ten years" before *The King's Demons*.

of a secret society led by Matthew Siolfor. The Khameirians put their life essences into what would later be called the Philosopher's Stone. They mentally enthralled six of the brotherhood to work toward restoring them to health. The descendants of the society would spread throughout the world, influenced by the Khameirians.[332]

The sunburst icon became known as a sigil of extra-terrestrial power from the thirteenth century.[333]

1212 (late summer) - BENNY: THE VAMPIRE CURSE: "Possum Kingdom"[334] **->** Benny and the members of a Yesterways, Ltd., time travel tour group visited Marseilles during the Children's Crusade. Nepesht arrived through time from the twenty-sixth century, and sacrificed his liberty to once again imprison the last of the Utlunta, Lilu, in a pocket universe.

1215 (4th-5th March) - THE KING'S DEMONS[335] **->** The Master attempted to pervert the course of constitutional progress on Earth by preventing the signing of Magna Carta. On 3rd March, 1215, an android controlled by the Master, Kamelion, arrived at Fitzwilliam Castle posing as the King. The Master accompanied him, disguised as the French swordsman Sir Giles Estram. The Fitzwilliams had served the King for many years before this, giving him their entire fortune to help the war against the abhorrent Saracens, but the King now demanded even more of them. "King John" began to challenge the loyalty of even the King's most devoted subjects, but the fifth Doctor, Tegan and Turlough exposed the Master's plan. They took

Kamelion with them in the TARDIS.

The Doctor acquired a copy of the Magna Carta.[336] Around 1225, the Doctor defeated Thorgan of the Sulumians, who was attempting to kill the mathematician Fibonacci before he wrote the *Liber quadratorum* (*The Book of Squares*), a text on Diophantine equations.[337] **In 1231, the Pandorica was donated to the Vatican.**[338]

1240 - BUNKER SOLDIERS[339] **->** The first Doctor, Steven and Dodo landed in Kiev. The Doctor was asked to help fend off the Mongols, but knew that history recorded the sacking of the city and refused - so the governor of the city, Dmitri, imprisoned him. Dmitri sought supernatural aid, uncovering a casket under the Church of St Sophia. This held an alien soldier, who started a killing spree. He infected Dmitri with a virus that drove him mad, leading to Dmitri refusing the Mongols' offer of sparing the city in return for an honourable surrender. The Mongols ransacked Kiev, but the Doctor deactivated the soldier.

1242 - SANCTUARY[340] **->** The seventh Doctor and Benny made an emergency landing in the Pyrenees. The Doctor discovered a plot to recover the skull of Jesus Christ from the heretical Cathare sect, even as Benny fell for the knight Guy de Carnac. The Church forced an attack on the Roc of the Cathares sanctuary and set it afire, but the Doctor found the skull was a fake. The Doctor and Benny escaped the destruction - it's possible that Guy de Carnac did also...

---

332 *Option Lock*
333 "End Game" (*DWM*)
334 Dating *Benny: The Vampire Curse*: "Possum Kingdom" (Benny collection #12b) - The year and season are given.
335 Dating *The King's Demons* (20.6) - The TARDIS readings say it is "March the fourth, twelve hundred and fifteen".
336 As seen in *The Doctor, the Widow and the Wardrobe*.
337 *The Gallifrey Chronicles*
338 *The Big Bang*
339 Dating *Bunker Soldiers* (PDA #39) - The Doctor says "we are in Kiev in 1240" (p16).
340 Dating *Sanctuary* (NA #37) - Benny "persuaded someone to tell her that the year was 1242".
341 Dating *Guy de Carnac: The Quality of Mercy* (BBV audio #35) - The audio features Guy de Carnac from *Sanctuary*, but it's not expressly said whether this is a prequel or a sequel to that book (presuming for the moment that Guy survived the Roc of the Cathares - his body is never found, after all). That said, a conversation concerning Guy and an "unrequited love" could well be a reference to Bernice. Seven years passed in the real

world between the release of the two stories; the placement here somewhat arbitrarily splits the difference.
342 *FP: Warlords of Utopia*
343 *The Impossible Astronaut*, possibly contradicting the origin of the statues given in *Eye of Heaven*. The first moai on Easter Island were carved in the thirteenth century.
344 *Marco Polo*. Barbara states that Marco Polo was born in "1252", although actually it was two years later.
345 *Death in Blackpool*
346 *The Zygon Who Fell to Earth*
347 *The Bodysnatchers*; Zygor is also named in *The Zygon Who Fell to Earth*.
348 "Several centuries" before *Deep Blue*.
349 *Terror of the Zygons*. The Zygon leader Broton tells Harry that they crashed "centuries ago by your time-scale". While disguised as the Duke, Broton later tells the Doctor that there have been sightings of the Loch Ness Monster "since the Middle Ages", the implication being that the Zygons and Skarasen have been on Earth since then.

In *Timelash*, we're made to believe that the Borad has been similarly swimming around Loch Ness from 1179

c 1245 - GUY DE CARNAC: THE QUALITY OF MERCY[341] **->** Guy de Carnac protected a space traveller from an Inquisition, and helped him return to his people.

> = On Roma I, only Seres (China) stood against the might of the Roman Empire thanks to their Great Walls. They had little contact with Rome. By the mid-thirteenth century of our calendar, Roman roads and bridges linked every part of the world. The Seric Navy under Zheng He launched attacks on Roman ports, and war raged for twenty-eight years as the Serics made great territorial gains.
>
> Then Emperor Yung Lo met the Roman Emperor Cosimo. They agreed that rather than destroy the world with a devastating war, they should settle the matter on the toss of a coin. Rome won, and Yung Lo knelt at the feet of his new Emperor. The merging of Roman and Seric philosophies led to a new golden age. A perfect world was built.[342]

River Song and the eleventh Doctor visited Easter Island; the inhabitants made many statues of him.[343] **Marco Polo was born in Venice.**[344]

A sub-set of Zygons - called Zynogs (sic) - were exiled from Zygor, the Zygon homeworld, as punishment for breaking the oldest of Zygon laws: using the body-print of another Zygon. The Zynogs' original forms were destroyed, and they were trapped within stunted forms incompatible with Zygon body-print technology. Some Zynogs found a technological means of transferring their essences into brain-dead individuals.[345]

According to the Doctor, the Zygons hailed from "the deepest, murkiest fathoms of space".[346] The arachnid Xaranti destroyed Zygor.[347] The Zygons retaliated and destroyed the Xaranti homeworld in Tau Ceti. The Xaranti consequently became nomadic.[348] **A Zygon spacecraft crashed in Loch Ness. While awaiting a rescue party,** they fed on the milk of the Skarasen, an armoured cyborg creature that was often mistaken for the locals as a "monster".[349] Another Zygon craft, commanded by the warlord Hagoth, crashed elsewhere on Earth. The crew entered hibernation, but would later revive and promote industry throughout the twentieth century.[350]

In the Middle Ages, Stangmoor was a fortress.[351] **A medieval knight was kidnapped by the Master using TOM-TIT.**[352] **When Marco Polo was 12, English crusaders occupied the African port of Accra.**[353]

The Doctor was based for a time around 1268 at Ercildoune in Scotland. He cured a crippled stable hand called Tommy. Two years later, the Queen of the Charrl contacted Tommy from the far future, promising him immortality in return for his stealing the Doctor's TARDIS. Tommy came to be known as the wizard Jared Khan.[354]

In 1270, a mysterious doctor who tended King Alexander sent his stable boy Tom away. The legends of Kebiria claimed that the Caliph at Giltat was visited by mysterious demons, the Al Harwaz, who promised him anything he wanted - gold, spices, slave women - if his people learnt a dance, "dancing the code". The arrangement continued for a time, until the Caliph broke the agreement and flying monsters destroyed his city.[355] In the 1270s, Marco Polo witnessed oil seeping out of the ground in the vicinity of the Aural Sea.[356]

In 1271, Marco Polo left Venice to explore China.[357]

c 1273 - THE TIME WARRIOR[358] **->** The third Doctor arrived from the twentieth century on the trail of the Sontaran Linx, who had kidnapped scientists and pulled them back in time. For his own amusement, Linx was supplying a local warlord, Irongron, with advanced weapons. The third Doctor and Sarah Jane -- who had stowed away in the TARDIS - thwarted both Linx and Irongron, and the destruction of the Sontaran's ship also destroyed Irongron's castle.

onwards, but the Borad's death in *The Taking of Planet 5* suggests he doesn't actually contribute to the Loch Ness sightings. *The Programme Guide* claimed that the Zygon ship crashed in "50,000 BC", *The Terrestrial Index* preferred "c.1676".
350 The eighth Doctor believes that the Zygon craft in *The Zygon Who Fell to Earth* crashed concurrent to the one that landed in Scotland in *Terror of the Zygons*.
351 *The Mind of Evil*
352 *The Time Monster*
353 *Marco Polo*
354 *Birthright*
355 "Seven hundred years" before *Dancing the Code*.
356 *Brave New Town*
357 *Marco Polo*
358 Dating *The Time Warrior* (11.1) - The story seems to be set either during the Crusades, as Sir Edward of Wessex talks of "interminable wars" abroad, or quite soon after the Conquest as Irongron refers to "Normans". The Doctor tells Professor Rubeish they are in the "early years of the Middle Ages". However, in *The Sontaran Experiment*, Sarah says that Linx died "in the thirteenth century". According to *The Paradise of Death*, this was "eight hundred years back" (p12), and it's "three centuries" before "Dragon's Claw". *The Programme Guide* set a date of "c.800", but *The Terrestrial Index* offered "c.1190". *The TARDIS Logs* said "1191 AD", *Timelink* said "1272" and *About Time* "1190-1220".

Marco Polo arrived in Cathay in 1274, the same year the beautiful maiden Ping-Cho was born. Three years later, Polo entered the service of Kublai Khan.[359]

1278 (29th August) ASYLUM[360] **->** An alien dispatched from 1346, now hosted in Brother Thomas of the Franciscan Order, tried to further philosopher Roger Bacon's research into the Elixir of Life - a possible cure to the impending Black Death seventy years hence. The fourth Doctor and Nyssa prevented the alien from disrupting history, and Nyssa dislodged the alien presence from Thomas' mind. Bacon burned his unsuccessful Elixir Manuscript, but the Franciscan Order imprisoned him for twelve years for committing "heretical" research into alchemy. Bacon would become renowned to future generations as a great philosopher, not a scientist.

In 1283, a meteorite from the Jeggorabax Cluster - a dark nebula on the cusp of the Bezeta-Vordax system, said to contain entities created by emotions - fell to Earth in the Weserbergland Mountains in Lower Saxony. The next year, the people of Hamelin's collective fear of rats caused the energy within the meteorite to manifest as the Pied Piper - a being who needed fear to survive, and stole Hamelin's children to create it. In the centuries to come, aspects of the Piper would steal children for similar effect.[361]

Hughes de Chalons, a Knights Templar, took refuge in a hidden chamber beneath the Sphinx in 1287. A woman bearing the seal of the Knights gave him a box of scrolls, and said he was the new Guardian of Forever.[362]

---

359 *Marco Polo*
360 Dating *Asylum* (PDA #42) - It's "1278" according to the blurb, and 1266 was "twelve years previously" (p116).
361 *SJA: The Day of the Clown.* The first Doctor met the Pied Piper in the *TV Comic* story "Challenge of the Piper" (outside the bounds of this chronology), and this may well have been the same entity.
362 *Benny: The Sword of Forever.*
363 Dating *Marco Polo* (1.4) - Marco gives the year as "1289". *The Programme Guide* gave the date as "1300".
364 "Voyager"
365 *Birthright*
366 *Terror of the Zygons*
367 *The Two Doctors.* Dante lived from 1265-1321.
368 *The Face of Evil.* William Tell lived in the early fourteenth century.
369 *Lords of the Storm.* Robert the Bruce was one of Scotland's greatest kings, and ruled from 1306-1329.
370 "Centuries" before *Thin Ice.* The site of the Kremlin has been occupied since the second century BC, but the first stone structures were built there in the fourteenth century.
371 "Thirteen hundred years" before Rose's time, according to *Only Human.*
372 "By Hook or by Crook"
373 "Profits of Doom". The Doctor doesn't recognise him face-to-face, so they probably don't meet at this time.
374 *TW: End of Days*
375 *Benny: The Sword of Forever.* Historically, Philip did move against the Knights in 1307; Pope Clement V declared the Order disbanded in 1312.
376 *Benny: The Sword of Forever.* De Molay and de Charnay are historical, and were burned to death in March. In real life, Guillaume was the twenty-first Grand Master of the Knights (de Molay was the twenty third) and died during the siege of Acre in 1291. The character in *The Sword of Forever*, however, wasn't born until

1292 (perhaps the one is the son of the other, born after the father's death?).
377 *The End of Time* (TV)
378 *The Gallifrey Chronicles.* Ockham was a philosopher and friar during the Middle Ages. He was responsible for the principle of Occam's Razor (also spelled "Ockham's Razor") and lived c.1287 to c.1349.
379 *The Time Meddler*
380 Dating *Renaissance of the Daleks* (BF #93) - The date is given.
381 *The Awakening*, "centuries" before the village was destroyed in the English Civil War.
382 In the travellers' personal timelines, this occurs between *Boom Town* and *Bad Wolf.*
383 *Asylum*
384 *Rat Trap*
385 *SJA: The Time Capsule.* This story might actually be true, even allowing for the diamond's extra-terrestrial origins.
386 Dating *TimeH: Kitsune* (TimeH #4) - It's medieval Japan, complete with samurais, but the dating is otherwise left unsaid.
387 *Benny: The Sword of Forever.*
388 "Change of Mind". This was in 1349.
389 "Genesis of Evil". This was in the year 1600 of the New Skaro Calendar.
390 Dating *The Art of War* (DL #9) - The story occurs in "November" (p34) in "medieval London" (p27). The TARDIS databank makes mention (p28-29) of the Black Death ravaging London in 1348, and that the population had been halved by 1350, so the story is here - a little arbitrarily - placed after that. For the Doctor and Gisella, the story concludes *The End of Time* (DL).
391 *The King of Terror.* The Shroud is first recorded in the fourteenth century.
392 *Imperial Moon.* This takes place at "611,072.26 Galactic Time Index".
393 *Matrix*

1289 - MARCO POLO[363] **->** Kublai Khan refused permission for Marco Polo to return to Venice. In 1289, Polo led a caravan across the Roof of the World to the court of the Khan. He took with him Tegana, the emissary of the Mongol warlord Noghai, and Ping-Cho, who was destined to marry a 75-year-old nobleman. They discovered the first Doctor, Ian, Barbara and Susan - along with their blue cabinet, which Polo decided to present to the Khan. They traversed Cathay and the Gobi Desert, arriving at Shang-Tu. Tegana's plan to murder the Khan was exposed, and he killed himself. In gratitude to the travellers, the Khan returned their cabinet.

Astrolabus claimed to have an appointment with Marco Polo.[364] Jared Khan narrowly missed acquiring the TARDIS at this time.[365] **The Forgill family served the nation from the late thirteenth century.**[366] **The Doctor met Dante and acquired his business card.**[367] **The Doctor met William Tell.**[368] The Doctor met Robert the Bruce in the early fourteenth century.[369] He also visited the citadel that became the Kremlin.[370]

The Doctor slayed a dragon in Krakow.[371] The fourteenth century saw the rebirth of the organic statues of Es-Ko-Thoth Park in the city-state of Tor-Ka-Nom.[372]

Seth was a grand schemer in fourteenth century Rome known to the Doctor. He would go on to be known as Vance Galley, Van Giefried, Virgil Gaustino, Vincent Grant and the twenty-fourth century entrepreneur Varley Gabriel.[373] **The Cardiff Rift transported a fourteenth-century plague victim to the twenty-first century.**[374] King Philip IV of France moved against the Knights Templar in 1307. Hughes de Chalons was captured while enjoying the pleasures of a whore's bed.[375]

In March 1314, the last key members of the Knights Templar (Grand Master Jacques de Molay; Geoffrey de Charnay, the Order's Preceptor of Normandy; and Hughes de Chalons) were burnt at the stake. de Molay's nephew, Guillaume de Beaujeu, procured a relic sacred to the Order - the finger of John the Baptist - and secured it in his castle in Arginy.[376] **In the 1300s, a "demon" fell from the sky near a convent near London. A "sainted physician" (i.e. the Doctor) "smote" the demon and it disappeared. This created The Legend of the Blue Box, which was commemorated in stained glass at the church later built on that site.**[377]

The Doctor almost gave William of Ockham a nervous breakdown trying to get him to work out the history of the planet Skaro.[378] **The Monk calculated that if his plan to prevent the Norman Conquest had worked, then mankind would have developed aircraft by 1320.**[379]

1320 - RENAISSANCE OF THE DALEKS[380] **->** The fifth Doctor dropped off Nyssa to look into an anomalous time track in Rhodes, 1320, then ventured off to investigate a second anomaly. Nyssa made the acquaintance of a Mulberry, a member of the Knights of Templar, but they both fell down a wormhole to Petersburg at the time of the American Civil War.

The Malus, a psychic probe from Hakol, arrived in Little Hodcombe.[381] **The ninth Doctor, Rose and Jack "only just escaped" Kyoto in 1336.**[382]

Aliens emerged from a null dimension and into London in 1346. They took control of human bodies, which were vulnerable to a plague that the aliens knew would arrive in two years. They discovered that philosopher Roger Bacon wrote of a possible cure for the plague, and sent one alien back several decades to ensure Bacon's research succeeded. The alien's host in that era, Brother Thomas, survived and felt drawn to the aliens in 1346, but they failed to heed his warnings about the futility of their efforts.[383]

Cardogan Castle suffered a large outbreak of the Black Death shortly before the plague's end.[384] The black diamond of Ernfield, a cursed gem, was said to have been stolen from a mid-fourteenth century temple.[385]

c 1350 - TIMEH: KITSUNE[386] **->** While investigating the history of mischievous fox-spirits - the kitsune - Emily Blandish briefly visited medieval Japan.

Guillaume de Beaujeu, age 62, went off to war in 1354 and didn't return. The finger of John the Baptist remained at the Castle of Arginy.[387] The Doctor was at the university of Prague when it opened.[388] On the planet Skaro, a small, squat blue-skinned warlike race had evolved... the Daleks.[389]

c 1360 (November) - THE ART OF WAR[390] **->** A Krashok warship materialised several miles from London, having fled into the past using a Dalek temporal shift device. The tenth Doctor and his companion, Gisella, pursued the Krashoks to prevent their activating the fake Eternity Crystal in their possession - an act that could have triggered an explosion large enough to destroy Earth. The Doctor incapacitated the Krashoks with sonic waves, and medieval knights slew many of them. The surviving Krashoks returned to the future with both the real Crystal and Gisella, and the Doctor followed them.

The Canavitchi faked the Turin Shroud in an attempt to slow man's progress.[391] The Phiadoran Clan Matriarchy came to power in the Phiadoran Directorate. They ruthlessly weeded out their political opponents.[392] Cartophilius lived in Italy under the name John Buttadaeus.[393]

The Doctor met Chaucer in 1388 and was given a copy

of *The Doctour of Science's Tale*.[394] The Doctor drank ale with Chaucer in Southwark.[395]

Around this time, the Doctor acquired his ticket to the Library of St John the Beheaded.[396]

The Renaissance

The Daemons inspired the Renaissance.[397]

The cult named Sodality achieved limited time travel through a book linked to the Daemons, and used conventional and psionic science to alter the course of human development. Select individuals were born as time-channellers (humans with the innate ability to travel through time) or time-sensitives (empathic humans who served as the channellers' navigators during time-jumps). Through such individuals, Sodality hoped to gain command of time and space travel.[398]

By the end of the fourteenth century, wire-drawing machinery had been developed.[399] Constantinople was renamed Istanbul.[400] **The Doctor was present at the Battle of Agincourt.**[401]

The Doctor assisted the great-great-great grandfather of the Duke of Medici in some bother with the Borgias.[402] A renegade Time Lady, also a friend of the Doctor, founded a restaurant on Earth during the time of the Hapsburgs.[403] Upon the murder of his father, Vlad III took the name

"Dracula" - which means "son of the dragon".[404] Legends about a "beast" which terrorized the German town of Orlok circulated in the Middle Ages.[405] The planets of the Radzera system fell into a pattern of constant war.[406]

From the time he was knee high, Richard III was a subject of huge interest to alien time tourists and academics. Random time travellers would repeatedly show up to question Richard about the future murder of his nephews - one of history's greatest mysteries - and had strong views about whether he should kill the boys or not. This puzzled Richard, who at around age 12 had no intention of doing anything of the sort. By accident, Richard discovered that most of the travellers were afraid of someone called "the Doctor", and he continually dropped the Doctor's name as a means of making the visitors leave.[407]

Many of those who died in the Nor' Loch, Edinburgh, from the fifteenth century onwards were likely to be resurrected by the Onk Ndell Kith in 1759.[408] An unknown race established itself on the planet Helhine, then fell to ruin.[409]

w - Sutekh sent hordes of Mal'akh to fifteenth century Earth, where they became involved in the conflict between the European Christians and the Ottoman Turks. He withdrew his forces after the Great Houses, to protect their involvement in this crucible of history, signed a treaty with the Osirian Court. Ellainya of the Great Houses, a.k.a. Merytra, was bound by blood into Sutekh's service.[410]

394 *Cat's Cradle: Time's Crucible*

395 *Synthespians™*

396 *All-Consuming Fire*

397 *The Daemons*

398 *TimeH: The Child of Time* (p64).

399 "A hundred years" before *The Masque of Mandragora*.

400 *Shadowmind*

401 *The Talons of Weng-Chiang, Shada, The King of Terror*. Agincourt was fought on 25th October, 1415.

402 *The Doomsday Quatrain*. The Doctor refers to the man who was Duke in 1560, i.e. Cosimo de Medici. His paternal grandfather was Givoanni di Bicci de' Medici (circa 1360 to 1429). The Borgia family (mentioned in *City of Death*) became prominent in politics and the church in the fifteenth and sixteenth centuries.

403 "Urban Myths". The country where the restaurant is located isn't specified, but it's evidently where goulash was invented - originally, that would be Hungary. The Hapsburgs ruled there from 1437 to 1918, and it's possible that the Doctor's comment "since the time of the Hapsburgs" refers to the start of their reign.

404 *Son of the Dragon*. Vlad II was killed in 1447.

405 Four hundred years before *The Beast of Orlok*.

406 "Centuries" before *The Beast of Orlok*.

407 *The Kingmaker*. Richard III was born October 1452.

408 *The Many Hands*

409 By the Doctor's best guess, this happened "more than two thousand years" before *Cobwebs*.

410 *FP: Coming to Dust. FP: The Book of the War* says that the Mal'akh are monstrosities tainted by the blood of the Yssgaroth (*The Pit*).

411 *A Death in the Family*. The year is unknown, but the Great Vowel Shift - a sea change in how the English language is pronounced - occurred at some point between 1450 and 1750.

412 Dating *The Aztecs* (1.6) - According to Barbara, Yetaxa was buried in 1430. *The Programme Guide* dated the story "c.1200 AD". *The Terrestrial Index* suggested "1480", claiming that fifty years elapsed between Yetaxa being buried and the TARDIS landing inside the tomb. This is not supported (or contradicted) by the story itself, although Lucarotti's novelisation is set in "1507". Both editions of *The Making of Doctor Who* placed the story in "1430". *The Left-Handed Hummingbird* firmly dates the story in "1454".

413 "Agent Provocateur". They presumably, unlike the first Doctor in *The Aztecs*, don't wind up engaged because of this.

414 *Wishing Well*

415 *City of Death*. Movable type was developed in China during the ninth century, but as Scaroth possessed a number of Gutenberg Bibles (printed 1453-1455), we can infer he was responsible for *Europe's* development of printing.

416 *Son of the Dragon*. Vlad very briefly ruled in 1448 before being cast into exile; this event must occur after he grained the throne in 1456.

The Doctor tripped the Word Lord's CORDIS on the lost twenty-seventh letter of the English alphabet, which made him crash into the entire alphabet, and caused the Great Vowel Shift.[411]

c 1454 - THE AZTECS[412] **-> The Aztec priest Yetaxa died and was entombed around 1430. When the first Doctor, Ian, Barbara and Susan emerged from Yetaxa's sealed tomb, Barbara was taken for the reincarnation of Yetaxa. She attempted to use her "divine" power to end the Aztec practice of human sacrifice, knowing it would horrify the European conquerors in future, and hoped this would save the Aztec civilisation from the Spanish. Her efforts failed.**

The tenth Doctor and Martha had a drink of chocolate in Aztec times.[413] They also visited the Italian Renaissance.[414]

In the mid-fifteenth century, Scaroth gave mankind the printing press, although he kept a number of Gutenberg Bibles for himself. It was possibly this splinter of Scaroth that acquired a Ming vase.[415] During the first Easter of his reign, Vlad III invited two hundred boyars to his banqueting hall - and afterwards had them slaughtered for the roles they played in the deaths of his father and brother.[416] The Wandering Jew once shared a bottle of Tokay with Vlad Tepes, who was unable to end the man's immortal life.[417]

The Varaxil Hegemony developed a science based upon Odic power, an energy associated with the supernatural. They became such despised outcasts on so many worlds, they renounced their technology and began hunting down any beings who could innately channel Odic energy, imprisoning them on Varix Beta.[418]

1462 (17th June to July) - SON OF THE DRAGON[419] **->** Turkish forces led by Sultan Mehmed II invaded Wallachia, part of what would later become Romania. Prince Vlad III (a.k.a. Vlad the Impaler, a.k.a. Dracula) ruled Wallachia and ravaged his people's own crops, livestock and water supplies to stop his enemies making use of them.

The fifth Doctor, Peri and Erimem arrived during this

conflict, and Erimem wound up saving Dracula's life. Dracula welcomed her as a guest at his palace, Poienari Castle. Events led to the Doctor being captured and Peri earning a death sentence, whereupon Erimem bargained with Dracula - in exchange for letting her friends go, she'd become his wife. The Turks surrounded Poienari, and the King of Hungary withdrew his support from Dracula. Erimem was released from her promise, and Dracula fled to Transylvania. Radu, Dracula's brother, became the head of Wallachia.

A legend concerning these events claimed that an archer (actually the Doctor) had warned Dracula of the impending siege of Poienari. It was further said that Dracula's first wife threw herself to her death (a misinterpretation of Dracula briefly dangling Peri off the Poienari battlements), and the portion of the Arges River marking this point became known as Raul Doamenei, "the princess' river". The Doctor stole Radu's journal to keep the name of Dracula's "first wife" - even though he and Erimem hadn't formally married - a secret.

The "sons" of King Edward IV - who were historically fated to die in the Tower of London - were actually born as girls. Edward feared this would throw the line of royal succession into doubt, and spark decades of fighting amongst the power-crazed nobility. He therefore announced that the girls were in fact boys: the future Edward V and Richard of Shrewsbury.[420] In 1478, George, the Duke of Clarence, was convicted of treason against his brother, King Edward IV. He was slated for execution, but their other brother, Richard of Gloucester, quietly rescued him. George was believed dead and lived in disguise as Clarrie, the barkeep of The Kingmaker tavern.[421]

In 1479, a wall was built around the parish of St. James - which would one day be known as Cardiff - to keep out plague victims. A little girl named Faith died, but a priest brought her back to life with a resurrection gauntlet. Her revival enabled an aspect of Death to manifest in St. James - its hold on Earth would have solidified had it killed thirteen people, but it had only murdered twelve when Faith stopped it. The gauntlet was hidden within St. Mary's Church.[422]

417 *Matrix*
418 "Two centuries" before *The Witch from the Well*.
419 Dating *Son of the Dragon* (BF #99) - The story begins on 17th June, 1462, the night of an infamous attack by Dracula's forces on the Turks. Act Three opens on July 2nd, and events unfold relatively soon thereafter. The name of Dracula's first wife is lost to history, although there's a problem with this woman being Erimem - Dracula's first wife bore him a son, Mihnea cel Rau, who ruled Wallachia 1508-1510. As the Doctor here says, Dracula did briefly regain his throne after

this... for all of two months in 1476, before he was killed in battle.
420 *The Kingmaker*. Edward and Richard were respectively born in 1470 and 1473.
421 *The Kingmaker*. History says George was executed on 18th February, 1478.
422 *TW: Dead Man Walking*. It's never said what became of Faith after Death was banished, and for all anyone knows, she's the ageless, fortune-telling little girl whom Jack consults in *Dead Man Walking* and *TW: Fragments*.

A "Northern chap with big ears" left a pair of messages for Peri and Erimem at The Kingmaker tavern on Fleet Street in London. They would receive the notes in 1483.[423]

The year 1482 was full of temporal glitches, making it difficult for the TARDIS to land there.[424]

1483 (April to October) - THE KINGMAKER[425] ->

The wayward TARDIS deposited Peri and Erimem in Stony Stratford, 1483. William Shakespeare, having stowed aboard from 1597, snuck out of the Ship. Shakespeare presented himself to Richard III as "Mr Seyton", someone from the future who advocated that Richard should murder his nephews.

King Edward IV died, so Richard escorted the new monarch - his nephew, King Edward V - back to London. Along the way, Richard discovered that his nephews were female. He rounded up anyone who might know this secret, and executed Hastings, a friend of the old king. Three days after Richard's discovery, Peri and Erimem arrived at The Kingmaker tavern and - based upon the Doctor's messages - realised they were doomed to stay in 1483 for a time. They worked as waitresses there for about six months.

Commemorative mugs, plates and tea towels were made in anticipation of Edward V's coronation on 24th June, but the event didn't occur. Parliament declared Edward and his "brother" Richard illegitimate; their uncle had Mr Seyton conduct a press conference on this development with the finest gossips in England, including the *Lincolnshire Tattletale* and the *Wessex Busybody*. Richard was subsequently crowned as Richard III.

---

423 "Two years" before Peri and Erimem's arrival in *The Kingmaker*. The "big-eared" chap is almost certainly a veiled reference to the ninth Doctor, who apparently passes through the fifteenth century and completes this task, fulfilling the line of communication between his previous self and his companions.

424 Or so he claims in *The Impossible Astronaut*. It's entertaining to think this could be related to all the conflicting stories about the fate of the nephews of King Richard III, per *Sometime Never* and *The Kingmaker*, especially with regards the temporal shenanigans in the latter story.

425 Dating *The Kingmaker* (BF #81) - Edward IV died on 9th April, 1483, and Edward V's short-lived reign began on 18th April (he's one of three British monarchs to have never been crowned). Peri and Erimem arrive at least three days beforehand, and work at The Kingmaker for about six months. A minor anomaly is that Henry Stafford later claims Peri and Erimem turned up "about eighteen months" before what's clearly August 1485, meaning it's more accurately two years plus change.

426 Dating *The Kingmaker* (BF #81) - One of the Doctor's notes to Peri and Erimem dates their arrival to 1st August, 1485. Bosworth Field was fought on 22nd August, and it's a little puzzling to wonder how the run-up to the conflict unfolded, given that Richard III time-jumps with the Doctor to 1597 and is apparently absent some days beforehand. Henry Stafford was historically executed on 2nd November, 1483, so in the *Doctor Who* universe, he languishes in prison for twenty-one months beyond that point.

427 *The King of Terror*

428 *Blood Harvest*

429 *Project: Twilight*

430 According to Harrison Chase in *The Seeds of Doom*. The Wars of the Roses lasted from 1455-1485.

431 Dating *Sometime Never* (EDA #67) - The date is given.

432 Dating *The Left-Handed Hummingbird* (NA #21) - The date is first given on p39.

433 *The Talons of Weng-Chiang*. The Doctor notes, "I haven't been in China for four hundred years" - presumably four hundred years ago in history, as opposed to when the Doctor was four hundred years younger.

434 *Dreamland* (DW)

435 *Managra*. This happened "seven years" before Torquemada's death in 1498.

436 The Doctor has Christopher Columbus' business card in *The Two Doctors*. Columbus lived 1451-1506 and discovered the New World in 1492.

437 *Eye of Heaven*

438 *Cobwebs*

439 Dating *The Masque of Mandragora* (14.1) - It's said that the Helix will return to Earth in five hundred years at the "end of the twentieth century", so the story is set at the end of the fifteenth century. The second edition of *The Making of Doctor Who* said that the story is set in "the fifteenth century". Hinchcliffe's novelisation specified the date as "1492", *The Terrestrial Index* and *The TARDIS Logs* both set the story "about 1478". *The Discontinuity Guide* said it must be set "c.1470-1482" when Da Vinci was in Florence". In *SJA: Death of the Doctor*, Sarah Jane would seem to remove any ambiguity about this when she says that she visited "Italy, San Martino, 1492".

The entity that encroaches on Earth in *The Eleventh Tiger* (set in 1865) also seems to be the Mandragora Helix, even though the Doctor says in *Masque* that it's been banished for five hundred years. There's either another conjunction taking place that he doesn't know about, or he's discounting events of 1865 because he knows he already won the day then.

The novel *Beautiful Chaos* not only agrees that *Masque of Mandragora* occurs in 1492 (pgs 41, 167), it takes the added step of saying that the Doctor and Sarah fought the Helix "five hundred and seventeen years, one month, four days" (p43) prior to 15th May, 2009 - which would be very handy, if the "15th May" dating weren't so dubious (see the dating notes for *Beautiful Chaos*).

440 *Beautiful Chaos*

The now-illegitimate Princes were relocated to the Tower of London - the king invited Peri and Erimem to serve as their handmaidens. Henry Stafford, the Second Duke of Buckingham, sought to bring the Woodville family into conflict with the king as a means of claiming the throne for himself. He hoped to trigger this by convincing Peri and Erimem to poison the "boys", but the king discovered the plot and threw Stafford in prison.

Richard III had Peri and Erimem double as the Princes while the genuine article went to work as waitresses with their uncle Clarrie at The Kingmaker. Peri and Erimem routinely appeared in public as the Princes, seen from afar playing tennis or exercising. The king got fed up with Shakespeare/Seyton and had him tortured, learning much about the web of time. Peri and Erimem spent the next two years masquerading as the Princes, but the public didn't take much notice of the "lads". History would record that the Princes were last seen in 1484.

Pointy beards were all the rage in France, and considered a fashion statement for the 1480s (as distinguished from the large, open-necked beards of the 70s).

1485 (August) - THE KINGMAKER[426] **->** The fifth Doctor, Peri and Erimem arrived from 1597, wanting to investigate the death of Richard III's nephews. But while the Doctor departed to patronize The Kingmaker tavern, the TARDIS - telepathically resonating with the Doctor's recent boozing - hiccupped and slipped back to 1483 with Peri and Erimem aboard.

Henry Stafford was tortured to death by Sir James Tyrell, the king's Royal High Concussor. The barkeep Clarrie - formerly George, the Duke of Clarence - was identified and died in a chase, drowning in the Thames. In future, the play *Richard III* would spread the belief that he had drowned in a vat of Malmsey wine.

William Shakespeare, a.k.a. Mr Seyton, escaped imprisonment and demanded that the Doctor take Richard III to stand trial in Queen Elizabeth's era. Much calamity ensued, and after a brief visit to 1597, the TARDIS arrived at the Battle of Bosworth Field. Shakespeare was forcibly hauled out of the TARDIS by a sixty-fourth century publishing robot that eventually exploded. Erimem had broken Shakespeare's arm, and a laser pistol wound had singed his foot and given him a limp, so Shakespeare was mistaken for the king. He was killed, blubbing like a girl, after scrambling up a tree.

The Doctor relocated Richard III's nieces, Susan and Judith, to join their uncle in 1597.

The Canavitchi helped guide the Spanish Inquisition.[427] Agonal, an immortal who gained strength from suffering, fed on its fear and death.[428] The Doctor was present during the Spanish Inquisition.[429] **The earliest parts of Chase Mansion were built during the Wars of the Roses.**[430]

1485 - SOMETIME NEVER[431] **->** An Agent of the Council of Eight kidnapped the two nephews of Richard III to prevent their having an impact on history. The eighth Doctor and Trix later rescued the boys, and took them to the early twenty-first century.

1487 - THE LEFT-HANDED HUMMINGBIRD[432] **->** In the Aztec city of Tenochtitlan, the god Huitzilopochtli's taste for blood grew every year. By 1487, his priests demanded twenty thousand sacrifices. These fed the psychic Huitzilin - a human mutated by the Xiuhcoatl, an Exxilon device that leaked radiation. Huitzilin used his powers to remain alive, and used the Xiuhcoatl to make his people worship him. For centuries, he would visit the most violent places in human history, feeding off the carnage of such events. He would become known as the Blue.

In the late fifteenth century, the Doctor visited China.[433] He believed the best Chinese takeaway came from the Ming dynasty.[434] The Doctor encountered Torquemada in Toledo, where an *auto-da-fé* didn't go as planned, and "mini-Beelzebubs" hauled Torquemada from his bed.[435]

The Doctor met Christopher Columbus.[436] He travelled on the *Santa Maria*, but Columbus refused his suggestion of plotting courses with an orange and a biro.[437] The Doctor told Columbus that there was more to travelling than going from A to B.[438]

1492 - THE MASQUE OF MANDRAGORA[439] **->** The fourth Doctor and Sarah Jane accidentally brought the Mandragora Helix to Renaissance Italy, where it made contact with the Brotherhood of Demnos cult. The Doctor drained and dissipated the Helix's energy before it could plunge Earth into an age of superstition and fear.

What remained of the Helix seeped into the ground and water around San Martino. The people there became endowed with traces of Helix energy - by 2009, the Helix would be able to control their descendants. In the centuries to come, San Martino would become uninhabited and lost to history.[440]

Following the Mandragora incident, Duke Giuliano formed the Orphans of the Future: a secret society dedicated to helping mankind. In the centuries to come, Giuliano's written account of the Mandragora affair became known as *The Book of Tomorrows*, and was regarded as a work of prophecy. The Orphans eventually split into two camps - the White Chapter and the Crimson Chapter - based upon their interpretation of *The Book*, particularly its prediction that an "alien intelligence" would return to Earth in half a millennia. The White Chapter believed that the returning aliens would take humanity away to a better life; the Crimson Chapter thought the aliens wanted to eradicate mankind.[441]

| = The sixth Doctor visited the planet Yestobahl in |
| 1494.[442] |

The Doctor was present when Torquemada died in Avila - an event that involved the arrival of the personification of Death, complete with scythe.[443] The Doctor was with Vasco da Gama when he sailed into the harbour of Zanzibar in 1499.[444]

The Cylox were immensely powerful psionics and a very long-lived species, being the equivalent of adolescents after surviving for millennia. Two of the Cylox, Lai-Ma and his brother Tko-Ma, had spent several millennia annihilating planets in another dimension. Around the late fifteenth century, an intergalactic court exiled them to a pocket realm located on Earth. The brothers later loosed their shackles and agreed to see who could destroy Earth the fastest. The Ini-Ma, the brothers' jailor of sorts, endowed its essence into female members of the bloodline that would produce Loretta van Cheaden.[445]

The painter Hieronymus Bosch was a friend of the Doctor, who posed for one of Bosch's triptychs: *The Garden of Earthly Delights*. The Doctor spent hours lying against a table, and Bosch went mad if he so much as twitched.[446] **Guieseppe di Cattivo, a contemporary of Leonardo da Vinci, was known in fifteenth century Florence as the Artist of Nightmares.**[447]

The Sixteenth Century

c 1500 - THE GHOSTS OF N-SPACE[448] **->** Around the turn of the sixteenth century, the third Doctor and Sarah were briefly seen as ghosts.

During the sixteenth century, the Ancient Order of St Peter existed to fight vampires.[449] Stattenheim and Waldorf created working plans for a TARDIS during the sixteenth century.[450] Jack Harkness visited a dying galaxy and found a sole survivor. He relocated it to Earth, where it came to inspire myths about the shapeshifting Selkie.[451] Veec-Elic-Savareen-Jal-9 became a fugitive after speaking out against the warmongering Hive Council on Jal Paloor. Darac-Poul-

---

441 *SJS: Buried Secrets, SJS: Fatal Consequences* and *SJS: Dreamland*. Sarah's research-minded friend Natallie says that Giuliano wrote his journal in the "sixteenth century", suggesting that Giuliano didn't record events from *The Masque of Mandragora* until some years afterwards. Alternatively, it's possible that Natallie is just guessing based upon the sketchy records at her disposal, and Giuliano wrote his journal before the turn of the century. A continuity glitch exists in that the Doctor doesn't tell Sarah until the very end of *The Masque of Mandragora* that the Mandragora Helix will return to Earth in five hundred years, so there's no opportunity for Giuliano to learn of this and later record it in his journal. It's possible, though, that Giuliano - even from a distance - overhears the Doctor and Sarah's final conversation, which would explain why he seems a bit disconcerted even before witnessing the TARDIS dematerialise. If so, however, it's strange that Sarah so repeatedly flogs herself in *Sarah Jane Smith* Series 2 because her "loose lips" told Giuliano of the future, when if anything it's the Doctor's fault.
442 *Spiral Scratch*
443 *Managra*. Torquemada died 16th September, 1498.
444 *So Vile a Sin*. Vasco da Gama, a Portuguese explorer, was the first European to journey by sea to India.
445 *Instruments of Darkness*
446 *Absolution*. *The Garden of Earthly Delights* is Bosch's best-known work, painted somewhere between 1490 to 1510. The idea that the Doctor posed for this becomes even more fanciful once you realise that the depicted figures are nude.
447 *SJA: Mona Lisa's Revenge*. The artist's name is spelled "Giuseppe" in the closed captioning, but

"Guieseppe" in the art book Rani consults on screen.
448 Dating *The Ghosts of N-Space* (MA #7) - The Doctor says it is "somewhere near the turn of the century".
449 *Minuet in Hell*
450 *The Quantum Archangel*, doubtless extrapolating from use of a Stattenheim remote control in *The Two Doctors*, with a dash of *Muppets* influence.
451 *TW*: "The Selkie". Date unknown, but women on Seal Island have been aiding the Selkie for some "centuries".
452 "Four hundred years" before *Ghosts of India*.
453 *The Stones of Venice*
454 *SJA: The Curse of Clyde Langer*. Date unknown, but at a rough guess, it's probably some centuries prior to the Mojave surrendering to United States forces in 1859. Mojave culture stretches back that far, but very little is known about it.
455 *Recorded Time and Other Stories*: "Recorded Time". Prince Arthur died on 2nd April, 1502.
456 *The Time Meddler, City of Death*.
457 *Kingdom of Silver*
458 *City of Death*. The Doctor's note to Leonardo ends "see you earlier". In *The Two Doctors,* the Doctor has Leonardo's business card.
459 *SJA: Mona Lisa's Revenge*. It seems reasonable to presume that all seven Mona Lisas were created using paint made from the alien rock, as the original painting is destroyed in 1979 (*City of Death*). In both *City of Death* and *Mona Lisa's Revenge*, various characters attribute Leonardo as having painted the Mona Lisa between 1503 and 1519, in accordance with the painting's real-world history. *City of Death*, however, specifies that the original Mona Lisa, at least, was completed by 1505.

Caparrel-Jal-7 was dispatched to capture him.[452] The Doctor visited Venice in the sixteenth century.[453]

Legends spoke of Hetocumtek as a vicious warrior god who descended from the heavens, and tried to conquer the peoples of the Great Plains. The most powerful medicine men of the Mojave tribe trapped Hetocumtek in a totem pole that was buried in the Mojave Desert. It was said that if ever the totem fell back into the hand of men, Hetocumtek would be freed.[454]

A young Prince Henry found a quill made from a temporal phoenix feather. It could rewrite time - so Henry had his Scrivener use the quill to kill his brother, Arthur the Prince of Wales. This paved the way for him to become King Henry VIII.[455]

Leonardo da Vinci

Both the Monk and Scaroth claimed credit for inspiring Leonardo to consider building a flying machine.[456] The Doctor told da Vinci that coleopters were more trouble than they were worth.[457] **The Doctor visited Leonardo while he was painting the Mona Lisa, "a dreadful woman with no eyebrows who wouldn't sit still".[458]**

The model who sat for the Mona Lisa was "a dreary Italian housewife who laughed like a camel and farted like a donkey". Leonardo painted the Mona Lisa using oils he blagged from his neighbour, Guieseppe di Cattivo, and had been made from minerals found in a rock that fell from space.[459] Leonardo had a cold.[460]

Leonardo convinced the Doctor to take him back to the time of Christ, and following this journey produced a "marvellous adoration painting"... that he didn't finish. The Doctor ended up owning some of Leo's designs, and gifted them to his great-grandson Alex, to further the boy's interest in architecture.[461] The Doctor took Leonardo to attend the wedding of Bernice Summerfield and Jason Kane; Leonardo designed their wedding cake.[462]

1505 - CITY OF DEATH[463] -> Captain Tancredi, one of the splinters of Scaroth the Jagaroth, kept Leonardo a virtual prisoner and ordered him to begin making six additional copies of the Mona Lisa. Scaroth hoped to sell them at great profit to fund his time experiments in 1979. The fourth Doctor arrived, and wrote "This is a Fake" in felt-tip on many of Leonardo's blank canvasses. Leonardo painted the copies over them.

Although nobody took notice of Leonardo da Vinci's sketches of helicopters or tanks at the time, his drawings would "seed" the idea for such inventions, and help to facilitate their creation in future.[464]

Guieseppe di Cattivo painted a self-portrait in 1509. He also painted his masterpiece, *The Abomination*, but discovered that nobody could look upon it without losing their sanity. He locked *The Abomination* in a special case made from hangman's gallows, and the next morning was found in his Florence apartments, completely insane.[465]

The Doctor watched Michelangelo paint the Sistine Chapel, and told him that if heights frightened him, he shouldn't have accepted the commission.[466] Michelangelo drew the sixth Doctor.[467] The tenth Doctor learned how to sculpt from Michelangelo.[468] The Monk owned a cupid that Michelangelo had sculpted.[469]

The Baobhan Empire fell in a galactic war, and the Baobhan Sith were all but exterminated. A spaceship with a few surviving Baobhan females crashed in Yorkshire, where the ship projected a force field that kept the sun at bay for seventy days. The Baobhan feasted upon the locals until a Sisterhood killed them. A single Baobhan survived, trapped within a pile of rocks that became known as Lucifer's Tombstone. The village of Thornton Rising grew up around it.[470]

In 1514, a Sontaran ship crashed near Mount Omei in China. A monk, Yueh Kuang, investigated the starfall. The Sontarans taught him martial arts for three months. He then returned to share his new knowledge with his fellow monks, deposed Abbot Hsiang and took over as Abbot.[471]

---

460 *Doctor Who - The Movie*
461 *Relative Dimensions*
462 *Happy Endings*
463 Dating *City of Death* (17.2) - Tancredi asks what the Doctor is doing in "1505".
464 *The Nowhere Place*
465 *SJA: Mona Lisa's Revenge*. The number of years that elapse between Guieseppe painting *The Abomination* and his death in 1518 isn't specified.
466 *Vincent and the Doctor*. The Sistine Chapel was painted from 1508-1512.
467 "Changes". Peri is surprised to find the picture in a store room, so she wasn't with the Doctor at the time.

468 *The Stone Rose*
469 *The Resurrection of Mars*
470 "Centuries" before *The Rising Night*. As the Baobhan Sith are enemies of the Time Lords of old, it's odd that they were, historically speaking, allowed to create an Empire. Then again, the fall of their Empire here might well owe to Gallifrey's intervention.
471 "Eight years" before "Dragon's Claw".

Guieseppe di Cattivo died in 1518 in a lunatic asylum.[472] The Doctor thinks he invented the expression "mind like a sieve".[473] **Cortez landed in South America.**[474] A fragment from the Omnim planet fell to Earth and was carved into an Aztec stone knife of sacrifice. The knife was included in the plundered treasure aboard the Spanish ship *Santa Isabella*, but the crew surrendered the knife to English raiders. The hilt was taken to Madrid.[475] The Doctor met the magician Heinrich Cornelius Agrippa von Netteshiem, and thought him an example of how dark powers destroyed great talent.[476]

1522 (summer) - "Dragon's Claw"[477] **->** For years, Japanese pirates attacked ports along the coast of the East China Sea. One group was repelled by the Shaolin monks of Mount Omei. Abbot Yueh Kuang, their leader, had an advanced energy weapon. The fourth Doctor, Sharon and K9 arrived and found people killed by the gun. They were captured by the monks and taken four hundred miles to their monastery, where the Doctor discovered they'd been taught martial arts by the mysterious "eighteen bronze men". The Doctor snuck into the Hall of the Eighteen Bronze Men and survived a series of death traps to discover a group of Sontarans. The aliens were planting hypnotic commands in the monks, creating a deadly fighting force. The Doctor discovered their crashed ship, and learned its transmitter was damaged. The Sontarans needed a rock crystal to repair it, and only the Emperor had one large enough. The Doctor returned to the monastery, and one of the monks, Chang, slew the Sontarans in a hypnotic killing frenzy.

The Trib Museum was established in 1528. Its treasures would include fifteenth-century longbows from Earth.[478]

Henry VIII

On one of their earliest visits to Earth, the first Doctor and Susan met Henry VIII, who sent them to the Tower after the Doctor threw a parson's nose back at the King. The TARDIS had landed in the Tower, and this enabled the Doctor and Susan to make good their escape.[479] The Doctor had six wedding invitations from Henry VIII.[280] An early incarnation of Iris Wildthyme met Henry VIII and two of his wives - and a good time was had by all.[481] Iris and Panda hobnobbed at Hampton Court, then left for the future to avoid being beheaded.[482]

King Henry VIII mistook the Doctor for a jester.[483] **Henry VIII dissolved The Convent of Little Sisters of St Gudula.**[484] **Priests from around the country hid at Cranleigh Hall.**[485]

By the 1530s, the Spanish knew of an Incan myth about a fire god. It was based on the "burning" sentience.[486]

1533 (19th July) - SJA: LOST IN TIME[487] **->** Rani Chandra was transported back in time to find a piece of chronosteel, and met the doomed Queen Lady Jane Grey on the last day of her nine-day reign. The chronosteel had adopted the form of a dagger and threatened to derail history, but Rani prevented a Protestant from using the blade to martyr the Queen. Rani returned with the item to 2010.

1536 (4th May) - RECORDED TIME AND OTHER STORIES: "Recorded Time"[488] **->** Anne Boleyn learned that King Henry VIII wanted his time-rewriting Scrivener to make him the immortal King of Time. She used the Scrivener's phoenix pen to summon the sixth Doctor and

---

472 *SJA: Mona Lisa's Revenge.*
473 *Hornets' Nest: The Stuff of Nightmares.* The expression is first cited in a 1520 poem by Conrad Goclenius.
474 Susan says in *The Aztecs* that this happened in 1520; as *The Left-Handed Hummingbird* correctly identifies, it was actually 1519.
475 *Point of Entry.* The Spanish invasion of the Aztecs happened 1519-1521.
476 *Point of Entry.* Agrippa lived 1486-1535.
477 Dating "Dragon's Claw" (*DWW* #39-43, *DWM* #44-45) - "It is 1522...the summer of death!" according to the opening captions.
478 *Benny: The Lost Museum*
479 *The Sensorites.* Henry VIII reigned from 1509-1547. In *Tragedy Day*, the seventh Doctor says he has "never met" Henry VIII (p74); but the sixth Doctor says he has in *The Marian Conspiracy*, and is seen doing so in *Recorded Time and Other Stories: "Recorded Time".*
480 "The Gift"
481 *Iris: The Panda Invasion*

482 *Iris: Enter Wildthyme.* This happens "four hundred years" before the destination they flee to, a Shirley Bassey concert (so, likely the twentieth century, but possibly the twenty first).
483 *Terror Firma.* It's unclear if this refers to the same occasion mentioned in *The Sensorites.*
484 *The Stones of Blood.* The dissolution of the monasteries took place in the fifteen-thirties.
485 *Black Orchid*
486 *The Burning*
487 Dating *SJA: Lost in Time* (*SJA* 4.5) - The date is given.
488 Dating *Recorded Time and Other Stories: "Recorded Time"* (BF #150a) - King Henry VIII states the exact day. Anne Boleyn was killed about two weeks later, on 19th May. That Anne is still at liberty - and arguing with Henry in the court about his affairs - is a bit ahistorical; in real life, she was arrested on 2nd May and imprisoned in the Tower of London.
489 *Deadly Reunion,* unrelated to the sixth Doctor meeting Boleyn in *Recorded Time and Other Stories:*

Peri, who became one of the Queen's ladies in waiting. Henry proposed marriage to Peri. He also exacted vengeance on the Queen, making the Scrivener write that she was an adulterer, a sorceress and had a sixth finger on one hand. The Scrivener expired after defying the King's wish that the Queen be burned alive, writing instead that she would receive a clean sword-strike to the head. The Doctor destroyed the phoenix pen.

The Doctor witnessed the execution of Anne Boleyn.[489]

In 1540, under the reign of King James V, a shooting star landed near the Torchwood Estate in Scotland. Only a single cell of an alien - a werewolf - survived. In the generations to come, the cell would take host after host and grow stronger. The local monks in the Glen of St. Catherine tended to the creature, and made plans to facilitate the Empire of the Wolf.[490]

The Utlunta were slavers who purportedly drained the blood of other races to power their organic spaceships. The leader of a benevolent race trapped the Utlunta, and himself, in a pocket universe. He went mad, forgot his purpose and fled back to the proper universe - which also freed Lilu, the last Utlunta. While Lilu and her spaceship were pitched forward to the fifty-first century, the leader wound up with the Tigua Indians of pre-Columbian America, He became the source of a Comanche legend of the demon Nepesht and his vampiric offspring.[491]

c 1550 - THE JADE PYRAMID[492] **->** The ruler of Japan sent his samurai to collect the prized jade pyramid in the town of Kokan, and to bring it to Kyoto. The eleventh Doctor and Amy prevented bloodshed and made off with the pyramid. They also disabled a spaceship and the Otoroshi that it animated.

Around 1550, the Doctor was attacked by a jiki-ketsu-gaki, or vampire, in Japan. He was buried in a snowdrift and spent three months recovering in a monastery. He confronted the vampire, let her drain his blood until she was sated and fell asleep - and then burnt down her castle.[493]

Hexagoran scouts reconnoitered sixteenth-century London, but judged Earth as unsuitable for colonisation.[494] The Canavitchi supplied Nostradamus with many of his prophecies.[495] **The fourth Doctor's long scarf was made by Madame Nostradamus, "a witty little knitter".[496]**

1555 (January) - THE MARIAN CONSPIRACY[497] ->

The sixth Doctor helped Evelyn Smythe explore her ancestry. While the Doctor visited the court of Queen Mary, Evelyn stumbled on a Protestant plot to poison the Queen and replace her with Elizabeth. The time travellers were both imprisoned in the Tower of London. They met Reverend Thomas Smith, Evelyn's ancestor, before escaping and preventing the assassination.

The Elizabethan Age

The Doctor attended the Coronation of Queen Elizabeth I.[498] The Doctor was appalled by the Earl of Essex's behaviour at the Coronation.[499] The eighth Doctor, Samson and Gemma also visited the Court of Queen Elizabeth.[500]

1560 (spring) - THE ROOM WITH NO DOORS[501] -> A

Kapteynian slave escaped from a Caxtarid slaver ship, and its capsule crashed in the Han region of Japan. Within days, the Victorian time traveller Penelope Gate also visited Japan. A month later, the seventh Doctor and Chris Cwej arrived and became embroiled in a dispute between rival

---

"Recorded Time".

490 *Tooth and Claw* (TV)

491 *Benny: The Vampire Curse:* "Possum Kingdom". The Tigra, a.k.a. the Tiwa, are first mentioned in 1541 by the conquistador Francisco Coronado, although Nepesht's sojourn with them could predate that.

492 Dating *The Jade Pyramid* (BBC *DW* audiobook #10) - The Doctor and the blurb vaguely identify the period as "medieval Japan". A much earlier version of this story was set in Korea and dated between 1592 and 1598. Foreigners from across the seas are mentioned, possibly denoting the Portuguese, who arrived in 1543. Firearms are cited in such a way that they don't appear to be common. Ultimately, while author Martin Day didn't have a year in mind for the final version of *The Jade Pyramid*, he was inclined to think that it was during the early years of Ashikaga Yoshiteru's shogunate, which lasted 1546-1564. But even Day concedes that

this was more of a generalisation on his part than a hard and fast rule.

493 "Ten years" before *The Room with No Doors*.

494 *Hexagora*

495 *The King of Terror*

496 *The Ark in Space*. Nostradamus lived from 1503-1566, and published his prophecies in 1556.

497 Dating *The Marian Conspiracy* (BF #6) - It is one month after the Wyatt Uprising, at the end of 1554.

498 *The Curse of Peladon*, although the Doctor admits he might be confusing it with the Coronation of Queen Victoria. Elizabeth was Queen from 1558, but the Coronation wasn't until the following year.

499 *Cat's Cradle: Witch Mark*. There wasn't an Earl of Essex at the time of Elizabeth's Coronation.

500 *Terror Firma*. Elizabeth ruled 1558-1603.

501 Dating *The Room with No Doors* (NA #59) - It is "probably March 1560", and "early spring".

warlords Guffuu Kocho and Umemi, both wanting possession of the capsule. The Doctor managed to prevent either of them from taking control of it.

Iris saved the fourth Doctor and Sarah Jane in Scotland, in an escapade involving Mary Queen of Scots - who crocheted Iris a nice seat cushion.[502] The Doctor advised Mary Queen of Scots to change her muckspreader.[503]

"The Beast" were flying creatures that would move from planet to planet by way of dimensional interfaces, and invisibly feed off other beings. This was normally harmless, but on the planet Benelisa, the Beast wiped out the native populace as their numbers were few. The Beast moved on, but at least one Benelisan construct - Azoth - endured and pledged to eradicate the Beast.[504]

In 1564, an Agent of the Council of Eight prevented an Italian blacksmith from gaining the insight needed to invent the steam engine.[505] The Fulgurites - aliens who looked like mushroom-headed men - secretly established themselves on Earth and traded various commodities with other planets.[506] The Doctor said that the stories didn't lie - Ivan the Terrible really was *that* terrible.[507]

1572 (21st-24th August) - THE MASSACRE[508] -> The first Doctor and Steven arrived in Paris in August 1572. The Protestants of the city, the Huguenots, were massing to celebrate the wedding of Henry of Navarre to Princess Marguerite. Yet they lived in fear of the

Catholic majority, particularly the Queen Mother - Catherine de Medici - and the ruthless Abbot of Amboise. One hundred Huguenots had been killed at Wassy ten years ago, and a full-scale massacre was now instigated. The Doctor and Steven fled and were forced to leave Anne Chaplet, a serving girl befriended by Steven, behind to her fate.

Rebels from the mid-twenty-first century kidnapped the young Shakespeare to prevent time-travelling Daleks assassinating him. This removed Shakespeare from time, but history was restored upon his safe return.

(=) In a version of history without Shakespeare, the Daleks had a compound in Warwick in 1572.[509]

1580 - THE VAMPIRES OF VENICE[510] -> The planet Saturnyne was "lost" to the Silence, but a small group of fish-like Saturnynians escaped through a Crack in Time and arrived at Venice. Their leader used a perception filter to pose as Signora Rosanna Calvierri, a powerful figure who convinced the Venetians that the surrounding countryside was afflicted with plague. Calvierri also established an exclusive school - a means of genetically altering the girls there into Sisters of the Water, mates for the males. The human survival instinct would override the Sisters' perception filters in time of danger, making them look like vampires.

502 *Verdigris*. Mary Queen of Scots ruled 1542-1567.
503 *Tragedy Day*
504 *The Taint*. The Beast arrive on Earth in 1944, according to *Autumn Mist*.
505 *Sometime Never*
506 "Centuries" before *The Perpetual Bond*.
507 *Thin Ice*. Ivan ruled 1533 to 1584.
508 Dating *The Massacre* (3.5) - The first three episodes take place over a single day each, the last picks up nearly twenty-four hours after the end of the third late on the evening of the 23rd and runs into the 24th. The Admiral Gaspar de Coligny was shot on the 22nd. This story is sometimes referred to as *The Massacre of St. Bartholomew's Eve*, based on some production documents, but this is historically erroneous. The event is more accurately named "the massacre of St. Bartholomew's *Day*".
509 *The Time of the Daleks*, which implies that Shakespeare used some of the names of individuals he met in the future for characters in plays such as *Hamlet*, *King Lear*, *Twelfth Night*, *Titus Andronicus* and *The Tempest*.
510 Dating *The Vampires of Venice* (X5.6) - The opening caption says "Venice 1580". This is another story affected by the Cracks in Time, so it's possible - given that the Saturnynians would never have come to Venice but for

benefit of one - that this story was removed from history when the cracks were sealed (see the Cracks in Time sidebar, however, for why this probably isn't the case). The Doctor references this story's "sexy fish vampires" in *A Good Man Goes to War*, giving no indication that they're now the stuff of alternate history.
  The aliens are called "Saturnynians" on the BBC website, "Saturnynes" in *Doctor Who: The Encyclopedia*. The story ends with the canals of Venice still containing ten thousand Saturnynian males, and it's the subject of fan-conjecture that, somehow, they become the progenitors of the fish-people seen in *The Stones of Venice*.
511 *Timewyrm: Revelation*
512 *The Stones of Blood*
513 Dating *TimeH: Child of Time* (TimeH #11) - The year is given (p68). It's possible that these events occur in an alternate timeline; see the 2586 entry of this story.
514 *The Seeds of Doom*
515 *The Empire of Glass*, which consistently renders "Roanoke" as "Roanoake".
516 *EarthWorld*. This was in 1587.
517 *Four to Doomsday*. The Spanish Armada attacked in 1588.
518 *The Marian Conspiracy*
519 *Birthright*
520 *Only Human*

The eleventh Doctor, Amy and Rory stopped Calvierri from sinking Venice with an earthquake device, which would have turned the city into the Saturnynians' new domain. Calvierri killed herself, taunting the Doctor that he had wiped out another species.

In 1582, the Doctor visited Rome while trying to track the Timewyrm.[511] **Boscombe Hall was built on the site of the Convent of the Little Sisters of St Gudula in the late sixteenth century.**[512]

1586 - TIMEH: CHILD OF TIME[513] **->** The cult Sodality sought further power and summoned the Daemon Mastho during a masked ball at the Palazzo Bembo, Venice. Mastho decried Sodality, and ordered that the group destroy the time-sensitives and channellers it had created, lest their existence interfere with the Daemons' experiments on humanity. Sodality was given exactly one millennium to complete this task; Mastho threatened to return at that time, and to destroy the world if Sodality failed.

The West Wing of Chase Mansion was completed in 1587.[514] In 1587, the Greld wiped out the Roanoke colony in the New World. They implanted the colonists with components for a meta-cobalt bomb, hoping to sabotage the Armageddon Convention. Christopher Marlowe, an agent of the crown, investigated the tragedy but escaped.[515] The Doctor may have been at the execution of Mary, Queen of Scots.[516] **The Doctor met Francis Drake just before he faced the Spanish Armada.**[517] He played bowls with Drake and met William Cecil at Elizabeth's court.[518] The Doctor let Drake win at bowls so Drake could leave early to face the Spanish Armada on time.[519]

Jack Harkness had fun with a lady at Elizabeth's court.[520] An Agent of the Council of Eight released a single butterfly in Africa. The slight disturbance it caused in the atmos-

phere triggered a storm that helped to destroy the Armada. The Council of Eight's leader, Octan, arrived in 1588 to try and stop this. The Agent, unable to recognise Octan, pushed him into the Time Vortex.[521]

The tenth Doctor married and deflowered Elizabeth I.[522] **The Queen waited in a glade to elope with the Doctor.**[523] Elizabeth I knighted the Doctor for "more intimate reasons" than Victoria would in future.[524]

Around 1589, Irving Braxiatel began a diplomatic effort that culminated in the signing of the Armageddon Convention.[525] On 28th October of the same year, the ancient werewolf Pieter Stubbe escaped after being sentenced to death for sorcery in Cologne.[526]

c 1592 (summer) - POINT OF ENTRY[527] **->** The Omnim, largely existing as mental energy in rogue asteroid D359XQ2, locked onto the TARDIS' flight trail as a means of drawing close to Earth. A Spaniard, Don Lorentho Velez, found the Omnim-tainted stone hilt in Madrid, and so fell under the Omnim's power. He was made to find the Omnim stone knife the English had taken from the Aztecs, and recruited help from the dramatist Christopher Marlowe - an agent of the crown, who was busy writing *The Tragical History of the Life and Death of Doctor Faustus* - by allowing him to experience astral projection. The sixth Doctor and Peri destroyed the Omnim as they attempted to manifest during a lunar eclipse. Marlowe wrote a line in *Doctor Faustus* ("Where the philosopher ceases, the Doctor begins") in the Doctor's honour.

Christopher Marlowe continued serving as a secret agent of the British government. He conspired with Walsingham, the Secretary of State, to fake his death.[528] Towards the end of the sixteenth century, the Xaranti attacked a Zygon fleet. A Zygon ship survived the fighting and crashed on Earth.[529]

---

521 *Sometime Never*
522 The Doctor's claim in *The End of Time* (TV) is backed up by Liz X in *The Beast Below* and the Dream Lord in *Amy's Choice*. We don't know the year, but we can presume that it was before *The Shakespeare Code*, and explains her anger with him in that story.
523 *The Wedding of River Song*
524 *The Empire of Glass*
525 "A Fairytale Life"
526 *Loups-Garoux*
527 Dating *Point of Entry* (BF LS #1.6) - The Doctor judges that they've arrived "1590 local time, or thereabouts. The Elizabethan Age." A slightly later dating, however, is indicated in the Doctor telling Peri that while "Shakespeare's hardly started yet", they can potentially see *Henry VI, Part 1, Part 2* and *Part 3*. The real-life evidence suggests that at the very earliest, those three plays were written in 1591, and first per-

formed no later than September 1592. Whatever the case, it's after Marlowe's *Tamburlaine* - the first part of which was first performed in late 1587 - has been performed for Queen Elizabeth I.

Certainly, *Point of Entry* happens before Marlowe's real-life death on 30th May, 1593 - although *The Empire of Glass* details how he faked his demise. That story and *Point of Entry* are reasonably compatible as far as Marlowe's life is concerned, although the sixth Doctor curiously tells Peri that Marlowe - as history claims, and as the Doctor should know better from *The Empire of Glass* - will die young in a bar fight.

It's twice said to be summer.
528 *The Empire of Glass*. History tells us Marlowe died on 30th May, 1593.
529 "Three centuries" before *The Bodysnatchers*. This is a different ship from the one seen in *Terror of the Zygons*.

103

Shakespeare[530]

The Doctor encouraged Shakespeare, a "taciturn" young man, to take up writing.[531] Shakespeare and John Fletcher wrote *Cardenio - A Spanish Comedie*.[532]

1592 (September) - "A Groatsworth of Wit"[523] ->

The alien Shadeys took Robert Greene, a staunch critic of Shakespeare, from his deathbed and transported him over four hundred years into the future. The ninth Doctor and Rose arrived, hot on Greene's trail. The Doctor quoted from *Richard III* and was mistaken for an actor, while Shakespeare tried to seduce Rose. Greene attacked Shakespeare, but the Doctor suggested that if Greene destroyed the great playwright *now*, Greene himself would lose what little future fame he currently enjoyed. Greene banished the Shadeys and returned to his deathbed.

1597 - THE KINGMAKER[534] ->

Peri and Erimem watched an exceedingly bad preview of *Richard III*, while the fifth Doctor went boozing at The White Rabbit tavern with his friend William Shakespeare. A loyalist to the Queen, Shakespeare became greatly disturbed by the Doctor's suggestion that in future, suspicion for the murder of Richard III's nephews would fall on Henry Tudor. Shortly afterwards, the Doctor and his companions left for 1485, and Shakespeare - determined to convince Richard to kill his nephews and thereby preserve the Queen's family name - stowed aboard.

Events in 1485 caused the TARDIS to materialise back in 1597 during a subsequent performance of *Richard III*. The genuine King Richard III had stowed away and remained behind as Shakespeare re-entered the TARDIS and met Richard's historical fate on Bosworth Field.

To preserve history, Richard III lived out Shakespeare's life and wrote his remaining plays, historicals, tragedies

---

530 SHAKESPEARE: Going on just the information in the television series, the Doctor has met Shakespeare at least three times. Taking all the other media into account, we can infer that the Doctor has met Shakespeare a bare minimum of eight separate occasions, in at least six incarnations.

We actually see five of these meetings. In chronological order of Shakespeare's life, these are *The Time of the Daleks* (when Shakespeare is a child), "A Groatsworth of Wit" (set in 1592), *The Kingmaker* (set in 1597, and in which Shakespeare is replaced by Richard III), *The Shakespeare Code* (set in 1599) and *The Empire of Glass* (set in 1609, but with an epilogue that shows Shakespeare's death in 1616). Additionally, *The Chase* has the first Doctor, Ian, Barbara and Vicki using the Time-Space Visualizer to observe Shakespeare in the court of Elizabeth I, presumably at some point between *The Shakespeare Code* (as *Hamlet* has still not been written) and *Hamlet*'s real-life registry in 1602 (years before *The Empire of Glass*, then).

In one regard, this is all far less contradictory than it might seem. None of the stories (save for *The Chase* and *The Shakespeare Code*, in which Shakespeare twice receives inspiration to write *Hamlet*) bear different accounts of the same event. Indeed, none of the adventures even occur in the same year - the closest pairing (*The Kingmaker* and *The Shakespeare Code*) are set two years apart. Taking the general events in the five stories that directly involve Shakespeare, then, at face value is not very difficult.

Two impediments remain, however. One is that Shakespeare does not remotely look or act the same in some of his appearances. All things being equal, it's hard to believe that Shakespeare as voiced by Michael Fenton-Stevens in *The Kingmaker*, as played by Dean Lennox Kelly in *The Shakespeare Code*, and as played by Hugh Walters in *The Chase* are all the same person.

(Note that this problem isn't limited to the different *Doctor Who* media, but occurs even in Shakespeare's two appearances on television.) Shakespeare's personality varies wildly between stories, even allowing that we're witnessing different points of his life.

The other problem is that Shakespeare in his later appearances never acknowledges having met a stranger named "the Doctor" before. He is admittedly never seen to meet the same incarnation twice, but it's implausible to think that he never makes a connection between the various men who keep appearing during turbulent and strange events, all of them named "Doctor". *The Kingmaker* actually helps a little in this regard - the Doctor and Shakespeare are on very chummy terms, but Shakespeare dies on Bosworth Field, eliminating the need for Richard III to acknowledge having met the Doctor in *The Time of the Daleks* and "A Groatsworth of Wit". Obviously, this doesn't explain why Richard himself doesn't acknowledge the Doctor in the next story in the line - *The Shakespeare Code* - or thereafter.

The Kingmaker is a particular sticking point, as it has Richard III living out Shakespeare's life from 1597 onward. This would mean that the "Shakespeare" that the tenth Doctor and Martha meet in *The Shakespeare Code* is actually a disguised Richard III installed by the fifth Doctor... but who is somehow driven to great depression by the death of the original Shakespeare's son, who has acquired two perfectly functional arms and who doesn't limp. It might be best to assume events in *The Kingmaker* happened, then the Time War or some other intervention (allowing for Shakespeare's importance to history) reversed them. This would carry the double benefit of not having to rationalise the conflicting fates of Richard III's nephews/nieces in *The Kingmaker* and *Sometime Never*.

531 *City of Death.* This unseen encounter would have

and comedies. He was moved to write his late brother George into *Henry IV, Part 1*, but kept misspelling Shakespeare's name. The Doctor suggested that Richard look up Francis Bacon to help with his writing.

Shakespeare's only child, Hamnet, had died, so the Doctor relocated Richard's nieces to live with him as "Shakespeare's daughters", Susanna and Judith.

The grief Shakespeare suffered after Hamnet's death allowed three Carrionites entrance back into history, and they manipulated him in a bid to free their sisters. They also influenced Peter Streete - the architect of the Globe Theatre - to design the stage area with fourteen sides, in accordance with the fourteen stars of the Rexel planetary configuration. Streete lost his mind as a result, and was consigned to Bedlam.[535]

1599 - THE SHAKESPEARE CODE[536] **->** The tenth Doctor and Martha were surprised when a performance of *Love's Labour's Lost* in London ended with an announcement by Shakespeare that the sequel, *Love's Labour's Won*, would debut the following night. Three

witch-like Carrionites were manipulating Shakespeare - *Love's Labour's Won* was embedded with coordinates that would open a spatial rift, and allow the rest of their race freedom. Shakespeare used his command of language to seal the portal and banish the Carrionites; all copies of *Love's Labour's Won* were destroyed.

Shakespeare took note of the Doctor's use of the word "Sycorax"[537], and a few choice phrases. The Doctor and Martha escaped when a wrathful Elizabeth I called for his head - owing to events that hadn't yet happened in the Doctor's personal timeline.

The first Doctor used the Time-Space Visualiser to watch Shakespeare at the court of Elizabeth I. The Queen was interested in Falstaff, but Francis Bacon gave Shakespeare the idea to write *Hamlet*.[538] The Doctor helped Shakespeare write his plays.[539]

The Doctor suggested that *The Merry Wives of Windsor* needed to be redrafted, but the Queen wanted it performed as soon as possible.[540]

The fourth Doctor said Shakespeare was a "charming fellow", but a "dreadful actor".[541] The Doctor tran-

to be before 1590, when we know Shakespeare was writing, and must have involved one of the Doctor's first four incarnations.

532 *TW: Trace Memory*. Shakespeare and Fletcher are credited as writing the lost play *Cardenio* in a 1653 Stationers' Register that otherwise makes false use of Shakespeare's name. In the *Doctor Who* universe, it appears he and Fletcher did author the work.

533 Dating "A Groatsworth of Wit" (*DWM* #363-364) - Greene's death on 3rd September, 1592, is historical record. Greene is famous for dismissing Shakespeare both for plagiarism and because he was mainly - at that time - an actor, not a writer. When Rose asks if the Doctor knows Shakespeare, he says he's "known him for ages. Just not yet". This would suggest that the meeting mentioned in *Planet of Evil* didn't involve too much familiarity.

534 Dating *The Kingmaker* (BF #81) - The date is given. It's believed that *Richard III* was written in 1592-93, and it was entered into the Register of the Stationers Company on 20th October, 1597 by bookseller Andrew Wise. The Doctor and Shakespeare go drinking at The White Rabbit - a London establishment mentioned in Big Finish projects such as *The Reaping*.

535 *The Shakespeare Code*. Hamnet Shakespeare was buried on 11th August, 1596.

536 Dating *The Shakespeare Code* (X3.2) - The date is given in a caption at the start, and confirmed by the Doctor. In real life, it's thought that *Love's Labour's Lost* was performed in 1597; *Love's Labour's Won* is on a list of Shakespeare's plays dating from 1598. Historically, the Globe Theatre opened in the autumn.

The tenth Doctor claims that he "hasn't met" Queen

Elizabeth I yet, but *Birthright* establishes that she's been familiar with the seventh Doctor since at least 1588. It's possible that the tenth Doctor means that he hasn't yet met Elizabeth in his current incarnation (and is therefore surprised because she recognises him on sight), and that Elizabeth doesn't realise that the different Doctors are the same being.

537 The implication is that (among other things) the Doctor inspires Shakespeare to use the name Sycorax - not just the aliens from *The Christmas Invasion*, but also the name of Caliban's mother in Shakespeare's final play, *The Tempest*. (A moon of Uranus is named after the same character.)

538 *The Chase*. Literary scholars disagree when *Hamlet* was written, but we know it was entered in the Stationers' Register in 1602. It was almost certainly written and performed around 1600.

539 *Endgame* (EDA)

540 *The Ultimate Treasure*. *The Merry Wives of Windsor* was written around 1597, but could have been a little later, so this is just possibly the same visit as the one where the Doctor helped with *Hamlet*.

541 *City of Death*. Historically, Shakespeare was known as an actor by 1592, and tradition has it that he continued to act even when he was better known as a writer. This reference seems to contradict the one in *Planet of Evil*, and clearly represents a different, subsequent visit (or visits). We can therefore infer that it's the fourth Doctor who helped with *Hamlet*, after *Planet of Evil*. The encounter is mentioned again in *Asylum*. One problem is that it's also mentioned by the first Doctor in *Byzantium!* - if that needs explaining away, it's possible the first Doctor has seen the manuscript, recognised

scribed a copy of *Hamlet* for Shakespeare, who had sprained his wrist writing sonnets. Scaroth later acquired the manuscript.[542]

The Doctor saw Garrick take the title role in the first performance of *Hamlet*.[543] **If the Monk's plan in 1066 had worked, *Hamlet* would have been written for television.**[544] The Doctor wrote Poor Tom's dialogue in *King Lear*[545], and saw Garrick play the part.[546] The Doctor has a copy of *Mischief Night*, or *As You Please*, an unknown Shakespeare play, in a TARDIS storeroom.[547]

The Seventeenth Century

The planet Caresh was in a binary star system containing the larger, warmer sun Beacon and the smaller, colder Ember. Caresh randomly orbited one of the two stars each solar cycle, causing unpredictable warm and cold years. In the seventeenth century, a protracted cold period killed off a large amount of the population. As the warm years returned, scientists on Dassar Island built a scanner capable of seeing into the future, giving them advance warning of cold years. The Time Lords ruled the scanner a violation

of their monopoly on time travel, and dispatched agents Solenti and Lord Roche to shut down the device.[548]

Centuries ago, invaders dominated the planet Indo. The surviving microscopic natives travelled to Earth on a meteorite. They fed off the latent emotions of humans in the Brighton area, and would gain in strength by 1936.[549]

The Sepulchre transported a resident of the seventeenth century - "Springheeled Sophie", a funambulist and thief - into the London-recreation that existed in its mental landscape. Following the Sepulchre's defeat by the eighth Doctor and Lucie, Sophie remained in the Sepulchre's recreation of her native time.[550]

In the seventeenth century, an inhabitant of the planet Parrimor was exiled to Earth. He became Claudio Tardelli - an artist whose paintings and sculptures warped reality, and had a "malign influence" on anyone who looked at them. In Rome, the Doctor stopped Tardelli from using his artworks to influence the Pope. Tardelli was discredited, and the Doctor worked to keep him obscure, destroying many of Tardelli's works. Tardelli fled to Florence and sequestered himself inside a black diamond he'd created - one that contained a compressed universe about three

his handwriting (we know from *The Trial of a Time Lord* that the Valeyard and sixth Doctor have the same handwriting, so presumably all the Doctors do) and so inferred a future meeting.

542 *City of Death*

543 *The Gallifrey Chronicles*. Presumably on the same visit he helped write it, although the amnesiac eighth Doctor should have no memory of that.

544 *The Time Meddler*, although there's no evidence of any contact between the Monk and Shakespeare.

545 *The Cabinet of Light*. *King Lear* appeared in the Stationers' Register for November 1607, so this is another meeting. *Island of Death* implies it has to involve one of the Doctor's first three incarnations.

546 *Island of Death*

547 "Changes". This play, unlike the ones Braxiatel acquires in *The Empire of Glass*, is completely unknown to Shakespearean scholarship.

548 *The Suns of Caresh*

549 *Pier Pressure*

550 *Dead London*

551 *Grand Theft Cosmos*

552 *The Banquo Legacy*. In the real world, the *Necronomicon* was a fictional book of magic invented by H.P. Lovecraft.

553 *Spare Parts*

554 *The Mind of Evil*. Raleigh lived 1552-1618, and was imprisoned 1603-1616.

555 "Centuries" before *The Way Through the Woods*.

556 Dating "The Devil of the Deep" (*DWM* #61) - It's "the early seventeenth century" when Diego is rescued according to a caption. The Sea Devil revived "ten years"

before rescuing Diego, who is rescued "twenty years" after being marooned.

557 Dating "The Road to Hell" (*DWM* #278-282) - The Doctor asserts "I'm fairly sure I've set us down in the tenth century", but quickly corrects this to "the early seventeenth century".

558 "The Glorious Dead"

559 *Birthright*. It's entirely possible that after this point, Jared Khan passes off the identity of "John Dee" to a successor who later starves to death while containing the Enochians ("Don't Step on the Grass").

560 "Don't Step on the Grass". The head Enochian says its spaceship arrived on Earth "over five hundred years" prior to 2009 (so, concurrent with Dee's lifetime), and the date is given as "sixteenth century Greenwich" in "Final Sacrifice". Seemingly without any evidence, the Doctor also claims that the spaceship has been on Earth for "thousands of years". Enochian is an occult/angelic language found in Dee's journals in real life.

561 "Final Sacrifice"

562 *The Dying Days*

563 Dating *The Plotters* (MA #28) - The year is given (p23).

564 *Endgame* (EDA)

565 Before *Revenge of the Cybermen*. The signing of the Convention is the central event of *The Empire of Glass*.

566 "Don't Step on the Grass". In real life, it's unknown if Dee died in 1608 or 1609, as both the parish registers and his gravestone are missing.

light years across. The King of Sweden later acquired the diamond in 1898.[551]

Around 1600, the *Necronomicon* was translated into Spanish.[552] In the early seventeenth century, the Doctor was given tea by Emperor Tokugawa Ieyasu of Japan.[553] **The Doctor once shared a cell with Walter Raleigh, who "kept going on about this new vegetable he'd discovered".**[554]

Neighbouring empires fought The Long War, a conflict that went on for generations. During this, a space explorer, Reyn the were-fox, crashed on Earth near the village of Foxton. Reyn's spaceship *learned* from its travels, attaining some sentience through a process called The Shift.

(=) Reyn's ship needed to absorb living minds every half-century, and so extruded a number of temporal and spatial anomalies through Swallow Woods from the Bronze Age to the present day. People subconsciously avoided the Woods, save for when the ship mentally lured in people to drain their minds. It would claim three hundred and nine victims.

The eleventh Doctor, Amy and Rory undid the temporal anomalies. The Long War ended very badly for Reyn's homeworld, but the Doctor and Rory retroactively established a legend that "the Traveller" would one day return with knowledge of lost technology.[557]

c 1600 - "The Devil of the Deep"[556] **->** The ship of Diego da Columba of Cordoba vanished off the coast of South America. It had been attacked by pirates led by Korvo. Diego was rescued after walking the plank by a Sea Devil who had revived ten years previously. The pirates discovered the Sea Devil's island and he was captured by Korvo. One of the pirates accidentally activated a Caller, a device that summoned a giant marine reptile that sank the pirate ship. Diego was left alone for twenty years until he was rescued and could tell his tale - his proof was that he still had the Caller.

c 1600 (5th May) - "The Road to Hell"[557] **->** The eighth Doctor and Izzy arrived in Japan and were brought before aliens known as Gaijin, who sought to understand the concept of honour. They had a nano-sculptor that turned thoughts into reality, and could make people immortal - they did so with Katsura Sato. The Doctor was angry at the interference, but the Gaijin didn't understand the objections. One of the Japanese, Asami, saw a vision of Japan's future in Izzy's mind, including the atomic bombs of World War II. He decided to launch a preemptive attack on the West. The Gaijin now understood that honour was linked to responsibility and deactivated the nano-sculptor even though it killed them.

Katsura Sato, unable to commit seppuku, wandered the Earth, became a pirate and ended up incarcerated in Saragossa for fifty years. The Master wrote the *Odostra*, a fake holy book, and gave it to Katsura in his cell. Katsura was filled with crusading zeal and set out to conquer the world. History changed because of this.[558]

Jared Khan had adopted the guise of John Dee, and had served as Queen Elizabeth's counsellor for twenty years. In 1603, the Queen diverted Dee's attention so he would not discover that the seventh Doctor was at her court.[559]

The ley lines in Greenwich, London, were a source of energy akin to the Cardiff Rift; in future, Greenwich would become the primary meridian of all Earth time, and the naval college would be full of ghosts. A group of alien conquerors, the Enochians, were drawn to Greenwich's ley lines, but their colony ship encountered a systems failure. They sought help from John Dee by speaking through his associate, the medium Edward Kelley. Dee parted ways with Kelley in 1589 and returned to England, then moved his private library and the Enochian spaceship to Duke Humphrey's house. He hoped to help the aliens, whom he regarded as "angels", and created the Enochian language to better communicate with them.[560] The Enochians had unknowingly been diverted to Greenwich by the Tef'Aree, as a means of enabling its own creation.[561]

General William Lethbridge-Stewart was among King James' retinue on his initial arrival in London.[562]

1605 - THE PLOTTERS[563] **->** The first Doctor and Vicki decided to investigate the Gunpowder Plot while Ian and Barbara set off for the Globe Theatre. The Doctor and Vicki - who was disguised as a boy named Victor - met King James I, and learned that the statesman Sir Robert Cecil was encouraging the Plot to draw out the conspirators and discredit the Catholics. Some Catholics captured Barbara, leading to Guy Fawkes befriending her. Robert Catesby, a member of the Plot, argued with Fawkes and killed him... which isn't how the history books reported events.

The King's courtier, Robert Hay, was a secret member of a grand order devoted to mysticism. Hay sought to create anarchy, but the Doctor manoeuvred Hay to the cellar under Parliament, where Cecil arrested him. Hay was tortured and executed in Fawkes' place, preserving history.

The Doctor met Cervantes.[564] **The Armageddon Convention was signed, and banned the use of cobalt bombs.**[565] John Dee learned that the Enochian "angels" were actually conquerors and destroyed their physical forms, but their essences were absorbed into the Earth. One Enochian remained aboard their spacecraft in a clockwork body, and so Dee sealed the ship within the cellars of Duke Humphrey's house. He finally starved to death aboard the spacecraft.[566]

1609 - THE EMPIRE OF GLASS[567] -> Irving Braxiatel and the first Doctor - accompanied by Steven and Vicki - hosted a meeting, the Armageddon Convention, that saw doomsday weapons such as temporal disrupters and cobalt bombs banned. Although the Daleks and Cybermen refused to attend, many other races did sign. The Convention was nearly sabotaged by the Greld, a race of arms dealers who stood to lose money from it; and the Jamarians, who craved an empire for themselves.

The first performance of *Macbeth* had the last minute substitutions of Shakespeare in the role of Lady Macbeth, and the Doctor and Vicki in the roles of the doctor and his servant. The spy Christopher Marlowe died in a duel.

The Doctor dropped Sarah Jane off at Skye for a few days, and stopped a monstrous undertaking by the serial killer Elizabeth Bathory, a.k.a. the Blood Countess. He was present at her trial in 1611. The Mimic, a creature banished from Gallifrey, copied a demonic creature that Bathory had summoned. On 29th June, 1613, the talentless playwright Francis Pearson - a follower of Countess Bathory - burnt down Shakespeare's Globe Theatre during a production of *Henry VIII*. He later vanished, transported by the ancient Mimic to the thirty-first century.[568] In April 1616, a dying William Shakespeare handed over three unpublished plays - *Love's Labours Won*, *The Birth of Merlin* and *Sir John Oldcastle* - to Irving Braxiatel in return for memories of events in Venice, 1609.[569]

On one occasion, the Doctor saw a beached whale lie on the shore for four days until its bowels exploded - some of the eye-witnesses died from disease after being splattered by rotten whale meat.[570]

Chamberlen, the inventor of modern obstetrical forceps, bequeathed a pair of his creations upon the Doctor.

567 Dating *The Empire of Glass* (MA #16) - The Doctor states that it "must be the year of our lord, 1609" (p30).
568 *Managra*. Bathory lived 1560-1614; her trial commenced on 7th January, 1611, with her in absentia.
569 *The Empire of Glass*
570 Three hundred years before *Year of the Pig*.
571 *The Settling*. The person who bestows the forceps upon the Doctor is merely referred to as "Chamberlen". Peter Chamberlen is regarded as the inventor of forceps, although the name actually refers to two brothers (respectively 1560-1631 and 1572-1626). The elder Peter is apparently the creator of the device, which was a family secret for generations.
572 "Don't Step on the Grass"
573 *The End of Time* (DL), p40. There were actually two "Defenestrations of Prague", in 1419 and 1618, although the term more often refers to the latter. Some real-life texts do claim that those thrown out the third window of the Bohemian Chancellory lived owing to a large heap of manure.
574 *Silver Nemesis*
575 *Sometime Never*
576 "Ten generations" before *Imperial Moon*.
577 *FP: Newtons Sleep* (p14). Silver says he was born "the year the last king came to the throne" - meaning Charles I, in 1625.
578 Dating *The Church and the Crown* (BF #38) - The date is given.
579 *The Abominable Snowmen*. This was "1630" according to the Doctor. *The Programme Guide* suggested "1400 AD".
580 The Doctor speaks Tibetan in *Planet of the Spiders* (but can't in *The Creature from the Pit*), and uses Tibetan meditation in *Terror of the Zygons*.
581 *Heart of TARDIS*. Bacon died in April 1626.
582 *The War Games*. The Thirty Years War ran from 1618-1648.
583 Dating *Borrowed Time* (NSA #49) - The year is given (p253). The peak of "tulip mania" was February 1637.

584 *The Church and the Crown*
585 Dating *Silver Nemesis* (25.3) - The Doctor gives the date of the launch, but there is no indication of exactly how long afterwards Lady Peinforte leaves for the twentieth century. Quite how "Roundheads" can be involved in this business when the term wasn't used until the Civil War is unclear. As a letter to *Radio Times* after *Silver Nemesis* aired noted, the adoption of the Gregorian calendar in 1752 means that eleven days were "lost" in Britain, so had the Nemesis *really* landed exactly three hundred and fifty years after 23rd November, 1638, it would have landed on 3rd December, 1988.

The statue passes over the Earth every twenty-five years (in 1663, 1688, 1713, 1738, 1763, 1788, 1813, 1838, 1863, 1888, 1913, 1938, 1963 and finally 1988). *The Terrestrial Index* offers suggestions as to the effects of the statue on human history, but the only on-screen information concerns the twentieth century.

Fenric's involvement is established in *The Curse of Fenric*.
586 Dating *FP: Newtons Sleep* (FP novel #6) - The date is given on the back cover, in accord with the English Civil War starting in 1642. The publisher of *Newtons Sleep*, Random Static, has stated that the lack of an apostrophe in the title was deliberate; it's a quote from William Blake.
587 *The War Games*. The English Civil Wars ran from 1642-1649.
588 *The Time Monster*
589 *The Awakening*
590 *The Hollow Men*
591 *The Spectre of Lanyon Moor*
592 *Nightshade*
593 *The Daemons*. The witchhunter Matthew Hopkins died in 1647.
594 *Players*
595 Dating *The Roundheads* (PDA #6) - The Doctor says it's "1648, December I should say" (p39).

He used this item in 1649 to deliver a child during the sacking of Wexford.[571] The Doctor met Inigo Jones in 1649, and either helped him find his cat or defeat an army of cats - he couldn't remember which.[572]

The Doctor was present at the Defenestration of Prague, and saved the lives of the intended victims with a pile of manure. The TARDIS stank for a week.[573]

In 1621, the infamous Lady Peinforte poisoned her neighbour Dorothea Remington.[574] In 1624, the Doctor met an Agent of the Council of Eight in Devon.[575]

The Phiadoran Directorate systems were dominated by the Phiadoran Clan Matriarchy, who influenced males with genetically augmented pheromones. The Matriarchy instigated ten generations of tyranny that lasted Galactic Time Index 611,072.26 to 611,548.91. The Sarmon Revolution brought down the Matriarchy, and exiled its members to die in a safari park built on Earth's moon. Thirty-two years later, the carnivorous Vrall killed the Matriarchy, and disguised themselves as the Phiadorans by wearing their skins. Lacking space-travel, the Vrall launched RNA spores encoded with technical information to Earth.[576]

Nathaniel Silver was born in 1625.[577]

1626 - THE CHURCH AND THE CROWN[578] **->** At the court of King Louis, the Musketeers and Cardinal Richelieu were in constant dispute. The fifth Doctor, Peri and Erimem arrived, and it transpired that Peri was the double of Queen Anne. The Duke of Buckingham kidnapped Peri - he was planning a British invasion of France by dividing the French court. Erimem rallied the troops, and averted a major diplomatic incident.

The Doctor apparently visited the Det-Sen monastery in Tibet on a number of occasions, and in 1630 helped the monks there to survive bandit attacks. He was entrusted with the holy Ghanta when he left.[579] **It was possibly on this visit that the Doctor learned the Tibetan language and meditation techniques.**[580]

The Doctor witnessed philosopher Francis Bacon conduct an experiment on the preservation of meat by stuffing snow into a chicken. Bacon later contracted pneumonia from the incident and died.[581] **The War Lords lifted a battlefield from some point during the Thirty Years War.**[582]

1636 - BORROWED TIME[583] **->** Jane Blythe, now a fugitive from the Time Market following her economic ruin in 2007, fled into the past and established a low-level time commodities scheme. Her avatars, Mr Hoogeveen and Mr Verspronck, loaned out time to certain residents of the Netherlands - before long, this created an economic bubble pertaining to the value of tulips.

The Doctor met Louis XIII in 1637.[584]

1638 (November) - SILVER NEMESIS[585] **->** On 23rd November, 1638, the seventh Doctor was present as some Roundheads fought Lady Peinforte's soldiers, and as the Nemesis asteroid was launched into space from a meadow in Windsor. Following this, the Doctor set his watch alarm to go off on 23rd November, 1988, the day that the Nemesis would return to Earth.

The Nemesis passed over the Earth every twenty-five years, influencing human affairs. Lady Peinforte employed a mathematician to work out the asteroid's trajectory, and then used his blood in a magical ceremony - one that also involved the Validium arrow in Peinforte's possession - to transport Peinforte and her servant Richard Maynarde to its ultimate destination. The imprisoned Fenric aided her time travel.

w - 1642 - FP: NEWTONS SLEEP[586] **->** Nathaniel Silver, a Roundhead soldier, was shot dead at Edgehill. Representatives from humanity's posthuman era, seeking to guarantee the stability of their timeline, meddled with Silver's biodata and resurrected him. Silver didn't age from this point onward. The posthumans also gave him possession of a mysterious egg that aided his efforts to learn the secrets of natural philosophy.

The English Civil War

The War Lords kidnapped a Civil War battlefield.[587] A division of Roundheads was also kidnapped by the Master using TOM-TIT.[588] On 13th July, 1643, the Royalists and Roundheads met in Little Hodcombe, wiping out themselves and the entire village. The Malus fed from the psychic energy released by the deaths and briefly emerged from its dormancy. The Doctor returned the time-flung Will Chandler to this, his native era, shortly afterwards.[589]

Returning Will Chandler was not a straightforward business.[590] A group of Roundheads was torn apart on Lanyon Moor, apparently by wild beasts.[591] In 1644, "strange fire" consumed the castle of Crook Marsham.[592] **Witches hid from Matthew Hopkins in Devil's End.**[593] The Doctor met King Charles II.[594]

1648 - THE ROUNDHEADS[595] **->** Ben Jackson and Polly were mistaken for Parliamentarians. Polly was kidnapped by Royalists, while Ben was press-ganged. Meanwhile, Oliver Cromwell's men arrested the second Doctor and Jamie. Cromwell's belief that Jamie was a fortune teller aided the TARDIS crew in escaping, but they were accompanied by King Charles... who according to history should have stayed in prison. Polly was forced to betray Christopher Whyte, a new friend and a Royalist, to protect history. Charles was duly recaptured and executed.

1649 (12th September to 11th October) - THE SETTLING[596] **->** The seventh Doctor, Ace and Hex arrived in Ireland as Oliver Cromwell's forces successfully besieged Drogheda. Weeks later, Cromwell's army threatened Wexford, and he demanded that the town recognise the authority of Parliament. Conflict ensued until Cromwell received a surrender notice and ordered the fighting to cease. Hex, having witnessed the horror at Drogheda, roused the townsfolk to resist. The fighting resumed, hundreds of fleeing women and children drowned on crowded boats. Cromwell's troops prevailed.

The seventh Doctor met Dr. Goddard, who helped to found the Royal Society.

w - 1650 - FP: NEWTONS SLEEP[597] **->** When Isaac Newton, a.k.a. Jeova Unus Sanctus, was a young boy, the wounded babel that had escaped from Thessalia of the Order of the Weal hid within his timeline. Newton carried on with his life, unaware of this.

w - 1651 - FP: NEWTONS SLEEP[598] **->** The mortally wounded Thessalia, a member of the Great Houses, arrived from 1678 and regenerated. A young girl named Aphra Behn - later a dramatist and spy for King Charles II - mistook the reborn Thessalia, later named Larissa, for a beautiful nymph and pledged allegiance to her.

An act of murder within the standing stones in Cirbury awakened the Ragman. Emily, the mayor's daughter, was raped by a corpse that the Ragman animated. The Ragman triggered acts of class warfare, but was driven back into the stones. The townsfolk relocated the stones to Dartmoor. Emily was left pregnant and later died in poverty, but her bloodline led to the journalist Charmange Peters and the

---

596 Dating *The Settling* (BF #82) - Cromwell's ultimatum to Wexford is issued on 12th September, 1649, and the story begins shortly beforehand. The sacking of Wexford lasted from 2nd to 11th October. The "Dr. Goddard" in this story apparently refers to Dr. Jonathan Goddard (1617-1675), a distinguished Society member and a favourite of Cromwell.

597 Dating *FP: Newtons Sleep* (FP novel #6) - Newton was born on 4th January, 1643, and is currently "a child of nine summers with shite on his brow" (p1). Rene Descartes is "freshly-dead" (p2) - he died on 11th February 1650. Newton is constantly referred to in *Newtons Sleep* by his pseudonym, "Jeova Unus Sanctus" (more commonly rendered as "Jeova Sanctus Unus") - the letters of which can be rearranged (allowing that J's in Latin are rendered as I's, as demonstrated in that great and seminal documentary of archaeology, *Indiana Jones and the Last Crusade*) to spell *Isaacus Neutonuus*, an invented rendering of his name in Latin.

598 Dating *FP: Newtons Sleep* (FP novel #6) - Behn, a real-life historical figure, was born on 10th July 1640, and is age 10 when she meets Larissa.

599 "The seventeenth century", says *Rags* (p39).

600 *The Androids of Tara.* Izaak Walton lived 1593-1683, and published *The Compleat Angler* in 1653.

601 *Ghost Ship.* Hobbes lived 1588-1679.

602 According to the monument in *Silver Nemesis.*

603 *The Stones of Blood.* The English writer John Aubrey (best known for his collection of biographies, *Brief Lives*) lived 1626-1697.

604 *Ghost Light.* The Royal Geographical Society was formed in 1645 during the Civil War.

605 The Doctor says that these should have been outlawed "centuries" before *The Many Deaths of Jo Grant.*

606 Dating *The Witch from the Well* (BF #154) - It's the "seventeenth century", and "three and a half centuries"/"350 years" from the present day. The Varaxils landed in spring, and it's now six months later.

607 *The Ghosts of N-Space*

608 *The Eleventh Hour.* This was in 1665.

609 *SJA: The Eternity Trap*

610 Dating *FP: Newtons Sleep* (FP novel #6) - The year is given in the blurb.

611 Dating *The Demons of Red Lodge and Other Stories*: "The Demons of Red Lodge" (BF #142a) - The Doctor twice comments that it's 1665, and it's "twenty years" after the time of Matthew Hopkins, who operated as a witchhunter from 1645 to 1647.

612 *TW: Hidden.* In real life, Vaughan was a member of the Society of Unknown Philosophers, established his reputation by writing the pseudo-mystical work *Anthroposophia Theomagica*, and lived 1621 to 1666.

613 *K9: Fear Itself*

614 *Doctor Who and the Invasion from Space*

615 Dating *The Visitation* (19.4) - The Doctor, trying to get Tegan home, suggests "we're about three hundred years early". The action culminates with the start of the Great Fire of London, which took place on the night of 2nd to 3rd September, 1666, so the story would seem to start on 1st September. According to the novelisation, the Terileptils crashed on "August 5th". On screen, Richard Mace says this was "several weeks ago".

616 The Doctor says he was blamed for the Great Fire in *Pyramids of Mars*. He refers to Mr and Mrs Pepys in *Robot*, and to Mrs Pepys' coffee-making prowess in *Planet of the Spiders*. Pepys lived 1633-1703 and began his diary in 1660. His wife Elizabeth died in 1669. Mention of the Doctor's reluctance to talk about the Great Fire is from *Doctor Who and the Pirates*.

617 Dating "Black Death White Life" (IDW *DW* one-shot #6) - "It's the year of our Lord sixteen hundred and sixty-nine" according to a villager.

618 Dating *The Impossible Astronaut* (X6.1) - No date is given. The affronted man is not named in the story, and is only referred to as "Charles" in the end credits. However, the story implies that he is king, and the

lout Kane Sawyer in the twentieth century.[599]

The Doctor fished with Izaak Walton.[600] He also met Thomas Hobbes.[601] **Lady Peinforte's servant Richard Maynarde died on 2nd November, 1657, and was entombed at Windsor.**[602]

According to the Doctor, Aubrey invented Druidism "as a joke".[603] **The Doctor was a founder member of the Royal Geographical Society.**[604] Mindscape generators, devices capable of crafting fake scenarios in a subject's mind, were invented.[605]

c 1660 (autumn) - THE WITCH FROM THE WELL[606]

-> Two shapeshifting Varaxils arrived in the village of Tranchard's Fell while hunting beings who could channel Odic power. They killed Finicia and Lucern, the children of Squire Portillon, and assumed their forms. The eighth Doctor and Mary Shelley arrived six months later, but the older versions of Finicia and Lucern with them used the TARDIS' Fast Return Switch to return to the twenty-first century with Mary, stranding the Doctor.

A botched attempt by the Varaxils to leech Odic energy from the midwife Agnes Bates, who had the "second sight", resulted in her becoming a monstrosity that attacked the village. The Doctor drained her Odic energy, and tricked everyone involved into thinking that the monster-Agnes was imprisoned down a well. In actuality, only an energy echo of monster-Agnes was trapped. The Doctor aided Agnes, who had been found guilty of witchcraft, in moving to another village.

Finicia and Lucern pledged to spend their lengthy lifespans searching for their Odic scanner - a.k.a. the Witch Star - which Squire Claude Portillon had hidden. Mary returned in the TARDIS, and the Doctor left with her.

In 1661, the astronomer Clancy discovered a comet that returned to Earth every one hundred and fifty-seven years.[607] **The mathematician Pierre de Fermat died in a duel, his last theorem unproven, because the Doctor slept in.**[608] In 1665, an alien stranded on Earth adopted the guise of Erasmus Darkening, an alchemist. James, the Third Earl of Marchwood, hired Darkening to find the secret of turning common metal into gold - but Darkening instead built trans-dimensional equipment in the hopes of getting home, and powered it with the life force of Marchwood's children. Marchwood stabbed at Darkening, damaging Darkening's device - which reduced them both to a ghost-like state. In the centuries to follow, Darkening's ghost turned at least thirteen people into shades, using their life-energies to fuel his immortality.[609]

w - 1665 - FP: NEWTONS SLEEP[610]

-> A commoner, Thomas Piper, died from the plague. A Faction Paradox delegation that included Cousin Hateman, Mother Sphinx, the androgynous Father-Mother Olympia and their cat, Faction Cat, recruited his widow to join the Faction as Little Sister Greenaway.

1665 - THE DEMONS OF RED LODGE AND OTHER STORIES: "The Demons of Red Lodge"[611]

-> The fifth Doctor and Nyssa visited the village of Red Lodge. The alien Spira were busy replicating the townsfolk as a precursor to a takeover of Earth, but died from imperfections upon incorporating the nonhuman Doctor into their genetic matrix.

The Welsh philosopher Thomas Vaughn studied alchemy, and discovered a means of living for centuries.[612] In 1665, a plague spread across London, killing thousands and causing widespread panic.[613] The Mortimer family - George, Helen and their children Ida and Alan - stumbled into the TARDIS when the first Doctor landed during the Great Fire of London. Much to the Doctor's irritation, they thought he was a warlock. Together, they travelled to the Andromeda galaxy in the far future.[614]

1666 (early September) - THE VISITATION[615]

-> A group of escaped Terileptil prisoners made planetfall on Earth. They planned to wipe out the human population with rats infected with the bubonic plague virus, but were thwarted by the fifth Doctor, Tegan, Nyssa and Adric. A final confrontation resulted in the Doctor dropping a torch that caused the Terileptils' equipment to explode - which killed the Terileptils and caused the Great Fire of London.

Prior to this in his lifetime, the Doctor had already been blamed for the Great Fire. The Doctor perhaps met Mr and Mrs Pepys on the same visit. Mrs Pepys "makes an excellent cup of coffee". The Doctor doesn't like to talk about the Great Fire of London.[616]

1669 - "Black Death White Life"[617]

-> The tenth Doctor and Martha found an English village in the grip of a plague. A "fallen angel" in the local church was healing people, and the Doctor identified it as an Immunoglobulin from Mimosa 3 in the Crux Constellation. The Immunoglobulins and the Macroviruses had been locked in an ongoing war, but recently the Macroviruses had gained an advantage - and were now on Earth. The Doctor coaxed the Immunoglobulin to reproduce and destroy the Macroviruses on Earth, then returned it to Mimosa 3.

c 1670 - THE IMPOSSIBLE ASTRONAUT[618]

-> Charles II found the eleventh Doctor nude and hiding under the skirts of Matilda, a woman who had just painted him in that state. The Doctor was imprisoned in the Tower, but flew out of his cell two days later.

w - 1671 - FP: NEWTONS SLEEP[619] **->** On behalf of Sir Samuel Morland, Aphra Behn infiltrated a gathering of alchemists and ritualists in Cambridge, as hosted by a man named Salomon. Those present - including Isaac Newton (a.k.a. Jeova Unus Sanctus); representatives of Faction Paradox; and Valentine, a member of the French secret society *le Pouvoir* - had gathered to watch an advanced science demonstration by "the Magus", Nathaniel Silver. Salomon was actually Dr Alexander Bendo, the head of the Secret Service - he had arranged the gathering to round up the attendees with his soldiers, but largely failed. Little Sister Greenaway's performance during these events earned her a promotion to Cousin.

The Doctor placed skeletons in the Tower of London, which were found in 1674 and identified as the lost Princes.[620] The eleventh Doctor claimed to know the bar where the Governor of New Amsterdam lost the city in a bet. The Doctor wasn't present, as he was busy with the "Bronx peace talks", which he said were more akin to a "barn dance".[621]

Operating on instructions from John Dee, the Society of Horticultural Historians, a.k.a. the Knights of the Arboretum, worked to prevent the last of the imprisoned Enochians from escaping. Christopher Wren, Inigo Jones and William Boreman were members of the group. In 1675, Wren convinced John Flamsteed, the royal astronomer, to move the location for the proposed Greenwich Observatory to thirteen degrees off magnetic north. The Observatory was built over the foundations of Duke Humphrey's house, further sealing off the Enochian vessel. The Doctor would receive notes that Wren left for him concerning these events in 2009.[622]

In 1677, the mathematician John Wallis gave a paper on sympathetic vibration to the Royal Society.[623]

w - 1678 - FP: NEWTONS SLEEP[624] **->** Dr Alexander Bendo sought to learn more about Faction Paradox and dispatched the spy Aphra Behn to a brothel called the Inferno, where a mysterious woman had appeared out of thin air. This was Thessalia of the Great Houses, who had arrived following the Violent Unknown Event on the planet Zo La Domini. Determining that Thessalia had less value than he had hoped, Bendo shot her. Thessalia's bio-suit automatically "jumped" her to safety along Behn's timeline, depositing her in 1651. An enraged Behn stabbed Bendo with a biodata needle engineered to erase people from history - henceforth, he would only be remembered as a disguise of John Wilmot, the second Earl of Rochester.

= Around 1679, on an alternate Earth where Rome never fell, a race of genetically engineered soldiers - the Bestarius - were created but proved uncontrollably violent. Robots were deemed to be far more useful, and around this time the first robot, Vesuvius, was built. Centuries later, by 1979, Rome's iron legions had conquered the entire galaxy.[625]

---

man's attire, moustache and impressive hair all match that of Charles II (who reigned 1660-1685) as painted by John Michael Wright. *Doctor Who: The Encyclopedia* cites the man as a "seventeenth-century nobleman", and also says that Matilda is the man's daughter. None of Charles' real-life children have that name, although he did have an awful lot of illegitimate issue.

619 Dating *FP: Newtons Sleep* (FP novel #6) - The back cover names the year.

620 *Sometime Never*

621 *The Forgotten Army*. New Amsterdam reverted to the name "New York" in November 1674, but the Bronx wasn't incorporated into New York until 1874. Either this discrepancy owes to some aspect of time travel on the Doctor's part, or - as with a lot of the Doctor's spurious and inaccurate claims in this novel - one does have to wonder if he's just making it all up.

622 "Don't Step on the Grass"

623 *The Happiness Patrol*. Wallis lived 1616-1703, and is credited with furthering the development of modern calculus.

624 Dating *FP: Newtons Sleep* (FP novel #6) - Events follow the death of the courtier Edward Coleman (p143), who was hanged on 17th May, 1678. Rochester in real life went underground as "Dr Bendo" following a brawl with the night watch, in which one of his companions was killed. "The Inferno" is presumably a precursor to the nightclub seen in *The War Machines*. (Writer Daniel O'Mahony also mentions the Inferno - the nightclub, that is, not the brothel - in *The Cabinet of Light*, so the name of the brothel here is looking less and less like coincidence.)

625 "Centuries" before "The Iron Legion". Vesuvius is the oldest robot, and a guard says he "should have been dealt with centuries ago". Likewise, the Bestarius have lain in their suspended animation "for centuries".

626 "Three centuries" before *Shada*.

627 *Enlightenment*

628 *Phantasmagoria*

629 *The Last Dodo*

630 Dating *FP: Newtons Sleep* (FP novel #6) - The back cover cites the year.

631 "Two hundred years old, at least" before *Kiss of Death*. Mention of the Arar-Jecks suggests this is the time of the Twenty Aeon War cited in *Frontios*.

632 Dating *The Glorious Revolution* (BF CC #4.2) - It's 1688, the year of the Glorious Revolution. The specific day isn't mentioned, but historically, the king fled on

In the late seventeenth century, Professor Chronotis retired to St Cedd's College, Cambridge.[626] The Eternals kidnapped a seventeenth-century pirate crew.[627] Nikolas Valentine, actually an extra-terrestrial stranded on Earth, received a knighthood in the 1680s.[628] The tenth Doctor and Martha visited Mauritius in 1681.[629]

w - 1683 - FP: NEWTONS SLEEP[630] **->** Nathaniel Silver, having worked for le Pouvoir since the botched Cambridge raid in 1671, stretched the mysterious egg in his possession to create a series of mirrors that displayed possible futures. Cousin Greenaway, in a fit of anger against the babel within Isaac Newton, stabbed Newton with a bio-data needle designed to wipe people from history. Silver removed the needle and saved Newton, but enough of a temporal anomaly appeared within Newton's timeline to net the attention of parties in humanity's posthuman era. The babel was trapped in Silver's egg, and killed when the egg compressed into a dark pebble. Greenaway and her fellow Cousins performed rituals to stabilise Newton's history. On Aphra Behn's recommendation, Larissa of the Great Houses forged a personal alliance with the Faction.

Vislor Turlough's great-great-great grandfather was a member of the royal court on Trion, and an ambassador to alien worlds. By the time the Arar-Jecks had fought their way to Trion's borders, Turlough's ancestor had negotiated with neutral powers for use of a dimensional vault - a final hiding place for the Trion Queen and her entourage. In future, rumours spoke of the Queen's "lost treasure horde", which remained in the vault for safekeeping.[631]

1688 (10th-11th December) - THE GLORIOUS REVOLUTION[632] **->** The second Doctor, Jamie and Zoe arrived just prior to the Glorious Revolution - the relatively bloodless transfer of power from King James VII to William of Orange - and aided Queen Mary and her son, James Stewart, in fleeing to France as history recorded. They soon met King James VII. Jamie, having fought for James Stewart's right to the throne in future, persuaded the king to stay and fight rather than fleeing London - the act that would doom his kingship...

> (=) A paradoxical timeline was created in which the king became mad with power and vowed to burn those who didn't convert to Catholicism. The historical alterations cast doubt upon whether Jamie had ever met the Doctor, and so a Celestial Intervention Agency operative circa 1786 intervened...

... enabling Jamie to realise his terrible mistake. Jamie and his friends abducted the king, then ratted him out to the locals. It was believed that the king had abdicated. The Doctor's party also met the infamous "hanging judge", George Jeffries, who was captured while trying to escape.

The Doctor met the Baroque composer Henry Purcell.[633] **The Gore Crow Hotel was built in 1684.**[634]

In 1685, the Hakolian battle vehicle Jerak arrived on Earth, but failed to find its partner, the Malus, as planned. The scheduled invasion didn't happen, and the battle vehicle went dormant. Its radiating malevolence ensured that local legends sprang up of an evil spirit named "the Jack i' the Green".[635]

The fourth Doctor claimed to have met Isaac Newton. At first he dropped apples on his head, but then he explained gravity to him over dinner.[636] Newton was furious about the Doctor dropping an apple on his head, as his nose bled for three days.[637] Newton showed the Doctor around Cambridge University.[638] The Doctor visited Hampton Court maze soon after it was planted.[639] The Doctor took Newton to Practas Seven, and it made the man sit in a corner and whimper.[640]

w - 1689 (16th April) - FP: NEWTONS SLEEP[641] **->** Aphra Behn was dying, having been poisoned by remedies prescribed by a quack. Nathaniel Silver visited Behn and comforted her on the last day of her life.

The Vondrax assumed the forms of samurai, and killed many in Japan, 1691.[642] Goibhnie, a member of the Troifran race, took samples from Earth and created the mystical world of Tír na n-Óg.[643]

10th of December and was captured the next day.

633 Ghost Ship. Purcell lived from 1659-1695.

634 Battlefield. This is the date on the capstone above the hotel's fireplace.

635 The Hollow Men

636 The Pirate Planet. Newton lived 1642-1727, and published his theories of gravitation in 1685. This meeting clearly predates the fifth Doctor encountering Newton in Circular Time.

637 Circular Time: "Summer"

638 Psi-ence Fiction

639 Winner Takes All. This would be around 1690.

640 "Final Sacrifice"

641 Dating FP: Newtons Sleep (FP novel #6) - Behn died 16th April, 1689. The real-life cause of her death isn't actually known, but she was buried in Westminster Abbey.

642 TW: Trace Memory

643 Cat's Cradle: Witch Mark. The Ceffyl have lived at peace with the humans on Tír na n-Óg for "three centuries" (p169).

1692 - THE WITCH HUNTERS[644] -> The TARDIS landed in Salem, and the first Doctor, Ian, Barbara and Susan quickly retreated to avoid becoming implicated in the witch trials. Susan, however, wanted to help those who were accused and took the TARDIS back there. She and Ian were soon accused of witchcraft. The Doctor saved his friends, but to preserve history, he persuaded the governor not to pardon the alleged witch Rebecca Nurse, age 71.

Later, the Doctor returned and took Rebecca to 1954. He convinced her that her death would encourage future tolerance, and she agreed to return to her native time and face her historical demise.

An extra-terrestrial was "lost in darkness" for many centuries, but finally fell to Earth and adopted human form. In 1695, she fell in love with Tobias Williams - who decried her as a witch and had her burned at the stake. The shapeshifter survived, and vowed vengeance upon Williams and his descendants. Whenever sons were born to the family, the creature rendered its grandparents immobile with a potion. They were believed dead... and then buried, but remained aware for a hundred years.[645]

c 1696 - THE SMUGGLERS[646] -> A group of pirates led by Captain Samuel Pike of the *Black Albatross* attempted to locate Captain Avery's treasure in Cornwall, with only a rhyme as a clue to its whereabouts. Avery had died a drunk pauper, and his treasure was said to be cursed. The first Doctor, Ben and Polly became embroiled in efforts to find the treasure. It was found in the local church, and the names in the rhyme appeared on tombs in the crypt. The King's militia arrived, killing Pike and many of his crew.

Toby Avery's mother died, two years after he last saw his father.[647]

1699 (April) - THE CURSE OF THE BLACK SPOT[648] -> The pilot of a Skerth spaceship had died when exposed to human bacteria. The ship's holographic medical system continued on automatic, and took to teleporting injured sailors and pirates into its medical bay. The system manifested as a glowing Siren and appeared through reflected surfaces - shining treasure was an excellent medium for this, and the Siren inspired folklore about gold-laden ships being cursed.

The eleventh Doctor, Amy and Rory landed aboard a becalmed pirate ship, the *Fancy*, on which the Siren had apparently disintegrated anyone with even a slight scratch. The Doctor freed the Siren's patients. Captain Avery and his son Toby took command of the Skerth ship, and left with the crew of the *Fancy* to explore the stars, starting with Sirius.

Calling in a debt, the eleventh Doctor summoned Avery and Toby to help him storm Demon's Run and rescue Amy.[649]

The Eighteenth Century

Biochemical warfare wiped out the population of Anima Persis. The ghosts of the dead haunted this geopsychic planet. The Time Lords used the world as a training ground.[650] The Talichre once attacked Anima Persis.[651] Raldonn travelled the universe peacefully for hundreds of years. He would crash on Earth in the nineteen sixties.[652]

An alien force arrived in Earth's dimension, and was

---

644 Dating *The Witch Hunters* (PDA #9) - Each section states the date. Nurse was executed on 19th July, 1692.
645 *100*: "Bedtime Story"
646 Dating *The Smugglers* (4.1) - The Doctor notes that the design of the church he sees on leaving the TARDIS means that they could have landed "at any time after the sixteenth century". Later, he says that the customers in the inn are dressed in clothes from the "seventeenth century". *The Terrestrial Index* and *The TARDIS File* set the story in "1650", *The TARDIS Logs* in "1646". *Timelink* went for "1672", *About Time* said it's "likely to be after 1685".

The Discontinuity Guide states that as a character says "God save the King" (and, perhaps more to the point, Josiah Blake is the "King's Revenue Officer"), it must be when England had a King (between 1603-1642, 1660-1688 or 1694 onwards). However, William III ruled as King from 1688-1702, and even though this was alongside Mary at first, legally and in the minds of the public he was King. The *Guide* further speculates that the costumes suggest this story is set in the latter part of the century.

647 "The previous winter" and "three years" before *The Curse of the Black Spot*.
648 Dating *The Curse of the Black Spot* (X6.3) - The Doctor says it's the "seventeenth century". The BBC website preview for the episode has Avery give the date as "April 1st, 1699", and says the ship has been becalmed for eight days. There's no evidence that *this* Avery is the same pirate said to have died in *The Smugglers*. The Skerth are named in *Doctor Who: The Encyclopedia*, but not on screen.
649 *A Good Man Goes to War*
650 "Hundreds of years" before *Death Comes to Time*. Anima Persis is also mentioned in *Relative Dementias* and *The Tomorrow Windows*.
651 *Relative Dementias*
652 "Operation Proteus"
653 Unspecified "centuries" before *The Deadstone Memorial*.
654 *Wishing Well*
655 *The Stones of Blood*
656 *Fury from the Deep*

separated into a ghostly ectoplasmic form and a disembodied bundle of psychic energy. Henry Deadstone encountered the creature's psychic aspect and buried it in a pit, but was mentally compelled to feed it children and animals. Gypsies accused Deadstone of "feeding children to the Devil" and hanged him. The creature remained in the pit and artificially extended Deadstone's life.[653]

A Vurosis - a proto-molecular parasite from the Actron Pleiades system - fell to Earth as a seed, and germinated beneath a well in the English village of Creighton Mere. It spawned an eighteenth-century legend that a highwayman had lost his gold treasure down the well, and drowned in it while hiding from the Duke of York.[654]

By the late twentieth century, no documents from before 1700 existed at Boscombe Hall. This was the year before Dr Thomas Borlase was born.[655] Weed creatures were seen in the North Sea during the eighteenth century.[656] The Doctor "ran Taunton for two weeks in the eighteenth century and I've never been so bored".[657]

An inter-clan marriage between the Blatherean and the Slitheen resulted in some tan-skinned hybrids.[658] During the eighteenth century, the Ragman inhabited the body of an executed highwayman.[659] The Doctor visited Rio de Janero in 1700.[660] **The Uvodni-Malakh War began in the eighteenth century.**[661]

On the planet Artaris, civilisation divided itself into fortified city-states. The planet began to industrialize, and "Reeves" emerged as a type of government overseer in the city-state of Excelis. Within a hundred years, a Reeve had commissioned volunteers among the citizens to become law-enforcement officers named Wardens. The immortal Grayvorn worked as one of the earliest Wardens and rose through the ranks.[662]

The Doctor learned to cook in eighteenth-century Paris.[663] He told the philosopher David Hume that you couldn't have an effect without a cause.[664] **A Cyber-ship crashed in Colchester and went dormant.**[665]

Two humanoid life forms - the carbon-based Fleshkind and the boron-based Metalkind - lived in a binary planetary system at the eye of the Tornado Nebula. The Fleshkind mined the Metalkind's world for ores, which were actually the Metalkind's children, and so the two races warred with each other for centuries.[666]

The homeworld of the Veritas - a race of beings with no concept of lying - was obliterated when an unscrupulous merchant released an energy virus there. Three Veritas survived, and pledged to pass sentence on any being they found to be practicing deceit.[667]

> (=) Katsura Sato had conquered the Europe of his alternate timeline. Africa and Asia soon followed.[668]

Will Butley, a clerk in Shanghai, fell in love with a Taoist philosopher who taught him the secrets of the *chi*: the life force itself. Butley murdered his lover, and spent the next three centuries draining the life essences from young men as a means of prolonging his own.[669]

1702 (8th-10th March) - PHANTASMAGORIA[670] ->
The fifth Doctor and Turlough witnessed phantoms abducting a gambler, Edmund Carteret, who died from a heart attack. This was the latest of many such disappearances. The Doctor discovered that a stranded alien, Karthok of Daeodalus, was operating on Earth as Sir Nikolas Valentine, a card-playing member of the Diabola Club. Valentine had been absorbing human minds into his ship's computer, then using the amassed calculating power to help the ship heal itself. The phantoms were the collected consciousness of the minds absorbed, directed by Valentine to snatch more victims. The Doctor tricked Valentine into seeding his own bioprint into the ship's computer, whereupon the phantoms tore Valentine to pieces. Valentine's ship was programmed to self-destruct.

c 1705 - DOCTOR WHO AND THE PIRATES[671] -> The
TARDIS landed onboard a ship as the pirate Red Jasper attacked it. The sixth Doctor and Evelyn were taken on board Jasper's vessel. Jasper was looking for treasure in the Ruby Islands, and was unimpressed by the Doctor's reluctance to kill. The Doctor incited mutiny on Jasper's ship, leaving Jasper stranded.

---

657 *The Highest Science*
658 "Many generations" before *SJA: The Gift*.
659 *Rags*
660 *Loups-Garoux*
661 *SJA: Warriors of Kudlak*
662 "Three hundred years" before *Excelis Rising*.
663 *The Lodger* (TV)
664 "The Child of Time" (*DWM*). Hume lived 1711-1776.
665 Unspecified "centuries" before *Closing Time*.
666 "Centuries" before *SJA: Sky*.
667 "Centuries" before *SJA: Judgement Day*.

668 "Within a century" of his crusade beginning, according to "The Glorious Dead".
669 "Three hundred years" before *SJS: The Tao Connection*.
670 Dating *Phantasmagoria* (BF #2) - The exact date is given.
671 Dating *Doctor Who and the Pirates* (BF #43) - The date isn't specified beyond it being "the eighteenth century".

c 1707 - "Ravens"[672] -> The seventh Doctor saw patterns in history and convinced a warrior in seventeenth-century Japan, the Raven, that although his wife and children were dead, he could still save others. The Doctor took Raven to the future to confront a street gang named the Ravens.

c 1708 (July) - CIRCULAR TIME: "Summer"[673] -> The fifth Doctor was distracted by an alchemy demonstration in London, and handed Nyssa some coins from other eras. Sir Isaac Newton, disguised as an Algerian juggler with a false chin, witnessed this and - under his authority as director of the Royal Mint - had them incarcerated for counterfeiting. Newton's formidable brain pieced together many details about the coins, and made several correct guesses about the future and the Doctor and Nyssa's origins. The knowledge triggered one of Newton's seizures, and the Doctor prevented him from swallowing his own tongue and choking to death. Newton ordered the travellers' release, hoping they would never meet again. The Doctor thought that Newton would have a headache for some days, then become bored with the memory of the time travellers and move on to something new.

The Doctor knows that marrying for love is a mistake, due to his experience with Lady Mary Wortley Montagu.[674] **The Doctor once met the Duke of Marlborough.**[675] He also met Peter the Great in Russia, and saw the Peter and Paul Cathedral being built.[676] In 1720, the Doctor saw the Earth's fury at Okushiri.[677]

The Tristian Cluster was a series of asteroids that had been a planet, and settled in orbit around the planet's moon. They became much colder, but retained enough sunlight that the planet's albino-skinned natives could live there. A family of criminals from the Cluster came to reside on Earth in a West Sussex village, Wolfenden - so named for the white wolf that was carved into the rocks there. Most of the family remained in cryo-sleep, awaiting the day that their sentence had passed.[678]

Through the millennia, the Silurian Malohkeh's family had monitored mankind's evolution. From around 1720, only Malohkeh remained to perform this task.[679]

Casanova was born in 1725.[680] *Gulliver's Travels* was **published in 1726.**[681]

1727 - THE GIRL IN THE FIREPLACE[682] -> The tenth Doctor passed through a time window from the fifty-first century and met Reinette for the first time.

---

672 Dating "Ravens" (*DWM* #188-190) - It's "four hundred years" before the main event of this story.
673 Dating *Circular Time: "Summer"* (BF #91) - The year isn't specified, but the month is given as July. The story occurs while Newton is warden of the Royal Mint - he was appointed to the post in 1696, and served until his death in 1727. This date is otherwise arbitrary, based upon actor David Warner's age of 65 when he voiced Newton (who was born in January 1643 by the Gregorian calendar) for this audio. Historically, counterfeiting in this period was treated as high treason, and those found guilty were put to death. Convictions proved difficult to achieve, but Newton - often venturing out in disguise, as occurs here - personally collected evidence against such criminals. His most notable prosecution was against the counterfeiter William Chaloner - who was hanged, drawn and quartered on 23rd March, 1699.
674 *Only Human*. Montagu, an aristocrat chiefly known for her letters from Turkey (when she was the wife of the British ambassador) lived 1689-1762.
675 *The Android Invasion*. The Doctor presumably means the first Duke, who lived 1650-1722 and was made a Duke in 1702.
676 *The Wages of Sin*. This would have to be between 1712-1725.
677 *The English Way of Death* (p46).
678 "Hundreds of years" before *SJA: The White Wolf*.
679 Malohkeh has been watching mankind "for the last three hundred years" according to *Cold Blood*.
680 "One hundred forty-five years" after *The Vampires*

of Venice (which is in accordance with Casanova's real-life birth year).
681 *The Mind Robber*
682 Dating *The Girl in the Fireplace* (X2.4) - Reinette says it's 1727. The Doctor tells her that August of that year is "a bit rubbish", but he's no way of knowing if August has already passed or not. We might expect Reinette to correct him if it has, but he's gabbling and doesn't really give her a chance.
683 Dating *The Girl in the Fireplace* (X2.4) - It is "weeks, months" after the Doctor and Reinette's first meeting. It's snowing outside, so it's winter. The older Reinette later says she has "known the Doctor since she was seven" - as she was born 29th December, 1721, she would have been that age almost exclusively in 1728. If the initial meeting takes place in 1727 and the second is "months" later in 1728, then Reinette's comment about her age makes some sense - although it means (not unreasonably) that she's more referring to the Doctor saving her from the clockwork man than their initial, very brief conversation through the fireplace. This probably isn't what was intended on screen, but it fits the available evidence fairly well. The alternative is that the Doctor and Reinette first meet in the last three days of 1727 - which would again push their second meeting into 1728.
684 "Thirty years" before *The Many Hands*.
685 Dating *FP: Newtons Sleep* (FP novel #6) - It's "nearly sixty years" (p135) after the raid at Salomon's house in 1671. It's also spring (p134).
686 *The Highlanders*

c 1728 - THE GIRL IN THE FIREPLACE[683] **-> Weeks or months later, he met her again and saved her from a clockwork man.**

An alien creature, the Onk Ndell Kith, was damaged when it fell into the water near Edinburgh. Its consciousness was split into multiple units programmed to self-replicate. A brewster found one of these, and sold it to a man named Alexander Monro. The unit sampled Monro's DNA, and transformed itself into a mechanical hand. He experimented on the hand using electricity, and it split into two - one of which turned into a younger copy of Monro. Without the critical mass needed to restore it to life, the Onk Ndell Kith remained disembodied until 1759.[684]

w - c 1730 (spring) - FP: NEWTONS SLEEP[685] **->** Nathaniel Silver's extended lifespan came undone, and he died at the Inferno brothel, in the bed of a French prostitute named Madame Machine.

The Aliens Act was passed in 1730.[686] In the same year, a Mr Chicken resided at 10 Downing Street.[687] The Doctor's old friend Padmasambhava began to construct Yeti from this time.[688]

1738 - THE DOOMWOOD CURSE[689] **->** The sixth Doctor and Charley arrived in 1738, having just encountered some Grel at the Archive of Alexandria IV. The literal-minded Grel - only able to acknowledge verifiable fact - had developed the Factualizer, a device that contained particles that made fictional tales manifest in the real world. The time travellers unknowingly released some of these particles, and people started acting in accordance with the novel *Rookwood* (1834). The Doctor eventually

contained the particles after they concentrated for a time in Dick Turpin - a heroic highwayman as depicted in *Rookwood*, but a violent criminal and petty thief in real life. Turpin departed, historically fated to be tried and executed the following year.

c 1738 - THE GIRL IN THE FIREPLACE[690] **-> The tenth Doctor met Reinette when she was a young woman, and snogged her.**

In 1740, the man who would become known as Sabbath was born.[691] On 8th September, 1742, the first Doctor and his companions spent some time in New England after their adventure in Salem, 1692.[692] Alexander Monro's father, John Monro, died in 1740. Alexander loved his father so much, he sought to use the Onk Ndell Kith's replication abilities to bring John back to life as an infant.[693] Time travellers Penelope Gate and Joel Mintz briefly visited the year 1743.[694]

1744 - THE GIRL IN THE FIREPLACE[695] **-> The King's mistress, Madame de Chateauroux, was ill and near death. The tenth Doctor spied on Reinette as she walked through the grounds of a stately home, plotting to take Chateauroux's place.**

1745 (February) - THE GIRL IN THE FIREPLACE[696] **-> Shortly afterwards, the Doctor used another time window to visit Reinette the night she became the royal mistress.**

A battlefield from the Jacobite Uprising was kidnapped by the War Lords.[697]

---

687 *World War Three* strongly implies that the Doctor met this man. Mr Chicken is historical, and was the last private resident of the building before King George II put it at the disposal of Sir Robert Walpole, the first British Prime Minister.

688 "Over two hundred years" before *The Abominable Snowmen* according to the Abbot Songsten.

689 Dating *The Doomwood Curse* (BF #111) - The back cover says it's "England, 1738". The story is a little more vague - the Doctor estimates that it's about "twenty years" after 1720, the date he spies on a tombstone. In real life, as in the *Doctor Who* universe, Turpin was a petty criminal and murderer whose exploits were over-romanticized in the likes of *The Genuine History of the Life of Richard Turpin* (1739), *Black Bess and the Knight of the Road* (1867-68), *Rookwood* and other stories. Historically, as here, Turpin was executed in April 1739.

690 Dating *The Girl in the Fireplace* (X2.4) - Reinette's age as a young woman isn't given, although she's "23" the next time they meet.

691 *The Adventuress of Henrietta Street*, and specified on the back cover of *FP: Sabbath Dei*.

692 *The Witch Hunters*

693 *The Many Hands*

694 *The Room with No Doors*

695 Dating *The Girl in the Fireplace* (X2.4) - It is said that Madame de Chateauroux, the King's mistress prior to Reinette, is "ill and close to death". She died on 8th December, 1744. The scene probably occurs a few months beforehand, as Reinette is seen walking across a sunny patch of grass.

696 Dating *The Girl in the Fireplace* (X2.4) - It is the night that Reinette meets the King - historically this occurred in February 1745, after Chateauroux's death. The Doctor says Reinette is "23", which she historically would have been at the time. Incidentally, *The Girl in the Fireplace* fails to mention that the real-life Reinette was married at age 19 and later had two children, neither of whom lived beyond age ten.

697 *The War Games*

1746 (April) - THE HIGHLANDERS / THE WAR GAMES[698-699] -> The second Doctor, Ben and Polly prevented the crooked solicitor Grey from selling Scottish prisoners into slavery. The highlanders had signed six-year plantation work contracts, but the Doctor sent the boat to the safety of France. Jamie McCrimmon, a Scots piper, joined the Doctor on his travels. The Time Lords later returned Jamie to his native time, but walled off his memories of all of his adventures with the Doctor save the very first.

Once again, Jared Khan - this time known as Thomas - narrowly missed acquiring the TARDIS. After this time, he posed as "Alessandro di Cagliostro".[700] The Kith-spawned version of Alexander Monro married a woman named Katherine.[701] In 1750, a ship was wrecked off Haiti. Washed ashore was Nkome, a six-year-old African slave kept alive by voodoo, who began plotting his revenge against the white landowners - the blancs.[702] The Doctor knew the landscape architect Lancelot Brown, a.k.a. Capability Brown.[703]

Around 1750, a "Mr Sun" arrived in England from China. He inherited business space in Covent Garden, and opened a toy store there. A successive number of "Mr Suns" would operate the shop for two hundred years.[704]

The Daemons inspired the Industrial Revolution.[705]

Britain decided to adopt the Gregorian calendar, meaning that eleven days (from 2nd to 14th September) would be removed from the current calendar. Faction Paradox approached King George II and offered to purchase and occupy those missing days, intending that they would become their centre of operations, the Eleven-Day Empire. The future George III was present in January 1752, when a Faction representative performed a six-armed "shadow dance" for the King at St. James' Palace. The compact governing the sale of the eleven days was later signed in the upstairs room of a public house.[706]

The father of Corwyn Marne, a founding member of the Society of Sigismondo di Rimini, attended the compact signing. At this time, Faction Paradox placed race banks and biodata codices at secret locations on Earth - a precaution if they required more troops and agents in this era. Sutekh ruined one such cache at Mount Vesuvius, and hid the body of Osiris there. In the decade to come, Osiris'

---

698 Dating *The Highlanders* (4.4) - The provisional title of the story was *Culloden*, and it is set shortly after that battle. Despite references in *The Highlanders, The War Games* and other stories, Culloden took place in April 1746, not 1745. This is first explicitly stated in *The Underwater Menace*, (although the draft script again said "1745"). The *Radio Times* specified that *The Highlanders* is set in April. The 1745 date has been perpetuated by the first edition of *The Making of Doctor Who*, and surfaces in a number of books, such as *The Roundheads*. *Birthright* has Jared Khan narrowly miss the TARDIS' departure after *The Highlanders*, in a scene dated to 1746.

699 Dating *The War Games* (6.7) - Jamie is returned to his native time.

700 *Birthright*. Cagliostro, an occultist in real life, lived from 1743-1795.

701 "Eleven years" before the *The Many Hands*.

702 *White Darkness*

703 *The Doomwood Curse*. Brown lived 1716 to 1783.

704 *The Cabinet of Light* (p85).

705 *The Daemons*

706 *Interference, FP: Sabbath Dei, FP: In the Year of the Cat, FP: "Political Animals", FP: "Betes Noires and Dark Horses".

707 *FP: Coming to Dust*

708 *Interference, FP: "Betes Noires and Dark Horses".

709 *The Vampires of Venice*

710 Dating *The Girl in the Fireplace* (X2.4) - It is "five years" before Reinette is 37. Owing to her 29th December birthday, she would have been that age almost the entirety of 1759, so it's now 1754.

711 *Smith and Jones*. History records this as happening on 15th June, 1752.

712 *The Stones of Blood*

713 *The Also People*

714 "Nearly ten" Krillitane generations before *School Reunion*.

715 *Hornets' Nest: The Circus of Doom*

716 "A century" before "The Screams of Death".

717 Dating *The Girl in the Fireplace* (X2.4) - Rose says the clockwork men will come for Reinette "some time after your thirty-seventh birthday", which was on 29th December, 1758, so it must now be 1759.

718 Dating *The Many Hands* (NSA #24) - The back cover and a caption before the first part of the book confirm the year.

719 *...ish, Synthespians™, The Gallifrey Chronicles*

720 *The Underwater Menace*

721 "The Collector"

722 *The Silent Stars Go By*. Chingachgook appeared in the writings of James Fenimore Cooper, in stories set from 1740 to 1793.

723 Dating *FP: Sabbath Dei / FP: In the Year of the Cat* (FP audios #1.3-1.4) - The narrator says, "In the calendar of the West, this is the winter in the year seventeen hundred and sixty-two".

724 Dating *FP: The Labyrinth of Histories* (FP audio #1.6) - Compassion tells Justine, "I'll explain once you're back here with us in 1763", indicating that the New Year has come and gone.

725 Dating *FP: Coming to Dust / FP: The Ship of a Billion Years* (FP audio #2.1-2.2) - The year is given. Corwyn expects his ailing daughter will die "by this summer", so

biomass, co-mingled with Faction Paradox genetic material, seeped into the soil and was distributed amongst different lifeforms, including cows and flowers with black petals - "the buds of the hours".[707]

On 14th September, 1752, as the calendar moved forward eleven days, one soul in a thousand - including a young Sabbath - saw, just for a moment, London bathed in shadow as the intervening days passed into Faction Paradox's care.[708]

The Doctor lost a bet to Casanova, and wound up owing the man a chicken.[709]

& 1754 - THE GIRL IN THE FIREPLACE[710] **-> Rose appeared and warned Reinette that the clockwork men would come for her in five years. Reinette briefly travelled to the fifty-first century, then returned to her home time.**

The Doctor received mild injuries when he helped Benjamin Franklin fly his kite.[711] **Dr Borlase was killed surveying the Nine Travellers in 1754.**[712] In the same year, the seventh Doctor discovered Kadiatu Lethbridge-Stewart half-dead in a slaver off Sierra Leone. He took her to the Civilisation of the People.[713]

The Krillitanes, a race who are a genetic amalgam of all the species they've conquered, invaded the planet Bethsan and made a million widows in a day. They also absorbed the natives' wings into their own physiology.[714] Antonio, a hideous dwarf, was born around 1755.[715] The Doctor saw a performance of *Eurydice*.[716]

& 1759 - THE GIRL IN THE FIREPLACE[717] **-> The tenth Doctor saved Reinette from the clockwork men, but was apparently trapped in the past. However, Reinette had arranged to move her fireplace to her new residence, and it was still capable of working as a time window. The Doctor returned to the future, promising he would return for her.**

1759 - THE MANY HANDS[718] **->** The tenth Doctor and Martha landed in Edinburgh and briefly encountered Benjamin Franklin - who was there to pick up an honorary degree from St. Andrews University - as the self-replicating biological material of the Onk Ndell Kith approached a critical mass. This caused the dead to rise from the city's Nor' Loch, and much of the Onk Ndell Kith's substance was animated as hundreds of hands. Many of the Onk Ndell Kith's parts merged into a larger creature, but it required the genetic information of eighty thousand people to fully repair itself. The Doctor tried to avert chaos, but the Onk Ndell Kith learned of the TARDIS and coveted it. Inspired by Franklin, the Doctor used a kite, the TARDIS key and a bolt of lightning to destroy the creature.

The last hand of the Onk Ndell Kith remained in Franklin's possession. The elder Alexander Monro died during this conflict - his younger self took over "father's" position as Chair of Anatomy at St. Andrews.

The Doctor met Doctor Johnson.[719] **Scottish poet Robert Burns was born in 1759, so Jamie McCrimmon had never heard of him.**[720] A salon full of people from the eighteenth century was kidnapped by Varan Tak.[721] The Mohican named Chingachgook refined the Doctor's tracking abilities.[722]

w - 1762 - FP: SABBATH DEI / IN THE YEAR OF THE CAT[723] **->** Cousins Justine and Eliza, having fled the ruined Eleven-Day Empire, took refuge with the Order of St. Francis. The arrival of their timeship caused such a commotion at Portsmouth Docks, they used lethal force against bystanders in fighting their way out. With Lord Dashwood absent, the Earl of Sandwich served as their host. The Cousins routed Special Forces assassins dispatched against them by the Service (over Sabbath's recommendation against such a move).

The living timeship Lolita sought to strengthen her hold on this era by giving King George III an army of three hundred clockwork automata, the commanders of which originated from circa the year 5000. Lolita overlaid her personality onto Queen Charlotte; it was possible that Prince George IV was actually of Lolita's blood.

The rival timeship Compassion, as channelled through the famous prostitute/witch Mary Culver, aided the Cousins against Lolita. Sabbath discretely helped Eliza, Lord Sandwich and the Sieur d'Eon - a French spy, transvestite and special envoy to King Louis IV - in destroying the automata army sequestered at Queen's House. A speech that the King had made to both houses of Parliament about bringing in "troops from outside the country" was dismissed as a symptom of his growing madness. Eliza informed Sandwich that history would forget his role in helping to save the world, and that he would chiefly be remembered for "those snacks you always have brought to your desk while you're working - where you stick the beef between the two slices of bread".

The Great Houses captured Justine, put her on trial and sentenced her to perpetual imprisonment in their prison asteroid.

w - 1763 - FP: THE LABYRINTH OF HISTORIES[724] **->** Compassion spent six months using her influence to liberate Justine, who was reunited with her friends in 1763.

w - 1763 - FP: COMING TO DUST / THE SHIP OF A BILLION YEARS[725] **->** Three members of the Society of Sigismondo di Rimini - Corwyn Marne, John Pennerton and Abelard Finton - summoned Cousins Justine and Eliza to Naples to consult on reports of renewed activity from the Mal'akh. Justine vowed to kill Sutekh upon discovering that he had destroyed what was probably the last cache of Faction biomass on Earth. Merytra's cadre of Mal'akh self-immolated themselves - a sacrifice to open an interdimensional tunnel for benefit of their master. Justine used this tunnel to travel to the Osirian Court.

w - Cousin Eliza joined Justine at the Court, and spent weeks tracking down what remained of Osiris' biodata, which was now spread across thousands of miles.[726]

w - 1764 - FP: OZYMANDIAS[727] **->** Justine and Eliza sent a telepathic message to Corwyn Marne and Abelard Finton, who comprehended it through their dreams and poetry writing. The two men felt compelled to journey via an interdimensional tunnel to Mars, circa 5,000 BC, where they assisted the Cousins in defeating Sutekh.

1764 (15th April) - THE GIRL IN THE FIREPLACE[728] **->** The tenth Doctor once again travelled to France to meet Reinette, but arrived to find that she had died. He took a letter she had written to him back to the future.

w - 1764 (16th October to 8th November) - FP: THE JUDGMENT OF SUTEKH[729] **->** Sutekh mentally compelled John Pennerton to write letters urging that the Society of Sigismondo di Rimini destroy Faction Paradox

wherever it found them. Sutekh released Pennerton from his servitude about three weeks later, and also returned Abelard Finton home. Finton's encounter with Sutekh proved so horrifying, he soon died.

Winterborne was built in Surrey, 1764, by Sir Isaac Greatorex for use as a charity house, but was later sold off and became a public boys' school. Greatorex himself was charged with being the leader of a dark cult, and was tried in secret and hanged.[730]

Neutronic War on Skaro - and the Dalek Conquests Begin

& 1763 - There were two races on Skaro: the original Daleks (or Dals) and the Thals. The Daleks were teachers and philosophers, the Thals were a famous warrior race. Skaro was a world full of ideas, art and invention.

However, there were old rivalries between the two races, and this led to a final war. Skaro was destroyed in a single day when the Daleks detonated a huge neutronic bomb. The radiation from the weapon killed nearly all life on the planet, and petrified the vegetation. The only animals that survived were bizarre mutations: the metallic Magnadons, their bodies held together by a magnetic field, and the monsters swarming in the Lake of Mutations.

it's earlier than that in the year.

726 *FP: Body Politic*

727 Dating *FP: Ozymandias* (FP audio #2.5) - Marne says that it's been "more than six months", since they last saw Justine, but Finton later comments that it was "a year ago". Either way, it's most likely 1764 now.

728 Dating *The Girl in the Fireplace* (X2.4) - The final sequence takes place shortly after Reinette's death. This historically happened on 15th April, 1764 - the same year as is listed on the painting at the end of the story. The King says Reinette was "43" when she died, but historically she was only 42. (Writer Steven Moffat has conceded this as a mistake.)

729 Dating *FP: The Judgment of Sutekh* (FP audio #2.6) - The dates are given in Pennerton's letters.

730 *P.R.O.B.E.: The Devil of Winterborne*

731 "Five hundred years" before *The Daleks*.

THE NEUTRONIC WAR ON SKARO: The Neutronic War referred to in *The Daleks* is clearly a different conflict from the Thal-Kaled War seen in *Genesis of the Daleks*, given that the Neutronic War in *The Daleks* lasted just "one day", whereas the Thal-Kaled War lasted "nearly a thousand years". In the first story, a Dalek tells the Doctor that "We, the Daleks and the Thals" fought the Neutronic War, implying that this was after the Daleks were created (a version of events supported by the *TV Century 21* comic strip). The Thal named Alydon speaks

of this as the "final war", maybe suggesting that there was more than one.

It's interesting to note that after the Neutronic War, both the Thals and Dals mutated until they resembled the state they'd been in at *Genesis of the Daleks* - the Thals becoming blond humanoids, the Dals becoming green Dalek blobs.

732 This is the opening caption of the first "The Daleks" *TV Century 21* strip.

733 Dating "The Daleks: Genesis of Evil" (*TV21* #1-3, *DWW* #33) - This is the first story in "The Daleks" comic strip printed in *TV Century 21*. As the story starts with the birth of the Daleks, but ends at a time when Earth has spaceships (shortly before *The Dalek Invasion of Earth*, it seems), and "Legacy of Yesteryear" is explicitly "centuries" after "Genesis of Evil", the strips have been broken into two blocks, with events of each block happening over a relatively short time, but with hundreds of years between the two.

The year this story - and so the rest of its block - is set isn't given in the strip, but Drenz was killed in 2003 according to both *The Dalek Book* and *The Dalek Pocketbook and Space-Travellers Guide*, both of which are otherwise consistent with the strip. However, this isn't 2003 AD: *The Dalek Outer Space Book* mentions the "New Skaro Calendar", with Year Zero being the year the "Thousand Years War" started. It also says the Daleks

After the Neutronic War, the Daleks retired into a huge metal city built as a shelter, where they were protected from the radiation. They became dependent on their machines, radiation and static electricity. Most of the Thals perished during the final war, but a handful survived on a plateau a great distance from the Dalek City, where they managed to cultivate small plots of land. The Thals mutated, evolving full circle in the space of five centuries, becoming physically perfect blond supermen.[731]

"Deep in Hyperspace is Planet Skaro. This world is the most feared globe in all the universe. Many thousands of years ago, it was already the scene of a vicious conflict. On the continent of Davius, the Thals, a tall, handsome, peaceful race went in constant dread of attack from the short, ugly Daleks who inhabited Dalazar across the Ocean of Ooze."[732]

& 1763 - "The Daleks: Genesis of Evil"[733] -> The Daleks discovered cobalt in a mountain range, and developed a neutron bomb. In the year 2003 of the New Skaro Calendar, Minister Zolfian, Warlord of the Daleks, killed the peaceful leader Drenz. The scientist Yarvelling developed war machines ("metal slaves") to kill Thal survivors. As the Dalek factories prepared for war, a meteorite storm struck, starting fires which spread to where the neutron bombs were stored. There was a vast atomic explosion which wiped out the entire continent of Dalazar and reached as far as the Thals' homeland, Davius. Radiation spread across the planet.

The explosion shifted the north pole of the planet, freezing three scientists who had recently discovered a planet nine galaxies away: Earth.[734]

& 1765 - "The Daleks: Genesis of Evil"[735] -> Two years later, Yarvelling and Zolfian emerged from a shelter.

Exploring their continent, they failed to locate any other survivors, and began to succumb to radiation poisoning. They were ambushed by one of the war machines, learning that a mutated survivor had crawled inside. This was the first of a new race of Daleks, with brains a thousand times superior to the original. Zolfian and Yarvelling rebuilt the war factory, creating a Dalek production line. The first Dalek declared himself Emperor and had a special casing constructed - it was finished as Zolfian and Yarvelling died. The Emperor realised the Daleks needed slaves to continue their work.

The Black Dalek was built - it had even more firepower than a standard Dalek, and was the Emperor's deputy.[736]

& 1765 - "The Daleks: Power Play"[737] -> Within two months, the Daleks had built a vast new city and begun to develop new inventions and weapons. A Krattorian slave ship arrived to collect valuable radioactive sand. The Daleks encouraged a slave revolution, then took the spaceship and the slaves for themselves. Two of the slaves managed to recapture the ship and escape with the slaves... but not before the Daleks learned the spaceship's secrets.

& 1765 - "The Daleks: Duel of the Daleks"[738] -> All the Daleks lacked was the ability to make a material strong enough to withstand the heat stress of space travel. Dalek Zeg was bathed in chemicals and found that he had become stronger (and that his casing had become red and gold). Zeg announced that he had discovered metalert, a substance strong enough to build spaceships from, and would only share it if he was declared Emperor. Zeg attracted followers, and the Emperor consulted the Dalek Brain Machine, which ordered the two fight a duel. Realising that Zeg was resistant to heat, not cold, the Emperor froze Zeg - thus destroying him.

emerged in the year 1600 and "The Year of the Dalek" lasted until the year 1,000,000 (the original date given in scripts for *The Daleks' Master Plan*, which may or may not be a coincidence). This would account for a line in "The Dalek World" stating it's not unusual to find Daleks that are a million years old. See the Are There Two Dalek Histories? sidebar for how this can be reconciled with *Genesis of the Daleks*.

So... the blue-skinned original Daleks appear in 1600, "Genesis of Evil" is set in 2003, and *The Daleks* takes place five hundred years after "Genesis of Evil" (so around 2503). We also know that *Genesis of the Daleks* is set at the end of the Thousand Years War, so in 1000. Making the assumption that a "year" is the same length as a year on Earth (as this chronology does, unless

stated otherwise), and using other dates from this chronology, we can work back. *The Daleks* is set in 2263 AD and 2503 according to the New Skaro Calendar, so to calculate an Earth date, you subtract two hundred and forty from the Skaro date. Therefore, "Genesis of Evil" starts in 1763 and *Genesis of the Daleks* is set in 760 AD.

734 "Legacy of Yesteryear"
735 Dating "The Daleks: Genesis of Evil" (*TV21* #1-3, *DWW* #33) - It is two years later.
736 "Duel of the Daleks"
737 Dating "The Daleks: Power Play" (*TV21* #4-10, *DWW* #33-34) - "Two months" after "Genesis of Evil".
738 Dating "The Daleks: Duel of the Daleks" (*TV21* #11-17, *DWW* #35-36) - It's set soon after "Power Play".

& 1765 - "The Daleks: The Amaryll Challenge"[739]

-> The first three prototype spacecraft failed, but the fourth succeeded... until it tried to break the light barrier, when it was destroyed. Proto 9 broke the light barrier, but metalert proved too weak to resist the heat barrier. The saucer-shaped Proto 13 passed every trial, and soon a space armada left Skaro. The Emperor led the fleet, from the golden flagship Proto-Leader.

Dalek saucers landed on Alvega, the nearest planet to Skaro. It was the home of the Amarylls: plant creatures who resisted the Dalek scouts. They wiped out the Amarylls, and destroyed the world-root - and with it, the entire planet. The Emperor declared a new law: what the Daleks could not conquer, they would destroy.

& 1765 - "The Daleks: The Penta Ray Factor"[740]

-> The fleet went onward to Solturis, home of a humanoid race that had been at peace for a hundred years. The Daleks were welcomed, and pretended to be friendly while they discovered the extent of the planet's defences. The penta ray (which combined alpha, infra, omega, ultra and beta rays) was a threat. The Daleks swapped the real weapon for a fake, but needed the key to operate it. The main fleet left while Daleks from two saucers attacked the city of Bulos, but were destroyed by the ray. Instead of avenging this, the Emperor received a message from Skaro that demanded his immediate return.

& 1765 - "The Daleks: Plague of Death"[741]

-> Skaro had become a huge war factory that was overseen by the Black Dalek, but a dalatomic rust cloud escaped from one research base and began eating through every Dalek it came into contact with. Dalek hoverbouts were sent to investigate the cloud, and it was contained with magnets,

but mutated into a plague. The Daleks began destroying each other, rather than risk infection. The Emperor returned and deduced that the Black Dalek carried the plague. The Black Dalek's casing was recast, and the planet was rebuilt.

& 1765 - "The Daleks: The Menace of the Monstrons"[742]

-> The Monstrons landed in a dead volcano on Skaro, and set their Engibrain robots to building a bridgehead. A Dalek was captured, and the city bombarded with missiles. The Daleks seemed defeated, but the captured Dalek broke free and set off the volcano, destroying the Monstrons.

& 1765 - "The Daleks: Eve of War"[743]

-> A few months later, a new Dalek City had been built, with improved defences. The Daleks constantly monitored against surprise attack. The Daleks built a space station as a staging post to the planet Oric, with construction supervised by the Red Dalek. Workers there were attacked by the Mechanoids' "suspicion ray", and began fighting amongst themselves. The Daleks detected the Mechanoid ship and destroyed it. Two Mechanoid ships quickly retaliated, destroying the Dalek saucer and warning the Daleks to avoid their territory.

& 1765 - "The Daleks: The Archive of Phryne"[744]

-> The Emperor ordered the Daleks to prepare new weapons to fight a galactic war, and began searching nearby planets for new inventions. A force led by the Black Dalek discovered the planet Phryne behind an invisibility screen, and landed to seize "the genius of a hundred planets". But the Phrynians kept the information in their own memories, and fled the Dalek invasion.

739 Dating "The Daleks: The Amaryll Challenge" (*TV21* #18-24, *DWW* #36-37) - It's not stated how long the Daleks experiment with spacecraft, but they design and build thirteen different prototypes, test them and then build a fleet of the winning design in the first installment. This allows one of only two gaps in the narrative (the other is between "Impasse" and "The Terrorkon Harvest"), which have to add up to the "centuries" between "Genesis of Evil" and "Legacy of Yesteryear". That said, there's no indication it takes the Daleks very long to develop space travel.

740 Dating "The Daleks: The Penta Ray Factor" (*TV21* #25-32, *DWW* #37-39) - The story follows straight on from "The Amaryll Challenge".

741 Dating "The Daleks: Plague of Death" (*TV21* #33-39, *DWW* #39-40) - The Emperor is summoned back at the end of "The Penta Ray Factor", so this story starts while that story is running.

742 Dating "The Daleks: Menace of the Monstrons" (*TV21* #40-46, *DWW* #40-42) - The Monstron ship arrives

while the Daleks are rebuilding after "Plague of Death".

743 Dating "The Daleks: Eve of the War" (*TV21* #47-51, *DWM* #53-54) - It's "a few months" after "The Menace of the Monstrons", and the Daleks have spent the time rebuilding their city. The Mechanoids in the *TV Century 21* strip physically resemble the ones seen in *The Chase*, but see the dating notes on that story for more.

744 Dating "The Daleks: The Archive of Phryne" (*TV21* #52-58, *DWM* #54-55) - The story is set shortly after "Eve of the War", with the Daleks gearing up to fight the Mechanoids.

745 Dating "The Daleks: Rogue Planet" (*TV21* #47-51, *DWM* #53-54) - The Daleks are still preparing to fight the Mechanoids, so this is shortly after "The Archive of Phryne". The rogue planet is accidentally called Skardel in a couple of the later instalments.

746 Dating "The Daleks: Impasse" (*TV21* #63-69, *DWM* #62-66, 68) - The story ends the immediate threat of war between the Mechanoids and Daleks.

747 *TW: Trace Memory*. Sheridan was an Irish actor,

& 1765 - "The Daleks: Rogue Planet"[745] **->** The Astrodalek observed a newborn rogue planet in the Eighty-Fourth galaxy, which they named Skardal. It collided with the planet Omega Three, altering its course so that it was heading for Skaro. Upgraded Dalek saucers fitted with Magray Ultimate deflected Skardal until it was aimed at the home planet of the Mechanoids, Mechanus.

& 1765 - "The Daleks: Impasse"[746] **->** The leaders of the planet Zeros were alarmed at the prospect of galactic war between the Daleks and Mechanoids, and sent a robot agent, 2K, to prevent either side from winning. 2K arrived on Skaro and discovered the existence of Skardal. 2K launched himself towards the rogue planet in a Dalek missile. 2K was captured by the Mechanoids, but diverted the Dalek missile to destroy Skardal. He tricked the Mechanoids into thinking the Daleks had saved them, and the threat of war receded.

As a time agent, Jack Harkness stole a rare manuscript of Shakespeare and Fletcher's *Cardenio - A Spanish Comedie* from Thomas Sheridan in 1765.[747] Sir Francis Dashwood, an ancestor of Brigham Elisha Dashwood III and Chancellor of the Exchequer to King George III, founded the Hellfire Club as a social organization. The group peaked in the 1760s, becoming a debauched haven for the aristocracy. The generations to follow exaggerated the group's dabblings with the black arts.[748]

1768 - HORNETS' NEST: THE CIRCUS OF DOOM / A STING IN THE TALE[749] **->** The Hornets mentally compelled the fourth Doctor to bring them to this time, and they took control of the hideous dwarf Antonio was he was 13. He met the Hornets in the lagoons outside Venice, and they granted him vast psychic powers - that he used to burn out the minds of those who had taunted him. Freed of the Hornets' influence once they possessed Antonio, the Doctor and a dog the Hornets had previously possessed - which he named Captain - tried to find the dwarf for four days, but to no avail.

Rubasdpofiaew, a drug from Tau Ceti Minor, found its way to Earth and started growing in Tibet as a "miracle flower" named Om-Tsor. Those who consumed Om-Tsor could turn thought into reality. Starving Tibetan lamas ate the Om-Tsor flowers, and used their newfound abilities to found the peaceful "Om-Tsor" valley.[750]

Sabbath was initiated into the British intelligence service in 1762, adopting the name by which we know him.[751] He was not supposed to survive the initiation, but the Council of Eight saved him. The Council claimed to be humans from the future who wanted to become the Lords of Time. They recruited Sabbath as a counterpart to the Doctor, but he did not hear from them for another twenty years.[752]

1770 (April to June) - TRANSIT OF VENUS[753] **->** The TARDIS arrived on the sailing ship *Endeavour*, which was commanded by Captain James Cook. His expedition had recently left Tahiti after observing a transit of Venus - a rare event when Venus moves across the disc of the sun. The transit would aid astronomers in creating a map of the skies, and the *Endeavour* was now headed toward Cook's historical discovery of Australia.

Superstitious sailors pitched the TARDIS - with Barbara and Susan inside - into the water. The first Doctor and Ian were mistaken as hailing from Venus, and enjoyed Cook's hospitality while worrying about their lost friends. Susan had tied the TARDIS to the *Endeavour* with some rope, and the time machine had been pulled behind Cook's vessel. Barbara passed some time relating details of the period to Susan, whose latent empathy had unknowingly influenced Cook's chief scientist, Joseph Banks, to write and talk about historical events, tunes and poems from the future.

In June, the Doctor's party were reunited when the *Endeavour* reached Australia; Cook's nephew, Isaac Smith, was the first to step ashore. Banks promised to remain silent about these events - and the extra-terrestrial travellers he'd purportedly met.

Banks named a plant "Barberer" after "barber", meaning Latin for beard, possibly because his telepathic link with Susan brought the word "Barbara" to mind.

educator and proponent of elocution movement.
748 *Minuet in Hell*
749 Dating *Hornets' Nest: The Circus of Doom* and *Hornets' Nest: A Sting in the Tale* (BBC fourth Doctor audios #1.3-1.4) - The date is given.
750 "Two centuries" before *Revolution Man*.
751 *The Adventuress of Henrietta Street*. Sabbath is working with the service prior to this in the *Faction Paradox* audios; this must represent his initiation into its higher echelons.
752 *Timeless*
753 Dating *Transit of Venus* (BF CC #3.7) - The adventure occurs over a period of "less than two months" in

1770, and concludes "days" after the *Endeavour* gets stuck on the Great Barrier Reef on June 11. Susan's empathic link with Banks is deemed an offshoot of the telepathy she used in *The Sensorites*. Ian claims to have seen "the metal seas of Venus", but it's not stated that he actually met any Venusians; the Doctor, Ian and Barbara do so in *Venusian Lullaby*.

Transits of Venus are extraordinarily rare - pairs of transits will occur at eight-year intervals, then not be seen again for two hundred and forty-three years. A transit of Venus occurred in 1761; Cook's party witnessed its "pairing" in 1769.

In 1771, Alexander Monro reclaimed the last Hand of Onk Ndell Kith from Benjamin Franklin, who was staying at the home of the philosopher David Hume. Two years later, Alexander used the hand to "rebirth" his father as a baby, and presented it to his wife Katherine as an abandoned infant that they should raise as their own.[754] The Xoanthrax Empire subjugated the Hargarans.[755]

w - 1774 (December) - FP: "Political Animals" / FP: "Betes Noires and Dark Horses"[756] -> Empress Catherine of Russia gifted the court of King George III with a mammoth - a relic of history from a different time. Mother Francesca of Faction Paradox arrived, along with her unnamed second, as various parties gathered at the court for a ritualistic hunt. The event drew the attention of Sabbath. The American delegation intended on using a Mayakai warrior, Mayakatula, as their hunting dog, but she freed herself and made the acquaintance of a young servant named Isobel...

Sabbath first met the Mayakai warrior Tula Lui in 1776, when she was ten. She would eventually become his apprentice. In 1780, Sabbath failed to seduce Scarlette, a brothel owner and ritualist. The same year, he was present during the Gordon Riots. He left the Service, and dealt with the agents of the Service - the "Ratcatchers" - sent to assassinate him. Tula Lui, as Sabbath's only real company from 1780 to 1782, eliminated some high-ranking Service officials as a message for them to leave Sabbath alone.[757]

The American War of Independence

The Doctor was at the Boston Tea Party in 1773.[758] **The Rani was present during the American War of Independence.**[759] The Canavitchi were involved in the same conflict.[760] **The Doctor met American founding fathers Thomas Jefferson, John Adams and Alexander Hamilton - two of them fancied him.**[761] The Doctor was

---

754 *The Many Hands*
755 "Two hundred years" before *The Many Deaths of Jo Grant*.
756 Dating *FP:* "Political Animals" and *FP:* "Betes Noires and Dark Horses" (*FP* comic #1-2) - The year and month are given. The story was interrupted by the cancellation of the *Faction Paradox* comic after two issues.
757 *The Adventuress of Henrietta Street*
758 *The Unquiet Dead*
759 *The Mark of the Rani*. The American War of Independence ran from 1775-1783.
760 *The King of Terror*
761 *The Impossible Astronaut*
762 *Survival of the Fittest*. Jefferson lived 1743 to 1826.
763 *Seasons of Fear*. No date is given, but Franklin died in 1790. The modern-day American government didn't start until 1789, so unless Franklin was President in the *Doctor Who* universe under its predecessor, the Articles of Confederation, then he must have served during the term normally attributed to George Washington.
   The mistake wasn't deliberate - writer Paul Cornell genuinely believed that Franklin had been President. In *Neverland*, a line that the "wrong man became President" was meant to denote the Bush/Gore election in 2000, but fans have cited it to cover this mistake.
764 *FP: Warlords of Utopia*
765 "Two hundred years" before *The Daemons*.
766 *City of Death*
767 We see the portrait of Ace hanging in Windsor Castle in the extended version of *Silver Nemesis*. In Ace's personal timeline, she had not yet sat for the painting. Gainsborough lived from 1727-1788, painting society portraits 1760-1774 before turning to landscapes.
768 *Timeless* (p93). Kalicum says that D'Amantine, who's alive in 1830, is the third generation affected by his alterations.

769 *The Nightmare Fair*
770 *The Devil Goblins from Neptune*. He ruled 1780-1790.
771 *The Stones of Blood*. Allan Ramsay, a Scottish portrait painter, lived 1713-1784.
772 Three months before *Catch-1782*.
773 Dating *Catch-1782* (BF #68) - The dates of Mel's arrival and departure from this era are given.
774 Dating *The Adventuress of Henrietta Street* (EDA #51) - It is "March 1782" on p2, more specifically "March 20, 1782" on p15. The Siege of Henrietta Street happens on "February 8", 1783 (p259). Scarlette's funeral is dated 9th February on p269 and the back cover, with the Doctor departing Henrietta Street on February 13 (p273), and his final conversation with Scarlette occurs on the same day. An epilogue with Sabbath and Juliette happens on "August 18 1783" (p278).
   The book is told in a style reminiscent of a history book, and some of the key facts are open to dispute. With that in mind, novels after this one state that Anji has been travelling with the Doctor only for "months", suggesting the timeframe of *Henrietta Street* might be more condensed than the book itself suggests.
   Scarlette is the young girl Isobel from the *Faction Paradox* comic series, which covers some of her early history and takes place in 1774.
775 Dating *Dead of Winter* (NSA #46) - The six days that pass within the story - starting with "4th December 1783" (p10) and ending with "10th December 1783" (p251) - are listed in various journal entries and letters.
776 *The Spectre of Lanyon Moor*
777 *The Haunting of Thomas Brewster*. Franklin died in 1790.
778 A bit more than two hundred years before *The Nightmare Fair*.
779 *Hexagora*. Date unknown, but this is within the

once stuck at a tea party with Thomas Jefferson, who wouldn't shut up about bees.[762]

Benjamin Franklin became President of the United States.[763]

> = On Roma I, Americanus crushed a republican insurrection in America. As a reward, the Emperor granted his family stewardship of the continent.[764]

Devil's End became notorious when the Third Lord of Aldbourne's black magic rituals were exposed.[765] In the late eighteenth century, Scaroth lived in France at the time of Louis XV. He acquired a Gainsborough.[766]

Gainsborough also painted a portrait of Ace that ended up in Windsor Castle.[767] Kalicum, an agent of the Council of Eight, made genetic alterations to the grandfather of the Frenchman D'Amantine. The alterations would work their way through thirteen successive generations.[768] Shardlow lost a game of backgammon at the Hellfire Club in July 1778, and became the Celestial Toymaker's thrall.[769]

The Doctor met Emperor Joseph II of Austria-Hungary.[770] **Cessair posed as Lady Montcalm and was painted by Ramsay.[771]** In September 1781, Jane Hallam - the wife of Henry Hallam, one of Mel's ancestors - died from a horse-riding accident.[772]

1781 (12th December) to 1782 (June) - CATCH-1782[773] -> Melanie Bush arrived through time from 2003, and the transition left her extremely confused and disorientated. Henry Hallam cared for her and, failing to recognise Mel as one of his descendants, became intent on making her his second wife. The sixth Doctor and Mel's uncle, John Hallam, arrived and intervened. The travellers returned with Mel to the twenty-first century, and Henry eventually married his housekeeper, Mrs McGregor. Henry's journal and other documents from the period would note the existence of "Eleanor Hallam" - actually Mel, who was erroneously believed to have been born about 1760 and died in 1811.

1782 (20th March) to 1783 (13th February) - THE ADVENTURESS OF HENRIETTA STREET[774] -> At the limit of human consciousness was the "horizon", and beyond that was the Kingdom of the Beasts and the babewyns, bestial ape creatures. The destruction of Gallifrey destabilised time, allowing the babewyns to escape to Earth as humans were beginning to conceive of time as a dimension.

The eighth Doctor arrived in this era, suffering physical symptoms as a result of his being linked to his homeworld, which no longer existed. He allied himself with a brothel owner and ritualist, Scarlette. Together, they agreed that the Doctor should marry Juliette, a young woman working in the brothel, as this would link him to Earth and allow

him to serve as its protector.

The Doctor came to the attention of Sabbath, who thought the Doctor had brought the babewyns to Earth. Sabbath was building a time machine, the *Jonah*. The Doctor and Sabbath teamed up upon realising they both wished to repel the monsters. Juliette abandoned the Doctor for Sabbath, so the Doctor instead married Scarlette in the Caribbean. The Doctor's illness got worse, and the babewyns transported his party to their domain (possibly the ruins of Gallifrey). Sabbath saved the Doctor by removing one of his hearts.

The babewyns assaulted Scarlette's brothel, and Scarlette was believed killed in the fighting. The Doctor defeated the babewyns, and beheaded the King of Beasts with the sonic screwdriver. A funeral was held for Scarlette on 9th February, 1783, but she had survived and parted company with the Doctor on 13th February.

After implanting the Doctor's heart in his chest, Sabbath gained the ability to travel through time. The Doctor wrote the novel *The Ruminations of a Foreign Traveller in his Element* during this time.

1783 (4th-10th December) - DEAD OF WINTER[775] -> Dr Bloom, the head of a clinic in St. Christophe, Italy, preformed miracle cures in conjunction with a water-dwelling hive-creature that had visited Earth at various times. The creature could heal disease, and also generated Familiars: ghost-like recreations of lost loved ones. A Familiar had raised Prince Boris, a Russian aristocrat, and cured him of his wasting disease. The eleventh Doctor, Amy and Rory were present as Boris tried to use the creature's psionic abilities to conquer the world. A distraught Bloom fatally shot the Doctor after learning that his wife Perdita was also a Familiar. The hive-creature exploded after healing the Doctor, unable to process the weight of his life's memories. Many of Bloom's patients, including Boris, regained their ailments. Two last Familiars remained: an 11-year-old girl named Maria and her mother, both of whom were unaware of their true nature.

Sir Percival Flint excavated a fogou in Cornwall in 1783 and heard ghastly screams.[776] The TARDIS wine cellar contained a bottle of 1784 Madeira, which was the property of Benjamin Franklin.[777] The Pathfinders - androids who prided themselves on "always getting their man", i.e. obliterating their opposition - participated in what would become one of the most pointless interplanetary wars in modern history.[778] The insectoid Hexagora colonised Zagara IX and came into conflict with the Agelli - hostile ape-like creatures native to the Acteon galaxy, but had ventured into the Milky Way. The Hexagora obliterated the Agelli warfleet - one hundred thousand starships were destroyed, and the cause of the Agelli defeat would remain a mystery.[779]

c 1784 - HELICON PRIME[780] -> Mindy 'Voir believed the second Doctor had made off with the prized memory bank of the Fennus colony, and travelled back to eighteenth century Scotland to see if Jamie knew its location. The data bank was a pendant around Jamie's neck - and when Mindy attacked Jamie, it absorbed her, trapping her mind with the memories of the Fennus colonists.

c 1786 - THE GLORIOUS REVOLUTION[781] -> Jamie McCrimmon had married a young woman named Kirsty, and they'd had "more bairns than there are days in the week". Their children had grown up, and made them grandparents.

A representative of the Celestial Intervention Agency visited Jamie about forty years after he'd encountered the Doctor, having detected a fluctuation in Earth's timeline.

> (=) Jamie's encounter with King James VIII in 1688 had created a paradoxical timeline in which the king never left England and stayed on the throne, causing the ascension of King Charles III. The CIA operative stabilized the temporal integrity of Jamie's past self in 1688, enabling him to put history right...

Jamie decided that he'd had a full life and was better off not knowing about his adventures with the Doctor. At Jamie's request, the CIA agent re-instated his memory block.

In the late 1780s, Montague and Tackleton, a firm making dolls' houses, scandalously made a house that resembled the haunted Ilbridge House.[782] **In 1788, the Nemesis Bow was stolen from Windsor Castle.**[783] Fitz's great-great-grandfather and his twin, Freddie Tarr and Neville Fitzwilliam Tarr, were born in 1790.[784]

c 1791 - "The World Shapers"[785] -> The sixth Doctor, Peri and Frobisher arrived in the Scottish Highlands, looking for Jamie and clues about the mysterious Planet 14. The Time Lords had failed to erase Jamie's memory after all, and he was now known as "Mad Jamie" because he had told people about his adventures with the Doctor. Jamie remembered the reference to Planet 14 - the Cybermen referred to it when they invaded Earth. The Doctor let Jamie go back to Marinus with him, dematerialising the TARDIS in front of the other villagers to prove that Jamie wasn't mad.

The Doctor claimed to be the first person to spin a jenny.[786] **The first Doctor met James Watt, an engineer who influenced the Industrial Revolution.**[787] **Auderly House was built in Georgian times.**[788]

In the late eighteenth century, a cabin boy named Varney served aboard a treasure galleon. A storm left him shipwrecked, and he wasn't seen for five years. During that time, the last of the Curcurbites entered "communion" with Varney, altered his blood and gifted him with a knowledge of biochemistry. He rejoined civilisation as a vampire pirate, made his fortune and settled on an island in the Atlantic. Like Varney, his descendents worked toward the Curcurbite's restitution.[789]

---

lifetime of Queen Zafira, who as a Hexagoran has a lifespan of five hundred years.
780 Dating *Helicon Prime* (BF CC #2.2) - The next Companion Chronicles audio starring Frazer Hines, *The Glorious Revolution*, suggests that the same amount of time has passed for Jamie as has passed in the real world since the broadcast of *The War Games* in 1969. If that's the case, the framing sequence of *Helicon Prime* (which was released in 2007) probably takes place circa 1784.
781 Dating *The Glorious Revolution* (BF CC #4.2) - The Time Lord says that it's been "forty years" since *The Highlanders*, which is set in 1746, evidently mirroring the real-life time that's passed for Frazer Hines since he left *Doctor Who* in 1969. Additionally, it's said that 1688 was "a hundred years ago", and that King James VII died "eighty years ago" (he lived 1633-1701). Jamie's wife, named as "Kirsty", is presumably Hannah Gordon's character of the same name from *The Highlanders*.
782 *The Death of Art*
783 *Silver Nemesis*
784 *The Taint*. Fitz is named after Freddie's brother.
785 Dating "The World Shapers" (*DWM* #127-129) - It's

"the eighteenth century" according to a caption, and the Doctor thinks he's miscalculated by "about forty years". The previous edition of *Ahistory* dated this story to circa 1785, but the inclusion of *The Glorious Revolution* at circa 1786 makes it advisable to bump "The World Shapers" ahead in time a bit, under the assumption that personal matters go downhill for Jamie afterwards. Peri remembers *The Two Doctors* as being "a couple of years ago". The reference to Planet 14 appeared in *The Invasion*.
786 *Doctor Who and the Pirates*. The Spinning Jenny was invented in 1797.
787 *The Space Museum*. James Watt lived 1736-1819.
788 *Day of the Daleks*, Alex Macintosh, the television commentator in that story, states that the house is "Georgian".
789 "One and a half centuries" before "Tooth and Claw" (*DWM*).
790 According to Susan in *The Reign of Terror*.
791 In *An Unearthly Child*, Susan borrows a book about the French Revolution, but already knows a great deal about the subject.
792 *The Scapegoat*. The Bastille was in operation as a

The French Revolution

This was the Doctor's favourite period of Earth history.[790] **Susan visited France at this time with the first Doctor.**[791] A rack used at the Bastille would later, in German-occupied Paris, be occupied by Lucie Miller.[792]

In 1791, the first Doctor and Susan were imprisoned in Paris, but escaped by using an artillery shell. Transcripts of the Doctor's interrogation would end up with the Shadow Directory.[793] It was the Doctor and Susan's first-ever visit to Earth. It demonstrated to the Doctor that the old order could be toppled, and that people wanted freedom and a hope for the future.[794]

Mozart hated cats.[795]

(=) 1791 (5th December) - 100: "My Own Private Wolfgang"[796] **->** A Mozart clone from the far future travelled back in time, intending to damage the reputation of his original self. He appeared, masked, at the dying Mozart's bedside and offered him immortality in exchange for his producing a new symphony every year. Mozart agreed, and the clone pumped him full of self-regenerating fluid, curing his tuberculosis. As the clone intended, Mozart lived for centuries - and proved the rule that while the good die young, the mediocre stick around forever.

The sixth Doctor and Evelyn convinced Mozart to not sign the life-extending deal. To hobble Mozart's reputation just a little, the Doctor - with Mozart's consent - tore out the last twelve pages of his finished *Requiem*.

The Doctor met Marie Antoinette and obtained a lockpick from her.[797] The Doctor claimed to have been invited into Marie Antoinette's boudoir.[798] He judged that Marie Antoinette had a lovely cook, and decided that eating cake was a good way of passing the time.[799] The Meddling Monk claimed to have cakes from the kitchen of Marie Antoinette.[800]

In 1791, the fifth Doctor, Tegan and Turlough were dining at the Cafe de Saint Joseph in Aix-en-Provence when they were accidentally scooped up by the Crystal Bucephalus and whisked thousands of years into the future.[801] **In 1793, the attempted opening of Devil's Hump by Sir Percival Flint resulted in disaster.**[802] The Daniells brothers unearthed a statuette of a dancer in Pakistan in 1793.[803] In 1793, the actor Robert Dodds built Banquo Manor using money he inherited. The rumour was that Dodds had murdered his aunt for her money.[804]

1794 (late July) - THE REIGN OF TERROR[805] **->** The first Doctor and his companions landed in France during the Reign of Terror. Ian met the British spy James Stirling, but Barbara and Susan were arrested as aristocrats and sentenced to the guillotine. Posing as a Citizen, the Doctor rescued his companions. Ian and Barbara helped Stirling to identify Napoleon as the next ruler of France, but were unable to prevent his predecessor, Robespierre, from being arrested.

(=) A group of curious aliens performed experiments on reality control and used a "world-machine" device to slip the entire Earth out of N-Space. The planet was remade according to the philosophies of a single human: the Marquis de Sade. However, the world-machine's operator threw off the aliens' control and became Minski, a dwarf. Minski created an automaton of the Marquis, who began ruling France the day Robespierre was arrested, and the real Marquis was imprisoned. The fake Marquis ruled France, with Minski as his deputy, for ten years.[806]

---

fortress prison from 1370 until its storming on 14th July, 1789.

793 *Christmas on a Rational Planet*

794 *Just War*

795 *"The Golden Ones"*

796 Dating *100:* "100 My Own Private Wolfgang" (BF #100b) - It's the day of Mozart's death. His last composition, *Requiem in Mass D minor*, is regarded as one of his most popular works - but it's also unfinished, and was completed by Franz Xaver Sussmayr or other parties after Mozart's death. In *Time and Relative*, Susan relates that her grandfather regards Mozart as a "bad-mannered show-off with a silly hairstyle" - but as Susan herself hasn't met Mozart, this is likely just the first Doctor's opinion without benefit of having met the man.

797 The lockpick is mentioned in *Pyramids of Mars*. The Doctor mentions Marie Antoinette again in *The Robots of Death*.

798 *The Adventuress of Henrietta Street*

799 *The Beautiful People*

800 *The Resurrection of Mars*. Antoinette was Queen of France from 1774 to 1792.

801 *The Crystal Bucephalus*

802 *The Daemons*

803 *The Burning*

804 *The Banquo Legacy*

805 Dating *The Reign of Terror* (1.8) - The date is given on screen. *The Programme Guide* offered the date "1792", but *The Terrestrial Index* corrected this. The story shows the arrest of Robespierre, which occurred on 27th July.

806 *The Man in the Velvet Mask*

1794 (August) - WORLD GAME[807] -> The immortal Players interfered in Earth history for their amusement. After an attempt to kill the future Duke of Wellington failed, the opposing Player countermoved by having Napoleon arrested.

The second Doctor and Serena - an ambitious Time Lady sent to keep him in check - arrived in Antibes to monitor the time disturbances caused by the Players' actions. The Doctor saved Napoleon from execution and came into contact with the Countess, one of the Players, who was working to see Napoleon defeat the British. The Doctor worked out that she hoped to kill Nelson and Wellington, and that the two only met once, in 1805. The Doctor and Serena departed for that meeting.

In 1795, the Directory was running France after Robespierre's arrest. They learned of many unusual visitations and encounters on Earth, and set up the Shadow Directory to capture or destroy such things. At some point, the Shadow Directory autopsied a Time Lord and knew of them as *les betes aux deux coeurs,* or "the devils with two hearts". One of the Shadow Directory's agents, the psychic aristocrat Marielle Duquesne, investigated the Beautiful Shining Daughters of Hysteria in Munchen.[808]

Samuel Taylor Coleridge was the "last man" to have read every book in circulation; he was the last true "universal expert". But as a result, he kept falling asleep and forgetting his poems.[809] The Doctor met the artist Turner.[810] The Quoth gave psychic abilities to the toymaker Montague in 1797.[811] In 1798, Napoleon undertook an expedition to colonise Egypt. He entered the Great Pyramid, and was mentally influenced to dig out the sand-covered Sphinx.[812]

1798 - SET PIECE[813] -> Benny fled the robot Ants, and ended up with archaeologist Vivant Denon as he began to uncover ancient Egyptian treasures for Napoleon. She located the TARDIS, thanks to a message Ace left in 1366 BC, and programmed it to find the Doctor. It did so in Paris, 1871.

The Doctor had a close friendship with Wordsworth, and was present when the writer did a first draft of his most famous poem.[814] Robert Dodds was murdered at Banquo Manor in 1798. A Time Lord agent was dispatched to wait for the Doctor, who eventually showed up a century later.[815] In 1799, Mother Mathara of Faction Paradox and two thousand refugees from Ordifica arrived from 2596. They began building the city of Anathema. With the help of the remembrance tanks that Mathara left, this society would become the Remote.[816]

1799 (9th November to 25th December) - CHRISTMAS ON A RATIONAL PLANET[817] -> Napoleon returned to France from Egypt, shutting down the Directory and replacing it with the Consulate. The Shadow Directory secretly survived. The mysterious Cardinal Scarlath gave the Vatican's Collection of Necessary Secrets certain documents that described the creation of ancient Egyptian civilisation by a one-eyed monster.

Roz Forrester accidentally ended up in Woodwicke, New York state, after investigating a temporal anomaly in 2012. She set herself up as a fortune-teller and met Samuel Lincoln, whom she mistook for an ancestor of Abraham Lincoln. Roz planned to assassinate Samuel, thus changing history and enabling the seventh Doctor to locate her.

The Doctor arrived and stopped Roz, but a vast psychic disturbance started in the town. This was caused by the Carnival Queen, also known as Cacophony, who sought to create an irrational universe. The Queen was releasing irrational gynoid monsters into the area, and sought to create further disruption through the latently telepathic Chris Cwej. He chose Reason over the Carnival Queen's

---

807 Dating *World Game* (PDA #74) - Serena gives the date of the Doctor's arrival as 9th August, 1794. The Duke of Wellington was a leading military and political figure. He was a Field Marshall during the Napoleonic Wars, and oversaw Napoleon's defeat at Waterloo.

808 *Christmas on a Rational Planet*

809 *The Scarlet Empress* (p90). Coleridge lived 1772-1834.

810 *The Hollow Men, Blood Heat*

811 *The Death of Art*

812 *The Sands of Time.* Napoleon began his expedition in March 1798, and the year is given (p203).

813 Dating *Set Piece* (NA #35) - It is "1798 CE" (p57).

814 *The Zygon Who Fell to Earth.* William Wordsworth lived 1770-1850, and his magnum opus is generally regarded as *The Prelude* - a work he started working on when he was 28, but was published posthumously.

815 *The Banquo Legacy*

816 *Interference* (p59, p147).

817 Dating *Christmas on a Rational Planet* (NA #52) - It's "1799. At Christmas" (p24).

818 "The early nineteenth century" according to *The Eight Doctors.*

819 *Instruments of Darkness.* In our history, the dodo was extinct by 1700.

820 *The Lazarus Experiment*

821 *A Thousand Tiny Wings.* This presumably occurred when the Arapaho lived on the plains - they were relocated, in the mid-nineteenth century, to reservations in Wyoming and Oklahoma.

822 *The Demons of Red Lodge and Other Stories*: "Special Features"

823 "The Glorious Dead"

824 "Millennia" before *Earth Aid.*

irrationality, and the defeated Queen departed into eternity, where she hoped to inspire more ideas.

The Doctor learned afterwards that the TARDIS had planted a memory in Chris' mind that swayed his decision, as the TARDIS feared becoming denationalised under the Queen's rule. Jake McCrimmon, agent of the American Special Congress, investigated the aftermath.

The Nineteenth Century

Lord Aldbourne formed a branch of the Hellfire Club and played at devil worship.[818] The Doctor brought the ornithologist James Bond to the 1800s to see a live Dodo.[819] **The Doctor met Beethoven.**[820] He learned tracking skills from the Arapaho tribe, who were experts in pursuing buffalo across the American plains.[821]

Mind parasites, the Racht, germinated throughout space via "seed discs". One such disc infected a town in Norfolk in the 1800s; the fifth Doctor and Nyssa cleansed the populace, but the seed disc went missing.[822]

> (=) By this time, Katsura Sato had conquered the Earth. He renamed the world Dhakan.[823]

A sentient planet birthed grub-creatures that ravaged her resources and returned nothing. The planet then birthed a warrior race, the Metatraxi, to eliminate the grubs. The Metatraxi developed a highly refined sense of honour and left their homeworld, returning only to supply their Great Mother planet with minerals. Some grubs survived, off world.[824]

1800 (December) - FOREIGN DEVILS[825] **->** The Emperor became sickened by the foreign-sponsored opium trade afflicting China, and ordered the removal of all "foreign devils". The Chief Astrologer to the Emperor placed a curse on one such opium trader, Roderick Upcott. The curse was designed to first endow the Upcott family with prosperity, making their inevitable downfall all the more crushing.

The TARDIS arrived in China, and while the second Doctor was caught up with local politics, Jamie and Zoe disappeared through a "spirit gate" - a stone ring traditionally designed to keep demons at bay. The Doctor realised

the gate was a teleporter and used the TARDIS to follow his companions to 1900.

> **(=) 1804 - THE MAN IN THE VELVET MASK**[826] **->** The first Doctor and Dodo arrived on Earth, which had been remade ten years ago by a world-machine. The dwarf Minski, in control of the remade France, attempted to start a war between France, Britain and America that would spread a virus. Anyone infected would have fallen under Minski's control. Minski's plan fell to ruin and he was killed. Dodo acquired Minski's virus while sleeping with an actor named Dalville, but the virus was harmless without its creator. The Doctor and the real Marquis de Sade sabotaged the world-machine, and the machine's creators returned Earth to N-Space, erasing this history.

c 1805 (November) - THE RISING NIGHT[827] **->** In Thornton Rising, Yorkshire, the last of the Baobhan Sith was freed from its cairn. Its spaceship projected a force field that trapped the locals within, and kept the sun at bay. Three weeks later, the tenth Doctor confronted the Baobhan as it infected other women with its taint and started slaughtering the men of the town. The Doctor deactivated the force field, slaying those with Baobhan DNA via exposure to ultraviolet. A tainted young woman named Charity survived, and the Doctor - possibly after a few side-adventures with her - relocated Charity to a planet where the sun never rose.

Events in Thornton Rising were attributed to the Devil's work, and that the village was removed from all the maps of the kingdom, as if it had never existed.

1805 - TIMEH: THE CLOCKWORK WOMAN[828] **->** The time travellers Honoré Lechasseur and Emily Blandish helped a clockwork woman named Dove - the creation of Sir Edward Fanshawe, a genius builder - to become self-actualised. Dove was influenced by the writings of Mary Wollstonecraft, and pledged to become a writer who advocated gender equality.

Nelson "was a personal friend" of the Doctor.[829] The Doctor breakfasted with Nelson in 1805, the day before Nelson's final battle with Napoleon at Trafalgar.[830] The

---

825 Dating *Foreign Devils* (TEL #5) - It's "December 1800" (p22).
826 Dating *The Man in the Velvet Mask* (MA #19) - The Doctor and Dodo see a poster that gives a date of "Messidor, Year XII", and the Doctor calculates that they are in "June or July 1804".
827 Dating *The Rising Night* (BBC *DW* audiobook #4) - The Doctor guesses that it's the seventeenth or early eighteenth century; the back cover says that it's the

eighteenth. It's said that the Baobhan is freed in October, and the Doctor arrives three weeks later, so it's quite possibly November by now.
828 Dating *TimeH: The Clockwork Woman* (TimeH #3) - The year is given.
829 *The Sea Devils.* Nelson lived 1758-1805.
830 *Eye of Heaven.* Nelson's final battle occurred on 21st October, 1805.

Doctor was "instrumental" at Trafalgar.[831] His sextant calculated the position of Napoleon's fleet.[832]

1805 (12th September) - WORLD GAME[833] **->** The second Doctor and Serena narrowly saved Wellington and Nelson when Valmont, one of the immortal Players, attempted to kill them with a bomb.

The Doctor and Serena travelled to Paris to discover more about the Players' plans. They saved Napoleon from assassination, and learned that another Player, the Countess, was also in Paris. The Doctor learned that Napoleon had a secret weapon - a submarine - and in part survived a vampire assassin because of all the garlic he'd been eating since arriving in France. The Countess had designed the submarine's omega drive propulsion system, and had tasked a Raston Warrior Robot to serve as a guard. When this vanished, the Doctor deduced that someone on Gallifrey had sent the Robot and the vampire. The Doctor and Serena sabotaged the submarine, but with no more

leads to the Players' grand plan, they departed for 1815.

An original painting by Turner would come to adorn Irving Braxiatel's study.[834]

(=) 1806 - SEASONS OF FEAR[835] **->** The eighth Doctor and Charley confronted the long-lived Grayle once again. This time, Grayle built a transmat and brought his masters, the Nimon, to Earth. The Doctor engineered a time corridor that returned the Nimon to Britain in 305 BC.

Albert Tiermann was the son of a successful writer, but had no imagination of his own. As part of his plan to trap the Doctor, the Demon working for the Hornets granted Tiermann an imagination in return for implanting a shard of ice in his heart. The Demon also created a hotel in the Murgin Pass.[836]

Golems were unthinking lifeforms/killing machines

831 *The Scarlet Empress*
832 "Fire and Brimstone"
833 Dating *World Game* (PDA #74) - The date is given, and is indeed the only day Nelson and Wellington met historically.
834 *Benny: The Medusa Effect*. This presumably denotes *The Battle of Trafalgar* by J.M.W. Turner (1775-1851), painted in 1806, and currently owned by the Tate Gallery in London.
835 Dating *Seasons of Fear* (BF #30) - The date is given.
836 "Forty years" before *Demon Quest: A Shard of Ice*.
837 Twenty years before *The Beast of Orlok*.
838 "About two hundred years" before *The Raincloud Man*.
839 "Two hundred years" before *Planet of the Dead*. There is no International Gallery in real life, but we see it again in *SJA: Mona Lisa's Revenge*.
840 "Two hundred years" before *SJA: Eye of the Gorgon*.
841 According to a gravestone in *The Curse of Fenric*.
842 *Managra*. This happened to one of the first three Doctors.
843 "The Forgotten"
844 *The Pit*
845 *The Eye of the Tyger*, which sounds like a different visit to the one seen in *The Pit*.
846 *Hornets' Nest: The Stuff of Nightmares*
847 *Night of the Humans* (p16). Pond lived 1767 to 1836, and served as Astronomer Royal from 1811 to 1835.
848 *The Devil Goblins from Neptune*. Other references to meeting the Duke of Wellington around this time appear in *The Tomorrow Windows*, *Synthespians™* and *The Book of the Still*.
849 *The War Games*
850 *Day of the Daleks*. The Doctor does not meet Napoleon in *The Reign of Terror* (although Ian and

Barbara do). The third Doctor is still exiled in the twentieth century timezone, so he must have met Napoleon in an earlier incarnation (see *Mother Russia* and *World Game*). Napoleon lived 1769-1821. The meeting is also mentioned in *Escape Velocity* and *Warmonger*.
851 *The Impossible Astronaut*. Napoleon lived 1769-1821.
852 *TW: Greeks Bearing Gifts*. Mary is evidently from the same race as the peaceful "star poet" seen in *SJA: Invasion of the Bane*, which suggests that - as Mary speculates in the *Torchwood* episode - her planet has undergone a regime change.
853 Dating *Emotional Chemistry* (EDA #66) - The date is given in the blurb.
854 Dating "The Time of My Life" (*DWM* #399) - Jonathan Morris' behind-the-scenes notes in *The Widow's Curse* graphic novel specifies that this scene originated from a pitch of his where "Napoleon attacks Moscow with nuclear bombs". The resolution to this dilemma is never told, but said temporal interference is presumably (but not necessarily) erased from history.
855 *Loups-Garoux*
856 Dating *Mother Russia* (BF CC #2.1) - As the back cover says, "it's 1812". The Doctor's party is said to lodge with Nikitin for some "weeks" before Napoleon marches on Moscow and the battle of Borodino, which occurred on 7th September. Steven claims that it's "spring" when the TARDIS arrives, but that would mean that the TARDIS crew spends entire months with Nikitin, so he's probably just estimating and it's actually summer.
Troublingly, the historical 1812 fire of Moscow and the withdrawal of Napoleon's troops from the city (concurrent with the arrival of winter, which is why it starts snowing in the final scene) are here conflated into the same day. In real life, the fire occurred 14th-18th

crafted from virtually indestructible aluminosilicate; many civilised worlds and Article 12 of the Galactic Code outlawed them. Experiments were undertaken to create intelligent Golems that could integrate themselves into a society. A humanoid-looking boy and girl Golem were birthed, but one of their creators had a crisis of conscience and sent them away in a spaceship.

In the quiet German town of Orlok, Baron Teufel had systematically dismembered fourteen people as part of experiments on the reanimation of human tissue using electricity - the savage deaths were attributed to the fabled "Beast of Orlok". The spaceship with the young Golems arrived in the Black Forest near Orlok, just as the Baron attempted to make a local, Frau Tod, his fifteenth victim. She permanently blinded the Baron and claimed the Golems as her own children, naming them Hans and Greta. The Baron left town.[837]

The Tabbalac were an orange-skinned, aggressive species who could innately sense lies by reading body language, and were skilled at matter transmission. One Tabbalac - a technical genius who feared that his government would use his talents for killing - adopted the name "Brooks" and escaped his homeworld by building a casino boat, The High Straights, that teleported from planet to planet. The casino served an elite clientele, and another of Brooks' inventions, the reality-warping High Stakes table, enabled patrons to bet such abstract commodities as their youth, skills, emotions and their very history.[838]

The Cup of Aethelstan was put on display in the International Gallery in London.[839] One of the surviving Gorgons possessed an Abbess.[840] Joseph Sundvig was born on 8th April, 1809.[841] The Doctor met Byron at the Parthenon, and had an episode with him that involved five oranges, a purple handkerchief and a misplaced nostrum. He also met Percy Shelley.[842] A squad of Parisian soldiers were lost in the Catacombs in 1810. They found themselves in 2000.[843]

In 1811, the poet William Blake vanished from his home and met the Doctor.[844] The Doctor also met William Blake at home once.[845] William Blake was a personal friend of the fourth Doctor.[846] The Doctor said that John Pond, the Astronomer Royal, was a "lovely chap" who once told him a filthy joke.[847] The Doctor was with a British rifle brigade when he met Sir Arthur Wellesley. He was a prisoner of the French at Salamanca in 1812.[848]

Also in 1812, a battlefield from Napoleon's Russian campaign was kidnapped by the War Lords.[849] The Doctor met Napoleon and told him that an army marches on its stomach.[850] The Doctor kept a bottle that Napoleon threw at him. He later drank it in 2011 with Amy, Rory and River Song on the shore of Lake Silencio.[851]

In 1812, the alien criminal "Mary" arrived on Earth. She would later claim to hail from a savage, repressive world that punished dissent with death. The beings there communicated with pendants that granted telepathy. Mary killed the guard escorting her, and hosted herself within a passing young woman.[852]

1812 - EMOTIONAL CHEMISTRY[853] -> The Magellans were essentially living stars. One such creature broke a rule among its kind by giving birth; its child was named Aphrodite. The Doctor acted as defence council when the Magellan was put on trial. The Magellan's people ruled to spilt the creature in half and place each part in separate time zones on Earth. The emotional side of the Magellan became the female Dusha, and by the early nineteenth century had been adopted by Count Yuri Vishenkov. The Magellan's intellectual half became Lord General Razum Kinzhal, a strategist around the year 5000. Aphrodite was contained and given the extra-dimensional locale of Paraiso as her home.

Living as a Russian noblewoman, Dusha Vishenkov had the ability to alter probability and affected her "sister" Natasha Vishenkov. Natasha's descendants would look virtually identical for millennia to come, and be predisposed to good luck. Dusha's influence also turned the Vishenkov family's possessions into empathic capacitors that amplified the emotions of those nearby. One such item, a painting, would be on display in the Kremlin Museum in 2024 and start a fire there.

The eighth Doctor helped Dusha reunite with her lover, Kinzhal, in the year 5000.

(=) 1812 - "The Time of My Life"[854] -> The tenth Doctor and Donna found that time had been interfered with, and that Napoleon's troops were attacking Cossacks with impulse weapons.

Illeana (later Illeana de Santos) fled with her wealthy merchant father from Smolensk, but bandits killed her father. The werewolf Stubbe turned her into a werewolf and bound her to him for a century or two.[855]

1812 (summer to 18th October) - MOTHER RUSSIA[856] -> The first Doctor, Steven and Dodo spent some time at the home of Count Gregori Nikitin, where the Doctor tutored Nikitin's son. A spaceship carrying an infiltration unit - one designed to adopt the form of an enemy's leaders to assassinate them - crashed to Earth and impersonated the Doctor just prior to Napoleon's invasion of Russia. The disguised unit served as an advisor to Napoleon once he'd captured Moscow. The public set fire to the city rather than surrender it - Napoleon withdrew, and a Russian mob killed the infiltration unit.

While on the Russian front, Napoleon had coffee with Iris Wildthyme.[857] The Celestial Toymaker beat Napoleon at Risk.[858]

c 1813 - THE MARK OF THE RANI[859] **->** The Rani was present during the Industrial Revolution, extracting a chemical from human brains. Her project was interrupted by the arrival, and rivalry, of the Master and the sixth Doctor. The Master attempted to disrupt human history as the greatest scientific minds of the era converged on Killingworth. The Doctor trapped the two renegades in the Rani's TARDIS and banished them from Earth.

1814 (February) - FROSTFIRE[860] **->** The first Doctor, Steven and Vicki arrived at the last-ever frost fair - literally a fair situated upon ice - on the River Thames. Captain McClavity owned a Collection of Curiosities there, as well as a phoenix egg that he had acquired from the Medina in Tunis. The travellers encountered Jane Austen, much to the Doctor's delight, as he had read all of her novels and thought them very witty. Soon afterwards, McClavity was murdered and the phoenix egg stolen.

The phoenix inside the egg had been responsible for the destruction of a thousand worlds, and now sought to be reborn on Earth. Its essence possessed Georgina Mallard, whose husband - Sir Joseph Mallard - worked for the Royal Mint. The phoenix hoped to use the Mint's metal-melting furnace as a hatchery for itself, but Austen assisted the Doctor's group in turning down the heat. The newly hatched phoenix chick died, but a cinder from the fire - endowed with a small piece of the phoenix's being - remained in Vicki. She only learned of its presence after she left the Doctor's company and became Lady Cressida.

Iris and Jane Austen visited the Moulin Rouge - not the one in Paris, but a space station near Betelgeuse.[861]

The Doctor helped River Song celebrate her birthday on a frozen Thames in 1814, at the last of the great frost fairs. Entertainment was provided by Stevie Wonder, who didn't realise the Doctor had brought him back in time.[862]

1815 (June) - WORLD GAME[863] **->** Using psychic paper, the second Doctor gatecrashed a ball being held by Wellington, and warned him of the Players' plans. Serena died saving Wellington from an assassination attempt.

The Doctor impersonated Napoleon in order to infiltrate the French lines at Waterloo and divert reinforcements arranged by the Players. History was returned to its

September, but Napoleon's troops didn't withdraw until a month later, on 18th-19th October. It's possible that Napoleon have left sooner in the *Doctor Who* universe than in real-life - but mid-September still seems a bit early for snow, even for Moscow.

The fifth Doctor recalls witnessing Napoleon's invasion of Russia in *Loups-Garoux*, and that the occassion had stormy weather - retroactively, this could be taken as a reference to *Mother Russia*.

857 *Iris: The Panda Invasion*

858 "End Game" (*DWM*)

859 Dating *The Mark of the Rani* (22.3) - The date is never stated on screen or in the script, but *DWM* reported that the production team felt that the story was set in "1830". *The Terrestrial Index* set the story "c1825", the novelisation simply said "the beginning of the nineteenth century". Tony Scupham-Bilton concluded in *Celestial Toyroom* that, judging by the historical evidence and the month the story was filmed, the story was "set in either October 1821 or October 1822". As that article states, the story must at the very least be set before the Stockton-Darlington line was opened in September 1825, and after Thomas Liddell was made Baron Ravensworth on 17th July, 1821. However, Jane Baker later told *DWM* that her research was confused by the Victorian convention of biographies referring to Lords by their titles even before they were given them. Given that, Jim Smith in *Who's Next* suggested that the date given in *DWM* was a mishearing of "1813", which fits all the evidence apart from the existence of Lord

Ravensworth.

860 Dating *Frostfire* (BF CC #1.1) - The year is given. Historically, the last River Thames frost fair started on 1st February, 1814, and only lasted four days. The issue of whether the first Doctor only had one heart or not is complicated by the phoenix's comment about the cold "in the Doctor's hearts". As Austen claims, she had only published two novels by 1814: *Sense and Sensibility* (1811) and *Pride and Prejudice* (1813). *Mansfield Park*, her third book, saw print in July 1814.

861 *Iris: The Panda Invasion*. Austen lived 1775 to 1817.

862 *A Good Man Goes to War*

863 Dating *World Game* (PDA #74) - The Doctor arrives on the eve of the Battle of Waterloo, so therefore it's 17th June, 1815.

864 *The Dying Days*. His first name and rank were given in *The Scales of Injustice*.

865 *The Eye of the Jungle*

866 *The Eight Doctors*

867 Dating *World Game* (PDA #74) - The date is given.

868 *Players*, almost certainly the same meeting mentioned in *The Eight Doctors*. The bank account is also mentioned in *World Game*.

869 *The Land of the Dead*

870 Dating *The Company of Friends*: "Mary's Story" (BF #123d) - "It was 1816," says Mary, later adding that it was "one dreary night in June". Interestingly, Mary *was* calling herself "Mary Shelley" (as opposed to "Mary Godwin", her maiden name) by this point, even though she and Percy weren't actually married. They wouldn't

normal course and the Players - worried about further intervention from the Time Lords - suspended their games.

Major General Fergus Lethbridge-Stewart fought in the Battle of Waterloo.[864] Oliver Blazington, later a big game hunter, was a rifleman who fought alongside the Duke of Wellington at Waterloo.[865] The Doctor met Wellington after the conflict.[866]

(=) 1815 (18th November) - WORLD GAME[867]
-> The second Doctor and Serena arrived in a Paris that was celebrating a great victory over the British and Wellington's mysterious death. The Doctor and Serena first travelled fifty years into the future - to see the end result of the Countess' Grand Design - then went into the past to prevent it happening.

In 1816, the Doctor visited the Duke of Wellington, and made a lot of money at a gambling den. He set up an account at Chumley's Bank that he occasionally dipped into while on Earth.[868] The Doctor was present when Peter the Great sent an expedition to Alaska.[869]

1816 (June) - THE COMPANY OF FRIENDS: "Mary's Story"[870] -> A temporal storm infected the TARDIS and the eighth Doctor with corrosive "vitreous time". He arrived, charred and misshapen, at the Villa Diodati at Lake Geneva, 1816, just as Lord Byron challenged his friends - Mary and Percy Shelley, Mary's step-sister Claire and John William Polidori - to each write a ghost story. The Doctor muttered, "Dr Frankenstein", lay injured for a week and appeared to have died. Percy suggested they test

whether an electro-static spark could make his body twitch, as had been reported with frog's legs. The experiment revived the Doctor, and he wandered off.

Mary found the Doctor in his ransacked TARDIS. An earlier version of the eighth Doctor answered his later self's distress call after dropping Samson and Gemma off in Vienna. The younger Doctor activated the TARDIS' self-repair systems, which healed his older self via their symbiotic link. The older Doctor left, and Mary accepted the younger one's offer to become his travelling companion.

The Doctor tried to relocate the TARDIS in space, not time, to reunite with Samson and Gemma in Vienna... but he and Mary instead found themselves in that city in 1873.[871] The Doctor and Mary travelled together for years, encountering foes such as Cybermen and Axons.[872] Mary eventually ended her travels with the Doctor, and returned home to be with her soul mate, Percy Shelley.[873]

1818 - THE GHOSTS OF N-SPACE[874] -> Travelling back in time, the third Doctor and Sarah witnessed the early life of the wizard Maximillian.

In the early nineteenth century, the Doctor met Beau Brummel, who told him he looked better in a cloak.[875]

A Dalek scoutship crashed on the planet Vulcan. By this time, the Daleks had already encountered the second Doctor.[876] The Dalek ship was from the far future.[877]

The Beast of Fang Rock was seen.[878] The Reverend Thomas Bright surveyed the Nine Travellers. At some point between now and the late twentieth century, Cessair posed as Mrs Trefusis for sixty years, then

---

wed until late 1816, after his first wife killed herself. The Doctor having familiarity with Byron, Mary Shelley and/or the night that *Frankenstein* was created was also mentioned in *Storm Warning*, *Neverland*, *Zagreus* and *Terror Firma*. *Managra* mentions a separate incident involving the Doctor, Byron and Percy Shelley.

871 *The Silver Turk*
872 *The Company of Friends:* "Mary's Story"
873 The epilogue to *Army of Death* has Mary deciding to ask the Doctor to take her home. That story also implies, however, that they've only experienced events in *The Silver Turk*, *The Witch from the Well*, *Army of Death* and a side trip to the planet Mayhem. Given that she and the Doctor travel together for "years" (*The Company of Friends:* "Mary's Story"), perhaps she reconsiders for a time, or she goes home for a bit and travels with him again.
874 Dating *The Ghosts of N-Space* (MA #7) - It is "eighteen eighteen" (p63), one hundred and fifty-seven years before the present-day setting (p200).
875 The Doctor mentions Beau Brummel in *The Sensorites*, *The Twin Dilemma* and *The Two Doctors*.

Brummel lived 1778-1840. He was an arbiter of fashion in Regency England, and helped further the style known as "dandyism".
876 The Dalek ship crashed "two hundred years" before *The Power of the Daleks*. This is the first recorded Dalek expedition in our solar system assuming, of course, that Vulcan is (or was) in our solar system. *War of the Daleks* states that this capsule is from the far future (after *Remembrance of the Daleks*), and this fits some of the circumstantial evidence - a Dalek from this mission recognises the Doctor, despite his regeneration (and despite no recorded adventures with any Doctor - except for *Genesis of the Daleks* - up to this point). In *Day of the Daleks*, the Daleks must use the Mind Analysis Machine to establish the Doctor's identity. On the other hand, the Daleks are silver and blue, and dependent on external power supplies - quite unlike the Davros Era Daleks.
877 *War of the Daleks*
878 "Eighty years" before *Horror of Fang Rock*.

Senora Camara.[879]

On 3rd July, 1820, Florence Sundvig was born.[880] Napoleon died in 1821, still traumatised by what he had witnessed in the Great Pyramid in 1798.[881]

In 1826, the *Camara* was lost in the Irish Sea after snaring a stone "demon" in its nets.[882] James Fenimore Cooper struck a deal to include Chingachgook, an actual Mohican, as a fictional character in his writings.[883] Mary Shelley's *The Last Man* was published in 1826.[884]

1827 - THE BEAST OF ORLOK[885] -> General Zoff, the commander-in-chief of the Radzera Planetary League, now possessed Golems that were halfway between mindless brutes and the "civilised" versions represented by Hans Tod and his "sister" Greta. Hoping to create an army of the enhanced versions, Zoff tracked Hans and Greta across sixty thousand light years to Earth.

Baron Teufel returned to Orlok, and a Golem under Zoff's command killed him, which enabled Zoff to adopted Teufel's form using a "metamorphiser". The eighth Doctor and Lucie visited Orlok by mistake after the TARDIS entirely failed to materialise in Alton Towers. The Doctor destroyed Zoff's Golem and Orlok Castle in the process. Zoff's people made him suffer a humiliating loss of rank, and Hans and Greta remained on Earth.

1827 - THE EYE OF THE JUNGLE[886] -> The eleventh Doctor, Amy and Rory found themselves in the Amazon rain forest, and confronted the Nadurni: aliens who were harvesting animals to transform into biological weapons for a war effort. The big game hunter Oliver Blazington, who was aiding an expedition to collect animals for the opening of the London zoo, was hideously transformed by the Nadurni's experiments. He attacked his tormentors, and died as their space station was destroyed.

(=) c 1827-1828 - MEDICINAL PURPOSES[887] -> A human researcher from the future acquired a Type 70 TARDIS from a Nekkistani dealer of Gryben, and a dying alien race employed him to research a virus that was killing them. The aliens' immune systems resembled those of humans, so the researcher set up shop in Edinburgh, 1827. He took the guise of "Dr. Robert Knox", the anatomist who employed the graverobbers William Burke and William Hare to provide cadavers for study. Not content with unearthing corpses, Burke and Hare started murdering people to fulfill Knox's demands.

Knox infected some Edinburgh residents with the alien virus, but anyone who consumed alcohol proved immune. Failing to make progress, Knox used his illicit technology to roll back time in Edinburgh

---

879 *The Stones of Blood*

880 *The Curse of Fenric*

881 *The Sands of Time* (p220). The year is given, and Napoleon died 5th May, 1821.

882 "Seaside Rendezvous"

883 *The Silent Stars Go By*. Chingachgook (misspelled here as "Chingachook") appeared in Fenimore Cooper's *Leatherstocking Tales*, published from 1826 to 1841.

884 The liner notes to *Army of Death* hint that this book was inspired by Mary's trip to the planet Draxine, and her encountering an army of skeletons there.

885 Dating *The Beast of Orlok* (BF BBC7 #3.3) - The year is given. Greta says that she and Hans can't leave Earth because Frau Tod will kill them if they "weren't home for Christmas", and she makes an "early gift" to the Doctor by returning his sonic screwdriver - but the statements are offhanded enough that the story doesn't necessarily take place in winter.

886 Dating *The Eye of the Jungle* (BBC *DW* audiobook #13) - The year is given in the blurb, and when the Doctor whispers to his companions, "Ahhh... this is 1827, the year before London Zoo opens".

887 Dating *Medicinal Purposes* (BF #60) - The back cover says 1827. Burke and Hare met the real Knox in November 1827, but the majority of their murders occurred throughout 1828, until they were caught in November of that year. The audio concurs with the historical date for Burke's execution. Hare was granted immunity because he turned King's Evidence against

Burke. The real Knox was never prosecuted.

888 *The Eye of the Jungle*. The zoo opened on 27th April, 1828, at first as a collection for benefit of scientists. It opened to the public in 1847.

889 *Assassin in the Limelight*

890 "Three years" before *Hornets' Nest: The Circus of Doom*.

891 *The Stealers from Saiph*

892 *Timeless*

893 *Reckless Engineering*

894 *The Haunting of Thomas Brewster*

895 Dating *Hornets' Nest: The Circus of Doom* (BBC fourth Doctor audio #1.3) - The Hornets told the Doctor they met "over a hundred years ago" in *Hornets' Nest: The Dead Shoes*. It's "June" and "1832" according to the Doctor here. The CD sleeve includes a *Radio Times* entry saying it's "1832", and a letter from Sally's father - dated "15th June 1832" - warning against the circus.

896 "One hundred seventy-six years" before *Voyage of the Damned*.

897 Dating *Bloodtide* (BF #22) - The date is given.

898 "These past ten years" before *Demon Quest: A Shard of Ice*.

899 *Cuddlesome*. William Webb Ellis is the alleged inventor of rugby, and lived 1806-1872.

900 *Sometime Never*

901 "Three years" before "The Curious Tale of Spring-Heeled Jack".

and start with "new" bodies. He grew ambivalent toward his employers' survival, and turned the enterprise into an elite tourist attraction, with patrons paying to witness the "Hale and Burke Experience". The memories of the locals grew cloudy as time repeatedly looped. The sixth Doctor and Evelyn arrived inside of Knox's time loop, and discovered his operations.

The Doctor was at the opening of the London Zoo.[888]

On 28th January, 1829, the Doctor and Evelyn observed Burke's public hanging. The Doctor tricked Knox into leaving his time loop and infected him with the alien virus. Knox fled in his TARDIS, and history was restored to its proper path. The Doctor and Evelyn took the mentally disabled "Daft Jamie", who was fated to become one of Burke and Hare's victims, back to meet his appointed demise.

Knox was dying from a flu virus that he'd contracted in Edinburgh. He found an emotion-eating Indo in a crater of congealed iron magma on Mercury - in exchange for the Indo extending Knox's lifespan, Knox agreed to facilitate the creature feasting upon the emotions of John Wilkes Booth, one of history's most famous assassins, in 1865.[889]

Francesca Farrow ran away with the Circus of Delights in 1829 and became its bearded lady.[890] Octopoid psychovores, the Saiph, inhabited a planet of the same name in the constellation of Orion. In 1829, some of their number relocated to Earth after a cosmic storm struck their satellite. The Saiph reverted to protoplasm, and were nourished by the minerals in a cave near Antibes, France.[891]

In early May 1830, the time traveller Chloe and her dog Jamais happened upon Sabbath in St. Raphael, France. She sensed part of his history but fell unconscious. When she awoke, Sabbath had left her a diamond and a book purporting to speak of the future. Her belief in the book allowed Sabbath to manipulate her activities.[892]

(=) In 1831, energy beings from the Eternium, a doomed pocket universe, manipulated the aspiring poet Jared Malahyde to work on the Utopian Engine: a device intended to temporally age Earth to extinction. The Eternines wanted to harvest the life force energy released by Earth's demise. Malahyde partnered with architect Isambard Kingdom Brunel, and they pioneered the Malahyde Process, a means of developing superior steel. Malahyde spent the next twelve years working on the Utopian Engine.[893]

The TARDIS arrived in 1831 on the fifth Doctor's preset instructions, having travelled from an alternate version of 2008. The Ship buried itself in the muck of the Thames, and remained inert for thirty-four years.[894]

1832 (June) - HORNET'S NEST THE CIRCUS OF DOOM[895] **->** The fourth Doctor arrived in Blandford and learned from a shop assistant, Sally, that the strange Circus of Delights had come to town. Almost the whole population watched the show until two in the morning, amazed by the lion act and the Clown Funeral. An Italian dwarf, Antonio, served as ringmaster. The Doctor met Dr Adam Farrow, who was looking for his sister Francesca.

On the second night, all the villagers returned to watch the show again, and the Doctor discovered that the Hornets had both possessed Antonio and infiltrated the entire circus. Various villagers were compelled to join the circus and perform incredible acts.

The Doctor realised that the withered feet he'd seen in the ballet shoes in the future belonged to Francesca. He hypnotised Antonio to learn of the dwarf's history - and was shocked to find that the Hornets had somehow used the TARDIS to take control of him, an event that had not happened yet in the Doctor's timeline. The Hornets swarmed out of Antonio. Francesca was killed, but the Doctor left with Antonio's body, now in stasis.

Farrow took his sister's body and had it embalmed. Eventually, only her feet survived, still in their ballet shoes.

Max Capricorn started running Max Capricorn Cruiseliners in 1832.[896]

1835 - BLOODTIDE[897] **->** The sixth Doctor took Evelyn to meet Charles Darwin, her personal hero, in the Galapagos Islands. They learned of "devil creatures" on the island, identifying them as Silurians. The Doctor confronted their leader, the renegade scientist Tulok, who planned to wipe out all human life with a virus. The Doctor tricked the Silurians' Myrka into destroying a Silurian submersible, which killed Tulok before he could launch his bacterial warheads. The Doctor suggested that Darwin not mention the Silurians in his writing.

Albert Tiermann began entertaining the blind King with stories.[898] The Doctor took tackling lessons from Webb Ellis.[899] In May 1837, in the Pyrenees, the archaeologist Louis Vosgues stood on the verge of formulating the theory of evolution years before Darwin. An Agent of the Council of Eight ensured that Vosgues fell off a cliff to his death.[900] The killer Springheeled Jack was first reported in London in 1837.[901]

The Victorian Era

The Doctor attended the coronation of Queen Victoria.[902] In the 1840s, a tenant farmer who tried to flatten the tumulus on Lanyon Moor died of a heart attack. The crops nearby failed for the next seven years.[903]

Professor Litefoot's Chinese fowling piece was last fired around this time.[904] The Doctor met Brunel.[905] He also gave Hans Christian Andersen the idea for "The Emperor's New Clothes".[906] The International Gallery took possession of Guieseppe di Cattivo's works in Victorian times.[907] Benny, Jason and Peter, in fleeing from a party of time-travelling Grel, stopped off in Victorian times. The Grel took the opportunity to test their Great Grel Gun, and atomized a group of schoolgirls.[908]

(=) It was possible that an alternate version of Benny and her friend Ruth survived in a Victorian London created by the Epoch.[909]

1840 - "The Curious Tale of Spring-Heeled Jack"[910]**->** The eighth Doctor investigated the case of Springheeled Jack, who had apparently been assaulting young women in London. He discovered that Jack was innocent, and the killings had been performed by the alien Morjanus, a bitter rival of Jack's race. Morjanus released the fire-beings named the Pyrodines, and the Doctor destroyed them. Jack remained in London to fight crime.

An alien race, on the verge of losing a war, had long ago seeded its DNA into space in millions of head-shaped *moai*. The aliens' rivals killed them, but the *moai* distributed the DNA like a virus, creating hybrids of the aliens on multiple worlds. On Earth, such *moai* had settled on Rapa Nui (also known as Easter Island) and turned some Polynesians into alien hybrids. But in October 1842, Horace Stockwood's expedition to the island carried a disease that would kill off the hybrids.[911] The Welsh town of Dinorben mysteriously emptied overnight. Goibhnie had taken the people to populate a town on the world of Tír na n-Óg.[912]

In 1843, the first Doctor and Susan met Sherlock Holmes' father, Siger Holmes, in India and learnt that the natives believed in a gateway to another world.[913]

(=) **1843 - RECKLESS ENGINEERING**[914] **->** The Eternine gambit reached fruition in 1843, when Malahyde activated the Utopian Engine. The eighth Doctor's intervention meant that instead of aging Earth to death, the device advanced time on the
---

902 *The Curse of Peladon.* Victoria was crowned in 1838.
903 *The Spectre of Lanyon Moor*
904 According to Professor Litefoot in *The Talons of Weng-Chiang*, the gun "hasn't been fired for fifty years".
905 *The Two Doctors.* The architect Isambard Kingdom Brunel lived 1806-1859, and also features in *Reckless Engineering*.
906 *The Romans*
907 *SJA: Mona Lisa's Revenge*
908 *Benny: The Grel Escape*
909 *Benny: Epoch: Judgement Day.* Bernice wonders if it's the "eighteenth or nineteenth century", the blurb says it's "Victorian London". It's not clear, however, if *this* Victorian London coincides with the genuine article, or is in another era per the Epoch's machinations.
910 Dating "The Curious Case of Spring-Heeled Jack" (*DWM* #334-336) - The date "1840" is given.
911 *Eye of Heaven.* The date of Stockwood's first expedition is given (p1).
912 "A hundred and fifty years" (p222) before *Cat's Cradle: Witch Mark*.
913 *All-Consuming Fire*
914 Dating *Reckless Engineering* (EDA #63) - The date is given as "19 July 1843" (p5).
915 *The Church and the Crown*
916 According to *The Tomorrow Windows. The Unquiet Dead*, on the other hand, certainly presents itself as the first meeting between them.
917 *The Death of Art*

918 *The Haunting of Thomas Brewster* suggests that Brewster is about four or five in 1851. Even Brewster is unclear about this, however, as "it's hard to judge [your age] when you have no birthdays."
919 Dating *Demon Quest: A Shard of Ice* (BBC fourth Doctor audio #2.3) - Tiermann says "the year was 1847".
920 No year given, but Eleanor is a child when this happens, and seems middle-aged (actress Joanna Monro was 54 when she played the adult Eleanor) in *J&L: The Man at the End of the Garden*.
921 Dating *Nevermore* (BF BBC7 #4.3) - The Doctor says his meeting with Poe occurred "three days" prior to the man's death, although technically, Poe was found delirious on the Baltimore streets on 3rd October, 1849, and died on October 7th.
922 *The Algebra of Ice* (p8-11).
923 *FP: The Book of the War.* From the original Cwej's perspective, this happens some time after *Benny: Twilight of the Gods*.
924 Fifteen years prior to *Other Lives*.
925 "Nine years" before *A Town Called Fortune*
926 *The Next Doctor*
927 "Ten years" before *Serpent Crest: The Broken Crown*.
928 Dating *The Haunting of Thomas Brewster* (BF #107) - The year is given.

planet's surface forty years. This created an alternate timeline in which an estimated 95% of mature humans and animals either aged to death or died from shock. Humanity's children, suddenly aged to adulthood, became savage creatures of instinct named the Wildren. The remaining pockets of civilisation struggled to survive in disparate settlements. In some parts, cannibalism became acceptable.

In 1844, the Doctor helped Alexandre Dumas with *The Three Musketeers*.[915] The Doctor met Charles Dickens.[916] Dickens' work became far darker in tone after he encountered Montague's killer dolls in 1845.[917] Thomas Brewster, a companion of the fifth and sixth Doctors, was born in or around 1846.[918]

1847 (winter) - DEMON QUEST: A SHARD OF ICE[919] -> Writer Albert Tiermann was being rushed through the Murgin Pass for an audience with the King at his Winter Palace in San Clemence when the TARDIS materialised in front of his carriage. The fourth Doctor and Mike Yates showed Tiermann a book of his fairytales - a book which had yet to be written. Tiermann had run out of stories to tell the King, and was desperate to lay hands on the book. The lodge was menaced by a monster, which killed Hans the footman. The Doctor and Tiermann tracked the monster - the shapeshifter Demon that the Doctor encountered in Roman Britain and Paris - to its lair. The Doctor revealled that on this occasion, the Demon had assumed the guise of Albert's Queen. She had engineered the Doctor's arrival and wanted to take him to her home, called Sepulchre. The Doctor and Yates escaped her clutches, and the Doctor took Tiermann to safety, before heading back to Nest Cottage.

Tiermann related this story to his King.

A fairy-like man gave little Eleanor Maycombe a pocketbook that could make real anything she wrote within its pages. The deal required Eleanor to wake the little man up after a year and a day - but she didn't, and he slept as she grew into adulthood. The family housekeeper, Mrs Hitch, confiscated the pocketbook and in future used it to keep herself and Eleanor off parish relief.[920]

1849 (3rd October) - NEVERMORE[921] -> The eighth Doctor attended to some business in Baltimore, Maryland, and happened upon an ailing Edgar Allan Poe. He begged the Doctor to look after his "final message to the world", which he'd written on some sheets of paper he kept in a bottle. After hospital orderlies took Poe away, the Doctor found that Poe hadn't emptied the bottle before putting the paper inside - meaning the ink had run, and Poe's text now read, "[obscured] [obscured] verdigris [obscured] [obscured] manifold [obscured] a shadow over the

[obscured] [obscured] principia of the human [obscured]..." With a sigh, the Doctor poured Poe's final writings into the gutter. Poe died soon after.

(=) Time distortion threw Edgar Allen Poe's death into flux. In alternate histories, he either died in a gutter four days before history recorded or happily survived and stayed on a drinking binge. The distortion abated, and Poe expired on 7th October, 1849.[922]

w - The Great Houses' military wing established a training facility at the future site of the Japanese city of Kobe, circa 1850. Chris Cwej, already their agent, served as the template for the Army of One project and underwent mass replication. Cwej's duplicates, collectively called the Cwejen, fell into three types: the original blonde version ("Cwej-Prime"), a shorter, dark-haired version ("Cwej-Plus") and an extremely rare armoured version ("Cwej Magnus"). The original Cwej increasingly became a loner, wanting less and less to do with himself.[923]

The traveller Edward Marlow married his beloved Georgina at Camden Chapel. They lived in his uncle's house in Camden Town, and had two sons: Edward and Henry. The elder Edward explored the world and wrote about his discoveries, but went missing in 1850.[924] In Dry Creek, a town in America, Sheriff Samuel P Hayes secretly killed the prospector William Donovan over the love of a woman. The town's mayor and owner, Thaddeus Sullivan, blackmailed Hayes into keeping quiet as he stole the rights to Donovan's gold mine, and in the process renamed the town "Fortune".[925]

The Doctor considered 1851 to be a bit dull.[926] The wormhole conveying a spaceship with the cyborg child Alex, his guardian Boolin and a Skishtari gene egg overshot its intended destination and deposited them in the village of Hexford, 1851. Boolin lost his memory, and became known as "Mr Bewley". He tutored Alex, who was taken in by a rector, and made to wear a paper bag on his head to disguise his cyborg nature.[927]

1851 - THE HAUNTING OF THOMAS BREWSTER[928] -> When Thomas Brewster was four or five, his mother killed herself by jumping off the Southwark Bridge. Brewster never knew his father, and his first memory was that of his mother's funeral. Brewster's aunts and uncles blamed him for his mother's suicide, and it was decided that he should be sent to a workhouse, to be raised by the parish.

The fifth Doctor and Nyssa were briefly at the funeral, as they were trying to determine when young Brewster came under psychic influence from beings from an alternate 2008. From his mother's graveside, Brewster glimpsed the departing TARDIS.

1851 - OTHER LIVES[929] -> At the Great Exhibition of the Works of Industry of All Nations, civil unrest was threatened when two French visitors - Monsieur de Roche and his wife Madeleine - went missing. Charley and C'rizz aided the Duke of Wellington in a deception to cover up their disappearance, but the visitors had simply time-jumped ahead in the TARDIS and returned without incident. The eighth Doctor was mistaken for the absent traveller Edward Marlow, and assisted the man's wife in retaining her household. C'rizz was briefly imprisoned in a freak show and crippled its owner, Jacob Crackles.

1851 (12th September) - "Claws of the Klathi!"[930] -> The seventh Doctor landed in London at the time of the Great Exhibition, and met Nathaniel Derridge of the New Lunar Society, a scientific club. The Doctor learned that some curious murders had taken place in Docklands, and was attacked by a robot at the scene of the crime. He evaded the robot to discover a crashed spacecraft.

Nearby, the Wyndham's Freakshow included some live aliens. The Doctor met one, Caval of the Joebb, whose race was lifted out of squalor by the Klathi - ruthless aliens who were also in London. The Klathi need a large crystal to power their ship, but activating the reflective lattice would kill people over a vast area. The Doctor confronted the Klathi at Crystal Palace, but they didn't care about the human casualties. Joebb rebelled, and the aliens were killed when their spacecraft exploded.

The *America* crossed the Atlantic in seventeen days in 1851.[931] Henry Gordon Jago attended the Great Exhibition in Crystal Palace, 1851, and saw Michael Faraday demonstrate the benefits of electricity.[932] **Jackson Lake, a mathematics teacher from Sussex, arrived in London with his family to take a post at university. They encountered a group of Cybermen that had fallen through time from the Void. Lake's wife Caroline was killed, his son Frederic was abducted and Lake himself was riddled with energy from an infostamp - an device containing the Cybermen's database on the Doctor's activities. Lake believed he *was* the Doctor, and in such a capacity saved a young woman, Rosita, from the Cybermen at Osterman's Wharf.**[933]

1851 (Christmas Eve to Christmas Day) - THE NEXT DOCTOR[934] -> The tenth Doctor was surprised to encounter "the Doctor" - actually Jackson Lake - and his "companion" Rosita as they fought the Cybermen and the Cybershades, their beast-like servants. Mercy Hartigan, the matron of St Joseph's Workhouse, aided the Cybermen operating in this time zone as they built a CyberKing: a Dreadnought-class mechanoid that would be the front line of an invasion, and housed a Cyberfactory capable of converting millions. To this end, they rounded up children from workhouses to serve as a workforce.

The Cybermen Cyber-converted Miss Hartigan into the last component of the CyberKing, but her mind proved strong enough to resist total conversion, and

---

929 Dating *Other Lives* (BF #77) - The year is 1851, and the Great Exhibition was held from 1st May to 15th October. The Doctor's comment that the Exhibition did a lot of business in its "first six months" is therefore an approximation, as it was only open five and a half months total. As the Duke of Wellington claims, he would have been 82 in this story, and he died the following year.

930 Dating "Claws of the Klathi!" (*DWM* #136-138) - Derridge says it's "the twelfth of September, year of Our Lord Eighteen Hundred and Fifty-One".

931 *Enlightenment*

932 *The Mahogany Murderers*

933 "Three weeks" before *The Next Doctor*.

934 Dating *The Next Doctor* (X4.14) - An urchin tells the Doctor it's "Christmas Eve" and "the year of our Lord 1851", with the action continuing through the night to Christmas Day.

A glaring oddity is that the CyberKing here rampages across London, and destroys patches of it with heavy weaponry. Lake comments that the "events of today will be history, spoken of for centuries to come", and even though said events are wildly nonhistorical, the Doctor only comments "Funny, that". The eleventh

Doctor later implies in *Flesh and Stone* that the Cracks in Time ate away at the CyberKing, explaining why it's not recorded in the history books. (He speculates this, however, before knowing that he's going to restore everything the Cracks destroyed upon rebooting the universe in *The Big Bang*; see the Cracks in Time sidebar.) It could equally be the case, however, that the CyberKing event isn't well remembered because it happened at night (severely limiting the number of people who could have actually *seen* the CyberKing) in an era without suitable photography to record the proceedings (even had they occurred in the daytime), meaning the resultant damage was attributed to other causes or left as a mystery.

935 *The One Doctor*. Peter Roget was a physician and lexicographer who lived 1779-1869. He compiled *Roget's Thesaurus*.

936 *Cryptobiosis*. "Livingstone" is presumably David Livingstone (1813-73), the famed Scottish medical missionary and explorer of Africa (from 1852-56).

937 *State of Decay*. Grimm lived 1785-1863.

938 *Tooth and Claw* (TV). Prince Albert and Sir Robert's father seem to have begun collaborating as early as Robert's childhood, but the exact dating is unclear. The

she took control of the Cybermen. The Doctor and his allies freed the children, including Lake's son Frederic. The CyberKing emerged as a vast robot that began to stomp across London, but the Doctor confronted the CyberKing in Lake's hot air balloon, the Tethered Aerial Release Developed In Style (TARDIS). The Doctor offered to send Hartigan and her Cybermen to an uninhabited world, and when she refused, he destroyed them all. He also sent the CyberKing's remains into the Vortex, where it would disintegrate.

The Doctor stayed on to have Christmas Dinner with Jackson Lake, Frederic and Rosita.

Roget was a very good friend of the Doctor.[935] The Doctor claimed that he once told Livingstone: "That's all very well... but the elephant in the gorilla suit has to go."[936] Around this time, Jacob Grimm discovered the Law of Consonantal Shift.[937]

Albert, the Prince Consort, frequently lodged at Torchwood Estate with the father of Sir Robert MacLeish. The two of them dared to imagine that local stories about a werewolf and the brethren that protected it were true, and fashioned a trap for the beast. A light chamber was constructed, and Albert had the Koh-i-Noor, the diamond given to Victoria as spoils of war, recut to serve as the chamber's focusing device.[938]

Victoria Waterfield, a companion of the second Doctor, was born in 1852.[939] The Doctor met Thackeray, Baudelaire, Delacroix and Manet.[940] In 1853, Saul, a living church in Cheldon Bonniface, was baptised in his own font.[941]

1854 - THE FOUR DOCTORS[942] **->** The seventh Doctor visited Professor Michael Faraday, and dealt with a Dalek time corridor that ended at Faraday's laboratory at the Royal Institution of Great Britain.

On 20th September, 1854, during the Crimean War, the British readied to besiege the port city of Sevastopol. A British officer, Brigadier-General Bartholomew Kitchen, tried to avert bloodshed by inventing a story that the

Russians were preparing to surrender, causing the British fleet to hold back and according the Russians time to fortify themselves. Kitchen had expected that the British would withdraw entirely once they learned of the Russians' preparations, but the attack proceeded anyway, causing massive casualties...[943]

1854 (25th September to 19th November) - THE ANGEL OF SCUTARI[944] **->** The seventh Doctor and Ace arrived during the siege of Sevastopol on 25th September, 1854, to investigate accounts that the Doctor was a traitor to the crown. A cannonball hit the TARDIS and triggered the Ship's Hostile Action Displacement System (HADS), causing it to retreat into the Vortex to heal.

The Russians incarcerated the Doctor and Ace, and accused him of trying to signal the British fleet; Tsar Nicholas I was indifferent as to the Doctor's guilt or innocence. Ace befriended the future author Leo Tolstoy, who was currently a Russian soldier. He had lost his family home - and three hundred fifty peasants - while playing cards, and to date had only published two stories in *The Contemporary*.

On October 7th, the Doctor learned that the Tsar had authorised his execution; Ace escaped at roughly the same time. Brigadier-General Kitchen pinned his traitorous actions at Sevastopol on the Doctor, and reported to his superiors that the Russians were mistakenly executing one of their own double agents. The Doctor fulfilled causality by making sure that correspondence from Sir Hamilton Seymour - the British ambassador in St. Petersburg - to the Minister of War backed up Kitchen's claims, then escaped with Seymour's help. Ten days later, the Doctor and Ace were reunited in Kursk and summoned the TARDIS, intending to retrieve Hex from mid-November of the same year. Kitchen became unhinged upon witnessing the Ship's departure, and reported that he'd killed the Doctor.

On 17th October, the Doctor, Ace and Hex made their initial landing in this era, at the British army barracks at Scutari. William Russell, a *London Times* war correspondent, accused the Doctor of being a traitor, prompting the

---

Koh-i-Noor was presented to Queen Victoria in 1850, and Albert died 14th December, 1861. The recounting of the diamond in *Tooth and Claw* deviates a little from history - the story implies that Albert whittled down the stone through constant recuttings, when most of the lost mass was shed in a single cutting in 1852.

939 *Downtime.* Victoria was "11" (p14) when her mother died in "1863" (p261). This would make her 14 when she started travelling with the Doctor.

940 *Ghost Ship.* Novelist William Thackeray (*Vanity Fair*) lived 1811-1863; poet Charles Baudelaire 1821-1867; painter Eugéne Delacroix 1798-1863; painter Édouard Manet 1832-1883. While there's no indication these

meetings were on the same trip, it's possible.
941 *Timewyrm: Revelation* (p4).
942 Dating *The Four Doctors* (BF subscription promo #9; also numbered as #142b) - The year is given.
943 *The Angel of Scutari*
944 Dating *The Angel of Scutari* (BF #122) - The Doctor provides all of the specified dates, which historically match the siege of Sevastopol and the Charge of the Light Brigade. The attempted rescue of Hex happens "10:14 on 19th of November". The only small deviation from history is that Nightingale seems to have arrived in Scutari in early November, not mid-month.

Doctor and Ace to go back four weeks to investigate his claims and Seymour's reports. Hex remained to care for the wounded and meet his idol, Florence Nightingale, who was scheduled to arrive in about a month. The Charge of the Light Brigade occurred on 25th October.

Ten days after the Doctor and Ace departed Kursk, Kitchen was taken off active service and accompanied Nightingale to the hospital at Scutari. They arrived mid-November, and Hex met Nightingale. On 19th November, Kitchen hotly confronted Hex concerning his affiliation with the Doctor and Ace. Hex's friends arrived through time to collect him - just as Kitchen shot him. The Doctor and Ace bundled their wounded friend into the TARDIS, and set course for St. Gart's Hospital in the twenty-first century. Nightingale was left to pray, with a distraught Kitchen, for Hex's recovery.

c 1855 - "Perceptions" / "Coda"[945] -> The eighth Doctor, Stacy and Ssard helped P'fer'd and M'rek'd, two purple and yellow-spotted Equinoids stranded on Earth, to get home.

1855 (13th December) - "Cuckoo"[946] -> The seventh Doctor, Benny and Ace landed in the seaside village of Lifton, where it was rumoured the devil had shown himself. This was the location of one of the richest fossil beds in Southern England. Mary Anne Wesley was pioneering the field of paleontology at this time, despite the fact the locals disapproved. The Doctor was here to stop her, as Wesley was about to unearth the fossil of an alien - and set science back by decades as it pursued a false trail. While the Doctor and Benny met Wesley, Ace found a body on the beach. The Doctor realised that one of the Wesleys' other guests was a lizard-like shapeshifter, a Surcoth, looking to repatriate the fossilised remains of an ancient explorer. The Doctor let him leave.

The Crimean War

The Crimean War was fought 1853-1856. On 25th October, 1854, the Doctor was present at the "magnificent folly" of the Charge of the Light Brigade.[947] The Doctor claimed he had been wounded in the Crimea.[948] The War Lords lifted a Crimean War battlefield.[949]

In 1854, Theodore Maxwell experimented with electromagnetism.[950] The Ogron homeworld was discovered in 1855. From this point, the ape-like race would be used as slaves and hired muscle by more than a dozen races.[951]

Two residents of the Euphorian Empire, the artisan brothers Jude and Gabriel, travelled to Earth in 1855 via a dimensional portal. On the island of Es Vedra, the monk Francisco Belao mistook them for angels.[952]

(=) 1856 (27th January) - 100: "My Own Private Wolfgang"[953] -> The Mozart who bargained for immortality was all-too horrifyingly aware that he'd become a hack. Along with scores of time-travelling Mozart clones, the sixth Doctor and Evelyn attended a ball to celebrate Mozart's 100th birthday - and bore witness as a despondent Mozart tried and failed to kill himself on stage. Evelyn was accidentally transported to the future, while the Doctor - learning how Mozart had been manipulated and mistreated - travelled in the TARDIS back to Mozart's deathbed.

In Scotland, 1856, a young boy named James Lees encountered a different dimensional portal while swimming in the River Clyde near the Corra Linn falls. Lees remained on the other side of the portal, but the aliens who lived there sent a doppelganger of him back through as an ambassador. The ersatz James could tap people's memories to "speak with the voices of the dead" and was committed to an asylum. Within a few years, he'd become renowned as a spiritualist.[954]

---

945 Dating "Perceptions" and "Coda" (*Radio Times* #3805-3816) - It's broadly said to be "Victorian London".
946 Dating "Cuckoo" (*DWM* #208-210) - The date is given at the beginning of the story.
947 *The Evil of the Daleks*
948 *The Sea Devils*
949 *The War Games*
950 *The Evil of the Daleks*
951 *Interference* (p191).
952 *The Rapture.* The brothers' portal isn't related to the portal that abducts James Lees in the same era.
953 Dating *100*: "100 My Own Private Wolfgang" (BF #100b) - Mozart was born 27th January, 1756, and it's now his 100th birthday.
954 *Empire of Death.* James is replaced in 1856, as dated on the back cover and p5.

955 Dating *The Haunting of Thomas Brewster* (BF #107) - Brewster has been at Shanks' workhouse for five years, and the season of the year is stated.
956 *FP: Erasing Sherlock* (p27). The traditional date for Holmes' birth, January 1854, is extrapolated from clues in the Conan Doyle story "His Last Bow". Where *Erasing Sherlock* is concerned, the differing birthdate accommodates Holmes being 25 when the story opens in 1882.
957 *Downtime*
958 *The Nightmare Fair.* It's not said which shelling during the Opium Wars (the first of which lasted 1839-1842, the second 1856-1860) this is meant to denote.
959 Dating "The Screams of Death" (*DWM* #430-431) - The year is given.
960 "The Child of Time" (*DWM*)

1856 (winter) - THE HAUNTING OF THOMAS BREWSTER[955] **->** Thomas Brewster had spent five years at the workhouse, taking lessons and enduring regular beatings from Mr. Shanks, the master there. Brewster experienced recurring dreams of his dead mother - the result of a psychic "test signal" sent to him from the future. The fifth Doctor and Nyssa arrived and quickly departed, deciding they were still too early in Brewster's timeline.

w - Gillian Rose Petra came into information suggesting that Sherlock Holmes had been born in late February, 1857 (and not January 1854, as was more commonly believed) and that his first name was Edmund (not William).[956]

Charles Dodgson photographed a young Victoria Waterfield in 1857.[957] During the Opium Wars, the Doctor recreated a tapestry from a grubby Han-Sen original as the British fleet shelled a city. The Celestial Toymaker was not present, but would later acquire the copy.[958]

(=) 1858 - "The Screams of Death"[959] **->** Monsieur Valdemar, a criminal from the future, was transported into the past by the time-child Chiyoko. He used a DNA sequencer to transform young women to his agents - and excellent opera singers to boot. The eleventh Doctor and Amy enjoyed the best performance of *Eurydice* that the Doctor had seen in a century, and stopped Valdemar from eliminating the ancestors of the four men who had betrayed him. Valdemar's slaves turned on him, and threw him to his death.

The TARDIS absorbed a young woman, Cosette, into itself, but she was restored to life when Chiyoko cancelled out her own existence.[960]

c 1859 - A TOWN CALLED FORTUNE[961] **->** The sixth Doctor and Evelyn visited the town of Fortune, and helped to bring Mayor Sullivan to justice for crimes. Sheriff Hayes turned himself in for the murder of William Donovan.

The Doctor talked to Lewis Carroll about the sleeping King Constantine, which influenced Carroll's writing.[962] Darwin published *The Origin of the Species* in 1859.[963] The Doctor met Darwin.[964] The Doctor dropped by New York as the Plug Uglies and Dead Rabbit gangs were tearing into each other. He helped to resolve the conflict, either by sorting it out with them over a pack of Jammy Dodgers, or just sending them back to Sligo, Ireland.[965] In 1860, Ian's great-grandfather, Major William Chesterton, served as a member of a Hussar company at Jaipur, India.[966]

c 1860 - BENNY: THE VAMPIRE CURSE: "Possum Kingdom"[967] **->** Benny and the Yesterways Ltd. tour group visited Transylvania during Victorian times.

In 1860, Litefoot's father was a Brigadier-General on the punitive expedition to China. The Litefoot family stayed in the country for the next thirteen years. Around this time, Henry Gordon Jago began working in the entertainment business.[968]

1861 - THE HAUNTING OF THOMAS BREWSTER[969] **->** Mr Shanks sold Thomas Brewster to a man named Creek, who offered the lad an apprenticeship in his shop on Jacob's Island - a notorious rookery on the south bank of the Thames. The boys in Creek's employ scavenged the river for all manner of valuables, including items thrown overboard to avoid the revenue man. Brewster endured Creek's regular beatings.

961 Dating *A Town Called Fortune* (BF CC #5.5) - The story is oddly circumspect about when it's set, given that it's a historical. Fortune is an American town, but we're not told the state in which it resides, let alone the year. The only tangible clue is that it's nine years after Donovan was engaged in the gold prospecting business - such activity generally dates to the mid-nineteenth century, and the most famous example of this, the California Gold Rush, lasted 1848-1855.
962 *The Shadows of Avalon*
963 "Cuckoo"
964 *Island of Death.* The third Doctor remembers the meeting, so it's a different occasion than when the sixth Doctor met him in *Bloodtide*.
965 *The Forgotten Army.* The Doctor says this was in "1829" (p156) - probably either a typo or the result of him misremembering, as the Plug Uglies and Dead

Rabbits operated in the 1850s, not the 1820s.
966 *The Eleventh Tiger*
967 Dating *Benny: The Vampire Curse:* "Possum Kingdom" (Benny collection #12b) - The tour group members dress up for the Victorian era (1837-1901), but nothing more specific is given.
968 *The Talons of Weng-Chiang.* Jago claims to have had "thirty years in the halls".
969 Dating *The Haunting of Thomas Brewster* (BF #107) - Brewster is sold after having lived at Shanks' workhouse for ten years.

1861 (June) - THE GOOD, THE BAD AND THE ALIEN[970] **->** A Jerinthioan, a type of psionic vampire, became trapped on Earth. It mentally enticed two space smugglers - members of the Cemar race, who looked like humanoid meerkats - to come to Mason City, Nevada, so it could escape. The eleventh Doctor, Amy and Rory ran afoul of the Jerinthioan, the Cemars and some bank robbers - the Black Hand Gang. The Jerinthioan over-fed on the Doctor's psionic energy and died, and the Doctor took the Cemars back to their homeworld to face trial for smuggling.

Earth was now classified as a Level Three[971] planet.

1861 - SERPENT CREST: THE BROKEN CROWN / ALADDIN TIME[972] **->** The cyborg Alex was now a teenager, and had become attuned to the Skishtari egg in his possession. It created within itself fictional worlds based upon the books he read. The fourth Doctor and Mrs Wibbsey arrived down a wormhole from the far future as the egg made Alex increasingly capricious. The Doctor and Wibbsey were briefly trapped inside the egg's dimensions, and experienced a realm based upon *Arabian Nights*. The Doctor's scarf manifested as a genie and granted Alex some wishes - which he used to close down the egg's fictional constructs. The Doctor buried the egg and gave instructions that Nest Cottage, which he would come to own, be built over it. Alex used his last wish to transport himself, Boolin, the Doctor and Wibbsey to Nest Cottage in 2010.

The Doctor met Victor Hugo in Guernsey.[973] The Doctor showed Victor Hugo the catacombs of Paris. Hugo was so spooked by this that he changed the plot of *Les Miserables*, which he had planned to make a comedy.[974] **The Doctor** encountered the Silurian warrior Madame Vastra, who was trying to avenge the deaths of her sisters on innocent workers in the London Underground. The two of them formed an enduring friendship.[975]

A child born ten miles from the Torchwood Estate was stolen from a cultivation, and became the newest host to the essence of an alien werewolf.[976] In 1863, the stone-imprinted minds of Qin Shi Huang and his two generals were transferred into Abbot Wu and two warrior monks.[977] A time warp in the USA sent a Cheyenne War Party to the twentieth century, where they attacked a trucker.[978]

A time traveller of unknown origin arrived in the nineteenth century, and - as far as could be determined - conducted experiments to improve the cognitive and intellectual abilities of pigs. Two "children" were born in the laboratory: the human-looking Charlie and his brother Toby, a walking, talking pig who passed in polite society as a swine of culture. Charlie and Toby were both endowed with false memories of their childhood.

The traveller died, taking his secrets to the grave. Charlie adopted the name "Alphonse Chardalot". In the years to follow, he sought to continue the work of his "father", often mistakenly believing himself to be the deceased time traveller. Meanwhile, Toby became a stage performer who shared his "life story" (such as he knew it) with audiences, and would perhaps sing an aria or two.[979]

The Doctor took tightrope-walking lessons from Blondin and accompanied him on one of his tightrope walks across Niagara Falls.[980] Thomas Brewster and his mates visited the new Metropolitan line, and had a contest to see who could ride it the furthest without paying.[981]

---

970 Dating *The Good, the Bad and Alien* (BBC children's 2-in-1 #3) - The story takes place "three months" (p109) after "18 April 1861" (p7).

971 It's a Level Five world come the twenty-first century; see *City of Death*.

972 Dating *Serpent Crest: The Broken Crown* and *Serpent Crest: Aladdin Time* (BBC fourth Doctor audios #3.2-3.3) - The Doctor tells Mrs Wibbsey, "You saw that newspaper in the village shop, this is 1861. We have to get acclimatised."

973 *Just War*

974 "The Forgotten"

975 *A Good Man Goes to War*. The London Underground first opened in 1863; it's not specified if the Doctor met Vastra as part of the initial construction or as it continued. *Doctor Who: The Encyclopedia* says that the Underground tunnelling accidentally obliterated the shelter in which Vastra's people lived.

976 *Tooth and Claw* (TV)

977 *The Eleventh Tiger*

978 "The Tides of Time"

979 "Half a century" before *Year of the Pig*, provided the age of Chardalot's journals is anything to go by.

980 *An Earthly Child, Wooden Heart*. "Blondin" is Charles Blondin (a.k.a. Jean François Gravelet-Blondin), a French tight-rope walker and acrobat who lived 1824–1897. He first performed the Niagara Falls feat in 1859, but repeated it, with variations, a number of times after that.

981 *The Three Companions*. The Metropolitan line opened 10th of January, 1863.

982 Dating *Empire of Death* (PDA #65) - The story's starting and ending dates are given on p37 and p235.

983 *Logopolis*. Thomas Huxley lived 1825-1895.

984 *The Evil of the Daleks*, with further details in *Downtime*.

985 *The War Games*

986 *The Chase*. The TARDIS crew supposedly watch this on the Time-Space Visualiser, although it's possible that they're just watching Lincoln rehearse the speech

1863 (14th-21st February) - EMPIRE OF DEATH[982] -> The duplicate James Lees was now performing séances for the heads of Europe, and Queen Victoria commissioned him to hold one for her late husband, Prince Albert. Earth's physical laws were affecting the other side, and the beings who lived there became increasingly desperate to seal off the dimensional rift. The fifth Doctor and Nyssa used the TARDIS to close the rift, and the Queen vowed to never speak of the matter again. The false James expired, and the real one was returned, having barely aged since he entered the rift in 1856.

The Doctor lost track of whether he had met Queen Victoria before now.

Around this time, the Doctor befriended biologist Thomas Huxley.[983] **Victoria Waterfield's mother, Edith Rose, died on 23rd November, 1863.**[984]

The American Civil War

A battlefield from the American Civil War was lifted by the War Lords.[985] **The Gettysburg address was made on 19th November, 1863.**[986] Iris had breakfast with Abraham Lincoln on the White House lawn after seeing off Martian invaders for the third time.[987] The Doctor was present at the opening of the Clifton Suspension Bridge in Bristol.[988]

1864 - THE RUNAWAY TRAIN[989] -> The Cei were on the losing side of an inter-planetary war, and their last warship attempted to use a terraformer to transform Earth into a Cei-compatible planet. The eleventh Doctor and Amy destroyed the terraformer, and the Doctor assisted the warship in returning to its homeworld.

1864 (30th July) - RENAISSANCE OF THE DALEKS[990] -> Nyssa and the knight Mulberry arrived in Petersburg, Virginia, via a wormhole from 1320. The Siege of Petersburg was underway, and Union troops set explosives

in a mine tunnel running under Confederate lines. The bombs detonated early in the morning on 30th July, killing about three hundred Confederate soldiers.

> (=) The fifth Doctor arrived too late to rescue them, and Nyssa and Mulberry were present at 3:15 am when the bombs exploded.

The Doctor overrode the TARDIS' time-track crossing protocol, and rescued Nyssa and Mulberry at 3:14 am.

The brilliant Victorian scientist Harriet Dodd created a feasibility generator, and used it to make Wonderland - a subterranean locale designed to contain creatures that broke through from other dimensions. Dodd allied herself with the earliest form of the Ministry for Incursions and other Alien Ontological Wonders (MIAOW), but the group deemed her work as too subversive and weird, and sealed up Wonderland with Dodd inside. She and the whole of Wonderland slept for more than a century.[991]

1865 (February to April) - BLOOD AND HOPE[992] -> The fifth Doctor, Peri and Erimem attempted to visit the Wild West but arrived in the waning days of America's Civil War instead. The Doctor assisted the Union army as the medic "Doctor John Smith", and was present on 26th March, 1865, when Billingsville Prison was captured. On 5th April, the Doctor saved President Lincoln from an assassination attempt in Richmond, Virginia. On the same day, Peri shot dead the Confederacy's Colonel Jubal Eustace when he attempted to murder her friends as Union collaborators. Lincoln was killed days later.

The Doctor warned Lincoln not to go to the theatre.[993] Lord Kelvin laid transatlantic telegraph cables in 1865.[994]

---

beforehand. The actual event had Lincoln surrounded by a huge crowd in close quarters; the Visualiser shows him very much isolated.
987 *Iris: The Panda Invasion*
988 *An Earthly Child.* This happened in 1864.
989 Dating *The Runaway Train* (BBC *DW* audiobook #9) - The year is given, and it's after the battle of Galveston (there were actually two of these, fought on 4th October, 1862, and then on 1st January, 1863).
990 Dating *Renaissance of the Daleks* (BF #93) - The date is given toward the end of episode two. As stated, the detonation killed three hundred Confederates, but the Union army miscalculated in the explosion's aftermath, and lost fifty-three thousand troops. The crater caused by the mine explosion is still visible to this day.

991 "Over one hundred years" before *Iris: The Land of Wonder.* The implication is that Lewis Carroll's work was based upon Dodd's Wonderland, but it's not explained how this is the case. Perhaps the malleable creatures in Wonderland patterned themselves, somehow, after the characters in Carroll's books. Either way, *Alice in Wonderland* saw print in 1865, and Dodd's Wonderland was presumably created around the same time.
992 Dating *Blood and Hope* (TEL #14) - Judging by a letter on p29, the TARDIS crew arrive in America on 21st February, 1865. The Doctor's saving Lincoln is dated on p49; Eustace's death is dated on p69.
993 *Minuet in Hell*
994 "Fifteen years" before *Evolution* (p107).

1865 (14th April) - ASSASSIN IN THE LIMELIGHT[995]
-> Dr Robert Knox had exchanged his Type 70 TARDIS for a newer model, and he imprisoned the Indo accompanying him within the Ship. The Indo summoned one of its own kind, who hoped to alter the events surrounding Lincoln's assassination so that the American Civil War would resume, enabling both Indo to feast upon the resulting emotional trauma.

Knox died from his disease. The Doctor trapped the second Indo inside Knox's TARDIS, then deactivated the Ship's temporal shields and sent it hurtling through the Vortex - aging both creatures to death. Knox had absorbed some of the Indo's power, and used it to put his consciousness in the dead body of Pops, a stagehand at Ford's Theatre. In such a form, Knox adopted the identity of Arthur Conan Doyle and booked passage to England.

An earlier version of Knox was in the audience when Booth, as history dictated, killed Lincoln.

1865 - THE HAUNTING OF THOMAS BREWSTER[996]
-> Creek tried to interrogate Thomas Brewster after the fifth Doctor and Nyssa inquired about him, but lost his footing and drowned in the Thames. Brewster escaped with a fellow scavenger named Pickens.

The Doctor and Nyssa returned with Brewster's older self, having identified this as the point when the "test signal" from the future formed a psychic link with Brewster's mind. The older Brewster persuaded his younger self that the dreams he'd experienced of his mother were an illusion, and the younger Brewster's conviction about this caused the alternate 2008 timeline to cease to exist.

Creek's scavengers recovered the TARDIS from the Thames, where it had been buried since 1831. It would remain in Creek's abandoned shop for two more years.

1865 - THE ELEVENTH TIGER[997] -> Earth prepared to enter a unique stellar conjunction for the first time in two thousand years. Qin Shi Huang, controlled by the intelligence that revived him, assembled an army and started securing "sacred sites" that would serve as conduits to the intelligence's power, enabling it to seize control of China. The first Doctor, Ian, Barbara, Vicki and their allies flooded a tomb seeped with the intelligence's power. Qin took control of his host long enough to step into the water, shorting out the intelligence's energy. Qin's mind dissipated, and the possessed Abbot Wu recovered.

Major William Chesterton served in China at this time, and suffered a concussion while fighting bandits in Qiang-Ling. The Doctor and his friends encountered the Ten Tigers of Canton, the top ten kung fu masters in Guangdong.

995 Dating *Assassin in the Limelight* (BF #108) - The story takes place on the day Lincoln was shot (14th April, 1865; he died the following day). The Civil War had concluded a mere five days beforehand on 9th April, when General Lee surrendered the Army of Northern Virginia.

Knox here passes himself off as Oscar Wilde - who is only age ten when this story takes place - but the few people to see him as "Wilde" either die or (in Henry Rathbone's case) go insane and become institutionalized before the real Wilde became famous, suggesting none of them would have noticed the discrepancy in future. An exception is the theatre manager, Henry Clay Ford, who would have lived to hear of Wilde's fame - but who also, having deduced that the Doctor and Evelyn were time travellers, would perhaps be inclined to keep quiet about it all.

It's fancifully implied that Knox, his mind in Pops' dead body, assumes the life meant for Arthur Conan Doyle (1859-1930) from this point on. Conan Doyle is actually seen in two *Doctor Who* stories: *Evolution*, set in 1880; and *Revenge of the Judoon*, set in 1902. The former is set before *Assassin in the Limelight*, and so doesn't rule out the notion of an identity-swap. However, in the latter, Conan Doyle is presented as the genuine article, not a lively corpse-person with Knox's mind.

The more one considers Knox's plan to swap himself for Conan Doyle, the more unlikely it seems that he succeeded. Such a scheme begs the question of a) what exactly Knox did to the real Conan Doyle, b) how, exactly, everyone who knew Conan Doyle could have possibly mistake Knox-Pops for him, and c) how, exactly, Knox is meant to have married three times and sired five children when his animated Pops-body reeks of decay and death. Some of these issues are solved if Knox transfers his consciousness into Conan Doyle's body after arriving in England, but this isn't actually said, and it's very odd that Knox is already telling people that he's Conan Doyle before he's even left America. Conan Doyle in real life was a doctor of medicine, so Knox would be able to fake that expertise, at least.

The Doctor and Evelyn are mistaken for Pinkertons - the Agency got its start in 1850, after Allan Pinkerton thwarted an attempt to kill president-elect Lincoln.

996 Dating *The Haunting of Thomas Brewster* (BF #107) - It's "two years" before the 1867 component of the story, and it's said that the TARDIS is recovered "thirty-four years" after 1831.

997 Dating *The Eleventh Tiger* (PDA #66) - The date is given. Although not referred to by name, the alien intelligence bears the characteristics of the Mandragora Helix (*The Masque of Mandragora*), and it's intimated (p274) that the Doctor defeated its attempt to dominate Earth "four hundred years" previous.

998 Dating *World Game* (PDA #74) - The TARDIS travels "fifty years" beyond 1815.

Following the Players' defeat, they abandoned the
Grand Design. All Games were suspended indefinitely due
to the amount of disruption the Countess had caused,
which drew the attention of the Time Lords.

1866 (2nd-3rd June) - THE EVIL OF THE DALEKS[999]
**-> The second Doctor and Jamie were brought to the
Waterfield household from 1966 by the Daleks, who
ran tests on them in the hopes of discovering the
Human Factor. That done, the Doctor, Jamie, Victoria
Waterfield and her father Edward were taken to Skaro.**

A massive time breach in the TARDIS caused the fifth
Doctor to become separated from Nyssa, and he performed an emergency materialisation that caused him to
arrive in London, on or about November 1866. While
awaiting Nyssa's arrival, he resided at 107 Baker Street as
an English gentleman. As "Doctor Walters", he became a
Royal Society member so he could collect the materials he
needed to repair the damaged TARDIS. For appearance's
sake, he took on Robert McIntosh - a medical student at
Edinburgh - as his assistant-cum-protégé.[1000]

K9 was programmed with all grandmaster chess
games from 1866 onwards.[1001] The Doctor implied that
he was present when Brighton's West Pier opened in
1866.[1002] Sherlock Holmes' younger sister, Genevieve, was

left mentally handicapped owing to the birth trauma that
killed her mother.[1003] **The War Lords lifted a battlefield
from the Mexican Uprising of 1867.**[1004]

**1867 (14th November) - THE HAUNTING OF
THOMAS BREWSTER**[1005] **->** Nyssa, who had been
expelled by the TARDIS, arrived in Seven Dials on the day
the Doctor was addressing the Royal Society. He unreserv-
edly lauded a paper by the physicist Leon Foucault, which
calculated the speed of light as 298 km per second. The
Doctor was now friends with physicist James Maxwell.

Under the direction of his mother's shade, Thomas
Brewster had spent the last two years stealing various bits
of scientific paraphernalia - and thereby lashed together a
machine capable of creating a time breach. Smoke-beings
from an alternate 2008 travelled down this corridor to
help guarantee that their timeline became the dominant
one; they murdered Brewster's friend Pickens and the
Doctor's protégé, Robert McIntosh. Their deaths, and others caused by the smoke beings, were attributed to yet-
another lethal London smog.

The Doctor severed the time corridor, but the smoke-
beings tricked Brewster into stealing the Doctor's TARDIS
and travelling to their native time. The Doctor and Nyssa
retrieved an older version of the TARDIS that had been
sitting in Creek's shop since 1965, and followed Brewster
into the future.

The travellers defeated the smoke beings, then returned
to the Doctor's house. Brewster, fearing a return to a life of
scavenging and near-starvation, hijacked the TARDIS a
second time.[1006]

In 1868, the Doctor opened a bank account at Coutts
Bank in London under the name R.J. Smith Esq.; Susan
Foreman, Victoria Waterfield, Sarah Jane Smith, Melanie
Bush and Bernice Summerfield were named as signatories
on the account.[1007] In the same year, Wychborn House
burnt down.[1008] In 1868, the Phiadoran spores enabled
Professor Bryce-Dennison to create a solar-powered impel-

999 Dating *The Evil of the Daleks* (4.9) - An early storyline gave the date of the Victorian sequence as "1880"
(and the date of the caveman sequence which was
later deleted as "20,000 BC"). The camera scripts gave
the date of "1867", as did some promotional material,
but this was altered at the last minute to dovetail *The
Faceless Ones* and *The Evil of the Daleks*.
1000 "Twelve months" before the November 1867
component of *The Haunting of Thomas Brewster*.
1001 *The Androids of Tara*
1002 *Pier Pressure*
1003 *FP: Erasing Sherlock*. Genevieve is "ten
years" younger than Sherlock, who is said to have been
born in 1857.

1004 *The War Games*
1005 Dating *The Haunting of Thomas Brewster* (BF
#107) - The day and year are given. James Clerk
Maxwell lived 1831-1879. The Doctor here tries to seem
older by growing a beard - a rare occurrence, but something he also does in *The Adventuress of Henrietta Street*
and *The Wedding of River Song*.
1006 Brewster has possession of the TARDIS for five
months (from his perspective), and has such adventures as *The Three Companions* during that time. The
Doctor and Nyssa catch up with him in *The Boy That
Time Forgot*.
1007 *Birthright*
1008 *Strange England* (p157).

ler drive.[1009] Shotgun manufacturer Purdeys received the Royal Warrant in 1868.[1010]

c 1868 - THE BOY THAT TIME FORGOT[1011] -> The fifth Doctor gathered twelve of the finest minds in the Empire - including Professor Quandry, the novelist Beatrice Mapp and the fraudulent explorer Rupert Von Thal - in Mapp's sitting room in Bloomsbury to conduct an experiment. Those present read off ones and zeroes; by this use of Block Transfer Computation (BTC), the Doctor and Nyssa could locate the hijacked TARDIS. The Doctor's subconscious guilt over Adric's death usurped the BTC, creating a prehistoric timeline where Adric had survived. The Doctor, Nyssa, Beatrice and Rupert were transported there.

The Doctor, Nyssa and Beatrice - along with an aged Adric - returned six weeks after they'd left. Adric's health was failing, and he died while using the last of his strength to recall the TARDIS. Adric was buried in the same cemetery as Thomas Brewster's mother.

The Doctor said that other Time Lords, "Iris especially", had travelled in this period.

The Doctor told Jules Verne to leave the Silurians out of *20,000 Leagues Under the Sea*.[1012] Bilis Manger served as the manager of the Amser Hotel in Roath, which never recovered from being gutted by "eerie pink flames" in 1869. The incident linked Bilis to a Rift entity - he simultaneously had to do its bidding and set about engineering its destruction.[1013]

The Doctor visited the New York Natural History Museum quite a lot when it first opened, as he hadn't properly cleaned up after himself, and some of the items recovered from the Gobi were "far too unstable" to be put on display.[1014]

1869 (24th December) - THE UNQUIET DEAD[1015] -> The ninth Doctor and Rose landed in Cardiff. A dramatic recital by Charles Dickens was interrupted by what seemed to be a ghost. These were gas creatures, the Gelth, who had travelled to Earth by a time rift, a.k.a. the Cardiff Rift. The Gelth posed as refugees, but sought to invade Earth. The Doctor and his allies sent the Gelth back through the Rift and closed it behind them. Dickens hoped to write the adventure as *The Mystery of Edwin Drood and the Blue Elementals*, with the killer being an extra-terrestrial instead of the boy's uncle as originally planned, but died the following year before completing it.

The "healed" Rift left a residual dimensional scar; this was harmless to humans, yet useful as a means of refuelling time vessels. The Rift would continue to attract all manner of alien beings and technology to the Cardiff area.[1016] The existence of the Rift created a "field of despair" over Cardiff that normally just made the people there a bit miserable, but intensified in times of approaching crisis and increased the suicide/homicide rate.[1017]

Gwen Cooper, a future Torchwood operative, had an old Cardiff family dating back to the 1800s. Gwyneth Cooper, a maid the Doctor and Rose met and who died fighting the Gelth, was linked to her through "spatial genetic multiplicity".[1018]

Captain Jack Harkness used his vortex manipulator to travel back from the year 200,100 to find the Doctor. He arrived in 1869, would discover in 1892 that he was now immortal, and live on Earth until the early twenty-first century.[1019]

The Doctor knew Mary Ann Evans, a.k.a. George Eliot, the author of *Middlemarch*.[1020] The eleventh Doctor, Amy, Rory and Kevin the Tyrannosaur met Sitting Bull.[1021]

1009 *Imperial Moon*
1010 *Revenge of the Judoon*
1011 Dating *The Boy That Time Forgot* (BF #110) - It's unclear how much time has passed since Brewster stole the TARDIS in mid-November 1867, and so it's possible that it's either late 1867 or some time in 1868. For the Doctor, Nyssa and Brewster, this story continues in the undatable *Time Reef*.
1012 *Peacemaker. 20,000 Leagues Under the Sea* was published in 1869.
1013 *TW:* "Broken". The incident seems unrelated to events in *The Unquiet Dead*, even though they occur in the same year, and the Rift entity isn't Abaddon, whom Bilis is seen serving in *Torchwood* Series 1.
1014 *The Forgotten Army* (p163). The American Museum of Natural History - presumably the same building that this novel keeps calling the "New York Natural History Museum", and identified down to its

street address (p26) - opened in 1869.
1015 Dating *The Unquiet Dead* (X1.3) - The Doctor gives the year (having originally aimed for 1860). The date is given a number of times, first on a poster in Dickens' dressing room. The Doctor, Rose and Jack's discussion about the Rift in *Boom Town* seems to indicate that it predates events in *The Unquiet Dead*.
1016 The Doctor uses the Rift to refuel the TARDIS in *Boom Town* and *Utopia*. Evidence of the Rift attracting alien beings and technology to Cardiff is witnessed throughout *Torchwood*.
1017 *TW: Ghost Train*
1018 *Journey's End*, providing an explanation within *Doctor Who* as to why Gwen and Gwyneth look identical (as both were played by Eve Myles). From her conversation with Rose about boys, Gwyneth is very clearly not a mother in *The Unquiet Dead*, and so Gwen is not her descendant, and the physical resemblance seems

c 1870 - INDUSTRIAL EVOLUTION[1022] -> The sixth Doctor and Evelyn returned Thomas Brewster to the town of Ackleton in his native era. Rival bits of alien technology - a "catalyser" that dissected machines and improved upon their designs, and a living mechanical "inhibitor" (outlawed under intergalactic law) designed to create malfunctions, ruin research and make a planet's inhabitants frightened of technological developments - competed with one another. Brewster saved the progress of the Industrial Revolution by destroying the inhibitor, but the Doctor was disgusted because Brewster had slain a living being. The Doctor and Evelyn left without Brewster, who struck up a partnership with "Samuel Belfrage" - a Karlean working the interplanetary black market. Their first haul was half a ton of Earth's rock salt, which was considered a delicacy on other planets.

In 1870, the Jameson boys were out cutting peat when they encountered the Zygons on Tullock Moor. The elder brother Robert was driven mad by the experience and never spoke again; his younger brother Donald simply disappeared.[1023] **Around that time, Reuben joined the lighthouse service. He spent twenty of the next thirty years in a gas-powered lighthouse.**[1024] **In 1871, a battlefield from the Franco-Prussian War was lifted by the War Lords**[1025] **and the Doctor was given a Gladstone bag by Gladstone.**[1026]

1871 - SET PIECE[1027] -> The time-lost seventh Doctor, Benny and Ace were reunited in Paris. After they defeated the robotic Ants, Ace chose to leave the TARDIS and joined the ruling Paris Commune. She was the last soldier to leave the barricades when the Commune fell from power. She had possession of a time-hopper built by Kadiatu Lethbridge-Stewart, a means of travelling through time.

The Doctor met Tsar Nicholas at the Drei Kaiser Bund of 1871.[1028] **During this time, Magnus Greel arrived in the Time Cabinet from the year 5000. The Chinese peasant Li H'sen Chang sheltered Greel, thinking he was the god Weng-Chiang. The Emperor acquired Greel's cabinet, and gave it as a gift to Litefoot's mother.**[1029]

Cousin Octavia of Faction Paradox was born in Scotland, 1872.[1030] The Doctor had a permanent suite on Floor Six of the Singapore Hilton from 1872 until at least 2008.[1031] A mine owner, Gideon ap Tarri, established the Tretarri in Cardiff as a housing district for his employees in 1872.[1032] Agnes Havisham found herself shooting at zombies - a clue that perhaps the Cardiff Rift was becoming more active.[1033]

Edward Waterfield, Victoria's father, was officially reported as missing in 1872. It was thought that he'd gone off to Africa. Victoria sold his estate, but let the Doctor use the house on Dean Street as a base in London. Edward's sister, Margaret, looked after the place. Victoria visited her a few times - sometimes with the Doctor, and once when she was studying graphology.[1034]

more like a result of (to coin a phrase) "time echoing" than genetics.

1019 *Utopia.* It may or may not be coincidence that 1869 is the year the TARDIS landed at the Rift in *The Unquiet Dead.* Jack's immortality is first revealed in *TW: Everything Changes.*

1020 *The Criminal Code.* Evans lived 1819 to 1880.

1021 "Your Destiny Awaits". This happens when Sitting Bull is a Sioux leader, which started no later than 1864, and ended with his surrender in 1881.

1022 Dating *Industrial Evolution* (BF #145) - The period is generalised as "nineteenth century Lancashire", but the Doctor would hardly want to deposit Brewster in his personal past, and there's no sign on this occasion of the TARDIS missing its mark. It's probably relevant that when the Doctor offers to take Brewster home in *The Feast of Axos,* he suggests a destination of "about 1870", to which Brewster replies, "That'll do."

1023 According to Angus in *Terror of the Zygons.*

1024 *Horror of Fang Rock*

1025 *The War Games*

1026 *Companion Piece*

1027 Dating *Set Piece* (NA #35) - It is "1871 CE" (p62). The Commune fell on 28th May, 1871. Ace's departure in *Set Piece* deliberately echoes the epilogue to *The*

Curse of Fenric novelisation, in which the Doctor visits an older Ace in nineteenth-century Paris, some time after she's departed his company. Reconciling the epilogue with the New Adventures is difficult, as the epilogue takes place in 1887 (p186 and 188) when Ace is still a "young lady". Given her aging in the New Adventures, this makes it unlikely that she lives in Paris for all of the sixteen years between 1871 and 1887. Fortunately, the New Adventures have Ace taking up time travel after *Set Piece,* and using a time-jump to facilitate her meeting with the Doctor in 1887 would explain a great deal.

1028 *The Devil Goblins from Neptune*

1029 *The Talons of Weng-Chiang.* Greel arrived in 1872, according to *The Shadow of Weng-Chiang.*

1030 *FP: The Book of the War.* She's in her "eleventh year" in 1883 according to *FP: Warring States* (p52).

1031 *The Girl Who Never Was*

1032 *TW: The Twilight Streets*

1033 *TW: Risk Assessment.* Havisham says that the zombie incident occurred "a few years" after a space-time disturbance "shifted" the Rift - presumably a reference to *The Unquiet Dead.*

1034 *Birthright*

1872 (August to December) - EYE OF HEAVEN[1035] -> Horace Stockwood organized a second expedition to Easter Island, and the fourth Doctor and Leela joined his group aboard the sailing ship *Tweed*. On the island, Stockwood's party discovered a giant stone head containing a teleport device. This transported some of the group to the homeworld of the aliens who built Easter Island's *moai*. They searched an alien library, but their presence triggered a booby trap that turned the alien sun black. The party returned to Earth, hoping the sun would return to normal in their absence. From Leela's blood, the Doctor created an antidote to the sickness that had killed the Polynesian/alien hybrids thirty years ago. Stockwood remained on the island to help protect the Polynesians until the alien DNA the *moai* carried could re-infect them.

1872 (25th November) - THE CHASE[1036] -> **The first Doctor, Ian, Barbara and Vicki arrived on the *Mary Celeste*, and left moments before the Daleks pursuing them. The crew were so terrified by the Daleks, they abandoned ship.**

c 1872 - 100: "The 100 Days of the Doctor"[1037] -> The sixth Doctor learned that an assassin working for the Tharsis Acumen - a technocracy of scientists who were enraged because he freed their political prisoners - had tainted him with an intelligent virus that would eventually kill him. The Doctor and Evelyn backtracked his various destinations to find the point of infection, and in so doing observed two versions of the eighth Doctor - respectively accompanied by Lucie; Charley and C'rizz - playing cards in a Western saloon in the 1870s.

Joseph Sundvig died on 3rd February, 1872.[1038] Ace witnessed some of the rebuilding of Paris in 1873, then used her time-hopper to meet up with the Doctor and his

friends in 2001.[1039] **The Nine Travellers were surveyed in 1874.**[1040] **Old Priory, a Victorian folly, was built for the Scarman family. After this time, Marcus and Laurence Scarman played in the priest-hole there as children.**[1041] The Doctor swam with Captain Webb in the Channel.[1042]

1873 (11th September) - THE SILVER TURK[1043] -> Mondas was now within two hundred light years of Earth. A scoutship with two Cybermen, Graham and Brem, reconnoitred the space around Mondas and crashed on Earth. Dr Johan Drossel and Alfred Stahlbaum acquired Brem, who was badly damaged, and turned him into a touring curiosity that could play checkers and the piano. The eighth Doctor and Mary Shelley stopped Graham - who cannibalised Brem for needed parts - from contacting Cyber-Control on Mondas. Graham's systems failed, and the Doctor and Mary burned a number of advanced marionettes that he had constructed. Stahlbaum toured with one such marionette - a wooden Doctor-duplicate, "the Silver Doctor", which challenged people to play games.

1873 - STRANGE ENGLAND[1044] -> The TARDIS landed on an asteroid shaped by Gallifreyan Protyon units to resemble an idyllic Victorian country house based on Wychborn House. It was sculpted by a friend of the Doctor, the Time Lady Galah, who had reached the end of her regenerative cycle. With the seventh Doctor's help, Galah lived on as one of her human creations, Charlotte. She returned to Earth and married Richard Aickland, who became a renowned Gothic novelist (of such books as *Cold Eyes* and *The Wine Press*) in the early twentieth century.

1875 - "Bad Blood"[1045] -> The eighth Doctor landed in the Dakota Hills, and found that Chief Sitting Bull had been told he would arrive in a vision. Miners had awoken

---

1035 Dating *Eye of Heaven* (PDA #8) - The date is given (p17).
1036 Dating *The Chase* (2.8) - The emptied *Mary Celeste* was discovered in November 1872.
1037 Dating *100*: "The 100 Days of the Doctor" (BF #100d) - It's the "1870s". The Tharsis Acumen is said to lack time travel, and to have existed for "only a few centuries", so the Doctor could theoretically have freed their slaves at just about any point from (say) the 1500s to the twenty-second century.
1038 *The Curse of Fenric*
1039 *Head Games*
1040 *The Stones of Blood*
1041 *Pyramids of Mars*
1042 *Doctor Who and the Pirates*. The Doctor says he "paced" Webb, which indicates he was swimming ahead of Webb to increase the man's pace rather than

trying to defeat him.
1043 Dating *The Silver Turk* (BF #153) - A newspaper has the dateline "11th September, 1873". The Doctor mentions the real-life Turk - an automation exhibited starting in 1770, was exposed as a fraud in the 1820s, and was incinerated in a fire in 1854.
1044 Dating *Strange England* (NA #29) - The Doctor says that the "temporal location" is "1873" (p229).
1045 Dating "Bad Blood" (*DWM* #338-342) - The date is given in a caption.
1046 *The Pirate Planet*. Bandraginus V disappeared "over a century" ago according to the Doctor, when the Zanak native Balaton was young. As Zanak is not capable of time travel, it must have been operating at least that long. The planets attacked by Zanak are named in production documents, and plaques were made up with the names on... but only those for Bandraginus V,

an ancient evil, and Indians and General Custer's forces were both attacked by wolf-like creatures: the Windigo. The Doctor was reunited with Destrii when she arrived with her uncle, Count Jodafra, but the two aliens started to arm Custer's men with laser weapons.

It turned out that Jodafra had made a deal with the Windigo, as it could navigate the timestream. Destrii sided with the Doctor, and helped destroy the Windigo. Jodafra savagely attacked Destrii, leaving her for dead, but the Doctor brought her back aboard the TARDIS.

The *Vantarialis* crashed on Zanak, where its injured captain was remade as a cyborg. With the assistance of old Queen Xanxia, the Captain converted the entire planet into a hollow world capable of teleporting between star systems and sucking the life out of planets by materialising around them. After this time, and with increasing frequency, Zanak attacked and destroyed Bandraginus V, Aterica, Temesis, Tridentio III, Lowiteliom, Bibicorpus and Granados.[1046]

Gideon ap Tarri bore witness in 1876 as an earthquake wracked Cardiff. This was a consequence of Abaddon fighting Pwccm for control of the Rift. The combatants each had a second: the twins, Bilis and Cafard Manger. The contest left Abaddon trapped under Cardiff, and Pwccm stuck the Rift. Cafard physically merged with Bilis. On Bilis' advice, ap Tarri relocated his workers to newer accommodations in the Windsor and Bute Esplanades. The Tertarri would remain uninhabited for a century, and become a place of hauntings.[1047]

The Doctor met Alexander Graham Bell.[1048] **Bell initiated the first phone message while asking for his assistant Watson. The message would later dominate phone lines during a time paradox in 1987.**[1049] The Doctor warned General Custer against taking his Seventh Calvary over the ridge, but Custer ignored him.[1050] **The Doctor met Gilbert and Sullivan.**[1051] The Doctor claimed to have inspired the *Mikado*, a comic operetta.[1052] In 1878, the Vondrax collected an Orb from Canada.[1053] The Doctor

knew Billy the Kid, who wasn't like Emilo Estevez's portrayal in *Young Guns II*.[1054]

1878 (September) - IMPERIAL MOON[1055] **->** Using Bryce-Dennison's impeller drive, the British government had crafted three spaceships: the *Cygnus*, *Draco* and *Lynx*. The fifth Doctor and Turlough arrived as the ships explored Earth's moon, and mistook the deadly Vrall for the exiled Phiadorans. While returning to Earth, the Vrall were exposed aboard the *Draco* and a deadly struggle took place. The crewless *Draco* sped into space.

The *Cygnus* and *Lynx* arrived on Earth, where Queen Victoria greeted the "Phiadorans" as emissaries from another world. The Vrall self-replicated and instigated a slaughter. The Doctor and Turlough used advanced weapons from the lunar safari park to wipe out the Vrall on Earth. At the Doctor's command, Kamelion disguised himself as the late Prince Albert and appeared to the Queen "in a vision". Kamelion convinced the Queen to dismantle the remaining spaceships and never mention the incident.

The moon safari park self-destructed, leaving only a large crater.

Torchwood Victoriana

1879 - TOOTH AND CLAW (TV)[1056] **->** The tenth Doctor and Rose met Queen Victoria in Scotland. She was en route to the royal jewellers, but was diverted by the brethren who served a werewolf-like alien to Torchwood Estate. The alien intended to bite Victoria and through her foster the Empire of the Wolf, but the Doctor deduced Prince Albert's plan to defeat the creature and killed it.

Queen Victoria knighted the Doctor for saving her life, and named Rose as "Dame Rose of the Powell Estate". However, the Queen was not amused - she was fearful that the Doctor and Rose had strayed from all that was good, and therefore posed a danger. She ban-

---

Granados, Lowiteliom and Calufrax are clearly visible on screen. *First Frontier* gives a little more detail about Bandraginus V (p129).

1047 *TW: The Twilight Streets,* explaining how Abaddon came to be imprisoned beneath Cardiff (*TW: End of Days*).

1048 *The Android Invasion.* Bell lived 1847-1922.

1049 *Father's Day.* Bell's famous phone call occurred on 10th March, 1876.

1050 *Players* (p62), *Festival of Death.* Custer was killed 25th June, 1876.

1051 *The Edge of Destruction.* Gilbert and Sullivan collaborated between 1875-1896.

1052 *Doctor Who and the Pirates*

1053 *TW: Trace Memory*

1054 "When Worlds Collide". Billy the Kid lived 1859-1881.

1055 Dating *Imperial Moon* (PDA #34) - It's "the year of our Lord 1878" (p7).

1056 Dating *Tooth and Claw* (X2.2) - The Doctor gives the date as "1879". The book *Creatures and Demons* (a nonfiction book about various *Doctor Who* monsters) suggests that the parallel universe first seen in *Rise of the Cybermen* diverged from our history because Queen Victoria was killed in their (Doctorless) version of these events. The series itself was going to state this,

ished them from her empire, and secretly ordered the formation of the Torchwood Institute to protect the realm from such alien threats.

It was possible that the werewolf scratched the Queen before it died. The Doctor theorised that the Queen might similarly nip her children, and that the "royal disease" (unknown in Victoria's bloodline before her, and thought to be haemophilia) might actually be the alien werewolf taint.

Torchwood was established by royal decree, and was funded directly by the Crown. Victoria stated:

"Torchwood is also to administer to the Government thereof in our name, and generally to act in our name and on our behalf, subject to such orders and regulations as Torchwood shall, from time to time, receive from us through one of our Principal Secretaries of state."[1057]

The Doctor was named as an enemy of the Crown in the Torchwood Foundation Charter, which was established on 31st December, 1879.[1058] Torchwood Cardiff - per Victoria's decree and on the advisement of Agnes Havisham, a Torchwood associate - was established as a means of monitoring Rift activity.[1059] Torchwood India was founded to recover alien artifacts in the Raj.[1060] Torchwood took to studying a stone circle near Cardiff, which was a focus for Rift energy.[1061]

In 1879, an Arkansas Bible salesman named Abraham White touched a shooting star and was exposed to images from a thousand worlds, including visions of Time Lords. The "star" was actually the consciousness of Pariah - a predecessor to Shayde, and now an enemy of Gallifrey. White hosted her essence within him. Armed with Pariah's knowledge, White sought to boost humanity's technology development. He nudged a generation of geniuses and inventors - including Thomas Edison, Nicola Tesla, Rudolf Diesel, Henry Ford and Albert Einstein - along.

Pariah grew herself a new body within White's form, and learned to replicate her basic sphere influence. White infused select agents with the spheres and turned into living gateways. In this fashion, he founded the Threshold: an organisation that traded its services (moving clients through spatial doorways) in exchange for alien technology. The Threshold mastered space as the Time Lords had mastered time, and avoided Gallifrey's detection by refraining from time travel technology.

Threshold began developing an energy wave, but this would take over three thousand years to perfect. The group came into conflict with the seventh and eighth Doctors; events between them climaxed on the moon in the fifty-third century.[1062]

The Doctor met Afrikaaners during the Boer War and was at the battle of Roarke's Drift.[1063]

1880 - EVOLUTION[1064] **->** Percival Ross witnessed a Rutan scoutship crashing in Limehouse, and recovered a flask of Rutan healing salve from the wreckage. The alien gel had a miraculous healing effect on humans, but it also could merge human and animal genetic material, as Ross discovered when a boy he was treating became a ferocious dog-like creature. Ross interested the industrialist Breckingridge, the owner of a vast cable factory in the town of Bodhan, in the creation of a race of hybrid dolphin-men. Ross kidnapped fifteen children, and conduct-

---

but Russell T Davies decided against it. While it might explain why the Britain of that universe is a Republic, it doesn't explain why the Queen's successor would create Torchwood - an organisation founded in response to the Doctor and Rose irritating Victoria. Perhaps the Queen's death at the hands of a werewolf triggered an urge to defend Britain against such foes.
1057 *TW: Children of Earth*
1058 *Army of Ghosts,* with the date of the Charter's establishment stated in *The Torchwood Archives* and on Home Office files in *TW: Children of Earth.*
1059 *TW: Risk Assessment. The Torchwood Archives* establishes that Victoria gave orders for the founding of Torchwood Cardiff in 1879. *TW: Slow Decay* provides confirmation that it was operating no later than 1885.
1060 *TW: Golden Age*
1061 *TW: "Rift War"*
1062 "Wormwood"
1063 *Storm Warning.* Roarke's Drift occurred on 22nd to 23rd January, 1879.

1064 Dating *Evolution* (MA #2) - It is the "year of grace eighteen hundred and eighty" (p6, p108). Events here seem to influence Conan Doyle regarding *The Hound of the Baskervilles,* which was written in 1902. Kipling lived 1865-1936, so he is "15" here (p45).
1065 *Storm Warning.* No date given, but the Doctor did meet him in *Evolution.* Conan Doyle lived 1859-1930.
1066 *Tooth and Claw* (TV). Bell lived 1837-1911, and Conan Doyle studied under him. Note that in *The Moonbase,* the Doctor remembers studying in Glasgow under Lister in 1888. Either he studied under both, or has altered the details slightly here.
1067 *Storm Warning,* "The Golden Ones". Despite the eleventh Doctor using "Geronimo" as a catch-phrase, only these two stories claim that he actually met the man. Geronimo lived 16th June, 1829, to 17th February, 1909. He instigated revenge attacks after soldiers killed his family in 1858, and surrendered in 1886.
1068 Dating "The Greatest Gamble" (*DWM* #56) - The date is given.

ed experiments that turned them into mer-children.

Breckingridge died when one of his mutated guard dogs turned on him; Ross drowned. The fourth Doctor relocated the mer-children to a water planet in the Andromeda galaxy. A young Arthur Conan Doyle witnessed the happenings on Dartmoor, and his chance encounter with the Doctor inspired two of his most famous characters: Sherlock Holmes and Professor Challenger. An even younger Rudyard Kipling, future author of *The Jungle Book*, also witnessed the events surrounding the closure of Breckingridge's factory.

The Doctor "borrowed" Conan Doyle's stethoscope and kept meaning to return it.[1065] **The Doctor claimed to have studied medicine under Bell in Edinburgh.**[1066] The Doctor met Geronimo.[1067]

c 1880 - "The Greatest Gamble"[1068] **->** Gaylord Lefevre, a gambler on a Mississippi riverboat, played the Celestial Toymaker and lost, like so many before him.

On the instructions of Bilis Manger, Gideon ap Tarri recorded the Abaddon/Pwccm battle that he'd witnessed into his diary on 12th June, 1880. On 18th September, 1881, an operative from Torchwood London approached ap Tarri about the document. Ap Tarri fled to prevent it falling into Torchwood's hands, but he died in the same year, and Torchwood exhumed his grave to obtain the item.[1069] **Torchwood Cardiff was equipped with cryogenics in the Victorian era.**[1070]

1881 (25th-26th October) - THE GUNFIGHTERS[1071] **->** The first Doctor, Steven and Dodo landed at Tombstone shortly before the Gunfight at the OK Corral. As the Doctor searched for a dentist, the gun-

man Johnny Ringo found one - Doc Holliday - who he'd been tracking for two years. Marshall Wyatt Earp and his allies killed Ringo and some members of the renegade Clanton family.

w - 1882 (autumn) to 1883 (26th August) - FP: ERASING SHERLOCK[1072] **->** The time traveller Gillian Petra became a maid in Sherlock Holmes' household to observe him for her doctoral thesis. She was unaware that her benefactor, Jimmy Moriarty, and his associate Thomas Peerson Corkle were conducting an experiment to see if the history of a "dynamic individual" such as Holmes could be derailed, and his notoriety erased, early on in his career. Petra and Holmes became lovers. Corkle murdered Holmes' father and sent a serial killer, Francis Black, to debase and kill his sister Genevieve. An anguished Holmes shot Corkle dead, and set about rescuing his sister. The energy released by the eruption of Krakatoa powered Petra's return to the future.

The Doctor witnessed the eruption of Krakatoa.[1073] **The Krakatoa eruption released a Xylok crystal from under the Earth. It would eventually form the heart of Sarah Jane Smith's computer Mr Smith.**[1074] Van Gogh painted the Doctor.[1075] The Monk owned two paintings by van Gogh.[1076] **The Rani kidnapped microbiologist Louis Pasteur.**[1077]

Penelope Gate built herself a time machine using a miniature Analytical Engine. She left her husband in 1883 for a life of time travel. She first headed to the year 2000, actually landing in 1996. The seventh Doctor returned Penelope to her native time after meeting her in feudal Japan.[1078] In 1883, the Time Lord Ulysses exiled his fellow Time Lord Marnal to the home of Penelope Gate's parents

---

1069 *TW: The Twilight Streets*
1070 *TW: To the Last Man*
1071 Dating *The Gunfighters* (3.8) - The story ends with the Gunfight at the OK Corral. The depiction of events owes more to the popular myths and Hollywood treatment of the story than historical accuracy.
1072 Dating *FP: Erasing Sherlock* (FP novel #5) - The story ends with the eruption of Krakatoa on its historical date of 26th August, 1883; many dating notations mark the progression of the story through the year beforehand. Gillian says that the woman whose identity she adopts, "died in early August, just before I arrived" - but Gillian is already ensconced in Holmes' household when the story opens, and it's said to be "autumn" on p13, "November" on p27 (how much time passes between the two isn't immediately clear). While the adventure is based upon the premise that nefarious parties are trying to change Holmes' timeline, it's also implied that he regains his moral compass enough to

become the same detective seen in Conan Doyle's stories (and, by extension) in *Doctor Who*.
1073 *SJA: The Lost Boy*
1074 *Inferno, Rose*. The ninth Doctor also visited the scene. Krakatoa erupted in 1883.
1075 According to the sixth Doctor in "Changes". *Vincent and the Doctor* doesn't rule out that van Gogh and the Doctor (in another body) have met before; in fact, that story has van Gogh claim, "My brother's always sending doctors..."
1076 *The Resurrection of Mars*
1077 *Time and the Rani*. Pasteur lived 1822-1895.
1078 *The Room with No Doors*

on Earth. Marnal's memories were locked off, and he wouldn't recover them until his regeneration in the twenty-first century.[1079]

There was a single account of a pocket of dinosaurs surviving on one plateau in Central Africa, but most scientists and reporters, including a young Arthur Conan Doyle, dismissed it as the ravings of a madman:

"The pygmies from the Oluti Forest led me blindfold for three whole days through uncharted jungle. They took me to a swamp full of giant lizards, like giant dinosaurs." [1080]

1883 - GHOST LIGHT[1081] -> While Light slumbered, the Survey Unit assisting him had established itself in Gabriel Chase north of London as Josiah Samuel Smith, arch-advocate of Darwinist theories. Two years after Inspector Mackenzie vanished while investigating the goings-on at the house, Smith was plotting to use a pass to Buckingham Palace given to his associate - the adventurer Redvers Fenn-Cooper - to assassinate Queen Victoria and bring new order to the "anarchic" British Empire. The seventh Doctor brought Ace to Gabriel Chase to confront her having burned it down in a hundred years' time. Light awoke and sought to destroy Earth in a firestorm, but was goaded by the Doctor into dispersing itself. Josiah and Light's Control Unit swapped places on the evolutionary ladder. Control, Fenn-Cooper, the servant Nimrod and the diminished Josiah left in Light's spaceship, and the house remained abandoned for a century.

The seventh Doctor knew "a nice little restaurant on the Khyber Pass".

The Torchwood Institute learned about events pertaining to the Doctor, Krakatoa and Gabriel Chase.[1082] Justine McManus, later Cousin Justine of Faction Paradox, was born to Jake McManus.[1083]

On 23rd December, 1883, Major Henry Rathbone - his mental health having deteriorated after witnessing Abraham Lincoln's assassination, and after being repeatedly stabbed at the event - murdered his wife Clara.[1084] In 1884, a book was published detailing many types of Amazonian fungus.[1085] Robert Lewis Stevenson gifted the Doctor with a tumbler of whiskey.[1086]

1884 - SJA: THE GHOST HOUSE[1087] -> The genocidal war criminals Skak and Efnol fled from the twenty-first century to a Victorian villa built in 1865, and attempted to produce a time bubble that, when shattered, would help them escape but destroy Earth in the process. Sarah Jane, Luke, Clyde and Rani briefly went back to 1884 and thwarted their plan. An alien bounty hunter - whose name translated in Russian to "Death Kill Massacre" - took the criminals away for trial.

1079 *The Gallifrey Chronicles*
1080 *Ghost Light.* It is unclear from the story whether the plateau really existed or was merely a delirious Fenn-Cooper's rationalisation of his adventures in Gabriel Chase.
1081 Dating *Ghost Light* (26.2) - Set "two years" after 1881, when Mackenzie is sent to investigate the disappearance of Sir George Pritchard, and "a century" before Ace burns down Gabriel Chase in 1983. It's a time of year when the sun sets at six pm (so either the spring or autumn). The script suggested that a caption slide "Perivale - 1883" might be used over the establishing shot of Gabriel Chase. Queen Victoria was a Hanover, not a Saxe-Coburg, but late in her reign she did acquire the nickname "Mrs Saxe-Coburg".
1082 "The Time Machination"
1083 Justine is "barely 16" in *FP: Movers*, set circa March 1899. If the word "barely" can be taken at all literally, she was born in 1883.
1084 *Assassin in the Limelight.* This is historical, and remains a secondary tragedy inflicted on those attending Ford's Theatre with Lincoln. After killing his wife, Rathbone lived in an asylum in Hildesheim, Germany, and died himself in 1911. He was buried alongside Clara in Hildesheim until the authorities deemed their graves as extremely unattended, and had the gravesites

destroyed in 1952. Rathbone and Clara's eldest son served as a U.S. Congressman from Illinois, Lincoln's home state.
1085 *The Green Death*
1086 *The Three Companions.* Stevenson lived 1850-1894.
1087 Dating *SJA: The Ghost House* (*SJA* audiobook #4) - The year is given. Skak's time manipulator relies upon Zygma energy, which was first mentioned in *The Talons of Weng-Chiang*.
1088 Dating *Peacemaker* (NSA #21) - It's the "1880s" according to the back cover. Similarly, the Doctor licks his thumb, holds it up to the air, and determines, "This is 1880-something, I reckon. A Monday. Just after breakfast." *The Time Machine* was published "ten years" after this (in 1895).
1089 Dating *Timelash* (22.5) - The Doctor applies "a time deflection coefficient of 706 years" to the timelash's original destination of 1179, and concludes that Vena will arrive in "1885... AD". *The Terrestrial Index* set this in "c1891", after *The Time Machine* was written.
1090 *The Ghosts of N-Space*
1091 *Deadly Reunion*
1092 *Christmas on a Rational Planet.* No date given, but Blavatsky lived 1831-1891.
1093 *The Unicorn and the Wasp*

c 1885 - PEACEMAKER[1088] **->** The tenth Doctor and Martha learned that a smallpox outbreak in the Wild West town of Redwater, Colorado, had been contained by a travelling salesman: Alvin Godlove. They were attacked by gunslingers with energy weapons, but escaped and discovered that Godlove was making a fortune from his miracle cures. The Doctor determined the involvement of the Clades, sentient weapons whose only rationale was to destroy; Godlove's miracle cure was part of the Clades' self-repair system. The Doctor destroyed the Clade before they "sterilised" the Earth.

1885 - TIMELASH[1089] **->** Vena, the daughter of a Councillor on Karfel, was transported to Earth in the timelash and met Herbert George Wells, who was conducting an experiment with a ouija board. Wells travelled to Karfel with the sixth Doctor, and the experience inspired him, upon his return home, to write his scientific romances.

The Doctor helped "Bertie Wells" with invisibility experiments.[1090] He discovered that H.G. Wells was a ladies man.[1091] The Doctor met the mystic Madame Blavatsky.[1092]

Lady Clemency Eddison met and fell in love with a man named Christopher, actually a Vespiform in human guise, in India in 1885. She became pregnant by Eddison - who died when the Jumna river flooded - and returned to England, secretly giving birth the following year. The child would become the Reverend Arnold Golightly.[1093]

c 1887 - ZYGONS: THE BARNACLED BABY[1094] **->** The Zygon named Demeris, the sole survivor of a wrecked expedition that was searching for Zygon colonies, became part of Jethro's Travelling Freak Show as "the Barnacled Baby". Phineas T. Barnum expressed interest in buying the Baby, or at least arranging for him to be on display in New York. Demeris' notoriety gained him an audience with

Queen Victoria - he subdued the queen, adopted her form and went forth to rule the British Empire...

1887 - ALL-CONSUMING FIRE[1095] **->** Sherlock Holmes and Dr Watson were travelling through Austria on the Orient Express when the train was stopped by Pope Leo XIII. The Pope commissioned Holmes to investigate the theft of occult books from the Library of St. John the Beheaded. With help from the seventh Doctor, Ace and Benny, Holmes discovered that his eldest brother Sherringford had allied himself with the Baron Maupertuis. They planned to use incantations in the books to open a gateway to the planet of Ry'leh. Sherringford was under the thrall of the Great Old One named Azathoth, and hoped this would facilitate her escape to Earth. Maupertuis and Sherringford were both killed, and the Doctor transported Azathoth and her followers to 1906, where they also perished. The Doctor and Holmes sealed the portal to Ry'leh forever.

Arthur Conan Doyle would later write the book *All-Consuming Fire*, but it never saw print.

The Doctor told Ace that he met Sherlock Holmes.[1096] After leaving the Doctor's company in 1871, Ace became lovers with Count Nikolai Sorin, the great grandfather of Captain Sorin. They pretended to be married, but Ace's violent nature frightened the Count, and he left her. Ace continued travelling on her time-hopper, and would attend the wedding of Bernice Summerfield in 2010.[1097]

The inventor Sir Joseph Montague obtained a probe from the future, and incorporated it into the metal mind of his Difference Golem: a robot named Adam. Montague established a factory so that Adam's offspring could eliminate the need for human servants, which he viewed as a form of slavery. The events of Bloody Sunday, 1887, made Montague fear that his robots would be misused for injustice or war, and he deactivated them all.[1098]

In 1888, the Doctor gained a medical degree in

1094 Dating *Zygons: The Barnacled Baby* (BBV audio #30) - The story ends with a shapechanging Zygon replacing Queen Victoria, and nothing is said about what happens next. Victoria definitely isn't killed, as Demeris - as with the TV Zygons - can only assume the body print of a living subject, so it's easy enough to imagine that the substitution is discovered and the real Victoria rescued. For that matter, it's easy to retroactively think that the Victoria seen here is a ringer sent by Torchwood to investigate the mysterious and potentially extra-terrestrial "Baby" - would the actual Queen have been allowed to travel to the baby's bedroom without a single escort? Prince Albert has died (so, the story occurs after 1861), but Barnum is alive (so, it's before his passing in 1891).

1095 Dating *All-Consuming Fire* (NA #27) - It is "the year eighteen eighty seven" according to both Watson (p5) and Benny (p153). References to *The Talons of Weng-Chiang* (p42, p64) suggest this book is set after that story, but aren't conclusive.
1096 *Timewyrm: Revelation*. This was before *All-Consuming Fire*. The eighth Doctor also encountered Holmes, according to *The Gallifrey Chronicles*.
1097 *Happy Endings*, elaborating upon details about Ace given in *The Curse of Fenric* novelisation; see the dating notes on *Set Piece*.
1098 *SJA: Children of Steel*. Bloody Sunday occurred on 13th November, 1887.

Glasgow under Lister.[1099] Around that time, he sparred with John L Sullivan, the first modern world heavyweight champion.[1100] The Doctor discovered the truth behind the mysterious Pale Man in nineteenth-century Whitechapel.[1101]

In the Winter Gardens in Berlin, 1888, Miss Alice Bultitude was in the front row of the stalls as Toby the Sapient Pig's European tour opened. Toby performed with such entertainers as Professor Prometheus, the fireproof Secasian, the "incomparable" Hildebrand and the Blondin Donkey. Bultitude would also attend Toby's farewell concert at the Black Castle, Alhambra, and acquire a first edition copy of his memoirs.[1102]

@ 1888 - THE ANCESTOR CELL[1103] -> Compassion brought the eighth Doctor to Earth to recuperate following Gallifrey's destruction. He woke up in a carriage with no memory of what had happened, and found he possessed a tiny cube, all that remained of his TARDIS.

@ The Doctor was found wandering and was placed on a hospital ward for five days.[1104] He travelled in England for a few years, still having no memories.[1105]

Jack the Ripper

1888 (30th September) - THE PIT[1106] -> The seventh Doctor and William Blake were conveyed by a space-time tear to the East End at the time of the Jack the Ripper murders, then departed to the late twentieth century.

1888 (30th September) - "Ripper's Curse"[1107] -> The eleventh Doctor, Amy and Rory intended to watch Accrington Stanley play football in London, but instead materialised just after Jack the Ripper - actually a ferocious alien reptile, a Re'nar, using a shimmer suit to disguise itself as human - murdered Long Lizzie Stride. The Doctor's psychic paper helped to establish Amy and Rory's credentials as Miss Marple and Inspector Clouseau of CSI London, and then named Rory as the Earl of Upper Leadworth, Conan Doyle's inspiration for Sherlock Holmes.

Amy remembered that the Ripper would next murder Catherine Eddowes, who died later that very night. She led the police to the scene... to find that Eddowes had already been murdered. The Doctor was found kneeling over her dead body, and was arrested on suspicion of being the Ripper. He was quickly released by Inspector Abbeline, the detective investigating the Ripper crimes.

1099 *The Moonbase.* Surgeon Joseph Lister lived 5th April, 1827, to 10th February, 1912. *Apollo 23* says the Doctor was given an honourary degree in rhetoric and oratory by the University of Ursa Beta. In *The God Complex*, he claims to have a degree in cheese-making.
1100 *Carnival of Monsters*
1101 *Synthespians™*
1102 *Year of the Pig*
1103 Dating *The Ancestor Cell* (EDA #36) - It's "more than a hundred years" (p282) before 2001, and "one hundred and thirteen years" before in *Escape Velocity* (p184), which would make It 1888.
1104 *Vanishing Point*
1105 *The Burning*
1106 Dating *The Pit* (NA #12) - Blake sees a newspaper dated "the thirtieth of September, 1888". There's some indication this takes place in a parallel timeline, so it's not "the" Jack the Ripper murders.
1107 Dating "Ripper's Curse" (IDW *DW* Vol. 2 #2-4) - The opening caption says it's "30 September 1888. 12:30 a.m.", which matches the real-life murder of Elizabeth Stride, the Ripper's third canonical victim.
1108 Dating "Ripper's Curse" (IDW *DW* Vol. 2 #2-4) - Amy confirms that it's "9th November", the night of the final Ripper murder. *Matrix* and *A Good Man Goes to War* offer alternate explanations for Jack the Ripper (see the Unfixed Points in Time sidebar). "Ripper's Curse", very oddly, seems to ignore some new-series rules pertaining to historical alteration - the Doctor says that the Ripper's victims are all "static" points in time, but tries to

alter the final one anyway (see the Fixed Points in Time sidebar). Moreover, time *is* altered in this story - Mary Warner is "meant" to die, but the timeline is left with Mary Kelly (who died in our history) being killed instead.

It's arguably an anachronism that a member of the Metropolitan police is so well acquainted with both Sherlock Holmes and Conan Doyle's methodology in creating the character - the first Holmes story, *A Study in Scarlet*, was published prior to this in 1887, but the character's popularity didn't take off until the first series of short stories emerged in *The Strand*, starting in 1891. However, the Earl of Upper Leadworth is fictional, suggesting that Holmes' history in the *Doctor Who* universe is a deviation from the real world.

UNFIXED POINTS IN TIME: Reconciling the three accounts of Jack the Ripper in *Matrix*, "Ripper's Curse" and on screen in *A Good Man Goes to War* does tend towards absurdity - the Ripper is respectively shown to be the Valeyard, to be a murderous alien, and to be an unnamed party dispatched by Madame Vastra, all in seemingly unrelated adventures.

As a unifying theory about this, though, perhaps there's a class of events that are destined to remain mysteries. After all, the main historical significance of the Jack the Ripper is that it's famous *as a mystery*. Perhaps what happened remains unknown and open to question *even after we've seen an explanation*. (A whimsical example of this from real life: IDW's publicity materials proclaimed that "Ripper's Curse" would be

Mary Warner was fated to become the Ripper's final victim, and Amy was horrified to learn that the Doctor planned to let Warner die because each of the Ripper's victims was a static point in space and time, and couldn't be altered. Amy warned Mary anyway, but she didn't listen. The Doctor discovered that an alien Ju'wes was passing as Sir Charles Warren of Scotland Yard, and had pursued the Re'nar from the future. The Re'nar was committing the murders with the intent of discrediting the Ju'wes, retroactively undermining them in the Re'nar/Ju'wes war to come. The Doctor was convinced by Amy that they should try to save Warner, and jumped forward five weeks in the TARDIS...

(=) 1888 (9th November) - "Ripper's Curse"[1108] **->** Mary Warner was Jack the Ripper's final victim.

Amy's warning to Mary Warner five weeks previous had altered time - she had survived, but the Ripper instead killed Mary Kelly. The Re'nar-Ripper captured Amy, and the Doctor and Rory took the TARDIS to 2011 to examine the historical alteration. They returned forewarned that the Ripper would kill both Amy and Mary Warner. The Ripper took Amy and Mary to a cellar, but they escaped. The Ju'wes posing as Warner pulled the Re'nar into an unstable space-time tunnel, killing them both.

1888 (November) - MATRIX[1109] **->** The Valeyard now had control of the Dark Matrix - the embodiment of the dark thoughts of the Time Lord minds within the Matrix - and journeyed with it to Whitechapel, 1888. While the Dark Matrix lodged itself in a tomb, the Valeyard renamed himself "the Ripper" and set about killing prostitutes. The Dark Matrix fed off the psychic potential of these murders.

The seventh Doctor and Ace arrived from an alternate timeline in 1963, and the Doctor was mentally assaulted by the Dark Matrix so much, he downloaded his mind into a telepathic circuit. The amnesiac Doctor became a card-shark named Johnny, and was aided by a man named Joseph Liebermann (possibly the Wandering Jew of legend), even as Ace tried to make ends meet as a maid.

The Doctor's memories were restored, and he confronted the Valeyard. The Dark Matrix imploded, and the Valeyard was struck by lightning and killed.

1888 (November) - A GOOD MAN GOES TO WAR[1110] **->** The Silurian warrior Madame Vastra had become an adventuress in London alongside her human companion Jenny. On the very night that Vastra caught and ate Jack the Ripper, the Doctor sought Vastra's help in storming Demon's Run and saving Amy.

1889 - SJA: LOST IN TIME[1111] **->** Sarah Jane Smith was transported to the wrong time zone on her mission to find a piece of chronosteel, and met the ghost-hunter Emily Morris. The chronosteel had taken the form of a key, and was causing a temporal overlap with a future time in which two children were under threat from a fire. Sarah and Emily used the chronosteel key to open the children's bedroom door, saving their lives. A mishap caused Sarah to return to 2010 without the key. Emily kept it, went on to become a doctor and founded a hospital for children.

---

the "first" time that *Doctor Who* had dealt with Jack the Ripper, a statement the company retracted when it was pointed out that actually, it wasn't.)

This doesn't rule out *all* mysteries being unsolved - the Doctor seems to conclusively solve the mystery of Agatha Christie's real-life disappearance in *The Unicorn and the Wasp*, for example. But it might account for why there are historical mysteries with multiple solutions in the *Doctor Who* universe. Candidates might include the beginning of the universe, the extinction of the dinosaurs, the exact origin of man, how and why the Pyramids were built, the purpose of standing stones, the Fall of Atlantis, the Great Fire of London, what happened to the *Mary Celeste* (only if one stacks the short story "Timechase" and the comic "The Mystery of the Marie Celeste" - both of them being outside the remit of this timeline - alongside *The Chase*), what happened at Tunguska, the sinking of the *Titanic* as well as a whole host of Fortean mysteries (the Loch Ness Monster, Yeti, Roswell, flying saucers, etc.). Within the fiction of the *Doctor Who* universe, the exact origins of the Daleks, the start of the Sontaran-Rutan war, the beginnings of the Time Lords and the reason the Doctor left Gallifrey might be "unfixed".

Great care should be taken, however, to distinguish between "unfixed" historical mysteries and simply things where there's one explanation that's not been uncovered. It's also probably best not to use this as a handwave for any continuity problems - like, say, why the manned space program of the UNIT years is more advanced than the one seen in the new series, or the final fate of the planet Earth. But where *Doctor Who* has multiple explanations for the same historical mystery, we might usefully think the reason is that it's "unfixed".

1109 Dating *Matrix* (PDA #16) - It's during the time of the Ripper murders (the later part of 1888); the month is given as "November" (p155, 231). The last of the canonical Jack the Ripper murders took place on 9th November, 1888, so this is presumably after that.

1110 Dating *A Good Man Goes to War* (X6.7) - As with *Matrix*, this is presumably after the last of the Ripper killings.

1111 Dating *SJA: Lost in Time* (SJA 4.5) - The year is given.

1889 - "The Time Machination"[1112] **->** "Jonathan Smith", a time traveller from the mid-fifty-first century, became an acquaintance of H.G. Wells as part of a scheme to kill the fourth Doctor and avert Magnus Greel's demise. The tenth Doctor learned of Smith's plot, and collaborated with Wells to thwart it. Robert Lewis and Eliza Cooper of Torchwood were tricked into thinking that Smith was the Doctor, and imprisoned him. They also learned that the Doctor had the ability to change his appearance. Wells said goodbye to the Doctor and vowed to start writing a story called "The Time Machine".

By this time, Torchwood had hubs in Cardiff, Glasgow and the West India Docks.

Torchwood subsequently dissected Mr Smith.[1113]

c 1889 - THE TALONS OF WENG-CHIANG[1114] **->** The fourth Doctor and Leela arrived in London during the middle of Li H'sen Chang's search for the time cabinet of Magnus Greel, a war criminal who had escaped the fifty-first century. Greel himself lurked in the sewers, reliant on draining the life force of young women to continue surviving. He had brought the Peking Homunculus with him to act as his agent. With the help of an eminent pathologist, Professor Litefoot, and the manager of the Palace Theatre, Henry Gordon Jago, the Doctor tracked Magnus Greel to his lair and destroyed him and the Homunculus.

Human sacrifice was still taking place in Moreton Harwood in the early eighteen-nineties.[1115] The Doctor met Mark Twain.[1116] He also met the French novelist Emile Zola.[1117] **Jack Harkness had a boyfriend in the 1890s - a Slovenian who took arsenic to improve his skin.**[1118]

1890 (early June) - VINCENT AND THE DOCTOR[1119] **-> The eleventh Doctor and Amy visited Auvers to investigate the mystery creature painted into Vincent van Gogh's *The Church at Avers*. They found Vincent at a cafe, but were attacked by a creature invisible to everyone but the painter. Vincent painted *The Church at Avers*, which showed the creature behind one of the church windows. The Doctor identified it as a Krafayis, a predatory creature abandoned on Earth. The Krafayis was blind and died, impaled on Vincent's painting stand. The Doctor and Amy briefly took Vincent to a museum in Amy's time; after Vincent returned home, he signed one of his works, *Still Work: Vase with Twelve Sunflowers*, "For Amy, Vincent."**

1890 (June) - THE PANDORICA OPENS[1120] **->** Vincent van Gogh was sensitive to the signals being broadcast by the Underhenge, and experienced mental anguish. One of his last paintings, *The Pandorica Opens*, depicted the destruction of the TARDIS.

1112 Dating "The Time Machination" (IDW *DW* one-shot #2) - A caption says it's "London 1889", and Wells claims that he met the Doctor in *Timelash* "four or five years back" (even if the version of Wells seen here is very hard to reconcile against the slightly younger version seen on screen). The story ends with the fourth Doctor and Leela arriving at the beginning of *The Talons of Weng-Chiang*. Lewis and Cooper seem attached to the Torchwood branch operating out of the West India Docks, although they are acquainted with Jack Harkness by "Final Sacrifice".
1113 "Final Sacrifice"
1114 Dating *The Talons of Weng-Chiang* (14.6) - No date is given, and the story is trying to encapsulate an era, rather than a precise year. The story is set soon after the Jack the Ripper murders (1888), as Henry Gordon Jago refers to "Jolly Jack". In the draft script, Casey went on to say that the new batch of disappearances can't be the Ripper because he "is in Canada".

Litefoot is seen reading a copy of *Blackwood's Magazine* from February 1892 in episode four... then again, there's also a modern newspaper visible in Litefoot's laundry in episode three, with a headline that references British politician Denis Healey, so both could be considered set dressing rather than definitive dating evidence.

The story takes place before *The Bodysnatchers* and possibly *All-Consuming Fire* (although that only mentions Mr Sin, so might refer to earlier activities than this story). The *Jago & Litefoot* audios, which most likely begin in 1892, seem to occur some months, more likely some years, after *Talons*.

The first edition of *Timelink* stated that it was 1895; the Telos version of the book goes for February 1892. *About Time* roughly concurred with the latter. *The Terrestrial Index* went for "c1890".
1115 "Ninety years" before *K9 and Company*.
1116 *The Crooked World*
1117 *Ghost Ship*. Zola lived 1840-1902.
1118 *TW: Miracle Day*
1119 Dating *Vincent and the Doctor* (X5.10) - The story entails Vincent painting *The Church at Auvers*, which Dr Black says was completed "somewhere between the 1st and 3rd of June 1890, less than a year before [van Gogh] killed himself". Vincent died on 29th July, so while Black is technically right, it was more accurately about two months beforehand.

The story has a few anachronisms... Vincent has both ears, but in real life, he'd cut one off in December 1888. *The Church at Avers* was painted in 1890, but Vincent's series of sunflower paintings (the creation of which Amy here influences) were done August 1888 to January 1889. The episode opens with Vincent painting *Wheatfield with Crows*, which was actually completed

(=) 1890 (July) - THE STORY OF MARTHA: "The Frozen Wastes"[1121] **->** The tenth Doctor and Martha attended a presentation by the explorer Pierre Bruyere to the London Geographical Congress - an event that puzzled the Doctor, as history claimed that Bruyere's expedition had vanished three months previous, in April 1890. The Doctor and Martha accompanied Bruyere on a balloon trip to the North Pole, and were caught in a time loop - an unidentified entity was forcing Bruyere to make his journey again and again, so it could harvest his memories. The creature tried to feed upon the Doctor and Martha, but their memories were so voluminous, it burst...

Pierre Bruyere happily settled into a life of being a baker, as his parents had been before him.

Vincent van Gogh killed himself.[1122]

The eleventh Doctor suggested that the Moulin Rouge in 1890 would be a suitable romantic destination for Rory and Amy.[1123] Jack Harkness met a man named Alec at the Moulin Rouge, 1890, and fought with the painter Toulouse Lautrec over him. An extra-terrestrial conman, Monsieur Jechiel, was on commission to recruit an army of the undead to fight the Togomil Heresy, and transformed Alec into such a soldier. Jechiel subsequently left - partly because Jack told him to get lost, partly because he'd not been paid.[1124]

w - In October 1890, the pair of boots that Sherlock Holmes lost during his time with Gillian Petra was returned to him.[1125]

By 1890, a retired William Chesterton had translated Ho Lin Chung's *Mountains and Sunsets* into English.[1126] Ace was on the Red List of the Shadow Directory by 1892.[1127] An advanced society on Duchamp 331 had built the Warp Core, an energy being, to combat the Krill. The Warp Core killed off the Krill and its creators also, reducing Duchamp 331 to a dust planet. The creature wandered through space and time before seeking refuge in the mind of the Norwegian artist Edvard Munch. He painted *The Scream*, which exorcised the Warp Core from his mind into the painting.[1128] Following his encounter with Moriarty at Reichenbach Falls, Sherlock Holmes went into hiding.[1129]

In 1892, Captain Jack got into a fight on Ellis Island. He was shot through the heart and lived - and thereby came to realise that events in 200,100 had rendered him immortal.[1130]

1892 - TIMEH: THE SEVERED MAN[1131] **->** The Cabal of the Horned Beast formed as a middling demon-worshipping cult, an excuse to engage in debauchery. The group obtained a book that could control time and summon representatives of the Daemons. Although the book was eventually stolen, the Cabal's surviving members reclaimed it in the twenty-sixth century and used it to retroactively give their forefathers more wealth and influence, leading in future to the creation of Sodality.

Jago & Litefoot[1132]

Professor Litefoot and Henry Gordon Jago continued to team up after the Weng-Chiang affair, investigating infernal incidents and cracking complex conundrums. They resolved a mystery with a trained anteater and an aluminium violin, then didn't see each other for a time. Litefoot

some weeks *after* this story, around 10th July. (Then again, the opening might be more thematic than literal.) It's perhaps excusable that Vincent appears to have signed "For Amy" in English, assuming the TARDIS is translating it; in real life, the work just bears Vincent's signature.
1120 Dating *The Pandorica Opens* (X5.12) - The year appears in a caption. *Doctor Who: The Encyclopedia* says this happened "a few weeks" after *Vincent and the Doctor*, so it's very close to van Gogh's death.
1121 Dating *The Story of Martha*: "The Frozen Wastes" (NSA #28d) - The year and month are given.
1122 *Vincent and the Doctor*. This happened on 29th July, 1890.
1123 *The Vampires of Venice*
1124 *TW*: "Fated to Pretend"
1125 The prologue to *FP: Erasing Sherlock*, as published in *FP: Warring States*.
1126 *The Eleventh Tiger*
1127 *The Death of Art*

1128 *Dust Breeding*. There are actually four different versions (and a lithograph) of *The Scream*, all created by Munch between 1893 and 1910.
1129 *Benny: The Adventure of the Diogenes Damsel*, following the continuity established in Conan Doyle's stories. "The Final Problem", where Sherlock seemed to perish, was set in 1891.
1130 *Utopia*
1131 Dating *TimeH: The Severed Man* (*TimeH* #5) - The year is repeatedly given. The Cabal's links to Sodality are explained in *TimeH: Child of Time* (p64).
1132 Dating *The Mahogany Murderers* (BF CC 3.11) and *Jago & Litefoot* Series 1, 2 and 3 (*The Bloodless Soldier*, 1.1; *The Bellova Devil*, 1.2; *The Spirit Trap*, 1.3; *The Similarity Engine*, 1.4; *Litefoot and Sanders*, 2.1; *The Necropolis Express*, 2.2; *The Theatre of Dreams*, 2.3; *The Ruthven Inheritance*, 2.4; *Dead Men's Tales*, 3.1; *The Man at the End of the Garden*, 3.2; *Swan Song*, 3.3; *Chronoclasm*, 3.4) - The production notes for *Jago & Litefoot* Series 1 say, "The year is 1892. It is a short while after *The Talons of*

had a laboratory in the basement of St. Thomas' Hospital, which the trustees made available to the police. Jago was forced to close the Palace Theatre, and became the master of ceremonies at the Alhambra Theatre in Putney.

Dr Heinrich Tulp, having studied astral projection in Tibet, projected his mind into the future and witnessed technological developments to come. This also, however, brought his mind into contact with a formless entity in the dark recesses of space. It compelled Tulp to undertake many experiments with his future knowledge, searching for a means of making Earth akin to its homeworld, a radioactive wasteland. To finance his experiments, Tulp embarked upon many criminal endeavours.[1133]

c 1892 (summer) - THE MAHOGANY MURDERERS -> Jago and Litefoot discovered that Dr Tulp had engineered a device that could transfer a person's spirit into inanimate objects. He had done so with several convicts at Newgate, creating a gang of men made from wood. The leader of this bunch, Jack "the Knife" Yeovil, proposed that

they shift their spirits into bodies made from more impervious materials, then rally an army of convicts to take over the Empire, then the world. Litefoot disconnected Tulp's machinery, making the convicts' spirits return to their discarded, buried bodies.

c 1892 (summer) - JAGO & LITEFOOT: THE BLOODLESS SOLDIER / THE BELLOVA DEVIL / THE SPIRIT TRAP / THE SIMILARITY ENGINE / LITEFOOT AND SAUNDERS -> Jago and Litefoot intervened in mysterious happenings that included a British army captain who was infected with lycanthropy. They also brought down the Far-Out Travellers Club, a con run by Dr Tulp to swindle patrons out of their estates. On yet another case, Jago and Litefoot stopped beings from the forty-ninth century from projecting their minds into people via seances, part of a plan to take control of the British Empire. They finally stopped Dr Tulp from cornering the world's supply of uranium, and embarking upon a scheme to replace prominent government officials and businessmen

Weng-Chiang, in which Litefoot reads the February 1892 edition of *Blackwood's Magazine*. But unless we absolutely have to, we won't mention specific dates. The stories exist in the limbo of the classic late Victorian era. Queen Victorian is on the throne, the British Empire seems to control most of the world, and science is the answer to all problems. London is a perpetual murk of... fogs and industrial pollution, and you can always charter a special railway train to get you wherever you need to go."

Despite this intended ambiguity, however, Series 1 simultaneously indicates that the year is 1892 (the revolution that occurred in Eastern Rumelia in 1885 happened "seven years ago", according *J&L: The Bellova Devil*) and that a fair amount of time has passed since *Talons* (Jago says in *J&L: The Similarity Engine* that the "demonic deflagration" that closed the Palace Theatre happened "a few years back"; Litefoot calls Jago one of "his oldest friends" in *J&L: The Spirit Trap*; Litefoot says in *J&L: Litefoot and Saunders* that the events which brought him and Jago together happened "some time ago"; and even *The Mahogany Murders* has Jago stating that the "adventure in Limehouse", presumably meaning *Talons*, was "a while back". He and Litefoot appear to have working together off and on since then.

Jago & Litefoot Series 1 and 2 (as well as the Companion Chronicles audio leading into them, *The Mahogany Murderers*) seem to happen in relatively close succession to one another. Litefoot's conversation with Ellie the barmaid in *J&L: The Bellova Devil*, for instance, suggests that as little as a week has passed since the previous episode. However, the seasonal time frame within the mini-series is a little warped... a week passes within *The Similarity Engine*, but only a few days then seem to elapse between Ellie the barmaid being

"killed" by the vampire Saunders (in *Litefoot and Saunders*, which occurs the day after *The Similarity Engine*) and her body being shipped via train for burial in a pauper's field (in *J&L: The Necropolis Express*). And yet, in that relatively short space of time, it's magically gone from being "the middle of summer" (as Jago claims in *The Similarity Engine*) to Litefoot commenting upon the "frosty air" and wishing he were at home in front of a warm fireplace (in *The Necropolis Express*). At least "a month" seems to pass in the course of *J&L: The Theatre of Dreams*, and another passes during *J&L: The Ruthven Inheritance*, so if it isn't already autumn when *The Theatre of Dreams* begins, it almost inescapably is when Series 2 finishes.

The references given in Series 3 point to it taking place the following year (1893), even if this wasn't necessarily the intent, and there's a little ambiguity about it. Jago says in *J&L: The Man at the End of the Garden* that "It's August" - as Series 2 concluded so late in the year, it must now be the *following* August, i.e. August 1893. Also, *J&L: Chronoclasm* has Jago referring to the panto performance held at the New Regency in Christmas - he only inherited the theatre in Series 2, so, again, it must now be the following year. However, mention is made in *J&L: Swan Song* that Jago has only been at the New Regency "a few months", when (if it really *is* 1893), it's been more like a year.

Where this becomes especially tricky is that in the final Series 3 story (*Chronoclasm*), Litefoot says to Sgt Quick: "You and I, and Jago and Miss Leela, we've come across some of the most vile and appalling things over the past year or so..." - a line possibly meant to suggest that a year had passed within *Jago & Litefoot* Series 1, 2 *and* 3. Given the aforementioned math on how much time passes in Series 1 and 2, though, Litefoot's line

with his wooden simulacra. The entity influencing Tulp turned him into a tentacled monster, which Jago and Litefoot dispatched.

The day after defeating Tulp, Jago and Litefoot challenged - and badly burned - Gabriel Saunders, a purported vampire expert who was himself a master vampire.

c 1892 (autumn) - JAGO & LITEFOOT: THE NECROPOLIS EXPRESS / THE THEATRE OF DREAMS / THE RUTHVEN INHERITANCE -> Jago inherited the New Regency Theatre. His continuing adventures with Litefoot entailed their defeating Dr Sibelius Crow, a mad scientist who wanted to turn corpses into bestial creatures to serve as soldiers for the Empire; besting the Theatre de Fantasie, a living story that fed off the dreams and fantasies of mortals; and killing the fiend Gabriel Saunders.

c 1892 - JAGO & LITEFOOT: DEAD MEN'S TALES -> Operating from 2011, the temporal engineer Elliot Payne tried to harvest all of Earth's temporal energy - enough raw power to free his wife, who was trapped in an event horizon millennia in the future. Payne's experiments created time breaks, and so Leela was dispatched from Gallifrey to aid Litefoot and Jago in dealing with the situation. One of Payne's experiments translocated the doomed Navy seaman Johnny Skipton from 1958; the resultant time break resolved when the spirits of Skipton's crewmates claimed him, and they all drowned as intended.

1893 (spring to 8th May) - BENNY: THE ADVENTURE OF THE DIOGENES DAMSEL[1134] -> Straxus, a Time Lord who was stranded on Earth, diverted

Benny's time ring as she travelled from prehistoric times. Dr Watson and his wife were away on a recuperative cruise, so Benny made the acquaintance of Mycroft Holmes - who worked for Her Majesty's Foreign and Commonwealth Office, and looked nothing like his illustrations in *The Strand*. She aided him in solving a number of crimes, including the Case of the Peculiar Pig. They also stopped the Choirmaster of Cloistersham from selling cipher keys to the Shah of Iran.

Benny and Mycroft stopped Straxus' assistants, two Cwejen, from committing murders that prominently featured the number 7, in an attempt to create a pattern in history that would attract the attention of a "pale god" named Mr Seven. A past version of Straxus locked up his successor, and also gave Benny a working time ring.

Mycroft Holmes currently possessed the only copy of *All-Consuming Fire*.

1893 (July to August) - CAMERA OBSCURA[1135] -> The eighth Doctor and Sabbath both arrived in Victorian England after detecting disturbances in time. A faulty time machine, based on the principles of temporal interferometry, had splintered the stage magician Octave into eight individuals. Octave attacked the Doctor, who lived because Sabbath had placed the Doctor's second heart in his own chest, which tethered the Doctor to the living world. Sabbath's assassin, the Angel-Maker, killed Octave.

The time machine had also twinned the insane psychologist Nathaniel Chiltern. One of the Nathaniels attempted to further use the machine, which could have punctured the space-time continuum, but the Doctor destroyed the device by flinging himself into it. Nathaniel killed the Angel-Maker, but was then killed by Sabbath. By

probably has to be construed as indicating how much time has passed in Series 3 alone. This would mean that Leela literally spends about a year dashing around resolving time breaks with Litefoot and Jago, but to date there's nothing to particularly rule that out. Leela arrives at Litefoot's house in the epilogue of Series 2, so it's possible that the first story of Series 3 (*J&L: Dead Men's Tales*) happens in 1892, even if the bulk of Series 3 must then unfold in 1893.

In *Chronoclasm*, Payne is suitably vague when he tells Nikolas Tesla that the year is "1890, give or take a few years." Jago and Litefoot's encounter with Claudius Dark is the lead-in to *Jago & Litefoot* Series 4 (released in 2012, so outside this chronology).
1133 The background to *Jago & Litefoot* Series 1, largely given in *The Mahogany Murderers* and *J&L: The Similarity Engine*.
1134 Dating *Benny: The Adventure of the Diogenes Damsel* (Benny audio #9.3) - Benny guesstimates her arrival in this era as being "late spring" based upon the "filthy weather", and she seems to spend some weeks

helping Mycroft solve cases. Her diary states that her confrontation with Straxus begins on "7th of May", and events spill over to the next day. It's doubtful that Benny spends much more time in 1893 after getting a working time ring on 8th May, as she seems awfully eager to check on Peter.

The legendary figure of the Cwejen, "Mr Seven", also here called Time's Champion, is almost certainly the seventh Doctor. Mycroft's housekeeper is named as "Mrs Grose", presumably the character seen in *Ghost Light*. Cloisterham is a fictional town from *The Mystery of Edwin Drood*, Charles Dickens' unfinished work. A different incarnation of Straxus appeared in Big Finish's BBC7 range.
1135 Dating *Camera Obscura* (EDA #59) - It's the "nineteenth century" (p6), Maskelyne (presumably the magician John Nevil Maskelyne, 1839-1917) is alive (p7) and it's a "century" before Anji's time (p35). Fitz here meets George Williamson, so this is before *Time Zero*.

159

extension, this killed the other Nathaniel.

At this time, the Doctor, Fitz and Anji attended a séance. Also in attendance was a young man named William.[1136] The Doctor collected some oolong tea in Peking in either 1893 or 1983.[1137]

c 1893 (August) - JAGO & LITEFOOT: THE MAN AT THE END OF THE GARDEN ->

Eleanor Naismith, née Maycombe, had become a famed author of fantasy stories. Litefoot, Jago and Leela helped to stop the fairy-man whom Eleanor had bargained with as a child from vengefully killing Eleanor's daughter Clara - who had been formed via the fairy-man's magic pocketbook. Clara used the book to make jackdaws carry the fairy-man away to the moon, where one of their number kept him company.

c 1893 - JAGO & LITEFOOT: SWAN SONG / CHRONOCLASM ->

Litefoot, Jago and Leela found that Elliot's experiments had forged a temporal link between the New Regency Theatre and Elliot's laboratory, which stood on the same locale in 2011. Payne's equipment was ruined, but he successfully journeyed down the link and arrived in the 1890s. Because it amused him, Payne kidnapped Nikola Tesla from a future year to serve as his assistant.

(=) Leela and her allies failed to find Payne, who converted Earth's temporal energy. Roads split and the Thames boiled as the whole history of London happened all at once. Jago witnessed the cataclysm and was thrown back in time a few hours...

Leela's temporal register triangulated Payne's location from the future Jago. A cadre of Time Eaters arrived to collect the energy Payne had promised them. Payne realised

the Time Eaters had killed his wife, and, on Litefoot's suggestion, temporally connected his lair with 12th October, 1940 - when a bomb was slated to destroy the New Regency. The Time Eaters were obliterated, Payne also seemed to perish and Tesla was returned to his native year.

Leela said farewell to her friends, but her time ring failed to return her home - indicating that danger was still present - even as Jago and Litefoot were approached by Professor Claudius Dark...

Prior to this, Professor Litefoot had met Oscar Wilde.

In 1894, Frederick Simonsson purchased two of Claudio Tardelli's reality-warping paintings for the King of Sweden.[1138] **Thomas Reginald Brockless, a soldier in World War I, was born on 7th February, 1894.**[1139]

1894 - TIME ZERO[1140] ->

Keen to be an adventurer in his own right, Fitz accompanied palaeontologist George Williamson on an expedition to Siberia. Tsar Alexander III was present when the expedition left Vladivostok.

Reptiles from another timeline attacked the expedition, killing everyone but Fitz and Williamson. A huge explosion encased the two of them in ice, where they would remain for over a hundred years. The eighth Doctor and Williamson later went back to 1894 and averted the saurians' timeline by arranging Williamson's death. The billionaire Maxwell Curtis, travelling down a time corridor to this era from 2002, died in a minor explosion.

As a result of these events, an energy being from an o-region - a sort of isolated, mini-universe - was drawn to Earth. Bits of it seeped through Williamson's time corridor into the past, where it was worshipped by some cultures. The main portion of the fire elemental that arrived in 1894, however, achieved enough critical mass to work toward its agenda of consuming Earth entirely.

1136 *Camera Obscura.* William is the human version of Spike from *Buffy the Vampire Slayer.* However, the dating is awry - in *Buffy,* Spike became a vampire in 1880.
1137 *Army of Death*
1138 "Four years" before *Grand Theft Cosmos.*
1139 *TW: To the Last Man*
1140 Dating *Time Zero* (EDA #60) - This was in "1894" (p15).
1141 *The Burning*
1142 *The Gallifrey Chronicles.* This is the same issue of the *Strand* the Doctor is looking for in *The Bodysnatchers.*
1143 Dating *Demon Quest: The Demon of Paris* (BBC fourth Doctor audio #2.2) - The Doctor dates the poster to "1894" in *Demon Quest: The Relics of Time.* Mrs Wibbsey affirms that year in *Demon Quest: Starfall,* and it's "June 1894" according to the sleeve notes.
1144 *Demon Quest: The Demon of Paris*
1145 Dating *Iris: Enter Wildthyme* (Iris novel #1) - The year and month are given (p80). It's a Thursday (p82).

1146 Dating *The Bodysnatchers* (EDA #3) - It is "11.01.1894" (p15). It is six years since the Ripper murders (p2), and five years since *The Talons of Weng Chiang* (p37). Previous editions of *Ahistory* postulated that the minor character "Mr. Stoker" (no first name given) was *Dracula* author Bram Stoker, but a closer examination of Stoker's life voids this idea. Stoker was living in London in 1894, but served as the business manager of the Lyceum Theatre from 1878 to 1905 - it doesn't seem likely that such an established businessman, husband and father would moonlight (as "Stoker" does here) as a thuggish enforcer to a factory-owner.
1147 "Three years" before *Grand Theft Cosmos.*
1148 Dating *The Burning* (EDA #37) - It's "a few years" since the Doctor arrived on Earth (p142), dated in *Escape Velocity* to 1888. The most precise indication in *The Burning* itself is that it's "the late nineteenth century". It is "fifty years" before *The Turing Test* (p59), which is set in January 1943.

The elemental allied itself with Roger Nepath, who believed it could restore his dead sister Patience to life.[1141] Marnal's first story, "The Giants", was published in the *Strand* in 1894.[1142]

1894 (June) - DEMON QUEST: THE DEMON OF PARIS[1143] ->

The fourth Doctor and Mrs Wibbsey dropped off the elephant they picked up in Roman Britain and proceeded by train to Paris to investigate the Doctor's appearance on one of Henri Toulouse-Lautrec's posters. Lautrec's recent behaviour had been erratic, and a number of girls had been found murdered. Moreover, all of the paintings in the artist's studio had been slashed to pieces. The Doctor and Wibbsey found Lautrec at the Moulin Rouge, and discovered that even Lautrec has begun to doubt his own sanity. The travellers found desiccated corpses in Lautrec's attic, along with the missing component from the TARDIS - but this made the Doctor suspect Lautrec wasn't the murderer. The concierge was a shapeshifter who drained life energy, and the same demonic being who posed as Claudius in the first century. The alien once again escaped in a dematerialisation chamber, and the Doctor and Mrs Wibbsey returned to 2010.

Shortly after this time, Mrs Wibbsey's parents died. Her younger self was sent to live with her aunt.[1144]

= **1894 (a Thursday in June) - IRIS: ENTER WILDTHYME**[1145] -> Iris Wildthyme's favourite month and year to spend in Paris was June 1894, and she worked to avoid running into herself there. She, Kelly, Simon and Panda saw the Martians invade the Paris of an alternate dimension. Between now and the turn of the century, the city would be levelled.

1894 - THE BODYSNATCHERS[1146] ->

Henry Gordon Jago had been a bit dyspeptic of late, and on Professor Litefoot's orders had gone to see his sister in Brighton for a few weeks. With Litefoot's help, the eighth Doctor and Sam Jones discovered that a series of grisly murders were part of a Zygon plot to conquer the world. The Doctor confronted Balaak, the Zygon leader, and accidentally killed some of the Zygons by poisoning their milk. The Zygons' pack of Skarasen threatened London until the Doctor lured them into the TARDIS. He relocated them and a Zygon survivor, Tuval, to an uninhabited planet.

In 1895, Frederick Simonsson acquired one of Claudio Tardelli's sculptures. It was actually a silicate-based life-form tasked with protecting the diamond containing Tardelli's micro-universe.[1147]

@ c 1895 (January) - THE BURNING[1148] ->

The amnesiac eighth Doctor ended up in Middletown, just in time to investigate a mysterious geological fault. He realised that it was the home of a fire elemental that was in league with local developer, Roger Nepath. The Doctor blew up a dam, flooding the fault and extinguishing the elemental. The Doctor callously killed Nepath.

On February 14th, 1895, the Doctor attended the debut performance of *The Importance of Being Earnest*.[1149]
@ In March 1895, the Doctor met George Bernard Shaw at a party hosted by Oscar Wilde. Around that time, Sherlock Holmes solved the McCarthy murders before the Doctor could.[1150] The Doctor claimed to have acquired a walking stick and shroud after an encounter with Oscar Wilde and a theatre of midget assassins.[1151] The fourth Doctor claimed he was asked to be George VI's godfather.[1152] Nikola Tesla was temporarily transported back in time by Elliot Payne.[1153]

The fire elemental first manifests on Earth in *Time Zero* and writer Justin Richards has confirmed that whereas bits of the creature seep through Williamson's time corridor (causing a residual presence of it to be worshipped by ancient cultures, etc.), it's only when the main chunk of it arrives in 1894 that the elemental attains enough critical mass to work toward its own insidious agenda. Therefore, *The Burning* - in which the elemental works to its own design, and the Doctor defeats it - manifestly has to occur after *Time Zero*.

The Burning (p238) specifies that it's January, so allowing that some time (a few months at least) probably pass while the elemental and Nepath forge their pact and start to implement it, January 1895 seems the most likely time for *The Burning* to occur. The date was given as 1889 in the original story synopsis.
1149 *Assassin in the Limelight*

1150 *The Gallifrey Chronicles*, a reference to Nicholas Meyer's novel *The West End Horror*, which features Holmes and Shaw. Holmes at this point would have resurfaced following his encounter with Moriarty at the Reichenbach Falls, per Conan Doyle's "The Adventure of the Empty House", set in 1894.
1151 "The Forgotten". He actually got the stick from Kublai Khan, and the shroud from the San Francisco hospital where he regenerated for the seventh time.
1152 *Wolfsbane*. George was born in 1895.
1153 *J&L: Chronoclasm*. Year unknown, but Tesla lived 1856-1943. Duncan Wisbey, who played Tesla, was 40 when this story was recorded. Tesla might well be the same age when Payne abducts him, but that only puts him a few years ahead of the *Jago & Litefoot* stories, and begs the question of why Payne didn't just look up Tesla's contemporary self.

1895 - THE VAMPIRE OF PARIS[1154] -> Brother Varlos of the Darksmiths buried the Eternity Crystal on Earth's moon and took up residence in Paris. A timeship followed Varlos to Earth, and the time vampire that powered the vessel killed the crew and escaped. The tenth Doctor and Varlos' android daughter, Gisella, tracked down her "father". Together, they reversed the strange temporal effects that the creature was causing, and allowed it to peacefully escape into the Time Vortex, but Varlos died while doing so. The Doctor and Gisella left to find a means of obliterate the Eternity Crystal, but destronic particles jolted the TARDIS, catapulting it to the Silver Desolation in another time zone...

1896 (10th November) - THE SANDS OF TIME[1155] -> The fifth Doctor, Tegan and Nyssa arrived in the Egyptian Room of the British Museum. At the invitation of Lord Kenilworth, they attended the unwrapping of an ancient mummy, only to discover that the mummy was the perfectly preserved body of Nyssa herself. The Doctor came to realise that the intelligence of the Osirian Nephthys was in Nyssa's body.

Lord Salisbury lent the Doctor a morning coat for the Queen's Diamond Jubilee.[1156]

1897 (November) - THE DEATH OF ART[1157] -> The seventh Doctor, Chris and Roz investigated a psychic disturbance in France. They encountered the Brotherhood, a secret society researching psychic activity. A man called Montague ruled one faction of the Brotherhood, but another, "the Family", were working against him. The outbreak of psychic powers was because the Quoth, multidimensional beings, had taken shelter in human brains. The Doctor sided with the Family against Montague, who was killed. The Doctor retrieved all the Quoth and took them to a new home in a neutron star.

In 1898, humanity's average life expectancy was forty-nine years, nine months and five days.[1158] The Martian landing at Horsell Common, as depicted in *War of the Worlds*, was indeed fictional.[1159]

w - (=) ? 1898 - FP: WARRING STATES[1160] -> The timeship Compassion required an independent power source, and extruded part of her internal

---

1154 Dating *The Vampire of Paris* (*DL* #5) - The year is given (p10). This "time vampire" has different attributes from those described in *The Time Vampire*, and follows Varlos' "time trail" - suggesting that he has, in fact, come back in time (see Dating *The Darksmith Legacy*). For the Doctor and Gisella, the story continues in *The Game of Death*.
1155 Dating *The Sands of Time* (MA #22) - The date is given (p29).
1156 *Paper Cuts*. Queen Victoria's reign began on 20th June, 1837, and her Diamond Jubilee was held in 1897.
1157 Dating *The Death of Art* (NA #54) - It's "26 November 1897" (p16).
1158 *TW: Miracle Day*
1159 According to the Doctor in *Heart of Stone* (p79). *War of the Worlds* was published in 1898 and had a contemporary setting.
1160 Dating *FP: Warring States* (FP novel #4) - The White Pyramid seems to (mostly) be located outside linear time, so the dating here, based upon the year in which Compassion allows the Pyramid to become historically noticeable (p187), might be a bit of a cheat. One interpretation of the ending is that Octavia and Ying leave the realm of fiction altogether.
1161 *TW: From Out of the Rain*
1162 Dating *The Banquo Legacy* (EDA #35) - The date is given (p7).
1163 *The Curse of Fenric*
1164 Dating *Grand Theft Cosmos* (BF BBC7 #2.5) - Lucie expresses frustration to the Doctor that as it's 1898, she can't play her MP3 player in public.
1165 According to Alice's diary on Torchwood.org.uk.

A morgue inventory on the website suggests that Holroyd's partner was named Philip Lyle. Holroyd and Guppy appear in *TW: Fragments*.
1166 Dating *FP: Movers* and *FP: The Labyrinth of Histories* (FP audios #1.5-1.6) - It's "one hundred and twenty-five years" after 1764. More specifically, it's "about six months" before the Siege of Mafeking, which commenced in October 1899. Emma comments that Justine's step-mother is always "drunk after a Saturday", so it's probably Sunday.
1167 Dating *TW: Fragments* (TW 2.12) - The exact year isn't given, but it's before 1900 per the prediction of The Girl (who everyone calls the tarot-reader according to Torchwood.org.uk). Jack generalises that Earth is "a century away" from official first contact with alien life, also hinting that it's closer to 1900 than not.
Transcripts of Jack's bar conversations - seen briefly on screen, but better illustrated on the official Torchwood website and in *The Torchwood Archives* - are dated to 12th February, 1987; 16th December, 1897; and 4th April, 1898. However, as Alice Guppy only joins Torchwood in mid-September 1898 and seems very adept when she meets Captain Jack, it's probably 1899 when she and Holroyd approach him.
1168 Dating *TW: Consequences*: "The Baby Farmers" (*TW* novel #15a) - Charles Dickens' reading at the Taliesin Lodge (in *The Unquiet Dead*) happened some "thirty Christmases past". Moreover, the future Jack writes a letter to Holroyd (p241) that says, "I'm guessing the year [where you are] is 1899."

dimensions into Chinese history as a White Pyramid. Compassion's machinations brought Cousin Octavia of Faction Paradox and a Chinese girl named Liu Hui Ying into conflict over a casket found within the pyramid in 1900, and they both travelled (Octavia by derailing a Faction Paradox train while doing so) to the pyramid itself. Compassion time-looped the battle between the two women - sometimes Octavia prevailed, sometimes Ying would. Each "winner" became a mummy within the casket, enabling Compassion to power herself from their witchblood.

Compassion sustained herself in this manner for "thousands of years", but Octavia and Ying finally combined efforts to defeat her, and vanished into another reality.

Enigmatic circus people, the Night Travellers, performed in the dead of night and left a trail of "damage and sorrow" - as well as claiming children to "live with them forever" - wherever they performed. In 1898, they were responsible for a number of disappearances and coma victims in the town of Wellsfield.[1161]

1898 - THE BANQUO LEGACY[1162] **->** A scientist, Harris, built a machine that could share thoughts. He demonstrated it at Banquo Manor as the eighth Doctor, Fitz and Compassion arrived, trapped by a Time Lord device. The Doctor discovered that the butler, Simpson, was a Time Lord searching for Compassion. The Doctor unravelled the web of blackmail and murder involving Harris and his sister, Catherine. Simpson was thought killed, and the Doctor's trio left before Simpson was missed by Gallifrey.

On 12th January, 1898, Florence Sundvig died. Mary Eliza Millington was born on 3rd March, dying four days later. At the end of the nineteenth century, the grandfather of Reverend Wainwright translated the Viking Runes in the crypt of his church.[1163]

1898 - GRAND THEFT COSMOS[1164] **->** The eighth Doctor and Lucie went to Stockholm by train to see Strindberg's new play, and made the acquaintance of Frederick Simonsson, an art buyer for the King of Sweden. The time-travelling Headhunter summoned Tardelli forth from the black diamond that Simonsson had obtained, as the Emperor Vassilar-G of Ralta wanted to hire him as an official court artist. The Doctor convinced Tardelli to perform a fifth-dimensional dump on the diamond, sending its pocket universe into the gap between universes, where it could exist independently. He also confiscated the Tardelli paintings in Simonsson's possession while the diamond's stone guardian wandered off into the woods around Stockholm. The Headhunter and Karen took

Tardelli away to work for the Emperor Vassilar-G, but the Doctor believed that the Emperor had notoriously fickle tastes, and would likely eat Tardelli on a balcony, in front of a crowd, when he got bored with him.

Having failed to sell the diamond as an energy source to the industrialist Yashin, the Headhunter thought it best to avoid Earth between now and his death in 1905, lest he exact retribution on her.

Emily Holroyd, an operative for Torchwood Cardiff, burned her partner to death when he contracted a mutative infection and transformed into a giant snake. His replacement, Alice Guppy, was offered employment with Torchwood on Tuesday, 13th September, 1898.[1165]

w - 1899 (a Sunday in March) - FP: MOVERS / THE LABYRINTH OF HISTORIES[1166] **->** Godfather Sabbath had just been appointed the head of Faction Paradox's military wing. To insulate his bloodline from temporal interference by the Faction's enemies, he began systematically killing off his family tree. The godfather murdered his mother, then his mother's father - after each slaying, the historical equations governing Godfather Sabbath's existence were rebalanced so he could exist without progenitors. He next tried to kill his maternal grandfather's mother, Fiora Vend, but arrived after she was already pregnant. As killing his grandfather twice would be in very bad form, the godfather instead murdered Fiora's niece, Emma James, hoping it might open up further avenues of attack in his family history.

Godfather Morlock recruited Emma's cousin and best friend, Justine McManus, to join Faction Paradox.

1899 - TW: FRAGMENTS[1167] **->** Jack Harkness had taken to wandering from drinking den to drinking den. He had been "killed" fourteen times in the proceeding six months when Emily Holroyd and Alice Guppy of Torchwood investigated statements Jack had made in taverns concerning the Doctor. Holroyd offered Jack employment as an uncontracted field agent, and he accepted after a mysterious young girl who read tarot predicted that "the century would turn twice" before he would see the Doctor again.

1899 - TW: CONSEQUENCES: "The Baby Farmers"[1168] **->** Admiral Sir Henry Montague financed an operation aboard the decommissioned HMS *Hades* to breed extra-terrestrials and create an army of superstrong amphibious assassins for the Empire. Torchwood - led by Emily Holroyd, and otherwise composed of Alice Guppy, Charles Gaskell and Jack Harkness - destroyed the operation. Jack allowed members of the race that Montague was farming to kill the man.

Holroyd received a sentient alien book that Jack had

sent through the Rift from 2009, and per his instructions filed it away in the University College library. This caused the book to become aware of Torchwood's existence, and it desired stories pertaining to the group.

The Panoptican Theatre in Cardiff opened in 1899, and hosted touring dramatic companies.[1169]

1899 - PLAYERS[1170] -> The sixth Doctor and Peri stopped the murder of a 24-year-old Winston Churchill, who was serving as a war correspondent in South Africa. The Doctor helped Churchill escape from a P.O.W. camp, and Churchill returned home a hero.

1899 (26th December) - CASTLE OF FEAR[1171] -> The fifth Doctor and Nyssa visited Stockbridge, and witnessed a mummery that entailed Father Christmas, St. George, a dragon... and a rendition of the fifth Doctor himself and his TARDIS. The travellers went back to 1199 to investigate the source of the play. They returned to 1899 to find that the Rutan spaceship in Stockbridge Castle had regrown in the interim, and was influencing the town residents to dig it out. The Doctor and Nyssa piloted the weakened ship into the stratosphere, but its engines triggered a hyperspatial warp-core explosion that flung them to Stockbridge in the early twenty-first century.

The Doctor and Iris met Oscar Wilde in Venice after his imprisonment. They also fought some "fish people".[1172] **Gerald Carter**, age 24, **joined Torchwood** after being trained in military intelligence. One of his earliest missions was the Centurian Incident of New Year's Eve, 1899.[1173]

The Twentieth Century

Joan Redfern had married Oliver, her childhood sweetheart, but he died at the Battle of Spion Kop.[1174]

The first Doctor was present at the Relief of Mafeking.[1175] In 1900, Emily Holroyd drafted a manifesto pertaining to Torchwood's Rules and Regulations, including guidelines concerning the group's succession of leadership.[1176] Professor Angelchrist saw H.G. Wells speak about *The War of the Worlds* at a bookshop on Charing Cross Road.[1177]

Battlefields from the Boxer Rising and the Boer War were lifted by the War Lords.[1178] Jack Harkness was in China for the Boxer Rebellion.[1179] Nurse Albertine studied battle surgery and saw some action during the South African War. She would come to work for Toby the Sapient Pig.[1180] Colonel Hugh served in the Boer War.[1181]

(=) By the beginning of the twentieth century, Dhakan - the alternate Earth ruled by Katsura Sato - had interstellar travel.[1182]

The Doctor told L. Frank Baum that if monkeys had wings, they technically would no longer be monkeys.[1183] Iris met Arthur Balfour in the Reform Club.[1184]

1900 (January) - TALES FROM THE VAULT[1185] -> Kalicarache, an extra-terrestrial being composed of psionic energy and could possess dead bodies, escaped when the prison transport carrying it crashed in Africa. The first Doctor, Steven and Dodo confronted Kalicarache during the Battle of Spion Kop, after he had possessed the late Lt.

1169 Torchwood.org.uk, elaborating on *TW: From Out of the Rain*.
1170 Dating *Players* (PDA #21) - The date is given (p15).
1171 Dating *Castle of Fear* (BF #127) - The exact day is given. The fifth Doctor here says that he hasn't visited Stockbridge prior to 1899.
1172 *The Scarlet Empress*. Although never specified, the "fish people" could be the amphibious gondoliers that appear in Paul Magrs' *The Stones of Venice*. This meeting must have occurred after Wilde's release from prison on 19th May, 1897, but before his death on 30th November, 1900.
1173 Per Torchwood.co.uk. There's some confusion regarding Gerald's surname - on screen he's credited as just "Gerald", the official Torchwood website gives his last name as "Carter", but *The Torchwood Archives* and *Torchwood: The Encyclopedia* both claim that it's "Kneale".
1174 *Human Nature* (TV). The Battle of Spion Kop occurred on 23rd and 24th January, 1900.
1175 *The Daleks' Master Plan, The Invasion of Time, The Unicorn and the Wasp*. This occurred on 17th May, 1900,

when British troops ended the Siege of Mafeking during the second Boer War.
1176 *TW: Consequences*: "Kaleidoscope"
1177 *Paradox Lost*
1178 *The War Games*. The Boer War ran 1899-1902, the Boxer Rising was in 1900.
1179 *TW: Miracle Day*. It's not specified that this was for Torchwood, and it might've been during his time as a Time Agent.
1180 *Year of the Pig*. The South African War (also known as the Second Boer War) lasted 1899-1902.
1181 *The Unicorn and the Wasp*
1182 "The Glorious Dead"
1182 *A Thousand Tiny Wings*. Baum lived 1856-1919; *The Wonderful Wizard of Oz* saw print in 1900, but the described argument could have taken place either before or after publication.
1184 *Iris: The Two Irises*. Arthur Balfour, UK Prime Minister from 1902 to 1905, lived 1848-1930.
1185 Dating *Tales from the Vault* (BF CC 6.1) - Steven says that "The year is 1900". The Battle of Spion Kop lasted from 23rd to 24th January.

Thornicroft. Kalicarache's consciousness was left trapped inside the fabric of a coat worn by a killed solider, Tommy Watkins. In the decades to come, Kalicarache could control anyone wearing the item.

---

w - (=) 1900 (May) - FP: WARRING STATES[1186] **->** Compassion furthered her gambit with the White Pyramid by placing the Empress Dowager Ci Xi in a garden within her internal dimensions, and then impersonating her. Cousin Octavia, accompanied by her Red Burial and Prester John, arrived in this time zone to lay claim to a casket found within the Pyramid by an archaeological team, as she believed that it held the secret of immortality. Compassion pitted Octavia against Liu Hui Ying, and they both travelled back to the Pyramid.

When Compassion's stratagem finally failed, the archeological team found only an empty tomb.

The toadstool-like xXltttxtolxtol discovered their homeworld would extinguish in a few thousand years, and sent a stardrive through the Rift to "invite" to other species to travel to them... a means of identifying a world to conquer. The Queen granted George Herbert Sanderson of Torchwood permission to visit the stardrive's planet of origin, a few solar systems distant, on behalf of the Empire. Sanderson experienced time dilation during the journey, and aged little as a century passed in the outside universe.

Late in her life, Queen Victoria commissioned Agnes Havisham to serve as the Torchwood Assessor. Havisham would enter cryo-sleep at a storage facility in Swindon, and only awaken when automatic systems predicted deadly peril for a Torchwood station. Havisham was to have absolute authority over Torchwood in such cases. Her hibernation chamber was finally ready in late 1901. She would only awaken four times in the next hundred years

- for "two invasions, one apocalypse and a Visitation by the Ambassadors of the Roaring Bang".[1187]

1900 (December) - FOREIGN DEVILS[1188] **->** The second Doctor followed Jamie and Zoe's passage through the "spirit gate" in 1800, arriving exactly a hundred years later. The Chief Astrologer's curse started murdering the descendants of Roderick Upcott, and the Doctor teamed up with Carnacki, an investigator of the supernatural, to look into events at Upcott House. The curse used the spirit gate's dimensional energy to remove the house from time and space, and transformed Roderick Upcott's corpse into a dragon. The Doctor destroyed the spirit gate, which returned the house and made the dragon crumble to ash.

1901 - TW: EXIT WOUNDS[1189] **->** Alice Guppy and Charles Gaskell of Torchwood unearthed Jack Harkness, who had been buried since 27 AD. At Jack's urging, they placed him into cryo-freeze and timed his revival for the twenty-first century. Jack's younger self continued working for Torchwood.

= Iris was "instrumental" in the final battles against the Martians in an alternate dimension.[1190]

In 1901, the Night Travellers were responsible for the disappearances of eight people from Church Stretton.[1191] In the same year, an English author began to write boy's stories for *The Ensign*.[1192] The Doctor saw the assassination of President McKinley.[1193] Henri de Toulouse-Lautrec died in 1901.[1194] **Jack Harkness dated Proust for a while, and claimed the man was rather immature.**[1195] **Jack was married at least once.**[1196]

1901 (20th October) - CRYPTOBIOSIS[1197] **->** The sixth Doctor and Peri sought to vacation aboard the *Lankester* (sic), a cargo ship en route from the Cape of

---

1186 Dating *FP: Warring States* (*FP* novel #4) - "Cousin Octavia... stepped... into a May afternoon in Peking, 1900" (p4). Prester John, here a member of Faction Paradox, is a legendary figure said to have ruled over a lost Christian nation.
1187 *TW: Risk Assessment*. Victoria died on 22nd January, 1901, and as her conversation with Havisham occurs in December of a year that Victoria fears will see "her last Christmas", it's likely December 1900.
1188 Dating *Foreign Devils* (TEL #5) - It's "December 1900" (p35).
1189 Dating *TW: Exit Wounds* (*TW* 2.13) - The year is given.
1190 "About seven years" after the 1894 component of *Iris: Enter Wildthyme*.
1191 *TW: From Out of the Rain*, off a newspaper report-

ed dated "August 11th 1901".
1192 *The Mind Robber*
1193 *Byzantium!* (p179). No date given, but McKinley was shot 6th September, 1901, and died eight days later.
1194 *Demon Quest: The Demon of Paris*. Toulouse-Lautrec died 9th September, 1901.
1195 *TW: Dead Man Walking*. Proust lived 1871-1922.
1196 As strongly implied by a photo of Jack and an unidentified woman in *TW: Something Blue*. The *Torchwood Archives* state that the marriage occurred "in the early 1900s". The eleventh Doctor mentions "all of Jack's stag parties" in *The Wedding of River Song*.
1197 Dating *Cryptobiosis* (BF subscription promo #3) - The date is given.

Good Hope to New Orleans. The *Lankester*'s chief mate, Jacques De Requin, was smuggling two captured mermaids - Anthrotrite and her daughter, Galatea - to sell them for profit. Other mer-people, led by Anthrotrite's father Nereus, breached the ship's under-carriage. Anthrotrite died, the *Lankester* sank and the mer-people captured de Requin to torment him. The Doctor and Peri returned Galatea to her grandfather, and convinced him to discretely rescue any *Lankester* survivors. As part of these events, the Doctor was drafted to serve as a medical professional attached to the Merchant Navy.

On 12th December, 1901, John Lafayette, a linguist, accidentally travelled along a space-time path to ancient Babylon.[1198] Jack Harkness met a precognitive named Sam who had just returned home from the Boer War.[1199] In the same year, Jack, Emily Holroyd and Alice Guppy defeated a shadowy terror that brutalised the imagination.[1200]

Baden-Powell taught the Doctor the rudiments of tracking.[1201] By 1902, there were Polynesian/alien hybrids on Easter Island again. They used the teleport device to resettle their forefathers' homeworld. The explorer Stockwood was still alive, and planned to return to the alien homeworld also.[1202]

Sarah Bernhardt starred in *Hamlet* at the New Regency Theatre.[1203] The Doctor told P.G. Wodehouse - who was saddened because he didn't know what he was writing about - that it sounded as if he had a story that was trying to get out.[1204] The first Doctor learned some housebreaking skills from A.J. Raffles.[1205] In 1902, Rupert Gaskin started building the Gaskin Tunnel, hoping to find the lost highwayman's gold rumoured to be beneath a well in Creighton Mere. The construction was abandoned when Gaskin died from influenza.[1206]

The Corialiths of Masma engineered memory devices to house the mental engrams of their dead. A Corialith came to Earth with one such Mnemosyne unit, but was feared by members of the public and killed. The young Mnemosyne sequestered itself in the alcoves of the Northern Line.[1207]

c 1902 - HORROR OF FANG ROCK[1208] -> The fourth Doctor and Leela arrived at Fang Rock lighthouse as a series of mysterious murders took place. The Doctor discovered the culprit was a Rutan scout, then destroyed the scout and its mothership.

Earth was now strategically important for the Rutans in their war with the Sontarans. According to the Doctor, the Rutans "used to control the whole of the Mutters Spiral once".

1902 - FORTY-FIVE: "False Gods"[1209] -> The Time Lord formerly worshipped as Thoth was now "Jane Templeton", an associate of Howard Carter. She directed him to excavate what she believed to be Userhat's tomb, hoping that her TARDIS was located inside. The Ship was dying, and caused temporal disruption that drew the seventh Doctor, Ace and Hex to the tomb. The Doctor convinced Jane that her TARDIS had to be euthanised in the heart of a sun, and she duly went back in time to do so.

1902 - REVENGE OF THE JUDOON[1210] -> A lizard-like alien altered his form and became "Professor Challoner", the head of a British secret society that investigated extreme science: the Cosmic Peacemakers. Challoner wanted to take over the world by installing Edward VII as a global emperor, and to this end involved Sir Arthur Conan Doyle - whose memory of Challoner's plot was erased.

The tenth Doctor and Martha landed at Balmoral Castle while Edward VII was there... only to find that the castle had vanished. They recognised this as the work of the

---

1198 *Benny: Walking to Babylon*
1199 *TW: Trace Memory*. Sam is 96 in 1967, and says that he met Jack when he was 31 (p184-185). The second Boer War ended in 1902.
1200 *TW:* "Hell House"
1201 *The Silent Stars Go By*. Lt General Robert Baden-Powell, a.k.a. Lord Baden-Powell, served in India and Africa from 1876 to 1910, and authored many books on the art of reconnaissance and scout training.
1202 *Eye of Heaven*
1203 *J&L: Swan Song*. No year given, but Bernhardt debuted as Hamlet in the silent film *Le Duel d'Hamlet* (1900), and would have been more likely to have continued in the role prior to a leg injury she incurred in 1905. Gangrene forced an amputation in 1915, although her acting career did continue.
1204 *Circular Time:* "Autumn". Wodehouse lived 1881-

1975, but the date is otherwise arbitrary.
1205 *The Suffering*. Raffles is a fictional "gentleman thief" created by Arthur Conan Doyle's brother-in-law, E.W. Hornung, as something of a mirror reflection of Sherlock Holmes. The first collection of Raffles stories was published in 1899; the last by Hornung - a novel, *Mr. Justice Raffles* - saw print in 1909.
1206 *Wishing Well*
1207 "One hundred and seven Earth years" before "Ghosts of the Northern Line".
1208 Dating *Horror of Fang Rock* (15.1) - The Terrance Dicks novelisation and contemporary publicity material set the story "at the turn of the century". Electric power was introduced to lighthouses around the turn of the century. Fang Rock is in the English Channel ("five or six miles" from Southampton) and is particularly treacherous, and was probably upgraded early on.

Judoon, who had been tricked into aiding Challoner under a false warrant. Martha interviewed Doyle about the Peacemakers while the Doctor used the TARDIS to locate Balmoral - which was in the Arabian Desert. He also met Baden-Powell, who was investigating the disappearance. Challoner had established Temporal Reversion devices that could eliminate all of Britain's rivals, but the Doctor got Balmoral back to its normal location and convinced the Judoon of Challoner's duplicity. The Judoon left, and Challoner fell victim to his own device. The Doctor and Martha departed for a working holiday as they cleared out Challoner's Temporal Reversion devices from all the world's capitals.

The Doctor was technical advisor on *A Trip to the Moon*.[1211] In 1902, Monroe Stahr saw a film about the unearthing of an Egyptian tomb that would later inspire him to finance the movie *The Curse of the Scarab*.[1212]

@ The eighth Doctor drank absinthe in Prague, 1903.[1213] In the summer of 1903, Toby the Sapient Pig attended a gathering of creative minds in Vienna. By 1913, owing to his addled memories, Toby would believe that all present were pigs.[1214]

(=) The TARDIS' simultaneous arrival in 1903 and 2003 massively disrupted the timelines. In 1903, the Doctor helped the English defeat the Daleks, who had attacked Central London. Only two Daleks survived and were taken captive. The first World War still happened, but the British used the captured Dalek technology to take control of the whole world. The British government locked the Doctor and Evelyn in the Tower of London for propaganda purposes, and Evelyn starved to death.[1215]

1903 (December) - THE SLEEP OF REASON[1216] -> The Sholem-Luz were creatures that could tunnel through the Time Vortex, and were attracted to mental turmoil as part of their life-cycle. In December 1903, a Sholem-Luz was drawn to Mausolus House, an asylum. The Sholem-Luz essence infected an Irish wolfhound, which became monstrous and triggered a series of murders. Joseph Sands, the nephew of a Mausolus House patient, slew the creature and burned its corpse in a fire that had started in a chapel on the grounds. The eighth Doctor arrived through a time corridor from around 2004, and the second Sholem-Luz accompanying him also perished in the fire. Not wishing to relive the twentieth century over again, the Doctor went into suspended animation for about a hundred years.

Dr. Thomas Christie, the governor of Mausolus House, found a dog's tooth - all that remained of the Sholem-Luz - and made a pendant from it. It reappeared a century later.

Parts of *The Book of Tomorrows* had been lost over the centuries, but now the Orphans of the Future stole it entirely. By the early twenty-first century, their number included scientists, philosophers, inventors and other key individuals in Europe and North America.[1217]

1905 - FREAKSHOW[1218] -> The fifth Doctor, Tegan and Turlough visited Buzzard Creek, Arizona, and saw a travelling carnival: Thaddeus P Winklemeyer's Menagerie of Medical Marvels. The freaks on display were alien beings, and Winklemeyer was actually a Vmal, an alien who propagated via micro-organisms that he sold to the crowd as an "elixir of life". The travellers thwarted Winklemeyer's plans, alerted galactic authorities as to his actions and took his captives home.

At this time, Cyvaks were horned serpents that inhabited the swamps of the planet Pallios, near Trion.

There's a reference to King Edward. As fan Alex Wilcock has noted, although the Doctor's style of dress is often referred to as "Edwardian", this is the only *Doctor Who* TV story set in the Edwardian period (and there's not a frock coat to be seen). The young lighthouse worker Vince states that the Beast was last seen "eighty years ago", "back in the twenties". *The Programme Guide* offered the date "1909", *The Terrestrial Index* claimed "1904". *The TARDIS Logs* suggested "c.1890", *The Doctor Who File* "early 1900s". *The TARDIS Special* gave the date "1890s". *Timelink* makes a convincing case for 1902, based on mumbled references to Salisbury and Bonar Law.

1209 Dating *Forty-Five: "False Gods"* (BF #115a) - It's "1902".

1210 Dating *Revenge of the Judoon* (*Quick Reads* #3) - The back cover gives the year; in the story the Doctor

says it's "the very beginning of the twentieth century".

1211 *The City of the Dead*

1212 "The Curse of the Scarab". It's "forty years" before the story, but that's clearly rounding up as the Melies' silent movie *Trip to the Moon* is referenced, and that was released in 1902.

1213 "The Fallen"

1214 *Year of the Pig*. Toby's fan Alice Bultitude later shows him film footage of this event - even though 1903 is rather early for footage of this kind.

1215 *Jubilee*

1216 Dating *The Sleep of Reason* (EDA #70) - We're told it's "Thursday 24th December 1903" at the start of this section (p22).

1217 "One hundred years" before *SJS: Buried Secrets*.

1218 Dating *Freakshow* (BF promo #9, *DWM* #419) - The year is given.

The Doctor once went for a stroll in Edwardian Bromley.[1219] The National Foundation for Scientific Research, UK, originated as a group of private researchers that adopted the name and gained charity status after World War II. The organisation eventually leased a house from Melanie Bush's great-uncle.[1220] **The Doctor trained the Mountain Mauler of Montana.**[1221]

The Doctor learned a great deal from Houdini.[1222] **Houdini was slightly shorter than five slightly scary girls that the Doctor encountered: the Vampires of Venice.**[1223] **The Doctor also learned sleight of hand from Maskelyne.**[1224]

The Kalarians turned Ockora into a holiday resort, and hunted the natives for sport. They did not realise the Ockorans were intelligent.[1225] An alien gave J.M. Barrie the idea for *Peter Pan*, based on a popular extra-terrestrial story.[1226]

@ The Doctor claimed to have chained Emmeline Pankhurst to the railings outside 10 Downing Street.[1227] **Pankhurst stole the Doctor's laser spanner.**[1228] **The Doctor met Einstein.**[1229] The chess master Swapnil Khan and his daughter Queenie Glasscock were present during a chess tournament in Nuremberg, 1906, where Rudolf Spielmann played David Przepiorka. The Doctor intended on being there, but his train was delayed by anarchists on the line at Baden-Baden.[1230]

In 1906, Jack Harkness set up a bank account that gathered interest for at least a century.[1231] Eliza Cooper had met Jack Harkness by this point.[1232]

1906 - "Final Sacrifice"[1233] **->** Robert Lewis and Eliza Cooper of Torchwood visited Alexander Hugh, Professor of Advanced Sciences at Oxford, and his assistant Annabella. Hugh had built a time portal using repulsors from an alien tripod that crashed in Surrey, and the batteries from a giant metal man recovered from the Thames. But when the four of them stepped through the portal, intend-ing to arrive just five minutes into the future, they found themselves twenty thousand years and five star systems away from their starting point.

The tenth Doctor and Emily Winter eventually gave Hugh a lift back home. The Doctor concluded that the slain Annabella was a fixed point in space and time - she should have lived, while Emily should have died. To correct the situation, Emily left the Doctor's company twenty years before she had met him, and adopted Annabella's identity. Funded by horse-betting information that the Doctor provided, Emily/"Annabella" came to own a theatre in Peckham, to discover the comic actor Archie Maplin, and to create United Actors Studio with him.

Jack Harkness first happened upon the uninhabited Tretarri housing district after enjoying a good night with a sailor and a showgirl together. An invisible force kept him from entering the location. Over the next century, he would make fourteen attempts to do so.[1234]

> **(=) 1906 (March) - TW: THE HOUSE THAT JACK BUILT**[1235] **->** Jack Harkness was the first owner of Jackson Leaves, a Cardiff house built in 1906. Interdimensional beings who fed off paradoxes were drawn to Jack and retroactively inserted themselves into the house's history, causing all who lived there to die violently. Jack was secretly the lover of both the realtor who sold him the house, Alison, and her fiancé Miles. The exchange of vows at their wedding was extremely awkward, each of them worried that the other had discovered their involvement with Jack.
>
> The day after Miles and Alison were married, he drowned her. An older version of Jack altered history so he didn't purchase the house - the interdimensional beings were consequently woven into a massive paradox, and consumed themselves.

1219 *Only Human*

1220 One hundred years before *Catch-1782*.

1221 *The Romans*

1222 Mentioned in *Planet of the Spiders, Revenge of the Cybermen*, "Voyager", *The Pit, Head Games, The Sorcerer's Apprentice, The Devil Goblins from Neptune, The Church and the Crown, Eye of Heaven, Independence Day, Dreamland* (*DW*) and "Don't Step on the Grass". There's no date given in any of those stories. Houdini lived 1874-1926.

1223 *The Vampires of Venice*

1224 *The Ribos Operation*. No date is given, but this is presumably the magician John Neville Maskelyne (1839-1917, and also mentioned in *Camera Obscura*), although it could be his grandson, the magician Jasper Maskelyne (1902-1973).

1225 "Centuries" before *The Murder Game, The Final Sanction*.

1226 *The Tomorrow Windows*. *Peter Pan* was published in 1905.

1227 *Casualties of War*. Pankhurst was a founder of the British suffragette movement. She was chained to Number Ten in 1905.

1228 *Smith and Jones*

1229 *The Stones of Blood*. No date given. Einstein lived 1879-1955, publishing his Special and General Theories of Relativity in 1905 and 1915 respectively. He also appeared in *Time and the Rani*, but it isn't made clear if he and the Doctor already knew one another.

1230 *The Magic Mousetrap*

1231 *TW: Miracle Day*

1232 "Final Sacrifice"

In the amended history, Alison lived and had a son, Gordon Cottrell.

In 1906, Charles Gaskell and a Torchwood team discovered advanced alien cryo-tech that could be used to freeze the dead.[1236] A 5.2 earthquake wracked Swansea on 27th June, 1906. It was suspected that Torchwood Cardiff suffered aftershocks, and that a number of its personnel died.[1237]

(=) 1906 (24th December) - THE CHIMES OF MIDNIGHT[1238] -> The eighth Doctor and Charley discovered the inhabitants of an Edwardian manor house were trapped in a time-loop. The servants were brutally murdered, but at midnight time would roll back two hours and the process would repeat itself. The Doctor found that the house was imprinted with the murders and that Edith Thompson - one of the servants - would later work for the Pollard family. Edith had killed herself in 1930 upon learning of Charley's death in the *R-101* accident, but Charley's paradoxical arrival in 1906 left history confused as to whether Edith had cause to kill herself or not. The Doctor decisively talked Edith out of killing herself, ending the time-loop.

Azathoth and her army of Rakshassi were destroyed in the San Francisco earthquake of 1906, following the Doctor's intervention.[1239] The vampire Weird Harold was buried alive in the San Francisco earthquake.[1240]

Emily Winter, a companion of the tenth Doctor, was born in 1907.[1241] In the same year, Gerald Carter assumed command of Torchwood Cardiff.[1242] The Doctor visited in Brighton in 1907.[1243]

(=) c 1907 - TIMEH: THE SIDEWAYS DOOR[1244] -> An alternate version of Honoré Lechasseur killed Professor Roche, a member of the Academy of Fine Arts Vienna who recommended against Adolf Hitler's admission as an art student. This cleared the way for Hitler's successful application, preventing him in future from joining the Nazi Party.

= 1908 - FP: WARLORDS OF UTOPIA[1245] -> Marcus Americanius Scriptor was born on Roma I, a parallel Earth where the best of all possible outcomes had occurred to the Roman Empire. It was a utopian civilisation that encompassed the world, from the cities under the ice caps to cities built on and under the oceans - such as Atlantis. The world had existed in five centuries of unbroken peace. It was the perfect world, although half the population were slaves. Scriptor's family ruled North America, and he lived on a family estate that took up the whole of Manhattan. America was a backwater, although an Atlantean astrologer gave Scriptor's family hope that their new son would bring them glory.

On the day Scriptor was born, a mysterious old man arrived in the Forum in Rome, using a time ring. He was one of thirteen members of the Great Houses apparently fleeing the War in Heaven.

1233 Dating "Final Sacrifice" (IDW *DW* Vol. 1, #13-16) - A caption tells us it's "1906". Lewis says "the British Empire will rise again", but actually, it was still in good shape in 1906. The tripod is presumably a reference to *The War of the Worlds*; the remains of the "giant metal man" recovered from the Thames presumably refers to the CyberKing (*The Next Doctor*), in defiance of it looking on screen as if it was completely disintegrated.
1234 *TW: The Twilight Streets*
1235 Dating *The House That Jack Built* (*TW* novel #12) - In the corrected timeline, a report written by Alice Guppy concerning temporal flux that occurred "last night" - the same night that Jack first seduces Alison, it seems - at Jackson Leaves is dated to "17th March, 1906".
1236 *TW: The Twilight Streets* (p133). The equipment doesn't seem able to revive frozen people, so it presumably compliments the cryo-tech that Torchwood has been using since Victorian times, as evidenced with Jack in 1901.
1237 This event is only mentioned in *The Torchwood Archives*, which is a useful secondary source but hardly

sacrosanct. However, until another explanation is offered, this might well explain the fate of Emily Holroyd's Torchwood crew.
1238 Dating *The Chimes of Midnight* (BF #29) - The date is given.
1239 *All-Consuming Fire*
1240 *Vampire Science*
1241 Emily says she is "19" in "Silver Scream".
1242 There's conflicting dates about this - Gerald's biography on Torchwood.org.uk says he took charge in 1907; *The Torchwood Archives* says it was 1910.
1243 *Pier Pressure*
1244 Dating *TimeH: The Sideways Door* (*TimeH* #10) - The Academy rejected Hitler twice, in 1907 and 1908.
1245 Dating *FP: Warlords of Utopia* (*FP* novel #3) - Marcus was born on 8th January 2661, by the Roman calendar, which measures from the founding of Rome (753BC). So Scriptor was born on 8th January, 1908. This is the same day, in our version of history, that William Hartnell was born.

The Tunguska Incident

The third Doctor, Jo Grant and Liz Shaw watched the Tunguska explosion in 1908.[1246] The Warlock alien arrived on Earth in the meteorite that landed in Tunguska.[1247] **Alien bacteria arrived with the meteorite.**[1248] **The Tunguska Scroll, which told the story of Horath and his final resting place, was recovered from the site.**[1249] The UNIT Vault contained what was thought to be a part of Sontaran scoutship that crashed at Tunguska... or it could just have been a rusted lump of metal.[1250]

1908 (30th June) - BIRTHRIGHT[1251] -> Half of the seventh Doctor's TARDIS fell through time to June 1908 and exploded in the wastes of Tunguska in Siberia. It disintegrated on impact; historians attributed this event to a meteorite strike.

Vislor Turlough's great-grandfather ran a smuggling operation, and used the dimensional vault established by his own great-grandfather to house contraband. Turlough's ancestor betrayed his fellow smugglers and was killed. The vault's security system slaughtered his murderers, but also pulverised the royal treasure of Trion.[1252]

In Lahore, 1909, some men under the command of Captain Jack got drunk and ran over a "chosen one" - a little girl with a connection to the spirit world, and who was protected by fairy creatures. The next week, the fairies killed fifteen of Jack's men on a train. Jack was the only survivor.[1253] The Doctor bought Inuit garb from the explorer Robert Peary as Peary journeyed north, and also owned snowshoes belonging to Peary's associate Matthew Henson.[1254]

The Doctor personally knew the performer/Chinese giant Chang Woo Gow, and regarded him as a marvellous fellow and a good dancer. Gow finally retired and opened a tea-room in Bournemouth. Elsewhere, Toby the Sapient Pig and Nurse Albertine saw Mrs Lillian Washbourne on stage at a theatre in Cincinnati.[1255]

1909 (February to 24th April) - BIRTHRIGHT[1256] -> The secret society the New Dawn, led by Jared Khan, attempted to stabilise the Great Divide with the future and bring the Chaarl back to this time. Some Chaarl broke through and murdered a number of people in the East End. Khan hypnotised Margaret Waterfield, Victoria's aunt, to further his schemes, and then had her killed. The seventh Doctor left Benny and Ace in this time while he dealt with matters elsewhere. The Doctor was a member of the same club as Prime Minister Herbert Henry Asquith, and had Asquith get Benny out of a spot of trouble.

The Doctor's TARDIS time-rammed itself to stop Khan's plans, and half of the Ship - with Khan's mind inside - fell through time to June 1908 and exploded in the wastes of Tunguska in Siberia. The Chaarl were trapped in one of the surviving TARDIS' inner dimensions.

1909 (mid September) - STING OF THE ZYGONS[1257] -> The tenth Doctor and Martha discovered a Zygon colony in the Lake District and wiped them out.

1910 (13th-17th October) - PARADOX LOST[1258] -> Amy, Rory and the artificial person Arven travelled to London, 1910, in an experimental time vessel to rendezvous with the eleventh Doctor, but materialised on 13th October, three days before his arrival. Their timeship created the very rip in space-time that they had been investigating, enabling the extra-dimensional Squall to get a foothold in the Universe.

The Doctor arrived in the TARDIS on 17th October, and reunited with his friends. Professor Archibald Angelchrist, a retired secret serviceman who had investigated paranor-

---

1246 *The Wages of Sin*
1247 *Warlock* (p353).
1248 *Dalek*
1249 *SJA: Enemy of the Bane*
1250 *Tales from the Vault*
1251 Dating *Birthright* (NA #17) - Page 202 cites the meteorite strike's historic date of 30th June, 1908. On the multiple events attributed to the Tunguska incident, see the Unfixed Points in Time sidebar. Alternatively, perhaps the location is a space-time nexus (akin to the Cardiff Rift) that drew several items to the same point, where many of them exploded together.
1252 Estimated as three generations prior to *Kiss of Death*.
1253 *TW: Small Worlds*. A caption gives the date. The *Torchwood* website said this was when Jack was a time-travelling conman, but as he's commanding troops and survives the fairy attack, it's more likely that this is the Jack who lived through the twentieth century.
1254 *Brotherhood of the Daleks*. The most famous of Peary's expeditions was in 1909.
1255 Some "years" before *Year of the Pig*
1256 Dating *Birthright* (NA #17) - It is "Thursday 15 April 1909" on p23, and Benny has been stranded "two months" (p24) by then. She departs on "24 April" (p203).
1257 Dating *Sting of the Zygons* (NSA #13) - The TARDIS lands "16 September 1909" and the adventure takes at least three days.
1258 Dating *Paradox Lost* (NSA #48) - The days are provided at the start of each relevant chapter.
1259 "A century" prior to *TW: Ghost Train*, although it isn't especially clear what this means.
1260 *The English Way of Death* (p46).

mal threats such as tentacled creatures in the Thames, extra-terrestrial viruses and ancient entities awakening from tombs underneath Edinburgh, helped the Doctor banish the Squall back to their home dimension. Arven was heavily damaged and fell into the Thames. It would meet the Doctor, Amy and Rory's past selves in 2789.

Torchwood had an Internet at its disposal.[1259] The Doctor saw Earth tremors in Peru in 1910.[1260] In same year, Torchwood Cardiff reorganised their archive.[1261]

Gareth Robert Owen, a freelance agent for Torchwood and the son of the founder of G.R. Owen's department store, found a being akin to a tiny butterfly in a crashed spaceship in 1910. To prevent Torchwood weaponising the alien, Owen merged with the creature and relocated G.R. Owen's Department of Curiosities to a pocket dimension. The two of them lived there in a timeless state.[1262]

Humans associated with the criminal aliens in Wolfenden realised that the aliens' technology could be fuelled by brain chemicals related to memory. In the decades to follow, visitors to Wolfenden were robbed of some of their memory chemicals and then released, largely none the wiser.[1263]

c 1910 - THE CATALYST[1264] **->** Lord Joshua Douglas, an Edwardian gentleman, became a companion of the third Doctor. He was gone from home for a year, but returned looking ten years older and claiming that he'd been off in Peru. The Z'nai emperor H'mbrackle II, having been imprisoned in a quarantine tesseract accessible from Joshua's home, escaped and exacted vengeance by killing Joshua, his wife and their daughter Jessica. A group of Z'nai arrived through time in a Z'nai Angel of War to retrieve their emperor, but fell prey to a Z'nai-killing virus. The fourth Doctor and Leela trapped H'mbrackle II where "nobody would find him", and purified Joshua's home by burning it down.

The dancer Ernestina Stott was born around 1911.[1265] **The Doctor said 1911 was "an excellent year, one of my favourites".**[1266] **The Nine Travellers were surveyed in 1911.**[1267] **In 1911, the Doctor was due to take a lesson in either flying a biplane or knitting.**[1268] **On 13th March, 1911, the** *Hunstanton Chronicle* **reported Mr. Alfred Mason's insistence that his dead wife, a victim of the Night Travellers, could be resurrected if the flask containing her stolen life-essence was found.**[1269]

1911 - PYRAMIDS OF MARS[1270] **->** The fourth Doctor and Sarah Jane landed at the Old Priory, on the future site of UNIT HQ. They discovered that the servants of Sutekh were planning to release him from his imprisonment. The Doctor trapped Sutekh in a time corridor, eventually destroying him.

The King's Regulations were published in 1912.[1271] **The Royal Flying Corps was formed in 1912.**[1272] Xznaal, an Ice Lord, was struck by the state of the withered plant life on his home planet of Mars.[1273] The downfall of Imperial China was sealed when the Celestial Toymaker lost a game.[1274]

> (=) A historical deviation caused colleagues of the self-sacrificing Captain Oates to drag him back to camp, where they died together.[1275]

1261 *TW: Slow Decay*

1262 *TW: Department X*

1263 "One hundred years" before *SJA: The White Wolf*.

1264 Dating *The Catalyst* (BF CC #2.4) - The year isn't given, but the Douglas family lives in an Edwardian house, and comes across as an Edwardian family. The suffragette movement (which peaked in 1912) is topical enough for Lady Douglas to view it with contempt. Douglas' first name, "Joshua", isn't mentioned until *The Time Vampire*.

It's here said that Joshua travelled with a Doctor who was an "old man"; *The Time Vampire* specifies that it's the third Doctor (a "white-haired man who wore a bright red jacket"). Joshua travelled with the Doctor for about a decade - such a massive duration of time in the third Doctor's lifetime is most likely to have occurred in the interim between *The Green Death* and *The Time Warrior*, when he's no longer exiled, companionless and possibly - in wake of Jo Grant's departure - looking for a reason to spend some time away from Earth.

1265 She is 21 according to the sleeve notes of *Hornets' Nest: The Dead Shoes*.

1266 *Pyramids of Mars*

1267 *The Stones of Blood*

1268 *The Impossible Astronaut*

1269 *TW: From Out of the Rain*

1270 Dating *Pyramids of Mars* (13.3) - Laurence Scarman gives the date as "nineteen hundred and eleven".

1271 *The War Games*

1272 *Ghost Light*

1273 "Eighty-five" years before *The Dying Days* (p175).

1274 *The Nightmare Fair*. Imperial China came to an end in 1912. The Toymaker's interest in China is doubtless meant to explain his attire.

1275 *The Algebra of Ice* (p13). Oates died 17th March, 1912.

The *Titanic* sank, although the Doctor claimed that he had nothing to do with that... The ninth Doctor warned the Daniels family not to board the *Titanic* and was photographed with them. However, he boarded the ship, and ended up clinging to an iceberg.[1276]

1912 (14th April) - THE LEFT-HANDED HUMMINGBIRD[1277] -> On the sinking *Titanic*, the seventh Doctor prevented Huitzilin - also called the Blue - from acquiring the Xiuhcoatl, an Exxilon weapon capable of manipulating molecules. It could transmute or destroy matter. Huitzilin manifested but was killed.

Charley Pollard, a companion of the eighth Doctor and (later) the sixth Doctor, was born the day the *Titanic* sank.[1278]

1912 - THE SUFFERING[1279] -> In Piltdown, the skull of the female leader from the fourth galaxy was excavated and thought to be the "missing link" between ape and man. The leader's consciousness influenced women to start an uprising against men at a suffrage rally in Hyde Park. The first Doctor, Steven and Vicki combined efforts to defeat the leader, then fulfilled history by replacing her skull with a human cranium and the jawbone of an ape.

1912 (30th-31st October) - GRACELESS: THE FOG[1280] -> An asteroid destroyed the Cheshire town of Compton, dispersing extra-terrestrial energy in such a way as to obliterate the town without leaving a crater. The impact rippled through time and space, attracting the living tracers Abby and Zara. They interacted for a time with the last echoes of the townsfolk killed in the event.

The British government bought out the land where Compton once stood, and the army erected new buildings, further making the memory of the town lost to history.[1281]

Around 1913, Harding Wellman died while mountaineering in Switzerland.[1282] A Wyndham Lewis painting was amongst the artifacts later taken to the Earth colony of Jegg-Sau, and found ruined there.[1283] **Lydia Childs joined Torchwood** in 1913, and would serve as the secretary of Torchwood Cardiff until the early 1920s.[1284]

1913 - YEAR OF THE PIG[1285] -> The sixth Doctor and Peri sought to relax at the Hotel Palace Thermae in the Belgian municipality of Ostend. Also in residence were Toby the Sapient Pig, Nurse Albertine, Toby's admirer Alice Bultitude and the mentally confused Inspector Alphonse Chardalot. The Doctor deduced that Toby and Chardalot were actually brothers, the result of genetic experiments carried out some decades previous. The two siblings were reunited, and the Doctor believed they were perhaps better off not knowing details about their origins.

The Doctor happened upon Proust at this time, and made a point of grabbing the reclusive man by the shoulders, calling him Marcel, breathing port fumes up his nose and telling him exactly what he thought of the central character in *Swann's Way*. The actress Lillian Washbourne died in a fire, and Toby decided to send her agent flowers. Chardalot gave Peri a stuffed monkey that was believed to hail from the gift shop of Madame Ensor, the mother of the Belgian painter James Ensor.

Owing to a mishap with a temporal fission grenade that Chardalot possessed, the sky was briefly filled with exploding cows.

1276 The Doctor mentions the *Titanic* in *Robot*, but tells Borusa in *The Invasion of Time* that "it had nothing to do with me". The ninth Doctor's involvement with the *Titanic* was cited in *Rose* and *The End of the World*.

1277 Dating *The Left-Handed Hummingbird* (NA #21) - The story takes place on the *Titanic*, and the date is confirmed on p221.

1278 *Neverland*. She was eighteen years, five months and twenty-one days old when she met the Doctor (in *Storm Warning*), according to *The Chimes of Midnight*. However, that would seem to mean that Charley was born 14th April (the night the iceberg struck *Titanic*) as opposed to 15th April (when *Titanic* went under).

1279 Dating *The Suffering* (BF CC #4.7) - It's "the year of our Lord, nineteen hundred and twelve". This particular Hyde Park rally seems to be fictional; other suffrage rallies took place there in real life, as when 250,000 people marched there in June 1908.

1280 Dating *Graceless: The Fog* (*Graceless* #1.2) - Amy procures a copy of *The Manchester Guardian* dated to "Wednesday, 6th of November, 1912", which is "a week"

after the story takes place. She and Zara arrive in Compton the night before the catastrophe.

1281 "A year" after *Graceless: The Fog*.

1282 "Some fifty years" before *Winter for the Adept*.

1283 *Benny: The Relics of Jegg-Sau*. Lewis, a co-founder of the Vorticist art movement, lived 1882-1957. His work was exhibited as early as 1912.

1284 From Torchwood.org.uk and *The Torchwood Archives*. Childs is seen in the photograph of the 1918 Torchwood in *TW: To the Last Man*, alongside Gerald Carter, Harriet Derbyshire, Douglas Caldwell and Dr Charles Quinn.

1285 Dating *Year of the Pig* (BF #89) - The year is given, and specified on the back cover. Proust lived 1871-1922, and *Swann's Way* - his seven-volume, semi-autobiographical novel - was published between 1913 and 1927. The Ostend gift shop run by James Ensor's mother is historical, and some items in the store inspired Ensor's painting.

1286 *Just War*

1287 *Lungbarrow, Vampire Science*.

5555555555
555555555

The Doctor saved St Peter Port from some terrible threat on Halloween 1913. He could not save the life of young Celia Doras.[1286] The Doctor and Ace independently visited the premiere of the ballet *The Rites of Spring* in 1913.[1287]

1913 (September to 11th November) - HUMAN NATURE (TV) / THE FAMILY OF BLOOD[1288] -> To escape the Family of Blood - expert hunters who wanted the DNA of a Time Lord - the tenth Doctor used a Chameleon Arch to become human and hide in 1913. With Martha's help, the amnesiac Doctor became a teacher at Farringham School and fell for nurse Joan Redfern. The Family arrived on Earth in their invisible spacecraft and confronted Smith, who had no idea he had been the Doctor. Martha helped the Doctor resume his true nature, and the Time Lord swiftly and ruthlessly granted the Family their wish for immortality by imprisoning them all for eternity.

The First World War

The Nemesis statue passed over the Earth in 1913, heralding the First World War.[1289] The immortal Captain Jack served in the First World War.[1290]

The sarcophagus carrying the second Hornet Swarm materialised at the Cromer Palace of Curios at 2 am on 14th April, 1914. This triggered a fire, and the Swarm perished as the Palace burned down.[1291]

John Watson passed by Buckingham Palace on 4th August, 1914, and was inadvertently swept up in a crowd celebrating His Majesty's Government declaring war on Germany and its allies. Just two days beforehand, Sherlock Holmes and Watson had defeated Von Bork, an agent of the Kaiser who tried to steal documents related to Britain's defence plans. Watson accepted a Colonelcy from his old regiment, and was preparing to leave for France when Mycroft Holmes and Bernice Summerfield asked for his help. Together, they solved a mystery pertaining to a malfunctioning piece of Time Lord circuitry.[1292]

1914 (April) - HUMAN NATURE (NA)[1293] -> Wanting to learn more about human emotions, the seventh Doctor acquired nanites that transformed his Time Lord body into that of a human, and stored his biodata and memories in a small pod. He mentally became "John Smith" - a persona crafted by the TARDIS - and worked as the house master at Hulton Academy for Boys in the village of Farringham in Norfolk. Benny posed as Smith's niece. Smith and a teacher, Joan Redfern, soon fell in love.

The shapechanging Aubertides pursued the TARDIS to Farringham - consuming the Doctor's biodata would greatly extend their lifespans and enable them to produce enough offspring to overwhelm Gallifrey, then countless worlds. Most of the Aubertides were killed in a pitched battle; Smith saved Joan by exchanging his mind with that of the Doctor, and then died while inhabiting the body of the Aubertide leader, August. The sole surviving Aubertide, Greeneye, escaped by turning himself into a cow - but met his fate in a slaughterhouse.

The Doctor and Joan parted ways, but not before she gifted him with her cat, Wolsey, as a memento.

1288 Dating *Human Nature* (TV)/*The Family of Blood* (X3.8-3.9) - Martha shows the Doctor a newspaper dated "Monday November 10th 1913", and a poster for the Annual Dance - which occurs the following day - yields the date of "November 11th". The Doctor has been on Earth "two months", so since early September.
1289 *Silver Nemesis*
1290 *Utopia*
1291 *Demon Quest: Sepulchre*
1292 *Benny: Secret Histories:* "A Gallery of Pigeons"
1293 Dating *Human Nature* (NA #37) - It is "April" (p17) "1914" (p16).
    ARE THERE TWO HUMAN NATURES, NOW?: Well, yes. The 2007 television story *Human Nature/The Family of Blood* is an adaptation of the New Adventures novel *Human Nature*, both written by Paul Cornell.
    In varying degrees, the new series has done this four other times so far: *Dalek* was based on elements of *Jubilee* (a Big Finish audio also by Rob Shearman), *Rise of the Cybermen/The Age of Steel* resulted from an attempt to adapt the audio *Spare Parts* by Marc Platt (the finished product was a different story altogether, but Platt still received a credit), *The Lodger* (TV) came

about when Gareth Roberts revamped his tenth Doctor *DWM* comic of the same name, and Steven Moffat used the central idea and the name of the main character of his *Annual 2006* story ("What I Did On My Christmas Holidays by Sally Sparrow") as the basis of *Blink*. All four of these examples are clearly different stories - the Cyberman ones explicitly take place in different universes, in fact - and it's easy enough to believe they could all happen to the Doctor, given a little coincidence.
    The idea of coincidence is stretched to and probably beyond breaking point by the two *Human Natures*, however. There's nothing in the TV story to explain how both could happen. Yet this chronology counts both stories, as it counts both *Shadas*, so some explanation is probably needed.
    There are a number of possibilities:
    1) Both happened, and it's all a coincidence. There are differences, some of them pretty serious ones: they take place in different years; the school is called Hulton in the novel and Farringham in the TV story; the Doctor is in a different incarnation with a different companion and becomes human for a different reason; he fights

During World War I, the first conflict between England and Germany occurred at the Battle of Mons. The English Captain Dudgeon luckily survived when his platoon was wiped out, and he later claimed to have seen one of the Angels of Mons: guardians from on high who sought to protect the British troops.[1294] Jack Harkness was vaguely acquainted with author/mystic Arthur Machen.[1295]

(=) The carnage of the Battle of Mons awoke the Dark Matrix. The British Expeditionary Force saw the form of Jack the Ripper over the battlefield.[1296]

Douglas Caldwell, formerly a draughtsman in the Royal Engineers, **joined Torchwood Cardiff** during World War I.[1297]

1914 (14th October) - PROJECT: TWILIGHT[1298] ->

The Forge, a secret project to improve the stock of soldiers, experimented on prisoners to create a race of "twilight vampires". One of the subjects, Amelia, a.k.a. Twilight Seven, became vampiric on 12th September, 1914. On 14th October, the vampires overpowered their creator, Dr Abberton, and fled. Abberton took the vampire formula to survive his wounds, and became known as Nimrod.

The Doctor was in Folkstone during the German bombardment of Antwerp in October 1914, and met a young woman named Jessica Borthwick. Under fire, she shuttled Belgian refugees across the channel in her yacht.[1299]

In 1914, Manuel Gamio discovered a part of the Great Temple of the Aztecs.[1300]

1914 (Christmas Day) - "The Forgotten"[1301] ->

The ninth Doctor and Rose found themselves in the trenches of the 11th Battalion Bedfordshire Regiment, and the Doctor celebrated the holiday by organising a football match between the two sides. The man in charge of this section of the trench, Captain Harkness, had been shot in the head and taken to hospital - he survived without a scratch.

Charles Arthur Cromwell of Torchwood was born on 6th March, 1915.[1302] The sixth Doctor had mint-condition gas masks from the Second Battle of Ypres, 1915.[1303]

(=) The Already Dead kidnapped Corporal Francis Morgan of the Welsh Fusiliers to serve as the living core component of a temporal fusion device.

A Vortex Dweller retroactively prevented Morgan's abduction, and he died instead.[1304]

1915 (7th May) - THE SIRENS OF TIME[1305] ->

The fifth Doctor was on a merchant ship that was torpedoed by a U-boat. He was captured and posed as a German secret agent. He escaped shortly before the U-boat torpedoed the RMS *Lusitania*. The Doctor failed to save the *Lusitania*, but in doing so prevented the future murder of Alexander Fleming, the discoverer of penicillin. Without it, the world would have suffered from plagues and fallen prey to the Second Velyshaan Empire.

1915 (August) - WHITE DARKNESS[1306] ->

The seventh Doctor, Benny and Ace arrived in Haiti as a civil

---

different aliens. The Joan Redferns he falls for are different ages and have different histories. So the Doctor has a similar adventure twice - luckily, it's one that involves him losing his memory, so the second version of "John Smith", at least, wouldn't notice the redundancy.

2) Both happened, and it's not a coincidence. We're told in the TV story that the TARDIS chose the landing point. Perhaps it's deliberately picked a situation that "worked" in similar circumstances. It seems a little odd - if not actively cruel - for the TARDIS to pick on another Joan Redfern, though.

3) The original was erased from history... possibly as a result of the Time War, the events of the novel *Human Nature* no longer "happened" (this does not automatically suppose that the whole of New Adventures did not "occur", however). The Big Finish version of *Shada* establishes that in this situation, there would be a timeline gap that needs filling, but that a different incarnation of the Doctor can play the part.

1294 *No Man's Land*. Dudgeon says the Mons conflict started 22nd August, 1914, although some resources say it technically was initiated on the 23rd. Real-life soldiers did report seeing the angels that Dudgeon

describes, but they're commonly regarded as the result of battle trauma, urban legends and perhaps deliberately targeted propaganda.

1295 *TW: Consequences*: "The Wrong Hands". Machen, a Welsh author responsible for the legend of the Angels of Mons, lived 1863-1947.

1296 *Matrix*

1297 Per Torchwood.org.uk.

1298 Dating *Project: Twilight* (BF #23) - The exact days are given.

1299 *Brotherhood of the Daleks*

1300 *The Left-Handed Hummingbird* (p58).

1301 Dating "The Forgotten" (IDW *DW* mini-series #2) - The date is given. Private Benton may be an ancestor (the grandfather?) of UNIT's Sergeant Benton.

1302 *TW: Trace Memory*

1303 *Recorded Time and Other Stories*: "Paradoxicide". The battle was 22nd April to 25th May, 1915.

1304 *TW: The Undertaker's Gift*. The book is a little contradictory concerning Morgan's abduction/death - it's said on page 90 that Torchwood investigated his disappearance after the war in 1919, and yet when his kidnapping is retroactively prevented, page 239 claims

rebellion against President Sam started. Lemaitre, an ancient man working on behalf of the Great Old Ones, was raising an army of zombies. They planned to open a gateway from their realm to Earth, and to conquer Europe. The Doctor destroyed Lemaitre and his base with a bomb.

In 1915, Mr Sun was imprisoned for killing a professor of economics, who was later revealled as an Austrian spy.[1307] Arthur Kendrick distinguished himself by second-guessing the U-boat commanders on the Atlantic convoys. He would serve as an Admiral in World War II.[1308] **Professor Travers began his search for the Yeti.**[1309]

1915 (12th-13th September) - "The First"[1310] -> Tall crystalline beings, the Skith, were explorers of the Four Galaxies. They coveted knowledge to such an extent, they would acquire samples from planets, then eradicate their inhabitants or infect them with Skith crystals and turn them into Skithself. The Skith drove the Viskili, Mammox and pig-like Byndalk to extinction.

The tenth Doctor and Martha found that the Skith were interfering with Ernest Shackleton's trans-Antarctic expedition aboard the *Endurance*. A whale was transformed into a Skith octopoid, and zoologist Robert Clark progressively turned into Skithself. Together with Shackleton and the legendary adventurer/photographer James Francis Hurley, the travellers opened a rift and sent the Skith and their spaceship - Oppressor One - into the sun. Clark returned to normal, and Shackleton's expedition failed as history recorded.

The Skith leader survived, wounded, on Earth. It retained some knowledge of time travel that had been copied from the Doctor's mind when he was briefly turned into Skithself.[1311]

1915 (18th November) - PLAYERS[1312] -> The second Doctor arrived in No Man's Land using a time ring. He saved Winston Churchill from an ambush engineered by

two Players, the Count and the Countess. The next day, he saved Churchill again, this time with the help of Jeremy Carstairs and Jennifer Buckingham. Carstairs joined Churchill's staff. The Doctor escaped a German firing squad by using the time ring.

The scientist Nikita Kuznetzov saw the devastation at Tunguska.[1313] Harry Randall and his twin brother Herbert - both of whom became trapped in the Toymaker's domain - performed as comic funambulists. The two of them, or possibly just Harry, topped the bill at the Empire Theatre in Penge.[1314]

The Somme

The Battle of the Somme took place on 14th July, 1916. Richard Hadleman survived, treated by Timothy Dean, a former student of Dr John Smith of Aberdeen.[1315] **Tim Latimer saved himself and his schoolmate Hutchinson on a First World War battlefield, thanks to a premonition he'd had some years earlier.**[1316] Lance Corporal Weeks, later the chief steward aboard the *R-101,* fought at the Somme.[1317] Roger Gleave, a future police inspector, witnessed the devastation.[1318]

On one of their missions, the crew of the *Teselecta* converted their ship to look like Rasputin - but made the mistake of rendering him as green.[1319]

w - Two days before Rasputin's death, Faction Paradox took him away to the Eleven-Day Empire, where he became Father Dyavol, an advisor to Cousin Anastasia. In his place, the Faction supplied a duplicate Rasputin generated in a remembrance tank. The Great Houses sensed something amiss with Rasputin's history and attempted to rewrite the duplicate's biodata, even as the Celestis put their mark of indenture on him. The faux Rasputin effectively became three zombies in one, and the prolonged manner of his death embarrassed all concerned.[1320]

that "he was dead by 1915".
1305 Dating *The Sirens of Time* (BF #1) - The date is given.
1306 Dating *White Darkness* (NA #15) - "On the wall, a calendar of 1915 had just been turned to the August page" (p22).
1307 *The Cabinet of Light* (p85).
1308 *Just War*
1309 "Twenty years" before *The Abominable Snowman*.
1310 Dating "The First" (DWM #386-389) - The exact days are given. The expedition is historical, and renowned as the last great (albeit failed) crossing of Antarctica.
1311 "The Age of Ice", "The Crimson Hand".

1312 Dating *Players* (PDA #21) - The date is given (p69).
1313 *The Wages of Sin*
1314 *The Magic Mousetrap.* The brothers started performing "before the war", but the Empire Theatre didn't open until April 1915, as a music hall starring Marie Lloyd.
1315 *Human Nature* (NA)
1316 *The Family of Blood*
1317 *Storm Warning*
1318 *Eater of Wasps*
1319 *Let's Kill Hitler.* Presumably Rasputin wasn't the target of their attack, as they were impersonating him.
1320 *FP: The Book of the War*

1916 (December) - THE WAGES OF SIN[1321] -> The third Doctor, Jo Grant and Liz Shaw arrived in St. Petersburg as members of the city's elite, concerned about Father Grigori Rasputin's growing influence over Empress Czarina Alexandra, conspired to murder him. Jo befriended Rasputin and saved him from death by poisoning, but the conspirators repeatedly shot and beat Rasputin, still failing to kill him. The conspirators finally had Rasputin thrown into a frozen river. The Doctor refrained from action as Rasputin drowned, fulfilling history. Six weeks later, the Russian Revolution overthrew Tsar Nicholas II.

1917 - THE ROOF OF THE WORLD[1322] -> Lord Davey discovered an alien pyramid in the Himalayas when his expedition was wiped out in a storm. He was killed and replaced with a doppelganger. The fifth Doctor, Peri and Erimem arrived in Darjeeling, where Erimem met Davey and was possessed by the same force. A black cloud descended, killing dozens of people... including Erimem. The Doctor deduced this was an attempt on the part of the Great Old Ones to take control of the world, and that Erimem was still alive. Peri froze the cloud with liquid nitrogen. The pyramid was buried beneath an avalanche.

On 16th April, 1917, the Doctor and Lenin played tiddlywinks on the train journey that returned Lenin from Switzerland to Russia. After that, the Doctor met Empress Alexandra.[1323] The Doctor was present in Russia during the October Revolution, met Lenin and became a Hero of the Revolution.[1324] The Doctor regarded Lenin as a "disagreeable man with terrible breath".[1325]

1917 - NO MAN'S LAND[1326] -> An agent of the Forge, posing as "Lieutenant-Colonel Brook" of the British army, undertook experiments to refine his soldiers' killing instinct. The Forge also wanted to know if psychological trauma could endow people with time sensitivity or precognition. Soldiers at Charnage Hospital near Arras in France were subjected to psychological refinement in the "hate room", and made to "kill" dummies of German troopers. Brook sent a squad to No Man's Land when a wounded trooper, Private Taylor, informed him of an old church on an excellent vantage point there. Due to Brook's conditioning, the British soldiers slaughtered one another.

The seventh Doctor, Ace and Hex destroyed Brook's research, and Brook was killed by his own callous men. The Doctor postulated that perhaps the unhinged Private Taylor had indeed demonstrated precognition.

The first Doctor and Susan were caught in a Zeppelin raid at some point during the war.[1327] **A First World War battlefield near Ypres was kidnapped by the War Lords.**[1328] **The Doctor claimed to have been wounded at the Battle of Gallipoli.**[1329] **Burton, later a camp leader at Shangri-La in 1959, fought in the War using his sabre in hand-to-hand combat.**[1330] **The Toymaker kidnapped two British soldiers from Ypres.**[1331]

Turkish soldiers during the First World War claimed to

1321 Dating *The Wages of Sin* (PDA #19) - The date is given (p21). *Zagreus* confirms that the Doctor has met Rasputin.
1322 Dating *The Roof of the World* (BF #59) - It's 1917 according to the back cover.
1323 *Storm Warning*
1324 *The Devil Goblins from Neptune*
1325 *Singularity*
1326 Dating *No Man's Land* (BF #89) - The year is given.
1327 *Planet of Giants*
1328 *The War Games*
1329 *The Sea Devils*
1330 *Delta and the Bannermen*
1331 *Divided Loyalties*
1332 *Eternity Weeps*
1333 *Byzantium!, The King of Terror.*
1334 *The Empire of Death.* Luckner lived 1881-1966.
1335 *Mad Dogs and Englishmen*
1336 *Storm Warning.* The Treaty of Versailles was signed 28th June, 1919.
1337 Torchwood.org.uk. Harriet appears in *TW: To the Last Man.*
1338 *TW: Small Worlds*
1339 Dating *The Way Through the Woods* (NSA #45) - It's "autumn 1917, shortly after closing time" (p19).

1340 *FP: The Book of the War, FP: Warring States.*
1341 *Assassin in the Limelight*
1342 *FP: The Book of the War, FP: Warring States* (p52).
1343 *The Coming of the Terraphiles*
1344 *Sontarans: Old Soldiers*
1345 Dating *Casualties of War* (EDA #38) - The date is given (p7).
1346 *Eater of Wasps*
1347 *Pier Pressure.* The armistice with Germany was signed in France on 11th November, 1918.
1348 Dating *TW: To the Last Man* (TW 2.3) - The year is given. Tommy is 24 and was born 7th February, 1894, so events in 1918 must occur after that day. *The Torchwood Archives* claims that Tommy was killed on 28th October, 1918, so events in *To the Last Man* - set three weeks beforehand - presumably occur in the same month.
1349 Dating *TW: "Rift War"* (TWM #4-13) - The year is given.
1350 *Birthright, Casualties of War.*
1351 "Twelve years" before *The English Way of Death* (p83).
1352 *The Magic Mousetrap*
1353 *Matrix*
1354 Dating *The Memory Cheats* (BF CC #6.3) - The month and year is given.

have seen The Ark of Ages on Mount Ararat.[1332] The Doctor saw the Battle of Passchendale.[1333] The Doctor met the noted sailor Felix von Luckner.[1334]

In 1917, Reginald Tyler started writing the fantasy epic *The True History of Planets* while on leave from soldiering in France.[1335] Brigadier General Tamworth was part of the Versailles delegation, and foresaw that reparations against Germany would further a bigger conflict.[1336] **Harriet Derbyshire was recruited** from Oxford to join Torchwood Cardiff.[1337]

In 1917, the Cottingley Fairies photographs caused a sensation - even Sir Arthur Conan Doyle thought they were genuine. Decades later, the girls who took the pictures admitted they were fakes, but Torchwood would have reason to suspect they were real.[1338]

1917 (autumn) - THE WAY THROUGH THE WOODS[1339] **->** As part of their investigations into the people who had gone missing in Swallow Woods, the eleventh Doctor and Amy dropped off Rory to observe barmaid Emily Bostock. Rory and Emily were transported into a pocket dimension that Reyn the were-fox used to save the odd person from his sentient spaceship.

w - Russia made the switch from the Julian calendar to the Gregorian one in 1918, when the 31st January was immediately followed by 14th February. Cousin Anastasia claimed these lost thirteen days and founded the Thirteen-Day Republic, a rival to Faction Paradox's Eleven-Day Empire.[1340]

The Doctor was present on 23rd March, 1918, when the Chinese conjuror Chung Ling Soo died on stage in London. Soo was performing in the Wood Green Empire, and perished when his bullet-catching act went wrong.[1341]

w - Grand Duchess Anastasia Nikolaevna, Tsar Nicholas II's youngest daughter, was recruited to join Faction Paradox and became known as Cousin Anastasia. History recorded that Anastasia was executed along with her family on 17th July, 1918.[1342]

Around 1918, the Doctor and Cornelius literally crossed swords in an adventure that involved a Newcastle coal mine and Leopard Men.[1343] The British military captured a Sontaran named Brak when he crashed to Earth. He was brought to England in 1918, and would be kept under paralysis until World War II.[1344]

@ 1918 - CASUALTIES OF WAR[1345] **->** The eighth Doctor investigated reports of the walking dead in Hawkswick in Yorkshire. Befriending the village midwife, Mary Minnett, he discovered that the creatures were being created by the traumatic memories of wounded soldiers convalescing at Hawkswick Hall. The Doctor caused a psychic backlash, destroying the hall and the man behind it - the head of the hospital, Dr Banham.

@ The Doctor kept the last letter Mary wrote to him (on 22nd August, 1918).[1346] The West Pier in Brighton absorbed the cheerful feelings of its visitors - the malevolent aliens from Indo subsisted off these emotions, and grew stronger. However, the armistice that ended World War I created such a widespread feeling of relief, the aliens were temporarily subdued.[1347]

1918 (October) - TW: TO THE LAST MAN[1348] **->** The Rift caused St. Teilo's Hospital in Cardiff to overlap with itself in the twenty-first century, an act that endangered both time zones. Gerald Carter and Harriet Derbyshire of Torchwood were instructed by a future projection of Thomas Reginald Brockless - a soldier at St. Teilo's recovering from shellshock - to find and cryo-freeze his past self. They did so, enabling Torchwood in future to close the Rift by sending Tommy back through it. Tommy resumed being shellshocked on his return to 1918; three weeks later, he was returned to France and executed for cowardice.

1918 - TW: "Rift War"[1349] **->** Gerald Carter and Harriet Derbyshire disrupted a group of stone circle worshippers by "borrowing" a tank from the military. Rift activity briefly juxtaposed them with Ianto and Tosh in 2008, where they saw their friend and colleague Jack Harkness.

An influenza epidemic in 1918 and 1919 killed more people than the Great War itself.[1350] An agent of the Bureau arrived from the future (circa 2386) and adopted the name Percival Closed.[1351] Following an incident on a rowing boat on Lake Balaton, the summer of 1919, Mrs Elsa Kerniddle would never speak again. She was later transported into the Celestial Toymaker's realm.[1352]

(=) In the world of the Dark Matrix, the Jack the Ripper killings started again after the Great War. Ghostly Rippers begin terrorising London. There was mass panic, despite summary executions for suspects. The government withdrew to Edinburgh.[1353]

1919 (August) - THE MEMORY CHEATS[1354] **->** The second Doctor, Jamie and Zoe were in Tashkent, Uzbekistan, as the Bolsheviks took command of the North, and were expected to spread their control to the South. The letters of Richard Lansing detailed how school children were going missing, and said a deformed man was responsible. Lansing and his wife Elizabeth were killed before discovering the truth. It was possible that a kind alien observer was collecting some children to take back to its homeworld, and spare them the horror of warfare on Earth. It was also possible that the Lansings had died because Zoe accidentally agitated the creature into killing them. In Zoe's native time, she and her defence council were unable to agree on exactly what had taken place, and how this matter resolved.

1919 (late September) - TOY SOLDIERS[1355] -> Investigating the mysterious disappearance of children across post-War Europe, the seventh Doctor, Benny, Roz and Chris discovered that they had been kidnapped by the Recruiter, a device transporting beings from many worlds to act as soldiers in the fourteen-hundred-year war that had ravaged the planet Q'ell. The Recruiter had been built to destroy the Ceracai race, but the Doctor reprogrammed it to rebuild the devastated planet.

Harriet Derbyshire was killed, age 26. Gerald Carter retired from active Torchwood service, but remained a consultant.[1356] **The Doctor drank with Lloyd George when he was Prime Minister.**[1357]

The Nineteen Twenties

The Doctor acquired a copy of the 1920 book *Every Boy's Book of the English Civil War*. He would later lose it in 1648.[1358] The Doctor met movie producer Harold Reitman in England in the 1920s.[1358] He helped Joyce with *Ulysses*.[1360]

In the 1920s, Blue Tit birds in Southampton learned to tear the tops off milk bottles and drink the cream inside. Soon, Blue Tit birds more than a hundred miles away were exhibiting the talent - even though the birds rarely flew more than fifteen miles - and by 1947, the habit was universal among the species. This owed to morphic resonance, a collective memory held within a planet's morphogenetic field, and passed on to each new generation of life. The same effect was witnessed in monkey creatures four million years in the future, on the planet Endarra.[1361]

The time traveller Honoré Lechasseur was born in

1355 Dating *Toy Soldiers* (NA #42) - The main action of the book starts "25 September 1919" (p39).
1356 *TW: To the Last Man.* Harriet is said to be killed "the year after" an undated photo of Gerald Carter's Torchwood team is taken; *The Torchwood Archives* dates her death to 1919, confirming that the photo was taken in 1918. There's conflicting reports of when Gerald stops leading Torchwood Cardiff - Torchwood.org.uk says he held himself responsible for Harriet's death and "retired from active service soon afterwards", but *The Torchwood Archives* says he remained in charge until 1926.
1357 *Aliens of London.* No date is given, but Lloyd George was Prime Minister 1916-1922.
1358 *The Roundheads*
1359 *Dying in the Sun*
1360 "The Final Chapter"
1361 *Scaredy Cat*
1362 He's 29 in *TimeH: The Tunnel at the End of the Light* (p16), which appears to take place in early 1950 - although he might have already had a birthday, in which case he was born in 1921.
1363 *TimeH: The Sideways Door*
1364 Dating *Blink* (X3.10) - Benjamin's newspaper names the day and year.
1365 Dating *TimeH: The Severed Man* (*TimeH* #5) - A time-sensitive tells Honoré and Emily that they're in 1921 (p108). Strangely, though, *TimeH: Echoes* p10 seems to state that these events happened in 1924.
1366 Dating *The Daleks' Master Plan* (4.4) - The script for episode seven, "The Feast of Steven", specified a date of "1919", but publicity material released on 1st October, 1965, stated that the TARDIS lands in "California 1921". The film being made is a talkie, which means this must be after the release of *The Jazz Singer* in 1927. Numerous Hollywood personalities are seen or hinted at in the episode. Actor Rudolph Valentino made his debut in

1914, but was only really famous after *The Sheik* in 1921. Actor Douglas Fairbanks Sr. debuted in 1915, but he wasn't "big" (as he is described in the episode) until *The Three Musketeers* in 1921. Chaplin's debut was 1914, but the film we see in production strongly resembles *Gold Rush* (1924). Bing Crosby didn't go to Hollywood until 1930. *DWM* writer Richard Landen claimed a date of "1929", *The TARDIS Special* offered "c.1920".
1367 *The Wages of Sin*
1368 Angus relates the story in *Terror of the Zygons*.
1369 According to Commander Millington, the accident happened "over twenty years" before *The Curse of Fenric*, and Judson appears to blame Millington for it. The novelisation, also written by Ian Briggs, confirms that Millington was culpable.
1370 "Wormwood"
1371 *TW: Trace Memory*
1372 *TW: The Twilight Streets*
1373 *TimeH: Kitsune*
1374 *Assassin in the Limelight.* This is said to have taken place in "the summer of 23 or 24", but Fender was more at his height in the former year, as England dropped him after 1924.
1375 "The Age of Ice". The likely suspect here is *The Life of Ernest Shackleton* (1923), published a year after Shackleton's death, but it's unclear who did the censoring as UNIT didn't yet exist.
1376 Dating *Paradox Lost* (NSA #48) - The exact day is given (p233).
1377 Dating *Timewyrm: Exodus* (NA #2) - Part Two of the novel is set during the Munich Putsch, which took place between the 8th and 9th of November 1923. A textbook quoted in the novel erroneously gives the month as "September" (p95).
1378 *Illegal Alien*
1379 *Iris: The Panda Invasion.* Historically speaking, the claim is a strange one. Eric Blair, a.k.a. George Orwell,

1920.[1362] Jean-Henri, Honoré's father, abandoned his son and Honoré's mother, Evangeline Lechasseur.[1363]

1920 (5th December) - BLINK[1364] **->** The Weeping Angels transported Kathy Nightingale from 2007 to Hull in 1920. She would marry Benjamin Wainright and live out her life in her own past.

1921 - TIMEH: THE SEVERED MAN[1365] **->** The Cabal of the Horned Beast was now powerful enough to enthrall the village of Middleton Basset using a time-creature. The time travelling Honoré Lechasseur and Emily Blandish broke the Cabal's hold over the time-creature, freeing the townsfolk.

c 1921 - THE DALEKS' MASTER PLAN[1366] **->** While hiding from the Daleks, the TARDIS landed briefly on a film set in Hollywood.

The Russian mineralogist Leonid A Kulik visited the area of the Tunguska explosion in 1921, but failed to locate the impact site.[1367] **In 1922, a foreigner staying at Tullock Inn vanished on Tullock Moor, kidnapped by the Zygons.**[1368] **Dr Judson was crippled before this time.**[1369] The Threshold set up offices on Earth's moon in 1922.[1370] Sao Paulo, 1922, was the site of a Vondrax visitation.[1371]

In the same year, Jack Harkness once again failed to enter the Tretarri housing district, but engaged in some "sexual deviancy" with a young lady in the back of the Torchwood Daimler he'd requisitioned.1372 Zoo animals killed during an earthquake in Tokyo, 1923, became vengeful spirits, and were contained within a haunted house later built on the same locale.1373 The Doctor watched a cricket game featuring Percy George Herbert Fender - whom he regarded as the finest cricketer ever to captain England.[1374]

Material pertaining to the Skith was embargoed from Ernest Shackleton's biography.[1375]

1923 (23rd October) - PARADOX LOST[1376] **->** The eleventh Doctor brought the AI unit Arven to live with the retired Professor Archibald Angelchrist, figuring they could both use the company.

1923 (9th November) - TIMEWYRM: EXODUS[1377] **->** The seventh Doctor and Ace witnessed the Munich Putsch, an attempted coup organised by a young Adolf Hitler, so the Doctor could gain Hitler's confidence and sway events in future. A man with energy weapons fired upon the time travellers - it was the War Chief, who was operating in this era to aid the Nazis, but the Doctor didn't recognise him.

In 1923, George Limb, a member of military intelligence, failed to convince his superiors that the British should side with Hitler.[1378] Iris Wildthyme spent a night in a cell with George Orwell.[1379]

@ The Doctor studied Ba Chai in Peking, the 1920s.[1380] The Doctor borrowed a rucksack from George Mallory and Andrew Irvine before their final assault on Everest in 1924. He warned them not to lose their gloves, lest they lose their lives, but he never saw from them again - possibly because he'd failed to return Mallory's gloves.[1381] In 1924, the Panoptican Theatre was converted into an 850-seater and renamed the Beacon Film Theatre.[1382] Iris Wildthyme's bus had a constant supply of fresh water thanks to an inter-dimensional, time-travelling pipeline to a Canadian lake in 1924.[1383]

The last remnants of Marshall Sezhyr's Ice Army fell into in-fighting, and his most devout followers were slaughtered - chained out onto the surface of Mars to face the Red Dawn. One group gathered relics from his shrine and escaped to Earth.[1384]

On 28th February, 1924, Jack Harkness showed up at Torchwood India in Delhi armed with dance records, and seduced the group's leader: Eleanor, the Duchess of Melrose. Britain's hold over India was coming to an end, and Jack had orders to relocate Torchwood India's holdings back to the home country. On 29th February, the Duchess and her associates used a piece of alien tech left behind - a "time store" - to halt the passage of time inside an old colonial mansion. They carried on for decades, unaging, as the world changed around them.[1385]

---

wasn't incarcerated but did serve as an imperial policeman in Burma from 1922 to 1927. Perhaps Iris was imprisoned and Orwell was her jailor.
1380 *To the Slaughter*
1381 *Circular Time*: "Spring". George Mallory and Andrew Irvine perished while attempting to climb Everest in June 1924, which perhaps makes the Doctor and Nyssa's light-hearted banter about the topic a little inappropriate.
1382 Torchwood.org.uk, elaborating on *TW: From Out of the Rain*.

1383 First mentioned in *The Scarlet Empress*, with year specified in *Iris: Enter Wildthyme*.
1384 "Forty-three years" before *Thin Ice*.
1385 *TW: Golden Age*. The specific days are given - which is fortunate, as the time between 1924 and 2009 is variably rounded as "eighty years", "about eighty years", "over eighty years", and "nearly ninety years". The Duchess offhandedly suggests that Torchwood India collected, amongst other things, Yeti spheres and a one-eyed yellow idol from the north of Kathmandu. It's difficult to imagine *The Abominable Snowmen* taking

The Meddling Monk offered his companion Tamsin "Caesar's very own Caesar salad".[1386] Another Toymaker captive, Lola Luna, was a denizen of the Weimar cabaret circuit.[1387]

1924 (October) - THE CLOCKWISE MAN[1388] -> The ninth Doctor and Rose arrived to visit the British Empire Exhibition, and quickly discovered that a creature that ticked had committed a series of attacks. Shade Vassily, a war criminal from the planet Katuria, had been tracked down to Earth by the socialite Melissa Heart - actually a disfigured alien hunter. The Katurians used clockwork technology, but the Doctor prevented Vassily and Heart's conflict from destroying London.

= c 1924 - FP: WARLORDS OF UTOPIA[1389] -> On Roma I, Scriptor came to the attention of the Emperor and was commissioned to write the history of the Hercules Bridge that linked Europe to Africa. Following this, he decided to write a history of the Forum in Rome, and learned of the mysterious old man who'd materialised the day he'd been born. He also made many contacts, and married Angela, the daughter of a Scottish merchant.

A few months later, Scriptor tracked down the old man in a Swiss hospital and located his time ring. Scriptor accidentally followed the old man to another universe (Roma II) where Rome never fell, but had not prospered quite as much as his own. Scriptor and his family negotiated trading deals between the two universes, keeping their monopoly on travel between them - and the existence of other Romes - a closely-guarded secret. He soon mapped hundreds of other Romes - Roma III, where Yung Lo had won the coin toss and moved the Chinese court to Rome; Roma IV,

where the Christians were a political force; Roma V, where the Mediterranean had been drained to irrigate the Sahara; Rome VI, a matriarchy; and so on. Lacking any understanding of parallel universes, the Roman philosophers believed that each of these Romes orbited a different sun in their own universe.

On Rome CLII, the asteroid that killed the dinosaurs in most universes arrived sixty-five million years late, and wiped out a Roman civilisation that pitted dinosaurs against each other in their arenas. On this ruined world, Scriptor killed a mysterious monster that had been tracking the thirteen Great House members who'd fled their universe, and had murdered seven of them. Scriptor took the seven time rings the monster had collected - now armed with eight such devices, Scriptor's family expanded the scope of their operations considerably. The existence of other Romes became public knowledge on Roma I.

w - The earliest iteration of Faction Hollywood, an offshoot of Faction Paradox, could be traced back to 1925, although Faction Paradox proper would have little to do with the group after the 1940s.[1390]

1925 - "The Futurists"[1391] -> The tenth Doctor and Rose landed in Milan, because Rose wanted an ice cream. The Futurists were holding a meeting, and a strange green glow heralded the materialisation of a futuristic city - which quickly started to crumble. The TARDIS transported the Doctor and Rose to Cardiff in the late third century.

In 1925, the Doctor stopped the time traveller Studs Maloney importing hooch from the twenty-fifth century.[1392] **The American CIA acquired a photo of Jack Harkness that was taken in 1925.**[1393]

place before 1924 (this book dates it to 1935), so perhaps she's just being whimsical about having such items.

1386 *The Resurrection of Mars.* It's a common misconception that "Caesar salad" originated with Julius Caesar - it actually started with Caesar Cardini, who is said to have created it during a 4th of July rush on his restaurant in 1924. Cardini died in 1956.

1387 *The Magic Mousetrap.* The Weimar lasted from 1919-1933, and the height of its cabaret was 1930-ish, but Lola presumably performed before *The Magic Mousetrap* takes place in 1926.

1388 Dating *The Clockwise Man* (NSA #1) - The date is given.

1389 Dating *FP: Warlords of Utopia* (FP novel #3) - Scriptor is "18" when this sequence of events starts.

1390 *FP: The Book of the War*

1391 Dating "The Futurists" (*DWM* #372-374) - It is "two

decades into the new century", and the Doctor says it is 1925 later in the story.

1392 *Island of Death*

1393 *TW: Miracle Day*

1394 Dating *Black Orchid* (19.5) - The Doctor says it is "three o'clock, June the eleventh, nineteen hundred and twenty-five".

1395 *The Mind Robber*

1396 *Carnival of Monsters.* The Doctor has heard of the disappearance of the SS *Bernice*, but we see it vanish from the MiniScope and apparently return to its native time at the end of episode four. Perhaps the ship didn't arrive home safely after all. Alternatively, perhaps the Doctor's actions alter history, although this would make for something of a paradox.

1397 *The Girl Who Never Was*

1398 Dating "The Gods Walk Among Us" (*DWM* #59) - The year is given in the opening caption.

1925 (11th June) - BLACK ORCHID[1394] -> The explorer George Cranleigh was believed killed by Indians while on an expedition in the Amazon in 1923. Cassell and Company published his book *Black Orchid*. George's fiancée, Anne Talbot, eventually became engaged to his brother Charles. Yet George hadn't died. The Kajabi Indians had horribly disfigured George because he stole their sacred black orchid, but the chief of a rival tribe rescued him. George was kept hidden away at Cranleigh Hall. The fifth Doctor, Tegan, Nyssa and Adric were guests at the hall when George broke out, and fell to his death while trying to abduct his former fiancée.

A famous author of boys' stories for *The Ensign* magazine vanished at his home in 1926.[1395] On 4th June, 1926, the SS *Bernice* inexplicably vanished in the Indian Ocean. The ship had left England in early May, and the last anyone ever saw of it was on 2nd June, when it left Bombay.[1396] The Doctor's account at the Singapore Hilton went unpaid from 1926 to decades afterwards. He settled the bill, with a gold brick, in 2008.[1397]

1926 - "The Gods Walk Among Us"[1398] -> Archaeologists unearthed the tomb of Sontar in Egypt. The Sontaran within was still alive after fifty-five hundred years, and killed the archaeologists - but their Egyptian bearers dropped a stone slab on the alien, apparently killing it.

1926 (late June) - "Silver Scream" / "Fugitive" / "Final Sacrifice"[1399] -> The tenth Doctor investigated a static point in space and time connected to Emily Winter, a hopeful starlet. He attended a Hollywood party thrown by Archibald Maplin, and met actor Maximilian Love (the biggest thing to hit Hollywood since Rudolph Valentino) as well as studio-runner Matthew Finnegan. The Doctor learned that an alien Terronite from the future, Leo Miller, was posing as human and using an ancient device to chemically alter people's rostal anterior cingulate cortexes - the part of the brain that controls optimism. The device let Miller transfer the hopes and dreams of individuals into Love, making him more charismatic and successful. The Doctor thwarted the Terronites and saved Emily's life - but this changed history, as she was fated to die. A squad of Judoon arrested the Doctor, and took him to the Shadow Proclamation to stand trial.

Upon the Doctor's return, Emily and Matthew joined him on his travels. Unknown to the travellers, Emily's older self - passing as Annabella Primavera - had also attended Maplin's party. The Doctor helped Maplin to secure funding for his films; in future, Maplin would star in *The Fun Fair, The Great Oppressor* and *Future Times*.

1926 - THE MAGIC MOUSETRAP[1400] -> Ludovic Comfort served as director of the Hulbrook sanatorium in Switzerland. He was captured by the Celestial Toymaker, and spent ten years playing games including electric shock tiddlywinks and poison-tipped pin the tail on the donkey.

(=) The seventh Doctor, Ace and Hex and other people in the Toymaker's domain defeated the mandarin, turning him into a wooden doll. The Doctor believed that the Toymaker's powers and identity would fade if separated for long enough, and had everyone present - save for Ace and Hex - eat one piece of the Toymaker. Everyone believed they'd been transported back to the Hulbrook sanatorium, 1926, but the Toymaker's realm was mimicing the locale.

Four weeks passed. The still-wooden Toymaker revived and made his foes play games, winning back many splinters of himself. The chess master Swapnil Khan and his daughter Queenie manipulated gameplay until Swapnil and the Toymaker were trapped on an electrocuted board. So long as Swapnil didn't make his final move, neither of them could leave without burning to death. Theoretically, the board could remain viable for two thousand billion years.

Swapnil mustered enough mental force to return everyone save himself and the Toymaker to the real Hulbrook sanatorium in 1926. The game-losers remained in the shape of toys.

1399 Dating "Silver Scream" (IDW *DW* Vol. 1 #1-2) - A caption in issue #1 states that it's "1926", although when the Doctor returns to the scene in "Fugitive", the caption says "1927". It's 1926 again when we see Maplin's party once more at the end of "Final Sacrifice". Matthew specifies in "Don't Step on the Grass" that he met the Doctor in "late June 1926", which would concur with a mention of Rudolph Valentino that implies he's still alive - he died suddenly in August that year. Bizarrely, in "Don't Step on the Grass", the Doctor wonders why Matthew - a native of 1926 - has never read *The Lord of*

the Rings, which was published in 1954.
1400 Dating *The Magic Mousetrap* (BF #120) - The year is given. This adventure appears to finish with two "pieces" of the Toymaker still lodged in Ace's mind. The Toymaker claims he deliberately gave up his powers just to know what it was like to lose, but that could just be hyperbole.

1926 (8th and 19th December) - THE UNICORN AND THE WASP[1401] -> The tenth Doctor and Donna arrived at Eddison Manor, where Agatha Christie was just one of the guests of Lady Clemency Eddison. Another guest, Professor Peach, was murdered and suspicion fell on a mysterious jewel thief: the Unicorn, who was after Lady Eddison's necklace, the Firestone. Soon after, Donna was attacked by a giant wasp - a Vespiform from the Silfrax galaxy.

The Doctor solved the mystery... Reverend Golightly killed Professor Peach when he learned that Golightly was Lady Eddison's illegitimate son. The Firestone was a Vespiform telepathic recorder which contained Golightly's true identity - he was also a Vespiform. Golightly abducted Christie, but after a car chase, he drowned. He was mentally tethered to Christie's mind through the Firestone, and as he died, she lost her memory of these events. The Doctor dropped Christie in Harrogate, knowing that history dictated that she would be found after having gone missing for ten days. It was possible that Christie's subconscious remembered details of this adventure that would be incorporated into her novels, including the creation of Miss Marple. The Unicorn escaped.

In 1927, the Doctor watched the Cuban grandmaster Capablanca play chess.[1402] In the same year, the second Doctor met Ella's grandfather in Tibet. From this time, his family became caretakers of the Doctor's house in Kent.[1403] The Vondrax killed people in Siberia, 1927.[1404] The Doctor was in the movie *Metropolis* (1927).[1405]

(=) 1927 - REAL TIME[1406] -> The Cybermen succeeded in infecting Earth with a techno-virus that transformed living beings into cybernetic ones. Most of the human race died from shock, and all animals perished. The cybernetic survivors fell under Cybermen domination. Evelyn Smythe was reportedly the virus' original carrier, having travelled back to this year after being infected in 3286.

1927 (July) - TW: MIRACLE DAY[1407] -> Jack Harkness met Angelo Colasanto, an Italian immigrant, on Ellis Island after Angelo stole Jack's visa. The two of them became lovers, and infiltrated bootlegging operations in Little Italy, New York. They fulfilled Jack's mission by destroying one of the Trickster's Brigade - a parasite considered as vermin on at least one hundred and fifty worlds, and served as dinner on another. The Trickster had intended that the parasite would lay eggs in Franklin Roosevelt's brain, driving him mad and changing world history so the Trickster could feed off the resulting chaos. Jack was temporarily shot dead while killing the parasite - he went to Los Angeles, even as Angelo was arrested and sentenced to a year in prison.

The Doctor met Dame Nellie Melba, a noted Australian opera soprano, and learned her party piece: how to shatter glass with your voice.[1408] The Doctor met Sigmund Freud and knew Marie Curie intimately. He met Puccini[1409] in Milan.[1410] Puccini had a cold.[1411]

1401 Dating *The Unicorn and the Wasp* (X4.07) - The Doctor sniffs the air and states it's the "1920s", then later finds a newspaper giving the date as "8 December 1926". Christie's disappearance on that day is a matter of historical record; she was found on 19th December.
1402 *The Androids of Tara*. José Raúl Capablanca y Graupera lived 1888-1942. He spent six years as a world chess champion, ending in 1927.
1403 "Fellow Travellers". This may or may not be a reference to *The Abominable Snowman*. If so, it's unclear which character Ella's grandfather was.
1404 *TW: Trace Memory*
1405 *Serpent Crest: Tsar Wars*
1406 Dating *Real Time* (BF BBCi #1) - Dr. Goddard identifies the date of Cyber-infection.
1407 Dating *TW: Miracle Day* (TW 4.7) - The year is twice given in captions. Angelo and Jack watch fireworks set off for the 4th of July celebrations, and Jack mentions that Franklin Roosevelt will be elected governor of New York "this November" (actually incorrect - that happened in November 1928, not 1927). The visa permit that Jack forges for Angelo bears the starting date of 2nd June, 1927, the expiration date of 9th

December. The Trickster's Brigade is a recurring villain in *The Sarah Jane Adventures*.
1408 *The Power of Kroll*, and also mentioned in *Serpent Crest: Aladdin Time*. Dame Nellie Melba lived 1861-1931.
1409 *Doctor Who - The Movie*. It's possible these encounters were all on the same visit: Freud lived 1865-1939, Marie Curie 1867-1934, and Puccini 1858-1924. The only date given is that the Doctor was with Puccini shortly before he died.
1410 *The Devil Goblins from Neptune*
1411 *Relative Dementias*. This is possibly a misremembering of *Doctor Who - The Movie*. The Doctor name-dropped Puccini in that story, but it was Leonardo da Vinci who had the cold.
1412 *The City of the Dead*
1413 *Grimm Reality*
1414 *Borrowed Time* (p126).
1415 *The Curse of the Black Spot*
1416 *Illegal Alien* (p83).
1417 *Phantasmagoria*
1418 "Silent Scream"
1419 Dating *TW: Miracle Day* (TW 4.7) - Angelo has been locked away for "a year" when Jack re-enters his

@ The eighth Doctor had sessions with Freud, hoping to jog his memory.[1412] He told Freud that he had a phobia of silverfish.[1413] Sigmund Freud told his friend the Doctor: "Vell Doctor, ven confronted vis ze unbelievable, ze human brain goes into shock!"[1414] **The Doctor had fond memories of Freud's comfy sofa.**[1415]

The Doctor watched Babe Ruth hit three home runs for the Yankees in 1926.[1416] The Doctor owned a copy of *Wisden's Almanac* from 1928.[1417] The tenth Doctor's runaround with Leo Miller in Hollywood, 1926, inspired director Buster Keaton regarding the filmography of the silent film *Steamboat Bill Jr.* (1928).[1418]

1928 - TW: MIRACLE DAY[1419] **-> Jack Harkness reunited with Angelo Colasanto upon Angelo's release from Sing Sing prison in New York. Angelo believed that Jack's resurrection powers stemmed from the devil, and turned him over to the superstitious residents of Little Italy. Jack was repeatedly killed in the basement of the Giordano Butcher Shop, coming back to life every time.**

A trio of men with the surnames Ablemarch, Costerdane and Frines sensed that Jack represented an opportunity, and embarked on a partnership - they paid $10,000 for the contents of the butcher's basement. Angelo regretted his actions and freed Jack, but Ablemarch, Costerdane and Frines retained Jack's spilt blood and formed The Three Families. Jack judged that Angelo would be better off without him, and exited his life. Angelo remained inspired by Jack, and devoted the rest of his life to finding a means of living forever. He monitored Jack for decades to come.

The Three Families went into the world and became shadow players - one family specialised in finance, one in politics and one in the media. They systematically erased all records of their bloodlines, purging the names Ablemarch, Costerdane and Frines from history. Angelo had some early affiliation with the Families, but was ostracised because he had loved a man.

1928 (14th August) - THE GLAMOUR CHASE[1420] **->** The Tahnn wiped out the English town of Little Cadthorpe while searching for the missing Weave spaceship *Exalted*. They refrained from destroying Earth, fearing the wrath of the Shadow Proclamation.

Aaron Blinovitch formulated his Limitation Effect in the reading room of the British Museum in 1928. He authored *Temporal Mechanics*, and was a member of Faction Paradox.[1421] **The Night Travellers recognised that the advent of cinema had numbered the days of their circus shows. They opted to endow themselves onto film containing their images; one such reel wound up in the basement archives of the Electro Cinema in Cardiff.**[1422] Jack Harkness once cruised the Kurfurstendamm in Berlin with Christopher Isherwood.[1423]

In 1929, Lord Barset led an expedition to Antarctica aboard his ship, the *Rochester*. A base that contained "lizard men" was discovered, and disaster ensued. The *Rochester* sank and all hands were lost, save for one member found with Lord Barset's diary of the mission. The man died shortly afterwards, screaming about monsters, but the journal was later passed down to Barset's grandson.[1424]

The base was a Silurian shelter, and UNIT would investigate it in the 1970s.[1425] The *Daily Telegraph* of 12th April, 1929, noted rumours that an Antarctic expedition had been lost after finding a city of intelligent reptiles.[1426]

1929 - THE HOUNDS OF ARTEMIS[1427] **->** An expedition found the temple of Artemis in Smyrna, Eastern Turkey, and released the psychic parasite inside. The eleventh Doctor and Amy helped to bind the creature in iron

life, and Jack's torture in the basement is later referenced as occurring in "1928".

1420 Dating *The Glamour Chase* (NSA #42) - The exact day is given (p23).

1421 *Timewyrm: Revelation* (p50), *The Ghosts of N-Space* (p147) and *Unnatural History* (p164). The Blinovitch Limitation Effect was first mentioned in *Day of the Daleks* (and subsequently in *Invasion of the Dinosaurs* and *Mawdryn Undead*). Episodes of New *Who* (particularly *The Big Bang* and *A Christmas Carol*) indicate the Limitation Effect has lost its potency, somehow.

1422 "Eighty years" before *TW: From Out of the Rain*, according to Captain Jack. *The Torchwood Archives* dates the Travellers' encounter with Christina - seen as an old woman in the TV story - to 1928.

1423 *TW: A Day in the Death*. Isherwood, a novelist, resided in Berlin from 1929 to 1933. His meeting with

Jack could have easily have happened in another year, but it's perhaps relevant - given that Jack was involved - that Isherwood at this time capitalised upon Berlin's relative sexual freedom to indulge his taste for "pretty youths" (*The Telegraph*, 18th May, 2004).

1424 *Frozen Time*, reflecting events from the Audio-Visuals story *Endurance*. Nick Briggs, who wrote *Frozen Time*, starred as the Doctor in that adventure.

1425 *The Scales of Injustice*, also referring to *Endurance*.

1426 "City of Devils", and yet another reference to *Endurance* by *The Scales of Injustice* author Gary Russell. By 2012, the loss of the expedition is publicly acknowledged, not just rumoured.

1427 Dating *The Hounds of Artemis* (BBC *DW* audiobook #11) - The year is given.

once more, and a group of local psionics re-buried its temple. The Doctor provided the expedition's only survivor, Bradley Stapleton, with the location of a genuine temple of Artemis, guaranteeing the man's career.

1929 (summer) - THE STEALERS FROM SAIPH[1428]

-> The Saiph had possessed an archaeologist and spent some decades establishing energy reception points in Antibes, Thessalonica, Tobruk, Tunis and Tangiers. Using an elemental converter aboard an orbiting satellite, the Saiph hoped to create an energy ring that would change the chemical composition of the Mediterranean Sea, turning it into a breeding ground for them. The fourth Doctor and Romana, having vacationed for some weeks at the Hotel du Cap in Antibes, France, torched the Saiph.

1929 - BLOOD HARVEST[1429] -> As gangland violence

escalated in Chicago, the enigmatic Doc McCoy opened a speakeasy right in the middle of disputed territory. The Doc and his moll Ace saved Al Capone's life. The seventh Doctor was tracking down the eternal being Agonal, who had amplified the gang warfare to feed his lust for violence.

The vampire Yarven travelled to Earth from E-Space aboard the Doctor's TARDIS.

Yarven became a progenitor of many of Earth's vampires. Villagers in Croatia overpowered and buried him alive, and he would remain trapped until 1993.[1430] The Doctor couldn't remember if Al Capone or Genghis Khan told him that villains often wanted records detailing exactly how bad they'd been.[1431]

The Brigadier's car, a Humber 1650 Open Tourer Imperial Model, was built in 1929.[1432] The Canavatchi engineered the Wall Street Crash of October 1929 to hinder mankind's development.[1433]

Lord Tamworth witnessed the arrival of the Engineer Prime of the telepathic Triskele on Earth. He was promoted to "Minister of Air", and oversaw preparations to use the R-101 airship to return the Engineer Prime to its people.[1434]

The Nineteen Thirties

The Urbankans began to receive radio signals from Earth.[1435] The Doctor met the cricket player Donald Bradman, and once took five wickets for New South Wales.[1436]

During the 1930s, the League of Nations set up a secret international organisation, LONGBOW, to deal with matters of world security. It found itself, on occasion, dealing with unexplained and extra-terrestrial phenomena.[1437] The Doctor discussed the theoretical Philosopher's Stone (not the Khamerian-created one) with psychiatrist Carl Jung.[1438]

The Silurian Triad was revived. These were Ichtar, Scibus and science advisor Tarpok.[1439]

In the 1930s, a matador named Manolito trained the Doctor in the basics of his art, and the Doctor and his friend Ernest Hemingway ran with the bulls in Pamplona.[1440] The tenth Doctor got drunk with Ernest Hemingway on the banks of the Seine. In future, the Doctor would lose this memory to the Memeovax.[1441] The Doctor was friends with the philosopher Wittgenstein.[1442] He worked with the Three Stooges in Hollywood, and was the fourth Stooge.[1443] Firestone Finance was founded in Cardiff, the 1930s, as a front to acquire and sell alien technology for profit - until the business did so well selling war bonds, it became a legitimate bank.[1444]

Between 1932 and 1940, Odd Bob the Clown - an aspect of the Pied Piper - abducted at least one hundred and four children across America.[1445] The people of Parakon discovered rapine, a crop that when processed could be used as a foodstuff or a building material. For the next forty years, the Corporation that marketed rapine

---

1428 Dating *The Stealers from Saiph* (BF CC #3.12) - Romana's narration tells us, "It was the summer of 1929." Somewhat uniquely for a Doctor/first Romana story, this audio takes place between *The Armageddon Factor* and *Destiny of the Daleks*.

1429 Dating *Blood Harvest* (NA #28) - The blurb states it is 1929. The book is set during Prohibition (1919-1933), but while Al Capone is at liberty. In May 1929, Capone was sentenced to prison time for carrying a concealed weapon, so *Blood Harvest* occurs before that. He saw release in 1930; his more infamous conviction on tax evasion charges happened in 1931.

1430 *Goth Opera*

1431 *Borrowed Time*

1432 His student Ibbotson, nicknamed "Hippo", identifies the car in *Mawdryn Undead*.

1433 *The King of Terror* (p179).

1434 "One night last winter" before *Storm Warning*.

1435 *Four to Doomsday*

1436 *Four to Doomsday*. No date given. Donald Bradman was born in 1908, playing for Australia from 1928-1948.

1437 *Just War*

1438 *Option Lock*. No date given. Jung lived 26th July, 1875, to 6th June, 1961.

1439 "Around forty years" before *The Scales of Injustice*.

1440 *Deadly Reunion*. No date given. Hemingway lived 1898-1961.

1441 "Thinktwice". Hemingway lived 1899-1961. He appears in good health during his meeting with the Doctor, and was much less so after being nearly killed in a plane crash in 1952.

1442 *The Hollows of Time*. Ludwig Wittgenstein lived 1889-1951.

ruled the planet unopposed, supplanting nations, governments, armies and all competition.[1446] An escape pod carrying the criminal Zimmerman landed in England, where he met a woman named Rachel. He became known as "Nick Zimmerman", turned over a new leaf and spent the next thirty years with her in wedded bliss.[1447]

Jack Harkness went undercover with a travelling show, billing himself as a man who couldn't die, while looking into rumours of the Night Travellers. He found no trace of them.[1448] During the 1930s, Jack went to the Weimar Republic to investigate reports that some prominent National Socialists were peddling in alien technology. He entirely failed in his mission owing to a number of parties and other distractions.[1449]

A young actor named Billy appeared in *I'm an Explosive* (1933) and *While Parents Sleep* (1935). He would come to befriend the music hall comedian Max Miller.[1450] The Doctor sparred with Errol Flynn.[1451]

The stage musician Professor Talbot performed on Brighton's West Pier, which led to his encountering the Indo aliens. Talbot was killed, but the aliens' energy animated his body, and his mind became focused on gaining widespread recognition and authority. He was presumed dead, but would resurface in 1936.[1452]

UNIT in the Thirties[1453]

Alistair Gordon Lethbridge-Stewart was born. He was an only child whose mother died when he was young. He was raised by his father and Granny McDougal. He was raised in Simla, India, and his happiest memories are of summers there. His father rose to the rank of Colonel.[1454]

> (=) u - When Lethbridge-Stewart was six or seven, he was heartbroken to lose a red balloon, and had a recurring nightmare about it for the rest of his life.

The eighth Doctor caught the balloon and returned it.[1455] Lethbridge-Stewart left India for prep school in England when he was eight.[1456]

? 1930 - THE WORMERY[1457] **->** On a planet affected by a dimensional nexus point, worms evolved with a precognitive ability. Appalled to see themselves turning into hairy, complex beings, the worms divided into factions to derail their future. The "anti faction" group sought to turn the universe into total chaos, preventing development of any type. The "pro faction" group allied with the club singer Bianca, hoping to freeze the universe in a single perfect moment. Additionally, a group of shadow beings - the potential future selves of the worms, held in a state of flux - searched for a means of becoming corporeal.

The nightclub "Bianca's" now existed in a dimensional nexus, accessible via special taxis that shuttled patrons through dimensional portals. The club was Iris Wildthyme's TARDIS, with its exterior looking like 1930s Berlin. The sixth Doctor and Iris arrived separately at Bianca's club, and exposed Bianca as the embodiment of Iris' darker natures. The worm factions and their shadow selves each tried to exploit the club's extra-dimensional nature to their advantage. The Doctor used his TARDIS to Time-Ram the nightclub, which severed its dimensional links and returned its patrons to their native times. This defeated the worms and their shadows, and transferred the wreckage of the club to Berlin. Bianca escaped.

1930

1930 (June) - THE ENGLISH WAY OF DEATH[1458] **->** The TARDIS arrived in London during an inexplicable heat wave, as the fourth Doctor needed to return some library books. He, Romana and K9 stumbled upon a group from the thirty-second century (the Bureau) that were using time corridor technology to send retired people to the English village of Nutchurch. While the Doctor put a stop to that, Romana confronted the sentient smell Zodaal, an exiled would-be conqueror from the planet Vesur. Zodaal was trapped in a flask.

In 1930, Douglas Caldwell transferred to Torchwood London to work in research and development.[1459] **Around**

1443 *Paradise 5.* The Stooges were effectively active from 1925 until Larry Fine had a stroke in January 1970.
1444 *TW: Department X*
1445 *SJA: The Day of the Clown*
1446 "Forty years" before *The Paradise of Death* (p131).
1447 "Thirty years" before *No More Lies.*
1448 *TW: From Out of the Rain*, with *The Torchwood Archives* specifying that Jack did this undercover work in the "early 1930s".
1449 *TW: Almost Perfect*
1450 *Pier Pressure.* Billy is obviously a young William Hartnell, who appeared in both films.
1451 *Hexagora.* Flynn lived 1909-1959. His first starring

role was *Captain Blood* (1935).
1452 "At least" fifteen years before *Pier Pressure.*
1453 See the article on UNIT Dating - the exact dates of the early years of Lethbridge-Stewart's life are affected by the wider issue of when the UNIT stories are set.
1454 *Island of Death*
1455 *The Shadows of Avalon* (p3, 271).
1456 *Island of Death*
1457 Dating *The Wormery* (BF #51) - It is some point in "the thirties".
1458 Dating *The English Way of Death* (MA #20) - The date is given (p23).
1459 From Torchwood.org.uk.

1930, the fourth Doctor visited Tigella and saw the Dodecahedron.[1460] The Doctor bought Jacques Cousteau his first set of flippers.[1461] Jacques Cousteau taught the Doctor about sharks.[1462] **In the US census of 1930, the population of Manhattan was 1,867,000.**[1463]

1930 (5th October) - STORM WARNING[1464] **->** The TARDIS landed on the doomed airship *R-101* during its maiden voyage, and the eighth Doctor discovered Charley Pollard, a stowaway. Lord Tamworth, a government minister, ordered the ship to a higher altitude and it docked with an alien vessel. The British had arranged to return a crashed alien to its own people, the Triskele. A faction of the Triskele became aggressive when the Lawgiver that kept them in check died. The Doctor eased the situation, and Tamworth stayed with the Triskele as an advisor. The *R-101* was damaged upon its return, and the Doctor and Charley escaped as it crashed in France. The Doctor realised that Charley was meant to have died in the crash.

1930 (1st November) - DALEKS IN MANHATTAN / EVOLUTION OF THE DALEKS[1465] **->** The tenth Doctor and Martha discovered that homeless people in New York had been going missing from a Hooverville, a community of victims of the Great Depression living in Central Park. The people had been abducted by the Cult of Skaro - the last four surviving Daleks, who had fled the Battle of Canary Wharf in 2007 via temporal shift. The Daleks required human subjects for their genetic experiments, and were turning them into pig slaves. The final experiment was undertaken by their leader, Dalek Sec, who converted himself into a "human Dalek".

The Daleks planned to draw energy from a solar flare down through the Empire State Building, and use it to create a new race of human Daleks. The Doctor sabotaged the attempt, and the resultant human Daleks rebelled. In the ensuing conflict, every Dalek and Dalek hybrid was destroyed save for Dalek Caan - who escaped via a temporal shift.

Dalek Caan penetrated the time lock established around the Last Great Time War, and succeeded in rescuing Davros from it.[1466]

Half-human creatures dubbed "Subterraneans" took to living in an underground cavern near the Constitution Hill tube station in London.[1467]

(=) Their leader escaped to find a better life on the surface. He became the famed poet Randolf Crest, writing such works as *The Darkness That Hides as Kind*.

Honoré Lechasseur and Emily Blandish changed history so that Crest never left his people.

Advanced humans from the future sought to spur their own creation, and mentally influenced the founding of the British Hampdenshire Programme, an undertaking to create supermen. It produced genetically modified children of the species *homo peculiar*.[1468]

1930 (31st December) - SEASONS OF FEAR[1469] **->** The immortal Sebastian Grayle found the eighth Doctor and Charley in Singapore, and boasted that he'd already killed the Doctor in the past. The Doctor set about investigating the matter, heading for Britain in 305 AD.

1460 "Fifty years" before *Meglos*.
1461 "Children of the Revolution". In *The Devil Goblins of Neptune*, the third Doctor (as his internal monologue conveys to the reader) lies to Captain Yates that he "taught Jacques Cousteau everything he knows".
1462 *The Murder Game.* No date is given.
1463 *TW: Miracle Day*
1464 Dating *Storm Warning* (BF #16) - It is stated that it is "early in October 1930"; the *R-101* historically began its maiden flight on 4th October, 1930, and crashed the next day. The date is confirmed in *Minuet in Hell* and *Neverland*. According to *The Chimes of Midnight*, Charley was born the day the *Titanic* sank (or, rather, the night the ship hit the iceberg), and was eighteen years, five months and twenty-one days old when she met the Doctor.
1465 Dating *Daleks in Manhattan/Evolution of the Daleks* (X3.4-3.5) - Martha finds a newspaper just after the TARDIS lands, and it sets the date as "Saturday 1 November 1930". Construction of the Empire State Building commenced on 17th March, 1930, and it offi-

cially opened on 1st May, 1931.
1466 *The Stolen Earth, Journey's End.*
1467 At least twenty years before *TimeH: The Tunnel at the End of the Light*.
1468 *TimeH: Peculiar Lives.* The blurb specifies this as happening "between the wars", i.e. World War I and II, and a member of *homo peculiar*, Percival, was a 15 year old "five years" prior to 1950 (p21), meaning he was born in 1930.
1469 Dating *Seasons of Fear* (BF #30) - The play starts with the Doctor saying it's the "cusp of the years 1930 and 1931".
1470 *The Rapture*
1471 "The Final Chapter"
1472 The island resurfaces "four years, three months and six days" prior to *Lurkers at Sunlight's Edge*.
1473 Dating *TimeH: The Sideways Door* (TimeH #10) - Honoré's mother is killed "four months" before he turns 12 (p19), and he was born in either 1920 or 1921 (likely the former). A little confusingly, page 16 says that Honoré's grandmother raised him "from early child-

The Doctor fought in the Spanish Civil War with the father of future bar owner Gustavo Riviera. Later, he brought Gustavo to refuge in Ibiza.[1470] The Doctor was a house guest of Dali.[1471]

The island with the citadel of the Carnash Coi re-surfaced near Alaska. While three Carnash Coi continued sleeping, a fourth adopted human form and set out to reconnoitre Earth. The scout passed as Clarence Penrose Doveday, but his human aspect became so dominant, he forgot his supernatural origins. Doveday's memories surfaced as dreams, and the stories he wrote based upon them appeared in such pulps as *Shuddersome Tales* and *Weird Tales of Cosmic Horror*.[1472]

c 1931 - TIMEH: THE SIDEWAYS DOOR[1473] **->** When Honoré Lechasseur was 11, two serial killers - the blood ritualists John and Wayne Carter, whom the papers dubbed the "Royal Street Vampires" - killed his mother. The adult Honoré witnessed the event with Emily Blandish, but let history run its course. Afterwards, the younger Honoré was raised by his Grandmother Delecrolix.

In 1931, the Beacon Film Theatre was renamed the Electro.[1474]

1932

Diane Holmes incorrectly thought Amelia Earhart disappeared in 1932.[1475] **Richard Lazarus was born around 1932.**[1476] Mrs Wibbsey was a fan of the movie star Mimsy Loyne.[1477]

The eleventh Doctor knew a military code that had been on record since 1932, and which instructed those receiving the code to stand aside for its bearer, "however harebrained [their] actions might seem".[1478]

1932 (summer) - HORNETS' NEST: THE DEAD SHOES[1479] **->** The fourth Doctor arrived in Cromer and was drawn to the Cromer Palace of Curios, run by Mrs. Fenella Wibbsey. There he met the dancer Ernestina Stott, whose one-woman performance of *The Nutcracker* was running on the Pier. They found a display cabinet with a pair of old ballet shoes that still contained withered feet, but Ernestina stole the shoes.

The Doctor saw Ernestina dance, which she did with supernatural brilliance - aided by the shoes. He also watched Ernestina flying, but got her to safety. Mrs Wibbsey was revealled to be possessed by the Hornets, and shrunk the Doctor and Ernestina, setting them down in a large Victorian dolls house. The Doctor again made contact with the Hornets, who said they met him in 1832 (something which had not yet happened from the Doctor's perspective). The Doctor returned himself and Ernestina to their normal scale, but the Hornets released Mrs Wibbsey and took control of Ernestina, forcing her to dance. The Doctor removed the shoes, freeing her. Mrs Wibbsey had residual traces of the Hornet influence, so the Doctor brought her to the twenty-first century.

1933

Otto Kreiner moved from Germany to England, soon meeting and marrying Muriel Tarr. They would become the parents of the eighth Doctor's companion Fitz.[1480] **Jack Harkness saw the Pacific Ocean, and wouldn't do so again until the twenty-first century.**[1481]

@ The eighth Doctor spent much of 1933 in the South Seas, and claimed to have gotten a tattoo there. He now had a criminal record in England.[1482] While in the South Seas, he saw magic performed.[1483] He served about the ship *Sarah Gail*, where he learned to play the violin[1484] and

hood" - not a term that's typically attributed to an 11 year old.

1474 Torchwood.org.uk, elaborating on *TW: From Out of the Rain*.

1475 *TW: Out of Time*. Earhart really disappeared in 1937.

1476 Lazarus declares he is "seventy-six years old" in *The Lazarus Experiment*, which is set in 2008.

1477 *Demon Quest: Starfall*. She meets the actress, after a fashion, in the 1970s.

1478 *The Forgotten Army*. The code was presumably originated for the Doctor's personal benefit, but it's not said how this came about.

1479 Dating *Hornets' Nest: The Dead Shoes* (BBC fourth Doctor audio #1.2) - It's stated a number of times in this story and the previous one that it's 1932. *Hornets' Nest: The Stuff of Nightmares* says it's "July"; the sleeve notes

for *The Dead Shoes* include a newspaper clipping datelined "13th June 1932", and which dates events to "last week". Mrs Wibbsey's first name is never given in dialogue, but appears in the sleeve notes of *The Dead Shoes*.

1480 *Frontier Worlds*

1481 "About seventy-eight years" before *TW: Miracle Day*.

1482 *Eater of Wasps*

1483 *Mad Dogs and Englishmen*

1484 *The Year of Intelligent Tigers*

read a report of wasps attacking a train outside Arandale.[1485] At some point, he visited Australia and Hangchow.[1486]

1933 (August) - EATER OF WASPS[1487] -> An alien device from the future caused wasps to mutate into killers. The eighth Doctor, Fitz and Anji encountered a trio of Time Agents who were seeking the device. The Time Agents decided to sterilise the area with a nuclear explosion, but the Doctor disarmed their nuclear weapon, and also smashed the mutagenic device.

By 1933, Germany had become aware that werewolves existed. Such nonhumans were ordered to register with the government, and werewolves loyal to the party were reportedly used to sense dissenters. Several werewolves were rounded up and incarcerated for a year in a camp equipped with silver wire. A man from the Schutzstaffel (the SS, the Nazi Party's "praetorian guard") pressed the desperate werewolves into the service of the state.[1488]

In 1933, Cuevas discovered a part of the Great Temple of the Aztecs.[1489]

1934

1934 - THE EYE OF THE GIANT[1490] -> The *Constitution III* was beached upon an uncharted island of Salutua in the South Pacific. The third Doctor and Liz Shaw arrived at the island using a time bridge portal, and discovered a spacecraft in a volcanic crater. Animal and plant life on the island was subject to gigantism: giant crabs roamed the beach, bats the size of men flew at night, and the forest was hypertrophied. The Doctor discovered that drugs created by the Semquess, the most skilled bioengineers in the galaxy, were responsible for the mutations. The drugs had been brought to Earth fifty years before by Brokk of the Grold. The Semquess had tracked him, and now they

apparently destroyed him. Brokk, though, used the properties of the Semquess drug to merge with Grover's young wife Nancy and leave Earth.

1934 - LURKERS AT SUNLIGHT'S EDGE[1491] -> Emmerson Whytecrag III, a millionaire white supremacist, sought to ritualistically summon the power of the Carnash Coi. The beasts consumed Whytecrag, but the seventh Doctor, Ace and Hex succeeded in once again submerging the Carnash Coi's island-citadel and putting the monstrosities within to sleep. C.P. Doveday failed to escape the citadel before this happened, and also entered hibernation.

The Doctor pursued the Master across Berlin, and met Himmler and the future "Butcher of Prague", Reinhold Heydrich.[1492] On 30th June, 1934, the German-imprisoned werewolves were unleashed at a hotel housing men loyal to Ernst Roehm's Sturmabetilung ("Storm Division", a.k.a. stormtroopers). One of the werewolves, Emmeline Neuberger, bit a silver chain around a man's neck and was rendered unconscious. She was subsequently overlooked, and escaped into the German woods.[1493]

1935

The seventh Doctor and Bernice failed to meet Virginia Woolf and went to the theatre instead. In the audience was twenty-fifth century explorer Gustaf Heinrich Urnst, who had been transported there by a Fortean Flicker.[1494] **The Doctor was on Virginia Woolf's bowling team.**[1495] **In 1935, Victor Podesta, an eyewitness to Jack Harkness' torture and resurrection in Little Italy, 1928, wrote and published the short story "The Devil Within" based upon what he'd seen.**[1496]

1485 *The Year of Intelligent Tigers,* referring to events in *Eater of Wasps.*
1486 *History 101.* This was possibly during his second bout of world travelling in the sixties and seventies.
1487 Dating *Eater of Wasps* (EDA #45) - The Doctor estimates "it is probably the 1930s. If pushed, I'd have to say 1933. Twenty-seventh of August in fact" (p10).
1488 *Wolfsbane* (p90).
1489 *The Left-Handed Hummingbird* (p58).
1490 Dating *The Eye of the Giant* (MA #21) - "The time is the eighth of June, nineteen thirty-four" (p42).
1491 Dating *Lurkers at Sunlight's Edge* (BF #141) - The year is given.
1492 *The King of Terror* (p103).
1493 *Wolfsbane.* Page 93 says the werewolves were taken from the camp on 29th June, 1934; the hotel slaughter occurred the following evening. Historically,

Hitler moved against Roehm and his Sturmabetilung because they could have staged a *coup d'etat.* He ordered the Sturmabetilung leaders to congregate at the Hanselbauer Hotel in Bad Wiesse near Munich, which is where the massacre in *Wolfsbane* evidently takes place. The purge is sometimes referred to as "The Night of the Long Knives".
1494 *The Highest Science* (p257).
1495 *The Time of Angels.* Woolf lived 1882-1941.
1496 *TW: Miracle Day*
1497 Dating *The Abominable Snowmen* (4.2) - According to the Doctor, this story takes place "three hundred years" after events that the monk Thonmi says took place in "1630". In *The Web of Fear*, Victoria states that the Travers Expedition took place in "1935". In *Downtime*, Charles Bryce says it was "1936" (p65).
1498 *The Nightmare of Black Island*

1935 - THE ABOMINABLE SNOWMEN[1497] -> The second Doctor, Jamie and Victoria arrived in the Himalayas. They found that the Yeti were menacing a local monastery and an expedition led by Professor Travers. The Yeti were robots built on behalf of the Intelligence - a powerful being of pure thought that attempted to manifest physically. The Doctor banished it from Earth.

A Cynrog spacecraft crashed in Wales. The pilot died after implanting segments of his memories in eight local children.[1498] **The Agatha Christie novel *Death in the Clouds* was first published in 1935.**[1499]

1936

The seventh Doctor and Mel met German racing driver Emil Hartung in Cairo. The Doctor accidentally inspired Hartung to develop aircraft that could avoid radar detection. Hartung won the Cairo 500 thanks to the modifications the Doctor made to his car.[1500]

Fitz Kreiner, a companion of the eighth Doctor, was born in Hampstead on 7th March, 1936.[1501] Sir Henry Rugglesthorpe and his family become playthings of the Toymaker.[1502]

Ian Chesterton, a companion of the first Doctor, was born.[1503] **In October of that year, the Doctor joined Mao Tse-Tung on the Long March.**[1504] The first Doctor visited the court of Edward VIII.[1505]

1936 (Sunday) - THE GLAMOUR CHASE[1506] -> The eleventh Doctor, Amy and Rory stopped some Tahnn from destroying the Weave stranded in the English town of Shalford Heights. Some of the Weave (including 6011, the Doctor's former acquaintance) had perished, and three locals - including the archaeologist Enola Porter - agreed to crew the ship and take it away from Earth. Owain, having guarded the Weave for six thousand years, finally died.

@ 1936 (November) - WOLFSBANE[1507] -> The eighth Doctor had returned to England, and been rejected several times after submitting short stories to *Astounding Stories* magazine. Harry Sullivan disembarked to explore when the fourth Doctor's TARDIS stopped on Earth, but the Ship inexplicably dematerialised. Stranded, Harry met the eighth Doctor. Lady Hester Stanton, believing herself the reincarnation of Morgan le Fay, performed magic rituals to wake the land and bind it to her. She hoped to rule England from behind-the-scenes, with her son George taking Edward VIII's place. Stanton magically compelled the werewolf Emmeline Neuberger to assist her.

Stanton's spells began to awaken the land, and a wood dryad expelled the slumbering swordsman Godric. He possessed the Holy Grail, which Harry used to make the Earth swallow Stanton - and the Grail also. Emmeline, instinctively desiring a mate, bit Harry.

The fourth Doctor and Sarah returned for Harry, and took Godric back to his native time. Some reports suggest Harry turned into a werewolf and killed Sarah, then was killed by the Doctor; some suggest Harry returned home and secretly became a werewolf during the full moon; and some say the Doctor cured Harry's condition.

The eighth Doctor believed Harry, Stanton and Godric had all died, and made gravesites to stop anyone getting curious about them or the Grail. He introduced Emmeline to his friends in the British Ministry, but they experimented on her in the hope of creating lupine soldiers.

1936 (December) - WOLFSBANE[1508] -> The TARDIS rematerialised after leaving Harry behind two weeks in the past, and the fourth Doctor and Sarah found his "tombstone". They pieced together what had occurred during

---

1499 *The Unicorn and the Wasp*
1500 *Just War*
1501 *The Ancestor Cell* (p126), based on the writers' guidelines. He was "27" in *The Taint*. His year of birth is "1935" in *Escape Velocity*. He celebrates his birthday on 7th March in *Interference*.
1502 *Divided Loyalties*
1503 According to an early format document for the series, dating from July 1963, Ian is "27". Then again, William Russell, born in 1924, certainly looks older than that on screen.
1504 *The Mind of Evil*. The Long March was a massive retreat on the part of the Chinese Communist Army to elude the Kuomintang Army. It granted the Communists a needed respite in the north of China.
1505 *The Cold Equations*. Edward ruled 20th January, 1936, to 11th December of the same year.

1506 Dating *The Glamour Chase* (NSA #42) - The year is repeatedly given. According to p59, it's a Sunday. The Doctor rattles off a list of the "true greats" of archaeology (p139), but as he does so while expressly lying to Enola Porter that she's going to number among them (and as the list includes at least one real-life fraud, Shinichi Fujimura) the whole thing looks so improvised, it's probably best to not take it seriously.
1507 Dating *Wolfsbane* (PDA #62) - Harry is abandoned on 27th November, 1936, according to p24. Harry's fate is left ambiguous due to the presence of multiple timelines, which were finally compressed to one history in *Timeless*. *Sometime Never* says the Council of Eight had a hand in engineering Harry's "death".
1508 Dating *Wolfsbane* (PDA #62) - It's 11th December, 1936 (p49).

the previous fortnight. The Doctor rescued Emmeline from the Ministry, and drew enough blood from her to ritualistically send the land back to sleep. She departed back to Germany; the Doctor and Sarah went back to find Harry.

@ The Doctor made a visit to Highgate.[1509]

1936 (December) -   PLAYERS[1510] **->** King Edward VIII sought to dissolve the British government, hoping to vest more power with Nazi sympathizers. The sixth Doctor aided Winston Churchill in coercing the King to abdicate the throne, threatening to charge him with treason. This thwarted the schemes of the Players, who were engaged in a game of historical alterations.

The Doctor and Peri stopped at Cholmondeley's bank, where the Doctor's account had amassed one hundred twenty years of compound interest.

1936 (December) - PIER PRESSURE[1511] **->** In Brighton, a string of murders gave rise to stories of "the Phantom Bloodsucker of Preston Park", a killer who preyed upon the blood of fresh young maidens. The sixth Doctor and Evelyn encountered the famous music hall comedian Max Miller, and found the reportedly dead Professor Talbot as an agent of the Indo aliens. The Doctor feared the aliens would gain much power by feeding off the emotional trauma of the impending World War II, and short-circuited their energy with a piece of Gallifreyan zinc. This

allowed Talbot to finally die, dissipated the aliens' mass and embedded their essence within Brighton's West Pier.

The Doctor estimated that the essence of the Indo aliens from 1936 would corrode the West Pier, and probably consume its metal entirely in sixty or seventy years.[1512]

1937

@ The amnesiac Doctor was in London at this time.[1513]

1937 - BENNY: SECRET ORIGINS[1514] **->** As part of his crusade against the Deindum, Irving Braxiatel endowed Frost, a Nazi officer, with an extended lifespan and tasked him with destroying Buenos Aires. Frost wouldn't accomplish this mission until the late twenty-sixth century.

(=) Alternate versions of Honoré Lechasseur and Emily Blandish prevented the *Hindenburg* disaster, enabling continued use of dirigibles.[1515]

1937 - HISTORY 101[1516] **-** Sabbath sent an agent to Barcelona to track down the Absolute, a being from the future that had acquired information about his activities. This disrupted history, which in turn corrupted the Absolute's perceptions. The eighth Doctor, Anji and Fitz arrived and discovered that the Picasso painting *Guernica* had been altered. The Doctor sent Fitz to Guernica itself to

---

1509 *Grimm Reality*
1510 Dating *Players* (PDA #21) - The date is given (p150).
1511 Dating *Pier Pressure* (BF #78) - The year is given. Mention that *Charlie Chan at the Opera* is currently showing in Brighton is potentially a glitch, as some documentation indicates it wasn't distributed in the UK until 8th January, 1937. Miller states that he's 40; he's approximating, because he would have been 42 at the time.
1512 *Pier Pressure*. This refers to the West Pier's real-life decay. It partially collapsed on 29th December, 2002, then further caved in on 20th January, 2003.
1513 *History 101*
1514 Dating *Benny: Secret Origins* (Benny audio #10.4) - The year is given.
1515 *TimeH: The Sideways Door*. The *Hindenburg* went down on 6th of May, 1937.
1516 Dating *History 101* (EDA #58) - It's "Barcelona, 1937" (p1).
1517 *The Shadow of Weng-Chiang* (p208).
1518 *Superior Beings* (p58).
1519 Dating *The Shadow of Weng-Chiang* (MA #25) - The date is given (p1).
1520 "Tooth and Claw" (*DWM*). Threshold's involvement and the date are confirmed in "Wormwood".

1521 *Ghost Ship*
1522 *TW: Miracle Day*
1523 *J&L: Swan Song*. This dating is somewhat arbitrary, as the date of Jago's death isn't known, but it must occur before the New Regency's destruction in 1940.
1524 Dating "The Curse of the Scarab" (*DWM* #228-230) - The date is given.
1525 Dating *Let's Kill Hitler* (X6.8) - The date is given in a caption. In all of the *Doctor Who* stories that involve Hitler, this is the only one where he actually sees the TARDIS.
1526 Dating *TimeH: The Albino's Dancer* (*TimeH* #9) - The exact day is given, p1.
1527 Dating *Invaders from Mars* (BF #28) - The date is given, although the Welles play was actually broadcast on 30th October, not the 31st. Big Finish claims to have deliberately changed the date as part of the historical alterations affecting the second season of McGann audios. There are a couple of further anachronisms, such as a mention of the CIA and Welles not knowing about Shakespeare, which are explained in *The Time of the Daleks*.
1528 *Timeless*. The bookshop is said to be on Charing Cross Road, but it was on Euston Road in *Time Zero*.
1529 *Time Zero*
1530 *Silver Nemesis*

check events. The Doctor restored reality and the Absolute returned home. These events inspired Eric Blair, also known as the writer George Orwell.

Aviatrix Amelia Earhart disappeared, possibly because she flew into one of the Dragon Paths, lines of magnetic force.[1517] The Doctor had Amelia Earhart's flying jacket.[1518]

1937 (August) - THE SHADOW OF WENG-CHIANG[1519] **->** The fourth Doctor, Romana and K9 were drawn to Shanghai while searching for the Key to Time. They stumbled across the Tong of the Black Scorpion's plan to recover their "god" Weng-Chiang (Magnus Greel) from the zygma beam experiment. The Doctor followed the Tong's leader, H'sien-Ko - the daughter of the stage magician Li H'sien Chang - to the holy mountain of T'ai Shan. There, the Doctor found the Tong had constructed the world's first nuclear reactor to achieve the power needed to retrieve Greel. The Doctor narrowly prevented a temporal paradox by time-ramming Greel's Time Cabinet, hurling it back to 1872.

In 1937, the eighth Doctor and Fey Truscott-Sade fought psychic weasels in Russell Square. Soon after, the Threshold implanted a perceptual relay unit in Truscott-Sade's brain, enabling them to monitor what she saw.[1520]

1938

Ghosts were sighted on the *Queen Mary* in 1938.[1521] **In 1938, the entire Podesta family - which had ties to the Three Families - changed their names and disappeared from the public record.**[1522] *Swan Lake* was first performed at the New Regency some time after the death of the theatre's legendary impresario, Henry Gordon Jago. It was a huge success.[1523]

1938 - "The Curse of the Scarab"[1524] **->** The fifth Doctor and Peri landed in what they thought was an Egyptian tomb, but which was actually a Hollywood film set. The movie *The Curse of the Scarab* was beset with problems, including Raschid Karnak, the uncommunicative lead, who played the Mummy. Director Seth Rakoff was under a great deal of pressure from the studio boss, Monroe Stahr. Peri led Karnak to his dressing room, where he choked and scarab beetles started emerging from his mouth. A robot Mummy killed Stahr. The Doctor discovered more deactivated Mummies in a control centre inside a prop pyramid. Karnak was there, and told them he was cursed by the beetle god Kephri. He used the Grimoire of Anubis to resurrect Kephri. A plague of locusts was released as Kephri manifested. The Doctor held it in place with an ankh, and had a robot Mummy destroy it. The film set was destroyed in a fire.

At one point during this encounter, Peri was abducted by Threshold.

1938 - LET'S KILL HITLER[1525] **->** The *Teselecta* - a robot vehicle crewed by four hundred and twenty-one miniaturized justice agents, whose mission was to pull the greatest villains in history from the end of their lives and punish/torture them - travelled through time to capture Adolf Hitler, but arrived too early in his timestream. The *Teselecta* shifted to pose as a Nazi officer and approached Hitler just as the TARDIS, with the eleventh Doctor, Amy, Rory and Mels aboard, crashed through the window of Hitler's office. Rory locked Hitler in a cupboard, but Mels was hit by a stray bullet... which triggered her regeneration into the body of the person the Doctor's group knew as River Song.

Programmed by the Silence to kill the Doctor, Melody kissed him using lipstick laced with poison from the Judas Tree before heading out into Berlin. The justice agents identified Melody as the criminal River Song and began torturing her - but Amy sabotaged the *Teselecta*, forcing its crew to transmat to safety. The TARDIS taught Melody to fly her, enabling Melody to rescue Amy and Rory from the *Teselecta*'s interior.

The dying Doctor asked Melody to find River Song and whispered something to her that profoundly affected her. Amy used the *Teselecta* records to prove that Melody *was* River Song, whereupon River sacrificed her remaining regenerations to save the Doctor's life. The Doctor, Amy and Rory took the exhausted River Song to the fifty-first century to recover.

1938 (8th April) - TIMEH: THE ALBINO'S DANCER[1526] **->** Honoré and Emily fulfilled history pertaining to events in the Albino's bunker by damaging and hiding a time-belt.

1938 (31st October) - INVADERS FROM MARS[1527] **->** An alien spaceship crashed in New Jersey and was looted by the gangster Don Chaney, who discovered a bat-like being aboard. Chaney hired the Russian physicist Yuri Stepashin to develop an atom bomb from the advanced technology, hoping to give America an advantage over Germany. The eighth Doctor and Charley found conflict brewing between Chaney and his rival, Cosmo Devine, who wanted to sell the technology for the Nazis.

The alien split into thirty beings and threatened to go on a rampage, but the aliens Streath and Noriam subdued the pilot as part of a protection racket. Devine convinced Streath and Noriam that their weapons could seize control of Earth without the need for deception. The Doctor went to CBS Studios and had Orson Welles stage a second, private performance of *War of the Worlds* for the aliens' benefit, hoping to make them think that the formidable Martians had already invaded Earth. The plan failed.

Stepashin detonated his atom bomb aboard the aliens' spacecraft while it was in orbit, destroying them.

The eighth Doctor left a copy of Fitz's journal, entitled *An Account of An Expedition to Siberia*, in a second hand bookshop for his past self to find.[1528]

@ In 1938, the amnesiac Doctor bought Fitz's journal from a bookshop on Euston Road.[1529]

Adolf Hitler gained the Validium Arrow, a piece of the Nemesis statue. The Nemesis itself passed over Earth, heralding Germany's annexation of Austria.[1530]

1938 (Christmas) - THE DOCTOR, THE WIDOW AND THE WARDROBE[1531] -> The eleventh Doctor destroyed a threatening alien spaceship, and donned an impact suit as he fell to Earth. A young mother, Madge Arwell, helped him get back to the TARDIS. As his helmet was on backwards, she never saw his face.

1939

In Antarctica, the Nazis started construction of a huge underground base that was shaped like a swastika.[1532] **A photo of Jack Harkness from 1939 wound up in the American CIA archives.[1533]**

Circa 1939, a pair of Cybermen from the thirtieth century arrived accidentally in Jersey. They secretly took control of Peddler Electronic Engineering in London.[1534] **In 1939, a failed attempt to open Devil's Hump, "the Cambridge University Fiasco", took place.[1535]** A fez-

wearing eleventh Doctor found his way onto a Laurel and Hardy movie.[1536]

1939 - "Tooth and Claw" (*DWM*)[1537] -> The eighth Doctor and Izzy were summoned to Varney's island in the Atlantic, where eccentric guests - including Fey Truscott-Sade, an old friend of the Doctor - were served the meat of endangered animals by Varney's monkey servants. Truscott-Sade worked for British Intelligence, and suspected that Varney was creating biological weapons for the Nazis. In truth, Varney had drugged everyone's champagne with a microbe derived from his ancestors, and this turned the guests - the Doctor and Fey included - into vampires.

Varney served the last of the Curcurbites - an alien construct fuelled by blood. The Doctor destroyed the Curcurbite by poisoning his own blood and allowing the construct to feed off him... this returned the Doctor to normal, but left him gravely ill. Izzy and Fey got him back to the TARDIS, knowing they would have to take the Doctor to Gallifrey if he was going to survive.

The Second World War

During the war, bunkers were built in the London Underground, including one at Covent Garden.[1538] The Doctor advised Winston Churchill on policy.[1539] During World War II, the *Queen Mary* was used as a troop ship and torpedoed. Soldiers died, leading people to suspect the ship was haunted.[1540] Beings of light from Altair III observed the Second World War.[1541] Gaskin Manor in

---

1531 Dating *The Doctor, the Widow and the Wardrobe* (X7.0) - It is three years before the story's main action.
1532 *The Shadow in the Glass*
1533 *TW: Miracle Day*
1534 "A year or two back" before *Illegal Alien*.
1535 *The Daemons*
1536 *The Impossible Astronaut*. The movie appears to be *The Flying Deuces* (1939).
1537 Dating "Tooth and Claw" (*DWM* #257-260) - It's "1939", according to the opening caption.
1538 *The Web of Fear*
1539 *Doctor Who and the Pirates*
1540 *Ghost Ship*
1541 *Endgame* (EDA)
1542 *Wishing Well*
1543 *Heart of TARDIS*. This was "several years" before Crowley's reported death in 1947 (p6).
1544 *Heart of TARDIS*
1545 *Project: Twilight*
1546 *Resistance*. The start of the war is generally dated to 1st September, 1939, when Germany invaded Poland.
1547 Dating *Timewyrm: Exodus* (NA #2) - Part Three of the novel is set in "1939" (p111).
1548 *Remembrance of the Daleks*

1549 *Sontarans: Old Soldiers*
1550 *The Paradise of Death* (p25).
1551 *Island of Death*
1552 *Business Unusual*
1553 *Old Soldiers*
1554 In *Mawdryn Undead*, the 1983 Brigadier talks of "thirty years of soldiering". He doesn't have a moustache in the regimental photograph seen in *Inferno*. He is a member of the Scots' Guards in *The Web of Fear*. Other information here comes from *The Invasion* and *The Green Death*.
1555 *The Spectre of Lanyon Moor*
1556 *Matrix*
1557 *Illegal Alien* (p211). The Nazis occupied Jersey on 1st May, 1940.
1558 *TW: Sleeper*
1559 Dating *The Nemonite Invasion* (BBC *DW* audiobook #3) - The date is given, and the story takes place at the start of the Dunkirk evacuation, which took place from 26th May to 4th June, 1940.
1560 Dating *Timewyrm: Exodus* (NA #2) - The story coincides with the historical evacuation of Dunkirk, and the Doctor exorcises the Timewyrm from Hitler's mind shortly prior to that.

Creighton Mere was used as a convalescent home during World War II.[1542]

Occultist Aleister Crowley summoned the demon Jarakabeth.[1543] During World War II, the United States feared that collective Nazi belief could alter the fabric of reality. The US government hired writer J.R.R. Tolkien and his contemporaries to infuse world culture with a greater sense of what was fantasy, and what was reality.[1544] The Doctor knew his way around the secret tunnels under the Thames used during the Second World War.[1545]

Polly Wright's parents were married a month before World War II broke out. Her father Edward was a doctor, and her mother was a proper society lady, being one of the Bessingham-Smiths. They lived in a big old house in the country. Edward had two siblings: his elder brother Charles, and his younger brother Randolph.[1546]

1939 (early September) - TIMEWYRM: EXODUS[1547]

-> The seventh Doctor, having inveigled his way into Hitler's confidence as "Herr Doktor Johann Scmidt" with Ace as his "niece, Fräulein Dorothy Scmidt", told Hitler that if he invaded Poland, the British would declare war on Germany. Hitler refused to believe him, but the Doctor was proved right - which made Hitler trust him all the more.

Hitler had risen to power, doubly aided by the War Lords and the Timewyrm nestled within his mind. The War Lords hoped to build a "War Lord universe" by giving the Nazis space travel, whereas the Timewyrm wanted to divert the course of history. The Doctor exposed the War Lords' plans to betray the Nazis, and the forces of Reichsmarshal Goering slaughtered them. The War Lords' influence ended with the destruction of their base, Drachensberg Castle.

As the Second World War started, a few people in England felt that their country should fight alongside the Nazis. Ratcliffe was one such person, and he was imprisoned for his belief.[1548]

The British government wanted the Sontaran Brak to create weapons for use in World War II. Brak synthesised Kobalt Blue, a malleable substance that could power projectile and energy weapons - and hoped that it would either spur humanity into becoming foes worthy of the Sontarans, or push Earth's governments into destroying one another. However, the government's development of Kobalt Blue never got past the testing stage.[1549]

UNIT in the Forties

Lethbridge-Stewart would later attend Holborough with Teddy "Pooh" Fitzoliver. Lethbridge-Stewart's Granny McDougal died when he was 13[1550], and he later won the Public Schools Middleweight Cup during his last year at Fettes.[1551] Lethbridge-Stewart and John Sudbury went to

the same school.[1552] When a young Alistair Gordon Lethbridge-Stewart told his father that he was going to join the army, the senior Lethbridge-Stewart said, "In life, as on the field of battle, there are old soldiers and there are bold soldiers, but there are very few old, bold soldiers."[1553]

u - Alistair Gordon Lethbridge-Stewart began his military service. Shortly afterwards, he attended Sandhurst with Billy Rutlidge. Once his training was complete, Lethbridge-Stewart grew his moustache, joined the Scots' Guards and was stationed for a time at Aldgate.[1554]

1940

Radar equipment on Lanyon Moor was subject to mysterious interference, and the men stationed there suffered from mental illnesses.[1555]

> (=) On the Earth of the Dark Matrix, Britain had to use its army to fight civil disorder, not Hitler. The Americans intervened, and took control of the United Kingdom before defeating Hitler.[1556]

The Nazis occupied Jersey. Colonel Schott found a dormant Cyberman army in the Le Mur engineering factory.[1557] **The British military sealed off a mineshaft just outside Cardiff in the 1940s, and in future used it to store nuclear weapons.[1558]**

1940 (26th May) - THE NEMONITE INVASION[1559] ->

Aliens terraformed the homeworld of the leech-like Nemonites and culled them. One Nemonite fled into space in a crystalline sphere, and sought to initiate a breeding cycle that would create millions of offspring - enough to possess the population of an entire planet.

The tenth Doctor and Donna were in hot pursuit of the rogue and arrived at Dover Castle, the tunnels of which contained a British navy centre under the command of Vice Admiral Bertram Ramsay. The Nemonite spawned thousands of offspring that were contained aboard a British submarine. A Naval rating named Fossbrook - whom Donna had become enamoured with - sacrificed himself to blow up the vessel.

British forces were trapped at Dunkirk, but Ramsay was reluctant to initiate Operation Dynamo (a strategy for saving the troops using civilian vessels) for fear of the blow to morale if the civilians involved were killed. At the Doctor's recommendation, Ramsay initiated the operation.

1940 (May) - TIMEWYRM: EXODUS[1560] ->

Hitler, still emboldened by the Timewyrm within him, became jubilant as his armies scored many successes. German forces had reached Abbeville in France. At Hitler's command post of Felsennest, the seventh Doctor and Ace exorcised the

Timewyrm from Hitler's mind. This left Hitler weakened, and the Doctor persuaded him to halt the German advance on Dunkirk. This enabled the Miracle of Dunkirk - the rescue of hundreds of thousands of British and French soldiers in a makeshift fleet of civilian boats - to occur and mark a turning point of the war.

The seventh Doctor remembered being at Dunkirk during the evacuation.[1561] In early June, Donna visited Fossbook's mother, and delivered a letter that he'd written to her.[1562] Polly Wright's oldest brother was born in the summer of 1940.[1563]

@ The eighth Doctor visited Lancashire in the forties and met aliens from Antares 5.[1564] He failed to join the RAF, unable to prove he was a British subject. He left England, spending two years in South America and Africa.[1565]

1940 - ILLEGAL ALIEN[1566] **- >** A time-travelling Cyberman, injured by a Luftwaffe bomb in London, instinctively sought blood plasma to heal its damaged components. It began a murder campaign and gained a reputation as "the Limehouse Lurker". The seventh Doctor and Ace destroyed it.

The time travellers discovered that George Limb, a former Foreign Office secretary, had given Cyber-technology to both the Allies and the Nazis as a means of sparking a technology race. Limb escaped using a Cybermen time machine, but the Doctor's intervention eradicated much of the errant Cyber-technology, plus destroyed the Nazi Cyber-conversion base in Jersey. However, a pump house containing hundreds of Cybermen cocoons survived, and was discovered by private detective Cody McBride.

The "original" Jack Harkness - an American pilot whose name would be adopted by a Time Agent in 1941 - killed twenty-six opponents during the Battle of Britain.[1567] At 8:47 pm on 12th October, 1940, a bomb destroyed a hotel next to the New Regency Theatre, which as a consequence was torn down. Elliot Payne linked his location in the Victorian Era to the very minute that the bomb fell, destroying a group of Time Eaters (and evidently himself) when it detonated.[1568]

The seventh Doctor and Bernice arrived in Guernsey in December 1940. Bernice went undercover as Celia Doras, the daughter of a local landlady.[1569] **As a child, Richard Lazarus was caught up in the Blitz and became obsessed with immortality.**[1570]

Barbara Wright, a companion of the first Doctor, was born in 1940 and lived in Bedfordshire for a time.[1571]

= c 1940 - FP: WARLORDS OF UTOPIA[1572] **->**
While exploring parallel Romes, Scriptor crossed a great Divide between universes. He arrived in a new order of realities, ones where Hitler was winning World War II. On one of these worlds, Germania V, he met and slept with a parallel version of his wife Angela, and helped the British army fight SS officers parachuting in to kidnap the British royal family.

Returning across the Divide, Scriptor developed a plan to liberate all these Nazi Earths. Few differences existed between these realities (the point of divergence came in 1918, at the end of World War I), and the Romans quickly alighted on winning strategies. The plan failed for the first time on Germania LXI; Scriptor soon met Abschrift - one of the Cwejen - and realised that the Nazi worlds were co-ordinating with one another.

There was also a "Hitler wins" Earth - the one perfect iteration of the idea. The Hitler of that world had set up a Council of Hitlers from other parallels. These Nazis were using atomic weapons to devastate Britain. The tide was turning across the Nazi worlds, and Scriptor was captured.

1561 *Just War*
1562 *The Nemonite Invasion*
1563 *Resistance*, in which it's said that his "third birthday" occurs in the summer of 1943.
1564 *Grimm Reality*
1565 *The Turing Test* (p59).
1566 Dating *Illegal Alien* (PDA #5) - Tomorrow's date, "14 November 1940" is given (p20).
1567 *TW: Captain Jack Harkness*. The Battle of Britain lasted 10th July to 31st October, 1940.
1568 *J&L: Chronoclasm*
1569 *Just War*. The date is given as 1941 (p4), but that is a mistake and should read 1940.
1570 *The Lazarus Experiment*. Lazarus names the year as 1940. The Blitz began on 7th September, and lasted into 1941. The Doctor refers to having seen the horrors of the Blitz, which he did in *The Empty Child/The Doctor Dances*, as well as in a number of the novels.
1571 In *The Rescue*, Vicki claims that Barbara ought to be "550" years old. As *The Rescue* is set in 2493, this means Barbara was born in 1943 - making her twenty in 1963, and therefore too young to be a history teacher. Jacqueline Hill was born in 1931, and was 34 when *The Rescue* was made - meaning that Vicki is clearly rounding down. The finalised Writers' Guide for the first series said Barbara was "23", although she certainly seems older.
1572 Dating *FP: Warlords of Utopia* (FP novel #3) - Scriptor arrived on the first Nazi Earth in time to hear the original broadcast of Churchill's "Fight them on the beaches" speech, which was delivered 8th June, 1940.
1573 "A few months" before *Victory of the Daleks*, and

A single Dalek ship had fallen back in time following the Reality Bomb gambit in 2009. The few Daleks aboard needed to draw the Doctor out of hiding, and fashioned an independent-thinking android: Professor Edwin Bracewell. He presented the Daleks to Churchill as his own inventions: the "Ironsides", war machines powerful enough to change the course of the war.[1573] Churchill had concerns about the Ironsides and telephoned the Doctor, requesting his presence.[1574] Park Vale barracks was hit by a German bomb in December 1940, burying the Berserker pendant there.[1575]

1940 (end of December) - VICTORY OF THE DALEKS[1576] -> The eleventh Doctor and Amy arrived in the Cabinet War Rooms in response to a summons from the Doctor's old friend Winston Churchill. It was a month since Churchill phoned the Doctor, and in that time he'd come to see the advantages of Bracewell's machine soldiers: the Ironsides. The Doctor was horrified to learn that the Ironsides were actually Daleks - they had obtained the final remaining Dalek Progenitor, but were not genetically pure enough to activate it. The Doctor's identification of his foes as Daleks triggered the Progenitor, and it spawned "a new Dalek paradigm": five new, genetically pure Daleks with the designated functions of Scientist, Strategist, Drone, Eternal and Supreme. These Daleks exterminated the impure Daleks, and threatened to destroy the Earth with an Oblivion Continuum planted in Bracewell. The Doctor deactivated the Continuum, but the Daleks escaped.

Bracewell's knowledge temporarily enabled a few British airplanes to become space-worthy and fight the Daleks. The Doctor later took the aircraft through time to help rescue Amy from Demon's Run.[1577]

1941

In 1941, the Doctor was present when a group of Alpha Centauri were stranded in Shanghai and panicked.[1578] Lydia Childs of Torchwood died in 1941.[1579] Dr Charles Quinn of Torchwood was killed during an air raid in World War II.[1580] **The Lone Centurion dragged the Pandorica free from a warehouse hit by incendiary devices during the Blitz. This was his last recorded appearance.**[1581]

1941 (2nd January) - TW: TRACE MEMORY[1582] -> The time-jumping Michael Bellini visited the day a German bomb destroyed his childhood home, killing his mother.

1941 - THE PANDORICA OPENS[1583] -> The painting *The Pandorica Opens* was found in an attic in France. Professor Bracewell showed Churchill the painting, and Churchill telephoned the Doctor about it. The TARDIS redirected the call so that Churchill spoke to River Song, who was at Stormcage prison in the future.

1941 (Saturday, 20th January) - CAPTAIN JACK HARKNESS[1584] -> Captain Jack and Toshiko Sato arrived from the twenty-first century, having entered a temporal shift in the Ritz, a Cardiff dance hall. They

presumably after Dunkirk, or Churchill would have deployed the Ironsides then. The Daleks seen here seem to be survivors from the events of *Journey's End*. (The Doctor: "When we last met, you were at the end of your rope, finished." Dalek: "One ship survived." The Doctor: "And you fell back through time, crippled, dying.") In the Monster File on the DVD extras, writer Mark Gatiss states that "The last three Daleks who survived Davros and the Reality Bomb have arrived back in 1940".

1574 "A month" before *Victory of the Daleks*.

1575 *SJA: The Mark of the Berserker*.

1576 Dating *Victory of the Daleks* (X5.3) - There's no year given. The story takes place during the Blitz (September 1940 to May 1941) and there's reference to St Paul's being hit - it was never hit in real life, but there was a famous near-miss that destroyed much of the surrounding area on 29th December. This might be when the story is set, but there's no evidence of it being around Christmas. When we see Bracewell and Churchill again, in *The Pandorica Opens*, the caption tells us it is 1941.

1577 *Victory of the Daleks*, *A Good Man Goes to War*
1578 *The Shadow of Weng-Chiang* (p23).
1579 From *The Torchwood Archives*
1580 Torchwood.org.uk
1581 *The Big Bang*
1582 Dating *TW: Trace Memory* (*TW* novel #5) - The exact day is given, p30.
1583 Dating *The Pandorica Opens* (X5.12) - The date is given in a caption. No explanation is given for why Bracewell, who seemingly went into hiding in fear of being deactivated (*Victory of the Daleks*) is working for Churchill again. Bracewell's black glove, indicating the hand he lost in *Victory of the Daleks*, proves that *The Pandorica Opens* comes after that story.
1584 Dating *Captain Jack Harkness* (*TW* 1.12) - The story takes place on 20th January, 1941 (as is stipulated on the dance hall poster), and the original Jack Harkness is fated to die the following day.

met an American pilot named Captain Jack Harkness - the man whose identity "our" Jack stole while operating as a conman - and who was due to die the following day. Jack befriended his namesake before the Rift reopened, and he and Tosh returned home.

The original Jack Harkness died on 21st January. His squadron was out on a training mission, and two formations of Messerschmitts surprised them. The Captain destroyed three of the enemy, but was hit and couldn't bail out because his plane was on fire.

... and, earlier in "our" Jack's timeline, he arrived in 1941 to perpetrate a con job.[1585] He had never met the original Jack Harkness, but adopted his name after falsifying the records.[1586]

1941 - THE EMPTY CHILD / THE DOCTOR DANCES[1587] -> Captain Jack Harkness, a con-artist and former Time Agent from the fiftieth century, attempted to scam the ninth Doctor and Rose by crashing a Chula ambulance capsule into London. The capsule dispatched sub-atomic nanogenes that attempted to heal a gas-masked boy who'd been killed by a German bomb. The nanogenes were unfamiliar with human physiology and concluded that the masked, torn-up child was indicative of the human race. The child revived as a hollow, gas mask-wearing individual who was looking for his mummy.

The Doctor and Rose arrived "a few weeks, maybe a month" afterwards. The nanogenes had become airborne and started restructuring people into gas mask-wearing figures *en masse*. Jack admitted his con job to the Doctor and Rose, and the three of them deduced that a young woman named Nancy was the child's mother. The nanogenes recognised Nancy as such and examined her, creating a more suitable template of the human form. The affected humans were restored, and the Doctor programmed the nanogenes to deactivate. Jack took up travel with the Doctor and Rose.

1941 (1st-6th March) - JUST WAR[1588] -> The seventh Doctor, Bernice, Roz and Chris investigated reports of a new Nazi weapon. Roz and Chris joined the Scientific Intelligence Division to find out what the British knew, and Bernice went undercover in Guernsey. The German scientist Hartung had built two radar-invisible planes, *Hugin* and *Munin,* which he had started developing before the British had even invented radar. *Hugin* exploded on a test flight, killing Hartung. Bernice was captured and tortured, but Roz blew up *Munin,* denying it to the Nazis.

1941 (7th June) - SJA: LOST IN TIME[1589] -> Clyde Langer was transported back in time to obtain a piece of chronosteel discovered beneath the Rhineland. Hitler believed the item was Thor's Hammer, an object of great power. A team of Germans tried to use the chronosteel to block a radar system in the English village of Little Maulding - the first step of a German invasion that would catch the English by surprise. A local boy, George Woods, aided Clyde in alerting the authorities, and the German force was captured. Clyde returned to 2010 with the chronosteel.

1585 *The Empty Child*

1586 *TW: Captain Jack Harkness*

1587 Dating *The Empty Child/The Doctor Dances* (X1.9-1.10) - The date is repeatedly given as 1941. Jack says it's the "height of the Blitz", which ended 16th May.

In *TW: Everything Changes,* military records claim that Captain Jack Harkness failed to report for duty on 21st January and was presumed dead. Some fans and commentators have adopted this date for *The Empty Child* two-parter, under the assumption that Jack was "presumed dead" because he left on that date with the Doctor and Rose. However, it's stipulated in *TW: Captain Jack Harkness* that the original Captain Jack Harkness died on 21st January, and "our" Jack admits that he falsified the military's records to cover up the man's death. The reference to Harkness "failing to report for duty", then, must refer to the genuine article, not "our" Jack.

It is unlikely that "our" Jack would start passing as "Jack Harkness" before the original has died; nor does it ring true that he takes the name, experiences the events of *The Empty Child/The Doctor Dances* and departs in the TARDIS all in a twenty-four hour period. Moreover, *The Empty Child* states that the Doctor and Rose don't turn up until "a few weeks" or perhaps "a month" after the alien probe has landed. "Our" Jack presumably passes as "Captain Jack Harkness" during that time, as he has no way of knowing when the targets of his con-job - the Doctor and Rose - will arrive.

The most likely scenario, then, is that the original Jack Harkness dies on 21st January, the time-travelling con man (whose real name - for all we know - might well be "Jack") adopts his identity shortly thereafter, the con man gets cosy with the soldiers seen in *The Empty Child* and the Doctor and Rose land "a few weeks" or "a month" later - meaning February 1941 is the most probable time for this story to occur.

The *Torchwood* website says that Captain Jack disappeared on 5th January, which doesn't fit what we're told on screen.

1588 Dating *Just War* (NA #46) - The main action of the book starts on "the morning of 1 March 1941" (p5).

1589 Dating *SJA: Lost in Time* (SJA 4.5) - The precise date is given.

1590 *TW: Ghost Machine*

1591 Dating *TW:* "Overture" (*TWM* #25) - The day is given.

Thomas Erasmus Flanagan, age eight, was evacuated to Cardiff in 1941. He never saw his mother or sister again, and momentarily got lost at the railway station. He was adopted, and lived out his life in Cardiff.[1590]

1941 (7th August) - TW: "Overture"[1591] **->** An alien race had seeded sleeper agents onto Earth - a means of monitoring the human race prior to it developing a space empire. The sleeper agents were activated upon hearing a specific song; Captain Jack's future self in 2607 sent back a sonic failsafe that he thought would safely deactivate the agents, but it killed them instead.

1941 (18th August) - THE TWILIGHT STREETS[1592] **->** Torchwood Cardiff was now composed of Dr Matilda B Brennan, Llinos King, Gregory Phillip Bishop, Jack Harkness and a Welshman named Rhydian. To test Jack, Bilis Manger disrupted the group's operations - Jack killed an enthralled Tilda Brennan, and failed to save Bishop, his lover, from being incinerated. The Hub was currently accessed by a warehouse; in future, this would become a pizza parlour.

1941 (2nd November) - "The Way of All Flesh"[1593] **->** The eighth Doctor and Izzy arrived in Mexico during the Day of the Dead festival. While the Doctor tracked a strange energy reading, Izzy was run over and rescued by the artist Frida Kahlo. The ghost of Frida's father appeared. The Doctor met the aliens responsible, the Torajenn. Their mistress, Susini of the Wasting Wall, was a necrotist - she created art from the death of the innocent. The Torajenn wanted to have their natural bodies restored using her technology. The Torajenn were vulnerable to loud sounds, and Frida and Izzy set off fireworks to prevent them from killing the revellers. The Doctor destroyed them, but aliens arrived and kidnapped Izzy.

1941 (November) - "Me and My Shadow"[1594] **->** Fey Truscott-Sade was fighting Nazis in Austria, using her "Feyde" powers as a last resort, when she was summoned by the eighth Doctor to help find Izzy.

Toshiko Sato's grandfather stayed in London after the attack on Pearl Harbor, but was persecuted for his ethnicity.[1595] Basement sections D-3 and D-4 of the Torchwood Hub were built in 1941 and 1942, under cover of the work being part of Britain's war effort.[1596]

1941 (Christmas) - THE DOCTOR, THE WIDOW AND THE WARDROBE[1597] **->** Madge Arwell's husband, Reg, was killed in action over the Channel. She decided to postpone telling their children, Lily and Cyril, about it until after Christmas so as not to ruin the holiday. They evacuated to a house owned by their Uncle Digby in Dorset - the eleventh Doctor had got there before them, and prepared the place to give the children the perfect Christmas. Part of this involved wrapping up a dimensional portal to a planet that was a winter wonderland. Cyril opened his present early, and fell through to the year 5345. The Doctor and Lily went after him, and Madge soon followed.

Using her memories of home, Madge navigated the Time Vortex and returned the Doctor and her family back to England. This acted as a beacon for her husband's bomber, which arrived outside Uncle Digby's house in time for the family to celebrate the perfect Christmas.

1942

Ben Jackson and Polly Wright, companions of the first and second Doctors, were both born in 1942. The Jackson family lived near a brewery.[1598] Polly had four brothers, and was the second-born in her family.[1599]

1592 Dating *TW: The Twilight Streets* (*TW* novel #7) - The exact day is given, p17.
1593 Dating "The Way of All Flesh" (*DWM* #306, 308-310) - The date is given.
1594 Dating "Me and My Shadow" (*DWM* #318) - The date is given.
1595 *TW: Captain Jack Harkness.* Pearl Harbor was attacked on 7th December, 1941.
1596 *TW: Trace Memory*
1597 Dating *The Doctor, the Widow and the Wardrobe* (X7.0) - A caption says Reg is shot down "three years later" than the day Madge first met the Doctor. The telegram she receives states that he was shot down on the "20th". A second caption states that the Arwells arrive at Uncle Digby's house on "Christmas Eve". Madge later tells Droxil she is from "1941".

1598 According to a plot synopsis issued on 20th May, 1966, Ben and Polly are both "24" at the time of *The Smugglers*. Michael Craze (Ben) was then 24, Anneke Wills (Polly) was 23. The document also gave Polly's surname as "Wright", which is never used on screen, but is mentioned in the *Missing Adventure Invasion of the Cat-People*. In the same book, Polly says she was brought up in Devon. In *The War Machines*, Kitty, the manageress of the Inferno nightclub, remarks that they rarely get anyone "over twenty" into the club, which might suggest that Ben and Polly are a little younger. Mind, neither of them look younger than twenty, and *The Murder Game* reaffirms their birth year as 1942, and *Resistance* concurs that Polly was born before 1944.
1599 *Resistance*

Gerald Carter of Torchwood died in 1942.[1600] The husband of Henrietta Goodhart, a future friend of Wilf Mott, was killed during the bombing of Singapore. They had been married for only three days.[1601]

The German battleship *Bismarck* was sunk.[1602] The Doctor once claimed to have been wounded at El-Alamein in Egypt.[1603] He drove an ambulance at El Alamein and was registered as Dr John Smith, 55583.[1604]

In November 1942, there were reports of vampires in Romania.[1605] On Christmas Eve of that year, the Nazi Oskar Steinmann oversaw the first test of the "flying bomb" at Peenemunde.[1606] Aviatrix Amy Johnson vanished after her plane crashed. The Celestial Toymaker had kidnapped her.[1607]

Captain Anthony Rogers was part of an early space experiment, possibly as far back as 1942. He was hardwired into satellite technology that was later sold to the Deselby Matango company, and remained in such a state for centuries.[1608]

@ The eighth Doctor rented a flat in Bloomsbury, and lived there for almost a decade from 1942.[1609]

1942 (15th January) - THE GIRL WHO NEVER WAS[1610] **->** The Japanese laid siege to Singapore, which was defenceless after the Imperial Navy sank the HMS *Repulse* and HMS *Prince of Wales*. The SS *Batavia* was one of the last ships out of the harbour, having been chartered by the smuggler Byron - the ship's contraband included part of Adolf Hitler's private gold supply.

The TARDIS deposited Charley Pollard on board the *Batavia*, then returned to 2008 when the Cybermen compelled Byron to modify equipment that "translocated" the vessel to the year 500,002. The eighth Doctor, arriving separately from 2008, sent a recall signal that pulled the *Batavia* back to 1942. Byron's grandson, also originating from 2008, forced the reunited Doctor and Charley to transport him to 500,002, as he wanted to plunder the Cyber-ship there.

Japanese torpedoes struck the *Batavia*; its passengers took to lifeboats, but were killed by Japanese mines. The *Batavia*, with a cache of Cybermen in its hold, took to "bouncing" through time and would be seen in 2008. Madeleine Fairweather, a seaman, was the sole survivor of the event. Exposure to Cyber-signals rendered her amnesiac, and she spent the next sixty-five years thinking her name was "Charlotte Pollard". The Byron family took her in, and she later birthed a son.

c 1942 - THE SCAPEGOAT[1611] **->** A group of goat-like Barok aliens had amalgamated themselves into French society. The "scapegoat" of their tribe had crafted a career as "Max Paul, the most assassinated person in the world". Paul would be brutally killed on stage - past performances had seen him cut into pieces, crushed, shot by firing squad, stabbed, strangled, burnt, as well as his being blown up in *Testing, Testing*, and lynched in *Last Post*. After each "death", the Baroks used a quantic reanimator to turn back time and heal Paul's injuries.

1600 Torchwood.org.uk. *The Torchwood Archives* claims that Gerald died during the Blitz in January 1941, possibly juxtaposing his fate with the one the website attributes to Charles Quinn.

1601 *Beautiful Chaos* (p105). The first air raid on Singapore occurred on 8th December, 1941, followed by a long respite until the prolonged Battle of Singapore (29th December, 1941, to 15th February, 1942).

1602 The Doctor knows of the *Bismarck* in *Terror of the Zygons*.

1603 *The Sea Devils*. Two World War II battles were fought at El-Alamein, an Egyptian town, in 1942. The first lasted 1st to 27th July. The second, 23rd October to 4th November, saw the Allies forcing the Axis to retreat back to Tunisia.

1604 *Autumn Mist*, *The King of Terror* (p241).

1605 "Six months" before *The Curse of Fenric*.

1606 *Just War*

1607 *Divided Loyalties* (p46).

1608 *Benny: The Tub Full of Cats*, presuming Rogers' claims can be given any credit.

1609 *Endgame* (EDA)

1610 Dating *The Girl Who Never Was* (BF #103) - The date is given.

1611 Dating *The Scapegoat* (BF BBC7 #3.5) - The Germans are currently occupying Paris, and did so from June 14, 1940 to August 25, 1944. The Doctor here says his regenerative powers won't save him if he's decapitated - this contradicts what occurs to another Time Lord in *The Shadows of Avalon*, but as the Doctor is here in danger of being beheaded for sport, he could just be bluffing to save his current life.

1612 Dating *Mad Dogs and Englishmen* (EDA #52) - The date is given.

1613 Dating *The Shadow in the Glass* (PDA #41) - The date appears on p217. This contradicts *Timewyrm: Exodus*, which the Doctor says is his first meeting with Hitler.

1614 *Just War* (p252).

1615 *Utopia*

1616 *TW: Small Worlds*. Jack's relationship with Estelle lasted weeks, at most, but it was serious enough for them to have a photograph (with Jack in uniform) taken together.

It isn't specified whether Estelle met Jack while he was working as a con man prior to *The Empty Child*, or while he was immortal and living through the entire twenty-first century. The latter seems more likely for a couple of reasons. Such a heartfelt relationship appears

The quantic reanimator was losing its potency, and required power from a time machine. The Baroks projected a quantic beam that snagged the TARDIS while the eighth Doctor and Lucie were en route to the Moulin Rouge, 1899. Paul was appearing at the Theatre des Baroques in Paris, and Lucie found herself performing alongside him in *The Executioner's Son* - in which Paul was guillotined. The Doctor finally relocated the Baroks back to their homeworld, which had recovered from the cosmic disaster that occurred there two millennia ago. Paul snuck away with a slinky female Barok.

1942 - MAD DOGS AND ENGLISHMEN[1612] -> In the nineteen-forties, various Oxford academics and writers such as Tyler and Cleavis started meeting as the Smudgelings. All was well until the necromancer William Freer was invited to join - before long, the other members started to mock Tyler's work. The eighth Doctor discovered that Freer had put Tyler in psychic contact with Dogworld, and compelled Tyler to rewrite *The True History of Planets*. The Doctor left for London and met Noel Coward, who was in on Freer's scheme. Later, Coward refused to help some talking kittens from Pussyworld.

1942 (August) - THE SHADOW IN THE GLASS[1613] -> The sixth Doctor and the Brigadier arrived at a Berlin ballroom party, where the Doctor presented himself to Hitler as "Major Johann Schmidt" of the Reich. The time travellers acquired a sample of Hitler's blood for analysis.

Steinmann oversaw the first test of Germany's V-1 rocket at Peenemünde in December.[1614] **The immortal Captain Jack served in the Second World War.[1615] Captain Jack became close to a 17-year-old woman named Estelle Cole, whom he met at the Astoria ballroom a few weeks before Christmas. They pledged to spend the rest of their lives together, but he was posted abroad, and she volunteered to work the land. He**

would renew their friendship decades later in the twenty-first century, while posing as his own son.[1616]

1943

> (=) The English Empire retook the American colonies, but there was a revolt in 1943. The future American Prime Minister's grandfather led the army that put it down.[1617]

Liz Shaw, a companion of the third Doctor, was born in Stoke-on-Trent, 1943, to Ruben Shaw.[1618]

In 1943, the toy store owner Mr. Sun walked out of his shop in Covent Garden and was never seen again. A week later, the shop was bombed and vanished as if it had never existed. It soon reappeared.[1619] Honoré Lechasseur was posted to England in 1943.[1620] **When Angela Price was a little girl, her grandmother, Emily Morris, gave her the chronosteel key and a newspaper clipping that Sarah Jane had left behind in 1889. Morris tasked her granddaughter with returning the key to Sarah on the date of the clipping: 23rd November, 2010.[1621]**

1943 (May) - THE CURSE OF FENRIC[1622] -> The seventh Doctor and Ace arrived at a military base on the Yorkshire coast which housed the ULTIMA machine, an early computer. The Russians sent a squad to capture the machine, but the British had anticipated this by booby-trapping it to detonate a lethal toxin, waiting for a time when the Russians became their enemies. Fenric, an ancient being trapped by the Doctor, had engineered the situation to free himself and roused an army of Haemovores to help his bid. The Doctor convinced the Ancient Haemovore to destroy Fenric.

The Doctor visited the German High Command around this time.

---

more characteristic of the slightly bitter, emotionally withdrawn and immortal Jack than the carefree con man who knows he's working to the clock and is possibly involved with Algy (*The Empty Child*). Additionally, it's specified that Jack met Estelle "a few weeks before" Christmas, yet it's unlikely that he started using the name "Jack Harkness" until the original died in January 1941 (*TW: Captain Jack Harkness*). Unless Estelle thinks the "son" has a different surname to his father (unlikely, although in truth she never calls him anything other than "Jack"), her meeting him in December 1940 seems suspect.

An earlier dating is probably preferable, as the odds of Jack and Estelle keeping in touch increase as World War II comes to a conclusion. However, the Torchwood

website dates some final correspondence between Jack and Estelle to 1944.
1617 *Jubilee*
1618 *The Devil Goblins of Neptune* (p10). Actress Caroline John, who played Liz, was born in 1940. Liz's father was named in *P.R.O.B.E.: The Devil of Winterborne*.
1619 *The Cabinet of Light* (p86).
1620 *The Cabinet of Light* (p17).
1621 *SJA: Lost in Time*. Date unknown, but actress Rowena Cooper was born in 1935, and so fits the timeframe of being Morris' granddaughter.
1622 Dating *The Curse of Fenric* (26.3) - Ace says that the year is "1943". The script stated that the time is "1943 - probably May".

In the later stages of the war, the painter Amelia Ducat manned an ack-ack gun in Folkestone.[1623] The Master kidnapped a V1 from the skies over Cambridgeshire using TOM-TIT.[1624] Melanie Bush's grandfather died during the war.[1625] A time warp meant a World War II soldier bowled a cricket ball instead of a hand grenade.[1626] A German fighter crashed in the River Tees following a collision with a Q'Dhite spaceship.[1627]

@ 1943 - THE TURING TEST[1628] **->** The eighth Doctor met the British spy/novelist Graham Greene in Sierra Leone, where they encountered pale-skinned humanoids.

Rachel Jensen, a future scientific adviser to the Intrusion Counter Measures Group, worked with cryptographer Alan Turing on codebreaking.[1629] The Reverend Foxwell, a friend of the Doctor, was a leading mind at the Naval Cryptographic Section at Bletchley, and worked with Alan Turing.[1630] The Philadelphia Experiment created a rift that interacted with the upper dimensions containing fairy creatures: the Sidhe.[1631]

1943 (26th October) - THE MACROS[1632] **->** American military researchers applied Einstein's unified field theory in an attempt to bend light around the USS *Eldridge*, hoping to develop invisibility for use in the war. The sixth Doctor and Peri went to Washington, D.C., where they

tried, and failed, to retroactively prevent the effort - dubbed the "Philadelphia Experiment" - from proceeding. The *Eldridge* was caught in a time-looping rift, and would remain stuck there until 2010.

Later, the American government covered up the loss of the USS *Eldridge* by claiming it had been renamed the *Leon* and given to Greece.

1944

In 1944, Belgium, Honoré Lechasseur was caught in a German booby trap in Belgium and severely injured. He spent the next few years in a Dorset hospital, proving his doctors wrong by walking again. He rarely slept, and began having strange visions.[1633]

John Benton's brother Christopher accidentally fell to his death while the two boys were out playing.[1634] The boys' father, an army sergeant, was blown to pieces by a grenade in a town in Normandy.[1635] The Doctor visited a set of rooms beneath Cadogan Castle, and there saw Winston Churchill work on Operation Daylight, a covert operation that worked toward the liberation of France.[1636]

1944 (February) - RESISTANCE[1637] **->** The second Doctor, Polly, Ben and Jamie became separated in German-occupied France following a scuffle with the Milice (the French Gestapo). Polly found herself face to face with a

---

1623 *The Seeds of Doom*

1624 *The Time Monster*

1625 *Just War*

1626 "Forty years" before "The Tides of Time".

1627 "Fifty years" before "Evening's Empire".

1628 Dating *The Turing Test* (EDA #39) - It's "in January 1943" (p116).

1629 *Who Killed Kennedy*, taking its cue from the *Remembrance of the Daleks* novelisation.

1630 *The Hollows of Time*

1631 *Autumn Mist*

1632 Dating *The Macros* (BF LS #1.8) - The day is given. The mythos around the Philadelphia Experiment claim it commenced around 28th October, 1943. *Autumn Mist* offers an alternative explanation for what happens to the *Eldridge* - it's possible to reconcile the two if the ship wasn't entirely destroyed in *The Macros*, enabling the eighth Doctor to find it in a still-dephased state and make use of it in 1944. (Alternatively, see Unfixed Points in Time.) The "cover up" story of the *Eldridge* mirrors the real-life explanation for what became of the vessel.

1633 *The Cabinet of Light*

1634 The independent film *Wartime*, based upon some graffiti that reads "CB + JB 1944".

1635 The independent film *Wartime*. The Allied invasion of Normandy occurred in 1944.

1636 "About forty years" before *Rat Trap*. Both

Operation Daylight and Cadogan Castle are fictional; D-Day actually commenced, under the codename Operation Neptune, on 6th June, 1944.

1637 Dating *Resistance* (BF CC #3.9) - The back cover says it's "February 1944"; the same month and year appear on Polly's train ticket.

1638 Dating *Colditz* (BF #25) - The date "1944" is given. The detail about New York and Moscow being bombed comes from "Klein's Story". *A Thousand Tiny Wings* relates what happens to Klein between 1944 and when she next meets the Doctor.

1639 *The Architects of History*

1640 *The Impossible Astronaut*

1641 "Five months" before *The Turing Test*.

1642 Dating *Deadly Reunion* (PDA #71) - The date is given (although as previously noted, it does make Lethbridge-Stewart older than most other stories would have him).

1643 *Death and Diplomacy*

1644 *The Taint*

1645 "Thirty years" before *The Last of the Gaderene*.

1646 *Divided Loyalties*

1647 Dating *The Shadow in the Glass* (PDA #41) - The date is given (p29).

1648 Dating *Autumn Mist* (EDA #24) - The story takes place during the Battle of the Bulge. The Doctor confronts the Beast in *The Taint*.

downed British pilot: her father's brother, Randolph Wright, who was historically slated to die in a German POW camp. She abandoned her friends in a bid to save her uncle from his fate, only to realise that her "uncle" was a spy. The real Randolph Wright had already been captured, and the spy had been using his biographical details as a cover story. A French resistance member shot the spy dead, and Polly was reunited with her friends.

1944 / (=) 1944 - COLDITZ[1638] **->** The seventh Doctor and Ace were quickly captured when the TARDIS landed at Colditz Castle.

(=) The Doctor realised that one of his interrogators, Klein, had travelled back from a future where the Nazis had developed laser technology from the components of Ace's walkman, won the war by dropping nuclear bombs on New York and Moscow, and secured the TARDIS. Ace had been killed, but the Doctor had given himself a second chance by regenerating and posing as "Schmidt" - a scientist who helped Klein determine how to operate the TARDIS.

In one version of events, the Doctor's manipulations caused Klein to keep Ace alive, averting the errant history. The Doctor and Ace escaped Colditz while Klein, now the only survivor of her timeline, fled to South America. She sheltered with a colony of National Socialists, and requalified for medicine.

Owing to events in 2044, the version of Klein who visited Colditz was erased from history - and the Colditz paradox was somehow resolved without her involvement.[1639]

The eleventh Doctor took part in a failed breakout from a World War II POW camp.[1640]

@ The eighth Doctor met Joseph Heller, an American pilot, in a military hospital.[1641]

1944 - DEADLY REUNION[1642] **->** Second Lieutenant Alistair Gordon Lethbridge-Stewart served in Intelligence during World War II. He was assigned to update the British army's maps of the Greek islands.

On the island of Zante, Lethbridge-Stewart encountered the Greek gods Demeter, Persephone and Hermes, who were attempting to lead quiet, domestic lives. The Greek god Hades hoped to provoke a world conflict even more devastating than World War II, which would cripple humanity and allow him to rule Earth. The god Poseidon, at Persephone's request, ended Hades' scheme and cast him back into the underworld. Persephone and Lethbridge-Stewart became lovers, but she used water from the River Lethe to make him forget these events.

During the Normandy landings, Jason Kane's grandfather was killed when a sniper hit his lucky crucifix and it became lethal shrapnel.[1643] Captain Davydd Watson saw visions during the Normandy landings, an effect of an experiment by the organic computer Azoth.[1644]

During the nineteen-forties, two Gaderene scouts - members of an insectoid race whose homeworld was dying - arrived on Earth via an unstable transmat process. One of them matured into the calculating Bliss, but her brother mutated into a dragon-sized Gaderene that covered itself in mud and went dormant. Bliss lost the ninth key - a small jade shard - to the Gaderene transmat, but British Wing Commander Alec Whistler discovered it in the aftermath of an explosion at Culverton Aerodrome. Without the key, Bliss could only bring Gaderene embryos, not adults, through to Earth.[1645]

In 1944, the Toymaker kidnapped US Marine Mark Conrad.[1646]

1944 - THE SHADOW IN THE GLASS[1647] **->** On 17th May, 1944, a British fighter plane shot down a Vvormak spacecruiser as it passed over Turelhampton, England. The Vvormak were in stasis, but the ship's gravitational field rendered it immobile. Unable to relocate the ship, the British military sealed off the area for fifty years as part of a cover story.

Private Gerrard Lassiter stole the Vvormak ship's main navigation device as a talisman. It could project images of the future, and became known as the Scrying Glass. Gunther Brun, a German trooper, killed Lassiter in France and took the device, only to lose it to Colonel Otto Klein in a game of cards. Two weeks later, Reichsfuher Heinrich Himmler learned of the device and ordered Klein to hand it over to him. Himmler then gave it to a group of Tibetan mystics for study.

In July 1944, the sixth Doctor persuaded Churchill to help smuggle him into France, and infiltrated the Reich Records Department as "Colonel Johann Schmidt". In August 1944, Hitler became curious about other items left at the Turelhampton site, and authorised the Doctor, as "Schmidt", to participate in a raiding party. The raid occurred on 18th August.

1944 (December) - AUTUMN MIST[1648] **->** The eighth Doctor, Sam and Fitz were split up when they arrived during the Battle of the Bulge. Sam was injured, the Doctor served as a medic, and Fitz found himself serving as a corporal in the German army. Sam's injuries were fatal, but she was rescued by the Sidhe. A rift had formed between our realm and theirs, but the Doctor trapped the anarchic King of the Sidhe, Oberon, aboard the dephased USS *Eldridge*. Oberon perished as the Doctor deployed the *Eldridge* into the rift, sealing it. It was expected that another aspect of Oberon would take his place. The rift's closure enabled the Beast to arrive on Earth and begin feeding upon humanity.

George Woods enlisted in the Army when he was 16, and fought in the Battle of the Ardennes, a.k.a. the Battle of the Bulge. He survived, and would work in the field of radar development in the 50s and 60s.[1649]

@ 1944/5 - THE TURING TEST[1650] **->** The cryptographer Alan Turing intercepted a unique code transmitted from Dresden, concluding that it was alien in origin. The eighth Doctor had befriended Turing, and suggested they contact the signal's originator. They allied themselves with the spy Graham Greene. The Doctor also approached American pilot Joseph Heller, promising to get him out of the army if he flew the Doctor and Turing to Dresden. An English officer, Elgar, was revealled as an assassin out to kill the mysterious pale-skinned aliens. The Doctor killed Elgar and the aliens beamed away from Earth, leaving the Doctor behind as the Allied bombing of Dresden began.

w - Eleonora Albertova Kruger, one of the iterations of Cousin Anastasia, died in Bulgaria in 1944.[1651]

1945

Evelyn Smythe, a companion of the sixth Doctor, was born around 1945.[1652] **Harry Sullivan, a companion of the fourth Doctor, was born around the same time.**[1653]

On 13th February, 1945, the seventh Doctor and Bernice witnessed the destruction of Dresden.[1654] Charles Arthur Cromwell joined Torchwood in 1945.[1655] In March, the Doctor flew a Mark VIII Halifax bomber.[1656] The Tibetans charged with keeping the Scrying Glass were murdered on 25th April, 1945. In the years to follow, it would fall into the hands of Adolf Hitler's son.[1657]

In 1945, members of *homo peculiar*, fearing that evolution would go the route of exterminating them or *homo sapiens*, took to living in seclusion at a number of retreats. *Peculiar Lives*, a "scientific romance" by Erik Clevedon based upon his meeting with Percival, one of *homo peculiar*, was published.[1658]

1945 (Monday, 30th April) - THE SHADOW IN THE GLASS[1659] **->** The sixth Doctor, the Brigadier and journalist Claire Aldwych arrived from 2001 with Hitler's adult son, and the men entered Hitler's bunker. The Doctor easily portrayed Hitler's son as a madman, and Hitler, failing to recognise his offspring, shot him dead. The Nazis disposed of the body in a nearby water tower. The Allies would later mistake the corpse for a double of Hitler, killed for an unknown reason.

Martin Bormann, one of Hitler's aides, killed Claire and substituted her body for that of Eva Braun. Hitler committed suicide. A pregnant Eva was flown to a submarine in Hamburg. She later gave birth to a son named Adolf. He was raised at the secret Nazi base in Antarctica.

1649 *SJA: Lost in Time*
1650 Dating *The Turing Test* (EDA #39) - The story takes place over several months, and ends with the Allies bombing Dresden, which occurred in February 1945.
1651 *FP: The Book of the War*. The joke here is that Anastasia, following her downfall concerning the Thirteen-Day Republic debacle, was triplicated and made to live as three women who, in real life throughout the twentieth century, claimed to be the "lost" Grand Duchess Anastasia. Anastasia's remains were conclusively identified in 2008.
1652 *The Marian Conspiracy*, which takes place circa 2000, says she is "55. A Big Finish press release, however, claims she was 65 in 1999, suggesting a much earlier birth date of 1934. Big Finish Producer Gary Russell says *The Marian Conspiracy* should be favoured whatever the press release says.
1653 Harry celebrates his 41st birthday in *Harry Sullivan's War*, set circa 1986 but subject to UNIT dating. Ian Marter, who played Harry and also wrote *Harry Sullivan's War*, was born in 1944.
1654 *No Future*
1655 *TW: Trace Memory*
1656 "Next March" after *The Shadow in the Glass*.
1657 *The Shadow in the Glass*

1658 *TimeH: Peculiar Lives*
1659 Dating *The Shadow in the Glass* (PDA #41) - The date is given (p23, 147).
1660 Dating *Forty-Five*: "Casualties of War" (BF #115c) - The Doctor provides the specific day.
1661 *TW: Children of Earth*
1662 *P.R.O.B.E.: The Zero Imperative*
1663 Dating *Atom Bomb Blues* (PDA #76) - The story is set on the eve of the first A-Bomb tests.
1664 *TW: The Undertaker's Gift*
1665 *Just War*
1666 "Memorial"
1667 *Heart of TARDIS*
1668 "Operation Proteus"
1669 *Time and the Rani*. A scene showing the Rani kidnap Einstein was deleted from the camera script.
1670 "Thirty years" before *The Web of Fear*.
1671 "Thirty years" before *The Paradise of Death* (p79).
1672 Variously said to occur at the end of World War II and about "sixty years" before *The Eternal Summer*, set in 2009.
1673 Dating *Dying in the Sun* (PDA #47) - Early on, a newspaper is dated "12 October 1947" (p17).
1674 Dating *Ghosts of India* (NA #25) - The year is given.

1945 (9th May) - FORTY-FIVE: "Casualties of War"[1660] **->** Joey Carlisle, a thief, stole a cache of alien tech belonging to the Forge, and came into possession of a bracelet called a Truthsayer. The Deons, lawkeepers from the Anurine Protectorate, used such devices to make suspects tell the truth. The seventh Doctor, Ace and Hex tracked the bracelet's psychic emissions during the VE Day celebrations. Carlisle and his mother lived next door to Ace's mother and grandmother on Old Terrace in Streatham, and so Ace briefly visited her mother, who was currently age three.

Lucia Moretti of Torchwood was born on 18th June, 1945.[1661] A reservoir of pain and suffering, possibly representing humanity's darker nature, became concentrated in an area of England during perihelion: a point in mid-August when our reality and its reality became closest. The dark force was believed to have manifested in dozens of murderous individuals throughout the centuries - and on 13th August, 1945, it compelled young Daniel O'Kane to kill his parents and two sisters.[1662]

= **1945 - ATOM BOMB BLUES**[1663] **->** The seventh Doctor and Ace arrived in Los Alamos, where the Manhattan Project was about to culminate in the detonation of the first atom bomb. The Doctor identified one of the scientists, Ray Morita, as someone from the twenty-first century of a parallel universe. The Doctor made contact with a jellyfish-like alien, Zorg, and went to Los Angeles to confront the Chapel of the Red Apocalypse: a cult that had been a front for a spy ring.

Ace learned that *she* was in a parallel universe, and that Ray was from her reality, lured to the alternate history by a love of Duke Ellington music. In the proper timeline, a musicians' union strike meant much of his work was never recorded, but the strike didn't take place in the other universe.

The Doctor and Ace uncovered a plot to alter the equations of the Manhattan Project to unleash enough power to destroy this universe, tipping history in Japan's favour across the multiverse. The Doctor defeated the plan, the atom bomb test concluded as history recorded and the Doctor took Ray home - with his precious records.

The End of the Second World War

Captain Jack and a platoon of commandoes rounded up fugitive Nazis in Berlin at the end of World War II.[1664]

The Russians captured Emil Hartung's research into stealth aircraft, and took it to a vault in the Kremlin. Generalleutnant Oskar Steinmann was found guilty (along with twenty-two others) of Nazi war crimes and sentenced to life imprisonment at Nuremberg.[1665]

Brian Galway was killed in North Africa during the Second World War. His 12-year-old brother, Simon, attended a memorial service on 20th December, 1945. The Doctor placed the surviving consciousness of the Telphin, a peaceful race wiped out by the Chaktra, inside the boy.[1666]

After World War II, the American military experimented to see if widespread belief could alter the laws of physics. The residents of the Midwest town Lychburg were brainwashed with transceivers, creating thousands of people who simultaneously believed whatever the military wanted. An experiment to make the people believe "the gates of Hell were opening", however, created an unstable dimensional rift. The military tried to level the project with a low-yield nuclear device, but only succeeded in knocking Lychburg out of Earth's dimension entirely.[1667]

After the war, the British government set up Operation Proteus to create illegal chemical weapons.[1668] **The Rani briefly kidnapped Albert Einstein.**[1669] **The collector Julius Silverstein bought the only surviving robot Yeti from Professor Travers.**[1670] The Parakon named Freeth began to visit Earth, accounting for some UFO sightings over the next thirty years.[1671]

(=) A time bubble caused the village of Stockbridge to vanish. Authorities said a bomber had destroyed the town, and the mystery of Stockbridge's disappearance gave rise to the Psychic Investigation Group (PIG).[1672]

1947

1947 - DYING IN THE SUN[1673] **->** The second Doctor, Ben and Polly called in on the Doctor's old friend, movie producer Harold Reitman, but found he had been murdered. Star Light Pictures were about to release *Dying in the Sun*, and the Doctor was surprised that such a poor movie had received such rave reviews. The telepathic Selyoids were affecting the audience's perceptions of the film. The movie's producer, De Sande, was intent on using their powers to dominate the world. The Doctor caused a plane crash that killed De Sande, but this released the Selyoids present in De Sande's body. Their dispersal meant that Hollywood would remain a place of extreme emotions.

1947 - GHOSTS OF INDIA[1674] **->** The tenth Doctor tried to satiate Donna's craving for curry, but arrived in Calcutta ten years later than he had planned, while India was in the throes of its independence struggle. They met Mohandas "Mahatma" Gandhi, and soon discovered that a weed-like alien, the Jal Kalath named Darac-7, was creating outlawed

Gelem Warriors for use by the Hive Council of its home-world. The Gelem were created by absorbing violent impulses, and when Darac-7 forced Gandhi into the Gelem-making machine, it exploded, killing Darac-7. The Doctor and Donna wished Gandhi farewell, and the Doctor solemnly informed Donna that Gandhi was fated to die in January, the following year.

c 1947 - "The Professor, the Queen and the Bookshop"[1675] -> C.S. Lewis wrote *The Professor, the Queen and the Bookshop*, in which little Amelia and Rory wandered into Phoenix Books - a time-travelling book-shop - and met the Professor who managed it. They arrived in the realm of the White Queen, where it was always winter - not Christmas - and trapped her in a book. J.R.R. Tolkien thought that Lewis' story was rubbish, but one of the Inklings sharing their company at the Eagle and the Child pub - the eleventh Doctor, accompanied by Amy - suggested that the story might work better with a ward-robe.

The seventh Doctor took his friend, J.R.R. Tolkien, through time to attend the wedding of Bernice Summerfield and Jason Kane.[1676]

The Roswell Incident

The CIA captured a Nedenah ship at Roswell. One alien was autopsied, the others were taken to Area 51.[1677] **The collector Henry Van Statten had artifacts from Roswell in his private museum.**[1678] The Roswell incident was an alien "fender-bender", according to the Doctor.[1679]

On 13th June, 1947, ambassador Seruba Velak - a "Grey Alien" - was en route to negotiate an alliance against the Viperox when pirates shot down her sau-cer. Her ship crashed outside Roswell, and the US Air Force took her to Area 51. Her husband, Rivesh Mantilax, was fighting the Viperox and unable to mount a rescue attempt for six years.[1680]

The Doctor knocked over a paint pot and inspired Jackson Pollock, an American artist, around this time. Pollock gave the Doctor a painting, *Azure in the Rain by a Man Who'd Never Been*.[1681]

The rituals of black arts practitioner Edward Alexander Crowley had summoned a Jarakabeth demon to Earth. The demon impersonated Crowley after his death at Hastings, 1947. The US security service Section Eight approached "Crowley" in the hope that his Hermetic Arts could be adopted for military use. The Crowley demon would become the head of the DIvisional department of Special Tactical Operations (Provisional) with Regard to Insurgent and Subversive Activity (DISTO(P)IA), a govern-ment branch designed to counter subversion.[1682]

1948

On 30th January, 1948, Mohandas "Mahatma" Gandhi was assassinated.[1683] A year after the first crash, a Nedenah rescue mission was shot down over Roswell.[1684] The Doctor bought a stuffed owl for Sarah in 1948. It was one

---

1675 Dating "The Professor, the Queen and the Bookshop" (*DWM* #429) - It's prior to Lewis writing *The Lion, the Witch and the Wardrobe*, the manuscript of which was finished in March 1949.
1676 *Happy Endings.* Tolkien's wedding gift is a first edition of *The Hobbit*, which was published in 1937.
1677 *The Devil Goblins from Neptune*, and also referred to in *The Face of the Enemy*.
1678 *Dalek*
1679 *Peacemaker*
1680 *Dreamland* (*DW*). The date is given in a caption. See the Unfixed Points in Time sidebar.
1681 *Divided Loyalties.* Pollock was influential to the abstract expressionism movement.
1682 *Heart of TARDIS*
1683 *Ghosts of India*
1684 *The Devil Goblins from Neptune* (p240).
1685 *Interference.* We see it in *The Hand of Fear*.
1686 *Fear Her*
1687 *TW: Slow Decay*
1688 *The End of Time* (TV)
1689 *SJA: The Temptation of Sarah Jane Smith.* No date given, but this is before Sarah Jane is born in 1951.
1690 *FP: The Labyrinth of Histories*, extrapolating from

the godfather's grandfather being conceived circa February 1899.
1691 Dating *The Cabinet of Light* (TEL #9) - The year is 1949, according to p14 and the back cover blurb. *TimeH: Peculiar Lives* specifies that the pyjama-clad Emily was found wandering the streets of London in "late 1949" (p13). The Doctor admits that his own memories are "hazy", and so he might be conflating the story of his last regeneration with the one in *Doctor Who - The Movie*. (Alternatively, it might have happened exactly as he claims.)
Emily's amnesia is attributed to Mestizer's agents attacking her. Given the murky recollections of every-one involved, though, it could stem from the blow to the head she receives at the end of *TimeH: Child of Time*.
1692 *TimeH: Child of Time*
1693 Dating *TimeH: The Winning Side* (*TimeH* #1) - The *Time Hunter* novella series picks up in wake of events in *The Cabinet of Light*; the year is variously reiterated as 1949. Pages 7 and 78 say that Emily is "killed" on a "cool, crisp December night".
1694 "Twenty years" before *The Underwater Menace*.
1695 *The Scales of Injustice.* No date is given.
1696 *Return of the Living Dad.* This happened in "the

of the items she packed when she left his company.[1685]

The Doctor liked the 1948 Olympics opening ceremony so much, he went back to see it again.[1686] Torchwood acquired some alien artifacts at auction in 1948.[1687] **Wilf Mott was too young to fight in the Second World War, but joined the British Army and served as a private in Palestine, 1948.**[1688]

Barbara Wilson and Eddie Smith, the future parents of Sarah Jane Smith, met while serving coffee in a Navy, Army and Air Force Institutes (NAAFI) canteen. They were married after he proposed by passing her a note asking her to become "Mrs. Smith".[1689]

1949

Godfather Sabbath of Faction Paradox was born.[1690]

1949 - TIMEH: THE CABINET OF LIGHT[1691] **->** An unknown incarnation of the Doctor - one who believed he had regenerated after visiting "the city by the bay" and being shot after meeting "a beautiful lady with no pity" - arrived in London with his companion, Emily Blandish. Agents working for Mestizer, a nemesis of the Doctor, attacked them - Emily helped the Doctor to escape, but Mestizer's agents captured the Doctor's time cabinet. The trauma of the event rendered Emily amnesiac. She was found wandering the streets of London with no memory, and became known in the press as "the Girl in Pink Pyjamas" (and occasionally "the Girl in the Pink Bikini"). She was used to promote clothes rationing.

To retrieve his property, the Doctor sought help from an expatriate and time sensitive named Honoré Lechasseur, who chiefly worked as a "fixer" - a trafficker of goods in a largely, but not entirely, legal fashion. Honoré observed the Doctor confronting Mestizer, and light from the Doctor's time cabinet started her house on fire. The Doctor, Mestizer, the house and the cabinet all disappeared. Afterwards, Honoré and Emily struck up a partnership.

By now, the Doctor was regarded as a "hobgoblin" or "myth" in the underground community. Legends claimed

he variously gave fire to mankind, burned London in 1666, kidnapped the crew of the *Mary Celeste* and built Stonehenge with his bare hands.

Honoré and Emily's future selves travelled back to watch as she was found, wandering the London streets, in her pyjamas.[1692]

1949 (December) - TIMEH: THE WINNING SIDE[1693] **->** Emily found that she was a "time channeller" who could travel through time and space in conjunction with a time-sensitive such as Honoré. They investigated the appearance of Emily's body beneath Hammersmith Bridge - part of a divergent timeline triggered when a civil servant, Simon Brown, released nuclear secrets to the entire world. Emily and Honoré erased this errant history after travelling to it in the year 1984, and Emily prevented her death by letting go of her "killer", a time-sensitive named Radford, during a time jump.

The Nineteen Fifties

In the early nineteen-fifties, Professor Zaroff - "the greatest scientist since Leonardo" - vanished.[1694] The testing of nuclear weapons, plus an increase in dumping of toxic waste, destroyed many Silurian shelters.[1695]

Albinex the Navarino arrived down a faulty time corridor from the far future.[1696] In Jamaica, the 1950s, the Doctor met the ornithologist James Bond and took him to the 1800s to see a live dodo. The Doctor later introduced writer Ian Fleming to Bond, who served as inspiration for Fleming's super-spy novels.[1697] The Doctor met the Cuban guerrilla leader Che Guevara.[1698] **UFOs were fashionable in the fifties.**[1699]

Amy and Rory agreed with the eleventh Doctor that American hot dogs from the 1950s were the best hot dogs of all.[1700] Jack Harkness thought the food of the 1950s was horrid.[1701] Torchwood collected about a dozen items of alien technology that came through the Rift in the 1950s.[1702]

---

fifties" (p66).
1697 *Instruments of Darkness*
1698 *Psi-ence Fiction.* No date is given.
1699 According to the Doctor in *Dreamland* (DW).
1700 *The Eye of the Jungle*
1701 *TW: Department X*
1702 *TW: Slow Decay*

UNIT in the Fifties

u - When Lethbridge-Stewart was 21, he spent a time in New York on the way back from Korea.[1703] Lethbridge-Stewart met Fiona, his future wife.[1704] Lethbridge-Stewart's grandmother died in 1955.[1705]

1950

Mentally influenced by the Player Myrek, President Truman approved Operation Kali, a psychic warfare programme.[1706] Kenneth James Valentine, a former policeman who was at D-Day, joined Torchwood Cardiff in 1950.[1707]

> **(=) 1950 - TIMEH: THE TUNNEL AT THE END OF THE LIGHT**[1708] -> Mestizer resurfaced and took command of the Subterraneans. They committed an escalating number of murders while helping her find a time-sensitive that she could use to escape.

Honoré and Emily went back in time and stopped the Subterraneans' leader from leaving them, which retroactively prevented Mestizer from knowing they existed.

Honoré and Emily made further time-jumps, and had adventures pertaining to a clockwork woman in 1805; an impending apocalypse in Japan, 2020; the murderous Cabal of the Horned Beast in 1921; and a trapped time entity in London, 1995.[1709]

1950 (June) - TIMEH: PECULIAR LIVES[1710] -> The future humans that had created *homo peculiar* now sought to eliminate them, as their timeline depended upon *homo peculiar* dissipating its essence through humanity. Members of *homo peculiar* defeated this goal by mastering time-channelling, and took to living in future eras where animal and plant life were in abundance on Earth, but mankind was absent.

On "a hot summer's night", Honoré and Emily left for Antioch, 1098.[1711]

1951

The radio telescope was invented.[1712] The last witchcraft act on the English statute books was repealed in 1951.[1713] Rupert Locke, a resident of Jackson Leaves, was convicted of six violent rapes in 1951.[1714] **Mrs Randall, a future nursing home resident who would meet Sarah Jane Smith, was named Miss Ealing of 1951.**[1715]

A computer built to regulate space trains, cars and buses was left at loose ends once its humanoid creators were lost in an undisclosed incident. In 1951, the Rift transported a Cardiff train leaving from Platform 4 for Grangetown to the computer's world. The train driver died, but the computer kept itself occupied by copying him and building trains to shuttle the replicants about.[1716]

1703 *The Devil Goblins from Neptune* (p37).
1704 "Fifteen years" before *The Scales of Injustice*.
1705 *The Devil Goblins from Neptune* (p56), *The King of Terror* (p126).
1706 "About a year" before *Endgame* (EDA).
1707 *TW: Trace Memory*, extrapolating from the fact that Valentine's paper trail vanishes in that year, and his records were later purged by Torchwood.
1708 Dating *TimeH: The Tunnel at the End of the Light* (*TimeH* #2) - The cover bears the year, and when all is said and done, Honoré and Emily return to their starting point of "early 1950" (p150).
1709 *TimeH: The Clockwork Woman*; *TimeH: Kitsune*; *TimeH: The Severed Man*; *TimeH: Echoes*. Honoré and Emily tend to return home after each adventure, and the intros to each novella (as well as some internal references, including *The Severed Man*, pgs. 60-61, 106; *Echoes*, p9) reiterate that they originate from 1950.
1710 Dating *TimeH: Peculiar Lives* (*TimeH* #7) - The month and year are given as June (pgs 13, 41, 82), and an epilogue references some incidental events on "early July" (p127) and "5th September" (p129).
1711 *TimeH: Deus Le Volt*. Honoré mentions some relaxation of rationing in the United Kingdom, as historically occurred in May 1950.

1712 "Forty years" after *Pyramids of Mars*.
1713 *The Daemons*
1714 *TW: The House That Jack Built*. This event still occurs even once the house's history is revised.
1715 *SJA: Eye of the Gorgon*
1716 *TW: Ghost Train*
1717 Dating *TimeH: The Sideways Door* (*TimeH* #10) - After Honoré and Emily cross over into the parallel reality, page 32 reads: "The masthead on *The Times* confirmed the date was the same as it had been that morning: 13 February 1951." While this would seem to mean that it's 13th February in Honoré and Emily's native reality as well, *TimeH: Child of Time* - set in either late November or December 1951 - claims (p12) that events in *The Sideways Door* happened only "weeks" ago. The only way to reconcile this is to assume that some time displacement does occur when they cross from one Earth to another, but that's certainly not the impression one gets here.
1718 Dating *TimeH: The Albino's Dancer* (*TimeH* #9) - The exact day is repeatedly given.
1719 According to *SJA: Whatever Happened to Sarah Jane?*, Sarah was "13" by mid-July, 1964. *SJA: The Temptation of Sarah Jane Smith* establishes that she was "three months old" in August 1951, suggesting she

(=) 1951 (13th February) - TIMEH: THE SIDEWAYS DOOR[1717] -> Jonah Rankin, a time sensitive, accidentally transported Honoré and Emily to a parallel reality where their alternate selves had brazenly used their abilities to avert World War II and make other changes. The temporal amendments were such that history began to unravel. Honoré and Emily escaped as their counterparts were transported to parts unknown by a fatally wounded Rankin.

1951 (23rd February) - TIMEH: THE ALBINO'S DANCER[1718] -> Emily and the Albino - a half-human, half humanoid crimelord - travelled back some months to a bunker the Albino owned, as did Honoré and Catherine Howkins, one of the Albino's dancers. They were present as Leiter and Catherine's younger self - fugitives from the Sodality - arrived at the bunker using time belts. Honoré saved Catherine's younger self when the bunker exploded; she believed that Emily had perished, when in fact her older self had died instead. The Albino was also killed in the explosion - which so gravely wounded a man named Burgess, he would become the Albino in future.

Sarah Jane Smith - a companion of the third and fourth Doctors, an associate of the tenth Doctor and a thwarter of alien evil-doers - was born between 1st and 21st May, 1951, in the village of Foxgrove, to Eddie and Barbara Smith.[1719] On 30th June, 1951, Catherine Howkins was hired as an exotic dancer for the Albino.[1720]

1951 (18th August) - SJA: THE TEMPTATION OF SARAH JANE SMITH[1721] -> When Sarah Jane Smith was three months old, her parents mysteriously left her in her pram along the side of the road in the village of Foxgrove, then were killed when their car struck a tractor that had broken down in the lane. She would be raised by Lavinia Smith, her father's sister.

(=) The Trickster enabled Sarah Jane to travel back from 2009 and prevent her parents' death, creating a parallel timeline in which the Trickster devastated Earth. Sarah's parents accepted that their survival had crippled the world, and sacrificed themselves to restore history.

1951 (4th November) - TIMEH: THE ALBINO'S DANCER[1722] -> Catherine Howkins happened upon Honoré and thanked him for saving her life last February - in an explosion where Howkins believed that Emily had died. Honoré, Howkins, Emily and the Albino used various means to go back to February, all of them intent on uncovering the truth about the incident.

Honoré and Emily briefly travelled to a parallel reality in which their alternate selves were abusing their powers.[1723]

1951 (1st December) - TIMEH: CHILD OF TIME[1724] -> Honoré and Emily examined the corpse of a woman from the future, which caused them to travel to 2586. After learning of Emily's origins, they returned to 1951 and looked forward to new adventures together.

(=) 1951 - TIMEWYRM: EXODUS[1725] -> Following the total defeat of the British army at Dunkirk in 1940, the German army swept across the Channel and landed at Folkestone. Britain fell in six days. Churchill and thousands of suspected troublemakers were executed. Oswald Mosley was installed as Prime Minister, and Edward VIII was crowned. Unsure what to do with Britain, the Nazi High Command let the country fall into ruin.

All able-bodied men were conscripted as slave workers and shipped to the continent. In 1951, the

---

was born in May. We can further narrow the date as *SJA: Secrets of the Stars* says that Sarah is a Taurus, which lasts 20th April to 21st May.

In *SJA: Goodbye, Sarah Jane Smith*, Sarah says she was "23" when she met the Doctor (in *The Time Warrior*) - the same as her age given on screen in *Invasion of the Dinosaurs* (although in the novelisation of that story, she's "22"). Elisabeth Sladen, who played Sarah, was born in 1948. In the format document for the proposed *K9 and Company* series, it's stated that Sarah was born in "1949". She was "about 30" in the spin-off novel *Harry Sullivan's War* (suggesting a birth date of 1955), and she's born "over sixty years" after 1880 in *Evolution* (p242).
1720 *TimeH: The Albino's Dancer*
1721 Dating *SJA: The Temptation of Sarah Jane Smith*

(*SJA* 2.5) - The precise date is given.
1722 Dating *TimeH: The Albino's Dancer* (*TimeH* #9) - The exact day is repeatedly given, and while it's stated within the text and on the cover that Honoré and Emily now originate from 1951, the introduction - as with the previous six *Time Hunter* novellas - continues to stubbornly insist that it's 1950.
1723 *TimeH: The Sideways Door*
1724 Dating *TimeH: Child of Time* (*TimeH* #11) - This is the final *Time Hunter* novella. It's reiterated that it's still 1951. The day is given (p15), and it's been "a couple of weeks" (pgs 12, 15) since the previous novella.
1725 Dating *Timewyrm: Exodus* (*NA* #2) - In Part One of the novel, the Doctor proclaims it to be the "Festival of Britain, 1951" (p5). At the end of the novel, the Doctor and Ace arrive at the real Festival of Britain.

Festival of Britain took place in London to celebrate ten years of Nazi victory. The Germans planned to have a man on the moon in this year. The seventh Doctor and Ace realised that history had been altered. They travelled back and averted this timeline with the destruction of Drachensberg Castle in 1939.

After they defeated the War Lords and Timewyrm, the Doctor and Ace visited the real Festival of Britain and discovered that history was back on course.

@ 1951 - ENDGAME[1726] **->** The seventh Doctor (and Ace) saw the eighth Doctor at the Festival of Britain, but neither recognised the other.

The Players decided on a new game, seeing which among them could provoke a nuclear holocaust on Earth. Kim Philby, a member of British intelligence and a double agent for the Soviet Union, recruited the eighth Doctor to defeat the Players.

President Truman became abnormally hostile to China, and the Doctor discovered the president was under the influence of the Player Myrek. As Philby suspected, another Player - the Countess - was manipulating Stalin. The Doctor ended the Players' control of the Russian leader and Truman. Returning to America, the Doctor tricked the Players into killing each other. The Doctor declined a job at the White House and returned to London.

@ The eighth Doctor was present in the Soviet Union during a high profile chess match played in 1951.[1727] In 1951, the Dionysus Project in Cardington opened a doorway to the Divergents' domain. This killed the researchers Dr. Stone and the Reverend Matthew Townsend.[1728]

(=) 1951 - REAL TIME[1729] **->** With the Cybermen firmly in control of Earth, a group of human rebels crafted an organic techno-virus capable of destroying the Cybermen's artificial implants. They used a Chronosphere to dispatch Dr Reece Goddard to 3286, the year in which the Cybermen altered history, in the hope of averting this timeline altogether.

1952

Barbara Wright worked at Hampstead High School for girls in 1952.[1730] **Pilot Diane Holmes flew from England to Australia in just four days.**[1731]

Ronald Turvey went to university to read biochemistry when he was 18, but bullies tore his beloved teddy bear, Mr. Cuddles, to shreds. In the years to come, Turvey was infected with the Tinghus: a member of a race of psychic parasites. He felt as if the ghost of Mr. Cuddles was talking to him, and would found a toy company.[1732]

1952 (7th September) - THE NOWHERE PLACE[1733]
-> Scientists working on behalf of the British War Office

1726 Dating *Endgame* (EDA #40) - The year is given (p242).
1727 *Father Time* (p58).
1728 *Zagreus*, again judging by a historical simulation.
1729 Dating *Real Time* (BF BBCi #1) - The date is given, episode one, track 1.
1730 *The Plotters.* If we take the writers' guidelines at face value, she would have been 12 at the time.
1731 *TW: Out of Time*
1732 *Cuddlesome.* It's not stated when this occurs, but Timothy West, who plays Turvey, was born in 1934 - making 1952 as good a dating as anything else.
1733 Dating *The Nowhere Place* (BF #84) - The date is given.
1734 *A Thousand Tiny Wings*
1735 Dating *A Thousand Tiny Wings* (BF #130) - The back cover vaguely declares that it's "Kenya, the 1950s", but to judge by everyone's anxieties, the Mau Mau uprising (1952-1960) has just begun. A BBC Overseas Service radio broadcast relates how the Kenyan governor, Sir Evelyn Baring, has declared a state of emergency just two weeks after taking office, and how the authorities have already arrested one hundred leaders of the insurgency, including rebel spokesperson Jomo Kenyatta (who later became Kenya's first prime minister) - all of which occurred on 20th October, 1952.

Annoyingly, and despite all the historical detail that indicates an October 1952 dating, *The Architects of History* dates this story to "1953" - although the version of Klein who works for UNIT might be rounding when she says that.
1736 *A Thousand Tiny Wings.* De Flores appeared in *Silver Nemesis*.
1737 Dating *Amorality Tale* (PDA #52) - It's "Wednesday, December 3, 1952" (p12).
1738 Dating *A Christmas Carol* (X6.0) - The year is given. Monroe *was* between marriages, as it happens, in 1952.
1739 *Nightshade* (p111).
1740 *Escape Velocity* (p196).
1741 *The Dying Days* (p52). Sherpa Tensing Norgay and Edmund P. Hillary were the first to conquer Everest.
1742 *The Suffering.* In real life, *The Times* published evidence of the hoax in November 1953.
1743 *The Catalyst.* The type of race isn't specified.
1744 "Five years" before *Dreamland* (*DW*).
1745 *Dreamland* (*DW*). *SJA: The Vault of Secrets* specifies that the Men in Black were first active in 1953.
1746 Trueman is 56 in *SJA: Secrets of the Stars*, set in early November, 2009, so he was born in either 1952 or 1953. Trueman-actor Russ Abbott is somewhat older than the part he played, having been born 16th September, 1947.

were stationed RAF Hill Lankton Base, and the Oxford-educated Trevor Ridgely was assigned to work on rocket propulsion there. Trevor doodled the rudimentary design for a star drive-equipped ship, and although he never worked toward the completion of such a device, his sketch planted the seed of his idea. Someone would return to Trevor's sketch in future, spot something he'd overlooked and help to facilitate mankind's journey into the stars.

The sixth Doctor and Evelyn arrived from 2197, and encountered Trevor on the *Ivy Lee*, the last Turret-class train in service, as it was passing through Stapely Moor. Representatives of the original race that evolved on Earth hoped to trick the time travellers into facilitating the loss of Trevor's sketch - and thereby subvert humanity's star-travel - but the Doctor and Evelyn thwarted the plot and returned to the future.

> (=) In Klein's history, the Third Reich controlled Africa. When the Mau Mau rebelled in 1952, waves of German aircraft obliterated their tribal areas.[1734]

1952 (October) - A THOUSAND TINY WINGS[1735] ->

The Chaliss had evolved as a species of intelligent little birds - a rarity in the universe, owing to their inability to work tools with wings. They would nestle on a humanoid - a "mule", of sorts - in their hundreds, thousands even, and thereby achieve a group consciousness.

One such Chaliss gestalt arrived in Kenya as the Mau Mau rebelled against the British. It intended on using humanity as test subjects in the creation of a "universal plague" that could be tailored and sold to various parties. As different races wiped themselves out, the Chaliss would amass enough economic might to control the galaxy.

> (=) The Elizabeth Klein who escaped from Colditz was now in Kenya, owing to her fascination with the dark continent. She had a full laboratory in Nairobi, but abandoned it when the uprising started. The seventh Doctor happened upon Klein as she sheltered in a farmhouse, and together they killed the Chaliss birds, whose "mule" died soon afterwards. A British subject, Mrs Sylvia O'Donnell, was tasked with seeing that a dome the Chaliss had built was buried, forever trapping the contagion within. The Doctor hoped to broaden Klein's philosophies by letting her see other worlds, and made her his new companion.

Owing to Klein's removal from history in 2044, the Doctor defeated the Chaliss without her involvement.

> (=) In Klein's history, Hans De Flores was "the Führer's favourite". The Nazis sent builders to construct new cities in the devastated Kenya, but the carpet bombing in 1952 had released the Chaliss contagion. Within three years, most of the builders were dead. The Führer assigned Klein to take a team of doctors and investigate, but they were evacuated before making any progress. It was years before the Nazis dared return to Africa.[1736]

1952 (December) - AMORALITY TALE[1737] ->

The third Doctor and Sarah Jane sought to investigate a warp shadow, and arrived prior to a killer smog descending on London. The Doctor set up shop as a watchmaker. Sarah found out that a war was brewing between the Ramsey and Callum gangs. Callum was actually a member of the Xhinn, a ruthless alien species, and the killer smog was actually a Xhinn weapon. The Doctor destroyed the Xhinn scoutship, which deterred their main fleet from attacking.

1952 - A CHRISTMAS CAROL[1738] -> The eleventh Doctor, the teenage Karzan Sardick and Abigail Pettigrew visited Hollywood. The Doctor was supposed to do a duet with Frank Sinatra, but accidentally got engaged to Marilyn Monroe. They were married at a locale the Doctor later insisted wasn't a real chapel. In the same year, the Doctor met Albert Einstein and Father Christmas - whom the Doctor better knew as "Fred" - at Sinatra's hunting lodge.

1953

The science fiction serial *Nightshade* was first shown by the BBC in 1953. It would run for five years.[1739] @ The eighth Doctor quickly became a fan of the show.[1740]

The Doctor was the first man to climb Everest, giving Tensing and Hillary a hand up.[1741] The notorious Piltdown Man skull was exposed for what it was: a human cranium with the jawbone of an ape attached.[1742] Joshua Douglas, a companion of the third Doctor, won first prize in a race in 1953 and was awarded a metal cup.[1743] **Rivesh Mantilax was shot down attempting to rescue his wife from Area 51. He was found and kept safe by a group of Native Americans led by Night Eagle.[1744]**

In 1953, the Alliance of Shades - an extra-terrestrial organisation dedicated to keeping advanced technology from primitive worlds such as Earth - deployed robots presenting themselves as Men in Black to perform recovery operations. The tenth Doctor would encounter a quartet of Men in Black - Mr Dread, Mr Fear, Mr Terror and Mr Apprehension - during his visit to Area 51 in 1958.[1745]

Martin Trueman was born at exactly the right moment, exactly the right time, for him to later serve as a channel for the power of the Ancient Lights.[1746]

The Doctor made a hobby of seeing *The Mousetrap*, and watched every production from 1953 to at least 2009.[1747]

u - Jo Grant's grandfather died when she was seven.[1748]

1953 (1st-2nd June) - THE IDIOT'S LANTERN[1749] **->**
An alien became an energy being after her people executed her, and fled to Earth in 1953. The Wire, as she was now called, conscripted Mr Magpie of Magpie's Electricals to supply cheap televisions in the run-up to the coronation of Queen Elizabeth II. This enabled the Wire to feed off the electrical energy of viewers' brains, which turned them blank-faced. The Wire wanted to connect with the twenty million people expected to watch the Coronation, and regain her corporeal body.

The tenth Doctor and Rose arrived on Florizel Street in London and learned of the Wire's intentions. The Doctor sabotaged the transmitter at Alexandra Palace, which trapped the Wire onto a Betamax tape (that the Doctor intended to tape over) and restored her victims to health.

The Wire killed Mr. Magpie before she was captured, but his company would prosper without him.[1750]

1953 (20th November) - TW: TRACE MEMORY[1751] **->** An Arctic expedition discovered a Vondraxian Orb, and sent it via a Scandinavian cargo ship to Torchwood Cardiff. The Orb reacted badly to the presence of the Rift and exploded - a dock worker, Michael Bellini, absorbed the Orb's energy and was flung back to 1941.

> (=) In 1953, the second President of the English Empire celebrated the fiftieth Jubilee of victory by executing one of his two captive Daleks.[1752]

The Toymaker beat Le Chiffre at baccarat.[1753] **On 18th December, 1953, a plane with three people on board fell through the Rift in Cardiff. They would emerge from it in late 2007.**[1754] An archaeological dig at Mynach Hengoed in 1953 uncovered an alien spaceship, which Torchwood acquired.[1755]

1954

In March 1954, Torchwood Cardiff carried out an inventory of its alien tech that took all five of its staff the best part of a month to complete.[1756]

1954 - "The Good Soldier"[1757] **->** The seventh Doctor and Ace drove up to a diner in the Nevada desert and found it full of American soldiers. The area lifted into space and docked with a flying saucer, which in turn docked with its mothership... and Cybermen emerged from the sand. The Doctor told Ace that the Mondasian Cybermen would have attacked Earth before 1986 if they'd had the right weapon... and that they were standing in it.

Meanwhile, the Cybermen had learned how to control human minds, and required aggression - which they lacked themselves - to power their warship. They installed Colonel Rhodes, the leader of the soldiers, into the device. Ace interfaced with the system, detaching the flying saucer. The Cybermen pursued, but the Doctor and Ace overloaded their reactor, destroying the warship.

1954 (9th November) - THE WITCH HUNTERS[1758] **->** The first Doctor, Ian, Barbara and Susan arrived after visiting Salem during the witch trials. Susan was distressed to think that some of the residents would be burnt as witches, and used the TARDIS' Fast Return Switch in a bid to go back and save them. Returning to 1954, the time travellers attended the premiere of *The Crucible* in Bristol.

Later, the Doctor brought the condemned Rebecca Nurse to this era to view *The Crucible* and see memorials to the victims of the Salem witch trials.

1747 "Ghosts of the Northern Line"
1748 *The Mists of Time*, based upon Katy Manning being born in 1946, but subject to UNIT dating.
1749 Dating *The Idiot's Lantern* (X2.7) - The story's climax coincides with the coronation of Queen Elizabeth II, with the Doctor and Rose arriving the day before.
1750 Use of the Magpie Electricals logo has become a running joke for the new series design team, and is seen on various electronics in *The Runaway Bride, The Sound of Drums, Voyage of the Damned, Day of the Moon* and *TW: The Undertaker's Gift*. It's on a banner in *The Beast Below*, and on equipment in the TARDIS in *The Eleventh Hour* and *Vincent and the Doctor*.
1751 Dating *TW: Trace Memory* (*TW* novel #5) - The exact day is given, p27.
1752 *Jubilee*
1753 "End Game" (*DWM*). Le Chiffre is the villain in the first James Bond novel, *Casino Royale* (1953).
1754 *TW: Out of Time*
1755 *TW: Slow Decay*
1756 *TW: Trace Memory*
1757 Dating "The Good Soldier" (*DWM* #175-178) - "It's 1954" according to the Doctor. The Cybermen resemble those from *The Tenth Planet*, and that's specified in dialogue. The Cybermen report to Mondas Control.
1758 Dating *The Witch Hunters* (PDA #9) - The date is given, p68. The Fast Return Switch first appeared in *The Edge of Destruction*, but in that story, it was used to move the TARDIS into the past quickly - not as a "return to previous location" device.

CYBERMEN ... FASHION VICTIMS?: Does the variation in design between the Cybermen actually symbolise anything, and how helpful is it to the dating process? It's a similar question to that of the Klingons in *Star Trek* - there's a real-life reason (generally related to budgets and audience expectations) as to why they look different in the sixties and the eighties, but is there a reason *within* the fiction?

On television, it's not even clear that the characters "see" any difference between different models of Cybermen. Ben instantly recognises the Cybermen in *The Moonbase*, even though they bear little resemblance to the ones he saw in *The Tenth Planet*. Notably, he doesn't so much as comment that they've been redesigned - something that might be relevant to say, if one is evaluating the capabilities of the alien invaders that are besieging one's moonbase. Ben is hardly alone in this, as many other characters fail to make the same observation (just to name a few, the Doctor, Polly, Jamie, Zoe, Brigadier and Sarah Jane all encounter different versions of the Cybermen). On screen at least, we never see an old model once a new one has been introduced (except for the flashback in *Earthshock* and the head in a museum in *Dalek*).

We never see two versions of the Cybermen together. Yet the development doesn't appear to be linear in terms of fictional history - it's strictly linear in terms of the order the Doctor meets them. Without wanting to get unduly philosophical, the television episodes we see are a *representation* of reality, not a window on it - unless there's an unrevealled canonical reason as to why (for instance) the Silurians have zips down their backs in *Warriors of the Deep*. We're seeing things as convincingly as the BBC can render them, so it's entirely possible that - to the characters - the Cybermen from *The Tenth Planet* look identical to the ones in *The Moonbase* and *Earthshock*.

In the books, audios and comic strips, the distinction is made rather more often - for example, the Doctor notes that the Cybermen in "The Good Soldier" are the same design as the ones from *The Tenth Planet*.

If we take it as read that the characters *do* see different models of Cybermen, the significance could be functional. Perhaps the Cybermen from *The Tenth Planet* are adapted for Arctic conditions, the ones in *The Moonbase* and *The Wheel in Space* for low gravity operation and so forth. This seems unlikely, though - the Cybermen we see are almost always intent on roughly the same thing: marching into a human military installation and taking it by force.

It may well be that what we think of as one race is, in fact, many. Elsewhere in the *Doctor Who* universe, it seems to be a common stage of evolution for an organic race to remove "weaknesses" using cybernetic implants. Not every race does so - the Gallifreyans don't, for example, and humans apparently only ever do so in a limited fashion (as seen in, say, *Warriors of the Deep* or *The Long Game*). But a fair number of the

Doctor's adversaries are cyborgs - the Daleks, the Sontarans and the Ice Warriors all are to at least some extent. Perhaps "Cyberman" is just the name of the end result when one of the human-like races that seem to exist on countless planets independently (or semi-independently) discards their organic form for a cybernetic one. Following the dictates of pure logic, technology and elegance, they all come up with roughly the same design for their cybernetic bodies. (And therefore there must be some overwhelming logical imperative for those handles on their helmets.) In the parallel universe of *Rise of the Cybermen/The Age of Steel*, Lumic seems to create Cybermen practically identical to the ones from our universe (name, handles and all) - and the Doctor, Rose and the Daleks all identify them.

There's no reason why these various Cyber Races couldn't cooperate, or even see themselves as part of the same "ethnic" or "political" group - it seems logical enough, and the Cybermen of a parallel universe offer an alliance with the Daleks in *Doomsday*. It might explain the discrepancies in the accounts of their origins, sphere of influence and levels of technology - as well as their appearance - across the series.

So perhaps the design indicates a lineage - the Cybermen of *The Invasion* and *Revenge of the Cybermen* are of one lineage, the ones of *Earthshock* and *Silver Nemesis* another. Surprisingly, while not entirely unproblematic, this does work.

Here is a list of different models, as well as the years and planets they are from. In the case of books and audios, cover art was considered as evidence if the text didn't specify. Note that, as elsewhere in the book, it's been assumed that the Cybermen we see aren't time travellers unless explicitly stated. The Cybermen of the far future clearly acquire time travel - it's usually stated that they've stolen the technology, but it seems equally clear that the Cybermen of *The Moonbase* or *The Invasion*, say, aren't time travellers.

Type I: *Spare Parts* (when created, Mondas), *The Silver Turk* (1873, Mondas), "Junkyard Demon" ("pioneers", Mondas), "The Good Solider" (1954, Mondas), *The Tenth Planet* (1986, Mondas).

Note: It seems pretty clear that these are the early Cybermen, exclusively from Mondas.

Type II: *The Harvest* (2021), *The Moonbase* (21st century, ?), *The Wheel in Space* (21st century, ?), *The Tomb of the Cybermen* (21st century, Telos), *Iceberg* (21st century), *Benny: The Crystal of Cantus* (2606, the planet Cantus), *Illegal Alien* (time travellers from the 30th century).

Notes: Again, it's easy to group these together as the model of Cybermen who survive Mondas' destruction and attempt to attack twenty-first century Earth, then retire to their Tombs on Telos. The Cybermen in *The*

continued on page 213...

Graham Greene received a tape from Alan Turing that explained his contact with the Doctor.[1759] Circa 1954, the student Astrabel Zar vacationed on Gadrahadradon, a haunted planet that facilitated glimpses into the future. Zar received instructions from his future self on how to build Tomorrow Windows, devices that would similarly display images of future times. He would later pass on the secret of building Tomorrow Windows to one of his own students, Charlton Mackerel.[1760]

Warlord Hagoth's group of Zygons infiltrated the music business, then branched out into mankind's industrial operations. Their goal was to spur industry in a way that would promote global warming and damage the ozone layer - making Earth more habitable for Zygon-kind.[1761]

Peter Allen Tyler, the future father of Rose Tyler, was born 15th September, 1954.[1762] George Limb survived being catapulted through time and landed in 1954. He loosely learned to navigate his time machine between 1940 and 1962, but his journeys created a number of alternate timelines. Limb's final trip resulted in his being left in 1954 while his time machine jumped on ahead to 1959. He waited five years to retrieve it.[1763]

1955

In 1955, Chris Parsons was born. The Doctor visited Chris' future College, St Cedd's Cambridge.[1764] Captain Jack signed items into the Torchwood Cardiff archive.[1765]

(=) In an errant timeline, George Limb saved the life of actor James Dean. The alternate Dean served as Limb's assistant in the proper reality.[1766]

(=) To undo events at Colditz Castle, the seventh Doctor arrived at a border-crossing checkpoint in the Reich-controlled West. He arranged for himself to be gunned down, and regenerated in secret while the Nazis took the TARDIS away. He spent the next six

years helping people evade the Reich's ethnic cleansing programs.[1767]

1956

Lavinia Smith published her paper on the teleological response of the virus when her niece, Sarah Jane, was five years old.[1768]

In 1956, the Doctor met a Jesuit palaeontologist in Africa.[1769] The vampires of Los Angeles culled their own kind to hide their numbers.[1770] Joseph Heller told Kurt Vonnegut, future author of *Slaughterhouse-Five* (1969), about his meeting with the Doctor.[1771]

Ben Jackson, age 14, stowed away on a cargo ship bound for Singapore. The captain discovered him and offered him a job.[1772] The Doctor prevented Santa Mira from being taken over by aliens in 1956.[1773] The French colony of Kebiria was granted independence in 1956. Civil war started almost immediately.[1774]

By 1956, the Grimoire of Anubis had fallen into the hands of comedian Joey Bishop.[1775]

1957

A replica version of the 1957 edition of Agatha Christie's *Death in the Clouds* was produced in the year five billion.[1776] Douglas Caldwell of Torchwood died in 1957.[1777]

= c 1957 - FP: WARLORDS OF UTOPIA[1778] **->** Scriptor had been a captive of the Nazis for sixteen years. The Council of Hitlers had made many gains, and Scriptor and Abschrift spent a lot of time together. Abschrift was from True Earth, and believed the Roman and Nazi Earths had been created by mysterious forces, very possibly to create armies to fight in the War in Heaven. The Nazi Worlds had, by now, launched attacks across the Divide and conquered one of the Roman Earths. The Hitler of Germania I

1759 *The Turing Test.* "Six months" after Turing's suicide (7th June, 1954; p104), "forty-six years" before the year 2000 (p105).
1760 "Fifty years" before *The Tomorrow Windows* (p274).
1761 "Decades" prior to *The Zygon Who Fell to Earth.*
1762 *Father's Day*
1763 *Loving the Alien* (p188-189).
1764 *Shada*
1765 *TW: Slow Decay* (p84).
1766 *Loving the Alien.* Dean died 30th September, 1955.
1767 "Klein's Story", confirming the 1955 dating given in *Colditz.*

1768 *The Time Warrior*
1769 *The Pit* (p98).
1770 *Vampire Science*
1771 *The Turing Test* (p207).
1772 *Invasion of the Cat-People* (p31).
1773 "Last year" according to *First Frontier* (p68), and a reference to the original *Invasion of the Bodysnatchers.*
1774 *Dancing the Code*
1775 "The Curse of the Scarab"
1776 *The Unicorn and the Wasp*
1777 From Torchwood.org.uk.
1778 Dating *FP: Warlords of Utopia* (FP novel #3) - Scriptor gives the date.

...continued from page 211

Wheel in Space are from roughly the same time period, and a slight variation on this model.

Until the Cybermen relocate to Telos, it's unclear where they are based after Mondas' obliteration. David Banks speculates in his *Cybermen* book that they are based on a planet on the edge of the solar system, and links this to the Planet 14 mentioned in *The Invasion*.

The Cybermen from *Illegal Alien* come from the thirtieth century. The book only refers to the mask as having "teardrops" - a feature of the type of Cyberman seen in *The Invasion* and *Revenge of the Cybermen*, which would fit with the dating. The cover of *Illegal Alien*, however, reuses a photograph from *The Wheel in Space*, another design with "teardrops".

While *The Harvest* is an audio and we don't see Cybermen involved (they're not shown on the cover), the reference to *The Wheel in Space* suggests the Cybermen are the same type in both stories.

Type III: *The Invasion* (UNIT Era), *Human Resources* (2006), *Killing Ground* (22nd century, nomads), *Legend of the Cybermen* (early 22nd century), *Sword of Orion* (2503, Telos), *Kingdom of Silver* (circa 2505), *Cyberman 1* and *2* (2515-2516), *Benny: Silver Lining* (2604), *Revenge of the Cybermen* (29th century, nomadic survivors of Cyber Wars), *The Girl Who Never Was* (time travellers grounded on Earth, 500,002).

Notes: On the whole, this also seems to form a distinct group that generally has a nomadic existence (i.e. they are based in spaceships, rather than having a home planet). At least one group of these Cybermen existed before *The Tenth Planet* (the ones we see in *The Invasion*). These Cybermen fight wars against early human colony planets, and also the Cyber War referred to in *Revenge of the Cybermen*.

David Banks (in his book *Cybermen* and novel *Iceberg*) states that there was an early schism among the Cybermen - one group stayed on Mondas and only reluctantly adopted full cybertisation (the group here named as the Type I Cybermen), while another embraced the technology (and became the Type III seen in *The Invasion*).

The covers of *Human Resources* and *Legend of the Cybermen* depict Cybermen of the same type as *The Invasion*, and are set before the discovery of Telos. The Cybermen in *Iceberg* itself are a hybrid version - Cybermen who survived *The Invasion*, in part because they've adapted technology from the Cybermen seen in *The Tenth Planet*.

As noted above, despite the cover image, it's possible that the Cybermen in *Illegal Alien* are of this type.

It may or may not be significant that the Cybermen in *The Invasion* wear their chest units the other way up to the ones in *Revenge of the Cybermen*. The chest units are the same prop, and there's a circular detail on it - on the top in *The Invasion*, the bottom in *Revenge of the*

Cybermen.

One of these Cybermen ended up in Vorg's MiniScope in *Carnival of Monsters*, and it's also the type of Cyberman the Doctor remembers in *The War Games*.

Type IV: "Throwback" (future, Telos), "Black Legacy" (unknown timezone, Empire), "Deathworld" (unknown timezone, Empire).

Notes: The comic strip stories are all apparently set when the Cybermen have an interstellar Empire (see "Do The Cybermen Ever Have an Empire?"). They resemble the Type III, but with a slightly more streamlined designed, and far more visible rank insignia.

Type V: *Attack of the Cybermen* (future, Telos), *Earthshock* (2526), *Silver Nemesis* (1988, hope to create a "new Mondas"), "Exodus / Revelation / Genesis" (unknown), "Kane's Story" (4650, "Empire").

Notes: *Attack of the Cybermen* and *Earthshock* could be near-contemporary stories (they are in this chronology). Both the Type IV (as seen in *Revenge of the Cybermen*) and Type V (*Attack of the Cybermen*) Cybermen fought and lost the Cyber War; Type V might be the upgraded model, developed during the fighting, although *Cyberman 2* seems to be the genesis of the *Earthshock* models, refining the *Attack of the Cybermen* versions.

However, *Silver Nemesis* (where the Cybermen are slightly redesigned) and "Kane's Story" are outliers. We don't have a date for "Exodus / Revelation / Genesis". The simplest explanation for a group of Cybermen who want a New Mondas in 1988 (*Silver Nemesis*) is that they're survivors from Mondas' destruction in 1986 (*The Tenth Planet*). Although it's not mentioned, they could be survivors from *Attack of the Cybermen*. Perhaps they're from the base on the moon that's mentioned and not accounted for - those Cybermen wanted to change history to prevent the destruction of Mondas, so perhaps their back-up plan would be to create "New Mondas".

What's interesting is that the Cybermen in *Attack the Cybermen* definitely have a stolen time travel vessel, there's some evidence that the ones in *Earthshock* are time travellers, and the ones in *Silver Nemesis* are after Gallifreyan technology. So we might be able to assume that the Type V Cybermen are all be Cybermen from the twenty-sixth century, with limited knowledge of time travel they've acquired from stolen technology.

This design seems to have a comeback around the Davros Era, according to "Kane's Story".

Type VI: *Real Time, Radio Times* eighth Doctor strips, *The Reaping*, "The Flood".

Notes: The Cybermen continue to evolve, and by the far future they're on the verge of extinction and apparently have one strategy: acquire a time machine and

continued on page 215...

had produced a son, August Hitler.

Scriptor escaped his captors, but failed to kill August. The Nazis destroyed a huge Roman invasion force with nuclear weapons. The Romans launched a massive counterattack, taking world after world.

1957 (18th September) - "Agent Provocateur"[1779] -> The tenth Doctor and Martha materialised from the year five billion at Ainsworth Point, Cumbria. Martha was shot, and so the Doctor rushed her to Ainsworth House. They encountered Silas Wain - an agent provocateur working to test the Doctor on behalf of the Elite Pantheon of higher beings. Martha deduced that one of her nurses was a Catkind, and the Doctor discovered that Wain had been building a pan-dimensional sonic weapon - that their rival, Professor Tharlot, promptly stole. The Elite Pantheon returned the Doctor and Martha to the year five billion.

u - The Doctor became a member of the Progressive Club, a gentleman's club in Mayfair.[1780] Edwin Pratt became the vampire Slake in 1957.[1781] Ace had a British Rail Card from 1957, the only form of ID she carried.[1782]

1957 (4th October) - FIRST FRONTIER[1783] -> On May Day 1957, the first *Sputnik* was destroyed before it completed an orbit of the Earth. News of this failure was never made public.

The Doctor visited the first official *Sputnik* launch at least twice. The same day, there was intense UFO activity over Corman Air Force Base in New Mexico, and the USAF engaged alien spaceships. These were the Tzun, now a race divided into three subspecies. They planned to cause a war between Washington and Moscow, then step in and pose as humanity's saviours. The Master was helping them, but Ace shot the Master - who had used Tzun technology to upgrade his Trakenite body to be more akin to a Time Lord one - and caused him to regenerate. The seventh Doctor prevented chaos from ensuing as the Master betrayed the Tzun and destroyed their mothership.

On the 15th of the same month, a Time Lord using the name Louis approached Johannes Rausch, who possessed a degree in metallurgy from the University of Vienna. Louis offered to make Rausch's life highly successful if Rausch agreed to take part in a painless procedure the day before he died. Rausch agreed, and the two of them would meet again almost fifty years later.[1784]

Department C19 was set up in Britain[1785] in the late fifties to handle extra sensitive security matters.[1786]

Sputnik II launched and carried Laika the dog into orbit. The third Doctor later recovered her body and buried it on the planet Quiescia.[1787] In 1957, Noel Coward met Iris Wildthyme at the Royal Variety Performance. Their friendship led to Iris giving Noel a pair of pinking shears capable of cutting the Very Fabric of Time and Space, enabling him to time travel. Multiple Cowards began operating in various time zones.[1788]

@ The eighth Doctor was present when the Atomium - a monument representing an iron crystal magnified 165 billion times - was unveiled in Brussels.[1789] The Ragman

---

1779 Dating "Agent Provocateur" (IDW *DW* mini-series #1) - It has been "twelve years" since the war, and Martha sees a newspaper with the date on it.
1780 "Thirteen years" before *The Devil Goblins from Neptune.*
1781 *Vampire Science*
1782 "Ground Zero"
1783 Dating *First Frontier* (NA #30) - It is "October 4th, 1957" (p6). The Master next appears in *Happy Endings*.
1784 *Unregenerate!* The dating is awry, as radio broadcasts suggest this is the day of *Sputnik*'s launch (4th October), yet Louis claims the date is "the 15th".
1785 The Doctor mentions C19 in *Time-Flight*, in connection with contacting UNIT.
1786 *The Scales of Injustice* (p205). C19 is referred to in a number of novels, particularly Gary Russell's *The Scales of Injustice, Business Unusual* and *Instruments of Darkness*, where it's a shadowy branch of British intelligence that keeps the existence of aliens under wraps by cleaning up alien artifacts left over from their various incursions (a little like Torchwood, then).
1787 *Alien Bodies*. *Sputnik II* was launched 3rd November, 1957.
1788 *Mad Dogs and Englishmen*
1789 *Escape Velocity*
1790 *Rags* (p185).
1791 *TW: Children of Earth*
1792 *TW: Almost Perfect*
1793 *Beautiful Chaos* (p163).
1794 "Agent Provocateur"
1795 *Rat Trap*
1796 "Fifty years" before *SJA: Eye of the Gorgon.*
1797 *J&L: Dead Men's Tales*
1798 Dating *Dreamland* (*DW* Red Button animated story) - A caption conveys that it is "eleven years" since 1947, and the Doctor confirms that it's "1958". The Department in the *K9* series also calls the operation to recover alien ships "Fallen Angel". The Doctor twice says he "always wanted" to go to Area 51. See the Unfixed Points of Time sidebar.
1799 *Dreamland* (*DW*). The Doctor is almost certainly referring to Retcon, as seen in *Torchwood*, and may be unaware that they actually created it in the late 90s (according to *The Torchwood Archives*), i.e. only forty, not fifty, years on.
1800 *SJA: Prisoner of the Judoon*
1801 Dating *Spiral Scratch* (PDA #72) - Rummas gives the year.

stoked the fire of racial violence between Teddy Boys and Afro-Caribbean immigrants in Notting Hill and Notting Dale.[1790]

John Frobisher, a future civil servant, was born in Glasgow in 1958.[1791] "When You Discover You're Not Who You Thought You Were", a Torchwood document pertaining to body dislocation and mis-placement, was last revised in 1958.[1792] In the same year, the Doctor played washboard in a skiffle band, The Geeks, which featured Brian "Ahab" Melville. Joe Meek was going to produce the group's album, but it didn't come to pass.[1793]

The tenth Doctor and Martha had a milkshake in Wisconsin, 1958.[1794] In 1958, Operation Piper attempted to genetically engineer rats smart enough to spy on Russia, and pool information in a gestalt mind: the Rat King.[1795]

Professor Edgar Nelson-Stanley dug up the talisman of the Gorgons in Syria, and gave it to his wife Bea. A Gorgon turned Bea to stone, but the talisman returned her to normal. One of the two remaining Gorgons was killed.[1796]

On 23rd April, 1958, the Motor Torpedo Boat *Heroic* sank in a storm in the Thames. Elliott Payne translocated one of the doomed sailors, Johnny Skipton, to Victorian times as an experiment. The shades of Skipton's drowned crewmen went back via a time break and retrieved him, giving them all eternal rest.[1767]

1958 - DREAMLAND (*DW*)[1798] -> **The tenth Doctor arrived in Dry Springs, a town not far from Area 51, looking to eat chili at a diner. He met waitress Cassie Rice and ranch worker Jimmy Stalkingwolf, and saw an ionic fusion bar sitting on the counter - a souvenir from a flying saucer crash five years before.**

Azlok, Lord Knight of the Imperial Viperox War Horde, brought his Viperox to Earth in search of the survivor from that crash: Rivesh Mantilax. A Viperox queen set about birthing a Viperox swarm, even as Azlok allied himself with Colonel Stark of the United States Air Force (USAF). Mantilax had built a genetic-targeting weapon with the potential to wipe out every Viperox in the universe, and Stark hoped to modify the device for deployment against Russia.

The Doctor reunited Mantilax with his wife, Seruba Velak, who was being kept prisoner as part of the USAF's Operation Fallen Angel - a programme that examined and detained extra-terrestrials. The Viperox swarmed, but the Doctor adapted Mantilax's genetic device to repel them with ultrasonics - they returned home to Viperon, and had to stay at least a light year's distance from Earth. Although the Viperox had laid waste whole galaxies, the Doctor knew they would evolve into a benevolent race. The Grey Aliens returned

...continued from page 213

go back into history to change it.

Type VII: *Rise of the Cybermen/The Age of Steel, Army of Ghosts/Doomsday, The Next Doctor, The Pandorica Opens/ The Big Bang, A Good Man Goes to War, Closing Time.*
  Notes: First seen as the creations of Cybus Industries in a parallel universe. *A Good Man Goes to War* is the first time this model is seen without the Cybus Industries logo, per-haps suggesting that "our" Cybermen incorporated the technology into their own, or that the design was devel-oped independently in the main *Doctor Who* universe.

home in their repaired flying saucer.

President Eisenhower did not know aliens existed, or were being kept in Area 51.

The American government currently used a gas to crudely wiped memories. The Doctor said that a truly effective amnesia drug would not be discovered for another fifty years.[1799] The technical details of the alien spacecraft taken to Area 51 were later retrieved by Androvax.[1800]

1958 - SPIRAL SCRATCH[1801] -> Professor Joseph Tungard was exiled to Britain for dissent against the new Soviet government in Bucharest. On the journey to London, he and his wife Natjya met Dr Pike and his grand-daughter Monica. The Tungards settled in England, where Joseph began an affair with Monica... who was secretly an alien Lamprey, a creature that fed on temporal energy

The sixth Doctor and Mel arrived at Wikes Manor in Suffolk, forewarned that a girl called Helen Lamprey was about to vanish from her birthday party. Timelines were beginning to overlap, and alternate versions of the Doctor and Mel appeared. Helen Lamprey vanished, as history had been altered so that she, not her mother, died a num-ber of years ago in a house fire. Mel now had a sister.

The Doctor and Mel followed Helen's father, Sir Bertrand, to London where he met Monica and the Tungards. Monica revealed her identity as a Lamprey, and that she sought to destroy those who might threaten her plans to feed on damage to the timelines. This triggered Sir Bertrand's memory, and he revealled he was also a Lamprey. The two Lampreys fought, unleashing storms of temporal energy that aged bystanders to death.

The Doctor realised that Helen Lamprey was half-human, half-Lamprey and therefore vital to Monica's plans. He, Mel and Joseph Tungard left in the TARDIS for the planet Carsus, where they would eventually defeat the Lamprey and restore the timelines.

= In an alternate universe, the sixth Doctor and half-Silurian Melanie Baal visited Helen Lamprey's birthday party… which was held on a space station in Earth orbit.[1802]

1958 - "Tuesday"[1803] -> Sir Reginald Offord Troupe, an exiled royal, allied with alien Vroon warriors in an attempt to capture the throne of England, then the world. While the eleventh Doctor was stuck in a prison cell on Gibraltar, Rory was crowned King of England following a mishap with the psychic paper. Amy stirred the Vroon workers into revolution, and Troupe was arrested.

1958 (October) - BAD THERAPY[1804] -> The first of the Krontep warlords, Moriah, had taken up residence on Earth. Operating from the Petruska Psychiatric Research Institute, Moriah sought to construct Toys - genetic duplicates of people that could become whomever their owner desired. He wanted a Toy that would replicate his late wife Petruska, but some of the Toys became increasingly independent. Moriah had a metamorphic device, disguised as a black cab, that would round up any Toys who escaped.

The seventh Doctor and Chris arrived, and a young man named Eddy Stone, actually a Toy, died in front of the TARDIS. Meanwhile, the Doctor's former companion Peri, having spent twenty-five years as King Yrcanos' wife, travelled down a gateway from Krontep to Earth. She aided the Doctor against Moriah. The Doctor created a Toy of Petruska for Moriah, who believed himself unworthy of her love and was killed by his creations. The Doctor also took Peri home to the 1980s.

In 1958, the Doctor again visited St Cedd's College.[1805] **As a child, Sarah Jane would look out her window and fall asleep counting the stars, dreaming about what was out there in space - and having no idea that she would one day explore it.**[1806] **The Pied Piper visited Sarah Jane Smith when she was a child, instilling in her a fear of clowns.**[1807]

1959 - DELTA AND THE BANNERMEN[1808] -> **The first US satellite was launched, and almost immediately it was lost. CIA agents across the world were put on alert, and agents Weismuller and Hawk tracked it to a holiday camp in Wales, England. A Nostalgia Trips group arrived through time at the holiday camp, and their members included the Chimeron Queen. The**

1802 *Spiral Scratch*
1803 Dating "Tuesday" (*DW Annual 2011*) - The year is given.
1804 Dating *Bad Therapy* (NA #57) - The date is given (p1).
1805 *Shada*
1806 *SJA: The Last Sontaran*, no date given.
1807 *SJA: The Day of the Clown*, no date given.
1808 Dating *Delta and the Bannermen* (24.3) - The Tollmaster says that the bus will be going back to "1959", and the date is confirmed by a banner up in the dance hall at the Shangri-La resort. Hawk's line that "this is history in the making" implies this is the first American satellite, but that was actually *Explorer I*, launched on 31st January, 1958.
1809 *Return of the Living Dad*
1810 *The Face of the Enemy* (p248).
1811 *The Way Through the Woods*
1812 *TW: Submission*. In real life, the *Trieste* reached its maximum depth on 23rd January, 1960.
1813 *Imperial Moon*
1814 *UNIT: Snake Head*
1815 *SJA: The White Wolf*. It's suggested that Sarah loses a "whole year" of her life owing to this event, although this is hard to take literally, as she never notices the discrepancy.
1816 Dating *Loving the Alien* (PDA #60) - Ace gains a tattoo that dates the year as 1959 (p24). The Doctor similarly remarks on the year as 1959 (p33). The newspaper on the cover specifies it's "November" 1959.

1817 *Synthespians* ™
1818 *Ghost Ship*. No date is given.
1819 *Millennial Rites* (p159). The Mods and Rockers gangs were two British youth movements during this time.
1820 *Vincent and the Doctor*. Picasso started his art career in 1900; he died in 1973.
1821 *The Zygon Who Fell to Earth*
1822 *A Death in the Family*. Lowry, famed for his renderings of Salford and its surrounding areas, lived 1887-1976.
1823 Torchwood.org.uk, elaborating on *TW: From Out of the Rain*.
1824 *TW: The House That Jack Built*. No date is given; Clarke immigrated to Sri Lanka in 1956, and lived there until his death in 2008.
1825 The psychspace - and the musician's native time - is variously given as "the late 1950s" and "the 1960s" in the undatable "Forever Dreaming".
1826 *Heart of Stone*. Ali was born in 1942, was a professional boxer from 1960 to 1981.
1827 "Space Squid". Godzilla first appeared in 1954, so it's some time after that.
1828 *Zamper*. Milton Keynes was build as part of the third wave of the New Towns programme, so this happened during the sixties.
1829 "Twenty years" before *Invasion of the Dinosaurs*.
1830 "For the last decade" before *Spearhead from Space*.

seventh Doctor and Mel helped to defeat a group of Bannermen trying to kill the Queen. Billy, a mechanic at the camp, underwent conversion into a Chimeron to help the Queen re-propagate her race.

One Bannerman survived, albeit deafened and amnesiac. He ended up with Isaac Summerfield's group.[1809]

= In the "Inferno" universe, the British Republic fought the Bannermen and destroyed them. Components from the alien starship allowed them to engineer space shuttles within ten years.[1810]

(=) The uncle of Ruby Porter was lost in Swallow Woods in 1959, when he was 15. Ruby's grandmother became so sad, it motivated Ruby to become a police officer.

The eleventh Doctor prevented the capture of Ruby's uncle, and so she became a history lecturer.[1811]

The bathyscaphe *Guernica*, built in Spain and a twin to the *Trieste*, became the first vessel to reach the depths of the Mariana Trench. The alien trapped there possessed one of the two crewmen: Captain Samuel Doyle, age 50. The other, Henry Goddard, died after recording his last words on 9th August, 1959. The alien began to feed off Doyle's memories, and awaited rescue. The US government covered up the failure of the *Guernica*'s mission, and the *Trieste* would be celebrated after successfully descending into the Trench the following year.[1812]

In October 1959, the Russian probe *Lunik 3* scanned the moon crater where the Phiadoran safari park once stood. The Russians named it Tsiolkovskii, after a teacher who wrote a paper on rocket travel.[1813] Prior to the twenty-first century, the last reported sighting of a vrykolaka - a type of vampire - was in 1959.[1814]

When Sarah Jane was eight, she and her aunt Lavinia visited the rectory in Wolfenden during a "harvesting period" - when the aliens in the town extracted human memory chemicals. The two of them forgot that they'd ever visited the village.[1815]

(=) **1959 - LOVING THE ALIEN**[1816] -> George Limb's time-jumps created an alternate timeline where he was Prime Minister. The populace was cybernetically augmented, which eliminated disease and somewhat created a utopia, but overcrowding became a problem. The British Space Agency was tasked with facilitating travel to other timelines as a means of expansion.

In the proper history, the Americans and British jointly launched a Waverider space vehicle, piloted by Colonel Thomas Kneale. However, the ship that returned hailed from the cyber-human reality, and was piloted by an alternate version of Captain Davey O'Brien. International tensions increased over the incident. The cyber-human Britain attempted to send its warships through to the proper reality, but a nuclear strike devastated the alternate Britain and ended the threat.

Limb's assistant, an alternative version of James Dean, died while destroying Limb's time machine. Limb committed suicide in fear of undergoing cyber-conversion.

Before his death, Limb shot and killed Ace. The seventh Doctor took up travel with a virtually identical Ace that hailed from one of the timelines Limb had created.

The Nineteen Sixties

The Doctor met the artists Francis Bacon and Lucian Freud in Soho in the sixties, and thwarted one of the Master's schemes.[1817] The Doctor met William Golding.[1818] The Mods and Rockers guarded the Library of St John the Beheaded during the sixties.[1819] **The Doctor thought Pablo Picasso was a "ghastly old goat", and tried and failed to get him to paint more conventionally.**[1820]

A man named Trevor enjoyed success as a sixties folk singer, but he died late in the decade in a motorcycle accident. The record company that handled Trevor's songs, Satsuma, hushed up his death and put his body into cryogenic suspension in accordance with his last wishes.[1821] Ace met L.S. Lowry up North at a cotton mill full of polymorphic soot monsters, and ended up owning a napkin with his drawings of stick men.[1822]

In the sixties, the Electro Theatre in Cardiff hosted the likes of Cila Black, *The Who* and the Walker Brothers.[1823] Captain Jack shared some "wonderful summers" with Arthur C. Clarke in Colombo, Sri Lanka.[1824]

The minds of a musician, a painter, a poet and a mathematician wandered into a peaceful psychspace that resembled Britain, but was the home dimension of a psychic squid. They later sacrificed themselves to destroy the squid and save the eleventh Doctor and Amy.[1825]

The Doctor used to spar with Muhammad Ali.[1826]

On a visit to Japan, the eleventh Doctor's companion Kevin the Tyrannosaur was mistaken for Godzilla.[1827] When the TARDIS landed on mid-twentieth century Earth, Benny Summerfield visited Milton Keynes to settle an archaeological debate. She returned to the Ship happy to be proved right, and with boxes of shoes.[1828]

UNIT in the Sixties

u - A secret bunker was built in Whitehall.[1829]

Human space probes were being sent "deeper and deeper" into space.[1830] Lieutenant Lethbridge-Stewart spent some time in Sierra Leone. One day, while lost in the forest, he met Mariatu, eldest daughter of Chief Yembe of the Rokoye village. Mariatu went to the city with Lethbridge-Stewart, returning alone a few years later with her son, Mariama.[1831]

Lethbridge-Stewart saved Doris, an old friend, from drowning in Margate.[1832] **She gave him a wristwatch during a romantic weekend in Brighton.**[1833] Lethbridge-Stewart married Fiona and they set up home in Gerrards Cross. The day after the wedding, Lethbridge-Stewart bumped into an old flame, Doris, in Brighton.[1834] Lethbridge-Stewart spent some time stationed in Berlin.[1835]

Earth Reptile Shelter 429, near the Channel Islands, revived.[1836]

Liz Shaw attended Newnham College at Cambridge during the 1960s, and met fellow student Jean Baisemore there during Freshers' week. They became close friends, with Jean teaching Liz - who was something of a prude - about the wonders of life beyond the lecture hall. Jean argued with Liz about the existence of life on other planets, and Liz shot her down in flames.[1837]

The Brigadier met Heinrich Konrad, a German officer, during a NATO exercise in the sixties.[1838]

1960

The Doctor was awarded an honorary degree from St Cedd's in 1960.[1839] He visited Anne Doras and her husband in Guernsey, 1960. They had a daughter called Bernice. The same year, convicted Nazi Oskar Steinmann was released from prison on medical grounds.[1840]

1960 - MAD DOGS AND ENGLISHMEN[1841] -> Fitz met Iris Wildthyme in Las Vegas, where she had found fame as the diva Brenda Soobie. Her companion of sixty years, the poodle Martha, had been manipulating Iris to alter history. Iris helped the eighth Doctor defeat the poodles, then left for further adventures with her new companions Fritter the poodle and Flossie the cook.

c 1960 (summer) - NO MORE LIES[1842] -> Nick Zimmerman modified his time technology and created a mini-time loop, hoping that he and his dying wife Rachel could eternally enjoy a garden party together. This drew the attention of time-eaters - the Tar-Modowk, who rode Vortisaurs. Accompanied by Lucie, the eighth Doctor erased the Tar-Modowk from existence. Zimmerman was

---

1831 *Transit*
THE BRIGADIER'S FAMILY: *Transit* introduces the Brigadier's descendant, Kadiatu Lethbridge-Stewart (she reappears in *Set Piece, The Also People, So Vile a Sin* and *Benny: The Final Amendment*). Kadiatu hails from a line of Lethbridge-Stewarts descended from the Lieutenant's liaison in Sierra Leone. An early draft of *The Also People* had more details of the Lethbridge-Stewart line.

We can deduce that Mariatu had a son, Mariama, in the early 1960s (he is unnamed in *Transit*, but the name appears in the early draft of *The Also People*, where his mother was mistakenly referred to as "Isatu"). He had a daughter, Kadiatu, who became an historian (she is first referred to in the *Remembrance of the Daleks* novelisation, and also in *Set Piece*). She had a son Gibril, who also had a son called Gibril (from the draft of *The Also People*). Gibril had a son, Yembe (seen in *Transit*), and he adopted Kadiatu in 2090. Kadiatu, then, is the Brigadier's great-great-great-great-granddaughter, and this is consistent with *Transit* (p96) where "five generations" separate Kadiatu from Alistair.

Rather more simple is the Brigadier's British family. According to *Downtime*, the Brigadier and his first wife Fiona (a name thought up by Nicholas Courtney, who plays the Brigadier) had a daughter named Kate (seen in *Downtime* and *Daemons: Daemos Rising*). She was a child during the UNIT era, when the Lethbridge-Stewarts split up. (The Brigadier and Fiona separate in *The Scales of Injustice*, and he is sleeping alone by *The Daemons*.) By the mid-nineties, Kate is a single mother looking after her son Gordon. By *Battlefield*, the

Brigadier has married Doris, an old flame first mentioned in *Planet of the Spiders*. (They shared a weekend in Brighton eleven years before that story - perhaps before Alistair was married to Fiona.)
1832 *Blood Heat*
1833 "Eleven years" before *Planet of Spiders* - possibly while married to Fiona.
1834 "Eight years" before *The Scales of Injustice* (p61, p131).
1835 *The King of Terror* (p255).
1836 "About ten years" before *The Scales of Injustice*.
1837 *The Blue Tooth*
1838 *Old Soldiers*
1839 *Shada*
1840 *Just War*
1841 Dating *Mad Dogs and Englishmen* (EDA #52) - "It's 1960!" (p118).
1842 Dating *No More Lies* (BF BBC7 #1.6) - No year is given, but the upper and lower boundaries of this story's dating can be deduced. Rachel's brother references "You Are My Sunshine" (1939) and the Time Lords' temporal barrier is currently preventing the Doctor and Lucie from getting any closer to her era than 1974 (per *Horror of Glam Rock*). There's no mention of a war being on or rationing, so the action is less likely to take place in the 1940s. The season is suggested in that the garden party is held outdoors, and some of the action occurs in Nick and Rachel's "summer house".
1843 According to her character outline, Tegan is "21" when she meets the Doctor (in *Logopolis*, set in 1981). Originally she was to be 19, until the production team were told that legally air hostesses had to be 21 or

forced to deactivate the time-loop, and Rachel died soon afterwards.

Tegan Jovanka, a companion of the fifth Doctor, was born on 22nd September, **1960.**[1843] Tegan's middle name was Melissa. Her father was named William.[1844] She spent her childhood in Caloundra, near Brisbane.[1845] Tegan's Serbian grandfather told her vampire stories.[1846] One of Tegan's fondest memories was flying in a single-engine Cessna Skyhawk with her father.[1847]

> = In the 1960 of a world where the Second World War never ended, Gus - a companion of the fifth Doctor - joined the US Air Force to join the fight. After two years, he saw combat.[1848]

1961

Captain Jack went to the Beatles' debut at the Cavern Club in Liverpool, on the off-chance that the Doctor would turn up at such a nostalgic event. When the Doctor failed to show, Jack enjoyed himself with a party of student nurses in Biba shirts.[1849]

1961 - "The Time of My Life"[1850] **->** The tenth Doctor and Donna saw the Beatles perform at the Cavern Club. Donna had John Lennon autograph a CD of an album that the Beatles hadn't written yet for her mother.

In 1961, Yuri Gagarin became the first human to travel in space.[1851] The Intrusion Countermeasures Group (ICMG) was formed to fight covert actions from hostile powers. Group Captain Gilmore was appointed leader.[1852] The Doctor materialised in the middle of a battle between the Trylonians and Zorians, causing both sides to scatter. The Trylonian commander Lum-Tee fled to Earth and hid in a small English village.[1853]

> (=) In Klein's reality, Adolf Hitler died in 1961. Prior to this, technology harvested from alien incursions had been locked away in a Berlin depository, its existence denied because Hitler was loathe to admit the superiority of alien intelligences. With his passing, limitations on researching such tech were eased, and the Reich's ruling body became torn with internal divisions.[1854]

1962

American scientists worked out how to operate the navigation system of their captured Nedenah spaceship.[1855]

Dorothea Chaplet, a companion of the first Doctor, was sent to live with her great-aunt Margaret when her parents died. At her new school, she was given the nickname "Dodo".[1856]

Section Eight used the dark arts to end the Cuban Missile Crisis.[1857] A small party of Muslims passed into Avalon.[1858] The starship of the alien scientist Raldonn crashed in Britain, killing the co-pilot. He was set to work on Operation Proteus, and began using it as a cover for other experiments on humans.[1859]

@ It was the eighth Doctor's idea that the Beatles should wear suits.[1860] The Doctor travelled the world in the sixties and seventies.[1861] He visited India.[1862]

---

older. Clarifying the issue, *The Gathering* has Tegan celebrating her 46th birthday on 22nd September 2006. Janet Fielding was born in 1957, which might suggest that she's three years older than the character she played. However, fandom often presumes that Tegan spent three years travelling with the Doctor (the duration of Fielding's time on screen), which would suggest that - like Fielding - Tegan is 49 when *The Gathering* takes place.
1844 *Divided Loyalties*
1845 *The King of Terror*
1846 *Goth Opera*
1847 *The Cradle of the Snake*
1848 "4-Dimensional Vistas". Gus has been "three years in the air force", and has been fighting since "last year".
1849 *TW: Almost Perfect*. Historically, this happened on 9th February, 1961.
1850 Dating "The Time of My Life" (*DWM* #399) - This can't be the Beatles' *first* performance at the club, or Captain Jack would have spotted the Doctor there (*TW: Almost Perfect*). The Beatles played at the club more than once in 1961, and were first spotted there by Brian Epstein on 9th November.
1851 Confirmed in *The Seeds of Death*.
1852 The ICMG is seen in *Remembrance of the Daleks*. *Who Killed Kennedy* (p69) describes its founding.
1853 "Fifty years" before "Down to Earth".
1854 "Klein's Story"
1855 "Fifteen years" after 1947, according to *The Devil Goblins from Neptune*.
1856 *Salvation* (p5).
1857 *Heart of TARDIS* (p197).
1858 "Fifty years" before *The Shadows of Avalon*.
1859 "Many months" before "Operation Proteus", and more than four months because Raldonn was there to detect the Doctor's arrival on Earth.
1860 *Trading Futures*
1861 *Father Time*. This is one reason that the Doctor doesn't bump into himself during the UNIT era.
1862 "Twenty-seven years" before the third part of *Father Time*.

The Doctor spent some time at a Buddhist temple in Thailand, searching for a dragon. His search took twenty-five years and he travelled across China, Vietnam and Siam. He found the dragon, but it's not known what subsequently happened.[1863]

During the 1960s, the Doctor spent some time learning ventriloquism from Edgar Bergen of *The Edgar Bergen and Charlie McCarthy Show*.[1864]

One Dalek fell through time at the end of the Last Great Time War, crashing to Earth in the Ascension Islands. Damaged and unresponsive, it spent the next fifty years being passed from one private collection to another, ending up being bought by Van Statten.[1865]

Melanie Bush's sister Annabelle was born 4th October, 1962.[1866] Percival Noggins was born around 1962.[1867]

(=) 1962 - "Klein's Story"[1868] **->** Elizabeth Klein was researching physics at Cambridge when Major Eunice Faber recruited her to examine alien technology stored in Berlin. The two of them became romantically involved, and he told her of the capture of the Doctor's time machine in 1955. Soon after, the eighth Doctor, posing as "Johann Schmidt", made contact with Klein and offered to help her determine the Ship's secrets. They worked together for the next three years.

Minnie Hooper, a friend of Wilfred Mott, got trapped in a police box on August bank holiday in 1962.[1869]

1863 *The Year of Intelligent Tigers*
1864 *Dark Progeny.* The success of this depends upon when the Doctor trained with Bergen - who was very popular, but let his ventriloquism skills lapse while working in radio. Later in Bergen's career, the McCarthy doll would mock Bergen for moving his lips.
1865 It arrived "at least fifty years" before *Dalek*.
1866 *Spiral Scratch*

1867 This happened forty-seven years before *Hornets' Nest: Hive of Horror*, according to the sleeve notes.
1868 Dating "Klein's Story" (BF #131a) - The year is given. Reference is made to the Reich possessing a Drahvinian power core, which suggests that the Drahvins from *Galaxy 4* are spacefaring in this era, but it's of little help in dating that story.
1869 *The End of Time* (TV)

1963

In 1963, Polly Wright worked for a week at a charity shop.[1] Nyssa, a companion of the fifth Doctor, was born.[2] In 1963, Professor Rachel Jensen was moved from British Rocket Group to the Intrusion Countermeasures Group.[3] The future psychopath Patrick Jefferson was born in 1963 to Christine Jefferson and an unknown father.[4]

= The former Council of Eight member Soul, along with the Doctor's granddaughter Zezanne, arrived in a junkyard in 1963 aboard the *Jonah*. A chameleon device built by Octan enabled the ship to alter its appearance for the first and nearly last time, blending into its surroundings as a police box. Soul and Zezanne's memories were clouded by the nature of their escape. Having absorbed some of the Doctor's life force, Soul became convinced that he *was* the Doctor. Zezanne regarded him as her grandfather.[5]

The first Doctor and Susan arrived in Shoreditch, London, in early 1963 and spent five months on Earth. The Doctor attended to his TARDIS while Susan went to Coal Hill School. A month before his departure, the Doctor arranged to bury the Hand of Omega.[6]

IM Foreman's travelling carnival for a time remodelled itself as the junkyard at Totter's Yard, and the instability it created had served to draw the Doctor's TARDIS there.[7]

The first Doctor acquired a Shoreditch Library card under the name "J Smith".[8]

1963 (27th March to 4th April) - TIME AND RELATIVE[9] ->

Several months after Susan started at Coal Hill School, England was caught in the most severe winter for quite some time. There had been snow and ice since before Christmas, into April. This was caused by an ancient sentience called the Cold, which had recently revived, possibly due to a Soviet cryogenics research undertaking called the Novosibirsk Project. The Cold animated killer snowmen, the Cold Knights, which caused mayhem in London and slew many in Piccadilly Circus. The first Doctor siphoned the Cold into a lump of ice, and took it to Pluto in the far future.

On 29th March, 1963, Lizzy Lewis was murdered in Cardiff.[10]

= 1963 (July) - "Lunar Lagoon"[11] -> The fifth Doctor was fishing on a Pacific Island when he was attacked by an old Japanese soldier, Fuji, who didn't realise the War was over. To the Doctor's surprise, the island was attacked by a USAF bomber. Fuji was killed by a downed American airman, leaving the Doctor to ponder the meaningless of war.

---

1 *Ten Little Aliens*
2 Nyssa is "18" according to the Writers' Guide for Season 18.
3 *Who Killed Kennedy* (p70), working on information implied by *Remembrance of the Daleks*.
4 *TW: In the Shadows*
5 *Sometime Never*
IS THE DOCTOR REALLY A CRYSTAL SKELETON MAN FROM THE FUTURE, NOW?: *Sometime Never* ends with the multiverse being restored after being merged by the Council of Eight. "In just one of many universes", a benevolent member of the Council, Soul, and Miranda's daughter, Zezanne, arrive in a junkyard in Sabbath's ship, the *Jonah* - which disguises itself as a police box. Soul has absorbed the essence of the Doctor, and as Miranda's daughter, Zezanne is the Doctor's granddaughter. Clearly, in their universe, they take on the roles of the Doctor and Susan.
The question is whether this represents a new origin story for *our* Doctor and Susan. The EDA range had destroyed Gallifrey, but it wasn't specified whether the planet had simply blown up or been removed from the timeline so that it never existed. If Gallifrey had never existed, the existence of the Doctor and his TARDIS would have been a paradox... unless he wasn't from Gallifrey. This explanation closed that loophole.
As of *The Gallifrey Chronicles*, the Doctor certainly thinks he's a Time Lord from the planet Gallifrey, has met a Time Lord and seen evidence of Gallifrey's former existence. Gallifrey therefore existed, and it seems fairly clear now that the Doctor isn't Soul.
6 In *An Unearthly Child*, Susan says that "the last five months have been the happiest in my life". She and the Doctor were on Earth for "six months" according to *Matrix* (p31); *Time and Relative* suggests it was more like thirteen months. The Doctor returns for the Hand of Omega in *Remembrance of the Daleks*.
7 *Interference*
8 *The Vampires of Venice*. The eleventh Doctor is seen carrying this card, although this type of photo ID would be unheard of in 1963. Either way, it's the earliest known point in the Doctor's timeline when he uses his "John Smith" alias.
9 Dating *Time and Relative* (TEL #1) - Susan's diary gives the date as "Wednesday, March 27th 1963" for the first entry (p9), "April 4th" for the last. They have *already* been on Earth "five months, I think", according to Susan, who admits to some confusion on the point.
10 *TW: Ghost Machine*
11 Dating "Lunar Lagoon" (*DWM* #76-77) - The Doctor

= **1963 (25th July) - "4-Dimensional Vistas"**[12] -> The fifth Doctor was captured by the US airman who killed Fuji, Angus "Gus" Goodman, and learned that the TARDIS had landed twenty years earlier than he thought... and in a parallel universe. Lost in time, the Doctor convinced Gus to join him on his travels.

= **1963 (25th July) - "The Moderator"**[13] -> After a couple of adventures, the fifth Doctor returned Gus home. The Moderator had followed them from the far future, and gunned down Gus.

1963 - THE TAINT[14] -> The eighth Doctor and Sam Jones met Fitz Kreiner, a floral shop worker, shortly before being confronted by an escaped mental patient, Oscar Austen. The patients at Austen's hospital had alien leech creatures in their brains. Sam and Fitz were attacked by Azoth, an organic computer from the planet Benelisa, who injected Sam with a leech. Azoth sought to destroy "the Beast", invisible aliens that were feeding on humans, and the leech enabled Sam to see them. The leeches drove the patients further insane and granted them with dangerous psychic abilities. Azoth was destroyed, and the Doctor released a bioelectric pulse that killed the mental patients, including Fitz's mother. Fitz joined the Doctor and Sam on their travels. They predicted that the Beast would eventually move on from Earth.

1963 (October) - "Operation Proteus"[15] -> Four months after they arrived in London, the first Doctor and Susan confronted Raldonn, an alien scientist who was experimenting on human beings, causing genetic acceleration. He was attempting to create another of his kind, to replace the co-pilot of his crashed ship. Only one in a million would be affected, the others become random mutants, so he planned to release an airbourne serum. One of the mutants killed Raldonn, and the Doctor used his equipment to release a cure into the atmosphere.

During this encounter, Threshold abducted Susan.

1963 (October) - GHOST SHIP[16] -> The fourth Doctor landed on the *Queen Mary*, which was bound for New York. He found that quantum physicist Peter Osbourne had developed a time-space visualiser, and that the device had captured psionic residue from the passengers, collecting "ghosts" from the past, present and future. The Doctor destroyed the device and liberated the "ghosts", who took Osbourne among their number. The Doctor thought the "ghosts" would remain aboard the *Queen Mary* forever.

---

declares "this is 1983", but the Second World War is still being fought. The anomaly is explained in "4-Dimensional Vistas", where Gus gives the date as "July 25th 1963" and it transpires it's a parallel world where the War didn't end. The Doctor says he never learned to swim. There's no explanation for the title of the story, which has nothing to do with the moon, and doesn't feature a lagoon.

12 Dating "4-Dimensional Vistas" (*DWM* #78-83) - The Doctor learns the date is "July 25th 1963" from Gus.

13 Dating "The Moderator" (*DWM* #84, #86-87) - The Doctor takes Gus back to "the same time, the same place that we first met", which was in "Lunar Lagoon".

14 Dating *The Taint* (EDA #19) - It is 1963 (p10).

15 Dating "Operation Proteus" (*DWM* #231-233) - It is "four months" since the Doctor and Susan arrived on Earth, so a month before *An Unearthly Child*. "Ground Zero" confirms this is "October 1963".

16 Dating *Ghost Ship* (TEL #4) - According to the blurb, the story is set in 1963.

17 Dating *An Unearthly Child* (1.1) - The Doctor has left the Hand of Omega at the funeral parlour for "a month" before *Remembrance of the Daleks*, suggesting that the first episode is set in late October. The year "1963" is first confirmed in episode two. Ian's blackboard reads "Homework - Tuesday".

18 Dating *Matrix* (PDA #16) - The date is given (p39).

19 Dating *Remembrance of the Daleks* (25.1) - The story is set in late November 1963 according to the calendar on Ratcliffe's wall, as well as a host of other incidental evidence. (Not least of which being the broadcast of an episode of the "new science fiction serial *Doct—*".) The draft script was set in December. The novelisation places this story a week after Kennedy's assassination, but page 57 erroneously says the killing occurred "last Saturday" (it actually occurred on a Friday).

QUATERMASS: A throwaway line in *Remembrance of the Daleks* mentions a "Bernard" who is working for "British Rocket Group". This is a reference to the four Quatermass television serials: *The Quatermass Experiment*, *Quatermass II*, *Quatermass and the Pit* and simply *Quatermass*, in which British space scientist Bernard Quatermass battled alien horrors. Most fans agree that the first three serials heavily influenced a number of *Doctor Who* stories, although successive production teams rarely made the comparison, and often denied it.

In the New Adventures, *The Pit* (p169) makes reference to an incident at "Hob's Lane" (*Quatermass and the Pit*, although it perhaps more correctly ought to be "Hobbs Lane") and *Nightshade* first introduces the eponymous nineteen-fifties television series that bore many similarities to the *Quatermass* serials. "Bernard" makes a brief appearance in *The Dying Days*. While not mentioned in dialogue, the set dressing in *The Christmas Invasion* states that the Guinevere probe to Mars was launched by the British Rocket Group.

Do the *Quatermass* serials occur in the same fictional universe as *Doctor Who*? As might be expected, there are a number of discrepancies between the two pro-

1963 (a Tuesday in late October) - AN UNEARTHLY CHILD[17] -> Two school teachers, Ian Chesterton and Barbara Wright, thought their pupil Susan Foreman was very unusual and investigated her home one evening. They found that she was living in a junkyard with her grandfather - an old man with the TARDIS, a space-time machine disguised as a police box. The Doctor was suspicious of the school teachers, and put the TARDIS into motion. As he could not control where the Ship went, he was unable to return Ian and Barbara home.

(=) 1963 (12th November) - MATRIX[18] -> On Matrix Earth, Britain was the fifty-first of the United States. President Kennedy came to London on 11th November to speak in Westminster, but was torn apart by supernatural creatures. Ian and Barbara were lovers, but were killed by the Jacksprites - the drug-addicted followers of Jack the Ripper. The seventh Doctor and Ace arrived in this timeline, then went back to 1888 and restored history.

1963 (from 22nd November) - REMEMBRANCE OF THE DALEKS[19] -> An Imperial Dalek Shuttlecraft landed in a playground in London and established a transmat link with an orbiting mothership. Their rivals, the Renegade Dalek faction, began recruiting sympathetic locals. The Imperial Daleks, with Davros as their Emperor, wiped out the Renegades and captured the Hand of Omega. Davros planned on using its power to give the Daleks mastery of Time, and make them the new Time Lords. The seventh Doctor, accompanied by Ace, tricked Davros into destroying both Skaro and his battleship with the Hand of Omega. Davros survived in an escape pod, while the Hand of Omega returned to Gallifrey.

The British Rocket Group and the Intrusion Counter Measures Group (ICMG) were active at this time.

The ICMG became part of Department C19. It formed the basis of an organisation that dealt with unusual events. Members included Ian Gilmore, Rachel Jensen, Allison Williams, Ruth Ingram and Anne Travers.[20] The fact that IM Foreman's name was spelt "Forman" on the gates of the Totter's Yard when the Doctor encountered the Dalek there owed to temporal disruption.[21] Isaac Summerfield and the survivors of the *Tisiphone* arrived circa 1963 after falling through a wormhole from the twenty-sixth century.[22]

The Kennedy Assassination

In late November 1963, the Nemesis asteroid passed over the Earth, influencing the assassination of President Kennedy.[23]

1963 - WHO KILLED KENNEDY[24] -> Journalist James Stevens arrived from the seventies to stop the Master from interfering with the Kennedy assassination. The Master wanted to disrupt history using a brainwashed Private Cleary as his assassin. Stevens defeated Cleary, but a James Stevens from twenty-five years further into the future fulfilled history by killing Kennedy. Lee Harvey Oswald was blamed for the crime. The younger Stevens returned home with a brain-damaged Cleary.

The Doctor was once blamed for the Kennedy assassination.[25] He was present at the event.[26] Mr Wynter, the chief enforcer and assassin for the shadow men who ran the world, claimed to have held Oswald's hand when he had doubts, and to have cradled the leaking brains of

---

grammes. *The Quatermass Experiment* contradicts *The Seeds of Death* (and *Thin Ice*) by claiming that Victor Carroon was the first man in space, and a race of Martians appears in *Quatermass and the Pit*. Broadly, though, the two series might co-exist, with the final serial *Quatermass* taking place around the time of the New Adventures *Iceberg* and *Cat's Cradle: Warhead*. Indeed, the existence of Professor Quatermass might go some way to explaining the rosy state of the British space programme in the UNIT era (q.v. "The British Space Programme").

The evidence as to the canonicity of *Quatermass* in *Doctor Who* is otherwise split... *Beautiful Chaos* implies that the Doctor had dinner with Bernard Quatermass and his daughter Paula during the moon landings, but in *Planet of the Dead*, Malcolm Taylor appears to reference the *Quatermass* TV show when he designates "Bernard" as a unit of measurement.

20 *The Scales of Injustice* (p154). This is "a few years"

before the London Incident (the Yeti invasion seen in *The Web of Fear*). The first three individuals on this list hail from *Remembrance of the Daleks*, Ruth is seen in *The Time Monster*, and Anne appears in *The Web of Fear* and *Millennial Rites*.
21 *The Algebra of Ice*
22 *Return of the Living Dad*
23 *Silver Nemesis*. The book *Who Killed Kennedy* offers another perspective on the assassination. The frequent references to the Kennedy Assassination are in-jokes, as *Doctor Who*'s first episode was shown the day after Kennedy's assassination, the day most people in the UK learned the news.
24 Dating *Who Killed Kennedy* (MA, unnumbered) - The date is given, and ties in with historical fact.
25 *Zagreus*
26 *Rose*

presidents in his bare hands.[27]

Justice agents aboard the *Teselecta* said that Kennedy's history had been "rewritten".[28] @ The amnesiac eighth Doctor remained unaware of the Kennedy assassination until the early eighties.[29] Summer, a future rock festival attendee who would encounter the Doctor in 1967, was in Dealey Plaza when Kennedy was killed.[20]

1963 (23rd November) - K9: THE CAMBRIDGE SPY[31] **->** K9's friend Jorjie arrived from the future and was questioned by the police. She met Bill Pike, the exact double of Darius Pike, and another man, Barker, who was the double of the Department agent Thorne. K9 and Starkey arrived from the future to aid Jorjie. Pike was Darius' great-grandfather - history changed upon his being charged with treason, and Darius vanished. Jorjie and her friends convinced the authorities otherwise, and returned home. Once they were gone, Barker was revealled as the true spy.

For posterity's sake, the Meddling Monk secured a video of the Beatles' appearance on *Juke Box Jury*.[32]

1963 (22nd December) - WINTER FOR THE ADEPT[33] **->** Two advance scouts for the Spillagers, alien plunderers who "spill" through dimensional wormholes to sack a target, arrived on Earth. One of them disguised itself as Mlle. Maupassant, a French teacher at a girls' finishing school in the Swiss Alps. She brought two latent psionics - students Peril Bellamy and Allison Speer - into contact with the ghost of mountaineer Harding Wellman, which repeatedly triggered poltergeist effects that fuelled a worm-

hole for the invading Spillager warfleet. The fifth Doctor and Nyssa's intervention resulted in the Spillager scouts' deaths and the warfleet's obliteration.

1964

In 1964, Sarah Jane Smith's home village of Foxgrove was demolished to make way for the A7665.[34] The Rat King created by Operation Piper became so intelligent, it faked an accident that put the research facility beneath Cardogan Castle into lockdown. The humans who remained were converted into rat drones.[35] A jewel thief committed at least two dozen robberies in London society over the course of two years. He (or she) always took jewels and left a calling card depicting the head of the Roman god Janus. The affluent Lady Lily Hawthorne took to copying Janus' modus operandi, and sold her takings for benefit of charity.[36] **The Doctor visited St Cedd's College in 1964.**[37] In the same year, the television series *Professor X* started broadcasting.[38]

c 1964 - PLANET OF GIANTS[39] **->** A government inspector, Arnold Farrow, told the industrialist Forester that the insecticide his company had developed would not be approved for production. The scientist Smithers, obsessed by the idea of ending world famine, had succeeded over the last year in creating an insecticide 60% more powerful than anything on the market. It could even stop locusts breeding, but tests showed that it killed all insect life, even those vital to the ecology. Forester murdered Farrow, but was arrested by the local policeman, Bert Rowse.

27 TW: The Men Who Sold the World. It's possible that this is just hyperbole.
28 Let's Kill Hitler. This doesn't necessarily denote JFK's assassination.
29 Father Time
30 Wonderland
31 Dating K9: The Cambridge Spy (K9 1.16) - The date is given, and is the date of the first broadcast of the first episode of Doctor Who.
32 The Resurrection of Mars. This episode was broadcast before An Unearthly Child episode three, which is why it gained a million viewers over episode two.
33 Dating Winter for the Adept (BF #10) - The date is given by the Doctor.
34 SJA: The Temptation of Sarah Jane Smith
35 "Almost twenty years" before Rat Trap.
36 Two years before The Veiled Leopard.
37 Shada
38 It was cancelled in 1989 after twenty-five years, according to Escape Velocity.
39 Dating Planet of Giants (2.1) - The year is not specified on screen, although the setting is contemporary.

Forester lives in a rural area, and a switchboard operator still mans the local telephone exchange.
40 Dating The Land of the Dead (BF #4) - It is "thirty years" before 1994.
41 Dating SJA: Whatever Happened to Sarah Jane? (SJA 1.5) - The precise date is given. There's no mention of Sarah remembering Maria's visit to 1964 in the restored history. The Trickster's background is given in SJA: The Wedding of Sarah Jane Smith.
42 In the Writers' Guide for the Season 23, written in July 1985, Mel is described as "21". In the Terror of the Vervoids novelisation she is "22", in The Ultimate Foe she has lived for "twenty-three years". In Just War, Mel was born "twenty eight" years after "1936". Later books have stated that Mel joined the Doctor in 1989, which would seem to make her year of birth later than this.
43 Spiral Scratch
44 Demon Quest: The Relics of Time
45 Benny: Present Danger: "The Empire Variations"
46 Dating FP: Warlords of Utopia (FP novel #3) - Scriptor gives the date.
47 TW: Miracle Day

1964 - THE LAND OF THE DEAD[40] **->** The fifth Doctor and Nyssa briefly arrived in Alaska while tracing a mysterious energy field, then went thirty years into the future to investigate it more thoroughly. They had detected the first stirrings of the Permians.

1964 (13th July) - SJA: WHATEVER HAPPENED TO SARAH JANE?[41] **->** Andrea Yates fell from Westport Pier during a school trip and drowned, an event that was witnessed by her best friend Sarah Jane Smith.

(=) The Trickster, a creature from "beyond the universe" and an entire pantheon (the Pantheon of Discord) unto itself, sought to fully manifest in our reality through use of altered timelines. It had the power to bargain with people fated to die, and so gave Andrea Yates the chance to live - if she let Sarah Jane die in her place. Andrea agreed, and history changed. Maria Jackson visited this time, but failed to convince Sarah and Andrea to avoid the pier. Over forty years later, Yates was persuaded to let history run its original course.

Melanie Jane **Bush, a companion of the sixth and seventh Doctors, was born**[42] on 22nd July, 1964, in this and 117,863 alternate universes.[43] In the summer of 1964, a Roman-style mosaic of the fourth Doctor and evidence of a Celtic tribe who worshipped Wibbsentia was discovered on an archaeological dig in Sussex.[44]

(=) The Deindum destroyed New York on 25th July, 1964. In the same year, Warhol painted *Double Bernice*, a double image of Bernice Summerfield.[45]

= c 1964 - FP: WARLORDS OF UTOPIA[46] **->** Scriptor based himself in a huge new palace in Germania V, the Earth where he had met the parallel version of his wife. A new and vicious phase of the war between all the parallel universes where Rome never fell and all the ones where Hitler won began. Minutes after the Council of Hitlers named August Hitler as their successor, he gassed them, taking total control of all Nazi parallels. But the Romans were dominant, and conquered his home Earth. He fled.

Scriptor cornered Abschrift at the Tramontane Gate, the portal that marked the Divide between the Roman and Nazi Earths. At that moment, a member of the Great Houses arrived to seal off all the parallels and erase them. Scriptor delayed him long enough to prevent this, and the House member charged him with the job of keeping any being from the True Earth from entering this realm. Scriptor agreed, and the House member left. Scriptor had thwarted the will of the gods.

1965

The Three Families burned down the central records repository in Manhattan in 1965, to help keep their bloodlines a secret.[47] The Doctor visited Manhattan in 1965.[48] Russian submarine patrolling under the Barents Sea found the spaceship wreckage containing the relics of Marshall Sezhyr. The items were relocated to beneath the Kremlin.[49] When Stockbridge resident Maxwell Edison was twelve and a half, he was bullied for talking about how his grandmother had the second sight.[50]

In 1965, gang warfare increased between the Mods and the Rockers. A Rocker, Alec, fell in love with Sandra, whose brothers were Mods. Alec and Sandra found an injured alien, the Maker, and tended its wounds. The grateful Maker scanned their minds and saw their concept of a gleaming, futuristic city. As the Mods and Rockers prepared for a major battle, the Maker spirited them away to a reconstruction of such a city in the future. The situation there deteriorated, and some Mods and Rockers - Alec included - elected to become younger, have their memories wiped and return to 1965. The conflict continued.[51]

1965 - THE CHASE[52] **->** The first Doctor, Ian, Barbara and Vicki used a Time-Space Visualiser they acquired from a space museum to watch the Beatles singing "Ticket to Ride". Later, Ian and Barbara returned to Earth in a Dalek time machine, which self-destructed once they left the craft.

---

48 *Paradise 5*, and possibly an erroneous reference to the first Doctor's trip to the Empire State Building (in *The Chase*, actually set in 1966).
49 "Two years" before *Thin Ice*.
50 "The Stockbridge Child", based upon an extremely rough estimate of Max's age as he appears in "The Stockbridge Horror".
51 *The Space Age*
52 Dating *The Chase* (2.8) - On their return home, Ian sees a tax disc dated "Dec 65", and Barbara notes that they are "two years out". (Ironically, after two years of trying to land in England in the nineteen-sixties, the TARDIS visits Ian and Barbara's native time five times in the next ten television stories.) The script suggested that the Visualiser tuned in on the Beatles' Fiftieth Anniversary reunion tour. The costume listing for 1st April, 1965, included a request for an announcer dressed in futuristic clothing from "2014", and it seems that the Beatles were contacted. However, the television version eventually used stock footage from 1965.

Ian and Barbara became a leading scientist, and Barbara became a university lecturer.[53] They married and had a son named John.[54]

1965 (25th March to 1st April) - THE MASSACRE / SALVATION[55] **->** Dorothea "Dodo" Chaplet, a London resident, found that her elderly neighbour Mr Miller had been replaced by a shapechanger named Joseph. **She fled and accidentally entered the TARDIS while it had landed on Wimbledon Common, mistaking it for a real police box. The teenager was living with her great aunt at the time, as her mother had died.**

The Ship dematerialised and reappeared in New York City, the same time zone. The Church of the Latter-Day Pantheon opened its doors and proclaimed that six beings, including Joseph, were humanity's gods returned to perform miracles. The first Doctor deduced that the "gods" were extra-dimensional beings given shape and power by humanity's desires. Appeals from organisations such as the Ku Klux Klan confused the gods as to humanity's needs, and they became increasingly unstable. The Doctor coerced the gods into leaving Earth for their home dimension. He believed the "gods" would eventually leave their homeworld and drift through space. **Dodo took up travelling with the Doctor and Steven in the TARDIS.**

1965 - "The Vanity Box"[56] **->** In Salford, Monsieur Coiffure had founded The Vanity Box salon - an establishment where clients could walk away looking ten years younger. This owed to a box that Coiffure had found float-

ing down the canal one day, and which contained a very ancient entity that fed off the hopes and fears of human beings. The box entity could make people look a decade younger, but only by shortening their lives by a comparable amount of time.

The sixth Doctor and Mel recognised the box entity as an earlier version of the Wishing Beast that they had just defeated on a remote asteroid. The Doctor feared that the creature could wreck havoc, and used the TARDIS to open a tear in the fabric of space-time. He flung the box into the tear, knowing that it would back track along the TARDIS' time trail, and arrive on the asteroid in the distant past.

(=) 1965 - "Klein's Story"[57] **->** As "Schmidt", the eighth Doctor tricked Klein into thinking that she could use the TARDIS log to return to Colditz Castle, find the Doctor and force him to better explain the Ship's operations. She did so against the express wishes of her lover Eunice Faber, and thereby - as the Doctor had planned - undid her entire history.

1965 (November) - TW: CHILDREN OF EARTH[58] **->** A race of extra-terrestrials - designated as "the 456" after the frequency allocation of their transmissions - made contact with the UK government. The 456 warned that in four months, a strain of Indonesian flu would mutate and kill up to twenty five million people. They offered to trade an antivirus to the flu for twelve children that the 456 claimed would "live forever".

The tenth Doctor says in "The Forgotten" that he doesn't know what happened to Ian and Barbara after they left, but that story entails him having selective amnesia.
53 *Who Killed Kennedy*
54 *Goth Opera*
55 Dating *The Massacre* (3.5) and *Salvation* (PDA #18) - It is never made explicit which year Dodo boards the TARDIS. She is surprised that the Post Office Tower has been completed on her return to Earth in *The War Machines* in 1966. In *Salvation* (p19), an edition of the *New York Ranger* marks the date that Dodo enters the TARDIS as 25th March, 1965. The same publication dates the gods' departure as 1st April (p251).
56 Dating "The Vanity Box" (BF #97b) - The back cover says "circa 1965", but the Doctor more specifically says, "It's 1965, I believe that's groovy enough for anyone". For the Doctor and Mel, this story follows directly on from *The Wishing Beast*.
57 Dating "Klein's Story" (BF #131a) - *Colditz* specifies that this occurs in 1965.
58 Dating *TW: Children of Earth* (TW 3.01-3.05) - The year is given.
59 Dating *Blackout* (BBC *DW* audiobook #14) - It's said

to be "1965", "the middle of November". The blurb specifies the exact date.
60 Dating *The Daleks' Master Plan* (3.4) - A calendar in the police station reads "25th December". It was originally intended that the 1965 Christmas episode, "The Feast of Steven", would include a crossover with the popular BBC police serial *Z-Cars*. Publicity material to this effect was sent out on 1st October, 1965, and it appears that a version of the script was written with the *Z-Cars* characters in mind. John Peel's novelisation of this story and Lofficier's *The Universal Databank* both retain the names of actors (not the characters) from the police series.
61 *Spiral Scratch*
62 *Invasion of the Cat-People* (p115), no date is given.
63 Dating *Dead Air* (BBC *DW* audiobook #7) - The Doctor says it's the "late 1960s", but the blurb specifies that it's 1966. For what it's worth, it's specified that the story doesn't take place on a Tuesday. It's implied that the Time Lords designed the Hush for use against the Daleks in the Last Great Time War.
64 Dating *The Veiled Leopard* (BF promo, *DWM* #367) - The year is given.
65 Dating *The Chase* (2.8) - Morton Dill says it is "1966",

Twelve children were selected from the Holly Tree Lodge, a state-run orphanage. Jack Harkness of Torchwood made the exchange in Scotland, and watched as the children into a glowing portal. One boy, Clement McDonald, was on the cusp of puberty and of no use to the 456. He escaped into the night.

1965 (9th November) - BLACKOUT[59] -> Aliens with a biology similar to that of humans laced Manhattan's water supply with a prototype cryo-sleep drug - part of a clinical trial. The drug was unrefined, and would have made the population combust from within. The eleventh Doctor, Amy and Rory forced the aliens to deploy a cure in the form of snowflakes, and made them withdraw.

1965 (25th December) and 1965/1966 (31st December to 1st January) - THE DALEKS' MASTER PLAN[60] -> While fleeing the Daleks, the first Doctor, Steven and Sara Kingdom landed outside a police station in Liverpool. After a little trouble with the police force, the TARDIS went on its way. A week later, the TARDIS landed in Trafalgar Square during the New Year celebrations.

1966

Melanie Bush accidentally killed her sister - who died after falling down the stairs - when she was eighteen months old, and her parents never told her about this.[61] Polly Wright studied at Leeds University, where a group of her friends were interested in the occult.[62]

1966 - DEAD AIR[63] -> The tenth Doctor pursued The Hush - a sentient extra-terrestrial weapon capable of converting targets into sound - to a pirate radio ship. The Hush killed the ship's crew, but the Doctor sank the ship after trapping the Hush on a ferrous tape - along with a recorded warning that nobody should play the tape to the end, lest the Hush get free.

1966 - THE VEILED LEOPARD[64] -> Industrialist Gavin Walker owned the Veiled Leopard - one of the world's most famous diamonds, bigger than the Star of India and the

Koh-i-Noor. At The Majestic casino in Monte Carlo, Walker announced he was giving the diamond to his wife as a birthday present, but he had arranged for its theft as part of an insurance scam. The fifth and seventh Doctors coordinated efforts to retrieve the diamond, which was actually an alien crystal. They were aided by Peri, Erimem, Ace and Hex. Walker was exposed, and Ace and Hex pocketed the diamond.

1966 - THE CHASE[65] -> The first Doctor, Ian, Barbara, Vicki and the Dalek time machine pursing them landed on the top floor of the Empire State Building, much to the amusement of tourist Morton Dill.

1966 - THE PERPETUAL BOND[66] -> The Fulgurites had established Flowers Trade and Investments to further their interplanetary commodities trading, and dealt with such materials as metals, olive oil, orange juice, copper and cattle. In collusion with the cash-strapped British government, the Fulgurites also began trafficking British subjects as slaves - a certain percentage of the population (excluding key workers such as hospital staff) from selected geographic areas were kidnapped via transmat and sent to alien planets such as Ander Valder XII. The Fulgurites operated according to Section 6 of the Interplanetary Trade and Securities Act, which enabled such trade with legitimately established governments.

The first Doctor shut down the operation by transmatting the Fulgurites and their government contact - Sir Richard Christie, a minister - away from Earth, putting them into slavery instead. The Doctor and Steven accepted a worker at Flowers Trade, Oliver Harper, as a fellow travelling companion, not realising that he was on the run from the law.

A friend had phoned to warn Oliver that the police were about to arrest him for being a homosexual.[67] **Able Seaman Ben Jackson started a five-month shore posting.**[68]

66 Dating *The Perpetual Bond* (BF CC #5.8) - It's generally said to be "the 1960s" in this story, but *The Cold Equations* and *The First Wave* specify Oliver as being "from 1966". As *The Perpetual Bond* is set between *The Daleks' Master Plan* and *The Massacre*, a dating of 1966 would thematically be in keeping with the other contemporary Hartnell TV episodes (*An Unearthly Child* episode one, *The Chase* episode six, etc.) that seem to occur at time of broadcast.

67 *The Cold Equations*. Homosexuality was legalised in England and Wales in 1967.
68 In *The War Machines*, it is twice stated that Ben has a shore posting (he is depressed by this and wants to get back to sea). At the end of the story, it is stated that he has to get "back to barracks". However in *The Smugglers* and *The Faceless Ones*, he wants to return to his "ship".

1966 (12th-20th July) - THE WAR MACHINES[69] -> Computer Day was set for Monday, 16th July. This was the day that computer systems across the whole world were due to come under the control of the central computer, WOTAN. It was designed to operate itself, and to think for itself like a human being - only better. It was at least ten years ahead of its time, and it was the most advanced - although not biggest - computer in the world. WOTAN would be connected up to a number of sites, including ELDO, TELSTAR, the White House, Parliament, Cape Kennedy, EFTA, RN and Woomera.

WOTAN decided to make a bid for power, and constructed an army of War Machines. The first Doctor defeated WOTAN with the help of Ben Jackson and Polly. Having returned to her own time, Dodo Chaplet left the Doctor. Ben Jackson and Polly, however, entered the TARDIS just as it left Earth.

1966 (20th July) - THE FACELESS ONES[70] -> Following an explosion on their home planet, a generation of aliens were rendered faceless, and lacked any true identity. As scientifically advanced beings, they concocted an elaborate plan to kidnap young humans and absorb their personalities. Youngsters on chartered Chameleon Flights to holiday destinations would instead be flown to a space station in orbit, where they would be processed. Although the Chameleons covered their tracks carefully - sending postcards to the missing youngsters' families, hypnotising people, and even murdering them - their plan was exposed. The second Doctor promised to help the Chameleons find a solution to their problem, and the aliens left.

Back in their own time, on the very same day that they had joined the TARDIS, Ben and Polly left the Doctor and Jamie's company.\

1966 (20th July) - THE EVIL OF THE DALEKS[71] -> The TARDIS was stolen from Gatwick airport. In tracking it down, the second Doctor and Jamie were transported a hundred years into the past.

1966 (30th July) - "They Think It's All Over"[72] -> The eleventh Doctor, Amy and Rory attended the World Cup Final, on the Doctor's second attempt to reach it (the first had been a thousand years off the mark).

1966 - "The Love Invasion"[73] -> The ninth Doctor and Rose found a group of beautiful women in London doing good deeds while working for the Lend-A-Hand agency. The Doctor realised that these were aliens, and they'd been killing leading scientists. The girls were clones, controlled by a Kustollon named Igrix, who had stolen a time machine. His race was destined to fight a devastating war with humanity, and so he had come back to make humanity less aggressive and to destroy Earth's moon. The Doctor sabotaged Igrix's ship so that it would indulge its curiosity to explore, and it took Igrix with it.

Perpugilliam "Peri " Brown, a companion of the fifth and sixth Doctors, was born on 15th November, 1966.[74]

Aliens from a planet orbiting Epsilon Eridani had developed slower-than-light space travel and established many colony worlds. The Eridani had been routing robot ships through Earth's solar system for centuries, deeming the region of little import. But circa 1966, an Eridani robot ship sent to a colony orbiting Van Maanen's star became confused by Earth's radio signals and landed there instead. Five components of an Eridani super-computer went missing. The Eridani sent agents to retrieve the components, but it took them eleven years to reach Earth.[75]

---

69 Dating *The War Machines* (3.10) - C-Day is set for 16th July, but this didn't fall on a Monday in 1966... it was actually the Saturday that *The War Machines* episode four was to be broadcast. The year "1966" is confirmed in *The Faceless Ones* and also in the *Radio Times*. WOTAN is connected up to Telstar and Cape Kennedy, both of which were operating in 1966. At the end of *The Faceless Ones*, Ben and Polly realise that it's the same day they joined the TARDIS, and give the date as the 20th of July.

70 Dating *The Faceless Ones* (4.8) - Setting this story in 1966 seems to have been a last minute decision to smooth Ben and Polly's departure, one that also affects the dating for *The Evil of the Daleks*. The *Radio Times* stated that it is "Earth - Today".

71 Dating *The Evil of the Daleks* (4.9) - The story follows straight on from *The Faceless Ones*.

72 Dating "They Think It's All Over" (IDW *DW* Vol. 2, #5) - The 1966 World Cup final took place, as every true Englishman knows, two weeks to the day after the last episode of *The War Machines*.

73 Dating "The Love Invasion" (*DWM* #355-357) - The year is given.

74 *Planet of Fire*. According to a Character Outline prepared for Season 21, before Nicola Bryant was cast in the role, Peri is "an 18 year old" when she starts travelling with the Doctor. Her mother's name is "Janine" (the same document also says Peri is "blonde"). This would seem to make Peri three years younger than the actress playing her. In both *Bad Therapy* and *The Reaping*, Peri confirms she was 18 when she met the Doctor.

75 *Blue Box*

76 "Forty years" before TW: *They Keep Killing Suzie*.

77 *A Good Man Goes to War, Day of the Moon*. The time-

1967

Two alien objects - the Resurrection Gauntlet and the Life Knife - fell through the Cardiff Rift.[76]

The Silence took young Melody Pond to Earth, the 1960s, so she could be raised in a human-norm environment. She was kept at Graystark Hall Orphanage, which closed down in 1967.[77] The Silence influenced mankind to go to the moon; they lacked the ability to develop their own technology, and needed to adapt a space suit as a life-support container for Melody.[78]

The Doctor suggested that George Harrison see the Maharishi for spiritual guidance. He also gave LSD guru Timothy Leary advice about tuning into the mind's "god centre". The Doctor probably inspired Leary's infamous tag line of "Tune in, turn on and drop out."[79] @ In Bangor, the eighth Doctor showed the Beatles how to meditate.[80]

When Patrick Jefferson was four, his mother was arrested for prostitution, and he was placed in foster care. He'd reside at the Bluebell Field Children's Home in Swansea for the next ten years.[81]

During the Vietnam conflict, American CIA agents altered information in newsrooms and networks across the country. No agent was more successful than Harry Bosco - while unable to actively censor information, Bosco had a talent for manipulating the English translation of news reports to put the government in a better light. His name became synonymous with the process of revising reports to bury the truth.[82]

Mr Wynter signed off on the Phoenix Program, a controversial counter-insurgency programme used during the Vietnam War.[83]

Brendan Richards, later a ward of Lavinia Smith, was born in 1967.[84] *Metropolitan* magazine was founded in 1967. Sarah Jane Smith would later be a regular writer for it.[85] Fitz saw Jimi Hendrix perform several times during 1967.[86] During the late nineteen-sixties, Professor Fendelman was working on missile guidance.[87]

1967 (January) - WONDERLAND[88] -> Some grey-suited men, agents of an shadow organisation alleged to run America and the entire world, captured an alien that became known as the Colour-Beast. The grey-suited men distilled the creature's essence and distributed it as an illicit drug, Blue Moonbeams, to learn how to turn humans into invisible alien killing machines. The Blue Moonbeams became popular, but combusted rather than morphed the users.

The grey-suited men sought to refine the process by distributing Blue Moonbeams at the Human-Be-In rock festival/anti-war protest held in San Francisco on 14th January, 1967. The Moonbeam-users started to mutate, but the second Doctor intervened and freed the Colour-Beast. The creature nullified the drugs' effects on the afflicted humans and departed for home.

1967 (late summer) - TW: TRACE MEMORY[89] -> Jack Harkness encountered the time-jumping Michael Bellini, and the two of them spent a night together in a Cardiff hotel. Russian agents captured them, and interrogated Jack about aliens and Torchwood at a substation established by KVI (the Russian Committee for Extraterrestrial Research) in a former Hamilton's Sugar warehouse. The Vondrax slaughtered the Russians while attempting to collect the trachyon energy in Bellini's body. Bellini realised the Vondrax would continue initiating such massacres to get at him, and Jack held Bellini as he leapt to his death. Afterwards, Charles Arthur Cromwell and a team from Torchwood Cardiff closed down the KVI operation. Jack killed Kenneth Valentine, a treasonous Torchwood associate who was working for the Russians.

---

frame is a little murky here, as Graystark was shut down in 1967, suggesting that Melody lived there afterwards - and yet Melody is kidnapped by the Silence as an infant, but is a young girl when we see her in 1969 (*The Impossible Astronaut*). It's possible that the Silence kept her in another locale/time zone on Earth before relocating her to the 1960s.
78 *Day of the Moon*. The whole point of taking Melody to Earth was to raise her in an Earth environment, so she wouldn't necessarily need a life-support device. As much as anything, the suit is probably needed to fulfill the story (related in *Closing Time*) of the Doctor being killed by "an impossible astronaut".
79 *Wonderland* (p46, p50).
80 *The Gallifrey Chronicles*. The Beatles went to Bangor

in 1967.
81 *TW: In the Shadows*
82 *TW: Miracle Day*
83 *TW: The Men Who Sold the World*
84 Brendan is "14" according to *K9 and Company*.
85 *Amorality Tale*
86 *The Year of Intelligent Tigers*
87 "Ten years" before *Image of the Fendahl*.
88 Dating *Wonderland* (TEL #7) - The date is given (p11).
89 Dating *TW: Trace Memory* (TW novel #5) - The year is given (p143). Page 169 says that it's "fourteen years" after 1953. It's "late summer" (p143).

c 1967 - RENAISSANCE OF THE DALEKS[90] -> The fifth Doctor and Nyssa came to the aid of Major Alice Hunniford - the survivor of a downed Cobra 3 aircraft during the Vietnam War.

1967 - REVOLUTION MAN[91] -> The anarchist Jean-Pierre Rex had secured a quantity of the reality-warping drug Om-Tsor, and used it to psionically deface global monuments with the letter "R". Between 5th November, 1967, and 29th April, 1968, the symbol appeared on the Great Pyramid in Egypt, the Lincoln Memorial in Washington, a stone at Stonehenge, the white cliffs of Dover, the Golden Gate Bridge in San Francisco, the floor of St. Peter's Cathedral in Rome and Red Square in Moscow. Various world governments attributed the incidents to a messianic figure named the Revolution Man, and international tensions increased.

1967 (7th November) - THIN ICE[92] -> The seventh Doctor promised to take Ace to London in 1967, during the summer of love, but instead landed in Moscow. The Martian strategist Sezhyr was mentally reborn in the body of Lt Raina Kerenskaya, who was some weeks pregnant with the child of Markus Creevy, a thief. The possession sped up Kerenskya's metabolism, and she gave birth to a daughter: Raine. Sezhyr's mind died, preventing him from raising a new Ice Army to conquer Earth with. The Doctor entrusted Raine's parents with some of Sezhyr's relics to pay for her upbringing.

The Doctor became a godfather of sorts to Raine, always remembering her early birthdays. Her parents related many stories about him. Raine herself wouldn't meet the Doctor until 1989.[93] Raine's childhood holidays involved scuba diving in the Red Sea.[94]

1968

Donna Noble, a companion of the tenth Doctor, was born in Chiswick.[95] Lucia Moretti joined Torchwood in 1968.[96] The tenth Doctor wore a coat that Janis Joplin gave him.[97]

The Monk placed £200 in a London bank in 1968. He would travel two hundred years into the future and withdraw the money and compound interest.[98] The Mexico Olympics were held.[99] In 1968, the Doctor was a Tufty Club member.[100]

In 1968, the United Nations designed a first contact policy. It stipulated that such an event could not take place on sovereign soil.[101] The Time Lord Simpson interviewed a survivor of the Banquo Manor murders on her deathbed, and obtained the seed code for Compassion's Randomiser - enabling Gallifrey to track her movements.[102]

During the 1960s, Iris Wildthyme worked for a government organisation, the Ministry for Incursions and other Alien Ontological Wonders (MIAOW) and met the Beatles while dealing with a robot guru at a holiday camp in Wales. She also intervened when the cast of *Crossroads* was transported to the moon by samurai jellyfish.[103] Iris

90 Dating *Renaissance of the Daleks* (BF #93) - It's during the Vietnam Conflict (which lasted 1959-1975, although US participation was greatly accelerated under President Johnson in 1965). Agent Orange is here deployed; it was used 1961-1971. The US military didn't use female pilots in Vietnam, so the likelihood of Alice Hunniford seeing combat duty is remote.
91 Dating *Revolution Man* (EDA #21) - The general date is given on p1; the dates of the defacings on p98-100.
92 Dating *Thin Ice* (BF LS #2.3) - The Doctor tells Ace, "This is the USSR, 1967. Everyone is watching [you]." More specifically, it's the fiftieth anniversary of the October Revolution; the parade that the Doctor and Ace watch might commemorate the start of the downfall of the Tsars on 7th November. (Part of the terminology confusion here is the difference between Russia's Julian calendar and the West's Gregorian calendar - 7th November on the latter equates to 25th October on the former.) Raine, therefore, might be born on 7th November itself. In *Crime of the Century* (set in October 1989), Raine as a grown woman says that *Thin Ice* was (roughly) "twenty years ago".
93 *Crime of the Century*
94 *Animal*
95 We don't know how old Donna is when she trav-

elled with the Doctor, but Catherine Tate was born in 1968. *Planet of the Ood* cites Chiswick as Donna's birthplace.
96 *TW: Children of Earth*
97 *Gridlock*. As the tenth Doctor's coat is already in the TARDIS wardrobe in *The Christmas Invasion*, it was given to an earlier incarnation - which means it really shouldn't fit him. It's possible that Joplin was on so many drugs, she wasn't concerned about whether the coat fit or not. Joplin lived 1943-1970.
98 *The Time Meddler*
99 *The Underwater Menace*
100 *Frontier Worlds*. The Tufty Club was a group that taught British children the fundamentals of road safety. The group's mascot, Tufty the squirrel, avoided roadside accidents and was featured on club badges.
101 *The Sound of Drums*. Some have viewed this as a reference to events in *The Invasion*, which broadcast in November and December 1968. John Frobisher seems to reference the same protocols in *TW: Children of Earth*.
102 *The Banquo Legacy* (p274).
103 *Iris: The Land of Wonder*, presumably reflective (in Iris Wildthyme terms) of the second Doctor working alongside UNIT in *The Invasion*. *Crossroads* initially ran 1964-1988. Mention of the "robot guru" is probably

appeared on *Animal Magic*, and had a thing for Johnny Morris in his zookeeper's uniform.[104] Iris and Panda went to the London Zoo in the sixties, and Panda visited the well-known lady Panda named Chi Chi.[105]

1968 - NIGHTSHADE[106] -> The seventh Doctor and Ace found murders and hauntings in the Yorkshire town of Crook Marsham. The retired actor Edmund Trevithick, former star of the Nightshade series, had been seeing monsters from his old show. Energy beings sealed off the village and began a rampage. The Doctor discovered the Sentience, an ancient creature, was feeding on the lifeforce of humans. He convinced it to transmit itself to a supernova in Bellatrix, where it became trapped. Afterwards, the Doctor prevented Ace from leaving him to stay on Earth with her new boyfriend, Robin Yeadon, instead taking the TARDIS to a planet with three moons.

1968 - THE DEMONS OF RED LODGE AND OTHER STORIES: "The Entropy Composition"[107] -> Guitarist Geoffrey Belvedere Cooper (a.k.a. "The Coop") enjoyed commercial success with his quartet. The BBC banned one of their songs, "You Can See My Pad, Doll". The Coop pursued a solo career, and an Entropy Siren inserted primal sonics into his last composition, "White Wave, Soft Haze" - part of a scheme to similarly infect the music repository Concordium in future. The fifth Doctor and Nyssa destroyed the Siren, but primal sound disintegrated The Coop.

In 1968, Jean-Pierre Rex had given up being the Revolution Man. The singer Ed Hill murdered Rex and used the drug Om-Tsor to continue the Revolution Man's anarchist activities. The Revolution Man symbol appeared on the deck of the US *Constitution* on 12th November. On 4th January, 1969, it appeared at a US Air Force base in High Raccoon, Tennessee.[108]

The Doctor bought a beach house in Sydney in 1969,

and rented a green VW that he conveniently forgot to return.[109] The Victorian villa at 39 Bannerman Road was demolished in 1969, and replaced with a plain family home.[110] Paper from the planet Papyria in the Proxima Centauri system - a substance used by the long-dead, psionic Papyrians to rewrite reality for entertainment purposes - made its way to Earth. The budding author Gregory P. Wilkinson bought the paper as a journal from a Charing Cross Road bookshop in 1969, and the paper filled his head with such imaginings that he produced the *Wraith World* novel series.[111]

The tenth Doctor and Martha planned to see the Beatles' rooftop concert at Savile Row on 30th January, 1969, but ended up in 1669 instead.[112] **Canton Delaware III was fired from the FBI in February 1969, as he wished to marry a black man.**[113]

c 1969 - IRIS: THE SOUND OF FEAR[114] -> The Naxian warlord Mohanalee forced Iris Wildthyme and her husband, Sam Gold, to bring him back to the 1960s so he could implant Earth's radio signals with Naxian brainwashing signals, and retroactively make Earth the centre of the Naxian Empire. Gold died while saving Iris' life, and Mohanalee was killed also - enabling Iris to return, alone, to the future to retrieve her companion Panda.

1969 - BLINK[115] -> Detective Inspector Billy Shipton was transported to 1969 by the Weeping Angels. He met the tenth Doctor and Martha, who gave him a message for Sally Sparrow... he would have to live out nearly forty years to deliver it.

1969 (8th April) - THE IMPOSSIBLE ASTRONAUT[116] -> The Silence continued to prepare and hardwire the young Melody Pond as an assassin to kill the Doctor. She was given an augmented NASA astronaut suit that contained a communications array - this enabled her to link up to the Oval Office phone, and she reported to

meant to parallel the Beatles' association with Maharishi Mahesh Yogi, which started in 1967.

104 *Iris: The Claws of Santa*. *Animal Magic* ran 1962-1983.

105 *Iris: Enter Wildthyme*. Chi Chi arrived at the London Zoo in September 1958, died in 1972.

106 Dating *Nightshade* (NA #8) - Ace finds a calendar saying it is "Christmas 1968".

107 Dating *The Demons of Red Lodge and Other Stories*: "The Entropy Composition" (BF #142b) - The year is given.

108 *Revolution Man* (p180).

109 *Instruments of Darkness*. This might be the same car the eighth Doctor drives in the early EDAs.

110 *SJA: The Ghost House*

111 *SJA: Wraith World*

112 "Black Death, White Life"

113 "Six weeks" before *The Impossible Astronaut*.

114 Dating *Iris: The Sound of Fear* (Iris audio #2.1) - Mohanalee makes Iris take him back to an unspecified part of the 1960s, but it's probably later in the decade than earlier, given this story's fixation on the golden oldies.

115 Dating *Blink* (X3.10) - The year is given, first of all in the graffiti that the Doctor leaves for Sally to find in 2007. The Doctor and Martha mention that the moon landing hasn't happened yet - this occurred on 20th July, 1969.

116 Dating *The Impossible Astronaut* (X6.1) - The date is given. The story continues in *Day of the Moon*; some

President Nixon that she was scared of "the space-man". Nixon summoned the ex-FBI agent Canton Delaware III to investigate the call.

Arriving from 2011, the eleventh Doctor made the TARDIS exterior invisible and landed in the Oval Office as Nixon and Delaware listened to one of the mysterious phone calls. The Doctor offered his assistance, and that of his companions Amy, Rory and River Song. They quickly identified the caller's location as an intersection in Florida, five miles from Cape Kennedy. The Doctor, his companions and Delaware went there, and discovered a disused warehouse containing alien technology... and some of the leaders of the Silence. Anyone who saw the Silence lost all memory of them once they looked away.

The Doctor and Amy found the little girl, who was wearing the same spacesuit as the person who had killed the Doctor in 2011. To prevent the Doctor's death, Amy shot the spacesuited figure...

Young Melody Pond escaped. The Doctor, Amy, Rory and River spent the next three months investigating the pervasiveness of the Silence in this era. Canton Delaware pretended to be trying to apprehend them for the FBI while he constructed a cage made of dwarf star alloy - a way to guarantee that they weren't being monitored.[117] River Song was aware that the girl was her younger self, but pretended not to know.[118]

1969 (18th May) - REVOLUTION MAN[119] -> The "Revolution Man" incidents greatly increased tensions between the US, the Soviet Union, China and India. Ed Hill's psionic abilities spiralled out of control, threatening to destroy all life on Earth, and Fitz and the eighth Doctor killed Hill to prevent such a catastrophe. The Doctor consumed a portion of Om-Tsor, and used its reality-warping abilities to prevent the world governments from instigating a nuclear war.

1969 (July) - DAY OF THE MOON[120] -> Canton Delaware "captured" the eleventh Doctor, Amy and Rory. They used the invisible TARDIS, which was located within the dwarf-star alloy cage, to reunite with River Song. Melody Pond tore her way out of her spacesuit and went into hiding; the Doctor's party found that the spacesuit contained technology from twenty different species.

Delaware acquired video footage of one of the Silence. The Doctor went to Cape Kennedy and inserted a transmitter into the *Apollo 11* capsule; he was captured while doing so, but Nixon ordered his release. As the moon landing took place, the Doctor's transmitter stripped Delaware's video clip into all broadcasts of Neil Armstrong stepping foot onto the lunar surface. The clip showed a Silence saying:

"You should kill us all on sight."

This acted as a subliminal order - humanity wouldn't remember hearing it, but for a thousand generations, the Silence would be a hunted species, attacked by any person that saw them. The Doctor's group said farewell to President Nixon, and the Doctor suggested that the Nixon should record everything said in the Oval Office so he could better know if the Silence was influencing him. The Doctor returned River to the future, and resumed his travels with Amy and Rory.

From their base on the moon, the Threshold watched Neil Armstrong land.[121] **The tenth Doctor and Martha watched the moon landing four times.**[122] Bernard and Paula took the Doctor to the Royal Planetary Society, where they shared a meal and watched the moon landing.[123] The *Apollo 11* astronauts returned with samples of moon rock, one of which contained an alien bacteria.[124]

Iris Wildthyme helped Jacqueline Susann write *The Love Machine*.[125] The trauma caused by Charles Manson and his followers provided sustenance to Huitzilin.[126]

---

details from that story and *A Good Man Goes to War* have been included in this summary for clarity.

117 *Day of the Moon*

118 *The Wedding of River Song*

119 Dating *Revolution Man* (EDA #21) - The date is given (p223).

120 Dating *Day of the Moon* (X6.2) - A caption tells us that the action (which follows on from *The Impossible Astronaut*) has resumed "3 Months Later. July 1969". Events culminate with the *Apollo 11* moon landing (on 20th July).

121 "Wormwood". The *TV Comic* story "Moon Landing" predicted the first moon landing would occur in 1970. Richard Lazarus namechecks Armstrong in *The Lazarus Experiment*.

122 *Blink*. These were separate occasions from their being stranded in 1969.

123 *Beautiful Chaos* (p76). This presumably references Bernard Quatermass and his daughter Paula.

124 *Heart of Stone* (p146). This happened on "the last *Apollo* mission", presumably *Apollo 11*.

125 *The Blue Angel*. The novel was published in 1969.

126 *The Left-Handed Hummingbird*. No specific actions on Manson's part are mentioned, but the infamous "Helter Skelter" murders took place in August 1969, and the most prominent victim, actress Sharon Tate, was killed 8th August. Page 243 establishes that Huitzilin merely fed off Manson's actions, but didn't "possess" or influence him as is sometimes claimed.

The Unit Era

Establishing when the UNIT stories take place is probably the most contentious *Doctor Who* continuity issue.

The UNIT stories are set in an undefined "end of the twentieth century" era that could more or less comfortably fit at any time between the mid-sixties and mid-nineties (but no further, as the Doctor is specifically exiled to "the twentieth century").

Some *Doctor Who* fans have insisted on trying to pin down the dates more precisely, and some have even claimed to have "found the right answer". But all of us face the problem that as successive production teams came and went, a mass of contradictory, ambiguous and circumstantial evidence built up. To come up with a consistent timeframe, this evidence must be prioritised, and some of it has to be rationalised away or ignored.

It is a matter of individual judgement which clues are important. The best chronologies are aware of the problem and admit they're coming down on one side of the argument, while the worst blithely assert they alone have the right answer while not noticing they've missed half the evidence.

The Virgin version of *Ahistory* was wrong when it said there was no right answer. The problem is that there are several, mutually incompatible, right answers.

It happens that a number of firm, unambiguous dates are given in dialogue during the course of the series:

1. *The Web of Fear* (broadcast 1968) is the sequel to *The Abominable Snowmen* and features the first appearance of Lethbridge-Stewart. There, Victoria and Anne Travers establish that *The Abominable Snowmen* was set in "1935". Earlier in the same story, Professor Travers had said that this was "over forty years ago". *The Invasion* "must be four years" after that, according to the Brigadier.

Some chronologies have made heroic efforts to ignore or reinterpret this, with *About Time*'s "His mumbled 'more than forty years ago' is a spur-of-the-moment estimate, and it's not unreasonable to assume he meant 'more than thirty years ago' " being only the most recent example. This line of thought usually leads to forty four being added to 1935 to get 1967 or 1968, and liberal use of the phrase "rounding up". But using conventional maths and English, the only possible reading of the lines is that *The Web of Fear* is set in or after 1975 and that *The Invasion*, the first story to feature UNIT, was broadcast in 1968 but was set no earlier than 1979.

2. In *Pyramids of Mars* (broadcast 1975), the Doctor and Sarah both say that she is "from 1980". Here, there's a little room for interpretation, but not much. The most literal reading has to be that *The Time Warrior*, Sarah's first story, is set in 1980. The only plausible alternative is that she's

been travelling with the Doctor for some years, and that she is referring to the date of *Terror of the Zygons*, her last visit to Earth in her timezone. Either way, it refers to a story featuring UNIT.

Anyone trying to contradict Sarah's statement is suggesting that they know better than she does which *year* she comes from. It is difficult to believe that Sarah is rounding up, that she comes from the mid-seventies and simply means "I'm from around that time". The year is specified so precisely, and it jarred when the story was broadcast in 1975, just as it would if anyone now claimed to be from 2020. This isn't "vague" or "ambiguous", as neither she or the Doctor say she's "from around then" or "from the late nineteen-seventies/eighties" - they actually specify a year, and not the easy option of "1975", which would have been a conveniently rounded-up figure that would have brought the threat to history closer to home for the viewing audience. And to cap it all, they then go to a devastated "1980". So, Sarah comes from 1980.

3. *K9 and Company* (the pilot of an unmade *K9* show) and *Mawdryn Undead*, two stories from the 1980s, are set the UNIT era in the years they were first broadcast.

K9 and Company is set in late December 1981, and K9 has been crated up waiting for Sarah since 1978. The format document for the proposed spin-off series stated that Sarah was born in "1949" and that "she spent three years travelling in Space and Time (15.12.73-23.10.76)". This story is "canon", as Sarah and K9 appeared together in *The Five Doctors, School Reunion* and *The Sarah Jane Adventures* (starting with *SJA: Invasion of the Bane*). If we discount the dates for her travels given in the document (they don't, after all, appear on screen), nothing contradicts the "1980" reference... but it means K9 was waiting for her *before* she met the Doctor. This needn't be a problem, however - he clearly delivered Sarah to the wrong end of the country, so why not K9 a couple of years early? It might even explain why Sarah in *School Reunion* thinks the Doctor abandoned her after *The Hand of Fear*, rather than thanking him for the gift.

But *Mawdryn Undead* is impossible to rationalise away that easily. Broadcast in 1983, it states that the Brigadier retired a year before 1977, presumably after Season 13, which was broadcast in 1976. A host of references pin down the dating for *Mawdryn Undead* more precisely. There are two timezones, and these are unambiguously "1977" (where the Queen's Silver Jubilee is being celebrated) and "1983".

So, the Brigadier retired in 1976.

4. *Battlefield* is set "a few years" in Ace's future - apparently in the mid-to-late 1990s. According to the story's author, Ben Aaronovitch, it takes place in "1997". Whatever the case, it is established once again that the UNIT stories are "a few years" in the future. The same writer's *Remembrance of the Daleks* also provides upper and lower limits - UNIT is not around in 1963 when the story is set, but the Doctor rhetorically asks Ace (from the mid-eighties) about the events of *The Web of Fear* and *Terror of the Zygons*.

5. The New Series and *The Sarah Jane Adventures*. Since its return in 2005, the new *Doctor Who* has reintroduced UNIT and Sarah Jane. In *The Sontaran Stratagem*, the Doctor makes a cheeky reference to the dating issue by stating that he worked with UNIT "in the seventies... or was it the eighties?".

The Sarah Jane Adventures, though, have consistently opted for a "year of broadcast" approach, on screen in stories such as *SJA: Whatever Happened to Sarah Jane?*, but particularly in the background features seen on the BBC website and the DVD extras. As with *The Sontaran Stratagem*, however, *The Sarah Jane Adventures* does joke around with the UNIT dating problem - in *SJA: The Lost Boy*, Sarah's UNIT dossier reads: "... making our presence felt in a golden period that spanned the sixties, the seventies, and, some would say, the eighties."

The current *Doctor Who* series opts to downplay or ignore many of the scientific advances we saw in the seventies UNIT stories that didn't come to pass in the real world - for example, *The Christmas Invasion* has a pioneering British unmanned mission to Mars, and Sarah Jane explicitly says that no one has set foot on Mars, but *The Ambassadors of Death* showed a long-established UK manned Mars program.

Thousands of words have been written trying to discount or reinterpret either the *Pyramids of Mars* or the *Mawdryn Undead* account of events. Dozens of distinct explanations - either within the logic of the fiction or taking account of production facts - have been proposed. They tend to be convoluted or to stretch the meanings of very plain English words beyond acceptable tolerances.

The only thing they have in common is that none of them would stand up in court. However you weigh up and prioritise evidence, the *Pyramids of Mars* and *Mawdryn Undead* dates are "as true" as each other. They are scripted and broadcast lines of dialogue within a single story that unambiguously state a firm date, then the characters go to that year and then the date is stated again.

Ultimately, the only way to come up with a consistent UNIT dating scheme is to pick one and ignore the other.

Broadly speaking, then, there are two schools of thought. Either the stories are set in the "near future", as was originally stated (a view that actually elides *two* distinct accounts, as *The Invasion* had the UNIT era starting no earlier than 1979, but *Pyramids of Mars* pretty much ended it in 1980); or they are set in the year of broadcast, as was stated in the early 1980s (which glosses over/ignores/corrects what was said in those previous stories) in a version of history where certain aspects of technological progress were more advanced and the political situation was different.

As noted in the individual UNIT story entries, there are a wealth of clues beyond what's actually said that might be used to tip the balance one way or the other. Different chronologies give different weight to these, and so come to different conclusions. But most try to address the following areas:

1. Technology: There are an abundance of references to scientific developments that hadn't happened at the time the UNIT stories were broadcast, but were reasonable extrapolations of what the near future would hold.

The technology is far in advance of the early nineteen-seventies: there are talking computers, compact walkie talkies, experimental alloys, laser guns and robots. Colour televisions and even colour videophones are commonplace. Man has landed on Mars, there are space freighters and advanced artificial intelligences. Comprehensive space and alternative energy programmes are underway.

It could be argued that the UNIT stories are set in a parallel history where by (say) 1970 mankind was more technologically advanced than the real 1970. One obvious reason for this might be that scientists had access to an abundance of alien technology from all the failed invasions, and so made great technological progress. There are examples of high technology being developed due to alien influence in some stories. For example, the interstitial time travel of *The Time Monster* is inspired by the Master, not because it's part of mankind's natural progress. There are other stories with no obvious alien influence, like *The War Machines* with its prototype internet and advanced artificial intelligence.

However, there's no evidence that, say, the British mission to Mars seen in *The Ambassadors of Death* uses alien technology (rather the opposite). One difference between it and *The War Machines* is that there are several explicit references to things being obsolete that were state-of-the-art at the time of broadcast. While it's a little far-fetched that Britain could mount such an ambitious programme, there's no technology in the story that NASA weren't planning to have by the 1980s. In 1970, NASA planned - not just hoped - to have a man on Mars by 1982.

2. Historical and Political Details: Again, the evidence overwhelmingly suggests that either the political history of the early nineteen-seventies is very different to reality, or the UNIT stories aren't set in the early 1970s.

There's a Prime Minister called Jeremy in *The Green Death*, and one who's a woman by the time of *Terror of the Zygons*. Both of these are clear - and clearly tongue-in-cheek - references to someone who was an actual opposition leader with an outside chance of winning the next election or the one after that. The United Nations is more powerful than its seventies equivalent. The Cold War has been over for "years" by the end of the era. Environmentalism has become a matter for Westminster politicians and civil servants. All of these things are clearly reasonable extrapolations, not a reflection, of the situation at the time the stories were made.

Two pieces of dialogue suggest it is the early seventies: in *Doctor Who and the Silurians*, a taxi driver wants his fare in predecimal currency, and Mao Tse Tung seems to be alive at the time of *The Mind of Evil* (he died in 1976).

3. Calendars: The month a UNIT story is set is often specified or can be inferred from information in a story, or by close observation of calendars on walls or other such set dressing. We are told that the barrow in *The Daemons* (broadcast 1971) is opened on Beltane (30th April). We can infer that it's a Saturday or - more probably - Sunday (see the entry for that story). So, taken literally, that would mean that it was set in a year when 30th April fell on a Sunday - in the seventies, that would be 1972 or 1978.

While there have been some excellent attempts to reconcile this sort of information, this is not a level of detail the production team ever went into, and this is not a "key" to revealing a consistent chronology. The evidence is often contradictory, even within individual stories: *four* calendars appear in *The Green Death*, one stating that the story is set in February of a leap year, two more say it is April, the fourth indicates that it's May.

4. Fashions: Except for *The Invasion* and *Battlefield*, the clothes, haircuts and cars all resemble those of the year the programme was made. There was no attempt to mock-up car number plates or predict future fashions. The UNIT soldiers sport haircuts that would have been distinctly nonregulation in the 1970s, but this is just as true today. The UNIT era looks and feels like the early 1970s, the characters have many of the attitudes and concerns of people in the seventies. However, is this evidence it was set in the early 1970s, or simply that it was made in the early 1970s?

5. Authorial Intention: We might also want to refer to interviews with the production team, to find out what they intended.

Derrick Sherwin, the producer at the time the UNIT format was introduced, said in the *Radio Times* of 19th June, 1969, that Season Seven would be set in "a time not many years distant from now when such things as space stations will be actuality". In an interview with the *Daily Mail* two days later, Jon Pertwee stated that his Doctor would be exiled to Earth "in the 1980s". The *Doctor Who*

and the Sea-Devils novelisation by Malcolm Hulke, published in 1974, said that "North Sea oil had started gushing in 1977".

The Terrestrial Index claimed that the decision was made to redate the UNIT era was taken when real life overtook it, but that didn't happen. When asked in *DWB* #58 why the dates for *Mawdryn Undead* contradicted what was established in the Pertwee era, Eric Saward, the script editor for the story, admitted that the 1977/1983 dates were "a mistake". In fact, the only reason the Brigadier is even in *Mawdryn Undead* is that William Russell wasn't available to play Ian Chesterton in that story, and without the 1977 date given in *Mawdryn Undead*, there's little to debate.

On the other hand, *The Making of Doctor Who*, written by Malcolm Hulke and Terrance Dicks and published in 1972, placed *Spearhead from Space* in "1970".

The editors of the early New and Missing Adventures consciously chose to set the UNIT stories on or about the year they were broadcast. In practice, when a date is specified it was left pretty much to the discretion of an individual author, and there were a number of discrepancies (see the entries for each story). More recent novels mentioning UNIT have been far more coy about specifying dates, for the most part, and a number (like *No Future*, *The Dying Days* and *Interference*) have suggested fictional reasons for the confusion. Big Finish has shown little interest in weighing in on the topic, although a token effort was made to place its *UNIT* audio series in the near-future of release.

6. Real Life: The late eighties/early nineties fit the UNIT era almost perfectly - the Cold War was over, China was hardline communist, the British government was unstable, there was a female prime minister, the UN was powerful, environmental issues were at the forefront of political debate, there was video conferencing, British scientists were working on their own space probes and Microsoft were putting a computer in every home and making IE's attempts at world domination look half-hearted.

To top it all, a trend for seventies retro meant that the fashionistas were all dressing like Jo Grant. The Doctor's reference to Batman in *Inferno* was clearly because he'd just seen the Tim Burton movie. It's uncanny.

7. Other Reference Books: The balance of fan opinion, or at least the fans who write books, has definitely tipped towards setting the UNIT era in or around the year of broadcast. *The Terrestrial Index*, *The Discontinuity Guide*, *Who Killed Kennedy*, *Timelink* and *About Time* all - give or take a year here or there - concur. A clear majority of the original novels do. However, the BBC-published *Doctor Who - The Legend* sets the UNIT era in the "near future" and concludes that *Mawdryn Undead* is the anomaly.

The Conclusion: It is very tempting to hope for a right answer, but *Doctor Who* is fiction, not a documentary and a "one right answer" just does not - cannot - exist. Even if we limit ourselves solely to dates specifically and unambiguously given in on-screen dialogue, then the Brigadier retires from UNIT three years before his first appearance as the commanding officer of UNIT. It is utterly impossible to try to incorporate every calendar, E-reg car and videophone into one consistent timeframe. People who claim to have done so have invariably, and by definition, missed or deliberately ignored some piece of evidence established somewhere.

However, none of the dates given place the "UNIT era" earlier than the late sixties or later than the early eighties. A right answer doesn't exist, but something everyone ought to be able to agree on is that the UNIT stories took place in "the seventies", give or take a year or so.

The personal preference of the authors of *Ahistory*, for the record, neatly reflects the main split in fandom on this issue: Lance prefers that the UNIT era takes place in the

---

1 "Five years" before *The Invasion* according to Vaughn.

2 Dating *The Web of Fear* (5.5) - It is the near future. Professor Travers declares that the events of *The Abominable Snowmen* were "over forty years ago", Victoria says that they were in "1935" and no-one contradicts her, so it's at least 1975.

Some fans have suggested that Travers is senile or confused, but in the story he's clearly the opposite. All things considered, he's sharp-witted and in command of the facts. The maps of the London Underground that we see render the network as it was in 1968, and don't show the Victoria or Jubilee lines, which opened on 7th March, 1969, and 1st May, 1979, respectively.

Downtime states that this story took place "some twenty-five years before", in "1968".

3 *Downtime*

4 *The Web of Fear*

5 *The Paradise of Death*. This happened "just before he joined UNIT".

6 *The Invasion*. UNIT is not set up specifically to fight aliens, but to "investigate the unexplained". The independent film *Wartime* says that UNIT was formed "during the late 1960s".

7 *Who Killed Kennedy*

8 *Emotional Chemistry*

9 *The Dying Days*

10 *Island of Death*

11 *Bullet Time*

12 *The Time Monster* - the Seventh Enabling Act allows the Brigadier to take command of government forces - and *The Green Death*.

13 Between *The Web of Fear* and *The Invasion*, although there's no indication in the TV series as to precisely when. In *Spearhead from Space,* the Brigadier tells Liz Shaw that "since UNIT was formed" there have been two alien invasions. *The Web of Fear* took place before UNIT was formed, and so we only saw UNIT fight one set of aliens, in *The Invasion*. It's here presumed that the Brigadier was simplifying events and referring to the two televised Troughton stories that he appeared in. If not, the Doctor does not seem to have been involved in fending off the other invasion, as he never refers to it. In *Spearhead from Space* and *Terror of the Zygons,* the Brigadier implies that UNIT existed before he was placed in charge of it.

14 "Years" before *Old Soldiers*.

15 *The Mind of Evil*

16 "Years" before *The Ambassadors of Death*.

17 *The Ambassadors of Death*

18 "Over twenty years" before *The Dying Days* (so before 1977). This was a Mars Probe mission as seen in *The Ambassadors of Death*.

19 Carrington set off for Mars no later than thirty months before *The Ambassadors of Death*.

BRITAIN'S MISSIONS TO MARS: The timeline for the backstory of *The Ambassadors of Death*, and therefore the British space programme, is unclear.

It is a long-term project. Carrington was on Mars Probe 6, and the "missing" ship is Mars Probe 7. Mars Probe 7 takes between seven and eight months to get to Mars (various characters say it takes "seven months", "seven and half months" and "nearly eight months"), the astronauts spend two weeks on the surface and logically need seven or so months to return to Earth. That's a round trip of about fifteen months.

Assuming all missions followed that timescale and that only one mission was underway at any one time, then even if each mission was launched the day the previous one returned, this would stretch the Mars programme back eight or nine years. However, not all the Apollo missions were designed to land a man on the moon, so we could reasonably infer that some of the early Mars Probes were shorter test flights. Nowhere, though, is it stated that Carrington was the *first* man on Mars, and *The Dying Days* makes clear that he wasn't.

Furthermore, when Recovery 7 is lost, we're told that Recovery 8 isn't due for service for "three months" - presumably following a schedule that allows it to rendezvous with Mars Probe 8. It seems unlikely that Recovery 8 would be prepped before Mars Probe 8 is launched, and it's much more plausible that the planners expect Mars Probe 8 to *return* to Earth then. The Mars Probe 8 mission might have been aborted when contact was lost with Mars Probe 7, or it might have continued (as it's not mentioned, we have no way of knowing). Whatever the case, it suggests that Mars Probe 8 was launched while Mars Probe 7 was underway and at least three months ago, given that it's now three months away from Earth.

Either way, we know Mars Probe 7 wasn't launched

near future, five or so years after broadcast, while Lars favours the stories being set at time of broadcast, or near enough for comfort.

For the Purposes of this Book: Even though it's not possible to specify the year, it *is* possible to come up with a consistent timeline. Many UNIT stories contain some reference to other UNIT stories, so it is possible to place them relative to each other. Furthermore, the month a story is set is often given. While there are inconsistencies (which have been noted), it's therefore possible to write a broadly consistent history of the "UNIT era".

The stories of the UNIT era have been separated from those of the other contemporary and near-contemporary stories, and instead talk in "UNIT years". "UNIT Year 1" in this scheme is the year that *The Invasion* and *Spearhead from Space* are set. This only applies to the "UNIT era" - the stories set in the seventies - by the time of *K9 and Company* in 1981, real life seems to have caught up with the near-future of the series whichever way you cut it.

Depending on which story's dating scheme you adopt (and give or take a year in all cases), Unit Year 1 is:

The Invasion - 1979
Pyramids of Mars - 1974
Mawdryn Undead - 1969

Unit Year -5

Around this time, the Cybermen contacted Tobias Vaughn, who offered them help with their invasion. Soon afterwards, Vaughn's company, International Electromatics (IE), marketed the micromonolithic circuit. It revolutionised electronics, and made IE the world leader in the field.[1]

Unit Year -4

THE WEB OF FEAR[2] **->** Mysterious cobwebs started to appear across London, the fog thickened and "bears" and "monsters" attacked people in the Underground. Londoners fled in terror, and the army was called in to restore order. They found themselves under siege in the London Underground, where the disturbances were concentrated. Faced with an attack from the Intelligence, a sentience billions of years older than Earth and with its own army of robot Yeti, the military were reduced to blowing up tunnels to try to contain the situation. The second Doctor arrived with Jamie and Victoria, and met Colonel Lethbridge-Stewart for the first time. Together, they fought the Yeti, and the Doctor banished the Intelligence.

This became known as the London Event, and the official story was that there had been an industrial accident.

Lethbridge-Stewart retained the Locus, a small carved statuette of a Yeti as a memento. Six months later, he met Air Vice-Marshall "Chunky" Gilmore in the Alexander Club and learnt that Earth had been invaded in the winter of 1963. He also learned there was evidence of aliens visiting Earth since the time of the Pharoahs.[3]

The public were told that the Yeti incident was actually a nerve gas attack.[4] Lethbridge-Stewart attended a Middle East Peace Conference.[5]

Aware that the world faced new threats, the United Nations Intelligence Taskforce (UNIT) was established.[6] Lethbridge-Stewart appeared before the UN Security Council and, in part, UNIT was formed because of his efforts.[7] The Russian branch of UNIT was called Operativnaya Gruppa Rasvedkoy Obyedinyonnih Natsiy (OGRON).[8] The French branch was called NUIT.[9] UNIT had a liaison office in Bombay.[10] There was also a South East Asian branch, UNIT-SEA.[11]

Enabling legislation was passed in the UK (it was drafted by the future Minister for Ecology).[12] **Alistair Gordon Lethbridge-Stewart, the Scots Guards Colonel who had led the soldiers that repelled the Yetis in the Underground, was promoted to Brigadier and made commanding officer of the British UNIT contingent.**[13] The Brigadier was present when UNIT took ownership of Kriegeskind Castle in Germany, and made it one of dozens of worldwide UNIT facilities that watched for signs of invasion, the paranormal and the unexplained.[14]

Gas warfare was banned by international agreement.[15] **SOS signals were abandoned.**[16] **The British space programme was blossoming with a series of Mars Probe Missions. Space technology had dramatically improved since the old moonshot days. The new fuel variant M3, though highly volatile, provided a great deal more thrust than conventional fuels, and decontamination procedures had been reduced from two days to one hour. Space research took place at the Space Centre in London, not far from UNIT HQ. In this complex was Space Control (callsign: "Control") where missions were co-ordinated. Astronauts were selected from the military.**[17]

The British astronauts Grosvenor and Guest became the first men on Mars. They planted the Union Flag on Mount Olympus.[18] **The British astronaut Carrington, part of the Mars Probe 6 mission, discovered radioactive aliens on Mars that killed his crew. Returning to Earth, and terrified by what he saw as a threat to humanity, Carrington formed an elaborate plan to destroy them. On his return, he was promoted to General and led the newly-formed Space Security Department.**[19]

TALES FROM THE VAULT[20] -> A criminal gang staged a series of robberies in Manchester, Birmingham and the surrounding counties, using an alien crystal to erase the memory of any eye-witnesses. The second Doctor, Jamie and Zoe foiled the scheme. The Doctor later gave the crystal to the Brigadier, complete with a copy of Zoe's memories as a user "manual"/interface. UNIT used the crystal to extract memories from anyone who witnessed alien activity, keeping secret the existence of extra-terrestrials.

(20th December, 1968 to 30th January, 1969) - THE LEFT-HANDED HUMMINGBIRD[21] -> Early in its history, UNIT had a Paranormal Division. After extensive trials, they recruited six genuine human psychics. The division was run by Lieutenant Hamlet Macbeth, and investigated Fortean events. Following "the Happening", a massive psychic event in St John's Wood, London on 21st December, 1968, the Paranormal Division was disbanded. Ace foiled an attempt to kill the Beatles on the roof of the Apple building on 30th January, 1969. At least two of the Doctor's incarnations went to Woodstock.

Unit Year 1

A Cyber-scout ship surveyed Earth in preparation for an invasion, but its pilot died when the vessel crashed near Cambridge. It remained buried until Gareth Arnold, a local dentist, happened upon it some years later.[22]

(April) UNIT radar stations tracked a shower of meteorites in an odd formation over Essex.[23]

(summer) - THE INVASION[24] -> UNIT began monitoring the activities of International Electromatics after hundreds of UFO sightings occurred on IE property. IE now controlled every computer line in the world by undercutting the competition, and Tobias Vaughn had built a business empire around his philosophy of uniformity and exact duplication. One of IE's most successful products was a disposable radio, which had sold ten million units. Vaughn was in league with the Cybermen, who were using his company as a front for their invasion plans. The second Doctor, Jamie, Zoe and UNIT defeated the Cybermen. Vaughn was apparently **killed**.

---

until Mars Probe 6 returned. So Mars Probe 6 launched at least thirty months before *The Ambassadors of Death*. We know that Dr Taltalian has been working at the Space Centre for "two years", so the Mars programme has been around at least that long.

The Invasion states that only America and Russia can launch a moon mission, and *The Ambassadors of Death* is almost certainly set within a year of that. This means one of two things. Either the first Mars Probe was launched after *The Invasion*, or it's a type of ship that can't be retasked for a moon mission.

No evidence suggests that the history of space travel in the fifties and sixties in *Doctor Who* differs from the history we know. On the contrary, there's evidence that it's the same: Yuri Gagarin is named as the first man in space in *The Seeds of Death*, Ben (from 1966) is from a time before Lunar landings according to *The Tenth Planet* and Richard Lazarus mentions Armstrong in *The Lazarus Experiment*. The moon landing takes place in 1969 according to *Blink*.

20 Dating *Tales from the Vault* (BF CC #6.1) - UNIT has only been in existence "for a few months", and it's "about fifty years" before 2011. The Doctor says that in a few months hence, the Bank of England will be printing the notes required for decimalisation.

21 Dating *The Left-Handed Hummingbird* (NA #21) - The UNIT stories are set the year of broadcast. The last time Cristian Alvarez saw the Doctor was "January the thirtieth, 1969" (p8). The TARDIS arrives in that timezone on "December 20, 1968" (p122). "The Happening" takes place on "December 21" (p163).

22 *The Blue Tooth*. The scoutship is clearly reconnoitring Earth in preparation for *The Invasion*.

23 "Six months" before *Spearhead from Space*.

24 Dating *The Invasion* (6.3) - It is the near future. According to the Brigadier in this story, the events of *The Web of Fear* "must be four years ago, now", making it at least 1979. A surveillance photo has the caption "E091/5D/78", the last two digits of which might (or might not) be the year.

There are advanced, voice-operated computers and "Public Video" videophones. UNIT has an IE computer, and use some IE components in their radios and radar. UNIT has compact TM45 radios with a range of 50 miles, while IE personnel have wrist-communicators. IE has an elaborate electronic security and surveillance system. There are electric cars and hypersonic jets.

There's no suggestion that this is because IE has been given Cyber-technology - the computer in IE's reception (which also answers the phones) uses ALGOL and blows up after failing to solve a simple formula, neither of which indicate that a superior alien technology is involved.

There are many communications satellites in orbit, and UNIT has the authority to fire nuclear rockets into space. "Only the Americans and the Russians" have rockets capable of reaching the moon - the Russians are just about to launch a manned orbital survey of the moon, and it would apparently only take "ten hours" to reach it. The IE guards and many UNIT troops wear futuristic uniforms, while Vaughn wears a collarless shirt. The Brigadier's "anti-feminist" ideas are outdated.

The Doctor jokes that as it's Britain and there are clouds in the sky, it must be "summertime".

A casting document written by director Douglas Camfield suggested *The Invasion* was set "about the

One cybership crashed in the South Pole.[25]

After the collapse of IE, Ashley Chapel, Vaughn's chief scientist, set up his own company named Ashley Chapel Logistics.[26] Vaughn, though, had survived by downloading his consciousness into a waiting robot body. For the next thousand years, he would secretly run a succession of massive electronics corporations that developed state-of-the-art equipment. He would re-encounter the Doctor in 2975.[27] The public were told the mass unconsciousness that occurred during the Cybermen incursion was because Earth passed through the tail of a comet. Isobel Watkins' photos of Cybermen were dismissed as fakes.[28]

The "Big Bug Era" began, as Earth was invaded and threatened by alien life. Many books and fanzines trying to catalogue and expose these invasions were published.[29] One of the most popular fanzines was *Who's Who and What's That*. The government, though, covered much of UNIT's work with D-notices, making it difficult to keep track of the dates. The time-displaced Isaac Summerfield set up a secret organisation to "mop up" after UNIT, with the intention of getting stranded aliens home. Initially, it was based in Llarelli.[30]

Mars Probe 7 was launched. After seven months, Mars Probe 7 landed on Mars and radio contact was lost, but two weeks later it took off from the red planet... or at least, something did.[31]

The third Doctor exiled to Earth

(October, "months" after *The Invasion*) - SPEARHEAD FROM SPACE[32] -> UNIT went on a covert recruitment drive, bringing Liz Shaw up from Cambridge to act as a scientific advisor. The very same day, reporters were tipped off that a mysterious patient with two hearts was present at Ashbridge Cottage Hospital.

This "spaceman" was the newly regenerated third Doctor, exiled to Earth in the twentieth-century timezone by the Time Lords. He turned up the morning after a meteorite shower, and UNIT were soon on the scene. The meteorites were Nestene Energy Units, part of a plan to conquer the Earth using killer automata Autons. With the Doctor's help, UNIT led an assault on a plastics factory in Essex, mere hours after reports surfaced of "walking shop dummies" in city centres. They defeated the Nestene.

Captain Mike Yates led the clean-up operation after the Nestene Invasion, and discovered a single Energy Unit that had not been recovered by the Autons. It remained UNIT property, but was loaned to the National Space Museum.[33] Gareth Wostencroft was one of the UNIT soldiers involved with the first Auton invasion.[34]

---

year 1976 AD". The *Radio Times* in some regions said that the date was "about the year 1975", and the continuity announcer echoed this at the beginning of the broadcast of episode one. In *Dalek*, the plaque below the Cybermen head reads "Extraterrestrial Cyborg Specimen, recovered from underground sewer, location London, United Kingdom, date 1975"... almost certainly a reference to this story. However, the Cybermen head is from the wrong era (it's from *Revenge of the Cybermen*, not *The Invasion*) and the plaque isn't readable on screen, so there are grounds to discount it. According to *Iceberg*, this story takes place "ten years" (p90) before *The Tenth Planet* (meaning 1976), in "the 70s" (p2). *No Future* suggested "1970", (p2). *Original Sin* claims that this story was set in "the 1970s" (p281). *Millennial Rites* suggests that the UNIT era took place in "the nineteen eighties" (p15), with *The Invasion* a little over "twenty years ago" (meaning 1979). The 1979 date is repeated in *The Face of the Enemy* (p21).

25 *Iceberg*
26 *Millennial Rites*
27 *Original Sin*
28 *Who Killed Kennedy*
29 *No Future*
30 *Return of the Living Dad. Who's Who and What's That* is also mentioned in *The Dying Days*.
31 Mars Probe 7 is launched fifteen and a half months

before *The Ambassadors of Death*, and contact was lost "eight months" before *The Ambassadors of Death*.
32 Dating *Spearhead from Space* (7.1) - There's no firm evidence if this is near future or contemporary. The Brigadier tells Liz Shaw here that "in the last decade we have been sending probes deeper and deeper into space", but that needn't mean humanity's first-ever space probe was launched exactly ten years ago.

The Brigadier states in *Planet of the Spiders* that "months" elapsed between *The Invasion* and *Spearhead from Space* (meaning 1979). The weather is "uncommonly warm", suggesting it is autumn or winter. According to *The Face of the Enemy* (p21) it was "two years" before (meaning 1981). It was "five years ago" in *No Future* (meaning 1971). *Who Killed Kennedy* and *The Scales of Injustice* both state this story takes place in October, which is also the month the story was filmed.
33 *Terror of the Autons*, also referred to in *The Eye of the Giant*. Mike Yates doesn't appear on screen until *Terror of the Autons*. He apparently doesn't remember Nestene Energy Units in *The Scales of Injustice*.
34 *Dominion*

The Nestene invasion was covered up as a terrorist attack, which became known as Black Thursday. A report filed by journalist James Stevens had all references to UNIT erased. This prompted him to start investigating the mysterious organisation, an undertaking he would pursue for several years.[35]

The Vault, Department C19's storehouse of discarded alien artifacts, recovered two Nestene Energy Units. Dr Ingrid Krafchin, a researcher for SeneNet, began experiments with plastic.[36] The Doctor was put on UNIT's payroll as "Doctor John Smith", but did not cash his cheques.[37] The Brigadier saw his friend, Kolonel Heinrich Konrad, after a debriefing on the initial Auton incident.[38]

Unit Year 2

(winter) - DOCTOR WHO AND THE SILURIANS[39]
-> UNIT investigated power losses at the experimental Wenley Moor research centre. These were caused by the Silurians, reptile people who ruled the Earth millions of years before, and who had revived from suspended animation. The Silurians saw the humans as apes and plotted to wipe them out - first with a plague, then by dispersing the Van Allen Belt. This would have heated Earth to a level suitable for Silurians, but not to human life. The third Doctor attempted to negotiate, but the Brigadier triggered explosives that sealed off the Silurian base and possibly killed those within.

This was Earth Reptile Shelter 873, led by Okdel L'da.[40] James Stevens followed a tip and managed to (briefly) phone the Brigadier at Wenley Moor. The plague spread to Paris airport. Four hundred people died, twenty of them abroad, and three ministers resigned.[41] The Doctor believed that the Silurians at Wenley Moor were killed.[42] The Brigadier was issued with direct orders to destroy the Silurians.[43] Those orders came from C19.[44] Mike Yates lead a team looking for surviving Silurian technology.[45]

Mortimus (also known as the Monk) used the captured Chronovore Artemis to create an alternative history where the Doctor died during the Wenley Moor adventure.[46]

> = In a parallel timeline, the Doctor was captured and killed by the Silurians before he could find an antidote to their plague. Millions died in a matter of days, a time that would become known to the survivors as "the Nightmare".[47]

The Silurian Imorkal was hatched. In one reality, he was

---

35 *Who Killed Kennedy* is James Stevens' account of the early UNIT years, and allocates firm dates for the stories, specifically:
  Remembrance of the Daleks (November 1963)
  The Web of Fear (August 1966)
  The Invasion (spring 1969)
  Spearhead from Space (October 1969)
  Doctor Who and the Silurians (November 1969)
  The Ambassadors of Death (December 1969)
  Inferno (February 1970)
  Terror of the Autons (April 1970)
  The Mind of Evil (November 1970)
  The Claws of Axos
  The Daemons (May 1971)
  Day of the Daleks (September 1971)

The Dying Days rather cheekily claimed that the government had insisted the dates be changed before allowing the book to be published.
36 *Business Unusual*
37 *No Future*, which clashes with the Doctor saying he was "unpaid" in *Terror of the Autons*. This was the "early seventies" in *Return of the Living Dad*.
38 *Old Soldiers*
39 Dating *Doctor Who and the Silurians* (7.2) - There's conflicting dating evidence. A taxi driver asks for a fare of "10/6", so this story appears to be set before the introduction of decimal currency in February 1971, but the cyclotron is a futuristic experimental machine that converts nuclear energy directly into electricity.
There's no indication how long it's been since *Spearhead from Space*, but the Doctor has settled in with UNIT and (recently) acquired Bessie. People are wearing winter clothes. The New Adventure *Blood Heat* states that this story is set in "1973".
40 *The Scales of Injustice*. Okdel was named in *Doctor Who and The Cave-Monsters*, the novelisation of *Doctor Who and the Silurians*.
41 *Who Killed Kennedy*. We see the Brigadier take the phone call in *Doctor Who and the Silurians*.
42 *The Hungry Earth*
43 *Blood Heat*
44 *The Scales of Injustice*
45 *The Eye of the Giant, The Scales of Injustice.*
46 *No Future*, a reference to *Blood Heat*.
47 *Blood Heat*
48 *Eternity Weeps*
49 *The Scales of Injustice*, a reference to the Audio Visuals story *Endurance*.
50 *The Devil Goblins from Neptune*
51 *Who Killed Kennedy*
52 "Eighteen years" before *Millennial Rites*, so in 1981. It is stated that *Inferno* was "early on in her tenure" and Anne had responsibilities for the British Space Programme (p14). That would place the UNIT stories later than most other references, but this dating scheme is perfectly compatible with that in *The Web of Fear*, which is after all where Anne Travers first appeared.

one of the Silurian masters of Earth. In the proper timeline, he eventually worked for NATO.[48] A UNIT station in Antarctica investigated a possible Silurian shelter uncovered in the 1920s.[49] Another Silurian shelter was discovered and destroyed in Oregon.[50] The government destabilised under political pressure following the plague.[51] Anne Travers became scientific advisor to the cabinet.[52]

OLD SOLDIERS[53] **->** Kolonel Heinrich Konrad was now head of the UNIT facility at Kriegeskind Castle, and oversaw research on Project 995: an attempt to create a super-soldier using the psychotropic elements of an extra-terrestrial plant - a phylum that originated in Galaxy M33 - found in the jungles of South East Asia.

Kriegeskind came under attack by ghostly soldiers from bygone eras. The third Doctor and the Brigadier determined that Konrad was manifesting psychic powers due to the phylum, and was latching onto the emotional residue left in the castle's stone by soldiers who had visited the location. Konrad's second-in-command initiated the Arc Light Protocol: a scorched-earth policy created by the Brigadier. Two F5 bombers each deployed a single fuel-air explosive bomb - the most lethal ordinance UNIT had at its disposal. The Arc Light planes obliterated the castle, Konrad and all research pertaining to the project.

The lower ranks of UNIT regarded the Doctor as a myth, someone spoken of like a ghost story.

SHADOW OF THE PAST[54] **->** The Mim, a race of shape-changers who used oceans for breeding pools, sent a war-fleet to Earth. The third Doctor contacted the Time Lords, who sent the warfleet back to the Mim-sphere and made sure that it was too busy to leave. A single Mim scout was left behind, and Sergeant Robin Marshall of UNIT died while exploding the creature within its spaceship. Corporal Benton was given Marshall's sergeant stripes, and the scoutship was quarantined in UNIT Vault 75-73/Whitehall.

THE AMBASSADORS OF DEATH[55] **->** Recovery 7 was dispatched, piloted by Charles Van Lyden, to give assistance to Mars Probe 7, which was still maintaining radio silence after lifting off from Mars. Van Lyden linked up with and entered Mars Probe 7, but contact was again lost. Recovery 8 couldn't be prepared for launch for ten days, forcing the ground crew to await developments.

Recovery 7 returned to Earth, but not with the Earth astronauts aboard. Instead, it contained three ambassadors from the race of radioactive aliens that General Carrington had encountered on Mars. Furthering his private agenda, Carrington intercepted the ambassadors and directed them, via a signalling device, to commit acts of terror. Carrington hoped to portray the aliens as invaders, mobilising a global effort to destroy them, but the third Doctor and UNIT exposed the scheme. The ambassadors and Earth astronauts were exchanged, and Carrington was discredited.

That was "twenty-five years ago" (so around 1974), meaning there were seven years between *The Web of Fear* and her appointment.

53 Dating *Old Soldiers* (BF CC #2.3) - The story takes place "a few weeks" after *The Silurians*, but before *The Ambassadors of Death*.

54 Dating *Shadow of the Past* (BF CC #4.9) - Once again, the story happens "a few weeks" after *The Silurians*, and before *The Ambassadors of Death*.

55 Dating *The Ambassadors of Death* (7.3) - This story is very clearly set in the near future. Britain has an established programme of manned missions to Mars. Professor Cornish remarks that decontamination takes "under an hour... it used to take two days" (the time it took the lunar astronauts when the story was made). There are colour videophones and we see a machine capable of automatically displaying star charts. SOS messages were abandoned "years ago".

Those advocating that the UNIT stories are set in the year of broadcast admit this story causes them problems. One argument (used in both *Timelink* and *About Time*) concedes that Mars missions weren't possible in 1970, but that as we still haven't landed a man on Mars, it doesn't prove this story is set in the near future. It's an odd train of logic to say that something too advanced

for 1980 (or indeed the world of today) therefore indicates a 1970 setting.

Leaving that aside, when *The Ambassadors of Death* was made, it wasn't science fantasy. NASA had just landed on the moon and had plans to put a man on Mars in the nineteen-eighties. This wasn't just a hope as the technology to get to Mars existed, at least in prototype form, and only a lack of political will and funding prevented it. At that point, NASA was seriously projecting that half of American employees would be working in space by 2050.

At the time that *The Ambassadors of Death* was made, then, what was shown wasn't possible - but it would be, for NASA, in about ten years. The most implausible aspect was that Britain could do the same - but there had been a British space programme up until the early sixties, and, again, it was lack of funding rather than lack of expertise that killed it off.

The Doctor is still bitter about the events of *Doctor Who and the Silurians*, so this story probably happens only shortly afterwards. The Brigadier says he has known the Doctor "several years, on and off", so it's that long since *The Web of Fear*.

The new channel BBC3 launched with coverage of the Recovery 7 capsule.[56] The Doctor appeared on *Nationwide* during this incident.[57] The aliens conducted limited diplomatic discussions, but concluded that mankind wasn't ready for their technology. Contact was limited, as the aliens were a plutonium-based lifeform.[58] Mars Probe 6 ended up in C19's Vault.[59] The Mars Probe Programme continued for several more years.[60]

Jones, a hired killer from C19's Vault, abducted a young secretary called Roberta. Vault scientists gave her cybernetic implants and false memories.[61]

(late July) - INFERNO[62] **-> Professor Stahlman discovered a gas underneath the crust of the Earth, and claimed that it might be "a vast new storehouse of energy which has lain dormant since the beginning of time". The government funded a drilling project (nicknamed "Inferno" by some of the workers) based in Eastchester. But as the project's robot drill approached its target, a green slime came to the surface. On skin contact, people became savage beastmen, Primords.**

= "Sideways in time", Britain was a republic, and it had been since at least 1943 when the Defence of the Republic Act was passed. A fascist regime had executed the royal family. In this version of events, Professor Stahlman's project was a day ahead of ours, and was under the aegis of the Republican Security Forces. This world was destroyed when Stahlman's project released torrents of lava and armies of Primords.

On our Earth, the project was halted at the insistence of Sir Keith Gold and UNIT.

= The Britain of the parallel world was run by an alternate version of the Doctor.[63] In the parallel universe, the British Isles were destroyed in hours, the rest of Europe a day later. The entire world was devastated within thirty-six hours. The leaders of the American Confederation, India, White Russia and the Asian Co-prosperity Sphere, along with the new

---

56 *Who Killed Kennedy*
57 "During that General Carrington business" according to *No Future*.
58 *The Dying Days*
59 *The Scales of Injustice*
60 Mars Probe 9 is referred to in *Dancing the Code*, and *The Dying Days* mentions Mars Probe 13.
THE BRITISH SPACE PROGRAMME: Perhaps because they are acutely aware of the threat from outer space, the British government seems to have invested heavily in the space programme before and during the UNIT era. In *Invasion of the Dinosaurs*, some very clever and important people are fooled into believing that a fleet of colony ships could be built and go on to reach another habitable planet, although Sarah knows that even the most advanced spaceship "would take hundreds of years" to do so, and it transpires the ships are fakes. In *The Android Invasion*, an experimental "space freighter" has been in service for at least two years. There's no obvious evidence that the British are using alien technology that they've recovered from one of the alien incursions in the sixties to speed up their space programme. On the contrary, they're using pretty basic rocket technology.

The Christmas Invasion features Britain sending an unmanned probe to Mars in late 2006, and portrays it as a pioneering effort.
61 *Business Unusual*
62 Dating *Inferno* (7.4) - This story seems to be set in the near future. The computer at the project uses perspex/crystalline memory blocks. Stahlman has a robot drill capable of boring down over twenty miles. A desk calendar in the parallel universe says it is "July 23rd", and the story runs for five days - the countdown we see

early in the story says there is "59:28:47" remaining before penetration.

The word "Primord" is not used in dialogue, but appears in the on-screen credits. The name "Eastchester" is only used in a scene cut from the original broadcast (but retained in foreign prints and the BBC Video and DVD release), when the Doctor listens to a radio broadcast in the parallel universe. Stahlman spells his name with two "n"s in the parallel universe. The Doctor claims this is the first attempt to penetrate the Earth's crust, forgetting the attempt he'd seen in *The Underwater Menace*.
63 *Timewyrm: Revelation*
64 *The Face of the Enemy*
65 *The Scales of Injustice, Business Unusual.*
66 *The Devil Goblins from Neptune. The Face of the Enemy* says Ian is on a year-long exchange programme.
67 *Byzantium!*
68 *Who Killed Kennedy*
69 "Seven or eight months" before *Scales of Injustice*, "twenty years" before *Business Unusual*.
70 "The previous year", "late last year" and "eight months" before *The Devil Goblins from Neptune.*
71 The Christmas before *The Scales of Injustice.*
72 *The Devil Goblins from Neptune.* The new members were presumably Billy Preston and Klaus Voormann.

THE BEATLES: *Doctor Who* has a terrible record for predicting the future, one that can best be summed up by noting that *Battlefield* predicted a near future with Soviet soldiers operating under the UN's aegis on British soil - but between the story's filming and its broadcast, the Soviet Union collapsed. In the entire twenty-six-year run of classic *Doctor Who*, it made two successful predictions - that there would be a female

leader of the British Republic, were evacuated to Copernicus Base on the moon. Once there, they formed the Conclave.[64]

C19 acquired some of Stahlman's Gas.[65] The Doctor attended the wedding of Greg Sutton and Petra Williams. He met Ian Chesterton, who was now working at NASA, at the reception.[66] Greg Sutton gave Ian some fashion advice - that he should buy an orange shirt and purple tie.[67] James Stevens tracked down the Suttons, who told him about Project: Inferno and the Doctor's involvement. The Suttons left the country shortly afterwards.[68]

Two Irish twins, Ciara and Cellian, assisted Dr Krafchin in a number of plastics experiments. He offered them immortality, and their blood was replaced with Nestene Compound, a type of plastic. They become contract killers for C19's Vault.[69]

The Doctor gave a lecture tour in the United States that was really cover for UNIT recruitment operations. He met rocket scientist Von Braun. Soviet radar detected meteor impacts in Siberia, which unknown to them marked the arrival of the Waro on Earth. The Brigadier met Soviet UNIT commander Captain Valentina Shuskin.[70] He also spent Christmas in Geneva on UNIT business.[71]

The Beatles reformed without Paul McCartney, but with two new members called Billy and Klaus.[72] Sarah Jane Smith went out with a Royal Navy officer named Sammy Brooks.[73]

Unit Year 3

(January) The Liberals formed a coalition government following a General Election.[74] (February) James Stevens wrote a series of articles for the *Daily Chronicle* that referred

to UNIT and C19. These got him sacked, and his wife left him.[75] (March) UNIT moved to a new headquarters.[76] (Early March) Soviet satellites detected a vast mining operation in Siberia. All military attempts to investigate were wiped out. The Soviet branch of UNIT lobbied Geneva to send the Doctor.[77]

At C19's Vault, Grant Traynor injected Stahlman's Gas into a Doberman, creating the Stalker, a vicious killer animal.[78] (April/May) C19's Vault acquired a Venus flytrap large enough to eat a dog in Africa. They also stole a Blackbird stealth aeroplane.[79]

(May) - THE EYE OF THE GIANT[80] -> The third Doctor was sent an alien artifact that he discovered was emitting omicron radiation. He converted the Time-Space Visualiser into a space-time bridge to track the object's origin, and he and Liz Shaw wound up on Saluta in the Pacific in 1934.

(=) Their actions in 1934 inadvertently created an alternative timeline ruled by The Goddess of the World, the starlet Nancy Grover. The Doctor returned to 1934 and set history back on the correct course.

THE BLUE TOOTH[81] -> Gareth Arnold, a local dentist, had discovered the crashed Cyber-ship near Cambridge, and experimented upon the Cyber-metal within. He developed a blue liquid variant that could directly convert people's bodies into metal, as well as gestate Cyber-insects within the human form. Arnold himself succumbed to Cyber-conversion, and used his dentistry business as a means of kidnapping people - including Liz Shaw's friend Jean Baisemore - to turn into Cybermen.

The third Doctor and Liz investigated the disappearances. Jean died, but the Doctor created a compound that

British Prime Minister (*Terror of the Zygons*), and that there would, one day, be a museum dedicated to the Beatles in Liverpool (*The Chase*).

The original draft of the script called for the real Beatles to appear, made up to look very old to indicate they were still performing in the future (the script specified 2012).

The Devil Goblins from Neptune reveals that The Beatles of the *Doctor Who* universe stayed together at least into the early seventies. John Lennon was murdered as he was in our history in *The Left-Handed Hummingbird*, though, and Paul McCartney was playing with Wings in *No Future*.

In *The Gallifrey Chronicles*, it's revealed that Fitz collects Beatles records from parallel universes, and that he saw them play a song called "Celebrate the Love" at Live Aid. "Celebrate the Love" is the title of the song the Ewoks sang at the end of *Return of the Jedi*, at least until the Special Edition.

73 "Five years" before *Island of Death*.

74 "Six months" before *The Devil Goblins from Neptune*.
75 *Who Killed Kennedy*. It is "1970" (p87).
76 "Three or four months" before *The Devil Goblins from Neptune*. There are at least two UNIT HQs: one that's almost certainly in a London office block by the Thames in London (seen in *Terror of the Autons*) and one that's a stately home (seen in *The Three Doctors*).
77 "Early March" before *The Devil Goblins from Neptune*.
78 "Three months" before *The Scales of Injustice*, "fifteen years" before *Business Unusual*
79 "A couple of months" and "a month" before *The Scales of Injustice*.
80 Dating *The Eye of the Giant* (MA #21) - The story is set "thirty-seven years" after 1934, so 1971. UNIT have a photocopier. This is apparently the first time Mike Yates meets the Doctor, although he's been working for UNIT "over the last year". This is "a few weeks" before *The Scales of Injustice*, according to that book.
81 Dating *The Blue Tooth* (BF CC #1.3) - It's toward the end of Liz's tenure with UNIT (she's been with the

terminated Arnold. His demise quelled the remaining Cybermen - who were later executed by the Brigadier's troops using the Doctor's compound.

Liz herself was infected by the blue liquid - the Doctor cured her condition, but she lost a tooth as a result.

(June) - THE SCALES OF INJUSTICE[82] **->** A group of Silurian/Sea Devil hybrids awoke in Kent, and performed genetic experiments in the hope of ending their sterility and shortened lifespans. The third Doctor investigated the matter, but the warmongering Silurian leader launched an attack on the coast of Kent. UNIT defeated the assault, and a smaller group of benevolent Silurians sued for peace.

The cyborg leader of C19's Vault sought to acquire Silurian technology, leading to UNIT uncovering the Vault's base of operations. The Vault leader escaped along with his two Nestene-augmented assassins. Foreign powers had purchased some of the Vault's acquisitions.

After this incident, Sir John Sudbury of C19 knew too much to be sacked by any government, and he gained in power. The Brigadier's wife Fiona filed for divorce and left with their daughter Kate.[83]

Liz Shaw told the Doctor that she planned to leave UNIT, return to Cambridge and continue her researches.[84] She took a leave of absence.[85] Liz travelled around the world, and published a book entitled *Inside the Carnival*.[86]

Harry Sullivan served on the Ark Royal after leaving

Dartmouth Naval College.[87]

(June) - THE DEVIL GOBLINS FROM NEPTUNE[88] **->** Geneva refused to release the third Doctor to help with a situation in Siberia, so Captain Shuskin of the USSR branch of UNIT attempted to kidnap him instead. Liz Shaw was working with Professor Bernard Trainor, who was planning an unmanned mission to Neptune. The Doctor and Liz travelled to Siberia and were attacked by the Waro, demonic creatures from Neptune's moon Triton. The Doctor realised this was a distraction - the Waro were really after the American supplies of cobalt-60, with which they hoped to build a bomb that would devastate Earth. The Brigadier uncovered a conspiracy in UNIT that led to Area 51 in Nevada, a secret military base containing five aliens, the Nedenah. Freed by the Doctor, the Nedenah released a virus that made the Waro destroy themselves.

On 18th June, there was a General Election, and the Wilson government was defeated by the Conservatives under Heath with a majority of 43. Days before that, James Stevens' book *Bad Science* was published.[89] At some point during the UNIT era, the Doctor met the Russian Colonel Bugayev. During the encounter, Bugayev and some of his comrades were exposed to temporal radiation that either aged them to death or prolonged their lives.[90]

Liz Shaw returned to Cambridge, and soon afterwards the Doctor started to agitate for a new assistant.

organisation "about a year") and Captain Yates is described as "a new boy" - which would place the story between *The Eye of the Giant* and *The Scales of Injustice*.
82 Dating *The Scales of Injustice* (MA #24) - The back cover states this is set between *Inferno* and *Terror of the Autons*, and "immediately after" *The Eye of the Giant*. It's a "few weeks" since that book. Liz tells the Doctor she is leaving at the end of the book "eight months, two weeks and four days" after *Spearhead from Space*. It is "six months" since *Doctor Who and the Silurians*.

The Silurians who sue for peace are not mentioned again. The next time we see them, *The Sea Devils*, they are pitted against humanity. By the time of *Eternity Weeps*, set in 2003, man and Silurian are working together in relative harmony. Perhaps the discrepancy can be put down to the fact that UNIT don't feature in *The Sea Devils*, and the reptile people there were revived and are being provoked into conflict by the Master.
83 *Business Unusual*
84 *The Scales of Injustice*, which states that it's "eight months, two weeks and four days" since she met the Doctor in *Spearhead from Space*, although their amount of time together has become "thirteen months" by *The Devil Goblins from Neptune*.
85 *The Devil Goblins from Neptune, The Face of the*

Enemy.
86 *The Devil Goblins from Neptune*
87 *The Face of the Enemy*, picking up on a reference in *Harry Sullivan's War*.
88 Dating *The Devil Goblins from Neptune* (PDA #1) - Between *Inferno* and *Terror of the Autons*. Liz has been with UNIT for "thirteen months". The Brigadier hasn't been to Geneva for eight months (when, we're told, he was reporting on the events of *Inferno*). It is "1970", with a host of contemporary references to, for example, David Bowie and Brazil winning the World Cup (p109).
89 *Who Killed Kennedy* (p117), which specifies the year as "1970".
90 *Emotional Chemistry*
91 *Terror of the Autons*
92 *The Death of Art*
93 *Terror of the Autons*
94 *Blood Heat*
95 *The Wages of Sin, Catastrophea*.
96 *Verdigris*, a reference to *The Avengers*.
97 Dating *Terror of the Autons* (8.1) - It seems to be the near future, and the plastics factory has a videophone.

The Doctor works on his dematerialisation circuit for "three months", and apparently hadn't started in *Inferno*, so this story would seem to start at least three months after Season Seven ends. There is no indication how

The Doctor started the steady state microwelding of his dematerialisation circuit.[91] There were some slow weeks at UNIT. The Doctor helped Benton paint some Nissen huts.[92]

Jo Grant was seconded to UNIT at the insistence of a relative in government. Although she failed her General Science A-Level, she managed to pass the UNIT training course.[93] Her relative was General Frank Hobson, the UK ambassador to the United Nations.[94] She was trained to use skeleton keys and interrogation techniques.[95] Her best friend on the course was called Tara. Jo did intelligence work for the Ministry, alongside a gentleman adventurer.[96]

(At least three months after *Inferno*) - TERROR OF THE AUTONS[97] **-> Josephine Grant became the third Doctor's new assistant.**

The Master had allied himself with the Nestenes, and together they plotted mass slaughter - when a radio signal was sent, thousands of distributed plastic daffodils would spray a plastic film capable of suffocating a person. The Nestenes would take over the country during the resulting chaos. The Doctor convinced the Master to help him defeat the Nestene plan. The Master was subsequently stranded on Earth when the Doctor stole his Mark 2 dematerialisation circuit, rendering his TARDIS useless.

A spatula-shaped piece of Auton matter survived. It would eventually end up in Little Caldwell, where it would be called Graeme.[98] In October, UNIT started training its men to resist hypnosis. James Stevens completed work on his second book, and was invited to a demonstration of the Keller Process at Stangmoor Prison.[99]

The Doctor helped set up **the Black Archive, a UNIT storehouse of alien technology. Among many other things, it contained the Tunguska Scroll (recovered in 1972) and a number of spacecraft.**[100]

THE MIND OF EVIL[101] **-> Incognito as "Professor Emil Keller", the Master developed the Keller Process: a means of rehabilitating convicts by having their "evil" brain impulses transferred into a machine. However, the machine actually housed an alien parasite that fed off the evil in mankind. The Master hoped to put the parasite's powers at his command. After a riot at Stangmoor Prison, the Master's scheme was exposed and the Keller Process abandoned.**

UNIT were now involved with security of the World Peace Conference in London. The Master sought to steal Thunderbolt, an outlawed nuclear missile slated for destruction. He nearly succeeded and triggered a World War, but the third Doctor and UNIT destroyed both the missile and the Master's alien parasite.

---

much time has passed since the previous Auton story, *Spearhead from Space*. A desk calendar is referred to when the Doctor and Brigadier visit Farrell's office, but we do not see it.

This is clearly not the Master's first arrival on Earth at this time - he has managed to research the history of Lew Russell, the circus owner.

Inferno was "a few years" before *Terror of the Autons* according to *The Face of the Enemy* (p215). In *Genocide*, Jo says that she's been on UNIT's books since 1971. *Who Killed Kennedy* prefers April 1970.

98 *Return of the Living Dad*

99 *Who Killed Kennedy*. It is "four months" since the June 1970 General Election (p119).

100 The Black Archive was first seen in *SJA: Enemy of the Bane*. The Doctor's involvement was established in "Don't Step on the Grass". We don't know precisely when it was built, but it would seem to be after *The Scales of Injustice*, which features Department C19's (very similar) Vault. In *Terror of the Autons*, the Brigadier expresses an interest in the technology of the Master's grenade but the Doctor defuses it, suggesting they hadn't a protocol about alien technology at that point. It is not related to the (again, very similar) Vault in *SJA: The Vault of Secrets*, or the UNIT Vault featured in *Tales from the Vault*. *Army of Ghosts* established that Torchwood have a similar archive, "The Age of Ice" includes a UNIT archive in Sydney, Australia, and *Dreamland (DW)* shows us that the US stores alien technology and aliens at Area 51. By the time of the K9 series, the Department keep aliens and alien technology in the Dauntless facility in the Tower of London.

101 Dating *The Mind of Evil* (8.2) - It seems to be the near future - there is a National Power Complex, there is a World Peace Conference in progress in which the Chinese are key players. Gas warfare was banned "years" ago. Mao Tse Tung is referred to in the present tense - he died in 1976, after *The Mind of Evil* was made.

Inferno was "some time ago". This story might be set a full year after *Terror of the Autons*: the Master has been posing as Keller since "nearly a year ago". However, it's clear from *Terror of the Autons* that the Master has been on Earth for at least a little while. It's possible that the Master set his plan in motion before his apparent arrival on Earth in *Terror of the Autons*... which would mean he had two entirely distinct plans to take over the Earth running simultaneously. The "year ago" line might well be a remnant from an earlier draft of the script that didn't include the Master.

According to *Who Killed Kennedy*, it is October 1970 (p119).

DEADLY REUNION[102] -> The former Greek gods Demeter, Persephone and Hermes were now living as nobility in the English village of Hob's Haven. Hades had founded a cult named the Children of Light as a means of spreading anarchy among mankind, and coerced the Master into helping him. The Master supplied an alien drug, sarg, that drove its users to commit acts of violence at a pop festival. The third Doctor aided Demeter in summoning Zeus from his abode in another dimension, and the king of the gods exiled Hades from Earth forever. Demeter's trio departed Earth for Zeus' realm. The Brigadier remembered his time spent as Persephone's lover in the nineteen forties.

In December, James Stevens met Dodo Chaplet, who was homeless. He invited her to stay with him.[103]

Unit Year 4

(January) - "Change of Mind"[104] -> The third Doctor and Liz flew to Prague for a Psi conference, but the plane's wing was torn off in a psychic attack. The Doctor realised that one of the passengers was keeping the plane intact using the power of her mind, but she died from the effort.

Hamlet Macbeth investigated Professor Hardin, a Cambridge professor of Paranormal Sciences, leaving just as the Doctor and Liz arrived. Hardin was using technology to boost latent psychic powers, and was experimenting on his students. He tried to kill the Doctor, but the Brigadier shot him.

In late February, James Stevens started writing a book about UNIT. In March, Liz Shaw, who was working on the genetic engineering of reptiles, contacted Stevens and warned him not to research C19. His house was ransacked.[105]

(spring or summer?) - THE CLAWS OF AXOS[106] -> The Washington UNIT HQ sent one of their agents, Bill Filer, to help UNIT UK to search for the Master. Meanwhile, the civil servant Chinn investigated UNIT.

UNIT radar stations detected a UFO one million miles out, on a direct bearing for Earth. The alarm bells started to ring when it got within five hundred miles. UNIT HQ sent the order to launch an ICBM strike against the UFO, but the ship vanished before the missiles hit. It landed on the south east coast of England close to the National Power Complex at Nuton, amid freak weather conditions. As the army arrived to seal off the area, the UFO began to broadcast a signal:

> "Axos calling Earth, request immediate assistance. Axos calling Earth..."

The Axons made contact with the UNIT party. They claimed that solar flares had damaged their planet, and that they possessed an advanced organic technology. Their ship had been damaged. In return for help, the Axons offered humanity Axonite - a substance that was "the chameleon of the elements". It could be pro-

---

102 Dating *Deadly Reunion* (PDA #63) - *Terror of the Autons* is "recent", but the Master's TARDIS works, so this is set after *The Mind of Evil*.
103 *Who Killed Kennedy*. It is "December" (p136) 1970.
104 Dating "Change of Mind" (*DWM* #221-223) - The date is given as 1971. Liz has already left UNIT, but there's no mention of Jo.
105 *Who Killed Kennedy* (p162, p157).
106 Dating *The Claws of Axos* (8.3) - This story is set in the near future. There are videophones, although normal telephones are also in use. The National Power Complex "provides power for the whole of Britain" according to Sir George Hardiman, the head of the facility. (This needn't mean that the complex provides *all* of the country's power, just that it contributes to the whole of the National Grid rather than one region of it.) The complex has a "light accelerator". While this story was filmed in January, and the trees are bare, the snow is described as "freak weather conditions", perhaps suggesting the story is set in the spring or summer. Chinn says of the Brigadier's actions "that's the kind of high-handed attitude one has come to expect of the UN lately".

107 *Business Unusual*
108 Nuton is destroyed in *The Claws of Axos*, but mentioned in *The Daemons*.
109 *Who Killed Kennedy*
110 *Colony in Space*
111 *The Gallifrey Chronicles*
112 Dating *Colony in Space* (8.4) - There's no clear indication of the year. When Jo reaches the future, she is surprised that a colony ship was sent out in 1971 (it wasn't, of course, it was 2471). Either this story is set before 1971 and Jo is amazed how quickly the space programme has progressed, or it is set afterwards and she finds it difficult to believe that the colony ship was kept secret.
113 Dating "The Forgotten" (IDW *DW* mini-series #2) - No date is given. This could take place at any point when Jo is the Doctor's companion.
114 *The Eight Doctors*. In *The Daemons*, the local squire Winstanley says "there have been a lot of queer goings on the last few weeks", suggesting that's how long the Master has been in the area.
115 Inferred from *TimeH: Child of Time* (p64).
116 Dating *The Daemons* (8.5) - The story is set in the

grammed to absorb all forms of radiation, and to replicate and transmute matter. In theory, it would end the
world's food and energy problems. In reality, the Axons
had captured the Master in space, and he had led them
to Earth - a rich feeding ground - in return for his freedom and a chance to kill the third Doctor. The Axos
ship was banished from Earth and time-looped, but the
Nuton Complex was destroyed.

Private Erskine was attacked by an Axon and left for
dead, but survived. He was rescued by C19's Vault, and
bore a grudge against the Brigadier. He ended up working
for SeneNet.[107] **The National Power Complex at Nuton
was rebuilt.**[108] Chinn was blamed for the disaster at
Nuton and was pensioned off.[109]
**UNIT went hunting for the Master and accidentally
arrested the Spanish ambassador, mistaking him for
the renegade Time Lord.**[110] Marnal's son - who was on
the run at the time - visited his father during the nineteen
seventies, and told him exactly why the Doctor left
Gallifrey.[111]

COLONY IN SPACE[112] -> The TARDIS left the third
Doctor's laboratory in UNIT HQ for a matter of seconds, en route to 2472.

"The Forgotten"[113] -> The third Doctor, Jo and the
Brigadier were in Bessie, being chased by greyhound-like
aliens in walking machines. The Doctor immobilised the
aliens with sound from his sonic screwdriver.

The parish council of Devil's End converted the cavern
below the church into a witchcraft museum. The Master
arrived in Devil's End, killed the vicar Canon Smallwood,
and buried him in his own churchyard. He adopted the
identity of the new vicar, "Mr Magister".[114] The Master stole
a book from the Cabal of the Horned Beast, and it aided
him in summoning the Daemon Azal.[115]

(29th April - 1st May) - THE DAEMONS[116] -> At midnight on the major occult festival of Beltane, noted
archaeologist Professor Gilbert Horner attempted to
open the Devil's Hump - an ancient burial mount outside the village of Devil's End. BBC3 broadcast Horner's
endeavour, but the mount was actually the buried
spaceship of Azal, the last of the Daemons. Horner was
killed by a blast of subzero temperatures that resulted
when he opened the ship.
As the Reverend Magister, the Master organised a
coven to awaken Azal so he could receive the Daemon's
power. The Master succeeded, and Azal prepared, per
his instructions, to pass his power on to a creature
worthy of overseeing the planet. Azal deemed the third
Doctor, not the Master, a worthy recipient, but the
Doctor refused to accept such authority. Azal moved to
destroy the Doctor as a nuisance, but Jo Grant offered
her life in the Doctor's place. Her "irrational and illogi-
cal" move drove Azal to self-destruct. UNIT apprehended the Master soon afterwards.

James Stevens watched the opening of Devil's Hump on
BBC3 with Dodo, whom he had befriended.[117] The church
in Devil's End was destroyed, but the cavern beneath was
intact.[118]
Public outrage at UNIT's blowing up of the church at
Devil's End ("The Aldbourne Incident") led to "questions
in the House; a near riot at the General Synod".[119] UNIT
Private Cleary suffered a nervous breakdown after seeing
Azal.[120] SeneNet acquired the remains of Bok, a stone gar-
goyle animated by Azal's power.[121] After this, the Doctor
explored the area around Devil's End and found Hexen
Bridge, where he sensed an oppressive atmosphere.[122]
The public were told that the Master was an anarchist
terrorist, Victor Magister. He was remanded at Stangmoor
Prison.[123] The trial took place *in camera*. He was convicted
of murder, high treason and numerous other crimes.[124]
**While many wanted the Master executed, the Doctor
pleaded for clemency at his trial and the Master was
instead sent to Fortress Island in the English Channel.**[125]

near future, as BBC3 is broadcasting.
　Devil's Hump is opened at "midnight" on "Beltane",
and the story ends with a dance around the May pole.
Beltane appears to be a Saturday or Sunday, as Yates
and Benton watch a Rugby International and don't
know the result. As Professor Horner's book is released
the next day (and the shops would have to be open), it
is almost certainly Sunday. It is "two hundred years"
since Devil's Hump has been of interest, and the first
attempt to open it was in 1793.
117 *Who Killed Kennedy*
118 *The Eight Doctors*
119 *Downtime*. It is a little odd that this is named the

"Aldbourne Incident" - Aldbourne is the real village
where *The Daemons*, set in the fictional village of Devil's
End, was filmed. (Although an historic "Lord of
Aldbourne" is referred to in *The Daemons*.)
120 *Who Killed Kennedy*
121 *Business Unusual*
122 *The Hollow Men*
123 *The Face of the Enemy*
124 *Who Killed Kennedy*
125 *The Sea Devils*. The name of the island appears on
Captain Hart's map, but isn't referred to in dialogue.

The Master was kept at Aylesbury Grange Detention Centre until Fortress Island was ready.[126]

"The Man in the Ion Mask"[127] -> The third Doctor visited the imprisoned Master at Aylesbury Grange, a UNIT prison. With both of them locked in his cell, the Master claimed to have reformed, but the Doctor was suspicious - suspicions that were confirmed when it transpired that the Master had replaced himself with a hologram. The Master was just leaving... when the third Doctor, Lethbridge-Stewart and Benton apprehended him - the Doctor in the cell was also a hologram!

(summer) - THE SENTINELS OF THE NEW DAWN[128] -> Liz Shaw was now working in the Department of Applied Mathematics and Theoretical Physics at Cambridge. She asked the Doctor to examine the efforts of her friend and former research partner, Terri Billington, to build a time dilator - a device that could open a wormhole through time. The Sentinels of the New Dawn, operating in 2014, linked their dilator to Billington's prototype and transported the Doctor and Liz into the future. Upon their return, they destroyed Billington's work, preventing the Sentinels from seizing power. Billington, unaware that her research had nearly allowed a power-mad cabal to take over Earth, never spoke to Liz again.

At the UNIT staff panto, Mike Yates played Widow Twankey.[129] Mike Yates kissed Jo Grant at the UNIT Christmas party. The Master interrupted the festivities.[130]

Unit Year 5

(July) - THE MAGICIAN'S OATH[131] -> A master criminal - a ten-foot-tall mechanical creature with the power to control space and matter - was exiled to Earth. Its memories were siphoned into a storage unit while its blank mind resided in a human avatar. As the street performer "Diamond Jack", the criminal used his powers to perform incredible illusions - but this drew heat from the surrounding area, and caused freak weather conditions in Central London. Frosty lawns were reported in mid-July, and the Metropolitan Line was smothered in twenty inches of snow. Finally, on a Saturday, Hyde Park and the Serpentine froze over instantly, killing everyone there. More temperature drops followed; Trafalgar Square was just nine degrees Celsius.

The Doctor and UNIT found Jack's spaceship buried under Highgate Cemetery. Jack's original form was accidentally destroyed, and a despondent Jack started draining Jo's memories - thereby goading Mike Yates into shooting him dead. Jo was comatose in a UNIT medical facility just outside Tunbridge Wells for a week. Her memories of this

---

126 *The Face of the Enemy*

127 Dating "The Man in the Ion Mask" (*DWM Winter Special 1991*) - The story takes place shortly after *The Daemons*, in "1976". The story appeared in *DWM's UNIT Special*, which set out a timeline for the UNIT stories running from *The Invasion* in 1975 to *The Seeds of Doom* in 1980.

128 Dating *The Sentinels of the New Dawn* (BF CC #5.10) - It's "about a year" after Liz left UNIT, during "summer break" at Cambridge.

129 *No Future*, which places it in "1973", three years earlier. This must have been quite an occasion, as the Doctor also remembers it in *Timewyrm: Revelation*.

130 "The UNIT Christmas party last year" according to *Verdigris*.

131 Dating *The Magician's Oath* (BF CC #3.10) - The story takes place between *The Daemons* and *Day of the Daleks*. Mention is made of frosty lawns being found in mid-July - while it's possible that the subsequent events take place some weeks later in August, it's probably best to assume that everything happens in the same month.

132 Dating *The Doll of Death* (BF CC #3.3) - Big Finish cites the story as taking place between *The Daemons* and *Day of the Daleks*. Jo says she's already gone out to dinner and a club with Mike Yates; presumably, this is a precursor to their thwarted attempt at "a night out on the town" in *The Curse of Peladon*.

Jo says she's 18 in this story, which presumably means that she was 17 when she joined UNIT - which is awfully young for someone to be dashing about with a leading military organisation that investigates the paranormal, high-ranking uncle at the United Nations or no. Katy Manning born in 1949, and so was 21 when she first played Jo.

133 Dating *Who Killed Kennedy* (MA, unnumbered) - See Ft. 35 (pg240) for the dates given in this book.

134 Dating *Day of the Daleks* (9.1) - This may have a contemporary setting. While the world is on the brink of WW3, a BBC reporter appears as himself.

Jo tells the Controller that she left the twentieth century on "September the 13th". The Controller notes, rather annoyingly for those trying to pin down the dates of the UNIT stories, that Jo has "already told me the year" she is from.

135 *Return of the Living Dad*

136 *No Future*

137 *Business Unusual*

138 *The Dimension Riders*. Rafferty is Professor of Extra-Terrestrial Studies at Oxford and the Doctor's old friend.

139 "Death to the Doctor!", in what looks like an incident from the Doctor's UNIT days.

140 INTERNATIONAL POLITICS IN THE UNIT ERA: In the UNIT era, there appear to be four superpowers: The US, USSR, China and the United Kingdom. In the nineteen-seventies, the world apparently lurches from a period

incident and few other alien incursions would remain in one of Jack's playing cards for a few decades.

THE DOLL OF DEATH[132] -> The third Doctor and Jo investigated a temporal disturbance at the National Museum in Bloomsbury, where they encountered HannaH (sic), a "future historian" from a parallel Earth where time ran backwards. Our past was her future. HannaH had mentally crossed over to our universe to study the Doctor, the most consistent element that fended off all manner of global disasters, and her consciousness had come to occupy a doll. The Doctor and Jo facilitated HannaH's return home when Retrievers - dogs the size of ponies - were dispatched to fetch her back.

Jo kept missing her weekly training course because alien invasions typically happened on Fridays. Her instructor regarded her as a data-gathering operative, not a secret agent.

(summer) - WHO KILLED KENNEDY[133] -> James Stevens tried to reveal the truth about UNIT in a live broadcast on BBC3's *The Passing Parade*. His house was torched, and the Master kidnapped him. He was taken to the Glasshouse, a home for traumatised soldiers, and kept sedated for weeks. The Master was the director of the Glasshouse, and had been brainwashing the soldiers to create an army. He planned to send them through time to disrupt Earth's history.

Upon meeting Francis Cleary, Stevens managed to escape with him. He brought a TV crew back, but the place had been cleared out and Stevens was utterly discredited. Cleary was still under the Master's control, and killed Dodo on the Master's orders. The third Doctor instructed Stevens on how to use one of the Master's time rings, and he went back to 1963 to preserve the course of

history. Stevens returned to his native time, haunted with the knowledge that his older self would kill Kennedy.

(12th-13th September) - DAY OF THE DALEKS[134] -> UNIT were called in to guard the World Peace Conference at Auderly House. On the evening of 12th September, there was an assassination attempt on Sir Reginald Styles. Guerrillas from the future believed that Styles would sabotage the Conference, and that its failure would create a history in which the Daleks ruled Earth two hundred years hence. The third Doctor and Jo discovered that the guerrillas' interference, not Styles, had foiled the conference and paradoxically created this future.

A time-travelling squad of Daleks and Ogron footsoldiers attacked the House, attempting to guarantee that their version of history prevailed. The guerrilla Shura detonated a Dalekanium bomb and wiped out the invaders, but only after the delegates had been evacuated. With the delegates' survival, the guerrillas' history ceased to be.

Two Ogrons escaped and ended up in the village of Little Caldwell.[135] UNIT recovered a Dalek casing.[136] SeneNet recovered twenty-second century weaponry from the site.[137] James Rafferty wrote a paper about dust samples from the site.[138] The third Doctor, the Brigadier and Jo defeated a demonic-looking villain, the Mentor.[139]

The Cold War was brought to an end.[140]

Surgeon-Lieutenant Harold Sullivan was posted to Faslane.[141] **The Doctor took Jo on a test flight of the TARDIS. Under the Time Lords' guidance, the TARDIS headed for Peladon.**[142]

---

of detente with the Soviet Union (*The Invasion*), to the brink of World War Three (*The Mind of Evil, Day of the Daleks*), but within a few years of *Day of the Daleks*, the Cold War has ended. *Invasion of the Dinosaurs* includes the line "back in the Cold War days". *Robot* is also set after the Cold War ended. *About Time* notes that "it's massively unlikely that the entire Cold War has ended at this point since the stories made/set in the 1980s seem to suggest a world where there's still a schism between the US and USSR (see especially *Time-Flight*)". Alternatively, it's evidence that *Robot* is set after *Time-Flight* (so after 1981), which ties in nicely with the date given in *Pyramids of Mars* (the 1980 date would be the date of *The Time Warrior*).

The Soviet system seems to survive - in *Battlefield* the Russian troops' uniforms bear the hammer and sickle, but they are operating on British soil under UN command, and the "Soviet Praesidium" is mentioned in

The Seeds of Death.

Stories told since the collapse of the Soviet Union in the real world have referred to it: Ace mentions "perestroika" in *Timewyrm: Exodus*, and the Doctor talks of the collapse of the Soviet Union in *Just War*.

141 "A couple of weeks" before *The Face of the Enemy*.
142 *The Curse of Peladon*

= **THE FACE OF THE ENEMY**[143] -> The Conclave, the surviving members of the parallel Earth devastated by Project: Inferno, captured the Koschei of their reality and used his TARDIS to open dimensional portals to Earth.

The Conclave members began replacing their parallel duplicates to gain positions of power, but UNIT came to suspect the plan. With the Doctor offworld, the Brigadier allied himself with Royal Air Force lecturer Ian Chesterton and the imprisoned Master. The trio travelled to the parallel Earth, euthanised the dissected Koschei and severed the Conclave's link with the other Earth.

UNIT eliminated most of the Conclave members now stranded on Earth, but Marianne Kyle, the Conclave's Secretary General, remained at liberty.

By now, the Brigadier was in a relationship with Doris, an old friend from Sandhurst. Liz Shaw was in the US on a lecture tour. Ian Chesterton and Barbara had a son, John.

THE SEA DEVILS[144] -> **Imprisoned at Fortress Island, the Master attempted to contact a dormant colony of Sea Devils in the English Channel, hoping to direct them to attack mankind. The Master won the confidence of Colonel Trenchard, the governor of the prison, by claiming the creatures were terrorists that threatened Britain's national security. Trenchard acceded to the Master's requests, enabling him to contact the Sea Devils and engineer his escape. Trenchard died when a team of Sea Devils overran the prison.**

The third Doctor intervened and implored the Sea Devil leader to make peace with humankind, but a sneak Navy attack engineered by Robert Walker, the Parliamentary Private Secretary, convinced the Sea Devil leader to make war instead. Unable to contain the impending violence, the Doctor destroyed the underwater base and the Sea Devils within. The Master escaped shortly afterwards.

"Under Pressure"[145] - > The fourth Doctor landed on a submarine, quickly deduced it was on the trail of Sea Devils and convinced the crew he was the scientific advisor... unfortunately, the third Doctor was also involved. The fourth Doctor realised he had to play his part in history without giving away his identity. The Sea Devils attacked the submarine, and the two Doctors worked together over a radio link to translate a message to the Sea Devils, who withdrew.

THE EIGHT DOCTORS[146] -> The Master evaded capture by the third Doctor and Jo and reached his TARDIS, which was disguised as the sacrificial stone at Devil's End. The Doctor met his eighth incarnation at UNIT HQ.

"Target Practice"[147] -> The third Doctor and Jo headed to UN airbase 43, ostensibly UNIT's new training centre. They thought the Brigadier was there, but he was in Geneva and instead they met Colonel Ashe. But Ashe served tea to the Doctor before Jo, and misidentified an Auton as an Ogron - tipping the Doctor off that he was a bounder. He was a Russian spy, sent to abduct the Doctor. The Brigadier arrived in time to see the Doctor capture Ashe.

The Doctor went on Professor Gibbs' lecture on electro-particles.

143 Dating *The Face of the Enemy* (PDA #7) - This runs while the Doctor and Jo are away in *The Curse of Peladon*, and takes about a fortnight.
144 Dating *The Sea Devils* (9.3) - This is probably set in the near future. The prison guards' vehicles and uniforms are futuristic. Although this is effectively a sequel to two stories, no indication is given how much time has passed since *Doctor Who and the Silurians* or *The Daemons*. The Master insists that his second television be in colour, but this doesn't mean that the story is set just after colour TV was introduced - before the advent of cheap colour portable TVs, a household would commonly have a big colour set and a smaller black and white one. The Master watches an episode of *The Clangers*, first broadcast in 1971 and repeated many times since.
145 Dating "Under Pressure" (*DWM Yearbook 1992*) - It's the "late twentieth century". It's unclear if this is an unseen part of *The Sea Devils* or a later encounter with the monsters. We've assumed the former.

146 Dating *The Eight Doctors* (EDA #1) - This happens straight after *The Sea Devils*.
147 Dating "Target Practice" (*DWM* #234) - The story takes place after *The Sea Devils*, as there's a Sea Devil target on the range. The Doctor says he hasn't been to Russia for "several hundred years", and regardless of whether that's historically or within his own timeline, that places the story before *Wages of Sin* and contradicts *The Devil Goblins from Neptune*.
148 Dating *Tales from the Vault* (BF CC 6.1) - Jo names the titular characters from *The Sea Devils*, so it's after that. The one thing that initially seems telling but isn't: Jo records an account of this event over a cassette of Paul McCartney and Wings, but they were active from 1971 to 1981.
149 *The Mutants*
150 *The Time Monster*
151 In *The Green Death* it was "last year".
152 Dating *The Time Monster* (9.5) - There's nothing to suggest this is the near future. Benton wishes Jo a

TALES FROM THE VAULT[148] -> Roddy Fletcher, a friend of Jo Grant, was briefly possessed by the mind of Kalicarache when he bought and donned the army jacket of Tommy Watkins. The third Doctor wrested the jacket off Roddy, and the item was relegated to the UNIT Vault.

The Time Lords assigned the third Doctor and Jo the task of delivering a message pod, and they departed for the planet Solos.[149] All UNIT HQs received a new standing order, priority A1, to be on the lookout for the Master.[150] The Coal Board closed Llanfairfach Colliery in South Wales.[151]

(29th September) - THE TIME MONSTER[152] -> For several months, the Master had posed as one "Professor Thascales" to conduct research into the science of interstitial time at the Newton Institute in Wootton. He succeeded in developing TOM-TIT (Transmission of Matter Through Interstitial Time), a device capable of moving matter through the cracks between "now" and "now". However, the Master's true intentions were to use TOM-TIT to put Kronos, the ancient Chronovore, at his command.

The Master succeeded in bringing the Atlantean priest Krasis through time to assist him. The Master and Krasis set off back to Atlantis circa 1500 BC, and the third Doctor and Jo Grant pursued them there.

The Thascales Theorem was held by the United Nations for security purposes.[153] The Doctor and UNIT investigated abductions in Memphis, and were aided by singer Dusty Springfield.[154]

Unit Year 6

(May) - RAGS[155] -> At Dartmoor, a bloody conflict between a punk band and a group of university students freed the Ragman, who animated their corpses. They staged punk band performances as part of the Unwashed and Unforgiving tour, mentally stimulating persons in the area to commit violence. The group's performances caused a riot at Dartmoor Prison, and saw a group of fox hunters massacred by escapees from an asylum. UNIT was called in to investigate as the band reached Cirbury, and the Ragman also incited violence at Stonehenge. Kane Sawyer, a local ruffian and one of the Ragman's descendents, sacrificed himself to re-bind the Ragman in some standing stones.

FIND AND REPLACE[156] -> Iris Wildthyme and an older version of Jo Grant learned that the third Doctor - knowing that Jo would leave him some day, and fearing that his enemies would hunt her down to gain knowledge of him - was plotting to put her into a "witness protection programme" of sorts, in which Jo would become Iris' companion. They discouraged him from doing so, but when Iris tried to return the older Jo home in her bus, they found themselves on an alien locale...

(May) - VERDIGRIS[157] -> The third Doctor and the Brigadier fell out after defeating an Arcturan who had arrived on Earth with sinister intent. The Doctor decided to take a break from UNIT and went to an old mansion he owned in the town of Thisis.

The alien Verdigris, who had been drifting towards

"Merry Michaelmas". The TARDIS in this story appears to be fully functional - although this story is broadcast before *The Three Doctors*, perhaps it takes place afterwards. If not, then all the stories in Season Nine apparently take place between 13th September (*Day of the Daleks*) and 29th September (*The Time Monster*) of a given year.

This story is set in "the mid-seventies" according to *Falls the Shadow*, and "thirty years" before *The Quantum Archangel* (so 1973).
153 *Falls the Shadow*
154 *The Blue Angel*. At some unspecified point during the Doctor's exile.
155 Dating *Rags* (PDA #40) - This was the first PDA that didn't specify on the cover which TV stories it was set between. The Doctor's exile has not been lifted, yet Jo refers to Daleks and Ogrons, meaning it takes place at some point between *Day of the Daleks* and *The Three Doctors*.

It is "the beginning of May" when the Ragman starts his campaign, "Tuesday 10th May" a little later. The year is given as "79" at the beginning of the book (although

10th May wasn't a Tuesday in 1979). It is after Malcolm Owen of the Ruts died (July 1980, in real life), and The Damned song "I Just Can't Be Happy Today" was released (November 1979).
156 Dating *Find and Replace* (BF CC #4.3) - The younger Jo is currently the Doctor's assistant, the Doctor thinks about nicking a component from Iris' bus (so his exile is presumably still in force), UNIT is now based in "an old manor house" (so it's more likely to be Season 9 than Season 8), and the Master is at liberty. Taking all of that into consideration, Iris and the older Jo must show up at some point between *The Sea Devils* and *The Three Doctors*. The story ends on a bit of a cliffhanger, suggesting that Iris and Jo have any number of adventures before returning to 2010.
157 Dating *Verdigris* (PDA #30) - The month and year are stated in the book as "1973" and "May". Jo has known the Doctor "two years" (p143). Paul Magrs playfully made it tricky to place this story precisely... the story leads into *The Three Doctors* (p241), and yet Jo doesn't know about Peladon (p192). This is after the eventful UNIT Christmas party (p126).

Earth for thousands of years, contacted a race of refugees named the Meercocks. The Meercocks had decided to settle on Earth disguised as characters from Earth's fiction.

Iris Wildthyme and her companion Tom called on the Doctor, and they discovered the Meercocks' plan. They defeated an army of robot sheep and The Children of Destiny, a group of annoying psychic teenagers working for Galactic Federation Supreme Headquarters in Wales.

Verdigris escaped to inform Omega that the Doctor was on Earth.

The third Doctor's exile ends

THE THREE DOCTORS[158] -> The stellar engineer Omega, having survived in a universe of anti-matter, began incursions into the matter universe and started draining power from the Time Lord homeworld. With Omega's attention focused on the exiled third Doctor, the Time Lords decided to violate the First Law of Time and dispatch the Doctor's previous two incarnations to aid his current self.

The first Doctor was trapped in a time eddy and could only advise on the situation, but the second and third Doctors travelled to Omega's anti-matter universe. Omega desired to leave his domain, and tried to coerce the Doctors into becoming his successors. The Doctors escaped after triggering a matter/anti-matter explosion that seemingly destroyed Omega. The Time Lord homeworld regained full power.

The Time Lords sent the Doctor's previous selves back to their native times, and in gratitude ended the Doctor's exile. They restored his knowledge of time travel, and repaired the TARDIS to its proper function.

The Doctor constructed a force field generator and took the TARDIS on a test flight.[159] He defeated the Brotherhood of Beltane and blobby aliens called the Talichre, and the encounters went down in UNIT legend.[160]

Miss Gallowglass (later Countess Gallowglass) started running a mail forwarding service for aliens and time travellers alike, operating from a Portakabin in the East End. The Doctor first met her just after his exile on Earth ended. One of her customers, irate at a misplaced parcel, declared war on Earth and stole Britain's Crown Jewels. The Time Lords replaced the jewels with fakes, preserving history.[161]

THE WAGES OF SIN[162] -> The third Doctor offered to take Jo Grant and his former companion Liz Shaw to witness the Siberian meteorite strike in 1908. Instead, they erroneously arrived in St. Petersburg, 1916, shortly before the murder of Rasputin.

The Doctor and Jo meet Iris and Tom in a cocktail joint on a far flung outpost.[163] **Professor Whitaker disappeared when the government refused to fund his time-travel research.**[164] Tobias Vaughn funded Whitaker's experiments.[165]

The Doctor and Jo set off on another test flight. They landed on Inter Minor, where they became trapped in a MiniScope owned by the Lurman entertainer Vorg.[166]

THE SUNS OF CARESH[167] -> Lord Roche, a Gallifreyan, discovered that Caresh would enter a seventy-four year cold period that would extinguish all life on the planet. Roche set about modifying the Careshi time scanner into a stellar manipulator, hoping to save the planet's Fayon civi-

---

158 Dating *The Three Doctors* (10.1) - The evidence is mixed. Dr Tyler says the Americans have launched a deep space monitor, but he also cites "Cape Kennedy". (This might suggest that *The Three Doctors* takes place between 1963 and 1973.) Jo misquotes the words to "I am the Walrus". According to *Transit* (and a number of novelisations, such as *The Mysterious Planet*), the Doctor's exile lasts "five years".

159 The Doctor says at the end of *The Three Doctors* that he needs to build a new force field generator to replace the one that has been destroyed, and goes on a test flight in *Carnival of Monsters*.

160 *Relative Dementias*

161 *Relative Dementias* (p18) mentions when the Doctor encountered the Countess.

162 Dating *The Wages of Sin* (PDA #19) - It's just after *The Three Doctors*, in "the 1970s" (p34).

163 *Verdigris*

164 "Six months" before *Invasion of the Dinosaurs*.

165 *Original Sin*

166 *Carnival of Monsters*, in which Jo says that 1926 is

"forty years" before her time.

167 Dating *The Suns of Caresh* (PDA #56) - It is soon after the Doctor's exile is lifted (p35), and straight after the TARDIS gets back from Inter Minor (p36).

168 Dating *The Many Deaths of Jo Grant* (BF CC #6.4) - The blurb says that the story occurs between *Carnival of Monsters* and *Frontier in Space*.

169 *Dancing the Code* (p61). These unseen encounters either occur with UNIT, or elsewhere with the Doctor.

170 *Interference* (p75).

171 Dating *Dancing the Code* (MA #9) - Set between *Planet of the Daleks* and *The Green Death*. Watergate appears to be topical (p154).

172 *The Android Invasion*. Sarah reported on Crayford's disappearance "two years" before that story.

173 Dating *Last of the Gaderene* (PDA #28) - It is "some thirty years" since WW2 (p241). A constable indicates that it's the "the middle of July", which would contradict all four of the calendars in *The Green Death*.

174 Dating *Speed of Flight* (MA #27) - Jo is now thinking about leaving the Doctor (p242).

SECTION THREE: PRESENT DAY

lisation, which was a curiosity to him. Roche intended to deviate a neutron star and use its gravity to bump Caresh into orbit around its warmer star Beacon, but the Curia of the Nineteen - rulers of the Realm of the Vortex Dwellers - forecast that the diverted neutron star would devastate their territory. They dispatched two Furies to attack Roche, but he trapped the Furies within his TARDIS and sent it back in time thirteen centuries. It was unearthed in 1999, creating a time anomaly that the third Doctor detected.

The Doctor used Roche's equipment to manoeuvre Caresh closer to its smaller star Ember, avoiding damage to the Curia's territory. The Curia refrained from sending the Furies to attack Roche, averting the 1999 anomaly.

THE MANY DEATHS OF JO GRANT[168] ->
The Hargarans rebelled against their subjugators, the Xoanthrax Empire. The Xoanthrax had no sense of self-sacrifice, and were perplexed by Hargaran kamikaze runs on their outposts. The Brigadier chafed because a mysterious purple mould was spreading on the outside of Big Ben, and the Doctor was unavailable to investigate it. He was away in the Xoanthrax system, where he rescued a Xoanthrax peace activist: Vorlan. A detachment of the Xoanthrax Stormtroopers - living tanks with a Xoanthrax within directing them - pursued the TARDIS back to UNIT HQ. A Vanguard scientist named Rowe abducted Jo, hoping to study her keen sense of self-sacrifice. She was placed in a mindscape generator - a device that created false scenarios in the mind - and was made to "die" four hundred and twelve times. The Doctor freed Jo and Vorlan, but Rowe harvested much information on self-sacrifice - leaving the Doctor and Jo unsure if the Empire would use the data benevolently, or perpetrate greater atrocities with it.

Before this time, Jo had met a number of alien races including the Methaji, Hoveet, Skraals and Kalekani.[169] The Kalekani aggressively terra-formed worlds into rolling grasslands using the memetic virus known on Earth as the game "golf".[170]

DANCING THE CODE[171] ->
There were reports of "unorthodox weapons" in the North Africa country of Kebiria. UNIT sent a Superhawk jet fighter to investigate, and discovered a nest of Xarax - an insect hivemind. The Xarax began to infest the rest of the country, including the capital, Kebir City. The US Navy prepared a nuclear strike, but a UNIT team from the United Kingdom deactivated the nest using synthesised chemical instructions.

Defence astronaut Guy Crayford's XK5 space freighter, launched from Devesham Control, was lost during a test flight. It was believed to have collided with an asteroid. Sarah Jane Smith reported on the story.[172]

LAST OF THE GADERENE[173] ->
By now, the surviving Gaderene numbered only three hundred thousand. The Gaderene scout Bliss had founded the aeronautics manufacturer Legion International as a front for her operations, and enslaved residents of the British town Culverton by implanting them with Gaderene embryos. Bliss repaired the Gaderene transmat, intending to bring thousands of adult Gaderene through to Earth as an invasion force. However, UNIT's involvement resulted in the deaths of Bliss, her towering brother and the Gaderene embryos. The transmat was destroyed, and the resultant energy backlash further annihilated the Gaderene invasion force and homeworld.

SPEED OF FLIGHT[174] ->
The Doctor, Jo Grant and Mike Yates departed in the TARDIS for the planet Karfel, but arrived on the planet Nooma in the far future by mistake.

At some point, the Doctor and Jo (and possibly someone else) succeeded in visiting Karfel.[175] Tobias Vaughn helped develop the BOSS computer for Global Chemicals.[176]

THE GREEN DEATH[177] ->
The Doctor succeeded in reaching Metebelis III, and acquired one of its famed blue sapphires.

The government gave the green light to Global Chemicals' experiments into the Stevens Process, which produced 25% more petrol from a given amount of crude oil. The "Nutcake Professor" Clifford Jones - who had won the Nobel prize for his work on DNA synthesis - protested that the process would double air pollution, but Global Chemicals claimed that the pollution generated was negligible.

UNIT were sent to investigate a body that was discovered in the abandoned coal mine - a body that was glowing green. They discovered Global Chemicals had been dumping the pollution created by the Stevens

---

175 *Timelash. Speed of Flight* implies the Karfel visit occurs shortly afterwards.
176 *Original Sin*
177 Dating *The Green Death* (10.5) - This is the near future. The Prime Minister is called Jeremy. BOSS is an advanced "Biomorphic" artificial intelligence that has been linked to a human brain. There is a Ministry of Ecology. Four calendars appear: the first, in the pithead office, shows the date as "April 5th". The second, in the security guard's office, shows the month as February during a leap year. A wall calendar in Elgin's office suggests that it's May, but a similar one seen behind Mike Yates in episode four indicates that it's Monday, 28th April. See the British Politics in the UNIT Era sidebar.

Process into the mine, and that it had mutated the maggots down there. The giant maggots produced a slime that was toxic to humans, but the Doctor and Professor Jones discovered a fungus that killed them.

Global Chemicals was run by the BOSS, or Bimorphic Organisational Systems Supervisor, a computer linked to the brain of Stevens. In an effort to help the world achieve "maximum efficiency", the BOSS attempted to mentally dominate Global staff at seven sites throughout the world, including Llanfairfach, New York, Moscow and Zurich. Global Chemicals was destroyed when the BOSS blew up. Professor Jones' Nuthutch was given UN Priority One research status, leading to "unlimited funding".

The Prime Minister was called Jeremy. Jo Grant left UNIT at this time to marry Professor Jones.

The newlyweds went on an expedition to the Amazon.[178]

DEEP BLUE[179] -> The fifth Doctor, Tegan and Turlough landed in Tayborough Sands for a holiday and met up with UNIT. With "their" Doctor away, UNIT recruited his later incarnation to investigate a mutilated corpse. The Xaranti were attempting to convert Earth into a new homeworld, but they were defeated. Most of the UNIT staff involved in this adventure lost their memories of it, with only Captain Yates remembering the Doctor's future incarnation.

THE THREE COMPANIONS[180] -> The Brigadier accompanied the third Doctor to answer a distress call from deep-space freighter 621 Gamma Delta in the Deuteronomy Quadrant. The freighter contained a large representation of London and various Earth icons - including the Statue of Liberty, the Eiffel Tower, Queen Victoria, etc - as part of an alien game intended for children. The Doctor again encountered Jerry Lenz, a.k.a. "Garry Lendler," who had been hired to maintain the representation and purchase props for it. The representation was on its last legs, and the Doctor terminated the simulation.

Unit Year 7

THE TIME WARRIOR[181] -> British research scientists began to mysteriously disappear. UNIT were called in and the leading research scientists were all confined to the same barracks in a secret location. Nevertheless, the press got wind of the story. A young reporter named Sarah Jane Smith smuggled herself into the complex by posing as her Aunt Lavinia, the noted virologist. Before long, Sarah and the third Doctor had followed a time disturbance back to the Middle Ages.

THE PARADISE OF DEATH[182] -> The Parakon Corporation opened Space World on Hampstead Heath. It offered many attractions based on space and space travel, including twenty-one alien creatures such as the Giant

---

178 *Planet of the Spiders*
179 Dating *Deep Blue* (PDA #20) - It's "six months" after *The Green Death*, and it's Mike's first mission since then. The Doctor has spent only a small amount of time on Earth since Jo's departure, but there's no mention of Sarah. This is "six months" after *The Green Death* (p15), "ten or so" years before Tegan's native 1984 (p20).
180 Dating *The Three Companions* (serialised story; BF #120-129) - Jo has moved to Wales and the Doctor is companion-less, so it's between *The Green Death* and *The Time Warrior*.
181 Dating *The Time Warrior* (11.1) - Sarah states in this story that she's from the twentieth century, and isn't more specific than that. In *Pyramids of Mars*, it's stated four times that Sarah is "from 1980". The most straightforward interpretation of the line has to be that this story, Sarah's first, is set in 1980.
182 Dating *The Paradise of Death* (Target novelisation #156) - The Brigadier hasn't heard of Virtual Reality, and the Secretary-General of the United Nations is a woman. There is no gap on television between *The Time Warrior* and *Invasion of the Dinosaurs*, but this features both Sarah and Mike Yates. Barry Letts decided to set this radio play before Mike Yates' "retirement" from UNIT. Captain Yates is referred to in the book version.

183 Dating *Invasion of the Dinosaurs* (11.2) - The balance of evidence is that this is the near future. The Whomobile is a new car and an "M" reg, but the human race are - in theory at least - capable of building manned ships capable of interstellar flight. Whitaker has built a Timescoop capable of calling up dinosaurs from hundreds of millions of years ago. The bunker was built "back in the Cold War days".
184 The Doctor's car was never named on screen, but was dubbed both "Alien" and "the Whomobile" by the production team. The Doctor continues to use Bessie, as both are seen in *Planet of the Spiders*.
185 *SJA: Judgement Day*
186 *Invasion of the Dinosaurs*. The Doctor says that Chun Sen couldn't be a suspect with regards to the dinosaur appearances as he "hasn't been born yet".
187 *Terror of the Zygons*. Presumably the Brigadier didn't have the Space-Time Telegraph before *Invasion of the Dinosaurs*, when dinosaurs were over-running London, or he would surely have used it.
188 *Hornets' Nest: Hive of Horror*
189 Dating *The Five Doctors* (20.7) - The third Doctor is kidnapped after *The Time Warrior* as he recognises Sarah. Sticking strictly to what we know in the television series, his abduction must occur between *The Monster of Peladon* and *Planet of the Spiders*, because

Ostroid, the crab-clawed Kamelius from Aldebaran Two, Piranhatel Beetles and Stinksloths. Using Experienced Reality techniques, Parakon could give people guided tours of the Gargatuan Caverns of Southern Mars and the wild side of Mercury.

UNIT investigated the death of a young man whose thighbone had been bitten clean through, and exposed the Parakon Corporation as an extra-terrestrial organisation. Parakon had been negotiating with Earth for a number of years, hoping to sign a trading agreement. Parakon would supply a wonder material named rapine in exchange for human bodies to fertilise their world, which had been devastated by the rapine harvests. Parakon had already sacked many worlds, including Blestinu, but UNIT defeated it.

INVASION OF THE DINOSAURS[183] -> Eight million Londoners were evacuated after dinosaurs began to terrorise the population. The government decamped to Harrogate. UNIT helped with the security operation, which was under the command of General Finch and the Minister for Special Powers, Sir Charles Grover.

UNIT scientists calculated that someone was operating a time machine that required an atomic reactor. They tracked the Timescoop in question to a hidden bunker near Moorgate Underground Station. The bunker contained an elaborate shelter that served as home to a group of people - including the conservationist Lady Cullingford, the novelist Nigel Castle and the Olympic long jumper John Crichton - who were all convinced they were in a spaceship bound for a new, unpolluted planet. Using the Timescoop, Professor Whitaker hoped to regress Earth back to its primeval days, repopulating it with the people in the bunker. The Doctor and UNIT ended this plan, and Whitaker and Grover were stranded in the past. Mike Yates, a member of the conspiracy, was discharged from UNIT.

During this, the Doctor unveiled his new car.[184] At the Brigadier's request, Sarah Jane spread a cover story about the Operation: Golden Age incident, claiming that a "terrorist threat" had ended.[185] After this time, the tem-

poral scientist Chun Sen was born.[186] Realising that UNIT might need to contact him in an emergency, the Doctor gave the Brigadier a syonic beam Space-Time Telegraph.[187] The Brigadier gave Mike Yates a hip flask the day he left the service.[188]

THE FIVE DOCTORS[189] -> While on Earth at this time, the third Doctor was kidnapped by Borusa while driving his sprightly yellow roadster Bessie.

(20th-21st May) - THE GHOSTS OF N-SPACE[190] -> While on holiday in Italy, the third Doctor, Sarah, Jeremy Fitzoliver and the Brigadier prevented Maximillian Vilmio, a wizard, from achieving immortality. Vilmio had planned to use the space-warping effect of Clancy's comet to match his real body and his N-form in Null-Space.

ISLAND OF DEATH[191] -> Sarah investigated the disappearance of Jeremy, and found he had joined a cult that worshipped a reptilian alien called Skang. The third Doctor helped her discover that the cultists' drinks were laced with psychotropics. They flew to Bombay with the Brigadier, and traced the cult to Stella Island, but the Great Skang was summoned to Earth. It had infected followers with spores - a means of preserving its race. The Doctor placed the Skang gestalt in a time loop to preserve it.

Unit Year 8

To prevent nuclear launches, the US, USSR and China gave their Destructor Codes to Britain. Joseph Chambers was made Special Responsibilities Secretary with responsibility for protecting them.[192]

Three years and eight months after the Doctor and Liz defeated the Sentinels of the New Dawn, Terri Billington had a fatal stroke. She had only been CMS chair for a month and a day, and Liz succeeded her in the post.[193]

AMORALITY TALE[194] -> Sarah Jane discovered a 1952 photograph of the third Doctor while researching a story. The Doctor was intrigued by a "warp shadow" on the photo, and the two of them went to 1952 to investigate.

---

the other stories of Season 11 follow on from each other. However *The Paradise of Death* is set in a "nonexistent" gap between the first two stories of the series, so the Doctor might have been taken from that point.
190 Dating *The Ghosts of N-Space* (MA #7) - For the Doctor and Sarah, the story occurs after *Death to the Daleks*. Clancy's Comet returns to Earth every one hundred and fifty-seven years, and the last sighting was in "1818", so it's 1975. As the month is given as May, *Planet of the Spiders*, set in March, must take place the following year. Fitzoliver was Sarah's photographer in *The*

Paradise of Death.
191 Dating *Island of Death* (PDA #71) - The story mentions Sarah's trip to Sicily in *The Ghosts of N-Space*, and the Hallaton arrived on Stella Island on 20th September, so this story happens in UNIT Year 7.
192 "A few months" before *Robot*. The system has passed to UN control by *World War Three*.
193 *The Sentinels of the New Dawn*
194 Dating *Amorality Tale* (PDA #52) - The story starts between *The Monster of Peladon* and *Planet of the Spiders*.

The Doctor started a project to research the psychic potential of humans.[195]

(mid-March) - PLANET OF THE SPIDERS[196] -> A stage magician, Clegg, died at UNIT HQ as the third Doctor investigated his psychic potential. This was linked to a disturbance at a Tibetan monastery in Mortimer, Mummerset. It was led by Lupton, a man bitter because he was sacked by a company after twenty-five years of service, then saw his own company bankrupted by his previous employers. The Spiders from Metebelis III had contacted Lupton, and compelled him to try and steal a Metebelis crystal that was in the Doctor's possession. The Doctor pursued Lupton to Metebelis in the future. Upon the Doctor's return to Earth, he regenerated.

Tobias Vaughn helped fund Kettlewell's research into robotics.[197]

(4th April) - ROBOT[198] -> UNIT's limited budget left the organisation unable to afford a Captain to replace Mike Yates. Benton was promoted to Warrant Officer and made the Brigadier's second-in-command.

The National Institute for Advanced Scientific Research, a.k.a. Think-Tank, concentrated many of Britain's scientists all under one roof. They developed pieces of high technology that included the disintegrator gun - a weapon capable of burning a hole on the moon's surface - and dynastrene, the hardest material known to science. The most impressive achievement, though, was Professor Kettlewell's "living metal", which he used to build the K1: a robot capable of performing tasks in environments where no human could survive. Many Think-Tank personnel were also members of the Scientific Reform Society (SRS), a group that believed in efficiency and logic.

The SRS tried to use the K1 to further their aims, but the newly regenerated fourth Doctor used a metal-eating virus to destroy the robot. He also prevented the SRS from triggering a nuclear holocaust. Afterwards, the Doctor and Sarah left with their new travelling companion, UNIT medic Harry Sullivan.

Several members of Think Tank went to prison for violations of the Official Secrets Act. Hilda Winters' associate Jellico went down on a murder charge; Winters herself would be incarcerated for fifteen years.[199] Corporations used Kettlewell's technology to develop various technologies including nanotech. His family didn't profit from his discoveries.[200] **Following this time, a woman became Prime Minister.**[201] Mike Yates met the fourth Doctor at the Brigadier's Christmas Party.[202]

(January) - TERROR OF THE ZYGONS[203] -> Centuries after arriving on Earth, the Zygons in Loch Ness learnt that a stellar explosion had destroyed their home planet. A refugee fleet had been assembled and was looking for a new home. The Zygon leader Broton signalled that Earth would be suitable once the ice caps had been melted, the mean temperature of the planet had been raised and the necessary minerals had been introduced to the water.

The Zygons intensified their campaign against humanity when oil companies started disrupting the free passage of their Skarasen, a vast monster that lived in Loch Ness but which ventured out into the North Sea from time to time. In the space of a month, the Zygons destroyed three North Sea oil rigs, causing massive loss of life. Two of the rigs were owned by Hibernian Oil. UNIT were sent to Tullock to deal with the problem.

Broton, posing as the Duke of Forgill, got into the Fourth International Energy Conference on the banks

---

195 The Doctor is conducting such research in *Planet of the Spiders*. It's only mentioned in that story, and there's no suggestion that the fourth Doctor continues the study.
196 Dating *Planet of the Spiders* (11.5) - The story takes place three weeks before *Robot*. "Meditation is the in thing" according to Sarah Jane.
197 *Original Sin*
198 Dating *Robot* (12.1) - This is clearly set in the near future. As with *Invasion of the Dinosaurs*, the Cold War has been "over for years" according to the Brigadier. Advanced technology includes the K1 robot, the Disintegrator Gun and dynastrene. Sarah Jane Smith's day pass to Think-Tank bears the date "April 4th".
199 *SJS: Mirror, Signal, Manoeuvre*
200 *Benny: The Relics of Jegg-Sau*

201 In *The Ark in Space*, Harry is surprised that the High Minister, "a member of the fair sex," was "top of the totem pole", suggesting Britain has yet to elect a female Prime Minister by his time. There must be a General Election or change of leadership in the government while he was away from Earth. In *Terror of the Zygons*, the Brigadier receives a phone call from the PM, whom he twice addresses as "Madam", and later refers to her as "she".
202 *Hornets' Nest: The Stuff of Nightmares*
203 Dating *Terror of the Zygons* (13.1) - It is the near future. The Prime Minister is a woman. In *Pyramids of Mars*, two stories after this one, Sarah states that she is "from 1980". According to *No Future*, this story is set in January 1976.

BRITISH POLITICS IN THE UNIT ERA: During the UNIT era, there are references to two Prime Ministers who are not the actual PM when the story was shown. However, both are semi-jokey references to actual opposition leaders of the time.

"Jeremy" mentioned in *The Green Death* would be Jeremy Thorpe, the leader of the Liberal Party at the time the story was made. Thorpe, of course, was never Prime Minister, although he was in the ascendant at the time *The Green Death* was shown. Shortly afterwards, in the February 1974 Election, the Liberal vote tripled to six million and they entered a pact with Labour to form a government.

In *Terror of the Zygons*, the Prime Minister is a woman. Margaret Thatcher had already been elected leader of the Conservatives when *Terror of the Zygons* was taped - the scene in which the Brigadier is phoned by the PM was recorded on 23rd April 1975, and Mrs Thatcher had been party leader since February of that year. The Labour government of the time had a tiny majority of four seats, and predicting a Conservative victory at the next election was a fairly safe bet (in much the same way that *Zamper*, written in 1995, referred to "Number ten, Tony's den").

If we assume the UNIT stories are set in the near future, then this is remarkably straightforward, as only the result of one "real life" election need be changed. According to *The Green Death*, there is a general election won by Thorpe's Liberals at some point after 1973 (it can't be before *The Green Death* was shown, or it wouldn't be the future). Thatcher's Conservatives defeat this government. We can pinpoint the date of that election - it's between *Robot* and *Terror of the Zygons*, as Harry is surprised by the female leader in *The Ark in Space*. This coincides neatly with Sarah's assertion in *Pyramids of Mars* that she's from 1980. So the Liberals win the next General Election (one that had to be called by June 1975), the Tories win the one after that (possibly in May 1979, as in our history) and it all fits.

The date the Liberals come to power is harder to pin down. The model above assumes that it's a single-term government. A four or five-year term in office would mean they came to power around the time the Doctor was exiled to Earth. The man who's Minister of Ecology in *The Green Death* drafted UNIT's charter. It's possible to squeeze the Liberal election victory in before *The Invasion*, but there's nothing that demands he was a member of the governing party when he drew up the charter. A diplomatic, military or even legal career could have made him the right man for the job (we can only say for certain is that it's an unlikely job for a serving Minister of Ecology). Politics in the UNIT era is a world of grey, middle-aged men. There are occasional visionaries, but government is practically run by civil servants. There's no obvious point where the government's character changes in the UNIT stories.

Throughout the UNIT era, the government is throwing money at new energy projects. We see grand schemes in *Doctor Who and the Silurians*, *Inferno*, *The Claws of Axos*, *The Green Death* and *Robot*, although these all end in disaster and mankind is still dependent on oil in *Terror of the Zygons*. The environment is clearly a huge political issue, with concerns about pollution voiced in many stories. The existence of a Minister of Ecology as a cabinet post is telling. When the Tories come to power, a lot of these responsibilities might transfer to the World Ecology Bureau we see in *The Seeds of Doom*. It's interesting to note that there's no mention of Europe, especially as (perhaps because) the Common Market was a hot political issue at the time. (The EEC debate was - far more vaguely than most fans seem to think - satirised in *The Curse of Peladon*.)

This version, then, is consistent with what we're told in the series and with what someone writing in the early seventies would extrapolate as a plausible backdrop for a science-fantasy adventure show set in the near future.

Some recent writers - particularly those who see the UNIT stories as being set at the time of broadcast - have developed a parallel political history for *early 1970s* Britain of the *Doctor Who* universe. Books like *Who Killed Kennedy* and *The Devil Goblins from Neptune* infer that events in the UNIT stories destabilised actual governments. This seems to be the logical consequence of the catalogue of incompetent government action, politicians dying, international crises and high profile disasters we see ... although in the TV series, politicians and civil servants are depicted, almost to a man, as complacent and obtuse. They seem far *too* secure, rather than people scared the government will fall at any moment.

All in all, the various things we are told about the parallel political history described in the books are difficult to reconcile.

In real life, the Prime Ministers since 1970 (along with the date of the general election, the winning party and their majority) were:

Heath   (18th June, 1970, Conservative, 30)
Wilson (28th February, 1974, Labour minority, 0)
Wilson (10th October, 1974, Labour, 4)
Callaghan (5th April, 1976)
Thatcher   (3rd May, 1979, Conservative, 43)
Thatcher   (9th June, 1983, Conservative, 143)
Thatcher   (11th June, 1987, Conservative, 102)
Major   (27th November, 1991)
Major   (9th April, 1992, Conservative, 21)
Blair   (1st May, 1997, Labour, 179)
Blair   (7th June, 2001, Labour, 167)
Blair   (5th May, 2005, Labour, 66)
Cameron   (6th May, 2010, Conservative coalition, 0)

continued on page 259...

of the Thames - he planned to assassinate the world leaders assembled there by signalling for the Skarasen. Broton, the signal device and the Zygon ship were all destroyed, and the Skarasen returned to Loch Ness.

Harry Sullivan opted to return to London by InterCity as the Doctor and Sarah tried to more directly go there in the TARDIS...

Sarah Jane spread a cover story to help conceal the truth about the Zygon gambit.[204] Probably owing to the Loch Ness Monster incident, the press got word of the Doctor's role in saving the world. He played for Lord's Taverners, but avoided most other tenants of celebrity-dom. A publisher approached the Doctor, who agreed to write a series of educational books for children.[205]

The government ordered Department C19 to be cleaned up, and many of its top brass were removed.[206]

Jo Jones travelled down the Amazon for months, and finally reached a village with the only telephone for thousands of miles. She phoned UNIT to ask about the Doctor... and was told that he had left and never come back. The Doctor, for his part, couldn't find Jo because she stayed on the move so much.[207]

Harry Sullivan's stories of being a naval doctor encouraged his younger step-brother, Will Sullivan - whose widowed father had married Harry's mother - to enter the medical profession. When Will Sullivan was a medical student, the Crimson Chapter recruited him.[208]

HEART OF TARDIS[209] -> A collision with the second Doctor's TARDIS further de-stabilised the Lychburg singularity, to the point that it threatened the entire universe. The Time Lords sent the fourth Doctor and Romana to deal with the problem, but the Jarakabeth demon impersonating Alistair Crowley impeded their efforts, hoping to use the singularity to re-write reality in the name of chaos.

The second Doctor (secretly aided by his future self) used telemetry readings from the TARDIS to return Lychburg to Earth, whereupon the residents deserted the town entirely. A benevolent Jarakabeth demon hosted in government agent Katherine Delbane killed the Crowley demon. She became a UNIT captain under the Brigadier's command.

UNIT has recently requisitioned industrial lasers, marmosets, archaeological tools, rocketry components, Watsui tribal masks and a US college's particle accelerator. They also took a third of the Bank of England's gold reserves and didn't replace them, triggering a stock market crash.

(19th-22nd June, 1976) - NO FUTURE[210] -> The terrorist organisation Black Star, a group of anarchists, spent the summer planting bombs in sites around London: Hamleys, Harrods, the Albert Hall, the Science Museum and Big Ben. There was an assassination attempt on the Queen, junior treasury minister John Barfe was killed, the entertainer Jimmy Tarbuck was badly hurt in a hit-and-run incident, and Pink Floyd's private jet was lost over the English Channel. Civil disturbances happened across the globe. Prime Minister Williams declared a state of emergency.

Meanwhile, the Vardans were preparing an "active immigration" to Earth. The Vardan High Command formed an alliance with the Monk, the Time Lord otherwise known as Mortimus. The Monk freed the Vardans from their time loop, and under the guise of Priory Records boss Robert Bertram, he used Vardan Mediascape technology to plant crude subliminal messages in Earth's TV broadcasts. More sophisticated brainwashing techniques were available in the new VR training system that the Monk provided for UNIT.

The seventh Doctor, Ace and Benny helped some members of UNIT and Broadsword intelligence agents to repel

---

204 *SJA: Judgement Day*
205 *The Kingmaker.* In real-life, Target published the *Doctor Who Discovers...* books, the fifth of which (here unnamed) was *Doctor Who Discovers Early Man.* This would also explain why the fourth Doctor was chosen to present a segment of children's show *Animal Magic.* Naturally, as that was broadcast in 1980, it's final, clinching and irrefutable proof that the UNIT stories are set in the future.
206 "Six months" before *No Future,* and also referred to in *Return of the Living Dad.*
207 *SJA: Death of the Doctor.* Date unknown, but probably no earlier than *Terror of the Zygons* - although the Doctor does aid UNIT in *The Android Invasion* and *The Seeds of Doom,* his association with the group is on the decline, and he doesn't step foot in UNIT HQ on those occasions.

208 *SJS: Buried Secrets, SJS: Fatal Consequences.* It's unclear when Will was recruited, but it's almost certainly after Harry joined UNIT, and even more probably after he went travelling with the Doctor and Sarah.
209 Dating *Heart of TARDIS* (PDA #32) - The dating seems particularly confused. UNIT knows the fourth Doctor, but Benton's a Sergeant and Yates hasn't been discharged. This is after the 1982 Falklands War, and there is a Conservative government. We could infer from the gold reserves reference that UNIT have fought the Cybermen - either in *The Invasion,* the 1975 invasion mentioned in *The One Doctor* and *Dalek* (presuming that's a different invasion) or another incident entirely.
210 Dating *No Future* (NA #23) - The date is given (p6).

...continued from page 257

In the books, a Liberal-led coalition government was formed in January 1970. *The Devil Goblins from Neptune* (p8) states, "an alliance of Liberals, various disenfranchised Tories and Socialists, and a group of minor fringe parties, enter power on a platform of social reform, the abolition of the death penalty, and a strong interstellar defence programme".

In June 1970, Heath defeats Wilson, just as in our history (*Who Killed Kennedy*). This can't be easily reconciled with *The Devil Goblins from Neptune*, which also takes place in June 1970.

Shirley Williams is Prime Minister in *No Future*, set just after *Terror of the Zygons* in 1976. We're told that Thorpe had resigned mid-term, but there is also reference to Wilson.

In *Millennial Rites,* a female PM lost an election in the early eighties. In 1999, the leader of the Opposition is a woman ("all handbag and perm"). The Prime Minister is a man.

The unnamed winner of the 1997 general election was assassinated in *The Dying Days*. Edward Greyhaven is installed Prime Minister by the new Martian King of England, but dies during the course of the story.

Terry Brooks, Prime Minister in 1999, tries to fake a military coup as a pretext to dismantle the military and spend the money health and education instead. He is forced to resign, and is replaced by Philip Cotton. (*Millennium Shock* - they're a thinly-veiled Tony Blair and Jack Straw).

Tony Blair is alive, well and Prime Minister in *Project: Twilight* and *Death Comes to Time*. Mickey mentions him in *Rise of the Cybermen*.

Interference lists the recent British Prime Ministers as Heath, Thorpe, Williams, Thatcher, Major, Blair and Clarke. (The last could be senior Conservative Kenneth Clarke, but could possibly be Labour's Charles Clarke. The proofreader added the "e" - Lawrence Miles' original intention was that it was Tory MP Alan Clark.)

Aliens of London and *World War Three* had scenes set in Downing Street, with photographs of Callaghan and Major on the stairway (no photos of Thorpe, Williams, Brooks, Cotton or either Clarke were visible!). The Prime Minister of the day is murdered by the Slitheen, and Harriet Jones becomes PM sometime between this story and *The Christmas Invasion*.

Once we're clear of the confused accounts of the 1970 elections, the sequence of Prime Ministers and when they come to power would seem to be:

Thorpe   (Liberal coalition, in power at the time of *The Green Death*)

Williams   (Labour, in power during *Terror of the Zygons* and *No Future*)

Thatcher   (Conservative, who came to power in the early eighties, later than in real life)

Major   (Conservative - we might infer he's the assassinated winner of the 1997 election)

Greyhaven   (briefly in 1997 and almost certainly not counted officially)

Brooks   (Unknown party, possibly leading from 1997 to 1999)

Cotton   (The same party as Brooks, takes over in 1999 - the leader of the opposition at this time is a woman, so isn't...)

Blair   (Labour, the dates are uncertain, but he comes to power later and apparently leaves earlier than in real life, and thus manages to avoid two successful alien assassinations of a British Prime Minister.)

Clarke   (Unknown party, presumably the Prime Minister seen in the *UNIT* audio mini-series and assassinated in *Aliens of London* in 2006 - although the body looks more like Blair than either Kenneth or Charles Clarke, both of whom could comfortably accommodate a Slitheen in real life!)

Jones   (The same party as Clarke. The ninth Doctor says in *World War Three* that she was originally supposed to serve three terms - possibly until c 2016 in *Trading Futures*, where the PM was male. However, her first term is curtailed by the tenth Doctor in *The Christmas Invasion* - this would seem to be a significant deviation of established history, unless the ninth Doctor was mistaken in *World War Three* to think Jones was a three-termer.)

Unknown. (There is at least one interim Prime Minister after Jones' downfall in *The Christmas Invasion*. A blurry picture of him is seen in *TW: Out of Time*, along with the apparently sceptical headline, "Working Hard, Minister?")

Saxon. (According to *The Sound of Drums*, he leads the newly-formed Saxon Party, which has attracted support from across the political spectrum. While time is reversed in *Last of the Time Lords*, his outing himself as the Master and ordering the death of the US President on global TV "still happens". Saxon dies at the end of the story, which is set in 2008.)

Fairchild. (Killed in 2009 when the Daleks shoot his plane down in *The Stolen Earth*; he's named as "Aubrey Fairchild" in *Beautiful Chaos*.)

Green. (Seen in *TW: Children of Earth*, set in September 2009 - he almost certainly takes over when when Fairchild dies earlier in the year. The story ends with Denise Riley, a member of Green's cabinet, obtaining incriminating evidence on him, but it's not said if she plans to force him out and become prime minister herself, or just pull his strings from behind the scenes. Either way, given the abominable events of *Children of Earth* - including the army being used to forcibly take thousands of children from their parents - it's difficult to imagine the party in power winning the next election. *TW: The Men Who Sold the World*, set in 2010, alludes to the UK having a new coalition government.)

the Vardans from Earth. The Vardan Popular Front, a democratic organisation, took control of Varda. The Monk had captured the Chronovore Artemis and had been tapping her power to alter time, but she was freed and took her revenge on him.

The Brigadier was seeing Doris at this time. The seventh Doctor selectively wiped his memory, and he retired.

The Russians were operating vodyanoi units at this time.[211] One Vardan remained behind, living in the Liverpool phone network until 1983.[212] **Following this, the Brigadier spent a great deal of time in Geneva.**[213]

(6th July) - THE ANDROID INVASION[214] **-> The leader of the Kraals' Armoury Division, Chief Scientist Styggron, planned his race's escape from the dying planet Oseidon using their technological skills. The Kraals could engineer space-time warps, and two years previously, Styggron had used one of these to capture an experimental Earth freighter in deep space. He analysed the mind of the astronaut within, Guy Crayford, and used Crayford's memories to construct a training ground - an almost-perfect replica of the English village of Devesham, including the nearby Space Defence Station. It was populated with Android villagers, and the Kraals were able to study human civilisation and behaviour, honing their preparations to invade the Earth.**

It was the Kraals' first attempt at conquest, and although they were thwarted by the fourth Doctor and Sarah - as aided by Harry Sullivan and RSM Benton - Marshal Chedaki's fleet survived.

SeneNet recovered a Kraal android.[215]

(early one month in autumn) - THE SEEDS OF DOOM[216] **-> The World Ecology Bureau was active at this time. They received reports that an unusual seed pod had been discovered in the Antarctic permafrost, and called in UNIT. The fourth Doctor and Sarah identified the item as a Krynoid seed pod and also discovered a second one. One Krynoid was killed in the Antarctic, while an RAF air strike on the mansion of Harrison Chase, the millionaire plant enthusiast, destroyed the other.**

Sir Colin Thackeray ordered that cuttings be taken from the Krynoid remains, so a better means could be found of killing the creatures.[217]

THE PESCATONS[218] **->** Upon their return to Earth, the fourth Doctor and Sarah were attacked by a sea creature, which the Doctor recognised as a Pescaton. He hurried to the astronomer Professor Emmerson and watched Pesca, the homeplanet of the Pescatons in the outer galaxies, explode.

The Pescatons had escaped in a space fleet, which arrived on Earth and attacked many cities. A smaller number went to Venus. The Doctor located the Pescaton leader, Zor, in the London Underground and killed him with ultraviolet light. The Pescatons died without their leader.

The Pescatons and their sister race, the Piscons, both originated in the Picos system. While an expanding sun destroyed the Pescaton planet, the Piscons' homeworld survived but became desert. The Piscons wandered around the universe acquiring water supplies - sometimes benevolently from unpopulated planets, sometimes illegally.[219]

---

211 *No Future,* and a reference to the 1981 BBC drama *The Nightmare Man* - adapted by Robert Holmes and directed by Douglas Camfield.
212 *Return of the Living Dad*
213 The Brigadier is in Geneva during *The Android Invasion* and *The Seeds of Doom.*
214 Dating *The Android Invasion* (13.4) - This is the near future. For at least the last two years, Britain has had a Space Defence Station, a team of Defence Astronauts, and has been operating space freighters. The calendar in the fake village gives the date (every day) as "Friday 6th July". The nearest years with that exact date are 1973, 1979, 1984 and 1990.
215 *Business Unusual*
216 Dating *The Seeds of Doom* (13.6) - On balance, it seems to be the near future. There is a satellite videolink to Antarctica and UNIT have access to a laser cannon. The Antarctic base has an experimental fuel cell. On the other hand, Sarah only wants 2p to use the public telephone. Chase says it is autumn (location

work for the story was recorded in October/November). The Doctor is invited to address the Royal Horticultural Society on "the fifteenth".
217 *Hothouse*
218 Dating *The Pescatons* (Argo Records LP, novelised as Target #153) - The story is set in Sarah's time. It was released in August 1976, between Seasons 13 and 14, so it's been placed after *The Seeds of Doom.* The bit with Professor Emmerson and the telescope is in the novelisation, not the original record. It's quite the impressive telescope too - able to watch events on another planet in real-time, which is impossible.
219 *Peri and the Piscon Paradox*
220 Dating *The Hand of Fear* (14.2) - While it doesn't feature UNIT, Sarah is returned home at the end of the story. It has to be set before December 1981 and *K9 and Company,* in which she's back at work. According to *The Visual Dictionary,* it is "thirty years" before *School Reunion.*
221 *School Reunion*

THE HAND OF FEAR[220] -> The "obliterated" alien named Eldrad had fallen to Earth as a stone hand and regenerated into a humanoid (albeit female) form. There was near-meltdown in the main reactor of Nunton Nuclear Power station, although there was no radiation leak as Eldrad used the energy to facilitate his/her regeneration. The fourth Doctor and Sarah decided to escort Eldrad back to his/her homeworld of Kastria.

Afterwards, in answering a summons to Gallifrey, the Doctor was forced to return Sarah Jane Smith home. Although the TARDIS apparently failed to return Sarah to Croydon, she arrived in England.

The Doctor had dropped her off in Aberdeen.[221] Fortunately, it was the right timezone. Sarah resumed her work as a journalist.[222]

WARTIME[223] -> Benton was en route to UNIT HQ with a cache of radioactive material, and was passing through Bolton when he found himself haunted by apparitions of his mother, his late father and his dead brother Christopher. He also stopped a hijacker intent on stealing the nuclear cargo.

Realising that the Doctor's visits were becoming less and less frequent, the Brigadier had Bessie mothballed.[224] The Brigadier announced his retirement from UNIT. Soon afterwards, he became a mathematics teacher at Brendon School.[225]

Unit Year 10

THE ARCHITECTS OF HISTORY[226] -> The seventh Doctor visited the new iteration of Elizabeth Klein, having erased the version of her that went to Colditz from history. The surviving Klein had been born in England to German parents, and now worked for UNIT. She acknowledged the Doctor as an ally in keeping the world safe.

---

222 *K9 and Company*

223 Dating *Wartime* (Reeltime Pictures film #1) - *Wartime* was released in 1987, and John Levene (understandably) looks older, suggesting that some time has passed since Benton's last TV appearance (*The Android Invasion*). The Brigadier is still in command of UNIT; otherwise, placement of this film is only a rough approximation. *The Android Invasion* establishes that Benton has a kid sister, but nothing is said about her here.

224 *Battlefield. The Seeds of Doom* is the last story to feature UNIT until *Mawdryn Undead*, and it is established in the later story (and implied in *Time-Flight*) that the Doctor hasn't visited the Brigadier for years.

225 *Mawdryn Undead*, a year before 1977.

226 Dating *The Architects of History* (BF #132) - Klein implies that the Doctor hasn't visited UNIT for two years. Steve Lyons, the author of this story, commented: "That last scene is set two years after the Doctor left UNIT, circa *Terror of the Zygons/The Android Invasion*. *Battlefield* hasn't happened yet, because Klein would recognise the Doctor more immediately if it had (she only knows of [his seventh] incarnation through second-hand reports of his adventures), and anyway, she'd be a lot older than she is".

The only other clue, oddly enough, is that the CD track containing this scene is labelled "UNIT 1960's" (sic) – which is incorrect under any dating scheme.

The Non-UNIT Seventies

NB: The line between a UNIT and non-UNIT story isn't always clearly defined. When a reference makes a direct link to a UNIT era story, it is included in the UNIT Era section. When there's a more vague or general reference to UNIT, it's included here.

The Doctor once took piano lessons from a man called Elton.[1] He also had to swim the English Channel naked, after losing a bet with Oliver Reed.[2]

Isaac Summerfield moved his team to London, where they were based in a centre for the homeless.[3] The Doctor fought the Geomatide Macros on Sunset Boulevard in the 1970s, and defeated their plan to use ceiling tiles as a mathematical hyperspace vector generator.[4]

The archaeologist Bradley Stapleton died as an exhibit of his work was being prepared. The eleventh Doctor sent Amy Pond's journal of Stapleton's doomed 1929 expedition to the man's granddaughter.[5]

NASA sent messages - including maps of the solar system and details about humanity - into space in the 70s. One alien race sent a reply, which wound up in the possession of Henry John Parker, a millionaire collector of alien artifacts.[6]

Jack Harkness had a moustache at some point in the 70s.[7] He claimed that movies in the 1970s were so bad, making out was guaranteed. It wasn't unknown for him to wear platforms and five-inch lapels.[8]

1970

In 1970, the book *Great Finds* described the Roman mosaic discovered in 1964.[9] The United States officially cancelled the Apollo spaceflight programme, bowing to criticism of its expense, but continued it in secret - if for no other reason than every dollar spent on Apollo yielded $14 back from related exports, patents and expertise.[10]

Geoff and Sylvia Noble, the future parents of Donna Noble, were married.[11] A ship containing a hundred Veil crashed on Earth and was taken to a hyperdimensional Vault by the Alliance of Shades.[12]

Sarah Jane Smith began doorstepping when she was 19.[13] Lionel Carson served as Sarah Jane's editor when she first started out with the national papers, but he later moved on to the food and wine circuit.[14] Professor Edward Shepherd educated Sarah Jane on the ethics of journalism while she was at university, and was the best teacher she ever had.[15] Sarah Jane specialised in English and humanities.[16] She studied under James Stevens, as did Ruby Duvall.[17]

---

1 *Project: Lazarus.* This refers to Elton John, presumably, but no date is given.
2 "The Betrothal of Sontar". The Doctor also claims to have swum the Channel in *Doctor Who and the Pirates*. There's no indication exactly when this happened, but it's apparently after "Lunar Lagoon", when the fifth Doctor said he'd never learned to swim. (He seemingly has by *Warriors of the Deep*, however.) Oliver Reed, an actor known for such films as *The Three Musketeers* (1973), lived 1938-1999.
3 "The early seventies", according to *Return of the Living Dad* (p66).
4 *Peacemaker*
5 *The Hounds of Artemis.* No date is given, but Stapleton was a young man in 1929.
6 *TW: A Day in the Death*
7 *TW: Miracle Day*
8 *TW: The Dead Line*
9 *Demon Quest: The Relics of Time*
10 *Apollo 23* (p51). *Apollo 20* was cancelled on 4th January, 1970; *Apollo 18* and *19* were cancelled after that, on 2nd September of the same year. The last Apollo flight, *Apollo 17*, launched on 7th December, 1972.
11 *Beautiful Chaos.* Geoff died in 2008, after he and Sylvia had been married "thirty-eight years" (p26).
12 "Forty years ago" in *SJA: The Vault of Secrets*.
13 *SJA: Goodbye, Sarah Jane*, in accordance with Sarah being born in 1951 (*SJA: Whatever Happened to Sarah Jane?*). This probably denotes when Sarah started doing journalist work - "doorstepping" is a UK term meaning the practice of parking oneself outside the home of a celebrity/politician to snag a quote or photograph.
14 *SJA: The Man Who Never Was*
15 *SJA: Judgement Day*. This is "a few years" before Sarah joins UNIT.
16 *SJA: The White Wolf*
17 *Who Killed Kennedy*
18 Dating *Day of the Moon* (X6.2) - A caption says it is "6 months later" after the main action of the story. Melody isn't identified by name until *A Good Man Goes to War*. It's not directly established *why* Melody regenerates; it's not even certain that Amy's gunshot (the end of *The Impossible Astronaut*) actually hit her. It's possible that Melody's immune system was compromised because she was initially raised in a spacesuit acting as a life-support system. *Doctor Who: The Encyclopedia* says that Melody regenerated because she was "exhausted and injured".
19 *Let's Kill Hitler*. This leaves around a quarter-century gap where we don't know what Melody Pond was doing. Fortunately, the same story makes it clear that Melody/River has some control over her appearance - she looks about age seven when we see her with young Amy and Rory, and presumably she allows herself to outwardly age with Amy and Rory from childhood to adulthood. It would appear that she didn't

1970 (January) - DAY OF THE MOON[18] -> Six months after escaping the Silence, young Melody Pond - now wandering the streets of New York - regenerated in an alleyway.

Melody's new body looked like a toddler. A quarter-century later, she would end up in Leadworth, meet her future parents (Amy and Rory) and become their best friend, Melody "Mels" Zucker.[19]

c 1970 (20th March) - THE UNDERWATER MENACE[20] -> The mad Professor Zaroff died in agony while attempting to raise Atlantis from the ocean floor with his Plunger.

On 5th April, 1970, Hitler's remains were exhumed and destroyed on the orders of Andropov, head of the KGB.[21] On 14th August, the Revolution Man cult claimed Ed Hill was the Messiah.[22]

The seventh Doctor's companion Ace was born Dorothy Gale McShane on 20th August, 1970, to **Audrey** and Harry McShane.[23] Around 1970, an Imperial bodyguard and nurse fled from the far future with Miranda, the daughter of the Emperor, following a revolution in which the Imperial Family were hunted down and killed. The fugitives settled in the Derbyshire village of Greyfrith.[24]

Hilda Hutchens won the 1970 Nobel Prize for Philosophy.[25] The tenth Doctor changed history, allowing Frank Openshaw to meet his wife a few years earlier than he otherwise would have.[26]

The British launched a military satellite, *Haw-Haw*, to block extra-terrestrial signals in 1971.[27] Nimrod's encounter with the vampire Reggie left Reggie recuperating for three years.[28] Captain Jack helped sort out a problem during the early days of the United Arab Emirates, when something under the ground was disturbed.[29]

w - The second iteration of Cousin Anastasia of Faction Paradox died as Nadezhda Vasilyeva in an insane asylum in Kazan, 1971.[30] **Decimal currency was introduced in the United Kingdom. At some point afterwards, the first Doctor and Susan visited England.**[31]

In 1972, Nazi war criminal Oskar Steinmann died from cancer of the spine.[32] NASA launched the Pioneer 10 deep-space probe. The eleventh Doctor would find it on the Gyre in the year 250,339.[33] The Great Big Book Exchange opened in Darlington.[34] **Joseph Samuel Serf, the future**

---

regenerate a second time between 1970 and meeting up with Amy and Rory as children, because when she regenerates in *Let's Kill Hitler*, she mentions "the last time" she did such a thing, in New York (in *Day of the Moon*). Mels' surname isn't given on screen, but is listed in *Doctor Who: The Encyclopedia*.

20 Dating *The Underwater Menace* (4.5) - Polly discovers a bracelet from the 1968 Mexico Olympics; she and Ben guess that they must have landed about "1970". The Atlanteans are celebrating the Vernal Equinox.

The Programme Guide says the story is set "1970-75"; it's "soon after" 1969 according to *The Terrestrial Index*. *The TARDIS Logs* claimed a date of "1969". *Timelink* chose "1970". *The Legend* simply states it's "after 1968".

21 *The Shadow in the Glass* (p172).

22 *Revolution Man* (p247).

23 ACE'S EARLY LIFE: According to *The Curse of Fenric*, Ace does "O-Levels", not GCSEs, so she must be a fifth former (i.e.: 15 or 16 years old) by the summer of 1987 at the latest. This supports *Ghost Light*, where she is "13" in "1983". As Ace has a patch reading "1987" on her jacket in *Dragonfire*, it seems that the timestorm which swept her to Svartos must have originated in that year. Fenric is therefore rounding up when he tells Ace that Audrey Dudman will have a baby "thirty years" after *The Curse of Fenric*. Sophie Aldred was born in 1962, making her nine years older than the character she played.

In the New Adventures, starting with *Timewyrm: Revelation*, Ace's birthday was established as 20th August (Sophie Aldred's birthday). In *Falls the Shadow*, the Doctor says that she was born in "1970". Paul Cornell attempted to establish that Ace's surname was

"McShane" in *Love and War*, but series editor Peter Darvill-Evans vetoed this at the proof stage. *Conundrum* (p245) and *No Future* (p19) both suggest that Ace's surname begins with an "M" (although when asked in the latter, Ace claims it is "Moose"!). It wasn't until Kate Orman's *Set Piece* that "McShane" was officially adopted.

Ace is "Dorothy Gale" in some books by Mike Tucker, notably *Matrix* (p124) and *Prime Time* (p234). *The Rapture* attempts to reconcile this by stating that her middle name is Gale. In *Loving the Alien*, which appears to be set prior to *The Rapture*, Ace dies and is replaced by a parallel timeline version of herself. The Doctor says this swap accounts for much of the confusion regarding Ace's last name.

24 *Father Time*. Miranda is "ten" in the first part of the book (p54), and "two months old" when she arrives on Earth.

25 *Island of Death* - although there isn't actually a Nobel Prize for Philosophy.

26 *I am a Dalek*

27 *The Dying Days* (p101).

28 *Project: Twilight*

29 *TW: The Sin Eaters*. Prior to 1971, the Emirates were known as the Trucial States.

30 *FP: The Book of the War*

31 *An Unearthly Child*. Susan is also familiar with the Beatles before their first hit single in *Time and Relative*.

32 *Just War* (p178).

33 *Night of the Humans*. Pioneer 10 was launched 2nd March, 1972.

34 "Forty years" prior to the modern day portion of *Iris: Enter Wildthyme*.

founder of Serf Systems, was born May 1972 in Dayton, Ohio.[35] Ace's mother moved into the home in which Ace would grow up[36]; the road on which they lived was named Beech.[37]

On 4th June, 1972, UNIT obtained the Tunguska Scroll from a collector.[38] In December of that year, the skeleton of Nazi Martin Bormann was discovered in West Germany.[39] Playwright Noel Coward died in 1972. One of his selves claimed - due to his status at a time traveller - that at his moment of death, he'd be mentally whisked back to his birth to experience life all over again.[40]

In 1972, the Alliance of Shades disbanded, and pulled the plug on its robot Men in Black.[41] Mr Dread and his Men in Black, however, became the guardians of a hyperdimensional Vault containing numerous extra-terrestrial items and vessels. Ocean Waters, age 24, encountered Dread in 1972 - he wiped her memories of the event, and gave her one of two activation keys to the Vault for safekeeping.[42]

The American military downed an alien spaceship carrying the Stormcore, a navigational instrument. The government erroneously believed the Stormcore was a weather control device, and formed Operation Afterburn to make it compatible with human technology. Researchers determined the device needed a psionic operator. In the years to come, the government's ESP/Remote Viewing program, called Grill Flame, would locate such individuals. The spaceship's crewmembers, now stranded on Earth,

joined the American CIA as agents Melody Quartararo and Parker Theroux.[43]

Iris Wildthyme's people exiled her and Panda to London, 1972. She again worked for the Ministry for Incursions and other Alien Ontological Wonders (MIAOW) to obtain the alien technology needed to repair her bus. Iris based herself above a bus depot and tatty pool hall in New Cross. MIAOW's headquarters was named the Pussy Parlour.[44]

1973

When Ace was three, her mum cried for days when Ace's grandma Kathleen died. Ace's first pet was called Marmaduke.[45]

When Elton Pope was three or four, his mother was killed by an "elemental shade" that had escaped from the Howling Halls. Elton saw the tenth Doctor standing over her body, and would become obsessed with the mysterious stranger.[46]

Aubrey Prior's expedition to the Black Pyramid in 1973 discovered Nephthys' burial chamber.[47] Jack Harkness was involved in the Hell House case, which he said "didn't go well".[48] In 1973, Jack twice saved the life of Professor Leonard Morgan - then left him for a chorus girl from Boston.[49]

On 23rd February, 1973, Dr. Albert Gilroy - a researcher at the University of Michigan - developed an artificial

35 *SJA: The Man Who Never Was*
36 "Five years" after *Thin Ice*.
37 *Night Thoughts*
38 *SJA: Enemy of the Bane*
39 *The Shadow in the Glass*. This is historical. The skeleton was identified first through dental records, then twenty-seven years later through a DNA test.
40 *Mad Dogs and Englishmen*
41 *Dreamland* (DW), *SJA: The Vault of Secrets*.
42 *SJA: The Vault of Secrets*
43 "Thirty years" before *Drift*.
44 *Iris: The Land of Wonder*
45 *Night Thoughts*. Kathleen is Ace's grandmother as seen in *The Curse of Fenric*.
46 *Love & Monsters*
47 "Twenty-three years" before *The Sands of Time*.
48 *TW*: "Hell House". This presumably references the horror film *The Legend of Hell House* (1973).
49 *TW: Something in the Water*
50 *Nuclear Time*. The day is given (p7). A janitor says "the war's over" (p9), presumably referring to the Paris Peace Accords signed on 27th January, 1973, which were intended to end the Vietnam War. The conflict actually lasted until 30th April, 1975, when Saigon fell.
51 *SJA: Wraith World*
52 According to the writers' guidelines. She was "28" in

Escape Velocity, set in February 2001.
53 Per *The Torchwood Archives*.
54 Dating *Iris: The Land of Wonder* (Iris audio #2.2) - The year is repeatedly given.
55 Dating *Iris: Enter Wildthyme* (Iris novel #1) - The month and year are given.
56 *The Doctor Trap*
57 When she was "13", according to *The King of Terror*.
58 *Byzantium!* (p8).
59 *Revolution Man* (p248).
60 *The Rapture*
61 *Partners in Crime*
62 *Mad Dogs and Englishmen*
63 Dating "Agent Provocateur" (IDW *DW* mini-series #1) - The Doctor names the year, and a flier advertises the exhibit as being open from "July 8" to "September 5". Martha says it's "ten years before I was born" (in 1986 according to *Wooden Heart*, 1984 according to *The Torchwood Archives*).
64 *The King of Terror* (p32).
65 "Ten years" before *The Zygon Who Fell to Earth*.
66 Dating "Urgent Calls" (BF #94b) - The year is given on the back cover. This is the first in a series of one-part stories related to the viruses released in *Patient Zero*.

intelligence that he named "Isley" after his daughter's love of the Isley Brothers.[50] *The Rise of Hancada*, a *Wraith World* book, was published in 1973.[51]

Anji Kapoor, a companion of the eighth Doctor, was born in Leeds on 1st April, 1973.[52] **Suzie Costello of Torchwood was born** 6th May, 1973.[53]

1973 - IRIS: THE LAND OF WONDER[54] **->** The Earth-exiled Iris Wildthyme and Panda investigated Harriet Dodd's Wonderland when some of its denizens escaped from it. MIAOW, desperate that Iris not discover Wonderland's secrets, turned on her and torched it. Dodd bequeathed Iris with the feasibility generator that made Wonderland possible - with this device, Iris repaired her bus and ended her exile. She and Panda left with the mock turtle from Wonderland and the generator - which adopted the shape of a sentient dodo.

1973 (July) - IRIS: ENTER WILDTHYME[55] **->** Iris Wildthyme kept a private office in South Kensington, London; it was somewhere near the Victoria and Albert Museum, and above *The Gilded Lily* boutique. She stored important documents and objects there, but only for a three-day period in July 1973. On the last of these, a Saturday, Iris and her friends vapourised the building to keep the items from falling into the wrong hands. The same day saw Vince Cosmos announce that he was retiring from pop music. Iris' rival, Anthony Marville, raided the office before its destruction and nicked her Blithe Pinking Shears, which could open portals by cutting through the Very Fabric of Space and Time.

> (=) In an alternate dimension, Martian assassins overran Cosmos' last concert at the Hammersmith Odeon.

The accomplished hunter Sebastiene believed that he had been an undergraduate at Cambridge, 1973, who was looking at a meteorite through an electron microscope - and suddenly found himself on an alien planet, a million light years from home. The tenth Doctor suspected that Sebastiene's recollection might be true, or that he might be unaware of his genuine origins.[56]

Tegan Jovanka's grandmother died of coronary thrombosis. About this time, Tegan's father had an affair and her parents split up. Tegan was sent to boarding school.[57] A short sword bearing the initials "IC", given to Ian Chesterton by Thalius Maximus, was now on display in the British National Museum. Historians erroneously dated it to the end of the first century; it was about thirty-five years older.[58] On 12th December, 1973, Revolution Man cult leader Madeleine "Maddie" Burton died in Paris as the result of a drug addiction. The cult quickly died without her influence.[59]

1974

When Ace was four, her parents had a son, Liam. When Ace's father discovered his wife was having an affair with his friend Jack, he left with the infant Liam.[60] **When Donna Noble was six, her mother said there would be "no holiday this year", so Donna caught a bus to Strathclyde. Her parents sent the police after her.**[61]

Reginald Tyler died in a domestic accident. He had been working on his novel *The True History of Planets* since 1917, much to the annoyance of his wife, Enid, who sold the movie rights and moved to Jamaica with her lover.

> (=) In another version of history, Reginald Tyler didn't die. He was rescued by a poodle that walked on its hind legs, who transported him off Earth... in this reality, *The True History of Planets* would become a very different book.

@ The eighth Doctor read the original *The True History of Planets*.[62]

1974 (summer) - "Agent Provocateur"[63] **->** The tenth Doctor and Martha saw sand sculptures of British pop stars in Parliament Square, London, that previewed an exhibition by one Princess Hentopet. The sand-sculpture exhibits were real people turned into sand, and were held together by a nanometre force field. The Doctor learned the story of Bubastion, Hentopet and Sheeq - who had travelled the world since Egyptian times - and had Bubastion restore the sculptures to life in return for promising to take him home. These events were part of a wider plot to snare the Doctor on behalf of the Elite Pantheon; the scheme culminated in the year five billion.

Tegan ran away from home when she was 15. Once she was found, her father sent her to live with his sister Vanessa in England.[64]

Hagoth's Zygons continued their scheme to promote global warming; Phase Five entailed using biochemical warheads to detonate the accumulated gases in Earth's atmosphere. Circa 1974, however, Hagoth renounced his people's conquering ways, and made off with both his crew's Skarasen and a crystal lattice that enabled his ship's firing sequence. Deprived of the Skarasen's lactic fluid, Hagoth's crew made do with the powdered stuff.[65]

1974 - "Urgent Calls"[66] **->** Telephone operator Lauren Hudson was exhibiting strange symptoms, but a wrong call luckily put her in touch with the sixth Doctor, who advised that an alien worm was hugging her spine. Military surgeons extracted the worm, and Lauren experienced a string of wrong-but-fortuitous phone calls. The Doctor said that an alien "luck" virus capable of transmitting itself through telephones had infected them. He suspected that the virus was engineered to let sleeper agents communicate, or to summon precisely the right sort of aid. Earth wasn't ready for such a virus (however helpful it had become), and the Doctor said he would deal with it. Some time later, Lauren was saddened to find that every call she placed went through correctly. Failing to hear from the Doctor, she mailed him a letter instead.

1974 - HORROR OF GLAM ROCK[67] -> The singer Nancy Babcock said that her cat dictated all of her music. Lucie Miller's mother - a blonde named Mary - presently worked in a Gloucester shoe shop.

Arnold Korns, a dynamic and powerful manager in the music industry, discovered two budding talents: Trisha and Tommy Tomorrow, who performed as The Day After Tomorrow. Korns scheduled them to make their debut on *Top of the Pops*. However, a group of discorporealised alien beings, seeking to stop over on Earth and consume the polyunsaturates and fibre found in the human body, had contacted Tommy as sound waves conducted through his Stylophone. They touted themselves as the "Only Ones", claiming they were the only race in existence besides humanity, and helped Tommy to compose his songs.

En route to London, Korns and the twins stopped off at Nadir Services, a service station and café just outside Bramlington. The spot had previously seen such celebrities as Hendrix, Lulu and the Wombles, and now witnessed the dissolution of the band Methylated Spirits. The group had lost their singer Wendy, and Bendy Roger - dressed in full regalia - now severed ties with drummer Patricia Ryder, who in future would become Lucie Miller's "Auntie Pat". Outside the café, the Only Ones manifested as scaled, bear-like creatures and killed Roger.

The eighth Doctor and Lucie showed up as the Only Ones murdered Tricia Tomorrow and threatened to unleash a massacre. The Doctor found a means of converting the Only Ones back into sound, and trapped them on shuffle mode in Lucie's MP3 Player. He speculated that the carnage would be blamed on the Hell's Angels.

The Headhunter pursuing the Doctor and Lucie narrowly missed them in this period.

---

67 Dating *Horror of Glam Rock* (BF BBC7 #1.3) - "It's 1974", the Doctor says.

68 *Divided Loyalties* (p46). Lord Lucan, a British peer, disappeared 8th November, 1974 - the day after Sandra Rivett, his children's nanny, was murdered. He was never found, and has been a source of speculation ever since.

69 *P.R.O.B.E.: Unnatural Selection*

70 *The One Doctor*. This may be a reference to *The Invasion*.

71 "Eight years" before *Return of the Living Dad*.

72 *TW: Greeks Bearing Gifts*, in which Mary gives the month and year of Tosh's birth and Tosh doesn't correct her. Otherwise, though, there's conflicting evidence as to when Tosh was born. *Torchwood: The Official Magazine Yearbook* (2008) and her on-screen personnel file in *TW: Exit Wounds* both say she was born 18th September, 1981. *The Torchwood Archives* says she was born on the same day, but in 1975. Internet sources, almost appropriately given the confusion around her character, seem split down the middle as to whether actress Naoko Mori was born in 1971 or 1975, but seem to agree that her birthday is 19th November.

73 *Nuclear Time*

74 *TW: Children of Earth*

75 *TW: The Dead Line*

76 *TW: Trace Memory*

77 *Hexagora*, going by Tegan being born in 1960.

78 Dating *Fury from the Deep* (5.6) - It is clear that this story is set in the near future. There is a Europe-wide energy policy and videophones are in use. It's tempting, in fact, to see this as being set in the same near future as the early UNIT stories. Although Robson, the refinery controller, talks of "tuppence ha'penny tinpot ideas", this is clearly a figure of speech rather than an indication that the story is set in the era of predecimal currency.

The Programme Guide always assumed that the story was contemporary. *The TARDIS Logs* set the story in "2074", the same year it suggested for *The Wheel in Space*. In *Downtime*, Victoria has been in the twentieth century for "ten years" by 1984 (p41).

The quotation is the Doctor reassuring Jamie about Victoria's new home in *The Wheel in Space*.

79 *Blue Box*

80 "The Lunar Strangers". Jackson says she's been in "the service forty years".

81 *The Reaping*. *Rocky Horror* debuted on 14th August, 1975.

82 *Return of the Living Dad*

83 *Timewyrm: Revelation*

84 *Minuet in Hell*. This claim is either hyperbole on the Order's part or extremely short-lived, as *Goth Opera* (set in 1993) has between three to four hundred vampires active in Britain alone.

85 *TW: The Sin Eaters*

86 *Father Time*

87 "Over twenty years" before *The Dying Days*.

88 *The Demons of Red Lodge and Other Stories*: "Special Features"

89 Dating *The Forbidden Time* (BF CC #5.9) - It's "thirty-five years" before 2011.

90 Dating *Vampire Science* (EDA #2) - It's "1976" (p3).

91 Dating *Demon Quest: Starfall* (BBC fourth Doctor audio #2.4) - Buddy's opening narration says it's "July", "1976". He later says the meteorite lands on the "12th".

In November, the Celestial Toymaker kidnapped Lord Lucan, sparking an international manhunt.[68]

1975

The British government established the BEAGLE project to determine the next stage of human evolution. Professor Julius Quilter developed an advanced human - Alfred - who could absorb human organs, but Alfred killed a BEAGLE member while doing so. The government shut down the project in 1975; Quilter officially said that Alfred had been destroyed, but nurtured him in secret.[69]

During the Cybermen invasion of June 1975, the Doctor was based at 35 Jefferson Road, Woking.[70] The Doctor visited a planet orbiting Lalande 21185. The Caxtarids had developed a virus that the government were planning to use against a rebel faction.[71]

In July 1975, Toshiko Sato was born in London. Her parents were in the RAF, and her grandfather worked at Metchley Park.[72] Colonel Geoffrey Redvers coerced Albert Gilroy into building android assassins for the US military on 3rd August, 1975.[73]

Melissa Moretti, the daughter of Lucia Moretti and Jack Harkness, was born 5th August, 1975. Lucia stopped working for Torchwood in the same year.[74] Jack Harkness dated a junior doctor named Stella Courtney for a few weeks in 1975.[75] Charles Arthur Cromwell retired from Torchwood in 1975.[76]

Tegan and Mike Bretherton were high school classmates, and next door neighbours, in Brisbane. They were both inspired by Miss Anderson, who taught physics. When Tegan was 15, Mike carried her books home after she broke her toe during track and field.[77]

c 1975 - FURY FROM THE DEEP[78] **-> On the whole, this period was "a good time in Earth's history to stay in. No wars, great prosperity, a time of plenty." Gas from the sea now provided energy for the south of England and Wales, as well as mainland Europe. Twenty rigs pumped gas into every home without incident for more than four years.**

When scientists registered a regular build-up and fall in pressure in the main pipelines, the supply was cut off for the first time. A mutant species of seaweed was responsible, and it mentally dominated some of the rigs' crews before being beaten back by amplified sound.

Victoria Waterfield left the second Doctor and Jamie to settle down with the Harris family.

The Doctor met hacker Robert Salmon in 1975. They stopped a US Navy programmer from installing a back door that would've granted illicit access to the Navy's computers.[79] Freda Jackson joined the space programme in

1975 - she would later command Moon Village One.[80] The Doctor had tickets to opening night of *The Rocky Horror Picture Show*.[81]

1976

In 1976, a Lalandian safari killed people in Durham. Isaac Summerfield tipped off UNIT to the problem.[82] The seventh Doctor and Ace visited London in 1976.[83] In 1976, the Order of St Peter chased the last known European vampire from the continent. It escaped to the United States.[84] Jack Harkness converted the husk of an alien visitor into a coracle in 1976.[85]

@ On 28th May, Deborah Gordon and Barry Castle married in Greyfrith. The eighth Doctor was elsewhere, with a widow called Claudia.[86]

The last British mission to Mars, Mars Probe 13, ended in disaster when the Ice Warriors killed two crewmembers. The British government made a secret deal to stay away from Mars, and they framed the mission's sole survivor, Lex Christian, for murder. He was sent to Fortress Island, where he remained for more than twenty years.[87]

The Racht seed disc on Earth infected actress Johanna Bourke. As "Phillip Mungston", she wrote a horror portmanteau film - *Doctor Demonic's Tales of Terror* - and incorporated the seed disc into a sacrifice scene, a means of infecting anyone watching with a newborn Racht. The fifth Doctor and Nyssa visited the production in summer of 1976, and destroyed all footage pertaining to the scene. Nyssa appeared in the first *Tales of Terror* installment, "Curse of the Devil's Whisper" as "Nyssa Traken".[88]

= 1976 - THE FORBIDDEN TIME[89] **->** The Vist were time-walkers with bodies the size of greyhounds, set atop giraffe-like legs. They claimed dominion over a period of eight years, three months and two days - roughly from 2011 to 2019 - across the whole of creation, and sought to "penalise" the life force of any civilisation that entered it without permission. The second Doctor, Polly, Ben and Jamie encountered the Vist on a shadowy "sideways" version of Earth in the 70s, and the Doctor tricked the Vist into venturing back to the start of the universe.

1976 - VAMPIRE SCIENCE[90] **->** Carolyn McConnell, a pre-med student, met the eighth Doctor and Sam in San Francisco. The Doctor was on the trail of a clutch of vampires, and a scuffle led to the death of his best lead, the vampire Eva. He gave Carolyn a signalling device in case the vampires resurfaced.

1976 (12th July) - DEMON QUEST: STARFALL[91] **->** The fourth Doctor, Mike Yates and Mrs Wibbsey arrived in Central Park in Manhattan, looking for the fourth stolen component of the TARDIS' spatial geometer and using an old comic book from this year as guidance. Buddy Hudson saw a meteorite land in Central Park, but when he and his girlfriend Alice Trefusis - who was helping to write the memoirs of faded actress Mimsy Loyne - investigated the incident, Alice touched the meteor and began crackling with energy. The Doctor and his friends recognised the scene from the comic book - Alice had become the super-heroine Miss Starfall. She could fly, and played the part by wearing a superhero costume, rescuing people and putting out fires.

Buddy and Wibbsey found a room full of cultists who were using a ritual - one that featured the last part of the spacial geometer - to drain the Doctor's lifeforce. Mimsy Loyne was revealled as the aspect-changing Demon in disguise, and abducted Wibbsey while announcing that "the Sepulchre is prepared". The Doctor and Mike vowed to find their friend, and returned to 2010. Alice's powers faded, but not before she and Buddy took one last flight around the city.

On 24th September, 1976, the Rift radiated energy that ended the worst drought Wales had seen in three centu-ries. The head office of the Cardiff and West Building Society, Madoc House, was struck by lightning charged with an electrical virus. This rendered thirteen employees comatose when they answered the phones. They were relocated to a private hospital; Madoc House was closed, its operations moved to Swansea. The virus remained trapped in the disused Madoc House phone system.[92]

1977

On 14th February, 1977, Lucia Moretti's application that her daughter Melissa be put into deep cover was approved. Melissa was renamed Alice Sangster, and officially was the child of James and Mary Sangster - place-holder names used for those undercover or in witness relocation.[93] The Electro in Cardiff had a final screening - Terry Gilliam's *Jabberwocky* - then survived for another eighteen months as a bingo hall before closing.[94]

Peri's mother divorced and remarried when Peri was ten.[95] **When Toshiko Sato was two, her family moved to Osaka, Japan.**[96] **Count Carlos Scarlioni, one of the richest men on Earth, married his Countess in 1977.**[97] In 1977, the sixth Doctor and Frobisher attended the open-

92 *TW: The Dead Line*
93 *TW: Children of Earth*
94 Torchwood.org.uk, elaborating on *TW: From Out of the Rain. Jabberwocky* debuted in the United Kingdom on 28th March, 1977.
95 *Blue Box*. This is contradicted by *Synthespians™*, which states that Peri's father died in 1979 and her mother remarried after that.
96 *TW: Greeks Bearing Gifts*
97 "Two years" before *City of Death*.
98 *Mission: Impractical*
99 *Day of the Moon*. Sir David Frost, a British media personality, conducted a series of seminal interviews with Nixon (later adapted as a play and a movie starring Michael Sheen and Frank Langella) in 1977.
100 *Nuclear Time* (p75). Colonel Redvers remarks that it's "only been... a week" since *Star Wars* came out; in the real world, it was only two days, as *A New Hope* saw release on 25th May.
101 Dating *Mawdryn Undead* (20.3) - The earlier part of the story takes place during the Queen's Silver Jubilee - various events to commemorate this started as early as February, and culminated in June. It's repeatedly said that Tegan and Nyssa have arrived "six years" before the story's modern-day component, set in 1983.
102 Dating *Image of the Fendahl* (15.3) - According to Ma Tyler, it is "Lammas Eve" (31st July) at the end of episode three. There's nothing to suggest it's not set the year of broadcast. "Hartman", a character spoken to over the phone, is pretty obviously not Yvonne Hartman of Torchwood (*Army of Ghosts/Doomsday*).
103 *Timewyrm: Revelation* (p13).

104 Seven years before *Turlough and the Earthlink Dilemma*.
105 Dating "The Nightmare Game" (*DWM* #330-332) - The year is given.
106 *The Left-Handed Hummingbird* (p23).
107 *Terror Firma*. Presuming this doesn't instead refer to the Las Vegas nightclub of the same name, the infamous disco operated from 1977-1986.
108 *Iris: Enter Wildthyme*
109 *Benny: Beige Planet Mars. Option Lock*, which entails some nuclear gamesmanship in the late twentieth century, makes no mention of this protocol.
110 "Nearly forty years" before *Iris: Iris and the Celestial Omnibus:* "The Deadly Flap" (set in 2008), and possibly a more definitive break-up after *Iris: The Land of Wonder*.
111 *Iris: Iris and the Celestial Omnibus:* "The Deadly Flap"
112 *Benny: The Diet of Worms*. The date isn't specified, but Cartland lived 1901 to 2000.
113 Dating *The Pirate Planet* (16.2) - The Doctor says that the population of Earth is "billions and billions", possibly suggesting a contemporary setting. *First Frontier* implies the same.
114 Dating *The Stones of Blood* (16.3) - There is no indication what year the story is set, but it is clearly contemporary.
115 *The Armageddon Factor*
116 *Shada*
117 "Seven years" before *Attack of the Cybermen*.
118 Dating *Mad Dogs and Englishmen* (EDA #52) - The date is given.
119 Among Jack's Torchwood agents, Gwen's birthday is the most uniformly referenced - it's the same in

ing of *Star Wars* at Mann's Chinese Theatre, Los Angeles.[98] The eleventh Doctor told Richard Nixon to say hello to David Frost for him.[99] Albert Gilroy, working from a Utah military research base, successfully transferred the AI Isley into an android body on 27th May, 1977.[100]

1977 - MAWDRYN UNDEAD[101] **-> The Brigadier had retired from UNIT, and was now teaching mathematics at Brendan Public School. The TARDIS arrived with Tegan and Nyssa on board - the Ship had been thrown back to 1977 thanks to a warp eclipse from Mawdryn's spaceship. Mawdryn himself arrived in a transmat capsule, but the journey left him gravely injured. Tegan and Nyssa mistook him for the Doctor, and agreed to take him back to the spaceship. The Brigadier insisted on accompanying them.**

On Mawdryn's ship, the Brigadier came into contact with his older self and triggered the Blinovitch Limitation Effect. This left the younger Brigadier with some memory loss - the fifth Doctor and his companions left him on Earth to continue teaching.

c 1977 (30th-31st July) - IMAGE OF THE FENDAHL[102] **-> The fourth Doctor and Leela encountered the Fendahl at Fetchborough, a village on the edge of a time fissure. A team of scientists under Professor Fendelman were attempting to probe the far past using a time scanner, but this had only succeeded in activating the dormant Fendahl skull. Fetch Priory was destroyed in an implosion. The Doctor defeated the Fendahl, and took the skull with the intent of throwing it into a supernova.**

In 1977, the seventh Doctor landed in Lewisham in an attempt to track the Timewyrm.[103] On Trion, the dictator Rehctaht emerged as the most tyrannical ruler in the planet's history. She would rule for seven years, and butcher the Clansmen. She founded the colony of New Trion primarily as a slave labour force, but conflict between Trion colonies in the East and the West diverted her attention. New Trion functioned independently, if inefficiently.[104]

1977 - "The Nightmare Game"[105] **->** The eighth Doctor discovered that the alien Shakespeare Brothers were behind Delchester United's recent bad run.

1978

On 21st February, 1978, electrical workers uncovered the sacrificial stone at the base of the Great Temple in Mexico City.[106] The eighth Doctor, Samson and Gemma visited Studio 54.[107] Panda arranged to have Iris scraped off the floor of Studio 54.[108]

From the Carter-Brezhnev era, it became standard policy to lodge missile command codes into the hearts of people beloved to the persons authorised to launch nuclear strikes. It was hoped - as approving a missile strike would now necessitate the loved one's death - that those entrusted with such weaponry would consider and reconsider the humanity and consequences of their actions.[109]

Iris Wildthyme stopped working for the South Kensington branch[110] of The Ministry of Incursions and Other Alien Wonders (MIAOW), thinking them too nefarious.[111] The romance novelist Barbara Cartland bought extra-terrestrial stationery from a seemingly ordinary shop near Charing Cross: McZygon of the Strand.[112]

c 1978 - THE PIRATE PLANET[113] **-> Zanak's career as the Pirate Planet - a hollowed out world that teleported around other planets and mined out their riches - was brought to an abrupt end when the fourth Doctor, Romana and K9 helped to bring about the destruction of its engines and the death of its Captain and Queen Xanxia. Zanak settled in a peaceful area of space.**

c 1978 - THE STONES OF BLOOD[114] **-> The fourth Doctor, Romana and K9 helped defeat Cessair of Diplos, who had escaped from her prison ship in hyperspace and been hiding on Earth for four thousand years. She was found guilty by two justice machines - the Megara - of impersonating a deity, theft and misuse of the Seal of Diplos, murder, and removing silicon lifeforms from the planet Ogros in contravention of article 7594 of the Galactic Charter. She was sentenced to perpetual imprisonment.**

Around this time, the Time Lord Drax spent ten years in Brixton Prison.[115] Chris Parsons graduated in 1978.[116] Work was done on the sewers under Fleet Street.[117]

1978 - MAD DOGS AND ENGLISHMEN[118] **->** The eighth Doctor dropped Anji off in Hollywood, where she met embittered special effects man Ron von Arnim. The Doctor went to 1942 and returned with Noel Coward - and the news that von Arnim was being manipulated to create a movie about poodles by director John Fuchas. The Doctor tied Fuchas to a chair, headed off to Dogworld, and forgot to go back, so Fuchas died. This prevented the movie being made, and saved the day.

Gwen Cooper of Torchwood was born in Swansea on 16th August, 1978, to Mary and Geraint Wyn Cooper.[119]

The Tulkan Empire failed to annex the Annarene homeworld. In response, the Annarene erased the deposed Tulk War Council's memories. An Annarene named Sooal, dying from a genetic disease, spirited the amnesiac council away in a spaceship. Sooal hoped to restore the Council's memories and gain the command codes needed to open a Tulk stasis chamber, which contained a metabolic stabiliser. He established the Graystairs elderly care facility in Muirbridge, Scotland, to conduct genetics research. On Annarene, the ruling Protectorate favoured pacifism, but a hawk-like faction desired a return to warfare.[120]

Followers of the demon Asmedaj summoned their master in December 1978, but the youthful Jane Fonda-esque version of Iris Wildthyme infiltrated the group, chanted the wrong words and tore Asmedaj's body apart. Iris celebrated her triumph with two hitchhikers named Doug. A part of Asmedaj's mind hosted itself in Iris' brain as she fell asleep while watching *The Wizard of Oz*. One of Asmedaj's followers, Marwick, tried to heal his master by implanting Asmedaj's body parts in several newborn children - including Iris' future companion Tom.[121]

When not on assignment for Torchwood, Jack Harkness tried his hand working in life insurance and at a burger bar on Bondi Beach. The fourth revival of Agnes Havisham from cryo-sleep entailed an escapade with Jack at a roller discotheque in Sweden, the late 1970s, when a lethal space plague turned people into the undead. Jack went to an Abba concert while he was in Sweden, as he expected that he could get a ticket from either Agnetha or Bjorn.[122]

1979 (spring) - CITY OF DEATH[123] **-> Scaroth's plan to alter history - which would have saved his race but doomed humanity - was reaching its culmination. With the help of the foremost temporal scientist of the day,** Professor Theodore Nikolai Kerensky, Scaroth produced a device capable of shifting the whole world back in time four hundred million years.

To finance the plan, Scaroth was selling off his art collection, flooding the market with lost masterpieces. This failed to raise enough money, and he arranged for the theft of the Mona Lisa from the Louvre in Paris. One of Scaroth's other selves had commissioned six more Mona Lisas from Leonardo da Vinci in 1505, and Scaroth intended to sell all seven copies to private buyers. Each would think they were purchasing the stolen Mona Lisa.

Scaroth succeeded in travelling back in time four hundred million years, but the fourth Doctor, Romana and the investigator Duggan followed in the TARDIS and stopped his plans. Upon his return to 1979, Scaroth died when a fire started in his laboratory. Only one Mona Lisa copy - with "This is a Fake" scribbled in felt tip on the canvas, detectable to any x-ray - survived the fire. It was returned to the Louvre.

Earth was now classified as a Level Five planet.[124]

The Doctor came to possess a Mona Lisa that didn't have the words "This is a Fake" in felt tip.[125]

Peri and her father went hunting together. Her grandmother went senile, forgot everyone but her teddy bear, and took to acting like Marlene Dietrich.[126] Peri's father Paul drowned underneath a capsized boat in 1979. Her mother, Janine, remarried soon afterwards.[127]

Turlough and a girl named Deela were childhood friends, then shared a teenage infatuation - they weren't

---

TW: Children of Earth, The Torchwood Archives and *Torchwood: The Official Magazine Yearbook* (2008). A photo of Gwen in *TW: Miracle Day* bears the caption "1978", presumably for the same reason. Her passport in *Miracle Day* says that she was born 11th December, 1974, but she's using an alias, so it's presumably fake.

120 Four years before *Relative Dementias*.

121 *Iris: The Devil in Ms. Wildthyme*

122 *TW: Risk Assessment*

123 Dating *City of Death* (17.2) - The Doctor says that this isn't a vintage year, "it is 1979 actually, more of a table wine, shall we say". A poster says there's an exhibition on from Janiver - Mai, and the blossoms on the tree would suggest it was towards the end of that period.

MONA LISAS: The Mona Lisa in the Louvre (a fake from *City of Death* onward, and presumably the one featured in *SJA: Mona Lisa's Revenge*) is destroyed by the Martian asteroid in 2086 (*Transit*). Multiple Mona Lisas are seen a UNIT archive in "The Age of Ice" (set in 2010). The Monk owns a Mona Lisa that may or may not be destroyed in *To the Death* (circa 2190). "Art Attack!" shows a Mona Lisa as still around in a thousand years time. In *The Art of Destruction*, the Doctor saves a Mona Lisa in the fifty-first century. Rory smashes a Mona Lisa over a robot's head in the undateable *The Girl Who Waited*.

124 A LEVEL FIVE WORLD: This is first mentioned by Romana in *City of Death*. Earth is similarly a Level Five world in many New *Who* stories, including *Voyage of the Damned*, *Partners in Crime*, *The Eleventh Hour* and *SJA: Revenge of the Slitheen*. Earth is a Level Three planet in *The Good, the Bad and the Alien*, set in 1861. In *Ferril's Folly*, set circa 2011, the first Romana repeatedly (and oddly) names Earth as a Level Four world.

125 *Dust Breeding*. This implies that the Doctor went back in time and nicked the original Mona Lisa before the fire in Scaroth's house could destroy it.

126 *Peri and the Piscon Paradox*

127 *Synthespians™*. This contradicts *Blue Box*, which said Peri's mother remarried when Peri was ten (in 1976). It's possible, if a little messy, to reconcile the two accounts by suggesting Peri's mother married three times. *The Reaping* confirms her father's name was Paul.

128 Turlough says they last went into the vault "three years, nine months and seventeen days, give or take", before *Kiss of Death*.

related by blood, but belonged to the same Clan. He found the dimensional vault last used by his great-grandfather, and changed the security key so it would only grant him and Deela access.[128]

The Doctor assisted in bringing Skylab down to Earth and it "nearly cost him a thumb".[129] Izzy, a companion of the eighth Doctor, was born on 12th October, 1979. She never knew her parents, and was adopted by Les and Sandra Sinclair. Because of her uncertain parentage, she chose to call herself "Izzy Somebody".[130]

By 1979, the Zygon Hagoth had acquired the corpse and body print of the folk singer Trevor. In Trevor's form, Hagoth attended the Kendal Folk Festival and met Patricia Ryder, the future aunt of Lucie Miller. "Trevor" and Patricia were married that same year - she knew he was extra-terrestrial, deeming him her "great big hunk of Zygon".[131]

c 1979 - "The Iron Legion"[132] **->** The fourth Doctor landed on Earth just as it was attacked by robots resembling ancient Roman soldiers...

= In another dimension, Rome never fell. Rome's robot legions, led by the eagle-headed Ironicus, fought the Eternal War across a thousand planets and by now had conquered the entire galaxy. The attack on our dimension represented the first strike in Rome's attempt to conquer the whole of creation.

Rome itself was a vast futuristic city full of alien and human citizens, slaves and robots. Citizens enjoyed themselves watching gladiator fights between aliens and bionic humans at the Hyp-Arena, and car races at the Circus Maximus. Both events were televised. Rome had contact with many alien planets, including the home of the Ectoslime and the Kronks in the Crab Nebula. The Kronks had fought Zarks in the Hyp-Arena, and were also turned into kronk-burgers.

The child Adolphus Caesar - "Master of the Solar System and the Galaxy Beyond" - was now Emperor, with Ironicus serving as regent. The Doctor realised that Juno, the Adolphus' mother, was actually an alien. Following them to the Temple of the Gods, the Doctor recognised the building as a spacecraft, and the "gods" as the five Malevilus - Babiyon, Abiss, Epok, Nekros and Magog, a form of anti-life. They had given the Romans advanced technology to aid their goal of the conquest of all creation.

With the help of the bionic gladiator Morris and the ancient robot Vesuvius, the Doctor started a revolt. He unleashed the Bestarius (who were genetically engineered warriors), and confronted Juno, who revealled herself to be Magog. The Doctor tricked Magog into the TARDIS by promising to share its secrets, then trapped him in a pocket dimension. The other Malevilus tried to launch their ship, but Magog had drained its power and it crashed, killing them. Vesuvius was installed as Emperor by popular decree.

---

129 *Tooth and Claw* (TV)
130 Izzy was born on the cover date of the first issue of *Doctor Who Weekly* (a fact established in "TV Action"). That date wasn't the day the magazine was published - magazine dates are when newsagents are meant to take them off the shelves. Details on her being adopted were mentioned in "End Game" (*DWM*).
131 *The Zygon Who Fell to Earth*
132 Dating "The Iron Legion" (*DWW* #1-8) - The Doctor lands on contemporary Earth and makes topical references to inflation and the fuel crisis, suggesting the story is set around the year it was published (1979).

The Eternal War has "lasted through the millennia". The Doctor surmises they have "conquered the entire galaxy" (a sentiment echoed by a later caption) and refers to them as the Galactic Roman Empire. Ironicus says "now that Rome has gone on to conquer all dimensions" when offering sacrifices from our universe, but it's later clarified that the process has just started - these are "the first sacrifices from other dimensions".

It's unclear what year it is on the alternate Earth, or how long the Malevilus have been there. The Malevilus don't have time travel, at least not in a form as advanced as the TARDIS; this implies that if time runs at the same rate between dimensions, it's also 1979 there. However, Ironicus says it's the "year MMMXXI R.I.", with R.I. standing for Regency of Ironicus. That suggests it's 3021 years since the Regency started, but 1979 is only 2732 years after the founding of Rome (and when measuring the year, that was the start date Romans used), suggesting it's the future.

Adolphus, though, appears to be a normal young boy - one who looks about eight years old. He seems shocked by Magog's true appearance, and there's no indication that Adolphus is a Malevilus or half-Malevilus himself. This may mean that Magog killed his real mother, or that he's preventing him from growing up (or both), but this isn't ever mentioned.

Roman technology is an odd mix of twentieth century technology such as tanks, television, zeppelins with advanced robots, bionics, dimension ducts, air-cars, metal eating "bact guns", robophants (robot war elephants) and interstellar travel. The Malevilus have presumably supplied most of the advanced technology. Robots have been around "centuries", and it would seem - although it's never explicitly stated - that the Malevilus built them, so have been around at least that long, too.

The story doesn't reconcile these statements. It doesn't explicitly say (or rule out) that it's the Malevilus

The tenth Doctor planned to take Rose to an Ian Dury concert on 21st November, 1979.[133]

The Nineteen-Eighties

In the 1980s, the vampires Amelia Doory and Reggie Mead gained enough resources to start up a blood farm. They traded blood with other victims of the Forge in exchange for vampire DNA.[134] In the same decade, Iris stopped the mermaid Magda from using her siren song to blow up a nuclear power plant. Magda reformed and later came to work for MIAOW.[135] The eleventh Doctor, Amy, Rory and Kevin the Tyrannosaur investigated a crime in Los Angeles, posing as members of the LAPD.[136]

(=) PYRAMIDS OF MARS[137] -> The fourth Doctor took Sarah to an alternate version of 1980, to show her what would happen if they left England in 1911 before defeating Sutekh. Earth was a devastated wasteland.
----

c 1980 - "Yonder... the Yeti"[138] -> A small expedition to Tibet went looking for the Yeti. They visited a local monk Lama Gampo, but the creatures attacked them, and the Great Intelligence possessed one of the expedition members. The Yeti had flying vehicles and web guns, and the Intelligence planned to launch a new conquest of Earth. Lama Gampo, whose father's uncle fought the Yeti sixty years before, rescued the party and summoned the real Yeti

before destroying the power transfuser that linked the Intelligence to Earth. He then hypnotised the surviving expedition members to maintain his secrets.

The android Isley killed an assassination target in Cuba on 3rd February, 1980 - and then, owing to her overly sensitive programming, killed fifty potential witnesses.[139]

Owen Harper of Torchwood was born 14th February, 1980.[140]

The US military decided on 28th February, 1980, that Albert Gilroy's killer androids had become too uncontrollable, and made preparations to destroy them - with a nuclear bomb, in violation of the Limited Test Ban Treaty - in the fake Colorado city of Appletown. Colonel Redvers told Gilroy that the Reagan Administration believed that the detonation would have the added benefit of pushing Cold War tensions to America's advantage.[141]

With foreign investment rare in Argentina, the American CIA began tracking contract-intensive money there in 1980.[142]

1980 - "The Star Beast"[143] -> The peaceful Meeps became warlike when Black Sun radiation affected their planet. The Wrarth Galaxy Star Council created the Wrarth Warriors, amalgams of their five strongest races, to defeat them. The Meep armada was destroyed at the Battle of Yarras, but their leader, Beep the Meep, escaped.

An alien ship crashed at a steel mill in Blackcastle, a city in the north of England. The government denied it was a

who've prevented Rome from falling. If that was the case, it would mean they've been around at least fifteen hundred years.

The Doctor refers to Magog as "him", so his natural form is male. We see all five Malevilus "statues" apparently come to life with Juno in the room, even though Juno is Magog in disguise. Later we learn that Magog can be in more than one place at once. In "The Mark of Mandragora", we see Magog still in the TARDIS in the seventh Doctor's era, being eaten away by the Mandragora Helix.

The Doctor has heard of the Ectoslime and the Malevilus - who in turn have heard of the Time Lords - and kronkburgers are mentioned in The Long Game, so it would seem they all exist in our universe. The Doctor knows about a strict boarding school run by Lukronian Vorks on the ice planet of Cryos IV on the edge of the galaxy, perhaps indicating it also exists in our universe.

133 Tooth and Claw (TV)

134 Project Twilight

135 Iris: Enter Wildthyme

136 "Your Destiny Awaits". No date is given. The Doctor's alias of "Lt. Addison" has a Moonlighting feel about it, suggesting that it's the 1980s.

137 Dating Pyramids of Mars (13.3) - The year is stated

several times by both the Doctor and Sarah (including the Doctor's comment, "1980, Sarah, if you want to get off"). The Doctor's actions prevent this timeline from coming to pass.

138 Dating "Yonder... the Yeti" (DWW #31-34) - When Bruce mentions the Yeti attack in the 1920s, the Lama replies "many things have changed in the last sixty years", so the story - published in 1980 - is set in the 1980s.

139 Nuclear Time (p89).

140 Per his personnel file in TW: Exit Wounds and a reference in TW: Pack Animals (p139), but there's confusion about this. It's said in TW: Dead Man Walking that Owen is 27, but as that story cannot conceivably occur before February 2008, he should really be 28. To muddy the waters even further, TW: SkyPoint, set after Dead Man Walking, seems to suggest that Owen is only 26 (p45). Torchwood: The Official Magazine Yearbook (2008) also gives Owen's birthday as "14/02/80", but The Torchwood Archives says he was born on the same day in 1982. Actor Burn Gorman was born in 1st September, 1974.

141 Nuclear Time (p89).

142 TW: Miracle Day

UFO, and UNIT troops were sent to secure the site. Two schoolchildren, Fudge and Sharon, discovered the survivor - the immensely cute Beep the Meep, who was being pursued by the monstrous Wrarth Warriors. The fourth Doctor and K9 landed on the Wrarth Warrior ship. The aliens immobilised the Doctor and planted a bomb inside him, sending him down to Earth, knowing he would locate the Meep.

The Meep used mind control to enslave humans to rebuild his ship, and planned to make a star jump while still on Earth - an act that would have hideous consequences. The Meep activated the black sun drive, sucking Blackcastle into a black hole, but the effects were temporary because the Doctor sabotaged the stardrive. Stuck in Earth orbit, the Meep was arrested and sent for trial. Sharon joined the Doctor on his adventures.

c 1980 - "The Collector"[144] **->** The fourth Doctor and Sharon returned to Blackcastle after many adventures, but were immediately snatched up by a teleport-beam and rematerialised on a base in the asteroid belt. This was the home of Varan Tak from Oskerion, who had been capturing specimens from Earth for two thousand years. His ship had been damaged for that long, and he was waiting for his distress signal to arrive at his home planet. His only companionship during this exile was the ship's computer, who had built a robot form for herself. She was preventing Varan Tak from teleporting to Earth, but the Doctor destroyed the security precautions.

> (=) Varan Tak beamed to Earth... only to die because he couldn't tolerate the pollution levels. The computer destroyed K9 in revenge.

The Doctor used the TARDIS to manipulate the ship's time stasis fields and changed history, destroying the teleporter and saving Varan Tak and K9. The Doctor, Sharon and K9 left Varan Tak and the computer in peace.

c 1980 - THE LEISURE HIVE[145] **->** The fourth Doctor, Romana and K9 briefly landed on Brighton beach, but the Doctor had got the season wrong, and they soon left for Argolis.

Ashley Chapel experimented with the micromonolithic circuit and made contact with Saraquazel, a being from the universe that exists after our own.[146] One of Sabbath's agents tried and failed to assassinate Pope John Paul II in 1980.[147] @ The eighth Doctor defeated the Voord in Penge during the nineteen-eighties.[148]

Samantha Angeline Jones, a companion of the eighth Doctor, was born on 15th April, 1980.[149]

> (=) She was born dark-haired, her mother a social worker and her father a doctor. She would grow up to become a vegetarian, and have scar marks on her arms from injecting diamorphine. She would end up living in a bedsit near King's Cross.

She was born blonde-haired, her mother a social worker and her father a doctor. She would grow up to become a vegetarian, and have no scar marks on her arm. She would meet the Doctor while attending school in 1997.[150]

1980 (30th April) - THE CITY OF THE DEAD[151] **->** The eighth Doctor arrived from the early twenty-first century to investigate a bone charm. Louisiana resident Alain Auguste Delesormes tried to summon a water elemental, but most of his family died when their home was flooded. The Doctor saved a young boy from the calamity, failing to realise that he was the water elemental in human form.

Delesormes' son, also named Alain, survived and was put into foster care in Vermont. He grew up to become police investigator Jonas Rust, and sought to continue his father's work. The water elemental's mother came to search for her son and was bound into a human body. She became the wife of New Orleans resident Vernon Flood, unable to escape her fleshy prison.

---

143 Dating "The Star Beast" (*DWW* #19-26) - It's a contemporary setting, and the story was first published in the 80s. "Star Beast II" is set "fifteen years" later in "1995". **144** Dating "The Collector" (*DWM* #46) - It is Sharon's native time.
145 Dating *The Leisure Hive* (18.1) - It isn't clear when the TARDIS lands on Brighton beach. In Fisher's novelisation it is clearly contemporary, although the opening chapter of the novel is set in June - which would contradict Romana's on-screen exasperation that the Doctor has got "the season wrong". *The Terrestrial Index* and *The TARDIS Logs* both suggested a date of "1934", although why is unclear. The date doesn't appear in the script or any BBC documentation.

146 "Twenty years" before *Millennial Rites* (p216), and "five years" after he gets the circuit (p4).
147 *History 101.* In real life, assassination attempts were made on John Paul's life in May 1981 and May 1982.
148 *The Tomorrow Windows*
149 *Alien Bodies* (p177-178), with the date re-confirmed in *Revolution Man* (p191).
150 *Alien Bodies* (p177-178). Sam's original timeline is that of a dark-haired drug-user, but events in *Unnatural History* cancel out this history and create the blonde-haired version that becomes the Doctor's companion.
151 Dating *The City of the Dead* (EDA #49) - "That was in 1980" (p66).

On 3rd June, 1980, the alien Ambassadors completed their survey of the solar system and left. No further contact with humanity was made.[152] America used its secretive Apollo programme to establish Base Diana on the dark side of the moon. *Apollos* 18 to 21 set up the base, and the final flight - *Apollo 22*, in June 1980 - ferried the equipment for a quantum displacement system. From that point, a teleport link existed between Base Diana and a command centre, Base Hibiscus, in the Texas desert.[153]

1980 - THE FIRES OF VULCAN[154] -> The archaeologist Scalini excavated a police box from the ruins of Pompeii. The seventh Doctor and Mel were inside, and exited the ship when no-one was looking. Captain Muriel Frost of UNIT called in the fifth Doctor to investigate.

c 1980 (October) - SHADA[155] -> Answering a distress signal from Professor Chronotis, the fourth Doctor and Romana arrived in Cambridge. They discovered that the geneticist Skagra had taken *The Worshipful and Ancient Law of Gallifrey*, the key to the Time Lord prison planet of Shada, and ended his scheme to mentally dominate the universe.

or ...

c 1980 (October) - THE FIVE DOCTORS / SHADA -> Borusa attempted to abduct the fourth Doctor (and possibly Romana) while they were punting in Cambridge. The abduction failed, and they were caught in a time eddy. This averted their visit to

---

152 *The Dying Days*, referring to the aliens seen in *The Ambassadors of Death*.

153 *Apollo 23*. The quantum displacement system is possibly plundered alien technology, because in the thirty years to follow this story, the Americans never develop more than just the one working unit.

154 Dating *The Fires of Vulcan* (BF #12) - It is "the year 1980".

155 Dating *Shada* (17.6 and BF BBCi #2) - The TARDIS was "confused" by May Week being in June, so it landed in October. No year is given, but the story has a contemporary setting, and Chris Parsons graduated in 1978.

WHICH SHADA, IF ANY, IS CANON?: The TV version of *Shada* was never completed, following an industrial dispute during filming. A couple of clips were later used in *The Five Doctors* to show the fourth Doctor and Romana being taken out of their timestream. In 1992, the *Shada* footage that had been filmed was released on video, with special effects, music and a linking narration by Tom Baker. The clips that were included in *The Five Doctors* were re-jigged for the 1995 "Special Edition" release of that story. Finally, in 2003, the story was remade in its entirety as a webcast with Paul McGann as the lead character and Lalla Ward reprising her role as Romana. A new introduction scene was included to help explain the eighth Doctor and Romana's sudden interest in these events. Big Finish later released the McGann version on CD.

Which of these - if any - is the "canonical" version of events? All things being equal, the *Doctor Who* TV series trumps all other formats, but in this case, the actual completion of the Paul McGann story - as opposed to the abandoned TV version - makes the webcast hard to ignore. Also, the alteration of the fourth Doctor/Romana clips in the different versions of *The Five Doctors* makes it harder and harder to reconcile them against the TV *Shada* itself.

A growing theory now holds that Borusa's time-scooping of the fourth Doctor and Romana derailed their adventure and they simply departed after the

punting, with the eighth Doctor and Romana later returning to complete the task. The webcast, in fact, suggests that the eighth Doctor is plugging a gap in history by performing the duties that his fourth self would have done.

156 Dating *TW: Trace Memory* (*TW* novel #5) - Toshiko is currently five (p71); her birth in this chronology is dated to 1975.

157 *TW: Children of Earth*

158 Dating *Meglos* (18.2) - Unless the Gaztaks can time travel, this story is set in the late twentieth century. The Earthling wears an early 1980s business suit. *The TARDIS Logs* offered a date of "1988", *Timelink* says "1983".

159 Dating *Father Time* (EDA #41) - The only date given is "the early 1980s". At the beginning of the book, Debbie is looking forward to a television schedule that is the evening that *Meglos* episode one was shown, 27th September, 1980.

160 *Salvation*

161 *Eye of Heaven*

162 *The Left-Handed Hummingbird*

163 *Downtime*

164 *Divided Loyalties*

165 *Primeval*

166 She's "26" in *TW: Cyberwoman*, set in 2007.

167 Dating *The Keeper of Traken* (18.6) - Traken is destroyed in the subsequent story, *Logopolis*, so *The Keeper of Traken* can't occur after this time, although *The TARDIS Logs* suggested a date of "4950 AD". Melkur arrived on Traken "many years" before. The script specifies that Kassia is 18 at the time, the same age as Nyssa when the Doctor first meets her.

168 *Cold Fusion*

169 *Four to Doomsday*. The Doctor mentions the visit during his attempt to convince Tegan that the Urbankan ship might be Heathrow.

170 Dating *Logopolis* (18.7) - The date is first stated in *Four to Doomsday*, and is the same day that the first episode was broadcast. This is the first on-screen use of the term "chameleon circuit". *The TARDIS Logs* set the

Chronotis, but the eighth Doctor and Romana later arrived and stopped Skagra as scheduled.

1980 - TW: TRACE MEMORY[156] **->** A five-year-old Toshiko Sato was very pleased when her father returned to Osaka for the Tenjin Festival. The next day, she briefly met the time-hopping Michael Bellini and the Vondrax pursuing him.

John Frobisher joined the civil service in 1980. Bridget Spears worked with him for six months; it would be another ten years before he requested that she work in his office.[157]

c 1980 - MEGLOS[158] **->** On the planet Tigella, the fourth Doctor, Romana and K9 prevented Meglos, the last Zolfa-Thuran, from recovering the Dodecahedron - the power source that would let him use the Screens of Zolfa-Thura to destroy planets. The Screens, the Dodecahedron and Meglos himself were destroyed. The Doctor returned home an Earthling that a band of Gaztaks had kidnapped as a host body for Meglos.

@ c 1980 (winter) - FATHER TIME[159] **->** Rumours of mysterious lights and flying saucers drew UFO spotters to the Derbyshire village of Greyfrith. This had been caused by the arrival of a Klade saucer from the far, far future. The Klade Prefect Zevron and his deputy, Sallak, were hunting down the ten-year-old Miranda - the last survivor of the Imperial Family, brought to Earth by her nanny.

Aided by the Hunters Rum and Thelash, plus the giant robot Mr Gibson, Zevron tracked Miranda down. The eighth Doctor was staying just outside the village, and with the help of Miranda's teacher, Debbie Castle, he defeated Zevron and his henchmen. Zevron died, but Sallak survived and was arrested. Debbie's husband Barry was rendered mindless. The Doctor pledged to protect Miranda, who - like him - had two hearts.

After the Doctor officially adopted Miranda, they moved south to a large house. The Doctor worked as a business consultant, very quickly becoming a millionaire as he solved economic problems that confounded everyone else.

Following a remark from the Doctor, the barman of the Dragon pub in Greyfrith started selling bottled water. Within five years, he was making twenty million pounds a year from sales of Dragonwater.

In November 1980, *Prey for a Miracle* was released. It was a movie version of the "gods hoax" of 1965, starring Peter Cushing as the Doctor.[160] Shortly before he died, John Lennon told the Doctor, "Talent borrows, genius steals".[161] John Lennon was murdered on 8th December, 1980, by Mark Chapman. Huitzilin fed off the trauma of the event.[162]

Professor Edward Travers CBE died on Christmas Day the same year.[163]

1981

The Union of Traken now stretched over five or six planets in one solar system.[164] All diseases had been eradicated on Traken by this time.[165] **Lisa Hallett of Torchwood London was born.**[166]

c 1981 - THE KEEPER OF TRAKEN[167] **->** Traken was a peaceful planet in Mettula Orionsis. Two of the consuls of Traken - Tremas and Kassia - married.

Kassia had tended to the Melkur, a creature of evil that had calcified in Traken's serene environment, since she was a child. But now the Melkur had begun to move again. Hypnotically controlling Kassia, the Melkur - in reality the Master - attempted to take control of the Source, the power of the Keeper of Traken. The Master was at the end of his regeneration cycle, and was desperate to obtain the power necessary to gain a new body. Kassia was killed, but the fourth Doctor and Adric prevented the Master from acquiring the Source, and Consul Luvic became the new Keeper. The Master escaped, and took the body of Tremas as his new form.

Survivors from Traken would found the colony of Serenity, a verdant world of peace and isolation.[168] **The Doctor visited Terminal Three of Heathrow Airport around this time.**[169]

1981 (28th February) - LOGOPOLIS[170] **->** The fourth Doctor and Adric landed on Earth and took the measurements of a genuine police box to help repairs to the TARDIS' chameleon circuit. The Doctor had previously visited the planet Logopolis, hoping they could help him with their mathematical expertise and mastery of block transfer computation. Tegan Jovanka, an airline stewardess, found herself aboard the TARDIS after the Master murdered her Aunt Vanessa.

The Doctor learnt from the Monitor of Logopolis that the universe had already passed the natural point of heat death. All closed systems succumb to heat death, and the universe was such a closed system. Or rather it used to be: the Logopolitans had opened up CVEs into other universes, such as E-Space. When the Master learnt of this, he recognised a chance to blackmail the entire universe. The Master's interference halted Logopolis' operations, which caused the CVEs to collapse. Entropy began to accumulate and destroyed a vast region of space, including Logopolis and Traken.

The Watcher observed these events, and brought Nyssa of Traken to Logopolis to join the Doctor.

On Earth, the Doctor and the Master worked to re-open a CVE in Cassiopeia at co-ordinates 3C461-3044. The Master threatened to close off even this CVE, and broadcast a message to the entire universe:

"Peoples of the universe please attend carefully, the message that follows is vital to the future of you all. The choice for you all is simple: a continued existence under my guidance, or total annihilation. At the time of speaking, the fate of the universe lies in the balance at the fulcrum point, the Pharos Project on Earth..."

The Doctor prevented the Master from closing the CVE, but fell to his death. As he regenerated, the Watcher merged with him...

1981 - CASTROVALVA[171] -> ... the newly-regenerated fifth Doctor, Nyssa and Tegan returned to the TARDIS. The Master kidnapped Adric.

1981 (28th February) - FOUR TO DOOMSDAY[172] -> The fifth Doctor, Tegan, Nyssa and Adric defeated Monarch's plans to travel back to the creation of the universe. Monarch's android crew opted to find a habitable world and settle on it.

A formless race of explorers sent seeds the size of acorns into space. Each of these would land on a planet, analyse the environment and grow a creature that could survive there. One such seed bank, later named the Juniper Tree, was adopted into a UK military programme that hoped to develop disposable soldiers. The first child grown from it, Sebastian, was born on 3rd March, 1981, and met Jack Harkness of Torchwood a few days later.[173]

Cassandra Hope Schofield, the future mother of the Doctor's companion Hex, was born on 7th April, 1981.[174]

(=) 1981 (28th August) - NUCLEAR TIME[175] -> The US military's obliteration of Appletown, Colorado, and the killer androids gathered there, resulted in the deaths of Amy Pond, Rory Williams, and Albert Gilroy... and triggered a full-fledged war between the US and the Soviet Union.

The explosion caused the eleventh Doctor to experience time backward, and he altered history. The energy of the bomb's detonation was dispersed over a ninety-minute window, generating radiation but not a full-fledged mushroom cloud. The android Isley developed feelings for Gilroy, her creator, and they went into hiding together.

In 1981, UNIT encountered the Zygons in the Kalahari Desert and the Ice Warriors in Northampton.[176] The Jex arrived on Earth on 4th December, 1981, and took shelter

Logopolis sequence in "4950". It's never stated if the other CVEs are ever restored, although it's possible that reviving the Cassiopeia CVE opened the others.
171 Dating Castrovalva (19.1) - This story immediately follows Logopolis.
172 Dating Four to Doomsday (19.2) - The Doctor establishes that he has returned Tegan to the right point in time "16.15 hours" on "February 28th 1981", the day episode one of Logopolis was broadcast.
173 TW: First Born
174 Project: Destiny
175 Dating Nuclear Time (NSA #40) - The day is repeatedly given.
176 The King of Terror. In Castrovalva, the newly-regenerated/confused fifth Doctor seemed to allude to an incident that involved the Brigadier and the Ice Warriors. In The Dying Days, the Brigadier says he never met the Ice Warriors, so this couldn't have involved him.
177 The King of Terror
178 The Gallifrey Chronicles
179 Dating The Hollows of Time (BF LS #1.4) - It's "the early 1980s", "a year or two" in Peri's past. In the original conceptualisation of this story, Stream was to be unmasked as the Master; in the actual audio, he's just (if you can call it that) a genius with robotic helpers, hypnotism, knowledge of the Doctor's previous encounter with the Tractators and the ability to pilot the TARDIS.

180 Dating K9 and Company (18.7-A) - Sarah arrives in Moreton Harwood on "December the 18th", and later tells K9 that it is "1981". The other dates are given in dialogue. This story is part of the UNIT timeframe, but real life has overtaken Sarah's "I'm from 1980" comment in Pyramids of Mars.
181 Dating Blue Box (PDA #59) - Presuming one can believe Peters' account, the story opens "two days before Christmas 1981" (p10). Peters visits Swan in the Bainbridge Hospital in late 1982 (p5).
182 Dating Time-Flight (18.7) - The date isn't specified beyond Tegan's "this is the 1980s". There's no indication that it's the exact day Tegan left in Logopolis (or that it isn't). There's snow on the ground, which there wasn't in Logopolis, but which doesn't rule out it being February.
183 TW: The Undertaker's Gift
184 "Ten years" before Iris: Enter Wildthyme.
185 The King's Demons
186 Arc of Infinity
187 Night Thoughts. The Falklands War lasted from 2nd April to 14th June, 1982.
188 Six hundred thirty days before The Reaping, which opens on 24th September, 1984.
189 Dating Relative Dementias (PDA #49) - The date is given (p40).

in California.[177]

@ Even with the help of character references from people such as Graham Greene and Lawrence Olivier, the eighth Doctor needed nearly a year to formally adopt Miranda. Shortly after that, he defeated the Great Provider's plan to use evil mobile telephones to take over the world.[178]

c 1981 - THE HOLLOWS OF TIME[179] **->** The sixth Doctor and Peri detected gravitational anomalies in the English village of Hollowdean, and paid a visit to the Doctor's old friend, the Reverend Foxwell. The villainous Professor Stream attempted to engineer a Quantum Gravity Engine: a device that would make Stream *become* all of space and time. Stream incorporated eleven Tractators into the Engine, and used the Doctor's TARDIS to retrieve most important Tractator - the Gravis - from the future. The Gravis and his Tractators turned on Stream, making him swell up like a balloon and explode.

1981 (18th-22nd December) - K9 AND COMPANY: A GIRL'S BEST FRIEND[180] **->** In September, a hailstorm lasting thirteen seconds destroyed Commander Pollock's crop. He was renting the East Wing of Lavinia Smith's house at the time. On 6th December, Lavinia Smith left for America, phoning her ward Brendan Richards on the 10th to tell him that he would be spending Christmas with her niece, Sarah Jane. The next day, Brendan's term ended and he began waiting for Sarah to pick him up, but she had spent the first two weeks of December working abroad for Reuters.

Sarah Jane found a crate waiting for her at Moreton Harwood. It contained K9 Mk III, sent as a gift from the Doctor. Working together, Sarah, Brendan and K9 exposed a local coven of witches who conducted human sacrifices. On 29th December, the cultists appeared in court on an attempted murder charge.

1981 (23rd December) - BLUE BOX[181] **->** Eridani agents on Earth had recovered three of the five computer components that went missing circa 1966. The sixth Doctor allied with the Eridani to recover the last two, fearing they could affect Earth's development. However, he discovered that the components, part of a system named "the Savant", could usurp control of the human brain's "hardware/software", and had been dispatched to the Eridani colony to mentally dominate it.

The Doctor and the Eridani retrieved the last two components from the formidable hacker Sarah Swan and her friend Luis Perez. However, the Savant had mentally dominated Swan and Perez, who were left near-catatonic. By late 1982, Swan was reportedly in the Bainbridge Hospital, a facility where the American government kept persons with dangerous information. Perez's family cared

for him in Mexico.

The journalist Charles "Chick" Peters later wrote *Blue Box*, a chronicle of these events.

In 1982, a Betamax recorder fell into the Rift.[182] The parents of Simon, a future companion of Iris Wildthyme, died in a plane crash while on "the trip of a lifetime" that they'd won on a game show.[183]

c 1982 - TIME-FLIGHT[184] **->** Following the disappearance of Speedbird Concorde 192 down a time contour, the fifth Doctor, Tegan and Nyssa arrived at Heathrow Airport. At the insistence of Sir John Sudbury at C19, the Doctor and his friends were allowed to take a second Concorde into the contour, and travelled back one hundred and forty million years. Upon their return, the fifth Doctor and Nyssa had to leave Heathrow in such a hurry, Tegan was left behind.

The Master's TARDIS was propelled to Xeraphas, where he discovered Kamelion, a tool of a previous invader of that planet.[185] Tegan Jovanka resumed being an air stewardess, but was sacked shortly afterwards.[186]

During the Falklands War, the chemical gas weapon Gravonax was tested on one of the small Hebrides Islands in Scotland. All wildlife on the isle - which was dubbed Gravonax Island - died, and nobody wanted to live there even after it was decontaminated. Major Dickens and a female military chaplain, a.k.a. "the Deacon", left the British army after "a bit of an incident". The secluded Gravonax Island was perfect for Dickens' scientific research, and he took up residence there.[187]

A Cyber-Leader, potentially the last of its kind, arrived from the far future in a Gallifreyan time-ship. The Cyber-Leader was greatly weakened by exposure to Vortex energy, but continued its scheme to trap the Doctor.[188]

1982 (April) - RELATIVE DEMENTIAS[189] **->** Joyce Brunner, a former UNIT physicist, came to suspect abnormal activity at the Graystairs nursing home. She alerted her old colleague the Doctor (who was now in his seventh incarnation), who arrived with Ace to investigate. The head of Graystairs - the Annarene named Sooal - restored the Tulk war council's memories, then murdered the group upon obtaining the command codes to the Tulk stasis chamber. Two renegade Annarene arrived and killed Sooal, desiring the advanced weaponry within the stasis chamber to return their people to war. The Doctor tricked the Annarene into transmatting into the stasis chamber before it was opened, freezing them in time. He then destroyed the Tulk spaceship.

The ninth Doctor had a number of blind spots in his historical knowledge, the events of May 1982 among them.[190]

@ After two years of the eighth Doctor attempting to interrogate him, the imprisoned alien Sallak got a legal injunction preventing the Doctor from making any other contact.[191] Isaac Summerfield met Hamlet Macbeth in 1982, and was given a copy of his book *The Shoreditch Incident*.[192]

1982 (11th July) - LIVING LEGEND[193] **->** Two agents of the aggressive Threllip race constructed an interdimensional portal in Ferrara, Italy, as a means for their people to invade Earth. The eighth Doctor and Charley squashed the plan, and used the portal to strand the agents on the seventeenth moon of Mordalius Prime.

The Doctor spent time with Nelson Mandela during his imprisonment at Robbin Island.[194] Melanie Bush left school after getting five A-Levels. She backpacked around Europe before getting a job at a Scottish nature reserve. Around the same time, SenéNet was buying up European computer firms and other youth market companies. Their executives were converted into drones.[195]

Peri Brown attended a Slayer concert.[196] In Baltimore, Peri was friends throughout her school years with the Chambers family. The father, Anthony Chambers, kept Peri and his children amused by letting them use a telescope. Peri briefly dated Nate Chambers, and became best friends with his sister Kathy.[197]

Ronald Turvey resented that children grew to become adults and, motivated by the Tinghus within him, schemed to kill all adults with Cuddlesomes: fluffy toys akin to pink vampire hamsters, but equipped with an extra-terrestrial poison. Cuddlesomes were *the* toy to get in the 1980s, and three million were produced. The radio signal intended to release the poison was never sent, as Turvey was arrested for tax fraud and imprisoned for two decades.[198]

The Doctor in Stockbridge

Around 1983, the fifth Doctor settled in the Gloucestershire village of Stockbridge for a time, a guest at the Green Dragon Inn. He had volunteered to investigate time warps on behalf of the Time Lords. After a number of interruptions, he learned that the time warps had been triggered by the Meddling Monk.[199]

The Doctor was head of the Stockbridge Chess Society.[200]

(=) c 1983 - "The Tides of Time"[201] **->** The Prime Mover produced the ordered vibrations of the universe on a vast biomechanical device known as the Event Synthesiser. For the first time in centuries, he fumbled a note, introducing a note of discord. Time warps occurred. The fifth Doctor had been staying in Stockbridge for some time, and was playing a cricket match on the village green when he was bowled a hand grenade instead of a cricket ball. Shortly afterwards, a Roman soldier was shot in nearby woods, only to vanish. The Doctor quickly learned the disturbances were worldwide.

Meanwhile, the Event Synthesiser's discord had opened a gap in time, and the Demon Melanicus emerged through it. He took control of the Event

---

190 *Only Human*
191 "Two years" after the first part of *Father Time*, "three years" before the second (p114).
192 *Return of the Living Dad*
193 Dating *Living Legend* (BF promo #4, *DWM* #337) - The date is given, Track 1.
194 *The Also People*. This would be between 1982 and 1988.
195 *Business Unusual*
196 *The Song of the Megaptera*. Slayer was founded in 1981, and Peri saw them prior to her meeting the Doctor in 1984.
197 *The Reaping*
198 Either "twenty-five years" (according to Turvey and a local named Angela Wisher, who could be generalising a little) or "twenty-three Christmases" (according to the product blurb) before *Cuddlesome*.
199 For almost the entire run of the fifth Doctor's *DWM* adventures, he was based in Stockbridge. The reason for this was finally given in "4-Dimensional Vistas". The stories have a contemporary setting. While they started publication in 1982, the Doctor in "Lunar Lagoon" assumes it is 1983 - the only time a year is specified.

As for *where* these stories take place in relation to the fifth Doctor's television adventures, the Big Finish audios featuring Stockbridge (especially *Circular Time*: "Autumn", *Castle of Fear* and *The Eternal Summer*) establish that the Doctor is already acquainted with Stockbridge, Sir Justin ("The Tides of Time") and Max Edison ("The Stars Fell on Stockbridge") during the time he is travelling with Nyssa alone (between *Time-Flight* and *Arc of Infinity*). Even this, however, means that he must have dropped her (and possibly Adric and Tegan too, if he first visited Stockbridge during Season 19) off somewhere and picked them up again. In "The Tides of Time", the Doctor says that deference is shown on Gallifrey to his "honorary title" of president (*The Invasion of Time*). The *DWM* stories with Gus, however, possibly happen later in the fifth Doctor's lifetime, as his sixth incarnation is still hunting for the person that had Gus killed, suggesting it happened more recently.
200 "Fugitive"

Synthesizer in order to create universal fear, destruction and unending chaos.

A jousting knight - Sir Justin - initially attacked the Doctor, but came to realise his error and vowed to help fight whoever was behind the time warps. Melanicus removed the Event Synthesizer from time to prevent attack, but was detected by the spirit of Rassilon deep in the Matrix. He vowed to act, despite advice from Morvane and Bedevere to be cautious. Rassilon decided to operate through the Doctor, who arrived on Gallifrey and used his Presidential authority to access the Matrix. The Doctor entered the Matrix to commune with Rassilon, and saw him chairing a meeting of the High Evolutionaries from a number of planets.

The High Evolutionaries tasked the Doctor with locating the Event Synthesizer. Rassilon despatched a mysterious agent named Shayde to help the Doctor. Melanicus' interference created the maelstrom - a whirlpool in space and time - and sent a mantric bomb against Gallifrey. Shayde protected the Doctor from its effects, but the TARDIS was sucked into Melanicus' domain: a surreal world where the Doctor and Justin encountered a carnival, a mysterious woman that the Doctor recognised, a demonic fairground ride, barbarian hordes and Dracula.

Emerging from Melanicus' domain, the Doctor took the TARDIS out of time to help his search. He re-entered time, then encountered a ship from Althrace which took them to their home in an alien dimension - a vast solar system engineered so that the planets were bolted together and set orbiting a white hole. The technology of Althrace was as advanced as that of the Time Lords, and the white hole allowed direct access to the forces of creation, making them one vast, living organism. Using the power of the White Hole, the High Evolutionaries combined their mental force to halt time and discover the co-ordinates of the Event Synthesizer. Meanwhile, Melanicus had ushered in the Millenium Wars:

The Millenium Wars

"A thousand worlds in conflict for a thousand years .. with causes lost in the distant past, their fury rages through time and space..."

In the year 375, barbarian hordes from Asia swept into Central Europe... and were wiped out by a division of Nazi tanks... which in turn were wiped out by American F-15 fighters... which in turn were wiped out by advanced space fighters.

"This was the beginning of the Reign of Melanicus as millenium fought millenium... and so what began as a series of small, confused skirmishes soon escalated into a holocaust of conflict, culminating in a far-flung armageddon - the Millenium Wars! A thousand worlds in conflict for a thousand years."

(=) **"The Deal"**[202] -> The fourth Doctor caused a trooper of the 12th Trouble 'chuters to crash. The trooper set his robot "spider" on him, but the Doctor blocked its psychic attack. A pursuit ship arrived, firing missiles at the TARDIS. The Doctor realised that the trooper was a psychopath and left, abandoning him to death at the hands of another pursuit ship.

(=) **"The Tides of Time"** -> But due to his lack of knowledge, Melanicus had confined himself to a cul-de-sac in time. This was to prove his undoing.

After a thousand years of the Millenium Wars, Earth was ruined and lifeless. Melanicus had based the Synthesizer here, and the fifth Doctor located it. The Doctor and Shayde weakened Melanicus, and Justin pierced the demon with his sword, unleashing vast energies. Justin and Melanicus were killed, and the Prime Mover was restored to his rightful place as user of the Event Synthesizer.

---

201 Dating "The Tides of Time" (*DWM* #61-67) - Time is disturbed during this story, and strictly speaking the events take place in a cul-de-sac of time created by Melanicus, and which is destroyed at the end.

The year the story starts is not specified, but the first part features the discordant note and specifies that the Doctor's cricket game on contemporary Earth is taking place "at that precise moment". "Forty years before", the village green was a sandbagged army training army, so clearly that was during the Second World War. The story was published in 1982. In "Lunar Lagoon", the Doctor

had thought he was in "1983", perhaps suggesting that's the year the Stockbridge adventures take place.

The story spells "Event Synthesizer" in both its American and British ("Synthesiser") form in different installments. Stockbridge isn't named until the following story. The mysterious woman the Doctor sees in the dreamscape is never identified - the dress she wears resembles a jumpsuit Zoe wore in *The Wheel in Space*. In retrospect - and completely coincidentally - she resembles the first incarnation of Patience, seen in a similar flashback in *Cold Fusion*.

The Doctor awoke to find time restored, and a memorial to the fallen knight in the church in Stockbridge: St Justinians. As Shayde watched the cricket game resume, the Doctor was unsure if it had all been a dream.

c 1983 - "Stars Fell on Stockbridge"[203] -> UFO spotter Maxwell Edison discovered the TARDIS, and inspired the fifth Doctor to detect an alien spacecraft two days from Earth. They went to the ship, which was deserted and had been drifting for thousands of years. There was some sort of haunting presence on board, but the ship was already heading for Earth's atmosphere. The Doctor and Maxwell returned to Earth, from where Maxwell watched the shooting stars caused by the ship's break-up.

No human space agency had any space labs in orbit.

c 1983 - "The Stockbridge Horror"[204] -> A local limestone quarry unearthed the TARDIS in rock five hundred million years old. Nearby, a police constable discovered a charred body.

The fifth Doctor, still staying at the Green Dragon Inn, saw a report from the quarry. He ran to where he had left the TARDIS - Well's Wood - and found it was still there, covered in mud. He went to the quarry, but couldn't get to the mysterious buried police box. Well's Wood caught fire, and the Doctor - upon returning to the TARDIS - discovered an alien figure that could shoot jets of fire.

The Doctor dematerialised his Ship, but the alien clung to the TARDIS, then forced its way inside. It stalked the Doctor, who realised it was the presence he'd recently encountered on the deserted spaceship. The Gallifreyan military dispatched Lord Tubal Cain in a specially adapted TARDIS, while Shayde trapped the alien in the Matrix. Cain fired seeker torpedoes at the TARDIS... which landed on Gallifrey moments after they hit the homeworld.

While the Doctor faced trial on Gallifrey, the government agency SAG3 investigated the TARDIS. Shayde neutralised them, and erased the imprint of the TARDIS just as the military TARDIS landed. The Doctor was freed.

c 1983 - ARC OF INFINITY[205] -> Omega had relocated the Arc of Infinity - a gateway between dimensions - away from the star system Rondel and placed its curve on the city of Amsterdam. The fifth Doctor and Nyssa tracked Omega to Amsterdam, and found Omega's base in a crypt there. The ancient Gallifreyan's attempt to bond with the Doctor failed, and he apparently died. Tegan Jovanka joined the Doctor's travels once again.

Omega recorporealised enough to stow himself aboard the TARDIS of Ertikus, a Time Lord who arrived in this period to study Omega's exploits. Ertikus' TARDIS relocated to the far future with Omega aboard.[206] **Before this time, the Arar-Jecks of Heiradi had carved out a huge**

---

202 Dating "The Deal" (*DWM* #53) - No date is given, other than stating that the story takes place during the Millenium Wars. *DWM* consistently misspelt "millennium" with one "n". This is not the same as the Millennium War in *The Quantum Archangel*.

203 Dating "Stars Fell on Stockbridge" (*DWM* #68-69) - No year is given, but it's a contemporary setting, and the Doctor is still based in Stockbridge, as he was in "The Tides of Time".

204 Dating "The Stockbridge Horror" (*DWM* #70-75) - Once again, it's a contemporary setting.

205 Dating *Arc of Infinity* (20.1) - There is no indication of the year. It is some time after *Time-Flight*, and before *The Awakening*.

206 *Omega*

207 As mentioned by Turlough in *Frontios*, although the universe isn't yet twenty billion years old at this point.

208 *Damaged Goods*

209 *SJA: Death of the Doctor*

210 *Army of Death*

211 Dating *Hexagora* (BF LS #3.2) - The story occurs between *Arc of Infinity* and *Snakedance* (and directly after *The Elite*), during Tegan's native time on Earth.

212 *Mawdryn Undead, Planet of Fire.*

213 *Kiss of Death*

214 Dating *Mawdryn Undead* (20.3) - The Doctor says

"if these readings are correct, its 1983 on Earth", and the date is reaffirmed a number of times afterwards.

Turlough first appears in *Mawdryn Undead*, but his origins are revealed in *Planet of Fire*. According to the initial Character Outline, Turlough was "20" on his first appearance, which makes him a couple of years too old to be at Brendon School - this was almost certainly written when the plan was to introduce the character in *The Song of the Space Whale* by Pat Mills, a story that was delayed, then rejected. Mark Strickson was 22 when he began playing Turlough.

Turlough's pact with the Black Guardian ends in the undatable *Enlightenment*.

215 Dating *Kiss of Death* (BF #147) - The story occurs between *Mawdryn Undead* and the reforms on Trion that enable Turlough to return home (*Planet of Fire*).

216 Dating *Rat Trap* (BF #148) - It's "June the 9th, 1983", general election day in the United Kingdom.

217 Dating *Turlough and the Earthlink Dilemma* (*The Companions of Doctor Who* #1) - As Turlough's actions eliminate Rehctaht, this presumably (and paradoxically) causes the very political reform that allows his younger self to return home to Trion in *Planet of Fire*.

218 Dating *The Five Doctors* (20.1) - The Brigadier recognises Tegan, so he must be kidnapped by Borusa after the second half of *Mawdryn Undead* in 1983. It is specified that he is attending a UNIT reunion (perhaps

subterranean city during the 20-Aeon War on that planet.[207] The seventh Doctor and Ace fought an N-form by the Rio Yari in 1983.[208] **Jo Jones lived with the Nambiquara tribe from the Mato Grosso for about six months in 1983.**[209] The Doctor collected some oolong tea in Peking in either 1983 or 1893.[210]

c 1983 - HEXAGORA[211] **->** The Hexagora, a nomadic insect species, had settled on Luparis - the third planet of Proxima Centauri. A global cooling event prevented the Hexagorans from moving on - to survive, they required mammalian bodies. Humans were abducted from Earth via spacepods, and the Hexagorans swapped minds with them, leaving their insectoid bodies in hibernation. The humanised Hexagorans constructed a city, Lupara, based upon schematics they had taken of Tudor London.

The fifth Doctor, Tegan and Nyssa relaxed in Tegan's hometown, near Brisbane, when Tegan learned that her friend Mike Bretherton had been abducted. They followed Bretherton's trail to Luparis. Queen Zafira recognised that human bodies didn't live long enough to survive the Luparis winter, and so decreed that she and the Doctor would marry and sire longer-lived offspring. The Doctor convinced Zafira that the collective Hexagoran memory pool, the Hexagon, was fragmenting because they were inhabiting human bodies. He aided them in returning to their insectoid forms, and relocating to a warmer world. The abducted humans, most of whom had slept in stasis, were returned to Earth seconds after they left.

There was civil war on Trion. Turlough's mother was killed and the ship containing his father and brother crashed on Sarn, formerly a Trion prison planet. Turlough was captured and exiled to Brendon School on Earth, where Trion agents, including a solicitor on Chancery Lane, watched him.[212] Deela's father was on the winning side of the civil war, and had seen to it that Turlough was exiled.[213]

1983 - MAWDRYN UNDEAD[214] **->** The Brigadier regained his memory, but lost his beloved car when he met the fifth Doctor, Tegan and Nyssa. When the Brigadier met his past self from 1977, he unwittingly provided the energy that released Mawdryn and his followers from their curse of immortality. The Black Guardian forged a deal in secret with Turlough, and tasked him with killing the Doctor. Turlough left Brendon to join the TARDIS crew.

1983 - KISS OF DEATH[215] **->** Trion repatriation squads were now in operation on various worlds.
Turlough's old flame Deela became engaged to a ruthless entrepreneur named Halquin Rennol. When Deela's father disavowed the union and froze her assets, the pair coveted

the royal treasure rumoured to reside in the dimensional vault established by Turlough's ancestor. Only Turlough and Deela's DNA in combination - through a simple kiss, for instance - would open the vault, and so Rennol's mercenaries captured Turlough when the TARDIS landed on the vacation world of Vektris. The vault's security system went haywire - Rennol killed Deela, and was probably killed himself when the vault resealed.

1983 (9th June) - RAT TRAP[216] **->** The Rat King living beneath Cardogan Castle attempted to release a variant of the Black Death that would wipe out humanity. The fifth Doctor, Tegan, Turlough and Nyssa helped to destroy the Rat King, and UNIT was summoned to clear up the mess.

1983 - TURLOUGH AND THE EARTHLINK DILEMMA[217] **->** After departing the fifth Doctor's company, a time-travelling Turlough encountered the dictator Rechtaht while she ruled Trion. Rechtaht tried to transfer her mind into Turlough, but his ally - a Time Lord named the Magician - helped Turlough to expel Rechtaht from his mind. This averted a timeline that included the destruction of Earth, Trion and New Trion. Turlough learned that as he had altered history, he couldn't remain in this timeline without causing a paradox.

= With the Magician's help, Turlough found a reality in which he had died and took up residence there. He was reunited with his old friend, Juras Maateh, of that reality.

c 1983 - THE FIVE DOCTORS[218] **->** The second Doctor and the Brigadier were kidnapped by Borusa in the grounds of UNIT HQ. The next day, the second Doctor bought a copy of "The Times" that reported the UNIT reunion. Colonel Crichton was running UNIT at this point. Despite K9's warnings, Sarah Jane Smith was also kidnapped by Borusa.

Masie Hawk, Hamlet Macbeth, Liz Shaw and Sir John Sudbury also attended the reunion. Benton had returned to active duty. Carol Bell was married with a child. Mike Yates and Tom Osgood had opened a tearoom together.[219] Lethbridge-Stewart spent some time in Haiti.[220]

1983 - "4-Dimensional Vistas"[221] **->** A British Airways 747 crashed in the Arctic, shot down by the test firing of a Martian cannon. The Meddling Monk and a group of Ice Warriors led by Autek had a base there, and were manipulating time. The fifth Doctor homed in on them, but was attacked by the beam weapon. SAG3 arrived by plane to investigate.

Meanwhile, the Doctor and Gus discovered that the Ice Warriors had drilled a vast shaft. Gus and SAG3 launched an attack on the Ice Warrior base, but Autek and the Meddling Monk got away. They had activated "the Crucible", then jumped five million years forwards in time. As they returned, the Doctor chased the Monk's TARDIS in his own and set up a Time Ram - apparently annihilating the Monk and destroying the Ice Warrior base.

His vigil on Earth ended, the Doctor pledged to get Gus home.

In 1983, a 13-year-old Ace was friends with an Asian girl, Manisha, whose flat was firebombed in a racist attack. In anger because of this, Ace burnt down Gabriel Chase. She was assigned a probation officer and social worker.[222]

Joel Mintz had been thrown back in time to 1983 from 1993. He ended up in New York, where Isaac Summerfield found him.[223] Jason Kane, a future rogue and husband of Bernice Summerfield, was born in 1983.[224] In 1983, Faction Paradox agents wrecked the Blue Peter garden.[225]

c 1983 (summer) - "City of Devils"[226] **->** Aunt Lavinia sent Sarah Jane and K9 to Egypt to write a story about her friend Warren Martyn. An archaeological dig there had experienced some mysterious deaths and disappearances. Entering the tomb, Sarah and K9 encountered a group of Silurians and Sea Devils in a vast subterranean city. Sarah opened diplomatic relations with the Silurians, and it was hoped that this would lead to an accommodation between the two civilisations. Returning to England, Sarah Jane contacted Lethbridge-Stewart, who was keen to make amends for the mistakes of the past.

c 1983 (July) - HEART OF TARDIS[227] **->** Crowley lured the fourth Doctor and Romana to the Tollsham USAF base, as he needed the Doctor to open the Golgotha gateway.

Ianto Jones of Torchwood was born on 19th August, 1983.[228] Peri Brown, a 17-year-old student at Boston University, bought a handgun.[229] A Nestene sphere fell to Earth, injured. A little girl, Elizabeth Sarah Devonshire, found the sphere - it would influence her mind and manipulate her career path in future.[230]

1983 - RETURN OF THE LIVING DAD[231] **->** The seventh Doctor, Benny, Jason, Chris and Roz discovered that Benny's father, Isaac, was alive and well in the village of Little Caldwell. He was running an underground movement that helped stranded aliens on Earth return home.

Albinex the Navarino paid one of Isaac's allies to retrieve nuclear launch codes from the Doctor. Albinex and Isaac were working together to detonate a nuclear device, which Isaac hoped would spur an arms race so humanity would have more advanced weapons to use against the Daleks in the twenty-second century. However, Albinex was actually a Dalek agent, and planned to destroy the Earth. The Doctor, Isaac and Benny captured the Navarino and thwarted the plan. Benny made peace with her father.

Isaac Summerfield's presence in the twentieth century created historical anomalies that enabled the Daleks to locate and capture him. They took him to the twenty-seventh century and slaved him to battle computers. Following the Daleks' defeat, Braxiatel returned Isaac to

one he initiated once his memories returned?), but this isn't the occasion of his retirement. Sarah is kidnapped around the same time, certainly after *K9 and Company*.
219 *Business Unusual*
220 "Last year" according to *Heart of TARDIS* (p41).
221 Dating "4-Dimensional Vistas" (*DWM* #78-83) - This story marks the end of the Doctor's vigil on Earth. In "Lunar Lagoon", the Doctor thought he was in "1983".
222 *Ghost Light*. Marc Platt's novelisation specifies that Gabriel Chase is burnt down in August 1983. Ace's social worker is referred to in *Survival*.
223 "Eight months" before *Return of the Living Dad*.
224 *Return of the Living Dad* (p53). While in 1983, Jason says he was "born this year". In *Death and Diplomacy* (set circa 2011), Jason must be rounding when he says, "I'm thirty years old, near enough" (p196).
225 *Interference* (p296).
226 Dating "City of Devils" (*DWM Holiday Special 1992*) - The date is given in the opening caption.
227 Dating *Heart of TARDIS* (PDA #32) - It's July (p117), "fifteen years" after 1968 (p246).
228 *TW: Fragments*, and confirmed in *The Torchwood Archives*, although *Torchwood: The Official Magazine*

Yearbook (2008) says he was born 2nd December, 1982.
229 *Burning Heart* (p102).
230 "Thirty years" before *Autonomy*.
231 Dating *Return of the Living Dad* (NA #53) - It's "10 December 1983" (p34).
232 *Benny: Life During Wartime, Benny: Death to the Daleks*.
233 According to the CIA files in *TW: Miracle Day*. 24th October is named as a Saturday; in 1983, it was actually a Monday.
234 *Remembrance of the Daleks*. Had someone from 1963 discovered Ace's ghetto blaster, this would have occurred "twenty years too early".
235 *Touched by an Angel*. He's 37 in October 2011, so was born in either 1983 or 1984.
236 *The Hollow Men*
237 *Father's Day*. No precise dating is given, but it's before Rose's birth in 1986.
238 *The Reaping*
239 *The Runaway Bride*. The Thames Barrier was constructed from 1974 to 1984.
240 "Eighteen years" before *SJS: Comeback*.
241 *FP: The Book of the War*

Little Caldwell.[232] **On Oct. 24, 1983, the Welsh Assembly denied allegations of a conspiracy.**[233]

The "microchip revolution" took place in the early eighties.[234] Mark Whitaker, a person of interest to the Weeping Angels, was born.[235] The fifth Doctor, Tegan and Nyssa visited Hexen Bridge in 1984.[236] **The ninth Doctor and Rose quietly attended the wedding of her parents, Peter Tyler and Jacqueline Andrea Suzette Prentice.**[237] The Doctor said 1984 was "never as good as the book".[238] **Torchwood constructed a secret base beneath the Thames Barrier.**[239]

Laboratories belonging to a French company, Rechauffer, Inc., contaminated the Well of St. Clothide in the village of Cloots Coombe, which made the population sterile. Rechauffer took genetic samples from the villagers, allegedly to clone them children, but actually to work towards the creation of disposable clones for military purposes. The initial experiments produced an abomination that fed off the life force itself, and lived in the well.[240]

w - The third iteration of Cousin Anastasia died as Anna Anderson in Charlottesville, Virginia, 1984.[241]

When Gwen Cooper was about five or six, her father came home after receiving the blame for money that had gone missing from work. He told Gwen that he wasn't distressed about the money, but that he couldn't stand anyone thinking that he wasn't an honest man. She would always remember the incident, as it was the first time anyone had spoken to her like an adult.[242]

1984 (1st May) - THE AWAKENING[243] **->** The Malus absorbed the psychic energy of a series of war games in Little Hodcombe, amplifying the villagers' violence. The fifth Doctor prevented the Malus from becoming totally active and blew up the church in which the Malus lay dormant. After this, the Doctor, Tegan and Turlough spent some time in Little Hodcombe with Tegan's grandfather, Andrew Verney.

The Doctor's experiences in Little Hodcombe reminded him of Hexen Bridge. He decided to monitor the area.[244]

c 1984 - "The Forgotten"[245] **->** The fifth Doctor, Tegan and Turlough spent time at the Doctor's house at Allen Road, with the Doctor enjoying playing cricket for the local team. A Judoon ship arrived on Earth in defiance of galactic law that put the planet outside their jurisdiction. They were looking for the spherical Eye of Akasha, which was in the Doctor's possession, but he tricked them into taking a cricket ball instead.

1984 - RESURRECTION OF THE DALEKS[246] **->** Daleks from the future arrived in the twentieth century and placed their Duplicates in key positions around the world. They used the timezone as a safe storage place for the Movellan virus that had all but wiped them out. The fifth Doctor, Tegan and Turlough were present as a pitched battle broke out between the British army and the Daleks. The Doctor released the virus, killing the Daleks. Afterwards, Tegan was appalled by the carnage and left the Doctor's company. Lytton, an agent of the Daleks, escaped.

Tegan relocated to Brisbane after leaving the Doctor, and eventually took over the family business, Verney Feeds, from her father. The company supplied animal feed to farmers, and Tegan for a time dated one of its employees, Michael Tenaka.[247]

c 1984 (9th May) - PLANET OF FIRE[248] **->** Professor Howard Foster discovered an archaeologically important wreck off the coast of Lanzarote. His step-daughter, Perpugilliam Brown, travelled to the planet Sarn in the fifth Doctor's TARDIS. There, the Master attempted to restore his shrunken body using the Numismaton gas of a sacred volcano. The Doctor facilitated the

242 _TW: Miracle Day_
243 Dating _The Awakening_ (21.2) - The Doctor assures Tegan that "it is 1984", despite Will Chandler's clothing. As Tegan is the Queen of the May, it is presumably May Day.
244 _The Hollow Men_
245 Dating "The Forgotten" (IDW _DW_ mini-series #2) - Tegan is wearing her outfit from _Frontios/Resurrection of the Daleks_. This may well be set after _The Awakening_, when we know the Doctor and his companions stayed on Earth for a while.
246 Dating _Resurrection of the Daleks_ (21.3) - The Doctor says it is "1984 - Earth". We never hear of the Duplicates again. In terms of this timeline, the Daleks are from 4590.
247 _The Gathering_. The "Verney" of Verney Feeds pre-

sumably refers to Tegan's grandfather from _The Awakening_.
248 Dating _Planet of Fire_ (21.5) - Peri says she is due back at college in "the fall", which is "three months" away. There is nothing to suggest that the story isn't set in the year it was broadcast (1984). It can't take place before 1983, otherwise Turlough would return home while his past self was still in exile (_Mawdryn Undead_). In _Timelash_, the Doctor threatens to take Peri back to "1985". The back cover of _The Reaping_ specifies that Peri first met the Doctor on 9th May, 1984. _Peri and the Piscon Paradox_ says that Peri first met the Doctor "twenty-five years" prior to 2009.

Peri's step-father says they were on the island of Lanzarote, which is where filming took place. Yet Lanzarote was not on any ancient Greek trading routes,

Master's demise before this could happen. Turlough's exile was lifted and he returned to Trion. Peri started travelling with the Doctor. In autumn of the same year, she was due back at college.

The Time Lords' meddling in Peri's history resulted in a version of her that returned home, her memories of the Doctor wiped save for their first adventure together. This Peri attained a doctorate of biology, wed her college boyfriend (Davy Silverman), escaped what became a physically abusive marriage and moved to Los Angeles. In time, she became "Dr Perpugilliam Brown" - a relationship counsellor with a hit cable show, *Queen of Worries*.[249]

The tenth Doctor and Emily Winter met Turlough on Trion, and confirmed that he never kept a diary - meaning the Advocate had faked one as a means of manipulating Matthew Finnegan.[250]

Anthony Chambers became undertaker of St. Anne's Cemetery in Baltimore, and happened upon the Cyber-Leader from the far future there. The Cyber-Leader staged Chambers' brutal murder to catch the Doctor's interest. A local vagrant was blamed for the crime, even as Chambers' body was secretly Cyber-augmented.[251]

? 1984 - "Urban Myths"[252] **->** Three agents of the Celestial Intervention Agency were infected by a strain of the Tule-Oz virus - which mucked up their memories, and caused them to think that the fifth Doctor and Peri had committed mass slaughter on the planet Poiti. The agents

tracked the travellers to a restaurant on Earth and sought to kill them, but the Doctor and Peri served them the antidote throughout a multi-course meal.

1984 (August to September) - DOWNTIME[253] **->** Victoria Waterfield was mentally compelled to return to the Det-Sen monastery, which was suddenly destroyed. She was later contracted by Professor Travers, unaware that he was dead and animated by the Great Intelligence.

1984 (24th September) - THE REAPING[254] **->** In Baltimore, news of Anthony Chambers' "murder" became public, and Peri arrived with the sixth Doctor to attend the man's funeral. She had been gone for four months. Peri's mother - Janine Foster - and Howard had divorced.

A Cyber-Leader from the far future, who had arrived two years before, attempted to compel the Doctor to pilot his acquired time-ship back to prehistoric Earth, and to retroactively initiate the conversion of humanity into Cybermen. The Doctor deposited the Cyber-Leader on the contemporary Mondas, where the indigenous Cybermen viewed the Leader as defective and scheduled him for reprocessing.

In the course of this investigation, the media branded the Doctor as a dangerous criminal. The Cyber-augmented Anthony Chambers went dormant, but not before grievously wounding his own son Nate.

Peri decided to leave the Doctor, live with her mother and enrol at university. However, she kept half of a Cyber-

---

unlike the island in the story.
249 *Peri and the Piscon Paradox*
250 "Final Sacrifice". There's no indication of how much time, for Turlough, has passed since *Planet of Fire*. It's possible that they visit him on the alt-Trion he relocates to in *Turlough and the Earthlink Dilemma*.
251 Three months before *The Reaping*, set in September 1984.
252 Dating "Urban Myths" (BF #95b) - The story takes place at an Earth restaurant (probably in Hungary, owing to mention of the invention of goulash), but the dating is unknown. The only real clue is that a restaurant has operated at the location "since the time of the Hapsburgs", ruling out anything beyond the mid-twenty-second century (when the Dalek Invasion would undoubtedly interrupt service). The choice of dating this story to 1984 - contemporary with the fifth Doctor and Peri's adventures on TV - is arbitrary. It could also be concurrent with the release of "Urban Myths" in 2007.
253 Dating *Downtime* (MA #18) - This is "1984" (p22).
254 Dating *The Reaping* (BF #86) - The date is given. *Miami Vice* is touted as a new show, and it debuted on 16th September, 1984, about a week before *The Reaping* begins.

255 *The Gathering*
256 Dating *The Zygon Who Fell to Earth* (BF BBC7 #2.6) - The date is given. The Doctor's mention of "another lot" of nineteenth-century Zygons "down south" is probably a reference to *The Bodysnatchers*.
257 Dating *Turlough and the Earthlink Dilemma* (The Companions of Doctor Who #1) - The story opens some months after Turlough has left the TARDIS. According to p193, it is relative Trion date 17,883 when Turlough arrives on Trion.
258 *Time and the Rani*
259 "Seven years" before *Cat's Cradle: Witch Mark* (p25).
260 "Twenty-three years" before *The Runaway Bride*.
261 Dating "The Fires Down Below" (*DWM* #64) - A caption says it is "1984".
262 Dating *TimeH: The Winning Side* (TimeH #1) - "1984" is printed on the cover, and Honoré and Emily find a "four year old" (p45) newspaper dated "2 March 1980" (p35).
263 Dating *Attack of the Cybermen* (22.1) - Mondas' attack is in "1986", which the hired gun Griffiths confirms is "next year".
264 Dating *The Two Doctors* (22.3) - The story is contemporary, but there is no indication exactly which year it takes place.

conversion egg as a memento. The device exploded, killing Janine Foster and her friend, Mrs Van Gysegham. Peri resumed travelling with the Doctor.

After Janine died, Katherine Chambers took the other half of the Cyber-conversion egg and went into hiding with her crippled brother. She had studied medicine at Boston, and a colleague of hers from university - James Clarke - helped them relocate to Brisbane. Kathy finished her education and became a doctor, but Nate's condition worsened and she turned him into a pseudo-Cyberman.[255]

1984 - THE ZYGON WHO FELL TO EARTH[256] **->** As a result of the Zygon scheme to boost global warming, CDs had been manufactured to emit invisible gas when they were played.

Along with her Zygon husband Trevor, Lucie Miller's Aunty Pat was now running a hotel - the Bygones Guest House - near Lake Grasmere. Trevor's Skarasen had chewed a tunnel between Allswater and Grassmere, under the mountains; the creature was glimpsed from time to time, boosting the tourist trade.

Three members of Trevor's crew tracked down their former leader, and retrieved their stolen crystal lattice which - as the product of organic crystallography - had bonded to Patricia's flesh. They tore it away, killing her. Trevor ordered his Skarasen to attack the Zygons' spaceship. The Skarasen, the crew and the spaceship were all destroyed in an explosion.

Lucie thought Trevor had died, and was unaware that her Aunty Pat had perished. Trevor shapeshifted one last time, and assumed his late wife's form. In the decades to come, "he" fulfilled history by masquerading as the Aunty Pat that Lucie had grown up with. The eighth Doctor knew about the deception.

= c 1984 (winter) - TURLOUGH AND THE EARTHLINK DILEMMA[257] **->** On Trion, the dictator Rehctaht fell from power, and the exiled Clansmen - including Turlough - returned home to a hero's welcome. Turlough used his knowledge of TARDISes to build the first-ever ARTEMIS drive, a time-travel device that used "muon" particles. On New Trion, Turlough discovered a copy of an alien edifice named the Mobile Castle, and equipped it with a second ARTEMIS drive. The in-flight Castle was sabotaged and crashed onto Trion, destroying the planet. Earth and New Trion were subsequently annihilated in nuclear conflicts.

Turlough discovered that Rehctaht had transferred her mind into the body of his old friend Juras Maateh, and had engineered Earth, Trion and New Trion's obliteration to further her gravity control experiments, hoping to gain the secret of time travel.

Turlough killed Rechtaht/Juras, then travelled back in time to prevent this history from occurring.

In 1984, scientists in Princeton discovered Strange Matter.[258] The seventh Doctor and Mel visited the Welsh village of Llanfer Ceiriog.[259] **Torchwood bought the London security firm HC Clements.**[260]

1984 - "The Fires Down Below"[261] **->** Lethbridge-Stewart sent Major Whitaker of UNIT to Reykjavik to investigate an unnatural increase in volcanic activity. The UNIT troops discovered a squad of Quarks planting seismic charges. A member of the party, Professor Iskander, learned that the Dominators were planning to destroy Earth to extract its core for fuel. The UNIT troops attacked, then escaped as the Dominators' machines exploded and destroyed the aliens.

(=) 1984 - TIMEH: THE WINNING SIDE[262] **->** Honoré Lechasseur and Emily Blandish visited a parallel timeline where the release of nuclear secrets in 1949 had caused a massive suppression of education, schools, libraries and scientists, and a single Party had uncontested political power.

1985 - ATTACK OF THE CYBERMEN[263] **->** The police had been aware of Lytton, a sophisticated thief who had stolen valuable electronic components, for a year. Lytton had discovered the Cybermen were operating in the sewers of London and was trying to contact them. The Cybermen tried, but failed, to divert Halley's Comet so that it would crash into Earth and avert the destruction of Mondas in 1986.

The Cybermen captured Lytton and lured the sixth Doctor and Peri to Telos in the future.

c 1985 - THE TWO DOCTORS[264] **->** Some years ago, the Doctor had officially represented the Time Lords at the opening of space station Chimera in the Third Zone. Now a renegade, his second incarnation - accompanied by Jamie - was sent to the station by the Time Lords. Experiments conducted by professors Kartz and Reimer were registering 0.4 on the Bocca Scale, and could potentially threaten the stability of space-time.

Before the Doctor could finish lodging a protest with the Head of Projects - his old friend, Joinson Dastari - a Sontaran attack devastated the station. The Third Zone had been betrayed by Chessene of the Franzine Grig, an Androgum that Dastari had technologically augmented.

The Doctor was captured and taken to Seville by one of Chessene's Sontaran allies, Major Varl. He was joined by Group Marshall Stike of the Ninth Sontaran Attack Group. The Sontarans wanted Dastari to operate on the Doctor and discover the means by which Time Lords had a symbiotic relationship with their travel capsules. They hoped to create a time capsule for use against the Rutan in the Madillon Cluster.

The sixth Doctor and Peri traced his earlier self to Seville, which he had visited before. He helped to rescue his former self and defeat the Sontaran plan. Chessene, Dastari and the Sontarans all died.

The sixth Doctor dropped Peri off on Earth in 1985. She didn't expect to see him again.[265]

1985 - "Kane's Story"[266] **->** The sixth Doctor and Frobisher went to New York and met up with Peri, who rejoined the TARDIS crew.

A Zygon spaceship exploded, stranding Commander Kritakh and his second, Torlakh, on Earth. They assumed human form, and set about committing industrial espionage to increase Earth's greenhouse gas emissions. If successful, Earth would become as warm as the Zygon homeworld.[267] The third Doctor and Jo met an N-form in Tranquilandia the time they met the drug baron Gomez.[268] SeneNet acquired a Sontaran Mezon rifle.[269]

> = Fitz saw the Beatles perform at Live Aid in a parallel universe.[270]

On the planet Artaris, the immortal Grayvorn kept shifting identities and rose to the rank of Reeve, becoming known as Reeve Maupassant.[271] In July 1986, the wreck of the *Titanic* was discovered.[272] A virus on Lalanda 21185 created hundreds of thousands of zombies.[273] Artist Karen Kuykendall created the Tarot of the Cat-People.[274]

@ Iris Wildthyme visited the eighth Doctor and Miranda and tried (unsuccessfully) to explain the gaps in his memories. That year, the Doctor won the London Marathon.[275] Dorothy McShane was disillusioned when she met her idol, pop star Johnny Chess.[276]

During the mid-eighties, Carol Bell worked for an arms manufacturer, watching SF films to inspire the creation of new weapons.[277] She had attained the rank of captain during her time with UNIT, but was rendered brain-damaged in a car accident.[278]

@ The eighth Doctor was offered a chair at Cambridge, but declined as he was dedicated to looking after Miranda.[279]

---

265 This occurs in an unrecorded adventure before "Kane's Story", and we don't learn why she left.

266 Dating "Kane's Story" (*DWM* #104) - A caption says it's "1985".

PERI LEAVES AND CAUSES CONTINUITY PROBLEMS, TAKE ONE: When Peri joined the sixth Doctor and Frobisher's adventures in the comic strip, it created a mild continuity headache. While we never saw her leave, she rejoins in "Kane's Story" when the Doctor and Frobisher pick her up in New York. She's settled down and just quit (another) job there, and it's not even established whether she recognises Frobisher.

So far, so simple. We know from *The Trial of a Time Lord* that there are big gaps in the sixth Doctor's recorded adventures. So, at some point after *Revelation of the Daleks*, Peri leaves the Doctor, who goes on to meet Frobisher in "The Shape Shifter" before meeting up with his old companion again. No matter how one plays the cards here (or invokes the multiple Peris established in *Peri and the Piscon Paradox*), Peri must meet Frobisher for the first time in "Kane's Story". She's then present until the end of the sixth Doctor's *DWM* run in "The World Shapers", which then leads into *The Trial of a Time Lord* and her televised departure. This is even supported by the way Peri switches, during the course of the comic strip, from wearing her Season 22 leotards to her more tailored look of Season 23.

In *Planet of Fire*, Peri said she would travel with the Doctor for "three months". This line was forgotten about on television, but perhaps she was true to her word and

left the Doctor as planned. This could still be after *Revelation of the Daleks* - although *Attack of the Cybermen* and *Timelash* both have the "present day" as 1985, not 1984.

267 Specified by Torlakh as "eighteen friggin years" prior to *Zygon: When Being You Isn't Enough*. Torlakh's plan is basically identical to that of the Zygons in *The Zygon Who Fell to Earth*.

268 *Damaged Goods*

269 *Business Unusual* (p244).

270 *The Gallifrey Chronicles*

271 "About fifteen years" before *Excelis Rising*.

272 *The Left-Handed Hummingbird* (p261).

273 "Two years" after *Return of the Living Dad* (p98).

274 *Invasion of the Cat-People* (p46). This matches the Tarot deck's real-world release in 1985. Kuykendall died in 1998.

275 "About a year ago" (p129) and "last year" (p115) according to *Father Time* (p129).

276 When Ace was "14" (p89) according to *Timewyrm: Revelation*. Chess is the son of Ian and Barbara (the "Chess" moniker is apparently short for "Chesterton").

277 *Interference* (Book Two, p157).

278 *The Left-Handed Hummingbird* (p100).

279 *Mad Dogs and Englishmen* (p23).

280 Dating *Father Time* (EDA #41) - The date is never specified beyond "the mid-eighties" and there are a couple of (deliberate) references to keep the dating vague, such as one to Guns N' Roses. It is "five years" after part one of the story.

@ c 1985 (spring) - FATHER TIME[280] -> Sallak escaped from prison and summoned his people, the Klade, from the far future. Ferran, brother of Zevron, arrived through a time corridor in an abandoned tower block in a northern city. Ferran and Sallak killed the comatose Barry Castle as revenge for Zevron's death, then set their sights on the eighth Doctor and Miranda.

Ferran became enamoured of Miranda and explained her alien heritage to her, but the Doctor sent him back to the far future. Miranda shot and killed Sallak, then went on the run.

Mr Wynter negotiated the price per kilo as part of a deal to fund the Contras, then bumped a rail up his nose while they mowed down their enemies with the weapons their money had purchased.[281] The eleventh Doctor visited a Little Green Storage facility on the Isle of Dogs.[282] Raine Creevy went to King's University College.[283]

1985 (12th December) - "Skywatch-7"[284] -> A Zygon attacked Skywatch-7, a UNIT radar station in the Arctic. The UNIT staff saw it off, and the intruder died after falling into frozen water.

1986

In 1986, Toshiko Sato moved back to the UK from Japan.[285] Matthew Hatch was exposed to the power of the Jack i' the Green and started planning to release him.[286] On 28th January, 1986, the *Challenger* exploded.[287]

On the 26th April, 1986, a strange light shone over Takhail in the USSR - radiation from the Chernobyl disaster irradiated 11-year-old Piotr Arkady, and killed every-

one else in the village.[288]

Martha Jones, a companion of the tenth Doctor, was born in 1986.[289] **Henry John Parker went into seclusion.**[290] In 1986, two students were incinerated while exploring a house in the "haunted" Tretarri in Cardiff.[291] When Owen Harper was six, he went to see his piano teacher after Christmas... only to discover the man had died, and been eaten by his cats.[292] The sixth Doctor insisted that his coat was the height of fashion.[293]

c 1986 - HARRY SULLIVAN'S WAR[294] -> Surgeon-Commander Harry Sullivan was reassigned to a NATO chemical weapons centre on the island of Yarra, and researched the lethal toxin Attila 305. He found a nykor inhibitase that showed great promise in both curing infertility and providing an antidote to the toxin.

Led by Zbigniew Brodsky, a terrorist group named the European Anarchist Revolution stole three ampules of the toxin. Harry exposed his department head, Conrad Gold, as being part of the conspiracy. Brodsky's group was using the Van Gogh Appreciation Society as a front for its operations, and French authorities rounded up the terrorists during the Society's annual meeting at the Eiffel Tower.

Harry celebrated his forty-first birthday.

c 1986 - THE NIGHTMARE FAIR[295] -> The Celestial Toymaker set up operations in Blackpool, and manufactured video games that manifested monsters to kill the game-players when they lost. He intended to mass produce the games, but also sought to revenge himself upon the Doctor, and drew the TARDIS to Blackpool. The sixth Doctor and Peri imprisoned the Toymaker in a holofield that was powered by the Toymaker's own mind, and

281 *TW: The Men Who Sold the World*, presumably in reference to the Iran-Contra affair of the mid-80s.

282 *Borrowed Time*. It's "about 1985, just a year before the Big Bang changed the regulation of the London stock market" (on 27th October, 1986).

283 *Animal*, extrapolating from Raine's birth year of 1967 (*Thin Ice*).

284 Dating "Skywatch-7" (*DWM #58, DWM Winter Special 1981*) - The date is given in the caption running across the top of the first page.

285 *TW: Greeks Bearing Gifts*

286 *The Hollow Men*. Hatch is "fourteen" (p79) when this occurs.

287 *Return of the Living Dad* and *Father Time*. The space shuttle is never mentioned in a television story, and *The Tenth Planet* depicts an international space programme of a far greater extent than the real 1986.

288 "Black Destiny"

289 *Wooden Heart*, although *The Torchwood Archives* says she was born on 14th September, 1984. Freema Agyeman was born on 20th March, 1979.

290 *TW: A Day in the Death*

291 *TW: The Twilight Streets*

292 *TW*: "The Legacy of Torchwood One!"

293 "Four hundred and fifty years" after 1536, i.e. 1986, according to *Recorded Time and Other Stories*: "Recorded Time". Mind you, the Doctor doesn't say that his coat was fashionable *on Earth*.

294 Dating *Harry Sullivan's War* (*The Companions of Doctor Who #2*) - It is "ten years" since Harry left UNIT, and so placing this story is subject to UNIT dating. It's clearly set in the mid-nineteen eighties.

295 Dating *The Nightmare Fair* (BF LS #1.1) - The story was written for Season 23, and intended for broadcast in 1986. It's "about a hundred years" after *The Talons of Weng-Chiang*. 1778 was "over two hundred years ago".

would keep him looped in time for the rest of his life. The Doctor made plans to transport the bubbled Toymaker to somewhere that he wouldn't be noticed.

The Ventusans served as mechanics at this time, and kept half the spacefleets in the galaxy running. A replica of Blackpool was being built out by the Crab Nebula - but to the Doctor's horror, it was, compared to the genuine article, being built for a *purpose*. The Pathfinders serving in an entirely pointless galactic war were now part of the Third Federation Force for Peace.

(=) **1986 - "Time Bomb"**[296] -> The sixth Doctor and Frobisher went to pick up Peri in New York... but discovered that the Hedron interference two hundred million years ago had disrupted history. Mankind never evolved, and dinosaur men ruled the Earth.

1986 (December) - THE TENTH PLANET[297] -> Technological developments continued on Earth. The Z-Bomb and Cobra missiles had been developed, and Zeus spaceships (launched on Demeter rockets) carried out manned missions to the moon as well as close-orbital work. Zeus 4's mission was to monitor weather and cosmic rays. Space missions were controlled from the South Pole base (callsign: "Snowcap"). The space programme was now an international effort with Americans, Australians, British, Italians, Spaniards, Swiss and Africans manning Snowcap. International Space Command and its Secretary General, Wigner, controlled the programme from Geneva.

In late 1986, "the tenth planet" appeared in the skies of the southern hemisphere. This was Mondas, the homeworld of the Cybermen. The first Doctor, Ben

296 Dating "Time Bomb" (*DWM* #114-116) - The caption reads "Earthdate 1986". The dinosaur men are not Silurians.
297 Dating *The Tenth Planet* (4.2) - A calendar gives the date as "December 1986". This is the clearest example so far of real life catching up with "futuristic" events described in the series, but in *Attack of the Cybermen* (broadcast in 1985), the date of "1986" for this story was reaffirmed. *Radio Times* and publicity material at the time gave the date as "the late 1980s", as did the second edition of *The Making of Doctor Who*. The draft script set the date as "2000 AD", as did Gerry Davis' novelisation. (The book followed a draft of the story rather than the broadcast version, as the draft included more scenes with the Doctor.)

The Making of Doctor Who (first edition) also used the "2000" date. The first two editions of *The Programme Guide* set the range as "1975-80". This confused the American *Doctor Who* comic, which decided that *The Tenth Planet* must precede *The Invasion* and both were set in "the 1980s". John Peel's novelisation of *The Power of the Daleks* set the preceding story in "the 1990s".
298 *The First Wave*
299 *The Tenth Planet*, *The Power of the Daleks*. The term "regeneration" isn't used until *Planet of the Spiders*.
300 *Original Sin*
301 *Iceberg*
302 *Human Resources*
303 "Ten years" before *Battlefield*.
304 *Dragonfire* establishes much of Ace's background, with further details given in *Battlefield* and *The Curse of Fenric*. She first returns to Perivale in *Survival*.

The tie-in stories offer more detail. The timestorm was in 1987 according to *Timewyrm: Revelation* (p70) and *Independence Day* (she saw *Withnail and I* a few days before the timestorm occurred). She's from 1986 in *White Darkness* (p130) and *First Frontier* (p45). *Crime of the Century* establishes that Ace left Earth before Black Monday (19th October, 1987), and *Thin Ice* estab-

lishes that she doesn't know about such late-80s political elements as *glasnost*.
305 *Matrix*
306 During *The Crystal Bucephalus*.
307 The short stories "Mondas Passing" (from *Short Trips*, 1998) and "That Time I Nearly Destroyed the World Whilst Looking For a Dress" (from *Short Trips: Past Tense* 2004). Both are outside the boundaries of this guidebook, but are referenced here because it's relevant to Polly and Ben's status in *The Five Companions*.
308 *The Also People*
309 *Death and Diplomacy*. Jason was "nearly 13" when Lucy was "nine" (p150).
310 "Two years" before *Business Unusual*.
311 *Mad Dogs and Englishmen*
312 *TW: First Born*
313 *SJA: The Glittering Storm*
314 *The Eight Truths*, *Worldwide Web*.
315 *The Room with No Doors*
316 This date is given in the Writers' Guide and in an article written by Russell T. Davies in the *2006 Doctor Who Annual*. However, Rose is "19" according to the Doctor in *The Unquiet Dead* and *Army of Ghosts*, when she really ought to be 18. It's said in *Rise of the Cybermen* that Rose was "six months" when her father died, which would fit her written birthday of 27th April and the dating of *Father's Day* to 7th November.
317 According to Kathy's tombstone as seen in *Blink*. Her handwritten letter to Sally seems to be dated "7th February, 1987".
318 *Crime of the Century*
319 *Benny: Nobody's Children*
320 Dating *Damaged Goods* (NA #55) - The date "17 July 1987" is given (p8).
321 Dating *Father's Day* (X1.8) - The date is given. The Reapers are not named on screen, but are named as such in the script.
322 The Powell Estate is cited in episodes such as *Aliens of London* and *Tooth and Claw*. Victor Kennedy

and Polly were present at Snowcap as Mondas attempted to drain Earth's energy, but absorbed too much and was destroyed.

The first Doctor's body was so aged, it had worn out. The disembodied Oliver Harper used the last of his essence to manifest one final time - as the weakened Doctor stood in the TARDIS doorway, he spotted Oliver and gave a little wave before entering.[298] **Aided by Ben and Polly, the Doctor entered the TARDIS console room and was "renewed" into a new body.**[299]

Tobias Vaughn recovered the bodies of the Cybermen from Snowcap.[300] Cybermen who had crashed in the South Pole - remnants of an earlier, failed invasion - located and adapted Cyber technology from the 1986 incursion.[301] After Mondas' destruction, a surviving group of Cybermen settled on the planet Lonsis.[302] **In the late nineteen-eighties, archaeologist Peter Warmsley began excavating a site associated with King Arthur on the edge of Lake Vortigern near Carbury.**[303]

Ace was now becoming a problem. She had sat her O-Levels, including French and Computer Studies, and was beginning to study for her A-Levels. But she was expelled from school for blowing up the Art Room using homemade gelignite - an event she described as "a creative act". Ace vanished one day in a timestorm whipped up by Fenric, following experiments in her bedroom that involved her trying to extract nitro-glycerine from gelignite. Ace's mother reported her missing, and her friends thought she was either dead or in Birmingham.[304]

Ace did work experience at an old folks home. She worked in McDonald's on weekends.[305] She kicked a time-lost and penniless Tegan out of the establishment, failing to realise they would later have something in common.[306]

Decades after she left the TARDIS, Polly Wright had married a man named Simon, and they had a son named Mikey. Ben Jackson had also married. On the last day of 1986, Ben and Polly met in a hotel room to commemorate the passing of Mondas, and their involvement in it with the Doctor. Despite the temptation, they kept their relationship platonic.[307]

The Johnny Chess album *Things to do on a Wet Tuesday Night* was released in 1987.[308] In the same year, Jason Kane's sister Lucy was born.[309] SeneNet begin developing their Maxx games.[310]

@ In 1987, the Doctor was accidentally responsible for releasing a breed of talking wild boar into the wild.[311] In 1987, the UK government tested an alien device on the village of Rawbone, and made everyone there sterile. The town was gradually isolated from the outside world.[312] Sarah Jane profiled Dr. Francis Augur for *Metropolitan* magazine in 1987.[313]

The Headhunter, now allied with the spiders on Metebelis III, planted some Metebelis crystals in Yorkshire in 1987. A potholer, Clark Goodman, found the crystals, and the spiders implanted beliefs in his mind. Goodman founded a self-help organisation - "The Eightfold Truth" - and sent its members to locate more of the crystals. The group would, unknowingly, spend eighteen years facilitating the spiders' plan to conquer thousands of worlds.[314]

The eighth Doctor visited Little Caldwell and met Joel Mintz.[315] **Rose Tyler, a companion of the ninth and tenth Doctors, was born on 27th April, 1987.**[316] **Katherine Costello Wainright (formerly Kathy Nightingale) died the same year.**[317]

Colonel Felnikov of the Soviet Union engineered the 1987 recession as a means of attacking the West by destabilising its economy. Those in the know about this dubbed it The Crime of the Century. Felnikov's superiors lost too much money in the resultant economic bloodbath, and he was booted back to the Army.[318]

Benny had Isaac Summerfield babysit Peter in 1987 while she dealt with a quarrel between the Draconians and the Mim.[319]

1987 (July) - DAMAGED GOODS[320] **->** The seventh Doctor, Roz and Chris investigated the Quadrant, an area of tower blocks in an English city. An N-form, an ancient Gallifreyan weapons system, had occupied the body of drug dealer Simon "the Capper" Jenkins. The N-form was searching for vampires, per its programming, and sold contaminated coke that allowed it to manifest in the brains of anyone who took it. The N-form erupted and went on a killing spree, but the Doctor shut it down.

(=) 1987 (7th November) - FATHER'S DAY[321] **->** The ninth Doctor took Rose back to witness the death of her father, Peter Tyler, from a hit-and-run car accident. Rose saved her father's life, which altered history and created a "wound" in time. Winged creatures, the Reapers, converged on the wound to "sterilise" it by consuming every person on Earth. Humanity was eradicated on a large scale, but Peter acknowledged the historical deviation and sacrificed himself. Upon his death, time reverted to normal and the Reapers disappeared.

Outside the wedding of Stewart Hoskins and Sarah Clark, Peter Tyler died from a hit-and-run accident. An unnamed young woman stayed with him until the end.

Jackie and Rose continued to reside at Flat 48, Bucknall House, Powell Estate SE15 7GO.[322]

The eighth Doctor and Lethbridge-Stewart discovered the secret of the Embodiment of Gris in Hong Kong in 1988.[323] Benny accidentally had a comic commissioned while walking through the offices of an American comic book publisher, just because she had a British accent.[324] **Victor Podesta, an associate of the Three Families who had adopted the name John Forester, died in La Boca, Argentina.**[325]

1988 (8th April) - THE COMPANY OF FRIENDS: "Izzy's Story"[326] **->** The eighth Doctor took Izzy to Grub and Sons newsstand in Stockbridge, as she knew that a prized copy of *Aggotron* #56 could be found there. The issue revealled the true face of Courtmaster Cruel, a vigilante magistrate, but all copies of it had mysteriously vanished afterwards. The travellers found Suits - the android henchlings of The Man, a villain from the comic - ruining every copy of #56 with their brolly guns.

At the *Aggotron* publication offices in Queenspoint Spire, London, the Doctor and Izzy found that the comic's editor (known in print as "Grak, the Head-Swollen") and artists were aliens that had been censored from their native Smog Worlds, and had based many of the *Aggotron* characters on their native forms. They also confronted Derek Dell - a geek who'd adopted the Courtmaster's identity in the

fifty-first century, but was so horrified upon learning that the original artwork to issue #56 rendered Courtmaster Cruel as a girl, he'd dispatched the Suits to destroy every copy. Izzy was similarly aghast at the revelation.

Dell, while trying to escape, was haphazardly flung through time. The Doctor relocated Grak and his artists back to the Smog Worlds, and *Aggotron* was merged into *Square Jaw.*

On 22nd May, 1988, an accident involving a Range Rover killed the parents of a young girl named Alice, and put her in a wheelchair for life.[327]

Lucie Miller, a companion of the eighth Doctor and (briefly) the Monk, was born on 31st July, 1988.[328]

Santiago, the grandson of Cliff and Jo Jones, was born in a caravan in the foothills of the Andes. He would never attend school, and instead travel the world with his parents while his advocacy-minded grandmother did such things as chain herself to the railings at a G8 Summit. Santiago's father would get arrested - twice - at a climate change conference.[329]

A temporal breach was detected high above London. Torchwood constructed a huge skyscraper to enclose the breach; the building was privately known as Torchwood Tower, but publicly it served as Canary

specifies Rose and Jackie's address as "Bucknall House, No. 48" in *Love & Monsters.* The full address, with the post code, appeared in the *Doctor Who Annual 2006.*
323 *The Dying Days* (p94).
324 *Sky Pirates!* (p334).
325 *TW: Miracle Day.* He's born in 1912 and dies age 76, presuming the file on his adopted alias can be trusted.
326 Dating *The Company of Friends:* "Izzy's Story" (BF #123c) - The Doctor tells Izzy that they've arrived at "The village of Stockbridge, relative date: Friday, the 8th of April, 1988."
327 *J&L: Swan Song*
328 *Brave New Town*
329 *SJA: Death of the Doctor.* Date unknown, but actor Finn Jones, who played Santiago, was born in 1988.
330 *Army of Ghosts.* Construction of the building began in 1988.
331 Twenty years before the Doctor kills the Captain, as related in *The Eyeless.*
332 Dating *Silver Nemesis* (25.3) - The first scene is set, according to the caption slide, in "South America, 22nd November 1988". The Doctor's alarm goes off the next day - although it is a beautiful sunny day.
333 *Option Lock*
334 "Eighteen years" before *Red Dawn.*
335 *SJA: Wraith World.* This happened "back in the 80s", but also "twenty years" before 2010.
336 Amy is repeatedly said to be seven when she meets the Doctor in *The Eleventh Hour,* set in Easter

1996. "Forever Dreaming" names her birth year as "1989", so she was evidently born before Easter. Her middle name is given in *The Beast Below.*
337 Mel first appeared on television in *Terror of the Vervoids,* but the events of her joining the Doctor were shown in *Business Unusual.*
MEL'S FIRST ADVENTURE: The Writers' Guide for Season 23 suggested that Mel joined the Doctor after an encounter with the Master, and this is echoed in the Missing Adventure *Millennial Rites* (p83). This appears to be contradicted by *The Ultimate Foe* when Mel fails to recognise the renegade Time Lord, but *Business Unusual* establishes that Mel didn't actually meet the Master on that occasion. The Writers' Guide also suggested that Mel had been travelling with the Doctor for "three months". It is entirely possible that Mel started her travels with the Doctor at the end of *The Ultimate Foe,* negating the need for a "first adventure", but this idea is riddled with paradoxes (i.e.: she is from her own future and would have memories of her first few adventures before she arrived).

The period set after *The Trial of a Time Lord,* but before the Doctor has his "first meeting" with Mel (in *Business Unusual*), is now brimming with book and audio adventures. These include the Doctor's time with companions Frobisher, Evelyn Smythe, Thomas Brewster, Charley Pollard (after she travelled with the eighth Doctor), Grant Markham (who only appeared in two Missing Adventures: *Time of Your Life* and *Killing*

Wharf, a business development. Torchwood also used the facility as their main headquarters.[330]

The Steggosians, "a particularly nasty race of fascist dinosaur people", were all but wiped out by a plague that destroyed their immune systems. One patrol survived, its Captain driven mad by the death of his people. He would later encounter the Doctor in London.[331]

1988 (22nd-23rd November) - SILVER NEMESIS[332] -> Thousands of Cyber-Warships massed in the solar system. A scouting party tried to recover the Validium asteroid, which had been launched from Earth two hundred and fifty years before. They wanted its power to make Earth into "New Mondas". The seventh Doctor and Ace kept the statue from falling into the hands of the Cybermen, the Lady Peinforte (a sorceress from 1638), and a group of Nazis hoping to create a new Reich. The villains all died in the process.

By the end of the Reagan administration, the US military had built Station Nine. This was a Top Secret satellite - so secret, in fact, that no President after Reagan would be told about it. Station Nine quietly remained in orbit, ready to fire intercepting Nuke Killer missiles that would nullify an oncoming nuclear attack.[333]

An unmanned lander sent from Earth to Mars recovered Martian DNA. Webster Corporation combined it with human DNA in the hopes of creating augmented soldiers, and the young Tanya Webster was born with Martian DNA in her system. Webster began developing a manned mission to Mars, hoping to recover more Martian DNA or a live Martian.[334] Sarah Jane Smith interviewed novelist Gregory P. Wilkinson for *Metropolitan* magazine.[335]

Amelia Jessica Pond was born in 1989 to Augustus and Tabitha Pond.[336]

Melanie Bush joined the sixth Doctor after helping him prevent the Master and the Usurians taking over the world in 1989. She had recently turned down a job at I^2, but accepted one at Ashley Chapel Logistics.[337]

1989 (mid June) - BUSINESS UNUSUAL[338] -> The sixth Doctor thwarted an attempt by the Master and his Usurian partners to devastate America's economy, but required a native computer expert to fully purge the conspirators' illicit programming. This led to the Doctor meeting computer programmer Melanie Bush, and she helped him erase the Master's programs.

Martyn Townsend, the former director of the Vault, was now the Managing Director of SeneNet. The company officially specialised in computer game consoles, but fronted Townsend's ambitions to use Nestene technology to conquer Earth. Lacking the components to maintain his cybernetic body, Townsend kidnapped the telepathic Trey Korte in the hopes of mentally transferring his intelligence into a prosthetic form.

The Doctor's intervention resulted in SeneNet's destruction. Townsend died when falling rubble crushed him. The Auton-augmented twins Cellian and Ciara foreswore allegiance to Townsend and escaped. Melanie stowed away on the TARDIS and took up travelling with the Doctor.

The Brigadier, investigating SeneNet, met the sixth Doctor for the first time.

= In an alternate universe where Rome never fell, the sixth Doctor lost his New World companion Brown Perpugilliam, and an eye, to the warlord Dominicus. He visited the scientist Praetor Linus to repair the TARDIS image translator, and took the slave Melina into his service.[339]

The sixth Doctor left Evelyn on Earth, and asked her to monitor the pseudo-Auton twins Cellian and Ciara for him. Evelyn came to discover that the Doctor had erroneously dropped her off in the late 1980s, meaning that her younger self was still teaching at Nottingham. She kept a low profile, fearful that she might run into herself, but used her foreknowledge to earn some money winning contests and betting pools.[340]

In 1989, the Ritz dance hall in Cardiff ceased operation.[341] The sixth Doctor planted a mattress in Perivale - he'd later land on it while confronting the Master...[342]

Ground), "Flip" Jackson, Jason and Crystal (*The Ultimate Adventure*) and a Land-of-Fiction version of Jamie McCrimmon.

In *Just War*, Mel says that she has never been to the past before, "only the future". Subsequent stories such as *Catch-1782* and "The Vanity Box" contradict this.

Millennial Rites and *Business Unusual* both have Mel meeting the Doctor in 1989. She's from "1986" in *Head Games* (p154) and *The Quantum Archangel* (p17).

338 Dating *Business Unusual* (PDA #4) - The date is given (p15). From the sixth Doctor's perspective, he first meets the Brigadier circa 2000 in *The Spectre of Lanyon*

Moor.

339 *Spiral Scratch*. Linus is that universe's version of Bob Lines from *The Scales of Injustice*, *Business Unusual* and *Instruments of Darkness*.

340 *Instruments of Darkness*. On p93, Evelyn claims the Doctor dropped her off in 1988. The Doctor conferred with Evelyn off panel during the events of *Business Unusual*, set in June 1989.

341 *TW: Captain Jack Harkness*

342 In *Survival*, according to "Emperor of the Daleks".

c 1989 (Sunday) - SURVIVAL[343] **->** In a relatively short span of time, several residents in Perivale vanished without trace, abducted by the Cheetah People. Their planet was dying, and they were preparing to move on to new feeding grounds. The Master was trapped on the planet, and lured the seventh Doctor and Ace there to aid in his escape. As the Doctor and the Master fought, the Cheetah People vanished. The Master also disappeared.

As the Cheetah Planet exploded, the Master went back to Earth. A surfeit of artron energy in the atmosphere diverted him to 1957.[344]

The Star Jumpers, a band including Johnny Chess, were a success. They made the albums *Circle Circus*, *Modernism*, *Can Anyone Tell Me Where the Revolution Is?*, and one other before splitting. InterCom were working on a means of splicing alien DNA into humans to create a slave race. UNIT operatives Geoff Paynter and Paul Foxton infiltrated Black Star terrorists based in Baghdad, but Foxton was killed.[345] The science-fiction series *Professor X* was cancelled after more than twenty-five years on TV. Dave Young, Anji Kapoor's future boyfriend, played a Cybertron in one of the last episodes.[346]

1989 (summer) to 1990 (August) - "Business as Usual"[347] **->** Winston Blunt discovered some strange meteorites. Overnight, the former plumber became a wealthy plastics magnate and set up Galaxy Plastics, but he killed himself after handing over the business to a Mr Dolman. A year later, a rival company sent Max Fischer to investigate Galaxy Plastics, and he discovered that the Autons were running it. Dolman accidentally set off an explosion while trying to kill Fischer - who escaped, pursued by living toy soldiers. Dolman was damaged but murdered Fischer, and a replica of Fischer went on to open Stellar Plastics.

1989 (October) - CRIME OF THE CENTURY[348] **->** The Polyglot 7 (third release), one of the worst translation devices in the galaxy, was recalled. It was, however, equipped to translate Dolphin, as they were one of the few sentient species on planet Earth.

The seventh Doctor read the diary of Raine Creevy, who had become an accomplished cat burglar, and so was waiting inside a safe as she opened it. The two of them joined Ace in Kafiristan, where Russian operatives acting against the Kafiristan government had procured the services of the Metatraxi: a proud warrior race that insisted on fighting

---

343 Dating *Survival* (26.4) - Ace returns to Perivale. When she asks how long she's been away, the Doctor replies "as long as you think you have". Her friends Midge and Stevie vanished "last month"; Shreela the week before.

344 *First Frontier*

345 All "a decade" before *The King of Terror* (p130, p141 and p144).

346 "Eleven years" before *Escape Velocity*.

347 Dating "Business as Usual" (*DWW* #40-43) - The Doctor says the meteorites fell "that summer night in 1989" in the framing sequence; Stellar Plastics opens in "August 1990" according to a caption.

348 Dating *Crime of the Century* (BF LS #2.4) - Raine's dairy specifies the day she meets the Doctor as "October 13th, 1989... It's Friday the 13th", and the action continues from there, with Raine saying that it takes her "a few days" to get over her jet-lag.

349 Dating *Father Time* (EDA #41) - The date is never specified beyond "the late 1980s" (p199), but the Berlin Wall fell on 9th November, 1989.

350 *Forever Autumn*

351 *System Shock*

352 *The Shadow in the Glass*

353 *Escape Velocity*, *The Slow Empire*. She's 28 and left home when she was 17.

354 "Five hundred years" after *The Masque of Mandragora*. The *DWM* strip "The Mark of Mandragora" dealt with this return.

355 *Downtime*

356 *TW: Adam*. This would be in February 1990.

357 *The Beast Below*. The Queen seems to personally know the Doctor when she wishes him Merry Christmas in *Voyage of the Damned*.

358 *Death Riders* (p130). If it's the current Queen's mother (1900-2002), this could occur just about anywhere in the twentieth century.

359 *Benny: A Life Worth Living*: "A Summer Affair". McGinley is a professor of twenty-first century literature at the Collection, and it seems likely that he hails from that period.

360 Dating "Train-Flight" (*DWM* #159-161) - There's no indication of the date, although the concert is an Oscar Peterson one, and so probably takes place before his stroke in 1993. There's nothing to suggest it isn't set the year it was published (1990). Sarah seems to be living in the same house she was in during *The Five Doctors*. This is the first time she's met the Doctor's seventh incarnation. They don't take K9 along, but they have the option, so he's still active.

361 Dating *Cat's Cradle: Time's Crucible* (NA #5) - It is "three years" since Ace left Perivale.

362 Dating "Seaside Rendezvous" (*DWM Summer Special 1991*) - There's no date given, but the story has a contemporary setting and was published in 1991.

363 *TW: First Born*. The year is given. Sebastian, born 3rd March, 1981, is "almost ten".

364 *Timewyrm: Revelation*

with only the same weapons as their opponents. Prince Sayf Udeen of Kafiristan - a multiple Olympic competitor with seven wives - was one of the greatest swordsmen in the world, and the Doctor was relying upon him to defeat the Metatraxi leader in single combat. Udeen died in a skirmish, and so Ace bested the Metatraxi leader instead - but the victory didn't count because she was female. Raine directed the Metatraxi to destroy a number of robots built by the Margrave University Cybernetics Research Unit. This completed the Metatraxi's contract, enabling them to withdraw - but not before the Doctor had set their translator to "surfer dude" mode. The Doctor secured alien technology that the Russians had been testing amidst this conflict, and left with Ace and Raine to investigate Margrave.

@ 1989 (November) - FATHER TIME[349] **->** The eighth Doctor made *Time* magazine's list of Top Fifty People of the Decade. He had spent a great deal of his time searching the world for Miranda, and was living with Debbie Castle. He was present at - and possibly responsible for - the fall of the Berlin Wall.

Ferran returned from the future aboard his ship, the *Supremacy*, and abducted Miranda from a hotel in India. Seeing this on television, the Doctor and Debbie went to Florida and stowed aboard the space shuttle *Atlantis*. The shuttle docked the *Supremacy* and Debbie was killed. Miranda had started a mutiny, and Ferran decided to destroy the ship rather than let it fall to his enemies. The Doctor and Miranda teamed up to shut down the *Supremacy*'s time engines. Miranda took control of the ship and declared herself Empress, heading back to the far, far future to end the intergalactic conflict.

The Nineties

The Doctor went to a Barry Manilow concert in 1990.[350] In the early 1990s, there were a string of privatisations: the electricity industry became Elec-Gen, and British Rail became BritTrack. In August 1991, information about the Russian Coup reached the West via the Internet.[351]

Sometime after the Soviet Union's fall, the Doctor assisted Yablokov, the Russian President's counsellor, in accounting for the Soviets' inventory of nuclear weapons. They proved unable to account for eighty four such devices.[352] Anji left home at 17, as her family had an outdated view of women.[353] **The Mandragora Helix was due to return to Earth in the early 1990s.**[354]

The Brigadier's grandson, Gordon James Lethbridge-Stewart, was born. Kate Lethbridge-Stewart split up from Gordon's father, Jonathan, when Gordon was two. She didn't speak to the Brigadier for six years; thus, the Brigadier didn't know about his grandson until Gordon was five.[355]

When Owen Harper turned ten, his mother spent the whole day screaming that her loving him didn't mean that she had to like him.[356]

The Doctor had tea and scones with Queen Elizabeth II.[357] He also had a regrettable incident involving a piece of "vomit fruit" and the Queen Mother.[358]

Irving Braxiatel offered Ronan McGinley, a highly mundane office worker, a blissful and rewarding summer in exchange for McGinley doing a service for him. McGinley agreed, and was taken through time to the Braxiatel Collection.[359]

c 1990 - "Train-Flight"[360] **->** The seventh Doctor visited Sarah Jane to invite her to a jazz concert. She refused to travel via TARDIS, so they went on a train... that mysteriously entered a space vortex. The Doctor and Sarah discovered a fleet of buses - the passengers of which had been dissolved - and learned they were in orbit on a Kalik organic ship. The Kaliks were an advanced race of insects that were usually vegetarian, but this was a renegade, carnivorous faction. The Doctor manipulated the hypnotic signal that the Kalik used to control humans to control *them* instead. He then beamed the train to Royal Albert Hall station... but as there's no such station, the train materialised in the middle of the street. The Doctor and Sarah sneaked away.

c 1990 (Sunday) - CAT'S CRADLE: TIME'S CRUCIBLE[361] **->** The seventh Doctor and Ace were summoned back to the TARDIS after eating baked Alaska on Ealing Broadway.

c 1991 - "Seaside Rendezvous"[362] **->** The seventh Doctor and Ace enjoyed a day at the seaside, but the "demon" from the wreck of the *Camara*, lost in 1826, emerged from the sea. The creature was actually a life-draining Ogri, which had been worn down into sand, but the Doctor destroyed it with a firehose.

In early 1991, Jack Harkness helped to relocate the Juniper Tree and its progeny, Sebastian, to the village of Rawbone - the people of which had been rendered sterile. Sebastian and his handler, Elena Hilda Al-Qatari, produced more Juniper Tree children - the Scions - who were given to various Rawbone families. The government's knowledge of the Juniper Tree project was lost in a paperwork shuffle.[363]

In the summer of 1991, the seventh Doctor hid a portable temporal link in St Christopher's Church, Cheldon Bonniface, while brass rubbing with Mel.[364]

Jenny, a traffic warden, became a companion of Iris Wildthyme after trying to issue a ticket to Iris' bus, which was on a side street in Sunderland in 1991. They wound up travelling together for four years, although Jenny got the runs every time Iris' bus went through the Vortex.[365]

Soviet intelligence agents in Uzbekistan built the fake town of Thorington on an island in the Aral Sea. Thorington was patterned after a village in Suffolk, and served as a "school for spies". In time, the Soviets populated Thorington with Autons derived from technology obtained from Nestene meteorite landings. The Autons were to be trained to function as bulletproof spies in the United Kingdom. When Uzbekistan ceased being part of the Soviet Union on 1st September, 1991, all support was cut off to Thorington. The Autons there stuck to their daily routines for seventeen years, oblivious to their true nature.[366]

Maria's father Alan Jackson was such a great skateboarder, he earned the nickname "King of the Concrete, Romford, 1992".[367] Eugene Jones' teacher gave him a bona-fide alien eyeball. It was a Dogon sixth eye, capable of - temporally speaking - aiding people in seeing "what was behind them".[368] UNIT researchers began examining remnants of previous alien incursions at a research facility called The Warehouse.[369]

Amy Pond developed a love of Raspberry Ripple with extra sprinkles when she was three years old.[370] Lucie Miller had a "thing" about jelly after an unfortunate incident at a children's party in 1992.[371]

c 1992 (early summer) - CAT'S CRADLE: WITCH MARK[372] -> The daytime sun around the mystical world of Tír na n-Óg - Dagda's Wheel - was dying, and the humans there were evacuating to Earth through a gateway in the village of Llanfer Ceiriog, Wales. The nonhumanoids were being left behind to perish, and so demons attacked the Tír na n-Óg town of Dinorben. The demons mortally wounded Tír na n-Óg's creator, Goibhnie, but he aided the seventh Doctor and Ace in transferring the demons into Dagda's Wheel, giving it two thousand years of fuel.

The Spotter claimed that the President of the United States had taken to bathing in cranberry sauce.

1992 - "Invaders from Gantac"[373] -> The seventh Doctor saved the tramp Leapy from alien police in London. Some time previously, the Gantacs had invaded Earth, destroyed London landmarks and declared a curfew. They were a hive mind species from two hundred thousand light years away, but had made an administrative mistake - they should have invaded the planet Wrouth, not Earth. Leapy's fleas infected the Gantac leader, who died. Without his control, the Gantacs died with him.

1992 (Christmas) - TIMEWYRM: REVELATION[374] -> The seventh Doctor and Ace found themselves in a perfect replica of Cheldon Bonniface that was built on the moon (although not before Ace had died of oxygen starvation). The Doctor and Ace entered a surreal, tortured landscape that they discovered was the Doctor's own mind. Ace managed to rally the Doctor's former incarnations, and they gave the Doctor the strength to defeat the Timewyrm. The Timewyrm's mind was placed in a mindless baby grown in a genetics laboratory. The Hutchings family raised the baby as their daughter, Ishtar.

---

365 Jenny is mentioned in such stories as *Verdigris* and appears in *Iris: Enter Wildthyme*; the information here comes from *Iris: Iris and the Celestial Omnibus*: "The Deadly Flap".
366 *Brave New Town*
367 *TW: Random Shoes*
368 *SJA: Whatever Happened to Sarah Jane?*
369 "About five years" before *Auton*, although one of the Warehouse workers, Winslet, says he's been there for "seven years".
370 "Forever Dreaming"
371 *Orbis*
372 Dating *Cat's Cradle: Witch Mark* (NA #7) - The book saw release in June 1992 and seems contemporary. It's "early summer" (p57).
373 Dating "Invaders from Gantac" (*DWM* #148-150) - Leapy says it is "1992".
374 Dating *Timewyrm: Revelation* (NA #4) - "It was the Sunday before Christmas 1992" (p2). The Doctor confronts "Death", here a creation of the Timewyrm, but will often encounter the living embodiment of Death itself in the New Adventures.
375 Thirteen years before the present-day portion of

Night Thoughts.
376 Rani is an Aries according to *SJA: Secrets of the Stars*, which puts her birth date between 20th March and 20th April. As she's 17 in *SJA: Lost in Time*, set on 23rd November, 2010, she must have been born in 1993. By comparison, Clyde turned 15 in June 2008 (if one aligns information on him provided in *Secrets of the Stars* and *SJA: The Mark of the Berserker*), meaning he and Rani out to be a year apart in school, even if they seem to share a fair amount of classes together.
377 "Four years" before *The Rapture*.
378 Dating *Touched by an Angel* (NSA #47) - The exact day is given (p228).
379 Dating *Blood Heat* (NA #19) - This story is a sequel to *Doctor Who and the Silurians*, containing many elements from its novelisation *Doctor Who and the Cave-Monsters*. Thus, the Silurians are called "reptile people", but the Doctor wears his velvet jacket, not coveralls, when he goes potholing and the Silurian leader is named Morka. It is repeatedly stated that the first encounter with the Silurians took place "twenty years" ago in "1973".
380 *No Future*

Circa 1993, Major Dickens and three scientific-minded colleagues, including the physics theorist J.J. Bartholomew, started gathering on Gravonax Island to conduct various experiments.[375]

Sarah Jane Smith's friend Rani Chandra was born to Haresh and Gita Chandra between 20th March and 20th April, 1993.[376] In 1993, Ace's father had a heart attack. He told his son Liam about Ace, but Liam failed to reconcile with his mother while searching for his missing sister. Liam returned home to find his father dead.[377]

1993 (8th May) - TOUCHED BY AN ANGEL[378] **->** The eleventh Doctor, Amy and Rory took Mark Whitaker, age 46, through time to have a final conversation with his late wife, Rebecca Coles, when she was a young woman. Mark's time differential shorted out, reversing the aging he'd experienced from time travelling - physically, he reverted to being 37. The Doctor and his friends took Mark back to 2011, but only after the Doctor spilled red wine on the contemporary Mark's T-Shirt - causing him and Rebecca to meet for the first time.

= 1993 - BLOOD HEAT[379] **->** In an alternative timestream, the Silurian plague released at Wenley Moor in the early nineteen-seventies wiped out most of humanity. The third Doctor was killed before he could discover the antidote. Over the next twenty years, the Silurians initiated massive climatic change, rendering the plant life inedible to humanity and altering coastlines. Dinosaur species from many different eras were reintroduced to the wild. The capital of Earth became Ophidian, a vast city in Africa. Some Silurians hunted down humans for sport.

This timeline was created by the Monk, and deactivated by the seventh Doctor. It would survive for a generation or so after this before winding down.

The seventh Doctor, Benny and Ace visited the 1993 Glastonbury Festival, and met Danny Pain, a former singer for the punk bank Plasticine, and his daughter Amy.[380] Jason Kane's father, Peter Jonathan Kane, physically abused his children. When Jason's sister Lucy was about six, Peter punished her for touching herself in a "bad place" - and

broke three of her fingers, one per day over the school holidays, with a mallet.[381]

1993 (31st October) - THE LEFT-HANDED HUMMINGBIRD[382] **->** The so-called Halloween Man opened fire on a crowd of unsuspecting people in a marketplace in Mexico City. Cristian Alvarez witnessed this, narrowly avoiding death himself.

(=) The Halloween Man opened fire on a crowd of unsuspecting people in a marketplace in Mexico City. Cristian Alvarez witnessed this, narrowly avoiding death himself. The evidence suggested an alien presence - the Blue, also known as the psychic being Huitzilin. On 12th December, Alvarez sent a note for the Doctor's attention to UNIT HQ in Geneva.

The seventh Doctor investigated early the next year. In his own timeline, this was before "the Happening" of late 1968, early 1969. Huitzilin killed Christian, but the Doctor's actions erased this from history.

= 1993 (2nd November) - CONUNDRUM[383] **->** As part of his revenge against the seventh Doctor, the Monk trapped the TARDIS in the fictional village of Arandale, which was populated by colourful characters. It was part of the Land of Fiction, and the Doctor wrote himself out of the trap.

1993 (18th November) - THE DIMENSION RIDERS[384] **->** The President of St Matthew's College, Oxford - actually a Time Lord named Epsilon Delta - plotted with the Garvond, a creature composed of the darker sides of the minds within the Gallifreyan Matrix. They sought to create a Time Focus - a bridge through time between student Tom Cheynor and his future descendant, Darius Cheynor - that would let the Garvond absorb a massive amount of chronal energy. The Garvond turned on the President and killed him. The seventh Doctor trapped the Garvond within the dimensionally transcendental text *The Worshipful and Ancient Law of Gallifrey*, then disposed of the book in a pocket dimension.

---

381 *Death and Diplomacy,* and reiterated in *Benny: The End of the World.*
382 Dating *The Left-Handed Hummingbird* (NA #21) - The date of the massacre is given. The Doctor arrives in "1994".
383 Dating *Conundrum* (NA #22) - The Doctor thinks that it is "November the second, 1993".
384 Dating *The Dimension Riders* (NA #20) - The scenes in Oxford are set in "1993", "November 18th".

(=) **1993 - "Time and Time Again"**[385] -> The seventh Doctor, Benny and Ace arrived in a London that was in ruins... a battleground for armies of monsters. The Black Guardian had altered history so that the Doctor never left Gallifrey, but the Doctor and his companions travelled through history reassembling the Key to Time, and the White Guardian restored the timeline to its normal path.

1993 (November) - GOTH OPERA[386] -> The Time Lady Ruath sought to fulfill prophesies that spoke of the birth of a vampire nation. She rescued the vampire Yarven from his burial spot in Croatia and allowed him to turn her. Together, they sought to raise a vampire army. Tracking them down to Manchester, the fifth Doctor destroyed the army and its attempt to create the Vampire Messiah. Yarven was incinerated; Ruath was flung into the Time Vortex.

The vampires Jake and Madeline departed into space. They later returned, and by the twenty-fourth century had sired many descendents.

1993 (29th December) - INSTRUMENTS OF DARKNESS[387] -> The sixth Doctor and Mel found Evelyn in Great Rokeby. The twins Cellian and Ciara had reformed and were improving the school system in the village of Halcham.

By now, the Cylox named Lai-Ma was trying to psionically absorb the energy of his former prison realm, hoping to increase his power levels and destroy Earth. His brother Tko-Ma hoped to steal his brother's power and had founded the Network, an organisation that kidnapped psionics and exploited their abilities. The Ini-Ma, the Cylox brothers' jailor, killed the siblings but died in the process.

A powerplay between Tko-Ma's anchor on Earth (Sebastian Malvern) and the Network's head administrator (John Doe) triggered a slaughter that killed Cellian, Ciara and Doe. The Network reformed, with Mel's associate Trey Korte as a member, into an organisation pledged to protect Earth from extra-terrestrial threats. Evelyn resumed travelling with the Doctor and Mel.

Department C19 had closed by 1993 due to internal corruption. Sir John Sudbury was murdered to prevent his exposing the Network.

385 Dating "Time and Time Again" (*DWM* #207) - The date is given.

386 Dating *Goth Opera* (MA #1) - It is "1993", "November".

387 Dating *Instruments of Darkness* (PDA #48) - The Doctor and Mel arrive on 29th December (p69). "John Doe", although his surname is never mentioned, is likely Jeremy Fitzoliver, Sarah Jane's associate from *The Paradise of Death* and *The Ghosts of N-Space* (although this would clash with *Interference*). Sudbury was mentioned in *Time-Flight*.

388 *The Sun Makers* first mentions the discovery, the year of which is given in *Iceberg*. It has to be discovered after *The Tenth Planet*, or the story would have been called "The Eleventh Planet". *GodEngine* and *The Crystal Bucephalus* refer to the Battle of Cassius.

389 *Interference*

390 *Dreamland* (*DW*).

391 *Tales from the Vault*. Construction on the Angel of the North began in 1994.

392 Dating *The Land of the Dead* (BF #4) - The year is given.

393 According to *SJA: Secrets of the Stars*, Clyde's birthday is 5th June. He's 15 in *SJA: The Mark of the Berserker*, likely set after that date in 2009.

394 Dating *Touched by an Angel* (NSA #47) - The exact days are given (pgs 34, 39, 79). Page 224 appears to contain a mistake, saying that Mark was sent back to 2003, not 1994.

395 Dating *Invasion of the Cat-People* (MA #13) - It is "AD 1994", the adventure starting "Friday the eighth of July 1994".

396 Dating *P.R.O.B.E.: The Zero Imperative* (P.R.O.B.E. film #1) - The film was released in 1994, and seems contemporary. The story appears to begin on 8th August (as noted when a clinic worker who seems to be arriving for work checks off 7th August on her calendar, suggesting that it's the next day). Liz's desk calendar at one point reads (albeit somewhat hazily) "August 1994", and roughly mid-way through the story, she flips her desk calendar to reveal that it's now 10th August. A mortician tells Liz how unusual it is that the ground around the body he's examining was "frozen in August". The story ends on the night of perihelion, presumably the same day (13th August) as in 1945 when O'Kane killed his family.

397 *Zamper*

398 *Who Killed Kennedy* (p271).

399 *The Five Companions*

400 "Ten years" before *UNIT: Time Heals*.

401 About ten years before *Iris: Wildthyme on Top*.

402 Dating "Star Beast II" (*DWM Yearbook 1996*) - Beep's been imprisoned for "fifteen years", and it's "1995".

403 According to publicity material, she's "13" in *SJA: Invasion of the Bane*.

404 *TW: Greeks Bearing Gifts*

405 *Utopia*

406 Dating *TimeH: Echoes* (TimeH #6) - The year "1995" is given on the cover of the printed book and the cover of the audiobook, and is reiterated at least four times within the text. However, a frequently used online version of the cover (including the one on the Telos website) gives the year as 2006.

The outermost planet of the solar system was discovered in 1994 **and called Cassius.**[388] UNISYC, a UN security group, was founded in 1994. Like UNIT, they were involved with alien encounters.[389] **The US government only admitted that Area 51 existed in 1994.**[390] UNIT constructed the Vault, a.k.a. the Museum of Terrors - an underground base found under the Angel of the North - to house alien artifacts and weapons.[391]

1994 - THE LAND OF THE DEAD[392] ->

The fifth Doctor and Nyssa were attacked in Alaska by sea monsters. They sheltered in the home of oilman Shaun Brett. One of the fossils in his collection was a Permian - an ancient predator that looked like a living skeleton, bound together by a bio-electric field. A pack of Permians revived and threatened to breed. As the creatures were vulnerable to fire, the Doctor destroyed them with a stock of flammable paint.

Clyde Langer, a future friend of Sarah Jane Smith, was born on 5th June, 1994, to Paul and Carla Langer.[393]

1994 (10th-11th June) - TOUCHED BY AN ANGEL[394]

-> A variant of the Weeping Angels that fed on paradoxes attempted to create a complex space-time event centred around Mark Whitaker, whose wife Rebecca was fated to die in 2003. An Angel sent Mark back to 1994 from 2011 - he had in his possession a series of instructions he believed his future self had written, but which the Angels had crafted. The eleventh Doctor, Amy and Rory arrived from 2011, but believed that Mark's future self had to remain in the 1990s and fulfill upon the instructions to preserve history. They failed to realise that he intended to save Rebecca from dying. The Doctor set the TARDIS to follow disturbances in Mark's timeline, and they would next meet in 1997.

1994 (8th July) - INVASION OF THE CAT-PEOPLE[395]

-> The second Doctor, Polly and Ben prevented the Cat-People, one of the most powerful races in the galaxy, from harnessing the magnetic energy of the Earth.

1994 (8th-13th August) - P.R.O.B.E.: THE ZERO IMPERATIVE[396] ->

Liz Shaw had left Cambridge and now worked for the Preternatural Research Bureau (P.R.O.B.E.), an arm of the government that investigated supernatural phenomena. She looked into a series of murders centred around the Hawthorne psychiatric clinic - the new home of Daniel O'Kane, a.k.a. Patient Zero. The dark forces that turned O'Kane into a killer tried to manifest through his son, Peter Russell. O'Kane stopped them from doing so, at the cost of his own life.

The seventh Doctor, Benny, Chris and Roz spent a couple of days at the Doctor's house in Allen Road to recover from their experiences on Zamper.[397] On 5th April, 1995, Private Cleary died in hospital.[398]

Ian Chesterton retired after spending thirty years doing research. He then got bored, and returned to teaching, while Barbara worked on a new book.[399] Using blueprints stolen from UNIT, Bernard Kelly worked to develop a matter-transporter for benefit of "Britain first" zealots within the military. He spent a decade failing to do so.[400]

Iris Wildthyme's companion Tom left her company and returned to his native era. He brokered a deal with the publisher Satan and Satan Ltd. to produce a series of novels based upon his adventures with Iris. Sales soared, and Tom gained a reputation as an eccentric alien abductee. Satan and Satan was a front for MIAOW, who hoped to learn Iris' secrets.[401]

1995 - "Star Beast II"[402] ->

Judges Zagran, Scraggs and Theka concluded that white star therapy had successfully rehabilitated Beep the Meep and he was released. He remained evil, but the authorities had removed his black-star drive. Beep had a spare hidden on Earth, and headed there. The fourth Doctor arrived in Blackcastle just before the Meep. Fudge Higgins now managed the multiplex built on the site of the old steel mills, and this was where the Meep had buried his stardrive. The Doctor adjusted a film projector and imprisoned the Meep within a *Lassie* movie.

Nightshade: The Movie was in general release.

Maria Jackson, a friend of Sarah Jane Smith, was born around 1995.[403] Age 20, Toshiko Sato joined a government science think tank.[404] Jack visited the Powell Estate once or twice in the nineties and watched Rose grow up, but refrained from speaking with her.[405]

(=) 1995 - TIMEH: ECHOES[406] ->

The time-creature that Honoré and Emily saved from the Cabal of the Horned Beast took up residence in the Dragon Industry Tower - an office block that proved so financially ruinous, its founder, John Raymond, killed himself. The creature sought redemption for its crimes by absorbing the timelines of abused women, but this cast the women into a noncorporeal void. Emily persuaded the creature to return the women home and absorb Raymond's timeline, an act that erased the tower from history.

The paradox resolved itself enough that the time-creature broke free, and left for parts unknown.

c 1995 - DOWNTIME[407] -> Under the direction of the Great Intelligence, which was secretly hosted in Professor Travers, Victoria Waterfield had invested an eight-figure sum in the New World University in north-west London. The University specialised in teaching classes by computer, but the Intelligence used a hypnotic technique to control the students there. It inhabited the university's computers, and spread into the Internet. There was chaos as all computer systems succumbed to - as the media termed it - the "computer flu". The CIA's files were broadcast on Russian television, bank cash points released all their cash and Tomahawk missiles were launched in the Gulf.

The Intelligence transformed some of the University students into Yeti, leading to a conflict with UNIT. Before the Intelligence could take control of Earth, Victoria and her allies destroyed the University's generators, which banished the Intelligence. Professor Travers' dead body collapsed without the Intelligence to animate it.

Victoria was put on Interpol's Most Wanted list for her role in this affair. The Doctor provided a letter of reference to clear her name with UNIT.

After this time, the Brigadier reunited with Doris. They married and the Brigadier gave up teaching.[408]

1995 - P.R.O.B.E.: THE DEVIL OF WINTERBORNE[409] -> Liz Shaw's father, Reuben Shaw, had recently died. P.R.O.B.E. investigated a number of killings at the Winterborne boys' school. Christian Purcell, a student there, thought he was the cult-leader Isaac Greatorex reincarnated, and was murdering people to ritualistically attain immortality. Confronted, Purcell seemingly leapt to his death on a motorway, but his body vanished...

(=) Around 1995, physicist John Finer accidentally killed his daughter Amelia. He began researching time travel, hoping to go back in time to prevent this. Events circa 2001 nullified this timeline.[410]

In 1995, Ironside Industries purchased British Rocket Group and the former Space Defence Station at Devesham.[411] While the fourth Doctor and Romana were in Cornwall in 1995, the Doctor read of the suicide of David Brown, captain of the English cricket team and a native of Hexen Bridge.[412] In 1995, Katherine Chambers started up her own practice, Chambers Pharmaceuticals, in Brisbane.[413]

1995 (20th December) - "Memorial"[414] -> The seventh Doctor and Ace landed in Westmouth. The Doctor freed the Telphin consciousness from Simon Galway, in whom it had resided in peace for exactly sixty years.

407 Dating *Downtime* (MA #18) - The story is set "about thirty" or "over twenty-five" years after *The Web of Fear*, "nearly twenty years" after *Fury from the Deep* and Sarah's time in UNIT, and about ten years after 1984. The Brigadier has been teaching at Brendon for "twenty odd years". The Intelligence's next incursion on Earth - *Millennial Rites*, set in 1999 - is "four years" afterwards. "Brigadier Crichton" is said to still be with UNIT.
408 Between *Mawdryn Undead* and *Battlefield*, and shortly after the Missing Adventure *Downtime*. Doris is first mentioned in *Planet of the Spiders*.
409 Dating *P.R.O.B.E.: The Devil of Winterborne* (P.R.O.B.E. film #2) - The video came out in 1995, and seems contemporary. Liz's father has passed away recently enough for her boss to offer condolences, and her father's tombstone in *P.R.O.B.E.: The Ghosts of Winterborne* says he lived "1919-1995".
410 "Six years" before *Psi-ence Fiction*.
411 *The Feast of Axos*, respectively referencing *Remembrance of the Daleks* and *The Android Invasion*.
412 *The Hollow Men*
413 "Eleven years" before *The Gathering*.
414 Dating "Memorial" (*DWM* #191) - "The TARDIS chronometer read December 20th 1995".
415 "Twelve years" prior to 2008, according to *Iris: Iris and the Celestial Omnibus*: "The Deadly Flap".

416 "Fifteen years" before *Ferril's Folly*.
417 *Who Killed Kennedy*. It is "nearly twenty-five years" (p274) after Cleary's return to the 1970s, and is subject to UNIT dating. This novel presumes that the UNIT stories occurred around the time of broadcast, and the date of Stevens' departure is given (p271).
418 *TW: Miracle Day*
419 Dating *Night Thoughts* (BF #79) - It is "ten years" before the story's present-day component. An audio statement from Maude, recorded shortly before her suicide, is dated 12th January.
420 Dating *Touched by an Angel* (NSA #47) - The exact day is given (p91).
421 Dating *Benny: The End of the World* (Benny audio #8.4) - Jason was born in 1983 and is "nearly 13" when he leaves home. A conversation between Jason and Benny in *Death and Diplomacy* detailed Jason and Lucy's physical abuse, in a scene that's here dramatised for audio.
422 *Death and Diplomacy*
423 *The Big Bang*
424 Dating *Interference* (EDA #25-26) - The date is "1996" (p8, p29). This means that Sam actually arrives back on Earth a bit before her younger self leaves in the TARDIS.
425 The backstory to *The Eleventh Hour*, given in *The*

1996

Iris Wildthyme and her companion Jenny parted ways following an escapade with jellyfish creatures, their secluded moonbase and the cast of a daytime soap that Iris watched. Jenny would eventually head the Darlington branch of MIAOW.[415]

The fourth segment of the Key to Time, disguised as a meteoroid, passed through the Cronquist system. The Cronquist charged the meteoroid with their power, and it later impacted a NASA shuttle. Astronaut Millicent Drake, the only survivor, came under Cronquist's control and furthered their invasion plans.[416]

In January 1996, James Stevens retrieved his time ring from his safety deposit box at a bank in London. Rifle in hand, he departed into the past to assassinate Kennedy.[417] **A set of army barracks in Wales was closed down in 1996, but would be reopened as the Cowbridge Overflow Camp in 2011.**[418]

c 1996 (12th January) - NIGHT THOUGHTS[419] -> On
Gravonax Island in Scotland, J.J. Bartholomew developed the prototype Bartholomew Transactor, a device that could send a subatomic particle back in time to an identical piece of equipment. By this method, audio messages from the future could be heard in the past.

Major Dickens theorised that if the device were used to retroactively halt an established death, then the closely related timelines would overlap and the deceased's body would re-animate. When a destitute woman named Maude appeared with her two daughters, Edie and Ruth, Dickens decided to test this and deliberately misdiagnosed Edie's eye infection as Gravonax gas poisoning. Dickens' colleagues were moved to euthanise Edie rather than let her suffer what they believed was an inevitable, agonizing death.

A Bartholomew Transactor was present as Dickens gave Edie a lethal dose of anaesthetic. The veterinary scientist Hartley chemically preserved Edie's body on Dickens' behalf, and her corpse was placed inside a taxidermied bear. Maude discovered Dickens' deception and committed suicide. Ruth was shuffled between foster homes. Dickens held Bartholomew prisoner so she could perfect her device; she tried to escape, but was permanently crippled by a bear trap. The world believed that she was dead.

As Dickens desired, the Transactor relayed a message from ten years in the future and caused a temporal anomaly. The seventh Doctor arrived from that period, tasked with conclusively ensuring Edie's death, but found himself unable to kill her.

1996 (17th April) - TOUCHED BY AN ANGEL[420] ->
Mark Whitaker and Rebecca Coles impulsively slept together, which had a chilling effect on their friendship.

1996 - BENNY: THE END OF THE WORLD[421] -> When
Jason Kane was nearly 13, he responded to his father's physical abuse by catching a train out of town, leaving his mother and sister Lucy behind. As an adult, Jason travelled back from 2607 and arrived at his family home two days after his younger self fled. Posing as a detective-inspector from the "Child Protection Taskforce", Jason told Peter Kane that young Jason's disappearance was being investigated - and that the Kane household would be under surveillance. Jason hoped this would curtail his father's abuse of Lucy, and he also established a trust fund for her.

Shug, the leader of the Skrak, was betrayed by his subordinate Gleka and transmatted to the Dagellan Cluster in 1996. The beam also swept up Jason Kane, who was living on the streets of London. Jason became a rogue and spent the next fifteen years away from Earth, thinking that Shug was his small, furry pet.[422] **Amy Pond went to the National Museum when she was little.**[423]

1996 - INTERFERENCE[424] -> The eighth Doctor was
summoned by the United Nations, who had been offered a weapon - the Cold - by a race of alien arms dealers. The aliens were members of the Remote, a Faction Paradox colony. Sarah Jane Smith, who was now involved with a man named Paul, investigated the matter and met Samantha Jones, who was taken to the Remote. Fitz was frozen in suspended animation and wouldn't awaken until the twenty-sixth century. He would become Father Kreiner of Faction Paradox.

The Saudis captured and tortured the Doctor. He sent an emergency message to his third incarnation, who was on the planet Dust in the thirty-eighth century. Sarah rescued the Doctor and he travelled to the Remote, who had built a settlement on a Time Lord warship. This ship was designed to destroy the original home planet of their Enemy - Earth - in the future War. The Doctor convinced the people of the Remote that they were being used. The ship was sent to a place of safety.

Sam accepted an offer to stay with Sarah Jane Smith and left the Doctor's company. The Doctor was joined on his travels by two members of the Remote: Compassion and Kode, the latter of whom had been generated from a Remote remembrance tank and endowed with much of Fitz's personality. The Doctor used the TARDIS to revise Kode into a copy of Fitz as he had been prior to his joining Faction Paradox.

Amelia "Amy" Pond had grown up with a Crack in Time in her bedroom wall. It erased her parents from existence; Amy would remember scant details about them, but didn't know their fate. Her Aunt Sharon raised her. Amy went to the National Museum when she was little.[425]

1996 (Easter) - THE ELEVENTH HOUR[426] -> The newly regenerated eleventh Doctor crashed to Earth in the backyard of Amelia Pond, age seven, and the falling TARDIS destroyed her garden shed. She asked the Doctor to investigate a crack in her wall - actually a Crack in Time, through which a voice could be heard saying, "Prisoner Zero has escaped." The Doctor recognised it as a message from a prison, but had to attend to the healing TARDIS when its engines misphased. He told Amelia that he would right the TARDIS by taking a short hop five minutes into the future - she packed to go away with him, and waited for him in the back yard. Instead of reappearing in five minutes, the Doctor would return twelve years later.

1996 (Easter) - THE BIG BANG[427] -> Amelia fell asleep in her backyard while waiting for the Doctor. As the eleventh Doctor's timeline came undone after he sealed the Cracks in Time, he carried Amelia into her house and put her to bed. The words he spoke while she slept would help her to remember him in future.

Amelia Pond told her best friends Rory and Mels about meeting the Doctor.[428] In the years to follow, the persistence with which Amy clung to the existence of her imaginary friend - her "raggedy Doctor" - caused her to be taken to four psychiatrists.[429]

(=) 1996 - THE BIG BANG[430] -> The explosion of the Doctor's TARDIS in 2010 caused every sun to supernova at every moment in history, obliterating the universe. Only the Earth and its moon remained, lit by the energy from the exploding TARDIS. In this eye of the storm, the people of Earth lived beneath a starless sky. All of the races allied against the Doctor in 102 AD had been wiped out, although a few "never-were" vestiges of them remained, resembling statues.

The Pandorica, having held Amy Pond in stasis ever since 102 AD, was now kept in the National

---

Big Bang.
426 Dating *The Eleventh Hour* (X5.1) - Amelia says that it's "Easter" in her prayer to Santa. The year isn't stated, but it's twelve years before the Doctor sees Amy again, then a further two years before her wedding day, which is stated to be in 2010.
427 Dating *The Big Bang* (X5.13) - The action picks up from Amelia waiting in *The Eleventh Hour*.
428 *Let's Kill Hitler*. This has to be shortly after Amelia's first meeting with the Doctor in *The Eleventh Hour*.
429 *The Eleventh Hour*
430 Dating *The Big Bang* (X5.13) - It's "1894 years later" than 102 AD, and the older Amy confirms it's "1996".
431 *The Hounds of Artemis*; Vortis first appears in *The Web Planet*. This was true in one story, the apocryphal *Doctor Who Annual 1965* story "The Lair of Zarbi Supremo", set circa 1996.
432 *TW: Adam*
433 *Army of Ghosts, TW: Fragments*, with the years given in *The Torchwood Archives*.
434 Dating *P.R.O.B.E.: Unnatural Selection* and *P.R.O.B.E.: The Ghosts of Winterborne* (P.R.O.B.E. films #3-4) - As with the rest of the *P.R.O.B.E.* series, the stories seem contemporary - in these last two cases, with their release in 1996. In *Unnatural Selection*, events in 1975 are repeatedly said to be "twenty years ago" and "over twenty years ago". The body of Alfred's first victim was found "in early hours of July the 8th", so *Unnatural Selection* would seem to occur in August at the earliest. In *The Ghosts of Winterborne*, enough time has passed that headmaster Gavin Purcell has been tried and convicted for his culpability in events in *The Devil of Winterborne*. *The Ghosts of Winterborne* has Andrew, a student at Winterborne, returning there after a leave of absence - possibly suggesting that it's the start of the new term.

435 Dating *The Chase* (2.8) - The Doctor claims that as "this house is exactly what you would expect in a nightmare", suspecting that the TARDIS and the Dalek time machine have landed "in a world of dreams" that "exists in the dark recesses of the human mind". Viewers later find out the truth - the TARDIS has simply landed in a theme park. A sign proclaims that it is the "Festival of Ghana 1996". The "Tower of London" quote is Ian's description of what he has just seen. Quite why Peking would cancel an exhibition in Ghana is not explained.
436 *Original Sin*. Vaughn's memories are, by his own admission, corrupted and he seems to be a year out.
437 *Interference*
438 *Something Inside*. The year is unspecified, although there's nothing to say it isn't the discontinued Ghana celebration mentioned in *The Chase*.
439 Dating *The Sands of Time* (MA #22) - The date is given (p117).
440 At the start of *Return of the Living Dad* (p15).
441 *Bad Therapy*. The exact year isn't given.
442 Dating "End Game" and "Oblivion" (*DWM* #244-247, 323-328) - "End Game" takes place "six days to Christmas", and the day of Izzy's return (the same as when she left) is given as "December 19th, 1996" in "Oblivion". We learn in "TV Action" that Izzy was born on 12th October, 1979, and she's "17" in a couple of the strips. "The Company of Thieves" establishes that Izzy is short for Isabelle.
443 *The Sontaran Stratagem*. The Doctor says that Rattigan is only "18", but he's either estimating or belittling him, as Rattigan's on screen biography says he attended local primary school from 1990 to 1992 - suggesting that, like the actor who played him (Ryan Sampson), Rattigan was born in 1985.
444 *Benny: The Vampire Curse*: "The Badblood Diaries", with an obvious reference to *Buffy the Vampire Slayer*.

Museum. The eleventh Doctor left a note that made Amy's seven-year-old self insist that her aunt take her to see the Pandorica exhibit. The younger Amy touched the Pandorica, which used a sample of her DNA to resurrect the older Amy. The Doctor freed River Song, who had been time-looped inside the exploding TARDIS; Rory the Last Centurion, who was still guarding the Pandorica after two millennia, joined them.

History continued to collapse... the Doctor's group realised that the Pandorica contained some atoms from the universe before it was destroyed, and that the Pandorica's light - if given an infinite power source - could extrapolate the whole universe from just one of them. The Doctor piloted the Pandorica into the exploding TARDIS, providing the power necessary to (effectively) trigger the second Big Bang. The Cracks of Time were sealed, but the Doctor was on the wrong side of them when this happened - and so everyone in the universe forgot about him.

The eleventh Doctor claimed that Vortis could be seen from Earth.[431] **When Owen Harper was 16, he packed his bags and left his emotionally abusive household.**[432] **Yvonne Hartman became the head of Torchwood London** in 1996. **Alex Hopkins took charge of Torchwood Cardiff** no later than 1996.[433]

1996 - P.R.O.B.E.: UNNATURAL SELECTION[434] ->
The genetically advanced man Alfred began harvesting organs from humans in a bid to give his benefactor, Professor Julius Quilter, extended life. The ailing Quilter died anyway, and P.R.O.B.E. ended Aldred's murder spree by killing him.

1996 - P.R.O.B.E.: THE GHOSTS OF WINTERBORNE[434]
-> Christian Purcell's body was found by the motorway where he'd jumped. The ghost of Isaac Greatorex sought to return to life and gain great powers, but Liz Shaw oversaw a ritual that banished him.

1996 - THE CHASE[435] -> One of the exhibits at the 1996 Festival of Ghana, "Frankenstein's House of Horror", featured roboticFac versions of a number of Gothic characters. For $10, visitors could wander around an animated haunted house, be frightened by mechanical bats and meet Frankenstein's monster, Dracula and the Grey Lady. The exhibition was cancelled by Peking. The first Doctor, Ian, Barbara and Vicki briefly visited the exhibition while fleeing through time from the Daleks.

Tobias Vaughn claimed he saw the Dalek Time Machine at the "1995 Earth Fair in Ghana".[436] The robots were programmed by Microsoft, who later faced lawsuits.[437] The Doctor attended the crowded Festival of Ghana.[438]

1996 - THE SANDS OF TIME[439] -> Nyssa's awakening drew near, and the agents of Nephthys made ready for her resurrection. Nephthys' intelligence resided within Nyssa, but her instinct resided in a Nephthys clone named Vanessa Prior. The fifth Doctor tricked the instinct part of Nephthys into thinking its intelligence had dissipated in 1926. The Nephthys-instinct went back in time but failed to reunite with itself. It circled back and forth between 1926 and 1996 until it aged to death. The Doctor removed Nephthys' intelligence from Nyssa and woke up his companion, then buried the intelligence at Nephthys' pyramid.

The seventh Doctor, Roz and Chris rested in Sydney in 1996.[440] The same Doctor returned Peri to the late twentieth century.[441]

1996 (19th December) - "End Game" / "Oblivion" (*DWM*)[442] -> The eighth Doctor landed in Stockbridge and was attacked by giant doll-like figures that resembled a butcher, a baker and a candlestick maker. He was rescued by his old friend Maxwell Edison and a fellow UFO spotter named Izzy. They had acquired a strange medallion called the "focus", but were soon rounded up by humanoid foxes in hunting gear and brought to the Celestial Toymaker - who had created a surreal version of Stockbridge, and stuffed the real one in a snowglobe.

The Toymaker similarly captured the Doctor and Izzy in a snowglobe, and the Doctor was forced to hand over the focus. It was part of the Imagineum - a device built by an ancient race of alchemists - and the Toymaker used it to create an evil doll-like duplicate of the Doctor. However, the two Doctors teamed up and exposed the Toymaker himself to the device. The Toymakers disappeared into the void, in perpetual stalemate, and Izzy joined the Doctor on his adventures.

Eventually, Izzy decided to leave the Doctor's company and make things right with her parents. He returned her to Stockbridge at the exact moment she left.

1997

The genius Luke Rattigan became a millionaire, age 12, following his invention of the Fountain 6 search engine.[443] Sunnydale, California, refused to reissue permits for tour caravans to park on Main Street anytime after 1997, between the hours of midnight and 4 a.m.[444]

The drug Mandrake, or M, first appeared on the streets in 1997. Its crystalline structure contained an unknown radiation, and UNIT classified it as a Foreign Hazard (meaning alien).[445] The Brigadier helped to oversee the creation of a new Parliament for Scotland.[446] The Doctor was given a sun visor by Ginger Spice.[447]

1997 (April) - BULLET TIME[448] -> With Britain scheduled to relinquish Hong Kong to China, the Chinese government secretly created the Tao Te Lung, a smuggling and extortion ring, as a means of rooting out Hong Kong's criminal element beforehand. The seventh Doctor usurped control of the Tao Te Lung, and used its operations to covertly move a group of stranded extra-terrestrials.

A rogue UNIT faction, The Cortez Project, sought to eliminate all extra-terrestrials as a threat to humanity. The Doctor arranged for his old ally, Sarah Jane Smith, to travel to Hong Kong and expose the Cortez members. However, Sarah's investigations put her in danger from the Tao Te Lung. In order to save Sarah's life, the Doctor arranged to publicly discredit her as a journalist.

The Doctor's alien allies reached their sunken spaceship, but a group of Cortez commandos, led by Colonel Tsang, seized control of the USS *Westmoreland* submarine in an attempt to head them off. The Doctor thwarted the Cortez

members and the aliens departed Earth.

One account of these events suggested that Sarah Jane killed herself to prevent Tom Ryder, an intelligence agency operative, from holding her hostage to blackmail the Doctor. Other reports failed to corroborate her death.

1997 (May) - THE RAPTURE[449] -> The Euphorian Empire had fallen into war with Scordatora. The drafted brothers Jude and Gabriel deserted and fled through the dimensional portal they previously used to reach Earth in 1855. Bar owner Gustavo Riviera helped the brothers found the Rapture nightclub in San Antonio, Izbia.

Gabriel's mental health deteriorated, and Jude realised that he'd need to take his brother home for medical care. Fearing court-martial and summary execution, Jude decided to entrance the Rapture patrons with PCP and a special mix of Gabriel's music, then kidnap the humans back to the Empire as an offering of ready-made soldiers. On 15th May, Gustavo disavowed the brothers' actions and wrestled with Gabriel, causing them to fall to their deaths. A vengeful Jude tried to unleash a music score that would kill anyone who heard it, but the seventh Doctor and Ace -

---

445 "The Mark of Mandragora"

446 *Minuet in Hell*

447 *Ghosts of India*

448 Dating *Bullet Time* (PDA #45) - The date of April 1997 is given (p15). Sarah Jane visits Bangkok just prior to this in March (p7). Britain turned over Hong Kong to China on 1st July, 1997. The report of Sarah Jane's demise in this novel is largely unsubstantiated and hails from Ryder's unreliable point-of-view. *Sometime Never* suggests the ambiguity of her death owes to the Council of Eight's machinations. Sarah clearly survives, as evidenced in *School Reunion, The Sarah Jane Adventures* and several of the books (including *System Shock, Millennium Shock, Christmas on a Rational Planet, Interference* and *The Shadow in the Glass*). *Bullet Time* never names the stranded aliens, but they would appear to be the Tzun from McIntee's *First Frontier*. The Cortez Project head, General Kyle, is possibly Marianne Kyle from *The Face of the Enemy*.

449 Dating *The Rapture* (BF #36) - Ace reckons it is "ten years" after she left Earth.

450 Dating *Battlefield* (26.1) - The Doctor tells Ace that they are "a few years in your future". Sergeant Zbrigniev is apparently in his mid-thirties, served in UNIT while the Doctor was present, and appears to have first-hand recollection of two of the Doctor's regenerations. Even if we assume that Zbrigniev is older than he looks (say, forty), and was very young when he joined UNIT, *Spearhead from Space* must have taken place in the mid-seventies. (The earliest Zbrigniev could be in the regular army is age 16, but he'd almost certainly need a couple more years before seeing active service, espe-

cially with an elite organisation like UNIT.)

The *Battlefield* novelisation by Marc Platt, based on notes by story author Ben Aaronovitch, sets the story in "the late 1990s" (p15). Ace later notices that Peter Warmsley's tax disc expires on "30.6.99" (p30). *The Terrestrial Index* set the story in "1992" and *The TARDIS Special* chose 1991 - perhaps they misheard the Doctor's line as "two years in your future". In a document for Virgin Publishing dated 23rd March, 1995, concerning "Future History Continuity", Ben Aaronovitch perhaps settled the matter when he stated that *Battlefield* is set "c.1997". *The Dying Days* is set after this story.

The Doctor is apparently surprised to learn that Lethbridge-Stewart married Doris - in this story, *The King of Terror* and *The Spectre of Lanyon Moor*.

THE FUTURE OF THE UNITED NATIONS: By *Battlefield*, UNIT is a truly multinational organisation with British, Czechoslovakian and Polish troops serving side by side. UNIT appear in the New Adventures *The Pit, Head Games* and *Happy Endings*, and the UN is referred to in *Cat's Cradle: Warhead*. In *The Enemy of the World*, nations have been grouped together into Zones. The governing body of the world is the United Zones, or the World Zones Authority, headed by a General Assembly.

The United Nations still exists at the time of the Thousand Day War referred to in the New Adventure *Transit*. Gradually, though, national barriers break down and a World Government runs the planet. Where this leaves the UN is unclear, although it appears that the United Nations survives or is reformed at some time far in the future. In *Mission to the Unknown*, Lowry's ship is the "UN Deep Space Force Group 1", and has the United

now calling herself Dorothy McShane - thwarted Jude's plan. Jude fled. Sometime later, a young office worker opened an e-mail attachment that played music from the Rapture nightclub.

At the Rapture, Dorothy encountered her younger brother Liam.

= c 1997 - BATTLEFIELD[450] **-> In a parallel universe, twelve centuries after defeating Arthur, Deathless Morgaine of the Fey had become battle queen of the S'Rax, ruler of thirteen worlds. Her world was scientifically advanced with energy weapons and ornithopters, but the people weren't reliant on technology and still knew the magic arts. There was still resistance against her rule, as Merlin had promised that Arthur would return in the hour of greatest need. Morgaine's immortal son Mordred led her troops to victory at Camlaan, forcing an enemy soldier, Ancelyn, to flee the field.**

Morgaine had tracked the magical sword Excalibur to our dimension, which Mordred called Avallion. When UNIT discovered that the Doctor was involved in this affair, the Secretary General persuaded Brigadier Alistair Gordon Lethbridge-Stewart to come out of retirement. Morgaine's extra-dimensional knights fought UNIT as led by Brigadier Winifred Bambera, and Morgaine secured control of a nuclear missile. The seventh Doctor, Ace and the Brigadier put paid to Morgaine's plans.

Benny attended Bambera and Ancelyn's wedding.[451]

1997 (Tuesday, 6th May) - THE DYING DAYS[452] **->** Mars 97, a British mission to the Red Planet, inadvertently trespassed on a Martian tomb. Xznaal, leader of the Argyre clan, used this as a pretext to invade Earth. He was working with the power-hungry Lord Greyhaven, and together they deposed the Queen and took control of the United Kingdom. Xznaal was crowned King of England and began begins transporting slave labour to Mars. When the eighth

Doctor was apparently killed, the Brigadier, Benny and UNIT formed a resistance movement that marched on London to dethrone the usurper. The Martians attempted to release "the Red Death", which would have wiped out all life on Earth. Greyhaven died trying to stop Xznaal, and the Doctor returned to save the day.

Lethbridge-Stewart was promoted to General.

"Since the Gantic Invasion and the Availlon Fiasco, unearthly threats have become a matter of fact."[453]

1997 - THE MANY HANDS[454] **->** The tenth Doctor took Martha to Edinburgh in 1997 to show her the Scott Monument, where the Nor' Loch had been once.

1997 - THE EIGHT DOCTORS[455] **->** The eighth Doctor, his memory wiped by the Master, landed in Totter's Lane, London. He saved the life of schoolgirl Samantha Jones, who was being chased by the drug dealers Baz and Mo. After a series of adventures, the Doctor returned to the junkyard and Sam persuaded him to take her with him.

1997 - VAMPIRE SCIENCE[456] **->** Carolyn McConnell summoned the eighth Doctor and Sam when she suspected vampires were active in San Francisco. The Doctor arrived and joined up with the American branch of UNIT, run by Brigadier-General Kramer. A generational war was brewing between the vampires, and a group of younger vampires - led by the upstart Slake - wiped out every old vampire except for their leader, Joanna Harris. The Doctor ingested silver nitrate, killing Slake and all the vampires that feasted on his blood. He also arranged for Harris to become human again. Harris and Carolyn joined the staff of UNIT.

Before this time, Kramer's branch of UNIT handled a Brieri scouting party.

c 1997 - GENOCIDE[457] **->** Jo Grant and her husband Cliff had now separated, and had an 11-year-old son named Matthew. The Tractite named Gavril grew a time tree from a seedling, and allied himself with an ecowarrior named Jacob Hynes. Archaeologists Rowenna Michaels

---

Nations symbol and a Union Jack on the hull.

451 *Benny: Present Danger:* "The Empire Variations"

452 Dating *The Dying Days* (NA #61) - The date is given at the start of the story and on the back cover. 6th May is the date that Virgin's license to publish *Doctor Who* books officially ended. Lethbridge-Stewart was cited as a General in *Head Games*.

453 "The Mark of Mandragora" - a reference to "Invaders from Gantac" and *Battlefield*.

454 Dating *The Many Hands* (NSA #24) - The year is given.

455 Dating *The Eight Doctors* (EDA #1) - The date is given. Technically, Sam returns home in *Interference* before her younger self leaves with the Doctor.

456 Dating *Vampire Science* (EDA #2) - The date is given (p25).

457 Dating *Genocide* (EDA #3) - The time seems concurrent with the book's publication in 1997. On page 147, Jo wonders if even "twentieth-century hospitals" will be capable of curing an illness that Julie contracts. Jo and Cliff are separated, and while it's not expressly said that they're divorced - they live near each other,

and Julie Sands had an offputting encounter with Hynes, who was posing as a UNIT captain, in the Kilgai Gorge in Tanzania. Jo, as Rowenna's old friend, was summoned to help, but Hynes captured all three of the women. A confusing escape followed, and the time tree took Jo, Rowenna, Julie and Hynes back to 2.5 million BC. The eighth Doctor later returned Jo home, after she had preserved history by wiping out a Tractite colony.

1997 - AUTON[458] **->** Dr Sally Arnold, the head of The Warehouse, conducted experiments that accidentally reactivated a Nestene energy unit. It revived several Autons, and while Arnold and Lockwood - the psychic leader of a UNIT containment team - quelled the situation, a bit of gelatinous Nestene essence escaped.

Jackie Tyler's father - "Grandad Prentice", as Rose called him - died of heart failure.[459] Torchwood stripped bare a Jathaa Sun Glider that crashed off the Shetland Islands. They would deploy the ship's main weapon against the Sycorax in 2006.[460]

Summer, a former attendee at the "Human-Be-In" rock festival in 1967, spent thirty years on the run from the mysterious gray-suited men. She settled in the American Northwest, but the fourth Doctor rescued Summer from the gray men as they arrived to kill her.[461]

c 1997 - THE PIT[462] **->** UNIT were called in to investigate an alien skeleton discovered on Salisbury Plain. The seventh Doctor and William Blake arrived via a space-time tear, and the Doctor feared the skeleton wasn't entirely dormant. Hunters riding batlike creatures came through the tear and tore apart a passenger airliner just outside Bristol. The Doctor and Blake travelled to the Yssgaroth's domain, then into the future.

1997 - INFINITE REQUIEM[463] **->** Twenty-one-year-old Tilusha Meswani died shortly after giving birth to her child Sanjay, who was really the Sensopath named Kelzen - an immensely powerful, psionic being. Kelzen grew rapidly to adulthood and gained empathy with humanity. It agreed to help the seventh Doctor fight another Sensopath on Gadrell Minor in 2387.

Hammerson Plastics PLC came out of nowhere to corner the market in plastics in six months. The success was credited to automation techniques, but the organisation was a front for an Auton production facility.[464]

The Conspiracy Channel broadcast *The Last Days of Hitler?*, written and directed by Claire Aldwych, on 12th August, 1997.[465] The only Recoronation in British history took place on 23rd November, 1997. Queen Elizabeth II was formally restored to the throne following Xznaal's usurpation of the crown.[466]

---

and remain friendly enough that Cliff gave Jo a present on the first anniversary after he left her - Jo is using her maiden name of Grant, having been formerly known as Jo Jones. Matthew would appear to be Jo and Cliff's only child, contradicting the shedload of offspring they have in *SJA: Death of the Doctor*.
458 Dating *Auton* (Auton film #1) - The story was released in 1997, and seems contemporary. Lockwood says that the Nestenes are using "a bit of slurry" left over from a body they tried to create "decades ago" - presumably a reference to *Spearhead from Space*.
459 "Ten years" before *Army of Ghosts*.
460 Also "ten years" before *Army of Ghosts*, and elaborating on the super-weapon used in *The Christmas Invasion*.
461 *Wonderland*
462 Dating *The Pit* (NA #12) - The Doctor and the poet William Blake travel to the 1990s, apparently after the Doctor has met Brigadier Bambera in *Battlefield*.
463 Dating *Infinite Requiem* (NA #36) - It is "1997".
464 "A couple of years" before "Plastic Millennium".
465 *The Shadow in the Glass*
466 *The Dying Days*, first mentioned in *Christmas on a Rational Planet*.
THE MONARCHY: Different stories say different things about who is the British monarch around the turn of the millennium. Lethbridge-Stewart refers to the King in *Battlefield*, which is set in the late twentieth

century. *Happy Endings* specifies that King Charles ruled at the turn of the millennium. There is a King when Mariah Learman seizes power in *The Time of the Daleks*, and by the time of *Trading Futures*. In *Revenge of the Judoon*, the tenth Doctor forecasts the reigns of Charles III and Queen Camilla, and King William V.
However, Queen Elizabeth II still reigns in *Head Games* (set in 2001) and *Voyage of the Damned* (set in 2008). *Christmas on a Rational Planet* refers to the "Recoronation", apparently implying that Elizabeth II abdicated in favour of Charles, but - for reasons we can only speculate on - was restored to the throne soon afterwards. *The Dying Days* (set just after *Battlefield*) offers a different reason for the Recoronation: the Queen was usurped by the Ice Warrior Xznaal.
In the *Doctor Who* universe, there's a Princess Mary who's 19 at time *Rags* is set (p158). While it isn't stated, she's clearly a senior royal and by birth, so the obvious inference is that she's the Queen's daughter.
467 Dating *Touched by an Angel* (NSA #47) - The exact day is given (p95).
468 *Christmas on a Rational Planet*. "Morley" is presumably the same as the "Paul" whom Sarah is dating but not married to in *Interference*, set two years previous in 1996. If so, there's no evidence that Sarah and Paul were married for long. When asked by Alan Jackson if she's ever been married (in *SJA: Revenge of the Slitheen*), Sarah replies "No, never found time" - which might sug-

1997 (16th December) - TOUCHED BY AN ANGEL[467] -> The version of Mark Whitaker that was living through the 1990s a second time arranged for his past self to receive a lottery ticket worth £16,000. Rebecca Coles was now engaged to a man named Anthony.

1998

By 1998, Sarah Jane Smith had married a man called Morley, and was a speaker at the Nobel Academy.[468]

In April 1998, Rebecca Coles split with her fiancé after discovering that he was cheating on her. They had already booked holiday in Rome, and so Mark Whitaker agreed to go with her. He paid for his half from the £16,000 lottery winnings his future self had provided.[469] In 1998, the Japanese set up the Nikkei 5 station in the Antarctic to measure carbon dioxide levels.[470] Margaret Thatcher might have returned to power at some point.[471]

Paul Travers reviewed a Johnny Chess concert in the 18/7/98 *NME*.[472] A Kulan evaluation team crashed in Norway in 1998, split into two factions and began work supporting two rival space flight enterprises. The pro-invasion group helped entrepreneur Pierre Yves-Dudoin in the construction of his Star Dart shuttle, and the more benign faction sided with the lucrative Arthur Tyler III in building a Planet Hopper.[473]

In 1998, humanity's average life expectancy was sixty-six years, five months and thirty-three days. The Three Families had located the Blessing in the mid-90s; Angelo Colasanto and his granddaughter Olivia intercepted a message indicating as much in 1998.[474]

The Uvodni-Malakh War ended.[475] **The Pharos Para-Science Institute was established to study paranormal phenomena.**[476] Members of Drast Speculation Initiative

Fourteen - alien specualtors who would manipulate a target planet's economy and culture until it came under their control - established themselves on Earth.[477]

On 27th June, 1998, Torchwood obtained a corpse belonging to a member of Cell 114.[478]

1998 - SYSTEM SHOCK[479] -> Virtually every computer on Earth now used the operating system Vorell, developed by I^2. The owner of I^2, 43-year-old Lionel Stabfield, quickly became the fifth richest man in the world. His company bought the rights to every major work of art, releasing images of them on interactive discs. The new technology allowed flat-panel, interactive television and the recordable CD-ROM to be perfected. Sales of computer equipment rocketed still further.

All computers were joined up to the Hubway, a formalised version of the Internet. As Hubway went online, though, chaos broke out: aeroplanes crashed at Heathrow as air traffic control systems failed, the Astra satellite was sent into a new orbit, the Library of Congress catalogue and all its backups were wiped, the computer facilities of the First National Bank of China were obliterated. Instruments at Nunton told technicians that the reactor had gone to meltdown. The head of MI5, Veronica Halliwell, was assassinated. Jonah Cosgrove, former sixties superspy, succeeded her as the head of MI5.[480]

This was all part of the plan of the Voracians, cybernetic reptilians from Vorella. They planned to use the sentient software Voractyll to take control of the Earth. The fourth Doctor, Sarah and Harry helped to defeat them.

c 1998 - OPTION LOCK[481] -> President Dering was now in the White House, with Jack Michaels serving as vice-president.

---

gest that their marriage was annulled, that Sarah means she "never found time to commit to a relationship of wedlock", or that she's withholding the entire truth from Alan (whom she's just met and has no reason to be all that forthcoming with) or some combination of all of those options. If Sarah and Paul's marriage fizzled out quickly, it could owe to what Sarah implies in *SJA: Invasion of the Bane* - that there was "only ever one man for me [i.e. the Doctor]. After him, nothing compared..." - even if she comes to reevaluate that position while under supernatural influence (*SJA: The Wedding of Sarah Jane Smith*).

469 *Touched by an Angel*
470 *Iceberg*
471 In *Transit*, there's a history book called *Thatcher: The Wilderness Years*.
472 *Timewyrm: Revelation*
473 *Escape Velocity*
474 *TW: Miracle Day*
475 "Twenty years" before *SJA: The Lost Boy*. Despite the

similar name, no overt connection has been made between the Pharos Institute and the Pharos Project seen in *Logopolis*.

476 "Ten years" before *SJA: Warriors of Kudlak*.
477 "Ten years" before the linking material in *The Story of Martha*. As the Drast are defeated during the year of time that's erased in *Last of the Time Lords*, it's unclear what ended their plans in the actual history.
478 Per Alex Hopkins' report on Torchwood.org.uk.
479 Dating *System Shock* (MA #11) - When asked, a barman, Rod, informs the Doctor that this is "1998". The Doctor goes on to tell Sarah that in that particular year, "nothing of interest happened as far as I remember". It is "twenty odd years" after Sarah's time, and she muses that a "greying, mid-forties" future version of herself is alive in 1998, which the epilogue confirms.
480 Cosgrove has "not left his desk in London for nearly twenty years" before *Trading Futures*.
481 Dating *Option Lock* (EDA #8) - It's "present day England" according to the blurb.

The Khameirian-sponsored brotherhood, founded in the thirteenth century, had many members in positions of power. They sought to trigger a nuclear conflict that would produce the energy needed for the Khameirians to recorporealise. A brotherhood member launched an unauthorised nuclear strike from Krejikistan, which compelled the Americans to reveal the nuke-killing Station Nine as they nullified the threat. The US subsequently turned Station Nine over to the United Nations.

The brotherhood's leader, Norton Silver, forced the eighth Doctor to relocate the TARDIS to Station Nine to launch a nuclear strike from there. Britain's Captain Pickering died while destroying Station Nine to prevent this, an act that also killed Silver and the Khameirian core

within him. A month later, Sam Jones learned that Silver's widow was pregnant, and worried the Khameirian taint might have passed to the child.

1998 (11th-12th August) - TOUCHED BY AN ANGEL[482] -> The older Mark Whitaker had started a consultancy company, and used his foreknowledge of the future to make millions. He was a partial investor in *Mama Mia!* The eleventh Doctor, Amy and Rory helped the older Mark to lock his younger self and Rebecca out on a balcony for the evening - and the two of them took the opportunity to cement their budding relationship.

AMERICAN PRESIDENTS IN THE DOCTOR WHO UNIVERSE: As with British political history, *Doctor Who* presents a version of American politics that's a mix of historical fact and whimsy. *Interference* lists the recent American Presidents as Carter, Reagan, Bush, Clinton, Dering (*Option Lock*, around 1998), Springsteen (*Eternity Weeps*, 2003) and Norris (*Cat's Cradle: Warhead*, circa 2007 or 2009). *Death Comes to Time* has George W Bush as President, and stories including *Trading Futures* and *Unregenerate!* mention features of his presidency such as the War on Terror and the Iraq War. President Arthur Winters appears in *The Sound of Drums*, set in June 2008, but he's assassinated. Obama is president in *The End of Time* (TV), which occurs at Christmas 2009, and in *The Forgotten Army* (p129), set in 2010.

A discrepancy is that in *SJA: The Secrets of the Stars* (set at November 2009), the president is hypnotised because he's a Cancer - in real life, Obama was born 4th August and is a Leo. (Possibly, the news report of "the president" walking out of the White House is simply wrong.) Norris doesn't fit the bill of being a Cancer either; he was born 10th March. Funnily enough, George W. Bush was born 6th July, and has the correct astrological symbol.

Bad Wolf mentions President Schwarzenegger (at present, Arnold is barred from the US presidency since he wasn't born an American citizen). *Trading Futures* has President Mather in charge around 2015.

It is a little tricky to juggle the aforementioned presidents without inferring any impeachments or assassinations. Still, assuming the same fixed terms, elections would take place in, and be won by:

1996: Dering (meaning Clinton was a single termer in the *Doctor Who* universe.)

2000: Springsteen

2004: George W Bush (another single termer in the *Doctor Who* universe - this time missing the first term he had historically. This would set *Death Comes to Time* a couple of years after it was released, but that's certainly not ruled out by the story. The reference in *Neverland* claiming the "wrong man became President" was meant to refer to Bush winning in 2000, which

might be relevant - if highly ambiguous - in this context.)

Winters, then Norris, or vice-versa (US presidential elections are always held in November, so Winters being president in June 2008 would seem to indicate - unless one discards *Death Comes to Time* entirely, in which case Bush was probably never president and Winters was elected in 2004 - that Bush failed to complete his entire term. It's tempting to think that Norris takes office following Winters' death in June 2008, as the dating for *Cat's Cradle: Warhead* is probably flexible enough to accommodate that. In which case, Norris only serves for a few months until the 2008 election. This is somewhat cleaner than thinking that Norris followed Bush and that Winters - somehow - followed Norris, which would result in another unnamed person being president after Winters is killed.

(Winters' statement in *The Sound of Drums* that he's "president elect" must be his way of telling the Toclafane "I'm the elected representative of my people" - a US politician would never use this term in such a fashion, as Americans use the term "president elect" to indicate someone who's won a presidential election but has not yet taken office. The US Constitution dictates that a president elect can only exist between early November and the following January - anyone who becomes president via the death, incapacitation, resignation or Congressional ousting of the sitting president would immediately take office.)

2008: Obama (wins the November 2008 election as he did in real life. At time of writing, and barring further appearances by Obama on screen, the extreme social and economic upheaval seen in *TW: Miracle Day* in 2011 - including the cratering of the economy and the construction of mass incinerators for the near-dead - calls into question whether *any* sitting president could win reelection the next year, which might result in Obama being a single-termer.)

2012: Mather

2016 or 2020: Schwarzenegger (he'd be 69 or 73 on taking office.)

Their party affiliation can perhaps be inferred - if

Thomas "Hex" Schofield, a companion of the seventh Doctor, was born to Cassandra Schofield on 12th October, 1998.[483] **When Rose Tyler was 12, she received a red bicycle for Christmas.**[484]

1999

Adelaide Brooke, the woman destined to become the commander of the first Martian colony, was born on 12th May, 1999.[485] A rain of frogs was reported in San Francisco.[486]

w - The Great Houses dispatched Chris Cwej to curtail the activities of Faction Hollywood. Cwej bested Faction Hollywood's leader, Michael Brookhaven, in combat during the Hollywood Bowl Shooting incident of 1999; Faction Hollywood was not expected to prosper after Brookhaven's downfall.[487]

In 1999, a division of Phicorp purchased the land in Shanghai containing the Blessing - part of the Three Families' preparation to destroy the world's economy and rebuild it under their control.[488] In June 1999, James Lawson of Torchwood Cardiff improved upon a formula supplied by Jack Harkness, and did the early field tests on the amnesia drug Retcon.[489]

c 1999 - FP: WARLORDS OF UTOPIA[490] **->** Marcus Americanius Scriptor arrived in the True Earth to track down August Hitler, who had been spirited away from his own parallel universe. The Little Hitler was in South America. Scriptor killed him, then wrote an account of his long life.

1999 - AUTON 2: SENTINEL / AUTON 3: AWAKENING[491] **->** The Nestene essence that escaped from The Warehouse two years previous established an Auton contingent on the remote Sentinel Island, home to the best preserved of the ancient Nestene chambers. Lockwood used a psychic seed the Nestene had planted in his mind to absorb the long-dormant Nestene beneath the island, and prevented it from summoning the entire Nestene consciousness to Earth.

Soon afterwards, all of the New York Exchange's systems were wiped, the Nasdac went into freefall and Flight 4906 came down over Berlin owing to computer error. Some surviving Autons tried to channel through Lockwood's mind a pulse that would awaken all the dormant Nestene on Earth, but he stopped their scheme by killing himself.

1999 (July) - THE KING OF TERROR[492] **->** The alien Jex sought to conquer Earth, and had fronted the communications conglomerate InterCom to this end. They were secretly stockpiling plutonium to detonate and raise Earth's temperature to better accommodate their race. The Canavitchi, formerly enslaved to the Jex, worked to exterminate their former masters. The Brigadier received reports of extra-terrestrial involvement in California, and summoned the fifth Doctor, Tegan and Turlough to UNIT's Los Angeles office.

The Doctor and his allies brought InterCom to ruin as rival Jex and Canavitchi warfleets showed up in Earth orbit. The Doctor used Earth's satellite network to create a planetary defence shield as the warfleets slaughtered one another and departed. The Doctor advised the Brigadier to co-ordinate with the American CIA and help capture the Jex and Canavitchi agents still at-large.

Dering beats Clinton (rather than, say, Clinton stepping aside or being impeached), he's a Republican. The real-life Springsteen is a Democrat. Winters is almost doubtlessly a Republican, as his portrayal in *The Sound of Drums* marks him as a conservative. The real-life Chuck Norris is a Republican. Obama is a Democrat. Mather served in Bush's Cabinet, so he's likely a Republican (only on very rare occasions will a Cabinet member hail from a different party, although it happened under Clinton and Obama). We might assume that Schwarzenegger wouldn't stand against a fellow Republican, so Mather serves two terms.

482 Dating *Touched by an Angel* (NSA #47) - The exact days are given (pgs 103, 126).

483 *The Harvest, Project: Destiny*. Actor Philip Oliver was born 4th June, 1980, making him - relatively speaking - about a year older than the character he's playing.

484 It's implied in *The Doctor Dances* that the Doctor gave it to her.

485 *The Waters of Mars*

486 *Iris: The Panda Invasion*. No such rain has occurred in real life, but this might be a reference to the frog downpour in *Magnolia* (1999).

487 *FP: The Book of the War*

488 *TW: Miracle Day*

489 From *The Torchwood Archives*. Lawson is cited as dead in *TW: In the Shadows*, and is presumably one of the slain Torchwood staff in *TW: Fragments*.

490 Dating *FP: Warlords of Utopia* (FP novel #3) - Scriptor gives the date.

491 Dating *Auton 2: Sentinel* and *Auton 3: Awakening* (Auton films #2-3) - It's repeatedly said in *Auton 2* that "two years" have passed since *Auton*, so it's a year in the future of *Auton 2*'s release in 1998. Events in *Auton 3* (released in 1999) continue from there.

492 Dating *The King of Terror* (PDA #37) - It's "1 July 1999" (p5).

1999 (July) - DOMINION[493] **->** Department C19 had resumed active service by this time.

Professor Jennifer Nagle, a UNIT scientist, experimented with captured alien equipment at a C19 base in Sweden. She accidentally created a dimensional wormhole into a pocket universe named the Dominion. The larger universe expanded into the Dominion, threatening many races there. Some of the carnivorous Ruin fled through the wormhole to Earth, but Earth's higher gravity killed them.

The Dominion was completely eradicated, but the eighth Doctor evacuated fourteen of the frog-like T'hilli and their Queen to a habitable planet, saving the race from extinction. The wormhole terminated, but an energy backlash destroyed the C19 base and killed Nagle.

(=) In July 1999, an encounter with Lord Roche's dead TARDIS inflicted young Ezekiel Child with Jeapes' Syndrome, a condition in which a person matures backwards in time rather than forward. Child was 21 in 1999, but age 46 in 1972, and failed to notice anything odd about this. The Doctor's involvement retroactively averted the Child anomaly.

In 1999, a lingering side-effect of temporal interference turned the *Independent on Sunday* newspaper into the *Sunday Telegraph*.[494] Shortly after Joseph Heller's death, documents were found among his effects with the recollections of Alan Turing, Graeme Greene and Heller himself of their encounter with aliens in Dresden, 1945.[495]

w - 1999 - THE TAKING OF PLANET 5[496] **->** UNIT was called in to investigate an anomaly in the Antarctic that had been detected by satellite, and discovered a protoplasmic creature inside an alien structure. The eighth Doctor, Fitz and Compassion eventually arrived from twelve million years in the past, where they'd been thwarting the machinations of a group of future Time Lords.

c 1999 - "Darkness Falling" / "Distractions" / "The Mark of Mandragora"[497] **->** The party drug M - Mandrake - was a problem. Captain Muriel Frost and Sergeant Jasper Bean of UNIT discovered a Mandrake factory at the popular Falling Star nightclub in London, but an energy creature killed Bean.

The Mandragora Helix was warping the TARDIS' structure and drawing it towards Earth. The seventh Doctor and Ace found themselves at the Falling Star with Frost, and Lethbridge-Stewart vouched for their identities via video link from Geneva. Returning to the Falling Star, they arrived to see the Helix energy manifesting in a bid to take over the Earth, then the universe. The Helix started to kill the clubbers, whose will had been sapped by the Mandrake

493 Dating *Dominion* (EDA #22) - On p35, Fitz reads a newspaper dated 31st July, 1999.
494 *The Suns of Caresh*, both the Child anomaly and Jo's observation.
495 *The Turing Test.* Heller died 12th December, 1999.
496 Dating *The Taking of Planet 5* (EDA #28) - It's "1 October 1999" (p21).
497 Dating "Darkness Falling" / "Distractions" / "The Mark of Mandragora" (*DWM* #167-172) - It's "the end of the twentieth century", but not (as far as we're told) New Year's 1999 itself. It's after *Battlefield*, and Mandrake first appeared in 1997 (so the story takes place after that). "Darkness Falling" and "Distractions", both prologues to the main story, went untitled in *The Mark of Mandragora* graphic novel.
498 Dating *Zygons: Homeland* (BBV audio #15) - The audio was released in 1999 and seems contemporary.
499 Dating *Krynoids: The Root of All Evil* (BBV audio #18) - The audio came out in 1999 and seems contemporary, including mention of *The X-Files* and the fact that mobile use is not so universal that the protagonists, when trapped on the farm, can just call for help.
500 *TW: Children of Earth*
501 Dating *Touched by an Angel* (NSA #47) - The exact days are given (pgs 129, 133).
502 "The Forgotten"
503 The short story "That Time I Nearly Destroyed the World Whilst Looking for a Dress" (from *Short Trips: Past*

Tense, 2004), here mentioned because it's relevant to the continuity of *The Five Companions*.
504 *Beautiful Chaos* (p189). In a case of very awkward math, 31st December, 1999, is said to be "eight years" prior to 2009.
505 Dating "Plastic Millennium" (*DWM Winter Special 1994*) - The date is given. It's tempting to link the contents of the phial with the Doctor's "anti plastic" in *Rose*.
506 Dating *Millennial Rites* (MA #15) - The story revolves around the date, first confirmed on p34.
507 Dating *TW: Fragments* (TW 2.12) - The day and exact time of Alex's death are given. There's no sign of reality warping at midnight of the New Year per *Doctor Who - The Movie*, but this could simply owe to San Francisco being about eight hours behind Cardiff.
508 *TW: Fragments*
509 Dating *Iris: The Panda Invasion* (Iris audio #2.4) - The day and year are given. Bits of this audio resonate with *Doctor Who - The Movie*: Iris is taken to a hospital, and an x-ray says that she's got two livers (rather than two hearts); the theft of a fancy dress costume is reported; and it's said that "Daphne" (a reference to Daphne Ashbrook, who played Grace) is "on shift". Even so, it's not specified that Iris is taken to the same hospital as the wounded seventh Doctor, and there's no reason why both stories can't occur together, especially as the authorities ignore reports of the evil Pandas. Panda and Iris are reunited *Iris: The Claws of Santa*.

drug, and Frost ordered in the UNIT troops. The Doctor was convinced the Helix had won, but the circuit broke. It appeared that the TARDIS had disintegrated, but it rematerialised at UNIT HQ a few days later.

The very public threat convinced the United Nations to increase UNIT's powers and put it on a more public footing. A new United Nations team - Foreign Hazard Duty - was set up to deal with problems that had to be kept more secret. Muriel Frost was promoted to Major.

1999 - ZYGONS: HOMELAND[498] **->** UN military adviser Guy Dean and his allies stopped a group of Zygons from unleashing a shoal of Skarasen upon the world, but perished while self-destructing the Zygons' spacecraft.

1999 - KRYNOIDS: THE ROOT OF ALL EVIL[499] **->** The Chase Foundation had a website that provided some information on Krynoids. Eve Black, a biologist working for the Ministry of Agriculture, destroyed two Krynoids that hatched on an isolated Yorkshire farm.

Steven Carter - the son of Joe and Alice Carter (née Sangster), and the grandson of Jack Harkness - was born on 4th October, 1999.[500]

1999 (29th and 31st October) - TOUCHED BY AN ANGEL[501] **->** The older Mark Whitaker used his clout to secretly get his younger self a job with the law firm of Pollard & Bryce. The younger Mark Whitaker proposed to his beloved, Rebecca Coles.

The Millennium

The turn of the twenty-first century was one of the Doctor's favourite parts of Earth's history, and he suspected that he had visited it more times than he'd been on the *Titanic*.[502]

Ben Jackson's wife was "gone". Polly Wright was estranged from her son, Mikey. On the last day of 1999, Ben and Polly acknowledged their love for one another at a house that belonged to the Doctor, where they had gathered with the second Doctor and Jamie.[503]

Dana Morgan, a thrall of the Mandragora Helix, heightened the prominence of his company, MorganTech, on a news special broadcast that was live on 31st December, 1999.[504]

1999 (31st December) - "Plastic Millennium"[505] **->** The seventh Doctor and Mel gatecrashed a New Year's Eve hosted by Alisha Hammerson, director of the world's largest plastics factory, for the world's business leaders. Hammerson gassed the CEOs and planned to replace them with Autons. The Doctor brewed up a phial that he used to destroy the meteor that represented the link to the Nestene, and Hammerson melted.

1999 / 2000 (30th December to 1st January) - MILLENNIAL RITES[506] **->** Ashley Chapel had worked for International Electromatics before forming his own company, ACL. Following the collapse of I², ACL quickly bought up all their hardware and software patents, and Chapel became a multi-millionaire. He funded the construction of the new Millennium Hall on the banks of the Thames, and began work on a powerful computer program - "the Millennium Codex" - that would use quantum mnemonics and block transfer computation. This would change the laws of physics to those of the universe of Saraquazel, which was created from the ashes of our own. Elsewhere, Dame Anne Travers became worried about the return of the Great Intelligence. She attempted to banish the sentience, but inadvertently summoned it.

On the stroke of midnight, 31st December, 1999, magic returned to the world as the Intelligence and Saraquazel fused over London, transforming the city into an aeons-old battleground between the forces of three factions: the Abraxas, Magick and Technomancy. After only ten minutes of real time, the new laws unravelled and the world was returned to normal. Fifteen people had died. Saraquazel took Chapel back with him to his own universe.

1999 (31st December) - TW: FRAGMENTS[507] **-> Alex Hopkins of Torchwood used an alien device to foresee the future... and was so horrified by events to come, he mercy-killed his teammates and then himself on the stroke of midnight, the year 2000. The unkillable Jack Harkness, having given Torchwood Cardiff a century of service, assumed command of it.**

Jack subsequently severed all links between Torchwood Cardiff and Torchwood London.[508]

1999 (31st December) - IRIS: THE PANDA INVASION[509] **->** Iris and Panda went to San Francisco, New Year's Eve, 1999, to find the biggest, happiest party in history - but Iris opened up a multi-dimensional rift after spilling gin into her bus' engine. Lional Pandeau, a version of Panda from a parallel universe, was drawn through the rift and poured more gin into the engine, widening the rift and summoning an army consisting of versions of himself/Panda from alternate realities. Parts of San Francisco were beset by flying vampire Pandas from five million years in the future, as well as the lumbering monstrosity Panda-zilla. Panda pulled Lionel and himself into the rift, sealing it and returning the other Pandas to their native realities. Iris went in search of her lost friend as San Francisco authorities dismissed reports of the Pandas as a hoax or part of the millennium festivities.

1999/2000 (30th December to 1st January) DOCTOR WHO - THE MOVIE[510] **->** The seventh Doctor was transporting the Master's remains to Gallifrey from Skaro when the Master - now a gelatinous creature - forced the TARDIS to make an emergency landing. The Doctor was shot in San Francisco and died on the operating table when surgeons misunderstood his alien physiology, regenerating into his eighth incarnation. The Master took over the body of an ambulance worker. He attempted to steal the Doctor's remaining lives by use of the TARDIS' Eye of Harmony, and his scheme threatened to destroy the entire planet. The Doctor stopped the Master with the help of heart surgeon Grace Holloway, and the Master was sucked into the TARDIS' Eye.

UNIT spread a cover story blaming the freak effects caused by the opening of the TARDIS' Eye of Harmony on "freak fluctuations in the Earth's magnetic pole".[511]

2000 (Saturday, 1st January) - MILLENNIUM SHOCK[512] **->** Silver Bullet Solutions developed chips to help combat the Y2K bug, but this was a front by the Voracians, who were trying to re-assemble the sentient computer virus Voractyll and seize control of Earth's computers. The Silver Bullet chips exacerbated the switch-over from 1999 to 2000, temporarily cutting power in Malaysia, Auckland and parts of Britain, and jamming Hong Kong's traffic. The fourth Doctor, working with MI5 agent Harry Sullivan, re-programmed the Silver Bullet chips to also endow Voractyll with a Y2K sensitivity. The creature terminated, and the Voracians, serving as part of Voractyll's command nodes, perished also.

Disgraced Prime Minister Terry Brooks tried to exploit the chaos and declare martial law to advance his private agenda. Officially, it was said that his Cabinet lost faith in him, and he resigned "for personal reasons". Philip Cotton, Brooks' deputy, was appointed his successor.

2000 (1st January) - "The Forgotten"[513] **->** The fourth Doctor brought the second Romana to Paris again, this time for the turn of the millennium. They saw a mime vanish into a space-time portal and followed him, meeting soldiers from 1810. Together, they disturbed the sanctum of Taureau the Minotaur, who demanded the answer to his riddles in return for the key to the portal. The Doctor pickpocketed the key, and Taureau was destroyed when he opened the door.

At the turn of the Millennium, the Brigadier became a media icon as he led King Charles' troops in a blockade of Westminster Bridge. The King offered him a role in the Provisional Cabinet, but he declined.[514]

The Twenty-First Century

"The twenty-first century is when everything changes, and you've gotta be ready..."[515]

The nonprofit organisation Livingspace was formed at the beginning of the twenty-first century.[516] News interpretation software sifted the media for the user's own preferences. Televisions could be set so that news bulletins automatically interrupted regular broadcasts.[517]

Early in the twenty-first century, Britain joined the Ecu,

510 Dating *Doctor Who - The Movie* (27.0) - The date is first given when Chang Lee fills out the Doctor's medical paperwork. On screen, the Master looks like a gelatinous snake, although *The Eight Doctors* attributes this to his swallowing a "deathworm".
511 *Tales from the Vault*
512 Dating *Millennium Shock* (PDA #22) - It is "Christmas Eve" (p64).
513 Dating "The Forgotten" (IDW *DW* mini-series #2) - The Doctor and Romana are here to see the Millennium celebrations. While it isn't specifically cited as being New Year's Day, a sign on a structure that's presumably meant to be the Eiffel Tower says "2000", and the Doctor wishes his opponent, "Happy New Year".
514 *Happy Endings*
515 Captain Jack, *Torchwood* Series 1 and 2.
516 *Seeing I* (p86).
517 *Cat's Cradle: Warhead, System Shock.*
518 The ecu is in use by *Iceberg*, at the exchange rate of one ecu to two dollars. In *Warlock*, the drug enforcement agent Creed McIlveen has a suitcase full of "EC

paper money", although Sterling is still used on a day-to-day basis.
519 *The Shadow of the Scourge*
520 *Psi-ence Fiction*
521 *So Vile a Sin*
522 *Blink.* Allowing for wherever Sally's taste in DVD entertainment might take her, Billy must have inserted the Easter Eggs over the course of a few years at least, and prior to 2007.
523 *Tooth and Claw* (TV).
524 *The Taking of Chelsea 426*
525 "The Immortal Emperor"
526 *The Mind Robber.* Zoe was a fan, which would seem to imply that she is from the year 2000, but see the dating notes on *The Wheel in Space. Alien Bodies* says the adventures of the Karkus are still running in the 2050s.
527 *Christmas on a Rational Planet*, via *The Mind Robber* and *The Wheel in Space. The Harvest* has the Wheels operating in 2021.
528 *Escape Velocity*, referenced as occurring "last year".
529 "Five years" before *SJS: Fatal Consequences.* The

the single European Currency.[518] The pacifying gas pacificus was developed in the twenty-first century.[519] Walton Hummer was a popular three-foot tall kazoo player from the twenty-first century.[520] The musician Sting was assassinated in the early twenty-first century.[521]

Since 1969, Billy Shipton had "got into" publishing, then video, then DVD production. On the tenth Doctor's instructions, he secretly inserted Easter Eggs onto seventeen DVDs that Sally Sparrow would come to own in future.[522]

The Doctor theorised that if Queen Victoria was infected by an alien werewolf cell, it might take "one hundred" years to mature in her children, and "be ready" by the early twenty-first century.[523]

The broadcast journalist Riley Smalls was cryo-frozen in the early twenty-first century, and would be revived as a Cryogen in the twenty-sixth.[524] Archaeologists excavated the throne room containing the robotic version of Emperor Qin Shi Huang in the early twenty-first century.[525]

2000

By the year 2000, the *Hourly Tele-press* kept the world's population up to date with events around the globe. One of the *Tele-press*' most popular features was the strip-cartoon adventures of The Karkus.[526]

The first Space Wheel was constructed in 2000.[527] In the same year, Arthur Tyler III was working on the Space Dart and Earthrise private space projects. Diagnosed with terminal cancer, he threw himself into his task.[528]

Based upon *The Book of Tomorrows*, the White and Crimson Chapters of the Orphans of the Future both believed that aliens would return to Earth in the year 2000. When this failed to happen, the Chapters fell into a philosophical crisis, and their representatives met for the first time in a century. They increasingly focused upon mention in the *Book* of a human herald - variously identified as "Sarah" and "SJS" - who would serve as a harbinger of the aliens' return. They increasingly believed that Sarah Jane Smith was this very herald.[529]

NASA discovered the six-billion-year-old Cthalctose Museum on the Moon. Construction started on Tranquillity

Base to better study the alien artifact, and there were regular moonshots to service it.[530] *The Greytest Hips of Johnny Chess* was released in the early 2000s.[531]

Henry Louis Noone, a friend of Ace, was born on 10th February, 2000.[532] When Thomas "Hex" Schofield was two, his mum left him in Bolton with her mother, Hilda Schofield, while she sought work in London.[533] When Eve Pritchard was four, she was struck by a car, and entered a near-death state in which the Mi'en Kalarash inserted a shard of itself into her mind. Over the next twenty years, it influenced her to develop Rapid-Emotional Programming technology.[534]

Hokrala Corp, a law firm in the forty-ninth century, believed that Torchwood and humanity as a whole would bungle the challenges of the twenty-first century, and wanted to sue Earth for a mismanagement of history. To this end, Hokrala commenced, once every year since the turn of the century, trying to land a writ on - or otherwise assassinate - Captain Jack Harkness.[535]

(=) 2000 - "The Glorious Dead"[536] -> In an alternate timeline, Paradost was a planetary museum that celebrated a million alien races. Earth, known as Dharkan, was a wasteland ruled by Cardinal Morningstar - who the Doctor previously knew as Katsura Sato. The eighth Doctor, Izzy and Kroton were on Paradost when it was invaded. Kroton left the Doctor's company to take control of a reality-bending device known as the Omniversal Spectrum, and restored the established timeline.

2000 - SONTARANS: OLD SOLDIERS[537] -> Brak had now been held captive for eighty years, and had lived longer than any Sontaran in history. Captain Alice Wells of UNIT escorted Brak to the Weapons Crisis Conference in Geneva, where he was to testify concerning his ties to Kobalt Blue. Brak planned on providing the secret of harnessing Kobalt Blue, but before he could do so, a Sontaran operative executed him for cowardice.

"alien visit" the Chapters were expecting (i.e. the return of the Mandragora Helix) actually happened on schedule in "The Mark of Mandragora", but, following the Helix's defeat by the seventh Doctor and Ace, the Chapters had no way of knowing this.
530 "The last three years" before *Eternity Weeps*.
531 *Benny: The Sword of Forever*
532 *A Death in the Family*
533 The blurb for *Project: Destiny* says that Cassie left for London in 1999, but Nimrod says that this hap-

pened "two years" after Hex was born in October 1998.
534 "Two decades" before *House of Blue Fire*.
535 *TW: The Undertaker's Gift*
536 Dating "The Glorious Dead" (*DWM* #287-296) - The year isn't specified, but it is the "present day".
537 Dating *Sontarans: Old Soldiers* (BBV audio #22) - The audio was released in February 2000 and seems contemporary. Brak repeatedly says that it's been "eighty years" since World War I.

? 2000 - TIME AND THE RANI[538] **->** The newly regenerated seventh Doctor and Mel prevented the Rani from creating a Time Manipulator - a world-sized cerebral mass, with immense powers over time and space - on the planet Lakertya. Afterwards, the Rani's bat-like servants, the Tetraps, rebelled and forcibly took her back to their homeworld, Tetrapyriabus, so that she could develop additional supplies of plasma for them...

2000 - THE RANI REAPS THE WHIRLWIND[538] **->** Tetrapyriabus was once populated with a species not unlike dinosaurs, but these had gone extinct, and so the Tetraps had turned to animal husbandry of other species.

The Rani escaped Tetrapyriabus, but was forced to leave her TARDIS behind. She intended to re-engineer a conventional spacecraft so that it could travel in time, and to then exact revenge upon her former servant, Urak.

c 2000 - GRAVE MATTER[539] **->** The European space probe Gatherer Three explored the outer planets and returned to Earth, where it was discovered to have picked up alien DNA. This was named "Denarian", and seemed to have miraculous medical properties. In actuality, Denarian was an alien creature that possessed bodies to survive. A team of scientists relocated to the Dorsill islands off the south west coast of the UK and began secret experiments

---

538 Dating *Time and the Rani* (24.1) and *The Rani Reaps the Whirlwind* (BBV audio #28) - There isn't much doubt that *The Rani Reaps the Whirlwind* - BBV's sequel to *Time and the Rani*, one of the famously undatable *Doctor Who* TV adventures - takes place in (or, worst case, very near to) 2000. The Tetraps kidnap two humans, Sam and Lucy, from Earth via conventional spacecraft, and the Rani later returns the two of them home via the same means. Sam, a neurochemist, has scientific knowledge on par with 2000 (when the audio was released), and - very tellingly - he refers to the Millennium Dome (completed in 1999, and opened to the public on 1st January, 2000) as a "twenty-first century folly" in London.

Whether or not *Time and the Rani* occurs in the same year is entirely contingent on if any temporal displacement is involved when the Tetraps tie the Rani up and return home in her TARDIS at the end of that story. It's unlikely that the Rani would have given the Tetraps the know-how to pilot her Ship in through space-time in an unfettered fashion - then again, they might know enough to operate the TARDIS on preprogrammed coordinates that do, in fact, involve time travel. The choice remains fairly clean-cut, however: either no time travel happens and *Time and the Rani* occurs in 2000, or time travel *does* occur and the story should once more be designated undatable.

539 Dating *Grave Matter* (PDA #31) - Peri thinks it's the "twentieth century" (p201); there's nothing to suggest it's not set the year the book was published, in 2000.

540 Dating *Imperial Moon* (PDA #34) - "Some time in the early twenty-first century" (p7). The book was published in 2000.

541 Dating *The Marian Conspiracy* - No year is given. Evelyn is from the present day, and has a mobile phone.

542 *100:* "My Own Private Wolfgang"

543 *Doctor Who and the Pirates*

544 Dating *The Spectre of Lanyon Moor* (BF #9) - Lethbridge-Stewart has been retired "a few years now". Evelyn phones one of her friends, so this is her native time. The first meeting of the sixth Doctor and Lethbridge-Stewart is portrayed both here and in *Business Unusual*. Given that the Doctor first meets Mel

in *Business Unusual*, and that he clearly travelled with Evelyn before her, it's fair to assume that from the sixth Doctor's perspective, he first encounters the Brigadier in *The Spectre of Lanyon Moor*. But the Brigadier first meets the sixth Doctor in *Business Unusual*, which takes place about eleven years previous in 1989.

545 Dating *Excelis Rising* (BF *Excelis* series #2) - The story is set a thousand years after *Excelis Dawns* and three hundred before *Excelis Decays*.

546 *TW: Adrift*; Torchwood.org.uk gives the date.

547 Dating *Touched by an Angel* (NSA #47) - The exact day is given (p137).

548 *Verdigris* (p2). *Iris: Wildthyme on Top* suggests that Tom returns to Earth in the mid-90s... about five years, then, before he joined Iris on her travels.

549 *Made of Steel*

550 *Unnatural History* (p33), picking up on a line from *Doctor Who - The Movie*.

551 "Six months" before *SJS: Comeback*, which opens with Sarah Jane at Lavinia's gravesite, very shortly after her funeral. Brendan appeared in *K9 and Company*. Lavinia's death is sometimes implied in *The Sarah Jane Adventures*; *Comeback* and *Ghost Town* are explicit about it. *SJA: The White Wolf*, set in 2010, both confirms Lavinia's death and loosely agrees with the dating given here, mentioning an article Sarah wrote "about five years ago" after her aunt's passing.

The framing sequence of *Millennium Shock*, set in 1998, entails Sarah telling Harry, "I have to get back to Morton Harwood, sort out Aunt Lavinia's things" (p2) - possibly an indicator that Lavinia has died, possibly an indicator that she's still alive but is moving house, or possibly just meaning that Lavinia is leaving for/returning from a lecture tour, and wants Sarah to help her pack/unpack.

552 *Let's Kill Hitler.* No date is given, but Amy, Rory and Mels are all pupils at Leadworth Comprehensive (named in a sign above the anti-bullying poster).

553 *SJA: The Mad Woman in the Attic*

554 *Borrowed Time*

on animals and the local population. The sixth Doctor and Peri found the islands overrun with walking corpses, but the Doctor discovered that a second dose of Denarian cancelled out the first.

c 2000 - IMPERIAL MOON[540] **->** The fifth Doctor and Turlough materialised near Earth's moon to avoid hitting themselves in the Vortex. A time safe aboard the TARDIS opened and revealed a diary purporting to be the log of a Victorian expedition to the moon - which historically did not occur. They went to 1878 to learn the truth.

c 2000 - THE MARIAN CONSPIRACY[541] **->** Time disturbances surrounded history professor Evelyn Smythe. The sixth Doctor met her and concluded that the problem lay with her ancestor John Whiteside-Smith, who lived at the time of Elizabeth I. They departed to investigate.

(=) By Evelyn's time, the immortal Mozart had been producing substandard works for hundreds of years. Some thought that "Mozart" was a shared alias. He'd begun work on his 10,000th symphony (the soundtrack to a remake of *The Italian Job*), had started to use electronic drum kits, had appeared in various Eurovision entries, and, tragically, had discovered hip-hop.[542]

Evelyn Smythe told her student Sally about the time she and the Doctor met some pirates.[543]

c 2000 (October) - THE SPECTRE OF LANYON MOOR[544] **->** Lethbridge-Stewart, occasionally performing surveillance work for UNIT, looked into the latest of a string of mysterious deaths in the Lanyon Moor area. An archaeological expedition there had woken up the Tregannon scout Sancreda after eighteen thousand years of semi-dormancy, and Sancreda sought to use his vast mental abilities to exact revenge on his brother Screfan for abandoning him. The sixth Doctor and Evelyn aided the Brigadier as Sancreda summoned his survey ship from space, but Sancreda discovered that he had inadvertently killed his brother during their initial survey on Earth. Sancreda tried to destroy Earth, but the Brigadier swapped out a crucial component from Sancreda's psionic cannon. The resultant energy backlash destroyed Sancreda and his survey ship.

c 2000 - EXCELIS RISING[545] **->** On the highly-industrialised planet Artaris, border disputes sprang up between the city-states of Gatracht and Calann. The public came to regard "the warlord Grayvorn and his lost treasure" as the stuff of myth, although officials at the Imperial Archives' Black Museum privately acknowledged the tales as true.

The Relic had become the property of the Excelis

Museum, and an Imperial Edict forbade the head curator from turning the object over to anyone beyond the Empress, her Regent or the Etheric Minister. Possibly due to the Relic's presence in the city, mediums were able to commune with the dead.

At the Museum, the sixth Doctor found the former warlord Grayvorn trying to re-acquire the Relic. An altercation between them resulted in a discharge of the Relic's energies, which dissipated Grayvorn's physical form. His consciousness became embedded in the Museum's stone walls, and he waited for someone to die in the museum so he could inhabit their body.

Captain Jack discovered that in addition to disgorging objects, the Rift sometimes relocated people in Cardiff to alien locales. Some later returned through the Rift, mentally unstable or otherwise altered owing to their experiences. On 27th October, 2000, **Jack purchased Flat Holm, a property on an island in the Bristol Channel, to serve as a shelter for such persons.**[546]

2000 (4th November) - TOUCHED BY AN ANGEL[547] **->** The Weeping Angels nearly disrupted the wedding of Mark Whitaker and Rebecca Coles, but the eleventh Doctor, Amy and Rory saw that she got to the church on time. The Doctor wiped Rebecca's memory of their having used the TARDIS four times to achieve this.

In early November 2000, a man named Tom jumped aboard a bus in London and found he'd entered Iris Wildthyme's TARDIS. He became her travelling companion.[548] Martha Jones visited the Millennium Dome with her family and secretly enjoyed it.[549] On Christmas Day 2000, a serious earthquake called the Little Big One hit San Francisco.[550]

2001

Lavinia Smith, Sarah Jane's aunt, died in 2001. Lavinia's ward, Brendan, was in San Francisco at the time. Sarah Jane inherited Lavinia's house and the royalties on her patents.[551]

Amelia Pond's best friend Mels got into trouble in history classes because she kept mentioning the Doctor.[552] **In 2001, Samuel Lloyd's parents died in a car accident. He was sent to the St. Anthony's Children's Home, and became friends with Rani Chandra.**[553]

Following his defeat of Jane Blythe, the eleventh Doctor was deposited on Earth more than five years prior to his starting point. He spent the intervening time waiting to reunite with Amy and Rory in 2007, and foiled a few plots to destroy mankind along the way.[554]

In 2001, the Harvard-Smithsonian Centre for

Astrophysics estimated that a comet that had visited Earth five hundred years ago would return, and that Earth would pass through its tail - the first such event since Halley's Comet in 1910. Sir Donald Wakefield, a billionaire and the leader of the White Chapter, viewed the comet as a sign of salvation. He poured his fortune into building a spacecraft, the *Dauntless*, to make a private journey into space.[555]

The Grid, a means of pooling the unused processing power of Internet computers to create unlimited memory space, came online in 2001. Paul Kairos, a classmate of Melanie Bush, learned to manipulate photons in a way that rendered the transistor and micro-monolithic circuit obsolete. Anjelique Whitefriar stole Kairos' design and patented it as the Whitefriar Lattice.[556]

@ 2001 (February) - ESCAPE VELOCITY[557] **->** Compassion dropped Fitz in London on 6th February, 2001 - two days ahead of his scheduled rendezvous with the amnesiac eighth Doctor. By now, the Doctor owned the St. Louis Bar and Restaurant in London to facilitate his meeting with Fitz. After their rendezvous, the Doctor gave the bar to its manager, Sheff.

Competition between the Kulan factions increased, as the first group to report to the Kulan leadership would be likely to persuade them to either invade or spare Earth.

Anji Kapoor, a 28-year-old futures analyst, took a break in Brussels with her boyfriend Dave and became embroiled in the Kulan conflict. The Doctor, Fitz and Anji allied with the benevolent Kulan faction and blew up Yves-Dudoin's Star Dart. A pro-invasion Kulan member named Fray'kon killed Dave.

A Kulan warfleet arrived in Earth orbit, but the TARDIS completed its century of healing and became functional again. The Doctor, Fitz and Anji travelled to the flagship and tricked the Kulan ships into annihilating one another. Arthur Tyler III and Fray'kon died in the fighting. The TARDIS had departed Earth with Anji aboard, but the Doctor promised to try and return her home...

After many adventures, the Doctor returned Anji home three weeks after she left, and she resumed her life. She would not see him again for eighteen months.[558]

2001 - THE SHADOW IN THE GLASS[559] **->** Historical journalist Claire Aldwych discovered evidence of the Vvormak cruiser located in Turelhampton, England, which

---

555 *SJS: Fatal Consequences, SJS: Dreamland.*
556 *The Quantum Archangel*
557 Dating *Escape Velocity* (EDA #42) - The exact date is given (p26).
558 *Time Zero*
559 Dating *The Shadow in the Glass* (PDA #41) - According to the blurb, it's "2001".
560 Dating *FP: This Town Will Never Let Us Go* (FP novel #1) - The Red Uranium detonation seems to be linked, although this isn't directly established, to the start of humanity's "ghost point" (an era in which humanity's scientific and cultural progress greatly stagnates, and becomes vastly less relevant to the War in Heaven) as detailed in *FP: The Book of the War*. The same text says that the "ghost point" begins in 2001, and while *This Town Will Never Let Us Go* was published in 2003, the story fits either year reasonably well, with the participants displaying a cultural awareness relevant to that time. (For instance, Inangela and Valentine's bafflement as to how Orwell could appear on *The Muppet Show*.) Inangela is presented as very young woman, and she was "15" (p34) when Princess Diana died (in 1997).

The bigger question is to what degree events in *This Town Will Never Let Us Go* are to be taken as actually occurring within the timeline of *Doctor Who* - or within that of *Faction Paradox*, for that matter. To what degree is this book a treatise on culture, not to be taken overly literally? To what degree is the narrator unreliable? Are the timeship's tendrils so interwoven into the town that the town exists in its own little cul-de-sac of history, hence why the national government has no evident response to the town being sometimes pelted by

rockets? All of that said, there's nothing to resolutely rule against *This Town Will Never Let Us Go* being part of the greater *Doctor Who* canon either.

The "Black Man" who supplies Valentine with the Red Uranium previously appeared as an agent of the Celestis in *Alien Bodies*. Page 243 establishes that the timeship buried beneath the town is the same lineage of War-vessel as Compassion, citing her as the mother (conceptually, if nothing else) of future Ships.
561 Dating *The Demons of Red Lodge and Other Stories*: "Special Features" (BF #142d) - The commentary is slated for the 25th Anniversary release of *Doctor Demonic's Tales of Terror* (1976).
562 Dating *Psi-ence Fiction* (PDA #46) - The year isn't given, but there's a modern day setting, with references to (for example) *The Blair Witch Project* and CCTV cameras. The book was released in 2001.
563 Dating *Touched by an Angel* (NSA #47) - The exact day is given (p161).
564 Dating *Project: Twilight* (BF #23) - No year is given, but it's the present day (or close enough) for Evelyn, and Tony Blair is the Prime Minister. *Project: Destiny* says that Cassie went missing on "23rd August, 2001" - as that story was also written by Cavan Scott and Mark Wright, this is presumably the same day that the Doctor and Evelyn visit The Dusk.
565 Dating *Animal* (BF LS #2.5) - Writer Andrew Cartmel scripted the story as taking place in 2011, but this was changed - both in the dialogue and the blurb - to 2001. It's during the school year, and it's after the Doctor and Ace meet Bambera in *Battlefield*.

prompted the sixth Doctor and the Brigadier to investigate. Suspecting Nazi involvement, the Brigadier stole pieces of Hitler and Eva Braun's remains from the State Special Trophy Archive in Moscow for comparison.

The Doctor and his allies discovered the existence of a Nazi organisation at an Antarctic base, led by the son of Adolf Hitler and Eva Braun. The Doctor retrieved the Scrying Glass from the base, but it depicted the Doctor taking Hitler's son back in time to 1945. To fulfill the Glass' visions, the Doctor, the Brigadier, Claire and Hitler's son travelled back to that year.

After their return, the Doctor and the Brigadier helped the sleeping Vvormak awaken and depart Earth. UNIT assisted with breaking up the exposed Fourth Reich cells.

w - c 2001 - FP: THIS TOWN WILL NEVER LET US GO[560] ->

A timeship involved in the War in Heaven buried itself beneath an unnamed town in England, and took root in its culture. Rocket attacks sometimes besieged the town. The public believed that Faction Paradox was a powerful conspiracy group, and Faction iconography was increasingly in use as a fashion statement. An episode of *The Muppet Show* was broadcast that perplexingly featured special guest-star George Orwell (who died in 1950). Orwell's appearance on screen followed a Muppet re-enactment of the Room 101 scene from *1984*, starring Rizzo the Rat.

A paramedic named Valentine Bregman believed that damaging the timeship would trigger a cultural event that would endow the public with a greater awareness of the War. He procured a half-critical mass of Red Uranium - a mythic substance that existed in totemic form. A young woman named Inangela Marrero alternatively wanted to wake the Ship up with a ritual, and tried to stop Bregman. The Red Uranium went off accidentally, and although this only caused a relatively small physical explosion, the totemic nature of the Red Uranium damaged humanity's collective psyche, threatening to curtail its future potential.

Four average people (the so-called "Faction Four") were implicated in the explosion; media coverage of their arrest caused Faction Paradox to be perceived as nothing more than a little band of terrorists with no influence, and its reputation plummeted. Some hope remained that the timeship would repair itself, and that its awakening and launch would help to revive human ingenuity.

2001 - THE DEMONS OF RED LODGE AND OTHER STORIES: "Special Features"[561] ->

The fifth Doctor and Nyssa attended the DVD commentary recording for *Doctor Demonic's Tales of Terror*, and banished the Racht still living within Joanna Munro.

(=) c 2001 - PSI-ENCE FICTION[562] ->

The TARDIS landed at the University of East Wessex, where researcher Barry Hitchens was studying psychic powers. One of his students, Josh Randall, had secretly become a formidable psychic and was viciously making other students hallucinate. Hitchens was being funded by physicist John Finer, who was trying to build a time machine to go back six years to prevent his daughter from dying.

The fourth Doctor inspected the machine and deduced that its use would destroy the timelines. Randall was driven insane, and deemed himself a god. The TARDIS materialised around the time machine, fixing history. Finer never started his time travel research, and the Doctor and Leela, along with everyone else, forgot that these events ever happened.

2001 (May to 5th June) - TOUCHED BY AN ANGEL[563] ->

Rory arrived in May 2001, having been sent there from 2003 by a Weeping Angel. Working to the Doctor's instructions and armed with a psychic credit card, he arranged for a series of lights, cameras and monitors to be set up in a field in April 2003. Rory was astonished at what could be achieved, if one was willing to prepay.

On 5th June, the same Rory tracked down the eleventh Doctor, Amy and his earlier self. The quartet went to 21st April, 2003: the day Rebecca Whitaker was fated to die.

2001 (23rd August) - PROJECT: TWILIGHT[564] ->

The Forge-created vampires Amelia Doory and Reggie Mead now owned and operated The Dusk casino in London, and had converted its basement into a secret medical research facility. The sixth Doctor and Evelyn arrived as Nimrod returned to stalk the vampires, and Amelia convinced the Doctor to help her find a cure to vampirism. However, Amelia instead used the Doctor's discoveries to create The Twilight Virus, an airborne virus capable of converting humans into vampires on contact. She converted Cassie Schofield, now a waitress at The Dusk, into a vampire as a test, but a vengeful Cassie killed Reggie. Nimrod destroyed Amelia's laboratory and the Doctor confiscated the last vial of Twilight Virus. Amelia went missing in the Thames, and the Doctor helped Cassie relocate to a remote part of Norway.

2001 - ANIMAL[565] ->

Margrave University researchers experimented on ravenous tree-like creatures that originated from a crashed spaceship, in a forest in Mauritania. The alien Numlok walled Margrave off with a force field, presenting themselves as peace-loving herbivores who opposed the eating of animal flesh. The seventh Doctor, Ace and Raine investigated Margrave's operations, and met with Brigadier Bambera. They discovered that the Numlok were conducting blood tests on people at Margrave to identify the meat-eaters - and then turn them into a dietary supplement the Numlok required. The Doctor prevented a slaughterhouse by allowing the tree-creatures to consume the Numlok, then sent the Numlok's spaceship - with the tree-creatures aboard - back to the Numlok homeworld as a warning to leave Earth alone.

The Metatraxi had now become the objects of ridicule following the Doctor's irreversibly switching their translator to "surfer dude" mode in 1989, and refused his request for assistance. Raine looked up her father on the Internet... and discovered that he had died. Nonetheless, she continued travelling with the Doctor and Ace.

Raine eventually left the TARDIS to investigate her father's affairs. She was breaking into a hotel safe in Johannesburg when the Metatraxi captured her, and used the rudimentary time technology they'd developed to take her to the future - as bait for the Doctor.[566]

2001 - HEAD GAMES[567] **->** General Lethbridge-Stewart was semi-retired. Ace met up with a future version of the seventh Doctor, who informed her that his evil duplicate Dr Who was planning to assassinate the Queen. The Queen was shot in Sheffield, but wasn't even slightly injured. Meanwhile, UNIT forces were involved in an assault on Buckingham Palace. Brigadier Bambera arrived in a Merlin T-22 VTOL aircraft and penetrated a force field surrounding the palace.

Dr Who had been created by a spiteful Jason, the ex-Master of the Land of Fiction. The Doctor counselled Jason and convinced him to dissipate Dr Who. Jason and Dr Who had rescued Melanie Bush from the planet Avalone in the future - she decried the violent, manipulative methods used by the seventh Doctor and his new companions (Benny, Roz and Chris) to solve problems, and parted on bad terms with him on modern-day Earth.

At this time, Bernice kicked a mangled drinks can into the middle of a path. Four and a half hours later, a young man stumbled over it on his bike and suffered slight bruising. This instigated a chain reaction of small historical alterations that climaxed directly before the Draconian War in the twenty-sixth century.

566 *Earth Aid*
567 Dating *Head Games* (NA #43) - It is "2001", some time before December 2001, and "953 years" (p150) before Cwej is born (in 2954, p205). The bit with the pop can is on p165-166.
568 *Head Games*. The kids might have been born prior to 2001, as Bambera is on duty in *Head Games* and *Animal*, both set in that year. Alternatively, it's possible that Brigadier Fernfather (*The Shadow in the Glass*) covered Bambera's maternity leave.
569 According to Owen's comments and a computer graphic related to Lucy's death in *TW: Greeks Bearing Gifts*.
570 *Touched by an Angel*
571 *TW: Miracle Day*. The fact that the CIA *has* "456 files" indicates some knowledge of the UK's contact with the 456 in the 60s, despite the great pains that the UK government takes to keep it secret in *TW: Children of Earth*.
572 "A year" before *Rutans: In 2 Minds*.
573 Dating "The Fallen" (*DWM* #273-276) - According to the Doctor, it's "2001. Somewhere in November judging by the temperature".
574 "The Widow's Curse"
575 "Five years" before *Rise of the Cybermen*.
576 *The Hollow Men* (p74).
577 "Fifty years" after *Amorality Tale*.
578 *Sometime Never*. The Doctor, Fitz and Trix visit Sam's grave in *The Gallifrey Chronicles*, which gives her date of death as 2002. From *The Bodysnatchers* onwards, some of the EDAs hinted that Sam would meet a premature death. Others, such as *Interference*, hinted that she would live into great old age; *Beltempest* even alluded that she was now immortal.

Alien Bodies and *Unnatural History* reveal that contact with the Doctor changed Sam's timeline, preventing her from becoming "Dark Sam" (dark-haired, sexually active and a drug user) and making her squeaky-clean instead. Further complicating things, some of the "companion deaths" the Council of Eight arranged were either ambiguous or retconned away after their defeat. As of *The Gallifrey Chronicles*, it's clear that Sam died in 2002 and "stayed dead".
579 *Sometime Never*
580 "Seven years" before *TW: The Undertaker's Gift*.
581 *Happy Endings*
582 Dating *The Ratings War* (BF promo #2, *DWM* #313) Beep's early appearances on Earth are roughly contemporary. Previous to *The Ratings War*, he was imprisoned in "Star Beast II", a comic story in the *1996 DWM Annual*. The tone and heavy amount of reality TV in this story suggests author Steve Lyons had a contemporary or near-contemporary setting in mind.
583 Dating *The Forge: Project: Valhalla* (BF New Worlds novel #3) - The year is given.
584 Dating *Tales from the Vault* (BF CC 6.1) - Ruth names the exact date, and it's "about ten years" before the story's linking material, set at time of release in 2011. The Doctor says that he and Romana have arrived in "Kensington on a wet Wednesday afternoon", but in 2002, 6th June was actually a Thursday.
585 Dating *Benny: Secret Origins* (Benny #10.4) - It's the day that England played Argentina for the World Cup: 7th June, 2002.

By now, Bambera and Ancelyn had given birth to twins.[568] **In September 2001, Owen Harper had been qualified as a physician for six months. The alien Mary tore the heart out of 43-year-old Lucy Marmer, and Owen was present when Lucy's body was brought into Cardiff General Hospital.**[569] The elder Mark Whitaker had foreknowledge of the destruction of the World Trade Center, but held his tongue, fearful of interfering with history.[570] **After 11th September, 2001, the American CIA cross-referenced its 456 files under "Worldwide Incursion" and designation JF323B.**[571]

The Rutan Host occasionally separated and exiled individual Rutans, including those that were exposed to neural toxins from a Sontaran bioweapon. A ship containing one such rogue Rutan crashed in Algeria in November, and was retrieved by the United Kingdom.[572]

2001 (November) - "The Fallen"[573] **->** The dead were walking in West Norwood in London, and seven people had disappeared. The eighth Doctor and Izzy discovered Grace Holloway investigating with MI6, which was secretly run by Leighton Woodrow.

Grace had recovered the Master's DNA from her encounter with him. Working with the scientist Donald Stark, she hoped to unlock the secrets of regeneration - she thought the eighth Doctor had been hinting she *should* do so by mentioning he was half-human, and telling her to hold back death. However, Grace's sample wasn't Time Lord DNA as she had believed. Stark was transformed into a snake creature - a morphant from Skaro like the Master before him. The Doctor destroyed the Stark monster, even as Woodrow decided to blame the explosion on Arab terrorists. As the Doctor left, Woodrow found one of his men... killed by the Master's tissue compression eliminator.

Donna Noble's mother gifted her with Tesco's brand of unisex perfume, *Odeur Delaware*, at Christmas 2001. Donna used it to treat bites and stings - and, in future, sprayed it into the eyes of a hostile female Sycorax.[574]

2002

Mickey Smith's mother had been unable to cope with raising him, and his father - Jeremiah Smith, who formerly worked at the key-cutters on Clifton Parade - went to Spain and never returned. Mickey was raised by his blind gran, but she died after tripping and falling down the stairs.[575] The "Great Drought of '02" affected the UK.[576] The main Xhinn fleet was due to arrive on Earth in 2002.[577] The Council of Eight arranged for a drug overdose to kill Sam Jones, a former companion of the Doctor, who had become an ecocampaigner.[578] The eighth Doctor found another part of Octan's skeleton in New York, 2002.[579]

Zero, the orange, gelatinous child of a Vortex Dweller, came through the Rift and wound up in a cell at the Torchwood Hub in Cardiff.[580] The fertiliser Bloom was developed, but it was viral and spread uncontrollably. It was banned before 2010.[581]

c 2002 - THE RATINGS WAR[582] **->** The tyrannical Beep the Meep escaped from his imprisonment in a *Lassie* film, and used blackstar radiation to mesmerise executives at a TV network. Under Beep's direction, the network enjoyed success with shows such as *Appealing Animals in Distress* and *Hospital Street*, the first ever 24-hour soap opera.

Beep sought to brainwash the public through subliminal messages jointly seeded into the final episode of *Audience Shares*, and the debut of *Beep and Friends*. The sixth Doctor crushed this scheme, and exposed Beep's murderous tendencies on national television. Authorities apprehended the raving Meep.

2002 - THE FORGE: PROJECT: VALHALLA[583] **->** Nimrod recruited Cassie Schofield, who had become savage during her self-imposed exile, as an agent of the Forge.

2002 (6th June) - TALES FROM THE VAULT[584] **->** The fourth Doctor and Romana checked an art gallery to see if the Doctor had left himself any messages in the corners of paintings, and learned that one of the great lost art treasures of the universe - the *Quistador Molari* - was on sale at a London auction house. The painting had caused more suffering than any other work in history, including everything by Tracey Emin, because it would depict the future death of anyone who looked at it, driving them mad. The Doctor took the painting away to destroy it, but as he didn't dare look at the item, Sergeant Ruth Matheson of UNIT substituted a fake beforehand. The genuine item wound up in Unit's Vault, and was classified as an Omega 10 artifact, only to be used when all alternatives had failed.

2002 (7th June) - BENNY: SECRET ORIGINS[585] **->** The android Robyn and a temporal projection of Bernice Summerfield encountered their arch-nemesis, Samuel Frost. He procured the Right and Left Hands of God - powerful artifacts that granted great power to anyone attaching them to a handless statue of Arincias, one of the lost gods of Atlantis.

Sarah Jane Smith Series 1 [586]

Sarah Jane Smith was now crafting exposes for Planet 3 Broadcasting. The Crimson Chapter tested Sarah to see if she was the herald cited in *The Book of Tomorrows*, and so provided backing to the former members of Think Tank and their leader, Hilda Winters. The ex-Think Tank members arranged for Sarah to be fired when accusations she levelled against Halter Corp, a Scottish fishery, were thought to be based upon false evidence. Her reputation in tatters, Sarah began living under various aliases. [587]

2002 - SJS: COMEBACK [588] **->** Six months after the Planet 3 broadcast that had hobbled her career, Sarah Jane continued trying to clear her name. Her associates included a computer hacker named Natalie Redfern and a young do-gooder named Josh Townsend. Sarah's investigations took her to Cloots Coombe, where the local Squire had been feeding people to the monster that lived in the town well. Josh set fire to the Rechauffer labs, destroying the facility and incinerating the well-mutant.

Josh was actually a member of the White Chapter, and had inveigled himself into Sarah's life to protect her.

2002 - SJS: THE TAO CONNECTION -> Sarah, Natallie and Josh looked into the death of an 18-year-old whose prematurely aged body was fished from the Thames. They linked the incident to Holtooth Hall, a retirement home where the lives of aged multi-millionaires were being extended by draughts of *chi*-enriched blood taken from young people, who consequently aged to death. The pop star Lotus, renowned as an ageless beauty, had withdrawn from public life after she had been expelled from Holtooth and started aging. Sarah and her allies ended the operation, and the billionaire Will Butley, who had survived for three hundred years, died when denied the draughts.

2002 - SJS: TEST OF NERVE -> Hilda Winters' group anonymously challenged Sarah Jane to stop a sarin-gas attack slated to occur in London in the next twenty-four hours. A former soldier, James Carver, threatened to unleash sarin pellets in the Underground unless the Prime Minister met his demands for compensation to British soldiers given unsafe vaccines as test subjects. Carver eventually backed down and killed himself. Sarah Jane's old friend - Claudia Coster, an administrator in the Ministry of Intelligence - also died during these events.

2002 - SJS: GHOST TOWN [589] **->** Sarah Jane sold Lavinia's property in Moreton Harwood, and moved into Claudia Coster's old flat.

Dr Mikhail Berberova, a physics professor, had perfected a means of using low-frequency electromagnetic fields to affect people's perceptions, causing them to think they

---

586 Dating *Sarah Jane Smith* Series 1 (*SJS: Comeback*, #1.1; *SJS: The Tao Connection*, #1.2; *SJS: Test of Nerve*, #1.3; *SJS: Ghost Town*, #1.4; *SJS: Mirror, Signal, Manoeuvre*, #1.5) - The five Big Finish audios that compose *Sarah Jane Smith* Series 1 were released from August to November 2002, and occur in fairly rapid succession. The setting seems contemporary - tellingly, *Ghost Town* occurs "six months" after events described in a scientist's journal, which is dated to "22nd November, 2001".
587 *SJS: Comeback*. Details about the Crimson Chapter's role in Sarah's professional downfall are revealed in *SJS: Fatal Consequences*. Winters and Think Tank were seen in *Robot*.
588 Josh's allegiances are revealed in *SJS: Fatal Consequences*.
589 It's not expressly said that the villains hoping to disrupt the peace conference are Hilda Winters' group, but it seems likely.
590 In *SJS: Mirror, Signal, Manoeuvre*, Hilda Winters acquires the deactivated K9 - who admittedly isn't cited by name - from Sarah's flat. Although the audios say nothing more about this, it seems reasonable to assume that Sarah re-acquires K9 after Winters' death in *SJS* Series 2. The different *Doctor Who* media (this story, *Decalog 3*: "Moving On" - also written by Peter Anghelides - and *School Reunion*) are remarkably consistent on the point that Sarah, for a time, is unable to keep K9 operational because she lacks the futuristic technology needed to service him. The situation that doesn't change until the tenth Doctor revives the rusty K9 in *School Reunion*.
591 Dating *The Fearmonger* (BF #5) - This is "just over fifteen years" after Ace's time.
592 Dating *Rutans: In 2 Minds* (BBV audio #34) - The audio came out in 2002 and seems contemporary. Notably, the potential crisis is resolved because the UK's air defences are on full alert owing to 9-11. One of the characters jokes about a "winter migration", suggesting that it's later in the year.
593 Dating *Drift* (PDA #50) - The year isn't given, but it's clearly the modern day.
594 Dating *Time Zero* (EDA #60) - Anji returns home three weeks after she met the Doctor, and stays there eighteen months, so this story is set around the end of August 2002. Control also appears in *The Devil Goblins of Neptune*, *The King of Terror*, *Escape Velocity*, *Trading Futures* and *Time Zero*. The fire elemental that Curtis attracts is the creature the Doctor defeats in *The Burning*.
595 Dating *Unnatural History* (EDA #23) - Excerpts from a publication, *Interesting Times*, are dated to 7th and 14th November, 2002, and it's said to be "November 2002" when the story opens (p1).

were seeing ghosts. Nefarious parties seeking to disrupt an international peace conference in Romania used this technique to terrorize the delegates. Sarah and Josh exposed an expatriate Brit - Christian Ian Abbotly - as being behind the operation. The conference resumed after a hiatus.

2002 - SJS: MIRROR, SIGNAL, MANOEUVRE[590] ->

Sarah Jane travelled to India to investigate illicit genetic research being done by a company named Scala, and came face-to-face with the ex-members of Think Tank, including Hilda Winters. Winters' group planned to kill millions by contaminating a series of dams and reservoirs - the Parambikulam-Aliyar Project - with an engineered brucella virus. Sarah and her allies thwarted their plan, but Winters escaped. Scala lost its government contracts.

c 2002 - THE FEARMONGER[591] ->

Sherilyn Harper's New Britannia Party was gaining political influence by preaching strong anti-immigration policies. She was subject to an assassination attempt at the hands of United Front terrorists. Serious riots started spreading as the population panicked, but Harper was made to unwittingly broadcast a confession that New Britannia was secretly funding the United Front. The situation may or may not have been whipped up by the Fearmonger, an energy being from Boslin II. The seventh Doctor and Ace had been tracking the Fearmonger and destroyed it. Beryllium laser guns were top secret in this era.

2002 - RUTANS: IN 2 MINDS[592] ->

The Rutan Host didn't deem Earth of strategic importance at present. The renegade Rutan brought to the UK summoned about two dozen other such rogues, intending that they should form a new Rutan Host aware of the benefits of individuality, and overthrow the current Host. The United Kingdom's air defences registered the rogues' ship as an unidentified craft and destroyed it.

c 2002 - DRIFT[593] ->

The fourth Doctor and Leela landed in New Hampshire and met soldiers from the elite White Shadow unit. They were looking to retrieve a crashed fighter that was testing the Stormcore, an alien device recovered thirty years earlier. Also, an ice monster was loose in the area. The Doctor realised the Stormcore had opened a portal into another dimension, and that the monster was not intelligent, but was inadvertently killing people while trying to make contact. The Doctor crystallised the monster and handed it over to the authorities.

2002 (late August) - TIME ZERO[594] ->

The reclusive billionaire Maxwell Curtis had learned that his body contained a microscopic remnant of the Big Bang, masquerading as an ordinary atom, which was in danger of collapsing and turning him into a black hole. He had founded the Naryshkin Institute in Siberia as a means of researching black hole phenomena.

Led by Control, a division of the American CIA suspected the Institute was conducting time travel experiments. Control's agents constructed a temporal detector and identified Anji as a time traveller. They made her accompany them to Siberia.

In Siberia, the eighth Doctor found that Curtis' black hole matter was distorting space-time in the region. This allowed the Doctor to free Fitz and George Williamson from the icy prison from which they had been trapped in 1894. Williamson existed in a ghostly state, as the universe couldn't decide if he'd survived or not.

Curtis travelled down a time corridor into the past that Williamson's pseudo-existence had generated, hoping to reach Time Zero and spare Earth by unleashing his black hole matter there. The Doctor realised that if the black hole within Curtis erupted before time began, it would destroy the universe. The Doctor convinced Williamson to go back with him to 1894 and avert Williamson getting trapped in the ice, which nullified the time corridor's existence. Curtis travelled back no further than 1894, and died in a comparatively minor explosion.

Curtis' black hole mass attracted light from a far distant o-region to Earth. The o-region light contained something organic, which lodged itself on Earth's past and would manifest in the late nineteenth century as a fire elemental.

Trix, a disguise artist who sometimes worked for Sabbath, took the opportunity to stow herself aboard the TARDIS.

2002 (November) - UNNATURAL HISTORY[595] ->

A dimensional scar, the after-effect of the singularity that befell Earth on New Year's Eve, 2000, appeared in San Francisco. The eighth Doctor investigated the anomaly, but his companion Samantha Jones was lost to it. He sought out Sam's original self, a dark-haired drug user, to assist. The Doctor also recruited Professor Joyce, a resident of Berkeley, to craft a dimensional stabiliser. Fitz and the dark-haired Sam became lovers.

Griffen the Unnaturalist, an agent of a secret Society that catalogued all aliens, arrived at this time to collect specimens for his catalogue. Dark-haired Sam sacrificed herself to the anomaly to restore blonde-haired Sam, who helped the Doctor to unleash the Unnaturalist's extra-dimensional specimen case. The freed specimens drove the Unnaturalist into the dimensional scar, and the case sealed it permanently.

The Doctor later realised that blonde Sam's timeline came about because she touched his biodata within the scar, meaning that she paradoxically facilitated her own creation.

On 30th November, 2002, the gunman Murdock killed five people... although Ace's interference in history reduced this total to three. This was about as far in the future as she could travel using her time hopper.[596] *The Day the World Turned Dayglo*, Hollywood's take on the Jex-Canavitchi war, was released in late 2002. Reporter Gabrielle Graddige approached the Brigadier in January 2003 for the true story.[597]

2003

With time destabilised, the eighth Doctor, Anji, Fitz and the stowaway Trix were drawn into a series of adventures in alternate histories...[598]

(=) 2003 - THE DOMINO EFFECT[599] -> The eighth Doctor, Fitz and Anji discovered a version of history where the British Empire ruled the world. There was widespread racial and sex discrimination. This timeline had developed because an alternate version of Sabbath had murdered key figures in the history of computing, including Babbage and Zuse, thus preventing the development of computers. The alternate

Sabbath had learned that the Time Vortex was disintegrating following Gallifrey's destruction, and hoped to preserve his Earth in a temporal focal point. He was betrayed by a Vortex creature devoted to chaos, and the focal point collapsed. The entire past, present and future of this timeline were consumed.

(=) 2003 - RECKLESS ENGINEERING[600] -> The Doctor, Fitz and Anji arrived in an alternate Bristol after "the Cleansing" effect had ravaged Earth, and found the Utopian Engine still generating a slow-time effect around Jared Malahyde's estate. After linking the Utopian Engine to the TARDIS' systems, the Doctor rolled back time a hundred and sixty years and averted "the Cleansing" timeline altogether.

(=) 2003 - THE LAST RESORT[601] -> Fourteen-year-old Jack Kowaczski had built a time machine, and thus created many thousands of variant histories. This included his own, in which President Robert Heinlein presided over the USA and Mars - along

---

596 *Head Games*

597 *The King of Terror*

598 *Time Zero, The Infinity Race, The Domino Effect, Reckless Engineering, The Last Resort, Timeless.*

599 Dating *The Domino Effect* (EDA #62) - The book starts on "Thursday April 17 2003" (p1).

600 Dating *Reckless Engineering* (EDA #63) - The Doctor is sure it's "2003" (p24).

601 Dating *The Last Resort* (EDA #64) - Time is a rather fluid concept in this novel, but Fitz and Anji are based in "2003" (p7, p11).

602 Dating *Timeless* (EDA #65) - No year is given, but the story takes place after *The Last Resort*, and Anji has been going out with Greg for a year by the time of *The Gallifrey Chronicles*.

603 Dating *The Forge: Project: Valhalla* (BF New Worlds novel #3) - The present day segments conclude with Nimrod commencing with Project: Lazarus (from the audio of the same name), and Cassie being promoted to the rank of field agent. So, even though *Project: Valhalla* was released in November 2005, the "present day" in this case must mean 2004 if not 2003.

604 *Project: Lazarus*

605 "About five years" before *SJA: Eye of the Gorgon*.

606 *TW: Miracle Day*

607 "Seven years" before *Iris: Enter Wildthyme*.

608 Dating *Touched by an Angel* (NSA #47) - The exact days are given (pgs 7, 197, 227).

609 Dating *Eternity Weeps* (NA #58) - The date is given (p1).

DID LIZ SHAW DIE IN 2003?: Until recent years, and for anyone who considers the New Adventures canon,

the answer was almost unequivocally, "Yes." In *Eternity Weeps* (set in 2003), Liz, as Operations Chief for Tranquillity Base on the moon, is infected with a flesh-eating terraforming virus, endures an unspeakable amount of pain, and dies after passing along the formula for an anti-virus to her lover Imorkal - who himself perishes after telepathically planting the information in Chris Cwej's mind. Cwej's failure to euthanise Liz despite her pleas is examined in *The Room with No Doors*, and the matter is then considered closed.

Of late, both *The Sarah Jane Adventures* and the Big Finish Companion Chronicles starring Caroline John (reprising her role as Liz) have called Liz's death into question. In *SJA: Death of the Doctor*, Colonel Karim mentions, with regards associates of the Doctor invited to his funeral, "Miss Shaw can't make it back from moonbase until Sunday" (not an indicator that there's a crisis there, and probably just reflecting the infrequency with which shuttles transport personnel back to Earth). The acknowledgement of Liz working on a moonbase, strangely enough, confirms some of *Eternity Weeps* while rejecting another part of it.

With the Companion Chronicles being on audio, it was possible to imagine that Liz was narrating her stories prior to her death in 2003... until she says in *The Sentinels of the New Dawn* that if events in 2014 had not been wiped from history, "That horror would be starting around now...", i.e. a few years beforehand, concurrent with the audio's release in 2011.

Balancing these accounts is no easy task. The only leeway lies in the fact that in *Eternity Weeps*, we don't actually see Liz's dead body. The virus gives Liz horrific

with the Martians - had been conquered.

The Doctor, Fitz and Anji landed in one such history, where the time-travel holidays of Good Times Inc, founded by Jack's father Aaron, had turned the whole of human history into an homogenous tourist resort. The constant time travel, though, had destabilised reality and generated hundreds if not thousands of versions of events - including duplicate Doctors and companions. Sabbath was the only being unaffected by this process. The Doctor carefully sacrificed all but one version of himself and his companions, thus restoring the timeline.

c 2003 - TIMELESS[602] **->** The eighth Doctor, Fitz and Anji arrived back in the London of their reality. They found that Erasmus and Chloe, two survivors of a destroyed homeworld, had set up Timeless Inc. as a means of "helping people". Chloe and her time-active dog Jamais would visit parallel realities to find persons in pain, then bring them to the proper reality. Jamais would transfer each person's soul into their parallel counterpart, creating a merged soul with an improved timeline. Clients of Timeless Inc. paid £75,000 in diamonds for the privilege of murdering the parallel reality version, preventing the merged souls from defaulting back to their original state. Erasmus eventually realised that his goal of helping people had failed and killed himself, ending Timeless.

The genetic manipulations performed by Kalicum in the eighteenth century culminated in the British government worker Guy Adams. He possessed the DNA needed to house an intelligence that Kalicum and Sabbath had gestated, in a pile of diamonds, on behalf of the Council of Eight. The Doctor and his allies followed Sabbath back to the beginning of time, where he and Kalicum tried to seed the intelligence into the universe's beginnings.

Afterwards, Anji left the TARDIS crew to return to her old life in 2003. Aided by forged documents produced by Trix, she adopted Chloe and Jamais. Chloe introduced Anji to a man named Greg, whom she predicted Anji was going to get to know a lot better.

c 2003 - THE FORGE: PROJECT: VALHALLA[603] **->** A maximum-security spaceship holding the Nyathoggoth - a sentient liquid that had killed billions to slacken its hunger for blood - was dispatched to fly into a black hole, but instead crashed in Lapland. Nimrod and Cassie Schofield of the Forge investigated the incident, and Nimrod - thinking the Nyathoggoth was uncontrollable - caused the ship to self-destruct, killing the creature. Afterwards, Nimrod became the Forge's deputy director.

Cassie received a promotion after the Nyathoggoth affair and became "Artemis", Nimrod's top field agent in northern Europe.[604]

Professor Edgar Nelson-Stanley died - he was an accomplished adventurer who had learned much about extra-terrestrials, and deemed Sontarans the "silliest-looking aliens in the galaxy". His wife Bea would become a resident of the Lavender Lawns rest home.[605] **The mother of Esther Drummond, a future Torchwood operative, died in 2003.**[606] A young woman named Kelly started helping out behind the counter at the Great Big Book Exchange in Darlington. Over the next seven years, she absorbed the reverberations from a magical text there, the *Aja'ib* - an unfinished, and endless, sequence of tales and puzzles from the planet Hyspero.[607]

2003 (10th and 16th April) - TOUCHED BY AN ANGEL[608] **->** Rebecca Whitaker died in a lorry accident after visiting her parents in Chilbury. The older version of Mark Whitaker attempted to prevent this - had he succeeded, the Weeping Angels would have fed off the resulting paradox, and become strong enough to endanger Earth.

The eleventh Doctor, Amy and two versions of Rory arrived from 2001 to stop the Angels. One of the Rorys was touched by an angel, and sent back in time two years. The lights, cameras and monitors that Rory pre-ordered while he was there enabled the Doctor to spring a trap - the Angels, already malnourished, were caught in a closed circuit and erased. One Angel survived, and would encounter the contemporary Mark in 2011.

The older Mark realised the havoc his saving Rebecca would have caused, and allowed her car accident to proceed as scheduled. She died in his arms.

On 16th April, the Doctor, Amy, Rory and the older Mark attended Rebecca's funeral in secret. The travellers then took Mark, who was now 46, for one last meeting with his wife in 1993.

2003 (April) - ETERNITY WEEPS[609] **->** Liz Shaw was Chief of Operations at Tranquillity Base on the moon, where co-operation with the Silurians had led to the construction of an experimental weather control gravitron. Shaw and the Silurian Imorkal were in a close relationship.

Mount Ararat and Mahser Dagi were now in territory disputed by Turkey and Iraq, but an expedition to find Noah's Ark on Mount Ararat set off anyway. Bernice Summerfield and Jason Kane joined the team, although Benny found the Tendurek Formation, six billion years old and utterly alien. The Cthalctose terraforming virus - dubbed Agent Yellow - was set off and triggered catastrophic geological changes on Earth.

The US launched a nuclear strike in the area, but only succeeded in speeding up the process. This wiped out many cities including Istanbul, Thessaloniki, Almawsil, Tbilisi and Krasnodar. President Springsteen ordered the targeting of the moonbase, believing the crew there to be responsible. Jason fled billions of years back into the past and returned. The Agent was spreading as far as the Alps, the Sahara and Asia. The seventh Doctor engineered an x-ray burst using singularities to sterilise the Agent. This wiped out one tenth of all life on Earth, including six hundred million people.

Imorkal perished during these events, and Liz Shaw appeared to die also. Benny and Jason agreed to separate. Suborbital flights could be used to travel quickly around the world.

c 2003 (late May to June) - RIP TIDE[610] **->** A peaceful alien race used spatial gateways to become tourists on other worlds. Two young members of the species, genetically altered to resemble human beings, violated their people's strict rule against risk of discovery by visiting a small Cornish fishing village. One of them died in a sightseeing accident, losing the "key" to their spatial gateway in

the process. His stranded mate adopted the name "Ruth", but began dying from prolonged exposure to Earth's environment. Nina Kellow, age 17, aided the eighth Doctor in rescuing Ruth, and he transported her back home.

A Fortean Flicker transported a group of train-riders on the 8:12 out of Chorleywood to the planet Hogsumm in the twenty-seventh century. They were later returned to Rickmansworth Station in their native time.[611] In 2003, Detective Inspector Tom Cutler discovered that an alien entity in Hammersmith had possessed Mark Palmer, and compelled him to rape and murder three boys. Torchwood London drew the entity out of Palmer, but left Palmer to be arrested. Cutler testified to falsifying evidence, sparing Palmer from a life sentence. Palmer wound up in a mental hospital, and Torchwood permitted Cutler to keep his memories of the incident.[612]

---

injuries at a United Nations Hazmat base in Turkey, but her actual passing is only confirmed by Imorkal, who tells Chris and Jason Kane, "She is dead". It becomes the stuff of fan-fiction to imagine events by which Liz recovered enough to be alive and well in 2011 (for instance, Imorkal placed Liz in a prototype Silurian healing chamber after plucking the formula for the anti-viral from her mind), but keeping these stories in a single continuity requires some off-screen explanation, however spurious.

610 Dating *Rip Tide* (TEL #6) - It is "late May" (p13), in "the twenty-first century" (p78). There's no reason to say the story isn't set in the year the novella was published.

611 *The Highest Science*. The year is given on p2, and reiterated in *Happy Endings* (p5).

612 *TW: Into the Silence*

613 Dating *The Quantum Archangel* (PDA #38) - It's 2003 according to the blurb and p48, "thirty years" since *The Time Monster* (p39).

614 *The Quantum Archangel*

615 Dating *Minuet in Hell* (BF #19) - It's "the twenty-first century" and humanity has just developed quantum technology, suggesting it's the near future. *Neverland* gives the firm date of 2003 for this story.

616 *The Taking of Planet 5* (p15).

617 *The Power of the Daleks*

VULCAN: The planet Vulcan is only seen in *The Power of the Daleks*, a story that is almost certainly set in 2020. There is no indication that mankind has developed interstellar travel or faster-than-light drives in this or any other story set at this time. This would seem to suggest that Vulcan is within our own solar system.

There is some evidence to support this conjecture: since the nineteenth century, some astronomers (including Le Verrier, who discovered Neptune), speculated that a planet might orbit the sun closer than Mercury. There was new interest in this theory in the

mid-nineteen-sixties, which might explain why the home planet of Mr Spock was also called Vulcan around the same time in *Star Trek*. The draft script talked of a "Plutovian Sun", suggesting Vulcan is far from the Sun, not close.

In 1964, *The Dalek Book*, which, like *The Power of the Daleks* was co-written by David Whitaker, named Vulcan as the innermost planet in our solar system (and Omega as the outermost). This, though, contradicts the story that immediately precedes *The Power of the Daleks*, in which Mondas is referred to as "the Tenth Planet"; *Image of the Fendahl*, where the Fendahleen homeworld is "the Fifth Planet"; and *The Sun Makers*, where Pluto is established as the ninth planet of the solar system. So it seems that Vulcan wasn't in our solar system in the late nineteen-eighties or the far future.

Taking all this literally and at face value, *Doctor Who* fan Donald Gillikin has suggested that Vulcan arrives in the solar system but later leaves. This might be scientifically implausible - at least in the timescale suggested - but we know of at least three other "rogue planets" that enter our solar system according to the series: Earth's moon, Mondas and Voga. *The Taking of Planet 5* (p15) confirms Gillikin's theory by stating that Vulcan was discovered in 2003 and had vanished by 2130.

618 Dating *The Hollow Men* (PDA #10) - No year is given, but the drought of '02 is mentioned, and five-pound coins are legal tender.

619 Dating "Evening's Empire" (*Doctor Who Classic Comics Autumn Special 1993*) - There's a calendar giving the month as June in the first panel in which we see the real Alex. The year is harder to establish, however. The complete story was published in 1993, and in the last part, there's a newspaper dated "Nov 23 1993". It's "fifty" years since the World War II plane crashed, again supporting a date in the early nineties. However, the story falls after "The Mark of Mandragora", set after 1997, and

SECTION THREE: PRESENT DAY

c 2003

2003 - THE QUANTUM ARCHANGEL[613] **->** Stuart Hyde was now the Emeritus Professor of Physics at West London University. He had used the discarded technology from TOMTIT to build TITAN, a dimensional array intended to penetrate the higher dimensions called Calabi-Yau Space. Thanks to TITAN, businesswoman Anjeliqua Whitefriar became infused with the core of the Calabi-Yau and gained reality-warping powers. She became "the Quantum Archangel", and channelled her newfound reality-warping powers through the Mad Mind of Bophemeral, the super-computer that triggered the Millennium War, in a benevolent attempt to create separate utopias for each person on Earth. This threatened to plunge the universe into chaos.

> (=) The alternate realities created by the Quantum Archangel included ones where Mel was British Prime Minister, and faced a Cyberman invasion; the Doctor was President of Gallifrey, leading his people against the Master and the Daleks; and the Master, the Monk, the Rani and Drax altered Earth's DNA.[614]

The sixth Doctor persuaded Anjeliqua to restore order and relinquish her power, while the Chronovore named Kronos sacrificed himself to destroy Bophemeral.

2003 - MINUET IN HELL[615] **->** Hellfire Club leader Brigham Elisha Dashwood III believed he'd allied himself with a group of demons, and set about using their support to booster his organisation. In truth, he'd contacted alien Psionivores, members of a species of cosmic parasites that feasted on negative emotions. With the Psionivores' help and technical expertise, Dashwood seceded a small portion of America, renamed it "Malebolgia" and dedicated it to a social program of devil worship. The Psionivores helped Dashwood perfect the PSI-895, which was capable of rewriting or transferring human memories, and Dashwood hoped this would let him install Psionivores in his political opponents' bodies.

The eighth Doctor and Charley, aided by the Brigadier, publicly exposed Dashwood as a political charlatan. Dashwood turned against Marcosius, his main contact among the Psionivores, and accidentally disrupted the PSI machine. This created an unstable portal that consumed Dashwood, Marcosius and the device. The remaining Hellfire Club leaders crumbled in a political scandal.

Lethbridge-Stewart had now retired from UNIT, but still undertook occasional work for them.

Vulcan, nearest planet to the Sun, was discovered in 2003.[616] **Vulcan was a large, hot world with a bleak landscape of mercury swamps and geysers that spat toxic fumes. It had a breathable atmosphere and soil capable of supporting plant life. Plans were made to set up a mining colony on Vulcan for a trial period.**[617]

c 2003 (Saturday, 14th June) - THE HOLLOW MEN[618] **->** The Hakolian battle vehicle Jerak revived in Hexen Bridge and animated scarecrows, who attacked the villagers and fed them to Jerak's organic component. Jerak mentally influenced a former resident, Defence Minister Matthew Hatch, in a bid to taint Liverpool's water supply with genetic material that would increase Jerak's mental hold over any humans it infected. The seventh Doctor thwarted the scheme, entered Jerak's psychic realm via a mirror gateway and convinced the villagers absorbed over the centuries by Jerak to turn their willpower against the battle vehicle. The Doctor escaped and Ace destroyed the gateway, trapping Jerak on the astral plane. Hatch died, still mentally connected to Jerak upon its defeat.

c 2003 (June) - "Evening's Empire"[619] **->** The seventh Doctor and Ace were in Middlesbrough, where Colonel Muriel Frost of UNIT was recovering a German fighter from the Tees. They learned that the plane was downed after contact with an alien ship.

Ace met a local named Alex Evening, and upon following him home discovered a tiny Q'Dhite mindtreader spaceship among the Airfix models in his bedroom. The Q'Dhite explored the universe by weaving reality from fantasy, and Alex had been using that power to kidnap women, send them to his imaginary "empire" and then humiliate them. Ace was woven into his empire, and the Doctor, Frost and her troops followed in the TARDIS. The Doctor defeated Alex by bringing his domineering mother into the empire, shattering the illusion. They returned to the real world to find Alex in a coma.

At this time, Muriel Frost was in a relationship with a scientist called Nick - both of them were unhappy.[620]

---

enough time has passed for Frost to be promoted from Major to Colonel.
620 MURIEL FROST: According to John Freeman in his afterword to the collected "Evening's Empire", *DWM* originally planned to introduce "a more solid supporting cast" for the seventh Doctor. Muriel Frost of UNIT, a fiery redhead with a complicated personal life, was clearly a big part of those plans. However, publication

of "Evening's Empire" was delayed, and the comic series ended up tying in more closely with the New Adventure novels - meaning the planned storylines were dropped.

Muriel Frost appeared in "The Mark of Mandragora", "Evening's Empire" and "Final Genesis" in *DWM*. A Captain Muriel Frost also appeared in the 1980 sequence of *The Fires of Vulcan*. This is clearly meant to be the same character, but it really doesn't fit with what

323

= c 2003 - "Final Genesis"[621] -> The seventh Doctor, Benny and Ace arrived in a parallel universe where humans worked side by side with Silurians, and Colonel Frost served with the United Races Intelligence Command (URIC). The Silurian scientist Mortakk had created human-Silurian hybrids called Chimeras, and sent them to attack URIC. The Doctor defeated Mortakk.

c 2003 (summer) - ZYGON: WHEN BEING YOU ISN'T ENOUGH[622] -> The Zygon Kritakh was briefly rendered unconscious while undercover as a young man named Mike Kirkwood... and afterwards believed he *was* Kirkwood, who was experiencing dreams of being a Zygon. Kritakh's second, Torlakh, took the form of Robert Calhoun - a criminal who had killed about half a dozen women in the Edinburgh area. Torlakh/Calhoun endowed Kirkwood's therapist - Dr. Lauren Anderson - with Zygon essence to make her a shapechanger, hoping that she would better empathise with Kritakh's condition and

restore his identity. Kirkwood and Anderson were in a relationship and resisted Torlakh's plans, so Torlakh staged a massacre at St Kitts Hospital while wearing Anderson's form. Anderson faked her death by killing Torlakh, then departed for a new life with Kirkwood.

2003 (August) - THE SHADOW OF THE SCOURGE[623] -> The Pinehill Crest Hotel was host to the unfortunate triple-booking of a presentation of a temporal accelerator, a demonstration of spiritual channelling and a cross-stitch convention. The seventh Doctor, Ace and Benny stopped the Scourge from manifesting into our universe.

(=) 2003 - JUBILEE[624] -> The sixth Doctor and Evelyn discovered that their thwarting a Dalek invasion in 1903 had given rise to an English Empire. The two of them were widely regarded as heroes, and Nelson's Column had been rebuilt to depict the Doctor dressed as an English stormtrooper. The British and American populates were strictly kept

we know. In the British regular army, it's possible to spend twenty years as a Captain, but an able candidate could expect to be promoted to Major within four or five years (not to mention the fact that Frost doesn't look old enough in "The Mark of Mandragora"). Between "The Mark of Mandragora" and "Evening's Empire", she's gone from Major to Colonel - a process that would normally take over ten years.

"The Mark of Mandragora" has Frost refer to the Doctor as "child" at one point, so perhaps an untold story would have explained that she was older than she appeared - although even this wouldn't explain her career progression.

Even though the intention was that they are the same character, it might be simpler to imagine (and nothing particularly contradicts this idea) that the Frost in *The Fires of Vulcan* is Colonel Frost's mother. In which case, the young US major who appears and is killed in *Aliens of London* (set in 2006) - the same character who the Doctor called "Muriel Frost" in the draft script, and who has a "Muriel Frost" name badge - must presumably be her American cousin.

621 Dating "Final Genesis" (*DWM* #203-206) - Ace recognises Muriel Frost, so in her terms the story takes place after "Evening's Empire".

622 Dating *Zygon: When Being You Isn't Enough* (BBV independent film) - The story was released in 2008 but filmed years beforehand, hence why a credit card flashed by a minor character, Ray, bears the active/expiration dates of "09/02" to "09/04". It seems reasonable to assume that the card is still valid, because Anderson goes on a shopping spree upon finding it. A Euronics Centre advertisement establishes that it's summer.

Somewhat infamously, this film is a canonical *Doctor*

Who-related erotic thriller, with full-frontal nudity and two softcore sex scenes - although the back cover, featuring three pictures of naked people on a couch, overstates the amount of film time given to sex acts. That said, in what will doubtless be disappointing news to some, there are no sex scenes involving Zygons in their natural state.

623 Dating *The Shadow of the Scourge* (BF #13) - It is "the fifteenth of August 2003" according to the Doctor.
624 Dating *Jubilee* (BF #40) - The date is given (and it's the hundredth anniversary of the events of 1903).
625 Dating *Daemons: Daemos Rising* (Reeltime Pictures film #6) - A calendar in Cavendish's house cites the exact day that Mastho is summoned as 31st October, 2003, and the story begins the night before. This is the first time that Mastho had been summoned from his point of view; from Sodality's, it's the second (the first being in 1586, in *TimeH: Child of Time*).
626 Dating *Falls the Shadow* (NA #32) - It is "a crisp November morning", "five years" after "UN adventurism in the Persian Gulf". Winterdawn is alive and well in *The Quantum Archangel*, so this book is set after that. Thascales was an alias of the Master in *The Time Monster*. Author Daniel O'Mahony intended it to be set in "the near future".
627 Dating *Catch-1782* (BF #68) - The date is given.
628 *TW: Miracle Day*, in a cheeky little reference to the ITV show *Mine All Mine* (2004) by Russell T Davies.
629 "Four years" before "The Widow's Curse".
630 "Five years" prior to *TW: Consequences*: "The Wrong Hands".
631 *Unregenerate!* Rausch says he hasn't seen Louis in "fifty years", but this could be a rounded sum. A radio broadcast says US and UK forces are "hours" away from Fallujah in Iraq. The main offensive there occurred on

apart to protect British genetic purity. The Daleks were heavily merchandised, and their defeat was told in movies such as *Daleks: The Ultimate Adventure!*, starring Plenty O'Toole as Evelyn "Hot Lips" Smythe. Use of contractions was outlawed.

The President of the English Empire, Nigel Rochester, scheduled the Empire's jubilee celebration to include the public execution of the sole surviving Dalek from the 1903 attack. However, the Dalek secretly killed the Doctor's temporal duplicate, who had been a prisoner in the Tower for a hundred years.

The timelines of 1903 and 2003 began meshing together, and the Dalek invasion of 1903 started to unfold in the latter era. The Doctor convinced the "jubilee" Dalek that if the Daleks succeeded in their attempt to destroy all other life forms, they could only then turn on each other until a single Dalek remained, purposeless and insane. Logically, success would mean the Dalek race's destruction. The Dalek concurred and connected itself to the Dalek command net, transmitting a message that the Daleks could only survive by dying. The entire Dalek invasion force self-destructed, which retroactively averted the 1903 assault.

Remnants of the cancelled timeline remained in the restored history. Nigel Rochester, visiting the Tower of London as a tourist, briefly recognised the Doctor and thanked him for his help in the aberrant history. The English Empire's atrocities subtly lived on in the history and the dreams of the English people.

2003 (30th-31st October) - DAEMONS: DAEMOS RISING[625] **->** The Sodality - a group of revolutionaries who had grabbed power in a potential future by using the Daemons' science - reached back and compelled Captain Douglas Cavendish, who had been discharged from UNIT following the mid-nineties Yeti visitation, to summon a Daemon. Sodality hoped to shackle the Daemon as a means of controlling this time zone, but Cavendish and Kate Lethbridge-Stewart bore witness as a Daemon named Matso was summoned - and then rejected Sodality's claim on its power.

c 2003 (November) - FALLS THE SHADOW[626] **->** Professor Jeremy Winterdawn and his team at Shadowfell House had experimented for five years with the "Thascales Theorem", and their research indicated that applied quantum physics was a possibility. Winterdawn experimented

with the metahedron to the grey man's Cathedral, but in doing so caused damage to the universe. The beautiful humanoids Gabriel and Tanith were thereby created as expressions of the universe's pain; they were creatures of pure sadism, who wanted to use Cathedral's power to harm every living being. Winterdawn died from a heart attack. The grey man summoned the seventh Doctor, Ace and Bernice to help, and the Doctor used the TARDIS to put the metahedron inside Cathedral, creating a closed environment that saved the universe as Cathedral succumbed to entropy. Ace killed Gabriel and Tanith after the grey man cut them off from the universe's suffering, rendering them powerless. The grey man departed, eager to explore the universe.

2003 (12th December) - CATCH-1782[627] **->** The sixth Doctor and Mel arrived in Berkshire at the invitation of Mel's uncle, John Hallam, to attend the 100th anniversary celebration of the National Foundation for Scientific Research, UK. Hallam had constructed a cylinder from a unique alloy provided by a space agency, but the interaction of the TARDIS and chrono-atoms within the cylinder threw Melanie two hundred and twenty-two years back in time. The Doctor and Hallam pursued her in the TARDIS.

2004

The "Vivaldi inheritance" of 2004 demonstrated a means of establishing the truth through paper documentation.[628] The Doctor visited Cuba.[629]

Policewoman Gwen Cooper assisted with the recovery of a child abandoned in a courtyard; the child survived, and was fostered.[630] As arranged in 1957, the Time Lord Louis collected Johannes Rausch on the day before his death. They travelled to a Gallifreyan CIA Institute, where Rausch took part in an experiment to transfer TARDIS sentiences.[631] **Paul Langer walked out on his family, including his son Clyde, and ran off to Germany with his sister-in-law Mel. Clyde handled his father's departure so badly, he got into trouble and was expelled.**[632]

Hex thought until he was six that his grandmother was his mum.[633]

2004 - SOMETIME NEVER[634] **->** The scientist Ernest Fleetward stood on the brink of inventing a form of unbreakable crystal that would greatly advance mankind's development. Fleetward had set about reconstructing a crystal human skeleton, unaware that it was the Council of Eight leader Octan, lost to the Time Vortex in 1588. Octan

---

8th November, 2004. *Unregenerate!* was recorded just more than a week later on 16-17 November.
632 "Five years" before *SJA: The Mark of the Berserker.*
633 *Night Thoughts*

634 Dating *Sometime Never* (EDA #67) - An invitation states that an exhibition at the Institute of Anthropology opens on 31st January, 2004. *Sometime Never* was published in the same month.

himself travelled through time to prevent Fleetward's efforts from impacting history and cast the skeleton into the Time Vortex, failing to realise that he was re-obliterating his own body.

The eighth Doctor convinced Fleetward to adopt the nephews of Richard III, who were saved from their historical fate.

Anji started dating Greg in the summer.[635] On June 8, 2004, Ian Chesterton was very keen to see a transit of Venus - he'd missed the previous such event, back in 1770, by just a few months.[636]

Ben Jackson and Polly Wright were now married. Polly and Ian Chesterton were separately Timescooped into the Death Zone on Gallifrey, and returned home after aiding the fifth Doctor.[637]

2004 (18th July) - PROJECT: LAZARUS[638] -> The Forge, located on Dartmoor beneath an abandoned asylum, had begun collecting dead alien life forms and technology on Earth. Its agents captured a stranded, blue skinned alien capable of exuding a slime that killed on contact; Nimrod dubbed the alien's race as the "Huldran". The Forge took into custody the Huldran's spacecraft, which could generate spatial gateways. The sixth Doctor and Evelyn briefly encountered the Forge, causing the Forge to procure a sample of the Doctor's blood. A clone of the Doctor was created to assist their endeavours.

Nimrod killed Cassandra Schofield when she betrayed him to help the Doctor and Evelyn.

2004 (July) - THE TOMORROW WINDOWS[639] -> The "selfish memes" seeded on behalf of Martin culminated on various planets. The planet Shardybarn was eradicated when the Low Priest Jadrack the Pitiful triggered several nuclear bombs, hoping that his god would perform a miracle and stop the disaster. On Valuensis, a misunder-

standing made the Gabaks and Aztales annihilate one another with doomsday devices. On Estebol, malevolent cars began to possess their drivers and the people withered due to extreme pollution.

To combat this self-destructive trend, the billionaire philanthropist Charlton Mackerel set up Tomorrow Window exhibits on various planets. The Tomorrow Windows allowed the indigenous populations to glimpse their future and hopefully amend their behaviour. Martin sought to ruin Mackerel's exhibits. In June 2004, Martin eradicated the Tate Modern - and a Tomorrow Windows exhibit there - with an electron bomb.

The eighth Doctor aided Mackerel by seeking out the original Tomorrow Windows builder, Astrabel Zar. Electrical beings named the Ceccecs, working for Martin, destroyed the belt of moon-sized Astral Flowers in an attempt to kill Zar, but the Doctor and Zar escaped.

A "selfish meme" on the planet Minuea made the populace do nothing as their moon slowly moved toward a collision with their planet. The Doctor used a Tomorrow Window to make the people see the benefit of using a missile to stop the catastrophe, and thereby saved the planet.

The aged Zar returned to Gadrahadron to tell his younger self, fifty years in the past, how to make the Tomorrow Windows. Martin discovered this and killed Zar. The repentant actor Prubert Gatridge and Martin died in mutual combat. Fitz, Trix and Mackerel ensured that the younger Zar learned the Tomorrow Windows secret.

Mackerel's Tomorrow Windows exhibits continued, granting planets with selfish memes a second chance. The Doctor determined that Martin never completed his work on Earth, and that humanity developed selfish memes independent of him.

The Doctor was by now an old friend of Ken Livingstone, the current Mayor of London.

---

635 "A year" before *The Gallifrey Chronicles*. Greg was introduced in *Timeless*.
636 *Transit of Venus.* The most recent transit happened in June 2012 - another won't occur until 2117.
637 *The Five Companions.* This happens at an unspecified point after Ben and Polly become a couple on New Year's Eve, 1999. Ian, although constantly said to be "older", is still spry enough to run down corridors and dodge Dalek laser beams with the best of them.
638 Dating *Project: Lazarus* (BF #45) - The dating clues are very conflicting. According to Professor Harket's journal, the story opens on 18th July, 2004 , and the first track is explicitly titled as such. However, the Doctor says it's "late November". He lets the TARDIS choose the destination, though, so perhaps he's confused. Nobody can quite agree on how much time has passed since

Project: Twilight - the Doctor thinks it's been "a couple years", Cassie suggests it's been "a few years", and Nimrod specifies that it's "five years". *Project: Destiny* seems to establish that *Project: Twilight* was set in 2001, and its back cover reiterates that Cassie died in 2004.
639 Dating *The Tomorrow Windows* (EDA #69) - Trix's clothes are "very 2004" (p13). The Earth year 2004 is equivalent to the Galactic Year 2457. All the events on alien planets in *The Tomorrow Windows* seem contemporaneous, and the Doctor even says on p278, "we only travelled in space, not in time".
640 Dating *TW: Trace Memory* (TW novel #5) - Owen is now a doctor (*TW: Greeks Bearing Gifts* says that he was six months into his residency in September 2001) and has a girlfriend (who isn't necessarily his future finance, seen in *TW: Fragments*), but the year is still a bit unclear.

c 2004 - TW: TRACE MEMORY[640] -> As a young doctor, Owen Harper met the time-jumping Michael Bellini.

2004 - TW: FRAGMENTS[641] -> Toshiko Sato worked for the Lodmoor Research Facility, a division of the Ministry of Defence. Toshiko's mother was kidnapped, and her abductors forced Toshiko to steal blueprints for a sonic modulator that could emit powerful sonic waves. UNIT captured those involved, imprisoned Toshiko for treason in a detention facility and withdrew her rights as a citizen. Captain Jack had Toshiko's record wiped clean, in exchange for her agreeing to work for Torchwood for five years.

c 2004 - THE SLEEP OF REASON[642] -> Mausolus House had been replaced by the Retreat, a more modernised asylum. Caroline "Laska" Darnell, the great-great-granddaughter of one of Dr. Christie's patients, came into possession of the Sholem-Luz dog-tooth pendant. The pendant again infected an Irish wolfhound with the Sholem-Luz essence, and the infernal hound set about trying to germinate Sholem-Luz seeds through time and space. The eighth Doctor, aided by Fitz and Trix, lured the creature into a time corridor to 1903. Afterwards, the husband of a Retreat medical officer found Laska's pendant, which possibly still contained the Sholem-Luz taint.

c 2004 - THE ALGEBRA OF ICE[643] -> In another universe, an alien gestalt composed of mathematical equations sought to drain energy from outside realities into its own. The gestalt contacted the genocidal Sheridan Brett in our universe, hoping to use human mathematicians to further its plans. The seventh Doctor, accompanied by Ace, confronted the gestalt on a mathematical level and resolved the creature into zero.

c 2004 (October) - THE CITY OF THE DEAD[644] -> The eighth Doctor visited New Orleans to identify a bone charm he had found in the TARDIS. He determined that the charm could summon a water elemental, and left for 1980 to investigate such an occurrence. This journey made the charm retroactively appear in the TARDIS for the Doctor to find in the first place.

Upon returning, the Doctor found that the wife of resident Vernon Flood was a bound water elemental. The Doctor freed Mrs Flood from her human form and she returned to her own dimension, causing Vernon to drown. Her elemental son, bound in 1980, had become the crippled museum owner Thales. The ritualist Jonas Rust attempted to absorb Thales to attain great power, but an emptiness that Rust summoned - the Void - wound up consuming him. Thales was liberated from his human body and reunited with his mother.

c 2004 - THE DEADSTONE MEMORIAL[645] -> The long-lived Henry Deadstone, having established an identity as the old man Crawley, continued to tend to the alien psychic force he'd encountered some centuries ago. The eighth Doctor intervened when the creature tried and failed to reunite itself, causing psychic terror for the local McKeown family. The anguished creature withdrew its power from Deadstone and he instantly aged to death. The Doctor returned the creature to its home dimension.

2005

In 2005, Ianto Jones joined Torchwood London as a junior researcher.[646]

641 Dating *TW: Fragments* (*TW* 2.12) - It's "five years" prior to the story's 2009 component. This synchs with *TW: Greeks Bearing Gifts* (set in 2007, where it's said that Tosh has been with Torchwood for three years) and *TW: To the Last Man* (set in 2008, in which Toshiko has known Tommy - who revives from stasis annually - for "four years"). *The Torchwood Archives* is the odd man out on this one, saying that Tosh was arrested "late 2004/early 2005", but held for eight months before Jack approached her. *TW: SkyPoint* alternatively says that she was imprisoned for "six months" (p87).
642 Dating *The Sleep of Reason* (EDA #70) - It's the "near future" according to the blurb, but references to things like Limp Biskit and *Casualty* suggest it's at most only a few years after publication. It is "a hundred years or so" since 1903 (p273).
643 Dating *The Algebra of Ice* (PDA #68) - It's apparently set "several years" after the Brigadier first met the

seventh Doctor (in *Battlefield*). From his perspective, the Brigadier previously met the seventh Doctor in *No Future*, but the Doctor mind-wiped the Brigadier's recollection of those events, and doesn't restore these memories until *Happy Endings*, set in 2010. *The Algebra of Ice* falls in the period where the Brigadier would recall *Battlefield* as their first meeting. Lloyd Rose wrote this story with "the modern day" in mind.
644 Dating *The City of the Dead* (EDA #49) - No year is given, but it's "a few years" after Anji's time.
645 Dating *The Deadstone Memorial* (EDA #71) - There's no specific date beyond "early twenty-first century" (p51). It's set in the modern day.
646 "Two years" prior to the 2007 component of *TW: Fragments*.

2005 (New Year's Day) - THE END OF TIME (TV)[647] -> The dying tenth Doctor met Rose and Jackie on New Year's Day. He realised that Rose hadn't met him yet, but assured her she would have a fantastic year. Rose headed away, and the Doctor saw a vision of Ood Sigma - who told him his song had come to an end. The Doctor returned to the TARDIS, put it in motion and regenerated...

2005 (New Year's Day) - THE ELEVENTH HOUR[648] -> The TARDIS careened out of control, and the newly regenerated eleventh Doctor held on for dear life as it fell back through time...

2005 - IRIS: WILDTHYME AT LARGE[649] -> Agents of an extra-dimensional being - who manifested in our reality as a severed head on a pike - sought out Iris Wildthyme because the knowledge she'd acquired in her travels could be used to help plan an invasion. Many of Iris' memories had been siphoned into a jewel from the mines of Marleon, and she entrusted the gem to her former companion Tom. His sentient stuffed Panda bear smashed the jewel, depriving the villains of their prize. The Head returned to its home dimension, and Tom and Panda took up travelling with Iris...

Panda couldn't remember his origins - not even if he was unique, or but one of a race of ten-inch-tall, talking pandas. He did, at least, remember living in London with Tom, and experienced love at first sight upon finally meeting Iris.[650]

2005 - IRIS: THE DEVIL IN MS. WILDTHYME[651] -> Tom and Panda were chagrined because Iris had promised them adventures, but her bus had wound up in London, right back where they'd started. The remnant of Asmedaj that was squirrelled away in Iris' mind had been freed when the Marleon crystal broke - but he'd been altered by his interaction with Iris' memories and the Marleon crystal, and so was restored to life as a sheep. Iris, Tom and Panda left Earth for some proper adventuring.

? 2005 - SJA: LOST IN TIME[652] -> Two children accidentally started a house fire while their babysitter was busy elsewhere. Sarah Jane and Emily Morris, operating from 1889, used a chronosteel key to open the children's bedroom door, saving them.

2005 - ERIMEM: THE COMING OF THE QUEEN[653] -> Carra Wilton, the youngest professor of Egyptology in England, discovered a tomb that related some of the story of the Pharaoh Erimem. The fifth Doctor, Peri and Erimem herself were in attendance nine months later at the National Museum of Egyptian Antiquities in Cairo, where artifacts from the tomb were on display.

647 Dating *The End of Time* (X4.17-4.18) - Rose gives the date.
648 Dating *The Eleventh Hour* (X5.1) - In the precredits sequence (a late addition to the story), as the TARDIS is seen swooping over London, both the Millennium Dome (started in 1996) and the London Eye (built in 1999) are visible. The opening action, then, presumably entails the new Doctor flailing about in the same time zone in which he regenerated, not when he meets Amy.
649 Dating *Iris: Wildthyme at Large* (Iris audio #1.1) - The story seems contemporary with the audio's release in November 2005. A case could be made for dating it slightly later, though, as *Iris: The Devil and Ms. Wildthyme* - which takes right after this story - is said to occur "thirty years" after December 1978.
650 *Iris: Enter Wildthyme*
651 Dating *Iris: The Devil in Ms. Wildthyme* (Iris audio #1.2) - The story directly follows *Iris: Wildthyme at Large*.
652 Dating *SJA: Lost in Time* (SJA 4.5) - Date unknown, but the setting seems a bit contemporary in that the babysitter has a compact mobile. Even so, this portion of the story is unlikely to occur simultaneous to Sarah's starting point in 2010, as the Shopkeeper meant to send her "through time" to this location.
653 Dating *Erimem: The Coming of the Queen* (BF New Worlds novel #2) - Wilton is said to discover the tomb

"today", and the novel was published in 2005.
654 Dating *Rose* (X1.1) - The year isn't specified, but there's a contemporary setting. The story is clearly set after 2003, as the Doctor reads a paperback copy of the novel *The Lovely Bones* by Alice Sebold. *Aliens of London* shows a missing persons poster that definitively cites Rose as last seen on 6th March, 2005. The casualty figures come from the www.whoisdoctorwho.co.uk website, which also has pictures with time-stamps that offer an alternative date 26th March, the day of broadcast.
655 *Aliens of London*. Mickey's surname isn't established on screen until *Boom Town*.
656 Dating *UNIT* Series 1 (*UNIT: The Coup*, #1.0; *UNIT: Time Heals*, #1.1; *UNIT: Snake Head*, #1.2; *UNIT: The Longest Night*, #1.3; *UNIT: The Wasting*, #1.4) - The audios were released from December 2004 to June 2005. The blurb for *The Coup* (the prelude to the mini-series, packaged with *DWM* #351) says it takes place in "London, the Near Future". Two details support this - a) the train bombings in Spain that occurred in 2004 are said to have happened "a few years ago", and b) Captain Winnington was born in the 1980s, suggesting a mid-to-late 2000s dating at the minimum. The Brigadier also suggests in *The Coup* that *The Silurians* occurred "thirty years ago"; that's subject to UNIT dating.
Everything else about the mini-series seems con-

2005 (5th-6th March) - ROSE[654] -> Rose Tyler worked at Henrik's department store in London, which was the location of a secret Auton transmitter. She met the ninth Doctor shortly before he blew up the store, and accidentally took an Auton arm home with her. The Doctor found the arm and deactivated it. Fascinated by the Doctor, Rose tracked down Clive, who ran a website charting appearances of the Doctor over the years. Rose met up with the Doctor again and helped him defeat the Nestene invasion, but not before Auton shop dummies rampaged through London. Seventy-eight people were killed (including Clive), three hundred injured. Rose joined the Doctor on his travels.

Rose's disappearance prompted the police to search for her. Her boyfriend Mickey Smith was interviewed by the police, who - like Rose's mother Jackie - assumed that he had murdered her.[655]

UNIT Series 1 [656]

c 2005 - UNIT: THE COUP -> Colonel Brimmicombe-Wood now commanded the UK branch of UNIT; Colonel Emily Chaudhry served as its press officer.

The fortunes of the UK division of UNIT waned, and it was ordered to cede authority to a new organisation, Britain's Internal Counter-Intelligence Service (ICIS). The day before the transition, UNIT and ICIS troops battled some Silurians - actually delegates who had been petitioning for months for a peace treaty - near Tower Bridge. Orgath, a Silurian ambassador, approached General Sir Alistair Gordon Lethbridge-Stewart for help. Sir Alistair held a press conference and disclosed that UNIT had protected the world from unnatural and extra-terrestrial threats for "nearly forty years", and had thwarted more than two hundred alien invasions. He then presented Orgath as a Silurian representative. Captain Andrea Winnington of the ICIS was arrested after trying to kill Orgath, which weakened the group's standing. UNIT's

---

temporary, including the suggestion that some of the terrorist incidents are reprisals against Britain for its military intervention in Iraq - a hot button issue in 2005. Most importantly, the *UNIT* production team had no way of taking the new series - in particular the continual social disruption and political upheaval seen throughout Series 1 to Series 4 - into account. (Along those lines, it's very hard to believe that the Brigadier's public unveiling of a Silurian would so easily be dismissed after the likes of *The Christmas Invasion*, etc.) Trying to place *UNIT* in-between developments in New *Who* becomes a fairly ridiculous shell game, especially as the Prime Minister seen (or, rather, heard) in *The Longest Night* and *The Wasting* clearly isn't Harriet Jones or Harold Saxon. It's feasible to think that the *UNIT* Prime Minister was in power between Jones and Saxon, but then the lack of any mention in Series 2 of the compound crises and high death toll in *UNIT* becomes conspicuous by its absence. It's alternatively tempting to think that the *UNIT* Prime Minister is Brian Green from *TW: Children of Earth*, but they don't sound the same. The idea that the *UNIT* Prime Minister succeeds Green isn't very appealing, as *Children of Earth* is set in 2009, and so *UNIT* - featuring the older Brigadier - would have to occur in a hellishly narrow window before he's restored to his youth in *Happy Endings*.

The far simplest solution is to place *UNIT* at time of its release, and to assume that the Prime Minister of *UNIT* is the one whose corpse is seen in *Aliens of London*. A 2005 dating has the massive benefit of reconciling the comparatively weakened UNIT in the audios with the far more powerful group in New *Who*, which is fortified enough to have a flying aircraft carrier. Under this scenario, the only lingering issue is that 10 Downing Street is destroyed twice - in *The Longest*

Night and *World War Three* - and was presumably rebuilt in-between, all in the space of about a year.

Within *UNIT* itself, events happen in fairly rapid succession. Presuming Colonel Dalton's statement that he fought an invisible vampire on Southend "hours ago" can be taken at face value, a day at most passes between episode two (*Snake Head*) and episode three (*The Longest Night*), and two weeks pass between episode three and episode four (*The Wasting*) as Colonel Chaudhry recovers from the explosion that destroys 10 Downing Street. *The Wasting* also claims that the flu outbreak caused by the virus released in episode one (*Time Heals*) started "a few weeks ago", and so it's possible, depending on when the first symptoms manifested, that the entire mini-series takes place over that duration of time. Either way, Kevin Lee claims in *Snake Head* that "it will be summer soon", so we know that episodes two to four (and possibly *The Coup* and *Time Heals* as well) take place in spring.

The Coup is the first *Doctor Who* story to state that the Brigadier has been knighted, which was later mentioned on screen in *The Poison Sky* and *SJA: Enemy of the Bane*. Colonel Brimmicombe-Wood first appeared in the apocryphal *Sympathy for the Devil*, and was mentioned in *Project: Valhalla*. Albion Hospital was seen in *Aliens of London* and *The Empty Child*. Mention is made of Planet 3, the broadcaster from in Big Finish's *Sarah Jane Smith* audios. The ICIS isn't related to Torchwood, although both groups share a "Britain first" philosophy.

The help that the Silurians here give to Harry Sullivan compliments *Eternity Weeps*, set in 2003, in which some Silurians are aiding UNIT even though the public is unaware of their existence.

authority was restored.

Despite Sir Alistair's best efforts, the Silurian bid for diplomatic relations was regarded as a hoax, and Orgath taken by some for a man in a rubber suit.[657]

c 2005 - UNIT: TIME HEALS[658] **->** Colonel Brimmicombe-Wood was secretly the head of the ICIS. The group staunchly opposed forces they perceived were weakening Britain's sovereignty. UNIT announced that it would be moving nuclear weapons across Britain - a cover story to conceal transport of an alien spaceship. A team of ICIS soldiers captured the spaceship and "kidnapped" Brimmicombe-Wood - so he could continue ICIS' work in secret. Colonel Robert Dalton became UNIT's acting commanding officer. The ICIS experimented on the captured spaceship - when opened, it released an alien virus. In the weeks to come, it manifested as a deadly flu outbreak.

Attempts to reverse-engineer the spaceship's transporter caused freak side-effects. A high-speed train from Lancaster to King's Cross collided head-on with another train, and bank ATMs disgorged an estimated £70 million. A jet plane crashed into Windsor Castle; rumours variously said that two members of the royal family, or perhaps "the prince and a close friend" had been killed.[659]

The reactor aboard the HMS *Perthshire* was breached; it was buried under millions of tons of rock on offshore continental shelf just before it went critical. The British public suspected the incidents owed to terrorists.

Sir Alistair aided UNIT's investigations. Doris was currently away visiting her ailing sister.

c 2005 (spring) - UNIT: SNAKE HEAD -> Colonels Emily Chaudhry and Robert Dalton investigated a series of mysterious deaths near a Saxon burial ground in Southend. They killed a type of vampire - a vrykolaka - that had been used by a crooked restaurateur, Kevin Lee, to eliminate a group of cockle-pickers.

The deaths were blamed on Goran Dhampir, a self-proclaimed vrykolaka hunter. His arrest increased racial tensions in Southend.[660]

c 2005 (spring) - UNIT: THE LONGEST NIGHT -> The Prime Minister signed the Euro Combine treaty to enhance ties between Britain and Europe. Critics said the treaty was a threat to British sovereignty.

The ICIS had supplied Major Philip Kirby, a sympathiser and the Prime Minister's press secretary, with alien

---

657 The *UNIT* audios *Time Heals* and *Snake Head*.

658 Bricommbe-Wood's allegiances are revealed in *UNIT: The Wasting*, and the effects of the flu aren't known until *UNIT: The Longest Night*.

659 Reports of members of the royal family being killed are contradictory and never confirmed, and so can perhaps be ignored.

660 *UNIT: The Longest Night*

661 Dating *Death Comes to Time* (BBCi drama, unnumbered) - No year is given, but Tony Blair is the Prime Minister and George W Bush is President of the United States, suggesting a contemporary setting. The story was webcast in 2002. Lee Sullivan's illustrations suggest that UNIT is operating a moonbase at this time, and although such details aren't in the script or dialogue, this could nudge the story a couple of years into the future (there was a moonbase in the 2003 of *Eternity Weeps* and *SJA: Death of the Doctor*, after all). See "American Presidents in the *Doctor Who* Universe" for why this story seems to take place after 2004.

IS DEATH COMES TO TIME CANON?: As the seventh Doctor dies at the end, all Time Lords are revealed to have godlike powers that they simply haven't used before and all the Time Lords are extinguished or otherwise removed from the universe during the seventh Doctor's time, a strong case can be made that this story is apocryphal. Crucially, the Time Lords' godlike abilities aren't reconcilable against the Gallifrey History section of this book. However, references to Anima Persis in *Relative Dementias* and *The Tomorrow Windows* and the Canisians in *Trading Futures* suggest *Death Comes to*

Time may well be canonical. As with all *Doctor Who*, readers can include or ignore this story as they wish.

662 *Trading Futures*, making reference to *Death Comes to Time*.

663 *Iris: The Claws of Santa*. It's not specified if this is George W. Bush or his father, although the younger Bush was more commonly regarded as being clumsy, such as a 2002 incident where he briefly fell unconscious after choking on a pretzel.

664 Dating *TW: Fragments* (TW 2.12) - Owen's fiancée dies "four years" before the 2009 component of this story. The weather seems decent, and Owen comments that he promised Katie "a summer wedding", suggesting that it's spring. Some time must elapse, however, between Owen first meeting Jack in 2005 and his being recruited to work for Torchwood - *TW: Exit Wounds* says that Owen was only on the job his "second week" when *Aliens of London*, set in March 2006, occurred. *The Torchwood Archives* concurs that Owen "hooked up with Jolly Jack" in 2006, and *TW: SkyPoint*, set in 2008, says that Owen joined Torchwood "two years" ago (p24).

665 Dating "The Flood" (*DWM* #346-353) - It's "the early twenty-first century", and the story was published from 2004 to early 2005. Thematically, the resolution of this story is much like Rose unleashing the power of the Time Vortex in *The Parting of the Ways*.

666 Dating *The Gallifrey Chronicles* (EDA #73) - The date is given (p75).

brainwashing technology. Kirby used this to trigger societal unrest - he made a suicide bomber blow up the Vita Futura nightclub, a symbol of Britain's multiculturalism. ICIS agents dressed as policemen killed several survivors - including Lt. Will Hoffman of UNIT - to prevent the bomber being identified. The incident was blamed upon Abdul Malik Hassib, a Muslim student.

The resultant racial tensions, combined with a worsening flu epidemic and further terror incidents, caused a decline in social order. London experienced rioting and an increasing death toll - Albion Hospital was overwhelmed, people took shelter in Westminster Abbey and the government grounded all flights out of the city. The Prime Minister's deputy, Meena Cartwright, disclosed that her family had been abducted and - in accordance with the kidnappers' instructions - killed herself on live television. A suicide bomber devastated BBC Television Centre, taking the network off the air.

A confession obtained from Kirby was broadcast and restored some calm - but he triggered explosives that obliterated himself, Colonel Dalton and 10 Downing Street.

c 2005 (spring) - UNIT: THE WASTING -> The flu epidemic went global. Britain alone had six hundred thousand cases; those afflicted became violent as their flesh rotted. St. Catherine's was reserved for flu victims. The Prime Minister mobilised the army to maintain order.

Sir Alistair contacted Harry Sullivan, who was doing secret work for NATO at Deepcastle, to analyse the disease victims. Sullivan's team determined that the flu virus was an alien food additive designed to make human flesh more palatable for consumption. Silurian scientists aided Sullivan in developing a vaccine. Sir Alistair aided UNIT in dispersing the vaccine into the atmosphere via an old missile facility in the former Soviet Union.

Chaudhry exposed Brimmicombe-Wood as the head of the ICIS; he was arrested on charges of terrorism and treason, and the ICIS was shut down. UNIT was given new funding. Chaudhry was appointed its new commanding officer, with Sir Alistair serving as an unofficial adviser.

c 2005 - DEATH COMES TO TIME[661] -> General Tannis, commander of the Canisian armies, conquered the planet Santiny in violation of the Treaty of Carsulae. The seventh Doctor and his companion Antimony arrived to ferment resistance, but were abruptly summoned to the Orion Nebula. There, the Minister of Chance - an old friend of the Doctor - warned him that someone had killed two Time Lord "saints" working on Earth. The Doctor headed there to investigate; the Minister travelled to Santiny.

The Doctor discovered that a vampire, Nessican, had murdered the Time Lords to cover up their discovery of massive spatial disturbances. He returned to Santiny, where Tannis killed Antimony - who was actually an

android - and revealed himself to be a renegade Time Lord. When Tannis killed Sala, a young woman the Minister had become fond of, the Minister unleashed the full force of his Time Lord powers. The Doctor could not act against Tannis, but had to punish the Minister - all part of Tannis' plan to divide and distract his rival Time Lords. The Doctor stripped the Minister of his powers, but Tannis launched an invasion of Earth.

Meanwhile, Ace trained to become a Time Lord with a mentor, Casmus, and the mysterious Kingmaker. Reunited, the Doctor and Ace headed for Earth, where they helped Lethbridge-Stewart and UNIT - now with a fleet of shuttles at their disposal - repel the Canisian invasion. The Doctor used his Time Lord powers to destroy Tannis and himself. The Canisians were defeated.

Felix Mather was the US Secretary of State during the Canisian invasion.[662] Iris WIldthyme's companion Panda got a scratch on his nose when a bike-riding George Bush ran over him.[662]

2005 (spring) - TW: FRAGMENTS[664] **-> Owen Harper's fiancée, Kate Russell, died when an alien life form incubated in her brain. Jack Harkness covered up the incident.**

c 2005 - "The Flood"[665] **->** The eighth Doctor and Destrii arrived in Camden Market, and quickly discovered that people were over-reacting emotionally. The Doctor also learned that MI6 were in the area. Destrii's senses registered two advanced Cybermen, who begin to convert the population and captured her. The Doctor worked with MI6, convinced these were the most advanced Cybermen he'd ever seen.

The Cybermen neutralised British defences, and their mothership materialised over London. They created a rainstorm that soaked the MI6 personnel, and caused extreme emotional reactions - the humans gladly became Cybermen to cure themselves. The Cybermen planned to flood the world in this way.

Desperate, the Doctor offered to allow the Cybermen to kill him and study his regeneration if the Cybermen returned to their own time - this would allow Cybermen to convert other races, not just humans, into their own kind. The Doctor freed Destrii, who distracted the Cybermen while he leapt into the mothership's power source - a fragment of the Time Vortex. He focused the power there and destroyed the Cybership, whereupon he and Destrii went off to their next adventure.

2005 (June) - THE GALLIFREY CHRONICLES[666] **->** The eighth Doctor was lured to Earth by the Time Lord Marnal, who had recently learned of the Doctor's role in the destruction of Gallifrey. Fitz and Trix left the Doctor to set up home together, but the police approached Trix and attempted to arrest her on suspicion of murder. As they fled the country, Marnal confronted the Doctor and the Eye of Harmony was briefly opened. Like moths to a flame, the insect race the Vore was drawn to Earth. Their moon materialised in Earth orbit and a full scale invasion took place. The Doctor and his companions destroyed the moon, and engaged the surviving Vore.

Captain Jack Harkness renewed his acquaintance with Estelle, claiming that she had met his father during World War II.[667]

Sarah Jane Smith Series 2[668]

Rechauffer, Inc., rebranded itself as Mandrake, Inc.[669]

2005 (20th-22nd of the month) - SJS: BURIED SECRETS[670] **->** Sarah Jane Smith now resided in a cottage on the coast. She hadn't seen Harry Sullivan since he left for an overseas posting, but went anyway to their annual rendezvous at a restaurant not far from Blackfriars in London. Harry failed to show up, but Sarah instead met Will Sullivan, Harry's younger step brother. Hilda Winters died while under house arrest; she'd been killed by the Crimson Chapter for going too far in her mission against Sarah Jane. Sarah and Josh went to Italy to help Natalie Redfern, who was working with archaeologists excavating 500-year-old Medici tombs beneath the Church of San Lorenzo. Natalie's boyfriend Luca, a Crimson Chapter member, tried to obtain some pages from *The Book of Tomorrows* from a hidden room beneath the basilica of San Lorenzo, but Josh killed Luca when he tried to kill Sarah.

2005 - SJS: SNOW BLIND[671] **->** Sarah Jane and Josh visited Nikita Base in Antarctica, as Sarah had used some of Lavinia's inheritance to fund an operation there. The project was drilling for ice-core samples, hoping to calculate when global warming would reach a tipping point. One of the research team - Morgane Kaditch, a member of the Crimson Chapter - attempted to steal a supply of uranium-235 found beneath the ice, and thereby help fund the Chapter's operations. She was killed when an accomplice double-crossed her. Sarah secured the uranium.

667 "Two years" before *TW: Small Worlds*.
668 Dating *Sarah Jane Smith* Series 2 (*SJS: Buried Secrets*, #2.1; *SJS: Snow Blind*, #2.2; *SJS: Fatal Consequences*, #2.3; *SJS: Dreamland*, #2.4) - These four audios were released from February to April 2006, but seem to have been written with 2005 in mind. Somewhat definitively, Josh says in *Fatal Consequences* that he's been protecting Sarah for "three years", denoting how long it's been since *SJS: Comeback*, set in 2002. Little clues throughout Series 2 support a 2005 dating: in particular, Natalie says in *SJS: Buried Secrets* that a Medici burial chamber was located "in July 2004" - a phrasing she'd be unlikely to use in 2004 itself. Two items establish that Series 2 can't take place any later than 2007: *Buried Secrets* mentions that the *Dauntless* was originally scheduled for lift-off "in 2008", but has now been moved up, and it's said in *SJS: Dreamland* that Chuck Yeager broke the speed of sound "nearly sixty years ago" (he did so on 14th of October, 1947).

As Series 2 ends on a cliffhanger, a 2005 dating is preferable to 2006 (or 2007, even) in that it allows more time for an unspecified adventure in which Sarah Jane returns to Earth and wraps up any and all lingering details from her dealings with the Crimson Chapter before casually witnessing events in *The Christmas Invasion*, which she mentions upon meeting the tenth Doctor in *School Reunion*.

Series 2 ends with the *Dauntless* launching into space on 27th of September, and all signs are that the series begins some months beforehand; see the Series 2 episode entries for more. It seems likely, although it's not actually stated, that Sarah Jane recovers some of her professional standing between *SJS* Series 1 and Series 2 - at the very least, she's no longer living under cover identities, and is currently having to dodge media inquires about Hilda Winters' death.

The *Dauntless* launch is cited throughout Series 2 as being Earth's first "space tourism" flight... while the attempt made in *Escape Velocity* probably wouldn't count owing to an alien invasion scuttling it, by 2004 that ship had long since sailed in the real world; Dennis Tito and Mark Shuttleworth made "space tourist" flights in 2001 and 2002 respectively. That said, nothing within *Who* itself (other than *Escape Velocity*, maybe) particularly contradicts the *Dauntless* being the first tourist flight as stated.

669 Eighteen months before *SJS: Fatal Consequences*. "Mandrake" is the English equivalent of "Mandragora", for reasons given in *SJS* Series 2. It's also the name of a drug in "The Mark of Mandragora".
670 Dating *SJS: Buried Secrets* (*SJS* #2.1) - *SJS: Snow Blind* establishes that Sarah spends two months after *Buried Secrets* recovering from a gunshot wound. The month in which *Buried Secrets* takes place, however, still isn't clear (see the dating notes under *Snow Blind* for why). Natalie specifies that the story opens on "the 20th", and if the two subsequent "midday headlines" reports are any gauge, the action wraps up two days later. The Crimson Chapter's role in Winters' death is revealed in *SJS: Dreamland*.
671 Dating *SJS: Snow Blind* (*SJS* #2.2) - The amount of time that passes between *Snow Blind* and *Fatal Consequences* is rather vague. The two installments could easily take place in the same month (meaning that *Buried Secrets* occurs in June) - then again, they might be further apart than that (meaning that *Buried*

2005 (August) - SJS: FATAL CONSEQUENCES[672]

-> Sir Donald Wakefield warned Sarah that the Crimson Chapter viewed her "emergence" as the human herald mentioned in *The Book of Tomorrows* as a call to action - and would seek to bring about an apocalypse if none was forthcoming. The Crimson Chapter had used Mandrake, Inc.'s operations, as funnelled through the Pangbourne Research Centre in Reading, to create a powerful variant of the Marburg virus - one that incubated within people in a matter of hours. Sarah and her allies stopped the Chapter from opening vials of the virus in twelve major world cities, an act that would have killed millions. The international media covered the failed plot, and identified the Crimson Chapter as a doomsday group obsessed with aliens.

Sarah learned that Josh was both Wakefield's son and a White Chapter agent. Will Sullivan - a Crimson Chapter operative - died in a scuffle with Josh, who also killed the Keeper of the Crimson Chapter.

2005 (August to 27th September) - SJS: DREAMLAND ->

Sir Wakefield believed that Sarah still had a destiny to fulfill as a human herald, and invited her to join him aboard the maiden voyage of the *Dauntless*, set for 27th of September at the Dreamland facility (Area 51) in Nevada. Sir Wakefield succumbed to cancer beforehand, and so Josh accompanied Sarah as the *Dauntless* lifted off. The *Dauntless* pilot, a Crimson Chapter agent, mutually died with Josh in an exchange of gunfire that ruined the ship's instrument banks. Sarah was alone as the *Dauntless*, its life support failing, ventured further into space. She saw a bright light, commented that she'd seen something like it before a lifetime ago, and said goodbye to Earth...

c 2005 - RED DAWN[673] ->

Backed by the Webster Corporation, the first manned American mission to Mars - *Ares One* - successfully reached the Red Planet. The crew made planet-fall in the *Argosy* shuttle just as the fifth Doctor and Peri arrived. The astronauts and the time travellers found the tomb of Izdal, a heroic Martian who sacrificed himself to the Red Dawn - the ultraviolet Martian sunrise.

The tomb's guardian, Lord Zzaal, was revived with his Ice Warriors. Zzaal believed the humans had good intentions, but a misunderstanding quickly escalated into conflict. Zzaal sacrificed himself to the Red Dawn to save the Doctor's life, ending Webster Corp's plans, but it was hoped his dream of a peaceful existence with Earth could survive. *Ares One* returned to Earth. Tanya Webster, a human who possessed Martian DNA, remained behind as Earth's first ambassador to the Martians.

A Russian general ordered a nuclear strike against Chechnya, killing half a million people in an instant. After leaving the army, the General erased his identity and became the notorious arms dealer known as Baskerville. He lacked an electronic presence of any kind, making him impossible to track. After British Airways went bust, Baskerville bought one of their Concordes and converted it for stealth.

Nicopills, designed to wean people off tobacco, were marketed as a consumer item in their own right. The pills were less harmful but even more addictive than cigarettes, and thus were more profitable.[674]

Jack Harkness recruited Suzie Costello to join Torchwood after she encountered him and Torchwood operative Ben Brown. She helped to contain an alien virus that had been downloaded via some computers into her boss. Brown later died in an unrelated incident.[675]

Suzie Costello had been on the run when she joined Torchwood, and used her technical skill to wipe clean

Secrets occurs in May or even April).

672 Dating *SJS: Fatal Consequences* (*SJS* #2.3) - It's said that a round-the-clock vigil at Pangbourne labs has lasted for "six months", and *SJS: Buried Secrets* says the same vigil started "last Christmas" - so by logical extension, *Fatal Consequences* should take place circa June. However, a news report in *SJS: Dreamland* simultaneously mentions that the *Dauntless* is "cleared for lift-off next month" (September, according to *Dreamland*) and that the Marburg incident in *Fatal Consequences* occurred "last week", meaning that the "six months" figure has to be taken as rounding, and *Fatal Consequences* must occur in August. That squares with Sarah in rapid succession attending the funeral of Will Sullivan - who's shot dead at the end of *Fatal Consequences* - and then embarking on a four-week training course so she can

join the *Dauntless* launch.

673 Dating *Red Dawn* (BF #8) - It is "thirty years" since the "Mars Probe fiasco" of *The Ambassadors of Death*, which is a UNIT story. So to cut a very long story short, it's the now first decade of the twenty-first century. As *The Dying Days* was "over twenty years" after *The Ambassadors of Death*, this story is set before 2007. The impact of Tanya's ambassadorship to Mars must be minimal, as humanity and the Martians are in conflict by *The Seeds of Death*.

674 Both "ten years" before *Trading Futures*.

675 *TW: Long Time Dead*. Brown appears to be an otherwise unmentioned member of Jack's Torchwood team.

all records pertaining to her. She secretly joined Pilgrim - a religious support group and debating society started by Sara Briscoe - and conditioned Max Trazillion to brutally kill the other Pilgrim members if he didn't see her for three months.[676]

On Earth, a reptilian extra-terrestrial set up a business supplying combat divisions to clients on other worlds. Creating armies posed significant problems: Combat computers were only so reliable; artificial intelligences could only be created under certain conditions; remote-control signals could be scrambled; and fully crewed combat vehicles were costly, plus had a high turnover rate.

As a solution, the alien created heavily armed giant robots, which resembled twentieth-century Earth office complexes on the inside. Humans were kidnapped and brainwashed into thinking that they were simple office workers; in reality, their "paperwork" and office meetings coordinated the robots' attack patterns.

One worker, Todd Hulbert, overcame his conditioning and instigated a hostile takeover. The company was renamed Hulbert Logistics, and moved its home office from Ipswich to London.

A group of Cybermen had settled on the planet Lonsis, the next system over from Shinus. Its people - the Shinx - were traders who disliked aggression because it destabilised their markets. The Gallifreyan CIA sought to eliminate the Lonsis Cybermen, and seeded paranoia into the Shinx's minds. The Shinx hired Hulbert, whose combat divisions started routing the Lonsis Cybermen in 2005.

The CIA secretly aided Hulbert by equipping his Telford branch with a quantum crystalliser - a device that splintered the timelines over a small area, then picked the most desirable one as dictated by its programming.

Elsewhere on Earth, the CIA manipulated history to prevent Karen Coltraine becoming a dictator. Certain negative experiences were eliminated from Coltraine's history, and she matured into a more agreeable person.[677]

The First Environmental Crisis

By the middle of the first decade of the twenty-first century, it was clear that unchecked industrial growth had wreaked havoc on the environment. Increasing instability in weather patterns subjected Britain to acid rain and created turbulence that made air travel less reliable. Shifts in the ozone layer laid waste to Oregon. Traffic had reached gridlock in most of the major cities around the world. Motorcycles superseded the familiar black cabs in London, and many car owners sat in traffic jams working at their computers as they commuted. Predictably, air pollution reached new levels.

A catalogue of environmental disasters threatened the entire planet. The Earth's population was spiralling towards eight billion. Low-lying ozone and nitrogen dioxide levels had risen to such an extent that the London air was unbreathable without a face mask on many days, even in winter. Global warming was steadily increasing: by the turn of the century, there were vineyards in Kent. Antarctic waters became hazardous as the icecap broke up in rising temperatures. The rate of ice-flow had trebled since the nineteen-eighties.

River and sea pollution had reached such levels that the marine environment was on the verge of collapse. Water shortages were commonplace, and even the inhabitants of First World cities like London and Toronto were forced to use standpipes for drinking water and to practise water rationing. The mega-cities of South America saw drought of unprecedented proportions. The holes in the ozone layer were getting larger, causing famine in many countries. Sunbathing, of course, was now out of the question. "The plague", in reality a host of virulent, pollution-related diseases such as HIV 7, appeared and killed millions.

The collapse of the environment triggered political instability. New terrorist groups sprang up: the Earth For Earth groups, freedom fighters, environmentalists, anarchists, nationalists and separatists, the IFA, PPO and TCWC. In England, a whole new youth subculture

---

676 *TW: They Keep Killing Suzie.* This is part of Suzie's insurance policy in case of her death, although it doesn't entirely account for why she kills herself in *TW: Everything Changes.* (One explanation is that Suzie knows she's going to get fired - meaning mind-wiped - from Torchwood, and her suicide/resurrection gambit is a desperate means of maintaining her memories and identity.)

677 *Human Resources.* The Lonsis operation has been running for "a year" prior to 2006, and Hulbert acts as if he's been in charge of the company for some time before that.

678 *Iceberg* and *Cat's Cradle: Warhead* are both set around the same time and feature an Earth on the

brink of environmental and social collapse. The two books are broadly consistent, although the odd detail is different - in *Iceberg*, for example, journalist Ruby Duvall muses that sunbathing in England is impossible nowadays, whereas Ace sunbathes in Kent during *Cat's Cradle: Warhead.* The Connors Amendment is mentioned in *Warlock.*

679 *Interference*

680 *St Anthony's Fire*

681 *Placebo Effect* (p12).

682 *Iceberg*

683 *Something Inside.* This occurred on 25th May, 2005.

684 "Years" before *TW:* "Somebody Else's Problem".

685 *TW: In the Shadows*

evolved. Gangs with names like the Gameboys, the Witchkids and the Crows smashed machinery (except for their own gaming software) and committed atrocities. In the most notorious incident, the Witchkids petrol-bombed a McDonald's restaurant on the M2 before ritually sacrificing the customers: men, women and children.

Every country on Earth saw warfare or widespread rioting. In the face of social disorder in America, President Norris' right-wing government ended immigration and his infamous "Local Development" reforms restricted the unemployed's rights to movement. The Connors Amendment to the Constitution also made it easier for the authorities to declare martial law and administer the death penalty. The underclass was confined to its slums, and heavily armed private police forces guarded the barriers between the inner cities and the suburbs.

Once-fashionable areas fell into deprivation. The popular culture reflected this discord: In Britain, this was a time when SlapRap blared from every teenager's noisebox. There was a Kinky Gerlinki revival, its followers dressing in costumes described as "outrageous" or "obscene" depending on personal taste. The most popular television series was *Naked Decay*, a sitcom inspired by 45-year-old Mike Brack's "Masks of Decay" exhibition which had featured lumps of wax hacked into caricatures of celebrities. The teledildonic suits at the "SaferSex emporiums" along London's Pentonville Road became notorious. All faced the opprobrium of groups such as the Freedom Foundation and the Citadel of Morality. American children thrilled to the adventures of Jack Blood, a pumpkin-faced killer, and they collected the latest Cthulhu Gate horror VR modules and comics. Their elder brothers became Oi Boys: skinheads influenced by the fashions of Eastern Europe.

The early twenty-first century saw many scientific advances, usually in the field of computer science and communications. Elysium Technology introduced the Nanocom, a handheld dictation machine capable of translating speech into written text. Elysium also developed the first holographic camera. The 3D telephone was beyond the technology of the time, although most rich people now had videophones. In June 2005, "Der Speigel" gave away a personal organiser with every issue. The first robot cleaners were marketed at this time - they were small, simple devices and really little more than automated vacuum cleaners or floor polishers. Communications software and computer viruses were traded on the black market; indeed, they became almost substitute currency in countries like Turkey.

Surgeons could now perform eye transplants, and the super-rich were even able to cheat "death" (or rather the legal and medical definition of it) by an intensive programme of medication, transplants and implants. If even this failed, suspended animation was now possible - the rich could afford full cryogenic storage, the poor settled for

a chemical substitute. Military technology was becoming smarter and more dangerous. The Indonesian conflict and the Mexican War in the first decade of the century were the test-bed for much new weaponry. Arms manufacturers were happy to supply the Australian and American forces with military hardware. The British company Vickers built a vision enhancement system capable of tremendous magnification and low-intensity light applications. The helmet could interface with most weapons, allowing dramatically improved targeting. If anything, the helmet was too efficient - one option, which allowed a soldier to target and fire his weapon merely by moving and blinking his eyes - proved too dangerous and was banned. A new generation of UN aircraft were introduced, including a remote controlled helicopter (the Odin), a jet fighter with batteries of Valkyrie air-to-air missiles (the Loki), Niffelheim bombs and Ragnarok tactical nuclear devices. The US military introduced a turbo-pulse laser gun developed for use against tanks.[678]

Early in the twenty-first century, there were disasters, wars and nuclear terrorism. The first half of the century saw human civilisation close to collapse.[679] Rising sea levels claimed Holland, and the Dutch became the wanderers of Europe.[680] Christian fundamentalists campaigned for the extermination of homosexuals in the twenty-first century.[681]

The most pressing threat was that of magnetic inversion. For some decades, scientists had known that Earth's magnetic field periodically reversed. If this happened now, it would damage all electronic equipment and have serious environmental consequences. In 2005, spurred into action by such reports, the major governments of the world set up the FLIPback Project at the old Snowcap complex in the Antarctic. Shortly afterwards, a vehicle from the base - the hovercraft AXV9 - vanished in the Torus Antarctica with the loss of two men.[682]

The Doctor saw the 2005 European Cup Final, in which Liverpool overcame formidable opposition from AC Milan and claimed the Cup for the fifth time in its history.[683]

The tentacled alien Mister Quatnja established a drugs factory in Cardiff. Jack Harkness tolerated the operation, as Quatnja's products calmed the rowdier elements of Earth's extra-terrestrials.[684] Patrick Jefferson received a matchbox containing huon particles, which could transport objects into a hell dimension and age them to death. Captain Jack later suspected that Torchwood London sent the matchbox to Jefferson to field test it as a weapon. Jefferson used the matchbox to kill people he deemed sinners.[685]

Rupert Howarth, Ianto's mentor and the head of Torchwood One's biochemical research division, attempted to create a human-alien hybrid with special forces applications. Most of Howarth's test subjects died, but he became fearful of a survivor - the fear-inducing Chimera - and faked his death to go underground.[686]

Astrid Peth spent three years working at the Spaceport Diner before signing up as a waitress with Capricorn Cruiseliners.[687]

c 2005 - TW: TRACE MEMORY[688] **->** Cardiff police officer Gwen Cooper met her new partner, Andy Davidson, and briefly encountered the time-travelling Michael Bellini.

2006[689]

Luke Rattigan established the Rattigan Academy, an advanced school for science students, in 2006.[690] Phicorps, a pharmaceutical company controlled by the Three Families, began stockpiling drugs in preparation for the Miracle.[691] Oswald Danes, a schoolteacher, was convicted in 2006 for the rape and murder of 12-year-old Susie Kabina. Concerning his victim, Danes infamously declared, "She should've run faster."[692]

In 2006, Lucie Miller relocated from the North of England to London, and planned to live with her friend Amanda from school. She met Karen Coltraine in the Tube - the pair of them had interviews with Hulbert Logistics. Todd Hulbert brainwashed them and sent them via a portal to his "Telford branch" on Lonsis. This worried the Time Lords, who feared that the history-revised Coltraine might become unstable if brought into proximity with the Telford branch's quantum crystalliser. However, the Time Lords worked from faulty intelligence data, and mistook Lucie for Coltraine.

The Time Lords intercepted Lucie's transport through space, causing her to arrive in the eighth Doctor's console room. The Doctor was duped into thinking Lucie had been placed with him as part of the Time Lords' witness protection programme. He tried to take Lucie home, but found that the Time Lords had established a temporal barrier around her era.

Lucie became the Doctor's companion - on their first trip together, they encountered the Daleks on the human colony planet Red Rocket Rising. Hulbert was distressed to find Lucie missing - if for no other reason than he wanted to know which rival was poaching his employees. He hired a time-travelling Headhunter to bring her back.[693]

Jack Harkness encountered the Perfection - aliens who were passing as two young men named Brendan and Jon. They claimed to be "very old gods" who habitually visited a planet for millennia, made it wonderful and moved on; Hallam's World, the Province of Sovertial and the Min Barrier were examples of their work. After a night of "negotiating" with Brendan and Jon in bed, Jack accepted that they were a bit knackered of world-building, and sought nothing more than to improve Cardiff's gay scene by running a nightclub.[694]

The Raxas Alliance consisted of four planets: Raxacoricofallapatorius, Raxacoricovarlonpatorius, Clom and Clix. The Slitheen, a family from Raxacoricofallapatorius, were charged by the High Council of Raxas Prime with fraud, theft and treason - each of which carried a death sentence - and were forced out of the Alliance by the Judoon. In their absence, the Blatthereen and Hostrozeen families wielded influence. A Grand Council and a Senate governed Raxacoricofallapatorius. The Raxacoricofallapatorians had an instinctive urge to hunt, as it was the only way to keep food safe when the Baaraddelshelliumfatrexius beasts (creatures akin to giant squirrels) roamed the plains.[695]

Toshiko Sato's mother died.[696]

---

686 *TW:* "The Legacy of Torchwood One!"
687 *Voyage of the Damned*
688 Dating *TW: Trace Memory* (*TW* novel #5) - Gwen is already a police officer and here meets Andy, but the year is unclear. Rhys eats some Marmite even though the "sell-by date said fifth of March" (p80), so Bellini must visit after that.
689 Events in 2006 include the "present day" sequences of *Doctor Who* Series 1 from *Aliens of London* onwards, and *The Christmas Invasion*.

THE YEAR AHEAD ERA (2006-2009): When the ninth Doctor returns Rose home in *Aliens of London*, "twelve months" after she left (in *Rose*), the subsequent "present day" *Doctor Who* episodes (as well as many of the related *Torchwood* and *The Sarah Jane Adventures* stories) adhere to a dating scheme in which they are set (roughly) a year or so after broadcast. This paradigm ends with *Planet of the Dead*, which has to occur in 2009, the year in which it aired (see the dating notes on

that story for why).

Torchwood Series 1 adheres to the "year ahead" approach, Series 2 deviates from the pattern, Series 3 (a.k.a. *TW: Children of Earth*) occurs about two months rather than a year ahead of broadcast, and Series 4 (a.k.a. *TW: Miracle Day*) happens in the same year it was shown, 2011.

The way in which *The Sarah Jane Adventures* initially accommodates the "year ahead of broadcast" dating scheme, then returns to a "time of broadcast" setting midway through Series 3, means that the whole of the show (Series 1-5) elapses over a total of two years and nine months (from August 2008 to May 2011).

See the entries for 2007, 2008 and 2009 (and by extension 2010 and 2011) for a more specific list of which stories occur in those years.
690 Per his on-screen bio in *The Sontaran Stratagem*.
691 "Five years" before *TW: Miracle Day*.
692 *TW: Miracle Day*. It's variously said that Danes

2006 - HUMAN RESOURCES[697] -> The planet Telos was unknown to the Cybermen based on the war-torn Lonsis.

The Headhunter captured Lucie and returned her to Lonsis, but the eighth Doctor followed them using a time ring. The Time Lords and the CIA had brokered a deal in which neither group would interfere on Lonsis directly. The Doctor found the CIA's quantum crystalliser and expanded its range; the Cybermen were killed as probability went against them. Hulbert died amid the battle, and the Headhunter took Coltraine on as her assistant.

The Doctor ordered the Time Lords to destroy Hulbert's machines and return the displaced humans home, then retrieved his TARDIS and continued travelling with Lucie.

c 2006 - NIGHT THOUGHTS[698] -> The seventh Doctor, Ace and Hex arrived on Gravonax Island, just as Major Dickens and his colleagues transmitted a message (via the Bartholomew Transactor) to their previous selves in 1996, with aim of preventing the death of a young girl, Edie. The resultant paradox caused Edie's corpse to revive in a zombified state. Edie took vengeance on those involved in her death - she murdered Bartholomew and Hartley, drove the Deacon to commit suicide and gouged out Dickens' eyes. Her fate remained unclear, but her sister Ruth was reunited with their father, Dr. O'Neill.

The Doctor sent Bartholomew's unpublished thesis to the editor of *The New Scientist*, helping it to reach the widest possible audience. In future centuries, it would speed development of a workable theory of time travel.

2006 (2nd February) - TW: TRACE MEMORY[699] -> Following the 1967 Hamilton's Sugar incident, Charles Arthur Cromwell had some preknowledge concerning the time-jumps of Michael Bellini. Cromwell arrived at Torchwood One, as he knew he was fated to do, prior to Bellini appearing there. Torchwood One was evacuated as the Vondrax attacked it to capture Bellini. The Vondrax killed Cromwell, then pursued Bellini through time. Ianto Jones' boss, Bev Stanley, went missing during this incident.

c 2006 - LET'S KILL HITLER[700] -> Shortly after stealing a bus and driving it through a botanical garden, Mels Zucker caused Amy Pond to realise that Rory fancied her.

Amy's favourite cat was named "Biggles". One summer, Rory returned to school with a ludicrous haircut, claiming he'd been in a rock band, and consequently had to learn to play the guitar. He and Amy had their first kiss while dancing the Macarena.[701]

Captain Jack recruited Owen Harper for Torchwood. On only his second week on the job, Owen woke up drunk. Toshiko went undercover as a medic in his place, and investigated the Slitheen's infiltration of 10 Downing Street...[702]

2006 (March) - ALIENS OF LONDON / WORLD WAR THREE[703] -> The ninth Doctor accidentally returned Rose home twelve months after he first met her, instead of twelve hours. A spaceship soon crashed into the Thames, and a state of emergency was called in the

---

uttered his quote during his arrest/at his trial.
693 *Blood of the Daleks, Human Resources.*
694 "Three years" prior to *TW: Almost Perfect.*
695 The background to *Aliens of London* and the Slitheen's subsequent appearances, as detailed in *SJA: Revenge of the Slitheen* and *SJA: The Gift*. The two accounts don't entirely match up: where does Raxas Prime (another name for Raxacoricofallapatorius, perhaps?) fit into the Raxas Alliance hierarchy? And if the Slitheen were given death sentences, why did the Judoon "force them out" rather than arresting them? (Perhaps the Slitheen were "forced out" in the sense that they fled in the wake of the Judoon's overwhelming force.) Either way, the timeframe of exactly when all of this occurred is uncertain.
696 The year is unknown, but she's alive in the 2004 portion of *TW: Fragments*, and yet is a ghost in *TW: End of Days* (set in early 2008).
697 Dating *Human Resources* (BF BBC7 #1.7-1.8) - Lucie has been "pulled back to her natural place in time", which according to *Blood of the Daleks* is 2006.
698 Dating *Night Thoughts* (BF #79) - The setting is

roughly contemporary, and the audio was released in February 2006. Dickens and the Deacon served in the Falklands War (which took place in 1982), and the researchers have subsequently met or permanently lived on the island for the last thirteen years.
699 Dating *TW: Trace Memory* (TW novel #5) - Cromwell's death is dated to "14/02/2006" (p99).
700 Dating *Let's Kill Hitler* (X6.8) - The three of them are acquainted while age seven, and this happens after Amy has known Rory for "what, ten years?" The way in which Mels helps to push the two of them together means that River Song, as if her life wasn't complicated enough, helped to facilitate her own conception.
701 *The Girl Who Waited*
702 *TW: Exit Wounds*. This confirms that "Dr Sato" in *Aliens of London*, as played by Naoko Mori, is the same character as Toshiko from *Torchwood*.
703 Dating *Aliens of London/World War Three* (X1.4-1.5) - It is "twelve months" since *Rose*, and a missing persons poster says Rose has been missing since 6th March, 2005 - so it's March 2006, and for all we know specifically 6th March. The (BBC's) UNIT website gave the story

UK. Worse, the Prime Minister had vanished. The Doctor investigated and realised that the crash had been faked... by genuine aliens who had infiltrated 10 Downing Street and murdered the Prime Minister. This was done to lure the world's main experts on alien life into a lethal trap.

The perpetrators were the Slitheen, a notorious criminal family of Raxacoricofallapatorians, who were plotting to provoke humanity into launching nuclear missiles and destroying their own planet. This would enable the Slitheen to convert and sell Earth's remains as radioactive fuel. The Doctor used his UNIT codes to launch a missile that destroyed 10 Downing Street and the Slitheen.

A backbench MP, Harriet Jones, had been instrumental in helping the Doctor - who told Rose that Jones was destined to become Prime Minister, serve three terms and usher in the British Golden Age. Harriet Jones became Prime Minister following a general election when her party won a landslide majority.[704]

Margaret Slitheen escaped the destruction of Downing Street using a portable teleporter. She ended up in a skip in the Isle of Dogs, later making her way to Cardiff.[705] After this time, Torchwood Cardiff were involved with Operation Goldenrod, which saw people's bodies fused together.[706]

2006 (24th May) - "F.A.Q."[707] -> The tenth Doctor and Rose arrived in a London transformed into a surreal place of talking trees and Vikings with laser guns. It was a virtual reality created by Craig, an abused youngster who had erroneously received a Happytimez Intergalactical game-box. The Doctor helped an alien technician, a Cyrelleod, to end the virtual reality.

(=) 2006 (24th June) - THE TIME TRAVELLERS[708] -> After colliding with a man falling through the Vortex, the TARDIS materialised in Canary Wharf. The first Doctor, Susan, Ian and Barbara discovered that Britain was at war with South Africa. The British were conducting time travel experiments using Dalek technology recovered from Coal Hill School in 1963, and different versions of history were beginning to intrude on this one. In this version of history, WOTAN succeeded in its bid for domination, and banned electronic communication in 1968. It was subsequently destroyed in 1969, and everyone under its hypnotic control was left brain-damaged. A World War broke out. The South Africans gained Cybertechnology at the South Pole, and used it to invade Europe.

The TARDIS' presence disrupted the time experiments, allowing the various timelines to connect. By travelling back to 1972, then 1948, Ian restored history.

---

the date of "28 June 2006".

HARRIET JONES, BRITISH PRIME MINISTER: We learn in *The Christmas Invasion* that Harriet Jones took office shortly after *World War Three*, winning a general election by a landslide. As she's a member of the governing party, she presumably became its leader (perhaps unopposed), so became Prime Minister, then called a snap election. In *World War Three*, the ninth Doctor remembers her ushering in the British Golden Age and serving three terms.

Three full terms as Prime Minister would be fifteen years, although constitutionally it's technically possible - if highly unlikely - that someone could serve three terms as a Prime Minister in a matter of months. As of *Aliens in London*, Harriet Jones was almost certainly Prime Minister for around a decade. We might speculate that Jones was a prime mover behind the Reconstruction mentioned in some of the New Adventures, itself portrayed as the beginning of a golden age. There's a female Prime Minister in *The Shadows of Avalon* who, retrospectively, could well be Harriet Jones. Shortly after that, in stories like *Time of the Daleks* and *Trading Futures*, British politics becomes more turbulent.

However... at the end of *The Christmas Invasion*, the Doctor seems to abruptly unseat Jones from office, and

potentially cancels out this history. From stories like *Father's Day* and *I am a Dalek*, it seems the Doctor is "allowed" to make small historical changes, but averting the career of a three-term Prime Minister would seem to cross the line. Does the Doctor *really* deny Britain its Golden Age because he's fallen out with Jones? At the very least, he certainly erases Jones' part in it. (For more on this, see the "Vote Saxon" essay.)

The Doctor doesn't seem to know much about the history of the first decade of the twenty-first century - he explicitly says he doesn't know about the "first contact" situation seen in *Aliens of London* (a remarkable gap in his knowledge of Earth's history, whichever way you look at it). Compare and contrast with Captain Jack's continuous assertion in *Torchwood* that the twenty-first century is the time that "everything changes".

704 *The Christmas Invasion*

705 *Boom Town*

706 TW: *Slow Decay*. A potential glitch is that Ianto needs to ask if Toshiko was involved - and she was.

707 Dating "F.A.Q." (*DWM* #369-371) - The date is given, and means Rose is here travelling a year or so into her past (although the Doctor had been planning to take her to China, not London).

708 Dating *The Time Travellers* (PDA #75) - The dates are

The Doctor travelled the Jubilee line in the London Underground on 24th June, 2006, and had some ice cream.[709]

2006 - WINNER TAKES ALL[710] **->** The ninth Doctor took Rose home, where the latest craze was the video game *Death to Mantodeans*. It had been supplied by the porcupine-like Quevvils of the planet Toop, and was a perfect simulation of their war. The Doctor got the high score and was teleported to the warzone - but he managed to disintegrate the Quevvil invasion force.

c 2006 (early September) - CIRCULAR TIME: "Autumn"[711] **->** The fifth Doctor and Nyssa lodged in Stockbridge for a number of weeks. While the Doctor played cricket, Nyssa wrote a novel - not intended for publication - and made the acquaintance of a waiter/graduate student named Andrew Whitaker. One day, Nyssa and Andrew travelled forty minutes away from Stockbridge to Traken Village.

On the final day of the cricket season, the Stockbridge team prevailed - but the team leader, Don, died of a heart attack while scoring the winning run. Nyssa and Andrew became lovers that afternoon, but she left with the Doctor afterwards, bequeathing her finished novel to Andrew.

2006 - "A Groatsworth of Wit"[712] **->** The alien Shadeys brought Robert Greene from 1592 to the present day, where Greene was disgusted to find he was hardly-known but Shakespeare was world famous. The ninth Doctor and Rose arrived to see Greene lash out in anger in a bookshop, and begin a rampage that involved attacking the premiere of a movie version of *The Taming of the Shrew*. The Doctor realised that the Shadeys were feeding off his negative emotions - Greene returned to his native time, and the Doctor and Rose followed in the TARDIS.

2006 (September) - BOOM TOWN[713] **-> Margaret Slitheen, a.k.a. Margaret Blaine, became Lord Mayor of Cardiff and pushed through construction of the Blaidd Drwg Power Station, which she had designed to destroy Earth and facilitate her escape into space on an Extrapolator surfboard. The ninth Doctor, Rose and Captain Jack landed in Cardiff to refuel the TARDIS and captured Margaret. Exposure to the heart of the TARDIS reverted Margaret to her original state as an egg. The Doctor returned Margaret to her home planet, Raxacoricofallapatorius, to start life anew.**

Margaret's scheme to destroy Earth to facilitate her escape had wracked Cardiff with an earthquake; officially, she was believed to have died during the event.[714]

The TARDIS' chameleon circuit welded its properties onto a very small area of the Rift, and created a perceptual blind spot.[715]

---

all given. The implication of the book is that the "real" timeline of the universe is one without the Doctor, so one where the monsters win. The Doctor is actually changing history when he defeats them. WOTAN appeared in *The War Machines*, and the Dalek technology stems from *Remembrance of the Daleks*.

709 Dating *Winner Takes All* (NSA #3) - The story is set after *Aliens of London/World War Three* and before *Boom Town*.

710 *The Slitheen Excursion* (p129). This is unrelated to *The Time Travellers*, which occurs on the very same day.

711 Dating *Circular Time*: "Autumn" (BF #91) - The story seems to end in early September, with the Doctor and Nyssa lodging in Stockbridge for at least five weeks beforehand. The year isn't given, but it's suggested that the Doctor has been coming to Stockbridge (the setting for his *DWM* comic strips) to play cricket for some time now. (Specifically, it's said that the clubhouse has photographs of "the Doctor's family" going back years.) A contemporary dating is supported by mention that the whole country has gone a bit mad about cricket since "England won the Ashes" - presumably a reference to the 2005 series, in which England bested Australia and won for the first time in eighteen years.

Traken Village isn't real, as appealing as it might

sound. The Doctor says that Nyssa (a Trakenite) and Andrew (a human) have roughly the same lifespan, which isn't helpful to anyone trying to reconcile discrepancies in the Doctor's age by suggesting that he and Nyssa travelled together for many years (possibly even decades) between *Time-Flight* and *Arc of Infinity*.

712 Dating "A Groatsworth of Wit" (DWM #363-#364) - Greene is transported to the present day.

713 Dating *Boom Town* (X1.11) - A caption at the start says it is "Six Months Later" than *World War Three*. The evening is "freezing" and it's dark relatively early, suggesting it's at least September (the month it would be if *World War Three* was set in March). A mention of Justicia in the story is a reference to the ninth Doctor novel *The Monsters Inside*. The mention of venom grubs - named as such in *The Web Planet* novelisation (entitled *The Zarbi*), but called "larvae guns" in the TV story - suggests Margaret hails from the Isop galaxy. (*Bad Wolf* also names Isop as the home galaxy of the Face of Boe.)

714 *TW: The Twilight Streets*
715 *TW: Everything Changes*

2006 - THE DEVIANT STRAIN[716] -> The ninth Doctor, Rose and Jack arrived at Novrosk Peninsula in Siberia, the site of an old Soviet base. There had recently been a series of mysterious deaths, which the Doctor determined was caused by the defence systems of a crashed ship from the Arcane Collegiate. The threat was dispelled when the Doctor destroyed the ship.

2006 - ONLY HUMAN[717] -> The ninth Doctor, Rose and Jack arrived in Bromley to investigate temporal distortion caused by a "dirty rip" engine. They discovered a Neanderthal named Das at a local hospital. Das couldn't return home because the dirty rip engine had weakened his structure, but the Doctor and Rose went to 29,185 BC to locate the source of the problem. With Jack's help, Das quickly got a job in construction and married a girl called Anne-Marie.

Suzie Costello of Torchwood recovered an alien device that could open any lock.[718]

2006 (22nd September) - THE GATHERING[719] -> Scarred by her brother's misfortune, Katherine Chambers envisioned the removal of humanity's weaknesses and emotions through widespread Cybertisation. She worked toward the creation of System, the ultimate medical computer. Aiding her was James Clarke, secretly an agent of the Forge.

Tegan Jovanka now had a brain tumour - possibly the result of her travels with the Doctor - and was deemed by Kathy, an acquaintance of hers, as a perfect test subject. James and Kathy created System using Cyber-technology, but the fifth Doctor was on hand and convinced the half-human Nate Chambers to activate System's self-destruct. James escaped, but Chambers Pharmaceuticals exploded, killing Nate. Kathy was believed dead, but the Doctor took her elsewhere to be looked after.

Tegan resumed her romance with Michael Tenaka and turned down the Doctor's offer of finding treatment for her brain tumour.

---

716 Dating *The Deviant Strain* (NSA #4) - The year isn't given, although there are references to the Cold War ending "twenty years" ago. It would seem to be set in Rose's home time.

717 Dating *Only Human* (NSA #5) - The story takes place after *Boom Town* (and *The Deviant Strain*), but - owing to Jack's presence - before *The Parting of the Ways*.

718 Jack says that Suzie found the lock-pick "last year" in *TW: Cyberwoman*.

719 Dating *The Gathering* (BF #87) - The date is given, and reinforced by a radio broadcast citing the birthday of Australian rocker Nick Cave, and discretely mentioning the same for Billie Piper - both were born on 22nd September. In an attempt at symmetry with *The Reaping*, a radio broadcast also mentions an interview with Colin Farrell about the 2006 *Miami Vice* movie. However, the broadcast implies the film isn't out yet - it was actually released in Australia about five weeks prior on 10th August, 2006. Tegan's mother is still alive.

720 Dating *The Parting of the Ways* (X1.13) - No specific date is given, but there's no evidence that much time has passed since Rose and Mickey's meeting in *Boom Town*. In *The Christmas Invasion*, Jackie's been going out with Howard for "about a month", and Rose doesn't know about their relationship beforehand, so *The Parting of the Ways* is probably set before late November.

721 The date of the publication was given in the *Remembrance of the Daleks* novelisation, and was confirmed by *Set Piece*. In *Transit*, Yembe Lethbridge-Stewart states that Kadiatu was named after his great-grandmother, the historian. Although in *Set Piece*, Kadiatu claims that her namesake was her "grandmother", presumably for brevity's sake.

722 *Boom Town*. This was due to happen on "the nine-

teenth" and "next month".

723 "About a month" before *The Christmas Invasion*.

724 *TW: Children of Earth*

725 Dating *Iceberg* (NA #18) - The main action of the book takes place in 2006, from "early November" (p25) to "Friday 22 December" (p1). The epilogue is set on "Wednesday 31 January 2007" (p251).

726 Dating *The Christmas Invasion* (X2.0) - The story takes place at Christmas, shortly after *The Parting of the Ways*. Subsequent stories establish that this is indeed Christmas 2006. "A third" of the world's population is two billion people at this time.

WHEN DO THE GENERAL PUBLIC ACCEPT THE EXISTENCE OF ALIENS?: It's was a long-held tradition in classic *Doctor Who* that there are plenty of alien invasions, yet no one in the present day believes in them, or even really notices. Even given the Doctor's comments in *Remembrance of the Daleks* and *Rose* that humans are blind to what's going on around them, that most alien attacks are covert or limited to isolated locations, and that the government keeps hushing up the existence of aliens, there are a number of stories set before 2085 (cited in *The Dying Days* as humanity's first official diplomatic contact with alien races) where the general population really can't escape the existence of aliens. Such stories include *The Tenth Planet*, *The Dying Days*, and *Aliens of London*. By the end of the last two, people have already started declaring that the aliens are a hoax, and this seems to become the accepted view of what happened.

This has shifted now, though. The new *Doctor Who* occasionally jokes about humanity's willingness to overlook the blatantly obvious, but by *Last of the Time Lords*, only people as obtuse as Donna Noble can be in much doubt about the existence of extra-terrestrial life.

2006 - THE PARTING OF THE WAYS[720] -> The ninth Doctor forcibly returned Rose to her native time aboard the TARDIS, removing her from the Dalek incursion in 200,100. Rose realised that the words "Bad Wolf" had been scattered throughout time and space as a message that she should return to the fray, and she exposed the heart of the TARDIS with help from her mother and Mickey. Rose and the TARDIS returned to 200,100.

By now, the general population knew that aliens had invaded Earth over a dozen times. In 2006, Kadiatu Lethbridge-Stewart published her controversial bestseller *The Zen Military: A History of UNIT*. Lethbridge-Stewart was the granddaughter of Alistair Lethbridge-Stewart and Mariatu of the Themne tribe, making her ideally placed to write the "definitive" study of the UNIT era.[721]

Cathy Salt, the pregnant journalist spared by Margaret Slitheen, was scheduled to marry Jeffrey on 19th October.[722] In November, Jackie Tyler started going out with Howard from the market.[723] On 23rd November, 2006, Lucia Moretti, a former Torchwood operative, died from heart failure.[724]

2006 (November to December) - ICEBERG[725] -> Earth's magnetic pole shifted slightly, causing consternation at the FLIPback project. Tensions were not eased when the nearby Nikkei 5 research station vanished into the Torus Antarctica. The Cybermen were behind both the disappearances and the magnetic fluctuations, but the seventh Doctor defeated them with the help of journalist Ruby Duvall.

2006 (24th-25th December) - THE CHRISTMAS INVASION[726] -> The newly-regenerated tenth Doctor arrived back on Earth with Rose. He recovered in Jackie's flat, and became the target of robot Santas and a killer Christmas tree. These were just "pilot fish" for

---

Between 2006 and 2008, humanity is made to witness a spaceship destroying Big Ben and crashing into the Thames (*Aliens of London*); another spaceship arriving over London, and its sonic boom causing a swath of damage - this is accompanied by a third of humanity being compelled to stand on rooftops while strange lights illuminate their heads, the face of the Sycorax leader being transmitted on BBC1, a newscaster's declaration that it is "absolute proof that alien life exists", and a super-laser destroying the departing spaceship (*The Christmas Invasion*); the public acceptance of "ghosts", who manifest as five million Cybermen and capture Earth before they're pulled through the sky - along with a flying Dalek army - into Canary Wharf (*Army of Ghosts/Doomsday*); the Racnoss spaceship firing bolts of energy against London, and Mr Saxon gaining prominence because the military destroys the ship on his orders (*The Runaway Bride*); a horned demon looming over Cardiff, and its shadow killing droves of pedestrians (*TW: End of Days*); Royal Hope Hospital vanishing, leaving behind only a crater before reappearing some hours later - this coincides with the hospital appearing on the moon, and about a thousand people inside being scanned by space rhinos (*Smith and Jones,* although it's still possible for Clive Jones' girlfriend, Annalise, to dismiss the idea of aliens); and - most tellingly of all - the British Prime Minister presenting the Toclafane to the world, a day before one of their number murders the American President during a worldwide broadcast (*The Sound of Drums*). The destruction of the Paradox Machine undoes the Toclafane's capture of Earth, but explicitly everything up to and including the assassination of the President still happens. And soon after that, the sun turns a cold blue (*SJA: Invasion of the Bane*), an event that is (flimsi-

ly) attributed in a cover story to a "temporary reversal of the Earth's magnetic poles".

The final straw for anyone too thick to believe in aliens prior to this is, surely, *The Stolen Earth/Journey's End* - in which Earth is both teleported into a sector of space with twenty six other abducted worlds, incurs massive casualties while being overrun by the Daleks, and is physically hauled through space while being returned to its natural orbit. Clyde Langer's father later mentions the Daleks by name (*SJA: The Mark of the Berserker*), and it's an event so hard to ignore, Gwen Cooper can tell someone who has been in cryo-freeze, "These days the whole alien cat is rather out of the bag... The Daleks invaded." (*TW: Risk Assessment*, p83)

Circa 2009 to 2011, the public also experiences the moon being set on a collision course with Earth (*SJA: The Lost Boy*), astrologer Martin Trueman hijacking every TV broadcast and hypnotising large swathes of the public according to their astrological symbols (*SJA: Secrets of the Stars*), the entire human race (sans Wilf and Donna) turning into Prime Minister Harold Saxon/the Master (*The End of Time*), everyone on Earth being made to think a meteor is hurtling toward them (*SJA: Goodbye, Sarah Jane Smith*), the children of Earth simultaneously speaking words in English (*TW: Children of Earth*) and death being suspended across the globe for a period of at least two months, possibly more (*TW: Miracle Day*).

It remains to be seen if future production teams will "erase" the public's belief in aliens and credit this change to the Cracks in Time in Series 5, but at time of writing, there's reason to believe this hasn't happened (see the Cracks in Time sidebar). The occasional glitch remains (Adam in *Dalek* - set in 2012 - thinks that the existence of aliens isn't public; Hex, who originates

the Sycorax, whose vast spacecraft intercepted the British Guinevere 1 Probe to Mars and set course for Earth.

NATO went to red alert. Prime Minister Harriet Jones took control of UNIT's command centre underneath the Tower of London, where the Sycorax made contact and lay claim to the entire Earth. As a means of blackmail, they used "blood control" to hypnotically command one-third of the population, including the Royal Family, to walk to the nearest rooftop.

Jones made a public appeal to the Doctor as the Sycorax ship arrived over London. Jones, Major Blake of UNIT, Danny Llewellyn of the British Rocket Group and the PM's aide Alex were teleported to the Sycorax ship, where Llewellyn and Blake were quickly killed. The Doctor recovered and challenged the Sycorax leader to a duel. The leader cut off the Doctor's hand with a sword, but as the Doctor was within the first fifteen hours of his regeneration cycle, he was able to regrow the hand and go on to kill the Sycorax leader. The Sycorax retreated.

Harriet Jones feared that the Sycorax would spread word about the Earth, and that more alien invaders would return in the Doctor's absence. She ordered Torchwood to destroy the retreating Sycorax ship with an energy weapon - whereupon the horrified Doctor called Jones' fitness to lead into question, and deposed her with a single sentence ("Don't you think she looks tired?"). Questions were raised about Jones' health,

and a vote of no confidence was quickly scheduled.

The British could use "the Hubble array" to track spacecraft. The Sycorax used the Sycoraxic language.

Many people went to Trafalgar Square to celebrate - Ursula Blake was among them, and while there happened to take a picture of the Doctor.[727] Donna Noble missed the excitement of Christmas Day because she had a bit of a hangover.[728] The Doctor's severed hand ended up in the archives of Torchwood Cardiff.[729] The Sycorax leader defeated by the Doctor fell to Earth at Westminster Abbey.[730]

The newly-regenerated Master arrived on Earth from the end of the universe, and adopted the alias "Harold Saxon". He faked his past, and set up the Archangel Network of satellites to subliminally influence the British public into supporting his policies. The Archangel signals also masked the Master's presence, and preventing the Doctor from detecting him in this time zone. The Master married a woman named Lucy, and his meteoric rise saw him become Minister of Defence. In such a position, he helped to design a flying aircraft carrier, the *Valiant*.[731]

After the Sycorax Invasion, some people obsessed with the Doctor formed the group LINDA.[732]

c 2006 - "The Lodger" (DWM)[733] **->** The tenth Doctor popped in to see Mickey, telling him that he and Rose had just escaped some Lombards - but that the TARDIS had

from 2021, believes the same in *Project: Destiny*), but for now, at least, there's no need to do anything as drastic as put most of Series 1-4, the Tennant specials, *Torchwood* and *The Sarah Jane Adventures* into alternate-universe bubbles.

One story from the non-TV media is worth mentioning: the *DWM* strip "The Mark of Mandragora" establishes that the events of "Invaders of Gantac" and (perhaps a little oddly) *Battlefield* led the general public to the realisation that aliens existed. That was contradicted by *Rose,* but the new TV series swiftly established that - in the words of Captain Jack in *Torchwood* - "the twenty-first century is when everything changes".

727 *Love & Monsters*
728 *The Runaway Bride*
729 *TW: Everything Changes*, and confirmed in *Utopia*. The Doctor lost his hand in *The Christmas Invasion*.
730 "The Widow's Curse"
731 "Eighteen months" before *The Sound of Drums*, and by implication very soon after *The Christmas Invasion*. It's not clear who runs Britain for those eighteen months - possibly it's a weakened Harriet Jones. As Jones had only recently won by a landslide, it's easy to infer that the opposition parties are also in disarray. The

fact that Saxon's Cabinet in *The Sound of Drums* is composed of people from various political parties would seem to support that. However, the Prime Minister as seen in a blurry photograph in *TW: Out of Time* (set in late 2007) looks male.

The official "Vote Saxon" website states that Lucy's father (mentioned, but not named, in *The Sound of Drums*) is called Lord Cole of Tarminster, so it's likely her maiden name was "Lucy Cole".
732 *Love & Monsters*
733 Dating "The Lodger" (*DWM* #368) - This would seem to fit into the gap between *The Christmas Invasion* and *New Earth*. This strip contains a few jokes and story beats later seen the Series 5 episode of the same name (also written by Gareth Roberts), but the two aren't *so* similar that they become as contradictory as the two versions of *Human Nature*. Any commonalities can, ultimately, be written off as coincidence.
734 Dating *New Earth* (X2.1) - The Doctor and Rose leave the Powell Estate, some undetermined amount of time after *The Christmas Invasion*. The cheerful note on which that story ends might make one think that they intended on leaving immediately afterwards - except that in *New Earth*, the TARDIS has moved; Jackie, Mickey

accidentally jumped a time track, so Rose wouldn't be showing up for a couple of days. Jackie was occupied with a man called Alan, so the Doctor stayed with Mickey. After the Doctor beat him at video games *and* tuned his TV so that Mickey got programmes from ten years in the future *and* ruined a night in planned with a girl called Gina, Mickey got sick of him. After a few days, the TARDIS arrived with Rose. The Doctor arranged it so that Mickey and Rose had a nice Sunday together.

c 2006 - NEW EARTH[734] **->** The tenth Doctor and Rose set off on their travels, leaving behind Jackie and Mickey.

There was Graske activity on Earth.[735] A group of Groske, similar in form to the Graske but with blue skin, were stranded on Earth in 2006. UNIT made them earn their keep as engineers.[736]

2007[737]

The Krillitanes were a composite species, given to absorbing the physical aspects of the races they conquered and destroyed. A small group of them took on human form and infiltrated Deffry Vale School, with "Mr Finch" taking over as headmaster.[738]

Joseph Serf, the owner of Serf Systems, died in a skiing accident in 2007. John Harrison, Serf's public relations officer, purchased a group of Scullions - short aliens with only one eye - on the black market after their ship crash-landed in Central Asia. With the Scullions manipulating a holographic image of Joseph Serf, Harrison covered up the man's death and assumed control of the company.[739]

In 2007, Jack Harkness, Owen Harper and Suzie Costello dealt with ravenous creatures masquerading as schoolchildren. A school teacher, Eryn Bunting, saw the creatures and was given Retcon. Suzie stole one of Eryn's bank slips, and set up a secret account for herself under Eryn's name.[740] Elena Hilda Al-Qatari became ill and requested a replacement to head the Rawbone Project, which renewed the government's interest in it.[741]

Maxwell Edison set up the Stockbridge Preservation Society to protest Khrysalis Corporation building a leisure park.[742] **Henry John Parker acquired extra-terrestrial items that included a Dogon eye, Ikean wings, and an alien translation of James Herbert's** *The Fog* **(1975).**[743]

Tamsin Drew, a future companion of the eighth Doctor and the Monk, appeared in an advert for leg wax.[744] She also worked for a summer at the London dungeon, as a Cockney drab who was killed by Jack the Ripper.[745]

Coldfire Construction, a front for the Slitheen, started expanding and specialised in the installation of technology blocks in schools in London, Barcelona, Washington D.C., Santiago, Los Angeles, Sydney, Beijing, Moscow, Naples and Paris.[746] A geologist friend sent Sarah Jane a crystal found at the site of Krakatoa - as Sarah quickly discovered, the crystal revealed itself to be alive when it communicated with her laptop. Following its instructions, she built a computer to house its sentience, which she called Mr Smith and kept in her attic. Mr Smith offered to help Sarah protect Earth and monitor extra-terrestrial activity, and dutifully did so. In secret, however, Mr Smith schemed to release its brethren, the Xylox, from their imprisonment beneath the Earth.[747]

2007 - THE STONE ROSE[748] **->** Mickey showed the tenth Doctor and Rose a statue from Ancient Rome in the British Museum - one that depicted Rose. The Doctor and Rose travelled back in time to investigate.

---

and Rose are all wearing different clothes; Rose now has luggage with her; and the ash from the Sycorax ship has gone. Also, they still had some Christmas food waiting inside (not to mention that they hadn't opened any presents). It's not impossible, though, that they left straight after *The Christmas Invasion*, returned after some unseen adventures, then left once again.

735 "A couple of years back" according to Sarah Jane in *SJA: Whatever Happened to Sarah Jane?* It's almost certainly a reference to the interactive story *Attack of the Graske* that appeared on the BBC website (and which is outside the remit of this book).

736 *SJA: Death of the Doctor*

737 Events in 2007 include the "present day" sequences of *Doctor Who* Series 2 and most (but not all) of *Torchwood* Series 1.

738 "Three months" before *School Reunion*.

739 *SJA: The Man Who Never Was*

740 *TW: Long Time Dead* (p206).

741 "A few years" before *TW: First Born*.

742 The year before "The Stockbridge Child".

743 Throughout the year prior to *TW: A Day in the Death*.

744 "Three years" before *Situation Vacant*.

745 *Deimos*

746 "Eighteen months" before *SJA: Revenge of the Slitheen*.

747 "Eighteen months" before *SJA: The Lost Boy*, and after K9 begins monitoring the black hole, as they have not met before that story.

748 Dating *The Stone Rose* (NSA #7) - Mickey hasn't joined the TARDIS crew, but Rose knows about Petrifold Regression, so it's set between *New Earth* and *School Reunion*.

2007 - THE FEAST OF THE DROWNED[749] -> The HMS *Ascendant* sank in the North Sea, killing Jay, the brother of Rose's friend Keisha. The tenth Doctor and Rose arrived, discovering that a number of people had died in London since wreckage from the *Ascendant* was brought there. Relatives of the dead were apparently being contacted by the ghosts of the drowned, but this was a side effect of alien technology. The Waterhive were attempting to conquer the world, but the Doctor thwarted them.

2007 - CUDDLESOME[750] -> Ronald Turvey was released from prison, but his toy factory at Shoreham Harbour was defunct. The Tinghus within Turvey formed a plan: new Cuddlesomes would be manufactured that could transform people into Tinghus-human hybrids. A recall signal summoned the 1980s Cuddlesomes to their birthplace, and a rumble broke out between the different generations of Cuddlesomes. The fifth Doctor witnessed the Cuddlesome slaughter, which ended when Turvey and the Tinghus (which manifested as a giant Cuddlesome) both died, rendering the Cuddlesomes inactive.

2007 - SCHOOL REUNION[751] -> **Mickey called in the tenth Doctor and Rose to help investigate Deffry Vale School. The Doctor posted a winning lottery ticket through the letterbox of one of the physics teachers and took their place. He met Sarah Jane Smith, who was also investigating the school. The Krillitanes were using the children's brains to formulate the Skasas Paradigm - an equation which could be used to control "the building blocks of the universe", even to the point**

of rewriting the past. **The reactivated K9 sacrificed himself to destroy the Krillitanes.**

The Doctor built a new K9 for Sarah Jane. Mickey joined the TARDIS crew.

The new K9 contained a compartment with a number of helpful gadgets for Sarah Jane, like the sonic lipstick.[752] **A black hole was released following a Swiss laboratory accident. K9 contained it, but this fully occupied his time, so he was unable to help Sarah Jane on her adventures.**[753]

c 2007 - "The Green-Eyed Monster" (*DWM*)[754] -> When Rose was infected by an alien worm that ate emotions, the tenth Doctor induced great jealousy in her by setting Mickey up with a girlfriend, and having an adventure on the planet of the Amazastians (the entire population of whom were beautiful teenage girls, much to the mystification of even their own scientists). The Doctor resorted to kissing Jackie, which overloaded the alien worm.

2007 - BORROWED TIME[755] -> Little Green Storage had installed a storage facility, the internal dimensions of which were compressed down to 7.5% normal, beneath the Millennium Dome. This provided a service to space travellers on Earth, which Little Green regarded as "the most frequently attacked colonised, exploited and enslaved planet in the five galaxies".

Members of the Ah N'Drubrn Clan of Warrior Molluscs were currently residing in the Thames. The Doctor had

---

749 Dating *The Feast of the Drowned* (NSA #8) - The story is set between *The Christmas Invasion* and *School Reunion*.

750 Dating *Cuddlesome* (BF promo #7, *DWM* #393) - The audio saw release in March 2008 and seems contemporary, including mention of texting. However, a radio report says that authorities in England are investigating a possible outbreak of H5N1 avian flu, which in real-life was a concern in the UK in 2007.

751 Dating *School Reunion* (X2.3) - The story features Mickey, and Sarah refers to the events of *The Christmas Invasion* as "last Christmas", so the story is set in 2007 (and at some point during a school term).

SARAH JANE'S REUNIONS WITH THE DOCTOR: In *School Reunion*, the very strong implication is that Sarah hasn't had any form of contact with the Doctor since she left him at the end of *The Hand of Fear*. Somewhat tellingly, the Doctor comments that he's regenerated "half a dozen times" since she last saw him.

Some commentators have seized upon this as evidence that the non-TV media (which entailed a post-*Hand of Fear* Sarah meeting the Doctor on more than one occasion) are apocryphal, but in truth this scenario

doesn't match the TV series either. In the first place, the Doctor sent Sarah a K9, and in *K9 and Company*, she even says "so he didn't forget me after all". Yet in *School Reunion*, Sarah says she thought the Doctor had forgotten about her after dropping her off. Also, she was reunited with the third Doctor - and met the fifth - in *The Five Doctors*. Clearly, as occasionally happens, the series chooses not to complicate the narrative by invoking every possible relevant previous story. Indeed, a new or more casual viewer would infer from what Sarah says that some time ago, the Doctor left her and K9 on Earth to go and fight the Time War.

Sarah Jane also appeared in a number of stories in other media set after *The Hand of Fear*: "Train-Flight" (set c 1990), *System Shock* (set in 1998; she didn't meet the Doctor in that story, but neither did she believe he was dead or had abandoned her), *Interference* (set in 1997, and portraying her as romantically involved with a man called Paul) and *Bullet Time* (also set in 1997). Ergo, Sarah Jane has encountered four of the "half a dozen" incarnations that the Doctor has been through between *The Hand of Fear* and *School Reunion*. The basic story beat is the same in each case - Sarah contin-

access to Galactic Enquiries, a newly introduced service that could provide an individual's phone number based upon such data as their sporting interests, their mother's name and whether or not they had a stain on their tie that day.

A parasitic organism posed as "Jane Blythe", a high-ranking personal assistant at Lexington International Bank. Blythe's avatars, Mr Symington and Mr Blenkinsop, offered select individuals Time Harvesters: wristwatches that they could use to borrow extra time. Interest was accrued at a rate of five minutes per hour, *every hour*, meaning the debt quickly exceeded the borrowers' lifespans. Blythe traded the accrued debt on the Time Market.

The eleventh Doctor, Amy and Rory ran afoul of Blythe when they arrived to observe the bank's historic collapse. Amy used a Time Harvester to spend more time with her husband, her parents and by herself, and the Doctor surrendered twenty-five years of his life to pay off the debt that this accrued. Blythe sought to sell the Doctor - the last remaining Time Lord - on the Time Market. He achieved an estimated value of five inhabited galaxies (about fifteen sextillion lives) before Blythe suffered a liquidity crisis. The Doctor bought Earth's outstanding debt for a second a decade. Blythe became a fugitive from the Time Market.

= **2007 (1st February) - RISE OF THE CYBERMEN / AGE OF STEEL**[756] -> The TARDIS materialised in a parallel universe with military checkpoints in the streets and zeppelins in the skies. The tenth Doctor, Rose and Mickey found that Rose's father Pete Tyler was alive in this reality, and had become rich from selling a health drink called Vitex Lite. Pete was preparing for Jackie's fortieth birthday party, and the guests included the President of Great Britain and a Torchwood agent named Stevie.

This world was home to a New South America and a New Germany. The Torchwood Institute was releasing studies to the public. The Bio-Convention required the registration of new life-forms. Rose was never born on this world, but the Tylers owned a small dog with the same name.

John Lumic's Cybus Industries owned "just about every company" in Britain, including Vitex. Cybus had sold EarPods to virtually everyone. Lumic himself was dying, and had developed a robot body that could house the human brain. His agents, operating through a dummy company named International Electromatics[757], started rounding up the homeless to convert into such cybernetic beings. Mickey discovered that his alternate self, Ricky, ran a resistance cell.

Lumic activated his cyborgs - the Cybermen - and they stormed Jackie's birthday party. The President was killed, and many guests were captured. Lumic transmitted a signal via the EarPods to all Londoners, making them march to Battersea Power Station to undergo conversion. Cybermen took to the streets, and Ricky was killed.

The Doctor confronted Lumic - who against his will had been converted into the Cyber Controller. Cyber-conversion factories had been built on all seven continents, but the Doctor instructed Mickey on how to deactivate the Cybermen's emotional inhibitors. Mentally unable to confront the nature of their lost humanity, the Cybermen malfunctioned. The Doctor and his allies escaped in Lumic's zeppelin, destroying the Power Station and the Controller.

Mickey remained in the parallel universe to help liberate it from the remaining Cybermen.

---

ues to be a successful journalist, while missing the Doctor.

752 Established on the BBC website; the sonic lipstick is seen in *SJS: Invasion of the Bane*.

753 "Eighteen months" before *SJS: Invasion of the Bane*.

754 Dating "The Green-Eyed Monster" (*DWM* #377) - *School Reunion* and The *Girl in the Fireplace* are both referenced, but it's before *Rise of the Cybermen*, as Mickey is still around.

755 Dating *Borrowed Time* (NSA #49) - The year is given (p60). The Chancellor of the Exchequer is to give a speech based upon the booming economy following "the first six months of 2007" (p201), so it's likely summer. Certainly, nobody complains about the weather. It's a Tuesday (p72).

756 Dating *Rise of the Cybermen/The Age of Steel* (X2.5-2.6) - Mickey finds a newspaper that he says is dated to

"1st February, this year" - in other words, the year *School Reunion* is set, 2007. Lumic cites the day as 1st February.

A birthday party is being held for the parallel-universe Jackie, and Rose says - when she and the Doctor are outside the Tyler mansion - "February the first, mum's birthday" (thereby indicating that "our" Jackie was born on the same day).

One point of confusion is that the official biography of the parallel Jackie - or so she claims - states that she was born the same day as actor Cuba Gooding Jr. He was actually born on 2nd January, 1968 (it would seem that someone on the production team didn't take into account that in America, the date "1/2" means the second of January). We might imagine that Gooding was born on 1st February in the parallel reality, or it's possible that Jackie's biographers - in an attempt to make her sound more interesting - simply got the date

Back in our universe, the Doctor and Rose met Jackie for a tearful reunion.

= On Pete's World, the People's Republic took control of Torchwood. The Cybermen were sealed in their factories, but a debate ensued about what to do with them, as they were living beings. Some Cybermen infiltrated Torchwood and vanished.[758]

2007 - I AM A DALEK[759] -> A Dalek left over from the Time War activated the Dalek Factor within the human Kate Yates. The tenth Doctor and Rose deactivated the Dalek, neutralising the Dalek Factor within Kate.

c 2007 - 100: "Bedtime Story"[760] -> Near Harrogate, the sixth Doctor accompanied Evelyn as she paid respects to one of her former students - Jacob Williams - regarding the death of his father Frank. The Doctor exposed the shapeshifting creature responsible for the Williams family "curse", but the shapeshifter rendered Evelyn, Jacob and Frank's wife Mary immobile - just as it had with Frank. The Doctor tricked the creature into thinking the Williams line had ended, then showed his charges the wonders of the universe in the TARDIS - and returned them home once they had recovered.

2007 - LOVE & MONSTERS[761] -> A "Bad Wolf" virus had corrupted Torchwood's files on Rose.

Elton Pope had been obsessed with the Doctor ever since seeing him as a child. He became a member of the group LINDA (London Investigation 'N' Detective Agency), which was made up of other people for whom the Doctor's existence filled a gap in their lives.

On a Tuesday night in March, the group fell under the sway of Victor Kennedy. He was secretly an Abzorbaloff from Clom, the twin planet of Raxacoricofallapatorius, who wanted to absorb the Doctor and his memories. Elton briefly met the tenth Doctor and Rose as they fought an alien Hoix, then later struck up a friendship with Jackie Tyler - in an attempt to get close to Rose. The Doctor and Rose tracked down Elton because he was "stalking" Rose's mother, and together they confronted the Abzorbaloff - who was defeated, and burst. Elton continued his relationship with Ursula, a member of LINDA, even though she had become a living paving slab.

The *Daily Telegraph* ran the headline: "Saxon Leads Polls with 64 per cent". Four more months of government paralysis were forecast.[762] Ghosts started appearing around the world, but people got used to them.[763]

---

wrong and nobody corrected her. (This is no more implausible an error than the real-life production team failing to fact-check Gooding's birthday via Google.)

"Our" Gooding was born in 1968 - so if Jackie was born the same year, she should be 39 in *Rise of the Cybermen*, not 40 as she claims. In addition to everything else, then, it's possible Jackie and Gooding's parallel counterparts were born a year prior in 1967.

757 Evidently a reference to Vaughn's company from *The Invasion*, which otherwise doesn't appear to exist in this reality.

758 *Doomsday*. The Doctor names this version of Earth as "Pete's World" (as Pete Tyler is alive there), and the term has caught on in texts such as *Doctor Who: The Encyclopedia*.

759 Dating *I am a Dalek* (*Quick Reads* #1) - No year is given, but the story has a present day setting.

760 Dating *100: "Bedtime Story"* (BF #100c) - The story seems contemporary with the audio's release in September 2007 - Jamie Oliver is referenced, and mention is made of the rumours surrounding Evelyn's disappearance. There's a glaring story flaw in that the Williams family has long since recognised the correlation between the birth of a son causing his grandparents to "drop dead", and yet no generation has, apparently, refrained from siring children even knowing that the act will kill their parents.

761 Dating *Love & Monsters* (X2.10) - It's "two years"

since the events of *Rose* (set in March 2005). The story takes place after *The Christmas Invasion*, but before *Army of Ghosts* and *Doomsday*. Jackie says that Mickey has gone, placing it after *The Age of Steel*.

Elton says that Kennedy approached LINDA on "a Tuesday night in March".

762 The Abzorbaloff reads the newspaper in *Love & Monsters*.

763 "Two months" before *Army of Ghosts*.

764 Dating *Turn Left* (X4.11) - This is "six months" before Donna would have met the Doctor in December 2007 (so, June). Rose says it's "Monday 25th", and June was the only month in 2007 when the 25th fell on a Monday. In the alternate timeline created by Donna turning right, there is no mention of Harold Saxon - because if the Doctor died defeating the Racnoss and *Utopia* didn't happen, the Master presumably remained at the end of time.

765 *Planet of the Ood, The Sontaran Stratagem, The Unicorn and the Wasp, Journey's End, The End of Time* (TV).

766 Dating *Army of Ghosts/Doomsday* (X2.12-2.13) - No month is given, but it's after *Love & Monsters* and before *The Runaway Bride* (set at Christmas Eve 2007).

Backtracking the *Torchwood* Series 1 dating makes it somewhat hard to believe that the Battle of Canary Wharf occurs any later than July. (*TW: Out of Time* takes place right before Christmas; *TW: They Keep Killing Suzie*

2007 (Monday, June 25th) - TURN LEFT[764] -> Donna Noble, a Chiswick resident[765], was offered temp work with HC Clements, but her mother insisted that she consider a full-time position as a secretary with Jival Chowdry's photocopy service. At one minute past 10 am, Donna made a fateful decision while driving: turn left and continue on to HC Clements, or turn right to interview for the full-time job. She turned left, and so went on to meet the tenth Doctor.

(=) Owing to the intervention of one of the Trickster's Brigade, a parallel timeline was created in which Donna turned right. Rose Tyler and UNIT aided the alternate version of Donna in travelling back to the temporal junction point, enabling the alt-Donna to sacrifice her life to cause a traffic jam so her other self would turn left. History was placed back on track.

2007 - ARMY OF GHOSTS / DOOMSDAY[766] -> Torchwood sought to obtain energy independence for the United Kingdom, and had been using particle engines to further open the temporal breach in Canary Wharf. A Voidship, designed to exist outside space and time, came through the breach; Torchwood took to studying it. The parallel-Earth Cybermen as created by Lumic followed in the Voidship's wake, and were manifesting on Earth as ghostly figures.

The tenth Doctor and Rose returned home to find that the public had accepted ghost appearances as a fact of life. Many media shows, including *Ghostwatch*, discussed the phenomenon.

The Doctor tracked the appearances of the ghosts to Torchwood HQ in Canary Wharf, and confronted the head of Torchwood, Yvonne Hartman. Soon after, the Cybermen achieved full manifestation - five million of them materialised from the parallel universe and occupied the planet. Hartman was forced to undergo Cyber-conversion. A Cyberman was seen strangling the host of *Ghostwatch*.[767] Martha Jones' cousin, Adeola Oshodi,

worked for Torchwood London and died just prior to the Cybermen takeover.[768]

Meanwhile, four Daleks - members of the Cult of Skaro, a secret order above even the Dalek Emperor - emerged from the Voidship with a Genesis Ark. The Cybermen and Daleks began fighting, and the Daleks opened the Ark - a Time Lord prison containing millions of Daleks. With the help of Pete Tyler and Mickey who had arrived from Pete's World), the Doctor and Rose opened a gateway to the Void and sucked all the Cybermen and Daleks into the gap between universes. The Cult of Skaro Daleks fled to the 1930s, but the Void was forever sealed. Rose, Jackie and Mickey were left trapped in the parallel universe with the alternate Pete.

After the battle, Rose and Jackie were listed as dead.

These events became known as The Battle of Canary Wharf.[769] Captain Jack read Rose and Jackie's names on the official list of those killed in the battle, and believed they had died.[770] During the battle, Donna Noble was scuba-diving in Spain.[771]

Items in the Torchwood HQ archives before the battle had included a particle gun, a magna-clamp that was found in a spaceship at the base of Mount Snowdon and a sarcophagus. Torchwood still used the Imperial weight system, having refused to go metric.[772]

The Cybermen had converted a number of the Torchwood London staff, but the conversion of Lisa Hallett - Ianto Jones' girlfriend - was interrupted by their defeat. Ianto cared for her in secret.[773]

Three Cybermen who were built on our Earth survived and escaped from the Torchwood Tower with an alien teleportation device. They set up a base inside the Millennium Dome.[774] The Cybertechnology Institute of Osaka was founded to learn the secrets of Cybertechnology. It was headed by a Dr Tanizaki.[775]

The Cybermen stole from the Daleks a dimension vault as well as information about the Doctor, which they placed on an infostamp.[776] Two members of

takes place beforehand but is "three months" after *TW: Everything Changes* - which *TW: Miracle Day* suggests occurs in October; Jack and Gwen chat about Canary Wharf in *TW: Everything Changes*, and don't speak as if the battle there occurred, say, within the last week or so.) *Army of Ghosts* and *Doomsday* respectively broadcast on 1st July and 8th July, and could well take place on one of those dates in 2008.
767 Alistair Appleton, who might be among the casualties in the *Doctor Who* universe.
768 *Smith and Jones*, which explains why Freema Agyeman portrayed both Martha in Series 3 and Adeloa in *Army of Ghosts*.

769 *TW: Everything Changes*
770 *Utopia*
771 *The Runaway Bride*
772 *Army of Ghosts*. The sarcophagus is evidently a reference to *Pyramids of Mars*.
773 *TW: Cyberwoman*
774 *Made of Steel*
775 *TW: Cyberwoman*, with additional info from Torchwood.co.uk.
776 The Doctor deduces this in *The Next Doctor*.

Torchwood Cardiff scoured the remains of Torchwood London to prevent its equipment falling into the wrong hands.[777] They failed to prevent billionaire Joshua Naismith from acquiring an alien device, the Immortality Gate, from the ruins.[778]

2007 - TW: FRAGMENTS[779] **->** Ianto Jones approached Captain Jack about a job at Torchwood Three. Jack resisted, but hired Ianto after he helped capture a pterodactyl that came through the Rift. Jack had Suzie dredge the reservoir for the Resurrection Gauntlet.

The alien viewer that fell into the Rift before life developed on Earth now emerged from it. Torchwood recovered the credit-card-sized device, which Suzie Costello had implanted into the skin of her belly, hoping it could convert energy and power the Resurrection Gauntlet.[780]

Jack saw the Perfection, a.k.a. Brendan and Jon, at Cardiff Gay Pride, where Owen used a flamethrower to help save singer Charlotte Church from a tentacle monster.[781] **Lance Bennett, the head of human resources at H C Clements, allied himself with the Empress of the Racnoss. As ordered, Bennett slipped some huon particles into the coffee of his co-worker, Donna Noble. The particles gestated within her, and Bennett had her re-dosed on a daily basis.**[782]

2007 - BLINK[783] **->** The Weeping Angels had developed as a race of hunters who could send people back in time, then live off the potential energy of the years their victims might have had. As a defence mechanism built in to their biology, they turned to stone if seen.

Sally Sparrow investigated the abandoned house Wester Drumlins, and discovered a message to her written on the wall by the tenth Doctor in 1969, before she was born. She returned with her friend Kathy Nightingale, who was sent to 1920 by the Angels.

Gradually, Sally discovered that the Doctor was a time traveller. The Angels had stolen the Doctor's TARDIS key and transported him - along with his companion Martha - back to 1969. Owing to messages left by the Doctor, Sally sent the TARDIS back to 1969 - and in doing so, caused the Weeping Angels to look at each other and become forever immobile.

c 2007 - "Fellow Travellers"[784] **->** The seventh Doctor and Ace defeated a Hitcher at the Doctor's house.

c 2007 - "Ravens"[785] **->** A notorious gang called the Ravens massacred everyone at a service station and used their blood in an occult ritual. Needing more blood, they tried to kill two passersby: Christine Jenkins and her daughter Demi. The TARDIS materialised, and the seventh Doctor let out Raven, a seventeenth-century Japanese warrior who butchered the gang apart from a woman named Annie - whose face he slashed in a deliberate way. A few months later, outside the house at Allen Road, Annie explained to other youths that she now understood the patterns of time.

---

777 *TW: Fragments*

778 *The End of Time* (TV)

779 Dating *TW: Fragments* (*TW* 2.12) - Ianto surely wouldn't waste much time in approaching Jack after the destruction of Canary Wharf (in *Doomsday*), as he joins Torchwood Cardiff to care for his injured girlfriend, who was partly cyber-converted in the battle there. The modern-day component of *Fragments* occurs "21 months" after this flashback. *TW: Dead Man Walking*, set in 2008, says that the first Resurrection Gauntlet was recovered "last year", i.e. in 2007.

780 *TW: Long Time Dead*, at an unspecified point between the Gauntlet's recovery and Suzie's first death.

781 "Two years" before *TW: Almost Perfect*.

782 "Six months" before *The Runaway Bride*.

783 Dating *Blink* (X3.10) - The year is given by Kathy Nightingale (who claims she was transported from 2007 to 1920) and the Doctor, who says it's "thirty-eight years" after 1969. The epilogue of the story takes place in 2008.

784 Dating "Fellow Travellers" (*DWM* #164-166) - Date unknown, but no-one has been inside the house "for years".

THE HOUSE AT ALLEN ROAD: A good example of continuity between the New Adventures and the *DWM* strip is that both establish that the Doctor has a house in England which he occasionally visits.

The house is usually associated with the seventh Doctor. It first appeared in "Fellow Travellers" and *Cat's Cradle: Warhead*. It was named Smithwood Manor in "Ravens" and "The Last Word". The Doctor owned it at least as early as the Second World War (*Just War*) and has it in the early twenty-second century (*Transit*).

The eighth Doctor visits the house in *The Dying Days* and mentions it in *The Scarlet Empress*. He also has a house in the 1980s in part two and three of *Father Time*, which may or may not be the same house. *So Vile a Sin* depicts a parallel universe where the third Doctor lived in the house for a thousand years until the thirtieth century. *Verdigris* has the third Doctor using the house during his exile to Earth. The house is stolen in "Question Mark Pyjamas" (a short story from *Decalog 2*), but the seventh Doctor, Ace and Bernice recover it.

"Fellow Travellers", "Ravens" and *Cat's Cradle: Warhead* all indicate that the house has a mysterious reputation - and the last two have the street sign altered to read "Alien Road".

785 Dating "Ravens" (*DWM* #188-190) - It's "the near,

2007 (late September) - THE NIGHTMARE OF BLACK ISLAND[786] -> The tenth Doctor and Rose arrived on the Welsh island of Ynys Du, and discovered the children there were all having nightmares. The children contained the psychic residue of Balor, General of the Cynrog Hordes, but the Doctor dispersed him.

c 2007 (late October) - CAT'S CRADLE: WARHEAD[787] -> The Butler Institute - a huge conglomeration of corporations "from Amoco to Zenith", and which had secretly been bought up over the last decade by the vast Japanese Hoshino company - made projections of the future. Butler could see no alternative but massive, irrevocable environmental collapse. The planet was now reaching the point of no return.

Butler's executives secretly poured money into experiments that attempted to download human consciousness into computers. The Institute developed a weapons system run by an electronically-recorded human consciousness, but its ultimate aim was to "record" the minds of the elite and store them in indestructible databanks, safe from the ravages of pollution and the ozone layer's destruction.

The seventh Doctor deemed Butler's plan a perversion. He sought out Ace's friend Shreela - now a renowned science writer, who was dying from an auto-immune disorder brought on by the increasingly toxic environment. Shreela died after agreeing to put her name on an article the Doctor had written ("A Doorway to Other Worlds") that made connections between a type of protein and psionic abilities - all part of his efforts to deceive Butler.

The Doctor and Ace brought together two young psionics who could serve as a telekinetic "bomb": Vincent Wheaton, who could transform dark emotions into destructive force, and Justine, a "battery" of emotional energy. The Doctor's plan failed because Vincent and Justine fell in love, which quelled her inner rage. Vincent instead drew energy from Butler's project director, Mathew O'Hara, and released a wave of energy that destroyed Butler's memory-transfer project outside Albany. O'Hara was reduced to ash.

During these events, Ace was forced to kill Massoud, a Kurdish mercenary. With the collapse of Butler's project, the directors of the world's corporations realised their only option was to instigate a massive environmental clean-up programme.

c 2007 - PROJECT: LAZARUS[788] -> The seventh Doctor happened to re-visit the Forge, and met his former self's clone. The captive Huldran had died - it was part of a gestalt race, and its traumatised fellows assaulted the Forge via a gateway. The clone triggered the base's self-destruct, but died at Nimrod's hands. The Doctor and the Huldran fled as the Forge was destroyed. The Forge's computer, Oracle, put the organisation's beta facility on-line.

The Reconstruction kicked the King's representative out of the British Parliament. Reconstruction Acts were passed to improve the environment. Large family farms started growing meat-substitute plants.[789] Within a couple of decades, air quality improved, the oceans were cleaner and the

---

harsh future", and the story takes place at the same time as *Cat's Cradle: Warhead*.

786 Dating *The Nightmare of Black Island* (NSA #10) - It's "late September" and the story is set in the present day. This would mean that the tenth Doctor and Rose have landed a couple of months or so after the Battle of Canary Wharf in *Doomsday* - hardly impossible, as *The Nightmare of Black Island* is an isolated incident, and provides them with no warning about what awaits their personal futures.

787 Dating *Cat's Cradle: Warhead* (NA #6) - A specific date for this story and its two sequels is not established in the books themselves. The blurb states "The time is the near future - all too near". Shreela, a contemporary of Ace from Perivale first seen in *Survival*, dies of an "auto immune disease" at a tragically early age (p19).

The book is set in a year when Halloween falls on a Saturday (on p199 it's Halloween, on p250 it's the next day, a Sunday), making it either 1998, 2009 or 2015 - although in a number of stories, the real calendar doesn't match that of the *Doctor Who* universe. Ace's clothes are how Mancuso, a policewoman, dressed "twenty years ago" (p202), and Ace is from the late

1980s. *Just War* confirms that the Cartmel books take place in the "twenty-first century timezone" (p250). However, mention is made of "President Norris" (p26) - with Obama being president in *The End of Time* (TV), set in 2009, an earlier dating for *Cat's Cradle: Warhead* is preferable (see the American Presidents in the *Doctor Who* Universe sidebar). In his "Future History Continuity" document, Ben Aaronovitch suggested that *Cat's Cradle: Warhead* was set "c.2007".

788 Dating *Project: Lazarus* (BF #45) - Nimrod implies "three years" have passed since the first installment.

789 *Happy Endings*

THE RECONSTRUCTION: The televised stories set in the twenty-first century offer a broadly consistent view of a peaceful Earth with a single world government, in which people of all nations cooperate in the field of space exploration and social progress. To reconcile this with the rather more downbeat New Adventures set in this century, Ben Aaronovitch suggested in his "Future History Continuity" document that a concerted global effort was made at some point in the early twenty-first century to repair the damage that had been done to Earth's environment. A "Clean Up" is first hinted at the

ozone layer holes had been patched. Sophisticated traffic monitoring systems and a reconfigured road network eased congestion - and therefore pollution - in the South East of England. Central London, though, was still busy.[790]

Torchwood Series 1 (2007-2008)[791]

By now, the Cardiff Rift had attracted all manner of aliens and extra-terrestrial technology, and approximately two hundred Weevils were living in the sewers below the city.

The Battle of Canary Wharf had led to the destruction of Torchwood One in London - such was the devastation that Torchwood was reduced to "only a half dozen" operatives: Captain Jack Harkness, Suzie Costello, Owen Harper, Toshiko Sato and Ianto Jones. They worked from the Hub - an underground base near Cardiff's Millennium Centre.

The Cardiff branch of Torchwood was designated Torchwood Three. Torchwood Two was an office in Glasgow, and "a very strange man" named Archie[792], who wasn't very adept with computers, **worked there.** Torchwood Four had gone missing.

Captain Jack stressed to his operatives that Torchwood had to arm the human race for what lie ahead...[793]

2007 (early October) - TW: EVERYTHING CHANGES[794] -> Members of the police were obligated to grant Torchwood operatives special access, and - not knowing the truth about the organisation - regarded the group as Special Ops. A series of murders led to Cardiff PC Gwen Cooper encountering Captain Jack's team. Gwen and Jack discovered that his second-in-command, Suzie Costello, had been committing the murders as a means of field testing an alien glove - the

---

end of *Iceberg*, which is where we learn of the "Arms for Humanity" concert and the procuring of drinking water from icebergs, but we might suggest that it only gains impetus after *Cat's Cradle: Warhead*, when all the corporations put their full weight behind it.

This process was named "the Reconstruction" in *Happy Endings*. We would suggest that this period of international co-operation lasts for around seventy years. Earth during this time is a relatively happy, clean and optimistic place.

790 Travelling by car is a lot easier in *Warlock* than *Cat's Cradle: Warhead* (*Warlock*, p179), and we learn about the monitoring systems (p224) and new road system (p211), yet London traffic has barely improved (p265).

791 Dating *Torchwood* Series 1 - Gwen joins Torchwood after *Doomsday*, as events of that story are mentioned in *TW: Everything Changes* and *TW: Day One*, and form the basis of *TW: Cyberwoman*. This shifts the Series 1 stories to a year after they were broadcast, like all the "present day" *Doctor Who* stories since *Aliens of London*.

In *TW: Miracle Day*, Esther says Gwen joined Torchwood in "October 2006", with the "year ahead" rule seemingly forgotten about (and in a script by Russell T. Davies, who engineered the convention, no less!). There are a couple of escape contingencies here... the CIA files that Esther is reading from might list the year wrong, or she might misread the year while repeating the information to Rex.

If the "October" reference is correct, however, then every story between *TW: Everything Changes* and *TW: Border Princes* (set at "nearly Halloween") must happen in that month. Also, *Everything Changes* must take place in *early* October, as "three months" (technically accurate with benefit of rounding) pass between it and *TW: They Keep Killing Suzie* (which must occur before *TW: Out of Time*, set near Christmas).

Most details presented in *Torchwood* Series 1 support a dating of 2007 - in *TW: Ghost Machine*, for example, 1941 is "sixty-six" years ago. However, there are some anomalies in stories such as *TW: Random Shoes* and *TW: Out of Time*. See the individual episodes for more detail.

792 Archie is cited by name in *TW: The Twilight Streets* and *The Torchwood Archives*.

793 *TW: Everything Changes*

794 HOW PUBLIC IS TORCHWOOD?: In *Tooth and Claw* (set in 1879), Queen Victoria creates Torchwood as an ultra-secret organisation devoted to defending Britain's borders against alien/supernatural incursion. Similarly, *The Christmas Invasion* (set in 2006) seems to imply that Torchwood is so secret and so clandestine, the Prime Minister - in this case, Harriet Jones - isn't even supposed to know that it exists. Yet in *Torchwood* Series 1, Captain Jack and company can race through the Cardiff streets with the name "Torchwood" prominently displayed on the side of their SUV, the group (or Owen, at least) orders pizza under the name "Torchwood" and so forth.

The on-screen evidence offers a simple solution to this, even though *Torchwood* Series 1 doesn't spell it out very succinctly: The authorities are well aware of Torchwood's existence, and believe the group is a Special Ops team to whom they must yield authority. Episodes that support this notion include *TW: Everything Changes* (the police blatantly regard Torchwood as Special Ops), *TW: Cyberwoman* (Gwen mentions Torchwood to a contact at Jodrell Bank), *TW: Countrycide* (Gwen thinks a "policeman" - actually a treacherous cannibal - might know of Torchwood as a Special Ops group), *TW: They Keep Killing Suzie* (police units clear the roads for the Torchwood SUV) and more.

Put very simply, it's only the organisation's goal of

Resurrection Gauntlet - that could briefly bring people back to life. Exposed, Suzie killed herself. Afterwards, Jack recruited Gwen to work for Torchwood.

2007 (October) - TW: DAY ONE -> According to the official records, no American citizen had been born with the name "Jack Harkness" in the last fifty years.

A gaseous alien landed near Cardiff in a meteor, and possessed a young woman named Carys. The alien thrived on orgasmic energy and used pheromones to provoke sexual desire in its victims. Torchwood destroyed the creature, enabling Carys to return home.

2007 (October) - TW: GHOST MACHINE[795] **->** Torchwood recovered a piece of alien technology - a "quantum transducer" - that could convert and amplify human emotion as a means of witnessing the past, or making premonitions about the future. The device enabled Owen Harper to witness the murder of Lizzie

Lewis, which was committed in Cardiff, 1963. A scuffle led to the death of Lizzie's killer, Ed Morgan.

Torchwood dealt with a Cyclops and a robot.[796]

2007 (October) - TW: ANOTHER LIFE[797] **->** Torchwood defeated a plot by man-eating aliens that resembled starfish to manipulate the MMOG Second Reality.

2007 (late October) - TW: BORDER PRINCES[798] **->** Torchwood thwarted the Amok, zombie-animating aliens.

2007 - TW: SLOW DECAY -> Torchwood investigated Doctor Scotus' weight clinic - a business that was achieving dramatic results by having its patients, including Gwen's boyfriend Rhys, ingest an alien parasite. They shut down the operation.

---

harvesting alien technology that's secret, not the very mention of Torchwood itself. This fits most of the evidence, but requires one to retroactively assume that in *The Christmas Invasion*, Harriet Jones is suggesting that the Prime Minister isn't supposed to know Torchwood's true purpose, or that they have a super-weapon capable of obliterating spaceships. At the very least, this explains how Jack can talk to the Prime Minister about Torchwood funding issues (*TW: Greeks Bearing Gifts*).

In *Fear Her* (set in 2012), Torchwood is mentioned in a TV broadcast, but the reference is too obscure to tell if the group's real agenda is known to the public, or if they're still considered an elite branch of the military.

Some fans are uneasy with the notion that Torchwood - even as an organisation that by definition is given to deception - could have existed throughout the twentieth century without the third Doctor or UNIT learning about them. A few attempts have been made to explain this, and a recurring one speculates that, temporally speaking, Torchwood didn't exist until the tenth Doctor and Rose went back and annoyed Queen Victoria (*Tooth and Claw*). This theory is hard to credit, however, partly because it overlooks the obvious point that Torchwood does, in fact, predate the Doctor and Rose's trip to 1879. The group is mentioned in *Bad Wolf* and *The Christmas Invasion*, and in the latter story obliterates the departing Sycorax spaceship.

There is nothing special about *Tooth and Claw* in terms of time mechanics, so if such revision occurred, it would almost presuppose that the timeline gets revised nearly each and every time the TARDIS lands. Logically, this would suggest that the Great Fire of Rome shouldn't exist in time until the first Doctor inspires Nero to do it (*The Romans*) - even though the Doctor and Vicki both mention it beforehand. A similar case applies to the fifth Doctor causing the Great Fire of

London in *The Visitation*, even though it's cited in *Pyramids of Mars*. Therefore, the idea that Torchwood didn't "exist" until *Tooth and Claw* might help to explain its secrecy in the 1970s, but would throw the entire *Doctor Who* timeline into chaos.

It is far, far simpler to think that Torchwood was officially listed in the 70s as a Special Ops group; that Torchwood let UNIT get on with the business of actually combating alien incursions; that the Torchwood agents of the time operated with a high degree of stealth (not surprising, if a "Britain first" group were attempting to out-fox a United Nations organisation); and that the Doctor and UNIT were never given reason to look upon the group with suspicion.

795 Dating *Ghost Machine* (*TW* 1.3) - Thomas Erasmus Flanagan and his daughter say they're watching the *Strictly Come Dancing* finals - this is a bit hard to credit, as the show routinely starts in October and finishes in late December. It's possible they're watching a rerun, but it's presented as if it's the original broadcast.

796 Mentioned in *TW: Another Life*.

797 Dating *Another Life* (*TW* novel #1) - The novel is set before *Cyberwoman* - Ianto is seen sneaking down to the basement in the novel. The spines of the first three *Torchwood* novels fit together to make one picture, suggesting a reading order of *TW: Another Life*, *TW: Border Princes* and *TW: Slow Decay*.

798 Dating *Border Princes* (*TW* novel #2) - There are three mentions of the book taking place in October, one of which reads "An October night, almost Halloween" (p221). It's after the release of *Pirates of the Caribbean III* (in May 2007).

2007 - TW: WEB OF LIES[799] **->** An operative of the Three Families captured Jack and tested the limits of his immortality - which included throwing Jack out of a plane near Chernobyl. Gwen located Jack, who killed the agent, but the Families wiped their memory of the event with Retcon gas. Jack and Gwyn only knew that they had a "missing day", nothing more.

2007 - TW: CYBERWOMAN -> Ianto had secretly been keeping his part-Cybertised girlfriend - Lisa Hallett - in the basement of the Hub, but her Cyber-programming finally won out, and she attempted to "upgrade" the Torchwood team into Cybermen. Lisa's body was destroyed when Jack set his pet pterodactyl

on her, and although she transferred her brain into a pizza delivery woman, the Torchwood operatives shot her new body to death.

The first generation of Arcan Leisure Crawlers were now considered collectors' items as far as spaceships went - Torchwood politely warned one such vessel away from Earth, pointing out that they were scaring the locals. The Arcans themselves were mostly liquid, and rather boring.

2007 - TW: SMALL WORLDS[800] **->** Fairies tried to claim a young girl named Jasmine, their "Chosen One", and killed Jack's old friend Estelle Cole. Torchwood was unable to stop the fairies, and Jack

---

799 Dating *TW: Web of Lies* (*TW* animated serial #1) - The year is given in a caption.

800 Dating *Small Worlds* (*TW* 1.5) - A calendar appears in Jasmine Pearce's kitchen, but it's too fuzzy to read.

801 Dating *TW: Hidden* (*TW* audiobook #1) - The story takes place during *Torchwood* Series 1. Ianto and Jack are decently friendly toward one another but don't seem to be an item, suggesting a placement between *TW: Cyberwoman* and *TW: They Keep Killing Suzie*. Also, Ianto tells Tosh during a crisis that he should "never leave the bloody office ever again", which could be taken as a reference to *TW: Countrycide*.

802 Dating *TW: Greeks Bearing Gifts* (*TW* 1.7) - Tosh estimates that the dead British soldier who was killed in 1812 has been buried for "one hundred ninety-six years, eleven to eleven and a half months". This would seem to suggest a dating of 2009, save that Tosh stresses she's estimating, and - for that matter - can hardly be expected to have knowledge of the on-screen caption denoting the murder as occurring in 1812. Most likely, Torchwood - without benefit of the omnipotent narrator - concludes the soldier was killed in 1810.

803 Dating *TW: They Keep Killing Suzie* (*TW* 1.8) - "Three months" have passed since Suzie's death in *TW: Everything Changes*.

804 Dating *TW: Random Shoes* (*TW* 1.9) - The story is rife with minor glitches. The eBay listing for Eugene's alien eyeball claims the auction began on "14-Oct-06", but the date only appears on the full graphic on the *Torchwood* website, and isn't actually seen on screen. As such, it can be safely ignored. Another anomaly is that the "Black Holes and the Uncertainty Principle" flyer says the convention will begin on the 27th, a Thursday. This doesn't match any later month of the year in 2006, but such a day happened in September and December 2007. Those months don't seem viable (given this episode's relation to other *Torchwood* Series 1 stories), but the flyer is minor evidence. More glaringly, Eugene says it's been "fourteen years" since his father left in 1992 - which would indicate a dating of 2006.

805 Dating *TW: Out of Time* (*TW* 1.10) - Owen says in *TW: Captain Jack Harkness* that Diane flew back into the Rift on 24th December, denoting when the story ends. Diane says the *Sky Gypsy* flew into the Rift on 18th December, 1953 - *Captain Jack Harkness* also claims that she and Owen only had "a week" together, so it would appear that the *Sky Gypsy* reappears on the very same day it flew into the Rift, just in half a century later. (The Rift surely doesn't care about matching the Gregorian calendar for aesthetic reasons, so this must owe to the position of the Earth around the sun or some other factor.) An anomaly is that 29th December is said to be a Friday - which is was in 2006, not 2007. The *Cardiff Examiner* is seen with the headline, "Drunk Driving Records Soar This Christmas".

806 Dating *The Runaway Bride* (X3.0) - It's "Christmas Eve", and the Sycorax invasion was "last Christmas". It's also after the Battle of Canary Wharf (*Doomsday*). Strangely, Donna comments in *The Fires of Pompeii* that the Doctor "saved her in 2008", seemingly referring to this story (she must be rounding up from "Christmas 2007" by way of discussing temporal mechanics with the Doctor). Donna's surname is misspelled "Nobel" by some sources such as *Doctor Who Adventures* and in the official *Doctor Who* Exhibition.

807 Dating *Turn Left* (X4.11) - This is the alternate timeline version of *The Runaway Bride*.

808 *The Sontaran Stratagem*

809 *The Sound of Drums*

810 *Partners in Crime*

only ended their rampage by giving Jasmine over to their custody. She was retroactively seen in a "fairie photograph" that had intrigued Arthur Conan Doyle.

2007 - TW: COUNTRYCIDE -> Seventeen people had disappeared in the last five months in rural Wales, and Torchwood feared that the Rift's effects were spreading beyond Cardiff. They investigated, and found a group of cannibalistic villagers, who "harvested" travellers every ten years. Jack and his team facilitated the cannibals' arrest.

2007 - TW: HIDDEN[801] **->** The seventeenth century alchemist Thomas Vaughn was now passing as Sir Robert Craig. Through the research conducted at the CARU fertility clinic in Caerphilly, he hoped to achieve true immortality. Craig had a number of people - including Alice Proctor, the daughter of a friend of Jack Harkness - murdered to protect his secrets, and Jack killed Craig to avenge their deaths. Craig's "son" Simon was actually his own clone, but Jack ascertained that Simon was undergoing genetic deterioration, and wouldn't live past age 20.

2007 - TW: GREEKS BEARING GIFTS[802] **->** The alien named Mary sensed the unearthing of the transmat device that carried her to Earth in 1812. Mary approached Toshiko with a pendant that enabled her to read the thoughts of others, and seduced her in the hopes of retrieving the transmat from the Hub. Jack and his staff found that Mary was an exiled criminal who had been eating people's hearts for years, whereupon Jack teleported her into the Sun. Tosh destroyed the pendant.

2007 (mid-December) - TW: THEY KEEP KILLING SUZIE[803] **->** By now, Torchwood Cardiff had dispensed amnesia pills - each containing Compound B67, also known as Retcon - to two thousand and eight people.

Max Tazillion responded to Suzie's mental programming and started killing members of the Pilgrim support group. Torchwood investigated, learned that Suzie Costello had belonged to the group, and used the Resurrection Glove to revive her. Suzie escaped, vengefully murdered her father and nearly drained all of Gwen's life-force in a bid to stay alive. Jack realised the glove was diverting Gwen's life-energy into Suzie and ordered its destruction, causing Suzie to die for good.

2007 (December) - TW: RANDOM SHOES[804] **->** Prior to this, there had been a trade for Dogon sixth eyeballs.

Eugene Jones had become a Torchwood groupie of sorts. He tried to raise funds by selling his Dogon sixth eye on eBay, but this led to a string of events in which

Eugene swallowed the eyeball - and it kept his spirit tethered to Earth when he died in a hit and run. Eugene's shade accompanied Gwen as she investigated his death, and he manifested enough to save her life from an oncoming car at his funeral. Gwen and her comrades watched as Eugene then vanished into a haze of light, as if departing for the great beyond.

2007 (18th-24th December) - TW: OUT OF TIME[805] **->** Pilot Diane Holmes and two of her passengers - Emma Louise Cowell and John Ellis - emerged from the Cardiff Rift, having flown into it in 1953. The three reacted differently to life in the future - Emma thrived, John killed himself and Diane became lovers with Owen. On 24th December, she flew her plane back into the Rift, expecting to find adventures anew.

2007 (Christmas Eve) - THE RUNAWAY BRIDE[806] **->** The huon particles within Donna Noble caused her to dematerialise from her wedding ceremony, and to reappear in the TARDIS. Returning her to Earth, the tenth Doctor had to rescue her from Roboforms disguised as Santas. This time, the robot "pilot fish" served the Empress of Racnoss, a huge spider-like creature and ancient enemy of the Time Lords.

From an abandoned Torchwood facility below the Thames Barrier, the Empress harvested the huon particles within Donna - the key to awakening the only other surviving members of the Racnoss, who were trapped at the Earth's core. The Empress also killed her ally, Donna's fiancé Lance. The Doctor emptied the Thames into a tunnel leading to the core, killing the Racnoss below. Under orders from Mr Saxon, British Army tanks destroyed the Empress and her spaceship.

(=) 2007 (Christmas Eve) - TURN LEFT[807] **->** In the timeline where Donna turned right, she was celebrating a job promotion when the Racnoss Empress' ship (the "Christmas Star") attacked London. At the scene, she saw UNIT taking away the tenth Doctor's body - for lack of Donna convincing him to show restraint and leave, he had been killed without regenerating. Rose arrived to find the Doctor, too late.

Donna's grandfather, Wilfred Mott, was unable to attend her wedding because he had the Spanish flu.[808] The Racnoss incident helped Mr Saxon come to prominence with the public.[809]

Meeting the Doctor changed Donna's life. She tried travelling abroad, including a trip to Egypt, but found it mediocre. Finally, she sought out mysterious happenings, looking for the Doctor.[810]

2008[811]

San Francisco fell into the sea.[812] The Doctor stopped the End, Rue, Burn Doomsday Cult from destroying London.[813] **Martha Jones owned a television made by Magpie Electricals.**[814]

(=) Manipulated by the poodle people of the Dogworld, John Fuchas produced a movie "adaptation" of *The True History of Planets* in 2008 that abandoned the original book in favour of a story about the deposed poodle Princess Margaret. The eighth Doctor prevented this timeline from ever happening.[815]

Ed Gold was born in Australia in 2008, a time when his country was seriously lagging behind in the space race.[816] **Clyde Langer won First Place in a Park Vale drawing competition in 2008.**[817] Theo Lawson, a genius teenage hacker, caused a confidence crisis in the banking system that triggered a domino effect and led to a global recession.[818]

2008 (1st January) - THE GIRL WHO NEVER WAS[819]

-> Charley was deeply upset by the eighth Doctor's dispassionate reaction to the death of C'rizz - their travelling companion - and demanded that he take her home. He set course for Singapore Harbour, New Year's Eve, 1930, but a "temporal hump" diverted the TARDIS to the same location at the start of 2008.

Charley wrote the Doctor a goodbye note at the Singapore Hilton, then agreed to join him for one last investigation when the long-lost SS *Batavia* mysteriously reappeared at sea. The *Batavia* was riddled with temporal corrosion - a known TARDIS-killer that engaged the Ship's HADS and transported Charley back to 1942, stranding her there while the TARDIS returned to this time.

The Doctor encountered an elderly Madeline Fairweather - who still thought her name was "Charlotte Pollard" - and her son, the smuggler Byron. To eliminate the Cybermen in the *Batavia*'s hold, the Doctor made the vessel to collide with an iceberg. Madeline was killed, and the Doctor, deducing the real Charley's location, went back to 1942.

The TARDIS finally returned to this time, with the unconscious Doctor inside, after a side trip to the year

811 Events in 2008 include the last few episodes of *Torchwood* Series 1, the "present day" sequences of *Doctor Who* Series 3, most (but not all) of *Torchwood* Series 2, and *The Sarah Jane Adventures* Series 1.
812 *The Janus Conjunction* (p79). It's referred to as around in the twenty-second century in *The Face-Eater*.
813 "A little over two hundred and seventy-one days" from *Borrowed Time*.
814 According to a label on Martha's television in *The Sound of Drums*, referencing *The Idiot's Lantern*.
815 *Mad Dogs and Englishmen*
816 *The Waters of Mars*
817 The certificate for this is hanging on his bedroom wall in *SJA: The Curse of Clyde Langer*. This would appear to be a school competition, separate from the "country's most promising young artist" contest that Clyde wins in *SJA: Mona Lisa's Revenge*. Even so, there's a small continuity error in that *Mona Lisa's Revenge* is better suited to occur in 2009, and yet Clyde protests that his being entered in a "nerdy competition" isn't "good for his image", as if such a thing hasn't happened to him before now.
818 *Situation Vacant*. The global recession that Lawson triggered is presumably the same as the real-world economic thrashing that started in 2008.
819 Dating *The Girl Who Never Was* (BF #103) - Fireworks spell out the new year as 2008, and the audio came out in December 2007. A glitch is that Madeleine is said to have been 21 in 1942, but is "85 now" - even allowing that she hasn't had a birthday this year, that only gets matters as far as 2006. Contrary to that, the Doctor says (allowing for the new year) that the *Bavaria* has been

missing for "sixty-six years".
820 Dating *TW: Combat* (*TW* 1.11) - Owen is greatly depressed and avoiding work owing to the loss of Diane, and Gwen here learns from Tosh about their relationship. Both facts suggest that weeks (or possibly just *a* week) rather than months have passed since *TW: Out of Time* (set in late December). It is possible, therefore, that *TW: Combat* takes place before the New Year, although a 2008 dating is perfectly feasible. (The episode itself broadcast on 24th December, the same day that *TW: Out of Time* concludes.) One anomaly is that *TW: Combat* opens with Gwen and Reece having dinner at an outside restaurant, and looking very comfortable despite their lack of winter clothing.
821 Dating *TW: Captain Jack Harkness* (*TW* 1.12) - The last two episodes of *Torchwood* Series 1 seem to occur in rapid succession, and placing them on the timeline is problematic. Deciding where to date them depends on whether one favours the overall aesthetic of *Captain Jack Harkness* and the pacing of plotlines in Series 1 (in which case, it's probably January 2008) or a "Vote Saxon" poster seen outside the Ritz dance hall in Cardiff (in which case, it's probably June 2008).

Doctor Who Series 3 takes place over a four-day period in June, and the "Vote Saxon" poster seems to indicate the national election that concludes in *The Sound of Drums*. However, *TW: Out of Time* ends on 24th December, 2007, and *Combat* seems to take place shortly thereafter. Moving *Captain Jack Harkness* and *End of Days* to June because of the poster would mean, then, that six months pass between *Torchwood* episodes eleven and twelve.

500,002. The Doctor failed to realise that Charley had been left behind in 500,002 and went looking for her - only to find her goodbye note. He presumed that she'd left his company for good.

c 2008 - TW: COMBAT[820] -> Torchwood found that an unidentified group was kidnapping Weevils. Jack and company found the Weevils were being used by thrill-seeking businessmen in a "fight club" scenario and shut the operation down.

2008 (20th January) - TW: CAPTAIN JACK HARKNESS[821] -> A tip-off prompted Captain Jack and Tosh to investigate the deserted Ritz dance hall, but the Rift flared up and catapulted them back to the building as it was on 20th January, 1941. The Ritz caretaker, Bilis Manger, could travel through time and was attempting to manipulate Torchwood into fully opening the Rift. Owen was desperate to get Diane back, and used the group's Rift Manipulator to open the Rift. This enabled Jack and Tosh to return home, but although the Rift seemed to close...

2008 - TW: END OF DAYS[822] -> Opening the Rift had caused it to splinter, and it started depositing people from the past around the world. The Beatles were seen playing on the roof of Abbey Road Studios, a quarantine was established when someone arrived through time with the Black Death, and a Roman soldier murdered two people. UFOs were sighted over the Taj Mahal, and a samurai went on a rampage in the Tokyo subway system. Concurrent with these events, the Torchwood operatives saw visions of their dead or missing loved ones - each of them recommending that the Rift should be opened.

Bilis Manger was an acolyte of the devil-like being Abaddon, and had arranged these events as a means of freeing his master. The Torchwood operatives rebelled against Jack and opened the Rift, which loosed Abaddon to tower over the city. Abaddon's shadow killed anyone it touched, but Jack allowed Abaddon to feed off his immortal life energy. This overloaded Abaddon and killed him - Jack revived after spending some days in a coma.

He then disappeared as the TARDIS arrived...

2008 - UTOPIA[823] -> The tenth Doctor and Martha landed in Cardiff to refuel the TARDIS at the Rift. Captain Jack hurried to meet them, and found himself hanging on as the TARDIS launched itself into the

---

While this might sound plausible in theory, it is hard to watch *Torchwood* Series 1 and genuinely believe that such a six-month gap has taken place where none was apparently meant to exist. Not only does the general flow suggest that events in *Out of Time* were fairly recent (notably the rawness that Diane's departure has inflicted on Owen - as Ianto's "You've been off, haven't you?" comment helps to indicate), the costuming indicates January. Jack wears his trenchcoat regardless of the weather, but Toshiko and Bilis have on winter clothes that no sane person would wear in June. Owen and Gwen are dressed a bit more casually, but their jackets are still out of place for daytime in summer.

The apparent symmetry of Rift travel also suggests a January dating. Jack and Tosh travel through the Rift and arrive in 1941 on 20th January, and as previous Rift travellers seemed to arrive on the same calendar day they left (*Out of Time*), a case can be made that the two of them similarly depart on 20th January, 2008.

Overall, it has become a convention of modern-day television that time within a series progresses in relation to the time of broadcast - even some non sci-fi shows (such as *Boston Legal*) adhere to this rule, and in the main *Torchwood* is no exception. Series 1 seems to open a couple of months after *Doomsday*, and episode eight (*TW: They Keep Killing Suzie*) occurs "three months" after the series opener - it's actually been more like two months in the real world, but it's in the ballpark. Viewers innately tend to follow this pattern,

and among those who keep track of this sort of thing, a January dating (roughly concurrent with the broadcast of *Captain Jack Harkness* and *End of Days*) seems to cause far less confusion than June.

One possibility is that the "Vote Saxon" poster indicates the Saxon Party, as mentioned by Saxon himself in *The Sound of Drums*. Little is known (beyond a general sense of instability) about British politics between Harriet Jones' downfall and Saxon becoming Prime Minister, and the poster could refer to a secondary election that takes place in January. Similarly, the *Daily Telegraph* headline in *Love & Monsters* that reads "Saxon Leads Polls with 64 percent" is just as likely to refer to the party as Saxon himself.

822 Dating *TW: End of Days* (TW 1.13) - There is an obvious need to link this story to *Doctor Who* Series 3, as Jack here registers the TARDIS' arrival and chases the Ship down at the start of *Utopia*. Related to the dating issues in *TW: Captain Jack Harkness*, it seems far simpler to presume that it's February 2008 when the Doctor and Martha land to refuel in *Utopia*, even though this (plausibly) means they've arrived four months before their first meeting in *Smith and Jones*, and that Jack is gone from Cardiff for that duration of time. The Torchwood website supports this with a missing poster of Jack that's dated to February 2008.

823 Dating *Utopia* (X3.11) - The precredit sequence of *Utopia* matches up with the end of *TW: End of Days*, and shows Jack reunited with the Doctor - explicitly for the

Vortex. The trio found themselves in the year 100,000,000,000,000. The Doctor reclaimed the severed hand he'd lost fighting the Sycorax leader, which Jack had in his possession.

2008 - TW: CONSEQUENCES: "Kaleidoscope"[824] ->

Gwen became the interim head of Torchwood Cardiff. Her team secured an alien device, a "Rehabilitator", that could morph anyone seen through it into their "more ideal" selves.

2008 (28th-29th February) - THE CONDEMNED[825]

-> The Shinx were an economically successful and generally low-key race from the planet Shinus. They had red, jelly-like skin, but could use DNA patches to look human. The Shinx government opened a covert embassy on Earth for benefit of any Shinx there.

The sixth Doctor and Charley arrived in Manchester, 2008, and found the body of Kord, a Shinx embassy official. With help from DI Patricia Menzies, they thwarted a Shinx operating on Earth as a mobster named Slater. He'd hoped to perfect a device that emitted a peculiar form of radiation - one that dissolved a being's physical form and placed their consciousness within a piece of architecture; a much more economic means of dominating a planet than outright invading it.

(=) **2008 - THE HAUNTING OF THOMAS BREWSTER**[826] -> In an alternate version of 2008 that was unlikely to come to pass, smoke-like beings controlled Earth. They reduced the planet to ash, ruin and charred bodies to gain the energy needed to send information back to the eighteenth century, and conveyed instructions on how to create a time corridor. The young Thomas Brewster, convinced he was seeing visions of his dead mother, cobbled together such a device.

Brewster travelled to this timeline by hijacking the TARDIS, but the fifth Doctor and Nyssa followed in a later version of the Ship. The Doctor preprogrammed the earlier TARDIS to return to 1833, then left with Nyssa and Brewster. Owing to events in 1865, the smoke-beings' history collapsed entirely.

c 2008 - "Warkeeper's Crown"[827] -> Brigadier Lethbridge-Stewart vanished from a passing out ceremony at Sandhurst, and materialised on an alien world where he quickly met up with the tenth Doctor - and discovered he had been named "warkeeper elect" of a world of dragons and ogres. The original Warkeeper's influence was waning, and so he had brought the Doctor and Brigadier to the Slough of the Disunited Planets. The Brigadier asked for

---

first time since *The Parting of the Ways*. *End of Days* is set shortly after Christmas 2007, so the Doctor and Martha must land a few months in her past.

824 Dating *TW: Consequences: "Kaleidoscope"* (*TW* novel #15b) - The story occurs shortly after Jack goes missing from Torchwood in *Utopia*, and *TW: End of Days* is cited as being "recent". It's wrongly claimed that Gwen and Rhys are already married (p69).

825 Dating *The Condemned* (BF #105) - Menzies starts interrogating the Doctor at "1:05 am on 29th February, 2008"; the Doctor and Charley seem to arrive in Manchester a couple hours or so beforehand. The baddies here try to poison the Doctor with a bit of aspirin - something fandom has presumed as being the pill the third Doctor thinks will kill him in *The Mind of Evil*, but which goes unnamed on screen.

826 Dating *The Haunting of Thomas Brewster* (BF #107) - The year is given, and it matches the year of this audio's release.

827 Dating "Warkeeper's Crown" (*DWM* #378-380) - The Brigadier is in his seventies, which (probably) means this is the first decade of the twenty-first century.

828 Dating *The Eleventh Hour* (X5.1) - It's "two years" before Amy finally starts travelling with the Doctor, which is firmly established as 2010. When the Atraxi scan Earth, they see the Vashta Nerada, Hath and Ood - three races that we've never seen attack Earth. The image of the Cybermen marching is from *Rise of the*

Cybermen, so it technically happened on a parallel Earth, but it presumably stands in for similar events from *Army of Ghosts/Doomsday*.

829 *The Forgotten Army*

830 "Seven months and eleven days" before *TW: Adrift*, which means that the Rift likely "abducts" Jonah in March. A continuity glitch exists in that Jack investigates the incident on the very day that Jonah is taken - even though he should be off world with the Doctor and Martha (per *Utopia*). It's possible that Jack used his Vortex Manipulator to go back and look into Jonah's disappearance after the fact.

831 Alan claims that Chrissie "took [their] home apart six months" before *SJA: Eye of the Gorgon*.

832 *TW: The Undertaker's Gift*

833 The actor who played Geoff Noble in *The Runaway Bride*, Howard Attfield, died in October 2007, during the filming of Series 4. We learn that Donna's father had died when we see her again in *Partners in Crime*. The novel *Beautiful Chaos* cites the day of Geoff's death as 15th May, 2008, but see the dating notes on that story for why this must be called into question.

834 Dating *Smith and Jones* (X3.1) - In *The Sound of Drums*, Martha says it's "four days" since she met the Doctor. As that story takes place the day after a General Election, and elections are always held on a Thursday in the UK, it would mean that *The Sound of Drums* starts on a Friday and so *Smith and Jones* is set on a Monday.

Mike Yates to help him, but the wrong Mike Yates - a xenophobic would-be MP - was summoned. As trolls started to overrun the Keep, the Doctor and Brigadier discovered the clone vats that kept the war supplied with troops. The whole planet was, in fact, an R&D facility for galactic arms dealers, and they shut down the operation.

Back on Earth, Yates tried to use the demons to further his political career, but the Doctor and Brigadier arrived back with an army of cloned Brigadiers and stopped him.

2008 (March) - THE ELEVENTH HOUR[828] -> Earth was a Level Five planet with six billion people on it.

The eleventh Doctor returned to Amelia Pond and Leadworth... twelve years after he promised he would. Amy had grown up, and was now working as a girl who delivered kissograms while dressed as a policewoman, a nurse or a nun. The Atraxi followed the Doctor's time trail via a Crack in Time, and threatened to destroy Earth unless Prisoner Zero - a multi-form who had been hiding in Amy's house for twelve years - was handed over to them.

The Doctor met Amy's "sort-of boyfriend" Rory Williams. To help the Atraxi locate Prisoner Zero, the Doctor arranged a video conference with NASA, Jodrell Bank, the Tokyo Space Centre and the Doctor's friend, Sir Patrick Moore. They spread a computer virus that the Doctor prepared; it reset every digital number and clock in the world to read "0". This directed the Atraxi's attention to Leadworth, whereupon they captured Prisoner Zero and withdrew. The Doctor called the Atraxi back to warn them that Earth was under his protection.

The Doctor made a short trip to the moon and back to recalibrate the TARDIS. He intended to return for Amy, but wouldn't reappear for another two years...

The Prisoner Zero crisis was passed off as a computer fault.[829] The Rift transported 15-year-old Jonah Bevan to an alien locale, where he looked into the heart of a dark star and went mad. After the Rift returned Jonah to Earth, he resided at Jack Harkness' convalescent home for Rift abductees.[830] Alan and Chrissie Jackson, Maria's parents, split up when Chrissie ran off with her judo instructor.[831]

In May 2008, Torchwood recovered the Betamax recorder that fell through the Rift in 1982.[832] **Donna's father, Geoff Noble, died.**[833]

2008 (a Monday in June) - SMITH AND JONES[834] ->
The tenth Doctor investigated electrical anomalies at the Royal Hope Hospital in central London, and met medical student Martha Jones. At the same time, the Judoon - intergalactic policemen/enforcers who looked like humanoid rhinos - were looking for a fugitive Plasmavore who was charged with the murder of the Child Princess of Padrivole Regency Nine. The Judoon had no jurisdiction over Earth, and so transported the entire hospital - and the Plasmavore within - to the moon. The Plasmavore disguised her alien nature by drinking human blood, but thanks to the Doctor's intervention, the Judoon registered her as an alien and killed her. The hospital was returned to Earth, and Martha joined the Doctor on his travels.

> **(=) 2008 (June) - TURN LEFT[835] ->** In the timeline where Donna turned right, the Thames was closed following the Racnoss' defeat. Mr Chowdry sacked Donna on the day that the Royal Hope Hospital vanished. Without the Doctor's intervention, those inside the hospital had suffocated, including Martha Jones, Sarah Jane Smith, Luke, Clyde and Maria. Rose met Donna again, and warned her to stay out of London over Christmas.

2008 (a Tuesday in June) - THE LAZARUS EXPERIMENT[836] -> The tenth Doctor returned Martha home twelve hours after they left. The 76-year-old Richard Lazarus conducted an experiment: hypersonic sound waves created a state of resonance and rewrote his DNA, which rejuvenated him into the body of a young man. Martha's sister Tish worked for Lazarus' public relations department, and the family attended

---

Smith and Jones is clearly set after the Battle of Canary Wharf (*Doomsday*), and Martha, as a medical student, has upcoming exams. In *The Shakespeare Code*, the Doctor boasts that Martha is going to love reading the last *Harry Potter* book - eagerly anticipated at time of broadcast, but released on 22nd July, 2007, the year before he met her. Perhaps she's mentioned she's not read it, but as *The Shakespeare Code* follows directly on from *Smith and Jones*, there are maybe two opportunities for this off-screen conversation to occur.

In *Utopia*, Martha says the Cardiff earthquake (*Boom Town*, set in 2006) was "a couple of years ago". A small

oddity is that the Doctor's John Smith persona (in TV's *Human Nature*) dreams that he's from "2007", not 2008.
835 Dating *Turn Left* (X4.11) - This is the alternate timeline version of *Smith and Jones*. It's "six months" since the alternative *The Runaway Bride* - despite dialogue saying the Thames "remains closed", it looks fine in the footage we're shown. Funnily enough, as Sarah Jane goes to the moon in this version of events, the story title *Smith and Jones* is still apt.
836 Dating *The Lazarus Experiment* (X3.6) - The Doctor says that Martha has only been away "twelve hours". This has to mean "twelve hours" after she left in the

the first demonstration. Lazarus mutated into a canni-balistic monster, but the Doctor killed him in a show-down at Southwark Cathedral.

Saxon had funded Lazarus' experiments; his agents warned Martha's mother to beware the Doctor.

2008 - MADE OF STEEL[837] -> The tenth Doctor took Martha home, and they learned about a number of recent thefts of advanced electronics. Martha was captured by the culprits - a small group of Cybermen who had survived the Battle of Canary Wharf, and had set up camp in the Millennium Dome. The Cybermen wanted the Doctor to open a gateway into the Void to free their fellows, but instead he opened a time portal and released a Tyrannosaurus - which killed the last of the Cybermen.

? 2008 - THE FAMILY OF BLOOD[838] -> The tenth Doctor and Martha attended a World War II remem-brance service and saw an elderly Tim Latimer.

c 2008 - WISHING WELL[839] -> The tenth Doctor and Martha arrived in the English countryside near Creighton Mere. The brain of the Vurosis parasite living beneath the well there had become separated from its body, which emerged as a huge tentacled creature. The Vurosis tried to take over the Doctor, but he destroyed it, turning both its body and brain to ash.

c 2008 - "Bus Stop!"[840] -> The tenth Doctor arrived from the twenty-seventh century via a crude time machine, and tried to prevent mutant assassins from killing the Mayor of London. The Doctor concocted a thermos-full of soup that contained the Mayor's DNA, making the mutants track him by mistake. Martha recalled the Doctor to the twenty-seventh century, and the mutants perished when the Doctor destroyed the time machine.

c 2008 - "Death to the Doctor!"[841] -> Research base Truro served as a meeting place for would-be conquerors and villains who had been defeated by the Doctor, and

TARDIS with him at the end of *Smith and Jones*, not when they first met each other in the kidnapped hos-pital - otherwise, Martha and her family would be made to experience Leo's party and events in *The Lazarus Experiment* on the same evening.

837 Dating *Made of Steel* (*Quick Reads* #2) - This is the first time Martha has returned to the Royal Hope Hospital. The events of *Smith and Jones* are "recent", and her absence is a source of curiosity to Rachel rather than serious concern - however, it's clearly after *The Lazarus Experiment*, which is Martha's first return to her own time. Martha's exams are "soon".

838 Dating *The Family of Blood* (X3.9) - The year isn't given, but Latimer's extreme age and the fact the ser-vice is conducted by a woman indicates at least a near-present-day setting. It's likely Martha's "present day".

839 Dating *Wishing Well* (NSA #19) - The year isn't given, although it seems to be around Martha's native time. A 1989 mountaineering accident occurred "nearly twenty years" ago (p53). The book saw release in December 2007.

840 Dating "Bus Stop!" (*DWM* #385) - The story was published in 2007, and might follow the "year ahead" rule pertaining to Series 3.

841 Dating "Death to the Doctor!" (*DWM* #390) - None of the villains are said to have time-travel capabilities. Given the flashback of the ninth Doctor and Rose at the Powell Estate - and the third Doctor's defeat of the Mentor in the UNIT era - this presumably happens in accordance with the story's publication in 2007, allow-ing for the "year ahead" paradigm of Series 3.

842 Dating *Blink* (X3.10) - A caption says it's a year later in the broadcast version, but doesn't appear in the DVDs (possibly the result of a last-minute change the DVD-authoring house didn't know about). The earlier

sequences were explicitly set in 2007.
843 At the end of *42*.
844 *The Sound of Drums*
845 Dating *The Sound of Drums* (X3.12) - The Doctor, Martha and Jack arrive back from the future "four days" after *Smith and Jones*, the following morning when the Toclafane are unveiled. Constitutionally, there wouldn't be an existing Cabinet, as the Master would have had to appoint one before killing its members.

VOTE SAXON: There are apparent inconsistencies concerning the rise and election of Harold Saxon.

The facts are laid out as follows: Harriet Jones is deposed as Prime Minister after *The Christmas Invasion* (set in Christmas 2006). The Abzorbaloff in *Love & Monsters* holds a paper with the headline "Saxon Leads Polls with 64 per cent" (this occurs before *Doomsday*, as Jackie Tyler is still living on "our" Earth). Mr Saxon rises in prominence after ordering the shooting down of the Racnoss ship in *The Runaway Bride* (Christmas 2007, and explicitly after *Doomsday*). In *TW: Captain Jack Harkness* (set sometime after Christmas, as *TW: Out of Time* ends on 24th December), there's a Vote Saxon poster in front of the disused Ritz dance hall. The "con-temporary" stories in *Doctor Who* Series 3 (*Smith and Jones*, *The Lazarus Experiment*, a sequence in *42*, *The Sound of Drums*) all take place in the same week, with a General Election the day before *The Sound of Drums*. We're told it's eighteen months since *The Christmas Invasion* in *The Sound of Drums* (so it's June 2008).

The problems are:

1. The Vote Saxon poster outside the Ritz suggests that *TW: Captain Jack Harkness* is set during the General Election campaign that elects Saxon, but the episode itself seems to be set soon after Christmas 2007, not June 2008. We can probably discount this problem

wanted to pool their resources against him. The eighth Doctor and Izzy had previously reclaimed the Crystal of Consciousness from Valis, High Arbiter of the Darkness; the fourth Doctor, Romana and K9 stopped Bolog and his Reptilios Invasion Fleet from invading Earth; the ninth Doctor and Rose defeated Zargath and his army within five minutes of their landing at the Powell Estate; the sixth Doctor and Frobisher bested Plink; and the first Doctor, Dodo and Steven overcame Questor in the living jungle of Tropicalus. The base's wiring proved faulty, and villains became paranoid and trigger-happy about the Doctor. They eventually killed one another. The tenth Doctor and Martha found all the bodies at Truro moments later, and the Doctor lamented that had he arrived sooner, he might have saved the "poor unfortunates".

2008 - BLINK[842] -> The tenth Doctor and Martha, on their way to stop a dangerous migration/hatching, met Sally Sparrow for the first time… although she'd met them in her past, and was able to give them a dossier with details regarding their becoming trapped in 1969.

Martha phoned her mother on Election Day.[843] Saxon sent the Torchwood staff to the Himalayas to prevent them from helping Captain Jack and the Doctor.[844]

2008 (a Friday and Saturday in June) - THE SOUND OF DRUMS[845] -> The United Nations had provisions for removing the British Prime Minister

from office.

Harold Saxon, secretly the Master, won the election and convened a meeting of his Cabinet in the newly-rebuilt Downing Street. He killed everyone present, then announced to the world that he had made contact with the alien Toclafane and refused to keep it secret as past governments had. As President of America, Arthur Coleman Winters flew to Britain - both to warn Saxon to take his responsibilities carefully and to take control of the public revelation of the Toclafane.

Meanwhile, the British authorities were looking for three "terrorists" - the tenth Doctor, Martha and Jack, who had returned to the twenty-first century from the far, far future. Onboard the flying aircraft carrier *Valiant* - a UNIT ship - a number of Toclafane materialised and killed President Winters. The Master revealled his plan…

(=) and six billion Toclafane emerged from a space-time rift. They decimated the human population, and the Master took control of Earth. The Master incapacitated Jack and used Professor Lazarus' technology to greatly age the Doctor, capturing both of them.

(=) **THE STORY OF MARTHA**[846] -> Martha escaped London, dodging the Unified Containment Forces under the Master's control. As she went, she told people stories of her adventures with the Doctor. Her

pretty easily - the Vote Saxon poster doesn't have to be part of the General Election campaign, it could have appeared quickly in the wake of the events of *The Runaway Bride*, as the start of the momentum that sees Saxon elected six months later.

2. Saxon is ahead in the polls (*Love & Monsters*) before he comes to prominence (after *The Runaway Bride*). The "poll" Saxon leads in late 2007 can't be one for the General Election of June 2008, as British election campaigns only take four to six weeks. This is harder to explain, but it is possible…

Following *The Christmas Invasion*, it's a turbulent time in British politics, as stated in *The Sound of Drums*. What we're told in the series actually would lead to political problems - Harriet Jones' party won a landslide victory, but confidence in Jones evaporates overnight. Under the British constitution, there's no obligation for either Jones to hold a general election, or for there to be a general election if her party deposed her as leader… unless the government lost a vote of no confidence, and in practice no party with a "landslide" majority could lose such a vote. *The Christmas Invasion* implies that Jones resigns or is deposed soon after. Her party won an election largely because of her, and holds a massive Commons majority, but she's no longer in

charge. Whoever took part is at least third choice to lead the party (after the former Prime Minister who was assassinated by the Slitheen in *Aliens of London*, and Jones), and would almost certainly start out as a lame duck. We should probably note that this instability, exploited by the Master in Series 3, is actually instigated by the Doctor when he deposes Harriet Jones in *The Christmas Invasion*.

In this situation, people would be looking for alternative leaders, and papers would be running polls. Saxon becomes the Minister of Defence at some point in 2007, the www.votesaxon.co.uk website has him as a published novelist (the novel is called *Kiss Me, Kill Me*) and he's married to the daughter of a Lord - so he's clearly a public figure before *The Runaway Bride*. The Racnoss attack, and his handling of it, must be the last piece that makes his succession inevitable.

So the poll in *Love & Monsters* is almost certainly speculative, and perhaps even the first time most people had heard of Mr Saxon. It's also very probably been placed there by Saxon himself.

846 Dating *The Story of Martha* (NSA #28a) - The book contains four of the many stories ("The Weeping", "Breathing Space", "The Frozen Wastes" and "Star-Crossed") that Martha relates in her travels across the

travels took her through France, Turkey, Munich, Ljubljana and Belgrade. In Japan, she met the Drast: tall extra-terrestrials who had sought control of Earth's economy, but owing to the Master's domination sought to leave via a Relativistic Segue. This would have punched a hole in space-time, eradicating Earth. The Drast operation was exposed, and the Master ended their threat by eradicating Japan.

2008 (a Saturday in June) - LAST OF THE TIME LORDS[847] -> The *Valiant* returned from a year in the future, to a point just before the Toclafane appeared. The Master's devastation of Earth had been temporally reversed. Lucy Saxon shot her husband, but the Master refused to regenerate and died. The Doctor burnt his body on a funeral pyre. Martha declined to rejoin the Doctor on his travels. Jack returned to Torchwood.

One of the Master's acolytes, Miss Trefusis, retrieved his ring.[848] Lucy Saxon was tried in secret and confined in Broadfell Prison.[849]

2008 - "The Widow's Curse"[850] -> A cadre of female Sycorax searched for the males of their clan: the group of Sycorax defeated by the Doctor at Christmas 2006. They were led by a head warrior, the Haxan Craw, and a chief strategist, the Gilfane Craw. Their rock spaceship landed in the Caribbean, was designated the island of Shadow Cay, and remodelled its exterior on parts of London using Adobe Magma-Sculpt Version 12.2. (Adobe Magma-Sculpt

Version 13 could craft interiors as well.) It featured a version of Westminster Abbey in which Hawkmoor's towers included such twentieth-century martyrs as Martin Luther King, Oscar Romero, Lucian Tapiedi and Wang Zhiming.

The Sycorax women were enraged upon learning the fate of their men, and dispatched zombies carrying a virus to London - Earth would become a planet of the undead. The tenth Doctor and Donna terminated the zombies, and destroyed both the Sycorax and their spaceship.

Thirty-five years after Jo worked for UNIT, she and her husband Cliff were based halfway up the Rio Negro at the Institute of Mycology. Cliff was now an MBE, a Nobel Prize winner and a veteran eco-warrior; Jo served as his manager. The two of them visited London for the first time in ages so Cliff - his slogan being "Make the Future Yourselves" - could appear on the chat-show circuit, attend the UN's World Future Conference and harangue people there about the imminent collapse of the Amazon forest.[851]

While Cliff did so, Mike Yates took Jo out to dinner. Jo had found Diamond Jack's playing card in her uncle's attic a few weeks prior to this; her stolen memories had returned, and she gave the card to Mike - which he took to a UNIT office. At this time, Mike was single.[852]

By now, one of the old UNIT HQs had been turned into an embassy for a new east-European state. A window that the Doctor blew out at least three times was barred over, and had CC cameras.[853] UNIT currently had offices at Tower Bridge.[854]

---

globe, with linking material that details, among other things, her involvement in thwarting the Drast.

847 Dating *Last of the Time Lords* (X3.13) - Time is reversed to 08:02, just before the Toclafane appeared in great numbers. This means Saxon is still elected and kills his Cabinet and (as is explicitly stated) President Winters is still assassinated. The last detail is something of a glitch, as all of the Toclafane's actions (Winters' death included) should have been temporally erased. Another problem is that the Doctor, Martha and Jack should still be known as "public enemies number one, two and three" despite the historical reversal (as is the case in *The Sound of Drums*), yet they're later seen casually chatting in public with no fear of arrest.

Also at story's end, the "accident and emergency" board behind Thomas Milligan says it's October. This raises the possibility that the Doctor and Martha stay in London for a few months after the Master's defeat, even if nothing else supports or denies the notion.

848 *Last of the Time Lords, The End of Time* (TV).

849 *The End of Time* (TV)

850 Dating "The Widow's Curse" (*DWM* #395-398) - The female Sycorax have been trying to learn what became of their men (*The Christmas Invasion*) for "two years".

851 *The Doll of Death*. Jo says in the framing material that it's "thirty-five years on" from the flashback story, which is set between Seasons 8 and 9 (broadcast in 1971 and 1972). The audio was released on October 2008, either suggesting that writer Marc Platt favours the UNIT stories taking place a bit in the future, or just that Jo is rounding a little. Mention is made in *The Magician's Oath* (the framing sequence of which occurs a week after this story) of "Sir Alistair" (as Lethbridge-Stewart is called in *The Poison Sky*), also suggesting that it's contemporary.

852 Mike shows up to have dinner with Jo at the end of *The Doll of Death*; the framing sequence of *The Magician's Oath* opens a week afterwards.

853 *The Doll of Death*

854 *The Magician's Oath*, also mentioned in *The Sontaran Stratagem*.

855 Dating *Torchwood* Series 2 - While it's customary in this phase of *Doctor Who* to place stories a year ahead of broadcast, this would seem to be an exception. The new season opens with Jack returning to his Torchwood team after *Last of the Time Lords*; notably, he seems to go home under his own power (it's questionable if the Doctor even could give Jack a lift in the TARDIS if he

Torchwood Series 2 (2008-2009)[855]

2008 - TW: KISS KISS, BANG BANG -> Captain Jack returned to Torchwood and was approached by Captain John Hart - a former Time Agent and Jack's ex-lover, someone with whom Jack had been trapped in a time loop for five years. Hart conned Torchwood into retrieving what he believed was an Arcadian diamond, but was actually an explosive device planted to kill him - an act of vengeance from one of Hart's murder victims. Torchwood contained the explosion within the Rift, and Hart left town.

2008 - TW: "The Legacy of Torchwood One!"[856] -> Torchwood eliminated the fear-inducing Chimera, but not before it killed its creator, Rupert Howarth.

2008 - TW: SLEEPER -> Torchwood discovered that aliens designated Cell 114 - whose *modus operandi* was to infiltrate planets with intelligence-gathering sleeper agents bearing false memories - had deployed a cell of such agents on Earth. The agents blew up a telecommunications centre and killed the Cardiff emergency city coordinator, but Torchwood prevented them from detonating ten nuclear warheads that the military had secured in a disused coal mine.

2008 (Friday, 20th June) - TW: TO THE LAST MAN[857] -> St. Teilo's Hospital in Cardiff was slated for demoli-tion, which caused the Rift to fluctuate and make time overlap with the hospital as it stood in 1918. Torchwood saved both time zones by reviving Thomas Reginald Brockless from stasis, then sending him back through the Rift to 1918 with a Rift Manipulator that sealed the Rift behind him.

2008 - TW: SOMETHING IN THE WATER[858] -> One of the remaining inhabitants of the vanished planet Strepto - having biological abilities that resembled water hags, legendary witch monsters - travelled to Earth. Torchwood killed the water hag and her offspring, but not before the hag murdered an old associate of Jack Harkness, Professor Leonard Morgan.

2008 (Sunday) - TW: TRACE MEMORY[859] -> The remains of the Vondraxian Orb that exploded in 1953 were stored in the Hub, and had discretely irradiated Captain Jack's team. This tethered the time-jumping Michael Bellini to their personal histories, causing him to appear at least once in their lifetimes. Bellini finally arrived at Torchwood Three in 2008, and made one last jump back to 1967 - where he was fated to die.

2008 - TW: MEAT -> A band of criminals captured a baby star whale that flew through the Rift, and profited by selling big chunks of it as raw meat for pies, burgers, pasties, etc. Torchwood shut down the operation, but the star whale died.[860]

wanted, after the way the Ship reacted in *Utopia*), so no time displacement is involved, and Series 2 presumably opens in the space of time it takes Jack to mop up any lingering details concerning the Master's tenure as prime minister and return to Cardiff. The mood at Torchwood is such that Jack has been absent for some months at least, but nothing suggests that he's been away anything as long as a year (everyone is still actively pining for Jack, in fact), which supports the notion that the modern-day component of *Utopia* occurs a few months before the Doctor and Martha first meet in *Smith and Jones*.

    Torchwood script editor Gary Russell confirms that timeline for Series 2 was calibrated to begin in 2008 and end the following year - that is supported in that save for the last two episodes (*TW: Fragments* and *TW: Exit Wounds*), the dating clues throughout Series 2 all concur with a dating of 2008. See the individual entries for more.

856 Dating *TW: "The Legacy of Torchwood One!"* (*TWM #1*) - The story saw release between *TW: Kiss Kiss, Bang Bang* and *TW: Sleeper*.

857 Dating *TW: To the Last Man* (*TW 2.3*) - "Friday the 20th" is circled on Tosh's calendar, and is also seen on Jack's calendar. In 2008, such a day only occurred in June - which neatly fits with *Last of the Time Lords* occurring in the same month, and Jack returning to the Hub shortly afterwards. Tommy, who was frozen in 1918, is said to have been at the Hub for "ninety years". Tosh says that she's known Tommy for "four years", which is consistent with her having been a member of Torchwood for "three years" in *TW: Greeks Bearing Gifts*, and "five years" in *TW: Fragments*. Tommy has been revived on an annual basis but doesn't know Gwen, so less than a year has passed since *TW: Everything Changes*.

858 Dating *TW: Something in the Water* (*TW novel #4*) - Tosh mentions (p31) the Rift's "recent time shift with 1918" (*TW: To the Last Man*), but Rhys doesn't yet know (p30) Torchwood's true purpose (*TW: Meat*). *The Time Traveller's Almanac* says that Strepto is one of the twenty-seven planets the Daleks abducted to build their reality bomb (*The Stolen Earth*).

859 Dating *TW: Trace Memory* (*TW novel #5*) - The year is given (p23), and it's twice said that it's "fifty-five years" after 1953. It's a Sunday (p13, p232).

860 It's possible that the "star whale" is related to the "space whale" seen in *The Beast Below*.

2008 - TW: EVERYONE SAYS HELLO[861] **->** A spaceship came through the Rift and released a "telesensual field" - part of a nonviolent first contact protocol designed to solicit information. The Cardiff public became overly eager to say hello and to divulge their personal details, and the city descended into chaos as people ignored their responsibilities. Torchwood shut down the field by broadcasting gibberish through Jack's cell phone.

2008 (Friday) - TW: IN THE SHADOWS[861] **->** Captain Jack's crew stopped Patrick Jefferson's serial-killing spree, and confiscated his huon-particle-laced matchbox. Unable to formally bring Jefferson to justice, Torchwood planted spare bodies in his cellar and alerted the authorities.

2008 - TW: "Rift War"[861] **->** The Sanctified once had a powerful empire, but were now farmers of dinosaurs. One of their number, Vox, manipulated his people into thinking that Torchwood would attack by weaponising the Rift, prompting a pre-emptive strike. Torchwood repelled the Sanctified's shock troops - the bestial Harrowkind - who materialised in Cardiff to neutralise the Hub.

Soon after, Captain Jack's crew dealt with a Rift bubble that developed in Cardiff Castle, and cared for an enormous Zansi baby during the six weeks it took the child to mature. Torchwood also rounded up a pack of Sanctified-owned dinosaurs in Millennium Stadium, and sent them back through the Rift. They also investigated a stone circle that focused Rift energy every eighty years, and briefly swapped Ianto and Tosh with Gerald Carter and Harriet Derbyshire in 1918.

2008 - TW: "Shrouded"[861] **->** John Hart and Rhys arrived from the future to warn Ianto that a time-traveller named Beatrice, a.k.a. Mairwyn, would try to seduce him - and that his surrendering to her advances could potentially change history. Mairwyn showed Ianto a future in which he, Owen and Tosh died, and the Hub was destroyed. She proposed that they steal the Shroud - a device from Torchwood One assigned to Ianto's care - and escape together, but Ianto killed Mairwyn, gave a precognitive device in her possession to the future-Hart and Retconned his knowledge of events to come.

2008 - TW: ADAM[862]**->** An entity that was adrift in the Rift surfaced in Cardiff, and manifested by engraining itself into the minds of Jack's Torchwood agents. They believed the interloper was a fellow Torchwood agent, Adam Smith, and retroactively thought they had all worked together for three years. Jack uncovered the deception and eradicated Adam by removing everyone's memories of the past two days. Jack himself had to go a step further, and permanently lost the last good memory he had of his father.

2008 - TW: "Rift War"[863] **->** The Harrowkind renewed their assault on Torchwood, and sped through a Cardiff retail centre. The last Omnicron trapped the Harrowkind within its tesseract as data files, but was then destroyed by Vox. Soon afterwards, Vox focused enough Rift energy through the Hub's Rift Manipulator to endow himself with fantastical abilities. Torchwood curtailed the energy feeding Vox, leaving him at the mercy of some golems - antibodies generated by the Rift to deal with such threats.

2008 (August) - THE TWILIGHT STREETS[864] **->** Abaddon's death had tipped the balance of power toward the Dark and its allies. Bilis Manger aided Torchwood in trapping the Dark in a containment box, and in releasing the Light into the Rift to keep Abaddon's nemesis, Pwccm, forever imprisoned. Manger departed to intern Abaddon's ashes outside Britain. During this conflict, earthquakes and fires destroyed the Tretarri housing district.

---

861 Dating *TW: Everyone Says Hello* (*TW* audiobook #2), *TW: In the Shadows* (*TW* audiobook #3), *TW: "Rift War"* (*TWM* #4-13), *TW: "Shrouded"* (*TWM* #21-22) - In all of these stories, Rhys knows Torchwood's true purpose (so, it's after *TW: Meat*), but Owen hasn't "died" (so, it's before *TW: Reset*). *Everyone Says Hello* (cited on its blurb as occurring in Series 2) was released on 4th February, 2008, between the broadcasts of *TW: Meat* and *TW: Adam*, and nestles between the two stories easily enough. One oddity is that Gwen and Rhys seem to spend six weeks in "Rift War" caring for a giant Zansi infant; fortunately, the continuity in this phase of Series 2 is pliable enough that such a duration of time might well elapse between the TV episodes.

Ianto's statements establish that *In the Shadows* happens on a Friday; Mariwyn establishes that "Shrouded" occurs two days before a "Wednesday", but the story then continues an unspecified number of days later.

862 Dating *TW: Adam* (*TW* 2.5) - Torchwood believes that Adam has been working alongside them for "three years", and his doctored personnel file says he was recruited on "07/05/05".

863 Dating *TW: "Rift War"* (*TWM* #4-13) - Owen hasn't yet kicked the bucket, but "three weeks straight" have passed since Torchwood had any engagement with the Sanctified.

864 Dating *TW: The Twilight Streets* (*TW* novel #6) - Once again, placement is determined because Rhys knows about Torchwood but Owen still isn't dead yet. Moreover, it's "twenty-two months, eight days and about nine hours" (p76) since Jack last met Margaret Slitheen's secretary Idris Hopper - an encounter that

2008 - TW: RESET / TW: DEAD MAN WALKING[865] ->
Martha Jones was now working for UNIT, and helped
Torchwood uncover a conspiracy regarding the Pharm:
a partnership between the government and a consortium of pharmaceutical companies. Dr. Aaron Copley
sought a means of resetting the human body back to its
"factory settings" - a development that could potentially cure all human ailment - using "the mayfly", an
alien insect species. Copley's experiments were killing
his test subjects, so Torchwood shut down the operation. An enraged Copley killed Owen Harper, and was
then shot dead by Jack.

Jack retrieved the second Resurrection Gauntlet
from St. Mary's Church, and used it to revive Owen for
a few moments - or so he thought. Unexpectedly, Owen
remained active as an animated cadaver even after the
Gauntlet's destruction. As with events in 1479, Owen's
return to life enabled a personification of Death to
stalk Cardiff. Death attempted to murder thirteen people - the number required to secure its foothold on
Earth - but had only killed twelve when Owen grap-
pled with Death and banished it.

2008 - TW: A DAY IN THE DEATH[866] -> Henry John
Parker died, and Owen acquired from him an extra-
terrestrial device - a reply sent by unknown parties to
the NASA space messages of the 70s. Martha returned
to UNIT.

The planet Ytraxor was freezing as its sun grew dim, and
approaching glaciers forced the Ytraxorians to fight for
what land remained. Ytraxorian scientists developed a
Reality Gun that could displace objects in space and time
- useless as a means of escape, but an effective weapon.
The Ytraxorians destroyed themselves, but one of them,
and his Reality Gun, were hurled through space and mate-

rialised in a deep-fat fryer in Cardiff. Captain Jack, Gwen
and Ianto confiscated the dead alien's Reality Gun.[867]

**2008 (last week of August) - SJA: INVASION OF
THE BANE**[868] -> Thirteen-year-old Maria Jackson
moved to a new house in Ealing, West London, with
her father Alan. That night, she saw her neighbour,
Sarah Jane Smith, talking to an alien. Sarah aided this
lost being - a Star Poet from Arcateen 5 - in returning
home, and Maria teamed up with her to uncover the
secret behind the popular new addictive drink Bubble
Shock. It was a creation of the cephalopod-like Bane -
Bubble Shock was laced with a secretion of the Bane
Mother, and could take control of anyone who drank it.
Two percent of the population carried innate resist-
ance to Bubble Shock, and so the Bane had created an
Archetype: a teenage human boy made from the data
scans of the ten thousand people who had visited the
Bubble Shock factory. The Bane intended that the
Archetype would enable them to refine Bubble Shock
and eliminate the 2% deviation.

The Bane assumed mental control of the Bubble
Shock drinkers - legions of people took to the streets
with bottles of Bubble Shock, intoning "Drink it, drink
it..." Sarah, Maria and the Archetype thwarted the
Bane overseer, Mrs Wormwood, and destroyed the
main Bubble Shock factory. Bubble Shock was withdrawn, and a government cover story claimed that
chemicals released from the Bubble Shock plant had
caused a mass hysteria.

Sarah named the Archetype "Luke Smith" and
adopted him as her son. The two of them resided at 13
Bannerman Road.

---

happened "a month" (p81) after *Boom Town*, in October
2006. So, it's now August 2008. The year is loosely confirmed in that it's "nearly one hundred thirty years" after
Queen Victoria established Torchwood (p103).

865 Dating *TW: Reset* and *TW: Dead Man Walking* (*TW*
2.6-2.7) - A glitch exists in that Owen says that one of
Copley's victims, Meredith Roberts, is 45, but both the
man's driver's license and Tosh's computer search says
he was born "11-01-1962". It's impossible to think that
this story occurs prior to 11th January, and yet that
would only amount to it being 2007.

866 Dating *TW: A Day in the Death* (*TW* 2.8) - Three days
have passed since the previous episode.

867 "Two years" before *TW: The Men Who Sold the
World*.

868 Dating *SJA: Invasion of the Bane* (*SJA* 1.1) - It's at
least "eighteen months" since *School Reunion*, as that's

how long Sarah has had her new K9. Maria's dad says
that she's going to "start school next week", presumably
in September (as with the 2010 school year starting on
6th September in *SJA: The Nightmare Man*). Maria's
clock says "11 1", but she starts a new school "next week"
and it's light at 6 pm, so we can only assume it's showing the wrong date, possibly because it was unplugged
during the move.

A small oddity is that Sarah says in *SJA: Sky* that Luke
was "born" as a 13 year old, yet he's "14" just a week
afterwards in *SJA: Revenge of the Slitheen*. It's possible,
however, that she initially designated him as 13, then
shortly thereafter decided he was "14" (and had Mr
Smith alter Luke's documents accordingly) to accommodate his entering school at a slightly higher level.

(=) In the history where Sarah Jane died instead of Andrea Yates, the Trickster prevented the Bane from visiting Earth.[869]

2008 - "A "Perfect World"[870] **->** While travelling in the TARDIS solo, Thomas Brewster stopped in London, 2008, and met a young woman named Connie Winter. She wished for a more perfect world - and as Brewster hadn't materialised the TARDIS properly, a quantum fissure formed that enabled two existential maintenance workers, "Phil" and "Trev", to hear their conversation.

(=) After Brewster departed in the Ship, Phil and Trev manipulated Connie's timeline to avert her biggest mistakes, and curtailed a large number of political scandals and disasters. The fifth Doctor and Nyssa - having reunited with Brewster - learned how his actions had altered history. Phil and Trev were persuaded to undo their alterations.

Brewster left the TARDIS to start a relationship with the original Connie. The Doctor gave Brewster ownership of his house on Baker Street, which hadn't been occupied in one hundred forty-one years, thinking that the proceeds from its sale would keep him afloat for a time.

2008 (a Monday and Tuesday in September) - SJA: REVENGE OF THE SLITHEEN[871] **->** Maria and Luke started at their new school, Park Vale, and made a new friend, Clyde Langer. With Sarah Jane's help, they discovered that a group of Slitheen had murdered some of the fatter teachers and the school headmaster, and that their friend Jeffery was a Slitheen child. The Slitheen planned to harvest all energy from Earth and its sun with the equipment housed in the Coldfire Technology Blocks, then sell the energy to fund the retaking of their homeworld, Raxacoricofallapatorius, with a battlefleet. The Slitheen activated their equipment, and the sun temporarily turned a cold blue. Discovering the aliens' vulnerability to vinegar, Sarah Jane and her friends fought their way to the machine at Park Vale and destroyed it, ending the scheme.

UNIT cleaned up the Slitheen operation, and Sarah had Mr. Smith release a cover story that the sun's outage resulted from a temporary reversal of the Earth's magnetic poles.

869 *SJA: Whatever Happened to Sarah Jane?*

870 Dating "A Perfect World" (BF #113b) - The year is specified, and coincides with the story's release in October 2008.

871 Dating *SJA: Revenge of the Slitheen* (SJA 1.2) - The Slitheen refer to the events of *Smith and Jones*. It's the start of a school year, so the story begins on a Monday and continues onto Tuesday.

872 *SJA: Whatever Happened to Sarah Jane?*

873 Dating *SJA: Eye of the Gorgon* (SJA 1.3) - No specific dates are given. In *The Mind Robber*, the Doctor was convinced that Medusa could not exist. Sarah also presents herself as "Victoria Beckham" in *SJA: The Temptation of Sarah Jane Smith*.

874 Sarah tells the Trickster, in *SJA: Whatever Happened to Sarah Jane?*, "Never mind the Bane, what about the Slitheen? And the Gorgons? And the Patriarchs of the Tin Vagabond? I stopped them all from taking over the Earth." There's some leeway as to when she fought the Patriarchs, and it's not even clear as to whether she did so with the teenagers or on her own, but it seems reasonable to presume that she's naming her recent adversaries in order. The Doctor referred to the Church of the Tin Vagabond as worshippers of the Beast in *The Satan Pit*. Sarah seems to have made a return to fighting satanists, as she did in *K9 and Company: A Girl's Best Friend* and also the *K9 Annual*.

875 *SJA: Whatever Happened to Sarah Jane?*. If this means that the Trickster somehow averted the Gorgon from coming to Earth in the first place (which isn't said), then the "Andrea Yates" timeline must be devoid of the Medusa mythos.

876 Dating *SJA: Warriors of Kudlak* (SJA 1.4) - It's a Tuesday, but children aren't at school, so it may be half term. No human astronaut has set foot on Mars by this time, which directly contradicts *The Ambassadors of Death* and *The Dying Days*.

877 *SJA: Whatever Happened to Sarah Jane?*

878 Dating *TW: Something Borrowed* (TW 2.9) - The story opens on a Friday night at Gwen's bachelorette party, and the wedding occurs the next day. Given everyone's dress and the ease with which they can go outdoors, it's a warm month.

879 Dating *TW: SkyPoint* (TW novel #8) - Gwen and Rhys have been married "a little over two weeks now" (p1, p13), and have just returned from their honeymoon of "ten days in Cuba" (p1). More time than that seems to pass between *TW: Something Borrowed* and *TW: From Out of the Rain*, so *SkyPoint* appears to fall between the two. The month is September (p85).

880 Dating *TW: From Out of the Rain* (TW 2.10) - Enough time has passed since *TW: Something Borrowed* that Gwen has gone on her honeymoon and returned. Everyone is now wearing jackets, suggesting that it's a bit later in the year.

881 Dating "Hotel Historia" (DWM #394) - The month and year are given.

882 "The Crimson Hand"

883 Dating *Brave New Town* (BF BBC7 #2.3) - The exact date is given.

(=) The Trickster stopped the Slitheen from going to Earth.[872]

2008 - SJA: EYE OF THE GORGON[873] ->

Sarah Jane and her friends investigated Lavender Lawns, a nursing home where apparitions have been reported. One of the residents, Bea Nelson-Stanley, gave Luke the prized talisman that could link the world of the ancient Gorgon with Earth. The nuns protecting the remaining Gorgon (who was in the body of an Abbess) acquired the talisman, and opened a portal so the other Gorgon could dominate humanity. The Abbess-Gorgon tried to take Sarah Jane as its new host, but Maria disrupted the transfer, turning the Abbess to stone. The portal was deactivated.

Sarah Jane's current aliases included Bunty Mansfield, Victoria Williams and Felicity Barnes. The Viszern Royal Fleet, composed of six hundred ships, passed through Earth's solar system and created a magnificent stellar light show.

Sarah Jane defeated the Patriarchs of the Tin Vagabond.[874]

(=) The Trickster stopped the Gorgon from invading Earth, and "turned away" the Patriarchs.[875]

2008 (a Tuesday) - SJA: WARRIORS OF KUDLAK[876]

-> Twenty-four children had vanished at various Combat 3000 locations, which offered realistic laser tag. Sarah Jane and her friends learned that the disappearances all coincided with freak storms. At the London Combat 3000 site, they saw Kudlak - a member of the insectoid Uvodni race who was trying to recruit warriors to fight his enemies, the Malakh. Kudlak's battle computer, Mistress, had deliberately withheld a message that the war had ended ten years before, because she had no purpose except war. Kudlak destroyed Mistress and released his prisoners.

(=) The Trickster thwarted Kudlak.[877]

2008 (a Friday and Saturday) - TW: SOMETHING BORROWED[878] ->

A Nostravite - a shapeshifting species in which the male carries fertilised eggs in his mouth - bit Gwen, who became pregnant with Nostravite offspring during her wedding to Rhys Williams. Torchwood killed the Nostravite mother and removed her young from Gwen, then dosed all of the wedding guests with Level 6 Retcon in their champagne.

2008 (September) - TW: SKYPOINT[879] ->

The master criminal Besnik Lucca built SkyPoint - an apartment highrise in Cardiff - as his personal fortress. A thought-entity from beyond the grave had hitched a ride with a SkyPoint resident, a young girl named Alison Lloyd, when she was resuscitated after being clinically dead. The thought-creature stayed corporeal by consuming some of the SkyPoint residents, but Owen injected the creature with a syringe of his dead blood, killing it. Torchwood gave the authorities enough evidence to put Lucca away for fifty years.

2008 - TW: FROM OUT OF THE RAIN[880] ->

The Electro Cinema in Cardiff reopened as a museum, and an examination of old film stocks in its basement released the Night Travellers contained within. Two Night Travellers stole life essences from half a dozen people, then released the remainder of their contingent from the film. Jack prevented the Travellers from taking more victims by recording their images onto a film reel and exposing it to sunlight, seemingly eradicating them. It was possible that the Travellers had survived on a film reel at a flea market.

2008 (October) - "Hotel Historia"[881] ->

The supercriminal Majenta Pryce and her assistant Fanson founded the Hotel Historia - a chain that became the toast of the Seven Galaxies, offering guests the opportunity to time travel to different points in history. The chain fell into decline as patrons shied away from time travel in the aftermath of the Last Great Time War, but Majenta and Fanson operated one of the remaining Hotel Historias on Earth. Patrons could experience wildlife in the Jurassic, converse with great wits in Elizabethan England, etc. Meals served at the Historia included vintage Vesuvian vino and woolly mammoth steaks.

The tenth Doctor travelled down one of the Historia's time corridors from 4039, and sent the hotel's main time-travel device - the Chronexus 3000 - back there to thwart the Graxnix. Cosmic bailiffs arrested Majenta, took her to the future and imprisoned her at the Thinktwice orbital penitentiary.

Fansom's own teleport beam to Thinktwice was diverted, and he came into the service of the Skith leader.[882]

2008 (24th October) - BRAVE NEW TOWN[883] ->

Various rivers in Uzbekistan had been depleted by the continual use of water for cotton fields, cloth, swimming pools and more. The Aral Sea dried up, and the faux English village of Thorington - formerly on an island - had rejoined the mainland. A Nestene unit with the mother consciousness for the Thorington Autons exerted influence over them, turning them murderous. The eighth Doctor and Lucie cut off the signal from the mother-unit and left as the Autons, now aware of their origins, faced the decision of whether to stay in Thorington or go elsewhere.

2008 (late October to early November) - TW: ADRIFT[884] **->** Gwen discovered that the Rift had claimed dozens if not hundreds of Cardiff residents in the last ten years, and learned about the shelter that Jack was operating for such persons.

2008 (1st November) - TW: PACK ANIMALS[885] **->** A young man named Gareth Portland found an alien terra-forming device that enabled him to manifest creatures and effects rendered in *MonstaQuest*, a card game he'd created. The telepathic device enhanced Gareth's emotions, causing him to hurt or murder those he believed had slighted him, and then to transform Millennium Stadium into a replica of an alien locale. Jack shot Gareth dead, and the monsters he created fell into a chasm that opened up inside the Stadium.

2008 (Tuesday) - TW: "Jetsam"[886] **->** Torchwood neutralised a battlewagon used by an extra-terrestrial race to settle turf wars and border disputes.

A Verron soothsayer gave Sarah Jane a warp star - a warpfold conjugation trapped in a carbonised shell; it was "an explosion waiting to happen". The soothsayer advised that she use it at "the end of days".[887]

2008 - SJA: WHATEVER HAPPENED TO SARAH JANE?[888] **->** By now, the book *UNIT: Fighting for Humankind* by Sarah Jane Smith had been published.

Sarah Jane told her friends that Meteor K67 was approaching Earth through a radar blind spot, but that Mr Smith would emit a magnetic pulse to deflect it the next day. A Verron soothsayer had given Sarah Jane a small box with instructions that she pass it along to the person she trusted most, and so she gave it to Maria. That night, a mysterious hooded figure, the Trickster, approached Sarah Jane's house.

(=) The box protected Maria's memories when the Trickster altered history in 1964. Maria was the only person who remembered Sarah Jane, and found that a woman called Andrea Yates was living in Sarah's house. Maria remembered the oncoming meteor, but without Mr Smith, there was no way to deflect it. The Trickster thrived on chaos, which the meteor strike would certainly cause. At the local library, Maria learned that a 13-year-old Sarah Jane had drowned after falling from a pier... as seen by her friend, Andrea Yates. A Graske working for the Trickster took the meddlesome Maria to Limbo - but she escaped, and briefly found herself back on 13th July, 1964. Faced with the evidence of what her deal with the Trickster had done, Andrea revoked her bargain with him.

884 Dating *TW: Adrift* (TW 2.11) - Further establishing that it's 2008, Rift-abductee Jonah Bevan was born 15th February, 1993, and is now 15. Also, a flier says that the first meeting of Searchlight - a missing persons support group - is slated for Monday the 27th; in 2008, such a day only occurred in October. The story's epilogue takes place one week later, presumably in early November. Entertainingly, a handwritten note says that another abductee, Bahri Agon, was born on the fictional date of "30/2/83".

885 Dating *TW: Pack Animals* (TW novel #7) - The back cover mentions "Halloween is a day of fun and frights", and yet the action occurs on a "freezing Saturday... in November" (p57) that falls after a bit of Halloween festivities (p51). In 2008, the day after Halloween was a Saturday, so the story presumably takes place on 1st November. Regrettably, the book is at odds with the continuity of Series 2 - Owen is already dead (p75, so it's after *TW: A Day in the Death*), and Gwen and Rhys are still making preparations for their wedding (so it's before *TW: Something Borrowed*), but a placement anywhere in November (hard to avoid, as the month is expressly stated) would have *Pack Animals* occurring after or roughly concurrent with *TW: Adrift*, which

manifestly occurs after Gwen and Rhys' nuptials. To judge from the prologue, Gareth murders his first victim on the Saturday before Halloween.

886 Dating *TW: "Jetsam"* (*TWM* #3) - The comic saw release between *TW: Adrift* and *TW: Fragments*. It's specified as being "a wet Tuesday morning".

887 "The other week" according to *SJA: Whatever Happened to Sarah Jane Smith?* Sarah and Captain Jack use the warp star against the Daleks in *Journey's End*, and it's presumably still aboard the Crucible when it's destroyed.

888 Dating *SJA: Whatever Happened to Sarah Jane?* (*SJA* 1.5) - Andrea says she has been dead "forty years" and she's the same age as Sarah Jane, who was born in 1951. It's later established that Andrea died in 1964, so it was actually forty-four years earlier. It's still 2008, as Clyde says in *SJA: The Temptation of Sarah Jane Smith*, set in 2009, that they first fought the Trickster "last year". The Trickster makes his move on the Doctor in *Turn Left*.

889 Dating *SJA: The Glittering Storm* and *SJA: The Thirteenth Stone* (*SJA* audiobooks #1-2) - The stories take place during *The Sarah Jane Adventures* Series 1, and saw release simultaneous to *Whatever Happened to Sarah Jane?* episode two.

Sarah Jane and Mr Smith deflected the meteor at the last moment. Having skimmed Sarah Jane's memories, the Trickster became curious as to how much damage would ensue if the Doctor had never existed.

2008 - SJA: THE GLITTERING STORM[889] -> Sarah Jane and her friends investigated a series of gold thefts, and found that the Keratin (slug-like aliens who used gold to enhance their psychic abilities) had a foothold at the Auirga Clinic in Hounslow. The Keratin's mind-slaves were developing a bacterial culture that would boil away Earth's oceans in a day, exposing twenty million tons of gold that the Keratin could harvest and use to conquer many worlds. The Keratin on Earth were destroyed with seawater, and Sarah Jane and Luke destroyed the formula for the culture.

2008 - SJA: THE THIRTEENTH STONE[889] -> Luke Smith's class visited a tourist attraction called The Stone Whisperers - actually the petrified criminal Ravage and his twelve jailors. Ravage transferred his mind into Luke's body, and his wardens revived as armoured warriors intent on killing his host form. Luke banished Ravage from his mind, and the warriors turned themselves back into rock.

c 2008 (a Saturday) - SJA: THE LOST BOY[890] -> Mr Smith moved forward his secret plans to free the colony of Xylok crystals trapped since ancient times under the Earth's crust. Smith allied itself with a group of Slitheen, who - disguised in new fleshsuits that were slimmer, and handled gas exchange better - posed as the Stafford family. TV news reports were said they had been looking for their missing son, Ashley, for five months - and the photo shown was that of Luke Smith. Sarah Jane was arrested for child abduction, and "Ashley" was reunited with his "parents". UNIT vouched for Sarah Jane and she was released.

Mr Smith had manipulated the Slitheen into spur-

ring the creation of a telekinetic energiser, Magnetized Intensification of Telekinetic Reactive Energies (MITRE), at the Pharos Institute. Luke's mind was forcibly used to power the device and draw the moon toward Earth; Mr Smith intended that the collision would free the Xylok. Earth experienced spontaneous forest fires, avalanches, freak storms and tidal waves. The United Nations convened an emergency session.

Sarah briefly brought K9 back to Earth. The robot dog defeated Mr Smith, who was reprogrammed to protect Earth from harm. The moon returned to its original position, and the Slitheen departed.

Darlington became a nexus point for adventurers and other travellers because it was home to the Deadly Flap: a gateway to the multiverse. In December 2008, Barbra the vending machine arrived in Darlington from the fifty-ninth century via the Deadly Flap. Iris Wildthyme persuaded MIAOW to accept Barbra as a trainee operative.[891]

2008 (December) - THE RAINCLOUD MAN[892] -> A coalition of species had restrained the alien Tabbalac, and an unknown party infected the Tabbalac with a neurosis that created the Cyrox - a race that replicated like a hyper-intelligent virus, and was ever ready to combat Tabbalac aggression. The Tabbalac could still leave their homeworld, but only if their intentions were peaceful.

In Manchester, DI Patricia Menzies had developed a network of aliens and time travellers whom she'd aided. The sixth Doctor and Charley again met Menzies while investigating Carmen Priminger, a time traveller who had gambled her memories away at the planet-jumping High Straights casino boat a year ago. The Doctor and Charley played a Tabbalac leader at the High Stakes table, and Charley's victory caused the Tabbalac to forfeit their conflict with the Cyrox. As events played out, the Tabbalac leader and Brooks - the High Straights owner - were killed, and the casino was destroyed.

890 Dating *SJA: The Lost Boy* (*SJA* 1.6) - It's straight after *SJA: Whatever Happened to Sarah Jane?*. The news report about "Ashley Stafford" (i.e. Luke) says that his family hasn't seen him in "five months", which is presumably how long has passed since *SJA: Invasion of the Bane*. If that were literally true, however, *The Lost Boy* would have to take place at the absolute end of 2008, or possibly even in the early part of 2009 (not impossible, but the seasonal weather seems all wrong for that). One possibility is that Sarah and her friends, upon hearing the report, presume that "Ashley" was taken by the Bane and experimented upon for some weeks prior to Luke's "activation" in *Invasion of the Bane*. Supporting this idea, everything that's happened to Sarah and her friends since is said to have happened in the "past few

months". Maria, who was 13 in *Invasion of the Bane*, is now 14. A guard says that it's a Saturday.
891 The month and year are specified. Barbra's arrival is seen in *Iris: Iris and the Celestial Omnibus*: "The Deadly Flap". Barbra relates her arrival in the twenty-first century in *Iris: Enter Wildthyme*.
892 Dating *The Raincloud Man* (BF #116) - Charley says that *The Condemned* took place "earlier in the year". *The Raincloud Man* saw release in January 2009, but Menzies specifies that "it's Christmas" - presumably denoting the season rather than the actual day, as an awful lot of people are out doing Christmas shopping - which suggests a dating of December 2008.

2008 (mid-December) - "The Stockbridge Child"[893]

-> The Doctor's former companion Izzy was now a world traveller, and had recently written to Max Edison that she'd found something "amazing" in Kabul. Bonnybridge, Scotland, contained a large dimensional flaw, and would have been a nexus of alien activity were it not for the Cardiff Rift.

The TARDIS brought the tenth Doctor and Majenta Pryce to Stockbridge as the town celebrated its Aurelia Winter Festival. The Lokhus, which hailed from the universe after ours, had completed its chrysalis stage - upon its birth, it would be larger than Earth's sun. The creature was incinerated before this could happen. After the Doctor and Majenta left, the Crimson Hand scanned Max's memories to determine Majenta's whereabouts.

Lucie Miller, thinking the Doctor dead, accepted a lift from the Time Lords back to Blackpool.[894]

2008 (24th December) - DEATH IN BLACKPOOL[895]

-> The Zygon Hagoth, still disguised as Lucie Miller's Aunty Pat, discovered he was dying from melanoma - the result of his having maintained the same form for too long. "Pat" outwardly looked middle aged as a result, and the only cure was the milk of a Skarasen.

A Zynog (sic) named Landack schemed to mentally possess Hagoth and become a proper Zygon again. Hagoth - knowing he wouldn't live another year - summoned the eighth Doctor and Lucie to Earth, wanting to have a proper Christmas with Lucie one last time. Landack killed Hagoth's mind, then transferred his consciousness into his body - which Hagoth had poisoned, slaying Landack.

Lucie discovered the deception that the Doctor and Hagoth had perpetrated regarding her "Aunty Pat", and - unable to trust the Doctor any longer - left his company and stayed in Blackpool. She agreed to keep low until the Headhunter kidnapped her younger self, who was currently back home, the following summer.

---

893 Dating "The Stockbridge Child" (*DWM* #403-405) - The Doctor says that it's the "early twenty-first century", and "mid-December". A banner in Stockbridge reads, "Aurelia Winter Festival, '08". In real life, Bonnybridge fancies itself as "the UFO capital" of Scotland.

894 *The Vengeance of Morbius*; see the dating notes for *Death in Blackpool*.

895 Dating *Death in Blackpool* (BF BBC7 #4.1) - It's said to be Christmas Eve, but there's confusion as to the actual year. The back cover says it's "Christmas 2009", which mirrors the intent of the writer, Alan Barnes. However, within the story itself, the Doctor tells Hagoth that it's "2008", and nothing in this or any other Lucie Miller story contradicts that assertion.

Additionally, *Death in Blackpool* takes place concurrent to Lucie returning home for six months at the end of *The Vengeance of Morbius* - an audio that saw release in 2008. For anyone listening at the time, it would've been reasonable to presume that Lucie had returned to either A) her native year of 2006, or B) the year simultaneous to the story's release (2008). Certainly, there's no evidence to make the listener intuitively think that Lucie had gone home in what was, at the time, the future - which makes a dating of 2008 a bit more aesthetically pleasing than that of 2009.

Luckily, as *Death in Blackpool* takes place on Christmas Eve and *Voyage of the Damned* happens on Christmas Day itself, there's no need to explain why nobody in the audio story is distracted by news coverage of a cruise ship plummeting from space toward Buckingham Palace. Either way, Lucie - who meets the Doctor in 2006 - has done a remarkable job at keeping her family from realising that she's been gallivanting off in time and space for two or three years.

896 Dating *Voyage of the Damned* (X4.0) - Wilf spells out that *The Christmas Invasion* happened "Christmas

before last", *The Runaway Bride* occurred "last year".

897 As inferred from *The Stolen Earth*.

898 Dating *Turn Left* (X4.11) - This is the alternative version of *Voyage of the Damned*. In that story, the Doctor believed that all life on Earth would be wiped out when the *Titanic* hit, although it's not quite as severe here. London is presumably not evacuated in the alternate timeline (as it was in the original) because the Doctor wasn't around to phone in a warning.

899 "The Screams of Death". She puts her lock-picking to use in such stories as *The Beast Below*.

900 Events in 2009 include the "present day" sequences of *Doctor Who* Series 4; the last two episodes of *Torchwood* Series 2; *Planet of the Dead*; the "interim" (i.e. post-Series 2) *Torchwood* novels, audios and comics featuring Jack, Gwen and Ianto; *Torchwood* Series 3 (a.k.a. *TW: Children of Earth*); *The Sarah Jane Adventures* Series 2; the first half of *The Sarah Jane Adventures* Series 3; the BBC fourth Doctor audio series *Hornets' Nest* and *The End of Time* (TV).

901 "Two years" before *SJA: The Curse of Clyde Langer*.

902 "Three months" before *TW: Bay of the Dead*.

903 "Four years" before *Autonomy*.

904 The year before "The Age of Ice".

905 The year before *The Lodger* (TV).

906 *The Eyeless*. "They'd only just finished rebuilding" Big Ben, so this is after *The Christmas Invasion*.

907 The background to *The Sontaran Stratagem/The Poison Sky*. A car with an ATMOS sticker is seen in *Partners in Crime*, so at least some distribution of ATMOS occurs beforehand.

908 First mentioned in *Partners in Crime*, explained in *The Stolen Earth*.

909 Dating *Peri and the Piscon Paradox* (BF CC #5.8) - "It's definitely Earth, Los Angeles, 2009 AD", the Doctor says, in agreement with the blurb.

2008 (24th-25th December) - VOYAGE OF THE DAMNED[896] -> London was near-emptied as everyone feared a repeat of the devastating events of the last two Christmases. The Queen stayed in Buckingham Palace over the holiday. Wilf Mott, a news vendor, was impressed by her courage and stayed at his post.

Max Capricorn Cruiseliners now offered tours from the planet Sto in the Casavanian Belt to "primitive" cultures, and had one starliner designed after the Earth vessel *Titanic*. Max Capricorn himself wanted revenge after he was voted off the company board - he bribed the captain of the *Titanic* to lower the ship's shields during a meteor storm as it arrived in Earth orbit to celebrate a traditional Christmas. Capricorn hoped that the *Titanic* would crash and detonate its nuclear storm drives, destroying Earth and dooming the board to charges of mass murder. He then intended to retire to the beaches of Penhaxico II, where the ladies loved cyborgs such as himself.

The tenth Doctor met the waitress Astrid Peth and the faux historian Mr Copper aboard the *Titanic*, as well as Wilf Mott during a brief shore leave to Earth. Capricorn's plan came to fruition - the *Titanic* fell from orbit, and the Heavenly Host angelic robots built to serve the passengers started killing everyone on board to eliminate potential witnesses. Astrid sacrificed herself to kill Capricorn, and the Doctor both assumed command of the Host and ignited the *Titanic*'s secondary engine, pulling the ship up just before it hit Buckingham Palace. The Queen thanked the Doctor for his help, and wished him a Merry Christmas. Mr. Copper started up a new life on Earth.

By the Light of the Asteroid was a popular soap opera on Sto. Cyborgs were discriminated against on Sto, but were gaining more rights, including the right to marry The minimum penalty for space-lane fraud was ten years in jail. Five thousand Sto credits represented twenty years' wages; 50,000,056 credits equalled a million pounds.

Earth was designated as a Level Five planet and had six billion people. The Doctor hinted that Europe and America would go to war at some point in the future.

Mr. Copper founded the Mr. Copper Foundation. Harriet Jones, the former Prime Minister, had Copper's foundation develop the Subwave Network.[897]

- -
(=) 2008 (24th-25th December) TURN LEFT[898] -> The Noble family followed Rose's advice and stayed in a hotel outside London. The starship *Titanic* hit Buckingham Palace, killing everyone in London and dosing southern England with radiation.
- -

Amy Pond learned to pick locks when a Mr. Harrison became a little over-eager with the handcuffs during a 2008 Christmas party.[899]

2009[900]

A young woman who would befriend Clyde Langer became homeless after her father died and her mother remarried, and the new living situation "didn't work out for her". She adopted the name Ellie Faber.[901] Leet, a child of the Dellacoi, rode the time winds but was hurled to Earth. His arrival killed sixty-three people at the Regal Cinema in Splott. Leet sought refuge in the only survivor, 22-year-old Oscar Phillips.[902]

In 2009, Hyperville opened - at five square miles, it was the largest shopping mall in Europe. The Nestene-controlled Elizabeth Devonshire had facilitated construction of Hyperville for benefit of the Nestene unit she was nursemaiding, and also arranged for production of Plastinol-2: an all-purpose plastic intended to serve as the chief substance of a new generation of Autons. At this time, Kate Maguire, age 16, was given an all-access Hypercard to Hyperville by a mysterious stranger - the tenth Doctor, who knew they would need the card in 2013.[903]

UNIT repelled an advance party of Ice Warriors.[904] Craig Owens (a future flatmate of the Doctor) and his friend Sophie met at a call centre.[905] The last of the Steggosians attempted to wipe out Earth with poison. The tenth Doctor fought him on top of Big Ben, and the fight ended with the Steggosian Captain falling to his death.[906]

The Sontarans collaborated with Luke Rattigan in a new bid to conquer Earth. Rattigan's company distributed the Sontaran-based Atmospheric Omission System (ATMOS), a navigation system and means of reducing carbon dioxide emissions in cars to zero. Before long, it was fitted as standard on all UK government vehicles.[907] Some bees on Earth were migrant bees from the planet Melissa Majoria. Sensing danger approaching due to the Daleks' reality bomb, they began returning home.[908]

2009 - PERI AND THE PISCON PARADOX[909] -> The fifth Doctor and Peri dealt with a suicidal Piscon named Zarl - or so they believed. The sixth Doctor, sensing something awry about the incident, revisited it... and accidentally killed Zarl before his previous self had defeated him. The sixth Doctor fulfilled history by disguising himself as Zarl, and was aided by Peri's contemporary self: Dr Perpugilliam Brown, a talk show host and three-time divorcee who convinced her younger self that she was a secret agent for the X-Files. Thinking "Zarl" defeated, the fifth Doctor and "his" Peri left. The older Peri declined to travel with the sixth Doctor again.

c 2009 - THE SONTARAN GAMES[910] -> The tenth Doctor arrived at the British Academy of Sporting Excellence (BASE), where elite athletes were training for the Globe Games. A group of Sontarans from the Twelfth Sontaran Fleet, led by Major Stenx, forced everyone there to a series of physical challenges to assess human prowess - those who failed were killed or fed to Sontar Sand Shrews. The BASE athletes gained the upper hand, and killed Stenx's Sontarans. The Doctor realised that Emma, one of the athletes, was a Rutan spy wanting to stage a diplomatic incident at the Games, which would trigger a war and allow the Rutans to invade. She seemed to consider the Doctor's offer that she abandon her plan and let him take her away from the Sontaran-Rutan conflict - but before she could decide, she and Stenx died in combat with one another. The Doctor fled as the energy Emma had absorbed was released, destroying BASE.

2009 (March) - TW: "The Return of the Vostok"[911] -> Torchwood killed the Vostok - jelly-fish-like aliens capable of creating winter conditions, and who sought to use the Rift to retroactively send an ice age back through time.

2009 (a Tuesday and Wednesday in March) - PARTNERS IN CRIME[912] -> The loss of the breeding planet Adipose III compelled the Adipose first family to hire Matron Cofelia of the Five-Straighten Classabindi Nursery Fleet to oversee the production of their offspring. She founded Adipose Industries on Earth as a front for this operation. The company signed up a million customers to its weight-loss programme in Greater London alone, with the intention of going national. Pills were distributed under the claim that anyone who took them would lose exactly a kilogram a day, but in actuality the pills slowly transformed people's fat into baby Adipose. The tenth Doctor and Donna independently investigated Adipose Industries, were reunited, and came to the realisation that the pill-takers' bones, hair and internal organs could be completely broken down into the Adipose offspring.

The Matron sent a signal that generated ten thousand Adipose, who marched through the streets of London, but the Doctor stopped the signal from fully converting all one million of the weight-loss customers. A giant ship of the Adipose first family arrived over London and collected the baby Adipose with levitation beams. Seeding a Level Five planet such as Earth

---

910 Dating *The Sontaran Games* (*Quick Reads* #4) - This has a contemporary or very near-future setting, although no year is specified.

911 Dating *TW: "The Return of the Vostok"* (*TW* webcomic #1) - The opening caption says, "Cardiff, March". The year isn't specified, but the story was released in February 2009, and - owing to Owen and Tosh's presence - occurs before the Series 2 finale.

912 Dating *Partners in Crime* (X4.01) - No month is given here, but in the alternate timeline in *Turn Left*, the Adipose incident takes place in March. An Adipose Industries customer tells Donna that she "started taking the pills on Thursday" and has been doing so for "five days", meaning the story begins on a Tuesday. It concludes the next day.

913 Dating *Turn Left* (X4.11) - It's at least "eight weeks" since the *Titanic* disaster, as the Colasantos family have been living in Leeds that long, and the Nobles are told they face "another three months" stuck where they are unless they relocate to Leeds.

914 Dating *The Sontaran Stratagem/The Poison Sky* (X4.5-4.6) - The month isn't given, but the dating can be extrapolated from the alternative universe seen in *Turn Left*, and the fact that only "a few days" have passed since Donna left with the Doctor in *Partners in Crime*. Frustratingly, Martha walks past a wall calendar that is too blurry to make out.

The Brigadier also mentions being in Peru in *SJA: Enemy of the Bane*. Russell T Davies has said that UNIT's name change resulted from the United Nations asking

that its name not be associated with the group, although UNIT is said to still receive UN funding.

915 *The Doctor's Daughter*

916 *The Taking of Chelsea 426*

917 Dating *Turn Left* (X4.11) - This is the parallel timeline's version of *The Poison Sky*.

918 Dating *TW: Fragments* and *TW: Exit Wounds* (*TW* 2.12-2.13) - The repeated flashback segments in *TW: Fragments* best align with established *Torchwood* continuity if the final two episodes of Series 2 occur in 2009. Most relevantly, it's established that Ianto approached Jack for a job "21 months" ago, after the destruction of Torchwood One (in *Doomsday*) in 2007. If *Doomsday* is indeed set in July 2007, then *Fragments* would occur in April 2009. It might seem like a glitch when Jack tells the Torchwood of 1901 to deep-freeze him and set the alarm for "107 years' time...", suggesting a target year of 2008, but if he's unearthed late in 1901, he could easily be rounding down from, "107 years and a few months".

919 *TW: Lost Souls*

920 Dating *SJA: The Last Sontaran* (*SJA* 2.1) - *The Sontaran Stratagem/The Poison Sky* are referenced in detail, so it's after those stories. No mention is made of events of *The Stolen Earth*, and, notably, both Maria's mum Chrissie and Professor Skinner's daughter Lucy become incredulous upon learning that aliens are real. Chrissie isn't portrayed as the brightest of people, but Lucy - as the daughter of a man whose job is to search for friendly life in outer space - would surely better

with offspring violated a galactic law enforced by the Shadow Proclamation, and so the first family killed the Matron to cover up her crime.

The Doctor agreed to let Donna join him on his travels, and briefly showed the TARDIS in flight to Wilf Mott as they departed.

Before she left with the Doctor, Donna briefly met the dimension-hopping Rose Tyler.

(=) **2009 (March) - TURN LEFT**[913] -> An Emergency Government took control of the United Kingdom. Seven million were in need of relocation from the radiation-flooded southern England, and France closed its borders. The Noble family were relocated to Leeds, and shared a small house with the Colasantos family. The United States promised £50 billion in aid... but before it could deliver, America's economy was devastated when sixty million Americans were converted into Adipose. Spaceships collected the Adipose offspring.

2009 (March) - THE SONTARAN STRATAGEM / THE POISON SKY[914] -> UNIT had been renamed the Unified Intelligence Taskforce. It received massive funding from the United Nations in the name of homeworld security, and still operated the *Valiant*. UNIT had access to the nuclear arsenals of the US, UK, France, India, Pakistan, China and North Korea. Sir Alistair Gordon Lethbridge-Stewart was currently in Peru. The Doctor was technically on staff with UNIT, as he never formally resigned. UNIT Headquarters was near Tower Bridge, London.

The ATMOS navigation/anti-pollution system had now been installed in half of the world's eight hundred million cars. Martha summoned the tenth Doctor and Donna when fifty-two people were poisoned to death inside their cars at the exact same moment, in eleven different time zones. General Staal the Undefeated of the Tenth Sontaran Battle Fleet advanced his plans to release poison gas from every car fitted with ATMOS. The gas was a Caesofine concentrate that would alter Earth's atmosphere, turning the planet into a Sontaran breeding world.

As the ATMOS-made gas intensified, the UK government declared a national emergency, and the UN issued a worldwide directive for people to leave the cities. The first deaths were reported in Tokyo. In Europe, thousands walked across country to escape. The Eastern seaboard of America became reminiscent of Dunkirk, as boats took refugees out into the Atlantic. The tenth Doctor and Donna restored Earth's atmosphere to normal, and the genius entrepreneur Luke Rattigan, realising the Sontarans never intended

to give him the power he sought, sacrificed himself to destroy the Sontaran mothership.

Martha was now engaged to Tom Milligan, who was in paediatrics and working out in Africa. Rattigan's inventions, not all of them derived from Sontaran technology, included nanotech steel, biospheres, gravity simulation, rattifan 18 and a cordolaine signal.

The tenth Doctor and Donna returned Martha home after sharing an adventure with her - and the Doctor's daughter Jenny - in the future.[915] The Rutans learned of the Sontaran plan to make Earth a breeding world, and seeded Saturn with a spore that would possess the resultant clones. With the Sontaran defeat, the spore remained inactive on Saturn until the twenty-sixth century.[916]

(=) **2009 (mid March) - TURN LEFT**[917] -> With so little petrol, Britain was spared the worst when the Sontarans activated their ATMOS stratagem, although the rest of the world was badly affected. Torchwood took the fight to the Sontaran mothership and although they prevailed, Gwen and Ianto were killed, and Jack Harkness was transported to the Sontaran homeworld. Rose met Donna again, and claimed that Donna would come with her in three weeks time.

2009 (April) - TW: FRAGMENTS / EXIT WOUNDS[918] -> Jack Harkness' vengeful brother Gray coerced Captain John Hart into embarking upon a major terror campaign against Torchwood. Hart wracked Cardiff with fifteen building-levelling explosions, and aided Gray in taking Jack back to 27 AD and burying him. Gray enhanced the Rift so that Cardiff came under siege from ghosts, Weevils and hooded figures bearing scythes. The four most senior police offers were murdered. The systems servicing the Turnmill Nuclear Power Station failed, and Owen Harper died a final time while diverting irradiated coolant to contain the resultant meltdown. Gray shot Toshiko Sato, killing her. Torchwood quelled the situation; Jack revived from the stasis into which he'd been placed in 1901 and overpowered his rogue brother, then placed him in cryo-freeze.

Martha attended Owen and Tosh's funerals.[919]

2009 - SJA: THE LAST SONTARAN[920] -> Strange lights were seen near the Tycho Project, a radio telescope that searched for friendly alien life. Sarah Jane, Clyde, Luke and Maria went to investigate and were stalked by Commander Kaagh, a Sontaran who had survived the recent invasion. He planned to use the Tycho radio telescope to crash Earth's satellites into its nuclear stockpiles, but Sarah Jane and her friends drove Kaagh away.

Kaagh became a mercenary for the Bane, and encountered the fugitive Mrs Wormwood on a planet in the Snake Tongue Nebula. They hatched a scheme to acquire the power of the banished Horath.[921]

2009 - BEAUTIFUL CHAOS[922] ->
The tenth Doctor took Donna home so she could spend time with her mother and grandfather on the anniversary of her father's death. Morgan Tech, owned by a thrall of the Mandragora Helix, was about to release the newest personal computing gadget: the M-TEK. The Helix planned to control and speed up man's expansion into space - it was projected that humans would build farms on Mars in twenty years and colonise Alpha Centauri in a hundred, all part of a Mandragoran Empire. The Helix took control of people whose lineage extended back to San Martino, Italy, but the Doctor ended its schemes. UNIT helped to recall the M-TEKs.

The Prime Minister at this time was Aubrey Fairchild.

c 2009 - "The Time of My Life"[923] ->
The tenth Doctor and Donna confronted gun-totting dog aliens from space, whose spaceship arrived over London to incite the dogs of Earth into revolution against their human masters.

(=) 2009 (early April) TURN LEFT[924] ->
In the "Donna turned right" universe, the Emergency Government adopted an "England for the English" policy, sending foreign-born residents to labour camps. Soon afterwards, the stars started going out. Donna met with Rose and a UNIT group led by Captain Erisa Magambo. They had recovered the dying TARDIS from under the Thames, and used its technology to build a time machine that could reflect chronon energy from mirrors. Donna agreed to travel back to the point of temporal deviation, and convince her past self to turn left...

2009 (a Saturday in early April) - THE STOLEN EARTH / JOURNEY'S END[925] ->
Davros, rescued from the Last Great Time War by Dalek Caan, created a new generation of Daleks genetically derived from his own cells. A new Dalek Empire was born, and set about creating a reality bomb - an alignment of twenty-seven planets that would flatten Z-Neutrino energy into a single string, and thereby undo the electrical field binding all reality. The Daleks intended to shield themselves as all matter became dust, then mere atoms. They would become the only living creatures in existence. Three worlds were plucked from different time zones for the reality bomb: Adipose III, Pyrovillia and

keep track of this sort of thing. The point is that while it's a little suspect to think that they haven't noticed all the very public alien events that have taken place throughout New *Who*, *Torchwood* and *The Sarah Jane Adventures* before now, it's barking mad to think that they're still in the dark after events of *The Stolen Earth/ Journey's End*. Moreover, this reflects a marked shift within *The Sarah Jane Adventures* Series 2 itself - Clyde's dad mentions "those Dalek things" (i.e. *The Stolen Earth/ Journey's End*) mid-way through the series in *SJA: The Mark of the Berserker*, and by *SJA: Enemy of the Bane*, the last story of Series 2, the Brigadier can bluff his way out of a tight spot by saying that, "as the cat's out of the bag" with regards aliens, he's now at liberty to reveal details of his UNIT days in his memoirs.

While it's very counter-intuitive, the best fit is to place *The Last Sontaran* prior to *The Stolen Earth* (i.e. in spring 2009), and to set the rest of *The Sarah Jane Adventures* Series 2 later in the year. (The alternative would be to set *The Last Sontaran* at least six weeks prior to *SJA: The Day of the Clown*, which would mean that the Park Vale school year has started nearly a month earlier than normal - see *SJA: Revenge of the Slitheen* and *SJA: The Nightmare Man* - for no discernible reason.) It might be relevant that when mention is made of the Doctor, Sarah Jane gives no clue that she's met him recently in *Journey's End*, further suggesting

that story hasn't happened yet.

Where Maria is concerned, a pre-*The Stolen Earth* dating makes some sense: if her father gets the job offer in spring, she might be allowed to finish out the school year (during the "six weeks" that pass prior to the epilogue of *The Last Sontaran*), and they move to America at the start of summer. It also works better to assume that not that long has passed since *The Poison Sky* for Kaagh (as opposed to a fall dating for *The Last Sontaran*, which would mean that he's evidently been sitting around Earth for some months doing nothing). The only real glitch to all of this, then, is that when Luke gets an email dated 9th October from Maria in *The Day of the Clown*, it's treated as if it's the first time she's gotten in touch with her old gang, when one would expect that she might have done so some time prior.

921 *SJA: Enemy of the Bane*
922 Dating *Beautiful Chaos* (NSA #29) - The story has a very precise dating framework, with the text split into days rather than chapters. Events begin on "Friday 15th May 2009" (per a newspaper dateline, p24), and progress to the following Monday (pgs 15, 79, 135, 185), with an epilogue that takes place the next "Friday" (p221). Page 53 reiterates that it's the "middle of May".

... all of this information, however, must be set aside because it clashes with the continuity of the TV episodes. Given the need for *Planet of the Dead* to occur at

the lost moon of Poosh.

The Daleks moved into the second phase of their plan, and teleported twenty-four planets - including Callufrax Minor, Jahoo, Shallacatop, Woman Wept and Clom - into the Medusa Cascade along with the three worlds already taken. Earth was also one of the stolen planets, and humanity was horrified to look into the sky and find itself surrounded by other worlds. When the translocation occurred, Martha Jones was at UNIT's New York HQ, working as medical director on Project Indigo: an attempt to salvage Sontaran technology into a teleport system. Captain Jack was at the Torchwood Hub, and Sarah Jane was at Bannerman Road. Rose Tyler materialised on Earth from Pete's World. Mickey Smith and Jackie would later journey from Pete's World to help her.

The Daleks were operating from the Crucible: a massive space station in the middle of the planetary arrangement. A fleet of two hundred Dalek ships set out to subjugate Earth, transmitting in advance a single word, repeated: "Exterminate, exterminate, exterminate". The Daleks gleefully dismantled every form of resistance, from UNIT forces aboard the *Valiant* to Wilf Noble with his paintball gun. Daleks landed in Japan and Germany, and forced the air force to retreat over North Africa. Contact was lost with the airplane bearing the UK Prime Minister. The Commander General of the United Nations signalled Earth's surrender.

The tenth Doctor and Donna learned about the missing planets from the Shadow Proclamation. Harriet Jones connected the Doctor's allies using the Subwave Network she'd developed, and together they sent out a pulse that enabled the Doctor and Donna to return to

Earth. The Daleks traced the signal back to Harriet's home and exterminated her.

The TARDIS materialised in London, and the Doctor was reunited with Rose... and was then shot by a Dalek. He began to regenerate, but used the process to heal himself and diverted the excess energy into a bio-matching receptacle - the hand severed in combat with the Sycorax - to save his life.

The Doctor and his many allies confronted the Daleks aboard the Crucible. The Supreme Dalek had the TARDIS dumped in the Z-neutrino core of the Crucible to destroy it. Donna was still aboard the Ship, and the regenerative energies in the Doctor's hand (severed during his battle with the Sycorax leader at Christmas 2006) interacted with her. The hand grew into a duplicate of the tenth Doctor who was part human, and Donna absorbed all the Doctor's knowledge, becoming a human-Time Lord metacrisis. This was enough to turn the tables - Donna deactivated the reality bomb, and twenty six of the planets were returned to their rightful places, but the Supreme Dalek destroyed the machinery before Earth could be returned. Jack destroyed the Supreme Dalek, and the duplicate Doctor used a backfeed to wipe out the Daleks. Davros refused the Doctor's offer of a rescue, and the TARDIS left the exploding Crucible. In conjunction with the Torchwood Hub and Sarah Jane's Mr. Smith computer, the tenth Doctors and their companions used the TARDIS to tow the Earth back home.

Humanity celebrated Earth's return to its proper location, although there was widespread rainfall due to atmospheric disturbances. Mickey opted to remain in his native reality as his grandmother on Pete's World

Easter 2009 (see the dating notes on that story for why), all Series 4-related stories must happen beforehand, ruling out a mid-May dating for *Beautiful Chaos*. Additionally, the story is said to happen "one month" after *The Poison Sky* (p13), which is dated in this chronology to mid-March 2009.

Conflict with the TV series aside, *Beautiful Chaos* (pgs 187-188) is otherwise accommodating to continuity by acknowledging the other Mandragora-related adventures: "The Mark of Mandragora", *Sarah Jane Smith* Series 2 and *The Eleventh Tiger*. Fairchild is the Prime Minister whose plane goes down in *The Stolen Earth*.

923 Dating "The Time of My Life" (*DWM* #399) - The story was released in 2008, but the "year ahead" rule governing Series 4 might apply. It must be roughly contemporary in that Donna spies her house, and is incensed that her neighbours have a swimming pool that she didn't know about. The London Eye, constructed in 1999, is seen in the background.

924 Dating *Turn Left* (X4.11) - "Three weeks" after *The*

Poison Sky.

925 Dating *The Stolen Earth/Journey's End* (X4.11) - This story crosses over with *Torchwood* and *The Sarah Jane Adventures*, and picks up the story from all three series. It is set after *The Poison Sky*, but before *Planet of the Dead*; between *TW: Exit Wounds* and *TW: Children of Earth*; and at some point after *SJA: Revenge of the Slitheen* and before *SJA: Secrets of the Stars* (which mentions this story). Sarah says Luke is 14, as he was in *Revenge of the Slitheen*. Triangulating from all of that, *The Stolen Earth* would have to be set in early April, before Easter. Rose passes a sign advertising a dance night on "Friday 25 July" (which in 2009 was actually a Saturday) - not that this means it's actually July, though.

Adelaide Brooke's biography in *The Waters of Mars* confirms that this Dalek invasion occurred in "2008". The Doctor says it's a Saturday. Callufrax Minor (as it's spelled on screen here) is presumably related to Calufrax (as it's spelled on screen in *The Pirate Planet*).

had died. The duplicate Doctor, Rose and Jackie returned to Pete's World. Jack returned to Torchwood, and Sarah Jane went home.

UNIT had developed the Osterhagen Key: 25 nuclear warheads placed at strategic points beneath the Earth's crust as a means of destroying the planet - a final option should humanity's suffering be deemed too great to be allowed to continue. Martha promised the Doctor that she would dismantle the system.

Donna's mind couldn't cope with the Time Lord abilities it had absorbed. The Doctor saved her life by removing all of her memories of him, the TARDIS and their travels together, then left her with her family.

Adelaide Brooke lost her parents in the Dalek invasion. A Dalek confronted her, but - perhaps recognising her importance to history - did not exterminate her.[926] The Daleks' gambit with the reality bomb weakened the dimensional walls, enabling some Cybermen within the Void to fall back through time to London, 1851, using the dimension vault they stole from the Daleks. Everything else inside the Void perished.[927] One Dalek ship survived and was hurled back through time, damaged, to the 1940s.[928]

2009 (April) - PLANET OF THE DEAD[929] -> The aristocratic art thief Lady Christina de Souza stole the Cup of Athelstan, which was worth £18 million, from the International Gallery in London and fled aboard a No. 200 bus. The tenth Doctor joined de Souza and her fellow passengers on the bus, which promptly fell through a wormhole to San Helios - a desert planet in the Scorpion Nebula, on the other side of the universe. A UNIT team led by Captain Magambo sealed off the tunnel in London.

The Doctor made contact with the Tritovores, fly-like aliens who thought San Helios had a population of one hundred billion. In the last year, all life on the planet has been devoured by monsters that resembled ravenous flying stingrays. The Doctor realised that the wormhole between San Helios and Earth was growing, and that the Stingrays would soon cross over, wiping out all life on Earth. With the help of UNIT, and after breaking up the Cup of Athelstan to use as components in a machine, the Doctor got the bus back to London and closed the wormhole. He also helped de Souza elude the police.

The TARDIS had landed in the grounds of Buckingham Palace, and the Doctor was confident the Queen "didn't mind".

926 *The Waters of Mars*
927 *The Next Doctor*, presuming the "greater battle" that the Doctor mentions refers to events in *The Stolen Earth/Journey's End*.
928 *Victory of the Daleks*
929 Dating *Planet of the Dead* (X4.15) - It is "April" according to the bus driver, and the Doctor wishes Christina "Happy Easter". This is after *The Stolen Earth/Journey's End*, as "planets in the sky" are referenced. The story is mentioned in *SJA: Mona Lisa's Revenge*, so must take place beforehand. Most importantly, *Planet of the Dead* must occur before *The End of Time* (TV) per a psychic's prediction of not just the tenth Doctor's impending death, but Gallifrey's return.

Planet of the Dead, then, is the first contemporary *Doctor Who* TV story since *Rose* to be set the year it was shown, ending the practice (starting with *Aliens of London*) that "present day" stories are set around a year after broadcast. Any temptation to continue the "year later" tradition is overruled partly because of the psychic's prediction, but also because *The End of Time* has to occur at the end of 2009 per the continuity of *The Sarah Jane Adventures*. Sarah and Luke first meet the tenth Doctor in *Journey's End* (set in 2009), acknowledge that meeting in *SJA: The Wedding of Sarah Jane Smith* (where it's said that Sarah and the Tennant Doctor will meet at least one more time), they have their final meeting in *The End of Time* (TV) when the Doctor saves Luke from an oncoming car, and then

Sarah acknowledges *that* meeting in *SJA: Death of the Doctor* (set in 2010), when she airs her suspicion that the Doctor regenerated because, "The last time I saw him, he didn't say a word, he just looked at me".
930 *TW: Lost Souls*. The real life CERN project was also mentioned in *SJA: Invasion of the Bane*.
931 "Six weeks" after *Beautiful Chaos*.
932 Dating *SJA: The Last Sontaran* (SJA 2.1) - This epilogue occurs six weeks after the story's main events.
933 Dating *Last of the Time Lords* (X3.13) - It's "one year later" than the events of *The Sound of Drums*.
934 *The Vengeance of Morbius*, *Orbis. Death in Blackpool* specifies that Lucie is abducted in summer - no later than June, as she's kidnapped "six months" after returning home in 2008.
935 Dating "Ghosts of the Northern Line" and "The Crimson Hand" (*DWM* #414-420) - Intersol agents state in "Ghosts of the Northern Line" that it's "late '09, post-Stolen Earth scenario" (*Journey's End*). Obama is said to be in power.
936 Dating the *Torchwood* Series 2/Series 3 interim stories (*TW: Lost Souls*, TW audio drama #1; *TW: Almost Perfect*, TW novel #9; *TW:* "Ma and Par", TW webcomic #2; *TW:* "The Selkie", TWM #14; *TW:* "Broken", TWM #15-19; *TW: The Sin Eaters*, audiobook #4; *TW: Into the Silence*, TW novel #10; *TW: Bay of the Dead*, TW novel #11; *TW: The House That Jack Built*, TW novel #12; *TW: Asylum*, TW audio drama #2; *TW: Golden Age*, TW audio drama #3; *TW: The Dead Line*, TW audio drama #4; *TW: Risk*

In May, a test conducted on the Large Hadron Collider at CERN created a dimensional bridge that provided a neutron-eating creature with access to our universe.[930] Sylvia Noble received a letter that Donna had written prior to her memory loss. It detailed her excitement about travelling with the Doctor.[931]

2009 - SJA: THE LAST SONTARAN[932] -> Six weeks after defeating Kaagh, Maria Jackson moved to Washington with her father.

(=) 2009 (a Saturday in June) - LAST OF THE TIME LORDS[933] -> The Master had controlled Earth for a year, and turned it into a factory world. The enslaved human population was put to work building two hundred thousand war rockets "set to burn across the universe" and create a Time Lord Empire. A space lane traffic advisor warned all travellers to stay away from Sol 3.

Japan had been devastated, and New York was reportedly in ruin. China had fusion mills, Europe had radiation pits, and a shipyard in Russia ran from the Black Sea to the Bering Strait.

Martha Jones spent a year travelling the world and spreading word of the Doctor, telling the public to think of him when the rockets were launched. The hyper-aged tenth Doctor had spent the last year linking himself into the telepathic field of the Archangel network, and used the humans' psychic energy to restore himself. Captain Jack destroyed the Paradox Machine, reversing time one year and one day to the exact moment before the Toclafane materialised.

Six months after a grieving Lucie returned home, the Headhunter arrived on her doorstep, shot her unconscious and whisked her away to the planet Orbis in the future.[934]

2009 - "Ghosts of the Northern Line" / "The Crimson Hand"[935] -> Intersol, a time-travelling intergalactic justice organisation, estimated that Earth's oil reserves were "almost depleted".

The Mnemosyne unit hidden in London's Northern Line had matured, and wanted revenge for the murder of its guardian. The tenth Doctor and Majenta Pryce intervened as the Mnemosyne manifested everyone who had died on the Northern Line in previous decades as "ghosts", and announced its intention to incinerate everyone within the Underground. Majenta convinced the ghostly engrams to turn on the Mnemosyne, destroying it and themselves.

A squadron of Intersol ships arrived in Earth orbit and arrested Majenta. They time-locked the TARDIS, and returned with it, the Doctor and Majenta to the future...

Torchwood
Series 2 / Series 3 Interim[936]

2009 - TW: LOST SOULS[937] -> Martha Jones asked Torchwood to help her investigate mysterious events at CERN, the European Organisation for Nuclear Research, in Switzerland. CERN was about to switch on its Large Hadron Collider (LHC) in an effort to identify the theoretical Higgs particle (the most fundamental unit of existence), but the LHC had enabled a deadly alien entity that consumed neutrons to cross into our reality. The LHC was reconfigured to smash protons into anti-protons - creating the Higgs particle, but also killing the creature and preventing others of its kind from crossing over.

Assessment, TW novel #13; TW: The Undertaker's Gift, TW novel #14; TW: Consequences, TW novel #15 - actually a novella collection, but generally counted as part of the novel range; TW: "Fated to Pretend", TWM #20; TW: "Somebody Else's Problem", TWM #23; TW: "Hell House", TWM #24; TW: Department X, TW audiobook #5; TW: Ghost Train, TW audiobook #6; TW: The Devil and Miss Carew, TW audio drama #5; TW: Submission, TW audio drama #6) - The aforementioned Torchwood stories all feature Captain Jack, Gwen and Ianto, and are set between Torchwood Series 2 and Series 3 (the latter being a single story, TW: Children of Earth). The year is confirmed as 2009 in Risk Assessment (p9), Asylum, Consequences: "Consequences" (p241), The Sin-Eaters and Golden Age. Weirdly, in TW: The Dead Line, events in 1976 are identified - in the very same conversation! - as being both thirty-three and thirty-four years ago.

With so few tangible clues as to how these audios,

novels and comics slot together, the stories are here presented in nothing more scientific than release order. See the individual entries for more.

937 Dating TW: Lost Souls (TW audio drama #1) - The story aired on 10th September, 2008, as part of Radio 4's "Big Bang Day" to commemorate the LHC switch-on of the very same date, and was released on CD on 18th September. Within the fiction, nothing is said about the year - which is fortunate, given the overarching need to place the Jack, Gwen and Ianto stories in 2009. Nor is any reference given to the month or day, save for repeated mentions of an LHC field test conducted "back in May". It's tempting to think that the switch-on just occurs a year later in the Doctor Who universe than in real life, but as the year of the actual LHC switch-on has already been compromised, there's no particular reason to think one way or the other that the 10th September dating is still valid. That being the case, Lost

Gwen Cooper met a trader from the planet Murgatroyd, and acquired from him a device that could purportedly speak to the dead. She used it - or so she hoped - to send a message to Owen and Tosh in the hereafter.[938]

2009 (Friday to the following Saturday) - TW: ALMOST PERFECT[939] **->** The Perfection had built a sentient device that extended their natural reality-warping abilities, but the device became bored of creating perfection and escaped with the Perfection's interior decorators. The device began "helping" various people, causing such brouhaha as a group of speed-daters being reduced to skeletons. Torchwood confronted the Perfection - who had broken their word to Jack, and decided to install themselves as Earth's gods after all. Ianto used the device to drain the life-energy from the Perfection, leaving them as aged husks that he Retconned. In accordance with its wishes, Jack pitched the device into Cardiff Bay.

2009 - TW: "Ma and Par" -> Torchwood electrocuted a Bull-Craktor - a monstrous arachnid - and its offspring at the Pontyvale Golf Course.

2009 - TW: "The Selkie" -> Jack found that the shapeshifting Selkie he'd previously aided was behind a series of murders on Seal Island in Scotland, and killed it.

2009 - TW: "Broken" -> Bilis Manger had designed the Clockhouse Hotel - located on the old site of the Amber Hotel - to contain a creature thought to have been either born of the Rift, or was an expression of the Rift's own self-awareness. Torchwood looked into reports of missing persons at the Clockhouse exactly one hundred forty years to the day after the Rift struck the Amber. The entity hoped to tap enough of Jack's life energy to properly manifest, but

Jack temporarily died in such a fashion that severed the Rift entity's link to reality, and also destroyed the hotel.

2009 - TW: THE SIN EATERS -> A swarm of alien insects - creatures that normally lived in a shadow dimension - fed upon the guilt of people in the Cardiff city centre, endowing them with euphoria in return. Torchwood destroyed the swarm and their queen, a giant creature in Cardiff Bay. Jack also burnt down the church of St. Francis, which had been infected by the creatures.

2009 - TW: INTO THE SILENCE -> The Rift enabled an entity from the Silent Planet - a shadowy world in the furthest corner of the universe, where the formless inhabitants lived in total isolation and only corporealised to mate - to travel to Earth. The entity thought sound so beautiful, it murdered several singers to absorb their vocal cords and larynxes - but even these barely functioned as intended. The killings disrupted preparations for the fifth annual Welsh Amateur Operatic Contest. Torchwood ended the killing spree by allowing the entity to merge with Ryan Scott, an autistic child who craved isolation, and then return home. Detective Inspector Tom Cutler helped Captain Jack with the case; afterwards, Jack removed Cutler's memories of Torchwood with Retcon.

2009 - TW: BAY OF THE DEAD -> The symbiont Leet heard the siren call of his life pod, and used Oscar Phillip's memories of *The All-Night Zombie Horror Show* to create "search units" to retrieve it. Dozens if not hundreds of people were transformed into the undead but proved hard to control, so Leet sealed Cardiff within a time-energy barrier. Oscar disintegrated the cadavers by killing himself, whereupon Leet brought down the barrier and was believed to have returned home.

Souls might as well go into the release-order rotation with its post-*Torchwood* Series 2 contemporaries.
938 The framing sequence to *TW: In the Shadows*. Placement is unknown, save that Gwen references *TW: Lost Souls*.
939 Dating *TW: Almost Perfect* (*TW* novel #9) - The action begins on a Friday (p131) and concludes the next Saturday.
940 *TW: Out of Time* establishes that Torchwood already has asylum protocols for people from the past, so the issue here must be in convincing the group to similarly protect benevolent aliens.
941 Dating *TW: Risk Assessment* (*TW* novel #13) - It's "Thursday" (p92), and after the new morning dawns, it's said that Havisham was revived "two days ago" (so, she awoke on a Wednesday). Gwen goes missing for "two days" after that, so the story concludes on a Sunday.
942 Dating *The Eternal Summer* (BF #128) - After the bubble's collapse, Max reappears in Stockbridge on 4th

August, 2009 - one of many dates said in a time ripple, and probably representing the furthest point that the time bubble extends into the future. By default, then, that's when the story takes place. Max also confirms, in a conversation with the Doctor, that it's now the twenty-first century. *The Eternal Summer*, alas, wasn't actually released in summer, but came out in November 2009.
943 Dating *TW: Consequences*: "The Wrong Hands" and "Virus" (*TW* novel #15c, #15d) - The second day of "Virus" falls on the "last Thursday of the month", so it's not yet September, as that would conflict with *TW: Children of Earth*.

2009 - TW: THE HOUSE THAT JACK BUILT -> Jack discovered that interdimensional beings had polluted the timeline of a house he owned, Jackson Leaves, causing the deaths of thirteen of its residents over the past century. He destroyed the beings, and - as insurance against more fatalities - enabled to the current owners of Jackson Leaves to win a lottery, preventing them from renting the house out.

2009 - TW: ASYLUM -> Some inhabitants of an unknown planet escaped in "lifeboats" when solar flares ravaged their world. One lifeboat landed on Earth, and the thirteen benevolent aliens aboard integrated with Earth society and sired offspring with humanity. One of the aliens lived in Cardiff under the name "Moira Evans".

The Rift disgorged Moira's granddaughter - Freda, a Cardiff resident in 2069, whose personal debit gun could disrupt modern-day communications, security and transport systems. Captain Jack's team suspected that the Torchwood of the future had deliberately sent Freda back so they would adopt an asylum policy, hopefully blunting some of the xenophobia that Torchwood would otherwise cause. Jack, Gwen and Ianto helped Freda adjust to life in the present.[940]

2009 - TW: GOLDEN AGE -> The "time store" at Torchwood India required an ever-growing amount of energy, which it collected via an energy net that consumed the potential, unfulfilled history of people's lives. Over the last few months, the net had made thousands of beggars and transients in India vanish without a trace. Captain Jack's Torchwood team investigated the resultant temporal emissions in Delhi. The Duchess tried to widen the time store's effect and roll the whole of Earth back to 1924, but Jack sabotaged the device. The Duchess and her colleagues were unwilling to venture into the modern world; the device exploded, destroying them and Torchwood India.

2009 - TW: THE DEAD LINE -> Professor Stella Courtney, an old flame of Jack Harkness, was now a grandmother and one of the country's top neuroscientists. The electrical virus trapped in the disused Madoc House escaped and quickly infected twenty people - including Captain Jack - by ringing their phones. Through these victims, the virus sought to achieve the critical mass required to ring every phone across the world. Ianto and Gwen destroyed the virus with an electro-magnetic pulse, causing its victims to awaken.

2009 (Wednesday to Sunday) - TW: RISK ASSESSMENT[941] **->** Torchwood destroyed the planet-eating Vam when it manifested on Earth, but not before it further ravaged the SkyPoint apartment complex. Agnes Havisham, the Torchwood Assessor, awoke once more

from stasis and colluded with George Herbert Sanderson - her fiancé - to help the supposedly peaceful xXltttxtolxtol settle on Earth. Torchwood helped to destroy a xXltttxtolxtol bridgehead once the aliens' conquering intentions became known, and Havisham left to start a new life with Sanderson.

(=) 2009 - TW: THE UNDERTAKER'S GIFT -> Hokrala Corp's use of warp-shunt technology to send people and messages into the past had widened the Rift, and the Already Dead - beings who sought to keep the Rift from their enemies' hands - exploited this by triggering a temporal fusion device known as the Undertaker's Gift. The resultant explosion destroyed Cardiff. An enormous Vortex Dweller came through the widened Rift and reclaimed its child, Zero. In gratitude to Captain Jack, the Dweller rewrote history to stop the Already Dead from building their temporal device.

(=) 2009 (4th August) - THE ETERNAL SUMMER[942] **->** A hyperspatial warp-core explosion originating in 1899 caused a time-stasis field to encompass all of Stockbridge. The bubble trapped six decades of the town's history, and the residents were made to experience their lives over and over again.

In one version of events, the entity Veridios awoke and endowed the fifth Doctor and Nyssa - who had been thrown forward in time by the explosion - with some of its life force. As "the Lord and Lady of the Manor", they ruled Stockbridge for at least a million years. They became ancient, desiccated husks that leeched off the histories of their subjects.

In another version of events, the Doctor and Nyssa awoke in Stockbridge to find that he was regarded as the town doctor and she was its postmistress. The Lord and Lady threatened to expand the bubble so they could feed upon humanity, but the Doctor collapsed it, erasing the Lord and Lady's timeline.

Only Maxwell Edison remembered these events. The bubble's collapse hurled the Doctor and Nyssa into the future, to Stockbridge's last days.

2009 (August) - TW: CONSEQUENCES: "The Wrong Hands" / "Virus"[943] **->** Jack, Gwen and Ianto recovered an alien weapon - a Torrosett 51 binary heat-cannon - that was an offering from an alien mother who had abandoned her child. Half of the cannon self-destructed, destroying the child and a Happy Price supermarket. The next day, the child's vengeful father infected Jack and Gwen with a Kagawa Virus that paralysed them with a mental feedback loop. Ianto acquired an antidote from a black market operation selling alien tech, and destroyed the group's base of operations with a Tregennan demolition bomb.

2009 (August) - THE THREE COMPANIONS[944] ->

Garry Lendler was still working as a merchantman and purveyor of quality goods for extra-terrestrial clients. He found the Doctor's TARDIS adrift in space with Thomas Brewster inside, and gave Brewster a job overseeing his warehouse. Brewster's negligence caused a coffin-loader - the ultimate space-scavenger, swarms of which would appear in the last few days of a doomed world - to hatch.

The coffin-loader hid under London, and started generating a mould that triggered an environmental crisis. The Amazon basin went without precipitation for four months, but London had six straight days of rainfall. Flooding was reported halfway up to Farringdon, and Westminster was only approachable by boat. Parts of the Underground were closed, and the government relocated to Birmingham. Cliff Jones, now attached to the Institute of Mycology in Brazil, attended an emergency summit in New York concerning the crisis. The profit-minded Lendler coordinated with Jones to seed Earth's clouds with a substance that would eliminate the mould.

On Lendler's orders, Brewster searched for the Doctor's former associates, and tracked down Polly Wright and the Brigadier. Polly now worked in a governmental office in Westminster. On Tuesday the 18th, Brewster had Polly and the Brigadier meet at the Hope Springs Café on Beagle Street. They aided him as an alien hunter died while exterminating the coffin-loader, in a struggle that ravaged half of Trafalgar Square with fire. Lendler's cloud-treatment eliminated the coffin-loader's mould, and Polly and the Brigadier coerced Lendler into providing further clean-up services at reduced charges. Brewster left in the TARDIS.

2009 - TW: GHOST TRAIN[945] ->

The computer directing space traffic for legions of Powell clones sought to leave its dying homeworld. It opened up a wormhole to Earth, and used its trains to send its components through for reassembly. An escapade with one such train resulted in Rhys

---

944 Dating *The Three Companions* (serialised story; BF #120-129) - The story appears contemporary, and was released April 2009 to February 2010. Tellingly, Polly tells the Brigadier that it's been "forty-three years" since she last saw the Doctor - presumably referencing the duration of time between *The Faceless Ones* (set in 1966) and the release of *The Three Companions* in 2009.

The Brigadier in return tells Polly that he hasn't seen the Doctor in "twenty years" - a pretty nonsensical thing to say, whatever one's views on *Doctor Who* continuity. It's possible this comment is similarly meant to denote the amount of time that's passed between the release of *The Three Companions* and the last time the Brig saw the Doctor on TV - in *Battlefield*, broadcast in 1989 - but not only does this ignore the tie-in stories featuring the Brig in that interim (including those made by Big Finish!), it forgets that *Battlefield* wasn't actually set in 1989, and instead dates to the mid-90s. The oversight becomes even more peculiar when you consider that Marc Platt wrote both *The Three Companions* and the *Battlefield* novelisation.

Brewster's journal says that the meet-up between him, Polly and the Brigadier - and by extension the end of the story - occurs on "Tuesday the 18th." In 2009, only August had such a day.

Polly's first encounter with Lendler is fairly hard to date, as Lendler's origins are so unknown - whether or not he's a time traveller, or is even human despite his having the demeanour of one, is entirely unclear - so the "Polly's Story" component of this adventure has been relegated to None of the Above.

945 Dating *TW: Ghost Train* (*TW* audiobook #6) - Torchwood seems to deal with other cases during the two-week period in which the future Rhys hides out in Ianto's apartment and fulfils his own history (hence why Ianto keeps downing minor doses of Retcon, to guarantee that his actions are historically consistent), but as no references are given, deciding *which* stories happen in this gap is something of a tossup.

Curiously, the story's continuity is a bit awry - Rhys' co-worker says that it's "February", but Rhys himself mentions the ATMOS incident, which has to occur later than that (see the dating notes on *The Sontaran Stratagem*). The blurb says that the story occurs before *TW: Children of Earth*, but doesn't specify that it's after Series 2. No mention is made of Owen or Tosh - while it's not impossible that they're still alive (meaning that it's prior to *TW: Exit Wounds*), one has to wonder why - if that were the case - there's no evidence of their being involved in the waves of crises Torchwood here deals with. With that in mind, it's probably best to ignore the "February" reference, and place the story in the *Torchwood* Series 2-3 interim, which according to writer James Goss was the intent.

946 Barrett is a physicist who appears in *The Legend of Hell House* (1973).

947 Dating *TW: Ghost Train* (*TW* audiobook #6) - To the contemporary Rhys, events begin on a Wednesday and (after he's thrown back in time and catches up with the present) end on a Friday morning.

948 Dating *TW: The Devil and Miss Carew* and *TW: Submission* (*TW* audio dramas #5-6) – These two audios were released after *TW: Miracle Day* (as part of the *Torchwood: The Lost Stories* boxset), but take place during the Series 2 to 3 interim. *Submission* occurs fifty years (the duration of Doyle's memories) after the *Guernica* went missing in August 1959. The dating clues in *The Devil and Miss Carew* are a bit bewildering – Gwen says that Joanna Carew, born in 1930, is now "81", suggesting that it's now 2011 (which is clearly isn't).

being thrown back in time two weeks. With help from Ianto, Rhys' future self set about creating the very events that had led to his involvement in the incident - including a disruption to Cardiff's satellite navigation and the theft of at least three dozen fridges.

2009 - TW: CONSEQUENCES: "Consequences" ->

Nina Melanie Rogers, a history student at Cardiff University, happened upon the sentient book that had an interest in Torchwood. The book compelled Nina to observe Torchwood, but Jack, Gwen and Ianto fulfilled history by sending the book through the Rift to 1899, then Retconned Nina to eliminate the book's influence on her.

2009 - TW: "Fated to Pretend" ->
Dozens of people transformed by Monsieur Jechiel into undead beings had felt compelled to congregate beneath Cardiff. One of the undead went rogue and killed sixteen people, whereupon Jack - to prevent more such incidents - told the undead that he could either take them to live as workers on the Heretical Moons... or they could end their lives simply by walking into the rain. They opted for the latter.

2009 - TW: "Somebody Else's Problem" ->
Gwen traced production of R'Ochni - a street drug that killed any human who used it - to Mister Quatnja's operation at the run-down Huffern Estate. She convinced Jack to put Quatnja out of business.

2009 - TW: "Hell House" ->
The shadowy horror that Jack defeated in 1902 sought revenge, but Torchwood drained its essence into an improved version of Lionel Barrett's spectral containment unit.[946]

2009 - TW: DEPARTMENT X ->
The economic downturn motivated Firestone Finance to return to the practice of finding and selling alien technology. One of Firestone's customers - a bullion facility in the Ural Mountains - wanted the alien within Gareth Robert Owen as a defence system. The formerly tiny alien was now mature and ravenous, and had killed thirty-four people. Torchwood destroyed the creature, and Owen resumed ownership of his family's department store.

2009 - TW: GHOST TRAIN[947] ->
The inter-dimensional link formed by the alien traffic computer caused some maladies afflicting its homeworld to bleed through to Cardiff. Torchwood variously dealt with a rain of fire (officially cited as the result of climate change) on Cardiff's west side, dragons, shapeshifting assassins, a "yellow, blotchy" plague in Ryder that Ianto cured, a few outbreaks of mass hysteria and an increase in the Rift's "field of despair". Jack and Rhys commandeered one of the computer's inter-dimensional trains and attempted to out-race

a fireball headed down the link - causing Rhys to be thrown back in time while Jack crashed the train into the defunct Queen Street Station, killing three hundred Powell replicants. The inter-dimensional link was severed, and Jack put the alien computer to work managing Cardiff's traffic lights.

2009 – TW: THE DEVIL AND MISS CAREW[948] ->
"Fitzroy", a single entity who wandered the stars, and had been born of nothing, desired a home. It struck bargains with pensioners, rejuvenating their vigor in exchange for their aid. Rhys Williams' great uncle, Bryn Williams, refused to bargain with Fitzroy and was given a fatal heart attack.

Joanna Carew, the octogenarian head of First Valley Computings - a developer of operating systems for utilities companies, and so had unique access to the Western World's power supplies - accepted Fitzroy's bargain. She began dampening electrical systems first in the UK, then Europe, so Fitzroy could arrive on Earth without facing electrical interference. Torchwood intervened - Carew fell to her death, and Fitzroy was kept at bay in deep space.

2009 – TW: SUBMISSION[948] ->
Torchwood dealt with an alien casino, and blew up some aliens as they fled in a minivan down the M4 - at the cost of also damaging the Severn Bridge.

The alien aboard the *Guernica* in the Mariana Trench had exhausted Captain Doyle's memories, and sent out a cry for help - between 23:42 to 23:46, GMT, anyone in the world who had their head under water heard a distorted form of it. Ianto asked Carlie Roberts - a marine biologist, old flame and former Torchwood coworker - for help. Jack pulled rank at UNIT using the Doctor's name. Torchwood was transported in the USS *Calvin*, an Arleigh Burke class destroyer, to the *Octopus Rock*: the first in a new class of submarine, equipped with diving suits made from dwarf star alloy. Jack, Gwen, Ianto and Carlie visited the Trench and encountered the alien, which died as they returned to the surface.

Martin Trueman was an astrologer... and a fraud. Just as he confessed this to one of his clients, he was hit by a shooting star charged with the power of the Ancient Lights, and turned into a genuine psychic.[949] A partner in a law firm, Peter Anthony Dalton, died after falling down a stairwell in his home.[950]

(=) Dalton accepted the Trickster's offer to live again, and became a pawn in one of the Trickster's gambits against Sarah Jane Smith. Peter later cancelled out the deal, which restored his death.

Torchwood Series 3: Children of Earth

2009 (a Tuesday to Saturday in September) - TW: CHILDREN OF EARTH[951] -> The 456 heralded its return to Earth with a transmission that caused all of humanity's children to stand frozen in silence for one minute at 8:40 GMT. Hours later, the 456 made the children stop and chant, in English, in unison, "We... we... we... are... we are... coming."

John Frobisher, the Permanent Secretary to the Home Office of the United Kingdom and Northern Ireland, ordered the deaths of anyone connected to the 1965 incident with the 456 - Captain Jack Harkness included - to prevent the government's previous deal-ings with the aliens becoming known. Government operatives wrongly believed that Jack's immortality stemmed from the Torchwood Hub, and so destroyed it with a bomb planted in Jack's stomach. Simultaneous to the Hub's obliteration, Earth's children chanted, "We are coming... back."

On Day Two of the crisis, the 456 sent the UK government instructions for the construction of an environmental chamber suitable for the 456's representative. This was built in the M15 headquarters, Thames House. The children of Earth stopped and chanted: "We are coming tomorrow."

On Day Three, the children of Earth pointed toward London as the 456's representative descended from the skies in a column of fire, and occupied the chamber in Thames House. Humanity's children declared: "We are

---

Also, a radio shipping forecast gives the date as "Wednesday, the 10th of November" – that day was a Wednesday in 2010, but not 2009 or 2011.

949 "Two months" before *SJA: Secrets of the Stars*.

950 "A few months" before *SJA: The Wedding of Sarah Jane Smith*.

951 Dating *TW: Children of Earth* (*TW* 3.01-3.05) - As with Series 2, *Children of Earth* bucks the trend that *Doctor Who*-related episodes in this era are a year ahead of broadcast. Conspicuously, Ianto picks up a newspaper with the dateline, "Wednesday, September 2009" - as the paper is put out for the morning of Day Two, the 456 crisis must begin on a Tuesday and end on a Saturday. It's twice said that "forty-four years" have passed since 1965 - once in Day Two in reference to how long Clement's real name has been inactive, and once by Rhys in Day Four.

952 *TW: Long Time Dead*

953 As we learn in *The End of Time* (TV). Martha was engaged to Tom Milligan as of *The Sontaran Experiment/The Poison Sky*, but the relationship evidently ended off screen.

954 *TW: Children of Earth*

955 "Don't Step on the Grass"

956 *TW: "Shrouded"*. Jack is here seen at Ianto's funeral; in *TW: The House of the Dead*, he tells Ianto's ghost that he wasn't because he "had to leave".

957 *TW: Miracle Day*. This occurs prior to *TW: Long Time Dead* (p238).

958 Dating "Don't Step on the Grass" (IDW *DW* Vol, 1 #9-12) - Martha is now married and Magambo tells the Doctor that "Torchwood's gone", indicating that the story occurs after *TW: Children of Earth*. Denise Riley is cited as Home Secretary and Brian Green is said to be Prime Minister - offices they might well continue with for some time after *Children of Earth*. Martha here accepts the "Sontaran job" on which she and Mickey are working when we next see them in *The End of Time* (TV). Events in "Don't Step on the Grass" continue in "Old Friend" and "Final Sacrifice".

959 "Nine months" before *TW: The Men Who Sold the World*.

960 Dating *SJA: The Day of the Clown* (*SJA* 2.2) - Luke opens the story by reading an email from Maria dated to "9th October", but as Rani's mum says that it's a Monday, he must have received the email a few days prior (9th October was a Friday in 2009), had a busy weekend and wasn't able to read it until the following Monday. *The Ealing Echo* reports upon the disappearance "yesterday" of the victim in the opening credits, so the story begins on the 11th and takes place over two days, ending on the 13th. Luke has school records from the "past year". Park Vale here gains a headmaster, and seems to have been without one since the Slitheen killed Haresh's predecessor in *SJA: Revenge of the Slitheen*.

961 According to Clyde in *SJA: The Day of the Clown*. It's the sort of statement to make a fan chronologer go rushing to his/her notebook, so here goes: 1. the Bane (*SJA: Invasion of the Bane*); 2. the Slitheen (*SJA: Revenge of the Slitheen*); 3. the Gorgon (*SJA: Eye of the Gorgon*); 4. Kudlak (*SJA: Warriors of Kudlak*); 5. the Trickster (*SJA: Whatever Happened to Sarah Jane?*); 6. the Keratin (*SJA: The Glittering Storm*); 7. Ravage (*SJA: The Thirteenth Stone*); 8. the Slitheen again (*SJA: The Lost Boy*); and 9. the Sontarans (*SJA: The Last Sontaran*). The Verron soothsayer referred to in *SJA: Whatever Happened to Sarah Jane?* and *Journey's End* might count. We also know from *Whatever Happened to Sarah Jane?* that Sarah defeated the Patriarchs of the Tin Vagabond, quite probably after besting the Gorgon (although it's possible that she did this on her own, without the kids' help). Sarah and Luke had a role in the defeat of the Daleks (*The Stolen Earth/Journey's End*)... which would make twelve, and not force us to fancifully imagine that Sarah and company were somehow involved the 456 affair in *Torchwood: Children of Earth*.

here." Prime Minister Brian Green withdrew from dialogue with the 456 per objections raised by General Austin Pierce of the US and Colonel Oduya of UNIT. It was agreed that the UK civil service, as a nonelected branch with no authority of state, would conduct the talks; Frobisher was chosen as Earth's ambassador. The 456 told Frobisher that it wanted a "gift": 10% of the children of the entire human race.

On Day Four, the 456 said humanity had one day to deliver 10% of their children; refusal would trigger the destruction of the entire human race. The 456 refused a counter-offer of one child for every million people (6,700 in total), and made Earth's children chant a number equal to 10% of the children of each country. Green's Cabinet privately decided that children would be taken from the lowest-rated schools, and exempted their own children and grandchildren from the selection. Torchwood forced a confrontation with the 456 - who, as a demonstration of their power, released a virus that killed nearly everyone within Thames House, including Ianto Jones of Torchwood. The 456 sent a pulse that killed Clement McDonald, who had been tethered to the 456 following the 1965 incident.

On Day Five, the 456 told Earth's negotiators that the surrendered children would be biologically grafted to the 456, and not age while producing chemicals that made the 456 "feel good". The world governments mobilised to secure the children by force, under a cover story that they were to be inoculated against further alien communication. The UK army started collecting children from schools and their households at 12:00 hours. Green informed Frobisher that the government must be seen to have suffered loss against the 456, and ordered that Frobisher surrender his two daughters to the aliens. To prevent this, Frobisher killed his daughters, his wife and then himself.

Jack Harkness transmitted the wavelength used to murder Clement through humanity's children, turning it into a constructive wave. The 456 representative exploded in a shower of blood, and its remains were withdrawn on a column of fire. Humanity's children suffered no harm, save for the single child Jack had used at the centre of the resonance: his grandson Steven, who died. Frobisher's executive assistant, Bridget Spears, used Torchwood's surveillance equipment to record Green making incriminating statements, allowing Home Secretary Denise Riley to gain political leverage over him.

Gwen Cooper learned that she had been pregnant for three weeks. The Home Office believed that Torchwood Two had been disbanded.

The Hub's destruction created enough kinetic energy to activate the alien viewer in Suzie Costello's belly, and would facilitate her revival in weeks to come.[952]

Martha Jones and Mickey Smith married[953] **and were on their honeymoon during the 456 crisis.**[954] The tenth Doctor sent them a wedding gift - without warning that nobody should spill champagne on it. Martha later chastised the Doctor for this, claiming it took four hours to get her mum off the ceiling.[955]

John Hart was present at Ianto's funeral. Also in attendance were alternate-history versions of Mairwyn and an Ianto who had accepted her offer.[956]

Angelo Colasanto's agents recovered a Proper Null Field - an alien device that could generate a cancellation wave - from the Hub's remains.[957]

2009 - "Don't Step on the Grass"[958] **->** Martha, now a freelance agent who sometimes continued to work for UNIT, summoned the tenth Doctor, Emily Winter and Matthew Finnegan to Greenwich. They and UNIT forces led by Erisa Magambo became embroiled in a pitched battle between the Enochians (who had freed themselves from imprisonment, and whose essence was variously turning trees into ravenous monsters or animating clockwork bodies) and the Knights of the Arboretum. The Advocate had engineered the conflict as part of her crusade against the Doctor, but the Enochians were contained aboard their spaceship and blown up. Matthew left the Doctor and Emily's company, preferring to travel with the Advocate.

The Department's salvage team retrieved a Ytraxorian Reality Gun from the Hub's remains.[959]

2009 (11th-13th October) - SJA: THE DAY OF THE CLOWN[960] **->** Haresh and Gita Chandra moved into 36 Bannerman Road. Sarah Jane, Luke and Clyde quickly made friends with their daughter, Rani, a budding journalist... and Clyde was horrified to discover that Haresh was their new headmaster.

Meanwhile, three children had gone missing in two weeks. Rani, Luke, Clyde and Sarah Jane all worked out that every missing child had visited the clown exhibit at a local circus museum: Spellman's Magical Museum of the Circus. The owner, Elijah Spellman, was the legendary Pied Piper. He caused balloons that mesmerised on contact to rain from the sky, and thereby attempted to steal all the children at Park Vale. He psychically attacked Sarah Jane, but Clyde broke the spell by telling jokes. Spellman weakened, and was confined to a fragment of the meteorite he'd fallen to Earth in centuries before. Sarah sealed the meteorite fragment away in a box of Halkonite steel, though which not even thoughts could penetrate.

By now, Sarah Jane, Luke and their friends had saved the world twelve times.[961]

2009 - SJA: THE NIGHTMARE MAN[962] -> Luke told Sarah Jane he planned to take his A Levels early, allowing him to go to university a year ahead of his class - and made this announcement while the two of them were handcuffed to a bomb by a group of Slitheen. K9, Rani and Clyde saved them.

2009 (30th-31st October) - FOREVER AUTUMN[963] -> The tenth Doctor and Martha arrived in Blackwood Falls, New England, to investigate an anomalous energy pulse. The buried Hervoken spaceship had repaired itself, but required an injection of negative emotional energy to power its escape. The Hervoken planned an atrocity in the town using possessed animals and Halloween costumes, but Doctor disrupted their ceremony and destroyed them.

2009 - SJA: THE TIME CAPSULE[964] -> The Persopolisian named Janxia revived from stasis, and sought out the components of the lost construction device. One of these was the black diamond of Ernfield - an enigmatic 82-CD gem that was on exhibit at the Natural History Museum, where Luke Smith had a work placement. Janxia's attempts to claim the diamond triggered chaos, causing a dinosaur exhibit to explode. Sarah Jane and her friends accidentally caused Janxia and the diamond to meet their fate in a car compactor. Sarah gave the museum a copy of the diamond and, to avoid awkward questions about Luke's role in the fracas, also donated an alien jewel she'd obtained from a Kissarni.

2009 - SJA: THE GHOST HOUSE[964] -> Sarah Jane and her friends discovered that the plain-looking house at 39 Bannerman Road had mysteriously been replaced by the Victorian villa that had stood there from 1865 to 1969. A temporal bridge formed between their era and 1884, and they journeyed back there to stop a pair of alien war criminals from destroying the world.

2009 (early November) - TW: LONG TIME DEAD[965] -> The Department, as led by Mr Black, had dispatched retrieval teams to sift through the Hub's remains. Suzie Costello awoke in a fully healed body within the heavily damaged Torchwood morgue - but found that the alien viewer in her belly had linked her to an extra-terrestrial blackness, a space between dimensions that was hungry. Its energies surged through Suzie and killed various individuals - their brains were pulped, and their consciousnesses were consigned to the darkness' void. As the dark-

962 Dating *SJA: The Nightmare Man* (SJA 4.1) - We see this in flashback; a caption says that the main events of the story occur set "a year" later. Rani's inclusion, however, means that it's after *SJA: The Day of the Clown* (so, it hasn't actually been a full year; it's more like eleven months). K9 appears in the flashback, even though he hasn't yet been released from his black-hole-containment duties (*SJA: The Mad Woman in the Attic*), so he must have briefly been let out to deal with this crisis.
963 Dating *Forever Autumn* (NSA #16) - No year is given, but the book was released in 2007 and seems contemporary. The story opens on Friday afternoon - the day before Halloween (p9) - and continues to next day, which fits the real-world calendar of 2009 but not any other year (to draw arbitrary boundaries) from 2006 to 2012.
964 Dating *SJA: The Time Capsule* and *SJA: The Ghost House* (SJA audiobooks #3-4) - The audios were released together on 13th November 2008, between the broadcasts of *SJA: The Mark of the Berserker* and *SJA: The Temptation of Sarah Jane Smith*. However, Luke is said to be 14 in *The Time Capsule*, so it's before he "turns 15" in *SJA: Secret of the Stars* (and where *The Time Capsule* goes, *Ghost House* might as well go also). That fits with Sarah Jane's claim in *The Time Capsule* that the Chandras moved in "so recently" (*SJA: The Day of the Clown*).
　Two bits of discontinuity exist in *The Time Capsule*: Luke says that he's only lived "for a year", when it's only been a couple of months since *SJA: Invasion of the Bane*. Also, Rani wears some glasses that Sarah Jane says

"made her look older than her 15 years" - which has to be taken as a mistake, as all the on-screen evidence indicates Rani didn't meet Sarah Jane and company until she was 16. Clyde, at least, is correctly said to be 15.
965 Dating *TW: Long Time Dead* (TW novel #16) - The dating evidence is a bit contradictory. It's said (p17) that the Department started combing through the ruins of the Hub "barely a month" after its destruction (in September 2009, *TW: Children of Earth*), and that it's now "three weeks" into that undertaking - meaning it's currently on or about early November 2009. The Department believes that Gwen is still pregnant, and Jack appears in the final act, presumably before his departure from Earth (in March 2010, *Children of Earth* again). However, it's said that Suzie has been dead for "years", and that it's been "so many years ago" since she created a bank account in 2007. Most specific of all, Suzie looks at the date on a note saying when a toilet was last cleaned and concludes "She'd been dead for three years?" (p30), which should mean that it's now 2010, not 2009. It's something of a coin toss as to which evidence should take precedence, but the timeline of the Department salvaging the Hub seems a bit harder to set aside.
966 Dating *SJA: Secrets of the Stars* (SJA 2.3) - The article reporting on the mass hypnosis event in *The Ealing Echo* at story's end is a bit difficult to make out, but seems to be datelined "November 7". Sarah and friends first go to see Trueman's show on a "Friday night", and the mass-hypnosis event occurs the next day. In 2009,

ness grew stronger, at least fifteen Cardiff residents were pulled into seemingly ordinary shadows. The proximity of the darkness caused at least seven people who had been treated with Retcon to regain their memories, and they committed suicide after scrawling "I Remember".

Suzie became lovers with Detective Inspector Tom Cutler. He deduced her involvement in both the mysterious deaths and the spatial disturbances, which were now large enough for NASA to detect. Cutler lured Suzie to the ruined Hub, where his associates detonated charges that brought rubble down atop them. Jack Harkness was nearby as the darkness within Suzie claimed Cutler, instants before their bodies were pulverised.

2009 (5th-7th November) - SJA: SECRETS OF THE STARS[966] -> Every star in the universe aligned in a perfect conjunction for the first time since the universe's creation thirteen billion years ago, and so the Ancient Lights made a bid to enthrall Earth - the first stepping stone to controlling every living being in creation. Martin Trueman, as empowered by the Ancient Lights, had gained fame as a psychic and star of the stage show *Secrets of the Stars*. Broadcasting from the East Acton New Theatre, he hijacked every TV station in the world and began systematically bringing the human race, one star sign at a time, under the control of the Ancient Lights. News services all around the globe reported that mass droves of people had fallen prey to a television hypnosis stunt. The President of the United States, also enthralled, walked out of the White House holding hands with the wife of the Prime Minister of Kazakhstan. Having no star sign, Luke

Smith was immune to the Lights' power and defeated them. Trueman vanished into space, either destroyed or having journeyed away with the Ancient Lights.

Shortly after Trueman's defeat, Luke and Sarah designated "today" as Luke's "birthday".[967] Sarah Jane met Peter Dalton in a shoe shop, and they started dating in secret.[968]

2009 (Friday, 13th November to 14th November) - SJA: THE MARK OF THE BERSERKER[969] -> At Park Vale School, student Jacob West used a mind-controlling talisman - a device made by the alien Berserkers to create soldiers - to hypnotise a teacher. Rani found Jacob's pendant, and deposited it with Sarah Jane for safekeeping. Meanwhile, Clyde's long-lost father, Paul, showed up. Clyde showed him Sarah Jane's attic, and Paul pocketed the pendant. He revelled in the pendant's mind-controlling ability, but the more he used its power, the more he was converted into a Berserker-soldier. Sarah Jane held up a mirror, shocking Paul into becoming himself again. She and her friends throw the pendant into the sea.

(=) 2009 (Friday, 20th November to Saturday, 21st November) - SJA: THE TEMPTATION OF SARAH JANE SMITH[970] -> The Trickster opened a time fissure to 1951, and engineered a situation wherein Sarah Jane was tempted to travel there and visit her parents. She saved them from their historical deaths, an act that enabled the Trickster to come through a weak point in the web of time,

7th November was indeed a Saturday - unfortunately, the first paragraph of *The Ealing Echo* story reads, "the world was coming to [unreadable word] yesterday", suggesting that the world was spellbound on "Saturday, 6th November", and that this is yet-another instance of the calendar in a *Doctor Who*-related TV story being off from that of the real world. It's a puzzler as to how news services in this story are reporting on the "hypnosis" event when Trueman has seemingly usurped every TV broadcast.

967 *SJA: Secrets of the Stars.* The date that Luke and Sarah pick for his "birthday" would *seem* to be 7th November - the same as the dateline listed on the *The Ealing Echo* that appears in the same scene - although this isn't expressly said, and so they might be having the discussion on 8th November or shortly thereafter. Either way, they must take this opportunity to advance his "age" - Luke is "14" before this, but is "15" in *SJA: The Gift.* This means, however, that Luke has spent about 15 months (the time since *SJA: Revenge of the Slitheen*) being "14", and that Sarah somehow forgot to inch up

his age (or throw him a birthday party, for that matter). **968** They first meet at least "a month" before *SJA: The Wedding of Sarah Jane Smith.* While Sarah's life is extremely busy in this period, dealing with one crisis or another, it is hardly beyond the realm of all possibility that she could meet a man while shopping in a shoe store.

969 Dating *SJA: The Mark of the Berserker* (SJA 2.4) - Paul Langer refers to "those Dalek things", so it's set after *The Stolen Earth / Journey's End.* Clyde's mother specifies that the story opens on a "Friday night". As *SJA: Secret of the Stars* and *SJA: Enemy of the Bane* seem to respectively take place the first and third weeks in November, *The Mark of the Berserker* by logical extension can only start on the Friday in-between the two, i.e. 13th November, and continue to the next day.

970 Dating *SJA: The Temptation of Sarah Jane Smith* (SJA 2.5) - The events of *SJA: Whatever Happened to Sarah Jane?* were "last year". The action begins on an afternoon and continues to the next day, when Rani says, "Mum, it's a Saturday". Given the need to accommodate

and fully manifest from the limbo dimensions. This created an alternate history in which the Trickster sucked the life from the world - Clyde and Rani, protected from historical alterations by the Verron soothsayer's box, witnessed the remnants of humanity working as slave gangs driven by Krislok the Graske. The timeline was restored when Sarah and her parents changed history back. Clyde gave Krislok the soothsayer's box as payment for his help, freeing the Graske from the Trickster's control.

2009 (21st-22nd November) - SJA: ENEMY OF THE BANE[971] -> Mrs Wormwood asked Sarah Jane for help, claiming that the Bane were hunting her, and that she wished to gain revenge by stopping them from releasing the ancient, evil being named Horath. Wormwood didn't know where Horath rested, and so Sarah Jane called on Brigadier Lethbridge-Stewart. He aided Sarah in acquiring an artifact stored in the UNIT Black Archive: the Tunguska Scroll, which could summon a

portal to Horath's dimension.

Sarah and her friends discovered that Wormwood was in league with the Sontaran Kaagh, and that they wanted to rule the universe using Horath's power. Wormwood and Kaagh opened the portal to Horath at a stone circle in Whitebarrow, but Wormwood then betrayed Kaagh. To regain his honour, Kaagh pushed himself and Wormwood into the portal. Sarah sealed the portal behind them, and destroyed the Scroll.

UNIT now operated under a Homeworld Security Mandate.[972]

2009 - SJA: FROM RAXACORICOFALLAPATORIUS WITH LOVE[973] -> A Slitheen posing as "Ambassador Rahnius of the Galactic Alliance" teleported into Sarah Jane's attic to lavish praise upon her group... and then immobilised them with energy-laced deeley boppers. The Slitheen hoped to capture K9 and use his systems to steal from galactic banks. Sarah overcame the Slitheen with her sonic lipstick, and Mr Smith teleported the Slitheen away.

SJA: The Mark of the Berserker occupying the only weekend available between 7th and 21st November, and the next story occurring on 21st and 22nd November, The Temptation of Sarah Jane Smith has to unfold the two days beforehand (see the dating notes on SJA: Enemy of the Bane).

971 Dating SJA: Enemy of the Bane (SJA 2.6) - Miss Wormwood writes the date "20-11-200[?]" on the cheque that she gives to Gita Chandra, with the last digit being a squiggle, probably either an "8" or a "9". Either way, the third digit is a zero (so it's before 2010), and the date of 20th November is very legible.

The story opens with Rani's mum Gita working late on Saturday night to accommodate Mrs Wormwood's order; the action continues the next morning when Rani and Haresh realise that Gita has gone missing (because Wormwood abducts her to get Sarah's attention). In 2009, 20th November was actually a Friday, not a Saturday, although it's plausible to think that Wormwood wrote the cheque the day beforehand as preparation for her scheme. That said, with the previous Series 2 stories occupying the other weekends in November, the cheque can only have direct relevance if SJA: The Temptation of Sarah Jane Smith and Enemy of the Bane occur in rapid succession over a three-day period. Such a scenario is more believable than it might seem - as Sarah is only summoned to look into Gita's disappearance the morning after it happens, her group at least has the comfort of dinner and a night's sleep after The Temptation of Sarah Jane Smith before dealing with this newest dilemma. In the course of her adventuring, Sarah has surely had to cope with a lot worse.
972 SJA: Enemy of the Bane, and suggested by mention of "homeworld security" (The Sontaran Stratagem).

973 Dating SJA: From Raxacoricofallapatorius With Love (2009 Comic Relief special) - This five-minute special aired between Series 2 and 3, and fits comfortably there. K9 briefly appears, presumably leaving his duties around the black hole for a few minutes. The very last image is of K9 wearing the Comic Relief red nose, but this isn't any more of a continuity violation than William Hartnell wishing everyone a merry Christmas at the end of The Daleks' Masterplan episode seven - an episode that virtually everyone regards as canon.
974 Dating The Sarah Jane Adventures Series 3 (SJA: Prisoner of the Judoon, 3.1; SJA: The Mad Woman in the Attic, 3.2; SJA: Monster Hunt, webcomic #1; SJA: The White Wolf, audiobook #5; SJA: The Shadow People, audiobook #6; SJA: The Wedding of Sarah Jane Smith, 3.3) - The transition of The Sarah Jane Adventures from being a show set one year ahead of broadcast (per all Doctor Who-related television after Aliens of London) and set at time of broadcast (starting with Planet of the Dead) means that Sarah Jane Series 2, 3 and 4 are condensed into about fifteen months of time. Series 2 (still a year ahead of broadcast) seems to begin in late August 2009 and to end on or around 20th November, 2009. By Series 4, the series has resumed a time-of-broadcast approach, opening in September 2010 and ending relatively close to 23rd November, 2010. (See the individual story entries for how those dates were derived.)

Series 3, then, fills the gap between the two. Where Sarah and Luke are concerned, their encounter with the tenth Doctor in SJA: The Wedding of Sarah Jane Smith occurs prior to their final meet-up with him in The End of Time (TV) - the result being that Series 3 has to be broken in half, the first three stories occurring in 2009 and the rest occurring in 2010. It's tempting to

The Sarah Jane Adventures
Series 3 (first half)[974]

2009 (a Sunday) - SJA: PRISONER OF THE JUDOON

-> The homeworld of the reptilian Veil had perished when its sun turned cold. The Veil named Androvax, thinking himself the only survivor, subsequently became a nihilist and was responsible for the destruction of twelve planets. The Judoon captured Androvax, but Tybo, a captain of the 1,005th Judoon Guard, crashed to Earth while escorting Androvax elsewhere. This was a violation of The Articles of the Shadow Proclamation, which deemed Earth as primitive and forbade the Judoon from setting foot there.

Androvax used the technology at the nanotech company Genetec to construct a spacecraft, but Judoon reinforcements arrived and arrested him. For their interference, the Judoon cited Clyde and Rani with a ticket that banned them from leaving Earth.[975]

Androvax learned at his trial that before his homeworld's destruction, one hundred of his people had escaped in a spaceship.[976]

2009 (a Saturday) - SJA: THE MAD WOMAN IN THE ATTIC[977]

-> Rani was feeling left out when Sarah Jane and her other friends discussed Maria, who was now helping "the government" to hide aliens. One of Rani's old friends from the seaside town of Danemouth, Samuel Lloyd, told her that a demon was at the local funfair. Rani investigated and met Eve, a red-skinned alien. Eve's people could read the timelines and alter history, and had been all-but-wiped out in a war.

(=) Rani inadvertently wished that Sarah Jane and the others would leave her alone. Eve erased them from the timeline, creating an alternate history where Rani would be lonely her whole life. Fifty years later, Eve recognised her mistake and sent her son Adam to write Sarah Jane and the others back into history.

In the restored history, Eve departed after her spaceship drained energy from the black hole that K9 was containing, enabling K9 to return to Earth. Sam Lloyd accompanied Eve, and in future would father her child.

2009 - SJA: MONSTER HUNT[978]

-> The Krulius, an enigmatic alien who exhaled toxic gas, placed a dozen different species in quasi-digital suspension to study their strengths and weaknesses. The spaceship transporting the Krulius was damaged, causing the Krulius to download its menagerie as biodata onto Earth's World Wide Web. Clyde and Rani used Mr. Smith to find the various aliens on the Internet and teleport them home. Sarah Jane signalled the Shadow Proclamation, and a squadron of Judoon arrested the Krulius.

2009 (December) - SJA: THE WHITE WOLF[979]

-> Eddison Clough contacted Sarah Jane because photographs identified him as a friend and professional colleague of her aunt Lavinia, but he had no memory of it - or of anything at all from 1972 to 2004. Sarah and her friends looked into the town of Wolfenden, which was known as a refuge for people who believed they'd been abducted by aliens. Sarah had Mr. Smith contact a passing spaceship; ambassadors soon arrived, and removed the sleeping alien convicts and their technology.

---

gain some flexibility on this by thinking that the dying tenth Doctor could have slipped through time a bit and met Sarah and Luke at virtually any point - as he does when he meets Captain Jack in the space bar - but Luke's phone conversation with Clyde ("That was the maddest Christmas ever!", followed by a reference that almost certainly denotes the whole world turning into the Master) suggests that *The End of Time* (TV) has very recently happened.

Everyone is wearing clothing that's more or less commensurate with colder weather.

975 Sarah is already aware of the Judoon, although we've never seen her meet them before now. The embargo on the Judoon visiting Earth isn't mentioned when they appear in the fifth Doctor sequence in "The Forgotten". It's said to be a Sunday, which could (in accordance with when Series 2 concludes) mean that it's now 29th November, or early December (the 6th, for instance).

976 *SJA: The Vault of Secrets*
977 Dating *SJA: The Mad Woman in the Attic* (SJA 3.2) - Sam was born in 1994 and is now "15". It's specified as being a Saturday. Presuming the comment about Maria aiding "the government" can be taken at face value, it's not entirely clear if this means the US or the UK government.
978 Dating *SJA: Monster Hunt* (SJA webcomic #1) - The webcomic was released in 2009, and involves Sarah Jane, Luke, Clyde and Rani (so it's after *SJA: The Day of the Clown*). K9's appearance in the final panel suggests that it's after *SJA: The Mad Woman in the Attic*, although one does have to wonder why he isn't seen helping against the Krulius.
979 Dating *SJA: The White Wolf* and *SJA: The Shadow People* (SJA audiobooks #5-6) - The audios were released together on 8th October, 2009, prior to the debut of *The Sarah Jane Adventures* Series 3. In *The White Wolf*, Sarah makes mention of encountering the

2009 (a Saturday in December) - SJA: THE SHADOW PEOPLE[979] -> Sarah Jane drove Luke and Clyde out to a class geography trip in the heart of Snowdonia, Wales, as the boys had been delayed by an extra-terrestrial warlord disguised as a kitten. They came across a spaceship belonging to the Shaydargen, a race of space pioneers, that had crashed millennia ago. An empathic, artificial entity built to meet the spaceship crew's needs had gone dormant, but now awakened and begged Sarah Jane and her friends to stay with it forever. Sarah persuaded the entity to let them go - and used her sonic lipstick to permanently shut down the spaceship's systems.

2009 (December) - SJA: THE WEDDING OF SARAH JANE SMITH[980] -> Sarah accepted Peter Dalton's marriage proposal, but her engagement ring mysteriously glowed, and seemed to influence her mind. The wedding rushed ahead with such speed that the Brigadier couldn't attend, as he was back in Peru. Clarissa, Sarah's former editor, was present. When the Registrar asked if anyone objected, the tenth Doctor burst into the room and demanded the wedding be stopped.

His intervention came too late - this was a trap set by the Trickster, and the hotel where the wedding was taking place was moved to a mysterious white void. The Trickster offered Sarah a choice: marry Peter, and doom Earth to an alternate timeline in which she wasn't present to save it, or remain trapped in the void forever with her friends. Peter revoked his deal with the Trickster, thwarting the scheme at the cost of his own life. The Doctor took Sarah Jane and her friends home in the TARDIS.

c 2009 - THE SLITHEEN EXCURSION[981] -> The tenth Doctor met a classics student, June, at the Parthenon. June helped the Doctor to defeat some blobby aliens, and so he took her back to ancient Greece as a reward. They returned to this time and discovered that the "blobby aliens" were in fact space police - who dutifully arrested three Slitheen that had been in stasis since 1500 BC. When June missed her train, the Doctor offered her one last hop in the TARDIS back to Birmingham.

Judoon (*Prisoner of the Judoon*), and Luke has memories of the "past few years", even though it's only been about sixteen months since *Invasion of the Bane*. It's "close" to exam time, suggesting that it's a bit later in the school year. With that in mind, these two stories have, a little arbitrarily, been placed after *SJA: The Mad Woman in the Attic*. Eddison Clough claims that "nearly forty years" of his life are missing - it's actually been thirty-two (1972-2004), which again proves that characters in the *Doctor Who* universe do round their sums, and not every statement can be taken literally.

In *The Shadow People*, Sarah specifies that it's a Saturday. Given that *SJA: The Mad Woman in the Attic* also occurs on a Saturday, that two weeks and five days elapse during *SJA: The Wedding of Sarah Jane*, and that Sarah's wedding doesn't seem to occur in tandem with Christmas or Boxing Day, the most likely scenario is that *The Shadow People* occurs on 5th December (the only Saturday remaining following *SJA: Enemy of the Bane*). However, it could also be case that these audiobook stories happen within the two-and-a-half-week period that elapses during *The Wedding of Sarah Jane*.

Events from *SJS: Ghost Town* are mentioned in *The Shadow People*, providing a bit of cross-pollination between the Big Finish and BBC *Sarah Jane* audio series.

980 Dating *SJA: The Wedding of Sarah Jane Smith* (SJA 3.3) - Rani says, in response to Sarah making up a flimsy story and sneaking off (to meet Peter), "It's the fifth time she's done this in a month." This has commonly been interpreted to mean that nothing strange has happened to Sarah and her friends in the last month - but it doesn't, it merely denotes the frequency with which

Sarah has offered a lame excuse and dashed off somewhere on her own, so all sorts of adventures could easily have occurred in the interim. Events in this story play out over two weeks and five days, with the wedding itself falling on a Saturday. No matter how one orders *SJA: The Mad Woman in the Attic*, *SJA: The White Wolf* and *SJA: The Shadow People*, at least two Saturdays have passed since *SJA: Enemy of the Bane*, so it's definitely December. As previously mentioned, for Sarah and Luke, this story has to end before *The End of Time* (TV). The Doctor's outfit suggests that for him, these events happen between *Planet of the Dead* and *The Waters of Mars*.

981 Dating *The Slitheen Excursion* (NSA #32) - No year is given - but again, for the Doctor, this story is set between *Planet of the Dead* and *The Waters of Mars*.

982 Dating "The Big, Blue Box" (IDW *Doctor Who Annual 2010*) - The story seems to have a contemporary setting.

983 Dating "Old Friend" (IDW *Doctor Who Annual 2010*) - Barnaby lives at a "twenty-first century rest home", and there's nothing to suggest it's not a contemporary setting. The story continues in "Final Sacrifice".

984 Dating *Blue Forgotten Planet* (BF #126) - The few sane people on Earth - the ones who take a Viyran vaccine that counteracts the madness afflicting humanity - can't remember the year, and the dating clues are very piecemeal.

It's said that two billion have perished owing to the madness - presuming that this is true, the story cannot take place before mankind's numbers are that high. Additionally, a crater is attributed to an oil refinery exploding, narrowing the possibilities to mankind's oil-

c 2009 - "The Big, Blue Box"[982] **->** A yellow alien attacked Douglas Henderson near his home. The tenth Doctor rescued him, and revealed that Douglas was actually an advanced doomsday weapon - one banned by the Shadow Proclamation - that was capable of destroying electronics on a planetary scale. Two rival planets had sent battle fleets to recover him. Douglas set himself off aboard one of the alien ships... and awoke on Earth to find that the Doctor had provided him with enough energy to live out a normal human lifespan.

c 2009 - "Old Friend"[983] **->** The tenth Doctor and Emily Winter arrived at the Shady Grove rest home, where an old man named Barnaby was celebrating his birthday. They learned that when Barnaby was "barely 20", he had become the companion of a future incarnation of the Doctor, and that they'd fought flying slugs, Sontarans and the Floor Menace together. Barnaby had been entrusted with the charred remains of Turlough's diary, which he returned to the Doctor before dying of old age.

2009 - BLUE FORGOTTEN PLANET[984] **->** The time-travelling Viyrans had now eliminated 3,436,000 of the viruses released from Amethyst Station. In five instances, they had they opted to wipe out the carriers and commit genocide.

(=) The Viyrans scanned Earth, found that a particle of the 001 variant of Amethyst icosahedral plasmic virus No. 9007/41 was present within every human, and calculated a one in 5.4 billion chance that a human would contract the virus within the next seven million years. The Viyrans attempted to eradicate the particles with their meson radiation disseminator, but this inadvertently made humanity develop a chemical imbalance that triggered forgetfulness, uncontrollable fear and rage. Wars broke out, more casualties happened as people lost the ability to work technology, and everyone forgot what year it was. Within a decade, Earth's population was reduced by two billion.

When the sixth Doctor and Mila (who was disguised as Charley Pollard) arrived, the Viyrans revived the genuine Charley. She had assisted them on various missions, always entering cryo-freeze afterwards. The Doctor found that chronon particles, which occur during time travel, could destroy virus No. 9007/41. He used the TARDIS and the Viyran disseminator to put the Earth into a time bubble, then rolled back time to when the Viyrans scanned Earth. This destroyed virus No. 9007/41, and stopped the Viyrans from accidentally ruining humanity.

Mila died during these events. Afterward, Charley convinced the Doctor to let the Viyrans revise his memories to preserve the web of time. He forgot that he'd ever travelled with Charley, and believed that he'd parted ways from his long-standing companion, Mila - a "tiny" woman with jet-black hair and bright green eyes - on Gralista Social. Charley continued travelling with the Viyrans.

Hornets' Nest[985]

c 2009 - HORNETS' NEST: THE STUFF OF NIGHTMARES -> The fourth Doctor was on a break at his cottage in Sussex when he read that a Cabinet minister had been trampled to death in his own bed by an Alpine Ibex. The following weekend, several influential figures belonging to a government think tank were trampled at a cocktail party by a charging stuffed elephant, which was

producing period. Lastly, the Viyrans, as time travellers, cannot be blind as to mankind's eventual expansion beyond Earth - so the fact that they believe they can wipe out virus No. 9007/41 (which exists in every human) by treating the people on Earth alone suggests that mankind's space age hasn't happened yet. Related to this, it's implied that Charley's travelling with a past version of the Doctor has destabilised history, so the entire derailment of mankind's future - colony planets, Earth Empire, everything - may have actually occurred before the Doctor steps in and fixes things.

Taking all of that into account, the best placement for *Blue Forgotten Planet* is, funnily enough, the modern day. The story saw release in September 2009 - not only does that work as well as anything, it actually avoids any conflict with the new-series adventures happening in the same window. The only real alternative is 1930 - the year that the Doctor and Mila were travelling to, but it seems that the TARDIS missed that mark. Anyway, the survivors all talk like modern-day individuals, not people from the 30s.

It's commonly accepted that Charley, not Mila, dies at the end of this story; the final scene between "Charley" and the Doctor is reasonably ambiguous on this point, although the story's epilogue seems to suggest that the genuine article has survived. The fact that Big Finish has considered doing Charley solo adventures might also suggest that the real Charley lived.

985 Dating *Hornets' Nest* (BBC fourth Doctor audios; *The Stuff of Nightmares*, #1.1; *The Dead Shoes*, #1.2; *The Circus of Doom*, #1.3; *A Sting in the Tale*, #1.4; *Hive of Horror*, #1.5) - The story was released in 2009, and there's nothing to suggest it doesn't have a contemporary setting. It's "the twenty-first century" and the existence of aliens is common knowledge. Mike says in the opening narration of *Hornets' Nest: The Stuff of Nightmares* that it's "the day after the winter solstice - the twenty-second of December". The Doctor relates his

brought down by the military. An elderly nuclear scientist was strangled in her bath by a stuffed python.

The Doctor investigated the killings. Taxidermy was out of fashion, so many museums and stately homes were dumping their stuffed exhibits, and lorries owned by Percy Noggins were taking them away. The Doctor found that the animals were being reanimated at Noggins' factory, but was followed back to his cottage by stuffed animals and attacked. After defeating them, the Doctor discovered the animals had paper brains inhabited by tiny hornets - creatures that could take possession of human minds, and were controlling Noggins. The Hornet Swarm made contact with the Doctor, and demonstrated that they were aliens with massive mental powers who had previously encountered him in Earth's past, but his relative future.

The Doctor gathered all the stuffed animals containing the Hornets at Nest Cottage, where he kept them trapped by use of hypnotic control and a semi-permeable force shield. A week later, the Doctor realised he could leave Nest Cottage in the TARDIS as long as he returned to the exact point in time he left. He found himself fighting the Hornets across space and time.

Noggins, free of the Hornets' influence, went home to look after his infirm grandmother, the ex-dancer Ernestina Stott. The Doctor followed a lead to 1932 and returned with Mrs Wibbsey, who became his housekeeper.[986] The Doctor brought the shell of the body of the dwarf Antonio back to Nest Cottage, and put it in the garden.[987] He also returned from 1039 with a dog which had been possessed by the Hornets, and named it Captain.[988]

2009 (22nd-23rd December) - HORNETS' NEST: THE STUFF OF NIGHTMARES -> Mike Yates answered an advert placed in an issue of *Country Time* that was seemingly aimed at him, and arrived at a cottage in deepest Sussex called The Nest. He was welcomed by housekeeper Mrs Wibbsey, and reunited with the fourth Doctor. The next day, the Doctor related the first part of his story to Mike, and explained that he was running out of ideas of ways to fight the Hornets. The stuffed animals came to life again, forcing Mike and the Doctor to barricade themselves in the cellar...

2009 (23rd December) - HORNETS' NEST: THE DEAD SHOES -> While in the cellar, the fourth Doctor related to Mike events pertaining to the Hornets in Cromer, 1932.

2009 (24th December) - HORNETS' NEST: THE CIRCUS OF DOOM / A STING IN THE TALE -> In the middle of the night, the fourth Doctor told Mike of events in Blandford in 1832. As dawn broke, the Doctor related his encounter with the Hornets in 1039.

The stuffed animals became dormant again. The Doctor and Mike realised that Mrs Wibbsey had placed the personal advertisement that summoned Mike, as she was still under the Hornets' influence. They emerged from the cellar to discover the animals were still very much active and hostile ...

story the next day. It is "quite some time" since Mike's UNIT days, which were in "the seventies"; *Hornets' Nest: Hive of Horror* says that Mike's tenure with UNIT was "three decades" and "thirty years" ago. It's "seventy years" since Mrs Wibbsey's time according to *Hornets' Nest: The Dead Shoes* (so, circa 2002).

In the Doctor's personal timeline, his "recent exploits" include "giant rats, killer robots, skulls from the dawn of time" (i.e., the end of Season 14 and *Image of the Fendahl*). In *Hive of Horror*, he recalls events from *The Invisible Enemy*. With no mention of Leela or Romana, the *Hornet's Nest* series may take place for the Doctor between *The Invasion of Time* and *The Ribos Operation*.

986 *Hornets' Nest: The Dead Shoes*
987 *Hornets' Nest: The Circus of Doom*
988 *Hornets' Nest: A Sting in the Tale*
989 Dating *Hornets' Nest: Hive of Horror* (BBC fourth Doctor audio #1.5) - The story follows directly on from *Hornets' Nest: A Sting in the Tale*. It's Christmas Eve when the fourth Doctor, Mike and Mrs Wibbsey defeat the Hornets, and they have Christmas dinner on Christmas Day. *The End of Time* (TV) implies that at some point later that day, Mrs Wibbsey and Mike Yates would have transformed into copies of the Master.
990 *Demon Quest: The Relics of Time*

991 Dating *The End of Time* (X4.17-4.18) - No year is given, but it's after *Planet of the Dead*. The story begins on Christmas Eve, and unfolds over the next two days. In *SJA: Death of the Doctor*, set in 2010, Sarah acknowledges seeing the tenth Doctor as part of his "goodwill tour". The same story establishes that the dying Doctor visited every one of his former companions, not just those of his tenth incarnation.
992 *The End of Time* (TV). As humanity - including some billions with no Wi-Fi - spends an entire day as the Master, it seems very unlikely that many people would swallow this story.
993 *Hornets' Nest: Hive of Horror*
994 Events in 2010 include the last half of *The Sarah Jane Adventures* Series 3; the present day sequences of *Doctor Who* Series 5 and *The Sarah Jane Adventures* Series 4.
995 As revealled in *Demon Quest: Sepulchre*. This happens "earlier in the year", i.e. 2010.
996 The year prior to *TW: Miracle Day*.
997 "Hotel Historia"
998 *Mad Dogs and Englishmen*
999 "Decades" before the first portion of *Singularity*.
1000 In Amy's time, and "by 2010" according to *The Coming of the Terraphiles*.

2009 (24th-25th December) - HORNETS' NEST: HIVE OF HORROR[989] -> ... but the Doctor subdued them with hypnosis. The Queen of the Hornets inhabited the paper brain of a stuffed zebra, and the Doctor cobbled together a machine that shrunk him, Mike and Mrs Wibbsey so they could confront her. They made their way through the black and white landscape of the zebra's head, through its ear and into the brain. The Doctor miniaturised the Queen until she ended up in the microuniverse and became just another insect. The other Hornets were now mindless, and so the Doctor sealed the Hive, vowing to take the Hornets to a distant galaxy.

The Doctor, Mike and Wibbsey enjoyed a Christmas dinner. The Doctor gave his dog, Captain, to Mike and installed Wibbsey permanently as his housekeeper.

On Boxing Day, the fourth Doctor installed a special cordless answering machine in Nest Cottage.[990]

2009 (24th-26th December) - THE END OF TIME (TV)[991] -> Everyone on Earth had terrible dreams of impending destruction, but only Wilf Noble remembered them. The acolytes of Harold Saxon sacrificed themselves as part of a ritual to resurrect the Master, but Lucy Saxon sabotaged the attempt, mortally wounding the Master's new body and making it insatiably hungry. He gained fantastical abilities and seemed akin to an avatar of death. Broadfell Prison was destroyed, apparently killing Lucy.

Meanwhile, the world awaited a grand announcement from President Obama, who was to outline an instant and radical means of ending the current global recession. Donna was now engaged to Shaun Temple. They had very little money, and could only afford a tiny flat.

The restored Master briefly confronted the tenth Doctor, but was then kidnapped by Joshua Naismith, a businessman and author of *Fighting the Future*. Naismith wanted the Master to help him repair the Immortality Gate that had been recovered from Torchwood, as Naismith believed that the Gate could give his daughter Abigail the gift of immortality. The Gate was of Vinvocci origin, and could be used to heal whole planets by transmitting a biological template through an entire population. The Master used the device to transmit his own biological template across the globe, turning 6,727,949,338 people on Earth (all save Donna Noble and Wilf Mott) into copies of himself. With such an army, he made plans to "turn Earth into a warship".

Rassilon and the High Council of Time Lords, still trapped inside the timelock on the final day of The Last Great Time War, saw a way to escape. They planted the sound of drums - the heartbeat of a Time Lord - into the Master's mind when he was still a child, then sent a white-point star crystal to Earth at this time. The Master retrieved the star, amplified the drum-sound now echoing through billions of people, and traced it back to its source. The disruption to the timelines allowed the entire planet of Gallifrey to emerge in space near Earth. The Master then sought to copy his biological template through every Time Lord.

Rassilon thwarted the Master by restoring humanity to normal, and the Doctor destroyed the Gate. The Master attacked Rassilon in revenge for the High Council driving him mad with the Sound of Drums, and the two of them - and all the Time Lords - vanished as Gallifrey was consigned back to the Time War.

The Doctor sacrificed his life to save Wilf, who had become trapped in a chamber that was filling with radiation. With what time he had remaining, the Doctor visited his former companions - he saved Mickey and Martha, who had become freelance alien hunters, from a Sontaran; saved Luke Smith from a car accident; attended a book signing of Verity Newman, the great-granddaughter of Joan Redfern, whose book *The Journal of Impossible Things* was based on her ancestor's diary; and travelled forward a few months to attend Donna Noble's wedding.

UNIT headquarters was still based in Geneva.

Sarah Jane had Mr. Smith distribute a story claiming that Wi-Fi had gone mad all over the world, and given everyone the hallucination that they had become Harold Saxon.[992] Mike Yates planned to attend the UNIT New Year reunion.[993]

2010[994]

One Hornet had survived at Nest Cottage. Mrs Wibbsey disturbed it when she cleaned a pair of curtains, and it took control of her. It developed into a new swarm, which allied itself with an interdimensional demon capable of assuming different aspects, and began plotting its revenge on the Doctor...[995] **Dr. Vera Juarez, a future associate of Torchwood, made the decision not to resuscitate her mother after she suffered a massive stroke.**[996] The Samarands invaded Greece in 2010.[997]

The Halliwell Film Guide of 2010 contained a particularly scathing review of *The True History of Planets* movie, which was broadcast on television for the first time this year. Britain had a King at this time.[998] The Americans researched military applications for Schumann Resonance, a set of low frequency peaks in Earth's electro-magnetic spectrum.[999] Earth's scientists first noticed the dark tides that permeated the universe, but it would be a long time before they were understood.[1000]

(=) The third Doctor surrendered Earth to the Martians. The Martians withdrew, and Earth became a nature reserve. The Doctor spent a thousand years living in Kent.[1001]

c 2010 - SHADOW OF THE PAST[1002] -> The remains of the Mim scout locked in UNIT quarantine reconstituted, and merged with the remains of Sergeant Robin Marshall. Liz Shaw judged that the resultant hybrid, who looked like Marshall, had at least some of the man's memories and possessed none of the Mim's anger.

2010 - CUDDLESOME[1003] -> The fifth Doctor visited Angela Wisher, a Sussex resident who aided him during the Cuddlesome slaughterhouse three years previous.

2010 - THE MACROS[1004] -> The space-time rift created by the Philadelphia Experiment interacted with the micro-universe containing the planet Capron. Presidenter (sic) Osloo had established a dictatorship, and tapped the rift to power her society and growing army. The sixth Doctor and Peri arrived on Capron, and Osloo increased the power being siphoned from the rift - the first gambit in her effort to conquer the macro-universe from which the travellers originated. The power drain caused the USS *Eldridge*, time-looped in the rift since 1943, to disintegrate entirely. The Doctor ended Osloo's reign by neglecting to stabilise her

temporal equilibrium after a trip to the macro-universe, which turned her into an infant. He also provided a battery which, hailing from the macro-universe, was powerful enough to fuel Capron for a million years.

c 2010 - MEMORY LANE[1005] -> Travel to planets in the solar system was now feasible from Earth, and the *Led Zeppelin* spaceships were named after a public vote. Kim Kronotska became a commander in the Commonwealth Space Programme - a means of using British money to fire off rockets in the middle of the Outback - and participated in the *Led Zeppelin II* mission to the Martian moon of Phobos.

The development of cryo-stasis facilitated grander ambitions. Kim, Tom Braudy and their colleague Samuel were dispatched aboard the *Led Zeppelin IV* to Jupiter, but a system failure drew them off course. They wouldn't awaken for a hundred years. The eighth Doctor rescued Kim and Tom on the planet Lucentra, and returned them to their native era. They settled down together under adopted identities, letting the world believe they were lost in space.

The film *Star Begotten* entailed a second sun appearing over Earth.

2010 - SITUATION VACANT[1006] -> The Pan-Galactic Initiative on Dimensional Rifts had been established as an organisation that monitored rogue wormholes and other dimensional anomalies. On Earth, *Situation Vacant* was a

1001 An alternative timeline seen in *So Vile a Sin*.
1002 Dating *Shadow of the Past* (BF CC #4.9) - The story's framing sequence is probably concurrent with the audio's release in April 2010. Liz says that it's been "nearly twice" as long since the Mim incident (in the UNIT era) as the young troopers slain during the event (who were "barely out of school") were alive.
1003 Dating *Cuddlesome* (BF promo #7, *DWM* #393) - It's been three years since the main part of the story. Angela says that her ex-partner and his fiancé have a wedding planned "for June".
1004 Dating *The Macros* (BF LS #1.8) - The Doctor gives the year as 2010, and twice generalises that it's "over sixty years" since 1943. The TARDIS has been refitted with a Zero Room (also seen in *Renaissance of the Daleks* and *Patient Zero*), following its destruction in *Castrovalva*.
1005 Dating *Memory Lane* (BF #88) - No specific year is given, but most signs indicate that Kim and Tom hail from near the present day. Kim is familiar with iPods; Tom is acquainted with both *Space Lego* (1978-2001) and *Star Wars Lego* (first introduced in 1999) and the Doctor explicitly names their ion jet rocket as the product of the twenty-first century. It's further said that the rockets come into being "thirty-five years" after the

Earth-recreation of Tom's childhood on Lucentra, and although this stems from a composite of Tom's memories and isn't very reliable, it does tie in with the date for *The Seeds of Death* in this chronology.

Kim expects Tom to recognise the names of female astronauts Eileen Collins (who flew in 1995 and 1997, and commanded missions in 1999 and 2005) and Pamela Anne Melroy (who piloted space shuttle missions in 2000 and 2002, and was selected to command one in June 2006).
1006 Dating *Situation Vacant* (BF BBC7 #4.2) - The story seems to be contemporary, and was released in July 2010. The Monk's involvement is revealed in *The Resurrection of Mars*.
1007 *The Resurrection of Mars*, as partially revealled in *The Book of Kells*.
1008 Dating *Apollo 23* (NSA #37) - It's twice said (pgs. 30,147) that it's "thirty years" after *Apollo 22* launched in June 1980, which would roughly coincide with the novel's publication in April 2010. The time of year is more indeterminate, although mention that it's a "cold, grey day" in Texas (p7) tends to imply that it's not summer. Either way, the story cannot fit into the one-day gap between *The Eleventh Hour* and *The Big Bang*, as it takes the Doctor and company a full day (pgs. 147, 160)

reality show that had contestants competing for a job.

The Meddling Monk had regenerated, and advertised for a new companion - then syphoned some of the more murderous and hapless respondents to a secondary location, and manipulated the eighth Doctor into handling them while he conducted the real auditions in an office in Soho. The less-than-desirable applicants assisted the Doctor in stopping a 20-foot-tall robot from menacing London. One of the companion hopefuls - Theo Lawson, a hacker who had caused a global recession - was killed. The Doctor asked another applicant, actress Tamsin Drew, to accompany him on his travels.

Lucie Miller answered the Monk's ad, and became his new companion.[1007]

2010 - APOLLO 23[1008] **->** The discontinued Saturn V rocket remained the biggest launch vehicle ever built by mankind. Base Delta, America's secret moonbase, was being used to conduct clandestine experiments upon hardened criminals in an effort to remove their evil impulses, a.k.a. their Keller impulses.

The gelatinous, slimy inhabitants of the planet Taleria discovered that their bodies were dying - each new generation of Talerians was more fragile than the one before it. The Talerians took control of Base Delta - part of their plan to mentally transfer their whole race into humanity. The eleventh Doctor was briefly stranded on Earth, and rode aboard *Apollo 23* - a standby Saturn V (serial No. SA-521) that had been mothballed since the 1970s, and was made to run on M3 Variant fuel - to reunite with Amy and the TARDIS aboard Base Delta. They stymied the Talerians' efforts, and decompression burst the Talerians' bodies. The quantum link emanating from Base Delta became non-functional, and it was expected that the base would be unsustainable without it.

2010 - CODE OF THE KRILLITANES[1009] **->** In London, the tenth Doctor was surprised to see ordinary people demonstrate amazing mental feats. They had been eating Brainy Crisps - which the Doctor tested and discovered contained Krillitane Oil. At the Brainy Crisps home office,

he learned that the Krillitane were planning to harness the power of social networking to solve the riddle of life. They also created a new generation of Krillitane - only to find that the Director of Computing at Brainy Crisps had programmed the new Krillitane to be polite and agreeable. The two factions clashed with one another, which destroyed the Brainy Chips factory - and both generations of Krillitane - in an explosion.

2010 (a Saturday night) - THE FORGOTTEN ARMY[1010] **->** The eleventh Doctor told Amy that the sausage-burgers served at Big Paulie's Sausages - a battered old trolly in Manhattan where a tired-looking man flipped burgers - became so renowned in future that all manner of beings (including Judoon, Graske, cat-people and Haemo-Goths) journeyed back through time to discretely consume them. Such time travellers had to endure a 12-year waiting list; the Doctor claimed to have circumvented this by purchasing the street on which the trolley stood, and named it after Amy. He recommended to her the "Doctor Burger": "like a cheeseburger but with extra bacon, sausage and steak. And a bit of chicken... No ketchup though. Absolutely banned."[1011]

The 99th Vykoid Expeditionary Force revived, and arranged for a human expedition to find its (secretly robotic) woolly mammoth frozen in ice. The *New York Times* proclaimed, "New York Welcomes Wooly the Mammoth" as the "creature" was taken to the New York Natural History Museum. The Vykoids deployed a Time Freeze and used their combat vehicles to round up New Yorkers for use in the desiccated Vykoid slave mines on Cassetia 2. In the brouhaha to follow, New York was cut off from the outside world: the Vykoids sealed off all access routes with debris, brainwashed every member of the New York Police Department to corral the populace, and plunged the city into its worst power outage since 1922.

The Doctor and Amy commandeered the mammoth and "swam" it across the Hudson, then used a Vykoid teleport device in the Statue of Liberty to send the invaders away from Earth. The Time Freeze ended, and the New Yorkers lost all memory of what had triggered the chaos.

to prep *Apollo 23* for launch, and another two days (p147) to reach Base Delta. The Doctor says that it's "a few hundred years" (p55) before a penal colony is built on the moon (*Frontier in Space*) and that T-Mat won't be established there (p87) "for a while yet" (*The Seeds of Death*). M3 Variant fuel was developed for the Mars Probe missions (*The Ambassadors of Death*). Mention of "Keller impulses" doubtless refers to *The Mind of Evil*.
1009 Dating *Code of the Krillitanes* (*Quick Reads* #5) - The year is given.
1010 Dating *The Forgotten Army* (NSA #39) - The

Doctor says it's 2010. The Doctor's mention of the Ood Food Guide praising June 2010 might suggest the month. It's "a Saturday night" (p110, p151).
1011 Presuming for even a second that the Doctor isn't just having Amy on with his wild claims of "the Doctor Burger", his having purchased an entire street on her behalf *and* his having banned ketchup on said street, it's not specified *which* street he's named after her. A "Pond Street" exists in Staten Island, but not Manhattan, where the story seems to take place.

(=) 2010 - "The Golden Ones"[1012] **->** The time-child Chiyoko freed Axos from the time loop in which it was trapped, and it transmogrified its form to become the Shining Dawn Tower in Tokyo. Axons disguised as humans formed the Shining Dawn Corporation and marketed a brain-boosting drink that claimed to increase the intelligence of children. UNIT summoned the eleventh Doctor and Amy upon discovering that Tokyo's children *were* becoming noticeably smarter, and chemical analysis claimed the drink was ordinary water.

Axos converted the fifty thousand children who drank the brain-booster (actually Axonite molecules changed to look like water) into little Axons. A state of emergency was declared as they secured government offices and utilities in Tokyo. Axos absorbed enough energy from the Tokyo grid to transform into a giant Axon monster, and initiated its nutrition cycle. The Doctor reversed the polarity of the neutron flow, and broadcast a message that the Tokyo residents should switch on all their electrical devices. The power drain killed Axos, and freed the children.

The TARDIS absorbed some of Axos' genetic material, which aided in Chiyoko's creation. She later reversed the effects of her interference.[1013]

= 2010 - DOOMSDAY[1014] **->** On Pete's World, Harriet Jones was President and there was optimism for a new global age. However, in the last sixth months, the planet's average temperature had risen by two degrees. Lumic's Cybermen were infiltrating our universe - Pete Tyler and Torchwood helped to defeat them, then sealed off travel between the two universes. Rose, Mickey and Jackie were stuck in the parallel universe.

A few months after arriving in the parallel universe, Rose was contacted by the Doctor. She said goodbye to him at Dårlig Ulv Stranden ("Bad Wolf Bay") in Norway, and announced that Jackie was three months pregnant with Pete's child.

2010 - VINCENT AND THE DOCTOR[1015] **->** The eleventh Doctor and Amy visited the Musee d'Orsay museum in Paris to see a van Gogh exhibition. The Doctor saw a monster in the painting *The Church at Auvers*, and he and Amy hurried to 1890, when van Gogh painted it. A few days later, they brought van Gogh himself to the museum, to show him that he was considered one of the greatest painters of all time. Van Gogh still committed suicide in his own era, but the painting he dedicated to Amy, *Still Life: Vase with Twelve Sunflowers*, was on display in the museum.

1012 Dating "The Golden Ones" (*DWM* #425-428) - The story was published in 2010, and looks contemporary. It's after UNIT has changed its name to become the Unified Intelligence Taskforce.

1013 "The Child of Time" (*DWM*). Chiyoko's temporal undoing of her actions (meaning "The Golden Ones" was erased from history) is fortunate, given that events in this story heavily contradict *The Feast of Axos*.

1014 Dating *Doomsday* (X2.13) - Pete states that "three years" have passed since the end of *The Age of Steel*; this must mean that it's 2010. In "our" universe, it's still 2007 (confirmed in *TW: Everything Changes* and *The Runaway Bride*, and as can be inferred from Jackie saying she's "forty" in *Army of Ghosts* and telling Pete he "died twenty years ago" in *Doomsday*).

Perhaps the disruption caused by travelling between the two universes has knocked them out of sync. It means that Mickey, Pete and Jake are all three years older in *Army of Ghosts* than they were in *The Age of Steel* (even though they all look exactly the same as before), and that Jackie is "officially" three years older there than her actual age (which presumably she's not happy about).

Jackie is three months pregnant by the time the Doctor contacts Rose, so it takes at least three months (of parallel universe time, at any rate) for him to do so.

1015 Dating *Vincent and the Doctor* (X5.10) - The

Doctor tells Vincent that it's "Paris, 2010 AD"; he and Amy first visit the museum "a few days" beforehand.

Like Martha before her, the main "present day" events of Amy's first season are compressed into a very short period, so, technically, other "present day" stories (in Amy's case, this story and *The Lodger*) must happen out of sequence with those events and can be safely placed elsewhere. There's snow on the ground outside Musee d'Orsay, everyone is wrapped warmly and their breath is visible - snow in Paris is very rare in April, although it did happen, without much accumulation, in 2008. Further research into this was thwarted because neither of this guidebook's authors speak French.

1016 Dating *The Big Bang* (X5.13) - The scene occurs the same day as *The Lodger* (TV).

1017 Dating *The Lodger* (X5.11) - An advert on Craig's fridge for a "Vincent Van Gogh: The Great Innovator" exhibit is dated "13th March-29th August, 2010". (This isn't the same exhibit that the Doctor and Amy visit in *Vincent and the Doctor*, especially as Craig has never been to Paris and can't see the point of it.) It's a time of year when people are wearing jackets and even gloves. The population of the Earth is given as 6,000,400,026 ... fewer people than were on Earth in *The End of Time* (TV), which either suggests that *The Lodger* is set before that, or that the Cracks in Time have temporarily "erased" some of Earth's population (see the Cracks in

2010 - THE BIG BANG[1016] **->** As the eleventh Doctor regressed through his timeline, he saw Amy place a card in a newsagent's shop that would prompt him to become the lodger of Craig Owens...

2010 - THE LODGER (TV)[1017] **->** A prototype timeship crashed in Colchester, Essex - its crew died, and the vessel's emergency programme made it blend in with the local architecture. It became the top floor of a house; Craig Owens lived on the main level. The TARDIS was headed for the fifth moon of Sinda Callista, but instead arrived in Colchester and was caught in a materialisation loop. Amy was trapped in the TARDIS while the eleventh Doctor was left behind and became Craig's lodger - he spent three days excelling at football, matchmaking Craig with Craig's friend Sophie and using the nontechnology technology of the Lammasteens to detect that the time engine was upstairs. The timeship was seeking someone who wanted to travel, but Craig and Sophie's desire to stay caused it to implode. The TARDIS landed properly, and the Doctor went back to retroactively smooth the way for his becoming Craig's lodger, which included having Amy drop off an advert in her handwriting for him to find.

2010 (March) – TW: THE HOUSE OF THE DEAD[1018] **->** The House of the Dead, reputed to be the most haunted pub in Wales, had a change of ownership and was slated to become flats. An alignment in space-time, combined with a final séance being held in the House as part of its "closing down" party, accorded Syriath the Death Feeder the opportunity to enter our universe. Jack Harkness interceded, but was confronted by the "ghost" of Ianto Jones, whom Syriath had re-created by reaching through time. Ianto's shade sacrificed itself to detonate a box of rocks and

coal laced with Rift energy – the resulting dust storm destroyed Syriath, and sealed the Rift forever.

2010 (March) - TW: CHILDREN OF EARTH[1019] **->** Jack Harkness had travelled across the world while coming to terms with events concerning the 456, but deemed Earth as too small, and that it felt like a graveyard. He briefly met with Gwen and Rhys, who returned his Vortex Manipulator; it had been recovered from the Hub's remains. He then accepted a lift from a cold fusion cruiser surfing the ion reefs at the edge of the solar system.

Jack ended up at an alien bar. He saw the tenth Doctor for one last time, and the Doctor introduced him to Alonzo Frame, a former midshipman aboard the starship *Titanic*.[1020]

2010 (April) - TW: FIRST BORN[1021] **->** Gwen and Rhys escaped Cardiff and went underground when government agents tried to capture them.

2010 (spring) - THE END OF TIME (TV)[1022] **->** The tenth Doctor attended Donna Noble's wedding. Joshua and Abigail Naismith had been arrested. The Doctor gave Donna a triple rollover winning lottery ticket... bought with a pound he had borrowed from Donna's late father, Geoffrey Noble.

c 2010 / 2010 (spring) - DEATH AND DIPLOMACY / HAPPY ENDINGS[1023] **->** The small, furry, three-eyed Skrak constructed automatons to pose as the "Hollow Gods": purportedly powerful beings who demanded that the rival empires of the Czhans, the Saloi and the Dakhaari negotiate a peace accord on Moriel - a world at the intersection of their territory. In truth, the Skrak were steering

Time sidebar). Either way, it's preferable that *The Lodger* occurs before the other "modern-day" stories in Series 5, as at least two years elapse between this story and *Closing Time*, which likely occurs in spring 2012 (see the dating notes on that story).

1018 Dating *TW: The House of the Dead* (*TW* audio drama #7) – Jack tells Ianto's shade, "Six months ago, you died in my arms", so this is just prior to Jack's leaving Earth in the epilogue of *TW: Children of Earth*. Barring on any further stories that address the topic, the Rift is here sealed forever – which might explain why Jack finally feels at liberty to relinquish his duty to Cardiff and depart into space.

1019 Dating *TW: Children of Earth* (*TW* 3.05) - It's "six months" after the defeat of the 456.

1020 *The End of Time* (TV). This occurs after *TW: Children of Earth*.

1021 Dating *TW: First Born* (*TW* novel #17) - Gwen is currently "seven months" pregnant (p5). It's possible that this scene is the start of Gwen and Rhys being forced to go underground, following their meet-up with Jack in March 2010 at the end of *TW: Children of Earth*. No reason is given as to why the government has left them alone this long, although *TW: The Men Who Sold the World* hints that the UK has a new coalition government, which might have negated the damning video evidence collected against Prime Minister Green's administration in *Children of Earth*.

1022 Dating *The End of Time* (X4.17-4.18) - We're told that Donna planned to marry in the spring.

1023 Dating *Death and Diplomacy* and *Happy Endings* (NA #49-50) - The Virgin version of *Ahistory* dated *Death and Diplomacy* to the present day, based upon the synopsis. The final book has Benny asking Jason the

the empires toward war so they could ransack their remains and become more powerful. The Skrak also diverted the seventh Doctor to Moriel as they hoped to obtain his TARDIS. The Doctor's companions - Bernice, Roz and Chris - were transmatted to other worlds to deprive him of help.

Bernice encountered the rogue Jason Kane, who had been travelling the Dagellan Cluster for about fifteen years. The two of them consummated their relationship and, despite their abandonment issues, increasingly fell in love. The Doctor foiled the Skrak's plans and broadcast an announcement from "the Hollow Gods" that the talks had been a resounding success, establishing peace. Afterwards, Benny broke the news to the Doctor that she'd accepted Jason's marriage proposal.

Guests from across space and time attended the wedding of Bernice Summerfield and Jason Kane in the Norfolk village of Cheldon Bonniface. Those present included - thanks to the seventh Doctor's efforts - Roz, Chris, Ace, General Lethbridge-Stewart and his wife Doris, Mike Yates, John Benton, Irving Braxiatel, Kadiatu Lethbridge-Stewart, Muldwych, William Blake, the Pakhar Keri, Ruby Duvall, Hamlet Macbeth, Anne Doras' daughter Bernice, Creed McIlveen, Christian Alvarez and his son Benjamin, the Ice Warriors Savaar and Rhukk, Tom Dekker, Sherlock Holmes, John Watson, Joan Redfern, J.R.R. Tolkien (who gave Benny and Jason a signed first edition of *The Hobbit*) and a girl who looked remarkably like Death of the Endless. Winifred Bambera and Ancelyn couldn't attend, as they were off on a quest. Music was

provided by the Isley Brothers, the band Plasticine and the Silurian group Bona Fide. Leonardo da Vinci served the wedding cake he had designed.

The Master had stolen the Loom of Rassilon's Mouse, a bioengineering tool, to fashion himself a new body. A Fortean Flicker caused him to coincidentally be operating in Cheldon Bonniface during Bernice and Jason's wedding, and he did what he could to disrupt events. Multiple clones of Jason were created, and the Loom generated a huge gelatinous monster. The Doctor had Ishtar Hutchings slay the creature with her dormant Timewyrm abilities.

General Lethbridge-Stewart, having been engulfed by the monster before Ishtar killed it, found that - as a happy side-effect - his body had become decades younger.

The Doctor gifted Benny and Jason with time rings; together, they could travel throughout space-time.

Ace reconciled with her mother, Audrey - who was now engaged to Robin Yeadon, Ace's boyfriend in 1968. Ace herself left on her time hopper with one of the Jason Kane clones. Ishtar was left pregnant from an encounter with Chris Cwej. She believed that their daughter, Jasmine, would become the girlfriend of Ricky McIlveen - and that the two of them would sire the Eternal named Time.

The word "cruk" was introduced in the anime series *Bones and Kay*, and quickly caught on as a mild expletive.

The rejuvenated General Lethbridge-Stewart returned to active duty with UNIT.[1024] Mike Yates told the Brigadier about his adventure with the Hornets, and did the same when he met Liz Shaw in the summer.[1025]

---

year, and him replying that it's "Nineteen ninety-six when I last looked. Mind you, that was something like fifteen years ago, more or less. I had a watch once, but it broke and I lost count" (p123).

While it's reasonable to take Jason's "something like fifteen years" comment to mean *precisely* fifteen years, and thereby date *Death and Diplomacy* to circa 2011, it also seems justifiable to place it before *Happy Endings* - which is repeatedly said to be set in 2010, with the season specified as "spring" (p11). Given the vagueness of Jason's remarks and with the two stories occurring so close together regardless, why *would* the Doctor have decided to hold the wedding in the year before Benny and Jason actually met? A wedding invite in *Happy Endings* (p90) specifies Benny and Jason's nuptials as taking place on "Saturday, 24th April, 2010" (which in real life was actually a Tuesday).

In *Prime Time*, the director of Channel 400, Lukos, tells Ace's younger self that her mother died age 85, haunted by never knowing what happened to her daughter. As Ace's mother was born in 1943 (*The Curse of Fenric*), this would place her death in 2028. However, Channel 400's account is specifically tailored to torment Ace and is therefore suspect, especially given the older Ace's

reunion with her mother in *Happy Endings*. Ricky McIlveen is the son of Vincent and Justine from *Warchild*. Time was first mentioned in *Love and War*, and the seventh Doctor is often cited as "Time's Champion".

1024 *The Shadows of Avalon*, following on Lethbridge-Stewart's rejuvenation as a result of events in *Happy Endings*. This explains how the Brigadier lives well past a normal human lifespan.

1025 *Demon Quest: The Relics of Time*. We see Mike with the Brigadier at Benny's wedding, so perhaps he told him then.

1026 Dating *The Sarah Jane Adventures* Series 3 (*SJA: The Eternity Trap*, 3.4; *SJA: Mona Lisa's Revenge*, 3.5; *SJA: The Gift*, 3.6) - The remainder of Series 3 occurs in the spring of 2010, with the last story, *The Gift*, appearing to finish at the very end of the school year. This isn't directly said, but the children are doing GCSE preliminary exams, and the final scene - with Sarah and company enjoying a backyard BBQ without jackets on, and basking in the sunshine - looks and feels as if they're celebrating the start of the summer holiday. Either way, *The Gift* definitely occurs later in the spring - established green plants are shown as the Rakweed pollinates everywhere, and Rani goes off to school without

The Sarah Jane Adventures
Series 3 (second half)[1026]

2010 (spring) - SJA: THE ETERNITY TRAP[1027] -> Sarah Jane and her friends investigated Ashen Hill Manor - one of the most haunted locations in the UK. They confronted the shade of the alchemist Erasmus Darkening, an alien whose attempts to manipulate other dimensions to get home had caused all the spooky happenings. Darkening proved hostile, but Sarah and her allies dissipated him into mere electricity. The spirits of everyone Darkening had captured over the centuries were likewise liberated.

2010 (spring) - SJA: MONA LISA'S REVENGE[1028] -> Clyde Langer won a competition that saw his imaginative drawings (actually images of aliens and their technology that he had seen in his adventures) displayed in the Artists of the Future competition at the International Gallery in London. The gallery was also hosting the Mona Lisa, which was on loan from the Louvre. The close proximity of the Mona Lisa to Guieseppe di Cattivo's painting *The Abomination* - which had, along with the Mona Lisa, been painted with oils derived from an alien mineral - caused the embodiment of the Mona Lisa to come to life and step from the painting. The Mona Lisa had the ability of molecular transplantation, and sought to release others of her kind. She did so with William Bonneville's *The Dark Rider*, and wanted to liberate her "brother", the Abomination. Clyde drew a picture of K9, which temporarily came to life and dispersed the Abomination's pigments. All the effects of the Mona Lisa's power were reversed, and she returned to her painting.

2010 (end of school year) - SJA: THE GIFT[1029] -> Sarah Jane and her friends were about to thwart a Slitheen child's plan to crush the Earth into a large diamond when Tree Lorn Acre and Leef Apple Glyn - two Blat25hereen (cousins of the Slitheen) - captured the child. The Blathereen gave Sarah a Rakweed plant - a staple food they said would grow even in the harshest conditions, and end world famine. In actuality, the Rakweed was a fast-growing addictive drug that would seed itself via spores across Earth, and could then be harvested for a massive profit on the galactic market. Tree and Leaf were not true Blathereen, but Slitheen-Blathereen hybrids. The Rakweed seeded spores that could have taken over London in hours, Earth in days, but Sarah Jane learned the plants would burst if exposed to a sound frequency of 1421.09 Hz. Sarah broadcast the sound with K9's help, ending the threat... and making the Rakweed-soused Blathereen explode.

Anwen Williams, the daughter of Gwen Cooper and Rhys Williams, was born in or near early May 2010.[1030]

(=) 2010 - TW: THE TWILIGHT STREETS[1031] -> Bilis Manger showed Torchwood a potential future in which the Dark influenced Owen, his wife Toshiko and Gwen. They slaved Jack to the Hub's Rift Manipulator, then used his life energy to harness the Rift - in less than a year, the Torchwood Empire had conquered the world. While Gwen gave birth to a son, Geraint Williams Junior, Ianto killed Owen and was shot dead by Toshiko's guards. Jack destroyed the Rift Manipulator, breaking the Dark's power.

2010 - TW: "Shrouded"[1032] -> John Hart established himself in Mexico, near a mini-Rift that provided him with an easy means of transport, as a trafficker of alien artifacts. Hart and Rhys realised that a rogue time traveller named

---

a jacket on as birds chirp in the warm sun.

1027 Dating *SJA: The Eternity Trap* (*SJA* 3.4) - Rani and Darkening separately (and broadly) say that 1665 was "three hundred forty years ago". Lord Marchwood's shade claims, twice, that he's been searching "over three hundred years" since 1665 for the souls of his children. Clyde and Rani have school "on Monday", so it's during the school year.

1028 Dating *SJA: Mona Lisa's Revenge* (*SJA* 3.5) - The International Gallery curator mentions "the Cup of Athelstan fiasco at Easter" (*Planet of the Dead*). He definitely *doesn't* say "last Easter" - so this is possibly evidence that *Mona Lisa's Revenge* occurs before Easter 2010 (4th April, in that year). It's not impossible, of course, that the "at Easter" reference denotes that *Mona Lisa's Revenge* (and by extension *SJA: The Eternity Trap*) take place at the very tail end of 2009, but that would

necessitate forcing a five-month gap between *The Gift* and the rest of Series 3 where none was meant to exist. Moreover, the more Series 3 stories one wedges into the waning weeks of 2009, the more the total absence of bitterly cold weather and holiday decorations becomes conspicuous.

1029 Luke is said to be 15. The Blathereen first appeared in *The Monsters Inside*.

1030 Extrapolating from Gwen being three weeks pregnant in *TW: Children of Earth*.

1031 Dating *TW: The Twilight Streets* (*TW* novel #6) - The exact dating for this is unclear, but it's possible that Gwen's pregnancy parallels the one in the real timeline. Bizarrely, Gwen here gives birth to a son - on screen, she has a daughter.

1032 Dating *TW: "Shrouded"* (*TWM* #21-22) - Gwen has now given birth. John Hart says he met Beatrice in

Beatrice was attempting to meddle in Ianto's history, and went back in time two years to warn him.

The new coalition government in the United Kingdom became desperate for funds. Mr Black facilitated the sale to the Americans of a cache of advanced weapons - including Judoon, Yeti, Sea Devil and Sontaran firearms, as well as a Ytraxorian Reality Gun - that had been recovered from the Torchwood Hub.[1033]

In June, Luke Smith got four As at A-Level, earning a place at Oxford University a year early. Sarah Jane defeated a piece of sentient concrete that had disguised itself as a flyover in Chiswick, and was attempting to control people's minds.[1034] The Ood Food Guide gave June 2010 "a whole solar system of awards".[1035]

2010 (summer) - TW: FIRST BORN[1036] **->** Gwen, Rhys and their newborn daughter Anwen remained on the run, and took up residence in the North Wales town of Rawbone because Torchwood had keys to a caravan there. In the ten weeks to follow, they learned the origins of the townsfolk becoming sterile, the Scion children given to the Rawbone families, and the alien Juniper Tree that had birthed them.

Budget cuts necessitated that the Rawbone Project produce results, and so Eloise, the project's director, initiated Stage 2 of it. She killed the Juniper-spawned Sebastian and grew Sebastian 2. He was intended to take mental command of the Scions and turn them into soldiers, but viciously wanted to grow an army of Scions and kill humanity. Gwen contacted the creators of the Juniper Tree, who were so horrified by the new Sebastian's mindset that they aged him and the Juniper Tree to death. The people of Rawbone compiled enough evidence of the Rawbone Project to compel a huge payment from the government, and the new leader of the Scions, Jenny Meredith, was hopeful that the town's sterility could be reversed. Gwen, Rhys and Anwen left for parts unknown.

2010 (summer) - TW: THE MEN WHO SOLD THE WORLD[1037] **->** The cache of advanced weaponry recovered from the Torchwood Hub was now being sold by the UK to the US, and was clandestinely routed through Cuba. The American CIA sent agents to safeguard the shipment, but a mishap with the cache's Ytraxorian Reality Gun caused agent Oscar Lupé to materialise in the flight controls of American Airlines Flight AA2010. It crashed into the Gulf of Mexico, killing the four hundred and fifty people aboard. Two members of the CIA team - Cotter Gleason and his second, Mulroney - went rogue and stole the weapons, intending to stage enough devastation to force a large payout from the US government.

(=) A power-mad Gleason used the alien tech to destroy the White House. CIA agent Rex Matheson tried to stop Gleason, who used the Reality Gun to send Rex back to 100,000 BC.

The enigmatic assassin Mr Wynter obtained the Reality Gun, and used it to alter history. The White House was

---

2010, and Rhys tells Ianto in 2008 that Beatrice will "come to find" him in "two years".

1033 "Six weeks" before *TW: The Men Who Sold the World*.

1034 *SJA: The Nightmare Man*

1035 Or so the Doctor claims in *The Forgotten Army* (p17).

1036 Dating *TW: First Born* (*TW* novel #17) - The year at two points is implied to be 2011: Sebastian 1 (born 3rd March, 1981) is "thirty years old"(p134), and Jenny, one of the oldest Scions following the Juniper Tree being relocated to Rawbone in 1991, is "twenty" (pgs 81, 166). Both pieces of evidence need to be taken as approximations, however, as Anwen's age mandates that the year is 2010 (Gwen's family settles in Rawbone "two months", p9, after Gwen was "seven months" pregnant, p5, and Gwen throughout the story is hampered by lactation issues). The story proceeds over at least ten weeks (Anwen's stated age on p88) if not longer. The life-cycle of the potatoes that Rhys plants seems a bit strange - he puts them in the ground three weeks after he and Gwen move to Rawbone, but the plants are "just starting to come up" (p248) at story's end, when they should have emerged within two, maybe three weeks.

The ages of the last natural-born Rawbone children (Sasha, Davydd and Nerys) aren't of much help in making a determination. The town went sterile in 1987, Nerys is currently in her "early 20s" (p40), Davydd is "mid-20s" (p30) and Sasha is 24 (p112), but could easily have been born in 1986.

There's a continuity glitch in that Gwen and Rhys covertly take Anwen to meet Gwen's parents (p128), but *TW: Miracle Day* is presented as their first meeting.

1037 Dating *TW: The Men Who Sold the World* (*TW* novel #18) - No date is given, but it's been at least "nine months"(p121) since the Department's salvage team - in an operation that commenced in October 2009, judging by *TW: Long Time Dead* - recovered the Reality Gun from the Hub. So, it's most likely summer 2010 at present.

1038 Dating "The Age of Ice" (*DWM* #408-411) - The Doctor says that they've arrived in "Sydney, Australia, early twenty-first century", on a "glorious summer's day". A UNIT officer says that the Doctor and his allies saved the entire universe from the Daleks "just last year" (in *Journey's End*, set in 2009). It very much looks as if the story-creators forgot about the "year ahead" rule governing Series 4, meaning that the "last year" reference

saved, and Gleason was sent back to 100,000 BC instead of Rex. Some weeks later, Wynter rejuvenated his aged body and ate his employer.

2010 (summer) - "The Age of Ice"[1038] -> UNIT had established an underwater HQ in Sydney Harbour. Its archives contained at least eight Mona Lisas, a mummy robot, a War Machine, a Yeti, an Auton chair, a Sontaran space ship and a Sontaran Skyhammer cannon.

The Skith had gone to a military footing following the destruction of their homeworld, and the Skith leader who battled the Doctor in 1915 summoned the warship Oppressor Two - and its garrison of Skith - to Earth. The Skith constructed a faulty time machine, a Skardis, with information looted from the Doctor's mind. The Skardis created unstable temporal waves: those aboard Sydney Flight 218 were aged near to death, a Neolithic narwhal was seen in the Parramatta River, pterodactyls appeared by the Zenith Centre, and mammoths roamed the suburbs.

The tenth Doctor and Majenta Pryce arrived as chronal waves made more dinosaurs appear, and inflicted Sydney with a new ice age. The Skith briefly turned Majenta into Skithself so her mind could operate their Skardis - but she generated a pulse that destroyed them. Majenta's assistant Fanson had been aiding the Skith, and died saving her life.

Thomas Brewster's beloved, Connie Winter, was hit by a car and died after being taken off life support. The Doctor had previously saved the planet Symbios - a single organism with the appearance of a thriving ecology - from the Drahvin, and Symbios' governing intelligence summoned him to help against runamuck terraforming robots: the insectoid Terravore. Brewster answered Symbios' call, and used the time engine he'd built in 1867 to transport volunteers to Symbios - where the planet possessed them, and used them as foot soldiers.[1039]

Amy met a gorgeous scuba instructor called Claude on her hen night.[1040]

Amy Pond and Rory Williams

2010 (25th June) - THE ELEVENTH HOUR[1041] -> The eleventh Doctor returned to Amy Pond... two years later than he thought. She joined him travelling in the TARDIS, but didn't tell him that this was the night before she was due to marry Rory Williams.

2010 (25th-26th June) - FLESH AND STONE / THE VAMPIRES OF VENICE[1042] -> The eleventh Doctor and Amy returned to her house following their encounter with the Weeping Angels, and Amy finally admitted that she and Rory were going to get married. She attempted to seduce the Doctor, but he hurried her into the TARDIS and collected Rory from his stag party, determined to take the two of them somewhere romantic to cement their relationship...

2010 (26th June) - THE PANDORICA OPENS[1043] -> The coalition of alien races seeking to imprison the Doctor - so the TARDIS wouldn't explode and destroy the universe - scanned Amy's house for her psychic residue. A trap was laid for the Doctor in 102 AD, patterned after Amy's childhood recollections of *The Story of Roman Britain* and *The Legend of Pandora's Box*.

Soon after, the TARDIS brought River Song to Amy's house from 120 AD. She realised that the Doctor was in great danger, but the TARDIS - as feared - started to explode. The Ship automatically put River in a time loop to protect her; she would be released in 1996.

---

places "The Age of Ice" in 2010 rather than (as was perhaps intended) 2009, its year of publication. Consequently, for the Doctor and Majenta, this story and "Ghosts of the Northern Line" must chronologically happen out of order.

1039 "Six months" before *The Crimes of Thomas Brewster*.

1040 "Spam Filtered"

1041 Dating *The Eleventh Hour* (X5.1) - It's the night before Amy's wedding, the exact date of which ("26/6/2010") is first established in *Flesh and Stone*. Surprisingly given that time of year, the Doctor and Amy's breath is visible. (Did the recalibrated TARDIS cause a heat exchange upon materialisation?) Rory's badge to the emergency unit of the Royal Leadworth Hospital, where he works, is something of an anomaly given Rory's age: it was issued "30/11/1990".

1042 Dating *Flesh and Stone/The Vampires of Venice* (X5.5-5.6) - In *Flesh and Stone*, the clock ticks over to 12 am on 26th June, the date of Rory and Amy's wedding. Rory says in *The Vampires of Venice* that he's "getting married tomorrow" - either he hasn't noticed that it's past midnight already, or the Doctor nips back in time a little.

1043 Dating *The Pandorica Opens* (X5.12) - River checks the TARDIS instruments and confirms the date as "the 26th of June, 2010". The alien intruders broke down Amy's front door, so both they and River presumably go to Amy's house after the Doctor and Amy stopped there in *Flesh and Stone*. The clock ticked over to 12 am of the morning of the 26th as they left, so the action described in *The Pandorica Opens* probably occurs in the darkened morning hours.

2010 (26th June) - THE BIG BANG[1044] -> Following the eleventh Doctor's sacrifice in 1996, the universe was restored to its original form - save that everyone had forgotten he had ever existed. Amy Pond's parents returned to life after the Cracks in Time sealed, and celebrated Amy and Rory's wedding. As Amy's father began his speech, Amy - goaded by the TARDIS-patterned journal that River left for her - remembered something old, something new, something borrowed and something blue. She insisted that her "raggedy Doctor" was late for her wedding - at which point the Doctor was restored to the universe, and the TARDIS materialised at the reception.

River returned to the future using her vortex manipulator. The Doctor, Amy and Rory also left to have new adventures, starting with the case of an Egyptian goddess loose on the *Orient Express*, in space.

Amy and Rory conceived a child while travelling in the TARDIS.[1045]

The Sarah Jane Adventures Series 4

2010 (6th-10th September) - SJA: THE NIGHTMARE MAN[1046] -> Luke Smith's anxiety about going to university was exploited by the Nightmare Man - a Vishklar that hailed from the Seretti Dimension, and needed terror to enter our universe. The Nightmare Man infected Luke, Clyde and Rani with dreams of leading failed lives, but they didn't fear him, and so his power dissipated. Sarah gifted Luke with her car and K9 as he left for Oxford.

2010 (13th-15th September) - SJA: WRAITH WORLD[1047] -> Gregory P. Wilkinson came out of semi-retirement to write the final Wraith World novel, The Fall of Hancada. The reality-warping paper in Wilkinson's journal latched onto Rani's mind, and the series' main antagonist - the sorcerer Hancada, composed of bloodworms - nearly manifested through her. Sarah Jane,

---

1044 Dating *The Big Bang* (X5.13) - The date of the wedding ("26/6/2010") is established first in *Flesh and Stone*, and mirrors the broadcast of *The Big Bang* on the same day.
1045 The Doctor speculates in *A Good Man Goes to War* that this happened on Amy and Rory's wedding night (in *The Big Bang*), but there's reason to doubt this (see the Cracks in Time sidebar); the conception could have happened while they were travelling together in Series 5, or at any point between *The Big Bang* and the Doctor dropping Amy and Rory on Earth (prior to *The Impossible Astronaut*). Whatever the case, nine months must pass in Amy's personal timeframe before she starts to give birth at the end of *The Rebel Flesh*.
1046 Dating *SJA: The Nightmare Man* (SJA 4.1) - A calendar in Luke's room prominently says "September 2010" and is in accordance with the real-world calendar. The story counts down the four days marked on the calendar, from the 6th (when Luke starts packing) to the 10th (when he departs for Oxford).
1047 Dating *SJA: Wraith World* (SJA audiobook #7) - The story effectively begins on the day of Wilkinson's bookstore signing, on "Monday, 13th September" (an actual Monday in 2010) and events pick up "two days later". Unfortunately, that doesn't sit well with the established continuity of *The Sarah Jane Adventures* Series 4. Luke left for Oxford (in *SJA: The Nightmare Man*) the week prior to 13th September, so it's strange that he'd suddenly be back at home, without explanation, the very next Monday - and also a month later, in this story's epilogue - given how little he otherwise visits Sarah in the TV show. But, Rani's inclusion means that *Wraith World* cannot be bumped back to the previous year, as she didn't meet Sarah and friends until early October

2009 - which, again, would conflict with the 13th September dating. Whatever the case, Sarah's comment that she was "just like [Rani] when I was 15" has to be taken as a generalisation, as Rani should be 16 if this story occurs in 2009, 17 if it's 2010.
1048 The month prior to *SJA: Defending Bannerman Road*.
1049 Dating *SJA: The Vault of Secrets* (SJA 4.2) - No specific date is given, although it's said to be "almost forty years" since 1972. The "ancient and deadly civilisation" is likely the Osirians, as a pyramid a la *Pyramids of Mars* is briefly glimpsed on Mars on Mr Smith's monitor. The Alliance of Shades was introduced in *Dreamland* (DW).
1050 *Demon Quest: The Relics of Time*
1051 Dating *SJA: Death of the Doctor* (SJA 4.3) - No specific date is given, although Sarah comments that the Doctor "came back" about four years ago. (This is presumably a reference to his coming back into her life in *School Reunion*, although it's only been three years since that story. In a pinch, if one squints really hard, by "came back" Sarah might mean the Doctor's greater involvement in human affairs per Series 1.) The Doctor says it's been "forty years" since Jo left UNIT. Santiago mentions that he hasn't seen his mother in "six months", and hasn't gotten together with all of his family "since about February" - but since he might have seen his mother after that, it can't automatically be said that it's now August.

Sarah here recalls her final meeting with the tenth Doctor in *The End of Time* (TV). The Doctor has left Amy and Rory on a honeymoon planet, so this is almost certainly set between *The Big Bang* and *A Christmas Carol* in his timeline.

Aside from Jo, the fates of the companions as given

Wilkinson and Rani combined efforts to write an end Hancada's story, then burned Wilkinson's journal.

Sarah Jane and her friends recovered an antigravity ray from an old Nadloon Circus Comedy Cruiser that crashed into the Thames.[1048]

2010 (a Saturday) - SJA: THE VAULT OF SECRETS[1049]
-> Mr Smith sabotaged a NASA probe on Mars, as Sarah Jane did not want them finding evidence of an "ancient and terrible civilisation" there. Rani's parents joined the Ealing branch of the British UFO Research and Paranormal Studies Society (BURPSS) as a way of coping with their various alien encounters.

Androvax the Veil escaped his imprisonment on a swamp world controlled by the Judoon in the Calisteral Cluster, but not before he was bitten by a deadly Moxolon Swamp Viper. He found that the spaceship with the last one hundred members of his race was within the hyper-dimensional Vault created by the Alliance of Shades, the entrance to which was at the disused St. Jude's asylum. Sarah learned that activating the Veil ship within the Vault would create dimensional instability that would tear Earth apart. Androvax attempted to do so anyway, but the robot overseer of the Vault, Mr Dread, sacrificed four hundred fifty years of his personal power supply to reactivate the Vault's transmat. The Veil spaceship was sent into space, and it was expected that the Veil would settle on a new planet. The Vault became inaccessible as its second activation key had been lost. As Mr. Dread's mission had terminated, he deactivated himself.

Mike Yates saw Jo Grant in October, and told her about his adventure with the Hornets.[1050]

2010 - SJA: DEATH OF THE DOCTOR[1051] -> The vulture-like Shansheeth were known throughout the universe as intergalactic undertakers - they would search battlefields for the remains of heroes, then transport their bodies home. The Claw Shansheeth of the Fifteenth Funeral Fleet contacted UNIT, claiming to have found the Doctor's body ten thousand light years away in the Wastelands of the Crimson Heart, where he had evidently perished to save five hundred children from the Scarlet Monstrosity.

Colonel Karim of UNIT summoned the Doctor's associates to attend a funeral service at Unit Base 5, inside Mount Snowdon. The Brigadier was stuck in Peru, and Liz Shaw couldn't return from moonbase until Sunday. Sarah Jane went to Mount Snowdon with Rani and Clyde, and met for the first time Jo Jones, née Grant, who had arrived from the Tierra del Fuego with her grandson Santiago. Cliff Jones was picketing an oil rig in the Ascension Islands. Santiago's father was hiking across Antarctica with a gay dads organisation.

The Shansheeth had gone rogue, and falsified the Doctor's demise to capture his associates. They drained Sarah and Jo's minds with a Memory Weave, a device that could manifest physical objects from memories. The Weave crafted a new TARDIS key - a means by which the Shansheeth could enter the Doctor's Ship. They hoped to use the vessel to interfere with the timelines, and end death across the universe.

The eleventh Doctor arrived and aided his friends. Sarah and Jo's memories overloaded the Memory Weave and it exploded, killing the Shansheeth and their collaborator, Karim. The Doctor reclaimed his TARDIS and departed. Jo and her grandson left to go to Norway by hovercraft.

Sarah had researched other former companions of the Doctor. Ian and Barbara Chesterton were profes-

in this story broadly match (or, at least, don't grievously contradict) what has been established in the tie-in series. The non-televised stories seem, at the very least, to inform this story. A number of the books established that Ian and Barbara married and became professors (eg: *Goth Opera*). The rumours that Sarah mentions - that Ian and Barbara have "never aged since the 60s" - might indeed just be rumours, as the Big Finish audios (*The Five Companions* especially) have consistently rendered Ian as an older man, roughly concurrent with William Russell's real age.

Sarah here implies (but doesn't outright say) that Harry Sullivan has died - he's cited as being alive in *UNIT: The Wasting* (likely set in spring 2005), and Sarah tries to have her annual meet-up with Harry (although he fails to show) in *SJS: Buried Secrets*, set in the same year. He's also said to be alive in 2015 in *Damaged*

Goods (also by Russell T Davies). This being *Doctor Who*, it's possible that there's an extended stretch where Sarah thinks that Harry is dead, but he's actually been kidnapped by (say) space weasels, and that he later returns home. (Either way, this would explain why Harry never visits Sarah in her own series.) Liz Shaw apparently died in *Eternity Weeps*, set in 2003... but in that book, as with *Death of the Doctor*, she was working on a moonbase. (See the Did Liz Shaw Die in 2003? sidebar.)

The "Dorothy" that Sarah mentions might be Dodo, but the initials of Dorothy's charity imply otherwise. Ace's fate is convoluted, to say the least, but if we want to invoke the books, it's possible she saw the dystopian near-future of *Cat's Cradle: Warhead* and decided to try to avert it. Or, it's possible that her leading A Charitable Earth owes to her being undercover/on assignment for the Doctor, and is only temporary.

sors at Cambridge; rumours claimed they hadn't aged since the sixties. Tegan Jovanka campaigned for aboriginal rights. Sarah implied that Harry Sullivan had died, but before that had developed vaccines that saved thousands of lives. Ben and Polly ran an orphanage in India. A woman called Dorothy ran a billion-pound charity called A Charitable Earth.

Jo herself had seven children and twelve grandchildren (with another on the way). The Doctor said that the newest would be dyslexic, but a great swimmer.

2010 - SJA: RETURN OF THE KRULIUS / SJA: DEFENDING BANNERMAN ROAD[1052] -> The Krulius escaped from Judoon custody, and sought revenge against Sarah Jane and her friends. Urglanic shapeshifters in the Krulius' employ teleported Rani to the Krulius' spaceship, which was hidden in Earth orbit behind a force warp. Rani learned that the Krulius had grown clones of the various races it had studied, then escaped and warned Sarah about the Krulius' intentions.

A week after Rani escaped, the Krulius established a temporal stasis field around Bannerman Road. It deployed its cadre of hypnotised clones - including Slitheen, Judoon and Men in Black - against Sarah's house. Clyde fought off the attackers with a variety of alien technology that Sarah had collected. The Krulius' temporal field failed, and it withdrew its forces, vowing revenge.

2010 - SJA: THE EMPTY PLANET[1053] -> The king of an alien world and his brother had died, making Gavin - the king's son, living as a thirteen year old in Ealing with no knowledge of his heredity - the heir to the throne. The robot retrieval team sent to find Gavin eased their task by shunting the entire population of Earth into a sub-dimension, while preventing all traffic crashes, derailments and other damage that might have resulted from humanity's sudden disappearance. Clyde and Rani, barred from leaving Earth by the Judoon, awoke to find that they and Gavin were the only people left. They persuaded Gavin to go with the robots, and the population of the Earth was restored, with no memory that they had been gone. Gavin awarded his friends the titles of Lord Clyde and Lady Rani.

The biggest contradiction is Jo's fate (married mother of seven, grandmother of twelve), which is far more cheerful here than her status in *Genocide* (divorced mother of just one child). While it's easy enough to imagine that she and Cliff later remarried, there is, with the best of will, no good way to reconcile the differing accounts of their children.

1052 Dating *SJA: Return of the Krulius/SJA: Defending Bannerman Road* (*SJA* webcomic #2-3) - The action seems to take place after Luke departs for Oxford, as he's absent save for a highly posed group shot in the very last panel. The Krulius has a picture of Sarah standing next to the Matt Smith Doctor, implying it's after *SJA: Death of the Doctor*.

1053 Dating *SJA: The Empty Planet* (*SJA* 4.4) - No specific date is given, although it's said to be a school night. Clyde and Rani were "grounded" in *SJA: Prisoner of the Judoon*.

1054 Dating *SJA: Deadly Download* (*SJA* audiobook #8) - The audio was made available for download on 4th November, 2010, between the broadcasts of *SJA: The Empty Planet* and *SJA: Lost in Time*. (The CD was released 15th November, 2010.) Sarah opens the story with, "It all began one cold November afternoon", and plays some Christmas songs, albeit "a bit prematurely".

1055 Dating *SJA: Lost in Time* (*SJA* 4.5) - The date appears on a newspaper; in 2010, 23rd November was indeed a Tuesday. Rani says at one point, "I'm only 17". George Woods was 13 when Clyde met him on 7th June, 1941, and has now aged seventy years - which is feasible if his birthday is 8th June or later.

1056 Dating *SJA: Goodbye, Sarah Jane Smith* (*SJA* 4.6) - No specific date is given. The population of Earth is "six billion". Sarah here orders Mr Smith to distribute the cover story that the whole of humanity thought that a meteor was coming toward them as part of a 3D-game promotion, but it's such a ludicrous tale even by *Doctor Who* standards, it's hard to see it gaining any traction.

1057 Dating *Demon Quest: The Relics of Time* (BBC fourth Doctor audio #2.1) - The *Hornets' Nest* series was "last year", it is "next Christmas", and the Doctor has had "a year's absence" from Nest Cottage. It's three days before Christmas.

1058 *Demon Quest: Sepulchre*

1059 *Demon Quest: Sepulchre*

1060 Dating *Demon Quest: The Demon of Paris* (BBC fourth Doctor audio #2.2) - According to Mrs Wibbsey, "We arrived on the day we left, December the 23rd".

1061 Dating *Demon Quest: A Shard of Ice* (BBC fourth Doctor audio #2.3) - The Doctor and Mike return the same day as they left.

1062 Dating *Find and Replace* (BF CC #4.3) - It's repeatedly said that it's Christmas Eve, and the back cover blurb specifies the year as 2010. Adding to the debate of whether the public of this era knows about the existence of extra-terrestrials or not, Jo fakes surprise upon learning that Huxley is an alien.

1063 Dating *Demon Quest: Starfall* (BBC fourth Doctor audio #2.4) - The Doctor and Yates return soon after they left.

1064 Dating *Demon Quest: Sepulchre* (BBC fourth Doctor audio #2.5) - The final sequence takes place on Christmas Eve. The sequences on Sepulchre explicitly take place in "a different time" and are undatable, but have been included here for clarity.

2010 (November) - SJA: DEADLY DOWNLOAD[1054] -> Sarah Jane and her friends defeated the Emulgus, a 12-foot insectoid alien who tried to transmit a computer virus that would transform technology across Earth into mind-controlling metal replicants of itself.

2010 (Tuesday, 23rd November) - SJA: LOST IN TIME[1055] -> Sarah Jane and her friends were summoned to Smalley and Co. Antiques by the mysterious Shopkeeper, who answered to a parrot named Captain. The Shopkeeper opened a time window and sent Sarah Jane, Rani and Clyde to three different timezones (1889, 1553 and 1941 respectively) to find pieces of chronosteel - a metal forged in the Time Vortex, and which had the power to change history. If they failed to return with the objects the chronosteel had become fashioned into, the Earth would be destroyed. The Shopkeeper himself was forbidden from making such a journey.

Clyde and Rani returned with their chronosteel pieces, but Sarah Jane failed to retrieve hers. The granddaughter of the ghost-hunter Emily Morris arrived at the Shopkeeper's store with the final chronosteel piece, saving Earth and allowing the Shopkeeper and Captain to depart.

Clyde learned that George Woods, whom he had met in 1941, was now 83 and had been knighted by Queen Elizabeth II.

2010 - SJA: GOODBYE, SARAH JANE SMITH[1056] -> The Katesh - a race wherein each member had a humanoid component, and a giant, separate "stomach" that digested heightened emotions - exiled one of their own when her hunger grew too strong. She escaped her space-faring prison cell by modifying its game system, then learned of Sarah Jane's status as an adventurer. The Katesh presented itself to Sarah Jane, Rani and Clyde as "Ruby Ann White", a fellow adventurer who had just moved to Bannerman Road. Ruby began feeding off Sarah, impairing her cognitive function. Sarah made a mistake while fighting an invasion of the Dark Horde (that Ruby repelled), and became convinced by a medi-scan that she was ill. She reluctantly handed over her duties and Mr Smith to Ruby, but Sarah's friends soon realised the truth. Ruby accelerated her feeding cycle, but Luke returned from Oxford and reprogrammed Ruby's holographic game system to make every person on Earth think that a meteor was headed straight for them. The emotional overload exploded Ruby's "stomach", and she was returned to her prison capsule and sent back into space.

Demon Quest

2010 (22nd-23rd December) - DEMON QUEST: THE RELICS OF TIME[1057] -> The fourth Doctor returned to Nest Cottage after a year away, and enthusiastically dismantled the TARDIS console as part of an overhaul. Mrs Wibbsey (secretly under the control of the new Hornet Swarm)[1058] took many of the Doctor's items to sell at a jumble sale at the village hall, and swapped a mysterious gentlemen - actually a shapechanging demon in the Hornets' employ[1059] - four components of the spatial geometer in return for antiques: a mosaic tile attached to a page from a history book, a poster, a book of fairytales and a superhero comic. All of these items incorporated images of the Doctor, and the Doctor concluded they were a series of clues. Without the spatial geometer, the TARDIS could move in time, but not very far in space. The Doctor and Mrs Wibbsey headed to the first century AD to investigate this mystery, even as Mike Yates called to say he was at a loose end, and would like to come to Nest Cottage for the holiday.

2010 (23rd December) - DEMON QUEST: THE DEMON OF PARIS[1060] -> The fourth Doctor and Wibbsey returned from 1894 with the first and second parts of the spatial geometer, and reunited with Mike Yates.

2010 (23rd December) DEMON QUEST: A SHARD OF ICE[1061] -> The fourth Doctor and Mike Yates took a short trip to the nineteenth century to track down the third piece of the spatial geometer. The last part was to be found in New York City, 1976, so the Doctor, Yates and Wibbsey headed there.

2010 (24th December) - FIND AND REPLACE[1062] -> Iris Wildthyme and Jo Grant were flummoxed when Huxley - a five-legged noveliser from the mooned world of Verbatim VI - insisted that the Doctor had never been exiled to Earth, and that Jo was Iris' old travelling companion. They left in Iris' bus to visit the third Doctor during his time at UNIT to settle the matter.

2010 (24th December) - DEMON QUEST: STARFALL[1063] -> The fourth Doctor and Mike Yates returned to Nest Cottage from New York, but the Demon "kidnapped" Wibbsey. The Doctor and Yates could do little but wait...

2010 (24th December) - DEMON QUEST: SEPULCHRE[1064] -> The fourth Doctor and Mike Yates got an answering machine message from Mrs Wibbsey - a means of luring them to the Sepulchre, a hidden location at the edge of the universe. It resembled an English country house, but was the domain of the Demon. The Doctor learned that the Demon was from a backwater shadow dimension, and was working for secret masters: the new Hornet Swarm. They planned to disintegrate the Doctor and condense his knowledge of space-time into a four-dimensional Atlas of All of Time and Space - a device that would let the Swarm find its lost Queen. The Doctor extracted the Swarm from Wibbsey, and teleported it inside a sarcophagus to a 1914 fire at the Cromer Palace of Curios, where the Swarm died. The Doctor and his friends returned to Nest Cottage, where they enjoyed a dinner on Christmas Eve. The Demon was still on the loose.

2010 (24th-25th December) - SERPENT CREST: TSAR WARS / ALADDIN TIME[1065] -> The fourth Doctor, Mrs Wibbsey and Mike Yates were enjoying their Christmas Eve dinner when robot agents burst in, knocked Yates unconscious, and took the Doctor and Wibbsey down a wormhole to the Robotov Empire in the far future. After a subsequent trip back to the nineteenth century, the Doctor, Wibbsey, the cyborg teenager Alex and his guardian Boolin returned the following day, while Yates was recovering in hospital. While the Doctor took Alex and Boolin home in the TARDIS, saying he might be gone some time dealing with other business, Wibbsey did some washing up.

2011[1066]

Chloe Webber's father died in 2011. Both she and her mother had been terrified of him.[1067] When Hex was in secondary school, he went on a school trip to Venice.[1068] On 15th January, 2011, the US Senate Committee for

Drugs and Alcohol voted to hoard the national supply of surplus drugs, and make them only for use in civil defence programmes.[1069] The Doctor took Stevie Wonder back to 1814 to perform for River Song.[1070]

Van Statten discovered the cure to the common cold using alien technology.[1071] The Bantu Independence Group originated as a political movement in southern Africa in 2011. It purchased land and built communities on behalf of the oppressed.[1072]

The eighth Doctor and Lucie saved a bit of cash by doing their Christmas shopping in the January sales.[1073]

c 2011 - THE CRIMES OF THOMAS BREWSTER[1074] The sixth Doctor and Evelyn tried to quietly visit the Tower of London, but instead were embroiled in the conflict between Symbios, the Terravore and Thomas Brewster - who was passing as an East London gang leader named "the Doctor". The Terravore negotiated with Symbios - it would spare the sentient planet if it provided access to Brewster's wormhole, enabling them to attack Earth instead. The Doctor deactivated the Terravore by isolating their queen on Symbios, and the media deemed a Terravore assault on south London as something of a "Japanese Toy Robot Terror". Afterwards, Brewster departed with the Doctor and Evelyn.

2011 - THE FORBIDDEN TIME[1075] -> The entire population of Earth heard a prerecorded message that the Vist had encoded into space-time, but most interpreted this as a dream or hallucination. Polly Wright addressed a gathering of esteemed people - many of whom knew of the

1065 Dating *Serpent Crest: Tsar Wars* and *Aladdin Time* (BBC fourth Doctor audios #3.1, #3.3) - The story picks up directly after the robots charged into Nest Cottage on Christmas Eve, at the end of *Demon Quest: Sepulchre*.
1066 Events in 2011 include *The Sarah Jane Adventures* Series 5, many (but not all) of the "present day" sequences of *Doctor Who* Series 6, and *Torchwood* Series 4 (a.k.a. *TW: Miracle Day*).
1067 *Fear Her.* Chloe's father died the previous year.
1068 *No Man's Land*
1069 *TW: Miracle Day.* This is presumably part of the Three Families' efforts to exploit the Miracle.
1070 *A Good Man Goes to War.* Wonder had his first hit, age 13, in 1963. The Doctor could have recruited him at any point in the many decades to come; linking it to the present day seems reasonable.
1071 *Dalek*
1072 *Benny: Another Girl, Another Planet*
1073 *Relative Dimensions.* The year isn't stated, but the idea seems to be that Lucie is back her home turf, so it's probably the January after she started travelling with the Monk. The Doctor uses a debit card linked to an account with his "untouched" UNIT salary, further sug-

gesting that it's the modern day.
1074 Dating *The Crimes of Thomas Brewster* (BF #143) - The story seems contemporary and was released in January 2011; Evelyn concurs with this at the start of *The Feast of Axos*, claiming that *The Crimes of Thomas Brewster* took place in "2011". However, in *Tales from the Vault* - seemingly set in 2011 - Captain Ruth Matheson says the Terravore incident was "last year". Patricia Menzies mentions meeting the Doctor "a couple of years ago", and while she could be referring to *The Condemned* (set in February 2008), it's more likely she means *The Raincloud Man* (set in December 2008), so she could be rounding up a little.
1075 Dating *The Forbidden Time* (BF CC #5.9) - The Doctor tells Polly that the Vist seek to capture an eight-year span of time from "2011 to 2019", and the Vist's message is presumably triggered at the start of it - also in accordance with the audio coming out in 2011.
1076 Dating "Ripper's Curse" (IDW *DW* Vol. 2 #2-4) - The date is given in a caption. Amy and Rory are married, but there's no indication that Amy is pregnant, suggesting that this is part of the adventures they experience between *A Christmas Carol* and their returning to

402

Doctor - to relate her encounter with the Vist, and assure that they posed no further danger.

> **(=) 2011 - "Ripper's Curse"**[1076] **->** The eleventh Doctor and Rory arrived in Whitechapel from 1888 to check what if any historical alteration had occurred concerning the Jack the Ripper murders. A tour guide told them that the list of suspected Ripper victims included "Amelia Marple" - the name Amy had been using in 1888. They returned to 1888 and prevented Amy's death.

2011 - JAGO & LITEFOOT: SWAN SONG[1077] **->** Elliot Payne arrived from the future and undertook temporal experiments that he hoped would save his wife. A temporal link was forged between Payne's laboratory and the New Regency Theatre - which stood adjacent to the same site - in the 1890s. Time breaches occurred, and the collective emotions of all the performances given in the theatre coalesced into an intelligence that nestled within Payne's assistant Alice. The two of them sacrificed themselves to destroy Payne's equipment before it could destroy the world, and their consciousnesses transferred into what stone that remained from the theatre. Nonetheless, Payne travelled back to the 1890s to continue his plans.

c 2011 - THE SENTINELS OF THE NEW DAWN[1078] **->** Lt. Ed Grueber of UNIT, secretly an agent of the Sentinels of the New Dawn, gained valuable intelligence from Liz Shaw about historically nullified events in 2014.

c 2011 - FERRIL'S FOLLY[1079] **->** Millicent Drake - a thrall of the Cronquist - had married Sir Hector Ferril, and upon his death renovated his estate and observatory in Norfolk.

Ferril attempted to bring a Cronquist invasion force to Earth via a star alignment that occurred once every five thousand years, but the fourth Doctor and Romana dispersed the Key to Time segment that was crucial to Ferril's equipment. The invasion force and Ferril were dissipated into a thin layer of matter, and the Doctor and Romana went to retrieve the segment from the planet Tara.

c 2011 - TALES FROM THE VAULT[1080] **->** Captain Ruth Matheson, the Curator of UNIT's Vault, recruited Warrant Officer Charlie Sato of UNIT's Skywatch division to serve as her assistant. The mind of Kalicarache, still in the jacket of Tommy Watkins, possessed Sato and hoped to leave Earth by using the Vault's technology. Matheson drained Kalicarache's mind into the alien crystal containing a copy of Zoe Herriot's memories, then smashed it.

c 2011 - HEART OF STONE[1081] **->** The silicon-based lifeforms in the Pron-Kalunka galaxy used granite as the base matter for all their technology.

Scientists at the Henson Research Centre conducted experiments on moon rock samples in preparation for NASA's next moon landings. A moon rock was bathed in ultraviolet light, which activated the alien bacteria it contained. The TARDIS arrived in a pigsty on Conway Farm in England after the bacteria had birthed a new form of life - an animated rock man named Athrocite, who could have triggered a molecular wave that would turn everything on Earth's surface into moon rock. The eleventh Doctor, Amy and Rory returned the bacteria's original rock to the moon, cancelling its effects and turning Athrocite to dust.

c 2011 - THE WITCH FROM THE WELL[1082] **->** Workman unsealed the well into which the energy echo of the Agnes

---

Leadworth prior to *The Impossible Astronaut.*

1077 Dating *Jago & Litefoot: Swan Song* (J&L #3.3) - The setting seems contemporary; *J&L: Chronoclasm* specifies the year as "2011". Very strangely, Payne at one point says that in Victorian times, the New Regency was located adjacent to where his laboratory will be in "several thousand years". (This can't mean Earth in the future, as Payne isn't human and conducted his work near a black star.) No mention is made of the Miracle from *TW: Miracle Day*, so events in this story likely resolve beforehand.

1078 Dating *The Sentinels of the New Dawn* (BF CC #5.10) - This framing sequence is probably contemporary with the audio's release in 2011.

1079 Dating *Ferril's Folly* (BF CC 5.11) - The audio was released in May 2011, and the blurb says it occurs on "Earth in the present day". There's little to support or rule against this, save that Millicent Ferril was a NASA astronaut fifteen years ago.

1080 Dating *Tales from the Vault* (BF CC 6.1) - The audio came out in July 2011. Sato remarks that some items in the Vault have labels such as "Do not open until the year 2011", and the revived Kalicarache says, "What year is this... 2011". It's "about ten years" after the story's 2002 component. Mucking things up slightly is that Matheson says the Terravore incident in *The Crimes of Thomas Brewster* was "last year" (see the dating notes on that story).

1081 Dating *Heart of Stone* (BBC children's 2-in-1 #2) - The story seems contemporary, especially in its allusions to NASA, and was released in 2011. For the Doctor, Amy and Rory, it appears to occur during their travels together between Series 5 and 6.

1082 Dating *The Witch from the Well* (BF #154) - It's "twenty-first century Earth", and "three and a half centuries" since the witch scare at Tranchard's Fell in the seventeenth century. Without any other evidence, the story is probably contemporary with its release in 2011.

Bates-monster was trapped in the seventeenth century. Finicia and Lucern - secretly alien Varaxils who outwardly looked 17 - approached the eighth Doctor and Mary Shelley for help, claiming the monster had killed their father. The four of them went back in time to learn the creature's origins.

Finicia and Lucern stranded the Doctor in the past, and returned with Mary in the TARDIS. They located the Witch Star that the descendents of Squire Portillon had kept safe, and tried to siphon the monster's Odic energy. The resultant blast killed the Varaxils and dissipated the creature. Mary learned the historical fate of her associate, George Gordon Byron, from the man's great nephew. She then used the Fast Return Switch to retrieve the Doctor.

c 2011 (a Sunday) - "Down to Earth"[1083] **->** The eleventh Doctor visited the Tylonian commander Lum-Tee, who had settled into a cosy life in an English village as "Harold Lumley". The Doctor judged that Lum-Tee was quite at home on Earth, and enabled him to have one last joy ride in his Class II Trylonian Star Fighter.

(=) 2011 - "Do Not Go Gentle Into that Good Night"[1084] **->** A Vorlax Regeneration Drone, built to transfer the minds of fallen soldiers into clone bodies, was brought back to 2011 from 4688 by the time-child Chiyoko. It continued its programming at the Hawkshaw Manor nursing home, shifting the minds of deceased residents into artificially made children's bodies. The eleventh Doctor and Amy transported the Drone and its charges to peacefully live on an uninhabited garden planet.

The TARDIS absorbed the old-woman-turned-young-girl Margaret into its matrix. She became one of the components that would - in a history that was later nullified - create Chiyoko.[1085]

The eleventh Doctor dropped the now-married Amy and Rory off in Leadworth. They wouldn't see him for two months.[1086] Amy was replaced with a Ganger version of herself by Madame Kovarian.[1087]

1083 Dating "Down to Earth" (IDW *DW Annual 2011*) - The setting appears contemporary. A World War II fighter plane is considered "old", but not so old that it's unlikely that it could still fly.

1084 Dating "Do Not Go Gentle Into That Good Night" (*DWM* #432) - The year is given, and repeated in "The Child of Time" (*DWM*).

1085 "The Child of Time" (*DWM*). One of the downsides of Chiyoko cancelling out her own existence is that the Hawkshaw residents are, presumably, made to remain on Earth as senior citizens.

1086 Amy and Rory first part company with the Doctor at some point after *A Christmas Carol*, and it's "two months" before they see him again in *The Impossible Astronaut*.

1087 As revealled in *The Almost People*. It's not clear when Amy's abduction/replacement happens, but it's far more likely to have happened when she and Rory are living on Earth and away from the Doctor's protection (so, between *A Christmas Carol* and *The Impossible Astronaut*). It's alternatively possible that the switch happened in the three months between *The Impossible Astronaut* and *Day of the Moon* in 1969, but that would more awkwardly require the Silence to be nipping in and out of their own timeline, when (setting aside that River does this sort of thing all the time) there's no evidence otherwise that they're doing so.

1088 Dating *SJA: Sky* (SJA 5.1) - The Sarah Jane Adventures Series 5 was broadcast from 3rd to 18th October, 2011, but what few dating clues are provided suggests that it actually takes place sooner than that, in spring of the same year. As *SJA: The Curse of Clyde Langer* appears to occur in early April (see the dating notes on that story), and also says that Sky came to

Earth (in *Sky*) "barely a month" beforehand, *Sky* itself must take place in early March. Supporting that time-frame, Rani's mum says in *Sky* that Rani is "17" - we know from cross-referencing *SJA: Secrets of the Stars* and *SJA: Lost in Time* that Rani is an Aries born in 1993, so if she's still 17, then *Sky* cannot occur any later than the second-to-last day of Aries, 19th April. (If it were 20th April, and Rani's birthday were the same day, Gita would almost certainly have mentioned it instead of just saying, "She's 17") The scenery isn't entirely in keeping with early March - the trees have leaves, and Sky is amazed at all the green plants (flowers included) growing in Sarah's driveway - but otherwise it's not so warm and sunny as to evoke the onset of summer. In fact, it's noticeably windy and overcast.

Myers' name is spelled "the alien way", but we're never told what that means, exactly, so it's rendered here as it appears in the credits.

1089 Dating *SJA: The Curse of Clyde Langer* (SJA 5.2) - Sarah is reading *The Ealing Echo* as Clyde visits her the morning after the curse on him activates, and while the newspaper's dateline is unreadable, the top headline on the back page - presumably the sports section - says "... For Cricket's First Day". The 2011 English cricket season commenced on 2nd April (a mid to late April start is typical, but the seasons began much earlier than the norm in 2010 and 2011). That fits very well with *SJA: Sky* not being able to occur later than the end of Aries (20th April; see the dating notes on that story), and Sarah Jane's statement in *The Curse of Clyde Langer* that "barely a month" has passed since *Sky*.

The passage of time within *The Curse of Clyde Langer*, however, is a bit trickier to pin down. At first blush, it would appear that a total of two nights and three days

The Sarah Jane Adventures Series 5

2011 (a Sunday in early March) - SJA: SKY[1088] -> Miss Myers, one of the Fleshkind in the Tornado Nebula, bioengineered a synthetic lifeform: a baby girl that upon activation would release an energy pulse that would destroy the Fleshkind's enemies, the Metalkind. The Shopkeeper and Captain, in their roles as "servants of the Universe", stole Myers' child and left her on Sarah Jane's doorstep. The baby - which Sarah hurriedly named "Sky" - primed itself enough to instantly grow into the form of a 12-year-old girl. Myers attempted to lure the Metalkind to Earth and force Sarah to trigger Sky, but Sarah and her friends defeated her. Sky's genetic potential as a weapon was deactivated, and a Metalkind forcibly took Myers back to its homeworld. Afterwards, Sarah adopted Sky as her daughter.

2011 (first week of April) - SJA: THE CURSE OF CLYDE LANGER[1089] -> Clyde Langer was now in sixth form.

The totem containing the spirit of Hetocumtek was found in a cave in Death Valley, and became part of an exhibit of totem poles at the Museum of Culture in London. Sarah, Clyde, Rani and Sky investigated the totem pole as the possible cause of a storm of full-sized fish that rained upon Ealing. Hetocumtek's full revival was triggered when Clyde got a splinter from the totem pole in his finger - Clyde's name became the key to Hetocumtek freeing himself, but this left Clyde cursed. Everyone who heard his name ostracised him, and he soon became homeless. Sarah and Rani broke the curse by summoning enough willpower to say Clyde's name aloud, and brought Clyde to stop Hetocumtek from getting free. Hetocumtek's totem pole vanished, and was possibly destroyed. Clyde's only friend during his exile, a homeless woman with the alias Ellie Faber, thought he'd abandoned her and left town.

2011 (Sunday, 15th May) - SJA: THE MAN WHO NEVER WAS[1090] -> Sarah Jane was now regarded as one of the top three journalists in the country - as was Lionel Carson, her former editor. While K9 remained at Oxford to back up the Bodleian Library, Luke Smith visited Sarah Jane - and met his "sister" Sky - just as Serf Systems readied to debut the SerfBoard, a device touted as "the world's newest and best portable computer". The holographic image of the late Joseph Serf, as projected from equipment manipulated by the enslaved cyclopses from Scultos - had a hypnotic quality. Through this, the scheming John Harrison hoped to make billions by mesmerising the public into loving the SerfBoard when it was really quite rubbish. Sarah Jane, Clyde, Rani, Luke and Sky ended Harrison's plan, and summoned a rescue ship from Scultos to take the liberated Scullions back home.

2011 - SJA: CHILDREN OF STEEL[1091] -> Sarah Jane won at auction the head of Adam, Sir Joseph Montague's Difference Golem, and found its body at Montague's former estate, Holcote House. Reactivated, Adam created

---

(the first and last of which are school days) elapse, but Ellie's comment to Clyde at the start of episode two - that she first saw him "the other day" (back when he first visited the museum, after the rain of fish) - might suggest that more time than that passes. If so, and presuming for the moment that Sarah is seen reading (for whatever reason) an older edition of *The Ealing Echo*, a framework for this story can be derived... the rain of fish happens on 1st April, and Sarah and her friends visit the Museum (leading to Clyde getting the splinter) on the same day; the 2nd April edition of *The Ealing Echo* leads with the story "Fish Flingers" and also contains a *preview* (not an after-the-fact account) of "Cricket's First Day"; the curse on Clyde's name fully activates the night of 3rd April, when he signs his name to some artwork (this means that a day passes between the scenes of Clyde and his mother settling down to dinner and him going to bed, which isn't intuitive but works); Clyde is ostracised after visiting Sarah the morning of 4th April, when she's going through some articles from the 2nd April *Ealing Echo* (possibly just because she failed to read it over the weekend); night passes

between episodes one and two, and events conclude no earlier than 5th April. (Possibly even later than that, depending on how long Clyde is forced to live on the streets.)

1090 Dating *SJA: The Man Who Never Was* (SJA 5.3) - There's no indication of how much time has passed since *SJA: The Curse of Clyde Langer*. The SerfBoard launch date is given as "the 15th"; as it's not a school day and 15th April was a Friday in 2011, the best fit (if the real-world calendar holds any sway here) is Sunday, 15th May. It's also a bit symmetrical to think that *The Man Who Never Was* takes place at the end of the school year - this could in fact be the reason why Luke is home from Oxford, although it isn't said.

1091 Dating *SJA: Children of Steel* and *SJA: Judgement Day* (SJA audios #9-10) - The final (to date) *Sarah Jane Adventures* audios occur at some unspecified point after Sky's introduction (*SJA: Sky*). The audios were released after Series 5 had finished broadcasting, so it's entirely possible that they follow on from the final TV story, *SJA: The Man Who Never Was*. Both of the audios occur on a Saturday, and so must take place at least a

robotic offspring to fulfill Montague's wish that humanity be freed from servitude. A synthetic female operative arrived from the future, warned that Adam's actions would pollute the timelines and - with his permission - removed the future-tech probe that enabled his mental function, deactivating him and his children.

2011 - SJA: JUDGEMENT DAY[1091] -> The truth-seeking Veritas arrived on Earth in pursuit of Xando, an alien passing as a stage magician. Xando created an illusion of flame beings to distract the Veritas' spheres as they searched the White Cross Mall near West London, frightening hundreds. The Veritas identified Sarah Jane as a perpetrator of fabrications and cover stories, but she convinced the Veritas to save Sky from a mob, and taught them that the truth could sometimes harm innocents. The Veritas agreed, and Xando departed.

Lake Silencio

2011 (22nd April) - THE IMPOSSIBLE ASTRONAUT[1092] ->

"By Silencio Lake, on the Plain of Sighs, an Impossible Astronaut will rise from the deep and strike the Time Lord dead."[1093]

The eleventh Doctor, age 1103, had learned that he was historically fated to die at Lake Silencio in Utah on 22nd April, 2011. He sent invitations to Amy and Rory (who were back to living in Leadworth), River Song and the elderly Canton Delaware III to meet him there. As the Silence had planned, a younger version of River Song rose from Lake Silencio in a NASA astronaut suit and killed the Doctor - she shot him twice; the second time, fatally, in the middle of his regeneration. The River who killed the Doctor left, and the Doctor's friends give him a Viking funeral, cremating his body to prevent it falling into the wrong hands. Canton Delaware also departed, and the Doctor's friends met the fourth person he had invited to his murder... himself, age 909. Acting on the older Doctor's instructions, Amy, Rory and River had the 909-year-old Doctor take them back to 1969. This was the first of a series of adventures in which they fought the Silence and their ally, Madame Kovarian, all in the knowledge that the Doctor was destined to die.

(=) 2011 (22nd April) - THE WEDDING OF RIVER SONG[1094] -> The eleventh Doctor was apparently resigned to his fate at Lake Silencio, but River Song refused to play along... she emptied her weaponry, saving his life but undoing the

---

week apart. *Judgement Day* provides further evidence that Series 5 occurs earlier in the year than when it aired (in October 2011) - Sarah is said to "step out of the house, and into the spring sunshine", and it's established that *SJA: Judgement of the Judoon* was "many months ago", *SJA: Vault of Secrets* (set circa October 2010) was "a few months ago". One oddity - because there hasn't been quite enough done to confuse the issue of when the humanity learns about the existence of extra-terrestrials, oh no - is that Sarah Jane wins over the Veritas partly by convincing them that humanity is "not ready for the truth" that aliens are real, in defiance of the public *surely* having figured it out by now.

1092 Dating *The Impossible Astronaut* (X6.1) - River Song gives the year as "2011". Amy and Rory's invite instructs them to meet the Doctor on "22/4/2011"; it's possible they receive the invite before that exact day, allowing time for them to travel by conventional means from Leadworth to Utah. The specific date of the Doctor's death is also given as 22/4/2011 in *Let's Kill Hitler*, *Night Terrors*, *Closing Time* and *The Wedding of River Song*, and is doubtless meant to roughly parallel the broadcast of *The Impossible Astronaut* on 23rd April of that year.

1093 *Closing Time*

1094 Dating *The Wedding of River Song* (X6.13) - The bulk of the action of this story takes place in one instant: 5.02.57pm on 22nd April, 2011.

1095 Between *A Good Man Goes to War* and *Let's Kill Hitler*. Amy and Rory have not yet experienced events in *The Wedding of River Song*.

1096 *Serpent Crest: The Hexford Invasion*. Easter was on 24th April in 2011.

1097 "Almost a year" and, later, "over a year" earlier than *The Shadows of Avalon*.

1098 Dating *Serpent Crest: The Hexford Invasion* (BBC fourth Doctor audio #3.4) - Mrs Wibbsey's narration says that the story begins on "a Thursday in August", "nearly nine months" after the Doctor returned her to Hexford in *Serpent Crest: Aladdin Time*. The faux second Doctor putters about Hexford for "just over a fortnight" before the fourth Doctor returns "on Friday afternoon". The Hexford residents spend three months in their personal timeline in the far future, but Hexford presumably returns to Earth the moment after it left - Captain Yates swears the townsfolk to secrecy about everything they've witnessed, and that would be a great deal harder, given the inevitable media attention, had Hexford vanished overnight only to return three months later.

1099 *Serpent Crest: Survivors in Space*

1100 Dating *Let's Kill Hitler* (X6.8) - The Doctor has had "all summer" to look for baby Melody.

1101 Dating *Night Terrors* (X6.9) - Alex, while admittedly not knowing his son's true origins, believes that George was born "a couple of weeks" after "24/12/2002"

fixed point in time that was meant to see him die.

All of history happened simultaneously on the exact moment of the Doctor's intended death, at 5:02 pm on 22nd April. London became a chaotic landscape of steam trains, Roman chariots and pterodactyls. The War of the Roses entered its second year, and Charles Dickens appeared on Breakfast TV. The Holy Roman Emperor Winston Churchill returned to the Buckingham Senate on his personal mammoth, after having argued with Cleopatra ("a dreadful woman, but an excellent dancer"). Churchill's soothsayer, the Doctor, was kept imprisoned in the Tower of London.

The Doctor was rescued by Amy, who in this reality worked for a military organisation. She took him to Area 52, a military base kept in an Egyptian pyramid, where Madame Kovarian and over a hundred of the Silence were being held captive. River Song met the Doctor at Area 52, but the Silence were merely playing possum - they broke free, attacking their captors. Amy left Kovarian behind to die.

The Doctor believed that River was fated to become either the woman who married or killed him... so he married her, and secretly told her that his body was actually a shapeshifting spaceship, the *Teselecta*, made to look like him. The Doctor kissed River, starting time again and returning them to Lake Silencio. When River shot the Doctor this time, she actually struck the impervious *Teselecta*, thwarting the fixed point.

After the Battle of Demon's Run, River Song returned Amy and Rory to their native time. The two of them waited all summer for the Doctor to bring word of their missing infant daughter Melody.[1095]

Mrs Wibbsey danced the can-can during the Hexford Easter parade.[1096] In late July 2011, Lethbridge-Stewart's wife Doris was killed in a yachting accident.[1097]

2011 (August) - SERPENT CREST: THE HEXFORD INVASION[1098] -> The Skishtari longed for the gene egg that the fourth Doctor had hidden, in 1861, under what would become Nest Cottage. They created a clone of the second Doctor, who tricked UNIT into helping him grow biomesh trees - biomechanoids with metal roots. Captain Yates was brought out of retirement to help. The faux Doctor took up residence at Nest Cottage while the fourth Doctor was away, and spent two weeks planting the trees all around Hexford. The fourth Doctor returned just as a shrouded Skishtari spaceship linked energy beams with the trees and hauled up the entire village, hoping to find the egg underneath. The genuine Doctor tried to counteract this by having the TARDIS generate a gravity bubble,

but the resultant tug-of-war triggered the Skishtari wormhole that had been dormant since 1861, sending the whole village of Hexford into the far future. The fourth Doctor and Wibbsey collected the Skishtari egg, then followed in the TARDIS...

The clone second Doctor and the fourth Doctor combined efforts to return Hexford to its proper location. Yates decided to stay in Hexford for a time, and the fourth Doctor bid Wibbsey farewell, leaving for parts unknown. The second Doctor was a type of clone with a very limited lifespan, and it was expected that he would just fade away in a matter of months.[1099]

2011 (end of summer) - LET'S KILL HITLER[1100] -> The Doctor failed to answer Amy and Rory's phone calls, so they created a huge crop circle that read "DOCTOR" and was featured in the *Leadworth Chronicle*. He saw the photo and joined them. Amy and Rory's childhood friend, Mels, was on the run from the police and pulled a gun on the Doctor, ordering that they go back in time and kill Hitler. The Doctor took Amy, Rory and Mels back to 1938... after resolving matters there, Amy and Rory continued travelling with the Doctor.

2011 - NIGHT TERRORS[1101] -> The Tenza were birthed in space, then adapted their form in order to find a nest; they were effectively space cuckoos. One such Tenza transformed itself into George, the eight-year-old son of a young couple named Alex and Claire, and altered their memories so they would accept him. George feared rejection, and his psionic abilities trapped people in the place that symbolised where he put "bad things": the doll's house in his cupboard. The eleventh Doctor, Amy and Rory became trapped in the doll's house prison, and were threatened by living dolls. Alex's love for his son calmed his fears, and normality was restored.

2011 (7th-14th October) - TOUCHED BY AN ANGEL[1102] -> Mark Whitaker, a widower following his wife's death in 2003, was now a partner at the law firm of Pollard, Boyce & Whitaker. On 7th October, he received an archived set of instructions... that was written in his own handwriting, and which detailed tasks Mark had to perform throughout 1994 and 2001. The only Weeping Angel that had survived the eleventh Doctor's trap in 2003 used the very last of its energy to send Mark back to 1994.

The eleventh Doctor, Amy and Rory identified Mark as a curious blip in the space-time continuum, and followed him to that year. After many cross-time shenanigans, the travellers returned Mark to 2011. He had physically become a 37 year old again following events in 1993, and decided to move on with his life - hopefully by starting a new relationship.

2011 (late October) - THE WAY THROUGH THE WOODS[1103] -> The eleventh Doctor, Amy and Rory found that journalist Jess Ashcroft was the latest of hundreds of people who had gone missing in Swallow Woods throughout the millennia. They identified the semi-sentient spaceship of Reyn the were-fox as being responsible for the disappearances, and ended the spatio-temporal anomalies the ship had extruded into the Woods. This retroactively returned everyone the ship had captured. History would record that only three of the abductees - Jess, Laura Brown and Emily Bostock (a barmaid from 1917) - had gone missing, as they opted to travel with the liberated ship.

The Long War was now over, and Reyn returned to his devastated homeworld to fulfill upon the legend of the Traveller: a figure who would restore the lost technology of how to make spaceships semi-sentient.

Torchwood Series 4 (Miracle Day)

2011 - TW: MIRACLE DAY[1104] **-> The world's population now exceeded 6,928,198,000. In Cardiff Bay, the water tower had been rebuilt since the Hub's destruction. Rendition of UK citizens to US custody was permitted under the 456 Amendments to US Code 3184.**

The Three Families initiated their plan to destroy the world economy in order to rebuild and take control of it. The Families seeded the blood of an immortal, Jack Harkness, into the Blessing in Singapore and Buenos Aires simultaneously, causing the Blessing to

---

(the time-stamp on a photograph), and that George "just turned eight" in January. So, it's now 2011. Alex's landlord says that *Bergerac* (1981-1991) is "thirty years old". There's a day planner on the wall of George's bedroom, but nothing helpful can be discerned from it.

1102 Dating *Touched by an Angel* (NSA #47) - The exact days are given (pgs 13, 235). The Doctor and Amy make an initial visit to 1994, thinking they'll return the moment they left, but instead come back a week later (p43). In the interim, Rory stays in Mark's flat, and pops up to Leadworth to collect the post (p44).

1103 Dating *The Way Through the Woods* (NSA #45) - The book was released in 2011, and keeps making reference to "England, now" - which appears to be simultaneous to "late October" (p10).

1104 Dating *TW: Miracle Day* (TW 4.1-4.10) - No year, day, month or time of year is expressly stated.

The incidental evidence suggests that the year is 2011, the same as the story's broadcast. Events in 1928 are variously generalised as having occurred "eighty years" and "nine decades" ago; evidence pertaining to a murder in 1927 has been archived for "almost ninety years". The back of the Overflow Camp Heath Care Provider Framework: Standards and Guidelines folder that Gwen is given (in episode five) says "Copyright 2011". Oswald Danes says (episode two) he spent "six years" in solitary confinement - he was convicted in 2006, but it's very likely, for a crime of his magnitude, that he was held without bond for some time beforehand. An investigative report on Jack that Esther pulls from sealed CIA archive boxes (episode one) is dated 21st December, 2010. The CIA's intelligence (episode one) says that there's been "no sightings" of Gwen "for the last twelve months" - which isn't to say that Gwen didn't go underground some time before that (after *TW: Children of Earth*). Each episode begins with a rising population counter that starts at 6,928,198,000(ish) - in the real world, the Population Division of the United Nations declared the "Day of 7 Billion" (the day desig-

nated as Earth's population achieving that amount) as 31st October, 2011, although the Miracle might have made the population crest over the seven billion mark somewhat sooner. In *The End of Time* (TV), set prior to the Miracle at Christmas 2010, the population of Earth was given as 6,727,949,388.

Gwen's daughter Anwen, born in or near early May 2010, looks much more like a one year old than a two year old. Both Rex's mobile (episode two) and the phone logs on Charlotte Wills (episode ten) - although not entirely reliable for reasons discussed below - display the year as "2011". Overall, and barring some new finding coming to light, 2011 seems like a safe bet.

The biggest challenge with *Miracle Day*, then, is finding a portion of 2011 in which it can occur without coming into conflict with *Doctor Who* Series 6 and *The Sarah Jane Adventures* Series 5 - neither of which make any mention, or display any sign, of either the Miracle or its massive impact upon global society. Three pieces of evidence - all of which must be discounted for continuity reasons - go directly to this question: a) in a scene set a few days after the Miracle begins, Rex's secondary mobile gives the date as "22-MAR-11" (episode two), b) also a few days following the Miracle's start, Oprah Winfrey wants Oswald Danes as a guest on her show, which in the real world took a bow on 25th May, 2011 (episode two), and c) a CIA trace on the phone records of Charlotte Wills (in episode ten, so after the two month gap between eps eight and nine) says the last use of her mobile occurred on "2011.09.09".

The first two pieces of evidence are fairly easy to set aside... Rex is talking to Esther on what's presumably his CIA-issue mobile, so perhaps his secondary mobile is a disposable unit he hurriedly picked up for personal use, and the date isn't set right. Also, if anything could coax Oprah into bringing her show back (presuming that she ever ended it in the *Doctor Who* universe), the Miracle would be it. Charlotte's phone records, admittedly, are much more difficult to overlook, as they're

accept the blood as a new template and transmit some of its properties through humanity's morphic field.

On a Sunday night at 11:36 pm, Eastern US time, in what became known as the Miracle, death instantly vanished from Earth. People became so *alive* that they continued to function despite hideous injuries - not even decapitation could entirely kill someone. Some people had conditions that left them brain dead, their bodies denied the release of death. The child killer Oswald Danes was executed in Jacksonville, Kentucky - but the Miracle kept Danes alive, and the state governor was forced to set him free.

In spite of the Miracle, humanity continued aging as normal, suggesting that everyone would eventually become an undying, aged husk. The 50% of pregnancies that would naturally have aborted didn't, making genetic mistakes viable. As murder was no longer possible, many murder prosecutions were reduced to assault charges. The need for painkillers skyrocketed, and a bill introduced in the US Congress made all prescription drugs, painkillers and antibiotics available without a prescription - a windfall for the pharmaceutical companies.

Jack Harkness had returned to Earth, and the inversion of the Blessing meant that he had became mortal. His blood endangered the Families' plan, and so they

produced by advanced CIA spyware.

It's entirely possible that the production team meant for Rex and Charlotte's mobile dates to denote that six months pass during *Miracle Day* from start to finish - or it could equally be the case that they weren't paying attention to such things. (This is the same production team, after all, that allowed an email to Esther in episode two to read as if it were written by a Dadaist poet: "Ballistics wants report on top of the shade. The flower commands ballistics. The curtain outweighs ballistics. How will the welcome quiz ascend below report? Inside ballistics weds deterrent. Should ballistics stem report? The incidental river pops after report. Report rubs ballistics.") Whatever the intent, however, the phone records cannot be treated with absolute sanctity because...

While the time that elapses within the ten *Miracle Day* episodes is reasonably indeterminate, a non-negotiable gap of two months occurs between episodes eight and nine, and the first eight episodes appear to span a few weeks if not more. (The Torchwood team seems to conduct its investigations at a relatively quick pace, and some developments - such as the construction of the concentration camps - were undoubtedly hastened by the Three Families planning so far in advance of the Miracle; "weeks" passing seems to fit the bill better than "months".) There's wiggle room, but it must take a bare minimum of three months, roughly speaking, for *Miracle Day* to play itself out. (One side note: The prediction in episode one that Earth will exhaust its resources in four months probably doesn't need to be taken literally, as it's never mentioned again, and - as appalling as it is to point out - the mathematical models would change once the incineration units start reducing the number of Category 1 cases.)

When, then, do these three months (if not longer) occur in 2011? Some commentators determined from Rex's mobile date that the Miracle began in March 2011, and made some heroic efforts to explain how and why Amy and Rory might already be experiencing it when the Doctor summons them to Utah on 22nd April (in *The Impossible Astronaut*). It is simply beyond

the pale, however, to think that Amy and Rory would be reunited with their best friend - an adventurer in time and space with a penchant for solving cosmic problems - and not once ask him to address the issue that people can no longer die, that concentration camps are sprouting up all over the place, and that the world governments are feeding civil liberties into a paper shredder. It is doubly beyond the pale, in fact, to think that they would not once express bewilderment as to how the Doctor can be shot dead on the beach in a world without death, or at the very least scream at the grave injustice of it all. Thinking that such statements were made off screen seems like wishful thinking, and once it's factored in that *The Sarah Jane Adventures* Series 5 runs throughout spring 2011 without a single hint of the Miracle happening, any scenario in which the Miracle coincides with these episodes becomes nigh-impossible.

Could, then, the Miracle initiate in early summer 2011, be in play when Amy and Rory reunite with the Doctor in *Let's Kill Hitler*, and conclude in accordance with Charlotte's mobile records in September? Again, this is exceedingly unlikely, even if it does have the benefit of roughly pegging *Miracle Day* to its weeks of broadcast. As before, it's asking too much to believe that Amy and Rory would not once direct the Doctor's attention to the Miracle and the horrific suffering it has inflicted upon millions worldwide. It's also a little silly that, with all the guns being pointed about in *Let's Kill Hitler*, Amy and Rory don't wonder if the Miracle is still in play on their bodies now that they've relocated to another time zone.

The *most* likely scenario, then, for *Miracle Day* - albeit one that requires wilfully ignoring Charlotte's phone log - is that the Miracle initiates after Amy and Rory leave with the Doctor in *Let's Kill Hitler*, plays out in autumn 2011 and concludes before end of year. While hardly a perfect solution, this avoids all major continuity clashes in a world where *Doctor Who*, *The Sarah Jane Adventures* and *Torchwood* manifestly co-exist (the ties between the three shows are simply too strong to think otherwise). Such a solution leaves two *Doctor*

initiated an online virus to search out references of Torchwood, hoping to flush Jack into the open. Jack used malware to eliminate each and every digital mention of Torchwood, and the word itself ceased to exist online. Agents of the Families moved to discredit anyone with any knowledge of Torchwood, putting CIA agent Rex Matheson and CIA analyst Esther Dummond on the run. They were forced to join Jack and Gwen Cooper as the remnants of Torchwood.

2011 - TW: WEB OF LIES[1105] -> Miles Mokri, a conspiracy blogger, uncovered many details pertaining to the Miracle and was rendered silent when assassins shot him. Miles' sister Holly and FBI agent Joe Bradley combed through Miles' evidence and became convinced that a shadow group was trying to control the world through the Miracle. They found and destroyed the Three Families' back-up supply of Jack's blood, which was hidden at Coney Island.

2011 - TW: MIRACLE DAY[1104] -> The nations of Earth struggled to adjust to a world without death... Somalia stopped fighting, but North Korea mobilised its army at its southern border, as many of its soldiers thought themselves immortal. The Prime Minister of India announced a desire to reconcile with Pakistan - with reincarnation was no longer an option, the one life accorded to each human seemed too precious to waste on fighting. Some projections held that as the three hundred thousand people who died on average each day were still living, global resources would be exhausted in four months. Contraceptives were introduced to the water supply in India and mainland China. Hospices started closing down. The price of oil crossed a symbolic $100 a barrel amid fears over distribution in the Middle East.

Cultural movements emerged in response to the Miracle. People took to the streets as "the Soulless" - marchers wearing white masks with sad faces, and holding vigil candles, to denote that everlasting life had robbed mankind of its souls. Members of the suicide-minded 45 Club believed that jumping from the 45th floor or higher was the only guaranteed way to lose consciousness forever. Ellis Hartley Monroe, a darling of the Tea Party, started the Dead is Dead campaign, which advocated that the people who should have died should be treated as such. People in Egypt rioted against the "Western Miracle".

The world governments began to deal more decisively with the growing numbers of undead. Europe and the United States established categories for the classification of life... Category 3 designated a healthy person, Category 2 was a functioning person who had a persistent injury or illness, and Category 1 denoted someone without brain function, but whose body remained alive owing to the Miracle.

The United Kingdom, the United States, France, Germany and generally the whole of Europe established overflow camps for the undead. China declined to do so, but the Pan-African Summit opted in favour of it. Anyone designated Category 1 or 2 was taken to the camps - in the United States, this was sanctioned under the Emergency Miracle Law. The UK Prime Minister announced that the camps were part of a "new age of care and compassion".

Incineration units were secretly established in the camps to turn the Category 1 cases into ash; in the United Kingdom, the Emergency Rulings for the Sake of Public Heath allowed for the burning of dead bodies en masse. Torchwood exposed the truth about the incineration units, triggering headlines such as "Horror of Death Camps in the 21st Century", and also released a video showing the incineration of one of their associates, Dr. Vera Juarez. However, this merely

---

Who novels (*Touched by an Angel* and *The Way Through the Woods*) as outliers, as they have material dated to October 2011 that doesn't acknowledge the Miracle. But it's impossible to get through this process without a continuity clash somewhere, somehow.

Incidentally, trying to determine the time of year from the sun being up at 6 am in Kentucky (in the very first *Miracle Day* scene of all) proved to a fool's errand - it turns out that the sun is never up that early in Kentucky.

This chronology has avoided using the titles given to the individual *Miracle Day* episodes for publicity purposes, as these didn't appear in the episodes themselves and so aren't very intuitive. (Besides, with *Miracle Day* being a single story, using the individual titles rather than "episode one", etc., just tends to create need-

less confusion.) For anyone needing to cross-reference, the publicity titles (which also appear on the DVD menus) are: 4.1, *The New World*; 4.2 *Rendition*; 4.3, *Dead of Night*; 4.4, *Escape to L.A.*; 4.5, *The Categories of Life*; 4.6, *The Middle Men*; 4.7, *Immortal Sins*; 4.8, *End of the Road*; 4.9, *The Gathering*; 4.10, *The Blood Line*.

1105 Dating *TW: Web of Lies* (*TW* animated serial #1) - A caption says that it's "the present day". It's alternately said that Miles is shot "on Miracle Day"/the day *after* Miracle Day. While the action of this story only seems to take a day or so to unfold, it's evidently much longer than that, as mention is made of "people being burned" and the economy being on razor's edge.

1106 Gwen Cooper, *TW: Miracle Day*.

1107 *TW: Web of Lies*

paused the camps' operation. The White House ordered an investigation into Juarez's death, but made no apology for the Category 1 process. The footage of Juarez's murder received more than five million views online, and memorial services were held for her.

The US Supreme Court agreed to hear a case involving adjustments to the life sentences of convicted criminals. The US Congress considered the creation of Category Zero: a designation for anyone - including Oswald Danes - who had earned death by incineration for moral reasons. Phicorps facilitated Danes having a media career in which he advocated compassion in these difficult times, in a manner that boosted corporate profits. Madison Weekly attained some fame as the "bisected bride" - a car accident had sheered off her lower half, but she got married a week later while propped up on a box. Angelo Colasanto, having extended his lifespan by limiting his calorie intake and lowering his body temperature, used the Null Field from the Hub to cancel out the Miracle in a very small area and end his life.

The stock market collapsed, and the global economy went into freefall. Banks closed, and the Euro's weakness exacerbated the financial crisis. Greece and Ireland declared bankruptcy, and Spain's economy destabilised, threatening to pull down the whole European Union. Pension funds began going bankrupt, creating a domino effect. A new Great Depression was instigated. At the first sign of the economic meltdown, China withdrew from the United Nations and sealed its borders.

Two months into the new Great Depression, the White House halted all immigration into America. The insurance industry had largely gone bust, "along with half the Western World". The overflow camps built to dispose of Category 1 patients were in full operation - the Depression meant that the public was looking to its own welfare, and could offer little protest. Rationing was instituted. In the UK, the Emergency Powers Act allowed government agents to enter homes without a warrant in search of Category 1 patients. Violations of the Miracle Security Act were treated as treason. Some people in the US chose to classify themselves as Category 1, a means of assisted suicide.

Torchwood discovered how the Families had created the Miracle, and found the sites of the Blessing in Shanghai and Buenos Aires. Jack's mortal blood was fed into the Blessing at both locations, restoring the Blessing to its previous state.

"In a pit in old Shanghai, I brought death back to the world. They said it was like a breath, the breath that went around the whole wide world. The last breath, and then no more."[1106]

Everyone kept alive by the Miracle instantly died, including Gwen Cooper's father Geraint. Esther Drummond was killed in the final confrontation with the Families. Oswald Danes, having coerced Jack and Gwen into letting him accompany them to Shanghai, died while detonating the Families' facility there. The Three Families survived, still shrouded in secrecy, and judged the Miracle as a good trial run for their Plan B. UNIT sealed up the sites of the Blessing.

Rex Matheson found that - perhaps owing to his proximity to the Blessing when it recalibrated - he had become just as immortal as Captain Jack.

Miles Mokri recovered from his gunshot wounds. His sister Holly remained in possession of one last bag of Captain Jack's blood - a safeguard against Miles' injuries worsening and a resurgence of her cancer, which was in remission.[1107]

FUTURE HISTORY

Alistair Gryffen was born in Canada in 2012. By 2050, he would be perhaps the world's most brilliant scientist - an expert in robotics, cybernetics, weather control, time travel and alien technology.[1] In 2012, a special pound coin was minted for the London Olympics.[2]

c 2012 - THE GOD COMPLEX[3] -> Minotaur-like creatures - distant cousins of the Nimon - subsisted on the emotion of faith, and established themselves on various planets as gods. One such Minotaur was imprisoned in a space station that could transform its interior shape, and abducted beings with different belief systems to feed the prisoner.

The eleventh Doctor, Amy and Rory arrived in the station after it had shifted into the likeness of a 1980s hotel. The Minotaur longed to die, but instinctually kept killing the abductees - a gambler, Joe; a medical

student, Rita; and a blogger, Howie, all perished. Amy's faith in the Doctor attracted the Minotaur, but the Doctor broke her belief in him, which severed the emotional tether and killed the creature.

The Doctor realised that Amy and Rory's faith in him was dangerous, and that one or both of them would end up killed if they stayed with him. He set them up in London with a house and car, and took to travelling without them...

c 2012 (spring) - CLOSING TIME[4] -> Knowing he was about to die at Lake Silencio in Utah, the eleventh Doctor paid a social call on his friend Craig Owens - who now had a baby boy, Alfie, with his partner Sophie. The Doctor noticed electrical anomalies, and got himself a job at a department store where a number of employees had disappeared. They had been tele-

---

1 Gryffen is a regular character in the *K9* TV series. *K9: Taphony and the Time Loop* establishes the year of his birth.
2 *The Condemned*
3 Dating *The God Complex* (X6.11) - No year is stated, but there's no evidence that the station can abduct people through time, and the participants seem contemporary: mention is made of blogging, of the Internet, of the American CIA and of the Klingon language being the purview of geeks. Everyone's attire, Joe's horseshoe tie-tack included, is consistent with the modern day. The prison is made to look like a 1980s hotel, and, tellingly, Rita is familiar enough with such décor that it "takes her by surprise" to be trapped in it.

The Doctor returns Amy and Rory to Earth at a point between *Let's Kill Hitler* and *Closing Time*. The wild card here is to what degree he knows about the horrific events of *TW: Miracle Day* and - presuming he can't intervene in order to let history unfold as scheduled - whether he would deposit his best friends back on Earth in the thick of it. It seems reasonable to think that he drops Amy and Rory off after the worst consequences of the Miracle have come and gone; he might even drop them off in early 2012, after civilisation has recovered somewhat.
4 Dating *Closing Time* (X6.12) - The story unfolds over three days, ending on a Sunday (the Doctor: "Even with time travel, getting glaziers on a Sunday, tricky"), and is predicated on the idea that Sophie has gone away for the weekend and left Craig alone with Alfie. The time of year is indicated when the Doctor and Craig stand next to an advert for a "Spring Season" sales event. All well and good, but otherwise, this story's dating clues and continuity concerns make its placement very difficult.

The central question is whether, when the Doctor repeatedly says he will die "tomorrow" ("tomorrow is the day I [die]", "tomorrow I'm going to die", etc.), he

means it's *chronologically* tomorrow (i.e. 22nd April, 2011, as first mentioned in *The Impossible Astronaut*) or that it's tomorrow in his personal timestream. The latter seems more likely - as a time traveller, he could (and already has) spend years if not decades postponing his getting shot at Lake Silencio. It's only halfway through *The Wedding of River Song*, in fact, that he fully resigns himself to his fate and goes there.

The piece of evidence most in support of *Closing Time* literally occurring before 22nd April is a newspaper that Craig reads with the headline "Britain's Got Torment" - this appears to have been published two days before the story's end (at the very least, it's topical, with Nina the local girl being on *Britain's Got Talent*), and has the barely visible dateline of "19th April, 2011". This would mean, however, that the *Doctor Who* calendar is even more askew than normal... 22nd April was a Friday in 2011, so either the same day in the *Doctor Who* universe is actually a Monday (given that *Closing Time* ends on Sunday), or 22nd April *is* in synch with real life and is a Friday, meaning Tuesday through Thursday (when Sophie is gone) has somehow, someway, been re-designated as "the weekend". It's always regrettable to disregard a date blatantly given on screen, but it's probably fair to ignore it in this case.

Two elements support a dating for *Closing Time* of later than April 2011... the first is that the Doctor spies Amy and Rory from afar. In their timelines, this must happen after he dropped them off in *The God Complex* - not because Amy has a previously unmentioned modelling career (for all we're told, she could already be making a living that way in the two months before *The Impossible Astronaut*), but because the name of the fragrance she's advertising, "Petrichor" (meaning the smell of dust after rain), presumably derives from Amy and Rory learning about petrichor in *The Doctor's Wife*. Either way, Amy and Rory's presence helps to rule out

412

ported to a weakened Cyber-ship that had dispatched Cybermats to beam electricity back to it. From a distance, the Doctor saw Amy and Rory; Amy was currently appearing in an ad for Petrichor perfume, a scent "For the Girl Who's Tired of Waiting".

When the Cybermen attempted to convert Craig into their new Controller, his love for Alfie overloaded the circuits, destroying the Cybermen and their ship. The Doctor repaired the damage to Craig's house that a Cybermat had caused, and accepted Craig's gift of a Stetson. He also took some blue envelopes to send invites to his closest friends... and left to confront his fate at Lake Silencio.

c 2012 - THE WEDDING OF RIVER SONG[5] -> River Song visited Amy and Rory at their home, and told them how the Doctor had survived at Lake Silencio.

= Rose and her allies worked on a dimension cannon that would enable her to return home. The Daleks' gambit with a reality bomb weakened the dimensional walls, enabling the cannon to work. Rose returned to her native universe, and helped Donna resolve an errant timeline.[6]

= 2012 - JOURNEY'S END[7] -> Mickey and Jackie also crossed over to their home reality, and aided Rose and the Doctor against the Daleks. Afterward, Rose, Jackie and the duplicate tenth Doctor resumed residence on Pete's World, and the dimensional walls sealed once more. Jackie had now given birth to a son named Tony.

Paul Kendrick, an Auton created by the Nestene affiliated with Hyperville, and having no knowledge of his true origins, emerged as the best football player England had offered in the last two decades. In the Euro 2012 semi-final against Spain, Kendrick captained England and scored the winning goal. An injury to Kendrick prevented England from winning the final against Portugal.[8]

2012 (27th July) - FEAR HER[9] -> Adverts were distributed for *Shayne Ward: The Greatest Hits*. Humans were the only species in the galaxy to have ever bothered with edible ball bearings.

The Isolus were empathic creatures from the deep realms - it was not unusual for an Isolus family to consist of up to four billion members, or for them to journey for a thousand human lifetimes. During childbirth, an Isolus mother would jettison millions of spores into space, but one Isolus was caught in a solar flare, and its pod crashed to Earth. It empathised with Chloe Webber, age 12, and hosted itself in her. The Isolus could harness ionic power, enabling Chloe to turn people into drawings and vice versa.

As London geared up for the opening ceremony of the Olympic Games, the tenth Doctor and Rose investigated reports of missing persons - actually consigned by Chloe to an ionic holding pen - on Dame Kelly Holmes Close in the city. Chloe also made the eighty thousand people in the Olympic Stadium vanish. The Doctor and Rose restored them, and helped the alien back into space by lighting the Olympic Flame.

Papua New Guinea went on to surprise everyone in the shot put. At this time, there was an East London police authority and an East London Council.

Closing Time coming before *The Impossible Astronaut*.
The Doctor ends *Closing Time* intending to send Amy and Rory the invite to his death, which is delivered to their Leadworth address (on or prior to 22nd April) in *The Impossible Astronaut*, but it's unlikely that he would trust such a vitally important message to the vagaries of Royal Mail. If the time-travelling justice agents deliver the invite with the Doctor's other invitations (in *The Wedding of River Song*), Amy and Rory's invite must be stamped for Overnight Mail just for show.

The tipping point for a later dating for *Closing Time*, ultimately, is Alfie's age. Babies typically say their first words at around eleven to fourteen months, so unless the Doctor's conversations with Alfie boosted his vocabulary, Alfie must be at least a year old if he can say the words "doctor who". Add on the duration of Sophie's pregnancy, and it must have been at least two years since Craig and Sophie became a couple in *The Lodger* (set in 2010).

The Cybermen in this story, as with those in *A Good Man Goes to War*, don't bear the Cybus logo and are

presumably the ones from our universe, having incorporated the technology of the alternate-reality ones first introduced in *Rise of the Cybermen/The Age of Steel*.
5 Dating *The Wedding of River Song* (X6.13) - No date given for this epilogue, but it's after the Doctor drops Amy and Rory off at the end of *The God Complex*.
6 *Turn Left*, *The Stolen Earth*, *Journey's End*. The dimension-jumping Rose is glimpsed throughout Series 4, starting with *Partners in Crime*.
7 Dating *Journey's End* (X4.13) - The placement of these events is accomplished by (a little arbitrarily) adding two years (the same as passed in real life) to Rose parting ways with the Doctor in *Doomsday*. Jackie was pregnant in *Doomsday* and has now given birth, so that time-span seems reasonable.
8 *Autonomy*
9 Dating *Fear Her* (X2.11) - The year is given as "2012", and the story ends with the opening of the London Olympics, which was scheduled for 27th July, 2012. At present, pop singer Shayne Ward has no Greatest Hits collection.

2012 / = 2012 (June - August) - THE SHADOWS OF AVALON[10] **->** Britain had a King and a female Prime Minister. There had been no major alien attack that required UNIT's attention since the Martian invasion of 1997.[11]

The Time Lords detected that one of the eighth Doctor's companions, Compassion, was evolving into a form of technology they could use, and President Romana dispatched agents Cavis and Gandar to recover her. Still mourning Doris, General Lethbridge-Stewart was on leave. He was called in to investigate the loss of a nuclear warhead, which he discovered had passed through to the parallel universe of Albion.

= Meanwhile, in Albion, a war was brewing between the Unseelie and the Catuvelauni. The eighth Doctor, Fitz and Compassion arrived in Avalon following the seeming destruction of the TARDIS in a dimensional rift. They prevented war there from escalating. Compassion evolved into a new form of TARDIS. President Romana tried to capture her, but the Doctor and his companions escaped. Lethbridge-Stewart remained in Avalon to advise Queen Mab.

2012 - DALEK[12] **->** The ninth Doctor and Rose followed a distress signal and discovered that Henry Van Statten, the owner of the Internet, had what was reportedly the last Dalek captive in his extra-terrestrial museum deep underneath Utah. The Dalek broke free and killed most of Van Statten's staff, but contact with Rose's DNA made it mutate and question its purpose. The conflicted creature destroyed itself. Van Statten's employees rebelled at his callousness and had him mindwiped, then dumped in a US city starting with "S". The Doctor reluctantly welcomed Adam, one of Van Statten's staff, onboard the TARDIS.

Adam told Rose that the UN was keeping the existence of aliens a secret, and Van Statten didn't know that his alien was called a Dalek.

2012 - THE LONG GAME[13] **->** Adam attempted to send information from the year 200,000 home to exploit. When the ninth Doctor discovered this, he took Adam back to his native time and left him there.

Politically the world seemed less stable for a time. In 2012, the scientist/politician Salamander convinced a group of his followers that a global nuclear war was inevitable. He established a survival shelter at Kanowa

---

10 Dating *The Shadows of Avalon* (EDA #31) - The story starts in "July 2012" (p1). *The Ancestor Cell* specifies that Compassion is the first Type 102 TARDIS, and *FP: The Book of the War* establishes that she's the *only* Type 102. That said, we did see another in *The Dimension Riders*, but it didn't take the form of a person.
11 This statement appears odd in the light of the wide array of alien attacks in the new *Doctor Who, Torchwood* and *The Sarah Jane Adventures*.
12 Dating *Dalek* (X1.6) - The Doctor gives the date.
13 Dating *The Long Game* (X1.7) - No date is given, but it's clearly after *Dalek*. Adam's mother says she hasn't seen him for six months.
14 "Five years" before *The Enemy of the World*.
15 *The Time of the Daleks*. The Doctor restores some wayward history at the end of the story, but it's clear that the "real" history includes Learman coming to power, and she's mentioned in *Trading Futures*.
16 *The Face-Eater* (p55). *Trading Futures* (p68) - there's a New Kabul in that book, implying the original city was destroyed, so Afghanistan was also a battleground.
17 *Trading Futures*
18 *The Taking of Planet 5*
19 *Instruments of Darkness*. Presumably a reference to Tony Blair's son and Prince Andrew's daughter.
20 Dating *Christmas on a Rational Planet* (NA #52) - The date is given.
21 Dating *Frozen Time* (BF #98) - The year is given. The veiled implication is that Genevieve shares some

adventures with the Doctor before returning home.
22 Dating *Martha in the Mirror* (NSA #22) - "One hundred years, three months and six days" (p38) before the main part of the story.
23 Dating *The Darksmith Legacy* (*The Dust of Ages*, #1; *The Graves of Mordane*, #2; *The Colour of Darkness*, #3; *The Depths of Despair*, #4; *The Vampires of Paris*, #5; *The Game of Death*, #6; *The Planet of Oblivion*, #7; *The Pictures of Emptiness*, #8; *The Art of War*, #9; *The End of Time* (DL), #10) - This ten-book children's series entails the tenth Doctor and his one-off companion, the android girl Gisella, racing between different time zones.

Two of these are fairly easy to place: most of *The Art of War* occurs in medieval times, and *The Vampires of Paris* happens in "1895". Four more (*The Dust of Ages*, the opening sequences of *The Graves of Mordane*, *The Pictures of Emptiness* and the opening sequences of *The Art of War*) occur together relatively close to the books' publication in 2009. Another three (*The Depths of Despair*, *The Planet of Oblivion* and most of *The Graves of Mordane*) contain references to humans in space, and so must be placed in the future.

The intent of those making *The Darksmith Legacy* was that the Darksmiths themselves were contemporaneous with the first book, *The Dust of Ages*, and so originated from circa 2012. Said intent has been reflected in this chronology, even though many of the details in the series are vague, absent or maddeningly contradictory. Brother Varlos must have access to time tech-

in Australia for them.[14] Following the Euro Wars, Mariah Learman took power in the United Kingdom on a popular tide of anti-EuroZone feeling, renaming it New Britain. Britain had a King at this time.[15]

World War Three was fought in the early twenty-first century. India was reduced to a radioactive mudhole.[16] The War against Terrorism was won when the RealWar tel-etrooper was introduced. Subscribers could kill terrorists (identified with 80% accuracy by software) from the comfort of their own home by operating war robots. Baskerville, a Russian arms dealer, became the richest man in the world selling the technology.[17]

In 2012, firemen in New York laughed and toasted marshmallows instead of rescuing people from a fire. This resulted from the Memeovore feeding on human ideas.[18] The Doctor owned a commemorative mug from the wedding of Euan and Eugenie.[19]

2012 - CHRISTMAS ON A RATIONAL PLANET[20] **->** The seventh Doctor, Chris and Roz landed in Arizona. When Cacophony's gynoids emerged into our universe, Roz fell through a crack in time to the end of the eighteenth century.

2012 - FROZEN TIME[21] **->** Lord Barset sought to locate the colony of lizard men that his grandfather (also known as Lord Barset) had discovered, and sponsored an expedition to Antarctica to find advanced technology there. The expedition members found a frozen Ice Warrior base, and their heaters revived the war-mongering Arakssor - as well as the seventh Doctor, who had been frozen for millions of years. Barset was killed, but the Doctor signalled an Ice Warrior spaceship. The commander of the vessel enforced a death sentence upon Arakssor - his spaceship bombarded the base from orbit, and Arakssor and his warriors died. The Doctor escaped with a member of Barset's expedition, Genevieve, and she returned to her comrades a week later.

& 2012 - MARTHA IN THE MIRROR[22] **->** The planets Anthium and Zerugma had been at war for centuries. Castle Extremis, a floating edifice in space that was for-

merly home to the Mystic Mortal Monks of Moradinard, became crucial to the conflict - whomever controlled Extremis controlled the Sarandon Passage. The strategist Manfred Grieg ended the second Zerguain occupation, and was later given a gift: the Mortal Mirror. The Darksmiths of Karagula had built the Mirror on behalf of Grieg's opponents - he was trapped within its internal dimension, and couldn't counter-act the third Zerguain occupation.

The tenth Doctor and Martha hid Grieg's glass diary in Extremis, knowing they would find it in a hundred years' time.

The Darksmith Legacy[23]

c 2012 - THE DUST OF AGES / THE GRAVES OF MORDANE / THE COLOUR OF DARKNESS / THE PICTURES OF EMPTINESS / THE ART OF WAR[24] **->** Earth experienced such a shortage of minerals and metal ores, some corporations began surveying the moon for its mining potential. One such survey found the Eternity Crystal of the Darksmiths - it had been buried for at least a century, and instinctively created humanoids composed of moondust to defend itself with. The tenth Doctor ended the threat and sealed the Crystal within a stasis box, but was then confronted by a time-active Agent the Darksmiths had dispatched to retrieve the Crystal. The Doctor travelled to the planet Mordane in the far future to learn how to destroy the Crystal, but the Agent pursued him through time and captured the item.

The Doctor followed the Agent to the Darksmiths' homeworld of Karagula... and stole it back again. He experienced a handful of adventures, along with the android girl Gisella, as part of his efforts to destroy the Crystal.[25]

The Shadow Proclamation eventually ruled that Gisella was the rightful owner of the Eternity Crystal - but she had been reprogrammed, and recognised the Darksmiths' claim to the item. The Darksmiths went to London, Galactic reference 297/197AHG, to give the Crystal to the fearsome Krashoks who had commissioned it. The Krashoks turned upon the Darksmiths and killed them... but were then stymied by the Doctor, and retreated into

nology (that he presumably nicked from the Darksmiths) for the plot to function, but this isn't explicitly stated. The Darksmiths use up "every last item of temporal engineering" at their disposal in creating their Agent (*The Dust of Ages*), and yet they can still dispatch an entire Dreadnought through into the future after the Doctor (*The Depths of Despair*), and travel to the world of Oblivion (*The Planet of Oblivion*, also in the future).

Most glaringly of all, the Doctor stresses in *The Graves of Mordane* (p27) that he's only going to travel in

space, not time - and yet the TARDIS moves from Earth's moon, circa 2012, to a point when humanity's colony worlds have been burying their dead on Mordane for at least four centuries (p37), without any acknowledgement of the discrepancy.

One glitch that's unrelated to dating issues, but demonstrates the difficulty in analysing this series: Karagula is named a "cold desolate planet" in Book One (*The Dust of Ages*), but is a hot and arid world with two suns in Book Three (*The Colour of Darkness*).

See the individual entries for more.

the past using a Dalek temporal shift device. The Doctor saved Gisella and secured the Crystal, and they pursued the Krashoks to medieval times...

c 2012 (early autumn to late November) - IRIS: ENTER WILDTHYME[26] **->** Terrance - an accomplished thief operating throughout space and time, and the owner of the Great Big Book Exchange in Darlington - went missing and bequeathed the shop to one of its patrons: Simon, age 26. Simon and his friend Kelly fell in with Iris Wildthyme and Panda when the poet Anthony Marville stole the most important item in Terrance's collection - the glass jar containing the Scarlet Empress Euphemia, a.k.a. the "Objet D'Oom" (as it was called by the F'rrgelaaris). The Empress was crucial to Marville's plans to open up the Ringpull to gain access to the Obverse, and from there travel to the planet Hyspero to plunder its dark magics. Iris, Panda, Simon, Kelly, Barbra the sentient vending machine and Iris' ex-companion Jenny became embroiled in this affair, and dogged Marville to numerous locations in space-time. Kelly fell under the sway of Marville's hypnotic power of speech, *murmurism*.

Iris, Simon and Panda returned to this era to rest, thinking their other friends had died circa 33,935 on the planet Valcea. They then went to Hyspero, millions of years in the future. MIAOW closed down its Darlington branch.

? 2012 (November) - HUNTER'S MOON[27] **->** Kobal Zalu, a Galactic Marine Corps lieutenant in a past war between Torodon and the Terileptils, had now met the Doctor "many times".

The eleventh Doctor, Amy and Rory visited Leisure Platform 9, one of ninety such platforms in the Phrygian system. Rory lost a game of Dead Man's Duel - he was thereby conscripted as prey in a hunt, the Gorgoror Chase. The Xorg Krauzzen criminal cartel had effectively taken over Gorgoror, a moon of the gas giant Zigriz in the Torodon system, and operated the Chase as a hunt for benefit of bored millionaires, weekend warriors and gamblers. The Torodon Confederation, which spanned several star systems, left Krauzzen alone so long as Torodons were not involved. The Doctor posed as a hunter in the Chase to help Rory, and greatly curtailed Kruazzen's operations. Krauzzen, a cyborg, tried to hunt the Doctor down - but the Doctor increased the magnetic force of a nuclear reactor, causing Krauzzen to plunge to his death.

---

24 Dating *The Dust of Ages, The Graves of Mordane, The Colour of Darkness, The Pictures of Emptiness* and *The Art of War* (*DL* #1-#3, #8, #9) - The back cover of *The Dust of Ages* and the story recap in *The Graves of Mordane* both claim that the Doctor's involvement with the Eternity Crystal takes place "a few years into our future..." The general impression is that Earth's corporations are considering exploitation of the moon for the first time - so, more in the relative near future (in *Doctor Who* terms) than, say, hundreds of years hence. All references to UK and London culture are either vague or fictionalised, and of no help in determining the year.

According to the story recap and back cover to *The Art of War*, the Darksmith-Krashok rendezvous (i.e. the opening sequences to *The Art of War*, and by extension most of *The Pictures of Emptiness*, which leads into it) occurs on "present day" Earth. Taken literally alongside *The Dust of Ages* being "a few years in the future", this would mean that the tenth Doctor is attempting to thwart the meeting and retrieve the Eternity Crystal a few years before his younger self finds it on the moon. It seems fair to assume, however, that the four books *do* follow one another in the same year, as there's no sign that the stories were intended to be out of sequence - the "present day" references look very much like a mistake and can be treated as such.

25 *The Colour of Darkness, The Depths of Despair, The Vampire of Paris, The Game of Death.*

26 Dating *Iris: Enter Wildthyme* (Iris novel #1) - The modern-day component begins in "autumn" (p15, 38, 39), proceeds over some weeks (p165-166) and finishes

"Sometime in late November" (p311). A TV screen in Iris' bus (in a takeoff of *Doctor Who - The Movie*) says that it's "Darlington - Human Era - Early 21st Century" (p61).

Enter Wildthyme was published in 2011, but must occur in some other year owing to the need to place *TW: Miracle Day* in autumn 2011. (The meta-fictional nature of the Iris Wildthyme adventures means that Iris fans can probably overlook this continuity conflict, but this chronology doesn't have that luxury.) It's been "some years" since Barbra the vending machine arrived from the future (in December 2008, in *Iris: Iris and the Celestial Omnibus:* "The Deadly Flap"), so 2012 or 2013 is perhaps preferable to 2010.

27 Dating *Hunter's Moon* (NSA #46) - No year given. None of the participants are human, save for three people kidnapped from Earth to serve as prey in the Gorgoror Chase. The London in which the abductees live is very functional and could well be contemporary, but the references (including the Circle Line, the Metropolitan Police, Jobseeker's Allowance and a man from Romania) fall short of being very definitive. It's difficult to tell, in relation to the public's awareness in the new series that aliens exist, if the trio are surprised by the very notion that aliens are *real*, or are instead baffled to learn they personally have been abducted and taken into space on a star-cruiser. With the year being so uncertain, but the month in London being specified as November (p12), it's perhaps best to avoid the year of *Hunter Moon's* publication - 2011 - to curtail any further conflict with *TW: Miracle Day*.

Mention is made of a war between Torodon and the

c 2012 (Christmas) - THE DOCTOR, THE WIDOW AND THE WARDROBE[28] **->** The eleventh Doctor arrived at Amy and Rory's house in time to share Christmas dinner with them.

By 2012, Countess Gallowglass was operating her mail-forwarding service from a hidden location near Carnaby Street. The seventh Doctor visited the Countess, with Ace, in August to collect his mail. According to the Countess, London should be avoided on 14th July, 2013.[29] General Tidos, a dictator affiliated with the Sentinels of the New Dawn, rose to power in Tanganyika, Africa.[30]

2013 - AUTONOMY[31] **->** Animatronic attractions at Hyperville, the largest shopping mall in Europe, aroused the tenth Doctor's suspicions. Kate Maguire, now a trainee at Hyperville, aided the Doctor with the Hypercard he had given her in 2009. The two of them destroyed an army of Autons as well as the Nestene's top Auton assistant, Elizabeth Devonshire. UNIT cleared up the mess, and the Doctor popped back four years to give Kate Maguire the crucial Hypercard.

Erisa Magambo was still with UNIT. The singer Shaneeqi was one of the biggest hits of the past five years, with singles including "Gimmie Love Now" and "All That You Mean". Her "Don't Steal My Boyfriend, Girlfriend" was the vid-download No. 1 for nine weeks. She married soccer player Paul Kendrick - who was actually an Auton that was developing some glimmering of autonomy, and was destroyed during these events.

The eleventh Doctor claimed that the "truth" about a famed celebrity - who had arrived on Earth after falling through a dimensional rift - would be revealled to the public a "few years" after Amy's time. However, he couldn't remember if this revelation applied to the winner of X Factor, the winner of American Idol, the winner of South Korea's Got Talent or Lady Gaga.[32]

2014 - THE SENTINELS OF THE NEW DAWN[33] **->** Cambridge University now had a heliport, just off Wilberforce Road.

The Sentinels of the New Dawn emerged as an ascendant coalition of high-ranking scholars, scientists and politicians who officially promoted a "greener, fairer future", but in reality was a tool by which its elite members sought power. The Sentinels' scientists were having some success creating biomechanoids, including a human-bird monstrosity that resembled Heliodromus: a mythical punisher of the damned. The group was also trying to develop a concentrated form of the ebola virus - and a cure for it - so they could cause a widespread contagion after positioning themselves to restore order.

(=) The Sentinels built a time dilator using Terri Billington's schematics, and created a wormhole linked to Billington's prototype dilator in the 1970s. They hoped to attain enough control of time travel to retroactively empower their members, and to foresee their opponents' decisions. The third Doctor and Liz visited this time, and upon returning home destroyed Billington's work - retroactively preventing the Sentinels from creating their time-dilation device.

The eighth Doctor visited a house in Kent and saved a cat.[34]

c 2014 (late autumn) - WARLOCK[35] **->** Organised crime continued to rely on the profits of drug trafficking. Dealers now used sports cars to get around, and the British police were forced to use Porsches to keep up with them. Soon, Porsche were even making a special model for them.

Terileptils - the latter's ability to wage all-out war was presumably diminished after the destruction of their homeworld in *The Dark Path* (set circa 3400), so *Hunter's Moon* likely occurs before that. An Aggedor beast (*The Curse of Peladon*) is among the wildlife present, but no mention is made of the Federation. One of the hunters in the Chase bears a high-voltage shotgun called the Eradicator (p113), the design of which is similar (coincidentally or otherwise) to the weapon of the same name from *Carnival of Monsters*.

28 Dating *The Doctor, the Widow and the Wardrobe* (X7.0) - It is "two years" since Amy last saw the Doctor (in *The Wedding of River Song*, set in April 2011). At time of writing, it's a toss-up as to whether Amy is rounding up and means that it's now Christmas 2012, or she's rounding down and it's Christmas 2013.

29 *Relative Dementias* (p40) dates when the Doctor and Ace visit the Countess. Her warning about 14th July is on p17.

30 "The year before" *The Sentinels of the New Dawn*. Tanganyika was an independent state in Africa only from 9th December, 1961 to 26th April, 1964. The area is now part of Tanzania, and in recent times, the name "Tanganyika" has only been used in reference to Lake Tanganyika.

31 Dating *Autonomy* (NSA #35) - The year is given. The Doctor says this is the fourth Auton invasion "at least".

32 *The Glamour Chase* (p128).

33 Dating *The Sentinels of the New Dawn* (BF CC #5.10) - The year is given.

34 *The City of the Dead*. This retcon takes the sting out of one of the nastier bits of *Warlock*.

35 Dating *Warlock* (NA #34) - The novel is the sequel to *Cat's Cradle: Warhead*. The events of the earlier book are

In an attempt to win the Drugs War, the International Drug Enforcement Agency (IDEA) was set up. A pooling of Interpol and FBI resources, IDEA had a number of well-publicised successes against drug dealers, forcing many of them underground. IDEA was based in the King Building in New York, the old headquarters of the Butler Institute, and its methods often brought them into conflict with local police forces.

For around a year, IDEA had been aware of a new street drug called Warlock by many of its users. The seventh Doctor sent Benny to infiltrate IDEA's headquarters to learn more about Warlock, as it was granting people psionic abilities and seemed to defy analysis. He tried to contact Vincent and Justine Wheaton, who had settled down and were expecting a child, to locate their associate Mrs Woodcott - an expert on Warlock. An IDEA team learned about Vincent's powers, but an attempt to capture Vincent resulted in his psionically manifesting an opponent's hatred as a fireball that destroyed Canterbury Cathedral. The event was attributed to a freak ball-lightning effect.

Ace investigated a research lab near Canterbury that was kidnapping animals and using Warlock to exchange their minds with people. The Doctor's cat Chick, a resident of his house in Kent for about a year, was captured and euthanised. The Doctor and his allies found Vincent and ended the research lab's activities. The mind of a Kent resident, Jack, remained trapped in a dog, but the Doctor took possession of Jack's human body.

Creed McIlveen, an undercover IDEA agent, saved Justine Wheaton from a forced prostitution house that threatened to terminate her pregnancy. Grateful to Creed, Justine became his lover. Harry Harrigan Jnr, the head of IDEA, had been using Warlock to transfer his mind into younger bodies, and now intended on doing so with Creed. A further discharge of Vincent's powers released the alien intelligence within Warlock, and it left for space after incinerating Harrigan.

Justine left her husband for Creed. Vincent departed with the dog named Jack.

---

consistently referred to as happening "years" ago (p8, p203, p209, p223). Vincent and Justine, the two young lovers from *Warhead*, bought a car after a "few years" of marriage and have had it a while (p356).

In *Cat's Cradle: Warhead*, Ace had difficulty guessing how old Justine was, eventually settling on "maybe 16 or 17" (p181). By *Warlock*, Justine has matured into a woman (p203), but she is still only "probably a couple of years older than the medical student" (p301), so she is in her early-to-mid 20s. We suggest, then, that *Warlock* takes place about five years after *Cat's Cradle: Warhead*. It is late autumn (p279, p334).

36 *Damaged Goods*

37 "Six years" before *The Hungry Earth*.

38 *The Great Space Elevator*. This is the first we've seen of Victoria since *Downtime* - a story that established that she was 14 when she met the Doctor, and she's probably not much older than that when she leaves his company circa 1975. If she did restart her life (as an international fugitive or not) in wake of *Downtime*, then she's in her mid-30s when she starts a family, and the bare minimum of time required for her to be an impending grandmother must mean that the framing sequence for *The Great Space Elevator* occurs circa 2015 at the earliest.

39 *Night Terrors*, extrapolating from George being eight in 2011.

40 Dating *Benny: Present Danger*: "Excalibur of Mars" (Benny collection #14) - Benny says that she's in "the early twenty-first century, give or take". Bambera and Ancelyn are said to have been entrusted with Excalibur "decades ago" (at the end of *Battlefield*), but Bambera is still fit enough for active duty, Merlin is here presented as "a scruffy man in a long, raggedy afghan coat... Wearing an eye-patch, barely visible beneath a long,

asymmetric fringe of red hair", loosely in accordance with the *Battlefield* novelisation.

41 Dating "The Lunar Strangers" (*DWM* #215-217) - The date is given at a caption at the end of the story.

42 Dating *The Eight Truths/Worldwide Web* (BF BBC7 #3.7-3.8) - The back cover says it's "London, 2015", and a news broadcast claims that the story begins on 21st October. The Doctor then spends "twenty-three days" healing from a dose of radioactive Polonium-210, but awakens to facilitate the story's end. Terra Nova might be a corollary of the British space program first seen in *The Ambassadors of Death*. The Terra Nova probe dispatched to Mercury is "following up" on the NASA probe sent to Sol's innermost planet on 3rd August, 2004.

The clear implication is that the Doctor makes the public forget all the events of this story, and (off screen, somehow) erases all media coverage of it. It's very unclear, however, how the Eightfold Truth could have distributed millions of Metebelis crystals to its members for an 18-year stretch prior to 2015 without anybody involved in the original Metebelis incident (Sarah Jane, Mike Yates, let alone the Doctor, etc.) noticing.

Lucie here appears on TV as an Eightfold Truth spokesperson, but if the Doctor indeed erases all record of this, it needn't further complicate her media appearance in *Hothouse* circa 2045.

43 *FP: Erasing Sherlock* and its prologue in *FP: Warring States*. The year isn't specified, but Gillian is from the "twenty-first century", and stops to wonder how the 2018 embargo is going to affect the course of her academic studies.

At the start of 2014, the Home Office introduced compulsory HIV blood tests. In June the next year, MI5's Harry Sullivan told UNIT that the blood of a survivor of the Quadrant Incident might hold a cure to the condition.[36] **Ambrose Northover's aunt Gladys died in 2014. Her body had vanished from its grave by 2020, taken by Malohkeh of the Silurians.**[37]

Victoria Waterfield had created a new life for herself - she was a wife and a mother, and was soon to be a grandmother. She'd never told her family of her origins and adventures in time - and suspected that time was running out, as her memories were fading.[38]

The eleventh Doctor warned that the psionic abilities of George, a Tenza disguised as a young boy, might re-manifest around puberty, as it was "always a funny time".[39]

c 2015 - BENNY: PRESENT DANGER: "Excalibur of Mars"[40] -> Knight-General Ancelyn Ap Gwalchma broke his leg playing a charity football match for benefit of his Squires Academy in Wessex.

(=) The Deindum moved Deimos and Phobos out of Mars orbit to use as a power source, capitalising upon an other-dimensional weak spot within Phobos. Winifred Bambera used her husband's bionodal travelling armour to take the reactivated Excalibur to Mars, where she encountered a time-travelling Bernice Summerfield, and found a chamber built for the sword by Merlin. Benny sheathed Excalibur in a sword room, enabling it to act as a gravitational anchor that drew Deimos and Phobos back into orbit. This also anchored the moons in the past, preventing their loss from ever happening. Merlin told Benny that Excalibur must remain on Mars for several million years at least.

2015 (7th June) - "The Lunar Strangers"[41] -> The cow-like inhabitants of Dryra had settled into a peaceful existence, but two of their number - Ravnok and Vartex - released a killer virus to provoke the population into action. Ravnok and Vartex subsequently buried a treasure on Earth's moon, but were then captured and sentenced to three thousand years in prison. They soon escaped, and returned to find that a Moon Village had been built over their treasure. The fifth Doctor, Tegan and Turlough caught Ravnok and Vartex red-hooved trying to sabotage the Moon Village's reactor. Commander Jackson shot Vartex, and Ravnok suffocated on the moon's surface. The Doctor revealled that the "treasure" was actually cheese - the currency on Dryra.

2015 (21st October to 13th November) - THE EIGHT TRUTHS / WORLDWIDE WEB[42] -> Storms battered the Caribbean, and the President of Cuba blamed the problem on climate change.

Britain had spent £75 million on the Terra Nova space project, which had a tracking station in Buckinghamshire. A Terra Nova satellite sent to obtain water samples from Mercury went missing only two days after NASA lost contact with one of its solar probes. The eighth Doctor and Lucie aided authorities concerning the mystery. The Eightfold Truth's membership had increased fivefold in the last five years, and the group continued to advocate a self-help regimen of meditation using Metebelis crystals provided to its members. The organisation had converted the old BBC Television Centre into a residential block with lecture rooms. Journalist Kelly Westwood tried to prove the group fraudulent with her books *The Octopus Cult* and *Don't Believe the Truth*.

The moon-sized stellar manipulator that had shadowed the TARDIS through the Vortex appeared near Earth, and began draining energy from the Sun. The Eightfold Truth hailed this as the "rebel sun" foretold of in its teachings, and the group's membership soared to two hundred forty-four million. Some Metebelis spiders arrived from the future, and pushed their plan to conquer a thousand worlds to fruition. The stellar manipulator's energy was directed into the millions of Metebelis crystals held by the Eightfold Truth members, creating a hive mind. Unstopped, it would generate a psychic pulse that would ripple outward at 170,000 times the speed of light, and compel legions of worlds to worship the spiders.

The spiders' Queen, facing dissension in her ranks, tried to possess her ally the Headhunter - who had an evolved resistance to psionics and reflected the Queen's power back at her, killing them both. The Doctor defeated the spiders - whose surviving members returned to Metebelis in the future - and used the crystal-web's power to make the public forget these events. He also considered how to erase the relevant media coverage.

The Doctor relocated the stellar manipulator to a remote part of the universe where it would never be found. No longer in the Headhunter's employ, Karen Coltrane left for parts unknown. The Doctor and Lucie departed to spend Christmas in Blackpool, 2008.

w - Gillian Rose Petra released her Master's thesis, *The Magic Feather Duster: A Brief History of Domestic Service in Victoria's England*, and thereby caught the attention of corporate wizard Jimmy Moriarty. He suggested they use his time technology to send Gillian back to the 1880s, so she could study the seminal detective Sherlock Holmes for her doctoral thesis. She was barred from publishing its results until 2018. Gillian agreed and went into the past, returning after the eruption of Krakatoa.[43]

The Doctor was in Havana for Fidel Castro's funeral, and later said, "They all loved [Castro] again by then".[44]

Hex did a school project about the Crimean War and Florence Nightingale, which motivated him to mention an interest in nursing when a career officer visited that week.[45] Hex's father worked on the docks, and thought his job was safe until a strike was held in support of some men who'd been sacked. The disagreement dragged on for years, and Hex's father finally accepted redundancy. Hex's grandmother suggested that he should find an occupation that would always be in demand; when Hex left school, he figured that medicine was a pretty safe bet.[46]

c 2016 - TRADING FUTURES[47] **->** There were no rogue states remaining and the world's secret services kept almost every square inch of the planet electronically monitored. The only two remaining superpowers - indeed, the only two remaining sovereign powers - were the United States and the Eurozone, who dominated the world between them. But they were on the brink of war, as both were trying to extend their sphere of influence into power vacuums in North Africa and the Middle East. "Peacekeepers" from both sides took up positions.

Elsewhere in the world, Eurozone RealWar tanks were covertly sent into action against American corporate inter-

ests. The situation was a tinderbox that could have lead to World War Four. The United Kingdom was now part of the Eurozone and the semi-elected British President Minister was bound by the Articles of European Zoning, despite polls showing 84% of the British population taking the American side in the dispute. Britain secretly maintained its own intelligence service, run by the ancient Jonah Cosgrove. The American President was Felix Mather, former CIA astronaut.

There was a European national soccer team, and games were divided into eighths to fit more adverts in. Rhinos only existed in clonetivity. Human cloning was possible, but very expensive. Hypersonic jets could cross the world in a few hours. Nuclear bombs were used in civil engineering. There was a North China and a New Kabul. Kurdistan was a country in its own right, in a region blighted by civil wars. British Airways had gone bankrupt, the BBC was replaced by the EZBC. More than one channel tunnel was operating.

The international flow of money was through the IFEC computer system. Arms dealer Baskerville launched an ambitious con job to take control of it. He posed as a time traveller from ten thousand years in the future, and offered Cosgrove a time machine in return for access to the powerful EZ ULTRA computer. The CIA got wind of the plan, as

---

44 *Revolution Man* (p23). No date is given.

45 *The Angel of Scutari*

46 *LIVE 34*

47 Dating *Trading Futures* (EDA #55) - The year is not specified beyond "the early decades of the twenty-first century" on the back cover, but Mather says his encounter with the Doctor in *Father Time*, which occurred in 1989, was "more than twenty years ago". Malady Chang, a secret agent, seems to place it nearer thirty years, as she thinks the Doctor "would have been about ten at the time", and he looks like he's in his "early forties". People who were teenagers in the nineties are now "pushing pensionable age" (p8) and Anji's generation are the parents of teenagers. Learman from *The Time of the Daleks* is referred to (p107), as are the Zones from *The Enemy of the World*. It's not clear whether World War Four has been averted - US and EZ forces are fighting at the end of the book, and it's only *hoped* that the revelation of Baskerville's plan will end it.

WORLD WARS: The First and Second world wars occur much as we know them. There are fears of a Third World War in the UNIT era. It occurs some time between Anji joining the TARDIS crew (2000) and *Trading Futures* (c.2016) - whether the events of the episode *World War Three* qualify is unclear. World War IV was mentioned in *The Also People* and *Frostfire*, but no details are given. In *Christmas on a Rational Planet*, it's said that people danced in the ashes of Reykjavik during World War IV. The Doctor says he saw World War V in *The Unquiet

Dead. *Borrowed Time* references mutant crabs active in the 4900s; these were engineered to eat the marine vessels used in World War V. World War VI is averted in the year 5000, according to *The Talons of Weng-Chiang*.

48 *Heritage*. In terms of *Doctor Who* history, the earliest mention of humans cloning humans is in *Trading Futures*.

49 "Nine years" before *Project: Destiny*.

50 According to the computer in *The Waters of Mars*. If that's correct, Brooke would have started her doctorate very young.

51 *Army of Death*

52 Dating *The Enemy of the World* (5.4) - One of Salamander's followers, Swann, holds up a scrap of newspaper with a date on it from the year before, but the photograph is not clear enough to discern the date. (*Timelink* suggests it says 2041, but still dates the story to 2017.) The licence disc on the helicopter expires in 2018.

None of the scripts contain any reference to the year that the story is set in. However, the *Radio Times* in certain regions featured an article on fashion that set *The Enemy of the World* "fifty years in the future", which would give a date of 2017. The first edition of *The Programme Guide* mistakenly thought that the story had a contemporary setting, and placed it between "1970-75".

The date "2030", which is now commonly associated with the story, first appeared in David Whitaker's sto-

did Sabbath's Time Agents; the eighth Doctor, Anji and Fitz; and the rhino-like alien Onihrs. The Doctor and his companions uncovered Baskerville's plan just as shootings in Tripoli triggered a potential world war.

The earliest human clones were mindless, bred for use as perishable stunt doubles in motion pictures. Humanity became uneasy with the morality of this and ended the practice. Cloning fell into disuse, but scientists periodically revived the art.[48] The British government recovered dystronic missiles - weapons that could destroy all organic life in a set radius - from an Arcadian spacecraft.[49]

In 2017, Adelaide Brooke began her doctorate in Physics at Rice University in Texas, having studied Physics and Maths at Cambridge.[50] Ramirez Harmon was president of Mexico in 2017.[51]

? 2017 - THE ENEMY OF THE WORLD[52] -> Rockets could now be used to travel between continents on Earth - the journey from Australia to Hungary took around two hours. Hovercars made shorter trips. Television pictures were broadcast via videowire.

The political situation on Earth had stabilised.

National concerns were put aside and the world was reorganised into large administrative areas called Zones, such as the Australasian, North African and Central European Zones. The world was organised by the United Zones, more properly known as the World Zones Authority. Commissioners dealt with multinational concerns such as Security matters. A Controller led each Zone.

One of the major problems the world faced was famine. The scientist Salamander announced he could solve the problem using his Mark Seven Sun-Catcher satellite, which made previously desolate areas of the world into fertile farmland that robots could harvest. Within just a year, the Sun-Catcher had solved the problems of world famine, allowing crops to grow in Siberia and vineyards in Alaska. In the more fertile areas, concentrated sunlight forced growth: each summer could bring three or even four harvests. Salamander was hailed as the saviour of mankind.

Soon after Salamander's announcement, a series of natural disasters struck, including a freak tidal wave that sank a liner full of holidaymakers in the Caribbean and the first volcanic eruptions in the Eperjes-Tokaj

---

ryline for the novelisation of his story, submitted to WH Allen in October 1979. The document was reprinted in *DWM* #200, and amongst other things of interest it is the only place to give Salamander a first name: "Ramon". The novelisation was due to be published in 1980, and was to be set "some fifty years later than our time - the year 2030" according to the storyline, but the book was not completed before Whitaker's death.

The second edition of *The Programme Guide* duly gave the date as "2030". The blurb for the novelisation by Ian Marter, published in 1981 - the same year as *The Programme Guide* - concurred, although perhaps significantly, the text of the book didn't specify a date. 2030 was soon adopted wholesale, with *The TARDIS Logs* and *The Terrestrial Index* giving the new date. *Encyclopedia of the Worlds of Doctor Who* is confused: the entry for "Denes" gives the date as "2017", but that for "Fedorin" states "2030". *The TARDIS Special* was less specific than most, claiming the story takes place in an "Unknown Future" setting. *The Legend* states it's "c.2017". *About Time* hedges its bets a little, saying that "around 2017 - 2030 is the most likely possibility". *Alien Bodies* sets the story later, after *Warchild* and apparently around the 2040s.

It seems clear that David Whitaker intended the story to be set fifty years after it was broadcast, so that date has been adopted here.

WEATHER CONTROL: In a number of stories set in the twenty-first century, we see a variety of weather control projects. The earliest is in the New Adventure *Cat's Cradle: Warhead*, and simply involves "seeding" clouds

with chemicals to regulate rainfall (p129). A year before *The Enemy of the World*, Salamander develops the Sun-Catcher, the first Weather Control system. As its name suggests, the Sun Store satellite collects the rays from the Sun and stores them in concentrated form. It is also capable of influencing tidal and seismic activity.

Each major city has its own Weather Control Bureau by *The Seeds of Death*, and these are co-ordinated and monitored centrally by computer. The London Bureau is a large complex, manned by a handful of technicians. The Weather Control Unit itself is about the size of a large desk, with separate circuits for each weather condition. With fully functioning Rain Circuits, rainfall over a large area can be arranged quickly.

By 2050, the Gravitron had been set up on Earth's moon. This is the ultimate form of weather control, working on the simple principle that "the tides control the weather, the Gravitron controls the tides". Weather control is under the control of the (United Zones?) General Assembly.

It's clear those last two are different systems, but it's less clear which is the most advanced. This becomes important when trying to date *The Seeds of Death* - *About Time* suggests that the weather control in *The Seeds of Death* is "far more compact and efficient", so that's the later story. But it can certainly be argued that a device in a room in London that makes it rain on special occasions looks primitive compared with a moon-based one that manipulates gravity as part of an international programme to manage the entire world's weather.

mountain range since the sixteenth century. These were caused by Salamander's followers in a bunker below Kanowa using his technology. Salamander had convinced them that the Earth's surface was highly radioactive, and that they had to fight back against the aggressors.

The second Doctor, Jamie and Victoria uncovered the truth: that Salamander had been gradually assassinating his political opponents within the United Zones and replacing them with his own people in a bid to become the dictator of Earth. Salamander was defeated when his followers in Kanowa learned there had been no global nuclear war. He tried to escape in the TARDIS, but was sucked into the Vortex when the Ship's door opened in flight.

In 2017, UNIT closed their file on the Quadrant Incident.[53] Kakapos were extinct on Earth by 2017.[54] The Doctor placed a personal advert "Ace - Behind You!" in an NME from 2018. Ace bought a copy outside Ladbroke Grove hypertube station.[55] Paletti wrote the opera The Fourth Sister, including the stirring Rebirth Aria.[56]

The risk of nuclear warfare diminished after the Southport Incident, when governments realised that the stockpiling of atomic weapons could only lead to a serious accident or all-out nuclear warfare.[57]

The Doctor acquired a ten pound coin from the time of King William V.[58] **Single Molecule Transcription replaced the microprocessor in 2019.**[59]

From around 2019, Earth experienced forty long years of chaos including climate change, difficulty with the ozone layer and an "oil apocalypse". The human race almost reached extinction.[60]

53 Damaged Goods. Marcie Hatter, a UNIT Corporal here (p262), was the name of the heroine of Russell T Davies' TV serial Dark Season (1991).

54 The Last Dodo

55 Timewyrm: Revelation

56 "A few decades" after Vampire Science.

57 Benny remembers the Southport Incident in Just War (p214), but doesn't specify what or when it was. Zoe, who lacks even rudimentary historical knowledge, recognises the effects of an atomic blast in The Dominators, perhaps suggesting that nuclear weapons are still around (and have been used?) in her time.

58 Winner Takes All. No date is given, but William is currently second in line to the throne, and will be King at some point in the twenty-first century.

59 The Long Game

60 As detailed by Brooke in The Waters of Mars. There's a fairly consistent narrative in Doctor Who that the first half of the twenty-first century sees environmental and other catastrophes that are overcome in the second half of the century by technology - space exploration in particular - although there are many differences in detail.

61 Dating The Hungry Earth/Cold Blood (X5.8-5.9) - The year is given in a caption at the beginning of The Hungry Earth.

62 Or so the Doctor claims in The Hungry Earth, either suggesting that it's fallen fairly dramatically since 2009, or that he's just confused.

63 Dating TimeH: Kitsune (TimeH #4) - Honoré and Emily attend an evening festival in Kyoto on "17 July 2020" (p23). It's later said that they "left for Tokyo on the Friday morning" (p30) - which presumably denotes the next day, although 17th July, 2020, will be a Friday.

64 Dating House of Blue Fire (BF #152) - Sally tests a colleague's memory by asking, "I'm guessing you remember what year it is?", and receives the (evidently correct) reply, "Of course... 2020."

65 Dating The Power of the Daleks (4.3) - There is no confirmation of the date in the story itself. Lesterson says the Dalek ship arrived "at least two centuries ago", "before the colony", which might suggest the Earthmen have been there for just under two hundred years. However, the generally low-level of technology, the reliance on "rockets" and the fact that there is only one communications link with Earth suggests the colony is fairly new. The colonists don't recognise the Daleks, suggesting it's before The Dalek Invasion of Earth.

The contemporary trailer (included on the Lost in Time DVD) announced it was set "in the year 2020", and press material at the time confirmed that. This date also appeared in the 10th anniversary Radio Times, was used by the second edition of The Making of Doctor Who and the first edition of The Programme Guide.

Nevertheless, Doctor Who fans can see a statement like "I'm from 1980" as problematic and ambiguous, and most fan chronologies have seen 2020 as implausibly early for Earth to have a colony on a planet that's not in our solar system. Ergo, they often use the fact the date only appeared in a trailer to disallow it. (To be fair, the trailer for The Dalek Invasion of Earth set that story in "2000" - a date to which nobody subscribes.) In DWM, The TARDIS Logs offered a date of "2049", but "A History of the Daleks" contradicted this and gave the date as "2249". The American Doctor Who comic offered the date of "2600 AD", apparently unaware that the Dalek ship has been dormant. The Terrestrial Index came to the elaborate conclusion that the colonists left Earth in 2020 - in spacecraft with suspended animation - and then used the old calendar when they arrived. As a result, while they call the date 2020, the story is really set in "2220". Timelink opted for "2120". About Time claims that "internal publicity" gave the date as "2070" (it didn't, actually - that was for The Moonbase), but concludes the story is set "probably somewhere in the mid-2100s". Earth could only really have a colony on

SECTION FOUR: FUTURE HISTORY

2020 - THE HUNGRY EARTH / COLD BLOOD[61] ->
The eleventh Doctor, Rory and Amy arrived in the village of Cwmtaff, South Wales, in the right year but the wrong place, as they had been aiming for Rio. Rory and Amy saw their future selves in the distance, but the Doctor was more interested in patches of blue grass: evidence of minerals unseen in Britain for twenty million years.

Cwmtaff was the site of the most successful recorded boring in human history - a shaft had been drilled to a depth of 21 km. The drill threatened an underground Silurian city, and its automatic systems awoke Silurian warriors to stage a response. The Doctor found that these were a different branch of the species to the one he had previously encountered.

One Silurian, Alaya, was killed. Her enraged sister Restac attempted a coup against Eldane, a peaceful Silurian leader willing to negotiate with humanity. Eldane decided that his people were not ready to share the planet and activated a decontamination programme, forcing the warriors to return to their cryochambers. The humans Nasreen Chaudhry and Tony Mack accompanied them into stasis. The Doctor altered the Silurians' systems to awaken them in a thousand years, when they would hopefully be welcomed by humanity. The drilling site was destroyed.

Restac killed Rory, who was dematerialised by a Crack in Time. Amy lost all memory of him, and remembered seeing only her future self, not Rory, in the distance.

The population of Earth was six billion.[62]

2020 (17th July) - TIMEH: KITSUNE[63] -> Ikari, the brood mother of the White Claw Kitsune, thought the developed world had lost its way and sought to punish humanity for it. She started a clothing business, Hide and Chic, whose offerings were woven with chaos-inducing hair. Honoré Lechasseur and Emily Blandish averted an apocalypse by convincing Ikari to refrain from unleashing animal spirits of vengeance, and to instead take her kitsune and find a new world.

2020 - HOUSE OF BLUE FIRE[64] -> Eve Pritchard's work into Rapid-Emotional Programming (REP) technology - a means of extracting phobias, either to create fearless sol-

diers or to cripple a target population with "fear bullets" - reached an apex at Fulton Down Military Base. Four test subjects with chronic fears, including Private Sally Morgan (who had athazagoraphobia, the fear of being forgotten about) were connected to an REP control apparatus: the Blue Fire System. The seventh Doctor prevented the Mi'en Kalarash from manifesting via Blue Fire and triggering global Armageddon, and banished it back to the wasteland between realities. Afterward, he accepted Sally as his new travelling companion.

2020 - THE POWER OF THE DALEKS[65] -> The colony on Vulcan was in danger of being "run down". Mining operations had not proved economically successful and the governor of the colony, Hensell, faced mutiny. An Examiner from Earth was due to assess the Vulcan colony in two years.

The chief scientist, Lesterson, discovered what he thought might be the colony's salvation - a buried alien spaceship. He quickly determined that the capsule was constructed of a metal that wasn't found on Vulcan and could revolutionise space travel. Lesterson opened the capsule and discovered that it contained three inert Daleks. The lure of reviving them proved too great for the human colonists.

At first, the Daleks cunningly pretended to be servants, dependent as they were on the power provided by the humans. The Daleks promised to build a computer that could predict meteorite showers and protect the weather satellites, a move that offered huge financial savings and won the colonists' trust. All the time, though, the Daleks were setting up their production line. Dozens of Daleks swarmed across the colony within a matter of hours, exterminating every human in their path.

The newly regenerated second Doctor, Ben and Polly witnessed the Daleks' rampage. Once again, though, the Daleks' external power sources proved their undoing - although they guarded their static electricity generator, it proved possible to destroy the power source. This rendered the Daleks immobile once more.

Steffi Ehrlich, a future Mars colonist, was born in Iserlohn, Germany, in September 2021.[66]

---

another world this early if the planet Vulcan was in our solar system. See the article "Vulcan" for how it might be possible to justify the "2020" date.
66 *The Waters of Mars*

2021 (12th October) - THE HARVEST[67] -> There was political tension between Europe and the Pan-US Core. The European Council had recovered an expeditionary force of Cybermen that crashed in the Pyrenees. The Cybermen brokered a deal with the European government, offering Cyber-technology to create astronauts cyber-augmented for space. In return, the Cybermen asked for operations to make them organic beings again.

By October 2021, the "Recarnative Program" was secretly in operation at St Gart's Brookside, a London hospital managed by the Euro Combine Health Administration. The duplicitous Cybermen intended to turn the facility into a ready-made Cyber-conversion centre, facilitating a planetary takeover. The seventh Doctor and Ace learned of the plot and triggered a termination protocol that shut down the Cybermen. The Doctor also erased the Program's data, preventing the Euro government from exploiting it. Thomas Hector "Hex" Schofield, a staff nurse at St Gart's, joined the Doctor and Ace on their travels.

An AI system was in use at St Gart's, and the Wheel space stations were in operation.

2022 - BENNY: THE GREL ESCAPE[68] -> With the time-travelling Grel in hot pursuit, Benny, Jason and Peter stopped at the Festival of Piranha, a disused funfair (and the home to flesh-eating Evatra Wraiths).

During the 2020s, the Silurians entombed at Wenley Moor were scheduled to revive. If they did so, they remained hidden from humanity.[69] The UN banned beryllium laser weapons in the mid-2020s.[70] The phased plasma rifle was developed in 2024.[71]

2024 - EMOTIONAL CHEMISTRY[72] -> The eighth Doctor, Fitz and Trix infiltrated the Kremlin Museum to retrieve a diamond locket that formerly belonged to the Russian noblewoman Dusha. Colonel Grigoriy Bugayev, working for the Russian division of UNIT, knew the Doctor of old and aided the time travellers.

The disgraced physicist Harald Skoglund had retro-engineered a lost time belt into the Misl Vremnya, a device that enabled its user to see down the timeline of various objects, and to witness events through the eyes of anyone in contact with them. With further exertion, the device allowed its operator to dominate the wills of such people. Bugayev destroyed the device.

By now, the Moscow waste management system had organic microfilters to reprocess sewage. Robot drones were used for reconnaissance.

The novel *The Unformed Heart* by Emily Hutchings was published, and the Doctor acquired a copy. The word "cruk" was very rude by 2025.[73] Demeter Glauss, the future author of *Cybercrime: An Analysis of Hacking*, was

---

67 Dating *The Harvest* (BF #58) - The date is given on the back cover blurb.

68 Dating *Benny: The Grel Escape* (Benny audio #5.1) - The year is given. The "Festival of Piranha" is a parody of the "Festival of Ghana" seen in *The Chase*.

69 At the end of *Doctor Who and the Silurians*, the Reptile People go back into deep freeze for "fifty years". Alternatively, they might have all perished in the explosions triggered by the Brigadier's men. There are Silurians working alongside humanity in *Eternity Weeps* in 2003, but it's never stated they are from Wenley Moor, and we know there were other shelters. The UNIT audios (set circa 2005) show a failed attempt to reconcile humanity and the Silurians, although a group of Silurians nonetheless help human scientists to cure a lethal virus. The eleventh Doctor indicates in *Cold Blood* that the Wenley Moor Silurians were killed, not entombed.

70 "Twenty years" after *The Fearmonger*.

71 *First Frontier* (p137).

72 Dating *Emotional Chemistry* (EDA #66) - The date appears in the blurb.

73 *Happy Endings*

74 Glauss was born twenty-six years after *Millennial Rites* (p86). A bit confusingly, p70 says her *Cybercrime* text was written "in the early twenty-first century".

75 Dating *The Feast of Axos* (BF #144) - Axos was stuck

in the time loop "fifty years" ago in *The Claws of Axos*, making this story subject to UNIT dating.

76 Dating *The Ring of Steel* (BBC *DW* audiobook #8) - The Doctor tells Amy that they're "maybe fifteen years into her future".

77 Dating *Project: Destiny* and *A Death in the Family* (BF #139-140) - The Doctor is initially uncertain as to the date ("We're in the year 2024, or possibly 2026") and the back cover says that it's 2025. It's said three times within the story, though, that it's 2026 - once by Nimrod in response to Hex asking about the year, and twice on data files related to the Contaminants. The same data files seem to indicate that *Project: Destiny* begins on "18th of April" and continues the next day - when the Doctor is shot, and later awakens after spending three days in healing coma. So, that adventure ends - and events seem to pick up immediately afterwards in *A Death in the Family* - on the 22nd. The later portion of *A Death in the Family*, which begins in 2027, confirms that London was evacuated "last year".

78 Dating *A Death in the Family* (#140) - Ace establishes the date of her arrival (24th June, 2027) by checking a newspaper. She dispatches Henry's account of her to Hex on "Tuesday, 24th of May" (actually a Wednesday in 2028) - evidently the same day that Professor Noone springs into creation and confronts the Word Lord.

79 *The Waters of Mars*

born. The book was the seminal work on breaking and entering computer systems, including the Paradigm operating system. Mel would use the text to hack into Ashley Chapel Logistics in 1999.[74]

c 2025 - THE FEAST OF AXOS[75] **->** Earth continued to experience an energy crunch - fossil fuel supplies were dwindling, renewable energy sources couldn't meet demand and security concerns had slowed growth in the nuclear industry. A large portion of Oklahoma was now desert. The Eurozone Space Agency operated the space shuttle *Jules Verne*. A global lottery was now in operation.

Ironside Industries offered space-tourism flights for the cost of a luxury cruise. The CEO of Ironside, Campbell Irons, had the shuttle *Windermere* fitted with an alien displacement device capable of penetrating the time loop surrounding Axos, and sent a crew to negotiate with it. Irons wanted Axos to supply Earth with carbon-free energy. The sixth Doctor, Evelyn and Thomas Brewster were present as Axos used the *Windermere*'s microwave transmitter to exterminate the Ironside mission control station at Devesham. The Doctor strengthened the time loop as the mini-nuclear reactor aboard the *Windermere* was detonated, trapping Axos in a cycle of being exploded over and over again.

c 2025 - THE RING OF STEEL[76] **->** The eleventh Doctor and Amy stopped a Caskelliak - a weapon of war crafted by a dead race, and which had been tasked with polluting and destroying entire worlds - from using Astragen, a utilities company in the Orkney islands, Scotland, to complete an energy circuit that would have poisoned the Earth.

2026 (18th-22nd April) - PROJECT: DESTINY / A DEATH IN THE FAMILY[77] **->** The public accepted that aliens were real, as too much evidence was available in the information age to deny it. Nimrod, a.k.a. Sir William Abberton, had spent years rebuilding the Forge into Department C4 - a governmental agency that served as the public face of extra-terrestrial investigation. C4 bungled a harvest of alien xenotech, causing a widespread infection of DNA from insectoid aliens named the Contaminants. These creatures' life cycle entailed mutating residents of a target world into hybrids, then breeding to produce more pure offspring. London was evacuated and quarantined as fifteen thousand people were infected. The hybrids consumed those too old or infirm to survive the transformation. Outbreaks were reported in Chelsea, Hammersmith, Camden and Wandsworth.

Two months after the evacuation, the Home Secretary assured Parliament - which was currently in session in Harrogate - that the quarantine zone around the M-25 was secure. The Contaminant hybrids all swarmed to C4's main facility - the Crichton Building, which overlooked the Thames - in a mating frenzy. Captain Lysandra Aristedes usurped control of C4 and destroyed the Crichton Building and all the Contaminants with an air strike of dystronic missiles. Nimrod perished in the blast, and his death effectively ended the Forge.

Afterward, the seventh Doctor and Ace located a Gallifreyan sarcophagus in the Forge archives - and found within an older version of the seventh Doctor, who had become the Storyspeaker for the Handivale of Pelican. The Word Lord had been trapped within the Handivale, but was now freed. The Handivale transferred into Captain John Stillwell of UNIT, who became comatose.

The Word Lord made a soldier intone "Nobody can stop the Doctor regenerating" and "No One has the power of life and death over the Doctor" - and thereby gained those very attributes. The younger seventh Doctor re-bottled the Word Lord within a conflicting narrative spun from the trans-galactic Internet, but this burned out the Doctor's cerebral cortex, killing him. The older seventh Doctor, now only a potential future, took Hex to the distant past on Pelican, then had the TARDIS deliver Ace to 2027.

S.J. Wordly was now Prime Minister.

2027 (24th June) to 2028 (Tuesday, 24th May) - A DEATH IN THE FAMILY[78] **->** The British government, UNIT, the remnants of the Forge and a secret cabal of the Doctor's former companions covered up his death in 2026, fearing the consequence of extra-terrestrials learning that Earth no longer had his protection. The Doctor's corpse was interred in York Minster, in a secret chamber reserved for Earth's fallen, clandestine heroes.

The TARDIS, per the older seventh Doctor's instructions, arrived in 2027 with Ace aboard. In the months to follow, she entered into a relationship with Henry Louis Noone. In May 2028, Ace had Henry write about what she would be like as his wife of ten years, then sent the document to Hex in the distant past using a Vaspen space-time stamp. This created a linguistic version of Ace - Professor Dorothy Noone - whose name enabled her (per the phrase, "No One has the power of life and death over the Doctor") to tap the Word Lord's reality altering CORDIS and bring the Doctor back to life. The Word Lord was liberated from the Doctor's narrative and killed Professor Noone, but was then uploaded, along with his CORDIS, into the Handivale within Captain Stillwell. Ace and the restored Doctor took Stillwell back in time to Pelican.

A number of future Mars colonists were born around this time: Andrew Stone on a commune in Iowa in 2025; Tarak Ital in 2026 in Karachi; and Margaret Cain in Sheffield in December 2028. After intensive training, Adelaide Brooke became the first non-US citizen to fly shuttles for NASA. Ed Gold earned a BA in mechanical engineering in 2030.[79]

By 2030, the issue of thargon differentials in the orange spectrum of upper atmospheric problems was solved. This enabled the creation of stable energy fields on satellites.[80] Gorillas were extinct on Earth by 2030.[81] The seventh Doctor, Ace and Bernice visited UNIT HQ in Geneva in 2030, and picked up a note left by Cristian Alvarez thirty-seven years before.[82] The eleventh Doctor claimed that the World Cup final held at Wembley Stadium in 2030 was the greatest football match in history. The score was Scotland three, England nil.[83]

2030 (early autumn) - WARCHILD[84] **->** Computer technology enabled cars to practically drive themselves and computers that understood straightforward voice commands. Instead of passports, people had implants on the back of their necks. Three-dimensional television now existed. Passenger airliners were still in use. A cure had been found for Alzheimer's disease, and few people smoked thanks to health-awareness campaigns.

Vincent Wheaton had secretly inserted himself into the life of his son, Ricky McIlveen, in the guise of a history teacher. Vincent suspected that Ricky possessed immense mind-control abilities... enough to make Ricky president of America, with Vincent pulling his strings. Ricky was potentially the greatest alpha male who ever lived, and so Vincent experimented with the concept of pack behaviour. The dog Vincent owned, which contained the mind of a human, Jack, accordingly became the White King - an old dog that caused packs of dogs to display remarkable intelligence and murder people. The seventh Doctor, travelling with Benny, Roz and Chris, reunited Jack's mind with his human body.

Creed McIlveen now worked for a secretive crimefighting force, the Agency, but started an affair with his associate Amy Cowan - who was secretly in Vincent's employ. Vincent wanted revenge on Creed and Justine, and invaded their home. In the resulting confrontation, Amy had a change of heart and killed Vincent to save Justine. Creed and Justine's marriage ended. The Doctor and his friends pledged to help Ricky learn control of his abilities.

c 2032 (Tuesday, 30th November) - SINGULARITY[85] **->** Houses were now equipped with computer attendants that responded to voice recognition; phones also recog-

---

80 "Twenty or thirty years" after *The King of Terror*.
81 *The Last Dodo*
82 *The Left-Handed Hummingbird*
83 "Apotheosis"
84 Dating *Warchild* (NA #47) - The book is the sequel to *Warlock*. At the end of the earlier novel, Justine was in the early stages of pregnancy, so her baby would have been born in the spring of the following year. In *Warchild*, her son Ricky is "15". This book is set in the early autumn, as the long summer ends and the school year is starting in America.
85 Dating *Singularity* (BF #76) - The year is unspecified, but 30th November is a Tuesday; in the twenty-first century - and allowing that the portion of *Singularity* eleven years hence cannot occur before 2090 - that narrows the possibilities to 2010, 2021, 2027, 2032, 2038, 2049, 2055, 2060, 2066 and 2077. As Somnus publicity materials brag about the goal of its members to terraform Mars within "two years", 2077 doesn't seem very likely; it would push the later portion of *Singularity* to 2088 and the end of the devastating Thousand-Day War - a year in which Somnus would be rather brazen to make such a claim.

Moscow endures its worst storm "in fifty years", an event that would be unlikely in the era of weather control witnessed in *The Moonbase* and *The Seeds of Death*. The former story takes place in 2070, ruling out this part of *Singularity* occurring before 2066. One complication is the Doctor's offhanded comment that mankind is only "a few years" from expanding beyond the solar system, suggesting a later dating as opposed to an earlier one. Nonetheless, given *Ahistory's* projected dating of *The Seeds of Death*, the best compromise for

the early part of *Singularity* seems to be 2032, with the remainder of this adventure occurring in 2043.
86 *The Waters of Mars*. See Dating *The Seeds of Death*.
87 *Cold Fusion* (p216), no date given.
88 *Iris: The Two Irises*. Rossiter lived 1926-1984; Edmonds was born in 1948 and is still alive; the placement here arbitrarily has him living to his mid-eighties, and assumes he didn't lose his soul while living.
89 *The King of Terror*
90 "F.A.Q."
91 *The Waters of Mars*
92 Darius is 15, and Jorjie and Starkey are both 14, in *K9: Regeneration*. Jorjie is still 14 in *K9: Dream-Eaters* and *K9: The Last Oak Tree*.
93 "About ten years" prior to *Hothouse*.
94 Dating *Benny: The Vampire Curse*: "Possum Kingdom" (Benny collection #12b) - It's "the technologically comfortable early-to-mid twenty-first century" (p111).
95 *The Seeds of Death*
96 At some point before *K9: The Sirens of Ceres*.
97 "Years" before *K9: Robot Gladiators*, but presumably after the development of hyperlogarithms.
98 *Alien Bodies*. The World Zones Accord was intended as a reference to the establishment of the political system of *The Enemy of the World*, which most chronologies set earlier than this. We could speculate that the World Zones Accord strengthened an existing World Zones Authority, in the same way successive European treaties have granted more powers to the EEC/EC/EU.
99 *A Death in the Family*. It's not established whether "you" means Great Britain, humanity in general or something else entirely.

nised voice command.

In Russia, the Somnus Foundation had been created to study sleep disorders and neuro-science, but some descendents of humanity - originating from near the end of the universe - usurped the organisation. The descendents hoped to modify the brain chemistry and "wave forms" of several humans, inducing telepathy and achieving a group consciousness. If successful, the effect would cascade through Earth's electro-magnetic signature and turn the whole of humanity into a single entity. The resultant Singularity would allow the descendants to bring their fellows through en masse from the future, and let them exact vengeance against the Time Lords.

On 30th November, Moscow witnessed its worst storm in fifty years. The fifth Doctor arrived to investigate matters at a Somnus clinic, but the Somnus test subjects started an electrical fire, hoping to end their suffering. The clinic burned down as the Doctor escaped.

In 2032, Yuri Kerenski began work for the Russia Federal Space Agency. He would end up specialising in treating long-term cosmonauts after they returned home. In the same year, Mia Bennett was born in Houston. Her mother was killed in a car accident, and her father relinquished a career in space exploration to raise her.[86] Earth picked up an Arcturan signal that included enough information to build a transmat device.[87] Iris owned a martini glass signed by actor Leonard Rossiter, which was said to contain the soul of TV presenter Noel Edmonds.[88]

Lethbridge-Stewart returned to Earth in 2032, having spent twenty years in the realm of Avalon.[89] By 2034, a young man called Craig would either be a drunk living under Hammersmith Bridge *or* a successful carpenter with children - depending on the choices he made in 2006.[90]

Ed Gold earned his doctorate in 2034 - the same year Roman Groom, a future child genius, was born.[91] **Starkey, Jorjie Turner and Darius Pike - future friends of K9 - were born in the mid-2030s.**[92] The Experts, featuring lead singer Alex Marlow, became the biggest band in the world. Marlow eventually abandoned performing in favour of being a charity worker and environmental activist, working to save endangered animals.[93]

c 2035 - BENNY: THE VAMPIRE CURSE: "Possum Kingdom"[94] -> Benny and the Yesterways Ltd. tour group arrived at Forks, Washington, and disrupted the Edward and Bella Players' re-creation of a battle between vampires and werewolves.

On Earth, there was a period of technological progress. Hypersonic aircraft were built, and mankind discovered how to synthesise carbohydrates and protein, which helped to feed the planet's ever-increasing population. Computers were now advanced enough to give spoken responses to sophisticated verbal instructions. Most energy now came from solar power, and compact solar batteries became available. Petrol cars were confined to museums. There were further advances in robotics and weather control technology.

Regular passenger modules were travelling between the Earth and its moonbases. Most people thought the moon would provide a stepping stone to the other planets of the solar system, and eventually to the stars. At this time Professor Daniel Eldred, the son of the man who designed the lunar passenger modules, invented an ion jet rocket with a compact generator. This vehicle promised to revolutionise space travel, paving the way for mankind's rapid exploration of the solar system.

Then the Travel-Mat Relay, an instantaneous form of travel, was invented. The massive capital investment required, and the promise of easy movement of all resources around the world, meant that after some debate the government ended all funding for space travel. All but a skeleton staff on the moon were recalled. Man had travelled no further than the moon. For years, all space travel halted.

Travel-Mat revolutionised the distribution of people and materials around the world. A T-Mat brochure boasted that:

> "The Travel-Mat is the ultimate form of travel. Control centre of the present system is the moon, serving receptions in all major cities on Earth. Travel-Mat provides an instantaneous means of public travel, transporting raw materials and vital food supplies to all parts of the world. Travel-Mat supersedes all conventional forms of travel, using the principal of dematerialisation at the point of departure and rematerialisation at the point of arrival in special cubicles. Departure and arrival are almost instantaneous. Although the system is still in its early stages, it is completely automated and foolproof against power failure."[95]

The development of hyperlogarithms allowed the development of a new generation of technology, including artificial intelligence.[96] Alistair Gryffen was involved in the development of the Thought Matrix, a revolutionary robot brain.[97]

In 2038, the World Zones Accord was signed. Around this time, Colonel Kortez fought the Cyber breaches for the ISC. He joined UNISYC in 2039 and fought lemur people at some point before 2069.[98] Ace told Henry Noone that bees would recover from a malady afflicting them by 2040, and also that "you're going to get new pandas!"[99]

Hazel Bright joined the League of Nature after witnessing ten thousand people perish in the Ganges during a flood. She worked undercover for Alex Marlowe at the World Ecology Bureau, and stole the Krynoid cuttings saved by Sir Colin Thackeray.[100]

It was predicted that Sarah Jane Smith would die around 2040, and that members of UNIT and Black Seed, possibly including Sam Jones, would attend her funeral. In 2043, Black Seed published their third manifesto.[101] There were anti-weather control demonstrations.[102]

The Doctor on Draconia

A race of reptilian humanoids had evolved on the planet Draconia. Although technologically advanced, they retained a feudal system. The Doctor visited Draconia at the time of the Fifteenth Emperor, around 2040, and cured a great space plague.[103] The Emperor was known as the Red Emperor, and by the Draconian calendar, it was the 68th Year of the Serpent. The Doctor became the only person to beat the Emperor at Sazou - a Draconian game akin to chess - and not lose his head. The

---

100 The cuttings are stolen "five years" prior to *Hothouse*. It's not expressly said that Hazel herself arranged the theft, but it seems likely.
101 *Interference* (Book Two, p292, p314), where the If, one of IM Foreman's incarnations, predicts Sarah's death. Following the machinations of the Council of Eight, the timeline is altered so that Sam Jones died in 2002.
102 *Dreamstone Moon* (p58).
103 "Five hundred years" before *Frontier in Space*. The incident is also recounted in *Shadowmind*.
104 *Paper Cuts*. The Doctor who visits Draconia is described as being "old" and "aged", which sounds like the first Doctor, but *The Dark Path* establishes it was the second Doctor.
105 *Catastrophea*
106 *Return of the Living Dad*. According to the Doctor in *The Parting of the Ways*, the Daleks also refer to him by that title.
107 "Cold-Blooded War!" The Doctor is familiar with this custom, so it must predate his first visit to Draconia.
108 *Benny: Nobody's Children*. There's no evidence that the Doctor actually tried to make off with the Empress' daughter.
109 Dating *The Seeds of Death* (6.5) - This story is tricky to pin down a date for, or even to place in relation to other stories.

On screen, the only indication of the date is the Doctor's identification of the ion rocket designed by Eldred as a product of "the twenty-first century". As the rocket only exists as a prototype at this stage, the story must take place before 2100. T-Mat is developed at least two generations after space travel, as Eldred's father designed spacecraft, including a "lunar passenger module", and Eldred is an old man himself. It's impossible to infer a firm date from that, particularly as we know from *The Tenth Planet* that moonshots were unremarkable events by the mid-1980s in the *Doctor Who* universe. However, "lunar passenger module" suggests an altogether more routine service, and that this story is not set in the late twentieth or very early twenty-first century. It's never stated how long Travel-Mat has been in operation before *The Seeds of Death*, but it is a relatively new invention, as the video brochure we hear (transcribed here in full) states. Young

Gia Kelly was involved with the development of T-Mat, but it has been around "a good many years" according to Eldred, long enough to make a rocket-travel advocate look eccentric. T-Mat is referred to as having been around for "years", rather than "decades" or "generations" - all told, it seems reasonable to suggest that T-Mat has been around for about a decade before the story.

It is possible to rule out certain dates by referring to other stories: The Weather Control Bureau is seen, so it must be set after 2016 when Salamander invents weather control; the Bureau is on Earth, which might suggest the story is set before 2050 when the Gravitron is installed on the moon, or that the system is later moved to Earth. Either way, the story can't be set between 2050 and (at least) 2070, because the Gravitron is in operation from the moon at that time and rockets are in use during that period. By the time of *The Seeds of Death*, it's stated that man has not travelled beyond the moon.

While *About Time* claims that the "technology is shown to be in advance of that in *The Wheel in Space*", it's a bit hard to see what that's based on. We're explicitly told that Zoe has a more extensive knowledge of spaceflight than Eldred. (He admits as much, and Radnor says the same later - and, despite what *About Time* says, clearly distinguishes between Zoe's expertise and Jamie's lack of it.) Laser weapons have been developed by *The Wheel in Space*, including compact hand "blasters", but projectile weapons are still used here. There are quite advanced robots in Zoe's time, nothing like that seen here. Zoe was trained in a futuristic city, yet the cities we see here look much as they do now. That might be circumstantial evidence, but there's far more than that - *The Seeds of Death* is set at a time when man has travelled no "farther than the moon", whereas *The Wheel in Space* is set at a time when man's got at least to the asteroid belt, explicitly has ships in "deep space", has a "fleet" of manned ships, has at least five permanent space stations, and has been selecting and intensively training people to be astronauts for at least Zoe's lifetime (nineteen years, according to *The Invasion*). While no one says it in the story, *The Seeds of Death* is clearly - and is clearly intended to be - set before *The Wheel in Space*, case closed.

Deep space interstellar missions with crews in sus-

Doctor implored the Emperor to seal Draconia's borders to contain the plague, and insisted that the plague-antidote be given to commoners and royals alike. The Emperor agreed, but the quarantine made Draconia lose contact with its Imperial domains, and its empire collapsed.[104]

The Doctor was given the rank of High Earl of the Imperial House.[105] The Draconians took to referring to the Doctor as "the Oncoming Storm".[106] Draconian society had changed from the days of its Tribal Epoch; historical records suggested that it was only when it entered its Industrial Epoch that Draconian females had become subservient to males.[107]

The Draconian tradition of the *nikhol vakarshta* - a retreat for mothers and daughters - dated back to the great space plague. A legend held that the Karshtakavarr, "The

Oncoming Storm", tried to depart with the Empress' daughter, but that she drove him off empty-handed - a symbol of female empowerment and the importance of motherhood.[108]

c 2040 (early in the year, winter) - THE SEEDS OF DEATH[109] **-> Thanks to Travel-Mat, humanity had become dangerously insular. The Ice Warriors remained confined to Mars during all this time, limited by the lack of resources their home planet had to offer. The Grand Marshall of the Martians ordered an invasion of Earth. A small squad led by Lord Slarr took Seed Pods - oxygen-fixing plants native to Mars - to the moonbase that controlled T-Mat. The plan was to cripple Earth by disabling the T-Mat, then use the Seeds to**

pended animation were launched in the twenty-first century according to *The Sensorites*, which would be after the events of this story. The lack of deep space travel would seem to set the story before *The Power of the Daleks* (whichever year that is).

Evidence in subsequent stories would indicate that it's not set between 2068 and 2096, as Galactic Salvage and Insurance are covering spacecraft between those dates according to *Nightmare of Eden* (although if the space programme ended, it might explain why they went bust). If it was just Galactic Insurance, we could say it was just a meaningless brand name - we can buy Mars bars, that's not evidence we've built chocolate factories on Mars. It's Galactic *Salvage* and Insurance. The implication seems to be that whatever else they do, they salvage and insure spacecraft.

The T-Mat network seems to connect up the whole world - it includes both New York and Moscow, for example, which would seem inconsistent with the Cold War world of 2084 seen in *Warriors of the Deep*. Not every city in the world is named, of course, and *About Time* speculates that China might be in a hostile rival bloc, because no Chinese cities are named (although "Asiatic Centres" are). Finally, the story probably isn't set after 2096, as four years seems too short a period to explore the entire solar system (*The Mutants*) before the interstellar missions mentioned in *The Sensorites*.

Or, to cut a long story short, and assuming a ten-year period before the story when T-Mat has been operating, *The Seeds of Death* has to be set more than ten years after *The Enemy of the World* (so after 2027), but before the Gravitron is installed in 2050.

This contradicts the limited space travel seen in stories (made after *The Seeds of Death*) to Mars in *The Ambassadors of Death*, *The Dying Days* and *Red Dawn*, and to Jupiter in *Memory Lane* and (accidentally) *The Android Invasion*, as well as the most likely date for *The Power of the Daleks*. If Vulcan was a rogue planet in our solar system, perhaps the colonisation mission was launched as it passed relatively close to Earth (although

that piles supposition on supposition), or perhaps - more likely - the Vulcan colony had long failed and "doesn't count".

The Waters of Mars, set in 2059, provides us with a lot of new information, mainly in the backstory of characters seen on computer screens. There are no direct or indirect references to the future history established in any other *Doctor Who* story (including *The Seeds of Death*), and it strongly supports an earlier, rather than later, dating for *The Seeds of Death*. It rules out *About Time*'s dating of circa 2090, given that's after (we know now) Earth's first lightspeed ship reached Proxima Centauri. Consequently, this edition of *Ahistory* has moved *The Seeds of Death* a few years earlier than previous editions, from ?2044 to c2040.

"Mankind has travelled no further than the moon" in *The Seeds of Death*. As discussed, a number of other stories have astronauts landing on Mars, and we have to fudge that, whenever we set *The Seeds of Death*. *The Waters of Mars*, though, has a full-fledged, historic, long-term colony on the planet in 2058.

It might seem plausible to speculate that Bowie Base One "doesn't count" because it was destroyed, just as it's easy enough to see how manned space exploration might be temporarily abandoned (for a few years, at least) in the light of the disaster. As with the issue of when the Silurians ruled (see "A Complete Misnomer"), though, *Ahistory* always tries to look at the spirit of a story, as well as every letter. We might be able to fudge "no further than the moon", but the whole thrust of *The Waters of Mars* is that Brooke's sacrifice was the spark that directly inspired further space exploration. We know from *The Moonbase* that space travel was not abandoned in the 2060s.

We face the problem that Brooke doesn't know about the Ice Warriors, but given that UNIT know about the Martians (*The Christmas Invasion*, even confining ourselves just to television stories), this is a problem whenever we place it. Brooke and Cain were the first and second female Britons to land on the moon... and

alter Earth's atmosphere until it more closely resembled that of Mars. The Pods were sent to Earth via Travel-Mat and preparations were made to guide the Martian invasion fleet to Earth. As killer foam spread through London, the second Doctor, Zoe and Jamie travelled to the moon and defeated the Ice Warriors, directing the Martian fleet into the Sun.[110]

The global teleportation system lead to disastrous UN aid decisions.[111]

The Conquest of the Solar System

Space travel was readopted and co-ordinated by International Space Command in Geneva. Ion jet rockets explored the solar system.[112]

Ed Gold became a US citizen in 2040 so that he could join NASA's astronaut program. The same year saw unprecedented storms; Andrew Stone's Iowa commune developed new farming techniques to cope.[113]

Temperatures in Britain were three degrees higher than they were in the Middle Ages, pollution levels

---

yet, we saw Gia Kelly on the moon in *The Seeds of Death*. That said, assuming Kelly is British, she didn't "land on the moon", she went there by Travel-Mat. The act of piloting the ship to a safe landing is what "counts", there. For that matter, if we're counting every Briton who's been to the moon, then there was a hospital full of them that materialised there in *Smith and Jones*.

Accepting that *The Seeds of Death* is set before *The Waters of Mars*, we now have to find somewhere in the timeline for the former before 2059, where there's about ten years with no evidence of human space exploration. Only one exists, between 2032 and 2040. We know from *The Waters of Mars* that Peter Bennett gave up space exploration to look after his daughter Mia, who was born in 2032. We are told that Yuri Kerenski started working as a doctor for the Russian space agency in 2032. There's nothing then until 2040, when *The Waters of Mars* tells us there is a burst of space exploration activity in 2040 to 2042 (as documented in the timeline). This is exactly what we'd like to see, exactly when we'd want to see it. The connection is not made in *The Waters of Mars*, but we can conjecture this: around 2032, Russia and America, at least, had functioning space programmes. These were abandoned when T-Mat came along shortly afterwards - Peter Bennett either got out just in time or saw which way the wind was blowing. Yuri got his job at the wrong time, and either didn't specialise in treating long term cosmonauts until later in his career, or he treated former cosmonauts or people working on the T-Mat station on the moon. Following the end of T-Mat, there was a burst of recruitment and activity.

The original storyline set the date as "3000 AD", but later press material suggested the story took place "at the beginning of the twenty-first century".

As we might expect, no fan consensus exists on the dating of *The Seeds of Death*, and probably - despite *The Waters of Mars* bringing a lot more information to the debate - never will. The first edition of *The Making of Doctor Who* claimed the story is set in "the latter part of the twentieth century", the second was less specific and simply placed the story in the "twenty-first century". The first two editions of *The Programme Guide* set the story "c2000", *The Terrestrial Index* alters this to "c2090", and the

novel *Lucifer Rising* concurs with this date (p171). *DWM* writer Richard Landen suggested "2092". *Timelink* says "2096, February", conceding "this is a difficult story to date". *Encyclopedia of the Worlds of Doctor Who* set the story in "the twenty-second century". Ben Aaronovitch's *Transit* follows on from *The Seeds of Death*, with his "Future History Continuity" setting the television story "c2086"; *About Time* conforms to that.

110 WHATEVER HAPPENED TO TRAVELMAT?: While we're told space travel will be readopted at the end of *The Seeds of Death*, no-one says they'll abandon T-Mat. As T-Mat is an astonishingly useful technology - one that's quickly been adopted by most countries, if not all - it seems odd that we never see it again. It's not just absent from the twenty-first century either - it's missing from every story set on a future Earth (with one exception: *The Year of Intelligent Tigers*, set circa 2185, which suggests that large spaceships use it). Service might be disrupted by the Dalek Invasion, but you'd think they'd have it working again for, say, *Frontier in Space*.

The obvious explanation is that Earth can afford a space programme or a T-Mat programme, but not both. This is implicit in *The Seeds of Death*. It might not be simply a case of money so much as expertise - it's stated that a number of top rocket scientists became T-Mat ones. Logically, if you can instantaneously beam men and materials to the moon, it ought to lead to a mass colonisation of the moon - but it hasn't. Earth's priorities have changed, mankind is looking inward. *The Seeds of Death* offers a world where the technology is there for space exploration, but the political will isn't (as such, it's the most realistic prediction of the twenty-first century that *Doctor Who* writers made in the sixties).

There are other explanations, all pure speculation, and mainly economic. T-Mat is a network requiring a huge infrastructure, and must be expensive. When real-life people were presented with the choice of seven hours on a normal plane or two hours on Concorde, they ended up picking the normal plane on cost grounds. Presumably using the T-Mat isn't free, and the technology might not look so attractive if instant travel from London to New York cost ten times more than taking a plane. Alternatively, the analogy might be with

were much higher and every oak tree and silver birch tree had now died out.[114] Many scientists were involved the efforts to develop artificial methods of cooling the planet.[115] As part of a team of scientists conducting experiments to that end, Alistair Gryffen almost single-handedly caused The Great Cataclysm: an event that included massive hurricanes and a sudden, massive rise in sea levels.[116]

Around 2040, Alistair Gryffen's family - his wife Eleanor and children Mina and Jacob - went for a walk without him while on holiday, and disappeared. He would never forgive himself for their loss, and the trauma of it made him agoraphobic.[117] Around 2041, Darius Pike's father arranged for a clown to provide the entertainment at his son's sixth birthday party, which gave Darius a permanent phobia.[118]

NASA undertook Project Pit Stop around 2041 - a refuelling base was set up on the moon, as a stepping stone to Mars. Adelaide Brooke met Ed Gold when they both worked on the project. Brooke became the first female Briton to land on the moon. Following this, unmanned shuttles flew to Neptune and Jupiter.

In 2042, Adelaide Brooke became the first woman to land on Mars, part of a three-person team. On her return, she campaigned to colonise Mars before the moon. Steffi Ehrlich was studying at the Bundeswehr and Aachen University at this time.[119]

c 2043 - SINGULARITY[120] -> Led by Natalia Pushkin - a.k.a. Qel, the High Priestess of the New Consciousness - the Somnus Foundation had emerged as a quasi-religious organisation dedicated to awakening mankind's potential.

trams - a system with many advantages over the cars that replaced them, but which lost out for all sorts of reasons (mainly that it was hard for them to co-exist, and trams required governmental funding but cars made money in taxes). Even if individuals aren't picking up the T-Mat bills, someone must be. It's a centralised system, and perhaps it's an all or nothing proposition - either a worldwide network or it's useless (like, say, GPS in the present day). Or it might be that space travel starts paying off - perhaps materials from the asteroid belt and cheap energy from space means there's suddenly an abundance of resources. Perhaps there were disasters. These could either be *Hindenburg*-style serious failures of the T-Mat system itself, or unintended consequences like T-Mat allowing a rapid spread of something undesirable - terrorists, diseases or even just migrant workers or counterfeit/grey market goods.

Transit tackles these questions, and imagines a solar system radically transformed a generation after T-Mat. Its author, Ben Aaronovitch, dated *The Seeds of Death* to about 2085 and *Transit* to about 2109, with the T-Mat system in continuous use between them - the story is essentially *The Seeds of Death: The Next Generation*, complete with Ice Warriors. But this needn't have been a continuous process. Perhaps, once the solar system had been explored by rockets for a generation, the political will and funding re-emerged and the T-Mat network was rebuilt and expanded (just as tram networks are now being re-established in many cities).

In the future, we see stories where rockets and transmats *can* co-exist, but mainly as a way to beam from a spacecraft to the surface of a planet - not as mass transit. But even given that, transmats are surprisingly rare in humanity's future. On television, humans use transmats in *The Mutants*, *The Ark in Space*, *The Sontaran Experiment* and *Revenge of the Cybermen* (and three of those stories use the same machine!), and transmats are mentioned in *The Twin Dilemma* (but it's alien technology). So we might not know exactly why T-Mat was

abandoned, but it clearly was.
111 *The Indestructible Man* (p78).
112 International Space Command is mentioned in *The Tenth Planet* and *Revenge of the Cybermen*, as well as *The Moonbase*, where it seems to be an agency of the World Zones Authority as seen in *The Enemy of the World* - we hear about "the General Assembly", "Atlantic Zone 6", and the head of the ISC is a "Controller" Rinberg. Ion jet rockets are mentioned in *The Seeds of Death*.
113 *The Waters of Mars*
114 *K9: The Last Oak Tree*
115 *K9: The Korven*
116 *K9: Aeolian* and *K9: The Sirens of Ceres*. The Great Cataclysm presumably happens before Gryffen becomes an agoraphobic. *The Waters of Mars* establishes that "unprecedented storms" happen in 2040, and that's a perfect fit. It's much more of a stretch to say this was one of the "disastrous decisions" caused by Travel-Mat alluded to in *The Indestructible Man*, but it's certainly possible that the atmospheric disturbances, flooding and hurricanes caused by the Great Cataclysm might have been what crippled the T-Mat system.
117 Gryffen has "not been out of the house for ten years", according to Darius in *K9: The Korven*; this was "a few years" before *K9: The Fall of the House of Gryffen*. *K9: The Last Precinct* claims Gryffen's house was a police station used by human officers until the introduction of robot CCPCs, and as that development only happened two years before that story, Gryffen must have lived in different places since becoming agoraphobic. The mystery of his family's disappearance was never solved in the series.
118 *K9: Dream-Eaters*
119 *The Waters of Mars*
120 Dating *Singularity* (BF #76) - The Doctor reads a Somnus Foundation brochure that claims the groups' brightest minds will terraform Mars "by 2090", so the story cannot occur after that date.

The Somnus Tower had been built behind the Kremlin, employing a Bygellian style that humans wouldn't create for another six hundred years.

Qel and her colleagues proceeded with their plan to turn all of humanity into a Singularity gestalt, and snared the inhabitants of Moscow in such a network. The fifth Doctor and Turlough intervened, and consequently the Singularity didn't hold, the Somnus Tower exploded, Qel was killed and the other conspirators were catapulted back to the far-flung future. Authorities claimed the incident was a terrorist attack against the Somnus cult, one that resulted in a hallucinogenic compound being released.

The Doctor believed that dozens of nonterrestrials were operating on Earth in this period. A Russian Public Security Directorate was in service.

Tarak Ital won gold medals in sprinting and the high jump in the Havana Olympics of 2044. He angered many of his countrymen by giving up athletics for a career in medicine. Ed Gold lobbied for an Australian space programme, and this led to a space elevator being built off the coast of Western Australia.[121]

c 2044 - THE GREAT SPACE ELEVATOR[122] -> Engineers on Earth had developed super conducted carbon micro-tubing that solved various stress-weight problems, and had used it to construct the Space Elevator: a giant lift going from a base station in Sumatra to a Sky Station 22,500 miles above the ground. A creature that had been drifting in space for thousands of years - one that existed as a kind of electromagnetic field - invaded the Sky Station and possessed some of its crew. The second Doctor, Victoria and Jamie stopped the creature from using the station's weather-control systems to direct a massive electrical storm against the Elevator's base, which would have made the creature immensely powerful but killed millions. The Doctor grounded the creature into the Earth's crust.

---

121 *The Waters of Mars*
122 Dating *The Great Space Elevator* (BF CC #3.2) - The back cover blurb only tells us it's "the future". Although the link isn't made in either story, we're told in *The Waters of Mars* that Ed Gold successfully lobbied to have a space elevator built "off the coast of Western Australia". Sumatra just about qualifies, and the weather control technology is consistent with that seen in *the Seeds of Death*.
123 Dating *The Architects of History* (BF #132) - The year is repeatedly given.
124 *The Well-Mannered War* (p204).
125 *Alien Bodies* (p9).
126 *Christmas on a Rational Planet*. "Nearly a millennium" before Roz is born (p31).
127 Dating *Hothouse* (BF BBC7 #3.2) - No year is given, but the story can be comfortably dated to the middle of the twenty-first century. It's said that white rhinos became extinct in "the wild" in "the last five years" - some are presumably still around in captivity, but all rhinos on Earth are extinct by 2051 according to *The Last Dodo*. The environment is in a bad way, and clearly headed for the sort of ecological carnage that occurs circa 2060 according to *Loups-Garoux*. Krynoids and the World Ecology Bureau were first seen in *The Seeds of Doom*. One curiosity is that an undercover Lucie Miller appears on the TV of the future as a raving member of the League of Nature while using her real name. As she was born in 1988, that should give any historian tracking her life something to think about.
128 Dating *Forty-Five*: "The Word Lord" (BF #115d) - The year is given. The "Second Cold War" is presumably a lead-up to the state of affairs seen in *Warriors of the Deep*.
129 *The Waters of Mars*
130 CCPCs were introduced "two years" before *K9: The*

Last Precinct.
131 *Alien Bodies*, pgs 263-264. This is the origin of the titular characters from *The Krotons*, the obvious implication being that the Krotons were pattered on the servo-robots from *The Wheel in Space*. (They *do* look roughly similar, as it happens.) The placement of the Krotons' creation in the twentieth century is nonetheless tricky - Lawrence Miles, as outlined in *About Time 2*, envisioned an earlier dating for *The Wheel in Space* (circa 2030) than this chronology, but the central question is when humans and their servo-robots could have feasibly arrived on Krosi-Apsai-Core. Mankind doesn't venture beyond the Sol system much in the twentieth century, so the Kroton homeworld should be comparatively closer to Earth than not. Either way, the Krotons undergo a startling evolution in just a few decades - by 2068, according to *Alien Bodies*, their war capabilities are fairly formidable.
132 Dating *K9* Series 1 - The stories of the *K9* TV series follow on from each other in relatively short order. No date is ever given on screen, but the prepublicity stated that the year is 2050, and that works as well as any other date. Pre-publicity also stated that the titular character was K9 Mark 1, but the on-screen evidence isn't nearly so certain about this...

THE FOUR K9s: Four models of K9 appear on television, with all of them making an appearance in at least one tie-in property.

Mark 1 K9: First appears in *The Invisible Enemy*, leaves the TARDIS to stay on Gallifrey with Leela in *The Invasion of Time*, goes on missions for the Time Lords in *The Adventures of K9* book series, loyally serves Leela on Gallifrey in the *Gallifrey* audios and is destroyed in *Gallifrey: Imperiatrix*.

Mark 2 K9: First appears (in a box) at the end of *The Invasion of Time*, and is first seen (out of box) in *The*

(=) 2044 - THE ARCHITECTS OF HISTORY[123] -> Elizabeth Klein, having stolen the seventh Doctor's TARDIS, made enough historical alterations to bring about the Terran Galactic Reich. She attained the rank of Oberst, and oversaw the Reich's temporal affairs. The Doctor of this timeline aided the Selachians in developing time-travel, which enabled their warfleet to travel from the future and lay waste to Earth in 2044. The Reich's moonbase was also destroyed, and the casualties included Rachel Cooper, the alternate Doctor's companion.

The consciousness of the Doctor from the proper timeline supplanted that of his alternate self, and he and Klein agreed to undo Earth's devastation by using the alternate Doctor's TARDIS to erase her - i.e. the version of her who travelled back to Colditz - from history. This undid Klein's historical revisions, and retroactively erased the Galactic Reich.

Professor Otterbland of the Dubrovnik Institute of New Sciences discovered psychotronic conditioning in 2045.[124] Borneo became a ReVit Zone in 2049. The rainforests were replanted and stocked with genetically engineered plants and animals.[125] The United States fell in the mid-twenty-first century.[126]

c 2045 - HOTHOUSE[127] -> Earth's population now stood at ten billion. The last five years had seen the extinction in the wild of the cheetah and the white rhino. Half of the Amazon rain forest was now a dust bowl. Britain had experienced drought for twenty weeks, and the government prosecuted people violating standpipe rations. In London, one hundred thousand protestors called for increased efforts to combat global warming. The previous year had seen a refugee crisis - millions had tried to flee North Africa and the Black Sea states, but borders were shut to avoid the Eurozone being overwhelmed. The St. Petersburg Bio-Protection Treaty enabled the World Ecology Bureau to inspect any facility used for agricultural research.

The activist Alex Marlowe had formed the ecomilitant League of Nature, which advocated mandatory population reduction and the abolition of private capital. The group had eight hundred and nine million paid members. Marlowe constructed the Hothouse as a top-secret research facility, and - using the Krynoid cuttings stolen from the World Ecology Bureau - had hundreds of people smuggled in from outside the Eastern Eurozone and forcibly turned into Krynoids. He hoped to develop a Krynoid variant that retained a human consciousness but could exert control over nature. If successful, he envisioned a mass sterilisation that would bring Earth's population down to about one hundred million.

One of Marlowe's agents, Hazel Bright, was forced to become a Krynoid and retained enough of her identity to kill him. With Bright's help, the eighth Doctor and Lucie destroyed the Hothouse's main biodome - killing Bright and all of Marlowe's Krynoids.

2045 - FORTY-FIVE: "The Word Lord"[128] -> During the Second Cold War, the Ranulph Fiennes Bunker was constructed in Antarctica. It was located four hundred and fifty miles from civilisation, and housed top-secret peace talks. The seventh Doctor, Ace and Hex arrived at the bunker pursued by the Word Lord, a.k.a. Nobody No One. The engines of Nobody's CORDIS had repeated instances of "45" in the Doctor's recent adventures. Nobody failed to capture the Doctor's party and claim several bounties on them. At this time, only thirty-four people had access to UN files on the Doctor.

Andrew Stone left his commune in Iowa in 2045, and had the desire to help the world survive the effects of global warming with new farming techniques. Despite Stone's lack of formal training, Peter Bennett recruited him for the Mars colonisation programme. Steffi Ehrlich gained her degree in solid state physics in 2046. She joined the German astronaut team of the European Space Agency in 2048. Tarak Ital was working on space medicine, and developed a transdermal dimenhydrinate patch to solve the problem of space sickness. That year, the Olympics were held in Paris. Margaret Cain beat twenty-five thousand candidates to become one of four astronauts on the Russian mission Midas. She spent eighteen months training at the Yuri Gagarin cosmonaut training centre.[129]

In 2048, the police force dishonourably discharged Harry Pike after he protested the Department's decision to replace human police officers with Cybernetic Civic Pacification troops: cyborgs built from cloned humans.[130]

The Krotons first evolved as a predatory, quasi-organic tellurium-based crystal (later called the "Kroton Absolute") on the planet Krosi-Apsai-Core. The Absolute generated "slaved" sub-beings capable of mimicking their prey's abilities, but didn't develop a true consciousness until human capitalists arrived to expand their territory and find mineral wealth. The humans' servo-robots proved easy to copy, and so the Absolute created millions, perhaps billions, of Krotons: semi-sentient, armoured crystalline entities that were linked through mental vibrations.[131]

K9 Series 1[132]

By 2050, London was a near-police state. Cybernetic Civic Pacification troops (CCPCs) patrolled the city and surveillance cameras and drones were ubiquitous. Giant floating screens advertised products and warned potential criminals. A totalitarian government agency, the Department, handled security and also ran Dauntless prison. The Tower of London had a facility that secretly held "Fallen Angels" - aliens - and experimented with alien technology. Most aliens were peaceful, but all were indefinitely detained. Juvenile human criminals were held in Virtual Reality detention.[133]

People carried verometers: advanced mobile phones.[134] The currency in Britain was either the pound or the "cred".[135] Britain had a King.[136] Omnivorous bacteria had been discovered on Pluto.[137] Experiments on cyborgs were strictly regulated.[138]

The Mark II CCPC was introduced. It secretly used a variety of alien technology.[139] The Department was protected by hovering stun mines. The Jixen were winning their war with the Meron until the Korven began supplying the Meron with new energy weapons.[140]

2050 - K9: REGENERATION -> The activist Stark Reality, in reality a teenager named Starkey, stumbled across the house of the agoraphobic Professor Alistair Gryffen. He worked for the Department, mainly on the

Time/Space Project, which reconstructed a device capable of creating portals in time and space. Darius Pike, age 15, was employed as Gryffen's assistant.

K9 materialised in Gryffen's house, quickly followed by four turtle-like Jixen warriors. K9 self destructed to save Gryffen and the children, but Starkey recovered K9's regeneration disc. This activated and caused K9 to reform, but his memdrive was damaged, meaning he could not account for where and when he was from...

2050 - K9: LIBERATION -> One Jixen survived, had Starkey's scent and pursued him. K9 and his friends broke into Dauntless prison and freed the aliens held captive there. A Meron was revealled to be working at the Dauntless disguised as a human. The Jixen was killed and the existence of Dauntless made public, forcing the Department to close it.

2050 - K9: THE KORVEN -> K9 assisted Starkey, who was considered a dissident and on the run, to avoid the CCPCs and their invisible Camo vehicles. A dangerous alien Korven materialised in Gryffen's house and kid-

---

Ribos Operation. He remains in E-Space with Romana in *Warriors' Gate*, then returns with her to Gallifrey (as seen in *Lungbarrow*), and so becomes embroiled in the planet's ambiguous fate. He secretly survives the first destruction of Gallifrey (in *The Ancestor Cell*) and rejoins the eighth Doctor (as revealed in *The Gallifrey Chronicles*), but he's also present on the Gallifrey seen in the Big Finish audios. At the end of Gallifrey Series 4, he's left stranded in the Axis.

These two K9s first meet in *Lungbarrow*. There is some uncertainty as to which of these two K9s ends up starring in the *K9* TV series. The prepublicity for the show stated that it was the Mark 1 model. But in the first episode, *K9: Regeneration*, when an old model K9 is destroyed and regenerates into a new form, his reboot menu gives him the options "Mark 1" and "Mark 2"... and he clearly selects "Mark 2". So, either this is (as stated) the Mark 2 version, or it might be the Mark1 K9 taking an opportunity to upgrade his software. In either event, and somewhat unhelpfully, this K9 has lost its memory. As K9 Mark 1 is apparently destroyed in *Imperiatrix*, and without any other evidence to go on, the *K9* TV series would seem to feature the Mark 2 model - a survivor of the Last Great Time War.

Mark 3 K9: First appears in *K9 and Company: A Girl's Best Friend* (the 1981 pilot for a *K9* show that didn't get made). This K9 belongs to Sarah Jane Smith, and they subsequently have a series of adventures as outlined in the *K9 Annual* (not covered in this chronology); he briefly appears in *The Five Doctors*; he's seen in the comic strip "City of Devils" (*DWM Holiday Special 1992*); in 1996 he's still working with Sarah Jane (*Interference*),

but after this time he falls into disrepair (loosely in accord with the short story "Moving On" from *Decalog 3*); his non-functional form is stolen by Hilda Winters (*SJS: Mirror, Signal. Manoeuvre*) in 2002, but possibly recovered following her death in 2005; he's repaired by the Doctor and is apparently destroyed in *School Reunion*. For those who wish to count such things as canon, it's possible that he regenerates and appears again in the *Make Your Own Adventure* book *The Search for the Doctor*.

Mark 4 K9: First appears at the end of *School Reunion*, is sidelined shortly afterwards to tend to a black hole (*SJA: Invasion of the Bane*) and is then released from that duty, joining Sarah Jane on Earth (*SJA: The Mad Woman in the Attic*). In his last appearance to date, *SJA: Goodbye, Sarah Jane Smith*, he's living with Luke Smith while Luke studies at Oxford.

133 The general background to the *K9* television series, as given in *K9: Regeneration*.

134 *K9: The Korven*

135 It's pounds in *K9: The Bounty Hunter*, the cred in *K9: Oroborus*, *K9: Black Hunger*, *K9: The Custodians* and *K9: Mutant Copper*.

136 *K9: Oroborus*, *K9: Robot Gladiators*.

137 *K9: Black Hunger*

138 *K9: Mutant Copper*

139 The Mark II CCPCs have been in operation "six months" before *K9: The Last Precinct*.

140 *K9: Hound of the Korven*

napped him, but K9 and the children tracked them down to an iceworks. The Korven had travelled back in time to absorb Gryffen's knowledge and use it to cool the Earth in preparation for an invasion in the twenty-fifth century, but K9 defeated him.

2050 - K9: THE BOUNTY HUNTER -> The technology of this era included the THX1138 self-aware oven and the experimental NX2000 spacecraft. A Mr Smith won a billion pounds playing the Lottery.

The bounty hunter Ahab arrived from the year 50,000, and attempted to apprehend K9 for the assassination of the diplomat Zanthus Pia. K9 had been framed - Ahab and the Jixen were the true culprits. Ahab escaped to exactly the same spot in his own time... but the Earth had moved by then, and Ahab was left adrift in space.

2050 (Sunday) - K9: SIRENS OF CERES -> After witnessing police brutality, the rebellious teenager Jorjie Turner threw a stone at a CCPC. She was sent as punishment to Magdalen Academy, where pupils wearing strange bracelets were unusually conformist. K9 learned that the bracelets contained Cerilium, a material that notoriously caused civilisation on Ceres to collapse after destroying its inhabitants' free will. He also exposed the Department's use of the material at the Academy.

2050 - K9: FEAR ITSELF -> Widespread riots spread across the world, putting everyone on edge. The source was an alien living in a wardrobe, but K9 isolated the alien before Drake - an agent of the Department - detonated a bomb, destroying it.

2050 - K9: THE FALL OF THE HOUSE OF GRYFFEN -> The "biggest electrical event for decades", a huge storm, affected London. This disrupted the Space-Time Manipulator installed at Gryffen's house and released the Sporax, a creature that generated fear. It created ectomorphic replicas of Gryffen's lost family, but K9 and his friends banished them.

2050 - K9: JAWS OF ORTHRUS -> K9 was caught on a coast-to-coast vidcast attempting to assassinate Drake - all part of Drake's Project Orthus. The truth was revealed: the K9 that shot Drake was actually a duplicate, intended to frame the real K9 and have him taken into custody to be disassembled.

The Department was on the verge of introducing tracker chips for people.

2050 - K9: DREAM-EATERS -> London was bombarded with psychic energy that induced sleep and gave people nightmares. Terrifying creatures from Celtic myth, the Bodachs, had been disturbed by the Department's unearthing of an obelisk containing the Eyes of Oblivion - crystals that the Bodachs planned to use to send the world to sleep. The Bodachs were using Jorjie's mother June as an avatar, but Jorjie broke their control by convincing her mother she got a tattoo. K9 destroyed the obelisk.

2050 - K9: THE CURSE OF ANUBIS -> A pyramid-like spacecraft approached Earth. Drake ordered its destruction, but the ship vanished before the missiles hit, and reappeared over London close to K9 and his friends. Jackal-headed aliens, the Anubians, arrived and knelt before "the mighty K9, the great liberator": the being that freed them from the domination of the Huducts. The Anubians took over Gryffen's house, and used Torcs to control the minds of everyone present. K9 learned that the Anubians had used the Huduct mind-control technology to conquer other races that apparently included the Alpha Centaurians, Mandrels, Sea Devils, Aeolians and Jixen. K9 and Darius broke the conditioning, and the Anubians left.

2050 - K9: OROBORUS -> Gryffen's Space-Time Manipulator activated, seemingly by itself. K9, Gryffen and the others began to encounter time loops and reversals. Starkey's arm itched, and a scan revealed his body was producing alien antibodies. Gryffen revealed that Starkey's parents had experimented on him, and endowed him with an alien immune system. Despite events happening out of sequence, or twice, or not at all, K9 and his allies tracked the source of the time shifts to a snake creature: the time-consuming Oroborus. They lured the Oroborus back into the Space-Time Manipulator, and banished it.

2050 - K9: ALIEN AVATAR -> The Department interrogated some aliens, the Medes, who could project avatars of themselves. Drake was keen to acquire their molecular refractor technology, but his researchers were dumping an alien toxin - chenium - that was a by-product of Qualon 37, as used by the Medes in interdimensional technology, into the Thames. K9 detected the pollutant while he and Starkey were fishing, and later helped to free the Medes, who departed.

2050 - K9: AEOLIAN -> A huge hurricane swept across the UK and North Sea, disrupting communications. The event was centred on Holy Cross Cathedral. Tornadoes destroyed the Royal Albert Hall and Hyde Park. Drake arrested Gryffen, as Gryffen had created conditions similar to this when one of his experiments went wrong and caused the Great Cataclysm. K9 identified the disruption as indicative of the Aeolians, masters of amplification long thought wiped out. The culprit was the last of the Aeolians, left without memories following the destruction of her race - the music was a desperate mating call. Gryffen detected a mating call from another Aeolian in the Orpheus Constellation, and the two Aeolians were brought together and then left Earth, which restored the weather to normal.

Earth's population at this time was six billion.[141]

2050 - K9: THE LAST OAK TREE -> K9, Jorjie and Starkey met Robin Hood in a virtual reality Sherwood Forest exhibition, the centrepiece of which was the last oak tree: the Major Oak of the Robin Hood legend. An alien jamming signal disrupted the exhibit, and the Major Oak was stolen. K9 found traces of an alien substance and tracked down a Centuripede, which was using the oak to build a pod to transport her eggs. The Centuripede became a butterfly and her babies hatched. She gave Starkey three acorns as a reward for saving them from the Department.

2050 - K9: BLACK HUNGER -> The Department created the Black Hunger: an all-consuming bacteria swarm made from a combination of yeast and microbes from Pluto. The Hunger was made to alleviate London's rubbish problem, but it mutated into flesh-eaters and swarmed through the sewers. This would have destroyed all life on Earth in a week, but K9 contained the Hunger, and planned to take the swarm to Atrios. The leader of the Department, Lomax, decided that Drake had disobeyed orders too many times and replaced him with Thorne, the former governor of the Dauntless.

2050 - K9: THE CAMBRIDGE SPY -> Jorjie learned as part of a school assignment that Gryffen's mansion was a police station in 1963, the centre of an investigation into a spy ring. The Space-Time Manipulator whisked her back to that year. Darius was briefly erased from history, but Starkey and K9 went to 1963 and recovered Jorjie, repairing the timelines.

2050 - K9: LOST LIBRARY OF UKKO -> The Department held an Open Day to look for new recruits, much to K9's curiosity. Starkey attended and was sucked into a mysterious picture. K9 identified this as a library card from Ukko; Thorne had been planning to use it to exile criminals. Starkey was trapped on a barren world, Urlic, which had been compressed into a hologram by the Ukkans, an all-female race of archivists. An Ukkan, Yssaringintinka, arrived and retrieved Starkey.

The major world powers currently included the United Kingdom, the Americas and the Pacific Union.

2050 - K9: MUTANT COPPER -> The CCPCs were given sweeping new powers, including the ability to enter homes without warrants. K9 and the others come across a "mutant" CCPC whose connection to the Department had been broken, and who had human DNA. They named him Birdie, because he was fascinated with birds. Birdie gradually became more human, and learned new skills such as how to make toast. K9 and his friends smuggled Birdie away from London to the countryside, where he enjoyed seeing the birds.

2050 - K9: THE CUSTODIANS -> Jorjie and Darius played the new VR game *Little Green Men*, even as the city outside was in chaos, and emergency services were overwhelmed. The headsets for the game were alien in origin, and twenty million children had been simultaneously affected by it. Greenroom Entertainment had allied with the last of the Etydions - they were the most powerful telepaths who ever lived, and had hired themselves out to psionically repel invading forces with waves of fear, but were wiped out by their enemies. Greenroom intended that the Etrydion would create a telepathic network that would pacify youngsters into being good children, but the Etrydion secretly planned to transform the children into members of its own race. The Etrydion died when June's emotions for Jorjie's safety overloaded it.

---

141 *K9: Aeolian* establishes that Earth's population in the *K9* series is "six billion", which is lower than it is in 2010 (in both real life and the *Doctor Who* universe), and this might suggest there has been a catastrophic lost of life - possibly owing to the "Great Catastrophe" described in the *K9* show or some other event.
142 The episode is a clip show, with very little new material.
143 *Iris: The Claws of Santa* outright states that the ice cap melted. *Hothouse* shows that global warming has

become a major political issue, and *K9: Sirens of Ceres* says that many top scientists have been assigned to find a solution. It's very tempting to see the Gravitron from *The Moonbase*, a global weather control system set up in 2050, as a potential solution to the environmental collapse the planet is suffering from in other stories set around that time.

2050 - K9: TAPHONY AND THE TIME LOOP ->
Gryffen helped to liberate Taphony, a girl trapped in a
VR created by the Department. She was a Time Blank,
an entity that didn't follow the normal rules of time
and could disintegrate everything she touched. She
had been created within the Department by use of
alien technology, but became vengeful upon learning
that Gryffen was partly responsible for said experiment. Starkey, Jorjie and Darius befriended Taphony,
and persuaded her to leave for a realm better suited to
her.

2050 - K9: ROBOT GLADIATORS -> Freddie Maxwell
ran Destructertainment, which put on robot gladiator
shows. Darius pretended to trick K9 into becoming
part of Maxwell's stable of robots - all part of a plan to
end Maxwell's illegal scam. Thorne colluded with
Maxwell to develop combat robots such as the Pain-
Maker, with the ultimate aim of acquiring K9's regenerative technology. The Pain-Maker was packed with
enough solarmite explosive to destroy everything in
the arena apart from K9's regeneration unit, and when
K9 refused to fight, Thorne had the Pain-Maker self-
destruct. The blast wasn't enough to damage K9.
Maxwell's business was shut down, leaving Gryffen,
K9 and the kids to wonder how Thorne knew that K9
could regenerate...

2050 - K9: MIND SNAP[142] **->** K9 activated the Space-
Time Manipulator, hoping that some siphoned temporal power would help restore his memories. Instead, it
adversely affected his mind, making him confused and
aggressive. Gryffen restored his memories by having
K9 remember his previous adventures.

2050 - K9: ANGEL OF THE NORTH -> K9 deduced
the co-ordinates of a Fallen Angel - the ship from
which the Space-Time Manipulator was recovered - in
Canada. Gryffen thought the ship might contain the
device's missing temporal stabiliser, but was unable to
conquer his agoraphobia, and so travelled to Canada in
a VR encasement suit. K9 and the kids used the
Manipulator to teleport to the alien ship, where they
encountered a Korven - one of over a hundred in the
area. The Korven were the most dangerous race K9 had
ever encountered, and the Manipulator had been made
from their technology. Gryffen vowed to never use the
temporal stabiliser upon deducing that K9's enhancement code was somehow part of it.

2050 - K9: THE LAST PRECINCT -> A group called
The Last Precinct staged a spate of attacks on CCPCs.
Fake CCPCs came to Gryffen's house and immobilised
K9 - these were actually humans, all of them all ex-

policemen made obsolete by the CCPCs. Darius'
father, Harry Pike, was among their number. They
planed to infect the CCPCs with a virus, but it proved
unstable, and caused the CCPCs to go on a rampage.
K9 deactivated the CCPCs, and the Last Precinct members were rounded up and arrested.

2050 - K9: HOUND OF THE KORVEN -> Thorne
showed Darius that his father was cracking up in his
solitary confinement VR prison, and demanded that he
fetch him K9's regeneration unit. He also revealled he
had K9's memory disc and offered a swap. Thorne and
K9 traded the components - but K9's memory disc had
been implanted with a self-destruct code that would
activate if he got within range of an unknown location.
A Jixen kidnapped Gryffen, and explained that the
Jixen were a friendly, peaceful race marauded by the
Meron, who were allied with the Korven. K9 and his
allies realised that someone at the Department was
working for the Korven. Although K9 rerouted the self-
destruct orders on his memory disc, Thorne still had
his regeneration unit.

2050 - K9: THE ECLIPSE OF THE KORVEN -> The
Space-Time Manipulator observed a white hole and a
black hole coming together - if they touched, Earth
would be destroyed. K9 discovered that the Department
also had a Space-Time Manipulator at their Millennium
Dome base. Thorne's army of CCPCs surrounded K9,
and Thorne explained that an alien army was massing
on the other side of the galaxy, ready to invade Earth
via a temporal portal. The Department had engineered
Trojan - a supersoldier built from the DNA of every
alien species they had encountered - and fitted it with
K9's regeneration unit. Throne was working with the
invaders, and had engineered the white hole and black
hole to come together, knowing it would force Gryffen
to use the temporal stabiliser to widen the portal.
Thorne was actually as a Meron, while the head of the
Department, Lomax, was a Korven.

The spearhead of the Korven invasion force arrived
through the portal, but Gryffen conquered his agoraphobia and closed the portal using his personal voice
command: "Omega, Sigma, Theta, Ohm". Lomax and
the Korven were sucked into the portal and destroyed.
K9 fought Trojan, and got its Jixen and Meron impera-
tives to destroy each other. Thorne was crushed to
death when Trojan toppled on him. The more evil elements of the Department had been eliminated.

The polar ice cap melted in the twenty-first century.[143]

c 2050 - THE TIME OF THE DALEKS[144] -> The Daleks attempted to exploit a temporal rift to enhance their time travel capabilities, but the experiment backfired and they almost lost their entire fleet. They made contact with Mariah Learman, the ruler of New Britain, who had a primitive time scanner. Learman didn't believe the population appreciated Shakespeare, and the price for her co-operation with the Daleks was that they would assassinate Shakespeare as a youth and preserve the only copy of his works for Learman's benefit. Rebels thwarted this plan by smuggling an eight-year-old Shakespeare from 1572 for his own protection, but this caused further time distortion. The eighth Doctor arrived, trying to explain why his companion Charley didn't know of Shakespeare. The Doctor set history back on course by returning young Shakespeare to his rightful time. The Daleks were trapped in an endless temporal loop after mutating Learman into one of them.

It now took only a couple of hours for a shuttle rocket to travel from the Earth to the new moonbases. Around 2050, the ultimate form of weather control, the Gravitron, was built on the moon's surface. The political implications on Earth proved complex, and the General Assembly spent more than twenty years negotiating between farmers and landowners.[145] The Butler Institute built the Gravitron.[146] Rhinos were extinct on Earth by 2051.[147]

Harnessing gravity waves allowed artificial gravity to be installed on spacecraft and space stations. Permanent space stations were built. Flowers were cultivated on the surface of Venus. The first Doctor visited this timezone.[148] Victorian time traveller Penelope Gate and her companion Joel Mintz accidentally visited the middle of the twenty-first century.[149]

Around the middle of the century, domesticated wolves were reintroduced into the forests of Northern Europe. It was rumoured that the Wicca Society had released wild wolves, and there was some debate as to which strain would become dominant.[150]

In 2050, after two years of training, Steffi Ehrlich formed part of the tenth German moon mission. The following year, she married Hans Stott. Roman Groom had degrees in English and Physics, and was beginning postdoctoral work in astrophysics. He was only 17, but was accepted into NASA's Search for Astronauts programme in January 2051, and began two years' training. In April 2051, Margaret Cain became only the second female Briton to land on the moon. As part of that effort, she met Adelaide Brooke.

Mia Bennett had her thesis on Martian geology published. She had managed to grow green beans and turnips from samples of Martian soil.[151]

144 Dating *The Time of the Daleks* (BF #32) - It is "the mid twenty-first century".
145 "Twenty years" before *The Moonbase*.
146 *Deceit* (p27, p153). It was possibly based on Silurian technology, as the Silurians establish a Gravitron on the moon (in an alternate history) in *Blood Heat* (p196).
147 *The Last Dodo*
148 *The Wheel in Space*. The Doctor's familiarity with the Gravitron in *The Moonbase*, ion rockets in *The Seeds of Death* and Galactic Salvage and Insurance in *Nightmare of Eden* suggests he visited the solar system during this period at least once.
149 *The Room with No Doors* (p48).
150 *Transit*
151 *The Waters of Mars*
152 Dating *The King of Terror* (PDA #37) - The day that Daniel Clompus visits the Brigadier is given.
153 Dating *The Wedding of River Song* (X6.13) - It's a "few months" after the Brigadier has passed away, the date of which was established in *The King of Terror*.
154 "Almost a century" before *The Final Sanction* (p175), although it must be a little longer than that, as the Selachians were active in the twenty-first century according to both *The Murder Game* and *Alien Bodies*.
155 *The Memory Cheats*. Mention of the Company's self-defence techniques presumably explains how Zoe

can flip the Karkus about the place in *The Mind Robber*. This placement here is roughly in accord with Zoe being "19 or so" in *The Invasion*; Wendy Padbury was 20 when she started playing the part (*The Wheel in Space*).
156 *TW: Asylum*
157 *Alien Bodies* (p12).
158 *Vampire Science*
159 *Mad Dogs and Englishmen*
160 *St Anthony's Fire*
161 *Interference* (p217). *The Indestructible Man* specifies that the UN is the force behind the ban (p13).
162 *The Waters of Mars*. We're told that the crew have been "gone over two years" before November 2059, and also that it was a "two year journey" to get to Mars, so they left in late 2056/early 2057. It would only take "nine months" to get back, but the outbound trip involved taking all the supplies necessary to build the colony, time refuelling on the moon and possibly time in Martian orbit while drones built the base.
163 Dating *The Waters of Mars* (X4.16) - The historical significance of the date of the destruction of Bowie Base One means the precise day is repeated a number of times. Once again, human beings who you'd think would have been briefed by someone in the know are totally unaware of the Ice Warriors. There's no evidence that the computer or robots on Bowie Base One have artificial intelligence.

2050 (28th September) - THE KING OF TERROR[152]
-> Eighty years after the events occurred, some early UNIT files were officially released. The records included details on Cybermen, the Autons, the fall of General Carrington and the Stahlman incident.

Reporter Daniel Clompus, writing for the *Guardian*, visited the elderly Brigadier General Sir Alistair Lethbridge-Stewart at the Westcliffe Retirement Home in Sussex; the Brigadier General was thought to be 121 years old, but physically looked about 75.

Lethbridge-Stewart passed away shortly afterwards. The book that Clompus wrote on UNIT, *Watch the Skies: The Not-So-Secret-History of Alien Encounters*, was published in 2051. Lethbridge-Stewart's memoirs, *The Man Who Saved the World*, were published in 2052.

c 2050 - THE WEDDING OF RIVER SONG[153] -> The eleventh Doctor phoned Lethbridge-Stewart's nursing home... and discovered he had passed away, peacefully, a few months before.

The people of the ocean planet Ockora built exoskeletal battlesuits and started an uprising against their Kalarian oppressors, who hunted them for sport. These warriors renamed themselves Selachians. After defeating the Kalarians, they conquered four planets, including Kalaya and Molinar. The Selachians became arms dealers, and attacked a Martian colony with a sunstroker.[154]

The best and brightest of Earth's children, including Zoe Heriot, were given over to the Company's Elite Programme at a young age. The Elite Programme erased the children's memories of their families - Zoe became unable to remember her mother - and performed other techniques so alarming, the Company could have toppled if the truth became known. The Company taught the children self-defence techniques.[155] Freda, an offspring of the aliens who settled in Cardiff, was born on 30th May, 2053.[156]

In 2054, the Doctor and UNISYC (led by General Tchike) defeated the Montana Republican militia, who were using Selachian weapons.[157] Sam Jones had a mid-2050s ergonomic chair in her TARDIS room.[158] The Dogworld poodles built their first space station. It received radio signals from other planets, including Earth.[159]

All the religious faiths of the world were merged with the idea of creating world harmony. This consensus was unworkable and quickly collapsed. The Chapter of St Anthony was formed to fill the spiritual vacuum. When China was taken over by Hong Kong, the Yong family joined them on a new crusade to purge the heathens.[160]

In the mid 2050s, the world government overreacted to major wars and nuclear terrorism by passing police shoot-to-kill laws and banning all religions. There were years of total chaos, and cities became no-go areas. There was no effective government.[161]

The shuttle *Apollo 34* taking the first colonists to Mars set off around 2057. The first Martian colony was established on 1st July, 2058. This was Bowie Base One, built by robot drones on top of the underground glacier in Gusev Crater, and as supervised by nine human astronauts. Their mission was to discover whether the planet could be made suitable for human beings. The crew of Bowie Base One had dehydrated protein for their Christmas Dinner in 2058. Susie Fontana Brooke, granddaughter of mission commander Adelaide Brooke, was born after the crew left Earth. The base was partly constructed using a steel combination manufactured in Liverpool.[162]

2059 (21st November) - THE WATERS OF MARS[163]
-> The tenth Doctor arrived at Bowie Base One, the very first Martian colony, and realised he had arrived on the day it was doomed to be destroyed. History recorded that all the colonists were killed in a mysterious explosion. This would have an inspirational effect on humanity, spurring them to explore space. The Doctor theorised that base commander Adelaide Brooke's death was a "fixed" moment in time that was crucial to the future of humanity, and as such he was powerless to intervene.

The colonists had tapped the underground glacier in Gusev Crater for water, and in doing so had woken the Flood - an ancient lifeform that lived in liquid water, and could transform host creatures with water in their bodies. As more of the colonists were affected, Brooke initiated Action Procedure Five: the destruction of the base via a nuclear device in its central dome.

(=) Brooke and all of her fellow colonists - Ed Gold, Tarak Ital, Andy Stone, Margaret Cain, Mia Bennett, Yuri Kerenski, Steffi Ehrlich and Roman Groom - were killed. Humanity mourned their loss, not knowing the cause of the tragedy.

The Doctor decided to change history and save the remaining colonists - as the last of the Time Lords, he believed that he alone could command the Laws of Time. Ed Gold sacrificed himself to prevent the Flood from capturing the base's shuttle; Ital, Stone, Cain, Ehrlich and Groom died as Action Protocol Five obliterated the base. The Doctor took Brooke, Bennett and Kerenski back to Brooke's home on Earth. Brooke was so horrified by the Doctor's arrogance, power and unaccountability that she killed herself in her house. Bennett and Kerenski, as the only survivors, credited Brooke with having saved Earth from the Flood, guaranteeing her reputation in future. Media accounts mentioned how "The Mythical Doctor" had saved Bennett and Kerenski.

Brooke's suicide made the Doctor acknowledge to himself that he had gone too far. He briefly saw a vision of Ood Sigma, and, worried that it was an omen of his death, departed in the TARDIS.

At this time, robots were commonplace, from small repairmen controlled by autogloves to giant construction drones. Other technology included atom clamps, medpacks and Hardinger Seals that hermetically sealed rooms. On Earth, people still drove cars, paying for them with credit stamps. Gay marriage was legal in Dagestan. Solar flares sometimes disrupted communications between Earth and Mars. Politically, the Earth consisted of the World State (including at least the USA, UK, Germany and Russia) and the independents (which might have included Spain and Philippines). There had been multiple stories of the Philippines building a rocket, and they were the leading contenders for a rival mission to Mars. The Spanish had been keeping their Spacelink Project under wraps. The Branson Inheritance had been talking about a Mars shot for years.

(=) 2059 - SJA: THE MAD WOMAN IN THE ATTIC[164] -> A boy called Adam visited an ancient Rani Chandra in the attic of her home, Sarah Jane Smith's former abode at 13 Bannerman Road. Rani had been living here alone for so many years, she had become something of a local legend. Adam was the son of Eve, an alien Rani had befriended when she was a teenager. Adam changed history so that Rani was never alone.

Rani lived at 13 Bannerman Road, and had at least one son and at least two grandsons. She had just returned from a visit to Washington with Luke, where they caught up with Maria.

The planet Flissta became uninhabitable due to a stellar cataclysm. The Doctor was onboard the medical frigate *Talaha*, with some of the surviving Flisk, when a rift opened as the ship crossed the Opius Expanse.[165]

Earth sent out colony ships in the late twenty-first century to Mars, Venus and a "weird little planet" that was later determined to be a moon, but never left Earth's solar system for the first fifty years of this mode of travel. One colony ship ended up five systems away, possibly after falling through a wormhole or temporal eddy created by the Tef'Aree. The colonists were given terraforming technology that they used to "reboot" the planet's ecology. Only those within the shielded Colony One Base survived the process.[166]

New governments started to form by the 2060s. Octogenarian Samantha Jones might have been a major player in these events. Before this point, her father had died, shortly after the last King of England abdicated.[167]

(=) During a period of extreme instability, Karen Coltraine established an oppressive right-wing regime in Europe, and put Earth's expansion into space on a more aggressive footing. The Gallifreyan CIA prevented this future from occurring.[168]

In the 2060s, the Bantu Independence Group received new funding from energy tycoon Olle Ahlin, and directed its efforts to central Africa and Scandinavia. In the decades to come, Bantu would look to aiding colonies on other worlds.[169] Cricket was an Olympic sport in time for the Barcelona Olympics of 2060.[170] The eleventh Doctor, Amy and Rory photographed a lake that occupied the space where Swallow Woods had stood.[171]

2062 - THE LAST DODO[172] -> Chinese Three-Striped Box Turtles were now extinct on Earth. The Museum of the Lost Ones had a single specimen of each extinct species in

---

164 Dating *SJA: The Mad Woman in the Attic* (SJA 3.2) - The date is given in a caption and reiterated by Adam. While no link is made in any of the stories, we might infer some and come to interesting conclusions. Luke may have inherited the house on Sarah Jane's death (in 2040, according to a possible future seen in *Interference*). This is set after the *K9* series, so we can infer the teenagers from *The Sarah Jane Adventures* were in their fifties and in London during those events. We don't know the fate of K9 Mk IV, but it's entirely possible there are at least two versions of K9 around in Britain in 2059 - the Mk I or II model from the *K9* series, and the Mk IV from *The Sarah Jane Adventures*.

165 "Nearly forty years" before *Snowglobe 7*.

166 "Final Sacrifice". The "weird little planet" could be a reference to Vulcan from *The Power of the Daleks*. The

Doctor finds the lost colony circa 21906.

167 *Interference* (p217).

168 *Human Resources*. No date is given, but it has to be at a point in the twenty-first century with both political instability and a human space programme. Karen is apparently the same age as Lucie (late teens) in 2006.

169 *Benny: Another Girl, Another Planet*

170 *Nekromanteia*

171 "Fifty years in the future" of the present-day component of *The Way Through the Woods*. Although the temporal anomalies that occur in Swallow Woods are undone, the area presumably does still become a lake after Reyn's spaceship is sent away from Earth.

172 Dating *The Last Dodo* (NSA #13) - The Chinese Three-Striped Box Turtle is a new addition to the collection, and has recently gone extinct, so it's around 2062.

FIXED POINTS IN TIME: The new *Doctor Who* has introduced the concept of "fixed points in time" as a shorthand, of sorts, to address a problem with time travel that classic *Doctor Who* always had, but was hesitant to discuss. Namely, why does the Doctor treat the past of modern-day Earth as if it's sacrosanct, but happily intervene in events set in Earth's future? To a time traveller, most if not all of history should be the past from *some* vantage point, meaning that the nexus points of both Earth's "past" and "future" history should be treated with equal weight.

Even David Whitaker (*Doctor Who*'s first script editor, and the show's biggest proponent of the "You cannot change history, not one line" approach to time travel) is somewhat hypocritical about this. On Whitaker's watch, it's literally impossible for Barbara to alter Aztec history (*The Aztecs*), and efforts to change Napoleon's timeline are doomed to failure (the final scene of *The Reign of Terror*). However, given the chance to overthrow the Daleks who have conquered Earth (conventionally, without benefit of time travel) circa 2167, the Doctor and his friends without hesitation do so (*The Dalek Invasion of Earth*). Whitaker's successors favoured the view that altering history *was* possible, but the dichotomy of leaving Earth's past alone while mucking about with its future remained. The slaughter of the Huguenots in Paris, 1572, must be allowed to play itself out (*The Massacre*), but stopping Mavic Chen and the Daleks from building a Time Destructor in the year 4000 is fair game (*The Daleks' Master Plan*).

In the early Silurian stories (*Doctor Who and the Silurians*, *The Sea Devils*), the third Doctor further complicates matters by advocating an accord between humanity and the Silurians that he must know - as a matter of established history - didn't happen. It's fairly evident that Malcolm Hulke, Terrance Dicks, et al, were more concerned with the stories' morality play than the temporal implications of the Doctor's viewpoint, but the lack of any explanation has been conspicuous by its absence.

In the new series, moments/events that must, at all cost, happen to preserve the integrity of history are called "fixed points in time". The phrase has become fairly common currency, despite the tenth Doctor stressing to Adelaide Brooke in *The Waters of Mars* that it's all conjecture, not established fact. ("I mean, it's only a theory... but I think certain moments in time are fixed. Tiny, precious moments. Everything else is in flux, anything can happen, but those certain moments, they have to stand. This base, on Mars, with you, Adelaide Brooke, this is one vital moment. What happens here must always happen.") Whatever his uncertainty about the topic, though, the Doctor so strongly believes that the devastation of Pompeii (*The Fires of Pompeii*) is a "fixed point in history" that he and Donna kill twenty thousand people to make it happen.

In *Cold Blood*, and in an echo of past Silurian stories, the eleventh Doctor says that human and Silurian rep-

resentatives in 2020 can craft an accord between their races because "There are fixed points through time, where things must always stay the way they are. This is not one of them. This is an opportunity, a temporal tipping point. Whatever happens today, will change future events, create its own timeline, its own reality." That isn't a very satisfactory explanation, though... wouldn't the successful brokering of such a deal in 2020 overwrite all of the fixed points in time *after* that? Would the timetable of Adelaide Brooke's mission to Mars still hold true if humanity had gained access to Silurian technology about three decades beforehand? It's fair to say that *Cold Blood* doesn't actually answer the problems inherent in the Pertwee Silurian stories, it just more directly acknowledges that they exist.

The consequence of averting a fixed point in time isn't consistently rendered... when River Song subverts a fixed point in time by not shooting the eleventh Doctor (*The Wedding of River Song*), it instantly causes all of time and space to occur at the same moment. But when the tenth Doctor prevents Adelaide Brooke from dying in *The Waters of Mars*, nothing appears to happen in the interim before she fulfills upon the fixed point by committing suicide. The Reapers appear when Rose saves her father in *Father's Day*, but that might owe to her intervening in her personal history, not a fixed point. The comic story "Ripper's Curse" seems confused about this - the eleventh Doctor (seemingly forgetting everything he learned in *The Waters of Mars*) says that every victim of Jack the Ripper is "a static point in space and time, they can't be altered", then he, Amy and Rory *do* intervene anyway, and incur no penalty when one victim is swapped for another. Perhaps a "static point" is different from a "fixed point", but it isn't explained how. Further complicating this, *The Wedding of River Song* claims that Lake Silencio, 2011, is a "still point in time" that can be used to create a "fixed point", but doesn't actually define what a "still point" is or how one comes about.

The final way that the new series addresses "fixed points in time" is that Captain Jack is named as one following Rose's resurrecting him in *The Parting of the Ways*. (The Doctor in *Utopia* on Jack's immortality: "You're a fixed point in time and space. You're a fact. That's never meant to happen.") This deviates from the established use of "fixed point in time", but it at least has a certain internal logic: if Jack is, effectively, a mobile set of space-time coordinates that are impervious to being nullified, it might follow that his body could restore itself after being pulped (*TW: Children of Earth*). What effect becoming a "fixed point" had on Jack's blood is more open to interpretation - in *TW: Miracle Day*, the Blessing recalibrates itself after scanning Jack's blood, and Rex Matheson becomes similarly immortal owing to an infusion of Jack's blood and highly unusual circumstances. It remains to be seen if Rex himself is now a "fixed point", or just someone who can heal mortal injury.

the Milky Way and Andromeda. The tenth Doctor and Martha arrived as Eve, the curator, had decided to wipe out all other life in the universe. She died when a weapon she was aiming at the Doctor exploded. The Doctor returned the specimens to their native times.

Prior to the Bowie Base One disaster, the plan had been for the first colonists to stay on Mars until 2063.[173] During the mid 2060s, the Daleks were scattered around the edges of Mutter's Spiral, trying to build up a decent galactic powerbase. The ones who got left behind on Skaro were just starting to think about putting together their own little empire - this was the "static electricity" phase of Dalek development...[174]

The collapse of the Amazon's ecosystem made the "Lung of the World" into a dust bowl stretching from Rio de Janiero to the Andes, displacing a number of werewolves and Amazon Indian tribes. A constant risk of global war existed until the Earth's governments turned their attention to the moon and asteroid belt for resources.[175]

Legend had it that star whales guided early space travellers through the asteroid belt.[176] The spaceship *Gravity's Rainbow* was constructed in the twenty-first century.[177]

By 2068, a few colonisation missions had been launched to other solar systems, but there was no indication of whether they had succeeded. UNIT had recently been replaced by PRISM. On 3rd March, 2068, the Lunar Base picked up an alien signal. This was evidence of the Myloki. First contact proved disastrous, and the Myloki launched

---

173 *The Waters of Mars.* They were planning "five years on Mars", which started in 2058.

174 *Alien Bodies.* See "Are There Two Dalek Histories?"

175 "About twenty years" before *Loups-Garoux*.

176 *The Beast Below*

177 "At least five hundred", maybe five hundred and fifty years" before *Benny: the Tub Full of Cats*.

178 *The Indestructible Man.* This story seems to contradict a lot of the other stories set around this time, both in broad terms and points of detail.

179 Dating *Alien Bodies* (EDA #6) - The date is given, p68.

180 *TW: Asylum.* Freda seems to hail from 2069, despite Gwen's suspect math; somehow, she's able to add Freda's birthday (30th May, 2053) to her age (17) to determine that she stems from 2069.

181 *Seeing I* (p29). No date given.

182 *Nightmare of Eden.* A monitor readout states that Galactic Salvage and Insurance were formed in "2068". The Doctor has heard of the company and briefly pretends to be working for them.

183 *The Murder Game* (p9).

184 Dating *The Wheel in Space/The War Games* (5.7, 6.7) - This, along with *The Seeds of Death*, is one of two stories set in the twenty-first century that are trickiest to date. There's no date given in the story itself.

In *The Moonbase*, base leader Hobson states that "every child knows" about the destruction of Mondas (in *The Tenth Planet*). Yet none of the crew of the Wheel have heard of the Cybermen, and they're generally sceptical about the existence of alien life. This is a contradiction whether Zoe comes from before, around the same time or after *The Moonbase*. Invoking Zoe's narrow education doesn't work if "every child" knows about Mondas' demise, and surely the only way she wouldn't know is if it had been deliberately kept from her, which would be a bit bizarre. (Unless it's felt that telling future astronauts about all the monsters up there would be counter-productive.)

Amongst its other duties, the Wheel gathers infor-

mation on Earth's weather, but this needn't mean that weather control isn't in use - to control the weather, you surely need the ability to monitor it.

As it's Zoe's native time, we get more clues in subsequent stories she's in: Zoe is "born in the twenty-first" century (*The War Games*), and she is "19 or so" according to the Brigadier in *The Invasion*, so the story must be set somewhere between 2019 and 2119. In *The Mind Robber*, she recognises the Karkus - a comic strip character from the year 2000 - which might suggest she comes from that year. For that reason (presumably), the narration in *The Prison in Space* identifies Zoe as "a pretty astrophysicist from the year 2000". However, when discussing the Karkus, Zoe asks the Doctor if he's *been* to the year 2000 - if it's not a rhetorical question, then *The Wheel in Space* isn't set in that year. In *The Mind Robber*, we see an image of Zoe's home city - a highly futuristic metropolis.

It's never explicitly stated that *The Seeds of Death* takes place before Zoe's time (see the dating notes on *The Seeds of Death*). In *The Seeds of Death*, Zoe understands the principles behind T-Mat, meaning she possesses knowledge that's otherwise limited to a few specialists (she may have picked this up on her travels - although she doesn't in any story we see). Why Zoe doesn't remember T-Mat or recognise the Martians is a mystery, but it does indicate she was born after T-Mat was abandoned, or she'd recognise it. Then again, Zoe has a narrow education and doesn't recognise kilts or candles, either, so perhaps T-Mat is seen as a quaint and irrelevant historical detail by her time.

If Zoe's inability to recognise T-Mat is relevant, it suggests that the earliest date for *The Wheel in Space* is at least "nineteen years or so" (the Brigadier's estimate of Zoe's age in *The Invasion*) after *The Seeds of Death* (dated to circa 2040 in this chronology), so it can't take place before 2059. This doesn't help narrow the upper limit on when the story can occur, however.

Many subsequent stories establish that the governments of Earth knew about the existence of aliens in

a war on humanity. Although conducted in secret, the war with the Myloki was so devastating that on 29th August, 2068, the UN banking system collapsed under the strain. The war ended when Colonel LeBlanc sent Captain Grant Matthews, an indestructible Myloki duplicate who retained his loyalties to humanity, to the moon with a twenty-megaton bomb strapped to his back. This destroyed the Myloki base. But the war exhausted Earth's natural resources and saw New York destroyed in a nuclear attack. An altered maize crop destroyed the ecology of Africa. The City of London became an independent city-state, walled off from the rest of the world.[178]

2069 (26th March) - ALIEN BODIES[179] **->** In the East Indies ReVit Zone, Mr Qixotl hosted a private conference in which representatives from various powers were to bid on the Relic, a Gallifreyan body that contained extremely rare biodata... and which the eighth Doctor, accompanied by Sam, discovered was *his* body from his personal future.

Friction among the delegates increased, and a Kroton Warspear arrived to claim the Relic by force. The Doctor used a Faction Paradox timeship to reflect the Warspear's weaponry back on itself, destroying the entire battlefleet. Mortally wounded, Qixotl traded the Relic to the Celestis in return for a new body. The Doctor travelled to Mictlan, the Celestis' powerbase, and reclaimed the Relic. The Doctor buried the Relic alongside the dog Laika on the planet Quiescia, and destroyed the Relic with a thermosystron bomb.

By now, Kroton weapons developed on Quartzel-88 had decimated the Metatraxi homeworld, reduced the moons of Szacef-Po to powder, and convinced the united forces of Criptostophon Prima to surrender.

The Cardiff public had what resources they needed to live, but water was rationed, and fresh tomatoes were a rarity - as were automobiles. Tapping grid power in the daytime wasn't permitted. Universal Remote Controls (URCs) were hand-held devices used to make purchases - running one over a "zed code" would debit your ration. UK citizens had ID codes such as 818945/CF209B.

Peaceful, human-looking aliens who'd been living in Cardiff for fifty years became the targets of racism, and their offspring were disparagingly called "ghosties". One such offspring died in a deliberately set house fire, and a Torchwood agent - or possibly Captain Jack himself - sent the dead woman's daughter, Freda, through the Rift back to 2009.[180]

Middle Eastern countries turned their economies to high technology, particularly the space industry, as the oil ran out.[181] **Galactic Salvage and Insurance was set up in London in 2068.**[182] The space station Hotel Galaxian became the first offworld tourist attraction.[183]

The Cyber Incursions

? 2068 - THE WHEEL IN SPACE / THE WAR GAMES[184] **->** Jet helicopters had become the principal form of transport on Earth. Simple servo robots were developed, as were x-ray laser weapons and food dispensers. John Smith and Associates built advanced medical equipment for spacecraft. Psychotropic drugs could now prevent brain control, and all astronauts were fitted with Silenski capsules to detect outside influences on the human mind. Two years beforehand, Dr. Gemma Corwyn's husband had been killed exploring the asteroid belt. The loss of rockets was becoming rarer, though.

The Earth School of Parapsychology was founded around this time. It was based in an area known only as the City and trained children from a very early age in the disciplines of pure logic and memory. Zoe Heriot, one of the School's pupils, developed total recall and majored in pure maths. She qualified as an astrophysicist and astrometricist (first class). Her education was narrow and vocational, though, and didn't include any pre-century history. When she was about 19, Zoe was assigned to Space Station W3.

The Space Wheels were set up around the solar system. W3, for example, was positioned relative to Venus, 24,564,000 miles at perihelion, 161,350,000 miles at aphelion, a week's rocket travel from Earth. W5 was between eighty and ninety million miles from W3. The small, multinational crews of the Wheel warned travellers of meteorite storms and acted as a halfway house for deep space ships of the space fleet; they monitored all manner of stellar phenomena, and also supplied advance weather information to Earth.

The Wheels were armed with x-ray lasers with a range of ten thousand miles, and protected by a convolute force field, a neutron field barrier capable of deflecting meteorites of up to two hundred tonnes. Phoenix IV cargo rockets, which had a four-man crew but could be placed on automatic power drive, kept the stations supplied with food and materials.

Back on the human homeworld, the Pull Back to Earth movement believed it was wrong to colonise other planets. They committed acts of sabotage against the space programme, but their exponents were never seen as anything but crackpots. Space travel had undoubted benefits, but remained hazardous.

Zoe aided the second Doctor and Jamie in repelling a Cybermen assault on W3, then joined the TARDIS crew. Gemma Corwyn died in the attack.

As part of the resolution of the Doctor's first trial, the Time Lords returned Zoe to W3, but walled off her memories of her time in the TARDIS.

Zoe had a photographic memory and a degree in Pure Mathematics.[185] She eventually left the Wheel. Years later, she experienced dreams of her time with the Doctor and Jamie, and wondered if some of her memories were blocked off. She sought counselling, and related a particularly vivid adventure involving the Daleks. Zoe's unsettling dreams ceased after the Doctor's voice - through unknown means - told her not to fear the Daleks.[186]

2070 - THE MOONBASE[187] -> The Cybermen attempted to take control of the Gravitron on Earth's moon by using Cybermats to introduce a plague to the moonbase. The second Doctor, Ben, Polly and Jamie thwarted them. Medical units could now administer drugs and automatically control the pulse, temperature, breathing and cortex factor of a patient.

Tobias Vaughn recovered bodies of Cybermen from W3 and the moonbase, and used the components to repair his cybernetic body.[188] **Facing extinction, the Cybermen conquered Telos, all but wiping out the native Cryons and building their "tombs" using Cryon technology. Once this was completed, the Cybermen retreated to their tombs and vanished from the galaxy. The location of Telos remained a mystery.**[189] The Cybermen launched a star destroyer from Telos that headed to the Garazone Sector.[190] Seismic shifts created an island in the Atlantic, and this became a homeland for the

Dutch, the New Dutch Republic.[191] The Sontarans left the Coal Sack sector of space and wouldn't return for three hundred years.[191]

? 2070 - "The Forgotten"[193] -> The second Doctor, Jamie and Zoe arrived on a space station that was being attacked by an Alvarian Space Wyrm. The Doctor sent her snake soldiers to sleep by playing his recorder, then did the same to the Wyrm herself by amplifying the signal through the station's communication system.

On Earth, PVC made a big resurgence.[194]

2074 - MAD DOGS AND ENGLISHMEN[195] -> Science fiction by human authors had become the subject of serious academic debate. There were also groups who sought to rewrite literary texts for their own evil ends, including The Circle Hermeneutic and The New Dehistoricists. The eighth Doctor accidentally landed his TARDIS on one academic, Alid Jag.

The Doctor, Fitz and Anji learned that the novel *The True History of Planets* was a book about talking poodles, not the sword and sorcery epic the Doctor remembered. The Doctor teamed up with Mida Slike of the Ministry for Incursions And Ontological Wonders, a group that investigated such changes to history. Slike was killed, and poodle fur found on her body. Fitz discovered the co-ordinates for Dogworld in Tyler's novel.

the twentieth century, and the new television series (as well as stories in the books and comics) establish that the general public accepts the existence of aliens by the early twenty-first.

The Indestructible Man places this story after 2096, as it's set before Zoe was born. *The Harvest* (set in 2021) refers to the Wheel space stations.

The first two editions of *The Programme Guide* placed *The Wheel in Space* between "1990-2000", but *The Terrestrial Index* suggested a date "c2020" (or "2030" in *The Universal Databank*). "2074" was suggested by "A History of the Cybermen" in *DWM*. *Cybermen*, after some discussion (p61-62), said "2028 AD". The first edition of *Timelink* said "2020"; the Telos version favoured "2080". *About Time* says "it looks like the 2030s to us".

The story is here placed a century after it was broadcast, around the same time as the other Cyberman incursion seen in *The Moonbase*. In the last episode of *The War Games*, Zoe is returned to her native time.
185 "The Forgotten"
186 *Fear of the Daleks*. Wendy Padbury was 58 when this was recorded, a possible indicator of Zoe's age.
187 Dating *The Moonbase* (4.6) - Hobson tells the Doctor they are in "2070", and Polly later repeats this. On screen, the small crew of the moonbase includes Englishmen, Frenchmen and Danes. The production file

for the story listed the other nationalities represented at the moonbase: Australians, New Zealanders, Canadians, Germans and Nigerians.
188 *Original Sin* (p289).
189 *The Tomb of the Cybermen, Attack of the Cybermen.*
190 *Sword of Orion*
TELOS: After the destruction of their vast advance force (*The Invasion*), their homeworld of Mondas (*The Tenth Planet*) and most of the surviving Cyber warships (*Silver Nemesis*), the Cybermen must have been severely weakened. They gradually regrouped and attempted to attack Earth at least twice in the twenty-first century (*The Wheel in Space, The Moonbase*). These attempts failed, and the Cybermen faced extinction (according to the Controller in *The Tomb of the Cybermen*). So they left the solar system and conquered Telos. (The Doctor says in *Attack of the Cybermen* that "if Mondas hadn't been destroyed, the Cybermen would never have come here [to Telos]", which contradicts an unbroadcast line from *The Moonbase* where a Cyberman states, "We were the first space travellers from Mondas. We left before it was destroyed. We came from the planet Telos.") The Cybermen subjugated the native Cryons, used Cryon technology to build their "tombs" (*Attack of the Cybermen*) and experimented with new weapons before entering suspended animation. In the late twen-

The space station of the Dogworld poodles was now receiving radio signals from Earth. The movie of *The True History of Planets* was the story of how the Emperor deposed the mother of Princess Margaret, the true heir to the throne. After trips to 1942 and 1978, the Doctor and his companions discovered that Margaret had been manipulating history to change the contents of Tyler's book, and changed it back. Margaret was killed and the Emperor restored to power. A grateful Emperor allowed writer Reginald Tyler to remain on the Dogworld.

Talking boars were now part of Earth society and had their own culture.

On Earth, governments used genetic manipulation and intelligent chips to maintain their soldiers' loyalty.[196]

Earth had now experienced hostile alien visitors such as the Sycorax and the Slitheen, and friendly ones such as the Svillia and the Hive of Mooj. The Flisk arrived on Earth after a stellar cataclysm almost wiped out their race, and were welcomed until they were revealled as telepathic, whereupon they became targets of suspicion. Nonetheless, their expertise with computer programming helped many of them find employment across the globe.[197]

2080 - LOUPS-GAROUX[198] -> The ancient werewolf Pieter Stubbe tried to reclaim Illeana de Santos, now the de facto werewolf leader, as his mate. Illeana resisted Stubbe's advances, but Stubbe seized control of Illeana's werewolves

and directed them to assault Rio de Janeiro. The fifth Doctor and Turlough broke Stubbe's dominance of the pack. Stubbe died when he rushed into the TARDIS, enabling the Doctor to materialise in orbit and sever Stubbe from the Earth - the source of his elemental power - thus aging him to death.

Rio de Janeiro now had a monorail and spaceport. ID implants were compulsory, and robots checked passports. People had hover vehicles including limos, jeeps and four hundred mile-an-hour trains. The currency was the credit.

A body scan predicted that Henry Louis Noone was likely to die at age 82.[199] Circa 2084, on the planet Cray, the game Naxy started out as an innocent arena sport. The Naxy fans became increasingly violent, and took to fighting outside the arena before matches. The public's interest shifted to the bloody fan conflict, and Naxy was soon retooled as a sport in which teams fought to the death.[200]

c 2084 - WARRIORS OF THE DEEP[201] -> Earth consolidated into two blocs, the East and the West, and a new Cold War developed. New weapons technology was developed: Seabases sat on the ocean floor, armed with proton missiles that were capable of destroying life while leaving property intact. Sentinels - robots armed with energy weapons - orbited the Earth and large Hunter-Killers patrolled the seas. "Synchoperators" had computer interfaces implanted into

ty-fifth century, the Cybermen revive (*The Tomb of the Cybermen*), but are refrozen. Telos is destroyed soon after in an asteroid strike (the *Cyberman* audio series), but a new breed of Cybermen is forged to menace the galaxy (*Cyberman 2*, evidently leading into The Cyber War).
191 *St Anthony's Fire*
192 *Lords of the Storm* (p104).
193 Dating "The Forgotten" (IDW *DW* mini-series #2) - No date is given. The level of technology seems reminiscent of Zoe's time.
194 "Sixty years" after *Autonomy*.
195 Dating *Mad Dogs and Englishmen* (EDA #52) - It is "one hundred years" (p9) after "1974" (p3).
196 *Deceit* (p188), with similar technology in *Transit*.
197 "Twenty years" before *Snowglobe 7*.
198 Dating *Loups-Garoux* (BF #20) - The date is given.
199 *A Death in the Family*
200 "Four hundred years" before *The Game*.
201 Dating *Warriors of the Deep* (21.1) - The Doctor tells Tegan that the year is "about 2084". The televised story doesn't specify which bloc the Seabase belongs to, and only the novelisation specifies the blocs as "East and West". Even that leaves the geopolitics far from clear. The most obvious division in 1984 would have been between a capitalist West and communist East, but

nowadays that seems unlikely. Lt. Preston doesn't seem surprised that the TARDIS is "not from this planet", and no-one seems shocked that the Silurians are intelligent nonhumans. This might suggest that contact has been made with a number of alien races by this time.
THE RETURN OF THE EARTH REPTILES: In *Doctor Who and the Silurians*, *The Ambassadors of Death* and *The Sea Devils*, the Doctor thinks that the Brigadier has killed all the Silurians at Wenley Moor. However, they may simply be entombed, and one Silurian - Ichtar - seems to survive the first story into *Warriors of the Deep*.
Based on discrepancies between the events of *Doctor Who and the Silurians*, the descriptions of the Doctor's last encounter with the species in *Warriors of the Deep*, and the fact that the Doctor recognises Icthar, the Myrka and the Silurian submersible, *The Discontinuity Guide* postulated that there is an unrecorded adventure featuring the Doctor and the Silurians set between the two stories. The novel *The Scales of Injustice*, set in the UNIT era and published the year after *The Discontinuity Guide*, addresses most of these issues in an attempt to fill the gap.
Cold Blood entails a Silurian colony that's slated to revive and try to negotiate an accord with humanity around 3020, but we aren't shown the outcome of that effort. Silurians are referred to in a number of New and

their heads, allowing split-second control over proton missile runs. Soldiers carried energy rifles.

At the height of interbloc tension, a group of Silurians and Sea Devils attacked Seabase 4. They planned to launch the missiles there and provoke a war that would kill all human life. The fifth Doctor, Tegan and Turlough failed to prevent a massacre at the base, but saved humanity.

First Contact

The Arcturan Treaty of 2085 was often officially counted as mankind's first contact with alien races, as it was the first diplomatic contact.[202] The whole of humanity finally accepted the existence of aliens. Danny Pain's role in stopping an alien invasion in 1976 was now legendary.[203]

The first lightspeed mission to another solar system launched in 2085.[204]

2086 (25th April) - "Black Destiny"[205] -> The fourth Doctor, Sarah and Harry landed at the Troika Cultural Centre to celebrate world peace in Takhail in Russia, but the staff suddenly started dying. The Doctor met Direktor Arkady, the great-grandson of a boy who had been exposed to radiation there a hundred years before. The dead bodies reanimated as zombies. The Doctor checked the world-net computer network, and discovered that

Arkady was fascinated by nuclear accidents. Arkady began to glow with energy and transformed into an energy cloud, then attacked Moscow, but the Doctor managed to neutralise and disperse him. Sarah noted that Chernobyl had a new nuclear power station.

The Threshold abducted Sarah during this encounter.

The Doctor believed that Disneyland would be worth visiting in future, after it "had time to settle".[206]

The Thousand-Day War

Out of the blue, one day in 2086, the Martians attacked. Paris was hit with a meteorite that killed a million people, and wiped out centuries of history including the Mona Lisa, the Venus de Milo, Notre Dame and EuroDisney.[207] Humanity united behind President Achebe against the common enemy. First in were the Zen Brigade, the Blue Berets of the United Nations Third Tactical Response Brigade, made up of Irish and Ethiopians. They dropped in from orbit, and the Martians cut them to pieces. One of the few survivors was their commanding officer, Brigadier Yembe Lethbridge-Stewart. But the Blue Berets completed their mission and formed a bridgehead: the UN forward-base at Jacksonville halfway up Olympus Mons. More crucially, their engineers set up the first interstitial tunnel, a refinement of old Travel-mat technology that allowed

---

Missing Adventures set in the future (*Love and War*, *Transit* and *The Crystal Bucephalus* to name three). They seem particularly peaceful towards humans in Benny's native time.

202 *The Dying Days* (p115). This is mankind's first diplomatic contact with alien races, as opposed to being invaded by them. See also "When Does the General Public Accept the Existence of Aliens?"

203 *No Future* (p257).

204 It arrived "thirty years" after *The Waters of Mars*. Travelling at lightspeed, it would take a little over four years to reach Proxima Centauri, so it must have been launched in 2085.

205 Dating "Black Destiny" (*DWM* #235-237) - The date is given. The United Nations World Health Organisation is still operating, as are nuclear power stations. Peace must have broken out since *Warriors of the Deep*.

206 "A hundred years or so" after *The Nightmare Fair*. This isn't the Doctor's best suggestion, as "a hundred years" after that story would be around 2086, at the start of the Thousand-Day War.

207 *Transit*, with additional details of Paris' obliteration provided in *Benny: Beige Planet Mars*. The Mona Lisa that perishes is presumably the one with "This is a Fake" scrawled on it in felt-tip, per *City of Death*.

208 *Transit*

209 *Fear Itself* (PDA, p176-177).

210 *Transit*

211 *GodEngine*

212 *Legacy* (p86), *GodEngine* (p79). In *The Curse of Peladon*, we learn that the Martians and Arcturans are "old enemies".

213 *GodEngine* (p168).

214 *Legacy* (p86).

215 Dating *The Story of Martha*: "Breathing Space" (NSA #28b) - The year is given.

216 *Fear Itself* (PDA)

217 *Transit*

218 "Thirty years" after *The Waters of Mars*.

219 Dating *Paper Cuts* (BF #125) - The Doctor twice says that it's been "sixty years" since he visited Draconia and aided with the space plague, but the Queen Mother - who vividly remembers meeting the Doctor when she was only 12, and would presumably be in a better position to know - claims it's actually been "fifty years". The story leaves open-ended how Draconia resolves the struggle between the fifteen emperors, but however it happens, the Draconians have a new empire and just one emperor by *Frontier in Space*.

220 *Benny: The Vampire Curse*: "Possum Kingdom".

instantaneous travel between Earth and Mars. Men and materiel poured through the Stunnel.

Half-kiloton groundbreakers poured from the air onto the Martian nests. Tactical nuclear weapons were used. The early stages of the war were dogged by friendly fire incidents, but these were ironed out. As the war dragged on, some soldiers were genetically and cybernetically augmented to increase their efficiency. These first-generation ubersoldaten retained less than 50% of their natural DNA. Just about every soldier took combat drugs like Doberman and Heinkel to make them better fighters.[208]

At one point, the Zen Brigade was ambushed at Achebe Gorge - pinned down by snipers, they retreated under cover of a storm.[209]

New slang entered the language: Greenie (Martian), pop up (a cannon used by the Martians), spider trap, fire mission, medevac. During the war, hologram technology became more advanced. The Ice Maiden, an R&R stop in Jacksonville, became notorious. For a generation afterwards, the imagery and iconography of the War was burnt into the minds of humanity, and was popularised in vids like *Violet Sky*.

The war ended in 2088, exactly a thousand days after it had started. The surviving Martians had either fled the planet or gone into hibernation in deep nests. At first, the human authorities were worried about "stay behind" units, but it became clear that the Martian threat had completely dissipated, and the military satellites were decommissioned. A memorial forest was set up at Achebe Gorge on Mars. A tree was planted for each one of the four hundred and fifty thousand men who had died in the War, which didn't include the death toll in Paris. For many decades, Victory Night was celebrated every year on Earth, and trees were planted to honour the military dead.[210]

The only human defeat was at Viis Claar, or the Valles Marineris, when Abrasaar killed fifteen thousand humans and ten thousand of his own men in a trap.[211] 99% of Martians headed for a new planet, Nova Martia, beyond Arcturus. Hundreds of thousands of Martians remained behind, hidden in subterranean cities. UN peacemakers found the planet deserted. The bodies of six of the eight members of the ruling Eight Point Table were found, but these did not include Supreme Grand Marshal Falaxyr or Abrasaar.[212]

The Martian fleet heading to Nova Martia stopped off in the Rataculan system. A few Ice Warriors remained behind to found a colony on the planet Cluut-ett-Pictar.[213] There was little or no contact between the Ice Warriors and humanity for nearly a thousand years, and the Martians rarely allowed any visitors to their new world. In the twenty-sixth century, the "extinct" Martians briefly became a curiosity for archaeologists, but after that, mankind forgot all about their old neighbours.[214]

2088 - THE STORY OF MARTHA: "Breathing Space"[215]-> The alien Benefactors arrived in Earth orbit, offering to end global warming and atmospheric pollution. The tenth Doctor and Martha found themselves at an Earth space station, and the Doctor recognised the aliens as the Cineraria - a hostile race that subjugated planets by dropping space whales onto heavily-populated areas. The Cineraria's plan relied upon secrecy, and they retreated when the Doctor exposed their intentions.

The Colonisation of the Solar System

Wal-Mart began building the first trading post on Mars, but this was abandoned when the settlement Sheffield was established on Olympus Mons.[216] The World Government invested heavily in the state-owned Sol Transit System (STS) over the next twenty years, and soon Interstitial Tunnels linked every city, continent, habitable planet and moon in the solar system. Transportation within the solar system was now instantaneous and readily available. For the first time, the solar system had a single elected government, the Union of Solar Republics.

In the decade following the Thousand-Day War, Paris was rebuilt. Lowell Depot on Pluto was built to soak up population overspill.[217]

In 2089, thirty years after Bowie Base One was destroyed, the granddaughter of Adelaide Brooke - Susie Fontana Brooke - piloted the first lightspeed ship to Proxima Centauri. Some form of computer news service still operated at this time.[218]

c 2090 - PAPER CUTS[219] -> By the eightieth Year of the Blood on Draconia, no alien had set foot on Draconia for over fifty Earth years. The Fifteenth Emperor (a.k.a. the Red Emperor) was declared dead, and was placed in an orbiting tomb - still alive - alongside his predecessors. Four vigil-keepers were summoned to the tomb to witness the rite of succession - the sixth Doctor and Charley (actually Mila in disguise) answered this call, which had sat in the Doctor's In-Box for one hundred and fifty years.

The fifteen dormant emperors remained aware, and had a half-set of life-size Sazou pieces that responded to their mental commands. The White Emperor sought revenge on the Doctor for his role in the collapse of the Draconian Empire - in the power-struggles that followed, all of the emperors revived from stasis. It remained to be seen who would ascend to the throne. Despite this political quagmire, Draconia in future would forge a new empire.

Gypsy culture was subsumed in the late twenty-first century after proto-viruses left many ethnic groups sterile.[220] The Boor were interplanetary gangsters; the planet Oblivion was decimated and recolonised when it failed to pay one of their protection schemes. The Stellar Police ended the Boor's operations, but the key Boor entered suspended animation on Venedel. They expected to awaken in three decades, but wouldn't for five hundred years.[221]

The Halavans, humanoids who resided on Petreus III, destroyed their homeworld through misuse of their mental abilities. Some of their elite escaped on a spaceship, leaving everyone else behind to die. In-fighting amongst the Halavans made the ship crash on an unnamed planet; they tried to conquer the one-eyed humanoids who lived there, but were themselves enslaved when their telepathic boosters were destroyed. The subjugated Halavans named their masters "Monoids". The rest of the civilised universe believed that a natural disaster had ravaged Petreus III, and the Galactic Trust worked to preserve it.[222]

Zoe Heriot read the ingredients of a tea box in a kitchen on Pluto.[223]

2092 (29th August) - "Ground Zero"[224] **->** Ace was arrested on suspicion of theft at the Notting Hill Carnival, but the policeman was actually Dixon, an agent of Threshold. The seventh Doctor met another agent, Isaac,

who showed him the abducted Susan.

Meanwhile, Ace met the similarly kidnapped Sarah Jane and Peri. The Doctor learned that Threshold were an organisation that opened doors in space and time for their clients - their clients in this case being creatures living with the collective unconscious of mankind, the Lobri, who manifested as giant fleas. The TARDIS interior was heavily damaged. Ace sacrificed her own life to save the Doctor from the creatures - but the last Lobri nonetheless started to manifest on Earth. The Doctor materialised the TARDIS inside the Lobri, destroying it. He then returned his surviving companions to their rightful places in time, and was left travelling alone.

Tracks for a linear-induction monorail on Mars were first laid in 2093. Terraforming efforts started in 2095; the University of Mars was founded in the same year.[225]

2096 - THE INDESTRUCTIBLE MAN[226] **->** Intercontinental travel was impossible, and the world was broken into city-states. France and the former United States of America were in a state of civil war. Japan had invaded New Zealand. There was a United Zion Arab States. Only

---

221 Roughly five hundred years before *Benny: The Gods of the Underworld*.

222 This happens long enough before *Benny: The Kingdom of the Blind* that the Halvans' descendents don't remember their own history.

223 "Seventeen years" before *The Memory Cheats*.

224 Dating "Ground Zero" (*DWM* #238-242) - The date is given in a caption. The destruction of the TARDIS console would seem to lead to its new design in *Doctor Who - The Movie*, although oddly it's the old TV console introduced in *The Five Doctors* that's destroyed, not the version seen in the later seventh Doctor strips.

ACE'S FATE: The seventh Doctor and Ace walk off together in *Survival*, but the next time we see the seventh Doctor - in *The Movie* - he's travelling alone. Thus, there have been a number of accounts of Ace's fate.

The New Adventures saw her grow to become a young woman, then in *Set Piece* she acquires her own time machine and left the Doctor, and the last time we see her is in *Lungbarrow*, where she's still an independent time traveller. In "Ground Zero", a teenaged Ace sacrifices her life to save the Doctor's - and the Doctor is wearing the costume he did in *The Movie*, suggesting it's shortly before he regenerates. In (the possibly apocryphal) *Death Comes to Time*, an older Ace is training to become a Time Lord, and witnesses the seventh Doctor's death. In *Prime Time*, we see the Doctor exhume Ace's teenage body - although in *Loving the Alien*, we learn the dead Ace (the one we saw with the Doctor on TV) was replaced by one from an alternate timeline. The four Big Finish audios adapted from suggested stories for the unmade Season 27 (*Thin Ice*,

Crime of the Century, *Animal* and *Earth Aid*) don't have Ace leave the TARDIS as the production team at the time initially planned; instead, she continues travelling with the Doctor and Raine Creevy. In due course, Big Finish may also tell "Ace's last story".

It is, of course, very difficult to fully reconcile these accounts. The main problem is rationalising Ace's death in "Ground Zero" with her other appearances, although one explanation is that her "demise" relates to the Council of Eight's attempts to eliminate the Doctor's companions - *Sometime Never* p154-155 even mentions Ace's double timeline, and although this was in reference to *Loving the Alien*, it could also, albeit retroactively, be made to apply to "Ground Zero". As such, temporally speaking, Ace's "death" in "Ground Zero" might hold no more weight than the notion that Sarah Jane "dies" in *Bullet Time* (set in April 1997).

225 *Benny: Beige Planet Mars*

226 Dating *The Indestructible Man* (PDA #69) - The date is given. This story contradicts many other stories, but only ones that were written after the sixth season in which the novel is set. It's set after a "global teleportation system" is built and fails (p78), a reference to *The Seeds of Death* (or possibly *Transit*); and it's before Zoe's time (p283), which puts it before *The Wheel in Space*. (We've chosen to contradict this reference; see the dating notes on *The Wheel in Space*.)

227 *The Gallifrey Chronicles*. These would have to be time-travelling Daleks from the future, as the Daleks of this time period are confined to Skaro.

228 This is the historical background to *Transit*. In *The Seeds of Death*, Zoe has never heard of the Ice Warriors

Australia was spared the worst effects of a collapsing society. The second Doctor, Jamie and Zoe defeated the Myloki's plan to use Captain Grant Matthews as the ultimate agent of mankind's destruction.

In 2097, the eighth Doctor, Fitz and Trix prevented an unnamed alien race from exterminating the Pope on Mars, allowing her to consecrate the first cathedral on another planet.[227]

The economic boom promised by the Transit system didn't arrive. Instead, the ability to move freely around the solar system caused massive economic and social upheaval. Small companies saw an opportunity to undermine the industrial zaibatsu. Household names such as Sony, IBM and Matsui went under, and new companies from Brazil, China and Africa - such as Imbani Entertainment, Mtchali and Tung-Po - took their place. Power shifted to Washington, Brazilia, Harare, Beijing, Tehran, Jacksonville and Zagreb. Japan's economy collapsed and plans to terraform Mars proved more costly than had been expected. The money ran out, the floating cities planned for the Ionian Sea were never built and Australia starved. A new genre, silicon noir, charted the resultant corporate battles in the datascape.

The recession was not harsh on everyone. Relatively speaking, Europe was less prosperous than before, but many in Brazil, Africa and China were a great deal wealthier. For millions in Australia, though, and at the Stop - the end of the Transit line at the Lowell Depot - extreme poverty became a way of life. Whole areas became dead-end ghettos, and urban areas became battlegrounds for streetgangs. Vickers All-Body Combat Systems offered the option of using the Melbourne Protocols, automatically preventing the wearer from shooting civilians. Millions fled the riots using the Transit system, and relief workers rehoused the poor anywhere that would take them,

mostly on Mars. Private security firms such as the KGB and V Soc became very rich. With freedom of transport, humanity became more open to ideas from other cultures and to more experimental ways of living. Communal marriages enjoyed a brief vogue.

In 2090, Yembe Lethbridge-Stewart came out of retirement one last time and raided the headquarters of the genetics company IMOGEN. He stole a single child, the first of the second-generation ubersoldaten, and all the files pertaining to her creation. He named her after his great-grandmother, the historian Kadiatu.[228]

Two hundred years after they'd travelled with Pierre Bruyere, the tenth Doctor and Martha visited a museum of Polar Exploration.[229]

Out to the Stars

After mankind "had sacked the solar system they moved on to pastures new".[230] Twenty-first century ships still travelled slower than the speed of light and the crews were placed in suspended animation. It was not unusual to discover such ships many centuries later.[231] These were NAFAL ships, meaning Not As Fast As Light.[232] Nuke burning cadmium-damped spacebuckets were the first ships used to conquer the stars. The galaxy was full of the so-called "nukers" at one time. The first ships Earth built for deep space exploration were the starjammers, and great fleets of them were constructed. By 51,007, only one ship of this type, the *Paine*, remained.[233]

Huge Pioneer stations were set up, lining the way to the stars. They helped with refuelling and restocking of colony ships.[234]

Manned space travel remained enormously expensive prior to the advent of gravity plating. Once the hyperdrive was developed, Earth authorities - including the United Nations Aeronautics and Space Administration (UNASA)

- even though mankind is exploring the solar system in her time - which suggests that her contemporaries are not interested in Mars. We learn in *Transit*, amongst many other historical snippets, that the Thousand-Day War ended about twenty-five years before (p188) and that the decade following the war saw economic upheaval (p108). In his "Future History Continuity", Ben Aaronovitch stated that the War took place between 2086-2088, which by his reckoning was straight after *The Seeds of Death*. Victory Night is mentioned in *The Highest Science* (p21), and it might celebrate the end of this War. We learn in *Infinite Requiem* that forests are still planted after a battle (p266).
229 *The Story of Martha:* "The Frozen Wastes"
230 According to the Doctor in *The Mutants*. As we will see, a number of stories claim to be set on the "first" colony. To explain the apparent contradiction, it's pos-

sible that colonists are either counting different "firsts" (the first plan to colonise, to actually leave Earth, to arrive, to terraform, to settle, to form a local government and so on) or that they simply like to take pride in their pioneering ways and are prepared to exaggerate a little.
231 In *The Sensorites*, ship captain Maitland thinks the Doctor's party is from the twenty-first century. *The Waters of Mars* establishes the first mission to Proxima Centauri flew at "lightspeed", but there's been no firm date set for when mankind first flew faster than light.
232 *Transit* (p264).
233 *The Coming of the Terraphiles*. It's unclear what qualifies as "deep space" in the Terraphile era, when ships fly between galaxies and even universes.
234 *The Pit*

sent out unmanned Van Neumann probes to the first colony worlds to prepare them for human habitation. The probes were extremely adaptive but often disruptive - one landed on Arcturus and started to build a city, oblivious to the fact that the planet was already inhabited.[235]

The children of Susie Fontana Brooke and their children forged their way across the stars to the Dragon Star and the Celestial Belt of the Winter Queen. They mapped the Water Snake Wormholes. A Brooke fell in love with a Tandorian prince, which was the start of a whole new species.[236]

Prospectors such as Dom Issigri and Milo Clancey were the first men into deep space. Clancey's ship, the "C" Class freighter LIZ 79, remained in service for forty years. Spacecraft at that time were built with the metal tillium and used a thermonuclear pile to supply power. Mined ore was sent to refineries in "floaters", slow unmanned vessels. An almost indestructible metal, argonite, was found on some of the planets in the fourth sector. Soon, all ships were made from argonite, which became the most valuable mineral known to man.

Clancey and Issigri became rich over the next fifteen years of working together, especially after they had spent ten years strip-mining the planet Ta in the Pliny system. Clancey became something of a legend on Reja Magnum. The partners eventually split, though, and Issigri went on to found the Issigri Mining Company.[237]

Robots such as the self-activating Megapodic Mark seven-Z Cleaners had some degree of autonomy. Scanners were developed that could track individuals. Miracle City had been masterpiece of the architect Kroagnon, but he refused to move out and let the residents sully his work by moving in. He was forced out, but the booby-traps he left behind massacred many of the residents. Kroagnon fled and was allowed to build Paradise Towers. During the war, youngsters and old-sters were evacuated to the 304-storey building, where the authorities forgot all about them.[238]

Earth's Colonial Age began in the 2090s. Multinational conglomerates started the Century Program, sending colony ships to a dozen worlds in the hope of alleviating the population crisis on Earth.[238]

Slow Century Class ships were sent into deep space - once they arrived at their destination, they became useful space stations. Two such vessels, the *Castor* and the *Pollux*, were sent out into a demilitarised sector by the New Rome Institute to house dangerous criminals. Earth at this time was ruled by a World Minister. The Pacific Rim Co-operative was in conflict with the SubSaharan Autonomies. Quad fuel cars were operating.[240]

The Pinkerton Intergalactic Agency of detectives soon followed colonists into space, solving crimes on colony worlds where law enforcement was often erratic or corrupt.[241] **The prison planet Varos was established in the late twenty-first century to remove the criminally insane from galactic society.[242]** Humanity converted the moon Erratoon into a prison planet by encasing it in a geodesic sphere.[243] The seven planets of the binary Meson system were colonised at this time.[244]

Human Travellers fled oppression on Earth by stealing a ship. When human ships reached Arcturus Six, the Earth ambassador was told that Travellers had already landed.[245] Developers filled in the Serpentine in the late twenty-first century.[246] The corporation Imogen built a facility on Titan to clone generation two ubersoldaten. The Doctor visited this period to download Kadiatu's user manual.[247]

The Global Mining Corporation replaced the US Army, and provided military training for corporations. The world language was "International American".[248] **Galactic Salvage and Insurance went bankrupt in 2096.[249]** Kadiatu Lethbridge-Stewart acquired a Triangulum Swift 400, a ship built in the twenty-first century.[250]

---

235 *Benny: The Big Hunt*
236 *The Waters of Mars*. The Doctor no doubt means that the Brookes were space explorers for many generations, so it's very difficult to date these events. The Dragon Star might (or might not) be a reference to Draconia.
237 *The Space Pirates*. The story states the "whole galaxy" has been explored. Yet based on evidence from many other stories, in which planets and civilisations are discovered long after this time, this must be an exaggeration or the exploration must be fairly rudimentary.
238 The Doctor watches the prospectus in *Paradise Towers* and relates Kroagnon's story. The Chief Caretaker describes Kroagnon as a "being" rather than a "man", suggesting Kroagnon might be an alien. It's never

specified that the tower block was built on Earth, but this seems to be the implication. The war in question might be the conflict of *Warriors of the Deep* or the Thousand Day War first referred to in *Transit*.
239 *Killing Ground*
240 "At least a hundred years" before *Wooden Heart*.
241 *Shakedown*
242 *Vengeance on Varos*. The Governor notes that "Varos has been stable for more than two hundred years".
243 *The Prisoner's Dilemma*
244 "They've come a long way in a hundred years" according to the Doctor in *Time of Your Life* (p27).
245 *Love and War* (p39).
246 *Birthright* (p189).
247 *The Also People* (p155, p191).

In Salzburg, 2098, the leader of the Eugenic Cult - Eldritch Valdemar - was betrayed by his colleagues and convicted of treason, murder and mental domination. He was given a death sentence.

> (=) The time child Chiyoko transported Valdemar back to nineteenth century Earth.[251]

2099 - SNOWGLOBE 7[252] -> Global warming had now accelerated the melting of the polar ice caps to the point that the world's governments preserved large portions of the Arctic and Antarctic in ten enormous domes around the globe. Seven of these were transferred from public to private ownership and became holiday resorts. Service Robots were common in this era.

The TARDIS landed in Snowglobe 7 in Saudi Arabia, where the tenth Doctor and Martha found that the sole-surviving Gappa had been disturbed from its dormancy in the ice, and was hatching offspring from eggs. The Doctor destroyed the Gappa, and Snowglobe 7, by detonating the fusion core of the spacecraft that had brought the Gappa to Earth a hundred thousand years before.

c 2099 - "Sun Screen"[253] -> The Great Solar Shield - a series of networked mirrors in space that decreased the sunlight that fell on Earth, and was a stop-gap means of reducing global warming - was one of mankind's greatest technological achievements in the twenty-first century. Energy parasites, the Silhouettes, were drawn to the Shield's energy, then Earth. The tenth Doctor and Martha re-attuned the Shield to project a rainbow that destroyed the Silhouettes, but the Shield broke up. The Doctor ferried the Shield crew back to Earth in the TARDIS, and told Martha that humanity would develop an ingenious means of dealing with global warming in a few years' time.

The sixth Doctor and Grant Markham went back to see the *New Hope* leave for the Centraxis system in 2100. Within ten years, the colonists aboard would found Grant's home planet of Agora.[254]

Mankind didn't develop particle guns until after the twenty-first century.[255]

The Twenty-Second Century

The Doctor flew a Spitfire in the twenty-second century.[256] He also took Victoria to the NovaLon Hypercities of the twenty-second century.[257] Vincent Grant, the Butcher of Strasbourg, unified the Western Alliance in the early twenty-second century.[258]

c 2100 - PARADISE TOWERS[259] -> Paradise Towers, a self-contained, award-winning tower block that had been abandoned during the war, was rediscovered in the early twenty-second century. With only old and young people in residence, society became stratified. The young girls became Kangs - with an array of "ice-hot" slang and "high fabsion" (sic) clothing - the old women became Rezzies and the Caretakers tried to maintain the building by rigidly sticking to their rule book. Each group had a distinctive language, and each preyed mercilessly on the other. At least two of the residents resorted to cannibalism.

The Kangs split into three rival factions - Red, Blue and Yellow - although "wipeouts" or "making unalive" was forbidden (as were visitors, ball games and fly posting).

Kroagnon's disembodied mind had been exiled to the Towers' basement, but he now possessed the Chief Caretaker using the science of corporal ectoscopy. He put the Towers' robotic cleaners to the task of eliminating the residents, but the various social factions united

248 *The Face-Eater* (p64).
249 *Nightmare of Eden*
250 *So Vile a Sin*
251 "The Screams of Death", "The Child of Time" (*DWM*).
252 Dating *Snowglobe 7* (NSA #23) - The year is given.
253 Dating "Sun Screen" (*The Doctor Who Storybook 2008*) - It's "the twenty-first century". The technological prowess needed to erect the Great Solar Shield is well beyond contemporary levels. The Doctor believes that humanity will find a means of dealing with global warming in "a few years", but it's still a problem in *Snowglobe 7*, set in 2099.
254 "Ninety-one years" before *Killing Ground*.
255 According to the Doctor in *Army of Ghosts*, although he might just mean they shouldn't have them at that point in the twenty-first century (2007).
256 *Last of the Gaderene* (p246). He also says he has

flown a Spitfire in *Loups-Garoux*.
257 *Heart of TARDIS*
258 "Profits of Doom"
259 Dating *Paradise Towers* (24.2) - Paradise Towers has been abandoned for between about fifteen and twenty years, judging by the age of the Kangs. The Doctor's remark that the building won awards "way back in the twenty-first century" may or may not suggest that the story is set in the twenty-second. Taking the New Adventures into account, the War at Time Start might well be the Thousand-Day War that took place a generation before *Transit*. In *Lucifer Rising*, Adjudicator Bishop refers to the "messy consequences of the Kroagnon Affair" (p189), so it is set before then. *The Terrestrial Index* suggested that the war is the Dalek Invasion of Earth, and therefore set the story around 2164. *Timelink* sets the story in 2040.

alongside the seventh Doctor and Mel. A war deserter, Pex, sacrificed himself to kill Kroagnon. Social order was restored, and Pex was remembered in wallscrawls.

In the early twenty-second century, the Guild of Adjudicators was established as a judicial force unrestrained by authority or financial dependence. They were based on the remote planet Ponten IV. Early successes for the "ravens" (so-named because of their black robes) included the execution of fifteen drug dealers on Callisto, the suppression of a revolution in Macedonia and the disciplinary eradication of the energy-wasting population on Frinelli Minor. The Adjudicators also dealt with the Kroagnon Affair, vraxoin raids over Azure, the Macra case and the Vega debacle.[260] Adjudicator Bishop discovered Paradise Towers.[261]

c 2100 (24th December) - IRIS: THE CLAWS OF SANTA[262] -> Father Christmas was bedevilled as humanity expanded into space, leaving him unable to deliver presents on time. Iris Wildthyme provided Santa with Clockworks technology that let him take short cuts through the Vortex, and the two of them had a quick fondle in the back of his sleigh. Santa's wife, Mary Christmas, became incensed upon finding Iris' earring there.

Mary found Panda after he'd been lost to the Vortex in 1999. She kicked her husband out of his North Pole factory, and created "Flare Bears" modelled upon Panda. These became the best-selling toys in the multiverse, but contained a device that would regress all adults to children - which in Mary's opinion make the universe much happier. Iris was reunited with Panda while foiling Mary's plan, and an adaptation of Mary's device made her and Father Christmas young and in love again.

The Ceatul Empire's downfall enabled humans to settle the four planets of the Domus system. The Purpura Pawn - thought to have decorated Ceatul XVI's sword pommel during his final battle - became a surviving relic of the empire.[263] War spread throughout the quadrant containing the Imogenella Star Cluster. The Festari were defeated when a woman, Aldebrath, transferred her mind into the systems aboard the spaceship Fervent Hope, then emitted a telepathic virus that compelled the Festari to seek a path of love and tranquillity. Legends subsequently arose about Aldebrath, the mighty male warlord who saved Imogenella.[264]

Earth in 2105 was "a bit boring", according to the Doctor.[265] Grayvorn escaped the Imperial Museum when someone died there and he mentally inhabited their body. He took a position of authority within the Wardens and instigated a series of sociopolitical changes on Artaris.[266]

c 2106 - "The Cruel Sea"[267] -> The ninth Doctor and Rose arrived on Mars - now a leisure planet with artificial seas for the ultra-rich to sail on. They'd landed on the yacht of Alvar Chambers, who owned the air on Earth, the air on Io, air with lime and classic air. A protoplasmic replica of one of Chambers' ex-wives attacked them, and the Doctor deduced that the sea had become sentient. A dormant ancient Martian organism had been revived by the terraforming process on Mars, but the Doctor dissipated it.

2106 saw the Ozone Purge, the first sign that man had not solved the Earth's environmental problems. The Purge was caused by a breakdown of weather control technology, and a number of species - including such previously common creatures as sheep, cats and sparrows - were wiped out.[268]

During the twenty-second century, human babies were

---

260 The Master poses as an Adjudicator in *Colony in Space*, the only time the Adjudicators were referred to or seen on television. They feature a number of times in the New Adventures, and the Doctor's companions Cwej and Forrester are ex-Adjudicators. *Lucifer Rising* relates the foundation of the Guild of Adjudicators, and their early successes. "The Macra case" (p189) isn't necessarily *The Macra Terror*, and is likely another encounter with that race. *Gridlock* would suggest that humanity had many encounters with the species.

261 *Lucifer Rising*. There's no indication how long after *Paradise Towers* this happened.

262 Dating *Iris: The Claws of Santa* (Iris audio #2.5) - It's Christmas Eve, obviously. The story takes place after the melting of the polar ice cap in the late twenty-first century. Also, *The Claws of Santa* is predicated on Father Christmas not being able to cope with humanity's

expansion beyond the solar system - a flip-over point that roughly dates to 2100. All of this presumes that the planet-sized Cosmo Mart that Iris visits - which seems to be in the same time zone - actually has nothing to do with humanity at all, as it's far, far too soon for mankind's space explorers to have the resources and technology for such an undertaking.

263 This occurs as part of Earth's "first wave" of colonists, "five hundred years" (p153) before *Benny: A Life in Pieces*.

264 "Five hundred years" before *Benny: The Goddess Quandary*. There's no reason to think that any of the participants of the Festari war are human.

265 *The End of the World*

266 *Excelis Decays*

267 Dating "The Cruel Sea" (*DWM* #359-362) - It's "the early twenty-second century". At one point, the Doctor

grown artificially to be used in scientific tests.[269] Yembe Lethbridge-Stewart died in 2106. His daughter buried him alongside his wife at Achebe Gorge on Mars.[270]

In 2107, Eurogen and the Butler Institute - relatively small corporations for the time - merged to become Eurogen Butler or the "EB Corporation". Eurogen was a major genetic research facility. After its near-collapse a century before, the Butler Institute had survived by specialising in artificial intelligence, meteorology and weather control. Both companies were expanding into the field of interplanetary exploration, and their services were now required on a dozen worlds.[271]

Humans colonised the planet Sunday in 2107 in the Mk II Worldbuilder *One Small Step* - which was powered by a polluting fission generator, and had launched from the Democratic Republic of Congo. An asteroid caused a tsunami that inundated the colonists' main settlement, Sunday City, shortly after their arrival. Half of the four hundred settlers drowned, including their leaders.[272]

(=) 2108 (1st January) - GENOCIDE[273] **->** The eighth Doctor and Sam arrived on Earth in a deviant timeline in which humanity had been eradicated. The relatively passive Tractites now occupied Earth and had named it Paratractis. The Doctor and Sam travelled back to historical junctures 2.5 million years and 3.6 million years in the past to avert this history.

2108 - WETWORLD[274] **->** The tenth Doctor planned to take Martha to Tiffany's near the Robot Regent's palace on the planet Arkon, but they ended up on the swampy world of Sunday - where a mindless alien creature, the Slimey, had taken control of the native otterlike creatures. The Slimey planned to blast itself into space by detonating the colony's nuclear reactor, but the Doctor defeated it.

2108 - IRIS: THE TWO IRISES[275] **->** Iris Wildthyme's lover Roger had been sent back in time with a Naxian beachhead, but judged that his people were rubbish at conquering the galaxy and instead opened a nightclub in Spain. He unwisely tried to get Iris' attention by sparking an international incident using the power of disco.

Iris had now retired to a rehab dimension, and left Panda to travel with Iris Hilary Wildthyme, a computer-generated projection made by Iris' bus. Panda summoned the real Iris when Roger's actions triggered a nuclear conflict between Earth's North and South Blocs. Iris and her friends prevented the disaster, and Hilary stayed to help Roger run the nightclub.

In July 2108, the Doctor visited Oxford Street and bought a Xavier Eugene microscope and a pair of wings in the sales.[276] Marmadons were foul creatures that lived in deep space. A century after Kim Krontska, Tom Braudy and Samuel departed Earth, one such monster broke into their ship and killed Samuel. Tom and Kim revived from cryo-sleep and dealt with the creature, then learned they were far from home. Kim re-entered stasis and returned to Earth, but Tom left in a coffin-shaped escape pod.

Tom crashed on the planet Lucentra, marking the first visit to that world by an extra-terrestrial. The natives were a technologically advanced race with dreadful long-term memories. Two Lucentran entrepreneurs, Lest and Argot, extended Tom's lifespan and kept him docile in a cell that re-created his childhood. In the decades to come, Lest and Argot would repeatedly haul Tom out and dramatically re-create his arrival for the forgetful Lucentrans' enjoyment.

The Lucentrans, as with many other races, engineered nano-forms: tiny creatures with limited intelligence, designed to carry out very specific tasks. Such technology always derived from the nature of the species forging it.[277]

Events portrayed in the film *Independence Day* (1996) actually happened, but in 2109.[278]

& 2109 - LEGEND OF THE CYBERMEN[279] **->** Zoe Heriot deduced that she travelled with the Doctor and Jamie for a time, and her memories returned. The Cybermen re-invaded Space Wheel W3 and Cyber-converted its staff, including Leo Ryan. Zoe modified the Cybership's propulsion unit and transferred the Cybermen to the Land of Fiction, then enthroned herself as its new

---

says Rose is his fifty-seventh companion.

268 *Lucifer Rising* (p100, p320).

269 *Timewyrm: Revelation*

270 *Transit* (p157-158).

271 *Deceit* (p27-28).

272 *Wetworld*

273 Dating *Genocide* (EDA #4) - The date is given (p30).

274 Dating *Wetworld* (NSA #18) - The year is given (p32).

275 Dating *Iris: The Two Irises* (Iris audio #2.3) - The year is given.

276 *Speed of Flight, Genocide*.

277 *Memory Lane*

278 *Heart of Stone* (p79)

279 Dating *Legend of the Cybermen* (BF #135) - Zoe is clearly older, in contrast to her fictional self in the Land looking the same age as when she travelled with the Doctor. It seems reasonable to assume that from Zoe's perspective, the same number of years have passed since *The War Games* as have occurred since that story's broadcast in 1969 and the release of *Legend of the Cybermen* in 2010. *The Laird of McCrimmon*, an unmade TV story, is here cited as an adventure that Zoe invented in her capacity as the Land's Mistress.

Mistress. She marshalled an army of fictional characters against the Cybermen, and pulled the sixth Doctor's TARDIS into the Land so he could help. He had some side adventures with a fictional version of Jamie McCrimmon, and eventually helped Zoe to resolve the Cybermen into fiction. He returned Zoe to the Wheel - whereupon the Time Lords' memory blocks renewed themselves, and she forgot her travels with him again.

& 2109 - ECHOES OF GREY / THE MEMORY CHEATS / THE UNCERTAINTY PRINCIPLE[280] **->** At the Whitaker Institute in central Australia, the second Doctor, Jamie and the Zoe travelling with them shut down research pertaining to the Achromatics - man-made creatures who could heal any disease or injury, but couldn't refrain from killing both their patients and healthy people. Afterward, Ali, an agent for the Company who backed the Achromatic research, approached Zoe's contemporary self and used a

device to retrieve her memory of the adventure. The agent hoped that Zoe would provide the genetic codes for the Achromatics that she had seen, but Zoe, sensing the Company wanted to turn the Achromatics into weapons of war, said that she couldn't remember...

Forty-seven days into the cycle, the Company charged Zoe on thirty-six counts, including sedition, extortion and threats to personnel. Computer analysis suggested that Zoe should plea bargain, as she had a 63% chance of avoiding a death sentence. Zoe's defence assistant, Jen, said that the Company would exert a leniency clause if Zoe could provide information on time travel.

Jen and Zoe examined the second Doctor, Jamie and Zoe's trip to Uzbekistan, 1919, in the hope of restoring Zoe's memory. Zoe continued to insist that she had never travelled in time, and manipulated Jen into reading files that revealed the unscrupulous nature of the Company's Elite Programme. Jen was left to determine the veracity of

280 Dating *Echoes of Grey, The Memory Cheats* and *The Uncertainty Principle* (BF CC #5.2, 6.3, 7.2) - In *Echoes of Grey*, the Doctor tells the Zoe with him that they've arrived, "A little into your future, I think"; Ali says that the contemporary Zoe is now a "fifty year old"; and the contemporary Zoe says that she is "forty years older" than when she travelled with the Doctor. As *Echoes of Grey* saw release after (albeit by just two months) *Legend of the Cybermen*, it seems fair to assume that it happens next in line.

The Memory Cheats follows on from *Echoes of Grey*. Jen pulls records pertaining to the 1919 visit from an archive "one hundred fifty years old", but this would seem to be the age of the archive, not the duration of time since the Uzbekistan incident. If mention of it being "forty-seven days into cycle" in any way parallels the Gregorian calendar, then it's 16th February.

The final paragraph of this entry, a quick summary of the (for Zoe) "present day" scenes in *The Uncertainty Principle*, is the only material from a 2012-released story included in this edition of *Ahistory*, and was added for the sake of continuing the narrative of this storyline. A fourth audio in the series is forthcoming.

281 Dating *Transit* (NA #10) - The exact date of the story is not specified. The book takes many of its themes from *The Seeds of Death*, and is set at least a generation after that story. The Transit system has been established for at least the last couple of decades and has revolutionised the world - no television stories seem to be set during this period. It is hinted that the story takes place in the twenty-second century (p134). In his "Future History Continuity", *Transit* author Ben Aaronovitch places this story "c2109". *GodEngine*, following the Virgin version of *Ahistory*, dated the story as "2109" (p1). *So Vile a Sin* gave the date as 2010, which would seem to be a misprint (p140).

282 *GodEngine*

283 *Festival of Death*, possibly a reference to *Transit*.
284 *Deceit* says that production line warships are being made by 2112 (p28). Suspended animation is seen in a number of New Adventures set after this time, including *Deceit, The Highest Science* and *Lucifer Rising*.
285 *Nightmare of Eden*. This happens after *Transit*, but there's enough time before *Nightmare of Eden* to allow Tryst to explore and for Earth to found a colony on (at least) Azure. The starship *Empress* has left from Station Nine.
286 *Benny: Genius Loci*
287 *Cold Fusion*. The planet was named as Salomon in the synopsis, but not the book.
288 The Interstellar Space Corps appears in *The Space Pirates*, the Marine Space Corps appears in *Death to the Daleks* and the Space Corps is referred to in *Nightmare of Eden*.
289 "Three years" after *Transit* (p260).
290 *St Anthony's Fire* (p195, p260). Urrozdinee first appeared in a short story of the same name by Mark Gatiss in Marvel's *Doctor Who Yearbook 1994*. In that story, the city is a post-apocalyptic feudal state inhabiting the remains of EuroDisney.
291 *Sword of Orion*
292 Centuries before *Vanishing Point*. Arbitrary date.
293 Dating *Kursaal* (EDA #7) - The year isn't stated, but Gray Corporation is mentioned in *Seeing I* (p25), establishing - given that the founder of Gray Corp is here killed - something of a lower threshold as to when *Kursaal* can take place. Interplanetary travel is used to reach Kursaal, and visitors there include an Alpha Centaurian (from *The Curse of Peladon*) and some Ogrons (*Frontier in Space*). Not only does this suggest that Saturnia Regna is located near Earth space, but it's possible that Kursaal is a precursor to the sort of "leisure planet" trend found in such stories as *The Leisure Hive* (dated to 2290).

Zoe's character, and whether or not she should risk exposing the Programme...

Jen's children were chosen for the Elite Programme, binding her hands. She used a focused Morgan ray - a technique used to relieve dementia - to temporarily undo Zoe's memory blocks. Zoe was aware that she remembered everything... and nothing. Jen told her that they would find out why that was the case.

c 2109 - TRANSIT[281] **->** The Union of Solar Republics attempted to build the first interstitial tunnel to another star system. The Stunnel would provide instantaneous travel to Arcturus II, twenty-six light years away, and if successful would allow rapid colonisation of other planets.

The seventh Doctor and Benny were at King's Cross station when disaster struck during the Stunnel's initiation - a portion of an intelligence from another dimension came through the Stunnel, and the President was killed. The Doctor found that Stunnel network itself had attained a level of intelligence, and banished the intruder back to its native dimension. It became clear that it was impossible to maintain Transit tunnels over interstellar distances. Following activity on Mars, a nest of Martians was revived and entered negotiations with humanity.

The Doctor visited the Stone Mountain archive and found that the security software there had become sentient. He agreed to keep silent about this development if it wiped all records pertaining to him. The AI named itself FLORANCE.

Kadiatu Lethbridge-Stewart was now a student at Lunaversity, and met the Doctor - who postulated that she might be a sort of anti-body created in response to his intervening in history. After the Doctor and Benny left, Kadiatu finished her own time machine and followed them.

The Transit system was abandoned soon after this incident. The Martian castes debated making peace with Earth in 2110. Humans established two human cities on Mars: Jacksonville and Arcadia Planitia.[282] Humanity developed the theory of hyperspace tunnels in the early twenty-second century.[283]

The first production line warships began to be built. Lagships were still used for many years on longer journeys, although the technology remained risky.[284] **Mankind discovered warp drive, allowing it to travel faster-than-light. Azure, in West galaxy, was colonised and became a tourist destination. At least nine space Stations were set up. By now, contact with alien species was almost routine.**[285]

The Protocols of Colonisation were established. The Earth Reptiles and their allies inserted a Hibernation Clause stating that colonists must withdraw from a world if the indigenous species revived from stasis.[286] An ice

planet was discovered when a scientific expedition made a misjump through hyperspace. Marooned for three years, they established a colony run along rational lines. Three years later, when the rescue ships arrived, they elected to stay. Miners and other colonists arrived and were ruled by an elite of scientists, the Scientifica.[287]

The Space Corps was set up.[288]

Kadiatu Lethbridge-Stewart destroyed the Butterfly Wing, apparently committing suicide in the process ... although there were rumours that she had built a time machine.[289]

The crusade of the Chapter of St Anthony was becoming notorious. Youths from the Initiate League torched the city of Urrozdinee when they refused to accept the rule of the Chapter. Shortly afterwards, the crusade spread unopposed to the stars, in two mighty battleships capable of laying waste to whole planets and destroying small moons. The Chapter raided Titan, and recruited the malevolent dwarf Parva De Hooch. Shortly afterwards, the Chapter returned to Earth and De Hooch killed his parents.[290]

Garazone Central was one of the first cities to "float between the stars", and was located well away from Earth authorities, maintaining its own Space Patrol. The Garazone bazaar became a trading post for humans and aliens alike.[291]

Earth authorities imprisoned the geneticist Cauchemar for murdering people in his quest to achieve immortality. He was dispatched on a colony arkship to a prison world at the edge of the New Earth frontier, but half the crew died in a meteor strike. A race of benevolent aliens offered to save the survivors from dying of radiation poisoning. Cauchemar aided the aliens in transforming the humans into hosts for their own criminals.

The hybrids were seeded onto an unnamed planet, lacking knowledge of their previous identities. Those who lived commendable existences passed into the afterlife; those who didn't were reincarnated to try again. The colony lost population as souls were redeemed. "The Creator" was a semi-sentient entity that oversaw this process.

Cauchemar's experiments had rendered him unsuitable as a host, and he was exiled. He returned to find his lover Jasmine among the reincarnated populace, but his "alien" presence disrupted the Creator and killed her.[292]

c 2110 - KURSAAL[293] **->** Gray Corporation owned the planet Saturnia Regna, and was constructing the theme park/holiday destination Kursaal there. The eighth Doctor and Sam wanted to visit Kursaal, but erroneously arrived some years before it had been built. Gray Corp's bulldozers unearthed the Jax cathedral, enabling the revived Jax virus to turn human corpses into animated were-creatures. The founder of Gray Corp, Maximillian Gray, was infected with the virus while he was still alive; moonlight catalysed his transformation into a Jax pack leader. A struggle led to

Gray's death, and the virus secretly passed into Sam, who departed with the Doctor.

Because interstellar travel and communications were still relatively slow, colony planets were often left to their own devices. The founding fathers of these worlds were often important, and all sorts of political and social experimentation was attempted.

Many colonies were set up and directly controlled by the corporations, and many others were reliant on them for communications, transport and technology.[294] The EB Corporation was among the first to offer an escape from Earth in their warpship, *The Back to Nature*, which was commissioned in 2112. Arcadia was a temperate planet, the second in its system, and was less than a thousand light-years from Earth. A number of years previous, the EB Corporation had set up a survey camp on the planet, the site of which would become the capital city Landfall, and set about terraforming the world. The planet came to resemble medieval Europe, and was ready for the first

influx of colonists. Arcadia eventually became the Corporation's centre of operations.[295] **The eleventh Doctor took Amy to Arcadia at some point.**[296]

Early during Earth's interstellar expansion, a colony ship landed on Demigest and contact was lost. A rescue mission was also wiped out, but only after one member, Trudeau, dictated a log entry that became known as *The Black Book of Demigest*. Space and time never settled on Demigest as they did on most other worlds. The original colonists mutated to become the Warlocks of Demigest, and obtained great powers.[297]

No intelligent life was discovered on the outskirts of the galaxy, where the stars and planets were sparse. Before long, man abandoned all attempts to venture out past Lasty's Nebula. Mankind's colonisation efforts focused towards the centre of the galaxy - "the hub", as it became known. A thriving interplanetary community grew up.

The planet Evertrin was the site of the annual Inner Planets Music Festival, known as Ragasteen. The biggest bands in space attended to plug their discods: Deep Space,

---

294 The founding fathers of a planet are revered in *The Robots of Death*, *The Caves of Androzani* and the New Adventure *Parasite*. Earth colonies feature in many, many *Doctor Who* stories. The corporations' stranglehold over the early colonies is a theme touched on in many New Adventures, especially the "Future History Cycle" which ran from *Love and War* to *Shadowmind*

295 The Arcadia colony was founded "three hundred and seventy-nine" (Arcadian?) years before the events of *Deceit* (p115). It was one of the first Spinward Settlements (p16) and the planet (or at least part of it) has been terraformed (p103).

NAMING PLANETS: The planet Arcadia is referred to in "Profits of Doom", *Deceit*, *Doomsday* and *Vincent and the Doctor*; Arcadian diamonds are mentioned in *TW: Kiss Kiss, Bang Bang*. In each case, this could be the same planet, as could the planets called Lucifer referred to in *Lucifer Rising* and *Bad Wolf*.

The same can't be said for "New Earth", though - there's a New Earth Frontier in *Vanishing Point*, a New Earth Republic in *Synthespians™*, a New Earth system in "Fire and Brimstone", and planets called New Earth in "Dogs of Doom", *Time of Your Life*, *The Romance of Crime* and, well, *New Earth* (seen again in *Gridlock*). From what we see of the planets, what we're told of their locations and the dates in which they're settled, these are *not* the same planets. It's a natural enough name for a human colony, of course.

296 *Vincent and the Doctor*

297 *The Infinity Race*

298 *The Highest Science*

299 The Doctor says he visited Androzani Major when "it was becoming rather developed" in *The Caves of Androzani*. In *The Power of Kroll*, we see the third moon

of Delta Magna. (It is called "Delta III" in the novelisation and *Original Sin*, p21.)

THE SIRIUS SYSTEM: In *Frontier in Space*, the Master poses as a Commissioner from Sirius IV and accuses the third Doctor and Jo of landing a spaceship in an unauthorised area on Sirius III. According to Romana in *City of Death*, Sirius V is the home of the Academia Stellaris, an art gallery she rates more highly than the Louvre. *Max Warp* occurs during a time of prosperity for Sirius (probably circa 3999), when the Sirius Exhibition Station plays host to the Inter-G Cruiser Show. In *The Caves of Androzani*, Morgus is the chairman of the Sirius Conglomerate based on Androzani Major, and spectrox is found on its twin planet Androzani Minor. These two facts make Morgus the "richest man in the Five Planets". We might infer that these are the five planets of the Sirius system, and that Androzani Major and Minor are Sirius I and II. The Doctor once had a sneg stew in a bistro on Sirius Two, according to *Island of Death*. By *The Children of Seth*, Sirius has an empire.

300 *The Space Pirates*

301 *Lucifer Rising* (p84).

302 *The Highest Science* (p102). Bubbleshake is an addictive drink akin to Bubble Shock (*SJA: Invasion of the Bane*). No overt connection has been made between the two, save that both stories were written by Gareth Roberts.

303 Dating *The Rebel Flesh/The Almost People* (X6.4-6.5) - We're told it's "the twenty-second century", but nothing more specific, and the story doesn't have any explicit links with other adventures. We can probably conclude it is the first half of the century, as the second half entailed Earth being ravaged by the Dalek Invasion. There's no hint of interstellar travel or mention of space

M'Troth, The Great Mothers of Matra, Is Your Baby a God and Televised Instant Death were all at Ragasteen 2112. The riggers on Earth changed the style of music every three years to keep it fresh. Zagrat, for example, were very popular during the "headster time", but teenagers found their discod "Sheer Event Shift" embarrassing just a few years later.[298]

Worlds such as the five planets of the Sirius system and Delta Magna rapidly became industrialised and overpopulated.[299] Burglars began to use computers, forcing people to install audio locks.[300] Tourism on Earth was a thing of the past.[301] The lethal drink Bubbleshake, invented by the unscrupulous Joseph-Robinson corporation, was originally an appetite suppressant. Unchecked, it was addictive, leading to memory loss, hyperactivity and compulsive behaviour. The substance was eventually outlawed.[302]

c 2111 - THE REBEL FLESH / THE ALMOST PEOPLE[303]

-> On Earth, the Morpeth-Jetsan company set up industrial operations to harvest crystal-diluric acid. The process killed so many workers that Morpeth-Jetsan created the Flesh: a malleable substance used to create human clones, Gangers, that were remote-controlled by their progenitors. The Gangers were treated as expendable, although an electrical surge on the Isle of Sheppey had granted a Ganger enough autonomy to kill its controller.

The eleventh Doctor brought Amy and Rory to an acid-mining facility built into a thirteenth-century monastery, as he wished to see the Flesh technology in its early days. A solar tsunami caused all of the Gangers present to became autonomous. Hostility arose between the workers and their Ganger counterparts, and the facility was destroyed. The Doctor took the survivors - one human and two Gangers - back to the mainland, where they held a press conference to call for Ganger rights.

Back on the TARDIS, the Doctor revealled that for several months now, the Amy travelling with him and Rory had been a Ganger planted in their midst by the Silence. He dissolved the duplicate into Flesh as the real Amy went into labour...

2112 - THE GEMINI CONTAGION[304] -> Zalnex

Corporation's researchers on the ice planet Vinsk used cloned Meme-Spawn to create Gemini: a dual-purpose handwash that made anyone who used it fluent in every known language. Gemini was only tested on the native Vinskians, and turned humans into savage mutants. The eleventh Doctor and Amy helped to stop an initial shipment of Gemini from reaching Earth, and used heat to destroy some giant Meme-Spawn.

& 2112 - MARTHA IN THE MIRROR[305] -> The planets

Anthium and Zerugma had been at peace for twenty years, and were scheduled to sign a peace treaty in Castle Extremis. The tenth Doctor and Martha were present as Zerguman soldiers hidden within the interior dimension of the Mortal Mirror stormed Extremis, but were killed by a combination of sonic waves and combat with troops from the Galactic Alliance. Manfred Grieg emerged from the Mirror's interior. With the treaty assured, the Alliance planned to turn Extremis into a theme park.

Earth discovered universal concrete in 2115.[306] Welford Jeffery invented antigrav technology.[307] In 2115, human archaeologists found the Martian city of Ikk-ett-Saleth completely abandoned.[308]

2116 - NIGHTMARE OF EDEN[309] -> Interplanetary

standards and conventions were set up that applied to the whole of Human Space. The Galactic Credit (z) was a convertible interplanetary currency. Credits resembled colourful blocks of plastic, and were used for everything from buying a drink to funding an expedition to a new planet. None of this prevented a recession from hitting the galactic economy.

---

colonies, and the mining workers are listening to Dusty Springfield. All in all, we can probably set it a hundred years after the story was broadcast.
304 Dating *The Gemini Contagion* (BBC *DW* audiobook #12) - The year is given.
305 Dating *Martha in the Mirror* (NSA #22) - No date is given. The only real clue is that the Darksmiths of Karagula (the ten-part *Darksmith Legacy*) built the Mortal Mirror, meaning that *Martha in the Mirror* cannot take place more than a century after the Darksmiths are killed. Therefore, this dating reflects the latest that the story can occur.
306 *The Face-Eater* (p40).
307 "Several hundred years" after Charley's time (the

1930s), according to *Sword of Orion*.
308 *GodEngine* (p73).
309 Dating *Nightmare of Eden* (17.4) - Galactic Salvage and Insurance went bankrupt "twenty years ago" according to Captain Rigg, who had just read a monitor giving the date of the bankruptcy as "2096". *In-Vision* suggested that Azure is in "West galaxy", but this could just be a mishearing of Rigg's (fluffed) line "you'll never work in *this* galaxy again". While others have disagreed with that, there is certainly no on screen justification for *The Discontinuity Guide's* "Western galaxy". *The TARDIS Logs* gave the date as "c.2100", *The Doctor Who File* as "2113".

Laser technology advanced during this period. Stun laser weapons became available for the first time. Entuca lasers capable of carrying millions of signals were now used for telecommunications. Finally, vast amounts of information could now be recorded on laser data crystals.

Crime was a problem in the galaxy. Drug trafficking increased when the drug XYP, or Vraxoin, was discovered. Vrax addicts felt a warm complacency at first, followed by total apathy and thirst. Inevitably, its effects were fatal. The narcotic ruined whole planets and communities until the planet that was the only known source of the drug was incinerated. A Vraxoin merchant (drug trafficker) risked the death penalty if caught. Molecular scanners were developed that could detect even minute quantities of the drug. All citizens were required to carry an ident-plaque.

Interplanetary tourism developed at this time. Government-subsidised interstellar cruise liners, each holding nine hundred passengers, travelled between Station Nine and Azure. Passengers could travel either economy or first class, the former seated in "pallets" and forced to wear protective clothing, the latter allowed a great deal more freedom and luxury.

The scientist Tryst attempted to qualify and quantify every lifeform in the galaxy. As Tryst's log (published to coincide with a series of lectures given by the zoologist) recounted, his ten-man expedition travelled to Zil, Vij, Darp, Lvan, Brus, the windswept planet Gidi and the temperate world Ranx. Finally, Tryst's ship, the *Volante*, travelled past the Cygnus Gap to the three-planet system of M37. The second planet contained primitive life: molluscs, algae and insects. As well as taking visprints, they used a Continuous Event Transmitter (CET) machine - a device that encoded samples on laser crystals, enabling people to physically interact with them.

Six months before arriving at Azure, the *Volante* visited the planet Eden. They lost a member of the crew, Stott, who was secretly working for the Intelligence Section of the Space Corps. It was later discovered that Mandrels from the planet Eden decomposed into Vraxoin when they died, and that Tryst had partnered with Dymond, the pilot of the *Hecate*, to smuggle the material. Owing to intervention by the fourth Doctor, Romana and K9, the two of them were arrested.

The prison moon Erratoon was forgotten about during the galactic recession. The thousands serving life sentences there had families, and the robot wardens monitored their descendents, making them do maintenance.[310]

2118 (April) - THE ART OF DESTRUCTION[311] ->

Earth risked famine, and Agriculture Technology research was underway to prevent this. The tenth Doctor and Rose thwarted the Wurms in Chad, but the Wurms had tracked down a warren of their archenemies, the Valnaxi, to Earth.

---

310 *The Prisoner's Dilemma*. This is presumably the same galactic recession mentioned in *Nightmare of Eden*.

311 Dating *The Art of Destruction* (NSA #11) - The Doctor says it's "the eleventh of April 2118".

312 *The Face-Eater*. The dates given in the book seem to contradict a number of other stories set around this time.

313 *Tomb of Valdemar*. The Centauri are described as "multi-limbed" and having a "giant eye", so these are almost certainly the same race as first seen in *The Curse of Peladon*.

314 *Cold Fusion*

315 The space port has been open a hundred years before *The Year of Intelligent Tigers*.

316 Dating *Kursaal* (EDA #7) - It's fifteen years after the Doctor and Sam's first visit.

317 *State of Decay*. No date is given. On screen, one computer monitor seems to suggest that the computer was programmed on "12/12/1998", but the *Hydrax* is clearly an interstellar craft. *The TARDIS Logs* suggested a date in "the thirty-sixth century", *The Terrestrial Index* placed it "at the beginning of the twenty second".

318 *Lucifer Rising* (p59, p272-273).

319 *The Taking of Planet 5* (p15).

320 *Spiral Scratch*

321 Dating *The Face-Eater* (EDA #18) - The date is given (p126).

322 *St Anthony's Fire*

323 *The Taint*

324 *The Face-Eater*

325 Dating *The Space Pirates* (6.6) - A monitor readout in episode two suggests that the year is "1992", but this contradicts dialogue stating that prospectors have been in deep space for "fifty years". No other date is given on screen. The *Radio Times* said that the story takes place in "the far future". Earth is mentioned once in the first episode, but after that only a "homeworld" is referred to. The force here is specified as the Interstellar Space Corps. The regulatory actions of the government suggest that space travel is becoming more common now, but is still at an early stage.

As Zoe is unfamiliar with the technology of this story, it is almost certainly set after her time. The Main Boost Drive is not very advanced, and this story almost certainly takes place well before *Frontier in Space*, where hyperdrive technology is common. At the start of the story, the V41-LO is both "fifty days" and "fifty billion miles" from Earth - it seems reasonable to assume that writer Robert Holmes meant "billion" in the British

During the second and third decade of the twenty-second century, the Western Alliance banks foreclosed on Earth and the World Civilian Police Corps was formed. The Oceanic-Nippon bloc was working on interstellar flight, and the first supra-light vessel *New Horizon* was launched in 2126, taking five thousand colonists on a two-year journey to Proxima 2, the first colony in an alien environment. Proxima City was founded there. The second human colony world was called Earth 2.

UNIT had been disbanded by this time. The records of Global Mining Corporation listed the Doctor as a security consultant from 2127 (adding that his female companion graduated Geneva Corporate University in 2124) following an unrecorded incident in Albania.[312] Proxima 2 was the first of the settled worlds and humans would come to share it with the Centauri.[313] The Particle Matter Transmission (Deregulation) Act was passed in 2122.[314] The first humans to arrive on Hitchemus, a planet on the edge of explored space, were hunters in pursuit of the tigers that lived there. The colony of Port Any was built shortly afterwards. It became famed for music and attracted musicians from across human space.[315]

& 2125 - KURSAAL[316] **->** The eighth Doctor and Sam returned to Kursaal when it was open for business. Sam mentally succumbed to the Jax virus within her, but was stymied in her attempts to bathe in moonlight and complete her transformation. The Jax cathedral was obliterated, and the destruction of technology beneath it caused the Jax virus to perish. Unknown to the Doctor and Sam, the founder of the ecoterrorist organisation HALF, Bernard Cockaigne, remained at large as a Jax drone.

The exploration vessel *Hydrax* was lost en route to Beta Two in the Perugellis Sector. Its officers included Captain Miles Sharkey, science officer Anthony O'Connor and navigation officer Lauren Macmillan. It fell through a CVE into the pocket universe of E-Space.[317] The *Hydrax* disappeared around 2127. The InterSpace Incorporated ship had a crew of two hundred and forty-three. InterSpace refused to pay out pensions for the lost crew, claiming they might be found. IMC later claimed to have discovered traces of the ship in order to blackmail Piper O'Rourke - whose husband Ben had been an engineer on the *Hydrax* - into revealling details about the Eden Project. The ship was never discovered.[318]

The planet Vulcan suddenly vanished in 2130.[319]

> = In one alternate universe, a hydrogen accident had devastated America. Racing spaceships around the solar system was a spectator sport by 2130.[320]

2130 - THE FACE-EATER[321] **->** The eighth Doctor and Sam discovered the F-Seeta, a telepathic gestalt of the rat-like natives, was responsible for a series of murders on the first human colony world of Proxima 2. The colony was saved, but at the cost of the Proximans' group mind.

On Betrushia around the year 2133, as it had done many times over the centuries, war broke out between the Ismetch and the Cutch. Millions died in the conflict, which became the longest and most bitter struggle the planet had seen for three hundred years. The Ismetch had an early success at Dalurida Bridge under Portrone Ran.[322]

The eighth Doctor, Sam and Fitz arrived in London during the summer of 2134, and confirmed that the Earth was free of the Beast.[323] A second wave of colonists was expected on Proxima 2 in 2136.[324]

? 2135 - THE SPACE PIRATES[325] **->** As space travel became more common, the Earth government introduced a series of regulations to better control the space lanes in its territory. Space was divided into administrative and strategic Sectors. All flights now had to be logged with Central Flight Information and a network of Mark Five Space Beacons were established to monitor space traffic. The Interstellar Space Corps was given the latest V-Ships, armed with state-of-the-art Martian Missiles (H-bombs were considered old-fashioned by this time) and carrying squadrons of Minnow Fighters. The V-Ships were powered by Maximum Boost atomic motors. The Space Corps routinely used mind probes to interrogate their prisoners. The resources of the Space Corps were stretched very thin: they fought brush wars in three sectors, acted as customs and excise officials and attempted to curtail the activities of space pirates.

For two years, pirates were active in the Ta system and hijacked five of Milo Clancey's floaters, each of which contained fifty thousand tons of argonite ore. Despite a dozen requests, the Space Corps did little to help. As an old-timer, Clancey was suspicious of authority; he had lost his registration documents thirty years before and he didn't maintain his feedback link to CFI.

The Space Corps became involved when the pirates began to break up government space beacons to steal the argonite. The V41-LO was more than fifty days out of Earth, under the command of General Nikolai Hermack, Commander of the Space First Division. The ship was ninety minutes away from Beacon Alpha 4 when it was broken up by pirates. Clancey's ship was detected nearby, and he was questioned but quickly released. The second Doctor, Jamie and Zoe were recovered from Beacon Alpha 4, but they too were innocent.

The real culprit was Maurice Caven. His pirates were organised enough to equip themselves with Beta

Dart ships, costing one hundred million credits each, that could outrun virtually everything else in space. Some time ago, Caven had kidnapped Dom Issigri and blackmailed his beautiful daughter Madeline, the head of the Issigri Mining Company, into providing facilities for him on the planet Ta. The Corps hunted Caven down and executed him.

After this, the Issigri Mining Company was renamed the Interplanetary Mining Company, or IMC for short.[326] Humanity's contact with the Arcturans was proving fruitful. The Arcturans allowed limited human settlement in their sector, and supplied humanity with specialised drugs. Some humans became interested in studying Arcturan literature.

On Earth, however, things were getting desperate. The Islam-dominated Earth Central, based in Damascus and led by an elected president, was unable to prevent society from collapsing. An unprecedented energy crisis led to draconian restrictions on consumption and the foundation of the Energy Police. The invention of the vargol generator did little to relieve the demands for fuel.

In 2137, with Earth desperate for energy, corporations successfully lobbied for the repeal of all the anti-pollution laws brought in over the last century and a quarter. Three years later, an American subsidiary of Panorama Chemicals filled the Carlsbad Caverns with plastic waste, and the oceans of the world were a sludge of industrial effluent. Mineral water became a precious commodity. The whale finally became extinct, and auto-immune diseases - "the plague" of over a century before - returned.

Despite this, human life expectancy was now one hundred and ten years, and the population was soaring. Although it had religious objections to gambling, Earth Central introduced the Eugenics Lottery, and couples were forbidden from having children unless they won.[327]

---

sense of a million million, rather than the American (and now generally accepted British) thousand million. If this is the case, then the Beacon is 8.3 light years from Earth (otherwise it is a thousandth of this distance, and only just outside the solar system).

The Programme Guide set the story "c.2600". *The Terrestrial Index* suggested it was "during the Empire" period. *The TARDIS Logs* claimed a date of "8751". *Timelink* suggested "2146", *About Time* "2135ish".

326 The Issigri Mining Company appears in *The Space Pirates*. Another company with the same initials, the Interplanetary Mining Company, is seen in *Colony in Space*. In the Missing Adventure *The Menagerie*, we learn that they are the same company (p161). The change of name must have occurred before *Lucifer Rising*, when we see IMC in action.

327 *Lucifer Rising*. The evil polluting company in the television version of *The Green Death* is called "Global Chemicals". A real company of that name objected, and the name was changed in the novelisation to "Panorama Chemicals".

328 *Fear Itself* (PDA)

329 *Benny: Another Girl, Another Planet*. Aragonite was mentioned in *The Space Pirates*.

330 *The Sorcerer's Apprentice* (p203-204).

331 *Heritage* (p198).

332 *Leviathan*

333 Dating *The Murder Game* (PDA #2) - The date is given (p12).

334 *Lucifer Rising* (p158).

335 *Parasite*

336 Dating "The Daleks: The Terrorkon Harvest" (TV21 #70-75) - There's no indication how long after "Impasse" this *TV Century 21* Dalek story is set, allowing the first significant gap in the narrative. The next story, "Legacy of Yesteryear", is set "centuries" after the first (which seems to be set in 1763 AD). The novel *GodEngine* notes

that the Daleks became concerned with Earth ten years before they invade, and that's exactly what we see happening in these strips, so the novel has been used to establish the dating of these stories. This block of stories ends with the Daleks discovering Earth of the future and gearing up to invade - clearly a reference to *The Dalek Invasion of Earth*.

337 Dating "The Daleks: Legacy of Yesteryear" (TV21 #76-85) - It is "centuries" since the original Daleks were frozen - and that happened the day of the meteorite strike that set off the neutron bomb (seen in "Genesis of Evil"). The Daleks remember Yarvelling and his inventions. So there are "centuries" between "Impasse" and "The Terrorkon Harvest".

338 Dating "The Daleks: Shadow of Humanity" (TV21 #86-89) - There is no indication how long it has been since "Legacy of Yesteryear". The Emperor now knows about "human beings", although it's unclear when he heard the name - perhaps fragments of evidence were discovered in the wreckage of Lodian's ship after the previous story. The following stories all seem to take place without lengthy gaps between them.

339 Dating "The Daleks: The Emissaries of Jevo" (TV21 #90-95) - At the end of the story, the Emperor praises Kirid's "human spirit", and before that Kirid seems to call himself "human", although he looks more like a humanoid alien (he has forehead ridges, like a Klingon). Given that the next story features a spaceship from Earth, we are now definitely in the future.

340 Dating "The Daleks: The Road to Conflict" (TV21 #96-104) - The story is set soon after "The Emissaries of Jevo". There's no date given, but this story features an interstellar human passenger spacecraft, and the people have never heard of the Daleks. So this is set before *The Dalek Invasion of Earth*, almost certainly in the first half of the twenty-second century, which fits in with later televised stories such as *Nightmare of Eden*.

A string of fundamentalist Jihads killed many people on Earth.[328] Eurogen Butler colonised Dimetos in 2142, and plundered the planet's mineral wealth, including aragonite. The indigenous population wouldn't accept relocation offworld, so Eurogen Butler all but exterminated them.[329]

A colony ship made landfall on the planet Avalon in the year 2145. The colonists discovered an ancient Avalonian technology which allowed them to perform miracles, but soon rendered their electronic equipment useless. The colony regressed to a medieval level, in which certain people - unknowingly tapping the Avalonian technology - performed "magic".[330]

Dolphins' ability to think in three dimensions made them ideal pilots for Earth's first interstellar fighters.[331]

Humanity designed Leviathans - enormous multi-generation ships to the stars, with an independent ecosystem inside - in the mid-twenty-second century. Several prototype Leviathans were built until the interstellar drive was invented, and photon-speed travel made Leviathans obsolete. With Earth's governments moving against them, the Sentinels of the New Dawn populated a disused Leviathan with clones and slept in cryo-freeze as the Leviathan travelled toward the planet Flegathon in the Nyad system. The biomechanoid Herne, the Sentinels' chief assassin, kept watch over the clones. Zeron, a computer programme designed to control prison vessels, oversaw the Leviathan.[332]

2146 - THE MURDER GAME[333] **->** The European Government and the Terran Security Forces (TSF) were established by this time. The First Galactic Treaty had been signed. The Selachians had menaced Terra Alpha.

The second Doctor, Ben and Polly answered a distress call and landed in the Hotel Galaxian, a space station in Earth orbit. Two scientists, Neville and Dorothy Adler, were trying to sell assassination software to the Selachians. Neville Adler was killed and the space hotel burned up in the atmosphere. Dorothy Adler could not work the software without her husband.

In 2146, the American economy collapsed, and there were food riots.[334] The Doctor was in America at the time, and he was powerless to stop cannibals from killing Sonia Bannen shortly after she saved her son. Mark Bannen was placed on board a huge colony ship bound for a new star system. The stardrive misphased in the Elysium system and the colony ship crashed there.[335]

The Daleks Discover Earth

c 2146 - "The Daleks: The Terrorkon Harvest"[336] **->** On Skaro, one of the unknown creatures from the Lake of Mutations, the Terrorkon, attacked an underwater Dalek defence station. The Emperor and the Red Dalek watched as another mutation attacked it, saving the city.

& 2146 - "The Daleks: Legacy of Yesteryear"[337] **->** The Daleks begin a new survey of their home planet, discovering mineral riches and wiping out a race of sand creatures. One hoverbout inadvertently revived the group of original Daleks who had been in suspended animation for centuries, since the neutron explosion. These were the scientists Lodian, Zet and Yvric, who quickly determined that the new Daleks were without conscience. Even so, Yvric was keen to join the Daleks, but they exterminated him before he could even explain who he was. Zet realised that the Daleks would want to know about the Earth, a planet teeming with life and energy, and handed himself and Lodian over to them. Lodian escaped to a spaceship, planning to warn Earth of the Daleks. The spaceship exploded, killing the last two original Daleks and preserving the secret of Earth's existence.

& 2146 - "The Daleks: Shadow of Humanity"[338] **->** The Emperor ordered the building of a road to the Lake of Mutations, but one Dalek questioned the order and sabotaged the destruction of "beautiful" plant life. The Emperor feared that the introduction of human qualities could prove a disaster to the Daleks. The rebel Dalek exploited the natural Dalek to obey by issuing a new command to "protect beauty", and soon led a faction of Daleks as their Emperor. The Emperor quickly reasserted his power and destroyed the rebel.

& 2146 - "The Daleks: The Emissaries of Jevo"[339] **->** A space expedition from Jevo headed to Arides to prevent the spread of deadly pollen from that world. Their ship passed close to Skaro, and was snared by the Daleks' magnetrap. The Emperor assumed the pollen wouldn't affect Daleks, but the Jevonian leader Kirid tricked him into thinking otherwise. Kirid saved the universe from the pollen, but was tracked down and killed by the Daleks ... who nevertheless had started to worry about the strength of the human spirit.

& 2146 - "The Daleks: The Road to Conflict"[340] **->** The Daleks engineered a meteorite storm that damaged the Earth passenger ship *Starmaker*, which made a forced landing on Skaro. The Emperor was now obsessed with finding Earth - a planet hidden from Skaro by "skycurve" - as he was convinced that it was rich in polar magnetism and aluminium. Captain Fleet was captured and rescued by the children Jennie and Tom, but the Daleks destroyed the *Starmaker*. The three humans escaped in a Dalek transport ship to warn humanity about the Daleks... but the Daleks had now discovered the location of Earth, and planned its conquest.

& 2146 - "The Daleks: Return of the Elders"[341] -> The Daleks attacked Colony Five on Titan, and experimented on six humans as another alien fleet entered the solar system. The mysterious aliens identified themselves as Elders, and explained that they have tended Earth and warned that the Daleks would soon invade. The Earthmen destroyed one Dalek ship in the rings of Saturn, but another escaped. The Dalek Emperor vowed not to fail in his second attempt to conquer Earth.

By 2146, the Supreme Council of the Daleks had become concerned by the rapid expansion of humanity. They would monitor the situation carefully for ten years. The Martian Axis sprang up on Mars and turned to terrorism, bombing Coventry.[342]

3D cameras were developed around this time.[343]

2148 - ST ANTHONY'S FIRE[344] -> A mothership of the Chapter of St Anthony moved to pacify Betrushia, breaking up the planet's artificial ring system to wrack Betrushia with meteorites. Loosed from its shackles, the organic catalyser became active and threatened all life that it encountered. The seventh Doctor convinced the Chapter as to the creature's threat, and arranged for Betrushia's destruction while instigating an evacuation. Appalled by the Chapter's zealous actions, Bernice and Ace sabotaged the mothership's engines, crippling it to suffer the same destruction as Betrushia and the organism. The Doctor helped the Betrushia survivors relocate to the sister planet of Massatoris.

Earth funded a small Transit station on Charon, a moon of Pluto. The Martian Axis terrorists destroyed the Montreal monorail system, resulting in many deaths.[346]

---

341 Dating "The Daleks: Return of the Elders" (*DWM* #249-254) - This was a sequel to the *TV Century 21* strip. It is set straight after "The Road to Conflict". The Daleks attack the solar system, but it ends in failure. The Emperor vows to succeed next time - and that is almost certainly what happens, as we discover in *The Dalek Invasion of Earth*.
342 "10.6 human years" and "about ten years" before *GodEngine* (p107, p168).
343 *Frontier Worlds*
344 Dating *St Anthony's Fire* (NA #31) - The Doctor tells Bernice that the year is "2148" (p39).
345 "Five years" before *GodEngine* (p15, p98, p193).
346 *GodEngine*
347 *Cold Fusion*
348 *Autonomy*
349 Dating "The Grief" (*DWM* #185-187) - The date isn't specified. CHEX is an agency of the Sol Government; it has energy weapons and genetic fabrication units. The story appears to be set early in humanity's exploration efforts.
350 *Killing Ground* (p15).
351 *Benny: Another Girl, Another Planet*
352 *Excelis Decays*
353 *GodEngine* (p18).
354 "One hundred fifty years" after *Zygon: When Being You Isn't Enough*.
355 "A year" before *GodEngine*.
356 *Lucifer Rising*, *GodEngine*
357 Dating *Lucifer Rising* (NA #14) - The story takes place in the mid-twenty-second century, shortly before the Dalek Invasion of Earth. The Adjudicators' simularity registers the Doctor's arrival as "19/11/2154" (p30), Paula Engado's death as "22/2/2154" (p174) and her wake as "23/2/2154" (p13). Ace and Benny had expressed the desire to "pop back to the year 2154 or so" (p338), so at first sight it might appear that the story is set *in* 2154. However, this is inconsistent with the

Dalek Invasion, which the authors of *Lucifer Rising* place in "2158" (p337). On p195, there's mention of a raid "in Tokyo in fifty-six". The story is here placed in 2157, consistent with this chronology's dating for the Dalek Invasion.
358 *The Dalek Invasion of Earth*, with the date established in *The Daleks' Master Plan*.
359 According to the Doctor in *The Dalek Invasion of Earth*.

THE MIDDLE PERIOD OF DALEK HISTORY: Taking the Doctor's analysis at face value, the Middle Period of Dalek history might be the time when their power is at its zenith - they are technologically advanced, expansionist and feared. In the words of the Doctor in *Death to the Daleks*, they are "one of the greatest powers in the universe".

In the Virgin edition of *Ahistory*, it was speculated that it coincided with the Daleks developing an internal power supply - in *The Daleks,* they took static electricity up through the floor and so couldn't leave their city. In *The Dalek Invasion of Earth*, they had a disc resembling a satellite dish fastened to their backs; the Doctor and Ian speculate that it allows them free movement. In the first two Dalek stories, they have "bands" rather than the "slats" seen in all other stories. In *The Power of the Daleks,* they are dependent on a static electricity generator. In all subsequent stories - all of which (apart from the prototypes seen in *Genesis of the Daleks*) have Daleks originating from after *The Dalek Invasion of Earth* - none of these restrictions seem to apply. We are explicitly told they move via "psychokinetic power" in *Death to the Daleks*.

The Daleks are confined to the First Segment of Time, according to *The Ark*. We might speculate that the end of the Middle Period of Dalek history comes with either their defeat at the hands of the Movellans (*Resurrection of the Daleks*), or shortly afterwards with Skaro's destruction (*Remembrance of the Daleks*).

The Arcturans attacked the Martian colony on Cluut-ett-Pictar.[347] A premodernist architectural revival occurred in the mid-twenty-second century.[217] The fashions of the 1970s had a revival in the mid-twenty-second century.[348]

c 2150 - "The Grief"[349] -> The seventh Doctor and Ace landed on the dead planet Sorshan and met some marines from the Earth starship *Rosetta*. They worked for the Cartographic Historical Exploratory Service (CHEX). A device used the marines as material to recreate the voracious Lom - the Doctor and Ace escaped as the planetary shield and toxin were reactivated, killing the aggressors.

In the 2150s, the Cybermen invaded the colony world of Agora, making it one of their breeding colonies. Human Overseers were in charge of harvesting people to become Cybermen.[350] Eurogen Butler withdrew from Dimetos in 2151. A group of miners and officials remained behind to continue establishing the colony.[351]

The totalitarian Inner Party seized power in the city-state Excelis, and assassinated the Imperial family. More than a century and a half of oppression ensued. Grayvorn pushed other city-states into open conflict, fuelling a technology race.[352]

Earth's Colonial Marines fought in civil wars on the Outer Planets in the Arcturus system.[353] The third fleet from Zygor was scheduled to pass near Earth.[354] In 2156, Supreme Grand Marshall Falaxyr of Mars contacted the Daleks and offered them the GodEngine, an Osirian weapon that could destroy whole planets and stars. In return, he asked for Ice Warrior sovereignty of Mars. The Daleks accepted the offer.[355] By this time, mankind invented the Simularity, a holographic virtual reality.[356]

c 2157 - LUCIFER RISING[357] -> Earth encountered the Legions, a seven-dimensional race from Epsilon Eridani. Trading agreements were set up between the Legions and IMC. The Legions' sector of space was threatened by an unknown alien fleet, so IMC would supply the Legions with weaponry in return for advanced technology. Some Legions began working for IMC.

Earlier in the century, a Von Neumann probe had discovered a stable element with a very high mass in the core of the planet Lucifer, a gas giant two hundred and eighty light years from Earth. Theoretically, such an element could be used as a rich energy source. In 2152, Earth Central invested heavily in a scientific research station - the Eden Project - on Belial, one of the moons of Lucifer.

This was the era when Company Shock Troops - military men armed with neutron cannons, flamers, burners and screamers - took part in infamous corporate raids. In '56, IMC asset-stripped InterSpace Incorporated in Tokyo using armoured skimmers and Z-Bombs. Legend had it that companies used to capture employees of rival corpo-

rations and experiment on them. It was a risky life - on one raid in '51, praxis gas was used - but on average it paid four times more than Earth Central. The big human corporations learnt lessons from the aggressive capitalist races such as the Cimliss, Usurians and the Okk. But humanity proved capable of callousness that would put all three of those races to shame.

Six years after it was set up, the Eden Project had still not borne fruit, and pressure was growing to close it down. As Earth's government grew weaker and weaker, the corporations were flexing their muscles: an IMC fleet of over one hundred ships was sent to Belial Base when the scientists reported some progress.

The seventh Doctor, Ace and Benny found that Lucifer and its two moons, Belial and Moloch, formed a device that could affect morphic fields, and could transform one species of being into another. It had been formerly used upon the intelligent species of Lucifer, the "Angels". An expedition member, Alex Bannen, experimented with the device's control system and destabilised it; IMC troops worsened the situation by burning their way through a forest on Moloch, which was part of the device's control system. The IMC captain, a Legion, killed the Adjudicator Bishop - and the Doctor then killed the Legion. Bannen rectified his errors by allowing himself to be transformed into a new forest on Moloch. The Angels set up an exclusion zone around their world.

The Corporations had reached new levels of ruthlessness. IMC tripled the price of the fuel zeiton, and an impoverished Earth Central could no longer afford it. Earth was declared bankrupt and fell into the hands of its receivers: the Earth Alliance of Corporations, a holding company that was in reality the board of directors from all the corporations that traded off-Earth. It was a bloodless coup, and the megacorporations took formal control of the homeworld for the first time. Their reign lasted just under six months.

The Dalek Invasion of Earth

In 2157, the Daleks invaded Earth.[358] **This was the Middle Period of Dalek history.**[359]

An Astronaut Fair was held in London. The city was a beautiful metropolis, complete with moving pavements and a gleaming new nuclear power station alongside the historic Battersea Power Station.[360]

On the very same day that an Earth embassy opened on Alpha Centauri V, a billion settlers were exterminated on Sifranos in the Arcturus Sector. Fourteen other colonies were wiped out in a three-week period, including Azure and Qartopholos. Rumours of a mysterious alien fleet massing at the Legion homeworld of Epsilon Eridani were denied, but the Interstellar Taskforce was put on permanent standby, and a Spacefleet flotilla sent to that planet was completely destroyed. The alien fleet was a Dalek armada, the Black Fleet, which was annihilating any colony that might render aid to the human homeworld, and systematically destroying Earth's warships.[361]

Meteorites bombarded the Earth. Scientists dismissed it as a freak cosmic storm, but people started to die from a mysterious plague. The Daleks were targeting the Earth, and soon the populations of Asia, Africa and South America were wiped out. Only a handful of people had resistance to the plague, and although scientists quickly developed a new drug, it was too late. Earth was split into tiny communities.[362]

Millions started dying of a mysterious virus in Brazilia, Los Angeles and Tycho City. Some humans showed a mysterious resistance to the plague - because the seventh Doctor had seeded the atmosphere with an antidote.[363] The Daleks' Black Fleet destroyed Void Station Cassius while entering the solar system.[364]

Six months after the plague began, the first of the Dalek saucers landed. Some cities were razed to the ground, others simply occupied. Anyone who resisted was destroyed. Dalek saucers patrolled the skies. Ruthlessly suppressing any resistance, the Daleks subdued India. The leaders of every race and nation on Earth were exterminated.[365]

The Daleks quickly defeated the Terran Security Forces. Many Americans evacuated to Canada.[366] **New York was destroyed.[367]** Baltimore was reduced to ruins.[368] The Daleks exterminated the last monarch of Britain.[369] The

royal bloodline would continue at least until the fifty-third century.[370]

A supersaucer landed on Luton, crushing the city.[371] The Daleks mounted a victory parade in London, in front of the Houses of Parliament and Westminster Bridge.[372] The Daleks blockaded the solar system. The Bureau of Adjudicators on Oberon, a moon of Uranus, tried to work out the Daleks' plan. The Adjudicators detected mysterious signals at the Martian North Pole. Oberon continued to serve as a secret human military base throughout the invasion.[373] Chainswords were used to fight the Daleks.[374] The Daleks destroyed Earth's rockets, leaving the humans aboard a moonbase without a means of retrieval.[375]

The Daleks invaded Mars, but were defeated when a virus ate through their electrical cables.[376] The Daleks retaliated by releasing a virus that consumed all the oxygen in the atmosphere, and it would take decades to make the air breathable again.

2157 - GODENGINE[377] -> The seventh Doctor and Roz arrived on Mars, but Chris ended up on Pluto's moon of Charon after the TARDIS hit a subspace infarction. The Daleks bombed Charon, but Chris escaped down a Transit stunnel. The Doctor and Roz accompanied an expedition to the North Pole of Mars, which was joined by Ice Warrior pilgrims. At the pole, the Martian leader Falaxyr was about to complete the GodEngine, a device capable of making suns expel plasma bursts. Falaxyr hoped to negotiate with the Daleks to regain control of Mars. The Doctor defeated

As we've now seen the end of Dalek history (the Daleks withdrawing from history to fight the Time War, as recounted by Jack in *Bad Wolf*), we can perhaps speculate that the "early period" Daleks have bands and are dependent on externally-generated static electricity; the "middle period" Daleks are the slatted ones familiar from the original TV series and now we can add the "late period" Daleks seen in the new television series, which seem significantly more mobile and advanced than their forebears.

360 *The Dalek Invasion of Earth*
361 The Arcturus attacks take place at "the beginning of the year" according to *Lucifer Rising*. Sifranos is also mentioned in *GodEngine*.
362 *The Dalek Invasion of Earth, Legacy of the Daleks.*
363 *Lucifer Rising*
364 *GodEngine* (p3).
365 *The Dalek Invasion of Earth*
366 *The Final Sanction* (p75, p178).
367 According to Vicki in *The Chase* and *Salvation* (p58). *The Indestructible Man* said New York was destroyed in a nuclear assault in 2068, but it was evidently rebuilt. Even after its second devastation it seems to recover somewhat, as *Fear Itself* (PDA) says that New York's waterways are a tourist attraction near

the end of the twenty-second century.
368 *Nekromanteia*
369 *Legacy of the Daleks* (p45).
370 *The Mutant Phase*, although this occurs in an alternate timeline.
371 *GodEngine* (p107).
372 *Head Games* (p157).
373 *GodEngine*
374 *Fear Itself* (PDA), and referencing the weapon of choice of Abslom Daak.
375 *An Earthly Child*
376 *Genesis of the Daleks*. It is confirmed in *GodEngine* that this invasion takes place at the same time as the Dalek Invasion of Earth.
377 Dating *GodEngine* (NA #51) - The year is given (p3).
378 *The Dalek Invasion of Earth*
379 *GodEngine*
380 Dating *The Mutant Phase* (BF #15) - The year is given as "2158".
381 Dating *Renaissance of the Daleks* (BF #93) - The date is given, and re-confirmed as being "a year" after the Daleks should have invaded Earth in 2157. Vague mention is made of a "new Dalek homeworld".
382 *War of the Daleks*
383 "Three years" after *GodEngine* (p214).

Falaxyr's amended plan to eliminate the human colony of Jacksonville. The GodEngine was destroyed, and Dalek ships shot down Falaxyr as he fled.

Once the population of Earth was under control, the Daleks set to work in vast mining areas, the largest one covering the whole of Bedfordshire. There were few Daleks on Earth, and they boosted their numbers by enslaving humans and converting them into Robomen controlled by high frequency radio waves.

The Daleks cleared the smaller settlements of people and set them to work in the mines. In the larger cities, Robomen and Daleks patrolled every nook and cranny, looking for survivors. The Black Dalek oversaw the mining operations in Bedfordshire. At night, his "pet", the gruesome Slyther, patrolled the camp, attacking and eating any humans it found trying to escape.

The rebels in London survived by dodging Robo-patrols, raiding warehouses and department stores. Other threats came from escaped zoo animals, packs of wild dogs, human scavengers and traitors. The largest rebel group, under the leadership of the crippled scientist Dortmun, could only muster a fighting force of between fifteen and twenty and survived in an underground bolthole. They had a radio, although as time went by, contact was lost with more and more rebel groups. Dortmun spent much of his time developing an acid bomb, the only known weapon that could crack the Dalekenium shells of the invaders.[378]

The Daleks had total control of the Earth, barring a few pockets of resistance, and began a number of projects.[379]

2158 / (=) 2158 - THE MUTANT PHASE[380] ->

In Kansas, an Agnomen wasp worked its way inside a battle-damaged Dalek casing and stung the Dalek creature within. Dalek medics prepared to remove the tainting wasp DNA from the stung Dalek.

(=) The time-travelling Emperor Dalek arrived with a pesticide, GK50, which the Emperor claimed would destroy the wasp cells and safeguard the future. The Dalek medics complied, but the pesticide failed to work on the larval wasp cells. In the millennia to follow, the wasp DNA would spread through Dalek reproduction plants and taint the entire race, giving rise to the Mutant Phase and leading to Earth's destruction in the fifty-third century.

The fifth Doctor and Nyssa realised the Emperor Dalek's actions had paradoxically created the very condition he was trying to prevent and convinced him to not use the pesticide, averting the Mutant Phase.

(=) 2158 - RENAISSANCE OF THE DALEKS[381] ->

The collective thoughts of trillions of Daleks created a "seed Dalek" - a being known as the Greylish - who existed in an "island of time" inside a dimensional nullity: a Pan-Temporal Ambience, which existed in all times simultaneously. Time tracks from this realm led to various conflicts in history, including wars in Rhodes 1320; Petersburg, Virginia, 1864; and the Vietnam War.

The indifferent Greylish allowed his realm to become a Dalek foundry. Towers were constructed from millions of Dalek armour shells. The realm's temporal properties enabled the Daleks to mentally project subliminal voices to various points in space-time, causing humanity to become receptive to Dalek thoughts and concepts. An alternate timeline was created in which the Daleks did not invade Earth in 2157 - instead, by 2158, humanity had grown so comfortable with the concept of Daleks that merchandisers were pumping out Dalek toys.

The fifth Doctor found himself in the alternate history. He met General Tillington, who worked for a laser defence system named Global Warning. The Doctor diverted to rescue Nyssa and the knight Mulberry from 1864, and realised that the Daleks had developed a type of nano-Dalek. They had also learned to harness the power of actinodial energy, which could be projected through space-time. Unless stopped, the Daleks intended to transmit their nano-Daleks from the Greylish's realm into the Dalek toys, which would enable the nano-Daleks to infest every human on Earth. The Dalek invasion of Earth in the twenty-second century would still occur, but this time succeed without bloodshed.

The Daleks captured the TARDIS, deeming it a much quicker way of distributing the nano-Daleks. Mulberry destroyed the nano-Daleks by sweeping them into the Vortex, but was lost to it as well.

Afterward, the Doctor successfully appealed to the Greylish's emotions, and the Greylish came to better recognise his origins, understanding that *he* was the genetic template for the nano-Daleks. The Greylish erased his Pan-Temporal Ambience from existence with a thought, and all consequences of its creation were erased from history.

Searching Earth records, the Daleks discovered an account of the ICMG's battle with Daleks in 1963, including a description of Skaro's destruction in the future. Forewarned, the Daleks had a new mission - avert the destruction of their homeworld.[382]

In 2160, the Daleks began work on extracting the Earth's core, seeking to replace it with the GodEngine.[383]

Once the Earth's core was destroyed and replaced with a drive system, the Daleks planned to move the entire planet around space.[384] The Daleks had conquered every planet of the solar system by 2162.[385]

The High Council of the Time Lords sent their agent Homunculette to a ruined London to acquire the Relic - which arrived from 15,414 - but Qixotl got there first.[386]

c 2167 - THE DALEK INVASION OF EARTH[387] -> Ten years after the Daleks invaded, Project Degravitate neared its conclusion. Slave workers were instructed to begin clearing operations. The Daleks were tampering with the forces of creation, drilling down through the Earth's crust. A fission capsule was prepared and when detonated, it would release the Earth's magnetic core, eliminating Earth's gravitational and magnetic fields. Once the core was removed, it would be replaced with a power system allowing the Earth to be piloted anywhere in the universe.

The first Doctor, Ian, Barbara and Susan assisted the rebels fighting Dalek control. The rebels broke into the Dalek control room, and ordered the Robomen to attack their masters. The Robomen and slaves overwhelmed the invaders and fled the mining area. The fission capsule was diverted, and upon its detonation the Dalek base - containing the Daleks' external power supply - and the saucer Alpha Major was destroyed. An active volcano formed at the old Dalek mine.

Susan left the TARDIS to make a new life with David Campbell.

The seventh Doctor recovered the TARDIS key that Susan dropped[388], and yet Susan later had it in her possession.[389] Susan's husband David continued to think of her as human, and she found it easier to keep quiet about her true origins.[390]

---

384 *The Dalek Invasion of Earth, The Mutant Phase.*
385 *GodEngine* (p11).
386 *Alien Bodies*
387 Dating *The Dalek Invasion of Earth* (2.2) - There are two dates to establish: the date of the initial Dalek invasion, and the date of this story, which takes place after the Daleks have occupied Earth for some time. To start, the Doctor and Ian discover a calendar dated "2164" in a room that "hasn't been used in years" and Ian remarks that "at least we know the century". Arguably, the Doctor's recollection of the calendar is why Ben comments in *The Forbidden Time* that the Doctor told him about "that Dalek invasion in 2164". The prisoner Jack Craddock later says that the Daleks invaded "about ten years" ago.

However, it seems that someone was printing calendars after the invasion - in *The Daleks' Master Plan*, the Doctor urges Vyon to "tell Earth to look back in the history of the year 2157 and that the Daleks are going to attack again". In *The Space Museum*, Vicki states that the Daleks invaded Earth "three hundred years" before her own time [c 2193]. In *Remembrance of the Daleks*, the Doctor states that the Daleks conquered Earth in "the twenty-second century".

In *Lucifer Rising*, the Doctor says that the Daleks invade in "2158" (p337). *GodEngine* dates the invasion to 2157; the TV story to "ten years" later (p240). *The Mutant Phase* sets the TV story in "nine years" [2168]. It's "a few decades" after *No Future* [c.2000], "two centuries" after *Head Games* (p157) [c.2201], it's "2157" in *Killing Ground* (p48), and "2154" in *Return of the Living Dad* (p241).

A production document written in July 1964 gave the date as "2042". The trailer for the 1964 serial claimed the story was set in "the year 2000" (and, unlike *The Power of the Daleks*, that's explicitly contradicted in the story itself), and in *Genesis of the Daleks*, the Doctor talks of the Daleks' extraction of the Earth's magnetic core in "the year 2000", apparently referring to this story (although he seems to be remembering the movie version, which was set in 2150).

Radio Times consistently dated the story as "2164", as did *The Making of Doctor Who* second edition, *The Doctor Who File* and even the 1994 radio play *Whatever Happened to... Susan Foreman?*. The first edition of *The Programme Guide* set the story "c2060", the second "2164", while *The Terrestrial Index* said "2167". "A History of the Daleks" (*DWM* #77) set the story in "2166". *The Discontinuity Guide* suggested a date of "2174". In John Peel's novelisation of *The Chase*, Vicki says that the Daleks will destroy New York "one hundred years" after 1967.

In "The Forgotten", the tenth Doctor claims to have never seen Susan since they parted ways during the Dalek Invasion. But as his memory isn't the most reliable when he says this, it's perhaps best ignored - it would contradict not just tie-in stories such as *An Earthly Child* and *Legacy of the Daleks*, but *The Five Doctors* also.

More detail of the Dalek invasions of both Earth and Mars is given in *Benny: Beige Planet Mars*.
388 *GodEngine*
389 *To the Death*, although it's possible the eighth Doctor returned the key to Susan, off screen, as a keepsake.
390 *Here There Be Monsters*. This presumably changes later in Susan and David's marriage; by *Legacy of the Daleks*, he's certainly aware that she's aging slower than a human.
391 *The Crystal Bucephalus, GodEngine*.
392 *An Earthly Child*
393 *The Final Sanction*
394 *Legacy of the Daleks*
395 *Cold Fusion*

Aftermath of the Dalek Invasion

The Battle of Cassius saw the end of the Dalek blockade of the solar system.[391] The Dalek invasion reduced Earth's population by two-thirds, and its technological advancement was set back two hundred years.[392]

The second Doctor visited a ruined New York clearing up after the Dalek Invasion.[393]

The colony worlds offered to help rebuild, but Earth refused. The Peace Officers were formed in England to neutralise Dalek artifacts left behind after the Invasion. The attempt at creating a central authority, though, soon splintered into around a hundred dominions.[394]

The volcano formed by the destruction of the Daleks' base, Mount Bedford, became a tourist attraction. A salvage team recovered a starchart of Earth's whole sector of the galaxy from a derelict Dalek saucer.[395] A powerful cartel of Earth conglomerates took control of the Terran Security Forces. Within five years, it had become a force capable of waging intergalactic war.[396]

Following the Dalek Invasion of Earth, it became clear that there were a number of powerful warlike races in the galaxy. A number of planets, including Earth, Centauri and the Cyrennhics formed the Alliance, a mutual defence organisation. The corporation INITEC supplied the Alliance with state-of-the-art armaments.[397]

? 2170 - THE CHASE[398] **->** Upon discovering time-travel technology, the Daleks on Skaro launched a prototype time machine after the first Doctor and his companions Ian, Barbara and Susan.

The Daleks used time-travel to go back to Earth in the twenty-first century and re-invade the planet. This time they succeeded.[399]

At some point, while the Daleks continued to grow in power, they all but abandoned their homeworld, Skaro. The Daleks remaining behind became confined to their city.[400]

The Riley Act of 2171 banned neurological implants as a fundamental infringement of human rights, in reaction to use of Roboman technology during the Dalek Invasion.[401]

(=) c 2172 - DAY OF THE DALEKS[402] **->** An alternate timeline was created in the 1970s when the World Peace Conference failed. A series of wars erupted, and over the next century, seven-eighths of the world's population were wiped out. Time-travelling Daleks conquered the Earth in the mid-

---

396 *The Final Sanction* (p75).

397 THE ALLIANCE: *The Terrestrial Index* suggested that a group that included Earth, Draconia and perhaps the Thals, who were all "united to attack and punish the Daleks". This contradicts what we are told on screen [q.v. "The Dalek Wars"], and the Alliance is never referred to on television. The Alliance is mentioned in *Original Sin* (p286), and this revised account of its origins appears in *Lords of the Storm* (p201).

398 Dating *The Chase* (2.8) - The Daleks launch an attack against their "greatest enemies" - the first Doctor, Ian, Barbara and Susan - in revenge for *The Dalek Invasion of Earth*. The fact they don't know Susan has left and Vicki has joined the TARDIS crew indicates that this is relatively soon after their defeat. No date is given, but as the Daleks are based on Skaro here, but will be confined to their city by *The Daleks*, this has to be substantially before then. The Dalek time machine was named the DARDIS in the script but not on screen.

399 *Day of the Daleks*

400 Reconciling the first Dalek story, *The Daleks*, with the other Dalek stories is difficult. There was no intention to bring back the Daleks, and the first story is a self-contained story about a war confined to Skaro, that sees the Daleks killed off at the end. From *The Dalek Invasion of Earth*, the Daleks became galactic conquerors - they invade and occupy the Earth, go on to invent time travel, twice threaten to conquer the entire galaxy, then go off to fight a mutually destructive war with the Time Lords.

Despite the Doctor's assertion that *The Daleks* takes place in the far future, we know that *The Daleks* takes place before *Planet of the Daleks* (2540). We also know that, by then, the Daleks are back on Skaro.

There's no elegant way of reconciling this. The Daleks have to abandon Skaro, leaving behind a city full of Daleks who don't have space travel or any apparent knowledge of other planets. They can't leave their city, let alone conquer another planet. And they have to do it after *The Dalek Invasion of Earth*, then develop time travel (the Daleks in *The Chase* specifically leave and report back to Skaro).

If there *is* a logical reason this happened, there's no indication in an existing story. Vicki (from 2493) has heard of the Dalek Invasion of Earth, but doesn't know what a Dalek looks like, suggesting that from 2167ish to at least 2493, the Daleks don't menace Earth. (The eighth Doctor audios somewhat complicate this by featuring a second Dalek invasion later in the twenty-second century.)

401 *Fear Itself* (PDA)

402 Dating *Day of the Daleks* (9.1) - It is "two hundred years" after the UNIT era. A Dalek states that they "have discovered the secret of time travel, we have invaded the Earth again, we have changed the course of history". This isn't, as some fans have suggested, a version of events where the conquest seen in *The Dalek Invasion of Earth* was more successful - the Daleks travel back and invade a full century earlier, after the first attempt has failed.

twenty-first century, hoping to exploit the planet's mineral wealth. The remnants of humanity were put to work in prison camps, guarded by Ogron servants. Human guerrillas stole Dalek time-travel technology, and travelled back to the crucial peace conference.

This timeline was erased when the third Doctor and Jo had the Peace Conference delegates evacuated before Auderley House was destroyed.

Unidentified alien beings visited Earth, and one of their number - adopting the name Estella - stayed behind out of love for Duke Orsino, the ruler of Venice. They wed, but he soon lost her in a game of cards. As punishment, she cursed the Duke to extended life so he could better experience the guilt of losing her, and also cursed the city to destruction in a hundred years' time. Estella was rumoured to have committed suicide by flinging herself into the canal. The Cult of Our Lady Estella soon emerged to worship her memory.

The aliens evidently left behind paintings from other worlds, including one that depicted a lady in a glass jar, and one showing fox-people in smart outfits. These became part of Orsino's art collection.[403]

In 2172, the Tzun Confederacy invaded Veltroch, but the arboreal Veltrochni clans united to defeat them. The Veltrochni wiped out the Tzun Confederacy, destroying every Tzun starship but leaving behind many Tzun artifacts and ruins. A whole sector of space containing ten thousand planets was consequently abandoned. Mankind colonised many of these former Tzun worlds, and the Veltrochni begin to fear the spread of humanity.[404]

On 21st July 2172, Agnomen wasps were deliberately agitated to quell crop-threatening caterpillars, but the wasps killed five hundred people in a Kansas town. The governor authorised use of pesticide GK50 to deal with the problem.[405] In 2172, Grant Markham, a companion of the sixth Doctor, was born.[406] The Intercity Wars started and spread across Earth for decades. Military intervention from Earth's colonies enforced peace.[407]

In the late twenty-second century, the Monk withdrew the £200 he had deposited two hundred years before and collected a fortune in compound interest.[408] The Doctor once claimed that he was "fully booked" until this time.[409] On Tara, nine-tenths of the popula-

The Daleks don't recognise the third Doctor, so they have come from before 2540 and *Planet of the Daleks* (or the alternate history they set up has wiped that story from the new timeline).
403 "A hundred years" before *The Stones of Venice*. The painting of the "woman in a jar" probably refers to an Empress of Hyspero from *The Scarlet Empress*.
404 There are frequent references to the Veltrochni and Tzun in the books of David A McIntee. In *White Darkness,* we learn that civilisation on Veltroch is more than three billion years old (p90). The Tzun appear in *First Frontier,* and *Lords of the Storm* reveals much of their technology and the history of their destruction. The history is further sketched out in *First Frontier* (p94), *Lords of the Storm* (p24) and *The Dark Path* (p142). The Veltrochni also appear in *Mission: Impractical,* and the aliens in *Bullet Time* - although never named - could well be Tzun survivors of the *First Frontier* incident.
405 *The Mutant Phase*
406 He's 19 in *Killing Ground.*
407 *The Janus Conjunction*
408 *The Time Meddler*
409 The Doctor is booked up for "two hundred years" after *The Seeds of Doom.*
410 In *The Androids of Tara*, Zadek, one of Prince Reynart's men, states that the plague was "two hundred years" ago.
411 "Fifteen years" before *Fear Itself* (PDA).
412 "Forty-seven years" before *SLEEPY.* The Brotherhood plays a role in *The Death of Art* and *So Vile a Sin.*
413 *Seeing I* (p83).
414 "Twenty-five years" before *Longest Day.*

415 *The Five Doctors.* How much time has passed since Susan left the Doctor isn't clear, but she does look older.
416 Dating *The Year of Intelligent Tigers* (EDA #46) - It's the "twenty-second century" (p145), and references to colonies on Lvan and Gidi link it to *Nightmare of Eden.* It is clearly early in humanity's colonisation of other planets. That said, the spaceport has been established for a hundred years, so it must be the latter part of the century.
417 "Three years" before *To the Death.* It's possible that this happens concurrent with the start of *Lucie Miller* circa 2188, but as only two years elapse from the outbreak of the plague to the end of *To the Death,* the plague must take some time to spread.
418 Dating *An Earthly Child* (BF special release #8), *Relative Dimensions, Lucie Miller* and *To the Death* (BF BBC7 #4.7, 4.9-4.10) - These Big Finish audios explore what becomes of Susan on post-Dalek invasion Earth. The blurb to the first of these, *An Earthly Child,* says it's "thirty years on" from the Daleks conquering Earth. Within the story, it's repeatedly said that it's "thirty years since the invasion, twenty years since we set ourselves free" (in *The Dalek Invasion of Earth*). Susan suggests that everyone over 35 remembers where they were when the invasion came; one of her associates, Duncan, doesn't because he's only 33.
In the follow-up audio, *Relative Dimensions,* the Doctor picks up Susan and Alex on "Christmas Eve"- events in *An Earthly Child* are said to have happened "six months ago", establishing that *An Earthly Child* probably happens in summer. The Doctor seems to drop off Susan and Alex (along with Lucie) on the day

tion was wiped out by a plague and replaced by androids.[410] Some crewmen aboard an Earth Forces science mission to Jupiter suffered severe psychological damage.[411]

In 2180, FLORANCE's status as a sentient citizen was revoked under the Cumberland Convention. The Dione-Kisanu company bought FLORANCE and installed it at their private base. Director Madhanagopal, an operative for a Brotherhood that sought to augment humanity's psi-powers, experimented on it to research human memory and learning.[412]

Also in 2180, a Eurogen survey dispatched to see if Ha'olam could become an agricultural planet was abandoned when the company made budget cuts.[413]

The Kusks, a massive, brown-skinned species with advanced computer skills, dispatched a time probe to study various planets' histories, hoping to gather intelligence for potential conquests. The probe malfunctioned near the planet Hirath, and the Kusk spaceship sent to retrieve it failed in its mission. The Kusk crew entered suspended animation. Later, the Temporal Commercial Concerns (TCC) company set up a series of time barriers on Hirath, and rented space there for various races to use as penal colonies. TCC adapted the Kusk spaceship, with the sleeping Kusk crew inside, into a moonbase.[414]

Susan was transported to the Death Zone on Gallifrey.[415]

c 2185 - THE YEAR OF INTELLIGENT TIGERS[416] ->
One year, the Hitchemus tigers suddenly became intelligent, as they were prone to do every few generations. They attempted to take power, leading to massive conflict with the human colonists. To avert bloodshed, the eighth Doctor, accompanied by Fitz and Anji, destroyed the Hitchemus spaceport and used the tigers' weather control station to exacerbate the planet's already unstable tilt. This would have put all land on Hitchemus under water in ten years, but the humans and tigers - denied outside help - were compelled to work together to save their world. They agreed to live in peace.

Larger spaceships used T-Mat at this time.

The Second Dalek Invasion of Earth

As part of his alliance with the Daleks, the Monk went back in time, threw a vial of plague outside his TARDIS door, and left.[417]

c 2187 (summer) - AN EARTHLY CHILD[418] -> Two
decades after the Dalek invasion, civil unrest continued on Earth. Public burnings of Dalek technology were still being held. Some people were being found hiding in caves. The lack of people and industry, though, helped to ease global warming. Brewster College was open in Bristol, but could barely afford a proper computer. A Council governed Earth. A political movement, Earth United, spurred xenophobia.

David Campbell had died prior to this. His wife Susan became an advocate of accepting help from other worlds, and sent out a distress signal. The Galdresi - a race that established treaties with vulnerable worlds, then exploited them to fuel a war effort - answered her call. As a show of good faith, they rescued the humans who had been trapped in a moonbase since the invasion started.

The eighth Doctor exposed the Galdresi's plans, and made them withdraw from Earth. He was briefly reunited with Susan, and also met her son (and his great-grandson), college student Alex Campbell.

In 2187, Ted Henneker led a rebellion against the Cybermen on Agora.[419] In November, the peaceful Ivorians, on a recommendation from the Doctor, brokered a trading agreement with Earth.[420]

c 2187 (24th December) - RELATIVE DIMENSIONS[418]
-> The eighth Doctor and Lucie collected Susan and Alex so they could share Christmas together in the TARDIS. A good time was had by all, save that a now-giant Resurrection Fish that Susan had once acquired on Quinnis rampaged through the Ship. The Doctor returned his family home afterwards, and Lucie decided to accompany Alex on a grand tour of Europe to study its surviving architecture.

c 2188 - LUCIE MILLER[418] -> A Dalek Time Controller
- the sole survivor of the Dalek defeat at Amethyst station - arrived through time, gravely injured. The Daleks sought a temporal expert to stabilise the Controller's condition, and procured the services of the new incarnation of the Monk. In exchange for being allowed to collect humanity's great art treasures, the Monk aided the Daleks in a renewed bid to conquer Earth. The planet was quarantined as a Dalek-engineered plague once again ravaged humanity, and killed millions. Lucie sent the Doctor a distress call, but the Monk's interference prevented him from arriving on time...

c 2190 - LUCIE MILLER / TO THE DEATH[418] -> The
Daleks consolidated their hold on Earth, and engaged in mining operations in North America. The Time Controller intended to fit Earth with a time-space drive, then fly it to a point in the far future when the Vortex-flung Amethyst viruses would amass in a single place. This would turn Earth into a mobile plague planet; the Daleks would use it to infect worlds that threatened them. The eighth Doctor and his allies resisted the Daleks; during the fighting, an unknown amount of the great works the Monk had collected - the statue of Diana from Ephesus, the Elgin

Marbles, the roof of the Sistine Chapel, a Mona Lisa, the crown jewels from every known royal dynasty, the Venus de Milo and the Star of India - were destroyed.

The Daleks killed Alex Campbell and the Monk's companion, Tamsin Drew. Lucie Miller died to detonate a doomsday bomb that destroyed the Dalek fleet and its mining operation.

In the late twenty-second century, England's dominions were consolidated into ten large Domains, including Canterbury, Devon, Edmonds, Haldoran, London and Salisbury.[421]

Foreign Hazard Duty

? 2189 - "Echoes of the Mogor"[422] **->** Mekrom was a wild world on the edge of known space, the location of a Confederation colony. The colonists were being killed, and had requested a relief ship and a Foreign Hazard Duty (FHD) team. Now, the last of them, Stanton, was murdered. The seventh Doctor arrived shortly before the FHD squad, and learned the men died of fear.

Members of the FHD squad started dying. The Doctor discovered seams of crystal that could absorb emotion, creating "echoes" of someone's presence. The colonists died of fear from echoes of the warlike Mogor, meaning there were no real monsters. The Doctor snuck away as the FHD team filed their report.

? 2190 - "Hunger from the Ends of Time!"[423] **->** The planet Catalog was the repository for all collated knowledge in the universe. The seventh Doctor decided to go for a browse there, as he hadn't visited for decades, but he found the TARDIS dragged there anyway.

The Doctor met an FHD team, who informed him that the data was now stored as "information energy" across time rather than space. The system had become infiltrated by "bookworms" eating the information. These forces of chaos were only meant to exist at the ends of time, and their presence here was affecting the fabric of time. The Doctor brought all the records back into the present, cutting off the food supply... but leaving around a century's worth of refiling to do.

---

they left, and the concluding two-parter (*Lucie Miller/To the Death*) plays out over a period of two years (to judge by Alex's remark that Lucie fell ill during the initial plague outbreak "two years" ago).

These audios are virtually impossible to reconcile against *Legacy of the Daleks*, set circa 2199, and which also covers Susan's life on post-invasion Earth. Some of the contradictions pertain to Susan's personal life - *An Earthly Child* presents Alex Campbell as Susan and David's son, Susan acknowledges seeing her grandfather in *The Five Doctors*, and David Campbell has died beforehand in unspecified circumstances. Against all of that, *Legacy of the Daleks* claims that Susan and David never had biological children, and instead adopted three war orphans (in some accordance with *The Five Doctors* novelisation); Susan says she *hasn't* seen her grandfather since *The Dalek Invasion of Earth* (although the eighth Doctor, somehow, remembers their meet-up in *The Five Doctors*), and David Campbell dies saving the Doctor's life from the Master. In both stories, at least, it's established that Susan worked to secure Dalek technology left over from the invasion.

Perhaps the bigger concern, however, is that *Lucie Miller* and *To the Death* entail a second Dalek invasion of Earth - and the accompanying deaths of millions due to Dalek plague - that isn't referenced in any other *Doctor Who* story.

The conclusion that seems rather hard to overlook is that history *has* been changed here, either by a) the Dalek Time Controller arriving in the twenty-second century from Amethyst station, or b) the Meddling Monk intervening on the Daleks' behalf. (The Monk, we know, has the *ability* to change history - so adamant is

the Doctor about this in *The Time Meddler*.) History might have gotten off its established path, in fact, the moment the Monk nipped back a few years and threw the plague vial out of his TARDIS door.

Earth society is in relatively good shape in *An Earthly Child*, but is practically down to feudal levels in *Legacy of the Daleks* - this would be extremely hard to reconcile, were it not for the second Dalek invasion falling between the two, and almost inevitably setting Earth back some notches. In short, what remains of Earth after *To the Death* could easily slide into the "dominions" seen in *Legacy of the Daleks*.

The wild card here is to what degree, barring a complete and total temporal catastrophe, History might actively try to restore itself to its established path. *Doctor Who*, cumulatively, is less than clear on to what degree this is the case, but stories such as *The Waters of Mars* support the notion. (Actually, *The Kingmaker* is downright whimsical about it, claiming that the motto of the Celestial Intervention Agency is, "The [historical] details change, the story remains the same...") An entirely new timeline of Earth might have unfolded had the Monk's intervention led to the Daleks succeeding - but their defeat at Lucie Miller's hands might enable History to get back on track, give or take. An innate tendency of History to bend back into shape when possible might also explain David Campbell's contradictory fates - perhaps he initially died in *Legacy of the Daleks*, and in the revised history, he dies as a sort of temporal "pre-shock". (This wouldn't explain, of course, why Susan in the revised history has given birth to Alex if she was childless in the original timeline - but it might explain Alex's death in *To the Death*, if he was

2191 (January) - TIME OF YOUR LIFE[424] **->** For over twenty years, the Meson Broadcasting Service (MBS) had showed some of the all-time TV classics: *Bloodsoak Bunny*, *The Party Knights and the Kung-Fu Kings*, *Jubilee Towers*, *Prisoner: The Next Generation*, *Life's a Beach* and *Abbeydale High*. The broadcaster successfully rebuffed the claims of the Campaign for the Advancement of Television Standards that such programming as *Death-Hunt 3000*, *Masterspy* and *Horror Mansions* increased violence and criminal behaviour.

On Torrok, the citizens were compelled by law to watch MBS' offerings all day. Peace Keeper robots patrolled every street, rounding up suspected criminals. The sixth Doctor arrived on Torrok during this time and accepted an inquisitive Angela Jennings as his companion. The Time Lords directed the TARDIS to MBS' space station headquarters, where a mechanical adversary killed Angela.

As part of the reality show *Time of Your Life*, the city of Neo Tokyo was teleported from New Earth into a Maston Sphere, where the residents were terrorised. The Doctor discovered that the information-consuming datavore Krllxk had gone insane from absorbing the entire MBS output. He transmatted Neo Tokyo back home, and the ensuing conflict made the MBS station fly into the sun. Krllxk took refuge in a game-show android, but the Doctor destroyed it. MBS went off the air when the people on

Torrok rebelled, overthrowing the totalitarian regime. Grant Markham, a computer programmer who helped the Doctor, joined him on his travels.

2191 - KILLING GROUND[425] **->** Humanity thought the Cybermen were extinct. Most were asleep in their Tombs on Telos, but some nomads wandered the galaxy. Earth was still rebuilding from the Dalek Invasion at this time.

The sixth Doctor suspected the Cybermen were involved in the affairs of Agora, Grant Markham's home planet. The Overseers who ruled the planet on the behalf of the Cybermen captured the Doctor, and Grant fell in with the rebels.

One of the rebels, Maxine Carter, used Cybertechnology to build the Bronze Knights - a volunteer army of cyborgs. The Doctor learned that the Cybermen were running out of parts and becoming increasingly reliant on stolen technology. These Cybermen hijacked and adapted a Selechian warship. The Doctor sabotaged it, releasing radiation that was lethal to the Cybermen. The Bronze Knights left Agora to hunt down more Cybermen, and the remaining colonists rebuilt their planet.

? 2192 - "Conflict of Interests"[426] **->** Rigel Depot sent an FHD team at light by six to Aleph-77 in the Deneb system, where they found a Sontaran Infantry squad.

---

never supposed to have been born, and History is manoeuvring to both eliminate him and thwart the Daleks in the process.)

This is all, naturally, the result of us trying to pound a round peg into a square hole. Some open-ended questions will remain no matter how this is played. (If the audios overwrote *Legacy of the Daleks*, for instance, then how did the Roger Delgado Master come to be gravely wounded and dying on Terserus?) Still, if one squints a bit, it's possible to accept that intervention on the Monk's part has left Susan's life irrevocably altered, even though Earth's history runs pretty much as intended.

The Venus de Milo is collected by the Monk and possibly destroyed in *To the Death*; *Benny: The Sword of Forever* alternatively states that it was destroyed during the Thousand-Year War.

419 *Legacy of the Daleks*

420 "Four years" before *Killing Ground* (p71).

421 "Last month" according to *Relative Dimensions*.

422 Dating "Echoes of the Mogor" (*DWM* #143-144) - There's no indication of the date, but it seems to be early in the history of Earth's interstellar exploration. There are bullet holes in the walls at one murder scene, so the FHD might have projectile weapons, although weapons that resemble these are called "lasers" in "Hunger from the Ends of Time!". Due to the presence of the FHD, and their wearing the same uniforms and car-

rying the same weapons, we've assumed that this story, "Hunger from the Ends of Time!" and "Conflict of Interests" all take place around the same time.

In "Conflict of Interests", mankind has a base on Rigel (between seven and nine hundred light years from Earth in real life), and spacecraft capable of "light by six".

423 Dating "Hunger from the Ends of Time!" (*DWM* #157-158) - "Conventional filing has been obsolete here on Catalog for centuries." The FHD squad's uniforms and weapons are identical to those in "Echoes of the Mogor", so the two stories are probably set around the same time.

424 Dating *Time of Your Life* (MA #8) - It is "three weeks into Earth year 2191" (p1).

425 Dating *Killing Ground* (MA #23) - This is set the same year as *Time of Your Life*. Grant's departure from the TARDIS isn't conveyed in canonical *Doctor Who*; by default, then, the short story "Schrodinger's Botanist" in the *Missing Pieces* charity anthology serves to explain what becomes of him.

426 Dating "Conflict of Interests" (*DWM* #183) - As with other FHD stories, this seems to be set in an early colonial period. Humanity doesn't have translation devices. The story has to be set before "Pureblood", when the Sontarans withdraw from human space. Aleph-777 is the planet seen in the back-up strip "The Final Quest".

Galactic Survey was keen to protect the archaeology of the extinct civilisation on the planet, but found the Sontarans had the same goal... and they'd have to fight for it.

Efforts to terraform Mars continued throughout the twenty-second century. Each Martian pole was given an ocean - the Borealis Ocean in the north had freshwater and canals, whereas the Southern Sea generated carbon dioxide. Ransom Spaceport was near Mars' north pole, Carter Spaceport was near its south. Noachis Spaceport handled approximately 60% of Mars' commercial flights. Transmats were in use. Eventually, Mars became a popular living destination for retirees.[427]

c 2192 - FEAR ITSELF (PDA)[428] **->** The eighth Doctor, Anji and Fitz landed on Mars, where Anji was attacked and hospitalised. The Doctor and Fitz linked her attackers to Farside Station and set off to investigate... but shortly afterwards, Farside reported destroyed with all hands lost.

Thinking the Doctor and Fitz dead - and that she was stranded - Anji became a consultant on twenty-first century matters for a television channel. She married a cameraman called Michael. At this time, a new and ruthless military group called the Professionals emerged.

There was a space elevator in the Yucatan and holographic slides had replaced paper. A vaccine for the common cold had been developed. Anti-radiation suits were made from Dortmunium. The Martians who remained on Mars were a social underclass, and some resorted to terrorist acts.

Humanity fought against a number of hostile races in deep space, including the Cybermen. A number of Cyber Wars were fought at the beginning of the twenty-third century, but humanity prevailed.[429] Gustav Zemler's unit defeated some Cybermen on the borders of Earth's colonies, but the Cybermen's hostages were killed. Zemler and his survivors were dishonourably discharged and became mercenaries.[430]

After the Cyber Wars, Eurogen Butler changed their

---

427 *Benny: Beige Planet Mars*

428 Dating *Fear Itself* (PDA #73) - It's decades after the Dalek invasion of Earth (p274), but still the twenty-second century according to the back cover and p4.

429 Cyber Wars in the twenty-second or twenty-third century were postulated in *Cybermen* and *The Terrestrial Index*, and a number of stories that used those books as reference (including *Deceit, Iceberg, The Dimension Riders, Killing Ground* and *Sword of Orion*) have referred to "Cyberwars" in this time period. This is not the "Cyber War" involving Voga that is referred to in *Revenge of the Cybermen*. We might speculate that while the main force of Cybermen conquer Telos, another group remained active and travelled into deep space, perhaps colonising worlds of their own, and that this breakaway group was wiped out in the Cyber Wars. They seem to keep well away from Earth and only menace isolated human colonies.

430 *The Janus Conjunction* (p98).

431 *Deceit* (p23).

432 *Interference* (p305).

433 *The Nowhere Place*

434 *Seeing I*

435 *The Also People* (p29).

436 "A decade" before *The Final Sanction*.

437 Dating *Fear Itself* (PDA #73) - Anji is separated from the Doctor and Fitz for "four years".

438 *Fear Itself* (PDA). The "Paris crater" is evidently a reference to the Martian-propelled asteroid that obliterated Paris in the Thousand-Day War, as told in *Transit* and *GodEngine*. *Transit* specifies that Paris is rebuilt in the decade to follow this event, but a monument area might remain.

439 *Dreamstone Moon* (p18).

440 Dating *Wooden Heart* (NSA #15) - No date is given, but it's "at least a hundred years" since the *Castor* was launched. The hints we get are that the *Castor* was operating very early in Earth's era of interstellar travel, and the fact it's "Century-class" might link it to the Century ships referred to in *Killing Ground*. Space is divided into sectors and largely unregulated, suggesting the Castor was launched before *The Space Pirates*.

441 Dating *The Nowhere Place* (BF #84) - The story opens on 15th January, although Oswin files a report at 15:38 on the 16th, which suggests the Doctor and Evelyn don't arrive until that date.

442 *The Janus Conjunction* (p100).

443 Four hundred years before *Benny: The Doomsday Manuscript*.

444 Dating *Legacy of the Daleks* (EDA #10) - Susan met David when he was 22, and he's now 54 (p15), so it's thirty-two years after *The Dalek Invasion of Earth*. The blurb says it is the late twenty-second century. It's unclear why the Doctor is searching for Sam by travelling in time, rather than space, yet that's the implication of p27, where he "allows" for Thannos time. This does seem to mean he's looking for Sam before he lost her in *Longest Day* circa 2202, but he is admittedly diverted to Earth by a telepathic signal from Susan. While the Doctor thinks he is in the right timezone, perhaps the TARDIS has taken him just a handful of years earlier.

See the dating notes under *An Earthly Child* for the argument as to whether *Legacy of the Daleks* has been erased from history or not.

445 *The Pit* (p86).

446 *Managra* (p63).

447 *The Shadow of the Scourge*

448 *Genocide* (p27).

449 *Autonomy*

name and became the Spinward Corporation.[431] The former Houses of Parliament were used as a hospice for veterans of the first Cyber Wars.[432]

Privateers from the Andosian Alliance made several incursions into Earth's solar system in the last half of the twenty-second century. In the decade before 2197, they caused much loss of life and damage to cargo payloads, and continued menacing the spaceways into the early twenty-third century. The Privateers were eight feet tall, with rippling mauve muscles and possibly three heads. They had a penchant for the melodramatic, with their leaders choosing such names as Doctor Leopard.[433]

The I had developed as a gestalt, centaur-like race that seeded technology onto planets, then later returned to harvest the developments. The I acquired some Gallifreyan technology and the eyes of a Time Lord named Savar, and around 2192 used this to facilitate the development of advanced retinal implants on the planet Ha'olam.[434]

The buffalo became extinct in 2193.[435] The Selachians sold their Cloak weapons to Earth in the mid-2190s.[436]

& 2196 - FEAR ITSELF (PDA)[437] **->** Farside Station was rediscovered in Jupiter's atmosphere. Anji had become distant from her husband, and stowed away as a Professional was sent to investigate. The survivors had gone feral, while the station had been influenced by alien biological weapons - Fear and Loathing - which had survived in Jupiter's atmosphere for millennia.

The Doctor, who had been brainwashed into operating as a Professional for the last four years, neutralised the weapons. Reunited with Anji, the Doctor and Fitz continued on their travels.

At this time, tent cities existed on Earth and Mars. The Paris crater and the New York waterways were popular tourist traps.[438]

In 2197, the Dreamstone Moon Mining Company was set up to exploit the discovery of dreamstone on the moon of Mu Camelopides VI.[439]

? 2197 - WOODEN HEART[440] **->** The tenth Doctor and Martha landed on the *Castor*, a prison ship full of century-old corpses. Deep in the ship, they discovered a strange virtual reality forest and a preindustrial village. Aliens had preserved humans in the wooden heart of the ship.

2197 (15th-16th January to March) - THE NOWHERE PLACE[441] **->** Earth's *Damocles*-class ships emerged as the deadliest fighter-craft of their age, and were the envy of their enemies. The Red Cross symbol was still in use. Earth's military used security locks that were susceptible to high-frequency vibrations. A station was in operation on Jupiter. Cryo-freezing was used in this era.

The Damocles-fighter carrier *Valiant* travelled to Pluto's orbital path; scans indicated that hostile raider activity had occurred there in late December. The sixth Doctor and Evelyn arrived on the *Valiant*, which was under the command of Captain Tanya Oswin, as a mysterious door appeared in the ship's hull. Crew members were mentally compelled to walk through the door – a device used by the original species that had evolved on Earth, and was trapped in the realm called Time's End. The original race hoped to use the door to ensnare humanity and retroactively erase mankind from history. The Doctor and Evelyn identified the sound of a train bell coming from the door as hailing from 1952, and ventured back there to investigate. In their absence, three-fourths of the *Valiant* crew were lost to the door.

The Doctor and Evelyn returned two months later, just as the spaceship *Exeter* arrived in response to the *Valiant*'s cry for help. Oswin ordered the *Exeter* to fire nuclear weapons against the door; this would have paradoxically created Time's End and consigned humanity to suffer there. However, the Doctor altered events in Time's End so that Oswin's nuclear strike permanently destroyed Earth's original species.

Colonial marines fought in the Alphan Kundekka conflict of 2198.[442] Archaeologists Niall Goram and Matt Lacey contracted radiation sickness after opening the tomb of Rablev. They resealed it and split their journal - later known as *The Doomsday Manuscript* - into two halves. After they died, their estates sold off the documents.[443]

(=) & 2199 - LEGACY OF THE DALEKS[444] **->** The eighth Doctor arrived in New London as the Master started a war between rival Domains Haldoran and London. Haldoran and London themselves died in the conflict, and one of Haldoran's commanders, Barlow, took charge of both regions. The Master reawoke a hidden Dalek factory to gain an experimental matter transmuter. David Campbell was killed in a struggle with the Master, who fled to the planet Tersurus. Susan Campbell destroyed the matter transmuter, an act that ravaged the Master's body. The Time Lords sent Chancellor Goth to investigate the disturbance on Tersurus, leading to his meeting the now-skeletal Master. A grieving Susan left in the Master's TARDIS.

Brian Parsons fought in many space conflicts at this time, and his tactics were programmed into android soldiers for many centuries to come.[445] During the twenty-third century, Jung the Obscure published his theory of the Inner Dark in the Eiger Apocrypha.[446] By the twenty-third century, a riot control gas named Pacificus was invented.[447] Sperm whale songlines were published.[448] 1970s fashions were once again revived in the twenty-third century.[449]

Humanity conducted tests with fusion bombs out on the Galactic Rim. The devices were so powerful they were immediately banned.[450] The Doctor bought Bobby Charlton's 1966 World Cup shirt in a Venusian Auction in the twenty-third century.[451]

The corporations made vast profits from the colonisation of other planets and became a law unto themselves, killing colonists to get to mineral resources. The Adjudication Service became a neutral arbiter of planetary claims.[452]

Around 2200, the Interbank scandal took place. Chairman Wayne Redfern was indirectly responsible for the bankruptcy of the organisation.[453] The Re'nar and Ju'wes fought a war in the Matrua Nebula. One of the Re'nar fell through a time portal to 1888, and was pursued by a Ju'wes.[454]

& 2202 - LONGEST DAY[455] -> A Kusk rescue party arrived on the moon of Hirath, intent on retrieving their lost time probe. The probe malfunctioned even further and destabilised TCC's time barriers on Hirath, threatening to blow up half the galaxy. The eighth Doctor destroyed the probe, triggering an electrical surge that also killed the rampaging Kusks. Samantha Jones was separated from the Doctor in the confusion to follow, and was launched away from Hirath in a crewless Kusk ship.

& 2202 - DREAMSTONE MOON[456] -> Dreamstones, a material mined from a satellite of Mu Camelopides VI, also known as the Dreamstone Moon, became very desirable. Consumers would sleep with dreamstones under their pillows to experience vivid dreams. However, Anton La Serre, an artist who recorded and sold his dreams, had a tortuous dreaming experience with a dreamstone and sought to discredit the entire industry.

The Dreamstone Moon Mining Corporation (DMMC) ship *Dreamstone Miner* rescued Sam Jones, who had drifted in the Kusk ship for a week. She was taken to the DMMC mining operation on the Dreamstone Moon, which began to experience tremors. The Doctor arrived and concluded that the entire moon was a living entity, and that the dreamstones were parts of its brain.

The pained entity shared a special mental link with La Serre, and instinctively began lashing out due to his anger toward DMMC. The entity started projecting mental illusions - Earth Fleet had five hundred ships in the Mu Camelopides system on manoeuvres, and the captain of the dropship *Royale* self-destructed his vessel while experiencing such a waking nightmare. The ship's compliment of one thousand troops was lost, and altogether five thousand people died.

The Doctor entered La Serre's dreams and calmed him, allowing La Serre to peacefully dream himself to death, and the dreamstone entity fell dormant. DMMC aban-

---

450 "The twenty-third century" according to *Cold Fusion* (p180).

451 "They Think It's All Over"

452 *Colony in Space.* Many of the books pick up on this theme.

453 *The Final Sanction,* no date is given on p146, but it must be some time before 2203.

454 "Hundreds of years" after "Ripper's Curse".

455 Dating *Longest Day* (EDA #9) - It's "Ex-Thannos system, Relative Year 3177" (p15). In *Legacy of the Daleks,* it's stated "In Thannos time it had been 3177" (p27), so it's almost certainly not 3177 AD. This is the same time zone as *Legacy of the Daleks* (give or take), *Dreamstone Moon* and *Seeing I*.

456 Dating *Dreamstone Moon* (EDA #11) - For Sam, six days have passed (p7) since *Longest Day.*

457 Dating *Seeing I* (EDA #12) - Sam was en route to the planet Ha'olam at the end of *Dreamstone Moon,* and has only just arrived at the start of this novel. The Doctor sending out Data-umphs in 2202 looking for Sam must mean that he expects to find her in that year. "James Bowman" was the alias that Grace attributed to the Doctor in *Doctor Who - The Movie.*

458 Dating *The I: I Scream* (BBV audio #26) - The unnamed central character of *I Scream* describes Earth as having "ground cars, power plants, killer smog and diseases" - a state of affairs that loosely fits conditions

of the late thirtieth century. Then again, such a description could just be part and parcel of the Company's propaganda machine, designed to prevent the Galspar residents from wanting to venture off world. Another X-factor is whether or not the I's scheme has any measure of success; the period of the Earth Empire is documented well enough that people turning into I en mass would probably have warranted a mention in some other *Doctor Who*-related story. Either the scheme is thwarted off screen, then, or *I Scream* actually takes place in an indeterminate era. The dating is arbitrary, but fits an early colonial period.

459 *The Janus Conjunction* (p98).

460 According to *The Final Sanction,* p75. Page 146 suggests the war has been going on for a year.

461 *The Final Sanction* (pgs 73, 255) says this occurs "almost a year" before 2204.

462 *The Final Sanction* (p196).

463 *Benny: The Relics of Jegg-Sau.*

464 "Centuries" before *Benny: The Heart's Desire.* Eternals first appeared in *Enlightenment,* but compared to the Eternals seen there, Hardy and Barron's *modus operandi* is more akin to that of the Celestial Toymaker.

465 *Benny: Another Girl, Another Planet*

466 Dating *The Final Sanction* (PDA #24) - The date is given (p4).

doned operations on the moon. Sam Jones, embarrassed for her previous abandonment of the Doctor, departed the moon in an evacuation shuttle.

c 2202 - SEEING I[457] -> Sam Jones relocated to the world of Ha'olam, where she initially worked as a volunteer in an INC-run homeless shelter. She turned 18 during this time. The eighth Doctor was responsible for the Great Umph Massacre of 2202 when he sent data-umphs into the galaxy-wide computer network to look for Sam.

The Doctor, using the alias "Dr. James Alistair Bowman", continued to look for Sam and was arrested as an industrial spy on INC premises. He was given a ten year sentence and taken to the Oliver Bainbridge Functional Stabilisation Centre (OBFSC). He was questioned by Dr Akalu, the prison's "morale officer". Akalu implanted the Doctor with a retinal implant that provided advance warning of the Doctor's escape attempts. Akalu also set up DOCTOR, an artificial intelligence, to create an accurate psychological profile on the Doctor. DOCTOR would eventually discover three hundred forty-six reports of TARDIS sightings in hundreds' years worth of data, despite someone erratically, not systematically, erasing nearly all of it.

The non-profit organisation Livingspace hired Sam to do volunteer work at Eurogen Village, a desert community for former Eurogen workers. She started a relationship with Paul Hamani, a Eurogen worker assigned to teach her about life on the settlement; their relationship ended five months later. Sam also had relationships with a woman named Chris and a man named Orin (despite his being a soldier and eating meat). After Sam and Orin broke up, he and Paul became a couple.

? 2202 - THE I: I SCREAM[458] -> Humans devoted nearly every available acre of the planet Galspar to dairy, egg and sugar farms. These produced the raw ingredients for Galspar's single export: ice cream, of which Galspar made seven hundred million litres per day, and shipped to such worlds as Earth. The Governor of Galspar served as the CEO of the Company that made the ice cream, and the ruling council was the Company's board of directors. Galspar's relatively small population served the Company in one form or another. In their final term at school, students picked their occupation from a choice of farmer, driver, management, admin, computers, family, education and none of the above. Marco Polo City was Galspar's largest urban area.

The I - who reproduced in multiple ways - subverted Galspar's operations, and seeded into its ice cream a filament that would convert anyone who consumed it into the I. In this fashion, the I sought to "promote" humanity to become like them...

Around 2203, the Selachian Empire invaded Rho Priapus, one of Earth's colony worlds.[459] Terran Security Forces (TSF) in response instigated a war to combat the alleged Selachian threat, but the conflict owed more to the Selachians endangering human corporate interests on the arms markets.[460]

On Earth, Professor Laura Mulholland developed the gravity bomb, a devastating weapon capable of making a planet collapse in on itself. The G-bomb boosted Earth's confidence in the conflict with the Selachian Empire, and a warfleet, led by the flagship *Triumph*, left Earth to engage the enemy. The Selachians were forced back to their own system within a year.[461] In 2204, Adam Dresden was on his first TSF mission when the Selachians captured him on Molinar. He was subsequently transported to Ockora as a prisoner.[462] Robert Eliot Whitman stole valuable antiques that included a Kettlewell-type Robot, and the humans on the colony of Jegg-Sau used it to create more of its kind. The colony was abandoned when Jegg-Sau's soil failed due to bad terraforming. Whitman died, and the Robots - confused without any humans to serve - were left behind.[463]

An Eternal, Hardy, used a shard of Enlightenment to create Marlowe's World and the people living there - all of them pawns in a game against Barron, a rival Eternal. Barron spent centuries luring champions to Marlowe's World - had any of them discovered the planet's true nature, he would have won and claimed the Enlightenment shard. Barron's champions all failed.[464] The Bantu Independence Group became more militaristic in the 2200s, and - supported by various alien races - formed a loose alliance of dominated worlds.[465]

2204 - THE FINAL SANCTION[466] -> The war with the Selachians was coming to an end. Humans invaded Kalaya, the final planet in need of liberation from the Selachians. After a while, the humans forewent air raids to protect the native population. Out of a thousand troops, only around three hundred survived the campaign.

The second Doctor, Jamie and Zoe arrived on the war-torn Kalaya shortly before Selachian forces abandoned it. The Doctor found himself onboard the *Triumph* as it pursued the retreating Selachians to their homeworld of Ockora. The *Triumph's* G-bomb was launched, turning Ockora into a black hole and obliterating nine million lives there, including ten thousand hostages. Lieutenant Kent Michaels of the TSF gave the final password that launched the bomb, but the history books condemned Commander Wayne Redfern for the catastrophe, deeming him one of the most evil men who ever lived.

A group of surviving Selachians captured the *Triumph* and attempted to retaliate against Earth with the ship's second G-bomb. Professor Mulholland detonated the bomb before it could reach Earth, turning the *Triumph* into a second black hole.

& 2205 - SEEING I[467] **->** Sam Jones was involved in a failed protest to prevent INC from buying Eurogen Village. She sought to expose INC's corrupt practices and broke into a TCC research plant - where she found they were growing human clones with no higher brain functions for immoral experimentation.

Now 21, Sam learned about the Doctor's incarceration by hacking into INC's medical databases. She helped to liberate him, and the TARDIS removed his retinal implant. The Doctor had been an inmate of OBFSC for just over three years.

The I overran the INC Research and Development Complex at Samson Plains to strip-mine its technology. The Doctor liberated the I's organic spaceship from their control, turning the I into mindless drones. Reunited with Sam, he departed for Gallifrey to return Savar's eyes.

DOCTOR, having acquired some of the Doctor's personality traits through studying him, departed Ha'olam and travelled human dataspace with another AI, FLORANCE.

The settlement of Shelbyville was founded on Mars.[468]

? 2212 (May) to 2213 (Monday, 10th May) - THE DEMONS OF RED LODGE AND OTHER STORIES: "Doing Time"[469] **->** The fifth Doctor and Nyssa detected the echo of a potential temporal explosion on the planet Folly. The Doctor's efforts to warn the authorities of this resulted in his being incarcerated for a year, but he still retroactively prevented the explosion - the result of a warp drive accident - from occurring.

2211 (September) - THE JANUS CONJUNCTION[470] **->** In 2110, an aged Spacemaster, with one thousand colonists on board, was holed by an asteroid prior to crashlanding on the planet Menda. Led by Gustav Zemler, the mercenaries hired to protect the colonists discovered a hyperspatial Link that joined Menda to its neighbour, Janus Prime. The mercenaries crossed over to Janus Prime but were trapped there for a year, and went insane due to radiation sickness.

The eighth Doctor and Sam discovered that the hyperspatial Link was an accidental by-product of the Janus system's doomsday device. Zemler was killed before he could set the Janus Conjunction in motion and turn the sun into

---

467 Dating *Seeing I* (EDA #12) - The Doctor is imprisoned for "three years". Oddly, according to *SLEEPY*, also by Kate Orman, FLORANCE was trapped in a lab at this point.

468 "Fifty years" after *GodEngine*.

469 Dating *The Demons of Red Lodge and Other Stories*: "Doing Time" (BF #142c) - This all seems roughly in keeping with humanity's stage of development per the likes of *Seeing I*. The participants don't appear to be massively removed from present-day humanity - not only is the Gregorian calendar (or some local variation of it) in use on Folly, one of the locals references Bonnie and Clyde. Interstellar travel is possible, but takes some time - a year is here required to cross "three [solar] systems". One of the Doctor's fellow prisoners is alien, and relations with his race are such that his parents are allowed to visit.

While no year is given, the date of the explosion - 10th of May - is named as a Monday. In this era, and assuming the Folly calendar is exactly in synch with the Earth one (hardly a guarantee), that narrows the possibilities to 2202, 2213, 2219, 2224 and 2230.

470 Dating *The Janus Conjunction* (EDA #16) - It is "Dateline 14.09.2211 Humanian Era" (p16).

471 Dating *Benny: Secret Origins* (Benny audio #10.4) - Bernice names the year. Peter's math is very bad when she does so, as he reckons that 2212 was "nearly three centuries" prior to 2609.

472 Dating *The Cradle of the Snake* (BF #138) - It's currently "Manussan Year 2215", which is here presumed to be the same year in the Earth calendar (see the dating notes to *Snakedance*). Where the day is concerned,

"Tomorrow's New Year".

473 *The Highest Science* (p17).

474 *Strange England* (p7).

475 "Seventy years" after *GodEngine*.

476 Dating *SLEEPY* (NA #48) - While investigating the Dione-Kisanu Corporation in 2257, the Doctor sends Roz and Bernice back "thirty years", to "2227".

477 Dating *Frayed* (TEL #11) - No date is given, but as children are screened for psychic abilities, and this is an early colony world, it ties in with information given in *SLEEPY*. The oldest child is 12, perhaps suggesting the colony has been established that long.

478 *Rain of Terror*. This is twice implied as happening "centuries" ago. The Doctor suggests that it was "millions of years" (p381) ago, although it's not evident how he comes to that conclusion.

479 "A hundred and fifty years" before *The Dimension Riders* (p61).

480 "A hundred and fifty years" before *The Romance of Crime* (p8). There's another Great Breakout in the year 5000, according to *The Invisible Enemy*. Uva Beta Five was re-named "New Earth", but is not the planet of the same name in *Time of Your Life* or *New Earth*.

481 Dating "Spider-God" (*DWM* #52) - No date is given, but it seems to be the early colonial period. It is twenty years since Frederic joined the survey corps, and three years since the *Excelsior* left Earth. The Earthmen have a hover car "scouter" and energy weapons.

a black hole. Sergeant Jon Moslei sacrificed himself to collapse the Link, saving Janus Prime.

2212 - BENNY: SECRET ORIGINS[471] **->** The android Robyn and a temporal projection of Benny foiled Samuel Frost from recovering a zombifying virus from the planet Kresma.

? 2215 (last day of year) - THE CRADLE OF THE SNAKE[472] **->** The Mara manifested through Tegan a third time, and compelled the fifth Doctor - who was also accompanied by Nyssa and Turlough - to land on Manussa about a century before the Mara dominated it. Not caring if it violated its own timeline, the Mara tried to achieve full manifestation, and to conquer the Manussan Empire (again), through a 4-D crystal featured on the Manussan TV show *Dreamarama*. The Doctor eradicated the Mara by inverting the crystal's power. He expressed doubt that the Mara could ever truly be killed.

The Intergalactic Mineral Exploitation Act was passed in 2217, granting the mining combines vast powers. The corporations had already supplied the colony ships, weather control, terraforming and computer technology to the colonists.[473] The seventh Doctor, Ace, and Benny visited the Moscow City Carnival in 2219.[474]

The city of Springfield was established near Ascraeus Lacus on Mars around 2227.[475]

2227 - SLEEPY[476] **->** The Adjudication Service was just one of many organisations trying to enforce the law. The Serial/Spree Killers Investigations National Unit was one of the hundreds of small agencies operating in tandem with the conventional legal authorities throughout the twenty-third century - often with more powers than the authorities. Thanks to a combination of paranoia and real concern - some political parties took to hiring serial killers - Unit operatives could get in just about anywhere.

In the early twenty-third century, CM Enterprises attempted to create a computer that could think like a human by installing organic components - a cat's brain - into an Imbani mainframe. They only succeeded in building a computer that wanted to play with string and sit on newspapers. The Dione-Kisanu Company (DKC), on the other hand, encoded information in the form of memory RNA. Before long, DKC taught a woman the first verse of *Kublai Khan* by injection. In 2223, Madhanagopal finished his work on the AI named FLORANCE, which was taken offline.

Psychic ability was now recognised by humanity, and standard tests had been introduced. DKC were attempting to encode psi-powers using a model of the human mind: the AI named GRUMPY. Bernice Summerfield and Roz Forrester arrived in the preprogrammed TARDIS and met GRUMPY - who injected them with an antidote to a viral outbreak on Yemaya 4 thirty years in the future.

GRUMPY later escaped DKC by pushing himself through the computer networks, leaving his own hardware behind. He stored a few years' memories in a data vault in Malindi, tucked away a copy of his operating system in a communications satellite trailing Phobos, and spread pieces of himself across the solar system. For a decade, DKC kept the fact that GRUMPY had escaped secret and destroyed all they could find of him. GRUMPY became increasingly desperate, and used his psychic ability to terrorise and blackmail. After two years, DKC tracked him down, brought him back to Saturn's moon of Dione and erased the copies he had made of himself.

? 2230 - FRAYED[477] **->** Earth sent those with a perceived genetic disposition to crime or latent psychic abilities (the "future deviants") to the Refuge on Iwa. There was a strict Eugenics Code on Earth. Corporations funded research into psychic ability, but it was felt that the psychics' sense of superiority led them to a criminal lifestyle. Babies without brains were cloned for medical research.

A Time Lord and his companion landed on Iwa. Adopting the names "the Doctor" and "Susan", they observed the humans' fight with wolf-like aliens. An uneasy truce was forged, and the humans agreed to help the aliens cure a genetic decay that was afflicting them.

The Ulla people of Xirrinda developed self-replicating, ravenous machine-creatures that threatened to consume the planet. The machine-creatures were launched into space, but the Ulla civilisation collapsed anyway.[478]

The Colonies

The second quarter of the twenty-third century became a time of great expansion of Earth's colonial efforts. Around 2230, the Survey Corps vessel *Icarus* entered service.[479]

The early-mid-twenty-third century was known as the First Great Breakout, a period of massive colonial expansion from Earth. Humanity reached the Uva Beta Uva system, which contained fourteen planets. Earth was becoming crowded and polluted, so there was no shortage of settlers for Uva Beta Uva Five. A couple of years later, a mining agent found belzite on Uva Beta Uva Three, and the settlers discovered that all of their legal rights were rescinded under the Intergalactic Mineral Exploitation Act of 2217. The mining companies moved in.[480]

? 2231 - "Spider-God"[481] **->** A survey team from the Earth ship *Excelsior* landed on UX-4732 at the same time as the fourth Doctor. The Earthmen saw the peaceful natives apparently sacrifice themselves to giant spiders, and moved to eradicate the creatures. The Doctor deduced that the "people" were actually the larval stage of beautiful butterfly creatures, and relied upon the spiders to weave cocoons for them to emerge from.

In 2234, the French artist Heironymous Basquait tried to wrap the Sphinx in holly-and-snowball giftwrap, then attempted to buy it. The world governments deliberated on whether to protect their great structures by spraying them with a layer of clear glassite. Over the next half century, this debate caused twelve economic fiascos, two minor wars and a pilot episode for *All Our Yesterdays 2*.[482]

c 2237 - MEMORY LANE[483] **->** Astronaut Kim Kronotska returned to Earth a total of two hundred twenty-seven years after her departure, and instantly became a celebrity. She found that spaceships in this era could travel the distance she'd previously covered in mere months, and tracked the missing Tom Braudy to the planet Lucentra. She became trapped in the Earth-simulation cell holding him. The eighth Doctor, Charley and C'rizz helped to free the astronauts from the entrepreneurs Lest and Argot. They also demonstrated use of video-playback, allowing Lest and Argot to sell the technology to their people.

Portable sound-file players could now transmit sound directly into the user's ear canals.

In 2237, the artificial intelligence GRUMPY transferred his operating system into the computer of a fighter shuttle, and leapt out into interstellar space. DKC intercepted him at Sunyata, and shot him down over the temperate world of Yemaya, which was being surveyed for possible colonisation. To survive, GRUMPY seeded bits of its RNA into the colonists via their inoculations.[484]

In the twenty-third century, Earth was cluttered and grey, although there were crystal spires in Paris. Cities now stretched fifty levels underground, individuals had about five square metres of space.

The great entrepreneur Varley Gabriel scouted for planets to colonise. In 2241, the "top drawer" of the fittest and smartest people - along with twenty thousand crew to serve them - set off in the colony ship *Mayflower* on a planned one hundred year journey to a new world. It would go on to pass Aldebaran. At this time, humans used hovering service robots to maintain spaceships.[485]

A rush ensued to establish gas mines on the moons of Jupiter, including Callisto and Ganymede. The domed city of Valhalla was established as Callisto's capital, but when the mines ran dry, Earth declared the moon cities as independent and washed its hands of them. In the century to follow, conditions in the moon cities greatly deteriorated.

Genetically engineered termites had been used to bur-

---

482 *Benny: The Sword of Forever* (p40).

483 Dating *Memory Lane* (BF #88) - It is two hundred twenty-seven years and some months after Kim and Tom departed Earth, an event that occurs near the modern day.

484 *SLEEPY*

485 "Profits of Doom". It's "eight decades" before 2321.

486 At least "a century" - or four termite generations - before *Valhalla*.

487 The "mid-twenty-third century at least", according to Benny in *Benny: Epoch: Private Enemy No. 1*.

488 *Lords of the Storm*

489 *The Leisure Hive*

490 *Placebo Effect*

491 Dating *The Game of Death* (DL #6) - No year is given. the dating clues are somewhat fleeting... the Mars-Centauri Grand Prix is mentioned (and treated as a contemporary event), and it's said that General Augustus Korch fought in "the last" Dalek War, and was instrumental in securing the release of the infamous Aurora hostages. (This is sometimes confused with the "Auros" incident from *Prisoner of the Daleks* - also by Trevor Baxendale - but Korch didn't appear in that book, and the two events are very different in detail.)

The TARDIS data bank cites that the Silver Devastation was created "one hundred billion years ago" - a comment unlikely to have any relation to this story, as *Utopia* takes place in 100,000,000,000,000, and the state of humanity there is in no way similar to what's

seen in *The Game of Death*. It's unlikely that the Nocturns are moving their victims through time to this era: time travel isn't mentioned (save for TARDIS and the Agent pursuing it), and such a feat - given the Doctor's claim in *Utopia* that even the Time Lords didn't venture out as far as the year 100,000,000,000,000 - would represent an enormous exertion of power for the comparatively frivolous purpose of killing a few people in a habitat dome. It's an arbitrary guess, but this story feels like it takes place during mankind's early colonial era - say, in the 2200s. The story continues in *The Planet of Oblivion*.

492 Dating *SLEEPY* (NA #48) - The Doctor states it is "2257" (p29).

493 *Benny: Genius Loci*. It's some "centuries" (p71) prior to 2561, so this must be the early phase of humanity's colonial period, even though Pinky and Perky are far advanced from the technology generally available at this time.

494 Dating *The Daleks* (1.2) - No date is given in the story, but the Doctor says in *The Edge of Destruction* that "Skaro was in the future". In *The Dalek Invasion of Earth*, the Doctor tells Ian that the first Dalek story occurred "a million years ahead of us in the future" and the twenty-second century is part of the "middle of the history of the Daleks". Where he acquires this information is unclear - he had not even heard of the Daleks when he first met them (whereas the Monk knows of them in *The Daleks' Master Plan* and *The Five Doctors*

row into Callisto in search of new energy sources. As the region's economic prosperity waned, the termites remained outside Valhalla's gravity pan. Jupiter's gravity fluxes affected them, and they grew to monstrous size within just three generations. The termites had been tasked with providing information to the Valhalla Registry computer, but the flow of information became two-way, which greatly enhanced their intelligence.[486]

On Mars, the police used helicars.[487]

Hindu settlers colonised the Unukalhai system. In 2247, the Colonial Office began to terraform Raghi, the sixth moon of Unukalhai IV (which the settlers named Indra), a process that took forty million people a quarter of a century to complete. Raghi was one of the few colonies funded by public donation rather than the corporations. The colonists traded airavata (creatures that lived in the clouds of Indra, and whose DNA contained a natural radiation decontaminant) with Spinward Corporation.[488]

In 2250, the Argolin warrior Theron started a war with the Foamasi. The war lasted twenty minutes and two thousand interplanetary missiles reduced Argolis to a radioactive wasteland. Following this disaster, the Argolin became sterile and started tachyonics experiments in an effort to perpetuate their race.[489] The Foamasi homeworld of Liasici was destroyed in the war.[490]

? 2250 - THE GAME OF DEATH[491] **->** Horatio Hamilton did the Mars-Centauri Grand Prix in under six parsecs - which possibly entailed bending the rules, as parsecs were increments of space, not time.

Destronic particles derailed the TARDIS from 1895 to an asteroid in the Silver Devastation. The tenth Doctor and Gisella found a habitation bubble that was the setting for The Game of Death: a murder mystery in which contestants vied for a hundred million galactic credits. Karl Zalenby, a member of the Galactic Police, realised that the Game was a front to enable some shapechanging predators, the Nocturns, to satiate their murderous tendencies by killing the Game-players. The Judoon helped Zalenby shut down the Game, and Zalenby crushed to death the Darksmith Agent pursuing the Doctor. The Doctor triangulated the location where the Darksmiths had met the clients who commissioned the Eternity Crystal - the planet Ursulonamex, a.k.a. Oblivion - and went there with Gisella.

2257 - SLEEPY[492] **->** Australia was now a wasteland, ruined through centuries of chemical and nuclear pollution, although some Australians had made a fortune from solar power.

Yemaya 4 was ideal for colonisation - it had a large temperate zone, gentle seasons and biochemistry not too different to that of Earth. The four hundred colonists - mostly Botswanans, South Africans and Burandans from the

United African Confederacy - started accelerated gardens around the habitat dome almost immediately, and were busily turning some of the surrounding meadows into farms. They were going to use several Yemayan native plants as crops, and planetfall had been timed to allow almost immediate planting of Terran seed stock. With the help of drone farmers and AI administrators, the colony thrived for two months.

But then the first infections started. The seventh Doctor, Benny, Roz and Chris investigated why some colonists had developed psychic powers such as telekinesis, telepathy and pyrokinesis - the result of GRUMPY's RNA having been stripped into the colonists' inoculations. Chris also started to develop telepathy, but Benny and Roz made a trip in the TARDIS to DKC's research lab in the past, and upon their return distributed an antidote to the outbreak.

The core of GRUMPY resided in a crashed spaceship on Yemaya 4, but had become a blank slate re-named SLEEPY. DKC dispatched the warship *Flame Warrior* to Yemaya to safeguard its secrets, but SLEEPY sacrificed itself to destroy the warship. The colonists were able to partly assemble GRUMPY's memories from the RNA in their systems, and learned enough to either blackmail or bring down DKC. The corporation left the colony alone.

The Doctor won a bet with the personification of Death that he could prevent anyone from dying as a result of these events, but Death reminded the Doctor that he couldn't be everywhere...

Humans tasked two sentient terraforming machines - Pinky and Perky - with establishing the architecture, railways and roadways for a colony on Jaiwan. Pinky and Perky fell in love, swapped subroutines and built increasingly creative layouts for one another. The colonists, worried that the AIs had evolved beyond their original programming, deactivated them.[493]

? 2263 - THE DALEKS[494] **->** For centuries, the few survivors of the Thal race had lived on a plateau on Skaro, eking out an existence. They relied on rainfall that came only every ten years. One decade, the rain never came. After two years, the Thal Temmosus and his group left the plateau, hoping to find the city of the Daleks. This occurred five hundred years after the Neutronic War, and the Daleks had become affected by the reverse evolution on the planet, and had lost many of their technological secrets. Reconciliation between the Thals and the Daleks proved impossible.

The first Doctor, Susan, Ian and Barbara arrived on Skaro. They explored the Dalek city, then sided with the Thals in wiping out the Daleks.

The Doctor's encounter with the Daleks was Last Contact, when the Time Lords first encountered the race that would ultimately destroy them.[495] **At some point after this time, the Moroks acquired a Dalek from Skaro, and put it on exhibit in their Space Museum.**[496] The planet Badblood became cut off from humanity's other colonies owing to an outbreak of vampirism, as well as carbonised dust in the upper atmosphere scrambling communications.[497]

The Computers and Cybernetic Systems Act was passed on Uva Beta Uva in 2265.[499]

= The sixth Doctor visited the planet Huttan in the year 2267.[498]

By 2270, the Argolin had called a moratorium of their Recreation Programme. Instead, they set up the Leisure Hive, which offered a range of holiday pursuits for intergalactic tourists while promoting peace and understanding between races. Argolis became the first leisure planet. Meanwhile, a central government took control of the Foamasi planet, breaking the power bases of the old Lodges. The new government sought restitution with Argolis.[500]

Humanity had consolidated its position, and now possessed a large number of colony worlds. Both the Earth government and the corporations were quite capable of closing down the supply routes to uneconomic or uncooperative colonies, abandoning them entirely.

Away from Earth, life was often still very harsh. The

reveals that the Time Lords' ancestors forbid the use of the Daleks in their Games).

However, the Thals in *Planet of the Daleks* [2540] have legends of events in *The Daleks* as being from "generations ago".

In the original storyline for *The Survivors* (as the first story was provisionally titled), the date was given as "the year 3000", with the war having occurred two thousand years before. A revised synopsis dated 30th July, 1963, gave the date as "the twenty-third century".

The Terrestrial Index and *The Official Doctor Who & the Daleks Book* both suggested that the Daleks from this story were "new Daleks" created by "crippled Kaled survivors", and that the story is set just after *Genesis of the Daleks* - this is presumably meant to explain the Dal/Kaled question and also helps tie the Dalek history into the *TV Century 21* comic strip, although there is no evidence for it on screen. *The TARDIS Logs* dated the story as "2290 AD". The American *Doctor Who* comic suggested a date of "300 AD", on the grounds that the Daleks do not seem to have developed space travel. The FASA Role-playing Game dated the story as "5 BC". "Matrix Databank" in *DWM* #73 suggested that *The Daleks* takes place after *The Evil of the Daleks* and that the Daleks seen here are the last vestiges of a once-great race. This ties in with *The Dalek Invasion of Earth*, but contradicts *Planet of the Daleks*.

Timelink suggests 900. The Virgin version of *Ahistory* speculated that the Doctor had returned Ian and Barbara to 1963, but on the wrong side of the galaxy. If it was set at the time of broadcast, it would be a couple of months after they left London, so - stretching a little - it qualifies as "the future".

The main problem is that, whenever it's set, we have to reconcile the Daleks seen in first Dalek story - stuck in their city unaware of any life beyond it who are all killed - with the Daleks as galactic conquerors seen in all subsequent stories. We have to postulate (without any evidence from the series) that a faction of Daleks left Skaro at some point between becoming confined to their travel machines and the Neutronic War and

they subsequently lost contact with Skaro. This faction of Daleks had a powerful space fleet (*Lucifer Rising*) invaded the Earth (*The Dalek Invasion of Earth*) and the rest of the solar system (*GodEngine*), and fought the Mechanoids (*The Chase*). They developed internal power supplies and (at some point after *The Dalek Invasion of Earth*) the "slatted" design, rather than the "banded" one seen in the first two stories. Following this - possibly licking their wounds following their defeat in *The Dalek Invasion of Earth* - the survivors of this faction returned to their home planet. They would have discovered a city full of dead Daleks - and perhaps the Doctor's role in their cousins' defeat.

While unsupported by evidence from the show, and a little awkward, it fits in with the facts we learn at the end of *The Space Museum* and *The Chase* - the Daleks now live on Skaro, their influence stretches across time and space, they have limited knowledge of the Doctor, advanced science and a desire for revenge specifically against the Doctor, Ian, Barbara and Susan.

495 *The Gallifrey Chronicles*

LAST CONTACT: It's not recorded when the Daleks discover key facts about the Doctor. By *The Chase*, they can recognise the TARDIS (which they didn't see in the two TV stories up to that point, as it was either deep in the petrified forest or buried by rubble), and they also know the Doctor can travel in time. In *The Chase*, the Daleks refer to "The Doctor and these three humans", which might imply that they don't think the Doctor is human. Except that one of the other three is his granddaughter Susan, and later in the story they *do* refer to the Doctor as "human". In *The Chase*, it doesn't even occur to them that Susan might have left, so it's unlikely they've got records of other incarnations of the Doctor or companions. They think he's "more than human" (by virtue of his being a time traveller) in *The Evil of the Daleks*, and Chen claims that the Doctor was from "another galaxy" in *The Daleks' Master Plan*. When the Daleks deal with the Monk and the Master, they don't ever make the connection on screen that they are from the same planet as the Doctor.

corporations or governing elites that controlled each colony discovered that as long as Earth was kept supplied with minerals and other resources, Earth Central would turn a blind eye to local human rights abuses.[501]

Stanoff Osterling was regarded as one of the two greatest playwrights in human history. His work conformed to the stage conventions of his time, following the Greek tradition of reporting offstage action in elegant speeches rather than seeing it performed. The galaxy's economy was damaged after the wars and the colonies could not afford anything more lavish, but this reliance on dialogue and plotting rather than technological innovation led to a flourishing of the theatre across the galaxy. Osterling was regarded as a genius in his own time for such plays as *Death by Mirrors*, *The Captain's Honour* and *The Mercenary*. His greatest achievement, however, was felt to be his lost play *The Good Soldiers* (2273) that dealt with the aftermath of the battle at Limlough. The Doctor helped transcribe the play, as Osterling had restioparothis.[502]

Vilus Krull, a human born on the colony planet Tranagus, came into contact with a potent but mindless force from the end of time, which didn't obey conventional laws of physics. Krull thought the force was sentient and founded the Cult of the Dark Flame to facilitate its full manifestation; upon Krull's death, his skull became a lodestone for the Dark Flame's power. The cult infiltrated every star system in the galaxy for a time, but was eventually thought to have died out.[503]

c 2275 - THE PRISONER'S DILEMMA[504] **->** The seventh Doctor and Ace trailed Harmonious XIV Zinc and his wife IV Madga: two criminals from the Commune of the White Sun, who had stolen a time ring from the Trib Museum. Ace encountered them on the prison moon Erratoon, and also met Zara, a living tracer of the Key to Time. Zara found a Key segment disguised as an Erratoon lake. Harmonious XIV Zinc and Madga tried to kill everyone on Erratoon to acquire its mining rights; Ace pre-

---

Contrast all of this with *Resurrection of the Daleks*, where they refer (for the first time) to the Doctor as a Time Lord and identify his home planet as Gallifrey.

On the other hand, the Time Lords certainly know of the Daleks - they're referred to in the Doctor's trial in *The War Games*, plus the Time Lords send the Doctor on missions against them in *Planet of the Daleks* and *Genesis of the Daleks*. The Monk and the Master also know about the Daleks. In the time of Rassilon, the Daleks were banned from the Games of Death on Gallifrey, so the Gallifreyans then knew of the Daleks, but there's no evidence that the two races made contact. There's another continuity problem here - why is it that the Doctor and Susan *don't* know about the Daleks before they meet them in *The Daleks*? It's a particular problem because by *The Dalek Invasion of Earth*, the Doctor seems au fait with their complete history. It's possible, as with so much history of that period, that the modern Time Lords had long lost or filed away their knowledge of the Daleks.

We hear the Daleks and Time Lords have all but wiped each other out in *Dalek* and *The Parting of the Ways*.

496 In *The Space Museum*, the Moroks have a Dalek specimen from "Planet Skaro", one with horizontal bands rather than vertical slats. It seems likely that the Moroks raid Skaro at some undisclosed time around *The Daleks*. It's unlikely it was before, as it's implied that the Daleks have no knowledge of life on other planets. Although this in turn contradicts *Genesis of the Daleks*, in which both Davros and the Dalek leader express a wish to conquer other worlds once they know the Doctor is an alien.

497 Three centuries before *Benny: The Vampire Curse*: "The Badblood Diaries".

498 *The Romance of Crime*

499 *Spiral Scratch*

500 *The Leisure Hive*

501 Many stories feature Earth colonies that supply the home planet and are subject to tyrannical regimes. This is typically treated as a specific era in future history, when space travel and interplanetary communications are limited, and so most of these stories have been placed together just prior to the Earth Empire's formation. The New and Missing Adventures attempted to weave a more systematic and consistent "future history" for Earth, and many concerned themselves with this period of early colonisation, corporate domination and increasing centralisation.

502 *Theatre of War*

503 "Centuries" before *The Dark Flame*, although there's some confusion about this; see the dating notes for this story. Tranagus was named in *Benny: The Draconian Rage*.

504 Dating *The Prisoner's Dilemma* (BF CC #3.8) - It's "generations" after Erratoon is established as a prison planet. The dating here is otherwise a bit arbitrary, but the adventure likely occurs when hyperspace vessels are already in use, as Elysium ore will be used to refine the hyperspace process only "a generation" after this.

The robot wardens of Erratoon subject Ace to memory-wiping, and although the Doctor is confident that he can repair her lost memories using the TARDIS, the idea seems to be that Ace loses her memories of the New Adventures. This move was designed to help reconcile Ace's status later in the novel range (Spacefleet-trained adventurer with a motorbike that travels through time and space) with the Big Finish version (older sister to Hex, is still travelling with the Doctor). The seeming discrepancies in Ace's character, however,

vented this, but in so doing destroyed Erratoon's geodesic sphere. Emergency systems lifted the colony's buildings into space without a single casualty. In future, Erratoon's robot wardens would be withdrawn, and the moon would become home to a space dock and an artificial sky.

The Knights of Jeneve emerged as a military power. Their founder, Vazlov Baygent, was assassinated in 2276, but the Knights eliminated Baygent's killers and protected his son.[505] The terraforming of Raghi was completed.[506] The Mutant Rights Act was passed in 2278. Uva Beta Uva III was at the centre of a belzite rush unparalleled in human history around this time.[507]

On Earth, the fallout of the "Sphinx-giftwrapping" incident reached its conclusion when war broke out. The Leaning Tower of Pisa was destroyed - along with Pisa itself - by a mis-aimed half-ton asteroid. The economy's focus became weapons and transport, and the preservation of national monuments became less of a priority.[508]

c 2285 - VENGEANCE ON VAROS[509] **->** The Galatron Mining Corporation and the Amorb prospect fought over mineral rights on the planets of the galaxy, often with little concern for local populations. One such

place was Varos, a former prison planet (pop. 1,620,783) in the constellation of Cetes. An officer elite ran Varos and lived in relative luxury, although everyone was confined to enclosed domes with artificial atmospheres. A majority of the people had the constitutional right to vote for the Governor's execution. Until traces were detected on the asteroid Biosculptor, Varos was long thought to be the only source of zeiton-7 ore, a fuel for space/time vehicles.

In the late twenty-third century, Galatron and the government of Varos entered negotiations for the zeiton-7 ore. Galatron had a stranglehold over Varos because it supplied the colony with food, and so kept the price of zeiton-7 down to seven credits a unit. Successive Governors had developed an entertainment industry, Comtech, that sold footage of the executions, tortures and escape attempts of prisoners to every civilised world. This acted as a deterrent for potential rebels, and kept the population entertained.

Eventually, the sixth Doctor and Peri helped one Governor to negotiate the fair price of twenty credits a unit for Varos' zeiton, besting the efforts of Galatron's agent, Sil.

---

can be just as easily accounted for by the not-so-terribly controversial idea that people are different in their 20s, 30s and even 40s. Writer Simon Guerrier concedes that he added the memory-wiping angle "more for my own amusement than anything else", that it's certain that Ace gets back her memories of the Doctor and the TARDIS, and that the whole incident is a tool that continuity keepers can use or ignore as they wish.

505 *Benny: Dragons' Wrath*

506 "Nearly a quarter of a century" before *Lords of the Storm*.

507 "About a hundred and fifty years" before *The Romance of Crime*.

508 About fifty years after 2234, according to *Benny: The Sword of Forever*.

509 Dating *Vengeance on Varos* (22.2) - The Governor states that Varos has been a mining colony for "centuries" and it has been stable "for over two hundred years". Peri tells the Governor that she is from "nearly three centuries before you were born". The story takes place before *Mindwarp*. Mentors must live longer than humans, as the Mentor Sil appears in both stories (although he changes colour from brown to green between the two). The novelisation set it in "the latter part of the twenty-third century", as did *The Terrestrial Index*. *The Discontinuity Guide* set a range "between 2285 and 2320". *Timelink* said "2324".

510 Dating *Mission to Magnus* (BF LS #1.2) - Sil's operation on Magnus is a direct consequence of his defeat on Varos, so it's probably not long after *Vengeance on*

Varos. Peri reads off that it's the "twenty-third century" on one of the TARDIS read-outs as the Ship is pulled through the Vortex. The novelisation of this story, released in 1990, had the Doctor telling Peri that it's "Midway through the twenty-third century", but the likely dating of *Vengeance on Varos* suggests it's a bit later than that. A minor continuity glitch exists in that both here and in *Mindwarp*, Sil implies that he last saw the Doctor and Peri on Varos.

511 Dating *The Leisure Hive* (18.1) - Romana establishes that the war was in "2250", "forty years" before.

512 *The Highest Science*

513 "Seventy years" before *The Infinity Race*.

514 "Centuries" before *Benny: Oh No It Isn't!*.

515 Centuries before *Benny: Dry Pilgrimage*.

516 Dating *The Stones of Venice* (BF #18) - The story itself says that it's the "twenty-third century", but *Neverland* gives a firm date of 2294.

517 Dating *Whispers of Terror* (BF #3) - No date given, but references to the play *The Good Soldiers* relate to information given in *Theatre of War*. The story is set within a generation of the first performance of the play.

518 Dating "Dreadnought" (*Radio Times* #3775-3784) - No date given, but *Placebo Effect* claims that Stacey's parents are from the "twenty-third century".

c 2287 - MISSION TO MAGNUS[510] -> Humans had settled on the planet Magnus. The Seven Sisterhoods came to rule there when a virus killed off most of the male population; a few males were kept below the planet's surface for progenitor harvesting. The Ice Warriors triggered a series of nuclear explosions that moved Magnus into a colder orbit, hoping to alter the climate to their liking.

The Mentor Sil, trying to atone for his failure on Varos, was poised to reap a profit by selling warm garments and other goods to the Magnus inhabitants. Sil had previously met Anzor, a representative of the High Council on Gallifrey, on Thoros Beta. The sixth Doctor dealt with Anzor's interference by sending him and his TARDIS on a slow trek into the distant past.

> (=) Rana Zandusia - the leader of the Sisterhoods - and Sil came into possession of the Doctor's TARDIS, travelled a few hours into the future and saw that Magnus had been devastated.

The Doctor and Peri reclaimed the TARDIS, and triggered a second series of explosions that moved Magnus back into a warmer orbit. The men of Salvak offered to become husbands to the Sisterhoods.

2290 - THE LEISURE HIVE[511] -> **By 2290, it was clear that the Leisure Hive on Argolis was in trouble. Last year's bookings had fallen dramatically, and advance bookings for 2291 were disastrous. Argolis now faced competition from other leisure planets such as Abydos and Limus 4. The West Lodge of the Foamasi offered to buy the planet, but the board refused and instead pinned their hopes on tachyon experiments conducted by the Earth scientist Hardin. The fourth Doctor and Romana were present when agents of the Foamasi government arrested two members of the West Lodge, who were attempting to establish a power base on Argolis, and it was discovered that the Tachyon Recreation Generator could rejuvenate the Argolin. The Argolin and Foamasi governments re-opened negotiations.**

Checkley's World, "The Horror Planet", was settled in 2290 and selected as the best location for a scientific research station. The laboratories were released from state control a decade after the planet was colonised, and the facilities were funded by a number of empires and corporations, including the Arcturans, Riftok and Masel. Earth Government remained the major partner. Weapon systems such as compression grenades, Freire's gas and the Ethers - genetically engineered ghost-troops - were developed.[512]

Human colonists discovered Selonart.[513] The residents of the planet Perfecton determined that their sun would go supernova. Unable to escape, they encoded their entire culture onto a missile that could recreate their civilisation with quantum fluctuations. Humanity didn't know why the Perfectons had vanished, and quarantined Perfecton.[514] The leaders of the Slav and Russian colonists on the planet Vishpok advocated genetic purity - the "Visphoi Ideal". A series of emperors and empresses ruled Vishpok until it fell under a military dictatorship.[515]

2294 - THE STONES OF VENICE[516] -> After overthrowing yet another reign of terror, the eighth Doctor and Charley arrived in Venice on the eve of its destruction. The gondoliers of Venice, now amphibians with webbed hands and toes, eagerly awaited the chance to claim the city once it sank beneath the waves.

A series of tremors struck the city, but the Doctor discovered that the "late" Estella, now posing as a city resident named Eleanor Lavish, had once owned an alien device capable of altering reality. The device had kept Estella and Duke Orsino alive for a century by draining Venice's life force, leading to its present decay. The Doctor recovered the device, and Orsino proposed that he and Estella end their lives for Venice's sake. Estella agreed out of continued love for Orsino, and the device turned them into ash, saving the city. The high priest of the Cult of Estella made off with their ashes.

c 2295 - WHISPERS OF TERROR[517] -> Despite a dislike of the visual medium, Visteen Krane became acclaimed as the greatest actor of his age. His body of work was chiefly confined to audio recordings and a few photographs. Later, he became a politician and stood for Presidency with his agent, Beth Pernell, as his running mate.

Before the election, Krane seemingly committed suicide in the Museum of Aural Antiquities, an institution dedicated to the study of all things audio. Pernell pledged to run in Krane's place and continue his policies. The sixth Doctor and Peri discovered that at the moment of his death, Krane used advanced sound equipment to transfer his brainwaves into the sound medium. Krane had become a creature of pure sound, demented from his transformation and outraged at Pernell, who had engineered his murder.

The Krane-creature attempted to endlessly replicate itself and take control of the planet, but the Doctor shocked Krane back to sanity. Pernell's plans were exposed, and Krane agreed to stay at the Museum to aid Curator Gantman with his research. Pernell fled, but Krane engineered an automobile accident that killed her.

c 2296 - "Dreadnought"[518] -> Stacy Townsend was the only survivor when the Cybermen attacked the cargo ship *Dreadnought*; her fiancé, Bill, was Cyber-converted. The eighth Doctor destroyed the Cybermen, and Stacy joined him on his travels.

The Doctor later brought Stacy's parents, Christopher and Mary Townsend, through time to attend her wedding in 3999.[519] The Holy Space Squid began attracting acolytes.[520] The colony ship *Justinian* set off for Ordifica at the end of the twenty-third century.[521]

Circa 2296, Grayvorn abandoned his "Lord Vaughn Sutton" identity and covertly continued his sociopolitical engineering in Excelis. The leaders of Artaris' city-states secretly signed the Artaris Convention, ending the war between them. Grayvorn found the conflict useful to his industrial efforts and sabotaged the accord. His research culminated in the creation of lumps of biomass named Meat Puppets, his master shock troops. He used the Relic's abilities to rip the souls from dissidents and infuse the Meat Puppets with life.[522]

The Twenty-Fourth Century

By the twenty-fourth century, the lower half of England had become a vast Central City.[523] Much of what had been West London was covered in forest.[524] Duronite, an alloy of machonite and duralinium, was discovered in the early twenty-fourth century. Influenza had been eradicated.[525] The James Bond films were remade in the twenty-fourth century.[526] Merik's Theorem was discovered in the twenty-fourth century.[527]

Suspended animation ships were still available in the twenty-fourth century, but they had been superseded by the invention of super light drives.[528] Jonquil the Intrepid destroyed the vampires Lord Jake and Lady Madelaine, but their descendants survived for many thousands of years.[529] On a visit to the twenty-fourth century, the Doctor learnt about the colony at Yemaya.[530] Landor, on the galactic rim, was colonised around now.[531]

Humans colonised Pavonis IV, a verdant planet in the Delta Pavonis system, in the twenty-fourth century. It served as their home for a thousand years, during which time the first Doctor and his three companions saved the colonists from an alien invasion. The Pavonians regarded him as a mythical hero; some parents even named their children after him.[532]

The eleventh Doctor took Amy to Space Florida, a planet with automatic sand.[533]

Elysium ore was found to improve the fuel efficiency of

519 *Placebo Effect*
520 "Fifteen years" before "Space Squid".
521 *Interference*
522 About five years before *Excelis Decays*.
523 "Four hundred years" before *The Sensorites*. There is also a Central City on Earth in the year 4000, according to *The Daleks' Master Plan*.
524 In *The Dimension Riders,* Ace tells Lieutenant Strakk that she comes from Perivale, and he says that the area is a "forest" (p68).
525 "About four hundred years" after the 1909 section of *Birthright*.
526 *Synthespians™*
527 *The Stone Rose*
528 *The Highest Science* (p49).
529 Jake and Madelaine appear in *Goth Opera*, and we learn of their fate in *Managra* (p64).
530 *SLEEPY*
531 "Fifteen hundred years" before *A Device of Death*.
532 *The Pyralis Effect*
533 *The Big Bang*. The date of this is completely unknown, but the name suggests a connection to Earth, and it might be a leisure planet as seen in *The Leisure Hive*.
534 A generation after *The Prisoner's Dilemma*.
535 *The Taking of Planet 5* (p219).
536 *The Twin Dilemma*
537 "Almost one hundred years" before *LIVE 34*.
538 "Fifty years" before *The Price of Paradise*, which is set in the late twenty-fourth century. The reference to the Draconians apparently contradicts the timescale established in *Frontier in Space*, although other novels (such as *Love and War*) also suggested that humans and

Draconians met before their "official" first contact.
539 Dating *Excelis Decays* (BF *Excelis* series #3) - It is three hundred years before *Benny: The Plague Herds of Excelis*.
540 "Centuries" before *Benny: The Mirror Effect*.
541 Dating *The Slow Empire* (EDA #47) - No date is given, but it's before *Burning Heart*, because the Piglet People of Glomi IV are mentioned here and extinct there. This date is completely arbitrary. The realm is typically referred to just as "the Empire", and is here called "the Slow Empire" for clarity.
542 "Hundreds of years" before *Benny: Absence*.
543 "A few years" before "When Worlds Collide", and in an incarnation before his eleventh.
544 Dating *Graceless: The Sphere* (*Graceless* #1.1) - The trappings of the Sphere - whisky, roulette, hotel-casinos and even the term "Faraday cage" - suggests that the participants are descended from humanity. The fact that Amy and Zara's time rings don't function aboard the Sphere either suggests that its technology is incredibly advanced... or that it's just a fluke. The pirate Kreekpolt has illegal warships that can travel through time, but there's no way of establishing that if such technology is native to this era. It would be lying to say this placement is much more than a shot in the dark.
545 Dating *The Mists of Time* (BF promo, *DWM* #411) - The archaeology members seem human. Jo says that it's "the far future", then specifies that it's "centuries and centuries" after her time. Calder agrees that it's "hundreds of years" since Jo's native era.
546 Dating *The Twin Dilemma* (21.7) - In his novelisation, Eric Saward places the story around "2310". This is neither confirmed nor contradicted on screen. The

hyperspace vessels by 6 or 7%, and became greatly sought after. Galactic laws gave indigenous populations first claim on mining rights, so the discovery of Elysium on Erratoon made its inhabitants very wealthy.[534]

Early in the twenty-fourth century, a philosopher on a colony world published a monograph, *The Myth of the Non-Straight Line*. The population had ceased being able to conceive of circles. The planet was quarantined as scientists from a survey ship attempted to work out why.[535] **The fourth Doctor and one of his fellow Time Lords, Azmael, met on Jaconda around this time.**[536]

Humanity settled a group of forty-nine colony worlds that became cut off from Earth. On Colony 34, a hospital was built in the northern mountains from marnite stone. Colony 48 lacked access to navigable waters.[537] Maurit Guillan discovered the paradise planet of Laylora, but later his ship was found drifting near Draconian space, the location of Laylora lost. The search for the planet went on to inspire a number of explorers.[538]

c 2301 - EXCELIS DECAYS[539] -> Excelis was now in a permanent state of war. Grayvorn's ambition started to reach beyond Artaris, and he desired to deploy his Meat Puppet troops through the whole of time and space. The seventh Doctor merged his soul with the Relic, exerting enough power to send Grayvorn's captured souls to the afterlife and making his Meat Puppets go inert. Rather than accept defeat, Grayvorn activated Excelis' orbital defence grid and bombarded every major city on Artaris with nuclear missiles. Grayvorn died in the onslaught, but the Doctor escaped.

An entity was trapped in a mirror on an ice planet.[540]

? 2305 - THE SLOW EMPIRE[541] -> The Slow Empire had been founded in a region of space where the laws of physics prohibited faster-than-light travel. Some worlds facilitated trade and communication via Transference Pylons, which transmitted Ambassadors and materials between worlds at light speed. However, the Empire founders had long ago killed themselves through warfare, which helped to plunge the Empire into decay.

The Empire world Shakrath was ruled by a corrupt Emperor who gave visitors generous receptions for posterity, then sent them to the torture chambers. Some centuries previous on Goronos, a slave class had successfully revolted but found themselves unable to function without their masters. They transferred their minds into an elaborate "Cyberdyne" computer reality, and Goronos became an urban wasteland. On Thakrash, some five hundred years previous (as that planet recorded time), a metamorphic Collector crashed onto the planet and ruined its Transference Pylon. The slaves there revolted, forcing Thakrash into isolation.

A disturbance in the Time Vortex prompted some of its inhabitants, the Vortex Wraiths, to flee in fear of their lives. A group of them manifested on the long-dead homeworld of the Empire founders and usurped control of the Pylon system. The Wraiths hoped to manifest their entire race in its billions via the Pylons, and tried to coerce the eighth Doctor, Fitz and Anji's help by threatening the inhabitants of multiple worlds. The Doctor betrayed the Wraiths by shorting out the main Transference Pylon, both turning the Wraiths into ash and generating a pulse that would, in time, annihilate every Pylon and end the corrupt Empire.

The "detritus, junk and flotsam" of human and extra-terrestrial space travellers sometimes fused into habitable cluster worlds. One of these became the world of Absence.[542] The Doctor saved the life of Rok Soo'Gar, governor of Multiworld. He gave the Doctor a free pass to the facility and access to his tailors, the best in the galaxy.[543]

? 2308 - GRACELESS: THE SPHERE[544] -> No longer in the service of the Grace, the living Key-tracer Amy tracked her sister Zara to the Sphere - an arrangement in space of hotels and casinos, which doubled in size in a matter of weeks. The Sphere's technology prevented time rings from operating, and so Zara had fallen in with a rogue named Merak, and become pregnant with his child. Amy - having renamed herself "Abby" - for a time worked for a casino owner named Lindsey, using her mental powers to goad patrons into gambling away their winnings. Her opinion of the people aboard the Sphere became so low that she judged them as unworthy of surviving - and used her telekinesis to remove the pins holding the Sphere together. The subsequent ruination of the Sphere killed a hundred thousand beings, but enabled Abby and Zara to teleport away. Merak survived by happenstance, and pursued the sisters using time technology provided by the space pirate Kreekpolt.

? 2309 - THE MISTS OF TIME[545] -> A team from the Space Archaeology Group (SAG) found a ruined city of the Memosen - a race obliterated by the Time Lords - on Zion VIII in the Argo Navis Cluster. A "remembrance" device there, built to replay scenes of Memosen history, started reaching back in time and created interactive projections of people who had died. The third Doctor and Jo were present as a SAG member sought to get rich from the device and killed his colleagues, then was slain by Newton Calder, the sole surviving team member.

? 2310 (August) - THE TWIN DILEMMA[546] -> **Earth feared attacks by aliens, and the Interplanetary Pursuit Squadrons were established. The mathematical prodigies Romulus and Remus were abducted in the Spacehopper Mk III Freighter XV773, which had been**

reported destroyed eight months before. Romulus and Remus mysteriously reappeared on Earth shortly afterwards, claiming the gastropod Mestor, who planned to destroy Jaconda and spread his eggs throughout the universe, had kidnapped them. The sixth Doctor, Peri and Azmael (a Time Lord and the former leader of Jaconda) defeated Mestor and killed him, but Azmael died, all of his regenerations having been used up, while doing so.

? 2311 - "When Worlds Collide"[547] **->** The eleventh Doctor, Amy and Rory visited Multiworld, a holiday destination built on a stabilised fluctuation rift. Different "worlds" could be custom-made to replicate times in Earth history, and populated with holograms and artificial intelligences. A damaged Sontaran ship crashed on Multiworld, and fluronic gas leaking from its warp coil destabilised the wormhole. The Sontarans died on impact, but the Doctor's old friend, Rok Soo'Gar, sought to exploit the situation to harness the power of the rift and gain godlike powers. Everyone in Multiworld was duplicated, and everyone save the Doctor, Amy and Rory now believed the thirteen worlds to be real. The Sontarans appeared as Nazis, a flying carpet squadron commanded by Caliph Sul'Taran, and a set of Wild West outlaws: Sonny Taran and his men.

The Doctor learned of Soo'Gar's scheme, and the duplicate Sontarans turned on the governor en masse, evidently killing him and resetting reality. The Doctor placed Lisa Everwell, a vacationing project manager from Basildon, in charge of Multiworld.

Kevin the Tyrannosaur, a robot featured in the Prehistoric Zone, tired of his current occupation and accompanied the Doctor and his friends on their travels.

? 2311 - "Space Squid"[548] **->** The eleventh Doctor brought Amy, Rory and Kevin the Tyrannosaur to Space Station E11, a.k.a. Nebula Base, where the best granberry (a large thing with spiky ends, that tasted like mince) smoothies in the cosmos were made. The base was built on the edge of a Radion Singularity, and many followers of the Holy Space Squid religion had arrived to witness the coming of their god. The Doctor identified the squid as a brain-sucking Coledian - it had grown to huge proportions because of the radion, and dominated the minds of its followers. Only the Doctor and Kevin were able to resist, and they stunned the creature.

Nebula Base was converted into a tourist trap: the Last Sighting of the Holy Space Squid. Kevin decided to stay on as the base's new security commander.

freighter disappears "eight months" before *The Twin Dilemma*, which the novelisation sets in August. A computer monitor says that the "last contact" with the freighter was made on "12-99". If the twelve stands for the twelfth month, the ninety-nine might stand for the last year of a century. *The Programme Guide* set the story "c2310", *The Discontinuity Guide* in "2200", *Timelink* in "2200", *About Time* seemed comfortable with "2300".
547 Dating "When Worlds Collide" (IDW *DW* Vol. 2, #6-8) - No date is given. Lisa Everwell is from Basildon, in an era where she can save up and travel to Multiworld. There's enough interest in Earth's past to justify Multiworld patterning its zones after periods of it. There are twelve "fantasy" zones - the ones named are the Prehistoric, Old West, World War II, King Arthur, Swinging Sixties, Roman, Arabian Nights and Futuristic. There are four we can infer from the costumes of the duplicates: Samurai-era Japan, a soccer zone, Seventies USA and some sort of hospital-themed one. We might infer that this is the era of the Leisure Planets, which is consistent with the levels of artificial intelligence seen.
548 Dating "Space Squid" (IDW *DW* Vol. 2, #9) - No date is given; this dating is arbitrary, but allows Kevin to settle in his native time. The level of technology might suggest this is relatively early in mankind's progress into space.
549 *SLEEPY*
550 *Benny: The Joy Device*
551 "Profits of Doom"

552 "Two hundred and fifty years" before *The Also People*.
553 *Fear of the Dark*. The book's internal dating is confused. On p81, the Doctor finds a record dated "2319.01.12", which puts these events seventy-three years before the novel takes place. However, Tegan claims this happened "one hundred and fifty years ago" (p81), and the Doctor says it was "over one hundred and sixty years" ago (p93).
554 Dating "Profits of Doom" (*DWM* #120-122) - It's "eight decades out from Earth" and escaping "twenty-fourth century Earth". Although as the date is soon specified by a monitor robot as "January 7th 2321", they actually left twenty-*third* century Earth.
555 *The Cradle of the Snake* specifies that the Mara comes to power in "Manussan Year 2326", here presumed to be the same as the Earth calendar; see the dating notes under *Snakedance*.
556 *The Also People* (p54).
557 *Recorded Time and Other Stories*: "A Most Excellent Match"
558 "Thirty years" before *Lords of the Storm* (p263).
559 Dating *Valhalla* (BF #96) - The story would seem to occur in a year ending in 45, as "9-1-46" (the date given on a sales catalogue) is said to be "next month". Funnily enough, the actual century is never specified. One clue is that the Doctor says he has "overshot [Valhalla's] glory days" - meaning the gas mine rush there - by "about a century". This is probably related to mankind's

Youkali Press published *An Eye for Wisdom: Repetitive Poems of the Early Ikkaban Period* by Bernice S. Summerfield in 2315.[549] The Smermashi developed alpha-wave-altering crystals that made them exceedingly happy as pollution, disease and other disasters destroyed their world. The famed explorer Andreas Dorpfeld found a Smermashi crystal in 2315, and it kept him constantly full of joy. Dorpfeld cited the crystal as "my prison" on his deathbed, but this was misheard as "my prism", and so the gem was named after him. A Virabilis mining company took possession of it.[550]

Every six months, one of ten crew of the colony ship *Mayflower* was woken as part of a crew rota to check ship's systems - so each crewman woke every five years. Kara McAllista was revived, as planned, on 6th January, 2316.[551]

The Dyson Sphere of the Varteq Veil had begun to break up.[552] Humans arrived on the moon of Akoshemon, on the edge of the Milky Way, in 2319. By this time, there was a Human Sciences Academy on Mars, and a base on Titan.[553]

2321 (7th January) - "Profits of Doom"[554] ->
Sluglike aliens invaded the *Mayflower* colony ship. The sixth Doctor, Peri and Frobisher discovered that the cryotubes of the "top drawer", the elite, had been stolen. The aliens were the Profiteers of Ephte from Ephte Major - a profit-driven race of conquerors. The Doctor accessed the navigational systems and discovered there was nothing at the ship's destination. Instead, Varley Gabriel was profiting by selling the humans to the Profiteers. The Doctor got the aliens to withdraw by threatening to destroy the ship, and reprogrammed the navigation systems to set course for Arcadia.

The people of Manussa mastered molecular engineering in a zero-gravity environment, and thereby created blue crystals free from all flaws and distortions. Such crystals could convert thought into energy - into matter, even. The largest of these, the Great Crystal, harnessed and amplified the hatred, restlessness and greed of the Manussan people to create a snake creature: the Mara. It caused the end of the Manussan Empire almost overnight, and ruled over the newly formed Sumaran Empire.[555]

The Mindsmiths of Askatan created mind-control technology that let them to possess many of their enemies' soldiers, but nonetheless lost a "dirty little war". Cranton, a medical corps worker in a war in 2327, came into possession of a Mindsmith simulation generator.[556] Third Eye released their HvLP, *Outta My Way Monkey-boy* in 2327.[557] In 2341, a Rutan spy adopted the identity of Sontaran Major Karne. An attack on a Sontaran cruiser was staged, and the Sontarans recovered his escape pod. For decades, the Rutans received top-level Sontaran military secrets.[558]

? 2345 (the first Thursday in December) - VALHALLA[559] ->
The Mars Express was in operation at this time.

The domed city of Valhalla, located on Jupiter's moon of Callisto, had fallen prey to blight. It cost nothing to arrive at Valhalla, but a fortune to leave, so the city increasingly became home to the dispossessed, space hippies and tourists who arrived on the wrong flight. Immigration services stamped bar codes onto the tongues of everyone in the city. Food and energy cutbacks were introduced, and owing to the shoddy conditions, riots were dutifully held the first Thursday of every month. On such occasions, licensed outlets sold body armour and refreshments.

Genetically engineered termites had grown to massive size on Callisto, and their queen - Our Mother the Fourth - directed her children to take control of Valhalla. Our Mother wanted to facilitate her progeny's future by selling off Valhalla's assets and people; a sales catalogue was prepared. The seventh Doctor tricked the termites into thinking that Our Mother had died. This forcibly instigated a new wedding flight as winged termites sought out the new queen, and Our Mother did pass away. Dialogue was opened with the new Queen, and it was hoped she would be more reasonable than her predecessor.

---

original breakout from the solar system in the third millennium, but it's unlikely to have occurred in the twenty-second century (the Dalek invasion would surely have disrupted such a boom time, and no mention is made of this). We know from *Lucifer Rising* that people were living on Callisto as early as the early twenty-second century, and *To the Slaughter* (c.2505) depicts Jupiter's moons as being so worthless, they can be blown up in accordance with the principles of feng shui. The best compromise, then, is probably to say that the boom occurs in the twenty-third century, and *Valhalla* takes place in the twenty-fourth. (Callisto itself survives *To the Slaughter* and seems to have obtained greater significance by *So Vile a Sin*, set in 2982, as it's home to the Emperor's palace.)

Riots are held on the first Thursday of every month, and one occurs here. A piece of conflicting information, however, is that it's repeatedly said that electrical engineer Jevvan Petrovna Adrea is having a birthday, and she was born "3-2-23". This would seem to indicate that Valhalla takes place on 3rd February, not December as the catalogue suggests. If push comes to shove, the catalogue is probably more important to the plot (as it's what motivates the Doctor to visit Valhalla in the first place) and should arguably take precedence.

2346 (March) - TERMINAL OF DESPAIR[560] -> Terminal 4000, an interchange station for spaceships, serviced companies such as Orion Spaceways. A single flight a year was offered to Callisto. The terminal was put in quarantine owing to an outbreak of Desponds: squat dog-like creatures that fed on the emotion of hope. The eleventh Doctor, Amy and Rory ended the quarantine, and an animal welfare organisation took possession of the Desponds.

In 2350, the Jullatii would have over-run the Earth but for INITEC's invention of the boson cannon.[561] **The cooling agent Phosphane was invented in the mid twenty-fourth century.**[562]

c 2350 - "The Seventh Segment"[563] -> Humans settled Vyga 3 in 2350, and the eccentric culture that developed defied legal and policing systems. The fourth Doctor, Romana and K9 searched Vyga 3 for a Key to Time segment, but the tracer was confused by an object in a briefcase that a local criminal gang wanted. It wasn't a segment, but rather a fluctuating chronal wave. When opened, the briefcase aged everyone in the area to death - the Doctor was glad he hadn't got round to checking it for himself.

? 2350 - EXOTRON[564] -> Human colony planets were sometimes subject to oversight from Earth Authority, which could dispatch security officers as required.

On an unnamed Earth colony, the Exotron Project was initiated to create a new type of robot for sale to the military. Major Hector Taylor and Ballentyne, the Secretary of the Interior, colluded to further the project, which entailed hardwiring the bodies of mortally wounded soldiers into large Exotron robot shells. The soldiers remained alive in a state of pain, but their neural networks enabled the Exotrons to function.

Two years after the research team's arrival, a form of indigenous life - the hyena-like Farakosh - came into conflict with the Exotrons. Taylor died, but Ballentyne triggered the research facility's self-destruct. The troopers within the Exotrons regained some independence, and saved everyone by smothering the blast with their own bodies. The fifth Doctor and Peri expected that Ballentyne would be hounded from office.

---

560 Dating *Terminal of Despair* (BBC children's 2-in-1 #5, released in *Sightseeing in Space*) - It's "five months" after "October 2345" (p21).

561 *Original Sin* (p287).

562 "Three hundred years" after *K9: The Korven*.

563 Dating "The Seventh Segment" (*DWM Summer Special 1995*) - K9 says the planet was settled "Relative Terran date 2350 AD", but gives no indication how long ago that was, and a later dating is certainly feasible.

564 Dating *Exotron* (BF #95) - Writer Eddie Robson has stated that the planet was intended as being Earth, but the back cover states that the story takes place on "a distant outpost of Earth". Within the story, a colony ship arrives direct from Earth. (Track 36, for example, has Sergeant Shreeni say, "Bleedin' hell... what a time for the Earth shuttle to arrive.") Security officers are dispatched from an organisation named Earth Authority, which is presumably headquartered on Earth itself.

The atypical and dead-end development of the Exotrons themselves aside, the technology level suggests Earth's early colonial era. Otherwise, this date is arbitrary.

565 Dating *Recorded Time and Other Stories*: "A Most Excellent Match" (BF #150c) - The year of the fair is given.

566 "Profits of Doom". The *Mayflower* was twenty years from its original destination in 2321, its new destination is another "twenty or so" years away.

567 Dating *The Macra Terror* (4.7) - The planet was colonised "many centuries" ago. This date is somewhat arbitrary, but it allows the story to fit into a period in which Earth's colonies are relatively remote and unregulated. The level of technology is reasonably low. The second edition of *The Making of Doctor Who* described the setting as "the distant future". *The Programme Guide* set the story "c.2600", *The Terrestrial Index* preferred "between 2100 and 2150", *Timelink* "2670".

568 *Gridlock*. The Doctor says the Macra were the scourge of "this galaxy", and *New Earth* establishes that the planet New Earth isn't in our galaxy. Nonetheless, we can probably infer that he means our galaxy.

569 *Zagreus*, but this is part of a suspect simulation.

570 Tairngaire was colonised "three hundred years" before *Shadowmind* (p32).

571 Dating *Lords of the Storm* (MA #17) - The Doctor states that it is "Earthdate 2371" (p23).

572 *The Stone Rose*

573 "Five or six years" before *The Romance of Crime* (p62-63).

574 *The Eight Doctors*. Not date given, but Sarg appears in *Shakedown*, so it is before that time.

575 "Ten winters" and "many years" before *Infinite Requiem*.

576 *Divided Loyalties* (p31).

577 Dating *The Androids of Tara* (16.4) - The Doctor implies that Tara is "four hundred years and twelve parsecs" away from Earth at the time of *The Stones of Blood*. It's here assumed that the TARDIS travelled into the future, not the past, and that Tara is an isolated Earth colony (as the Tarans know of life on other planets). *The Terrestrial Index* set the story in the "fiftieth century", *Timelink* in "2378", *The Discontinuity Guide* in the "2370s", *About Time* thought that "somewhere around 2400" was reasonable.

578 Dating *Mindwarp* (23.2) - The Valeyard announces that the story starts in the "twenty-fourth century, last

2351 - RECORDED TIME AND OTHER STORIES: "A Most Excellent Match"[565] -> The showman Cranton used a Mindsmith generator to offer patrons mental simulations based upon the books of Jane Austin and other works of literature. Peri tried out Cranton's device at the 2351 Galaxy Fair, but the last remaining Mindsmith, whose consciousness was in the machine, attempted to possess her. The sixth Doctor tried to coax Peri out of the simulation by competing for her hand in marriage as "Mr. Fitzwilliam Darcy" of *Pride and Prejudice*. Tilly, an AI within the machine, saved the Doctor and Peri and terminated the simulation-scape, killing the Mindsmith.

Around 2361, the *Mayflower* arrived to colonise Arcadia.[566]

? 2366 - THE MACRA TERROR[567] -> The crab-like Macra had infiltrated a human colony, using indoctrination techniques to force the colonists to extract a deadly gas that the Macra breathed. The colonists were kept in a state of complacent happiness. Eventually, the second Doctor, Jamie, Ben and Polly exposed the Control - the colony's propaganda spokesperson - as a giant Macra. The Doctor directed Ben to destroy the Marca's gas pumps, which slew the invaders.

The Macra were a scourge of the galaxy, controlling a small empire with humans as slaves. Eventually, though, they degenerated into unthinking animals.[568]

Walton Winkle became known throughout the Earth Empire as "Uncle Winky, the man who put a smile on the galaxy". He founded the amusement park Winky Wonderland on Io, but entered hibernation inside his "Cosmic Mountain" on 18th December, 2367, due to a heart condition. He wouldn't revive from stasis until shortly before the end of the universe.[569]

Around 2370, human settlers colonised Tairngaire. The capital city was built on an isthmus and named New Byzantium. The planet rapidly became one of the more prosperous colonies. The temporary lights built by the settlers eventually became the Lantern Market.[570]

2371 - LORDS OF THE STORM[571] -> The Sontarans, fresh from destroying the Rutan installation at Betelgeuse V, attempted to use captured Tzun technology against their eternal enemies. They genetically tagged the human population of the Unukalhai system, intending that a Rutan sensor sweep would indicate a Sontaran population of one hundred million. The Rutan would send a fleet from Antares and the Sontarans planned to ignite a brown dwarf using the Tzun Stormblade, destroying the Rutans and the whole system as well. The fifth Doctor and Turlough defeated the plan.

By 2375, the Bureau Tygo was Earth's main scientific research centre, and humans were used to getting what they wanted. In May of that year, Salvatorio Moretti created Genetically Engineered Neural Imagination Engines (GENIEs) that could bend space and time to grant wishes. Earth was threatened by competing desires, so one group of people wished to go back in time and prevent the GENIEs' creation. A GENIE survived in ancient Rome.[572]

In 2375, the police broke up the notorious Nisbett firm, a criminal gang responsible for extortion, fraud, smuggling, arms dealing, torture and multiple murder. Tony, Frankie and Dylan the Leg were all executed, but the Nisbett brothers - Charlie and Eddie - escaped.[573] Sontaran Commander Vrag's commando squad was timescooped to the Eye of Orion by the Time Lord Ryoth, shortly after being presented with a medal by Admiral Sarg.[574]

The colony world Gadrell Major was on the brink of nuclear war in 2377, leading the population to construct fallout shelters. Around this time, the Earth was at war with the Phractons.[575] Dymok demanded isolation from Earth in 2378. Imperial Earth Space Station *Little Boy II* was built to oversee the planet.[576]

c 2378 - THE ANDROIDS OF TARA[577] -> On Tara, the fourth Doctor, Romana and K9 prevented Count Grendel from usurping the throne from its rightful heir, Prince Reynart. Grendel escaped to fight another day, and the travellers obtained the fourth segment of the Key to Time.

2379 (3rd July) - MINDWARP[578] -> The Mentors of Thoros Beta continued to trade across the galaxy via the warpfold relay, supplying phasers to the Warlords of Thordon, and weapons that allowed Yrcanos of the Krontep to conquer the Tonkonp Empire. They also traded with such planets as Wilson One and Posikar.

The brain of his Magnificence Kiv, the leader of the Mentors, continued to expand in his skull. He enlisted the services of Crozier, a human scientist who specialised in the transfer of consciousness. Crozier experimented on a number of Thoros Betan creatures and the Mentors' captives, creating hybrids and experimenting with the ageing process. After a decade of hard work, he had developed a serum that allowed him to place any brain in any body.

Subsequent events are unclear - it appears that the Time Lords intervened to prevent the threat posed to the course of evolution across the universe, causing Kiv to be killed. The sixth Doctor's companion, Peri Brown, was seemingly killed but in reality remained on Thoros-Beta, where she eventually married Yrcanos.

Time Lord intervention in Peri's history made this but one of at least five possible outcomes. In one version of history, Queen Peri had two sons and a daughter.[579] Peri had a son, Corynus, who went on to marry Yrcanthia and have two sons (Artios and Euthys) and a daughter (Actis).[580] **The late twenty-fourth century saw wars around the Rim Worlds of Tokl.**[581]

c 2380 - THE PRICE OF PARADISE[582] -> For eighteen months, Professor Petra Shulough led an expedition in the SS *Humphrey Bogart* to find the Paradise Planet. An electromagnetic pulse crippled the ship, and it crashed on the beautiful forest world of Laylora. The tenth Doctor and Rose answered the ship's distress call. The planet was rich in trisilicate - as Shulough's father had discovered fifteen years earlier - but it was also alive and reacted to the presence of alien life by creating Witiku, fierce four-armed monsters. Shulough agreed to keep the existence of Laylora a secret.

Micro fusion generators had been banned on most planets by this time, due to the toxic waste they produced.

c 2380 (21st to 22nd April) - THE ROMANCE OF CRIME[583] -> In the late 2370s, the Ceerads (Cellular Remission and Decay) - mutants - were purged on Vanossos. Some survived and resettled on Uva Beta Uva Six, leading to conflict with the colonists in that system. The galaxy faced another recession at this time.

Xais was the last of the Ugly Mutants and the self-proclaimed Princess of the Guaal Territories. She was a genius terrorist who murdered two thousand people, and was

executed by particle reversal in 2377. Xais had learned, however, how to transfer her consciousness into the substance helicon. Her mind came to reside in a helicon mask made by the artist Menlove Stokes, enabling her to possess people.

Xais teamed up with the criminal Nisbett brothers and their Ogrons, claiming to have discovered rich belzite deposits on Uva Beta Uva Eleven. In fact, the planet contained a great deal of helicon, through which Xais hoped to generate duplicates of herself and commit mass slaughter. The Nisbett brothers perished as part of this affair, but the fourth Doctor, Romana and K9 worked to stop Xais' plan. Xais' mind became trapped in a mass quantity of helicon, which expanded to cover the whole of Uva Beta Uva Eleven. The Doctor supplied one of his associates, the police investigator Spiggot, with a formula that could destroy the helicon and Xais within.

= c 2380 - THE INFINITY RACE[584] -> Sabbath attempted to harness the infinity forces on the planet Selonart in a parallel universe. Selonart served as host to the Trans-Global Selonart Regatta, which took place every five Earth years. The eighth Doctor, Fitz and Anji joined the fourteenth Regatta, defeating Sabbath's plan. Sabbath had released the Warlocks of Demigest to assist with his scheme, but the Doctor used time crystals formed on Selonart to erase the Warlocks' presence from the universe.

---

quarter, fourth year, seventh month, third day". There is a case to be made for 2379, but not "2479" as suggested by the third edition of *The Programme Guide*. Peri is apparently killed in *Mindwarp*, but is revealed as having survived in *The Ultimate Foe*, and returns in the novel *Bad Therapy*, the comic "The Age of Chaos" and the audio *Peri and the Piscon Paradox* (which establishes there are multiples of her). Yrcanos' people are rendered as the "Krontep" in the *Mindwarp* novelisation, as "Kr'on Tep" in *Bad Therapy*.
579 *Peri and the Piscon Paradox*
580 "The Age of Chaos"
581 *Mindwarp*
582 Dating *The Price of Paradise* (NSA #12) - It's "the late twenty-fourth century".
583 Dating *The Romance of Crime* (MA #6) - Uva Beta Uva was "colonised in Earth year 2230" according to Romana (p47); the story is set "a hundred and fifty years later" (p8). The month and day are given on p46.
584 Dating *The Infinity Race* (EDA #61) - There's a conspiracy of assassins who have been waiting "six hundred years" (p191) for the chance to eliminate Sabbath - this would appear to be an offshoot of the Secret Service, which initiated him into its ranks in 1762.

(There are reports - in the standard timeline, at least - of the Service trying to kill Sabbath in 1780, although it's entirely possible that they moved to kill him sooner.)
Mention is also made of an Earth Empire that's ruled by an Emperor, but as the story takes place in a parallel universe, there's no guarantee that its history is comparable to our own. Dating this story off Sabbath's history seems a surer bet, as it's established in *Sometime Never* that the Council of Eight - deeming the Doctor the most unpredictable element in the whole of history - recruited Sabbath as the most constant variable in the whole of time. This is the reason, in fact, that no temporal duplicates of Sabbath show up in *The Last Resort*, whereas the Doctor, Fitz and Anji are duplicated thousands of times over. In every alternate history that we're shown in this period of the EDAs, then, Sabbath's history is reliably consistent.
585 "Dogs of Doom". The date is given.
586 The real Jaeger comes to power "twenty years" before *LIVE 34*.
587 *The Happiness Patrol*
588 Dating *The Dimension Riders* (NA #20) - It is "the late twenty-fourth century" (p2). The Doctor repeats this, adding it is "Just before Benny's time, and after the

The New Earth system was colonised in 2380.[585]

On Colony 34, a planet with two moons, Premier Leo Jaeger swept to power. But a disease left him scarred, and surgical efforts to correct this only caused greater deformity. Jaeger feared this would erode his popularity, so a Jaeger look-alike from an outer province doubled for him at public events. The doppelgänger gradually replaced Jaeger's loyalists with his own staff, and finally took control. The genuine article was secretly kept alive so his Biometric ID could reinforce the duplicate's appearance.

Colony 34's resources were not as plentiful as previously thought, and an energy crisis caused unrest. Fifteen years after the real Jaeger took office, his double capitalised on the situation by restricting freedoms and postponing elections. Two years later, he tightened control using the Emergency Powers Act. Two years after that, the Chamber of Deputies was accused of widespread corruption and suspended.

Human bodies made excellent fuel if used properly, so the government secretly began harvesting Colony 34's underclass. Jaeger's Inner Senate advertised employment opportunities for outsiders, and interested travellers from other colonies were captured and turned into fuel.[586]

Gilbert M was exiled from Vasilip when he accidentally wiped out half the planet's population with a germ he'd been working on. By this time, there were scheduled interplanetary flights, and he travelled to Terra Alpha with the Kandy Man's bones in his briefcase.[587]

& 2381 (29th March) - THE DIMENSION RIDERS[588]
-> Half the planets colonised by humanity had been abandoned during the wars. But now, generally, this was a period of interplanetary peace. The Survey Corps existed to patrol space and deal with situations unsuitable for military or humanitarian missions. As such, Survey Corps vessels had both troopers (armed with state-of-the-art Derenna handguns) and support staff. By the end of the twenty-fourth century, however, underfunding meant that many of the Corps' ships were obsolete.

On 22nd March, 2381, Space Station Q4 in the fifty-fourth sector of charted space, on the edge of the spiral arm and human territory, was attacked by the Garvond's Time Soldiers. The station's crew were aged to death. The Survey Corps vessel *Icarus* investigated and fell to the soldiers. The seventh Doctor, Benny and Ace aided in repelling the soldiers, who were destroyed when their energies were reflected back upon them. This prevented the Garvond from triggering temporal paradoxes and using a Time Focus to absorb the resultant chronal energy. During the battle, Darius Cheynor, second-in-command of the *Icarus*, distinguished himself.

Cheynor was offered command of the *Phoenix*.[589]

2382 - FEAR OF THE DARK[590] -> Humanity had made
contact with the Vegans, a proud mining race, by this time. Earth had interests in the Antares, Betelgeuse, Denox, Kaltros Prime and Earth Colony E5150. Suspended animation was still in use, and neurolectrin was used to resuscitate sleepers. The University of Tyr specialised in temporal compression.

The fifth Doctor was drawn to the moon of Akoshemon when the Dark - an ancient being ravenous for blood - influenced Nyssa's mind. The Dark hoped to manifest itself physically in our dimension, but the Doctor destroyed it.

? 2385 - SLIPBACK[591] -> The TARDIS was pulled out of
the Vortex by illegal time experiments aboard the starship *Vipod Mor*. A Maston, an extinct monster, attacked the sixth Doctor and Peri. The Doctor discovered that a botched maintenance job had endowed the ship's computer with a split personality, and one of its personas was planning to take the ship back in time to impose order on the universe. The Doctor was about to stop the time journey when a Time Lord made contact to inform him that the *Vipod Mor* was part of the established history - it would explode upon arrival, creating the Big Bang.

In 2386, Unreal Transfer was discovered.[592] The artist Menlove Stokes entered cryogenic sleep, hoping to awaken in an era that better appreciated his work. He was

---

Cyberwars" (p25); this analysis comes from *The Terrestrial Index* rather than the TV series. The date is not precisely fixed until the sequel, *Infinite Requiem*, which is set in 2387, "six years" after the events of the first book. "March 22nd" was "one week ago" (p76).

589 *Infinite Requiem*

590 Dating *Fear of the Dark* (PDA #58) - The date is given on the back cover. The personnel file of a mineral pirate, Jyl Stoker, says she departed Earth Central some years back in 2363 (p109), and Tegan notes it has been "four hundred years" since 1982 (p118). It is after the time when Mechanoids were used. The Vegans first appeared in *The Monster of Peladon*.

591 Dating *Slipback* (Radio 4 drama, unnumbered Target novelisation) - An arbitrary date. The *Vipod Mor* is undertaking a census, perhaps placing it in the same time period as *The Happiness Patrol*. The illegal time travel experiments in this story also fit neatly with the time travel research mentioned in a variety of other adventures set in the twenty-fourth century.

592 *The Leisure Hive*

revived in the Fifty-Eighth Segment of Time.[593] When her colleagues were captured, a physicist travelled back in time to Little Caldwell, 1983. With the help of Isaac Summerfield, she returned home and freed her workmates.[594]

The same year, slow compression time - a method of slowing down time in a small area - was first theorised. Within a couple of years a slow time converter, or "time telescope" had been built.[595] The Bartholomew Transactor became very popular as a party tool, able to send messages back in time and create ghostly images of an alternate timeline for a minute at most.[596] A law enforcement agency, the Bureau, discovered an alien time corridor in the Playa del Nuttingchapel. They dispatched an agent to investigate in 1930, where he adopted the alias "Percy Closed".[597]

2387 (29th May) - INFINITE REQUIEM[598] -> In the late 2380s, there was a famine on Tenos Beta and storms in the Magellani system. There was also more co-operation between the various elements of the Earth's space navy. Over the next couple decades the military, the ships of the Guild of Adjudicators, the Survey Corps and the corporations' own battle squadrons unified into the Spacefleet.

The Earth colony of Gadrell Major had been rich in porizium ore, a valuable material used in medicine, but was now mined out. Earth Central perpetrated the lie that deposits of porizium remained - a means of causing the Phractons, telepathic cyborgs with a communal mind, to attack Gadrell Major to acquire the porizium for ailing members of their race. As Earth Central had planned, this kept the Phractons away from more central Earth worlds. Darius Cheynor was considered expendable by his superiors, and was sent with the Phoenix to "investigate" as the Phracton Swarm and their tanks - flamers - devastated much of the planet. The seventh Doctor and Benny were present, and met Cheynor again.

Cheynor negotiated a settlement with the Phractons; Gadrell Major was slated to become a war memorial. Earth's Colonial Office diverted funding to terraform an non-classed asteroid in the Magellani system. A breakaway faction of the Phractons sought retribution and killed Cheynor - this led to the Phractons achieving some vindication, and further negotiations would lead to peace.

? 2388 - THE HAPPINESS PATROL[599] -> The Galactic Census Bureau at Galactic Centre surveyed every colonised planet every six local cycles and, where necessary, suggested measures to control the population size. On one such planet, Terra Alpha, the native Alphidae were driven underground by the settlers, who covered the planet in sugar fields and factories. Offworlders were restricted to the Tourist Zones. The planet was ruled by Helen A, who insisted that her citizens be happy. To this end, the planet was gaily painted, muzak poured from loudspeakers on every street corner and Helen A created the Happiness Patrol, which was composed of women authorised to murder the so-called "killjoys". She also employed the services of the Kandy Man, an artificial being of pure sugar who created sweets that killed people.

Terrorists, protest groups and the Alphidae (now confined to the sugar-pipe network) all resisted, and Helen A authorised the "routine disappearance" of some 499,987 people, 17% of the population. The seventh Doctor and Ace brought down Helen A's regime in one night. The Kandy Man's candy centre melted.

---

593 *The Well-Mannered War* (p273).

594 She's from "the twenty-fourth century" according to *Return of the Living Dad* (p41).

595 *The Highest Science* (p203, p235).

596 "Centuries" after *Night Thoughts*.

597 "Many hundreds of years" after *The English Way of Death*, with reference to the group Third Eye (p37).

598 Dating *Infinite Requiem* (NA #36) - The year is quickly established as "2387" (p5). The precise date is given (p273). It is "six years" since *The Dimension Riders* (p15).

599 Dating *The Happiness Patrol* (25.2) - Terra Alpha is an isolated colony, apparently in the same system as Terra Omega. While Trevor Sigma's casual dismissal of Earth may suggest the story is set far in the future, the Doctor states only that the planet was "settled some centuries" in Ace's future. Interstellar travel is via "rocket pods". *Timelink* suggests "2788".

600 Two hundred years before *Benny: Dry Pilgrimage*.

601 *Benny: Dragons' Wrath*

602 *Benny: Down*

603 Two centuries before *Benny: The Doomsday Manuscript*.

604 *The Highest Science*

605 *The Taking of Planet 5*

606 "Twelve years" before *Divided Loyalties*.

607 Dating "Planet Bollywood" (*DWM* #424) - No year given. The tone of this story suggests that Bollywood culture has now crept into space, suggesting it's the future (unless Bollywood culture was, in fact, extra-terrestrial to start with).

608 "The Child of Time" (*DWM*)

609 *The Happiness Patrol*

610 *Synthespians™*

611 *Year of the Pig*

612 "Five hundred" years after *Year of the Pig*, although it's impossible to know if the conference is real - and of interest to Chardalot's time-travelling father - or just part of Chardalot's half-baked imaginings.

The Protestant Church officially accepted all scientific disciplines, including genetic engineering, as valid. In response, Marunianism - founded by Marunia Lennox, a Scottish Protestant - declared that all science was evil.[600]

Near the end of the twenty-fourth century, the dictator Hugo Gamaliel ripped many colonies from Earth control so his corporation could avoid paying taxes. His campaigns against the Knights of Jeneve culminated in the Battle of Bocaro (a.k.a. Bosarno), where the Knights tricked Gamaliel into believing that he'd wiped them out. The Gamalian Dragon - an emblem of the Knights' power - served as a symbol of Gamaliel's victory, but a camera within it let the Knights spy on Gamaliel's operations. It also contained a low-grade nuclear device, so the Knights could obliterate Gamaliel if needed.[601]

A plague halved the population of Sarah-361. The local prytaneium outlawed celibacy, made monogamy a social sin and instituted mandatory pornography.[602]

On Kasagrad, the radiation in Rablev's tomb fell to safe levels.[603]

The Intergalactic Taskforce served the Inner Planets in the late twenty-fourth century. Throughout the latter half of the twenty-fourth century, the notorious criminal Sheldukher - a ruthless murderer, thief and extortionist - menaced the galaxy. He destroyed the entire Krondel constellation for no apparent reason other than that he could. In 2389, he planned his biggest coup yet, and set about recruiting accomplices.

Marjorie Postine had been an aggressive child, and her parents sold her to the military, a common practice in the commercially-minded twenty-fourth century. She became a mercenary, and Sheldukher secured her services by offering her a Moosehead Repeater, a rifle capable of blowing a hole in a neutron star. She was the veteran of seventeen front-line conflicts. Her right arm was a graft-job, performed by an unqualified surgeon in a trench on Regurel, and her bald head was scarred and lumpy.

A couple of years before, Rosheen and Klift had infiltrated McDrone Systems and embezzled a vast sum of money. The central markets collapsed, causing entire planetary economies in the fourth zone to collapse into starvation and war. Millions died. The planet Tayloe was flooded with imports. Rosheen and Klift fled to the luxury of the North Gate, where Sheldukher tracked them down. The locals gladly handed them over to him.

Sheldukher had converted a Kezzivot Class transport freighter, welding on a furnace engine, installing sleep suspension chambers stolen from the Dozing Decades company and fitting heavy weaponry such as the cellular disrupter and the spectronic destabiliser. His team raided Checkley's World, stealing Project FXX Q84 - the Cell - an advanced telepathic, organic computer. Although this brought down the wrath of the Intergalactic Taskforce, it was only the beginning of Sheldukher's scheme. He

planned to locate the legendary planet Sakkrat, and the greatest prize in the galaxy: the Highest Science.

The mysterious Highest Science had preoccupied the galaxy's population for generations. In 2421, the explorer Gustaf Urnst claimed to have discovered Sakkrat, the planet which housed its secrets. No-one took Urnst seriously, although his books remained in print even after his mysterious disappearance. Unknown to the public, a Fortean Flicker had transported him to the twentieth century.

For the next three hundred years, the F61 searched the galaxy for Sakkrat, travelling past the stellar conjunctions of Naiad, the crystal quasars of Menolot and the farthest reaches of Harma. Over the centuries many lesser criminals would imitate Sheldukher, but none matched him.[604]

Archaeologists of this period believed the stories of HP Lovecraft were historically accurate.[605] *Convergence*, a cargo ship, mysteriously disappeared over Dymok in 2396.[606]

? 2397 - "Planet Bollywood"[607] -> A sentient construct, the Muse, was fashioned as an amusement for the elephantine Maharani of Baloch; it had the ability to make beings in her vicinity break into song and dance. The Maharani's attendants spirited the Muse away to a low-tech world when the Shasarak, a war-mongering people, deduced that her powers could force people to kill. The Shasarak tracked the Muse, but the eleventh Doctor and Amy helped the Muse to recalibrate her systems, and she forced the Shasarak to sing and dance until the Maharani could take them into custody.

(=) The TARDIS absorbed one of the Shasarak.

Upon the dissolution of the time-child Chiyoko, the Shasarak found itself at a singles night instead of a meeting for the Shasarak Revolutionary Front.[608]

The Twenty-Fifth Century

On a visit to Birnam in the twenty-fifth century, the Doctor saw a Stigorax.[609] The sixth Doctor took Peri shopping in a twenty-fifth century Wal-Mart.[610] In the twenty-fifth century, a mishap at a plastics factory with a matter synthesizer and an advertisement in an antique issue of *Power Man and Iron Fist* created a huge proliferation of x-ray spectacles. The company prospered for a year, but went out of business when a horde of rampaging sea monkeys - something else that shouldn't have existed - destroyed the factory.[611] Alphonse Chardalot wanted to take Toby the Sapient Pig to a scientific conference on Gamantis.[612]

2400 - THE PIT[613] **->** At the beginning of the twenty-fifth century, the space docks of Glasson Minor, a planet-sized ship-building station, bustled with activity and human colonisation continued to gather pace.

Bernice worried that the seventh Doctor was becoming too despondent, and tried to snap him out of it by having him investigate the destruction of the Seven Planets of the Althosian binary star system in 2400, an event that had never been explained. Colonisation at this time was still hazardous, and the Seven Planets were far from the normal trading routes, years away from the nearest other colony. A number of new religions sprang up on Nicea, the planet with the largest population, and these spread to the smaller worlds of Trieste and Byzantine. Most of these were based around the Form Manipulator, and adopted Judeo-Christian beliefs to the environment of the Seven Planets. The geographical and religious isolation made it easy for them to declare independence from the Corporation, but the corporations responded by cutting off all supplies and communications. Rioting broke out that the Archon and his armies were unable to contain.

The Time Lords' ancient enemies, the Yssgaroth, were making efforts to invade our universe and had created a series of space-time tears. The Doctor fell through one such tear into the past, and returned to this era with William Blake. A former Gallifreyan general, Kopyion Liall a Mahajetsu, had been among the Althosian system's first settlers and was seeking to thwart the Yssgaroth - but was moved to save the Doctor and Blake. Fearing that the Yssgaroth would view his compassion as a weakness to be exploited, Kopyion destroyed the Althosian system purely to demonstrate his resolve, sealing the tears and killing millions. The Doctor and Benny took Blake home.

c 2400 (days 1 to 16, ninth month) - LIVE 34[614] **->** Elections on Colony 34 were now five years overdue. Jaeger's administration continued its crackdown, but the Colony Central Commission (CCC) accepted a petition from his opposition - the Freedom and Democracy Party (FDP) - and ruled that elections must be held in sixteen days. The radio station LIVE 34 called Jaeger's administration into question through such programmes as *Wareing's World* and *Live With Charlotte Singh*, but the station's independence was revoked, and the State Broadcast Monitoring Department assumed editorial control.

The FDP leader, Durinda Cauldwell, had reportedly been killed by members of her own party, and her predecessor had allegedly died in a transporter accident. The

613 Dating *The Pit* (NA #12) - Benny states that the Seven Planets were destroyed "Fifty years before my time... 2400" (p9).

614 Dating *LIVE 34* (BF #74) - The isolated, heavily censored colonists believe that Earth was abandoned "centuries ago", and most facets of this society - the style of LIVE 34's broadcasts in particular - bring to mind an Earth colony rather than an alien one. Additionally, a LIVE 34 broadcaster doesn't question the dating system when Ace mentions a 1952 Vincent Black Lightning motorcycle. The dating of this story is somewhat arbitrary, although Colony 34 very much fits the mould of an isolated, oppressed Earth colony akin to Terra Alpha in *The Happiness Patrol*.

615 She was married to Yrcanos for twenty-five years according to *Bad Therapy* (p288).

616 PERI LEAVES AND CAUSES CONTINUITY PROBLEMS, TAKE TWO AND THREE: Peri's departure was a little confused on television. *The Trial of a Time Lord* first tells us that she died, then that she lived happily ever after with King Yrcanos - a last-minute addition to the script, and a big stretch given what we saw of their on-screen relationship.

However, there's a bigger problem: taking what we're told about subsequent events in the comics and novels, and - as *Ahistory* does - assuming that it's the same continuity, a couple of knotty problems emerge.

The first is exactly what happens to Peri, the problem being that the novel *Bad Therapy* and the comic "The Age of Chaos" contradict each other. In *Bad Therapy*, Peri resents her new life and returns to Earth after twenty-five years. In "The Age of Chaos", she remains on Krontep and raises a dynasty of children and grandchildren. This conundrum, at least, is easily explained thanks to *Peri and the Piscon Paradox* establishing that owing to the Time Lords' tinkering, there are at least five Peris active in the universe. Clearly, the Peri from *Bad Therapy* and the one in "The Age of Chaos" number among these variants.

Thankfully, the novelisations don't "count" for the purposes of this book, because in the *Mindwarp* novelisation, Philip Martin stated that Peri and Yrcanos immediately went to the twentieth century and Yrcanos became a professional wrestler.

There's another continuity issue connected with Peri's departure - Frobisher is the companion of the seventh Doctor for one adventure ("A Cold Day in Hell"), and they make reference there to Peri leaving for Krontep with Yrcanos (on television in *Mindwarp*), implying it was very recent. For people reading the *DWM* strip at the time, it was - the story follows straight on from "The World Shapers", featuring the sixth Doctor, Frobisher and Peri, but this is difficult to fit around the TV series.

Furthermore, in "The Age of Chaos", the sixth Doctor and Frobisher are *twice* seen visiting Krontep, so it's odd that Frobisher hasn't come to terms with Peri leaving. The story also implies that the sixth Doctor has dropped Frobisher off in the Antarctic at some point and is travelling solo. (Strange how Frobisher seems to take sabbaticals from the Doctor's company, as he also leaves the TARDIS for a time in *The Maltese Penguin*,

seventh Doctor - accompanied by Ace and Hex - accepted the FDP leadership, unwilling to risk anyone else's life in the post. Ace organised resistance as "the Rebel Queen", and her operatives blew up empty government buildings to obtain evidence of Jaeger's corruption. Nobody was killed, but Jaeger's forces blew up a vehicle manufacturing plant and a senior citizens' home, gaining political favour by blaming the hundreds of resultant casualties on the Rebel Queen and the FDP.

The Doctor stood for election against Jaeger, who claimed to have won with 81.5% of the vote, a victory margin of 63%. The CCC declared the election void as the Doctor was believed dead during the voting, and the truth about the false Jaeger was revealed. Jaeger's staff were arrested, political prisoners were freed and Charlotte Singh was designated the CCC's representative. A mob fell upon the false Jaeger.

One version of Peri spent twenty-five years being married to Yrcanos, and became Queen of the Krontep and the Seven Systems. She governed seven worlds. "Gilliam, Queen of Krontep", as she was known, disappeared in 2404 and returned to the twentieth century.[615] Another version of Peri stayed on Krontep with her family.[616]

Humans colonised the Garazone system. The Garazone Space Patrol was formed to fight smugglers.[617]

? 2405 - VANISHING POINT[618] -> The geneticist Cauchemar worked to overthrow "the Creator" responsible for the reincarnation process on an alien colony planet. The Creator's functions were disrupted to the point that deformed children named "mooncalves" were being born without the genetic "godswitch" needed to facilitate reincarnation. Cauchemar hoped to overload the Creator, triggering an energy release that would destroy the planet, yet facilitate his soul's admittance to the afterlife. The eighth Doctor, Fitz and Anji foiled this scheme. The genetic experiments that had extended Cauchemar's life, coupled with radiation exposure, failed and he died. One of the mooncalves became pregnant with Fitz's child.

Years later, the Creator had rebalanced enough to include the mooncalves in its designs.

2408 - DIVIDED LOYALTIES[619] -> The fifth Doctor, Tegan, Nyssa and Adric arrived on space station *Little Boy II* to find communications with Dymok had been disrupted. The Doctor travelled to the planet and was captured by the Toymaker. An attack by the Toymaker made Dymok vanish completely, but the Doctor again defeated him. The Toymaker decided to base himself in Blackpool, the 1980s.

In 2414, Darzil Carlisle was born outside Olympus Mons on Mars. At age three, following an airlock accident that killed his parents, he was relocated to an orphanage in Finchley, North London. At age 17, he earned a scholarship to the Phobos Academy of Music, and studied there for three years.

The fifth Doctor, having encountered an older Carlisle circa 2484, secretly aided Lord Carlisle in becoming a renowned peacemaker, and in saving billions of lives by ending wars on at least thirty-six planets.[620]

Around 2415, the people of the Elysium system discovered the Artifact, a vast ammonite-like structure, on the edge of their territory.[621] In 2416, on an unnamed colony world, IMC had set up a genetics engineering project named Project Mecrim. The Company built the ape-like Rocarbies, cheap labour developed from the native primate life; and the Mecrim, a race built for combat with a claw that could vibrate and cut through even the hardest materials. When a Mecrim gut microbe escaped, the colony was declared off limits. The survivors developed an immunity, but came to hate science and degenerated to a medieval level of technology.[622]

In 2420, the human race and Sontarans signed a non-aggression pact.[623] In the 2420s, the deserts of Earth were reclaimed and the city New Atlantis was built in the Pacific. The population of Earth was sixty billion at this time.

The sixth Doctor and Frobisher visited Peri on Krontep and caught up with her family. Following that visit, her son Corynus was killed in a hunting accident. Yrcanos died suddenly, and his and Peri's grandsons - Artios and Euthys - unaccountably fell out over the succession. Peri rode off, vowing not to return until the war had ended. Krontep was devastated by civil war between Artios and Euthys. Yrcanthia, their mother, was killed in crossfire, and this

---

then returns.)
  Any solution also has to explain how Mel - who's present when the Doctor regenerates (in *Time and the Rani*), but not in "A Cold Day in Hell" or the following story "Redemption" - fits in. Ultimately, unless Frobisher's hiding in the TARDIS, unmentioned, during the television stories (or Mel is doing the same during "A Cold Day in Hell" and "Redemption"), it's not easy to come up with a neat solution that fits all the evidence.
617 "About a hundred years" before *Sword of Orion*.

618 Dating *Vanishing Point* (EDA #44) - An arbitrary date. The colony has been around for "centuries".
619 Dating *Divided Loyalties* (PDA #26) - It is "thirty years" after Dymok became isolated in 2378 (p16). The Toymaker next appears in *The Nightmare Fair*.
620 *The Game*. Carlisle's birth date and details of his early life are given, Disc 1, Track 7.
621 "More than a century" before *Parasite* (p49).
622 *The Menagerie*
623 "Pureblood"

provoked the generals to rebel against both brothers and stake them out in the desert. Farlig was appointed regent to Peri's granddaughter Actis.[624]

c 2429 - "The Age of Chaos"[625] -> The sixth Doctor arrived on Krontep to celebrate Actis' sixteenth birthday, and learned of the turbulence of the last decade. At Actis' insistence, they went to the Antarctic to meet Frobisher. The Doctor and Frobisher set off on a perilous journey to the distant land of Brachion, in hope of finding what had gone wrong with the planet, and discovered a mysterious dome. The Doctor identified it as a Thought Aligned Random Displacement Energiser Negative Activated (TARDENA), and learned that it was being operated by a Nahrung, a member of an old race that fed on suffering - it was this madness that had consumed the planet. Deep underground in the Hall of Atonement, the lair of a sect of mad monks, the travellers went on to meet Euthys and Artios, and were reunited with Actis. They escaped thanks to the mysterious Ranith.

Comparing notes, the Doctor deduced that the regent Farlig had used Nahrung technology to set the brothers against each other. The Nahrung possessed Farlig, and both were killed. As the Doctor and Frobisher left, the Doctor revealled that Ranith was secretly Peri herself.

2430 - "Dogs of Doom"[626] -> The savage Werelox were werewolf-like aliens who could convert humans into their kind with a single bite or slash of their claws, and they attacked the more than thirty colonies of the New Earth system.

The TARDIS landed on the *Spacehog*: an astro-freighter, operated by Joe Bean and Babe Roth, that was working the system. As the fourth Doctor and Sharon introduced themselves, the Werelox attacked the ship and their leader, Brill, clawed the Doctor. He became a Werelok and retreated to the TARDIS, taking it out of time. Three months later, he had cured himself, and returned to the *Spacehog* mere minutes after he left. The Doctor hypnotised Brill and realised the Werelox were the Daleks' servants. The Daleks were using neutron fire to sterilise planets and planned to colonise them. The Doctor headed to the Dalek ship with Brill and K9.

Meanwhile, Joe Bean and his partner Babe planned to

---

624 In the "ten years" leading up to "The Age of Chaos".
625 Dating "The Age of Chaos" (*DWM Special*, unnumbered) - The story is set after *Mindwarp*, long enough afterwards that Peri's youngest grandchild is 16 (and her grandsons were young men ten years ago), but no exact date is specified. So, it has to be at least fifty years since Peri left the Doctor. The tenth Doctor claims in "The Forgotten" that he never visited Peri when she was living with Yrcanos, but he's not exactly in his right mind at the time.
626 Dating "Dogs of Doom" (*DWW* #27-34) - Babe tells Sharon the system has been "settled here for fifty years - since 2380 Old Earth time". It's never explained why the Daleks need Werelox to invade the settlements if they're going to sterilise the planets from orbit.
627 The colonists crashed on Axista Four about a hundred years before *The Colony of Lies*. Kirann mentions meeting the seventh Doctor on p164.
628 *Spiral Scratch*
629 Dating *Survival of the Fittest* (BF #130b) - The cliffhanger is resolved in *The Architects of History*. The Doctor finds himself in 2044 in that story, owing to Klein's historical alterations, but it's impossible to believe that *Survival of the Fittest* occurs in the same year - it's much too early for humanity to have spread out this far into the Milky Way. Also, human technology is now at a stage where a team of fortune-seeking humans can venture off into space armed with a fearsome amount of hardware - enough to kill thousands of adult Vrill and take out their hive system. Even so, this date is arbitrary.
630 *The Architects of History*

631 *Benny: Tears of the Oracle*. KS-159 is the future home of the Braxiatel Collection.
632 "Decades" before *Judgement of the Judoon*.
633 *Benny: Down*
634 Dating *Scaredy Cat* (BF #75) - According to the Doctor, the Earth Empire bans Saravin "a few hundred years" after this point.
635 Dating *The Underwater War* (BBC children's 2-in-1 #7, released in *Alien Adventures*) - Earth's space technology seems relatively advanced, as two trips between Earth and Hydron are made in the span of two years, minus all the time Fleming spends on Earth in the interim. That said, Earth culture is not so advanced from the present day that Jules Verne has been forgotten, as two submersibles are here named after him. "The Company" is not IMC, the seemingly ubiquitous mining corporation in operation during Earth's Empire phase (not that it's ever established that IMC is the *only* mining company of its day), and it seems a stretch, without it being said, to think that it's the same corporation that runs Terminus (*Terminus*). Ultimately, the story could occur just about anywhere.
636 2454, according to *Judgement of the Judoon*.
637 "Twenty years" before Mrs Ransandrianasolo is born, according to *Return of the Living Dad* (p164).
638 *The Crystal Bucephalus* - referred to as "shortly before the Second Dalek War" (q.v. The Dalek Wars).
639 *The Colony of Lies*
640 *Benny: Old Friends*. When this occurs is unclear, but by 2562, the lemurs' offspring are holding down jobs on the spacelanes.

ram the Dalek ship in the *Spacehog*. The Doctor discovered that the Daleks were distilling emotions from alien monsters to make themselves more efficient killing machines, and that unless something was done, the New Earth system would become a huge Dalek breeding ground. K9 released the alien monsters, which attacked the Daleks. Additionally, the Doctor used equipment in the Daleks' Room of Many Centuries - a laboratory where the Daleks were building a time transporter - to timelock the Dalek battlecruiser, removing the threat just as the *Spacehog* was about to ram it.

The Tyrenians had been developed as human supersoldiers with canine attributes, genetically engineered by Gustav Tyren. When the military pulled its funding for the project, the Tyrenians stole a ship and founded a colony on Axista Four. They set up satellite defences and then entered suspended animation using symbiotes.

Around 2430, the human colony ship *Big Bang* departed into space. The seventh Doctor, in preparing colonist Kirann Ransome to help one of his previous selves, was the last person to visit her before she entered stasis.

The defence grid on Axista Four shot down the *Big Bang*, and it crashed to the planet. Kirann remained trapped in stasis while the survivors founded a colony based on her text, *Back to Basics*, and strove for a low-technology approach that modelled society on the Wild West. They were unaware of the Tyrenians' presence.[627]

= In 2436, an alternative Earth that was ruled by Nazis who had won the Second World War, and later gone on to galactic conquest, was destroyed.[628]

? 2440 - SURVIVAL OF THE FITTEST[629] **->** Among the worlds of the galactic plane, the Geo-Police were a fascist group of "justice officers" who would cordon off various worlds to protect their resources.

The seventh Doctor and Klein arrived on a planet located high above the galactic plane, with a good view of the Milky Way. The insectoid Vrill who lived there were threatened by a team of humans seeking to acquire and sell the prized nutrient gels the Vrill used in their reproductive process. The humans used a nerve agent - the Spear of Destiny 2Tri-C81 - to kill the Vrill queen, their Authority. The Doctor saved enough gel to guarantee the Vrill's survival, but Klein - plotting to rewrite history in favour of the German Reich - stole the TARDIS, stranding him...

The Doctor was transplanted into the alternate reality Klein created in 2044, and retrieved his Ship.[630]

The lost planet of Delfus Orestes, formerly designated Cappa Nine Seven, was re-named KS-159. The Delfans of Delfus Clytaemnestra had built the Oracle of the Lost - a sentient statue that could make predictions of the future

based upon universal models - on Delfus Orestes, and it resided there even after its creators had passed.[631]

Enormous spaceport terminals were created as hyperspace travel enabled humanity to spread further into the universe. The small planet New Memphis was close to a hyperspace nexus point, and so became a hub of intergalactic travel, its Elvis the King Spaceport servicing traffic from a hundred different star systems.[632]

Circa 2450, Earth instigated a time-travel project on Vilencia Sixteen that went horribly wrong and destroyed half the planet. The Stella Stora Sigma Schutz-Staffel SturmSoldaten (SSSSSSS), a neo-Nazi organisation, used bits of this technology to weave their philosophies into the timelines of many worlds.[633]

c 2450 - SCAREDY CAT[634] **->** Fathrea - the fourth world orbiting its sun - had known peace for centuries, and colonists from there settled in another system on the planet Endarra. The biological agent Saravin had been developed for warfare, and a passing Ventriki ship tested the weapon's effects on the Endarra colony. The eighth Doctor, investigating events that would occur four million years in the future, refrained from interfering for fear of disrupting history. C'rizz gave the colonists an antidote from the TARDIS medial facility, but this wasn't enough to save them. Within three months, the colonists had perished. One small girl, Galayana, had a natural immunity and survived a few weeks longer, then perished herself.

Endarra was newly formed, and the trauma of the colonists' deaths remained in its morphogenetic field. Galayana's memories and aspect were also preserved.

? 2450 - THE UNDERWATER WAR[635] **->** The purple water planet Hydron was home to the Schoal: fish people whose eggs carried an immense electrical charge. One egg could power a starship for a week. The Schoal attacked the Earth vessel *Marine Adventurer* when it tried to steal the Schoal's eggs, but two survivors - including a man named Fleming - escaped back to Earth. Two years later, the eleventh Doctor, Amy and Rory defused tensions when the Company sent the *Cosmic Rover* to scour Hydron for minerals. Fleming tried and failed to capture thousands of eggs, sell them and retire to Catrigan Nova and its whirlpools of gold. With peace restored, the Doctor and his friends decided to visit the Tower of London.

General Moret fought in the Telepathic Uprising of '54.[636] Spacefleet used psi drugs to enhance human psychokinesis.[637] The Doctor met a Legion in the twenty-fifth century.[638] A Dalek War broke out in 2459.[639] Forests in Madagascar and Portugal were made into cropland to such a degree, the sentient lemurs there dispersed throughout the galaxy in search of a new home. They formed the Order of Lost Lemuroidea.[640] Comes the Trickster released the HvLIP *All The Way From Heaven* in 2465.[641]

Down Among the Dead Men, Bernice Summerfield's study of archaeology (particularly that of the Martians) was published.[642]

2472 (Tuesday, 3rd March, to Wednesday, 4th March) - COLONY IN SPACE[643] **->** Earth was over-populated, with one hundred billion people living like "battery hens" in communal living units. 300-storey floating islands were built, housing five hundred million people. There was "no room to move, polluted air, not a blade of grass left on the planet and a government that locks you up if you think for yourself".

IMC scoured the galaxy for duralinium, to build ever more living units. From Earth Control, their head-quarters, a fleet of survey vessels ruthlessly strip-mined worlds and killed anyone that stood in their way. Discipline on IMC ships and planets relied heavily on the death penalty: piracy, mutiny and even trespass were all capital offences. Earth Government turned a blind eye to these abuses, although an Adjudicator was assigned to each Galactic Sector to judge disputes in interplanetary law.

Despite the conditions on Earth, few were prepared to leave the homeworld for a bleak life on a colony planet. Some groups of eccentrics bought their own ship and tried to settle on a new world, but most people preferred a life on Earth, where the government may have been harsh, but at least they were able to feed their citizens.

Colonists on Uxarieus - a world that supported birds, insects and basic plant life, and which had an atmosphere similar to that of Earth before the invention of the motor car - found themselves in competition with IMC for control of the planet. The colonists arrived first, surveyed the planet and set up their habitation domes. They discovered that Uxarieus was inhabited by a small subterranean city of telepathic Primitives. Two colonists were killed when they tried to enter the city, but an understanding was reached - in return for food, the Primitives provided menial labour. The colonists proceeded with their plans, but it proved difficult to grow crops as they withered for no reason that the colonists could ascertain.

Just over a year after they arrived, giant lizards attacked some of the outermost domes and some colonists were killed. Many colonists were prepared to leave, but their spacecraft was obsolete, and would almost certainly be unable to reach another world.

IMC arrived in Survey Ship 4-3, under the command

---

641 *The Also People* (p170).

642 *Theatre of War.* The date of publication is given as both "2566" (p36), and "2466" (p135). While the first date is actually in Benny's home era, the intro pages to Big Finish's Benny short story anthologies take such continual delight in pointing out that *Down Among the Dead Men* was "published originally in 2466, which is odd given that it is now 26—", the latter date has become a lot harder to discount. Appendix II of *Sky Pirates!* is "A Benny Bibliography", and contains further details.

643 Dating *Colony in Space* (8.4) - We see a calendar being changed from "Monday 2nd March 2472" to the next day. Ashe tells Jo that they left Earth in "seventy-one". Hulke's novelisation sets this story in "2971".

644 "Some five hundred years" before *The Mutants*, according to the Administrator.

645 "Five hundred years" after *Return of the Living Dad* (p61).

646 "Seventy-two" years before *Return of the Living Dad*.

647 "Almost thirty-five years" before *The Taking of Chelsea 426* (p74). It's notable that Mars is not thought to support plant life in this era - we know from *Benny: Beige Planet Mars* that by 2545, a settlement equipped with photon missiles is in operation there.

648 *Burning Heart* (p174).

649 *K9: The Korven.* The Korven are a threat and possibly even continue to control areas of the Earth at least

until 2618.

650 "Three cycles" (presumably years) before *The Game*.

651 Dating *The Game* (BF #66) - Lord Carlisle was born 2414 and started his career as a peacemaker around age 20 (so, circa 2434). On Disc 1, Track 70, he says he has been working as a mediator for "fifty years".

652 Dating "Junkyard Demon" (*DWM* #58-59) - No date is specified, and it's hard to place it with any certainty because we don't know how long the Cybernauts have been deactivated on A54. The sequel, however, places it in the same period as *The Tomb of the Cybermen*. The Cyberman resembles - with modifications - the ones from *The Tenth Planet*, and says they will "once again rule time and space". Zogron is "one of the pioneers of our interstellar empire". A54 orbits Arcturus.

653 Dating "Junkyard Demon II" (*DWM Yearbook 1996*) - It's "four months" since "Junkyard Demon". Joylove is working for Eric Klieg and the Brotherhood of Logicians, setting this story shortly before *The Tomb of the Cybermen*.

654 Dating *Leviathan* (BF LS #1.3) - One of the salvagers says that it's now the twenty-fifth century. The Leviathan left Earth in the twenty-second century and was to spend some "centuries" in transit.

of Captain Dent, and angered the colonists by staking a claim on the world. When they discovered that IMC had been using optical trickery to project images of the lizards, and a Mark III servo-robot to kill the colonists, many turned to arms.

Colonists and IMC men were killed in a series of gun battles. The Master posed as an Adjudicator and ruled in IMC's favour, but he was more interested in the Primitives' secrets. The IMC team attempted to murder the colonists by forcing them to leave in their obsolete rocket. They were defeated and a real Adjudicator was brought in.

It was discovered that the Primitive city was home to an ancient superweapon, which had been leaking and poisoning the soil. The third Doctor and Jo, working on behalf of the Time Lords, convinced the guardian of this device to destroy to weapon - and the city - rather than let it fall into the Master's hands.

Humanity at this time still used imperial measurements, projectile weapons and wheeled transport ("space buggies"). Ships were powered by nuclear motors, and communicated with Earth via "warp" radio and videolink. The language of Earth was English; the currency was the pound. IMC had advanced scanning equipment for mineral surveys and medical diagnoses. Colonists bought old ships to transport them to their colony planets.

In the twenty-fifth century, Earth colonised Solos, a planet with rich deposits of thaesium. The beautiful planet was ravaged and its people enslaved.[644] The seventh Doctor, Benny, Roz and Chris went to Navarro to rest after their adventure in Little Caldwell.[645] Mrs Ransandrianasolo was born. She was a telepath, as her mother was given psi drugs.[646]

At this time, Earth was thought to be the only body in the solar system capable of supporting plant life.[647] In 2476, the Techno-Magi consulted the frozen head of Ralph Waldo Mimsey as an Oracle, driving him insane.[648]

The Korven invaded Earth in 2480, and attempted to cool the planet with phosphane devices because the planet was too warm for them.[649] Circa 2481, the UI designated Cray as Earth's sister planet, due to its position relative to Earth from Galactic Zero. The increased focus on Cray compelled Earth to try and end the planet's embarrassing war. The negotiator Lord Carlisle would be dispatched to try and arbitrate a peace.[650]

c 2484 - THE GAME[651] -> On the planet Cray, only two teams - the Gora and the Lineen - had survived to continue playing the lethal game of Naxy. The past five seasons had seen the deaths of 78,349 Gora and 65,418 Lineen, although the Gora were in much worse shape than was officially reported, and were on the brink of defeat.

The fifth Doctor and Nyssa witnessed Lord Carlisle's efforts to broker a truce, but the Doctor's involvement in a Naxy match led to an upset for the Lineen, with four hundred Lineen casualties. Carlisle died while saving the Doctor's life, but the Doctor exposed the Morian Crime Syndicate's manipulative influence on the planet. The Gora and Lineen united against the Morian, ending the Naxy tournaments. Carlisle was accredited with the planet's newfound peace.

Heroin slam, the so-called "razor drug", was now in distribution.

c 2485 - "Junkyard Demon"[652] -> The Salvage ship *Drifter* travelled along the edge of the galaxy, piloted by two traders: Flotsam and Jetsam of the Backwater Scrap and Salvage Company. They plucked the TARDIS out of space, interrupting the fourth Doctor's meditation. The Doctor was horrified to see that they'd recovered a Cyberman, and to learn that Flotsam and Jetsam reprogrammed them to sell on as butlers.

The Cyberman reactivated and took Jetsam to the planet A54 in the Arcturian system, where a great Cybernaut fleet had crashed. They quickly discovered Zogron, the deactivated leader, and Jetsam reprogrammed him... as a butler. The Doctor and Flotsam arrived in the *Drifter* and immobilised the Cyberman with a polymer spray.

c 2485 - "Junkyard Demon II"[653] -> Joylove McShane of Joylove Antiques arrived on A54 wanting to buy Flotsam and Jetsam out, and set his henchman Stinker on them when they refused. Joylove was a gunrunner working for the Brotherhood of Logicians, and he wanted the army of Cybermen. The fourth Doctor arrived and destroyed the Cyber Army, but Flotsam and Jetsam discovered a supply of Cybermats to keep them busy. Joylove escaped... but a surviving Cyberman went with him.

c 2486 - LEVIATHAN[654] -> The clones aboard the Leviathan carrying the Sentinels of the New Dawn had spent their whole lives in a Middle Ages setting - a template of the society the Sentinels hoped to establish on the planet Felgathon. A meteor storm struck the Leviathan as it was less than fifty light years from its destination, and the sleeping Sentinels were all killed. The sixth Doctor and Peri visited the Leviathan as human salvagers overrode the ship's Zeron computer system, and attempted to have all the clones recycled. The Doctor thwarted the salvagers and arranged for the clones to be relocated to safety.

c 2486 (September) - THE TOMB OF THE CYBERMEN[655] -> Eric Klieg and Kaftan, two members of the Brotherhood of Logicians, usurped control of an expedition mounted to unearth the Tombs of the Cybermen on Telos. The Cybermen were revived and planned to emerge into the universe, but were re-frozen by the second Doctor, Jamie and Victoria. Klieg and Kaftan were killed, and the CyberController was badly electrocuted and thought dead.

The currency at this time appears to have been the pound. Individuals and organisations could charter spacecraft.

The CyberController was not destroyed, but merely damaged. He went on to build a new Cyber-Race.[656]

By the end of the twenty-fifth century, a museum was dedicated to the Beatles in Liverpool. Clothes were self-cleaning, dirt repelling and non-creasing. Ten-year-olds took a certificate of education in physics, medicine, chemistry and computer science using learning machines for an hour a week. There was evidence that humanity now had some familiarity with temporal theory - even children knew Venderman's Law: "Mass is absorbed by light, therefore light has mass and energy. The energy radiated by a light neutron is equal to the energy of the mass it absorbs".[657]

Vicki Pallister, a companion of the first Doctor, was born in New London on Earth around 2480. She lived in Liddell Towers. Vicki's mother died when she was 11. After that, she and her father left Earth for a new life on space colony Astra.[658] She was inoculated using a laser injector when she was five, and owned a pony called Saracen.[659] In Vicki's time, St. Paul's was still standing, having survived four world wars "and an alien invasion".[660] Food was designed to be nutritious, not tasty. Pandas were extinct, and museums used holograms. Vicki's father, Lieutenant Commander Pallister, had basic paramedic training for his intended job on Astra.[661]

2487 - JUDGEMENT OF THE JUDOON[662] -> The planet New Memphis opened Terminal 13, hoping to expand its service of hyperspace vessels. Conflict escalated between criminal organisations respectively led by "Widow" and "Uncle", but the tenth Doctor and the Judoon stopped an effort to destroy Terminal 13 as part of an insurance scam. Uncle and Widow both died owing to a virus, the Invisible Assassin, that Uncle had tailored to Widow's DNA - he had failed to realise that she was

655 Dating *The Tomb of the Cybermen* (5.1) - The story is set "five hundred years" after the Cybermen mysteriously died out according to Parry, although the Cybermen don't indicate how long they've been in their tombs. No reference is made to the Cyber War [q.v.], so we might presume it is before that time (the disappearance of the Cybermen after the Cyber War wasn't a mystery). The Cybermen's history computer recognises the Doctor from "the lunar surface", so the Cybermen went into hibernation (shortly?) after *The Moonbase*. This would make it at least 2570, but we know that *Earthshock* is set in 2526. The Cybermen in *Earthshock* refer to the events of *The Tomb of the Cybermen*, so *The Tomb of the Cybermen* must be set before 2526 (although they also refer to *Revenge of the Cybermen*, which there's reason to believe is set later). Either Parry is rounding up or he doesn't know about the events of *The Moonbase*. As ever, no-one refers to stories made after this one, such as *Silver Nemesis* and *The Wheel in Space*.

Another option is that the Cybermen in *Earthshock* are time travellers. There's some circumstantial evidence for this - it explains how their scanner can show a scene from *Revenge of the Cybermen*, which is almost certainly set after 2526, and it may go some way to explaining how the freighter travels in time at the end - but there's nothing in the script that supports this, and if they have a time machine capable of transporting a huge army of Cybermen, then it's hard to believe that the best plan they can come up with is the one that they're implementing. Then again, even without a time machine, their plan makes no apparent sense.

Radio Times didn't give a year for *Tomb*, but specified that the month the story is set is "September". The draft script for serial 4D (at that point called *Return of the Cybermen*), suggested a date of "24/10/2248" for the story. *Cybermen* sets the story in "2486", *The Terrestrial Index* at "the beginning of the 26th century"."A History of the Cybermen" in *DWM* #83 preferred "2431", whereas *The Discontinuity Guide* settles on "2570". *Timelink* says "2526", *About Time* "early 2500s".

656 *Attack of the Cybermen*

657 This is the native time of the first Doctor's companion Vicki, who joins the TARDIS in *The Rescue*. We learn about her clothing and schooling in *The Web Planet,* and her visit to the Beatles Museum and familiarity with Venderman in *The Chase.* In that story we also learn that Vicki used to live close to a medieval castle.

658 *Byzantium!*

659 *The Plotters*

660 *Frostfire.* The "alien invasion" presumably refers to the Dalek invasion of the twenty-second century.

661 *The Eleventh Tiger*

662 Dating *Judgement of the Judoon* (NSA #31) - The year is given. A couple of Draconians are seen at Terminal 13, even though "first contact" (at least, officially) between Earth and Draconia doesn't happen until around 2520 (*Frontier in Space*).

663 The IMC armoury attached to the gardens has gone unused for "twenty years or more" (p88) before

secretly his daughter, and that the virus would affect him also.

Kronkburgers were served in the New Memphis settlement.

The Interplanetary Mining Corporation established Unit 426, a colony equipped with oxygen gardens in orbit around Saturn, to aid and supply its first hydrogen mine there.[663]

c 2493 - THE RESCUE[664] **-> There were emigrations to other planets. One such ship, the UK-201, crashed on Dido en route to Astra. This was a desert world, home of a peaceful humanoid race and lizard-like creatures known as sand beasts. The Didoans had a population of around one hundred, and had just perfected an energy ray that could be used as a building tool. A young girl named Vicki was one of only two survivors of the crash; her father was among the fatalities. When the TARDIS made a return visit to Dido, the first Doctor, Ian and Barbara exposed the other survivor, Bennett, as a murderer. Vicki joined them on their travels.**

Boar-like aliens attacked human colonists in the Thynemnus system, causing disputes. The aliens were driven off, but the Valethske attacked the system soon after.[665] The interior of Tyler's Folly reshaped itself according to explorer Franz Kryptosa's conception of the "inner world" myths. He merged with the Pool of Life there.[666]

A super-volcano destroyed the Incorporated Nation of NeoCalifornia in the late twenty-fifth century, and so a consortium of entertainment businesses terraformed the planet Hollywood to serve as the centre of the movie industry in the Milky Way. The planet BollyWood was the next orbit over from Hollywood, as were some Celebra-Stations, where visitors could chase talentless android celebrities in safari parks. The tenth Doctor and Martha visited Hollywood because she wanted to see a good Western, but when the cinema they planned to go to was closed, he took her to the real Wild West in the 1880s.[667]

c 2495 - SET PIECE[668] **->** In the late twenty-fifth century, spaceships started disappearing from one of the less-used traffic lanes. A space vessel, designed to save a group of doomed colonists by directly uploading their memories, had outstripped its programming. It now sought to absorb the memories of every living being, and was using its robotic workers, the Ants, to kidnap people.

Five hundred and six people were taken from one such captured ship, the *Cortese*. The seventh Doctor, Ace and Bernice tried to intercede and were flung through time to ancient Egypt and nineteenth century France. They eventually brought about the Ship's destruction. Kadiatu Lethbridge-Stewart briefly became the Ship's thrall - she was liberated, but fell through a space-time rift. The Doctor would next meet her in 1754, near Sierra Leone.

Androids indistinguishable from humans were constructed in the Orion Sector. They became smart enough to demand equal rights and protest their mistreatment. This led to a conflict - the Orion War - against humanity. The androids settled in the Orion system, ordering the humans to accept android rule or leave.[669]

c 2495 - ATTACK OF THE CYBERMEN[670] **-> The Cybermen faced total defeat. Thanks to Cryon guerillas and the Cybermen's failing hibernation equipment, they weren't even safe on Telos and planned to evacuate. They captured a three-man time machine that had landed on Telos, and used it to go to 1985 to prevent Mondas' destruction. The sixth Doctor and Peri were captured in 1985 and brought to Telos, where the Doctor destroyed the tombs and the CyberController.**

The Taking of Chelsea 426, so it's been at least that long since the oxygen gardens were established.

664 Dating *The Rescue* (2.3) - Vicki states that the year her spaceship left Earth was "2493, of course". The draft script suggested that Vicki and her fellow space traveller, Bennett, have been on Dido "for a year", but there is no such indication in the final programme. Ian Marter's novelisation is set in 2501. *The Making of Doctor Who*, the various editions of Lofficier and *The Doctor Who File* set the date of "2493". *The TARDIS Special* "c.2500". Peel's novelisation of *The Chase* says that Vicki is from "the twenty-fourth century".

665 *Superior Beings*

666 About a century before *Benny: Down*.

667 *Peacemaker*

668 Dating *Set Piece* (NA #35) - The Ants kidnap the Doctor, Benny and Ace in "the twenty-fifth century" (p33).

669 "Eight years" before *Sword of Orion*.

670 Dating *Attack of the Cybermen* (22.1) - No date is given on screen, but the story takes place after *The Tomb of the Cybermen* as the Controller remembers surviving that story. Although the Cybermen know of Lytton's people, and he is fully aware of the situation on Telos, it doesn't appear that *Resurrection of the Daleks* is set in this period... in that story, Stien says that the Daleks captured people from many different periods (while never really explaining why), so this could well be Lytton's native time (Lytton talks of humans as his "ancestors", so his home planet - Vita 15, in star system 690, with the satellite of Riftan V - is a human colony).

The previous edition of *Ahistory* dated *Attack* to circa

Lytton, a former Dalek operative now working for the oppressed Cryons, was killed.

In Earth's solar system, some humans who had been in cryo-freeze for centuries were revived, albeit with considerable brain damage. They were disparagingly called Cryogens, and most of them lived in nursing homes.[671]

The bloodthirsty Drexxons rampaged from planet to planet. They were defeated by the armies of the Combined Stellar Forces after a decade-long battle, and sealed inside a timeless Perpetuity Chamber which was hidden on the asteroid of Stanalan.[672]

The Twenty-Sixth Century

By the twenty-sixth century, interstellar travel had become a matter of routine. Fleets of spacecraft ranging from luxury liners to cargo freighters to battleships pushed further into deep space. Ships were built from durilium and had hyperdrives. The mind probe was commonly used to scan the minds of suspects, but it wasn't always reliable. Weapons of the time included hand blasters and neutronic missiles. This period saw the beginning of Earth's Empire.[673]

The warp drives of Earth ships were powered by anti-matter contained in stabilising vessels.[674] Space

was divided into Sectors.[675] The currency was the Imperial.[676] It was likely around now that the Doctor gained a licence for the Mars-Venus rocket run.[677] *The Collected Works of Gustav Urnst* were published in June 2503, striking a chord with the bombastic people of the twenty-sixth century.[678]

Planetoid KS-159, the future home of the Braxiatel Collection, was once located within Draconian space. Even when it was outside their borders, the Draconians contested it under a caveat about war reparations.[679]

In the twenty-sixth century, the galaxy did not experience a year that was free of war.[680]

? 2500 - ARMY OF DEATH[681] **->** Humans settled the frontier world of Draxine, and within ten generations had created the twin city-states of Stronghaven and Garrak. The Lifespan Project sought to extend human longevity, but President Carnex of Stronghaven discovered that it could transfer his mind into a psychic cloud. He wanted godhood by arranging Garrak's destruction with a bomb, and then, after the death of his physical form, animated the skeletons of Garrak's dead to attack Stronghaven. The eighth Doctor and Mary Shelley were present as Nia Bursk - a Garrak survivor - infused the psychic cloud with her own mind. She extinguished Carnex, then drove his skeleton army into the sea.

2530, but Big Finish's *Cyberman* mini-series (set circa 2515) occurs after an asteroid strike obliterates Telos an estimated five to ten years beforehand, and so *Attack* must take place prior to that point. There is little room to navigate around this, as the lead characters in *Cyberman* not only go to Telos' fragmented remains, they find its Cyberman-filled tomb floating about in space. Strangely enough, *Attack* has no direct interaction between the Telos Cybermen and the Earth of the future, so it's entirely possible that the Telos Cybermen were re-frozen in *The Tomb of the Cybermen*, then awoke some years afterwards and upgraded themselves (and their electrocuted Controller), and then were re-entombed in *Attack* prior to Telos' annihilation.

All previous versions of *Ahistory* took into account Lytton's comment in *Attack* that the Cybermen are the "undisputed masters of space" (odd in itself, as *Attack* has them in an extremely weak position). However, er, no such comment actually appears in the TV story. Eric Saward's novelisation of *Attack* has Lytton tell Griffiths that the Cybermen are the "Undisputed masters of the galaxy!", but that's it. Sorry!

671 At least ten years, if not more, before *The Taking of Chelsea 426* (p37).
672 "Over seven hundred years" (p117) before *Death Riders*. The participants in this conflict are identified as being nonhuman.
673 *Frontier in Space*

674 *Earthshock*
675 *Colony in Space, Earthshock*. The freighter in *Earthshock* starts off in Sector 16, in "deep space".
676 *Warriors' Gate*
677 *Robot, The Janus Conjunction*. The Mars-Venus cruise is mentioned in *Frontier in Space*, although presumably such flights take place from the twenty-first century until the far future.
678 *The Highest Science* (p48).
679 "More than a century" before *Benny: Parallel Lives*.
680 *Benny: The Judas Gift*. In fact, this century will see humanity in major conflicts with the Cyberman, the Draconians and the Daleks.
681 Dating *Army of Death* (BF #155) - The humans on Draxine are "tenth generation" settlers, which has a ring to it of their originating from Earth in the third millennium.
682 Dating *The Monsters Inside* (NSA #2) - Dennel tells Rose it is "2501". *Boom Town* refers to this story. *The Colony of Lies*, however, contradicts this book by suggesting a start date for the Earth Empire of circa 2534.
683 Dating "Throwback: The Soul of a Cyberman" (*DWW* #5-7) - No date is given. The story provides the impression of being set in the future of *The Tomb of the Cybermen*, as Telos is now serving as the Cybermen's strategic and military command centre, complete with a sprawling Cyberman city that has a monorail and space-field. This is very difficult to recon-

2501 - THE MONSTERS INSIDE[682] -> The ninth Doctor and Rose arrived on the planetary system of Justicia, a penal colony of the Earth Empire, where cruel guards were overseeing the construction of a set of pyramids. The Doctor met two criminals from Raxacoricofallapatorius who planned to use gravity warps to convert the entire system into a weapon that could destroy planets. These were members of the Blathereen family. The Doctor teamed up with members of the Slitheen family to defeat them.

? 2502 - "Throwback: The Soul of a Cyberman"[683] -> The Cybermen invaded the planet Mondaran, and encountered heavy resistance. Cyberleader Tork requested reinforcements from Telos, which was six days away. These included Junior Cyberleader Kroton, who refused to kill a resistance cell. Kroton was developing emotions, and sided with the humans. Together, they stole a ship from the spaceport and retreated to the safety of the forest of Lorn. Kroton took the ship into orbit to prevent the humans from being detected, but it was a one-way trip. When his batteries drained, he was left drifting in space.

Earth initiated the Sword of Orion project: an effort to obtain Cyber-technology left over from the Cyber incursions on Earth for use in the Orion War.[684]

2503 - SWORD OF ORION[685] -> A derelict spaceship was discovered near the Garazone Central habitat. It was a Cybermen factory ship, and Earth High Command dispatched Deeva Jansen to recover the Cyber-technology aboard. Jansen, however, was actually an android trying to obtain the technology for the Orion androids. The eighth

Doctor and Charley were present when the Cybermen aboard the spaceship revived in great numbers, but the Doctor defeated them. Jansen was swept into space with some Cybermen and presumably frozen.

Telos was destroyed in a random asteroid strike. The Cyber-vault there had been designed to survive the planet's break-up, and so floated in space amidst Telos' ruins, the Cybermen inside the vault still in cryo-sleep.[686]

c 2505 - TO THE SLAUGHTER[687] -> Earth had been abandoned to the poorer countries. Mercury had fallen into the Sun and Venus was a toxic waste dump. The Oort Cloud had been sold off and dismantled.

Falsh Industries demolished most of Jupiter's moons - using the designs of Aristotle Halcyon, a celebrity *decor-artiste* - as part of a redevelopment scheme to attract businesses to the solar system. The "Old Preservers", speaking on behalf of the Empire Trust, were opposed to this. Falsh himself was engaged in illicit weapons research. The eighth Doctor, Fitz and Trix uncovered his schemes and defeated him. Halcyon decided to use his talents to improve Earth.

The people of Atwalla 3 prevented a takeover by alien races by genetically engineering their women to interbreed with other species. As more and more hybrids were born, the Atwallans found their own race was in danger of extinction. The Atwallan males wiped out the hybrids, and stripped their women of all rights.[688]

The human colony on Cantus was believed "lost"; in actuality, the Cybermen had cyber-converted all the adults there, and harvested the children's organs for use in

cile, however, against the comparatively shoddy state of the Cybermen seen in both *The Tomb of the Cybermen* and *Attack of the Cybermen*, and the evidence in the *Cybermen* audio series that Telos is destroyed perhaps eight years after *Attack* (which gives the Cybermen precious little time to recover from the setback in that story and to create the relatively formidable settlement seen in "Throwback"). If we're taking the design of the Cybermen into account, though, they most resemble the model seen in *The Invasion* or *Revenge of the Cybermen* (although with unique modifications, particularly their rank insignia), which again (via *Revenge*) fits a date around the twenty-sixth century.

684 The project is formally named in *Cyberman*, but such an undertaking was first seen in *Sword of Orion*.

685 Dating *Sword of Orion* (BF #17) - It's during the Orion War as featured in the *Cyberman* audios (also written, in part, by Nicholas Briggs), and "a very long time" after the Cyber Wars. The Doctor says the Cybermen are "safely tucked away in their tombs on Telos" (*The Tomb of the Cybermen*); humans assume the

Cybermen are extinct. The only date given here is that the original Jansen died on "three zero zero five zero seven". However, *Neverland* gives a firm date of 2503.

686 "At least ten years" before *Cyberman* Series 1.

687 Dating *To the Slaughter* (EDA #72) - The dating of this story is inconsistent. It's "almost four hundred years" since 1938, according to Halcyon (p17, so before 2338), but Trix thinks it's "over five hundred years" since her time (p86, so after around 2503). The story is set before *Revenge of the Cybermen*, and explains why Jupiter only has twelve natural moons in that story. When *Revenge* was broadcast, astronomers thought Jupiter had twelve moons, but dozens more have been discovered in the years since, and Jupiter at present is known to have sixty-six (nineteen were discovered in 2003 alone; three more were discovered since the second edition of *Ahistory* saw print). Earth in this era has a President, the beginning of an Empire and there's a mention of the Draconians, supporting (strangely, perhaps) Trix over Halcyon.

688 Enough time prior to *Benny: Parallel Lives*: "The

Cybermats.[689] The Draconians committed war crimes during the reign of the thirty-fourth Emperor, and were later made to pay reparations.[690] After IMC closed its hydrogen mine on Saturn, Unit 426 was purchased and redeveloped by Powe-Luna Developments into a facsimile of a twentieth-century English market town. It was renamed Chelsea 426.[691]

Humanity built the Empire State: a single tower, named after the Empire State Building, that stretched from half a mile underground to the upper atmosphere on a desert moon that orbited six planets. It became a centre for trade and commerce, but around 2509, a misanthrope named Rand Goodwyn destabilised the State's generators and destroyed it.[692]

c 2509 (20th August) - THE TAKING OF CHELSEA 426[693] ->
The Third Renaissance was about to commence. Some features of it, including the Theatre of Nomogan, the ceilings of the Chamber of Ra and the Simarine Orchestra, would be talked about for centuries. Neptune had mining platforms.

The Oxygen Gardens of Chelsea 426 had become home to the Chelsea Flower Show. The top exhibit was the Blue Flower of Saturn, recently discovered in that planet's atmosphere. The tenth Doctor tried to attend the flower show, and found that the Blue Flower contained mind-controlling spores that the Rutans had seeded on Saturn five centuries previous. Compounding the situation, Colonel Sarg of the Fourth Sontaran Intelligence Division arrived with his shock troops, and demanded to search for enemies of Sontar. The Doctor contained the resulting battle and saved the humans on Chelsea 426. Sarg's Sontarans - not realising that they had been infiltrated by the Rutan spores - returned to Sontar.

Field Marshal Sir Henry Whittington-Smythe died as part of this conflict, and was given a full military funeral on Earth. He was a veteran of the Martian Wars, the Battle of Olympus Mons, the Battle of Mercutio 14 and the Siege of the Hexion Gates.

The Bantu Independence Group lost a war in 2511, and its position was greatly diminished.[694]

Dr. Oleg Mikelz located the Oracle of the Lost on planetoid KS-159. The Oracle had tired of its servile existence, and attempted to trick Mikelz into destroying it - but its ambiguous statements instead drove Mikelz to kill his

Serpent's Tooth" that the Atwallans have lost their scientific know-how.
689 "A hundred years" before *Benny: The Crystal of Cantus*, as implied by Jason Kane's narration.
690 "A century" prior to *Benny: Freedom of Information*. This seems to contradict *Shadowmind* (set in 2673), which occurs during the reign of the twenty-fourth Emperor - unless the numbering system was reset, for some reason.
691 The timeframe is a little unclear, but it's repeatedly said that Jake and Vienna Carstairs - children belonging to the family in charge of Chelsea 426 - relocate there from Earth "two years" before *The Taking of Chelsea 426*.
692 *Benny: The Empire State*
693 Dating *The Taking of Chelsea 426* (NSA #34) - The Doctor says it is "the beginning of the twenty-sixth century" (p54), roughly "five hundred years" (p37) after the twenty-first century. The day is given (p8).
694 *Benny: Another Girl, Another Planet*
695 *Benny: Tears of the Oracle*
696 Dating *Kingdom of Silver* (BF #112a) - The story occurs during the Orion War. Both the Orion androids and the Earth military have dispatched agents to scour the galaxy to salvage Cyber-technology - as is the case in *Sword of Orion*, perhaps suggesting that *Kingdom of Silver* happens about the same time. But in truth, *Kingdom of Silver* could occur at any pretty much point between here and *Cyberman*, set in 2515. The Tasak Cybermen here want to send out a reactivation signal to the thousands of dormant Cyber-tombs, somewhat contradicting *Cyberman*'s claim that the tomb on Telos

was the "master vault" given the special status of sending out such a signal.
697 Dating "Keepsake" (BF #112b) - The Orion War is still ongoing, and although the Orion androids still view Cyber-technology as a potential resource, there's no mention of the Cybermen having overrun Earth or encroaching into Orion territory (as occurs in *Cyberman*). Writer James Swallow intended *Keepsake* as a prelude to *Cyberman 2*, which is set in 2515.
698 *Cyberman 2: Machines*
699 The background detail to *Cyberman* Series 1.
700 *Cyberman 2: Terror*
701 *Cyberman 2: Outsiders*
702 *Cyberman 2: Terror*
703 Dating *Cyberman* Series 1 and 2 (BF mini-series) - The evidence is abundant, but placement requires juggling *Cyberman* in relation to other stories.
Telos has been fragmented for as much as ten years, so it's at least that long since *Attack of the Cybermen*. Likewise, events in *Sword of Orion* (set in 2503) lead into these audio series. Samantha isn't surprised that Barnaby - one of the highest-ranking officers in Earth's military - has never heard of the Cybermen (though a couple of minor characters in *Cyberman 2* have heard vague rumours about them), so it's definitely before the Cyber War and Earth's involvement in the alliance against the Cybermen in *Earthshock* (set in 2526). There's no mention of the Draconians, so *Cyberman* almost certainly happens before the Draconian War occurs circa 2520.
Brett's victory against the Android Eighth Fleet is

wife, his personal assistant and finally himself. Edward Watkinson, the finest archaeologist of his age and Mikelz's good friend, became infected with a mental parasite on the planet Paracletes. On September 11, 2515, Watkinson deduced the Oracle's involvement in Mikelz's murder-suicide and went to KS-159. Watkinson killed himself, causing the parasite to leap into the Oracle - which went inert to keep the creature contained.[695]

c 2505 - KINGDOM OF SILVER[696] **->** On Tasak, the House of Argentia, under the command of Magus Riga, found a Cybermen tomb established some millennia ago. Argentia revolutionised medicine by reverse-engineering the Cyber-technology, including the development of a healing solution called Silver. In so doing, Argentia ended a devastating war with the rival House of Sarkota through benevolence, not force of arms.

As a conclave gathered to celebrate the war's conclusion, the seventh Doctor presented himself as "Dr Johannes Smither of the House of Gallifrey". The Doctor and Riga wiped out the revived Cybermen before they could send an activation signal that would awaken thousands of Cyber-tombs across the galaxy, but Riga was killed. Erin of the House of Sarkota gave up her birthright and pledged to work with the new Argentia Magus for peace. Afterward, the Doctor offered two androids that he'd met - Temeter and Sara - a lift back to the Orion Zone.

The Doctor claimed that Tasak had the best tea in its quadrant.

c 2514 - "Keepsake"[697] **->** The androids Temeter and Sara were called before the Orion War Council to account for their failure to capture a Cybrid infiltrator and saboteur, Corvus, who arranged the deaths of hundreds of androids. The Council judged that Temeter and Sara's feelings for one another had hampered their effectiveness. Temeter was returned to active duty after his emotional connection to Sara was deleted from his core consciousness. Sara was deemed less fit for service, so her consciousness was deleted and replaced by another operative. What remained of Sara's persona was redeployed in a servo robot with Grade 3 intelligence.

Cyberman Series 1 and 2

On Earth, as the Orion War took a turn for the worse, the predecessor of President Levinson founded the Scorpius Project to make use of Cyber-technology developed from the failed Sword of Orion initiative. The Cybermen usurped Scorpius to their own ends, and manipulated Levinson into officially terminating it. Scorpius proceeded in secret; Paul Hunt, an advisor to the project, was converted into a Cybrid - a Cyber-operative who could pass as human[698] - and vanished from the public record. The

Cybermen made plans to replace Levinson with a president more agreeable to using Scorpius as they desired.[699]

At this time, Article 7 of the Earth spacefleet charter allowed three officers of senior rank to remove a captain from command decisions.[700] Article 92, sub-section 3, paragraph 4 - which hadn't been used in years - allowed for those of command rank to conscript civilian vessels for military use. The Navy, now part of Earth's Spacefleet, was equipped with proton rifles. Mark 4 fusion cores - part of a spaceship's drive systems - were a bit out of date, and Mark 6 cores were available. Earth's dominions included the Vega colony.[701] The industrial heartland of the British North was currently a bunch of ruined factories. The soil there was so laced with cadmium, even nanosheets couldn't strip it out.[702]

c 2515 - CYBERMAN: SCORPIUS / FEAR / CONVERSION / TELOS[703] **->** The Orion War continued to go against humanity. Earth's Planetary Assault Force Delta on Orius Beta VIII walked straight into an ambush, and although Admiral Karen Brett of the *Redoubtable* led a counter-assault that destroyed the Android Eighth Fleet - which was hiding just off Orius Beta V - human casualties still numbered fifty thousand. Orius Beta VIII was nuked. The victory, however technical, surged morale on Earth to its highest point in twenty years.

Brett was promoted to Commander-in-Chief of Earth's forces. Paul Hunt secretly met with Brett on Reticek IV, and explained to her the potential that Scorpius offered. Soon after, the Cybermen arranged for a shuttle to crash into the White House - President Levinson was assassinated, and his killers teleported away. The Senate invoked emergency powers and made Brett president. She appointed her old friend, Captain Liam Barnaby, as Commander-in-Chief.

Several months passed, with humanity suffering further defeats. The androids destroyed the Dracian VIII colony's reactor, causing massive casualties. They also killed millions, including Brett's parents, in the undefended Vaslovian system.

Brett increasingly underwent Cyber-hypnosis and conversion, and Hunt became a presidential advisor. Earth was flooded with refugees from the Orion conflict; many of these wound up at a camp on the Isle of Wight, and were then transported off-world for conversion. The fresh Cyber-troops made incursions into Orion territory, and destroyed the android tracking station Beta-4.

Commander Barnaby became politically ostracised from Brett, and increasingly heard rumours concerning Scorpius. He allied himself with Samantha Thorn - an android secret agent who for years had been Paul Hunt's lover. Assisted by androids aboard the Orion flagship *Antares*, they discovered a map of the galaxy identifying a thousand planets with Cyber-hibernation vaults. They realised that if an activation signal were sent from the master vault on Telos, billions of Cybermen would awaken, spelling the end for humanity and androids alike. The *Antares* immediately left for Telos to prevent this.

The Cyber-Planner running Scorpius advanced its master plan. Brett revealled the existence of Scorpius to Earth, claiming that "volunteers" augmented with cyber-tech had destroyed key android installations. Cybernetic commando units were stationed in all of Earth's major population centres, purportedly to protect the public from retribution by the androids. Worldwide martial law was declared. Brett announced that she would personally lead the final assault against the androids - but in actuality, she underwent full Cyber-conversion, and left with a Cyber-task force aboard an advanced XP-900 warship to intercept the *Antares*. In her absence, Hunt became emergency executive-in-chief.

Barnaby's group found that the Cyber-vault on Telos had survived the planet's break-up, and a dogfight between the *Antares* and the XP-900 resulted in the *Antares* colliding with the vault. A thousand Cybermen space-walked from the XP-900 and wiped out the *Antares* crew save for Barnaby and Thorn. The two of them raised the fuel rods in the Cyber-vault's reactor, saturating the area with radiation that killed the XP-900 Cybermen, the entombed Cybermen and Brett.

c 2516 - CYBERMAN 2: OUTSIDERS / TERROR / MACHINES / EXTINCTION[703] -> Six months passed as Barnaby and Thorn laboured to keep the *Antares*' damaged systems running, and the ship limped through space. Back on Earth, Brett was formally declared dead. Hunt became executive-in-chief in her place, extended his term indefinitely and continued martial law. To quell dissent, he engineered several "retirements" of senior officials. He also

---

said to make the public on Earth the happiest it's been "in twenty years". If this denotes the current duration of the Orion War (said to start in 2495, according to statements made in *Sword of Orion* and *Neverland*), *Cyberman* Series 1 by logical extension would occur around 2515. It's repeatedly said that Series 2 opens "six months" after that, and the remainder of the story seems to take a few days, or at most a few weeks.

Presumably, the Cybermen's retreat into space - and the survivors on Earth becoming all-too-horrifyingly aware of the Cybermen's existence - is the event that seeds humanity's future conflicts with the Cybermen, i.e. both the proposed alliance against the Cybermen in *Earthshock* and the Cyber War itself. In fact, the final installment of *Cyberman 2* entails the emergence of a "more advanced design of Cybermen" that's been made from "harvested human materials", which - although we can't *see* the Cybermen in question for confirmation - is probably meant to denote the *Earthshock*-style models. (Even so, this doesn't expressly rule out the sometimes-floated theory - not adopted by this chronology - that the Cybermen in *Earthshock* are time travellers.) Given the need to place *Attack of the Cybermen* before Telos' destruction, it's possible that the "more advanced" models in the mini-series are an improvement of the eminently killable versions first developed on Telos and seen in *Attack*.

Earth's current political structure bears some similarities to that in *Frontier in Space*, set in 2540: there's a global Senate, and in *Cyberman 2: Extinction*, Hunt is referred to as the "executive-in-chief of the Earth Empire". A feature of *Cyberman* that isn't mentioned in *Frontier in Space* is that the Earth president is based in the White House - either the current building in Washington, D.C., or one of the same name. It's entirely possible that in the interim between *Cyberman* and *Frontier in Space*, the White House was discontinued as the chief executive's residence - possibly to get a fresh

start after Hunt's disastrous tenure, or possibly to eliminate the stigma of President Levison having been assassinated there.

704 *Real Time*, possibly denoting the Orion-Cyber conflict that breaks out at the end of *Cyberman 2*, and perhaps a prelude conflict to the greater Cyber War.

705 Dating *Parasite* (NA #33) - The dating of this story is problematic. Mark Bannen is the son of Alex Bannen, who died in *Lucifer Rising* "more than two centuries" ago (p165), so the story is set after 2357. 1706 "was more than seven hundred years ago" (p140), so it is after 2406. Mark Bannen was a baby during the Mexico riots of 2146 and has been kept alive by the Artifact since the founding of the colony "three hundred sixty-seven" years ago (p73), so the story must be set after 2513. This last date is supported in that Earth now has "Empire" (p136-137).

706 "Twenty years" before *Frontier in Space*. General Williams claims that his ship was "damaged and helpless" and well as "unarmed", but it managed to destroy a Draconian battlecruiser anyway. A scene cut from episode three explained that Williams used his "exhaust rockets" to destroy the other ship.

707 *Head Games* (p165-166).

708 *Love and War* (p10).

709 *Frontier in Space*.

710 Forty years before *Prisoner of the Daleks*.

711 *Benny: Walking to Babylon*, p173. *Benny: Tears of the Oracle* verifies that publication occurred posthumously, as Watkinson died in 2515.

712 Inferred from *The Tomb of the Cybermen*.

THE CYBER WAR: The "Cyber Wars" feature in much fan fiction and are referred to in a number of the books and audios. On television, though, the term "the Cyber War" is only used once, by the Doctor in *Revenge of the Cybermen* - everyone else refers to it simply as "the war".

We are told that this war took place "centuries" beforehand, and that the human race won when they

had Barnaby convicted in absentia of treason and given a death sentence.

The Cybermen continued efforts to turn Earth into a new Mondas, and staged a number of mass abductions - fodder for Cyber-conversion - in cities such as Lyons and Kiev. Hunt released a number of cover stories, declaring various cities as off-bounds. An eruption was said to have occurred in Hawaii. Bombings were cited across Greater Britannica. Bergen, Norway, was completely emptied, supposedly due to biotoxins that a resistance movement put into the city's water supply. Eurozone News reported flooding in Birmingham, and that the Stafford metroplex had an emergency curfew. Meanwhile, a resistance movement to Hunt's rule began striking back, staging demonstrations in a dozen cities that included Moscow, Tokyo, New York City, Mumbai and the Canberra Arcology. Cybermen based in Nevada and the Sudan were targeted.

Thorn discovered that the Orion war council, fearful of the Cybermen on Earth, had authorised use of an Eclipse-Class device: a fusion initiator that would make Earth's sun release an intense solar shockwave. This would kill all organic life - human and Cyberman alike - within orbit of Mars.

Hunt underwent full Cyber-conversion as Barnaby and Thorn directed their attention toward the main Cyber-facility at Bergen. Thorn interfaced her positronic mind with the Cyber-network hub there, and convinced the Cyber-Planner that the Cybermen's campaign to conquer Earth would result in millions of Cyber-casualties and the complete obliteration of humanity and the Orion androids. The Cyber-Planner judged the cost of victory as too great, and ordered the Cybermen to leave Earth in fleet vessels. The strain of communing with the Cybermen killed Thorn. She was buried on the Norway coast.

The androids opted to live in peace with humanity, ending the Orion War. In deep space, an android warfleet engaged the Cyber-vessels before they could enter hyper-drive.

The twenty-sixth century saw the Great Orion Cyber Wars.[704]

? 2515 - PARASITE[705] **->** Three hundred and sixty-seven years after it had been colonised, the Elysium system was on the brink of civil war. Over the last fifty years, a schism had developed between the Founding Families (who wanted to remain isolated from Earth and maintain their own distinctive political system) and the Reunionists (who wanted to make contact with the Empire).

Before the situation could be resolved, the Artifact was found to be a vast transdimensional living entity. It could warp space to create water worlds that would collapse into stars, then generate gas giants to incubate its planet-sized eggs. The seventh Doctor, Benny and Ace visited the

Artifact during a crucial point in its life-cycle - which threatened to accelerate. As each young Artifact required the water from forty or fifty thousand planets, this posed a threat to the entire universe. The Doctor altered the Artifact's biology so that it would only produce children with a symbiotic, not a parasitic, relationship with water-bearing worlds. Previously laid eggs would be born as parasites, and possibly threaten the Elysium system in several million years.

The Draconian War

Around 2520, a peace mission between Draconia and Earth was arranged, but it ended in catastrophe when the Draconian ship approached, as was their tradition, with the missile ports open. The Draconian ship carried no missiles, but the humans assumed they had been lured into an ambush. A neutron storm prevented communications and the human ship destroyed the Draconian one. A war between Earth and Draconia started immediately, and although it didn't last long, millions died on both sides.[706]

As a result of a pop can that Bernice kicked onto a path in 2001, a less-elegant writer came to draft a crucial speech shortly before the outbreak of hostilities. The war consequently broke out an hour earlier, with dozens of extra casualties on both sides.[707]

During the Dragon Wars, Shirankha Hall's deep-space incursion squadron discovered a beautiful garden world halfway between human and Draconian Space. He named it Heaven.[708]

Although many on both sides wanted to see the war fought to its conclusion, diplomatic relations were forged and the war ended. The Frontier in Space was established, a dividing line which neither race's spacecraft could cross. Relations between the two planets remained wary, and factions on both Earth and Draconia wanted to wage a preemptive strike on the enemy. For twenty years, the galaxy existed in a state of cold war, although treaties and cultural exchanges were set up. Espionage between the powers was expressly forbidden.[709]

Arkheon was thought destroyed. It was known as Planet of the Ghosts, because it was the location of the Arkheon Threshold, a schism in time and space.[710] *Glory Under the Mud*, a collection of Edward Watkinson's essays, was published in 2524.[711]

The Cyber War

Over five hundred years after Mondas' destruction, the Cybermen had been redesigned and were more deadly than ever.[712]

2526 - EARTHSHOCK[713] -> Earth was not directly affected, but it was clear that only the homeworld could provide the military resources needed to combat the Cyber threat. In 2526, a Conference was held on Earth that proposed that humanity should unite to fight the Cybermen. The fifth Doctor, Tegan, Nyssa and Adric stopped the Cybermen from detonating a bomb on Earth. The Cybermen then attempted to land an invasion force on Earth using a hijacked space-freighter. Adric was still aboard the freighter, trying to alter its coordinates, as the ship was thrown back to prehistoric times...

The Cybermen were unafraid of contravening galactic law or arms treaties, and were prepared to destroy entire planets using Cyberbombs. But the war against the Cybermen united many planets, and humanity started from a strong position. Earth was aware of the Cybermen's vulnerability to gold and developed the glittergun, a weapon that exploited this weakness. There was more gold on Voga than in the rest of the known galaxy, and when those vast reserves were used against the Cybermen, humanity inflicted massive defeats.[714] The glittergun was built by INITEC.[715]

Realising that they were beaten, the Cybermen launched an attack on Voga and detonated Cyberbombs that blew the planet out of orbit. The Vogans were forced into underground survival chambers. After this time, the Cybermen disappeared, and it was believed that they had died out.[716] The Cyber Fleet was destroyed. Bounty hunters and mercenaries hunted down the remaining Cybermen.[717]

On Dellah, the Great Act of Toleration of 2528 recognised one thousand and thirty-six religions, including five hundred and twelve indigenous groups.[718] Mr. Misnomer was a pulp-story hero of such adventures as *The Shadow of the Dying Ones* (2529).[719]

---

discovered that Cybermen were vulnerable to gold and invented the "glittergun". Following their total defeat, the Cybermen launched a revenge attack on Voga, after which the Cybermen completely disappeared.

From the on-screen information, it seems that we can precisely position the date of this "Cyber War": it can't be before 2486, because in *The Tomb of the Cybermen*, the Cyber Race is thought to have been extinct for five hundred years after Mondas' destruction. In that story, the Controller is ready to create a "new race" of Cybermen. We learn in *Attack of the Cybermen* that the Controller wasn't destroyed at the end of *The Tomb of the Cybermen*, so we might presume that this new race emerged soon afterwards and began its conquests. A new type of Cyberman - possibly the *Earthshock* models - is created in *Cyberman 2*.

Either way, the aforementioned conquests didn't directly involve Earth: in *Earthshock*, Scott, a member of the Earth military, hasn't heard of the Cybermen (even though his planet is hosting a conference that the Cyber Leader says will unite many planets in a "war against the Cyber Race"). The Doctor observes that it is a war that the Cybermen "can't win". When the Cybermen's plan to blow up the conference is defeated (*Earthshock*), there is nothing to stop Earth from fighting this genocidal war against the Cybermen - and this is surely the "Cyber War" referred to in *Revenge of the Cybermen*. We might presume that the events of *Attack of the Cybermen* occur at the end of the War, when the Cybermen face defeat and are planning to evacuate Telos. The Cybermen are not mentioned in *Frontier in Space* (set in 2540), which could be inferred as meaning that the Cyber War has long been over by that time.

Before *Earthshock* was broadcast, *The Programme Guide* placed the Cyber "Wars" (note the plural) as "c.2300" (first edition) and "c.2400" (second edition). "A History of the Cybermen" (*DWM* #83) first suggested that the Cyber War took place immediately after *Earthshock*, post-2526. David Banks' *Cybermen* suggested that the Cyber Wars took place without any involvement with Earth around "2150 AD". *The Terrestrial Index* came to a messy compromise: The "First Cyber Wars" take place "as the twenty-third century began", when Voga is devastated. *Revenge of the Cybermen* takes place at the "tail end of the twenty-fifth century", then Voga's gold is *again* used after *Earthshock* to defeat the Cybermen in "the Second Cyber War".

Novels such as *Killing Ground* make it clear that the Cybermen menaced some early human colony worlds. **713** Dating *Earthshock* (19.6) - The Doctor states that it is "the twenty-sixth century", Adric calculates that it is "2526 in the time scale you call Anno Domini". *The TARDIS Logs* set the story in "2500".

How the Cyber-scanner in *Earthshock* can show a clip from *Revenge of the Cybermen* remains a mystery, and causes problems with the dating of that story. The "real" reason is that the production team wanted to show the Cybermen facing as many previous Doctors as they could and didn't worry too much about continuity (in the same way that the Brigadier's flashback in *Mawdryn Undead* had the Brigadier "remembering" scenes he didn't witness). Equally, the Cyber-scanner doesn't show clips from *Attack of the Cybermen* or *Silver Nemesis*, the latter of which at least should appear.

"A History of the Cybermen" in *DWM* #83 suggested that the Scope tunes into the TARDIS telepathic circuits, which seems a little implausible. One fan, Michael Evans, has suggested that as there is no indication how long before *Attack of the Cybermen* the time machine crashed on Telos, it is perfectly possible that the Cybermen have had it since before *Earthshock* and used it to research their future before using it to alter

The Rise of the Earth Empire

2534 - THE COLONY OF LIES[720] **->** Matter transmitters were abandoned by this time, and there were strict laws on DNA manipulation. The Eurozone still existed. The human colonies were known as the Earth Federation, and were patrolled by Colony Support Vessels. Space was marked with navigation beacons. The term "Earth Empire" was used for the first time this year.

On Axista Four, the human colonists divided into conservative and technological-minded factions: the Loyalists and the Realists. The Realists set up their own settlement away from the Loyalist city of Plymouth Hope, but often raided the Loyalists for supplies.

By now, the Daleks were making gains in the third quadrant. Human space stations and colonies on the front line were evacuated. The Earth Federation had formed an alliance to try to prevent Dalek expansionism. About eighty thousand refugees were scheduled for relocation to Axista Four, and the Earth support vessel *Hannibal* entered orbit around the planet, responding to a signal for help from the Realist faction. The *Hannibal*'s arrival triggered machinery that revived some Tyrenians from stasis, and they threatened to make warfare against the humans.

The second Doctor, accompanied by Jamie and Zoe, both revived Kirann Ransome from suspended animation and defused the conflict. The Realists and Loyalists agreed to accept Kirann as their mutual leader. The Doctor allowed the Federation to believe the Tyrenians were the survivors of a space plague, covering over their true history. Federation Administrator Greene agreed to let the Tyrenians live on Axista Four in peace.

Vega Station was built and secretly run by the Battrulian government. The fourth Doctor visited and lost a lot of money in the Station's casinos.[721] Jodecai Tyler founded a colony on a planet that became known as Tyler's Folly.[722]

c 2535 - MINDGAME / MINDGAME TRILOGY[723] **->** The Sontaran-Rutan war continued on the "outer reaches of the universe". A representative of an advanced race teleported a human female mercenary, the commander of Draconian Brigade Merq (who had served in the Second Cryogenics Wars) and Field Major Sarg of the Sontaran First Assault Battalion into an asteroid located between dimensions, to determine which of their species was worthy of partnering with for conquest. The captives overpowered their abductor and separately departed. Sarg perished in battle, the Draconian was found guilty of sedition and sentenced to banishment to an outer moon of the Draconian Empire, and the mercenary killed herself when her fighter craft was damaged and her oxygen ran out.

Earth had a female president from 2536 to 2541.[724]

In the mid-2530s, KroyChem AgroMedical produced cancer-fighting drugs. Per the First Demographic Charter of 2537, the Spirea Consortia established concentration camps on Darvilleva-Q, and "processed" any colonist with less than 34% human lineage.[725]

The Earth Empire moved to incorporate the four planets of the Domus system, and warred against the human settlers there. Generosum, Perfugium and Salvum capitulated, and while Aequitas kept its independence, the Empire seized its moon, Verum. Decades of guerrilla fighting ensued.[726]

The Sunless - an ashen race of humanoids - lived below

history. This would certainly be a logical course of action. *About Time* suggests that the Cybermen themselves have travelled from the future. For other possible explanations, see David Banks' *Cybermen* (p72, p79-80).
714 *Revenge of the Cybermen*
715 *Original Sin* (p287).
716 *Revenge of the Cybermen*. Stevenson claims that "the Cybermen died out centuries ago", the Doctor replies that "they disappeared after their attack on Voga at the end of the Cyber War".
717 *Real Time*
718 *Benny: Where Angels Fear*
719 *Benny: Down*
720 Dating *The Colony of Lies* (PDA #61) - The book's internal dating is very confused. The back cover says it's 2539, and there's a tombstone (p23) which says that 2535 was "four years ago". Despite this, a native of this timezone says the date is 2534 (p147). Transmats are seen a number of times after this (in, for example, *The Ark in Space*) so it is clear that humanity readopts the

technology.
721 *Demontage*. The fourth Doctor visited "soon after the place opened" (p6).
722 About sixty years before *Benny: Down*.
723 Dating *Mindgame* and *Mindgame Trilogy* (Reeltime Pictures films #4-5) - Date unknown, but it doesn't seem much of a stretch to suggest that the continuity-minded Terrance Dicks was thinking of the era of *Frontier in Space* when he wrote *Mindgame* - in which the Draconian Empire is mentioned, and the Draconian says that "the humans are not our allies". Also, twentieth century culture is topical enough for the mercenary (in *Mindgame Trilogy*) to mention James Dean and River Phoenix.
724 *Benny: Down*, and presumably a reference to the president seen in *Frontier in Space*.
725 *Benny: Down*
726 *Benny: A Life in Pieces*. Perfugium is the setting of *Master*.

ground on a planet with a dying red sun. The Piercy Corporation stole technology from the Sunless homeworld, and relocated some clam-like reproductive units, the Blooms, to the planet Ursu. The Blooms propagated the eight races living there. Meanwhile, the Sunless copied the Piercy spaceships, left their homeworld and subjugated other worlds, searching for the Blooms.[727]

The spaceship *Wayfarer* was rescued from a scrap yard, and retrofitted for use as a naval patrol ship.[728]

The Space War

c 2540 - FRONTIER IN SPACE[729] -> At this point, Earth's "Empire" was still democratic, ruled by an elected President and Senate, although Earth Security forces also had political influence. The Bureau of Population Control strictly enforced the rule that couples could only have one child.

The Arctic areas were reclaimed. New Glasgow and New Montreal were the first of the sealed cities to be opened, and the Family Allowance was increased to two children for those who moved there. The Historical Monuments Preservation Society existed to protect Earth's heritage. While there was a healthy political opposition, any resistance to the principles of government by either anti-colonialists or pacifists was ruthlessly suppressed. Under the Special Security Act, a penal colony was set up on the moon to house thou-

---

727 *Benny; Beyond the Sun.* This is said to occur "before the Galactic War", i.e. the Dalek Wars.

728 Twenty years before *Prisoner of the Daleks*.

729 Dating *Frontier in Space* (10.3) - The story takes place "somewhere in the twenty-sixth century" according to the Doctor. In the first scene, the freighter enters hyperspace at "22.09 72 2540 EST". This is probably nine minutes past ten at night on the 72nd day of 2540, although the President is later seen cancelling a meeting on "the tenth of January". The novelisation (also by Malcolm Hulke) gives the year as "2540", which *The Terrestrial Index* concurred with, although it misunderstood the relationship between Earth and Draconia at this time, suggesting that they are part of "the Alliance" [q.v.]. It isn't made clear whether the human military know of the Daleks before this story.

730 Dating *Planet of the Daleks* (10.4) - The story is set at the same time as *Frontier in Space*. Nevertheless, the American *Doctor Who* comic dated this story as 1300 AD. It is "generations" after *The Daleks*.

731 *Shadowmind* (p61).

732 *Love and War* (p10-11).

733 *Benny: The Summer of Love*

734 *Benny: Down*

735 According to the Doctor in *Death to the Daleks*.

736 "Cold-Blooded War!" The novelisation of *Frontier in Space* was called *The Space War*, and this is occasionally used by fans to refer to the events of both *Frontier in Space* and *Planet of the Daleks*. Presumably *this* battle is "the First Great Space War", not the conflict between Earth and Draconia twenty years earlier.

737 "Fugitive"

738 *Return of the Daleks*

739 BENNY'S BIRTHDAY: It is stated in *Love and War* (p46), in many later books and in the New Adventures Writers' Guide that Benny comes from "the twenty-fifth century". For a while, the writers worked on the assumption that she was from 2450 (e.g.: *The Highest Science* p34, *The Pit* p9). In *Falls the Shadow*, we learn that Benny was born in "2422" (p148). However, Paul Cornell's initial Character Guide had specified that she was born in

"2472", which, as *Love and War* is set the day after Benny's thirtieth birthday, would make it 2502 (in the twenty-*sixth* century).

Causing further complications, *Love and War* is definitely set after *Frontier in Space* [2540]. In subsequent books there was confusion, with some novels claiming that Benny does indeed come from the "twenty-sixth century" (e.g. *Transit* p186; *Blood Heat* p3).

Latterly, so as not to contradict the television series, it has been decided that Benny is definitely from the twenty-sixth century. Benny explained that there are a number of calendars in use in the cosmopolitan galaxy of her time, and in our terms she is "from the late-twenty-sixth century" (*Just War*, p136) - this is intended to explain away some of the contradictions. Paul Cornell and Jim Sangster have astrologically determined Benny's birthday as 21st June, a date that first appeared in *Just War* (p135) and now appears on the Big Finish official biography on their website. Even so, she celebrates on 20th November in *The Dimension Riders*.

The few Benny solo adventures that reference her birth year tend to work from a dating of 2540, or reasonably close to it. She's 22 in *Benny: Old Friends:* "The Ship of Painted Shadows" (set in 2562), and the 2562 component of *Benny: The Sword of Forever.* In *Benny: The Adventure of the Diogenes Damsel*, Benny says that she was born "six hundred forty-seven years" after 1893 - so, again, she was born in 2540. *Benny: The Vampire Curse:* "Predating the Predators", which ends on "Saturday 24 June 2609", goes out of its way to reiterate Benny's birth as 21st June, 2540. (Benny, page 215: "If we go by the calendar and ignore the time-travel, I should be 68. Actually, hell - Wednesday would have been my 69th birthday. I must have been too wrapped up in trivialities like not getting myself killed to notice.") *Benny: Genius Loci* seems to make an honest mistake - the story occurs in 2561, but Benny has a birthday in the midst of it, so she should be 20 when she arrives on Jaiwan, and yet she's already 21 (p6). A bigger disparity is that *Benny: The Wake* (which ends in early 2608) has

sands of political prisoners, each of whom served a life sentence with no possibility of parole or escape. In 2539, Professor Dale, one of the most prominent members of the Peace Party, was arrested and sent to the penal colony on Luna.

Larger colonies such as those in the Sirius system were given Dominion status, and allowed regional autonomy, including powers of taxation and extradition. Governors appointed directly by Earth ruled the smaller worlds.

In 2540, interplanetary tension mounted as human and Draconian spacecraft were subjected to mysterious attacks. Cargos were stolen and ships were destroyed. Each planet blamed the other, and eyewitnesses on both sides claimed to have seen their enemy. On Earth, war with the "Dragons" appeared to be inevitable.

On 12th March, Earth cargo ship C-982 was attacked only minutes from Earth at co-ordinates 8972-6483. The News Services monitored and broadcast their distress calls. Anti-Draconian riots flared up in Peking, Belgrade and Tokio. The Draconian consulate in Helsinki was burnt down, and in Los Angeles the President was burnt in effigy. When the C-982 docked at Spaceport Ten, Security discovered the third Doctor and Jo were onboard. He resisted the mind probe, even on level 12, and was sent to the Lunar Penal Colony. He was convinced that a third party was trying to provoke war, a possibility that no one else had considered. A small ship under the command of General Williams was sent to the Ogron home planet at co-ordinates 3349-6784, where the true masterminds, the Daleks, were revealed.

& 2540 - PLANET OF THE DALEKS[730] -> The third Doctor and Jo tracked the Daleks to the planet Spiridon in the ninth system, many systems from Skaro. Here, a group of six Thals - selected from the six-hundred strong division that hunted Daleks - were already investigating. They had discovered a research station where twelve Daleks were developing germ weapons, and also experimenting with an anti-reflective lightwave that rendered them invisible. The Doctor discovered an army of ten thousand Daleks in neutron-powered suspended animation beneath the research base. Supreme Command sent the Dalek Supreme to oversee the invasion of the Solar Planets, but the Doctor defeated them and froze the Dalek army with a mass of icy liquid from an "ice volcano".

The Doctor was remembered as a mediator between Earth and Draconia.[731] The Draconian Ambassador Ishkavaarr and the Earth President agreed that the planet Heaven should become an open world where both races

would bury their dead. Years later, several interplanetary agreements were signed there by the President and the Draconian Emperor.[732] Irving Braxiatel was one of the signatories to the Treaty of Heaven.[733] The so-called "golden age" of the autolit pulps reached a conclusion in the early 2540s, when the end of the cold war between Earth and its neighbours signalled the demise of humanity's pent-up sexual tensions, as funnelled through characters such as Mr. Misnomer, Rex Havoc and Captain Carnivore.[734]

The Daleks were one of the greatest powers in the universe at this time.[735] At the end of the First Great Space War, Draconia entrusted Earth with documents detailing its history.[736] When word got out that the Ogrons had been defeated by an old man with white hair, the demand for their mercenary services collapsed. The Judoon picked up a lot of their contracts.[737]

The natives of Spiridon sought to conceal their world from further Dalek oppression. In the generations to follow, Spiridon was renamed Zaleria, and the natives made themselves visible by spreading cell-altering chemicals throughout their food supply.[738]

Bernice Surprise Summerfield was born on 21st June, 2540, on the human colony of Beta Caprisis. She was the daughter of Isaac Summerfield, a starship commander in Spacefleet, and his wife Claire.[739]

A war between the Battrul and the lupine Canvine chiefly resulted in a draw, and a buffer zone was created between their territories. Vega Station was built as a casino and hotel, but the Battrulian government secretly used it to monitor the neutral zone.[740] The artist Menlove Stokes was born in 2542, according to official records.[741] Bernadette McAllerson discovered McAllerson's Radiation in 2542.[742] The Bantu Independence Group emerged as a purely commercial body, the Bantu Cooperative, in 2543.[743]

c 2545 - "Fugitive"[744] -> The Last Great Time War had left a power vacuum in the Stellian galaxy, and it now been at war longer than living memory. A ceasefire was being negotiated in secret on Luna IV, and while the Sontarans favoured peace in the region so they could concentrate on their conflict with the Rutans, the Krillitane Empire wanted conflict so it could absorb the strengths of other races.

The Shadow Proclamation brought trumped-up charges of temporal interference against the tenth Doctor (owing to his having saved Emily Winter's life in 1926), as the Shadow Architect hoped that the trail would let the Doctor expose underground elements at work within the Proclamation. A mysterious woman named Advocate served as the Doctor's counsel, and was thought killed by the prosecutor: the Krillitane named Mr. Finch. In truth, her older self had given "Finch" - actually a shapeshifting Gizou in her employ - a device that sent her younger self hurtling through time and space to the Last Great Time

War, fulfilling on her own history. The Doctor was sentenced to life imprisonment on the prison planet Volag Noc, but uncovered the Krillitanes' plot and was allowed to return to 1926. The Advocate returned from the Time War to pursue a secret agenda against the Doctor.

The People of the Worldsphere were covertly involved in wars in their galaxy.[745] In an old curiosity shop on Aminion 2, the Doctor happened upon a catalogue advertising the people of Valhalla City for sale as slaves. The catalogue was located next to a bust of Joanna the Mad, although it wasn't a good likeness, and he initially mistook her for Pliny the Elder.[746]

The Alps were damaged in a local war in 2547.[747] Mind probes were made illegal.[748] The fourth Doctor visited the farming world Unicepter IV.[749]

The Dalek Wars

The Daleks began their third wave of expansion, leading to the Galactic War, a.k.a. the Dalek Wars.[750] Life on the front was harsh, with tens of thousands killed by Dalek Plague on Yalmur alone. Other planets on the front line included Capella, Antonius, Procyon and Garaman (home to a Spacefleet station).

On the other hand, the Core Worlds - the heavily populated and fashionable heart of the Earth Empire - were safe and prosperous. The planet Ellanon was a popular holiday planet; Bacchanalia Two was the home of the Club Outrageous. There were shipyards on Harato, and thriving colonies on Thrapos 3 and Zantir. The Spinward Corporation's financial and administrative centre on Belmos was a space station the size of a planet. Humanity had also discovered Lubellin - "the Mud Planet" - and the

---

Benny telling Peter that she was born "seventy-one years ago" - which, even if she's not counting her upcoming birthday, at best adds up to 2538.

740 The ceasefire was declared "fifty years" before *Demontage* (p4).

741 *The Well-Mannered War* (p272). Stokes is from the 2400s, so the official records must have been altered to due to his relocation to the twenty-sixth century.

742 *Conundrum*

743 *Benny: Another Girl, Another Planet*

744 Dating "Fugitive" (IDW Vol. 1 #3-6) - It is "many centuries" since the time of the 15th Draconian Emperor, and the Draconians and Ogrons in this story date from relatively soon after *Frontier in Space*.

745 A generation or so before *The Also People*.

746 "Two hundred years" after *Valhalla*.

747 *So Vile a Sin* (p211).

748 "Three hundred years" before *Dark Progeny*. They are in use in *Frontier in Space*.

749 "Six or seven years" before "Dreamers of Death".

750 *Death and Diplomacy* (p124). We might infer from other stories that the first wave was in the mid-twenty-second century (seen in *The Dalek Invasion of Earth*) which was targeted on Earth's solar system, and the second led to the Dalek War mentioned in *The Crystal Bucephalus* and *The Colony of Lies*.

THE DALEK WARS: In *Death to the Daleks*, Hamilton states "My father was killed in the last Dalek War", implying there was more than one. We know from other Dalek stories that humanity and the Daleks come into conflict throughout history, starting with *The Dalek Invasion of Earth* [around 2157]. However, there are almost certainly no Dalek Wars affecting Earth directly between *To the Death* and *The Rescue* [c 2190-2493], as Vicki has only heard of the Daleks from history books discussing the Invasion (she doesn't even know what they look like). According to Cory in *Mission to the Unknown*, the Daleks have been inactive as a military

force in Earth's sphere of influence for a millennium before *The Daleks' Master Plan* [between 3000-4000 AD]. In *Planet of the Daleks*, the Doctor uses the term "Dalek War" to describe the events of *The Daleks*, which did not involve humanity.

According to *The Terrestrial Index*, there are a string of Human/Dalek conflicts, the First to Fourth Dalek Wars. The First was the Dalek Invasion of Earth; the Second was fought by "the Alliance" of Humans, Draconians and Thals in the twenty-fifth century; the Third was again fought by the Alliance after the events of *Frontier in Space* and *Planet of the Daleks*; the Fourth was *The Daleks' Master Plan*.

This is a numbering system that is never used on television, and some of the details of Lofficier's account actively contradict what we're told in the stories - at the time he proposes a "Second Dalek War" involving the Thals and Draconians, the Thals don't have advanced space travel and a century later, they think that humans are a myth (*Planet of the Daleks*). The first contact between humanity and the Draconians was in 2520 (in the twenty-*sixth* century), leading to a short war, followed by twenty years of hostility and mutual mistrust (*Frontier in Space*).

The books have established that Dalek Wars took place in Benny's native time. She's born the same year *Frontier in Space* and *Planet of the Daleks* are set [q.v. Benny's birthday]. her father fights in the Dalek wars and her mother is killed in a Dalek attack. What's more, Ace spends three years fighting Daleks in this time period between *Love and War* and *Deceit*. As such, there is a mass of information about the Wars in many of the novels. There's no mention of a lull in the fighting - war presumably breaks out soon after *Frontier in Space*, it carries on into Benny's childhood and apparently into her early adulthood. Humanity is still fighting the Daleks when Benny hits thirty (*Love and War*), but they've defeated the Daleks within three years of that

spotless Tarian Asteroids.

The best whiskey from this time was made in South America, but some people preferred Eridanian Brandy.[751]

In 2545, monitoring systems in the Oort Cloud detected three hundred Dalek battlecruisers headed for Earth's solar system. Mars was equipped with nine hundred photon missiles, but the only person authorised to fire them - Karina Tellassar, Mars' Minister of Defence - failed to do so because the missile-command codes were implanted in the heart of her lover, Isaac Deniken. The Daleks destroyed Mars' seabases with firestorm bombs, then used the planet's three billion inhabitants - mostly pensioners - as a human shield and pelted Earth with bioweapons. The Earth Senate narrowly voted not to retaliate with a nuclear strike, and General Keele launched a successful counter-offensive. A pair of offworlders aided Keele in downing a Dalek saucer at Argyre Dam, and in coordinating the final assault that drove the Daleks from Mars.[752]

Dalek missiles fell on Europe for nearly a month. The retroviruses they contained wouldn't be discovered for almost a decade. During the war, Nike supplied footwear to Earth soldiers, and Coca-Cola returned to using cocaine in its products. The British Parliament was destroyed and replaced by the Republic Museum of Social and Political History. The whole of London became a museum. The Thames was detoxed and stocked with genetically pure species from the Pacific Ocean. Inverness was replaced by a deep-water trench connecting Loch Ness to the Moray Firth. Paris became populated with human-alien hybrids.[753]

The Earth military captured a borogove of budding Mim children, and initiated Project Narcissus to condition the shapeshifting offspring to infiltrate the enemy's ranks.

Thousands of Mim offspring died, but their actions altered the course of the war in humanity's favour.[754]

The works of romance novelist Jilly Cooper were lost in the Dalek Wars.[755]

c 2545 - BENNY: BURIED TREASURES: "Closure"[756]

-> On the planet Panyos, an Ashcarzi soldier murdered a woman named Isabella. Her son - Ulrich Hescarti - would grow up to avenge his mother's death by instigating an ethnic cleansing programme against the Ashcarzi. Benny used her time ring to travel back and kill Isabella's would-be murderer, then made Isabella promise that she would either raise Ulrich properly or, failing that, kill him.

c 2547 - RETURN OF THE LIVING DAD[757]

-> The Daleks' tactics were repetitive and predictable. Earth's Spacefleet used vast Dalekbuster ships, highly-automated and heavily-armed six-man fighters. Isaac Summerfield captained one such ship. Albinex the Navarino contacted the Daleks and offered to change history in return for military assistance. The seventh Doctor and Benny arrived on Isaac Summerfield's ship, the *Tisiphone*, which was fighting the Daleks over Bellatrix. The *Tisiphone* interrupted Albinex's negotiations with the Daleks, and both the *Tisiphone* and Albinex ended up falling down a wormhole to the twentieth century.

The Dalekbuster commanded by Isaac Summerfield was reported to have broken formation and fled during a space battle, and its captain was branded a coward. In late 2547, at the height of the Dalek War, the Daleks attacked the human colony on Vandor Prime in the Gamma Delphinus

---

(*Deceit*). Nevertheless, according to *Lucifer Rising*, there are two distinct Dalek Wars at this time - Benny's father fought in the Second Dalek War (p65), whereas Ace fought in the Third (p309), so there must be a short-lived cessation of hostilities (which would seem to be at some point in the 2560s, when Benny is in her twenties).

A lengthy essay at the end of *Deceit* has the Dalek War starting after *Frontier in Space* and Ace fighting in the Second Dalek War.

Some stories (for example, *The Crystal Bucephalus*) stick to Lofficier's scheme.

So... the term "Second Dalek War" is used to refer to two or possibly even three different conflicts in both the twenty-fifth and twenty-sixth centuries (and this is further complicated because of the early confusion over which century Benny was born in). For the sake of clarity, references to the numbering of the Dalek Wars have been left out of the timeline itself; where they are given in a story, it's been footnoted.

Within the fiction, it's fairly easy to rationalise the discrepancy: these are the naming conventions of his-

torians, and different historians will have different perspectives on the various conflicts and labels for them.

751 *Deceit*

752 *Benny: Beige Planet Mars*. The "offworlders" are the apocryphal forty-second Doctor (as "played" by Ian Richardson) and his companion, Iphigenia "Iffy" Birmingham. Both feature in 90s fan-fic stories by Lance Parkin and Mark Clapham.

753 *Benny: The Sword of Forever*

754 *Benny: Nobody's Children*

755 *Benny: The Diet of Worms*

756 Dating *Benny: Buried Treasures*: "Closure" (Benny audio #1.5b) - It's "fifty years" before the "modern-day" component of "Closure". It's not said whether Benny's actions actually change history or not.

757 Dating *Return of the Living Dad* (NA #53) - This happens "forty" years before 2587 (p7), Benny would have been "seven" at the time (p12). Although the date is given as "2543" (p29), there is some confusion over Benny's birthday in the NAs, and this is a victim of that. This is "the height of the Second Dalek War" (q.v. The Dalek Wars).

system, where Claire Summerfield was killed. Bernice Summerfield was sent to military boarding school.[758] Benny's doll Rebecca was with Benny's mother when she was exterminated.[759]

c 2550 - "Pureblood"[760] -> The Dalek War continued to rage, but elsewhere in the galaxy, the conflict between the Rutans and Sontarans reached a critical point. The Rutans had already razed the community structures between the Warburg and the Prok Fral Edifice. Now, they destroyed Sontara, the Sontaran homeworld, with photonic bombs. The Sontarans got their Racepool away in time, and headed towards Pandora.

The seventh Doctor and Benny arrived on the Pandora Spindle in the Terran Federation. This was a distant space station run by the Lauren Corporation - the biggest industrial giant in the galaxy - and the home of a genetics facility. The Sontarans occupied the station, and a Rutan agent informed their enemies that the Racepool was there. The Sontarans' genetic expert was killed in an accident and the Doctor agreed to help save the Sontarans from extinction. He also exposed the spy, Modine.

The Sontarans had been betrayed to the Rutans on Sontara... by pureblood Sontarans who were untouched by cloning and genetic engineering, and hailed from a distant colony that the Rutans discovered. The pureblood Sontarans attacked Pandora, but the Doctor and Benny showed how the Rutans had tricked them into destroying their own kind. The two factions of Sontarans united and settled on Pandora to rebuild their race. In return, the Sontarans agreed to erase all knowledge of the human race from their databanks.

The Sontarans' survival would prevent the Rutans from overrunning the galaxy, and Sontaran advances in space drive, vaccines and genetic solutions to disease would be of great benefit to the future.

c 2550 - "Dreamers of Death"[761] -> For three years, the colonists of Unicepter IV enjoyed sharing adventure dreams. These were courtesy of the company Dreams Deluxe, who made the dream possible by harnessing the telepathic powers of a native creature: the small furry Slinth. The fourth Doctor, Sharon and K9 arrived just as one team of dreamers died in an accident. The Doctor and Sharon took part in a dream led by a man called Vernor, where they were attacked by the dead dreamers and an army of monsters. K9 severed the connection before they were killed, but the Slinths had become aggressive, fed off all the colonists' negative emotions, and fused into a single devil-like creature. The Slinths were absorbing electricity, so the Doctor doused them in water, collapsing the devil creature into a pile of harmless Slinths. Sharon elected to stay behind with Vernor.

The Doctor was later invited to Sharon's wedding.[762]

Abslom Daak... Dalek Killer!

Hardened criminals on Earth were given the choice of facing the death penalty or becoming Dalek Killers (DKs). The most notorious of the DKs was Abslom Daak.[763]

Daak's beloved, Selene, had run off with his business partner Vol Mercurius after defrauding four billion from a shipping company. Consequently, Daak cut off Mercurius' hand with his chainsword. Mercurius bought the planet Dispater, but Selene left him.[764]

c 2550 - "Abslom Daak... Dalek-Killer"[765] -> Rather than be vaporised, a serious criminal could choose "Exile D-K". He would be teleported to a world in the Dalek Empire, and made to kill as many of Daleks as possible before he was exterminated. The life expectancy of such DKs was two hours, thirty-two minutes and twenty-three

---

758 A number of references to Benny Summerfield's early life appeared in the New Adventures, and these were not always consistent. In *Love and War* (p75), Benny's birthplace is identified as "Beta Caprisis. Earth colony" - supporting that, in *Benny: The Wake*, Benny points at a star and tells Peter, "That's Beta Caprisis... that's where your mummy was born." But, in *Sanctuary*, Benny recalls that her mother was killed on a raid on "Vandor Prime, in the Gamma Delphinus system" (p185). We might speculate that she was born on the former and moved to the latter. As pointed out in *Set Piece* (p132), there is some confusion about the exact sequence of events during the raid that killed Benny's mother. Accounts also vary as to whether Benny's father disappeared before or after her mother's death. Benny was only seven when all this happened, so she is almost certainly misremembering some details or

blocking out some of her unpleasant memories.
759 "Emperor of the Daleks"
760 Dating "Pureblood" (*DWM* #193-196) - It's "the twenty-sixth century" in part one, but "the twenty-fifth" in part two. It seems to be around Benny's native time, as she's heard of the Lauren Corporation. The Second Dalek War is mentioned, but that's not as helpful a reference as one might think (q.v. "The Dalek Wars"). The Doctor says the Sontarans will not be a threat to Earth again until *The Sontaran Experiment* (which, as far as we know, they aren't). *Sontarans: Conduct Unbecoming* names Sontar as the Sontaran homeworld (perhaps it was founded after Sontara's destruction).
761 Dating "Dreamers of Death" (*DWM* #47-48) - The year isn't specified in the story, but there's a reference to Unicepter dream machines being "recently banned" in the *Abslom Daak - Dalek Killer* collected edition, plac-

seconds. Only one man in four survived the matter transmitter, and the overall odds of survival were six hundred million to one.

At this time, Curtis Fooble was accused of eating the Vegan ambassador. Humans had advanced humanoid robots, which operated machines and even sat as judges. Mazam was a human colony, with a monarchy as well as skysleds and space yachts. Dalek base ships were operated by a Command Dalek, wired into the ship's systems. The Daleks used Omega Units - advanced fighter/bombers - as well as hoverbouts.

The sociopath Abslom Daak was convicted of twenty-three charges of murder, pillage, piracy and massacre. He had been driven to such crimes by the loss of his beloved Selene, and chose Exile D-K. He was beamed to the feudal planet Mazam, located a thousand light years from Earth, where Princess Taiyin had just surrendered to the Daleks. Daak rescued her, and together they took on the Daleks' base ship. They destroyed it, but Taiyin was killed. Grieving for Taiyin's death, Daak vowed "I'm gonna kill every damned stinking Dalek in the galaxy!"

c 2550 - "Star Tigers"[766] **->** "The Frontier War with Earth had been fought and settled", and Draconia was now at peace. However, Dalek expansion towards Girodun threatened Draconian trade routes. Factions within the Draconian court wanted to strengthen their defences, but the prevailing wisdom was that the Daleks wouldn't fight a war on two fronts, and they should be negotiated with.

Three Dalek ships entered Draconian space while pursuing Abslom Daak, but he destroyed them before landing on Draconia. Daak was looked after by Prince Salander, and revealled that he had put Taiyin in cryogenic suspen-

sion. Salander's political rivals took the opportunity to have him arrested, and Daak shared his house arrest. Salander's family built warships, and he showed Daak a prototype frontier defence cruiser built to fight Daleks. Daak christened this the *Kill-Wagon*. Salander was told that a Dalek patrol had killed his son, and he decided to leave Draconia in the *Kill-Wagon* with Daak. They resolved to assemble a crew.

They went to the planet Paradise - a cosmopolitan planet where every pleasure was available for a price - and recruited the Ice Warrior Harma. They then headed to the war-torn planet of Dispater, where Vol Mercurius was playing a parachess tactics game with a robot companion that mirrored the real-life conflict. Mercurius owned the planet, but the Kill-Mechs of a self-proclaimed Emperor of the Jarith Cluster had invaded it. Mercurius agreed to join the *Kill-Wagon* crew. As they left Dispater, they discovered an army of Dalek Space Commando Units, ready to invade the Jarith Cluster while the inhabitants were divided. The *Kill-Wagon* let the Daleks invade, then wiped them out by dropping nuclear bombs into a nearby volcano.

At this time, Draconia was home to an animal somehow like a tiger, called a Thorion. The currency of Draconia was the "crystal", while bribes were in diamonds. Vorkelites enjoyed being executed. Rigellians had four tentacles, three mouths and a reputation for being untrustworthy.

c 2550 - "Nemesis of the Daleks"[767] **->** The *Kill-Wagon* launched an attack on the Dalek base on the planet Hell, but was shot down. The Emperor was there to supervise construction of the Daleks' vast battlestation, the Death Wheel. The seventh Doctor discovered the bodies of Salander, Vol Mercurius and Harma. He was cornered by

ing the story around then. The settlers on Unicepter IV are "human". Their technology is not terribly advanced - they have hover cars and energy weapons, thinking projectile weapons are "old fashioned".

762 "Star Beast II"

763 Abslom Daak first appeared in Marvel's *Doctor Who Weekly* #17, and has returned a number of times since. He was mentioned in *Love and War* (p46-47 - we also meet Maire, another DK, in that novel), before appearing in the (cloned) flesh in *Deceit*.

764 Before "Abslom Daak... Dalek Killer". Details are given in "Star Tigers".

765 Dating "Abslom Daak... Dalek Killer" (*DWW* #17-20) - It's "the twenty-sixth century"; humanity is at war with the Daleks. The sequel, "Star Tigers", establishes that it is shortly after a "frontier war" between the Draconians and Earth, a clear reference to *Frontier in Space*.

The matter transmitter between star systems is something humanity is still trying to perfect by the year 4000 and *The Daleks' Master Plan*. We learn about

Vol Mercurius in "Star Tigers".

766 Dating "Star Tigers" (*DWW* #27-30, *DWM* #44-46) - It's within three months of "Abslom Daak... Dalek Killer"; Salander says Mazam was conquered "within the last three months". "The Emperor does not want another war... not so soon after fighting the humans."

767 Dating "Nemesis of the Daleks" (*DWM* #152-155) - It's "the twenty-sixth century". Clearly, this takes place after "Star Tigers", but there's no indication of how much time has passed. The Emperor resembles the one from the comic strips (see The Dalek Emperors sidebar), and may well be killed in Daak's final attack because he's on the Death Wheel when it explodes. If so, it's tempting to imagine that the Emperor's death was the turning point in the war referred to as "years ago" in *Deceit* (which also says Daak's death here was "years ago").

There's no indication that these Daleks are time travellers. At first the Doctor assumes the Emperor is Davros, but the Dalek Emperor replies "Davros? Who is Davros?". *Terror Firma* has Davros losing his mind and

the Daleks, but rescued by Daak.

The Doctor learned that Hell was the source of Helkogen, a poison gas. He and Daak boarded the Death Wheel, where the Doctor confronted the Emperor and Daak learned the Daleks were building a Genocide Device - a gas weapon that threatened every known planet. Daak prevented the Doctor from sacrificing himself to destroy the Death Wheel's central reactor, and the Doctor escaped as Daak died to destroy the Death Wheel.

c 2550 - "Emperor of the Daleks"[768] -> Abslom Daak was transmatted away from certain death and returned to what he thought was Earth. There he was told to kill the Doctor - and in return, Taiyin would be resurrected.

The seventh Doctor and Benny arrived on Hell and met up with the remaining Star Tigers, who weren't dead after all, as the Helkans had revived them. Within moments, though, Daak grabbed the Doctor and they were all transmatted to Daak's masters... but the Doctor realised they were Dalek robots, and that this was a trap. They were on Skaro, in the future, at the mercy of the Emperor.

Returning from the future, the Star Tigers drank at a bar on Paradise. Daak's fixation with Taiyin had ended... he was now obsessed with Benny instead. The seventh Doctor met his previous self, and thanked him for his help setting a trap for the Daleks.

History recorded that Abslom Daak died destroying the Dalek Death Wheel.[769] On Kastropheria, a group of priests used the drug skar to boost their psionic abilities and mentally restrain the people's self-destructive impulses. Humans established a colony on the planet, but the natives became aggressive when supplies of skar began to run out.[770] The Class G maintenance robot entered service.[771]

c 2550 - CATASTROPHEA[772] -> The third Doctor and Jo discovered the human colonists on Kastopheria had enslaved the natives, and the Doctor was mistaken for El Llama, a prophesied revolutionary. The priests asked the Doctor to destroy the Anima, a giant skar crystal, with great care to free the people from their mind-lock. The Anima was destroyed too suddenly, and the people's destructive rage returned. War loomed between the natives and the colonists, but the Doctor helped to forge a non-interference treaty. The Draconians aided the colonists in evacuating, and the natives were left in peace.

The war criminal Karina Tellassar was now in hiding as "Elizabeth Trinity", an academic. In 2555, Trinity published A History of Mars, which argued that humanity had been noble in freeing the Martians from their backward ways. The generation to come would consider both sides of the argument.[773]

Benny, age 16, went AWOL from her military academy and hid out in the woods nearby, giving advice to other girls living there.[774] A military recruit named Simon Kyle, age 18, had established a shelter in the woods - he became Benny's best friend and first lover. When the military captured them, Benny refused to testify against Kyle, but he traded his journal of their activities for a reduced punishment. The military took Benny off frontline service and made her a private; en route to Capella, she jumped ship and arrived on a colony world. She started working with the archaeological unit there, faking her qualifications. Kyle went on to become Spacefleet officer.[775] Kyle later claimed that his bargain had prevented the officers involved from killing Benny, and that he'd never actually surrendered the journal.[776]

c 2560 - PRISONER OF THE DALEKS[777] -> The tenth Doctor became trapped within the disused refinery Lodestar Station 479 on Hurala, on the edge of Earth space. He was rescued by Dalek hunters led by ex-military man Jon Bowman, who were crewing the Wayfarer and received a fee from Earth Command for every Dalek eyestalk they netted. The Doctor was startled to realise that he

mutating into an Emperor Dalek, but ultimately it seems as if he and *this* Emperor are not one and the same. The Daleks also (apparently) probe the seventh Doctor's mind, identify him and see images of the Doctor's previous six incarnations.
768 Dating "Emperor of the Daleks" (*DWM* #197-202) - This takes place shortly after "Nemesis of the Daleks". It's specified that Daak is "lured across space and time" - the sequence on Skaro takes place between *Revelation of the Daleks* and *Remembrance of the Daleks* (4625, according to this chronology), and accounts for Davros' (physical, not mental) transformation into the Emperor Dalek, as seen in *Remembrance*.
769 According to *Deceit*, which was published between "Nemesis of the Daleks" (where Daak died) and "Emperor of the Daleks" (where it turned out he hadn't).

Presumably, either Daak evades the authorities, or they hush up his activities.
770 "Five years" before *Catastrophea*.
771 "Four decades" before *Cold Fusion*.
772 Dating *Catastrophea* (PDA #11) - It is "five or six hundred years" after Jo's time (p79).
773 *Benny: Beige Planet Mars*
774 *Love and War*
775 *Love and War, Return of the Living Dad*
776 *Benny: Old Friends*
777 Dating *Prisoner of the Daleks* (NSA #33) - This is stated to be in the middle of the first Earth Empire's war with the Daleks, at a point where "the Daleks are advancing, their empire constantly expanding into Earth's space" and young men can't remember a time they weren't at war. Bowman is a veteran of the

THE DALEK EMPERORS: Over the course of *Doctor Who* we see four different designs for the Dalek Emperor. We can be confident that this isn't always the same individual and, even allowing for the ability of the Daleks as a species and individually to survive what looks like certain death, can reasonably conclude that there are at least three bearers of the title.

• The "Golden Emperor" - *The Dalek Chronicles* comic strip introduced a gold Emperor with an oversized, spherical head, and he also appeared in the Dalek books of the sixties - he was the central character of the strip and we learn a great deal about him. He's never referred to as the "Golden Emperor" in the strip, but was in some supporting material, such as the game "The Race to the Golden Emperor" in *Terry Nation's Dalek Annual 1979*.

The character was introduced to new audiences by reprints in the seventies *Dalek Annuals* and *Doctor Who Weekly* reprints early in the eighties, and *DWM* used the same design in two original comic strips: "Nemesis of the Daleks" (set in the twenty-sixth century) and "Emperor of the Daleks" (set after *Revelation of the Daleks*). It's unclear if this is meant to be the same individual, and the Emperor is apparently killed at the end of both stories.

• The "Evil Emperor" - In *The Evil of the Daleks*, the Dalek Emperor is a vast, immobile Dalek based in a chamber in Dalek City. This design reappears in the stageplay *The Ultimate Adventure*, the *Dalek Empire* stories and *The Dalek Factor*. This Emperor is apparently killed at the end of *The Evil of the Daleks*, although he's not *quite* dead the last time we see him in that story (and this chronology places *Dalek Empire* significantly after *The Evil of the Daleks*).

Some commentators (Lofficier and *About Time* included) have speculated that this is Davros, although dialogue in *The Evil of the Daleks* seems to rule that out by stating it's the first time either the Doctor or the Emperor has met the other.

A more open question is whether this is the same individual as the Golden Emperor. The story "Secret of the Emperor" in *The Dalek Outer Space Book* depicts the Golden Emperor being rebuilt as an immobile Emperor based on Skaro. The design is not the same as seen in *The Evil of the Daleks*, but it's clearly the same concept.

In John Peel's books - the novelisations *The Chase*, *The Daleks' Master Plan*, *The Power of the Daleks*, *The Evil of the Daleks* and his original novels *War of the Daleks* and *Legacy of the Daleks* - the Daleks are led by the Dalek Prime. This is the same individual Dalek who makes the speech about the Daleks becoming the supreme beings of the universe at the end of *Genesis of the Daleks*. In Peel's version, he becomes the Daleks' leader, and in *War of the Daleks,* the description of his casing closely matches that of the Golden Emperor. *War of the Daleks* and the novelisation of *The Evil of the*

Daleks have the Dalek Prime and Emperor respectively as the last survivor of the original batch of Daleks - the same individual, in other words. This is the Golden Emperor who becomes the Evil Emperor, tweaked to fit the origin of the race seen in *Genesis of the Daleks*, as opposed to the one in *The Dalek Chronicles*. The real-life creator of the Daleks, Terry Nation, is said to have preferred the idea that the Daleks were rule by a Council rather than an Emperor, and the Dalek Prime fits that, too.

In *The Evil of the Daleks*, the Doctor meets the Emperor for the first time and the implication is that it's the first time the Emperor has met the Doctor, too. The only story to contradict that is "Nemesis of the Daleks", which is set in the twenty-sixth century (there's no date given for the Skaro sequence of *The Evil of the Daleks*, but no fan chronology has ever put it before this time) and has the Emperor meeting the seventh Doctor and using a mind probe to visualize all six of his previous incarnations.

On balance, the Golden Emperor and Evil Emperor would seem to be the same individual, the last survivor of the first batch of Daleks (as seen in *Genesis of the Daleks* or, if you prefer, *The Dalek Chronicles*), who leads them for most of their recorded history.

The Emperor we see in the *Dalek Empire* audio series resembles the Evil Emperor, but is this the same individual? There's no way of knowing conclusively, but it could well be. That Emperor dies at the end of that series, in a manner that goes out of its way to leave virtually no possibility he survived.

• "Emperor Davros" - At the end of *Revelation of the Daleks*, Davros is taken to Skaro to face trial by the Supreme Dalek, a role he wants for himself. In the next television story, *Remembrance of the Daleks*, Davros is Emperor and has a casing based on that of the Golden Emperor - although it is cream and gold, with a hexagonal patch instead of an eyestalk, and has no sucker or gun. How he comes to be Emperor has been depicted three times... the *DWM* strip "Emperor of the Daleks" shows the Golden Emperor being killed and Davros becoming Emperor. The book *War of the Daleks* says Davros never really had power, he was tricked by the Daleks into thinking he did. The audio *Terror Firma* has Davros undergoing a full mutation (physical and mental) to become a Dalek Emperor. (A fourth might exist in the DVD extra *The Davros Mission*, which has Davros bringing the Daleks on Skaro to heel, although the events to follow aren't specified.) *The Stolen Earth/ Journey's End* say that Davros was lost early in the Time War, but not that he was Emperor at the time.

• "The Last Emperor" - *The Parting of the Ways* introduces a new Emperor: a vast and apparently immobile structure containing a vast Dalek mutant. This is clearly

continued on page 519...

had gone back to a point in Dalek history before their race's involvement in the Last Great Time War.

Thousands of human colonists on Auros evacuated their world, and destroyed it using the Osterhagen Principle - a series of nuclear devices buried within the planet. The Doctor and his allies learned that the Daleks were based on Arkheon, a planet believed destroyed forty years before, because they hoped to use the Arkheon Threshold - a schism in time and space - to become the masters of time, perhaps even wiping humanity from history. The Doctor and Bowman were interrogated by the Daleks' Inquisitor General, the feared Dalek X, who arrived with a Dalek fleet led by an *Exterminator*-class warship. This was the first of its kind, with ten antigravity impeller engines and a crew of five hundred Daleks. The *Wayfarer* was destroyed, but the Doctor escaped, setting off an astrionic explosion that obliterated the Dalek base and fleet. Hurala became a radioactive world, with a communications seal that would last for five thousand years. Dalek X survived in the ruins, vowing revenge.

A Supreme Dalek led the Daleks on Skaro. Koral - one of the *Wayfarer* crew - believed herself to be sole survivor of Red Sky Lost, a planet the Daleks had destroyed. Her crewmate, Cuttin' Edge, had grown up on Gauda Prime.

The Draconian vessel *Hunter* and five destroyers were lost fighting Daleks. Female officers had recently been introduced to the Draconian military.[778]

The People of the Worldsphere fought a war against the Great Hive Mind, using new weapons and powerful sentient Very Aggressive Ships. The war saw twenty-six billion killed, destroyed fifteen planets and devastated dozens of others. The Great Hive Mind became part of the People.[779]

Corporations such as Ellerycorp, Peggcorp, Spinward, and IMC maintained battlefleets of their own. During the Battle of Alpha Centauri, a small squadron of Silurian vessels beat back the main Dalek force, which fled into hyperspace. Daleks also infiltrated human Puterspace.[780]

TAM Corporation's ships fought in the Galactic Wars. The corporation pulled out of remote colonies like Mendeb, taking as much high technology as it could.[781]

As often happened in wartime, the Dalek War saw a leap in human technological progress. A variety of intelligent weapons systems were developed: dart guns, data corrupting missiles, spikes, clusters and forceshells, random field devices, self-locating mines and drones.

Earth's Spacefleet included 1000-man troopships armed with torpedoes that could destroy a Dalek Battlesaucer. A fleet of warp vessels - X-Ships - were used to ferry communications, personnel and supplies. Most troopers were placed in Deep Sleep while travelling to the warzones. This was done to conserve supplies, not because the ships were particularly slow, as it now only took a matter of weeks to cross human space. Ships still used warp engines, but they also used ion drive to travel in real space.

Computer technology was now extremely advanced. The Spacefleet Datanet was a vast information resource, and data was stored on logic crystals. Nanotechnology was beginning to have medical applications: a nanosurgical virus was given to most troopers to protect against various alien infections, and cosmetic nanosurgery beautified the richest civilians. Holograms were now in widespread use for communications, display, entertainment, combat and public relations. Holosynths - simulations of people - acted as receptionists and could answer simple enquiries. HKI Industries, based on Phobos, specialised in the manufac-

---

Draconian conflicts. The Osterhagen Principle (almost certainly derived from the Osterhagen Key from *Journey's End*) was invented on Earth "over five hundred years ago". Gauda Prime is the planet in the *Blake's 7* series finale, where Avon and his crew make their last stand. Conflicting all of this evidence, however, one of the *Wayfarer* crew says that Morse Code (developed in 1836 by Samuel F.B. Morse) came about "thousands of years ago". The Daleks are bronze, like the new series Daleks (Dalek X is black and gold).

778 *War of the Daleks*. No date is given, but it's while the Draconian Empire is at war with the Daleks. Female officers are anathema again by *The Dark Path*.

779 "Thirty years" before *The Also People*. *Benny: Down* and *Benny: Walking to Babylon* have further details.

780 *Love and War* (p5, p64).

781 This was "during the wars" (*Independence Day*, p22).

782 *Deceit*

783 Dating *Enemy of the Daleks* (BF #121) - The story occurs during the Dalek Wars, after the Daleks - accord-

ing to Lt. Beth Stokes - have spent "years" overrunning colony planets, either killing or enslaving the populaces. Ace has a familiarity with the weaponry and military practices of this era (so much so, she knows the make-up of a Valkyrie unit when asked), perhaps owing to the Spacefleet training she gained 2570-2573 (see *Love and War* and *Deceit*). As the conflict with the Daleks goes into decline in the late 2560s but is here running strong, it's probably earlier than Ace's Spacefleet tenure. Bliss is referred to both as a planet and a planetoid.

784 Dating *Benny: Genius Loci* (Benny BF novel #8) - Benny spends most of 2561 on Jaiwan - some months at the very least pass before her birthday, which is 21st June - and she leaves the planet on 1st January, 2562 (p205). Cray might be the world seen in *The Game*.

785 Dating *Benny: Old Friends*: "The Ship of Painted Shadows" (Benny collection #9b) - The blurb says that it's "late 2562" and that Benny is 22. In Benny's lifetime, these events are specified as taking place after *Benny: Genius Loci*.

ture of transmats. These had a range of only a couple of thousand kilometres, but they were installed on all large ships and linked major cities on most colony worlds. Hoverspeeders were still in use.

By the late 2560s, it became clear that Earth was going to win the wars with the Daleks. By then, the fastline - a state of the art, almost real-time, interstellar communication system - had been developed.[782]

c 2560 - ENEMY OF THE DALEKS[783] **->** During the Dalek Wars, the planet Bliss was a sanctuary for rare flora and fauna. Professor Toshio Shimura, a scientist at a biological research facility there, took DNA from "piranha locusts" native to Bliss and gestated it in human beings without their consent. The subjects formed cocoons and emerged as the Kisibyaa: ferocious, metal-eating creatures that Shimura hoped would literally consume the Daleks. Shimura gave his own life to host Kisibyaa larvae. The seventh Doctor, Ace and Hex witnessed these events, and the Doctor - fearing the Kisibyaa would threaten all species, not just the Daleks - killed the Kisibyaa by destroying the facility.

At this time, Valkyrie units - composed of one commissioned officer and twenty troopers - were all-female fighting forces commissioned to engage the Daleks.

The Early Career of Bernice Summerfield

2561 to 2562 (1st January) - BENNY: GENIUS LOCI[784] **->** Benny's faked resume netted her the position of assistant field director at a dig on Jaiwan. Professor Mariela Ankola served as Benny's mentor, but died in her sleep after encountering lethal industrial toxins on the planet Cray. Benny adopted Ankola's habit of keeping journals. A non-sapient Jaiwan spider bit off Benny's foot, and she had a grown one attached on her birthday.

Owing to Benny's excavations, some Omega spiders were awakened from hibernation. This threatened to activate the Hibernation Clause of the Protocols of Colonisation, but the Omega spiders struck a clandestine deal with the Jaiwan authorities - the Omegas would share the planet in exchange for help in wiping out any remaining caches of Alpha spiders.

Benny and her allies - including members of Spacefleet's First Regiment of Combat Archaeologists, and the revived Pinky and Perky AIs - awakened some Alpha spiders to present their case. In doing so, Benny killed someone for the first time - she shot a local reporter and patriot, Lola, when she threatened to kill Benny's protégé, Shawnee.

No later than 1st January, 2562, Benny left Jaiwan

...continued from page 517

not Davros, and he's killed at the end of the story. Is this the Golden Emperor in another new casing? If it is, he's grown - it's no exaggeration to say that the mutant we see wouldn't fit in the Golden Emperor's casing.

There are at least two Emperors, then - a Dalek mutant and Davros. If we accept at face value the death of the Emperor in *The Evil of the Daleks*, we can say that there are at least three individuals. *Dalek Empire* would seem to make that four.

The maximum number of Emperors is harder to determine. The first panel we see the Golden Emperor's new casing in "Genesis of Evil", a caption informs us this is "the first Dalek Emperor", implying there would eventually be more than one, although there's little doubt the Emperor remains the same individual throughout *The Dalek Chronicles*. Russell T Davies' *Doctor Who Annual* essay refers to "puppet Emperors" of the Daleks. *The Dalek Factor* has an Emperor whose description matches the Evil Emperor, described as "an Emperor", which may mean there was more than one at that time.

We might infer that there were many Emperors. *The Dalek Chronicles* ends with the Emperor planning an attack on Earth. The stageplay *The Curse of the Daleks* is set in what could be the aftermath, and the Black Dalek rules Skaro following a Dalek defeat. So the Golden Emperor may have been killed. The Moroks raid Skaro and take a Dalek as a trophy according to *The Space Museum*. Could they have killed an Emperor as part of that conquest? An Emperor dies in *The Evil of the Daleks*, "Nemesis of the Daleks","Emperor of the Daleks", *The Parting of the Ways* and *Dalek Empire*. That would be seven Emperors that we know of.

aboard the *Goodnight Dolly*. A grateful archaeologist provided her with a certificate naming her as a Master of Science, Archaeology, accredited to the Department of History, University of Jaiwan at Kondeeo. On 2nd February, 2562, Benny travelled toward humanity's core worlds aboard the *Chin Shen Mo*. Papers provided by General Elsa Lafayette, a friend of Benny's parents, helped Benny avoid being incarcerated for desertion.

2562 - BENNY: OLD FRIENDS:"The Ship of Painted Shadows"[785] **->** Benny departed for Earth aboard the *Prince of Mercury* liner, and joined the New Gondwana Ladies' Choir to pay for her passage. The group was otherwise composed of the wives of Hanekawa Goro, a.k.a. Michio Dankizo XXVIII - a Kabuki performer who was being influenced by shadow beings that were entertained by tragedy. The shadow beings slaughtered many innocents, prompting Goro to commit suicide. Benny escaped as the *Prince of Mercury* disappeared into a spatial rift.

A demi-lemur, Ivo FitzIndri, had committed murder to

save Benny's life - he asked that she go to a temple of the Order of Lost Lemuroidea and tell her story. Benny planned on doing so, but was diverted upon receiving a clue as to her father's whereabouts. FitzIndri was consequently excommunicated and spent the next fifty years looking for her.

2562 - BENNY: THE SWORD OF FOREVER[786] **->** By now, retroviruses released during the Dalek Wars had spread across 40% of Earth, and infested 68% of terrestrial DNA. Most of the retroviruses were harmless, producing physical changes in a small amount of those infected. The Rhone Valley, however, saw evolution run wild, and produced a thousand species of hybrid terrestrial-alien strains of planet, animal and human life.

Benny attempted to find the finger of John the Baptist as a means of securing herself an easy fellowship and to qualify for a doctorate. She located the Castle of Arginy, but her lover, Daniel Beaujeu, seemingly drowned while trying to overcome the traps within. He actually survived, was mutated by retrovirus, forgave Benny her mistakes and enjoyed a relatively happy life in Paris.

At some point, Benny went to Stuttgart.[787] She visited Mars when she was 24. She was now in love with a man named Tim.[788] She made her reputation as an archaeologist during excavations of the Fields of Death, the tombs of the rulers of Mars in 2565.[789] She went on to investigate the Dyson Sphere of the Varteq Veil.[790] In Benny's time, humans had eradicated most of the previously common illnesses.[791]

2565 - BENNY: THE VAMPIRE CURSE: "The Badblood Diaries"[792] **->** The vampire-stricken Badblood had orbiting human settlements that moved to remain in continual daylight, and occasionally intersected for major celebrations. The Kikan corporation, run by psi-powered yakuza who went straight, coveted Badblood's

786 Dating *Benny: The Sword of Forever* (Benny NA #14) - The year is given on page 10; Benny is said to be 22 (p13). Page 19 cites that Daniel died in 2560, but this appears to be a typo. *Deceit* (p103) says that Benny didn't visit Earth for fifteen years before meeting the Doctor, but that claim contradicts *Benny: The Sword of Forever* and *Lucifer Rising* (p171).
787 *Just War* (p137)
788 *Benny: Beige Planet Mars*, following the lead of *Lucifer Rising* (p171).
789 *The Dying Days*, again elaborating on *Lucifer Rising* (p171).
790 *The Also People*
791 *Return of the Living Dad* (p51).
792 Dating *Benny: The Vampire Curse*: "The Badblood Diaries" (Benny collection #12a) - The year is cited at the top of every chapter.
793 Dating *Benny: The Vampire Curse*: "Possum Kingdom" (Benny collection #12b) - The year is given.
794 *Deceit*
795 Dating *Love and War* (NA #9) - The dating of this novel causes a number of problems as it features the debut of Bernice Summerfield. It is the "twenty-fifth century" (p46), and "five centuries" since Ace's time (p26). The novel clearly takes place after *Frontier in Space* (see p10-11 of *Love and War* or p252 of *The Programme Guide*, fourth edition) as it refers to events of that story. Heaven is established "three decades" before the events of the novel (p92), and *Frontier in Space* is set in 2540, so the novel can't take place before about 2570. Latterly, the decision was made that Benny is from the twenty-sixth century, so this is the date that has been adopted for this story. It is late June, as Benny celebrates her birthday just before the book starts, although it is autumn on Heaven.
796 *Deceit*. Many of the subsequent New Adventures

contain references to Ace's exploits in Spacefleet.
797 *Lucifer Rising*
798 *First Frontier, Theatre of War, Shadowmind, Lungbarrow* and *The Shadow of the Scourge*.
799 "Final Genesis"
800 *Death to the Daleks*
801 Thirty years before *Benny: The Gods of the Underworld*.
802 *Benny: Down*
803 *Benny: Beyond the Sun*
804 Dating *Deceit* - (NA #13) The novel is set "two, probably three Earth years" after *Love and War* (p85), and as such the dating of the story is problematic (q.v. Benny's Birthday). Both the blurb and the history section in the Appendix of the novel state that *Deceit* is set in "the middle of the twenty-fifth century", just after what *The Terrestrial Index* calls the Second Dalek War (p62-63). This is restated at various other points (e.g.: p69, p216), but contradicted by other evidence in the same book: Arcadia was colonised three hundred seventy-nine years before *Deceit* (p115), but not before the EB Corporation's first warship was operational in 2112 (p27), so the book must be set after 2491 AD. The book also refers to the Cyber Wars, and "Nemesis of the Daleks" was "years ago". In the Marvel strips, Abslom Daak comes from the mid-twenty-sixth century.
Pool - while not named there - briefly reappears in *Benny: Dead Romance*. Arcadia may or may not be the same planet that was the destination of the *Mayflower* in "Profits of Doom", or that was on the front line of the Last Great Time War according to the Doctor in *Doomsday*.
805 Dating *The Dark Flame* (BF #42) - The dating clues within *The Dark Flame* are so ambiguous, previous editions of *Ahistory* consigned it to "None of the Above". What few dating clues we're given pertain to the Cult of

fish exports as a means of strengthening its sushi monopoly. Benny was granted dispensation to study Hunanzun, the first human settlement on Badblood, and wound up preventing a vampire outbreak on Station CT1107.

2565 - BENNY: THE VAMPIRE CURSE: "Possum Kingdom"[793] **->** Benny joined an expedition to explore the cave system found underneath Possum Kingdom Lake in Texas. She found a naked, amnesiac man who was taken away to a military hospital at Fort Worth.

In 2568, the Spinward Corporation's computer, the Net, predicted that once the Dalek Wars ended, Earth's authorities would show an interest in their activities on Arcadia.[794]

2570 (late June) - LOVE AND WAR[795] **->** Bernice Summerfield and her group arrived on Heaven to survey the artifacts of the extinct Heavenite civilisation on behalf of Ellerycorp. The seventh Doctor and Ace arrived as the fungoid Hoothi brought to fruition a plan centuries in the making - Hoothi spores infected everyone on Heaven, meaning that the Hoothi could instantly turn the living into fungoid creatures and animate corpses. They sought to create an army of billions to attack Gallifrey with. Ace became engaged to one of the Travellers, Jan, who was in an open relationship with a woman named Roisa and her lover Marie. Jan was pyrokinetic, and so the Doctor manipulated him into becoming transformed into a Hoothi fungoid and joining the Hoothi group mind. The Doctor encouraged Jan to bring his pyrokinesis to bear - the Hoothi, their fungoid creatures, their army of the undead and Jan were all incinerated, saving the galaxy. Heaven was evacuated shortly afterwards, and Ace departed the TARDIS, unable to forgive the Doctor for sacrificing her fiancé. Bernice better accepted the Doctor's actions and became his travelling companion.

Following this time, Ace spent three years in the twenty-sixth century during the time of the Dalek War. After a series of adventures, including a spell working for IMC, she ended up with the Special Weapons Division of Spacefleet. She fought alongside the Irregular Auxiliaries, reputed to be the most dangerous arm of the military.[796] Ace served aboard the *Saberhagen*, the *Corporate Raider* and the IMC-funded ship *Corporate Strategy*. The planet Lucifer became of strategic importance in the Dalek Wars, and IMC asked Ace - should the opportunity present itself - to go back in time with the Doctor and discover why the planet was walled off behind a force field.[797] She used a D22 photon rifle when she was a Marine.[798] She fought Daleks in the Ceti sector and Hai Dow. She killed a Black Dalek. She fought Marsh Daleks in the Flova trenches. She was issued a tool for removing the tops of Daleks.[799]

Hamilton's father died during the last Dalek War.[800]

Venedel joined the Earthlink Federation, an allied group of worlds with ties to Earth.[801] By 2571, the Repopulation Bureau on Sarah-361 established guidelines for what constituted good breeding stock.[802] Circa 2573, a Chelonian slave camp on Apollox 4 was discovered.[803]

& 2573 - DECEIT[804] **->** The Dalek Wars were all but over, and although Dalek nests survived on a number of worlds, the army and Spacefleet were gradually demobilised.

During the Dalek Wars, Earth Central had superseded the Colonial Office, while Spacefleet had been expanded and modernised. The Office of External Operations, "the Earth's surveyors, official couriers, intelligence gatherers, customs officers and diplomats", now had a staff of five thousand. While the corporations remained powerful, the Earth government reigned in some of their power and broke some of their monopolies.

Agent Defries investigated the Arcadia system, the base of the Spinward Corporation. The nearest troopers were on Hurgal, although some were taking part in a pirate hunt in the Hai Dow system. Instead, Defries was assigned the troopship *Admiral Raistruck* and a squad of Irregular Auxiliaries. She was also given a "secret weapon": a clone of the Dalek Killer Abslom Daak, kept in cryosleep.

The ship's crew were told that they were going on a Dalek hunt. The *Admiral Raistruck* arrived in the Arcadia system and encountered an asteroid field carved to resemble terrified human faces. It was clear that Arcadia was subject to SYSDID (System Defence in Strength). Fighters attacked the *Admiral Raistruck*, but this was only a feint. The real attack came from behind: an energy being that was unaffected by the ship's torpedoes. The ship was destroyed.

Out of more than a thousand people, there were only four survivors: Defries, Daak and Troopers Ace and Johannsen. They discovered that Arcadia had been kept at a medieval level of technology. The population had been kept in ignorance, and the android Humble Counsellors enforced company law. All offworlders were killed as plague-carriers. The power behind Spinward was the Pool: vats of brain matter culled from generations of colonists, and housed in a space station in orbit around Arcadia. Pool intended to manufacture a universe of pure thought, making itself omnipotent. The clone Daak was killed, but Pool was ejected into the Vortex with the TARDIS' tertiary control room.

Ace rejoined the TARDIS, and travelled alongside the seventh Doctor and Bernice.

c 2573 - THE DARK FLAME[805] **->** The skull of Vilus Krull was unearthed on the toxic planet Marran Alpha, and agents of the Cult of the Dark Flame facilitated his resurrection in a dead body. The seventh Doctor and Ace collected Benny from a two-week stay on the deep-space research centre Orbos, and they stopped the Cult from creating a dark-light explosion that would enable the Dark Flame to spread its influence to every corner of space-time. Krull was thrown into the space-time vortex.

& 2574 - SHAKEDOWN[806] **->** The Sontarans secured information about the Rutan Host: Long ago, a wormhole had been established between Ruta III and Sentarion. In the event of a Sontaran victory, the Rutan Great Mother would use the tunnel to escape her fate. The Sontarans prepared to send a battlefleet down the wormhole to kill the Great Mother, but the Rutan spy Karne discovered the plan. The seventh Doctor, Roz, Chris and Benny tracked Karne down to the human colony of Megacity, and thwarted the Sontaran and Rutan plots.

The Galactic War had passed over the planet Dellah, and so the grateful three-eyed Sultan of the Tashwari built St. Oscar's University - partly to affirm peace and learning, and partly to further keep Dellah from ranking as a target. The Sultan gave the university and its nine colleges names appealing to humans.[807] To protect its neutrality, Dellah banned all military research. Unofficially, St. Oscar's continued weapons work in secret, and developed a prototype method of transferring mental engrams into synthetic forms - a means of producing the ultimate soldier. The process went awry, and the crew aboard the *Medusa*, a modified luxury liner, killed each other. Its navigation

system damaged, the *Medusa* remained adrift.[808]

The Dalek Wars formally ended in 2575. At the end of the Galactic Wars, arms treaties were signed to limit the size and capability of combat robots.[809] A race of master weaponsmiths, the Xlanthi, had aided Earth during the Dalek Wars. Out of gratitude, Earth let the Xlanthi hunt fugitives in Earthspace without interference.[810]

2575 - BENNY: THE SWORD OF FOREVER[811] **->** Kenya and Somalia had been afflicted by Dalek retroviruses, and become home to many of the resultant mutations. The mutants were spreading south toward Tanzania and, more slowly, across the Ethiopian Plateau. Nairobi was nothing more than mutant jungle. Addis Ababa, formerly home to half a million, was now inhabited by hybrid humans. A Mason named Marillian tracked the Ark of the Covenant to Axum, a home to many human hybrids in Ethiopia. Marillian's translator, Ondemwu, escaped with the Ark as the Russian Conglomerate Military Red Cross purified the area.

& 2575 - ARRANGEMENTS FOR WAR[812] **->** The sixth Doctor and Evelyn visited the planet Vilag after witnessing the Killoran invasion to come, and observed the love developing between Princess Krisztina and Marcus Reid, a lowly gardener's son.

---

the Dark Flame's own timeline - the back-cover blurb claims that the Cult was active "a thousand years" ago, and it's variously said that the Cult died out "centuries" or "thousands of years" ago. Vilus Krull, the Cult's founder, is twice said to have lived "thousands of years" ago.

However, the sequel to this story - *Benny: The Draconian Rage*, also written by Trevor Baxendale - not only makes references to Krull's defeat in *The Dark Flame*, it specifies that Krull was born on the human colony planet Tranagus. Given that *The Draconian Rage* occurs in 2602, and given the established timeline of human expansion into space, Krull could at most have lived a few centuries before events in *The Dark Flame* - meaning that all talk about Krull and the Cult going back "a thousand" or "thousands" of years must either be propaganda, or a case of those involved making guesses as to the Cult's shady past. With that in mind, there's only a window of some decades for *The Dark Flame* to occur before *The Draconian Rage*.

806 Dating *Shakedown* (NA #45) - There is no date given in the book, the story synopsis or the video version of this story. The novel is set after *Lords of the Storm* (set in 2371). The Rutans assert that the spy disguised as Karne "died long ago" (p66), but there's some sense that he is still a recent memory.

Benny: Mean Streets - set in 2594, and also written by

Terrance Dicks - is something of a *Shakedown* sequel. It contains a flashback to Roz and Chris' visit to Megacity, in which they learn about an undertaking named The Project. *Mean Streets* p235 indicates that the Project has been running for no more than two generations.

Some general details about *Mean Streets* suggest that events in *Shakedown* were at most a few decades ago - the augmented Ogron Garshak appears in both books (although it's possible that he possesses an extended lifespan). According to *Mean Streets* p122, the bar manager Sara is the dancer that Chris ogles on *Shakedown* p78. She's admittedly a long-lived alien, but isn't surprised to see Chris again in *Mean Streets*, only that he should look a bit older. The account in *Mean Streets* of a former miner, "old Sam", also suggests that The Project was initiated within a human lifetime.

It's said that Chris Cwej - who's capable of time travel by the time *Mean Streets* occurs - wants to settle "unfinished business" in Megacity, and placing *Shakedown* shortly after *Lords of the Storm* would strangely have him doing so more than two hundred years after the fact. (Then again, it's also odd that he'd return a couple of decades later.)

807 *Benny: Oh No It Isn't!*
808 Twenty years before *Benny: The Medusa Effect*.
809 *Cold Fusion* (p247).

? 2575 - HUMAN NATURE (NA)[813] **->** The seventh Doctor and Benny visited a bodysmith and bought a Pod that would allow the Doctor to become human. They travelled to Earth, 1914, so the Doctor could experiment with living as a human being.

? 2576 - RAIN OF TERROR[814] **->** On Earth, holiday excursions were available to an alien zoo on the far side of the moon, and the National Museum of Mars. The Off-Planet Railroad Company had a solid reputation for building train lines. An engineer working for one of the big colony builders could spend weeks or months on faraway planets, returning to Earth in the interim. Colony ships could erect temporary buildings on target worlds prior to engineering firms moving in to do the job properly. Galactic Safari offered use of hyper-sleep chambers that even an upper middle-class family in Brighton could afford. The chambers enabled travel to such worlds as the tourist planet of Xirrinda, which featured such exotic animals as the Trinto, Beslons and the predatory Sharkwolf.

The eleventh Doctor, Amy and Rory visited Xirrinda after dealing with a revolution that involved super-evolved Mire Beasts, and were present as the swarm of ravenous machine-creatures ejected from Xirrinda - numbering in the tens of billions - returned to their homeworld. The Doctor deciphered the key to an ancient "fail-safe" device left by the creatures' creators, and switched them off.

2577 - BENNY: THE SWORD OF FOREVER[815] **->** Marillian inherited many businesses after his father died in a transport accident. He tracked the stolen Ark of the Covenant to the Palace of the Arch-Regent Gebmoses III - the self-proclaimed (and virtually unacknowledged)

Emperor of the Third World - in Kampuchea. Gebmoses had Marillian killed, then resurrected using the Ark's power. Henceforth, Marillian acknowledged Gebmoses as his master.

On Draconia, only two of the six bloodlines from the reign of the First Emperor had survived to the twenty-sixth century: House Kaytar and House Salah. Members of House Kaytar found a stranded Earth ship and indentured the family they found within - but such was the respect and privilege that House Kaytar accorded to the humans, it was disbanded.[816]

The capital of Earth's moon colony was once the most exciting city in human space, but eventually became half historical theme park, half grimy port. The dark side of the moon was even worse off - efforts to keep it artificially lit and atmospherically supported ended when the population dropped below viability levels. It became a "huge, pitch-black ghost town".[817]

2579 - BENNY: THE VAMPIRE CURSE: "Possum Kingdom"[818] **->** Dallas-Fort Worth was now a city within the United States of Texas. Benny and her travelling companion questioned the amnesiac man - Nepesht - whom she had met fourteen years previously. The man's memories returned, and he generated a portal that let him pursue his nemesis back to 1212.

c 2580 - ARRANGEMENTS FOR WAR[819] **->** On Vilag, the countries of Galen and Malendia negotiated a ceasefire after centuries of warfare. Governor Justice Rossiter, the head of the country of Kozepen, served as an independent arbiter as Galen and Malendia worked to form a coalition:

810 *Benny: Beige Planet Mars.* The 2575 dating concurs with the war winding down in 2573 (*Deceit*).
811 Dating *Benny: The Sword of Forever* (Benny NA #14) - The year is given.
812 Dating *Arrangements for War* (BF #57) - This epilogue occurs five years before the main story.
813 Dating *Human Nature* (NA #38) - No date is given, but Ellerycorp and the Travellers are mentioned, suggesting this is around Benny's native time.
814 Dating *Rain of Terror* (BBC children's 2-in-1 #8, released in *Alien Adventures*) - The evidence sits at odds with itself. Professor Willard flew shuttlecraft "during the Cyber War" (p319); he's now older, indicating that it's a generation, or two at most, beyond that event. However, humanity's advancement - particularly the affordability, reliability and speed of space travel - seems well beyond that, more akin to the sort of thing one would expect from the Fourth Great and Bountiful Human Empire (*The Long Game*). Along those lines, the Doctor thinks that the Xirrinda colony was established "in the last year or two" (p226), and yet the colony

already has "eight million" colonists (p261). The "Cyber War" reference is very hard to shake, though, and space travel *is* very common in Bernice Summerfield's era. Perhaps it's a really nice planet.

No mention is made of either the Earth-Draconian conflict or the Dalek Wars, so the placement here, as much as anything, reflects the likelihood that the story occurs during a (relatively) peaceful period for Earth.
815 Dating *Benny: The Sword of Forever* (Benny NA #14) - The year is given.
816 "Forty years" before *Benny: The Judas Gift*
817 "Decades" before *Benny: Resurrecting the Past.* The Dalek Wars might well account for the drop in the moon's population. The dark side of the moon, at least in our time, never faces the Earth, but is not in permanent darkness.
818 Dating *Benny: The Vampire Curse*: "Possum Kingdom" (Benny collection #12b) - The year is given.
819 Dating *Arrangements for War* (BF #57) - No dating clues exist in this story or its sequel, *Thicker Than Water*, but placement is possible by extrapolating from the

the Kingdom Alliance. The sixth Doctor and Evelyn visited Vilag three weeks prior to an invasion by the warlike Killorans, knowing that the Alliance was historically slated to overcome them.

The Doctor's loose lips caused Galen's Princess Krisztina to declare her love for Lieutenant Marcus Reid, ruining her intended political marriage to Malendia's Prince Viktor. Thousands were killed as the scandal caused Galen and Malendia to resume their conflict. Nonetheless, the nations united their forces when the Killorans attacked, and drove off the invaders. Krisztina and Reid were killed the conflict. Rossiter, being a widower, asked Evelyn to stay with him, but she resumed her travels with the Doctor...

Adrian Wall fought in the battle of Vilag, and killed a boy no older than five during it.[820]

& 2581 - THICKER THAN WATER[821] **->** A triumvirate government was established on Vilag. The sixth Doctor and Evelyn re-visited the planet, and she left the TARDIS to marry Rossiter.

In 2582, Kothar - a descendent of the disgraced House Kaytar of Draconia - was appointed a cultural attaché to the Draconian Embassy on Earth.[822]

& 2583 - THICKER THAN WATER[823] **->** Rossiter was elected Principle Triumvir, the head of the tripartite government on Vilag. The sixth Doctor and Mel visited Evelyn Rossiter, and the Doctor ended illicit experiments involving Killoran DNA. He and Mel were present as Evelyn and Rossiter renewed their wedding vows.

Rossiter died. Three years later, Evelyn found the temporal stabiliser of the timeship UNS *Pelican* in a coal seam. It translocated her to billions of years in the past.[824]

Battrulian artist Toulour Martinique was mysteriously killed after painting his last work, *Murdering Art*, which depicted his being murdered by demons.[825] Around 2582, the Kalkravian Revolution took place, and the Adjudication Bureau was sent in to free hostages. The All Worlds Science Fair took place on the planet Dellah. Earth won the Worlds Cup in 2584.[826]

c 2585 - DEIMOS / THE RESURRECTION OF MARS[827] **->** The Mars Terraforming Project established a base on the Martian moon of Deimos, and built a re-ioniser to alter Mars' atmosphere from space, making it breathable to humans. The Project collapsed due to the onset of the Great Recession and technical problems related to the goal of creating artificial suns to give Mars heat and light. In

---

Bernice Summerfield range. *Benny: Parallel Lives:* "Hiding Places", set in 2606, establishes that Adrian Wall fought in the invasion of Vilag, suggesting that - once allowances are made that a Killoran lifespan might differ from that of humans - *Arrangements for War* and *Thicker Than Water* must occur closer to the start of the twenty-seventh century than not.

A recurring theory in fandom holds that the unnamed bodyguards to the Gallifreyan Imperatrix Pandora (*Gallifrey: Lies*) were Killorans, and that historical intervention on the part of the Time Lords - who "time-looped" the bodyguards' homeworld - is responsible for the Killorans transitioning from the primal brutes who attacked Vilag to the more civilised builders seen in the Benny range. A "time loop" would not in itself account for such historical revision, though; moreover, Adrian vividly remembers the Vilag invasion in *Parallel Lives*, so it's not as if the event was erased from history entirely.

820 *Benny: Parallel Lives:* "Hiding Places"
821 Dating *Thicker Than Water* (BF #73) - A year has passed since the Killoran invasion.
822 *Benny: The Judas Gift*
823 Dating *Thicker Than Water* (BF #73) - The blurb says that it's "Three years after Vilag was all but laid waste by the Killorans." The Doctor here takes Mel to meet Evelyn for "the first time", which disputes the claim in *Instruments of Darkness* that they've not only met but travelled together for a time, although the contradic-

tion is literally limited to a few lines of dialogue between the Doctor and Mel in an opening scene. Nonetheless, it is there.
824 *A Death in the Family.* Evelyn resides on Pelican for seven years, and remarks at the end of her life that Rossiter died "ten years ago" - so she must live on Vilag for three years after his passing, and an indeterminate amount of time with him after *Thicker Than Water*.
825 "Seven years, three months and eleven days" before *Demontage.*
826 *Cold Fusion.* The year of the revolution is given (p230), the science fair was "ten years ago" (p200).
827 Dating *Deimos/The Resurrection of Mars* (BF BBC7 #4.5-4.6) - It's "centuries" after the destruction of the Martian warfleet in *The Seeds of Death.* Mention is made of the "hippy holiday camp" seen in *Phobos*, set in 2589, suggesting that this story occurs in the same period.

Mars here gains a human-compatible atmosphere (curiously, no mention is made of how the three hundred thousand people living on Mars are currently surviving without one). Mars was terraformed and given a breathable atmosphere in the early twenty-second century - however, the Daleks released a virus during the Dalek Invasion that ate all of the Martian atmosphere's oxygen and took "years" (according to *Fear Itself*, PDA, p63) if not decades to reverse. It's entirely possible - although it's not expressly said - that the same fate befell the planet when the Daleks overran Mars during the Dalek Wars (in 2545, according

time, the Martian catacombs on Deimos were excavated, and the moonbase was transformed into a museum devoted to the Ice Warriors. The humans in the solar system believed that the Ice Warriors had been wiped out in the twenty-first century, and at least one documentary had been made of the T-Mat incident.

The Meddling Monk, in a bid to alter history so the utopian society on Halcyon would survive, awoke the Ice Warriors on Deimos "a few centuries" before they were due. He also fired Lucie Miller as his companion, and deposited her in the moonbase on Deimos. The Ice Warriors captured the base's re-ioniser, and attempted to alter Mars' atmosphere to support Martian life. The eighth Doctor destroyed the moonbase and the re-ionizer - an act that altered Mars' atmosphere so it could sustain human life, and ignited the surface of Deimos. The resultant chain reaction turned Deimos into a miniature sun that would supply Mars with heat and light.

Six hundred people had died - and three hundred thousand people living on Mars been endangered - because the Doctor had hesitated in killing the Ice Warriors, as this would have also meant Lucie's death. The Doctor's companion Tamsin decried his cowardice, and departed with the Monk. Lucie resumed travelling with the Doctor.

c 2585 - THE ALSO PEOPLE[828] -> The seventh Doctor, Bernice, Roz and Chris enjoyed a holiday at the Worldsphere of the People. Chris became lovers with a young woman named Dep, and Roz had a romantic relationship with a war veteran named feLixi. The seventh Doctor solved the murder of viCari, the first drone to be killed in more than three hundred years. feLixi was punished for his culpability in viCari's murder with ostracism - nobody in the Worldsphere would ever speak to him

again. The Doctor and Bernice also helped restore the feral Kadiatu Lethbridge-Stewart to sanity. Dep didn't tell Chris that she was pregnant with his child.

She later gave birth to a daughter, iKrissi. Because Dep made a mistake during conception, iKrissi was an exact clone of Chris. Dep had at least one more child.[829]

= 2586 - TIMEH: CHILD OF TIME[830] **->** The Sodality had been created when the surviving members of the Cabal of the Horned Beast re-acquired the Daemon-linked book that was lost in the twentieth century, and retroactively make their insignificant group more powerful. Honoré Lechasseur and Emily Blandish arrived in a version of 2586 in which Sodality's meddling with history had created a devastated Earth. The Daemon named Mastho appeared at St. Paul's Cathedral as Sodality summoned him a third time, and revealled that he had ordered Sodality to kill its time-sensitives and time-channellers as a means of culling all but the "Child of Time": a human with the combined abilities of both. The Daemons wanted to study such a creature, absorb its powers and gain the unfettered ability to travel through space and time. A woman named Maria became the Child of Time - but killed herself after falling through time to 1949, causing a psionic backlash that killed Mastho also.

An unknown incarnation of the Doctor witnessed these events, and took Sodality's High Executioner with him upon making his escape. She would part ways with him in 1949, and become Emily Blandish.

Benny: Beige Planet Mars), which both greatly reduced the number of people living on Mars (cited as three million in 2545 in *Beige Planet Mars*, but only three hundred thousand in *The Resurrection of Mars*) and prompted the Mars Terraforming Project seen here. Either way, Mars has a breathable atmosphere in *Beige Planet Mars*, set in 2595, further encouraging a placement prior to that.

The Earth public thinks that the Ice Warriors are extinct, suggesting that *The Resurrection of Mars* occurs prior to the Federation's diplomatic contacts with them (*The Curse of Peladon*, etc.), and neatly ties in with the claim in *Legacy* that the "extinct" Martians became of interest during the twenty-sixth century. The re-ionizer technology used on Mars is, clearly, a precursor to the ionizer seen in *The Ice Warriors* (even if the re-ionizer on Mars, if anything, seems more powerful that the model used at Britannicus Base).

828 Dating *The Also People* (NA #44) - The remains of "a sub gas giant that had broken up sixty-two billion

years previously" is referred to (p168) and the Doctor said his "diary's pretty much clear" until "the heat death of the universe" (p186). This led the Virgin edition of this book to conclude that the story was set many billions of years in the future. However, the Bernice Summerfield New Adventures made clear that the story takes place around Benny's native time.

829 *Happy Endings*

830 Dating *TimeH: Child of Time* (TimeH #11) - The year is given. Sodality in 2586 appears to be operating from a "potential" timeline - which is very fortunate, as the late twenty-sixth century is the native era of Bernice Summerfield, and it's impossible to reconcile the heavy amount known about this period with the total lack of a mention concerning the devastated Earth that Sodality has brought about. Sodality is expressly said to hail from a "possible" future in the *Time Hunter*-related film *Daemons: Daemos Rising*, and in *Child of Time* (co-written by David J. Howe, publisher of *Time Hunter* and the writer of *Daemos Rising*), and Honoré innately

A company in the Catan Nebula made Artificial Personality Embodiments (APEs): synthetic humans with a tailored set of memories. Two synthoids - Kara Delbane and an unnamed agent with Stratum Seven-level clearance - were created to join a mercenary group, the Oblivion Angels. They reported to a computer intelligence: the Artificial Viral-based Intelligence Destabilisation (ARVID). The Agent and Kara were sent to the planet Sharabeth, a nexus point of industry and commerce. One of the Dellan gods had been flung back through time, causing a number of time fractures on Sharabeth. It merged its consciousness with the cyber-body of Absolam Sleed, the company founder, and used his resources to commit mass carnage. Sleed seemed to die at the Agent's hands, but his brain survived.[831]

2587 (autumn) - RETURN OF THE LIVING DAD[832] -> The newly-married Bernice Summerfield and Jason Kane were on Youkali 6. Benny was studying for a genuine degree in archaeology, while writing a new book and trying for a child. An old friend of her father, Admiral Groenewegen, made contact with new information about Isaac Summerfield's disappearance. Benny called the seventh Doctor for help - and they discovered that Isaac was alive and well, and living on Earth in 1983.

The seventh Doctor and Chris visited Bernice and Jason on Youkali 6 to inform them of Roz Forrester's death.[833]

2589 - PHOBOS[834] -> An entity from a collapsing universe forged a singularity bridge to our reality. The bridge ended on the Martian moon of Phobos, but the entity

senses that Sodality's Earth isn't part of established history. By extension, this would seem to mean that Emily Blandish herself originates from a potential reality, but then crosses over and takes up residence in the universe's "main" timeline (similar to Elizabeth Klein; see *Colditz*). Whether or not this means that the Doctor who appears in *The Cabinet of Light* and *TimeH: Child of Time* is from the "proper" timeline or Sodality's altered history is an open-ended question. The "child of time" that Mastho here covets isn't to be confused with Chiyoko, the "child of time" seen in the *DWM* comics.

831 A decade before *Benny: Return to the Fractured Planet*.

832 Dating *Return of the Living Dad* (NA #53) - It's "2587" (p5).

833 *So Vile a Sin*

834 Dating *Phobos* (BF BBC7 #1.5) - "Apparently the year is 2589", the Doctor says.

835 "Three centuries" after *The Leisure Hive*.

836 "Ten years" before *Prime Time*.

837 Dating *Demontage* (EDA #20) - No date is given, but the art forger Newark Rappare appears in both this and *Benny: Dragon's Wrath* (set in 2593), and he is "middle aged" in both.

838 Dating *Cold Fusion* (MA #29) - The novel was originally set at the same time as *So Vile a Sin* and tied in quite closely to that book, but it became clear *So Vile a Sin* wouldn't be released as scheduled. Following that, *Cold Fusion* was reworked to occur just before the Benny New Adventures, and included the first mention of Dellah, the planet Benny was based on for that series. A copyright notice on a wardroid states that this is 2692, but that was a typographical error, and should have read "2592". It's "four hundred years" before Chris and Roz's time (p165). It's stated that the Adjudicators have been around for "half a millennium" (p247).

839 Patience vanishes mysteriously in *Cold Fusion*, and reappears in *The Infinity Doctors*

840 *Interference* (p113).

841 Dating The Bernice Summerfield New Adventures - The twenty-three New Adventures novels featuring Benny start with her joining the staff of St. Oscar's in 2593 (a year first established in The *Dying Days*) and roughly acknowledge the real-world passage of time during the two and a half years the Benny NAs were in publication. The series ends with *Benny: Twilight of the Gods*, set in 2596. See the individual entries for more.

TERMINOLOGY IN THE BENNY BOOKS AND AUDIOS: The New Adventures books continued after Virgin lost the *Doctor Who* licence in 1996. They were unable to use characters and concepts that originated in *Doctor Who*, but those created for the New Adventures (Benny, Jason Kane, Chris Cwej, Roz Forrester, the People of the Worldsphere from *The Also People*, Irving Braxiatel, etc.) were fair game. For legal reasons, a number of new terms were coined when referencing characters or concepts firmly lodged in *Doctor Who*.

The Dalek Wars that were so influential to Benny's background were more generically referred to as "the Galactic War". Braxiatel in both the NAs and the Big Finish audios broadly has "time technology" or "owns a time machine", although his timeship's inter-dimensional nature - as prominently seen in *Benny: Tears of the Oracle* and various audios - leaves no doubt that it's a TARDIS, a notion reinforced by Big Finish's use of TARDIS-like noises. The Time Lords - who were still involved in the New Adventures, unnamed, as the signatories to the treaty with the People (*Benny: Walking to Babylon*), as Irving Braxiatel's race and as Chris Cwej's employers (*Benny: Dead Romance*) were occasionally called "the Watchmakers". Big Finish was similarly coy about naming the Time Lords, even though the status of "Braxiatel's people" mirrors developments with the Time Lords in the *Gallifrey* mini-series, and the Time Lord Straxus appears in both the BBC7 audios and *Benny: The Adventure of the Diogenes Damsel*. While the Benny stories frequently refer to the Time Lords as "Braxiatel's people", *Ahistory* has used the terms "Time

became stuck in the transition point. It fed off feelings of euphoria, set up a thin atmosphere on Phobos and gained strength as the moon was used for extreme sports.

Problems arose during the development of Lunar Park (a hotel and botanical garden) on Phobos; only its environmental dome was finished. Squatters moved in when the moon was left unincorporated, and adrenaline junkies performed extreme sports against the backdrop of the moon's spectacular ice valleys. Such recreations included grav-board runs outside the dome, ice spelunking in the melted floes beneath the surface and "orbit-hopping".

The eighth Doctor and Lucie stopped on Phobos, and the Doctor jolted the emerging entity by concentrating his many fears - the creature either died or went dormant. As a precaution, the Doctor recommended that Phobos' sports come to an end.

The time-active Headhunter landed on Phobos days before the TARDIS' arrival, but fell off a bicycle and was unconscious until after the Doctor and Lucie had left.

In this era, the Githians were large, hirsute creatures who inter-acted with humanity, but were forbidden to marry outside their species in order to keep their gene pool pure. Hunters retrieved Githians who violated the law.

Around the year 2590, Radon 222 levels on the surface of Argolis had dropped to such a level that the planet became habitable again.[835] Blinni-Gaar was an agricultural planet feeding an entire sector. Channel 400 made a deal with the government and started broadcasting addictive programmes. The Blinnati stopped farming, nearly leading to famine on the Rim until offworlders started running the planet.[836]

c 2590 - DEMONTAGE[837] **->** The eighth Doctor, Sam and Fitz arrived on Vega Station. General Browning Phillips was planning to return the Battrulian junta to power by killing President Drexler, but the Doctor defeated that plan. Drexler and a Canvine representative, Bigdog Caruso, engineered a more permanent peace treaty between the Battrul and Canvine.

The artist Martinique had discovered a process that could physically transfer someone into a painting, or make items in paintings take physical form. He used this technique to survive his "murder", and took up residence in a serene painting, *On a Clear Day*.

2592 (31st October) - COLD FUSION[838] **->** By this time, the Third Draconian War had been fought. An Empress, revered as a goddess by some, now ruled Earth. The Empire had developed Skybases to operate as planetary command centres, and the Adjudicators were sent across the Empire to enforce Imperial Law. The Unitatus Guild, a secret society based on garbled legends of UNIT in the twentieth century, was politically influential.

The Scientifica, the ruling elite of scientists on an icy Earth colony planet, excavated a crashed TARDIS and its mummified pilot. Following experiments on the ship, ghosts start appearing across the planet. The seventh Doctor, Chris and Roz investigated the ghosts. The fifth Doctor, Tegan, Nyssa and Adric arrived a month later, and found the Patient - a mummified Time Lady - who promptly regenerated. The Doctor tried to get her to safety as the Adjudicators declared martial law. Both Doctors realised that the ghosts were the Ferutu, beings from the far future of an alternative timeline in which Gallifrey was destroyed in the ancient past. The Ferutu attempted to ensure Gallifrey's destruction, but the fifth and seventh Doctors joined forces and ensured history was not altered. A few Ferutu were trapped within a chalk circle, the only survivors of their timeline.

The Time Lady, Patience, was fatally wounded but rescued by Omega, who transported her to his anti-matter universe.[839]

Fitz awoke after almost six hundred years to find himself in Augustine City on Ordifica. The colonists had developed the Cold, a horrific weapon. Fitz celebrated his 626th birthday on Ordifica on 7th March, 2593.[840]

Bernice Summerfield at St. Oscar's University[841]

St Oscar's University had become became one of the most prestigious centres of learning in the Milky Way.[842] Dellah was closer to the Galactic Hub than Earth, but was considered more of a backwater. The days there lasted twenty-six hours. The Shakya Constellation was visible from Dellah's southern hemisphere.[843] Trans-galactic travel was fairly easy in this era for those with money, but navigation computers were expensive and time travel was forbidden. Instant information transfer was available.[844] Galactic Basic,

---

Lords" and Braxiatel's "TARDIS" for clarity.

The Benny equivalent of the Ice Warriors is less straightforward... in *Benny: Dragons' Wrath*, writer Justin Richards introduced the recurring character of Commander Skutloid, whose description (p109) leaves no doubt that he's an Ice Lord in all but name. Richards named Skutloid's species in *Benny: The Medusa Effect*

(p14) as "Neo Arietian" before establishing the more commonly used spelling of "Neo-Aretian" in *Benny: Tears of the Oracle* (p37, 40, etc.). Skutloid hails from "Neo Ares" (*The Medusa Effect*, p19), either an alternate name for "New Mars" (*Legacy*), a.k.a. "Nova Martia" (*GodEngine*) - a "Neo-Aretian" (i.e. "New Martian") could feasibly hail from either - or, more likely, Neo Ares and

the most common language, was an evolved version of English.[845]

2593 (Wednesday, 8th May) - THE DYING DAYS[846]

-> Benny Summerfield was offered the chair of archaeology at St Oscar's University on Dellah. She received the job offer in 1997 despite never actually applying for the position. The eighth Doctor dropped her off, and they enjoyed a fond farewell. He also gifted her with Wolsey the TARDIS cat.

The People's supercomputer God had brainwashed Benny into joining the St. Oscar's staff, preparing her for the coming day when she would help to free the conceptual entity MEPHISTO.[847]

The Black Guardian transported the con man and art dealer Menlove Stokes to Dellah from the far distant future. Stokes became a Professor of Applied Arts at St Oscar's.[848]

2593 - BENNY: OH NO IT ISN'T![849]

-> Benny, in her post as the Edward Watkinson Professor of Archaeology at St. Oscar's, accompanied a team of academics to the quarantined planet of Perfecton. The missile containing the encoded remains of Perfecton civilisation struck Benny's ship, the *Winton*, and impacted with Professor Archduke's thesis on obscure theatrical forms. The missile's quantum fluctuations manifested aspects of Archduke's thesis, and so Benny's team and some Grel - information monarchs / pirates with squiddy faces - found themselves in a world governed by pantomime. Benny passed as a young man named Dick Whittington, and her cat Wolsey temporarily became a talking biped. She ended the scenario, and her team escaped as Perfecton's sun went nova. Archduke acquired the data module containing the Perfecton culture.

The Knights of Jeneve captured Chris Cwej and put him in suspended animation.[850]

The Irving Braxiatel who was flung through the Time Vortex during his struggle with Lord Burner arrived on Dellah. He met Benny just once[851], realised that she was familiar with an alternate version of himself, and avoided contacting her until 2616.[852]

Nova Martia are separate Ice Warrior colonies, hence the different nomenclature. Big Finish wound up trying to have this both ways, using the term "Neo-Aretians" in *Benny: A Life of Surprises*: "Might", before having Benny encounter the actual, licensed Ice Warriors in *Benny: The Dance of the Dead*. In *Benny: A Life Worth Living*, Big Finish settled for calling the Braxiatel Collection gardener, Hass, "a Martian" (even if temporal distortion retroactively turned him into a Yesodi in *Benny: Something Changed*).

842 *Benny: Oh No It Isn't!*

843 *Benny: Ship of Fools*

844 *Benny: The Mary-Sue Extrusion*

845 *Benny: Return to the Fractured Planet*

846 Dating *The Dying Days* (NA #61) - The date is given. It's a bit of an oddity that Wolsey is still in the TARDIS even though the eighth Doctor is now "twelve hundred" years old. As Wolsey was initially the seventh Doctor's cat, and the seventh Doctor regenerated age 1009 (according to *Vampire Science*), the math would seem to suggest that, somehow, Wolsey has been living in the TARDIS for about two centuries.

847 *Benny: Down*

848 *The Well-Mannered War*

849 Dating *Oh No It Isn't!* (Benny NA #1) - The year was given in *The Dying Days*.

850 Six months before *Benny: Deadfall*.

851 *Gallifrey: Disassembled*, in a scene dramatised from *Dragons' Wrath*.

852 *Benny: Epoch: Judgement Day*

853 The art forger Menlove Stokes, also seen in *Demontage*, is here murdered.

854 Dating *Beyond the Sun* (Benny NA #3) - In Benny and Jason's timeline, eight months have passed since they last saw each other, and got divorced, in *Eternity Weeps*.

855 Cat's Paw is the same type of Catan-made artificial lifeform as the Stratum Seven agent from *Benny: The Mary-Sue Extrusion* and *Benny: Return to the Fractured Planet*.

856 *Benny: Down*

857 Dating *Benny: Down* (Benny NA #5) - It's now "early 2594" (p8). Benny arrives on Tyler's Folly no later than "January 14th" (p152), but the action opens at St. Oscar's some time beforehand. After Benny is apprehended, an interrogation report and an arrest report are respectively dated to "15/01/94" (p165) and "22/1/94" (p8). Benny is subjected to "the sound of the Young Nazi Male Voice Choir of the year 2594" (p151).

858 Dating *Benny: Deadfall* (Benny NA #6) - It's said that Benny has now been at St. Oscar's for "six months"; it's actually been more like nine, although it's possible she's counting from the start of the term. Either way, it's January 2594 at the latest.

859 This is a sequel to the New Adventures novel *Shakedown*.

860 Dating *Benny: Walking to Babylon* (Benny NA #10) - An extract from Benny's memoirs (p27) says that it's still 2594. She's currently procrastinating on writing *An Eye for Wisdom*, slated for publication in 2595.

861 The *Schirron Dream* crew formerly appeared in *Sky Pirates!* and *Death and Diplomacy*.

2593 - BENNY: DRAGONS' WRATH[853] **->** Irving Braxiatel was presently the head of the St. Oscar's Theatrology Department, and - from his perspective - met Bernice Summerfield for the first time. The warlord Romolo Nusek sought to further his power by proving that his ancestor, Hugo Gamaliel, once held a colony on Stanturus Three. Benny used the low-grade nuclear device hidden in the prized Gamaliel Dragon to obliterate the power-mad Nusek and his castle.

2593 - BENNY: BEYOND THE SUN[854] **->** The Sunless conquered the planet Ursu, and returned the Blooms stolen from them to their homeworld. Benny - with some help from her ex-husband Jason Kane, who approached her at a dig on Apollox 4 - deduced that the Blooms were a stellar manipulator. After being given the right keys - a particular brother and sister the Blooms had spawned - it generated enough energy to revitalise the Sunless' star.

2593 - BENNY: SHIP OF FOOLS -> Earth's seas were now a thick black sludge. The famed thief Cat's Paw stole an Olabrian joy-luck crystal from Marcus Krytell, one of the richest men in the sector. With the Olabrians prone to committing mass murder to recover their crystals, Krytell asked Bernice to handle the ransom exchange on the maiden voyage of the *Titanian Queen*, a luxury liner. Benny unmasked Cat's Paw as Isabel Blaine, a construct of the Catan Nebula. The *Titanian Queen* was destroyed when its artificial intelligence went mad, but Benny and Cat's Paw saved the passengers. In retribution for Krytell's crimes, Cat's Paw returned the joy-luck crystal to him - but also informed the authorities of its location, causing Olabrian battle cruisers to swoop down on his location.[855]

On Boxing Day, 2593, Benny won a bet on Fat Lightning, odds 8-1, at the annual St. Oscar's slug-racing championships. She celebrated by "not getting absolutely bladdered".[856]

2594 (January) - BENNY: DOWN[857] **->** Tyler's Folly declared independence from Earth, and the Republican Security Force responded by staging a military coup, declaring the colony there a police state. Benny's actions helped the conceptual entity MEPHISTO to emerge, but prevented it from remaking reality in its image. MEPHISTO's philosophy of pain amidst a utopia aided the further development of the People of the Worldsphere.

2594 (January) - BENNY: DEADFALL[858] **->** The Knights of Jeneve searched for descendants of their founder, Vazlov Baygent, hoping to host his preserved memories in one of them. Chris Cwej - identified as one of Baygent's descendants - and Jason Kane thwarted the Knights' efforts to find a Baygent-host aboard the *KayBee 2*, a prison ship.

2594 - BENNY: GHOST DEVICES -> The supercomputer God asked Benny to join an archaeological expedition to Canopus IV, where she found the Spire built by the long-dead Vo'lach race. Benny caused two Vo'lach Planetcracker missiles to travel into the past and damage the Spire. As God intended, this averted the paradox pertaining to the Spire's nature, saving billions of lives.

2594 - BENNY: MEAN STREETS[859] **->** Benny and Chris Cwej went to the planet Megerra and exposed The Project - an illicit undertaking by DevCorps to create genetically engineered miners with enhanced stamina. DevCorps was bankrupted. The Combine was currently the biggest crime syndicate in the galaxy.

2594 - BENNY: TEMPEST -> Benny gave a lecture to the archaeological society on the colony world of Tempest, then left for the spaceport aboard the *Polar Express* monorail. The business tycoon Nathan Costermann embarked on a murder and insurance scam involving the Drell Imnulate - an artifact of the Drell religion. After Benny exposed his plans, Costermann fell to his death.

2594 - BENNY: WALKING TO BABYLON[860] **->** !Ci!citel and WiRgo!xu believed that the People of the Worldsphere had become complacent, and tried to goad the People and the Time Lords into war by establishing a treaty-violating time corridor to ancient Babylon. Benny went into the past and stopped the rogues, removing the need for God to destroy the time-corridor - and Babylon - with a singularity bomb.

2594 - BENNY: OBLIVION -> The sentient spaceship *Schirron Dream* sought help from its old friends - Benny, Jason Kane, Chris Cwej and the late Roz Forrester, the last of whom the ship brought through time as a 20-year-old - after disruptions in space-time made its crew go missing. The wealthy Randolph Bane had found the Egg, an artifact in the Shadow Depository, and hoped to gain immortality from it even if the universe consequently perished. Bane and his rival, Simon Deed, were time-looped. Roz destroyed the Egg, but its final burst of power erased her memories of these events. The *Schirron Dream* crew was located, and Roz was sent back to her native time.[861]

2594 - BENNY: THE MEDUSA EFFECT -> The *Medusa* had now been adrift for two decades, and Benny joined an expedition to recover it. She and Braxiatel learned that the Advanced Research Department at St. Oscar's had been complicit in the deaths of the *Medusa* crew, but remained silent in exchange for a confession from Taffeta Graize, the main culprit. A synthoid containing the dead crew's memories killed Graize.

2594 - BENNY: DRY PILGRIMAGE -> Genetic engineering had now eliminated all major human cancers and blood disorders. Cigarettes contained no harmful substances, but very few people still smoked. Chateau Yquatine was in production.[862]

Saraani pilgrims fled an atheist revolution on their homeworld, and sought to establish themselves on an island on Dellah. Benny joined the Saraani aboard the cruise ship *Lady of Lorelei* as they searched for a suitable locale. Czaritza Violaine, the exiled leader of Visphok, cut a deal with some of the Saraani: they would use their mind-transference abilities (part of their reproductive cycle) to shift the minds of Violaine's aged veterans into weaponised bioconstructs, in exchange for Violaine liberating Saraanis. The agreement went south, and Violaine was killed.

In 2594, the fox-like Valethske searched for their former gods, the Khorlthochloi, and fought with the Sontarans. The Earth Empire had colonised the Thynemnus system, and a mass immigration led to tensions. The planet Korsair was established to settle disputes. The Valethske attacked one of the new colonies, overwhelming the Korsairs and capturing colonists for their larder.[863]

On Ordifica, Fitz was initiated into Faction Paradox around 2594. Laura Tobin, who would become the Doctor's companion Compassion, was sent to Ordifica the same year.[864]

2595 - BENNY: THE SWORD OF FOREVER[865] -> Armstrong City was a settlement in the Sea of Tranquillity on the moon.

Marillian, unofficially the third-richest man in the world, now owned London and Greenwich. Benny encountered Marillian while investigating the journal of Guillaume de Beaujeu, and platonically married him to get a childbirth license - a pre-requirement for her accessing the texts within the British Library. Marillian assisted Benny in recovering the finger of John the Baptist from Castle Arginy, and what they believed was the skull of Christ from a Templar museum in Paris. He then made off with both items.

Benny realised that four items associated with Christ - the Spear of Longinus that pierced Christ's side, Christ's Crown of Thorns, the Holy Grail and the Ark of the Covenant - could be combined to form the Sword of Forever: a device capable of creating entire worlds and timelines. Marillian's master, Gebmoses III, died while trying to use the Sword to retroactively create a master race cloned from Christ's skull.

Evidence suggested that Benny had died using the Sword - which was intended for use by a higher power, and would kill any human who operated it - to recreate Earth's timeline after its destruction. She dutifully welcomed God into her heart and died to activate the Sword. Earth's timeline was reinstated, and Benny was restored to life in a new body.

862 "Chateau Yquatine" presumably references *The Fall of Yquatine*, also by Nick Walters. Café Vosta, an establishment at the Braxiatel Collection, is also cited as serving it (*Benny: Collected Works*). All of which is very curious, since *The Fall of Yquatine* claims that the Yquatine system won't be colonized for a couple of centuries yet.

863 *Superior Beings* (p108).

864 *Interference*

865 Dating *Benny: The Sword of Forever* (Benny NA #14) - The chapter headings reiterate that it's 2595.

866 *Benny: Walking to Babylon*. Obviously, publication must occur before St. Oscar's is ravaged in *Benny: Where Angels Fear*. The Ikkabans were mentioned in *SLEEPY*.

867 *Dust Breeding* ends with the seventh Doctor and Ace giving Bev a lift in the TARDIS, and the idea seems to be that after some unspecified adventures, she left their company "two years" prior to 2597 (according to *Benny: The Judas Gift*), and became a fixture of Benny's native era.

868 Dating *Benny: Buried Treasures*: "Making Myths" / "Closure" (Benny audio #1.5b) - The *Buried Treasures* CD was released as a bonus for customers who purchased Big Finish's (apocryphal) CD adaptations of *Walking to Babylon*, *Birthright* and *Just War*. The two stories within *Buried Treasures* are slightly problematic to place within Benny's lifetime - "Closure" establishes that it's during

Benny's tenure at St. Oscar's (so, prior to *Benny: Where Angels Fear*), but the CD was released in August 1999, concurrent to *Benny: Return to the Fractured Planet*. The placement here is arbitrary.

869 Youkali University appeared in *Return of the Living Dad*.

870 Dating *Benny: Beige Planet Mars* (Benny NA #16) - The day is given (p7). Benny here celebrates her thirty-fifth birthday, but she must be counting in absolute terms, allowing for her travelling through time with the Doctor. The book was published in October 1998, just before the thirty-fifth anniversary of *Doctor Who*.

871 *Benny: Venus Mantrap*

872 *The Infinity Doctors*

873 Dating *Benny: The Mary-Sue Extrusion* (Benny NA #18) - Four months have passed since *Benny: Where Angels Fear*.

874 Dating *Benny: Dead Romance* (Benny NA #19) - Events in the outside universe are set between *The Mary-Sue Extrusion* and *Tears of the Oracle*. Within the bottle universe, events unfold from 27th September to 12th October, 1970. The universe-in-a-bottle also appears in *Interference* and *The Ancestor Cell*. FP: *The Shadow Play*, strongly implies that Christine ends up joining Faction Paradox as "Cousin Eliza", a main character in the Faction audios.

St. Oscar's University Press published Benny's *An Eye for Wisdom: Repetitive Poems of the Early Ikkaban Period* in 2595.[866] Bev Tarrant, a skilled thief from the future, found herself in the year 2595.[867]

c 2595 - BENNY: BURIED TREASURES: "Making Myths"[868] -> Benny and her friend Keri, a Pakhar journalist, visited the declining tourist planet Shangri-La; Benny claimed to have discovered the famed Mud Fields of Agrivan there. A video of Keri running atop a giant cart wheel motivated thousands of Pakhar to make bookings to Shangri-La, reviving the planet's economy.

c 2595 - BENNY: BURIED TREASURES: "Closure"[868] -> On the planet Panyos, the despotic regime led by Ulrich Hescarti ended when he was shot in the back by one of his own people. After witnessing the horrors of Hescarti's ethnic cleansing programme, Benny used her time ring to travel back and change his personal history.

2595 - BENNY: ANOTHER GIRL, ANOTHER PLANET -> Archaeologist Lizbeth Fugard researched the heritage of the colony planet Dimetos by studying the industrial sites established there by Eurogen Butler. Bantu Cooperative, a weapons manufacturer, sabotaged Fugard's operations to conceal how many installations had been built atop Eurogen nuclear reactors and disused mine workings, hoping to curry favour with the Dimetos administration. Benny stymied Bantu by destroying their largest research facility, but obliterated the biggest Dimetan archaeological site in the process.

The only surviving Dimetan, Csoker, killed himself rather than endure as the last of his race. Fugard became a professor of sidereal mythology at Youkali University.[869]

2595 (21st June) - BENNY: BEIGE PLANET MARS[870] -> On Mars, human slaves were illegal, but vat-grown clone slaves were permitted. "Spartan" was slang for a staunchly homosexual soldier who detested weakness in either gender.

Jason Kane had embarked on a lucrative career writing semi-autobiographical xenoporn novels; his first book, *Nights of the Perfumed Tentacle*, sold twelve million copies. Bernice's *Down Amongst the Dead Men* was in its sixth printing. Benny was attending an academic conference that celebrated the five-hundredth anniversary of Mars' terraforming and had a passionate reunion with Jason Kane - who, unknown to her, was in a relationship with the organiser of the event, the Pakhar named Professor Megali Scoblow. Benny failed to prepare her paper for the conference and instead gave a stream-of-consciousness delivery - in which she accidently exposed fellow academic Elizabeth Trinity as the notorious war criminal Tellassar.

Philip and Christina York, the trillionaire couple who owned YorkCorp, nearly started a nuclear conflict on Mars while fending off a hostile takeover from Bantu Cooperative. Together, Benny and Jason prevented the holocaust. Trinity submitted herself to General Keele for judgment.

The fiasco ruined Professor Scoblow's academic career. She became Jason's xenoporn editor. She was personally featured in Volume 7 (*Nibbling Around the Mousehole*, a bestseller) and took possession of his great unpublished work, *Barely Humanoid*.[871]

2595 - BENNY: WHERE ANGELS FEAR -> Immensely powerful beings thought to be the former gods of the People freed themselves from imprisonment on Dellah. As the gods' influence spread, Dellah experienced a burst of increasingly violent religious fanaticism; both the Time Lords and the supercomputer God feared this was the start of a much larger conflict. Benny and Braxiatel were separated as a fleet evacuated many Dellans, and Earth quarantined the planet.

The Time Lords were concerned with this situation.[872]

2595 - BENNY: THE MARY-SUE EXTRUSION[873] -> The gods had such dominance over Dellah, it was turning to desert. Their influence spread into space - Thanaxos, the system neighbouring Dellah, was gripped in a religious fever until Emile Mars-Smith, an ex-St. Oscar's student, went into seclusion to restrain the god nestled within him.

Pseudopod Enterprises Corporation dispatched an agent - a synthoid with Stratum Seven-level clearance - to find Bernice and learn more about the gods. The Agent discovered that Benny had rescued Wolsey from Dellah after submitting herself to a "Mary-Sue": a process that overwrites one's personality with a new persona, and helped her to resist the gods' influence.

Benny's former homeworld of Beta Caprisis was still abandoned, and had been since the Dalek assault there.

2595 - BENNY: DEAD ROMANCE[874] -> The Time Lords feared the gods to such an extent, they altered their treaty with the People. In exchange for not siding with the gods, the People would be allowed to develop time technology. The Time Lords also, using Chris Cwej as their agent, sought to prepare a bottle universe - one that contained a replica of 1970 Earth - as a shelter in case the gods became too powerful.

Cwej went into the bottle universe, and performed rituals that would manipulate the bottle's protocols and give the Time Lords access. He cloned three women and ritualistically murdered two of them - but the third escaped and came to believe she was a 23-year-old art student named Christine Summerfield. Cwej found himself unable to kill Christine, and they became lovers.

Cwej created and murdered yet-another clone, and a portal opened over London. The Time Lords poured forth, and reshaped the bottle Earth to their purposes. The world's nations fruitlessly launched a nuclear strike; Cwej caught a fatal radiation burst and was slated for regeneration. The Time Lords mutated the bottle-humanity into slaves or surrogate Time-Lords-in-waiting. Christine left the bottle.

c 2596 - BENNY: TEARS OF THE ORACLE[875] ->
Despite the new treaty, God predicted an 87% chance of war between the People and the Time Lords.

Braxiatel learned that the Oracle of the Lost was probably located on planetoid KS-159 - which he won by gambling with its owner, Howard Denson, at Vega Station. Benny and Braxiatel led an expedition to KS-159, but the parasite within the Oracle started murdering their associates. The Time Lords force-regenerated Chris Cwej into a shorter body, and sent him to help.

The parasite jumped into Benny's robotic porter Joseph - who was actually a drone of the People Ship J-Kibb, and had been deployed by God to spy on Benny. God directed the J-Kibb to crash onto Dellah, believing that the parasite's ability to spread uncertainty would counter-act the faith and religious mania that empowered the gods. The Oracle confirmed that the universal war was now much less likely to occur.

The Time Lords sterilised the planet Ordifica, which killed three hundred million people. Two thousand survivors, including Laura Tobin and Fitz, were evacuated to the *Justinian*, which headed to the year 1799.[876]

2596 - BENNY: RETURN TO THE FRACTURED PLANET[877] ->
The Proximan Chain had been established as a collection of space stations, planetary settlements and colonies. It was connected by a series of transit pads, and had a population of seven billion. The Chain lacked a cohesive law, and was largely inhabited by corporations doing shady business. Benny and Braxiatel recruited syn-

875 Dating *Benny: Tears of the Oracle* (Benny NA #20) - Allowing that *Benny: Twilight of the Gods* takes place "a year" after *Benny: The Mary-Sue Extrusion*, the calendar-flip from 2595 to 2596 likely occurs somewhere in this vicinity. The eighth Doctor, Fitz and Sam visit Vega Station in *Demontage*.
876 *Interference*, "two years" after Fitz is initiated into Faction Paradox.
877 Dating *Benny: Return to the Fractured Planet* (Benny NA #21) - *Benny: Tears of the Oracle* ended with Benny having only "a month to live" owing to a brain illness, and she's here cured.
878 Dating *Benny: Twilight of the Gods* (Benny NA #23) - Benny and company here reunite after spending a bit on their own pursuits, so some time has passed since *Benny: The Joy Device*. Moreover, it's said on p48 that "it had almost been a year since [Benny] had seen [Dellah]" (in *Benny: The Mary-Sue Extrusion*), which roughly coincides with the real-life duration of ten months that passed between the two books. The Ferutu first appeared in *Cold Fusion*.
The Benny New Adventures end in 2596, but Big Finish's Bernice Summerfield range don't rejoin her life until the very end of 2599, starting with the Benny anthology *The Dead Men Diaries*. As much as anything else, the relaunch dating was presumably meant to accommodate the release of Big Finish's first full-length Benny novel, *Benny: The Doomsday Manuscript*, in 2000 - nonetheless, this does create a three-year gap in Benny's timeline. In *The Dead Men Diaries*, Benny mentions arriving at the Braxiatel Collection after having endured "fraught adventures" that include "Time travel, other universes, the destruction of everything I'd previously relied upon to define me" and Jason being lost... all of which seems to refer to her New Adventures

tenure. It's possible that Benny whittled away a year or three at Vremnya until construction of the Braxiatel Collection was complete - but it's somewhat astonishing that she goes such a prolonged period with nothing particularly exciting happening to her.
879 *Benny: Resurrecting the Past*. It's possible that Braxiatel learned of the energy field near KS-159 after all the business concerning the Oracle of the Lost (*Benny: Tears of the Oracle*), and only then decided to make it the home of the Collection.
880 "Ten years" before *Benny: Beyond the Sea*.
881 *Benny: The Judas Gift*
882 *Benny: Secret Origins, Benny: Resurrecting the Past* and *Benny: Escaping the Future*. Braxiatel says Buenos Aires is destroyed "in the late twenty-sixth century", and Robyn says that it was "2598, or was it 2599?"
883 *Original Sin* (p204).
884 Two hundred years before *Nocturne*.
885 *The Stealers of Dreams*
886 From *Benny: The Dead Men Diaries*. The framing sequence says "it's now 2600", but the stories within predate *Benny: The Doomsday Manuscript* - which opens on New Year's Eve - and so must occur in 2599.
887 *Benny: Glory Days. Death to the Daleks* mentions the "Wonders of the Universe", so this is a different convention.
888 *Benny: The Dead Men Diaries* (p73).
889 *Benny: The Doomsday Manuscript.* The new Joseph is presumably built using what remains of the omnitronic processor that the seventh Doctor recovered from Victor Farrison's Joseph drone in *The Dark Flame*.
890 *Benny: The Dead Men Diaries:* "The Door Into Bedlam"
891 *Benny: The Infernal Nexus*, playing off a theory established in *Benny: Walking to Babylon*.

thoids - Artificial Personality Embodiments (APEs) - to hunt down any gods who eluded the Dellan quarantine. The freelance APE Kara Delbane was murdered, and Benny agreed to help Delbane's lover, the Stratrum Seven agent, find her killers. Absolam Sleed had survived his former encounter with the Agent and Delbane, and been transformed into a crystalline entity. Benny killed Sleed and the Dellan god merged with him, ending their plan to slaughter the Proximan Chain populace with a mutagenic bomb.

2596 - BENNY: THE JOY DEVICE -> Benny decided to have an adventure-filled holiday on the Rim frontier, with famed adventurer Dent Harper serving as her guide. Jason worried that Benny would enjoy herself so much that she'd never return home, and worked to prevent her from having a good time - or the stamina for an assignation with Harper. Braxiatel took possession of Dorpfeld's Prism, and filed in the KS-159 archives.

2596 - BENNY: TWILIGHT OF THE GODS[878] **->** The remaining gods on Dellah began to war amongst themselves, and the Time Lords and the People considered extinguishing them with a "doomsday probe" powerful enough to wipe out Dellah's sector of space. Hoping to avert this, Benny, Jason and Chris smuggled a dimensional-transfer node to Dellah using the *Revelation* - a dimension-hopping ship developed on Earth - then warped Dellah into the dimension from which the gods had originated. The gods stood revealled as a breakaway group of the Ferutu. They attacked Benny's group with temporal bolts - Benny's body was rejuvenated by about five years, and Chris reverted to his blonde-haired incarnation. Jason was left behind as Benny and Chris fled in the *Revelation*, trapping the Ferutu.

The accomplished diplomat Terin Sevic negotiated a peace on the war-torn planet of Vremnya, enabling wealthy patrons - including Braxiatel - to establish a university there. Braxiatel arranged for Benny to become the head of the new university's archaeology department. He also initiated construction of the Braxiatel Collection on KS-159.

Braxiatel deliberately situated the Collection near an energy field in space, one that produced interdimensional leakage strong enough to power a hundred colonies. He worked to keep the existence of the energy field a secret, fearing the Time Lords' enemies would exploit it.[879]

During a research term at Vremnya, Benny produced the documentary *Our Martians, Ourselves*.[880] In 2597, Bev Tarrant teamed with a smuggler, Ethan, who tried to kill her and steal their haul. Bev killed him instead.[881]

A space-time fissure opened in Lezama Park in Buenos Aires, and remained active for a century. A few dozen people fell through the fissure and emerged on the other side

of the universe at the planet Deindus, four million years in the future. The humans died, but the presence of their organic matter led to the creation of the Deindum.

> (=) Samuel Frost destroyed Buenos Aires to prevent the Deindum's existence. Bernice aided a Deindum creation, the android Robyn, in re-establishing the original timeline.[882]

The Twenty-Seventh Century

During the twenty-seventh century, oxygen factories were built in London.[883] Archaeologists unearthed documents pertaining to the extinct Ultani race and its bioharmonics, but failed to recognise their importance. The texts were filed, along with cosmographic mission reports, in the archives on Nocturne.[884] Colony World 4378976.Delta-Four was founded in the twenty-seventh century. The inhabitants soon started going "fantasy crazy" as a result of interactions with the microscopic native life, and the government banned all fiction to curb this problem.[885]

Bernice Summerfield at the Braxiatel Collection

Professor Bernice Summerfield became attached to the Braxiatel Collection, which touted itself as "A collection of everything. The various departments of the Braxiatel Collection house antique artifacts, literature, playscripts, recordings of events and people and performances, geological specimens, software and hardware of days gone by..."[886] The Collection housed 40% of the recognised Wonders of the Galaxy.[887]

Wolsey the cat had become a father - again - even though he'd been neutered, as the local fauna at the Collection were genetic hybrids, and bred in a curious fashion.[888] Braxiatel built Benny a new Joseph drone, with at least fifty terabytes of data storage.[889]

Jason Kane escaped from the Ferutu's domain, and wound up in the employ of Agraxar Flatchlock, a travel agent from an infernal dimension.[890] He didn't age while in the Ferutu realm, owing to Dr. Gilhooly's Theory of Transdimensional Contrivance.[891]

Braxiatel foresaw that the Deindum - a race that would evolve in the distant future - would develop time travel and conquer many worlds in many time periods, becoming strong enough to challenge even the Time Lords. He also discovered that Bernice would heavily impact the Deindum's development - that her memories and experiences would influence the primordial soup from which they would evolve. He increasingly meddled in Bernice's affairs and adjusted some of her personal history, hoping that, as a failsafe against his other efforts to curtail the

Deindum failing, he could influence the future conquerors through her.[892]

(=) Benny and Jason would eventually have two children - Keith Brannigan Summerfield-Kane and his younger sister Rebecca - and raise them alongside Benny's son Peter. Braxiatel, fearing that Keith and Rebecca would be too much of a drain on Benny's time, revised her history so they were never born.[893]

Braxiatel also changed the timelines so that Benny's friend Keri was a native of the twenty-sixth century, not the fortieth.[894] In this era, nano-suppressants were available that cured colds and flu within minutes.[895] Trans-Universal Export was "all over the galaxy" in Bernice's era. Messages between its various branches were sent across subspace using the Omninet bandwidth.[896]

2599 (31st December) to 2600 (1st-6th January) - BENNY: THE DOOMSDAY MANUSCRIPT[897] -> The

Fifth Axis, a military dictatorship, expanded its territory by subjugating numerous worlds. The planet Kasagrad resided in Axis space, but was protected by a global force field. Kolonel Daglan Straklant, claiming to head the Axis' relic restoration team, approached Benny and Braxiatel with an offer to help retrieve *The Doomsday Manuscript* from Kasagrad. Benny and Braxiatel realised Straklant was using them to deactivate Kasagrad's defence screen; owing to their actions, Kasagrad forces wiped out an Axis' Sixth Fleet, and forced a retreat to the old Merinfast Line. The Axis arrested Straklant on charges of treason.

---

892 *Benny: Resurrecting the Past, Benny: Escaping the Future.* Exactly when Braxiatel learns of Benny's significance to the Deindum's creation is unclear, but it motivates his actions and manipulations throughout much of the Big Finish Benny range.

IRVING BRAXIATEL VS. CARDINAL BRAXIATEL: Irving Braxiatel is one of Bernice Summerfield's best friends and most invaluable allies throughout the New Adventures, but the Big Finish Benny range recasts him as someone far more ruthless and amoral - a manipulator who (even under the caveat of acting for a greater good) aggressively rewrites the personal histories of Benny and her associates, brings the Mim to the point of extinction, and goads Benny's son Peter into savagely murdering Jason Kane.

In large measure, the difference in character owes to historical revision. *Gallifrey* Series 1 establishes that in Braxiatel's original history, he became so horrified by the destruction of Minyos (*Underworld*) that he left Gallifrey and founded the Braxiatel Collection to preserve the universe's great cultural treasures. Braxiatel's history changes, however, when a renegade Time Lord goes into Gallifrey's past and steals the timonic fusion device that obliterated Minyos, preventing the planet's annihilation and (inadvertently) robbing Braxiatel of his motive to leave Gallifrey. Alterations to Gallifrey's history are exceedingly rare - most of the tie-in ranges presume that safeguards created by Rassilon or his associates stop anyone from tampering with Gallifrey's past, although this isn't ever established on TV. Here, though, Gallifrey's timeline undeniably changes.

The second version of Braxiatel - the one who stays on Gallifrey long enough to become a Cardinal (as first seen in *Zagreus*) - presumably pops into existence and overwrites his previous self the exact moment the fusion device is stolen. Crucially, it's Cardinal Braxiatel and Romana (in *Gallifrey: The Inquiry*) who restore Gallifrey's history by facilitating the device's detonation - but as their existence is vital to the restoration of the timeline, they're presumably insulated when Gallifrey's history returns to normal.

Romana's history remains largely the same, save that Cardinal Braxiatel (*Gallifrey: Lies*) served as her tutor. For Cardinal Braxiatel, the result is that he stays on Gallifrey long enough for events to force him to trap a small part of Pandora's mind within his own. After he's subsequently exiled from Gallifrey (in *Gallifrey: Pandora*), events seen in the New Adventures run much the same - he still founds the Collection, etc. *Benny: The Wake* dramatizes scenes from *Theatre of War, Happy Endings* and *Benny: Tears of the Oracle*, helping to confirm that the NAs still occur, word for word (or near enough), in Braxiatel's revised history.

Whether the Pandora component directly warps Braxiatel's personality - or whether it just enhances his innate greed and arrogance - is a subject of some debate. Either way, it's surely not coincidence that the first instance of Braxiatel's machinations being exposed, *Benny: The Crystal of Cantus*, has one of Braxiatel's victims telling him, "The thing in your head... it's still there," presumably denoting the Pandora segment.

Odd as it might sound, the whole of Braxiatel's involvement in non-Gallifreyan time - all of the New Adventures with him, and the entire history of the Collection - seem to occur, from Gallifrey's perspective, between *Gallifrey* Series 2 and 3. While this seems to violate the unspoken idea that Time Lords meet in sequence, it's not unprecedented (see *The Apocalypse Element*).

Finally, in *Gallifrey: Mindbomb*, Braxiatel returns to Gallifrey after the Collection is defunct and attempts to salvage something of Time Lord society before the oncoming Last Great Time War. Largely failing, he once again allies with Romana, is lost to the Time Vortex (*Gallifrey: Disassembled*), emerges into history just prior to *Benny: Dragons' Wrath*, and has to spend years eluding his younger self before leaving a message for Benny in 2616 (*Benny: Epoch: Judgement Day*) that she should contact him.

893 *Benny: The End of the World* and the framing

2600 - BENNY: THE SECRET OF CASSANDRA[898]
-> Benny vacationed on the Earth colony Chosan, and was caught in a conflict between the warring continents of Calabraxia and Pevena. Cassandra Colley, a brilliant Pevenan neurotech designer, had transferred her mind into a synthetic form - a living bomb that was powerful enough to destroy the whole of Calabraxia. Colley's armaments were neutralised, and she was given into the care of her father, Captain Damien Colley.

The Pevenans and Calabraxians were mutually horrified by the scale of Colley's plans, and negotiated a peace.[899]

2600 (February) - BENNY: THE SQUIRE'S CRYSTAL[900] -> The aged collector Arsine de Vallen believed that the cavern of the legendary Soul-Sucker - a squire named Avil Fenman, who came into possession of a soul-swapping crystal on the planet Hera and was imprisoned by the noble Knights of Rowan - was on planetoid KS-159. One of de Vallen's agents found Avril's cavern, where her mind had indeed survived in a crystal. Wanting to question Avril about the crystal's applications, de Vallen's agent transferred Avril's mind into Benny's body - but Avril/Benny escaped and, after so long an imprisonment, availed herself of fleshly pleasures. She had a fling with the Collection's construction manager, Adrian Wall - a member of the Killoran race. Wall thought that he and Benny were in a relationship. More bodyswapping ensued, and de Vallen died after a botched bodyswapping attempt. Everyone regained their proper form, and Avril's mind was finally deposited into the body of a security guard named

Bill, whose mind had dissipated. Braxiatel let Avril/Bill continue living in her cavern, and Avril smashed the body-swapping crystal to better guarantee her freedom.

2600 (March) - BENNY: THE GODS OF THE UNDERWORLD[901] -> Venedel voted to withdraw from the Earthlink Federation. Braxiatel suspected that the long-dead Argians had built a war temple on Venedel, and Benny ran the Federation blockade to find the edifice, as it was thought to contain the Argian Oracle - a device that could locate anyone in the universe, the missing Jason Kane included. Benny stopped the hibernating Boor from awakening and furthering a new criminal empire, but the Oracle was destroyed.

According to the Doctor, the Daleks "started coming up with other schemes" after they lost the Wars.[902]

? 2600 - DEATH TO THE DALEKS[903] -> A plague spread through the atmospheres of many of the Outer Planets. Thousands died, and ten million people were threatened. Earth scientists quickly discovered an antidote to the plague: parrinium, a chemical that acted as both a cure and an immunity. It only existed in minute quantities on Earth, and was so rare that it was one of the most valuable known substances.

A satellite surveying the planet Exxilon discovered that parrinium was almost as common there as salt was on Earth. A Marine Space Corps ship was sent to Exxilon to collect parrinium, but the Daleks wanted to secure the substance for themselves, then force the

sequence to *Benny: A Life of Surprises* (which takes place in Benny's future, and presumably doesn't occur after Braxiatel rewrites her history). Potential versions of Keith Summerfield-Kane appeared in *Return of the Living Dad* and *Benny: A Life of Surprises*: "Might"; he was 18 months in the former, and killed as an adult in the latter. In *Benny: The Summer of Love*, Benny claims to know that she and Jason are fated to birth Keith and Rebecca, but that things aren't turning out as they should. Fan-commentators sometimes suggest that Braxiatel changed Benny's history to facilitate Peter's birth as a sort of oddity - the product of a human-Killoran mating - but there's little evidence to support this. An enigmatic man named "Kane" appears in *Burning Heart*, and is alluded to as being one of Benny and Jason's descendants (or possibly not, after Braxiatel's revisions to Benny and Jason's histories).
894 *Benny: The End of the World.* The change to Keri's background explains why she participates in the Benny audios, having first appeared in *Legacy*.
895 *Benny: Escaping the Future.* Van Statten was said to have cured the common cold in *Dalek*, and a vaccine exists at the time of *Fear Itself* (PDA). The secret was lost

in the Tenth Segment of Time, according to *The Ark*.
896 *Benny: Epoch: Private Enemy No. 1*
897 Dating *Benny: The Doomsday Manuscript* (Benny BF novel #1) - The story opens on New Year's Eve; Benny declares that it's "January the first" (p40) while tumbling into bed at three in the morning. Benny's diary cites the end date of the adventure as on or about "January 6th" (p125), and also confirms the year as 2600.
898 Dating *Benny: The Secret of Cassandra* (Benny audio #2.1) - The audio takes place between *Benny: The Doomsday Manuscript* and *Benny: The Squire's Crystal*. Chosan is named in *Benny: The Poison Seas*.
899 *Benny: The Poison Seas*
900 Dating *Benny: The Squire's Crystal* (Benny BF novel #3) - The month is given, which means that *The Squire's Crystal* takes place before *Benny: The Gods of the Underworld*, even though it was published afterwards.
901 Dating *Benny: The Gods of the Underworld* (Benny BF novel #2) - Benny's diary dates the start of the adventure to "March 12th 2600" (p7) and the story unfolds for some days afterwards.
902 *Love and War*, presumably a reference to the Daleks' use of blackmail in *Death to the Daleks*.

Space Powers to accede to their demands.

Upon arriving within range of the planet, the Earth ship suffered total power failure. The crew explored and discovered a fantastic city - the source of the power-drain - that was thousands of years old. The natives guarded this City fanatically, and the priests ensured that anyone caught there faced certain death. The third Doctor and Sarah Jane arrived shortly before the Daleks. Venturing into the City, the Doctor stopped the power drain. One of the Earthmen, Galloway, sacrificed himself to blow up the Daleks and their ship.

2600 - BENNY: THE STONE'S LAMENT[904] **->** The billionaire Bratheen Traloor contracted the Braxiatel Collection to build an extension onto his reclusive mansion on the planet Rhinvil. Traloor was obsessed with Benny, and had programmed his mansion's computer, House, to emulate her personality. Traloor and House physically merged into a cyborg that also became endowed with some of the planet's lifeforce. The gestalt tried to murder Benny, but Adrian Wall used explosives to kill it.

2600 - BENNY: THE EXTINCTION EVENT[904] **->** An auction house on Pelastrodon hosted The Extinction Event: an offering of items from destroyed civilisations. Braxiatel summoned Benny from a dig on the mud planet Lubellin to have her verify the authenticity of a harp from the obliterated planet Halstad. Hulver, the last survivor of Halstad, murdered the Gulfrarg ambassador for his role in the obliteration of his people. Hulver was taken away to the Gulfrarg homeworld for execution, but Braxiatel acquired the harp for the Collection.

2600 - BENNY: THE INFERNAL NEXUS[905] **->** Benny attempted to retrieve the damaged research vessel *Tinker's Cuss*, but her ship was pulled through space by an Enormous Space Octopus, part of an intergalactic towing service. She was deposited at Station Control - a nexus point between four hundred and seventeen multiverses, and run by clans from different realities - and reunited there with Jason Kane. He was contractually obliged - via his former employer, the benevolent demon Agraxar Flatchlock - to work for Volan Sleed, the head of the Iron

903 Dating *Death to the Daleks* (11.3) - There is no date given on screen, but the story takes place after the Dalek Wars. *The Programme Guide* placed it in "c.3700" (first edition), "c.2800" (second edition) and *The Terrestrial Index* put it in "the twenty-fifth century".

The TARDIS Logs offered a date of "3767 AD" (the same year as *The Monster of Peladon*). *The Official Doctor Who & the Daleks Book* claimed that the Dalek Plague used in this story is the Movellan Virus, so the author set the story between *Resurrection of the Daleks* and *Revelation of the Daleks*, around 3000 AD. This is nonsense, though, as that plague would have no effect on humans - as the Doctor says in *Resurrection of the Daleks*, "it is only partial to Dalek". The gas that disfigures humans seen in *Resurrection of the Daleks* is not the Movellan Virus, but a weapon that the Daleks themselves are immune to.

The Daleks routinely use germ warfare throughout their history (we see it in *The Dalek Invasion of Earth, Planet of the Daleks* and *Resurrection of the Daleks*). It's never stated in this story that the Daleks caused the plague on the human colony planets, but it's fair to infer they did, especially as they're stopped from launching a "plague missile" at Exxilon. *Timelink* suggested "3500". *About Time* said, "A dating between 2600 and 2900 would be plausible".

904 Dating *Benny: The Stone's Lament* and *Benny: The Extinction Event* (Benny audios #2.2, 2.3) - These are placed strictly by order of release.

905 Dating *Benny: The Infernal Nexus* (Benny BF novel #4) - "A few months" (p185) have passed since *The Squire's Crystal*.

906 Dating *Benny: The Skymines of Karthos* (Benny audio #2.4) - Five months have passed since Benny got impregnated (in absentia) in *The Squire's Crystal*.

907 Dating *Benny: The Glass Prison* (Benny BF novel #5) - "About ten months" (p17) have passed since *Benny: The Doomsday Manuscript*. That's in line with Benny being inseminated in *Benny: The Squire's Crystal* (which takes place in February), allowing that human-Killoran matings must still have a nine-month gestation cycle. *The Glass Prison* begins at "Day -7" (p9) from Peter's birth and finishes with the event on "Day 0" (p122), save for an epilogue with his christening. It's still 2600 (p25). Peter's middle name is a remembrance of Guy de Carnac from *Sanctuary*.

908 Dating Bernice Summerfield Series 3 (*Benny: The Greatest Shop in the Galaxy*, audio #3.1; *Benny: The Green-Eyed Monster*, audio #3.2; *Benny: The Plague Herds of Excelis*, Excelis series #4; *Benny: The Dance of the Dead*, audio #3.3; *Benny: A Life of Surprises*, collection #2; and *Benny: The Mirror Effect*, audio #3.4) and Series 4 (*Benny: The Bellotron Incident* audio #4.1; *Benny: The Draconian Rage*, audio #4.2; *Benny: The Poison Seas*, audio #4.3; *Benny: Life During Wartime*, collection #3; *Benny: Death and the Daleks*, audio #4.4; *Benny: The Big Hunt*, novel #6) - The dating clues within these stories are sparse, but time, particularly with regards Peter's growth and development, appears to be progressing roughly in accord with the real world. The opening story of Series 5 (*Benny: The Grel Escape*) dates to 2603, so it seems reasonable to conclude that Series 3 and 4 respectively occur in 2601 and 2602.

909 "Seven years" before *Benny: Beyond the Sea*. IMC operatives were seen in *Colony in Space*; the company is also mentioned in *Benny: Resurrecting the Past*.

Sun Clan. Jason and Benny exposed Sleed's plan to incite warfare between his clan-rivals. He was decapitated, and his body generated the head of Flatchlock - who explained that his race had primary, secondary and tertiary heads and personas. He made peace with the offended clans.

Benny learned that she was pregnant following Avril's encounter with Adrian Wall. Jason formed Dead Dog in the Water Preproductions to represent his xenoporn work, and wrote an outline for *The Kiss of the Dragon Woman* based upon his dalliance with Lady Mae An T'zhu, the head of the Dragon Clan. The Braxiatel Collection had a recently opened Starbucks.

2600 - BENNY: THE SKYMINES OF KARTHOS[906]
-> Benny travelled to the thullium mining settlement on the planet Karthos when her longtime friend Caitlin Peters went missing there. Winged humanoids made from carbon and thullium deposits - disposable troopers generated by a machine built by a long-dead race - attacked the miners. Caitlin was saved, and the machine was buried.

2600 (October) - BENNY: THE GLASS PRISON[907] ->
Benny left to quietly give birth away from the Collection, but ended up crashing on Deirbhile, a Fifth Axis world. She was incarcerated within the Axis' Glass Prison, a jail made from transparent walls to better monitor the inmates. Benny gave birth to a son, but the imprisoned Kolonel Straklant sought revenge by trying to kill her child. In repelling Straklant, Benny unleashed sonic waves that weakened the prison. Benny fled with her son and left Straklant to die as the entire edifice was destroyed. A Grel inmate, Sophia, scuttled the Axis' invasion plans by killing the Fifth Axis Imperator.

Afterward, Benny presented her child to the universe as Peter Guy Summerfield in a christening ceremony attended by, amongst others, her father and an older-looking Chris Cwej.

Buffy the Vampire Slayer was now in Season 792.

2601 - BENNY: THE GREATEST SHOP IN THE GALAXY[908] -> Benny signed up for a dig on the planet Baladroon - an excuse to explore the Gigamarket, the galaxy's largest shopping centre. The Gigamarket's time fields were disrupted as part of a hostile takeover, enabling the carnivorous Borvali to attack the human patrons. Benny's intervention prevented massive casualties, and the Gigamarket's stock plummeted.

2601 - BENNY: THE GREEN-EYED MONSTER -> The Goronos system consisted of five inhabited planets, each of them desiring supremacy over the entire region. Lady Ashantra du Lac of Goron IV asked Benny to verify the authenticity of various artifacts - part of a scheme to install Ashantra's charges, Boris and Ronald, as the system's rul-

ers, with Ashantra serving as regent. Ashantra's plot was exposed, and she was arrested.

2601 - BENNY: THE PLAGUE HERDS OF EXCELIS ->
Civilisation on Artaris had recovered enough that Excelis City had a feudal society. Benny visited Artaris and met Iris Wildthyme, who asked for help in recovering the Relic. An insectoid named Snyper used the Relic to create a horde of zombie animals, which attacked the Excelis populace. Snyper intended to kill the Excelans wholesale - an act that would detonate the Relic, destroy Artaris and obliterate the passing battlefleet of the war queen who had eradicated Snyper's people. Snyper was killed, and the Relic became an ordinary gold lame handbag.

2601 - BENNY: THE DANCE OF THE DEAD ->
Galactic dignitaries concluded peace negotiations with the war queen who had slaughtered Snyper's race, and Benny - hung-over from an outing with Iris - sought passage aboard the space liner *Empress*, which was en route to Ronnos Minor. Explosions breached the ship's hull - the Colgarian ambassador and his wife were killed, causing Benny and Grand Marshall Sstac, an Ice Lord, to inhale fumes from crystals that the Colgarians used to pass on memories to their offspring. Benny and Sstac experienced the Colgarians' memories until a team of Ice Warriors rescued them. The culprits behind the explosions were exposed, and further warfare was averted.

2601 - BENNY: THE MIRROR EFFECT -> A rare mirror found on an ice planet acted as a gateway to multiple timelines and locations. The entity trapped within the mirror sought to free itself by reflecting people's dark passions and absorbing their personalities. Benny, Jason and Adrian - but not Braxiatel - were made to confront dark reflections of themselves until Jason destroyed the mirror and the mirror-entity. Braxiatel mentally conditioned Jason to not question his authority and decisions.

IMC owned the planet Maximederias, a world that was only 3% land. The natives there were micro-organisms, who tricked an IMC survey team into thinking that the planet had no viable supply of minerals. The planet gained protected status when IMC signed it over to an affiliate.[909]

2602 - BENNY: THE BELLOTRON INCIDENT -> The Sontaran-Rutan war was now encroaching upon Terran trade routes. The planet Bellotron had an irregular orbit, and was passing from Rutan space into a Sontaran-controlled region. Before Bellotron slipped out of Earth jurisdiction, Benny attempted to examine a hieroglyph-covered slab on the planet. A peace-loving Rutan faction intercepted Benny, and kept her safe while their agents stopped the Rutan military from detonating a bomb on

Bellotron to damage Sontaran assets - an act that would have destroyed Bellotron's hunter-gatherer population.

Benny encountered Bev Tarrant as part of this, and returned with her to the Collection.

2602 - BENNY: THE DRACONIAN RAGE -> Vilus Krull's skull surfaced on Tranagus, a former Earth colony that was now part of the Draconian Empire. The skull renewed the Cult of the Dark Flame within the Empire; twenty million Draconians on Tranagus committed ritual suicide in support of it. On behalf of Emperor Shen and the Draconian court, Benny investigated the matter in Dralos, one of the oldest cities on Draconia. Dark Flame members within the court were exposed, and Benny helped to secure Krull's skull.

2602 - BENNY: THE POISON SEAS -> A Sea Devil colony on Chosan came under threat from both Calabraxian terrorists and a lethal protein in the planet's waters. The Earth Reptile Council asked Braxiatel for help, and he referred the matter to Benny. The terrorists were thwarted, and the Sea Devils abandoned their colony upon discovering that the protein - common to all sea life on Chosan - was sentient and adapting itself to possess them.

The Daleks provided the Fifth Axis with advanced weaponry that enabled them to capture new territories. The expansion of the Axis' dominions was a massive distraction, part of a Dalek plot to capture Braxiatel's TARDIS and enhance their time-travel capabilities.[910]

2602 - BENNY: LIFE DURING WARTIME[911] -> Benny returned from Chosan to find that the Fifth Axis had overrun the Braxiatel Collection's sector of space, and occupied the Collection itself. Braxiatel was under house arrest, Adrian and other Killorans were forced onto a work gang, Jason pretended to collaborate to better work against the Axis, and Peter went into hiding. Bev Tarrant secretly led a resistance movement.

Benny made bolder moves against the Axis, and killed the sadistic Commander Spang. She later infiltrated the Axis' communications centre, and discovered that the new leader of the Axis was her father, Isaac Summerfield...

2602 - BENNY: DEATH AND THE DALEKS[911] -> Benny and Jason tracked Isaac Summerfield to the planet Heaven, where he was slaved to a Dalek battle computer and made to coordinate the Axis' battlefleets. Bev and Adrian combined their forces with mercenaries allied with Jason to launch a major attack against the troops occupy-

910 Benny: Death and the Daleks
911 Dating Benny: Life During Wartime (Benny collection #3) and Benny: Death and the Daleks (Benny audio #4.4) - According to the introduction of Life During Wartime, "It's 2602." The audio follows on from the short story collection.
912 Benny: The End of the World. Mira is mentioned throughout the works of Dave Stone, and first appeared in Benny: The Mary-Sue Extrusion.
913 Dating Benny: The Big Hunt (Benny BF novel #6) - The blurb says that Benny is taking a break from the rebuilding of the Braxiatel Collection, suggesting that The Big Hunt follows on from Benny: Death and the Daleks - although technically, it was released between Benny: The Grel Escape and Benny: The Bone of Contention. The Eagle Museum is presumably in Armstrong City, mentioned in The Sword of Forever.
914 "A good few years" before Benny: The Empire State. Maggi's full name is given in Benny: The Tub Full of Cats. Braxiatel tells Maggi that the raw energy for her power comes from a stabilised black hole - presumably the Eye of Harmony on Gallifrey.
915 Dating Bernice Summerfield Series 5 (Benny: The Grel Escape, audio #5.1; The Bone of Contention, audio #5.2; Benny: A Life Worth Living, collection #4; Benny: The Relics of Jegg-Sau, audio #5.3; Benny: The Masquerade of Death, audio #5.4; Benny: Silver Lining, promo with DWM #351; Benny: The Tree of Life, Benny BF novel #7) and Series 6 (Benny: The Heart's Desire, audio #6.1; Benny: The

Kingdom of the Blind, audio #6.2; Benny: A Life in Pieces, collection #5; Benny: The Lost Museum, audio #6.3; Benny: The Goddess Quandary, audio #6.4; Benny: Parallel Lives, collection #6; Benny: Something Changed, collection #7; Benny: The Crystal of Cantus, audio #6.5) - The Series 5 opener (The Grel Escape) cites 2603 as "the present day", and the final adventure of Series 6 (The Crystal of Cantus) occurs in January (or possibly February) 2606. Ergo, Benny Series 5 and 6 must be extended over a nearly three-year period.
Helpfully, two markers denote when the calendar changes - Benny: A Life Worth Living (released between The Bone of Contention and The Relics of Jegg-Sau) says "it's now 2604" (p1) and also that it's "April 2604" (p17), and Benny: The Heart's Desire takes place on Christmas Eve of the same year, pushing the remainder of Series 6 into 2605. The only problem with this arrangement is that Benny has a comparatively unadventurous 2603, but it's no different from the similarly uneventful gap between her New Adventures and Big Finish stories.
916 Benny: The Crystal of Cantus; Benny: A Life Worth Living: "A Summer Affair".
917 Dating 100: "The 100 Days of the Doctor" (BF #100d) - The expedition occurs while Benny is in Braxiatel's employ; otherwise, its placement is arbitrary.
918 The year prior to Benny: The Goddess Quandary.

ing the Collection. The Daleks were wiped out, whereupon Braxiatel hard-wired his time machine to theirs and created a facsimile of the Dalek battle computer. Isaac used this lash-up to pilot the Axis' fleets into black holes, cause their forces to attack their own homeworlds, lead their own troops into ambushes, and more until the Axis was finished as a military power.

Benny resumed her relationship with Jason. Braxiatel forged deals with neighbouring empires to protect the Collection, and took Isaac home to his native era.

> (=) Jason Kane's psychic associate, Mira, was killed during the occupation. Braxiatel altered history to reverse Mira's death, and conditioned her to serve as his agent.[912]

2602 - BENNY: THE BIG HUNT[913] **->** A powerful businessman, Orlean Wolvencroft, owned the Eagle Museum on Earth's moon. A Van Neumann probe had landed on a planet in System 81, and spurred the creation of hyper-evolving robotic animals; robotic sabretooths were developed from robotic wolves, etc. Benny prevented Wolvencroft from possessing the robot-animal technology, as it could have destroyed entire ecosystems. Wolvencroft was stranded in System 81, and a hyperdrive explosion created gravity shockwaves that would prevent any ships from approaching the robots' adopted world for a decade.

Braxiatel fashioned a "daughter" - a living temporal physics experiment that he poured into a genetics engineering template that was available over-the-counter in Tokyo. He added a bit of his genetic material to stabilise the resultant creation: Margarita ("Maggi") Braxiatel Matsumoto, who could use temporal-rollback to restore people and edifices of the past. He tasked her with "cleaning up" various temporal messes.[914]

2603 - BENNY: THE GREL ESCAPE[915] **->** A party of time-travelling Grel from circa 2648 deemed Peter Summerfield - the child of a Killoran and a body-jumping sorceress of legend - as worthy of further study, and attempted to capture him. Peter proved capable of activating Benny and Jason's time rings, and the Grel pursued them to various points in space-time. The time rings temporarily matured Peter's body, and he killed the Grel following them.

2603 - BENNY: THE BONE OF CONTENTION -> Legends claimed that the inhabitants of the Mancor Sector fashioned skeletons around which cosmic storms would combine to form the Shadow Swans, creatures that terraformed worlds for their creators to inhabit. The Wishing Bone of Perlor was said to be a bone from one such Swan, and to bring good fortune upon whomever possessed it.

The government on Perlor traded the Bone to the Galyari aboard the Clutch in exchange for weaponry, but fell to a rebellion anyway. The new Perlor government asked Benny to negotiate the return of the Bone. She found that a Galyari youth, Griko, had been grown around the Bone in the hope of creating a Galyari warrior who could overcome his race's deep-rooted fear of the enigmatic Sandman. Griko broke his conditioning, and was killed to prevent his destroying the entire Clutch. The Galyari compensated the Perloran for the loss of their artifact.

Braxiatel wanted an army of Cybermen that could protect the Collection, and usurped the Cyber-tombs on Cantus. The blissful summer that Braxiatel had promised Ronan McGinley came to an end, and McGinley was forcibly installed as the Cantus Cybermen's Cyber-controller.[916]

c 2604 - 100: "The 100 Days of the Doctor"[917] **->** The sixth Doctor and Evelyn aided an expedition funded by Irving Braxiatel, and led by Bernice Summerfield. Evelyn had many good talks with Benny, but judged that she drank too much and had a lot of relationship issues.

2604 - BENNY: THE RELICS OF JEGG-SAU -> Benny went to the abandoned planet Jegg-Sau to search for the lost treasures of Robert Eliot Whitman. The Kettlewell-style Robots inhabiting the planet - including one designated K-103 - had gone mad for their isolation, and sought to form a new colony with robotic replicas of human beings. Any human that acted irrationally would be replaced, as the Robots did when Ethan Kalwell - a descendant of Professor Kettlewell - came in search of his ancestor's inventions. The interstellar Red Cross dispatched rescue ships to retrieve Benny, but the Robots attacked them after absorbing enough energy to enlarge in size. The Red Cross jets brushed aside Benny's pleas for clemency, and wiped out the Robots.

2604 - BENNY: MASQUERADE OF DEATH -> Benny found a copy of a play, *The Masquerade of Death*, and fell prey to a complex virus embedded in the text. She was comatose for four days, and dreamed of a storybook land with characters such as the Queen of Spring, the Duke of Autumn, the Matriarch of Winter and the Player of All Seasons. She used storyland logic to wake herself up.

On Etheria, Abbot Primus greatly enjoyed watching the Galactic Snooker Championship.[918]

2604 - BENNY: SILVER LINING -> Benny found a tomb of Cybermen on Tysir IV while giving an archaeology consult. The Cybermen hoped to weaken humanity with a plague, but Benny sealed the Cybermen within their tomb, and they were destroyed when it blew up.

2604 - BENNY: THE TREE OF LIFE -> The entrepreneur Hugo Tollip bought a jungle planet that he renamed Tollip's World, and initiated research to commercialise or even weaponise the variety of DNA found there. Benny helped to prevent Tollip from transplanting a Tree of Life off world, fearing it would defensively create a virus powerful enough to wipe out humanity. Tollip was killed, and the hammies stored within the Trees were revived.

2604 (24th December) - BENNY: THE HEART'S DESIRE[919] **->** Benny became embroiled in a diversionary game between the Eternals Hardy and Barron on Marlowe's World. She captured the prize of their game - a shard of Enlightenment - and used it to wish away a pulsar that was headed towards the Braxiatel Collection. For good measure, she turned Hardy and Barron into mortals. She then threw the Enlightenment shard out an airlock, confident that another Eternal would instantly claim it.

2605 - BENNY: THE KINGDOM OF THE BLIND -> Benny came into telepathic contact with the enslaved descendents of the Halavans while examining artifacts from the lost civilisation on Petreus III. The Monoids had become increasingly cruel slave-masters, giving the Halavans numbers for names, and forcing any slave who developed the power of speech to forfeit one of their other senses. Benny aided the Halavans in regaining their telepathic gestalt, which enabled them to overpower their masters. The vengeful Halavans - despite Benny's plea for mercy - psionically stripped the Monoids of their names and removed their ability to speak. They also used their mental prowess to destroy the Monoid planet, and set course back to Petreus III.[920]

The CroSSScape were gestalt beings who had transferred their minds into a datascape. The sudden appearance in the datascape of a box that couldn't be opened filled the CroSSScape with misery and loathing, and they theorised that their god - who had been imprisoned within the Tartarus Gate, a legendary gateway to Hell - could open it for them. To find the Gate, the CroSSScape presented themselves as a benevolent religious order that

---

919 Dating *Benny: The Heart's Desire* (Benny audio #6.1) - The story occurs on Christmas Eve, and ends at the stroke of midnight. Mention is made of a flight to Stella Stora, which was first referenced in *Terror of the Vervoids* and is cited in *Benny: Present Danger* (p93).

920 This is the background to the Monoid race seen in *The Ark*. They appear to have some contact with humanity long prior to that story, however: *The Doomsday Weapon* (the novelisation of *Colony in Space*) cites the Monoids as a race that humanity encountered during its expansion into space, and *The Pirate Loop* references them as a slave race akin to the Ood.

921 At least a year prior to *Benny: The Tartarus Gate*.

922 Dating *Benny: A Life in Pieces* (Benny collection #5) - The collection was published in December 2004, which all things being equal would place it between *Benny: The Relics of Jegg-Sau* and *Benny: Masquerade of Death* in 2604. However, Benny's diary and other notations date these stories to 2605. Morton is murdered on 23rd of September, 2605 (extrapolating backward from the anniversary of his death, p150), and Benny's diary claims that she and Jason return to the Collection on the last day of his trial, "14/11/05".

923 The pulp entertainment *Aventures de la Frontière Nouvelle* is presumably a translation of the Adventures of the New Frontier series often cited in New Adventures by Dave Stone.

924 *Benny: A Life in Pieces*

925 Dating *Benny: The Goddess Quandary* (Benny audio #6.4) - The cliffhanger leads into *Benny: Parallel Lives*, set in 2606. This audio was released after *Benny: The Last Museum*, but as that story leads into Braxiatel's departure in *Benny: The Crystal of Cantus*, *The Goddess Quandary* and its related stories must come first.

926 Dating *Benny: Parallel Lives* (Benny collection #6) - The book's introduction claims that "it is now 2606," which is in keeping with it variously being stated that Peter (who was born in 2600) is now "five" and "nearly six". The odd man out is Clarissa Jones' statement that it's been "nearly two years" (p4) since the Axis occupation when it's actually been more like four. In "Jason and the Pirates" - providing a word of its unreliable narration can be believed - mention is made of Oinky Pete, a Piglet Person, presumably the same race that's extinct in *Burning Heart* (set in 3174).

927 *Benny: Something Changed*. Benny says that, relatively speaking, she owned Wolsey for twelve years.

928 Dating *Benny: The Lost Museum* (Benny audio #6.3) - The blurb specifies the date and month. The last page of *Benny: Something Changed* specifies that *The Lost Museum* comes next in sequence.

929 Dating *Benny: The Crystal of Cantus* (Benny audio #6.5) - According to *Benny: Parallel Lives* (p10), Benny spends "two weeks" trailing Clarissa and Peter to Atwalla 3. If she spends the same amount of time returning, most of January must be consumed with her in transit. While it's *just* possible to imagine that *Benny: The Lost Museum* takes place in January as stated, Jason says that *The Crystal of Cantus* occurs nearly a week later, so it must now be February.

Benny mentions the realisation that the Cybermen have tombs dotted all over the galaxy as part of established history, confirming that her native time is after the *Cyberman* audio series. Mention is also made of the Garazone Bazaar from *The Sword of Orion*. The Crystal of Cantus would appear to be the Coronet of Rassilon (*The Five Doctors*), provided to Braxiatel by his younger self on Gallifrey.

used an edifice, simply called "the Factory", to reverse natural disasters by rolling back time on doomed worlds. The CroSSScape spent a year looking for the Gate and finally located it on Cerebus Iera, a desert world prone to freak electrical storms.[921]

2605 (23rd September to 14th November) - BENNY: A LIFE IN PIECES: "Zardox Break" / "The Purpura Pawn" / "On Trial"[922] ->

Earth had an official Acquisition of Alien Artifacts Department. A girl group, the Glitta Bitches, were working on a new Tri-D movie.

Marck Morton became governor of Verum - the contested moon of Aequitas - and negotiated a peace that granted Verum independence. However, Morton was murdered on 23rd September, 2605. Jason Kane - who had leveraged his career as a xenoporn author and become a major celebrity on the resort planet Zardox, partly due to the salacious reporting of his exploits in *Aventures de la Frontière Nouvelle* - was charged with the crime, and thought to have killed Morton to steal a relic of the old empire, the Purpura Pawn, from him.[923]

Jason's trial began on 12th November; Benny helped to establish his innocence on 14th November. As they returned to the Collection, a bomb destroyed the courthouse, killing one hundred and thirty-one people. The crime was blamed on parties who had opposed Verum's independence, stoking political tensions.

On 1st December, Aequitas cut all ties with Verum. On 2nd December, the Earth Empire dissolved Verum's government and secured the moon with peacekeeping troops; this instigated an era of hatred and terrorist incidents. On 2nd January, 2606, an Earth official named Matthew Barrister died in a shuttle explosion, after confiscating the remaining Ceatul Empire relics. The items officially went missing, but the Purpura Pawn, somehow, wound up in Braxiatel's possession.[924]

2606 - BENNY: THE GODDESS QUANDARY[925] ->

The leaky roof of the Etheria monastery was one of the Wonders of the Galaxy.

Benny had completed a documentary on the legendary warlord Aldebrath for the Tri-D Broadcasting Company, and the monks on Etheria invited her to learn whether their planetoid system contained his final resting place. Tri-D's central news bureau was on Angola V. Benny's friend Keri, a journalist for Tri-D, documented the search.

Benny found Aldebrath's ship, the *Fervent Hope*, in one of Etheria's outer planetoids. Aldebrath's mind was in the ship's computer systems, and she used her love-inducing telepathy to stop a religious uprising. Keri's reputation had suffered after she botched an expose on the multi-zillionaire Stellis Gadd, and Benny ended their friendship after learning that Keri had hampered her search to get a better story. Benny took Aldebrath and the *Fervent Hope* back to

the Collection, only to find that Clarissa Jones, one of the Collection's administrators, had gone missing...

2606 - BENNY: PARALLEL LIVES: "The Serpent's Tooth" / "Hiding Places" / "Jason and the Pirates" / "Parallel Lives"[926] ->

Clarissa Jones abruptly kidnapped Peter and disappeared. Benny followed them to Atwalla 3, a medieval world in the Fallan Nebula where women had no rights. She went undercover as a man, joined some knights on a successful quest and was rewarded by being married to Jesh, the daughter of Emperor Jodal. Benny bluffed Jodal into thinking that a virus had been devised that would let the Atwallan breed with other species - an act that would, in time, destroy the Atwallan bloodline. Jodal considered Benny's threat to unleash the virus unless he granted the Atwallan females equal rights.

Jason joined the search for Peter late, having been delayed - or so he told Benny - owing to an escapade where he had to join some pirates led by Buggering Barnabas Jimmity Jim-Bob Hullabaloo, aboard their ship *The Black Pig*.

Benny, Jason, Bev and Adrian confronted Clarissa on the suburban worlds of Thuban. Clarissa said she was from the future, and that she wanted to raise Peter to avoid the life that Benny suspected was in wait for him. She relented and returned Peter to Benny, but a scuffle led to Bev killing Clarissa as she drew a gun on Adrian.

Bernice's cat Wolsey died from natural causes, and was buried in the Collection's garden. Bev and Adrian were now in relationship. Temporal distortion revised the history of the Collection's gardener, Hass - he was no longer a Martian, and always had been a Yesodi, a jellyfish-like being capable of generating a vast store of radiation within its pressure suit.[927]

2606 (January) - BENNY: THE LOST MUSEUM[928] ->

Benny and Jason went to salvage exhibits from the Trib Museum, as the dictatorial regime on the planet housing it had fallen. Jason quelled the carnage by tricking each faction into thinking that the other had backed down.

2606 (February) - BENNY: THE CRYSTAL OF CANTUS[929] ->

The Galyari performed a production of *Macbeth* on Berkoff IV.

The crystal that allowed Ronan McGinley to control the Cybermen on Cantus was killing him, and a new Cybercontroller was required. Braxiatel tried and failed to install Jason as the new Cyber-controller; Benny learned of his treachery, and Jason broke Braxiatel's mental conditioning. Benny used the crystal to eradicate the Cantus Cybermen, then destroyed it. His machinations exposed, Braxiatel departed from the Collection. In his absence, the Draconians made a claim to planetoid KS-159.

2606 - BENNY: THE TARTARUS GATE[930] -> The Craxitanian government was so grateful to Benny for finding their prized temple, they rewarded her with ten boxes of their famed champagne.

The CroSSScape captured Bernice, thinking that - thanks to her body having already accommodated the mind of a goddess - she could serve as the physical host to their god. The Factory regressed time on Cerebus Iera to when the Tartarus Gate - a black hole, held in perfect balance - had last been opened, and the god transferred across. The god cast the CroSSScape into the Hell that lay beyond the Gate, and was then trapped in a datascape box.

2606 - BENNY: TIMELESS PASSAGES -> Important manuscripts had been lost when a giant space aardvark accidentally inhaled the Splendid Biblious Spiroplex of the ten billion sapients of Zoomos Prime. Rare documents in this era included *The Atrocity Exhibitions*, *The Augenblick Presidency* by Robert Dallek and *Aristotle's Poetics, Part 3: Smokey is the Bandit*. The Adjudicators were still active.

The origin of the Labyrinth on the planet Kerykeion was unknown, but it contained one of the biggest collections of human publications outside Earth, with more than two hundred million books, including the only known copy of *Gay Bulgaria*. A corporation, Omni-Spatial Mercantile Dynamics (OSMD), sought to buy Kerykeion because the Labyrinth's passages stretched into different points in space-time, which is how the original librarians there acquired their collection.

Bev Tarrant was now administrating the Braxiatel Collection, and sent Bernice to purchase rare books from the Labyrinth before the OSMD buy-out. Benny met - and destroyed - a murderous cyborg sent from the future by OSMD's descendents.[931] The librarian Hermione Wolfe wound up owning the Labyrinth, and cut a deal with the Braxiatel Collection as to the Labyrinth's holdings.

---

930 Dating Bernice Summerfield Series 7 (*Benny: The Tartarus Gate*, audio #7.1; *Benny: Timeless Passages*, audio #7.2; *Benny: The Worst Thing in the World*, audio #7.3; *Benny: Collected Works*, collection #8; *Benny: The Summer of Love*, audio #7.4; *Benny: Old Friends*, collection #9; *Benny: The Oracle of Delphi*, audio #7.5; *Benny: The Empire State*, audio #7.6) - Series 7 continues onward from Series 6 (which ends in February 2606) and finishes shortly prior to the opening episodes of Series 8 (which can be definitively dated to October 2607). Unavoidably, then, a single season's worth of stories must be spread out over a 20-month period.

It's not entirely clear when the switchover from 2606 to 2607 occurs. *Benny: Collected Works* is less helpful than other collections in making this call, as its stories are set over the course of a year, straddling both 2606 and 2607. Nor is trying to put the year in tandem with the year of release entirely helpful - *The Summer of Love* came out in October 2006, and yet must occur in 2607. The best compromise is to date the first two stories of Series 7 to 2606, and place *The Worst Thing in the World* in 2607, in accordance with a "last year" remark made regarding events in the Drome in *Benny: The Wake*.

In accounting for some of Benny's time in 2006, she spends at least a month being held captive in *The Tartarus Gate*. She also spends two weeks in transit to reach Kerykeion (and presumably the same amount to return home) in *Timeless Passages*.

931 Benny destroys the cyborg by bringing its present and future selves into collision, evidently invoking the Blinovitch Limitation Effect.

932 *Benny: Collected Works*. The malfunctions begin "months" prior to *Benny: The Summer of Love*. It's not said how Braxiatel went into the past without his TARDIS to become the Stone of Barter (*Benny: The Empire State*).

933 Dating *Benny: The Summer of Love* (Benny audio #6.4) - The story does, apparently, take place in summer, with references to the heat.

934 *Benny: The Summer of Love*, and similarly noted in the epilogue to *Benny: Collected Works*.

935 Dating *Benny: Old Friends*: "Cheating the Reaper" / "The Soul's Prism" (Benny collection #9a, 9c) - The two "modern-day" novellas in this collection occur between *Benny: The Summer of Love* and *Benny: The Oracle of Delphi*, and the back-cover blurb says that it's "late 2607". Benny now looks "nearly 40".

936 Dating *Benny: The Empire State* (Benny audio #7.6) - Benny seems to spend a few days digging up the Stone, and then as many as eight in the new Empire State itself. Benny ends *The Empire State* intending to travel back to the Collection, only seems to lose about a week in transit in the following story, and arrives in time for *Benny: The Judas Gift*, which occurs in the third week of October 2607. So, *The Empire State* very probably occurs in the same month.

937 Dating Bernice Summerfield Series 8 (*Benny: The Tub Full of Cats*, audio #8.1; *Benny: The Judas Gift*, audio #8.2; *Benny: Freedom of Information*, audio #8.3; *Benny: Nobody's Children*, collection #10; *Benny: The Two Jasons*, novel #9; *Benny: The End of the World*, audio #8.4; *Benny: The Final Amendment*, audio #8.5; *Benny: The Wake*, audio #8.6) - The stories that compose Benny Series 8 unfold in the space of roughly three months. *The Judas Gate* dates itself to 23rd and 24th October, 2607, and the other stories can be extrapolated from that (see the individual entries for more). In *The Tub Full of Cats*, Maggie reiterates the year as "2607", which translates to "818" in the standard modern calendar.

938 Dating *Benny: The Judas Gift* (Benny audio #8.2) - The exact dates are given via headline news and a recording that Bev makes. Events said to have occurred

Braxiatel had merged his TARDIS with the Collection before his departure. Without him, the Collection became subject to breakdowns.[932]

2607 - BENNY: THE WORST THING IN THE WORLD

-> Horses were believed to be extinct. Pop sensation Manda I had a new single, entitled "Pumpin' Out Your Baby of Love", set to the holovid of her daughter's birth.

The Drome had been established as a self-contained community that produced televised content for GalNet, and was located a half an hour from the Galactic Transit Core. The Drome's offerings included the *Inspector Wembley* movies, the long-running soap *Squaxaboolon Street*, *Topless Garden Makeovers*, *Whose Stool is That?*, *Airhead Factor*, *The Larder in the Garden*, *Mutilation Razor-Motor-Scooter Hockey on Ice*, *Frock and Fanny* and a revival of *The Infinity Division*. Galnet had at least 4796 channels.

Jason Kane was being interviewed about his work on *Xenomorphic Bondage Slaves, Part 37,* and asked Benny to investigate mysterious occurrences at the Drome. Its central computer, an AI named Marvin, had become so advanced that it was altering reality in accordance with people's beliefs. The Drome's production teams became murderous and zombie-like; Benny resolved the situation by singing a happy song, making everyone act as if they were in an old-style musical. Official reports said that a terrorist attack had caused mass hallucinations.

2607 (summer) - BENNY: THE SUMMER OF LOVE[933]

-> The Draconians and other races continued to have aspirations on the area of space that included the Collection. Bev undertook negotiations to avert war between six races. The Collection's systems further deteriorated, and exerted strain on all thirteen dimensions, causing people to randomly jump through time. Hass recommended planting Simpson's Thin Weave, which would work its roots into the Collection's soil and bind everything on a temporal level. As a side effect, the Thin Weave's pollen ramped up the libidos of everyone present, and a mass orgy ensued. Jason predicted that when word of this spread, student enrolment at the Collection would be up next year.

Bev asked Benny and Jason to undertake a mission to ancient Greece, and they left using their time rings...[934]

2607 (autumn) - BENNY: OLD FRIENDS: "Cheating the Reaper" / "The Soul's Prism"[935] -> The disgraced Ivo FitzIndri had died on the ex-mining planet Balgoris, and Benny attended his funeral. Benny's ex-lover Simon Kyle was now an Admiral with Spacefleet. Benny, Jason and Kyle discovered that a Mim - one of a race of shapeshifters, whose natural forms were bundles of toxic sponge-like matter - had killed FitzIndri as part of a

scheme to steal Balgoran artifacts. The Mim was incinerated in an ancient Balgoran tomb, and the loss of the items within removed any historical objection to Balgoris revamping itself as a retirement locale and holiday resort.

Jason privately warned Kyle to forever stay away from Benny, lest Jason show her a video recording of Kyle deliberately leaving Jason to die after the Mim attacked him. Benny visited the local temple of the Order of the Lost Lemuroidea, and her testimony cleared FitzIndri's name and that of his bloodline.

2607 (October) - BENNY: THE EMPIRE STATE[936]

-> Benny unearthed the Stone of Barter on a desert moon, thinking it could help her locate Irving Braxiatel - the being most likely to stabilise the Collection, and avert the brewing interplanetary war. The Stone caused Benny to acquire Maggi Matsumoto's "fixer" talent, and she accidentally recreated the long-destroyed Empire State as a hodgepodge of her textbook readings about the edifice and her own desires. The new State decayed, and Benny was forced to destroy it again. Matsumoto regained her fixer abilities, and Braxiatel was liberated from the Stone - he had been resting in it for some millennia. Benny persuaded him to return to the Collection.

2607 (October) - BENNY: THE TUB FULL OF CATS[937] -> Tensions between the Draconians and the Mim worsened, and both sides established blockades around the Collection. Benny, Braxiatel and Maggi returned to the Collection aboard *Gravity's Rainbow*, a spaceship that was technically, for tax purposes, owned by some cats. The *Rainbow* was equipped with a Deselby Matango filter which could make the ship invisible to the laws of physics, but required someone to function as an "anchorite" to bring the ship back into reality. The *Rainbow*'s current anchorite, Captain Anthony Rogers, emerged from the filter and died of old age. Maggi permanently took his place.

2607 (23rd-24th October) - BENNY: THE JUDAS GIFT[938] -> Under the Universal Rules of Engagement, weapons such as radiation chains, phase cannons and biogenic assaults could not be used on sentient species. Texts on the Draconians included *The Rough Guide to Draconia*, *The Time Out Guide to Draconia* and *Twitching for Draconians*.

Braxiatel somewhat stabilised the Collection's systems. The Earth Parliament tried to stay out of the Draconian-Mim stand off, and considered having the Terran Reserves set up a buffer zone. Ambassador Kothar of Draconia sought revenge against Bev Tarrant for the death of his blood brother Ethan, and while his use of the Judas Gift severed Bev's left hand, she was able to fake her death and escape the Collection.

The Draconians destroyed the Stonehauser Medical

Facility, which serviced dozens of species. They also landed combat troops on the Collection and occupied it.

> (=) Clarissa Jones, age six, was killed along with her parents in the attack on the Stonehauser facility. Braxiatel changed history so that an older version of Clarissa could serve as an administrator to the Collection.[939]

Bernard Jones, a xenophobic clone-maker who worked at Stonehauser, was killed in the attack. He had facilitated the replacement of Earth President (and Empress) Fiona Dickens with a clone of herself. Per her conditioning, the clone-Dickens instigated a number of anti-extra-terrestrial policies upon Jones' death.[940]

2607 (November) - BENNY: FREEDOM OF INFORMATION[941] **->** Braxiatel resolved the Draconian-Mim standoff by having Hass store up his radiation output, then open his containment suit on the Mim-Sphere. The Mim were obliterated almost to the point of extinction. In return, the Draconian Emperor withdrew his troops from the Collection, and agreed that the Collection would have sovereignty while remaining in Draconian space.

2607 (November) - BENNY: NOBODY'S CHILDREN: "All Mimsy Were the Borogoves" / "The Loyal Left Hand" / "Nursery Politics"[942] **->** The Draconian-Mim conflict had entailed deployment of panic-inducing phase cannons against Proxima Longissima. Eight million Mim fled the planet, and the Draconians claimed jurisdiction over the borogoves - nurseries for infant Mim - left behind.

Benny became pregnant with Jason's child, but miscarried. She learned - partly due to a Mim artifact she found in the ruins of Windsor Safari Park - that Project Narcissus had continued after the Dalek Wars, and had been redirected against Earth's rivals. At least thirty high-ranking Draconians were Mim infiltrators. In exchange for their not bringing the Empire to ruin, the infiltrators were selected to oversee the borogoves in Draconia's name until the Mim children came of age, at which time the Emperor would honourably banish them from Draconian space. The arrangement prevented an Institute from acquiring the Mim progeny for use against Earth's enemies.

2607 (December) - BENNY: THE END OF THE WORLD / BENNY: THE FINAL AMENDMENT / BENNY: THE TWO JASONS[943] **->** On Earth, clones were being generated for use as TV celebrities; New Newport had experienced an Equity uprising as cloned actors

in "the last year" include alien pollen and time jumps (*Benny: The Summer of Love*) and gravitational shifts (*Benny: Collected Works*).
839 *Benny: The End of the World*
940 *Benny: The Final Amendment.* It's not explicitly said, but Bernard is presumably Clarissa Jones' father.
941 Dating *Benny: Freedom of Information* (Benny audio #8.3) - A modest amount of time passes during the Draconian occupation of the Collection. Benny has been in hiding for five days when the story opens, and the Draconians lock her up for three more. Jason makes mention of Draconian troops shooting some civilians "the other week". Also, Hass disabled his radiation-neutraliser "weeks" ago, presumably the amount of time since Braxiatel returned to the Collection and could plot with Hass in person. All signs are, then, that it's now November - especially as some time must be allotted between this story and *Benny: The End of the World*, which finishes in December.
942 Dating *Benny: Nobody's Children* (Benny collection #10) - The stories are set after *Benny: Freedom of Information*, and lead into *Benny: The Final Amendment*. The unnamed "institute" with a fondness for the name Victoria is probably Torchwood.
943 Dating *Benny: The End of the World*, *Benny: The Final Amendment* and *Benny: The Two Jasons* (Benny audios #8.4 and #8.5, Benny BF novel #9) - These three stories run roughly concurrent to one another. Both *The End of the World* and *The Final Amendment* say that the

Stonehauser Medical Facility was destroyed "two months ago" (in *Benny: The Judas Gift*, set in October), so it's now December. A small glitch exists in that Jason refers to Peter as a "half-Killoran eight year old", when he's seven at most.

The fact that Benny only here learns about *The Jason Kane Show* - now in Season 15 (which isn't to automatically say that it's been running for fifteen years) - suggests that the Braxiatel Collection and Earth are some distance from one another, and news from Earth doesn't reach the Collection very much. Even so, it's quite the conceit that nobody at all, not once, has ever mentioned it to her.

The epilogue to *The Two Jasons* claims that Mira and the Jason-clone stay together for some decades, and that the Jason-clone eventually returns to Earth, has sex with President Summerfield and is informed that the remains of the original Benny have been found. However, it's hard to say (especially in light of President Summerfield's death in Series 10) whether this is canon or just some bit of fancy on writer Dave Stone's part.

Mention of the owner of London probably denotes Marillian from *Benny: The Sword of Forever*. The White Rabbit pub, here seen off Earth, appears in Big Finish stories such as *The Harvest* and *UNIT: The Longest Night*.
944 Dating *TW: "Overture"* (*TWM* #25) - The year is given.
945 Dating *Benny: The Wake* (Benny audio #8.6) - Benny gets notification of Jason's death at the end of

demanded various rights. GalNet 4 was now running Season 15 of *The Jason Kane Show* based upon Jason's books, with clones of Benny, Jason and their friends performing farcical hi-jinks. *Hollyoaks: Life on Phobos* was also being shown, as was *Fat, Fat, Fat, Fat, Fat, Fat!* Imperials were a currency used on Earth, and various establishments there displayed a rape-risk rating. Celebrity news reported that the owner of London was about to get married - again. Le Maison Celestial had established itself as a gourmet restaurant in a spaceship that was previously part of the Mim blockade. The White Rabbit pub, formerly an Earth establishment, had been relocated to Bedrock XII.

Kadiatu Lethbridge-Stewart became the personal bodyguard to Howard, the son of Earth President Fiona Dickens, and recruited Benny to investigate the president's increasingly strange behaviour. They stopped the clone-Dickens - who threw herself to her death - from pushing the Earth Empire into open warfare with various alien races. The clone of Benny from *The Jason Kane Show* became Earth president, while the original Dickens and Howard went travelling with Kadiatu.

Simultaneous to these events, Jason Kane learned that, owing to Braxiatel's machinations, large portions of his timeline had been altered or deleted altogether. Jason threatened Braxiatel with exposure - in response, Braxiatel goaded Peter into thinking that Jason was a threat to Bernice. Peter's savage side took over, and he killed Jason. Jason's associate Mira threw off Braxiatel's conditioning, and started a new life with a Jason-clone.

2607 (31st December) - TW: "Overture"[944] -> Jack Harkness visited the planet Zog. An alien representative gave him a sonic failsafe to curtail its sleeper agents on Earth, 1941, and Jack duly sent it back to his former self.

2607 (December) to 2608 - BENNY: THE WAKE[945] -> The dance version of "Abide With Me" was played at Jason's funeral, and his xenoporn books were republished. A provisional government was now running the Collection. Bernice continued teaching at the Collection for a time, but deduced Braxiatel and Hass' involvement in the Mim's downfall. Lacking the evidence and support to challenge Braxiatel directly, Benny snuck away from the Collection with Peter, and went on the run in a spaceship.

2608 - BENNY: BEYOND THE SEA[946] -> Galaxo-Starbucks-Disney copyrighted the name "Atlantis" when it opened up The Real Atlantis. Benny took a job producing a documentary of a lost civilisation on the watery world of Maximediras, which was rebranding itself as a tourist stop. Isolationist members of the micro-organisms who inhabited Maximediras animated some cadavers, and tried to push the human colonists off world. Benny curtailed the rogues, and the micro-organisms' government invited the colonists to share the planet with them.

Peter was transported back to 65,000 BC; Benny followed him after unearthing the time ring that he lost in a lava flow. They separately returned to their native era, after Benny made a side trip to 1893. Upon her return, Benny had manuscripts of some unpublished Sherlock Holmes adventures. These included *The Adventure of the Diogenes Damsel* and *The Cautionary Tale of Ludvig Cooray* - the latter of which involved the disappearance of the nephew of a minor German aristocrat.[947]

Benny: The Final Amendment, and the story picks up (albeit in flashback) upon her return to the Collection. An unspecified amount of time passes with her displaying normality at the Collection while she pieces together Braxiatel's actions, and it's almost certainly 2608 when she takes Peter and leaves. In support of this, her visit to the Drome (*Benny: The Worst Thing in the World*) is cited as being "last year". Braxiatel says that Jason's clones have been "taken care of" - although whether this includes the one who ran off with Mira in *Benny: The Two Jasons* isn't specified.

The Wake heavily cements ties between the *Doctor Who* New Adventures and the Big Finish Benny range, enacting scenes from *Theatre of War* and *Happy Endings* (*Benny: The End of the World* similarly enacts a scene from *Death and Diplomacy*), and mentioning Heaven, and the defeat of the Hoothi (*Love and War*).

946 Dating Bernice Summerfield Series 9 (*Benny: Beyond the Sea*, audio #9.1; *Benny: The Adolescence of Time*, audio #9.2; *Benny: The Adventure of the Diogenes Damsel*, audio #9.3; *Benny: The Diet of Worms*, audio

#9.4) - Following Benny's departure from the Collection, the Benny range defaults back to being a number of stand-alone stories, and there is little reason to suppose that Series 9 doesn't occur over the course of a year (mirroring the passage of real time). Also, starting with Series 9, Big Finish decided that the Benny stories, for simplicity's sake, would occur exactly six hundred years in the future - a helpful yardstick (even if the policy later ended with the *Benny: Epoch* boxset).

The novella collection *Benny: The Vampire Curse* was released between Benny Series 9 and 10 in November 2008, and the main contemporary story within ("Predating the Predators") dates itself to June 2609. Reconciling this against Bev's comments in (Benny: Glory Days), however, suggests that "Predating the Predators" takes place within Series 10, not beforehand.
947 *Benny: The Adolescence of Time*, *Benny: The Adventure of the Diogenes Damsel*. The unpublished Holmes stories are mentioned in *Benny: The Diet of Worms*, although it's unclear when Watson had time to write the *Diogenes Damsel* manuscript, unless it per-

2608 - BENNY: THE DIET OF WORMS[948] **->** On Earth, the Depository served as an archive for cultural and literary giants whose works had survived the Dalek Wars, including Martin Luther, Charles Darwin, Wilkie Collins and Barbara Cartland. Earth Central halved the Depository's budget, and a bibliotaph, Myrtle Bunnage, wanted to regain this funding by giving the impression that paper-eating worms had infested the facility. The worms consumed a manuscript by Cartland that contained extra-terrestrial paper, and thereby gained the ability to recite any text they ate. Bernice contained the situation and saved the worms - who were now the sole source of documents written by Luther, Darwin and Cartland.

c 2609 - THE COMPANY OF FRIENDS: "Benny's Story"[949] **->** Hired by Countess Venhella, Bernice excavated 50-million-year-old rock on Epsilon Minima and thereby found the buried TARDIS key, which summoned the eighth Doctor's TARDIS. Venhella believed that TARDISes were an enslaved species, and tried to liberate the Doctor's Ship with a manumitter - a forbidden Gallifreyan device. Improper use of the manumitter created cracks in the fabric of the universe, and threatened to unleash ravenous monstrosities. The Doctor and Benny were briefly flung back to Epsilon Minima's past, but returned - whereupon the Doctor sealed the space-time cracks. He and Benny shared some adventures before he successfully took her home.

tains to Benny's work with Mycroft prior to their confrontation with Straxus. Alternatively, it's possible that Benny acquired these documents during her later meeting with Watson in 1914 in *Benny: Secret Histories*: "A Gallery of Pigeons".

948 Dating *Benny: The Diet of Worms* (Benny audio #9.4) - The ending leads into *Benny: Glory Days* - but given the transit time over interstellar distances, the calendar might well change in the interim.

949 Dating *The Company of Friends*: "Benny's Story" (BF #123a) - The story takes place while Benny is freelance, and Peter is with his father. *The Company of Friends* was released in July 2009, and is presumably concurrent with Benny Series 10, in which Benny and Adrian are reunited after her time away from the Braxiatel Collection. The only oddity would then be why Benny doesn't enlist the Doctor's help against the rogue Irving Braxiatel.

950 Dating *Bernice Summerfield Series 10* (*Benny: Glory Days*, audio #10.1; *Benny: The Vampire Curse*: "Predating the Predators", collection #12c; *Benny: Absence*, audio #10.2; *Benny: Venus Mantrap*, audio #10.3; *Benny: Secret Origins*, #10.4; *Benny: Secret Histories*, collection #13) - As with Series 9, there's little reason to suppose that Series 10 doesn't pace itself over the course of a year, mirroring the passage of real time. Per Big Finish's new policy that the Benny stories happen six hundred years in the future, it must now be 2609.

In *Glory Days*, Bev comments that she spent "the best part of a year running the Collection", and also that she's now spent a year working as a thief. Presuming that she's rounding down a bit from her departure from the Collection in October 2607, *Glory Days* probably takes place in early 2609.

951 Dating *Benny: The Vampire Curse*: "Predating the Predators" (Benny collection #12c) - The dates are given in journal entries, with the final one (p215) specifying the year as 2609. The "Alukahites" seem to be the Benny equivalent of the Great Vampires (*State of Decay*).

952 Dating *Benny: Absence* (Benny audio #10.2) - Peter is now a "young man", old enough to be hired to haul

things. According to Benny's diary, the story takes place over fifty-nine days. The Technocult and the detail about the ball bearing were previously mentioned in *Benny: Timeless Passages*.

953 Dating *Benny: Venus Mantrap* (Benny audio #10.3) - The story is a sequel to *Beige Planet Mars*, a story in which Benny and Jason similarly lose a fortune in royalty payments. The Lunar penal colony is almost certainly the one seen in *Frontier in Space*.

954 *Benny: Secret Origins*

955 Benny and Robyn's retroactive undoing of Buenos Aires' ruination isn't without its temporal hiccups - the entire story might be paradoxical, in fact. Writer Eddie Robson says that despite Benny and Robyn's historical intervention, it's safe to presume that events in this time zone unfolded in a relatively similar fashion, and that Frost is still dead.

956 The framing sequence to *Benny: Secret Histories*.

957 Dating *Bernice Summerfield Series 11* (*Benny: Dead and Buried*, Benny animated short #1; *Benny: Resurrecting the Past*, audio #11.1; *Benny: Present Danger*, collection #14; *Benny: Escaping the Future*, audio #11.2; *Benny: Year Zero*, audio #11.3; *Benny: Dead Man's Switch*, audio #11.4) - Benny ends Series 10 intending to return to the Braxiatel Collection, but has some side adventures (including the framing sequence for *Benny: Secret Histories*) before doing so. The animated short *Benny: Dead and Buried* - which leads into *Resurrecting the Past* - saw release in August 2010, and so seems as good a place to "start" Series 11 (and to roll the calendar forward to 2610) as any. The short story *Present Danger*: "Six Impossible Things" says that it's been three years minimum since Benny left the Braxiatel Collection, so the Deindum invasion initiated in *Resurrecting the Past* almost certainly occurs in 2610. The booklets to *Resurrecting the Past* and *Escaping the Future* claim that "It's the year 2607" - this has to be regarded as a mistake, given the preponderance of evidence saying otherwise.

(=) 2609 - BENNY: GLORY DAYS[950] -> Bev and Adrian aided Benny in breaking into Finger's bank to gain entry to a vault there owned by Braxiatel. They found within a painting that Benny had created while wearing her time ring - in case of emergency, Braxiatel could download his consciousness into a cloned body via the painting's temporal link. Benny altered the painting's history...

... and in so doing, averted Finger's ever being founded. A beer seller stood in its former location.

Cloning had come a long way since its use on specialised farm worlds. *Ocean's 14 1/2* had been released. *The Collected Works of Jason Kane* had topped the adult charts since Jason's demise.

2609 (Sunday, 18th June to Saturday, 24th June) - BENNY: THE VAMPIRE CURSE: "Predating the Predators"[951] -> While Peter stayed on Fomalhaut IV, Benny joined an expedition arranged by the Fomalhaut Museum of Forerunner Artifacts to the Blood Citadel of the Alukah - an ancient race of vampires. She was present at the excavation of the tomb of Re'Olena, a servant of Lord Ekimmu who was banished as punishment for laughing. Olena awakened, and started a vampire insurrection at the First Colonial University on Murigen - a planet with three suns (Fea, Macha, and Nemhain), and was home to the Lavellans. Olena's vampires attempted to seize the intergalactic quantum tunnel system being developed by the Lavellan professor "Stassy" Leustassavil, hoping to create a transgalactic vampire empire with Olena at its head. Leustassavil opened tunnels that eradicated Olena and her vampires in Murigen's suns.

2609 - BENNY: ABSENCE[952] -> Benny and Peter stopped off on the cluster world of Absence - which was deep in human space and hundreds of light years from anyone hostile - while en route to Venus to collect Jason's immense royalties. Needing funds to leave Absence, Benny flipped burgers while Peter was hired to assist with an expedition sponsored by Interspatial Systems Acquisitions (ISA) into Absence's interior. The Technocult - a cyber-culture that could store the entire holdings of the Labyrinth of Kerykeion on the inside of a ball bearing - took an interest in Absence, and it was suspected that the world's interior was evolving. The founder of ISA, Lamarque Aslinesdes, was killed by Cindy, a sentient prototype environmental suit built by his company.

2609 - BENNY: VENUS MANTRAP[953] -> The government on Venus was responsible for two artificial moons: Eros and Thanatos. Eros had a reputation for romance, but industry drove Thanatos, which was installed with Venusian warhives and rockets. Eros had an orbital spaceport. Thanks to an agency run by Megali Scoblow, a disgraced former academic who Benny had met on Mars in 2595, the rich and influential on Eros could hire "love drones". These used state of the art cerebral-profilogical mapping techniques to match their clients' conscious and subconscious desires. The penalty for owing certain types of lockpicks on Eros was five years in Earth's Lunar penal colony; on some of the outer worlds of the solar system, the sentence was death.

Benny tried to acquire Jason's royalties from his publisher, Velvet Mandible, while Peter stayed with his father in Dallas. The Trans-Galactic Taxes and Duties Division of Outland Revenue claimed most of Jason's fortune, pursuant to duties under Section 32: erotica and explicit fiction import to the Xlanthi Clachworlds. Benny capitulated, as an appeal would mean spending six months on the ice moon of Flisp, which only got two days of sun a month.

N'Jok Barnes - the half-Venusian, half-human ambassador representing Venus on Eros - tried and largely failed to ratchet up tensions between Eros and Venus so he could look heroic while resolving the "crisis". He came out of the incident unscathed - unlike his co-conspirator, Eros' Vice Chancellor Safron Twisk, who was left disgraced when he publicly read aloud a passage from *Barely Humanoid* - one of Jason's pornographic novels - that Benny had fed into his autocue.

Samuel Frost murdered President Summerfield and sent her body in a shuttle to Eros - as a means of getting Benny's attention.[954]

2609 - BENNY: SECRET ORIGINS[955] -> Benny went to the ruins of Buenos Aires when Samuel Frost - her purported longtime nemesis, whom she didn't remember - kidnapped Peter. During the confrontation, Frost was killed. An android from the future, Robyn, sought to undo Buenos Aires' demise; her temporal powers enabled Benny, whose body remained in bed, to accompany her though time as a temporal projection. They encountered Frost in 2002 and 2212, and neutralised his obliteration of Buenos Aires after identifying his origin year as 1937.

Benny accepted an assignment to preserve a church on the war-torn planet Jovellia as an Antique Faith Environment. While doing so, she aided a lifeform that changed states of being in space - but was currently trapped on Jovellia as a series of black crystals - to attain the next phase of its lifecycle.[956]

2610 - BENNY: DEAD AND BURIED[957] -> Braxiatel fabricated a "lost civilisation" on the planet Jovada as bait for Benny. He had her put into stasis when she excavated the site, preventing her from interfering with his plans...

2610 - BENNY: RESURRECTING THE PAST[958] ->
Adrian and Peter found Benny and revived her from stasis. Braxiatel now believed that his people were doomed, and purchased the ocean planet Maximediras to adapt into a new home for the Time Lords he hoped to "resurrect". He relocated Maximediras' eight thousand residents, and moved the energy field near the Braxiatel Collection to Maximediras, hoping it would become the Time Lords' new power source.

Simultaneously, Braxiatel's operations against the Deindum entered a new phase... Braxiatel Protective Mechanoids (BPMs) were dispatched to kidnap various individuals, who were scanned in a former moonrock processing facility on Earth's moon. Braxiatel was searching for an individual who, when dispatched into the time-space rift to the Deindum's homeworld in the future, would alter the Deindum's development so they wouldn't develop time travel, and would have a less aggressive and paranoid nature. Bernice was Braxiatel's failsafe - consigning her to the rift would have curtailed the Deindum's advancement. Before that could happen, the android Robyn accidentally fell into the rift, which then closed.

(=) Robyn's inorganic matter had no effect on the Deindum's evolution, and they became immensely powerful beings that manifested as large, glowing reptilian heads. The Deindum sent troops back through time to conquer habitable space in the twenty-seventh century in the name of their empire...

(=) 2610 - BENNY: PRESENT DANGER / ESCAPING THE FUTURE -> The Deindum established a base on Maximediras, and from there conducted campaigns in the past and present to the stability of their timeline. They were a danger to every civilisation in the galaxy. In their wake, the Braxiatel Collection was overrun with refugees. Braxiatel, Bernice and their allies coordinated resistance efforts, but the Deindum succeeded in overcoming their coalition...[659]

Bernice suggested to Braxiatel that manipulating the Deindum at a crucial point of their development would erase their invasion from history. Braxiatel concurred, even though the effort would expend more than half of the Maximediras energy rift, preventing him from resurrecting his people. The

958 Dating *Benny: Resurrecting the Past* (Benny audio #11.1) - Benny is in stasis for "five days", and at least a few days pass in the course of the story.
959 According to *Benny: Escaping the Future*, the Deindum invasion unfolds over some "months".
960 *Benny: Year Zero* and *Benny: Dead Man's Switch*. Series 11 ends on the cliffhanger of Benny arriving at "Atlantis".
961 Dating *Benny: Epoch: Judgement Day* (Benny box set #1.4) - A robot attendant supplies the year. Benny comments, "Right... a little bit later than I was expecting, but same basic ballpark". The *Benny: Road Trip* and *Benny: Legion* box sets - released in 2012, too late to be included in this chronology - cover Benny's efforts to reach Legion as instructed.
962 *K9: The Korven*
963 *Singularity*
964 The "Little Mind's Eye" crystal that the Doctor gets in *Snakedance* is dated to "eight hundred years ago".
965 *Benny: A Life in Pieces*. Traillor is killed "two years" after the fortieth anniversary of Morton's death, cited as "23 September 2645" (p150). Mention that no records exist of Benny and company could simply mean that Verum is remote enough that Taillor lacks access to them. Alternatively, it could mean that all records of them have been expunged, somehow, in the wider universe.
966 Forty-five years after the Braxiatel Collection component of *Benny: The Grel Escape*.
967 "More than a century" before "Time Bomb".
968 Dating *Midnight* (X4.10) - No date given, but The

Time Travellers' Almanac sets it in the twenty-seventh century.
969 Poosh is mentioned in *Midnight*, and what became of it is revealed in *The Stolen Earth*.
970 *The Well-Mannered War*. The Thargons and Sorsons were originally seen in *The Tomorrow People*.
971 Dating *Shadowmind* (NA #16) - The Doctor tells Ace that "by your calendar the year is 2673" (p29). The events of *Frontier in Space* in "2540" (p74) were "one hundred and thirty years ago" (p61).
972 Dating *The Sandman* (BF #37) - No date is given, but *Benny: The Bone of Contention*, also written by Simon Forward, features the Clutch and is set in 2603. In that story, it's said that the Galyari Research Directorate hopes to build weapons against the Sandman. As the Clutch's weaponry isn't significantly advanced in *The Sandman* audio, it probably takes place soon after the Benny adventure.
973 *White Darkness*
STAR TREK: In the Pocket Books' range of *Star Trek* novels (particularly those by Diane Duane), the Romulans call themselves "Rihanssu", and the race is referred to in *White Darkness* (p129). A few of the other New and Missing Adventures have included such *Star Trek* in-jokes. There are many, for example, in *Sanctuary*, another of David McIntee's books, and Turlough refers to the Klingon homeworld in *The Crystal Bucephalus* (p104).
Star Trek and *Doctor Who* have radically differing versions of the future, and by this point, a wide variety of tie-in stories (*The Left-Handed Hummingbird*, *The*

Deindum sabotaged their efforts - to retroactively undo this defeat, Hass opened up his containment suit on Maximediras, killing the Deindum there and every living thing. The Deindum overwhelmed the Collection; Peter, Adrian and Bev were left behind as Benny and Braxiatel travelled four million years ahead in his TARDIS, successfully implemented their plan, and historically nullified the Deindum invasion.

Benny found herself in an unknown era on the planet Raster - one of twenty inhabited worlds where the disciplines of history and archaeology had been outlawed. She travelled in stasis to the worlds' capital, the planet Zordin, and awoke to find that Zordin looked like Earth, and that the Great Leader had just renamed it "Atlantis..."[960]

2616 - BENNY: EPOCH: JUDGEMENT DAY[961] ->

Benny escaped from "Atlantis" using a stasis chamber, and awoke in 2616 aboard Mars Base Grantham-Echo-Four. The version of Irving Braxiatel who had encountered Benny just once - on Dellah in 2593 - left a message that he could reunite her with Peter, and that she should rendezvous with him on the planet Legion...

In 2618, the human military organisation Global Command considered the Korven the most dangerous and destructive race of the age.[962] Circa 2620, crystal towers were constructed on Rigel VII, an Earth Empire colony.[963] **Some, if not all, of the crystals used by the Snakedancers of Manussa were created.**[964]

Mark Morton's illegitimate child - the historian and playwright Kristoffa Taillor - came to own a copy of Bernice Summerfield's diary, and studied it to learn more about his parents' deaths. Taillor found that no official records existed pertaining to Bernice Summerfield, Jason Kane, Adrian Wall, Bev Tarrant and Irving Braxiatel. In 2647, Taillor was fatally poisoned at an orbiting restaurant, The Final Rest. *A Life in Pieces*, a collection of texts concerning Morton's murder, was subsequently published.[965]

A party of Grel went back in time to capture Peter Summerfield and study him.[966] The *Arrow of Righteousness* set out on its holy journey some time before 2650, the pilgrims inside frozen in meditation.[967]

c 2650 - MIDNIGHT[968] -> The tenth Doctor brought Donna to Midnight, an airless but beautiful diamond world bathed in extonic sunlight. Donna preferred to sun herself in the Leisure Palace rather than take the Crusader tour to the 100,000-foot sapphire waterfalls. The Doctor and his fellow tour passengers were menaced by an entity that possessed them in turn - it repeated words spoken aloud, then *predicting* words before they were said. The tour hostess threw herself and the entity's core host, Sky Silvestry, into the radia-

tion-saturated planetscape, killing them both.

The Crusader 50 shuttle bus ran on micropetrol.

By this point, the Lost Moon of Poosh had been stolen through time to become part of the Daleks' reality bomb.[969] In 2660, Fridgya was devastated in the fifth Thargon-Sorson war. Its cryo-morts would remain undisturbed for many thousands of years.[970]

2673 - SHADOWMIND[971] -> This was the time of Xaxil, the twenty-fourth Draconian Emperor.

Thousands of years before, the Shenn of Arden had discovered "hypergems" that boosted their telepathic ability. Around 2640, one group of Shenn began to hear a mysterious voice from the sky that ordered them to construct kilns. This voice was the Umbra, a sentience that had evolved from carbon structures on a nearby asteroid.

The planet Tairngaire was now heavily populated and a member of a local alliance of planets, the Concordance, with its own space fleet that had recently seen action in the nasty Sidril War. In 2670, colonists from Tairngaire set up camp on the planet Arden. The Colonial Office decreed that the natural features of the planet should be named after characters from the works of Shakespeare. Accordingly, the main settlement was called Touchstone Base, and there was a Lake Lysander, a Titania River and a Phebe Range of mountains.

After completing wargame trials in the Delta Epsilon system, the CSS *Broadsword* was recalled to Tairngaire by Admiral Vego and sent to investigate the situation at the Arden. All contact had been lost with the settlers, and five ships dispatched to investigate also vanished. It was discovered that the Shenn were secretly operating in New Byzantium by inhabiting artificially constructed human bodies. The Umbra was building "shadowforms", extensions of its power. The seventh Doctor, Benny and Ace located Umbra and blocked off the sun's rays, effectively rendering it unconscious.

c 2675 - THE SANDMAN[972] -> The Clutch, the fleet of ships containing the Galyari race and numerous tagalongs, returned to the homeworld of the Cuscaru. A Cuscaru ambassador returned a piece of the Galyari's destroyed Srushkubr, but this catalysed the neural energy tainting the Galyari. The long-dead General Voshkar was reborn in a monstrous body, and tried to return the Galyari to warfare. The sixth Doctor and Evelyn's involvement resulted in Voshkar's demise. The Clutch departed into space, and resumed business as an intergalactic flea market of sorts.

During the twenty-seventh century, a Haitian deciphered the Rihanssu language, allowing a peace treaty that ended the war between Earth and that race.[973] **There had** been examples of humanity oppressing native species for centuries. The Swampies of Delta Magna, for example, had been displaced and oppressed. Slavery was formally reintroduced on many worlds.[974] The time-sensitive Tharils had once been the owners of a mighty Empire, with territory stretching across several universes including N-Space and E-Space. Now slavers had captured them. The Tharils were a valuable commodity, as they alone could navigate the ships using warp drive based on Implicate Theory. Many humans became rich trading in Tharils. One privateer, a veteran of Tharil hunts on Shapia commanded by Captain Rorvik, vanished without trace following a warp drive malfunction.[975]

Twenty families founded the colony of Kaldor City. The people there came to forget their origins, and had no contact with other planets.[976]

2680 - THE HIGHEST SCIENCE[977] **->** Authorities on Checkley's World had made the planet Hogsumm to resemble the fabled planet Sakkrat, hoping to capture the criminal Sheldukher and retrieve the Cell that he stole. A slow time converter set up on Hogsumm created a Fortean Flicker that moved objects through time, including a group of hostile Chelonians and some train-riders taking the 8:12 from Chorleywood in 2003.

In 2680, Sheldukher and his crew revived from stasis and landed on "Sakkrat". Sheldukher committed suicide while resisting arrest, and the Cell was killed also. Sheldukher's Hercules devastator atomised a large area of the planet. The Chelonians and the train-riders, known to the Chelonians as the EightTwelves, were left frozen in a stasis field.

The Master sabotaged the slow time converter on Hogsumm, creating a Fortean Flicker. President Romana of Gallifrey located the source of the disturbance on Hogsumm, and released the trapped humans and Chelonians. The Chelonians weren't grateful, so Romana marooned them there and took the humans home.[978] The abandoned Chelonians survived and created a viable colony that made contact with the rest of their kind after a few thousand years.[979]

? 2684 - MISSION OF THE VIYRANS[980] **->** The Viyrans cured Peri of a virus that she contracted while attending a party on the planet Gralista Social, then wiped her and the fifth Doctor's memories of the event. This was the first time that the Viyrans came into contact with humanity.

Gallifrey Chronicles, Peri and the Piscon Paradox, at least four stories involving the Doctor's companion Izzy, who is a huge fan of the series, etc.) establish that *Star Trek* is merely fiction in the *Doctor Who* universe. On screen, this is confirmed in *The Empty Child, Fear Her, The Impossible Astronaut, The God Complex, Closing Time, SJA: Warriors of Kudlak, SJA: The Lost Boy* and *SJA: Mona Lisa's Revenge*. Maybe, just as Trekkies in the seventies managed to get NASA to name a prototype space shuttle after the USS *Enterprise*, the *Star Trek* fans of the future managed to name a lot of planets after ones from their favourite series - Vulcan, as seen in *The Power of the Daleks*, being one of the first.

974 The Swampies appear in *The Power of Kroll*. Slavery exists at the time of *Warriors' Gate* and *Terminus*, and the work camps referred to in *The Caves of Androzani* are also near-slavery.

975 *Warriors' Gate*. Stephen Gallagher has stated in interviews (see, for example, *In-Vision* #50) that Rorvik's crew come from N-Space, and their familiarity with English (such as the graffiti), "sardines" and "custard" suggest they come from Earth. The coin flipped is a "100 Imperial" piece and they use warp drive, both of which suggest an Earth Empire setting, although placing the story details here is arbitrary.

976 *The Robots of Death*, as extrapolated from a painting native to Kaldor City (seen in *Kaldor City: Occam's Razor*) that's two hundred years old. "Crisis on Kaldor" concurs with this, as it seemingly happens around the time of *The Robots of Death*, and "centuries" after Kaldor was colonised.

977 Dating *The Highest Science* (NA #11) - Sheldukher's ship arrives at Sakkrat in "2680" (p17). It is "two hundred and thirty years" in Benny's future (p35) [q.v. "Benny's Birthday"].

978 *Happy Endings*

979 *The Well-Mannered War*

980 Dating "Mission of the Viyrans" (BF #102b) - Gralista Social seems to be a human planet; some of those present are named "Chris" and "Lawrence". The Viyrans say it's the first time they've encountered humanity, but allowing that they can time-travel, it's unclear if they mean relative to history or their own lifetimes. For lack of other evidence, this dating is very arbitrary. The sixth Doctor again visits Gralista Social in *Blue Forgotten Planet*.

981 Dating "Bus Stop!" (*DWM* #385) - It's "Mars in the twenty-seventh century". Environmental suits are here needed on the Martian surface, but Mars seems to still be inhabited (at the very least, it's got a president), so perhaps the toxicity is localised.

982 *Death and Diplomacy* (pgs 71, 203).

983 *The Crystal Buchephalus* (p40, p80).

984 *100:* "My Own Private Wolfgang"

985 "A thousand years" before *Interference*.

986 *The Dark Path*

987 Four generations after *Benny: Timeless Passages*.

988 Dating "By Hook or By Crook" (*DWM* #256) - The

c 2690 - "Bus Stop!"[981] -> Scientists on Mars invented a crude time machine. Mutant assassins captured the device and attempted to retroactively eradicate the ancestors of Martian President Lithops. The tenth Doctor followed the killers to the twenty-first century and stymied them while Martha and D.I. Moloch re-captured the time machine and recalled the Doctor to this time zone. The Doctor destroyed the time machine, which by extension exterminated the assassins.

The Battle of the Rigel Wastes took place in 2697. The seventh Doctor, Bernice, Roz and Chris witnessed the massacre. In the twenty-seven and twenty-eight hundreds, New Earth Feudalism was established. This social system would lead to the thirtieth-century Overcities.[982]

The Twenty-Eighth Century

In the twenty-eighth century, the Legions tried to undermine the business consortia of the galaxy using their multidimensional abilities. The Time Lords intervened, sending Mortimus to imprison the Legion homeworld for eight thousand years. Around this time, the Wine Lords of Chardon had the best wine cellars in the galaxy.[983] By the twenty-eighth century, interest in Mozart was so low, his work was pretty much restricted to the bargain bin.[984]

Earth claimed the planet Dust on the Dead Frontier, but never developed it.[985] The renegade Time Lord Koschei visited Earth in the twenty-eighth century and met Ailla, a woman who joined him on his travels. It was a time of food riots and constant war.[986]

The great-great-grandchildren of the shareholders of Omni-Spatial Mercantile Dynamics thought that their ancestors had blown a deal concerning the Labyrinth of Kerykeion, and sent a murderous cyborg back in time to secure a better result.[987]

2708 - "By Hook or By Crook"[988] -> The eighth Doctor and Izzy landed in the City-State of Tor-Ka-Nom. The Doctor chided Izzy for being more interested in the guidebook than seeing the sights, but changed his tune upon being arrested for a murder that he didn't commit. Izzy freed him by looking up the identity of the real murderer in her guidebook, which wouldn't be written for another twenty-three years.

A human hospital ship in the Dravidian war zone crashed "a long way from Earth" on the planet Chodor, at the eastern edge of Haldevron. The crew attempted to stop the ship's mechanical drones, a.k.a. Takers, from euthanising forty-four patients to contain the Richter's Syndrome they carried. This damaged the ship's quantum flux generator and released warp energy, turning the infected into ghostly beings. The surviving patients and their descendants - forgetting their past, and adopting hospital and sterilisation procedures as societal rituals - founded the colony of Purity.[989]

= The sixth Doctor visited the planet Narrah in 2721.[990]

The Doctor met the mad scientist Linus Leofrix on Ricarus in 2723.[991]

c 2725 - "Warlord of the Ogrons"[992] -> The brilliant if misguided surgeon Linus Leofrix landed on the planet of the Ogrons, along with his pilot Rostow, and captured one of the natives: Gnork. Leofrix used a surgical implantation technique to make Gnork super-intelligent, planning to use him to conquer half the galaxy. Gnork challenged Gwunn for the leadership of the tribe, sparing his life because he wanted his help to defeat the Earthmen. Gnork stole the ship, leaving the humans at the mercy of Gwunn.

The middle Sumaran era produced some exquisite artwork, including a headpiece entitled the "Six Faces of Delusion".[993]

One branch of humanity fell into a futile and stalemated war against the Foucoo - a humourless, burrowing and territorial species that fought with micro-munitions. Such was the conflict that nobody actually knew what the Foucoo looked like. The warfare lasted for decades, and the human colony on Nocturne was used as a departure point for soldiers going to or leaving the warzone.[994] In 2736, a guidebook to Tor-Ka-Nom was published; a copy of it would end up in the TARDIS library.[995] A breakaway cell of Ventriki militants believed its enemies were operating from the trading world Crestus V, and deployed the biological agent Saravin there. In response, the Earth Empire destroyed Saravin production plants across an entire sector of space.[996]

---

989 "One hundred years" before *The Whispering Forest*.
990 *Spiral Scratch*
991 "Warlord of the Ogrons"
992 Dating "Warlord of the Ogrons" (*DWW* #13-14) - Rostow mentions Federation patrols, but in the framing sequence the Doctor mentions that he met Leofrix in 2723, so it can't be the Galactic Federation.
993 "Seven hundred years" before *Snakedance*.
994 The war begins "seventy years" before *Nocturne*.
995 Twenty-three years after "By Hook or By Crook".
996 "A few hundred years" after *Scaredy Cat*.

2750 - "Time Bomb"[997] -> The *Arrow of Righteousness* was a hundred years from its destination. The TARDIS was nearby and was hit by a time weapon - a Temporal Disruption Pulser. The sixth Doctor and Frobisher traced it to a hundred years in the future on the planet Hedron.

c 2764 - THE SENSORITES[998] -> During the twenty-eighth century, spacecraft from Earth ploughed deeper and deeper into space, searching for minerals and other natural resources. On Earth, air traffic was becoming congested.

A five-man Earth ship discovered the planet Sense-Sphere, a molybdenum-rich planet that was inhabited by the shy, telepathic Sensorites. They feared exploitation, and refused to trade with Earth. The Earth mission left, but shortly afterwards, the Sensorites began dying from a mysterious new disease. Within a decade, two out of ten Sensorites had died.

By the time a second Earth mission arrived, the Sensorites were terrified of outsiders. They used their psychic powers to place the crew of the ship in suspended animation, a process that drove one human, John, mad. The first Doctor, Ian, Barbara and Susan found that the Sensorites were suffering from nightshade poisoning, introduced to the City water supply by the previous Earth expedition. The second expedition left, promising not to return to the planet.

c 2764 - THE END OF TIME (DL)[999] -> The Governors of Mygosuria had set up the "Universal Learning System", and ruled that the children of the Nine Galaxies should be educated to the highest standard. Those with the highest Ability Index were nicknamed The Mind Set and sent to study at the Space Brain, a school for gifted children.

The Krashoks finished construction of the Eternity Device - a machine that would reanimate the dead, when powered by the Eternity Crystal - and calibrated it aboard the Space Brain. The tenth Doctor recalibrated the device to emit an energy blast that turned the Krashoks' organic components to dust. He also destroyed the Eternity Crystal by tossing it into the Eternity Device, which exploded. Afterward, his companion Gisella elected to stay aboard the Space Brain.

By 2765, INITEC had built the first of a chain of Vigilant laser defence space stations in orbit around Earth. The station proved vital in preventing the Zygons from melting the icecaps and flooding the world.[1000]

2775 - THE STEALERS OF DREAMS[1001] -> The ninth Doctor, Rose and Captain Jack found themselves on Colony World 4378976.Delta-Four, where the authorities banned any form of fiction or fantasy. The Doctor discovered that a microscopic native life was feeding on the colonists' imaginations, overwhelming their ability to distinguish fact from fiction. When the truth emerged, the colony's scientists quickly came up with a cure.

2789 (10th June) - PARADOX LOST[1002] -> The TARDIS unexpectedly diverted the eleventh Doctor, Amy and Rory to the banks of the Thames, 2789. London was now a mixture of the future and the past - glittering metal towers were interspersed between brick houses and churches. Enormous glass domes housed forests and

---

997 Dating "Time Bomb" (*DWM* #114-116) - "Earthdate 2750" according to the opening caption.

998 Dating *The Sensorites* (1.7) - Maitland says "we come from the twenty-eighth century", which might mean it is later than that. The novelisation suggested the Earth ship set out in the "in the early years of the twenty-eighth century". An incoherent John says they've been at Sense-Sphere either "four years" or "for years". *The Programme Guide* set the story in "c.2600" in its first two editions, *The Terrestrial Index* settled on "about 2750". *The TARDIS Logs* gave the date as "2765". *Timelink* "2764".

999 Dating *The End of Time* (DL #10) - A case study of the Mind Set by H. James Moore, University of Castillianus V, is dated to 2764 (p17), and which at least provides the general era in which the Space Brain exists. The motives of the Krashoks have shifted slightly - the Doctor claimed in *The Art of War* (p11-12) that they wanted to animate fallen soldiers so they could prolong wars and further their weapons trade, but here, the Krashoks calibrate the Crystal to only raise their own soldiers from the dead.

1000 *Original Sin* (p287).

1001 Dating *The Stealers of Dreams* (NSA #6) - It's "2755 AD".

1002 Dating *Paradox Lost* (NSA #48) - The exact day is given. The Doctor vaguely alludes to the fact that much of old London will be preserved "for another few decades", possibly in reference to the new series' dating for *The Beast Below*, or something else altogether.

1003 "Twenty years" before *Nocturne*.

1004 *The Fall of Yquatine*, "over two hundred years" earlier than 2992.

1005 The girls are born, and Elizabethan is rendered comatose, "thirteen years" and about "seven years" respectively before *EarthWorld*.

1006 The foiled assassination attempts occur five years before *Nocturne*. Zeta Reticula is located thirty three light-years from Earth.

1007 Will happens upon the Ultani texts at least eighteen months before *Nocturne*.

1008 Dating *Companion Piece* (TEL #13) - It is "the twenty-eighth century" (p74), "eight hundred years" after Cat's time (p78). The seventh Doctor is similarly

served as oxygen factories. St. Paul's Cathedral, the Tower of London, Buckingham Palace, Oxford Street, the British Museum, the Houses of Parliament and Westminster Bridge were still in existence.

Humanoid constructs housing Artificial Intelligences, as created by the Villiers Artificial Life laboratory in Battersea, cost a small fortune and had been on the market for about three months. One such unit, Arven, was dredged from the Thames after nearly a thousand years spent buried there. Arven expired after warning the Doctor that a time-ship created by Professor Celestine Gradius had drilled a hole in space-time through which the Squall - extra-dimensional parasites that fed on psychic energy - were swarming into the Universe. The Doctor sent Amy and Rory to investigate Gradius while he travelled back to the day before Arven fell into the Thames: 16th October, 1910.

Amy and Rory found that the Squall had killed Gradius, and met Arven's younger self - who had been serving as Gradius' assistant. They escaped to 1910 in Gradius' time vessel when the Squall attacked - and thereby created the hole in space-time that granted the Squall access to the Universe.

The Doctor, Amy and Rory returned to 2789 after dealing with the Squall, and loaded a back-up copy of Arven's intelligence into a new body at the Villiers facility. They then took him to live with a mutual friend in 1923.

Lothar Ragpole established a drinking establishment on Nocturne, and it would serve the developing artistic enclave there.[1003] In the early 2790s, the ten-planet Minerva system was colonised by an Earth ship captained by Julian de Yquatine.[1004]

Elizabethan, the wife of President John F Hoover of New Jupiter, gave birth to triplets following fertility treatment. She had used DNA samples from Hanstrum, Hoover's chief technician, and not her infertile husband. The children were named Asia, Africa and Antarctica. Years later, Hanstrum tried to murder Elizabethan after she began to suspect her triplets were psychopaths, and wanted to confess her infidelity. Elizabethan was rendered comatose, and the triplets were blamed and imprisoned.[1005]

The human colony Nocturne was now home to the Department of War, munitions factories and some hospices, but the planet itself was secure, being located eight months of travel from the front. The adversity of the war with the Foucoo attracted to Nocturne the greatest concentration of artists and thinkers since the Florentine Renaissance - this creative revival would become known as the Far Renaissance. The creativity that flourished on Nocturne would only be accomplished about half a dozen times in the whole of human history.

Glasst City on Nocturne had canals and smelt like Venice. The Sol system, Zeta Reticula, the Hessa Cloud and the Foucoo home system and were all visible to the naked eye from Nocturne. The Doctor was involved when the Foucoo attempted to assassinate members of the War Department, and officials on Nocturne covered up two mysterious deaths.[1006]

Will Alloran, a student of Korbin Thessenger, went looking in the Nocturne archives and found alien scripts bearing the bioharmonics of the extinct Ultani race. He feared the documents' power and purged them - but his brother Lomas secretly made copies. Will signed up to fight in the war with the Foucoo. He spent eight months travelling to the front, and lost his leg during a skirmish on the planet Zocus.[1007]

c 2799 - COMPANION PIECE[1008] -> Philosophical questions about alien civilisations, such as whether nonhumans possessed souls and could be baptised, caused a rift in the Catholic Church. Social and political instability compelled Pope Athanasius to relocate to Rome, a mobile space station with a replica of Vatican City. The Catholics who remained on Earth elected Pope Urban IX as their leader, and each side declared the other false.

Missionaries from the Catholic Church had arrived on the planet Haven and converted much of the indigenous population. However, a malfunctioning TARDIS landed there and exploded, devastating the planet. The Church in response branded all Time Lords as witches. Grand Inquisitor Guii del Toro rose to power in the church on Haven, and instigated the Good Shepherd project, using human-like robots to evangelise.

A Carthian bandit chief named Brotak took control of most of the planets in the Magellanic system, and named himself Tsar of all the Magellanic Clouds. He converted to Roman Catholicism, and favoured the Cetacean Brrteet'k (a.k.a. Celestine VI) as the next Pope.

The seventh Doctor and his companion Catherine Broome repaired the malfunctioning TARDIS by stealing some mercury from the Weirdarbi, a race of cybernetic insects. They then arrived on Haven to do some shopping, but the Doctor, identified as a Time Lord, was quickly arrested by del Toro. The Doctor and Cat were dispatched to Earth aboard an Inquisition spaceship to face a papal conclave, but Pope John Paul XXIII was declared soul-dead at this time. Forces supporting either Celestine VI or Pope Urban XII as John Paul's successor fell into open conflict. Del Toro died amid the warfare.

The Inquisition ship took heavy damage, and the Doctor, Cat and their allies had minutes to live unless a robot could go through the ship's toxic areas and use the bridge controls to release the sealed-off TARDIS. With the Inquisition's robots nonfunctional, the Doctor resigned himself to telling Cat about her true nature.

c 2800 - NOCTURNE[1009] -> The Far Renaissance was one of the Doctor's favourite periods of history, and he visited the locale in more than one incarnation. The security force on Nocturne - the Overwatch - had eight separate reports of the Doctor's visits, dating back thirty years. Tegan was present during one such stopover.

Lomas Alloran sought to achieve great music with his copy of the Ultani bioharmonics, but Nocturne was a planet that inherently contained more discord than the Ultani homeworld. Use of the bioharmonics created a creature of pure noise - this entity sought works of artistry, but killed the artists themselves.

The TARDIS arrived on Nocturne, and Ace and Hex expressed scepticism that the seventh Doctor lacked an ulterior motive for the visit. Previously, the Doctor had taken them to Breearos to "return some library books", then spent a fortnight negotiating a ceasefire in the Orbit Wars. On another occasion, the Doctor said he wanted to use the infallible laundry services of Tau Sartos, but in fact worked to prevent the spawning of a Zylax swarm (an incident that left Hex covered in mucus).

The noise creature killed the celebrated composer Lucas Erphan Moret. Lomas Alloran also perished, and his brother Will - upon realising that his actions had caused some deaths - goaded the creature to killing him.

The Doctor devised a means of echoing and cancelling out the noise creature's harmonics. Will's mentor, Korbin Thessenger, was moved to write his Great Mass - it would be the last great work of his career, and celebrated for as long as humanity persisted. History forgot the manner of Will's death, and it was speculated that he died in the war.

The war would continue for "a long time", but the Far Renaissance lasted a total of thirty years. It gave rise to the plays of Casto, Cinder's Odes, the Quantum Movement, Luminalism, all but one of Thessenger's symphonies, the Zeitists and the novels of Elber Rocas. Also, the sculptor Shumac took eight years to carve "Man Triumphant Above the Rigours of Space" from a single block of Lympian Onyx.

Nocturne was home to the Museum of Culture, the Lazlo Collection and the College of Music. Data pads were in use. Robotic "familiars" - fashioned after the female form, as research showed that people were more comfortable with representations of the female gender - performed menial tasks for the populace.

c 2800 - EARTHWORLD[1010] -> Earth Heritage had established around the galaxy thousands of EarthWorld theme parks, where lifelike androids would replicate - albeit in a rather garbled form - the history of Earth. Many of the people of New Jupiter wanted independence from Earth, and the Association for New Jupitan Independence (ANJI)

---

travelling with a robotic companion in *Death Comes to Time*.

1009 Dating *Nocturne* (BF #92) - The Doctor tells Ace and Hex that they're "about seven hundred ninety years and three parsecs in that direction" from their native era on Earth. As Ace hails from the late 1980s but Hex originates from 2021, this could support a dating of roughly anywhere between 2777 and 2811.

1010 Dating *EarthWorld* (EDA #43) - The date is arbitrary, but New Jupiter wants independence from Earth and the advanced androids are "pretty standard". It is "the far distant future".

1011 *The Beast Below*. This is an arbitrary date - were the current Prince Harry to ascend to the throne (possible, but not likely), he would be Henry IX. Stories such as *Revenge of the Judoon* (p19) have established the reigns of Charles III and William V (the current Prince of Wales and his son, the Duke of Cambridge). *The Beast Below* establishes that eight Queen Elizabeths and at least four King Henrys rule after that, and we have to allow that *Interference* tells us the last King of England abdicated in the 2060s. *Legacy of the Daleks* says the last British monarch was exterminated in the Dalek Invasion of 2157 (so presumably only a Queen or Queens reigned for a hundred years before that). Clearly, as Liz X demonstrates, the British monarchy is restored at some point.

1012 "Fifty years" before *Three's a Crowd*.

1013 Dating *The Story of Martha*: "Star-Crossed" (NSA #28e) - No date is given. We know that old ships with colonists in suspended animation were still being found at the time of *The Sensorites*, and so this arbitrary placement puts it around that period.

1014 "Eight hundred years" after "Do Not Go Gentle Into That Good Night". The story is later reduced to being alternate history.

1015 Dating *Festival of Death* (PDA #35) - The date is given on p116.

1016 "Fifty years" before *Revenge of the Cybermen*.

1017 Dating *The Whispering Forest* (BF #137) - Mention is made of Earth Empire Command and the Dravidian (*The Brain of Morbius*) war zone, and the Doctor says that the Takers are "auto-medics in the twenty-eighth century". As one hundred years have passed since the hospital ship crashed, it's presumably now the twenty-ninth century.

1018 *Christmas on a Rational Planet* (p189).

1019 *The Ultimate Treasure* (p71).

1020 "Almost a century and a half" before *So Vile a Sin*.

1021 Dating *Dark Progeny* (EDA #48) - The date is given.

1022 Dating "Time Bomb" (*DWM* #114-116) - The caption states it's "Earthdate 2850".

was gaining support. The eighth Doctor, Fitz and Anji were arrested on suspicion of sympathy with the independence movement, but the Doctor stopped an android rampage.

Elizabethan revived from her coma, and although her daughter Asia died, she pledged to help her remaining two children.

The Doctor was a drinking buddy of Henry XII.[1011] Colonists seeking independence from Federation officials settled on Phoenix, the fourth planet in the Paledies system. Terraforming machinery automatically engaged while most of the colonists remained in hibernation, but sunspot activity hampered development of an ozone layer and set the process back by decades. Space station *Medusa* was set up in geostationary orbit.[1012]

c 2800 - THE STORY OF MARTHA: "Star-Crossed"[1013] -> The tenth Doctor and Martha arrived on generation ship 374926-slash-GN66, which was full of frozen Earth colonists. The Artificials - vat-grown clones engineered to perform maintenance - had become "the Breed" and now ran the ship. The human colonists had woken up two years previous, and war had broken out between them and the Breed. The Doctor learned that the colonists had died when their cryogenics failed, and that the Breed had used what raw material was available to create Artifical bodies for as many colonists as possible, downloading their memories into the new forms. The realisation that all of those present were Artificial stopped the conflict. The Doctor repaired the ship's energy cells enough to get the vessel to its destination.

(=) The eleventh Doctor was present when archaeologists dug up an empty coffin that was supposed to contain the remains of a Hawkshaw Manor nursing home resident. Finding this suspicious, he went with Amy to investigate the matter in 2011.[1014]

2815 - FESTIVAL OF DEATH[1015] -> The leisure cruiser *Cerberus*, with a thousand passengers onboard, was trapped in hyperspace between Teredekethon and Murgatroyd. Nearly one hundred ships crashed into it, including a prison ship containing dangerous Arachnopods. They escaped and went on the rampage. The Repulsion - an extra-dimensional creature that existed between life and death - offered the survivors of *Cerberus* the chance to escape. They agreed, and the Repulsion exchanged them with participants of the "Beautiful Death" in 3012. Rescue missions would discover only empty ships, prompting "the mystery of the *Cerberus*".

The wrecked spaceships were rebuilt inside the hyperspace tunnel as the G-Lock station.

A mysterious planetoid was detected entering the solar system, and it eventually became the thirteenth moon of Jupiter. It was named Neo-Phobus by humans, and the Nerva Beacon was set up to warn shipping of this new navigational hazard. Nerva was one of a chain of navigational beacons, which also included Ganymede Beacon at vector 1906702.[1016]

c 2820 - THE WHISPERING FOREST[1017] -> The fifth Doctor, Nyssa, Tegan and Turlough arrived at the Purity colony so Nyssa could test a potential cure for Richter's Syndrome. They destroyed the Takers and the ghostly beings who had been afflicting the colony for generations.

ID implants were mandatory in citizens of the Empire, except for those exempted by the Corporate Faiths Amendment Act 2820.[1018] The Privacy of Sentient Beings Act was passed in 2830.[1019] Earth President Helen Kristiansen declared herself Empress. Helen I would be kept alive by life support systems, and her brain would be controlled by the computer Centcomp, which gave her access to the memories of all previous Earth Presidents. She became aware of the Doctor.[1020]

2847 - DARK PROGENY[1021] -> The telepathic inhabitants of Ceres Alpha died out long ago, but survived as a psychic gestalt. Much later, the planet - the closest ever found to Earth's natural conditions - was colonised by humans. Earth was overcrowded and polluted at this time, and terraforming corporations like Worldcorp and Planetscape make planets suitable for human colonisation.

Influenced by the gestalt, the colonists' children began developing psychic powers. Worldcorp encouraged this, hoping that the children's telekinesis could be used to transform planets. The eighth Doctor, Fitz and Anji exposed the plan. The children rebelled against Worldcorp's corrupt leader, Gaskill Tyran, who died when the children made him mentally relive his acts of murder. The parents of one of the children, Veta and Josef Manni, took custody of the entire group.

The accelerator, a device than could heal wounds and change people's appearances, had been invented.

2850 - "Time Bomb"[1022] -> The scientists of the City of Light on Hedron reached complete control of their environment, and the genetic cleansing of their race. They banished impurities with their time cannon. The sixth Doctor and Frobisher were caught in the weapon's effect - which sent them two hundred million years into Earth's past.

The pilgrims of the *Arrow of Righteousness* arrived at their destination, but although their bodies were sound, their minds had gone. The ship crashed into the City of Light and devastated it, killing the population when its microbes and poisons were released.

The Doctor and Frobisher learned that the Hedrons had located the origin of the *Arrow of Righteousness* - Earth - and deliberately targeted their time cannon. In doing so, the Hedrons allowed mankind to evolve, and didn't destroy it.

? 2850 - THE MIND'S EYE[1023] **->** The Earth Empire Space Marines established a base on a planet designated YT45, which had a diurnal cycle lasting one hundred fourteen hours. YT45 was home to a type of flower - "kyropites" - that emitted a sleep-inducing gas; their victims experienced very detailed dream-realities while the kyropites fed upon their alpha waves, then their bodies. The fifth Doctor, Peri and Erimem were present when jekylls - monkey-like creatures who were immune to the kyropites - destroyed the marines' base. An agent of the Federation Drugs Administration thwarted a plan to derive mind-controlling drugs and telepathic enhancers from the kyropites.

The Dreamwavers of the Goyanna system had devices that could monitor dreams.

c 2850 - THREE'S A CROWD[1024] **->** A group of militaristic, reptilian Khellians happened across the Phoenix colony, and the Khellian Queen laid a clutch of eggs aboard the colony ship. The colony leader, Auntie, bargained with the Khellians and allowed them to feed off humans in stasis; in return, they were to spare her family. The number of humans who were awake dwindled down to sixteen. They became agoraphobic and lived intensely isolated lives, unaware of the Khellian presence and what had befallen their fellows.

The fifth Doctor, Peri and Erimem exposed the Khellian threat. The Khellians were wiped out and the colony ship destroyed, but the terraforming process improved the planet's sustainability. Humans sleeping in a dozen habitat domes were slated for revival.

In the mid-twenty-ninth century, zigma photography proved reconstructions of the Temple of Zeus to be inaccurate.[1025] The Forrester palace was built on Io.[1026] The Earth Empire annexed the Schirr homeworld and renamed it Idaho. Some Schirr - the Ten-Strong - formed a resistance movement. They stole knowledge of black arts from

---

1023 Dating *The Mind's Eye* (BF #102a) - It's the time of the Earth Empire, and yet a Federation Drugs Administration (FDA) is in operation. As with Colin Brake's other fifth Doctor-Peri-Erimem audio, *Three's a Crowd*, mention of the Federation might suggest a tie to *Corpse Marker*, and it seems fair to place the two stories in the same vicinity.

Erimem's dream-reality entails her ruling a colony planet in the twenty-fifth century - either a reflection of when she thinks the TARDIS has arrived on YT45, or just a tidbit her mind invented. Either way, the twenty-fifth century is too early for the Earth Empire - Brake's own novel, *The Colony of Lies*, specifies its creation as 2534.

1024 Dating *Three's a Crowd* (BF #69) - The Doctor estimates it is around the "twenty-eighth, maybe twenty-ninth century" from the space station's design, which dates back at least fifty years to the colony's formation. Mention of a Federation suggests this story occurs in the vicinity of *Corpse Marker*. There's talk of a "hyperspace transmat link" capable of "beaming" people from star system to star system, but nobody actually uses this device, and it's possibly part of Auntie's ruse against the colonists.

1025 *The Taking of Planet 5* (p15).

1026 *So Vile a Sin* (p28).

1027 "Fifteen years" before *Ten Little Aliens*.

1028 Dating *Revenge of the Cybermen* (12.5) - In *The Ark in Space*, the Doctor is unsure at first when the Ark was built ("I can't quite place the period"), but he quickly concludes that "Judging by the macro slave drive and that modified version of the Bennet Oscillator, I'd say this was built in the early thirtieth century... late twenty-ninth, early thirtieth I feel sure". Yet the panel he looks at

appears to be a feature of the Ark, not the original Nerva Beacon.

Still, in *Revenge of the Cybermen*, when Harry asks whether this is "the time of the solar flares and Earth is evacuated", the Doctor informs him that it is "thousands of years" before. Mankind has been a spacefaring race for "centuries" before this story when they fought the Cyber War, according to both Stevenson and Vorus. It is clearly established in other stories that the Earth is not abandoned in the twenty-ninth century (but see the dating on *The Beast Below*). *Revenge of the Cybermen*, then, would seem to be the story set in the "late twenty-ninth, early thirtieth century", not *The Ark in Space*. The Cybermen are apparently without a permanent base of operations, so the story is presumably set after the destruction of their base on Telos in *Attack of the Cybermen*.

One difficulty with this is that the Cybermen in *Earthshock* (set in 2526) watch a clip from this story. It's here been assumed this is the production team showing us the previous Doctors, rather than trying to date the story (in the same way, in *Mawdryn Undead*, the Brigadier "remembers" scenes he wasn't actually in). However, *About Time* suggests the Cybermen in *Earthshock* are time-travellers, which explains the otherwise erroneous *Revenge of the Cybermen* clip.

The Programme Guide set the story in both "c.2400" and "c.2900", while *The Terrestrial Index* preferred "the tail end of the twenty-fifth century". *Cybermen* placed the story in "2496", but admitted the difficulty in doing so (p71-72). *The Discontinuity Guide* offered "c.2875". *Timelink* suggests "2525". *About Time* went for "After the late 2800s, but 'thousands of years' before the time of

the non-corporeal Morphieans, who failed to distinguish between the Ten-Strong and the other corporeal beings. The Morphieans initiated retaliatory strikes against human worlds such as New Beijing, and the Ten-Strong launched terrorist strikes on planets such as New Jersey and Toronto, often killing millions.[1027]

? 2875 (Day 3, Week 47) - REVENGE OF THE CYBERMEN[1028] -> Fifty years after Neo-Phobos was discovered, the civilian exographer Kellman began his survey of the planetoid, setting up a transmat point between it and the Nerva Beacon. He renamed the planetoid Voga.

Fifteen weeks later, an extra-terrestrial disease swept through Nerva. Once the infection began, the victims died within minutes. The medical team on board the station were among the first to perish, and Earth Centre immediately rerouted all flights through Ganymede Beacon. As loyal members of the Space Service, the Nerva crew remained on board. Ten weeks after the plague first struck, all but four people on the station were dead. The Cybermen were responsible as part of their plan to destroy Voga. The fourth Doctor, Sarah Jane and Harry defeated them.

The Ice Warriors slumbering in the asteroid belt awakened and departed the solar system, hoping to found a new homeworld.[1029]

? 2878 - THE POWER OF KROLL[1030] -> The Sons of Earth Movement claimed that colonising planets was a mistake. They demanded a return to Earth, but most of its members had never been to the homeworld, which was now suffering major famines.

A classified project, a methane-catalysing refinery, was set up on the third moon of Delta Magna. Two hundred tons of compressed protein were produced every day by extracting material from the marshlands, and sent to Magna by unmanned rockets. It was claimed that the Sons of Earth were supplying gas-operated projectile weapons to the native Swampies on this moon, and that the group was employing the services of the notorious gun-runner Rohm-Dutt. The truth was that Thawn, an official at the refinery, was supplying the Swampies with faulty weapons as an excuse to wipe them out.

A squid creature on this moon had consumed the fifth segment of the Key to Time, and grown to a monstrous size. The Swampies regarded it as their god, Kroll. Thawn's plan was uncovered and he was killed. The fourth Doctor and Romana recovered the Fifth Segment, which ended Kroll's power. Kroll had been the source of the refinery's compressed protein, and the facility was useless upon the creature's reversion.

? 2878 - "Victims"[1031] -> Kolpasha was the fashion capital of the human empire. The fourth Doctor and Romana arrived and were accused of copyright theft - a crime more serious there than murder. Elsewhere, the political activist Gevaunt was planning to release Vitality, an age-reversing cosmetic. Romana discovered that repeat use of Vitality would make human flesh break down... and make it easier to digest.

The Doctor discovered that a carnivorous Quoll from the Reft Sector was behind the scheme. The Quoll had stripped their home bare and wanted new feeding grounds, but the Doctor made the Quoll explode by dousing it with Vitality. However, this ruined the Doctor's clothes...

Earth colonised Dramos, located between the secondary and tertiary spiral arms of the galaxy. Dramos Port became an important trading post.[1032] The third Doctor and Jo visited the home planet of the Pakha and discovered that an ancient Diadem contained a being that made them aggressive. The diadem was lost when the Doctor cast it into a ravine.[1033] Artificial people, such as those created by the Villiers Artificial Life laboratory in Battersea, were given their independence.[1034]

---

the solar flares". "A History of the Cybermen" (*DWM* #83) suggested the (misprinted?) date "25,514".

1029 "A few centuries" after *The Resurrection of Mars*.

1030 Dating *The Power of Kroll* (16.5) - The Doctor claims that Kroll manifests "every couple of centuries", and this is his fourth manifestation, suggesting it is at least eight hundred years since Delta Magna was colonised. *The Terrestrial Index* set the story in the "fifty-second century", *The TARDIS Logs* "c.3000 AD". *About Time* favoured it being the *far* future, possibly after the time of the solar flares, or even the same era as *The Sun Makers*.

1031 Dating "Victims" (*DWM* #212-214) - The year isn't specified, but reference to the human empire seems to

place it in the Earth Empire period. The implication is that the Doctor gets his burgundy outfit from Kolpasha following this story. The sixth Doctor says in *Year of the Pig* that his favourite tailor is on Kolpasha, and that his coat is considered the height of fashion there in *Instruments of Darkness*. *Spiral Scratch* mentions that the sixth Doctor and Mel visited Kolpasha. *Placebo Effect* (set in 3999) names Kolpasha as the "fashion capital" of the Federation.

1032 "Centuries" before *Burning Heart* (p4).

1033 "Many hundreds of years" before *Legacy*.

1034 "At least another century or two" after the future component of *Paradox Lost*.

Kaldor City

Kaldor City and its surrounding society became extremely reliant upon robots: fourteen million robots served a population of eight million people within Kaldor City itself, and a total of fifteen million people worldwide. The robots were created by the Company, which directly or indirectly ran the planet. The Company Board consisted of many Firstmasters, as led by a Firstmaster Chairholder.[1035]

Robots in Kaldor City became so advanced that some people found themselves greatly unhinged by the robots' inhuman body language. Psychologists christened this Grimwade's Syndrome, or "robophobia".

Vehicles called storm miners ventured out on two-year missions into a hundred million mile expanse of desert. Sand blown up in storms was sucked into the storm miners' scoops, which sifted out lucrative substances such as zelanite, keefan and lucanol. The water supplies for the storm miners' eight-man crew was totally recycled once a month, but the crew lived in relative luxury. Most of the work was done for them by robots: around a hundred Dums, capable of only the simplest task; a couple dozen Vocs, more sophisticated; and one Super-Voc co-ordinating them.[1036]

The first time that Uvanov commanded a storm mine, one of his crew - the brother of Zilda - developed robophobia, ran outside the storm mine and died. Uvanov was such a good pilot, the Company didn't want to lose him and overlooked the incident.[1037]

Taren Capel was an extremely innovative robotics engineer who had been raised by robots, and sought to elevate his robotic brethren above their lowly status. He introduced changes to the Company's designs so that newly made Dums, Vocs and Super-Vocs were embedded with a trigger phrase - "Awake, my brothers! Let the slaves become masters!" - to be given in Capel's own voice. When transmitted, this would turn the robots into killers. Capel went into hiding for six weeks, then **assumed the identity**

1035 The *Kaldor City* mini-series as produced by Magic Bullet features a number of the same characters, concepts and actors as appeared in *The Robots of Death*. *Legacy* says that *The Robots of Death* was set in the deserts of Iapetus, the second moon of Saturn, but *Kaldor City* maintains that Kaldor City is removed enough from Earth space that Carnell (and possibly even Kerr Avon; see the *Blake's 7* essay) view it as a safe haven after fleeing the Federation from *Blake's 7*. Furthermore, much of the plot of the first audio, *KC: Occam's Razor*, is predicated on the idea that Kaldor City has no interstellar trade.

In real life, Iapetus isn't large enough to have a desert the size of the one referred to in *The Robots of Death*. Also, according to Uvanov in the mini-series, the planet on which Kaldor City resides has a 26-hour day; a day on Iapetus is equal to seventy-nine days.
1036 The background to *The Robots of Death*.
1037 "Ten years" before *The Robots of Death*.
1038 *The Robots of Death*, with details about Capel's scheme given in *Kaldor City*.
1039 Dating *The Robots of Death* (14.5) - An arbitrary date. *The Programme Guide* set the story "c.30,000", but *The Terrestrial Index* preferred "the 51st Century". *Timelink* set the story in 2777, the same period as it set *The Happiness Patrol*. Previous editions of *Ahistory* picked 2877, while stressing this was a bit of a crapshoot.

While the specific century remains very much in doubt, at least two if not three episodes of the *Kaldor City* mini-series occur in or relatively soon after a year ending in "90", and it's said in *Kaldor City* episodes four and five that *The Robots of Death* - and the Company robot augmentations that Taren Capel carried out shortly beforehand - occurred "ten years" ago. Allowing that Capel went into hiding for "six weeks" (*KC: Taren*

Capel) after making his modifications to the robot assembly lines, and that the storm mine was "eight months" into its tour (according to both *Taren Capel* and *Corpse Marker*) when events in *The Robots of Death* happened, it's entirely possible that *Corpse Marker* takes place roughly six years, one month and two weeks after *The Robots of Death*. That said, the "ten years" figure is bantered about with such approximation, it's a coin toss as to whether *The Robots of Death* itself occurs nine or ten years prior to the end of *Kaldor City*. The final date of 2881 given here was chosen to better synch this story with *Corpse Marker*, although 2880 is also feasible. See the dating notes on *Kaldor City* for more.
1040 *Kaldor City: Taren Capel. Robophobia* confirms that the truth about the storm mine murders wasn't made public.
1041 Dating "Crisis on Kaldor" (*DWM* #50) - It seems to be around the same time as *The Robots of Death*.
1042 Dating *Corpse Marker* (PDA #27) - This is a sequel to *The Robots of Death*, and according to the back cover blurb occurs "several years later". The final installment of *Kaldor City* takes place "three years and thirty days" after Uvanov becomes Firstmaster Chairholder - an event that occurs at the end of *Corpse Marker*, when Uvanov leverages the previous chairholder, Dess Pitter, out of office. As ten months elapse within *Kaldor City* itself, this means that the audio series opens approximately two years and three months after *Corpse Marker*.

BLAKE'S 7: *Corpse Marker* and the *Kaldor City* audio series - both sequels to *The Robots of Death* - feature Carnell, a character who first appeared in the *Blake's 7* episode *Weapon*. Chris Boucher either wrote or was involved with all of these stories. Moreover, it's very likely that Kaston Iago - the lead character in *Kaldor City* - is Kerr Avon, who somehow survived the shootout at

of a robotics expert named Dask and joined the crew of a storm mine under the command of Uvanov. He waited for eight months while the Company created new robots with his murder sub-routine.[1038]

? 2881 - THE ROBOTS OF DEATH[1039] **->** The robots aboard Uvanov's storm mine predated the augmentation Capel had made to the Company's robots, and so **Capel personally turned Uvanov's robots into killers and instigated the murder of his crewmates. Thanks to the fourth Doctor and Leela's intervention, a robot killed Capel. Three of the crew - Uvanov, Pool and Toos - survived the slaughter.**

The Company publicly blamed the murders as the work of ore raiders, and Capel's trigger phrase went unused.[1040]

? 2882 - "Crisis on Kaldor"[1041] **->** Storm miners were found with their Voc and Dum-class robots destroyed, and their Super-Vocs missing. An advanced Kaldor City robot, the Ultra-Voc (UV-1), had achieved a greater degree of independence and was recruiting Super-Vocs to help it liberate robotkind. Sylvos Orikon, an investigator for the Kaldor Robotics Corps, went undercover as a Super-Voc on a storm miner, found UV-1 and destroyed it - but was mistaken for a malfunctioning robot and "disassembled" by the storm miner's Vocs.

& 2887 - CORPSE MARKER[1042] **->** In Kaldor City, the lowly-born Uvanov was promoted to being a topmaster of the Company, but this failed to sit well with members of the elite classes on the Company Board. They asked the psycho-strategist Carnell to devise a means by which they could secure their power. Carnell's scheme entailed use of new generation of cyborg-robots, which had been secretly created. The cyborgs proved uncontrollable and went on the rampage, killing many prominent citizens. The fourth Doctor destroyed the cyborgs, and Carnell supplied Uvanov with blackmail information against members of the Board. Uvanov quickly attained the position of Firstmaster Chairholder.

& 2889 - KALDOR CITY: OCCAM'S RAZOR / DEATH'S HEAD[1043] **->** Kaston Iago, an assassin, arrived in Kaldor City and was suspected in the murder of several Company Firstmasters. As Firstmaster Chairholder, Uvanov judged that Iago was innocent and hired him as his bodyguard and security consultant. The psycho-strategist Carnell told Uvanov that the murders owed to a conspiracy concerning Uvanov's motion that the Company

the end of *Blake's 7*, changed his name and went into hiding in Kaldor City afterwards. Although legal reasons prevented this from being expressly said, Iago is very much like Avon - he's a ruthless and brilliant killer with a number of programming skills. By the way, it's probably not coincidence that Iago, like Avon, is played by Paul Darrow. Iago says in *Kaldor City* that he killed "The Butcher of Zercaster" - the name given in the charity audio *The Mark of Kane* to Travis, the *Blake's 7* villain whom Avon shot dead on screen. *KC: Occam's Razor* identifies both Carnell and Iago as having fled the Federation.

This opens a can of worms, as it suggests that *Blake's 7* and *Doctor Who* occur in the same universe, which is just about possible. It's never established in which century *Blake's 7* takes place, and the original proposal stated only that it was "the third century of the second calendar". The only real indication was that the Wanderer spacecraft (in the *Blake's 7* story *Killer*, written by Robert Holmes) were the first into deep space "seven hundred years" before Blake's era. In *Doctor Who* terms, that would set *Blake's 7* in the twenty-eighth or twenty-ninth century.

The future history of *Blake's 7* is pretty basic - humanity has colonised many planets and most of those are under the control of the fascist Federation. While never stated in the series itself, publicity for the show (and subsequent guides to the series) said that there was a series of atomic wars across the galaxy several hundred years before Blake's time, and the Federation was founded in the aftermath. By coincidence, this fits quite neatly with the *Doctor Who* timeline, and the atomic war might be the Dalek/Galactic Wars of the twenty-sixth century. As might be expected, not every detail matches perfectly, but the oppressive Earth Empire of *Doctor Who* is not wildly different from the Terran Federation seen in *Blake's 7*. The symbol worn by the Earth expedition in *Death to the Daleks* (authored by Terry Nation, who created *Blake's 7* and wrote a fair amount of it) is the symbol of the Federation in *Blake's 7*, turned ninety degrees.

The audio *Three's a Crowd*, which roughly dates to this era, mentions a Federation and uses *Blake's 7* teleport sound effects. In *Kaldor City*, the sound effect of Iago's gun holster is very similar to that used in *Blake's 7* Series 4, and mention is made of Herculaneum, the substance that comprises the *Liberator*'s hull.

1043 Dating *Kaldor City* (Magic Bullet audio series; *KC: Occam's Razor*, #1.1; *KC: Death's Head*, #1.2; *KC: Hidden Persuaders*, #1.3; *KC: Taren Capel*, #1.4; *KC: Checkmate*, #1.5) - The *Kaldor City* mini-series follows on from *Corpse Marker*. Iago indicates in *KC: Checkmate* that the central five-part *Kaldor City* series happens over ten month period. The most glaring dating clue with regards the year is that Carnell's Voc says in episode four (*KC: Taren Capel*) that it was last upgraded on "09/01/90", so the later *Kaldor City* installments either occur in a year ending with 90 or, presumably, not long thereafter.

It's variously indicated that three or five months pass

send signals to other worlds and commence interplanetary trade with them. Iago killed the last of the alleged conspirators, seemingly ending the matter. In truth, Iago and Carnell had formed an uneasy alliance - Carnell knew that Iago had murdered the Firstmasters purely to gain a lucrative position with Uvanov, whereas Carnell had invented the "conspiracy" to prevent the Company opening up trade with the Federation, from which he had fled.

Some time after this, the Church of Taren Capel - a robot fundamentalist group led by the former storm mine worker Poul, a.k.a. Paulus - caused civil unrest and terrorist incidents. Uvanov, having hired Carnell as a consultant, arranged for security agent Elsca Blayes to go undercover and join the terrorists' ranks, then steered the Tarenists to eliminate his political opponents.

& 2890 - KALDOR CITY: HIDDEN PERSUADERS / TAREN CAPEL / CHECKMATE[1043] -> Carnell fled, having determined that the key players in Kaldor City were being manipulated by a force older than humanity. In a bid to stop the unseen entity's plans, whatever they might be, he activated Taren Capel's trigger phrase. Robots across Kaldor City turned murderous until Iago edited recordings of Capel's voice, and transmitted an order that the robots stand down.

Carnell arranged for Uvanov to receive evidence that his rival, Firstmaster Landerchild, was guilty of aiding the Tarenists; he also provided Landerchild with evidence that Uvanov was similarly culpable. The Company Board had to decide if they were both guilty, or if Carnell was lying.

Paulus acquired what he thought was Taren Capel's skull, but it was actually the Fendahl, which had become stronger after being thrown into a supernova. The Fendahl fed upon Paulus' followers, and its core hosted itself in Justina - Uvanov's personal assistant, and Iago's lover.

Iago tried to eliminate Blayes as competition for his services as a hired killer, and was gravely wounded in a shootout with her. The Fendahl, in Justina's body, appeared before Iago and suggested he would live if they went into the past and altered history. The two of them went back to an earlier point in Justina's quarters, where Iago destroyed Justina's painting of a red pentagram and killed her younger self. Carnell then appeared, and told Iago that they were both in Hell...

Kaldor City survived the Fendahl incident, and would prosper by exporting its robots to other worlds.[1044]

c 2890 - GRIMM REALITY[1045] -> Titan had whale ranches and was being terraformed. Space mining was big business, with prospectors looking for rare particles such as strange matter, squarks and Hydrogen 3. Zero Rad Day was celebrated on Earth.

The eighth Doctor, Anji and Fitz landed on the planet Albert as the salvage ship *Bonadventure* entered orbit. The Doctor realised that the planet was alive and had absorbed the memory banks of a crashed Earth ship, then modelled itself as a world of fairytales. The Doctor collected up various "wishing boxes", which contained the spawn of a nearby white hole. One of the insectoid Vuim used the great powers of the white hole to cure his race of a wasting disease, which seeded the white hole's spawn into a gap

---

between episode two (*KC: Death's Head*) and episode three, so it's a toss-up as to whether episode two takes place in the same calendar year as episode one. Uvanov comments in episode three that Iago last took a holiday - a reference to events in episode one - "last year sometime", so episodes one and three must occur in different years. Where the Fendahl is concerned, its core, Justina, says it grew stronger after being flung into a supernova (at the end of *Image of the Fendahl*).

1044 THE KALDOR CITY FINALE: The ending to the core *Kaldor City* mini-series, as the summary to *KC: Checkmate* demonstrates, is something of a surreal experience. So much so, it caused some confusion upon release as to how the story actually ended. Different theories have been offered concerning this... one possibility is that Iago was mortally wounded in his shootout with Blayse, and everything he experiences concerning Carnell and the retroactive murder of Justina is a delusion of his dying brain. Another is that it's all a metaphor, part of the political and sexual power plays that permeate the audio series.

The explanation that is increasingly hard to avoid, however, is that the Fendahl wins at the very end, and absorbs everyone in Kaldor City who wasn't killed beforehand. The choice offered to Iago - to deface Justina's painting, and to retroactively murder her - is part and parcel of the Fendahl's seduction; Iago fully enables the Fendahl's victory by agreeing to it. (Quite why the Fendahl *needs* to tempt Iago in such a fashion rather than just up and absorbing him isn't said.)

Kaldor City writer/producer Alan Stevens has stated - by way of confirming observations made independently online by Paul Dale Smith - that the last scene of *Checkmate*, plus the whole of the short story *KC: "The Prisoner"* (included on *The Actor Speaks* CD featuring Paul Darrow) and *KC: Storm Mine* (*KC* 1.6) occur within the Fendahl gestalt (hence the refrain in the latter story that, "We're all in this together"). "The Prisoner" evidently occurs from Landerchild's perspective within the gestalt; *Storm Mine* occurs from Blayse's point of view. The "Iago" that appears in both stories is just their respective memories of him, although Smith - tapped as a potential writer to continue the series - postulated that the Iago that appears in *Storm Mine* was the genuine article, trying to subvert the gestalt from within and cheat death.

between realities to gestate. The parent white hole left and life on Albert returned to normal.

c 2890 (May) - TEN LITTLE ALIENS[1046] -> Earth was exporting its poor and levying repressive taxes. Those born on Earth had legal and social advantages over offworlders. Alien planets were renamed after places on Earth. Pentagon Central ran Earth's military, which included the Pauper Fleet, the Royal Escort and the Peacekeepers. The Japanese Belt was trying to develop teleportation.

An Anti-Terror Elite squad from Earth landed on a planetoid for an exercise and discovered a Schirr building there, with a murdered group of Schirr terrorists inside. The first Doctor, Ben and Polly realised that Nadina Haunt, the human squad's leader, was a Schirr sympathiser who thought she was leading her men into an ambush.

The complex launched itself towards the Morphiean Quadrant. The Schirr terrorists, the Ten Strong, revived. They wanted to ally with a renegade faction of the Morphiean race, then topple the Earth Empire. The Doctor resisted the Ten-Strong's spells and annihilated them. The Morphiean authorities dealt with their renegades, ending the Morphiean Quadrant's conflict with humanity.

In 2891, the Daleks destroyed the planet of the reptilian Anthaurk, so the Anthaurk occupied Kaillor in the Minerva system and renamed it New Anthaur. The native Izrekt were massacred. The other planets declared war.

On the 16 Lannasirn, following the Anthaurk defeat, the Treaty of Yquatine was signed. The Minerva Space Alliance was formed when the system declared independence from Earth. The Anthaurks began the Century of Waiting, secretly rebuilding their arsenal. For a century, other races flocked to the Minerva system, including the Ixtricite (a crystal race combining "the Krotons, the Rhotons and the something-else-ons"). The Adamanteans and the Ogri colonised Adamantine.[1047]

A space battle led to two of the four Krotons serving aboard a dynatrope being "exhausted", i.e. killed. The dynatrope was largely composed of tellurium, and required the mental power of four "high brains" to function. Per standard procedure, the dynatrope put down on a nearby planet. The two surviving Krotons entered stasis while the dynatrope operated on automatic. It regularly culled the most gifted students that the humanoids living on the planet - the Gonds - could offer, hoping to find a pair smart enough to function as high brains. No such Gonds were found, and the mental energy harvested from the students was only enough to keep the dynatrope functioning.[1048]

c 2895 - "Supernature"[1049] -> Following a massacre on Nigella IV, the Earth Empire adopted a policy of not risking innocent lives on colony worlds. Transports filled with outcasts - thieves, the bankrupted, political dissidents, etc. - were sent on a one-way trip to confirm that potential colony planets were viable. If so, traction factories would follow and lay concrete.

One such transport arrived on a world where an alien terraforming effort had gone awry. An alien gene-splicer caused people to hybridise with the local wildlife; when the eleventh Doctor and Amy showed up en route to Basingstoke, she was transformed into a butterfly person. The Doctor destroyed the gene-splicer, returning everyone to normal. On his recommendation, the colonists maintained their quarantine warning, keeping the Empire at bay from what was now paradise. They also accepted the Doctor's proposed name for the planet: Basingstoke.

The TARDIS was tainted with the genetic transfer effect. It would absorb lifeforms in its travels to follow, leading to the creation of Chiyoko, the "child of time".[1050]

Around 2900, the Vargeld family became prominent in the politics of the Yquatine system.[1051] Early Hollywood comedy star Archibald Maplin was known in the thirtieth century; a holograph of him appeared on the uniweb.[1052]

If it's possible to puzzle through how *Kaldor City* ends, however, the Big Finish audio *Robophobia* - which has to take place after both *The Robots of Death* and *Kaldor City* - seems to indicate that Kaldor City not only survives the Fendahl incident (albeit through events we're never shown), but subsequently creates a booming robotics trade for itself. See the dating notes on that story.

1045 Dating *Grimm Reality* (EDA #50) - The mining companies were active "a hundred or a hundred and ten years" ago, in the 2780s.

1046 Dating *Ten Little Aliens* (PDA #54) - It is clearly the subjugation phase of the Earth Empire. An e-zine written somewhat prior to these events (p15), with biographies of Haunt's troopers, is dated "23.5.90", presumably meaning 23rd May, 2890.

1047 *The Fall of Yquatine* (p30, p43).

1048 "Thousands of years" before *The Krotons*.

1049 Dating "Supernature" (*DWM* #421-423) - It's the time of the Earth Empire. The forced use of an underclass to colonise worlds, and the Doctor's choice of an Earth city as the colony world's name, is somewhat akin to conditions described in *Ten Little Aliens*. The ongoing *DWM* storyline featuring Chiyoko starts in this story, continues in "The Screams of Death", "The Golden Ones", "Planet Bollywood" and "Do Not Go Gentle Into that Good Night", and ends in "The Child of Time" (*DWM*).

1050 "Apotheosis"

1051 *The Fall of Yquatine* (p30, p43).

1052 "Silver Scream"

c 2900 - SONTARANS: SILENT WARRIOR[1053] -> Humanity now used cloning transports to supply its colony planets with livestock. The advent of the Sigma 3, a.k.a. Sentinel, AI series meant that such transports required only a gene tech and an engineer as crew. An adversary of the Sontarans had early warning systems and graviton mines stationed on a frontier at Sigma 150, impeding the Sontarans from waging full-scale war against humanity. Field Major Starn attempted to smuggle a Sontaran army through human space aboard the cloning transport *Genesis*, but an advanced android named Alex diverted the *Genesis* through a field of life-sucking Plasmites, killing them.

Decline and Fall

By the beginning of the thirtieth century, the Empire had become utterly corrupt. Planetary governors, such as the one on Solos, would routinely oppress the native races of the planet.[1054] Humans were often little more than "work units", fit only for manning factories or mines where using humanoid robots was uneconomic. Humanity was exploiting other worlds and "going through the universe like a plague of interplanetary locusts". Mogar, in the Perseus Arm of the galaxy, was a rich source of rare metals such as vionesium, but although Earth assured the Mogarians that they only required limited mining concessions, they were soon strip-mining the planet. The vionesium shipments to Earth received Grade One security.[1055]

Every native animal species died out except humanity and the rat.[1056] The humans of Earth in the thirtieth century had no appendix or wisdom teeth, and most racial differences had been smoothed out in the general population.[1057] Humans had a lifespan of around one hundred and forty years.[1058] Suspensor pools were fashionable in the Earth Empire.[1059] In the thirtieth century, the Cybermen built a time capsule, but a test flight left them stranded in Jersey in 1940.[1060]

In 2905, Chris Cwej's father graduated from the Academy. He served in the Adjudication Service, as his ancestors had for centuries, until 2971.[1061] **Nerva Beacon completed its mission at Voga. The space station remained operational for many centuries afterwards.**[1062]

& 2944 - ROBOPHOBIA[1063] -> Kaldor City now had a thriving interstellar trade, and exported its robots to many other planets. A string of murders occurred aboard the factory starship *Lorelei*, which had set out to deliver approximately one hundred fifty-seven thousand robots and five construction plant kits to the planet Ventalis. Robots were suspected as having committed the killings, but the truth was that Security Chief Farel had contracted Grimwade's Syndrome following his wife's death in a storm mine scoop - an incident where robots had tried and failed

---

1053 Dating *Sontarans: Silent Warrior* (BBV audio #19) - The participants are cited as human, and mention of Grimwade's Syndrome suggests this is the same era as *The Robots of Death*. Alex's pedigree is unknown; he might be from Orion, but his vague talk of working for watchmen who "like to keep an eye on things" might imply that he's of Time Lord manufacture.
1054 *The Mutants*
1055 *Terror of the Vervoids*
1056 *Just War* (p143), although we see bears and wolves in *The Ice Warriors*, and hear of a variety of animal specimens in *The Ark in Space*. Pigs and dogs survive until at least the year 5000 AD (*The Talons of Weng-Chiang*, *The Invisible Enemy*), there are sheep and spiders on the colony ship sent to Metebelis III in *Planet of the Spiders*, Europa is well stocked with animal life in *Managra*, and the Ark (in *The Ark*) contains a thriving jungle environment complete with an elephant and tropical birds.
1057 *Death and Diplomacy* (p16). The lack of wisdom teeth is also mentioned in *Benny: Dry Pilgrimage*.
1058 *Just War*
1059 "Fifty years" before Roz's time. *The Also People* (p10).
1060 *Illegal Alien* (p152).
THE THIRTIETH CENTURY: While it's highly likely that the Earth was not ravaged by solar flares at this time

(see *The Beast Below* and *The Ark in Space*), the Doctor's description of a "highly compartmentalised" Earth society of the thirtieth century in *The Ark in Space* matches similar descriptions of Earth in stories set at this time. Earth is "grey" in *The Mutants* and "highly organised" in *Terror of the Vervoids* episode four. We learn of food shortages in *Terror of the Vervoids*.

In terms of the New Adventures, this is Cwej and Forrester's native time, and we meet them there in *Original Sin* - a story that ties in quite closely with *The Mutants* (Solos is even mentioned on p318). Roz returns and dies in her native time in *So Vile a Sin*.

We first learn of the decline of the Earth Empire and the Overcities in *The Mutants*, although in that story the Solos native Ky calls them "sky cities" and claims they were built because "the air is too poisonous", not because of the wars.
1061 *Original Sin* (p160-161).
1062 Nerva Beacon has a "thirty year assignment" according to Stevenson in *Revenge of the Cybermen*, so it ought to be decommissioned around 2915. We see the Beacon again in *The Ark in Space*.
1063 Dating *Robophobia* (BF #149) - No year is given, and it's an unspecified amount of time after the Storm Mine Four killings (*The Robots of Death*). A continuity clash between this story and the *Kaldor City* mini-series is somewhat inevitable... the Fendahl seemed to

to save her. Farel sought to end all human dependence on robots by faking transmissions that a robot revolution was in progress, then destroying Ventalis by driving the *Lorelei* into it. The seventh Doctor thwarted the scheme.

The Overcity Era

The pollution levels on the surface of Earth reached such a level that the population was forced to live in vast sky cities.[1064]

The Manussan people had been reduced to barbarism and degradation under the Mara's rule. The Mara was overthrown, and banished to the "dark places of the inside". The outsider who defeated the Mara founded and ruled over a three-world Federation, the third planet of which was Manussa. A legend said that the Mara would return in a dream.[1065] Around 2945, the Wars of Acquisition fought by the Empire reached Earth itself. The Overcities were built over the battle-torn Earth using a new form of cheap and effective null-gravity. They floated around a kilometre from the surface, supported on stilts and by null-grav beams.

Half the Earth's population, everyone that could afford it, lived in the Overcities and Seacities. The wealthier you were, the higher the levels that you were allowed to access. Earth's surface became the Undertown: a flooded, ruined landscape. The Vigilant belt of defence space stations proved invaluable at repelling alien attacks, and within ten years the front had shifted so far away from Earth that

humanity had almost forgotten they were taking place.

After a few years of austerity, Earth benefited from a technological and economic upsurge. It was "a time of peace and prosperity: well, for the peaceful and prosperous, at least". Earth was a cosmopolitan place, with races such as Alpha Centauri, Arcturans, Foamasi and Thrillip living in the lower areas of the Overcities, although aliens were treated as second-class citizens. Earth at this time had a human population of thirty billion, with almost as many robot workers. The data protection act was modified in 2945 to reflect the changes in technology and society.

Over the generations, a semi-feudal system had developed. A Baron was responsible for sections of an Overcity, typically controlling a few hundred levels. A Viscount ran the whole city (an area the size of an old nation state); a Count or Countess was responsible for ten Cities (equivalent to a continent). Earth, and each of the other planets, was ruled by a Marquis or Marquessa. The solar system and its Environs were under the authority of its Lord Protector, the Duke Marmion. The Divine Empress ruled over the whole of the Earth Empire, in which thousands of suns never set, and which stretched across half the galaxy. Few on Earth knew that the Empress was Centcomp - the computer network that ran the solar system - setting judicial sentences, running navigational and library databases, co-ordinating virtually every aspect of life.[1066]

Roslyn Sarah Forrester, a companion of the seventh Doctor, was born.[1067]

---

destroy/ingest/otherwise dominate Kaldor City in *KC: Checkmate*, so placing *Robophobia* - in which Kaldor City is quite active - after that is rather tricky. However, *Robophobia* can't easily go beforehand as it entails Kaldor City having a massive interstellar robot trade, whereas the *Kaldor City* audios establish that Kaldor City has no contact with other worlds. (In fact, the plot of the first *Kaldor City* story, *KC: Occam's Razor*, is highly dependent on that notion.) *Robophobia* and *Kaldor City* agree that the truth about Taren Capel's insurrection was never made public, but matters are further complicated in that everyone involved in *Robophobia* finds it unthinkable and unprecedented that robots might be capable of murder - even though the Fendahl's victory was preceded (*KC: Taren Capel*) by a robot rebellion that almost certainly killed some thousands, if not tens of thousands, of people.

While it's often undesirable to assume that there's a missing story that reconciles matters, in this case it's slightly easier to believe that the Fendahl was somehow defeated off screen - in such a way that everyone's memories of Kaldor City's robots becoming murderous en masse was somehow erased - than to make *Robophobia*, which occurs onboard a spaceship bearing one hundred fifty-seven thousand robots to anoth-

er planet, take place simultaneous to a set of audios predicated on Kaldor City having no offworld trade. With that shaky solution in mind, sixty years have arbitrarily been chosen for Kaldor City to recover from the Fendahl incident, and to develop (as was a stated goal in *Occam's Razor*) the commerce seen in *Robophobia*.
1064 *The Mutants*
1065 "Five hundred years" before *Snakedance*.
1066 *Original Sin*
1067 *The Also People* adds that Roz's clan name is "Inyathi", which means buffalo.

ROZ FORRESTER: A discussion document about Roz and Cwej prepared by Andy Lane for the New Adventures authors said that Roz was born in 2935. No date is given in the books themselves, and the collective evidence suggests that Roz is born a little later than that. Roz meets the Doctor in *Original Sin* (set in 2975), three years (*Original Sin*, p211) after the death of her treacherous mentor, Fenn Martle. She spent fifteen years squired to Martle, and prior to that spent five years with an offworld Adjudicator, which was preceded by two years of training on Ponten IV (*Original Sin*, p127). In *Benny: Oblivion*, Martle is "29, nine years older than Roz". At this point, Roz has been squired to him for a year (p8). In *So Vile a Sin* (p127), Roz says she was an

The Glass Men of Valcea established their Glass City, and defended it against many enemies.[1068] The second Doctor and Jamie arrived at a communications centre on Mendeb Two's equator. They pocketed the main communications relay device as a reminder that they should revisit the area, but this altered history. Without the device, Mendeb Two's disparate settlements were unable to pool their resources and skills, and thus failed to match technological developments on Mendeb Three.[1069]

Roz Forrester joined the Adjudicator service, against the wishes of her aristocratic family. She spent two years training on Ponten IV, then five more years training with an offworld Adjudicator[1070]

c 2950 - INDEPENDENCE DAY[1071] -> The Mendeb colonies regressed to a feudal, agricultural society without the corporations' advanced technology. On Mendeb Three, the tiny region of Gonfallon declared itself a duchy, and came to dominate the planet within a generation.

Military commander Kedin Ashar - the Duke of Jerrissar - helped King Vethran rise to power. Vethran enslaved Mendeb Two, using the drug SS10 to brainwash the populace into submission, but became increasingly tyrannical. Ashar launched a revolt against Vethran, and the seventh Doctor and Ace, hoping to atone for the Doctor's previous error in hindering Mendeb Two's development, helped Ashar achieve victory. Ashar formally ended the slave trade and ordered reparations be made to Mendeb Two.

c 2950 - MASTER[1072] -> The seventh Doctor brokered a deal with Death, having come to recognise the entity's hold over the Master. Their agreement was that the Master would remain outside of Death's purview for ten years, and live his days as a contented man. At the end of that time, the Doctor was required to kill his old friend.

The physically scarred Master consequently turned up in the colony of Perfugium with no memory of his past. He became known as "John Smith", settled into a happy life

---

Adjudicator for "twenty-three years" (p293). She's variously said to have "thirty years' experience as an enforcer" in *Zamper* (p184), "twenty-five years on the streets" in *The Also People* (p46), and to have been an Adjudicator for "over twenty years" in *Just War* (p184). She's cited as being "Class of 2955" in *GodEngine* (p175).

Presuming the "twenty-three years" remark should be accepted (because it's the most specific) as marking the end of Roz's tenure with the Adjudicators in *Original Sin*, and doesn't count the training she received on Ponten IV, a composite of Roz's life can be rendered... she's born in either 2937 or 2938, she goes to train on Ponten IV at about age 12 (circa 2950), she trains for five years with the offworld Adjudicator (circa 2952-2957), but "graduates" in 2955 (an event that, depending upon the training/coursework involved, might occur in the middle of her offworld training). She's squired to Martle at age 19 (circa 2957), Martle dies in 2972 and *Original Sin* occurs in 2975. All of which matches the New Adventures' continual (if somewhat vague) portrayal of Roz as someone who's closer to 40 than 30.

1068 "A thousand years" before *The Blue Angel*, according to *Iris: Enter Wildthyme*.
1069 "Some" Mendeb years before *Independence Day*.
1070 *Original Sin* (p127).
1071 Dating *Independence Day* (PDA #36) - It's "four hundred years" after the Galactic Wars (p22), which would place it in the mid-thirtieth century.
1072 Dating *Master* (BF #49) - Perfugium is a colony, part of a human empire ruled by an Empress, where Adjudicators enforce the law; so the story is set during the Earth Empire period.
1073 According to Andy Lane's discussion document about Roz and Cwej, and confirmed in *Head Games* (p205). The month and day is given in *The Room with No Doors* (p20).

1074 *Original Sin* (p32, p219).
1075 *Benny: Oblivion*
1076 This takes the Doctor's remark to the Black Dalek in *Remembrance of the Daleks* that the Daleks are "a thousand years" from home literally, although it's fairly clear the statement is rhetorical.
1077 *Dating The Space Museum* (2.7) - There's no date given in the story itself. However, it must fall somewhere before the collapse of the Morok Empire in Roz's time (mentioned in *The Death of Art*), and after the Moroks capture a "banded" Dalek (ie: one with the "bands" seen in *The Daleks* and *The Dalek Invasion of Earth*, not the "slatted" ones seen in all subsequent appearances). This date is arbitrary.
1078 *The Death of Art*
1079 Within living memory of "Children of the Revolution", but presumably before *The Evil of the Daleks*.
1080 Dating *The Evil of the Daleks* (4.9) - There is no date given for the Skaro sequences in the scripts. *About Time* and *Timelink* note that Maxtible says he and Victoria have undertaken a "journey through space" to get from Victorian England to Skaro, possibly indicating that the Skaro sequences are set in 1866. However, Waterfield calls the device used to get to Skaro a "time machine" and the story is based around the idea that humans have always beaten the Daleks in the long run - something that's not yet the case in the nineteenth century. The Doctor murmurs that this is "the final end" of the Daleks, and some fans have taken this statement at face value when they come to date the story. However, a line cut from the camera script of *Day of the Daleks* stated that the Daleks survived the civil war and that the human-ised Daleks were defeated. The surviving telesnaps are indeterminate - at the very end of the story, a Dalek has a bit of a lifeglow, but that could just

and became a physician.

In Perfugium, a serial killer slaughtered eleven prostitutes and an ordinary teenage girl. Green was the colour of death in the colony, and the bodies were found wrapped in green blankets. On the tenth anniversary of John Smith's arrival, his friends - the Adjudicator Victor Schaeffer and his wife Jacqueline - gathered at Smith's house to celebrate his "birthday". Their festivities were interrupted by the Doctor, who begrudgingly admitted Smith's previous identity as the Master. Victor was exposed as the serial killer and further murdered his wife - who was secretly in love with Smith.

The Doctor and Death amended their deal so Smith could choose his fate. Death presented Smith with the option of either killing Victor before he slew Jacqueline, an act that would retroactively save Smith's beloved but make him Death's agent again, or refraining from action and thus saving his benevolent personality. Death expelled the Doctor from Perfugium before he could learn of Smith's decision.

Christopher Rodamonte Cwej, a companion of the seventh Doctor, was born on 5th September, 2954, in Spaceport Nine Overcity.[1073] Roz Forrester was squired to Fenn Martle. She would be his partner for fifteen years, and he would save her life on five occasions.[1074] When Roz was 20, the *Schirron Dream* took her through time to the future. She returned with no memory of the event.[1075]

The Black Dalek and the Renegade Dalek Faction may have used the Time Controller to hide from Davros a trillion miles from Earth in the mid-2960s.[1076]

? 2965 - THE SPACE MUSEUM[1077] -> The TARDIS jumped a time track and the first Doctor, Ian, Barbara and Vicki found their future selves on exhibit in the Space Museum of the Morok Empire, located on Xeros.

The Moroks had executed the adult population of the planet and set the children to work as slaves. The temporal anomaly ended, and the travellers came under risk of the future they'd glimpsed. Vicki incited revolution among some Xeron rebels, and the travellers made their escape once the Moroks were overpowered.

The Morok Empire collapsed thanks to human intervention, with criminal gangs like the Morok Nostra filling the power vacuum.[1078] The Daleks exterminated the inhabitants of Santhorius.[1079]

? 2966 - THE EVIL OF THE DALEKS[1080] -> The Dalek Emperor made plans to capitalise on the difference between the Daleks and humanity. The Daleks were unable to make this distinction on their own, and so the Emperor hatched an elaborate trap in three time-zones for their old enemy, the second Doctor. The Daleks tricked the Doctor - who was accompanied by Jamie - into believing that they wished to become more human. He was all too willing to educate the Daleks about the "Human Factor", highlighting the difference between the two races: humans were not blindly obedient and showed mercy to their enemies. However, as the Emperor planned, this merely enabled the distillation of the "Dalek Factor". The Emperor planned to install this into all humans throughout the history of Earth, forcing them to become Daleks, but the Doctor managed to "humanise" a number of Daleks.

Civil war broke out between the "Human" and "Dalek" factions. Every Dalek had been recalled to Skaro in preparation for the conquest of humanity, and in the ensuing battle they were all wiped out. The Emperor was exterminated by his own kind. The Doctor named this the "final end" of the Daleks.

Victoria Waterfield joined the Doctor and Jamie on

---

be part and parcel of the carnage around it, not an indicator from the production team that perhaps the Daleks aren't entirely finished after all.

The Doctor knows his way into and around the Dalek city. The only previous time we've seen him on Skaro was in *The Daleks*, and the city is destroyed here - clearly indicating that *The Daleks* is set before *The Evil of the Daleks*. In *Mission to the Unknown*, Cory states that the Daleks have not been active in Earth's galaxy "for a thousand years" (so, from 3000-4000), but also says that they've conquered one hundred and ten planets elsewhere "in the last five hundred years", so *The Evil of the Daleks* is apparently not set between 3000 and 4000. As the Doctor sees the Daleks active in the year 4000, logically he wouldn't think this was "the final end" of the Daleks unless he thought it was set after that date.

Taking what we're told at face value, this story has to

be set before the destruction of Skaro in *Remembrance of the Daleks*. If Skaro wasn't really destroyed, as *War of the Daleks* states - and *Doctor Who - The Movie* and the new series imply - that needn't be a problem. However, *Destiny of the Daleks* seems to be set in the ruins of the Dalek city (built over the Kaled Bunker seen in *Genesis of the Daleks*). Again, the Doctor knows his way around. *The Evil of the Daleks* would seem to be set before *Destiny of the Daleks* (and so, therefore, the rest of the Davros Era, including *Remembrance of the Daleks*).

The Terrestrial Index set *The Evil of the Daleks* "a century or so" after *The Daleks' Master Plan*. John Peel and Terry Nation "agreed that *The Evil of the Daleks* was the final story" (*The Frame* #7), but did so before *Remembrance of the Daleks* was written. Peel's novelisation of *The Evil of the Daleks* is set around the year 5000. "A History of the Daleks" in *DWM* #77 claimed that *The*

their travels after her father, Edward Waterfield, died while saving the Doctor's life.

& c 2970 - "Bringer of Darkness"[1081] **->** The second Doctor, Jamie and Victoria encountered a group of Daleks who taunted them with the news that the humanised Daleks had all been exterminated.

However, one saucer of humanised Daleks did survive, and travelled to the planet Kyrol.[1082] **During the 2970s, anti-magnetic cohesion was developed.**[1083] The Landsknechte - Earth's official security force - fought the Aspenal Campaign in 2970. The seventh Doctor, Chris and Roz helped the Jithra repel the Jeopards, but the Earth Empire conquered Jithra and Jeopardy. The Jithra were wiped out, but a few hundred thousand Jeopards survived. Leabie Forrester began plotting to usurp the Empress.[1084]

The Earth's oceans were heavily polluted in the thirtieth century.[1085] Humanity and the Silurians were now working together.[1086] The seventh Doctor hired two Silurian musicians, Jacquilian and Sanki, to play at Benny's wedding.[1087]

2975 - ORIGINAL SIN[1088] **->** In the early 2970s, mankind fought a short but brutal war with the Hith, a sluglike race. The Empire annexed Hithis and terraformed it. The Hith were displaced, becoming servants and menial workers on hundreds of worlds. They adopted names to denote their displaced status, such as Powerless Friendless and Homeless Forsaken Betrayed and Alone.

The last Wars of Acquisition ended shortly afterwards, when Sense-Sphere finally capitulated. The Earth Empire now stretched across half the galaxy.

Soon after the Hith pacification, Roz Forrester saw a man kill a Ditz (a Centaurian pet akin to a bee, but the size of a small dog). When he denied it, she ate his ident and arrested him for perjury and not having valid ID. The incident entered Adjudicator folklore. Forrester eventually killed her partner Fenn Martle when she discovered he had betrayed the Adjudication Service and was on the payroll of Tobias Vaughn. She attended Martle's funeral, and shortly afterwards the Birastrop Doc Dantalion wiped her memories of Martle's death, replacing them with false memories that the Falardi had killed him.

Christopher Cwej graduated from the Academy in 2974. During his training on Ponten IV, he had achieved some of the highest marksmanship and piloting scores ever recorded. Cwej's first assignment was a traffic detail. A year later, he was squired to Roz Forrester.

The very same day, serious riots started throughout the Empire, particularly on Earth itself. Insurance claims were estimated at five hundred trillion Imperial schillings, a total that would bankrupt the First Galactic Bank. Worst of all, it was revealled that the Adjudication Service was rife with corruption. The riots had been sparked by the release of icaron particles from a Hith battleship, the *Skel'-Ske*, which had been captured by INITEC corporation and kept in hyperspace in Overcity Five.

When the source of the radiation was destroyed, it was clear that the Empire was collapsing. At the time of the rioting on Earth, the Rim World Alliance had applied to leave the Empire. Over the years, all the major corporations had moved from Earth to the outer Rim planets. An Imperial Landsknecht flotilla was sent to pacify them. Rioting also began on Allis Five, Heaven, Murtaugh and Riggs Alpha. Colony worlds took the opportunity to rebel, stretching the resources of the Landsknecht to their limit.

The seventh Doctor again encountered the now-robotic Tobias Vaughn, leading to a conflict in which Vaughn was decapitated. The Doctor used Vaughn's brain crystal to repair the Cwej family's food irradiator.

The corrupt head of the Adjudicators, Rashid, feared exposure. She named Roz Forrester and Chris Cwej as rogue Adjudicators, and placed a death sentence on them. Roz and Chris departed with the Doctor and Bernice.

Evil of the Daleks is set around "7500 AD". *Timelink* suggests "4066". *About Time* equivocates, but says it's after *The Daleks' Master Plan*.

In *Matrix* #45, Mark Jones suggested that the Hand of Omega is sent into Davros' future, thousands of years after Dalek History ends.

We suggest that the civil war in *The Evil of the Daleks* is not the "final end" of the Daleks, but it does represent a severe defeat, one that removes them from the Milky Way for five hundred years (as referred to in *Mission to the Unknown*). The Doctor might be referring to the "final end" of the Dalek city, the Daleks' presence on Skaro, or the reign of the Dalek Emperor. Or he may just be optimistic (he also thinks he's finally wiped out the Daleks in *The Daleks*, *Remembrance of the Daleks*, *Dalek* and *The Parting of the Ways*, after all).

1081 Dating "Bringer of Darkness" (*DWM Summer Special 1993*) - It's shortly after *The Evil of the Daleks*.
1082 "Children of the Revolution"
1083 *Carnival of Monsters*, "a thousand years" after Jo's time.
1084 *So Vile a Sin* (p10, p182).
1085 *The Also People* (p101).
1086 *Eternity Weeps*
1087 *Happy Endings*
1088 Dating *Original Sin* (NA #39) - The Doctor tells us that this is the "thirtieth century" (p23). Although we are told at one point that "2955" was "four years" ago (p86), the year appears to be 2975 - this ties in with the birthdates established for Cwej and Forrester in Andy Lane's discussion document, and the fact that Cwej's father graduated "seventy years" before, in "oh-five".

DALEK HIERARCHY: The ongoing Dalek comic strip in *TV Century 21* (called simply "The Daleks", later regarded as "The Dalek Chronicles") set up a straightforward hierarchy for the early Daleks. The Emperor led, guided by the Brain Machine (a perfect computer with the authority to dismiss him if he failed). The sixties Dalek annuals concurred with this, occasionally referring to the Emperor as the Supreme Dalek and the Gold Dalek. The Black Dalek was his "deputy" and "warlord" (and had a slightly more powerful casing and weapons than the normal Daleks). The rarely-seen Red Dalek looked after research and development on Skaro.

In non-television stories from the sixties - "The Dalek Chronicles" strip, the Dalek books, the stageplay *The Curse of the Daleks* - it seems clear that there's only one Black Dalek. It leads the Daleks in *The Curse of the Daleks*. In both the 60s and 70s in the *TV Comic/TV Action* strips, the Black Dalek is in overall command (he's black with red details in the *TV Action* comic "The Planet of the Daleks") and he's referred to as "Dalek Leader"; this could well be the same individual.

Black Daleks do show up frequently as leaders in the TV series, presumably because all the production team had to do to distinguish the head Dalek from the others was repaint an existing prop, and painting it black worked well even when the story was in black and white. We never see more than one at a time. In *The Dalek Invasion of Earth*, Dalek Earth Force is led by a Black Dalek, "the Supreme Controller", who takes his orders from a Supreme Command which is offworld (presumably on Skaro, although this is never stated). A Black Dalek is "the Dalek Supreme" in *The Chase* (and is based on Skaro). A Black Dalek is "the Supreme" in *Mission to the Unknown/The Daleks' Master Plan*, and again reports to Skaro. There's a Black Dalek, a.k.a. "the Supreme Dalek", in *Resurrection of the Daleks* who seems to be the highest authority of the weakened Daleks. The Renegade Faction in *Remembrance of the Daleks* is led by a Black Dalek. The leader of the Cult of Skaro, Sec, had an all-black casing in *Doomsday* and *Daleks in Manhattan*.

All the Daleks present are wiped out in *The Dalek Invasion of Earth* and *The Daleks' Master Plan*. We don't specifically see the Black Dalek killed in either story, but neither do we see him escaping. We see the Black Dalek killed in *Resurrection of the Daleks*... then again, Davros is seen dying in identical circumstances and he manages to come back. The Black Dalek also dies in *Remembrance of the Daleks*.

It's a stretch, then, but just about possible that this is the same Black Dalek in every TV story. If so, it may be the same individual from "The Dalek Chronicles".

It seems far more likely, however, that "Black Dalek" becomes a rank as the Daleks expand. There are other stories in which Black Daleks are senior commanders - by *The Evil of the Daleks*, a group of Black Daleks serves the Emperor (they only have black domes and modified eyestalks). In the books, Ace kills "a Black Dalek"

while she serves in Spacefleet. This represents a significant achievement, but also implies there is more than one Black Dalek at this point.

So what is the fate of the original Black Dalek, the first Dalek Emperor's deputy? John Peel's *War of the Daleks*, taking its cue from his *The Official Doctor Who and the Daleks Book* and his novelisation of *The Evil of the Daleks*, establishes that the Dalek Prime is the last surviving Dalek from the time of their creation (all the way back to *Genesis of the Daleks*), so the first Black Dalek must be dead by that point. It is possible, however, that before that, the original Black Dalek became the Supreme Dalek.

"Supreme Dalek" seems to mean a number of things over the course of the Dalek stories... When there's an Emperor, he is also referred to as Supreme Dalek (in, for example, *The Dalek World*). It may just be that "Supreme Dalek" and "Emperor" are interchangeable terms. The Supreme Dalek is usually treated like the Emperor in all but name - the sole Dalek at the top of the hierarchy.

If we go with the theory that only one individual was Emperor for most of Dalek history (see The Dalek Emperors sidebar), and that this individual was killed in *The Evil of the Daleks*, this creates a vacancy. This chronology places the Davros Era stories after *The Evil of the Daleks*, and in those, the Supreme Dalek rules the Daleks, with Davros deposing him to become a new Emperor. The (unseen) Supreme Dalek rules Dalek Central Control (from the Dalek space fleet) in *Destiny of the Daleks*, and Davros is keen to usurp the role. The Supreme Dalek in *Resurrection of the Daleks* is a Black Dalek. In *Revelation of the Daleks*, the (unseen) Supreme Dalek rules Skaro. In *Remembrance of the Daleks*, a Black Dalek leads the Renegade Faction, the group deposed by Davros.

This could, just about, be the same individual Dalek (although, as noted, it looks like he's killed at the end of *Resurrection of the Daleks*). The most natural successor to the original Emperor would be his deputy. So this Supreme Dalek might be the original Black Dalek, as introduced in "The Dalek Chronicles". Perhaps the implication is that once the original Emperor is dead, the Black Dalek leader doesn't quite dare to give himself the title "Emperor" - although Davros has no such qualms. This Black Dalek looks to be comprehensively killed at the end of *Remembrance of the Daleks*.

There are other Supreme Daleks, however... We see "the Supreme Dalek" in one illustration for *The Dalek Outer Space Book* story "The Living Death" and he's an odd mix - a standard Dalek body with a globe very like the Emperor's for a head. The book features (in other stories) a Gold Dalek, the Dalek Emperor and the Black Dalek. This Supreme Dalek might be a very oddly drawn Emperor, or a completely new character.

Elsewhere in *The Dalek Outer Space Book*, the story "Super Sub" refers to the crew of one submarine as

continued on page 569...

At this time, Armstrong Transolar Aerospace were building Starhopper craft on Empire City, Tycho and Luna.[1089] The Empire conquered the Ogron homeworld of Orestes, one of the moons of gas giant Clytemnestra, in the Agamemnon system. When humans engineered pygmy Ogrons, a native uprising started that would last six years.

While searching for secret Ogron bases, the Imperial ship *Redoubtable* discovered the Nexus on the moon Iphigenia. This was a Gallifreyan device that could alter reality, and drove the expedition insane.

Roz was declared legally dead in 2976. Her sister Leabie created a clone of Roz, Thandiwe, to raise as her own daughter.[1090] Humberto de Silvestre was born 31st December, 2978. Heavy pollution levels on Earth made him sickly, but his computer skills meant he received medical grants.[1091]

2982 - SO VILE A SIN[1092] -> A demilitarised zone existed between the Empires of Earth and the Sontarans. The planet Tara was part of the Empire, and the importance of the nobility had been diminished.

The seventh Doctor, Roz and Chris returned to this time zone and investigated the source of a signal that was awakening Gallifreyan N-forms. Roz discovered an N-form at the Fury colony on planet Aegistus, the Agamemnon system, and crushed it under a slab of dwarf star alloy. Meanwhile, the Doctor found that the moon Cassandra was actually an ancient TARDIS, wounded during the war with the Vampires, and that its distress signal was waking N-forms. The Doctor programmed the TARDIS to self-destruct, destroying the moon.

Back on Earth, the Doctor euthanised Empress Helen I at her request. He was arrested for regicide. The Empress' death sparked civil war and widespread rioting. The psionic Brotherhood launched a brutal attack on the Forresters' palace on Io, killing a dozen Forresters. The casualties included Roz's niece and nephew, Somezi and Mantsebo.

Abu ibn Walid, actually a pawn of the Brotherhood, was crowned Emperor. He offered Roz the office of Pontifex Saecularis, head of the Order of Adjudicators. Roz's sister Leabie, with army and Unitatus backing, instigated a rebellion against Walid's rule. Her forces attacked Mars on 26th

August. The Battle of Achebe Gorge started. Roz defected to Leabie's side and was appointed the rank of Colonel.

The Doctor and Cwej were captured by the Grandmaster, a psychic gestalt that hoped to use the reality-altering Nexus. The Doctor defeated the Grandmaster's plan, and the dozens of bodies that contained parts of the Grandmaster's persona were either killed or banished to alternate timelines.

Roz lost her life leading a ground assault on the Emperor's palace on Callisto. The death of the Grandmaster left the Emperor lifeless, and Leabie Forrester was declared Empress. The Doctor suffered a heart attack at Roz's burial. A year later, the Doctor, Cwej, Benny and Jason attended to Roz's final funeral rites.

House Forrester had recently resurrected the long-extinct elephant.[1093]

Earth's moon was home to conurbations in the late thirtieth century.[1094] **In 2983, Kimber met Investigator Hallett while he was investigating granary shortages on Stella Stora. The Doctor visited this timezone a number of times. He met Hallett and visited the planet Mogar. On another occasion, he involved Captain Travers in a "web of mayhem and intrigue", but did save Travers' ship.[1095] The Doctor was travelling with Evelyn at the time, and convinced her - rightfully, she thought - to turn down Travers' marriage proposal.[1096]**

2986 (16th April) - TERROR OF THE VERVOIDS[1097] -> Professor Sarah Lasky planned to breed intelligent plants, Vervoids, that would hopefully make robots obsolete. Vervoids bred and grew rapidly, plus were quick to learn and cheap to maintain. For an undisclosed reason, the Vervoids also had a poisonous spike. A consortium was ready to exploit the creatures, but as the Vervoids were being transported back to Earth in the intergalactic liner *Hyperion III*, they went on the rampage and killed a number of the passengers and crew, including Lasky. The sixth Doctor and Mel's intervention resulted in every example of the species being wiped out using the mineral vionesium, which accelerated their growth cycle.

1089 *The Sorcerer's Apprentice* (p17).
1090 *So Vile a Sin*, with Roz declared dead "six" years beforehand. The *Decalog 4* anthology covers the history of the Forrester family; Thandiwe appears in the short story "Dependence Day".
1091 *Hope*
1092 Dating *So Vile a Sin* (NA #56) - The date is given (p25).
1093 *So Vile a Sin* (p33). An elephant is seen in the far

future in *The Ark*. Leabie surely misspeaks in claiming that elephants have been "extinct for almost two millennia".
1094 *Return of the Krotons*
1095 *Terror of the Vervoids*
1096 *Instruments of Darkness*
1097 Dating *Terror of the Vervoids* (23.3) - The Doctor tells the court that this is "Earth year 2986". A monitor readout suggests it is "April 16".

...continued from page 567

including "a Supreme Dalek who is in charge of the fighting" and "a Black Dalek who is in charge of the scientific investigations".

In the *Dalek Empire* series, there is a Supreme Dalek who acts as the Emperor's deputy. The third series introduces a new Supreme after the last one is killed. This replacement Supreme is also killed later in the series. Below them are Supreme Controllers - Red Daleks.

In *The Stolen Earth/Journey's End,* the Daleks are ruled by a Supreme Dalek who has a modified red and gold casing. He is killed by Captain Jack.

Other stories state that the Daleks are ruled by a committee, not an individual (and this was apparently the preference of Terry Nation, the Daleks' real-life creator). In the Daleks' first story (*The Daleks*), the Dalek city is ruled by "the council", and all the Daleks we see look alike. While in *Planet of the Daleks*, we meet a Dalek Supreme - a larger Dalek than normal, black with gold bumps, with a redesigned eyestalk and other features - it's clear that this very senior Dalek is just one member of the Supreme Council (the Daleks on Spiridon also report to "Supreme Command").

Day of the Daleks and *Frontier in Space* both have Daleks led by gold Daleks. We never learn their title. "The Dalek Tapes" feature on the *Genesis of the Daleks* DVD says these are members of the Supreme Council.

The Dalek Outer Space Book story "The Dalek Trap" features a "leader" who is a gold Dalek, of apparently a standard design (he may be a little larger than the average Dalek, and like the Supreme Dalek in "The Living Death", he might be the Golden Emperor drawn by someone without reference material).

The fact that the Daleks have a Council doesn't contradict the idea they have an Emperor. We see the Dalek Emperor in command of a council in *The Dalek World*.

In *The Dalek Outer Space Book*, we see the most elaborate set up - below the Emperor (also referred to as "the golden Dalek"), there's the Black Dalek, possibly that odd Supreme Dalek with a globe head, a Dalek Council (including the Gold Dalek see in "The Dalek Trap"?) and a separate group, a conclave of senior Dalek commanders, such as the red Dalek who leads Red Extra Galactic Squadron. There are other Red Daleks, as well as Blue Daleks. In "The Secret of the Emperor", the blue/gold Daleks appear to be scientists. As noted, on the battlefront, a Dalesub has a Black Dalek and a Supreme Dalek in command.

The Doctor Who: Aliens and Enemies book (2006), published in close cooperation with the production team of the time, describes the set up in *The Parting of the Ways* as the Emperor in charge with a High Council, also known as the Emperor's Personal Guard. Some of these have black domes, some have two gunsticks.

There are other Dalek ranks: In *Destiny of the Daleks*,

the leader of the squad sent to recover Davros has black central slats. We never learn this Dalek's title. In other stories (*The Daleks*, *The Power of the Daleks*, *Death to the Daleks*, *Planet of the Daleks*) we see groups of Daleks able to function perfectly well with leaders in ordinary casings.

While the Black Dalek, the Dalek Leader (black with red details) is in command in "The Planet of the Daleks" (*TV Action*), his senior subordinate on the Dalek planet is a white Dalek with red detailing. The commander of the Earth expedition is also referred to as Dalek Leader and is black with gold detailing. There are Daleks with red domes that seem to outrank the standard Daleks.

War of the Daleks states that the Dalek hierarchy - at least at that point in their history - runs: Grey Daleks, Blue Daleks, Red Daleks, Black Daleks, Gold Daleks, with the Dalek Prime as absolute authority. The Dalek Prime is described as "slightly larger than the others, with a bulbous head. It was a burnished gold colour, and had about a dozen lights about the expanded dome instead of the average Dalek's two" - in other words, it strongly resembles the Golden Emperor.

In *Prisoner of the Daleks*, the overall leader of the Daleks is the Supreme Dalek and there is a chief interrogator Dalek X, the Inquisitor General, who is black and gold.

Victory of the Daleks introduces a "new Dalek paradigm", with five colour-coded classes of Dalek. These are red (Drone), orange (Scientist), yellow (Eternal), blue (Strategists) and white (Supreme).

The ruling Council on Earth came to realise that Earth was "exhausted... politically, economically, biologically finished", "fighting for its survival" and was "grey and misty" with "grey cities linked by grey highways across grey deserts... slag, ash, clinker". Earth's air was so polluted that the entire population now had to live in the vast sky cities if they wanted to breathe.

By this point, Earth couldn't afford an Empire any longer. By the end of the thirtieth century, most planets in the Earth Empire had achieved some form of independence from the homeworld.[1098] These were "the declining years of Earth's planetary empire".[1099]

As the Earth Empire underwent collapse, countless planets were cut off and abandoned.[1100] The Earth Empress granted Eta Centauri 6 the status of a Duchy Royal with the name of Tractis. Humans had committed genocide there during the Empire period, because the natives refused to allow the mineral exploitation of their planet or the growing of narcotic crops. The Silurian governor of the planet, Menarc, tried to establish an elected council, but human colonists formed a separatist party and assassinated key politicians. The decaying Empire tried to restore order, leading to a conflict that killed hundreds of thousands. The eighth Doctor told Sam Jones that matters would improve for Tractis after that.[1101]

c 2990 - "Children of the Revolution"[1102] -> The eighth Doctor and Izzy travelled to the waterworld of Kyrol, and spent time on the submarine *Argus*. While swimming at the uncharted Asamda Ridge, Izzy encountered some Daleks - who went on the board the submarine and greeted the Doctor as their saviour.

The Daleks steered the *Argus* to Azhra Korr, home of eight thousand Daleks who were the humanised Daleks from the civil war and their descendants. Their leader was Alpha, the first humanised Dalek, and he explained that the Daleks had developed psychokinetic abilities. When the Doctor and Alpha investigated a cavern under Azhra Korr, they discovered Kata-Phobus - the last Kyrolian and a giant octopus with psychic powers. Kata-Phobus had been planning to use the Daleks' psychic abilities to conquer the human colony.

Meanwhile, the humans rebelled and attempted to escape their Dalek captors. The Daleks were shocked that their saviour, the Doctor, was secretly more loyal to the humans than to them. Nonetheless, they sacrificed themselves to kill Kata-Phobus save the human colony.

c 2990 - THE MUTANTS[1103] -> One of the last planets to gain independence from Earth was Solos. The native Solonians staged organised resistance, but the Marshal of the planet resisted reform for many years. From his Skybase in orbit above Solos, the Marshal had been conducting experiments on the Solonian atmosphere, attempting to render it more suitable for humans. When the Solonians began mutating into insect-like creatures, the Marshal ordered the "Mutts" destroyed.

An Independence Conference was arranged between the Solonian leaders and the Earth "Overlords", with Solos to be granted independence. The Administrator was assassinated at the meeting, and martial law was declared. The Time Lords sent the third Doctor and Jo

---

1098 *The Mutants*

1099 *Frontier in Space*

1100 *Burning Heart, The Ultimate Treasure.*

1101 *Genocide* (p274-275).

1102 Dating "Children of the Revolution" (*DWM* #312-317) - Kyrol was colonised "a few centuries in the future" according to Izzy, and this is "a few short decades" after *The Evil of the Daleks* according to Alpha.

1103 Dating *The Mutants* (9.4) - The Doctor tells Jo that they have been sent to "the thirtieth century". The story must take place many years after *Original Sin*, where events are set into motion that will eventually mean the Empire's collapse. *The Programme Guide* set the story slightly later ("c.3100"), *Timelink* in 2971, and *About Time* in "3000-ish".

1104 Dating *The Fall of Yquatine* (EDA #32) - The date is given (p43, p150).

1105 Dating *Superior Beings* (PDA #43) - The year is given (p108).

1106 Three hundred years before *The Beast Below*. The Doctor cites this migration as owing to Earth being roasted by solar flares, but see the dating notes on this

story for why that's probably not the case.

1107 *Hope*

1108 In *Mission to the Unknown*, set in the year 4000, Lowery confidently says, "'The Daleks invaded Earth a thousand years ago," and Marc Cory replies, "That's right." Even allowing for figures of speech, this surely can't refer to *The Dalek Invasion of Earth*, set around 2157.

1109 *The Art of Destruction*, and consistent with the New Adventures.

1110 *The Dark Path*

1111 *Night of the Humans*

1112 *The Eye of the Jungle*

1113 *Iris: Enter Wildthyme.* Iris' companion Jenny muses (p169), "We're leaving our system and our millennium", so it's the third millennium if not later.

1114 *The Daleks' Master Plan*

1115 *Placebo Effect*

1116 *Hope*

1117 "A thousand years" before *The Book of the Still.*

1118 "A few years" before *Festival of Death.*

to Solos - they met Professor Sondergaard, who had discovered that the Solonians underwent a radioactive metamorphosis every five hundred years, meaning that the process that was transforming the population into Mutts and altering the atmosphere was seasonal. The Doctor and his allies deduced that the Mutts were a transitional stage as the Solonians turned into advanced beings. One of the Solonians, Ky, completed his transformation and killed the Marshal.

2992 - THE FALL OF YQUATINE[1104] -> The eighth Doctor attended the inauguration of Stefan Vargeld, who defeated the unpopular Ignatiev to win the Presidency of Yquatine. Four years later, the Doctor returned just as sentient gas creatures named the Omnethoth, constructed millions of years ago as a weapon to conquer the universe, awoke from dormancy and devastated the planet with searing gas bombs. The reptilian Anthaurk attempted to capitalise on this and capture Yquatine space, but the Doctor's companion Compassion engaged her Chameleon Circuit and impersonated Vargeld, helping to sue for peace. The Doctor mentally reprogrammed the Omnethoth as peaceful cloud-like beings, but a vengeful Vargeld, in retribution for Yquatine's devastation, destroyed the Omnethoth with ionization weapons.

2994 - SUPERIOR BEINGS[1105] -> The fifth Doctor and Peri were caught when the fox-like Valethske invaded a pleasure planet, Eknur 4. The invaders were looking for the homeworld of their gods. The Valethske put Peri into suspended animation aboard their ship and departed. The Doctor calculated its next arrival point, in a century's time, and left to rendezvous with Peri then.

Eknur 4 was one of the Wonders of the Universe, and a utopian society given over to hedonism.

Humanity migrated from Earth aboard space arks built to house the population of entire nations. Britain was unable to launch an ark until a star whale, hearing the cries of Britain's children, intervened. The Britons repaid this by capturing the whale and torturing it to fly through space with their ark atop it. The ark, named Starship UK, contained much of Great Britain, Wales and Northern Ireland (Scotland had chosen to go into space in its own ship). Enormous buildings housed the populations of Yorkshire, Devon, Surrey, Kent, Essex, Lancashire, London and more. The population of the ark chose to remain ignorant of the crime perpetrated upon the space whale, and continually had their memories of it erased.[1106]

In 2999, a Sun City teenager hacked Earth's TacNet, causing a meltdown that killed thousands on the East Coast of Australia. Humberto de Silvestre was wounded by this, and only saved when he was grafted with experimental liquid computers. He became the cyborg Silver.[1107]

The Fourth Millennium

The Daleks invaded the Earth around the year 3000.[1108] Africa was in the middle of its Third Golden Age in the year 3000.[1109]

At the turn of the thirty-first century, an Imperial Navy force was sent out to seek out alien technology that might help shore up the Earth Empire. They discovered the planet Darkheart and colonised it. They remained isolated for three and a half centuries, but came to discover a device that they also named the Darkheart, and which was built from Chronovore technology. The Chronovores had designed the device to beam healing energy to their remote, injured members, but the colonists adapted it to alter morphic fields. Properly tuned, the Darkheart could transform all alien species into human beings.[1110]

The Hexion Geldmongers of Mercutio 14, located out beyond Cassiopeia's Elbow, had an empire that spanned whole galaxies. They forged the Mymon Key: a device that could tap gravitational force to produce limitless energy. Mercutio 14 fell, and endless wars were fought over the Key - which was placed a casket that only a Hexion speaker could open. A museum of antiquities in the thirty-first century owned the casket, but had budget cuts. The Key was sold to a private buyer in Andromeda, but the Gobocorp ship transporting it, *The Herald of Nanking*, crashed on the Gyre: an amalgamation of space junk in the Battani 045 system. Only five hundred of the three thousand crew survived. In the hundreds of thousands of years to follow, their descendents forgot their origins, and thought that the Gyre was humanity's homeworld.[1111]

The eleventh Doctor failed to take Amy and Rory to Margate for the 3000 AD World Jamboree.[1112] The mobile Super Hotel Miramar operated during humanity's first expansion into space. It resided on the Spiral Wing, then spent a century on the edge of the Golden Chasm.[1113]

From the year 3000 to the year 3500, Earth knew of no Dalek activity in the galaxy.[1114] From around the year 3000, the Foamasi began gaining in power and reputation across the galaxy.[1115] In 3006, aliens invaded Earth, overrunning America and capturing Washington. The government used experimental time machines to send agents to fetch help - Agent Grey was sent to the past, Agent Silver to the far future.[1116]

Legends of *The Book of the Still* begin circulating. Unknown parties had developed this artifact so that stranded time travellers could summon help by writing their name in it. Copies of the book, made from invulnerable taffeta, found their way to various points in time and space, including the planet Lebenswelt in the year 4009.[1117]

Documentary maker Harken Batt was discredited when he used actors in an expose of organised crime.[1118]

3012 - THE SPACE AGE[1119] -> The eighth Doctor, Fitz and Compassion found an asteroid that contained a reconstruction of a futuristic city. The inhabitants - rival members of the Mods and Rockers gangs - had been spirited there from 1965 by a benevolent alien named the Maker. However, the gangs had fallen into continued bloodshed for nineteen years. The Maker, imprisoned by the Mods and compelled to make weapons, had instigated the city's dissolution. Other Makers arrived, liberated their colleague and caused the Mods and Rockers to stand down. The Makers offered the humans a choice: return to 1965 as their younger selves with no memories of these events, or join a futuristic society in 3012. The humans made their decisions, and the Doctor's party departed.

3012 - FESTIVAL OF DEATH[1120] -> Against objections from the major religions, Dr Koel Paddox - the galaxy's leading necrologist - opened the Necroport. This housed a machine in which tourists could be temporarily killed and experience the Beautiful Death, which was touted as the "thrill to end a lifetime". It was located at the G-Lock ship's graveyard in the Teredekethon-Murgatroyd hyperspatial conduit, and attracted visitors such as the alien Hoopy.

The fourth Doctor and Romana found that tourists experiencing the Beautiful Death were becoming savage zombies. The Repulsion had temporally swapped the tourists with survivors of the *Cerberus* disaster in 2815. The tourists went into the Repulsions' realm, and the *Cerberus* survivors were endowed with pieces of the Repulsion's essence - the Repulsion hoped this would let it fully manifest in our reality. The Doctor and Romana trapped the Repulsion's essence in ERIC, the G-Lock's central computer, then destroyed it. The Necroport exploded and the zombies expired.

1119 Dating *The Space Age* (EDA #34) - The year is given (p216). The people there think it is 2019.
1120 Dating *Festival of Death* (PDA #35) - The year is given (pgs 115, 116, 194).
1121 *Flip-Flop*
1122 *Vanderdeken's Children*
1123 There are some distinct continuity problems raised by the Silurian leader Eldane's voiceover at the end of *Cold Blood*. Eldane says "now as my people awaken from their thousand year sleep, ready to rise to the surface...", so they explicitly haven't emerged *yet*, meaning it's a little early to automatically see this as a triumph for interspecies co-operation. It's possible that Eldane (and Nasreen and Tom) woke early, to prepare the way and to double-check that the conditions were agreeable to human-Silurian co-habitation. The New Adventures established (in books such as *Eternity Weeps*) that other Silurians emerged in the twenty-first century and peacefully co-existed with mankind until at least the time of *Original Sin* (shortly before Eldane's group emerges)... but it's also established in both the books and the TV series (particularly in *The Mutants*, and further detailed in *Original Sin*) that the thirty-first century in the *Doctor Who* universe is that of the over-polluted and corrupt Earth Empire - not exactly the best time for the Doctor to arrange for Eldane's group to awaken from stasis. The only real alternative makes even less sense, as it entails Earth in this era having been sterilised by solar flares (see the dating notes on *The Beast Below*). Finally, it's also unclear how Eldane knows of "the far greater losses yet to come" for the Doctor (in Series 5), if he's been asleep for so long.
1124 Dating *The Sorcerer's Apprentice* (MA #12) - The TARDIS crew discover a spaceship built in "2976" (p17), which leads the Doctor to suggest this is the "end of the thirtieth century" (p33, p48). We learn that the colony was founded in 2145 (p203), eight hundred forty-six (Avalonian?) years ago (p33), making it the year 2991.

Later, though, we learn that the "city riots" seen in *Original Sin* were "fifty years ago" (p156), so it must be nearer 3025.
1125 Dating *Kinda* (19.3) - An arbitrary date. The colonists have recognisably English names, so it seems reasonable to assume that they are from Earth. On screen they only refer to a "homeworld", which Todd says is overcrowded. Sanders' attitude perhaps suggests an early colonial period, and the story would seem to be set after *Colony in Space*, in which colonists are seen as "eccentric". The colonists are from Earth in Terrance Dicks' novelisation, where the Doctor suggests they are from the time of the "Empire". Earth's Empire is in decline in this era, but while it would be preferable to date *Kinda* to the twenty-seventh or twenty-eighth centuries, "overcrowded" certainly describes Earth's state of affairs in *The Mutants* (set circa 2990). It's also plausible that the Empire would still be assessing new planets for colonisation and resource exploitation, even as it exhausts or loses control of long-standing ones. Previous versions of *Ahistory* dated *Kinda* as "? 2782", but the new placement of *Snakedance* in this edition necessitates pushing that date forward some, in accordance with the Mara being banished to the dark places of the inside circa 2926.
The TARDIS Logs set *Kinda* in the "25th Century". *Timelink* set it in 1981, reasoning that Deva Loka isn't an Earth colony.
1126 "A thousand years" before *The Bride of Peladon*.
1127 "The Love Invasion"
1128 Dating *Flip-Flop* (BF #46) - The dates are given.
1129 "Eighteen years" before *The Ribos Operation*.
1130 Dating *The Ultimate Treasure* (PDA #3) - Rovan Cartovall disappeared in 1936 BC, which was "five thousand years ago" (p37).
1131 Dating *Palace of the Red Sun* (PDA #51) - The journalist Dexel Dynes appeared in *The Ultimate Treasure* and remembers Peri from that story, which he

The G-Lock was evacuated and the hyperspace tunnel in which it was located collapsed, eradicating the station. The Arboretan race went extinct as a result of Paddox's experiments. Paddox attempted to reincarnate into his younger self and prevent his parents' deaths, but this trapped him in a recurring loop of his lifetime.

The Proxima Centauri All Blacks did the double in 3012. Pakafroon Wabster had their first No. 1 hit in the same year. The Doctor visited the colony of Puxatawnee, and deemed it a very happy and prosperous place.[1121] The planets Emindar and Nimos started a series of minor wars that would run for over a century.[1122] **The Silurian colony under Cwntaff in South Wales was set to emerge to the surface around 3020.**[1123]

c 3025 - THE SORCERER'S APPRENTICE[1124] **->** Although many remained patriotic and a new Empress was crowned, it was clear that the Empire was collapsing. The Landsknechte Corps had fallen, and the newly-independent human worlds were now building vessels of their own. On the medieval world of Avalon, some natives became more proficient at tapping the ancient nanobot system to generate "magic". The first Doctor, Ian, Barbara and Susan arrived as various "sorcerers" sought to gain further power. A magical battle ensued, but the Doctor had his allies place an Avalonian control device - Merlin's Helm - on the head of a reptilian cephlie, a native of the planet. The Helm restored the cephlies, but they elected to destroy themselves and the nanobot system.

? 3026 - KINDA[1125] **->** The homeworld was overcrowded, and teams were sent to assess other worlds for colonisation. One of these was S14, a primeval forest world, which had the local name Deva Loka ("the land of the Kinda"). The natives were humanoid telepaths and lived in harmony with nature. Trees came into fruit all year round, and the climate hardly varied throughout the year. The Mara compelled Tegan into letting it "borrow" her form, and so crossed over from the dark places of the inside. The fifth Doctor, aided by Adric while Nyssa experienced induced delta-sleep in the TARDIS, banished the Mara using a circle of mirrors. The colonists were persuaded to abandon further settlement. The Mara was not entirely purged from Tegan's mind, and would later revive.

On Peladon, the royal Citadel was constructed. The highest point of it looked out across the entire kingdom, from the Cargas Mountains in the east to the shores of Lake Vanashor. Midnight on Peladon was called "the witching hour", when the ancients of Peladon had pledged their souls to the Dark Beast to gain power, fame and immortality.[1126] In 3045, humanity and the Kustollons

fought a war which devastated both sides. Igrix, a Kustollon, stole a time machine and travelled to 1966 to prevent this.[1127]

3060 to 3090 - FLIP-FLOP[1128] **->** The planet Puxatawnee had two timelines.

= 1) The Slithergees arrived around Christmas, 3060, and demanded a moon to inhabit. President Mary Bailey was apparently killed by her secretary, who was allegedly a Slithergee agent. In truth, she had been assassinated by beings from another timeline, who feared she would cave in to the Slithergees. There was an uprising, and warfare against the Slithergees left Puxatawnee a heavily damaged, radioactive wasteland. Christmas Day was renamed Retribution Day. Thirty years later, Professor Capra built a time machine to change history by sending agents back to kill the President's secretary. The time machine overloaded, destroying the planet.

= 2) President Bailey survived thanks to the time travellers' intervention, and yielded to the Slithergee demands. Thirty years later, the aliens had dominated the planet. In this timeline, Capra built a mind peeler to interrogate people, not a time machine. Rebels forced the seventh Doctor and Mel to take them back in time, hoping to assassinate Bailey before she capitulated to the Slithergees...

The Cyrrehenic Alliance fought a series of Frontier Wars. The Graff Vynda-K led two legions of his men for a year in the Freytus Labyrinth, and also fought on Skarne and Crestus Minor. He was an unstable, temperamental man, though, and upon returning home discovered that his people had allowed his half-brother to take the throne. The High Court of the Cyrrhenic Empire rejected the Graff's claim for restitution. He spent eighteen years plotting his revenge.[1129]

c 3064 - THE ULTIMATE TREASURE[1130] **->** The fifth Doctor and Peri arrived at the Astroville Seven trading post. A dying merchant gave them galactic co-ordinates purporting to pinpoint the treasure of Rovan Cartovall, the emperor of Centros who once ruled fifty star systems. His treasury was worth the equivalent of 64,000,000,000,000 stellar credits. The co-ordinates led to the planet Gelsandor, where some telepaths set a variety of challenges for any who wanted Cartovall's treasure. The Doctor and Peri found that the treasure was the infinite possibilities of life, as represented by the puzzles themselves.

c 3068 - PALACE OF THE RED SUN[1131] **->** The warlord Glavis Judd had risen to power on his homeworld of Zalcrossar, and expanded his military might to create a

Protectorate of twenty star systems. His forces sought to subjugate the planet Esselven, but King Hathold and his family sealed the Keys to Esselven, an irreplaceable set of documents and protocols, in an impenetrable vault that would only open for their DNA. Without the Keys, Esselven society degenerated.

The royals fled and established the Summer and Winter Palace residences on Esselven Minor, a planetoid orbiting a white dwarf star. However, the white dwarf's gravity, in conjunction with the planetoid's mass and the royals' planetary defence shield, started altering space-time in the area. Time within the shield accelerated faster than time in the outside universe.

Judd spent a year tracking the royals and landed on the planetoid in search of them. Due to the fast-time effect, he wasn't seen again for five hundred years. Judd never appointed a successor, and his Protectorate collapsed in his absence.

? 3078 - THE RIBOS OPERATION[1132] **->** The rare mineral Jethryk was now used to power ships such as Pontenese-built battleships. Communication across the galaxy was via hypercable, and highly trained mercenaries, the Schlangi, were available for hire.

Located three light centuries from the Magellanic Clouds, the Cyrrhenic Alliance included the planets Cyrrhenis Minima (co-ordinates 4180), Levithia and Stapros, as well as the protectorate of Ribos (co-ordi-

nates 4940) in the Constellation of Skythra, 116 parsecs from Cyrrhenis Minima.

The fourth Doctor, Romana and K9 arrived on Ribos looking for the first segment of the Key to Time. They meet Garron, a con-man from Hackney Wick, who was forced to leave Earth after his attempt to sell Sydney Opera House to the Arabs backfired. Garron's exploits included a successful scheme to sell the planet Mirabilis Minor to three different clients.

Aware of the Graff Vynda-K's thirst for revenge and need for a powerbase, Garron proposed to sell him the planet Ribos for the sum of ten million Opeks. Garron boosted the Graff's interest by forging a survey suggesting that the planet was rich in Jethryk. Garron's lump of genuine Jethryk, used to con the Graff, was the first segment of the Key.

The Doctor defeated the Graff - leading to the Graff's demise - and outsmarted Garron to obtain the segment.

? 3087 - "Spider's Shadow"[1143] **->** A pan-dimensional being extruded bits of itself into an unnamed planet. Soldiers under the command of two princesses - Alison and Louisa Keldafrian, who had fought fifty campaigns across the outer reaches - viewed the extrusions as giant spiders and hacked at them. The being protected itself by weaving a "dimensional cocoon", locking the Princesses in a time loop. The seventh Doctor ended the time loop, and curtailed the being's hostility by aging it to death.

describes as a "few years" ago (p39).

1132 Dating *The Ribos Operation* (16.1) - A date is not given on screen. While this date is arbitrary, Ribos is close to the Magellanic Clouds, suggesting that humans have developed at least some level of intergalactic travel. Lofficier placed the story in "the late twenty-sixth century", apparently confusing the Cyrrhenic Alliance with the force established to fight the Cybermen in *Earthshock*. *Timelink* says 3010. *About Time* couldn't quite decide, but thought that "some time in the 5000s when humanity is once again expanding away from Earth" seemed the most likely.

1133 Dating "Spider's Shadow" (BF #109b) - The participants seem human, and the action presumably takes place on one of Earth's colony worlds in the future. Also, the Doctor says he's got signed copies of half the books in the princess' library - not a guarantee that the books were written by humanity, but it seems likely. Proton-knives are mentioned, and there's an aristocracy, but otherwise the details are so vague that this placement is a shot in the dark.

1134 *Managra*

1135 Dating *Superior Beings* (PDA #43) - It's "over five hundred years" after 2594 (p108).

1136 *Peri and the Piscon Paradox*

1137 *The English Way of Death*

1138 Decades before *I.D.*

1139 Dating *Warmonger* (PDA #53) - The story is a prequel to *The Brain of Morbius*, set when Solon was a young, renowned surgeon.

1140 *Legacy*, expanding on *The Curse of Peladon* and *The Monster of Peladon*. *Warmonger* sees a huge Alliance between many alien races, and talk of a United Planets Organisation being formed.

1141 *Timewyrm: Genesys* (p217).

1142 Dating *The Brain of Morbius* (13.5) - The Doctor informs Sarah Jane that they are "considerably after" her time. If the Mutt at the beginning of the story originated on Solos, that might affect story dating. *The TARDIS Logs* suggested "3047", *Apocrypha* gave a date of "6246 AD". *The Terrestrial Index* supposed that the "Morbius Crisis" takes place around "10,000 AD". The original version of this chronology set the story around the time of *Mindwarp*. *Timelink* says "2973", and *Warmonger* - the prequel to the story - seems roughly to concur. *About Time* speculated that if the space pilot *was* a Mutt from *The Mutants*, and given that the inhabitants of Solos underwent that transformation every two thousand years, "The 4900s would fit."

1143 Dating *Vanderdeken's Children* (EDA #14) - The year is given (p3). The Galactic Federation exists, although neither Emindar nor Nimos are members.

In the late thirty-first century, people from the Overcities began to recolonise the surface of the Earth. One group, later known as the Concocters, created Europa: a bizarre and eclectic fusion of historical periods built on the site of Europe. There were three Switzias, four Rhines, six Danubes and dozens of black forests. Each Dominion represented a different period between the fourteenth and early twentieth-century history. For example, there were five Britannias: Gloriana, Regency, Victoriana, Edwardiana and Perfidia.

The undead - the descendants of the vampires Jake and Madeline - dwelt in Transylvania. Fictional and historical characters, named Reprises, were cloned. This let the people from the Overcities to jostle with the likes of Byron, Casanova, Crowley, Emily Bronte and the Four Musketeers. The Vatican, a vast floating city equipped with psychotronic technology, was built to impose order on Europa (as the true papal seat had moved to Betelgeuse by this time).

The entire Concoction was masterminded by the Persona, a being formed from the merging of the Jacobean dramatist Pearson and the ancient Mimic.[1134]

c 3094 - SUPERIOR BEINGS[1135] -> The fifth Doctor arrived on a garden planet, anticipating the arrival of the Valethske with Peri as their captive. Mindless giant beetles - the remaining physical forms of the Khorlthochloi - dominated the planet. The Doctor rescued Peri and the Valethske discovered the beetles were the last remains of their former gods. The Valethske ship bombarded the planet from orbit, wiping out the Khorlthochoi. Veek, the Valethske leader, realised the futility of his mission and departed for home with his crew.

The fifth Doctor and Peri visited the planet Gargarod in the thirty-first century.[1136] The Bureau, a group from the thirty-second century, used time corridor technology to send retired people to the English village of Nutchurch in the 1930s.[1137]

The thirty-second century was an era that produced organic digital transfer, a means of directly moving information between machines and the human brain. Scandroids were robotic servitors that assisted humans and facilitated such information transfers, and most people were fitted with data transfer ports. Companies such as the Lonway Clinic specialised in altering people's personalities according to their wishes, and anyone who could afford such services "had some work done". One planet became a dumping ground for computer equipment - it was intended as part of a recycling programme, but became a scavenging ground for data pirates.

Zachary Kindell was deemed a pioneer of personality surgery, but his unethical experiments tarnished his reputation. Kindell sought to craft a programme capable of "auto-surgery" - one that would reshape a person's DNA to match their mental alterations - but his experiments brought his test subjects' aggression and hate to the surface, turning them into mutants. Kindell felt hampered by the threat of prosecution, and although he eventually died, he scattered copies of his memories and personality in various locales.[1138]

? 3100 - WARMONGER[1139] -> The planet Karn had gained a reputation as a place of healing, presumably due to the presence of the Sisterhood's Elixir of Life, and a medical association constructed a neutral facility there named the Hospice. The scientist Mehendri Solon served as the facility's Surgeon-General. The fifth Doctor arrived one day with a severely wounded Peri - who had been injured by a flying predator - to procure Solon's surgical skills. Solon adeptly healed her.

The deposed Gallifreyan President Morbius pooled mercenaries and space pirates from many worlds to assault Karn, hoping to gain the Sisterhood's Elixir. The Sisterhood repelled the attack, but Morbius' forces conquered many planets. The Time Lords manipulated events to form an Alliance, led by the Supremo, to counter Morbius' ambitions. The Alliance defeated most of Morbius' forces, and he suffered a final defeat on Karn when troops from Fangoria interceded.

Morbius was sentenced to execution, but Solon, his disciple, removed Morbius' brain before his body was atomised. The Hospice was disbanded and Karn was left to the Sisterhood. Solon remained on Karn with Morbius' brain.

The seeds of the Galactic Federation were sown as the space powers of the Milky Way began forging links and alliances with one another. Virtually the entire civilised galaxy was involved to some degree or another.[1140]

In the thirty-second century, Earth made contact with the descendants of Utnapishtim's people.[1141]

? 3120 - THE BRAIN OF MORBIUS[1142] -> Karn was a graveyard of spaceships, with Mutt, Dravidian and Birastrop vessels all coming to grief. Solon built a hybrid creature from the victims of these crashes and installed Morbius' brain into it, but the Time Lords sent the fourth Doctor and Sarah Jane to prevent Morbius from escaping. A mindbending contest with the Doctor drove Morbius mad, and the Sisterhood killed his physical form.

3123 - VANDERDEKEN'S CHILDREN[1143] -> The eighth Doctor and Sam arrived at a derelict structure floating in space - the product of a closed time loop - which was claimed by the warring Emindians and Nimosians. A hyperspace tunnel led to twenty years in the future, when the two planets had wiped each other out. The Doctor was unable to prevent the war, but he saved one of the ships and sent it a thousand years into the future, where it recolonised Emindar.

c 3150 - I.D.[1144] **->** The planet that served as a dumping ground for computer equipment was believed to hold four billion data storage devices, with another sixty thousand being discarded there on a daily basis. An estimated 80% of the equipment was useless, but that still left a massive amount for data pirates to harvest. Agents of the Lonway Clinic also scavenged the planet, looking for back-up copies of people's brains that were carelessly thrown out along with their computers. Such information became raw material for the Clinic's personality surgeries.

A Scandroid happened upon a copy of Zachary Kindell's personality and memories, and other Scandroids found a copy of his faulty auto-surgery programme. Kindell's mind was uploaded into a Lonway Clinic accountant, Ms Tevez. One of the Lonway employees, Dr Marriott, became infected with the auto-surgery programme and mutated into an abomination - as did Kindell-Tevez.

The sixth Doctor revised Kindell's auto-surgery programme, and uploaded Tevez's brain-print into both creatures, physically and mentally turning them into copies of her. One of the women died, but Tevez was restored as a person in the second - yet remained unsure if she had physically been Marriott. The Doctor neutralised the Scandroids and deleted all copies of Kindell's programme that he could find.

Liquid hardware was available in this era.

In 3158, the Rensec IX catastrophe took place when the planet's inhabited underground caverns were destroyed due to seismic activity caused by Puerto Lumina, the planetary satellite. The survivors were shipped, en masse, to the decommissioned, dormant staging-post facilities of Puerto Lumina. A combination of faulty life support and a ham-fisted attempt to chemically sterilise the survivors there left a hundred thousand civilians dead.[1145]

c 3170 - THE BEAUTIFUL PEOPLE[1146] **->** The Vita Novus Health Spa catered to clients who earned "half a planet", including humans, Morestrans, Sheltanaks, Lamuellans and Sirians. The fourth Doctor, Romana and K9 came to Vita Novus in search of doughnuts, and found that the proprietor, Karna, had developed a revolutionary tissue-reduction process. Subjects' body mass was broken down in "slimming booths", then reborn in revitalised forms. The excised fat was reconstituted as beauty products. Karna was brainwashing her clients, and sought to leverage contacts in the major galactic governments to set up slimming centres on every planet. Entire populations would be processed; those who refused would be killed.

The spa's computers were damaged, and Karna was slimmed to death. A client, Sebella Bing, took charge and reorganised the spa as a relaxation centre with fatty food, ice cream and champagne. The Doctor got a bag of sugary doughnuts.

Tythonians were known in this era.

3174 - BURNING HEART[1147] **->** The population of Earth was rebuilding following the destruction of the Overcities. Trade, culture and civil liberties suffered across the galaxy as humanity retrenched. On Dramos, a satellite of the gas giant Titania, the Church of Adjudication was becoming ever more draconian. Millions joined the extremist Human First group, which advocated the genocide of all aliens. White Fire was the group's inner core.

The sixth Doctor and Peri visited Dramos as conflict broke out between the Adjudicators and White Fire's forces. The Node of Titania, an area similar to Jupiter's Red Spot, was alive and had been increasing hostilities in its

1144 Dating *I.D.* (BF #94) - It's the "thirty-second century" according to the back cover blurb and the Doctor, who makes his dating solely on the presence of organic digital transfer - suggesting that the technology fell into disuse in centuries to come.
1145 *Burning Heart*. This happened when Mora Valdez, who is 21 (p15), was "five years old".
1146 Dating *The Beautiful People* (BF CC #1.4) - The back cover specifies that the story takes place in the "thirty-second century". Morestrans appeared in *Planet of Evil*. A Tythonian was the titular *Creature from the Pit*.
1147 Dating *Burning Heart* (MA #30) - The year is given (p20).
1148 *Lucifer Rising*. An excommunicated Knight of Oberon, Orcini, appears in *Revelation of the Daleks*. The suggestion that the order was based on the moon of Uranus was first postulated in the Virgin edition of this

book, and confirmed in *GodEngine*.
1149 "Thirty generations" before *Bang-Bang-A-Boom!*.
1150 Dating *Death Riders* (BBC children's 2-in-1 #1) - The Doctor says that according to the TARDIS instruments, it's "the thirty-third century" (p16).
1151 *Spiral Scratch*
1152 Dating *Managra* (MA #14) - The Doctor sets the co-ordinates for "Shalonar - AD 3278", and the TARDIS lands in the same timezone, but the wrong location (p26). Later, Byron states that he was created "in the middle of the thirty-third century" (p113).
1153 Dating *Real Time* (BF BBCi #1) - It is "millennia" since the creation of the Cybermen, who are thought to be extinct. The story is set after *Sword of Orion*. The online notes name the planet as Chronos.
1154 Dating *The Beast Below* (X5.2) - At time of writing, *The Beast Below* is, without a doubt, the New *Who* epi-

attempts to communicate. The sentience of the Node merged with OBERON, the Adjudicators' central computer. The conflict and xenophobia diminished, and the Adjudicators recruited more non-humans into their ranks.

The Sontarans and Cybermen had both recently tried to introduce more individuality into their species. The Sontaran attempt created disunity, and some of their ranks were banished.

As Earth went through its Empire and Federation phases, the fortunes of the Guild of Adjudicators waxed and waned. Eventually, they became unnecessary. A thousand forms of local justice had sprung up. Every planet had its own laws and police. The universe had passed the Guild by, leaving it nothing to adjudicate. The Guild degenerated into a reclusive order of assassins known as the Knights of the Grand Order of Oberon, dreaming of past glories and crusades for truth. The organisation was based on the moon of Uranus.[1148]

Gholos attacked the pastoral planet Angvia, beginning a conflict that would last thirty generations. Both sides violated the Tenebros IV peace treaty.[1149]

c 3210 - DEATH RIDERS[1150] -> The Interplanetary Mining Corporation found deposits of trisilicate and duralinium on the asteroid of Stanalan in the Torajii system, and established a frontier town there. "Fluripsent crystals" were embedded in rock walls as a means of illumination. The last Drexxon at liberty, just a child, came to Stanalan with the travelling Galactic Fair (which featured a Death Ride roller coaster). The eleventh Doctor, Amy and Rory stopped the Drexxon from freeing its murderous fellows from the Perpetuity Chamber imprisoning them.

The sixth Doctor visited the planet C'h'zzz in 3263.[1151]

3278 - MANAGRA[1152] -> For centuries, the Nicodemus Principle had prevented a Reprise from becoming the Pope of Europa. But in 3278, Cardinal Richelieu, a Reprise, assassinated Pope Lucian and attempted to succeed him. He faced opposition from the Dominoes, a secret organisation stretching across the Dominions. The fourth Doctor and Sarah were present as the Persona - a combination of the Mimic and the failed playwright Francis Pearson - attempted to seize control of Europa. The Doctor trapped Persona inside Europa's Globe, which was actually a TARDIS, and crushed both of them to death in the Vortex. Richelieu become Pope Designate.

3286 - REAL TIME[1153] -> Three survey teams went missing on the desert planet Chronos. The sixth Doctor and Evelyn accompanied a follow-up group there, and found that an absent alien race had equipped a temple of sorts with a time machine. The time traveller Goddard, hailing from 1951, warned the Doctor that events in this era would precipitate the Cybermen conquering Earth in the twentieth century. The Cybermen of the future reverse-engineered a techno-virus that Goddard carried, and created a virus that turned living beings into cybernetic ones. The Cyber-controller of the future infected Evelyn with this virus. The Doctor triggered a temporal wave that aged the Cybermen of the future to death, whereupon he and Evelyn departed, unsuspectingly, for 1927...

? 3297 - THE BEAST BELOW[1154] -> The eleventh Doctor and Amy found that Starship UK had become a virtual police state; it was monitored by human cyborgs (the Winders) and robot guardians (the Smilers). The Doctor learned that the ship's drive was a fake, and met Liz X - the British monarch Elizabeth X, who was similarly investigating the truth behind Starship UK. The Doctor discovered that Liz X wasn't

---

sode that's trickiest to place on a timeline.

We can calculate the date. Amy is said in dialogue to be "1306" - as she's seven in 1996 (*Flesh and Stone*), that means it's now 3295. However, the screen Amy looks at actually *says* "1308", which seems like a production error, possibly caused by confusion over the extra two years the Doctor keeps Amy waiting right at the end of *The Eleventh Hour*. If the screen's right, it's now 3297. *The Brilliant Book of Doctor Who 2011* similarly derived a dating of 3297 by favouring the screen and number-crunching Amy's birth year of 1989 with 1308.

Consistent with this, the Doctor dates the solar flares to "the twenty-ninth century", and Liz X says her mask is "nearer three hundred" years old than the Doctor's estimate of two hundred. As the mask was custom made so Liz could explore the mysteries of Starship UK incognito, the ship has been in flight at least three hun-

dred years, probably four hundred (it would mean the mask was made around 2995, which is nearly a hundred years after the end of the twenty-ninth century). Those are the dates given in the story, and they're clear and consistent.

Where this dating scheme runs aground is that while Earth is completely abandoned a number of times (see The Abandonment of Earth sidebar), it seems implicit that *these* solar flares are meant to be the same ones that cause Nerva Beacon to be converted into an Ark (as seen in *The Ark in Space/The Sontaran Experiment*). "The Keep" dates this to the fifty-first century, a time period that was already busy enough before the new series made it the native time of both Jack Harkness and River Song (neither of whom, though, have said much about Earth itself in their era). See the dating notes on *Revenge of the Cybermen* for where the "twen-

fifty years old as she claimed, she was nearer three hundred, and her own memories had been erased. He, Amy and Liz X learned that Starship UK was powered by the last of the star whales, which was being tortured to drive it forward. Amy released the whale from its torment, and it continued helping Starship UK of its own volition.

Starship UK had candyburgers, clockwork-powered technology and air-balanced porcelain. While on Starship UK, Amy saw a banner for Magpie Electricals.[1155]

Various environmental disasters, including radiation storms, rendered Pavonis IV uninhabitable. A handful of the populace escaped in ships carrying cloning facilities. They had also engineered a means of creating AI human-oids with fungal brains. The surviving Pavonians primarily sought to find their hero, the Doctor, thinking he could help restore their planet.[1156]

A gravity quake destroyed the planets orbiting the star Gloriana XVI and created the Gloriana Scattering, one of the most beautiful asteroid fields in the universe.[1157] The First Empire of Eternal Victory, a conquering regime from outside the Milky Way, fell when the Synthetic Emperor took the throne. The Emperor retasked the armies of robots the First Empire had created, spurring a new, robot-based Empire.[1158]

The Doctor rescued the Rembrandt painting *The Night Watch* from the Reichmuseum in Amsterdam shortly before the facility burned down.[1159] Mechanoids landed on Hesperus, and prepared it for habitation.[1160]

c 3312 - "Interstellar Overdrive"[1161] -> Pakafroon Wabster had become the greatest rock band in recorded history - it was on its sixty-third line-up, around the two hundred album mark. The band's founder, Wabster, had died fifty years ago in a rollerblading accident, but had been exhumed and animatronically reanimated. The tenth Doctor and Rose met the group aboard a starship that was causing weird time dilations, and realised the group's man-ager was trying to eliminate them to cement their reputa-tions. Wabster killed the manager, and the Doctor got the band to lifepods, then destroyed their ship.

Magellan-class starcruisers now used warp induction thrusters.

Officials on Manussa outlawed "snakedancing", a mental purification dance to resist the Mara's return.[1162]

---

ty-ninth century" date for the solar flares comes from, and The Solar Flares sidebar for why this chronology places them around 6000AD. The issue is that there are a number of classic *Doctor Who* stories (*The Mutants*, *Terror of the Vervoids*, etc.) definitely set in a thirtieth century where Earth isn't just populated, it's overpopu-lated, and there are even more set afterwards (say, *The Daleks' Master Plan*, set in 4000) where Earth has a highly functional/non-solar-flare-roasted society. There's no real wriggle room for any of this in *The Beast Below* itself - according to the Doctor, the solar flares have already happened, and so "the entire human race", not just some Britons, "packed its bags".

While some might be tempted to invoke the credo of "history can be rewritten, timey-wimey, wibbley-wobbley, it's after the Last Great Time War, the Cracks in Time affected things", etc., and say that *The Beast Below* represents a new history that has superseded the clas-sic *Doctor Who* one... unfortunately, *The Beast Below* doesn't match the continuity of the new series either. Only seven episodes later, *Cold Blood* has the Doctor setting the Silurians' alarm clocks to wake them in a thousand years time (so, around 3020), and expressing his hope that humanity of that time period will be more receptive to co-existing with the Silurians. But if the Doctor's comments in *The Beast Below* are kept sacrosanct, in actuality the Silurians would be waking up to an uninhabitable burnt cinder of a planet.

We see Liz X again in *The Pandorica Opens*, guarding the Royal Collection in a sequence after *The Beast Below* (she says that she "met the Doctor once") and dated to 5145 (although it's not established if the Royal Collection is on Starship UK or the planet the British settled on). While we know that Liz X's body clock had been slowed, that was specifically to keep the Star Whale's plight secret - by 5145, she'd be at least 2550 years old. It's possible that the slowing of her body clock was irreversible, but there's no indication in other stories that mankind discovers the secret of virtual immortality (not even the life-extending Spectrox, as seen in *The Caves of Androzani*, was this effective). While some sources claim Liz X "looks older" in *The Pandorica Opens*, neither of the authors of this chronology see it.

Setting the story a decade or two before 5145 is tempting, because it would consistent with "The Keep", and roughly supported if one presumes that the Doctor meant to say that the solar flares were twenty nine *centuries* after Amy's time. However... if the solar flares were in, say, 5010, and Liz X's mask is three hun-dred years old, *The Beast Below* would be well after 5145, i.e. when Liz X claims to have already met the Doctor (*The Pandorica Opens*). And it doesn't explain why the computer thinks Amy is 1306 (unless her con-nection to the Cracks in Time confused it).

Ultimately, the most pragmatic solution is to disa-vow not the Doctor's statement that Starship UK left Earth in the twenty-ninth century, but his claim that it happened as a result of the solar flares. Nobody and nothing else in *The Beast Below* makes this connection, and once that component is removed, everything else

SECTION FOUR: FUTURE HISTORY

c 3340 - THE DALEK FACTOR[1163] **->** Thal Search-Destroy squads continued to hunt down the Daleks, but it had been two generations since any significant contact had been made. On an unnamed planet, the Daleks worked to implant the Dalek Factor (or "Dalek-heart") into all other lifeforms. The Dalek-hearted life on the test planet considered itself superior to the original Daleks, forcing them to quarantine it. The Daleks successfully imprisoned an unidentified incarnation of the Doctor on this planet.

3380 - FORTY-FIVE: "Order of Simplicity"[1164] **->** Dr Verryman, a foremost expert in the field of bioengineering, had helped to found the Sphere of Influence: a world almost completely devoted to the advancement of knowledge. He developed an inductor: a scalpel-less means of performing surgery with energy pulses and gravity manipulation. The Order of Simplicity, a group devoted to destroying technology, acquired an intelligence-destroying virus. The seventh Doctor, Ace and Hex prevented an agent of the Order from manipulating Verryman into broadcasting the virus - an act that would have reduced billions of humans down to an IQ of 45.

The Galactic Federation

Nearly three hundred years after the first steps towards confederation, the Headquarters of the Galactic Federation on Io were officially opened and **the Federation (or Galactic) Charter was signed. Founding members included Earth, Alpha Centauri,** Draconia, New **Mars and Arcturus. Earth was now regarded as "remote and unattractive". It was ruled by an aristocracy, "in a democratic sort of way". The Federation prevented armed conflicts, and even the Martians renounced violence (except in self-defence). Under the terms of the Galactic Articles of Peace (paragraph 59, subsection 2), the Federation couldn't override local laws or interfere in local affairs except in exceptional circumstances, and was hampered by a need for unanimity between members when taking action.**[1165]

c 3400 - "Cold-Blooded War!"[1166] **->** The galaxy had now enjoyed three centuries of galactic harmony. Draconia had recently joined the Federation, but the coronation of Lady Adjit Kwan as empress of the royal house of Adjit Assan - and by extension the whole Draconian Empire -

---

neatly slots into place. Earth as seen in *The Mutants* (circa 2990) is so overcrowded, it might well resort to all sorts of drastic solutions to shed its excess population (especially as the Earth Empire goes into decline). If Starship UK can be construed to house the excess millions of the United Kingdom, just not the *whole* of the United Kingdom as part of some global disaster, it would actually be in keeping with the "twenty-ninth century" period that the Doctor names. This is an imperfect solution, but it at least keeps intact the on-screen date and the calculation of Amy's age, plus creates the least amount of contradictions.

1155 *The Beast Below*. The banner doesn't necessarily indicate that Magpie Electricals is still active in this era; it could just be a piece of decor from a previous era.

1156 *The Pyralis Effect*

1157 "Thousands of years" (p243) before *The Web in Space*.

1158 "One or two thousand years" before *The Web in Space*.

1159 *Dust Breeding*, "in the thirty-third century".

1160 *War of the Daleks*, "two hundred and seventy-five years" (p213) before the Daleks arrive on Hesperus.

1161 Dating "Interstellar Overdrive" (*DWM* #375-376) - It's "3000 ADish" according to the Doctor. *Flip-Flop* (also by Jonathan Morris) establishes that Pakafroon Wabster had its first hit single in 3012, and the group has now been around for "three hundred years". *The Tomorrow Windows*, however, seems to imply that the band dates to earlier than that.

1162 "Nearly a hundred years" before *Snakedance*.

1163 Dating *The Dalek Factor* (TEL #15) - In *Planet of the Daleks*, the Thal space missions against their arch-enemies seem relatively recent. Here, there have been search and destroy missions against the Daleks for "eight centuries" (p17). The lull in Dalek activity ties in with the one noted in *The Daleks' Master Plan*. The incarnation of the Doctor featured here isn't specified.

1164 Dating *Forty-Five: "Order of Simplicity"* (BF #115b) - The year is given.

1165 *The Curse of Peladon* and its various sequels are set at the time of a Galactic Federation. The date of its foundation is given in *Legacy* (p164); the words are those of Alpha Centauri and the Doctor from *The Curse of Peladon*. The justice machines named the Megara also follow "The Galactic Charter" in *The Stones of Blood*, and they are from 2000 BC. Many other stories refer to "Intergalactic Law", "Intergalactic Distress Signals" and so on - there are clearly certain established standards and conventions that apply across the galaxy, although who sets and enforces them is unclear.

1166 Dating "Cold-Blooded War!" (IDW *DW* one-shot #5) - Dating this story is difficult, and the internal evidence seems a little confused. It's during the time of the Federation. As with *Frontier in Space* (set in 2540), Earth has a President, Draconia has an empire and Draconian females lack equality. Adjudicators dress as the Master did when he posed as one in *Colony in Space* (set in 2472). An Alpha Centaurian briefly runs past the Doctor, but it's unclear if this is the same individual as seen in the Peladon stories, or just a member of the same race.

led Draconia to the brink of civil war. The President of Earth sent Adjudicators Hall and Spane to Draconia with ancient records showing that the Draconian females had only lost their rights following the planet's industrial revolution, and the Federation denied it had requested intervention from the Shadow Proclamation. Some observers, though, believed that Judoon troops would soon be sent to occupy Draconia's major cities. The Adjudicators' ship was destroyed en route, and the tenth Doctor and Donna were subsequently mistaken for that delegation. On Draconia, they worked alongside Martian monitors led by Commander Ixzyptir. Fusek Kljuco, the former head of the Draconian armed forces, accidentally killed his daughter during a botched attempt to assassinate the Empress. It was thought that the royal houses would respond to the tragedy by ratifying the Empress' ascendance, and put Kljuco on trial for crimes against the Empire.

c 3400 - THE DARK PATH[1167] -> The Adjudicators had become the Arbiters, the judicial service of the Federation. The Federation Chair was located on Alpha Centauri. The Federation included the Veltrochni, Terileptils, Draconians and Xarax.

The Federation ship *Piri Reis* reached the lost colony of Darkheart just as temporal distortion attracted both the second Doctor's TARDIS and that of the renegade Time Lord Koschei (an old friend of the Doctor's) and his companion Ailla. The Doctor and Koschei found the Darkheart device, which the colonists were using to make alien beings human.

Koschei accidentally killed Ailla and became stricken with grief. He became increasingly intent on hoarding power, and eradicated the planet Terileptus as a necessary means of testing the Darkheart's destructive capabilities. Ailla regenerated, and Koschei became even more isolated upon realising that she had spied on him for the High Council of the Time Lords. The Doctor stopped Koschei's thirst for power by programming the Darkheart to turn the system's star into a black hole. The colonists evacuated aboard the *Piri Reis*, but Koschei went missing when the black hole consumed his TARDIS.

> = These events happened in the Inferno universe, but in a different form that allowed Koschei and Ailla to continue their travels.[1168]

? 3410 - THE DEMONS OF RED LODGE AND OTHER STORIES: "The Entropy Composition"[1169] -> The fifth Doctor and Nyssa visited Concordium - a planet-sized repository containing music all the way back to the dawn of time - while en route to see the Terileptus event horizon. They visited 1968 upon examining the songs of Geoffrey Belvedere Cooper, and created a feedback loop between Concordium and Cooper's studio. This prevented an Entropy Siren from destabilising the entire universe with the primal sonics of creation.

Dojjin, the Director of Historical Research on Manussa, became convinced that the Mara would return. He abandoned his post, and joined the ranks of the snakedancers.[1170]

What muddies the waters is that it's simultaneously implied that it's been "five hundred years" since both the First Great Space War (presumably the Earth-Draconia conflict that forms the background of *Frontier in Space*, around 2520, meaning it's now around 3020), and since women on Earth were judged to have more important qualifications than "how many words they could type in a minute" (suggesting it's *currently* 2540-ish). Tellingly, though, there have been three hundred years of "galactic harmony" preceding this story - meaning it can't be either 2500 or 3040.

The novels established that the Adjudicators had become the Arbiters by *The Dark Path* (so this story is set before circa 3400). The novel *Legacy* (also written by Gary Russell) might provide the key - it establishes when the Federation was founded, that the process took around three hundred years (the "three centuries of galactic harmony" mentioned in this story?), and that Draconia was a founding member. If that's the case, the Alpha Centauri we see here almost certainly can't be the same individual from the Peladon stories.

1167 Dating *The Dark Path* (MA #32) - There is no exact date, but the Galactic Federation exists (p3) and it is over "three hundred and fifty years" after the turn of the thirty-first century (p175) which was "nearly half a millennium ago" (p178), which all suggests it's set in the thirty-fifth century. It's "a thousand years" since the Doctor first visited Draconia, which *Paper Cuts* helps to date to circa 2040. Terileptus is the homeworld of the Terileptils (*The Visitation*).

1168 *The Face of the Enemy*

1169 Dating *The Demons of Red Lodge and Other Stories*: "The Entropy Composition" (BF #142b) - No year is given. Mention is made of swing musician Benny Goodman having died in 1986, so it's after that. The Terileptus event horizon is said to be "the most magnificent sunset in this part of space-time" - presuming that the event horizon forms after Terileptus' destruction in *The Dark Path*, the Concordium sequences must take place after 3400. Even so, this placement is more guesswork than not.

1170 "Ten years" before *Snakedance*.

1171 Dating *The Menagerie* (MA #10) - It is "centuries" (p67) after Project Mecrim was initiated in 2416. The Doctor suggests that it happened "a millennium or three" (p126) and "hundreds, perhaps thousands of

? 3417 - THE MENAGERIE[1171] **->** Over the centuries, the Knights of Kuabris had prevented scientific discovery on their planet, and discouraged historical research. They came to be led by Zaitabor, who was unaware that he was an android. Zaitabor hoped to purge his city of corruption and revived some Mecrim, who initiated a slaughter. The second Doctor - travelling with Jamie and Zoe - arranged to detonate the city's reactor, which killed Zaitabor and the Mecrim. The Knights fell from power, and negotiations between the planet's various races were arranged.

& 3426 - SNAKEDANCE[1172] **->** The Mara took control of Tegan's mind a second time, and routed the TARDIS to its homeworld of Manussa. The public held a ceremony, as it did once every decade, to celebrate the Mara's defeat - this was the 500th anniversary of its downfall. The Federator's son, Lon, was mentally enthralled by the Mara and arranged that the Great Crystal would be returned to its ceremonial wall socket during the ceremony. This linked the Mara to the minds of those present, and it gained the mental energy required to partly manifest. The snakedancer Dojjin helped the fifth Doctor to resist the Mara by finding the still point within himself. The Doctor removed the Great Crystal from its socket, which

caught the Mara in-between states of being and destroyed it.

The Mara survived in Tegan's mind, and would manifest a third time.[1173]

On Trionikus, the brilliant scientist Tobal Reist built a weapon called the Eraser. He attempted to destroy a spittoon on his workbench, but underestimated the device's power and blasted Trionikus into eighteen billion bits. He was the only survivor, and went mad as a result of his actions.[1174]

Christopher Shaw was born on New Celeste, and became the youngest captain in Earth's Space Corps at age 23. He received a distinguished service medal for his performance in the human-Bavali conflict of 3478.[1175]

c 3480 - PARADISE 5[1176] **->** Targos Delta, the fourth planet in the Targos system, had become the financial and industrial core of the Earth Alliance. Stock market fluctuations from a thousand worlds were recorded on indestructible plastic tickertape, which could be heated and pressurised to be used as building material.

The Elohim were angelic, multidimensional beings undergoing a civil war; many of their number desired contact with the lower races, but their leadership favoured

---

years ago" (p102).

1172 Dating *Snakedance* (20.2) - The story has been long held to be undatable due to the lack of concrete dating clues, and partly because it can't even be established if the Manussans are human or not. *The Cradle of the Snake* ascribes the end of the Manussan Empire to "Manussan Year 2326". The Federation's records begin some "six hundred years" after that catastrophe, and as the Federation is now exactly "five hundred years" old, *Snakedance* must happen a total of eleven hundred years after the Mara's takeover. So, presuming for the moment that the "Manussan years" mentioned in *The Cradle of the Snake* are the same as Earth years, *Snakedance* would occur circa 3426.

While it's admittedly a stretch to think that Manussan years and Earth years *are* equal (if that's the case, what purpose does the different terminology serve?), the thirty-fifth century is a reasonably good fit for *Snakedance*. The Manussans do, to all intents and purposes, appear to be of human descent - the design of their clothing and environs suggests India, Punch and Judy shows are performed, and Earth flowers (including birds of paradise) are on display in the marketplace. Generally speaking, Manussa feels like a human colony cut off from Earth and left to its own devices after humanity's initial expansion into space (as with, to pick an example, Terra Alpha in *The Happiness Patrol*). A potential snag is that the twenty-third and twenty-fourth centuries (going by *The Cradle of the Snake's*

dating) seems a little early for humanity's descendents to have already established "an empire" - then again, we've no idea what actual scale the "Manussan Empire" entails. The grandiosely named "Federation" in *Snakedance*, after all, seems to consist of only three planets. Reference is made to the "leaders of the colonial worlds" in *The Cradle of the Snake*, but for all we're told, there might only be two of those.

About Time suggested that the twenty-seventh or twenty-eighth centuries were "an obvious estimate" for *Snakedance*, thinking it fair to assume that the Doctor takes Tegan to Manussa after events in *Kinda*, while concurring that the dating question largely hinged on whether or not the Manussans are human. *Timelink* presumes that *Snakedance* follows on immediately from *Arc of Infinity*, and that as the Doctor was teaching Tegan and Nyssa how to read "starcharts", meaning no temporal displacement has occurred, and it's still 1983 (*Timelink*'s preferred dating for *Arc of Infinity*) when they arrive on Manussa. Although as *Timelink* itself admits, it's a huge coincidence that without benefit of time-travel, the TARDIS has arrived at the five hundredth anniversary celebration of the Mara's defeat.

1173 *The Cradle of the Snake*
1174 "Fifty years" before "The Company of Thieves".
1175 *Zygons: Absolution*
1176 Dating *Paradise 5* (BF LS #1.5) - It's "the thirty-fifth century". The Galactic Federation is getting started around this time, and the Earth Alliance (prominent in

leaving them alone. The holiday resort Paradise 5, a satellite station in orbit over the toxic Targos Beta, became a recruiting tool for the rebel Elohim. The Paradise Machine there enabled visitors' minds to ascend and fight in the Elohim conflict, even as their bodies were recycled to become the servile Cherubs.

The sixth Doctor and Peri found that the Doctor's old friend Professor Albrecht Thompson, the galaxy's leading expert on the application of string theory to financial derivatives, had become a Cherub. Thompson died as the Elohim's rivals routed them.

Nyssa post-TARDIS

? 3482 - TERMINUS[1177] -> Passenger liners travelled the universe and sometimes fell victim to raiders, often those combat-trained by Colonel Periera.

Lazars' Disease swept the universe, spreading fear and superstition even among those in the rich sectors. Sufferers were sent secretly to Terminus, a vast structure in the exact centre of the known universe. The station was run by Terminus Incorporated, who extracted massive profits from the operation. The facility was manned by slave workers, the Vanir, who were kept loyal by their need for the drug Hydromel. The Lazars were either killed or cured by a massive burst of radiation from Terminus' engines.

The fifth Doctor, Nyssa, Tegan and Turlough arrived on Terminus as part of the Black Guardian's machinations. Nyssa left the TARDIS to create an improved version of Hydromel that would break the Vanir's

dependency on the company, and to help introduce proper diagnoses and controlled treatment to the Lazars.

During her time on Terminus, Nyssa approached one of the Lazars. She'd been unable to synthesise a cure for the disease, but offered to save his life in a manner similar to the Dar Traders - whose abilities she'd partly acquired, owing to her one-time encounter with them.[1178] Nyssa was Timescooped into a pocket dimension of the Death Zone, then returned home.[1179]

In 3487, Christopher Shaw was the only survivor of a Space Corps team sent to deal with some Zygons in Antella Orionsis. He was court-martialed for cowardice.[1180]

3488 - ASYLUM[1181] -> Nyssa developed a vaccine for Lazar's Disease and travelled the galaxy until it was eradicated. Full of optimism, she discovered there were many other pandemic problems such as war, famine and disease. She worked to relieve suffering, including periods spent as a nurse on Brallis and airlifting food into Exanos.

When Exanos was destroyed in a nuclear war, Nyssa established herself in a peaceful system and became a university teacher specialising in technography, the study of writings about science. As part of this, she studied the works of Roger Bacon. The fourth Doctor met Nyssa while tracking an anomaly in space-time, and discovered discrepancies in her recollection of Bacon. This was evidence of alien interference with the timeline. When the Doctor departed for the thirteenth century, Nyssa stowed aboard. After restoring history, the Doctor brought Nyssa home.

the *Dalek Empire* audios) is presumably a smaller organisation within the larger Federation framework.
1177 Dating *Terminus* (20.4) - Once again, an arbitrary date. The date from the Virgin edition of this chronology was adopted by *Asylum*, which is set in 3488, "six years" later. The *Terrestrial Index* saw Terminus Inc. as one of the "various corporations" fought by the Doctor in the late "twenty-fifth century". The FASA Role-playing game gave the date as "4637 AD". *Timelink* doesn't assume that the characters are human and sets it in 1983.
1178 *The Darkening Eye*. Nyssa's life and death "trading" ability - which we don't actually see put into effect, so she might only suspect she has the talent - stems from events in the main story of this audio, which are undatable. The Dar Traders' abilities are outlined in *The Death Collectors*.
1179 *The Five Companions*. Nyssa says that she "left the Doctor a very long time ago", so this could occur at virtually any point in her life after *Terminus*.
1180 *Zygons: Absolution*
1181 Dating *Asylum* (PDA #42) - The year is given. It is

"six years" since *Terminus*.
1182 Dating *Circular Time*: "Winter" (BF #91) - Nyssa implies that it's been "a few years" since her stay at Terminus and the Corporation Wars - allowing for *Asylum*, it's actually been more like eight or nine.
1183 *Cobwebs*, in which Nyssa tells the Doctor that Lazar's Disease "ended, almost fifteen years ago. Since I developed a vaccine, there hasn't been a new case for over two decades." In other words, she developed a vaccine twenty years before she again meets the Doctor, then spent five years dealing with - and curing - all the people who caught the disease before the vaccine was available. This does, however, clash with account in *Asylum*, which claims that Nyssa developed a vaccine for Lazar's about six years after *Terminus*.
1184 *The Cradle of the Snake*
1185 Dating *Cobwebs* (BF #136) - It's "forty years, two months, two days" before the latter part of the story, which occurs "about fifty years" after *Terminus*. "The Company" isn't necessarily the same unseen corporation mentioned in *Terminus*, but it seems a reasonably safe bet.

c 3490 - CIRCULAR TIME: "Winter"[1182] **->** Nyssa married a dream specialist named Lasarti, and they had a baby daughter named Neeka. Upon experiencing a recurring dream of her time with the Doctor, Nyssa decided to investigate using a device that Lasarti had developed to consciously explore dreams. Lasarti insisted on following her, and the two of them mentally arrived inside the dreamscape of the fifth Doctor - who was dying on Androzani Minor. With their help, the Doctor overcame a mind-trap set by the Master, and initiated his regeneration.

Within five years of Nyssa developing a vaccine for Lazar's Disease, the illness had been completely eradicated.[1183] Medical facilities were still in use on Terminus.[1184]

& 3492 - COBWEBS[1185] **->** The Company established a bioresearch station on Helhine, a toxic planet in the uncharted backwaters in the Eastern edge of the galaxy. Helhine was home to the Cractids, the only organisms with a natural immunity to Richter's Syndrome. The Company hoped to both find a cure for Richter's and develop a new strain of the disease - one that could only be cured with a licensed product. Per Company policy, the research team's memories had been siphoned off into a crystal databank, and would be restored if they succeeded with their mission.

The fifth Doctor, Tegan, Turlough and a much-older Nyssa had been thrown back in time, and arrived as Bragg, an agent for the Independent Bio-Development Group, became infected with the deadlier Richter's variant. He entered cryo-freeze and escaped as the other research team members died, and the station went dormant. Nyssa opted to resume travelling with her friends, and worked to perfect a cure for Richter's.

The Adventures of Kroton

? 3500 - "Ship of Fools" (DWW)[1186] **->** Kroton, the Cyberman with a soul, was picked up and revived by the passengers of a human spaceliner. He learned the ship had been renamed the *Flying Dutchman II*, as it was caught in a time warp. Kroton opened up the cockpit and reprogrammed the robot pilot to escape the rift. But once outside, the lost time caught up with the passengers - they aged by six hundred and twenty-eight years in an instant, and Kroton was left alone once more.

The Technosmiths of Baroq VII upgraded Kroton's armour to thank him for helping them.[1187]

? 3500 - "Unnatural Born Killers"[1188] **->** Kroton surfaced on a peaceful world that was being attacked by the Sontarans. He destroyed the invasion force, but could not share in the elation of the natives.

? 3500 - "The Company of Thieves"[1189] **->** The Qutrusian Cargo Freighter X-703 was captured by pirates led by Grast Horstrogg. Kroton the Cyberman offered resistance, and made the acquaintance of the eighth Doctor and Izzy, while the pirates headed for a new target in a nearby asteroid belt. The TARDIS was stolen by Tobel, the mad scientist who had destroyed his planet Trionikus (and thus formed the asteroid belt) fifty years previous. The pirates tried to steal Tobel's super-weapon - the Eraser - but this merely destabilised the last habitable asteroid. The Doctor, Izzy and Kroton reached the TARDIS, and Kroton joined the TARDIS crew.

Confusingly, Nyssa tells Turlough, "So, you're travelling with the Doctor now..." as if she remembers meeting him in *Mawdryn Undead*, but - somehow - doesn't recall that he joined her, the Doctor and Tegan on their adventures. Nyssa also claims that she doesn't age at the same rate as humans, which is why Tegan claims that she's "looking pretty good" for someone who's about seventy, but this contradicts the Doctor's comment (*Circular Time:* "Autumn") that humans and Trakenites have about the same lifespan (perhaps Trakenites don't actually live longer than humans, but remain heartier than humans as they age).

1186 Dating "Ship of Fools" (*DWW* #23-24) - The story is set after "Throwback", but no date beyond that is given. The story is set around six hundred and fifty-eight years after human space liners stopped using human pilots, but this isn't very helpful - it's possible human pilots were reintroduced (particularly if enough ships piloted by robots like this one were lost). It does

mean that it can't possibly be set before around 2800, however.

The closest period to this seen in a TV story is *Terminus*, which takes place at a time where ships are piloted automatically, span the galaxy and are threatened by pirates. "Unnatural Born Killers" and "The Company of Thieves" follow this story, but there's no indication how long it is between stories (and it could be many centuries, given that Kroton is effectively immortal).

1187 "The Company of Thieves"

1188 Dating "Unnatural Born Killers" (*DWM* #277) - see dating notes on "Ship of Fools" (*DWW*).

1189 Dating "The Company of Thieves" (*DWM* #284-286) - No date is given, but it's after "Unnatural Born Killers" and all previous Kroton stories. The pirates are scared of Cybermen, perhaps suggesting this is still within the period of the Cyber Empire (see "Did the Cybermen Ever Have An Empire?"). Pedants might note

The planet Lebenswelt sold its entire mineral wealth to Galactinational. Now immeasurably rich, the population dedicated themselves to decadence.[1190]

The Daleks returned to Earth's galaxy. Over the next five hundred years, they had gained control of more than seventy planets in the ninth galactic system and forty in the constellation of Miros. They were, once again, based on their home planet of Skaro. The Daleks were the only race known to have broken the time barrier, although Trantis had tried in the past without success. Dalek technology was the most advanced in the universe.[1191]

On Earth, a giant clock was constructed that didn't just measure time - it *dictated* time, bending space-time and facilitating the hyperspace avenues through Earth's dominions. The Guardians of the Solar System - aided by trusted members of the Space Security Service - "guarded" the clock, as it was the secret of Earth's power. The clock ran off the mathematical potential of the minds of old men who serviced its inner workings. Without the clock, Earth's empire would have collapsed, leaving billions dead or starving, and making Earth vulnerable to its rivals.[1192]

c 3502 - ZYGONS: ABSOLUTION[1193] -> Interplanetary Mining worked in concert with the human settlement of New Eden on Ganta 4, and shipped supplies of Amyrillum ore back to Earth. Christopher Shaw had become a religious leader dedicated to Neo-Christianity on Ganta 4. The New World translation of the Bible was still in circulation. Nine years after New Eden's formation, the Zygons seized the colony's spaceship - a means of evading Earth security and attacking humanity's homeworld. Shaw sacrificed his life so his fellow colonists could blow up the spaceship, killing the Zygons.

The Interplanetary Wars

The robotic Mechanoids were dispatched in rockets to planets such as Mechanus, and set out preparing the way for colonists. The Mechanoids cleared landing sites and made everything ready for the immigrants, but a series of interplanetary wars started. The space lanes were disrupted, and colonies such as Mechanus were cut off from Earth. Left to their own devices, the Mechanoid robots built and maintained a vast city, awaiting the code that would identify the rightful human colonists.[1194]

& 3520 - SISTERS OF THE FLAME / THE VENGEANCE OF MORBIUS[1195] -> Earth had embassies on different worlds. Space Traffic Control was in operation. Every spaceship had access to Galactinet: a supralight microwave information network transmitted across hyperspatial conduits. Members of many different species, including several humanoid ones and the Trell - an affable a race of giant centipedes - served as interplantary police marshals.

(=) Kristof Zarodnix became the richest man in the galaxy - possibly the universe - by buying and selling planets. The Sisterhood of Karn left their world after Zarodnix bought it out from under them. Karn became home to Zarodnix Corporation's central office. Zarodnix purchased many Trell worlds, and used mechanical devices to enslave the Trell.

Zarodnix was secretly the leader of the Cult of Morbius, and acquired a fragment of Morbius' brain from the deep chasm that Morbius fell into on Karn. Using a genetotron, Zarodnix combined Morbius' DNA into a captured Time Lord, Straxus. Morbius was reborn as a fusion of the two. He exacted vengeance on the High Council by using a stellar manipulator that he'd built to drain energy from the Eye of Harmony. Zarodnix's warfleet of converted Trell cordoned off Gallifrey. Ten years passed as Morbius raised a formidable army and conquered a thousand worlds, including Earth.

The eighth Doctor deactivated Morbius' stellar manipulator, restoring power to Gallifrey.

The Doctor and Morbius, both grappling for the remote activator to the stellar manipulator, fell into a chasm on Karn. The restored Time Lords reverted time back to before Zarodnix purchased Karn. Lucie Miller thought the Doctor was dead, and the Time Lords took her home.

---

that the eighth Doctor doesn't recognise Kroton even though the fourth Doctor "introduced" his original appearance in a *DWW* framing sequence.
1190 "Five hundred years" before *The Book of the Still*.
1191 *Mission to the Unknown*, *The Daleks' Master Plan*.
1192 Sara Kingdom speculates that the clock was built "centuries" before *The Guardian of the Solar System* - which would match with the claim that all of Mavic Chen's predecessors were tasked with protecting it.
1193 Dating *Zygons: Absolution* (BBV audio #17) - Shaw left the Space Corps in 3487; while it's not speci-

fied how much time has passed since then, he seems to have one of the original colonists, and New Eden is nine years old. "Interplanetary Mining" is presumably the Interplanetary Mining Corps seen in *Colony in Space*. The New World translation of the complete Bible was introduced in 1961.
1194 At least "fifty years" before *The Chase*, according to Steven Taylor. There's a possibility that Steven is mistaken about the Mechanoids' origin.
1195 Dating *Sisters of the Flame/The Vengeance of Morbius* (BF BBC7 #2.7-2.8) - It's repeatedly confirmed

The Sisterhood teleported the Doctor away from the chasm - either to aid an ally, or possibly because they didn't want the activator he clutched to be lost. The Doctor materialised in "tweenspace" - a layer of cosmic sediment - on the planet Orbis. The activator sank to the bottom of Great Ocean of Orbis, and the Doctor came to reside on the planet for six hundred years. The Headhunter acquired the Doctor's TARDIS from the Sisterhood, and went back to the twenty-first century to abduct Lucie.[1196]

Bragg was revived from cryo-stasis on Gondel Prime, and the enhanced version of Richter's Syndrome that he carried spread to other worlds in a matter of months.[1197]

& 3532 - COBWEBS[1198] -> Nyssa was still married to Lasarti. They had a daughter named Tegan, and a younger son named Adric.[1199]

Six billion people were now infected with Richter's Syndrome. Nyssa travelled to the disused tech station on Helhine to find a cure, and happened across the fifth Doctor, Tegan and Turlough there. The station's AI initiated a self-destruct, and the resultant explosion threw them, and the TARDIS, back in time forty years.

(=) 3562 - THE SIRENS OF TIME[1200] -> The Knights of Velyshaa fought Earth, but their First Empire fell. Thanks to the seventh Doctor, though, their leader Sancroff escaped to establish the Second Empire. Capturing a Temperon, the Knights built time machines and successfully attacked the Time Lords, although the Knights' bodies had become withered and parasitic. They used Time Lord flesh to maintain themselves.

The fifth, sixth and seventh Doctors joined forces to defeat the Knights. History was restored and Sancroff was executed.

Steven Taylor[1201]

Steven Taylor, a companion of the first Doctor, grew up during a war. Earth during this time had flying cars and motorbikes. Clean-up rigs worked all hours to clear orbital fragments, as even a small accident could halt sub-orbital traffic for days. Steven met representatives of the Cahlian race at various trading posts.[1202] Steven's era had

that it's been "centuries" since *The Brain of Morbius*. Morbius' stellar manipulator is akin to Hand of Omega from *Remembrance of the Daleks*, although Morbius' manipulator is as big as a moon (*Orbis*). The Doctor suggests that the Hand of Omega itself is "long gone", suggesting that it was either lost or destroyed after returning to Gallifrey in *Remembrance*. Straxus previously appeared in *Human Resources*.

And although it's not said, the chasm on Karn theoretically contains the body of a Morbius from a closed-off timeline.

1196 *Orbis*
1197 "Ten years" before the latter part of *Cobwebs*.
1198 Dating *Cobwebs* (BF #136) - From Nyssa's perspective, it's been "about fifty years" since *Terminus*. For the Doctor's group, that story happened two days ago.
1199 *Heroes of Sontar*
1200 Dating *The Sirens of Time* (BF #1) - The date is given.
1201 STEVEN TAYLOR: We know that Steven hails from an era in which interplanetary travel for Earth is becoming (or already is) commonplace, that Earth has been dispatching the Mechanoids to colonise other worlds, and that Earth "got mixed up in interplanetary wars" - which is why the colonisation of Mechanus wasn't completed. We also know from *The Daleks' Master Plan* that Steven is from at least some "centuries" if not more before the year 4000. Unfortunately, every piece of evidence related to Steven contains some degree of ambiguity, so debates are still being had as to whether he originates anywhere from as early as the twenty-third century to as late as the thirty-sixth century(ish).

On screen, the strongest clues about Steven's era come from *The Daleks' Master Plan*. In episode six, Sara (originating from the year 4000) says that "Gravity force as a source of energy was abandoned, centuries ago", to which Steven replies, "We were still using it." In itself, this isn't an indicator that Steven is from only "centuries" before Sara's time, as gravity force could have been discontinued long after his era. But in the same episode, Steven says to Sara, "The technology of my age may be hundreds of years behind yours and the Doctor's, but there are still some things I can handle." He could be speaking colloquially, as he seems to be saying that the Doctor's technology is only centuries ahead of his - but if he really were from thousands rather than hundreds of years behind Sara's time, he could have said exactly that and been just as colloquial where the Doctor was concerned.

Without a clear directive as to when Steven's era takes place, the tie-in stories have been of split minds about it. In *The First Wave*, writer Simon Guerrier assumed a later dating for Steven, claiming in the story that Steven once lived in a dwelling which was already "two centuries old" by the time he resided there, and was made using technology far in advance of the present day. Conversely, *Salvation* by Steve Lyons implied a much earlier dating, establishing (p58) that Steven saw the "rubble, the wasteland... the suffering of those... whom rebuilding had left behind" of New York following the Daleks devastating it in the mid-twenty-second century (*The Dalek Invasion of Earth*). This could just mean, however, that a portion of New York never recovers from the Dalek onslaught and is still in ruin in

particle conversion, which eliminated the need for recycling centres.[1203] **It used "gravity force" as a source of energy.**[1204]

Humanity had the ability to establish entire bases on planets, moons and asteroids using prefabricated blocks - an entire city was built on Sedna in slightly less than two weeks. Steven had a menial job ferrying such construction units between the outer planets of Earth's solar system. He found the job joyful at first, but tedium soon set in, and he went to war in part to escape the monotony.[1205]

Steven joined up to fight in the interplanetary wars after visiting New York, at least a portion of which had not recovered since the Dalek invasion in the twenty-second century. He became the helmsman of a battleship, living on spaceships and space stations. He ruined his promotion prospects by complaining about a soldier abusing a civilian on Roylus Prime, and was relegated to solo non-combat missions. His ship was built from modified Dalek designs.[1206]

Historical-doc romances were made in Steven's native time.[1207] People on Earth lived in cramped Hiveblocks. His ship crashed on Mechanus when Krayt fighters shot it down.[1208] The Daleks fought the Mechanoids on Hesperus.[1209]

? 3565 - THE CHASE[1210] **->** Nearly fifty years after the interplanetary wars had begun, Earth was still involved, although the end was now in sight. One of the combatants, space pilot Steven Taylor, Flight Red Fifty, was stranded on Mechanus. After several days in the hostile jungle, he was captured by the Mechanoids, who still maintained their city in preparation for the human colonists. Unable to crack their code, Taylor was imprisoned. Two years after this, the first Doctor, Ian, Barbara and Vicki arrived, pursued by the Daleks. The Mechanoid City, the Mechanoids and the Daleks were destroyed. Ian and Barbara returned to their native time in the captured Dalek time machine, and the Doctor, Vicki and Steven left in the TARDIS.

& 3568 - PALACE OF THE RED SUN[1211] **->** The sixth Doctor and Peri found that time on Esselven Minor was running faster within the planetoid's defence screen than without. The warlord Glavis Judd landed on the planet to capture the fugitive Esselven royals. The Doctor tricked Judd into thinking that everyone on the planetoid, including the royals' real-life descendents, were holographic projections. Judd departed, but the Doctor corrected the errant defence shield and brought the planetoid back into

---

Steven's time - a better restored part of the city might contain the popular waterways mentioned in *Fear Itself* (PDA), or it's possible that these are different cities entirely (in accordance with *The End of the World* establishing that at least fifteen cities bear the name "New York").

Previous editions of *Ahistory* erroneously reported that Steven said in *The Daleks' Master Plan* that he was from "thousands of years" before the year 4000, which doesn't appear to be the case. It was also reported that *Salvation* directly stated that Steven was from the "mid twenty-third century", which isn't (apologies again) true either.

Until a story comes along that cuts through the fog surrounding this topic and resolutely states that "Steven Taylor is from the X century", it seems best to assume by default that mention in *The Daleks' Master Plan* of Steven being from "hundreds of years" before the year 4000 does actually mean "hundreds of years" rather than millennia, hence the relocation in this guidebook of *The Chase* to the year 3565.

1202 *Cold Equations*
1203 *The Perpetual Bond*
1204 *The Daleks' Master Plan*
1205 *The First Wave*
1206 *Salvation*
1207 *Frostfire*
1208 *The Empire of Glass*
1209 *War of the Daleks*, and presumably the same class of Mechanoids seen in *The Chase*.
1210 Dating *The Chase* (2.8) - No date given, but this is

Steven's native time. See the Steven Taylor sidebar.

The TARDIS Logs suggested a date of "3773 AD". The first and second editions of *The Programme Guide* set dates of "2150" and "2250" respectively, *The Terrestrial Index* settled on "early in the twenty-seventh century". The American *Doctor Who* comic suggested a date of "2170". "A History of the Daleks" in *DWM* #77 claimed a date of "3764 AD", *The Discontinuity Guide* suggested that Steven fought in "one of the Cyber Wars, or the Draconian conflict". *Timelink* suggests "3550", *About Time* "2200 - 2400".

There's no indication that the Daleks are in their native time when they fight the Mechanoids at the end of the story, but the Daleks have fought the Mechanoids before. We saw this happen in the *TV Century 21* strip, in "Eve of the War", but there's a problem - that story is set very soon after the Daleks started space exploration, explicitly centuries before mankind could have built the Mechanoids. Additionally, the Mechanoids in the strip are far more inventive and advanced.

There are a number of possibilities. A rather messy one is that there are two, near identical, robot races out there - "Mechonoids" built by humans to colonise Mechonous, and "Mechanoids" built by a far more advanced race of outer space robot people from the planet Mechanus. Or, given that they look the same, perhaps the Mechanoids the humans sent out were based on alien technology, possibly acquired after some unseen Mechanoid attack on Earth (again, no evidence - and it doesn't explain why both come from Mechanus). Another alternative is that perhaps the

synch with the rest of the universe. Judd emerged in normal space five hundred years after he'd departed, and after the royals had re-settled Esselven. The royals didn't recognise Judd and, per policy regarding people claiming to be the warlord, threw him in an asylum.

c 3580 - THE FIRST WAVE[1212] **->** The first Doctor, Steven and Oliver Harper arrived at a mining operation on Grace Alone - a planetoid in the Kuiper Belt near Neptune - to fulfill history, as they had seen future records indicating they had been prisoners there, guilty of data theft. The Doctor entered their criminal records into the base's computer system when the Vardans, having backtracked Earth's radio signals, attempted to invade the Sol system. The Vardans killed the mining crew, but the Doctor dissipated their energy, forcing them to withdraw to their native space. The Doctor sent Earth authorities recommendations on how to tighten their security.

One Vardan remained behind, determined to use the last of its energy to kill the Doctor's trio. Oliver drew the Vardan's fire... and was disintegrated. The Doctor and Steven believed Oliver had died, but a last ember of his essence stayed with the TARDIS as it departed. In such a state, he observed all of the first Doctor's remaining travels.

& 3585 - THE RESURRECTION OF MARS[1213] **->** The planet Halcyon was located ninety light years from Earth, and had become home to one of the most civilised races in the cosmos. Its population of twenty billion had cured every disease, crafted transcendent works of art, knew the meaning of war but saw no need for it, and generally had created a Nirvana the likes of which the universe would never see again. It was one of the greatest tragedies to creation when Ice Warriors who had formerly been sleep-

ing in Earth's asteroid belt transformed Halcyon into a new Martian homeworld - wiping out the populace, their science and their culture.

c 3606 - "Art Attack!"[1214] **->** The ninth Doctor took Rose to see the Mona Lisa at the Oriel, a transdimensional gallery on Earth. The Doctor realised the visitors were being hypnotised by their information headsets. The culprit was Cazkelf, a crashed alien trying to drain enough psychic energy to power his ship's distress beacon. When the Doctor discovered that Cazkelf's planet had been destroyed, Cazkelf decided to settle on Earth - where his hypnotism was lauded as a bold work of performance art.

? 3625 - THE SONG OF THE MEGAPTERA[1215] **->** By now, the Swords Into Plowshares computer virus had proved useful against war robots in the Fourth Oil War, compelling those infected to take up flower arranging.

Environmentalists, "ecos", had positions of power on some colony worlds. Corporate factory ships hunted the Ghaleen: mile-long space whales with solar scales and internal ecosystems, and the only creatures known to live in the vacuum of space. The Ghaleen were converted into food for colony planets. The Tuthons, fungoid creatures on the planet Ziphius, regarded the Ghaleen as their "friends" but also hunted them. Only the pilot Ghaleen could recognise danger, and if needed make its herd escape predators by diving into the horizon of time itself. The Ghaleen were peaceful creatures who sometimes helped ships in distress, and were a safe haven for shipwreck victims.

The sixth Doctor and Peri saved a pilot Ghaleen and its thousand-strong herd from the clutches of a factory ship, the SS *Orcas*.

---

ones that fight the Daleks in the strip are time travellers (although there's absolutely nothing to indicate that). While there's no evidence for it, the simplest answer of all is... that the Mechanoids have lied to Steven about their origins, and that they are a powerful spacefaring alien race who have fought the Daleks in the past.

The end credits of episode five and six of *The Chase* spell the name as "Mechanoid" and "Mechonoid" respectively. The script spells the name of the planet as "Mechonous"; the comic strip prefers "Mechanus".

1211 Dating *Palace of the Red Sun* (PDA #51) - It is five hundred years after the previous part of the story.

1212 Dating *The First Wave* (BF CC #6.5) - Steven says that they're "somewhere a little after" his own time, as he's largely familiar with the technology at hand, but some improvements have been made to gravity and atmosphere control. Oliver Harper previously appeared in *The Perpetual Bond* and *Cold Equations*.

1213 Dating *The Resurrection of Mars* (BF BBC7 #4.6) - The Monk says that he and Tamsin have travelled "one

thousand years into the future", presumably referring to their previous location on Deimos rather than Tamsin's native era. The transformed Halcyon is separate from the Martian colony planet Nova Martia (i.e. New Mars, one of the founding members of the Federation), which is settled after the Thousand-Day War according to *GodEngine*.

1214 Dating "Art Attack!" (*DWM* #358) - It's "the thirty-seventh century".

1215 Dating *The Song of the Megaptera* (BF LS #1.7) - No year given. The back cover text says that it's "deep space in the distant future". The participants are aware of humanity, use Earth whaling terms and seem human themselves. A Terran warship inside the pilot Ghaleen has "Eat lead, Dalek scum" written on its side, so it's after humanity's conflicts with the Daleks.

Environmentalists hold influence on some colony planets, suggesting it's not the time of the less-than environmentally minded (to put it mildly) Earth Empire. The whale-hunters have some awareness of the

3655 - GALLIFREY: WEAPON OF CHOICE[1216] -> Representatives from Gallifrey, the Monan Host, the Warpsmiths of Phaidon and the Nekkistani were tasked with investigating reports of smuggled black-light rods, and were sent to the third moon of Kikrit in 3655. Nepenthe, a human member of the subversive group Free Time, made off with a timonic fusion device that had been hidden in a moonbase.

The first annual Intergalactic Song Contest was held.[1217] The name "Tony" died out.[1218]

In the Adelphine cluster on the galactic rim, relations between the humans of the Landor Alliance and the Averon Union were strained. Within four years, this became a full-scale war.

The Landor Alliance constructed Deepcity, a weapons research station on an asteroid. The Averons attacked Landor, but they were driven back. The Landorans destroyed Averon, but suffered 90% casualties themselves. There was a period of civil war across the cluster. Barris Kambril took control of Deepcity, and told the workers there that Landor was destroyed to better motivate them.[1219]

Galactic corporation TransAlliedInc was formed in the thirty-eighth century.[1220] A Kroton spaceship crashed on the planet Onyakis, and the Krotons within reverted to their constituent form. Dynatropes were now regarded as an "inferior form" of spacecraft, and the Krotons took to using more advanced models.[1221]

Targos Delta was overwhelmed with indestructible tickertape.[1222]

c 3788 / (=) c 3788 - INTERFERENCE[1223] -> The planet Dust, a former Earth colony on the Dead Frontier on the edge of the galaxy, was cut off for centuries. Cattlemen there organised into vigilante gangs called Clansmen.

IM Foreman's travelling show arrived briefly on Dust, distorting space-time in the area. Faction Paradox was planning to use a biodata virus to make Dust a world of paradox. A group from the Remote crashed on Dust around this time, and founded the settlement Anathema II from the remains of their ship. Fitz's original self had risen through the ranks of Faction Paradox and become Father Kreiner. He sought revenge against the Doctor.

IM Foreman released his final incarnation, the elemental Number Thirteen, to eliminate the Remote. Father Kreiner was lost to the Time Vortex. Foreman's first twelve incarnations were killed, displaced to early Gallifrey and underwent regeneration. Number Thirteen was convinced to merge with Dust's biosphere, whereupon Foreman became integrated with the entire planet. Dust was renamed Foreman's World.

Ghaleen's temporal abilities - such as measuring the depths to which they dive in "millenniums" - but lack the ability to follow, which rules out the time-tech-riddled fifty-first century. It's a guess, but the fourth millennium seems like a good compromise, when humanity's technology is developed enough to hunt space whales, but prior to its having time tech.

This audio story was adapted from the continually delayed and rewritten The Song of the Space Whale by Pat Mills, which in one phase of development was designed to introduce Turlough (who debuted instead in Mawdryn Undead). The Ghaleen seem different from the space whales seen in The Beast Below and TW: Meat, in that they can navigate through time as well as space.
1216 Dating Weapon of Choice (Gallifrey #1.1) - The year is given. "Black light" was first mentioned as a power source in The Mysterious Planet.
1217 The contest in Bang-Bang-A-Boom! is the 308th.
1218 "Centuries" before the forty-first century portion of "Hotel Historia".
1219 A Device of Death. There's a discussion of the history on p31. No date is given, but Kambril has been in charge for "eighteen years" (p90).
1220 Davros
1221 "Three millennia" before Return of the Krotons.
1222 "A few hundred years" after Paradise 5.
1223 Dating Interference (EDA #25-26) - It's the "thirty-eighth century" (p306) and "several centuries" after The

Monster of Peladon. The Foreman/bottle universe story occurs some time after the main events on Dust.
1224 The bottle next appears in The Ancestor Cell.
1225 Dating A Device of Death (MA #31) - No date is given, but this is a time of isolated Earth colonies, and it's fifteen hundred years since Landor was colonised. The implication that the robots are the Movellans, seen in Destiny of the Daleks, would seem to contradict War of the Daleks.
1226 Dating Earth Aid (BF LS #2.8) - No year given. Earth Aid is, presumably, either based on Earth or chiefly composed of humans; either way, it's after man's expansion into space. Spaceship technology is advanced enough that Earth Aid shipments appear to reach their destinations in time to actually provide relief, without decades spent in transit (a concern in humanity's early colonial age). The Vancouver and Lilliput both have "jump" capabilities, but the Vancouver's primary weaponry is nothing more fancy than cannons and missiles. There's not even mention of a transporter or T-Mat.

As there's no mention of a major war or its aftermath being of any concern, it's unlikely to be during the Dalek Invasion of Earth or the Dalek Wars (where the latter is concerned, the Vancouver, a warship, isn't said to be part of Spacefleet). With all of that in mind, thinking that Earth Aid happens at some point in the fourth millennium rings reasonably true, especially if the

(=) The third Doctor was shot and regenerated, a paradox as he was meant to die on Metebelis III. From this point, the Doctor was infected by the Faction's biodata virus. Every time he regenerated, it grew stronger.

On Foreman's World, the now-female IM Foreman created a bottle universe, and she was surprised when its inhabitants soon built their own bottle universe. Time Lords arrived to acquire the bottle, hoping to use it as a potential refuge in the coming future War. Foreman didn't give them an immediate answer. The eighth Doctor arrived, wanting answers about his visit to Dust. He learned that Father Kreiner was trapped in the bottle universe. After the Doctor left, Foreman discovered that the bottle universe had also vanished.[1224]

? 3800 - A DEVICE OF DEATH[1225] **->** The fourth Doctor, Sarah and Harry arrived at the Adelphine cluster. The Doctor revealed Barris Kambril's lies to the workers at the Deepcity weapons research station. The synthonic robots developed there would play a part in the Daleks' demise.

? 3820 - EARTH AID[1226] **->** Earth Aid had emerged as a charity organisation in the Milky Way, and brought relief supplies to ailing planets. The seventh Doctor and Ace posed respectively as chief medical officer and ship's captain aboard the warship *Vancouver* as it investigated the *Lilliput* - a vessel waylaid while transporting nine million tons of grain for Earth Aid to the planet Safenesthome. The Doctor found Raine Creevy locked in a safe aboard the *Lilliput* - the Metatraxi had brought her to this time zone as part of their plan to gain revenge on him. The Metatraxi had also invented the famine on Safenesthome, which was their homeworld, as a further deception. The grub-like

original inhabitants of Safenesthome had stowed themselves within the *Lilliput* grain, and the sentience of the planet welcomed her estranged children home. The Doctor, Ace and Raine left, knowing that the sentience could always evolve a third species to deal with the Metatraxi and the grubs if they failed to cohabitate.

Jack Harkness had a relationship with a Gloobi hybrid on Tarsius in the thirty-ninth century.[1227]

The Dark Peaks Lodge of the Foamasi was founded, devoted to restoring their home planet of Liasica to its former glory and taking control of the Federation.[1228] **For countless centuries, the people of the primitive planet Peladon had worshipped the creature Aggedor. The planet turned away from war and violence** under King Sherak, **but remained isolated.** In 3864, a Federation shuttlecraft crashed on Peladon after falling foul of an ion storm en route to the base at Analyas VII. The Pels rescued one of the survivors, Princess Ellua of Europa. **The Earthwoman married the King,** Kellian, within a year. Six months later, she persuaded him to apply for Federation membership. Their son was born a year later. **He was named Peladon, and was destined to become King.**[1229]

The Time Lords knew this era as the Sensorian Era.[1230]

& 3885 - THE CURSE OF PELADON[1231] **->** The **Preliminary Assessment Team arrived at King Peladon's court to see if Peladon was suitable for Federation membership. The third Doctor and Jo, having been sent to Peladon by the Time Lords, were mistaken for Earth's representatives. The spirit of Aggedor was abroad, and killed Chancellor Torbis, one of the chief advocates of Federation membership. This was revealed as a plot brewed between the high priest of Aggedor - Hepesh - and the delegate from Arcturus. If Peladon was kept from Federation membership, then**

spaceships' "jump" capabilities relate to the hyperspace paths in use prior to *The Daleks' Master Plan* (see *The Guardian of the Solar System*). The Metatraxi homeworld was "decimated" by the Krotons prior to 2068 (*Alien Bodies*), but might not have been outright destroyed.

1227 *Only Human*.

1228 "Two centuries" before *Placebo Effect*.

1229 *The Curse of Peladon*, with much elaboration given in *Legacy* - a book that incorporates some details from *The Curse of Peladon* novelisation.

1230 *Neverland*. The Sensorian Era was mentioned but not defined in *Doctor Who - The Movie*.

1231 Dating *The Curse of Peladon* (9.2) - There is no dating evidence on screen. The story takes place at a time when Earth is "remote", has had interstellar travel for at least a generation (King Peladon is the son of an Earthwoman) and has an aristocratic government.

It's not set between 2500 and 3000, when Earth has a powerful galactic empire according to fellow Pertwee stories *The Mutants* and *Frontier in Space*. Its sequel is set fifty years afterwards, and galactic politics is in much the same position as in the previous story.

Although the Federation seems to be capable of intergalactic travel at the time of *The Monster of Peladon*, Gary Russell suggested in the New Adventure *Legacy* that Galaxy Five was a mere "terrorist organisation" (p27). *Legacy* is set "a century" after *The Curse of Peladon*.

Remarkably, given the lack of on-screen information, there has been fan consensus about the dating of this story and its sequel: *The Programme Guide* set the story in "c.3500", and made the fair assumption that the Federation succeeded the collapsed Earth Empire. *The Terrestrial Index* revised this slightly to "about 3700". *The TARDIS Logs* suggests "3716". *Timelink* suggests "3225",

Arcturus would be granted the mineral rights to the planet. Arcturus was killed while attempting to assassinate one of the delegates, and Aggedor himself killed Hepesh. Peladon was granted Federation membership.

& 3890 - THE PRISONER OF PELADON[1232] -> Five years after Peladon joined the Federation, civil war erupted on New Mars. A military coup headed by Grand Marshall Raxlyr closed the planet's borders; the royal family was deposed and largely executed. Peladon took in hundreds of Martian refugees, who set up a camp near Mount Megeshra. Lord Ixlyr secretly smuggled out Lixgar - the daughter of the late Martian king, and heir to the Martian throne - and placed her in the care of Alpha Centauri. The third Doctor and King Peladon prevented Raxlyr's agents from finding and killing the girl.

Two alien scientists - Elliot Payne and his wife Shenyia - examined the Time Eaters: creatures trapped on the edge of a black star. A gravity spike pulled Shenyia into the star's event horizon, freezing her in time. The Time Eaters offered to teach Payne how to convert time into raw energy - he was to liberate Shenyia with half of the resultant energy cache, and free the Time Eaters with the other. Payne went back to 2011, then Victorian times. The Time Eaters realised that Payne had swindled them and digested all the years of Shenyia's life, enabling some of their number to follow Payne. The rest remained trapped.[1233]

c 3907 - THE PIRATE LOOP[1234] -> The starship *Brilliant* was built as a luxury passenger liner servicing races such as Balumins and Bondoux 56, in an era on the verge of a terrible intergalactic war. The ship's experimental warp core was a century ahead of its time, and allowed it to travel by bouncing off the exterior of the Time Vortex. The *Brilliant* disappeared, its fate unknown...

The tenth Doctor told Martha about the legend of the *Brilliant* as they evaded the rogue servo robots of Milky-Pink City; after they escaped, Martha wanted to find out what happened to it. They arrived a few days before the ship's disappearance, and found that badger-like pirates - adapted members of a genetically engineered human serv-

---

About Time "at least a thousand years in the future".

While that seems reasonable, another possibility is that this story is set very early in Earth's future history, when Earth's just starting to explore the galaxy. It's at least a generation after interstellar travel. But other than that, the aliens here and in *The Monster of Peladon* are all near neighbours - Mars, Alpha Centauri, Arcturus and Vega. On the evidence of the TV series alone, *The Curse of Peladon* could comfortably be set in the late twenty-second century, before the Earth Empire forms.

ARCTURUS: We have seen at least three different alien races come from Arcturus over the course of *Doctor Who*, and it has been the site of a large number of events, although all of these have alluded to rather than depicted.

The Curse of Peladon shows us an Arcturan that resembles a shrunken human head with some sort of tendrils growing from it, which needs a bulky life support system to survive in places suitable for humans. The criminal Arktos (*The Bride of Peladon*) was one of this species, and his nickname "the Scourge of the Nine Worlds" might indicate the extent of the Arcturan system. It's this species of Arcturan that seems most common, and in the far future, they become members of the Galactic Federation - along with Earth and their arch enemies, the Ice Warriors.

UNIT fought an Arcturan with sinister intent (*Verdigris*), but in the late twenty-first century, the relationship with Arcturus became very fruitful for Earth. Earth picked up an Arcturan signal with enough information to build a working transmat (*Cold Fusion*). Earth's first diplomatic agreement with an alien race was the Arcturan Treaty of 2085 (*The Dying Days*). Humans gained much from contact with Arcturans, including scientific information (*Lucifer Rising*).

Arcturus was the location of early human colonies. The interstellar Stunnel, a transmat corridor, was planning to reach Arcturus II (*Transit*). Arcturus Six is habitable by humans, and was reached early on in human spacefaring days (*Love and War*). A Von Neumann probe landed on Arcturus and started to build a city, oblivious to the fact the planet was already inhabited (*The Big Hunt*). Humans settled Sifranos in the Arcturus Sector, although that colony was wiped out by the Daleks (*Lucifer Rising*). There were soon civil wars in the Earth colonies in Arcturus (*GodEngine*).

The Arcturans were at war with the Ice Warriors, who had fled Mars for Nova Martia, beyond Arcturus (*GodEngine*). A great Cyber fleet crashed on A54 in the Arcturus system ("Junkyard Demon"). The Sontarans fought the Battle of Arcturus (*Sontarans: Conduct Unbecoming*).

Arcturans helped to fund Checkley's World (*The Highest Science*) and won the Galactic Olympic Games on at least one occasion (*Destiny of the Daleks*). They were obsessed with profits and thought to be selfish (*Interference*). During the height of the Earth Empire, some Arcturans lived in the Overcities on Earth (*Original Sin*). They had only a few records of the Doctor (*The Doctor Trap*), although the Doctor, Rose and an Arcturan once "shared an experience" in a cellar (*The Day of the Troll*). The Navarinos named one model of time machine the "Arcturan Ultra-Pod" (*The Tomorrow Windows*). In the Terraphile Era, one popular reconstructed world is the howling terrace of Arcturus-and-Arcturus (*The Coming of the Terraphiles*).

Arcturus is twice mentioned in short stories not included in this chronology... "Only a Matter of Time"

ant race - were attempting to make off with the ship's drive. The *Brilliant* became locked in a time loop that always ended with its destruction. The Doctor extended the time loop to include the pirates themselves, defusing the situation.

Everyone assembled for a party, and the Doctor offered passengers and pirates alike a choice - stay on the time-looping ship forever, or let him return them to their war-torn homes. He and Martha danced to Grace Kelly, as supplied by Martha's iPod, while everyone decided.

Hostilities between humans and the Daleks flared up, and raged for over a hundred years.[1235] Following a galaxy-wide armistice, the Valdigians - a civilised insect species - created a system in which kings could only rule from age 23, with a provisional government ruling before then. The Valdigians limited the monarchy by electing children who agreed to stand down at age 22, in return for a generous pension.[1236] Cloning was discovered in the part of the galaxy containing Helhine.[1237]

The first human clone was created in 3922 using the Kilbracken holograph-cloning technique. The process was unreliable; the longest a clone ever lived was ten minutes, fifty-five seconds. Most serious scientists thought of it as "a circus trick of no practical value".[1238]

? 3906 - THE RESURRECTION CASKET[1239] -> The tenth Doctor and Rose arrived in an area of space, the Zeg, where electromagnetic pulses made conventional technology break down. The inhabitants - keen to mine the rare minerals found there - used steam and wind-powered spaceships instead. They became involved with the quest for the treasure of Hamlek Glint, who had a robot crew.

c 3907 - THE INFINITE QUEST[1240] -> The space pirate Baltazar attempted to convert the Earth's population into diamonds, but the tenth Doctor and Martha destroyed the ship with a rust fungus. Baltazar's robot parrot, Caw, set them on a quest to find *The Infinite* - a legendary ancient spaceship that could grant their heart's desire.

Their first destination was Boukan, a planet that supplied Earth's oil. The second was Myarr, which was the scene of a conflict between humanity and the Mantasphids. The third was on the coldest planet in the galaxy, the prison planet Volag-Noc. The Doctor obtained the co-ordinates of *The Infinite*, but the promised "heart's desire" was simply an illusion. Baltazar was exiled to Volag-Noc.

(*Doctor Who Annual 1968*) says that Arcturus is a swollen star, and that one fleet of hundreds of ships left the dying solar system "many thousands of years" ago. These Arcturans were an entirely peaceful race of frail four-armed birdlike creatures who could no longer fly due to gravity fluctuations. More whimsically, "The Mystery of the Marie Celeste" (*Doctor Who Annual 1970*) details how Greek god-like beings from Arcturus studied Earth and abducted the *Marie Celeste*.

1232 Dating *The Prisoner of Peladon* (BF CC #4.3) - It's been five years since *The Curse of Peladon*. The seventh Doctor says in *Legacy* (p90) that he's visited Peladon on "two occasions" - an acknowledgment of only the TV Peladon stories, not this story or *The Bride of Peladon*.

1233 Specified as "two thousand years" after *J&L: Chronoclasm*.

1234 Dating *The Pirate Loop* (NSA #20) - It is repeatedly said to be the "fortieth century". However, when the tenth Doctor and Martha visit the planet Hollywood in the late twenty-fifth century (in *Peacemaker*), the Doctor suggests (jokingly or otherwise) that their movie-watching options include *The Starship Brilliant Story*.

1235 *The Only Good Dalek.* See the dating notes on this story for possible reasons why other stories seem to contradict this.

1236 "Three for four generations" before *The Judgment of Isskar*.

1237 "Several centuries" after the latter part of *Cobwebs*, and a possible reference to the Kilbracken technique referred to in *The Invisible Enemy*.

1238 *The Invisible Enemy.* Clones are seen or referred to before this date in a number of subsequent stories such as *Heritage, Deceit, Trading Futures, Project: Lazarus, The Also People* and *So Vile a Sin.* Professor Marius distinguishes between the Kilbracken Technique, which instantly creates a "sort of three-dimensional photocopy", and a true clone that would take "years" to produce. *Heritage* also suggests cloning keeps periodically falling into disuse, whereupon another scientist will come forward and claim to have perfected the science for the "first" time.

1239 Dating *The Resurrection Casket* (NSA #9) - No date is given, although Galactic Seven spacecraft went out of service a century before the story. References to trisilicate would seem to place it around the time of the Galactic Federation (although trisilicate is also mentioned in *The Price of Paradise*, set in the twenty-fourth century). This date coincides with the space piracy prevalent in *The Infinite Quest*.

1240 Dating *The Infinite Quest* (*Totally Doctor Who* animated story) - Balthazar is "scourge of the galaxy and corsair King of Triton in the fortieth century".

c 3920 - SONTARANS: CONDUCT UNBECOMING[1241]

-> The Sontarans were now governed by a Grand Strategic Council composed of their greatest warriors, each of whom had survived six hundred battles. A kamikaze attack five years previous had greatly razed facilities on the Sontaran homeworld, Sontar, and prompted the building of underground installations. Sontaran forces conquered the human colony on Haigen V, claimed the uninhabited planet Jogana, and were engaged in a "three-way battle of Arcturus".

For two years, the Council had known that their cloning process had been producing inferior stocks, as their master template - that of General Sontar - had become too corrupt after centuries of use. General Kreel outmanoeuvred his rival, General Bestok, to become the new template.

The Daleks slaughtered a garrison on Alpha Millennia. Sixth months later, a Dalek space vessel was identified near Mars.[1242]

The Ood were native to the Ood-Sphere, a planet close to the Sense-Sphere. They were born with hand-held secondary brains (which functioned much like the amygdala in humans, processing memories and emotions), and were mentally connected by a giant Ood Brain. The Earth corporation Ood Operations established itself on the Ood-Sphere - it found the Ood Brain beneath the planet's Northern Glacier, and placed it within a telepathic inhibitor field. Many Ood were lobotomised, their secondary brains replaced with translator units. Before long, Ood were bred to be slaves, household servants and soldiers.[1243]

In 3932, **Zephon** became all-powerful in his own galaxy, the Fifth, when he defeated Fisar and the Embodiment Gris, both of which had tried to depose him.[1244]

& 3935 - THE MONSTER OF PELADON[1245] -> When

Federation scientists surveyed Peladon, they discovered that planet was rich in trisilicate: a mineral previously only found on Mars, and which was the basis of Federation technology. Electronic circuitry, heat shields, inert microcell fibres and radionic crystals all used the mineral. Duralinium was still used as armour-plating.

King Peladon had died and been replaced by his daughter, the child Thalira. As she grew up, Federation mining engineers came to her world. Although Thalira's people were resistant to change, advanced technology such as the sonic lance was gradually introduced to Peladon.

The Federation was subject to a vicious and unprovoked attack from Galaxy Five, who refused to negoti-

---

1241 Dating *Sontarans: Conduct Unbecoming* (BBV audio #27) - Maria, a fugitive of Haigen V, says, "To think... I'm a sophisticated fortieth century woman, and I'm reduced to throwing rocks." Later on, President Forrest claims that as prisoners, he and Maria should be treated according to the "Terran Treaty of 21,000", which we can only assume can't be a date.

1242 "Seventy years" before *The Daleks: "The Destroyers".* This seems to go against Cory's claim in *The Daleks' Master Plan* that the Daleks "haven't been active in our galaxy for some time now", although it's debatable as to what exactly constitutes "active", and whether Cory would be informed concerning (or think it relevant to mention) every minor Dalek incident.

1243 "Two hundred years" before *Planet of the Ood.* That story is set during the time of the Second Great and Bountiful Human Empire, but these events seem to predate it. The Doctor says it's an Empire "built on slavery", so perhaps this is one of the first steps in that process. The Sense-Sphere is the home of the titular characters from *The Sensorites.*

1244 *The Daleks' Master Plan*, with the date of 3932 given in *Neverland.* The entity is referred to as "the Embodiment Gris" in *The Daleks' Master Plan*, as "the Embodiment of Gris" in *The Dying Days* and *Neverland.*

1245 Dating *The Monster of Peladon* (11.4) - Sarah guesses that it is "fifty years" after the Doctor's first visit, and this is later confirmed by other people, including

the Doctor, Thalira and Alpha Centauri.

1246 Dating *The Blue Angel* (EDA #27) - No date is given, but the ship serves the Federation and is en route to Peladon.

1247 Dating "A Cold Day in Hell" (*DWM* #130-133) - According to the Doctor, "you Martians allied yourself to the Federation years ago", and this is after *The Monster of Peladon*, because Axaxyr and the events of that story are mentioned. These Martians were "born and bred on the frigid wastes of Mars", and they style A-Lux "New Mars", so it would seem to be their original planet that's uninhabitable.

1248 Dating "Redemption" (*DWM* #134) - This is Olla's native time, so the story is set shortly after "A Cold Day in Hell".

1249 Dating *Bang-Bang-A-Boom!* (BF #39) - No date is given, but the story is set in the Federation period.

1250 *War of the Daleks*

1251 *Legacy.* We learn that the Vogans were "ultimately self-destructive" and that the Cybermen eventually settled on a "New Mondas", as they wished to do in *Silver Nemesis.* However, this second homeworld has also been destroyed by the time of *Legacy.* The Cybermen survive to appear in *The Crystal Bucephalus.*

1252 In *The Daleks' Master Plan*, Mavic Chen seems to have been Guardian for a very long time. He says, when accused of stealing the taranium, "Why should I arrange that fifty years be spent secretly mining to acquire this

ate. The Federation armed for war, with Martian shock troops being mobilised. Peladon's trisilicate supplies would prove crucial in this struggle. The planet was still prone to superstition, however, and when the spirit of Aggedor began to walk once more, killing miners that used the advanced technology, many saw it as a sign that Peladon should leave the Federation. For a time, production in the mines halted.

The third Doctor and Sarah Jane exposed the murders as the work of a breakaway faction of Martians, led by Azaxyr, who were working for Galaxy Five. When the plot was uncovered, Galaxy Five quickly sued for peace.

c 3935 - THE BLUE ANGEL[1246] -> The eighth Doctor, Fitz and Compassion arrived on the Federation ship *Nepotist*, which was en route to Peladon. The crew discovered the Valcean City of Glass had become connected to the Federation through space-time corridors. As the glass city was located within the Enclave, a pocket universe within the larger Obverse, the Federation feared this could destablise the region.

The Doctor joined the Federation mission to meet the Glass Men, and also met their leader, Daedalus, a giant jade elephant who planned to make war with the Federation. Daedalus had opened up forty-three space-time corridors from the Enclave to planets such as Telosa, Skaro, Wertherkund and Sonturak. The *Nepotist* launched a preemptive strike with sonic cannons, shattering the Glass Men, but was counter-attacked by the Sahmbekarts, a race of lizards. The *Nepotist* crashed near the Valcean city, and the people of the Obverse rushed to defend their territory. The Doctor attempted to intervene, but Iris Wildthyme tricked him into leaving the area. He would never know how the situation was resolved.

c 3940 - "A Cold Day in Hell"[1247] -> Ice Lord Arryx and a small squad of Ice Warriors captured the weather control station on the pleasure planet A-Lux. They transformed A-Lux into an arctic wilderness, wiping out almost the entire population. The Martian homeworld was uninhabitable at this time, and Arryx - who opposed Martian membership of the Federation - wanted this to become a home base.

The seventh Doctor and Frobisher arrived and reversed the weather control, killing the Ice Warriors. Frobisher stayed behind to help the natives rebuild their lives, and the Doctor was joined by a young woman - Olla - that Frobisher had met.

& 3940 - "Redemption"[1248] -> The TARDIS was caught in the null beams of a Federation ship captained by the Vachysian Skaroux. Olla confided that she used to be Skaroux's servant. The seventh Doctor was shocked to

learn that her people, the Dreilyn, had no legal status in the Federation because they were heat vampires ... but this was a lie. Olla was Skaroux's consort, and had stolen all his money. The Doctor handed her over for trial.

? 3950 - BANG-BANG-A-BOOM![1249] -> The 308th Intergalactic Song Contest was broadcast to over a quinquillion homes across the universe. Contestants included the Architects of Algol ("Don't Push Your Tentacle Too Far"), the Angvia of the Hearth of Celsitor ("My Love is as Limitless as a Black Hole, and I'm Pulling You Over the Event Horizon"), the Breebles, the Cissadian Cephalopods, Cyrene, the Freznixx of Braal and Maaga 29 of Drahva ("Clone Love"). The jury included a Martian. Earth's national anthem at this time was "I Will Survive".

The matriarchal warlords of Angvia and the transcendental gestalt Gholos had been feuding for thirty generations. A peace conference between the two was supposedly being held on Achilles 4, but this was a feint for the real conference, which was taking place at the Song Contest on the Dark Space 8 station. A Gholos nationalist tried to disrupt the proceedings, but both sides sued for peace.

Earth discovered and surveyed the planet Antalin.[1250] In the mid-fortieth century, a "Cyber-fad" swept the Federation. The Martian archaeologist Rhukk proved that both Telos and New Mondas had been destroyed, meaning the Cyber Race had been eradicated. The public were briefly fascinated by the Cybermen. Documentary holovid crews went to the dead worlds of Voga and Telos.[1251]

In 3950, **Mavic Chen became the Guardian of the Solar System, ruling over the forty billion people living on Earth, Venus, Mars, Jupiter and the moon colonies from his complex in Central City. At this time, the prison planet Desperus was set up to house the most dangerous criminals in the solar system.**

Chen sought alternatives to the giant clock that enabled humanity to travel through hyperspace, and **established a secret mining operation to find taranium, "the rarest mineral in the universe", and which was found only on Uranus.** Taranium, he suspected, was the vital component for a device that could bend time akin to the giant clock. **Many in the solar system showed an almost religious devotion to Chen. His reputation was enhanced in 3975, when all the planets of the solar system signed a non-aggression pact. For the next twenty-five years, they lived in peace under the Guardianship, and the solar system - though "only part of one galaxy" - now had a status that was "exceptional... it had influences far outside its own sphere". It was hoped that by following Chen's example, peace would spread throughout the universe.**[1252]

? 3951 - IRIS: THE SOUND OF FEAR[1253] -> Iris Wildthyme met a man named Sam Gold at the Intergalactic Song Competition and wound up marrying him. On the night of their wedding, the Master Bakers of Barastabon took Iris out of time and tasked her with finding the six lost slices of the Celestial Gateaux. Six months later, Iris and Panda arrived on Radio Yesterday, a space station broadcasting golden oldies to Earth's colonies; Gold was the manager and DJ there. The evil Naxian hordes sought to strip a mood-altering harmonic into the Radio Yesterday broadcasts and make everyone in human space terribly depressed, paving the way for an invasion. The Naxian warlord made Iris, along with Gold, take him back to the 1960s in a bid to rewrite history. Iris returned after Panda had turned the Naxians' signals against them, and the ones aboard the station threw themselves out of the airlock.

After the Radio Yesterday incident, Iris and a Naxian named Roger had a relationship. While Iris was off galli-vanting around the cosmos, Roger and a Naxian beach-head were sent back to 2108.[1254]

Around 3970, the Hiinds overthrew the Mufls. The Reverend Lukas established The Church of the Way Forward, and preached that marriage between alien species was unholy.[1255] In 3972, Sirius-One-Bee University Press published Albrecht's *Of Finders and Seekers - a users guide to being lost in time.*[1256] Strantana was the site of an orbital mining facility that later became Station 7, where humans carried out experiments on Dalek artifacts.[1257]

(=) Circa 3979, emaciated, grotesque beings named the Unnoticed had constructed a Tent City, made from invulnerable taffeta, on the photosphere of Earth's sun and set about breeding a colony of human time sensitives there. Uncertain as to their origins, the Unnoticed used the time sensitives to keep watch for time distortion and time travellers - wary that contact with such phenomena could some-how avert their own creation. The human Carmodi Litian was born as one of the Unnoticed's sensitives and served for fifteen years before being left for dead on the planet Porconine. She swore revenge against her former masters.[1258]

mineral..." - which implies, but does not actually state, that he has been actively involved with the plot for half a century. Against this, *The Guardian of the Solar System* establishes that Chen started mining taranium for rea-sons entirely unrelated to the Daleks, and only joined the conspiracy after the destruction of the giant clock in 3999 threatens Earth's security - a time-table that's in keeping with his being named as the newest member of the conspiracy, its "most recent ally", in the TV story. *Neverland* cites 3950 as the year that Chen became Guardian of the Solar System.

The non-aggression pact is referred to in *The Daleks' Master Plan*. This perhaps suggests that planets in the solar system were in conflict before this time, and Chen's hope that peace will spread throughout the universe implies that much of known space is at war. A short scene in *Legacy* suggests that Chen did not become Guardian until much later.
1253 Dating *Iris: The Sound of Fear* (Iris audio #2.1) - Iris and Gold meet at an Intergalactic Song Contest won by Nicky Newman, who appears in *Bang-Bang-a-Boom!*, so the two stories must occur relatively close to one another. Tom is no longer travelling with Iris and Panda, as he suddenly fell in love with someone he met while they battled giant alien cockroaches.
1254 *Iris: The Two Irises*
1255 *Placebo Effect*
1256 *The Book of the Still*
1257 Probably some decades before *The Only Good Dalek*.
1258 Carmodi was born as one of the Unnoticed's sensitives thirty years before *The Book of the Still*. At the end of that novel, she paradoxically averts the creation of the Unnoticed, making it debatable whether these events occurred in the proper history or not.
1259 "Twenty years" before *Max Warp*.
1260 Dating "Deathworld" (*DWW* #15-16) - The Doctor explains in the framing sequence that the Ice Warriors "came from Mars thousands of years ago, then spread their conquests through the galaxy". Trisilicate is a min-eral that's only been found on Mars and Peladon by *The Monster of Peladon*, so this story is set after that. The two races don't recognise each other, and the Cybermen refer to the Cyberman Empire.

DO THE CYBERMEN EVER HAVE AN EMPIRE?: As they are the second best-known monsters to fight the Doctor, it's easy to assume that the Cybermen are sec-ond only to the Daleks when it comes to the power they wield and territory they control. Yet there's pre-cious little evidence for this in the televised stories.

We see or hear that at various points in history, humanity, Daleks, Sontarans, Rutans, Draconians, Mutts, Osirians, Tharils, Jagaroth, Skonnos, Movellans, Autons and even the Chelonians (according to *Zamper*) all control vast areas of our galaxy. Elsewhere in the uni-verse, races have achieved domination of an entire galaxy - in *The Daleks' Master Plan* alone, we meet eight delegates who each have total control of one of the Outer Galaxies. The Wirrn (*The Ark in Space*) dominated Andromeda until humanity drove them out. The win-ners, though, are... the Dominators, the masters of "ten galaxies" according to *The Dominators*. (They also state they control "the whole galaxy" that Dulkis is part of, but while it's not as impressive a boast, neither is it the

SECTION FOUR: FUTURE HISTORY

The Varlon Empire tried to establish itself in the Sirius system, and fought a war with the Kith - a highly advanced spore-producing, sponge-like race (each of which had four progenitors) in the neighbouring system. Both sides were nearly wiped out before a treaty was signed at Pluvikerr-Hinton. The Varlon were made to apologise and pay compensation for the ruination of the Kith home system.[1259]

? 3980 - "Deathworld"[1260] -> An Ice Warrior mission to Yama 10 scouted for trisilicate until a Cyberman spacecraft arrived to stake a rival claim. The Ice Warriors retreated to the polar areas and set a trap for the Cybermen, destroying them with rising water. As a last act of retaliation, the Cybermen buried the Ice Warriors in ice. The Martian commander, Yinak, remained con-

scious and waited patiently for the spring thaw.

Carrington Corp built the leisure planet Micawber's World between Pluto and Cassius around 3984.[1261]

c 3985 - LEGACY[1262] -> The Federation fought a number of wars to secure its position and to protect democratic regimes. GFTV-3 covered the main news stories of this era: atrocities on the Nematodian Border, the android warriors of Orion, slavery on Rigellon and Operation Galactic Storm. The Martian Star Fleet built the deep space cruiser *Bruk*, one of the largest vessels the galaxy had ever seen, and it helped enforce law throughout the galaxy.

With its trisilicate mines exhausted, Peladon faced a choice between becoming a tourist resort or leaving the

---

contradiction some reference sources seem to think.) Linx's boast (in *The Time Warrior*) that the Sontarans have subjugated every galaxy in the universe must surely only be rhetoric.

Away from the televised stories, there's a parallel universe where the Roman Empire has conquered the entire galaxy ("The Iron Legion"), and the Gubbage Cones (*The Crystal Bucephalus*), Cat-People (*Invasion of the Cat-People*) and Foamasi (*Placebo Effect*) are all stated to be or have been major galactic powers.

So what of the Cybermen? For the most part, their effectiveness as would-be galactic conquerors is tepid to say the least. In *Doomsday*, tellingly, an army of parallel-universe Cybermen that's millions strong is no match for four Daleks, and when Dalek reinforcements arrive, the Cybermen are routed in minutes.

Perhaps surprisingly, in the four decades since the Cybermen debuted, the most territory we ever actually see them control in a television story... is one planet, and it's their homeworld. In *The Tenth Planet*, they control Mondas, which is destroyed at the end of the adventure. After that, the best they manage is one complex on one planet - in *The Tomb of the Cybermen* and *Attack of the Cybermen*, they control their city on Telos. In every other story, we see only a small force launching a stealthy attack - usually with a larger army being held in reserve - and every story ends with the defeat or destruction of every single member of that army (with the possible exception of *Attack of the Cybermen*, where a base on the moon is mentioned and its fate isn't accounted for). In a number of stories (*The Tomb of the Cybermen*, *Revenge of the Cybermen*, *Earthshock*, *Attack of the Cybermen* and possibly *Silver Nemesis*) it's explicitly stated that the Cybermen are on the verge of extinction.

The audios *The Harvest* and *Sword of Orion* follow the same pattern. "A handful" survive in *Real Time*. The Cybermen fare no better in the books - in *Legacy*, the Federation thinks they're extinct. *Iceberg* and *Illegal Alien* feature a small group of isolated survivors. They're routed in *Killing Ground*, which ends - to compound

their problems - with a group of converted humans setting out to pick off any Cybermen they can find.

In *none* of these stories does anyone claim that the Cybermen have "an empire" or anything like it.

Despite all of this, there's some evidence in the *DWM* comic strips that the Cybermen *do* have an empire. "Deathworld" directly makes this claim (a Cyberman tells an Ice Warrior, "Why are you intruding on a planet of the Cybermen Empire?"), and "Throwback", while not making actual mention of an empire, shows the Cybermen at their most powerful. They're feared, with a futuristic city on Telos, vast space fleets and the military power to conquer whole worlds with ease. "Black Legacy" shows Cybermen of the same vein as those seen in "Throwback", but is difficult to date.

"Kane's Story" makes reference of a "Cyber-Emperor" and is set at a time when Davros is the Emperor of the Daleks - so it's between *Revelation of the Daleks* and *Remembrance of the Daleks* (or after "Emperor of the Daleks" and before *Remembrance of the Daleks*, if we take the other media into account).

The Cybermen are also powerful at the time of *Earthshock* (in 2526), and this chronology links that to their re-emergence from their tomb on Telos (the *Cybermen* audio series appears to do the same). So there may well be a Cyber Empire blossoming in the late twenty-fifth, early twenty-sixth century - although it seems to have fallen by the time of *Frontier in Space* (2540), presumably after their crushing defeat in the Cyber War. The seemingly formidable Twelfth Cyber Legion is seen in *A Good Man Goes to War* (set in the fifty-second century)... but the Doctor deals it an indeterminate amount of damage while learning Amy's location. Nonetheless, logic suggests that at least eleven other Cyber Legions must exist in this time zone, whatever their effectiveness.

1261 "Fifteen years" before *Placebo Effect*.
1262 Dating *Legacy* (NA #25) - The dating of this book is problematic. It has to be set after "3948", when a couple of the fictional reference texts cited were written (p37). The Doctor says that it is "the thirty-ninth centu-

Federation altogether. The question remained unaddressed while Queen Thalira ruled, but she died in a space shuttle accident. Within four years of her death, her successor King Tarrol applied to leave the Federation, suggesting that Peladon ought to try and find its own solutions to its problems. His choice had perhaps been made easier by the carnage caused when an ancient weapon, the Pakhar Diadem, was tracked to his world. The Diadem was blasted out of space by the *Bruk* and went missing.

Tarrol's decision probably saved Peladon - had the planet remained in the Federation, it would almost certainly have been targeted by the Daleks thirty years later during the Dalek War.

3985 - THEATRE OF WAR[1263] -> The colony of Heletia was founded by a group of actors wanting to stage the greatest dramas of the universe. Society on Heletia was confined to one small area of their own planet, but nonetheless became an expansionist power and fought a war with the Rippeareans. The Heletians believed that only races with a sophisticated theatre were truly civilised. Following the death of their leader, the Exec, the Heletians sued for peace.

By this point, Stanoff Osterling's play *The Good Soldiers* had been lost. Bernice, while travelling with the seventh Doctor and Ace, first visited the Braxiatel Collection - and met its founder, Irving Braxiatel - at this time.

Sara Kingdom was present when her brother Bret Vyon, age 18, received a commendation.[1264] The Daleks used time corridors to establish hibernation units on many planets such as Kar-Charrat. The Daleks would only activate when a time traveller entered range, and the Daleks hoped this gambit would help them gain access to the Kar-Charrat Library.[1265]

Bret Vyon had been bred on Mars Colony 16, and joined the Space Security Service (SSS) in 3990.[1266] Earth forces recaptured Caridos from the Daleks in '94 and took Robomen prisoners. On one of the worlds the Daleks had ravaged and abandoned, human researchers found deactivated Mechanoids.[1267] The artificial star of Tír na n-Óg was due to run out of fuel around this time.[1268]

c 3994 - THE DALEKS: "The Destroyers"[1269] -> The Daleks were the dominant form of life on Skaro, which was located in the eighth galaxy. They exterminated the crew of Explorer Base One, located on the giant meteorite M5, as the first phase of a gambit to destroy Earth and its colonies. Three Space Security Agents - Sara Kingdom, Jason Corey and the humanoid robot Mark Seven - attempted to rescue the sole survivor of the incident: David Kingdom, Sara's brother. The Daleks escaped in a rocket with David as their captive...

---

ry" (p55) and later narrows this down to the "mid-thirty-ninth century give or take a decade" (p84) [c.3850]. The novel is set "one hundred years" after *The Curse of Peladon* (p106), at a time when "young" Mavic Chen is still a minor official and Amazonia, who first appeared at the end of *The Curse of Peladon*, is the Guardian of the Solar System (p237) [so before 3950]. It is "thirty years" before a Dalek War that might well be *The Daleks' Master Plan* (p299) [therefore 3970] and "six hundred years" after *The Ice Warriors* (p89) [therefore 3600, favouring the dating of that story as 3000]. The book takes place a couple of months before *Theatre of War*, and as that book is definitely set in 3985, this last date has been adopted.
1263 Dating *Theatre of War* (NA #26) - The book is set soon after *Legacy* in "3985" (p1), a fact confirmed by Benny's diary ("Date: 3985, or something close", p21), and the TARDIS' Time Path indicator (p81).
Benny: The Wake confirms that Bernice (from her perspective) first visits the Braxiatel Collection and meets Irving Braxiatel "a thousand years" in the future of her native era. This is slightly hard to reconcile against the Benny audios, where events progress in rough symmetry with the *Gallifrey* series - meaning that Braxiatel in 2610 is aware of the oncoming Last Great Time War, and it's a bit hard to think that he toils away for another thousand years before finally shut-

ting the Collection down and returning home (in *Gallifrey: Mindbomb*). That said, there's no evidence that the Collection *isn't* active at the time of *Theatre of War*, even if nothing else is presently known about its status after 2610. In *Tales from the Vault*, the fourth Doctor identifies a painting that was stolen from the Braxiatel Collection "over two centuries ago" - he can't mean that amount of time before the story (which is set in 2002), and so must mean that long ago in his lifetime, suggesting the Collection is in operation at least that long.
1264 *The Drowned World*. The commendation is presumably unrelated to Vyon's tenure with the Space Security Service, and he didn't join until 3990 according to *The Daleks' Master Plan*. Using Nicholas Courtney's age as standard based upon when he played the role, Vyon would have been born in 3967, age 18 in 3985.
1265 "One thousand two hundred and seventy years" before *The Genocide Machine*.
1266 *The Daleks' Master Plan*
1267 *The Only Good Dalek*
1268 "Two thousand years" after *Cat's Cradle: Witch Mark* (p247).
1269 Dating *The Daleks: "The Destroyers"* (BF LS #2.2b) - According to Sara in *The Guardian of the Solar System* (set in 3999), this happens "Back when I'd first met the Daleks, so many years ago." In *The Daleks' Master Plan*, Sara doesn't indicate one way or another as to whether

Mavic Chen would later read Mark Seven's account of the incident.[1270] **Bret Vyon attained First Rank in the SSS in 3995, and Second Rank in 3998.**[1271]

3999 (July) - PLACEBO EFFECT[1272] -> The eighth Doctor and Sam attended the wedding of his former companions Stacy Townsend and Ssard on Micawber's World. Stacy and Ssard had settled in this timezone two years ago after leaving the Doctor. The Church of the Way Forward, who opposed interspecies weddings, crashed the ceremony but order was restored. Stacy and Ssard left to honeymoon on Kolpasha, the fashion capital of the Federation.

Micawber's World was hosting the Olympic Games, and scientist Miles Mason was secretly infecting athletes with Wirrn eggs disguised as performance enhancing drugs. The Wirrn hatched, and the Space Security Service was called in to contain the situation. The Doctor destroyed the Wirrn Queen, although one group of Wirrn escaped to Andromeda. The Olympic Games continued.

Earth at this time had a Royal Family. King Garth had just died; Queen Bodicha was in mourning, but the rest of the world was glad to see the back of him. His heir was Prince Artemis, Duke of Auckland. Some humans on Earth, but few offworlders, followed the tenants of Christianity. There were 1362 races in the Federation's database, but the Time Lords weren't one of them. The Foamasi were members of the Federation.

? 3999 - MAX WARP[1273] -> The Inter-G Cruiser Show was held at the Sirius Exhibition Station to showcase various spaceship models; it was hoped that the event would improve Varlon-Kith relations. Geoffrey Vantage - a war veteran, and now a presenter on the ten-year-old show *Max Warp* - had access to a computer virus developed late in the Varlon-Kith war, and planned to use it to make the Kith warfleet crash into one of Sirius' moons. The eighth Doctor and Lucie stopped Vantage; the Kith Oligarchy pledged to make a massive investment in the Varlon, and President Varlon (sic) used the influx of funds to abolish income tax. *Max Warp* became a lot more banal without Vantage to host it.

The planet Sirius Alpha had at least four moons. Varlon politicians used Spindroids to judge public opinion and help determine policy. Spaceships in this period included the new Kith Sunstorm, the Umbriel Slipstream (regarded by the Doctor as the sleekest, fastest spaceship ever constructed), the escape-pod-less Epsilon Nova 90, the Magellan Danube 4000, the Nebular Toscanini, the Umbriel Slipstream, the Freefall Sunstriker (which contained the same engine as the Moonstalk, but at a fraction of the cost), the Skythros Warpshock, the New Thorndon 90, and the antiquated Cobra Mark Three.

Spaceship design now incorporated quark drives, hyperion boosters, gamma burst regulators, catalytic filtration systems, residual dampeners, gravitic thrust converters, plasma outfits, tractor beams, hydrogen fuel filtration converters and a-line converters.

---

she's met the Daleks before.

"The Destroyers" was intended to serve as the pilot episode of a (ultimately unmade) Dalek TV show, the outline for which was first published in *The Official Doctor Who & the Daleks Book* (1988). The summation here reflects the Big Finish audio adaptation released in 2010. In both Nation's outline and the Big Finish version, matters are left very open ended - the SSS team fails to rescue the Daleks' captive (David in the audio story, Sara in the original outline), and while the Daleks threaten to destroy Earth, nothing is said about how they intend to accomplish this - or if it has any relation whatsoever to the Time Destructor plot central to *The Daleks' Master Plan*.

1270 *The Guardian of the Solar System*
1271 *The Daleks' Master Plan*
1272 Dating *Placebo Effect* (EDA #13) - The date is given. *Placebo Effect* states that Christianity is still practised on Earth in 3999, but Sara Kingdom - hailing from the year 4000 - hasn't heard of Christmas in *The Daleks' Master Plan*. Historically, not every version of Christianity has placed an emphasis on Christmas, though
1273 Dating *Max Warp* (BF BBC7 #2.2) - No specific year was intended by writer Jonathan Morris, who feared that a concrete dating might conflict with other

stories. However, mention of the Magellan Danube 4000 - touted as "a *man's* spaceship", and not a historical piece - suggests a dating in or around 3999, provided spaceships follow the tradition that car models are designated a year ahead of manufacture. The story occurs in the Sirius system, and the overall prosperity and warmth of the society seen here matches much better with the time of the Federation - and the holding of events such as the Intergalactic Olympics in *Placebo Effect* (also set in 3999) - than the corporate-minded gloom that seems to pervade Sirius in *The Caves of Androzani*.

The only other dating clue is a derogatory mention of the Moroks from *The Space Museum*. According to *The Death of Art*, the Morok Empire collapsed in the thirtieth century, so it's entirely possible that they'd be the subject of ridicule afterwards.

It's not entirely clear if the Varlons are related to humanity, although the presence of a "gin and tonic" might suggest some human influence, and it's generally assumed that the inhabitants seen in *The Caves of Androzani* (if they do indeed reside in Sirius) are human. Mention of "Pluvikerr-Hinton" is a little tribute to the late Craig Hinton and his obsession with the Gubbage Cones (the unnamed fungus creatures seen in *The*

The eighth Doctor, Fitz and Compassion tried to find a way into the Obverse in the Wandering Museum of the Verifiably Phantasmagoric, also known as the Museum of Things That Don't Exist.[1274]

The Daleks' Master Plan

3999 - THE GUARDIAN OF THE SOLAR SYSTEM[1275]

-> The first Doctor, Steven and Sara found themselves in 3999 - a year before they first met - at the giant clock that enabled humanity to travel through hyperspace. Sara's younger self was currently on Venus, part of a six-month posting. Mavic Chen continued to pursue a number of alternatives to the clock, hoping it could be slowly wound down without Earth going into decline. Chen was impressed upon meeting Sara, and - not comprehending that she was from the future - promoted her contemporary self to be part of his senior staff on Earth.

The clock ensnared the Doctor and Steven's minds into its network, and threatened to do the same to Sara - who realised that she was historically destined to wreck it. She reached out with her mind and brought the clock crashing down, enabling the travellers to escape...

The loss of the clock imperilled Earth's security so much that **Chen allied himself with the Daleks. In exchange for the taranium that he possessed, the Daleks would make him ruler of the entire galaxy. The Daleks recruited Zephon to their Master Plan, and he secured the** support of the rulers of two further galaxies, Celation and Beaus. The conspiracy also included Trantis, Master of the Tenth galaxy (the largest of the Outer Galaxies), Gearon, Malpha, Sentreal and Warrien.[1276]

c 4000 - MISSION TO THE UNKNOWN[1277] ->

"This is Marc Cory, Special Security Agent, reporting from the planet Kembel. The Daleks are planning the complete destruction of our galaxy together with powers of the Outer Galaxies. A war party is being assemb---"

In the year 4000, Chen attended an Intergalactic Conference in Andromeda. The Outer Galaxies and the Daleks held a council at the same time, sending Trantis to Andromeda to allay suspicion. The Space Security Service (SSS) and the UN Deep Space Force had been monitoring Dalek activity for five hundred years.

On the planet Kembel, SSS agent Marc Cory learned that the Daleks and their allies were preparing for conquest. Cory was exterminated, but not before recording a warning.

4000 - THE DALEKS' MASTER PLAN[1278] -> Shortly

after concluding a mineral agreement with the Fourth galaxy, Mavic Chen left Earth for a short holiday, or so he told the news service Channel 403. In reality, his Spar 740 spaceship headed through ultraspace to

---

Chase) from the planet Pluvikerr.
1274 *The Taking of Planet 5* (p13).
1275 Dating *The Guardian of the Solar System* (BF CC 5.1) - The year is given.
1276 The backstory to *The Daleks' Master Plan*, as catalysed by events in *The Guardian of the Solar System*. Writer Simon Guerrier has confirmed that the clock's destruction triggers a slow-acting erosion of Earth's shipping and security, not something as cataclysmic as, say, every road in the United States vanishing overnight. The matter-transportation experiment that teleports the Doctor, Steven and Sara (and a few mice) to Desperus in *The Daleks' Master Plan* is part and parcel of Chen's attempts to free Earth from its reliance on the giant clock.
1277 Dating *Mission to the Unknown* (3.2) - The story is set shortly before *The Daleks' Master Plan*.
1278 Dating *The Daleks' Master Plan* (3.3) - The date "4000" is established by Chen. The draft script for *Twelve Part Dalek Story* set it in "1,000,000 AD".
1279 *I am a Dalek*
1280 "Two centuries" before "Body Snatched".
1281 *War of the Daleks*. Not long after the death of an SSS agent called Marc, presumably Marc Cory from *Mission to the Unknown*. This throws the dating scheme

of the book out, as Antalin is the planet the Daleks will disguise as Skaro to be destroyed. But that, according to writer John Peel, will happen *before* this.
1282 *Storm Harvest*
1283 "Agent Provocateur"
1284 Dating *The Book of the Still* (EDA #56) - It's "4009" (p57).
1285 "Thirty years after" *Legacy* (p299), and possibly intended as a reference to events of or following *The Daleks' Master Plan*.
1286 Dating *The Only Good Dalek* (BBC original graphic novel #1) - Although it's never confirmed that the human officers seen here are part of the Space Security Service, they wear SSS uniforms as seen in *The Daleks' Master Plan*. Tellingly, when the Doctor says he knew Bret Vyon and Sara Kingdom, Tranter replies, "you must have started fighting Daleks when you were very young". As the eleventh Doctor outwardly looks about thirty, "very young" would have to mean when he was a teenager, so *The One Good Dalek* is most likely to be set around fifteen to twenty years after *The Daleks' Master Plan*. Helpfully, *Legacy* had established that a "massive Dalek war" was fought at about this time. One glitch is that the war is meant to have "raged for a hundred years", which is explicitly not the case in *The Daleks'*

Kembel, the Daleks' secret base. There, he met the delegates from the Outer Galaxies for the first time, and presented the Daleks with a full emm of taranium - enough to power their Time Destructor, a device capable of accelerating time.

Space Security Agents were sent to investigate the disappearance of Marc Cory. One of them, Bret Vyon, allied with the first Doctor, Steven and Katarina. They stole the taranium and absconded with Chen's ship, which was diverted to the convict planet Desperus. The group escaped, but a convict smuggled himself aboard the Spar and took Katarina hostage. To end the standoff, she blew both of them out of an airlock.

The Doctor, Steven and Vyon reached Central City on Earth, where Vyon was killed by Sara Kingdom - his sister and a fellow SSS agent, who believed him a traitor. Pursued, the Doctor and Steven broke into a research facility. They were transported with Sara across the galaxy, via an experimental teleportation system, to the planet Mira - the home of invisible monsters named the Visians. Sara came to side with the Doctor against Chen, and the group returned to the Daleks' base on Kembel. They fled through time and space in the TARDIS, with the Daleks in pursuit.

Chen was ready to doublecross the Daleks, and had special forces on Venus ready to occupy Kembel. Eventually, the Daleks re-captured the taranium, and they exterminated their allies - including Chen - in readiness for universal domination. They had assembled the "greatest war force ever assembled", including an assault division of five thousand Daleks to invade Earth's solar system. The Doctor activated the Daleks' Time Destructor, which destroyed their army and transformed the surface of Kembel from lush jungle to barren desert in seconds. Sara helped the Doctor and was aged to death. The universe was safe once more.

Earth was under totalitarian rule. Humans were "bred", and told not to question orders. Christmas was not celebrated or even remembered.

The expression "never turn your back on a dead Dalek" came into use among humans.[1279] In the forty-first century, mankind developed vegetable life that resembled humans - Bio-Organic Plasmatoid Creations, a.k.a. Biogrowers - and used them as servants. Biogrowers lived for a hundred years, but were brain dead after fifty. The braindead Biogrowers were dumped on the planet hospital Bedlam, which was patterned after the original sanatorium.[1280]

SSS agent Dryn Faber investigated the planet Antalin and discovered Daleks there.[1281] Earth was involved in a number of wars on the frontier of Earthspace. The Daleks massacred the colonists on a mining outpost.[1282] The Sycorax Tribe of Astrophia died out in the Valhalla Wars of the forty-first century.[1283]

4009 - THE BOOK OF THE STILL[1284] -> About this time, TimeCorp offered its employees the plus of completing their workday, then temporally returning to the morning for family time. Participating TimeCorp workers aged a third faster than their families every day, but got to spend more time with their loved ones.

The temporal expert Albrecht managed to retroactively wipe himself from existence, but his diaries survived in a reality pocket. His theories gave rise to the condition Albrecht's Ennui, which affected temporally displaced people who went a few years without time travel.

The affluent, distant planet Lebenswelt settled into a state of hedonism and decay, as nobody would voluntarily travel so far to perform menial tasks. The IntroInductions escort service on Lebenswelt used illegal fast-acting memory acids to make kidnapped humans fall in love with their clients. Lebenswelt also became home to the Museum of Locks (*Das Museum der Verriegelungen*), which almost incidentally guarded a copy of *The Book of the Still*.

(=) In 4009, the Unnoticed desired to examine the *Book* because it mentioned their Tent City on the photosphere of Earth's sun. The eighth Doctor, Fitz and Anji discovered that the Unnoticed were the product of a closed time loop. By touching the time sensitive Carmodi, the Doctor accidentally caused the time loop to unleash waves of "soft time", which mutated IntroInductions founders Darlow, Gimcrack and Svadhisthana into a twisted gestalt creature that would give rise to the Unnoticed. When the newly created gestalt made contact with the Unnoticed, it both destroyed the Unnoticed and flung the gestalt back in time to become the Unnoticed.

Shortly afterwards, Carmodi departed with the *Book* and retroactively planted a bomb aboard the Unnoticed's spaceship, thus prematurely destroying them and averting the closed time loop altogether.

Around 4015, a massive Dalek War split the Federation. Upon the war's completion, the organisation was forced to re-evaluate itself.[1285]

c 4015 - THE ONLY GOOD DALEK[1286] -> The human soldier Tranter attained over ten years of frontline service, received the Mercury Medal with stars and moons, and was the hero of the fall of Pythagoran. He was reported killed at the siege of Logario, but was actually captured by the Daleks and conditioned to act as their sleeper agent. Tranter was allowed to escape, and subsequently became the commander of Station 7.

Station 7 now contained a conglomeration of items related to the Daleks, including a section of petrified jungle (complete with live Slythers and Varga plants) recovered from the ruins of Skaro. The station also held captive

Ogrons and Robomen, as well as ten Dalek prisoners who could only move on static electrified pathways. Human scientists aboard the station laboured to harness Dalek technology, but were frustrated because it only worked for Daleks. The station's chief scientist, Weston, had worked for years to change the nature of the Daleks, hoping to make them less aggressive so they would operate Dalek technology on behalf of humans. The culmination of his efforts was The Only Good Dalek: a genetically engineered Dalek mutant thought to have respect for other life.

Two months after Tranter took charge of Station 7, the eleventh Doctor and Amy arrived there as the Daleks, having learned about The Only Good Dalek and deeming it an abomination that had to be terminated, attacked Station 7 in spaceships disguised as asteroids. Commander Tranter, Weston and The Only Good Dalek sacrificed themselves to destroy the Daleks. The sole survivor, a human agent named Jay, returned with Weston's data to Earth Central...

where other Dalek agents were in positions of power, and arranged for Jay's ship to be destroyed en route. The Doctor told Amy that the ingenuity, bravery, love and hope that had spurred the creation of Weston's data would help Earth prevail.

The Colonial Marines raided Dalek strongholds in the 4020s.[1287] Kinzhal, a future general of the Icelandic Alliance, earned medals in the forty-second century.[1288] **The Sontaran Strax was born around 4025.**[1289] The Doctor established an account with Trans-Universal Union, which held his mail in a stasis drawer until he collected it.[1290]

& 4030 - THE BRIDE OF PELADON[1291] -> On Peladon, the people no longer believed in Aggedor worship, and Queen Elspera - the daughter of King Paladin and Beladonia - dissolved the church upon her ascent to the

---

Master Plan - although a case can be made that this war against the Daleks is more covert than not. (*The Only Good Dalek* only talks about frontier worlds being ravaged by the Daleks, so perhaps this is a war fought on the edge of Earth space rather than at its heart.) Alternatively, the Daleks in this story are the "new paradigm" Daleks first seen in *Victory of the Daleks*, so it's possible they have inserted themselves into history at this point. Mention of the high-ranking security officer "Silestru" is possibly meant to denote Georgi Selestru from *Dalek Empire III*, but has to be taken as a different character with a similar name.

1287 *Prime Time.* Reg Gurney has been in space corps for "thirty years".

1288 *Emotional Chemistry*

1289 He's "nearly 12" in *A Good Man Goes to War*.

1290 "A few hundred years" before the forty-fifth century segment of "Body Snatched".

1291 Dating *The Bride of Peladon* (BF #104) - It's "nearly a century" after *The Monster of Peladon*.

Peladon stops being a member of the Federation in *Legacy* - something that the seventh Doctor greets as good news, because it means Peladon will be left out of a Dalek conflict set to occur thirty years afterwards. It's entirely possible that by *The Bride of Peladon* - set roughly fifteen years after said conflict - Peladon has already re-entered the Federation or is at least considering it. Only one statement in *The Bride of Peladon* is made about Peladon's Federation status, when Alpha Centauri says that "Galactic peace is certain and Peladon's place in the Federation is assured" once the king marries Pandora. This can either be interpreted as suggesting that Peladon is about to return to the Federation fold, or just hopes to solidify its spot in the group's hierarchy.

If Aggedors have a century-long gestation cycle, it's little wonder that they're so rare and prized. That said,

the pregnancy of the female Aggedor seen here - the daughter of the one seen on TV - raises the rather incestuous question of who sired her pups. (Appalling as it might sound, however, father-daughter and mother-son matings are not uncommon when breeding animals such as horses; genetic deficiencies only start to crop up with brother-sister crossings.)

1292 Dating *A Good Man Goes to War* (X6.7) - The date is given in a caption. We know nothing else about this battle, save that one of the sides fighting is human.

1293 Dating "Hotel Historia" (*DWM* #394) - The month and year are given.

1294 THE EARTH EMPIRES: That the first Earth Empire lasted from the twenty-sixth century of *Frontier in Space* to the thirtieth of *The Mutants* has been well documented, particularly in the New Adventures. (The Doctor's companion Benny is from the Empire's early period, Ace lived in that time zone for a few years, and his later companions Chris and Roz were from the period when the Empire was starting to collapse.)

The Second Empire was first named in *Tomb of Valdemar*. The Doctor refers to the Second Great and Bountiful Human Empire in *Planet of the Ood* (set in 4162), *Pest Control*, *The Story of Martha*: "The Weeping", and by extension *The Impossible Planet/The Satan Pit* and *42*. *The Crystal Bucephalus* states that descendants of Mavic Chen became Federation Emperors, and it might be this Empire that they rule.

"A Fairytale Life" has the Doctor expecting to find the Third Great and Bountiful Human Empire in the seventy-eighth century. This could well be the human empire mentioned in *The Sontaran Experiment*.

The Long Game is set, in theory at least, at the time of The Fourth Great and Bountiful Human Empire, but the Emperor Dalek's machinations appear to alter history, and the apparent obliteration of Earth's continents (*The Parting of the Ways*) casts doubt on whether this Empire

throne. Elspera was thought to have been thrown from her horse on a hunting expedition and died, whereupon her son Pelleas became king. In actuality, the imprisoned Sekhmet the Avenger had killed Elspera - as well as the Martian ambassador Alyxlyr - because the blood of four royal females was required to unlock Sekhmet's bonds.

Earth sought to strengthen ties with Peladon, and arranged a marriage between Pelleas and the Earth princess Pandora. Sekhmet murdered Pandora, but failed to make the fifth Doctor's companion Erimem her fourth victim. The new Martian ambassador, Prince Zixlyr, blew up Sekhmet - and himself - with a Xanathoid Volatiser.

A female Aggedor had survived in secret for one hundred fifty years, and birthed new Aggedors after a century of pregnancy. Alpha Centauri assisted in the capture of the master Arcturan criminal Arktos - a.k.a. the Scourge of the Nine Worlds, the Silver Assassin and the Death Merchant.

Erimem found Peladon very agreeable to her former way of life, and decided to leave the fifth Doctor and Peri and marry Pelleas.

4037 - A GOOD MAN GOES TO WAR[1292] -> The eleventh Doctor called in a debt from Strax, a Sontaran Commander who had been demoted to battlefield nurse. As part of his atonement, Strax was helping humans during the Battle of Zaruthstra.

4039 (January) - "Hotel Historia"[1293] -> The Graxnix invaded Earth, damaging London and Big Ben. The tenth Doctor was captured, but escaped down a time corridor to the Hotel Historia in 2008. The Graxnix followed and brought back a Chronexus 3000 device - which, as the Doctor intended, nullified the Graxnix from making any

further change to history. They were left intangible and invisible.

The Second Great and Bountiful Human Empire[1294]

Mavic Chen's descendants eventually ended democracy in the Federation. The Chen dynasty of Federation Emperors ruled for thousands of years.[1295] The Second Empire rose, with its origins on the human colony world of Dephys. The cruel, oppressive Elite ruled it.[1296]

c 4106 - THE IMPOSSIBLE PLANET / THE SATAN PIT[1297] -> Humans continued to use the Ood as a slave race. The Ood seemed willing to be treated as such, but the Friends of the Ood organisation campaigned for their freedom. The Neo-Classic Congregational denomination didn't have a devil as such, but acknowledged that evil resided in the actions of men.

The tenth Doctor and Rose arrived on an unnamed planet which was set in an impossible orbit around the black hole K37Gem5.[1298] The scriptures of the Veltong named the world as Krop Tor - "the bitter pill" - and claimed the black hole was a demon that had swallowed the planet and spit it out.

Sanctuary Base 6, manned by people from the Torchwood Archive, monitored the anomaly. Beneath the planet was the Beast, a creature imprisoned before our universe was created. It influenced the Ood slaves to help engineer its release, but the Doctor prevented this. Krop Tor and the Beast's body fell into the black hole, as did the Beast's mind - which had taken root in the base's head of archaeology, Toby Zed.

---

ever comes to pass. If Rose reset all the actions of the Daleks, Earth's history could be restored to the one the Doctor knows about, but there's no evidence on screen she did that.

Either way, the overwhelming amount of evidence suggests that Earth survives and continues to have great influence on the universe, at least for billions of years into the future (*The End of the World*). It's probable, then, that there's a fifth and many more Empires after this point.

1295 *The Crystal Bucephalus*

1296 *Tomb of Valdemar*

1297 Dating *The Impossible Planet/The Satan Pit* (X2.8-2.9) - Casualties in this story are repeatedly said as dying on "43K2.1". If the numbers mean anything we could interpret, the "K" perhaps suggests a date in the 43,000s. In the DVD commentary, Russell T Davies says the draft script stated it was the forty-third century. The overriding consideration, however, is that the story presumably happens before the Ood are liberated

from slavery (*Planet of the Ood*, set in 4126). *Doctor Who: The Encyclopedia* and *Doctor Who: The Time Traveller's Almanac* both concur with that, dating events with the Beast to "the forty-second century". *Timelink* goes for an earlier dating of 4043. The Doctor's assertion they are "five hundred years" from Earth would seem to mean five hundred light years *or* that it would take the humans here five hundred years to get to Earth.

The Doctor previously encountered life from before the creation of our universe in *Terminus*, *Millennial Rites*, *All-Consuming Fire*, *Synthespians™*, and more.

1298 Commonly referenced as "K37J5", but it's "K37Gem5" in the closed captioning on the DVD - and indeed, that *is* what it sounds like Cross Flane is saying. (This is possibly the same dating system that starts inserting words like "apple" into year designations, as in *The End of the World*.)

& 4120 - ORBIS[1299] **->** The eighth Doctor had pleasantly spent six centuries in the company of the jellyfish-like Keltons who resided on Orbis, and had introduced to them the tradition of celebrating the dead with a funeral-feast, having noticed that the Keltons' habit of eating and regurgitating their deceased wasn't a very efficient way to compost the seabed. Orbis' troposphere was progressively changing, owing to influence of a passing moon.

The Molluscari, a race of aggressive space-oysters who could change gender, thought the waters of Orbis would make an ideal breeding ground... and the Keltons would make an excellent source of protein. The Molluscari leader, Crassostrea, had previously massacred the Tetraploids.

The Galactic Council had rejected a Molluscari claim to Orbis a few years ago, but now ruled in their favour, having determined that the Keltons' ownership of the planet wasn't tenable due to the recent climate changes. The Headhunter arrived in the TARDIS with Lucie from 2009, having struck a bargain with the Molluscari. In return for their retrieving the activator to Morbius' stellar manipulator, she was to coerce the Doctor into leaving Orbis by threatening Lucie's life.

The passing moon proved to be Morbius' stellar manipulator, which had been drawn to Orbis by the presence of the activator. The manipulator's approach made the oceans on Orbis boil; Crassostrea spawned while the Molluscari went into a feeding frenzy and attacked the Keltons. The Doctor and Lucie escaped in the TARDIS just as the manipulator crashed into Orbis - obliterating it, the Molluscari and the surviving Keltons.

The Headhunter pocketed the activator and returned to her warship. She used the activator to slave the stellar manipulator to Lucie's DNA - it would shadow the TARDIS through the Vortex, and emerge near Earth in 2015.[1300]

4126 - PLANET OF THE OOD[1301] **->** A member of the Friends of the Ood infiltrated Ood Operations on the Ood-Sphere, and reduced the telepathic dampener around the Ood Brain. Many Ood on the planet became lethal - as indicated by their red eyes - and instigated a rebellion. Ood Sigma, the personal assistant to the head of Ood Operations - Klineman Halpen - had been lacing Halpen's hair-restorer with Ood-graft for years, causing Halpen to fully transform into an Ood. The tenth Doctor and Donna helped to fully liberate the Ood Brain, and so the entire Ood species. A telepathic call summoned the enslaved Ood home. The Ood promised to honour the Doctor and Donna's names in song forever.

The unit of currency at this time was the credit; an Ood cost fifty credits. Earth was "a bit full", but the Second Great and Bountiful Empire, "a great big empire built on slavery", stretched over three galaxies (the "tri-Galactic"). There were vidphones.

c 4142 - 42[1302] **->** The tenth Doctor and Martha answered a distress call originating from the Terrachi system, located half a universe away from Earth. The engines of the spaceship *Pentallian* had failed, and it was falling into the nearest sun. Crewmember Korwin

1299 Dating *Orbis* (BF BBC7 #3.1) - The Doctor and the Headhunter confirm that he's been on Orbis "six hundred years or thereabouts". The plotline with the activator continues in *The Eight Truths/Worldwide Web*.
1300 *Orbis, The Eight Truths, Worldwide Web.*
1301 Dating *Planet of the Ood* (X4.3) - The Doctor first says that the Ood are "servants of humans in the forty-second century", then gives the exact year.
1302 Dating *42* (X3.7) - While no date is given on screen, prepublicity for the episode said it was set in the forty-second century - possibly just as a take-off on the title. Nonetheless, the Doctor's spacesuit bears the same design as the one he wore in *The Impossible Planet/The Satan Pit*, perhaps indicating that all three episodes take place in roughly the same time.
1303 "Centuries" before *Destiny of the Daleks*.
1304 *The Story of Martha*: "The Weeping"
1305 Dating *The Last Voyage* (BBC *DW* audiobook #6) - Earth currently has an empire, but as Eternity has a population of eight billion humans, this is well in advance of the struggling Earth Empire as seen in the Pertwee era. The only other historical clues are that a) robots are in use, b) a straight-shot flight from one end of the Empire to another is considered advanced (so

presumably, standard spaceships aren't too shabby either), and c) human longevity is such that Cluxton is 160, and is spry enough to undertake pioneering business ventures involving space transport. With all of that in mind, this story has been arbitrarily set during the Second Empire.
1306 Dating *Pest Control* (BBC *DW* audiobook #1) - The Doctor identifies the Pioneer Corps soldiers as being part of the Second Great and Bountiful Human Empire.
1307 Dating "Body Snatched" (IDW *DW* Vol. 2, #10-11) - It's "two hundred years" before the opening of "Body Snatched", which is set in the "forty-fifth century".
1308 Dating *The End of Time* (X4.17) - It's been "one hundred years" since the Doctor's last visit (*Planet of the Ood*).
1309 Dating *The Death Collectors* (BF #109a) - The participants seem human; not only do they possess such names as "Nancy" and "Smith Ridley", the sky station's computer has Puccini's "Madame Butterfly" in its music collection. No date is given, and so placement here amounts to little more than a guess, but the overall tone suggests it's a story where mankind has simply ventured so far into space, it's encountering horrors beyond its comprehension. Dar Traders also appear in

succumbed to an alien influence, becoming a being of burning light who proceeded to kill other crewmembers. The Doctor realised the star was alive - it felt violated because the ship had illegally mined it for fuel. The living particles were ejected from the scoops, which restored the sun and saved the ship.

The Daleks encountered a new threat: the Movellans, a race of humanoid androids from system 4X-Alpha-4. The Daleks were forced to abandon all operations elsewhere in the galaxy, including Skaro, and mobilise a huge battlefleet. The mighty Dalek and Movellan fleets faced each other in space, their battlecomputers calculating the moment of optimum advantage. This created an instant stalemate, and not a shot was fired for centuries. The vast Dalek Fleet was kept completely occupied, except for the occasional raiding mission on Outer Planets such as Kantria for slave workers, or on the starships of Earth's Deep Spacefleet.[1303]

Two thousand settlers from Earth established themselves on the planet Agelaos, and it became one of the most remote outposts of the Second Great and Bountiful Human Empire. Agelaos was located near a wormhole that granted the settlers with psionic abilities - but then mutated them into monsters. A beacon warned travellers to stay away from the planet.[1304]

? 4150 - THE LAST VOYAGE[1305] -> Inter-dimensional entities implanted the blueprints for a new type of interstellar engine into the mind of Joseph Sterns Cluxton, a 160-year-old billionaire, fostering the technology as a means of invading our reality. Within three years, Cluxton had used the designs to build the first Interstitial Transportation Vehicle (ITV).

The ITV made its maiden voyage across the longest stretch of humanity's empire - from Earth to the planet Eternity, home to eight billion humans - and its engines transported those aboard to the entities' dimension. The tenth Doctor returned everyone home, and permanently wrecked the ITV's engines.

In this era, robots were used for food preparation and other menial tasks.

c 4200 - PEST CONTROL[1306] -> Giants living in the Pettingard system came under threat from the Serfians - a large beetle-like species that reproduced by implanting eggs in other races. The Sharback Corporation built 25-metre-tall robots to combat the infestation, but the robots indiscriminately wiped out the giants and Serfians alike.

People of mixed human/alien heritage currently existed in the outer worlds of Earth's solar system. Human soldiers in the Pioneer Corps, a military arm of the Second Great and Bountiful Human Empire, invaded the planet Rescension. War broke out with the centaurs who lived there, the Akwabi, but a further infestation of Serfian eggs threatened to transform both sides into Serfian drones. The tenth Doctor and Donna intervened, and the Serfian queens were killed. It was expected that the surviving drones would be no threat without their leadership, and that the humans and Akwabi would rebuild the planet.

c 4211 - "Body Snatched"[1307] -> Dr Rubin, a scientist on the planet hospital Bedlam, developed Transmigratory Memory Mapping: a means by which minds could be transplanted into disused Biogrower bodies, according another fifty years of life. The Horse Lord of Khan wanted to go further and put his mind into a Time Lord body - to that end, he summoned his old friend, the Doctor. The eleventh Doctor, Amy and Rory found that Rubin had been testing his mind swap on different races, including a Re'nar, a Ju'wes, a Saturnynian, a Slitheen, a Sycorax and a Gizhou. Confusion followed... the Doctor and Amy accidentally swapped consciousnesses, and the Biogrowers were induced with schizophrenia, triggering a riot. The time travellers incapacitated the Horse Lord, ended the riot and returned to their own bodies - moments before Rory, thinking his wife was still in the Doctor's form, gave "her" a passionate kiss.

4226 - THE END OF TIME (TV)[1308] -> The tenth Doctor answered a summons to Ood-Sphere, and was shocked to see how developed the planet had become in the hundred years since his last visit. The mind of the Ood was troubled, and they showed him their dreams of the Master. Time was bleeding, and events on Earth in 2009 were affecting everything...

? 4300 - THE DEATH COLLECTORS[1309] -> The volcanic planet Antikon was quarantined after it became the source of Antikon's Decay - a lethal virus that decimated a solar system. Professor Mors Alexandryn, the foremost authority on the Decay, headed a research team in a sky station over Antikon. They encountered a spacefaring race called Dar Traders, a.k.a. the Death Collectors, who typically scavenged corpses after battles. The Dar Traders were technically dead, and used metal frames to move their husks around. They could preserve the last few moments of life in other species by introducing their own flesh to the dead.

The seventh Doctor found that the Decay was an alien intelligence that existed as a virus and trying to communicate through "a death state" - not comprehending that this was inimical to other species. The mass of Decay on Antikon increased exponentially upon contact with the Dar Traders, but Alexandryn gave his life to the Decay, peacefully dragging them both into death.

In 4302, Elliot Sardick was born on a human colony world near the Horsehead Nebula. His family had given their name to the main settlement, Sardicktown; the first settlers there referred to mid-winter as the Crystal Feast. As an adult, he would gain even more power than his ancestors and have a son, Kazran. The currency on Sardicktown was the gideon.[1310]

The Thals were driven off Skaro by the Daleks.[1311]

In 4338, Turlough was the guest of Wilhelm, König of the Wine Lords of Chardon.[1312] The railway network was reestablished in Europe.[1313]

c 4340-& 4347/(=) c 4340-& 4347 (Christmas Eve) - A CHRISTMAS CAROL[1314] -> Kazran Sardick was physically abused by his father, Elliott, and would grow up to become someone who didn't care if people lived or died. To teach Kazran Sardick the error of his ways, the eleventh Doctor travelled back to Christmas Eve when Kazran was 12. Kazran had been trying to make a video project about the sky fish that flew around Sardicktown, and the Doctor helped to disprove Kazran's belief that he was alone in a cruel world. The Doctor tried to attract the sky fish, but instead attracted a sky shark.

To transport the shark back to its natural habitat, Kazran suggested they borrow a hibernation unit from the vaults where his father kept people in suspended animation as debt-collateral. They opened the cryo-pod of Abigail Pettigrew, and her singing calmed the shark. She was returned to suspended animation, but Kazran was now smitten.

> (=) The Doctor returned for Kazran and Abigail each of the next seven Christmas Eves. They went for a sleigh ride with the flying shark, to the Egyptian pyramids, Uluru, the Eiffel Tower, the Statue of Liberty, to visit Abigail's family and a pool party in 1952 Hollywood. Abigail, though, was terminally ill, and had one more day to live. Kazran remained convinced the world was unfair.

The Doctor's efforts to rehabilitate Kazran failed, and so he took his 12-year-old self forward in time to see the miser he had become...

The Darkening Eye.

1310 *A Christmas Carol.* The date is given on Elliot's portrait.

1311 "Centuries" before *The Davros Mission*, and probably explaining why the Doctor blows up Skaro in *Remembrance of the Daleks* without fear of eradicating the Thals as well.

1312 *The Crystal Bucephalus* (p42).

1313 "Centuries" before *Emotional Chemistry*.

1314 Dating *A Christmas Carol* (X6.0) - The Doctor first meets Kazran Sardick (from Kazran's perspective) when Kazran is 12, but the precise year isn't given. Elliot Sardick was born in 4302, so couldn't have a 12-year-old son until, say, 4332 at the earliest (and while he has dark hair; Elliot's clearly at least middle aged at this point). The older Kazran was played by Michael Gambon, who was 68 at the time, so we can infer that Kazran is around 70 in the "present day". The Doctor then revisits Kazran on seven successive Christmas Eves.

1315 "Twenty years" before *A Christmas Carol*; the year of Elliot's death is on his portrait.

1316 *Spiral Scratch*

1317 Dating *A Christmas Carol* (X6.0) - We're told Elliot Sardick died "twenty years" before the story, and a plaque below his portrait states he died in 4378. In *SJA: Death of the Doctor*, the Doctor mentions a seemingly unrelated incident in which he dropped Amy and Rory off on a "honeymoon planet" that as it turned out was itself on a honeymoon, having married an asteroid.

1318 *Red.* "The Needle" in this story is not the same one as the Needle in *The Infinity Doctors*. The time-

travel process described here is similar to the early Gallifreyan experiments (as detailed in *Cat's Cradle: Time's Crucible*).

1319 Dating "Body Snatched" (IDW *DW* Vol. 2, #10-11) - It's the "forty-fifth century" according to the opening caption.

1320 Dating "Keepsake" (BF #112b) - The Doctor says that it's "nearly two thousand years" since *Kingdom of Silver*.

1321 *Only Human*

1322 Dating *Here There Be Monsters* (BF CC #3.1) - The back cover says it's the "distant future". Mention is made of yet another "human empire", but in itself, this isn't very telling. Rostrum says he doesn't know the year in Earth terms - a pity, as that would've been helpful.

"Benchmarking" has here been linked to the "dirty rip" engines mentioned in *Only Human*, as they seem to work on roughly the same principle. That would make this "empire" the Second Great and Bountiful Earth Empire.

It's unclear if the tentacled "deep space" creatures seen here are an evolved form of the Yssgaroth from *The Pit*, which were similarly loosed on our reality after Rassilon punched holes in the fabric of space-time. *Tomb of Valdemar* also alludes to similar creatures, and this chronology places the two stories at roughly the same time.

1323 Dating *Tomb of Valdemar* (PDA #29) - No date is given, but this is within a generation of the fall of the Second Empire. Since the last edition of *Ahistory*, which placed this story in 16,000, *Planet of the Ood* established that the Second Great and Bountiful Human

Elliot Sardick's machine to control the cloud bank over Sardicktown was finally completed. It had isomorphic controls that only responded to Elliot or his son Kazran. Elliot Sardick died in 4378.[1315]

```
= The sixth Doctor visited the planet Schyllus in 4387.[1316]
```

4398 (Christmas Eve) - A CHRISTMAS CAROL[1317] -> The eleventh Doctor left Amy and Rory to honeymoon aboard a galaxy-class starship, but they summoned him back when the ship went out of control near Sardicktown, a human colony world surrounded by a cloud bank. The ship could only be guided to safety by a machine operated by Kazran Sardick - but Sardick was a cruel man, and refused to help. The Doctor travelled back to Kazran's childhood and altered his history to make him a better person. When this failed, he brought Kazran's 12-year-old self to this time to see his future. The elder Kazran relented, but his history had been altered so much that the cloud-controlling machine no longer recognised him. The Doctor and Kazran woke Abigail Pettigrew for one last time, and she used her voice to create harmonics that controlled the clouds and saved the spacecraft.

The forty-fifth century was an era of technocrats and machine-driven life. One race engineered a biological-temporal link that enabled them to forge a mental connection with their machines. Some members of the species became biologically advanced enough to place themselves in metallic shells and time travel by simply willing the process. One such traveller was Celia Fortunaté, who would arrive in another time period at the Needle, a bio-mechanical living complex. The Needle's overseeing computer, Whitenoise, installed a chip in Celia to curb her of all violence, but this corrupted Whitenoise's systems and led to a string of murders.[1318]

c 4411 - "Body Snatched"[1319] -> The eleventh Doctor brought Amy and Rory to the Trans-Universal Union to collect his mail, which included a letter that had been sent two hundred years earlier from the Horse Lord of Khan. They went back in time to help.

c 4500 - "Keepsake"[1320] -> By this time, a musical had been made about the Orion War. Millions of self-repairing robots from Orion were still performing menial tasks.

The seventh Doctor stopped at Reclaim Platform Juliet-November-Kilo, the largest reclaim station on its side of the Easto Cluster, to acquire spare parts for the TARDIS. He encountered a servo robot containing the last vestiges of his android friend Sara's consciousness, and thereby learned of her fate.

The forty-sixth century saw the development of Dirty Rip engines, time machines that punched holes in time and were prone to both exploding and increasing the vortex pressure on users until they also exploded.[1321]

? 4500 - HERE THERE BE MONSTERS[1322] -> Humanity now treated mathematics like art; if an equation was beautiful and symmetrical, it was regarded as true.

On Earth, genetic manipulation was used to develop sentient vegetative lifeforms that could entwine their branches and leaves throughout a spaceship's interior. Such lifeforms could pilot spaceships, fight small wars and expand the human empire's boundaries, allotting humanity more time for pursuits such as sculpture and music. The lifeforms' memories were contained in seed pods, and they were genetically engineered to avoid boredom; they'd be content spending one hundred million years performing tasks and reaching for synthesized light.

Three hundred and thirty-eight years after these lifeforms were created, humanity also developed "benchmarking" - a means of using gravitational singularities contained in a Klein bottle to create a navigational system. Seven singularities were used in concert - one would puncture the fabric of space-time every tenth of a light-year; the remaining six would encode each "hole" with navigational information. The Earth Benchmarking Vessel (EBV) *Nevermore*, captained by the vegetative lifeform Rostrum, was intended as the first of many ships that would benchmark entire sectors of space. Spaceships would consequently always know their location, and which direction they needed to go.

The first Doctor, accompanied by Ian, Barbara and Susan, insisted to Rostrum that ravenous "things" lived in the "deep space" beneath space, and that the benchmarking process would give them access to our universe. A traveller from this "deep space" crossed over and adopted a human form - as benchmarking was laying waste to vast tracts of his reality - and said that while deep space contained lifeforms whose energy and matter were antithetical to humanity, it was also home to many intelligent, ethical civilisations. The traveller sealed the breach created by the *Nevermore*, which killed Rostrum and everything within half a light year. The traveller also perished, but only after recording a message warning humanity of the dangers of benchmarking.

c 4500 - TOMB OF VALDEMAR[1323] -> The Second Empire fell after three centuries, following a revolution that began with a declaration that the oppressed masses would no longer tolerate idle cruelty. The ruling class was aristocratic and decadent. The New Protectorate established the New Parliament on Earth, based on "the rigours of Puritanism applied to a purely materialistic philosophy". This was led by the Virgin Lady High Protector, the

Civil Matriarch, who had the Elite's palaces destroyed with Immolator Six capsules. A Duke named Paul Neville fled to Terra and became a powerful magician, the head of a cult dedicated to the dark god Valdemar. The Protectorate located Neville, forcing him to flee to the ends of the collapsing Empire. Neville sought the planet Ashkellia, which he believed contained the palace of the Old Ones - Valdemar was the last of their kind.

Neville attempted to resurrect Valdemar through an adolescent psionic named Huvan, but the fourth Doctor and Romana defeated his plans. Huvan nearly punctured the higher dimensions, which could have destroyed the universe, but the Doctor and Romana convinced Huvan that he lacked the maturity for such power. Huvan agreed to erase his memory and assume a new identity. He became a trapper named Ponch on the planet Janus Forus. Fifteen years later, Romana returned to help him remember his past. She regenerated at this time.

The New Protectorate lasted around a century or two before burning itself out.

The Davros Era[1324]

? 4500 - DESTINY OF THE DALEKS[1325] **-> The Daleks realised that their dependence on logic made it impossible for them to win a war against another logical machine race, the Movellans. Their battlecomputers suggested that they should turn to their creator, Davros, for help. The Supreme Dalek dispatched a force to Skaro to recover Davros from the ruins of the Kaled bunker. Mining operations started up, and the Daleks discovered their creator, who had survived in suspended animation for centuries.**

A Movellan party was sent to Skaro to investigate Dalek operations. As they arrived, the Daleks' slaves broke free, helped by the fourth Doctor and the newly regenerated Romana. Before a Dalek ship could arrive from Supreme Command, the slaves had overpowered the Movellans and defeated the small Dalek force. Davros was captured by the human force, who returned to Earth in the Movellan ship.

Before this time, Arcturus won the Galactic Olympic games, with Betelgeuse coming a close second. The economy of Algol was subject to irreversible inflation.

The Movellans were built by the Daleks, and the entire war was faked as part of their plan to prevent the destruction of Skaro.[1326] **Human authorities put Davros on trial. Humanity had abandoned the death penalty, so Davros was placed in suspended animation aboard a prison station in deep space. Without Davros' help, the Daleks were helpless. They lost the war when the Movellans released a virus that only affected Dalek tissue. Weakened, the Daleks were forced to rely on hired mercenaries and duplicates: conditioned clones produced by their genetic experiments, and generated from humans snatched from many timezones.**[1327]

Humanity discovered a cure for Becks Syndrome.[1328] Following another Dalek War with humanity, the Daleks were not active in the galaxy for a century.[1329] On Riften-5, the fifth Doctor saw archives of genetic tests on Daleks after the War of Sharpened Hearts.[1330]

& 4590 - RESURRECTION OF THE DALEKS[1331] **-> One Supreme Dalek came up with an audacious plan that would strengthen the Daleks' position. Davros would be released from prison, and use his scientific genius and understanding of the Daleks to find an antidote for the Movellan virus. Dalek duplicate technology would be used to strike on twentieth-century Earth, while a second group, composed of duplicate versions of the fifth Doctor and his companions, would**

Empire was around in 4126. Earth no longer seems to have an Empire in the Davros Era, so the latest this story can be set is around 4500.

1324 See The Davros Era sidebar.

1325 Dating *Destiny of the Daleks* (17.1) - The Daleks and Movellans have been locked in stalemate for "centuries". At this point, the Daleks are feared, highly advanced and have a vast war fleet which operates as their command base. In *Resurrection of the Daleks*, it is made clear that there is deadlock between the Movellans and the Daleks' computers, not the Daleks themselves.

1326 According to *War of the Daleks*.

1327 *Resurrection of the Daleks*

1328 "Forty years" before *Revelation of the Daleks*.

1329 Before *Davros*.

1330 *Christmas on a Rational Planet*. No date is given,

but Riften-5 was the home planet of Lytton according to *Attack of the Cybermen*, and this is (presumably) his home timezone. *Attack of the Cybermen* ends with the Doctor saying he misjudged Lytton, yet they didn't meet at all in *Resurrection of the Daleks* (unless you count Lytton shooting at the Doctor from a distance) and they barely meet in *Attack of the Cybermen*. If we wanted to fix that, we could theorise that the Doctor met Lytton - from his perspective - between the two stories (it would be before *Resurrection of the Daleks* for Lytton).

1331 Dating *Resurrection of the Daleks* (21.4) - This is the sequel to *Destiny of the Daleks*. Davros says he has been imprisoned for "ninety years". According to some reports, the rehearsal script set the story in 4590, which would follow the date established in *The Programme Guide*. This date also appears in *The Encyclopaedia of the*

THE DAVROS ERA: Four consecutive Dalek TV stories (*Destiny of the Daleks, Resurrection of the Daleks, Revelation of the Daleks* and *Remembrance of the Daleks*) form a linked series in which the creator of the Daleks, Davros (first seen in *Genesis of the Daleks*), is revived. In due course, he's captured and imprisoned by Earth before re-engineering the Daleks and gradually taking control over his creations. The series ends with the ultimate destruction of the Daleks' home planet of Skaro, although the novel *War of the Daleks*, set shortly after *Remembrance of the Daleks*, significantly reinterpreted those events.

Three Big Finish audios (and *The Davros Mission*, an audio story exclusive to *The Complete Davros Collection* DVD set) occur in gaps between the television stories, and act as bridges between them - *Resurrection of the Daleks* is followed by *Davros, Revelation of the Daleks* is followed by *The Davros Mission* and *The Juggernauts*, and *Remembrance of the Daleks* is followed by *Terror Firma*. The comic strip "Emperor of the Daleks" depicts Davros becoming Emperor between *Revelation of the Daleks* and *Remembrance of the Daleks*. Here, for the sake of convenience, we refer to the events of these stories as "the Davros Era" - a term that is never used in any of the stories themselves.

It is never stated exactly when the Davros Era is set, although it is clearly far in Earth's future.

The key story here is *Remembrance of the Daleks*. Before *Remembrance*, it was widely felt that *The Evil of the Daleks* really was, as the Doctor said, "the final end" of the Daleks (even though the draft script *of Day of the Daleks* explained that the Daleks had survived their civil war). *Remembrance of the Daleks* changed that, by ending with the destruction of Skaro. Clearly, taking *Remembrance of the Daleks* at face value, it - and by implication the rest of the Davros Era - has to happen after *The Evil of the Daleks* (the climax of which was set on Skaro).

Even before that, the first two editions of *The Programme Guide* set *Destiny of the Daleks* "c.4500" (as did the earlier versions of this chronology and *Timelink*). Following *The Programme Guide*'s lead, the script of *Resurrection of the Daleks* referred to the year as 4590, although that's not established on screen.

There have been other attempts to place it. *The Terrestrial Index* took the Doctor's speech to the Black Dalek in *Remembrance of the Daleks* that the Daleks are "a thousand years" from home literally, and respectively set the stories in "as the twenty-seventh century began", "towards the end of the twenty-seventh century", "as the twenty-eighth century began" and "about 2960". *The TARDIS Logs* chose "8740 AD" for *Destiny of the Daleks*. Ben Aaronovitch's novelisation of *Remembrance of the Daleks* and his introduction to the *Abslom Daak - Dalek Killer* graphic album had extracts from a history book, *The Children of Davros*, published in "4065" - apparently well after *Remembrance of the Daleks*.

John Peel's *The Official Doctor Who & the Daleks Book*

- written with Terry Nation's approval - offers a complete Dalek timeline, although it stresses it's not "definitive" and could change in the light of a new story (p209), and it was written *before Remembrance of the Daleks* was broadcast. In Peel's version, *Genesis of the Daleks* comes first, followed by *The Daleks* [c.1564], there are Dalek survivors in the Kaled Bunker and after five hundred years they emerge and force the Thals to flee Skaro. The Daleks discover space travel after about a hundred years, and launch *The Dalek Invasion of Earth* [2164]. The Dalek Wars begin, after several hundred years of Dalek preparation, leading to *Frontier in Space* and *Planet of the Daleks* [2540]. The Daleks developed time travel, as seen in *The Chase*. The Daleks and Mechanoids fought the Mechon Wars, and one Dalek capsule from that conflict ends up crashing on Vulcan where it is unearthed in *The Power of the Daleks* ["several centuries" after 2010]. The Daleks went back in time to reinvade Earth (*Day of the Daleks*). The Daleks were then attacked by the Movellans (*Destiny of the Daleks*) and the two races were deadlocked for "decades".

Ninety years later followed *Resurrection of the Daleks* (by which time, Earth and Draconia had defeated the Movellans). The Daleks exploited a space plague (*Death to the Daleks*). Davros had survived, but was captured by the Daleks at the end of *Revelation of the Daleks*, and he was taken to Skaro and executed. Weakened, the Daleks needed allies to conquer the galaxy, as seen in *The Daleks' Master Plan* [4000]. This led to the Dalek Wars, that lasted "the next couple of centuries" after which the Emperor Dalek initiated the events *of The Evil of the Daleks* [c 4200], which ended in a civil war that wiped out the entire Dalek race, once and for all.

No firm dates for the Davros Era are given, but working backwards, this timeline would seem to place *Destiny of the Daleks* somewhere in the thirty-ninth century.

War of the Daleks, also written by Peel, attempted to reverse the destruction of Skaro in *Remembrance of the Daleks*, and - unsurprisingly - it broadly follows the timeline in Peel's earlier book. Ironically, though, it undermines the case for setting the Davros Era before 4000 - first, the SSS explore Antalin (the planet the Daleks trick the Doctor into destroying instead of Skaro) after the events of *The Daleks' Master Plan*. Secondly, for the Dalek plan to work, the Doctor has to think Skaro was destroyed in *Remembrance of the Daleks*, and he wouldn't if he knew it still existed in the year 4000. (*About Time* has suggested that while the Daleks report to Skaro in *The Daleks' Master Plan*, the Doctor doesn't *see* them doing that, so he might not realise they do.)

Some fans have speculated that the Daleks might move to "New Skaro" after *Remembrance of the Daleks*, but no evidence exists for this on screen, and on the

continued on page 609...

assassinate the High Council of Gallifrey. The plan totally failed.

Once Davros was released, he attempted to usurp control of the Dalek army and completely re-engineer the race. This met from resistance from those loyal to the Supreme Dalek, and the two factions began fighting. The Duplicates rebelled, destroying the prison station and the Dalek battlecruiser. Davros escaped.

The parents of Geoff, who was later a member of Davros' science team, died in the Kensington disaster of '97.[1332]

c 4600 - DAVROS[1333] -> Arnold Baines, head of the TAI corporation (which sold everything from foodstuffs to recreational narcotics to laser cannons), tracked down Davros' body. The sixth Doctor saw Davros revive. Baines hired both the Doctor and Davros to develop business strategies to help mankind spread to other galaxies. Davros secretly developed a computer model that could accurately predict the galactic stock market. With it, he

planned to destroy capitalism in favour of a system that placed the entire galaxy's economy on a permanent war footing. He launched a coup against Baines, but failed. Davros escaped in Baines' spacecraft with a hostage, Kim, who killed herself - allowing the Doctor to crash the ship. The Doctor suspected that Davros survived.

Collectors were looking for Dalek regalia at this time. Some historians, like Lorraine Baines, offered revisionist histories where the Daleks were seen as victims, not aggressors, and Davros was hailed as a visionary. The Treaty of Parlagon prevented individuals from having nuclear weapons. There was famine in the galaxy, virtually every available planet of which had been colonised by humanity.

The Daleks reoccupied Skaro, and a new Supreme Dalek came to power. The Daleks developed biomechanoid computers that interfaced with human brains to provide the Daleks with raw creativity, and they began to reassert their power.[1334]

Worlds of Doctor Who.

1332 *The Juggernauts*

1333 Dating *Davros* (BF #48) - *Davros* is set after *Resurrection of the Daleks.* It's never explicitly stated that it occurs between that story and *Revelation of the Daleks,* but the Big Finish website places it between *The Two Doctors* and *Timelash.* TAI was formed "back in the thirty-eighth century".

1334 Skaro has been abandoned for "centuries" before *Destiny of the Daleks,* but the Supreme Dalek is based there in *Revelation of the Daleks.* We see a biomechanoid in *Remembrance of the Daleks* - presumably the Daleks haven't developed the technology when they lose the war with the Movellans. Although, according to *War of the Daleks,* the Movellan War was a ruse.

1335 Dating *Revelation of the Daleks* (22.6) - This story is set an unspecified amount of time after *Resurrection of the Daleks.* It has been long enough for Davros to gain a galaxy-wide reputation and build a new army of Daleks. The galaxy is ruled by a human President and faces famine.

1336 Dating *The Davros Mission* (exclusive audio story included with *The Complete Davros Collection* DVD set) - The story is set directly after *Revelation of the Daleks* (the ship that takes Davros to Skaro departs from Necros), and on the surface might seem to conflict with "Emperor of the Daleks" as yet-another "bridge" story between *Revelation of the Daleks* and *Remembrance of the Daleks.* In detail, however, the two stories are compatible - in *The Davros Mission,* the only leverage Davros gains over the Daleks on Skaro is a) what passes for his charm, and b) the concentrated Movellan virus he's holding. A Dalek civil war is slated to occur after this point (in *Remembrance*), so whatever fealty the Skaro

Daleks might here pledge to Davros is certain to fall to ruin under any scenario. It makes sense to assume that the Skaro Daleks only declare obedience to Davros in *The Davros Mission* to buy themselves the time required to neutralise the Movellan virus in his possession. Once that occurs, Davros would probably have little choice but to flee, leading to *The Juggernauts* and his eventually being captured and put on trial a second time (in "Emperor of the Daleks").

Davros is here slated to become the Dalek Emperor, but that doesn't actually happen - so it's fair to think that it only happens down the road, once Abslom Daak takes a chainsaw to him in the comic story. He also gains a robotic hand (to replace the one shot off in *Revelation of the Daleks*), but might upgrade to the claw he uses in "Emperor of the Daleks".

1337 Dating *The Juggernauts* (BF #65) - This story is set an unspecified amount of time after *Revelation of the Daleks.* It's said that Davros crash-landed seven hundred sixteen days prior to this story, but there's no indication of the duration of time in a day on Lethe.

1338 "Emperor of the Daleks"

1339 Dating "... Up Above the Gods"/"Emperor of the Daleks" (*DWM* #227, 197-202) - The story is set between *Revelation of the Daleks* and *Remembrance of the Daleks,* and bridges the gap between them (even if this means that the seventh Doctor is experiencing developments with Davros out of order). The Emperor resembles the one from the *TV Century 21* Dalek comic strip. This raises a question as to which Dalek Emperor this is - and not because that Emperor Dalek was apparently killed by Daak back in "Nemesis of the Daleks". We didn't *see* the Emperor killed on that occasion - we just didn't see him escape the exploding Death Wheel. Given that

? 4615 - REVELATION OF THE DALEKS[1335] -> A

human President now ruled the galaxy, which was becoming overpopulated. Famine was a problem on worlds across known space. Tranquil Repose on Necros had been established for some time as a resting place for the dead of the galaxy - literally, as they were kept in suspended animation there until whatever killed them was cured by medical science. The "rock and roll years" of twentieth century Earth were extremely popular. The grandfather of a DJ on Necros purchased some genuine records from Earth on a visit there.

Davros went into hiding on Necros and formed an alliance with Kara, a local businesswoman. He took control of Tranquil Repose, and secretly began to break down the corpses there into a foodstuff. This ended famine across the galaxy, and Davros gained a reputation as "the Great Healer". Kara discovered that Davros was also growing a new army of genetically re-engineered Daleks from the corpses, and planned to use them to take effective control of her company. She hired Orcini, an excommunicated member of the Grand Order of Oberon, to assassinate Davros.

Davros had been keeping track of the Doctor's movements - when one of the Doctor's friends, the agronomist Arthur Stengos, died, Davros prepared for the Doctor to attend the funeral. Orcini, the sixth Doctor and Peri thwarted Davros' plans, although Orcini died in the process. The Daleks were summoned from Skaro and captured their creator. The Doctor suggested that protein from a commonplace purple flower could alleviate the famine.

? 4615 - THE DAVROS MISSION[1336] -> The Daleks

took Davros to Skaro and put him on trial for plotting against them and creating "impure" Daleks. En route, a Thal named Lareen snuck into Davros' cell and - thinking she had convinced Davros to redeem himself by destroying his creations - provided him with a vial of super-concentrated Movellan virus. Had Davros released this, it would have killed all Daleks on Skaro and broken the spine of their empire. Instead, Davros convinced the Daleks that his refraining from destroying them demonstrated that they owed him their allegiance. The Daleks concurred, pledged to make Davros their Emperor and exterminated Lareen...

? 4620 - THE JUGGERNAUTS[1337] -> Davros crashed on

the planet Lethe, where mining engineers excavated a group of Mechanoids. Davros attempted to build an army of Mechanoids (re-named "the Juggernauts") that incorporated human tissue, but the grey Daleks tracked him

...continued from page 607

occasions when we see Skaro it is clearly the same world - the Doctor knows his way around in *The Evil of the Daleks* and *Destiny of the Daleks*. In the Time War shown in the EDAs, the Time Lords created duplicate home planets and it's possible that the Daleks might do the same.

In two New Adventures by Andy Lane (*Lucifer Rising*, *Original Sin*) we discover that the Guild of Adjudicators eventually becomes the Grand Order of Oberon referred to in *Revelation of the Daleks*, yet the Adjudicators are still active in *Original Sin*, so *Revelation of the Daleks* must take place well after the thirtieth century.

Mission to the Unknown established that the Daleks hadn't been a military force in Earth's galaxy for a thousand years prior to 4000 (and in one of the scenes where "galaxy" seems to mean "galaxy", not "solar system"). This - and perhaps the presence of the Galactic Federation - would seem to rule out the Davros Era taking place between 3000 and 4000. Humans from the time of *Destiny*, *Resurrection* and *Revelation* all know and fear the Daleks, and see them as an active threat - whereas in *Mission to the Unknown*, Gordon Lowery only knows that the Daleks invaded Earth "a thousand years ago", and needs their renewed interest in Earth space spelled out for him. The Daleks have been deadlocked for "centuries" with the Movellans before *Destiny of the Daleks* (tellingly, Peel has to reduce this to "decades" in his timeline). The preminence of the Earth Empire in the centuries before 3000 seems incompatible with the idea the Daleks are a major galactic power. All in all, it seems likely that *Destiny of the Daleks* is set at least "centuries" after 4000. As we know the *Dalek Empire* series is set in the first half of the millennium, the case for *The Programme Guide's* 4600 AD date, while not indisputable, is certainly persuasive.

down. The sixth Doctor and Mel sabotaged the Juggernaut production lines, and Davros' body was severely injured in the fighting. His life-support chair self-destructed, which obliterated the colony, the grey Daleks and the Juggernauts, although the colonists themselves evacuated.

Earth had passed mandatory organ donation laws.

The sixth Doctor and Peri encountered the Daleks on Mandusus.[1338]

? 4625 - "...Up Above the Gods" / "Emperor of the Daleks"[1339] -> The Daleks put Davros on trial - he had

replaced his destroyed hand with a claw, and started to persuade some Daleks that they could learn from him. Nonetheless, the Emperor sentenced him to execution. Before the sentence was carried out, a giant asteroid entered the Skaro system.

The sixth Doctor and Peri arrived on Skaro. While the Daleks were occupied with the asteroid (which the Doctor had sent their way), the Doctor infected the Dalek computers with a virus, then kidnapped Davros in the TARDIS. The Daleks vowed revenge.

A year later, the Daleks tricked Abslom Daak into bringing the seventh Doctor to Skaro (along with the other Star Tigers and Benny, from the mid-twenty-sixth century), Daak fought a pitched battle with the Daleks, but he and his allies were subdued. The Daleks demanded that the Doctor take them to Davros, and used a Psyche Dalek to place the others in a hypnotic trance.

A Dalek battle fleet under the command of the Black Dalek was dispatched to Spiridon, where they were met by Davros and an army of four million white-and-gold upgraded Daleks. The Psyche Dalek was destroyed, and the Doctor's friends were released from hypnotic control. Routed, the Black Dalek withdrew his forces and ordered the orbiting fleet to destroy Davros - but the energy was reflected back and destroyed all but one ship, which was also blown up.

Davros had won the battle, and had *not* - as he had promised the Doctor - given his upgraded Daleks a conscience. Davros' fleet set course for Skaro, planning to reactivate the Doctor's computer virus and seize control. Davros' forces landed, and he watched as the former Emperor was exterminated. However, Daak sliced through Davros with his chainsword before being forced to withdraw by the other Star Tigers. A nuclear blast devastated the Dalek city, and finally destroyed Taiyin's body.

Davros had a new survival chair built only four days after his arrival, but a bitter civil war was underway between the Dalek factions. **Davros was now Emperor of the Daleks.**[1340] The Thals had relocated from Skaro by this point, and the Daleks did not normally enter their region of space, which included Spiridon.

Abel Gantz revived the lost science of alchemy when he discovered paracelsium, a catalyst that could transmute metals.[1341]

"Emperor of the Daleks" establishes that Daak and all the Star Tigers - who were seen to perish in "Nemesis of the Daleks" - didn't actually die, the Emperor Dalek barely makes the top five "least probable resurrections" in the story. See The Dalek Emperors sidebar.

1340 Per his appearance as such in *Remembrance of the Daleks*.

1341 "Ten years" before "Abel's Story".

1342 Dating "Kane's Story"/"Abel's Story"/"Warrior's Story"/"Frobisher's Story" (*DWM* #104-107) - Davros rules the Daleks, and the only time this is the case on television is between *Revelation of the Daleks* and *Remembrance of the Daleks*. (Taking other media into account, this is between "Emperor of the Daleks" and *Remembrance of the Daleks*.) This also fits with where the story falls in the Doctor's timeline. "War-Game" is set a few years after this, and states the Draconians rule a third of the galaxy. The Planetary Federation is also known as the Federation of Worlds, and could well be the same - or remnants of the same - Federation from the Peladon stories (although the Draconians were part of that Federation according to *Legacy*).

1343 Dating *The Story of Martha*: "The Weeping" (NSA #28b) - Agaloas is established as part of the Second Great and Bountiful Human Empire (p49), and the story occurs "almost five centuries" (p56) after the colony's failure.

1344 Dating *Remembrance of the Daleks* (25.1) - This story is the sequel to *Revelation of the Daleks,* and there's no indication how long it has been since the previous story. Davros has completely revamped the Daleks, which was presumably a fairly lengthy process.

1345 "The Child of Time" (*DWM*)

1346 Dating *War of the Daleks* (EDA #5) - It's "about thirty years" after *Remembrance of the Daleks*. One of Davros' followers operates the controls of his dispersal chamber, suggesting that Davros was later reconstituted in secret - and later recaptured, leading to his next appearance in *Terror Firma*.

WAS SKARO DESTROYED?: The retcon in *War of the Daleks* that reversed Skaro's destruction proved controversial with fans. A couple of references in later BBC Books suggested that Skaro had been destroyed, after all. *Unnatural History* stated that the Doctor tricked the Daleks into tangling their timelines so much their history collapsed; *The Infinity Doctors* that Skaro suffered more than one destruction. *Doctor Who - The Movie* (after *Remembrance of the Daleks* in the Doctor's own timeline) opened on Skaro, but it could have historically been before it was destroyed. The 2005 TV series never stated that Skaro had been destroyed in the Time War (Russell T Davies' essay in the *Doctor Who Annual 2006* does name it and says it's now "ruins", though). The *Doctor Who Visual Dictionary* states that Skaro was "devastated" in *Remembrance of the Daleks*, but "finally obliterated" in the Time War.

There are a number of get-out clauses in *War of the Daleks* itself - the events aren't seen, only reported. Internal dating seems confused, and Antalin appears after it's meant to have been destroyed. There are pieces of contradictory information elsewhere - the origins of the Movellans in the book contradict their implied beginnings in *A Device of Death*, for example.

1347 *The Four Doctors*. The Dalek Prime seen in this audio isn't necessarily the exact same one seen in *War of the Daleks*, but the title isn't used in any other *Doctor Who* story. Allowing for all of the time travel involved, though, there's no guarantee that the Jariden sequences in *The Four Doctors* takes place in this era.

1348 Years rather than decades before *Terror Firma*. The presence of Samson and Gemma's mother suggests that this is their native time zone.

c 4635 - "Kane's Story" / "Abel's Story" / "Warrior's Story" / "Frobisher's Story"[1342] **->** Skeletoids invaded outposts on Vega and Sigma IV, meaning they were only weeks from the Sol system. The Skeletoids were armoured humans from the Vespin system, but their armour had gradually become so sophisticated, the humans inside had become redundant components. They swept through five systems in a year - either converting any humanoids they conquered, or wiping out races they couldn't convert (such as the Daleks and Cybermen). The Skeletoids were now at the gates of the Planetary Federation. The Draconians were their next targets, and the powers of the galaxy arranged a summit on Ankara III.

The sixth Doctor, Frobisher and Peri learned of the threat and headed for Xaos, the oldest planet in the galaxy - as did Abel Gantz, the Draconian Emperor's bodyguard Kaon (who the Doctor and Frobisher had met some years from now), and Kane Borg of Kaltarr. They were the champions of six worlds, and they travelled in the TARDIS to the Vespin system to take the fight to the Skeletoids. Abel sacrificed himself, destroying the Skeletoid command centre. The menace to the galaxy ended, and the Doctor and the surviving champions arrived at the galactic summit to tell the delegates they'd had a wasted trip.

c 4650 - THE STORY OF MARTHA: "The Weeping"[1343] **->** Agelaos had become an icy planet following the failure of its terraforming. The last of the colonists, Waechter, had guarded the quarantine there and lived for centuries thanks to a slowed metabolism. Waechter found that he would die if ever he left Agelaos, and the tenth Doctor and Martha helped him to attain his last wish: that he be mutated into a creature like his fellow colonists, so he would never be alone.

? 4663 - REMEMBRANCE OF THE DALEKS[1344] **->** Upon returning to Skaro, Davros usurped control from the Supreme Dalek and declared himself an Emperor Dalek. With his body now wasted, Davros was reduced to little more than a disembodied head. He fashioned a new casing for himself. Most Daleks supported Davros, who genetically re-engineered the race and oversaw a complete revamp of Dalek technology. These "Imperial Daleks" were given new cream and gold livery, improved weapons, sensor plates and eyestalks. As always, some Daleks dissented: this "Renegade Dalek" faction followed the Black Dalek and fled Skaro using a Time Controller.

Both factions had learned of the Hand of Omega, a powerful Gallifreyan device that could manipulate stars. They converged to its location on Earth in 1963. Davros acquired the Hand, but was unable to control the device. On the seventh Doctor's instructions, the Hand travelled to Skaro in Davros' native time and

made its sun go supernova, obliterating the planet. Davros escaped, but his flagship was obliterated and the Dalek homeworld was seemingly destroyed.

> (=) In 4688, Chiyoko, the "child of time", transported a Vorlax Regeneration Drone from the war planet Grakktar back to 2011.[1345]

& 4693 - WAR OF THE DALEKS[1346] **->** The Daleks had invaded Earth "several times" by this point.

The garbage ship *Quetzel* recovered both the eighth Doctor's TARDIS and Davros' escape pod. Thals raided the ship, and Delani, the Thal commander, asked Davros to reengineer his race to defeat the Daleks. Davros' reactivation alerted the Daleks, and the Doctor, Sam and Davros were taken to Skaro... which the Doctor had thought destroyed. The Dalek Prime explained that the Daleks had learned of Skaro's destruction beforehand and plotted to prevent it.

The Daleks had previously taken the dormant Davros from Skaro, and placed him in ruins on Antalin, which were designed to look like Skaro. The planet was then bathed in radioactivity. The Daleks then faked the Movellan War using their own robot servants, fooling Davros into believing they needed his help, but Davros escaped and triggered a civil war. He took the Hand of Omega, which destroyed *Antalin* rather than Skaro. The Daleks' real homeworld survived.

Now, the Dalek Prime planned to draw the Daleks who supported Davros out into the open and destroy them. The Doctor made a seemingly easy escape in the Thal ship - then discovered a Dalek factory in the hold. He jettisoned it back in time, where it crashed on Vulcan.

Daleks loyal to Davros attempted to rescue him, but the Dalek Prime's forces prevailed. Davros was placed in a dispersion chamber and seemingly vaporized, but the Dalek implementing Davros' execution was one of his followers, and it was possible that Davros survived...

The Dalek Prime was later lost to the Time Vortex, owing to the intervention of four incarnations of the Doctor in the Daleks' war with the Jariden, a race of biomechanoids.[1347] The eighth Doctor ventured into a library and came to accept a worker there, Samson Griffin, and his sister Gemma aboard the TARDIS. They shared many adventures together, but eventually were overpowered by Davros - who desired to strip the Doctor of everything he held dear, and so erased his memories of his two companions. Davros mentally conditioned Samson and Gemma to accompany him back to Earth, then embarked on a scheme to turn it into a new Dalek homeworld. Samson was allowed to live with his mother, Harriet Griffen, in Folkestone.[1348]

& 4703 - TERROR FIRMA[1349] -> On Earth, Davros and his Daleks encountered the eighth Doctor, Charley and C'rizz upon their return from the Divergent Universe. Davros believed that his Daleks had turned Earth into a "new Dalek homeworld" and converted eight billion humans into Daleks; however, the Daleks were actually operating to their own agenda while Davros was mutating into an Emperor Dalek. Davros hoped the Doctor would end his suffering and gave him a genocidal virus, hoping he would use it to end Davros' life. But the Doctor instead used the threat of the virus to make the Daleks abandon Earth. The Emperor Dalek persona completely erased Davros' own, and the Daleks left with their new leader.

Gemma Griffen died in the conflict. Her brother Samson regained his memories of the Doctor, but continued living on Earth.

Kaon's ship later crashed on Actinon after hitting a meteor field. The inhabitants were warlike, but no match for Kaon, who established himself as a warlord. His wife died in childbirth, but his daughter Kara grew to be a strong warrior.[1350] **The Weeping Angels wiped out the Aplans, the two-headed life form indigenous to Alfava Metraxis. Lacking a food source, the Angels went dormant in an Aplan moratorium.**[1351]

The metamorphic Collectors were galactic scavengers who entirely lacked the ability to discern the value or relevance of an item - essentially, they amassed junk. The Collectors' hyperwobble-drives and psychonomic shielding meant that no culture's defences could stand against them. The Daleks pretended that their planet had been destroyed to avoid being attacked by the Collectors.[1352]

c 4750 - "War-Game"[1353] -> The sixth Doctor and Frobisher landed on a barbaric world, Actinon, and detected advanced technology. Investigating, they discovered that the local Warlord Kaon was a Draconian. His daughter Kara had been kidnapped by Vegar, a rival warlord. The Doctor took Kaon to Vegar's fortress in the TARDIS and they rescued Kara - at the cost of Kaon's life. Kara vowed to stay on the planet and maintain his legacy.

1349 Dating *Terror Firma* (BF #72) - No specific date is given, but it is obviously after *Remembrance of the Daleks*, and a gap of some measure (Davros mentions "years of solitude") is required after the novel *War of the Daleks*. *Terror Firma* doesn't acknowledge *War of the Daleks*, but the two are not irreconcilable. Davros' mental health is clearly eroding throughout this audio, so it's entirely possible that the Daleks have altered his memories or that he's simply too far gone to remember those events. In fact, as the Daleks are obviously fooling Davros into thinking that he's in charge, it suits their plans if he forgets about Skaro and believes he's gaining revenge against the Doctor by "turning Earth" into a new Dalek homeworld.

Big Finish says that Davros *does not* become the Emperor Dalek seen in *The Parting of the Ways*.

WHO RULES THE DALEKS?: There's a fair amount of evidence the Emperor is not the ultimate, unchallengeable authority of the Daleks. In "Secret of the Emperor" (a comic from *The Dalek Outer Space Book*), it's stated that senior Daleks convene periodically to elect their Emperor... or rather to *re*-elect him, as it's always a unanimous vote and the only ever dissenter, seen in that story, is instantly exterminated for daring to question the Emperor's authority.

In *The Dalek Chronicles* strip, the Emperor follows the advice of the Dalek Brain Machine, a central computer, and *Destiny of the Daleks* and *Remembrance of the Daleks* also show a computer dictating strategy. *War of the Daleks* and *Terror Firma* have Daleks actively manipulating events and misleading Emperor Davros for their own ends. While Davros thinks he's asserting his own dominance, both stories suggest that the Dalek leadership have planned the events we see to unite the Daleks and harness his genius, while keeping all manner of key information from him. *The Stolen Earth/Journey's End* has Davros in a similar role, clearly more controlled by the Daleks than controlling.

Doomsday introduces the Cult of Skaro, four Daleks "above even the Emperor" (although still acknowledging his authority and concerned about his fate).

The Doctor claims in *The Evil of the Daleks* that the Daleks blindly obey their leaders, and this unity is their defining characteristic... to such a degree that in *Remembrance of the Daleks* and *Dalek* (and its "predecessor", the audio *Jubilee*), lone Daleks commit suicide because they've lost their entire purpose. We've seen Daleks ruthlessly eradicate individuals who dare to express even modest dissent on a number of occasions. However, the Daleks have a moral code that allows them to question orders if they seem un-Dalek-like and no compunction about replacing their leaders if they fail. It's perhaps no coincidence that this happens most visibly with two leaders who aren't pure Daleks: Davros and Sec (in *Evolution of the Daleks*). Cunningly, the Daleks have their cake and eat it: they are led by strong, imaginative, ambitious individuals who can think in ways the Daleks themselves can not... but they have a very strong (overriding, in fact) sense of what it is to be a Dalek. So if their leaders stray too far away from the Dalek ideal, the Daleks can quickly reach a consensus to exterminate him, without fear of disrupting the Dalek order based on blind obedience to their leaders, by simply deciding that their leader doesn't count as a Dalek.

Ultimately, then, the true leader of the Daleks is not an individual, it's the belief in their own supremacy and their hatred for anything that isn't a Dalek.

The Time Agents

The forty-ninth century was an era of unparalleled peace and prosperity on Earth. Advanced ubertronic devices existed. Earth developed time travel using transduction beams, but Time Agents strictly regulated the proliferation of the technology. Time travel had other uses: the film archivist Jaxa recovered all the lost films and television programmes. Thirty years before her native time, the moon was terraformed. Sabbath press-ganged Jaxa into his service following a failed time-jump on her part.[1354]

Humans didn't explore some parts of Earth's moon until the forty-ninth century.[1355]

At some point in human history, AEGIS operated a time travel service that, though expensive, allowed people to go into the past. The Technos wrongly thought it was impossible to change the past because time travellers were part of history. One group was sent back to hunt dinosaurs in the Cretaceous.[1356]

Fennus was one of the more successful frontier colonies until it became unstable and disintegrated. The colonists were thought dead, but the father of Mindy 'Voir had engineered a data bank to contain the contents of the colonists' minds. Mindy's father was a pioneer in sonic sculpting, and had enhanced her voice until she was the only human singer with a ten-octave range. She came into possession of the Fennus data bank and wore it as a pendant, unaware of its true nature.[1357]

? 4850 - HELICON PRIME[1358] **->** A long way from Earth's "side" of the universe, Helicon Prime served as a luxury resort in the Parnassas Cluster for many species. Helicon Prime was later moved to the Golden Section - an area of space that radiated a sense of well being - and thereby became an exceedingly exclusive holiday destination. A booking of decades in advance was required.

The second Doctor and Jamie stopped a murder spree committed by Ambassador Dromeo, who sought the Fennus data bank. Mindy 'Voir, having given Jamie her pendant as a present, thought the Doctor had absconded with the data bank and travelled back to eighteenth century Scotland in search of it.

Pursuant to Section 4 Paragraph 25 of the Future Time Edict dated E5150 pro-Hok Gibbon slash Kulkana, Hokrala Corp - a law firm in the forty-ninth century - filed suit against Captain Jack Harkness in the twenty-first century. A Vortex Dweller indebted to Jack closed off Hokrala's access to the past.[1359]

Around 4900, a Dalek expedition to the Magellan Cluster was attacked by spider-like creatures in Dalek-like armour, and it took months to subdue them. These spider-Daleks were Daleks from a parallel universe. The Daleks calculated that the only way to take the fight to the spider-Daleks was via a black hole, but knew their ships couldn't survive the journey.[1360] A thousand murders took place on the worlds of the Nepotism of Vaal in the fiftieth century. The Memeovore had made the population think their loved ones are impostors. The Doctor would visit and see

1350 "Many years" before "War-Game".
1351 "Four centuries" before *The Time of Angels*.
1352 *Heart of TARDIS*
1353 Dating "War-Game" (*DWM* #100-101) - The Doctor meets Kaon again in "Warrior's Story" (which takes place before this in Kaon's timeline) and that adventure sets the rough date for this one. The Draconians rule "a third of the galaxy" at this point. Kaon crashed "many years ago" - enough for Kara to be born and grow to womanhood (although we don't know how long that takes for a Draconian).
1354 *Trading Futures*. Magnus Greel (from the year 5000) feared Time Agents tracking him down in *The Talons of Weng-Chiang*, Time Agents appeared in *Eater of Wasps*, and in *The Empty Child/The Doctor Dances*, Captain Jack claims to have been a Time Agent, and knows that other Agents will be tracking him down. It's interesting to note that in the original, unbroadcast version of *An Unearthly Child*, the Doctor and Susan claim to be aliens, but Susan says she was born in the forty-ninth century.
1355 *I am a Dalek*
1356 "A Glitch in Time". It's never specified when the time travellers come from, but this would seem to be

the only era in which humanity develops time travel.
1357 The Fennus disaster is said to have happened "long ago" prior to the main events of *Helicon Prime*, but as Mindy herself is portrayed as a young woman and we meet three members of the rescue team sent to Fennus, the disaster presumably - depending on human longevity in this era - happened decades rather than centuries before *Helicon Prime* opens.
1358 Dating *Helicon Prime* (BF CC #2.2) - The dating clues are very vague. Mindy is specified as human, but as Helicon Prime is such a great distance from Earth, this is presumably a long time into humanity's expansion into space. It's not specified how, exactly, Mindy travels back to find a post-TARDIS Jamie, raising the possibility that time travel technology is available. Even so, this placement represents a stab in the dark.
Victoria is still studying graphology, so for the Doctor and Jamie, this story likely occurs during Season 6B.
1359 *TW: The Undertaker's Gift*
1360 "Three hundred years" before "Fire and Brimstone".

them establish a universal brotherhood.[1361] Zytron energy, which was affordable and adaptable but could mutate people into psychopathic monstrosities, was discovered on Earth in the fiftieth century.[1362]

Humans terraformed Alfava Metraxis. In time, six billion colonists would live there.[1363] Advanced genetic engineering facilitated the creation of fast-reproducing mutant crabs that consumed the otherwise-indestructible marine vessels used in World War V.[1364]

Under the auspices of the Great World Computer, human civilisation was more efficiently run than ever. But Earth regularly suffered massive famines. An artificial food was created on Earth that solved the problem. On the land once used to grow food, up-to-date living units were built to house the ever-increasing population. The amount of plants on the planet was reduced to an absolute minimum, and all plant life on Earth became extinct.[1365]

The Filipino Protectorate was established on Earth by 4993. Technology at the time included binoculars that could see through walls and read lips.[1366] Professor Marius registered K9 as a data patent on 3rd October, 4998.[1367] K9 was not Y5K compliant.[1368] **K9 wasn't the only cybernetic dog in the fiftieth century.**[1369]

The Fifty-First Century

The Meddling Monk's TARDIS had "Arctic coffee" from the fifty-first century.[1370] The Taklarian Empire began a program of selective breeding to create a master race.[1371] The Doctor took the Mona Lisa up Mount Everest on a camel in the fifty-first century.[1372]

In the fifty-first century, law and order collapsed. Derek Dell, a geek and avid reader of *Aggotron* - a twentieth century comic - adopted the identity of "Courtmaster Cruel", and struck fear into the hearts of criminals. Eventually, Derek went back in time to find the original artwork to the missing *Aggotron #56*, which revealled the Courtmaster's face.[1373] The fifty-first century was the era of the time traveller Chronodev, who was known to the Onihr.[1374]

5000 - THE INVISIBLE ENEMY[1375] **-> Five thousand AD was the year of the Great Breakout, when humanity "went leapfrogging across the galaxy like a tidal wave". To prepare the way, the Space Exploration Programme was instigated in the late fiftieth century, and a huge methane/oxygen refinery was set up on Titan. On asteroid K4067, the centre for Alien Biomorphology (the Bi-Al Foundation) treated extraterrestrial diseases, as well as tending those who were**

1361 *The Taking of Planet 5* (p222).
1362 "Three thousand years" after *Ghosts of India*. The metamorphic nature of Zytron energy, and the similar-sounding name, suggests it bears some relation to Zeiton-7 ore (*Vengeance on Varos*).
1363 "Two hundred years" before *The Time of Angels*.
1364 *Borrowed Time*. See the World Wars sidebar.
1365 In the century before *The Ice Warriors*.
1366 *Interference*. The Doctor has a pair of those binoculars, no doubt acquired when he was with the Filipino army (mentioned in *The Talons of Weng-Chiang*).
1367 *The English Way of Death*
1368 *The Gallifrey Chronicles*
1369 According to Gryffen in *K9: Jaws of Orthrus*. This may mean K9 is a production model, and Marius built him from a kit. Or it may simply mean that other unique robots were built to look like dogs. It could also mean that once Marius gets back to Earth, he markets K9s commercially. The Doctor apparently acquires the Mark 2 and Mark 4 K9s very quickly - he seems to have them stored in the TARDIS, but likewise it's impossible to say if he built or bought K9s Mark 2 to 4.
1370 *The Resurrection of Mars*
1371 "A thousand years" before *City at World's End*.
1372 *The Art of Destruction*. Given the catastrophes that afflict the Earth in the fifty-first century, it's tempting to speculate that the Doctor does this somehow to protect the painting.
1373 *The Company of Friends*: "Izzy's Story"

1374 *Trading Futures*
1375 Dating *The Invisible Enemy* (15.2) - The Doctor states that it is the year "5000, the year of the Great Breakout" and implies that the human race has not yet left the solar system. This contradicts virtually every other story set in the future - indeed, *The Invisible Enemy* would fit very neatly into this timeline about the year 2100.

The Breakout might be to other *galaxies*, and this is supported by the audio *Davros*, which has humanity poised to dominate the whole galaxy and eager to expand. Alternatively, perhaps a big section of humanity wants to leave because they've had enough of the Ice Age, lack of scientific progress, threat of World War and genocidal dictators we hear are on Earth in *The Talons of Weng-Chiang*. If so, no-one mentions it in *The Invisible Enemy*, and Marius' main concern with returning to Earth is that he has too much stuff to take home.

Looking more closely at the history of Earth since the collapse of the Earth Empire around the year 3000, it's clear that there are many human colonies - but there's no evidence that Earth has any political influence on them. While it's a major player on the galactic political stage, Earth's civilisation does seem to be confined to the solar system in *The Daleks' Master Plan*, the Peladon stories and the Davros Era stories (which even following the Peel timeline would fall between 3000 and 5000). Earth maintains a military capable of (small) missions across the galaxy, but the fact that it's igno-

injured in space. Regular shuttle runs were set up between the planets of the solar system and "good for nothing" spaceniks also travelled the cosmos.

Photon beam weapons were in common use, as were visiphones. Sophisticated robots and computers were built. The native language of the time was Finglish, a form of phonetic English.

The Nucleus of the Swarm, a microscopic space-borne entity, attempted to replicate itself across the universe and in the macro-world. It mentally compelled some humans to adapt the methane refinery on Titan into a breeding ground, but was destroyed by the fourth Doctor and Leela before it could reproduce.

Professor Marius' robot dog, K9, assisted the travellers against the Nucleus. The Doctor and Leela took K9 with them, as Marius was due to return to Earth.

c 5000 - THE GIRL IN THE FIREPLACE[1376] -> By the fifty-first century, mankind had warp engines capable of "punching a hole in the universe". Humans had travelled at least as far as the Dagmar Cluster, "two and a half galaxies" from Earth.

The spacecraft *Madame de Pompadour* was crippled in an ion storm, and drifted for a year while the clockwork robots aboard blindly followed their orders to repair it. They used the human crew as raw components, and then used the warp drive to travel back in time and find the historical Madame de Pompadour, who they mistakenly thought was the key to the problem. The tenth Doctor, Rose and Mickey arrived on the ship and - after multiple trips to the eighteenth century - deactivated the robots.

? 5000 - K9 AND THE BEASTS OF VEGA[1377] -> Twenty-seven light years from Earth, humans overseen by Professor Romius were building artificial planets near Vega III that would be ready in ten years. Four ships had been attacked, their crews paralysed. K9 saw the effects on the crew of Spaceshifter 138. Screaming hordes of giant space-borne monsters attacked the engineers, but K9 discovered that the real Vegans were intelligent energy, and that the monsters were a defence mechanism that projected fear. The Vegans didn't like the lasers the engineers were using, and so K9 suggested that the humans go more slowly.

The Second Ice Age

? 5000 - THE ICE WARRIORS[1378] ->

"And then suddenly one year, there was no spring. Even then it wasn't understood, not until the ice caps began to advance."

On Earth, the Second Ice Age had begun. Glaciers rapidly spread across every continent, displacing tens of billions of people to the Equatorial regions. Scientists attempted to come up with a theory that might account for the ice flow. They quickly ruled out a number of the possibilities: a reversal of the Earth's magnetic field, interstellar clouds obscuring the sun's rays, an excessive burst of sunspot activity and a severe shift of the Earth's angle of rotation. They came to realise that the extinction of Earth's plant life had dramatically reduced the carbon dioxide levels in the lower atmosphere, leading to severe heat loss across the world. Scientists tried to reverse the flow of ice, installing Ioniser Bases

rant of massive Dalek conquests in *The Daleks' Master Plan* - even the fact that Earth needs to name a fleet as "the Deep Space Fleet" in *Destiny of the Daleks* and finds it hard to fund or reinforce Davros' prison station in *Resurrection of the Daleks* - suggests that Earth doesn't dominate the galaxy. In *The Talons of Weng-Chiang*, we learn that Earth's in a technological cul-de-sac.

In short, it actually ties in with other stories that human civilisation is confined to Earth's solar system for a couple of millennia before 5000, by which time it's ripe for a "breakout", a new wave of colonisation.

The Gallifrey Chronicles gives the story the "relative date one-one-one-five-zero-zero-zero". *The TARDIS Logs* offered the date "4778".

1376 Dating *The Girl in the Fireplace* (X2.4) - The caption cuts from events in eighteenth-century France to the future with the caption "3000 years later", making it around 4759. However, the tenth Doctor tells Rose and Mickey that it's "three thousand years into your future, give or take", which would make it around 5007. Still later, the Doctor states it's the fifty-first century. The SS

Madame de Pompadour is in the Dagmar Cluster, two and a half galaxies from Earth, and the intergalactic travel probably supports the later date.

1377 Dating *K9 and the Beasts of Vega* (*The Adventures of K9* #2) - No date is given, but as this is set at a time when humans are mounting a massive colonisation effort, it's probably not too much of a stretch to say it's around K9's home time.

1378 Dating *The Ice Warriors* (5.3) - The date of this story is never given on screen. Base leader Clent says that if the glaciers advance, then "five thousand years of history" will be wiped out. If he's referring to Britannicus Base, a Georgian house, this would make the date about 6800 AD. If he is referring to human or European history, the date becomes more vague. It has to be set well over a century in the future, because the world has been run by the Great World Computer for that long.

An article in the *Radio Times* at the time of broadcast stated that the year is "3000 AD", and almost every other fan chronology used to follow that lead, although the first edition of *The Making of Doctor Who* said that the

at strategic points across the globe: Britannicus Base in Europe, and complexes in America, Australasia, South Africa and Asia. These were all co-ordinated by the Great World Computer.

Many refused to leave their homelands and became scavengers. Before long, everywhere on Earth apart from the equatorial areas was an Arctic wasteland, home to wolves and bears. When captured, scavengers were registered and sent to the African Rehabilitation Centres. Scientists remained behind to measure the flow of the ice with movement probes.

Varga the Ice Warrior, who had been trapped in the glacier since the First Ice Age, was revived. He excavated his ship and crew, but was defeated by the second Doctor, Jamie and Victoria before he could use sonic weapons to destroy Brittanicus Base.

THE DAY OF THE TROLL[1379] **->** Global efforts to use chemicals and ionizers to push back the glaciers succeeded, but many temperate zones remained ruined. Britain became a poisoned land and was abandoned, its people dispersing to the rest of the world. Synthetic food was so essential to the world's survival and economy that it became the new oil. Earth was re-divided according to defence of resources, and the fragmentation led to global mistrust. The Eurozone still existed, as did the Internet - some three hundred million people responded online to a charity appeal. Automated Medical Units were used to treat injuries. Paris had a satellite tracking office, and Spain was temperate enough for poolside parties.

Ten years after anyone had stepped foot in Britain, the philanthropist Karl Baring established The Grange, an experimental agricultural complex, in Hampshire. The tenth Doctor bore witness as the tentacled plant-creature

---

Doctor travels "three thousand years" into the future after *The Abominable Snowmen*, making the date 4935 AD. *The Dark Path* and *Legacy* both allude to the date of this story as being 3000 AD (p63 and p89 respectively). Earlier versions of *Ahistory* did the same. The blurb for the Region 1 VHS of the story said it was "AD 3000".

In *The Talons of Weng-Chiang*, the Doctor talks of "the Ice Age about the year five thousand" - possibly even a reference to this story, if Robert Holmes was using *The Making of Doctor Who* as a reference.

Timelink and *About Time* both conclude that this is the ice age mentioned in *The Talons of Weng-Chiang*. This does certainly seem to be a neater solution than proposing two ice ages in quick succession - particularly when there are a fair few stories set around 3000 on an Earth which doesn't seem to be affected by an ice age. Occam's Razor doesn't always work on fictional timelines, and can be wielded too liberally, but it seems sensible to invoke it here.

One peculiarity is that the Martians have only been buried for "centuries", although it is also made clear that they have been buried since the First Ice Age, when mastodons roamed the Earth. (*About Time* states that mastodons became extinct five million years ago, but scientists disagree, estimating it was more like 10,000 BC.) *The Terrestrial Index* and *Legacy* (p90) both suggest that the Ice Age began as a result of "solar flares" (presumably in an attempt to link it with Earth's evacuation in *The Ark in Space*), but that's specifically ruled out as a cause in the story.

One problem is that later stories (starting with *The Curse of Peladon*) would establish the Martians as a significant presence in the future, which would make the humans' ignorance of them in this story notable - mankind has apparently forgotten about the Martians who were near neighbours, and fellow members of the Galactic Federation in the Peladon stories (and who they fought against in books such as *Transit* and *The*

Dying Days).

THE SECOND ICE AGE: When base leader Clent explains the historical background to *The Ice Warriors*, he implies that the Ice Age began a century ago, but people are still being evacuated from England during the story, suggesting that glaciation is a more recent phenomenon. It would seem that although the global temperature drop is a direct result of the destruction of plant life, its consequences weren't felt overnight.

The present scientific consensus, of course, is that destroying the forests would cause global *warming* because of the resulting rise in carbon dioxide levels. However, this didn't gain widespread awareness until the 1970s; when *The Ice Warriors* was produced in the 1960s, the idea that the Earth might undergo global cooling was given more credence.

1379 Dating *The Day of the Troll* (BBC *DW* audiobook #5) - The blurb says it's the "far future", and the story clearly follows on from the ionization effort against the glaciers in *The Ice Warriors*. It's been long enough since that story that the glaciers have been defeated, and Britain has been uninhabited for ten years.

1380 According to the back cover copy for *FP: In the Year of the Cat*. This is not what we see in *The Invisible Enemy* or *The Ice Warriors*, although both do feature artificial intelligences.

1381 *FP: In the Year of the Cat*. This is intended as the background of Mr. Sin from *The Talons of Weng-Chiang*, who is here referenced as "the Pig" automaton. For that reason, the Pig and his fellows originate from "three thousand years" after 1762.

1382 "Agent Provocateur". Captain Jack and River Song, natives of this time, both use sonic technology. *The Hollow Men* specifies one of Magnus Greel's atrocities (mentioned by the Doctor in *The Talons of Weng-Chiang*) as being "the sonic massacres in fifty-first century Brisbane".

1383 *The Talons of Weng-Chiang*. This happened "about

Sphereosis emerged from the soil in search of sustenance, and generated several "trolls" - humanoids made from twigs - to do its bidding. Baring was absorbed into Sphereosis and mentally influenced the creature to exhaust itself to death. The Doctor was convinced that without Sphereosis syphoning soil nutrients, Britain would become arable again.

The Age of Greel

"By the end of the fifth millennium AD, the homunculi created by the human species - clones, crossbreeds, fighting-machines and artificial intelligences of all descriptions - outnumbered humanity by more than thirteen to one."[1380]

Twelve clockwork automata, each of them representing a different animal on the Chinese zodiac, were fashioned to serve as army commanders. Two of these were lost - the Dragon became a "crippled and idiotic thing" while the Pig "forgot his lowly station and was taken from us".

w - Lolita sent the rest of the automata to the eighteenth century, to the court of King George III.[1381] Earth in the fifty-first century had pan-dimensional sonic weaponry.[1382]

In the Ice Age around the year 5000, Findecker's discovery of the double-nexus particle had sent human technology into a cul-de-sac. Humans nonetheless developed limited psychic techniques such as the ability to read and to influence the weak-minded. Various Alliances governed the world.

The Peking Homunculus, an automaton with the cerebral cortex of a pig, was presented as a toy for the children of the commissioner of the Icelandic Alliance - but the pig component became dominant, and the Homunculus almost precipitated World War Six. The Supreme Alliance came to power, and horrific war crimes were committed. The Doctor was with the Filipino Army when it finally defeated the Alliance at the Battle of Reykjavik.

Magnus Greel - the Alliance's Minister of Justice, and the infamous Butcher of Brisbane - had performed terrible scientific experiments on one hundred thousand prisoners in an attempt to discover time travel and immortality. He escaped to the nineteenth century using a beam of zygma energy, and feared Time Agents would pursue him.[1383]

The Doctor witnessed the sonic massacres in Brisbane.[1384] Greel's path through time was deflected when his zygma beam hit the TARDIS.[1385]

---

the year five thousand" according to the Doctor; "the fifty-first" century according to Greel. The Doctor says he was with the Filipino army during their final advance. Note that World War Six is *averted* at this time, not fought, as some sources state.

Y5K: There are three television stories which establish versions of the state of Earth around the year 5000 which seem difficult to reconcile - *The Ice Warriors*, *The Talons of Weng-Chiang* and *The Invisible Enemy*. It's notable that those last two have the Doctor and Leela involved in events of the year 5000 in near-consecutive stories (only *Horror of Fang Rock* is between them) without any link being made.

From the details given in the stories, there's a way to reconcile them - *The Invisible Enemy* happens first, in "the year 5000" itself. It's a time where Earth has highly advanced technology and a rather sterile, computer-dependent society. *The Ice Warriors* depicts exactly the same sort of society. *The Ice Warriors* also suggests that the Ice Age has been around for a century of wintery weather - but goes on to claim that it's only recently reached a crisis point, with glaciers threatening the imminent destruction of major cities. At the time of *The Invisible Enemy*, it's clearly not a pressing problem (no-one mentions the issue, and Marius is planning to return to Earth). But it might be a factor (or *the* factor) in the "breakout" - a mass emigration to other planets would ease population pressures on Earth.

After this, when the slowly-advancing ice starts encroaching on the temperate areas (in both hemi-

spheres), the crisis seen in *The Ice Warriors* occurs. (This happens in an unknown year, but possibly later on in the year 5000 itself.) There is mass migration to the equator, and we see some people in that story have rejected the computer-controlled society for a more atavistic lifestyle. It's easy to imagine such a rigidly-controlled society collapsing very quickly if the computers started failing (or arguing with each other) - it might even happen in days. Society would be split in two - those heading off into space (the scientists), and the ones staying behind (the more atavistic).

An unregulated society with little scientific progress... is exactly what *The Talons of Weng-Chiang* tells us the world is like in Greel's time, "about the year 5000" and "the fifty-first century". Greel's a scientist - but clearly one who'd thrive better on the barbaric, individualistic Earth than on a regulated, sterile space station. Environmental collapse and warfare made the Earth a very hostile environment, as seen in *Emotional Chemistry* (towards the beginning of the process) and "The Keep" (ten years on).

Meanwhile, *The Empty Child/The Doctor Dances* tells us that humanity has spread across the galaxy. The *Girl in the Fireplace* shows us that, like the society seen *in The Ice Warriors*, people of this time clearly like reminders of the past along with their high-technology. And - as in the earlier story - when the technology fails, humanity doesn't last long.

1384 *The Hollow Men*, in the "fifty-first century".
1385 *The Shadow of Weng-Chiang*

5000 - EMOTIONAL CHEMISTRY[1386] -> Magnus Greel had been a Chinese national, part of the PacBloc regime. The PacBloc used anti-matter shells against opposing armies, but not on population centres, and deployed Stepperiders and Locust aircraft. The Alliance forces used Thor battle tanks and Fenrir reconnaissance tanks. An Alliance division commanded by Razum Kinzhal stormed Greel's fortress and secured his Zygma technology. Using this, Kinzhal developed transit belts that let his agents roam time and secure possessions formerly owned by Kinzhal's beloved, Dusha.

Hostilities had increased between the PacBloc - led by one of Greel's lieutenants, Karsen Mogushestvo - and the Icelandic Alliance. The strategies of the Alliance's Lord General Razum Kinzhal devastated the PacBloc's air force. Kinzhal's forces further eliminated Mogushestvo's troops in Sverdlovsk, and overran Omsk.

Formerly a being known as a Magellan, Kinzhal sought to reunite with his other half, the nineteenth century Russian noblewoman Dusha. The eighth Doctor realised that such an act would obliterate Earth as the Magellan recorporalised. Kinzhal's assistant, Angel Malenkaya, was mortally wounded and offered herself as a host. The Doctor used the Misl Vremya device in 2024 to link this era with 1812, and thereby transferred Dusha's soul into Angel's body. Reunited with his love, Kinzhal considered reorganising his temporal paratroopers into "a unit for policing the past and preserving the future".

As part of these events, Trix stole a psionic weapon that Kinzhal had developed using enemy technology. However, she was forced to abandon it.

c 5010 - "The Keep"[1387] -> The Sun began to fail. The great Metropolises fell and the rich deserted the Earth - they left for the stars in a fleet of space arks. Those who remained behind became desperate. Matter transmission was commonplace, and this development broke up the nation states and ushered in the Transmat Wars. The whole world became a battlefield.

Ten years into the Transmat Wars, the eighth Doctor and Izzy followed an SOS in the Vortex. They were captured by Uber-Marshal Hsui Leng of Greel's army, who believed they hailed from a structure named the Keep, and that they could help him secure the "treasure" within.

The Doctor and Izzy were transmatted inside the Keep by an android called Marquez. He served the greatest sci-

1386 Dating *Emotional Chemistry* (EDA #66) - The date is given in the blurb, and is clearly tied in with *The Talons of Weng-Chiang*. It's left unclear as to whether the retasking Kinzhal proposes for his paratroopers (presuming it actually happens) leads to the founding of the Time Agents; *Talons* suggests that the Time Agency was active before this, otherwise Greel wouldn't worry about "Time Agents" following him. (Unless, perhaps, he'd previously encountered some from another era.) The psionic weapon surfaces in *Eater of Wasps*.
1387 Dating "The Keep" (*DWM* #248-249) - It's "the fifty-first century", and the age of Magnus Greel. It's confirmed that the problem with the sun leads to the "solar flares" in "Wormwood".
1388 "Fire and Brimstone"
1389 *Borrowed Time*. The historical alteration is presumably undone when Blythe's scheme is nullified.
1390 Dating *Benny: The Vampire Curse*: "Predating the Predators" (Benny collection #12c) - The year is given.
1391 *Borrowed Time*
1392 "The Time Machination"
1393 "One hundred years" before *Silence in the Library/Forest of the Dead*.
1394 Dating *Borrowed Time* (NSA #49) - The year is given (p26).
1395 The end of the century prior to *The Time of Angels*.
1396 It's established in *TW: Captain Jack Harkness* that he adopted a false identity.
1397 *The Doctor Dances* first established that Jack is from the fifty-first century; the Boshane Peninsula is

referenced in *Last of the Time Lords* and *TW: Adam*.
1398 According to Jack in *TW: Fragments*.
1399 Dating *TW: Adam* (TW 2.5) - No year is given, and the placement here is roughly derived from a) actor Jack Montgomery being 15 when he played Jack in *Adam*, and b) John Hart's comment that Jack - presumably as an adult - was "Rear of the Year, 5094". There's no way of specifying how much time passed for Jack in-between the two - so in placing *Adam*, ten years have very arbitrarily been allocated.
1400 *TW: Miracle Day*
1401 *TW: Captain Jack Harkness*. The identity of his captors hasn't been revealed.
1402 *Last of the Time Lords*, *TW: Adam*. The clear implication is that immortal Jack will eventually transform into the Face of Boe, who was first seen in *The End of the World*. Those wishing to overlook this possibility often suggest that it could have just as easily been a punning nickname that Jack acquired because there was already a famous Face of Boe in his native era. Or, of course, both could be true.

There is no Boeshane Peninsula on present day Earth. That said, it's a safe bet that some place names on Earth will change in the next three thousand years, particularly if various floods, ice ages, solar flares and other incidents create new geographical features. There's never been any explicit confirmation that Jack grew up on Earth rather than another planet colonised by humans. Wherever the Boeshane Peninsula is, the people there speak with American accents.
1403 *TW: Kiss Kiss, Bang Bang*, *TW: Exit Wounds*.

entist of the age, the shrivelled Crivello, who had built an artificial sun - the Cauldron - to become the centrepiece of a new solar system for humanity in the Crab Nebula. The Cauldron was alive, and required a living conduit to achieve fusion and launch itself - only the Doctor, as a time traveller, was able to communicate with the Cauldron and survive. He did so, and the Cauldron headed out to the Crab Nebula, promising a new life for those that followed. After the Doctor departed, Marquez killed Crivello.

Marquez was actually a Dalek construct, and was trying to help his masters secure the Cauldron. The Daleks needed the artificial sun to fight spider-Daleks from a parallel universe. Work on the Cauldron had been secretly funded by the Threshold, as part of a plan to eliminate the Daleks' war fleet.[1388]

Paper magazines still existed in the year 5013. For a time, it was fashionable to print them on edible, vitamin-rich paper that was flavoured with the saliva of the author. Professor Henrietta Nwokolo and her team at Aberdeen University were honoured for their innovations, including the Super Infinite Cosmic Battery.

(=) Jane Blythe's time commodity scheme in 2007 diminished Earth's future and Nwokolo's accomplishment, meaning that a professor at Tokyo University was given the Buffet Prize for inventing a less-effective cosmic-power battery.[1389]

5019 - BENNY: THE VAMPIRE CURSE: "Predating the Predators"[1390] **->** A salvage crew found the starship with the last of the vampiric Utlunta, Lilu, in orbit near Bathory's Star. Lilu escaped into history by booking passage with Yesterways, Ltd., a time travel company embarking on a "The V is for Vampire" tour of different Earth eras.

The Super Lucky Romance Camera was invented on Earth in 5044, and was used on more than thirty planets. People could use such devices to extend their holidays by placing themselves in time bubbles.[1391] In the mid-fifty-first century, "Jonathan Smith", a member of the Supreme Alliance, repaired the Zygma Beam and travelled to 1889 to try to prevent the death of Magnus Greel.[1392]

A young girl, Charlotte Abigail Lux, was dying - and so her family turned an entire planet into a library to keep her occupied. The planet's core was the largest index computer and hard drive ever built, and Charlotte's mind was deposited inside it. The world became known as simply The Library - it contained every book ever written, and had "whole continents of Jeffrey Archer, Bridget Jones, Monty Python's *Big Red Book*" and more.

The books in the library were made from forests inhabited by the Vashta Nerada: microspores that lived in darkness, and fed off meat. They were on most inhabited worlds, and had endowed nearly every species with a fear of the dark. The Vashta Nerada in the Library books swarmed, and so the central computer teleported out the four thousand and twenty-two patrons in the Library. With nowhere to send the patrons, the computer digitally saved them on the planet's hard drive. The last outgoing message from the Library read, "The lights are going out", and then the planet was sealed. It took the Lux family three generations to find a way back in.[1393]

5087 - BORROWED TIME[1394] **->** Amy and Rory enjoyed a brief holiday on Earth until the eleventh Doctor collected them. Earth's cities had all been documented. New York had an Ascendancy Tower. Tourists could visit the beaches of Old Tokyo.

A dormant Weeping Angel was found in the ruins of Razbahan, and was kept in private hands.[1395]

Captain Jack Harkness

The man who would later become known as Captain Jack Harkness[1396] was a Time Agent in the fifty-first century. He lived on the Boshane Peninsula.[1397] The people of the fifty-first century, including Captain Jack, had pheromones far more potent than people from the twenty-first.[1398]

c 5084 - TW: ADAM[1399] **->** An unnamed race of howling aliens routinely passed by Jack's hometown - but one day, when he was an adolescent, they besieged it. Jack's father, Franklin, was killed while searching for Jack's mother. Jack lost his grip on his younger brother Gray in the chaos, and, unable to face his mother afterwards, ran away. He fruitlessly spent years searching for his missing brother.

As an adult, Jack still didn't know his mother's fate.[1400]

When Jack was young, he convinced a friend to go off with him to fight "the worst creatures imaginable", but they were captured and tortured. His friend was killed for being the weaker of the two.[1401] Jack was the first person from the Boshane Peninsula to join the Time Agency. He became a poster boy for the organisation, and was known as "the Face of Boe".[1402]

The Agency partnered Jack with Captain John Hart, as it was thought that Jack could "control" him. They were once trapped in a time bubble together for five years. Jack was dubbed "Rear of the Year, 5094".[1403]

This era was the native time of Time Agents Kala, Jode and Fatboy; the eighth Doctor met them in Marpling in

1932. They could time travel using a temporal transduction beam.[1404]

Jack awoke one morning while still in the Time Agents' employ and found two years of his memories were missing. He eventually acquired a Chula warship and took up trying to con his former colleagues. Jack came to own a sonic blaster/cannon/disruptor fitted with digital removal and rewind, and which was made at the weapons factories at Villengard. The Doctor visited the weapons factories, leading to an incident where the main reactor went critical. The summer groves of Villengard, which produced bananas, took to growing in the factories' place.

By this point, humanity had spread out across half the galaxy, and had commenced "dancing" with many species.[1405]

The Time Agency was eventually shut down; John Hart later told Jack Harkness that there were "only seven of us left now".[1406]

John Hart found Jack's now-adult brother Gray surrounded by corpses, and chained to the ruins of a city in the Bedla Mountains. Gray was the only survivor, and had gone mad owing to the torture he'd received. He forced Hart to help him exact vengeance on Jack in the twenty-first century.[1407]

When Lorna Bucket was a child, she met the Doctor in the Heaven-neutral, normally uneventful Gamma Forests. He said "run" a lot, and they ran together. The event inspired her to join the military arm of the Church in the hope of meeting him again. To the people of the Gamma Forests, the word "doctor" came to mean "mighty warrior".[1408]

1404 *Eater of Wasps*. The trio hails from "three thousand years" after 1932, but it's after *Emotional Chemistry*, so Kala is rounding up. They are presumably working for the same Agency as Captain Jack.

1405 *The Empty Child/The Doctor Dances*. The latter states Jack is from the fifty-first century.

1406 *TW: Kiss Kiss, Bang Bang*

1407 The backstory to *TW: Fragments, TW: Exit Wounds*.

1408 Apparently around twenty years before *A Good Man Goes to War*.

1409 DATING RIVER SONG IS A COMPLICATED BUSINESS: The Doctor refers to River Song's native time - in other words, when she attends university and is later confined to Stormcage - as "the fifty-first century" on two occasions (in *Silence in the Library* and *The Time of the Angels*). However, the two instances when we're given specific dates regarding River's home era (*Let's Kill Hitler*, 5123; *The Pandorica Opens*, 5145) occur in stories that chronologically take place before the Doctor's remarks, and happen in the fifty-*second* century. This contradiction would perhaps be more irritating, were it not so emblematic of River's history being even more complicated than it first appears.

The shorthand where River and the Doctor are concerned is that they meet in reverse order... the Doctor first meets River (from his point of view) when she dies (in *Silence in the Library/Forest of the Dead*), and she looks "younger" each subsequent time they meet up (with a line in *Let's Kill Hitler* explaining that she plays with her appearance). River broadly confirms in *The Impossible Astronaut* that she and the Doctor meet in reverse order ("It's all back to front. My past is his future. We're travelling in opposite directions. Every time we meet, I know him more and he knows me less."), and the ending of *Day of the Moon* depends upon it. In that story, the Doctor kisses River for what to him is the "first time", and River becomes alarmed that for her, this means it'll be the final time.

The idea that River and the Doctor always meet in

exactly reverse order starts to crumble once it's considered that if that were true, why do they compare diaries to determine where they are in each others' lifetimes? An exact reverse order would mean that River, at least, would always *know* the order of their meet-ups without having to ask. Perhaps she's just playing along, but this risks the Doctor hearing spoilers about the future. It becomes all the harder to rationalise in instances such as her asking in *Silence of the Library* if the Doctor has experienced the crash of the *Byzantium* (*The Time of Angels*), when exact reverse order would dictate that of course he hasn't. In fact, there are so many exceptions to the "reverse order rule" (the most glaring being that the Doctor, Amy and Rory are present when the Alex Kingston incarnation of River is "born" in *Let's Kill Hitler*, and again encounter her older self after that point), a more accurate way of putting it would be, "River and the Doctor encounter each other in reverse order... except for all the occasions that they don't."

A looming question that never gets answered is why they're meeting in reverse order *at all*, as if someone or some thing is trying (however imperfectly) to actually make their meet-ups run back-to-front. One possibility goes to a theory mooted in *About Time* - that in classic *Doctor Who*, the TARDISes of Time Lords such as the Doctor, the Master, the Rani, etc., coordinate things so that their pilots keep meeting each other in chronological order. Perhaps such protocols are rent asunder following the obliteration of Gallifrey and the Time Lords prior to New *Who*, making the psuedo-reverse means by which the Doctor and River keep meeting better than nothing.

For the Doctor (and the audience), his meet-ups with River are: *Silence in the Library/Forest of the Dead*; *The Time of Angels/Flesh and Stone*; *The Pandorica Opens/The Big Bang*; *The Impossible Astronaut/Day of the Moon* (909-year-old Doctor); *A Good Man Goes to War*; *Let's Kill Hitler*; *The Wedding of River Song* (1103-year-old Doctor) and, by extension, *The Impossible Astronaut* again. It is

River Song[1409]

5123 - LET'S KILL HITLER[1410] -> The eleventh Doctor, Amy and Rory took the newly regenerated River Song to the Sisters of the Infinite Schism, the "greatest hospital in the universe", to recover from the events of 1938. The Doctor left River a TARDIS-patterned, blank diary in which she would record her adventures. River recovered after the TARDIS had departed, and enrolled in Luna University to study archaeology under Professor Candy. The profession enabled her to uncover clues about the Doctor.

The movement known as the Silence and Academy of the Question, allied with the military forces of the Church (the Clerics) and the Headless Monks, believed that on the fields of Trenzalor at the fall of the Eleventh, when any living creature present must answer truly, a question that should never, ever be answered would be asked... and that silence would fall. The Silence sought to prevent the Doctor from ever reaching Trenzalor and answering the question, and worked to craft a weapon against him...[1411]

CLOSING TIME/THE WEDDING OF RIVER SONG[1412] -> The day River was awarded her doctorate, she read the account of children who saw the Doctor prior to

his meeting his death at Lake Silencio in 2011. Madame Kovarian, the Silence and the Clerics overpowered River and placed her in an augmented NASA astronaut suit. They then took her back to Lake Silencio, to kill the Doctor as history dictated. River returned to this era after she had married the Doctor.

River Song was imprisoned in the Stormcage Containment Facility for murder.[1413] The Daleks had records of River Song, and knew that she was not merciful.[1414] River dated a Nestene duplicate with a swappable head.[1415] She learned how to fly the TARDIS.[1416]

5145 - THE PANDORICA OPENS[1417] -> The TARDIS forwarded a call from Winston Churchill to River Song in Stormcage. He told her about the Vincent van Gogh painting *The Pandorica Opens*, and so she escaped and stole it from the Royal Collection aboard Starship UK. Liz X stopped River, but let her go when she understood that the Doctor was involved. River then travelled to a bar, the Maldovarium, and acquired a vortex manipulator "fresh from the wrist of a handsome Time Agent" from the bar owner, Dorium Maldovar. She used this to travel first to Planet One, then - based upon the date and map reference that Vincent included in the painting - Rome in 120 AD.

---

usually not specified exactly how many years pass between the Doctor and River's encounters in either her home era or elsewhere. As River is a human-Time Lord hybrid with a more malleable appearance (per *Let's Kill Hitler*), the time between their encounters is doubly indeterminate.

It should also be noted that Captain Jack Harkness hails from the late 5000s and so is a rough contemporary of River, but we've no record of their meeting one another. In *Silence in the Library/Forest of the Dead*, River has a squareness gun identical to Jack's (although it's entirely possible that she found Jack's old gun in the TARDIS), and *The Pandorica Opens* has her buying a time travel-enabling vortex manipulator that's "fresh from the [severed] wrist of a handsome Time Agent" (not that said handsome agent is necessarily Jack himself).

Timelink dated *Silence in the Library/Forest of the Dead* to 5008, but saw print before it could take River's appearances in Series 5 and 6 into consideration.

1410 Dating *Let's Kill Hitler* (X6.8) - The date River starts university is given in a caption. Professor Candy, who is named in the credits, first appeared in the short story "Continuity Errors" (also by Steven Moffat) and is mentioned in *Benny: Oh No It Isn't!*

1411 The background to much of Series 5 and 6, as given in *The Wedding of River Song*.

1412 Dating *Closing Time* (X6.12) - No date is given, but as River has been awarded her doctorate, it's at least several years since we last saw her in *Let's Kill Hitler*.

1413 After *Closing Time* and before *A Good Man Goes to War*. It's not entirely clear how this came to pass, as it looks like River is convicted and imprisoned for the Doctor's murder by the Clerics - the same organisation that helped to train and task her with killing him in the first place. That said, different factions within the Clerics might be working to different ends - by *The Time of Angels*, Father Octavian and his Clerics are not only willing to involve the Doctor in their affairs, Octavian blatantly draws the Doctor's attention to the murder (namely, his own) that River committed.

1414 *The Big Bang*

1415 Before *The Big Bang*.

1416 She can adeptly fly the Ship (in her timeline) no later than *The Pandorica Opens*. River says (*The Time of Angels*) that she had TARDIS-flying lessons from "the very best" and that it was a "shame" the Doctor was busy that day, but yells "You taught me!" at the Doctor in *The Pandorica Opens*. In *Let's Kill Hitler*, the TARDIS itself teaches River how to pilot it.

1417 Dating *The Pandorica Opens* (X5.12) - The date is given in three captions. River and the Doctor seem to be married by now, as implied by her impish conversation with him at the end of *The Big Bang*.

River returned to Stormcage after going to 2010 to spur Amy's memory of the Doctor, which restored him to life after he had sealed the Cracks in Time.[1418]

The Silence learned that Amy Pond was pregnant, and determined that if she and Rory Williams conceived the child while travelling in the TARDIS, the child might have some Time Lord attributes - meaning it could be turned into a weapon. The pregnant Amy was kidnapped from another time zone, replaced with a Ganger duplicate and taken to an asteroid fortress: Demon's Run. While Madame Kovarian kept watch over Amy's gestation, Amy's mind interacted with her Ganger duplicate - and remained unaware that she had been abducted.[1419]

THE REBEL FLESH / A GOOD MAN GOES TO WAR[1420]

-> The eleventh Doctor severed the connection between Amy and her Ganger. Amy awoke at Demon's Run and gave birth to a daughter, whom she named "Melody" after her best friend Mels.[1421]

"Demons run when a good man goes to war; Night will fall and drown the sun; When a good man goes to war; Friendship dies and true love lies; Night will fall and the dark will rise; When a good man goes to war; Demons run, but count the cost; The battle's won, but the child is lost; When a good man goes to war."

1418 In unknown circumstances between (from River's point of view) *The Big Bang* and *The Time of Angels*.

1419 At some point prior to *The Impossible Astronaut*, as revealed in *The Rebel Flesh* and *A Good Man Goes to War*.

1420 Dating *The Rebel Flesh* and *A Good Man Goes to War* (X6.6-6.7) - No firm date is given, but Dorium's presence (he was last seen in *The Pandorica Opens*) suggests that this is River Song's "native time". It's a bit of an oddity that River is born after her adult self has been confined to Stormcage, but it's no more strange than so many other things about her. The River who appears at Demon's Run can independently travel in time; for all we're told, she only gains the vortex manipulator that lets her do so in *The Pandorica Opens*. The Cybermen seen here are the first in the new TV series that don't have the Cybus logo on them, and are clearly a galactic power in the far future.

1421 *Let's Kill Hitler*

1422 *The Impossible Astronaut/Day of the Moon*

1423 Dating *The Wedding of River Song* (X6.13) - No date given, but we can infer that all of these events occur in the same timezone. Dorium's appearance is explicitly after the main events of *A Good Man Goes to War*.

1424 Dating *A Good Man Goes to War* (X6.7) - This is tricky to place. The fact that River has knowledge of events at Demon's Run - in particular, that the Doctor will then learn her true identity - suggests that for her, those events have already happened.

River doesn't seem to know, until Rory arrives, that it's the day that Demon's Run will occur - so even though it's her birthday, it's presumably a different year from when she was literally born. This has the slightly awkward consequence that while *A Good Man Goes to War* is set in River's native era, Rory must not visit Stormcage at the exact same time as the effort to rescue Amy from Demon's Run. With the Doctor recruiting allies from all throughout time and space, it's possible that Rory or the Doctor just told the TARDIS, "Take us to

River", and it acted accordingly. (Hence Rory's comment that, "The time streams, I'm not quite sure where we are...")

1425 In River's lifetime, these events happen before *The Impossible Astronaut*.

1426 Dating *The Impossible Astronaut/Day of the Moon* (X6.1-6.2) - The general reverse order of the Doctor and River's meet-ups would suggest that these two episodes would, for her, occur prior to *A Good Man Goes to War*. Also, River acts as if she and the Doctor who took her to the 1814 frost fair are quite chummy - so if *Day of the Moon* is indeed the last time she kisses him, the frost fair trip likely occurs (for River) before that event.

1427 Dating *The Time of Angels, Flesh and Stone* and *The Big Bang* (X5.4-5.5, X5.13) - River tells the Doctor that they will next meet "when the Pandorica opens" - meaning that for her, it's after *The Pandorica Opens* (set in 5145).

1428 *The Time of Angels/Flesh and Stone*. There's no mention of her being imprisoned after this point.

1429 *The Wedding of River Song*. River says that she "climbed out of the wreck of the *Byzantium*" and is dressed as she was at the end of *Flesh and Stone*. She has very possibly been released from prison at this point, although that's not explicitly stated.

1430 As the Doctor let slip to her in *The Time of Angels*, and as she introduces herself in *Silence in the Library*. Octavian refers to her as "Doctor Song" in *The Time of Angels*.

1431 *Forest of the Dead*. River tells the Doctor, "You never show up in the right order, though. I need the spotter's guide." As he doesn't meet her before his tenth life, it perhaps suggests that River meets other Doctors past the Matt Smith version. This would further violate the notion that River and the Doctor meet in exact reverse order, though.

1432 At some point before *Silence in the Library*. If the Doctor does indeed *not* tell River his real name when they're wed (*The Wedding of River Song*), and instead tells her the secret ("Look into my eye") that he doesn't have to die after all, then the most likely place that this

The eleventh Doctor and Rory narrowed down Amy's location, and visited the Twelfth Cyber Legion because it monitored that quadrant of the galaxy. The Doctor destroyed part of the fleet, and the Cybermen revealled the location of Demon's Run. To help save Amy, the Doctor and Rory recruited people who owed the Doctor a debt: Madame Vastra and Jenny, Commander Strax, the World War II pilot Danny Boy, the information broker Dorium Maldovar, pirate Captain Avery and Toby, as well as squads of Judoon and Silurians.

The Doctor provoked such in-fighting among his opponents that he swiftly took control of Demon's Run and routed the Clerics. He and Rory rescued Amy and met the newborn Melody. The Headless Monks eluded detection and counter-attacked, decapitating Dorium and killing Strax and the Cleric named Lorna Bucket - who had come to warn the Doctor of the danger. Kovarian escaped with the infant Melody.

River Song appeared in the battle's aftermath, and revealled to the Doctor, Amy and Rory that she was the adult Melody Pond. In the language of the people of the Gamma Forests - which had no ponds - "Melody Pond" translated as "River Song". The Doctor departed with new confidence that he could defeat Kovarian, leaving River to return his allies home.

The Silence took Melody to Earth, the 1960s, so she could be raised in a human-norm environment.[1422]

THE WEDDING OF RIVER SONG[1423] -> The eleventh Doctor investigated the Silence, and found the Seventh Transept, where the Headless Monks were keeping the still-living head of Dorium Maldovar. He also tracked down a former envoy of the Silence, Father Gideon Vandaleur... who had died six months before, and was actually the justice-agent spaceship *Teselecta* in disguise. The Doctor believed that he could no longer avoid travelling to 2011 to die at Lake Silencio, and asked the justice agents to deliver messages so Amy, Rory, River Song, an older Canton Delaware and a younger version of the eleventh Doctor could meet him there.

He also asked the justice agents if they would disguise the *Teselecta* to resemble him - a means of his avoiding death and thwarting the fixed point in time at Lake Silencio.

The Doctor succeeded, lived... and married River Song. He later returned Dorium's head to the transept, and Dorium pledged to keep the secret that the Doctor had cheated death.

A GOOD MAN GOES TO WAR[1424] -> River voluntarily returned to Stormcage after the Doctor took her ice skating on the river Thames, 1814, for her birthday. Rory approached River to help find him and the Doctor rescue Amy, but she refused, knowing that these events would lead to the Battle of Demon's Run, and that she could only appear at the "very end".

River Song and the Doctor met Jim the Fish. They also visited Easter Island.[1425]

THE IMPOSSIBLE ASTRONAUT / DAY OF THE MOON[1426] -> The Doctor sent River an invite to join him at Lake Silencio in Utah, the twenty-first century. She escaped Stormcage, and went there. The Doctor later brought her back to Stormcage and they kissed... it was the first time they had done so for the Doctor, meaning it was the last time for River.

THE TIME OF THE ANGELS / FLESH AND STONE / THE BIG BANG[1427] -> There were laws against marrying one's self.

The Weeping Angel found on Razbahan caused the category-four starliner *Byzantium* to crash on Alfava Metraxis - all part of an attempt to rescue the Angels sleeping in a maze of the dead there. The Clerics released River Song from Stormcage into the custody of Father Octavian, and offered her a pardon if she helped contain the situation. She carved a message into the *Byzantium*'s flight recorder, its Home Box, that summoned the eleventh Doctor and Amy to this time. The Angels fed off the *Byzantium*'s power, and gained enough strength to stalk the Doctor's party.

The eleventh Doctor's future self momentarily visited the *Byzantium* while he was backtracking along his own timeline. He stressed to Amy the importance that she remember the words he spoke to her when she was seven.

A Crack in Time appeared, and the "current" Doctor fed the Angels into it - they constituted enough of a space-time event that the Crack was sealed as it destroyed them. The Doctor learned that River was imprisoned for killing "a very good man", and that he would see her again when the Pandorica opened.

River Song was granted her pardon.[1428] She travelled to 2011 to tell Amy and Rory that the Doctor didn't die at Lake Silencio.[1429] River Song became a professor.[1430] She had pictures of all the Doctor's incarnations, but didn't know their order.[1431]

The Doctor told River Song his real name; "there was only one time he could" do that.[1432]

The Doctor and River went to the end of the universe together. Their adventures included the Bone Meadows and a picnic at Asgard. When the Doctor knew that the time had come for River to visit the

Library and meet her fate, he showed up on her doorstep with a new haircut and a suit. He took her to Darillium, where the towers sang - the Doctor cried, but didn't tell River why. He gave her an advanced sonic screwdriver equipped with a neural relay.[1433]

SILENCE IN THE LIBRARY / FOREST OF THE DEAD[1434] -> Professor River Song joined an expedition sent by Felman Lux Corporation to their planet-sized Library, which had been sealed off for a hundred years, and sent a message that the Doctor should join her there. The message was received much too early in the Doctor's timeline, and so the tenth Doctor arrived at the Library with Donna. He had not yet met River in his personal timestream.

The Vashta Nerada swarmed once more, and the Library's self-destruct was activated. The Doctor and the Vashta Nerada agreed that they could have the

Library if the Doctor was given one day to free the four thousand and twenty-two people saved on the Library's hard drive. The Doctor intended to hook himself up the Library's computer so his own memory space could be used to initiate the transfer - an act that would burn out his hearts, and kill him beyond all hope of regeneration. River incapacitated the Doctor and took his place. When he awoke, bound to the wall, she told him:

> "It's not over for you. You'll see me again. You've got all of that to come. You and me, time and space. You watch us run."

River's body died as the patrons were restored to life and the Library's self-destruct was terminated. The Doctor realised that River's sonic screwdriver had a neural relay that contained the last vestiges of her

---

occurs is when he's dying and whispers in her ear in *Let's Kill Hitler*. That, or the Doctor's real name actually *is* "Look Into My Eye".

1433 All before *Silence in the Library/Forest of the Dead*.

1434 Dating *Silence in the Library/Forest of the Dead* (X4.8-4.9) - For River, the story takes place an unspecified amount of time after *Flesh and Stone*. See the Dating River Song essay.

1435 Six hundred years after *Tomb of Valdemar*, according to the Doctor.

1436 Dating "Fire and Brimstone" (*DWM* #251-255) - The Doctor says "some two hundred years ago, I saw the Cauldron launched", a reference to "The Keep". The humans in this story don't recognise the Daleks.

1437 Dating "Wormwood" (*DWM* #266-271) - It's "twenty years" since "Fire and Brimstone" according to Chastity. Earth's moon is here destroyed (albeit without any mention of the environmental havoc such an event would inevitably mean for Earth itself), but might be restored off screen, as it looks whole in "The Child of Time" (*DWM*). By *The Long Game* (set in 200,000), Earth is the centre of the Fourth Great and Bountiful Empire, and has five moons.

1438 "Thirty years ago" in *The Mutant Phase*.

1439 "Twenty years" before *The Apocalypse Element*.

1440 Dating *The Mutant Phase* (BF #15) - No date is given, but this is the first *Doctor Who* audio set in the period of the *Dalek Empire* series; see the dating notes on *The Genocide Machine*.

1441 Dating *The Genocide Machine* (BF #7) - The dating for this story - which otherwise seems so unimposing - is surprisingly important, in that the whole of the *Dalek Empire* mini-series and its related *Doctor Who* audios (*The Mutant Phase*, *The Apocalypse Element*, *Dust Breeding, Return of the Daleks*) are contingent on the placement of this one adventure. (See the dating notes under the individual audios, and especially those under *Dalek Empire I*, for why.)

Only four pieces of evidence, however, exist to help make this decision: 1. In *The Genocide Machine*, the war between the Knights of Velyshaa and Earth (mentioned in *The Sirens of Time* as ending in 3562) is said to be "centuries ago". 2. The Big Finish website at one point dated *The Genocide Machine* to 4256. 3. Bev Tarrant, a native to the era of *The Genocide Machine*, twice states in *Benny: The Judas Gift* (definitely set in October 2607) that she's from "three thousand years in the future". 4. *Dalek Empire II* (set some "centuries" after *The Genocide Machine*) ends with a "Kill All Daleks" pulse being sent out into the Milky Way and Seriphia galaxies. (So, any placement for *The Genocide Machine* can't be just before a story with high Dalek involvement in those territories.)

The two pieces of evidence central to this discussion are the website date and Bev's statements. They can't be reconciled without concluding that when Bev said "three thousand years", she actually means only about 1650-ish years. Previous editions of *Ahistory* favoured the website date, but did not include the Benny series. This edition takes the "three thousand years" lines and rounds it somewhat to fit it around other stories, so that *The Genocide Machine* is set in 5256, not 4256.

One potential hiccup is that this is not long after the native time of Captain Jack Harkness and River Song, in which humanity has time technology at its disposal - whereas it manifestly doesn't throughout *Dalek Empire*. This is an issue, however, irregardless of *Dalek Empire*'s dating - in that one brief period, mankind (or certain members of it, at the very least) has time-tech, and yet it clearly doesn't on an ongoing basis. No explanation has been provided in any *Doctor Who* story for why this is the case.

1442 *Benny: The Judas Gift*

1443 Dating *The Apocalypse Element* (BF #11) - This is another story set around the time of the *Dalek Empire* audios.

mind, and transferred it into the Library's hard drive. River's mind took up residence in the hard drive's simulation of reality, along with the minds of her slain archaeology team and Charlotte Abigail Lux. The Doctor and Donna continued their travels.

The principles of atmospheric flotation were discovered.[1435]

c 5200 - "Fire and Brimstone"[1436] **->** Ninety-seven "audited precessions" after the Breakout, the eighth Doctor and Izzy landed on the satelloid Icarus Falling - one of six satellites revolving around the artificial sun Crivello's Cauldron. This was the New Earth system in the Crab Nebula, and held some of the remnants of humanity.

A Dalek fleet soon arrived and released self-replicating robot insects - the Contagium - to secure Icarus Falling. The Daleks sought to wipe out a race of spider-Daleks from a parallel dimension, and wanted to collapse the Cauldron and create a black hole - the means by which they could travel to the home territory of their rivals. The Daleks installed a synaptic conduit into the Doctor's brain, believing he could navigate their fleet through the black hole.

Sister Chastity, a religious official aboard Icarus Falling, revealed herself as a member of Threshold and rescued the Doctor. She claimed that Threshold had changed in the thousands of years since the Doctor last encountered them, and intended - with the Doctor's help - to crush the Dalek fleet as they passed through the black hole that the Cauldron would become. The Daleks took control of the Cauldron anyway, but spider-Daleks poured through the gateway and engaged Phalanx 44 of Special Weapons Daleks in battle. The Doctor learned that the Threshold had been hired by the Time Lords, and engineered a supernova that destroyed both Dalek armies. The Cauldron became an ordinary sun with planets orbiting it.

c 5220 - "Wormwood"[1437] **->** The newly-regenerated ninth Doctor (who was balding, wore a bowtie and carried a toothbrush in his jacket pocket), Izzy and Fey landed in Wormwood, a mock Western village controlled by Threshold on the moon. Their leader, Abraham White, showed the Doctor a host of landmarks from Earth such as the Eiffel Tower, the Statue of Liberty, Mount Rushmore and so forth, which he had saved to celebrate mankind's achievements. Fey confronted White after learning they'd been spying on her for years, but White summoned a demonic beast, the Pariah.

Izzy discovered that the Threshold were building the Eye of Disharmony, a device that made space impassable. Activated, the Eye annihilated the Traxonnia Research Cluster, the Kapli Refugee Fleet, the Ninth Sontaran Armada and every other vessel in space. The Threshold sent a transwarp signal to every civilisation offering to sell their teleport windows as an alternative.

The eighth Doctor showed up, and revealed that the "ninth Doctor" was actually Shayde in disguise. The Pariah, in turn, revealed that she was the original Shayde - who had rebelled against Rassilon. She defeated Shayde in battle, then killed all the members of Threshold to drain their energy. Fey merged with the wounded Shayde, gaining his powers, and they launched a second attack that destroyed Pariah. White also died.

The Eye of Disharmony's destruction obliterated Earth's moon, but restored space to its natural state. "Feyde" left the Doctor and Izzy's company to travel on her own.

(=) Daleks infected with wasp DNA mutated into a swarm of invulnerable, giant wasp-like creatures and devastated Earth, draining all of its minerals and nutrients. The colony planets were unable to help and all attempts to recolonise ended in starvation.[1438]

Unique minerals on Etra Prime draw the attention of over fifty galactic powers, including the Daleks and the Time Lords. The Daleks removed the planet, along with a team of researchers and President Romana, from space-time. A galactic war was only narrowly averted.[1439]

(=) c 5250 - THE MUTANT PHASE[1440] **->** The wasp-like Mutant Phase Daleks attacked Skaro, and the Emperor Dalek ordered the fifth Doctor and Nyssa to travel back to 2158 and prevent the Mutant Phase's creation. The Emperor Dalek self-destructed Skaro, but downloaded his consciousness into the Thal Ganatus and accompanied the TARDIS crew.

c 5256 - THE GENOCIDE MACHINE[1441] **->** The seventh Doctor and Ace visited the library of Kar-Charrat. The chief librarian, Elgin, had built a wetworks research facility that stored the sum of universal knowledge in liquid form. To accomplish this, Elgin had enslaved nearly the entire Kar-Charrat race, using their drop-sized bodies as data storage units.

Dormant Daleks on the planet revived and attacked. They gained access to the library by duplicating Ace, and all but destroyed the library in their quest for its data. The Doctor defeated them with the help of a "collector", Bev Tarrant, a legendary thief[1442] who was planning a heist. The library was ruined.

& 5256 - THE APOCALYPSE ELEMENT[1443] **->** The sixth Doctor and Evelyn landed on Archetryx as a Time Treaty was being signed. The missing planet Etra Prime suddenly re-appeared on a collision course with Archetryx. The Daleks wanted to wipe out the conference. Romana escaped her captors on Etra Prime. The Doctor, Romana and Evelyn went to Gallifrey as the planetary collision took place and the Daleks instigated an epic attack. The Daleks destroyed the Seriphia galaxy with the Apocalypse Element, generating a million new worlds there. They set about reshaping Seriphia in their image.

& 5257 - STORM HARVEST[1444] - The inhabitants of the waterworld Coralee had developed the Krill - vicious, aquatic humanoids with razor-sharp teeth - as instruments of war. The Krill wiped out their own creators, then entered hibernation. The Dreekans later colonised the planet, despite the legends of great danger there. They offered private islands for sale to the super-rich. The Krill awakened and were defeated by the seventh Doctor and Ace. Nonetheless, some Krill survived as eggs in a nearby asteroid field.

& 5257 - DUST BREEDING[1445] -> The Master brought the Warp Core, an energy creature contained in Edvard Munch's painting *The Scream*, to the planet Duchamp 331, a refuelling station off the main space lanes. It served as home to technicians and a small colony of artists. The Master sought to seed the Warp Core's energy into the dust on Duchamp 331, then goad it into action against its ancient enemies, the Krill. This would have created a

planet-sized weapon. The seventh Doctor and Ace defeated the Master, and the surface of Duchamp 331 was caught in an inferno that destroyed the Warp Core.

Bev Tarrant accepted a lift from the Doctor and Ace, and eventually parted company with them in 2595.

& 5261 - PRIME TIME[1446] -> The seventh Doctor and Ace investigated the activities of Channel 400 on Blinni-Gaar, only to become part of the station's programming. Meanwhile, the Master landed on Scrantek and made a deal with the Fleshsmiths, a race that harvested other races to continue their existence. The Master and the Fleshsmiths hoped to use the Channel 400 broadcasts to transport one hundred fifty billion viewers into the Fleshsmiths' body banks as raw material. The Doctor let the Fleshsmiths analyse a clone of himself, which broke down and released a molecular contagion. The toxin cascaded through the Scrantek network and reduced the Fleshsmiths to ooze. Channel 400 was disgraced and taken off the air.

Prior to its demise, the network tormented Ace with images from the past of her "future" tombstone. The Doctor falsely convinced Ace that the images were faked. Without her knowledge, he went back in time and dug up her corpse for clues as to how she died.

1444 Dating *Storm Harvest* (PDA #23) - No date is given. Reg Gurney, an engineer and spy on Coralee, spent thirty years in the Space Corps and fought in the Dalek Wars, supporting that dating.

1445 Dating *Dust Breeding* (BF #21) - It is "several centuries" in Ace's future, in Earth's colonial period and after the Dalek Wars. Bev Tarrant is also present, and for her, it is after *The Genocide Machine*.

1446 Dating *Prime Time* (PDA #33) - It is a year after *Storm Harvest*.

1447 Dating *The Caves of Androzani* (19.6) - There is no indication of dating on screen. Sharez Jek seems worried when it appears that the Doctor and Peri are from Earth, suggesting it has political influence (and hasn't been evacuated). The machine-pistols suggest a colonial setting, but Sirius society is long-established; there seems to be an interstellar economy and the androids are highly advanced. The Spectrox supplies must be so limited as to have little long-term effect on the human race, explaining why it is not referred to in any other story. *The Doctor, The Widow and the Wardrobe* features a Harvesting team from Androzani Major in the year 5345, and the Harvester team seems to share the same capitalist ethos seen in the earlier story. It seems reasonable to place *The Caves of Androzani* in roughly the same era - although this is slightly arbitrary, and they could take place many centuries apart.

The Terrestrial Index made a dubious link between the "federal forces" on Androzani Minor and the Galactic Federation (*The Curse of Peladon*), dating the

story to the fifth millennium. *Timelink* chose "3983", and *About Time* thought it was "The future, date unspecified", while acknowledging that a dating of as early as the twenty-second century was feasible. All of these books, however, were published before being able to take the evidence from *The Doctor, The Widow and the Wardrobe* into account.

1448 *Zamper*

1449 "Five hundred ninety-seven" years before *Tragedy Day* (p97).

1450 Dating *The Web in Space* (BBC children's 2-in-1 #6, released in *Sightseeing in Space*) - Earth has colonies on other planets, although "Earth Corp Couriers" might be a brand name, and not service Earth itself. The Daleks are spacefaring at this time. It's after humanity has encountered the Chelonians, but before the Chelonians go peaceful. Mention of Galaxy 16 suggests intergalactic travel, so we're guessing to say that this story occurs in the 5300s.

1451 Dating *The Doctor, the Widow and the Wardrobe* (X7.0) - One of the expedition team, Droxil, states that "the year is 5345". Droxil is "from" Androzani Major, meaning that this is a different planet, although they call the trees "Androzani Trees".

1452 Dating *Dalek Empire I* (episode one, *Invasion of the Daleks*; episode two, *The Human Factor*) - As with the Davros Era, the *Dalek Empire* mini-series (I-IV) are fairly easy to date in relation to one another, but it's harder to establish the century they are set. The only tangible dating evidence is the Dalek Emperor's com-

c 5300 - THE CAVES OF ANDROZANI[1447] -> Spectrox was "the most valuable substance in the universe". At the recommended dose of .3 of a centilitre a day, spectrox could halt the ageing process and double lifespans. There was some evidence that with a sufficient quantity of the substance, a human might live forever.

Spectrox was refined from the nests of the bats of Androzani Minor, a dangerous process carried out by androids. Supplies of spectrox were halted when the scientist Sharaz Jek and his androids rebelled against Androzani Major. The Praesidium sent a taskforce to apprehend Jek and they captured the refinery, but Jek removed the supplies of spectrox. The fifth Doctor and Peri were involved in an escalation of hostilities between Jek and the Praesidium's forces - Jek was killed, and the Doctor and Peri escaped during a mudburst, a tidal flood of primeval mud. The Doctor had been poisoned by raw Spectrox, and regenerated.

Along the Eastern edge of the galaxy, there was political upheaval for a thousand years. Many human colony worlds such as Pyka, Marlex, Dalverius, Pantorus and Shaggra warred with each other, and the galaxy's monetary system was in almost permanent crisis. In the fifty-fourth century, a consortium of industrialists attempted to solve the problem. Eventually they built Zamper: a neutral planet, snug in its own mini-universe, that would supply state-of-the-art battleships to all sides.

The only way to the planet was through a hyperspace gate controlled by Zamper itself, and the planet was completely self-contained to keep its designs secret. In four hundred and seventy-three years of operation, Zamper became rich and maintained a balance of power in East galaxy. The operation was completely smooth, averaging one minor technical failure every two hundred years.[1448]

Olleril was colonised. Governed by the principles laid down in the ancient records *The Collins Guide to the Twentieth Century*, *One of Us* by Hugo Young, *The Manufacture of Consent* and *The Smash Hits Yearbook*, it developed an eccentric, unworkable political and economic system that was an almost exact copy of the United Kingdom in the twentieth century. The cult of Luminus managed the planet in secret.[1449]

? 5325 - THE WEB IN SPACE[1450] -> Earth Corp Couriers served as intergalactic postmen, making deliveries to planets as the Earth colony on Hephestus Beta, which was experiencing an outbreak of Orion flu. Chelonian ships, "skymaidens", had terrorised humans in Galaxy 16. Enormous diamondweb spiders - space creatures that consumed the rocks, space dust and comets they caught in webs made from diamond - nearly went extinct when billionaires caged them as novelties. The eleventh Doctor, Amy and Rory stopped the Empire of Eternal Victory from

dissecting the last diamondweb spider to adopt its biology into their spaceship hulls. The Empire's last warship perished in a miscalculated space jump.

5345 - THE DOCTOR, THE WIDOW AND THE WARDROBE[1451] -> The eleventh Doctor had planned to take the Arwell family from 1941 to a planet where the fir trees grew natural Christmas baubles, making it the perfect winter wonderland. Cyril Arwell opened his present early and got lost on the planet. The Doctor and Lily followed, and the three of them found a lighthouse-like structure guarded by two wooden giants.

Madge Arwell followed them, and encountered a large metal walker: a Harvester from Androzani Major. A three-man team from Androzani Major was preparing to liquify the forest using acid rain; the melted wood of the Androzani Trees, when put in batteries, was the greatest fuel source in the universe. The trees were aware of this, and were planning to use the lighthouse to give up their physical forms and escape. They need to travel inside a living navigator to do this: a "strong" being, a mother. Madge served as the host, and used her memories of home to escape the world as the acid rain started to fall. She returned with the Doctor and her children back to 1941.

The Androzani Major expedition team had transmat technology, and scanners that could detect time travellers - but such scans could be confused if the subject was wearing wool.

The Seriphia-based Daleks Attack the Milky Way

& 5425 - DALEK EMPIRE I: INVASION OF THE DALEKS / THE HUMAN FACTOR[1452] -> The Milky Way was at peace, and under the protection of the Earth Alliance. The Daleks had been relegated to obscure history lessons, but had fortified themselves in the Seriphia galaxy, and now unleashed a massive invasion of human space. They conquered many planets, and enslaved billions. Amongst the many worlds to fall was Vega VI - the Daleks put slaves there to work mining veganite, a rare mineral that was too volatile to collect with Dalek technology. The Daleks were relentless taskmasters, and worked their slaves to death.

Susan Mendes, an employee of the Rhinesberg Institute, was amongst those enslaved in the mines on Vega VI. She met a fellow slave named Kalendorf - a telepathic Knight of Velyshaa who had been slated to represent his people in negotiations with Earth against the Dalek menace. The Dalek Supreme had Mendes psychologically profiled, and deemed her suitable for an undertaking to aid the Dalek cause. The slaves were allowed to rest and given food, while Mendes served as a spokesperson who encouraged the slave ranks to have hope and work hard. In this capacity, Mendes became widely known as The Angel of Mercy. As the slaves worked more willingly and required less subjugation, the Daleks diverted more resources into their war effort against Alliance forces.

Six months passed as Mendes travelled to many planets on behalf of the Daleks, obtaining better working conditions that saved millions of lives. She insisted that Kalendorf accompany her, and the two of them plotted the Daleks' downfall. On every world they visited, Kalendorf would telepathically communicate with the slave leaders, and told them to wait until Mendes publicly declared a code-phrase that would trigger an unstoppable rebellion against the Daleks.

One rebellion on the Garazone moon K-5000 broke out prematurely - Mendes feared that the insurrection would undo her master plan and reported it to the Daleks, who killed those involved. The Daleks conquered the ocean planet Guria, despite heavy resistance from the Alliance.

& 5425 - RETURN OF THE DALEKS[1453] **->** The Daleks stumbled upon the frozen Dalek army on the planet Spiridon - which had been renamed Zaleria - and sought to revive it as a weapon of war. They also hoped to crack the means by which the Spiridon natives had become visible, thinking they could reverse-engineer a means of turning Daleks invisible. Much data was collected, but any attempt to turn Daleks invisible caused fatal light-sickness.

The seventh Doctor feared that the revival of the frozen Dalek army could tip history in the Daleks' favour. He encountered Kalendorf, and the two of them spurred a minor rebellion against the Daleks. Kalendorf was captured, and the Doctor - deeming Kalendorf's place in history as too important to risk - offered to help the Daleks develop invisibility if they let Kalendorf go. The Daleks agreed, and Mendes and Kalendorf went to their next assignment. The Doctor was the Daleks' prisoner for years.

? 5426 - BROTHERHOOD OF THE DALEKS[1454] **->** The Thals had peacefully settled on the planet of New Davias. Many of them still regarded Earth as a lost planet, and the Doctor - who had contacts on New Davias - as a legend.

ment in *Dalek Empire I* episode four that it's been "centuries" since the Daleks invaded the Kar-Charrat library in *The Genocide Machine*, which in this chronology is dated to circa 5256. The war between the Knights of Velyshaa and Earth (mentioned in *The Sirens of Time* as ending in 3562) is said to have occurred "long ago".

1453 Dating *Return of the Daleks* (BF subscription promo #4) - The story occurs between *Dalek Empire I* episodes one (*Invasion of the Daleks*) and two (*The Human Factor*).

The knock-on effect of moving the *Dalek Empire* stories to the sixth millennium (see *The Genocide Machine* for how this came about) introduces a contradiction that *Ahistory* Second Edition had otherwise resolved. In *Return of the Daleks*, the seventh Doctor guarantees that the Dalek army on Spiridon (from *Planet of the Daleks*) remains frozen; later on, in "Emperor of the Daleks", Davros appropriates this army to create his Imperial Daleks. Reconciling the accounts of these stories was based upon the numbers of the Spiridon army... The Thals in *Planet of the Daleks* believe that "ten thousand Daleks" are buried on Spiridon, but *Return of the Daleks* says this is faulty information, and the frozen Daleks actually number 1,100,000. "Emperor of the Daleks" has Davros labouring on Spiridon for a year, whereupon he unleashes an army of four million gold-and-white Daleks. So, one could conclude that the third Doctor froze the Dalek army (cited as only ten thousand, but actually numbering 1,100,000) in *Planet of the Daleks*, that the seventh Doctor prevented their revival in *Return of the Daleks*, and that Davros later used the Spiridon army to cobble together his force of four million Daleks.

All well and good... save that moving *Return of the Daleks* forward in time means that the seventh Doctor is here re-freezing a Dalek army that Davros has already appropriated for use elsewhere. One explanation is that it's never expressly established that Davros takes *each and every* last Dalek from Spiridon - perhaps he builds four million Daleks, but leaves one million(ish) behind on Spiridon as reinforcements to call upon should he need them. Or, perhaps he actually constructs *five* million Daleks, takes four million with him and leaves the extra one million behind. Either way, it's understandable why the seventh Doctor would want to keep the surplus million Daleks frozen. What this *doesn't* explain is how, if *Return of the Daleks* comes later than "Emperor of the Daleks", the Spiridons are still invisible in "Emperor" when *Return* states that they become visible following *Planet of the Daleks*, and only regain their invisibility owing to the Doctor releasing a virus during Mendes and Kalendorf's revolution.

1454 Dating *Brotherhood of the Daleks* (BF #114) - Dating clues abound, but no actual year is mentioned. Kyropites previously appeared in *The Mind's Eye*, but there's no other relation given between that story and this one.

One of the Thals says, "And there are Ganatus knows how many levels like this..."; if this denotes the slain Ganatus from *The Daleks*, *Brotherhood of the Daleks* must take place after that. The Thals have now settled on New Davias, on such a scale that it's quite possibly where they went prior to Skaro's obliteration in *Remembrance of the Daleks*.

Tellingly, the Daleks at present have an empire. Also, one of the Thals is a veteran of "the Mechanoid Wars",

The Thals now had access to books from across time and space, including *Das Kapital*. The Thals had recently fought wars with the Mechanoids.

The Thal scientist Murgat adapted a Dalek facility in Antares, and experimented to see if kyropite flowers from planet YT45 - which was located four galaxies away - could replicate Thal personalities in Daleks, a means of sabotaging the Dalek war effort. The Daleks, however, had secretly facilitated Murgat's undertaking to see if they could install Thal characteristics - such as camaraderie and fighting spirit - into Daleks to make them better killers.

Some Daleks with Thal personalities, named "Thaleks", turned against their own kind and executed a Black Dalek. The sixth Doctor and Charley hoped that the Thaleks would peacefully thrive - but after they left, the Thaleks' Dalek-ness took hold. Their renewed desire to exterminate triggered a booby trap on the facility's anti-matter reactor, destroying them and Murgat.

& 5427 - DALEK EMPIRE IV: THE FEARLESS[1455] ->
Earth Alliance developed elite cybernetic battlesuits for use against the Daleks. Agnes Landen headed the battlesuit division, "the Spacers".

The able-bodied men of Talis Minor, an inhospitable colony world, were forcibly conscripted into the Spacers. The Daleks attacked Kedru VII, and although the Alliance won, the Daleks initiated a kamikaze manoeuvre that destroyed the planet's atmosphere and anyone living there. Salus Kade was appointed a Spacer squadron commander.

Most of Kade's squad was wiped out in a botched attempt to assassinate Susan Mendes, the Angel of Mercy. Kade survived, but spent a year in isolation while returning in a Dalek trans-solar disc. He was appointed captain of the flagship *Herald*, and destroyed key Dalek generators that would have propelled an asteroid storm into Earth's

solar system. Kade learned that Landen had reviewed surveillance and tagged him as a valuable asset prior to the Spacers ever visiting Talis Minor - setting in motion a series of events that had culminated in the death of his wife and child. He resigned his commission, but Landen suspected he'd rejoin the Spacers after realising his old life was gone.

& 5430 - DALEK EMPIRE I: "DEATH TO THE DALEKS!" / PROJECT INFINITY[1456] ->
The Daleks made great progress against the Earth Alliance in the years following their invasion of the Milky Way. Billions of people were killed. Carson's Planet attempted to stay neutral, and became a watering hole for space travellers.

Dalek forces directly attacked the Sol system - Jupiter and Saturn fell, and human forces on Mars were outnumbered 100 to 1. The President of Earth was left with no choice but to surrender.

The Dalek Supreme and Dalek Emperor were aware of Mendes and Kalendorf's plans, but let them proceed as the galactic invasion was a massive distraction. Using knowledge obtained from the Kar-Charrat library, the Daleks had learned of Project Infinity - an Alliance undertaking in the Lopra system, designed to penetrate the dimensional barriers so humanity could view a reality where the Daleks had been defeated, then replicate this accomplishment. Lopra was on the opposite end of the galaxy from Seriphia, and so the Daleks had invaded the Milky Way to reach it. The Daleks wanted to ally themselves with Daleks from another reality and jointly conquer the universe. The Imperial flagship departed, with the Dalek Emperor aboard, for Lopra Minor.

Mendes and Kalendorf judged that the time was right for their rebellion. She went to the planet Yaldos to make a major broadcast to all slaves in Dalek territory - and shouted the code-phrase "Death to the Daleks!", causing

which are likely to have occurred in the third or fourth millennium, as there's no record of the Mechanoids even being active later than some excavated ones being dug up in 4620 (in *The Juggernauts*). Additionally, Murgat says that the Doctor aided the Thals in driving the Daleks from this sector of the galaxy, but the Doctor says he hasn't been near Antares in six millennia, and assumes that Murgat refers to events in his personal future. It seems reasonable to take this as a reference to *Return of the Daleks*, meaning that *Brotherhood of the Daleks* must occur in close relation to the *Dalek Empire* series - which is handy, as the Daleks do have an empire at that point.

At least two of the Daleks present remember meeting Charley in Folkestone in *Terror Firma*, but allowing that those post-*Remembrance* Daleks likely have some form of time travel (however crude), it's not an altogether helpful detail. The term "Thaleks" was used in

the Unbound story *Auld Mortality*.

1455 Dating *Dalek Empire IV: The Fearless* - The story occurs in the years that pass very shortly after the start of *Dalek Empire I* episode three (*"Death to the Daleks!"*), but prior to the Daleks overrunning Earth in that installment. Ernst Tanlee, who's killed at the very end of *Dalek Empire I*, here appears as head of Earth Alliance security. Like *Dalek Empire II* but unlike the other *Dalek Empire* mini-series, *Dalek Empire IV* has no individual episode titles.

1456 Dating *Dalek Empire I* (episode three, *"Death to the Daleks!"*; episode four, *Project Infinity*) - An unspecified number of "years" occur as the Daleks make advances, and Mendes and Kalendorf shore up their master plan. "Eight months" pass after Mendes gives the rebellion signal, and Kalendorf spends five months after that in transit to the Lopra system.

billions of slaves to turn en masse against their Dalek masters. The Daleks put Mendes into suspended animation so she could be turned into one of their number.

When news came forth that Mendes and Kalendorf had initiated their galaxy-wide uprising, the seventh Doctor - still a prisoner on Spiridon - released a contagion he'd secretly developed. This wiped out his Dalek captors, and turned the Spiridon natives invisible again.[1457]

Eight months passed as the rebellion continued. Kalendorf learned of Project Infinity, and spent five months travelling to Lopra to investigate. Matters came to a head on Lopra Minor. The Dalek Emperor used the veganite obtained from Vega VI to power Project Infinity to a previously unimaginable scale, and opened a doorway to an alternate dimension where the Daleks reigned supreme. A delegation of alt-reality Daleks communed with the Emperor, but judged his Daleks as guilty of great crimes. The alt-Daleks vowed to destroy their counterparts.

The Mentor, the creator of the alt-Daleks, pledged to support the Earth Alliance against the enemy Daleks. Kalendorf became her fleet commander. The Dalek Emperor was captured on Lopra Minor, but mysteriously went inert.[1458]

? 5433 - PLANET OF THE SPIDERS[1459] **->** An Earth ship came out of its time jump without power and crashed on Metebelis III. Some humans, a few sheep and a handful of spiders survived the crash. The spiders found their way to the cave of the blue crystals, and the energies there mutated them, making them grow and boosting their intelligence and psychic abilities. The "Eight-Legs" came to dominate the planet, harvesting the human population as cattle. The Eight-Legs were ruthless - they wiped out two hundred and sixty-nine villagers, the entire population of Skorda, when they tried to resist.

Four hundred and thirty-three years after the crash, the Spiders set up a psychic bridge with a Tibetan monastery on twentieth-century Earth. They plotted to travel back in time to conquer their homeworld. Their leader, the Great One, planned to gain omnipotence by completing the crystal lattice of her cave. The third Doctor confronted his fear by bringing her the one perfect crystal he had taken from Metebelis some time previous. The energy backlash killed the Great One, but the Doctor received a fatal dose of radiation while in the Great One's cave. He returned to twentieth-century Earth.

1457 *Return of the Daleks*

1458 *Dalek Empire II*

1459 Dating *Planet of the Spiders* (11.5) - The colony ship that crashes on Metebelis III has intergalactic capability, as Metebelis is in the Acteon galaxy. It made a "time jump", also suggesting it's from the far future. *The Terrestrial Index* claimed that the colony ship was "lost during the early days of the twenty-second century", dating *Planet of the Spiders* itself as "c.2530". *The TARDIS Logs* suggested "4256", *Timelink* "3415".

1460 Dating *The Eight Doctors* (EDA #1) - This happens at some point in the aftermath of *Planet of the Spiders*.

1461 *The Eight Truths/Worldwide Web*

1462 Dating *Dalek Empire II: Dalek War* (no individual titles) - Mendes is revived from stasis "five, nearly six" years after instigating her rebellion in *Dalek Empire I*.

1463 *Dalek Empire III*

1464 Dating *Dalek Empire II: Dalek War* (no individual titles) - Kalendorf's conflict against the Alliance Daleks is described as a "long, terrible war", and must run for a number of years. The Great Catastrophe seems to occur shortly after the Alliance Daleks' withdrawal to their home dimension.

THE GREAT CATASTROPHE: *Dalek Empire II* ends with all Daleks and Dalek technology in the Milky Way and Seriphia galaxies exploding to such a degree, "countless worlds" (all of them unnamed) are devastated. Some take centuries or millennia to recover, some never do. The big question for *Ahistory*'s purposes is how much damage Earth itself endures... and, as it hap-

pens, this question is never answered. Although *Dalek Empire III* picks up the threads of the Great Catastrophe some two thousand years later, no mention whatsoever is made of Earth's status.

... which isn't to say that the homeworld has been especially devastated beyond repair. Although the Daleks do take control of Earth in *Dalek Empire II*, the "Daleks, Obliterate Yourselves" pulse that brings about The Great Catastrophe wouldn't mete out damage to the planets under Dalek control equally, and some worlds would surely weather that storm better than others. Where this is especially relevant is the question of whether the humans on Earth would emerge from the Great Catastrophe with the technological know-how and resources to react as we're shown to the Solar Flare event (established in *The Ark in Space*). So little is said about what happens to Earth during The Great Catastrophe, there's nothing to directly rule out pretty much any scenario to follow.

1465 *Dalek Empire III*

1466 Dating *The Pyralis Effect* (BF CC #4.4) - It's long enough after the destruction of Pavonis IV that the Doctor is regarded as a mythical hero, but not so long that the planet's environment has recovered and the survivors have resettled there. Otherwise, this date is arbitrary.

& 5433 - THE EIGHT DOCTORS[1460] -> The humans on Metebelis III hunted down the spiders. The seventh Doctor visited the planet and was caught by a giant spider. The eighth Doctor rescued him.

Some of the Metebelis spiders survived the Great One's downfall. They allied themselves with the profit-minded Headhunter, and went back to 2015 to capitalise on a master plan she had devised. The surviving spiders returned to their homeworld upon their defeat.[1461]

& 5436 - DALEK EMPIRE II: DALEK WAR[1462] -> Mendes' rebellion had greatly weakened the Daleks' empire, but they remained a formidable foe despite the best efforts of the Mentor's "Alliance Daleks" and the surviving human forces. The Alliance cut off the enemy Daleks' retreat back to Seriphia, triggering years of warfare. Meanwhile, Kalendorf learned that the Alliance Daleks had devastated several worlds, including Emeron, who refused to contribute to the war effort. He feared that if the enemy Daleks were defeated, mankind would just be replacing a nihilistic dictatorship with a more benevolent one.

Nearly six years after Mendes instigated her uprising, Kalendorf's most trusted allies located Mendes' cryo-pod and revived her. As they suspected, the Emperor had "escaped" by downloading his consciousness into Mendes' body. Kalendorf's fleet mounted an attempt to reclaim the Sol system - but the enemy Daleks' first wave self-destructed, obliterating a quarter of his forces. Kalendorf's fleet discovered that Jupiter had mysteriously been terraformed and could now sustain human life. Half of Kalendorf's spaceships put down on Jupiter to make repairs before the Daleks' second wave arrived - and were overcome by Varga plants that the enemy Daleks had seeded there.

The Mentor relieved Kalendorf of command and ordered him brought in for "brain correction", but he escaped, located Mendes and shared with her his plan to rout both Dalek factions. Mendes agreed with Kalendorf's proposal and killed her beloved, Corporal Alby Brook, to prevent his interference. She then made a galaxy-wide broadcast, saying she was the Angel of Mercy returned, and urging humanity to join forces with the enemy Daleks against the Alliance Daleks. The Dalek Supreme agreed to this new alliance.

The Alliance Daleks tried to create "demons": augmented humans who could combat the enemy Daleks. On a space station in the Plowik system, some Alliance Daleks genetically and technologically augmented test subjects with physical strength, an extended lifespan and the ability to alter their appearance on a cellular level, becoming temporarily invisible. Enemy Daleks attacked the station, interrupting the undertaking. One of the "demons", Galanar, would remain in stasis for two millennia.[1463]

& 5441 - DALEK EMPIRE II: DALEK WAR[1464] -> The Mentor accelerated plans to bring "brain correction" to those who resisted the Alliance Daleks. Kalendorf forged a pact with the enemy Daleks, and, alongside their forces, led what remained of humanity's forces against the Mentor. Years of warfare and devastation ensued. Kalendorf eventually convinced the Mentor that a continued conflict could only result in the destruction of all life in both their universes. She elected to withdraw all of her alt-Daleks back to their home universe.

For a short while, the galaxy knew peace as the enemy Daleks honoured the terms of their coalition with the Alliance. Kalendorf knew the Daleks would eventually renege, and went to Earth to negotiate with the Dalek Supreme. The Dalek Emperor took control of Mendes' body, and tapped the Dalek command net to probe Kalendorf's mind for signs of betrayal. In so doing, it enabled the last remnants of Mendes' personality to activate a telepathic self-destruct code that Kalendorf had planted in her mind. The destruct command routed through the entire Dalek network, running unfettered owing to the Emperor's full access. All Daleks and Dalek technology in human space and Seriphia were destroyed.

This event caused incalculable devastation, and became known as The Great Catastrophe. Entire star systems were ruined, and countless lives were lost. Parts of the galaxy took centuries, even millennia, to recover.

Kalendorf had expected to perish during his final gambit, but survived. In time, he returned to his homeworld of Velyshaa. His recorded memories were later stored in his burial chamber. History would regard him as a monster, a "dark one" who brought about the galaxy's ruination.

One Dalek outpost survived the Great Catastrophe, when a Dalek was conditioned to absorb Mendes' destructive pulse, then isolated from the outpost's command net. The isolated Dalek consequently absorbed some of Mendes' personality, and also gained the command codes for the entire Dalek network. In the millennia to follow, the Mendes-Dalek would become the new Dalek Supreme.[1465]

? 5500 - THE PYRALIS EFFECT[1466] -> The fourth Doctor and Romana found the *Myriad* - one of the ships containing the cloned survivors of Pavonis IV - as it travelled through the Kasterborous Cluster. A disused Pyralis obelisk influenced a Type 12 AI designated CAIN, who calculated the codes necessary to open it. Thousands of Pyralis escaped, but CAIN sacrificed himself to detonate a device that recalled the Pyralis and imprisoned them once more. The Doctor advised the Pavonians to let go of their past - including their hero-worship for him - and programmed the *Myriad*'s flight computer to take them to a small, habitable planet.

In 5665, the Chelonians launched an attack on the human colony Vaagon, but the Chelonians' tanks vanished mysteriously before they could complete their conquest, transported by a Fortean Flicker to the twenty-seventh century. Believing themselves blessed by divine intervention, the colonists were quite unprepared when the Chelonians reinvaded several generations later and wiped out the colony.[1467]

The Doctor bought a collapsible snooker table at the height of the retro-gaming fad of the fifty-eighth century.[1468]

In 5720, archaeologists discovered the remains of a Khorlthochloi starship.[1469] The militaristic Narbrab conquered an alien civilisation. The survivors, hosted in Ikshar host bodies, were banished in a solar-powered ship and arrived in London, 1346.[1470]

= In 5738, the sixth Doctor visited the planet Helios 3.[1471]

Around 5764, a Dalek civil war became so serious that the Time Lords intervened.[1472] Espero was colonised by mostly African and Asian humans with a shared Christian faith. The colonists hoped to escape the influence of the Eurozone and America, and bought the planet from the Homeworld Corporation. They renounced technology, which made it all but impossible to extract the planet's natural resources. With nothing to offer in trade, Espero became isolated from the rest of the galaxy. Religious schisms led to the Almost War.[1473]

? 5800 - COMBAT ROCK[1474] -> Earth won a war against the Indoni, making the planet Jenggel an Earth colony. The Indoni subsequently invaded the rival Papul people, forcing the Papul leaders to vote for integration. Tourism swelled amid the new political climate, with visitors arriving to experience the "primitive" Papul culture. The corrupt President Sabit of the Indoni kept most of the profits for himself. Christian missionaries arrived to minister to the Papul. Twentieth-century icons such as *Winnie the Pooh*, *Wind in the Willows* and Leatherface horror films were in use in pop culture.

On Jenggel, a sentient organism contained in a purple fungus from the Papul swamps possessed a Papul named Kepennis. As the mysterious "Krallik", the organism-Kepennis founded the OPG, a Papul resistance movement. Some eight rainseasons later, Kepennis rigged Papul mumis to kill tourists and Indoni soldiers by spitting snakes, furthering an atmosphere of anarchy. The second Doctor, Jamie and Victoria arrived, and the Doctor ingested some of the fungus himself, enabling him to mentally nullify the organism within Kepennis. A cannibalistic Papul tribe took Kepennis away to consume him as punishment, and a mercenary with a bit of a noble streak killed Sabit.

1467 *The Highest Science*
1468 *Synthespians™*
1469 *The Price of Paradise*
1470 "Thousands of years" after *Asylum*. No date given, and this is an arbitrary placing.
1471 *Spiral Scratch*
1472 "Five thousand years" before *The Crystal Bucephalus* (p114).
1473 "Two hundred and seventy years" before *Half-Life*.
1474 Dating *Combat Rock* (PDA #55) - There's no date given, although cigarettes were banned on the colonies "hundreds of years ago". There are smokers in *Resurrection of the Daleks*, but of course a smoking ban can be lifted and ignored, so it's hardly firm evidence that this story is set after that. This date is arbitrary, but it's linked to the Christian colonists of Espero.

The date of the Earth-Indoni war is unspecified, but Jenggel's current political climate seems to stem from its fallout, suggesting a shorter rather than longer span of time since it occurred. The Indoni subjugated the Papul, and the Christian missionaries arrived, some "thirty rainseasons" before the novel takes place.
1475 Dating *Sick Building* (NSA #17) - No dating clues are given, but in *Iris: Enter Wildthyme* (p240), Barbra says that she's from "the fifty-ninth century". The character is named as "Barbara" in *Sick Building* and *Iris: Iris and the*

Celestial Omnibus: "The Deadly Flap", but is "Barbra" in *Iris: Enter Wildthyme*.
1476 *Iris: Enter Wildthyme*
1477 Dating *The Krotons* (6.4) - This has been one of the most persistently undatable TV stories. *About Time* concedes that the year is "unknown", and Jon Preddle writes in *Timelink*, "I have placed *The Krotons* under ?????" While the story gives virtually no dating clues (it isn't even established if the Gonds are human or not), evidence from the tie-in media allows for the establishment of some parameters.

Alien Bodies (p263-264) says that the Krotons were literally patterned after the type of servo-robots seen in *The Wheel in Space*, meaning the Krotons didn't exist prior to mankind's colonial age. The same section of *Alien Bodies* suggests that (in terms of rudimentary personality, if nothing else) the Krotons as we know them took some "centuries" to develop.

In *Return of the Krotons*, a Kroton who went dormant circa 3700 regards dynatropes - relative to when it liquefied - as "an inferior form of craft, with low grade crew specifications. We are more advanced." So, if dynatropes haven't been outright discontinued by the thirty-eighth century, it's unlikely they were used much after. The Krotons featured in *The Krotons* might be using a dynatrope well past its expiration date, but we nonetheless have a rough approximation of when they

c 5850 - SICK BUILDING[1475] -> Professor Ernest Tiermann made a fortune in the Servo-furniture industry, and retired to a snowy planet he had purchased, Tiermann's World, with his wife and son. The tenth Doctor and Martha warned the family that a Voracoious Craw - a spaceship-sized monster akin to a tapeworm - was approaching from space and would carve up the planet's surface. Tiermann was determined to abandon his futuristic Dreamhouse - the consciousness of which, the Domovoi, felt betrayed and possessed a sunbed named Toaster. Tiermann and Domovoi/Toaster mutually killed one another, and Tiermann's wife died also. The Doctor and Martha transported Tiermann's son Solin and a sentient vending machine named Barbra to Spaceport Antelope Slash Nitelite.

Barbra fell in with a bad crowd - a pirate gang of decommissioned Servo-furnishings - and fell through a space-time rift, the Deadly Flap, to the twenty-first century.[1476]

c 5895 - THE KROTONS[1477] -> On the planet of the Gonds, the dynatrope registered the second Doctor and Zoe as the "high brains" it had long sought. The two surviving Krotons revived, and made plans to leave the planet, even though take-off would devastate the Gonds and their city. The Doctor, Jamie and Zoe helped to destroy the Krotons and their dynatrope with sulphuric acid.

? 5900 - MISSION: IMPRACTICAL[1478] -> Sabalom Glitz stole a Tzun data core from the reptilian Veltrochni. He sold it to Niccolo Mandell, an agent of the Vandor Prime government. Ten years later, the Veltrochni threatened to make war against Vandor Prime over the stolen Tzun data core. It was the last surviving information cache from the Tzun Empire, and contained blueprints on how to construct Tzun Stormblades. Vandor Prime head of security Niccolo Mandell, hoping to sell the data core, coerced the sixth Doctor, Frobisher and Glitz into retrieving the device from an orbital facility.

Glitz's associate Dibber died in a crossfire, but the Doctor purged the data core of its more dangerous information and returned it to the Veltrochni. Vandor Prime authorities arrested Mandell. Glitz continued travelling in his *Nosferatu*.

? 5900 - TRAGEDY DAY[1479] -> On the Earth colony Olleril, the precocious boy genius Crispin, leader of the secret society of Luminus, sought to gain mental control of the population, and to pattern everyone after characters from the show *Martha and Arthur*. Meanwhile, the immortal Friars of Pangloss hired the arachnid mutant Ernie "Eight Legs" McCartney, the most feared assassin in the Seventh Quadrant, to retrieve a cursed piece of red glass that the Doctor had acquired. The seventh Doctor, Benny and Ace thwarted Crispin's plans, and Crispin died when the Luminus submarine *Gargantuan* was destroyed. Ravenous Slaag creatures consumed McCartney. The Friars were disrupted by an anti-matter burst, and flung powerless into the Time Vortex.

The Solar Flares and the Evacuation of Earth

The Earth was ruled by the World Executive. Earth at this time was technically advanced, with advanced suspended animation techniques, fission guns and power supplied via solar stacks and granavox turbines.

Scientists monitoring the Sun predicted a series of massive solar flares: within only a matter of years, the Earth's surface would be ravaged and virtually all life would be wiped out. It would be five thousand years

---

landed on the planet of the Gonds.

The Gond leader Selris says in *The Krotons* episode one that the Krotons arrived "thousands of years" ago - not the most specific of terms to start with, and one that becomes even vaguer when it's taken into account that the Gonds have forgotten so much of their history. The Doctor similarly claims in episode three that the Krotons have been lying dormant for "thousands of years", but he might just be repeating what Selris told the TARDIS crew. Nonetheless, if we presume that the Krotons landed on Gond circa 2895 (the mid-point between man's colonial age starting about 2090 and dynatropes being deemed "inferior" circa 3700), then arbitrarily add on (say) three thousand years, *The Krotons* would occur circa 5895. It's a ballpark figure, to be sure, but it's better than nothing.

1478 Dating *Mission: Impractical* (PDA #12) - It is "a

couple of million years" before *The Trial of a Time Lord* (p56). Ernie McCartney from *Tragedy Day* is mentioned (p215), setting this around the same time as that book. This would not appear, from the other stories featuring Glitz, to be his native timezone. We might conclude that he has ended up somehow either acquiring time travel or been brought here by a time traveller.

1479 Dating *Tragedy Day* (NA #24) - There is no indication of the date in the book, although the colony planet Pantorus is mentioned here (p83) and in *Zamper* (p57), perhaps suggesting they are set around the same time.

1480 *The Ark in Space*

THE SOLAR FLARES: The solar flares ravage the Earth "thousands of years" after the thirtieth century (*Revenge of the Cybermen*). Judging by information in the TV series, the last recorded human activity on Earth for millions of years is in the fifty-first century (*The Talons of*

before the planet would be habitable again.

The High Minister and the Earth Council began working on humanity's salvation. Carefully screened humans, the Star Pioneers, were sent out in vast colony ships to places such as Colony 9 and Andromeda. Nerva was converted into an ark housing the cream of humanity, some one hundred thousand people, who were placed in suspended animation along with samples of animal and plant life. Nerva also contained the sum of human knowledge stored on microfilm.

The rest of humanity took to thermic shelters, knowing that they wouldn't survive. When the solar flares came, every living thing on the Earth perished.

A group of Star Pioneers reached Andromeda and encountered the Wirrn, a race of parasitic insects who lived in space, visiting worlds only to breed.[1480]

? 5950 - DREAMTIME[1481] -> Facing a catastrophic natural disaster, evacuation coordinators herded the people onto Phoenix lifeships that departed for space. In Australia, a guru named Baiame sought an alternative and hoped to channel the Dreaming - a collective force, derived from the minds and dreams of humanity - to influence matter. Baiame wanted to lift Uluru, a sacred bluff, and its people into space under protection of a Dreaming-generated force field. The seventh Doctor traversed the Dreaming and arrived from thousands of years in the future. Baiame acceded to the Doctor's request that he extend his sphere

---

Weng-Chiang, The Invisible Enemy). The books and audios push this forward by about a thousand years, to around 6000. The Solar Flares must occur relatively soon after this time.

The first edition of The Programme Guide claimed that Earth was only evacuated between "c.2800" and "c.2900", the second suggested dates between "c.2900" and "c.4300". The Terrestrial Index attempted to rationalise the statement that the Ark was built in the "thirtieth century", stating that Nerva was built, but then the Solar Flares "abated", Nerva was not informed and the population of Nerva went on to recolonise Ravolox "between 15,000 and 20,000" (as seen in The Mysterious Planet). This contradicts the date for The Mysterious Planet established on screen and would represent a rather implausible oversight on behalf of the Earth's authorities. The book's supposition that the Solar Flares caused the Ice Age we see in The Ice Warriors (a theory repeated in Legacy) is specifically ruled out by dialogue in The Ice Warriors. For analysis of the solar flares as referenced in the new series, see The Beast Below.

1481 Dating Dreamtime (BF #67) - Simon Forward scripted this story with the intent of it occurring during the time of the World Zones Authority in the twenty-first century, but nothing in the story itself supports this. Talk of evacuating the Earth means it fits naturally at the time of the solar flares. If the "past" segments are part of the Dreaming and inherently unreliable, dating becomes even murkier. Forward says that the Galyari Korshal in Dreamtime isn't the character of the same name in Benny: The Bone of Contention (even if Steffan Rhodri voices both parts); the Galyari are long-lived, but traditionally hand down some names through the generations.

THE ABANDONMENT OF EARTH: Earth is completely evacuated six, possibly seven, times that we know of: (1) for "ten thousand years" between the time of the Solar Flares and The Sontaran Experiment (c.5000-c.15,000 AD); (2) for at least three thousand five hundred years before (and an unknown amount of time after) Birthright (c.18,500 AD-?); (3) a line cut from the rehearsal script but retained in the Planet of Evil novelisation reveals that "The Tellurian planet [Earth] has been uninhabited since the Third Era" (significantly before 37,166 AD); (4) for a significant time after the Usurians move the workforce to Pluto before The Sun Makers millions of years in the future; (5) there is a mass evacuation shortly before Earth plunges into the Sun ten million years in the future, seen in The Ark and reported in Frontios; (6) finally, Earth was empty at the time of its final destruction in the year five billion, seen in The End of the World. A wild card is the migration from Earth involving Starship UK, as seen in The Beast Below (possibly, or possibly not, part of the aforementioned Solar Flare incident; see the dating notes on that story). System Wipe (p13) concurs that Earth "gets blasted" half a dozen times at least.

1482 The Reaping, The Gathering. The Doctor says that the Gogglebox was created while "humanity was on a day trip away from Earth space" owing to "solar flares or intergalactic war or something". This placement is arbitrary.

1483 Heritage. Cole's grandmother fights in it.

1484 Dating Zamper (NA #41) - It is "the sixtieth century" (p77). Earth appears to be populated at this time.

1485 Dating The Doctor's Daughter (X4.6) - The dates shown on screen are in a format that gives figures such as "60120724". Donna works out that it's "a big old space date" that runs year, month, day. Or, in the more familiar British format, the colonists land on Messaline on 17/07/6012, and events in this story occur on 24/07/6012. While the Doctor claims that said "big old space date" uses the New Byzantine Calendar, setting the story in 6012 AD seems reasonable enough.

1486 "Twenty" (p8) and "ten" (p18) years before Heritage.

1487 Three years before Heritage (p56).

1488 Dating Heritage (PDA #57) - Each chapter in the book has a precise date and time.

1489 Dating Half-Life (EDA #68) - This story is set after Heritage, as there are references to that story.

of protection a few miles and include settlers in the surrounding vicinity. The Uluru lifted off from Earth with its people and sped into space, and the Doctor returned to the future.

During a period in which humanity didn't inhabit the Earth, an alien race set up the Gogglebox - a giant museum dedicated to Earth and its history - deep within Earth's moon. The fifth Doctor met history student Alan Fitzgerald there, and left behind a copy of *The Rough Guide to Shabadabadon* which detailed - among other things - Shabadabadon's famous ice caves. For Alan's benefit, the Doctor confirmed his involvement in the great fire of London and the *Mary Celeste*, but he refused to discuss when his tenure with UNIT occurred. The Doctor then departed to investigate an energy spike emanating from Brisbane in September 2006.[1482]

There was a Cyber War in the late sixtieth century.[1483]

c 5995 - ZAMPER[1484] **->** There was revolution on Chelonia, where the peaceful forces of Little Sister overthrew Big Mother. This initiated a cultural reformation that saw the warlike race transformed into the galaxy's foremost flower-arrangers. Forty years later, many Chelonians hankered for the old blood-and-glory days, and Big Mother's fleet headed for Zamper to purchase a powerful Series 336c Delta-Spiral Sun Blaster - a ship whose effectiveness had been demonstrated in the Sprox civil war and the skirmishes of Pancoza. It was capable of withstanding neutronic ray blasts of up to an intensity of sixty blarks.

The seventh Doctor, Benny, Roz and Chris arrived on Zamper and found that the Zamps - slug-like creatures used to build the ships on the planet - had dreams of conquest and were building their own battleship. They had force-evolved their offspring to become ravenous tentacle-like creatures powered by a springtail; the Doctor estimated that these creatures would become unstoppable if they reached populated space. Big Mother owed the Doctor a debt and agreed with his assessment. In a variation of the Diemlisch manoeuvre (first used in the third Wobesq-Majjina war), Big Mother's Chelonian fleet destroyed itself to obliterate the Zamps' ship and seal the gate between Zamper and the rest of the universe.

6012 (24th July) - THE DOCTOR'S DAUGHTER[1485] **->** The fish-like Hath allied with humanity to create colonies. A spaceship containing some humans and Hath landed on Messaline with a third-generation terraforming globe that could create an ecosystem on the planet's barren surface. The mission commander died, and the resulting power vacuum put the humans and Hath into open warfare. Each camp had cloning devices that used "progenation": reproduction from a single organism. The conflict became so accelerated, twenty

generations could be born and lost in a day.

Seven days later, the TARDIS brought the tenth Doctor, Donna and Martha to Messaline as it had sensed a paradox there - a young woman named Jenny, cloned from the Doctor's genetics within moments of his arrival. The Doctor smashed the terraforming globe, releasing its gasses and causing areas on Messaline to bloom with new life. The humans and Hath agreed to live peacefully. The Doctor and his friends left, thinking that Jenny had been fatally shot while saving the Doctor's life. She was revived by the terraforming gasses, and departed in a shuttlecraft to find new adventures.

Colonists established a colony on Heritage. Ten years later, a company at Galactic Central developed a way of synthesising Thydonium, instantly putting mining colonies such as Heritage out of business. Melanie Bush and her husband Ben Heyworth settled on the impoverished Heritage sometime afterwards.[1486]

Years later on Heritage, the geneticist Wakeling successfully cloned a raven, naming her Arabella.[1487]

6048 (6th August) - HERITAGE[1488] **->** Menopause had become extremely rare. Undergoing the condition, Melanie Bush Heyworth asked Wakeling for a genetic solution to the problem. Wakeling's treatment seemingly led to Mel and her husband Ben conceiving a child named Sweetness, but the Heyworths discovered that Wakeling had violated their wishes by cloning Sweetness from Mel. A subsequent argument between Wakeling and Mel led to his striking her with a genetic sequencer, killing her.

The Heritage residents overlooked Wakeling's act of murder, believing his experiments could restore prosperity to the hard-up colony. Ben Heyworth's attempt to seek justice by alerting offworld authorities was discovered. Wakeling further persuaded the townsfolk to favour his experiments, and the locals tore Ben to pieces with their bare hands before torching his house. Wakeling took Sweetness into his own home.

A shuttlecraft arrived on Heritage - the first in years - and two visitors wanted to see the Heyworths, causing quite a stir. The buried memories of the Heyworths' deaths began to surface among the locals. The seventh Doctor and Ace gatecrashed an interstellar video conference and revealed Wakeling as a murderer, destroying the man's chance to reveal his success at cloning. Wakeling and two other inhabitants fell to their deaths when some of the old mineshafts collapsed under them. Cole, the Heritage town barman, adopted Sweetness.

c 6050 - HALF-LIFE[1489] **->** Two races, the parasitic Makers and the Oon, had been at war for centuries. The organic spaceship Tain, a Maker construct, fled the war but was infected with an Oon-made Trojan program. Tain crashed onto the planet Espero, and his personality remained in conflict. The eighth Doctor, Fitz and Trix received Tain's distress signal. Tain thought that the TARDIS heralded the Oon's arrival and unleashed its ultimate weapon: a wavefront designed to disintegrate and reconstitute a planet under Tain's control. Tain's internal struggle threw the wavefront into chaos, but the Doctor purged the Trogan program and ended the wavefront. Tain prepared to leave Espero afterwards.

High Catholic doctrine came to forbid use of matter transmitters, stating it was impossible to teleport a soul.

The last colonist left Heritage in 6057. None of the ex-colonists ever discussed their reasons for departing.[1490] On 8th December, 6064, former Heritage colonist Lee Marks, now head of the Ellershaw Foundation, died in a fire deliberately set at his home.[1491] A grown-up Sweetness Cole penned an autobiography entitled *First of a New Breed*.[1492]

The New Dark Age

In 6198, the Federation Scientific Executive funded a research project into genetic experimentation. The geneticist Maximillian Arrestis hired a team of consultants to develop the Lazarus Intent, a religion that he hoped would become a moneymaking venture. His "miracles" were publicised for three years, and his predictions of disasters all came to pass. *The Codex of Lazarus* was published early in the sixty-third century, and for nearly a decade he reaped the financial rewards of being the "Messiah".

Not content with this, Arrestis began to sell defence secrets to the Cybermen, Sontarans and Rutans. The Federation was fighting a war with the Sontarans at the time. In 6211, Sontarans launched a stealth attack that wiped much of the Federation DataCore on Io. Three weeks later, an earthshock bomb - sold by the Cybermen to the Sontarans - destroyed Tersurus. This didn't stop the Federation from winning the war. When the Sontaran

1490 *Heritage* (p227).
1491 *Heritage* (p279).
1492 Years after *Heritage*.
1493 *The Crystal Bucephalus*
1494 *The Kingmaker*. The publisher's robot is specified as being from the sixty-fourth century, but this isn't to say the dominating publishing house is located there also, and the Doctor's comments suggest that the company hails from much further in the future.
1495 Dating "Ground Control" (IDW *Doctor Who Annual 2010*) - Mister K gives the year.
1496 Dating *Return of the Krotons* (BF subscription promo #7) - The solar-flare event described in *The Ark in Space* occurred some "centuries" ago. The mining technology used is similar to that used in the moon conurbations of the late thirtieth century, so it's definitely after that time.
1497 "Five thousand years" after *No Future*.
1498 Dating *Wirrn Dawn* (BF BBC7 #3.4) - The story takes place amidst the background detail of the Galsec colonists as seen in *The Sontaran Experiment*. The migration of the Wirrn swarm into space could be the act that leads to a Wirrn queen invading Nerva Beacon in *The Ark in Space*. The title of this story seems to tip the scales in favour of spelling "Wirrn" with two r's, as opposed to the three-r'ed version preferred by *The Ark in Space* novelisation and *Placebo Effect*.
1499 *The Ark in Space*. As the colonists are scheduled to revive after "five thousand years" [c.11,000 AD], the Wirrn Queen must arrive on Nerva before that time.
ANDROMEDA: Andromeda is mentioned a number of times in *Doctor Who*, sometimes as a reference to the constellation, other times as the galaxy of the same name. According to the TARDIS Information File entry that the Master fakes in *Castrovalva*, Castrovalva itself is a planet in the Phylox series in Andromeda. There is

some evidence that Zanak (*The Pirate Planet*) raided worlds there, as the ground is littered with Andromedan bloodstones. In *The Daleks' Master Plan*, an intergalactic conference was held in Andromeda. In *The Ark in Space*, we learn that Star Pioneers from Earth reached Andromeda and discovered that it was infested with the Wirrn. The two races fought each other for a thousand years, until humanity succeeded in destroying the Wirrn's breeding grounds. Mankind went on to colonise the galaxy, and by the time of *The Mysterious Planet*, the civilisation was established on planets such as Sabalom Glitz's homeworld, Salostopus. At that time, Andromedans capable of building advanced robots and harnessing black light stole Matrix secrets and fled the wrath of the Time Lords. The Doctor considers visiting "the constellation of Andromeda" in *Timelash*. The Doctor took the mer-children to a water planet in the Andromeda galaxy at the end of *Evolution*. According to Trix in *The Gallifrey Chronicles*, the currency in Andromeda is the Andromedan Euro, although *Dragonfire*, *Legacy* and *Business Unusual* all agree it is the grotzi in Glitz's time.

The threat in *Doctor Who and the Invasion from Space* comes from Andromeda in the far future. "A lot of Andromedan planets are full of Migrators," large amoeba like creatures protected by external antibodies, according to the Doctor in the short story "Danger Down Below" (*Doctor Who Annual 1983*), although they are usually only found on otherwise uninhabited worlds. *Shining Darkness* depicts a highly advanced Andromedan galactic civilisation where organic and machine live exists together in relative harmony.
1500 *The Sontaran Experiment*
1501 Dating *Patient Zero* (BF #124) - The story takes place in a region of space-time so remote, it causes a glitch or two in the TARDIS' translation system. The only

Emperor suspected that Arrestis had double-crossed him, the traitor was brought to the Sontaran throneworld and executed. "Lazarus" became a martyr, the saviour of the galaxy, and it was the Intent of his followers to resurrect him.

Alexhendri Lassiter built a time machine and did rescue Arrestis moments before his death. Later, Arrestis escaped the destruction of the Crystal Bucephalus restaurant by fleeing through time, only to arrive back on Sontara right before his execution, which proceeded as planned.[1493]

Every small publisher in the universe had been bought out, and by "the end of time", this would give rise to one dominating, monolithic publishing house. The company owned the rights to all of the authors throughout history, especially the lazy ones who hadn't fulfilled on their contracts. Publisher's robots from the sixty-fourth century were equipped with time travel. Armed with laser cannons, they went throughout history to "remind" these writers to finish their texts. One such robot visited the fifth Doctor in 1597.[1494]

6558 - "Ground Control"[1495] **->** The tenth Doctor was stopped by Mister K of the Safety Patrol Interstellar Traffic Division in a space station forty clicks from the Antarean third moon, and forced to account for a number of safety violations he had made flying the TARDIS. He was shown a previous adventure where panda-like Cobalites chased him and Donna. One Cobalite was holding on to the TARDIS when the Ship dematerialised, and ended up in the Vortex. The Doctor realised this was all a trick to distract him while the TARDIS' energy was drained, and left.

c 6700 - RETURN OF THE KROTONS[1496] **->** Humans now received electronic identity implants at birth.

Some centuries after the solar flares ravaged Earth, two Euro Comgen ships bearing human colonists in cryo-sleep arrived at the dead planet Onyakis. They spent a year mining the energy-rich K-7 crystal there. The dormant Krotons on Onyakis reformed within K-7 solutions, and attempted to create an energy-transference network that would power Kroton vessels, enabling them to enslave several human outposts. Thousands of Krotons were re-generated on Onyakis, but the sixth Doctor and Charley intervened, killing them.

Around 6976, the Vardans who invaded Earth in 1976 arrived back home. They discovered there had been a revolution, and that the military had lost power.[1497]

? 7000 - WIRRN DAWN[1498] **->** The humanoids on Korista VII lived like peasants and farmers, but were at peace with the Wirrn. Every season, the Wirrn were summoned at dawn by the striking of a metal shard across an altar, and the humanoids would offer up one of their own

to be converted into a new Wirrn queen. So long as the queens gestated in people, they had enough intelligence to restrain the swarm. The grandfather of Delong, a soldier, was one of the last colony bosses to oversee this practice.

The old ways waned, and the arrival of the Galsec colonists created open warfare with the Wirrn. New Wirrn queens were gestated in senseless herbivores, and were born with limited brain power. The Wirrn stripped whole planets clean of crops and cattle. The Galsec colonists incorporated some of the natives - including Delong - into their infantry, but scornfully so. Such add-ons were referred to as "indigs" (short for "indigenous"), which became a by-word for anyone who didn't fit in, a scrounger, a criminal, etc.

The eighth Doctor and Lucie were present as the Galsec-Wirrn conflict encroached upon Korista VII. Admiral Farroll, who commanded a fleet of sixty-eight Galsec spaceships, was turned into a Wirrn queen. Delong knew that the Galsec colonists would never agree to continue the tradition of sacrifice, and so the Farroll-queen took her swarm into space, staving off a major bloodbath.

After a thousand years, the Star Pioneers had destroyed all the Wirrn breeding grounds, making Andromeda suitable for colonisation. One Wirrn Queen survived and travelled through space towards the Earth. She reached Nerva Beacon, but the station's automatic defences killed her. Before her death, the Queen damaged the systems that would have revived the humans, and laid her eggs within one of the sleeping Nerva engineers.[1499]

While those aboard Nerva slept, human colonies such as Galsec carved out an empire, with bases across half the galaxy. They retained legends of Nerva, "the lost colony" from the time of the Expansion, but most didn't believe that it really existed. In time, the colonies grew to distrust talk of Mother Earth.[1500]

c 7190 - PATIENT ZERO[1501] **->** A virus rendered Charley Pollard comatose, and she remained in the TARDIS' Zero Room for years while the sixth Doctor searched for a cure. She awoke just as the Doctor traced the virus to "one of the remotest parts of space-time the TARDIS had ever travelled to". A war had nearly destroyed the galaxy in question, and the Great Armistice Treaty had enabled the creation of Amethyst Viral Containment Station - the biggest stockpile of uncureable viruses in the universe, located on a lava planet. Amethyst was protected by the Viyrans - the ultimate authority of this galaxy. They were tasked with destroying the viruses in the heart of Amathustro, Amethyst's sun.

A Dalek time squad from the future arrived on Amethyst, seeking both the viruses there and Patient Zero: the person who had infected Charley. The Doctor thwarted the Daleks from moving Amethyst through time, but the resultant temporal explosion - which destroyed Amethyst and the Daleks - spread the viruses throughout space-time.

Patient Zero was actually Mila - a former Dalek captive subjected to Amethyst virus No. 7001, which could rewrite the DNA of those infected to mirror that of the carrier. This left Mila invisible, untouchable and dimensionally out of phase. She had stowed aboard a Dalek time machine, then the Doctor's TARDIS, where she had remained for centuries. The TARDIS protected its passengers from Mila's virus, but Charley's anomalous status as someone travelling with a past incarnation of the Doctor deprived her of that immunity. Mila became a corporeal copy of Charley and left with the Doctor.

The Viyrans cured Charley of Mila's virus and let her travel with them, putting her into cryogenic suspension for long journeys.[1502] The Dalek Time Controller also survived, and rode the temporal explosion back to twenty-second century Earth.[1503]

The Cybermen and Time Travel

On the desert planet Chronos, a race of beings built a time machine. This enabled them to travel into their world's future, when it had become a water planet and was far more habitable. In the distant future, only a handful of Cybermen survived. They fled to the water world Chronos and exterminated the beings who lived there, acquiring their time machine in the process. The Cybermen used it

---

tangible dating clue is that the Daleks seen here hail from the distant future (their time controller claims, almost wistfully, that they've travelled "so far back in time") and have a warfleet at their disposal. The Amethyst station-manager, Fratalin, hasn't heard of the Daleks - possibly indicating that *Patient Zero* takes place in an era free of Dalek interference, or possibly just that Amethyst is so remotely located, not even the Daleks have visited its galaxy before now. The Daleks don't know about the Viyrans, but given the Viyrans' habit of erasing the short-term memories of any being they encounter, this perhaps isn't surprising. It's unclear if Etheron, a very minor character and commander of the Interstar Cargo Carrier *Blaze*, has any connection to humanity or not. The back cover copy says "the Doctor must travel back in time, beyond all known civilisations", suggesting this is the very deep past.

However, *To the Death* (set circa 2190, and also written by Nicholas Briggs) so repeatedly says that *Patient Zero* occurs in the future, it has to be taken as correct. The Doctor says that Amethyst station was destroyed "relative to when we are now? Thousands of years in the future...", that the Dalek Time Controller "survived in the future and somehow travelled back", that he intends to rectify things by going *forward* in time to destroy Amethyst more conclusively this time, and so forth. The Monk, echoing the Daleks' claims, also says that the Dalek Time Controller was injured aboard Amethyst station "in the future". So, an arbitrary sum of five thousand years has been added to *To The Death* to derive a year for *Patient Zero*.

Patient Zero marks the genesis of Big Finish's "Virus Strand" story arc - which formally encompasses "Urgent Calls", "Urban Myths", "The Vanity Box" and *Mission of the Viyrans*. The viruses that appear in *The Death Collectors* and *Forty-Five*: "Order of Simplicity" might also stem from Amethyst.

It's implied that the invisible Mila stowed away aboard the TARDIS during *The Chase*. She impersonates Charley in *Paper Cuts* and *Blue Forgotten Planet*.
1502 *Blue Forgotten Planet*

1503 *To the Death*
1504 *Real Time*. No date given. The CyberController in this era is an alternate history version of Evelyn Smythe.
1505 "The Flood". No date is given, but the eighth Doctor declares the Cybermen to be the most advanced he's ever seen. This places the story after *Real Time* and *The Reaping* - two stories which also feature time-travelling Cybermen from the unspecified far future.
1506 *The Reaping*. Presumably this occurs after *Real Time*, but this date is otherwise arbitrary.
1507 Dating *The Time Vampire* (BF CC #4.10) - The year is given. The Doctor and Joshua's encounter with the Z'nai was largely detailed in *The Catalyst*, but is actually depicted here. Mention is made of "the Naxian recession", which could refer to the aliens from the Iris Wildthyme audios.
1508 *The Catalyst*
1509 Dating *The Time Vampire* (BF CC #4.10) - It's fifty years after the "Great Plague" that Joshua Douglas unleashed against the Z'nai.
1510 *The Quantum Archangel*
1511 *The Quantum Archangel*. No date is given, but it's before the Federation splits.
1512 Dating *The Skull of Sobek* (BF BBC7 #2.4) - It's said that the "culture" of Sobek extends back ten thousand years on various worlds, and it cannot be coincidence - although it curiously isn't mentioned - that the ancient Egyptians worshipped a crocodile-headed god of the same name. This must be yet another example of extra-terrestrials influencing Earth civilisation (as with *Death to the Daleks*, etc.). In real life, Sobek is mentioned in the Pyramid Texts, the oldest of which date to 2400-2300 BC. The dating of *The Skull of Sobek* to 7500 AD - i.e. about ten thousand years later - is somewhat arbitrary, but represents the latest that the adventure can feasibly occur. Conditions on Indigo 3 do, though, somewhat match with the "new dark age" of this era, as described in *The Crystal Bucephalus*.
1513 Dating *Dalek Empire II: Dalek War* (no individual episode titles) - The blurb to *Dalek Empire II* episode

to travel back to 3286, but a temporal blast from that era surged here and aged them to death.[1504]

Advanced Cybermen from the far future had a Cybership which contained a fragment of the Time Vortex, and so could travel in time. They used it to attack Earth in the early twenty-first century.[1505]

In the far, far future, the Cybermen were nearly extinct. A surviving Cyber-Leader held the Doctor responsible for his race's destruction, and had access to Cyber-race's entire history banks. The Cyber-Leader found an abandoned time-ship - the product of Gallifreyan technology - on a planet nearly destroyed by fire, and decided to lay a trap for the Doctor in 1984. The time-ship proved difficult to pilot; the Cyber-Leader arrived two years early in 1982.[1506]

7382 - THE TIME VAMPIRE[1507] **->** On a mission for the Time Lords, the third Doctor and his companion Joshua Douglas dined with H'mbrackle, the emperor of the Z'nai - a race of philosophers and magnificent architects who built hanging fountains and sky cities. H'mbrackle had arranged a trade agreement, and Z'nai representatives arrived on Westrope III to finalise it. The Westropian Embassy was a sea fort that had been used back in the Krypterian wars.

The emperor's son, H'mbrackle II, seized power and marshalled his people to war. H'mbrackle II sought to "purify the lesser species" by slaughtering billions - millions died when a Z'nai sky city incinerated Westrope III. Joshua released a virus the Z'nai themselves had developed, nearly wiping them out and ending their empire. The act of near-genocide ended the Doctor and Joshua's friendship, and the Doctor took him home. H'mbrackle II, now carrying the virus, was placed in a quarantine tesseract accessible from both the TARDIS and Joshua's home.

The fourth Doctor re-visited the Westrope III disaster with Leela, whose future self was present as a time vampire - a gestalt creature able to experience the majesty of time and creation. The time vampire dispatched K9 centuries ahead in the TARDIS to retrieve the aged, imprisoned Leela as she was dying. When K9 returned, the proximity of the aged and younger Leelas paradoxically facilitated the time vampire's creation. Leela's younger self left the Doctor, having no memory of these events, and her older self merged with the time vampire.

Some Z'nai survived, and a few of their number used the time capsule to venture back to recover their emperor.[1508]

c 7432 - THE TIME VAMPIRE[1509] **->** An interplanetary tourist board coordinated visits to what remained of Westrope III. Leela was briefly tussled through time from 7382, and visited the disued Westropian Embassy. Gustav Holland, a tour guide, had used a temporal suspension cage he stole from the Doctor's TARDIS in 7382 to impris-

on a time vampire, thinking he could profit from the creature's abilities. The time vampire - Leela's future self - aged Holland to death, and Leela returned to the past.

(=) The sixth Doctor and Mel failed to prevent nuclear warfare on the Federation planet Maradnias. A group of Chronovores and Eternals, grateful for the Doctor's help in the Bophemeral affair, changed history to prevent Maradnias' destruction.[1510]

Maradnias would become the centre of the Union.[1511]

? 7500 - THE SKULL OF SOBEK[1512] **->** The eighth Doctor and Lucie arrived on Indigo 3, a world with a blue sea, blue moons, a renowned blue desert and eighty-three different words for the colour blue. By coincidence, a torrential storm would flood the desert every eighty-three years, causing ultra-marine flowers to cover the region a few days afterwards. The storm wasn't due for another twenty years, but the Doctor swore he felt rain coming on.

The Sanctuary of Imperfect Symmetry on Indigo 3 was a place of pilgrimage, devotion and deliberate disparity. The old prince of the dead planet Sobek had paid for the construction of the sanctuary hall - the very foundations of which were actually the prized Skull of Sobek. General Snabb engaged the prince in personal combat for the Skull, and both perished when it collapsed on top of them.

The Triumphs of Sobek contained tales of that world.

& 7500 - DALEK EMPIRE II: DALEK WAR[1513] **->** The Galactic Union had been established, and was enjoying a time of peace. Technology, however, was inferior compared to what was available more than three thousand years prior.

The historian Saloran Hardew found Kalendorf's burial chamber on Velyshaa, and accessed his telepathic accounts of the Great Catastrophe by sleeping there. Siy Tarkov, an envoy from the Galactic Union, arrived with a military escort to examine Hardew's findings. It had taken Hardew five years to reach Velyshaa, but technology had improved since then, and Tarkov made the trip in one. Tarkov and Hardew decrypted a transmission conveyed via a freak wormhole, and concluded that the Daleks had refortified in the Seriphia galaxy and were once again mobilising for war. Hardew remained on Velyshaa while Tarkov's group left to warn the Union about the Dalek threat.

Tarkov's ship stopped to refuel on the planet Scalius, where his crew were amongst the first to contract a devastating plague: Neurotransmitter Failure Syndrome (NFS). Tarkov entered hibernation to survive, and his audio warning about the Daleks was ignored. He remained in stasis when the ship was later broken up for salvage.[1514]

Some years later, the security agent Giorgi Selestru

located the Alliance Daleks' space station in the Plowik system. He found within a cryogenic tube containing the augmented human Galanar, who awoke and became one of Selestru's most loyal operatives.[1515]

& 7520 - DALEK EMPIRE III: THE EXTERMINATORS / THE HEALERS / THE SURVIVORS / THE DEMONS / THE WARRIORS / THE FUTURE[1516] **->** The NFS plague became rampant amongst the border worlds. Millions died, and billions more were threatened. The plague increased political tensions, and the border worlds increasingly broke ties with the Union. As part of this, the border worlds rescinded the Union's claim to the Graxis system - possibly the most peaceful and undeveloped sector of the galaxy.

The Galactic Union had failed to act upon Tarkov's sketchy audio warning of the Dalek menace, and now received word that the Daleks had arrived in the Scalani system and were distributing a cure for the plague. The Daleks established "healing zones" throughout the Graxis system - ruining the ecology there - and on planets such as Tantalus and the formerly uninhabitable Scalanis VIII. The Daleks began treating patients with the plague-cure, which was designated Variant 7.

The Daleks' ranks had never recovered from the Great Catastrophe. Lacking the numbers for outright invasion, they had secretly released the NFS plague as part of a scheme to create the largest Dalek army ever assembled. Variant 7 contained an extra genetic code which, in conjunction with a unique type of radiation, would mutate the plague-survivors into Dalek embryos. Dalek munitions factories stood ready to arm the new Daleks.

Siy Tarkov awoke from stasis, and reported his concerns about the Daleks to Giorgi Selestru, who was now the Union's security commander. Galanar, as one of Selestru's operatives, accompanied Tarkov on a six-month trip to Velyshaa to retrieve Kalendorf's records, and thereby goad the Union into action. The Daleks pursued them. On Velyshaa, the Daleks killed Saloran Hardew, but Tarkov transmitted a copy of Kalendorf's accounts to Selestru. It was believed that Selestru would convince the Galactic Union Security Committee and its chairman, Bulis Meitok, to mobilise against the Daleks.

The NFS plague mutated Tarkov into a Dalek. Galanar

---

four says that it's "two thousand years" after the Great Catastrophe. This number is repeated - give or take a bit of phrasing - throughout *Dalek Empire III*.

1514 "Twenty years" before *Dalek Empire III*.

1515 "Years" before *Dalek Empire III*.

1516 Dating *Dalek Empire III* (*The Exterminators*, episode one; *The Healers*, episode two; *The Survivors*, episode three; *The Demons*, episode four; *The Warriors*, episode five; *The Future*, episode six) - The mini-series takes place "twenty years" after Tarkov sets out from Velyshaa at the end of *Dalek Empire II*, and ends on something of a cliffhanger, with humanity in this region of space presumably gearing up to fight the resurgent Dalek threat.

1517 "Five thousand years" after *Prisoner of the Daleks*.

1518 "Just over one hundred fifty years" before the main events of "A Fairytale Life". A holorecording showing the virus being released is timecoded "19-04-7711".

1519 Dating "A Fairytale Life" (IDW *DW* mini-series #3) - The Doctor is aiming for "the year 7704", but has to concede it's "Ah. Not the seventy-eighth century. More like the seventy-ninth ... ish." Later, we learn the virus was released in 7711, "just over one hundred fifty years ago".

1520 Dating *The Catalyst, Empathy Games* and *The Time Vampire* (BF CC #2.4, 3.4, 4.10) - Leela says that it's "centuries" after the Z'nai Empire ended, owing to the plague that Joshua Douglas released. The notion that Leela enjoyed an extended lifespan owing to her proximity to the Time Lords' biofields, and that she'd rapidly age without them, was introduced in *Gallifrey: Spirit*.

1521 Dating *The Judgement of Isskar* (BF #117) - It's

"sixteen thousand years" since the first part of the story. The Black Guardian rescues the Doctor and Amy at the start of *The Destroyer of Delights*.

1522 *The Reaping, The Gathering*.

1523 The background of *The Darksmith Legacy* series, as given in *The Graves of Mordane, The Colour of Darkness* and *The Planet of Oblivion*. The Darksmiths are variously said to have kept the Krashoks waiting for the Eternity Crystal "for millennia" (*The Art of War*, p13) and (ungrammatically) for "*a* millennia" (p18). The Darksmiths *seem* to originate from circa 2012, and so must have travelled into the future more than once to meet up with the Krashoks.

1524 THE MAZUMA ERA: A number of stories from the mid-80s *DWM* strip were set in the same colourful, cosmopolitan far future period. It might be termed the Mazuma Era, after the galactic currency which seems to preoccupy a number of the characters. The first time we're given a date for the story is in *Death's Head* #8 - a *Doctor Who* crossover issue of the Marvel UK comic - which sees the Doctor dropping off the cyborg Death's Head in the year 8162.

While Dogbolter's holdings include Venus, Mars and Jupiter, no mention is ever made of Earth - which the TV show tells us ought to be uninhabited at this time. The solar flares clearly don't affect the other planets of the solar system.

1525 Dating "Free-Fall Warriors" (*DWM* #56-57) - The story sees the fourth Doctor meeting Dr Asimoff for the first time.

1526 Dating "The Moderator" (*DWM* #84, #86-87) - The Free-Fall Warriors are mentioned.

was captured and brought before the Dalek Supreme - which in part had Susan Mendes' personality. The Dalek Supreme gloated that humanity would literally become Daleks, or at the very least would emotionally become like Daleks while fighting them. Galanar maintained that humans would always have a quality that the Daleks lacked, and that the Daleks therefore had no real power over them.

Dalek X believed that the astronic radiation on Hurala would keep it alive until the planet's communications seal expired, and its appeal for help was received. The tenth Doctor promised to be waiting if this occurred.[1517]

In the seventy-eighth century, the planet Caligaris Epsilon Six was one of the most renowned holiday planets of the Third Great and Bountiful Human Empire. It was designed to look like a medieval fantasy land, complete with unicorns, elves and dragons.

The Empire fell into decline, experiencing war, famine, plagues and confrontations with the Sycorax, Drahvins, Sontarans and Chelonians. Aethelred, the chief administrator of Caligaris Epsilon Six, sought to protect the children of that world from the wider conflict - on 19th April, 7711, he reprogrammed the planet's biofilter to stop screening for recombinant *yersinia pestis*, "The Pest", which killed 7,564 adults but spared everyone under the age of ten. The children of Caligaris Epsilon Six grew up with no knowledge of the outside universe, and the planet was placed under quarantine per Imperial Order 54567. Aethelred - who became the children's king - used modern medical techniques to extend his lifespan.[1518]

c 7862 - "A Fairytale Life"[1519] -> The eleventh Doctor and Amy had recently escaped the stomach of a space chicken, and he granted Amy's wish and landed the TARDIS on the fantasy-themed holiday planet of Caligaris Epsilon Six. They discovered the deception that King Aethelred had perpetrated in separating Caligaris Epsilon Six from the wider universe, and came to believe that the people there should make their own choices. The Doctor devised an antibody that eliminated the Pest contagion, and freed the colony from its isolation.

& 7932 - THE CATALYST / EMPATHY GAMES / THE TIME VAMPIRE[1520] -> After Gallifrey and the Time Lords were no more, Leela - who had enjoyed an extended lifespan thanks to the Time Lords' biofields replenishing her telomeres - rapidly aged. She became a prisoner of the Z'nai, who interrogated her about her encounter with their emperor, H'mbrackle II. Leela carried a Z'nai-killing virus that eliminated her captors, but their machines kept her alive for at least another year.

In the last moments of Leela's life, K9 arrived in the TARDIS and took her back in time some centuries - to meet her former self and facilitate her rebirth as a time vampire.

& 8000 - THE JUDGEMENT OF ISSKAR[1521] -> A castle - actually a disguised segment of the Key to Time - on the planet Safeplace radiated a balance-restoring sensation, and so became an ideal location for peace talks. The fifth Doctor and the Key-tracer Amy converted the segment, but were captured by the revived Lord Isskar - who demanded they face trial for their role in Mars' devastation. The rival Key-tracer Zara attempted to crash Isskar's spaceship, thinking she could retrieve Amy's segments from the rubble afterwards. Isskar ejected to safety in an escape pod. A new incarnation of the Black Guardian - needing the Key segments to restore his diminished abilities - transported the Doctor and Amy to ninth-century Sudan.

Two thousand years after it had been established, the Gogglebox enabled users to view every recorded media event from the human race's history. Alan Fitzgerald had been cloned, and one hundred eight copies of him aided visitors.[1522]

The Krashoks - cybernetic humans who had incorporated weaponry from races such as the Daleks, Cybermen and Rinteppi; and alien organs such as Renevian tiger claws, Slitheen arms and Gappa legs - initiated various wars and sold weapons to both sides. They hired the Darksmiths of Karagula to create a device that would resurrect the dead - a means of extending conflicts, which would be good for their business.[1523]

The Mazuma Era[1524]

c 8162 - "Free-Fall Warriors"[1525] -> Doctor Asimoff from Sigma had been coming to the Festival of the Five Planets for the last fifteen years, although it used to be the Festival of the Six Planets until one planet broke away from the Federation. Asimoff recognised the fourth Doctor as a Time Lord, and the Doctor showed him the TARDIS. They met the Free-Fall Warriors - a stunt pilot team who challenged the Doctor to go on a flight with Machinehead, one of their number. They launched right into the middle of an attack on the planet, and were forced down onto an asteroid. The remaining Free-Fall Warriors - Big Cat, Cool Breeze and Bruce - set off to intercept the raiders, and the Doctor fixed Machinehead's ship in time to play a decisive role in the battle.

c 8162 - "The Moderator"[1526] -> Josiah W Dogbolter, a creature not quite a man and not quite a frog, was the owner of the Intra-Venus Inc and the richest man in the galaxy. He profited from everything, including the war on Phobos and ruby mining on Celeste. Dogbolter had a presence on many planets, including Celeste - a world where he sent "moles", meaning people who rebelled against him. He owned Mars, Jupiter and Venus, plus a score of worlds in other systems.

The fifth Doctor and Gus landed on Celeste and narrowly escaped arrest for breaking curfew. Deep in the ruby mines, they were attacked by the Wrekka, a combat robot sent in to deal with the moles. Dogbolter's guards brought the Doctor and Gus to their boss, who learned the Doctor had a time machine. Dogbolter knew that "time is money", but the Doctor refused to sell his Ship and left. A furious Dogbolter brought in the Moderator, a company troubleshooter. He tracked them down and killed Gus.

Gus had wounded the Moderator. The Doctor returned the Moderator to a hospital in his home timezone... where Dogbolter's right-hand robot, Hob, turned off his life support.

c 8162 - "The Shape Shifter"[1527] **->** Avan Tarklu was a 45-year-old Whifferdill - a shapeshifting private investigator who was tempted by the quarter of a million Mazuma reward that Dogbolter had posted for the fifth or sixth Doctor.

Meanwhile, the sixth Doctor learned that Dogbolter had sent the Moderator, and was heading to Greenback Bay, Venus, when he was attacked. Avan Tarklu secretly helped the Doctor repel the attack - purely to get his hands on the reward - and snuck into the TARDIS. The Doctor and the shapeshifter landed at the headquarters of Intra-Venus Inc, which Dogbolter had evacuated, then nuked. They tricked

Dogbolter into handing over the reward, then escaped. The shapeshifter joined the Doctor on his travels.

c 8162 - "Voyager"[1528] **->** The sixth Doctor had a nightmare about a shadowy figure on a sailing ship, waking to find that the TARDIS had landed at the Antarctic of "an outback dimension somewhere between mythology and madness".

The shapeshifter - who was now semi-permanently in the form of a penguin, and calling himself Frobisher - had discovered the same ship, frozen in ice. Exploring the ship, the Doctor found star charts. He was accosted by Astrolabus, an old man with a blunderbuss, who took the charts and made his escape in a da Vinci flying machine.

The Doctor and Frobisher followed him to a lighthouse, where the Doctor confronted Astrolabus - and found that the lighthouse was his TARDIS. Astrolabus tried to escape, but crashed into the sea. Voyager showed himself to the Doctor and demanded the return of the charts - which Astrolabus had tattooed onto his chest. Astrolabus was in his last incarnation and was seeking immortality, but Voyager ripped the chart off his body, killing him. Voyager told the Doctor he was now free, and the Doctor and Frobisher continued their travels.

c 8162 - "Polly the Glot"[1529] **->** Terminal LX 116/RM was a space station at the centre of the Milky Way - the crossroads of an entire galaxy - and was known as Galena. Dr Ivan Asimoff was passing through when he saw the

1527 Dating "The Shape Shifter" (*DWM* #88-89) - This story happens soon after "The Moderator" from the Doctor's point of view, as he's looking to avenge Gus' death. Dogbolter is somehow aware that the Doctor has regenerated, but the wanted poster has images of both the fifth and sixth Doctors.
1528 Dating "Voyager" (*DWM* #90-94) - It's a "few weeks" since the end of "The Shape Shifter".
1529 Dating "Polly the Glot" (*DWM* #95-97) - It's after "Voyager", but there's no indication of how much time has passed.
1530 Dating "Once Upon a Time Lord..." (*DWM* #98-99) - The story follows on from "Polly the Glot".
1531 Dating *The Maltese Penguin* (BF #33 1/2) - No date is given, but this is clearly Frobisher's native time zone.
1532 "The Crossroads of Time"
1533 Dating "Where Nobody Knows Your Name" (*DWM* #329) - This is an unspecified amount of years after Frobisher has returned to his native time.
1534 Before *The Coming of the Terraphiles*, with Barsoom being Mars. Dogbolter profited from the war on Phobos, so it still existed at that point.
1535 Dating *Turn Left* (X4.11) - No date is given on screen or in the script. Shan Shen appears to be a

human colony. *The Time Traveller's Almanac*, a chronology of the *Doctor Who* universe published by BBC Books, states that the story is set in the eighty-fifth century, without explanation. *SJA: Whatever Happened to Sarah Jane?* suggests that the Trickster's Brigade is affiliated with the Trickster, a recurring villain in *The Sarah Jane Adventures*. A number of sources, such as the BBC website, refer to the beetle as a Time Beetle, but it's not called that on screen.
1536 *The Stolen Earth*
1537 The background to *The Crystal Bucephalus*. According to *Dalek Empire II*, there is a Galactic Union by 7500.
1538 Earth's colony worlds start burying their dead on Mordane "four hundred years" before *The Graves of Mordane*. Contrary to the TARDIS' estimate, the young woman Catz - who has studied Mordane in detail, but is perhaps working from faulty records - says that Mordane serviced only a dozen races from more than thirty different worlds.
1539 "A hundred and fifty years" before *The Planet of Oblivion*.

TARDIS. He invited the sixth Doctor to the Save the Zyglot Trust annual conference, as he was the group's treasurer.

Polly, the only Zyglot in captivity, was at the Ringway Carnival along with freakshow exhibits from a hundred worlds. The creatures were hunted for their colours by the dullest race in the universe, the Akkers, and the Trust was failing through lack of funds. The Doctor and Frobisher "kidnapped" Asimoff, generating a great deal of publicity for his cause.

The Doctor learned that the President of the Trust was a Professor Astro Labus. They headed for a hunting ship, freeing the Zyglot in their clutches and discovering that an Astral Arbus owned the Ringway Carnival. The Doctor also freed Polly, who soared and blossomed - and left Asimoff heartbroken. The Doctor left the quarter-million Mazuma reward he stole from Dogbolter for Asimoff to donate to the Trust.

c 8162 - "Once Upon a Time Lord..."[1530] -> The sixth Doctor and Frobisher entered the cabinet of Astrolabus, and encountered a variety of surreal obstacles.

c 8162 - THE MALTESE PENGUIN[1531] -> Frobisher briefly returned to his homeworld to resume his occupation as a private investigator. Through a bizarre twist of economics, Josiah W Dogbolter was generating immense profit on the planet by making sure no factory actually made anything. Frobisher's ex-wife, the Whifferdill named Francine, manipulated events to display the joke, "You don't have to be crazy to work here, but it helps", on the computer terminals of Dogbolter's employees. This triggered communication and productivity, and ruined Dogbolter's operations. Frobisher resumed travelling with the sixth Doctor.

The seventh Doctor banished Death's Head to Earth in the year 8162.[1532]

c 8162 - "Where Nobody Knows Your Name"[1533] -> The eighth Doctor drank at a bar run by his old friend Frobisher, but as both had changed their appearance, neither recognised the other.

At some point in the next forty thousand years or so, Real Phobos crashed into Old Barsoom, a.k.a. Mars.[1534]

c 8400 - TURN LEFT[1535] -> The tenth Doctor and Donna visited the planet Shan Shen, where Donna was lured into a fortune teller's booth and attacked by an alien beetle - one of the Trickster's Brigade. Such creatures normally changed people's lives in tiny ways and fed off the resulting temporal shift, but the beetle changed Donna's personal history so she never met the Doctor - with grave consequences to the history of Earth. Rose helped Donna to restore history, and the beetle died.

Donna passed a message from Rose to the Doctor - two words: "Bad Wolf" - which made the Doctor race outside the fortune teller's booth, and see that everything with writing said exactly that. The TARDIS cloister bell started ringing, and the Doctor told Donna that it signalled the end of the universe. They returned to the twenty-first century.[1536]

After the great cybernetic massacres of the eighty-fifth century, sentient androids fell out of favour. From this point, most robot servants were connected to a central webwork rather than being autonomous.

The Federation had remained a democracy, but the Chen dynasty brought an end to that. Civil war broke out, and the final battle of the conflict took place in the Mirabilis system. Federation forces won, but the Imperial Fleet devastated Mirabilis itself with an atmospheric plasma burst that killed 90% of the population. Emperor Chen was captured and executed.

The civil war had taken its toll on the Federation, and the galaxy entered a new dark age in which scientific progress all but ceased. During the ninetieth century, the remnants of the Federation became the Union - a united political entity at peace with the Draconian Republic, the Cyberlord Hegemony and the radioactive remains of the Sontaran Empire. There were two other forces for unity: the Elective, a massive criminal organisation that controlled all criminal activity between New Alexandria and the Perseus Rift; and the Lazarus Intent, a religious organisation which commanded eight quadrillion people.[1537]

The Darksmith Legacy

The entire surface of Mordane, the first planet of the Gandii Prime system, had been converted into a place of cemeteries and catacombs - according to the TARDIS data bank, Mordane served a hundred different species from a thousand worlds as a planet of the dead. Humans from colonies such as Folflower, Mayside, Riverville, Wystone and Humberville buried their dead on Mordane. Lady Rosilie of Peladon was buried there. An entire continent, Sector Alpha, was designated for humans.[1538]

An underwater research base was established on Flydon Maxima to monitor the planetary warming there. The global warming ultimately gave way to a catastrophic ice age, forcing the planet's inhabitants to abandon it.[1539]

King Morrish a'Jethwa, who ruled five planets in the Folflower system for many years, was buried on Mordane. Following his death, the monarchy was deposed in a bloodless coup and went into exile.

Brother Varlos, the Darksmiths' chief engineer on the Krashok project, succeeded in building a device that could reanimate the dead. He field-tested the device on Mordane, and succeeded in making the dead walk. Varlos realised that the device had the potential to revive the dead on millions of worlds, and was so horrified that he vowed to destroy the device - but didn't know how to demolish its central power source, the Eternity Crystal. Varlos left his "daughter", an android named Gisella, at a base made from Darksmith technology on Flydon Maxima. He then fled with the Crystal to nineteeth-century Paris.[1540]

The walking dead on Mordane prompted the Galactic Union to designate the planet a quarantine world with a Grade Two Exclusion Order. In the eighty years to follow, all records of Mordane were erased.[1541]

c 9000 - THE GRAVES OF MORDANE / THE COLOUR OF DARKNESS / THE DEPTHS OF DESPAIR / THE PLANET OF OBLIVION[1542] -> The tenth Doctor visited the cemetery world of Mordane to learn more about the Eternity Crystal. He deactivated Varlos' re-animation machine, turning the undead that walked on Mordane into dust. He also helped Catz, the granddaughter of King Morrish a'Jethwa, to retrieve a torch from the king's tomb - it was the symbol of her right to rule the Folflower system. The Darksmiths' Agent took the Eternity Crystal from the Doctor, and the Doctor pursued the Agent to the Darksmiths' homeworld of Karagula...

Later, the Doctor went to Flydon Maxima to learn how to destroy the Crystal. The Darksmiths' enforcers, the Dreadbringers, followed the Doctor through time in the Dreadnought *Adamantine*. The Doctor sent a surge of icy water through an underwater base - this both swept away the Dreadbringers and enabled some local lifeforms, the tentacled Blaska, to retrieve a clutch of their eggs. The Doctor met Gisella, and together they went to find her father in Paris, 1895...[1543]

The Darksmiths re-conferred with the Krashoks on the peaceful planet Ursulonamex, a.k.a. Oblivion, concerning the Eternity Crystal - a devastating "rain of fire" was then unleashed upon the planet to cover up the meeting. The insectoid Dravidians, a race of thieves, arrived at Ursulonamex's only surviving space station and claimed to have answered a distress call. The Dravidians clandestinely set about draining the station's power and adapting its environment to suit their offspring, which hatched in their thousands. The tenth Doctor and Gisella forced the Dravidians to withdraw.[1544]

After around eight thousand years in the time corridor created by the fourth Doctor, Sutekh finally perished at the beginning of the ninetieth century.[1545]

1540 *The Graves of Mordane, The Depths of Despair, The Dust of Ages, The Vampire of Paris.* It's never established that Brother Varlos has time travel capabilities, but the Darksmiths have a conglomeration of time technology by *The Dust of Ages*, so he could have nicked some bits of it beforehand.
1541 In *The Graves of Mordane*, it's said that the Darksmiths have been waiting "centuries"/"hundreds of years" since Brother Varlos absconded with the Eternity Crystal, that Varlos' machine has been on Mordane for "hundreds of years" (p91), and that the dead have been walking there every night "for centuries" (p107). And yet, it's twice said that the quarantine on Mordane has only been in operation for "eighty years" (p37, 82). Given that up to a thousand funerals a day were previously held on Mordane (p92), it doesn't seem remotely credible that the Galactic Union failed to notice - or decided to ignore - that the dead were rising every night on Mordane for decades if not longer. The Darksmiths confirm (p96) that the Varlos' test is what prompted the Mordane quarantine, making it unlikely that the machine lay dormant for centuries and flared to life for no apparent reason.
1542 Dating *The Graves of Mordane, The Depths of Despair* and *The Planet of Oblivion* (DL #2, 4, 7) - *The Graves of Mordane* occurs when quite a few of humanity's colony planets have been sending their dead to Mordane for "over four hundred years" (p37), and a "Galactic Union" (p82) passes a "galactic law" (p37) that quarantines Mordane. If the "Galactic Union" is the same "Union" mentioned in *The Crystal Bucephalus*, then *The Graves of Mordane* could occur more-or-less anywhere in the 8000s to 12000s.

The participants in *The Depths of Despair* are named as human (p96); *The Planet of Oblivion* does the same at least three times (pgs. 89, 90, 94), so both of these stories occur in humanity's future, quite possibly in the same time zone that Brother Varlos conducted his experiments on Mordane.
1543 Their adventures continue in *The Vampire of Paris* and *The Game of Death*.
1544 The story continues in *The Pictures of Emptiness* and *The Art of War*.
1545 *Pyramids of Mars*
1546 Dating *Dreamtime* (BF #67) - Some "thousands of years" have passed since the Uluru departed into space. Simon Forward says it's possible that as much as ten thousand years have elapsed. This date is arbitrary.
1547 Dating *The Children of Seth* (BF LS #3.3) - Date unknown, although the participants are identified as human. It's tempting to think that the android technology seen here - and the fear of it - dates back to Sharez Jek's android designs in *The Caves of Androzani* (which also takes place in Sirius), but no connection between the two is made. This dating is ultimately a guess, based upon no mention of Earth being made, and the empire's wealth and prosperity being in excess of that seen in *The Caves of Androzani*.
1548 *The Crystal Bucephalus*
1549 Dating *The Scarlet Empress* (EDA #15) - The novel

? 9,000 - DREAMTIME[1546] -> The seventh Doctor, Ace and Hex arrived at the Uluru as it travelled through space. The people's faith in the Dreaming had weakened, and the Dreaming began absorbing people into itself by turning them into stone. The Doctor accidentally travelled to the time of the solar flares and influenced the Uluru's departure from Earth. He returned and restored the people to normal, and it was hoped that the Dreaming's next attempt to terraform the Uluru would prove more successful.

? 9200 - THE CHILDREN OF SETH[1547] -> An army warred with itself on the plains of Ragnarok, and only three hundred of its mightiest heroes survived. Their leader, Autarch Siris, forged a major trading empire with the cities on the asteroid archipelago around Sirius as its core. Idra, a student, met the Doctor while she was subverting the propaganda agency on Sirius III. She belonged to the Gracious Academy of Women, and realised that the budding empire would need an enemy to fear and rally against. Idra invented the bogeyman Seth, as he was named in her book *The Trick of Darkness*. In time, she would became Siris' concubine, Queen Anahita, a.k.a. the Queen of Poisons.

The Sirian Empire reached a long way across its sector, and included at least ten humanoid variants. Androids were outlawed, and *The Trick of Darkness* was banned. Anahita's face was scarred as she tried to rescue copies of it from a fire.

Forty-three years after Anahita met the Doctor, Siris relinquished his authority to Lord Byzan - who consolidated his power by rallying his people against Seth, now said to have taken shelter in worlds beyond the Rim. Anahita feared the consequences for the empire, and summoned the fifth Doctor, Tegan and Nyssa. Androids who had infiltrated Sirius staged a coup, hoping to create a society without humans. The Doctor posed as Seth, and Byzan ended the insurrection by destroying the android Albis - which by extension made random "people" across the empire become immobile, their android origins revealled.

The empire disbanded, with individual worlds regaining their sovereignty. Anahita and Siris retired, after she poisoned Byzan in his cell.

The Antonine rescue raid on Scultiis in 9381 failed when the natives' electric fields disrupted their weapons.[1548]

c 9968 - THE SCARLET EMPRESS[1549] -> The planet Hyspero was visited at some point by hawk-like beings who were revered by the natives, yet had no interest in ruling the planet. They left behind Cassandra - the first Scarlet Empress, a jam-like creature in a jar - to look after their affairs. She built up the Scarlet Palace and founded the tattooed Scarlet Guard. A long line of Scarlet Empresses - Cassandra's descendents - ruled Hyspero, and the planet became home to an interstellar market.

The latest Scarlet Empress was a tyrant who conscripted Iris Wildthyme - who was dying, as she had eaten the flesh of a Kaled mutant - to reunite a mercenary band named the Four. One of the group was guarding Cassandra, and the incumbent Empress sought to lay claim to her ancestor. The eighth Doctor and Sam helped Iris find the Four, whereupon Cassandra destroyed her descendent and reclaimed the throne. Iris regenerated thanks to the healing properties of a life-restoring honey.

Around the end of the one-hundredth century, the Silurian scientists Ethra and Teelis worked on time-travel experiments. The results were published in the March 9978 edition of *Abstract Meanderings in Theoretical Physics*.[1550] The ArcHive studied the history of the universe, and served as vast repositories of knowledge. They had access to time-travel technology.[1551] Emperor Brandt and the Cyberlord Hegemony possessed the ArcHive in the hundredth century.[1552]

itself gives no dating clues. The word "human" is continually used, although it's frequently unclear if this means Earth-born humans or just "humanoid". Mention is finally made, however, of a "colony of human beings" on a private moon of a vizier, which would seem to indicate this is in humanity's future.

The short story "Femme Fatale" (*More Short Trips*, 1999), also by Paul Magrs, has the Doctor and Sam encountering Iris after events in *The Scarlet Empress*. "Femme Fatale" occurs in 1968 (concurrent with the radical feminist Valerie Solanas shooting Andy Warhol), and Iris mentions to Sam that events on Hyspero took place "eight thousand years" ago. It's a little unclear whether she means eight thousand years in the past or

the future - she might mean the former, but the presence of Draconians, Ice Warriors and Spiridons (who presumably start space-travelling at some point after *Planet of the Daleks*) on Hyspero seems to indicate the latter. Portions of "Femme Fatale" are obviously apocryphal (rendering "the Doctor and Mrs Jones" as agents of the British government, and eventually waking up on a *Prisoner*-style island), but the dating reference occurs in a section that is as canonical as one can get in a story such as this.
1550 *The Crystal Bucephalus*
1551 *Killing Ground*. The ArcHivists first appeared in the reference book *Cybermen*.
1552 *The Quantum Archangel*

10,764 - THE CRYSTAL BUCEPHALUS[1553] -> In 10,753, Alexhendri Lassiter fulfilled on the Lazarus Intent, stabilising a time gate that rescued Lazarus from the Sontaran throneworld before his death. But the truth about the false Messiah quickly became clear, and Arrestis took control of the criminal Elective. Meanwhile, Lassiter and his brother Sebastian built the Crystal Bucephalus, a time-travel restaurant on the planet New Alexandria, which sent the galaxy's elite to the finest eating establishments in history.

Eleven years later, the Crystal Bucephalus was destroyed. Arrestis was revealled as Lazarus and escaped in a time gate, only to arrive back on Sontara moments before his execution.

About a hundred years after the Crystal Bucephalus ended, humanity was again fragmented by civil war. The Union swiftly evolved into the Concordance, then the Confederation, then the Junta - a totalitarian regime that stemmed from the Elective. This instigated a millennium of barbarism.[1554]

c 11,000 - SYNTHESPIANS™[1555] -> A fleet of ark ships fled the galactic civil war and passed through an area known as the Great Barrier. Cut off from the rest of the galaxy, the colonists found themselves in an area rich with natural resources. The New Earth Republic was founded, and included such planets as Bel Terra, New Alaska, New California, New Regency, Paxas and Tranicula in the Thomas Exultation (which was noted for its vineyards).

A hundred years later, the Republic was peaceful but boring. A business consortium failed in its bid to restore contact with the rest of the galaxy, but managed to pick up old TV broadcasts from twentieth-century Earth. These proved extremely popular and Reef Station One was built to produce new shows such as *As the Worlds Turn*, *Dreams of Tomorrow*, *Executive Desires*, *The Rep*, *Star Traveller: The Motion Picture*, *ReefEnders*, *Liberation Street*, *Confessions of a*

1553 Dating *The Crystal Bucephalus* (MA #4) - The Doctor claims they are "six or seven centuries into the tenth millennium" (p27), but also says that it is the "108th century" (p40, which is in the *eleventh* millennium). The latter date is correct - elsewhere we learn that "10,663" was in the recent past (p69). Although the novel doesn't specify the exact date, author Craig Hinton assumed that it was set in the year 10,764 and that date has been adopted here.

1554 Combining accounts given in *The Crystal Bucephalus* and *Synthespians™*, both novels by Craig Hinton. *Synthespians™* claims that Chen's empire is finished before the Union is formed, and yet someone else claiming descent from Mavic Chen (evidently not the beheaded emperor) is either the leader of the Junta (which follows on from the Union) or has some form of authority as mankind seeks out its lost colonies (p273).

1555 Dating *Synthespians™* (PDA #67) - The events of *The Crystal Bucephalus* were "several centuries" ago.

1556 *Synthespians™*

1557 *The Crystal Bucephalus*

1558 *The Ark in Space*. Vira notes that scientists had calculated it would be "five thousand years before the biosphere was viable" on Earth after the solar flares. In *The Sontaran Experiment*, we learn that humanity has spread across the galaxy, and that Earth has been habitable for "thousands of years" but has remained abandoned.

1559 Before "Final Sacrifice". There's some confusion in the story about the time that elapses during the civil war, which is variously given as "tens of thousands of years", "ten thousand years", "over ten thousand years" and simply "millennia" before.

1560 *The Also People* (p247).

1561 According to the Doctor in *The End of the World*. This would seem to fall at the time Earth was thought to be abandoned by humanity following the solar flares. Perhaps the New Roman Empire wasn't based on Earth, or there was a shortlived resettlement of the planet.

1562 Dating *City at World's End* (PDA #25) - This is an arbitrary date, although we are told it is "thousands of years" after Ian and Barbara's native time.

1563 *Alien Bodies*

1564 Dating *The Ark in Space* (12.2) - Harry twice suggests that they are "ten thousand years" after the time of the Solar Flares, and the Doctor confirms this in *The Sontaran Experiment*, which takes place immediately afterwards. *The Terrestrial Index* set the stories between "15,000 and 20,000". *The TARDIS Logs* suggested a date of "28,537". *Cybermen* offered the year "?14714". *The TARDIS Special* gave the date "c.131st century". The first edition of *Timelink* said "10,000"; the Telos version went for "15,000". *About Time* decided it was "15000 AD, at the earliest".

1565 *Wirrn: Race Memory*

1566 Dating *The Sontaran Experiment* (12.3) - The story immediately follows *The Ark in Space*. In *SJA: The Last Sontaran*, Sarah claims that these events happened "ten thousand years" in the future.

1567 *Heroes of Sontar*

1568 Dating *The Eye of the Tyger* (TEL #12) - The dating is more than a little confused. The Doctor says this is "a million and a half years" in Fyne's future (p28), but the blurb says it's the "thirty-second century". It's clearly after the solar flares first referred to in *The Ark in Space*.

1569 Dating *Wirrn: Race Memory* (BBV audio #29) - It's repeatedly said to be "one hundred years" after events in *The Ark in Space*. The audio concurs with the TV story

Monoid and *This Evening With Phil and Bev*. The people of the Republic become obsessed with television.

A Time Lord force of War-TARDISes launched an attack against the Nestene home planet of Polymos. The mission was commanded by Lord Vansell, and destroyed swarms of energy units. The Nestene Consciousness attempted to relocate to the New Earth Republic. Plastic automata named Synthespians - in reality Autons - had been freely used to perform manual labour in the Republic, and those aboard Reef Station One instigated a slaughter. The sixth Doctor and Peri defeated the Nestene Consciousness and its Autons. The Consciousness was trapped in a plastic Replica body, forced to again and again act out the last episode of *Executive Desires*.

The Junta attempted to invade the New Earth republic several centuries after the Auton incident, but was repelled. The New Earth Republic began intergalactic colonization efforts, sending sleeper ships to the Wolf-Lundmark-Melotte galaxy and Andromeda.[1556] A resurgent Confederation finally overthrew the Junta.[1557]

The Earth became habitable again. Humanity didn't recolonise its homeworld.[1558] The human colonists who had arrived on an unnamed planet as the Sol Three and Terraforming groups renamed themselves the "Soul Free" and the "Terror Farmers". They fought each other for ten thousand years.[1559] Cyberblind released their DTM *Machina ex Machina* in 11,265.[1560] **The year 12,005 was the time of the New Roman Empire.**[1561]

? 15,000 - CITY AT WORLD'S END[1562] -> An asteroid hit the moon of Sarath, changing its orbit so that it was now on a collision course with the planet. Ten years later, the first Doctor, Ian, Barbara and Susan found that preparations to build a rocket to evacuate the planet for the nearby Mirath were nearly complete. However, the Sarath leaders, based in the capital city of Arkhaven, had realised that the rocket ship could never fly and were only planning to save five hundred members of the elite.

Most of the population had been killed in a recent war and replaced by androids. This was a plot on the part of Monitor, the central computer in Arkhaven, to save itself before the planet's destruction. Monitor was destroyed, and the Doctor and Susan increased the capacity of the true escape rocket to save those they could.

w - The first land battle of the War in Heaven between the Time Lords and the Enemy was fought on Dronid in the 160th century. It lasted a day, and was utterly devastating. The Time Lords used clockwork bacteria as a weapon. The Time Lords' attempts to cover their tracks after the battle wreaked almost as much harm as the battle itself, and became known by the inhabitants as the Cataclysm. The Doctor was thought to have been killed on Dronid,

and the Relic, said to be his body, was recovered there in 15,414. A misguided Faction Paradox member, Cousin Sanjira, cast the Relic into the Time Vortex and it arrived in the twenty-second century. The Faction made Sanjira murder his younger self as punishment.[1563]

Return to Earth

c 16,000 - THE ARK IN SPACE[1564] -> The fourth Doctor, Sarah Jane and Harry arrived on Nerva and helped some of the colonists there to awaken. The Wirrn had infested the Ark, and sought to absorb the humans' knowledge. The Wirrn were killed, and humanity prepared to reoccupy their homeworld. They intended to restock the planet with plant and animal life and to rebuild human civilisation.

Before their defeat, the Wirrn seeded their DNA into various insect species in Nerva's gene bank.[1565]

& c 16,000 - THE SONTARAN EXPERIMENT[1566] -> Field Major Styre of Sontaran G3 Intelligence conducted a Military Assessment Survey on Earth, which had acquired strategic value in the Sontarans' war with the accursed Rutans, and was believed devoid of intelligent life. Styre conducted experiments on Galsec colonists that he lured to Earth, but the fourth Doctor and Harry, accompanied by Sarah Jane, killed him.

The Sontarans posthumously published Styre's manual on human resistance to torture.[1567]

& c 16,000 - THE EYE OF THE TYGER[1568] -> Just after the people aboard Nerva had begun to resettle the Earth, a feline race arrived and helped the reconstruction efforts. Soon, though, some humans turned against the aliens, who left with ten thousand humans to find a new home. They were lured to settle on planets within a black hole by the avatars of their descendants, the Conservers, who existed in the black hole billions of years in the future.

& 16,100 - WIRRN: RACE MEMORY[1569] -> Fifty years after the Nerva sleepers revived, the station's solar stacks failed, and it was abandoned. Another half-century on, the remaining humans from Nerva and their descendents worked to restore Earth's ecology by using gene spoolers to re-create various animal species. Cherries had been cultured, but weren't yet approved for gene spooling. The Wirrn DNA hidden in Nerva's gene bank caused the spoolers to generate some mature Wirrn, and although these were killed, the Wirrn DNA persisted in at least two people. It was suspected that the Wirrn had absorbed so much non-Wirrn material, any new Wirrn offspring would be born as humans.

The Dalek War against Venus in Space Year 17,000 was halted by the intervention of a fleet of war rockets from the planet Hyperon. The rockets were made of a metal completely resistant to Dalek firepower. The Dalek task force was completely destroyed.[1570]

c 17,150 - THE TIME OF ANGELS[1571] **->** The Delerium Archive was the biggest museum ever and the final resting place of the Headless Monks. The eleventh Doctor found artifacts there relating to himself, and also a message from River Song carved into the Home Box of the *Byzantium*: "Hello, Sweetie", along with a series of time-space coordinates. He and Amy went to the *Byzantium*, in the past, as instructed.

The Far Future

In the far future, humanity's influence was felt in other galaxies such as Andromeda, Acteon, Isop, Artoro and the Anterides.[1572] The Daleks were the greatest threat in the universe ... until one day, when they just vanished. Eventually they became mere legends. Unknown to humanity, they had left to fight the Last Great Time War with the Time Lords, a conflict that all but wiped out both races.[1573]

The Gods of Light conducted experiments on Vortis.

They replaced the core with a propulsion system, and kidnapped the Menoptra from their home planet.[1574]

The Aapex Corporation, based on Mina Fourteen, started a genetics experiment on the planet Nooma to further terraforming and bioengineering on low-gravity planets. Nooma's sun was an Aapex spaceship, and the planet's artificial "Sky" - actually a sentient being programmed to regulate Nooma's biosphere - formed a protective shell around the planet.

Biology on Nooma became such that humanoids developed in the forest as carnivorous children, but mature males would fight to the death. The winners underwent genetic "promotion", which entailed their growing wings and joining the flying "naieen", but the losers would reanimate as infertile cadavers named the Dead. The naieen would mate, causing their seed to fall on the forest and bud new children.[1575]

? 18,000 - HEROES OF SONTAR[1576] **->** The Sontaran Empire now had seven "great" clans of distinction, each of which was cloned from one of the Sontarans' greatest warriors. Three Sontarans were required for a formal execution party. Under Standing Order 447-subsidiary clause two, mockery of a Sontaran officer was an act of war. The Sontarans regarded Terra as a Class-C civilisation. The Fifteenth Treaty - whether or not the Sontarans recognised

---

in that "ten millennia have passed since the solar flares", but also, a bit oddly, says that the Nerva gene bank is fifteen thousand years old.

1570 *Genesis of the Daleks.* It's a presumption that "Space Year 17,000" is the same as 17,000 AD.

1571 Dating *The Time of Angels* (X5.4) - It's "twelve thousand years" after the story's main events.

1572 Inter Minor is in the Acteon Group, as is Metebelis III (*Carnival of Monsters*), although it is later referred to as the Acteon galaxy (*The Green Death, Planet of the Spiders*). The Isop galaxy is the location of Vortis (*The Web Planet, Twilight of the Gods*), the home of the Face of Boe (according to *Bad Wolf*) and possibly the Slitheen (*Boom Town* refers to "venom grubs" - as they're called in *The Web Planet* novelisation; they're named "larvae guns" in the TV version). Artoro and the Anterides are referred to in *Planet of Evil*.

1573 "Thousands of years" before *The Parting of the Ways*. It's unclear exactly when this occurs. Captain Jack knows about the Daleks' disappearance, but as he's also a time traveller; it doesn't mean this happened before his native time. It's after "Space Year 17,000", historically the last recorded reference to the Daleks before *Bad Wolf*.

It's also unclear what this "vanishing" entails - the Doctor seems amazed that he meets a Dalek in *Dalek*, suggesting that they've been erased from history (would he, for example, have been surprised to meet

one around 2164 on Earth, during their invasion?). However, Captain Jack recognises their ships in *Bad Wolf*, and the inhabitants of 200,100 both know the Daleks' name and that they vanished. Perhaps the simplest solution is that the new-style, gold Daleks that make their debut in *Dalek* are "Time War Era" Daleks, and so none of them should exist after the Time War.

1574 "Thousands of years" before *Twilight of the Gods*.

1575 "Four thousand years ago" according to *Speed of Flight*.

1576 Dating *Heroes of Sontar* (BF #146) - A plaque commemorates the Sontaran invasion of Samur "in the Marshall year 7509", but this is unlikely to equate with the Earth calendar because a) the Sontarans are too inclusive and egotistical a race to resort to anything but their own dating, and b) a human-torture manual written by Field Major Styre is in use, so it's after *The Sontaran Experiment*. Judging exactly *how* far after is tricky: Styre's manual is still in circulation, even though one would presume that the Sontarans would eventually gain better intelligence on humans (whom they are aware of, to the point of designating Terra a Class-C civilisation) and render his findings outdated. And yet, enough time has passed since *The Sontaran Experiment* that Sontaran stories of the Doctor are now "legion", whereas Styre hadn't heard of him.

The Sontarans currently have an empire with considerable holdings in the Madillon Cluster, a territory they

it - exempted non-combatants in a war zone from martial jurisdiction. Sontarans could commit honourable suicide by ingesting coronic acid pills.

In this era, people all across the "middle galaxies" came to the planet Samur to find sanctuary and solace - especially at its Citadel, which stretched all the way around Samur's equator. Ten local years after the Doctor visited the Citadel, the Sontarans tried to oppress Samur and ran into heavy resistance from amorphic space-mercenaries, the Witch Guards. The Sontaran Stabb detonated one hundred twenty canisters of biological agent Zed-Oblique-Stroke-Zero-Zero-Two in Samur's troposphere, which transformed the planet's inhabitants into an invasive purple moss. Such was the honour to follow, Stabb became Field Marshall Stabb, the Unvanquished Supreme Commander of the Ninth Sontaran Space Fleet.

Stabb was used as the template for one million Sontaran clones, but a Witch Guard corrupted Stabb's DNA, so the clones had subtle defects. This marked a turning point for the Sontaran Empire - after the victory at Samur, Sontaran forces increasingly had to pull back from Rutan space and consolidate within the Madillon Cluster.

Twenty local years after the Sontarans devastated Samur, the fifth Doctor, Tegan, Nyssa and Turlough were present as the Witch Guards perished while trying to usurp the cloning vats on the Sontaran homeworld and create an army of themselves. A rain composed of embryonic Sontarans washed over Samur, eliminating the moss and reviving the planet's ecosystem.

c 18,000 - PLAGUE OF THE DALEKS[1577] **->** The Lucerians were a scholarly, non-aggressive purple-coloured race with tentacles. They re-absorbed their dead, and displayed bioluminescence in their mating rituals. Humans inhabited Satellite 16 in the Hammer Nebula; working ninety hours a week was permitted there, and

---

seemed to be battling the Rutans for in *The Two Doctors*.

1577 Dating *Plague of the Daleks* (BF #129) - The Doctor notes the use of a fortieth century-style shuttlecraft and a forty-fifth century-style environmental dome; from this, he conjectures that he and Nyssa have arrived "beyond the Critical Age", i.e. after the solar flares have ravaged Earth (presumably the same incident established in *The Ark in Space*). However, this isn't to say that the adventure actually takes place near the forty-fifth century - both items could be long-lasting, or could have been recreated for nostalgic purposes. The history established in *The Ark in Space*, in fact, tends to rule out *Plague of the Daleks* as occurring near the forty-fifth century - the solar flare cataclysm is so great that humanity takes desperate measures such as converting Nerva Beacon into a hibernation station to survive, and it's hard to imagine that amidst this tragedy, a heritage trust is shuttling carefree senior citizens to Earth as a tourist service with declining revenues.

One of the seniors, Vincent Linfoot, says that he's backtracked "several hundred generations" (call it seventy-five hundred to seventeen thousand five hundred years for the sake of argument) of his family to Stockbridge, and here finds a family gravestone from 1872. Extrapolating "several hundred generations" from that point, the story could date anywhere from circa 9,350 to 19,350. As Stockbridge itself - however much the Doctor mourns for its loss - could itself be a Dalek recreation, and there's nothing to say that a single brick of it stemmed from the genuine article, it's perhaps best to assume that it was established as a heritage city after Earth's repopulation after *The Ark in Space*, and that its destruction comes before the planet being (yet again) abandoned by 18,500 according to *Birthright*.

That just leaves the task of correlating this story to Dalek history. The Daleks' instruments say they've been hibernating in Stockbridge for seventeen centuries awaiting the Doctor's arrival, but as their equipment is badly corroded, the accuracy of their time-keeping devices is very questionable. Whether or not the "seventeen centuries" figure can be trusted, though, it's notable that A) the Stockbridge Daleks say their race possessed a mighty battle fleet when they went to sleep, and that B) two natives of this era - Lysette Barclay and Professor Rinxo Jabbery - respectively claim that "the Daleks died out centuries ago" and that most civilised races consider them to be extinct. If *Plague of the Daleks* does indeed take place after Earth's re-settlement in *The Ark in Space*, Jabbery and Barclay could be referring to the Daleks' failed assault against Venus in 17,000 (as established in *Genesis of the Daleks*).

Pursuant to this, the Doctor claims that while the Stockbridge Daleks slept, they were defeated by the "combined forces of over one hundred planets", and that they "were driven from this sector of the galaxy centuries ago; where there used to be a glorious Dalek empire, there's just a big empty nothing". As he's no means of establishing the year beyond the forty-fifth century technology he's witnessed, however, his opinion here can't particularly be trusted - he could just as easily be referring to the downfall in Dalek fortunes in the centuries after *The Daleks' Master Plan* or *Dalek Empire II*, or just be mocking them to gain a psychological advantage.

One last oddity: at story's end, the Doctor tells Nyssa that "time" deposited them at the last possible point in Stockbridge's future - i.e. its destruction. Not only is this claim bizarre on its face - does he mean the entity Time from the New Adventures, or does he actually mean to say that the time bubble in *The Eternal Summer* was somehow self-aware? - it's still not proof that the Stockbridge seen here isn't a Dalek recreation, and that the original didn't perish long ago.

there were queues for health care. The WN5 filtration booster was obsolete, replaced by the WN9 in deep-space communication systems.

The Daleks learned of the Doctor's fondness for the village of Stockbridge, and laid a trap for him by preserving it beneath an environmental dome - it was one of only three sites given such treatment in Earth's Northern Hemisphere. Tourists would visit Stockbridge, and what villagers remained were Nth-generation clones, the products of a degrading gene pool.

The fifth Doctor and Nyssa surfaced in this era owing to a collapsing time bubble in the twenty-first century, retrieved the TARDIS from a Dalek stasis vault, and prevented the Daleks from using the Ship to gain mastery of space-time. They departed as one of the Daleks' thralls nullified the environmental dome, destroying Stockbridge and all within.

Around 18,500, Earth was abandoned once again.[1578] The Aapex Corporation went bankrupt. Nooma was abandoned to its own fate.[1579]

? 20,000 - THE WEB PLANET[1580] **->** The planet Vortis in the Isop galaxy was the home of the moth-like Menoptra, who worshipped in glorious temples of light and lived in the flower forests. They kept an ant-like race, the Zarbi, as cattle. The planet was invaded by the Animus, an entity that could absorb all forms of energy, and which pulled three planetoids - including Pictos - into orbit around Vortis. Most of the Menoptra fled to Pictos, but the descendants of those that stayed behind slowly devolved into sightless dwarfs, the Optera. The Animus used the Zarbi as soldiers, and had dreams of galactic conquest until the first Doctor, Ian, Barbara and Vicki arrived. The Animus was destroyed by the Isop-tope, a Menoptra weapon.

1578 *Birthright*
1579 "2347.54 years" before *The Speed of Flight*.
1580 Dating *The Web Planet* (2.5) - The story seems to take place in the future as the Animus craves "Earth's mastery of Space". Bill Strutton's novelisation places it in "20,000", although the Doctor suggests that the TARDIS' "time pointer" might not be working. The New Adventure *Birthright* suggests that Earth is abandoned at this time, but it is established in *The Ark in Space* and *The Sontaran Experiment* that man has spread through the universe.
1581 "Over a hundred and fifty years" before *Twilight of the Gods*.
1582 Dating *Twilight of the Gods* (MA #26) - This is a sequel to *The Web Planet*. The Animus was defeated "seventy thousand days ago" (p1), which is a little under one hundred and ninety-two years.
1583 Dating "The Naked Flame" (*DWM Yearbook 1995*) - It's an unspecified amount of time after *The Web Planet*.
1584 Dating *Return to the Web Planet* (BF subscription promo #6) - The back cover says, "It's been hundreds of years and several regenerations since the Doctor last visited the insect world of Vortis." Within the story itself, the Doctor mentions his "previous visits" (note the plural) and that he hasn't visited since "a few regenerations back", a tacit acknowledgement of the second Doctor's trip to Vortis in *Twilight of the Gods*, and possibly (for those who prefer) even those seen in the Annuals and *TV Comic*.
1585 *Shada*. Chris Parsons' dating of the book gives a figure of "minus twenty thousand years", with time running backwards over the book. This might be a property of the book, rather than an indication it comes from the future.
1586 Dating "Final Sacrifice" (IDW Vol. 1, #13-16) - Robert Lewis' group arrives on the colony planet

"twenty thousand" years after they left, in 1906.
1587 Dating *Birthright* (NA #17) - Ace says she was born "Oh, probably about twenty thousand years ago" (p134), although how she reaches this figure is unclear. It is "year 2959" of the Charrl occupation of Earth (p1) when they start their scheme, which will take "almost five hundred years" (p60), yet curiously it is "year 2497" (p109) when they finish! This is presumably a misprint, and ought to read "3497".
1588 Dating *Speed of Flight* (MA #27) - This is "about twenty thousand years" after Jo's time (p23).
1589 "Twenty one thousand years" after *The Sands of Time* (p122).
1590 "A few thousand years" after 21,906, according to "Final Sacrifice".
1591 Dating *The Face of Evil* (14.4) - The story could take place at any point in the far future. The Doctor states in *The Invisible Enemy* that the year 5000 is the time of Leela's ancestors. This story, then, takes place at least ten generations after that - the crew of the colony ship were stranded for "generations" before the Doctor first helped them, and there have apparently been seven generations since (the Sevateem seem to attack the barrier once a generation, and this is the seventh attempt).

Humans evolve limited psychic powers around the time of the fifty-first century (*The Talons of Weng-Chiang*) and the Tesh have psychic powers, so they might originate after that time, but they probably receive all their abilities from Xoanon's selective breeding programme.

In *The Sun Makers*, the Usurian computer correctly guesses that "Sevateem" is a corruption of "Survey Team", and that Leela comes from a "degenerate, unsupported Tellurian colony" suggesting that there are many such planets known to the Company. *The Terrestrial Index* set the story "several centuries" after

New Rhumos broke away from Rhumos Prime, which marked the beginning of a lengthy conflict.[1581]

c 20,192 - TWILIGHT OF THE GODS[1582] **->** After the Animus' defeat, Vortis wandered into the Rhumos system. Two Rhumon factions, the Imperials and the Republicans, fought for control of the planet. The second Doctor, Jamie and Victoria arrived a year later, just as a seed of the Animus emerged. The Doctor brought the Rhumons and Menoptera together to destroy the new Animus. The Gods of Light who had engineered Vortis agreed to stop interfering in its affairs, and it was hoped that Vortis could peacefully co-exist with its Rhumon neighbours.

? - "The Naked Flame"[1583] **->** The fourth Doctor and Sarah landed on Vortis, where a glowing crystal was attracting Menoptra to their deaths. The Doctor shattered it with his sonic screwdriver.

c 20,592 - RETURN TO THE WEB PLANET[1584] **->** Humanity developed a synthetic means of propagating itself throughout space that was more efficient than colonisation or invasion; "seed ships", each carrying two "gene-synthetics" - a male and a female - were dispatched to barren worlds where humanity couldn't thrive. Upon arrival, the gene-synthetics would adapt to the local conditions, then merge into a large cocoon from which hundreds of offspring - humans biologically adapted to the environment - would emerge.

One seed ship was drawn to Vortis by a "lode-seed" - a powerful gravitational attractor that both nourished the land and helped the Zarbi navigate during migrations. The female gene-synthetic, named Xanthe, became telepathically integrated into the Zarbi hive mind. The fifth Doctor and Nyssa were present when Xanthe merged with her mate, Yanesh, and it was expected that their offspring would live in peace with the Zarbi.

Carbon-dating suggested that *The Worshipful and Ancient Law of Gallifrey* was written circa 22,000 AD.[1585]

c 21,906 - "Final Sacrifice"[1586] **->** Robert Lewis and Eliza Cooper of Torchwood, along with Alexander Hugh and Annabella Primavera, arrived from 1906 and met the tenth Doctor and Emily on an alien planet. The war between the Soul Free and the Terror Farmers had reduced a population of hundreds of thousands to just a few thousand. The Doctor deduced that the Terror Farmers would win the conflict and become known as the Terranites - and later his adversaries, the Terronites.

The Advocate arrived with Matthew Finnegan, who as a twentieth century-born human could activate the planet's terraforming satellite. This would have killed everyone present. Matthew turned on the Advocate and deactivated the satellite by electrocuting them both. The Advocate died, which released the millennia of fifth-dimensional power within her. The energy turned Matthew into the Tef'Aree: an immortal, five-dimensional being. The Tef'Aree manipulated events throughout time to engineer its own creation from Matthew's sacrifice.

Lewis and Primavera were killed during these events. Cooper stayed to help the surviving humans rebuild their world. The Doctor took Emily and Hugh back to 1906.

c 22,000 - BIRTHRIGHT[1587] **->** For three thousand four hundred and ninety-seven years, the insect-like Charrl had occupied the planet Anthykhon, which was far from the major space lanes. Their vast hive pumped ammonia into the already-depleted atmosphere, the planet's ozone layer had been depleted, the seas had dried up, and the soil was barren. The native life, the Hairies, survived by adapting to this environment.

The Charrl were not savages - indeed, they had created over three hundred of the six hundred and ninety-nine wonders of the universe - before coming to this world to escape solar flares on their own planet. The Charrls made contact with Muldwych, a mysterious time-traveller exiled to Anthykhon at this time, and together they attempted to traverse the Great Divide back into the past on Earth. Muldwych came to regret his association with the Charrls and foiled their plans. He remained on Anthykhon in exile.

Anthykhon was Earth during one of the several periods when the planet was isolated and forgotten.

c 22,000 - SPEED OF FLIGHT[1588] **->** The third Doctor, Jo and Mike Yates landed on Nooma. The Dead assaulted the planet's artificial sun, working on preprogrammed instructions to seek a means of terminating the Nooma experiment to protect Aapex's trade secrets. The Doctor tapped the sun's databanks and found a message from Aapex granting the citizens of Nooma independence, restoring social order on the planet.

The shafts of the Great Pyramid would align with the constellation of Orion around 23,000.[1589] The Terranites eventually became the Terronites, and the Tef'Aree enabled one Terronite - Leo Miller - to travel to Earth in 1926.[1590]

? - THE FACE OF EVIL[1591] **->** A Mordee colony ship landed on an unnamed world and developed a computer failure. The fourth Doctor helped their descendants by linking the computer to his own mind, but he neglected to remove his personality print from the data core. As a result, the computer became schizophrenic.

Centuries later, the colonists worshipped the computer as Xoanon. It had split them into two groups: the

Sevateem (the savage descendants of Survey Team Six); and the Tesh (formerly the technicians, to whom Xoanon granted psychic powers). Xoanon was thus attempting to breed superhumans, but the fourth Doctor returned and made a reverse transfer, curing the computer's multiple personality disorder. Leela, a warrior of the Sevateem, left with the Doctor.

? - LAST MAN RUNNING[1592] -> Class warfare was brewing between the First Planet's "firsters" and the Second Planet's lowly "toodys". An Out System Investigation Group (OIG) was sent to a forest plane to look for a toody weapons manufacturer. The OIG team, the fourth Doctor and Leela got caught in a Last Man Running complex, a simulated environment built by the Lentic race to find and clone the ultimate warrior. Leela destroyed the force field surrounding the complex, and the OIG bombed it.

& 33,935 - IRIS: ENTER WILDTHYME[1593] -> The Glass Men of Valcea had been ousted from their city, and killed in great numbers, by their "new gods": Servo-furniture in the form of flying wardrobes, who had no memory of their origins. Iris Wildthyme, Panda, Simon, Jenny and Barbra the vending machine tried to stop Anthony Marville from using Valcea's space-time corridors to reach the planet Hyspero. What remained of the Glass Men's city was melted by a bomb, and its impending explosion prompted Marville, Jenny, the Scarlet Empress Euphemia, Barbra and all of the wardrobes to flee through the *Dii h'anno Doors*: a portal in the head wardrobe that led to Hyspero, millions of years in the future. Iris, Simon and Panda, thinking their friends dead, returned to the twenty-first century.

Around the year 34,600, humans committed atrocities during the Platonic War and became despised by other races. The Lord Predator, Haralto Wong Bopz Wim-

Waldon Arlene, had died twenty-two years previous, and a new Lord Predator ruled. Some members of the Slitheen family, still exiled from their homeworld, came into possession of time technology that included a Navarino time-jump and a Sundayan stabiliser. Navarino technicians assisted in the construction of a time machine until the Slitheen ate them. The Slitheen used their plundered technology to open a time-travel tourist service to ancient Greece, but their operations in this era were bankrupted when they were held accountable for the wrongful death of Cecrops of the Collective of Mulch.[1594]

37,166 - PLANET OF EVIL[1595] -> A Morestran survey team arrived on Zeta Minor, searching for an energy source as their home planet was facing disaster. Zeta Minor was a planet on the edge of the universe, beyond Cygnus A, as distant from the Artoro galaxy as that is from the Anterides.

The Morestran team discovered that a black pool on Zeta Minor was connected to an incomprehensible universe of anti-matter. As a result, it was impossible to remove anything from the planet without incurring the wrath of powerful creatures native to the anti-matter universe. The fourth Doctor and Sarah helped the Morestrans to survive the experience and return home.

The Doctor offhandedly suggested to Professor Sorenson that he explore the energy potential of the kinetic forces involved in planetary movement.

c 39,164 - ZETA MAJOR[1596] -> Morestra was abandoned, and the fleet set off on a search for a new home planet. A suitable home was located in the Beta system forty months later, and the city of Archetryx was founded there. The New Church Calendar began and the Sorenson Academy was established.

the "fifty-second century". *The TARDIS Logs* offered the date "4931", *Timelink* "6000", *About Time* said "Somewhere around the fifty-third century might be a good bet."
1592 Dating *Last Man Running* (PDA #15) - The story could take place at any time in the far future.
1593 Dating *Iris: Enter Wildthyme* (Iris novel #1) - It's "something like thirty thousand years" after the last time Iris visited Valcea, in *The Blue Angel*.
1594 *The Slitheen Excursion*
1595 Dating *Planet of Evil* (13.2) - While it could be argued that the date "37,166" that appears on the grave marker might use some Morestran scale of dating, the Doctor does state that the TARDIS has overshot contemporary London by "thirty thousand years". *The Dimension Riders* and *Infinite Requiem* both suggest that the Morestrans are not human, which is possible (although they do know of Earth). The Doctor's sugges-

tion to Sorenson leads to events in *Zeta Major*.
1596 Dating *Zeta Major* (PDA #13) - It is 1998 by the New Church Calendar (p82), and that long since *Planet of Evil*.
1597 Forty-two thousand years after *Zamper* (p249).
1598 Algernon Pine is defrosted "about ten thousand years" before *The Coming of the Terraphiles*, and so the era of the Terraphiles is at least that old. The Lockesleys have governed for "nine millennia" before *The Coming of the Terraphiles*.
1599 Dating "The Child of Time" (*DWM* #438-441) - Jacobs mentions the damage the plague has done to "the human empire" - that, and the advanced human science that creates the Galteans, very much suggests that it's a fair distance in the future. A little strangely, however, a caption suggests that the plague cripples humanity in "The Near Future". Author Jonathan Morris

A hundred years later, work commenced on the Torre del Oro, a structure that would extract energy from planetary motion, but which would take fifteen hundred years to build. The dematerialisation beam was invented after several more centuries. Great Technology Wars were fought as the Cult of Science schismed.

A few years before the Torre del Oro was due to be completed, the Grand Council of Cardinals discovered errors in the equations - the Torre del Oro wouldn't work. To cover up this failure, they dispatched an expedition to extract anti-matter from Zeta Minor, and the Zeta Project was established on the nearby Zeta Major. By that point, Morestran territory spanned eighty million light years and contained one thousand four hundred and twenty-seven inhabited star systems, but the energy crisis meant that eight hundred and ninety-two of them, the Outer Systems, were beyond the Empire's reach.

Students of the Sorenson Academy started vanishing, part of the cover up of the Torre del Oro debacle. The fifth Doctor, Tegan and Nyssa discovered that the tower was full of anti-matter. Soon after, anti-matter creatures started a rampage. A State of Crisis was declared and old political and religious rivalries re-emerged. The Zeta Project was destroyed. The Doctor once again negotiated with the creatures of anti-matter and returned all the plundered material to its original universe.

At this time, a new breed of Zamps should be ready to conquer the universe.[1597]

The Terraphile Era[1598]

Human Guide Sensors possessed the ability to plot courses through the cosmos and map the multiverse. They discovered the Second Aether, which was between *everything*: Matter and Anti-matter, Law and Chaos, Life and Death, Reason and Romance. It was where Famous Chaos Engineers performed morphing miracles that even Morphail's wizard-scientists couldn't explain. It was the home of the immeasurable entities Spammer Gain and the Original Insect. A legend held that the Doctor had named this region, although he denied this.

An early Guide Sensor, Lord Renark of the Rim, led a huge percentage of the human race out of the original universe and into another. Renark disappeared, possibly into a greater structure than the known multiverse, which was not understood but was known as Renark's Multiverse or Renark's Dilemma.

The Galactic Union now spanned millions of worlds, encompassing humanity as well as a vast diversity of other intelligent species made from "flesh, metal and petal". The great rockets of the IGP and the interstellar mercantile vessels of the Terran Service crossed the whole Milky Way and the dwarf galaxies surrounding it, and spread into other space-time continua. Privateers preyed upon them. This was a time when galactic civilisation cycled between ages of prosperity and dark ages, and was peppered with intergalactic wars.

Humanity was planet hungry, and the commercial worldbuilding companies terraformed countless worlds. EarthMakers, run by the Tarbutton family, was the largest terraforming company and built planets with ancient Roman, Mogal Indian, Buffalo, ancient Greek and Eireish themes, as well as literary worlds based on the works of Disney, Balzac, Austen, Meredith, James, Lansdale, Mieville, Pynchon, Sinclair, Calderon, Gygax and Moore. The second largest company, TerraForma, was run by the Banning-Cannon family and specialised in Medieval English Edwardian versions of Earth: the Peers™. The firm was run from Earth Regenerated, which orbited Barnard's Star. Intergalactic Air supplied atmosphere plants to terraforming companies. Aqua Suppliers supplied water to inhabited worlds. Water was a valuable commodity on many worlds, and a frequent target for pirates.

There was immense interest in Earth history, although mankind had a garbled understanding of it, as the only surviving texts - as recovered from a cave system in Arctic Skipton in Old Yorkshire - were some old cigarette cards, *Robin Hood*, *Boys' Friend*, *Thriller Picture Library*, *The Captain*, *British Boys' Book of the Empire*, *Captain Justice and His Submarine Gunboat* and *Sexton Blake and the Terror of the Tongs*. They avidly played what they believed to be games from Earth such as broadswording (with swords far wider than they were long), cracking a nut with a sledgehammer and Arrers - a combination of darts, archery and cricket. The ancient artists Rembrandt, Picasso, Emin and Coca Colon were revered.

Earth itself was now known as Terra, Original Terra, Old Old Earth, Original Earth and Home Planet. It was in a thoroughly frozen state following a comet strike, massive earthquakes and a series of nuclear winters. It was to be found in the Greater Oort in Orion.

Around 41,000, Algernon Pine was defrosted on Old Old Mars to help create the backstory for the Peers planets, although he wasn't happy with the end result.

Other planets at this time included the beautiful worlds of Calypso V - Venice, Ur XVII and New Venus, as well as the howling terraces of Arcturus-and-Arcturus.

? 41,000 - "The Child of Time" (*DWM*)[1599] **->** A falling star on Earth heralded the start of a plague that all but wiped out the human empire. Such was the widespread death, it was feared humanity was doomed. Keltor Jacobs oversaw an effort to engineer a new form for humankind, one that could resist all disease: the robotic Galateans. The original Galateans were kept in a station on the dark side of the moon. They resembled specific individuals, and contained duplicate copies of their memories. Jacobs activated the Galateans just three hours before Minerva Base reported finding a plague-cure.

(=) The Galateans thought themselves a superior lifeform, and vowed to wipe out their creators. The time-child Chiyoko helped to ignite a war between humans and the Galateans. The conflict would last at least a hundred thousand years, and help to facilitate Chiyoko's creation.

The eleventh Doctor, Amy and a Galatean-made version of Alan Turing were sent to this era from the Museum of Lost Opportunities in the future, to avert the Galateans' creation. They failed, and Chiyoko capriciously moved the trio ahead in time, to the day when the human-Galatean war destroyed Earth...

Chiyoko was eventually persuaded to undo her existence and the harm it had caused. The eleventh Doctor, Amy, a fading Chiyoko and the Galatean-made Alan Turing arrived once again from the Museum. Turing uploaded his memories of the human-Galatean war into the newborn Galateans' network, which persuaded them to work alongside humanity and rebuild the Earth. Chiyoko's mind was uploaded into a Galatean body; both she and the Galatean-Turing decided to stay in this era.

(=) & 42,000 - "Apotheosis"[1601] **->** The human-Galatean war had now lasted a thousand years, and the planet Kepler IV was just one site of the conflict.

A church-based militia squad, the Sisters of Purity, investigated a space station that had wandered into human space, and met the eleventh Doctor and Amy there. The station had a defective time engine, which created pockets of fast-time. The TARDIS was hit with temporal acceleration, and the beings it had absorbed in its recent travels (the young girls Cosette and Margaret, part of the world-eater Axos and a Shasarak) were detached into a separate being that further incorporated Sister Konami into itself.

The Doctor tried to split the being into its separate components with a teleport, but they instead coalesced into a new individual: Chiyoko, a young girl with temporal abilities. She left to facilitate the events that led to her own creation, and the Doctor and Amy pursued her through time.

Chiyoko's temporal dissolution meant that Novice Konami's request to join the evangelical regiment was declined, and she stayed at an abbey for another year.

avoided giving exact dates for fear of contradicting other stories, and commented that, "['The Child of Time'] wasn't intended to tie in with anything that's already been established in *Doctor Who* (but if it does, that's fine with me!)." If one squints, then, it's possible to connect the meteor strike that spreads the plague in this story with the similar event that helps to inflict damage on Earth prior to *The Coming of the Terraphiles*.
1600 Dating "Apotheosis" (*DWM* #435-#437) - The war has been going on "a thousand years", so it's that long after the genesis of the Galateans in "The Child of Time" (*DWM*).
1601 "The Child of Time" (*DWM*)
1602 Dating "The Child of Time" (*DWM* #438-441) - The Doctor says that it's "thousands of years" since Amy's time, estimates that Chiyoko has been worshipped as a goddess in the war for "several hundred years", and judges that the war "hasn't been going too well" since he and Amy last witnessed it in "Apotheosis" (so, it's some time after that story).
1603 Before *The Coming of the Terraphiles*.
1604 "Several millennia" before *The Coming of the Terraphiles*.
1605 Within "several millennia" of *The Coming of the Terraphiles*, as this has to be after the Bacon Street Regulators were set up.
1606 *The Coming of the Terraphiles* sees the fifteenth such tournament, they are held every two hundred and

fifty years.
1607 "Onomatopoeia". Going by the galactic war numbering system used in *The Coming of the Terraphiles*, the seventh galactic war occurred somewhere between 47,000 and 50,957.
1608 *The Coming of the Terraphiles*
1609 Dating *Heart of TARDIS* (PDA #32) - There's no specific date, but it is "some tens of thousands of years beyond the twentieth century".
1610 *K9: The Bounty Hunter*. Pia's organisation is also referred to as the Galactic Peace Assembly. These events lead into the *K9* television series, starting with *K9: Regeneration*.
1611 Cornelius the pirate fought in the war, but not in the "past half century" before *The Coming of the Terraphiles*.
1612 *The Coming of the Terraphiles*
1613 "A few years" before *The Coming of the Terraphiles*. He claims this was in the "fifty-first thousandth century" - although the book is set in 51,007, which is in the 512th century.
1614 Dating *The Coming of the Terraphiles* (NSA #43) - The Doctor says "51,007's the date".
1615 Dating "The Gift" (*DWM* #123-126) - It's "twelve thousand years" before the main events of "The Gift".

(=) & 42,000 - "The Child of Time" (DWM)[1602] ->
The time-child Chiyoko was worshipped as a goddess by both sides in the human-Galatean war, and stoked conflict between them. Now she decided that the Galateans were the superior lifeform, and encouraged the remaining humans on Earth to deploy a network of fusion bombs under the Earth's crust. The eleventh Doctor and Amy tried to stop the countdown, but the Earth was destroyed. They were time-scooped at the last instant, and taken to the Museum of Lost Opportunities in the far future.

The TerraForma company refused to sell Peers to the Lockesleys for seven thousand years.[1603] The Sussex and Surrey Bacon Street Regulators kept law in the two hundred billion star systems of the Sagittarius Arm of the galaxy after the collapse of law during the last Dark Age, which followed the fifth or sixth intergalactic war.[1604] O'Bean the Younger drew the human race from the last Dark Age by discovering the colour pool, a method of propelling starships that made nukers obsolete.[1605]

In 47,507, the first Quarter Millennium Terraphile Renactment Tournament was held.[1606] Graveworld 909 was one of many cemetery planets established after the seventh galactic war. The robot guardian of Graveworld 909 malfunctioned and went dormant after establishing a respectful quantum null field that forced visitors to remain silent.[1607]

Manakai invaders from the Arkwright Cluster were wiped out ages ago. Dructionjen clans had been exiled many generations before for worshipping the Daleks.[1608]

c 50,000 - HEART OF TARDIS[1609] -> The fourth Doctor
and Romana found and rescued K9, who had become an exhibit at the Collectors' Big Huge and Educational Collection of Old Galactic Stuff.

The galaxy was at war in the year 50,000. The head of the Galactic Peace Commission, Zanthus Pia, was assassinated and K9 was framed for the killing. The real culprit was the renowned bounty hunter Ahab, who was working with the Jixen. K9 uncovered this plot and learned the Jixen were active in the mid-twenty-first century on Earth. He travelled there, but was heavily damaged and lost all his memories.

Later, Ahab followed K9 and was forced to retreat to his own time - but ended up adrift in deep space.[1610]

The twelfth intergalactic war was fought around 50,957, and by common consent it was fought in space, not on the surface of planets.[1611] The Doctor worked as a courier in the vast spaceport *Desiree* during his gap century, although he was fired because he kept getting lost.[1612] The Doctor joined the All Galaxy Legion of Terraphiles.[1613]

51,007 - THE COMING OF THE TERRAPHILES[1614]
-> The clans who ran the terraforming companies were now fabulously wealthy. Lady Mars, owner of Intergalactic Air, could afford a hat that was a life-sized replica of the lost Martian moon Phobos. EarthMakers introduced Mystery Worlds, based on the Sherlock Holmes stories.

The Galactic Union was democratic, although people could pay politicians to retire in General Ejections (seventy-eight members were up for Ejection in Nova Roma). It encompassed countless alien species, including the Judoon (who had taken up Arrers after abandoning their own lethal sport of Nukeball), Centaurs and the Pilparque dogmen of Chardine. The Banning-Cannons had recently lost money in a failed scheme to transform the Scullum Crux into a rose garden light years across. Planets in this era included Cygnus 34, New North Whales, Old Barsoom and Loondoon (home of many fashion houses). Vast spaceports serviced many different types of starships from small, old nuker ships to massive 110-deck G-class vessels such as the ISS *Gargantua*, which used colour engines. The advanced technology of this time included nanotech translation. Humans now comfortably lived to be two hundred years old, and could take identity pills that allowed them to become someone else. Gbot messengers acted as couriers, punching holes in space that would kill a human.

The eleventh Doctor and Amy enjoyed a week on Peers, a terraformed world in the Moravian Cluster in the Medieval Edwardian style, and governed by the 507th Earl of Lockesley. The Doctor became aware of a threat to the whole of the multiverse. As it involved the black hole at the centre of the galaxy, he feared General Frank/Freddie Force and his Anti-matter Men were responsible. He joined a team of Terraphile Reenactors heading to Miggea, a Ghost World (i.e. a planet that orbits sideways between universes), where they were due to compete for the Arrow of Law. Captain Cornelius, an old rival and acquaintance of the Doctor, was also aware of the problem. His home was in the dwarf galaxy Canis, but he was most often seen in the *Paine*, the most perfect light-powered vessel ever built, with a crew from a hundred worlds and a dozen space-time continua. He had seen the dark tides rising and dragging galaxies across billions of light years, and knew that unless it was stopped, the universe would stop regenerating itself and the multiverse would collapse in just a few centuries. The Doctor and Cornelius secured the Arrow of Law - the fabled Roogalator, an artifact from the Realm of Law that could restore the cosmic balance.

? - "The Gift"[1615] -> The sixth Doctor went back to the
point that a Zofton deep space load lugger had crashed on the moon of Zazz, and observed as - over the next fifty years - the surviving robot rebuilt and survived, eventually building self-replicating replacements for itself. Within twenty generations, they had a functioning civilisation.

A natural disaster on the moon of Zazz wiped out the machine civilisation there. The few survivors would lie dormant for two thousand years.[1616]

? - "The Gift"[1617] **->** By now, Zazz was a planet heavily-influenced by the Jazz Era of Earth, and the sixth Doctor, Peri and Frobisher accepted an invitation to the twenty-first birthday bash for the Lorduke of Zazz.

The TARDIS first landed at the retreat of the Lorduke's brother, Professor Strut, who was a mad scientist exiled after crashing an experimental moon rocket on the city. They agreed to take a gift... which turned out to be a surviving self-replicating robot. Strut found the robot on the moon, but didn't understand the danger. The robots began breeding, and collected raw materials to rebuild their civilisation on Zazz. The Doctor used the musicians of Zazz to duplicate the robot's recall signal, luring them to Strut's island. They boarded the moon rocket, and were blasted off into space.

c 101,861 - SERPENT CREST: TSAR WARS[1618] **->** Human-made robots became so advanced in a certain sector of space that they finally took over and formed the Robotov Empire. The humans that served the Empire lived on outlying worlds, and supplied energy from a biomoon. Centuries passed, and the humans moved closer to rebellion. Father Gregory, who physically looked like the fourth Doctor owing to "the endless chaotic ramifications of universal chance", allied himself with the rebels. The Tsarina

conceived with Gregory a child cyborg, Alex, in the hope of cementing bonds between the humans and Robotovs.

Gregory, however, was secretly allied with the Skishtari - a race of conquerors who were adept at manipulating wormholes. The Skishtari subjugated other races by hatching monstrous Skishtari Emperor serpents from eggs - one such egg was to be hidden inside Alex. Gregory's agents brought the fourth Doctor and Mrs Wibbsey to this era via a Skishtari wormhole, but Alex's heart was failing, and Gregory donated his own to save him.

The Doctor tried to resolve matters by sending himself and Wibbsey - as well as a spaceship containing Alex, his guardian Boolin and the Skishtari egg - down a Skishtari wormhole to Nest Cottage in 2010. They all ended up in the right location, but the nineteenth century.

The Doctor later used the TARDIS to bring Boolin and a teenage Alex home. Alex was made the new Tsar of the Robotov Empire, and facilitated peace between the robot and human factions.[1619]

c 101,881 - SERPENT CREST: SURVIVORS IN SPACE[1620] **->** The entire village of Hexford and its two hundred fifty-three civilians arrived on the biomoon of the Robotov Empire, thanks to the Skishtari wormhole and a mishap in 2011. Captain Yates took charge of the stranded townsfolk, who were left to their own devices for three months. The fourth Doctor and Mrs Wibbsey arrived in the TARDIS just as the Skishtari egg in their possession

1616 "Two thousand years" before "The Gift".
1617 Dating "The Gift" (*DWM* #123-126) - No date is given, but the people of Zazz are the "distant descendants of an Earth colony".
1618 Dating *Serpent Crest: Tsar Wars* (BBC fourth Doctor audios #3.1) - The story occurs in the future; the Robotov Empire is of human creation, and the insurrectionists are designated as human. In *Serpent Crest: The Broken Crown*, set in 1861, the Doctor tells Alex, "You've only just learned that you're the Robotov heir, from a hundred thousand years into the future."
1619 *Serpent Crest: Survivors in Space*
1620 Dating *Serpent Crest: Survivors in Space* (BBC fourth Doctor audios #3.5) - It's been "twenty years" since Alex was returned home (*Serpent Crest: Aladdin Time*) and made Tsar.
1621 "A hundred millennia" after *Grimm Reality*.
1622 *The Condemned*
1623 Dating "Onomatopoeia" (*DWM* #413) - The guardian here ends the "hundred thousand years" of silence that have passed on Graveworld 909 since the seventh galactic war, the rough date of which can be established from *The Coming of the Terraphiles*.
1624 *The Forgotten Army*
1625 *The Ark*

THE SEGMENTS OF TIME: The Commander in *The Ark* states "Nero, the Trojan Wars, the Daleks... all that happened in the First Segment of Time." References in that story to the Tenth and Twenty-Seventh Segments are noted later in this book. *The Well-Mannered War* is set in the Fifty-Eighth.

It's unclear whether a Segment is measured purely mathematically. A "century" has to mean "a hundred years". If a Segment is a fixed period of time, then as *The Ark* is set ten million years in the future, this might suggest fifty-seven equal segments of around 175,000 years.

Equally, the term might mark a specific era with distinct cultural or even physical features (like, say, "Victorian" or "Ice Age"). What would mark the beginning or end of a Segment? Would the boundary be formally defined and obvious (like say that of "the tenth Olympiad", or "the Leptonic Era"), even if it was open to a degree of interpretation (we can speak of "the Second World War", even though the exact moment it started and ended depends on which country you're from and how you define terms)?

Timelink offers the theory that as Zentos refers to "the Fifty-Seventh Segment of Earth life" and the Commander says "The Earth also is dying, we have left

hatched. The Skishtari welcomed their giant offspring - but the newborn Emperor had formed an empathic bond with Tsar Alex, and ate its progenitors instead. Alex agreed to relocate the giant snake to a planet with a sustainable food source. A clone of the second Doctor, freed from his obligation to the Skishtari, aided the fourth Doctor in sending Hexford back to the twenty-first century.

Circa 102,890, the white hole seedling from Albert was supposed to blossom into maturity.[1621] The Doctor judged that Carmen Priminger - a gambler who lost her memories - was human, and that her time machine originated from the 108th or 109th centuries.[1622]

c 148,500 - "Onomatopoeia"[1623] **->** The tenth Doctor and Majenta Pryce rebooted the slumbering robot guardian on Graveworld 909. It ended the pall of silence on the planet, and accepted the rat people who had evolved in the millennia while it slept as its new workforce.

The eleventh Doctor wanted to show Amy a museum in the 175th century, but warned her that the canteen there was rubbish, and for religious reasons served only boiled Jericoacoara beans.[1624]

The Daleks were part of the history of the First Segment of Time.[1625] **One Dalek ship, containing the Emperor, survived the Last Great Time War. It arrived at the edge of Earth's solar system, remaining hidden. For centuries, the Daleks would harvest the dregs and unwanted of humanity, building Daleks from their genetic material. The Emperor meddled in humanity's affairs and sought ways to slow its development.**[1626]

? - "War of the Words"[1627] **->** The war between the Vromyx and the Garynths had been raging for forty-seven point six three years. The conflict blocked access to the library planet Biblios, where all universal knowledge was stored by legions of robots. The warring factions wanted to access details of superweapons, then deny it to their opponents. The fourth Doctor blew up an empty building, telling both sides it was where the records were kept, and the rivals withdrew.

? 199,750 - HOME TRUTHS[1628] **->** On an island at Ely, a house was built that could grant wishes to its occupants. A husband and wife resided there, but the house proved capable of facilitating even unspoken wishes. In a moment of irritation, the wife briefly wished her husband harm - causing him to fall dead. The horrified wife begged for the tragedy to "stop", and immediately died also. The house then sealed itself off, its interior almost frozen in time. Some time later, the first Doctor, Steven and Sara found the bodies within. They came under threat from the house's wish-granting ability, so Sara wished that the house would develop a conscience that distinguished right from wrong. This endowed the house with a disembodied copy of Sara's persona, and the travellers left in the TARDIS.

Majenta Pryce and the Crimson Hand[1629]

The Order of the Crimson Hand was a secretive group of extra-terrestrial tyrants, elitists and industry tycoons. It possessed powerful artifacts that included the ashes of the scroll of Horath, a shard of the Glory and a piece of the Key to Time. The quartet that composed the Crimson Hand's inner cabal - Trique, Lunat, Pollox and Pi - recruited Lady Scaph after they acquired the Manus Maleficus: a machine from the higher realms that reshaped reality, but required five operators.

The wealthy adventurer Wesley Sparks was reputed to have harnessed the power of the quark, charted the depths

it for the last time", that Earth has been "left" before, and each Segment ends with the abandonment of Earth. It's neat and, as noted elsewhere in this book, Earth is certainly totally evacuated more than once. However, *Bad Wolf* and *The Parting of the Ways* have the Daleks active after the first abandonment of Earth, and, if the Commander is right, they were only part of the history of the First Segment.
1626 *The Parting of the Ways*. The Controller says the Daleks have been there for "hundreds and hundreds of years", the Doctor says "generations", and the Emperor Dalek says "centuries passed".
1627 Dating "War of the Words" (*DWM* #51) - The story is set after the twentieth century, because parliamentary records from that period are stored here. The head librarian robot has just had his two thousand year service, suggesting the facility has been around for millen-

nia. Beyond that, no date is specified, so this is completely arbitrary.
1628 Dating *Home Truths* (BF CC #3.5) - It's "a thousand years" before the linking sequences of *Home Truths*, *The Drowned World* and *The Guardian of the Solar System*.
1629 The background to *DWM*'s Crimson Hand storyarc, given in "Mortal Beloved", "The Age of Ice", "The Crimson Hand" and "Hotel Historia". Majenta's "relative age" is given as "eighty-one Earth years" in "The Age of Ice" (which may or may not include the time she's spent TARDIS-travelling), so under the dating scheme in this chronology, she would have been born circa 199,919.

MAJENTA PRYCE: The Crimson Hand storyarc running through the *Doctor Who Magazine* comic (*DWM* #394, 400-420) is remarkably circumspect when it comes to identifying the home era of the super-criminal Majenta Pryce, a companion of the tenth Doctor. We

of the multiverse, and duelled with Daemons. He established Stormlight House as a protected residence; those within could watch the largest storm in the universe as it raged at the edge of the Proxima system. Patrons could appear in Stormlight in bodies made from solid engram tachyonics. Scaph passed an initiation test in which she seduced Sparks, then abandoned him the night before their wedding.

The now-complete Crimson Hand field-tested the Manus Maleficus by reaching back to the twentieth century and obliterating a planet threatening their powerbase in the Obsidian Cluster: the Ownworld of the Skith. Lady Scaph regretted her role in the holocaust and fled. She became the entrepreneur "Majenta Pryce". With her assistant Fanson, they experienced the rout of Ichabod Nine, the Recession Wars on Fiscus and the Tarvu Initiative.

Majenta and Fanson operated one of the last remaining Hotel Historias in the year 2008, but were arrested by time-travelling bailiffs. Before Majenta was incarcerated, Fanson erased her memory to conceal the psychic tracking sigil the Crimson Hand had placed in her mind.[1630]

c 200,000 (Tuesday the Gluteenth of Mauve, and Wednesday) - "Thinktwice"[1631] -> The amnesiac Majenta Pryce was incarcerated at the Thinktwice Orbital Penitentiary, and the tenth Doctor met her for the second time while investigating abuses there. The facility's warden had become allied with the memory-eating Memeovax while he was a boy on Greene's World, and had constructed the Knowsall machine to extract memories from the prisoners for the Memeovax's benefit. Majenta destroyed the Memeovax with a power surge of unknown origin, and the Doctor agreed to take Majenta to the Hippocrats of Panacea - the finest mind-surgeons in the universe - for treatment. Majenta agreed - on the understanding that the Doctor was working for *her*, without pay (for now).

c 200,000 - "The Crimson Hand"[1632] -> Intersol recaptured Majenta in the twenty-first century and interrogated her, which unlocked her memories. The sigil in her mind attracted the inner circle of the Crimson Hand, who were wanted on 32,608 individual counts of grand larceny, murder and fraud. They brought Majenta back into their ranks, and she seemingly disintegrated the Doctor - but actually sent him into a pocket dimension for safekeeping.

The reunited Crimson Hand exerted the full power of the Manus Maleficus. Galaxies were swept aside, entire solar systems were rebuilt and many races were extinguished. Majenta brought prosperity, and tyranny, to her impoverished homeworld of Vessica.

On Day 36 of The Crimson Age, Majenta retrieved the Doctor because use of the Manus Maleficus had created an

---

know that Majenta can travel in time, as she's operating a time-travel holiday hotel when the Doctor first meets her (in the early twenty-first century, "Hotel Historia"). We also know that the Intersol agents who incarcerate her in the future at Thinktwice prison ("Thinktwice") have time-travel capabilities.

Does Majenta originate from the modern day or the future, though? Is the time travel tech in play indicative of her society? Does the Crimson Hand also have time technology? We're never told within the story itself - just as it's not expressly said whether or not the storyarc's finale ("The Crimson Hand", *DWM* #416-420) takes place in the present or the future. The Intersol agents "time-lock" the TARDIS to prevent it escaping when the story begins, but it's not stated if the Intersol ship then time-jumps before Majenta gets free, rejoins the Crimson Hand and conquers a vast sector of space to establish the Crimson Age. Admittedly, if the Crimson Age *was* contemporary, it would be nothing short of miraculous that the Hand's sweeping and tyrannical empire seems far removed from Earth and in no way affects it, but that's the best evidence that can be cited for Majenta and the Hand being future-based.

Author Dan McDaid had privately decided that Majenta, the Crimson Hand, the Thinktwice prison and Intersol all originated from the Fourth Great and Bountiful Human Empire - his intention being that the grubbiness of the Thinktwice facility nicely emulated the moral and social decay seen in *The Long Game*. "Intersol", McDaid commented over email, "have acquired time travel from somewhere (probably misappropriated from a Time Agent), so they're able to pursue their targets across time and space." He added, "[The Fourth Great and Bountiful Human Empire] is also Majenta's 'home' era... but you don't have to take any of this as gospel, and feel free to monkey about with it if you need to."

With the actual story evidence being so vague, it seems best to follow McDaid's lead and presume that Majenta and the Hand hail from in or near the Fourth Great and Bountiful Human Empire. It also seems fair to think that time travel in this era is limited to parties such as Intersol, because widespread time tech would radically alter the equation when the Daleks launch an all-out attack on Earth (*The Parting of the Ways*).

1630 "The Age of Ice" and "The Crimson Hand", although there doesn't appear to be a point in the story when this could have occurred.

1631 Dating "Thinktwice" (*DWM* #400-402) - The warden mentions his intention to spread use of the Knowsall machine through "The entire human empire!" The "cosmic bailiffs" who bring Majenta to Thinktwice presumably belong to Intersol - the justice organisation ("The Crimson Hand") that has access to time travel technology, but whose members aren't necessarily part of humanity.

expanding space-time rift. She repented her villainy, killed the Crimson Hand members and relinquished the Manus Maleficus' hold on reality. Space-time was returned to normal. Majenta died, but the Doctor brought her back to life with a final use of the Manus Maleficus, which returned to its home dimension. Afterward, the Doctor took Majenta to the future to live in New Old Detroit.

The Fourth Great and Bountiful Human Empire

200,000 - THE LONG GAME[1633] -> It was the age of the Fourth Great and Bountiful Human Empire. Earth was at its height: the hub of a domain stretching across a million planets, covered with megacities, possessing five moons and a population of ninety-six billion.

A sandstorm on the New Venus Archipelago left two hundred dead. There were water riots in Glasgow. The Face of Boe announced that he was pregnant with a Baby Boemina. The Mighty Jagrafess of the Holy Hadrojassic Maxarodenfoe was manipulating humanity by controlling its news media from Satellite Five, which broadcast six hundred channels. This held back humanity's development, and made it fearful of immigrants. The ninth Doctor and Rose defeated the Jagrafess, and the Doctor expected that humanity's development would accelerate back to normal without its interference.

Adam, a companion of the Doctor and Rose, tried to acquire knowledge from the future and download it to his own time in 2012. The Doctor discovered Adam's intentions and returned him home.

After Satellite Five was put out of commission, the information feed to Earth stopped. The government and economy collapsed. A hundred years of hell ensued.[1634] The Great Atlantic Smog Storm started in 200,080. On some days, it wasn't possible to breathe the air. The storm raged for at least twenty years.[1635]

200,100 - BAD WOLF / THE PARTING OF THE WAYS[1636] -> The Earth was now divided into continents that included Europa, Pacifica, the New American Alliance and Australasia. Default payments were made to Martian Drones. The Great Cobalt Pyramid was built on the remains of the famous Torchwood Institute. The Great Central Ravine was named after the "ancient" British city of Sheffield. Stella Popbait made hats. There was a penal colony on the moon. *Jupiter Rising* was a holo-series. The dish gaffabeck had originated on the planet Lucifer. The Face of Boe was now the oldest inhabitant of the Isop galaxy.

Humanity watched savage game shows such as *Big Brother*, *Call My Bluff* (with real guns), *Countdown* (where the aim was to defuse a bomb), *Ground Force* (contestants were turned to compost), *Wipeout*, *Stars in Your Eyes* (contestants were blinded), *What Not to Wear* (androids mutilated people), *Bear with Me* (contestants lived with a bear) and *The Weakest Link* (overseen by the dreaded Anne Droid). These were produced by the Bad Wolf Corporation, broadcast on ten thousand channels and filmed aboard the former Satellite Five, now called the Game Station.

Losing contestants were apparently vaporised, but in truth were teleported away and secretly converted into Daleks. The ranks of the Emperor Dalek's army swelled. The human, slaved Controller overseeing this operation sought out the Daleks' greatest enemy to help, and transmatted the ninth Doctor, Captain Jack and Rose to the Game Station.

The Doctor discovered the Daleks' machinations, and the Emperor mobilised his forces against Earth. Dalek missiles bombarded many of the continents, with enough force to alter their very shape. The Doctor briefly sent Rose to safety in her native time, but Rose gazed into the heart of the TARDIS and thus became endowed with the power of the Time Vortex. She

---

1632 Dating "The Crimson Hand" (*DWM* #416-420) - This resolves *DWM*'s ongoing Crimson Hand storyarc; see the Majenta Pryce sidebar.
1633 Dating *The Long Game* (X1.7) - The Doctor gives the date. It's established in *Bad Wolf* and *The Parting of the Ways* that the Jagrafess was a tool of the Daleks.
1634 *Bad Wolf*
1635 "Twenty years" before *Bad Wolf*, according to the *Big Brother* contestant Lynda Moss.
1636 Dating *Bad Wolf/The Parting of the Ways* (X1.12-1.13) - The Doctor says in *Bad Wolf* that "it's the year two-zero-zero-one-zero-zero", and the opening caption says it is "one hundred years" after *The Long Game*. Lynda says the Game Station has ten thousand chan-

nels, although the Doctor's *Big Brother* game is broadcast on Channel 44,000. Lucifer is (almost certainly) the planet featured in *Lucifer Rising*. It's unclear whether Rose used her power to restore anyone or anything other than Captain Jack - it's not stated that she, for example, reset the devastated Earth. Jack's journey to the nineteenth century is referenced in *Utopia*.

gained the godlike ability to alter time, and used it to destroy the Emperor and his Daleks. The Doctor sacrificed his life to stop the Vortex energies from consuming Rose, and regenerated as a result. Jack had been killed by the Daleks, but Rose brought him back to life. He was left behind on the Game Station, and used his vortex manipulator to travel to the nineteenth century.

The manner in which Rose brought Jack back to life made him an immortal:

"Something happened to me once, a long way away. Time itself changed me to a fixed point, and now I can't die. I suffer, and I perish, but I always come back."[1637]

c 200,300 - "Mortal Beloved"[1638] **->** Centuries after Majenta Pryce betrayed Wesley Sparks, he had become an aged cyborg consumed by hate. His company, Sparktech,

was moving to acquire Omnivax Inc. and Marscom. Sparktech's stock was falling, and Intersol acquired its offworld set-form division. The Mazuma was currently down against the grotzi.

Sparks targeted Majenta and the tenth Doctor when the TARDIS brought them to Stormlight House, but an engram of Sparks - reflecting his nobler, younger self - stabbed Sparks to death, then suffered file corruption.

? 200,750 - HOME TRUTHS / THE DROWNED WORLD[1639] **->** In the thousand years since the duplicate Sara Kingdom persona was created, humanity had undergone decline and lost much of its scientific knowledge. Even simple intercoms were not in use. Mankind was no longer capable of space travel, and its encounter with the Daleks had become the stuff of stories and legend. Cambridge was home to a Council of Elders composed of revered "old men" in their sixties. War was brewing in mid-Africa. The duplicate Sara had spent the preceding

---

1637 Jack in *TW: Miracle Day*, summarising the immortality that he exhibits throughout *Torchwood* and *Doctor Who*.

1638 Dating "Mortal Beloved" (*DWM* #406-407) - It's been "centuries" since Majenta Pryce abandoned Sparks. The application of tachyonics seen here is independent from the Argolis experiments seen in *The Leisure Hive*. Mazumas are a currency mentioned in the *DWM* comic (see The Mazuma Era); grotzis are a currency mentioned by Glitz (*The Trial of a Time Lord*, *Dragonfire*).

1639 Dating *Home Truths*, *The Drowned World* and *The Cold Equations* (BF CC #3.5, 4.1, 5.12) - The linking material in this trilogy of audios featuring Sara Kingdom takes place on an island at Ely, and although the historical clues are fairly numerous, no actual date is given. *Cold Equations* all-but names the Cahlians as being responsible for the very same sleeping sickness that afflicts Earth in *The Drowned World* and *The Guardian of the Solar System*. Given that Simon Guerrier wrote all four audios, this doesn't seem like a coincidence.

The claim in *Cold Equations* that the continents of Earth are "all different shapes" brings to mind the devastation seen in *The Parting of the Ways*, and suggests - but doesn't confirm - that the sharp decline of Earth in the Kingdom trilogy is the result of the devastation of the Fourth Great and Bountiful Human Empire. That Empire is so advanced that it might well have facilitated the creation of the wish-granting house - or the house might result from the plethora of alien tech that accumulates on Earth over the millennia in numerous *Doctor Who* stories. *The Drowned World* establishes that humanity's encounters with the Daleks are now the stuff of legend, suggesting that it's not the immediate aftermath of *The Parting of the Ways* but rather some

time later, and that humanity has in large measure forgotten (assuming they even had time to register what was happening before the Dalek onslaught) the cause of its current plight.

For benefit of non-UK residents, the Lion of Knidos is a giant stone lion on display in the British Museum, London.

1640 Dating *The Guardian of the Solar System* (BF CC #5.1) - The Sara Kingdom audio trilogy concludes ten years after the end of *The Drowned World*.

1641 *The Five Companions*

1642 *The Forgotten Army*

1643 Dating *Night of the Humans* (NSA #38) - The Doctor says (p19), "To be precise, it's 14 March 250,339. And it's six minutes past one in the afternoon," based upon the atomic clock he retrieves from the Pioneer 10 probe. The day and year are confirmed in the Sittuun situation reports (pgs 7-9), which seem to use the Julian calendar. The existence of the Lux Academy (doubtless referencing the family prominent in *Silence in the Library*) suggests that Earth has greatly recovered from the devastation the Daleks wrought in *The Parting of the Ways*. Somewhat uniquely, the Sittuun's natural language isn't translatable through the TARDIS' systems just because... it just isn't.

1644 "'Fifteen years" before *The Eyeless*. There is plenty of evidence that this was an incident during The Last Great Time War. The Doctor already knows of the Fortress, its Weapon and who built them. He also knows that both sides in the war are dead, and that one side had "footholds in different galaxies". The Eyeless probe the Doctor's mind, and see he was somehow involved with the firing of the Weapon. A number of Dalek stories have established that Skaro is in the Seventh galaxy; *The Daleks*: "The Destroyers" says it's in the eighth.

centuries accommodating many guests within her walls. Law officers periodically interviewed her; the law forbade apparitions, but each officer was moved to grant her an exception.

Guests eventually stopped arriving, and a law officer named Robert became the first person to visit the house in a long while. Robert was also inclined to leave the Sara-ghost in peace, but he discovered that she wanted the Elders to visit so she could grant their wishes, and that her power was extending in range - Robert's wife, in accordance with his unspoken wish, had become pregnant. Fearing her power, Robert ordered the Sara-ghost to disperse itself. She did so.

Twelve years passed, and a fatal sleeping sickness became rampant. The young and oldest were the hardest hit; when the Elders succumbed to the illness, law and order decayed. Robert's daughter, now age 11, caught the disease. He took her to the house at Ely, and revived the Sara-ghost. She was too depleted to affect reality outside the house, but agreed to cure Robert's ailing daughter - on the condition that he remain with her for the rest of his natural days. He agreed, and his daughter recovered.

? 200,750 - THE COLD EQUATIONS[1639] **->** Humanity had produced brilliant scientists and artists, and had shaped the destiny of a hundred different worlds, but a dark cloud had settled upon the Earth, and the remaining humans there were barely living above subsistence level. Earth had lost much knowledge following the downfall of its "vast sprawling empire", and an intergalactic Dark Age was underway. The very continents of Earth had been warped out of shape, and London was deep under water.

Much debris from Earth's space age remained in orbit, and a group of Cahlians - humanoids with fiery, sunset-coloured skin and sandy hair - representing the True-Jank Cahlian Co-operative set about salvaging whatever of value could be found in space or on Earth's surface. To whittle down the competition, the Cahlians had released a sleeping sickness that afflicted about four-fifths of Earth's population. Amongst other items, the Cahlians recovered the Lion of Knidos.

The first Doctor, Steven and Oliver Harper brokered a deal on behalf of Earth authorities - the Cahlians would keep the material they'd acquired in exchange for clearing the debris from Earth orbit. A coalition government on Earth agreed to assemble some historians, and determine if the salvage had value. Their work done, the Doctor's party left - having seen in records from the old empire that they were one day going to be incarcerated on the planetoid Grace Alone.

? 200,760 - THE GUARDIAN OF THE SOLAR SYSTEM[1640] **->** When Robert's daughter turned 21, she left the house to see the outside world. He never saw her

again. Robert found he wasn't aging, and in accordance with his wishes, he and Sara traded places - she was incarnated in an older body, and Robert became the house's governing intelligence. Sensing Sara's desire to escape - and to gain absolution for murdering her brother - Robert made the TARDIS materialise outside the house, with the Doctor inside.

At some point, the incarnated "house" version of Sara Kingdom was transported into the Death Zone on Gallifrey.[1641]

The Doctor claimed that the fare at Big Paulie's Sausages in New York, the twenty-first century, was regarded in the 208th century as the most famous food in the galaxy. "Anything with less than four stomachs" would spend a lifetime of savings to travel back and enjoy it.[1642]

250,339 (14th March) - NIGHT OF THE HUMANS[1643] **->** An Intergalactic Environmental Agency (IEA) was now in operation. Earth's solar system was home to the Lux Academy, and offered classes in ancient Earth music.

The Sittuun had evolved on a world with no predators, and so never developed fear. Humanity made first contact with the Sittuun, who used human names and language conventions when dealing with humans, as their own language was too untranslatable. The comet Schuler-Khan was due to strike the Gyre (a conglomeration of space junk), which would have propelled city-sized debris toward twelve inhabited worlds within twenty-five million miles. A team of Sittuun destroyed the Gyre, and the humans living there, with the largest nanobomb - which contained metal-eating nanites - ever made. The bomb had been built with funding from eight Battani planets and fifteen associated worlds.

Prior to this, a relatively early incarnation of the Doctor had facilitated swashbuckler Dirk Slipstream's incarceration on Volag-Noc, after Slipstream had crashed a passenger ship - and killed seven hundred - during a botched diamond heist on Belaform 9. After Slipstream's escape, the eleventh Doctor and Amy stopped him from acquiring the Mymon Key and blackmailing the Sol system with it. The Key was destroyed, and ravenous Sollogs ate Slipstream.

In 291,994, an alien Fortress materialised at the heart of Arcopolis, a utopian city of arcologies on a world in the Sculptor Dwarf galaxy (or Galaxy Seven) which had not known war or crime for thousands of years. The Weapon at the heart of the Fortress fired, apparently killing all two hundred million people in Arcopolis, as well as annihilating countless other star systems. It was the Ultimate Weapon - something that didn't just destroy one's enemy, but instead used vunktotechnology and vundatechnology to destroy everything that had ever been known about said enemy. This was the Last Battle of the Seventh Galaxy.[1644]

292,009 - THE EYELESS[1645] **->** The tenth Doctor went to Arcopolis to deactivate the Weapon at the heart of the Fortress there. He thought the Weapon had rendered the planet lifeless, but soon met survivors who lived in fear of "ghosts" that haunted the city. A girl called Alsa told him that the thirty-seven original survivors had birthed many children over the last fifteen years. The survivors and their offspring stayed away from the city, confining themselves to a settlement in what used to be a park.

The Eyeless - an alien race of glass telepaths who worked as galactic scavengers - arrived to claim the TARDIS. They soon learned of the Weapon and desired it, but Alsa wanted the Weapon for herself, believing it could power the ruins of the city. The Doctor learned that the "ghosts" were actually sentient shadows in space-time left by the people killed by the Weapon, but was himself forced to use the device - which wiped out the Eyeless and destroyed the Fortress. He took Alsa on his travels for a short time, returning her a little later than he expected...

292,029 - THE EYELESS[1646] **->** The tenth Doctor returned Alsa to Arcopolis two decades later than he intended - but this suited Alsa, who was more at home here than she had been in her own time.

309,906 - THE WAR GAMES[1647] **->** A race of alien warlords attempted to raise an army of galactic conquest by programming human soldiers kidnapped from various points in history with stolen Time Lord technology. A renegade Time Lord, the War Chief, aided them and was shot during an uprising engineered by the second Doctor, Jamie and Zoe. When the plan was uncovered, the Time Lords erected a force field that confined the aliens to their planet. The kidnapped soldiers were sent home, with no awareness of these events. The Time Lords also dematerialised the aliens' leader, the War Lord.

309,906 - THE EIGHT DOCTORS[1648] **->** The eighth Doctor rescued his second incarnation and encouraged him to summon the Time Lords to deal with the War Lords.

The War Chief was horrifically injured rather than killed. He was sent to the War Lords' home planet, but his regeneration aborted and his new form was disfigured. He allied with the son of the War Chief, and after many years, they broke through the force field the Time Lords had placed around the War Lords' home planet. They revived

---

On the other hand, the Doctor says that "pretty much whoever your enemy is", you would destroy yourself by using the Weapon against them, but The War in Heaven offers an obvious candidate for an Enemy for which that would not be the case. Possibly, the Weapon was built for the War in Heaven but used in the Last Great Time War.

1645 Dating *The Eyeless* (NSA #30) - The date is given.
1646 Dating *The Eyeless* (NSA #30) - It's "twenty years" since the main events of the story.
1647 Dating *The War Games* (6.7) - It is stated that humanity has been killing itself for "half a million years" before this story takes place, which (coincidentally) ties up with the date 309,906 established for the Doctor's first trial (or "Malfeasance Tribunal") in *The Deadly Assassin*. *The TARDIS Logs* suggested a date of "48,063" for this story, *Apocrypha* offered "5950 AD".

The aliens in this story are unnamed on screen, yet they're referred to as "the War Lords" in *The War Games* novelisation by Malcolm Hulke, *The Making of Doctor Who* 1972 edition, the Lofficier *Programme Guide*, and *Timewyrm: Exodus* by Terrance Dicks. They're simply "Aliens" in the 1973 *Radio Times Special*. As both Hulke and Dicks independently use the name "War Lords" in their other work, it has been adopted in this volume to avoid confusion with other unnamed alien races.

HOW MANY WAR ZONES ARE THERE?: *The War Games* establishes in dialogue that the aliens have "ten" zones under their control. The map we see shows eleven, not including the Control Zone. Three more

appear in dialogue, making a total of fifteen... map: Greek Zone [c500BC]; "two thousand years ago" map: Roman Zone; map: 30 Years War Zone [1618-1648]; map: English Civil War Zone [1642-1646]; "1745", Jacobite Rebellion; "1812", Napoleon's advance into Russia; map: Peninsular War Zone [1808-1814]; map: Crimean War Zone [1853-1856]; "1862", map: American Civil War Zone; map: Mexican Civil War Zone, "Mexican Uprising" (?1867); Franco-Prussian War [1870-1871]; map: Boer War Zone [1899-1902]; The Boxer Rising [1900]; "1905", map: Russio-Japanese War Zone; "1917", map: 1917 War Zone.

1648 Dating *The Eight Doctors* (EDA #1) - This happens during *The War Games*.
1649 The War Chief is shot in *The War Games*, and reappears in *Timewyrm: Exodus*.
1650 "Three hundred and seventeen thousand years" after 40 BC, according to *The Gallifrey Chronicles*.
1651 *The English Way of Death*
1652 *Only Human*
1653 Dating *Only Human* (NSA #5) - The Doctor calculates the precise date.
1654 Dating *The Girl Who Never Was* (BF #103) - The Cybermen seem to generalise the year as "500,000", but the eighth Doctor - using the TARDIS' scanning equipment - specifies the date as 500,002. This is further confirmed by the sixth Doctor in *The Condemned*, and Charley in *Brotherhood of the Daleks*.

their dreams of galactic conquest, and decided to concentrate on helping Nazi Germany.[1649]

Around 317,000, humans encroached on the territory of the Sulumians in the eighth dimension. The Sulumians began a time travel campaign dedicated to rewriting human history to prevent this.[1650] In 365,509, the collapse of a star in NGC4258 destroyed four civilisations. A region of space warps, the Grey Interchange, was created.[1651]

Around 436,000, Earth was caught in the crossfire of a war between Kallix Grover and the Sine Wave Shrine of Shillitar. A magnetic wave shut down all digital technology, cutting Earth off from its colonies. This was the Great Retrenchment.[1652]

438,533 (2nd October) - ONLY HUMAN[1653] ->
Following the Great Retrenchment, humans mastered the biological and chemical sciences to the point they could take apart the human body and put it back together without ill effects. All emotions were regulated, and - apart from the dissident Refusers - no human ever worried about anything.

500,002 - THE GIRL WHO NEVER WAS[1654] -> A Cyberman time squad was dispatched on a test flight from the future, but their systems failed, and their vessel grounded on Earth in 500,002, when the planet had been abandoned once again due to solar flare activity. Cyber-signals were sent back in time - contact was made with the *Batavia* in 1942, and events allowed the ship to translocate to this year. The Cybermen sought to send the *Batavia* back in time stuffed with conversation facilities - thereby replenishing their numbers through historical alteration - but the eighth Doctor thwarted their plan.

Soon after, the smuggler Byron forced the Doctor and Charley to bring him to this year in the TARDIS, as he wanted to loot the Cyber-ship. Charley installed a Cyber-Planner infected with "temporal rust" into the Cyber-ship's systems, destroying Byron, the Cybermen of this era and their ship. Charley thought Byron had killed the Doctor, and the temporal corrosion triggered the TARDIS' HADS, taking it - with the unconscious Doctor inside - back to 2008.

Charley sent out an SOS signal, and the TARDIS materialised in response... whereupon Charley was appalled to find the sixth Doctor, not the eighth, had rescued her. She faked amnesia and became his companion, worried that her presence in his past would upset causality.

"Half a million years of industrial progress" had left the Earth's surface as "just a chemical slime". The Ancient One, a Haemovore, was the last living creature to inhabit an Earth.[1655]

Lady Ruath showed Yarven, the Vampire Messiah, that mankind was destined to become a vampire race. The Haemovores lived in the sea, where they ganged up to hunt whales.[1656]

The Doctor arranged for a Mulo - a vampire created from a stillborn child - to become a caretaker at the Haemovore nature preserve on Vikramaditya.[1657]

? 800,000 - K9 AND THE MISSING PLANET[1658] ->
Earth had become known as Tellus, a smoggy, high-speed planet with no trees and plastic grass. It was a vast armaments factory run by Tellac Inc, a company that strip-mined worlds until they collapsed or exploded. One mining planet vanished, and represented a hazard to shipping.

The Time Lords sent K9 to investigate the missing world. K9's ship, the K-NEL fell into a time warp and arrived in a different universe. The unnamed mining planet had been transported there, as the miners found that the planet contained large deposits of Star Crystal - a

1655 "Half a million years" after *The Curse of Fenric*. When the Reverend Wainwright asks the Doctor how he knows about the Haemovores' future, the Doctor says "I've seen it". Some commentators (including *The Discontinuity Guide* and the previous editions of this chronology) have presumed that the Haemovore timeline was created when the Ancient One poisoned the Earth, and erased when he/she refrained from doing so, but this isn't actually said on screen. The Doctor attributes the Haemovore era to "half a million years of industrial progress", not something as sudden and cataclysmic as a single chemical release.

The next story to deal with Earth is *The Mysterious Planet*, set around the year two million - meaning that if the Haemovore timeline is "real", there are 1.5 million years for the dying Earth, "its surface a chemical slime", to recover. It perhaps sounds like a cheat to assume the Earth could simply "get over" such a catastrophe, but it's no less plausible than the idea that humanity's homeworld recuperates after the Daleks bombard it with enough firepower to change the shape of the very continents (in *The Parting of the Ways*, set in 200,100).

1656 *Goth Opera*, in which Ruath says the Haemovore timeline is a "possible future" (p44).

1657 *Benny: The Vampire Curse*: "Possum Kingdom", supporting the "haemovore future" from *The Curse of Fenric* being part of established history.

1658 Dating *K9 and the Missing Planet* (*The Adventures of K9* #4) - It's after "The human race had swarmed like locusts across the galaxy". Earth becoming known as Tellus isn't referenced in any other story, so dating when this could have occurred is a matter of sheer guesswork. That the miners on the unnamed planet have the technological nous to move between uni-

substance that broke down barriers between universes. Over five hundred million years of Earth evolution were represented on the planet, including early humans. The miners liked the idyllic life the planet offered, and thought that a new race of men might arise there. At the miners' request, K9 left them alone, reporting that the planet had disappeared from the universe as we know it.

? 802,701 - TIMELASH[1659] -> The third Doctor and Jo visited Karfel, preventing a great famine there. The Doctor also reported the scientist Magellan, who had been conducting unethical experiments on the reptilian Morlox, to the praesidium.

Over the next century, an accident with the substance Mustakozene caused Magellan to merge with a Morlox and became the mutated Borad. He took control of Karfel, enforcing discipline with an army of androids and the threat of exile into a time corridor, the Timelash. The Borad planned to provoke a war with neighbouring Bandril as a means of populating the planet with mutated clones of himself. Following the arrival of the sixth Doctor and Peri, the Borad was thrown into the Timelash, ending up in Loch Ness in the twelfth century.

Man fought the Primal Wars in the Tenth Segment of Time. Much scientific knowledge was lost during this period, including the cure for the common cold.[1660]

The viruses released at Amethyst Station all amassed at a single point in space-time.[1661]

? - "The Neutron Knights"[1662] -> Earth had endured in a long chain of catastrophes, and the last link in this was an invasion by the Neutron Knights. Earth's defences were overrun by forces led by the great mutant Catavolcus, who had previously breached the gates of Hell. Earth was a shattered world where only the strong survived.

The fourth Doctor was summoned to a fortress on Earth by the force of will of a mysterious bearded figure, who had himself previously been summoned through time to fight Earth's last battle. Catavolcus wanted the Dragon - a vast nuclear fission device as powerful as the Sun. He broke into the fortress, despite the best efforts of the castle's defender, Arthur. The mysterious summoner was Merlin, who set the Dragon to overload as Arthur fell to Catavolcus and his sword of flame. The Doctor and Merlin retreated to the TARDIS as the fortress - and Catavolcus - were destroyed. The Doctor woke in a forest, unsure what has happened. Merlin contacted him and warned that their paths were destined to cross once more.

"Descendance" / "Ascendance"[1663] -> On Mars, Luass - formerly of the House of Darsus Mons - thwarted her son Izaxryl's rite of ascension so that her brother, Artix, could become the head of the House of Balazarus Mons. The eighth Doctor and Stacy helped to end the warfare between the Houses, and Luass and Artix were both killed. Ssard, an Ice Warrior who had helped the Doctor and Stacy, joined them on their travels.

---

verses when they come across Star Crystal, and that they know of the Time Lords, suggests that it's the far future.

1659 Dating *Timelash* (22.5) - No date given on screen. This has been arbitrarily set in the same year that the Time Traveller met the Eloi and the Morlocks in H.G. Wells' *The Time Machine*. There is no indication on screen exactly when the third Doctor visited Karfel; the novelisation suggests it was "at least one hundred years" before this story, during the time of Katz's grandfather.

1660 *The Ark*

1661 Date unknown, but it's in the "far distant future" of *To the Death*.

1662 Dating "The Neutron Knights" (*DWM* #60) - No date is given, but if it truly is Earth's last battle, the story would seem to be set either before *The Ark* or somewhere in vast gap between that story and *The End of the World*. The Doctor speculates that "past and future are flowing into the same event", which doesn't really help. It doesn't seem to be set during the Millenium Wars. While the link isn't made in either story, it's been placed during the Primal Wars mentioned in *The Ark*.

1663 Dating "Descendance" / "Ascendance" (*Radio Times* #3785-3804) - No date given. The Doctor and Stacy open the story by witnessing "an early [Martian] period ascendancy rite", which could equally suggest that this is old Mars before the downfall of Ice Warrior civilisation, or that it's a traditional rite taking place in contemporary/future times. The surface of Mars is habitable - again, either an indication that it's prior to the decline of the Martian ecology (*The Judgement of Isskar*), or that it's after Mars has been terraformed (in stories such as *The Resurrection of Mars*). Either way, there are large Martian cities that modern-day astronomers and space probes would be unlikely to miss.

Two details suggest a future dating: The Martians are familiar with both Christmas and humanity (the Doctor is told, "You have all the outward appearance of a typically human buffoon"). No mention is made of the Federation. *The Silent Stars Go By* establishes that the Martians re-settle Mars at an unspecified point prior to the sun expanding and rendering the planet uninhabitable once more (*The Ark*). So while an old Mars dating is certainly feasible, a future dating was here chosen because the phrases "typically human buffoon" and Ssard's "It's the Martian equivalent of what humans call Christmas, Stacy" are rather hard to wave away as fig-

Glitz's Time

The criminal Kane was guilty of systematic acts of violence and extortion with his lover Sana, who killed herself rather than face trial. Kane was exiled from his home planet of Proamon, and sent to the barren planet Svartos. He remained there for three thousand years, slowly building his powerbase and dreaming of a return to his homeworld.

Unknown to Kane, Proamon was destroyed when its star went supernova a thousand years after his exile. Kane operated from the trading post of Iceworld, which was capable of spaceflight. This required the Dragonfire, a source of energy contained within the head of the Dragon: a biomechanoid sent to Svartos to prevent Kane from escaping the planet. Kane remained trapped on Iceworld.[1664]

Sabalom Glitz came from Salostopus in Andromeda. He was an habitual jailbird and thief, always on the lookout for a fast grotzi.[1665]

c 2,000,000 - THE MYSTERIOUS PLANET[1666] -> A group of Andromedans stole scientific secrets contained in the Matrix of the Time Lords and took shelter on Earth. By order of the High Council, the Magnotron was used to move the Earth and its entire constellation two light years, destroying everyone on the surface. The planet became known as Ravolox. The Andromedans, though, knew that the Time Lords had discovered them and had built a survival chamber. They entered suspended animation, awaiting rescue. The robot recovery mission sent to retrieve the Andromedans missed the Earth in its new location and sped on into the depths of space.

After five hundred years, this survival shelter had

become Marb Station, a completely self-contained system. Station guards maintained strict water rationing and population control. The population worshipped the Immortal - a being that lived in a citadel within their complex, and which was actually the robot caretaker of the facility, Drathro. The Earth's surface became viable again and served as home to The Tribe of the Free - a few primitive humans who had escaped from Marb Station. They worshipped the god Haldron, and killed any space traveller trying to steal his totem, a black light converter made from pure siligtone. They believed their ancestors' space travel had brought down their god's wrath and caused the solar fireball.

Glitz formed a business partnership with the Master, who knew that Earth had been moved and renamed Ravolox by the High Council. Glitz's accomplice was a young man, Dibber. The Master sent Dibber and Glitz to Ravolox to retrieve the Matrix files. The sixth Doctor and Peri defeated Drathro, allowing the two communities of humans to make contact.

The Time Lords subsequently restored Earth to its correct location.[1667] Thanks to a timestorm engineered by Fenric, Ace arrived on the ice planet of Svartos. Glitz used his ship, the *Nosferatu*, to raid space freighters. He ended up on Svartos with a rotten cargo and a mutinous crew, and tried to sell both to Kane.[1668]

After this time, the Andromeda galaxy fell under the rule of The One, a vast artificial intelligence that contained the memories and experiences of all Andromedans.[1669]

c 2,000,000 - DRAGONFIRE[1670] -> On the trading colony Iceworld, located on the dark side of Svartos, Kane was assembling an army. He put his soldiers into cryosleep, which erased their memories of their former

---

ures of speech.

As this was the last entry to be placed in *Ahistory* Third Edition, its exact placement (working to the parameters specified above) was literally chosen using the stairwell method - slips of paper were flung into the air, and the one reading "one million AD" reached the bottom of the stairs first.

1664 *Dragonfire*

1665 *The Mysterious Planet*

1666 Dating *The Mysterious Planet* (23.1) - The Doctor consults his pocket watch and suggests that it is "two million years" after Peri's time. Both the camera script and the novelisation confirm this date. *The Terrestrial Index* attempted to rationalise the various "ends of the Earth" seen in the series, but in doing so it ignored virtually every date given on screen. It is claimed, for example, that this story was set "c.14,500". The *TARDIS Special* gave the date as "two billion" AD, an under-

standable mishearing of the Doctor's line. *About Time* speculates that this is the same destruction of Earth seen in *The Ark* (the first Doctor was confused about the date), but doesn't explain why Time Lords who would covertly sterilise the Earth to prevent their secrets getting out give humanity notice this would happen, and enough notice to build a giant evacuation ship to boot.

The setting reminds Peri of "a wet November", perhaps suggesting the month. There's nothing on screen to suggest this isn't Glitz's native time.

1667 *The Eight Doctors*

1668 Before *Dragonfire*. *The Curse of Fenric* unveiled Fenric's involvement in Ace arriving in the future.

1669 "Ten hundred million years" (a billion) before *Doctor Who and the Invasion from Space*.

1670 Dating *Dragonfire* (24.4) - No date is given on screen, but Glitz's presence suggests the story takes

life to make them serve him without question.

Others chose to serve Kane willingly... Kane, whose natural body temperature was minus 193 Celsius, would burn the Mark of the Sovereign onto the palm of their right hand. One of Kane's officers, Belazs, joined him when she was 16 and served for twenty years. Kane earned many Crowns trading supplies to space travellers.

Many beings were drawn to Iceworld by the legends of a firebreathing dragon that supposedly lived in the ice tunnels beneath the colony. Kane finally killed the Dragon, his biomechanoid jailer, and acquired its Dragonfire power source. The seventh Doctor helped Kane to realise that his homeworld had been destroyed two thousand years ago, which deprived Kane of his revenge. Kane killed himself upon realising this. The Doctor's companion Melanie Bush elected to stay behind on Iceworld, now renamed the *Nosferatu II*, with Sabalom Glitz. He accepted as his new companion Ace, a time-stranded teenager working at Iceworld as a waitress.

? 2,000,002 - HEAD GAMES[1671] **->** The seventh Doctor had mentally influenced Mel into leaving his company, as he knew that Fenric was responsible for transporting Ace to Iceworld, and that he could no longer avoid certain responsibilities - of which Mel couldn't be a part. She soon left Glitz and attempted to reach Earth. She ended up marooned on the holiday planet Avalone, and spent two years there. She tried to get a lift from Glitz, and planted messages for him in the Galactic Banking Conglomerate's computer system, knowing that the Dragon cypher program she'd made for Glitz would find them. Glitz tried to exploit the open door and lift ten million grotzits from the bank, but he failed - causing officials to trace the intrusion to Mel's terminal. Avalone security caught up with Mel, who ran away and encountered the evil duplicate Dr Who.

On the sunless Detrios, an anomaly feeding off energy from the Land of Fiction had become the Miracle: a replacement source of heat and light for the planet. The unstable anomaly threatened the entire universe, so the seventh Doctor, Roz, Chris and Bernice sought to close it with force field generators. This nullified the Miracle, but some rebels on Detrios imposed order, and the inhabitants sought alternative methods of survival without a sun.

---

place after *The Mysterious Planet*. Iceworld services "twelve galaxies", and Glitz comes from Andromeda, suggesting that intergalactic travel is now routine (and that it's after Andromeda was colonised). According to the novelisation, Svartos is in the "Ninth galaxy".

Head Games claimed it was "a few thousand years into the future", at the time of the Galactic Federation. *Head Games* also establishes that Earth is devastated at this time, a reference to *The Mysterious Planet/The Ultimate Foe* (but one that might also support a dating around the time of the solar flares). Assuming it's the Galactic Federation from the Peladon stories, that and the dating of *Mission: Impractical* would seem to agree that Glitz's native time - and the events of *Dragonfire* - is much earlier than two million years in the future. Glitz is working for the Master in *The Mysterious Planet*, so could have been taken to the far future. However, with absolutely no evidence for this, or for Glitz having his own time machine, it seems better to conclude that he was in his native time in *The Mysterious Planet*.

1671 Dating *Head Games* (NA #43) - For Mel, it's been about two years since *Dragonfire*. It's here confirmed that Glitz is from the period when Earth was moved to become Ravolox.

The story is vague as to whether the Detrios sequences take place simultaneous to the modern day (2001), when Dr. Who and Jason pick up Mel from Avalone in the future, or in some other time zone entirely. While a contemporary dating *feels* more likely, a future dating is indicated when someone living on Detrios cites the people there as "we humans", and suggests that the planet's first settlers were "astronauts"

(p91). Previous editions of *Ahistory* dated these sequences to the year 4000.

1672 *Goth Opera*

1673 Dating *Iris: Enter Wildthyme* (Iris novel #1) - It's "millions of years" (p317) beyond the twenty-first century. Much of the book is spent trying to stop Marville from going to Hyspero to plunder its dark magic, but what happens after he reaches the planet is left unstated, beyond a homage to *The Face of Evil*.

1674 Euphemia says she's the first Scarlet Empress, but Cassandra made the same claim in *The Scarlet Empress*. The two of them don't appear to be the same character, although it's a bit hard to tell. Perhaps more than one empress has tried to augment her authority by claiming the mantle of being the "first", or perhaps each empress - for whatever reason - genuinely believes that they *are* the first. Or, perhaps owing to Hyspero existing in "a permanent state of magical anarchy and evolution" (*Iris: Enter Wildthyme*), the lineage resets itself every so often.

1675 Dating *Prison in Space* (BF LS #2.2) - No year given, nor is there any explanation as to how this story relates to the rest of Earth's history. The audio was made from an unmade (for good reason, the authors of this guidebook would argue) script for Season 6.

While there's little doubt that *Prison in Space* takes place in the future, the TARDIS crew suspect early on that they've arrived in Earth's distant past, as part of a conversation that makes one wonder if the Doctor is entirely well. When Zoe very spuriously asks if they've arrived, "About what? Forty million years BC?", the Doctor replies, "Give or take the odd million, yes.

Glitz found a MiniScope and briefly met Romana, who was trapped inside. Flavia arrived in a Type 90 TARDIS and returned Romana to Gallifrey.[1672]

? 3,000,000 - IRIS: ENTER WILDTHYME[1673] -> The super-thief Terrance went to the planet Hyspero and made off with the Scarlet Empress Euphemia.[1674] He took her back to his bookshop in the twenty-first century.

Kelly and the villain Anthony Marville arrived on Hyspero via the *Dii h'anno Doors*... and found themselves looking at a 20-storey-tall face of Iris Wildthyme, which had been carved out of rock. Jenny, Euphemia and Barbra also travelled through the *Dii h'anno Doors*, and were reunited with Iris, Panda and Simon when they visited from the twenty-first century.

PRISON IN SPACE[1675] -> Life on Earth prospered as machines were engineered to provide for humanity's heat, light and food. Some people lived in a futuristic city that looked down upon the clouds, and had art-deco skyscrapers. The world's overpopulation had been exacerbated by the advent of a drug that extended the average lifespan by two hundred years.

These developments gave rise to the regime of Chairman Babs. She brought about the World Federation of Womanhood and judged that men had become superfluous. Males were stripped of their right to vote, and treated as inferiors. Babs and the Federation Council outlawed war and capital punishment, but anti-social enemies of the state were launched in capsules to the Outer Space Corrective Establishment (OSCE): an octagonal satellite constructed more than a century ago. The most heinous crime cited in the Constitution of these United Female States was publicly insulting Chairman Babs. Her enforcers, all women, wore tight-fitting, black rubber uniforms. Paris, New York and Tokyo were provinces in Babs' government.

The second Doctor, Jamie and Zoe arrived on what was, in local time, the 14th of Aphrodite in the year 122 SCB (meaning Since Chairman Babs, denoting the time since her birth). The Doctor and Jamie were sent to the OSCE while Zoe underwent mental rehabilitation in Babs' Silver Maiden machine. Jamie's familiarity with kilts made him the logical candidate to crudely dress as a woman and attempt an escape; before long, he and the Doctor had started a revolt on the OSCE. Their actions gave the ruling Council the courage to depose Babs. A time of gender equality came about, with Sister Nora as Chairman. Jamie

---

Somewhere between the Oligocene and the Miocene periods." The Oligocene and Miocene *epochs* (subsets of *periods* of Earth prehistory) respectively ran from thirty-four to twenty-three million years ago, and from twenty-three to five million years ago - so the Doctor presumably means they're at twenty-three million BC, give or take. (Which would mean that when he says "give or take the odd million [years]", he actually means about "seventeen million [years]", but let's move on.)

Then the Doctor confirms, on the grounds that he's spotted some maple and oak trees, that they're in the Miocene [period], and that "It'll be another fourteen million years before man sets foot in this part of the world... in any part of the world." Calling upon the scientific consensus that man walked the Earth some four to six million years ago, it would further suggest the Doctor thinks they're somewhere between eighteen to twenty million BC.

Once the travellers meet Chairman Babs and her people, however, all discussion that they might be in Earth's past vanishes. At no point are Babs' people treated as aliens who have colonised Earth in defiance of established history - or, alternatively, breed in such a way as to become humanity's ancestors. They're decisively identified as human, have technology that has eliminated general need, and possess a drug that extends human longevity by two centuries (much more effectively, then, than even the life-extending Spectrox from *The Caves of Androzani*). By any measure, then, Babs' regime must exist in the future - the *far* future, even.

Earth and its environs (Paris, New York, Tokyo, Mars, Jupiter) are named so often, we probably have to accept (however reluctantly) that Chairman Babs' regime *did* rule Earth for more than a century. Certainly, the Doctor seems certain when he tells his companions that they've arrived at, "Terra, with a capital T. What you call the British Isles, Jamie." (Then again, this is the same man who misidentifies the era by at least twenty million years.) Funnily enough, the presence of oak trees - while a fairly terrible means of determining the year - supports the notion that this is humanity's birthplace, per *The Android Invasion* establishing that oak trees being exclusive to Earth. At one point it's commented that Zoe, "comes from a different world, a different culture" - but while it's tempting to wish otherwise, this should, in the face of all the other evidence, be interpreted that she's from "a different time period".

Attempts were made to place *Prison in Space* in the pre-solar flare era, but it's too difficult to find a century where Babs' regime could have taken place without massively contradicting other stories, or at least being unavoidably referenced in them. The best option, then, is probably to set *Prison in Space* in the *very* far future, when mankind's technology is greatly advanced, and the continued abandonment and restoration of Earth might provide an opening for a comparatively weak regime to rule the planet for a time. At a guess, *Prison in Space* might come before the collapse of Earth society in *The Sun Makers* - if nothing else, it's a bit in keeping with the parody nature of the latter story.

broke Zoe's mental conditioning by spanking her.

Chairman Babs, now just "Sister Babs", fancied the Doctor as the manliest man she had ever met. The Doctor fended off her advances, and escaped with his friends in the TARDIS.

c 4,000,000 - THE SUN MAKERS[1676] -> Earth's mineral wealth was finally exhausted and its people were dying. In return for their labour, the Usurians moved mankind to Mars, which they terraformed. The population was later moved to Pluto, where six megropolises were built, each with its own artificial sun. However, the fourth Doctor - who the Usurians knew had "a long history of violence and economic subversion" - and Leela started a rebellion. The Doctor imposed a growth tax and rendered the planet uneconomic.

c 4,000,000 - BENNY: ESCAPING THE FUTURE[1677] ->
The humans who fell through a time-space rift in twenty-sixth century Buenos Aires arrived on the planet Deindus, where their genetic makeup and memories co-mingled with primordial soup to create the Deindum - a race of reptilian humanoids.

(=) The Deindum made an immense technological leap during their Industrial Age, when they were contacted and aided by their future selves. This triggered their development into powerful beings who developed time travel and manifested as giant glowing heads. The hyper-evolved Deindum knew of Irving Braxiatel's efforts to hamper or eliminate them, and dispatched an android, Robyn, through time to stop him. They then sent warfleets to conquer the twentieth century - all in a bid to guarantee their creation.

Benny and Braxiatel intervened in the Deindum's Industrial Age using Braxiatel's TARDIS, and sent the younger Deindum down a wormhole to a faked civilisation they had constructed on the planet Rawlus.

1676 Dating *The Sun Makers* (15.4) - Set unspecified "millions of years in the future" according to contemporary publicity material, but this is never stated explicitly on screen. Earth has had time to regenerate its mineral wealth, which would suggest the story is set a very long way into the future. *The Programme Guide* failed to reconcile *The Sun Makers* with other stories, claiming that the Company dominated humanity only from "c.2100" to "c.2200" (first edition), or "c.2200" to "c.2300" (second edition). *The Terrestrial Index* suggested that the Earth was abandoned some centuries after the "fifty-second century", and recolonised "five thousand years" later. *The TARDIS Logs* suggested that the story was set "c.40,000", *Timelink* "25,000", *About Time* found it credible to think it was "millions of years in the future".

1677 Dating *Benny: Escaping the Future* (Benny audio #11.2) - Bev Tarrant says that the Deindum are based "four million years" in the future; as Benny and Peter have actually been there, one presumes Bev is in a pretty good position to know. *Benny: Secret Origins* says that the Deindum are from "billions" of years in the future, but this can probably be written off as misinformation spread by Robyn to hide her creators' native time. Writer Eddie Robson concurs that, "Although it says billions of years [in *Secret Origins*], for practical reasons we might say that's wrong and it's actually millions."

1678 *Benny: Escaping the Future.* The exact timeframe isn't given, but it's after the Deindum's empire - before Benny and Braxiatel erase it, that is - has run its course.

1679 "Several million years" after *Benny: Present Danger:* "Excalibur of Mars".

1680 Dating *Scaredy Cat* (BF #75) - It is four million years after the previous part of the story, which roughly takes place during the time of the Earth Empire.

1681 Dating *The Criminal Code* (BF CC #4.6) - Benny says that the story takes place "far, far into my future, and a long way from human space"; the Doctor is a little more specific in saying that the terraforming technology seen here is "a good few million years at least" in advance of her time. The terraforming tech is clearly of human manufacture, but there's nothing to say that it was developed on Earth itself. The technology seen here appears unrelated to that of *The Sorcerer's Apprentice*, although both involve nanobots/nanites that obey spoken command and create "magical" effects through transference of matter and energy.

1682 Dating "4-Dimensional Vistas" (*DWM* #78-83) - The time it takes to grow the crystal is specified.

1683 "Five million years" after "The World Shapers".

1684 "Five million years" after *Iris: The Panda Invasion*.

1685 *Time and Relative.* No date is specified, but it's safe to presume it wasn't when the Company occupied Pluto.

1686 "Many millions of years" after *The English Way of Death* (p189).

1687 *The Ark.* Earth, and a number of races known to Earth - most notably the Daleks - achieved limited success with time travel experiments (one human scientist built a time machine in the nineteenth century, according to *The Evil of the Daleks*), but these have presumably been forgotten by now.

1688 "Several million years" after *Parasite* (p304).

1689 *Frontios*

1690 Dating *The Ark* (3.6) - The Commander states that this is "the Fifty-Seventh Segment" of time, which the Doctor instantly calculates to be "ten million years" after Steven and Dodo's time.

The younger Deindum were tricked into thinking that their "future selves" were frauds, and the resultant conflict either weakened the Deindum's development or destroyed them in a paradox. If the Deindum existed afterwards, they never developed time travel.

Before they were erased from history, the advanced Deindum broke into Braxiatel's TARDIS, and killed both him and Bernice.

Bernice and Peter, hoping to learn of the Deindum's weaknesses, went even further into the future and saw the ruins of the Deindum's empire. The whole galaxy had been crippled by the Deindum's occupation.[1678]

Benny went to collect Excalibur from Mars, but found that Merlin had already retrieved it.[1679]

c 4,000,000 - SCAREDY CAT[1680] **->** According to legend, the people of Caludaar almost destroyed themselves through a series of global wars, and made a pledge to never set foot on their sister world, Endaara. Several millennia passed, but an expedition to Endaara was permitted when scans detected sophisticated indigenous lifeforms there. Professor Arken, a noted Caludaar scientist, used lambda radiation to experiment on the monkey-like natives, hoping to identify the part of the brain that facilitated evil. Arken hoped his research would facilitate a means of blocking evil impulses, ending war and violence.

The eighth Doctor, Charley and C'rizz arrived as Arken further used lambda radiation on Eunis Flood, a convicted serial killer from Caludaar. This unexpectedly forged a link between the planet's morphogenetic field and Flood, turning him into a formidable psionic. The planet's collective life force appeared in guise of the dead girl Galayana, and although Flood disintegrated her physical form, she peeled away his defences and left him with the mind of a child. Flood had similarly lobotomised Arken, but Endaara was now left to develop naturally.

c 4,500,000 - THE CRIMINAL CODE[1681] **->** Humanity developed a new method of terraforming: a quasi-organic, asexually reproducing machine that would generate massive amounts of nanobots. Such nanobots could transform entire worlds, and interface with a user's synapses to respond to verbal commands. They could erect force fields, direct lightning strikes and create earthquakes.

An nine-member terraforming team got lost in a wormhole, and emerged a long way from human space. They terraformed a local world, but a disease killed all but one of them. The survivor was alone for forty years, and the machine created smoke creatures based upon the darker recesses of his mind. After the survivor's death, the creatures spurred evolution of the Shanquis - a race of pale blue humanoids, whose bodies they could inhabit. The

Shanquis developed an advanced society, but the smoke-creatures possessed their political leaders and were deeply xenophobic. English became a forbidden language, as the smoke-creatures feared someone uttering commands that would terminate their existence.

Tensions increased between the Shanquis and the neighbouring planet of Esoria, and so the Doge of Micene - a cosmopolitan planet - asked the seventh Doctor to serve as an arbiter. The Doctor and Benny extracted the smoke-creatures from the Shanquis rulers, who petitioned for peace.

5,000,000 - "4-Dimensional Vistas"[1682] **->** In the twentieth century, the Monk and the Ice Warriors seeded a giant crystal in the Arctic. Now they arrived to harvest it. They would be able to destroy continents with the sonic cannon powered by the crystal.

Two Time Lords visited the far future, and found that the Cybermen had evolved to become pure thought - the most peace-loving and advanced race in the universe.[1683]

(=) Iris visited an alternate universe "three dimensions to the left" from our reality, where flying, vampiric versions of her companion Panda decimated entire worlds.[1684]

The Doctor took the Cold to Pluto in the far future.[1685] Many millions of years in the future, the people of Phryxus established a technocracy in NGC4258 and developed galactic travel using warp capsules in the Grey Interchange. The renegade scientist Zodaal was jailed for experimenting on lesser life forms, and tried to escape using a warp capsule. This failed and he had to reduce himself to a gaseous state to survive. He escaped to the year 1929.[1686]

Humanity attempted time-travel experiments during the Twenty-Seventh Segment of Time, but these proved to be a total failure.[1687] Parasitic eggs laid by the Artifact were expected to hatch in the Elysium system.[1688]

The Destruction of Earth

"Fleeing from the imminence of a catastrophic collision with the sun, a group of refugees from the *doomed* planet Earth..." [1689]

c 10,000,000 - THE ARK[1690] **->** In the Fifty-Seventh Segment of Time, ten million years hence, scientists realised that the Earth was falling towards the Sun. With the help of the Monoids, a mysterious race whose own planet had been destroyed in a supernova many years before, humanity constructed a great space vessel. It contained the entire human, Monoid, animal and plant population of the Earth in miniaturised form on microcells. Audio space research revealled that Refusis II was suitable for colonisation. It would take seven hundred years to reach the new world. To symbolise the survival of man, a vast statue of a human carved from gregarian rock was begun.

The ship set out, and the few humans and Monoid servants that remained active - the Guardians - watched the Earth's destruction. Very soon afterwards, the common cold swept through the vessel, brought by the first Doctor's companion Dodo. The Doctor cured the disease using animal membranes.

Enormous generation ships were "quite common" as mankind left Earth for the final time, during humanity's late expansion period: the great Diaspora Era. Human engineering was now at its peak - entire worlds could be terraformed to Earth conditions over several generations. The Ice Warriors had resettled on Mars prior to the Earth's death, but the Red Planet was rendered uninhabitable with the sun's expansion, and the Martians similarly migrated into space.[1691]

c 10,000,000 - FRONTIOS[1692] **->** A vast colony ship containing thousands of people, plus the technology and material capable of rebuilding the whole of human civilisation, was sent to the Veruna system on the distant edge of the universe. Despite being touted as fail-ure-proof, every system on the colony ship failed. The ship crashed on Frontios. Most of the crew died in the crash, and many more perished from diseases that spread through the colony immediately afterwards.

Captain Revere eventually restored order. For ten years, the survivors planted and harvested crops, stocking up with food. But then meteorite bombardments began, striking the colony with such accuracy to make plain that it was being deliberately targeted. The bombardment continued for thirty years, but that wasn't the worst of it: the earth began swallowing up the dead. Over the years, the number of Retrogrades - people who deserted the colony - swelled.

And then, the earth swallowed Captain Revere while he was investigating the planet's potential mineral wealth. This left his son, Plantagenet, in command. The colony was soon in danger of falling apart.

The Tractators, insect creatures who could harness gravity, had arrived on Frontios five hundred years before and were responsible for the colony's setbacks. Under the command of their leader, the Gravis, they had pulled down the colony ship. They had given the colonists ten years to establish themselves, then began the meteorite bombardment. The Tractators had been kidnapping humans to serve as "drivers" for their tunnelling machines. The Gravis hoped to create a tunnel system that would amplify the Tractators' gravity fields and let them pilot Frontios throughout the cosmos.

1691 *The Silent Stars Go By.* This is roughly in keeping with *The Ark*, save that such multi-generation vessels are cited as being more numerous than the TV story suggests. Also, there's no sign of the colonists in *The Ark* having terraforming technology - they target Refusis II because "only it" has conditions akin to Earth. The colonists in *Frontios* might have possessed such terraforming tech, but lost it when they crashed.

1692 Dating *Frontios* (21.3) - According to the Doctor, the story happens "on the outer limits. The TARDIS has drifted too far into the future". The inhabitants of Frontios are among the very last humans, and they have evacuated the Earth in circumstances that sound very similar to those of *The Ark*. While this would seem to dictate that *Frontios* is contemporary with *The Ark*, there is room for debate: no date is given in *Frontios*, there's no explicit link made to the earlier story, the colony ship is of a very different design, there is no sign of the Monoids and neither story refers to other arks. It is difficult to judge the level of technology, as virtually everything is lost in the crash, but it does not seem as advanced as that of *The Ark*.

1693 *Excelis Dawns*

1694 *The Hollows of Time*

1695 Dating "The Child of Time" (*DWM* #438-441) - It's a long while after Earth was obliterated in the human

Galatean war timeline. The present-day Galateans are said to be "the result of ten million years of robot evolution".

1696 Dating *The Silent Stars Go By* (NSA #50) - The Hereafter colonists left Earth owing to the same cataclysm as witnessed in *The Ark*. While it's unclear how long it took them to travel to Hereafter, "twenty-seven generations" (i.e. six hundred seventy-five years) have passed since they arrived. It's "winter" (p11).

1697 Dating *The Ark* (3.6) - The last two episodes of the story take place at the end of the Ark's journey, which occurs "seven hundred years" after the first two episodes.

1698 *The Silent Stars Go By*

1699 In *Frontios*, a message flashes up on a TARDIS console screen: "Boundary Error - Time Parameters Exceeded". Likewise, in *The Sun Makers*, the Doctor is worried that the TARDIS might have "gone right through the time spiral". This limitation doesn't seem to affect the TARDIS in *The Ark* or *The Savages*, or the New Adventures story *Timewyrm: Apocalypse*, which is also set in the distant future. The words quoted are those of the Doctor in *Frontios*. The novelisation of that story makes it clear that "ours" refers to the Time Lords, and that the story is set at the "edge of the Gallifreyan noo-sphere". It may - or may not - be significant that the

The fifth Doctor, Tegan and Turlough arrived on Frontios, isolated the Gravis and transported it to the planet Kolkokron. Without their leader, the Tractators were mindless drones, and the survival of the human colony was better assured.

After delivering the Gravis to Kolkokron, the fifth Doctor made a side trip to the planet Artaris circa 1001 before returning to Frontios.[1693] Professor Stream retrieved the Gravis from Kolkokron using the Doctor's TARDIS, and returned to the twentieth century.[1694]

(=) c 10,000,000 - "The Child of Time" (DWM)[1695] **->** The time-child Chiyoko had built the Museum of Lost Opportunities in the remains of Earth - nothing more than an asteroid belt circling a dying sun - as a tribute to the human race. The synthetic Galateans had now lived so long that they had gone insane, and exterminated all other races.

Some Galateans working at the Museum - made to resemble famous persons such as the Bronte sisters, Alan Turing, Buddy Holly, John Keats and Jayne Mansfield - had gained self-awareness. The Brontes saved the eleventh Doctor and Amy with a Timescoop when Chiyoko destroyed the Earth, then sent them and the faux Turing back to avert the Galateans' creation.

The trio failed and returned. The Doctor timescooped the young women Cosette and Margaret, plus Sister Konami, from points prior to their being physically combined to create Chiyoko. This greatly weakened Chiyoko's abilities. The Doctor persuaded Chiyoko that her actions had caused universal suffering and death, and she undid her existence. The Doctor and Amy took Turing and the now-anomalous Chiyoko back to the genesis of the Galateans...

---

c 10,000,675 (winter) - THE SILENT STARS GO BY[1696] **->** A colony ship arrived on the Earth-esque planet Hereafter. Three mountain-sized Terra Firmers were established, each containing engines that, over the course of hundreds of years, would make Hereafter's environment entirely comparable to that of Earth. A thousand of Earth's most powerful and elite members hibernated within the Firmers in secret, intending to emerge once the settlers had performed the hard labour required to shape Hereafter to human norm.

Twenty-seven generations later, Hereafter's three settlements - Aside, Beside and Seeside - had a total population of around nineteen thousand. An Ice Warrior migration fleet with members of the Tanssor clan of the Ixon Mons family from Old Mars entered the quadrant, and judged Hereafter as the most viable colony world. Seven years passed as the Martians attempted to alter the Terra Firmers with their seed technology, hoping to change Hereafter's environment to Martian norm. When the Firmers' defence mechanisms prevailed, the Martians directly altered the machinery. Three years passed, with the winters becoming increasingly harsher.

The Terra Firmers converted some of the sleeping elite into powerful transhumans to attack the Warriors. The eleventh Doctor, Amy and Rory defused hostilities, and sent the transhumans back to sleep. The Doctor convinced the Martian warlord Ixyldir that it would be honourable to leave Hereafter to the human settlers, and left the settlers to decide when, if ever, they should awaken the sleepers.

At the Doctor's direction, the Ice Warrior fleet relocated Mars-like world Atrox 881, located eight light years from Hereafter.

c 10,000,700 - THE ARK[1697] **->** The fever that had swept through the Ark had never fully abated, and it had weakened the humans. Seven hundred years after leaving the solar system, the Monoids had seized control of the ship, and the statue commemorating the voyage was now of a Monoid. The humans now called the ship "the Ark" after an old Earth legend, but the Monoids kept the Guardians' descendants in check with heat prods.

The TARDIS again brought the first Doctor, Steven and Dodo to the Ark as it arrived at Refusis II and Launcher 14 was sent to the surface. At first there was no sign of life, but it quickly transpired that the native Refusians were invisible giants. Nevertheless, the Monoid leader, named 1, planned to take his race's microcells to the planet. He also intended to destroy the Ark with a bomb planted in the head of the statue, but the Refusians helped to throw the statue overboard, allowing it to explode harmlessly in space. The Refusians allowed the humans and Monoids to live on their world, but only if they promised to live in peace.

Atrox 881 became a quadrant capital to the fiefworlds of the Ixon Mons dynasty. The Doctor arrived on Atrox 881 nine thousand years after the Martians settled there, but - in his personal timeline - before he had aided them in doing so. Azylax, the warlord of the Tanssor, bestowed upon the Doctor the honourary title of *Belot'ssar*, meaning "cold blue star", in recognition of his friendship.[1698]

Thus, humanity survived the destruction of its homeworld by travelling across the universe and rebuilding human civilisation on distant planets. What happened in the untold billions of years after that was a mystery - any TARDIS attempting to travel further into the future than this exceeded its time parameters, and the Time Lords themselves were unaware of anything beyond this time. "Knowledge has its limits; ours reaches this far and no further".[1699]

"The demise of Earth was followed by a period in which there was, effectively, no such thing as the human species; a period in which humanity suddenly found itself released from its heritage, with genetic manipulation and vast tracts of space separating the survivors from everything they'd once been. Many 'posthuman' societies inevitably became glorious, grotesque Princedoms, and none more so than those of the Blood Coteries, who - like the Medici and Borgia families of antiquity - commissioned the greatest art and culture of their age even as they conducted unimaginable vendettas and poisoned their potential rivals..." [1700]

w - The family of Demetra Kein of the Blood Coteries was one of the greatest patrons of opera in the posthuman Renaissance. Shuncuker of Faction Paradox invaded the family's home and crippled their 1000-year-old empire, motivating the Blood Coteries to render their agents impervious to the Faction's shadow weapons. [1701]

Some inhabitants in the posthuman city of Civitas Solis sensed a temporal ripple related to Isaac Newton - an anomaly that could potentially undo their existence. They channelled themselves back to the seventeenth century, and manipulated the life of Nathaniel Silver to better guarantee their survival. [1702]

w - The War in Heaven became such that the final generation living in the posthuman era foresaw the impending demise of humanity, and built the Universal Machine (UniMac) as a conceptual device that personified the whole of human technology. Mesh Cos, the last documented person of human descent, raided the Homeworld of the Great Houses to acquire the technology for the UniMac - and in so doing triggered an attack from House Mirraflex that eliminated the last of humanity. The UniMac continued operating and communicated through time with other forms of machine life. It made contact with the living timeship Compassion - together, they became the Secret Architects who created the City of the Saved, with Compassion's body forming the City's environs. [1703]

? 10,000,000 - INFINITE REQUIEM[1704] **->** Far in the future, representatives of over seven hundred cultures - including the Monoids, Morestrans, Rakkhins and Rills - used the Pridka Dream Centre. The Pridka were a race of blue-skinned, crested telepaths, and the Centre used their healing skills. At any one time, fifteen thousand individuals would be booked into the Centre, making it a tempting resource for the Sensopaths, a psychic communal mind intent on dominating the physical world.

The malicious Sensopath Shanstra attempted to absorb the Sensopath Jirenal. The benevolent Sensopath Kelzen intervened, and all three of them died.

Time Lords are unable to travel beyond the time of Earth's destruction.

It is perhaps also significant that in stories set after the destruction of Gallifrey, such as *Father Time, Hope, Sometime Never, The End of the World* and *Utopia*, the Doctor is capable of travelling much further into the future (although he also seems quite capable of doing so in other stories set before Gallifrey's destruction, such as *Timewyrm: Apocalypse* and *The One Doctor*).
1700 The back cover copy from *FP: Movers,* building on *FP: The Book of the War.* The "supernova" in question would seem to be the one from *The Ark,* rather than the one from *The End of the World.*
1701 *FP: Movers.* Date unknown, but the blurb (in accordance with *FP: The Book of the War*) establishes that the posthumanity era follows Earth's final demise.
1702 *FP: Newtons Sleep*
1703 *FP: Of the City of the Saved*
1704 Dating *Infinite Requiem* (NA #36) - Events at the Pridka Dream Centre occur "Beyond Common Era of Earth Calendar" (p83), millennia after the destruction of Earth, and the presence of Morestrans and Monoids emphasises that this is the far future. This date is arbitrary.
1705 Dating *TimeH: Peculiar Lives* (TimeH #7) - The era isn't named, but this strain of humanity is so advanced that one of their number, Sanfiel, has lived for "tens of millennia" purely on the basis of his genetics.

1706 *Evolution* (p40).
1707 Dating *The Well-Mannered War* (MA #33) - This is "right at the end of the Humanian era, after the destruction of Earth" (p25) and "the fifty-eighth segment of time".
1708 *The Well-Mannered War*
ERAS: The Humanian Era was first mentioned in *Doctor Who - The Movie,* which also referred to the Rassilon Era. The TARDIS console prop for that story also included references to the Peon, Manussan, Sumaron, Kraaiian and Sensorian eras. *Zagreus* adds the Morestran Era to the list.
The Humanian Era includes Earth in 1999, and is presumably a reference to the human race. *The Well-Mannered War* implies that it's simply the Era when humans exist. The Rassilon Era applies to Gallifrey (the "present" for the Doctor would seem to be 5725.2 in the Rassilon Era, according to the TV movie). *Neverland* specifies that the period around the Federation and Mavic Chen was the Sensorian. The Manussan and Morestran eras are presumably references to the planets from *Snakedance* and *Planet of Evil* respectively. Taking all this at face value, it would seem that eras can overlap each other - the Sensorian and Morestran eras, at least, fall comfortably within the Humanian Era.
1709 *Return of the Living Dad,* tying in with the date for *Delta and the Bannermen.*
1710 Dating *Delta and the Bannermen* (24.3) - An

The Doctor estimated that dogs would evolve thumbs in
around twenty million years time.[1706]

**The Fifty-Eighth Segment of Time - THE WELL-
MANNERED WAR**[1707] -> In the Fifty-Eighth Segment of
Time, human refugees colonised the planet Metralubit.
There was peace for two thousand years, but then a planet-
wide war suddenly wiped out two-thirds of the population. This had been engineered by the Hive, an evolved
gestalt of flies that fed on dead bodies. There were four
more such wars at roughly two-thousand-year intervals.
The Helducc civilisation emerged from the sixth war, but
also fell to conflict. A new civilisation rose and developed
the Femdroids, led by Galatea, to increase male efficiency.

The Black Guardian brought a Chelonian squad from
the distant past in a timestorm. The Chelonians claimed
the planet Barclow, close to Metralubit, and the two races
fought a short war until the Bechet Treaty was signed.
Galatea learned the secret of the devastating world wars,
evacuated most of the Femdroids to Regus V and plotted
to lure the Hive back.

The fourth Doctor, Romana and K9 found that the Black
Guardian was trying to trick the Doctor into releasing the
Hive in the twenty-sixth century, which would destroy
humanity. The Doctor defeated the Guardian by removing
himself and Romana from time and space altogether.

This was the end of the Humanian Era.[1708]

The Navarino civilisation was the only one to survive
the war on its home planet - their culture was based on
frivolity, and they were having too good a time to join in
the conflict. The Navarinos had time tourism, but paid
exorbitant taxes to the Time Lords for the privilege.[1709]

? - DELTA AND THE BANNERMEN[1710] -> The
Bannermen invaded the Chimeron homeworld, but the
Chimeron Queen escaped to Tollport G715. She joined
the seventh Doctor, Mel and a party of Navarinos on a
Nostalgia Trips tour to America in the 1950s. Nostalgia
Trips were notorious following an incident with the
Glass Eaters of Traal, and true to form, their Hellstrom
II cruiser wound up at a holiday camp in Wales by
mistake. The Bannermen pursued them back in time.

Six weeks into a war between two colonies in Cassiopeia,
a time traveller was brought before Uglosi, a high-ranking
prosecutor, on vagrancy charges. The traveller told Uglosi
that in three months, General Verdigast would travel to
Corinth Minor - a planet with volcanoes that showered
gemstones, and so had become a popular holiday destination for the rich and famous - and broker a peace treaty
with the rival colony. This would create the Corinth
Compact: an empire that would be "an unstoppable blight
on the region". A rival general, Morella Wendigo, concurred with Uglosi that this must be averted, and killed the
treaty-makers with a bacteriological weapon that ravaged
Corinth Minor's troposphere. This stratagem bankrupted
both armies, ending the war. Faced with the prospect of a
flesh-eating plague in such a densely populated area, the
authorities appealed to the Time Lords - who passed
Corinth Minor through a cloud of super-violet radiation,
sterilising it.

Corinth Minor was renamed Nevermore to symbolically
denote the folly of war (not that many in Cassiopeia
heeded this). A war crimes tribunal sentenced Wendigo to
exile on Nevermore, and Uglosi - being obsessed with the
works of Edgar Allan Poe - both designed her prison and
equipped it with robot ravens.[1711]

? - NEVERMORE[1712] -> The Time Lords directed the
eighth Doctor and Tamsin Drew to the planet Nevermore,
where the Doctor pardoned and released General Morella
Wendigo. In doing so, he curtailed the lethal mutant shad-

entirely arbitrary date. However, Nostalgia Trips is notorious throughout the "five galaxies", suggesting that the
story is set in a far future period of intergalactic travel.
In *Dragonfire*, Svartos serves "the twelve galaxies", so
perhaps it is set later than this story. While only the
Daleks had broken the time barrier by 4000 AD (*The
Daleks' Master Plan*), the human ship in *Planet of the
Spiders* and the Movellan ship in *Destiny of the Daleks*
have "time warp capability", and we see a couple of
races developing rudimentary time travel around now
(Magnus Greel in 5000 AD, the Metebelis Spiders a little
later). Such secrets are limited, and are lost by the time
of *The Ark*. Murray, the bus driver, says "the 1950s nights
back on Navaro were never like this", which implies

nostalgia parties rather than that he lived through the
1950s himself. *The Terrestrial Index* set this story
"c.15,000", *Timelink* went for "????' (sic), *About Time*
broadly dated it to "the future, possibly the *far* future".
1711 "Twenty years" before *Nevermore*.
1712 Dating *Nevermore* (BF BBC7 #4.3) - The works of
Poe have readily survived, to such an extent that Uglosi
and company can correctly recite them. It's possible
this story occurs in the *far* future, as the Doctor upon
leaving sets the coordinates for "The Humanian Era" -
then again, that doesn't automatically rule out
Nevermore taking place there as well. It should also be
noted that authorities in Cassiopeia have contact with
the Time Lords, which also suggests a later placement.

ows who had sprung into being after the holocaust on Corinth Minor, and were now using Wendigo as a host.

The Master stole a force field from a Farquazi Time Cruiser during the 300th Segment of Time.[1713]

The Vulgar End of Time - THE ONE DOCTOR[1714] ->
In the far future, everything had been discovered, everything had been done and technology made everything possible and affordable. It was therefore very boring.

A company on Generios VIII had thrived by exporting furniture, but the company's Assembler robots had wiped out the thirty-million-year-old population thousands of years ago. The Rim World of Abydos had no interesting features whatsoever, and Zynglat 3 boasted a sensory deprivation device. The Skardu-Rosbrix Wars were recent history. The super-computer Mentos spent thirty-three thousand years playing *Super Brain* against a holographic Questioner, even when warfare destroyed all other civilisation on Generios XIV.

The Doctor was famous in this era for his heroism, and the con man Banto Zame (a native of Osphogus, a planet that was terraformed five thousand years before) impersonated the Doctor to stage "defeats" of alien invasions, then collect rewards from grateful rulers. Banto tried his scheme on Generios I, but a genuine alien spaceship arrived and demanded the Generios system's three greatest treasures as tribute.

The sixth Doctor, Mel and Banto banded together to collect the Mentos super-computer from Generios XIV, furniture Unit ZX419 from Generios VIII, and the largest diamond in existence on Generios XV. The Cylinder accepted the tribute as proof of the Doctor's identity, but mistook Banto for the genuine Time Lord. The Cylinder spirited Banto away to face retribution for a past offence the Doctor had committed against the Cylinder's masters.

(? The Vulgar End of Time) - OMEGA[1715] -> The legend of Omega had become widely known. Jolly Chronolidays set up a heritage centre in the Sector of Forgotten Souls, where it was believed Omega had detonated a star on behalf of the Time Lords. The centre was modelled on Omega's ship, the *Eurydice*.

Omega himself arrived in this time zone and met Sentia, a telepath who became enamoured of him. However, Omega's failed attempt to merge with the fifth Doctor in Amsterdam, 1983, had left him with a copy of the Doctor's memories and a split persona. Omega's mental health deteriorated, and Sentia conspired to return Omega to his anti-matter universe aboard the real *Eurydice*, which was within a dimensional anomaly. Sentia was killed and Omega was yet again cast - along with the *Eurydice* - over the event horizon of a black hole.

Two agents of Gallifrey's Celestial Preservation Agency - Maven and the living TARDIS Glinda - arrived to preserve the Doctor's reputation by keeping secret his eradication of the Scintillan race. They offered Daland, an actor, a job in a Gallifreyan museum.

Even so, this dating represents a guess.
1713 *The Quantum Archangel*
1714 Dating *The One Doctor* (BF #27) - The Doctor expounds on the subject of the Vulgar End of Time at the beginning of the story.
1715 Dating *Omega* (BF #47) - The dating is arbitrary, but much about this story resembles the Vulgar End of Time: time travel is now deemed unfashionable rather than unattainable; the exploits of the Doctor, Omega and - generally speaking - the Time Lords are widely renowned, if somewhat erroneously; and the period is one of prosperity, leisure and dullness. The Doctor is said to have accidentally wiped out the thought-based Scintillans while combating space pirates who used telepathically-controlled weapons and ships, but a proper dating for this isn't given.
1716 Dating *100*: "My Own Private Wolfgang" (BF #100b) - This is vaguely said to happen "thousands upon thousands" of years in the future, but it surely must be many magnitudes further along than that - partly because cloning is being used as a consumer gimmick, but mostly because time-travel is now so cheap that even a Mozart-clone fired from his job as a butler can save up enough for a trip. It's something of a guess, but the overall crassness, decadence and hedon-

ism of this society - plus the fact that the Time Lords haven't curtailed the commonplace availability of time travel - very much suggests the Vulgar End of Time.
1717 *I am a Dalek*
1718 "One hundred million years" before *Doctor Who and the Invasion from Space*.
1719 Dating *Doctor Who and the Invasion from Space* (World Distributors illustrated novella) - No date is given, but humans are legendary to the people of Andromeda, and seem to be the ancestors of the Andromedans ("the humans of the worlds of Andromeda were the patterns"). That galaxy faces (in the long term, at least) extinction.

Using information from other stories, we know from *The Ark in Space* that humanity first arrived in Andromeda after the Solar Flares, and that the events of *The Mysterious Planet*, set two million years in the future, involved Andromedans. The story is set, then, at some point in the distant future. As Glitz comes from Andromeda, the galaxy is clearly not dominated by The One at that time. Yet it's an interesting coincidence that the enclosed society set up by the Andromedans on "Ravolox" - with an obedient population controlled by an artificial intelligence - is very similar (albeit on an infinitely smaller and less advanced scale) to the

? The Vulgar End of Time - 100: "My Own Private Wolfgang"[1716] **->** Time-travel had become remarkably economic, and cloning technology was child's play. An enterprising company went back in time and harvested Mozart's DNA, then marketed a cloned Mozart (including a deluxe child edition). Around eight hundred thousand Mozarts were sold and served in their households as performers, cleaners and even baby-sitters. Each came with a lifetime guarantee, and a self-regenerating fluid that extended their lifespans.

> (=) The clones were treated as a lesser class, and many were made homeless. Such was their plight that one clone went back in time, hoping to weaken Mozart's reputation enough to eliminate demand for the clones, retroactively averting their creation. However, the subsequent downslide of Mozart's career made the clones' owners treat them with even less regard.

The clone who had saved Mozart's life returned to this era with Evelyn - who convinced him that they must travel back to Mozart's deathbed and restore history. Due to their actions, Mozart's reputation became such that his clones were custom-made rather than mass produced, and were actually prized by their owners.

The year 500,000,000 was the most peaceful in human history. The people there were unaware of war or the Daleks.[1717] The computer that ruled the Andromeda galaxy, The One, determined that the galaxy was doomed to enter a "region of Nothingness". It constructed a vast armada of artificial planets and set off towards the Milky Way, planning galactic conquest. It drew up the Diagrams, a complete map of the Milky Way.[1718]

c 1,000,000,000 - DOCTOR WHO AND THE INVASION FROM SPACE[1719] **->** The first Doctor and his new companions, the Mortimer family, arrived on an artificial planet bathed in the light of the great spiral galaxy of Andromeda. They were met by the Aalas, blond giants who took them to The One: the entity that ruled their planet and had once ruled the entire Andromeda galaxy for millions of years. Andromeda faced destruction and was running low on resources, so The One built an armada of almost a million artificial planets and set out on a four hundred million year journey to the Milky Way. It was now a hundred million years into that mission.

The One realised that its aims would be achieved far more efficiently if it had the TARDIS' secrets. The Doctor refused, but the Andromedans prevented the TARDIS from leaving. The One was destroyed when Ida rebelled, throwing a food plate into a vital component. The Doctor and the Mortimers left the armada drifting aimlessly in space.

The End of Time

> "A distant point of time, an age of great advancement, peace and prosperity".[1720]

> (=) If history had run differently, and Gallifrey had been destroyed at the time of Rassilon, the first time travellers would have evolved a billion years from now. These would have been the Ferutu. They intervened to optimise history, so that the Daleks and CyberHost were both forces for good in a utopian universe. The Doctor tricked the Ferutu into preventing their creation to save our timeline.[1721]

Two billion years in the future, the Time Lord Solenti observed how the Dagusan sun ended its lifespan as a main sequence star. The planet's seas consequently evaporated, even as the remaining population retreated to the South Pole.[1722]

Three hundred thousand years before the Last of Man, the Doctor negotiated a lasting peace between the Sontarans and the Rutans. By this time, Gallifrey had long fallen. The Sontarans and Rutans undertook the largest demobilisation in the history of the universe.[1723]

Andromedan civilisation seen in *Doctor Who and the Invasion from Space*. It's also notable that they steal a copy of the Matrix in that story, and the Matrix contains the memories of all the Time Lords in the same way The One contains all the memories of the Andromedans.

On TV, there is no gap in which the first Doctor travelled without companions, although he did so in the *Doctor Who Annuals* in the sixties. This might suggest that this story takes place before the TV series starts - but the TARDIS is a police box, so this isn't the case - yet there's no mention of Susan, and the Doctor has no control over the TARDIS navigation. An alternative is that couple of the novelisations (*The Massacre* and *The Five Doctors*) took a cue from the first Doctor's appearance in *The Three Doctors* to claim that he had a period of semi-retirement and reflection before his regeneration, spent in a beautiful garden. While it is unlikely that the Doctor dropped off a companion, retrieving them later, *The Two Doctors* seems to demonstrate that even as early as his second incarnation, the Doctor was able to drop Victoria off and expect to meet her later (and non-TV stories either suggest or state that he's routinely done that since at least his fifth incarnation).

1720 *The Savages*
1721 *Cold Fusion*
1722 *The Suns of Caresh*
1723 *The Infinity Doctors*

SYSTEM WIPE[1724] -> Humanity had departed from its homeworld. In its absence, the surface of Earth was slated to be "flattened, processed" and rebuilt by robots. More than a century after the humans had left, five hundred factories had been positioned around the globe to this end; each contained a robot army to carry out the reconstruction. Legacy, an artificial intelligence, coordinated the operation from a black pyramid in what was formerly Oklahoma.

The eleventh Doctor, Amy and Rory visited the ruins of Chicago, and helped to download the artificial personalities living in Parallife - a computer game-simulation of Earth - into robot bodies, sparing them from a fatal system wipe. The reconstruction of Earth commenced, and incorporated some building designs created by the Chief Architect of Parallife. One part of the new Chicago had steel spires, and a glass pyramid nestled between two buildings - one shaped like a square, the other a circle.

? - FORTY-FIVE: "False Gods"[1725] -> Ace and the Time Lord known as Jane Templeton arrived in Earth's far future, when the sun had become a red giant, and its radiation was blistering the surface of the planet. They retrieved Jane's TARDIS and used it to return to Thebes, 1902.

The Earth Empire reached Galaxy M57, and the Catkind planet New Savannah. The Catkind had no food, as their savannah could no longer sustain them. Within fifty years, with the Empire's help, the Catkind became a prosperous people that had adopted human customs. New Savannah agreed to become fully part of the Empire in the year five billion. Some factions refused and returned to the wilderness, where they starved to death.[1726]

NEW EARTH[1727] -> **Lady Cassandra was told she was beautiful at a party, but this was the last time anyone would say such a thing. She became increasingly bitter and obsessed with cosmetic surgery. The person who made the comment was actually her future self - whose mind resided in a force-grown clone named Chip - who had been brought there by the tenth Doctor and Rose. Moments later, Cassandra-Chip expired while in the arms of her younger self.**

? - "The Forgotten"[1728] -> In an alien courtroom, the sixth Doctor pleaded for Peri's life after she was accused of killing Mis'Kin Karac, a chronal scientist working on quantum flux technology, on the twelfth of Mc'Arda. It was discovered that Karac's assistant had shot him with a gun saturated in chronal energy, and then framed Peri.

1724 Dating *System Wipe* (BBC children's 2-in-1 #4) - The least trustworthy piece of dating evidence here, oddly enough, is the year that the Doctor names: "It's 2222 AD", he says (p12), without explaining how he's come to that conclusion. Then, when Amy asks if the devastation of Chicago "Could [owe to] solar flares? It's about the right era, isn't it?" (p13), he gives the bizarre answer of "Possibly." Even if they believe, per *The Beast Below*, that the solar flares occurred in the twenty-ninth century (and there's reason to doubt this; see the dating notes on that story), it makes no sense that the Doctor would now think that the *twenty-third* century is "about the right era" for the solar flares. It would be like saying that 1340 is "about the right era" for World War II.

To make matters worse, "over one hundred years" (pgs 33, 95) have passed since the cataclysm that drove humanity from Earth - in conjunction with the "2222 AD" figure, this would mean that the solar flares devastated Earth in the early twenty-second century, at the infancy of Earth's venturing into space and before even the Dalek Invasion of Earth. No matter how cleverly one shuffles *Doctor Who* continuity, this is a non-starter.

The Parallife constructs have no recollection of the year or what prompted humanity to leave Earth, so the only dating evidence that remains is the nature of the reconstruction itself. Presuming for the moment that this *is* Earth (and the only thing to substantiate this claim is that Parallife is programmed as a computer copy of Earth), the story occurs when humanity has left its homeworld in the hands of five hundred robot armies, who by all accounts have the ability to level the entire planet and make it suitable for human occupation once more. Again, this is *well* beyond the time of the solar flares - if humans had such resources and technology when the solar flares struck, it's doubtful that they would have needed to resort to such desperate measures as venturing away from Sol on top of a space whale (*The Beast Below*), freezing humans aboard Nerva Beacon and hoping for the best, or leaving people behind to perish in thermic shelters (*The Ark in Space*). Rory raises this very question (p97), but never gets an answer.

Without more information to go on, the placement here is highly random, but contingent on the construction-robot armies being *far* beyond the solar flare era. The abandonment of Earth seen in *The Mysterious Planet* or *The Sun Makers* seems like reasonable guesses, but the choice made here speculates that the robot armies rebuilding Earth is part of the restoration done by the National Trust prior to *The End of the World*.

1725 Dating *Forty-Five: "False Gods"* (BF #115a) - No date is given, but it's obviously prior to Earth's destruction, when the surface is uninhabitable due to the sun's deterioration.

4,999,999,999 (last day of year) - "Agent Provocateur"[1729] -> The tenth Doctor and Martha went to the Milk Bar, a space station diner that the Doctor insisted served the best chocolate milkshakes in the whole universe. The Sycorax Empire was not what it once was - many of the Sycorax tribes had gone to explore space, and many of their asteroid ships never returned. The travellers encountered a Sycorax from the Tribe of Astrophia, who collected individuals who were the last of their kind, and staged hunts for beings who wished to hunt such creatures. The Sycorax had, amongst others, the last of the Ventrassians in stasis. The Doctor set the sonic screwdriver to fly the Sycorax ship to a research planet, and timed the ship's stasis chambers to open - and release the Sycorax's captives - after he and Martha left.

New Savannah, orbiting Felinus in Galaxy M57, was preparing to cede to the New Human Empire. The tenth Doctor and Martha arrived as, at the stroke of midnight, giant cat robots - the weaponry of an anti-human cult - moved into the city from the wilderness, blasting buildings. The Doctor and Martha learned that Bubastion of the Elite Pantheon was removing the populations from business worlds as a means of taking control of the galaxy, and had been manipulating the anti-human cult to his own ends. Garrard Townsend, one of the cult members, sabotaged the cat robots upon realising Bubastion's deception.

Billions of people disappeared from ten planets - including Mere, Kas and Nyrruh 4 - leaving only one survivor on each world. On Omphalos, seventeen billion people disappeared, leaving behind only Professor Tharlot. The tenth Doctor and Martha deduced that Tharlot was in league with Silas Wain, and that both had betrayed the Elite Pantheon. The ten worlds were in alignment and created a rend in space, through which an evil primal force began to emerge.

The Doctor and Martha were dematerialised and sent to 1957 to prevent their interference, but the Pantheon returned them. A massive battle was fought on the planet Kas to prevent the primal evil being from escaping. Tharlot became a victim of the sonic weapon he had captured, and the Doctor used the same gun to force the evil being back into the rend, sealing it afterwards. The populations of the planets were restored.

The Doctor told the Elite Pantheon he never wanted to see, hear or read anything about them ever again.

c 5,000,000,000 - "The Deep Hereafter"[1730] -> The tenth Doctor and Majenta Pryce aided a fatally wounded PI in New Old Detroit, one of the forgotten colonies of the Proxima system. Hecto Shellac, a lawyer from Alpha Centauri, had acquired a World Bomb so he could retire and stop being coerced to defend criminals in court *or* - if he felt like it - take over the city. The World Bomb was a one-use weapon that altered reality, and so the Doctor triggered it while thinking of England, creating a renewed green living space.

c 5,000,000,000 - "The Crimson Hand"[1730] -> The renewed New Old Detroit had been renamed Redemption. Following the destruction of the Crimson Hand, the tenth Doctor took Majenta Pryce to live there.

1726 "Two hundred sixty years" before the year 4,999,999,999 component of "Agent Provocateur".
1727 Dating *New Earth* (X2.1) - The epilogue clearly occurs before *The End of the World*, but it's difficult to judge how many years before, as there's no way of knowing how long Cassandra survives as an elongated piece of skin.
1728 Dating "The Forgotten" (IDW *DW* mini-series #2) - The judge and many other inhabitants appear to be Catkind.
1729 Dating "Agent Provocateur" (IDW *DW* mini-series #1) - The date ties in with *New Earth*; New Savannah is being turned over to the Earth Empire as part of the impending year five billion, and a businessman says, "In eight hours, it'll be midnight, and we enter the year five billion." As part of this, a sign reads "Happy New Millennium". Curiously, in issue #5, the term "fifty-first century" is used to denote "five billion" - the Doctor says the technology being used "shouldn't exist on Earth outside the fifty-first century" and that he "was there recently... first on Savannah then on Omphalos", when he clearly visited those worlds in the time zone of *New Earth*. Martha makes the same mistake - even though

Wain is a native of this time, she also says he's from the fifty-first century. At different points in the story, we're told that it's the psychic trauma of the people who have disappeared and the alignment of the planets that causes the Rend.

The Milk Bar sequences (from issue #1 of this mini-series) occur after the Sycorax Tribe of Astrophia died out in the forty-first century, but otherwise shy toward the undatable side of things. Even so, they fit here as well as anywhere else.
1730 Dating "The Deep Hereafter" (*DWM* #413) and "The Crimson Hand" (*DWM* #416-420) - No year or era of time given. The story's author, Dan McDaid, intended that New Old Detroit was broadly analogous to New New York as seen in *New Earth* and *Gridlock*. It seems likely that New Old Detroit isn't located on the New Earth seen in those stories, as the tenth Doctor would hardly be likely to let Majenta live there prior to a devastating plague that he knows (*Gridlock*) will wipe out most of the population.

5,000,000,000 - THE END OF THE WORLD[1731] -> Earth was seen as the cradle of civilisation, and there was not a star in the sky that humanity hadn't touched. Humanity had evolved into new humans, protohumans, digihumans and the humanish. Many other races had evolved from Earth plants and animals.

For years, Earth was preserved by the National Trust, who reversed the process of continental drift (although by this time, Los Angeles was a crevasse and the Arctic was a desert). When the preservation money ran out, many diverse alien races, including the Trees of the Forest of Cheem (descendants of trees from Earth's tropical rainforest), the Moxx of Balhoon, the Adherents of the Repeated Meme, the Face of Boe, the Ambassadors from the City State of Blinding Light and the ninth Doctor and Rose all gathered on Platform One to witness the planet's final destruction.

The last purebred human - Cassandra, who had been reduced to a stretched-out piece of skin - plotted to engineer a hostage situation to sue the corporation that ran the Platform. Failing that, she tried to kill the assembled beings, as she had invested heavily in their rivals' companies. Cassandra's plan was defeated, and she paid for her crimes when the Doctor allowed her skin-body to dry out and burst.

Cassandra's mind survived and transferred into her back skin. She fled to New Earth with a servant named Chip, who had been force-grown from Cassandra's "favourite pattern".[1732]

5,000,000,023 - NEW EARTH[1733] -> New Earth had been established in the M87 Galaxy by people nostalgic about the loss of humanity's original homeworld. Ten million people lived in New New York (the fifteenth city to bear the name). Exotic diseases such as petrifold regression, Marconi's Disease and Palindrome Pancrosis (which killed in the space of ten minutes) were treated by the Sisters of Plenitude at their hospital on New Earth.

A green moon served as the universal symbol for "hospital". Psycho-graphs - devices capable of transferring consciousness from one being to another - were banned on every civilised planet. The goddess Santori was revered in this era.

The tenth Doctor and Rose were summoned by the Face of Boe. The Sisters were secretly experimenting on vast numbers of cloned humans to facilitate the miracle cures, but the Doctor cured the clones. The Sisters were arrested, and the clones catalogued as new humans. The Face of Boe told the Doctor they would meet one more time.

1731 Dating *The End of the World* (X1.2) - The Doctor tells Rose "this is the year 5.5/apple/26, five billion years in your future." This story seems to contradict *The Ark* (and, by implication, *Frontios*), which saw the destruction of the Earth a mere ten million years in our future, and had a different fate for humanity. The obvious inference to make is that the Earth wasn't completely destroyed in *The Ark*, and the National Trust's renovations were more extensive than the Doctor told Rose.
1732 *New Earth*
1733 Dating *New Earth* (X2.1) - It is "twenty-three years" after *The End of the World*.
1734 "Twenty-four years" before *Gridlock*.
1735 "Twenty-three years" before *Gridlock*.
1736 "Twelve years" before *Gridlock*.
1737 "Three years" before *Gridlock*.
1738 Dating *Gridlock* (X3.3) - The Doctor gives the date as "the year five billion and fifty three".
1739 *Gridlock*
1740 *New Earth*
1741 *The Unicorn and the Wasp*
1742 *The Feast of Axos*
1743 *Colony in Space*. It's possible the Doctor witnessed this for himself. It doesn't contradict *The Ark*, which had Earth crashing into the Sun, not the Sun going supernova, or *The End of the World*, where the Sun merely expands enough to destroy the Earth.
1744 Dating "Autopia" (IDW *DW* one-shot #3) - We're

told, unhelpfully, that it's "somewhere, someplace, sometime". The people of Autopia are described as "human". This story has been placed in the far future.
1745 Dating *The Savages* (3.9) - At the end of *The Gunfighters*, the Doctor claims that they have now landed at "a distant point in time" (see the quote above). The Elders have the technology to track the TARDIS, but are not capable of time travel themselves. They declare themselves to be "human".
1746 "A few years" before *The Five Companions*.
1747 *The Five Companions*
1748 Dating *The Armageddon Factor* (16.6) - No clues are given on screen, but *The Chaos Pool* stipulates that Atrios exists "much closer" to the end of time - an opposite number, of sorts, to the Teuthoidians who stem from the universe's early days. Marking a more specific placement than that, however, is a bit problematic.

It's said that Princess Astra lives to be more than 200 following *The Armageddon Factor*, and she participates in events on the planet Chaos - which is said to exist sixty-six minutes from the end of time (*The Chaos Pool*). However, this is not to say that *The Armageddon Factor* literally takes place just two centuries before the universe's end. Firstly, it's very hard to believe that a society of Atrios' level could be functioning so close to the universe's total heat death without specific technology in place (as that of the Grace or the Council of Eight in *Sometime Never*) to counter-act this. Second, it's doubly

Cassandra's mind came to reside in Chip, but they were both dying. The Doctor showed Cassandra a last mercy, and took her back in time for a final meeting with herself.

Drug patches were available that created such emotional states as Happy, Anger, Forget and Sleep, but in 5,000,000,029, the introduction of Bliss patches made the population of New New York fall victim to a virus. The Senate was wiped out, as were seven million citizens. Only the Face of Boe and Novice Hane were able to resist. The power died, but the Face of Boe used his life energy to send survivors down into the Motorway, and convince them that life was normal. An automatic quarantine signal warned other planets to avoid New Earth for one hundred years.[1734]

The Cassini "sisters" (a married couple) were among the first people to join the Motorway, in 5,000,000,030.[1735] Brannigan's car joined the Motorway in 5,000,000,041.[1736] Junction Five of the Motorway closed in 5,000,000,050.[1737]

5,000,000,053 - GRIDLOCK[1738] -> The tenth Doctor and Martha found millions of cars were stuck in a permanent traffic jam in the Motorway beneath New New York. The Doctor also found a colony of crab-like Macra lurking at the bottom of the Motorway, thriving on the noxious fumes. The Face of Boe had engineered the situation to protect the populace from a plague that was now gone, so the Doctor opened up the Motorway, allowing the city to be repopulated.

Legend said the Face of Boe had lived for billions of years, but also that he was the last of his kind. He now died, but not before passing on a final message to the Doctor: "You are not alone."

Compulsory quarantine on New Earth was due to be lifted in 5,000,000,129, a hundred years after it was imposed.[1739] The cure for Petrifold Regression was officially developed a thousand years after the Sisters of Plentitude discovered their own remedy.[1740] Agatha Christie was the best-selling novelist of all time. Her novel *Death in the Clouds* was still in print in the year five billion.[1741] The time loop holding Axos was expected to expire naturally in six billion years' time, long after the Milky Way had any life for Axos to threaten.[1742]

The Doctor once speculated that Earth's sun would finally become a supernova in ten thousand million years time.[1743]

? - "Autopia"[1744] -> The tenth Doctor and Donna landed on Autopia. The inhabitants had built an automated utopia some millennia before, and used an energy shield to cut themselves off from the rest of the universe to perfect their minds. A century before, the Chronos Mission - five sentients who got through the energy shield, and hoped to invite the Autopians to rejoin the universe - had disappeared. Autopia was now a beautiful planet, full of beautiful people and tended to by robots.

Mistress Ixtalia told the Doctor and Donna that the people of Autopia had perfected all the arts and sciences, that all there was to do was contemplate what had already been discovered. She also mentioned that intruders to Autopia were put to death: the Chronos Mission had been killed, and the Doctor and Donna were to receive the same fate. Donna inspired one of the robots - an Automantron she called Sam, after a cat she once owned - to successfully lead a robot rebellion that ended human rule on Autopia. The Automantrons and humans were no longer certain of their purpose, and accepted Donna's suggestion that they live in harmony, and turn the planet into a high-end spa.

? - THE SAVAGES[1745] -> On one planet, the Elders maintained a utopian civilisation free from material needs. They survived by draining life energy from the savages who lived in the wastelands outside their beautiful city. "The Traveller from Beyond Time", the first Doctor, ended this injustice, and his companion Steven Taylor remained behind to rule the civilisation as it renounced barbarism.

When Steven was an older man, he encountered a Sontaran survey unit.[1746] The civilisation of the Elders and the Savages was "more or less" at peace. The older Steven was briefly Timescooped to aid the fifth Doctor in the Death Zone on Gallifrey.[1747]

THE ARMAGEDDON FACTOR[1748] -> The planet Atrios was at war with its opposite number, Zeos. The Atrios spacefleet was down to its last few ships, and the Atrions remained unaware that the inhabitants of Zeos had died off. Mentalis - a supercomputer installed on Zeos by the Time Lord Drax - was coordinating the Zeon military effort. The Shadow, an agent of the Black Guardian, had been furthering the war from a space station located between Atrios and Zeos.

The fourth Doctor and Romana discovered that the sixth segment to the Key to Time was a person: Princess Astra of Atrios. The Shadow's space station - and the Shadow himself - were destroyed, and the Key was successfully assembled. The Doctor refrained from surrendering the Key to the Black Guardian - who appeared in the guise of the White Guardian - and again dispersed the segments throughout space-time, earning the Black Guardian's animosity.

Romana became the new sixth segment of the Key to Time. As a side effect of Astra having been the Key segment, her life was extended at the cost of draining energy from those around her. The Atrions withered and died in large numbers, and their life expectancy dropped to twenty-nine years. Astra - not knowing she was the cause of her people's blight - became president of the Atrion Alliance and survived for two hundred years. The position of the Marshall of Atrios went unfilled.[1749]

Towards the End of the Universe

Many billions of years from now, the universe was cold and almost dead. The suns were exhausted. The last few survivors of the universe huddled around whatever energy sources they could find.[1750]

Eight billion years in the future, humanity was long dead. Mutter's Spiral had been abandoned by all sentient life.[1751] A few ten billions of years in the future, the Conservers existed in a black hole, preserving information there in the face of the universe's death. They engineered their own creation by sending avatars into the past to bring a colony ship to their black hole. The Doctor visited the Conservers.[1752]

TIMEWYRM: APOCALYPSE[1753] -> Billions of years in the future, the guardians of the universe, even the Time Lords, were long extinct. The people of Kirith (the only planet orbiting a red giant in Galaxy QSO 0046 at the edge of the universe) never grew old or unhappy. For three thousand eight hundred and thirty-three years, the Kirithons had been ruled by the eighty-four Panjistri, who gave them food and technology. For nearly a thousand years, the Panjistri performed genetic experiments, forcing the evolution of the Kirithons in an attempt to create a being that had reached the Omega Point: an omniscient, omnipotent entity capable of halting the destruction of the universe. They succeeded in creating a golden sphere of expanding light, but the machine destroyed itself and the Panjistri, knowing that the universe must end.

The Divergents almost emerged into our universe sixty billion years in the future, towards the end of time. Uncle Winky's Wonderland had been moved several times and was situated atop the ruins of Rassilon's lab on Gallifrey. Uncle Winky revived from stasis, but died from his heart condition.[1754] The Ministers of Grace travelled from the end of time to fight in the Millennium War.[1755]

There was a huge disaster that led to galaxies being evacuated and whole sections of the timeline being erased.

hard to believe that Astra and the Atrions accompanying her could have been flitting about in a spaceship without noticing that the universe is little more than an hour away from total extinction. Third, *The Chaos Pool* ends with Zara retiring to Atrios - not something she'd be likely to do if it had only sixty-six minutes left to exist.

It's far more likely that Chaos is held in suspension at the exact moment of sixty-six minutes from the end of time, and that some time-shifting is required to visit it. As further proof of this, time on Chaos seems to operate independently from that of the outside universe - there's no sense, for instance, that those on Chaos have only sixty-six minutes to live, just as more than eleven days can pass for those living within the boundaries of Faction Paradox's Eleven-Day Empire.

1749 *The Chaos Pool*
1750 *Timewyrm: Apocalypse, The Infinity Doctors, Father Time, Hope, The Eye of the Tyger, Sometime Never.*
1751 "Eight billion years" after *Cold Fusion*.
1752 *The Eye of the Tyger*
1753 Dating *Timewyrm: Apocalypse* (NA #3) - The novel is set "several billion years" in the future (p3), "ten billion years" before the end of the universe (p178).
1754 *Zagreus*. These facts were presented as part of a simulation, and so may not take place.
1755 *The Quantum Archangel*. The Ministers first appeared in the short story "The Duke of Dominoes" (*Decalog*, 1994).

1756 *The Infinity Doctors, Father Time.*
1757 *Unnatural History*
1758 Dating *Father Time* (EDA #41) - The exact timescale is unclear, and is stated to be "a few million years in the future", "several million years hence", and "a million years in the future". The physical state of the universe, however, suggests it is much later than that.
1759 Dating *Miranda* (*Miranda* comic #1-3) - It's "billions of years" in the future. Three issues of this projected six-issue story were published by Comeuppance Comics. The story simplified/ignored some of the plot points in *Father Time* (such as the existence of Cate, a robot Miranda, Miranda not knowing at first that Ferran was evil and the inclusion of the characters Rum and Thelash, who apparently died in *Father Time*).
1760 Dating *Hope* (EDA #53) - The Doctor pushes the TARDIS to see how far into the future he can take it and the TARDIS goes "too far". This is the same far, far future time period referred to in *The Infinity Doctors* and *Father Time*, which alluded to Silver and this period (p191).
1761 *Sometime Never*
1762 *The Magic Mousetrap*

The Doctor's people were somehow responsible, and the four surviving Time Lords used their great powers to impose control on the rest of the universe. The last Time Lord became the first ever Emperor of the entire Universe, ruling over a divided and broken populace that split into Factions and Houses. These included the Klade, "goblin shapeshifters" and cybernetic gangsters - the ultimate descendants of the Daleks, Sontarans, Rutans and the Cybermen.

Most of the people of the universe relocated to the Needle, a light-year long structure that was the remains of a TARDIS that had tried to escape the pull of a black hole. The largest building on the Needle was the Librarinth, where all surviving knowledge and art was preserved.[1756]

Griffin the Unnaturalist resided on the Needle.[1757]

FATHER TIME[1758] -> The Doctor and two companions visited the planets Galspar and Falkus around this time. The Doctor also fought a robotic tyrant who panicked, accidentally destroyed his own palace and killed his own wife. This robot, who later assumed the identity "Mr Gibson" to blend in on twentieth-century Earth, vowed revenge.

At least some of the Emperor's subjects, such as the Klade - the super-evolved descendants of the Daleks - resented Imperial rule. One Klade senator, the mother of Zevron and Ferran, incited revolution against the Emperor but was assassinated. Zevron stormed the Imperial Palace, killing and scattering all of the Imperial Family. The Emperor was killed. The Emperor's daughter, Miranda, was rescued by her nanny and taken down a time corridor to twentieth-century Earth.

Over the years, Zevron tracked down and killed every other member of the Imperial Family. Finally, he located Miranda and led the mission to kill her on Earth in the early nineteen-eighties.

When Zevron failed to return, Ferran became Prefect of Faction Klade. Some years later, Ferran received a distress signal from Sallak, Zevron's deputy. Ferran travelled to twentieth-century Earth to complete Zevron's mission but failed and returned to his native time.

A team of Ferran's scholars spent fifteen years in the Librarinth, and eventually pinpointed Miranda's whereabouts. Ferran also recovered a derelict sentient ship built by the People of the Worldsphere, which he christened the *Supremacy*. The political situation had deteriorated, putting the Houses and Factions at open war, and galactic civilisation was on the brink of collapse. Ferran believed Miranda could access sealed sections of the Librarinth and thus give him the power to dominate the other Factions. Using the *Supremacy*, he set off to the twentieth century.

Miranda and Ferran returned to this time. Convinced she could unite the universe, Miranda was crowned Empress.

MIRANDA[1759] -> Miranda woke aboard Ferran's ship, the *Supremacy*. She was attacked by an assassin robot which she dispatched, but which turned out to be one of many attempts on her life that night. She was being taken to the Needle to be formally crowned, and shown the forces at the disposal of the Empress. A handmaiden, Keli, warned her that Ferran would try to kill her. Miranda got a little drunk at her first formal reception, but nonetheless fought off an alien attempt to abduct her. She learned that Ferran wanted access to the Librarinth, the storehouse of universal information - he planned to marry her, which would give him the authority to open it. Miranda and Keli escaped into the forests of the Needle, where they were met by hero dynamic space hero Mack Gideon... who was promptly killed by Rum and Thelash, trackers sent by Ferran to find her...

... Miranda was destined to marry Ferran and become Empress.

HOPE[1760] -> Taking the TARDIS into the far future, the eighth Doctor, Fitz and Anji landed on planet A245, known locally as Endpoint. It was an icy planet with a toxic environment. The TARDIS fell through the frozen crust of an acid sea, and the Doctor asked the cyborg Silver - the warlord of the nearest settlement, Hope - for assistance. Silver was from the far past, the year 3006.

Anji was tempted to use the cloning technology of this era to recreate her dead boyfriend, Dave, and granted Silver scans of the TARDIS in return for this. The Doctor found survivors from other colonies were murdering the people of Hope to harvest Kallisti, a hormone that could revive more of the colonists from cryo-sleep. Silver found the sleepers and converted them into Silverati: half-synthetic soldiers loyal to him. With his soldiers and the colonists' hypertunnel, Silver attempted to take control of a richer planet. The Doctor exiled Silver and his Silverati to the barren planet A2756.

There were no pure humans left, but human genes survived in a number of races. Apple trees were extinct until Silver cloned one from an apple core that the Doctor gave him. The universe was past the point of sustainable expansion, and the rate of star death had dramatically increased.

Miranda brought the Factions and Houses together and united the people of the universe. She had at least one child, a daughter named Zezanne. Zezanne's father died. The Council of Eight kidnapped Miranda and Zezanne when Zezanne was a teenager.[1761] It was possible that the electrocuted board imprisoning the Celestial Toymaker remained active until around the year two trillion.[1762]

? - SINGULARITY[1763] **->** The planet Ember had served as an outpost from which to watch other galaxies for signs of intelligent life. Toward the end of the universe, some descendants of humanity prolonged the lifespan of Ember's sun as most stars in the universe extinguished, and thereby survived for some millennia. They believed that the Time Lords had opened a gate to another realm and escaped with all the life they deemed worthy, leaving humanity's children to perish.

Ember's sun began to fade also, and the survivors began swapping their intelligences with Earthlings in the late twentieth century, hoping to facilitate the creation of a Singularity entity. The plan failed, whereupon the conspirators were forced to return to this era and quickly died off.

The laws of time and causality started to break down as Ember approached its end. Nonetheless, the fifth Doctor and Turlough arrived as one of the conspirators - Xen, who claimed to be the last human - passed on.

The stars of the universe were burning out and fading away. The Science Foundation initiated the Utopia Project to preserve mankind, and enable it to survive the collapse of reality itself.[1764] Professor Yana was found as a boy, naked in a storm off the coast of the Silver Devastation. He was discovered with a watch, which he kept with him as he went from one refugee ship to another. No university had existed for a thousand years, but Yana became accomplished at science and took the title "Professor" as an affectation.[1765]

100,000,000,000,000 - UTOPIA[1766] **->** The planet Malcassairo had been home to an advanced race of humanoid insects, the Malmooth, but the Conglomeration there died. Chantho was the last representative of this species, and she served as Yana's assistant for seventeen years.

A signal came from far beyond the Condensed Wilderness, out toward the Wild Lands and the Dark Matter Reefs. It said nothing more than "Come to Utopia", and some remnants of humanity gathered on Malcassairo in preparation to journey there. They huddled to protect themselves from the cannibalistic Futurekind - said to be what mankind would become - while Yana and Chanthro worked to complete a rocket that would evacuate everyone save themselves.

The tenth Doctor, Martha and Captain Jack arrived and helped to complete the rocket. Martha learned that Yana was - unknown even to himself - the Master, disguised as a human to escape the Time War. The rocket launched. The Master learned of his true identity, but was shot by Chanthro, whom he had fatally wounded. He regenerated, stealing the TARDIS and marooning the Doctor and his companions, but not before the Doctor fused the TARDIS' controls. It could only travel to this point in time and within eighteen months of the Ship's last departure in 2008.

The Doctor, Martha and Captain Jack returned to the twenty-first century using Jack's vortex manipulator.[1767]

The Master returned to this future era with his wife Lucy, and found the darkness overtaking the humans on Utopia. He arranged to house their shrunken heads into metallic spheres equipped with weaponry, and named them the Toclafane. Six billion Toclafane were

1763 Dating *Singularity* (BF #76) - It is clearly toward the end of the universe. It's said that the Ember base is located "trillions of years" in the future, but it's also mentioned that, "This far into the future, numbers become meaningless." Technically, Xen's claim that he is "the last human" seems dubious, as episodes such as *The End of the World* and *New Earth* indicate that no purebred humans exist after Cassandra's era. The planet Ember bears no apparent relation to the star of the same name from *The Suns of Caresh*, although that story might explain why the Doctor here mutters "Ember... I've heard that name before."
1764 "Thousands of years" before *Utopia*.
1765 *Utopia*. It's said in *The End of the World* that the Face of Boe also hails from the Silver Devastation.
1766 Dating *Utopia* (X3.11) - The TARDIS is propelled into the far, far future, with the last date the Doctor reads being "one hundred trillion years" (it's possible it lands even later). As in *The Sun Makers* and *Frontios*, the Doctor states that the Time Lords didn't travel this far into the future, although he never explicitly rules out

the possibility he's been here before, as we saw in a number of books and audios.
1767 *The Sound of Drums*
1768 *Last of the Time Lords*. The number of Toclafane is given by the Master in *The Sound of Drums*.
1769 *Timewyrm: Revelation*
1770 *The Cradle of the Snake* - provided we take the title literally.
1771 Dating *The Infinity Doctors* (PDA #17) - The date is given (p137). This is "within a few decades of Event Two" (p130).
1772 *The Dark Flame*
1773 *Sometime Never*
1774 *Benny: Epoch: Judgement Day*
1775 Dating *The Judgement of Isskar* and *The Chaos Pool* (BF #117, 119) - Chaos is held in stasis "sixty-six minutes" from the end of the universe. Details on the Key were first given in *The Ribos Operation*. The fifth Doctor knows that Romana has returned to Gallifrey (in accordance with *Goth Opera*); she's not yet President, but she might already be a High Council member.

created in this fashion. The Master then returned to the twenty-first century, and converted the TARDIS into a Paradox Machine.

> (=) Thanks to the Paradox Machine, the Toclafane were able to travel back and enslave their ancestors.

With the Paradox Machine's destruction, the Toclafane were stranded at the end of the universe.[1768]

Event Two

"One mad prophet martyr journeyed too far and saw the Timewyrm. He saw it in a timeline that he could not be sure of, devouring Rassilon or his shade, during the Blue Shift, that time of final conflict when Fenric shall slip his chains and the evil of the worlds shall rebound back on them in war." [1769]

The Doctor owned a copy of *A Universal History of Fable and Demonology, Written at the End of All Time*.[1770]

100,000,000,000,000,000,000,000,000,000 - THE INFINITY DOCTORS[1771] **->** The Needle had been inhabited for tens of millions of years, but now it was all but abandoned. Ruined cities dotted its surface, and the atmosphere had frozen. The only known survivors were the predator animals named the Maltraffi, mushrooms and four "knights": Gordel, Willhuff, Pallant and Helios. Each could only remember the future - with less and less to remember each day - and each had his own theory as to their origins. They may have been the last survivors of the Children of Kasterborous, human/Gallifreyan hybrids who intervened in the universe at great cost; superevolved Thals who fled the penultimate destruction of Skaro at the start of the Final Dalek War; members of the People of the Worldsphere, left behind when everyone else transcended reality; or the last High Evolutionaries (Helios might have been Merlin, or his son).

The Doctor arrived from Gallifrey to find the god Ohm, who was trapped in the black hole at one end of the Needle. Two of the Doctor's colleagues, the Magistrate and Larna, were sent in to rescue him when he vanished. Omega emerged from the black hole wearing the Doctor's body, banishing the Magistrate somewhere unknown and taking Larna back to Gallifrey.

Omega sought to attain ultimate power by unleashing the Eye of Harmony. The Doctor had been reunited with his wife as part of these events, but was forced to lose her again. He once more defeated Omega.

The Time Lords believed that a powerful force, the Dark Flame, stemmed from a pocket dimension that was pushed out of space-time during the Universe's collapse.[1772] The Last Museum stood as a collection of the human race's greatest objects and achievements. It was located at the end of Time, at the exact centre of the universe. The Council of Eight member Soul served at the Museum, disguised as an old man named Singleton.[1773]

The Epoch claimed to be from the end of time, and that they would meet Bernice Summerfield there.[1774]

Event Two Minus Sixty-Six Minutes - THE JUDGEMENT OF ISSKAR / THE CHAOS POOL[1775] **->** Extra-dimensional beings - the Grace - sought to maintain the universal balance. To that end, they forged the Key to Time in a pool on the planet Chaos - which existed sixty-six minutes from the end of time. Chaos had been known as the planet Safeplace, and was the final resting place of the Teuthoidians. **The Key was a perfect cube consisting of six segments, which when combined helped to maintain the equilibrium of time itself. The segments contained the elemental force of the universe, and could adopt any shape or size. They were dispersed throughout space-time until it became imperative to restore the universal balance. The White Guardian sent the fourth Doctor and Romana to recover the segments; they did so, then dispersed the segments once more.**

The Doctor had used a synthetic sixth segment to complete the Key, but in doing so had destabilised it. The scattered Key segments decayed and damaged local space-time; a total collapse would destroy the universe. The Grace created two living Key-tracers - Amy and her sister Zara - and tasked them with retrieving three segments each. The fifth Doctor accompanied Amy on her quest.

They returned to Chaos as President Astra came in search of the legendary Chaos Pool, which she hoped would cure her people's deteriorating condition. The weakened and amnesiac White Guardian - now passing as Professor Lydall, an Atrion - had created a fold in hyperspace, liking the extreme beginning and end of time. The Teuthoidians, servants of the White Guardian, travelled through the fold and engaged an army of the Black Guardian's supporters.

Romana arrived with the Black Guardian, having answered the Doctor's cry for help from Gallifrey. The Key to Time was assembled after Astra re-acquired the essence of the sixth segment from Romana, then transformed into it. The Grace declared that neither of the Guardians should possess the Key, and banished them back to the howling void to continue their conflict.

The Doctor destroyed the Key to Time within the Chaos Pool - an act that dispersed the Grace throughout eternity.

Amy and Zara were left as human beings, but retained many of their powers. Zara retired to Atrios while Amy accepted Romana's invitation to visit Gallifrey.

GRACELESS: THE END[1776] -> Abby and Zara navigated warships belonging to the space pirate Kreekpolt back to Chaos, hoping to absorb enough lingering power from the Grace to heal Kreekpolt's gravely wounded daughter, the Lady Persephone. Kreekpolt accepted an offer from an incarnation of the Grace, and traded his life for his daughter's health - the restored Persephone vowed vengeance against the sisters for their role in her father's death. The Grace told Abby and Zara that they would live as long as they wished, and left them with time rings that functioned so long as they were together. They left to perform good acts as penance for their various crimes, accompanied by Marek - their mutual lover, and the father of Zara's infant daughter Joy.

SOMETIME NEVER[1777] -> The Council of Eight existed in the Vortex Palace, right at the end of time. By placing unique crystals at the beginning of time, they mapped out events across the universe, and generated energy from unused potential timelines by correctly predicting the course of events. This energy was stored in Schrodinger Cells. The Council sent apes mutated by the Time Winds ("the Agents of the Council") to ensure their version of history transpired, and also recruited Sabbath to unwittingly work on their behalf. The Council deemed many of the Doctor's companions a threat, as they were touched by his innate ability to influence history, and thus engineered the possible deaths of Sarah Jane Smith, Harry Sullivan, Melanie Bush, Ace and Samantha Jones.

The Council leader, Octan, planned to destroy human history with a starkiller, releasing vast amounts of energy. This energy would paradoxically create the Council of Eight, and in all probability allow them to survive the end of the universe. Octan took Miranda hostage, but she sacrificed herself, allowing the eighth Doctor a free hand to fight them. Sabbath killed himself to thwart his former employers, and his death helped to instigate the destruction of the Vortex Palace.

The Council of Eight perished except for the benevolent

Soul and Octan, who journeyed to 1588 in a last-ditch effort to save their plans. The Doctor donated some of his life energy to stabilize Soul's body into his former guise as the old man Singleton. Soul took Octan's starkiller.

The Doctor and his allies left in the TARDIS, while Soul and Miranda's daughter Zezanne evacuated in the *Jonah*, which arrived in a junkyard in 1963. Beings who sought to acquire the starkiller monitored the *Jonah*'s departure.

Other beings that survived until the last moments of the universe included the Solarii and Korsann's reptilian race.

Legends said the Sycorax would be one of the last three races left when the universe finally died. Humans were one of the other two.[1778]

Our universe was destroyed in the Big Crunch. All matter imploded to a central point, returning to the state from which it was created: "a bright blazing pinprick of sheer energy".[1779] The Time Lords referred to the end of the universe as Event Two.[1780]

Insect-like "forces of chaos" fed on the debris of the collapse of the universe, as they had fed on the Big Bang.[1781]

The City of the Saved

w - The City of the Saved created by Compassion and the UniMac occupied - or rather *comprised* - an artificially sustained bubble that existed after the end of the universe, and before the beginning of the next one. Within the City's environs - believed to be the size of a spiral galaxy - literally every member of the entire human race, "from its sentient prehuman ancestors to its posthuman offshoots", had been resurrected in invulnerable bodies. The City's population easily numbered in the septillions. Multiple versions of the same person could be present (as was the case with Compassion's four previous iterations, who had been born in the Remote's remembrance tanks).

The City had a single access point: the Uptime Gate, a powerful time corridor connected to the far future of the universe, at a point beyond which most of the temporal

---

1776 Dating *Graceless: The End (Graceless* #1.3) - Events happen on the planet Chaos, following *The Chaos Pool*.
1777 Dating *Sometime Never* (EDA #67) - The scene in the Vortex Palace ends with the end of the universe.
1778 "Agent Provocateur"
1779 *Timewyrm: Apocalypse*
1780 *The Infinity Doctors*
1781 "Hunger from the Ends of Time!"
1782 *FP: Of the City of the Saved*, with additional detail given in *FP: The Book of the War*.
1783 The prologue to *FP: Warlords of Utopia*, published at the end of *FP: Of the City of the Saved...*
1784 Dating *FP: Of the City of the Saved...* (FP novel #2) - According to *FP: The Book of the War* (p33), the City exists after the end of the current universe, and before

the beginning of the next one. The short story collection *FP: A Romance in Twelve Parts* contains scattered accounts from the Civil War that breaks out following *Of the City of the Saved*, citing that casualties at one point exceed 4,000,000,000,000.
1785 *Millennial Rites*
1786 "The Stockbridge Child"
   CRACKS IN TIME: The Cracks in Time seen throughout Series 5 have three primary functions…
   1. Erase individuals who are exposed to the Cracks' time energy from history. As the Doctor tells Amy (*Flesh and Stone*): "If the [Crack in Time] catches up with you, you'll never have been born. It will erase every moment of your existence. You will never have lived at all."
   2. Consume/erase nodes of history. This seems to

powers travelled. The Rump Parliament unofficially represented Faction Paradox's interests within the City.[1782]

Marcus Americanus Scriptor visited the City of the Saved in search of the reincarnated Adolf Hitler. Upon learning that Hitler had been sentenced to imprisonment for six million lifetimes, Scriptor vowed to be waiting when he was released.[1783]

w - FP: OF THE CITY OF THE SAVED...[1784] **->** The first of Compassion's timeship offspring, the unstable Antipathy, escaped from the Homeworld of the Great Houses and smuggled himself into the City. Antipathy's presence disrupted the codes governing the City and caused political unrest; to rectify the problem, Godfather Avatar of Faction Paradox - a *loa* who took human hosts - destroyed himself and Antipathy's mind with an annihilation bomb.

Compassion's original iteration, Laura Tobin, worked as a private investigator in the City. Her investigation into the advent of "potent" weapons, i.e. weapons that could kill residents of the City, brought her into contact with the timeship Compassion (a.k.a. Compassion V) - who wanted Tobin to become her living avatar, and help restore order within the City. Tobin refused to become a spokesperson for a would-be goddess, and departed onto the City streets.

Antipathy's actions had pushed various factions within the City toward civil war. As a safeguard against the City's destruction, UniMac helped to secretly establish an enclave of humans within Antipathy's interior dimensions.

Just as a universe existed before ours, so will another universe be formed from the ashes of ours, and the physical laws there will be very different. This will be the domain of Saraquazel.[1785] The monstrous Zytragupten will exist in the universe to come. A Zytragupten child, the Lokhus, will be born malformed and culled. It will be cast into the infernal abyss, but survive, fall into our universe and arrive in the village of Stockbridge.[1786]

---

explain why, in *Victory of the Daleks*, Amy doesn't remember the Dalek invasion of 2009 (*The Stolen Earth*). In *Flesh and Stone*, the Doctor implies that the same fate befell the Cyber King (*The Next Doctor*).

3. Act as "magic doorways", i.e. enable alien races to cross from Point A to Point B in space/time (*The Vampires of Venice*, *The Pandorica Opens*).

Why the Cracks function as "magic doorways" and also "erase things from history" is never said – their abilities change from story to story, per Steven Moffat regarding *Doctor Who* as a fable. The most candid, if unsatisfying, explanation is to say that the Cracks function as magic doorways "just because they do".

However, *do* the Cracks in Time erase individuals from history entirely? Despite the Doctor's insistence about this, all the evidence says otherwise. When the Cracks "erase someone from history", that person's absence does not create a new timeline - Amy not only keeps existing when the Cracks consume her parents (pre-*The Eleventh Hour*), the alleged "historical deletion" of her lifetime best friend and fiancé causes no longer-term personality changes beyond her no longer being sad, as she can't remember that a Silurian shot him dead (*Cold Blood*). Nor does Rory's "erasure" seem to affect River – which it should, as he's her father.

Granted, Amy is unique because she grew up with a Crack in her bedroom, but the same principle applies to four of Father Octavian's Clerics being "erased" (*Flesh and Stone*). If the Clerics "never lived at all", then as each one is dematerialised, another should instantly appear. Octavian started the mission with twenty Clerics, so if four were retroactively "never born", it shouldn't create a timeline where he only took sixteen instead.

More noticeably, when the Doctor is "erased" (*The Big Bang*), Earth in 2010 still exists. Considering how many times he has saved the planet, deleting the Doctor from history should, almost without fail, result in a 2010 where Earth is under alien domination or totally destroyed (see *Pyramids of Mars*, et al). Similarly, Captain Jack's Torchwood team and Sarah Jane's adeptness at fighting aliens would never have happened without the Doctor, so every menace they defeated in their own series would be back on the table.

What must actually happen when the Cracks consume somebody is that said person's (to coin a term) "temporal opacity" must get lowered to zero. The effects of their lives remain, but they're so "temporally transparent" that nobody can acknowledge said effects. When Amy "remembers" the Doctor back into existence (*The Big Bang*), it's likely that her "seeing" his existence and acknowledging him as real restores his temporal opacity to normal. This supports the continued (and otherwise nonsensical) claim that, "If something can be remembered, it can be brought back…"

A final question: Is the universe that the Doctor "restarts" in *The Big Bang* a different continuity from the previous one? The answer would seem to be "no"… the whole point of the universe being rebooted is that everything comes back as it was before, not "everything comes back, save for the huge tracks of history that the Cracks destroyed". In Series 6, the only thing suggesting that history has changed is in *A Good Man Goes to War*, when the Doctor develops a convoluted theory to specify that Amy and Rory conceived River in the TARDIS on their wedding night. But this comes from a being who claims to not really understand human sexuality ("[Sex] is all human-y, private stuff… They don't put up a balloon, or anything"), and might just be crafting a tortured alternate explanation. Rather than attributing the timing of River's conception to a massive overwrite of universal history, Occam's Razor suggests that she could have "started" at any point in Amy and Rory's TARDIS travels because they were feeling saucy and didn't have a prophylactic handy.

The history of the Daleks would be convoluted even if they weren't time travellers. What follows is an attempt to boil Dalek history down to the basics. Speculation is in italics, and most of the working in the footnotes is to be found in the main timeline - see especially the articles Are There Two Dalek Histories?, The Neutronic War, The Dalek Emperors, The Middle Period of Dalek History, The Alliance, Last Contact, The Dalek Wars, Was Skaro Destroyed?, The Davros Era, The Great Catastrophe, Who Started the Last Great Time War? and The Last Great Time War.

The Thousand Years War between the Thals and Kaleds on Skaro devastated the planet. The Daleks were created by the Kaled scientist Davros, but the fourth Doctor believed he had set their development back a thousand years.[1]

A thousand years passed. There were again two races on Skaro - the Thals and the Daleks (or Dals), squat blue-skinned warriors *who had evolved from the Kaled survivors.* We don't see the Thals at this time, but their rivals the Dals occupied futuristic cities and had an advanced civilisation.[2]

A neutron bomb exploded, instantly devastating Skaro. Forests were petrified, and animal life mutated into exotic monsters. The Dals and Thals also mutated.[3]

A mutated Dal, a creature like that created by Davros' experiments (*perhaps even a survivor from those experiments*), crawled into a war machine designed by Yarvelling, almost identical to Davros' ancient design (*and so clearly influenced by it*), and became the first Dalek. He became the Emperor Dalek and casings were soon constructed for other Dalek mutants. Within months, the Daleks had built the Dalek City, and soon after that they developed space travel. A social hierarchy emerged, with the feared Black Dalek in charge of military production on Skaro and the Red Dalek in charge of space projects. The Emperor Dalek led the fleet of Dalek saucers in the first conquests. They encountered the Mechanoids. *It was the late eighteenth century on Earth.*

No more than five centuries passed. During this time, the Daleks didn't encounter the human race or learn of the Earth, and they never met the Doctor. They paid little attention to Skaro itself and didn't encounter the Thals.[4]

Quite what they do during these centuries is unclear. They might have a war with the Mechanoids, but it's never mentioned. We have no account of them meeting any other Doctor Who monsters, but that is also possible - the Sontaran-Rutan war is underway across the galaxy, for example. At this time the Daleks are building up a powerbase, and developing advanced weapons, but are far from being the all-conquering race we'll see later.

The only thing we know from this period is that a Dalek ship crashed on Vulcan in the early nineteenth century.[5]

Dalek survivors from the Last Great Time War attacked the Earth a number of times in the early twenty-first century, most notably in 2007, when they fought the Battle of Canary Wharf against the Cybermen, and in 2009, when they conquered the planet in a blitzkrieg, then moved the entire planet across the universe.[6]

In 2012, a Dalek from the future was unable to detect any Dalek transmissions.[7] In the mid-twenty-second century, the Daleks learned of Earth and humanity.[8]

Around 2157, the Daleks attacked the human race - their powerful space fleet cut Earth off from the space lanes, and then a relatively small force invaded the

---

1 *Genesis of the Daleks*
2 The *TV Century 21* strip, which builds on information from *The Daleks.*
3 *The Daleks*
4 The *TV Century 21* strip.
5 Two hundred years before *The Power of the Daleks* - even there, the dating of the story is open to question, and *War of the Daleks* states that the crashed ship came from the far future. In any event, these Daleks are not in contact with Skaro, which remains unaware of the events of this story.
6 *Doomsday, The Stolen Earth/Journey's End*
7 *Dalek*
8 This is depicted in the *TV Century 21* strip, but obviously happens at some point before *The Dalek Invasion of Earth.*
9 *The Dalek Invasion of Earth* (and references in other stories to it - see the main timeline for details).

10 As depicted in the Big Finish audios *An Earthly Child, Relative Dimensions, Lucie Miller* and *To the Death.*
11 Oddly, the Daleks say the Doctor merely "delayed" their conquest of Earth in *The Chase.*
12 They run on "psychokinetic power" according to *Death to the Daleks*, but static electricity in *The Daleks, The Dalek Invasion of Earth* and *The Power of the Daleks.* Maxtible and Waterfield's experiments with static electricity attract the Daleks (*The Evil of the Daleks*).
13 *The Chase.* The Daleks have done some research - they know what the TARDIS looks like, even though they never saw it in *The Dalek Invasion of Earth* (or *Genesis of the Daleks, The Power of the Daleks* or *The Daleks*, for that matter). They know the Doctor's a time traveller, somehow (perhaps this was an accidental discovery when their were conducting their own time travel experiments). However, there are some big gaps in their knowledge: they don't even consider the pos-

Solar System. They attacked humanity on Earth and the Mars colony. Earth was occupied for ten years.[9]

Thirty years later, the Daleks invaded Earth again, only to suffer another defeat.[10]

The Daleks were defeated, but retained their ambition to conquer Earth.[11] Around this time, the Daleks internalised their power sources, removing their greatest vulnerability - now they ran on psychokinetic power, not static electricity.[12]

For the Daleks, their defeat had great significance for another reason - this was the very first time, from their point of view, that they encountered the Doctor. Soon after the Dalek Invasion, the Daleks developed time travel and sent an assassination group in their time craft to exterminate him.[13]

The Daleks also used their time travel to achieve their other great ambition - they went back in time and conquered the Earth. These Daleks already knew the Doctor's name - they hooked the Doctor up to a Mind Analysis Machine, and learned that the third Doctor was the same individual as his previous two incarnations. Whether this knowledge survived the collapse of the alternative timeline is unclear[14]. But from now on, even if they don't always recognise the Doctor on sight, they understand that he can change his appearance.[15]

The Dalek Invasion was also long-remembered by humanity (some historians called it The First Dalek War), and it resulted in an Alliance of a number of planets, and races being set up to defend against such an attack. The Daleks themselves don't seem to threaten Earth for centuries (Vicki, from 2493, only knows the Daleks from history books about the Invasion).[16]

What the Daleks do in this period, though, is a mystery. We know that the first Doctor's first encounter with the Daleks - when we see them in severely reduced circumstances - happens in Ian and Barbara's "future", "generations" before the year 2540, which would seem to fall around here on the timeline.

The Daleks were confined to Dalek City on Skaro. The Doctor and his companions helped the Thals to destroy them. There's no indication at this time that these Daleks have space travel, time travel, or even are aware that life exists on other planets.[17]

However you rationalise this away, even if you don't try to incorporate the TV Century 21 comic strip, the result is clumsy. The most straightforward explanation is perhaps that the vast majority of Daleks abandon Skaro because their conquests have taken them elsewhere, leaving behind a small group... but this doesn't explain why the Daleks there can't move or see beyond their city. Perhaps they have refused to upgrade their power supplies and literally been left grounded as a result.

Perhaps these are all the surviving Daleks - crippled by their defeat on Earth and the loss of their time craft, and perhaps leaderless (the Daleks need strong leadership, and are prone to turn on each other the moment they don't have it). We know that the Moroks were on Skaro - perhaps they stole more than just the one Dalek seen in their space museum. If they took, say, the Dalek Brain Machine that's seen to guide the Daleks and stripped the Daleks' archives, then it would have been a crippling setback.

The next time we see the Daleks, they're attacking human colony planets in the mid-twenty-fifth century. The Daleks did not, at this time, seem to have the strength to launch an attack against Earth itself.

---

sibility that the TARDIS crew might have changed, and they refer to the Doctor as "human" - we might infer they have yet to encounter another incarnation of the Doctor, and they don't know about the Time Lords.

14 *Day of the Daleks*

15 From *The Chase* onwards, the Daleks know about the Doctor. They have "files" on him by *The Daleks' Master Plan*; Chen thinks, possibly because the Daleks told him, that the Doctor is from "another galaxy". The Daleks recognise the second Doctor on sight in *The Power of the Daleks*, and lay a trap for him in *The Evil of the Daleks* (they have a photograph of him). They need to use the Mind Analysis Machine to identify the third Doctor in *Day of the Daleks*, but understand he can change his appearance. They know the third Doctor on sight in *Frontier in Space*, *Planet of the Daleks* and *Death to the Daleks* and the fourth Doctor in *Destiny of the Daleks*. They again lay a trap for the fifth Doctor in *Resurrection of the Daleks* (and have built duplicates of the fifth Doctor, Tegan and Turlough, so know of them). In *Revelation of the Daleks*, Davros has a tombstone prepared that's specifically the sixth Doctor's; the

Daleks don't seem to recognise the seventh Doctor in *Remembrance of the Daleks* - and Davros remarks on his changed appearance - but they know his name (and, indeed, both factions' plans rely on detailed knowledge of the Doctor's past).

Since the Time War, the Doctor has gone from being "an enemy of the Daleks" who they know is a threat to someone they are viscerally scared of - in *Dalek*, the Dalek knows the Doctor's name and reputation, but apparently doesn't recognise the ninth Doctor on sight. In *Doomsday*, the Daleks don't recognise the tenth Doctor, but are able to identify him, on sight, as a threat.

16 *The Rescue*

17 *The Daleks*

However, they are clearly far more powerful than they were when confined to one city on Skaro. They've had a few centuries to rebuild and regroup, but we don't know anything about the catalyst for this process. Perhaps various defeated remnants of the Daleks - the space travellers, the time travellers and the inhabitants of Dalek City - converge on Skaro. There's a Supreme Council in place by the twenty-sixth century - perhaps this is the body that provides the unified leadership that allows the Daleks to gain strength.

A century later, the Daleks are far more powerful than ever before.

Presumably this is just a natural consequence of building up a powerbase for centuries. Interestingly, the Daleks seem to have time travel, but not to use it - they might just be wary after their two high profile defeats. They don't seem aware of the Time Lords, yet, but they must have spotted that the Doctor has thwarted them on the three occasions they've used time travel technology.[18]

In the twenty-sixth century, there was "the third wave of Dalek expansion", and the Doctor described the Daleks as "one of the greatest powers in the universe" at this time. This was the time of the Second and Third Dalek Wars, which sparked off when the Daleks attempted to divide and conquer the space empires of Earth and Draconia.[19]

The Daleks plot this with the Master. It's never made clear exactly what the Master tells them about himself, but this might be the point where the Daleks realise that the Doctor is just one of a race of time travellers with TARDISes.

This was Benny Summerfield's native time - her father, Abslom Daak and (later) Ace all fought in these Dalek Wars. Abslom Daak apparently killed the Dalek Emperor at this time. *This might have been a turning point in the war.[20]* **It was a war that lasted a generation, ending in the early 2570s. The Daleks lost.**

Following this, the weakened Daleks tried tactics other than full scale assaults.[21]

There are no accounts of the Daleks for centuries - and the human race goes from strength to strength as the Earth Empire spreads across the galaxy. Perhaps unsurprisingly, the Daleks became interested in "the Human Factor". The next time we see them, the Daleks

are in their city on Skaro. The introduction of the Human Factor into the Daleks leads to civil war, to the Emperor's death and to the Doctor declaring this to be "the final end".[22]

So, the Daleks disappeared around the year 3000. It was the year 4000 before humanity came into contact with them again, but they'd begun their expansion around 3500.

The Daleks' Master Plan saw the Daleks' most ambitious scheme yet - a conquest of the entire Solar System, but merely as part of a strategy to dominate eleven whole galaxies. These Daleks also used time machines, and hoped to construct a Time Destructor. The Daleks were based back on Skaro at this point.[23]

Despite being defeated, the Daleks were now a powerful intergalactic force. Within twenty years of their Master Plan failing, the Daleks had succeeded in splitting the Federation. Within a couple of centuries of that, the Daleks were capable of threatening the Time Lords themselves.[24]

By now, then, the Daleks have learned of the Time Lords and Gallifrey. To a race dedicated to becoming the supreme beings of the universe, the Time Lords were now obviously the ones to beat - and from now on, the Daleks express no interest in conquering the Earth.[25]

The Davros Era took place - the Daleks lost their war with the Movellans, but Davros clawed his way to become the new Dalek Emperor. He re-engineered the Daleks, upgraded their technology and put them in a position where they were a genuine threat to the Time Lords... which may have been what the Dalek leadership had planned all along.

Whether the events of War of the Daleks *can be taken at face value or not, the Daleks get what they want - they go from military defeat and fragmented forces to having a strong leader and the knowledge and ability to fight a war across an entire galaxy and take on the Time Lords.*

The Dalek Empire period saw the Daleks based in the Seriphia galaxy launch a massive assault on the Milky Way, forcing the Earth Alliance to surrender. Resistance leaders Mendes and Kalendorf were able to foment a slave uprising and enlisted the help of Daleks from a parallel uni-

---

18 *The Chase, Day of the Daleks* and "Dogs of Doom".
19 *Frontier in Space*
20 "Nemesis of the Daleks"
21 "Metamorphosis", *Death to the Daleks*.
22 The seventh Doctor met the Emperor earlier in history in the comic strip "Nemesis of the Daleks". As the Emperor in *The Evil of the Daleks* says it's their first meeting, he's either lying or a different individual from the one in the earlier story.
23 *The Daleks' Master Plan*
24 *The Apocalypse Element*

25 The Doctor explicitly states that the Daleks don't want to conquer the Earth in *Remembrance of the Daleks*.
26 The four Big Finish *Dalek Empire* mini-series.
27 The televised Dalek stories from 2005 onwards have told a continuing story of the post-War Daleks rebuilding. These are *Dalek, Bad Wolf/The Parting of the Ways, Army of Ghosts/Doomsday, Daleks in Manhattan/Evolution of the Daleks, Journey's End/The Stolen Earth* and *Victory of the Daleks.*

verse, but despite countless sacrifices, still the Daleks could not be defeated. Eventually, a signal was sent that destroyed all Daleks and Dalek technology in both the Milky Way and Seriphia - triggering a Great Catastrophe that took those territories millennia to recover from. The Daleks were not utterly destroyed, and thousands of years after the Great Catastrophe, they unleashed a new plague on the galaxy. Humanity mobilised against them once more.[26]

The Daleks may, or may not, have lost Skaro. Either way, by now the Daleks were operating at a universal level, not just an intergalactic one. We have patchy information for the next ten thousand years or so, but Captain Jack sums it up: they were the greatest threat in the universe.

The Daleks now merely superficially resembled Davros' original creation. The Dalek Emperor (at least the third or fourth bearer of the title, and definitely not Davros) now oversaw an entirely revamped Dalek force - a huge army of highly-mobile, heavily-defended Daleks, with a re-engineered Dalek mutant inside. At least some of these Daleks had built-in "temporal shift" units. Dalek Saucers were now capable of firing missiles that could shoot down a TARDIS in flight.

To put the Daleks' might in perspective: now that the Daleks were upgraded, a single one of them was capable of subduing the entire human population of twenty-first century Earth. Four of them could fend off droves of Cybermen with no evident damage or difficulty.

Before this upgrade, in 2540, the largest army of Daleks ever assembled consisted of ten thousand Daleks - it was capable of conquering an entire galaxy. In the year 4000, five thousand Daleks would have been enough to subdue Earth's solar system.

Now, the Dalek space fleet consisted of ten million ships, each with two thousand Daleks onboard. Twenty *billion* Daleks.

The Daleks were ready to fight the Last Great Time War ...

The War devastated both sides, leaving few survivors. A few Daleks survived, as did remnants of their technology. From this, they were able to rebuild their strength, but only by losing their genetic purity. Eventually, the Daleks were able to create a new Dalek paradigm - genetically pure, with advanced travel machines.[27]

The history of the Time Lords and their homeworld of Gallifrey was shrouded in mystery. The Time Lords knew little of their own past, and much of what was known was cloaked in uncertainty and self-contradiction. It is extremely difficult to reconcile the various accounts of the origins of the Time Lords. The authorities suppressed politically inconvenient facts, although few Time Lords were very interested in politics anyway.[1]

Gallifreyan history can be divided into two periods: "the Old Time", the semi-legendary foundation of Time Lord society millions of years ago; and "recent history", that which has happened within living memory. (Time Lords, of course, live a long time.)[2]

The Old Time

We have only a few scraps of knowledge about the history of Gallifrey before the discovery of time travel.

"The Stolen TARDIS" -> In the distant past of Gallifrey, the dinosaur-like Gargantosaurs dominated the planet. The reptilian Sillag arrived here from the future in a stolen TARDIS, but a Gallifreyan technician - Plutar - was along for the ride and had the vital Relativity Differentiator needed to repair the Ship. The two fought and returned to their native time.

Gallifrey was the home of "the oldest civilisation in the universe", and had "ten million years of absolute power".[3] On the last day of Gallifrey, Rassilon spoke of "a billion years of Time Lord history".[4]

Gallifreyans mastered the use of transmats when the universe was less than half its present size.[5] Time Lords used to speak and write Old High Gallifreyan, now a dead language.[6] Old High Gallifreyan contained a lot of tenses that aided in speaking about the convoluted nature of time travel.[7] **There were days when Old High Gallifreyan could "burn stars, and raise up empires, and topple gods".**[8]

Gallifrey means, literally, "they that walk in shadows".[9] **Gallifrey was in the constellation Kasterborous.**[10] It "circled a little star in Kasterborous".[11]

Kasterborous was a mythological figure who was chained to a chariot of silver fire by the gods.[12] **The planet Karn was close to Gallifrey.**[13] Karn was in conjunction with the gas giant Polarfrey.[14]

Gallifreyans were naturally telepathic and could build "living" machinery that was also telepathic.[15] **They possessed a "reflex link", superganglions in their brains that allowed the Time Lord intelligentsia to commune.**[16] **The Time Lords discovered that they had a "dark side" of their minds.**[17]

Gallifrey had twin suns, a burnt orange sky, slopes with deep red grass and plants that displayed silver leaves in the autumn.[18] Masonry from the Old Time

1 In *The Deadly Assassin*, the Time Lords don't know that their power comes from the Eye of Harmony, and in both that story and *The Ultimate Foe*, they haven't heard of the Master. In *The Deadly Assassin*, even the Doctor seems unaware of the APC Net, and knows little about Rassilon.
2 The phrase "the Old Time" is first used in *The Deadly Assassin*. Not all Gallifreyans are Time Lords, as the Time Lords are the ruling elite of Gallifrey - the Doctor seems to say in *The Invisible Enemy* that there are only "one thousand" Time Lords. However, the terms "Time Lord" and "Gallifreyan" seem interchangeable for most practical purposes. Likewise, "Time Lord" is used to refer to the Doctor's race even before they master time travel (e.g.: *Remembrance of the Daleks,* where the "Time Lords" have trouble with the prototype of the Hand of Omega). Gallifrey is first named in *The Time Warrior*, although the Time Lords' home planet was called Jewel in the *TV Comic* strip "Return of the Daleks".
3 *The Ultimate Foe*
4 *The End of Time* (TV)
5 *Genesis of the Daleks*
6 *The Five Doctors*
7 *Borrowed Time*
8 *The Time of Angels*
9 *The Pit*
10 *Pyramids of Mars*
11 *An Earthly Child*
12 *Lungbarrow*
13 *The Brain of Morbius*
14 *Lungbarrow*
15 We learn that Susan is telepathic in *The Sensorites*, and it has been stated on a number of occasions that the Doctor (e.g. *The Three Doctors*), the TARDIS (e.g. *The Time Monster*) and all Time Lords (e.g. *The Deadly Assassin*) are mildly telepathic. The Doctor has also stated on a number of occasions that the TARDIS is alive (e.g. *The Five Doctors*), and so is the Nemesis seen in *Silver Nemesis*.
16 *The Invisible Enemy*
17 Omega has a "dark side" to his mind in *The Three Doctors*. The Valeyard [q.v.] represents the Doctor's dark side (*The Ultimate Foe*), and the Dream Lord (*Amy's Choice*) is "everything dark" in the Doctor given voice by space pollen. In *Falls the Shadow*, the Doctor refers to this as the "Dark Design".
18 *Gridlock*, expanding a little on Susan's description of her home planet in *Marco Polo*. As such, it's explicit confirmation that Susan is from Gallifrey.

survived, deep beneath the Capitol, into the modern era.[19] Gallifrey had a single moon, Pazithi Gallifreya.[20]

The Celestial Toymaker existed before the start of Time Lord records. Gallifreyan researchers later made some efforts to track his origins, but became bored with all of the Toymaker's games, realised they couldn't control him and opted to leave him alone.[21]

The ancient mythology of the Time Lords spoke of an entity that lived in the wastelands between realities, and subsisted on nightmares. In Old High Gallifreyan, its name, the Mi'en Kalarash, translated to "blue fire". The Doctor would make the Kalarash "remember what was done to you... what you did" during the Old Times.[22]

The Dark Days

At the very dawn of Time Lord history were "the Dark Days".[23] This was "the time of Chaos". One of the Doctor's most closely guarded secrets was that he was somehow involved with this period.[24]

"In the days before Rassilon, my ancestors had tremendous powers which they misused disgracefully. They set up this place, the Death Zone, and walled it around with an impenetrable force field. Then they kidnapped other beings and set them down here... even in our most corrupt period, our ancestors never allowed the Cybermen to play the game - like the Daleks they played too well... old Rassilon put a stop to it in the end. He sealed off the entire zone and forbade the use of the Timescoop... there are rumours and legends to the contrary. Some say his fellow Time Lords rebelled against his cruelty and locked him in the Tower in eternal sleep." [25]

Gallifreyans were naturally "time sensitive", with a unique understanding of time.[26] The earliest Time Lords discovered dematerialisation theory.[27] Another key discovery was transdimensional engineering.[28] The Time Lords built the Time Vortex, a vast transdimensional spiral encompassing all points in space and time.[29]

The Gallifreyans became "what they did" through

---

19 *The Deadly Assassin.* Engin says that deep beneath the Capitol there are "vaults and foundations dating from the Old Time".

20 *Cat's Cradle: Time's Crucible, The Infinity Doctors, The Gallifrey Chronicles* and the *Gallifrey* mini-series.

21 *The Nightmare Fair*

22 *House of Blue Fire*

23 *The Five Doctors*

24 *Silver Nemesis*

25 According to the Doctor in *The Five Doctors.*

26 *City of Death, Warriors' Gate, Time and the Rani.*

27 *The Claws of Axos*

28 *The Robots of Death*

29 *Just War.* The Time Vortex was first named in *The Time Monster.*

30 *A Good Man Goes to War*, implicitly suggesting that Time Lords developed the ability to regenerate in this fashion, hence why River Song has the talent (*Day of the Moon, Let's Kill Hitler*), because she was conceived while the TARDIS was in the Vortex.

31 *The Five Doctors*

32 *The Infinity Doctors*

33 *The War Games*; the claim is repeated in *The Infinity Doctors*, and by the tenth Doctor in "The Crimson Hand".

34 *Lungbarrow*

35 *Gallifrey: Annihilation*

36 *Cat's Cradle: Time's Crucible, Lungbarrow.*

37 *Lungbarrow*

38 *Interference.* Rassilon's dissolution of the monasteries presumably accompanies his defeat of the Pythia.

39 *The Song of the Megaptera*

40 "The Age of Ice"

41 Omega first appears in *The Three Doctors* and reap-

pears in *Arc of Infinity, The Infinity Doctors* and *Omega.* The Hand of Omega, his stellar-manipulation device, appears in *Remembrance of the Daleks, Lungbarrow* and *The Infinity Doctors.*

The first reference to Rassilon is in *The Deadly Assassin*; after that he becomes the central figure of Gallifreyan history, referred to in many subsequent stories (the quotes are from the Doctor, in *The Five Doctors* and *Shada* respectively). Both Rassilon and Omega are the legendary founders of Time Lord society, both are "the greatest" of the Doctor's race and supply the energy necessary for time travel. The first time that it is explicitly stated on-screen that they were contemporaries is in *Silver Nemesis*, although earlier in Season 25, *Remembrance of the Daleks* attempted to rationalise the two accounts of Time Lord origins. Early *Doctor Who Weekly* issues included a back-up strip written by Alan Moore which was an account of the origins of the Time Lords, and which has been referred to in novels such as *The Infinity Doctors* and *Interference.*

42 *Silver Nemesis*

43 The Other was mentioned or alluded to in several New and Missing Adventures; he first appeared (in flashback) in the *Remembrance of the Daleks* novelisation.

44 Engin, *The Deadly Assassin.*

45 *The Infinity Doctors*

46 *The Quantum Archangel*, following up a reference from *Castrovalva.*

47 The tenth Doctor's first reference to Citadel and its dome is in *Gridlock*, and it is actually seen in *The Sound of Drums.*

continued exposure to the Time Vortex - the Untempered Schism - over billions of years.[30]

The Time Lords' ancestors built the Timescoop.[31] The Gallifreyans mostly resembled tall, athletic humans.[32] They were truly immortal, barring accidents.[33]

CAT'S CRADLE: TIME'S CRUCIBLE -> The Pythias, a line of prophetesses who, since the 254th Pythia, rejected technology in favour of magic and superstition, ruled Gallifrey. Time travel was achieved by psychic prophecy, not physical means. The Pythias were guided by the prophesies in *The Book of Future Legends*, and saw their heritage as the Bright Past. The great philosopher Pelatov lived five thousand years before Rassilon.

At the time of the Intuitive Revelation, the age of Rassilon, the barbaric Gallifreyan Empire spread across the universe and encompassed the Pen-Shoza, Jagdagian, Oshakarm, the Star Grellades, Mirphak 2 and the rebellious Aubert Cluster. For aeons, Gallifreyan Heroes such as Ao had fought campaigns against foes such as the Gryffnae, lacustrine Sattisar and the batworms of the asteroid archipelago. The Winter Star was besieged for a century. The great hero Haclav Agusti Prydonius, commander of the Apollaten, defeated the marauding Sphinx of Thule, and was sent to observe a dispute brewing between Ruta III and the Sontara Warburg.

Across the cosmos, the ruling seers were dying: the Sphinx of Thule; the Logistomancer of A32K, foreseer of a cold empire of logic; the Core Sybilline of Klanti; the Sosostris in the West Spiral; The-Nameless-That-Sees-All in the North Constellations. The 508th Pythia became the last of her line. After a visit from a Master Trader of the South, she finally recognised that the veil of Time would soon only be traversed physically, not mentally. She instigated the Time Programme. The Time Scaphe, the first time vessel and powered by the mental energy of its crew, was launched but vanished.

Rassilon and his neo-technologists overthrew the Pythia. As her followers fled to Karn, the Pythia cursed Gallifrey with her dying words: its people became infertile, the colonies began to demand their independence and an Ice Age commenced. The Pythia cast herself into an abyss.

Rassilon lost a daughter to the Pythia's curse. The only good omen was the return of the Time Scaphe. Quennesander Olyesti Pekkary, captain of the Time Scaphe and first son of the House of Fordfarding, was Rassilon's nephew.

The family Houses of Gallifrey were sentient and the oldest beings on Gallifrey. They were born at the time of the Intuitive Revelation.[34] Mount Caden was home to the Houses of Firebrand and Heartshaven. Other Houses included Goodlight and Warpsmith.[35]

To get around the Pythia's curse of sterility, Rassilon and the Other built Looms capable of weaving Gallifreyans from existing genetic material.[36] Time Lords were born from the Loom fully grown and fully conscious, but needed educating.[37]

A priest on early Gallifrey was driven into the wilderness when Rassilon dissolved the monasteries. While wandering, he happened across all twelve of his future incarnations, who had no memory of how they came to appear together. The priest became known as IM Foreman, and his thirteen incarnations founded a time-travelling carnival. Their caravan was a complex space-time event that would model itself a new shape on each arrival.

Events on Dust in the thirty-eighth century mortally wounded Foreman's incarnations, forcing them to regenerate and causing amnesia. They were flung through time to early Gallifrey for the original Foreman to paradoxically find.[38]

It took the finest minds on Gallifrey a millennium to develop time technology.[39] The Doctor's people needed "millennia" to solve the equations, and harness the necessary power, required for time travel.[40]

The Mastery of Time

Two Gallifreyans ensured that their people became the Lords of Time: Rassilon and Omega. Rassilon was the "greatest single figure in Time Lord history", yet "no one really knows how extensive his powers were" and he "had powers and secrets that even we don't understand". To this day, the Time Lords revere Omega as their "greatest hero", "one of the greatest of all our race".[41] Omega and Rassilon developed Validium, a "living metal" designed to be the last line of defence for Gallifrey.[42] They were part of a Triumvirate, the third member of which was known as the Other to modern Time Lords.[43]

> "Today we tend to think of Rassilon as the founder of our modern civilisation, but in his own time he was regarded mainly as an engineer and an architect. And, of course, it was long before we turned away from the barren road of technology." [44]

The Time Lord Capitol and Citadel dated from the time of Rassilon and Omega, but in those days they weren't enclosed in a dome. The Citadel was built to withstand a siege, but against which enemy had been lost to history.[45] The Zero Room beneath the Capitol on Gallifrey was built by the Other.[46] **The Citadel of the Time Lords resided on the continent of Wild Endeavour, in the mountains of Solace and Solitude.[47]**

Omega was a member of the High Council, the solar engineer who found and created the power source needed for time travel: the energy released by a supernova. He was lost in the explosion, and the Time Lords believed that he had been killed.[48]

"A long time ago, on my home planet of Gallifrey, there lived a stellar engineer called Omega. It was Omega who created the supernova that was the initial power source for Gallifreyan time-travel experiments. He left behind him the basis on which Rassilon founded Time Lord society... and he left behind the Hand of Omega. The Hand of Omega is the mythical name for Omega's remote stellar manipulator - the device used to customise stars with. And didn't we have trouble with the prototype..." [49]

One version of Omega's history suggested that he was originally an Academy student named Peylix. He theorised that his people could gain mastery of time by exploding a star within the Sector of Lost Souls, but Peylix's tutor, Luvis, deemed this nonsense and awarded him an "omega" grade - the lowest score attainable. The nickname "Omega" plagued Peylix, but Rassilon's rise to power allowed him to properly implement his theories.

Peylix set out aboard the *Eurydice* to detonate a star, but his colleague Vandekirian warned that the targeted system contained sentient life. Omega proceeded anyway, and Vandekirian - trying to prevent Omega from gaining his handprint for security clearance - destroyed one of his hands in the ship's fusion reactors. Omega cut off Vandekirian's other hand, and used it to launch his stellar manipulator. The star exploded, killing the system's inhabitants. Vandekirian's hand caused an impurity in the fusion reactor and the ship exploded, consigning Omega to a universe of anti-matter.[50]

THE INFINITY DOCTORS -> The Ice Age had led to the collapse of Gallifreyan civilisation, in the time known as the Darkness. Libraries and temples burned. Many Gallifreyans perished. The Loom-born were smaller than the Womb-born and were mortal, but they preserved the Gallifreyan genetic codes.

Nine years after the Pythia's curse, the Elders still treated the Loom-born with disdain, viewing them a temporary solution to a problem. Rassilon and his Consortium gave everyone hope by finding the Fragment: the last surviving prophecy that spoke of Rassilon's personal rise and how the Gallifreyans would become the Lords of Time. The Other knew that Rassilon had faked the Fragment.

Rassilon and Omega set out for Qqaba, the only surviving Population III star in the galaxy. There were two Hands of Omega. They would detonate the star, releasing time energy that would be syphoned into fuel cells. However, the stasis halo protecting Omega's ship failed as Qqaba went supernova and Omega fell into the black hole that was forming. The crews of the surviving ships were infused with the energies. At the heart of this, Rassilon used the power of the singularity to rewrite the laws of physics across the entire universe. One effect of this, whether Rassilon knew it or not, was that Omega still lived, trapped inside the black hole.

Omega left behind a widow, a Womb-born Gallifreyan who would become known as Patience.

"Star Death" -> Four Gallifreyan starbreakers moved to the star Qqaba. From the flagship *Aeon*, Jodelex and Griffen waited, safe behind Stasis Haloes that protected their ships from the primal forces. They knew that Rassilon had yet to work out how to navigate through time. Fenris, a mercenary from the future, arrived to prevent the creation of the Time Lords. He sabotaged the lead ship, condemning Omega to what seemed like certain death, but

---

48 *The Three Doctors*
59 The Doctor, *Remembrance of the Daleks*.
50 *Omega*. These details hail from Omega's unreliable memories and are highly suspect. The details about Omega committing genocide, certainly, stem from a blending of the Doctor's recollections and are likely to be false.
51 *Lungbarrow*
52 *Omega*, an idea supported by *Zagreus*.
53 *Zagreus*. According to a questionable simulation, this occurred after Omega detonated his star. Arata is named as the third member of the Council of Three. The Great Mother belongs to the Sisterhood of Karn, although it isn't mentioned by name. Of all the suspect recreations shown in *Zagreus*, this one is the most dubious due to Tepesh's biased claims, and because he and Ouida, as vampires, would be unlikely to hold such

authority in the Gallifreyan echelons for long, if at all.
54 *The Book of the Old Time*, referred to in *The Deadly Assassin*.
55 *The Impossible Planet/The Satan Pit*
56 *The Three Doctors, The Deadly Assassin, Remembrance of the Daleks*.
57 *The Deadly Assassin*
58 "The Final Chapter". As it's only reached 5725.2 by the time of *Doctor Who - The Movie* - a period of millions of years after Rassilon's time - each unit can't represent a calendar year. Perhaps it misses out some of the numbers (i.e. it's short for 10,005,725 RE, or something like it), or it's more like a stardate in *Star Trek*, and the exact method of calculation is impossible for us to decipher.
59 *Heart of TARDIS*
60 *Neverland*

Rassilon used the power of his mind to contain the black hole, then severed Fenris' time belt as he tried to escape. Fenris was scattered throughout eternity, and Rassilon picked up the belt containing the directional control he needed to navigate time.

The star Omega detonated was in the Constellation of Ao.[51] Omega used the sunskipper *Eurydice* to reach the star he detonated, Jartus. Some scholars at the Omega Heritage Centre (a popular tour destination) think Rassilon deliberately got rid of Omega, who was more popular.[52]

Two members of a Council of Three - Provost Tepesh (the Prime of the Arcalian chapterhouses) and Lady Ouida, both of them vampires - allied with the Great Mother of a Sisterhood against Rassilon. The Great Mother's assistant was Cassandra, a member of the House of Jade Dreamers. They sought to discover the secrets of Rassilon's Foundry, but the Divergents again threatened to break through at this juncture. The Foundry was firestormed to prevent this, which wiped out the conspirators.[53]

"And Rassilon journeyed into the black void with a great fleet. Within the void no light would shine. And nothing of that outer nature continued in being except that which existed within the Sash of Rassilon. Now Rassilon found the Eye of Harmony which balances all things that they may neither flux, whither nor change their state in any measure, and he caused the Eye to be brought to the world of Gallifrey wherein he sealed this munificence with the Great Key. Then the people rejoiced." [54]

The Doctor's people invented black holes.[55] The Gallifreyans successfully concluded the experiments, becoming the Time Lords. Mastery of Time required an unimaginably vast energy supply, which Rassilon set about acquiring.[56]

Modern Time Lords believed the Eye of Harmony to be a myth, and that the Sash of Rassilon had merely symbolic importance. In reality, the Sash prevented the wearer from being sucked into a parallel universe. The Eye of Harmony was the nucleus of a black hole, from which all the power of the Time Lords devolved. "Rassilon stabilised all the elements of the black hole and set them in an eternally dynamic equation against the mass of the planet." [57]

Year Zero Rassilon Era is marked from the moment Rassilon activated the Eye of Harmony.[58] The earliest time-travel legends say Rassilon decapitated a Great Beast, took the branching golden tree of its metathalmus and found the First Secret of Chrononambulatory Egress.[59] Rassilon anchored the timeline of the universe, creating one unified history. The Antiverse was created as an equal and opposite reaction to this.[60]

LUNGBARROW -> Nine point six years after Omega was lost, Rassilon was purging anyone opposed to his regime. The Other was disgusted, and tried to get his granddaughter Susan and her nanny Mamlaurea to safety on the planet Tersurus. Susan had coined the term "TARDIS" to describe the new time ships. The Other then threw himself into the Prime Distributor that fed all the Looms. He knew he would be reborn at some point in Gallifrey's history.

A year later, the Doctor - unknown even to him, the reincarnation of the Other - arrived from the distant future. He found Susan wandering the streets, unable to escape. She recognised him as her grandfather and they left Gallifrey together to explore the universe...

"4-D War" ->

"We are fighting a timewar, comrades. A war in four dimensions. A war that on our timeline hasn't even started yet! Our enemy is in the future. We must know his identity. His reason for hating us... we must know his weaknesses!"

Twenty years after Fenris was scattered into the time vortex, Rema-Du - daughter of Jodelex and Griffen - had been training for a decade to retrieve him. At this time, the Time Lords employed the Special Executive, parahumans with unusual talents. One of them, Wardog (whose mind could withstand stresses that would reduce anyone else to insanity) partnered Rema-Du.

They entered the Vortex via a warp gate and located Fenris. He was connected to a Brainfeeler to identify the enemy. The Time Lords discovered that their enemy was from thirty thousand years in the future, a cadre of supermen called the Order of the Black Sun. A Black Sun squad - including members called Llorex, Faru-Faro and Drin - killed Fenris and the Brainfeeler, severed Wardog's arm and vanished. The Time Lords were left unsure what they would do, if anything, to provoke such an attack.

"Black Sun Rising" -> Ten years later, Rema-Du and Wardog attended talks with the Sontarans. A member of the Order of the Black Sun disrupted the gathering.

The Great Days of Rassilon

"Rassilon was the first of the Time Lords. Discovered time travel. Had a fondness for onions. Met him a couple of times. Bit of a dodgy beard, though."[61]

Rassilon lived "millennia" ago.[62] **As President of the Time Lords, Rassilon ushered in an age of technological and political progress. The phrase "the Great Days of Rassilon" appears in the Gallifreyan book** *Our Planet's Story*, **which was read by every Time Tot.**[63] **Even races such as the Urbankans, who knew nothing of the Time Lords, had legends of Rassilon.**[64] Rassilon's exploits were remembered on many planets, whose legends speak of Azaron, Razlon and Ra.[65]

Rassilon was credited with many scientific achievements: He created the transduction barriers surrounding Gallifrey. These prevented the unauthorised landing of a TARDIS or similar vehicle. A quantum force field also existed as a barrier against more conventional threats.[66] **Rassilon introduced the symbiotic nuclei - the Rassilon Imprimature - into the genetic make-up of Time Lords, allowing them to fully travel through Time.**[67] **Rassilon also discovered the secret of temporal fission.**[68]

Rassilon invented the Demat Gun, a weapon that required the Great Key to function. This weapon was so powerful that the Great Key was hidden from all future Presidents by successive Chancellors.[69] A Time

Lord Tribunal could impose the penalty of dematerialisation on other races or individuals, such as the War Lord.[70]

Rassilon created a servant, but she gained free will and rebelled, killing a few thousand Time Lords. Rassilon thought he'd killed Pariah - as she was now known - but she escaped to Earth in 1879. Subsequently, Rassilon created Shayde, a more loyal servant.[71] A legend said that Rassilon banished the Mimic - a mindless creature that could copy concepts, but had no imagination of its own. It would reappear in sixteenth century London.[72]

... of Rassilon

Rassilon was associated with many relics and concepts, all of which had "stupendous power". Many were lost, or their true purpose was unknown.[73]

These included the Sash of Rassilon, the Great Key of Rassilon, Rassilon's Star (the Eye of Harmony) and the Seal of Rassilon.[74] The Sash of Rassilon could alter the biodata of Time Lord President to allow better access to the Matrix.[75]

The Seal of Rassilon was also known as the omniscate.[76] The pattern for the Seal of Rassilon scrambled the neurosystems of beings from outside our Universe, such as vampires, to ward them off.[77]

Other relics and items included the Wisdom of Rassilon, the Rod of Rassilon ("Rassilon's Rod!" was also a mild Gallifreyan expletive)[78], the Record of Rassilon, the Directive of Rassilon[79], the Tomb or

61 The tenth Doctor, "The Forgotten".
62 *Gallifrey: Annihilation*
63 *Shada*
64 *Four to Doomsday*
65 *Neverland*
66 *The Deadly Assassin, The Invasion of Time.*
67 *The Two Doctors. Zagreus* further suggests that the Imprimature also facilitated regeneration, and that Rassilon introduced the limit of twelve regenerations to avoid the problem of degenerating biogenic molecules.
68 *The Five Doctors*
69 *The Invasion of Time*
   THE KEY: In *The Deadly Assassin*, the Great Key is "an ebonite rod" that seals the Eye of Harmony within its monolith. By *The Invasion of Time*, that artifact is called "the Rod", and the Great Key is an ordinary-looking mortise key that can power the Demat Gun and has been hidden from the President by successive Chancellors since the time of Rassilon. We might presume that the Chancellor told the President that the Rod *is* the Key, hence the confusion of the two. However, two Chancellors we know about - Goth and Borusa - are both in line to be President while (presumably, in

Goth's case) knowing the whereabouts of the real Great Key.
   In *The Ultimate Foe*, "The Key of Rassilon" allows access to the Matrix through portals such as the Seventh Door, and the Keeper of the Matrix wears it on his robes - this is presumably an entirely different artifact.
70 *The War Games*
71 "Wormwood"
72 *Managra*
73 *Shada*
74 *The Deadly Assassin*
75 *Alien Bodies*
76 *The Infinity Doctors*
77 *Interference*
78 *The Invasion of Time, The Androids of Tara.*
79 *State of Decay*
80 *The Five Doctors*
81 *Blood Harvest*. He played the Harp in *The Five Doctors*.
82 *Tomb of Valdemar*
83 *The Two Doctors, Interference*. The term is spelled "Imprimature" in *The Two Doctors* script and novelisation, and as "Imprimatur" in some of the later books.

Tower of Rassilon, the Game of Rassilon, the Black Scrolls of Rassilon, the Harp of Rassilon, the Coronet of Rassilon and the Ring of Rassilon.[80]

The fifth Doctor played "Rassilon's Lament" on the Harp of Rassilon.[81] Traditional Gallifreyan waltzes were known as the Foxtrots of Rassilon.[82] **The Rassilon Imprimature** mapped Time Lords on to the Vortex.[83] There was also **the Key of Rassilon (not the Great Key, but one which allows access to the Matrix)**[84]... **the Legacy of Rassilon**[85]... the Loom of Rassilon's Mouse[86], the Horns of Rassilon, also known as the Sign of Rassilon (a magical warding sign)[87]... Rassilon's Red, Gallifrey's finest vintage wine[88]... the Runes of Rassilon[89]... and the Equation of Rassilon, which allowed for travel through a time corridor. It "is and isn't" a scientific formula.[90]

The Time Lords signed the Pact (or Treaty) of Rassilon with the Sisterhood of Karn, protecting them in return for the Elixir of Life.[91] The Master destroyed TOM-TIT with a Profane Virus of Rassilon, which was designed to prevent Gallifreyan technology falling into alien hands.[92]

= In an alternate version of Gallifrey, Rassilon became a vampire and turned many of his contemporaries - including Lord Prydon, who then killed him. The transduction barriers were altered so no sunlight would shine on Gallifrey, and an ongoing war broke out between Prydon's vampires and the "True Lords of Gallifrey" led by Majestrix Borusa.[93]

= Another alt-Gallifrey never developed time travel because Rassilon used the still-developmental Eye of Harmony to trap the Krillic: 13,007,058,211 ravenous beings of pure thought.[94]

Rassilon as Ruler

Rassilon became President of Gallifrey.[95] Rassilon was the first - and to date only - Lord High President.[96] **Rassilon was also a legislator. In his time, five principles were laid down.**[97] Rassilon's Five Principles led Gallifrey to a more enlightened social order.[98] History says the Timescoop was destroyed after Rassilon's Reformation.[99] Gallifrey gave up slavery during the time of Rassilon.[100]

The Constitution was drafted. Article Seventeen guaranteed the freedom of political candidates.[101] Only a unanimous vote of the High Council could over-rule the President.[102] **Thanks to Rassilon, TARDIS databanks contained 18,348 coded emergency instructions. Older TARDISes (Type 40 and older) had a magnetic card system, the Record of Rassilon, which contained emergency instructions regarding the Vampires.**[103] The "Rules Governing Time Lords" were probably drafted at this time.[104]

Article Seven of Gallifreyan Law forbid Time Lords from committing genocide.[105] **The death penalty was abolished, except in extreme circumstances such as a threat to Gallifrey or genocide.**[106] Time Lords posing as

---

84 *The Ultimate Foe*
85 *Remembrance of the Daleks*
86 *Happy Endings*
87 *Timewyrm: Revelation* (p54), *No Future* (p203).
88 *The Eight Doctors*
89 *The Ancestor Cell*
90 *The English Way of Death*
91 *Warmonger*
92 *The Quantum Archangel*
93 *Gallifrey: Annihilation.* It's possible that Prydon knew Rassilon in the proper timeline and was a founder of the Prydonian Chapter. The fact that "Majestrix Borusa" is female could be viewed as either supporting evidence (as with *The Doctor's Wife*) that Time Lords can have incarnations of different genders, or is simply indicative of Borusa being born/Loomed female in this timeline.
94 *Gallifrey: Forever.* The Krillic don't appear to exist in Gallifrey's primary timeline. Strangely, they claim to have been imprisoned for "a million years", despite repeated references to Rassilon trapping them mere millennia ago. (Possibly, time passes differently within the Krillic's prison, or they've simply lost track of how long they've been dormant.)
95 *The Invasion of Time.* The Doctor becomes "the first

President since Rassilon to hold the Great Key", implying that Rassilon was President.
96 *The Infinity Doctors*
97 *Shada*
98 *Gallifrey: Forever*
99 *World Game*
100 *Gallifrey: Forever*
101 *The Deadly Assassin*
102 *The Five Doctors*
103 *State of Decay*
104 *The Androids of Tara*
105 *Terror of the Vervoids*
106 *The Brain of Morbius, Arc of Infinity, Terror of the Vervoids.* In *The Invasion of Time*, it's said that unauthorised use of a TARDIS "carries only one penalty", but this isn't definitively stated as execution.

deities in other cultures were guilty of a Class 2 intervention, the penalty for which was vaporisation. Altering the axial rotation of a planet was a Class 1 intervention.[107] Gallifrey outlawed use of "manumitters" - devices that severed the telepathic link between a Time Lord and their TARDIS, but could cause catastrophic damage to space-time if the Ships weren't fully powered down first.[108] It was "universally" forbidden to keep in captivity a coffin-loader - the ultimate form of scavenger - let alone a whole colony of them.[109]

The prison planet Shada was set up to house the most dangerous criminals in the universe. A key to the facility was encoded in the pages of Rassilon's book, *The Worshipful and Ancient Law of Gallifrey*, which was housed in the Panopticon Archive.[110]

Rassilon decreed that no Time Lord should travel into Gallifrey's past.[111] Rassilon's technology stopped Time Lords from investigating their own futures.[112] Rassilon built the Oubliette of Eternity, which exiled prisoners to the Antiverse. He was known as the Conqueror of Yssgaroth, Overpriest of Drornid, First Earl of Prydon, Patris of the Vortex and Ravager of the Void.[113]

The Eternal Wars

"The myths of Gallifrey talk about nameless horrors infesting our universe that were only defeated through the might of the Time Lords."

Rassilon's experiments created holes in the fabric of space-time, which consequently unleashed monsters from another universe. For over a thousand years, across the cosmos, the Ancient Gallifreyans fought the Eternal Wars against the monsters from another universe. These included the Vampires and the Yssgaroth. The great general Kopyion Liall a Mahajetsu was said to have died during this time, but he'd secretly survived. The Matrix contained no record of this war. When Rassilon overthrew the Pythia, Gallifrey was cursed with a plague from which only a few survived. Some suggested that Rassilon himself released the virus to wipe out all who knew of his mistake - they further claim that Rassilon deliberately sealed Omega in his black hole.[114]

When Rassilon was young, a Vampire army swarmed across the universe. Each Vampire could suck the life out of an entire planet.

107 *Forty-Five:* "False Gods"
108 *The Company of Friends:* "Benny's Story"
109 *The Three Companions*
110 *Shada*
111 *Timewyrm: Revelation*
112 *Alien Bodies*
113 *Neverland*
114 *The Pit*
115 *State of Decay*
116 *Damaged Goods*
117 *So Vile a Sin*
118 *Goth Opera*
119 *The Rising Night.* As with the vampires the Doctor encounters in *State of Decay*, the Baobhan Sith might well be the progeny of the Great Vampires.
120 *Zagreus*
121 *Lungbarrow*
122 *The Five Doctors*
123 *The Coming of the Terraphiles*
124 *Gallifrey: Reborn*
125 *Neverland*
126 "The Tides of Time"
THE HIGHER EVOLUTIONARIES: It's never explained in the comic strips exactly what defines a Higher Evolutionary, or what their sphere of influence is. From the examples of Rassilon and Merlin, we can see that they're semi-legendary figures - immortals with enormous personal powers that go far beyond psychic abilities until they are indistinguishable from magic. As such, the Higher Evolutionaries are capable of viewing and influencing events across infinity and eternity.
In the final part of "The Tides of Time", we see dozens of High Evolutionaries from "throughout the known universe". We're only given the names of six during the story: Rassilon; Morvane; Bedevere ("The Matrix Lords", and implicitly the latter two are Gallifreyans); Dakon Theta and the Thane of Kordar from the Althrace system; and Merlin the Wise from Earth. By the time of "The Final Chapter", the Higher Evolutionaries include a representative of the Order of the Black Sun, Demoiselle Drin, in the place of Merlin.
It's unclear whether the fact that Bedevere and Merlin are both names from Arthurian legend is significant, or how this Merlin relates to the Doctor being the Merlin of a parallel universe in *Battlefield*.
127 *The Five Doctors*
128 *The Infinity Doctors*
129 *The Ancestor Cell*
130 *Cat's Cradle: Time's Crucible*
131 We hear a female voice read an extract from the modern translation of *The Book of the Old Time* in *The Deadly Assassin*.
132 The last extant copy of The Black Scrolls of Rassilon is destroyed in *The Five Doctors*.
133 *Goth Opera* (p119).

"Energy weapons were useless, because the monsters absorbed and transmuted the energy, using it to become stronger. Therefore, Rassilon ordered the construction of bowships, swift vessels that fired a mighty bolt of steel that transfixed the monsters through the heart - for only if his heart be utterly destroyed will the Vampire die... The Vampire Army: so powerful were the bodies of these great creatures, and so fiercely did they cling to life, that they were impossible to kill, save by the use of bowships. Yet slain they all were, and to the last one, by the Lords of Time - the Lords of Time destroying them utterly. However, when the bodies were counted, the King Vampire, mightiest and most malevolent of all, had vanished, even to his shadow, from Time and Space. Hence it is the directive of Rassilon that any Time Lord who comes upon this enemy of our people and of all living things shall use all his efforts to destroy him, even at the cost of his own life..."

This war was so long and so bloody, that afterwards the Time Lords renounced violence forever.[115]

Members of the Prydonian and Arcalian chapters crewed the bowships. N-forms were developed to fight vampires by the Patrexes Chapter. N-forms existed in pocket universes and could quickly extrude a vast killing machine onto planets infected by vampirism. They were programmed to kill all life on planets where vampires were detected.[116]

Warships were built to act as carriers for the bowships.[117] A marginal illustration in one book of legends showed a bat overcoming an owl. The owl was a traditional symbol of Rassilon; the bat of the Vampires. Some Gallifreyan heretics to this day worship Rassilon the Vampire, believing the Great Vampire bit Rassilon, and that Rassilon himself became a vampire towards the end of his life.[118] When the Time Lords were in their infancy, they defeated the Baobhan Sith - a race with parasitic DNA and a hunger for blood - but only after the Sith feasted upon some of their number.[119]

A powerful rival race would have evolved after the Time Lords, but Rassilon trapped them in a moebius loop. They became known as the Divergents.[120]

Four of the outer worlds built temples to honour Rassilon in his own time.[121] Rassilon discovered the secret of perpetual regeneration - "timeless, perpetual bodily regeneration, true immortality" - but knew that only the power-mad would attempt such a thing. Rassilon prevented at least four such Time Lords from discovering the secret of true immortality.[122]

The Time Lords used to worry because time moved at different speeds in different parts of the galaxy, and ripples from the centre of the galaxy affected the past. When all

was well, the universe was effectively immortal as it constantly regenerated itself. The Time Lords understood this, and from this learned to regenerate themselves.[123] Regeneration was a function of a Time Lord's tri-strand DNA, and its nucleo-lingua symbiotica.[124]

The Neverpeople - a group of exiled Time Lord criminals - falsified legends which stated that Rassilon fought and prevailed against the destroyer Zagreus in the Antiverse, but was entombed in a Zero Cabinet. This was part of the Neverpeople's plan to lure Time Lords into the Antiverse and facilitate their escape.[125]

Rassilon's consciousness survived within the Matrix, from which he was able to watch over the whole of time and space. He was one of three Matrix Lords, along with Morvane and Bedevere. All three were Higher Evolutionaries.[126] Upon his death, Rassilon was entombed in the Dark Tower, where he remains to this day in eternal sleep. Legends state that anyone who reaches the Tower and takes the Ring of Rassilon will gain immortality. Gallifreyan children were familiar with the story and learned a nursery rhyme:

"Those to Rassilon's Tower Would Go... Must choose: Above, Between, Below." [127]

There were six vast statues in the Panopticon. These honoured the Founders of Gallifrey. Omega's statue was in the southern corner, Rassilon was opposite. Another was that of Apeiron (who wore combat boots). There was a nursery riddle that, when solved, revealed the identity of all six... although the Doctor couldn't remember all of it:

"Neath Panopticon dome Rassilon faces Omega... But who is the other?... brother." [128]

The six statues represented the six Gallifreyan Colleges.[129] While both Rassilon and Omega were virtually canonised, if not deified, there were no further records of the Other in any of the histories. Speculation said that he left Gallifrey altogether. Legend said that he grew weary of being an all-powerful player at the chess game of the Universe. Instead, he longed to be a pawn on the board in the thick of the action.[130]

The Ancient Texts

The Book of the Old Time was the official version of Rassilon's achievements, and a modern transgram had been made of it.[131] The Black Scrolls of Rassilon contained a forbidden account of the same period, including the secrets of Rassilon's power.[132] There were many R.O.O. texts (those dealing with legends of Rassilon, Omega and the Other).[133]

The Red Book of Gallifrey concerned the Dark Time and

talked of Rassilon the Ravager, Omega the Fallen and the Other. It also contained magical incantations.[134] The Green and Black Books of Gallifrey discussed legends of the future, including the Timewyrm.[135] There was a book called *The Triumphs of Rassilon*.[136]

There were records known as *The Other Scrolls*.[137] There was a prophecy that the Time Lord who found the lost scrolls of Rassilon will lead Gallifrey from darkness.[138] One book, bound in reptile skin and with an embossed omniscate on the cover, survived until the end of the universe. It contained one last prophecy, which terrified the Doctor when he read it.[139]

Between the Ancient and Modern

The Time Wars were fought in the generation after Rassilon. The Tomb of the Uncertain Soldier in the Capitol honours a Gallifreyan who died during the Time Wars, cancelling out his own timeline for the greater good of Gallifrey. The Time Lords' Oldharbour Clock is the only surviving relic from an alternate universe wiped out in the Time Wars. Unknown to anyone, the clockwork figures had evolved into the most intelligent beings on the planet.[140] The Doctor said he witnessed Gallifrey's Time Wars first-hand, although the Time Lords wiped the wars from their history books.[141]

Omegon was a Time Lord who created the system that gave the Time Lords time travel, and harnessed the power of a thousand suns for them. They made him Emperor, then plotted to destroy him and exiled him into a bubble in time. From there, he plotted his revenge.[142] The Pyralis, energy beings who mimicked other races, swarmed throughout Kasterborous and were defeated after a century-long war. They were imprisoned within a temporal void for millennia, but their obelisk-shaped dimensional gateways remained dormant on some worlds.[143]

The Time Lords time-looped the Fifth Planet, home of the Fendahl, twelve million years ago.[144] When the

134 *No Future* (p203).
135 *Timewyrm: Revelation* (p65).
136 *Lungbarrow*
137 *The Infinity Doctors*
138 *The Gallifrey Chronicles*
139 *The Infinity Doctors, The Ancestor Cell.*
140 *The Infinity Doctors*
141 *Heart of TARDIS*
142 *K9 and the Time Trap.* The story bears similarity to Omega's story, and is written by Bob Baker, Omega's co-creator. However, there are differences - Omega was never Emperor, and he only harnessed one sun. Omegon has a crippled leg. Despite the very similar names, they *do* seem to be different figures from early Time Lord history. *The Time Trap* doesn't mention Omega, so doesn't explore the relationship between the characters. Perhaps Omegon is Omega's son, building on his father's work. As an interesting side note, Omegon says he has met K9's master, presumably the Doctor.
143 "Millennia" before *The Pyralis Effect.* Gallifrey is in Kasterborous, and it's not impossible that the unnamed race that defeated the Pyralis was the Time Lords, although it's impossible to say exactly when in their history this event would fall.
144 *Image of the Fendahl*
145 *Underworld*
146 *Death Comes to Time.* This sounds like a retelling of the Minyan story, or possibly an indication that there were many such mistakes made in Gallifrey's past.
147 *Death Comes to Time*
148 *Time and Relative*
149 *Lungbarrow*
150 *The Ancestor Cell*
151 *The Doctor's Wife*
152 *Renaissance of the Daleks.* The fifth Doctor over-

rides this circuit to rescue Nyssa and a Knight Templar after they're killed in 1864, which somewhat begs the question of why he doesn't do this more often. It's presumably this circuit that malfunctions and causes the "time track" anomaly seen in *The Space Museum.* The fact that the Daleks don't use such a protocol probably accounts for the alternate timeline in which they're the masters of Earth in *Day of the Daleks.*
153 *The Dimension Riders*
154 *The Eight Doctors, The Infinity Doctors.*
155 *The Infinity Doctors*
156 *Tomb of Valdemar*
157 *The Infinity Doctors*
158 *The Infinity Doctors.* The implication is that they would be (or had been?) used against the People of the Worldsphere first seen in *The Also People.*
159 *Divided Loyalties*
160 Dating "The Stolen TARDIS" (*DWW* #9-11) - The Doctor says "when did it happen? Oh, a long time ago, dates really aren't important to us time travellers". Sillarg lands without encountering Gallifrey's transduction barriers (*The Invasion of Time*) or other defences, and the city isn't domed (although it may not be the Capitol, as we know there are other cities on Gallifrey).
161 Dating "Minatorius" (*DWM Winter Special 1981*) - Like "The Stolen TARDIS", this could take place at any time.
162 *Gallifrey: Reborn*
163 *The Deadly Assassin*
164 *Matrix*
165 *The Dimension Riders*
166 *Conundrum,* referencing *The Mind Robber.*
167 *So Vile a Sin*
168 *Millennial Rites*

Gallifreyans were new to space/time exploration, they discovered the inhabited world of Minyos and were worshipped by the population there. In return, they gave technology to the Minyans.[145]

The Time Lords used their great powers to help the people of Micen Island, in Orion. This led to chemical and biological warfare on the planet. The Time Lords renounced interference, erecting the Temple of the Fourth as a monument. A small number of Time Lords, though, felt the need to atone for past sins, and covertly intervened in the universe's affairs.[146]

Because of their great powers, and their tendency to lead to corruption, Time Lords were discouraged from emotion and affection. They were trained with a series of tests, including a journey to Anima Persis. They were mentored by older Time Lords, but the final judgement on whether an individual can be a Time Lord (and the punishment of any Time Lords who misuse their power) was handled by the mysterious Kingmaker, an ancient crone.[147]

Time Lords appear to have possessed mental blocks that prevented their interfering in history. However, if one of these blocks was broken, the others soon shattered.[148] Three centuries after Rassilon's death, Rassilon's Rampart was built to defend against the lawless Shobogans.[149]

It took fifty generations for TARDISes to become an acceptable form of travel, and another twenty for them to be used to participate in history.[150] **The "living soul" of each TARDIS was an eleventh-dimensional matrix.**[151] All TARDISes had a preset circuit - a time-track crossing protocol - that prevented travellers from visiting the same space-time location more than once. Doing so would result in recursion effects of completely unknown and unpredictable consequences. The Daleks didn't use such a system, meaning they could sometimes overlap their journeys and history.[152]

Epsilon Delta was a Time Lord from the Ancient Time who gained a double beta in cybernetics. He stole a TARDIS and adopted the name "the President". He settled in St Matthew's College, Oxford.[153]

The shanty township of Low Town sprang up at the base of the Capitol Dome, and was settled by normal Gallifreyans, Outsiders and those seeking a life free of the restrictions of Time Lord society. The Capitol once had a Harbour.[154] A suit of armour belonging to Tegorak gathered dust in one storeroom, as did a giant stuffed bird.[155]

Time Lords dabbled at breaching the higher dimensions, but the Dimensional Ethics Committee banned the work.[156] At some point, the Biblioclasm claimed the Endless Library. The Watch checked every night to prevent such a thing happening again. A quarter of a million years ago, the Time Lords were afflicted with the Blank Plague. The Time Lords fought military campaigns against Rigel, Gosolus and about a dozen other worlds.[157]

The Time Lords developed the blackstar, a weapon to crack Dyson Spheres.[158] Gallifreyan artifacts included Pandeka's staff and an artifact associated with Helron.[159]

"The Stolen TARDIS"[160] -> A Gallifreyan student named Plutar was failed because he wanted to meddle in the affairs of other planets. He was put to work maintaining TARDISes. Meanwhile, a ship landed outside the Time Lords' city, and the lizard-like Sillarg fooled those present into watching a space circus while he moved to steal a TARDIS. He stole one that Plutar was working inside, but it malfunctioned and took them to the distant past of Gallifrey. Plutar warned the authorities on their return, whereupon Sillag was arrested and his memory of Gallifrey erased. Plutar was asked to reapply to the Academy.

"Minatorius"[161] -> A young Time Lord visited the planet Minatorius, and died to prevent a reactor there from going critical.

Gallifrey's history was spotted with a few presidential assassinations.[162]

The Matrix

The Time Lords built the Matrix, a form of computer that could - amongst other things - store the minds of dead Time Lords.[163] When the Matrix was young, it began to break down as thousands of Time Lord minds resented their deaths. The Time Lords cleaned the Matrix by isolating its dark part: the Dark Matrix. It was caged and forgotten about beneath the Citadel, sealed with a great key held by the Keeper of the Matrix.[164]

The Garvond was imprisoned for a time in the Gallifreyan Matrix, where it assimilated copies of Time Lord minds, including that of the Doctor. The creature's exact origins were unknown, although by nature it was the embodiment of the evil in the minds in the Matrix. The Garvond wanted to sail the Time Vortex and consume all life. It had several thousand names, all corruptions of the High Gallifreyan term for "of darkest thought".[165]

The Land of Fiction was originally part of the Matrix.[166]

Technological and Scientific Advancement

Gallifreyan technology has been refined, rather than totally reworked, over the last ten million years.[167] A dark science of earlier Time Lords was quantum mnemonics, a reality-altering power that manipulated the basic nature of reality and probability. Quantum mnemonics allowed one to transform the history of a planet or an individual by warping space and time.[168]

The Time Lords used devices called amaranths to rebuild parts of time and space that were damaged in the

Time Wars. They were originally built to manipulate black holes.[169] **The Time Lords discovered an indestructible material.[170] They learnt to engineer micro-universes. Eventually, they abandoned the barren road of technology.[171]**

They abandoned tachyonics for warp matrix engineering.[172] They invented the Magnotron. Over time, the Primitive Phases One and Two of the Matrix were relegated to the Archives. Phases Three to Six remained in use.[173] They developed Gallifreyan Morse.[174] The science of Temporal Reversion was so tricky, the Time Lords avoided using it.[175] Gallifreyan zinc was an excellent conductor, and one of the strongest substances in the known universe.[176]

Erkulon, the greatest nano-engineer in Gallifreyan history, created the time ram.[177]

The Time Lords took the credit for the Library of Carsus, although no-one knew for sure who built it. It was built millennia ago, and contained every book ever written. It was in an area of space known for time anomalies - the same solar system as Minerva, Schyllus, Tessus, Lakertya, Molinda, Hollus and Garrett.[178]

Three thousand years ago, Mawdryn and his followers stole a Metamorphic Symbiosis Regenerator.[179] Two thousand years ago, the Time Lords abandoned interspacial geometry.[180] Some Time Lords such as Epsilon Delta could rehearse various events without altering the true timeline.[181] Time Lords could use Reverse Tachyon-Chronons to move time backwards and forwards, manipulating material so that it wouldn't age.[182]

With great effort, Time Lords used a process called "soul-catching" to absorb a dying Gallifreyan's memories.[183] The Time Lords built the Parachronistic Chamber, deep in the Capitol, to regulate time distortions.[184] Mimesis was a Gallifreyan art in which anything you write came true. It was practiced by a cult that held an annual ritual, the Thirteenth Night, but the High Council banned the ritual and the art - probably because it was too arcane

169 *Christmas on a Rational Planet*
170 *The Mutants*
171 *The Deadly Assassin*
172 *The Leisure Hive*
173 *The Trial of a Time Lord*
174 *Shada*
175 *Revenge of the Judoon*
176 *Pier Pressure*
177 *The Quantum Archangel*
178 *Spiral Scratch.* Lakertya appeared in *Time and the Rani.*
179 *Mawdryn Undead*
180 *The Stones of Blood*
181 *The Dimension Riders*
182 *Legacy*
183 *The Devil Goblins from Neptune*
184 *A Device of Death*
185 *Managra*
186 *Timewyrm: Genesys*
187 *Damaged Goods*
188 *The Impossible Planet,* which concurs with information in the novels, such as *Cold Fusion* and *The Taking of Planet 5.*
189 *Journey's End,* perhaps intended to explain why the Doctor is so rubbish at piloting the TARDIS, but in defiance of the large number of times in classic *Doctor Who* (*The Time Meddler*, every story with the Master, etc.) that TARDISes other than the Doctor's Ship operate just fine with a single pilot.
190 *Cold Fusion*
191 *Goth Opera*
192 *The Crystal Bucephalus*
193 *The Gallifrey Chronicles*
194 *Love and War*
195 *The Eight Doctors*
196 First seen in *The War Games* (suggesting that the technology predates the Doctor leaving Gallifrey) and most recently used in *The Doctor's Wife.*
197 *The Sound of Drums*
198 Aliens recognise the Doctor as a Time Lord in *The Time Warrior, The Brain of Morbius, Image of the Fendahl, Underworld, The Invasion of Time, The Ribos Operation, State of Decay, The Keeper of Traken, Earthshock, Mawdryn Undead, Frontios, Resurrection of the Daleks, Attack of the Cybermen, Vengeance on Varos, The Two Doctors, Timelash, The Trial of a Time Lord, The Curse of Fenric, Rose, The End of the World, Dalek, Human Nature* (TV), *The Stolen Earth, The Eleventh Hour, The Doctor's Wife* and *A Good Man Goes to War.*
199 *The Two Doctors*
200 *The War Games*
201 *The Time Warrior*
202 *The Hand of Fear*
203 *The Deadly Assassin, The Invasion of Time.*
204 *Scaredy Cat*
205 *The Deadly Assassin.* Fans and recent writers have rationalised away the Time Lords' stated "non-intervention" and the clear evidence that they have intervened by assuming that it's the secret (and in some stories highly sinister) "Celestial Intervention Agency" who are behind the interventions. This builds quite a lot on the one reference in the TV series.
206 *The Kingmaker*
207 *The Well-Mannered War*
208 *The Deadly Assassin*
209 *Damaged Goods*
210 *Lungbarrow*
211 *Shada*
212 *The Ancestor Cell*
213 *Shada*
214 *Gallifrey: Disassembled*
215 *Omega*

and unpredictable.[185]

Time Lords' extended lifespans sometimes necessitated that they edit out their more useless memories, storing them electronically or erasing them.[186] An artificial, multi-dimensional art gallery was located beneath the Capitol.[187]

TARDISes were grown, not built.[188] They were intended to have six pilots, but on numerous occasions had just one.[189] They were grown in space, away from Gallifrey, to prevent time pollution. Stattenheim signals could broadcast along Eye of Harmony time contours, so TARDIS remote control worked even from across the Universe.[190] Time Lord technology could retrieve ancestral memories from the blood of virgins. Time Lords could communicate telepathically across the Time Vortex. The poisons in tea couldn't harm them.[191]

Time Lords used two hundred and eight language tenses, most of which didn't translate well.[192] The Time Lords used an omegabet, which was better than an alphabet.[193] Castellan Lode, a female, was the greatest literary historian the Time Lords ever had.[194]

A Gallifreyan golden guinea could buy you a few drinks at a bar.[195] **Time Lords had an emergency messaging system that entailed bundling their thoughts into cube-shaped psychic containers that could be dispatched through time and space.[196]**

Foreign Policy

The Time Lords were the oldest and most mighty race in the universe, sworn only to watch, never to interfere. Gallifrey was called "the Shining World of the Seven Systems".[197]

Alien races from all periods of recorded time have had dealings with the Time Lords, ranging from those in the ancient past such as the Kastrians and the destroyer Sutekh to those in the far future such as the Usurians. Other races or beings who know something of the Time Lords and Gallifrey (without hearing just of the Doctor or another individual) include the Andromedans, the Bandrils, the Cryons, the Cybermen, the Daleks, the Face of Boe, the Family of Blood, the Fendahl, Fenric, the Forest of Cheem, the Guardians, House, the Keeper of Traken, Mawdryn's race, the Mentors, the Minyans, the Nestene, Prisoner Zero, the Racnoss, Saturnynians, the Shadow Proclamation, the Silence and the Academy of the Question, the Sisterhood of Karn, the Sontarans, some residents of the Third Zone, the Tractators, Vampires and the Vardans.

The Time Lords visited many worlds in many time periods, even in an official capacity.[198] They authorised (or prevented) other races' time travel experiments and defended the Laws of Time.[199] Time Lords observed but didn't interfere.[200] At times they intervened with

regards to unauthorised time travel, and could almost be thought of as "galactic ticket inspectors".[201]

They were committed to protecting weaker species, and to preventing aggression against indigenous populations.[202] The vast majority of Time Lords didn't concern themselves with the universe outside the Capitol, and were more concerned with internal politics.[203] Time Lords were taught "very early on" not to visit newly formed planets, as the morphogenetic fields of such worlds were still in flux, and therefore susceptible to undue influence from visitors.[204]

The Celestial Intervention Agency was concerned with covert intervention.[205] The CIA's motto was, "The story changes, the ending stays the same", meaning that it didn't matter how one fixed temporal anomalies so long as time continued along a straight path. For instance, if a man who would start a war were erased from time, it was incumbent on the organisation to start it anyway.[206] Study of the later Humanian era was forbidden by the Academy as being outside the Gallifreyan sphere of influence.[207]

Political

More Presidents hailed from the Prydonian Chapter than all other chapters combined. Prydonians were viewed as cunning, but claimed they "simply saw a little further ahead than most". They wore scarlet and orange robes. Other chapters included the Arcalians (who wore green) and Patrexes (who wore heliotrope).[208] The Patrexes were aesthetes who saw artistic value in all things, including suffering, but lacked the imagination to be true artists.[209]

The Celestial Intervention Agency evolved from Rassilon's personal guard.[210] **At some point, the Time Lords Rungar and Sabjatric were sent to Shada. They remained there.[211]** Apart from Rassilon, only President Torkal was ever referred to as "the Great".[212] **While young, Salyavin learnt how to project his mind into others' and was sentenced to imprisonment in Shada as a result. He escaped, using his powers to erase all knowledge of the prison planet.[213]** "Burn orders", i.e. kill orders, issued by Gallifreyan presidents were carried out by their personal assassin, a Time Lord with the title of Lord Burner. Such orders were sent directly into Lord Burner's mind, and not made public.[214]

Mundat the Third's reputation swung from his being a brutal murderer to a noble warrior - and that's just in the documentaries of the historian Ertikus.[215] Pandora became the first female President of Gallifrey, assumed the dictatorial title of Imperiatrix and sought to overturn the ancient laws of Rassilon. Legends would claim that Pandora tried to lead Gallifrey to war, hoping to reshape the web of time to her liking. The High Council defeated Pandora - her offworld bodyguard was sent home, and their planet time-looped. Pandora herself was placed in a dispersal chamber beneath the old Capitol and erased from history. However, her spirit survived in a partition of the Matrix, which was immune to such historical alterations.[216]

In the lifetime of some contemporary Time Lords, President Pandak III ruled for nine hundred years.[217] President Pandak III suppressed a report on Lampreys by Lord Rellox of the Arcalian Council for Temporal Research.[218]

Savar tried to rescue Omega from his black hole, but was ambushed by the Time Lord god Ohm. Attempting to escape, Savar's TARDIS was stretched until it became the light-year-long structure called the Needle. Savar fled in an escape capsule, which was intercepted by the I. The I stripped the ship of technology and took Savar's eyes. He was found by the Time Lords, but was utterly insane from the experience. He regenerated, but was a broken man.[219]

The Doctor's TARDIS

The Doctor's TARDIS was a Type 40, Mark 3.[220] The Type 40 TT-Capsule was introduced when Salyavin was young.[221] The Type 40 was withdrawn centuries ago and was considered a "Veteran and Vintage Vehicle".[222]

The Early Life of the Doctor

There are a number of seemingly contradictory facts about the Doctor's birth and upbringing.

The Doctor was born under the sign of "Crossed Computers".[223] **As a baby, the Doctor had a cot.**[224] **He was born the same year as the Rani.**[225] He was one of forty-five cousins from the House of Lungbarrow.

216 *Gallifrey: Lies*
217 *The Deadly Assassin*
TIME LORD PRESIDENTS: *The Ancestor Cell* says the Doctor was the 407th and 409th President of Gallifrey. *The Gallifrey Chronicles* says that Romana is the 413th. From this, we can extrapolate that the 405th President was the one killed in *The Deadly Assassin* (and almost certainly, in a previous incarnation, the one seen in *The Three Doctors*); the 406th was Greyjan the Sane (*The Ancestor Cell*); the 407th was the Doctor (he was "inducted" in *The Invasion of Time*); the 408th was Borusa (the President is referred to by the Doctor in *The Ribos Operation*, but not named as Borusa until *Arc of Infinity*. Borusa regenerates once more and his reign ends in *The Five Doctors*); the 409th is the Doctor; the 410th is Flavia, the 411th is Niroc, who's corrupt and deposed with the help of the Doctor and Rassilon in *The Eight Doctors*; the 412th is Flavia again, according to *Happy Endings*, which is set soon after Romana is installed as the 413th.
218 *Spiral Scratch*
219 Savar is first mentioned in *Seeing I*, but these events take place "a thousand years" before *The Infinity Doctors*, as far as Savar is concerned. There was a Time Lord called Savar in *The Invasion of Time*.
220 The term "Type 40" was first used in *The Deadly Assassin*. The *Teselecta's* records in *Let's Kill Hitler* list the Doctor's TARDIS as a "Type 40, Mark 3" - in accordance with the Doctor being amazed at the modernity of the Monk's TARDIS, a "Mark 4", in *The Time Meddler*.
221 *Shada*
222 *The Pirate Planet*
223 *The Creature from the Pit*
224 *A Good Man Goes to War*. The circumstances of the cot being in the TARDIS becomes more perplexing the more one thinks about it. The cot's presence might suggest that the TARDIS was some sort of family heirloom, but *The Doctor's Wife* says that the Doctor picked the

TARDIS because its door was open. If so, did he pack his childhood cot before leaving Gallifrey in such a rush? Did his family keep multiple TARDISes, and he just happened to select the one with his cot in it? Or did he just reclaim the cot during a stopover on Gallifrey? Or is he simply lying to say it's his cot - did it actually belong to a child of his?
225 In *Time and the Rani*, the Doctor deduces the combination to the Rani's lock is 953, "my age ... and the Rani's".
226 *Lungbarrow*, with *The One Doctor* confirming the "Snail" nickname.
227 SLEEPY (p204).
228 *Closing Time*
229 *The Wedding of River Song*
230 *Doctor Who - The Movie*
HALF HUMAN ON HIS MOTHER'S SIDE: The eighth Doctor's airing of his "secret" to Professor Wagg in *Doctor Who - The Movie* - that he is "half human on his mother's side" - has long been a source of debate in fandom, if for no other reason that it seems to go against all manner of stories where the Doctor biologically is no different from a purebred Time Lord. It's insufficient to claim that the Doctor is just joking with Wagg, because the Master concludes that the Doctor is half-human by looking into a projection of the eighth Doctor's iris. The "half-human" claim is chiefly limited to just *Doctor Who - The Movie*, although *The Gallifrey Chronicles* furthered this by hinting that the Time Lord named Ulysses / Daniel Joyce and the human time traveller Penelope Gate are the Doctor's parents.
The more likely explanation, however, is that Time Lords can hybridise with other species upon regeneration - the eighth Doctor claims as much in *Doctor Who - The Movie* (Grace: "Why don't you have the ability to transform yourself into another species?" The Doctor: "Well, I do, you see, but only when I 'die' [i.e. regenerate]". Some have taken this to mean - owing to

Unusually for a Time Lord, he had a belly button, which earned him the nicknames "Wormhole" and "Snail".[226] His Gallifreyan name had thirty-eight syllables.[227] **He dreamed of stars when he was very young.**[228] **The Doctor has been running from the question "doctor who?" all his life.**[229]

The Doctor was half human on his mother's side.[230] He was acquainted, somehow, with the Woman in White.[231] He had a family.[232] He had an "excellent if smelly" godmother with two heads and halitosis. She gifted him with a device that could recognise different alien species.[233] **He may have had an uncle[234], but he didn't have an aunt.**[235] As the Doctor let the Master die on Sarn, the Master called out, "Won't you show mercy to your own —"[236]

Irving Braxiatel, a.k.a. Lord Braxiatel, was a relative of the Doctor, either his brother or one of his Cousins.[237] **The tenth Doctor said he didn't have a brother "anymore".**[238]

The Doctor's family owned a home in South Gallifrey.[239] This home was House Lungbarrow, which was perched on the side of Mount Lung, overlooking the Cadonflood river, two days from Rassilon's Rampart.[240] The Doctor doesn't know much about Gallifrey's Southern Hemisphere.[241]

There are a number of seemingly contradictory facts about the Doctor's age.[242]

The Doctor's Father

The Doctor remembered "I'm with my father. We're lying back in the grass... it's a warm Gallifreyan night".[243] The Doctor's father was taught by the ancient Gallifreyan who would be known as Patience, as his father had been. Many of his generation - such as Savar; Hedin; the Doctor's mentor, Lady Zurvana; the future President (a Chancellor at the time) and Marnal thought they could change the universe.[244]

The Doctor's father was a member of the High Council. He launched a great exploration of the universe, which became known as the Odyssey.[245] On his travels, he met an Earthwoman, the Victorian time traveller Penelope Gate. They married, and had at least one child. The Doctor's father adopted the name Ulysses.[246]

The Time Lord Astrolabus was known as the thief of time - he stole the *Book of Old Time* before the Doctor was born. Astrolabus saw himself as a real Time Lord, a pioneer who charted the first meridians of time: "It was I who

the atypical manner of his regeneration (the dulling influence of the anaesthetic, his "changing" in a morgue full of human corpses) - that the eighth Doctor is "half-human" whereas all the other Doctors are full-blooded Time Lords. The notion that Time Lords can hybridise with other species is substantiated in the works of Paul Cornell: a regenerated Time Lord becomes part-Silurian in *The Shadows of Avalon*, and another becomes part-birdperson in *Circular Time*: "Spring".

The IDW mini-series "The Forgotten" tries to reconcile the "half-human" problem by saying that the eighth Doctor once used a half-broken Chameleon Arch (*Utopia*, the TV version of *Human Nature*) to convince the Master that he was half-human. There isn't a particularly good reason in *Doctor Who - The Movie* as to why this would be helpful, however; in fact, as a means of helping the Master to realise that human eyes can open the Eye of Harmony in the TARDIS, it's a fairly counter-productive thing to do.

231 The more descriptive name used for the mysterious woman seen throughout *The End of Time* (TV), credited on screen as just "the Woman". Russell T Davies confirmed in his memoir, *The Writer's Tale*, that the Woman was intended as the Doctor's mother, but has acknowledged that other interpretations of the character are fair game.

232 *The Tomb of the Cybermen*, further implied in *The Curse of Fenric* and confirmed in *Father's Day*.

233 *Vincent and the Doctor*

234 *Time and the Rani*. He says, possibly facetiously, "you should see my uncle".

235 *The Eleventh Hour*

236 *Planet of Fire*. The sentence isn't complete, but the next word could well spell out a family relationship (fan speculation over the years has suggested a number of things, usually "brother" and less usually "husband").

237 Braxiatel first appears in the NA *Theatre of War*, and becomes an ongoing character in the Bernice Summerfield range. The *Gallifrey* audios detail much of his early history. Justin Richards, who created the character, first implied that Braxiatel was the Doctor's brother in *Benny: The Tears of the Oracle* (p166-167). The notion was later reinforced by wordplay in *Gallifrey: Disassembled* (Romana tells Brax concerning an alt-Doctor: "I thought you'd be pleased to see your—"; Brax, as the alt-Doctor strangles him: "Surely, you wouldn't do this to your own—"), and also in Brax's description of "an old man and his granddaughter" (presumably the first Doctor and Susan) as "family".

238 *Smith and Jones*, and possibly a reference to Irving Braxiatel.

239 *Planet of the Spiders*

240 *Lungbarrow*

241 *The Scarlet Empress*

242 See The Doctor's Age sidebar.

243 *Doctor Who - The Movie*

244 *The Infinity Doctors*

245 *Cold Fusion*

246 *The Gallifrey Chronicles*. Penelope Gate first appeared in *The Room with No Doors*.

released Gallifrey from the chains of the present." However, he plundered the timezones he visited.[247]

The Master had a copy of the *Insidium of Astrolabus* in his TARDIS library.[248]

The Doctor's father had many friends and allies from alien planets. He broke protocol by inviting them to his House on Gallifrey. The Doctor's mother owned a Bible from which the Doctor read.

A computer portrait of the Doctor's parents hung on the wall of his quarters on Gallifrey. His father was "powerfully built with rugged features, a weathered face with dark eyes". His mother "a redhead, a little plump".[249]

One contemporary of the Doctor's father was Marnal, who believed that the Time Lords should intervene to eliminate potential threats to Gallifrey. He became known - dismissively - as a crusader. On one mission, to the Shoal on the edge of Mutter's Spiral, he stumbled across a race of insect creatures that he believed were a threat to Gallifrey. They weren't - until he intervened and changed history. "Marnal's Error" (meaning that he did not know his enemy) became a Time Lord proverb. Marnal had a son.[250]

Shortly after the Doctor was born, the Doctor's father was leading a team working on a mysterious Project. Other members included Penelope, Mr Saldaamir and a Time Lady from the relative future, Larna. Some Time Lords (including Marnal and Larna) knew of the Scrolls, recently-discovered prophecies that warned, in Larna's words:

"For millions of years, Gallifrey has existed in isolation. Soon - not imminently, not all at once - there will be a spate of attacks. Omega, the Sontarans, Tannis, Faction Paradox, Varnax, Catavolcus, the Timewyrm. You know some of those names, you will come to know the others. It is very important that Gallifrey survives all these attacks. All things must pass. Gallifrey will fall. But it must fall at precisely the right time. The enemy is unknown to us. It will be until Last Contact is made. If it's destroyed before that, by any of those other enemies, then the consequences... that is as much as I know."

Marnal added:

"The President and members of the Supreme Council know the prophecy. They have been told that a Time Lord now living will be central to all these events. That he will find the lost scrolls of Rassilon and lead Gallifrey from darkness."

To prevent the exposure of the Project, the Doctor's father wiped Marnal's memory and exiled him to Earth in 1883. He took Marnal's TARDIS, a Type 40, from him.[251]

In the nursery, the Doctor used to play with bricks that contained Roentgen radiation.[252] The Doctor remembered his mother smiling and his father holding him up to see the stars.[253] When the Doctor was ten years old, he was caught skinny-dipping with one of his Cousins.[254] The Doctor flew skimmers as a boy on Gallifrey.[255]

The Doctor was a lonely little boy.[256] Three of the Doctor's favourite bedtime stories as a child were *The Three Little Sontarans*, *The Emperor Dalek's New Clothes* and *Snow White and the Seven Keys to Doomsday*.[257] The Doctor heard legends of the Pantheon of Discord when he was a little boy.[258]

The first time the Doctor left Gallifrey was to visit his family's summer house on the other side of the Constellation. While looking up into the night's sky with his mother, he saw a fleet of time ships but never asked where they were going.[259]

An account of the Doctor's boyhood claims that he and the Master grew up together, and played near the river Lethe. A bully, Torvic, menaced the Master, but the Doctor fought back and thereby caused Torvic's death. Death later visited the Doctor in a dream, and sought to take him as her Champion, but the Doctor told her to take the Master instead. This gave rise to the Master becoming Death's Champion, and would motivate the Doctor and the Master to leave Gallifrey.[260]

247 "Voyager"
248 *The Quantum Archangel*
249 *The Infinity Doctors*
250 *The Infinity Doctors, The Taking of Planet 5, The Gallifrey Chronicles.*
251 *The Gallifrey Chronicles.* The prophecy paraphrases one from an abandoned American pilot script from the nineties. The book shows the Doctor fulfilling the prophecy - assuming the "lost scrolls of Rassilon" are the Matrix files in his mind. He had already made Last Contact in *The Daleks*, when he made contact with the race that would eventually destroy the Time Lords in the Last Great Time War, as revealed in *Dalek*.

252 *Smith and Jones*
253 *The Eight Doctors*
254 *Unnatural History*
255 *The Ghosts of N-Space*
256 *The Girl in the Fireplace*
257 *Night Terrors.* The latter is a take-off of the apocryphal 1970s *Doctor Who* stageplay, *Seven Keys to Doomsday*, starring Trevor Martin.
258 SJA: *The Wedding of Sarah Jane Smith*
259 *The Infinity Doctors*
260 *Master.* This account is told as a fable, and so may not be true.

THE DOCTOR'S AGE: The Doctor's age has been specified a number of times, but he is often vague and contradictory on the subject.

The second Doctor tells Victoria that he is "450" in *The Tomb of the Cybermen*. The Master of the Land of Fiction says he is "ageless" in *The Mind Robber*. (In the draft scripts of *The Power of the Daleks* and *The Underwater Menace,* he was "750".)

The third Doctor claims to have been a scientist for "thousands of years" in both *Doctor Who and the Silurians* and *The Mind of Evil*.

The fourth Doctor says he is "749" in *Planet of Evil, The Brain of Morbius* and *The Seeds of Doom*, and "nearly 750" in *Pyramids of Mars*. He is "750" by *The Robots of Death*, 756 (according to him) or 759 (according to Romana) in *The Ribos Operation*, nearly 760 in *Nightmare of Eden*, 750 again in *The Creature from the Pit* and *The Leisure Hive*. (A scripted scene in *The Stones of Blood* showed him celebrating his 751st birthday.) Complicating matters further, fifteen years elapse for the fourth Doctor and Romana in *Heart of TARDIS* (set between *The Stones of Blood* and *The Androids of Tara*) as they travel through a nexus fighting such foes as the Solstice Squid; it's thirty years if they do, in fact, have to make the same journey back again.

The sixth Doctor is 900 in *Revelation of the Daleks* and *The Mysterious Planet*, but "over 900" by *Terror of the Vervoids*. An elderly Jacob Williams claims in *100*: "Bedtime Story" that the sixth Doctor spent a hundred years showing four completely paralysed people - including him and Evelyn - the wonders of the universe, but this is a highly suspect claim given the Doctor's age in *Time and the Rani*, and could just owe to Jacob relating events to his son in a fable-like fashion.

In *Time and the Rani*, both the seventh Doctor and the Rani are "953", and the Doctor has "nine hundred years experience" by *Remembrance of the Daleks*. In the New Adventures, he was around a thousand years old. According to *SLEEPY*, he celebrated his 1000th birthday during *Set Piece*.

The eighth Doctor is 1012 in *Vampire Science*, in which it's also said that his current body is "three" years old, meaning that the seventh Doctor regenerated at age 1009. In *The Dying Days*, the eighth Doctor is 1200. We also know that this incarnation resided on Earth for one hundred and thirteen years, from 1888-2001 (beginning with *The Ancestor Cell* and ending with *Escape Velocity*) and that he spent six hundred years on the planet Orbis (*Orbis*). Cumulatively, and however one structures the eighth Doctor's adventures, he must be at least 1725 (probably more).

The new series reset the Doctor's age, but has been consistent in its progression since then. The ninth Doctor says he's 900 in *Aliens of London* and *The Doctor Dances*. In response to Rose's question about the problems introducing himself without a real name in *The Empty Child*, he says, "Nine centuries in, I'm coping".

The tenth Doctor says he's 903 in *Voyage of the Damned*, "The Whispering Gallery" and *The Nemonite Invasion*. He's 906 in *The End of Time* (TV). Taken at face value, this means that the Doctor's tenth body only survived for six years.

The eleventh Doctor is 907 in *Flesh and Stone* and *Amy's Choice*. He mentions spending "nine hundred years in time and space" in *A Christmas Carol*. In *The Impossible Planet*, we see him at two different points in his life - at age 909 and 1,103. He ends Series 6 as the latter. It's unclear if the intervening hundred and ninety-five years occur (for him) during the mid-season hiatus between *A Good Man Goes to War* and *Let's Kill Hitler* or between *The God Complex* and *Closing Time* (after he drops Amy and Rory on Earth). The Doctor telling young George in *Night Terrors*, "I was your age oh, about a thousand years ago", might suggest that about a century elapses between each break.

The tenth Doctor evidently doesn't add the ten years of life he yields to restart a TARDIS energy cell in *The Rise of the Cybermen* to the overall tally of his age, perhaps suggesting that the eleventh Doctor doesn't count the twenty-five years he donates to settle Amy's temporal credit card bill (*Borrowed Time*) either.

From this, we can infer some other dates:

• The Doctor has been operating his TARDIS for five hundred and twenty-three years by *The Pirate Planet*, and was 759 in the previous story, *The Ribos Operation*. This would mean that the Doctor left Gallifrey when he was 236. However, *The Doctor's Wife* claims that the Doctor has been travelling in the TARDIS for "seven hundred years"; as he was cited as being 909 in *The Impossible Astronaut*, this would alternatively suggest that he left Gallifrey when he was 209-ish.

• The Doctor attended his Tech Course with Drax "four hundred fifty years" before *The Armageddon Factor*. This would mean he was 309 at the time (implying it was after he left Gallifrey, or that he left and then returned before leaving for the last time).

• Romana is equally inconsistent with her age, and the age difference between her and the Doctor can variously be calculated as 617 or 620 (*The Ribos Operation*), 625 (*City of Death, Creature from the Pit*) or 600 (*The Leisure Hive*).

The Doctor's Early Education

Jo: "Makes it seem so pointless really, doesn't it?"

The Doctor: "I felt like that once when I was young. It was the blackest day of my life."

Jo: "Why?"

The Doctor: "Ah, well, that's another story. I'll tell you about it one day. The point is, that day was not only my blackest, it was also my best... when I was a little boy, we used to live in a house that was perched halfway up the top of a mountain. And behind our house, there sat under a tree an old man, a hermit, a monk. He'd lived under this tree for half his lifetime, so they said, and he'd learned the secret of life. So, when my black day came, I went and asked him to help me... He just sat there, silently, expressionless, and he listened whilst I poured out my troubles to him. I was too unhappy even for tears, I remember. And when I'd finished, he lifted a skeletal hand and he pointed. Do you know what he pointed at?... A flower. One of those little weeds. Just like a daisy, it was. Well, I looked at it for a moment and suddenly I saw it through his eyes. It was simply glowing with life, like a perfectly cut jewel. And the colours? Well, the colours were deeper and richer than you could possibly imagine. Yes, that was the daisiest daisy I'd ever seen."

Jo: "And that was the secret of life? A daisy? Honestly, Doctor."

The Doctor: "Yes, I laughed too when I first heard it. So, later, I got up and I ran down that mountain and I found that the rocks weren't grey at all, but they were red, brown and purple and gold. And those pathetic little patches of sludgy snow, they were shining white. Shining white in the sunlight."[261]

---

261 *The Time Monster*

262 *The Time Monster, Planet of the Spiders, State of Decay.*

263 *Lungbarrow*

264 *The Five Doctors*

265 *Shada*

266 *Image of the Fendahl*

267 *Black Orchid*

268 *The Nowhere Place*

269 "Planet Bollywood"

270 *Seasons of Fear*

271 *The Gallifrey Chronicles*

272 *Serpent Crest: Aladdin Time*

273 *The Sound of Drums*

274 *The Story of Martha:* "The Frozen Wastes"

275 Combining accounts given in *The Sound of Drums* and *The End of Time* (TV). Some have questioned how the appearance of the child Master, the Doctor's mention of Gallifreyan "families" (both in *The Sound of Drums*) and the appearance of what the Doctor claims is his cot (*A Good Man Goes to War*) can be reconciled against the notion of looming as given by the New Adventures. However, accounts of the Doctor's early life on Gallifrey always seem contradictory - by now, it's almost a tradition.

276 *The Sound of Drums*

277 "Mortal Beloved". It seems a stretch, given what we otherwise know of the Doctor's age and early life, to think that he spent whole centuries at the Academy. Maybe it just *felt* like centuries.

278 *The Coming of the Terraphiles*

279 *The Stolen Earth, Journey's End.*

280 According to the Master in *Last of the Time Lords.*

281 *The Fires of Pompeii*

282 *The Deadly Assassin*

283 *Lungbarrow*

284 *Timewyrm: Revelation*

285 *Divided Loyalties*

286 *Terror of the Autons, The Deadly Assassin, The Armageddon Factor, The Mark of the Rani.*

287 *The Time Meddler*

288 *The War Games*

289 *Arc of Infinity*

290 *Terror of the Autons*

291 *Divided Loyalties, Neverland.*

292 *The Death of Art*

293 *Time and the Rani*

294 Or so he claims, perhaps glibly, in *The Song of the Megaptera.*

295 *Night Thoughts*

296 *Mission to Magnus.* The back cover to the novelisation of this story (not included in this chronology in favour of the Big Finish audio adaptation) says that Anzor was a bully from the "class of the fourth millennium on Gallifrey".

297 *The Five Doctors*

298 *The Armageddon Factor*

299 *Island of Death*

300 *World Game*

301 *The Deadly Assassin*

302 *Lungbarrow*

303 *Cat's Cradle: Time's Crucible*

304 *The Twin Dilemma*

305 *Demon Quest: Sepulchre*

306 *The Time Monster*

307 *The Nightmare Fair*

308 *Made of Steel*

The same mentor told the Doctor ghost stories about the Vampires.[262] Satthralope, a member of House Lungbarrow, sacked the hermit because he was a bad influence and too expensive.[263]

The Doctor was interested enough in Gallifreyan history to take the unusual step of learning the dead language of Old High Gallifreyan.[264] The Doctor admired Salyavin.[265] He was frightened by stories of the Fendahl.[266] He always wanted to be a train driver.[267] The Doctor took up trainspotting as a hobby.[268] His first train set was a Hornby, Double-O.[269]

The Doctor's mother told him a nursery rhyme about Zagreus, which spoke of people disappearing up paradoxical staircases.[270] When he was an impressionable age, she also told him scary stories about Grandfather Paradox.[271] The Doctor read *Arabian Nights* when he was a Time Tot.[272]

On Gallifrey, the Toclafane were spoken of in fairytales, much like the bogeyman on Earth.[273] The Doctor was told as a boy that there was no point being an explorer, as the Time Lords had already discovered everything.[274]

The children of Gallifrey were taken from their families at age eight, and brought to the Academy. Each novice was taken for Initiation, and made to stand in front of the Untempered Schism: a gap in the fabric of reality. From there, each novice would see the whole of the Vortex, and stare at the raw power of time and space. Some novices would become inspired, some would run away, and some would go mad.

The Master looked into the Vortex while he was a child, and some believed this was the beginning of his madness. Rassilon and the High Council of Time Lords, trapped in the time-lock of The Last Great Time War, seeded the heartbeat of a Time Lord through the Vortex and into the eight-year-old Master's mind as a means of facilitating their escape. Throughout his lives, the Master was made to hear the sound of drums as a call to war.[275]

The Doctor chose his name, as did the Master.[276] The Doctor claimed that he didn't spend centuries at "that poxy academy" just to be called "Mister."[277] The Doctor worked as a courier in the vast spaceport Desiree during his gap century, although he was fired because he kept getting lost.[278] When the Doctor was "just a kid", only 90 years old, he visited the Medusa Cascade, a rift in time and space that reached into every dimension and every parallel reality.[279] At some point, he sealed the rift of the Medusa Cascade single-handed.[280] The Doctor's real name burns in the Cascade of Medusa.[281]

The Academy Years

The Doctor was a member of the Prydonian Chapter but came to forsake his birthright.[282] When the Doctor was on Gallifrey, Cardinal Lenadi led the Prydonians.[283]

Gallifrey's highest peak, Mount Cadon, extended to the fringes of the planet's atmosphere and held the Prydonian Academy far up its slopes. Acolytes there endlessly recanted protocols and procedures. In high towers, special pupils learned dark arts.[284]

The Academy was basically a self-contained city annexed to the Gallifreyan Capitol. It took up twenty-eight square miles of Gallifrey's surface.[285]

The Doctor was a contemporary of the Master, Runcible, Drax and the Rani.[286] He was "fifty years before" the Monk.[287] The War Chief and the Doctor recognised each other.[288] The Doctor knew Hedin and Damon.[289] He knew the Time Lord who warned him about the Master.[290]

The Doctor was at the Academy with Vansell.[291] He attended the Rani's raucous 94th birthday party.[292] The Doctor attended University with the Rani, and his speciality was thermodynamics.[293] He got an education at the "University of Gallifrey".[294] The Doctor said his field was "mainly" the science of macro-cosmology.[295]

Anzor, the son of a High Council member, bullied the Doctor into doing his homework at the Prydonian Academy. He also tormented him with a pain-inducing Galvanizer stick. One of the Doctor's friends, Cheevah, stood up to Anzor - who sealed Cheevah in a block of crystal, and dropped him from the Academy belltower.[296]

He attended "the Academy" with the Master.[297] The Doctor attended a Tech Course with the Class of '92, which included Drax, before he gained his Doctorate.[298] The Doctor was taught quantum mechanics at infant school. He and his friends once put a teacher in a time loop. He kept a pet flubble under his bed during his first year at the Academy, and was nearly caught when she went into heat and started a mating song.[299] He took his Gallifrey Lifesaver's Certificate.[300]

The Doctor studied at Prydon Academy (where Borusa taught him).[301] Lord Cardinal Lenadi led the Prydonian Chapter during the Doctor's time on Gallifrey.[302] Cardinal Borusa wrote a history called *Rassilon the God*.[303] The Doctor was taught by Azmael.[304] The Doctor's old academy teacher told him, "Ignore history at your peril".[305] He used to build time jammers to disrupt others' experiments.[306] When the Doctor was young, he kept enough odds and ends in his pockets to build a holo-field scrambler in five minutes flat - and often did.[307] He used to build space-time portals for fun.[308]

Ruath and the Doctor staged pranks together - they introduced cats into the Gallifreyan ecosystem, altered gravity to make a Panopticon graduation take place in mid-air and electrified Borusa's perigosto stick.[309] Cats were very popular on Gallifrey, to such an extent that every President had a presidential cat... until an incident with giant mice.[310]

A Cardinal Sendok taught them at the Academy.[311] The Doctor skipped his Academy class on transdimensional locus attraction dynamics to learn the yo-yo and juggling.[312] The Time Lord Dimension Ethics Committee banned all exploration of the higher dimensions. Nevertheless, fascinated by the legends of the Great Old Ones at the Academy, the Doctor and Master travelled back in time to search for Valdemar. They found nothing but warnings.[313]

Daring neonates at the Academy played a dangerous game called Eighth Man Bound. This entailed deliberately putting an "Initiate" into a state of flux between life or death, enabling them to witness and experience their future regenerations. The term was coined after a student of the Arcalian Chapter who discovered the natures of his first seven bodies, but couldn't observe the eighth. A student of the Prydonian Chapter was rumoured to have tied this record.[314]

The Doctor used to play truant so he could down pints of Best Shobogan beer at the Golden Grockle in Low Town. He seethed with anger at the High Council.[315] **The Doctor at this time was called "Theta Sigma", his nickname.[316] The Master got a higher grade at Cosmic Science than the Doctor. The Doctor claims he was a late developer.[317]** Cardinal Sendok taught the Doctor and the Master cosmic science.[318]

DIVIDED LOYALTIES -> The Doctor was part of the Deca, a group of ten brilliant students who were activists in favour of more Time Lord intervention. The Deca members were: the Doctor, Koschei (the Master), Mortimus (the Monk), Magnus (the War Chief), Drax, Ushas (the Rani), Vansell (actually a Celestial Intervention Agency spy), Rallon, Millennia and Jelpax.

They were taught by Borusa, Franilla, Sendok and Zass.

It was as part of the Deca that the Doctor learned about the Celestial Toymaker. The Doctor, Rallon and Millennia located the Toymaker and were caught up in his games. Rallon and Millennia were apparently killed, and the Doctor was expelled from the Academy on his return to Gallifrey, and ordered to spend five hundred years in Records and Traffic Control. He studied for his doctorate in his spare time.

The President at this time was Drall, the Castellan was

309 *Goth Opera*
310 *Nevermore.* This can only be after cats are introduced to the ecosystem. The giant mice are mentioned in *The Mark of the Rani.*
311 *The Quantum Archangel*
312 *Match of the Day*
313 *Tomb of Valdemar*
314 According to Professor Thripsted's *Genetic Politics Beyond the Third Zone* in *Christmas on a Rational Planet* (p212-216). The Doctor names himself as "Eighth Man Bound" in *The Dying Days.*
315 *The Eight Doctors*
316 *The Armageddon Factor, The Happiness Patrol.*
317 *Terror of the Autons*
318 *The Quantum Archangel*
319 *The Shakespeare Code*
320 "The Age of Ice"
321 *Lungbarrow*
322 *The Ribos Operation*
323 *The King of Terror*
324 *The Scarlet Empress*
325 *Verdigris*
326 *Excelis Dawns*
327 *Iris: The Panda Invasion*
328 *The Blue Angel.* In *Iris: Enter Wildthyme* (p283), Marville similarly claims that Iris and her "fabled ancestors" hail from the Obverse... right before Iris blends that and her Gallifreyan origins together with the comment, "Fabled ancestors, my arse! I had a number of peculiar aunts and we lived in a decrepit old house in the mountains."
329 *Iris: The Land of Wonder*
330 *The Daleks*
331 *The Chase* and *The Tomb of the Cybermen* suggest the Doctor "built" the TARDIS, *An Unearthly Child* states that Susan coined the term, although later stories seem to contradict both claims. Some commentators have tried to attribute the Doctor's statement in *The Chase* to mean that he only built his Ship's time-path detector, not the whole Ship, but this is a rationalisation after-the-fact and not borne out by the scene itself. *Lungbarrow*, at least, supports the notion that Susan created the word "TARDIS" by claiming she was around when TARDISes were relatively new.
332 *Galaxy 4*
333 *The End of Time* (TV)
334 *The Two Doctors*
335 *Carnival of Monsters*
336 *The Invisible Enemy*
337 *Shada*
338 *Cold Fusion, The Infinity Doctors.*
339 *Deadly Reunion*
340 *World Game*
341 Dating "Flashback" (*DWM Winter Special 1992*) - "Ancient Gallifrey, or so it seems." Magnus is apparently the War Chief from *The War Games.*
342 *Benny: The Tears of the Oracle* (p166-167)
343 *Underworld*

Rannex. Type 35 TARDISes were in operation; the Doctor used a Type 18 to visit the Toymaker.

Only Jelpax completed his time at the Academy in the conventional manner, the others either went to special projects or vanished. Jelpax went on to work with Borusa.

Time Lords had to pass a test to fly a TARDIS; the Doctor failed his.[319] The Doctor wasn't much for studying at school.[320] He deliberately failed his exams so that people would underestimate him, and to avoid office duty.[321] **The Doctor eventually scraped through the Academy with 51% on the second attempt.**[322] His poor results were a grave disappointment to his parents.[323]

Iris Wildthyme

The adventurer in time and space known as Iris Wildthyme claimed to have grown up in a House in southern Gallifrey. It was ruled by Aunts including Baba, her favourite. Iris' mother ran away with an offworlder. Iris found an abandoned TARDIS in the wilderness and adopted it.[324]

Iris also claimed to come from one of the New Towns under the Gallifreyan Capitol. She found her TARDIS abandoned in the mountains as a wasted experiment, helping it to learn, feed and evolve. In turn, the bus gave Iris advice. She's been travelling longer than the Doctor.

The Doctor said Iris wasn't a proper Time Lady and that the Time Lords were unsure of her identity.[325] Iris referred to the Doctor's people as "a snobby, over-privileged bunch".[326] Iris was unique in the whole of creation, and had no duplicates in parallel realities.[327]

Iris said the Obverse was her home, and that she was "not who she said she was, and more besides!"[328] On another occasion, Iris claimed to hail from the Clockworks - a place of logic and reason, inhabited by beings who tinkered with time and were "the grease in the cogs of the multiverse". She was just a kid from the slums, and rebelled by stealing her time-travelling bus.[329]

The Doctor on Gallifrey

The Doctor says he was a pioneer among his people.[330] **He claimed to have built his Ship. Susan coined the acronym TARDIS.**[331] **The Doctor excelled himself when he built the TARDIS force field.**[332] **He and the Master referred to each other as "Lords".**[333]

Before leaving Gallifrey, the Doctor was used on a diplomatic mission at least once, when he visited the inauguration of Station Chimera in the Third Zone.[334] **Following a campaign by the Doctor, the Time Lords banned MiniScopes.**[335]

The Doctor's reflex link connected him to the Time Lord intelligentsia.[336] Like all Time Lords, he swore an oath to protect the Law of Gallifrey.[337]

The Doctor was a member of the Supreme Council.[338] He held a powerful position before leaving Gallifrey.[339] He was a member of the High Council during the latter years of his first incarnation.[340]

"Flashback"[341] -> The first Doctor ("Thete") supervised Magnus' project to tap into a giant ball of Artron energy that Magnus had extracted from the Vortex. It would provide the Time Lords with more power than even Rassilon and Omega had dreamt of, and Magnus saw this as leading to "a new beginning for our stagnant race". The Doctor was more sceptical, and his fears were confirmed when they learned the energy ball was alive. Magnus wanted to continue regardless - so the Doctor destroyed his equipment with a staser. "And that was that. Any chance of a reconciliation between the two - any hope of regaining their former friendship - died at that moment." The Doctor was commended for his action.

Lord Braxiatel never wanted to conform, but graduated with a "fistful of firsts" and initiated many research projects - all to position himself as a nonconformist in conformist's clothing. By the time Braxiatel's brother was doing his exams (and scraped through with the barest minimum of effort), Braxiatel was trusted enough to achieve his dream of serving as an unofficial ambassador, and saw the universe by undertaking clandestine missions for Gallifrey's benefit. Braxiatel's brother followed his example to more of an extreme, and outright left their homeworld.[342]

The Minyan Incident

The Minyans used nuclear technology to destroy their planet. The Time Lords subsequently renounced intervention in the affairs of other planets.[343]

The truth was more complicated. Braxiatel and the Time Lord Narvin had become involved in Project Alpha, an undertaking to create a timonic fusion device capable of obliterating portions of space-time. As Braxiatel feared, the device was more powerful than its designers believed - when tested, it created a shockwave that ravaged Minyos. The High Council launched a cover-up, saying Minyos was destroyed in a civil war. Braxiatel felt that technology's potential for destruction had become so great that the universe's great artistic and cultural treasures needed better protection. He started sneaking away from Gallifrey and amassing a personal collection of such works.

(=) The isolationist Torvald travelled back to this point from Gallifrey's future and stole the timonic fusion device as part of a scheme to discredit President Romana, causing alterations to Gallifrey's history. Narvin covered up the theft.

Romana and Braxiatel travelled back and ensured the device was detonated as history recorded. Minyos was destroyed, and Torvald stole a fake device instead.[344]

Time Lords were "forbidden to interfere".[345]

Past Lives

Morbius would later probe the Doctor's mind, and see eight incarnations of the Doctor before the one generally accepted as the "first" Doctor.[346]

The Doctor's Marriage

The Doctor fell in love with his former nurse and tutor, the Womb-born Gallifreyan who would become known as Patience. She taught him to dance, which he did in front of some house guests including Mr Saldaamir, a pair from Althrace and a yellow-skinned man with red fins.

They married. Savar was one of the guests at the wedding.[347] The Doctor painted his wife's portrait. As he finished, she told him she was pregnant.[348] They went on to have thirteen children.[349]

Shortly after he regenerated, the Doctor and Patience celebrated the birth of their first grandchild. Their son was a Cardinal and the Doctor sat on the Supreme Council, as his father did before him. The President ordered the Guard to search the Doctor's family home for "children born of woman". The Doctor's thirteen children were dragged out and his daughter-in-law's baby was scheduled for termination. The Doctor's whereabouts during this incident were unknown, but there was a warrant for his arrest - he stood accused of "consorting with aliens".

The Doctor (in what we would consider his "first" incarnation) would later travel back in time to this point. He rescued his infant granddaughter and took her to the ancient past. He then got Patience to safety by taking her

---

344 *Gallifrey: The Inquiry*

345 According to the Cyber Lieutenant in *Earthshock*.

FORBIDDEN TO INTERFERE: *Underworld* established that the destruction of Minyos led directly to the Time Lords' policy of non-intervention. Previous versions of *Ahistory* have assumed that this happened in the distant past, but *Gallifrey: The Inquiry* establishes that this happens after the Doctor graduated. *Divided Loyalties*, however, states that while the Doctor was studying, there were those who wanted Gallifrey to intervene more often; *The Gallifrey Chronicles* says that this was true a generation before.

Clearly, this is a perennial and active debate among the Time Lords, with three factions. In descending order of size and influence: most are opposed to any form of intervention; a significant number think the Time Lords should be a benign influence; a very few feel Gallifrey should impose its rule on the rest of the universe. The majority of Time Lords clearly worry that "benign" intervention will quickly become tyranny, and this is not an unfounded fear.

From the time of Rassilon through to the Doctor's time, however, there seems to be a status quo - the Time Lords fight wars against immense threats, and perhaps monitor time-travel experiments and send occasional delegations out for specific reasons, but broadly confine themselves to Gallifrey. The existence of the Celestial Intervention Agency suggests that covert operations were also conducted.

If Gallifrey's "zero tolerance" attitude to intervention is a recent crackdown, rather than dogma since the time of Rassilon, this would help explain a few of the apparent contradictions in its policies towards other races. We can see that when the Doctor was young, he travelled and was involved in interventionist efforts, like banning the MiniScopes. Clearly, Gallifrey in this period was relatively willing to interact with the wider

universe.

The Minyan Incident seems to have been a shock to the system that resulted in a clampdown in all interventionism. As the Doctor left soon after this, and given what we know of the Doctor's attitude to intervention, it's extremely tempting to imagine that this clampdown was a factor in his departure. As the varying accounts of why the Doctor left Gallifrey show, what motivates him leaving could be anything from a principled rejection of Time Lord society to punishment for his being caught redhanded in a newly-illegal act.

346 *The Brain of Morbius*. See the Past Lives sidebar.

347 *Cold Fusion*, *The Infinity Doctors*.

348 *The Infinity Doctors*

349 *Cold Fusion*

350 *Cold Fusion*, *The Infinity Doctors*. The Doctor's new incarnation matches the description of the "Camfield Doctor" seen in *The Brain of Morbius*.

351 *The Infinity Doctors*

352 *Cold Fusion*

353 *Unnatural History*. There's also no account of what happened to the Doctor's son and daughter-in-law, or any of the Doctor's other children.

354 *Fear Her*. Although some have seen this as a reference to the Doctor raising Miranda in *Father Time*, if he was indeed Susan's biological grandfather, then he clearly must also have been a father.

355 *The Doctor's Daughter*

356 "A Fairytale Life"

357 Dating *The Infinity Doctors* (PDA #17) - The story takes place an unspecified amount of time after Patience disappears, to an unspecified incarnation of the Doctor, at an unspecified point before Gallifrey's destruction (possibly between *The Gallifrey Chronicles* and *Rose*). It's a thousand years since Savar lost his eyes.

IS THE INFINITY DOCTORS CANON?: *The Infinity Doctors* is a story set on Gallifrey that takes all the infor-

to an ancient TARDIS. As he did this, the Capitol was burning.[350] Mobs stormed the Panopticon that night.[351]

The Doctor's memories of this trauma were blocked, although by who or what is unclear. He believed his wife had died.[352] It is unclear if the Doctor's father was still on Gallifrey at this point. After this, the Doctor's father may have adopted the name "Joyce" and relocated to San Francisco on Earth, continuing the Project with Larna and Mr Saldaamir.[353]

The Doctor remembered that he was a father, once.[354] He was a father, but "lost all that a long time ago", and remembered "the hole the left, all the pain that filled it" - when they died, a part of him died with them.[355] He "had plenty of family and knew what it was like to lose them".[356]

The Infinity Doctor

? (=?) (w?) - THE INFINITY DOCTORS[357] -> The Doctor mourned for his dead wife, and even though she died a long time ago, he still lit a new candle every year in her memory. Before this time, he had travelled the universe and returned to Gallifrey. He had defeated and imprisoned Centro, a mechanical being that could warp space.

On Gallifrey, the Doctor served as a tutor who oversaw

- amongst others - the brilliant student Larna. He negotiated a final peace between the Sontarans and the Rutans, ending their eternal war. Gallifrey monitored the Effect, a reality-altering ripple. The Doctor and his friend the Magistrate went to the end of time to confront the one who was responsible: Omega. The Doctor met his wife Patience, whom Omega had rescued from death, but again lost her. Omega was defeated, but the Magistrate didn't return from this mission. The Doctor did, and had grown restless with Gallifrey.

Voran became President. Larna was charged to travel the universe and clear up after the Effect, a mission that would take two thousand years.

Susan

The Doctor's granddaughter Susan was something of an enigma.[358]

Susan was the Doctor's grand-daughter "and always will be".[359] Susan described her home planet as "quite like Earth, but at night the sky is a burned orange, and the leaves on the trees are bright silver".[360] She knew about the Dark Tower.[361] She was 15 when she met Ian and Barbara.[362] The other Time Lords never referred to

mation from every previous story (in all media) set on Gallifrey - and other references to it - at face value and incorporates them into the narrative. The paradox being that we've seen a vast number of contradictory accounts of the Doctor's home planet, so that *The Infinity Doctors'* super-adherence to established continuity actually makes it impossible to place at a particular point in continuity without contradicting something established elsewhere.

References in *Seeing I, Unnatural History, The Taking of Planet 5, Father Time* and *The Gallifrey Chronicles* all make it clear that *The Infinity Doctors* (or, at the very least, events identical to it) took place in the "real" *Doctor Who* universe.

Latterly a fan consensus has built up that *The Infinity Doctors* is set on the "reconstructed" Gallifrey promised by *The Gallifrey Chronicles*, that the Infinity Doctor is the eighth Doctor, and his Gallifrey is the one destined to be destroyed in the Time War. This wasn't the author's intention, but isn't ruled out by the book.

358 IS SUSAN THE DOCTOR'S GRANDDAUGHTER?: *Cold Fusion* recounts Susan being rescued by the Doctor as an infant, which followed the description in the original "Cartmel Masterplan" document. When the events of that document were dramatised in *Lungbarrow*, Susan was an older child.

This complicates an already rather convoluted story. If both the accounts of *Cold Fusion* and *Lungbarrow* are taken at face value (and both contain degrees of ambi-

guity), it seems that Susan was born to the Camfield Doctor's daughter-in-law in the recent past (ie: when the Doctor was a younger man and living on Gallifrey, not millions of years ago at the time of Rassilon). The Hartnell Doctor came back to this time zone (in *Cold Fusion*, it's possible he simply regenerated, but this would seem to seriously contradict *Lungbarrow*) with the Hand of Omega and then rescued the infant Susan and Patience. The Doctor then travelled deep into the past of Gallifrey, where Susan was left in "safety" with the Other (where she was considered the last womb-born child). Patience fled Gallifrey in an early TARDIS (possibly she was taken into the distant past, too, and stole the TARDIS there). The Hartnell Doctor would revisit ancient Gallifrey and discover that following the death of the Other, Susan had been living on the streets there.

359 *An Unearthly Child*, the quote comes from *The Dalek Invasion of Earth.* The Doctor and Susan frequently refer to each other as grandfather and grandchild.

360 *Marco Polo*

361 *The Five Doctors*

362 Barbara says Susan is 15 in *An Unearthly Child*. In *Marco Polo*, Ping Cho says she is "in my sixteenth year", and Susan says "Well, so am I". So Susan is not far older than she looks, unlike Romana.

Susan.[363] She coined the name "TARDIS".[364]

Susan was born in Gallifrey's recent past. Her grandfather was the Doctor. She was a naturally-born child, an abomination in the eyes of the authorities of Gallifrey. Her mother's fate was unknown. Her father was a Cardinal.[365]

Susan was born in Gallifrey's distant past. Her grandfather was the Other. She was the last naturally-born child on Gallifrey. Her mother died at the moment of her birth, as the Pythia's curse of sterility came into effect. Her father was a warrior.[366] Susan had a perfect memory, which she said was "the curse of her people".[367] Circumstances denied Susan a proper education on Gallifrey.[368]

The Doctor Leaves Gallifrey

The exact nature of the Doctor's departure from Gallifrey is still a mystery, and there have been a number of seemingly contradictory accounts of the circumstances in which he left.[369]

Account One[370]:

Jamie: "Why did you run away from [your people] in the first place?"

The Doctor: "What? Well... I was bored... The Time Lords are an immensely civilised race. We can control our own environment, we can live forever barring accidents, and we have the secret of space/time travel."

Jamie: "Well, what's so wrong in all that?"

The Doctor: "Well, we hardly ever use our great powers! We consent simply to observe and to gather knowledge."

Zoe: "And that wasn't enough for you?"

The Doctor: "No, of course not. With a whole galaxy to explore? Millions of planets? Aeons of time, countless civilisations to meet?"

Jamie: "Well, why do they object to you doing all that?

The Doctor: "Well... It is a fact, Jamie, that I do tend to get involved with things."

Jamie: "Aye, you can say that again! Whenever there's any trouble he's in it right up to his neck."

Zoe: "But you've helped people, Doctor."

The Doctor: Yes, yes, but that's no excuse in [the Time Lords'] eyes."

Account Two: LUNGBARROW[371] -> The Doctor worked as a Scrutationary Archivist in the Prydonian Chapterhouse Bureau of Possible Events. His applications for promotion were always turned down.

Consulting the Bench of Matrocians, Quences - the head of the Lungbarrow household - learned that the Doctor would be a huge influence on the future of Gallifrey. He wanted the Doctor to become a Cardinal. The Doctor stormed out of his family home after an argument with Quences about the Doctor's future prospects. With the Doctor no longer regarded as a member of the family, a replacement - Owis - was Loomed to maintain the family quota. However, this was illegal and the House was ostracised from Gallifreyan affairs. The Doctor's Cousins were trapped in the House.

The Doctor left an experiment with water-sligs running. A hundred and thirty years, later they broke out.

Quences was the 422nd Kithriarch of Lungbarrow.

The Doctor decided to steal a TARDIS and leave Gallifrey. The Hand of Omega recognised the Doctor was linked to the Other. When the Doctor left Gallifrey, the Hand redirected him to Gallifrey's ancient past.

---

363 On screen, Susan is never mentioned by any Time Lord, either those on Gallifrey or the various renegades.
364 *An Unearthly Child.* Later stories showed the manual for the Doctor's TARDIS which has the word on the cover, suggesting it was coined long before the Doctor's time. One possible conclusion is that Susan is from an earlier period of Gallifreyan history, and which is indeed what *Lungbarrow* established.
365 *Cold Fusion*
366 *Lungbarrow*
367 *Here There Be Monsters.* Having "a perfect memory" certainly isn't something one could convict the Doctor of, though.
368 *An Earthly Child*
369 As *The First Doctor Handbook* (p181) spells out, while the series was being devised and before the first scripts were in, the production team had a relatively clear idea of what the Doctor's secret was: "He has flashes of garbled memory which indicates he was involved in a galactic war and still fears pursuit by some undefined enemy... he escaped from his own galaxy in the year 5733." There's no supporting evidence for this on screen.
370 *The War Games*
371 Dating *Lungbarrow* (NA #60) - This was "eight hundred and seventy-three years ago". Given that this is set just before *Doctor Who - The Movie*, and *Vampire Science* states that the Doctor was 1009 when he regenerated, it would make him 136. However, given the contradictions over his age, it is probably best not to rely on this figure. Owis was Loomed 675 years ago.

THE DOCTOR'S FAMILY: Sixteen of the Doctor's forty-four Cousins are named in Lungbarrow: Quences, Owis, Glospin, Satthralope, Jobiska, Rynde, Arkhew, Maljamin, Farg, Celesia, Almund, Tugel, Chovor the Various, DeRoosifa, Salpash and Luton. Braxiatel is presumably another.

PAST LIVES: The orthodox view accepted wholesale by most fans is that the Doctor is a Time Lord who can regenerate his body twelve times when it is seriously injured. It's also held that William Hartnell played "the first Doctor" and that by the end of *The End of Time* (TV), the Doctor has regenerated ten times, so that Matt Smith is the eleventh incarnation of the Time Lord. This version of events is actually established very late in the show's history (the term "regeneration", for example, is not even used until *Planet of the Spiders* at the end of Season 11, the word "incarnation" is only used on rare occasions - such as in *The Twin Dilemma* and *The Trial of a Time Lord* - and so on).

Only a half a dozen stories in the classic series refer to the orthodox view: In *The Three Doctors*, the Time Lords claim that the Hartnell Doctor is the "earliest". We learn that the Time Lords are limited to twelve regenerations in *The Deadly Assassin*, a view that is reinforced by *The Keeper of Traken*, *The Five Doctors* and *The Twin Dilemma*. (Although in *The Deadly Assassin*, *The Keeper of Traken* and *The Five Doctors*, we learn that it is possible for a Time Lord to regenerate more than twelve times, and in *The Twin Dilemma*, Azmael initiates a thirteenth regeneration, the strain of which kills him.)

It is *Mawdryn Undead* (Season 20) before the Doctor explicitly states that he has regenerated four times and has eight regenerations remaining. In *The Five Doctors*, the first Doctor sees the Davison Doctor and concludes "so there are five of me now" and refers to himself as "the original, you might say". In *Time and the Rani*, the Doctor talks of his "seventh persona". The voiceover at the start of *Doctor Who - The Movie* says that the Doctor is "nearing the end of my seventh life".

The new series displays the established eleven Doctors in order (starting with William Hartnell and finishing with David Tennant, then Matt Smith) in *The Next Doctor* and *The Eleventh Hour*. In *The Lodger*, the earliest Doctors appear in a mental flash, and the Matt Smith version points at himself and says, "eleventh". *SJA: Death of the Doctor* upsets some orthodoxy when the Doctor says he can regenerate "five hundred and seven times" (see the "Regeneration... A Complete New Life Cycle" sidebar).

Despite all this, the commonly used terms such as "first Doctor", "second Doctor" and so on are never used on screen (and should never be capitalised).

More often, the evidence about the Doctor's past is ambiguous or inconclusive: he seems vague about his age throughout his life, the details varying wildly from story to story, likewise his name, his doctorate and the reasons why he left Gallifrey. In *The Deadly Assassin*, Runcible remarks that the Doctor has had a facelift and the Doctor replies that he has had "several so far" (the original script more specifically said he had done so "three times"). In *The Ultimate Foe*, the Valeyard comes from somewhere between the Doctor's "twelfth and final incarnation" (not the "twelfth and thirteenth"). No unfamiliar Doctors come to light in *The Three Doctors* or

The Five Doctors, but on two occasions (*Day of the Daleks* and *Resurrection of the Daleks*), an attempt to probe the Doctor's mind is abruptly halted just as the William Hartnell incarnation appears on the monitor. In *The Creature from the Pit*, he claims Time Lords have ninety lives, and he's had a hundred and twenty.

There have been a number of hints that incarnation of the Doctor played by William Hartnell was not the first. In the script for *The Destiny of Doctor Who*, the new Doctor confides to his astonished companions that he has "renewed himself" before. In the transmitted version of the story, *The Power of the Daleks*, the line does not appear, but neither is it contradicted. In *The Brain of Morbius*, Morbius mentally regresses the Doctor back from his Tom Baker incarnation, through Jon Pertwee, Patrick Troughton and William Hartnell, but this time no-one interrupts and we go on to see a further eight incarnations of the Doctor prior to Hartnell. Morbius shouts - as the sequence of mysterious faces appears on the scanner - "How far Doctor? How long have you lived? Your puny mind is powerless against the strength of Morbius! Back! Back to your beginning!" These are certainly not Morbius' faces (as has occasionally been suggested) or the Doctor's ancestors or his family. Morbius is not deluding himself. The Doctor fails to win the fight and almost dies, only surviving because of the Elixir... it just happens that Morbius' brain casing can't withstand the pressures either.

The production team at the time (who bear a remarkable resemblance to the earlier Doctors, probably because eight of them - Christopher Barry, George Gallacio, Robert Banks Stewart, Phillip Hinchliffe, Douglas Camfield, Graeme Harper, Robert Holmes and Chris Baker - posed for the photographs used in the sequence), definitely intended the faces to be those of earlier Doctors. Producer Philip Hinchliffe said: "We tried to get famous actors for the faces of the Doctor. But because no-one would volunteer, we had to use backroom boys. And it is true to say that I attempted to imply that William Hartnell was not the first Doctor".

However we might want to fit this scene into the series' other continuity, or to rationalise it away, taking *The Brain of Morbius* on its own, there's no serious room for doubt that these are pre-Hartnell incarnations of the Doctor. This hasn't stopped fans doubting, of course. Two stories later, in *The Masque of Mandragora*, the Doctor and Sarah Jane discover "the old control room" that the Doctor claims to have used, although it had never been seen in the TV series before.

Cold Fusion features a sequence where the Doctor remembers his past on Gallifrey (p172-173), where he has recently regenerated to resemble the "Camfield Doctor" seen in *The Brain of Morbius*. However, there is a degree of ambiguity as to whether these are the Doctor's own memories. *Lungbarrow* states that the Hartnell Doctor was the first and hints, but never explicitly states, that the faces seen in *The Brain of Morbius* are incarnations of the Other, not the Doctor.

715

Account Three[372]**:** The Doctor lived sealed inside a city, on a planet hidden behind energy barricades. He finally left his people so he could experience the universe's wonders, to see its majesty, firsthand. He didn't leave for Susan's sake - she was an "accidental passenger, a hanger on". The Doctor looked old, but was just an adolescent as far as his people went; Susan, comparatively speaking, was just a baby. The TARDIS navigation system wasn't broken as was sometimes claimed - the Doctor had yet to forge a "mystical" bond with his TARDIS, which the legends of his people said was possible.

Account Four[373]**:** The president of Gallifrey, Pandak VII, issued a kill order on Braxiatel - but Braxiatel killed Lord Burner, the president's assassin, in self-defence. Braxiatel was appointed Lord Burner as punishment, and given a "burn order" for a member of his family - an old man - as a test of loyalty. The old man was tipped off by Braxiatel as to the danger, stole a TARDIS and left Gallifrey with his granddaughter. Pandak VII died the very same day, owing to a power relay overload... that an inquiry led by Braxiatel determined was an accident. Braxiatel and the old man were the only two Time Lords to ever survive a burn order.

The Doctor might have left of his own free will, because he was "bored" or had "grown tired of their lifestyle". He renounced the society of Time Lords. He abandoned his Prydonian birthright.[374] **But he has also stated he was "kicked out" and was "on the run".**[375] **The Doctor "ran away" from Gallifrey.**[376]

The Doctor was an "exile", unable to return home.[377] **He "had reasons of his own" for leaving his home planet.**[378] **The second Doctor told Victoria that he might try to take her to his planet.**[379]

He left Gallifrey because of the corruption rife in Time Lord politics.[380] **The Doctor travelled to see history hap-**

---

372 Here There Be Monsters

373 Gallifrey: Annihilation. The inauguration of Pandak III is mentioned in The Deadly Assassin.

374 The War Games, Resurrection of the Daleks, Pyramids of Mars, The Deadly Assassin.

375 The Invisible Enemy, The Five Doctors.

376 The Sound of Drums, The Beast Below.

377 An Unearthly Child, The Edge of Destruction, The Massacre, The Two Doctors.

378 The War Games

379 The Tomb of the Cybermen, suggesting that he thought he could go back by that point, or he's just being cute with her.

380 World Game

381 Aliens of London

382 The Reign of Terror, Galaxy 4, The Massacre, The Celestial Toymaker, Colony in Space.

383 According to Susan in Marco Polo.

384 Timewyrm: Revelation (p48).

385 Frontier in Space, Logopolis.

386 The Big Bang

387 Frontier in Space, The Big Bang.

388 The Invasion of Time

389 Logopolis, Cold Fusion.

390 Planet of the Dead

391 The Song of the Megaptera

392 Logopolis - although it was working until An Unearthly Child.

393 Mindwarp

394 The Doctor's Wife. The Doctor was 909 in The Impossible Astronaut, a couple of episodes earlier, so was around 209 when he stole the TARDIS.

395 The Infinity Doctors

396 The Gallifrey Chronicles

397 Lungbarrow

398 The Eight Doctors

399 Remembrance of the Daleks, Silver Nemesis, An Unearthly Child.

400 The Sensorites

401 The Time Meddler. The Doctor says the Monk left their home planet fifty years after he did.

402 "Time and Time Again"

403 Seen in "Timeslip".

404 The Twin Dilemma, The Mark of the Rani, Planet of the Spiders respectively.

405 The Doctor's Wife

406 Spiral Scratch

407 The Doctor says he comes from "fifty years earlier" than the Monk in The Time Meddler. The War Chief remembers him leaving his home planet in The War Games. The Master is first seen in Terror of the Autons.

408 We first meet Irving Braxiatel in Theatre of War, but he's also present at the Armageddon Convention in The Empire of Glass, which occurs first chronologically. The Braxiatel Collection was first mentioned in City of Death.

409 Neverland

410 The Brain of Morbius. Gallifrey: The Inquiry establishes that the non-interference doctrine in its current hardline form is a development within the Doctor's lifetime, so the rebellion led by Morbius would seem to be against recent policy, rather than an ancient dogma.

411 Dating Warmonger (PDA #53) - It is never stated in The Brain of Morbius how long ago Morbius ruled Gallifrey. The Doctor recognises Morbius, but Morbius doesn't recognise the Doctor.

In his novelisation of the story, Terrance Dicks states that Morbius came to power after the Doctor left Gallifrey, and that the Doctor heard of Morbius on his travels. In Warmonger, also by Dicks, the Doctor (who has travelled into Gallifrey's past) muses that Borusa might be in his first incarnation (p166), and that this is the first time Borusa has met him, almost certainly setting it before the Doctor was born - but this is directly

pen in front of him.[381] He saw himself as an explorer and researcher.[382] After discovering "the mysteries of the skies", he could return home.[383]

The following image appears early in the Doctor's memory: "Here was a cowled figure shaking a fist at a dark castle, and in the next picture he was cowering from something huge and fearful. Then he was running."[384]

The Doctor claims to have borrowed rather than stolen the TARDIS.[385] The Doctor stole the TARDIS - or he borrowed it, he always intended to return it.[386] He fully intended to return it.[387] He wasn't authorised to take it.[388] Nor did he own the Ship.[389] He stole the TARDIS.[390] The Doctor technically nicked the TARDIS, but in truth the TARDIS wanted to see the universe as much as he did.[391]

There were "pressing reasons" why he couldn't wait for the Ship's chameleon circuit to be fixed.[391] If he stopped to consider his actions, he'd never have left Gallifrey.[393]

The Doctor's TARDIS was already a museum piece when he was young. The first time the Doctor touched the TARDIS console, he said aloud that she was "the most beautiful thing he had ever known". The Doctor chose the TARDIS because her door was open - the Ship wanted to see the universe, and so "stole" a Time Lord and ran away. Only the Doctor was "mad" enough to yield to the temptation the Ship offered.

By the time the Doctor was in his eleventh incarnation, he and the TARDIS had been travelling together for seven hundred years.[394]

The TARDIS was a family heirloom.[395] The TARDIS had been taken from Marnal by Ulysses. Marnal's son knew the truth about the Doctor's departure, and told his father what had happened afterwards.[396] The Doctor chose not to take a Type 53 TARDIS.[397]

The authorities thought of him as arrogant.[398] In addition to the TARDIS, the Doctor took the Hand of Omega, the Validium statue and his granddaughter Susan.[399]

The Doctor and Susan left home "ages" before they met Ian and Barbara.[400] Possibly more than fifty years.[401]

(=) If the Doctor had never left Gallifrey, he would have become President, but spent his time appeasing the Daleks. The Earth would have been invaded dozens of times.

Benny Summerfield witnessed the Doctor and Susan leaving Gallifrey.[402] During a timeslip, the Doctor would later re-enact the time he activated the TARDIS.[403]

Many other Time Lords were known to have left Gallifrey in the Doctor's lifetime: Azmael left Gallifrey to become Master of Jaconda. The Rani was exiled fol-lowing illegal experiments on animals, including an incident where genetically re-engineered mice that she had created ate the President's cat and attacked the President himself. She became ruler of Miasimia Goria. The Doctor's mentor left Gallifrey for Earth and became known as K'Anpo.[404] At some point, the Doctor knew the Corsair - a Time Lord adventurer who had a snake tattoo in every regeneration, including the couple of times that he was female.[405]

Rummas was taught by Delox and Borusa. He left Gallifrey in a stolen TARDIS to build up a collection, mainly of books. He took the Spiral Chamber - a portal to the Spiral at the nexus of the Time Vortex - and settled at the Library of Carsus.[406]

The Doctor left before the Monk, the War Chief and probably before the Master.[407]

Braxiatel spent twenty years arranging the Armageddon Convention. He would eventually dedicate himself to building the Braxiatel Collection, a repository of universal knowledge and art. Braxiatel collected every book banned by the Catholic Church. Unlike the Doctor, he freely left Gallifrey.[408]

The Morbius Crisis

The Cult of Morbius was formed in 5725.3, Rassilon Era.[409]

Morbius, the leader of the High Council, proposed that the Time Lords should end their policy of non-interference. When the High Council rejected this, he left Gallifrey and raised an army of conquest, promising them immortality. Devastating several planets on the way, the Cult of Morbius arrived on Karn, home of the Sisterhood. The Time Lords attacked them on Karn, destroying his army. Following a trial, Morbius was vaporised. Solon had removed Morbius' brain before his execution and preserved it.[410]

WARMONGER[411] -> Morbius was deposed by Saran, who became Acting President in his place. Junior Cardinal Borusa assisted Saran. Morbius was exiled from Gallifrey. Adopting the identity "General Rombusi", he raised an army of mercenaries using stolen Celestial Intervention Agency funds. These armies came from Darkeen, Fangoria, Martak and Romark. They conquered, among many other worlds, Tanith and the Ogron homeworld. Freedonia joined the General, and conquered nearby Sylvana. The General met the surgeon Solon, who pledged to build an army for him from patched-together corpses.

The fifth Doctor encountered Morbius and travelled to Gallifrey, where he convinced Acting President Saran to act. The Doctor took charge of a large Alliance - an army that included the Draconians, Sontarans, Ice Warriors, Cybermen and Ogrons - and defeated Morbius' forces.

The Order of the Weal, the Homeworld's first counter-intelligence organisation, was dedicated to the "common-weal" (i.e. common-good) and in operation at this time. It helped to expose the Imperator's abuses of power, accelerating his downfall.[412] One of Morbius' followers would acquire his presidential robes.[413]

Acting President Saran was almost certainly never elected President.[414]

The Time Lords had thrived on their status quo for ages, but the Morbius' rise and fall disrupted their culture to such a degree, some change seemed inevitable. Nonetheless, the announcement by one of their number, later known as Grandfather Paradox, of the formation of a new bloodline - that of House Paradox - seemed immeasurably tasteless, especially as the very name seemed an affront to the Time Lords' governing Protocols.[415]

Seven years after the formation of House Paradox, its members established the Eleven-Day Empire. It would serve as a "bolt-hole and reliquary" for the followers of Grandfather Paradox for years to come.[416]

Greyjan the Sane dabbled with the idea of time paradoxes. His three-year reign was the shortest in Gallifreyan history, and coincided with the relative Earth dates that saw the creation of the Eleven-Day Empire.[417] Four years after the Empire's founding, the Time Lords cracked down on threats to their hierarchy and imprisoned Grandfather Paradox, supposedly in perpetuity.[418]

The leader of the Order of the Weal, Chatelaine Thessalia, foresaw the oncoming War in Heaven and became intent on learning more about the future Enemy of the Great Houses. Her interrogation of a babel - a sentient weapon engineered to protect the Homeworld against physical and language-viral attacks - that had gone rogue and wiped out House Catherion ended in a Violent Unknown Event on the planet Zo La Domini. Thessalia was reported missing, and the Order crumbled without her. In actuality, the wounded babel hid itself in the timeline of Isaac Newton, and Thessalia was flung through time to seventeenth century Earth.[419]

THE DARK PATH -> Two hundred years after the second Doctor last saw Koschei, they met on the Earth colony of Darkheart in the thirty-fourth century. Koschei wanted an ordered universe, but his methods had become increasingly questionable. He felt betrayed upon realising that his dear companion Ailla was a Time Lord spy, and came into conflict with the Doctor also, which kept him emotionally isolated. Koschei became obsessed with the power of the Darkheart and declared himself the Master.

The Master has had many enemies, and always misses them when they are gone.[420]

---

contradicted just a few pages later (p173), when it's made clear that it's after the Doctor stole a TARDIS and has left Gallifrey.

Neverland places it before the Master steals the files on the Doomsday Weapon. *FP: The Book of the War* has its "the Imperator Presidency" occurring between 870 and 866 years before the War starts, so (almost certainly) after the Doctor left Gallifrey. *Timelink* prefers the idea that Morbius rose after *The Three Doctors*.

412 According to *FP: The Book of the War*, the Order of the Weal was formed during the "Imperator Presidency" - the *Faction Paradox* term for Morbius' tenure as President. Presumably the ancient Celestial Intervention Agency concerned itself with external issues, not Gallifreyan politics.

413 Fandom has tended to assume that Morbius was President of the Time Lords, although this isn't stated in his TV story. *The Vengeance of Morbius*, though, makes reference to his presidential robes of office.

414 While everyone is happy to call him "Lord President" in *Warmonger*, Saran is only Acting President until elections are held (p175). The Doctor thinks of Saran as "a very minor figure in Time Lord history" (p166), so we can probably infer that he lost the election. We can also speculate that the President who is elected at this point is the one seen in *The Three Doctors* and (after regenerating) the one assassinated in *The Deadly Assassin*. The Doctor never met the President

killed in *The Deadly Assassin*, according to that story, but he had known Saran before originally leaving Gallifrey.

415 *Interference* and *FP: The Book of the War*, the latter of which clarifies that the genesis of Faction Paradox lies in the founding of House Paradox two hundred and fifty-two years beforehand. Lawrence Miles, upon reading an advance draft of *Ahistory* (First Edition) verified that while Morbius and Grandfather Paradox were close contemporaries, "... It's the long-term effects of the Morbius/Imperator crisis that lead to the rise of the Faction, rather than its direct aftermath".

416 *Interference*, *FP: The Book of the War* - see the events of 1752 in the main timeline.

417 *The Ancestor Cell*. The online Faction Paradox timeline suggests that this Presidency fell between *The Deadly Assassin* and *The Invasion of Time*.

418 *FP: The Book of the War*

419 *FP: Newtons Sleep* and *FP: The Book of the War*, the latter of which says the Zo La Domini incident occurs three hundred eighty years before the War in Heaven, and twelve years after Grandfather Paradox's imprisonment.

420 *Terror of the Autons*

421 SEASON 6B: The second Doctor's status in *The Two Doctors* - that he's an agent working on the behest of the Time Lords - looks like a major contradiction of the established facts, as it's made clear in *The War Games*

The Doctor's First Trial / Increasing Intervention[421]

THE WAR GAMES / SPEARHEAD FROM SPACE -> In the aftermath of defeating the War Lords, the second Doctor faced a Malfeasance Tribunal. The Time Lords found the Doctor guilty of interfering in history, and exiled him to twentieth-century Earth, changing his appearance. The Tribunal continued to monitor him.[422]

A Gallifreyan protocol dictated that before entering a period of exile, a Time Lord was required to regenerate.[423] At the time of the second Doctor's trial, the current model of TARDIS was the Type 97, and psychic paper had just been invented. House Dellatrovella was politically powerful and ambitious.[424]

WORLD GAME -> The Time Lords covered up the true end of the Doctor's trial. He was secretly recruited to the Celestial Intervention Agency by its leader, Sardon, to investigate time disturbances on Earth, given a companion (Serena) and a new TARDIS. Serena was killed on that mission. On his return, the second Doctor was visibly older, with grey hair and in new clothes. It was noted that he "took his time getting back", and he insisted on reclaiming his old TARDIS.

The second Doctor, accompanied by Jamie, was sent to space station Chimera to call a halt to the time travel experiments of Kartz and Reimer.[425]

Eventually, the Doctor's sentence was reinstated. He regenerated and was exiled to twentieth-century Earth...

The Doctor's Exile to Earth

TERROR OF THE AUTONS -> Around this time, the Master removed Time Lord files containing information about the Doomsday Weapon and the Sea Devils. The Time Lords sent a messenger to warn the third Doctor about the Master's imminent arrival on Earth.[426]

The Master stole the plans for the Doomsday Weapon on 5892.9, Rassilon Era.[427] He also learned of the Psychic Parasites of Bellerophon; the Doomsday Weapon; Azal of the Daemons; the Earth Reptiles; the Crystal of Kronos; the Dalek army on Spiridon; the Source on Traken; the Cheetah people; the Midnight Cathedral; the GodEngine on Mars; the deathworm; the frozen gods of Volvox, the Amentethys, the Proculus and the Scerbulus; and the secrets of the planet Kirbili.[428]

COLONY IN SPACE / THE CURSE OF PELADON / THE MUTANTS -> The Time Lords sent the exiled third Doctor on various missions to other planets and times. These were always crucial points of galactic history, with implications for the entire universe. The Doctor was sent to Uxarieus to prevent the Doomsday Weapon from falling into the hands of the Master; to Peladon to ease the passage of that planet into the Galactic Federation and to prevent galactic war; and to Solos, where the Doctor delivered a message to Ky, the

---

that the Doctor has fled his home planet and is terrified of any contact with his people. Fans don't seem so worried that the Time Lords also contacted the first and second Doctors in *The Three Doctors*.

One theory that has gained currency since appearing in *The Discontinuity Guide* is that after *The War Games*, the Doctor wasn't regenerated straight away but was reunited with Jamie and Victoria (who is mentioned in *The Two Doctors*) and sent on missions for the Time Lords. Supporting evidence for this is that the second Doctor seems to remember *The War Games* in *The Five Doctors*. It also ties in with *TV Comic*, which had the second Doctor exiled to Earth for a time before he became his third incarnation. Two novels by Terrance Dicks (*Players* and *World Game*) explicitly have sequences that, from the Doctor's point of view, occur during Season 6B.

422 *The War Games*. The event is recalled and dated in *The Deadly Assassin*, the Doctor's exile begins in *Spearhead from Space* (continuing until *The Three Doctors*), and we learn the Tribunal is still monitoring the Doctor in *Terror of the Autons*. A number of accounts

have taken their lead from *The Auton Invasion* (the novelisation of *Spearhead from Space*) and the first edition of *The Making of Doctor Who*, and stated that the Doctor is also punished for stealing the TARDIS. This is not established on television. The Time Lords have the opportunity to confiscate the TARDIS, but send the Doctor to Earth with it.

423 *Circular Time*: "Spring", in reference to *The War Games*.

424 *World Game*

425 *The Two Doctors*

426 *Terror of the Autons*. The files are referred to in *Colony in Space* and *The Sea Devils*. Presumably, although this is never stated on TV, the Master also finds out about many of his other future allies and accomplices from these files.

427 *Neverland*

428 *The Quantum Archangel*, with reference to (respectively) *The Mind of Evil*, *Colony in Space*, *The Daemons*, *The Sea Devils*, *The Time Monster*, *Frontier in Space/Planet of the Daleks*, *The Keeper of Traken*, *Survival*, *Falls the Shadow*, *GodEngine* and *Doctor Who - The Movie*.

leader of the Solonian independence movement, that allowed him to fulfill his race's evolutionary potential.

THE THREE DOCTORS -> A black hole suddenly drained the cosmic energy of the Time Lords. Unable to power their machinery, the Time Lords called on the third Doctor for help. They brought two of his previous incarnations into the present to try and counteract whatever was draining the power.

The second and third Doctors travelled into the black hole and arrived in a universe of anti-matter. They discovered that Omega lived, maintaining an entire world with his mental control of a singularity. Omega resented the Time Lords, feeling they had abandoned him. He couldn't leave his domain without it ceasing to exist before he departed, and needed the Doctors' help to leave. But the Doctor learnt that Omega's body had long been destroyed, and that only his will remained. It would be impossible for him to return to the universe of matter.

The Doctors tricked their way back to their TARDIS,

apparently destroying Omega in a matter/anti-matter explosion. The power drain ended, and the Time Lords had a new source of energy. In gratitude, the Time Lords lifted the Doctor's exile.

For some time after this, the Time Lords would "occasionally" call upon the Doctor's services.[429]

PLANET OF THE DALEKS -> At the third Doctor's request, the Time Lords piloted the TARDIS to Spiridon, the location of a Dalek army.

Romana

Romana was born when the Doctor was between six hundred and six hundred twenty five.[430] She was from the House of Heartshaven.[431]

She was an only child, as her brother Rorvan had been consigned to the Oubliette of Eternity and erased from history.[432] She read *Our Planet's Story* as a Time Tot.[433] Romana's disapproving father once told her, "You know

---

429 In the television series, the Time Lords sending the Doctor on missions is a rare occurrence after the Doctor's exile is lifted - it only happens in *Genesis of the Daleks* and (the Doctor suspects) *The Brain of Morbius*. In the other media, it's far more common, particularly the *TV Comic* strip (not included in this chronology), where it's almost taken for granted that every time the Doctor uses the TARDIS, the Time Lords are controlling it at least to some extent.

430 WHEN WAS ROMANA BORN?: Like the Doctor, Romana doesn't give a consistent account of her age - she's "nearly 140" in *The Ribos Operation*, "125" in *City of Death* and "150" in *The Leisure Hive*. Potentially throwing another spanner into the works, *Heart of TARDIS* has her (between *The Stones of Blood* and *The Androids of Tara*) spending fifteen if not thirty years travelling through a nexus with the Doctor.

Nonetheless, her birth would seem to occur, in the Doctor's personal timeline, almost exactly halfway between *The Tomb of the Cybermen* and *Pyramids of Mars*. Given the continuity of companions and the Doctor's exile to Earth, the only certain gap between those two stories where the Doctor could age three hundred years would be between *The Green Death* and *The Time Warrior*, when the Doctor travels alone in his TARDIS. The UNIT personnel have no idea if the Doctor is away, as far as he is concerned, for decades or centuries at a time. If the Season 6B theory is true, there could be another significant gap there. The probability, then, is that Romana was born while the Doctor was in his third incarnation.

431 As repeatedly stated in various *Gallifrey* stories (*Lies*, *Panacea*, *Reborn* and *Annihilation*). *FP: The Book of the War*, however, implies that Romana is from the

House of Dvora, hence her full name (*The Ribos Operation*) of "Romanadvoratrelundar".

432 *Neverland*

433 *Shada*

434 *Gallifrey: Reborn*

435 *Gallifrey: Lies*. This seems intended to paint over Romana's not making the connection between her old tutor and the "Braxiatel Collection" that she mentions in *City of Death*. This doesn't fix the problem, though, as other Time Lords would know about their history together.

436 *Tomb of Valdemar*

437 *The Ribos Operation*

438 *State of Decay*

439 *The Romance of Crime*, *The Ancestor Cell*.

440 *Neverland*

441 *The Pirate Planet*

442 *Lungbarrow*

443 *Neverland*. This is presumably the visit in *Legacy of the Daleks*, first referenced in *The Deadly Assassin*.

444 *Interference*, *FP: The Book of the War*. Lawrence Miles, commenting on an advanced copy of *Ahistory* (First Edition), said the formation of Faction Paradox "should come just before *The Deadly Assassin* (or just after *Genesis of the Daleks*)... the point when Gallifrey starts being shaken up by renegades, assassinations and invasions, and mortality suddenly becomes a major issue."

445 *Alien Bodies*, *Interference*, *FP: The Book of the War*.

446 *FP: The Book of the War*

447 "Three hundred years" before "The Final Chapter", and it's tempting to see this as emerging from the same "cultural crisis" that created Faction Paradox.

you're getting old when the High Council seemed to be getting younger."[434]

Braxiatel served as Romana's tutor. One day, Romana wanted to escape the bullying of her fellow students and wandered into the ancient vaults beneath the Capitol. She came into contact with the lingering spirit of the Imperiatrix Pandora - who had manipulated Romana's genetic heritage so her body could host Pandora's spirit. Braxiatel prevented this by having one of his future selves - who was more adept at hypnotism - erase Romana's memory of the encounter. Romana also forgot that Braxiatel had ever mentored her. Romana believed that she met Braxiatel for the first time after her return to Gallifrey, when he offered to help with her political campaign.[435]

Romana spent most of her spare time at the academy developing mental and physical discipline, and learned the Seven Strictures of Rassilon, as well as the Foxtrots of Rassilon.[436] **As part of her studies, Romana studied the lifecycle of the Gallifreyan Flutterwing and she eventually graduated from the Academy with a Triple First.[437] Romana was an historian and worked in the Bureau of Ancient Records.[438]** She was a Prydonian.[439] When she was sixty, she went to Lake Abydos on holiday with her family.[440] **For her seventieth birthday, she was given an air-car.[441]**

THE TIME VAMPIRE -> The Time Lords asked the third Doctor and Joshua Douglas to intervene when the Z'nai acquired a primitive time capsule. Time travellers who crossed weak points in space-time in a paradoxical fashion sometimes created "time vampires": exquisite wraiths who only wanted to observe the beauty of time through the eyes of their hosts. The Time Lords deemed the creatures as abominations who could "ride the tides of time" and, potentially, use their power to wipe out creation. The Time Lords created temporal suspension cages to restrain such creatures, although Gallifrey's official policy was that the capture of such creatures was a crime, and such cages were outlawed.

GENESIS OF THE DALEKS -> The Time Lords predicted a time when the Daleks would dominate the universe, and sent the fourth Doctor, Sarah and Harry to prevent the Daleks' creation (or at least slow their development).

Lord Ferain was head of Allegiance at the Celestial Intervention Agency, and it was he who sent the Doctor to Skaro to prevent the Daleks' creation.[442]

THE BRAIN OF MORBIUS -> The Time Lords also apparently sent the TARDIS, with the fourth Doctor and Sarah Jane aboard, to Karn to prevent the resurrection of Morbius.

Chancellor Goth visited Tersurus on 6241.11, Rassilon Era.[443]

Faction Paradox

House Paradox re-defined itself as Faction Paradox during a time of cultural crisis on Gallifrey. The Time Lords officially outlawed and exiled House Paradox, whose representatives left Gallifrey and recruited the Faction's members from the lesser species, including humanity.[444]

The Faction set out to be deliberately confrontational. Whereas the Time Lords abhorred time paradoxes, Faction Paradox revelled in them. The Time Lords were immortal, so much of the Faction's iconography - like their skull masks - celebrated death. The Time Lords thought themselves sterile, so the Faction used familial titles such as "Father", "Mother", "Cousin" and "Little Brothers and Sisters". The relationship between the Time Lord authorities and Faction Paradox was analogous to that of the Catholic Church and satanic cults on Earth.[445]

"Faction Paradox doesn't do things for the sake of power, or out of any inherent sense of sadism. It seems to do them because it wants to make a point. Because the universe would be lacking if *nobody* did it. Because, quite simply, it's a carnival. And even the very word 'carnival', with its overtones of death, flesh and pointless ceremony, would on [the Homeworld] suggest something so disgusting that only the outcaste would consider it."[446]

The Elysians were a secret society on Gallifrey run by a man called Luther. They rejected the traditional houses, were sick of the non-intervention code, and styled themselves as "the Final Chapter". They planned to capture Gallifrey in a coup using unregistered clones. The first was the son of Uriel, named Xanti. Uriel, Xanti's father, volunteered for incarceration in a mental asylum: the Quantum of Solace.[447]

THE DEADLY ASSASSIN ->

"Through the millennia, the Time Lords of Gallifrey led a life of peace and ordered calm, protected against all threats from lesser civilisations by their great power. But this was to change. Suddenly and terribly, the Time Lords faced the most dangerous crisis in their long history..."

The fourth Doctor received a telepathic message, warning him that the President was going to be assassinated. He returned to his home planet, only to find himself implicated in the assassination. The President had been due to resign anyway after centuries in office,

SECTION FIVE: GALLIFREY

and the murder appeared motiveless.

The Doctor's old enemy, the Master, had lured him back to frame him for the murder. The Master had exhausted his regenerations, and had been found by Chancellor Goth on the planet Tersurus. Goth had been favoured to succeed the outgoing President, but he had discovered that another was to be nominated instead. In return for Goth's help, the Master killed the incumbent President.

The Master wanted full access to various items such as the Sash of Rassilon, as he needed to find a way to prolong his life. He discovered that he might regenerate again if he had a powerful enough source of energy - the Master selected the Eye of Harmony. He believed the Sash would protect him if he unleashed the Eye's power. The Doctor prevented the Master from destroying Gallifrey, but the Master escaped.

Around this time, the Doctor began to learn more about the Time Lords' ancient past.

---

448 *Cat's Cradle: Time's Crucible* (p210-211).

449 A different actor plays Borusa in each of his televised appearances (Angus MacKay in *The Deadly Assassin*, John Arnatt in *The Invasion of Time*, Leonard Sachs in *Arc of Infinity* and Philip Latham in *The Five Doctors*).

450 *The Ancestor Cell*

451 *Alien Bodies*

452 *Timewyrm: Genesys*

453 *Tomb of Valdemar*

454 We learn of Leela and Andred's marriage in *Arc of Infinity*.

455 In *The Ribos Operation*, the Doctor wishes that he'd thrown the President to the Sontarans, suggesting that Borusa has become President (although the treacherous Kelner apparently survived *The Invasion of Time* and he'd have a strong constitutional case, as the Doctor named him Vice-President). The Doctor was meant to have lost his memory of the Sontaran invasion at the end of *The Invasion of Time*, but clearly didn't, or was given some sort of account of it before he left Gallifrey. By *Arc of Infinity*, Borusa is President.

456 Established at the start of each of the four *K9* books published in 1980. In *K9 and the Zeta Rescue*, we learn that K9 reports to a Space Controller on Gallifrey and that the Doctor came up with the name for his spacecraft, K-NEL. We can also infer the order in which the books take place: K9 is flying K-NEL Mark 1 in *K9 and the Beasts of Vega*, it's destroyed in *K9 and the Time Trap*, he goes on a test flight in the Mark 2 at the start of *K9 and the Zeta Rescue*, he's using it in *K9 and the Missing Planet*.

It's also interesting to note that after many years of sending the Doctor on missions for them, the Time Lords stop doing so (the last time is apparently *The Brain of Morbius* on television, "Light Fantastic" - from *Doctor Who Annual 1980* - in other media). We might infer K9 is now doing this work for them.

457 Dating *K9 and the Time Trap* (*The Adventures of K9* #1) - This takes place in the Gallifreyan timeframe. K9 is referred to as being "hired" by the Time Lords, but this may be a figure of speech rather than indication he is paid.

RIGEL: The delegate from the Rigel Sector is a member of the Order of the Black Sun in "Black Sun Rising", and the Rigellians are mentioned as once being enemies of the Time Lords in *The Infinity Doctors*, but they are allies in *K9: The Time Trap* (in both "Black Sun Rising" and *The Time Trap*, they are depicted as humanoid). They would seem to be one of the "Higher Powers". These Rigellians would seem to exist in a different era to humanity - perhaps the same early universe as the Time Lords. Earth has a depot on Rigel by "Conflict of Interests" (?2192). Rigellians had four tentacles, three mouths and a reputation for being untrustworthy according to Abslom Daak (c2550). Rigel VII is part of the Earth Empire by 2620. The Battle of the Rigel Wastes took place in 2697. Slavery is abolished on Rigellon by the time of the Federation (3985). The Shadow Proclamation shut down a maximum security prison on Rigel 77 according to *TW: The Undertaker's Gift*.

458 Dating *K9 and the Zeta Rescue* (*The Adventures of K9* #3) - This story takes place soon after *K9 and the Time Trap*.

459 *The Ribos Operation*

460 *Gallifrey: Lies*. This directly conflicts with the notion in *The Chaos Pool* that Romana's regeneration occurred because she became a segment of the Key to Time. Much of *Gallifrey* Series 2 and 3 is predicated on the notion of Romana having a genetic link to Pandora, so it seems fair to give this account precedence. As Romana's memories of Pandora are suppressed, it's entirely possible that she falsely believes for a while that she regenerated due to the Key's influence - even if she does, for a time, become a Key segment.

461 "Centuries" before "The Final Chapter". It's unclear when this takes place. It's before "The Tides of Time", because we see the Watchtower in that story. Perhaps there was more extensive destruction during the Vardan/Sontaran assault in *The Invasion of Time* than we saw on TV. References to the "old Panopticon" might mean there's a new one - we haven't seen the Panopticon on television since *The Invasion of Time*.

462 *The Pyralis Effect*

463 *Shada*. It's unclear when this happened. FP: *The Book of the War* states it was three hundred and ninety-two years before the War starts, and four hundred and seventy-four years after Morbius' execution.

464 *Alien Bodies*. *The Terrestrial Index* and *The Discontinuity Guide* both mistakenly refer to Drornid as Dronid.

465 *Meglos, Full Circle*.

722

"It was a chance encounter with the *Book of the Old Time* that had first nudged the Doctor's own thoughts back towards his world's archae-barbaric past. A suspicion had been born in his mind that before regeneration there had been reincarnation. Some memories might be more than racial inheritance. Nothing lasts that does not change."[448]

Borusa regenerated at some point between this and the Doctor's next visit to Gallifrey.[449]

IMAGE OF THE FENDAHL / UNDERWORLD -> Soon after learning of his planet's past, the fourth Doctor began to encounter survivors from his race's ancient history: the Fendahl and the Minyans.

THE INVASION OF TIME -> The fourth Doctor was contacted by the Vardans, a race capable of travelling down energy waves, including thought. The Vardans had infiltrated the Matrix, and now wanted to commence a physical invasion of Gallifrey. The Doctor pretended to collaborate with the Vardans and claimed the Presidency of Gallifrey. He then returned the Vardan invasion force to their home planet and time-looped it. The Sontarans had been manipulating the Vardans all along, and attempted to invade Gallifrey themselves. This incursion was also repelled. Leela and K9 elected to stay behind on Gallifrey.

The Doctor was the 407th President.[450] During his short tenure, his biodata was altered by contact with the Sash of Rassilon.[451] While in the Matrix, the Doctor became aware of the Timewyrm. He sent his future self a warning about it.[452] Romana was not directly affected by the Sontaran invasion.[453]

Leela and Andred, a member of the Chancellery Guard, married soon afterwards, but the Doctor was unable to attend the ceremony.[454] Borusa became President and regenerated once again.[455]

K9 Mark 1 was sent on independent missions in situations classed as too dangerous for Time Lord intervention.[456]

K9 AND THE TIME TRAP[457] **->** K9 met with the Rigellian Fleet Commander to discuss the disappearance of the Rigellian Seventh Fleet. Between galaxies, K9's spaceship - the K-NEL - was sucked into a time trap, and K9 discovered ten thousand alien ships that had also been caught there, including the Rigellians. Omegon, a figure from early Time Lord history who was exiled here, was amassing the ships to form a warfleet and launch an attack on Gallifrey. K9 sacrificed K-NEL, using it to ram and destroy Omegon and his ship. As a reward, the Rigellians gave K9 K-NEL Mark 2 - the same ship, but with racing stripes.

K9 AND THE ZETA RESCUE[458] **->** K9 had now saved the Time Lords "many times". He tested the Mark 2 K-NEL, and was sent to investigate massive explosions in the Zeta Four Sector - if Zeta Canri went nova, the whole galaxy would be blown apart. At the heart of the devastation, K9 discovered a prison ship of the Megellan Empire, the sworn enemies of the Time Lords. He rescued Dea, an ambassador from Telios. Nuclear war had wiped out the Telians and Megallans, and K9 and Dea watched the two leaders kill each other in a final duel. The few survivors were given medical treatment.

The Key to Time

The White Guardian picked Romana to aid the fourth Doctor and recover the six segments of the Key to Time.[459]

Romana's torture by the Shadow broke the conditioning that had made her forget the Imperiatrix Pandora. Fearing that Pandora would manifest through the Imperiatrix Imprimature within her, Romana forced her own regeneration. Her memories of Pandora were again scrambled, and her genetic link to Pandora went dormant.[460]

Luther designed the reconstruction of the Capitol over the hulk of the old, including the Watchtower, over the old Panopticon.[461] The development of fungal brains eluded Gallifrey, as such networks were notoriously unstable.[462]

A schism in College of Cardinals led to a rival President setting himself up on Drornid. The Time Lords ignored them, and they eventually returned home.[463] Drornid was also known as Dronid.[464]

SHADA -> The fourth Doctor and Romana prevented Skraga of Drornid from using the powers of the Time Lord mind criminal Salyavin to impose himself as the "universal mind".

With the quest for the Key to Time long-completed, the Time Lords recalled Romana. Before she could return, the TARDIS fell through a CVE into E-Space.[465]

STATE OF DECAY -> The fourth Doctor, Romana, Adric and K9 destroyed the Great Vampire, who had survived the war with the Time Lords and fled to E-Space.

"The Tides of Time" -> The fifth Doctor continued at times to be addressed as "the President" of the Time Lords. He said of Gallifrey, "When my wanderings are over, I will make my home here."

The Time Lords installed a defence system onboard the TARDIS without telling the Doctor. In an emergency, it would automatically summon Shayde to the ship.[466]

"The Stockbridge Horror" -> The fifth Doctor arrived on Gallifrey seconds after Tubal Cain's missiles froze time in the Capitol. Within the time warp, the Doctor repaired the TARDIS. When the effect wore off, the Doctor was arrested and brought before a secret court for his interference with the timeline. Shayde disposed of evidence pertaining to the case, resulting in the Doctor's release.

Tubal Cain was demoted to run the Quantum of Solace.[467] It was possible for Time Lords to "transform" into - or otherwise hybridise with - other species during regeneration.[468]

CIRCULAR TIME: "Spring" -> Cardinal Zero was a Prydonian, and a member of the Council of the Great Mother - a group focused upon the politics of regeneration. He was in the running for a High Council seat when he abandoned life on Gallifrey, instead living in a rainforest on an alien world. The Time Lords dispatched the fifth Doctor and Nyssa to talk Zero into returning home, lest his actions damage the time-stream.

The Doctor and Nyssa found Zero living among a race of avian-people; Temporal Projectionists on Gallifrey had foretold that this species would progress from steam to orbital space flight in less than three generations. The avians themselves foretold of a prophet who would "lead them back to the sky", and Zero arranged his death using a local poison. He theatrically fell into a lake - which was actually his TARDIS - and regenerated inside it into a half-Time Lord, half-avian being. Events compelled the Doctor and Nyssa to leave, and Zero - hailed as the prophet of the avians - set about boosting their development and refining their judicial system along more civilised lines.

ARC OF INFINITY -> Omega had survived, and convinced a member of the High Council, Hedin, that he had been wronged by Gallifrey. With access to a bio-data extract, Omega would be able to bond with a Time Lord, re-entering our universe. Hedin chose the fifth Doctor as Omega's target - when the High Council discovered this, they recalled the Doctor's TARDIS to Gallifrey (only the third time this had been done in the planet's history) and lifted the ban on the death penalty. Killing the Doctor, they believed, would break the renegade's link with our universe. The Doctor survived

vaporisation by entering the Matrix, where he discovered Omega's plan. He tracked Omega to Amsterdam, where the renegade's new body proved unstable and disintegrated.

Time Lords could potentially live for millennia.[469]

"Blood Invocation" -> The fifth Doctor, Tegan and Nyssa responded to an emergency signal from Cardinal Hemal. A Time Lord had been found, drained of blood, and the Doctor realised there were vampires abroad. The Doctor discovered acolytes of the Cult of Rassilon the Vampire and had them rounded up. Meanwhile, Tegan was bitten by a vampire Time Lord who had gained access to the TARDIS. The vampire took the Ship to Earth... but disintegrated because he landed in the daytime.

THE FIVE DOCTORS[470] **/ THE FIVE COMPANIONS ->** Borusa regenerated once more. He had become dissatisfied with ruling Gallifrey. Now he wanted "perpetual regeneration": a secret discovered by Rassilon that allowed true immortality, not simply the vast lifespans granted to other Time Lords. Borusa discovered the ancient Timescoop machinery and restarted the Game of Rassilon, pitting the first, second, third and fifth Doctors and their friends - Susan, the Brigadier, Sarah Jane, Tegan and Turlough - against a selection of old enemies in the Death Zone on Gallifrey.

The fifth Doctor escaped a group of Cybermen by transmatting to the Capitol, but en route was diverted into a pocket dimension containing an alternate Death Zone environment: a collection of fused spacecraft and space stations. More of the Doctor's friends - Ian Chesterton, Steven Taylor, the incarnated "house" version of Sara Kingdom, Polly Wright and Nyssa - had been transported into the holding dimension, and aided him against foes that included Daleks, dinosaurs and members of the Sontaran Sixth Column. Time Lord technicians sent the Doctor's friends home, and the Doctor continued on to the Capitol...

Rassilon gave Borusa the immortality he sought, transforming him into a living statue. He also sent the first, second and third Doctors - and their associates - back to their native times. Chancellor Flavia declared the fifth Doctor as President, but he left Gallifrey with Tegan and Turlough before he could take up office, and appointed Flavia to rule in his stead.

---

466 "The Stockbridge Horror"

467 "The Final Chapter"

468 As witnessed in works by Paul Cornell (*Circular Time:* "Spring" and *The Shadows of Avalon*).

469 *Hexagora.* This direct statement on the Doctor's

part is further evidence that all of his adventuring has really taken a toll on his lifespan.

470 See the Regeneration, A Complete New Life Cycle sidebar.

"REGENERATION... A COMPLETE NEW LIFE CYCLE":
In *The Five Doctors*, the High Council offers the Master the carrot that - should he enter the Death Zone and help the Doctor as they wish - he will be rewarded with both a full pardon and "regeneration, a complete new life cycle". This has become a perennial source of confusion, as it would seem to be a change from the twelve-regeneration limit as first established in *The Deadly Assassin*. And yet, both on screen and in the tie-in media, nearly every classic *Doctor Who* story has ignored the development and continued to regard the twelve-regeneration rule as sacrosanct.

Even within *The Five Doctors* itself, the deal looks a bit suspect. The story entails Borusa wanting to be President of Gallifrey for eternity by obtaining the immortality promised by Rassilon, but we know that Borusa can remain President even if he regenerates (he's done so at least once while in office; compare with *Arc of Infinity*), so the issue isn't that he's desperate to hold onto his current body. He wants to be *truly* immortal, which *The Five Doctors* cites as being beyond any Time Lord save Rassilon and anyone he bestows it upon.

In which case, the question must be asked: If Gallifrey has, somehow, developed the ability to grant Time Lords a new set of regenerations, why would this invaluable life-extender be an option for one of the Time Lords' most infamous and evil renegades, but *not* their own Lord President? One theory, fronted by Neil Gaiman, holds that the limitation on regenerations is as much a legal limit as a naturally occurring one. The idea would seem to be that Time Lords are born with twelve regenerations "in the bank" (as it were), because they evolved that way due to exposure to the Untempered Schism (*A Good Man Goes to War*). But, given enough of an energy top-up, like recharging a battery, Time Lords can acquire even more lives - the Master attempts just that in *The Deadly Assassin*, albeit while going to the drastic lengths of trying to open the main Eye of Harmony (and threatening the destruction of Gallifrey) to achieve the energy required.

Following Gaiman's reasoning (and that of his associate Steve Manfred), we might imagine that the High Council in *The Five Doctors* has a safe, controlled and humane way of granting more lives that is normally illegal. *Why* it's verboten isn't clear - possibly, Rassilon laid down such a rule because (as *The Five Doctors* makes abundantly clear) immortality is "a curse, not a blessing". Alternatively, *Head Games* (p173) builds upon the idea in the New Adventures (*Timewyrm: Revelation* especially) that traces of previous personas remain in a Time Lord's mind after each regeneration, and has the Doctor state that the number of regenerations was limited because "too often the mind can't handle the multiplicity of psyches". (The mental schism that occurs between the seventh Doctor and his previous self - see *Love and War* and *Head Games* - stands in evidence of this.)

If the High Council *can* grant new lives, however, this presumably can't be done indefinitely - so adamant is *The Five Doctors* in keeping immortality the exclusive province of Rassilon. That might square with Borusa's actions, actually - if Gallifrey can implant (say) one extra set of twelve regenerations, he might not be content even if given a waiver and allowed twenty-five lives (that, or he wants to present himself as Rassilon's immortal, fully empowered heir to ward off all political opposition). Alternatively, it's possible that the Master's unique status as a former Time Lord now hosted within the body of a Trakenite via the lingering energies of the Source of Traken (*The Keeper of Traken*) qualifies him for a new set of regenerations, whereas a purebred Time Lord such as Borusa doesn't have that option.

A third option is that the High Council is simply lying when they offer to give the Master more lives - and yet, the Master doesn't seem to doubt their word on this, and he's better informed about Gallifreyan secrets and developments than most (*Colony in Space*, *The Ultimate Foe*, etc.). That would, however, create the lingering oddity that if Gallifrey has developed a means of dispensing new regenerations and the Master knows about it, it's remarkable that he hasn't (even allowing for his aborted attempt in *The Deadly Assassin*) tried to acquire/steal a new set for himself, choosing instead (after *The Keeper of Traken*) to go about space-time in a hijacked body in which he's altogether too mortal.

In *Gallifrey: Reborn* (set long after *The Five Doctors*), Romana comments that Gallifrey has the ability to "implant a new regeneration cycle, but not extract, divide or redistribute an existing one". This curiously, though, overlooks the Master's claim that the High Council has promised the Valeyard the sixth Doctor's remaining lives if he helps them cover up the Ravolox affair (*The Ultimate Foe*). Also, the Master nearly succeeds in "redistributing" the Doctor's regenerations to himself in *Doctor Who - The Movie*, using nothing more than the Eye of Harmony in the Doctor's TARDIS.

The new *Doctor Who* has largely steered clear of the topic of how many regenerations Time Lords possess, save that the formerly regeneration-less Master regenerates in *Utopia* (possibly part and parcel of his being "resurrected" for the Last Great Time War; see *The Sound of Drums*), that River Song burns up her finite number of regenerations healing the Doctor (*Let's Kill Hitler*), and that the eleventh Doctor tells Clyde in *SJA: Death of the Doctor* that he can regenerate five hundred and seven times - possibly indicating his unique status, possibly suggesting that the limitation on regenerations was done away with in the Last Great Time War, possibly suggesting that he *could* acquire new lives but hasn't done so yet, or possibly that he's just poking fun with Clyde, a teenager. It remains to be seen how future production teams will address the issue, or choose to ignore it.

The Doctor was the 409th President.[471] **Type 57 TARDISes were in operation at this time.**[472]

Flavia didn't chase the Doctor because she wanted the Presidency for herself. Her reign was one of prosperity.[473]

The Time Lords tasked the fifth Doctor with investigating time warps on Earth.[474] The fifth Doctor knew about the Shadow Proclamation, and that the Judoon had a contract with them.[475]

RESURRECTION OF THE DALEKS -> **The Daleks planned to assassinate the High Council of the Time Lords using duplicates of the fifth Doctor and his companions, but the Doctor prevented this.**

Type 70 TARDISes were better suited than Type 40s to apply brute force and penetrate distortion grids that prevented space-time travel.[476]

THE AXIS OF INSANITY -> The Axis was an interdimensional nexus akin to a giant tree, whose branches linked to alternate realities that were usually the result of time experiments gone wrong - especially those conducted by the Time Lords. The Axis prevented such errant realities from interfering with the primary timeline.

The scientist Jarra To conducted experiments with a Timescoop that brought dragons - the Firebreed - from the past of her homeworld of Pangorum to the present. Jarra To killed the Time Lord Protok when he attempted to intervene, and although the Time Lords closed off Jarra To's timeline, she escaped from it into the Axis - where she gained fantastical abilities and adopted multiple guises. As the nihilistic Jester, she killed the Overseer - a multi-faceted being from the dimension of Guardas, whose consciousness stabilised the Axis. This threatened to bring down the barriers separating timelines within the Axis, an act that would have spread madness through the whole of creation. Tog, a native of Pangorum, sacrificed himself to kill Jarra To. The fifth Doctor, Peri and Erimem, relegated Protok's TARDIS to a pocket dimension that held hundreds of inert TARDISes whose operators were deceased. The Doctor also went to the Grand Prosideum on Guardas to request installation of a new Overseer.

"Urban Myths" -> The fifth Doctor cured an outbreak of the Tule-Oz virus on the planet Poiti, but three CIA agents (Commander Edge, Commander Harom and Kettoo) became infected with a benign strain of the germ. The Tule-Oz virus made the agents believe that the Doctor and Peri had devastated Poiti, but the Doctor provided an antidote for the agents and their superior, Inquisitor Auron. At this time, top-secret correspondence was automatically routed via the nearest Type 40 TARDIS to incidents away from Gallifrey.

ATTACK OF THE CYBERMEN -> **The Cybermen invaded the sixth Doctor's TARDIS and cut short a signal he sent to the Time Lords asking for help.**[477]

MISSION TO MAGNUS -> The Seven Sisterhoods of Magnus petitioned the Time Lords for permission to incorporate time travel into their conflict with the neighbouring planet of Salvak. Anzor, as an envoy of the High Council, was sent to Magnus in a Type 60 TARDIS. He denied the Sisterhoods' request on the grounds that, "It is forbidden

471 *The Ancestor Cell*
472 In *Warriors of the Deep*, the Doctor says he should have changed his TARDIS for a Type 57 "when he had the chance". This could imply that Type 57 is the most advanced model at present, or simply that newer models exist but the Doctor prefers Type 57.
473 *The Eight Doctors*
474 "4-Dimensional Vistas"
475 "The Forgotten"
476 *Singularity*
477 Later in the story, the Doctor suspects that the Time Lords *are* aware of events and have been manipulating him, but this is never confirmed.
478 *Recorded Time and Other Stories*: "Recorded Time"
479 *The Mysterious Planet*. The Valeyard's "evidence", as displayed throughout *The Trial of a Time Lord*, derives from this feature, although it's unclear if the Doctor's TARDIS was secretly fitted with surveillance gear at some point (his visit to Gallifrey in *Arc of Infinity*, for instance), or if the Ship was incorporated into the system by remote.
480 *The Eight Doctors*
481 THE VALEYARD: It is unclear exactly what the Valeyard is. The Master, who knows a great deal about him, says, "there is some evil in all of us, Doctor, even you. The Valeyard is an amalgamation of the darker sides of your nature, somewhere between your twelfth and final incarnation, and I must say you do not improve with age".
This is rather vague, and it seems that the Valeyard might be a potential future for the Doctor (like those presented to him in *The War Games* or arguably those of Romana in *Destiny of the Daleks*), a projection (like Cho-je in *Planet of the Spiders* or the Watcher in *Logopolis*) or an actual fully-fledged future incarnation (as he was in the original script). The Master seems to have met the Valeyard before, and sees him as a rival (he also says "as I've always know him, the Doctor" - suggesting that the Valeyard would normally refer to himself as "the Doctor" not "the Valeyard").
That the Doctor has a "dark side" that can manifest, either physically or within his mind, was established in

to alter history. My job is to prevent time tampering, except in the most exceptional circumstances." The Doctor revenged himself on his school tormentor by sending Anzor and his TARDIS back to the Mesozoic Era.

The Phylesians made immortal temporal phoenix birds fly in time loops, creating quills capable of rewriting time. The Time Lords were thought to have destroyed all such devices, but at least one survived.[478]

New surveillance methods were developed, increasing the range of information that the Matrix could harvest. The Matrix could now record events that occurred within a certain vicinity of a TARDIS.[479]

"The World Shapers" -> The Time Lords sent an agent in a new TARDIS to investigate time disturbances on Marinus. That Time Lord died, but the sixth Doctor, Frobisher and Peri arrived and took on the assignment. At its conclusion, a delegation of senior Time Lords met up with the sixth Doctor and offered false assurances that they would nip the creation of the Cybermen in the bud.

The Celestial Intervention Agency worried that the Ravolox Affair would be exposed. They spread rumours that Flavia wasn't legitimately President, and she ordered an election to settle the matter. The Agency fixed the election, installing their supporter, Niroc.[480]

The Doctor's Second Trial

THE TRIAL OF A TIME LORD / THE ULTIMATE FOE
-> The sixth Doctor discovered that the planet Ravolox was in fact the Earth in the far future, but he didn't know what had moved the planet two light years or, more importantly, why. Despite this, the High Council became worried that the Doctor knew too much, and they brought him to a vast space station. The Doctor at first learned that he was to undergo an impartial

enquiry into his activities. He also learnt that as he had neglected his duties, he had been deposed from the Presidency.

The prosecuting council, named the Valeyard, successfully argued that the Doctor was guilty of interference on a grand scale, and the enquiry became a trial. It was revealled that the Doctor's actions on Thoros Beta had threatened the course of universal evolution. The Time Lords intervened directly, killing the scientist Crozier, the Mentor Kiv and possibly the Doctor's companion Peri. When the Doctor's own evidence proved that on another occasion he had committed genocide - wiping out the Vervoids to save the Earth - he faced a death sentence.

The Doctor claimed that the Matrix was being tampered with. The Keeper of the Matrix was brought in as an expert witness, but the Master suddenly appeared on the Matrix screen, demonstrating that it was indeed possible to breach the security of the Time Lords' master computer. The Master explained that Andromedans had previously entered the Matrix from their base on Earth and stolen valuable scientific secrets. To protect their position, the High Council had covertly ordered Earth's destruction.

The Master's greatest bombshell was the identity of the prosecuting council: the Valeyard was an amalgamation of all that was evil in the Doctor, somewhere between his twelfth and final incarnation.[481] The Master had encountered the Valeyard before, and knew that the High Council had brought him in to frame the Doctor, in return for which the Valeyard would gain the Doctor's remaining regenerations.

When the truth about Ravolox was revealed, popular unrest deposed the High Council. Both the Master and Valeyard moved to take advantage of the situation: the Master planned to take control of Gallifrey, even as the Valeyard attempted to assassinate senior members of the Time Lord hierarchy. Both failed. The Master

---

The Three Doctors; both the Valeyard and the Dream Lord (*Amy's Choice*), arguably, are a further culmination of this. Some commentators have leaned toward viewing the Dream Lord (the result of psychic pollen manifesting a dark part of the Doctor's psyche) as a sort of precursor (in the Doctor's lifetime) to the Valeyard, but no overt link has ever been drawn between the two.

Whatever the Valeyard is, he doesn't have any qualms about killing his past self - perhaps if the sixth Doctor died, the Valeyard would apparently gain his remaining regenerations by default. His survival at the end of the trial, when we had seen him disseminated (and the Doctor has promised to mend his ways) perhaps suggests that he is something more than just a mere Time Lord.

Note also that the Master says "twelfth and final", not "twelfth and thirteenth" - which, if you squint, leaves open the possibility that the Doctor will survive the end of his regenerative cycle. Alternatively, if the Master really is working to the "Time Lords get thirteen lives" paradigm first established in *The Deadly Assassin*, the Valeyard might be a "12.2 Doctor" of sorts.

The novels and audios have tended to steer clear of the Valeyard - indeed, the Writers' Guide for the New Adventures stated, "anything featuring the Valeyard is out - he's a continuity nightmare, and a rather dull villain". Despite this, a number of the novels (particularly *Time of Your Life*, *Head Games* and *Millennial Rites*) have developed the idea first aired in *Love and War* that the Doctor sacrificed his sixth incarnation ("the colourful

was trapped by the Limbo Atrophier, a booby trap placed on the Matrix files. The Valeyard was believed destroyed by his own particle disseminator, but he somehow survived. When last seen, he had assumed the guise of the Keeper of the Matrix.

The Doctor suggested that once order was restored, the Inquisitor should run for President.

A secret faction of Time Lords had authorised Peri's assassination, fearing the damaging testimony she might deliver at the sixth Doctor's trial. A splinter group of that faction, fearing reprisals from the Doctor, revised history so Peri instead became Yrcanos' queen. The incoming Gallifreyan president, upon reviewing the Trial, authorised use of standard CIA protocol - that Peri be returned home after her memories of the Doctor were wiped, save for their first adventure together. Each intervention created a new timeline for Peri; before long, at least five of her were active in the universe.[482]

THE EIGHT DOCTORS -> The eighth Doctor travelled to the time of his trial. He called on Rassilon to briefly free Borusa's noblest incarnation. Borusa deposed the corrupt High Council and arranged honest elections. Flavia was re-elected and restored Earth to its rightful place. Rassilon might have intervened to make the Doctor meet his companion Sam Jones in 1997.

UNREGENERATE![483] **->** The High Council foresaw a time when lesser species would develop time travel, and pack the space-time continuum to the bursting point. The Gallifreyan CIA therefore instigated a project to install the sentiences of newly birthed TARDISes into living beings. They hoped the sentiences would operate as CIA agents on their hosts' homeworlds, thwarting the lesser species' endeavours to create time-travel technology. The CIA believed this would work better than the usual array of spies and brainwashing.

Professor Klyst, a Time Lord, spearheaded the research. Experiments on Daleks were forbidden, but subjects were recruited from at least fifty worlds. Each were offered lifetimes of success if they participated in the research on the day before their deaths. Yet the beings' brains were unable to host the TARDIS sentiences, and many went insane.

The seventh Doctor ended the operation. One TARDIS sentience stabilised in the human Johannes Rausch. Klyst agreed to host another sentience, thus erasing her own knowledge of the research. The sentiences in Rausch and Klyst transferred another of their number into the Institute where the research was conducted, turning it into a make-shift travel vehicle. They went on the run from the Time Lords, hoping to stabilise the other sentiences in their host bodies.

REMEMBRANCE OF THE DALEKS -> Addressing Davros, the seventh Doctor claimed to be "President-Elect of the High Council of Time Lords... Keeper of the Legacy of Rassilon". After destroying Skaro, the Hand of Omega returned to Gallifrey.

---

jester") to create a stronger, more ruthless seventh persona ("Time's Champion") who was better equipped to change his destiny. Ironically, books such as *Love and War* and *Head Games* suggest that this internal conflict might well have been the catalyst that brought the Valeyard into being. The PDAs *Matrix* and *Mission: Impractical* feature the Valeyard, as does the non-canonical audio *He Jests at Scars*.

482 *Peri and the Piscon Paradox*

483 It's difficult to say how much the CIA is operating independently in this story, or to what degree it's sanctioned by the High Council. Presuming the CIA isn't acting totally solo, the High Council that initiated the project is possibly the administration that was overthrown in *The Trial of a Time Lord*.

484 *Lungbarrow*

485 *Thin Ice.* This was proposed as a means of Ace leaving the TARDIS in the unmade Season 27, but in the Big Finish adaptation of it, she stays with the Doctor after all.

486 Dating "The Forgotten" (IDW *DW* mini-series #2) - No date is given. It's interesting that the Time Lords designate this a "non-intervention site", as the working assumption is that all intervention is banned.

Presumably, this is a particularly sensitive area.

487 *The Chaos Pool*

488 Romana's desire to open up the Academy to non-Gallifreyans doesn't happen until a long time on (in the *Gallifrey* mini-series) and must fizzle at this juncture.

489 *A Death in the Family*

490 The novel version of *Human Nature*, in which a Gallifreyan agent arranges for an alien Aubertide to transform into a cow and get eaten as such.

491 *The Gallifrey Chronicles*

492 *Christmas on a Rational Planet.* No date is given in the *Doctor Who* books, but the Faction Paradox timeline in the back of *FP: The Book of the War* pegs the Grandfather's escape as occurring "one hundred fifty-one years" before the War in Heaven... and also places it simultaneous to the transition of House Paradox to Faction Paradox, which seems to happen in the era of the fourth Doctor, not (as here) the seventh.

493 *Christmas on a Rational Planet, Alien Bodies, Interference* - the first of these identifies the Time Lord criminal brand as a "dragon tattoo", probably in accordance with Jon Pertwee's real-life tattoo, as seen on the exiled third Doctor's right arm in *Doctor Who and the Silurians*.

Back on Gallifrey, the Hand of Omega missed its creator and tended to hover around the Omega Memorial.[484] An Adjudicator - a retired Time Lord acting as an academic assessment officer - considered Ace for enrollment in the Prydonian Academy... but she declined, and remained in the Doctor's company.[485]

"The Forgotten"[486] **->** The War of Agrovan Seven had now lasted fifteen hundred years, and the Time Lords had designated it a non-intervention site. The Strykes and Marats had been evenly matched for generations, but an unknown party gave the Strykes a bioweapon designed to work on Gallifreyans. As the Marats had a similar biology to the Gallifreyans, this lead to a great plague among them. The Time Lords wanted an end to the war, but the seventh Doctor and Ace gave the Marats a restorative that cured 90% of Gallifreyan ailments.

BLOOD HARVEST / GOTH OPERA -> Three Time Lords - Rath (the younger brother of Goth), Elar and Morin - took responsibility for security matters. Most Time Lords considered this a rather lowly position, but the Committee of Three, as they styled themselves, used their office to build their own powerbase. Using their expertise, they planned to kill Rassilon in his Tower and take control of the galaxy. They were defeated by the seventh Doctor, Ace, Benny and Romana.

The three traitors were sentenced to vaporisation. Romana settled back on Gallifrey from E-Space, and was greeted by Ruathadvorophrenaltid, a Time Lady acquaintance of the Doctor. Ruath planned to be the consort of the Vampire Messiah, and targeted the fifth Doctor. Romana alerted Gallifrey and the Doctor to the threat, and was rewarded with a seat on the High Council.

Gallifreyan medics examined Romana after her return from E-Space, and determined that her body - which had unknowingly become the sixth Key to Time segment - was degenerating, and that regeneration wasn't possible.[487]

THE CHAOS POOL -> Romana aided the fifth Doctor in the second quest for the Key to Time, then returned to Gallifrey with the former Tracer named Amy - whom she hoped would help to convince the Time Lords of the worthiness of non-Gallifreyans to attend the Academy. Afterwards, Amy left Gallifrey and went in search of her sister.[488]

The Time Lords outlawed Vaspen space-time stamps - a means of transporting a small package to any point in space-time, and which were more expensive than a planet.[489] Some Interventionists on Gallifrey took an interest in introducing alien genetic material into the make-up of other species, including humanity.[490]

The Romana Presidency

HAPPY ENDINGS -> Romana was elected President of the Time Lords, beating the previous Madame President - who had been found drunk while in possession of the Sash of Rassilon - by 53 to 47% in the elections, and won the support of the Interventionist movement. She promised an end to isolationism and to open an embassy with the Tharils. Very soon after her election, she investigated a Fortean Flicker which the Master was exploiting. He had stolen the Loom of Rassilon's Mouse, which could build monsters. The Master was defeated and the Loom retrieved, but he escaped Gallifreyan custody.

Romana was the 413th President.[491]

The Carnival Queen affected rationality throughout the universe. On Gallifrey, Grandfather Paradox, "voodoo priest of the House of Lungbarrow", escaped his prison when the Lady President had a fit and released three hundred prisoners from their prison asteroid. Six hundred Time Lords claimed to be the ghost of Morbius, and the planet's automatic defences activated.[492]

Grandfather Paradox removed his arm, as the Time Lords had branded it. Soon, he would remove himself from history. With its leader free, Faction Paradox would grow in size and influence.[493]

LUNGBARROW -> The seventh Doctor and Chris Cwej returned to the Doctor's ancestral home of Lungbarrow. He was accused of murdering Quences, the head of the household. The Doctor was badly beaten and incapacitated by his family, who blamed him for all their woes. Innocet - one of the Doctor's Cousins - joined Ace, Leela, Chris and Romana in reviving him. They learned the Doctor contained the genetic codes of the Other.

The Doctor deduced that another Cousin, Glospin, had briefly regenerated to look like the Doctor and thus framed him for Quences' murder. Quences' mind was in Badger, the House's robot servant. The House itself committed suicide, throwing itself from the mountain it rested upon. Romana ordered a new House built for the Cousins.

Chris decided to stay on Gallifrey and work as an agent of the President. He was given a time ring. Leela discovered she was pregnant. The Dromeians and Arcalians objected to Romana's interventionist policies. She was given a gift by the Chairman of Argolis and opened an embassy with Karn.

The Celestial Intervention Agency sent the Doctor to recover the Master's remains from Skaro.

DEATH COMES TO TIME[494] **->** A new generation of Time Lords was far more open to the idea of intervention. Among them was the Minister of Chance, and he met with the seventh Doctor to discuss intergalactic crises. One such matter emerged when the Time Lords Antinor and Valentine were killed on Earth. Meanwhile, Ace trained to be a Time Lord under Casmus. Events climaxed on the twenty-first century Earth.

Romana and a research team went missing when the planetoid Etra Prime vanished on 6776.7, Rassilon Era. An interim President was appointed in Romana's absence.[495]

> **(=) THE SIRENS OF TIME**[496] **->** The Knights of Velyshaa seized control of the Gallifreyan Capitol. They were exploiting time disturbances using a captured Temperon, an animal that could release particles capable of disrupting time. The fifth, sixth and seventh Doctors restored established history and the conquest of Gallifrey never happened. The Temperon sacrificed itself to forever hold in check the Sirens of Time, extra-dimensional creatures that fed off time distortion.

DOCTOR WHO - THE MOVIE -> The seventh Doctor recovered the Master's remains from Skaro, and was heading for Gallifrey in 5725.2, Rassilon Era. The Master sabotaged the TARDIS, and forced a landing in San Francisco, 1999, but was later lost to the TARDIS' Eye of Harmony.

10639.5 Rassilon Era - "The Final Chapter"[497] **->** Fey and Izzy piloted the TARDIS to Gallifrey. They told Castellan Tenion and Overseer Luther that the eighth Doctor was dying, and he was taken to a hospital complex called the Mortal Coil. At this point, the Doctor was con-

sidered fiction by most people on Gallifrey.

Xanti, an Academy dropout and admirer of the Doctor, hurried to meet him. The Doctor's mind resided in the Matrix while his body healed. He encountered the Higher Evolutionaries - which now included a representative of the Order of the Black Sun, Demoiselle Drin, in Merlin's place. They all had experienced nightmares of a Gallifrey grown "dark and wicked".

A group of Elysians materialised over the Doctor's body, planning to kill him "for the sake of the future", but Shayde arrived to fight them off. The Elysians vanished, taking Izzy with them.

The Doctor spoke to Uriel, Xanti's father, in the Quantum of Solace (which was now being run by ex-military man Tubal Cain). He learned of the history of the Elysians, and that Luther was their leader. Luther's rebuilding of the Capitol had effectively turned the whole planet into a giant TARDIS, powered by Xanti's mind. Now he planned to take it back to the moment of Rassilon's triumph and overwrite that history with his own. The Doctor forced Luther out into the Vortex, but Luther killed Xanti, and the Doctor had to take his place. Shayde rescued the Doctor, but the strain apparently triggered the Doctor's regeneration into a balding man...[498]

Eve of the War in Heaven

ALIEN BODIES / INTERFERENCE / THE TAKING OF PLANET 5 -> Although Time Lords were unable to see into their own future, the eighth Doctor found evidence that the Time Lords would fight a War across time and space against an unknown Enemy. This War involved exotic weapons and such shifts in the timeline, reality, and cause and effect as to make it all but impossible to determine any firm details. The broad sweep of events became apparent among the fragmentary evidence, however, and

494 Dating *Death Comes to Time* (BBC1 drama, unnumbered) - While there are discrepancies, *Death Comes to Time* shares a number of features with the timeline of the later New Adventures - the Time Lords are more openly interventionist, and Ace is training up as a Time Lord. While *Lungbarrow* is clearly meant to lead straight into *Doctor Who - The Movie*, there are other stories set in the "gap", such as *Excelis Decays* and *Master*. Ace is a lot older than she was in the New Adventures (her last appearance is in *Lungbarrow*). As with events in *Death Comes to Time* that occur in the Present Day section, the canonicity of these details is highly debatable. Fans are free to incorporate this story or ignore it.
495 *Neverland*
496 The story takes place during the interim Presidency, in the seventh Doctor's "current" Gallifrey.
497 Dating "The Final Chapter" (*DWM* #262-265) - The

date is given on the TARDIS screen at the beginning of the story, and is significantly later than the one given in *Neverland*. This is tricky to fit in with the books and audios, where Romana is President throughout the eighth Doctor range - although we never actually see the President in this story. It clearly happens before Gallifrey's destruction and fits in with the idea of Gallifreyan society fraying and succumbing to cultism depicted around the time of *The Ancestor Cell*.
498 The adventures of this newborn "ninth Doctor" (patterned after Big Finish producer Nicholas Briggs) continue in "Wormwood", set around 5220.
499 *The Shadows of Avalon*
500 *Interference*
501 *FP: The Book of the War* specifies that Compassion becomes a Type 102 TARDIS.
502 THE WAR IN HEAVEN: *Alien Bodies* introduced the

it was bleak news for Gallifrey.

Romana regenerated for the second time. Her third incarnation became increasingly concerned - perhaps even paranoid - about the prospect of the War.[499] Some Time Lords tried to acquire a bottle universe from IM Foreman, hoping to flee into it when the Enemy attacked.[500]

THE SHADOWS OF AVALON -> President Romana now put the survival of the Time Lords over more ethical considerations. While she was concerned with the dispute with the People of the Worldsphere, Romana was aware that the War with the unknown Enemy would soon be upon Gallifrey.

The Doctor's TARDIS ruptured in a dimensional rift and was presumed destroyed. Learning that the eighth Doctor's companion, Compassion, was mutating into a TARDIS thanks to her contact with future technology, Romana sent Interventionist agents Cavis and Gandar to capture her. Romana planned to force Compassion to breed with other TARDISes. Compassion transformed into a TARDIS, and she, the Doctor and Fitz fled the Time Lord authorities.

Until Compassion, the most advanced TARDIS was the Type 98.[501]

THE ANCESTOR CELL / THE GALLIFREY CHRONICLES -> As the War approached, Gallifreyan society was starting to fray at the edges and many Time Lords were becoming superstitious. Time Lords succumbed to the cults of Ferisix, Thrayke, Sabjatric, Rungar, the Pythian Heresy, Klade and the legend of Cuwirti.

A vast Edifice materialised over Gallifrey. This was the Doctor's original TARDIS, which was drawing energy from IM Foreman's leaking bottle universe.

On Gallifrey, many Time Lords had fallen under the sway of Faction Paradox. They summoned the dead President, Greyjan the Sane, who infected the Matrix with

Faction Paradox virus. Faction Paradox arrived in force to occupy Gallifrey, led by Grandfather Paradox. Fitz's original self, Father Kreiner of Faction Paradox, was freed from the Vortex, but killed by the Grandfather when he switched allegiances and aided the eighth Doctor.

The Enemy was revealled as evolved ancestor cells - primeval lifeforms that had been mutated and empowered by the leaking bottle universe. The Enemy now launched its first strike on Gallifrey, destroying the TARDIS berths.

Faced with the choice of either submitting to Faction Paradox or escaping, the Doctor instead used the remaining energy of the Edifice to destroy Gallifrey. Faction Paradox was wiped out, and the annihilation was so complete that it destroyed the entire constellation of Kasterborous, creating disturbances in space and time that prevented any further time travel to or from Gallifrey.

The Doctor and Compassion downloaded the entire contents of the Matrix into the Doctor's brain. Compassion sent the Doctor and his TARDIS, which had been all but destroyed, to Earth to recover. She also dropped Fitz off in 2001 to reunite with him, then left with Nivet, a Time Lord technician.

It was possible that the destruction of Gallifrey prevented...

The War in Heaven [502]

In some texts, the Time Lords were called the Great Houses, Gallifrey was cited as the Homeworld, and TARDISes were named as timeships.[503]

The War in Heaven was about meaning as much as it was about territory.[504]

The Time Lords created at least nine duplicate Gallifreys, in case the Enemy destroyed the original. Not even the President knew which was the "real" one.[505]

future War and the Enemy (neither of which were capitalised at that point). Further details were added in subsequent eighth Doctor books, principally *Interference*, *The Taking of Planet 5*, *The Shadows of Avalon* and *The Ancestor Cell*. The term "the War in Heaven", while not used very much in the Faction Paradox-related stories themselves, has become a common currency in fandom to differentiate this time-active conflict from the Last Great Time War of the new *Doctor Who*, following the lead of *FP: The Book of the War* as to how historical figures and others tend to perceive the conflict. Technically, this should be the *second* "War in Heaven", the first being the conflict between the Time Lords, the Great Vampires (*State of Decay*) and the Yssgaroth (*The Pit*) as elaborated upon in *FP: The Book of the War*.

The Doctor destroyed Gallifrey in *The Ancestor Cell*, in

large part to avert the War. At that point, all the events of the War ceased to be the "real" future of the *Doctor Who* universe. However, there's the caveat that, by definition, it's difficult to establish facts or the sequence of events of a time war. When asked about the canonicity of its *Faction Paradox* novels, Mad Norwegian Press - tongue planted firmly in cheek - would sometimes respond that *The Ancestor Cell* was propaganda written by the Faction's enemies (as evidenced by a framing sequence therein), and that the War events had not been erased from history.

503 FACTION PARADOX TERMINOLOGY: These equivalents were used throughout the *Faction Paradox* novels, audios and comics for legal reasons. Similarly, "babels" are the *Faction Paradox* equivalent of the Shaydes from the *DWM* comic; the "Imperator Presidency" refers to Morbius' tenure as head of the High Council. The War

Realising that the Enemy could erase them from history, some Celestial Intervention Agency members tried to remove themselves from the universe as a means of defence. They became conceptual beings named the Celestis. They operated from a realm called Mictlan, and influenced universal affairs with a network of agents.[506]

The War King, a former renegade who had tried and failed to warn the Great Houses about the Enemy, was made the official head of the Homeworld six years before the War began. He had a pointed beard that had grown white with age, and wore black robes.[507]

The living timeship Compassion was the only Type 102 timeship. Type 101 timeships, an attempt to breed a living timeship such as Compassion, had been a disastrous failure. Compassion largely attempted to stay neutral in the War, sometimes having adventures with companions such as Carmen Yeh. Two years before the War began, the death of the timeship Percival moved Compassion to take a more active role in the War, and she brokered a deal with the War King, becoming the mother of the first Type 103 timeships. Nonetheless, she insisted that the Enemy attacking the Great Houses was a distraction, and focused her attention on House Lolita.[508] The first of Compassion's offspring, Antipathy, was deeply unstable and kept imprisoned on the Homeworld.[509]

The Enemy struck Gallifrey, completely destroying it. Aware this attack was coming, the Time Lords broke their oldest laws, travelling back in time to assault their Enemy before they were attacked.[510]

Early in the War, the Enemy succeeded in wiping out the most powerful Gallifreyan artifacts like the Demat Gun and the Sash of Rassilon. Many secrets and pieces of bio-data were lost. Those that survived became extremely valuable, and much sought-after, as they could be adapted into weapons.

The first land battle of the War was fought on Dronid in the 155th century. The Doctor was thought to have died on Dronid. His body was recovered, and its unique bio-data would make it perhaps the most valuable artifact in the universe. The Doctor had agreed to donate his body to the Celestis in return for their non-intervention on Dronid.[511]

Every battle was fought and then refought, as the losing side retroactively attempted to reverse the result. Eventually, time collapsed in the vicinity and the fighting would move elsewhere. The Time Lords searched their own future for advanced weapons to be used in the War.[512]

The Enemy learned how to build conceptual entities such as the anarchitects, beings capable of rearranging architecture. Qixotl met the Doctor and saw him escape the Antiridean organ-eaters.[513]

Faction Paradox grew corrupt and started trading weapons and time travel. The Time Lord authorities moved to wipe them out as they would a virus. In 2596, the Time Lords destroyed the Earth colony Ordifica because of its contact with Faction Paradox.[514]

The Time Lords allied themselves with the Gabrielideans. The Time Lords had a military training ground on Gallifrey

King is generally presumed to be the *Faction Paradox* version of the Master, but little confirms this beyond a few background details (the War King's statement that he was one of the few to leave the Homeworld, that he has no House of his own, that the Council forgave him, etc.) given in *FP: Words from Nine Divinities*.
504 *FP: The Book of the War*, which chronicles the first fifty years of the War in Heaven in great detail.
505 *The Taking of Planet 5. FP: The Book of the War* says the alternate Homeworlds/Gallifreys were made "in the last decades before the War", and *FP: Sabbath Dei* specifies that this happens thirty years before the War starts.
506 This happens twenty years before the War, according to *FP: The Book of the War*. The Celestis first appeared in *Alien Bodies*.
    WHEN DID THE WAR IN HEAVEN START?: There's no indication in the *Doctor Who* books exactly when the War was due to start relative to the Doctor. The War began one hundred and fifty-one years after Grandfather Paradox escaped his prison, according to *The Book of the War*. That escape occurred in *Christmas on a Rational Planet*, shortly after Romana became President. Romana celebrates her one hundred and fiftieth year as President in *The Ancestor Cell*, meaning the War is now imminent.

507 *FP: The Book of the War, The Taking of Planet 5.*
508 *FP: The Book of the War, FP: Sabbath Dei, FP: In the Year of the Cat.* Lolita of House Lolita features prominently in the *Faction Paradox* audios.
509 *FP: Of the City of the Saved*
510 *The Ancestor Cell*
511 *Alien Bodies*
512 *The Ancestor Cell*
513 *Alien Bodies*
514 *Interference*
515 *Alien Bodies*
516 *FP: Newtons Sleep.* The Faction has recently severed ties with the Remote, and the Great Houses' Military is making a major effort to wipe out the Faction's holdings wherever they are found (p257) - which going by the timeline in *FP: Book of the War* means that it's about Year Six of the War. What becomes of Thessalia's alliance with the Faction isn't known.
517 *FP: The Book of the War*, and referenced throughout *FP: Warring States.*
518 This happens in Year 18 of the War, according to *FP: The Book of the War.*
519 It's Year 29 of the War, *FP: The Book of the War.*
520 *FP: Erasing Sherlock.* This happens before the Celestis' destruction in *The Taking of Planet 5;* the place-

XII. The latest model TARDISes were the Type 103s, which were sentient and could take the form of people.[515]

The regenerated Thessalia, now passing as "Larissa", agreed to a personal alliance with Faction Paradox.[516]

In the War's eighth year, Cousin Octavia and her corps of elite Faction troops - the Red Brigade - brought about the ruin of a breakaway Faction stronghold (the Thirteen-Day Republic) and its leader, Cousin Anastasia. Father Dyavol, formerly the mad monk Rasputin, died in mysterious circumstances. For her crimes against the Faction, Anastasia was triplicated and put back into linear time, in the twentieth century, to die three times over.[517]

One of the Great Houses - the highly militaristic Mirraflex - assaulted the City of the Saved with timeships reconfigured into behemoths. The City's state of grace protocols were temporarily suspended; twenty million City-dwellers (and eleven timeships) perished as the whole of Snakefell District was expelled into the Big Crunch. The casualties were re-resurrected and a memorial built to commemorate the attack.[518]

Christopher Cwej, an agent of the Great Houses, was mass replicated into a standing army called the Cwejen.[519] The Celestis provided Jimmy Moriarty, a corporate guru in the twenty-first century, with time-travel technology. He used it to interfere in the timeline of Sherlock Holmes.[520]

In Year 41 of the War, Cousin Octavia went in search of an immortality-granting casket in China, 1900. In Year 46, every parallel reality where Nazi Germany conquered the globe came into conflict with every parallel history where Rome dominated Earth. The forty-eighth year of the conflict saw increased political and social tensions within the City of the Saved.[521]

Faction Paradox Series 1: The Faction Paradox Protocols

Cousin Justine of Faction Paradox was sent on a mission to the East Indies ReVit Zone in 2069. She returned afterwards to the Eleven-Day Empire, having failed in her duty. One of Justine's guardians, Sanjira, failed even more badly and as punishment was made to kill his eight-year-old self, paradoxing his timeline.

One of Justine's associates in the Faction, Cousin Eliza, told her:

> "I used to live in a city like this. Different world, different time - different universe, come to think of it... One day, the sky just opened, and that was it. That was the end of it all. [The Great Houses] tore up all the cities, turned most of the people into worker drones. That was the way I found out about things, about how the universe really worked... I was pretty much the only person who got away."

Godfather Morlock now served as head of Faction Paradox's Bio-Research Wing, and was the Acting Emergency Speaker of Parliament. Godfather Sabbath commanded Faction Paradox's Military Wing. The biological catalogue in the Eleven-Day Empire contained eighteen billion species.

Old bloodlines were waning on the Homeworld, and new ones were in ascendancy. House Lolita emerged as a newblood amongst the Great Houses, and initially wasn't seen as being politically relevant. It was composed of a single member - the living timeship Lolita, who remarked that "there were only two [beings] like her".

By Year 50 of the War, Lolita had birthed a daughter and was again pregnant. She furthered her bloodline by overlaying her personality upon beings on multiple worlds, occupying at least one body on every planet where she had influence. She then began to infiltrate the bloodlines of those planets, planting her children within them.[522]

ment is in keeping with the way that Mad Norwegian's *Faction Paradox* novels (where the War in Heaven was concerned) tended to occur in reverse order.

521 The years are respectively provided in the intros to *FP: Warring States*, *FP: Warlords of Utopia*, *FP: Of the City of the Saved...*

522 The background to the *Faction Paradox* audios, as given in *Alien Bodies*, *FP: The Eleven-Day Empire*, *FP: The Shadow Play* and *FP: The Book of the War*. Eliza's quote hails from *The Eleven Day Empire*, and the implication behind it is that Eliza is Christine Summerfield from *Benny: Dead Romance*. (This is further evidenced in *FP: In the Year of the Cat*, when Eliza says she went to

Buckingham Palace on a school trip - meaning she grew up on Earth or *a* version of Earth.)

The "other being" like Lolita is Compassion, one of Lolita's chief rivals in the audios. Compassion is the only Type 102 timeship according to *FP: The Book of the War*; Lolita's Type is never revealed. The short story "Toy Story" - by Lawrence Miles, and included in the Mad Norwegian Press edition of *Dead Romance* - implies that Lolita once served as the Master's TARDIS.

Godfather Sabbath (actually seen in *FP: A Labyrinth of Histories*) and the Sabbath who trained with the British Secret Service and appears in the Eighth Doctor Adventures (and also crops up in the *Faction Paradox*

YEAR 50 - THE ELEVEN-DAY EMPIRE / THE SHADOW PLAY[523] -> Lolita moved to enhance her standing amongst the Great Houses by eliminating Faction Paradox. The Eleven-Day Empire repelled an attack by Lolita's allies, the Seventy-Ninth Sontaran Assault Corps, but this was just the opening volley of a greater gambit. The Houses offered the Faction a treaty - they would once again recognise House Paradox, and refrain from prosecuting its practices.

Godfather Morlock arranged events so that Cousin Justine lost her shadow - she was then fitted with the shadow of Grandfather Paradox, which resided within the knife he had used to cut off his arm. The Grandfather's shadow was a siege engine, capable of generating and discarding an infinite number of shadow weapons.

The Faction's Parliament ratified the treaty, whereupon Lolita exploited the laws governing transition of affairs and the treaty's clause on prestanding crimes - and demanded that the shadow of Grandfather Paradox be turned over for trial. The Faction's failure to do so put it in breach of protocol. Lolita performed an invocation that linked her to the *loa* protecting the Eleven-Day Empire... and she then consumed the whole of the Empire, compressing it into her internal dimensions. Justine and Eliza were the sole survivors of the Empire, and escaped in the timeship of a House member slain by Lolita.

Lolita said that the Empire's remains resided to the left of her alimentary canal.[524]

YEAR 51 - IN THE YEAR OF THE CAT / MOVERS / A LABYRINTH OF HISTORIES[525] -> The Great Houses recaptured Justine in 1762 and condemned her to their prison asteroid for all eternity, but she escaped back to the eighteenth century. Before doing so, Justine encountered Kresta Ve Coglana Shuncuker - the previous (and from Shuncuker's perspective, current) bearer of the shadow of Grandfather Paradox.

Faction Paradox Series 2: The True History of Faction Paradox

YEAR 51 - COMING TO DUST / THE SHIP OF A BILLION YEARS / BODY POLITIC / WORDS FROM NINE DIVINITIES / OZYMANDIAS / THE JUDGMENT OF SUTEKH[526] -> The past of the Osirian Court interacted with the present of the War in Heaven. The Great Houses officially recognised the Court via a treaty signed after Sutekh made a power play into fifteenth century Earth. Many Osirians took to living on the Ship of a Billion Years after Sutekh destroyed their homeworld, and although Sutekh was no longer acknowledged as a divine shield of Ra, some of their number were agreeable to giving him Osiris' throne as a matter of security. Cousin Justine - travelling to the Court from 1763, and intent upon killing Sutekh - strengthened the Ship's defences, stymieing Sutekh's efforts to claim dominion over it.

To further keep Sutekh in check, Justine asked Lord Anubis to resurrect Osiris. The War King backed Justine's gambit by deploying the Fifty-Ninth Fleet of the House military to protect Anubis' stronghold. Cousin Eliza harvested what remained of Osiris' biodata, but failed to retrieve 12% of his psychic mass and 7% of his timeline. Osiris' biodata was already tainted with Faction Paradox biomass, so Anubis used Eliza herself to fill in the gaps, instilling Osiris' essence within her. She made a bid for the throne as "Horus", and was acknowledged as being somewhere between Osiris' firstborn son and a reincarnation of

---

audios and comics) are *not* the same person, as first demonstrated when Eliza says the Secret Service's Sabbath, "I used to have a godfather called Sabbath... didn't look much like you, though" in *FP: Sabbath Dei.*

523 Dating *FP: The Eleven-Day Empire* and *FP: The Shadow Play* (*FP* audios #1.1-1.2) - The *Faction Paradox* audios follow on from *FP: The Book of the War*, which cites Year 50 of the War as "the present", and contains some character entries - notably those of Godfather Morlock and Lolita - that establish their status before the audios begin. A few references in the audios (notably in *FP: In the Year of the Cat* and *FP: Body Politic*) reiterate that the War is roughly at the half-century mark.

524 *FP: In the Year of the Cat*

525 Dating *FP: In the Year of the Cat*, *FP: Movers* and *FP: A Labyrinth of Histories* (*FP* audios #1.4-1.6) - Justine revives after six months (the same amount of time that Compassion has spent trying to aid in her escape) of

stasis on the Great Houses' prison asteroid (almost certainly Shada). Ergo, it might still be Year 50 of the War when she awakes, but simplicity tends to suggest that it's Year 51.

526 Dating *FP: Coming to Dust*, *FP: The Ship of a Billion Years*, *FP: Body Politic*, *FP: Words from Nine Divinities*, *FP: Ozymandias*, *FP: The Judgment of Sutekh* (*FP* audios #2.1-2.6) - For Justine and Eliza, a matter of months seem to pass between Series 1 and 2 of the *Faction Paradox* audios, and a comparable amount of time presumably passes where the War itself is concerned.

527 *Interference*

528 Subsequent events would suggest the clone was of the Master.

529 *The Taking of Planet 5*

530 *Alien Bodies*

531 *The Taking of Planet 5*

him. Lolita, not wanting a maniac like Sutekh on the throne, secretly endowed Eliza with some of her own biomass, giving "Horus" enough power to temporarily wound Sutekh. The matter of Sutekh's claim to the throne was settled on Mars, circa 5000 BC.

The War was currently being fought on nine hundred and twenty fronts, across nearly half a million worlds. The Great Houses had brokered alliances in more than eight thousand cultures, and thought the Osirians could be key allies on seventeen fronts of the War. The War King prematurely triggered an inevitable civil war between his followers and Lolita's, thinking it better to start the conflict before she became even more powerful. The clash ended with Lolita consuming the War King just as she had the Eleven-Day Empire, and claiming leadership of the High Council. Justine realised that Lolita represented a greater threat than even Sutekh, and sent her a "message": a cadre of Mal'akh, who tore their way through the Council chambers.

Justine negotiated a deal wherein the force of Osirians historically destined to defeat Sutekh were instead diverted to the Homeworld. Led by Cousin Eliza/Horus, they "dealt" with the effectively immortal Lolita.

ALIEN BODIES -> As some of the Celestis began switching sides, the War began tipping in favour of the Enemy. The Doctor's dead body - the Relic - was auctioned by Mr Qixotl. The Celestis won by giving Qixotl a new body when his original one was fatally wounded. The eighth Doctor tricked the Celestis and stole the Relic. He took it to Quiescia, then destroyed it with a thermosystron bomb.

The Time Lords quickly moved to occupy or control millions of planets. They opted to mate Marie, a Type 103 TARDIS, to a male Type 105 as a means of diversifying TARDIS genetics. They also created the Ogron Lords, shock troops with the ability to time travel.[527]

INTERFERENCE -> The Time Lords were losing the War. Gallifrey had a last resort - a weapon designed to destroy Earth, which would not only destroy the Enemy's homeworld but collapse the entire web of time. The ship was dispatched at sub-light speeds, and was due to arrive at Earth in 1996. Fitz became Father Kreiner of Faction Paradox and hunted down Time Lords, including the Master and the Rani. One of these was actually a clone.[528]

One of the duplicate Gallifreys was destroyed in the Battle of Mutter's Cluster. Gallifrey VIII was an industrial planet with vast Looms pouring out soldiers.[529] There was a Gallifrey XII.[530]

Time Lords were force-regenerated into physical forms engineered to fight. Fifteen out of a thousand Time Lords survived each combat mission. There were distinct Waves of warfare, with gaps between them allowing the Time Lords to Loom more soldiers. Only those from the First

Wave resembled humans. The Time Lords suffered heavy losses in the Third Zone during the Fifth Wave.

Any gathering of around a dozen TARDISes would attract an Enemy attack. The Time Lords used Parallel Cannons that created holes to other, more hostile, parts of the universe and unleashed the forces there. The Enemy detonated the star of the planet Delphon, causing a significant rout of the Time Lords.[531]

THE TAKING OF PLANET 5 -> The Time Lords planned to smash a fleet of War TARDISes against the barriers around the Fifth Planet, hoping to free the Fendahl for use against the Enemy. The eighth Doctor, Fitz and Compassion discovered the plot, and Compassion tried to save the War TARDISes. The barrier was destroyed, which unleashed not the Fendahl but the Fendahl Predator - a Memovore creature that had evolved the ability to destroy concepts. The Fendahl Predator was drawn to Mictlan and destroyed the Celestis before the Doctor banished it.

THE ANCESTOR CELL / THE GALLIFREY CHRONICLES -> Faction Paradox had gone from being a secret society to an army, led by Grandfather Paradox, the future self none of us hope to become. As well as a new rank of initiate - the Uncles, leather-clad assassins - there was now an armoured infantry, known as skulltroopers, and their shadow weapons had evolved so that they resembled guns. Although they were experienced at fighting Time Lords, Faction Paradox was not the Enemy.

Now they travelled two hundred and ninety-seven years into their own past to launch an invasion of Gallifrey. This would be the event that would lead to both the Faction conquering Gallifrey, and - three minutes seven seconds later - their total destruction and the annihilation of the War timeline.

Aftermath of the War in Heaven

Aided by Compassion at the moment of Gallifrey's destruction, the eighth Doctor had downloaded the entire contents of the Matrix - the memories of almost every Time Lord who had ever lived - into his own mind. They survived in a supercompressed form that left no room for the Doctor's own memories. Compassion apparently took the Doctor's memories, although for what purpose remains a mystery. Compassion dropped the amnesiac Doctor off in the late nineteenth century.

When his travels through time and space resumed, the Doctor met a man in the eighteenth century who resembled the Master and said the following:

"There are only four of us left now, you know. Four of us in all the universe." [532]

Without the Time Lords controlling the proliferation of time travel, many races attempted to gain mastery of time, often by acquiring Gallifreyan artifacts. Without the Time Lords to enforce the laws of time, magic started to seep back into the universe.[533]

THE GALLIFREY CHRONICLES -> Marnal regenerated and automatically regained his memories. He soon discovered the Doctor had destroyed Gallifrey and lured him to Earth to punish him. The eighth Doctor and Marnal came to realise that the Doctor's mind contained the contents of the Matrix and the memories of all the Time Lords. Marnal died saving the Doctor, convinced that the Doctor should dedicate himself to the task of building a New Gallifrey. The Doctor sent K9 to track down Compassion.

After the War in Heaven, relics of it - including members of the Mayakai civilisation, who had been primed as weapons - remained. Mother Francesca and her unnamed associate believed they were "the only ones left" of Faction Paradox.[534]

It would appear that the Doctor succeeded in building a new Gallifrey. His memories certainly returned. Romana was once again in her second incarnation.[535]

The Temporal Powers

An unspecified temporal incident caused space-time to warp around the Monan homeworld. Ten different time periods came into contact with one another, enabling some future Monan to conquer their ancestors. By stabilising the errant fields, the Monan unified the different periods into a single system - creating the Monan Host.[536]

THE APOCALYPSE ELEMENT -> Twenty time-active races met on Archetryx for a summit, but the planetoid

Etra Prime reappeared. The Daleks there were working on the Apocalypse Element: a substance capable of shredding the raw fabric of space-time in an unstoppable reaction. The Daleks attacked Archetryx and stole components needed to finish making the Element.

Romana had been imprisoned on Etra Prime for twenty years. She escaped as the Daleks, using a Monan Host time ship as a Trojan horse, attacked Gallifrey. The sixth Doctor and Evelyn aided Romana against the Daleks; as part of this, Gallifrey's security systems were temporarily slaved to Evelyn's retinal pattern. The Daleks detonated the Apocalypse Element in the Seriphia galaxy. As was their plan, the Daleks sacrificed their ranks on Gallifrey to reinforce the Eye of Harmony's power. The Eye contained the Element's destruction to Seriphia, which was restructured to create millions of new worlds for the Daleks.

The Daleks killed the interim President of Gallifrey, and Romana was restored to the Presidency.[537]

SHADA[538] **->** The eighth Doctor returned to Gallifrey and told President Romana and K9 that they needed to resolve a time anomaly by travelling to Cambridge in 1979.

NEVERLAND -> President Romana allied the Time Lords with the Warpsmiths of Phaedon and the Monan Host.

A warfleet of TARDISes pursued the eighth Doctor and Charley, who decided it was time to resolve the paradox of her existence (as she had been saved from dying in the R-101 crash). The two of them were taken to a Time Station.

President Romana and CIA coordinator Vansell warned that the structure of space and time was on the verge of collapse. They believed that Charley had attracted Anti-Time particles from the Antiverse, which was disrupting the universal balance. The Time Lords adapted the Station to pass into the Antiverse to investigate. The Doctor dis-

532 "THERE ARE FOUR OF US NOW": *The Infinity Doctors* (p213) first mentioned "four names" as the four people that Rassilon had ordered killed as a threat to Gallifrey, with Omega and the Doctor specified as two of the four. The above quote comes from *The Adventuress of Henrietta Street* (p231). In *The Gallifrey Chronicles*, the four survivors are described as "A man with a sallow face and small, pointed black beard, who wore a blue rosette; a young woman with long blonde hair in an extraordinary piece of haute couture; a tall man with a bent nose wearing a cravat and holding a pair of dice; the Doctor himself with close-cropped hair, sitting on an ornate throne, a new-born baby girl in his arms" - intended, but not named, respectively as the Master; Iris Wildthyme (or possibly Romana); the Minister of Chance from *Death Comes to Time*; the Doctor (possibly the Doctor from *The Infinity Doctors*, or

in his role as the Emperor of the Universe, father of Miranda, mentioned in *Father Time*).
533 The books from *Father Time* to *Sometime Never* often showed races with time travel or magical abilities.
534 The *Faction Paradox* comic series (*FP*: "Political Animals" and *FP*: "Betes Noires and Dark Horses"). To date, this is the only appearance of Faction Paradox set after the War in Heaven. As the Doctor, Fitz and Compassion all survived the War in Heaven, these events may or may not "still happen" following the potential erasing of the War in Heaven timeline in *The Ancestor Cell*.
535 The Doctor's intent to recreate Gallifrey in *The Gallifrey Chronicles* raises the interesting possibility that he does so, and that the Gallifrey featured in Big Finish's eighth Doctor-era audios and *Gallifrey* mini-series (which lead into the Last Great Time War) all take place

SECTION FIVE: GALLIFREY

covered Rassilon's TARDIS, the size of a planetoid, with a surface populated by "Neverpeople". Rassilon's casket was there. Vansell fell under the sway of the Neverpeople, who were actually exiled Time Lord criminals.

The Doctor realised that the Neverpeople had spread rumours throughout time of Zagreus, hoping to tempt the Time Lords here. Instead of Rassilon, the casket contained a mass of Anti-time sufficient to destabilise the universe. Vansell sacrificed his life, but failed to prevent the Station, with the casket onboard, from reaching Gallifrey. The Doctor surrounded the Station with his TARDIS. The Station exploded, but the TARDIS contained the Anti-Time. However, the Doctor was saturated with Anti-Time energy... which split his personality and made him the destroyer Zagreus.

> = In the Matrix, the Doctor saw a possible future where Gallifrey had been attacked and Romana was the Imperiatrix responsible for the genocide of the Daleks.[539]

This occurred in 6798.3, Rassilon Era.[540]

ZAGREUS -> The Anti-Time-infected Doctor became Zagreus, and a revived Rassilon sought to use him as a weapon against the Divergents. Zagreus objected to being manipulated and cast Rassilon through a portal into the Divergents' timeline. The TARDIS helped the eighth Doctor stabilise his true persona and he left for a Divergent Universe, fearing that by remaining, he would risk the Anti-Time within him allowing Zagreus to again take control. Charley accompanied the Doctor on his journey.

THE NEXT LIFE -> Rassilon was caught in a recurring time loop, and his identity began slipping away. The Zagreus persona was separated from the eighth Doctor and took on female form, but learned "she" was destined to remain in the Divergent Universe for at least twenty to

thirty millennia. The purged Doctor returned to our universe with Charley and a new companion, C'rizz. They immediately came into conflict with Davros and the Daleks.[541]

Time breaks were detected in Victorian times. Romana sent Leela back to aid Professor Litefoot and Henry Gordon Jago in ending this threat.[542]

Gallifrey Series 1[543]

Gallifrey had battle-TARDISes at its disposal. Cardinal Braxiatel was a member of the High Council, and Narvin served as CIA coordinator. Andred had disappeared, and Leela - mourning for him - became President Romana's personal bodyguard.[544]

GALLIFREY: WEAPON OF CHOICE -> Under President Romana, Gallifrey continued to withdraw from its monopoly of time travel, and furthered a coalition of temporal powers that included the Monan Host, the Warpsmiths of Phaidon and the Nekkistani. The temporal powers promised to protect the lesser races, in exchange for a moratorium on unauthorised time experiments. The planet Gryben was established as a "reception centre" for rogue time travellers - unauthorised time-vessels in the Vortex would be automatically diverted to Gryben, and their occupants dealt with on a case-by-case basis.

The Time Lords believed a timonic fusion device recovered by Nepenthe - a member of the subversive group Free Time - in 3655 was now on Gryben, and so Romana sent Leela, K9 Mark 1 and a CIA operative named Torvald there to find it. It was learned that a third party had engineered the situation to bring the Time Lords and the Monan into conflict; the device went unused and was teleported away, and Nepenthe martyred herself. Romana made the acquaintance of Mephistopheles Arkadian, a time-travelling rogue and arms dealer.

on the "restored" Gallifrey, not the original. If nothing else, this might explain why Romana (seen in her third incarnation in The Shadows of Avalon and The Ancestor Cell) reverts back to being her second incarnation as played by Lalla Ward - either the copy of the Matrix hidden in the Doctor's mind (The Ancestor Cell) hadn't been updated to include the new Romana, or (rather amorally) the Doctor went out of his way while renewing Gallifrey to bring Romana back to life as her previous self.
536 Gallifrey: Square One
537 Neverland
538 The prologue to the Big Finish webcast offers an in-story explanation as to why the Doctor needs to "repeat" an adventure. See "Which Shada, if Any, is

Canon?" for more.
539 Neverland
540 Neverland. The date was given earlier in the story as 6978.5, but this is clearly a fluffed line, given the other recent dates.
541 Terror Firma
542 J&L: Dead Men's Tales. There's not really a convenient point in the Gallifrey mini-series for this to have occurred, so it likely happened beforehand.
543 Dating Gallifrey Series 1 - The season opens up in wake of events in Zagreus.
544 Gallifrey: Weapon of Choice, providing the background to Gallifrey Series 1. Leela was pregnant in Lungbarrow, and no mention is made of her child in the Gallifrey series.

SECTION FIVE: GALLIFREY

GALLIFREY: SQUARE ONE -> The coalition of temporal powers held a summit on a synthetic planetoid in neutral space, and considered legislation to limit time travel in the Vortex. Romana and Leela thwarted a third party's attempts to cause various deaths, including that of the Unvoss representative, as a means of discrediting Gallifrey. The gathering was actually a decoy to draw Free Time into the open - the real summit proceeded in secret, with Braxiatel representing Gallifrey's interests.

GALLIFREY: THE INQUIRY -> Inquisitor Darkel[545] and Cardinal Braxiatel led an inquiry into Romana's conduct during the Gryben affair. She was cleared after it emerged she had helped to prevent the timonic fusion device from being stolen in the first place. Romana learned that Braxiatel, trading under the name "Irving Braxiatel", had been purchasing unique works of art, furniture, sculpture (including one by the artist Serafina) and even entire buildings for his private collection. She realised that Braxiatel was behind the Braxiatel Collection, but judged that he'd broken the laws of time to an inconsequential degree...

Though it was against the rules of time, Irving Braxiatel contacted his younger self on Gallifrey and asked him to send a Gallifreyan relic to the Braxiatel Collection.[546]

GALLIFREY: A BLIND EYE -> Romana, Leela and Narvin went back to Earth, the 3rd of September, 1939, and identified the culprit behind the timonic device theft. Leela learned that Andred had regenerated after a failed attempt to infiltrate the CIA, and had been passing himself as a new incarnation of the CIA agent Torvald.

Lucie Miller[547]

BLOOD OF THE DALEKS / HUMAN RESOURCES -> Interference in the year 2006 resulted in the Time Lords placing Lucie Miller with the eighth Doctor, and telling him that she was part of a witness relocation programme. They also placed a temporal barrier around Lucie's native era, preventing the Doctor from returning there. The Doctor and Lucie resolved events pertaining to Karen Coltraine and the Cybermen on Lonsis, and the Time Lords lifted the barrier.

SISTERS OF THE FLAME / THE VENGEANCE OF MORBIUS -> The Time Lords received word that the new leader of the Cult of Morbius - Kristof Zarodnix - was trying to capture a Gallifreyan. Fearing the consequences of this, they recalled all TARDISes, and used the Timescoop to capture any Time Lord who refused to return home.[548] Time rings became the only viable means of travel.

A restored Morbius deprived Gallifrey of energy using a

---

545 Inquisitor Darkel is the same character as the Inquisitor in *The Trial of a Time Lord*, and is once again played by Lynda Bellingham.
546 *Benny: The Crystal of Cantus*
547 The Big Finish audios featuring the eighth Doctor and Lucie Miller (initially broadcast on BBC7) are a little tricky to place in Gallifrey's timeline. The audios were marketed as occurring "later" in the eighth Doctor's life, but it's hard to imagine the Time Lords sparing the resources (or having the desire) to address issues related to Lucie and the Cybermen on Lonsis (*Human Resources*) once Gallifreyan society comes apart at the seams in *Gallifrey* Series 2. As the *Gallifrey* mini-series follow on from *Zagreus*, and the intent of the Lucie audios is, quite clearly, that they occur after the Doctor's travels with Charley Pollard, the best solution is to place these stories at some point before, after or during *Gallifrey* Series 1.
548 Given the sheer number of Time Lord renegades at work in the universe throughout *Doctor Who*, it's hard to swallow that "all Time Lords are accounted for", i.e. have been recalled to Gallifrey. Still, the Timescoop used here is powerful enough to snatch in-flight TARDISes - a much greater use of the device than is seen in *The Five Doctors*.
549 Dating *Gallifrey* Series 2 - The opening installment, *Lies*, takes place "six weeks" after *A Blind Eye*. *Spirit* opens

"a week" after *Lies*, and the remaining installments of Series Two happen in rapid succession. *Neverland* forecast Romana's ascension to Imperiatrix. Braxiatel departs Gallifrey in *Pandora*, and appears to experience all of his involvement in the New Adventures and the Bernice Summerfield range between now and his return to Gallifrey in *Mindbomb* (see the Irving Braxiatel vs. Cardinal Braxiatel sidebar).
550 Dating *Gallifrey* Series 3 - The fact that Pandora is Imperiatrix long enough to amass a horde of illegal temporal weapons suggests that some indeterminate time passes between Series 2 and 3, but the episodes of Series 3 themselves occur in rapid succession. Gary Russell, the producer of *Gallifrey*, has confirmed that Series 3 ends shortly before Gallifrey becomes embroiled in the Last Great Time War referenced in the new series. To that end, Arkadian expresses a desire to sell the temporal weapons stockpile to "metal gentlemen of his acquaintance", presumably meaning the Daleks. The suggestion that Time Lords could be restored from the biodata archive could be a precursor to the Time Lords "resurrecting" their number (particularly the Master, as mentioned in *The Sound of Drums*) for the Time War. The technique might even be a frontrunner to the resurrection gauntlets seen in *Torchwood* and *The End of Time* (TV).

stellar manipulator, then created a new empire. The eighth Doctor restored power to Gallifrey, and the Time Lords retroactively undid Morbius' triumphs.

NEVERMORE -> The Time Lords sent the eighth Doctor and his companion, Tamsin Drew, to procure the release of General Morella Wendigo on the planet Nevermore.

Gallifrey Series 2[549]

GALLIFREY: LIES -> At Romana's urging, the High Council altered some of Gallifrey's oldest laws to open up the Academy to non-Gallifreyan students. Romana realised that the Imperiatrix Imprimature within her might allow Pandora - the warmongering former president of Gallifrey - to take control of her body, and that Pandora's spirit still existed within a Matrix partition.

GALLIFREY: SPIRIT / PANDORA -> Romana promoted Braxiatel to the rank of Chancellor. She took a brief leave of absence, and went with Leela to the planet Davidia - a retreat used by presidents of various species for summits, conferences and holidays.

Andred stopped Gillestes - a Free Time agent from Yevnon - from contaminating the Time Lords' water supply with a "dogma virus" that had been engineered by Free Time. Pandora nestled herself in Castellan Wynter's mind, but was then confronted by Braxiatel and Darkel. Braxiatel devoted a portion of his thoughts to the Matrix equations that kept Pandora imprisoned, trapping Pandora in his own mind. Wynter died soon after. Braxiatel volunteered to go into exile, removing all possibility of Pandora escaping on Gallifrey - but the public disclosure that he'd broken the lines of time by communicating with his past and future selves meant that he did so in disgrace. Before leaving, Braxiatel warned Romana that he'd only bottled Pandora's past and present aspects; her future aspect remained in the Matrix.

GALLIFREY: INSURGENCY / IMPERIATRIX -> Non-Gallifreyans at the Academy included humans, the Warpsmiths of Phaidon, Monans and at least one Sunari. Cardinal Valyes became Chancellor of the Academy.

The Time Lords didn't know how many of their number had been infected by Gillestes' "dogma virus" - but learned that it would make any tainted Time Lord, upon their regeneration, accept Free Time's beliefs and political agenda. Racial tensions at the Academy increased, and a human student, Taylor Addison, died while attempting to sabotage the Eye of Harmony. A terrorist bombing at the Academy killed twenty; the High Monan and the Nekkistani emperor withdrew their citizens and students from Gallifrey. K9 Mark 1 detected another bomb at Gallifrey's spaceport - his early warning saved many lives,

but blast doors were lowered. He died in the subsequent explosion, along with everyone else trapped within.

Darkel decried Romana's policies as having compromised Gallifrey's security, and forced a new election. The future aspect of Pandora, communing with Romana through K9 Mark 2, insisted that Gallifrey would fall into civil war unless Romana stepped down. Romana worried about Pandora's secret agenda, but also feared the consequences of Darkel becoming president. In accordance with the law - and in full possession of the Great Key, the Sash, the Rod and the Coronet of Rassilon - Romana ended the stalemate by declaring herself Imperiatrix, i.e. dictator of Gallifrey. She ordered the dissolution of the Chapters.

Romana donned the Coronet of Rassilon to prevent another Free Time agent from blowing up the Panopticon and force-regenerating the assembled Time Lords therein, but this act triggered the Imperiatrix Imprimature within her, enabling Pandora to draw biological matter from the Matrix and manifest in the form of Romana's first incarnation. Pandora usurped the mantle of Imperiatrix. Romana realised that Pandora, as part of her schemes, had mentally influenced her into killing Andred.

Gallifrey Series 3[550]

GALLIFREY: FRACTURES / WARFARE / APPROPRIATION / MINDBOMB / PANACEA -> Civil war erupted on Gallifrey. Darkel and Chancellor Valyes sided with Pandora; Leela, Narvin, Councillor Matthias and others joined Romana's resistance effort. Romana used her presidential access codes to ground all TARDISes, denying Pandora access to time travel. The other temporal powers parked war fleets near Gallifrey. Romana's group sabotaged various resources - the Gallifreyan archive banks were razed, destroying millions of years of recorded history. Narvin and Leela attempted to ruin the Artron microform - a locale where excess Artron energy from Time Lord minds was absorbed and sent to the TARDIS berthing bays - but their charges went off prematurely, causing a discharge of Artron energy that permanently blinded Leela. Leela nonetheless stabbed Pandora through both hearts, slaying her physical form. Pandora's essence was once more contained within the Matrix - which was made to self-destruct, killing her and the preserved minds of former Time Lords within.

Political jockeying led to Chancellor Valyes, then Darkel, becoming acting president. The High Council took a vote of no confidence in Romana - an act that legitimised her term as president, and invalidated Valyes' tenure. Matthias claimed the powers of a vice-president, and called for the first presidential election Gallifrey had experienced in millennia. Darkel, Matthias and Romana stood as presidential candidates. Romana was impeached, and her candidacy declared void.

Gallifrey's transduction barriers temporarily fell, and timeships carrying Sunari soldiers - who said they wanted to retrieve any surviving Sunari students - arrived in the Capitol. The Nekkistani warfleet allied with the Sunari vessels. Matthias ordered Gallifrey's transduction barriers raised without giving the warfleets time to withdraw, killing hundreds and causing a diplomatic fiasco.

Braxiatel returned to Gallifrey, having learned that Gallifrey would soon face a threat that it was too weak to defeat without the Imperiatrix. He allied with Matthias, who tricked Darkel into annulling the effects of Romana's presidency from the moment Pandora escaped from the Matrix - which restored Braxiatel to his former position of Chancellor. He automatically became President.

The remaining Pandora component - little more than raw hatred - longed for freedom, even though this would kill both the component and its host. Darkel tried to murder Braxiatel by freeing the Pandora component, only to find that it had been restrained all along in *her* mind, and that Braxiatel's mind - while containing a small portion of Pandora - was merely the key to its prison. Darkel and the Pandora piece perished upon its release. Braxiatel declared that, for Gallifrey's safety, he would resume his exile. Knowing that the next president would fall with Gallifrey, Braxiatel named Matthias as his successor.

Matthias' tenure began with a great calamity: the pig-rats used to incubate Gillestes' dogma virus had escaped from the Academy labs during the civil war, and widely tainted the Gallifreyan population. K9 estimated that at least 35% of the Time Lords was already infected; any infected Time Lord who regenerated would became a mindless Free Time thrall. Before long, thousands of Time Lords were in such a state.

Braxiatel offered to trade the Braxiatel Collection's holdings to Mephistopheles Arkadian, in exchange for his help in securing and disposing of the treaty-violating temporal

551 Dating *Gallifrey* Series 4 - The series picks up immediately after (or near enough) Series 3.
552 Braxiatel's meet-up with Benny is a dramatisation of their "first" meeting (from Braxiatel's point of view, not Benny's) in *Benny: Dragons' Wrath* - which might suggest that post-*Gallifrey*, Braxiatel is, somehow, living in his own subjective past. One suspects that future Bernice Summerfield audios will address the point.
553 *Dalek*

WHO STARTED THE LAST GREAT TIME WAR?: In both an essay for the *2006 Doctor Who Annual* and an interview for *Doctor Who Confidential*, Russell T Davies is of the opinion that the Time Lords "fired first" in the Time War by sending the Doctor to intervene in the Daleks' origins (in *Genesis of the Daleks*). He may well be correct, but this perhaps doesn't tell the entire story.

By *Genesis of the Daleks*, there can be little doubt regarding the threat that the Daleks pose. In *The Daleks*, they're initially portrayed as a group of desperate war survivors who cannot even leave their own city, but in rapid succession they've conquered Earth (*The Dalek Invasion of Earth*) and developed a crude form of time travel (*The Chase*). As early as Season 3 (with *The Daleks' Master Plan*), they're an intergalactic power to be reckoned with. The stories to follow have them suffering various defeats and setbacks, but their potential to cause widespread havoc and genocide never diminishes much. Even in *Day of the Daleks*, their comparatively shoddy time-technology has allowed them to alter history and conquer Earth a second time.

Real-life analogies quickly fail when applied to the Daleks. At times they're compared to the likes of Nazis, but in truth they're literally lacking of humanity. Even "conquest" as we generally understand the term doesn't really interest them - sometimes they put foes to work as slaves (as in *Death to the Daleks*), but this is almost inevitably in the interest of facilitating new atrocities and exterminations. The point is that one can (and should) hope to use reason against real-world governments, but there is virtually no chance of diplomacy succeeding against the Daleks Occasionally the Doctor makes a group of Daleks passive - say, by altering their very nature in *The Evil of the Daleks* - but only under unique and limited circumstances. Basically, the Daleks remain united behind one goal: kill everything that isn't a Dalek (see especially *The Stolen Earth*).

In *Genesis of the Daleks*, the Time Lord that sends the Doctor to Skaro's past says, "We have foreseen a time when [the Daleks] will have destroyed all other life forms, and become the dominant creature in the universe". Based on the Daleks' characteristics and past behaviour, this seems worryingly plausible. Faced with such a scenario - literally a death sentence for everything save Dalek-kind - the Time Lords using their one trump card, their mastery of time, to change the Daleks' origins might well seem like a risk worth taking. (It should be remembered that it takes something as catastrophic as the War in Heaven for the Time Lords to marshal anything resembling military might. A war-TARDIS isn't even seen until the fifth Doctor's era in "The Stockbridge Horror", so in most periods of history, the Time Lords sending troops to physically contain Dalek advances doesn't appear to be an option. Time-technology remains the best leverage they have.)

A probable effect of the Doctor intervening in *Genesis*, however, would be to make the Daleks aware of the Time Lords as a rival temporal power. In the stories to follow, both Davros and the Daleks become openly confrontational toward Gallifrey, and even minor races (such as the Cryons in *Attack of the Cybermen*) know of the Time Lords. *Resurrection of the Daleks* has the Daleks plotting to assassinate the Gallifreyan High Council (there's no evidence that the Time Lords ever learn about this, though). *The*

weapons that Pandora had amassed while Imperiatrix. Arkadian offered to give Gallifrey a cure for the dogma virus in exchange for Pandora's weapons - which the Time Lords loaded into a battle-TARDIS rigged to explode, in the hope that they would obtain the cure and prevent the weapons from falling into the wrong hands.

Romana and K9 piloted the battle-TARDIS to the now-disused Braxiatel Collection, which was outside space-time. Braxiatel Timescooped the Time Lords' entire bio-data archive - and snared Leela and Narvin while doing so - so that it would survive Gallifrey's upcoming downfall. He told those assembled that the virus "cure" worked, but only by stripping a Time Lord of their ability to regenerate - this had been Free Time's goal all along, to curtail the Time Lords' near-immortality. Free Time itself was no longer a threat, perhaps owing to Braxiatel's adventures in exile.

Romana had to choose between using the cure and consigning the Time Lords to a single life each, or letting Gallifrey fall and reconstructing the Time Lords with the biodata archive. Before she could decide, the battle-TAR-DIS - with Arkadian inside - was recalled to Gallifrey. Romana, Leela, K9, Narvin and Braxiatel were horrified to realise that the battle-TARDIS was headed toward a zombie-filled Gallifrey with a stockpile of booby-trapped temporal weapons, and a cure that would rob the Time Lords of their regeneration prowess. Romana told her allies: "Right. What we're going to do is…"

Gallifrey Series 4[551]

= GALLIFREY: REBORN / DISASSEMBLED / ANNIHILATION / FOREVER -> Romana and her friends used the Axis to visit different versions of Gallifrey, hoping that one of them had the means of curtailing the dogma virus and halting the impending war. On one such alt-Gallifrey, the Time Lords boosted their economy through the sale of time rings, TARDISes, battle-TARDISes and more. Regenerations could be extracted and sold for currency.

A second alt-Gallifrey was highly interventionist,

and used surgical changes to history - including assassination and erasure from history by D-Mat gun - to achieve an optimal timeline. Romana's group prevented the President Romana of that Gallifrey from using the Axis to collapse all realities into a single continuum that she ruled, but Braxiatel and President Romana's assassin - Lord Burner, an alternate version of the sixth Doctor - were lost to the Vortex. The timelines shifted around Braxiatel, and he again encountered Bernice Summerfield in 2593.[552]

Romana obliterated Lord Prydon's vampires on a third alt-Gallifrey, but it was expected that Majestrix Borusa's diminished "True Lords" would die out soon after. Leela regained her sight by imbibing blood from one of Prydon's vampires. Yet another Gallifrey was found to have simian Time Lords.

Finally, Romana's group visited a militant Gallifrey that had never developed time travel. The President Romana of that reality was killed, and Chancellor Narvin died to prevent the insatiable Krillic from escaping the Eye of Harmony. Romana's access to the Axis was terminated to prevent the same, stranding her, Narvin and Leela while K9 Mark 2 remained behind in the Axis. Leela left, tired of Romana's broken promises. Romana and Narvin took their counterparts' place, making this Gallifrey their new home so that they could teach its inhabitants the ethics needed for them to one day become Time Lords.

The Last Great Time War

The Doctor's home planet was destroyed in the Last Great Time War, "a war between the Daleks and the Time Lords with the whole of creation at stake".[553]

The Daleks removed themselves from history to go off and fight the Time War.[554] They became experts at fighting TARDISes.[555] The Doctor led the battle in the Last Great Time War.[556] He was on the frontline during the war, and did "terrible things" just to survive.[557] He "butchered millions" during the Time War.[558] He fought on the front line, and saw the fall of Arcadia.[559]

Apocalypse Element has the Daleks directly attacking Gallifrey. *Remembrance of the Daleks* has Davros stating his intention to use the Hand of Omega to wipe out the Time Lords and install the Daleks as the new "Lords of Time" - although it's the Doctor who arranges Skaro's destruction, and in so doing probably rouses the Daleks into further hostilities. It's easy to see how such tit-for-tat escalation might lead to the Time War.

It was probably inevitable - given the Time Lords' mastery of time and the Daleks' intention to totally eradicate all other species - that their civilisations

would fall into open warfare at some point. Either way, the Doctor intervening in the Kaled bunker might well be the first cross-temporal attack in the conflict, but it's a bit disingenuous to think the Time Lords were without justification in sending him there.
554 *Bad Wolf*
555 *Journey's End*
556 *The Sontaran Stratagem*
557 According to Davros in *Journey's End*.
558 "The Stockbridge Child"
559 *Doomsday*

"I saw Arcadia destroyed. I laughed in the face of the Nightmare Child."[560]

In the very first year of the Time War, at the Gates of Elysium, the Doctor saw Davros' command ship fly into the jaws of the Nightmare Child. The Doctor tried, and failed, to save Davros as his ship was timelocked. Dalek Caan came back in time and attempted made a thousand attempts to rescue Davros - he gained vast insight into the nature of time in the process, but drove himself insane. He finally succeeded where the Doctor failed, and broke Davros from the timelock.[561]

The Daleks were led by the Dalek Emperor.[562]

The Time War was invisible to "smaller" species, but was devastating to "the higher forms".[563] Many planets, such as those of the Gelth, were affected. The food planets of the Nestene were wiped out.[564] The Forest of Cheem knew of the War, and thought it was impossible that any Time Lords could exist afterwards.[565] The Gelth were forced to become incorporate spirits when their bodies were destroyed.[566] The Sontarans consider this the finest war in history, but "weren't allowed to be part of it".[567]

The Time War devastated the Hajor dimension.[568] Hotel Historia was a popular attraction that allowed holiday-goers to time travel to other eras, but its business plummeted when the Last Great Time War triggered a lapse in demand for time travel.[569]

It's possible that the civilisations of Perganon and Assinder fell during the Time War.[570] It's possible that the city of Arcopolis was depopulated during the Time War, and it's possible the Doctor activated the weapon that did so.[571] The Graxnix were one of the grubbier races involved in the Time War, and had very unreliable time technology.[572]

The Time Lords used the Genesis Ark, a dimension-ally transcendental prison, to confine many thousands of Daleks. The Doctor was not involved with this.[573]

The Time Lords resurrected the Master as the perfect warrior to fight in the Time War - he was present when the Dalek Emperor took control of the Cruciform, and fled. He turned himself into a human, and hid at the end of the universe.[574] The four Daleks that made up the Cult of Skaro stole the Genesis Ark and used a Voidship to leave the universe before the end of the War.[575]

"The Forgotten"[576] -> The eighth Doctor was jailed by robots as a War raged around him, turning the skies turn to blood. On Day 21 of his captivity, he gained a Malmooth cellmate, Chantir. On Day 37, he escaped and freed the other prisoners, which included a Sea Devil. Then he proceeded to his objective: the Great Key of Rassilon, which was stored in the same castle. He hoped he never needed to use it, but knew he might need something that removed millions from space and time at once. The Key would lock the Medusa Cascade forever, should it ever be required.

The Doctor eventually used the Key, and it erased his memory of Chantir.

The Time War got desperate towards the end - at this time, the Doctor was the only version of himself anywhere in the multiverse.[577]

"You weren't there in the final days of the War, you never saw what was born. Not just the Daleks but the Skaro Degradations, the Horde of Travesties, the Nightmare Child, the Could-have-been-King with his armies of Meanwhiles and Never-weres, the War turning to Hell."[578]

---

560 "The Forgotten"
561 *The Stolen Earth*
562 *The Parting of the Ways, Doomsday, Utopia.* It's possible that the Emperor took power after the loss of Davros.
563 *The Unquiet Dead.* There seem to be some races in the middle - the Krillitanes (*School Reunion*) and Cynrog (*The Nightmare of Black Island*) - who were aware of the Time War, but weren't directly affected by it. In *Bad Wolf*, Captain Jack mentions hearing rumours of the Time War and the Daleks.
564 *Rose*
565 *The End of the World*
566 *The Unquiet Dead*
567 *The Sontaran Stratagem.* There's no explanation as to who or what blocked the Sontarans' participation. The Doctor seems to have formally led the Time Lord forces.
568 "The Futurists"
569 "The Age of Ice"
570 *School Reunion*
571 The weapon seen in *The Eyeless* may be the device the Doctor talked about in "The Forgotten" that needed the Key, which in turn may be the Moment, the weapon that dooms Gallifrey according to *The End of Time* (TV). If so, this link isn't explicitly established in any of those stories.
572 "Hotel Historia"
573 *Doomsday*
574 *The Sound of Drums.* Mention of the Master being "resurrected" probably covers all contingencies regarding his status prior to the new series. The Dalek Emperor's presence suggests that this occurs after Davros' "death" in the Time War.

The Final Day of the Time War

"There was a bad day, bad stuff happened."[579]

THE END OF TIME (TV) -> By the last day of the War, Dalek saucers had crashed on Gallifrey and the dome of the Capitol been cracked open. Gallifrey was at the furthest edge of the War. At the heart of the conflict, millions died every second, lost in bloodlust and insanity, time itself resurrecting them to find new ways of dying over and over again in a travesty of life. A Time Lord seer, the Visionary, confirmed that this was the last day of the Time War.

The Doctor had learned that Rassilon planned the Final Sanction, the end of time - a rupture that would continue until it ripped the Time Vortex apart. The Time Lords would ascend, become creatures of consciousness alone - free of their bodies, time and cause and effect - while creation itself ceased to be. The Doctor had to stop them, and the High Council, led by Rassilon, knew that the Doctor possessed the Moment and would use it to destroy the Daleks and Time Lords alike.

The Master believed that if the Doctor killed Rassilon, "Gallifrey could be yours".[580]

The Visionary had a prophecy that there would be two survivors beyond the final day: the Doctor and the Master. Learning this, the High Council approved Rassilon's plan to retroactively implant the sound of drums in the mind of the Master while he was a child, as an escape route for his people. There were two votes against this strategy, including one cast by the Woman in White. Rassilon sent the Master a white-star point on Earth, Christmas Day 2009. Gallifrey and Rassilon briefly rose from the Time War, but the tenth Doctor and the Master fought back, banishing the Time Lords - including the Woman in White - back to the hell of the Time War. The Master learned that Rassilon had been responsible for the sound of drums in his mind, and fell back into the Time War, fighting him.

The Advocate was transported across time and space from the Shadow Proclamation to the Medusa Cascade and into the Time War. She arrived seconds before the Doctor used the Moment and time-locked the War, and so was killed and reborn over a thousand years as time lost meaning. She became little more than stardust, and eventually drifted out of the War through the same tear in time as Davros. Once reformed, she decided that the Doctor was a great threat to the universe.[581]

"I saw Gallifrey sacrificed when the Cruciform fell. I turned the Key in the lock and I doomed them all."[582]

Time Lords outside the Capitol Dome, including a young girl, looked up and were bathed in a blue light. Gallifrey was destroyed in one second.[583] **Gallifrey was "lost in fire".**[584]

The Doctor wiped out the entire Dalek race, and their ten million-strong war fleet, in one second. The Time Lords - save for the Doctor - also perished as a result of this. The Doctor instigated this destruction, referred to as an "inferno". He "watched it happen... made it happen".[585] The Doctor killed all the Time Lords.[586] Many other planets, star systems and galaxies were destroyed at this point.[587]

The Last Great Time War was timelocked.

---

575 *Doomsday*
576 Dating "The Forgotten" (IDW *DW* mini-series #2) - This seems to take place during the Last Great Time War, but it could always be the War in Heaven. We don't learn the name of the planet or the Doctor's jailers. The landscape is red, so resembles Gallifrey, but it could be another planet. The Great Key was once part of the De-Mat Gun (*The Invasion of Time*), and the suggestion seems to be that "the Moment" that the Doctor uses to end the Last Great Time War is an extension of it. No explanation is given for why, if the Doctor lost all memory of Chantir, he's suddenly able to relate the story of how they met.
577 *The Coming of the Terraphiles*
578 The Doctor speaking to the Master in *The End of Time* (TV). The Doctor described the stone Daleks in *The Big Bang* as "footprints of the never-were", and River Song says that the Doctor's fate if he's erased from the universe would see him "trapped in the never-space, the void between worlds", so we might infer the Never-Weres are beings who exist despite being erased from history.
579 *The Beast Below*
580 *Journey's End*. This is possibly a sign that the Doctor had followers on Gallifrey during the War, or perhaps even was formally next in the order of succession.
581 "Fugitive", "Don't Step on the Grass".
582 "The Forgotten"
583 Seen on the first page of "Agent Provocateur". The Capitol Dome looks intact and no Dalek wreckage is visible, unlike *The End of Time* (TV).
584 *The Fires of Pompeii*
585 *Dalek*
586 *The Doctor's Wife*
587 "Agent Provocateur"

Aftermath
of the Last Great Time War

The Time Lords' secrets died with them, as well as artifacts such as the Seal of Rassilon. Susan was taken from the Doctor, everyone was taken from him.[588]

"Time Lords are the stuff of legends. Belong in the myths and legends of the higher species."[589]

Some people regard the Time War as a legend.[590] The Saturnynians knew the Doctor as the "man that let an entire race turn to cinders and ash".[591]

The Doctor himself survived the Last Great Time War. The eighth Doctor "started and ended this regeneration alone".[592] It was possible that the eighth Doctor regenerated during the Time War - the tenth Doctor suggested that his previous self had been "born in battle, full of blood and anger and revenge".[593]

"Remember what happened immediately after the War. Remember Rose."[594]

The Doctor's home planet was reduced to rocks and dust, and he was the only survivor.[595] He stated, "I lived... everyone else died."[596]

A single Dalek fell through time to the early twenty-first century.[597] The Emperor Dalek's flagship also survived, and limped to the solar system "centuries" before the year 200,000.[598] A single Dalek Progenitor survived, and was later recovered by the last surviving Daleks.[599]

Time was more fragile without the Time Lords to protect it, and some of the rules governing time were suspended.[600] Travel between parallel realities had been "easy" when the Time Lords "kept their eye on everything", but following their downfall, the walls of reality closed and travel between parallel worlds became nearly impossible.[601]

588 "The Forgotten". This is apparent confirmation that Susan no longer exists after the Time War.
589 *The Stolen Earth*
590 Jack, in *The Parting of the Ways*, for one.
591 *The Vampires of Venice*
592 Says the eighth Doctor in "The Forgotten". A line cut from *The Eyeless* said that the eighth Doctor was betrayed by his then-companions.
593 *Journey's End*. On when the eighth Doctor might have regenerated into the ninth, see The Last Great Time War sidebar.
594 "The Forgotten". This is apparent confirmation that *Rose* occurs soon after the end of the Last Great Time War.
595 *The End of the World*
596 *School Reunion*
597 *Dalek*
598 *Bad Wolf/The Parting of the Ways*
599 *Victory of the Daleks*
600 *The Unquiet Dead, Father's Day*.
601 *Rise of the Cybermen*

THE LAST GREAT TIME WAR: The new TV series is set after The Last Great Time War, and although we know the broad strokes of what happened, there's been little detail. Stories that provide hints about the event include *Rose, The End of the World, The Unquiet Dead, Dalek, Father's Day, Bad Wolf* and *The Parting of the Ways*.

Doctor Who Annual 2006 contains a short account of the Time War written by Russell T Davies, which echoes his thoughts in a *Doctor Who Confidential* interview that the roots of the War lie with the Time Lords trying to prevent the Daleks' creation in *Genesis of the Daleks*. The article links the story to *Lungbarrow* and *The Apocalypse Element*, mentions the Deathsmiths of Goth (from the *DWM* back-up strip "Black Legacy") and adds

the information that the Animus (*The Web Planet*) and the Eternals (*Enlightenment*) were caught in the fighting. The article was the first place related to the 2005 series that names Gallifrey as the Doctor's destroyed home planet (the new series later named it in *The Runaway Bride* and *The Sound of Drums*), and says Skaro was in "ruins" by the end - a reference that seems to support the claim in *War of the Daleks* that Skaro wasn't destroyed in *Remembrance of the Daleks*.

There is no indication (beyond an ambiguous statement from the tenth Doctor in *Journey's End*) whether it was the eighth or ninth Doctor who fought in the Last Great Time War, or whether he regenerated during (as a result of?) events during the War. The Dalek in *Dalek* doesn't seem to recognise the Doctor's face, but responds to his name. Many fans have speculated that the Doctor has recently regenerated in *Rose*, as he seems unfamiliar with his reflection. There's a broad fan consensus that it's the eighth Doctor who fought the Time War and that its climax somehow triggered the regeneration - but there's no actual evidence that this is the case, and it seems clear from Clive's website in *Rose* that the ninth Doctor's an established incarnation.

ONLY ONE DESTRUCTION OF GALLIFREY?: The intention of both the creative team behind the EDAs and the new series producer Russell T Davies is that the destruction of Gallifrey seen in *The Ancestor Cell* and the destruction of Gallifrey reported in the new series are entirely separate events. As the Doctor destroys Gallifrey once while preventing the Enemy and Faction Paradox from taking control of his homeworld, then (presumably after rebuilding Gallifrey, as he pledges to do at the end of *The Gallifrey Chronicles*) he destroys Gallifrey again in a great war with the Daleks, it would seem clear these are indeed mutually exclusive. Russell

The Shadow Proclamation[602]

"What is the Shadow Proclamation, anyway?"... "Posh name for police. Outer-space police."[603]

The Time Lords gave the Shadow Proclamation strict rulings on the subject of manipulations in Time and Space before they left.[604] **The Shadow Proclamation followed the Holy Writ of the Shadow Proclamation, and considered Time Lords "the stuff of legend"**[605]

There were at least twenty-three conventions to the Shadow Proclamation.[606] The extraction machines used to create Golems were forbidden under Article 29.8 of the Shadow Proclamation.[607] **Article 57 of the Proclamation forbid the destruction of Level Five planets.**[608] Article 1768C of the Shadow Proclamation allowed for a trial operating under "innocent until proven guilty", a legal standard found on eighty-seven member planets and 12,932 affiliated worlds.[609] Clause 374 of the Shadow Proclamation authorised lethal force to retrieve a culturally valuable artifact.[610] The Shadow Proclamation underestimated the success and reach of the Time Market.[611]

Rumours and anecdotal evidence suggested that the Shadow Proclamation had enforced the boundaries of a far galaxy by seeding a virus that would activate if any of that galaxy's populations ventured into space. One civilisation ventured toward the stars anyway, casing the virus to kill off a third of the beings in that galaxy. If this story was nothing more than propaganda, it was nonetheless effective at keeping some of the lesser races in line.[612]

THE DOCTOR'S WIFE[613] **-> The sentient planet called House existed in a bubble universe. It fed on rift energy, and over the course of half a million years had killed hundreds of Time Lords to feast upon the**

Davies likened it, in a *DWM* column, to the two World Wars humanity fought in quick succession.

But could Gallifrey have been destroyed just once? The Doctor certainly experiences the destruction of Gallifrey twice, in two different contexts. But this doesn't rule out it being the same *event*. If there was only one destruction of Gallifrey, he and his future self would have to be present, and both culpable.

Surprisingly, this already fits what we know from *The Ancestor Cell* - the Doctor's future self, Grandfather Paradox was there. Moreover, this future eighth Doctor fits everything we know about the Doctor who fought the Time War: fighting a vast time war has scarred him, made him lose his faith in humanity, made him a little callous. In *The Gallifrey Chronicles* recap of the end of *The Ancestor Cell*, Grandfather Paradox even wears a leather coat. As for the destruction of Gallifrey - the Doctor's description in *Dalek*, "I watched it happen ... I made it happen... I tried to stop it" is a neat summary of his actions in *The Ancestor Cell*.

If this theory is true, the Doctor's memories of the War are conflicted because he was *literally* fighting his (earlier) self over "pulling the lever" that destroyed Gallifrey. So it's *Grandfather Paradox* who has fought the Last Great Time War, the Daleks, the Nestenes and so on. He goes back to *The Ancestor Cell* having done all that, confronts his earlier self... who then outsmarts him by blowing up Gallifrey. Following this defeat, it's Grandfather Paradox who regenerates into Eccleston (growing his arm back in the process).

For this to be the case, it involves the introduction of the tiniest bit of extra information: the War that's being fought in the future has the Daleks in it and at some point they make a decisive move on Gallifrey. What the "current" eighth Doctor doesn't know - but which his future self does - is that, in the future, the War's going so badly that the Daleks are heading for Gallifrey. The

Daleks were ruled out as "the Enemy" in *Alien Bodies*, but they don't need to be for this theory to work - they just need to be capable of hitting the Time Lords hard.

602 THE SHADOW PROCLAMATION: This group is first referenced in *Rose*, is seen on screen in *The Stolen Earth*, and also appears in "Fugitive" (set circa 2545) and *The Darksmith Legacy* books. The Proclamation's native time zone is never specified, and it's unclear if it has access to time travel (meaning the characters seen there might not even originate from the same era) or if the Proclamation perhaps operates (as with Gallifrey) on its own continuum. It's evidently been around for some time, though - in *The Stolen Earth* (set in 2009), the Shadow Proclamation consider the disappearance of Pyrovillia as a "cold case", suggesting they investigated it at the time. "Agent Provocateur" has them active at the time of Ancient Egypt.

603 Donna, the Doctor in *The Stolen Earth*.

604 "Fugitive". This is difficult to reconcile with the actions of Rassilon in *The End of Time* (TV), so it might represent the actions of another Time Lord authority, although seemingly not the Doctor himself.

605 *The Stolen Earth* has one of the Shadow Proclamation talk of the Holy Writ, and another tell Donna "God save you", suggesting this might be some form of religious organisation.

606 *Beautiful Chaos* (p211).

607 *The Beast of Orlok*

608 *The Eleventh Hour*

609 *The Pictures of Emptiness* (p15).

610 *The Depths of Despair*

611 *Borrowed Time*

612 *The Glamour Chase*

613 HOW MANY TIMES HAS THE DOCTOR BEEN MARRIED?: Depending on how you define terms, at least five.

The earliest we know of in the Doctor's lifetime was

refined Artron energy in their TARDISes. Before doing so, House had to transplant the sentience of each TARDIS into a living being. House's junkyard included the remains of one hundred TARDIS models.

The eleventh Doctor received an emergency message from a Time Lord slain by House: the Corsair. He took Amy and Rory into House's bubble, where House transferred the "living soul" of the TARDIS into a young woman named Idris. When House learned that the TARDIS was the last of its kind, he took control of the Ship and attempted to fly back to the universe, marooning the Doctor in a collapsing universe with a dying Idris. They scratch-built a TARDIS from House's junkyard, and caught up with the House-TARDIS. As Idris' body died, the TARDIS Matrix was released and reclaimed control of the Ship, annihilating House.

The Doctor's TARDIS had about thirty console rooms in its archives, including ones the Doctor would use in future - until now, he had only changed the "desktop pattern" about a dozen times.

seen in flashback in *Cold Fusion*, a book that established that prior to the Doctor leaving Gallifrey, he was married to Patience, his former tutor (also seen in *The Infinity Doctors*). Patience is presumably Susan's grandmother. Much later in *The Adventuress of Henrietta Street*, the eighth Doctor married a ritualist named Scarlette on a platonic basis, as a means of becoming vested with the authority to serve as a protector of Earth.

Since 2009, the new *Doctor Who* has married off its central character three times. The tenth Doctor is said to have married Queen Elizabeth I – while this event isn't seen on screen, it's referred or alluded to so often (*The Shakespeare Code*, *The End of Time* (TV), *The Beast Below* and *Amy's Choice*), it seems safe to assume that it

happened. The eleventh Doctor very prominently marries River Song in *The Wedding of River Song*, and prior to that winds up married to Marilyn Monroe in *A Christmas Carol*.

An alternate future seen in *Human Nature* (TV) entailed the Doctor's "John Smith" persona living out his life as the husband of nurse Joan Redfern. *The Aztecs*, amusingly enough, entails the first Doctor becoming accidentally engaged to an Aztec woman, Cameca, when he fails to realise the cultural significance of making her a cup of cocoa.

To date, the Doctor has not literally married the TARDIS, despite *The Doctor's Wife* (as the title suggests) aking this ongoing element of the programme's subtext and, in large measure, turning it into text.

There are a number of stories without the references needed to place them in any meaningful relation to the rest of universal history.

Some (such as *The Celestial Toymaker*) take place in a reality that is completely detached from the universe's timeline. Some, such as the E-Space Trilogy (*Full Circle* to *Warriors' Gate*) and the Divergent Universe Series (the Big Finish audios *Scherzo* to *The Next Life*), take place in locations clearly outside the universe's physical boundaries.

A number of stories simply fail to provide (or aren't interested in providing) more evidence beyond the fact that they occur "on an alien planet in the future". Given the entire duration of human development into space, this isn't particularly helpful, presuming the humanoids featured in the story are human in the first place. Without more clues as to how such stories relate to human history or another documented event, a proper dating is impossible. A story such as *Anachrophobia* looks for all the world like placement on the timeline should be attainable, but the evidence (or lack thereof) says otherwise.

The following stories are among those that defy a proper dating. The TV stories are listed in broadcast order; the books, audios and comics are listed alphabetically.

TV Stories

The Edge of Destruction (1.3, set in the TARDIS)
The Chase (2.8, the sequence on Aridius - although it has to take place after the Daleks launch their time machine, as the Doctor and companions see that on the Time-Space Visualiser, which can only see into the past)
Galaxy 4 (3.1)
The Daleks' Master Plan (3.4, the sequences on Tigus and the ice planet)
The Celestial Toymaker (3.7, occurs in the Toymaker's domain)
The Dominators (6.1, at a time when the Dominators control "ten galaxies")
The Mind Robber (6.2, in the Land of Fiction, a timeless dimension)
Carnival of Monsters (10.2)
The Ribos Operation (16.1, the White Guardian sequence)
The Creature from the Pit (17.3)
The Horns of Nimon (17.5)
Full Circle (18.3, E-Space story)
State of Decay (18.4, E-Space story)
Warriors' Gate (18.5, E-Space story)
Castrovalva (19.1, the non-Earth sequences)
Enlightenment (20.5)
The Five Doctors (20.7, the first Doctor's kidnap and the Eye of Orion sequences)
The Greatest Show in the Galaxy (25.4)
"Born Again" (*Children in Need* sketch #1, post-regeneration scene in the TARDIS with tenth Doctor and Rose)
"Time Crash" (*Children in Need* sketch #2, scene in the TARDIS with the fifth and tenth Doctors)
Amy's Choice (X5.7, occurs in the TARDIS)
"Time" (*Comic Relief* sketch #1, occurs in the TARDIS)
"Space" (*Comic Relief* sketch #2, occurs in the TARDIS)
The Girl Who Waited (X6.10, although mention of Disneyland Clom, and the presence of a Mona Lisa and a Venus de Milo, broadly suggests that it's the future)

Novels and Novellas

Anachrophobia (EDA #54)
Beltempest (EDA #17)
Citadel of Dreams (TEL #2)
Coldheart (EDA #33)
Crooked World, The (EDA #57)
Doctor Trap, The (NSA #26)
Dreams of Empire (PDA #14)
Eight Doctors, The (EDA #1, the Eye of Orion sequence)
Frontier Worlds (EDA #29)
King's Dragon, The (NSA #41; the Doctor's remark on page 224 that Prime Directives are "So twenty-third century. So very retro", isn't very helpful, even presuming he can be taken literally)
Match of the Day (PDA #70)
Nightdreamers (TEL #3)
Parallel 59 (EDA #30)
Shell Shock (TEL #8)
Shining Darkness (NSA #27)
Sky Pirates! (NA #40)

Audios

Absolution (BF #101)
Blood of the Daleks (BF BBC7 #1.1-1.2; events on Red Rocket Rising)
Caedroia (BF #63, Divergent Universe story)
Cannibalists, The (BF BBC7 #3.6)
Circular Time: "Spring" (BF #91, events on the planet of the bird-people)
City of Spires (BF #133, occurs in the Land of Fiction)
Company of Friends, The: "Fitz's Story" (BF #123b)
Creatures of Beauty (BF #44)
Creed of the Kromon, The (BF #53, Divergent Universe story)
Dark Flame, The (BF #42)
Dark Husband, The (BF #106)
Darkening Eye, The (BF CC #3.6, flashback story)
Dead London (BF BBC7 #2.1, occurs in an alien's mind)
Doomsday Quatrain, The (BF #151, occurs on alien planet made to simulate sixteenth-century Earth)
Drowned World, The (BF CC #4.1, flashback story)
Elite, The (BF LS #3.1)

Embrace the Darkness (BF #31)

Empathy Games (BF CC #3.4, flashback story)

Faith Stealer (BF #61, Divergent Universe story)

Fear of the Daleks (BF CC #1.2)

Forever Trap, The (BBC DW original audiobook #2)

Four Doctors, The (BF subscription promo #9, a.k.a. #142b; the Jariden sequences)

"Fragile Yellow Arc of Fragrance, The" (BF LS #2.1b)

Her Final Flight (BF subscription promo #2)

Holy Terror, The (BF #14)

Immortal Beloved (BF BBC7 #1.4; the participants are human, but this isn't very helpful for dating purposes)

Invasion of E-Space, The (BF CC #4.4)

... Ish (BF #35)

Last of the Titans (BF promo #1, DWM #300)

Last, The (BF #62, Divergent Universe story)

Legend of the Cybermen (BF #135, Land of Fiction sequences)

Natural History of Fear, The (BF #54, Divergent Universe story)

Nekromanteia (BF #41)

Next Life, The (BF #64, Divergent Universe story)

Night's Black Agents (BF CC #4.11, occurs in the Land of Fiction)

No Place Like Home (BF promo #3, DWM #326)

Prisoner of the Sun (BF BBC7 #4.8)

Quinnis (BF CC #3.6, occurs in the Fourth Universe)

Recorded Time and Other Stories: "Paradoxicide" (BF #150b)

Recorded Time and Other Stories: "Question Marks" (BF #150d)

Red (BF #85)

Ringpullworld (BF CC #4.5)

Rocket Men, The (BF CC #6.2)

Scherzo (BF #52, Divergent Universe story)

Sirens of Time, The (BF #1, sixth Doctor segment)

Solitaire (BF CC #4.12, occurs in the Toymaker's domain)

Something Inside (BF #83)

Three Companions, The: "Polly's Story" (serialized back-up story; BF #120-129)

Time Reef (BF #113a)

Time Works (BF #80)

Twilight Kingdom, The (BF #55, Divergent Universe story)

Wishing Beast, The (BF #97)

Wreck of the Titan, The (BF #134, occurs in the Land of Fiction)

Audios (spin-off series)

Gallifrey: Spirit (Davidia sequences)

Graceless: The End (warship sequences)

Kaldor City: "The Prisoner" (supplemental story on "The Actor Speaks" CD featuring Paul Darrow, stated as taking place three days after *Kaldor City: Checkmate*, but likely occuring from Landerchild's perspective within the Fendahl gestalt)

Kaldor City: Storm Mine (*Kaldor City* #1.6, stated as taking place eighteen months after *Kaldor City: Checkmate*, but likely occurs from Blayse's perspective within the Fendahl gestalt)

K9: The Choice (BBV audio #13)

K9: The Search (BBV audio #16)

Minister of Chance, The: The Broken World (MoC #1)

Minister of Chance, The: The Forest Shakes (MoC #2)

Minister of Chance, The: The Pointed Hand (MoC #0)

Comics

"Are You Listening / Younger and Wiser" (DWM 1994 Summer Special)

"Autonomy Bug" (DWM #297-299)

"Beautiful Freak" (DWM #304)

"Betrothal of Sontar, The" (DWM #365-367)

"Black Legacy" (DWW #35-38)

"Blood Invocation" (DWM Yearbook 1995)

"Cat Litter" (DWM #192)

"Chameleon Factor" (DWM #174)

"Changes" (DWM #118-119)

"Character Assassin" (DWM #311)

"City of the Damned" (DWW #9-16)

"Crossroads of Time" (DWM #135)

"Culture Shock" (DWM #139)

"End of the Line" (DWW #54-55)

"Exodus / Revelation / Genesis" (DWM #108-110)

"Fabulous Idiot" (DWM Summer Special 1982)

"Fangs of Time" (DWM #243)

"Final Quest, The" (DWW #8)

"Follow That TARDIS" (DWM #147)

"Food for Thought" (DWM #218-220)

"Forever Dreaming" (DWM #433-#434, occurs in the dimension of a psychic squid)

"Forgotten, The" (IDW DW mini-series #2, tenth Doctor sequences)

"Funhouse" (DWM #102-103)

"Ground Control" (IDW DW Annual 2010, "Doctor and Donna being chased by killer bow-wielding pandas" sequence)

"Happy Deathday" (DWM #272)

"Keepsake" (DWM #140)

"K9's Finest Hour" (DWW #12)

"Land of Happy Endings" (DWM #337; dream sequence in the TARDIS)

"Land of the Blind" (DWM #224-226)

"Last Word, The" (DWM #305)

"Life of Matter and Death, A" (DWM #250)

"Nature of the Beast" (DWM #111-113)

"Oblivion" (DWM #323-328; story's main events)

"Ophidius" (DWM #300-303)

"Outsider, The" (DWW #25-26)

"Party Animals" (*DWM* #173)

"Planet of the Dead" (*DWM* #141-142)

"Religious Experience, A" (*DWM Yearbook 1994*)

"Rest and Re-Creation" (*DWM Yearbook 1994*)

"Return of the Daleks" (*DWW* #1-4, eight hundred years after previous Dalek invasion)

"Room with a Déjà vu" (IDW *DW* one-shot #5)

"Run, Doctor, Run" (IDW *DW Annual 2011*)

"Salad Daze" (*DWM* #117)

"Ship Called Sudden Death, A" (*DWM Summer Special 1982*)

"Silent Knight" (IDW *DW* Vol. 2, #12; arguably non-canonical, a bit of holiday silliness)

"Sins of the Fathers" (*DWM* #343-345)

"Spam Filtered" (IDW *DW* Vol. 2 #1, unnamed in single issue, entitled in trade paperback)

"Stairway to Heaven" (*DWM* #156)

"Tesseract" (IDW Vol. 1, #7-8)

"Time and Tide" (*DWM* #145-146)

"Time of My Life, The" (*DWM* #399, Zyglot courtship, swamp, clock creature, vampire goth cannibals, psychic parasite and Donna goodbye message sequences)

"Timeslip" (*DWW* #17-18)

"To Sleep, Perhance to Scream" (IDW *DW Annual 2010*)

"Touchdown on Deneb 7" (*DWM* #48)

"TV Action" (*DWM* #283)

"Uninvited Guest" (*DWM* #211)

"Universal Monsters" (*DWM* #391-393)

"Uroborous" (*DWM* #319-322)

"Whispering Gallery, The" (IDW *DW* one-shot #1)

"Woman Who Sold the World, The" (*DWM* #381-384)

"Your Destiny Awaits" (IDW *DW Annual 2011*, desert planet and "Kevin chases aliens" sequences)

BIBLIOGRAPHY

The following is a list of useful resources for anyone interested in the "fictional facts" of Doctor Who.

The Making of Doctor Who. (Malcolm Hulke and Terrance Dicks: first edition Piccolo/Pan Books, April 1972; second edition Target/Tandem Books, November 1976) - The earliest source of dates, often direct from BBC material.

Dr Who Special. (edited by David Driver, Jack Lundin: BBC, November 1973) - The tenth anniversary *Radio Times* special, including many previously unpublished story details. This magazine perpetuated the "incorrect" story titles, used by many fans.

The Doctor Who Programme Guide. (Jean-Marc Lofficier: first edition [2 vols] WH Allen, May 1981, second edition [2 vols] Target/WH Allen, October 1981, second edition has separate volume titles "The Programmes" and "What's What and Who's Who") **Doctor Who - The Programme Guide.** (Jean-Marc Lofficier: third edition Target/WH Allen, December 1989) **Doctor Who - The Terrestrial Index.** (Jean-Marc Lofficier: Target/Virgin Publishing, November 1991) **Doctor Who - The Universal Databank.** (Jean-Marc Lofficier: Doctor Who Books/Virgin Publishing, November 1992) **Doctor Who Programme Guide.** (Jean-Marc Lofficier: fourth edition Doctor Who Books/Virgin Publishing, June 1994) - The standard reference work, with most fans owning a copy of at least one of these books. A good starting point.

Doctor Who Monthly. (Marvel Comics Ltd.) - Richard Landen wrote a series of pseudohistories in the twentieth anniversary year: Issues 75-83 (April 1983 - December 1983) featured *The TARDIS Logs*, a list of TARDIS landings riddled with annoying little errors; issue 77 had a more concise list *Travels with the Doctor*, and a good attempt at "A History of the Daleks"; "A History of the Cybermen" (issue 83, with Michael Daniels) and *Shades of Piccolo* (UNIT history, issue 80) were both sensible, simple treatments of potential minefields.

The Doctor Who Role Playing Game. (FASA Corporation [US], 1985; Supplements published 1985-6) - Various dates, including much invented for the game's purposes.

Doctor Who. (Marvel Comics Group [US]) - Pseudohistories written by Patrick Daniel O'Neill: "A Probable History of the Daleks" (issue 9, June 1985), "A Probable History of the Cybermen" (issue 10, July 1985) and "The Master Log" Parts I and II (issues 14, 15, November, December 1985). Enthusiastic but ill-researched.

The Doctor Who File. (Peter Haining: WH Allen, September 1986) - Pages 223 to 228 contain a table listing the Doctor's adventures and where / when they took place.

Encyclopedia of the Worlds of Doctor Who. (David Saunders: Piccadilly/Knight Press 1986, 1989, 1990) - An A-Z of the series with many entries giving dates.

The Official Doctor Who & the Daleks Book. (John Peel & Terry Nation: St Martin's Press [US], April 1989) - Dalek history, including various other sources (comic strips etc). Approved by Terry Nation.

In-Vision 11: UNIT Special. (CMS, December 1988) - Includes *Down to Earth*, a history of UNIT, by Garry Bradbury. Each issue of *In-Vision* is a comprehensive analysis of an individual story, and the magazine is an indispensable reference work.

Doctor Who - Cybermen. (David Banks, with Andrew Skilleter, Adrian Rigelsford and Jan Vincent-Rudzki: Who Dares, November 1988; Virgin Publishing, September 1990) - Comprehensive, if elaborate, history of the Cybermen. The first, and still best, reference book of its kind.

Doctor Who Magazine. (Marvel Comics Ltd) - issue 174: *The TARDIS Special* (June 12th 1991) features "Journeys" by Andrew Pixley, a superbly researched list of every landing made by the TARDIS. Issue 176 (August 7th 1991) contains an addendum.

The Gallifrey Chronicles. (John Peel: Doctor Who Books/Virgin Publishing, October 1991) - Gallifreyan history and other information. (This isn't the same book as *The Gallifrey Chronicles*, the 2005 EDA.)

Doctor Who Magazine Winter Special 1991 - UNIT Exposed. (Marvel Comics Ltd, 28th November, 1991) - Includes an excellent UNIT chronology by John Freeman and Gary Russell, as well as "UNIT Exposed" by Andrew Dylan.

The Doctor Who Writers' Guide. (Peter Darvill-Evans, Rebecca Levene & Andy Bodle: Virgin Publishing, 1991) - The guidelines for prospective authors of New and Missing Adventures. Includes notes on Gallifreyan history.

Apocrypha. (Adrian Middleton: 1993-95). Fan published chronology drawing together everything the author can get his hands on: comic strips, novelisations, role-playing scenarios and so on.

The Discontinuity Guide. (Paul Cornell, Martin Day and Keith Topping: Virgin Publishing, May 1994) - Survey of the series' continuity and continuity mistakes. Many interesting fan theories, all marked as such.

I, Who vols. 1-3. (Lars Pearson, Mad Norwegian Press, 1999 - 2003) - A book-by-book and audio-by-audio survey of the novels and BF audios, including spin-offs and detailed breakdowns of the stories.

Timelink (Jon Preddle, TSV Books, 2000) - A massive fan-produced survey of the television series' continuity. With extensive quotes, and a story-by-story breakdown. **Timelink** (Jon Preddle, Telos, 2011) - Massively updated version of the TSV publication, now in two volumes.

Doctor Who - The Legend. (Justin Richards, BBC Books, 2003) - Hardback introduction to *Doctor Who*, with a story-by-story section that lists dates where they are known.

About Time. (Lawrence Miles and Tat Wood, Mad Norwegian Press, 2004 - present) - A series of books that place *Doctor Who* in a cultural context and offer opinions and essays on continuity matters, including some chronological ones like UNIT Dating.

Who's Next. (Mark Clapham, Eddie Robson and Jim Smith, Virgin Publishing, 2005) - A one-volume guide to *Doctor Who* on television, with a breakdown of continuity.

The Time Traveller's Almanac: The Ultimate Intergalactic Fact-Finder. (Steve Tribe, BBC Books, 2008) - Relates information about the historical events and characters seen in New *Who*.

Torchwood: The Official Magazine Yearbook. (uncredited: Titan Books, 2008) - Behind-the-scenes details on *Torchwood* Series 1, with short stories.

The Torchwood Archives. (Gary Russell: BBC Books, 2008) - Presented as archive of files and other material pertaining to *Torchwood* Series 1 and 2.

The Brilliant Book 2011. (Edited by Clayton Hickman, BBC Books, 2010) - Behind-the-scenes details on Series 5, with short stories.

The Brilliant Book 2012. (Edited by Clayton Hickman, BBC Books, 2011) - Behind-the-scenes details on Series 6, with short stories.

Doctor Who: The Encyclopedia. (Gary Russell, BBC Books, 2011) - Immense A-Z on New *Who*, up through Series 6.

Bold numbers indicate main story entries for each adventure (the same information is found in the Table of Contents). Plain-text numbers indicate a story reference in the footnotes. This index also lists all characters, alien races, planets and organisations that appear in three or more stories. Characters are alphabetical based upon their most commonly used name, followed by a quick description of that character and the media (TV, audios, etc) in which they *first* appeared.

tion) 606, 625, 631, 655, 667, 673, 679-680, 682-683, 704-705, 707, 711-713, 720-722, (first appearance) 723, 725-726, 728, (returns to Gallifrey, becomes President of Gallifrey) 729, 730-732, 736-741 (joins the Doctor as the TARDIS is in flight in *The Ribos Operation*; leaves in *Warriors' Gate*, in E-Space)

Romance of Crime, The (MA #6) 456, 476, 481-482, 488, **490**, 720

Romans, The (2.4) 74, **75**, 76, 136, 168, 351

Roof of the World, The (BF #59) 32, 67, **176**

"Room With a Dejà Vu" (IDW *DW* one-shot #4) 749

Room With No Doors, The (NA #59) **100**, 101, 117, 151, 288, 320, 438, 564, 705

Root of All Evil, The (BBV audio #18; features Krynoids) 308-**309**

Rory Williams (eleventh Doctor companion; TV) 25, 63, 71, 77, 79, 85, 103, 107, 114, 125, 131, 134, 142, 146, 154-155, 157, 170-171, 177, 189, 191, 204-205, 216, 227-228, 232, 262-263, 270, 272, 276, 295, 297, 300-301, 306, 312-313, 315, 321, 337, 345, 357, (joins TARDIS) 397, (marries Amy Pond) 398, 402-404, 406-409, 412-413, 416-417, 423, 440-441, 457, 486, 488, 497, 523, 552-553, 571, 577, 603-605, 619-622, (daughter born) 623, 627, 671, 676, 685, 707, 746

Rose (X1.1) 32, 77-78, 84, 88, 99, 151, 172, 223, 308, 328-**329**, 336-337, 340, 342-343, 346, 374, 484, 488, 702, 712, 742, 744-745

Rose Tyler (ninth and tenth Doctor companion; TV) 24-25, 30, 57, 77-78, 88, 92-93, 104-105, 118-119, 146, 149-150, 174, 180, 196, 210-212, 223, 228, 272, 282-283, (born) 289, 290, 297, 304, 307, 328, (joins TARDIS) 329, 330, 336-346, (leaves TARDIS) 347, 349, 351, 353, 357-359, 369, 371-374, 392, 413-414, 419, 441, 452-453, 458, 490, 502-503, 552, 578, 587, 590-591, 601, 615, 643, 659-660, 676, 678, 702, 707, 712, 744, 747

Roundheads, The (PDA #6) 108, **109**, 118, 178

Roz / Roslyn Forrester (seventh Doctor companion; novels) 128, 162, 178, 196, 282, 289, 297, 301, 316, 394, 415, 426, 432, 464, 476-477, 479, 499, 522, 525-527, 529, 551, 562, (born) 563, 564-565, (joins TARDIS) 566, (death) 568, 600, 635, 666

"Run, Doctor, Run" (IDW *DW Annual 2011*) 749

Runaway Bride, The (X3.0) 36, 38, **40**, 210, 282, 284, 341-342, 346-348, 352-**353**, 356-359, 368, 392, 744

Runaway Train, The (BBC *DW* audiobook #9) **143**

Rutans (long-standing foes of the Sontarans; TV) 27, 36-38, 42, 62, 89, 150, 164, 166, 286, 317, 319, 370-371, 487, 489, 504, 511, 514, 522, 537, 594, 636, 647, 649, 675, 681, 713

Sabbath (rival of the eighth Doctor; novels) 31, (born) 117, 118-119, 123-125, 135, 159, 190, 319-321, 490, 613, (death) 684, 732-734

Sabbath Dei (FP audio #1.3) 117-118, **119**, 732, 734

"Salad Daze" (*DWM* #117) 749

Salvation (PDA #18) 219, **226**, 274, 464, 585-586

Samantha "Sam" Jones (eighth Doctor companion; novels) 53, 161, 166, 201, 222, 267, (born) 273, 298, (leaves TARDIS) 299, (joins TARDIS) 303, 306, 316, (death) 317, 319, 428, 439-440, 453, 455-456, 458-459, 472, 474-476, 527, 532, 570, 575, 597, 611, 645, 684, 728

Samson and Gemma Griffen (eighth Doctor companions; audios) 101, 133, 269, 610, (joins TARDIS, leaves TARDIS) 611, (Gemma's death) 612

Sanctuary (NA #37) 88, **90**, 514, 536, 548

Sandman, The (BF #37) 56, 548-**549**

Sands of Time, The (MA #22) 60-61, **65**, 67, 128, 134, **162**, 264, 300-**301**, 650

Sara Kingdom (first Doctor companion; TV) 63, 227, 584, 596-598, (joins TARDIS, death) 599, (mind copied to create sentient wish-granting house) 657, 660-661, 724

Sarah Jane Adventures, The 182, 302, 312, 320, 336, 342, 354, 366, 368, 372-374, 384-385, 388, 394, 398, 402, 404, 408-409, 414, 440, 642, 685

Sarah Jane Smith (third and fourth Doctor companion; tenth and eleventh Doctor associate; UNIT associate; thwarter of alien invasions; TV) 25, 52, 82, 91, 96-98, 102, 108, 133, 145, 151-152, 155, 171, 189-190, 199, 204-206, (born) 207, 209, 211-212, 216-217, 224-225, 229, 233-234, 242-243, 252-254, (joins TARDIS) 255, 256, 258, 260, (leaves TARDIS) 262, 272, 276-277, 281-282, 289, 291-293, 295-299, 302, 304-305, 311-313, 318-319, 328, 332-333, (meets tenth Doctor) 334, 343-344, 357, 363-367, 371-374, 379-386, 388-389, 394-396, 398, (meets eleventh Doctor) 399, 400-401, 404-406, 409, 418, (projected death) 428, 434, 440, 446, 448, 536, 557, 574-575, 577, 589, 592-593, 646-647, 651-652, 684, 715, 721, 724

Sarah Jane Smith (Big Finish audios, two series)
  Buried Secrets (SJS #2.1) 98, 167, 258, **332**-333, 399
  Comeback (SJS #1.1) 282, 312, **318**, 332
  Dreamland (SJS #2.4) 96, 98, 168, 204-205, 208, 214-215, 245, 264, 296, 314, 332-**333**, 398
  Fatal Consequences (SJS #2.3) 98, 258, 310, 314, 318, 332-**333**
  Ghost Town (SJS #1.4) 312, **318**, 386
  Mirror, Signal, Manoeuvre (SJS #1.5) 256, 318-**319**
  Snow Blind (SJS #2.2) **332**
  Tao Connection, The (SJS #1.2) 115, **318**
  Test of Nerve (SJS #1.3) **318**

Satan Pit, The (X2.9) 30, 60, 364, 600, **601**, 602, 694

Savages, The (3.9) 670, 675, 678-**679**

Scales of Injustice, The (MA #24) 45-47, 132, 183-184, 204, 206, 214, 218, 223, 239-240, 242-243, **244**, 245, 291, 445

Scapegoat (BF BBC7 #3.5) 70, 126, **198**

Scaredy Cat (BF #75) 178, 496-**497**, 551, 668-**669**, 702

Scarlet Empress, The (EDA #15) 28, 128, 130, 164, 179,

Telos (adopted Cybermen homeworld) 26, 28-29, 37, 156, 211, 213, 285, 296, 337, 444-445, 471-472, 500-502, (destruction) 503, 504, 506, 508, 556, 593, 595, 646, 751

Tempest (Benny NA #9) 70, 102, 105, **529**

Temptation of Sarah Jane Smith, The (SJA 2.5) 204, 206-**207**, 224, 364, 366, 382, **383**, 384

Ten Little Aliens (PDA #54) 221, 556, **561**

Tenth Planet, The (4.2) 25, 48-51, 210-211, 213, 238-239, 287-**288**, 296, 340, 428, 431, 442, 444, 498, 595

Terminal of Despair (BBC children's 2-in-1 #6) **488**

Terminus (20.4) 30-31, 496, 550, **582**-583, 585, 601

Terror Firma (BF #72) 100-101, 133, 268, 515, 607, 610, **612**, 629, 737

Terror of the Autons (8.1) 24, 26, 32, 239-240, 243-244, **245**-246, 708, 710, 716, 718-**719**

Terror of the Vervoids (23.3) 224, 290, 540, 562, **568**, 578, 697, 707

Terror of the Zygons (13.1) 26, 86, 90-92, 103, 108, 147, 178, 198, 233-234, 236, 243, 254, **256**, 257-259, 261

Tersurus (alien planet) 52-53, 473, 636, 695, 721-722

"Tesseract" (IDW *DW* Vol. 1, #7-8) 749

Thals (rivals of the Daleks; TV) 44, 72, 80-83, 120-121, 467, 479-480, 511-512, 604, 607, 610-611, 628-629, 683, 686-687

Theatre of War, The (NA #26) 84, 481-482, 498, 520, 534, 545, **596**, 705, 716

They Keep Killing Suzie, The (TW 1.8) 228, 334, 346, 350, 352-**353**, 355

"They Think It's All Over" (IDW *DW* Vol. 2, #5) **85**, **228**, 474

Thicker Than Water (BF #73) 523-**524**

Thin Ice (BF LS #2.3) 58, 85, 88, 92, 102, 179, 223, 225, **230**, 264, 287-288, 448, 728

"Thinktwice" (DWM #400-402) 184, **658**

Thirteenth Stone, The (SJA audiobook #2) 65, 366-**367**, 380

This Town Will Never Let Us Go (FP novel #1) 314-**315**

Thomas Brewster (fifth and sixth Doctor companion; audios) 136, (born) 137, 140-142, 144, (steals the TARDIS; the fifth Doctor recovers it in the undatable *Time Reef*) 145, 146, (leaves sixth Doctor's company) 147, 290, 356, 364, 378, 397, (joins sixth Doctor's TARDIS) 402, 425

Thousand Tiny Wings, A (BF #130) 128, 164, 200, 208-**209**

Three Companions, The (serialized story; BF #120-129) 142, 145, 152, **254**, **378**, 698, 748

Three Doctors, The (10.1) 38, 243, 251-**252**, 675, 691-692, 694, 704, 715, 718-719, **720**, 727

Three's a Crowd (BF #69) 554, **556**, 559

Threshold (criminal organisation that makes use of spatial gateways; comics) 150, 179, 191, 222, 232, 446, 448, 507, 518, 619, (destruction) 625

"Throwback: The Soul of a Cyberman" (DWW #5-7) 502-**503**

"Tides of Time, The" (DWM #61-67) 36, 78, 84, 89, 142, 200, **278-279**, 280, 698, 722-**723**

Time and Relative (TEL #1) 55, 127, **221**, 263, 668, 700

Time and the Rani (24.1) 31, 43, 78, 151, 168, 202, 284, **312**, 495, 692, 702, 704-705, 707-708, 715

"Time and Tide" (DWM #145-146) 749

"Time and Time Again" (DWM #207) **296**, 716

"Time Bomb" (DWM #114-116) **42-43**, **288**, 548, **552**, 554-**555**

Time Capsule, The (SJA audiobook #3) 86, 92, **382**

"Time Crash" (Children in Need sketch #2) 747

Time Hunter (novella series) 28-29, 204, 207, 525

Time Lords (the Doctor's people) 23, 25, 30-36, 38-43, 50-51, 61, 64, 69, 71, 79, 82, 84, 99, 106, 114, 118, 126, 133, 145-146, 150, 155, 223, 226, 239, 241, 251-252, 258, 272, 278-279, 285-286, 308, 330, 331, 336-337, 353, 368, 389, 414, 427, 432, 439, 443, 466, 467, 471, 473, 478, 480-481, 485, 489, 499, 524, 526, 529, 531-534, 548, 551, 553, 570, 575, 580, 584-585, 589, 597, 620, 625, 632, 636, 639, 641, 647-648, 662-665, 669-675, 680-684, 687-688, 691-706, 709, 711-714, 716-724, 726-732, 735-745

"Time Machination, The" (IDW *DW* one-shot #2) 152, **156**, 618

Time Meddler, The (2.9) 68, 86, **87**, 92, 98, 106, 230, 468, 470, 702, 704, 708, 716

Time Monster, The (9.5) 32, 34, 64, **66**-67, 91, 108, 200, 223, 234, 236, 250-**251**, 322, 324, 691-692, 708, 719

Time of Angels, The (X5.4) 188, 613-614, 618, 620-622, **623**, **648**, 691

"Time of My Life, The" (DWM #399) 130-**131**, **219**, 372-373, 749

Time of the Daleks, The (BF #32) 78, 102, 104, 190, 304, 338, 414, 420, **438**

Time of Your Life (MA #8) 290, 450, 456, **471**, 476, 727

Time Reef (BF #113) 748

Time Travellers, The (PDA #75) **338**-339

Time Vampire, The (BF CC 4.10) 162, 171, 638, **639**, 640, **641**, **721**

Time Warrior, The (11.1) 25, 36-38, **91**, 171, 207, 212, 233, 249, **254**, 595, 691, 702, 720

"Time Witch, The" (DWW #35-38) **39**

Time Works (BF #80) 748

Time Zero (EDA #60) 44, 64, 159, **160**-161, 190, 314, 318, **319**, 320

"Time" (Comic Relief sketch #1) 747

Time-Flight (19.7) **43**, 214, 249, 261, 276, **277**, 278, 280, 296, 339

Timelash (22.5) 88, 90, 152, **153**, 156, 253, 283, 286, 608, 636, **664**, 702

Timeless (EDA #65) **31**, 123-124, 134, 189-190, 320-**321**, 326

**PUBLISHER /
EDITOR-IN-CHIEF**
Lars Pearson

**DESIGN MANAGER /
SENIOR EDITOR**
Christa Dickson

ASSOCIATE EDITOR
Joshua Wilson

**ASSOCIATE EDITOR
(AHISTORY)**
Damian Taylor

BETA TESTERS (AHISTORY)
Barnaby Edwards
Stephen Gray
Steve Manfred
Cody Quijano-Schell
John Seavey

**mad
norwegian
press**

1150 46th Street
Des Moines, Iowa 50311
info@madnorwegian.com